THE NORTON ANTHOLOGY OF

WORLD LITERATURE

SHORTER FOURTH EDITION

VOLUME 2

THE NORTON ANTHOLOGY OF

WORLD LITERATURE

SHORTER FOURTH EDITION

MARTIN PUCHNER, *General Editor*
HARVARD UNIVERSITY

SUZANNE AKBARI
UNIVERSITY OF TORONTO

WIEBKE DENECKE
BOSTON UNIVERSITY

BARBARA FUCHS
UNIVERSITY OF CALIFORNIA, LOS ANGELES

CAROLINE LEVINE
CORNELL UNIVERSITY

PERICLES LEWIS
YALE UNIVERSITY

EMILY WILSON
UNIVERSITY OF PENNSYLVANIA

VOLUME 2

W. W. NORTON & COMPANY | New York · London

W. W. Norton & Company has been independent since its founding in 1923, when William Warder Norton and Mary D. Herter Norton first published lectures delivered at the People's Institute, the adult education division of New York City's Cooper Union. The firm soon expanded its program beyond the Institute, publishing books by celebrated academics from America and abroad. By midcentury, the two major pillars of Norton's publishing program—trade books and college texts—were firmly established. In the 1950s, the Norton family transferred control of the company to its employees, and today—with a staff of four hundred and a comparable number of trade, college, and professional titles published each year—W. W. Norton & Company stands as the largest and oldest publishing house owned wholly by its employees.

Copyright © 2019, 2018, 2013, 2012, 2009, 2002, 1999, 1997, 1995, 1992, 1985, 1979, 1973, 1965, 1956 by W. W. Norton & Company, Inc.

Editor: Peter Simon
Project Editor: Taylere Peterson
Editorial Assistant: Katie Pak
Managing Editor, College: Marian Johnson
Managing Editor, College Digital Media: Kim Yi
Production Manager: Sean Mintus
Media Editor: Carly Fraser-Doria
Media Project Editor: Cooper Wilhelm
Assistant Media Editor: Ava Bramson
Editorial Assistant, Media: Joshua Bianchi
Marketing Manager, Literature: Kimberly Bowers
Art Direction: Rubina Yeh
Book Design: Jo Anne Metsch
Permissions Manager: Megan Schindel
Permissions Clearing: Margaret Gorenstein
Composition: Westchester Publishing Services
Cartographer: Adrian Kitzinger
Manufacturing: LSC Communications—Crawfordsville

Permission to use copyrighted material is included in the backmatter of this book.

ISBN: 978-0-393-60288-3 (pbk.)

Library of Congress Cataloging-in-Publication Data

Names: Puchner, Martin, 1969– editor. | Akbari, Suzanne Conklin, editor. | Denecke,
   Wiebke, editor. | Fuchs, Barbara, 1970– editor. | Levine, Caroline, 1970– editor. | Lewis,
   Pericles, editor. | Wilson, Emily R., 1971– editor.
Title: The Norton anthology of world literature / Martin Puchner, general editor ; Suzanne
   Akbari, Wiebke Denecke, Barbara Fuchs, Caroline Levine, Pericles Lewis, Emily Wilson.
Description: Shorter fourth edition. | New York : W. W. Norton & Company, 2019. | Includes
   bibliographical references and index.
Identifiers: LCCN 2018033851 | ISBN 9780393602876 (v. 1; pbk.) | ISBN 9780393602883
   (v. 2; pbk.)
Subjects: LCSH: Literature—Collections.
Classification: LCC PN6014 .N66 2019 | DDC 808.8—dc23 LC record available at
   https://lccn.loc.gov/2018033851

W. W. Norton & Company, Inc., 500 Fifth Avenue, New York, NY 10110
wwnorton.com
W. W. Norton & Company Ltd., 15 Carlisle Street, London W1D 3BS

1 2 3 4 5 6 7 8 9 0

Contents

IV. AT THE CROSSROADS OF EMPIRE   577

V. REALISM ACROSS THE GLOBE   655

VII. POSTWAR AND POSTCOLONIAL LITERATURE, 1945–68

VIII. CONTEMPORARY WORLD LITERATURE 1271

Preface

They arrive in boats, men exhausted from years of warfare and travel. As they approach the shore, their leader spots signs of habitation: flocks of goats and sheep, smoke rising from dwellings. A natural harbor permits them to anchor their boats so that they will be safe from storms. The leader takes an advance team with him to explore the island. It is rich in soil and vegetation, and natural springs flow with cool, clear water. With luck, they will be able to replenish their provisions and be on their way.

In the world of these men, welcoming travelers is a sacred custom, sanctioned by the gods themselves. It is also good policy among seafaring people. Someday, the roles may very well be reversed: today's host may be tomorrow's guest. Yet the travelers can never be certain whether a particular people will honor this custom. Wondering what to expect, the thirteen men enter one of the caves dotting the coastline.

The owner isn't home, but the men enter anyway, without any compunction. There are pens for sheep and goats, and there is plenty of cheese and milk, so the men begin eating. When the owner returns, they are terrified, but their leader, boldly, asks for gifts. The owner is not pleased. Instead of giving the intruders what they demand, he kills two of them and eats them for dinner. And then two more the next day. All the while, he keeps the men trapped in his cave.

A wily man, the leader devises a scheme to escape. He offers the owner wine, enough to make him drunk and sleepy. Once he dozes off, the men take a staff that they have secretly sharpened and plunge it into the owner's eye, blinding him. Without sight, he cannot see the men clinging to the undersides of his prized sheep as they stroll, one by one, out of the cave to graze, and cleverly the men cling only to the male sheep, not the females, which get milked.

*   *   *

This story of hospitality gone wrong comes from the *Odyssey*, one of the best-known works in all of world literature. We learn of this strange encounter of Greek soldiers with the one-eyed Cyclops named Polyphemus from Odysseus, the protagonist of the epic, when he recounts his exploits at the court of another host, the king of the Phaeacians. Unsurprisingly, Polyphemus isn't presented in the best light. Odysseus describes the Cyclopes as a people without a "proper" community, without agriculture, without hospitality. Is Odysseus, who has been wined and dined by his current host, trying to curry favor with the king of the Phaeacians by telling him how terribly he was treated by these non-Greek others? Reading the passage closely, we can see that Polyphemus and the other Cyclopes are adroit makers of cheese, so they can't be all that lazy. When the blinded Polyphemus cries out for help, his associates come to help him as a matter of course, so they don't live quite as isolated from one another as Odysseus claims. Even though Odysseus asserts that Polyphemus is godless, the land is blessed by the gods with fertility, and Polyphemus's divine father comes to his aid when he prays. Odysseus says that the Cyclopes lack laws and custom, yet we are also shown the careful, regular, customary way that Polyphemus takes care of his household. In a touching scene toward the end of his encounter with Odysseus, after he is blinded, Polyphemus speaks gently and respectfully to his favorite ram, so he can't be all that monstrous. The one-eyed giants assist one another, they are shepherds and artisans, and they are capable of kindness. The passage's ambiguities suggest that perhaps it was partly Odysseus's fault that this encounter between cultures went so badly. Were he and his companions simply travelers badly in need of food, or were they looters hoping to enrich themselves? The passage suggests that it's a matter of narrative perspective, from whose point of view the story is told.

Scenes of hospitality (or the lack thereof) are everywhere in world literature, and questions about hospitality, about the courtesies that we owe to strangers and that strangers owe to us (whether we are guests or hosts), are as important today as they were in the ancient world. Although many writers and thinkers today are fond of saying that our era is the first "truly global" one, stories such as this episode from Homer's *Odyssey* remind us that travel, trade, exile, migration, and cultural encounters of all kinds have been features of human experience for thousands of years.

The experience of reading world literature, too, is a form of travel—a mode of cultural encounter that presents us with languages, cultural norms, customs, and ideas that may be unfamiliar to us, even strange. As readers, each time we begin to read a new work, we put ourselves in the role of a traveler in a foreign land, trying to understand its practices and values and hoping to feel, to some degree and in some way, connected to and welcome among the people we meet there. *The Epic of Gilgamesh*, for example, takes its readers on a tour of Uruk, the first large city in human history, in today's Iraq, boasting of its city walls, its buildings and temples with their stairways and foundations, all made of clay bricks. Like a tour guide, the text even lets its readers inspect the city's clay pits, over one square mile large, that provided the material for this miraculous city made from clay. The greatest marvel of them all is of course *The Epic of Gilgamesh* itself, which was inscribed on clay tablets—the first monument of literature.

Foundational Texts

From its beginnings, *The Norton Anthology of World Literature* has been committed to offering students and teachers as many complete or substantially represented texts as possible. This Shorter Fourth Edition emphasizes the importance of *foundational* texts as never before by offering new translations of some of the best-known and most-loved works in the history of world literature. *The Epic of Gilgamesh* stands first in line of these foundational texts, which capture the story of an entire people, telling them where they came from and who they are. Some foundational texts become an object of worship and are deemed sacred, while others are revered as the most consequential story of an entire civilization. Because foundational texts inspire countless retellings—as Homer did for the Greek tragedians—these texts are reference points for the entire subsequent history of literature.

Perhaps no text is more foundational than the one with which we opened this preface: Homer's *Odyssey*. In this Shorter Fourth Edition, we feature the *Odyssey* in a new translation by our classics editor, Emily Wilson. This version captures the fast pace and rhythmic regularity of the original and offers a fresh perspective on cultural encounters such as the one between Odysseus and Polyphemus that is described above. Astonishingly, Wilson's translation is the first translation of the *Odyssey* into English by a woman. For centuries, commentators have remarked that the *Odyssey* is unusually attuned to the lives of women, especially in its portrait of Odysseus's wife, Penelope, a compelling and powerful character who cunningly holds a rowdy group of suitors at bay. Wilson's translation pays special attention to the poem's characterization of this remarkable woman, who is every bit as intriguing as the "complicated man" who is the eponymous hero of the tale. Other female characters, too, are given a new voice in this translation. For example, Helen, wife of the Greek king Menelaus and (according to legend) possessor of "the face that launched a thousand ships," is revealed through Wilson's translation to speak of herself not as a "whore" for whose sake so many young Greek men fought, suffered, and died (as she does in most other translations) but instead as a perceptive, clever person onto whom the Greeks, already eager to fight the Trojans, projected their own aggressive impulses: "They made my face the cause that hounded them," she says. The central conflicts of the epic, the very origin of the Trojan War, appear here in a startling new light.

This example highlights an exciting dimension of our emphasis on new translations. The first half of this anthology has always been dominated by male voices because men enjoyed privileged access to literacy and cultural influence in the centuries prior to modernity. Our focus on new translations has allowed us to introduce into these volumes more female voices—the voices of translators. So, for example, we present Homer's *Iliad* in a new translation by Caroline Alexander and Euripides' *Medea* in a new, specially commissioned translation by Sheila H. Murnaghan, and we continue to offer work in the first volume translated by female translators such as Dorothy Gilbert (Marie de France's *Lais*), Sheila Fisher (Chaucer's *Canterbury Tales*), and Rosalind Brown-Grant (Christine de Pizan's *Book of the City of Ladies*), among others. This commitment to featuring the work of female translators extends beyond these early centuries as well, for example in the brilliant new translation by Susan Bernofsky of a foundational text of literary modernity—Kafka's *Metamorphosis*. The result throughout the anthology is that these works now speak to today's readers in new and sometimes surprising ways.

Our emphasis in this edition on new translations is based on and amplifies the conviction expressed by the original editors of this anthology over fifty years ago: that world literature gains its power when it travels from its place of origin and speaks to people in different places. While purists sometimes insist on studying literature only in the original language, a dogma that radically shrinks what one can read, world literature not only relies on translation but actually thrives on it. Translation is a necessity; it is what enables a worldwide circulation of literature. It also is an art. One need only think of the way in which translations of the Bible shaped the history of Latin or English or German. Translations are re-creations of works for new readers. This edition pays keen attention to translation, featuring new translations that make classic texts newly readable and capture the originals in compelling ways. With each choice of translation, we have sought a version that would spark a sense of wonder while still being accessible to a contemporary reader.

Among other foundational texts presented in new translations and selections is the Qur'an, in a verse translation that is the product of a collaboration between M. A. Rafey Habib, a poet, literary scholar, and Muslim, and Bruce Lawrence, a renowned scholar of Islam. Their team effort captures some of the beauty of this extraordinary, and extraordinarily influential, sacred text. Augustine's *Confessions* are newly presented in a version by Peter Constantine, and Dante's *Inferno* is featured in the long-respected and highly readable translation by the American poet John Ciardi.

We have also maintained our commitment to exciting epics that deserve wider recognition such as the Maya *Popol Vuh* and *Sunjata*, which commemorates the founding of a West African empire in the late Middle Ages. Like the *Odyssey*, *Sunjata* was transmitted for centuries in purely oral form. But while the *Odyssey* was written down around 800 B.C.E., *Sunjata* was written down only in the twentieth century. We feature it here in a new prose translation by David C. Conrad, who personally recorded this version from a Mande storyteller, Djanka Tassey Condé, in 1994. In this way, *Sunjata* speaks to the continuing importance of oral storytelling, the origin of all foundational epics, from South Asia via Greece and Africa to Central America. Throughout the anthology, we remind readers that writing has coexisted with oral storytelling since the invention of literature and that it will continue to do so in the future.

A Network of Stories

In addition to foundational texts, we include in this edition a great number of stories and story collections. The origins of this form of literature reach deep into the ancient world, as scribes collected oral stories and assembled them in larger works. Consider what is undoubtedly the most famous of these collections, *The Thousand and One Nights*, with its stories within stories within stories, all neatly framed by the overarching narrative of Shahrazad, who is telling them to her sister and the king to avoid being put to death. What is most notable about this story collection is that it draws its material from India, Persia, and Greece. There existed a continent-spanning network of stories that allowed storytellers and scribes to recycle and reframe what they learned in ever new ways; it proved so compelling that later writers, from Marie de France to Chaucer, borrowed from it frequently.

Expanded Selections

Along with our focus on making foundational texts and story collections fresh and accessible, we have pruned the overall number of authors and are therefore able to increase our offerings from major texts that feature in many world literature courses. *Don Quixote* now includes the compelling "Story of Captivity in North Africa," in which Cervantes draws on his own experiences as a slave in Algiers, where he spent five years after having been captured by pirates. Other major texts with increased selections include the *Iliad*, Sappho, Ovid, the Qur'an, Murasaki's *Tale of Genji*, Machiavelli's *The Prince*, Baudelaire, and authors Tagore, and Borges, and we have introduced complete new texts, such as Aphra Behn's *Oroonoko*, Wole Soyinka's *Death and the King's Horseman*, Mo Yan's "The Old Gun," and Orhan Pamuk's "To Look Out the Window." We are particularly excited to now close the anthology with a story by the Nigerian writer Chimamanda Ngozi Adichie called "The Headstrong Historian," which, since its publication in 2008, has already become a favorite in world literature classrooms. This compact work introduces us to three generations of Nigerians as they navigate a complicated series of personal and cultural displacements. A thought-provoking exploration of the complex results of cultural contact and influence, this probing, searching journey seemed to us the most fitting conclusion to the anthology's survey of 4,000 years of literature.

The Birth of World Literature

In 1827, a provincial German writer, living in small-town Weimar, recognized that he was in the privileged position of having access not only to European literature but also to literature from much further afield, including Persian poetry, Chinese novels, and Sanskrit drama. The writer was Johann Wolfgang von Goethe, and in 1827, he coined a term to capture this new force of globalization in literature: "world literature." (We now include the "prologue" to Goethe's play *Faust*, which he wrote after encountering a similar prologue in the classical Sanskrit play *Śhakuntalā*.)

Since 1827, for less than 200 years, we have been living in an era of world literature. This era has brought many lost masterpieces back to life, including *The Epic of Gilgamesh*, which was rediscovered in the nineteenth century, and the *Popol Vuh*, which languished in a library until well into the twentieth century. Other works of world literature weren't translated and therefore didn't begin to circulate outside their sphere of origin until the last 200 years, including *The Tale of Genji*. With more literature becoming more widely available than ever before, Goethe's vision of world literature has become a reality today.

In presenting world literature from the dawn of writing to the early twenty-first century, and from oral storytelling to the literary experiments of modernism, this anthology raises the question not only of what world literature is but also of the nature of literature itself. Greek tragedies are experienced by modern students as a literary genre, encountered in written texts; but for the ancient Athenians, they were primarily dramas, experienced live in an outdoor theater in the context of a religious and civic ritual. Other texts, such as the Qur'an or the Bible, are sacred pieces of writing, central to many people's religious faith, while others appreciate them primarily or exclusively as literature. Some texts, such as those by Laozi or Augustine, belong in philosophy, while others, such as Machiavelli's *The Prince*, are also political documents. Our modern conception of literature as imaginative literature, as fiction, is very recent, about 200 years old. We have therefore opted for a much-expanded conception of literature that includes creation myths, wisdom literature, religious texts, philosophy, and political writing in addition to poems, plays, and narrative fiction. This speaks to an older definition of literature as writing of high quality or of great cultural significance. There are many texts of philosophy or religion or politics that are not remarkable or influential for their literary qualities and that would therefore have no place in an anthology of world literature. But the works presented here do: in addition to or as part of their other functions, they have acquired the status of literature.

This brings us to the last and perhaps most important question: When we study the world, why study it through its literature? Hasn't literature lost some of its luster for us, we who are faced with so many competing media and art forms? Like no other art form or medium, literature offers us a deep history of human thinking. As our illustration program shows, writing was invented not for the composition of literature but for much more mundane purposes, such as the recording of ownership, contracts, or astronomical observations. But literature is writing's most glorious by-product. Literature can be reactivated with each reading. Many of the great architectural monuments of the past are now in ruins. Literature, too, often has to be excavated, as with many classical texts. But once a text has been found or reconstructed it can be experienced as if for the first time by new readers. Even though many of the literary texts collected in this anthology are at first strange, because they originated so very long ago, they still speak to today's readers with great eloquence and freshness. No other art form can capture the human past with the precision and scope of literature because language expresses human consciousness. Language shapes our thinking, and literature, the highest expression of language, plays an important role in that process, pushing the boundaries of what we can think and how we think it. This is especially true with great, complex, and contradictory works that allow us to explore different narrative perspectives, different points of view.

Works of world literature continue to elicit strong emotions and investments. The epic *Rāmāyaṇa*, for example, plays an important role in the politics of India, where it has been used to bolster Hindu nationalism, just as the *Bhagavad-gītā* continues to be a moral touchstone in the ethical deliberation about war. The so-called religions of the book, Judaism, Christianity, and Islam, make our selections from their scriptures a more than historical exercise as well. China has recently elevated the sayings of Confucius, whose influence on Chinese attitudes about the state had waned in the twentieth century, creating Confucius Institutes all over the world to promote Chinese culture in what is now called New Confucianism. World literature is never neutral. We know its relevance precisely by the controversies it inspires.

There are many ways of studying other cultures and of understanding the place of our own culture in the world. Archaeologists can show us objects and buildings from the past and speculate, through material remains, how people in the past ate, fought, lived, died, and were buried; scientists can date layers of soil. Literature is capable of something much more extraordinary: it allows us a glimpse into the imaginative lives, the thoughts and feelings of humans from thousands of years ago or living halfway around the world. This is the true magic of world literature as captured in this anthology, our shared human inheritance.

About the Shorter Fourth Edition

New Selections and Translations

Following is a list of the new translations, selections, and works in the Shorter Fourth Edition, in order:

VOLUME 1

A new translation of Homer's *The Iliad* by Caroline Alexander and Book XVIII newly included • A new translation of Homer's *The Odyssey* by Emily Wilson • New translations of Sappho's poetry by Philip Freeman, including ten new poems • New translations of *Oedipus the King* by David Grene and *Medea* by Sheila H. Murnaghan • A new selection from *The Aeneid*, including Book VI and an excerpt from Book VIII • New selections from Ovid's *Metamorphoses*, including the stories of Jove and Europa, Ceres and Proserpina, and Iphis and Isis • A new translation of Augustine's *Confessions* by Peter Constantine with a new selection from "Book XI [Time]" • A new translation of the Qur'an by M. A. R. Habib and Bruce Lawrence with new selections from "Light," "Ya Sin," and "The Sun" • A new translation of Marie de France's *Lais* by Dorothy Gilbert, including the new selection "Bisclavret" • John Ciardi's translation of *The Divine Comedy*, newly included • Selections from Christine de Pizan's *The Book of the City of Ladies*, translated by Rosalind Brown-Grant, newly included • New poems by Li Bo • Selections from Sei Shōnagon's *The Pillow Book*, translated by Meredith McKinney, newly included • New selections from *The Tale of Genji*: "*Sakaki*: A Branch of Sacred Evergreen," "*Maboroshi*: Spirit Summoner," "*Hashihime*: The Divine Princess at Uji Bridge," "*Agemaki*: A Bowknot Tied in Maiden's Loops," "*Yadoriki*: Trees Encoiled in Vines of Ivy," and "*Tenarai*: Practicing Calligraphy" • A new prose translation of *Sunjata: A West African Epic of the Mande* by David C. Conrad • New selections from *The Prince*: "On Liberality and Parsimony," "On Cruelty and Pity," "In What Way Faith Should Be Kept," "On Avoiding Contempt and Hatred," "[The Best Defense]," "[Ferdinand of Spain, Exemplary Prince]," "[Good Counsel vs. Flattery]," and "[Why Princes Fail]" • A new selection from *Don Quixote*, "[A Story of Captivity in North Africa, Told to Don Quixote at the Inn]"

VOLUME 2

Aphra Behn's *Oroonoko; or, The Royal Slave*, newly included • A new translation of Sor Juana Inés de la Cruz's *Response* by Edith Grossman • A new selection from *Faust*, "Prelude in the Theatre" • New poems by William Wordsworth and Charles Baudelaire • Nguyễn Du's *The Tale of Kiều* A new translation of *The Death of Ivan Ilyich* by Peter Carson • Anton Chekhov's "The Lady with the Dog" translated by Ivy Litvinov • Rabindranath Tagore's *Kabuliwala*, translated by Madhuchhanda Karlekar • A new translation of *The Metamorphosis* by Susan Bernofsky • Eric Bentley's translation, new to this edition, of Pirandello's *Six Characters in Search of an Author* • Chapter 2 of Virginia Woolf's *A Room of One's Own* • Jorge Luis Borges's "The Library of Babel," translated by James E. Irby • W. B. Yeats's "Among School Children" • M. D. Herder Norton's translations of Rainer Maria Rilke's poems, newly included • Seamus Heaney's "Digging" • Wole Soyinka's *Death and the King's Horseman* • Mo Yan's "The Old Gun" • Orhan Pamuk's "To Look Out the Window" • Chimamanda Ngozi Adichie's "The Headstrong Historian"

Resources for Students and Instructors

Norton provides students and instructors with abundant resources to make the teaching and study of world literature an even more interesting and rewarding experience.

With the Shorter Fourth Edition, are pleased to launch the new *Norton Anthology of World Literature* website, found at digital.wwnorton.com /worldlit4pre1650 (for volume 1) and digital.wwnorton.com/worldlit4post1650 (for volume 2). This searchable and sortable site contains thousands of resources for students and instructors in one centralized place at no additional cost. Following are some highlights:

- A series of eight brand-new video modules are designed to enhance classroom presentation and spark student interest in the anthology's works. These videos, conceived of and narrated by the anthology editors, ask students to consider why it is important for them to read and engage with this literature.
- Hundreds of images—maps, author portraits, literary places, and manuscripts—are available for student browsing or instructor download for in-class presentation.
- Several hours of audio recordings are available, including a 10,000-term audio glossary that helps students pronounce the character and place names in the anthologized works.

The site also provides a wealth of teaching resources that are unlocked with an instructor's log-in:

- "Quick read" summaries, teaching notes, discussion questions, and suggested resources for every work in the anthology, from the much-praised *Teaching with* The Norton Anthology of World Literature: *A Guide for Instructors*

- Downloadable Lecture PowerPoints featuring images, quotations from the texts, and lecture notes in the notes view for in-class presentation

In addition to the wealth of resources in *The Norton Anthology of World Literature* website, Norton offers a downloadable Coursepack that allows instructors to easily add high-quality Norton digital media to online, hybrid, or lecture courses—all at no cost. Norton Coursepacks work within existing learning management systems; there's no new system to learn, and access is free and easy. Content is customizable and includes over seventy reading-comprehension quizzes, short-answer questions, links to the videos, and more.

Acknowledgments

The editors would like to thank the following people, who have provided invaluable assistance by giving us sage advice, important encouragement, and help with the preparation of the manuscript: Sara Akbari, Alannah de Barra, Wendy Belcher, Jodi Bilinkoff, Daniel Boucher, Freya Brackett, Psyche Brackett, Michaela Bronstein, Rachel Carroll, Sookja Cho, Kyeong-Hee Choi, Amanda Claybaugh, Lewis Cook, David Damrosch, Dick Davis, Burghild Denecke, Amanda Detry, Anthony Domestico, Megan Eckerle, Marion Eggert, Merve Emre, Maria Fackler, Guillermina de Ferrari, Alyssa Findley, Karina Galperín, Stanton B. Garner, Kimberly Dara Gordon, Elyse Graham, Stephen Greenblatt, Sara Guyer, Langdon Hammer, Emily Hayman, Iain Higgins, Paulo Lemos Horta, Mohja Kahf, Peter Kornicki, Paul W. Kroll, Peter H. Lee, Sung-il Lee, Lydia Liu, Bala Venkat Mani, Ann Matter, Barry McCrea, Alexandra McCullough-Garcia, Rachel McGuiness, Jon McKenzie, Mary Mullen, Djibril Tamsir Niane, Johann Noh, Felicity Nussbaum, Andy Orchard, John Peters, Michael Pettid, Daniel Taro Poch, Daniel Potts, Megan Quigley, Payton Phillips Quintanilla, Catherine de Rose, Imogen Roth, Katherine Rupp, Ellen Sapega, Jesse Schotter, Stephen Scully, Kyung-ho Sim, Sarah Star, Brian Stock, Tomi Suzuki, Joshua Taft, Sara Torres, J. Keith Vincent, Lisa Voigt, Kristen Wanner, Emily Weissbourd, Karoline Xu, Yoon Sun Yang, and Catherine Vance Yeh.

All the editors would like to thank the wonderful people at Norton, principally our editor Pete Simon, the driving force behind this whole undertaking, as well as Marian Johnson (Managing Editor, College), Christine D'Antonio and Kurt Wildermuth (Project Editors), Michael Fleming (Copyeditor), Gerra Goff (Associate Editor), Katia Pak (Editorial Assistant), Megan Jackson (College Permissions Manager), Margaret Gorenstein (Permissions), Catherine Abelman (Photo Editor), Debra Morton Hoyt (Art Director; cover design), Rubina Yeh (Design Director), Jo Anne Metsch (Designer; interior text design), Adrian Kitzinger (cartography), Agnieszka Gasparska (timeline design), Carly Fraser-Doria (Media Editor), Ava Bramson (Assistant Editor, Media), Ashley Horna and Sean Mintus (Production Managers), and Kim Bowers (Marketing Manager, Literature). We'd also like to thank our Instructor's Guide authors: Colleen Clemens (Kutztown University), Elizabeth Watkins (Loyola University New Orleans), and Janet Zong (Harvard University).

This anthology represents a collaboration not only among the editors and their close advisers but also among the thousands of instructors who teach from the anthology and provide valuable and constructive guidance to the publisher and editors. *The Norton Anthology of World Literature* is as much their book as it is ours, and we are grateful to everyone who has cared enough about this anthology to help make it better. We're especially grateful to the professors of world literature who responded to an online survey in 2014, whom we have listed below. Thank you all.

Michelle Abbott (Georgia Highlands College), Elizabeth Ashworth (Castleton State College), Clinton Atchley (Henderson State University), Amber Barnes (Trinity Valley Community College), Rosemary Baxter (Clarendon College), Khani Begum (Bowling Green State University), Joyce Boss (Wartburg College), Floyd Brigdon (Trinity Valley Community College), James Bryant-Trerise (Clackamas Community College), Barbara Cade (Texas College), Kellie Cannon (Coastal Carolina Community College), Amee Carmines (Hampton University), Farrah Cato (University of Central Florida), Brandon Chitwood (Marquette University), Paul Cohen (Texas State University), Judith Cortelloni (Lincoln College), Randall Crump (Kennesaw State University), Sunni Davis (Cossatot Community College), Michael Demson (Sam Houston State University), Richard Diguette (Georgia Perimeter College, Dunwoody), Daniel Dooghan (University of Tampa), Jeff Doty (West Texas A&M University), Myrto Drizou (Valdosta State University), Ashley Dugas (Copiah-Lincoln Community College), Richmond Eustis (Nicholls State University), David Fell (Carroll Community College), Allison Fetters (Chattanooga State Community College), Francis Fletcher (Folsom Lake College), Kathleen D. Fowler (Surry Community College), Louisa Franklin (Young Harris College), James Gamble (University of Arkansas), Antoinette Gazda (Averett University), Adam Golaski (Central Connecticut State University), Anissa Graham (University of North Alabama), Eric Gray (St. Gregory's University), Jared Griffin (Kodiak College), Marne Griffin (Hilbert College), Frank Gruber (Bergen Community College), Laura Hammons (Hinds Community College), Nancy G. Hancock (Austin Peay State University), C. E. Harding (Western Oregon University), Leslie Harrelson (Dalton State College), Eleanor J. Harrington-Austin (North Carolina Central University), Matthew Hokom (Fairmont State University), Scott Hollifield (University of Nevada, Las Vegas), Catherine Howard (University of Houston, Downtown), Jack Kelnhofer (Ocean County College), Katherine King (University of California, Los Angeles), Pam Kingsbury (University of North Alabama), Sophia Kowalski (Hillsborough Community College), Roger Ladd (University of North Carolina at Pembroke), Jameela Lares (University of Southern Mississippi), Susan Lewis (Delaware Technical Community College), Christina Lovin (Eastern Kentucky University), Richard Mace (Pace University), Nicholas R. Marino (Borough of Manhattan Community College, CUNY), Brandi Martinez (Mountain Empire Community College), Kathy Martinez (Sandhills Community College), Matthew Masucci (State College of Florida), Kelli McBride (Seminole State College), Melissa McCoy (Clarendon College), Geoffrey McNeil (Notre Dame de Namur University), Renee Moore (Mississippi Delta Community College), Anna C. Oldfield (Coastal Carolina University), Keri Overall (Texas Woman's University), Maggie Piccolo (Rutgers University), Oana Popescu-Sandu (University of Southern Indiana), Jonathan Purkiss (Pulaski Technical College), Rocio Quispe-Agnoli (Michigan State University), Evan Radcliffe (Villanova University), Ken Raines (Eastern Arizona College), Jonathan Randle (Mississippi College), Kirk G. Rasmussen (Utah Valley University), Helaine Razovsky (Northwestern State University of Louisiana), Karin Rhodes (Salem State University), Stephanie Roberts (Georgia Military College), Allen Salerno (Auburn University), Shannin Schroeder (Southern Arkansas University), Heather

Seratt (University of Houston, Downtown), Conrad Shumaker (University of Central Arkansas), Edward Soloff (St. John's University), Eric Sterling (Auburn University Montgomery), Ron Stormer (Culver-Stockton College), Marianne Szlyk (Montgomery College), Tim Tarkington (Georgia Perimeter College), Allison Tharp (University of Southern Mississippi), Diane Thompson (Northern Virginia Community College), Sevinc Turkkan (College at Brockport, State University of New York), Verne Underwood (Rogue Community College), Patricia Vazquez (College of Southern Nevada), William Wallis (Los Angeles Valley College), Eric Weil (Elizabeth City State University), Denise C. White (Kennesaw State University), Tamora Whitney (Creighton University), Todd Williams (Kutztown University of Pennsylvania), Bertha Wise (Oklahoma City Community College), and Lindsey Zanchettin (Auburn University).

THE NORTON ANTHOLOGY OF

WORLD
LITERATURE

SHORTER FOURTH EDITION

VOLUME 2

I

Literatures of Early Modern East Asia

When did "modernity" begin? Many features of what we today consider quintessentially "modern" started to emerge in Europe and around the world in the fourteenth century. The age of discovery and exploration, of European colonization and the spread of Christianity, created global interconnections on an unprecedented scale: scientific and technological progress in mathematics, physics, astronomy, and engineering changed people's view of the world and their ability to change it; the new scholarly cultures of the Renaissance and the Baroque developed new ideas about national sovereignty in contrast to the shared Latin high culture of the European Middle Ages. Along with this new age came the gradual process of "vernacularization," the increasing use of spoken local languages—such as Italian, English, French, or German—instead of Latin. This allowed a much broader slice of the population to become

The *Eight-fold Bridge of Mikawa*, depicted here by the renowned woodblock-print artist Hokusai (1760–1849) in a series of famous views of bridges in various provinces of Japan, takes its unique shape from a myth that eight rivers join in this spot. Travel became increasingly popular in early modern East Asia and people recorded their adventures in travelogues, poems, and pictures. The eight-fold bridge did not exist anymore in Hokusai's time, but literary references and historical nostalgia inspired him to paint what reality could no longer offer.

literate, start reading, and consume the books made available by the print revolution set off by Gutenberg in the fifteenth century.

In East Asia and particular China, modernity began half a millennium earlier than in Europe, in the eleventh century, with the spread of print technology across society, which transformed the ways people read, wrote, and circulated books and knowledge. Like later in Europe, printing was used not only for the mass circulation of texts and information, but also for the mass production of Buddhist scriptures and Buddha images, which gained the commissioner good karma. At the same time, literacy expanded to social classes beyond the elites as cheaper access to written texts exponentially increased production and consumption of knowledge and art.

Within East Asia—China, Korea, Japan—early modernity took different shapes, depending on the governments, ruling ideologies, policies, and social structures of these various societies. China's dynastic shift from the Chinese Ming dynasty (1368–1644) to the non-Chinese Manchu Qing dynasty (1644–1912) occurred during a period of intense interest in Western science and scholarship, when some European missionaries worked as astronomers, or later as painters and architects at the Chinese court, while attempting to convert the Chinese emperor to Christianity, which ultimately failed and led to the ban of Christianity.

Japan was reunited in the seventeenth century after a period of civil war, and the new military rulers of the Tokugawa shogunate (1600–1868) were interested in boosting foreign trade, though within the limits of their notion of law and order. The shoguns quickly decided to closely control trade with European merchants and ban Christianity. They allowed Chinese merchants to trade in the southern Japanese city of Nagasaki, and they built Dejima, a smallish artificial island created off the Japanese coast where only Dutch traders could live and conduct business. This tiny enclave became the heart of "Dutch learning," the study of European science, technology, and medicine in early modern Japan, which no doubt contributed to Japan's quick modernization in the late nineteenth and early twentieth centuries. The Tokugawa shoguns created peace and order, imposed strict social hierarchies and forceful policies, and laid the foundations for economic prosperity and a new cultural flourishing. As the traditional elites and great military clans lost their influence and power, social newcomers such as craftsmen and merchants became influential: These urban commoners, a crucial driving force in Japan's commercial revolution, could make their fortune in the rapidly growing grand cities of Edo (Tokyo), Osaka, and Kyoto. In this environment, commoners, among them also women, for the first time in Japanese history could acquire basic literacy and elementary education in the numerous *terakoya* "temple schools" that dotted Tokugawa Japan.

EARLY MODERN CHINESE VERNACULAR LITERATURE

Although the vernacular stories and novels written in this period are now regarded as unquestionable masterpieces, the status of vernacular literature was until recently far below that of the ancient and authoritative genres of classical poetry, prose, and tales. The last two dynasties of imperial China, the Ming (1368–1644) and Qing (1644–1911), bristled with artistic and literary creativity, and the classical genres thrived in an intellectual climate of unprecedented variety and sophistication. At the same time, new literatures formed, written not in the scholastic classical language but in the living vernacular of everyday speech. This literature was much more adept at handling themes and topics that had been outside the purview of classical literature, such as sex, violence, corruption, social satire, and slapstick humor. Vernacular literature in China could lay claim to a richer, or at least more wide-ranging, portrait of the lives of Chinese readers, and thus had a broad appeal across class lines. With the Ming dynasty, the civil service examinations regained their importance as a venue for a political career and thus created again a national culture of shared elite education, leading to a renewal of classical literature. At the same time, an emergent urban bourgeoisie, increasingly literate and influential, provided an eager market for literature in the vernacular, such as plays, stories, and prose fiction. The print culture in the

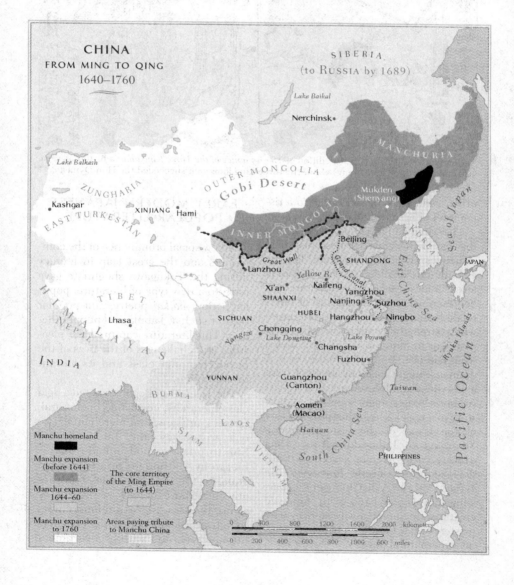

CHINA
FROM MING TO QING
1640–1760

SIBERIA
(to RUSSIA by 1689)

Lake Baikal

Nerchinsk

MANCHURIA

Lake Balkash

ZUNGHARIA

Kashgar

EAST TURKESTAN

XINJIANG Hami

OUTER MONGOLIA
Gobi Desert

INNER MONGOLIA

Mukden
(Shenyang)

Sea of Japan

KOREA

JAPAN

Great Wall
Lanzhou

Beijing

Grand Canal

SHANDONG

East China Sea

Ryukyu Islands

HIMALAYAS

TIBET

NEPAL

Lhasa

INDIA

Yellow R.

Xi'an
SHAANXI

Kaifeng
Yangzhou
Nanjing Suzhou
Hangzhou Ningbo

SICHUAN

HUBEI

Yangtze
Chongqing
Lake Dongting

Lake Poyang

Changsha

Fuzhou

YUNNAN

BURMA

Guangzhou
(Canton)

Taiwan

Pacific Ocean

LAOS

SIAM

VIETNAM

Aomen
(Macao)

Hainan

South China Sea

PHILIPPINES

Manchu homeland

Manchu expansion
(before 1644)

Manchu expansion
1644–60

Manchu expansion
to 1760

The core territory
of the Ming Empire
(to 1644)

Areas paying tribute
to Manchu China

0   400   800   1200   1600   2000 kilometers

0   200   400   600   800   1000   600 miles

An illustrated page from a 1581 edition of *The Romance of the Three Kingdoms*, a historical saga (attributed to Luo Guanzhong) about the three kingdoms that succeeded the Han Dynasty.

urban centers also contributed to a rising level of literacy and education.

The Ming and the Qing dynasties are the age of the great Chinese historical romances, which were often lengthy elaborations of older stories. On some level Chinese vernacular literature can be described as a vast tapestry of interrelated stories. This was a literature whose strength lay not in inventing new plots but in filling in details and saying what had been omitted in older ones. A dramatist might take one incident from a story cycle and develop it into a play. A fiction writer might spin out a short story in a novel. The rather prosaic story of the travel of the historical monk Xuanzang to India during the Tang dynasty (618–907) in search of Buddhist scriptures became *Journey to the West* (1592) by **Wu Cheng'en**, a sparkling novel populated with fantastic creatures, including a wily monkey who masters larger-than-life challenges with his supernatural powers.

EARLY MODERN JAPANESE POPULAR LITERATURE

The new social prominence of the commoners and the great leap in literacy during the Tokugawa shogunate gave birth to a new type of literature: popular fiction, *haikai* poetry, and popular theater such as kabuki and puppet theater. This literature captured the pleasures and challenges of the lives of the new commoner class and its vibrant urban milieu.

The Tokugawa shoguns created a rigid class hierarchy, consisting of samurai, farmers, artisans, and merchants. The old aristocracy and Buddhist and Shinto priests stood outside of this hierarchy, although priests ranked equal to the samurai class. The shoguns' vast bureaucracy was staffed by samurai retainers. With no more wars to fight, these former soldiers became bureaucrats, and with a government

RUSSIAN
EMPIRE

Hokkaidō

HOKKAIDO

Matsumae

TOKUGAWA JAPAN
1603–1867

0   50   100   200 kilometers

0   20 40   60 80 100 120 miles

TOHOKU

Regional name
and boundary

Oxford

Domain name
and boundary

Ōgaki

Bashō's 1689 journey
from Edo to Ōgaki as
recorded in *The Narrow
Road to the Deep North*

Akita   Morioka

Kisakata   Hiraizumi
Dewagoe (Naruko)
Sakata Obanazawa   Ishi-no-maki
                            Matsushima
Mount Haguro   Oishida Shiogama
Yamagata Ryūshakoji   Sendai
                  Iizuka
Echigo (Niigata)   Asaka (Fukushima)

                            Sukagawa
Shirakawa Barrier   Nasu
Nikkō   Kurobane
                            Muronoyashima
Ichiburi Barrier
                  Honshū   KANTO

Kanazawa   Edo (Tokyo)   Soka
Komatsu
Daishoji   CHUBU
Maruoka   Kamakura
Fukui
Iro-no-hama   Mount Fuji
Tsuruga
                  Ōgaki
KINKI
Kyoto
Nara
Osaka   ★ Ise Shrine

Sea of Japan

KOREA

Tsushima

CHUGOKU

Chōshū

Inland Sea

SHIKOKU

Shikoku

Pacific Ocean

KYUSHU

Kumamoto

Nagasaki
Dejima •Shimabara

Satsuma

Kyūshū

East China Sea

•Tanegashima

to run they clustered in the cities. Removed from the land and their previous military and agricultural pursuits, the urban samurai developed new needs, which were promptly met by enterprising urban commoners—such as merchants and artisans—whose numbers swelled in response to economic opportunity. Even the traditional ways of commerce evolved under the Tokugawa. Because rice, which had long been the traditional standard of exchange, was unwieldy and inconvenient in an urban setting, coined money took its place in business transactions. The development of a money economy had a slow but irreversible effect on every aspect of Japanese life.

Cities grew into bustling centers of commercial activity and changed under the impact of new policies. To prevent power challenges from the provinces, the shogun required his most prestigious retainers, the so-called "domain lords" (daimyō), to keep estates in Edo in addition to their castles in the provinces. Their women and children were held as hostages of sorts in Edo, while the domain lords lived in alternating years in the provinces and in Edo. This policy changed the face of Edo, as wealth from the provinces flooded into the city and commercial and cultural exchange between the provinces and the political center increased. The shoguns were also worried about public morals. To control prostitution, they consolidated brothels into officially licensed "pleasure quarters." The pleasure quarters were surrounded by a moat and only accessible through a main gate, to monitor entering clients and to prevent courtesans from leaving at their own will. The largest pleasure quarters—Yoshiwara in Edo, Shimabara in Kyoto, and Shinmachi in Osaka—quickly became proverbial. They appear again and again in popular literature as sites where fortunes were spent on music, dance, songs, seductive glances, and sex; purses and families ruined; hearts broken; and double love suicides planned.

The Tokugawa shoguns were also worried about outside threats. Portuguese traders had first reached Japan in 1543 when blown ashore by a typhoon. European merchants brought a few products that would have a major impact on Japan and the region: firearms and New World crops such as corn, sweet potatoes, and tobacco or chili (so crucial for Korea's distinctively spicy cuisine). Catholic missionaries who were seeking converts outside of Europe to combat the reformation movements in Europe followed in the wake of these merchants and traders. Francis Xavier, a priest of the recently founded Jesuit order, reached Japan in 1549 and, like many missionaries who followed him, had a keen interest in Asian cultures. The Jesuits were particularly sensitive to indigenous beliefs and practices. But ultimately quarrels between different Catholic orders over how to present Christianity in East Asia and how to accommodate radically different religious practices, in particular Confucian ancestor worship, damaged the credibility of the missionaries in the eyes of East Asian rulers. Repressions against Christianity began in Japan in 1587. By 1639 the shoguns had forbidden the practice of Christianity, overseas travel, and the importation of foreign books. European traders and Christian missionaries were expelled under threat of execution. Japanese converts were sometimes tortured or killed if they refused to abjure their Christian beliefs.

Although the period when Christian missionaries worked in Japan was relatively brief, they helped inspire a development that altered the face of Japan within a century: mass printing.

This late eighteenth-century woodblock print by Katsukawa Shunshō depicts a street scene in Edo's Yoshiwara pleasure quarter.

Japanese had imported printed texts from China as early as the eighth century and had subsequently used the technology of woodblock printing to print Buddhist sutras. But until the late sixteenth century, all books except for Buddhist texts circulated in extremely small, restricted numbers in manuscript format. Manuscripts were expensive, because they had to be copied by an expert hand; therefore, access to book knowledge was limited to those few who owned copies as members of elite families or who had the means to have them copied. After Christian missionaries set up a printing press with movable type and published among others a Japanese translation of Aesop's Fables in 1594, the first shogun, Tokugawa Ieyasu, had central Confucian texts, along with administrative and military works, printed with movable type in the early 1600s. Classical works of vernacular literature, such as an abridged version of *The Tale of Genji*, followed soon in luxury editions. In the 1630s, movable-type printing was replaced again with woodblock printing, which was more suitable to print the cursive Japanese *kana* syllabary, and commercial publishing houses opened. Classical Chinese and Japanese texts were printed quickly and sold to the urban population in the dozens of bookstores that sprang up in response.

As a result, literacy levels rose dramatically. Until 1600 only aristocrats and the Buddhist clergy received an extensive education, while peasants and many samurai could not read or write. By the mid-seventeenth century, most of the samurai, artisans, merchants, and even some farmers had gained basic literacy. A growing network of private schools for the merchant class and domain schools for the samurai class made this drastic change possible.

The advent of mass printing accelerated the speed of both reading and writing. At one point, for example, in 1680, Saikaku composed in a frenzied single one-day sitting a four-thousand-verse sequence. But not everybody liked the acceleration in literary life brought about by the printing revolution. The entire oeuvre of **Matsuo Bashō** (1644–1694), the most famous haiku writer of all time, contains only about a thousand verses and Bashō seems to have disdained Saikaku's prolific literary output as well as the commercialization of literature he saw gaining ground around him.

Despite their different outlook, both Bashō and Saikaku belonged to the new world of early modern popular literature. There was a strong awareness of the polar dynamic between popular (*zoku*) literature and highbrow or refined (*ga*) literature. Refined literature was rooted in the classical traditions: Chinese-style poetry and classical *waka* poetry continued to stress aristocratic topics and relied on a fixed vocabulary of acceptable themes and diction—romantic love (in the case of *waka*), the seasons, spring warblers, or cherry blossoms. Writers of popular literature, in contrast, became expert in depicting "bad" places such as the theater districts and the pleasure quarters in vulgar language or celebrating themes and earthy expressions of simple commoner life—courtesans, potatoes, or piss. Popular linked verse (*haikai no renga*), which gave birth to the genre of haiku, became a major ground for experimenting with novel combinations of high and low diction, classical and popular themes, and Chinese and Japanese styles. Bashō's **The Narrow Road to the Deep North**, a poetic diary of his travels through northeastern Japan, is a brilliant example of how the literary tradition could be recaptured and recast through a new poetic language, while preserving all the rich resonances of that tradition.

Early modern popular literature was one part of the revolution in lifestyles and forms of entertainment of this era. Actors, courtesans, adventurers, shopkeepers, rice brokers, moneylenders, fashion-plate wives, and precocious sons and daughters all created their own new cosmopolitan habits. Kabuki playwrights, haiku poets, woodblock artists, and best-selling novelists all captured in their own genres an intimate glimpse of kinetic bourgeois life—blunt, expansive, iconoclastic, irrepressibly playful. For the first time, ordinary people became standard literary characters, and the material and sexual aspects of life were deemed worthy and profitable subjects of literature.

Though politically and culturally deeply intertwined, various East Asian countries and their literatures developed along their own distinctive trajectory during the early modern period. With the late nineteenth century, the Western encroachments on China and the entire region, and the rise of Japanese imperialism, which led to the annexation of Korea in 1910 and resulted in the disastrous Pacific War in the mid-twentieth century, the East Asian region became more closely and, to this day, contentiously intertwined. Yet during this very period of political and military contention and collision in East Asia, the enthusiastic reception of Western literature in East Asia gave Japanese, Chinese, and Korean writers a new common denominator. This was to change the languages and traditional literatures of East Asia forever, resulting in today's modern Chinese, Japanese, and Korean literary scenes, which emerged and kept evolving in vivid dialogue with Western cultural and literary trends.

WU CHENG'EN
ca. 1500–1582

Nothing is impossible in *The Journey to the West*. People and fantastic creatures are whisked through the universe, a magic monkey can create thousands of companions by blowing on a wisp of his hair, and virgin monks can become pregnant. The novel has won over generations of readers with its unusual blend of a fast-paced, suspenseful martial-arts narrative and religious allegory, as well as its vivid satirical portrait of the workings and failings of human and heavenly bureaucracies.

The Journey to the West was not the work of a single person. First published in 1592, the novel is a product of the cumulative retelling of the story, which circulated orally and was adapted and transformed through the centuries. The final form of these stories in this vast, sprawling compendium of one hundred chapters transformed the traditional material into a great work of literature. Scholars are not entirely certain whether Wu Cheng'en did indeed give final shape to the story and was the author of the 1592 edition of *The Journey to the West*. But a local gazetteer of his home prefecture connects this title to his name. This piece of evidence is further supported by the fact that Wu had a reputation for being a versatile poet (there are over 1,700 poems in the novel), and for writing on mythical and supernatural subjects in a satirical style. Also, he was a native of a region in southeast China, whose dialect appears in the novel. We do not know much more about Wu than that he was a minor official serving under the Ming dynasty (1368–1644).

The core of the story had a historical basis in the journey of the monk Xuanzang, or Tripitaka (596–664), who traveled from China to India in search of Buddhist scriptures during the reign of Emperor Taizong, one of the most influential emperors of the Tang dynasty (618–907). At the time, travel to the Western territories was forbidden and Tripitaka could have faced arrest and execution for his transgression. But when he returned seventeen years later with the coveted scriptures, he earned immediate imperial patronage and was allowed to settle down, translate the new scriptures, and propagate them. He spent the last twenty years of his life in the Tang capital of Chang'an (modern-day Xi'an), translating hundreds of sutras and other Buddhist texts from Sanskrit into Chinese, more than any other person before him had ever done. He did write a brief record of his experience during his travels. The account of the historical Xuanzang had virtually nothing to do with the much-later novel, but it may have served as the early basis from which the story began to be retold. Pilgrimages to India were by no means unique among Chinese monks of this era, but Tripitaka's journey somehow captured the popular imagination; it was retold in stories and plays, until it finally emerged as *The Journey to the West*.

As Xuanzang's journey was retold, the most important addition was his acquisition of a wondrous disciple named Sun Wukong, "Monkey Aware-of-Vacuity." Monkey had already made his appearance in a twelfth-century version of the story and came to so dominate the full novel version that the first major English translation of the novel, published in 1943, was named after this character: *Monkey*. An argument can be made, from a Buddhist point of view, that Tripitaka, however inept and timorous, is the novel's true hero. But for most readers, the monkey's splendid vitality and boundless humor remain the center of interest. Tripitaka is also accompanied by the ever-hungry and lustful Bajie (alternately called "Pigsy"), a Daoist immortal who was banned to the human world for flirting with a goddess and who becomes increasingly unsympathetic as the journey progresses. Tripitaka's third disciple and protector is the gentle Sha monk (also called "Sandy"), a former marshal of the hosts of Heaven who was sent to the bottom of a river to expiate the sin of having broken the crystal cup of the Jade Emperor, the central deity of the Daoist pantheon.

Throughout their journey, the four travelers are watched over, and sometimes interact with, a number of otherworldly beings: an assortment of benign bodhisattvas (buddhas who linger in this world to help others) and a Daoist pantheon of unruly and sometimes dangerous deities. On the earthly plane, the pilgrims move through a landscape of strange kingdoms and monsters, stopping sometimes to help those in need or to protect themselves from harm. Some of the earthly monsters belong to the places where the pilgrims find them, but many of the demons and temptresses that the travelers encounter are either exiles and escapees from the heavenly realm or are sent on purpose to test the pilgrims. Although the story of the Buddhist monk at times shows the traditional hostility of Buddhism against Daoist, Xuanzang's quest has a broader, conciliatory message that sees Confucianism, Buddhism, and Daoist as complementary truths. As the Buddha says about the scriptures before the monk and his companions set out to India, they "are for the cultivation of immortality and the gate to ultimate virtue." Thus Buddhist scriptures also serve the purpose of fulfilling the Daoist desire for self-preservation and immortality as well as the Confucian quest for moral virtue.

Surrounded by three guardian disciples who are endowed with a more general, allegorical meaning, Tripitaka is the only truly human character in *The Journey to the West*. He is easily frightened, sometimes petulant, and never knows what to do. He is not so much driven on the pilgrimage by determined resolve as merely carried along by it. Yet he alone is the character destined for full Buddhahood at the end, and his apparent lack of concern for the quest and for his disciples has been interpreted as the true manifestation of Buddhist detachment. Although "Pilgrim," the monkey king, grows increasingly devoted to his master through the course of the novel, Tripitaka never fully trusts him, however much he depends on him. If there is a difficult Buddhist lesson in the novel, it is to grasp how Tripitaka, the ordinary man as saint, can be the novel's true hero. He is the empty center of the group, kept alive and carried forward by his more powerful and active disciples, both willing and unwilling. Yet he remains the master, and without him, the pilgrimage would not exist.

Both Pilgrim and Bajie are creatures of desire, though the nature of their desires differs greatly. Pilgrim, who had once lived an idyllic life with his monkey subjects in Water Curtain Cave at Flower-Fruit Mountain, is, in the novel's early chapters, driven by a hunger for knowledge and immortality, which takes him around the earth and the heavens. In the first stage of his existence, Pilgrim's curiosity is never perfectly directed; it is a turbulence of spirit that always leads to mischief and an urge to create chaos. He acquires skills and magic tools that make him more powerful, but since he uses them unwisely, they only lead him to ever more outrageous escapades. After wreaking havoc in Heaven and being subdued by the god Erlang, he is imprisoned by the Buddha under a mountain for five hundred years. Finally, Monkey is given a chance to redeem himself by guarding Tripitaka on his pilgrimage to India as "Pilgrim."

During the course of the pilgrimage, the monkey becomes increasingly bound both to his master and to the quest itself, without ever losing his energy and humor. Despite occasional outbursts of his former mischief making, the quest becomes for Pilgrim a structured series of challenges by which he can focus and discipline his rambunctious intellect. The journey is driven forward by Pilgrim alone, with Tripitaka ever willing to give up in despair and Bajie always ready to be seduced or return to his wife. Monkey understands the world with a comic detachment that is in some ways akin to Buddhist detachment, and this detachment makes him always more resourceful and often wiser than Tripitaka. Yet in his fierce energy and sheer joy in the use of his mind, Monkey falls short of the Buddhist ideal of true tranquility, while remaining the hero for unenlightened mortals.

Pilgrim is a complex character with many contradictions, as is perhaps fitting for a creature that may be seen in some sense as an allegory of the human mind. Bajie, on the other hand, is a straightforward and predictable emblem of human sensual appetites. In his initial domestic setting, as the unwelcome son-in-law on Mr. Gao's farm, Bajie was at least reliable and hardworking. But in the enforced celibacy of the pilgrimage, he grows increasingly slothful and undependable. Now and then on the journey he is permitted to gorge himself, but every time he finds a beautiful woman, something prevents him from satisfying his sexual appetite. Never having freely chosen the quest, Bajie is always distracted by his desire to go home to his wife—or to take another along the way. Yet his preoccupation with food and sex often makes him an endearing character.

The selections printed here treat the monkey's birth and early apprenticeship, and Tripitaka's dispatch to India, which is destined by the Buddha, overseen by the Bodhisattva Guanyin, and endorsed by Emperor Taizong. The next two sequences show the adventures and challenges Tripitaka and his companions encounter in two peculiar countries: one, a Daoist kingdom that suppresses Buddhists, where the Buddhist pilgrims straighten out the record with hilarious interventions for the sake of their brothers in faith, and the other, a kingdom of women in which the monk is erroneously impregnated by the water of a stream crossing its territory. While searching for a cure, they have to resist the attack of female charms and a female scorpion monster. Finally, in the last sections of our selection, they reach their goal in India and receive the scriptures. Whisked back to China by divine winds, they are rewarded in a solemn ceremony by the emperor back home in the capital of Chang'an, according to their merits.

Critics count *The Journey to the West* among the greatest novels of traditional China. In the modern period, it has inspired films, musicals, television series, comic books, anime adaptations, and computer games. They all capture facets of *The Journey to the West*, whose sprawling imagination and playful esprit make it unlike any other book.

From The Journey to the West[1]

From *Chapter 1*

The divine root being conceived, the origin appears;
The moral nature cultivated, the Great Dao is born.

* * *

There was on top of that very mountain[2] an immortal stone, which measured thirty-six feet and five inches in height and twenty-four feet in circumference. The height of thirty-six feet and five inches corresponded to the three hundred and sixty-five cyclical degrees, while the circumference of twenty-four feet corresponded to the twenty-four solar terms of the calendar. On the stone were also nine perforations and eight holes, which corresponded to the Palaces of the Nine Constellations and the Eight Trigrams. Though it lacked the shade of trees on all sides, it was set off by epidendrums on the left and right. Since the creation of the world, it had been nourished for a long period by the seeds of Heaven and Earth and by the essences of the sun and the moon, until, quickened by divine inspiration, it became pregnant with a divine embryo. One day, it split open, giving birth to a stone egg about the size of a playing ball. Exposed to the wind, it was transformed into a stone monkey endowed with fully developed features and limbs. Having learned at once to climb and run, this monkey also bowed to the four quarters, while two beams of golden light flashed from his eyes to reach even the Palace of the Polestar. The light disturbed the Great Benevolent Sage of Heaven, the Celestial Jade Emperor[3] of the Most Venerable Deva, who, attended by his divine ministers, was sitting in the Cloud Palace of the Golden Arches, in the Treasure Hall of the Divine Mists. Upon seeing the glimmer of the golden beams, he ordered Thousand-Mile Eye and Fair-Wind Ear to open the South Heaven Gate and to look out. At this command the two captains went out to the gate, and, having looked intently and listened clearly, they returned presently to report. "Your subjects, obeying your command to locate the beams, discovered that they came from the Flower-Fruit Mountain at the border of the small Aolai Country, which lies to the east of the East Pūrvavideha Continent. On this mountain is an immortal stone which has given birth to an egg. Exposed to the wind, it has been transformed into a monkey, who, when bowing to the four quarters, has flashed from his eyes those golden beams that reached the Palace of the Polestar. Now that he is taking some food and drink, the light is about to grow dim." With compassionate mercy the Jade Emperor declared, "These creatures from the world below are born of the essences of Heaven and Earth, and they need not surprise us."

That monkey in the mountain was able to walk, run, and leap about; he fed on grass and shrubs, drank from the brooks and streams, gathered mountain flowers, and searched out fruits from trees. He made his companions the tiger and the lizard, the wolf and the leopard; he befriended the civet and the deer, and he called the gibbon and the baboon his kin. At night he slept beneath

---

1. Translated by Anthony Yu.
2. Flower-Fruit-Mountain.

3. The chief deity in the Daoist pantheon.

stony ridges, and in the morning he sauntered about the caves and the peaks,
Truly,

> In the mountain there is no passing of time;
> The cold recedes, but one knows not the year.

One very hot morning, he was playing with a group of monkeys under the
shade of some pine trees to escape the heat. Look at them, each amusing himself in his own way by

> Swinging from branches to branches,
> Searching for flowers and fruits;
> They played two games or three
> With pebbles and with pellets;
> They circled sandy pits;
> They built rare pagodas;
> They chased the dragonflies;
> They ran down small lizards:
> Bowing low to the sky,
> They worshiped Bodhisattvas;
> They pulled the creeping vines;
> They plaited mats with grass;
> They searched to catch the louse
> They bit or crushed with their nails;
> They dressed their furry coats;
> They scraped their fingernails;
> Some leaned and leaned;
> Some rubbed and rubbed;
> Some pushed and pushed;
> Some pressed and pressed;
> Some pulled and pulled;
> Some tugged and tugged.
> Beneath the pine forest they played without a care,
> Washing themselves in the green-water stream.

So, after the monkeys had frolicked for a while, they went to bathe in the
mountain stream and saw that its currents bounced and splashed like rumbling
melons. As the old saying goes,

> Fowls have their fowl speech,
> And beasts have their beast language.

The monkeys said to each other, "We don't know where this water comes
from. Since we have nothing to do today, let us follow the stream up to its source
to have some fun." With a shriek of joy, they dragged along males and females,
calling out to brothers and sisters, and scrambled up the mountain alongside the
stream. Reaching its source, they found a great waterfall. What they saw was

> A column of rising white rainbows,
> A thousand fathoms of dancing waves—

Which the sea wind buffets but cannot sever,
On which the river moon shines and reposes.
Its cold breath divides the green ranges;
Its tributaries moisten the blue-green hillsides.
This torrential body, its name a cascade,
Seems truly like a hanging curtain.

All the monkeys clapped their hands in acclaim: "Marvelous water! Marvelous water! So this waterfall is distantly connected with the stream at the base of the mountain, and flows directly out, even to the great ocean." They said also, "If any of us had the ability to penetrate the curtain and find out where the water comes from without hurting himself, we would honor him as king." They gave the call three times, when suddenly the stone monkey leaped out from the crowd. He answered the challenge with a loud voice. "I'll go in! I'll go in!" What a monkey! For

Today his fame will spread wide.
His fortune arrives with the time;
He's fated to live in this place,
Sent by a king to this godly palace.

Look at him! He closed his eyes, crouched low, and with one leap he jumped straight through the waterfall. Opening his eyes at once and raising his head to look around, he saw that there was neither water not waves inside, only a gleaming, shining bridge. He paused to collect himself and looked more carefully again: it was a bridge made of sheet iron. The water beneath it surged through a hole in the rock to reach the outside, filling in all the space under the arch. With bent body he climbed on the bridge, looking about as he walked, and discovered a beautiful place that seemed to be some kind of residence. Then he saw

Fresh mosses piling up indigo,
White clouds like jade afloat,
And luminous sheens of mist and smoke;
Empty windows, quiet rooms,
And carved flowers growing smoothly on benches;
Stalactites suspended in milky caves;
Rare blossoms voluminous over the ground.
Pans and stoves near the wall show traces of fire;
Bottles and cups on the table contain leftovers.
The stone seats and beds were truly lovable;
The stone pots and bowls were more praiseworthy.
There were, furthermore, a stalk or two of tall bamboos,
And three or five sprigs of plum flowers.
With a few green pines always draped in rain,
This whole place indeed resembled a home.

After staring at the place for a long time, he jumped across the middle of the bridge and looked left and right. There in the middle was a stone tablet on which was inscribed in regular, large letters:

> *The Blessed Land of Flower-Fruit Mountain,*
> *The Cave Heaven of Water-Curtain Cave.*

Beside himself with delight, the stone monkey quickly turned around to go back out and, closing his eyes and crouching again, leaped out of the water. "A great stroke of luck," he exclaimed with two loud guffaws, "a great stroke of luck." The other monkeys surrounded him and asked, "How is it inside? How deep is the water?" The stone monkey replied, "There isn't any water at all. There's a sheet iron bridge, and beyond it is a piece of Heaven-sent property." "What do you mean that there's property in there?" asked the monkeys.

Laughing, the stone monkey said, "This water splashes through a hole in the rock and fills the space under the bridge. Beside the bridge there is a stone mansion with trees and flowers. Inside are stone ovens and stoves, stone pots and pans, stone beds and benches. A stone tablet in the middle has the inscription,

> *"The Blessed Land of the Flower-Fruit Mountain,*
> *The Cave Heaven of the Water-Curtain Cave.*

This is truly the place for us to settle in. It is, moreover, very spacious inside and can hold thousands of the young and old. Let's all go live in there, and spare ourselves from being subject to the whims of Heaven. For we have in there

> *A retreat from the wind,*
> *A shelter from the rain.*
> *You fear no frost or snow;*
> *You hear no thunderclap.*
> *Mist and smoke are brightened,*
> *Warmed by a holy light—*
> *The pines are ever green:*
> *Rare flowers, daily new."*

When the monkeys heard that, they were delighted, saying. "You go in first and lead the way." The stone monkey closed his eyes again, crouched low, and jumped inside. "All of you," he cried. "Follow me in! Follow me in!" The braver of the monkeys leaped in at once, but the more timid ones stuck out their heads and then drew them back, scratched their ears, rubbed their jaws, and chattered noisily. After milling around for some time, they too bounded inside. Jumping across the bridge, they were all soon snatching dishes, clutching bowls, or fighting for stoves and beds—shoving and pushing things hither and thither. Befitting their stubbornly prankish nature, the monkeys could not keep still for a moment and stopped only when they were utterly exhausted. The stone monkey then solemnly took a seat above and spoke to them: "Gentlemen! 'If a man lacks trustworthiness, it is difficult to know what he can accomplish!'[4] You yourselves promised just now that whoever could get in here and leave again without hurting himself would be honored as king. Now that I have come in and gone out, gone out and come in, and have found for all of you this Heavenly grotto in which you may reside securely and enjoy the privilege of raising a family, why don't you honor me as your king?" When the monkeys heard this, they all folded their hands

---

4. From the Confucian *Analects*.

on their breasts and obediently prostrated themselves. Each one of them then lined up according to rank and age, and, bowing reverently, they intoned. "Long live our great king!" From that moment, the stone monkey ascended the throne of kingship. He did away with the word "stone" in his name and assumed the title, Handsome Monkey King. There is a testimonial poem which says:

> *When triple spring mated to produce all things,*
> *A divine stone was quickened by the sun and moon.*
> *The egg changed to a monkey, perfecting the Great Way.*
> *He took a name, matching elixir's success.*
> *Formless, his inward shape is thus concealed:*
> *His outer frame by action is plainly known.*
> *In every age all persons will yield to him;*
> *Named a king, a sage, he is free to roam.*

The Handsome Monkey King thus led a flock of gibbons and baboons, some of whom were appointed by him as his officers and ministers. They toured the Flower-Fruit Mountain in the morning, and they lived in the Water-Curtain Cave by night. Living in concord and sympathy, they did not mingle with bird or beast but enjoyed their independence in perfect happiness. For such were their activities:

> *In the spring they gathered flowers for food and drink.*
> *In the summer they went in quest of fruits for sustenance.*
> *In the autumn they amassed taros and chestnuts to ward off time.*
> *In the winter they searched for yellow-sperms⁵ to live out the year.*

The Handsome Monkey King had enjoyed this insouciant existence for three or four hundred years when one day, while feasting with the rest of the monkeys, he suddenly grew sad and shed a few tears. Alarmed, the monkeys surrounded him, bowed down, and asked, "What is disturbing the Great King?" The Monkey King replied, "Though I am very happy at the moment, I am a little concerned about the future. Hence I'm distressed." The monkeys all laughed and said, "The Great King indeed does not know contentment! Here we daily have a banquet on an immortal mountain in a blessed land, in an ancient cave on a divine continent. We are not subject to the unicorn or the phoenix, nor are we governed by the rulers of mankind. Such independence and comfort are immeasurable blessings. Why, then, does he worry about the future?" The Monkey King said, "Though we are not subject to the laws of man today, nor need we be threatened by the rule of any bird or beast, old age and physical decay in the future will disclose the secret sovereignty of Yama, King of the Underworld. If we die, shall we not have lived in vain, not being able to rank forever among the Heavenly beings?"

When the monkeys heard this, they all covered their faces and wept mournfully, each one troubled by his own impermanence. But look! From among the ranks a bareback monkey suddenly leaped forth and cried aloud, "If the Great King is so farsighted, it may well indicate the sprouting of his religious inclination. There are, among the five major divisions of all living creatures, only

5. Plant whose roots were used for medicinal purposes.

three species that are not subject to Yama, King of the Underworld." The Monkey King said, "Do you know who they are?" The monkey said, "They are the Buddhas, the immortals, and the holy sages; these three alone can avoid the Wheel of Transmigration as well as the process of birth and destruction, and live as long as Heaven and Earth, the mountains and the streams." "Where do they live?" asked the Monkey King. The monkey said, "They do not live beyond the world of the Jambūdvīpa for they dwell within ancient caves on immortal mountains." When the Monkey King heard this, he was filled with delight, saying, "Tomorrow I shall take leave of you all and go down the mountain. Even if I have to wander with the clouds to the corners of the sea or journey to the distant edges of Heaven, I intend to find these three kinds of people. I will learn from them how to be young forever and escape the calamity inflicted by King Yama." Lo, this utterance at once led him

> To leap free of the Transmigration Net,
> And be the Great Sage, Equal to Heaven.

All the monkeys clapped their hands in acclamation, saying, "Wonderful! Wonderful! Tomorrow we shall scour the mountain ranges to gather plenty of fruits, so that we may send the Great King off with a great banquet."

Next day the monkeys duly went to gather immortal peaches, to pick rare fruits, to dig out mountain herbs, and to chop yellow-sperms. They brought in an orderly manner every variety of orchids and epidendrums, exotic plants and strange flowers. They set out the stone chairs and stone tables, covering the tables with immortal wines and food. Look at the

> Golden balls and pearly pellets,
> Red ripeness and yellow plumpness.
> Golden balls and pearly pellets are the cherries,
> Their colors truly luscious.
> Red ripeness and yellow plumpness are the plums,
> Their taste—a fragrant tartness.
> Fresh lungans
> Of sweet pulps and thin skins.
> Fiery lychees
> Of small pits and red sacks.
> Green fruits of the Pyrus are presented by the branches.
> The loquats yellow with buds are held with their leaves.
> Pears like rabbit heads and dates like chicken hearts
> Dispel your thirst, your sorrow, and the effects of wine.
> Fragrant peaches and soft almonds
> Are sweet as the elixir of life:
> Crisply fresh plums and strawberries
> Are sour like cheese and buttermilk.
> Red pulps and black seeds compose the ripe watermelons.
> Four cloves of yellow rind enfold the big persimmons.
> When the pomegranates are split wide,
> Cinnabar grains glisten like specks of ruby:
> When the chestnuts are cracked open,
> Their tough brawns are hard like cornelian.

> *Walnut and silver almonds fare well with tea.*
> *Coconuts and grapes may be pressed into wine.*
> *Hazelnuts, yews, and crabapples overfill the dishes.*
> *Kumquats, sugarcanes, tangerines, and oranges crowd the tables.*
> *Sweet yams are baked,*
> *Yellow-sperms overboiled,*
> *The tubers minced with seeds of waterlily,*
> *And soup in stone pots simmers on a gentle fire.*
> *Mankind may boast its delicious dainties,*
> *But what can best the pleasure of mountain monkeys.*

The monkeys honored the Monkey King with the seat at the head of the table, while they sat below according to their age and rank. They drank for a whole day, each of the monkeys taking a turn to go forward and present the Monkey King with wine, flowers, and fruits. Next day the Monkey King rose early and gave the instruction, "Little ones, cut me some pinewood and make me a raft. Then find me a bamboo for the pole, and gather some fruits and the like. I'm about to leave." When all was ready, he got onto the raft by himself. Pushing off with all his might, he drifted out toward the great ocean and, taking advantage of the wind, set sail for the border of South Jambūdvīpa Continent. Here is the consequence of this journey:

> *The Heaven-born monkey, strong in magic might,*
> *He left the mount and rode the raft to catch fair wind:*
> *He drifted across the sea to seek immortals' way,*
> *Determined in heart and mind to achieve great things.*
> *It's his lot, his portion, to quit earthly zeals:*
> *Calm and carefree, he'll face a lofty sage.*
> *He'd meet, I think, a true, discerning friend:*
> *The source disclosed, all dharma will be known.*

It was indeed his fortune that, after he had boarded the wooden raft, a strong southeast wind which lasted for days sent him to the northwestern coast, the border of the South Jambūdvīpa Continent. He took the pole to test the water, and, finding it shallow one day, he abandoned the raft and jumped ashore. On the beach there were people fishing, hunting wild geese, digging clams, and draining salt. He approached them and, making a weird face and some strange antics, he scared them into dropping their baskets and nets and scattering in all directions. One of them could not run and was caught by the Monkey King, who stripped him of his clothes and put them on himself, aping the way humans wore them. With a swagger he walked through counties and prefectures, imitating human speech and human manners in the marketplaces. He rested by night and dined in the morning, but he was bent on finding the way of the Buddhas, immortals, and holy sages, on discovering the formula for eternal youth. He saw, however, that the people of the world were all seekers after profit and fame: there was not one who showed concern for his appointed end. This is their condition:

> *When will end this quest for fortune and fame,*
> *This tyrant of early rising and retiring late?*

Riding on mules they long for noble steeds;
By now prime ministers, they hope to be kings.
For food and raiment they suffer stress and strain,
Never fearing Yama's call to reckoning.
Seeking wealth and power to give to sons of sons,
There's not one ever willing to turn back.

The Monkey King searched diligently for the way of immortality, but he had no chance of meeting it. Going through big cities and visiting small towns, he unwittingly spent eight or nine years on the South Jambūdvīpa Continent before he suddenly came upon the Great Western Ocean. He thought that there would certainly be immortals living beyond the ocean; so, having built himself a raft like the previous one, he once again drifted across the Western Ocean until he reached the West Aparagodānīya Continent. After landing, he searched for a long time, when all at once he came upon a tall and beautiful mountain with thick forests at its base. Since he was afraid neither of wolves and lizards nor of tigers and leopards, he went straight to the top to look around. It was indeed a magnificent mountain:

A thousand peaks stand like rows of spears,
Like ten thousand cubits of screen widespread.
The sun's beams lightly enclose the azure mist;
In darkening rain, the mount's color turns cool and green.
Dry creepers entwine old trees;
Ancient fords edge secluded paths.
Rare flowers and luxuriant grass.
Tall bamboos and lofty pines.
Tall bamboos and lofty pines
For ten thousand years grow green in this blessed land.
Rare flowers and luxuriant grass
In all seasons bloom as in the Isles of the Blest.
The calls of birds hidden are near.
The sounds of streams rushing are clear.
Deep inside deep canyons the orchids interweave.
On every ridge and crag sprout lichens and mosses.
Rising and falling, the ranges show a fine dragon's pulse.[6]
Here in reclusion must an eminent man reside.

As he was looking about, he suddenly heard the sound of a man speaking deep within the woods. Hurriedly he dashed into the forest and cocked his ear to listen. It was someone singing, and the song went thus:

I watch chess games, my ax handle's rotted.
I crop at wood, zheng zheng the sound.
I walk slowly by the cloud's fringe at the valley's entrance.
Selling my firewood to buy some wine.
I am happy and laugh without restraint.
When the path is frosted in autumn's height,

---

6. One of the magnetic currents recognized by geomancers.

I face the moon, my pillow the pine root.
Sleeping till dawn
I find my familiar woods.
I climb the plateaus and scale the peaks
To cut dry creepers with my ax.

When I gather enough to make a load,
I stroll singing through the marketplace
And trade it for three pints of rice,
With nary the slightest bickering
Over a price so modest.
Plots and schemes I do not know;
Without vainglory or attaint
My life's prolonged in simplicity.
Those I meet,
If not immortals, would be Daoists,
Seated quietly to expound the Yellow Court.

When the Handsome Monkey King heard this, he was filled with delight, saying, "So the immortals are hiding in this place." He leaped at once into the forest. Looking again carefully, he found a woodcutter chopping firewood with his ax. The man he saw was very strangely attired.

On his head he wore a wide splint hat
Of seed-leaves freshly cast from new bamboos.
On his body he wore a cloth garment
Of gauze woven from the native cotton.
Around his waist he tied a winding sash
Of silk spun from an old silkworm.
On his feet he had a pair of straw sandals,
With laces rolled from withered sedge.
In his hands he held a fine steel ax;
A sturdy rope coiled round and round his load.
In breaking pines or chopping trees
Where's the man to equal him?

The Monkey King drew near and called out: "Reverend immortal! Your disciple raises his hands." The woodcutter was so flustered that he dropped his ax as he turned to return the salutation. "Blasphemy! Blasphemy!" he said, "I, a foolish fellow with hardly enough clothes or food! How can I beat the title of immortal?" The Monkey King said, "If you are not an immortal, how is it that you speak his language?" The woodcutter said, "What did I say that sounded like the language of an immortal?" The Monkey King said, "When I came just now to the forest's edge, I heard you singing, 'Those I meet, if not immortals, would be Daoists, seated quietly to expound the *Yellow Court*.' The *Yellow Court* contains the perfected words of the Way and Virtue.[7] What can you be but an immortal?"

---

7. Also the title of the ancient Chinese Daoist classic, the *Daodejing* (*The Classic of the Way and Virtue*).

Laughing, the woodcutter said, "I can tell you this much: the tune of that lyric is named 'A Court Full of Blossoms,' and it was taught to me by an immortal, a neighbor of mine. He saw that I had to struggle to make a living and that my days were full of worries: so he told me to recite the poem whenever I was troubled. This, he said, would both comfort me and rid me of my difficulties. It happened that I was anxious about something just now; so I sang the song. It didn't occur to me that I would be overheard."

The Monkey King said, "If you are a neighbor of the immortal, why don't you follow him in the cultivation of the Way? Wouldn't it be nice to learn from him the formula for eternal youth?" The woodcutter said, "My lot has been a hard one all my life. When I was young, I was indebted to my parents' nurture until I was eight or nine. As soon as I began to have some understanding of human affairs, my father unfortunately died, and my mother remained a widow. I had no brothers or sisters; so there was no alternative but for me alone to support and care for my mother. Now that my mother is growing old, all the more I dare not leave her. Moreover, my fields are rather barren and desolate, and we haven't enough food or clothing. I can't do more than chop two bundles of firewood to take to the market in exchange for a few pennies to buy a few pints of rice. I cook that myself, serving it to my mother with the tea that I make. That's why I can't practice austerities."

The Monkey King said, "According to what you have said, you are indeed a gentleman of filial piety, and you will certainly be rewarded in the future. I hope, however, that you will show me the way to the immortal's abode, so that I may reverently call upon him." "It's not far. It's not far," the woodcutter said. "This mountain is called the Mountain of Mind and Heart, and in it is the Cave of Slanting Moon and Three Stars. Inside the cave is an immortal by the name of the Patriarch Subodhi, who has already sent out innumerable disciples. Even now there are thirty or forty persons who are practicing austerities with him. Follow this narrow path and travel south for about seven or eight miles, and you will come to his home." Grabbing at the woodcutter, the Monkey King said. "Honored brother, go with me. If I receive any benefit, I will not forget the favor of your guidance." "What a boneheaded fellow you are!" the woodcutter said, "I have just finished telling you these things, and you still don't understand. If I go with you, won't I be neglecting my livelihood? And who will take care of my mother? I must chop my firewood. You go on by yourself!"

When the Monkey King heard this, he had to take his leave. Emerging from the deep forest, he found the path and went past the slope of a hill. After he had traveled seven or eight miles, a cave dwelling indeed came into sight. He stood up straight to take a better look at this splendid place, and this was what he saw:

> Mist and smoke in diffusive brilliance,
> Flashing lights from the sun and moon,
> A thousand stalks of old cypress,
> Ten thousand stems of tall bamboo.
> A thousand stalks of old cypress
> Draped in rain half fill the air with tender green;
> Ten thousand stems of tall bamboo
> Held in smoke will paint the glen chartreuse.

Strange flowers spread brocades before the door.
Jadelike grass emits fragrance beside the bridge.
On ridges protruding grow moist green lichens;
On hanging cliffs cling the long blue mosses.
The cries of immortal cranes are often heard.
Once in a while a phoenix soars overhead.
When the cranes cry,
Their sounds reach through the marsh to the distant sky.
When the phoenix soars up,
Its plume with five bright colors embroiders the clouds.
Black apes and white deer may come or hide:
Gold lions and jade elephants may leave or hide.
Look with care at this blessed, holy place:
It has the true semblance of Paradise.

He noticed that the door of the cave was tightly shut; all was quiet, and there was no sign of any human inhabitant. He turned around and suddenly perceived, at the top of the clif, a stone slab approximately eight feet wide and over thirty feet tall. On it was written in large letters:

The Mountain of Mind and Heart;
The Cave of Slanting Moon and Three Stars.

Immensely pleased, the Handsome Monkey King said, "People here are truly honest. This mountain and this cave really do exist!" He stared at the place for a long time but dared not knock. Instead, he jumped onto the branch of a pine tree, picked a few pine seeds and ate them, and began to play.

After a moment he heard the door of the cave open with a squeak, and an immortal youth walked out. His bearing was exceedingly graceful; his features were highly refined. This was certainly no ordinary young mortal, for he had

His hair bound with two cords of silk,
A wide robe with two sleeves of wind.
His body and face seemed most distinct,
For visage and mind were both detached.
Long a stranger to all worldly things
He was the mountain's ageless boy.
Untainted even with a speck of dust,
He feared no havoc by the seasons wrought.

After coming through the door, the boy shouted, "Who is causing disturbance here?" With a bound the Monkey King leaped down from the tree, and went up to him bowing. "Immortal boy," he said, "I am a seeker of the way of immortality. I would never dare cause any disturbance." With a chuckle, the immortal youth asked, "Are you a seeker of the Way?" "I am indeed," answered the Monkey King. "My master at the house," the boy said, "has just left his couch to give a lecture on the platform. Before even announcing his theme, however, he told me to go out and open the door, saying, 'There is someone outside who wants to practice austerities. You may go and receive him.' It must be you, I suppose." The Monkey King said, smiling, "It is I, most assuredly!" "Follow me in then," said the boy. With solemnity the Monkey King set his clothes in order

and followed the boy into the depths of the cave. They passed rows and rows of lofty towers and huge alcoves, of pearly chambers and carved arches. After walking through innumerable quiet chambers and empty studios, they finally reached the base of the green jade platform. Patriarch Subodhi was seen seated solemnly on the platform, with thirty lesser immortals standing below in rows. He was truly

> An immortal of great ken and purest mien,
> Master Subodhi, whose wondrous form of the West
> Had no end or birth for the work of Double Three.[8]
> His whole spirit and breath were with mercy filled.
> Empty, spontaneous, it could change at will,
> His Buddha-nature able to do all things.
> The same age as Heaven had his majestic frame.
> Fully tried and enlightened was this grand priest.

As soon as the Handsome Monkey King saw him, he prostrated himself and kowtowed times without number, saying, "Master! Master! I, your pupil, pay you my sincere homage." The Patriarch said, "Where do you come from? Let's hear you state clearly your name and country before you kowtow again." The Monkey King said, "Your pupil came from the Water-Curtain Cave of the Flower-Fruit Mountain, in the Aolai Country of the East Pūrvavideha Continent." "Chase him out of here!" the Patriarch shouted. "He is nothing but a liar and a fabricator of falsehood. How can he possibly be interested in attaining enlightenment?" The Monkey King hastened to kowtow unceasingly and to say, "Your pupil's word is an honest one, without any deceit." The Patriarch said, "If you are telling the truth, how is it that you mention the East Pūrvavideha Continent? Separating that place and mine are two great oceans and the entire region of the South Jambūdvīpa Continent. How could you possibly get here?" Again kowtowing, the Monkey King said, "Your pupil drifted across the oceans and trudged through many regions for more than ten years before finding this place." The Patriarch said, "If you have come on a long journey in many stages, I'll let that pass. What is your xing?" The Monkey King again replied, "I have no xing.[9] If a man rebukes me, I am not offended; if he hits me, I am not angered. In fact, I simply repay him with a ceremonial greeting and that's all. My whole life's without ill temper." "I'm not speaking of your temper," the Patriarch said, "I'm asking after the name of your parents." "I have no parents either," said the Monkey King. The Patriarch said, "If you have no parents, you must have been born from a tree." "Not from a tree," said the Monkey King, "but from a rock. I recall that there used to be an immortal stone on the Flower-Fruit Mountain. I was born the year the stone split open."

When the Patriarch heard this, he was secretly pleased, and said, "Well, evidently you have been created by Heaven and Earth. Get up and show me how you walk." Snapping erect, the Monkey King scurried around a couple of times. The Patriarch laughed and said. "Though your features are not the most

---

8. A higher form of meditation, reflecting a doubling of the three standard practices.

9. A pun on xing meaning both "surname" and "temper."

attractive, you do resemble a monkey (*husun*) that feeds on pine seeds. This gives me the idea of deriving your surname from your appearance. I intended to call you by the name *Hu*. Now, when the accompanying animal radical is dropped from this word, what's left is a compound made up of the two characters, *gu* and *yue*. *Gu* means aged and *yue* means female, but an aged female cannot reproduce. Therefore, it is better to give you the surname of *Sun*. When the accompanying animal radical is dropped from this word, we have the compound of *zi* and *xi*. *Zi* means a boy and *xi* means a baby, so that the name exactly accords with the Doctrine of the Baby. So your surname will be 'Sun.' "

When the Monkey King heard this, he was filled with delight. "Splendid! Splendid!" he cried, kowtowing, "At last I know my surname. May the master be even more gracious! Since I have received the surname, let me be given also a personal name, so that it may facilitate your calling and commanding me." The Patriarch said, "Within my tradition are twelve characters which have been used to name the pupils according to their divisions. You are one who belongs to the tenth generation." "Which twelve characters are they?" asked the Monkey King. The Patriarch said, "They are: wide (*guang*), great (*da*), wise (*zhi*), intelligence (*hui*), true (*zhen*), conforming (*ru*), nature (*xing*), sea (*hai*), sharp (*ying*), wake-to (*wu*), complete (*yuan*), and awakening (*jue*). Your rank falls precisely on the word 'wake-to' (*wu*). You will hence be given the religious name 'Wake-to-Vacuity' (*wukong*). All right?" "Splendid! Splendid!" said the Monkey King, laughing, "henceforth I shall be called Sun Wukong." So it was thus:

> At nebula's first clearing there was no name;
> Smashing stubborn vacuity requires wake-to-vacuity.

We do not know what fruit of Daoist cultivation he succeeded in attaining afterward; let's listen to the explanation in the next chapter.

* * *

From *Chapter 12*

The Tang emperor, firm in sincerity, convenes the Grand Mass;
Guanyin, revealing herself, converts Gold Cicada.[1]

* * *

The work was finished and reported; Taizong[2] was exceedingly pleased. He then gathered many officials together in order that a public notice be issued to invite monks for the celebration of the Grand Mass of Land and Water, so that those orphaned souls in the Region of Darkness might find salvation. The notice went throughout the empire, and officials of all regions were asked to recommend monks illustrious for their holiness to go to Chang'an for the Mass. In less than a month's time, the various monks from the empire had arrived. The Tang emperor ordered the court historian, Fu Yi, to select an

---

1. Refers to the monk Xuanzang who was considered the reincarnation of the Buddha's second disciple, named Master Gold Cicada. Because he failed to follow the master's teachings, he was banished and reborn in China. His acquisition of the scriptures and adher- ence to Buddhism allow him in the end to reach Buddhahood. "Guanyin": the Bodhisattva of Mercy.
2. Emperor Taizong of the Tang dynasty, who ruled from 626 to 649 and dispatched Xuanzang to India.

illustrious priest to take charge of the ceremonies. When Fu Yi received the order, however, he presented a memorial to the Throne which attempted to dispute the worth of Buddha. The memorial said:

> The teachings of the Western Territory deny the relations of ruler and subject, of father and son.[3] With the doctrines of the Three Ways and the Sixfold Path, they beguile and seduce the foolish and the simpleminded. They emphasize the sins of the past in order to ensure the felicities of the future. By chanting in Sanskrit, they seek a way of escape. We submit, however, that birth, death, and the length of one's life are ordered by nature; but the conditions of public disgrace or honor are determined by human volition. These phenomena are not, as some philistines would now maintain, ordained by Buddha. The teachings of Buddha did not exist in the time of the Three Kings and the Five Emperors,[4] and yet those rulers were wise, their subjects loyal, and their reigns long-lasting. It was not until the period of Emperor Ming in the Han dynasty that the worship of foreign gods was established, but this meant only that priests of the Western Territory were permitted to propagate their faith. The event, in fact, represented a foreign intrusion in China, and the teachings are hardly worthy to be believed.

When Taizong saw the memorial, he had it distributed among the various officials for discussion. At that time the Prime Minister Xiao Yu came forward and prostrated himself to address the Throne, saying, "The teachings of Buddha, which have flourished in several previous dynasties, seek to exalt the good and to restrain what is evil. In this way they are covertly an aid to the nation, and there is no reason why they should be rejected. For Buddha after all is also a sage, and he who spurns a sage is himself lawless. I urge that the dissenter be severely punished."

Taking up the debate with Xiao Yu, Fu Yi contended that propriety had its foundation in service to one's parents and ruler. Yet Buddha forsook his parents and left his family; indeed, he defied the Son of Heaven[5] all by himself, just as he used an inherited body to rebel against his parents. Xiao Yu, Fu Yi went on to say, was not born in the wilds, but by his adherence to this doctrine of parental denial, he confirmed the saying that an unfilial son had in fact no parents. Xiao Yu, however, folded his hands in front of him and declared, "Hell was established precisely for people of this kind." Taizong thereupon called on the Lord High Chamberlain, Zhang Daoyuan, and the President of the Grand Secretariat, Zhang Shiheng, and asked how efficacious the Buddhist exercises were in the procurement of blessings. The two officials replied, "The emphasis of Buddha is on purity, benevolence, compassion, the proper fruits, and the unreality of things. It was Emperor Wu of the Northern Zhou dynasty who set the Three Religions in order. The Chan Master, Da Hui, also had extolled those concepts of the dark and the distant. Generations of people revered such saints as the Fifth Patriarch, who became man, or the Bodhidharma, who appeared in his sacred form; none of them proved to be inconspicuous in grace and power. Moreover, it has been held since antiquity that the Three Religions are most honorable, not to be destroyed or abolished. We beseech therefore, Your Majesty to exercise your clear and sagacious judgment." Highly pleased,

---

3. "Buddhism denies the principles of our Confucianism." The "teachings of the Western Territory" refer to Buddhism and the "relations of ruler and subject, of father and son" stands for the Confucian emphasis on social hierarchies.
4. Sage rulers of High Antiquity, long before Buddhism reached China from India.
5. The Chinese emperor.

Taizong said, "The words of our worthy subjects are not unreasonable. Anyone who disputes them further will be punished." He thereupon ordered Wei Zheng, Xiao Yu, and Zhang Daoyuan to invite the various Buddhist priests to prepare the site for the Grand Mass and to select from among them someone of great merit and virtue to preside over the ceremonies. All the officials then bowed their heads to the ground to thank the emperor before withdrawing. From that time also came the law that any person who denounces a monk or Buddhism will have his arms broken.

Next day the three court officials began the process of selection at the Mountain-River Platform, and from among the priests gathered there they chose an illustrious monk of great merit. "Who is this person?" you ask.

> Gold Cicada was his former divine name.
> As heedless he was of the Buddha's talk,
> He had to suffer in this world of dust,
> To fall in the net by being born a man.
> He met misfortune as he came to Earth,
> And evildoers even before his birth.
> His father: Chen, a zhuangyuan from Haizhou.
> His mother's sire: chief of this dynasty's court.
> Fated by his natal star to fall in the stream,
> He followed tide and current, chased by mighty waves.
> At Gold Mountain, the island, he had great fortune;
> For the abbot, Qian'an, raised him up.
> He met his true mother at age eighteen,
> And called on her father at the capital.
> A great army was sent by Chief Kaishan
> To stamp out the vicious crew at Hongzhou.
> The zhuangyuan Guangrui escaped his doom:
> Son united with sire—how worthy of praise!
> They saw the king to receive his favor;
> Their names resounded in Lingyan Tower.
> Declining office, he wished to be a monk,
> To seek at Hongfu Temple the Way of Truth,
> A former child of Buddha, nicknamed River Float,
> Had a religious name of Chen Xuanzang.

So that very day the multitude selected the priest Xuanzang, a man who had been a monk since childhood, who maintained a vegetarian diet, and who had received the commandments the moment he left his mother's womb. His maternal grandfather was Yin Kaishan, one of the chief army commanders of the present dynasty. His father, Chen Guangrui, had taken the prize of zhuangyuan and was appointed Grand Secretary of the Wenyuan Chamber. Xuanzang, however, had no love for glory or wealth, being dedicated wholly to the pursuit of Nirvāna. Their investigations revealed that he had an excellent family background and the highest moral character. Not one of the thousands of classics and sūtras had he failed to master; none of the Buddhist chants and hymns was unknown to him. The three officials led Xuanzang before the Throne. After going through elaborate court ritual, they bowed to report, "Your subjects, in obedience to your holy decree, have selected an illustrious monk by the name of Chen Xuanzang." Hearing the name, Taizong thought silently for a long time and said, "Can Xuanzang be the son of Grand Secretary Chen Guangrui?" Child River Float kowtowed and replied, "That is indeed your subject." "This is a most appropriate choice," said Taizong, delighted. "You are truly a monk of great virtue and devotion. We therefore appoint you the Grand Expositor of the Faith, Supreme Vicar of Priests." Xuanzang touched his forehead to the ground to express his gratitude and to receive his appointment. He was given, furthermore, a cassock of knitted gold and five colors, a Vairocana hat, and the instruction diligently to seek out all worthy monks and to rank all these ācāryas[6] in order. They were to follow the imperial decree and proceed to the Temple of Transformation, where they would begin the ceremony after selecting a propitious day and hour.

Xuanzang bowed again to receive the decree and left. He went to the Temple of Transformation and gathered many monks together; they made ready the beds, built the platforms, and rehearsed the music. A total of one thousand two hundred worthy monks, young and old, were chosen, who were further separated into three divisions, occupying the rear, middle, and front portions of the hall. All the preparations were completed and everything was put in order before the Buddhas.

* * *

We shall now tell you about the Bodhisattva Guanyin of the Potalaka Mountain in the South Sea, who, since receiving the command of Tathāgata,[7] was searching in the city of Chang'an for a worthy person to be the seeker of scriptures. For a long time, however, she did not encounter anyone truly virtuous. Then she learned that Taizong was extolling merit and virtue and selecting illustrious monks to hold the Grand Mass. When she discovered, moreover, that the chief priest and celebrant was the monk Child River Float, who was a child of Buddha born from paradise and who happened also to be the very elder whom she had sent to this incarnation, the Bodhisattva was exceedingly pleased. She immediately took the treasures bestowed by Buddha and carried them out with Moksa to sell them on the main streets of the city. "What were these treasures?" you ask. There were the embroidered cassock with rare jewels and the nine-ring priestly staff. But she kept hidden the Golden, the Constrictive, and the Prohibitive Fillets for use in a later time, putting up for sale only the cassock and the priestly staff.

Now in the city of Chang'an there was one of those foolish monks who had not been selected to participate in the Grand Mass but who happened to possess a few strands of pelf. Seeing the Bodhisattva, who had changed herself into a monk covered with scabs and sores, bare-footed and bare-headed, dressed in rags, and holding up for sale the glowing cassock, he approached and asked, "You filthy monk, how much do you want for your cassock?" "The price of the cassock," said the Bodhisattva, "is five thousand taels of silver; for the staff, two thousand." The foolish monk laughed and said, "This filthy monk is mad! A lunatic! You want seven thousand taels of silver for two such common articles? They are not worth that much even if wearing them would make

6. Spiritual masters, another word for Bud-   7. The Buddha.
dhist priests.

you immortal or turn you into a buddha. Take them away! You'll never be able to sell them!" The Bodhisattva did not bother to argue with him; she walked away and proceeded on her journey with Moksa.

After a long while, they came to the Eastern Flower Gate and ran right into the Chief Minister Xiao Yu, who was just returning from court. His outriders were shouting to clear the streets, but the Bodhisattva boldly refused to step aside. She stood on the street holding the cassock and met the chief minister head on. The chief minister pulled in his reins to look at this bright, luminous cassock, and asked his subordinates to inquire about the price of the garment. "I want five thousand taels for the cassock," said the Bodhisattva, "and two thousand for the staff." "What is so good about them," said Xiao Yu, "that they should be so expensive?" "This cassock," said the Bodhisattva, "has something good about it, and something bad, too. For some people it may be very expensive, but for others it may cost nothing at all."

"What's good about it," asked Xiao Yu, "and what's bad about it?"

"He who wears my cassock," said the Bodhisattva, "will not fall into perdition, will not suffer in Hell, will not encounter violence, and will not meet tigers and wolves. That's how good it is! But if the person happens to be a foolish monk who relishes pleasures and rejoices in iniquities, or a priest who obeys neither the dietary laws nor the commandments, or a worldly fellow who attacks the sūtras and slanders the Buddha, he will never even get to see my cassock. That's what's bad about it!" The chief minister asked again, "What do you mean, it will be expensive for some and not expensive for others?" "He who does not follow the Law of Buddha," said the Bodhisattva, "or revere the Three Jewels will be required to pay seven thousand taels if he insists on buying my cassock and my staff. That's how expensive it'll be! But if he honors the Three Jewels, rejoices in doing good deeds, and obeys our Buddha, he is a person worthy of these things. I shall willingly give him the cassock and the staff to establish an affinity of goodness with him. That's what I meant when I said that for some it would cost nothing."

When Xiao Yu heard these words, his face could not hide his pleasure, for he knew that this was a good person. He dismounted at once and greeted the Bodhisattva ceremoniously, saying, "Your Holy Eminence, please pardon whatever offense Xiao Yu might have caused. Our Great Tang Emperor is a most religious person, and all the officials of his court are like-minded. In fact, we have just begun a Grand Mass of Land and Water, and this cassock will be most appropriate for the use of Chen Xuanzang, the Grand Expositor of the Faith. Let me go with you to have an audience with the Throne."

The Bodhisattva was happy to comply with the suggestion. They turned around and went into the Eastern Flower Gate. The Custodian of the Yellow Door went inside to make the report, and they were summoned to the Treasure Hall, where Xiao Yu and the two monks covered with scabs and sores stood below the steps. "What does Xiao Yu want to report to us?" asked the Tang emperor. Prostrating himself before the steps, Xiao Yu said, "Your subject going out of the Eastern Flower Gate met by chance these two monks, selling a cassock and a priestly staff. I thought of the priest, Xuanzang, who might wear this garment. For this reason, we asked to have an audience with Your Majesty."

Highly pleased, Taizong asked for the price of the cassock. The Bodhisattva and Moksa stood at the foot of the steps but did not bow at all. When asked the price of the cassock, the Bodhisattva replied, "Five thousand taels for the cassock and two thousand for the priestly staff." "What's so good about the cassock," said Taizong, "that it should cost so much?" The Bodhisattva said:

> "Of this cassock,
> A dragon which wears but one shred
> Will miss the woe of being devoured by the great roc;
> Or a crane on which one thread is hung
> Will transcend this world and reach the place of the gods.
> Sit in it:
> Ten thousand gods will salute you!
> Move with it:
> Seven Buddhas will follow you!
> This cassock was made of silk drawn from ice silkworm
> And threads spun by skilled craftsmen.
> Immortal girls did the weaving;
> Divine maidens helped at the loom.
> Bit by bit, the parts were sewn and embroidered.
> Stitch by stitch, it arose—a brocade from the heddle,
> Its pellucid weave finer than ornate blooms.
> Its colors, brilliant, emit precious light.
> Wear it, and crimson mist will surround your frame.
> Doff it, and see the colored clouds take flight.
> Outside the Three Heavens' door its primal light was seen;
> Before the Five Mountains its magic aura grew.
> Inlaid are layers of lotus from the West,
> And hanging pearls shine like planets and stars.
> On four corners are pearls which glow at night;
> On top stays fastened an emerald.
> Though lacking the all-seeing primal form.
> It's held by Eight Treasures all aglow.
> This cassock
> You keep folded at leisure;
> You wear it to meet sages.
> When it's kept folded at leisure,
> Its rainbowlike hues cut through a thousand wrappings.
> When you wear it to meet sages,
> All Heaven takes fright—both demons and gods!
> On top are the rddhi pearl,
> The māni pearl,
> The dust-clearing pearl,
> The wind-stopping pearl.
> There are also the red cornelian,
> The purple coral,
> The luminescent pearl,
> The Sāriputra.
> They rob the moon of its whiteness;
> They match the sun in its redness.
> In waves its divine aura imbues the sky;
> In flashes its brightness lifts up its perfection.
> In waves its divine aura imbues the sky,

Flooding the Gate of Heaven.
In flashes its brightness lifts up its perfection,
Lighting up the whole world.
Shining upon the mountains and the streams.
It wakens tigers and leopards;
Lighting up the isles and the seas,
It moves dragons and fishes,
Along its edges hang two chains of melted gold,
And joins the collars a ring of snow-white jade.
The poem says:
The august Three Jewels, this venerable Truth—
It judges all Four Creatures on the Sixfold Path.
The mind enlightened knows and holds God's Law and man's;
The soul illumined can transmit the lamp of wisdom.
The solemn guard of one's body is Vajradhātu;[8]
Like ice in a jade pitcher is the purified mind.
Since Buddha caused this cassock to be made,
Which of ten thousand kalpas can harm a monk?"

When the Tang emperor, who was up in the Treasure Hall, heard these words, he was highly pleased. "Tell me, priest," he asked again, "What's so good about the nine-ring priestly staff?" "My staff," said the Bodhisattva, "has on it

Nine joined-rings made of iron and set in bronze,
And nine joints of vine immortal ever young.
When held, it scorns the sight of aging bones:
It leaves the mount to return with fleecy clouds.
It roamed through Heaven with the Fifth Patriarch:
It broke Hell's gate where Lo Bo sought his Mom.
Not soiled by the fifth of this red-dust world,
It gladly trails the god-monk up Mount Jade."[9]

When the Tang emperor heard these words, he gave the order to have the cassock spread open so that he might examine it carefully from top to bottom. It was indeed a marvelous thing! "Venerable Elder of the Great Law,"[1] he said, "we shall not deceive you. At this very moment we have exalted the Religion of Mercy and planted abundantly in the fields of blessing. You may see many priests assembled in the Temple of Transformation to perform the Law and the sūtras. In their midst is a man of great merit and virtue, whose religious name is Xuanzang. We wish, therefore, to purchase these two treasure objects from you to give them to him. How much do you really want for these things?" Hearing these words, the Bodhisattva and Moksa folded their hands and gave praise to the Buddha. "If he is a man of virtue and merit," she said to the Throne, bowing, "this humble cleric is willing to give them to him. I shall not accept any money." She finished speaking and turned at once to leave. The Tang emperor quickly asked Xiao Yu to hold her back. Standing up in the Hall, he bowed low before saying, "Previously you claimed that the cassock was worth five thousand

8. Golden or diamond element in the universe, signifying the indestructible wisdom of a particular Buddha.

9. Abode of the Queen Mother of the West, a Daoist deity.
1. The "Great Law" of Buddhism.

taels of silver, and the staff two thousand. Now that you see we want to buy them, you refuse to accept payment. Are you implying that we would bank on our position and take your possession by force? That's absurd! We shall pay you according to the original sum you asked for: please do not refuse it."

Raising her hands for a salutation, the Bodhisattva said, "This humble cleric made a vow before, stating that anyone who reveres the Three Treasures, rejoices in virtue, and submits to our Buddha will be given these treasures free. Since it is clear that Your Majesty is eager to magnify virtues to rest in excellence, and to honor our Buddhist faith by having an illustrious monk proclaim the Great Law, it is my duty to present these gifts to you. I shall take no money for them. They will be left here and this humble cleric will take leave of you." When the Tang emperor saw that she was so insistent, he was very pleased. He ordered the Court of Banquets to prepare a huge vegetarian feast to thank the Bodhisattva, who firmly declined that also. She left amiably and went back to her hiding place at the Temple of the Local Spirit, which we shall mention no further.

* * *

Time went by like the snapping of fingers, and the formal celebration of the Grand Mass on the seventh day was to take place. Xuanzang presented the Tang emperor with a memorial, inviting him to raise the incense. News of these good works was circulating throughout the empire. Upon receiving the notice, Taizong sent for his carriage and led many of his officials, both civil and military, as well as his relatives and the ladies of the court, to the temple. All the people of the city—young and old, nobles and commoners—went along also to hear the preaching. At the same time the Bodhisattva said to Moksa, "Today is the formal celebration of the Grand Mass, the first seventh of seven such occasions. It's about time for you and me to join the crowd. First, we want to see how the mass is going; second, we want to find out whether Gold Cicada is worthy of my treasures; and third, we can discover what division of Buddhism he is preaching about."

* * *

On the platform, that Master of the Law recited for a while the *Sūtra of Life and Deliverance for the Dead*; he then lectured for a while on the *Heavenly Treasure Chronicle for Peace in the Nation*, after which he preached for a while on the *Scroll on Merit and Self-Cultivation*. The Bodhisattva drew near and thumped her hands on the platform, calling out in a loud voice, "Hey, monk! You only know how to talk about the teachings of the Little Vehicle. Don't you know anything about the Great Vehicle?"[2] When Xuanzang heard this question, he was filled with delight. He turned and leaped down from the platform, raised his hands and saluted the Bodhisattva, saying, "Venerable Teacher, please pardon your pupil for much disrespect. I only know that the priests who came before me all talk about the teachings of the Little Vehicle. I have no idea what the Great Vehicle teaches." "The doctrines of your Little Vehicle,"

---

2. "Little Vehicle" and "Great Vehicle" refer to two forms of Buddhism. Hīnayāna Buddhism, the "Little Vehicle," is focused more on ascetic practices and individual salvation, while Mahāyāna Buddhism, the "Great Vehicle," which became dominant in East Asia, emphasizes care for others.

said the Bodhisattva, "cannot save the damned by leading them up to Heaven; they can only mislead and confuse mortals. I have in my possession Tripitaka, three collections of the Great Vehicle Laws of Buddha, which are able to send the lost to Heaven, to deliver the afflicted from their sufferings, to fashion ageless bodies, and to break the cycles of coming and going."

As they were speaking, the officer in charge of incense and the inspection of halls went to report to the emperor, saying, "The Master was just in the process of lecturing on the wondrous Law when he was pulled down by two scabby mendicants, babbling some kind of nonsense." The king ordered them to be arrested, and the two monks were taken by many people and pushed into the hall in the rear. When the monk saw Taizong, she neither raised her hands nor made a bow; instead, she lifted her face and said, "What do you want of me, Your Majesty?" Recognizing her, the Tang emperor said, "Aren't you the monk who brought us the cassock the other day?" "I am," said the Bodhisattva. "If you have come to listen to the lecture," said Taizong, "you may as well take some vegetarian food. Why indulge in this wanton discussion with our Master and disturb the lecture hall, delaying our religious service?"

"What that Master of yours was lecturing on," said the Bodhisattva, "happens to be the teachings of the Little Vehicle, which cannot lead the lost up to Heaven. In my possession is the Tripitaka, the Great Vehicle Law of Buddha, which is able to save the damned, deliver the afflicted, and fashion the indestructible body." Delighted, Taizong asked eagerly, "Where is your Great Vehicle Law of Buddha?" "At the place of our lord, Tathāgata," said the Bodhisattva, "in the Great Temple of Thunderclap, located in India of the Great Western Heaven.[3] It can untie the knot of a hundred enmities; it can dispel unexpected misfortunes." "Can you remember any of it?" said Taizong. "Certainly," said the Bodhisattva. Taizong was overjoyed and said, "Let the Master lead this monk to the platform to begin a lecture at once."

Our Bodhisattva led Moksa and flew up onto the high platform. She then trod on the hallowed clouds to rise up into the air and revealed her true salvific form, holding the pure vase with the willow branch. At her left stood the virile figure of Moksa carrying the rod. The Tang emperor was so overcome that he bowed to the sky and worshiped, as civil and military officials all knelt on the ground and burned incense. Throughout the temple, there was not one of the monks, nuns, Daoists, secular persons, scholars, craftsmen, and merchants, who did not bow down and exclaim, "Dear Bodhisattva! Dear Bodhisattva!" We have a song as a testimony. They saw only

> Auspicious mist in diffusion
> And dharmakāya[4] veiled by holy light.
> In the bright air of ninefold Heaven
> A lady immortal appeared.
> That Bodhisattva
> Wore on her head a cap
> Fastened by leaves of gold
> And set with flowers of jade,
> With tassels of dangling pearls,

---

3. Destination of Xuanzang's trip to India.　　4. The spiritual form embodying Buddhahood.

All aglow with golden light.
On her body she had
A robe of fine blue silk.
Lightly colored
And simply fretted
By circling dragons
And soaring phoenixes.
Down in front was hung
A pair of fragrant girdle-jade,
Which glowed with the moon
And danced with the wind,
Overlaid with precious pearls
And with imperial jade.
Around her waist was tied
An embroidered velvet skirt
Of ice-worm silk
And piped in gold,
In which she topped the colored clouds
And crossed the jasper sea.
Before her she led
A cockatoo with red beak and yellow plumes,
Which had roamed the Eastern Ocean
And throughout the world
To foster deeds of mercy and filial piety.
She held in her hands
A grace-dispensing and world-sustaining precious vase,
In which was planted
A twig of pliant willow,
That could moisten the blue sky,
And sweep aside all evil—
All clinging fog and smoke.
Her jade rings joined the embroidered loops,
And gold lotus grew thick beneath her feet.
In three days how often she came and went:
This very Guanshiyin[5] who saves from pain and woe.

So pleased by the vision was Tang Taizong that he forgot about his empire; so enthralled were the civil and military officials that they completely ignored court etiquette. Everyone was chanting, "Namo Bodhisattva Guanshiyin!"

Taizong at once gave the order for a skilled painter to sketch the true form of the Bodhisattva. No sooner had he spoken than a certain Wu Daozi was selected, who could portray gods and sages and was a master of the noble perspective and lofty vision. (This man, in fact, was the one who would later paint the portraits of meritorious officials in the Lingyan Tower.) Immediately he opened up his magnificent brush to record the true form. The hallowed clouds of the Bodhisattva gradually drifted away, and in a little while the golden light disappeared. From midair came floating down a slip of paper on which were plainly written several lines in the style of the gāthā:[6]

5. Full name of Guanyin, meaning "She who listens to the voices of the world."

6. A verse.

We greet the great Ruler of Tang
With scripts most sublime of the West.
The way: a hundred and eight thousand miles.
Seek earnestly this Mahāyāna,[7]
These Books, when they reach your fair state,
Can redeem damned spirits from Hell.
If someone is willing to go,
He'll become a Buddha of gold.

When Taizong saw the *gāthā*, he said to the various monks: "Let's stop the Mass. Wait until I have sent someone to bring back the scriptures of the Great Vehicle. We shall then renew our sincere effort to cultivate the fruits of virtue." Not one of the officials disagreed with the emperor, who then asked in the temple, "Who is willing to accept our commission to seek scriptures from Buddha in the Western Heaven?" Hardly had he finished speaking when the Master of the Law stepped from the side and saluted him, saying, "Though your poor monk has no talents, he is ready to perform the service of a dog and a horse. I shall seek these true scriptures on behalf of Your Majesty, that the empire of our king may be firm and everlasting." Highly pleased, the Tang emperor went forward to raise up the monk with his royal hands, saying, "If the Master is willing to express his loyalty this way, undaunted by the great distance or by the journey over mountains and streams, we are willing to become bond brothers with you." Xuanzang touched his forehead to the ground to express his gratitude. Being indeed a righteous man, the Tang emperor went at once before Buddha's image in the temple and bowed to Xuanzang four times, addressing him as "our brother and holy monk."

Deeply moved, Xuanzang said, "Your Majesty, what ability and what virtue does your poor monk possess that he should merit such affection from your Heavenly Grace? I shall not spare myself in this journey, but I shall proceed with all diligence until I reach the Western Heaven. If I do not attain my goal, or the true scriptures, I shall not return to our land even if I have to die. I would rather fall into eternal perdition in Hell." He thereupon lifted the incense before Buddha and made that his vow. Highly pleased, the Tang emperor ordered his carriage back to the palace to wait for the auspicious day and hour, when official documents could be issued for the journey to begin. And so the Throne withdrew as everyone dispersed.

Xuanzang also went back to the Temple of Great Blessing. The many monks of that temple and his several disciples, who had heard about the quest for the scriptures, all came to see him. They asked, "Is it true that you have vowed to go to the Western Heaven?" "It is," said Xuanzang. "O Master," one of his disciples said, "I have heard people say that the way to the Western Heaven is long, filled with tigers, leopards, and all kinds of monsters. I fear that there will be departure but no return for you, as it will be difficult to safeguard your life."

"I have already made a great vow and a profound promise," said Xuanzang, "that if I do not acquire the true scriptures, I shall fall into eternal perdition in Hell. Since I have received such grace and favor from the king, I have no alternative but to serve my country to the utmost of my loyalty. It is true, of course, that I have no knowledge of how I shall fare on this journey or whether good or

---

7. Again, this refers to Mahāyāna Buddhism common in East Asia.

evil awaits me." He said to them again, "My disciples, after I leave, wait for two or three years, or six or seven years. If you see the branches of the pine trees within our gate pointing eastward, you will know that I am about to return. If not, I shall not be coming back." The disciples all committed his words firmly to memory.

The next morning Taizong held court and gathered all the officials together. They wrote up the formal rescript stating the intent to acquire scriptures and stamped it with the seal of free passage. The President of the Imperial Board of Astronomy then came with the report, "Today the positions of the planets are especially favorable for men to make a journey of great length." The Tang emperor was most delighted. Thereafter the custodian of the Yellow Gate also made a report, saying, "The Master of the Law awaits your pleasure outside the court." The emperor summoned him up to the treasure hall and said, "Royal Brother, today is an auspicious day for the journey, and your rescript for free passage is ready. We also present you with a bowl made of purple gold for you to collect alms on your way. Two attendants have been selected to accompany you, and a horse will be your means of travel. You may begin your journey at once."

Highly pleased, Xuanzang expressed his gratitude and received his gifts, not displaying the least desire to linger. The Tang emperor called for his carriage and led many officials outside the city gate to see him off. The monks in the Temple of Great Blessing and the disciples were already waiting there with Xuanzang's winter and summer clothing. When the emperor saw them, he ordered the bags to be packed on the horses first, and then asked an officer to bring a pitcher of wine. Taizong lifted his cup to toast the pilgrim saying, "What is the byname of our Royal Brother?" "Your poor monk," said Xuanzang, "is a person who has left the family. He dares not assume a byname." "The Bodhisat-tva said earlier," said Taizong, "that there were three collections of scriptures in the Western Heaven. Our Brother can take that as a byname and call himself Tripitaka.[8] How about it?" Thanking him, Xuanzang accepted the wine and said, "Your Majesty, wine is the first prohibition of priesthood. Your poor monk has practiced abstinence since birth." "Today's journey," said Taizong, "is not to be compared with any ordinary event. Please drink one cup of this dietary wine, and accept our good wishes that go along with the toast." Xuanzang dared not refuse; he took the wine and was about to drink, when he saw Taizong stoop down to scoop up a handful of dirt with his fingers and sprinkle it in the wine. Tripitaka had no idea what this gesture meant.

"Dear Brother," said Taizong, laughing, "how long will it take you to come back from this trip to the Western Heaven?" "Probably in three years time," said Tripitaka, "I'll be returning to our noble nation." "The years are long and the journey is great," said Taizong. "Drink this, Royal Brother, and remember: Treasure a handful of dirt from your home, but love not ten thousand taels of foreign gold." Then Tripitaka understood the meaning of the handful of dirt sprinkled in his cup: he thanked the emperor once more and drained the cup. He went out of the gate and left, as the Tang emperor returned in his carriage. We do not know what will happen to him on this journey; let's listen to the explanation in the next chapter.

* * *

8. The monk carries hereafter the name "Buddhist Canon."

From *Chapter 44*

The dharma-body in primary cycle meets the force of the cart;
The mind, righting monstrous deviates, crosses the spine-ridge pass.

* * *

When the monks saw the two Daoists, they were terrified;[1] every one of them redoubled his effort to pull desperately at the cart. "So, that's it!" said Pilgrim, comprehending the situation all at once. "These monks must be awfully afraid of the Daoists, for if not, why should they be tugging so hard at the carts? I have heard someone say that there is a place on the road to the West where Daoism is revered and Buddhism is set for destruction. This must be the place. I would like to go back and report this to Master, but I still don't know the whole truth and he might blame me for bringing him surmises, saying that even a smart person like me can't be counted on for a reliable report. Let me go down there and question them thoroughly before I give Master an answer."

"Whom would he question?" you ask. Dear Great Sage! He lowered his cloud and with a shake of his torso, he changed at the foot of the city into a wandering Daoist of the Completed Authenticity sect, with an exorcist hamper hung on his left arm. Striking a hollow wooden fish with his hands and chanting lyrics of Daoist themes, he walked up to the two Daoists near the city gate. "Masters," he said, bowing, "this humble Daoist raises his hand." Returning his salute, one of the Daoists said, "Sir, where did you come from?" "This disciple," said Pilgrim, "has wandered to the corners of the sea and to the edges of Heaven. I arrived here this morning with the sole purpose of collecting subscriptions for good works. May I ask the two masters which street in this city is favorable towards the Dao, and which alley is inclined towards piety? This humble Daoist would like to go there and beg for some vegetarian food." Smiling, the Daoist said, "O Sir! Why do you speak in such a disgraceful manner?" "What do you mean by disgraceful?" said Pilgrim. "If you want to *beg* for vegetarian food," said the Daoist, "isn't that disgraceful?" Pilgrim said, "Those who have left the family live by begging. If I didn't beg, where would I have money to buy food?"

Chuckling, the Daoist said, "You've come from afar, and you don't know anything about our city. In this city of ours, not only the civil and military officials are fond of the Dao, the rich merchants and men of prominence devoted to piety, but even the ordinary citizens, young and old, will bow to present us food once they see us. It is, in fact, a trivia matter, hardly worth mentioning. What's most important about our city is that His Majesty, the king, is also fond of the Dao and devoted to piety." "This humble cleric is first of all quite young," said Pilgrim, "and second, he is indeed from afar. In truth I'm ignorant of the situation here. May I trouble the two masters to tell me the name of this place and give me a thorough account of how the king has come to be so devoted to the cause of Dao—for the sake of fraternal feelings among us Daoists?" The Daoist said, "This city has the name of the Cart Slow Kingdom, and the ruler on the precious throne is a relative of ours."

1. In the intervening chapters Tripitaka, the monk Xuanzang, has gained his three disciples: Pilgrim (the monkey, Sun Wukong), Sha Monk (or Sha Wujing), and Zhu Bajie. Having been subjected to numerous ordeals on the way to India in pursuit of the scriptures, they here enter a land where Buddhists are enslaved by Daoists.

When Pilgrim heard these words, he broke into loud guffaws, saying, "I suppose that a Daoist has become king." "No," said the Daoist. "What happened was that twenty years ago, this region had a drought, so severe that not a single drop of rain fell from the sky and all grains and plants perished. The king and his subjects, the rich as well as the poor—every person was burning incense and praying to Heaven for relief. Just when it seemed that nothing else could preserve their lives, three immortals suddenly descended from the sky and saved us all." "Who were these immortals?" asked Pilgrim. "Our masters," said the Daoist. "What are their names?" said Pilgrim. The Daoist replied, "The eldest master is called the Tiger-Strength Great Immortal; the second master, the Deer-Strength Great Immortal; and the third master, Goat-Strength Great Immortal." "What kinds of magic power do your esteemed teachers possess?" asked Pilgrim. The Daoist said, "Summoning the wind and the rain for my masters would be as easy as flipping over one's palms; they point at water and it will change into oil; they touch stones and change them into gold, as quickly as one turns over in bed. With this kind of magic power, they are thus able to rob the creative genius of Heaven and Earth, to alter the mysteries of the stars and constellations. The king and his subjects have such profound respect for them that all of us Daoists are claimed as royal kin." Pilgrim said, "This ruler is lucky, all right. After all, the proverb says, 'Magic moves ministers!' He certainly can't lose to claim kinship with your old masters, if they possess such powers. Alas! I wonder if I had even that tiniest spark of affinity, such that I could have an audience with the old masters?" Chuckling, the Daoist replied, "If you want to see our masters, it's not difficult at all. The two of us are their bosom disciples. Moreover, our masters are so devoted to the Way and so deferential to the pious that the mere mention of the word 'Dao' would bring them out of the door, full of welcome. If we two were to introduce you, we would need to exert ourselves no more vigorously than to blow away some ashes."

Bowing deeply, Pilgrim said, "I am indebted to you for your introduction. Let us go into the city then." "Let's wait a moment," said one of the Daoists. "You sit here while we two finish our official business first. Then we'll go with you." Pilgrim said, "Those of us who have left the family are without cares or ties; we are completely free. What do you mean by official business?" The Daoist pointed with his finger at the monks on the beach and said, "Their work happens to be the means of livelihood for us. Lest they become indolent, we have come to check them off the roll before we go with you." Smiling, Pilgrim said, "You must be mistaken, Masters. Buddhists and Daoists are all people who have left the family. For what reason are they working for our support? Why are they willing to submit to our roll call?"

The Daoist said, "You have no idea that in the year when we were all praying for rain, the monks bowed to Buddha on one side while the Daoists petitioned the Pole Star on the other, all for the sake of finding some food for the country. The monks, however, were useless, their empty chants of sūtras wholly without efficacy. As soon as our masters arrived on the scene, they summoned the wind and the rain and the bitter affliction was removed from the multitudes. It was then that the Court became terribly vexed at the monks, saying that they were completely ineffective and that they deserved to have their monasteries wrecked and their Buddha images destroyed. Their travel rescripts were revoked and they were not permitted to return to their native regions. His Majesty gave them to us instead and they were to serve as bondsmen: they are the ones who tend the fires in our temple, who sweep the grounds, and who guard the gates. Since we have some buildings in the rear which are not completely finished, we have ordered these monks here to haul bricks, tiles, and timber for the construction. But for fear of their mischief, indolence, and unwillingness to pull the cart, we have come to investigate and make the roll call."

When Pilgrim heard that, he tugged at the Daoist as tears rolled from his eyes. "I said that I might not have the good affinity to see your old masters," he said, "and true enough I don't." "Why not?" asked the Daoist. "This humble Daoist is making a wide tour of the world," said Pilgrim, "both for the sake of eking out a living and for finding a relative." "What sort of relative do you have?" said the Daoist. Pilgrim said, "I have an uncle, who since his youth had left the family and shorn his hair to become a monk. Because of famine some years ago he had to go abroad to beg for alms and hadn't returned since. As I remembered our ancestral benevolence, I decided that I would make a special effort to find him along the way. It's very likely, I suppose, that he is detained here and cannot go home. I must find him somehow and get to see him before I can go inside the city with you." "That's easy," said the Daoist. "The two of us can sit here while you go down to the beach to make the roll call for us. There should be five hundred of them on the roll. Take a look and see if your uncle is among them. If he is, we'll let him go for the sake of the fact that you, too, are a fellow Daoist. Then we'll go inside the city with you. How about that?"

Pilgrim thanked them profusely, and with a deep bow he took leave of the Daoists. Striking up his wooden fish, he headed down to the beach, passing the double passes as he walked down the narrow path from the steep ridge. All those monks knelt down at once and kowtowed, saying in unison, "Father, we have not been indolent. Not even half a person from the five hundred is missing—we are all here pulling the cart." Snickering to himself, Pilgrim thought: "These monks must have been awfully abused by the Daoists. They are terrified even when they see a fake Daoist like me. If a real Daoist goes near them, they will probably die of fear." Waving his hand, Pilgrim said, "Get up, and don't be afraid! I'm not here to inspect your work, I'm here to find a relative." When those monks heard that he was looking for a relative, they surrounded him on all sides, every one of them sticking out his head and coughing, hoping that he would be claimed as kin. "Which of us is his relative?" they said. After he had looked at them for a while, Pilgrim burst into laughter. "Father," said the monks, "you don't seem to have found your relative. Why are you laughing instead?" Pilgrim said, "You want to know why I'm laughing? I'm laughing at how immature you monks are! It was because of your having been born under an unlucky star that your parents, for fear of your bringing misfortune upon them or for not bringing with you additional brothers and sisters, turned you out of the family and made you priests. How could you then not follow the Three Jewels and not revere the law of Buddha? Why aren't you reading the sūtras and chanting the litanies? Why do you serve the Daoists and allow them to exploit you as bondsmen and slaves?" "Venerable Father," said the monks, "are you here to ridicule us? You must have come from abroad, and you have no idea of our plight." "Indeed I'm from abroad," said Pilgrim, "and I truly have no idea of what sort of plight you have."

As they began to weep, the monks said, "The ruler of our country is wicked and partial. All he cares for are those persons like you, Venerable Father, and those whom he hates are us Buddhists." "Why is that?" asked Pilgrim. "Because the need for wind and rain," said one of the monks, "caused three immortal elders to come here. They deceived our ruler and persuaded him to tear down our monasteries and revoke our travel rescripts, forbidding us to return to our native regions. He would not, moreover, permit us to serve even in any secular capacity except as slaves in the household of those immortal elders. Our agony is unbearable! If any Daoist mendicant shows up in this region, they would immediately request the king to grant him an audience and a handsome reward; but if a monk appears, regardless of whether he is from nearby or afar, he will be seized and sent to be a servant in the house of the immortals." Pilgrim said, "Could it be that those Daoists are truly in possession of some mighty magic, potent enough to seduce the king? If it's only a matter of summoning the wind and the rain, then it is merely a trivial trick of heterodoxy. How could it sway a ruler's heart?" The monks said, "They know how to manipulate cinnabar and refine lead, to sit in meditation in order to nourish their spirits. They point to water and it changes into oil; they touch stones and transform them into pieces of gold. Now they are in the process of building a huge temple for the Three Pure Ones, in which they can perform rites to Heaven and Earth and read scriptures night and day, to the end that the king will remain youthful for ten thousand years. Such enterprise undoubtedly pleases the king."

"So that's how it is!" said Pilgrim. "Why don't you all run away and be done with it?" "Father, we can't!" said the monks. "Those immortal elders have obtained permission from the king to have our portraits painted and hung up in all four quarters of the kingdom. Although the territory of this Cart Slow Kingdom is quite large, there is a picture of monks displayed in the marketplace of every village, town, county, and province. It bears on top the royal inscription that any official who catches a monk will be elevated three grades, and any private citizen who does so will receive a reward of fifty taels of white silver. That's why we can never escape. Let's not say monks—but even those who have cut their hair short or are getting bald will find it difficult to get past the officials. They are everywhere, the detectives and the runners! No matter what you do, you simply can't flee. We have no alternative but to remain here and suffer."

* * *

There were three old Daoists resplendent in their ritual robes, and Pilgrim thought they had to be the Tiger-Strength, Deer-Strength, and Goat-Strength Immortals. Below them there was a motley crew of some seven or eight hundred Daoists; lined up on opposite sides, they were beating drums and gongs, offering incense, and saying prayers. Secretly pleased, Pilgrim said to himself, "I would like to go down there and fool with them a bit, but as the proverb says,

A silk fiber is no thread;
A single hand cannot clap.

Let me go back and alert Bajie and Sha Monk. Then we can return and have some fun."

He dropped down from the auspicious cloud and went straight back to the abbot's hall, where he found Bajie and Sha Monk asleep head to foot in one bed. Pilgrim tried to wake Wujing first, and as he stirred, Sha Monk said, "Elder Brother, you aren't asleep yet?" "Get up now," said Pilgrim, "for you and I are going to enjoy ourselves." "In the dead of night," said Sha Monk, "how could we enjoy ourselves when our mouths are dried and our eyes won't stay open?" Pilgrim said, "There is indeed in this city a Temple of the Three Pure Ones. Right now the Daoists in the temple are conducting a mass, and their main hall is filled with all kinds of offerings. The buns are big as barrels, and their cakes must weigh fifty or sixty pounds each. There are also countless rice condiments and fresh fruits. Come with me and we'll go enjoy ourselves!" When Zhu Bajie heard in his sleep that there were good things to eat, he immediately woke up, saying, "Elder Brother, aren't you going to take care of me too?" "Brother," said Pilgrim, "if you want to eat, don't make all these noises and wake up Master. Just follow me."

The two of them slipped on their clothes and walked quietly out the door. They trod on the cloud with Pilgrim and rose into the air. When Idiot saw the flare of lights, he wanted immediately to go down there had not Pilgrim pulled him back. "Don't be so impatient," said Pilgrim, "wait till they disperse. Then we can go down there." Bajie said, "But obviously they are having such a good time praying. Why would they want to disperse? "Let me use a little magic," said Pilgrim, "and they will."

Dear Great Sage! He made the magic sign with his fingers and recited a spell before he drew in his breath facing the ground toward the southwest. Then he blew it out and at once a violent whirlwind assailed the Three Pure Ones Hall, smashing flower vases and candle stands and tearing up all the ex-votos hanging on the four walls. As lights and torches were all blown out, the Daoists became terrified. Tiger-Strength Immortal said, "Disciples, let's disperse. Since this divine wind has extinguished all our lamps, torches, and incense, each of us should retire. We can rise earlier tomorrow morning to recite a few more scrolls of scriptures and make up for what we miss tonight." The various Daoists indeed retreated.

Our Pilgrim leading Bajie and Sha Monk lowered the clouds and dashed up to the Three Pure Ones Hall. Without bothering to find out whether it was raw or cooked, Idiot grabbed one of the cakes and gave it a fierce bite. Pilgrim whipped out the iron rod and tried to give his hand a whack. Hastily withdrawing his hand to dodge the blow, Bajie said, "I haven't even found out the taste yet, and you're trying to hit me already?" "Don't be so rude," said Pilgrim. "Let's sit down with proper manners and then we may treat ourselves." "Aren't you embarrassed?" said Bajie. "You are stealing food, you know, and you still want proper manners! If you were invited here, what would you do then?" Pilgrim said, "Who are these bodhisattvas sitting up there?" "What do you mean by who are these bodhisattvas?" chuckled Bajie. "Can't you recognize the Three Pure Ones?" "Which Three Pure Ones?" said Pilgrim. "The one in the middle," said Bajie, "is the Honorable Divine of the Origin; the one on the left is the Enlightened Lord of Spiritual Treasures; and the one on the right is Laozi."[2] Pilgrim said, "We have to take on their appearances. Only then can we

2. Famous ancient philosophical master, to whom the book *Laozi* is ascribed, and central deity of the Daoist pantheon.

eat safely and comfortably." When he caught hold of the delicious fragrance coming from the offerings, Idiot could wait no longer. Climbing up onto the tall platform, he gave the figure of Laozi a shove with his snout and pushed it to the floor, saying, "Old fellow, you have sat here long enough! Now let old Hog take your place for a while!" So Bajie changed himself into Laozi, while Pilgrim took on the appearance of the Honorable Divine of the Origin and Sha Monk became the Enlightened Lord of Spiritual Treasures. All the original images were pushed down to the floor. The moment they sat down, Bajie began to gorge himself with the huge buns. "Could you wait one moment?" said Pilgrim. "Elder Brother," said Bajie, "we have changed into their forms. Why wait any longer?"

"Brother," said Pilgrim, "it's small thing to eat, but giving ourselves away is no small matter! These holy images we pushed on the floor could be found by those Daoists who had to rise early to strike the bell or sweep the grounds. If they stumbled over them, wouldn't our secret be revealed? Why don't you see if you can hide them somewhere?" Bajie said, "This is an unfamiliar place, and I don't even know where to begin to look for a hiding spot." "Just now when we entered the hall," Pilgrim said, "I chanced to notice a little door on our right. Judging from the foul stench coming through it, I think it must be a Bureau of Five-Grain Transmigration. Send them in there."

Idiot, in truth, was rather good at crude labor! He leaped down, threw the three images over his shoulder, and carried them out of the hall. When be kicked open the door, he found a huge privy inside. Chuckling to himself he said, "This Bimawen truly has a way with words! He even bestows on a privy a sacred title! The Bureau of Five-Grain Transmigration, what a name!" Still hauling the images on this shoulders, Idiot began to mumble this prayer to them:

"O Pure Ones Three,
I'll confide in thee:
From afar we came,
Staunch foes of bogies.
We'd like a treat,
But nowhere's cozy.
We borrow your seats
For a while only.
You've sat too long,
Now go to the privy.
In times past you've enjoyed countless good things
By being pure and clean Daoists.
Today you can't avoid facing something dirty
When you become Honorable Divines Most Smelly!"

After he had made his supplication, he threw them inside with a splash and half of his robe was soiled by the muck. As he walked back into the hall, Pilgrim said, "Did you hide them well?" "Well enough," said Bajie, "but some of the filth stained my robe. It still stinks. I hope it won't make you retch." "Never mind," said Pilgrim, laughing, "you just come and enjoy yourself. I wonder if we could all make a clean getaway!" After Idiot changed back into the form of

Laozi, the three of them took their seats and abandoned themselves to enjoyment. They ate the huge buns first; then they gobbled down the side dishes, the rice condiments, the dumplings, the baked goods, the cakes, the deep-fried dishes, and the steamed pastries—regardless of whether these were hot or cold. Pilgrim Sun, however, was not too fond of anything cooked; all he had were a few pieces of fruit, just to keep the other two company. Meanwhile Bajie and Sha Monk went after the offerings like comets chasing the moon, like wind mopping up the clouds! In no time at all, they were completely devoured. When there was nothing left for them to eat, they, instead of leaving, remained seated there to chat and wait for the food to digest.

* * *

From *Chapter 46*

Heresy flaunts its strength to make orthodoxy;
Mind Monkey shows his saintliness to slay the deviates.

We were telling you that when the king saw Pilgrim Sun's ability to summon dragons and command sages, he immediately applied his treasure seal to the travel rescript. He was about to hand it back to the Tang monk and permit him to take up the journey once more, when the three Daoists went forward and prostrated themselves before the steps of the Hall of Golden Chimes. The king left his dragon throne hurriedly and tried to raise them with his hands. "National Preceptors," he said, "why do you three go through such a great ceremony with us today?" "Your Majesty," said the Daoists, "we have been upholding your reign and providing security for your people here for these twenty years. Today this priest has made use of some paltry tricks of magic and robbed us of all our credit and ruined our reputation. Just because of one rainstorm, Your Majesty has pardoned even their crime of murder. Are we not being treated lightly? Let Your Majesty withhold their rescript for the moment and allow us brothers to wage another contest with them. We shall see what happens then."

* * *

Just then, the Tiger-Strength Great Immortal walked out from the Pavilion of Cultural Florescence after he had been washed and combed. "Your Majesty," he said as he walked up the hall, "this monk knows the magic of object removal. Give me the chest, and I'll destroy his magic. Then we can have another contest with him." "What do you want to do?" said the king. Tiger-Strength said, "His magic can remove only lifeless objects but not a human body. Put this Daoist youth in the chest, and he'll never be able to remove him." The youth indeed was hidden in the chest, which was then brought down again from the hall to be placed before the steps. "You, monk," said the king, "guess again what sort of treasure we have inside." Tripitaka said, "Here it comes again!" "Let me go and have another look." said Pilgrim. With a buzz, he flew off and crawled inside, where he found a Daoist lad. Marvelous Great Sage! What readiness of mind! Truly

Such agility is rare in the world!
Such cleverness is uncommon indeed!

Shaking his body once, he changed himself into the form of one of those old Daoists, whispering as he entered the chest, "Disciple."

"Master," said the lad, "how did you come in here?" "With the magic of invisibility," said Pilgrim. The lad said, "Do you have some instructions for me?" "The priest saw you enter the chest," said Pilgrim, "and if he made his guess a Daoist lad, wouldn't we lose to him again? That's why I came here to discuss the matter with you. Let's shave your head, and we'll then make them guess that you are a monk." The Daoist lad said, "Do whatever you want, Master, just so that we win. For if we lose to them again, not only our reputation will be ruined, but the court also may no longer revere us." "Exactly," said Pilgrim. "Come over here, my child. When we defeat them, I'll reward you handsomely." He changed his golden-hooped rod into a sharp razor, and hugging the lad, he said, "Darling, try to endure the pain for a moment. Don't make any noise! I'll shave your head." In a little while, the lad's hair was completely shorn, rolled into a ball, and stuffed into one of the corners of the chest. He put away the razor, and rubbing the lad's bald head, he said, "My child, your head looks like a monk's all right, but your clothes don't fit. Take them off and let me change them for you." What the Daoist lad had on was a crane's-down robe of spring-onion white silk, embroidered with the cloud pattern and trimmed with brocade. When he took it off, Pilgrim blew on it his immortal breath, crying, "Change!" It changed instantly into a monk shirt of brown color, which Pilgrim helped him put on. He then pulled off two pieces of hair which he changed into a wooden fish and a tap. "Disciple," said Pilgrim, as he handed over the fish and the tap to the lad, "you must listen carefully. If you hear someone call for the Daoist youth, don't ever leave this chest. If someone calls 'Monk,' then you may push open the chest door, strike up the wooden fish, and walk out chanting a Buddhist sūtra. Then it'll be complete success for us." "I only know," said the lad, "how to recite the *Three Officials Scripture*, the *Northern Dipper Scripture*, or the *Woe-Dispelling Scripture*. I don't know how to recite any Buddhist sūtra." Pilgrim said, "Can you chant the name of Buddha?" "You mean Amitābha,"[1] said the lad. "Who doesn't know that?" "Good enough! Good enough!" said Pilgrim. "You may chant the name of Buddha. It'll spare me from having to teach you anything new. Remember what I've told you. I'm leaving." He changed back into a mole-cricket and crawled out, after which, he flew back to the ear of the Tang monk and said, "Master, just guess it's a monk." Tripitaka said, "This time I know I'll win." "How could you be so sure?" said Pilgrim, and Tripitaka replied, "The sūtras said, 'The Buddha, the Dharma, and the Sangha are the Three Jewels.' A monk therefore is a treasure."

As they were thus talking among themselves, the Tiger-Strength Great Immortal said, "Your Majesty, this third time it is a Daoist youth." He made the declaration several times, but nothing happened nor did anyone make an appearance. Pressing his palms together, Tripitaka said, "It's a monk." With all his might, Bajie screamed: "It's a monk in the chest!" All at once the youth kicked open the chest and walked out, striking the wooden fish and chanting the name of Buddha. So delighted were the two rows of civil and military officials

---

1. "Buddha of Infinite Light," who presides over the Pure Land Paradise in the West, where believers who call his name can be reborn.

that they shouted bravos repeatedly; so astonished were the three Daoists that they could not utter a sound. "These priests must have the assistance from spirits and gods," said the king. "How could a Daoist enter the chest and come out a monk? Even if he had an attendant with him, he might have been able to have his head shaved. How could he know how to take up the chanting of Buddha's name? O Preceptors! Please let them go!"

"Your Majesty," said the Tiger-Strength Great Immortal, "as the proverb says, 'The warrior has found his equal, the chess player his match.' We might as well make use of what we learned in our youth at Zhongnan Mountain and challenge them to a greater competition." "What did you learn?" said the king. Tiger-Strength said, "We three brothers all have acquired some magic abilities: cut off our heads, and we can put them back on our necks; open our chests and gouge out our hearts, and they will grow back again; inside a cauldron of boiling oil, we can take baths." Highly startled the king said, "These three things are all roads leading to certain death!" "Only because we have such magic power," said Tiger-Strength, "do we dare make so bold a claim. We won't quit until we have waged this contest with them." The king said in a loud voice, "You priests from the Land of the East, our National Preceptors are unwilling to let you go. They wish to wage one more contest with you in head cutting, stomach ripping, and going into a cauldron of boiling oil to take a bath."

Pilgrim was still assuming the form of the mole-cricket, flying back and forth to make his secret report. When he heard this, he retrieved his hair, which had been changed into his substitute, and he himself changed at once back into his true form. "Lucky! Lucky!" he cried with loud guffaws. "Business has come to my door!" "These three things," said Bajie, "will certainly make you lose your life. How could you say that business has come to your door?" "You still have no idea of my abilities!" said Pilgrim. "Elder Brother," said Bajie, "you are quite clever, quite capable in those transformations. Aren't those skills something already? What more abilities do you have?" Pilgrim said,

> "Cut off my head and I still can speak.
> Sever my arms, I still can beat you up!
> My legs amputated, I still can walk.
> My belly, ripped open, will heal again,
> Smooth and snug as a wonton people make:
> A tiny pinch and it's completely formed.
> To bathe in boiling oil is easier still;
> It's like warm liquid cleansing me of dirt."

When Bajie and Sha Monk heard these words, they roared with laughter. Pilgrim went forward and said, "Your Majesty, this young priest knows how to have his head cut off." "How did you acquire such an ability?" asked the king. "When I was practicing austerities in a monastery some years ago," said Pilgrim, "I met a mendicant Chan[2] master, who taught me the magic of head cutting. I don't know whether it works or not, and that's why I want to try it out right now." "This priest is so young and ignorant!" said the king, chuckling. "Is head cutting something to try out? The head is, after all, the very fountain of the six kinds of *yang* energies[3] in one's body. If you cut it off. you'll die." "That's

2. Also known as Zen (Japanese). A Buddhist sect.

3. According to traditional medicine the body consists of a mixture of *yin* and *yang* energies.

what we want," said Tiger-Strength. "Only then can our feelings be relieved!" Besotted by the Daoist's words, the foolish ruler immediately gave the decree for an execution site to be prepared.

Once the command was given, three thousand imperial guards took up their positions outside the gate of the court. The king said, "Monk, go and cut off your head first." "I'll go first! I'll go first!" said Pilgrim merrily. He folded his hands before his chest and shouted, "National Preceptors, pardon my presumption for taking my turn first!" He turned swiftly and was about to dash out. The Tang monk grabbed him, saying, "O Disciple! Be careful! Where you are going isn't a playground!" "No fear!" said Pilgrim. "Take off your hands! Let me go!"

The Great Sage went straight to the execution site, where he was caught hold of by the executioner and bound with ropes. He was then led to a tall mound and pinned down on top of it. At the cry "Kill," his head came off with a swishing sound. Then the executioner gave the head a kick, and it rolled off like a watermelon to a distance of some forty paces away. No blood, however, spurted from the neck of Pilgrim. Instead, a voice came from inside his stomach, crying, "Come, head!" So alarmed was the Deer-Strength Great Immortal by the sight of such ability that he at once recited a spell and gave this charge to the local spirit and patron deity: "Hold down that head. When I have defeated the monk, I'll persuade the king to turn your little shrines into huge temples, your idols of clay into true bodies of gold." The local spirit and the god, you see, had to serve him since he knew the magic of the five thunders. Secretly, they indeed held Pilgrim's head down. Once more Pilgrim cried, "Come, head!" But the head stayed on the ground as if it had taken root; it would not move at all. Somewhat anxious, Pilgrim rolled his hands into fists and wrenched his body violently. The ropes all snapped and fell off; at the cry "Grow," a head sprang up instantly from his neck. Every one of the executioners and every member of the imperial guards became terrified, while the officer in charge of the execution dashed inside the court to make this report: "Your Majesty, that young priest had his head cut off, but another head has grown up." "Sha Monk," said Bajie, giggling, "we truly had no idea that Elder Brother has this kind of talent!" "If he knows seventy-two ways of transformation," said Sha Monk, "he may have altogether seventy-two heads!"

Hardly had he finished speaking when Pilgrim came walking back, saying, "Master." Exceedingly pleased, Tripitaka said, "Disciple, did it hurt?" "Hardly," said Pilgrim, "it's sort of fun!" "Elder Brother," said Bajie, "do you need ointment for the scar?" "Touch me," said Pilgrim, "and see if there's any scar." Idiot touched him and he was dumbfounded. "Marvelous! Marvelous!" he giggled. "It healed perfectly. You can't feel even the slightest scar!"

As the brothers were chatting happily among themselves, they heard the king say, "Receive your rescript. We give you a complete pardon. Go away!" Pilgrim said, "We'll take the rescript all right, but we want the National Preceptor to go there and cut his head off too! He should try something new!" "Great National Preceptor," said the king, "the priest is not willing to pass you up. If you want to compete with him, please try not to frighten us." Tiger-Strength had no choice but to go up to the site, where he was bound and pinned to the ground by several executioners. One of them lifted the sword and cut off his head, which was then kicked some thirty paces away. Blood did not spurt from his trunk either, and he, too, gave a cry, "Come, head!" Hurriedly pulling off a piece of hair, Pilgrim blew on it his immortal breath, crying, "Change!" It changed into a yellow hound, which dashed into the execution site, picked up the Daoist's head with its mouth, and ran to drop it into the imperial moat. The Daoist, meanwhile, called for his head three times without success. He did not, you see, have the ability of Pilgrim, and there was no possibility that he could produce another head. All at once, bright crimson gushed out from his trunk. Alas!

> Though he could send for wind and call for rain,
> How could he match an immortal of the right fruit?

In a moment, he fell to the dust, and those gathered about him discovered that he was actually a headless tiger with yellow fur.

* * *

We tell you now instead about those monks who succeeded in escaping with their lives. When they heard of the decree that was promulgated, every one of them was delighted and began to return to the city to search for the Great Sage Sun,[4] to thank him, and to return his hairs. Meanwhile, the elder, after the banquet was over, obtained the rescript from the king, who led the queen, the concubines, and two rows of civil and military officials out the gate of the court to see the priests off, As they came out, they found many monks kneeling on both sides of the road, saying "Father Great Sage, Equal to Heaven, we are the monks who escaped with our lives on the beach. When we heard that Father had wiped out the demons and rescued us, and when we further heard that our king had issued a decree commanding our return, we came here to present to you the hairs and to thank you for your Heavenly grace." "How many of you came back?" asked Pilgrim, chuckling, and they replied, "All five hundred. None's missing." Pilgrim shook his body once and immediately retrieved his hairs. Then he said to the king and the laypeople, "These monks indeed were released by old Monkey. The cart was smashed after old Monkey tossed it through the double passes and up the steep ridge, and it was Monkey also who beat to death those two perverse Daoists. After such pestilence has been exterminated this day, you should realize that the true way is the gate of Chan. Hereafter you should never believe in false doctrines. I hope you will honor the unity of the Three Religions: revere the monks, revere also the Daoists, and take care to nurture the talented. Your kingdom, I assure you, will be secure forever." The king gave his assent and his thanks repeatedly before he escorted the Tang monk out of the city. And so, this was the purpose of their journey:

> A diligent search for the three canons;
> A strenuous quest for the primal light.

We do not know what will happen to master and disciples; let's listen to the explanation in the next chapter.

* * *

4. Sun Wukong, the monkey.

From *Chapter 53*

The Chan[1] Master, taking food, is demonically conceived;
Yellow Hag brings water to dissolve the perverse pregnancy.

* * *

Walking to the side of the boat, Pilgrim said, "You are the one ferrying the boat?" "Yes," said the woman. "Why is the ferryman not here?" asked Pilgrim. "Why is the ferrywoman punting the boat?" The woman smiled and did not reply; she pulled out the gangplank instead and set it up. Sha Monk then poled the luggage into the boat, followed by the master holding onto Pilgrim. Then they moved the boat sideways so that Bajie could lead the horse to step into it. After the gangplank was put away, the woman punted the boat away from shore and, in a moment, rowed it across the river.

After they reached the western shore, the elder asked Sha Monk to untie one of the wraps and take out a few pennies for the woman. Without disputing the price, the woman tied the boat to a wooden pillar by the water and walked into one of the village huts nearby, giggling loudly all the time. When Tripitaka saw how clear the water was, he felt thirsty and told Bajie: "Get the almsbowl and fetch some water for me to drink." "I was just about to drink some myself," said Idiot, who took out the almsbowl and bailed out a full bowl of water to hand over to the master. The master drank less than half of the water, and when Idiot took the bowl back, he drank the rest of it in one gulp before he helped his master to mount the horse once more.

After master and disciples resumed their journey to the West, they had hardly traveled half an hour when the elder began to groan as he rode. "Stomachache!" he said, and Bajie behind him also said, "I have a stomachache, too." Sha Monk said, "It must be the cold water you drank." But before he even finished speaking, the elder cried out: "The pain's awful!" Bajie also screamed: "The pain's awful!" As the two of them struggled with this unbearable pain, their bellies began to swell in size steadily. Inside their abdomens, there seemed to be a clot of blood or a lump of flesh, which could be felt clearly by the hand, kicking and jumping wildly about. Tripitaka was in great discomfort when they came upon a small village by the road; two bundles of hay were tied to some branches on a tall tree nearby. "Master, that's good!" said Pilgrim. "The house over there must be an inn. Let me go over there to beg some hot liquid for you. I'll ask them also whether there is an apothecary around, so that I can get some ointment for your stomachache."

Delighted by what he heard, Tripitaka whipped his white horse and soon arrived at the village. As he dismounted, he saw an old woman sitting on a grass mound outside the village gate and knitting hemp. Pilgrim went forward and bowed to her with palms pressed together saying, "Popo,[2] this poor monk has come from the Great Tang in the Land of the East. My master is the royal brother of the Tang court. Because he drank some water from the river back there after we crossed it, he is having a stomachache." Breaking into loud guffaws, the woman said, "You people drank some water from the river?" "Yes," replied Pilgrim, "we drank some of the clean river water east of here." Giggling

---

1. Again, Zen (Japanese), a Buddhist sect.   2. Granny.

loudly, the old woman said, "What a joke! What a joke! Come in, all of you. I'll explain to you."

Pilgrim went to take hold of Tang monk while Sha Monk held up Bajie; moaning with every step the two sick men walked into the thatched hut to take a seat, their stomachs protruding and their faces turning yellow from the pain. "Popo," Pilgrim kept saying, "please make some hot liquid for my master. We'll thank you." Instead of boiling water, however, the old woman dashed inside, laughing and yelling, "Come and look, all of you!"

With loud clip-clops, several middle-aged women ran out from within to stare at the Tang monk, grinning stupidly all the time. Enraged, Pilgrim gave a yell and ground his teeth together, so frightening the whole crowd of them that they turned to flee, stumbling all over. Pilgrim darted forward and caught hold of the old woman, crying, "Boil some water quick and I'll spare you!" "O Father!" said the old woman, shaking violently, "boiling water is useless, because it won't cure their stomachaches. Let me go, and I'll tell you." Pilgrim released her, and she said, "This is the Nation of Women of Western Liang.[3] There are only women in our country, and not even a single male can be found here. That's why we were amused when we saw you. That water your master drank is not the best, for the river is called Child-and-Mother River. Outside our capital we also have a Male Reception Post-house, by the side of which there is also a Pregnancy Reflection Stream. Only after reaching her twentieth year would someone from this region dare go and drink that river's water, for she would feel the pain of conception soon after she took a drink. After three days, she would go to the Male Reception Post-house and look at her reflection in the stream. If a double reflection appears, it means that she will give birth to a child. Since your master drank some water from the Child-and-Mother River, he too has become pregnant and will give birth to a child. How could hot water cure him?"

When Tripitaka heard this, he paled with fright. "O disciple," he cried, "what shall we do?" "O father!" groaned Bajie as he twisted to spread his legs further apart, "we are men, and we have to give birth to babies? Where can we find a birth canal? How could the fetus come out?" With a chuckle Pilgrim said, "According to the ancients, 'A ripe melon will fall by itself.' When the time comes, you may have a gaping hole at your armpit and the baby will crawl out."

When Bajie heard this, he shook with fright, and that made the pain all the more unbearable. "Finished! Finished!" he cried. "I'm dead! I'm dead!" "Second Elder Brother," said Sha Monk, laughing, "stop writhing! Stop writhing! You may hurt the umbilical cord and end up with some sort of prenatal sickness." Our Idiot became more alarmed than ever. Tears welling up in his eyes, he tugged at Pilgrim and said, "Elder Brother, please ask the Popo to see if they have some midwives here who are not too heavy-handed. Let's find a few right away. The movement inside is becoming more frequent now. It must be labor pain. It's coming! It's coming!" Again Sha Monk said chuckling, "Second Elder Brother, if it's labor pain, you'd better sit still. I fear you may puncture the water bag."

"O Popo," said Tripitaka with a moan, "do you have a physician here? I'll ask my disciple to go there and ask for a prescription. We'll take the drug and have

---

3. In the *Record of the Western Territories of the Great Tang*, a diary by the historical Xuanzang, he mentions a Western kingdom of women.

an abortion." "Even drugs are useless," said the old woman, "but due south of here there is a Male-Undoing Mountain. In it there is a Child Destruction Cave, and inside the cave there is an Abortion Stream. You must drink a mouthful of water from the stream before the pregnancy can be terminated. But nowadays, it's not easy to get that water. Last year, a Daoist by the name of True Immortal Compliant came on the scene and he changed the name of the Child Destruction Cave to the Shrine of Immortal Assembly. Claiming the water from the Abortion Stream as his possession, he refused to give it out freely. Anyone who wants the water must present monetary offerings together with meats, wines, and fruit baskets. After bowing to him in complete reverence, you will receive a tiny bowl of the water. But all of you are mendicants. Where could you find the kind of money you need to spend for something like this? You might as well suffer here and wait for the births." When Pilgrim heard this, he was filled with delight. "Popo," he said, "how far is it from here to the Male-Undoing Mountain?" "About three thousand miles," replied the old woman. "Excellent! Excellent!" said Pilgrim. "Relax, Master! Let old Monkey go and fetch some of that water for you to drink."

*　*　*

When Pilgrim saw him, he pressed his palms together before him and bowed, saying, "This poor monk is Sun Wukong." "Are you the real Sun Wukong," said the master with a laugh, "or are you merely assuming his name and surname?" "Look at the way the master speaks!" said Pilgrim. "As the proverb says, 'A gentleman changes neither his name when he stands, nor his surname when he sits.' What would be the reason for me to assume someone else's name?" The master asked, "Do you recognize me?" "Since I made repentance in the Buddhist gate and embraced with all sincerity the teaching of the monks," said Pilgrim, "I have only been climbing mountains and fording waters. I have lost contact with all the friends of my youth. Because I have never been able to visit you, I have never beheld your honorable countenance before. When we asked for our way in a village household west of the Child-and-Mother River, they told me that the master is called the True Immortal Compliant. That's how I know your name." The master said, "You are walking on your way, and I'm cultivating my realized immortality. Why did you come to visit me?" "Because my master drank by mistake the water of the Child-and-Mother River," replied Pilgrim, "and his stomachache turned into a pregnancy. I came especially to your immortal mansion to beg you for a bowl of water from the Abortion Stream, in order that my master might be freed from this ordeal."

"Is your master Tripitaka Tang?" asked the master, his eyes glowering. "Yes, indeed!" answered Pilgrim. Grinding his teeth together, the master said spitefully, "Have you run into a Great King Holy Child?" "That's the nickname of the fiend, Red Boy," said Pilgrim, "who lived in the Fiery Cloud Cave by the Dried Pine Stream, in the Roaring Mountain. Why does the True Immortal ask after him?" "He happens to be my nephew," replied the master, "and the Bull Demon King is my brother. Some time ago my elder brother told me in a letter that Sun Wukong, the eldest disciple of Tripitaka Tang, was such a rascal that he brought his son great harm. I didn't know where to find you for vengeance, but you came instead to seek me out. And you're asking me for water?" Trying to placate him with a smile, Pilgrim said, "You are wrong, Sir. Your elder brother used to be my friend, for both of us belonged to a league of seven bond brothers when we were young. I just didn't know about you, and so I did not come to pay my respect in your mansion. Your nephew is very well off, for he is now the attendant of the Bodhisattva Guanyin. He has become the Boy of Goodly Wealth, with whom even we cannot compare. Why do you blame me instead?"

"You brazen monkey!" shouted the master. "Still waxing your tongue! Is my nephew better off being a king by himself, or being a slave to someone? Stop this insolence and have a taste of my hook!" Using the iron rod to parry the blow, the Great Sage said, "Please don't use the language of war, Sir. Give me some water and I'll leave." "Brazen monkey!" scolded the master. "You don't know any better! If you can withstand me for three rounds, I'll give you the water. If not, I'll chop you up as meat sauce to avenge my nephew." "You damned fool!" scolded Pilgrim. "You don't know what's good for you! If you want to fight, get up here and watch my rod!" The master at once countered with his compliant hook, and the two of them had quite a fight before the Shrine of Immortal Assembly.

> The sage monk drinks from this procreant stream,
> And Pilgrim must th' Immortal Compliant seek.
> Who knows the True Immortal is a fiend,
> Who safeguards by force the Abortion Stream?
> When these two meet, they speak as enemies
> Feuding, and resolved not to give one whit.
> The words thus traded engender distress;
> Rancor and malice so bent on revenge.
> This one, whose master's life is threatened, comes seeking water;
> That one for losing his nephew refuses to yield.
> Fierce as a scorpion's the compliant hook;
> Wild like a dragon's the golden-hooped rod.
> Madly it stabs the chest, what savagery!
> Aslant, it hooks the legs, what subtlety!
> The rod aiming down there[4] inflicts grave wounds;
> The hook, passing shoulders, will whip the head.
> The rod slaps the waist—"a hawk holds a bird."
> The hook swipes the head—"a mantis hits its prey."
> They move here and there, both striving to win;
> They turn and close in again and again.
> The hook hooks, the rod strikes, without letup—
> On either side victory cannot be seen.

* * *

The two of them began their fighting outside the shrine, and as they struggled and danced together, they gradually moved to the mountain slope below. We shall leave this bitter contest for a moment.

We tell you instead about our Sha Monk, who crashed inside the door, holding the bucket. He was met by the Daoist, who barred the way at the well and said, "Who are you that you dare come to get our water?" Dropping the bucket, Sha Monk took out his fiend-routing treasure staff and, without a word, brought it down on the Daoist's head. The Daoist was unable to dodge fast

4. I.e., the genitals.

enough, and his left arm and shoulder were broken by this one blow. Falling to the ground, he lay there struggling for his life. "I wanted to slaughter you, cursed beast," scolded Sha Monk, "but you are, after all, a human being. I still have some pity for you, and I'll spare you. Let me bail out the water." Crying for Heaven and Earth to help him, the Daoist crawled slowly to the rear, while Sha Monk lowered the bucket into the well and filled it to the brim. He then walked out of the shrine and mounted the cloud and fog before he shouted to Pilgrim, "Big Brother, I have gotten the water and I'm leaving. Spare him! Spare him!" When the Great Sage heard this, he stopped the hook with his iron rod and said, "I was about to exterminate you, but you have not committed a crime. Moreover, I still have regard for the feelings of your brother, the Bull Demon King. When I first came here, I was hooked by you twice and didn't get my water. When I returned, I came with the trick of enticing the tiger to leave the mountain and deceived you into fighting me, so that my brother could go inside to get the water. If old Monkey is willing to use his real abilities to fight with you, don't say there is only one of you so-called True Immortal Compliants; even if there were several of you, I would beat you all to death. But to kill is not as good as to let live, and so I'm going to spare you and permit you to have a few more years. From now on if anyone wishes to obtain the water, you must not blackmail the person."

Not knowing anything better, that bogus immortal brandished his hook and once more attempted to catch Pilgrim's legs. The Great Sage evaded the blade of his hook and then rushed forward, crying, "Don't run!" The bogus immortal was caught unprepared and he was pushed head over heels to the ground, unable to get up. Grabbing the compliant hook the Great Sage snapped it in two; then he bundled the pieces together and, with another bend, broke them into four segments. Throwing them on the ground, he said, "Brazen, cursed beast! Still dare to be unruly?" Trembling all over, the bogus immortal took the insult and dared not utter a word. Our Great Sage, in peals of laughter, mounted the cloud to rise into the air, and we have a testimonial poem. The poem says:

> You need true water to smelt true lead;
> With dried mercury true water mixes well.
> True mercury and lead have no maternal breath;
> Elixir is divine drug and cinnabar.
> In vain the child conceived attains a form;
> Earth Mother has achieved merit with ease.
> Heresy pushed down, right faith's affirmed;
> The lord of the mind, all smiles, now goes back.

Mounting the auspicious luminosity, the Great Sage caught up with Sha Monk. Having acquired the true water, they were filled with delight as they returned to where they belonged. After they lowered the clouds and went up to the village hut, they found Zhu Bajie leaning on the door post and groaning, his belly huge and protruding. Walking quietly up to him, Pilgrim said, "Idiot, when did you enter the delivery room?" Horrified, Idiot said, "Elder Brother, don't make fun of me. Did you bring the water?" Pilgrim was about to tease him some more when Sha Monk followed him in, laughing as he said, "Water's coming! Water's coming!" Enduring the pain, Tripitaka rose slightly and said, "O disciples, I've caused you a lot of trouble." That old woman, too, was most delighted, and all of her relatives came out to kowtow, crying, "O bodhisattva! This is our luck! This is our luck!" She took a goblet of flowered porcelain, filled it half full, and handed it to Tripitaka, saying, "Old master, drink it slowly. All you need is a mouthful and the pregnancy will dissolve." "I don't need any goblet," said Bajie, "I'll just finish the bucket." "O Venerable Father, don't scare people to death!" said the old woman. "If you drink this bucket of water, your stomach and your intestines will all be dissolved."

Idiot was so taken aback that he dared not misbehave; he drank only half a goblet. In less than the time of a meal, the two of them experienced sharp pain and cramps in their bellies, and then their intestines growled four or five times. After that, Idiot could no longer contain himself: both waste and urine poured out of him. The Tang monk, too, felt the urge to relieve himself and wanted to go to a quiet place. "Master," said Pilgrim, "you mustn't go out to a place where there is a draft. If you are exposed to the wind, I fear that you may catch some postnatal illness." At once the old woman brought to them two night pots so that the two of them could find relief. After several bowel movements, the pain stopped and the swelling of their bellies gradually subsided as the lump of blood and flesh dissolved. The relatives of the old woman also boiled some white rice congee and presented it to them to strengthen their postnatal weakness.

"Popo," said Bajie, "I have a healthy constitution, and I have no need to strengthen any postnatal weakness. You go and boil me some water, so that I can take a bath before I eat the congee." "Second Elder Brother," said Sha Monk, "you can't take a bath. If water gets inside someone within a month after birth, the person will be sick." Bajie said, "But I have not given proper birth to anything; at most, I only have had a miscarriage. What's there to be afraid of? I must wash and clean up." Indeed, the old woman prepared some hot water for them to clean their hands and feet. The Tang monk then ate about two bowls of congee, but Bajie consumed over fifteen bowls and he still wanted more. "Coolie," chuckled Pilgrim, "don't eat so much. If you get a sandbag belly, you'll look quite awful." "Don't worry, don't worry," replied Bajie. "I'm no female hog. So, what's there to be afraid of?" The family members indeed went to prepare some more rice.

The old woman then said to the Tang monk, "Old master, please bestow this water on me." Pilgrim said, "Idiot, you are not drinking the water anymore?" "My stomachache is gone," said Bajie, "and the pregnancy, I suppose, must be dissolved. I'm quite fine now. Why should I drink any more water?" "Since the two of them have recovered," said Pilgrim, "we'll give this water to your family." After thanking Pilgrim, the old woman poured what was left of the water into a porcelain jar, which she buried in the rear garden. She said to the rest of the family, "This jar of water will take care of my funeral expenses." Everyone in that family, young and old, was delighted. A vegetarian meal was prepared and tables were set out to serve to the Tang monk. He and his disciples had a leisurely dinner and then rested.

* * *

From *Chapter 54*

Dharma-nature, going west, reaches the Women Nation;
Mind Monkey devises a plan to flee the fair sex.

We tell you now about Tripitaka and his disciples, who left the household at the village and followed the road westward. In less than forty miles, they came upon the boundary of Western Liang. Pointing ahead as he rode along, the Tang monk said, "Wukong, we are approaching a city, and from the noise and hubbub coming from the markets, I suppose it must be the Nation of Women. All of you must take care to behave properly. Keep your desires under control and don't let them violate the teachings of our gate of Law." When the three disciples heard this, they obeyed the strict admonition. Soon they reached the head of the street that opened to the eastern gate. The people there, with long skirts and short blouses, powdered faces and oily heads, were all women regardless of whether they were young or old. Many of them were doing business on the streets, and when they saw the four of them walking by, they all clapped their hands in acclaim and laughed aloud, crying happily, "Human seeds are coming! Human seeds are coming!" Tripitaka was so startled that he reined in his horse; all at once the street was blocked, completely filled with women, and all you could hear were laughter and chatter. Bajie began to holler wildly: "I'm a pig for sale! I'm a pig for sale!" "Idiot," said Pilgrim, "stop this nonsense. Bring out your old features, that's all!" Indeed, Bajie shook his head a couple of times and stuck up his two rush-leaf fan ears; then he wriggled his lips like two hanging lotus roots and gave a yell, so frightening those women that they all fell and stumbled. We have a testimonial poem, and the poem says:

> The sage monk, seeking Buddha, reached Western Liang,
> A land full of females but without one male.
> Farmers, scholars, workers, and those in trade,
> The fishers and plowers were women all.
> Maidens lined the streets, crying "Human seeds!"
> Young girls filled the roads to greet the comely men.
> If Wuneng did not show his ugly face,
> The siege by the fair sex would be pain indeed.

In this way, the people became frightened and none dared go forward; everyone was rubbing her hands and squatting down. They shook their heads, bit their fingers, and crowded both sides of the street, trembling all over but still eager to stare at the Tang monk. The Great Sage Sun had to display his hideous face in order to open up the road, while Sha Monk, too, played monster to keep order. Leading the horse, Bajie stuck out his snout and waved his ears. As the whole entourage proceeded, the pilgrims discovered that the houses in the city were built in orderly rows while the shops had lavish displays. There were merchants selling rice and salt; there were wine and tea houses.

> There were bell and drum towers with goods piled high;
> Bannered pavilions with screens hung low.

As master and disciples followed the street through its several turns, they came upon a woman official standing in the street and crying, "Visitors from afar should not enter the city gate without permission. Please go to the post-house and enter your names on the register. Allow this humble official to announce you to the Throne. After your rescript is certified, you will be permitted to pass through." Hearing this, Tripitaka dismounted; then he saw a horizontal plaque hung over the gate of an official mansion nearby, and on the plaque were the three words, Male Reception Post-house. "Wukong," said the elder; "what that family in the village said is true. There is indeed a Male Reception Post-house." "Second Elder Brother," said Sha Monk, laughing, "go and show yourself at the Pregnancy Reflection Stream and see if there's a double reflection." Bajie replied, "Don't play with me! Since I drank that cup of water from the Abortion Stream, the pregnancy has been dissolved. Why should I show myself?" Turning around, Tripitaka said to him, "Wuneng, be careful with your words." He then went forward to greet the woman official, who led them inside the post-house.

*　*　*

They had hardly finished speaking when the two women officials arrived and bowed deeply to the elder, who returned their salutations one by one, saying, "This humble cleric is someone who has left the family. What virtue or talent do I have that I dare let you bow to me?" When the Grand Preceptor saw how impressive the elder looked, she was delighted and thought to herself: "Our nation is truly quite lucky! Such a man is most worthy to be the husband of our ruler." After the officials made their greetings, they stood on either side of the Tang monk and said, "Father royal brother, we wish you ten thousand happinesses!" "I'm someone who has left the family," replied Tripitaka. "Where do those happinesses come from?" Again bending low, the Grand Preceptor said, "This is the Nation of Women in the Western Liang, and since time immemorial, there is not a single male in our country. We are lucky at this time to have the arrival of father royal brother. Your subject, by the decree of my ruler, has come especially to offer a proposal of marriage." "My goodness! My goodness!" said Tripitaka. "This poor monk has arrived at your esteemed region all by himself, without the attendance of either son or daughter. I have with me only three mischievous disciples, and I wonder to which of us is offered this marriage proposal." The post-house clerk said, "Your lowly official just now went into court to present my report, and my ruler, in great delight, told us of an auspicious dream she had last night. She dreamed that

> Luminous hues grew from the screens of gold,
> Refulgent rays spread from the mirrors of jade.

When she learned that the royal brother is a man from the noble nation of China, she was willing to use the wealth of her entire nation to ask you to be her live-in husband. You would take the royal seat facing south to be called the man set apart from others,[1] and our ruler would be the queen. That was why she gave the decree for the Grand Preceptor to serve as the marriage go-between and this lowly official to officiate at the wedding. We came especially to offer you this proposal." When Tripitaka heard these words, he bowed his head and fell into complete silence. "When a man finds the time propitious,"

---

1. The "man set apart from others" is an elevated expression for the emperor.

said the Grand Preceptor, "he should not pass up such an opportunity. Though there is, to be sure, such a thing in the world as asking a husband to live in the wife's family, the dowry of a nation's wealth is rare indeed. May we ask the royal brother to give his quick consent, so that we may report to our ruler." The elder, however, became more dumb and deaf than ever.

Sticking out his pestlelike snout, Bajie shouted, "Grand Preceptor, go back and tell your ruler that my master happens to be an arhat who has attained the Way after a long process of cultivation. He will never fall in love with the dowry of a nation's wealth, nor will he be enamored with even beauty that can topple an empire. You may as well certify the travel rescript quickly and send them off to the West. Let me stay here to be the live-in husband. How's that?" When the Grand Preceptor heard this, her heart quivered and her gall shook, unable to answer at all. The clerk of the post-house said, "Though you may be a male, your looks are hideous. Our ruler will not find you attractive." "You are much too inflexible," said Bajie, laughing. "As the proverb says,

> The thick willow's a basket, the thin, a barrel—
> Who in the world will take a man as an ugly fellow?"

Pilgrim said, "Idiot, stop this foolish talk. Let Master make up his mind: if he wants to leave, let him leave, and if he wants to stay, let him stay. Let's not waste the time of the marriage go-between."

"Wukong," said Tripitaka, "What do you think I ought to do?" "In old Monkey's opinion," replied Pilgrim, "perhaps it's good that you stay here. As the ancients said, 'One thread can tie up a distant marriage.' Where will you ever find such a marvelous opportunity?" Tripitaka said, "Disciple, if we remain here to dote on riches and glory, who will go to acquire scriptures in the Western Heaven? Won't the waiting kill my emperor of the Great Tang?" The Grand Preceptor said, "In the presence of the royal brother, your humble official dares not hide the truth. The wish of our ruler is only to offer you the proposal of marriage. After your disciples have attended the wedding banquet, provisions will be given them and the travel rescript will be certified, so that they may proceed to the Western Heaven to acquire the scriptures." "What the Grand Preceptor said is most reasonable," said Pilgrim, "and we need not be difficult about this. We are willing to let our master remain here to become the husband of your mistress. Certify our rescript quickly and send us off to the West. When we have acquired the scriptures, we will return here to visit father and mother and ask for travel expenses so that we may go back to the Great Tang." Both the Grand Preceptor and the clerk of the post-house bowed to Pilgrim as they said, "We thank this teacher for his kind assistance in concluding this marriage." Bajie said, "Grand Preceptor, don't use only your mouth to set the table! Since we have given our consent, tell your mistress to prepare us a banquet first. Let us have an engagement drink. How about it?" "Of course! Of course!" said the Grand Preceptor. "We'll send you a feast at once." In great delight, the Grand Preceptor left with the clerk of the post-house.

We tell you now about our elder Tang, who caught hold of Pilgrim immediately and berated him, crying, "Monkey head! Your tricks are killing me! How could you say such things and ask me to get married here while you people go to the Western Heaven to see Buddha? Even if I were to die, I would not dare do this." "Relax, Master," said Pilgrim, "old Monkey's not ignorant of how you feel.

But since we have reached this place and met this kind of people, we have no alternative but to meet plot with plot." "What do you mean by that?" asked Tripitaka.

Pilgrim said, "If you persist in refusing them, they will not certify our travel rescript nor will they permit us to pass through. If they grow vicious and order many people to cut you up and use your flesh to make those so-called fragrant bags, do you think that we will treat them with kindness? We will, of course, bring out our abilities which are meant to subdue demons and dispel fiends. Our hands and feet are quite heavy, you know, and our weapons ferocious. Once we lift our hands, the people of this entire nation will be wiped out. But you must think of this, however. Although they are now blocking our path, they are no fiendish creatures or monster-spirits; all of them in this country are humans. And you have always been a man committed to kindness and compassion, refusing to hurt even one sentient being on our way. If we slaughter all these common folk here, can you bear it? That would be true wickedness."

When Tripitaka heard this, he said, "Wukong, what you have just said is most virtuous. But I fear that if the queen asks me to enter the palace, she will want me to perform the conjugal rite with her. How could I consent to lose my original *yang* and destroy the virtue of Buddhism, to leak my true sperm and fall from the humanity of our faith?" "Once we have agreed to the marriage," said Pilgrim, "she will no doubt follow royal etiquette and send her carriage out of the capital to receive you. Don't refuse her. Take a ride in her phoenix carriage and dragon chariot to go up to the treasure hall, and then sit down on the throne facing south. Ask the queen to take out her imperial seal and summon us brothers to go into court. After you have stamped the seal on the rescript, tell the queen to sign the document also and give it back to us. Meanwhile, you can also tell them to prepare a huge banquet; call it a wedding feast as well as a farewell party for us. After the banquet, ask for the chariot once more on the excuse that you want to see us off outside the capital before you return to consummate the marriage with the queen. In this way, both ruler and subjects will be duped into false happiness; they will no longer try to block our way, nor will they have any cause to become vicious. Once we reach the outskirts of the capital, you will come down from the dragon chariot and Sha Monk will help you to mount the white horse immediately. Old Monkey will then use his magic of immobility to make all of them, ruler and subjects, unable to move. We can then follow the main road to the West. After one day and one night, I will recite a spell to recall the magic and release all of them, so that they can wake up and return to the city. For one thing, their lives will be preserved, and for another, your primal soul will not be hurt. This is a plot called Fleeing the Net by a False Marriage. Isn't it a doubly advantageous act?" When Tripitaka heard these words, he seemed as if he were snapping out of a stupor or waking up from a dream. So delighted was he that he forgot all his worries and thanked Pilgrim profusely, saying, "I'm deeply grateful for my worthy disciple's lofty intelligence." And so, the four of them were united in their decision, and we shall leave them for the moment.

* * *

After putting everything in order, Pilgrim, Bajie, and Sha Monk faced the imperial carriage and cried out in unison, "The queen need not go any further. We shall take our leave now." Descending slowly from the dragon chariot, the elder raised his hands toward the queen and said, "Please go back, Your Majesty, and let this poor monk go to acquire scriptures." When the queen heard this, she paled with fright and tugged at the Tang monk. "Royal brother darling," she cried, "I'm willing to use the wealth of my entire nation to ask you to be my husband. Tomorrow you shall ascend the tall treasure throne to call yourself king, and I am to be your queen. You have even eaten the wedding feast. Why are you changing your mind now?" When Bajie heard what she said, he became slightly mad. Pouting his snout and flapping his ears wildly, he charged up to the carriage, shouting, "How could we monks marry a powdered skeleton like you? Let my master go on his journey!" When the queen saw that hideous face and ugly behavior, she was scared out of her wits and fell back into the carriage. Sha Monk pulled Tripitaka out of the crowd and was just helping him to mount the horse when another girl dashed out from somewhere and shouted, "Royal brother Tang, where are you going? Let's you and I make some love!" "You stupid hussy!" cried Sha Monk and, whipping out his treasure staff, brought it down hard on the head of the girl. Suddenly calling up a cyclone, the girl carried away the Tang monk with a loud whoosh and both of them vanished without a trace. Alas! Thus it was that

> Having just left the fair sex net,
> Then the demon of love he met.

We do not know whether that girl is a human or a fiend, or whether the old master will die or live; let's listen to the explanation in the next chapter.

From *Chapter 55*

Deviant form makes lustful play for Tripitaka Tang;
Upright nature safeguards the uncorrupted self.

* * *

We now tell you about Sha Monk, who was grazing the horse before the mountain slope when he heard some hog-grunting. As he raised his head, he saw Bajie dashing back, lips pouted and grunting as he ran. "What in the world . . . ?" said Sha Monk, and our Idiot blurted out: "It's awful! It's awful! This pain! This pain!" Hardly had he finished speaking when Pilgrim also arrived. "Dear Idiot!" he chuckled. "Yesterday you said I had a brain tumor, but now you are suffering from the plague of the swollen lip!" "I can't bear it!" cried Bajie. "The pain's acute! It's terrible! It's terrible!"

The three of them were thus in sad straits when they saw an old woman approaching from the south on the mountain road, her left hand carrying a little bamboo basket with vegetables in it. "Big Brother," said Sha Monk, "look at that old lady approaching. Let me find out from her what sort of a monster-spirit this is and what kind of weapon she has that can inflict a wound like this." "You stay where you are," said Pilgrim, "and let old Monkey question her." When Pilgrim stared at the old woman carefully, he saw that there were auspicious clouds covering her head and fragrant mists encircling her body. Recognizing all at once who she was, Pilgrim shouted. "Brothers, kowtow quickly! The lady is Bodhisattva!" Ignoring his pain, Bajie hurriedly went to his knees while Sha Monk bent low, still holding the reins of the horse. The Great Sage Sun, too, pressed his palms together and knelt down, all crying. "We submit to the great and compassionate, the efficacious savior, Bodhisattva Guanshiyin."

When the Bodhisattva saw that they recognized her primal light, she at once trod on the auspicious clouds and rose to midair to reveal her true form, the one which carried the fish basket. Pilgrim rushed up there also to say to her, bowing. "Bodhisattva, pardon us for not receiving you properly. We were desperately trying to rescue our master and we had no idea that the Bodhisattva was descending to earth. Our present demonic ordeal is hard to overcome indeed, and we beg the Bodhisattva to help us." "This monster-spirit," said the Bodhisattva "is most formidable. Those tridents of hers happen to be two front claws, and what gave you such a painful stab is actually a stinger on her tail. It's called the Horse-Felling Poison, for she herself is a scorpion spirit. Once upon a time she happened to be listening to a lecture in the Thunderclap Monastery. When Tathāgata[1] saw her, he wanted to push her away with his hand, but she turned around and gave the left thumb of the Buddha a stab. Even Tathāgata found the pain unbearable! When he ordered the arhats to seize her, she fled here. If you want to rescue the Tang monk, you must find a special friend of mine for even I cannot go near her." Bowing again, Pilgrim said, "I beg the Bodhisattva to reveal to whom it is that your disciple should go to ask for assistance." "Go to the East Heaven Gate," replied the Bodhisattva, "and ask for help from the Star Lord Orionis in the Luminescent Palace. He is the one to subdue this monster-spirit." When she finished speaking, she changed into a beam of golden light to return to South Sea.

Dropping down from the clouds, the Great Sage Sun said to Bajie and Sha Monk, "Relax, Brothers, we've found someone to rescue Master." "From where?" asked Sha Monk, and Pilgrim replied, "Just now the Bodhisattva told me to seek the assistance of the Star Lord Orionis. Old Monkey will go immediately." With swollen lips, Bajie grunted: "Elder Brother, please ask the god for some medicine for the pain." "No need for medicine," said Pilgrim with a laugh. "After one night, the pain will go away like mine." "Stop talking," said Sha Monk. "Go quickly!"

Dear Pilgrim! Mounting his cloud-somersault, he arrived instantly at the East Heaven Gate, where he was met by the Devarāja Virūḍhaka. "Great Sage," said the devarāja, bowing, "where are you going?" "On our way to acquire scriptures in the West," replied Pilgrim, "the Tang monk ran into another demonic obstacle. I must go to the Luminescent Palace to find the Star God of the Rising Sun." As he spoke, Tao, Zhang, Xin, and Deng, the four Grand Marshals, also approached him to ask where he was going. "I have to find the Star Lord Orionis," said Pilgrim, "and ask him to rescue my master from a monster-spirit." One of the grand marshals said, "By the decree of the Jade Emperor this morning, the god went to patrol the Star-Gazing Terrace." "Is that true?" asked Pilgrim. "All of us humble warriors," replied Grand Marshal Xin, "left the Dipper Palace with him at the same time. Would we dare speak falsehood?" "It has been a long time," said Grand Marshal Tao, "and he might be back already. The Great Sage should go to the Luminescent Palace first, and if he's not there, then you can go to the Star-Gazing Terrace."

Delighted, the Great Sage took leave of them and arrived at the gate of the Luminescent Palace. Indeed, there was no one in sight, and as he turned to

---

1. Again, the Buddha.

leave, he saw a troop of soldiers approaching, followed by the god, who still had on his court regalia made of golden threads. Look at

His cap of five folds ablaze with gold;
His court tablet of most lustrous jade.
A seven-star sword, cloud patterned, hung from his robe;
An eight-treasure belt, lucent, wrapped around his waist.
His pendant jangled as if striking a tune;
It rang like a bell in a strong gust of wind.
Kingfisher fans parted and Orionis came
As celestial fragrance the courtyard filled.

Those soldiers walking in front saw Pilgrim standing outside the Luminescent Palace, and they turned quickly to report: "My lord, the Great Sage Sun is here." Stopping his cloud and straightening his court attire, the god ordered the soldiers to stand on both sides in two rows while he went forward to salute his visitor, saying, "Why has the Great Sage come here?"

"I have come here," replied Pilgrim, "especially to ask you to save my master from an ordeal." "Which ordeal," asked the god, "and where?" "In the Cave of the Lute at the Toxic Foe Mountain," Pilgrim answered "which is located in the State of Western Liang." "What sort of monster is there in the cave," asked the god again, "that has made it necessary for you to call on this humble deity?"

Pilgrim said, "Just now the Bodhisattva Guanyin, in her epiphany, revealed to us that it was a scorpion spirit. She told us further that only you, sir, could overcome it. That is why I have come to call on you." "I should first go back and report to the Jade Emperor," said the god, "but the Great Sage is already here, and you have, moreover, the Bodhisattva's recommendation. Since I don't want to cause you delay, I dare not ask you for tea. I shall go with you to subdue the monster-spirit first before I report to the Throne."

When the Great Sage heard this, he at once went out of the East Heaven Gate with the god and sped to the State of Western Liang. Seeing the mountain ahead, Pilgrim pointed at it and said, "This is it." The god lowered his cloud and walked with Pilgrim up to the stone screen beneath the mountain slope. When Sha Monk saw them, he said, "Second Elder Brother, please rise. Big Brother has brought back the star god." His lips still pouting, Idiot said, "Pardon! Pardon! I'm ill, and I cannot salute you." "You are a man who practices self-cultivation," said the star god. "What kind of sickness do you have?" "Earlier in the morning," replied Bajie, "we fought with the monster-spirit, who gave me a stab on my lip. It still hurts."

The star god said, "Come up here, and I'll cure it for you." Taking his hand away from his snout, Idiot said, "I beg you to cure it, and I'll thank you most heartily." The star god used his hand to give Bajie's lip a stroke before blowing a mouthful of breath on it. At once, the pain ceased. In great delight, our Idiot went to his knees, crying, "Marvelous! Marvelous!" "May I trouble the star god to touch the top of my head also?" said Pilgrim with a grin. "You weren't poisoned," said the star god. "Why should I touch you?" Pilgrim replied, "Yesterday, I was poisoned, but after one night the pain is gone. The spot, however, still feels somewhat numb and itchy, and I fear that it may act up when the weather changes. Please cure it for me." The star god indeed touched the top of his head and blew a mouthful of breath on it. The remaining poison was thus eliminated, and Pilgrim no longer felt the numbness or the itch. "Elder Brother," said Bajie, growing ferocious, "let's go and beat up that bitch!" "Exactly!" said the star god. "You provoke her to come out, the two of you, and I'll subdue her."

Leaping up the mountain slope, Pilgrim and Bajie again went behind the stone screen. With his mouth spewing abuses and his hands working like a pair of fuel-gatherer hooks, our Idiot used his rake to remove the rocks piled up in front of the cave in no time at all. He then dashed up to the second-level door, and one blow of his rake reduced it to powder. The little fiends inside were so terrified that they fled inside to report: "Madam, those two ugly men have destroyed even our second-level door!" The fiend was just about to untie the Tang monk so that he could be fed some tea and rice. When she heard that the door had been broken down, she jumped out of the flower arbor and stabbed Bajie with the trident. Bajie met her with the rake, while Pilgrim assisted him with his iron rod. Rushing at her opponents, the fiend wanted to use her poisonous trick again, but Pilgrim and Bajie perceived her intentions and retreated immediately.

The fiend chased them beyond the stone screen, and Pilgrim shouted: "Orionis, where are you?" Standing erect on the mountain slope, the star god revealed his true form. He was, you see, actually a huge, double-combed rooster, about seven feet tall when he held up his head. He faced the fiend and crowed once: immediately the fiend revealed her true form, which was that of a scorpion about the size of a lute. The star god crowed again, and the fiend, whose whole body became paralyzed, died before the slope. We have a testimonial poem for you, and the poem says:

> Like tasseled balls his embroidered neck and comb,
> With long, hard claws and angry, bulging eyes,
> He perfects the Five Virtues forcefully;
> His three crows are done heroically.
> No common, clucking fowl about the hut,
> He's Heaven's star showing his holy name.
> In vain the scorpion seeks the human ways;
> She now her true, original form displays.

Bajie went forward and placed one foot on the back of the creature, saying, "Cursed beast! You can't use your Horse-Felling Poison this time!" Unable to make even a twitch, the fiend was pounded into a paste by the rake of the Idiot. Gathering up again his golden beams, the star god mounted the clouds and left, while Pilgrim led Bajie and Sha Monk to bow to the sky, saying, "Sorry for all your inconvenience! In another day, we shall go to your palace to thank you in person."

* * *

From *Chapter 98*

Only when ape and horse are tamed will shells be cast;
With merit and work perfected, they see the Real.

We shall now tell you about the Tang monk and his three disciples, who set out on the main road.

In truth the land of Buddha in the West[1] was quite different from other regions. What they saw everywhere were gemlike flowers and jasperlike grasses, aged cypresses and hoary pines. In the regions they passed through, every family was devoted to good works, and every household would feed the monks.

> They met people in cultivation beneath the hills
> And saw travellers reciting sūtras in the woods.

Resting at night and journeying at dawn, master and disciples proceeded for some six or seven days when they suddenly caught sight of a row of tall buildings and noble lofts. Truly

> They soar skyward a hundred feet,
> Tall and towering in the air.
> You look down to see the setting sun
> And reach out to pluck the shooting stars.
> Spacious windows engulf the universe;
> Lofty pillars join with the cloudy screens.
> Yellow cranes bring letters[2] as autumn trees age;
> Phoenix-sheets come with the cool evening breeze.
> These are the treasure arches of a spirit palace,
> The pearly courts and jeweled edifices,
> The immortal hall where the Way is preached,
> The cosmos where sūtras are taught.
> The flowers bloom in the spring;
> Pines grow green after the rain.
> Purple agaric and divine fruits, fresh every year.
> Phoenixes gambol, potent in every manner.

Lifting his whip to point ahead, Tripitaka said, "Wukong, what a lovely place!"

"Master," said Pilgrim, "you insisted on bowing down even in a specious region, before false images of Buddha. Today you have arrived at a true region with real images of Buddha, and you still haven't dismounted. What's your excuse?"

So taken aback was Tripitaka when he heard these words that he leaped down from the horse. Soon they arrived at the entrance to the buildings. A Daoist lad, standing before the gate, called out, "Are you the scripture seeker from the Land of the East?" Hurriedly tidying his clothes, the elder raised his head and looked at his interrogator.

> He wore a robe of silk
> And held a jade duster.
> He wore a robe of silk
> Often to feast at treasure lofts and jasper pools;
> He held a jade yak's-tail

1. The pilgrims have now reached India, the destination of their trip.
2. Immortals are thought to send their communications through magic birds like yellow cranes and blue phoenixes.

> *To wave and dust in the purple mansions.*
> *From his arm hangs a sacred register,*
> *And his feet are shod in sandals.*
> *He floats—a true feathered-one;[3]*
> *He's winsome—indeed uncanny!*
> *Long life attained, he lives in this fine place;*
> *Immortal, he can leave the world of dust.*
> *The sage monk knows not our Mount Spirit guest:*
> *The Immortal Golden Head of former years.*

The Great Sage, however, recognized the person. "Master," he cried, "this is the Great Immortal of the Golden Head, who resides in the Yuzhen Daoist Temple at the foot of the Spirit Mountain."

Only then did Tripitaka realize the truth, and he walked forward to make his bow. With laughter, the great immortal said, "So the sage monk has finally arrived this year. I have been deceived by the Bodhisattva Guanyin. When she received the gold decree from Buddha over ten years ago to find a scripture seeker in the Land of the East, she told me that he would be here after two or three years. I waited year after year for you, but no news came at all. Hardly have I anticipated that I would meet you this year!"

Pressing his palms together, Tripitaka said, "I'm greatly indebted to the great immortal's kindness. Thank you! Thank you!" The four pilgrims, leading the horse and toting the luggage, all went inside the temple before each of them greeted the great immortal once more. Tea and a vegetarian meal were ordered. The immortal also asked the lads to heat some scented liquid for the sage monk to bathe, so that he could ascend the land of Buddha. Truly,

> *It's good to bathe when merit and work are done,*
> *When nature's tamed and the natural state is won.*
> *All toils and labors are now at rest;*
> *Law and obedience have renewed their zest.*
> *At māra's end they reach indeed Buddha-land;*
> *Their woes dispelled, before Śramana[4] they stand.*
> *Unstained, they are washed of all filth and dust.*
> *To a diamond body[5] return they must.*

After master and disciples had bathed, it became late and they rested in the Yuzhen Temple.

Next morning the Tang monk changed his clothing and put on his brocade cassock and his Vairocana hat. Holding the priestly staff, he ascended the main hall to take leave of the great immortal. "Yesterday you seemed rather dowdy," said the great immortal, chuckling, "but today everything is fresh and bright. As I look at you now, you are a true of son of Buddha!" After a bow, Tripitaka wanted to set out at once.

"Wait a moment," said the great immortal. "Allow me to escort you." "There's no need for that," said Pilgrim. "Old Monkey knows the way."

---

3. Immortal or transcendent being.
4. Wandering ascetic.

5. The incorruptible body of Buddhahood.

"What you know happens to be the way in the clouds," said the great immortal, "a means of travel to which the sage monk has not yet been elevated. You must still stick to the main road."

"What you say is quite right," replied Pilgrim. "Though old Monkey has been to this place several times, he has always come and gone on the clouds and he has never stepped on the ground. If we must stick to the main road, we must trouble you to escort us a distance. My master's most eager to bow to Buddha. Let's not dally." Smiling broadly, the great immortal held the Tang monk's hand

> To lead Candana up the gate of Law.

The way that they had to go, you see, did not lead back to the front gate. Instead, they had to go through the central hall of the temple to go out the rear door. Immediately behind the temple, in fact, was the Spirit Mountain, to which the great immortal pointed and said, "Sage Monk, look at the spot halfway up the sky, shrouded by auspicious luminosity of five colors and a thousand folds of hallowed mists. That's the tall Spirit Vulture Peak, the holy region of the Buddhist Patriarch."

The moment the Tang monk saw it, he began to bend low. With a chuckle, Pilgrim said, "Master, you haven't reached that place where you should bow down. As the proverb says, 'Even within sight of a mountain you can ride a horse to death!' You are still quite far from that principality. Why do you want to bow down now? How many times does your head need to touch the ground if you kowtow all the way to the summit?"

"Sage Monk," said the great immortal, "you, along with the Great Sage, Heavenly Reeds, and Curtain-Raising, have arrived at the blessed land when you can see Mount Spirit. I'm going back." Thereupon Tripitaka bowed to take leave of him.

* * *

Highly pleased, the elder said, "Disciples, stop your frivolity! There's a boat coming." The three of them leaped up and stood still to stare at the boat. When it drew near, they found that it was a bottomless one. With his fiery eyes and diamond pupils, Pilgrim at once recognized that the ferryman was in fact the Conductor Buddha, also named the Light of Ratnadhvaja. Without revealing the Buddha's identity, however, Pilgrim simply said, "Over here! Punt it this way!"

Immediately the boatman punted it up to the shore. "Ahoy! Ahoy!" he cried. Terrified by what he saw, Tripitaka said, "How could this bottomless boat of yours carry anybody?" The Buddhist Patriarch said, "This boat of mine

> Since creation's dawn has achieved great fame;
> Punted by me, it has e'er been the same.
> Upon the wind and wave it's still secure:
> With no end or beginning its joy is sure.
> It can return to One, completely clean,
> Through ten thousand kalpas a sail serene.
> Though bottomless boats may ne'er cross the sea,
> This ferries all souls through eternity."

Pressing his palms together to thank him, the Great Sage Sun said, "I thank you for your great kindness in coming to receive and lead my master. Master, get on the boat. Though it is bottomless, it is safe. Even if there are wind and waves, it will not capsize."

The elder still hesistated, but Pilgrim took him by the shoulder and gave him a shove. With nothing to stand on, that master tumbled straight into the water, but the boatman swiftly pulled him out. As he stood on the side of the boat, the master kept shaking out his clothes and stamping his feet as he grumbled at Pilgrim. Pilgrim, however, helped Sha Monk and Bajie to lead the horse and tote the luggage into the boat. As they all stood on the gunwale, the Buddhist Patriarch gently punted the vessel away from shore. All at once they saw a corpse floating down the upstream, the sight of which filled the elder with terror.

"Don't be afraid, Master," said Pilgrim, laughing. "It's actually you!"

"It's you! It's you!" said Bajie also.

Clapping his hands, Sha Monk also said, "It's you! It's you!"

Adding his voice to the chorus, the boatman also said, "That's you! Congratulations! Congratulations!" Then the three disciples repeated this chanting in unison as the boat was punted across the water. In no time at all, they crossed the Divine Cloud-Transcending Stream all safe and sound. Only then did Tripitaka turn and skip lightly onto the other shore. We have here a testimonial poem, which says:

> Delivered from their mortal flesh and bone,
> A primal spirit of mutual love has grown.
> Their work done, they become Buddhas this day,
> Free of their former six-six senses[6] sway.

Truly this is what is meant by the profound wisdom and the boundless dharma which enable a person to reach the other shore.

The moment the four pilgrims went ashore and turned around, the boatman and even the bottomless boat had disappeared. Only then did Pilgrim point out that it was the Conductor Buddha, and immediately Tripitaka awoke to the truth. Turning quickly, he thanked his three disciples instead.

* * *

Highly pleased, Holy Father Buddha at once asked the Eight Bodhisattvas, the Four Vajra Guardians, the Five Hundred Arhats, the Three Thousand Guardians, the Eleven Great Orbs, and the Eighteen Guardians of Monasteries to form two rows for the reception. Then he issued the golden decree to summon in the Tang monk. Again the word was passed from section to section, from gate to gate: "Let the sage monk enter." Meticulously observing the rules of ritual propriety, our Tang monk walked through the monastery gate with Wukong, Wuneng, and Wujing, still leading the horse and toting the luggage. Thus it was that

> Commissioned that year, a resolve he made
> To leave with rescript the royal steps of jade.

---

6. Intensive form of the six impure qualities engendered by the objects and organs of sense: sight, sound, smell, taste, touch, and idea.

The hills he'd climb to face the morning dew
Or rest on a boulder when the twilight fades.
He totes his faith to ford three thousand streams,
His staff trailing o'er endless palisades.
His every thought's on seeking the right fruit.
Homage to Buddha will this day be paid.

The four pilgrims, on reaching the Great Hero Treasure Hall, prostrated themselves before Tathāgata. Thereafter, they bowed to all the attendants of Buddha on the left and right. This they repeated three times before kneeling again before the Buddhist Patriarch to present their traveling rescript to him. After reading it carefully, Tathāgata handed it back to Tripitaka, who touched his head to the ground once more to say, "By the decree of the Great Tang Emperor in the Land of the East, your disciple Xuanzang has come to this treasure monastery to beg you for the true scriptures for the redemption of the multitude. I implore the Buddhist Patriarch to vouchsafe his grace and grant me my wish, so that I may soon return to my country."

To express the compassion of his heart, Tathāgata opened his mouth of mercy and said to Tripitaka, "Your Land of the East belongs to the South Jambūdvīpa Continent. Because of your size and your fertile land, your prosperity and population, there is a great deal of greed and killing, lust and lying, oppression and deceit. People neither honor the teachings of Buddha nor cultivate virtuous karma; they neither revere the three lights nor respect the five grains. They are disloyal and unfilial, unrighteous and unkind, unscrupulous and self-deceiving. Through all manners of injustice and taking of lives, they have committed boundless transgressions. The fullness of their iniquities therefore has brought on them the ordeal of hell and sent them into eternal darkness and perdition to suffer the pains of pounding and grinding and of being transformed into beasts. Many of them will assume the forms of creatures with fur and horns; in this manner they will repay their debts by having their flesh made for food for mankind. These are the reasons for their eternal perdition in Avīci without deliverance.

"Though Confucius had promoted his teachings of benevolence, righteousness, ritual, and wisdom, and though a succession of kings and emperors had established such penalties as transportation, banishment, hanging, and beheading, these institutions had little effect on the foolish and the blind, the reckless and the antinomian.

"Now, I have here three baskets of scriptures which can deliver humanity from its afflictions and dispel its calamities. There is one basket of vinaya, which speak of Heaven; a basket of śāstras, which tell of the Earth; and a basket of sūtras, which redeem the damned. Altogether these three baskets of scriptures contain thirty-five titles written in fifteen thousand one hundred and forty-four scrolls. They are truly the pathway to the realization of immortality and the gate to ultimate virtue. Every concern of astronomy, geography, biography, flora and fauna, utensils, and human affairs within the Four Great Continents of this world is recorded therein. Since all of you have traveled such a great distance to come here, I would have liked to give the entire set to you. Unfortunately, the people of your region are both stupid and headstrong. Mocking the true words, they refuse to recognize the profound significance of our teachings of Śramana."

Then Buddha turned to call out: "Ānanda[7] and Kāśyapa, take the four of them to the space beneath the precious tower. Give them a vegetarian meal first. After the maigre, open our treasure loft for them and select a few scrolls from each of the thirty-five divisions of our three canons, so that they may take them back to the Land of the East as a perpetual token of grace."

The two Honored Ones obeyed and took the four pilgrims to the space beneath the tower, where countless rare dainties and exotic treasures were laid out in a seemingly endless spread. Those deities in charge of offerings and sacrifices began to serve a magnificent feast of divine food, tea, and fruit—viands of a hundred flavors completely different from those of the mortal world. After master and disciples had bowed to give thanks to Buddha, they abandoned themselves to enjoyment. In truth

> Treasure flames, gold beams on their eyes have shined;
> Strange fragrance and feed even more refined.
> Boundlessly fair the tow'r of gold appears;
> There's immortal music that clears the ears.
> Such divine fare and flower humans rarely see;
> Long life's attained through strange food and fragrant tea.
> Long have they endured a thousand forms of pain.
> This day in glory the Way they're glad to gain.

This time it was Bajie who was in luck and Sha Monk who had the advantage, for what the Buddhist Patriarch had provided for their complete enjoyment was nothing less than such viands as could grant them longevity and health and enable them to transform their mortal substance into immortal flesh and bones.

When the four pilgrims had finished their meal, the two Honored Ones who had kept them company led them up to the treasure loft. The moment the door was opened, they found the room enveloped in a thousand layers of auspicious air and magic beams, in ten thousand folds of colored fog and hallowed clouds. On the sūtra cases and jeweled chests red labels were attached, on which the titles of the books were written in clerkly script. After Ānanda and Kāśyapa had shown all the titles to the Tang monk, they said to him, "Sage Monk, having come all this distance from the Land of the East, what sort of small gifts have you brought for us? Take them out quickly! We'll be pleased to hand over the scriptures to you."

On hearing this, Tripitaka said, "Because of the great distance, your disciple, Xuanzang, has not been able to make such preparation."

"How nice! How nice!" said the two Honored Ones, snickering. "If we imparted the scriptures to you gratis, our posterity would starve to death!"

When Pilgrim saw them fidgeting and fussing, refusing to hand over the scriptures, he could not refrain from yelling, "Master, let's go tell Tathāgata about this! Let's make him come himself and hand over the scriptures to old Monkey!"

"Stop shouting!" said Ānanda. "Where do you think you are that you dare indulge in such mischief and waggery? Get over here and receive the scriptures!" Controlling their annoyance, Bajie and Sha Monk managed to restrain

7. Devout disciple of the Buddha.

leave, he saw a troop of soldiers approaching, followed by the god, who still had on his court regalia made of golden threads. Look at

His cap of five folds ablaze with gold;
His court tablet of most lustrous jade.
A seven-star sword, cloud patterned, hung from his robe;
An eight-treasure belt, lucent, wrapped around his waist.
His pendant jangled as if striking a tune;
It rang like a bell in a strong gust of wind.
Kingfisher fans parted and Orionis came
As celestial fragrance the courtyard filled.

Those soldiers walking in front saw Pilgrim standing outside the Luminescent Palace, and they turned quickly to report: "My lord, the Great Sage Sun is here." Stopping his cloud and straightening his court attire, the god ordered the soldiers to stand on both sides in two rows while he went forward to salute his visitor, saying, "Why has the Great Sage come here?"

"I have come here," replied Pilgrim, "especially to ask you to save my master from an ordeal." "Which ordeal," asked the god, "and where?" "In the Cave of the Lute at the Toxic Foe Mountain," Pilgrim answered "which is located in the State of Western Liang." "What sort of monster is there in the cave," asked the god again, "that has made it necessary for you to call on this humble deity?"

Pilgrim said, "Just now the Bodhisattva Guanyin, in her epiphany, revealed to us that it was a scorpion spirit. She told us further that only you, sir, could overcome it. That is why I have come to call on you." "I should first go back and report to the Jade Emperor," said the god, "but the Great Sage is already here, and you have, moreover, the Bodhisattva's recommendation. Since I don't want to cause you delay, I dare not ask you for tea. I shall go with you to subdue the monster-spirit first before I report to the Throne."

When the Great Sage heard this, he at once went out of the East Heaven Gate with the god and sped to the State of Western Liang. Seeing the mountain ahead, Pilgrim pointed at it and said, "This is it." The god lowered his cloud and walked with Pilgrim up to the stone screen beneath the mountain slope. When Sha Monk saw them, he said, "Second Elder Brother, please rise. Big Brother has brought back the star god." His lips still pouting, Idiot said, "Pardon! Pardon! I'm ill, and I cannot salute you." "You are a man who practices self-cultivation," said the star god. "What kind of sickness do you have?" "Earlier in the morning," replied Bajie, "we fought with the monster-spirit, who gave me a stab on my lip. It still hurts."

The star god said, "Come up here, and I'll cure it for you." Taking his hand away from his snout, Idiot said, "I beg you to cure it, and I'll thank you most heartily." The star god used his hand to give Bajie's lip a stroke before blowing a mouthful of breath on it. At once, the pain ceased. In great delight, our Idiot went to his knees, crying, "Marvelous! Marvelous!" "May I trouble the star god to touch the top of my head also?" said Pilgrim with a grin. "You weren't poisoned," said the star god. "Why should I touch you?" Pilgrim replied, "Yesterday, I was poisoned, but after one night the pain is gone. The spot, however, still feels somewhat numb and itchy, and I fear that it may act up when the weather changes. Please cure it for me." The star god indeed touched the top of his head and blew a mouthful of breath on it. The remaining poison was thus eliminated, and Pilgrim no longer felt the numbness or the itch. "Elder Brother," said Bajie, growing ferocious, "let's go and beat up that bitch!" "Exactly!" said the star god. "You provoke her to come out, the two of you, and I'll subdue her."

Leaping up the mountain slope, Pilgrim and Bajie again went behind the stone screen. With his mouth spewing abuses and his hands working like a pair of fuel-gatherer hooks, our Idiot used his rake to remove the rocks piled up in front of the cave in no time at all. He then dashed up to the second-level door, and one blow of his rake reduced it to powder. The little fiends inside were so terrified that they fled inside to report: "Madam, those two ugly men have destroyed even our second-level door!" The fiend was just about to untie the Tang monk so that he could be fed some tea and rice. When she heard that the door had been broken down, she jumped out of the flower arbor and stabbed Bajie with the trident. Bajie met her with the rake, while Pilgrim assisted him with his iron rod. Rushing at her opponents, the fiend wanted to use her poisonous trick again, but Pilgrim and Bajie perceived her intentions and retreated immediately.

The fiend chased them beyond the stone screen, and Pilgrim shouted: "Orionis, where are you?" Standing erect on the mountain slope, the star god revealed his true form. He was, you see, actually a huge, double-combed rooster, about seven feet tall when he held up his head. He faced the fiend and crowed once: immediately the fiend revealed her true form, which was that of a scorpion about the size of a lute. The star god crowed again, and the fiend, whose whole body became paralyzed, died before the slope. We have a testimonial poem for you, and the poem says:

> Like tasseled balls his embroidered neck and comb,
> With long, hard claws and angry, bulging eyes,
> He perfects the Five Virtues forcefully;
> His three crows are done heroically.
> No common, clucking fowl about the hut,
> He's Heaven's star showing his holy name.
> In vain the scorpion seeks the human ways;
> She now her true, original form displays.

Bajie went forward and placed one foot on the back of the creature, saying, "Cursed beast! You can't use your Horse-Felling Poison this time!" Unable to make even a twitch, the fiend was pounded into a paste by the rake of the Idiot. Gathering up again his golden beams, the star god mounted the clouds and left, while Pilgrim led Bajie and Sha Monk to bow to the sky, saying, "Sorry for all your inconvenience! In another day, we shall go to your palace to thank you in person."

* * *

From *Chapter 98*

> *Only when ape and horse are tamed will shells be cast;*
> *With merit and work perfected, they see the Real.*

We shall now tell you about the Tang monk and his three disciples, who set out on the main road.

hisattva. The Tang monk, after all, had endured unspeakable sufferings. Indeed, all the ordeals which he had to undergo throughout his journey have been recorded by your disciples. Here is the complete account." The Bodhisattva started to read the registry from its beginning, and this was the content:

> The Guardians in obedience to your decree
> Record with care the Tang monk's calamities.
> Gold Cicada banished is the first ordeal;
> Being almost killed after birth is the second ordeal;
> Delivered of mortal stock at Cloud-Transcending Stream
>   is the eightieth ordeal;
> The journey: one hundred and eight thousand miles.
> The sage monk's ordeals are clearly on file.

After the Bodhisattva had read through the entire registry of ordeals, she said hurriedly, "Within our order of Buddhism, nine times nine is the crucial means by which one returns to immortality. The sage monk has undergone eighty ordeals. Because one ordeal, therefore, is still lacking, the sacred number is not yet complete."

At once she gave this order to one of the Guardians: "Catch the Vajra Guardians and create one more ordeal." Having received this command, the Guardian soared toward the east astride the clouds. After a night and a day he caught the Vajra Guardians and whispered in their ears, "Do this and this . . . ! Don't fail to obey the dharma decree of the Bodhisattva." On hearing these words, the Eight Vajra Guardians immediately retrieved the wind that had borne aloft the four pilgrims, dropping them and the horse bearing the scriptures to the ground. Alas! Truly such is

> Nine times nine, hard task of immortality!
> Firmness of will yields the mysterious key.
> By bitter toil you must the demons spurn;
> Cultivation will the proper way return.
> Regard not the scriptures as easy things.
> So many are the sage monk's sufferings!
> Learn of the old, wondrous Kinship of the Three:[2]
> Elixir won't gel if there's slight errancy.

When his feet touched profane ground, Tripitaka became terribly frightened. Bajie, however, roared with laughter, saying, "Good! Good! Good! This is exactly a case of 'More haste, less speed'!"

"Good! Good! Good!" said Sha Monk. "Because we've speeded up too much, they want us to take a little rest here." "Have no worry," said the Great Sage. "As the proverb says,

> For ten days you sit on the shore;
> In one day you may pass nine beaches."

---

2. Reputedly the earliest book on alchemy; from the 2nd century C.E.

"Stop matching your wits, you three!" said Tripitaka. "Let's see if we can tell where we are." Looking all around, Sha Monk said, "I know the place! I know the place! Master, listen to the sound of water!"

Pilgrim said, "The sound of water, I suppose, reminds you of your ancestral home." "Which is the Flowing-Sand River," said Bajie. "No! No!" said Sha Monk. "This happens to be the Heaven-Reaching River." Tripitaka said, "O Disciples! Take a careful look and see which side of the river we're on."

Vaulting into the air, Pilgrim shielded his eyes with his hand and took a careful survey of the place before dropping down once more. "Master," he said, "this is the west bank of the Heaven-Reaching River."

"Now I remember,"[4] said Tripitaka. "There was a Chen Village on the east bank. When we arrived here that year, you rescued their son and daughter. In their gratitude to us, they wanted to make a boat to take us across. Eventually we were fortunate enough to get across on the back of a white turtle. I recall, too, that there was no human habitation whatever on the west bank. What shall we do this time?"

"I thought that only profane people would practice this sort of fraud," said Bajie. "Now I know that even the Vajra Guardians before the face of Buddha can practice fraud! Buddha commanded them to take us back east. How could they just abandon us in mid-journey? Now we're in quite a bind! How are we going to get across?" "Stop grumbling, Second Elder Brother!" said Sha Monk. "Our master has already attained the Way, for he had already been delivered from his mortal frame previously at the Cloud-Transcending Stream. This time he can't possibly sink in water. Let's all of us exercise our magic of Displacement and take Master across."

"You can't take him over! You can't take him over!" said Pilgrim, chuckling to himself. Now, why did he say that? If he were willing to exercise his magic powers and reveal the mystery of flight, master and disciples could cross even a thousand rivers. He knew, however, that the Tang monk had not yet perfected the sacred number of nine times nine. That one remaining ordeal made it necessary for them to be detained at the spot.

As master and disciples conversed and walked slowly up to the edge of the water, they suddenly heard someone calling, "Tang Sage Monk! Tang Sage Monk! Come this way! Come this way!" Startled, the four of them looked all around but could not see any sign of a human being or a boat. Then they caught sight of a huge, white, scabby-headed turtle at the shoreline. "Old Master," he cried with outstretched neck, "I have waited for you for so many years! Have you returned only at this time?"

"Old Turtle," replied Pilgrim, smiling, "we troubled you in a year past, and today we meet again." Tripitaka, Bajie, and Sha Monk could not have been more pleased. "If indeed you want to serve us," said Pilgrim, "come up on the shore." The turtle crawled up the bank. Pilgrim told his companions to guide the horse onto the turtle's back. As before, Bajie squatted at the rear of the horse, while the Tang monk and Sha Monk took up positions to the left and to the right of the horse. With one foot on the turtle's head and another on his neck, Pilgrim said, "Old Turtle, go steadily."

His four legs outstretched, the old turtle moved through the water as if he were on dry level ground, carrying all five of them—master, disciples, and the horse—straight toward the eastern shore. Thus it is that

In Advaya's[3] gate the dharma profound
Reveals Heav'n and Earth and demons confounds.
The original visage now they see;
Causes find perfection in one body.
Freely they move when Triyāna's won,
And when the elixir's nine turns are done.
The luggage and the staff there's no need to tote,
Glad to return on old turtle afloat.

Carrying the pilgrims on his back, the old turtle trod on the waves and proceeded for more than half a day. Late in the afternoon they were near the
eastern shore when he suddenly asked this question: "Old Master, in that year
when I took you across, I begged you to question Tathāgata, once you got to
see him, when I would find my sought-after refuge and how much longer
would I live. Did you do that?"

Now, that elder, since his arrival at the Western Heaven, had been preoccupied with bathing in the Yuzhen Temple, being renewed at Cloud-Transcending
Stream, and bowing to the various sage monks, Bodhisattvas, and Buddhas.
When he walked up the Spirit Mountain, he fixed his thought on the worship of
Buddha and on the acquisition of scriptures, completely banishing from his
mind all other concerns. He did not, of course, ask about the allotted age of the
old turtle. Not daring to lie, however, he fell silent and did not answer the question for a long time. Perceiving that Tripitaka had not asked the Buddha for
him, the old turtle shook his body once and dove with a splash into the depths.
The four pilgrims, the horse, and the scriptures all fell into the water as well.
Ah! It was fortunate that the Tang monk had cast off his mortal frame and
attained the Way. If he were like the person he had been before, he would have
sunk straight to the bottom. The white horse, moreover, was originally a dragon,
while Bajie and Sha Monk both were quite at home in the water. Smiling
broadly, Pilgrim made a great display of his magic powers by hauling the Tang
monk right out of the water and onto the eastern shore. But the scriptures,
the clothing, and the saddle were completely soaked.

* * *

From *Chapter 100*

They return to the Land of the East;
The five sages attain immortality.

* * *

We tell you now instead about the Eight Vajra Guardians, who employed the
second gust of fragrant wind to carry the four pilgrims back to the Land of the
East. In less than a day, the capital, Chang'an, gradually came into view. That
Emperor Taizong, you see, had escorted the Tang monk out of the city three
days before the full moon in the ninth month of the thirteenth year of the
Zhenguan reign period. By the sixteenth year, he had already asked the Bureau
of Labor to erect a Scripture-Watch Tower outside the Western-Peace Pass to
receive the holy books. Each year Taizong would go personally to that place for

---

3. Gateway to Buddha-nature.

a visit. It so happened that he had gone again to the tower that day when he caught sight of a skyful of auspicious mists drifting near from the West, and he noticed at the same time strong gusts of fragrant wind.

Halting in midair, the Vajra Guardians cried, "Sage Monk, this is the city Chang'an. It's not convenient for us to go down there, for the people of this region are quite intelligent, and our true identity may become known to them. Even the Great Sage Sun and his two companions needn't go; you yourself can go, hand over the scriptures, and return at once. We'll wait for you in the air so that we may all go back to report to Buddha."

"What the Honored Ones say may be most appropriate," said the Great Sage, "but how could my master tote all those scriptures? How could he lead the horse at the same time? We will have to escort him down there. May we trouble you to wait a while in the air? We dare not tarry."

"When the Bodhisattva Guanyin spoke to Tathāgata the other day," said the Vajra Guardians, "she assured him that the whole trip should take only eight days, so that the canonical number would be fulfilled. It's already more than four days now. We fear that Bajie might become so enamored of the riches down below that we will not be able to meet our appointed schedule."

"When Master attains Buddhahood," said Bajie, chuckling, "I, too, will attain Buddhahood. How could I become enamored of riches down below? Stupid old ruffians! Wait for me here, all of you! As soon as we have handed over the scriptures, I'll return with you and be canonized." Idiot took up the pole, Sha Monk led the horse, and Pilgrim supported the sage monk. Lowering their cloud, they dropped down beside the Scripture-Watch Tower.

When Taizong and his officials saw them, they all descended the tower to receive them. "Has the royal brother returned?" said the emperor. The Tang monk immediately prostrated himself, but he was raised by the emperor's own hands. "Who are these three persons?" asked the emperor once more.

"They are my disciples made during our journey," replied the Tang monk. Highly pleased, Taizong at once ordered his attendants, "Saddle one of our chariot horses for our royal brother to ride. We'll go back to the court together." The Tang monk thanked him and mounted the horse, closely followed by the Great Sage wielding his golden-hooped rod and by Bajie and Sha Monk toting the luggage and supporting the other horse. The entire entourage thus entered together the city of Chang'an. Truly

> A banquet of peace was held years ago.
> When lords, civil and martial, made a grand show.
> A priest preached the law in a great event;
> From Golden Chimes the king his subject sent.
> Tripitaka was given a royal rescript,
> For Five Phases matched the cause of holy script.
> Through bitter smelting all demons were purged.
> Merit done, they now on the court converged.

The Tang monk and his three disciples followed the Throne into the court, and soon there was not a single person in the city of Chang'an who had not learned of the scripture seekers' return.

We tell you now about those priests, young and old, of the Temple of Great Blessing, which was also the old residence of the Tang monk in Chang'an. That day they suddenly discovered that the branches of a few pine trees within the temple gate were pointing eastward. Astonished, they cried, "Strange! Strange! There was no strong wind to speak of last night. Why are all the tops of these trees twisted in this manner?"

One of the former disciples of Tripitaka said, "Quickly, let's get our proper clerical garb. The old master who went away to acquire scriptures must have returned."

"How do you know that?" asked the other priests.

"At the time of his departure," the old disciple said, "he made the remark that he might be away for two or three years, or for six or seven years. Whenever we noticed that these pine-tree tops were pointing to the east, it would mean that he has returned. Since my master spoke the holy words of a true Buddha, I know that the truth has been confirmed this day."

They put on their clothing hurriedly and left; by the time they reached the street to the west, people were already saying that the scripture seeker had just arrived and been received into the city by His Majesty. When they heard the news, the various monks dashed forward and ran right into the imperial chariot. Not daring to approach the emperor, they followed the entourage instead to the gate of the court. The Tang monk dismounted and entered the court with the emperor. The dragon horse, the scripture packs, Pilgrim, Bajie, and Sha Monk were all placed beneath the steps of jade, while Taizong commanded the royal brother to ascend the hall and take a seat.

After thanking the emperor and taking his seat, the Tang monk asked that the scripture scrolls be brought up. Pilgrim and his companions handed them over to the imperial attendants, who presented them in turn to the emperor for inspection. "How many scrolls of scriptures are there," asked Taizong, "and how did you acquire them?"

"When your subject arrived at the Spirit Mountain and bowed to the Buddhist Patriarch," replied Tripitaka, "he was kind enough to ask Ānanda and Kāśyapa, the two Honored Ones, to lead us to the precious tower first for a meal. Then we were brought to the treasure loft, where the scriptures were bestowed on us. Those Honored Ones asked for a gift, but we were not prepared and did not give them any. They gave us some scriptures anyway, and after thanking the Buddhist Patriarch, we headed east, but a monstrous wind snatched away the scriptures. My humble disciple fortunately had a little magic power; he gave chase at once, and the scriptures were thrown and scattered all over. When we unrolled the scrolls, we saw that they were all wordless, blank texts. Your subjects in great fear went again to bow and plead before Buddha. The Buddhist Patriarch said, 'When these scriptures were created, some Bhikṣu sage monks left the monastery and recited some scrolls for one Elder Zhao in the Śrāvastī Kingdom. As a result, the living members of that family were granted safety and protection, while the deceased attained redemption. For such great service they only managed to ask the elder for three pecks and three pints of rice and a little gold. I told them that it was too cheap a sale, and that their descendants would have no money to spend.' Since we learned that even the Buddhist Patriarch anticipated that the two Honored Ones would demand a gift, we had little choice but to offer them that alms bowl of purple gold which Your Majesty had bestowed on me. Only then did they willingly turn over the true scriptures with writing to us. There are thirty-five titles of these scriptures, and several scrolls were selected from each title. Altogether, there are now five thousand and forty-eight scrolls, the number of which makes up one canonical sum."

More delighted than ever, Taizong gave this command: "Let the Court of Imperial Entertainments prepare a banquet in the East Hall so that we may thank our royal brother." Then he happened to notice Tripitaka's three disciples standing beneath the steps, all with extraordinary looks, and he therefore asked, "Are your noble disciples foreigners?"

Prostrating himself, the elder said, "My eldest disciple has the surname of Sun, and his religious name is Wukong. Your subject also addresses him as Pilgrim Sun. He comes from the Water Curtain Cave of the Flower-Fruit Mountain, located in the Aolai Country in the East Pūrvavideha Continent. Because he caused great disturbance in the Celestial Palace, he was imprisoned in a stone box by the Buddhist Patriarch and pressed beneath the Mountain of Two Frontiers in the region of the Western barbarians. Thanks to the admonitions of the Bodhisattva Guanyin, he was converted to Buddhism and became my disciple when I freed him. Throughout my journey I relied heavily on his protection.

"My second disciple has the surname of Zhu, and his religious name is Wuneng. Your subject also addresses him as Zhu Bajie. He comes from the Cloudy Paths Cave of Fuling Mountain. He was playing the fiend at the Old Gao Village of Tibet when the admonitions of the Bodhisattva and the power of the Pilgrim caused him to become my disciple. He made his merit on our journey by toting the luggage and helping us to ford the waters.

"My third disciple has the surname of Sha, and his religious name is Wujing. Your subject also addresses him as Sha Monk. Originally he was a fiend at the Flowing-Sand River. Again the admonitions of the Bodhisattva persuaded him to take the vows of Buddhism. By the way, the horse is not the one my Lord bestowed on me."

Taizong said, "The color and the coat seem all the same. Why isn't it the same horse?"

"When your subject reached the Eagle Grief Stream in the Serpent Coil Mountain and tried to cross it," replied Tripitaka, "the original horse was devoured by this horse. Pilgrim managed to learn from the Bodhisattva that this horse was originally the prince of the Dragon King of the Western Ocean. Convicted of a crime, he would have been executed had it not been for the intervention of the Bodhisattva, who ordered him to be the steed of your subject. It was then that he changed into a horse with exactly the same coat as that of my original mount. I am greatly indebted to him for taking me over mountains and summits and through the most treacherous passages. Whether it be carrying me on my way there or bearing the scriptures upon our return, we are much beholden to his strength."

On hearing these words, Taizong complimented him profusely before asking again, "This long trek to the Western Region, exactly how far is it?"

Tripitaka said, "I recall that the Bodhisattva told us that the distance was a hundred and eight thousand miles. I did not make a careful record on the way. All I know is that we have experienced fourteen seasons of heat and cold. We encountered mountains and ridges daily; the forests we came upon were not small, and the waters we met were wide and swift. We also went through many kingdoms, whose rulers had affixed their seals and signatures on our document." Then he called out: "Disciples, bring up the travel rescript and present it to our Lord."

It was handed over immediately. Taizong took a look and realized that the document had been issued on the third day before the full moon, in the ninth month of the thirteenth year during the Zhenguan reign period. Smiling, Taizong said, "We have caused you the trouble of taking a long journey. This is now the twenty-seventh year of the Zhenguan period!" The travel rescript bore the seals of the Precious Image Kingdom, the Black Rooster Kingdom, the Cart Slow Kingdom, the Kingdom of Women in Western Liang, the Sacrifice Kingdom, the Scarlet-Purple Kingdom, the Bhikṣu Kingdom, the Dharma-Destroying Kingdom. There were also the seals of the Phoenix-Immortal Prefecture, the Jade-Flower County, and the Gold-Level Prefecture. After reading through the document, Taizong put it away.

Soon the officer in attendance to the Throne arrived to invite them to the banquet. As the emperor took the hand of Tripitaka and walked down the steps of the hall, he asked once more, "Are your noble disciples familiar with the etiquette of the court?"

"My humble disciples," replied Tripitaka, "all began their careers as monsters deep in the wilds or a mountain village, and they have never been instructed in the etiquette of China's sage court. I beg my Lord to pardon them."

Smiling, Taizong said, "We won't blame them! We won't blame them! Let's all go to the feast set up in the East Hall." Tripitaka thanked him once more before calling for his three disciples to join them. Upon their arrival at the hall, they saw that the opulence of the great nation of China was indeed different from all ordinary kingdoms. You see

> *The doorway o'erhung with brocade.*
> *The floor adorned with red carpets,*
> *The whirls of exotic incense,*
> *And fresh victuals most rare.*
> *The amber cups*
> *And crystal goblets*
> *Are gold-trimmed and jade-set;*
> *The gold platters*
> *And white-jade bowls*
> *Are patterned and silver-rimmed.*
> *The tubers thoroughly cooked,*
> *The taros sugar-coated;*
> *Sweet, lovely button mushrooms,*
> *Unusual, pure seaweeds.*
> *Bamboo shoots, ginger-spiced, are served a few times;*
> *Malva leafs, honey-drenched, are mixed several ways.*
> *Wheat-glutens fried with xiangchun leaves:*[1]
> *Wood-ears cooked with bean-curd skins.*

---

1. From a fragrant, slightly spicy plant.

Rock ferns and fairy plants;
Fern flour and dried wei-leaves.
Radishes cooked with Sichuan peppercorns;
Melon strands stirred with mustard powder.
These few vegetarian dishes are so-so,
But the many rare fruits quite steal the show!
Walnuts and persimmons,
Lung-ans and lychees.
The chestnuts of Yizhou and Shandong's dates;
The South's ginko fruits and hare-head pears.
Pine-seeds, lotus-seeds, and giant grapes;
Fei-nuts, melon seeds, and water chestnuts.
"Chinese olives" and wild apples;
Crabapples and Pyrus-pears;
Tender stalks and young lotus roots;
Crisp plums and "Chinese strawberries."
Not one species is missing;
Not one kind is wanting.
There are, moreover, the steamed mille-feuilles, honeyed pastries, and
    fine viands;
And there are also the lovely wines, fragrant teas, and strange dainties.
An endless spread of a hundred flavors, true noble fare.
Western barbarians with great China can never compare!

Master and three disciples were grouped together with the officials, both civil and military, on both sides of the emperor Taizong, who took the seat in the middle. The dancing and the music proceeded in an orderly and solemn manner, and in this way they enjoyed themselves thoroughly for one whole day. Truly

The royal banquet rivals the sage kings':
True scriptures acquired excess blessings bring.
Forever these will prosper and remain
As Buddha's light shines on the king's domain.

When it became late, the officials thanked the emperor; while Taizong withdrew into his palace, the various officials returned to their residences. The Tang monk and his disciples, however, went to the Temple of Great Blessing, where they were met by the resident priests kowtowing. As they entered the temple gate, the priests said, "Master, the top of these trees were all suddenly pointing eastward this morning. We remembered your words and hurried out to the city to meet you. Indeed, you did arrive!" The elder could not have been more pleased as they were ushered into the abbot's quarters. By then, Bajie was not clamoring at all for food or tea, nor did he indulge in any mischief. Both Pilgrim and Sha Monk behaved most properly, for they had become naturally quiet and reserved since the Dao in them had come to fruition. They rested that night.

Taizong held court next morning and said to the officials, "We did not sleep the whole night when we reflected on how great and profound has been the merit of our brother, such that no compensation is quite adequate. We finally composed in our head several homely sentences as a mere token of our gratitude, but they have not yet been written down." Calling for one of the secretaries from the Central Drafting Office, he said, "Come, let us recite our composition for you, and you take it down sentence by sentence." The composition was as follows:

We have heard how the Two Primary Forces[2] which manifest themselves in Heaven and Earth in the production of life are represented by images, whereas the invisible powers of the four seasons bring about transformation of things through the hidden action of heat and cold. By scanning Heaven and Earth, even the most ignorant may perceive their rudimentary laws. Even the thorough understanding of yin and yang, however, has seldom enabled the worthy and wise to comprehend fully their ultimate principle. It is easy to recognize that Heaven and Earth do contain yin and yang because there are images. It is difficult to comprehend fully how yin and yang pervade Heaven and Earth because the forces themselves are invisible. That images may manifest the minute is a fact that does not perplex even the foolish, whereas forms hidden in what is invisible are what confuse even the learned.

How much more difficult it is, therefore, to understand the way of Buddhism, which exalts the void, uses the dark, and exploits the silent in order to succor the myriad grades of living things and exercise control over the entire world. Its spiritual authority is the highest, and its divine potency has no equal. Its magnitude impregnates the entire cosmos; there is no space so tiny that it does not permeate it. Birthless and deathless, it does not age after a thousand kalpas; half-hidden and half-manifest, it brings a hundred blessings even now. A wondrous way most mysterious, those who follow it cannot know its limit. A law flowing silent and deep, those who draw on it cannot fathom its source. How, therefore, could those benighted ordinary mortals not be perplexed if they tried to plumb its depths?

Now, this great Religion arose in the Land of the West. It soared to the court of the Han period in the form of a radiant dream,[3] which flowed with its mercy to enlighten the Eastern territory. In antiquity, during the time when form and abstraction were clearly distinguished, the words of the Buddha, even before spreading, had already established their goodly influence. In a generation when he was both frequently active in and withdrawn from the world, the people beheld his virtue and honored it. But when he returned to Nirvāṇa and generations passed by, the golden images concealed his true form and did not reflect the light of the universe. The beautiful paintings, though unfolding lovely portraits, vainly held up the figure of thirty-two marks.[4] Nonetheless his subtle doctrines spread far and wide to save men and beasts from the three unhappy paths, and his traditions were widely proclaimed to lead all creatures through the ten stages toward Buddhahood. Moreover, the Buddha made scriptures, which could be divided into the Great and the Small Vehicles. He also possessed the Law, which could be transmitted either in the correct or in the deviant method.

2. Probably forces of darkness and light, of yin and yang.
3. Reference to a famous legend about China's first contact with Buddhism. Emperor Ming of the Han (r. 58–75 B.C.E.) dreamed that a golden deity was flying in front of his palace. The next morning one minister identified the deity in the dream as the flying Buddha from India.
4. Special physical marks on the body of the Buddha.

Our priest Xuanzang, a Master of the Law, is a leader within the Gate of Law. Devoted and intelligent as a youth, he realized at an early age the merit of the three forms of immateriality. When grown he comprehended the principles of the spiritual, including first the practice of the four forms of patience.[5] Neither the pine in the wind nor the moon mirrored in water can compare with his purity and radiance. Even the dew of Heaven and luminous gems cannot surpass the clarity and refinement of his person. His intelligence encompassed even those elements which seemingly had no relations, and his spirit could perceive that which had yet to take visible forms. Having transcended the lure of the six senses, he was such an outstanding figure that in all the past he had no rival. He concentrated his mind on the internal verities, mourning all the time the mutilation of the correct doctrines. Worrying over the mysteries, he lamented that even the most profound treatises had errors.

He thought of revising the teachings and reviving certain arguments, so as to disseminate what he had received to a wider audience. He would, moreover, strike out the erroneous and preserve the true to enlighten the students. For this reason he longed for the Pure Land and a pilgrimage to the Western Territories. Risking dangers he set out on a long journey, with only his staff for his companion on this solitary expedition. Snow drifts in the morning would blanket his roadway; sand storms at dusk would blot out the horizon. Over ten thousand miles of mountains and streams he proceeded, pushing aside mist and smoke. Through a thousand alternations of heat and cold he advanced amidst frost and rain. As his zeal was great, he considered his task a light one, for he was determined to succeed.

He toured throughout the Western World for fourteen years,[6] going to all the foreign nations in quest of the proper doctrines. He led the life of an ascetic beneath twin śāla trees[7] and by the eight rivers of India. At the Deer Park and on the Vulture Peak he beheld the strange and searched out the different. He received ultimate truths from the senior sages and was taught the true doctrines by the highest worthies. Penetrating into the mysteries, he mastered the most profound lessons. The way of the Triyāna and Six Commandments he learned by heart; a hundred cases of scriptures forming the canon flowed like waves from his lips.

Though the countries he visited were innumerable, the scriptures he succeeded in acquiring had a definite number. Of those important texts of the Mahāyāna he received, there are thirty-five titles in altogether five thousand and forty-eight scrolls. When they are translated and spread through China, they will proclaim the surpassing merit of Buddhism, drawing the cloud of mercy from the Western extremity to shower the dharma-rain on the Eastern region. The Holy Religion, once incomplete, is now returned to perfection. The multitudes, once full of sins, are now brought back to blessing. Like that which quenches the fire in a burning house, Buddhism works to save humanity lost on its way to perdition. Like a golden beam shining on darkened waters, it leads the voyagers to climb the other shore safely.

Thus we know that the wicked will fall because of their iniquities, but the virtuous will rise because of their affinities. The causes of such rise and fall are all self-made by man. Consider the cinnamon flourishing high on the mountain, its

---

5. Four forms of patience: endurance under shame, hatred, physical hardship, and in pursuit of faith [translator's note].
6. Perhaps a deliberate deviation from the

nearly seventeen years of the pilgrimage indicated in the historical sources.
7. Trees under which the Buddha died and passed into nirvana.

flowers nourished by cloud and mist, or the lotus growing atop the green waves, its leaves unsoiled by dust. This is not because the lotus is by nature clean or because the cinnamon itself is chaste, but because what the cinnamon depends on for its existence is lofty, and thus it will not be weighed down by trivia; and because what the lotus relies on is pure, and thus impurity cannot stain it. Since even the vegetable kingdom, which is itself without intelligence, knows that excellence comes from an environment of excellence, how can humans who understand the great relations not search for well-being by following well-being?

May these scriptures abide forever as the sun and moon and may the blessings they confer spread throughout the universe!

After the secretary had finished writing this treatise, the sage monk was summoned. At the time, the elder was already waiting outside the gate of the court. When he heard the summons, he hurried inside and prostrated himself to pay homage to the emperor.

Taizong asked him to ascend the hall and handed him the document. When he had finished reading it, the priest went to his knees again to express his gratitude. "The style and rhetoric of my Lord," said the priest, "are lofty and classical, while the reasoning in the treatise is both profound and subtle. I would like to know, however, whether a title has been chosen for this composition."

"We composed it orally last night,"[8] replied Taizong, "as a token of thanks to our royal brother. Will it be acceptable if I title this 'Preface to the Holy Religion'?" The elder kowtowed and thanked him profusely. Once more Taizong said,

> *"Our talents pale before the imperial tablets,*
> *And our words cannot match the bronze and stone inscriptions.*
> *As for the esoteric texts,*
> *Our ignorance thereof is even greater.*
> *Our treatise orally composed*
> *Is actually quite unpolished—*
> *Like mere spilled ink on tablets of gold.*
> *Or broken tiles in a forest of pearls.*
> *Writing it in self-interest,*
> *We have quite ignored even embarrassment.*
> *It is not worth your notice,*
> *And you should not thank us."*

All the officials present, however, congratulated the emperor and made arrangements immediately to promulgate the royal essay on Holy Religion inside and outside the capital.

Taizong said, "We would like to ask the royal brother to recite the true scriptures for us. How about it?"

"My Lord," said the elder, "if you want me to recite the true scriptures, we must find the proper religious site. The treasure palace is no place for recitation." Exceedingly pleased, Taizong asked his attendants, "Among the monasteries of Chang'an, which is the purest one?"

From among the ranks stepped forth the Grand Secretary, Xiao Yu, who said, "The Wild-Goose Pagoda Temple in the city is purest of all." At once Taizong

---

8. The emperor's declaration here was actually a note written in reply to a formal memorial of thanks submitted to the historical Xuanzang [translator's note].

gave this command to the various officials: "Each of you take several scrolls of these true scriptures and go reverently with us to the Wild-Goose Pagoda Temple. We want to ask our royal brother to expound the scriptures to us." Each of the officials indeed took up several scrolls and followed the emperor's carriage to the temple. A lofty platform with proper appointments was then erected. As before, the elder told Bajie and Sha Monk to hold the dragon horse and mind the luggage, while Pilgrim was to serve him by his side. Then he said to Taizong, "If my Lord would like to circulate the true scriptures throughout his empire, copies should be made before they are dispersed. We should treasure the originals and not handle them lightly."

Smiling, Taizong said, "The words of our royal brother are most appropriate! Most appropriate!" He thereupon ordered the officials in the Hanlin Academy and the Central Drafting Office to make copies of the true scriptures. For them he also erected another temple east of the capital and named it the Temple for Imperial Transcription.

* * *

We must tell you now about those Eight Great Vajra Guardians, who mounted the fragrant wind to lead the elder, his three disciples, and the white horse back to Spirit Mountain. The round trip was made precisely within a period of eight days. At that time the various divinities of Spirit Mountain were all assembled before Buddha to listen to his lecture. Ushering master and disciples before his presence, the Eight Vajra Guardians said, "Your disciples by your golden decree have escorted the sage monk and his companions back to the Tang nation. The scriptures have been handed over. We now return to surrender your decree." The Tang monk and his disciples were then told to approach the throne of Buddha to receive their appointments.

"Sage Monk," said Tathāgata, "in your previous incarnation you were originally my second disciple named Master Gold Cicada. Because you failed to listen to my exposition of the law and slighted my great teaching, your true spirit was banished to find another incarnation in the Land of the East. Happily you submitted and, by remaining faithful to our teaching, succeeded in acquiring the true scriptures. For such magnificent merit, you will receive a great promotion to become the Buddha of Candana Merit.

"Sun Wukong, when you caused great disturbance at the Celestial Palace, I had to exercise enormous dharma power to have you pressed beneath the Mountain of Five Phases. Fortunately your Heaven-sent calamity came to an end, and you embraced the Buddhist religion. I am pleased even more by the fact that you were devoted to the scourging of evil and the exaltation of good. Throughout your journey you made great merit by smelting the demons and defeating the fiends. For being faithful in the end as you were in the beginning, I hereby give you the grand promotion and appoint you the Buddha Victorious in Strife.

"Zhu Wuneng, you were originally an aquatic deity of the Heavenly River, the Marshal of Heavenly Reeds. For getting drunk during the Festival of Immortal Peaches and insulting the divine maiden, you were banished to an incarnation in the Region Below which would give you the body of a beast. Fortunately you still cherished and loved the human form, so that even when you sinned at the Cloudy Paths Cave in Fuling Mountain, you eventually submitted to our great religion and embraced our vows. Although you protected the sage monk on his way, you were still quite mischievous, for greed and lust were never wholly extinguished in you. For the merit of toting the luggage, however, I hereby grant you promotion and appoint you Janitor of the Altars."

"They have all become Buddhas!" shouted Bajie. "Why am I alone made Janitor of the Altars?"

"Because you are still talkative and lazy," replied Tathāgata, "and you retain an enormous appetite. Within the four great continents of the world, there are many people who observe our religion. Whenever there are Buddhist services, you will be asked to clear the altars. That's an appointment which offers you plenty of enjoyment. How could it be bad?

"Sha Wujing, you were originally the Great Curtain-Raising Captain. Because you broke a crystal chalice during the Festival of Immortal Peaches, you were banished to the Region Below, where at the River of Flowing-Sand you sinned by devouring humans. Fortunately you submitted to our religion and remained firm in your faith. As you escorted the sage monk, you made merit by leading his horse over all those mountains. I hereby grant you promotion and appoint you the Golden-Bodied Arhat."

Then he said to the white horse, "You were originally the prince of Dragon King Guangjin of the Western Ocean. Because you disobeyed your father's command and committed the crime of unfiliality, you were to be executed. Fortunately you made submission to the Law and accepted our vows. Because you carried the sage monk daily on your back during his journey to the West and because you also took the holy scriptures back to the East, you too have made merit. I hereby grant you promotion and appoint you one of the dragons belonging to the Eight Classes of Supernatural Beings."

The elder, his three disciples, and the horse all kowtowed to thank the Buddha, who ordered some of the guardians to take the horse to the Dragon-Transforming Pool at the back of the Spirit Mountain. After being pushed into the pool, the horse stretched himself, and in a little while he shed his coat, horns began to grow on his head, golden scales appeared all over his body, and silver whiskers emerged on his cheeks. His whole body shrouded in auspicious air and his four paws wrapped in hallowed clouds, he soared out of the pool and circled inside the monastery gate, on top of one of the Pillars that Support Heaven.

As the various Buddhas gave praise to the great dharma of Tathāgata, Pilgrim Sun said also to the Tang monk, "Master, I've become a Buddha now, just like you. It can't be that I still must wear a golden fillet! And you wouldn't want to clamp my head still by reciting that so-called Tight-Fillet Spell, would you? Recite the Loose-Fillet Spell quickly and get it off my head. I'm going to smash it to pieces, so that that so-called Bodhisattva can't use it any more to play tricks on other people."

"Because you were difficult to control previously," said the Tang monk, "this method had to be used to keep you in hand. Now that you have become a Buddha, naturally it will be gone. How could it be still on your head? Try touching your head and see." Pilgrim raised his hand and felt along his head, and indeed the fillet had vanished. So at that time, Buddha Candana, Buddha Victorious in Strife, Janitor of the Altars, and Golden-Bodied Arhat all assumed the position of their own rightful fruition. The Heavenly dragon-horse too returned to immortality, and we have a testimonial poem for them. The poem says:

One reality fallen to the dusty plain
Fuses with Four Signs and cultivates self again.
In Five Phases terms forms are but silent and void;
The hundred fiends' false names one should all avoid.
The great Bodhi's the right Candana fruition;
Appointments complete their rise from perdition.
When scriptures spread throughout the world the gracious light,
Henceforth five sages live within Advaya's heights.

At the time when these five sages assumed their positions, the various Buddhist Patriarchs, Bodhisattvas, sage priests, arhats, guardians, bhikṣus, upāsakas and upāsikās, the immortals of various mountains and caves, the grand divinities, the Gods of Darkness and Light, the Sentinels, the Guardians of Monasteries, and all the immortals and preceptors who had attained the Way all came to listen to the proclamation before retiring to their proper stations. Look now at

Colored mists crowding the Spirit Vulture Peak,
And hallowed clouds gathered in the world of bliss.
Gold dragons safely sleeping,
Jade tigers resting in peace;
Black hares scampering freely,
Snakes and turtles circling at will.
Phoenixes, red and blue, gambol pleasantly;
Black apes and white deer saunter happily.
Strange flowers of eight periods,
Divine fruits of four seasons,
Hoary pines and old junipers,
Jade cypresses and aged bamboos.
Five-colored plums often blossoming and bearing fruit;
Millennial peaches frequently ripening and fresh.
A thousand flowers and fruits vying for beauty;
A whole sky full of auspicious mists.

Pressing their palms together to indicate their devotion, the holy congregation all chanted:

I submit to Dipamkara, the Buddha of Antiquity.
I submit to Bhaiṣajya-vaidūrya-prabhāṣa, the Physician and Buddha of Crystal Lights.
I submit to the Buddha Śākyamuni.
I submit to the Buddha of the Past, Present, and Future.
I submit to the Buddha of Pure Joy.
I submit to the Buddha Vairocana.
I submit to the Buddha, King of the Precious Banner.
I submit to the Maitreya, the Honored Buddha.
I submit to the Buddha Amitābha.
I submit to Sukhāvativyūha, the Buddha of Infinite Life.
I submit to the Buddha who Receives and Leads to Immorality.
I submit to the Buddha of Diamond Indestructibility.
I submit to Sūrya, the Buddha of Precious Light.
I submit to Mañjuśrī, the Buddha of the Race of Honorable Dragon Kings.

I submit to the Buddha of Zealous Progress and Virtue.
I submit to Candraprabha, the Buddha of Precious Moonlight.
I submit to the Buddha of Presence without Ignorance.
I submit to Varuna, the Buddha of Sky and Water.
I submit to the Buddha Nārāyaṇa.
I submit to the Buddha of Radiant Meritorious Works.
I submit to the Buddha of Talented Meritorious Works.
I submit to Svāgata, the Buddha of the Well-Departed.
I submit to the Buddha of Candana Light.
I submit to the Buddha of Jeweled Banner.
I submit to the Buddha of the Light of Wisdom Torch.
I submit to the Buddha of the Light of Sea-Virtue.
I submit to the Buddha of Great Mercy Light.
I submit to the Buddha, King of Compassion-Power.
I submit to the Buddha, Leader of the Sages.
I submit to the Buddha of Vast Solemnity.
I submit to the Buddha of Golden Radiance.
I submit to the Buddha of Luminous Gifts.
I submit to the Buddha Victorious in Wisdom.
I submit to the Buddha, Quiescent Light of the World.
I submit to the Buddha, Light of the Sun and Moon.
I submit to the Buddha, Light of the Sun-and-Moon Pearl.
I submit to the Buddha, King of the Victorious Banner.
I submit to the Buddha of Wondrous Tone and Sound.
I submit to the Buddha, Banner of Permanent Light.
I submit to the Buddha, Lamp that Scans the World.
I submit to the Buddha, King of Surpassing Dharma.
I submit to the Buddha of Sumeru Light.
I submit to the Buddha, King of Great Wisdom.
I submit to the Buddha of Golden Sea Light.
I submit to the Buddha of Great Perfect Light.
I submit to the Buddha of the Gift of Light.
I submit to the Buddha of Candana Merit.
I submit to the Buddha Victorious in Strife.
I submit to the Bodhisattva Guanshiyin.
I submit to the Bodhisattva, Great Power-Coming.
I submit to the Bodhisattva Mañjuśrī.
I submit to the Bodhisattva Viśvabhadra and other Bodhisattvas.
I submit to the various Bodhisattvas of the Great Pure Ocean.
I submit to the Bodhisattva, the Buddha of Lotus Pool and Ocean
    Assembly.
I submit to the various Bodhisattvas in the Western Heaven of
    Ultimate Bliss.
I submit to the Great Bodhisattvas, the Three Thousand Guardians.
I submit to the Great Bodhisattvas, the Five Hundred Arhats.
I submit to the Bodhisattva, Bhikṣu-īkṣaṇi.
I submit to the Bodhisattva of Boundless and Limitless Dharma.
I submit to the Bodhisattva, Diamond Great Scholar-Sage.
I submit to the Bodhisattva, Janitor of the Altars.
I submit to the Bodhisattva, Golden-Bodied Arhat of Eight Jewels.
I submit to the Bodhisattva of Vast Strength, the Heavenly Dragon
    of Eight Divisions of Supernatural Beings.

Such are these various Buddhas in all the worlds.

I wish to use these merits
To adorn Buddha's pure land—
To repay fourfold grace above
And save those on three paths below.
If there are those who see and hear,
Their minds will find enlightenment.
Their births with us in paradise
Will be this body's recompense.
All the Buddhas of past, present, future in all the world,
The various Honored Bodhisattvas and Mahāsattvas,
Mahā-prajñā-pāramitā![9]

9. The Great Perfection of Wisdom.

MATSUO BASHŌ
1644–1694

During his lifetime Matsuo Bashō was only one of many haikai masters. He was not even part of the prominent haikai circles in the major cities of Kyoto, Osaka, or Edo, but spent much time on the road and eventually settled on the outskirts of Edo, supported by patrons and friends. Although Bashō was a socially marginal figure, like the travelers, outcasts, beggars, and old people who feature in his poetry, he and his school of haikai came to embody the art of haiku.

Bashō was born into a former samurai family that had fallen low in a small castle town thirty miles southeast of Kyoto. After serving the lord of the local castle, where he also developed his tastes for haikai poetry, he moved to Edo at the age of twenty-nine and installed himself as a haikai master, making his living from teaching poetry. A few years later, in 1680,

Bashō retreated to a "Banana plant hut" (Bashō-an), from which he took his pen-name, on the Sumida River in the outskirts of Edo. For the next four years he would write in a style heavily tinged by Chinese recluse poetry, before setting out on travels in 1684, during which he wrote poetic travel diaries.

In 1689 he set out with his travel companion Sora on a five-month journey to explore the Northeast, a trip which resulted in *The Narrow Road to the Deep North*, included in the selections here. The journey depicted in *Narrow Road* is a pilgrimage through nature, but it is also a very conscious emulation of the conventions of the past as Bashō seeks inspiration from famous poetic sites. It is also a travel through language. Some places evoke the frail aesthetics of Heian waka, while others are tinged with reminiscences of Chinese poets, such as **Du Fu** and **Li Bo**. Both Bashō and his travel companion Sora kept a travel diary of sorts. Sora's diary, not published until 1943, shows that the majority of the fifty haiku in Bashō's travelogue were actually written after the journey or were revisions of earlier poems, and that Bashō made himself look far more ascetic and contemplative in the process of revision. *The Narrow Road to the Deep North* is thus not a diary but an idealized version of his travels.

Bashō was always on the move in search for new poetic themes, new languages, and new objects. In his travel diaries he accomplished nothing less than influencing how people saw some of the most defining sites of Japanese identity. He gave the haikai movement a distinctive prose style. Previous classical linked verse had always stayed in the aristocratic realm of waka, never developing a prose language of its own. But with the innovations of haikai prose, haikai poetry reached a new degree of freedom, where poetry, prose, painting, and lifestyle flowed seamlessly into one another.

From The Narrow Road to the Deep North[1]

* * *

The months and days, the travelers of a hundred ages;
the years that come and go, voyagers too.
floating away their lives on boats,
growing old as they lead horses by the bit,
for them, each day a journey, travel their home.
Many, too, are the ancients who perished on the road.
Some years ago, seized by wanderlust, I wandered along the shores
     of the sea.

Then, last autumn, I swept away the old cobwebs in my dilapidated dwelling on the river's edge. As the year gradually came to an end and spring arrived, filling the sky with mist, I longed to cross the Shirakawa Barrier, the most revered of poetic places. Somehow or other, I became possessed by a spirit, which crazed my soul. Unable to sit still, I accepted the summons of the Deity of the Road. No sooner had I repaired the holes in my trousers, attached a new cord to my rain hat, and cauterized my legs with moxa than my thoughts were on the famous moon at Matsushima. I turned my dwelling over to others and moved to Sanpū's villa.

> Time even for the grass hut
> to change owners—
> house of dolls[2]

I left a sheet of eight linked verses on the pillar of the hermitage.

I started out on the twenty-seventh day of the Third Month.

The dawn sky was misting over; the moon lingered, giving off a pale light; the peak of Mount Fuji appeared faintly in the distance. I felt uncertain, wondering

1. Translated by Haruo Shirane. For the route of Bashō's travels, see the map on p. 7.
2. It is the time of the Doll Festival, in the Third Month, when dolls representing the emperor, the empress, and their attendants are displayed in every household.

whether I would see again the cherry blossoms on the boughs at Ueno and Yanaka. My friends had gathered the night before to see me off and joined me on the boat. When I disembarked at a place called Senju, my breast was overwhelmed by thoughts of the "three thousand leagues ahead," and standing at the crossroads of the illusory world, I wept at the parting.

> Spring going—
> birds crying and tears
> in the eyes of the fish

Making this my first journal entry, we set off but made little progress. People lined the sides of the street, seeing us off, it seemed, as long as they could see our backs.

Was it the second year of Genroku?[3] On a mere whim, I had resolved that I would make a long journey to the Deep North. Although I knew I would probably suffer, my hair growing white under the distant skies of Wu, I wanted to view those places that I had heard of but never seen and placed my faith in an uncertain future, not knowing if I would return alive. We barely managed to reach the Sōka post station that night. The luggage that I carried over my bony shoulders began to cause me pain. I had departed on the journey thinking that I need bring only myself, but I ended up carrying a coat to keep me warm at night, a night robe, rain gear, inkstone, brush, and the like, as well as the farewell presents that I could not refuse. All these became a burden on the road.

We paid our respects to the shrine at Muro-no-yashima, Eight Islands of the Sealed Room. Sora, my travel companion, noted: "This deity is called the Goddess of the Blooming Cherry Tree and is the same as that worshiped at Mount Fuji. Since the goddess entered a sealed hut and burned herself giving birth to Hohodemi, the God of Emitting Fire, and proving her vow, they call the place Eight Islands of the Sealed Room. The custom of including smoke in poems on this place also derives from this story. It is forbidden to consume a fish called *konoshiro*, or shad, which is thought to smell like flesh when burned. The essence of this shrine history is already known to the world."

On the thirtieth, we stopped at the foot of Nikkō Mountain. The owner said, "My name is Buddha Gozaemon. People have given me this name because I make honesty my first concern in all matters. As a consequence, you can relax for one night on the road. Please stay here." I wondered what kind of buddha had manifested itself in this soiled world to help someone like me, traveling like a beggar priest on a pilgrimage. I observed the actions of the innkeeper carefully and saw that he was neither clever nor calculating. He was nothing but honesty—the type of person that Confucius referred to when he said, "Those who are strong in will and without pretension are close to humanity." I had nothing but respect for the purity of his character.

On the first of the Fourth Month, we paid our respects to the holy mountain. In the distant past, the name of this sacred mountain was written with the characters Nikkōzan, Two Rough Mountain, but when Priest Kūkai[4] established a temple here, he changed the name to Nikkō, Light of the Sun. Perhaps he was able to see a thousand years into the future. Now this venerable light shines throughout the land, and its benevolence flows to the eight corners of the earth, and the four classes—warrior, samurai, artisan, and merchant—all live in peace. Out of a sense of reverence and awe, I put my brush down here.

> Awe inspiring!
> on the green leaves, budding leaves
> light of the sun

Black Hair Mountain, enshrouded in mist, the snow still white.

> Shaving my head
> at Black Hair Mountain—
> time for summer clothes
>
> Sora

Sora's family name is Kawai; his personal name is Sōgoro. He lived near me, helping me gather wood and heat water, and was delighted at the thought of sharing with me the sights of Matsushima and Kisagata. At the same time, he wanted to help me overcome the hardships of travel. On the morning of the departure, he shaved his hair, changed to dark black robes, and took on the Buddhist name of Sōgō. That is why he wrote the Black Hair Mountain poem. I thought that the words "time for summer clothes"[5] were particularly effective.

Climbing more than a mile up a mountain, we came to a waterfall. From the top of the cavern, the water flew down a hundred feet, falling into a blue pool of a thousand rocks. I squeezed into a hole in the rocks and entered the cavern: they say that this is called Back-View Falls because you can see the waterfall from the back, from inside the cavern.

> Secluded for a while
> in a waterfall—
> beginning of summer austerities[6]

. . .

There is a mountain-priest temple called Kōmyōji. We were invited there and prayed at the Hall of Gyōja.

> Summer mountains—
> praying to the tall clogs
> at journey's start[7]

. . .

The willow that was the subject of Saigyō's[8] poem, "Where a Crystal Stream Flows," still stood in the village of Ashino, on a footpath in a rice field. The lord of

---

5. The first day of the Fourth Month was the date for changing from winter to summer clothing.
6. Period in which Buddhist practitioners remained indoors, fasting, reciting scripture, and practicing austerities.
7. At the beginning of the journey, the traveler bows before the high clogs, a prayer for the foot strength of En no Gyōja, the founder

of a mountain priest sect believed to have gained superhuman powers from rigorous mountain training.
8. Celebrated 12th-century poet. Bashō thinks here of the following poem: "I thought to pause on the roadside where a crystal stream flows beneath a willow and stood rooted to the spot."

the manor of this village had repeatedly said, "I would like to show you this willow," and I had wondered where it was. Today I was able to stand in its very shade.

> Whole field of
> rice seedlings planted—I part
> from the willow

The days of uncertainty piled one on the other, and when we came upon the Shirakawa Barrier, I finally felt as if I had settled into the journey. I can understand why that poet had written, "Had I a messenger, I would send a missive to the capital!" One of three noted barriers, the Shirakawa Barrier captured the hearts of poets. With the sound of the autumn wind in my ears and the image of the autumn leaves in my mind, I was moved all the more by the tops of the green-leafed trees. The flowering of the wild rose amid the white deutzia clusters made me feel as if I were crossing over snow. . . .

At the Sukagawa post station, we visited a man named Tōkyū. He insisted that we stay for four or five days and asked me how I had found the Shirakawa Barrier. I replied, "My body and spirit were tired from the pain of the long journey; my heart overwhelmed by the landscape. The thoughts of the distant past tore through me, and I couldn't think straight." But feeling it would be a pity to cross the barrier without producing a single verse, I wrote:

> Beginnings of poetry—
> rice-planting songs
> of the Deep North

This opening verse was followed by a second verse and then a third; before we knew it, three sequences. . . .

The next day we went to Shinobu[9] Village and visited Shinobu Mottling Rock. The rock was in a small village, half buried, deep in the shade of the mountain. A child from the village came and told us, "In the distant past, the rock was on top of this mountain, but the villagers, angered by the visitors who had been tearing up the barley grass to test the rock, pushed it down into the valley, where it lies face down." Perhaps that was the way it had to be.

> Planting rice seedlings
> the hands—in the distant past pressing
> the grass of longing

. . .

The Courtyard Inscribed-Stone was in Taga Castle in the village of Ichikawa. More than six feet high and about three feet wide; the moss had eaten away the rock, and the letters were faint. On the memorial, which listed the number of miles to the four borders of the province: "This castle was built in 724 by Lord Ono no Azumabito, the Provincial Governor and General of the Barbarian-Subduing Headquarters. In 762, on the first of the Twelfth Month, it was rebuilt by the Councillor and Military Commander of the Eastern Seaboard, Lord Emi Asakari." The memorial belonged to the era of the sovereign Shōmu. Famous

9. One of the place names with the longest poetic history in the Deep North. The "Mottling Rock" was thought to have been used to imprint cloth with patterns of *Shinobugusa*, literally "longing grass," a typical local product. The plant was associated with wild and uncontrollable longing.

places in poetry have been collected and preserved; but mountains crumble, rivers shift, roads change, rock are buried in dirt; trees age, saplings replace them; times change, generations come and go. But here, without a doubt, was a memorial of a thousand years: I was peering into the heart of the ancients. The virtues of travel, the joys of life, forgetting the weariness of travel, I shed only tears. . . .

It was already close to noon when we borrowed a boat and crossed over to Matsushima. The distance was more than two leagues, and we landed on the shore of Ojima. It has been said many times, but Matsushima is the most beautiful place in all of Japan. First of all, it can hold its head up to Dongting Lake or West Lake. Letting in the sea from the southeast, it fills the bay, three leagues wide, with the tide of Zhejiang.[1] Matsushima has gathered countless islands: the high ones point their fingers to heaven; those lying down crawl over the waves. Some are piled two deep; some, three deep. To the left, the islands are separated from one another; to the right, they are linked. Some seem to be carrying islands on their backs; others, to be embracing them like a person caressing a child. The green of the pine is dark and dense, the branches and leaves bent by the salty sea breeze—as if they were deliberately twisted. A soft, tranquil landscape, like a beautiful lady powdering her face. Did the god of the mountain create this long ago, in the age of the gods? Is this the work of the Creator? What words to describe this?

The rocky shore of Ojima extended out from the coast and became an island protruding into the sea. Here were the remains of Priest Ungo's dwelling and the rock on which he meditated. Again, one could see, scattered widely in the shadow of the pines, people who had turned their backs on the world. They lived quietly in grass huts, the smoke from burning rice ears and pinecones rising from the huts. I didn't know what kind of people they were, but I was drawn to them, and when I approached, the moon was reflected on the sea, and the scenery changed again, different from the afternoon landscape. When we returned to the shore and took lodgings, I opened the window. It was a two-story building, and I felt like a traveler sleeping amid the wind and the clouds: to a strange degree it was a good feeling.

> Matsushima—
> borrow the body of a crane
> cuckoo!![2]

> Sora

I closed my mouth and tried to sleep but couldn't. When I left my old hermitage, Sodō had given me a Chinese poem on Matsushima, and Hara Anteki had sent me a waka on Matsugaurashima. Opening my knapsack, I made those poems my friends for the night. There also were hokku by Sanpū and Jokushi.[3]

* * *

On the twelfth we headed for Hiraizumi. We had heard of such places as the Pine at Anewa and the Thread-Broken Bridge, but there were few human traces, and finding it difficult to recognize the path normally used by the rabbit hunters and woodcutters, we ended up losing our way and came out at a harbor called Ishi no maki.

1. Flattering comparisons to well-known scenic sites in China. The tidal bore in Hangzhou, Zhejiang Province, was already famous in ancient China.
2. Typical summer bird. The gist of the poem is: "Your song is appealing, cuckoo, but the stately white crane is the bird we expect to see at Matsushima [Pine Isles]." Pines and cranes were a conventional pair, both symbols of longevity.
3. Bashō's disciples. "Hokku": the first three lines of a linked-verse sequence, from which haiku evolved.

Across the water we could see Kinkazan the Golden Flower Mountain, where the "Blooming of the Golden Flower"[4] poem had been composed as an offering to the emperor. Several hundred ferry boats gathered in the inlet; human dwellings fought for space on the shore; and the smoke from the ovens rose high. It never occurred to me that I would come across such a prosperous place. We attempted to find a lodging, but no one gave us a place for the night. Finally, we spent the night in an impoverished hovel and, at dawn, wandered off again onto an unknown road. Looking afar at Sode no watari, Obuchi no maki, Mano no kayahara, and other famous places, we made our way over a dike that extended into the distance. We followed the edge of a lonely and narrow marsh, lodged for the night at a place called Toima, and then arrived at Hiraizumi: a distance, I think, of more than twenty leagues.

The glory of three generations of Fujiwara[5] vanished in the space of a dream; the remains of the Great Gate stood two miles in the distance. Hidehira's headquarters had turned into rice paddies and wild fields. Only Kinkeizan, Golden Fowl Hill, remained as it was. First, we climbed Takadachi, Castle-on-the-Heights, from where we could see the Kitakami, a broad river that flowed from the south. The Koromo River rounded Izumi Castle, and at a point beneath Castle-on-the-Heights, it dropped into the broad river. The ancient ruins of Yasuhira[6] and others, lying behind Koromo Barrier, appear to close off the southern entrance and guard against the Ainu barbarians. Selecting his loyal retainers, Yoshitsune fortified himself in the castle, but his glory quickly turned to grass. "The state is destroyed; rivers and hills remain. The city walls turn to spring; grasses and trees are green." With these lines from Du Fu[7] in my head, I lay down my bamboo hat, letting the time and tears flow.

> Summer grasses—
> the traces of dreams
> of ancient warriors
>
> In the deutzia
> Kanefusa[8] appears
> white haired
>
> Sora

4. Ōtomo no Yakamochi, an important poet in the *Man'yōshū*, composed a poem for the emperor when gold was discovered in the area: "For our sovereign's reign, / an auspicious augury: / among the mountains of the Deep North / in the east, / golden flowers have blossomed."

5. In the 12th century, members of a local branch of the powerful Fujiwara family— Kiyohira, Motohira, and Hidehira—had built up a flourishing power base in the north. Hiraizumi was the tragic site of the forced suicide of Minamoto no Yoshitsune, a heroic warrior of the Genpei Wars (1180–85) fought between the Taira/Heike and the Minamoto/ Genji.

6. Son of Fujiwara Hidehira, whose fight with his brother destroyed the clan's prosperity in the region. After killing his brother, Yasuhira was in turn killed by the Minamoto/Genji

chieftain Yoritomo, the founder of the Kamakura shogunate in 1185.

7. Minamoto no Yoshitsune won the crucial battles in the Genpei Wars, chronicled in *The Tales of the Heike*, and gave the Heike/Taira their death blow in 1185. Since his half-brother Yoritomo had become ever more suspicious of him, he sought refuge with the Fujiwara in Hiraizumi. Fujiwara no Yasuhira eventually betrayed him to Yoritomo and Yoshitsune was forced into suicide in 1189. Bashō compares Yoshitsune's tragedy to Du Fu's poem "View in Spring," written in a tragic moment when the Chinese capital was taken by rebels.

8. A loyal retainer of Yoshitsune. Some legends claim that he helped Yoshitsune's wife and children commit suicide and also saw his master to his end, before himself dying. "Deutzia": a white summer flower.

The two halls about which we had heard such wonderful things were open. The Sutra Hall held the statues of the three chieftains, and the Hall of Light contained the coffins of three generations, preserving three sacred images.[9] The seven precious substances were scattered and lost; the doors of jewels, torn by the wind; the pillars of gold, rotted in the snow. The hall should have turned into a mound of empty, abandoned grass, but the four sides were enclosed, covering the roof with shingles, surviving the snow and rain. For a while, it became a memorial to a thousand years.

> Have the summer rains
> come and gone, sparing
> the Hall of Light?

Gazing afar at the road that extended to the south, we stopped at the village of Iwade. We passed Ogurazaki and Mizu no ojima, and from Narugo Hot Springs we proceeded to Passing-Water Barrier and attempted to cross into Dewa Province. Since there were few travelers on this road, we were regarded with suspicion by the barrier guards, and it was only after considerable effort that we were able to cross the barrier. We climbed a large mountain, and since it had already grown dark, we caught sight of a house of a border guard and asked for lodging. For three days, the wind and rain were severe, forcing us to stay in the middle of a boring mountain.

> Fleas, lice—
> a horse passes water
> by my pillow

...

I visited a person named Seifū at Obanazawa. Though wealthy, he had the spirit of a recluse. Having traveled repeatedly to the capital, he understood the tribulations of travel and gave me shelter for a number of days. He eased the pain of the long journey.

> Taking coolness
> for my lodging
> I relax

...

In Yamagata there was a mountain temple, the Ryūshaku-ji,[1] founded by the high priest Jikaku,[1] an especially pure and tranquil place. People had urged us to see this place at least once, so we backtracked from Obanazawa, a distance of about seven leagues. It was still light when we arrived. We borrowed a room at a temple at the mountain foot and climbed to the Buddha hall at the top. Boulders were piled on boulders; the pines and cypress had grown old; the soil and rocks were aged, covered with smooth moss. The doors to the temple buildings at the top were closed, not a sound to be heard. I followed the edge of the cliff, crawling over the boulders, and then prayed at the Buddhist hall. It was a stunning scene wrapped in quiet—I felt my spirit being purified.

9. Of Amida Buddha, the Buddha presiding over the Pure Land Paradise in the West, and his attendants Kannon and Seishi. The coffins contained the mummified remains of Hide-hira, his father, and his grandfather.

1. Better known as Ennin (794–864), a famous Japanese priest who studied in China and helped establish Tendai Buddhism in Japan.

Stillness—
sinking deep into the rocks
cries of the cicada

The Mogami River originates in the Deep North; its upper reaches are in Yamagata. As we descended, we encountered frightening rapids with names like Scattered Go Stones and Flying Eagle. The river skirts the north side of Mount Itajiki and then finally pours into the sea at Sakata. As I descended, passing through the dense foliage, I felt as if the mountains were covering the river on both sides. When filled with rice, these boats are apparently called "rice boats." Through the green leaves, I could see the falling waters of White-Thread Cascade. Sennindō, Hall of the Wizard, stood on the banks, directly facing the water. The river was swollen with rain, making the boat journey perilous.

Gathering the rains
of the wet season—swift
the Mogami River

. . .

Haguroyama, Gassan, and Yudono are called the Three Mountains of Dewa. At Haguroyama, Feather Black Mountain—which belongs to the Tōeizan Temple in Edo, in Musashi Province—the moon of Tendai[2] concentration and contemplation shines, and the lamp of the Buddhist Law of instant enlightenment glows. The temple quarters stand side by side, and the ascetics devote themselves to their calling. The efficacy of the divine mountain, whose prosperity will last forever, fills people with awe and fear.

On the eighth, we climbed Gassan, Moon Mountain. With purification cords around our necks and white cloth wrapped around our heads, we were led up the mountain by a person called a strongman. Surrounded by clouds and mist, we walked over ice and snow and climbed for twenty miles. Wondering if we had passed Cloud Barrier, beyond which the sun and moon move back and forth, I ran out of breath, my body frozen. By the time we reached the top, the sun had set and the moon had come out. We spread bamboo grass on the ground and lay down, waiting for the dawn. When the sun emerged and the clouds cleared away, we descended to Yudono, Bathhouse Mountain.

On the side of the valley were the so-called Blacksmith Huts. Here blacksmiths collect divine water, purify their bodies and minds, forge swords admired by the world, and engrave them with "Moon Mountain." I hear that in China they harden swords in the sacred water at Dragon Spring, and I was reminded of the ancient story of Gan Jiang and Mo Ye, the two Chinese who crafted famous swords.[3] The devotion of these masters to the art was extraordinary. Sitting down on a large rock for a short rest, I saw a cherry tree about three feet high, its buds half open. The tough spirit of the late-blooming cherry tree, buried beneath the accumulated snow, remembering the spring, moved me. It was as if I could smell the "plum blossom in the summer heat," and I remembered the pathos of the poem by Priest Gyōson.[4] Forbidden to speak of the details of this sacred mountain, I put down my brush.

---

2. A Buddhist sect that originated from Tiantai (Japanese Tendai) Mountain in southern China and was established in Japan in the 9th century.
3. Gan Jiang was a Chinese swordsmith who forged two famous swords with his wife, Moye.
4. "Plum blossoms in summer heat" is a Zen phrase for the unusual ability to achieve enlightenment. The plum tree blossoms open in early spring and never last until the summer. The poem by Gyōson (1055–1135), composed when he discovered cherries blooming out of season, reads: "Let us sympathize / with one another, /

When we returned to the temple quarters, at Priest Egaku's behest, we wrote down verses about our pilgrimage to the Three Mountains.

Coolness—
faintly a crescent moon over
Feather Black Mountain

Cloud peaks
crumbling one after another—
Moon Mountain

Forbidden to speak—
wetting my sleeves
at Bathhouse Mountain!

Left Haguro and at the castle town of Tsurugaoka were welcomed by the samurai Nagayama Shigeyuki. Composed a round of haikai. Sakichi accompanied us this far. Boarded a boat and went down to the port of Sakata. Stayed at the house of a doctor named En'an Fugyoku.

From Hot Springs Mountain
to the Bay of Breezes,
the evening cool

Pouring the hot day
into the sea—
Mogami River

Having seen all the beautiful landscapes—rivers, mountains, seas, and coasts— I now prepared my heart for Kisagata. From the port at Sakata moving northeast, we crossed over a mountain, followed the rocky shore, and walked across the sand—all for a distance of ten miles. The sun was on the verge of setting when we arrived. The sea wind blew sand into the air; the rain turned everything to mist, hiding Chōkai Mountain. I groped in the darkness. Having heard that the landscape was exceptional in the rain,[5] I decided that it must also be worth seeing after the rain, too, and squeezed into a fisherman's thatched hut to wait for the rain to pass.

By the next morning the skies had cleared, and with the morning sun shining brightly, we took a boat to Kisagata. Our first stop was Nōin Island, where we visited the place where Nōin had secluded himself for three years. We docked our boat on the far shore and visited the old cherry tree on which Saigyō had written the poem about "a fisherman's boat rowing over the flowers."[6] On the shore of the river was an imperial mausoleum, the gravestone of Empress Jingū.[7] The temple was called Kanmanju Temple. I wondered why I had yet to hear of an imperial procession to this place.

---

cherry tree on the mountain: / were it not for your blossoms, / I would have no friend at all."
5. Bashō compares Kisakata to the famous West Lake in China, of which the Chinese poet Su Shi (or Su Dongpo, 1037–1101) wrote: "The sparkling, brimming waters are beautiful in sunshine; / The view when a misty rain veils the mountains is exceptional too."
6. From a poem attributed to Saigyō: "The cherry trees at Kisakata are buried in waves—a fisherman's boat rowing over the flowers."
7. Legendary empress said to have ruled in the second half of the 4th century.

We sat down in the front room of the temple and raised the blinds, taking in the entire landscape at one glance. To the south, Chōkai Mountain held up the heavens, its shadow reflected on the bay of Kisagata; to the west, the road came to an end at Muyamuya Barrier; and to the east, there was a dike. The road to Akita stretched into the distance. To the north was the sea, the waves pounding into the bay at Shiogoshi, Tide-Crossing. The face of the bay, about two and a half miles in width and length, resembled Matsushima but with a different mood. If Matsushima was like someone laughing, Kisagata resembled a resentful person filled with sorrow and loneliness. The land was as if in a state of anguish.

> Kisagata—
> Xi Shi[8] asleep in the rain
> flowers of the silk tree

> In the shallows—
> cranes wetting their legs
> coolness of the sea

> . . .

Reluctant to leave Sakata, the days piled up; now I turn my gaze to the far-off clouds of the northern provinces. Thoughts of the distant road ahead fill me with anxiety; I hear it is more than 325 miles to the castle town in Kaga. After we crossed Nezu-no-seki, Mouse Barrier, we hurried toward Echigo and came to Ichiburi, in Etchū Province. Over these nine days, I suffered from the extreme heat, fell ill, and did not record anything.

> The Seventh Month—
> the sixth day, too, is different
> from the usual night[9]

> A wild sea—
> stretching to Sado Isle
> the River of Heaven

Today, exhausted from crossing the most dangerous places in the north country—places with names like Children Forget Parents, Parents Forget Children, Dogs Turn Back, Horses Sent Back—I drew up my pillow and lay down to sleep, only to hear in the adjoining room the voices of two young women. An elderly man joined in the conversation, and I gathered that they were women of pleasure from a place called Niigata in Echigo Province. They were on a pilgrimage to Ise Shrine, and the man was seeing them off as far as the barrier here at Ichiburi. They seemed to be writing letters and giving him other trivial messages to take back to Niigata tomorrow. Like "the daughters of the fishermen, passing their lives on the shore where the white waves roll in,"[1] they had fallen low in this

8. A legendary beauty of early China, whose charms were used to bring down an enemy state. Xi Shi was known for a constant frown, which enhanced her beauty.

9. Because people were preparing for the Tanabata Festival, which was held on the 7th day of the 7th month in honor of the stars Altair (the herd boy) and Vega (the weaver maiden). Leg-

end held that the two lovers were separated by the Milky Way, except for this one night, when they would meet for their annual rendezvous.

1. From an anonymous poem: "Since I am the daughter of a fisherman, passing my life on the shore where the white waves roll in, I have no home."

world, exchanging vows with every passerby. What terrible lives they must have had in their previous existence for this to occur. I fell asleep as I listened to them talk. The next morning, they came up to us as we departed. "The difficulties of road, not knowing our destination, the uncertainty and sorrow—it makes us want to follow your tracks. We'll be inconspicuous. Please bless us with your robes of compassion, link us to the Buddha," they said tearfully.

"We sympathize with you, but we have many stops on the way. Just follow the others. The gods will make sure that no harm occurs to you." Shaking them off with these remarks, we left, but the pathos of their situation lingered with us.

> Under the same roof
> women of pleasure also sleep—
> bush clover and moon[2]

I dictated this to Sora, who wrote it down. . . .

We visited Tada Shrine where Sanemori's helmet and a piece of his bro- cade robe were stored. They say that long ago when Sanemori belonged to the Genji clan, Lord Yoshitomo offered him the helmet. Indeed, it was not the armor of a common soldier. A chrysanthemum and vine carved design inlaid with gold extended from the visor to the ear flaps, and a two-horn frontpiece was attached to the dragon head. After Sanemori died in battle, Kiso Yoshinaka attached a prayer sheet to the helmet and offered it to the shrine. Higuchi Jirō acted as Kiso's messenger. It was as if the past were appearing before my very eyes.

> "How pitiful!"
> beneath the warrior helmet
> cries of a cricket[3]
> . . .

The sixteenth. The skies had cleared, and we decided to gather little red shells at Iro-no-hama, Color Beach, seven leagues across the water. A man named Ten'ya made elaborate preparations—lunch boxes, wine flasks, and the like—and ordered a number of servants to go with us on the boat. Enjoying a tailwind, we arrived quickly. The beach was dotted with a few fisherman's huts and a dilapidated Lotus Flower temple. We drank tea, warmed up saké, and were overwhelmed by the loneliness of the evening.

> Loneliness—
> an autumn beach judged
> superior to Suma's[4]

2. Bashō shows surprise that two very different parties—the young prostitutes and the male priest-travelers—have something in common. The bush clover, the object of love in classical poetry, suggests the prostitutes, while the moon, associated with enlightenment and clar- ity, implies Bashō and his priest friend.
3. An allusion to a scene from *The Tales of the Heike*, in which the warrior Sanemori, who did not want other soldiers to realize his advanced age, dyed his white hair black and fought valiantly to death, slain by retainers of Yoshinaka. A Noh play connects the washing and identification of Sanemori's head, which occurred at the place Bashō is visiting here, to the cry of a cricket, a poetic image of autumn, decline, and loneliness.
4. A coastal town well known for people who spent their time in exile, such as the poet Ari- wara no Yukihira (ca. 893) and Genji, the pro- tagonist of *The Tale of Genji*.

> Between the waves—
> mixed with small shells
> petals of bush clover

I had Tōsai write down the main events of that day and left it at the temple.

Rotsū came as far as the Tsuruga harbor to greet me, and together we went to Mino Province. With the aid of horses, we traveled to Ōgaki. Sora joined us from Ise. Etsujin galloped in on horseback, and we gathered at the house of Jokō. Zensenshi, Keiko, Keiko's sons, and other intimate acquaintances visited day and night. For them, it was like meeting someone who had returned from the dead. They were both overjoyed and sympathetic. Although I had not yet recovered from the weariness of the journey, we set off again on the sixth of the Ninth Month. Thinking to pay our respects to the great shrine at Ise, we boarded a boat.

> Autumn going—
> parting for Futami
> a clam pried from its shell

CHIKAMATSU MONZAEMON
1653–1725

The early eighteenth century in Japan was perhaps the only period in the history of theater when puppets performing for adult audiences were more popular than real-life actors. Although puppetry exists in many cultures and often has a long history as a folk art, in Japan it became a major literary form with acclaimed playwrights and sophisticated puppeteers. No playwright in this tradition was more popular or influential than Chikamatsu Monzaemon, and his play *The Love Suicides at Amijima* (1721) is considered one of his greatest masterpieces.

THE RISE OF PUPPET
THEATER IN JAPAN

Beginning with the Heian Period (794–1185) puppeteer troupes roamed the capital and the provinces in search for audiences, competing with other low-class entertainers who thrived on the fringes of the aristocratic culture at the court in Kyoto. But puppet theater entered a new stage as a literary art form in 1684, when Takemoto Gidayū, a famous chanter, founded his own puppet theater in Osaka. Gidayū was an acclaimed performer of *jōruri*, popular narrative chanting that took its name from the heroine of a well-known tale and that was accompanied by a banjo-like instrument called a *shamisen* ("three flavor strings"). The shamisen had recently been imported from Okinawa, then an independent kingdom south of Japan, and had become a popular instrument in the demimonde of the pleasure quarters. Gidayū convinced Chikamatsu to collaborate with him. Gidayū's invitation was fortunate: Chikamatsu would become the most brilliant playwright in the history of puppet theater.

Puppet theater thrived in the early modern milieu of the Tokugawa shogunate (1600–1868), the military regime of the Tokugawa family that ruled from Edo, modern-day Tokyo. Also called the "Edo Period," this era saw an unprecedented growth of commercial culture. Urbanization accelerated, book printing caught on and fostered various genres of popular literature, while also enabling the spread of education and the flourishing of Confucianism and scholarship. Licensed pleasure quarters thrived, attracting customers of all social classes. Yet Tokugawa society was based on a strict status order. Under the symbolic authority of the emperor, who resided in Kyoto, and the Tokugawa shoguns, the de facto power holders in Edo, there were four social classes: samurai (warriors), peasants, artisans, and merchants. Actors and entertainers were considered outcasts, together with prostitutes and beggars. Marriage outside one's class was forbidden, although in practice the boundaries were more fluid. Medieval Noh theater often borrowed themes and language from classical literature and addressed the higher rungs of Edo society, mostly samurai and rich merchants; it was sponsored by the shoguns as official state theater. In contrast to the high-class Noh theater, the new popular theater of the Edo Period—Kabuki and puppet theater—attracted commoners by staging current events and addressing concerns of contemporary society.

THE ELEMENTS OF PUPPET THEATER

Puppet theater performances include three elements: puppets, shamisen music, and jōruri chanting. The puppets are up to three-quarters of life-size. At first they were handled by one person, but they quickly became more complex creatures requiring the manipulation of three men, a head puppeteer in charge of the head and right hand, and two assistants responsible in turn for the left hand and the feet. Unlike puppetry that uses strings or other devices to make the puppeteers invisible to the audience, Japanese puppeteers are in full view on stage, dressed in black. The assistants' heads are covered with black hoods, while the calm face of the main puppeteer is visible above the heads of the puppet. During the eighteenth century, the puppets became ever more sophisticated, as the genre competed with other forms of popular theater such as Kabuki, an opulent popular genre of dance-drama with live actors. Crucial technical inventions that enhanced the puppets' appeal were the introduction of movable eyelids and mouths, and prehensile hands that could now wield swords, tissue paper, and other props.

During performance, the shamisen player and the chanter sit on an auxiliary stage protruding into the theater at stage left. Although the puppeteers, the shamisen player, and the chanter usually do not make eye contact, their performance is carefully synchronized and the percussive strumming of the shamisen helps pace the narrative and timing of the action. The central star of puppet theater is the chanter. He intones the entire text of the play, taking in turn the roles of all puppet protagonists and of the narrator. At times he must switch among the voices of a timid child, a swashbuckling warrior, and an enamored lady within a few sentences. A master chanter uttering the last dramatic words of a famed young beauty in utmost despair before taking her life can make an audience forget that he is an old man who is turning the script's pages with his coarse and wrinkled hands.

Although in its heyday puppet theater had raging success and reached a broad spectrum of early modern Japanese society, it has long since been eclipsed by other forms of mass entertainment. Today the Japanese government sponsors puppet theater as a traditional art form

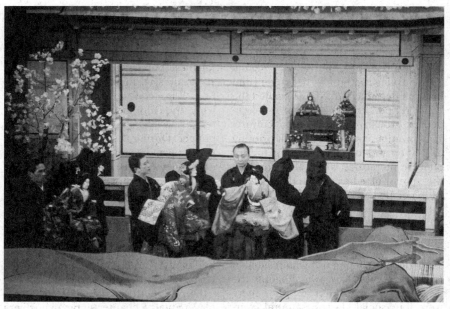

A contemporary puppet-theater performance in Osaka.

that is struggling in the modern world. But its reputation has spread beyond Japan, and it dazzles even those first-time spectators outside Japan who consider themselves immune to the perplexing power of puppets to evoke the deepest human feelings.

THE LOVE SUICIDES AT AMIJIMA

Chikamatsu was born into a provincial samurai family. He served in the households of the imperial aristocracy in Kyoto before moving to Osaka, a bustling commercial hub at the time. He produced his first plays in the 1680s. Although after 1693 he devoted most of his energies to kabuki, in 1703 he reconnected with Gidayū and wrote exclusively for Gidayū's puppet theater during the last two decades of his life.

Chikamatsu wrote about one hundred puppet plays. His earlier plays were mostly historical dramas common at the time, but this subject changed in 1703, when he pioneered a new subgenre: the "contemporary-life play." In that year a shopkeeper from Osaka had committed double suicide with a prostitute from the Sonezaki pleasure quarters, because at the time people believed that they could be reborn with their lover "on the same lotus" in the Buddhist Pure Land if they committed suicide together. Three weeks after the event, Chikamatsu's The Love Suicides at Sonezaki premiered with roaring success. It was the first time that such a scandalous contemporary event was depicted on the puppet theater stage. Chikamatsu would write twenty-four contemporary-life plays inspired by contemporary incidents during his lifetime.

The Love Suicides at Amijima, Chikamatsu's masterwork, was first performed in Osaka in 1721, and quickly adapted for the Kabuki stage, as happened often with successful plays. In the play the Osaka paper merchant Jihei, with a wife and children, falls desperately in love with Koharu, a prostitute under contract at a Sonezaki establishment. This situation upsets a complicated network of social relationships and obligations between husband and wife, parent and child, and even among prostitute, madam, and customer. Koharu, a prostitute far below Jihei's social status, refuses other customers, Jihei squanders the sparse resources of his shop, his father-in-law demands a divorce, his brother tries to save him, while his wife develops an admirable bond of loyalty with Koharu. The clashes between social obligations and the desire for personal happiness are irreconcilable. Unlike in other "love suicide" plays, where suicide is the unforeseen final outcome, in *The Love Suicides at Amijima* suicide is on the horizon from the beginning and nobody can in the end avert the tragic end of the lovers, however hard they try. Despite the dark subject matter, the play glistens with moments of social comedy.

The play became so successful that the authorities intervened. While Noh theater was patronized by the shoguns and the warrior elite, popular theater was seen by the elite classes as potentially subversive and incendiary and was often subject to censorship. Some of the prohibitions concerned the actors; for example, women and young boys were banned from the stage in 1629 and 1652, respectively, because of the seductive appeal they had for adult male audiences. Other prohibitions concerned the plays' subject matter: a year after *The Love Suicides at Amijima* premiered, the government prohibited plays on "love suicide" since they seemed to inspire waves of real-live suicides of lovers whose social class and life circumstances forbade their union. Prohibitions fostered inventiveness, and playwrights started to disguise their staging of current events by setting the action in the distant past. Yet, since everybody in the audience knew what lay behind the historical veil, these plays remained contemporary-life plays of sorts and thus sustained the immense popularity of puppet theater.

From The Love Suicides at Amijima[1]

CHARACTERS

JIHEI, *a paper merchant, age twenty-eight*
MAGOEMON, *a flour merchant, Jihei's brother*
GOZAEMON, *Jihei's father-in-law*
TAHEI, *Jihei's rival for Koharu*
DEMBEI, *Proprietor of the Yamato House*
SANGORŌ, *Jihei's servant*

KANTARŌ, *Jihei's son, age six*
OSUE, *Jihei's daughter, age four*
KOHARU, *a courtesan belonging to the Kinokuni House in Sonezaki, a pleasure quarter in the northern part of Ōsaka*
OSAN, *Jihei's wife*
OSAN'S MOTHER (*also Jihei's aunt*), *age fifty-six*

1. Translated by Donald Keene. A rarely performed opening scene, omitted here, shows Koharu making her way to the teahouse in Sonezaki to meet a samurai customer (the disguised Magoemon, Jihei's brother). The audience learns that Koharu is in love with Jihei, while Tahei, a man she dislikes, is trying to buy out her contract. When Koharu sees Tahei in the street, she escapes.

ACT I

* * *

SCENE: *The Kawachi House, a Sonezaki teahouse.*

NARRATOR Koharu slips away, under cover of the crowd, and hurries into the Kawachi House.

PROPRIETRESS Well, well, I hadn't expected you so soon.—It's been ages even since I've heard your name mentioned. What a rare visitor you are, Koharu! And what a long time it's been!

NARRATOR The proprietress greets Koharu cheerfully.

KOHARU Oh—you can be heard as far as the gate. Please don't call me Koharu in such a loud voice. That horrible Ri Tōten[2] is out there. I beg you, keep your voice down.

NARRATOR Were her words overheard? In bursts a party of three men.

TAHEI I must thank you first of all, dear Koharu, for bestowing a new name on me, Ri Tōten. I never was called *that* before. Well, friends, this is the Koharu I've confided to you about—the good-hearted, good-natured, good-in-bed Koharu. Step up and meet the whore who's started all the rivalry! Will I soon be the lucky man and get Koharu for my wife? Or will Kamiya Jihei ransom her?

NARRATOR He swaggers up.

KOHARU I don't want to hear another word. If you think it's such an achievement to start unfounded rumors about someone you don't even know, throw yourself into it, say what you please. But I don't want to hear.

NARRATOR She steps away suddenly, but he sidles up again.

TAHEI You may not want to hear me, but the clink of my gold coins will make you listen! What a lucky girl you are! Just think—of all the many men in Temma and the rest of Osaka, you chose Jihei the paper dealer, the father of two children, with his cousin for his wife and his uncle for his father-in-law! A man whose business is so tight he's at his wits' ends every sixty days merely to pay the wholesalers' bills! Do you think he'll be able to fork over nearly ten *kamme* to ransom you? That reminds me of the mantis who picked a fight with an oncoming vehicle![3] But look at me—I haven't a wife, a father-in-law, a father, or even an uncle, for that matter. Tahei the Lone Wolf—that's the name I'm known by. I admit that I'm no match for Jihei when it comes to bragging about myself in the Quarter, but when it comes to money, I'm an easy winner. If I pushed with all the strength of my money, who knows what I might conquer?—How about it, men?—Your customer tonight, I'm sure, is none other than Jihei, but I'm taking over. The Lone Wolf's taking over. Hostess! Bring on the saké! On with the saké!

PROPRIETRESS What are you saying? Her customer tonight is a samurai, and he'll be here any moment. Please amuse yourself elsewhere.

NARRATOR But Tahei's look is playful.

TAHEI A customer's a customer, whether he's a samurai or a townsman. The only difference is that one wears swords and the other doesn't. But even if this samurai wears his swords he won't have five or six—there'll only be two,

---

2. Villain in another puppet play.
3. Allusion to an ancient Chinese text, where it is an image for someone who does not know his own limitations. "*Kamme*": one *kamme* corresponded to 3.75 kilograms (or 8.3 pounds) of silver. The price is extremely high.

the broadsword and dirk. I'll take care of the samurai and borrow Koharu afterwards. (*To* KOHARU.) You may try to avoid me all you please, but some special connection from a former life must have brought us together. I owe everything to that ballad-singing priest—what a wonderful thing the power of prayer is! I think I'll recite a prayer of my own. Here, this ashtray will be my bell, and my pipe the hammer. This is fun.

Chan Chan Cha Chan Chan.
Ei Ei Ei Ei Ei.
Jihei the paper dealer—
Too much love for Koharu
Has made him a foolscap,
He wastepapers sheets of gold
Till his fortune's shredded to confetti
And Jihei himself is like scrap paper
You can't even blow your nose on!
Hail, Hail Amida Buddha!
Namaida Namaida Namaida.

NARRATOR   As he prances wildly, roaring his song, a man appears at the gate, so anxious not to be recognized that he wears, even at night, a wicker hat.[4]

TAHEI   Well, Toilet paper's showed up! That's quite a disguise! Why don't you come in, Toilet paper? If my prayer's frightened you, say a Hail Amida![5] Here, I'll take off your hat!

NARRATOR   He drags the man in and examines him: it is the genuine article, a two-sworded samurai, somber in dress and expression, who glares at Tahei through his woven hat, his eyeballs round as gongs. Tahei, unable to utter either a Hail or an Amida, gasps "Haaa!" in dismay, but his face is unflinching.

TAHEI   Koharu, I'm a townsman. I've never worn a sword, but I've lots of New Silver[6] at my place, and I think that the glint could twist a mere couple of swords out of joint. Imagine that wretch from the toilet paper shop, with a capital as thin as tissue, trying to compete with the Lone Wolf! That's the height of impertinence! I'll wander down now from Sakura Bridge to Middle Street, and if I meet that Wastepaper along the way, I'll trample him under foot. Come on, men.

NARRATOR   Their gestures, at least, have a cavalier assurance as they swagger off, taking up the whole street.

The samurai customer patiently endures the fool, indifferent to his remarks because of the surroundings, but every word of gossip about Jihei, whether for good or ill, affects Koharu. She is so depressed that she stands there blankly, unable even to greet her guest. Sugi, the maid from the Kinokuni House, runs up from home, looking annoyed.

SUGI   When I left you here a while ago, Miss Koharu, your guest hadn't appeared yet, and they gave me a terrible scolding when I got back for not having checked on him. I'm very sorry, sir, but please excuse me a minute.

NARRATOR   She lifts the woven hat and examines the face.

---

4. Customers visiting the pleasure quarter by day usually wore deep wicker hats, concealing their faces, in order to preserve the secrecy of their visits; this customer wears the hat even at night.

5. A word play on *ami*, part of the name of *Amida* Buddha (the "Buddha of Infinite Light" promising rebirth in the Western Paradise of the Pure Land) and *ami*gasa, meaning "woven hat."

6. Good-quality coinage common around 1720.

SUGI   Oh—it's not him! There's nothing to worry about, Koharu. Ask your guest to keep you for the whole night, and show him how sweet you can be. Give him a barrelful of nectar![7] Good-by, madam, I'll see you later, honey.

NARRATOR   She takes her leave with a cloying stream of puns. The extremely hard-baked[8] samurai is furious.

SAMURAI   What's the meaning of this? You'd think from the way she appraised my face that I was a tea canister or a porcelain cup! I didn't come here to be trifled with. It's difficult enough for me to leave the Residence even by day, and in order to spend the night away I had to ask the senior officer's permission and sign the register. You can see how complicated the regulations make things. But I'm in love, miss, just from hearing about you, and I wanted very badly to spend a night with you. I came here a while ago without an escort and made the arrangements with the teahouse. I had been looking forward to your kind reception, a memory to last me a lifetime, but you haven't so much as smiled at me or said a word of greeting. You keep your head down, as if you were counting money in your lap. Aren't you afraid of getting a stiff neck? Madam—I've never heard the like. Here I come to a teahouse, and I must play the part of night nurse in a maternity room!

PROPRIETRESS   You're quite right, sir. Your surprise is entirely justified, considering that you don't know the reasons. This girl is deeply in love with a customer named Kamiji. It's been Kamiji today and Kamiji tomorrow, with nobody else allowed a chance at her. Her other customers have scattered in every direction, like leaves in a storm. When two people get so carried away with each other, it often leads to trouble, for both the customer and the girl. In the first place, it inteferes with business, and the owner, whoever he may be, is bound to prevent it. That's why all her guests are examined. Koharu is naturally depressed—it's only to be expected. You are annoyed, which is equally to be expected. But, speaking as the proprietress here, it seems to me that the essential thing is for you to meet each other halfway and cheer up. Come, have a drink.—Act a little more lively, Koharu.

NARRATOR   Koharu, without answering, lifts her tear-stained face.

KOHARU   Tell me, samurai, they say that, if you're going to kill yourself anyway, people who die during the Ten Nights[9] are sure to become Buddhas. Is that really true?

SAMURAI   How should I know? Ask the priest at your family temple.

KOHARU   Yes, that's right. But there's something I'd like to ask a samurai. If you're committing suicide, it'd be a lot more painful, wouldn't it, to cut your throat rather than hang yourself?

SAMURAI   I've never tried cutting my throat to see whether or not it hurt. Please ask more sensible questions.—What an unpleasant girl!

NARRATOR   Samurai though he is, he looks nonplussed.

PROPRIETRESS   Koharu, that's a shocking way to treat a guest the first time you meet him. I'll go and get my husband. We'll have some saké together. That ought to liven things a bit.

---

7. The translator has changed the imagery from puns on saltiness in the original (soy sauce, green vegetables, etc.) to puns on sweetness.
8. Technical term from pottery making, meaning "hard-fired."

9. A period in the Tenth Month when special Buddhist services were conducted in temples of the Pure Land sect. It was believed that people who died during this period immediately became Buddhas.

NARRATOR The gate she leaves is illumined by the evening moon low in the sky; the clouds and the passers in the street have thinned.

For long years there has lived in Temma, the seat of the mighty god, though not a god himself, Kamiji, a name often bruited by the gongs of worldly gossip, so deeply, hopelessly, is he tied to Koharu by the ropes[1] of an ill-starred love. Now is the tenth moon, the month when no gods will unite them;[2] they are thwarted in their love, unable to meet. They swore in the last letters they exchanged that if only they could meet, that day would be their last. Night after night Jihei, ready for death, trudges to the Quarter, distractedly, as though his soul had left a body consumed by the fires of love.

At a roadside eating stand he hears people gossiping about Koharu. "She's at Kawashō with a samurai customer," someone says, and immediately Jihei decides, "It will be tonight!"

He peers through the latticework window and sees a guest in the inside room, his face obscured by a hood. Only the moving chin is visible, and Jihei cannot hear what is said.

JIHEI Poor Koharu! How thin her face is! She keeps it averted from the lamp. In her heart she's thinking only of me. I'll signal her that I'm here, and we'll run off together. Then which will it be—Umeda or Kitano?[3] Oh—I want to tell her I'm here. I want to call her.

NARRATOR He beckons with his heart, his spirit flies to her, but his body, like a cicada's cast-off shell, clings to the latticework. He weeps with impatience.

The guest in the inside room gives a great yawn.

SAMURAI What a bore, playing nursemaid to a prostitute with worries on her mind!—The street seems quiet now. Let's go to the end room. We can at least distract ourselves by looking at the lanterns. Come with me.

NARRATOR They go together to the outer room. Jihei, alarmed, squeezes into the patch of shadow under the lattice window. Inside they do not realize that anyone cavesdrops.

SAMURAI I've been noticing your behavior and the little things you've said this evening. It's plain to me that you intend a love suicide with Kamiji, or whatever his name is—the man the hostess mentioned. I'm sure I'm right. I realize that no amount of advice or reasoning is likely to penetrate the ears of somebody bewitched by the god of death, but I must say that you're exceedingly foolish. The boy's family won't blame him for his recklessness, but they will blame and hate you. You'll be shamed by the public exposure of your body. Your parents may be dead, for all I know, but if they're alive, you'll be punished in hell as a wicked daughter. Do you suppose that you'll become a Buddha? You and your lover won't even be able to fall smoothly into hell together! What a pity—and what a tragedy! This is only our first meeting but, as a samurai, I can't let you die without trying to save you. No doubt money's the problem. I'd like to help, if five or ten ryō would be of service. I swear by the god Hachiman and by my good fortune as a samurai that I will never reveal to anyone what you tell me. Open your heart without fear.

---

1. The sacred ropes at a Shintō shrine. "Temma . . . god": one of the main districts of Ōsaka, Temma was the site of the Tenjin Shrine, dedicated to the deified poet-official Sugawara no Michizane (845–903). "Kamiji": the word *kami*, for "paper," sounds like *kami*, "god."

2. The Tenth Month was when the gods were believed to gather at Izumo, an ancient province on Japan's southwestern shore; they thus were absent from the rest of Japan.
3. Both places had well-known cemeteries.

NARRATOR   He whispers these words. She joins her hands and bows.

KOHARU   I'm extremely grateful. Thank you for your kind words and for swear-ing an oath to me, someone you've never had for a lover or even a friend. I'm so grateful that I'm crying.—Yes, it's as they say, when you've something on your mind it shows on your face. You were right. I have promised Kamiji to die with him. But we've been completely prevented from meeting by my master, and Jihei, for various reasons, can't ransom me at once. My con-tracts with my former master[4] and my present one still have five years to run. If somebody else claimed me during that time, it would be a blow to me, of course, but a worse disgrace to Jihei's honor. He suggested that it would be better if we killed ourselves, and I agreed. I was caught by obliga-tions from which I could not withdraw, and I promised him before I knew what I was doing. I said, "We'll watch for a chance, and I'll slip out when you give the signal." "Yes," he said, "slip out somehow." Ever since then I've been leading a life of uncertainty, never knowing from one day to the next when my last hour will come.

I have a mother living in a back alley south of here. She has no one but me to depend on, and she does piecework to eke out a living. I keep thinking that after I'm dead she'll become a beggar or an outcast, and maybe she'll die of starvation. That's the only sad part about dying. I have just this one life. I'm ashamed that you may think me a coldhearted woman, but I must endure the shame. The most important thing is that I don't want to die. I beg you, please help me to stay alive.

NARRATOR   As she speaks the samurai nods thoughtfully. Jihei, crouching outside, hears her words with astonishment; they are so unexpected to his manly heart that he feels like a monkey who has tumbled from a tree. He is frantic with agitation.

JIHEI (*to himself*)   Then was everything a lie? Ahhh—I'm furious! For two whole years I've been bewitched by that rotten she-fox! Shall I break in and kill her with one blow of my sword? Or shall I satisfy my anger by shaming her to her face?

NARRATOR   He gnashes his teeth and weeps in chagrin. Inside the house Koharu speaks through her tears.

KOHARU   It's a curious thing to ask, but would you please show the kindness of a samurai and become my customer for the rest of this year and into next spring? Whenever Jihei comes, intent on death, please interfere and force him to postpone and postpone his plan. In this way our relations can be broken quite naturally. He won't have to kill himself, and my life will also be saved.—What evil connection from a former existence made us promise to die? How I regret it now!

NARRATOR   She weeps, leaning on the samurai's knee.

SAMURAI   Very well, I'll do as you ask. I think I can help you.—But there's a draft blowing. Somebody may be watching.

NARRATOR   He slams shut the latticework *shōji*. Jihei, listening outside, is in a frenzy.

JIHEI   Exactly what you'd expect from a whore, a cheap whore! I misjudged her foul nature. She robbed the soul from my body, the thieving harlot! Shall I slash her down or run her through? What am I to do?

---

4. The master at the bathhouse where Koharu worked before.

NARRATOR The shadows of two profiles fall on the *shōji*.

JIHEI I'd like to give her a taste of my fist and trample her.—What are they chattering about? See how they nod to each other! Now she's bowing to him, whispering and sniveling. I've tried to control myself—I've pressed my chest, I've stroked it—but I can't stand any more. This is too much to endure!

NARRATOR His heart pounds wildly as he unsheathes his dirk, a Magoroku of Seki. "Koharu's side must be here," he judges, and stabs through an opening in the latticework. But Koharu is too far away for his thrust, and though she cries out in terror, she remains unharmed. Her guest instantly leaps at Jihei, grabs his hands, and jerks them through the latticework. With his sword knot he quickly and securely fastens Jihei's hands to the window upright.

SAMURAI Don't make any outcry, Koharu. You are not to look at him.

NARRATOR At this moment the proprietor and his wife return. They exclaim in alarm.

SAMURAI This needn't concern you. Some ruffian ran his sword through the *shōji*, and I've tied his arms to the latticework. I have my own way of dealing with him. Don't untie the cord. If you attract a crowd, the place is sure to be thrown in an uproar. Let's all go inside. Come with me, Koharu. We'll go to bed.

NARRATOR Koharu answers, "Yes," but she recognizes the handle of the dirk, and the memory—if not the blade—transfixes her breast.

KOHARU There're always people doing crazy things in the Quarter when they've had too much to drink. Why don't you let him go without making any trouble? I think that's best, don't you, Kawashō?

SAMURAI Out of the question. Do as I say—inside, all of you. Koharu, come along.

NARRATOR Jihei can still see their shadows even after they enter the inner room, but he is bound to the spot, his hands held in fetters which grip him the tighter as he struggles, his body beset by suffering as he tastes a living shame worse than a dog's.[5] More determined than ever to die, he sheds tears of blood, a pitiful sight.

Tahei the Lone Wolf returns from his carousing.

TAHEI That's Jihei standing by Kawashō's window. I'll give him a tossing.

NARRATOR He catches Jihei by the collar and starts to lift him over his back.

JIHEI Owww!

TAHEI Owww? What kind of weakling are you? Oh, I see—you're tied here. You must've been pulling off a robbery. You dirty pickpocket! You rotten pickpocket!

NARRATOR He drubs Jihei mercilessly.

TAHEI You burglar! You convict!

NARRATOR He kicks him wildly.

TAHEI Kamiya Jihei's been caught burgling, and they've tied him up!

NARRATOR Passersby and people of the neighborhood, attracted by his shouts, quickly gather. The samurai rushes from the house.

SAMURAI Who's calling him a burglar? You? Tell what Jihei's stolen! Out with it!

NARRATOR He seizes Tahei and forces him into the dirt. Tahei rises to his feet only for the samurai to kick him down again and again. He grips Tahei.

---

5. Allusion to a proverb of Buddhist origin: "Suffering follows one like a dog."

SAMURAI   Jihei! Trample him to your heart's content!

NARRATOR   He pushes Tahei under Jihei's feet. Bound though he is, Jihei stamps furiously over Tahei's face. Tahei, thoroughly trampled and covered with mire, gets to his feet and glares around him.

TAHEI (*to bystander*)   How could you fools stand there calmly and let him step on me? I've memorized every one of your faces, and I intend to pay you back. Remember that!

NARRATOR   He makes his escape, still determined to have the last word. The spectators burst out laughing.

VOICES   Listen to him brag, even after he's been trampled on! Let's throw him from the bridge and give him a drink of water! Don't let him get away!

NARRATOR   They chase after him. When the crowd has dispersed, the samurai approaches Jihei and unfastens the knots. He shows his face with his hood removed.

JIHEI   Magoemon! My brother! How shaming!

NARRATOR   He sinks to the ground and weeps, prostrating himself in the dirt.

KOHARU   Are you his brother, sir?

NARRATOR   Koharu runs to them. Jihei, catching her by the front of the kimono, forces her to the ground.

JIHEI   Beast! She-fox! I'd sooner trample on you than on Tahei!

NARRATOR   He raises his foot, but Magoemon calls out.

MAGOEMON   That's the kind of foolishness responsible for all your trouble. A prostitute's business is to deceive men. Have you just now waked up to that? I've seen to the bottom of her heart the very first time I met her, but you're so scatter-brained that in over two years of intimacy with the woman you never discovered what she was thinking. Instead of stamping on Koharu, why don't you use your feet on your own misguided disposition?—It's deplorable. You're my younger brother, but you're almost thirty, and you've got a six-year-old boy and a four-year-old girl, Kantarō and Osue. You run a shop with a thirty-six-foot frontage,[6] but you don't seem to realize that your whole fortune's collapsing. You shouldn't have to be lectured to by your brother. Your father-in-law is your aunt's husband, and your mother-in-law is your aunt. They've always been like real parents to you. Your wife Osan is my cousin too. The ties of marriage are multiplied by those of blood. But when the family has a reunion the only subject of discussion is our mortification over your incessant visits to Sonezaki. I feel sorry for our poor aunt. You know what a stiff-necked gentleman of the old school her husband Gozaemon is. He's forever flying into a rage and saying, "We've been tricked by your nephew. He's deserted our daughter. I'll take Osan back and ruin Jihei's reputation throughout Temma." Our aunt, with all the heartache to bear herself, sometimes sides with him and sometimes with you. She's worried herself sick. What an ingrate, not to appreciate how she's defended you in your shame! This one offense is enough to make you the target for Heaven's future punishment!

I realized that your marriage couldn't last much longer at this rate. I decided, in the hopes of relieving our aunt's worries, that I'd see with my own eyes what kind of woman Koharu was, and work out some sort of solu-

---

6. A large shop.

tion afterwards. I consulted the proprietor here, then came myself to investigate the cause of your sickness. I see now how natural it was that you should desert your wife and children. What a faithful prostitute you discovered! I congratulate you!

And here I am, Magoemon the Miller,[7] known far and wide for my paragon of a brother, dressed up like a masquerader at a festival or maybe a lunatic! I put on swords for the first time in my life, and announced myself, like a bit player in a costume piece, as an officer at a residence. I feel like an absolute idiot with these swords, but there's nowhere I can dispose of them now.—It's so infuriating—and ridiculous—that it's given me a pain in the chest.

NARRATOR   He gnashes his teeth and grimaces, attempting to hide his tears. Koharu, choking the while with emotion, can only say:

KOHARU   Yes, you're entirely right.

NARRATOR   The rest is lost in tears. Jihei pounds the earth with his fist.

JIHEI   I was wrong. Forgive me, Magoemon. For three years I've been possessed by that witch. I've neglected my parents, relatives—even my wife and children—and wrecked my fortune, all because I was deceived by Koharu, that sneak thief! I'm utterly mortified. But I'm through with her now, and I'll never set foot here again. Weasel! Vixen! Sneak thief! Here's proof that I've broken with her!

NARRATOR   He pulls out the amulet bag which has rested next to his skin.

JIHEI   Here are the written oaths we've exchanged, one at the beginning of each month, twenty-nine in all. I return them. This means our love and affection are over. Take them.

NARRATOR   He flings the notes at her.

JIHEI   Magoemon, collect from her my pledges. Please make sure you get them all. Then burn them with your own hands. (*To* KOHARU.) Hand them to my brother.

KOHARU   As you wish.

NARRATOR   In tears, she surrenders the amulet bag. Magoemon opens it.

MAGOEMON   One, two, three, four . . . ten . . . twenty-nine. They're all here. There's also a letter from a woman. What's this?

NARRATOR   He starts to unfold it.

KOHARU   That's an important letter. I can't let you see it.

NARRATOR   She clings to Magoemon's arm, but he pushes her away. He holds the letter to the lamplight and examines the address, "To Miss Koharu from Kamiya Osan." As soon as he reads the words, he casually thrusts the letter into his kimono.

MAGOEMON   Koharu. A while ago I swore by my good fortune as a samurai, but now Magoemon the Miller swears by his good fortune as a businessman that he will show this letter to no one, not even his wife. I alone will read it, then burn it with the oaths. You can trust me. I will not break this oath.

KOHARU   Thank you. You save my honor.

NARRATOR   She bursts into tears again.

JIHEI (*laughs contemptuously*)   Save your honor! You talk like a human being!

---

7. A dealer in flour (for noodles). His shop name Konaya—"the flour merchant"—is used almost as a surname.

(*To* MAGOEMON.) I don't want to see her cursed face another minute. Let's go. No—I can't hold so much resentment and bitterness! I'll kick her one in the face, a memory to treasure for the rest of my life. Excuse me, please.

NARRATOR   He strides up to Koharu and stamps on the ground.

JIHEI   For three years I've loved you, delighted in you, longed for you, adored you, but today my foot will say my only farewells.

NARRATOR   He kicks her sharply on the forehead and bursts into tears. The brothers leave, forlorn figures. Koharu, unhappy woman, raises her voice in lament as she watches them go. Is she faithful or unfaithful? Her true feelings are hidden in the words penned by Jihei's wife, a letter no one has seen. Jihei goes his separate way without learning the truth.

ACT 2

SCENE: *The house and shop of Kamiya* JIHEI.

TIME: *Ten days later.*

NARRATOR   The busy street that runs straight to Tenjin Bridge named for the god of Temma, bringer of good fortune, is known as the Street Before the Kami,[8] and here a paper shop does business under the name Kamiya Jihei. The paper is honestly sold, the shop well situated; it is a long established firm, and customers come thick as raindrops.

Outside crowds pass in the street, on their way to the Ten Nights service, while inside the husband dozes in the *kotatsu*,[9] shielded from draughts by a screen at his pillow. His wife Osan keeps solitary, anxious watch over shop and house.

OSAN   The days are so short—it's dinnertime already, but Tama still hasn't returned from her errand to Ichinokawa.[1] I wonder what can be keeping her. That scamp Sangorō isn't back either. The wind is freezing. I'm sure the children will both be cold. He doesn't even realize that it's time for Osue to be nursed. Heaven preserve me from ever becoming such a fool! What an infuriating creature!

NARRATOR   She speaks to herself.

KANTARŌ   Mama, I've come back all by myself.

NARRATOR   Her son, the older child, runs up to the house.

OSAN   Kantarō—is that you? What's happened to Osue and Sangorō?

KANTARŌ   They're playing by the shrine. Osue wanted her milk and she was bawling her head off.

OSAN   I was sure she would. Oh—your hands and feet are frozen stiff as nails! Go and warm yourself at the *kotatsu*. Your father's sleeping there.—What am I to do with that idiot?

NARRATOR   She runs out impatiently to the shop just as Sangorō shuffles back, alone.

OSAN   Come here, you fool! Where have you left Osue?

8. Again, wordplay on *kami* (god) and *kami* (paper).
9. A low, quilt-covered table under which a charcoal burner is placed as a source of heat.

1. Site of a large vegetable market near the north end of Tenjin Bridge, named, again, after the god "Tenjin," the deified Michizane.

SANGORŌ   You know, I must've lost her somewhere. Maybe somebody's picked her up. Should I go back for her?

OSAN   How could you? If any harm has come to my precious child, I'll beat you to death!

NARRATOR   But even as she screams at him, the maid Tama returns with Osue on her back.

TAMA   The poor child—I found her in tears at the corner. Sangorō, when you're supposed to look after the child, do it properly.

OSAN   You poor dear. You must want your milk.

NARRATOR   She joins the others by the *kotatsu* and suckles the child.

OSAN   Tama—give that fool a taste of something that he'll remember![2]

NARRATOR   Sangorō shakes his head.

SANGORŌ   No, thanks. I gave each of the children two tangerines just a while ago at the shrine, and I tasted five myself.

NARRATOR   Fool though he is, bad puns come from him nimbly enough, and the others can only smile despite themselves.

TAMA   Oh—I've become so involved with this half-wit that I almost forgot to tell you, ma'am, that Mr. Magoemon and his aunt[3] are on their way here from the west.

OSAN   Oh dear! I'll have to wake Jihei in that case. (*To* JIHEI.) Please get up. Mother and Magoemon are coming. They'll be upset again if they let them see you, a businessman, sleeping in the afternoon, with the day so short as it is.

JIHEI   All right.

NARRATOR   He struggles to a sitting position and, with his abacus in one hand, pulls his account book to him with the other.

JIHEI   Two into ten goes five, three into nine goes three, three into six goes two, seven times eight is fifty-six.

NARRATOR   His fifty-six-year old aunt enters with Magoemon.

JIHEI   Magoemon, aunt. How good of you. Please come in. I was in the midst of some urgent calculations. Four nines makes thirty-six *momme*. Three sixes make eighteen *fun*. That's two *momme* less two *fun*.[4] Kantarō! Osue! Granny and Uncle have come! Bring the tobacco tray! One times three makes three. Osan,[5] serve the tea!

NARRATOR   He jabbers away.

AUNT   We haven't come for tea or tobacco. Osan, you're young I know, but you're the mother of two children, and your excessive forbearance does you no credit. A man's dissipation can always be traced to his wife's careless-ness. Remember, it's not only the man who's disgraced when he goes bank-rupt and his marriage breaks up. You'd do well to take notice of what's going on and assert yourself a bit more.

MAGOEMON   It's foolish to hope for any results, aunt. The scoundrel even deceives me, his elder brother. Why should he take to heart criticism from his wife? Jihei—you played me for a fool. After showing me how you returned Koharu's pledges, here you are, not ten days later, redeeming her!

2. A pun on two meanings of *kurawasu*: "to make eat" and "to beat."
3. Magoemon's and Jihei's aunt, who is also Osan's mother.
4. Meaningless calculations. Twenty *fun* made two *momme* (and one *kamme* made one thousand *momme*).
5. The name Osan echoes the word "three" (*san*).

What does this mean? I suppose your urgent calulations are of Koharu's debts! I've had enough!

NARRATOR   He snatches away the abacus and flings it clattering into the hallway.

JIHEI   You're making an enormous fuss without any cause. I haven't crossed the threshold since the last time I saw you except to go twice to the wholesalers in Imabashi and once to the Tenjin Shrine. I haven't even thought of Koharu, much less redeemed her.

AUNT   None of your evasions! Last evening at the Ten Nights service I heard the people in the congregation gossiping. Everybody was talking about the great patron from Temma who'd fallen in love with a prostitute named Koharu from the Kinokuni House in Sonezaki. They said he'd driven away her other guests and was going to ransom her in the next couple of days. There was all kinds of gossip about the abundance of money and fools even in these days of high prices.

My husband Gozaemon has been hearing about Koharu constantly, and he's sure that her great patron from Temma must be you, Jihei. He told me, "He's your nepbew, but for me he's a stranger, and my daughter's happiness is my chief concern. Once he ransoms the prostitute he'll no doubt sell his wife to a brothel. I intend to take her back before he starts selling her clothes."

He was halfway out of the house before I could restrain him. "Don't get so excited. We can settle this calmly. First we must make sure whether or not the rumors are true."

That's why Magoemon and I are here now. He was telling me a while ago that the Jihei of today was not the Jihei of yesterday—that you'd broken all connections with Sonezaki and completely reformed. But now I hear that you've had a relapse. What disease can this be?

Your father was my brother. When the poor man was on his deathbed, he lifted his head from the pillow and begged me to look after you, as my son-in-law and nephew. I've never forgotten those last words, but your perversity has made a mockery of his request!

NARRATOR   She collapses in tears of resentment. Jihei claps his hands in sudden recognition.

JIHEI   I have it! The Koharu everybody's gossiping about is the same Koharu, but the great patron who's to redeem her is a different man. The other day, as my brother can tell you, Tahei—they call him the Lone Wolf because he hasn't any family or relations—started a fight and was trampled on. He gets all the money he needs from his home town, and he's been trying for a long time to redeem Koharu. I've always prevented him, but I'm sure he's decided that now is his chance. I have nothing to do with it.

NARRATOR   Osan brightens at his words.

OSAN   No matter how forbearing I might be—even if I were an angel—you don't suppose I'd encourage my husband to redeem a prostitute! In this instance at any rate there's not a word of untruth in what my husband has said. I'll be a witness to that, Mother.

NARRATOR   Husband's and wife's words tally perfectly.

AUNT   Then it's true?

NARRATOR   The aunt and nephew clap their hands with relief.

MAGOEMON   Well, I'm happy it's over, anyway. To make us feel doubly reassured, will you write an affidavit which will dispel any doubts your stubborn uncle may have?

JIHEI   Certainly. I'll write a thousand if you like.

MAGOEMON   Splendid! I happen to have bought this on the way here.

NARRATOR   Magoemon takes from the fold of his kimono a sheet of oath-paper from Kumano, the sacred characters formed by flocks of crows.[6] Instead of vows of eternal love, Jihei now signs under penalty of Heaven's wrath an oath that he will sever all ties and affections with Koharu. "If I should lie, may Bonten and Taishaku above, and the Four Great Kings below afflict me!"[7] So the text runs, and to it is appended the names of many Buddhas and gods. He signs his name, Kamiya Jihei, in bold characters, imprints the oath with a seal of blood, and proffers it.

OSAN   It's a great relief to me too. Mother, I have you and Magoemon to thank. Jihei and I have had two children, but this is his firmest pledge of affection. I hope you share my joy.

AUNT   Indeed we do. I'm sure that Jihei will settle down and his business will improve, now that he's in this frame of mind. It's been entirely for his sake and for love of the grandchildren that we've intervened. Come, Magoemon, let's be on our way. I'm anxious to set my husband's mind at ease.—It's become chilly here. See that the children don't catch cold.—This too we owe to the Buddha of the Ten Nights. I'll say a prayer of thanks before I go. Hail, Amida Buddha!

NARRATOR   She leaves, her heart innocent as Buddha's. Jihei is perfunctory even about seeing them to the door. Hardly have they crossed the threshold than he slumps down again at the *kotatsu*. He pulls the checked quilting over his head.

OSAN   You still haven't forgotton Sonezaki, have you?

NARRATOR   She goes up to him in disgust and tears away the quilting. He is weeping; a waterfall of tears streams along the pillow, deep enough to bear him afloat. She tugs him upright and props his body against the *kotatsu* frame. She stares into his face.

OSAN   You're acting outrageously, Jihei. You shouldn't have signed that oath if you felt so reluctant to leave her. The year before last, on the middle day of the Boar of the tenth moon,[8] we lit the first fire in the *kotatsu* and celebrated by sleeping here together, pillow to pillow. Ever since then—did some demon or snake creep into my bosom that night?—for two whole years I've been condemned to keep watch over an empty nest. I thought that tonight at least, thanks to Mother and Magoemon, we'd share sweet words in bed as husbands and wives do, but my pleasure didn't last long. How cruel of you, how utterly heartless! Go ahead, cry your eyes out, if you're so attached to her. Your tears will flow into Shijimi River and Koharu, no doubt, will ladle them out and drink them! You're ignoble, inhuman.

6. The charms issued by the Shintō shrine at Kumano were printed on the face with six Chinese characters, the strokes of which were in the shape of crows. The reverse side of the charms was used for writing oaths.
7. A formal oath. Bonten (Brahma) and Taishaku (Indra), though Hindu gods, were considered protective deities of the Buddhist law. The four Deva kings served under Indra and were also protectors of Buddhism.
8. It was customary to light the first fire of the winter on this day.

NARRATOR   She embraces his knees and throws herself over him, moaning in supplication. Jihei wipes his eyes.

JIHEI   If tears of grief flowed from the eyes and tears of anger from the ears, I could show my heart without saying a word. But my tears all pour in the same way from my eyes, and there's no difference in their color. It's not surprising that you can't tell what's in my heart. I have not a shred of attachment left for that vampire in human skin, but I bear a grudge against Tahei. He has all the money he wants, no wife or children. He's schemed again and again to redeem her, but Koharu refused to give in, at least until I broke with her. She told me time and again, "You have nothing to worry about. I'll never let myself be redeemed by Tahei, not even if my ties with you are ended and I can no longer stay by your side. If my master is induced by Tahei's money to deliver me to him, I'll kill myself in a way that'll do you credit!" But think—not ten days have passed since I broke with her, and she's to be redeemed by Tahei! That rotten whore! That animal! No, I haven't a trace of affection left for her, but I can just hear how Tahei will be boasting. He'll spread the word around Osaka that my business has come to a standstill and I'm hard pressed for money. I'll meet with contemptuous stares from the wholesalers. I'll be dishonored. My heart is broken and my body burns with shame. What a disgrace! How maddening! I've passed the stage of shedding hot tears, tears of blood, sticky tears—my tears now are of molten iron!

NARRATOR   He collapses with weeping. Osan pales with alarm.

OSAN   If that's the situation, poor Koharu will surely kill herself.

JIHEI   You're too well bred, despite your intelligence, to understand her likes! What makes you suppose that faithless creature would kill herself? Far from it—she's probably taking moxa treatments and medicine to prolong her life!

OSAN   No, that's not true. I was determined never to tell you so long as I lived, but I'm afraid of the crime I'd be committing if I concealed the facts and let her die with my knowledge. I will reveal my great secret. There is not a grain of deceit in Koharu. It was I who schemed to end the relations between you. I could see signs that you were drifting towards suicide. I felt so unhappy that I wrote a letter, begging her as one woman to another to break with you, though I knew how painful it would be. I asked her to save your life. The letter must have moved her. She answered that she would give you up, though you were more precious than life itself, because she could not shirk her duty to me. I've kept her letter with me ever since—it's been like a protective charm. Could such a noble-hearted woman violate her promise and brazenly marry Tahei? When a woman—I no less than another—has given herself completely to a man, she does not change. I'm sure she'll kill herself. I'm sure of it. Ahhh—what a dreadful thing to have happened! Save her, please.

NARRATOR   Her voice rises in agitation. Her husband is thrown into a turmoil.

JIHEI   There was a letter in an unknown woman's hand among the written oaths she surrendered to my brother. It must have been from you. If that's the case, Koharu will surely commit suicide.

OSAN   Alas! I'd be failing in the obligations I owe her as another woman if I allowed her to die. Please go to her at once. Don't let her kill herself.

NARRATOR   Clinging to her husband, she melts in tears.

JIHEI   But what can I possibly do? It'd take half the amount of her ransom in earnest money merely to keep her out of Tahei's clutches. I can't save Koharu's life without administering a dose of 750 *momme* in New Silver.[9] How could I raise that much money in my present financial straits? Even if I crush my body to powder, where will the money come from?

OSAN   Don't exaggerate the difficulties. If that's all you need, it's simple enough.

NARRATOR   She goes to the wardrobe, and opening a small drawer takes out a bag fastened with cords of twisted silk. She unhesitantly tears it open and throws down a packet which Jihei retrieves.

JIHEI   What's this? Money? Four hundred *momme* in New Silver? How in the world—

NARRATOR   He stares astonished at this money he never put there.

OSAN   I'll tell you later where this money came from. I've scraped it together to pay the bill for Iwakuni paper that falls due the day after tomorrow. We'll have to ask Magoemon to help us keep the business from betraying its insolvency. But Koharu comes first. The packet contains 400 *momme*. That leaves 350 *momme* to raise.

NARRATOR   She unlocks a large drawer. From the wardrobe lightly fly kite-colored Hachijō silks;[1] a Kyoto crepe kimono lined in pale brown, insubstantial as her husband's life which flickers today and may vanish tomorrow; a padded kimono of Osue's, a flaming scarlet inside and out—Osan flushes with pain to part with it; Kantarō's sleeveless, unlined jacket—if she pawns this, he'll be cold this winter. Next comes a garment of striped Gunnai silk lined in pale blue and never worn, and then her best formal costume—heavy black silk dyed with her family crest, an ivy leaf in a ring. They say that those joined by marriage ties can even go naked at home, though outside the house clothes make the man she snatches up even her husband's finery, a silken cloak, making fifteen articles in all.

OSAN   The very least the pawnshop can offer is 350 *momme* in New Silver.

NARRATOR   Her face glows as though she already held the money she needs; she hides in the one bundle her husband's shame and her own obligation, and puts her love in besides.

OSAN   It doesn't matter if the children and I have nothing to wear. My husband's reputation concerns me more. Ransom Koharu. Save her. Assert your honor before Tahei.

NARRATOR   But Jihei's eyes remain downcast all the while, and he is silently weeping.

JIHEI   Yes, I can pay the earnest money and keep her out of Tahei's hands. But once I've redeemed her, I'll either have to maintain her in a separate establishment or bring her here. Then what will become of you?

9. Koharu's situation is described in terms of the money needed to cure a sickness. If 750 *me* is half the sum needed to redeem Koharu, the total of 1,500 *me*, 6,000 *me* in Old Silver, is considerably less than 10,000 *me* in Old Silver (equivalent to the 10 *kamme* previously mentioned by Tahei).

1. Woven with a warp of brown and a woof of yellow thread to give a color like that of a kite. "Kite" also suggests that the material "flies" out of the cupboard.

NARRATOR   Osan is at a loss to answer.

OSAN   Yes, what shall I do? Shall I become your children's nurse or the cook? Or perhaps the retired mistress of the house?

NARRATOR   She falls to the floor with a cry of woe.

JIHEI   That would be too selfish. I'd be afraid to accept such generosity. Even if the punishment for my crimes against my parents, against Heaven, against the gods and the Buddhas fails to strike me, the punishment for my crimes against my wife alone will be sufficient to destroy all hope for the future life. Forgive me, I beg you.

NARRATOR   He joins his hands in tearful entreaty.

OSAN   Why should you bow before me? I don't deserve it. I'd be glad to rip the nails from my fingers and toes, to do anything which might serve my husband. I've been pawning my clothes for some time in order to scrape together the money for the paper wholesalers' bills. My wardrobe is empty, but I don't regret it in the least. But it's too late now to talk of such things. Hurry, change your cloak and go to her with a smile.

NARRATOR   He puts on an under kimono of Gunnai silk, a robe of heavy black silk, and a striped cloak. His sash of figured damask holds a dirk of middle length worked in gold: Buddha surely knows that tonight it will be stained with Koharu's blood.

JIHEI   Sangorō! Come here!

NARRATOR   Jihei loads the bundle on the servant's back, intending to take him along. Then he firmly thrusts the wallet next to his skin and starts towards the gate.

VOICE   Is Jihei at home?

NARRATOR   A man enters, removing his fur cap. They see—good heavens!— that it is Gozaemon.

OSAN and JIHEI   Ahhh—how fortunate that you should come at this moment!

NARRATOR   Husband and wife are upset and confused. Gozaemon snatches away Sangorō's bundle and sits heavily. His voice is sharp.

GOZAEMON   Stay where you are, harlot!—My esteemed son-in-law, what a rare pleasure to see you dressed in your finest attire, with a dirk and a silken cloak! Ahhh—that's how a gentleman of means spends his money! No one would take you for a paper dealer. Are you perchance on your way to the New Quarter? What commendable perseverance! You have no need for your wife, I take it—Give her a divorce. I've come to take her home with me.

NARRATOR   He speaks needles and his voice is bitter. Jihei has not a word to reply.

OSAN   How kind of you, Father, to walk here on such a cold day. Do have a cup of tea.

NARRATOR   Offering the teacup serves as an excuse for edging closer.

OSAN   Mother and Magoemon came here a while ago, and they told my husband how much they disapproved of his visits to the New Quarter. Jihei was in tears and he wrote out an oath swearing he had reformed. He gave it to Mother. Haven't you seen it yet?

GOZAEMON   His written oath? Do you mean this?

NARRATOR   He takes the paper from his kimono.

GOZAEMON   Libertines scatter vows and oaths wherever they go, as if they were monthly statements of accounts. I thought there was something peculiar about this oath, and now that I am here I can see I was right. Do you still swear to Bonten and Taishaku? Instead of such nonsense, write out a bill of divorcement!

NARRATOR   He rips the oath to shreds and throws down the pieces. Husband and wife exchange looks of alarm, stunned into silence. Jihei touches his hands to the floor and bows his head.

JIHEI   Your anger is justified. If I were still my former self, I would try to offer explanations, but today I appeal entirely to your generosity. Please let me stay with Osan. I promise that even if I become a beggar or an outcast and must sustain life with the scraps that fall from other people's chopsticks, I will hold Osan in high honor and protect her from every harsh and bitter experience. I feel so deeply indebted to Osan that I cannot divorce her. You will understand that this is true as time passes and I show you how I apply myself to my work and restore my fortune. Until then please shut your eyes and allow us to remain together.

NARRATOR   Tears of blood stream from his eyes and his face is pressed to the matting in contrition.

GOZAEMON   The wife of an outcast! That's all the worse. Write the bill of divorcement at once! I will verify and seal the furniture and clothes Osan brought in her dowry.

NARRATOR   He goes to the wardrobe. Osan is alarmed.

OSAN   My clothes are all here. There's no need to examine them.

NARRATOR   She runs up to forestall him, but Gozaemon pushes her aside and jerks open a drawer.

GOZAEMON   What does this mean?

NARRATOR   He opens another drawer: it too is empty. He pulls out every last drawer, but not so much as a foot of patchwork cloth is to be seen. He tears open the wicker hampers, long boxes, and clothes chests.

GOZAEMON   Stripped bare, are they?

NARRATOR   His eyes set in fury. Jihei and Osan huddle under the striped *kotatsu* quilts, ready to sink into the fire with humiliation.

GOZAEMON   This bundle looks suspicious.

NARRATOR   He unties the knots and dumps out the contents.

GOZAEMON   As I thought! You were sending these to the pawnshop, I take it. Jihei—you'd strip the skin from your wife's and your children's bodies to squander the money on your whore! Dirty thief! You're my wife's nephew, but an utter stranger to me, and I'm under no obligation to suffer for your sake. I'll explain to Magoemon what has happened and ask him to make good whatever inroads you've already made on Osan's belongings. But first, the bill of divorcement!

NARRATOR   Even if Jihei could escape through seven padlocked doors, eight thicknesses of chains, and a hundred girdling walls, he could not evade so stringent a demand.

JIHEI   I won't use a brush to write the bill of divorcement. Here's what I'll do instead! Good-by, Osan.

NARRATOR   He lays his hand on his dirk, but Osan clings to him.

OSAN   Father—Jihei admits that he's done wrong and he's apologized in every way. You press your advantage too hard. Jihei may be a stranger, but his children are your grandchildren. Have you no affection for them? I will not accept a bill of divorcement.

NARRATOR She embraces her husband and raises her voice in tears.

GOZAEMON Very well. I won't insist on it. Come with me, woman.

NARRATOR He pulls her to her feet.

OSAN No, I won't go. What bitterness makes you expose to such shame a man and wife who still love each other? I will not suffer it.

NARRATOR She pleads with him, weeping, but he pays her no heed.

GOZAEMON Is there some greater shame? I'll shout it through the town!

NARRATOR He pulls her up, but she shakes free. Caught by the wrist she totters forward when—alas!—her toes brush against her sleeping children. They open their eyes.

CHILDREN Mother dear, why is Grandfather, the bad man, taking you away? Whom will we sleep beside now?

NARRATOR They call out after her.

OSAN My poor dears! You've never spent a night away from Mother's side since you were born. Sleep tonight beside your father. (*To* JIHEI.) Please don't forget to give the children their tonic before breakfast.—Oh, my heart is broken!

NARRATOR These are her parting words. She leaves her children behind, abandoned as in the woods; the twin-trunked bamboo of conjugal love is sundered forever.

ACT 3

SCENE 1: *Sonezaki New Quarter, in front of the Yamato House.*

TIME: *That night.*

NARRATOR This is Shijimi River, the haunt of love and affection. Its flowing water and the feet of passersby are stilled now at two in the morning, and the full moon shines clear in the sky. Here in the street a dim doorway lantern is marked "Yamatoya Dembei" in a single scrawl. The night watchman's clappers take on a sleepy cadence as he totters by on uncertain legs. The very thickness of his voice crying, "Beware of fire! Beware of fire!" tells how far advanced the night is. A serving woman from the upper town comes along, followed by a palanquin. "It's terribly late," she remarks to the bearers as she clatters open the side door of the Yamato House and steps inside.

SERVANT I've come to take back Koharu of the Kinokuni House.

NARRATOR Her voice is faintly heard outside. A few moments later, after hardly time enough to exchange three or four words of greeting, she emerges.

SERVANT Koharu is spending the night. Bearers, you may leave now and get some rest. (*To proprietress, inside the doorway.*) Oh, I forgot to tell you, madam. Please keep an eye on Koharu. Now that the ransom to Tahei has been arranged and the money's been accepted, we're merely her custodians. Please don't let her drink too much saké.

NARRATOR She leaves, having scattered at the doorway the seeds that before morning will turn Jihei and Koharu to dust.

At night between two and four even the teahouse kettle rests; the flame flickering in the low candle stand narrows; and the frost spreads in the cold river-wind of the deepening night. The master's voice breaks the stillness.

DEMBEI (*to* JIHEI) It's still the middle of the night. I'll send somebody with you. (*To servants.*) Mr. Jihei is leaving. Wake Koharu. Call her here.

NARRATOR   Jihei slides open the side door.

JIHEI   No, Dembei, not a word to Koharu. I'll be trapped here till dawn if she hears I'm leaving. That's why I'm letting her sleep and slipping off this way. Wake her up after sunrise and send her back then. I'm returning home now and will leave for Kyoto immediately on business. I have so many engagements that I may not be able to return in time for the interim payment.[2] Please use the money I gave you earlier this evening to clear my account. I'd like you also to send 150 *me* of Old Silver to Kawashō for the moon-viewing party last month. Please get a receipt. Give Saietsubō[3] from Fukushima one piece of silver as a contribution to the Buddhist altar he's bought, and tell him to use it for a memorial service. Wasn't there something else? Oh yes—give Isoichi a tip of four silver coins. That's the lot. Now you can close up and get to bed. Good-by. I'll see you when I return from Kyoto.

NARRATOR   Hardly has he taken two or three steps than he turns back.

JIHEI   I forgot my dirk. Fetch it for me, won't you?—Yes, Dembei, this is one respect in which it's easier being a townsman. If I were a samurai and forgot my sword, I'd probably commit suicide on the spot!

DEMBEI   I completely forgot that I was keeping it for you. Yes, here's the knife with it.

NARRATOR   He gives the dirk to Jihei, who fastens it firmly into his sash.

JIHEI   I feel secure as long as I have this. Good night!

NARRATOR   He goes off.

DEMBEI   Please come back to Osaka soon! Thank you for your patronage!

NARRATOR   With this hasty farewell Dembei rattles the door bolt shut; then not another sound is heard as the silence deepens. Jihei pretends to leave, only to creep back again with stealthy steps. He clings to the door of the Yamato House. As he peeps within he is startled by shadows moving towards him. He takes cover at the house across the way until the figures pass.

Magoemon the Miller, his heart pulverized with anxiety over his younger brother, comes first, followed by the apprentice Sangorō with Jihei's son Kantarō on his back. They hurry along until they spy the lantern of the Yamato House. Magoemon pounds on the door.

MAGOEMON   Excuse me. Kamiya Jihei's here, isn't he? I'd like to see him a moment.

NARRATOR   Jihei thinks, "It's my brother!" but dares not stir from his place of concealment. From inside a man's sleep-laden voice is heard.

DEMBEI   Jihei left a while ago saying he was going up to Kyoto. He's not here.

NARRATOR   Not another sound is heard. Magoemon's tears fall unchecked.

MAGOEMON   (*to himself*)   I ought to have met him on the way if he'd been going home. I can't understand what takes him to Kyoto. Ahhh—I'm trembling all over with worry. I wonder if he didn't take Koharu with him.

NARRATOR   The thought pierces his heart; unable to bear the pain, he pounds again on the door.

DEMBEI   Who is it, so late at night? We've gone to bed.

MAGOEMON   I'm sorry to disturb you, but I'd like to ask one more thing. Has Koharu of the Kinokuni House left? I was wondering if she mightn't have gone with Jihei.

---

2. On the last day of the Tenth Month, one of the times during the year for making payments.   3. Name of a male entertainer in the Fukushima quarter, west of Sonezaki.

DEMBEI   What's that? Koharu's upstairs, fast asleep.

MAGOEMON   That's a relief, anyway. There's no fear of a lovers' suicide. But where is he hiding himself causing me all this anxiety? He can't imagine the agony of suspense that the whole family is going through on his account. I'm afraid that bitterness towards his father-in-law may make him forget himself and do something rash. I brought Kantarō along, hoping he would help to dissuade Jihei, but the gesture was in vain. I wonder why I failed to meet him?

NARRATOR   He murmurs to himself, his eyes moist with tears. Jihei's hiding place is close enough for him to hear every word. He chokes with emotion, but can only swallow his tears.

MAGOEMON   Sangorō! Where does the fool go night after night? Don't you know anywhere else?

NARRATOR   Sangorō imagines that he himself is the fool referred to.

SANGORŌ   I know a couple of places, but I'm too embarrassed to mention them.

MAGOEMON   You know them? Where are they? Tell me.

SANGORŌ   Please don't scold me when you've heard. Every night I wander down below the warehouses by the market.

MAGOEMON   Imbecile! Who's asking about that? Come on, let's search the back streets. Don't let Kantarō catch a chill. The poor kid's having a cold time of it, thanks to that useless father of his. Still, if the worst the boy experiences is the cold I won't complain. I'm afraid that Jihei may cause him much greater pain. The scoundrel!

NARRATOR   But beneath the rancor in his heart of hearts is profound pity.

MAGOEMON   Let's look at the back street!

NARRATOR   They pass on. As soon as their figures have gone off a distance Jihei runs from his hiding place. Standing on tiptoes he gazes with yearning after them and cries out in his heart.

JIHEI   He cannot leave me to my death, though I am the worst of sinners! I remain to the last a burden to him! I'm unworthy of such kindness!

NARRATOR   He joins his hands and kneels in prayer.

JIHEI   If I may make one further request of your mercy, look after my children!

NARRATOR   These are his only words; for a while he chokes with tears.

JIHEI   At any rate, our decision's been made. Koharu must be waiting.

NARRATOR   He peers through a crack in the side door of the Yamato House and glimpses a figure.

JIHEI   That's Koharu, isn't it? I'll let her know I'm here.

NARRATOR   He clears his throat, their signal. "Ahem, ahem"—the sound blends with the clack of wooden clappers as the watchman comes from the upper street, coughing in the night wind. He hurries on his round of fire warning, "Take care! Beware!" Even this cry has a dismal sound to one in hiding. Jihei, concealing himself like the god of Katsuragi,[4] lets the watchman pass. He sees his chance and rushes to the side door, which softly opens from within.

JIHEI   Koharu?

KOHARU   Were you waiting? Jihei—I want to leave quickly.

---

4. The god was so ashamed of his ugliness that he ventured forth only at night.

NARRATOR   She is all impatience, but the more hastily they open the door, the more likely people will be to hear the casters turning. They lift the door; it gives a moaning that thunders in their ears and in their hearts. Jihei lends a hand from the outside, but his fingertips tremble with the trembling of his heart. The door opens a quarter of an inch, a half, an inch—an inch ahead are the tortures of hell, but more than hell itself they fear the guardian-demon's eyes. At last the door opens, and with the joy of New Year's morn[5] Koharu slips out. They catch each other's hands. Shall they go north or south, west or east? Their pounding hearts urge them on, though they know not to what destination: turning their backs on the moon reflected in Shijimi River, they hurry eastward as fast as their legs will carry them.

SCENE 2: *The farewell journey of many bridges.*

NARRATOR
The running hand in texts of Nō is always Konoe style;
An actor in a woman's part is sure to wear a purple hat.[6]
Does some teaching of the Buddha as rigidly decree
That men who spend their days in evil haunts must end like this?
Poor creatures, though they would discover today their destiny in the Sutra of Cause and Effect, tomorrow the gossip of the world will scatter like blossoms the scandal of Kamiya Jihei's love suicide, and, carved in cherry wood, his story to the last detail will be printed in illustrated sheets.[7]
Jihei, led on by the spirit of death—if such there be among the gods—is resigned to this punishment for neglect of his trade. But at times—who could blame him?—his heart is drawn to those he has left behind, and it is hard to keep walking on. Even in the full moon's light, this fifteenth night of the tenth moon,[8] he cannot see his way ahead—a sign perhaps of the darkness in his heart? The frost now falling will melt by dawn but, even more quickly than this symbol of human frailty, the lovers themselves will melt away. What will become of the fragrance that lingered when he held her tenderly at night in their bedchamber?
This bridge, Tenjin Bridge, he has crossed every day, morning and night, gazing at Shijimi River to the west. Long ago, when Tenjin, then called Michizane,[9] was exiled to Tsukushi, his plum tree, following its master, flew in one bound to Dazaifu, and here is Plum-field Bridge. Green Bridge recalls the aged pine that followed later, and Cherry Bridge the tree that

5. Mention of the New Year is connected with Koharu's name, with *haru* meaning "spring."
6. The Konoe style of calligraphy was used in books with Noh texts. Custom also decreed that young male actors playing the parts of women cover their foreheads with a square of purple cloth to disguise the fact that they were shaven.
7. These sheets mentioned here featured current scandals, such as lovers' suicides. "Cause and Effect": a sacred scripture of Buddhism, which says: "If you wish to know the past cause, look at the present effect; if you wish to know the future effect, look at the present cause." "Cherry wood": the blocks from which illustrated books were printed were often of cherry wood.

8. November 14, 1720. In the lunar calendar the full moon occurs on the fifteenth of the month.
9. Sugawara no Michizane, unfairly slandered at court, was exiled to Dazaifu on Japan's southernmost main island of Kyushu. When he was about to depart, he composed a poem of farewell to his favorite plum tree. Legend has it that the tree, moved by his master's poem, flew after him to Kyushu, while the cherry tree in Michizane's garden withered away in grief. Only the pine seemed indifferent, but after Michizane complained in a poem, the pine tree also flew to Kyushu to join his master.

withered away in grief over parting. Such are the tales still told, bespeaking the power of a single poem.

JIHEI Though born the parishioner of so holy and mighty a god, I shall kill you and then myself. If you ask the cause, it was that I lacked even the wisdom that might fill a tiny Shell Bridge.[1] Our stay in this world has been short as an autumn day. This evening will be the last of your nineteen, of my twenty-eight years. The time has come to cast away our lives. We promised we'd remain together faithfully, till you were an old woman and I an old man, but before we knew each other three full years, we have met this disaster. Look, here is Ōe Bridge. We follow the river from Little Naniwa Bridge to Funairi Bridge. The farther we journey, the closer we approach the road to death.

NARRATOR He laments. She clings to him.

KOHARU Is this already the road to death?

NARRATOR Falling tears obscure from each the other's face and threaten to immerse even the Horikawa bridges.

JIHEI A few steps north and I could glimpse my house, but I will not turn back. I will bury in my breast all thoughts of my children's future, all pity for my wife. We cross southward over the river. Why did they call a place with as many buildings as a bridge has piers "Eight Houses"? Hurry, we want to arrive before the down-river boat from Fushimi comes—with what happy couples sleeping aboard!

Next is Temma Bridge, a frightening name[2] for us about to depart this world. Here the two streams Yodo and Yamato join in one great river, as fish with water, and as Koharu and I, dying on one blade will cross together the River of Three Fords.[3] I would like this water for our tomb offering!

KOHARU What have we to grieve about? Though in this world we could not stay together, in the next and through each successive world to come until the end of time we shall be husband and wife. Every summer for my devotions[4] I have copied the All Compassionate and All Merciful Chapter of the Lotus Sutra, in the hope that we may be reborn on one lotus.

NARRATOR They cross over Kyō Bridge and reach the opposite shore.[5]

KOHARU If I can save living creatures at will when once I mount a lotus calyx in Paradise and become a Buddha, I want to protect women of my profession, so that never again will there be love suicides.

NARRATOR This unattainable prayer stems from worldly attachment, but it touchingly reveals her heart. They cross Onari Bridge.[6] The waters of Noda

1. The lovers' journey takes them over twelve bridges altogether. They proceed first along the north bank of Shijimi River ("Shell River") to Shijimi Bridge, where they cross to Dōjima. At Little Naniwa Bridge they cross back again to Sonezaki. Continuing eastward, they cross Horikawa, then cross the Temma Bridge over the Ōkawa. At "Eight Houses" (Hakkenya) they journey eastward along the south bank of the river as far as Kyō Bridge (Sutra Bridge). They cross this bridge to the tip of land at Katamachi and then take the Onari Bridge to the final destination, Amijima.

2. The characters used for Temma mean literally "demon."
3. A river in the Buddhist underworld that had to be crossed to reach the world of the dead. One blade plus two people equal "Three Fords."
4. It was customary for Buddhist monks and some of the laity in Japan to observe a summer retreat to practice austerities.
5. This location implies Nirvana. "Kyō Bridge": called "Sutra Bridge."
6. The word "Onari" implies "to become a Buddha."

Creek are shrouded with morning haze; the mountain tips show faintly white.

JIHEI Listen—the voices of the temple bells begin to boom. How much farther can we go on this way? We are not fated to live any longer—let us make an end quickly. Come this way.

NARRATOR Tears are strung with the 108 beads of the rosaries in their hands. They have come now to Amijima, to the Daichō Temple; the overflowing sluice gate of a little stream beside a bamboo thicket will be their place of death.

SCENE 3: *Amijima.*

JIHEI No matter how far we walk, there'll never be a spot marked "For Suicides." Let us kill ourselves here.

NARRATOR He takes her hand and sits on the ground.

KOHARU Yes, that's true. One place is as good as another to die. But I've been thinking on the way that if they find our dead bodies together people will say that Koharu and Jihei committed a lovers' suicide. Osan will think then that I treated as mere scrap paper the letter I sent promising her, when she asked me not to kill you, that I would not, and vowing to break all relations. She will be sure that I lured her precious husband into a lovers' suicide. She will despise me as a one-night prostitute, a false woman with no sense of decency. I fear her contempt more than the slander of a thousand or ten thousand strangers. I can imagine how she will resent and envy me. That is the greatest obstacle to my salvation. Kill me here, then choose another spot, far away, for yourself.

NARRATOR She leans against him. Jihei joins in her tears of pleading.

JIHEI What foolish worries! Osan has been taken back by my father-in-law. I've divorced her. She and I are strangers now. Why should you feel obliged to a divorced woman? You were saying on the way that you and I will be husband and wife through each successive world until the end of time. Who can criticize us, who can be jealous if we die side by side?

KOHARU But who is responsible for your divorce? You're even less reasonable than I. Do you suppose that our bodies will accompany us to the afterworld? We may die in different places, our bodies may be pecked by kites and crows, but what does it matter as long as our souls are twined together? Take me with you to heaven or to hell!

NARRATOR She sinks again in tears.

JIHEI You're right. Our bodies are made of earth, water, fire, and wind, and when we die they revert to emptiness. But our souls will not decay, no matter how often reborn. And here's a guarantee that our souls will be married and never part!

NARRATOR He whips out his dirk and slashes off his black locks at the base of the top knot.

JIHEI Look, Koharu. As long as I had this hair I was Kamiya Jihei, Osan's husband, but cutting it has made me a monk. I have fled the burning house of the three worlds of delusion; I am a priest, unencumbered by wife, children, or worldly possessions. Now that I no longer have a wife named Osan, you owe her no obligations either.

NARRATOR In tears he flings away the hair.

KOHARU I am happy.

NARRATOR Koharu takes up the dirk and ruthlessly, unhesitantly, slices through her flowing Shimada coiffure. She casts aside the tresses she has so often washed and combed and stroked. How heartbreaking to see their locks tangled with the weeds and midnight frost of this desolate field!

JIHEI We have escaped the inconstant world, a nun and a priest. Our duties as husband and wife belong to our profane past. It would be best to choose quite separate places for our deaths, a mountain for one, the river for the other. We will pretend that the ground above this sluice gate is a mountain. You will die there. I shall hang myself by this stream. The time of our deaths will be the same, but the method and place will differ. In this way we can honor to the end our duty to Osan. Give me your under sash.

NARRATOR Its fresh violet color and fragrance will be lost in the winds of impermanence; the crinkled silk long enough to wind twice round her body will bind two worlds, this and the next. He firmly fastens one end to the crosspiece of the sluice, then twists the other into a noose for his neck. He will hang for love of his wife like the "pheasant in the hunting grounds."[7]

Koharu watches Jihei prepare for his death. Her eyes swim with tears, her mind is distraught.

KOHARU Is that how you're going to kill yourself?—If we are to die apart, I have only a little while longer by your side. Come near me.

NARRATOR They take each other's hands.

KOHARU It's over in a moment with a sword, but I'm sure you'll suffer. My poor darling!

NARRATOR She cannot stop the silent tears.

JIHEI Can suicide ever be pleasant, whether by hanging or cutting the throat? You mustn't let worries over trifles disturb the prayers of your last moments. Keep your eyes on the westward-moving moon, and worship it as Amida himself.[8] Concentrate your thoughts on the Western Paradise. If you have any regrets about leaving the world, tell me now, then die.

KOHARU I have none at all, none at all. But I'm sure you must be worried about your children.

JIHEI You make me cry all over again by mentioning them. I can almost see their faces, sleeping peacefully, unaware, poor dears, that their father is about to kill himself. They're the one thing I can't forget.

NARRATOR He droops to the ground with weeping. The voices of the crows leaving their nests at dawn rival his sobs. Are the crows mourning his fate? The thought brings more tears.

JIHEI Listen to them. The crows have come to guide us to the world of the dead. There's an old saying that every time somebody writes an oath on the back of a Kumano charm, three crows of Kumano die on the holy mountain. The first words we've written each New Year have been vows of love, and how often we've inscribed oaths at the beginning of the month! If each oath has killed three crows, what a multitude must have perished! Their cries have always sounded like "beloved, beloved," but hatred for our crime of taking life

---

7. A reference to a poem from the 8th-century anthology *Collection of Myriad Leaves* (*Man'yōshū*): "The pheasant foraging in the fields of spring reveals his whereabouts to man as he cries for his mate."

8. Amida's Western Paradise of the Pure Land lies in the west. The moon is frequently used as a symbol of Buddhist enlightenment.

makes their voices ring tonight "revenge, revenge!"[9] Whose fault is it they demand revenge? Because of me you will die a painful death. Forgive me!

NARRATOR   He takes her in his arms.

KOHARU   No, it's my fault!

NARRATOR   They cling to each other, face pressed to face; their sidelocks, drenched with tears, freeze in the winds blowing over the fields. Behind them echoes the voice of the Daichō Temple.

JIHEI   Even the long winter night seems short as our lives.

NARRATOR   Dawn is already breaking, and matins can be heard. He draws her to him.

JIHEI   The moment has come for our glorious end. Let there be no tears on your face when they find you later.

KOHARU   There won't be any.

NARRATOR   She smiles. His hands, numbed by the frost, tremble before the pale vision of her face, and his eyes are first to cloud. He is weeping so profusely that he cannot control the blade.

KOHARU   Compose yourself—but be quick!

NARRATOR   Her encouragement lends him strength; the invocations to Amida carried by the wind urge a final prayer. *Namu Amida Butsu*. He thrusts in the saving sword.[1] Stabbed, she falls backwards, despite his staying hand, and struggles in terrible pain. The point of the blade has missed her windpipe, and these are the final tortures before she can die. He writhes with her in agony, then painfully summons his strength again. He draws her to him, and plunges his dirk to the hilt. He twists the blade in the wound, and her life fades away like an unfinished dream at dawning.

He arranges her corpse head to the north, face to the west, lying on her right side,[2] and throws his cloak over her. He turns away at last, unable to exhaust with tears his grief over parting. He pulls the sash to him and fastens the noose around his neck. The service in the temple has reached the closing section, the prayers for the dead. "Believers and unbelievers will equally share in the divine grace," the voices proclaim, and at the final words Jihei jumps from the sluice gate.

JIHEI   May we be reborn on one lotus! Hail Amida Buddha!

NARRATOR   For a few moments he writhes like a gourd swinging in the wind, but gradually the passage of his breath is blocked as the stream is dammed by the sluice gate, where his ties with this life are snapped.

Fishermen out for the morning catch find the body in their net.[3]

FISHERMEN   A dead man! Look, a dead man! Come here, everybody!

NARRATOR   The tale is spread from mouth to mouth. People say that they who were caught in the net of Buddha's vow immediately gained salvation and deliverance, and all who hear the tale of the Love Suicides at Amijima are moved to tears.

9. The cries have always sounded like *kawai, kawai* ("beloved"), but now they sound like *mukui, mukui* ("revenge").
1. The invocations of Amida's name freed one from spiritual obstacles, just as a sword freed one from physical obstacles.
2. The dead were arranged in this manner because the historical Buddha, Shakyamuni Buddha, chose this position when he died and passed into Nirvana.
3. The vow of the Buddha to save all sentient beings is likened to a net that catches people in its meshes. "Net" (*ami*) is echoed a few lines later in the name "Amijima."

II

The Enlightenment in Europe and the Americas

I s the latest thing always the best? On the whole, our society assumes that progress is likely and desirable. We move and communicate ever faster; we pursue the newest and shiniest things—our appetite for the modern knows no bounds. Yet we also indulge in moments of nostalgia, worrying that things are no longer what they used to be, that something has been lost in our tremendous rush. Before, we tell ourselves, there were standards; now all is confusion. Although the pace of change is now swifter, this ambivalence is nothing new.

The quarrel between "ancients" and "moderns"—those who believed, respectively, that old ideas or new ones were likely to prove superior to any alternatives—proved especially virulent in France and England during the late seventeenth and eighteenth centuries. Those who espoused the cause of the ancients feared—understandably—that the new commitment to individualism promoted by the moderns might lead to social alienation, unscrupulous self-seeking, and lack of moral responsibility. Believing in the universality of truth, they wished to uphold established values, not to invent new ones. On the other side, the moderns upheld the impor-

A Philosopher Giving a Lecture in the Orrery, 1766, by Joseph Wright of Derby.

tance of individual autonomy, broad education for women, and intellectual and geographical exploration. They stood for the new and are the recognizable forebears of what we even now call "modernity."

On both sides of the ancient/modern divide, thinkers believed in reason as a dependable guide. Both sides insisted that one should not take any assertion of truth on faith, blindly following the authority of others; instead, one should think skeptically about causes and effects, subjecting all truth-claims to logic and rational inquiry. Dr. Johnson's famous *Dictionary* defined reason as "the power by which man deduces one proposition from another, or proceeds from premises to consequences." By this definition, illumination occurs not by divine inspiration or by order of kings but by the reasoning powers of the ordinary human mind. Reason, some people argued, would lead human beings back to eternal truths. For others, reason provided a means for discovering fresh solutions to scientific, philosophical, and political questions.

In the realm of philosophy, thinkers turned their attention to defining what it meant to be human. "I think, therefore I am," René Descartes pronounced, declaring the mind the source of truth and meaning. But this idea proved less reassuring than it initially seemed. Subsequent philosophers, exploring the concept's implications, realized the possibility of the mind's isolation in its own constructions. Perhaps, Gottfried Wilhelm Leibniz suggested, no real communication can take place between one consciousness and another. Possibly, according to David Hume, the idea of individual identity is a fiction constructed by our minds to make discontinuous experiences and memories seem continuous and whole. Philosophers pointed out the impossibility of knowing for sure even the reality of the external world: the only certainty is that we think it exists.

If contemplating the nature of human reason led philosophic skeptics to doubt our ability to know anything with certainty, other thinkers insisted on the existence, beyond ourselves, of an entirely rational physical and moral universe. Isaac Newton's demonstrations of the order of natural law greatly encouraged this line of thought, leading many to believe that the fullness and complexity of the perceived physical world testified to the sublime rationality of a divine plan. The Planner, however, did not necessarily supervise the day-to-day operations of His arrangements; He might rather, as a popular analogy had it, resemble the watchmaker who winds the watch and leaves it running.

God as a watchmaker was the central image for thinkers known as deists, who justified evil in the world by arguing that God never interfered with nature or with human action. Deism encouraged the separation of ethics from religion, as ethics was increasingly understood as a matter of reason. Human beings, Enlightenment thinkers argued, could rely on their own authority—rather than looking to priests or princes—to decide how to act well in the world. Yet no one could fail to recognize that men and women embodied a capacity for passion as well as reason: "On life's vast ocean diversely we sail, / Reason the card, but Passion is the gale," Alexander Pope's *Essay on Man* (1733) pointed out. One could hope to steer with reason as guide, but one had to face the omnipresence of unreasonable passions. Life could be understood as a struggle between rationality and emotion, with feeling frequently exercising controlling force. Those who believed in the desirability of reason's governance often worried

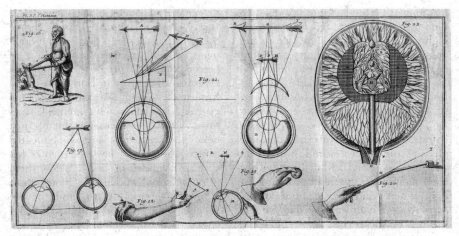

An illustration from an early eighteenth-century edition of the French philosopher René Descartes's unfinished book on the human body. Descartes saw the body as a machine whose operations could be understood mathematically.

that it rarely prevailed over feelings of greed, lust, or the desire for power. For them as for us, the gap between the ideal and the actual caused frustration and often despair.

The questions raised by Enlightenment thinkers about human powers and limitations have left a legacy so lasting that it is hard to imagine our world without the Enlightenment. They are the ones who urged us to trust our own judgments and our own senses—while insisting on the need to think skeptically and critically—and they were the ones who shifted the dominant model of truth from divine revelation to human forms of knowledge: science, statistics, history, literature. They imagined conquering nature with ever-increasing knowledge—allowing humans to control their environment and harness nature's power for their own gain. And they ushered in a new sense of the equality of all human beings, launching the demand for universal human rights.

SOCIETY

The late seventeenth century, when the Enlightenment began, was a period of great turmoil, which persisted at intervals throughout the succeeding century. Reason had led many thinkers to the conclusion that kings and queens were ordinary mortals, and that conclusion implied new kinds of uncertainty. Civil war in England had ended in the king's execution in 1649; the French would guillotine their ruler before the end of the eighteenth century. The notion of divine right, the belief that monarchs governed with authority from God, had been effectively destroyed. God seemed to be moving further away. Religion still figured as a political reality, as it did in the struggle of Cavaliers and Puritans in England, which ended with the restoration of Charles II to the throne in 1660. But the most significant social divisions were now those of class and of political conviction—divisions no less powerful for lacking any claim of God-given authority. To England, the eighteenth century brought two unsuccessful but bitter rebellions on behalf of the deposed Stuart monarchs as well as the cataclysmic American Revolution. Throughout the eighteenth century, wars erupted over succession to European thrones and over nationalistic claims. In Europe, internal divisions often assumed greater importance than struggles between nations. In the Americas, meanwhile, the ideas of the Enlightenment and the example of the American Revolution spread widely, leading to the revolts of creole elites against their European masters and to the birth of new nations.

Although revolution, civil war, and other forms of social instability dominated this period, the idea of civil society retained great power during the Enlightenment. Seventeenth-century English philosopher Thomas Hobbes, who believed that human life before the formation of societies was inevitably "nasty, mean, brutish, and short," thought that men and women had originally banded together for the sake of preservation and progress. By the late seventeenth century in Europe as in the Americas, social organization had evolved into elaborate hierarchical structures with the aristocracy at the top. Just below the aristocrats were the educated gentry—clergymen, lawyers, men of leisure with landed property. Below them were masses of workers of various kinds, many of them illiterate, and, in the Americas, the large populations of indigenous or *mestizo* (mixed-race) peoples, as well as slaves of African descent. Although literacy rates grew dramatically during the eighteenth century, those who wrote (and, for a long time, those who read) belonged almost entirely to the two upper classes. As new forms of commerce generated new wealth, and with it, newly wealthy people who felt entitled to their share of social power,

The Topsy-Turvy World, 1663, by the Dutch genre painter Jan Steen, presents a satirical picture of the disarray in the household of a newly wealthy middle-class family.

the traditional social order faced increasing challenges. In the Americas, white creoles chafed at European entitlements while insisting on their own privilege over other races. By the eighteenth century, the abolitionist movement would begin to question whether slavery could be ethical, a challenge anticipated by **Aphra Behn**'s *Oroonoko*, the story of an African prince tricked into slavery and spirited to the New World.

Among the privileged classes, men had many opportunities: for education, for service in government or diplomacy, for the exercise of political and economic power. Both men and women generally accepted as necessary the subordination of women, who, even in the upper classes, had few opportunities for education and occupation beyond the household. But the increasing value attached to individualism had implications for women as well as men. In the late seventeenth century, **Sor Juana Inés de la Cruz**, a Mexican nun, articulated her own passion for thought and reading, and became an eloquent advocate of the right of women to education and a life of the mind. During the next century, a number of women and an occasional man made the same case. It became increasingly common to argue that limiting women solely to childbearing and childrearing might not conform to the dictates of reason. If God had given all human beings reason, then women were just as entitled to develop and exercise their minds as their male counterparts. The emphasis on education in virtually all of the period's tracts about women provides proof that the concept of rational progress offered a device that could be used to gain at least some rights for women—if not civil rights, which were long in coming, at least the right to thought and knowledge.

Women of the upper classes occupied an important place in Enlightenment society, presiding over "salons," gatherings whose participants engaged in intellectual as well as frivolous conversation. In France as in England, by the late seventeenth century women also began writing novels, their books widely read by men and women alike. Although novels by women often focused attention on the domestic scene, they also ranged further, as in Behn's *Oroonoko*. Women published translations from the Greek as well as volumes of literary criticism, and were the most prolific writers in certain genres, such as Gothic fiction. Even if society as a whole did not acknowledge their full intellectual and moral capacities, individual women were beginning to claim for themselves more rights than those of motherhood.

Society in this period operated, as societies always do, by means of well-defined codes of behavior. Commentators at the time frequently showed themselves troubled by the possibility of sharp discrepancies between social appearance and the "truth" of human nature: **Molière**'s *Tartuffe* provides a vivid example, with its exposé of religious sham. Jonathan Swift, lashing the English for institutionalized hypocrisy; Pope, calling attention to ambiguous sexual mores; **Voltaire** and Johnson, sending naive fictional protagonists to find that moralists don't always practice what they preach—all of these writers call attention to the deceptiveness and the possible misuses of social norms as well as to their necessity. While the social codes may themselves not be at fault, people fail to live up to what they profess. The world would be a better place, these writers suggest, if people examined not only their standards of behavior but also their tendency to hide behind them.

In fiction, drama, poetry, and prose satire, writers of the Enlightenment in one way or another make society their subject. On occasion, they use domestic situations to provide microcosms of a wider social universe. Molière focuses on a private family to suggest how professed sentiment can obscure the

Molière Reading Tartuffe *at the Home of Ninon de L'Enclos,* by Nicolas Andre Monsiau. This eighteenth-century painting of the seventeenth-century playwright is a tribute both to Molière and to L'Enclos, an author, courtesan, and patron of the arts who was host to some of the era's most celebrated literary salons.

operations of ambition; marriage comes to represent a society in miniature, not merely a structure for the fulfillment of personal desire. Marriage, an institution at once social and personal, provides a useful image for human relationship as social and emotional fact. The developing eighteenth-century novel would assume marriage as the normal goal for men and women.

Other writers focus on a broader panorama. Voltaire's world travelers witness and participate in a vast range of sobering experiences. In general, women fill subordinate roles in the harsh social environments evoked by these satiric works: erotic love plays a less important part and the position of women becomes increasingly insignificant as the public life is privileged over the home. It is perhaps relevant to note that no literary work in this section describes or evokes children, an omission that the generation of writers to follow— the Romantics—were eager to correct.

But for the thinkers of the Enlightenment, it was only in adulthood that people assumed social responsibility; and so it was only then that they could provide interesting substance for social commentary.

HUMANITY AND NATURE

If the subject of human beings' relation to society occupied many writers, the problem of humankind's relation to the universe also perplexed them. Deism assumed the existence of a God who provided evidence of Himself only in His created works. Studying the natural world, therefore, might be seen as a religious act; the powers of reason would enable fruitful study. But how, exactly, should humanity's position in the created universe be understood? Alexander Pope, who in *An Essay on Man* investigates his subject in relation both to society and to the universe, understood creation as a great continuum, with man at the apex of the animal world. This view, sometimes described as belief in a Great Chain of Being, was widely shared. But if one turned the eye of reason on generic man himself, his dominance might seem questionable.

Yet the natural order—however incomplete our grasp of it—remains a comfort. It suggests a *system*, a structure of relationships that makes sense at least in theory; rationality thus lies below all apparently irrational experience. It supplies a means of evaluating the natural world: every flower, every minnow, has meaning beyond itself as part of the great pattern. The passion with which the period's thinkers cling to belief in such a system suggests anxiety about what human reason could not do.

The notion of a permanent natural order corresponds to the notion of a permanent human nature, as conceived in the eighteenth century. It was generally believed that human nature remains in all times and places the same: all people hope and fear, are envious and lustful, and possess the capacity to reason. All suffer loss, all face death. Thinkers of the Enlightenment emphasized these common aspects of humanity far more than they considered cultural dissimilarities. Readers and writers alike could draw on this conviction about universality. It provided a test of excellence: if an author's imagining of character failed to conform to what eighteenth-century readers understood as human nature, a work might be securely judged inadequate. Conversely, the idea of a constant human nature held out the hope of longevity for writers who successfully evoked it. Moral philosophers could define human obligation and possibility, convinced that they, too, wrote for all time; ethical standards would never change. Like the vision of order in the physical universe, the notion of constancy in human nature provided bedrock.

CONVENTION AND AUTHORITY

Guides to manners proliferated in the eighteenth century, emphasizing the idea that commitment to decorum helped preserve society's standards. Literary conventions—agreed-on systems of verbal behavior—served comparable purposes in their own sphere, providing continuity between present and past. While these conventions may strike modern readers as antiquated and artificial, to contemporary readers they seemed both natural and proper, much as the plaintive lyrics of current country music or the extravagances of rap operate within restrictive conventions that appear "natural" only because they are familiar to us. Eighteenth-century writers had at their disposal an established set of conventions for every traditional literary genre. As the repetitive rhythms of the country ballad tell listeners what to expect, these literary conventions provided readers with clues about the kind of experience they could anticipate in a given poem or play.

Underlying all the conventions of this era was the classical assumption that literature existed to delight and instruct its readers. The various genres of this period embody such belief in literature's dual function. Stage comedy and tragedy, the early novel, satire in prose and verse, didactic poetry, the philosophical tale: each form developed its own set of devices for creating pleasure as well as for involving audiences and readers in situations requiring moral choice. The insistence in drama on unity of time and place (stage action occupying no more time than its representation, with no change of scene) exemplifies one such set of conventions, intended to produce in their audiences the maximum emotional and moral effect. The two-dimensional characters of Voltaire's tales provide clues about whether the author intends us to read "straight" or to recognize a satirical intention.

One dominant convention of twenty-first-century poetry and prose is something we call "realism." In fiction, verse, and drama, writers often attempt to convey the literal feel of experience, the shape in which events actually occur in the world, the way people really talk. Behn and Voltaire pursued no such goal. Despite their concern with permanent patterns of thought and feeling, they employed deliberate and obvious forms of artifice as modes of emphasis and of indirection. The sonorous lines in which Behn's characters reflect on their passions ("Since I have sacrificed Imoinda to my revenge, shall I lose that Glory which I have purchased so dear, as at the Price of the fairest, dearest, softest Creature that ever Nature made?") embodies a characteristic form of stylization. Artistic transformation of life, the period's writers believed, involves the imposition of formal order on the endless flux of event and feeling. The formalities of this literature constitute part of its meaning: its statement that what experience shows as unstable, art makes stable.

By relying on convention, eighteenth-century writers attempted to control an unstable world. The classical past, for many, provided an emblem of that stability, a standard of permanence. But some felt that overvaluing the past was problematic, the problem epitomized by the quarrel of ancients versus moderns in England and France. At stake in this controversy was, among other things, the value of permanence as opposed to the value of change. Proponents of the ancients believed that the giants of Greece and Rome had not only established standards applicable to all future works but had provided models of achievement never to be excelled. Homer wrote the first great epics; subsequent epics could only imitate him. When innovation came, it came by making the old new.

Those proud to be moderns, on the other hand, held that men (possibly even women) standing on the shoulders of the ancients could see further than their predecessors. The new was conceivably more valuable than the old. One might discover flaws even in revered figures of the classic past, and not everything had yet been accomplished. This view, of course, corresponds to one widely current since the eighteenth century, but it did not triumph easily: many powerful thinkers of the late seventeenth and early eighteenth centuries adhered to the more conservative position.

Also at issue in this debate was the question of authority, which was to prove so perilous in the political sphere. What position should be assumed by one who hoped to write and be read? Did authority reside only in tradition? If so, must one write in classical forms, rely on classical allusions? Until late in the eighteenth century, virtually all important writers attempted to ally themselves with the authority of tradition, declaring themselves part of a community extending through time as well as space. The problems of authority became particularly important in connection with satire, a popular Enlightenment form. Satire involves criticism of vice and folly; Molière, Pope, Swift, Voltaire, and Johnson at least on occasion wrote in the satiric mode. The fact that satire flourished so richly in this period suggests another version of the central conflict between reason and passion: that of the forces of stability and of instability. In its heightened description of the world (people eating babies, young women initiating epic battles over the loss of a lock of hair), satire calls attention to the powerful presence of the irrational, opposing that presence with the clarity of the satirist's own claim to reason and tradition. As it chastises human beings for their eruptions of passion, urging resistance and control, satire reminds its readers of the universality of the irrational as well as of opposition to it.

MOLIÈRE
(JEAN-BAPTISTE POQUELIN)
1622–1673

Jean-Baptiste Molière, one of the great comic dramatists in the Western tradition, wrote both broad farce and comedies of character in which he caricatured some form of vice or folly by embodying it in a single figure. His targets included the miser, the aspiring but vulgar middle class, female would-be intellectuals, the hypochondriac, and in *Tartuffe*, the religious hypocrite. Yet Molière's questioning goes far beyond witty farce: his works suggest not only the fallibility of specific types but also the foolishness of trusting reason to arrange human affairs.

LIFE AND TIMES

Son of a prosperous Paris merchant, Molière (originally named Poquelin) devoted his entire adult life to the creation of stage illusion, as playwright and as actor. He was educated at a prestigious Jesuit school and seems to have studied law for some time, though without taking a degree. At about the age of twenty-five, he took his stage name and abandoned the comfortable life of a bourgeois to join the Illustre Théâtre, a company of traveling players established by the Béjart family. With them he toured the provinces for about twelve years, and, in 1662, he married Armande Béjart. Molière's lengthy experience as an actor doubtless honed his dramatic writing skills, although he first became known not for the tragedies that he preferred but for the short farces that he appended to them.

Molière's particular talents, it would soon become clear, lay in satirizing an overly sophisticated society that was heavily invested in fashion, appearances, and proper behavior. Molière's skepticism about religious devotion, which he exposed as hypocrisy, would prove hugely controversial in a France that had recently been led by the powerful Cardinal Mazarin, chief minister while Louis XIV was a young boy, and where the Catholic Church still wielded considerable power.

Over the course of his long reign, Louis XIV, the "Sun King," consolidated royal power by upholding the divine right of kings, and became an important patron of the visual and literary arts. In Louis's France, the true measure of cultural worth was the approval of the court and the Paris stage. After years of courting noble patrons, in 1658 Molière's theatrical company was finally ordered to perform for the king in Paris; a year later, the playwright's first great success, *The High-Brow Ladies* (*Les Précieuses ridicules*), was produced. The company, now patronized by the king, became increasingly successful, developing finally (1680) into the Comédie Française. With success came opposition: the *parti des Devots* (party of the faithful) banded together to protest Molière's irreverence, as he took on more and more of his society's sacred cows. Yet the king continued to protect him, granting him a pension and allowing Molière to evade the censorship often demanded by the Church or the more conservative voices in society.

Molière became increasingly famous—and infamous—as his works met with increasing resistance, culminating in the furor over *Tartuffe*, discussed below. Over the course of his years in Paris, Molière wrote over thirty plays and produced many more on his stage. Ever the man of the theater, he died a few hours after performing in the lead role of his own play *The Imaginary Invalid*.

TARTUFFE

In *Tartuffe* (1664), as in his other plays, Molière employs classic comic devices of plot and character—here, a foolish, stubborn father blocking the course of young love; an impudent servant commenting on her superiors' actions; a happy ending involving a marriage facilitated by implausible means. He often uses such devices, however, to comment on his own immediate social scene, imagining how universal patterns play themselves out in a specific historical context. *Tartuffe* targeted the hypocrisy of piety so directly and transparently that the Catholic Church forced the king to ban it, although Molière managed to have it published and produced once more by 1669.

The play's emotional energy derives not from the simple discrepancy of man and mask in Tartuffe ("Is not a face quite different from a mask?" inquires Cléante, who has no trouble making such distinctions) but from the struggle for erotic, psychic, and economic power in which people employ their masks. Orgon, an aging man with grown children, seeks ways to preserve control and instead falls for the ploys of the hypocritical Tartuffe. A domestic tyrant, Orgon insists on submission from the women in the play, even when they prove far more perceptive than he about Tartuffe's deceptions.

Tartuffe's lust, one of those passions forever eluding human mastery, disturbs Orgon's arrangements; in the end, the will of the offstage king orders everything, as though a benevolent god had intervened.

To make Tartuffe a specifically religious hypocrite is an act of inventive daring. Although one may easily accept Molière's defense of his intentions (not to mock faith but to attack its misuse), it is not hard to see why the play might trouble religious authorities. Molière suggests how readily religious faith lends itself to misuse, how high-sounding pieties allow men and women to evade self-examination and immediate responsibilities. Tartuffe deceives others by his grand gestures of mortification ("Hang up my hair shirt") and charity; he encourages his victims in their own grandiosities. Religion offers ready justification for a course as destructive as it is self-seeking.

Throughout the play, Orgon's brother-in-law Cléante speaks in the voice of wisdom, counseling moderation, common sense, and self-control, calling attention to folly. More important, he emphasizes how the issues Molière examines in this comedy relate to dominant late seventeenth-century themes:

> Ah, Brother, man's a strangely
>   fashioned creature
> Who seldom is content to follow
>   Nature,
> But recklessly pursues his inclination
> Beyond the narrow bounds of
>   moderation,
> And often, by transgressing Reason's
>   laws,
> Perverts a lofty aim or noble cause.

To follow Nature means to act appropriately to the human situation in the created universe, recognizing the limitations inherent in the human condition. As Cléante's observations suggest, "to follow Nature," given the rationality of the universe, implies adherence to "Reason's laws." All transgression involves failure to submit to reason's dictates, a point that Molière's stylized comic plot makes insistently.

Although the comedy suggests a social world in which women exist in utter subordination to fathers and husbands, in the plot, two women bring about the unmasking of the villain. The virtuous wife, Elmire, object of Tartuffe's lust, and the clever servant girl, Dorine, confront the immediate situation with pragmatic inventiveness. Both women have a clear sense of right and wrong, although they express it in less resounding terms than does Cléante. Their concrete insistence on facing what is really going on, cutting through all obfuscation, rescues the men from entanglement in their own abstract formulations.

Molière achieves comic effects above all through style and language. Devoted to exposing the follies of his society, his plays use a number of devices that have become the gold standard of comic writing. His characters are often in the grip of a fixed idea, rigidly following a single principle of action, such as extreme religious devotion or sexual rejuvenation. These fixed ideas also manifest themselves in the characters' speech patterns, which are full of ticks and repetitions. Adher-ing to single abstractions, Molière's comic protagonists often seem like marionettes, whose rigid bearing, behavior and language is controlled by an outside force as if by a puppet master. Yet despite their singlemind-edness, his characters are also recognizable portraits of human folly, closely observed and humorously rendered.

Comedies conventionally end in the restoration of order, declaring that good inevitably triumphs; rationality renews itself despite the temporary deviations of the foolish and the vicious. Although at the end of *Tartuffe* order is restored, the arbitrary intervention of the king leaves a disturbing emotional residue. The play has demonstrated that Tartuffe's corrupt will to power can ruthlessly aggrandize itself. Money speaks, in this society as in ours; possession of wealth implies total control over others. In the benign world of comedy, the play reminds its readers of the extreme precariousness with which reason finally triumphs. Tartuffe's monstrous lust, for women, money, power, genuinely endangers the social structure. The play forces us to recognize the constant threats to rationality, and how much we have at stake in trying to use reason as a principle of action.

Tartuffe[1]

CHARACTERS

MADAME PERNELLE, *mother of Orgon*
ORGON, *husband of Elmire*
ELMIRE, *wife of Orgon*
DAMIS, *son of Orgon*
MARIANE, *daughter of Orgon*
VALÈRE, *fiancé of Mariane*
CLÉANTE, *brother-in-law of Orgon*

TARTUFFE,[2] *a religious hypocrite*
DORINE, *lady's maid to Mariane*
MONSIEUR LOYAL, *a bailiff*
THE EXEMPT, *an officer of the king*
FLIPOTE, *lady's maid to Madame Pernelle*
LAURENT, *a servant of Tartuffe*

The scene is Paris, in ORGON's *house.*

1.1

[MADAME PERNELLE, FLIPOTE, ELMIRE,
MARIANE, DORINE, DAMIS, CLÉANTE]

MADAME PERNELLE[3]   Flipote, come on! My visit here is through!
ELMIRE   You walk so fast I can't keep up with you!
MADAME PERNELLE   Then stop! That's your last step! Don't take another.
  After all, I'm just your husband's mother.
ELMIRE   And, as his wife, I have to see you out—   5
  Agreed? Now, what is this about?
MADAME PERNELLE   I cannot bear the way this house is run—
  As if I don't know how things should be done!
  No one even thinks about my pleasure,
  And, if I ask, I'm served at someone's leisure.   10
  It's obvious—the values here aren't good
  Or everyone would treat me as they should.
  The Lord of Misrule here has his dominion—
DORINE   But—
MADAME PERNELLE   See? A servant with an opinion.
  You're the former nanny, nothing more.   15
  Were I in charge here, you'd be out the door.
DAMIS   If—
MADAME PERNELLE   —You—be quiet. Now let Grandma spell
  Her special word for you: "F-O-O-L."
  Oh yes! Your dear grandmother tells you that,

---

1. Versification by Constance Congdon, from a translation by Virginia Scott.
2. The name Tartuffe is similar both to the Italian word *tartufo*, meaning "truffle," and to the French word for truffle, *truffe*, from which is derived the French verb *truffer*—one mean-

ing of which in Molière's day was "to deceive or cheat."
3. The role of Madame Pernelle was originally played by a male actor, a practice that was already a comic convention in Molière's time.

Just as I told my son, "Your son's a brat.   20
He won't become a drunkard or a thief,
And yet, he'll be a lifetime full of grief."
MARIANE   I think—
MADAME PERNELLE   —Oh, don't do that, my dear grandchild.
You'll hurt your brain. You think that we're beguiled
By your quietude, you fragile flower,   25
But as they say, still waters do run sour.
ELMIRE   But Mother—
MADAME PERNELLE   —Daughter-in-law, please take this well—
Behavior such as yours leads straight to hell.
You spend money like it grows on trees
Then wear it on your back in clothes like these.   30
Are you a princess? No? You're dressed like one!
One wonders whom you dress for—not my son.
Look to these children whom you have corrupted
When their mama's life was interrupted.
She spun in her grave when you were wed;   35
She's still a better mother, even dead.
CLÉANTE   Madame, I do insist—
MADAME PERNELLE   —You do? On what?
That we live life as you do, caring not
For morals? I hear each time you give that speech
Your sister memorizing what you teach.   40
I'd slam the door on you. Forgive my frankness.
That is how I am! And it is thankless.
DAMIS   Tartuffe would, from the bottom of his heart,
If he had one, thank you.
MADAME PERNELLE   Oh, now you start.
Grandson, it's "Monsieur Tartuffe" to you.   45
And he's a man who should be listened to.
If you provoke him with ungodly chat,
I will not tolerate it, and that's that.
DAMIS   Yet I should tolerate this trickster who
Has become the voice we answer to.   50
And I'm to be as quiet as a mouse
About this tyrant's power in our house?
All the fun things lately we have planned,
We couldn't do. And why? Because they're banned—
DORINE   By him! Anything we take pleasure in   55
Suddenly becomes a mortal sin.
MADAME PERNELLE   Then "he's here just in time" is what I say!
Don't you see? He's showing you the way
To heaven! Yes! So follow where he leads!
My son knows he is just what this house needs.   60
DAMIS   Now Grandmother, listen. Not Father, not you,
No one can make me follow this man who
Rules this house, yet came here as a peasant.
I'll put him in his place. It won't be pleasant.

DORINE   When he came here he wasn't wearing shoes.   65
But he's no village saint—it's all a ruse.
There was no vow of poverty—he's poor!
And he was just some beggar at the door
Whom we should have tossed. He's a disaster!
To think this street bum now plays the master.   70
MADAME PERNELLE   May God have mercy on me. You're all blind.
A nobler, kinder man you'll never find.
DORINE   So you think he's a saint. That's what he wants.
But he's a hypocrite and merely flaunts
This so-called godliness.   75
MADAME PERNELLE   Will you be quiet!?
DORINE   And that man of his—I just don't buy it—
He's supposed to be his servant? No.
They're in cahoots, I bet.
MADAME PERNELLE   How would you know?
When, clearly, you don't understand, in fact,
How a servant is supposed to act?   80
This holy man you think of as uncouth,
Tries to help by telling you the truth
About yourself. But you can't hear it.
He knows what heaven wants and that you fear it.
DORINE   So "heaven" hates these visits by our friends?   85
I see! And that's why Tartuffe's gone to any ends
To ruin our fun? But it is he who's zealous
About "privacy"—and why? He's jealous.
You can't miss it, whenever men come near—
He's lusting for our own Madame Elmire.   90
MADAME PERNELLE   Since you, Dorine, have never understood
Your place, or the concepts of "should"
And "should not," one can't expect you to see
Tartuffe's awareness of propriety.
When these men visit, they bring noise and more—   95
Valets and servants planted at the door,
Carriages and horses, constant chatter.
What must the neighbors think? These things matter.
Is something going on? Well, I hope not.
You know you're being talked about a lot.   100
CLÉANTE   Really, Madame, you think you can prevent
Gossip? When most human beings are bent
On rumormongering and defamation,
And gathering or faking information
To make us all look bad—what can we do?   105
The fools who gossip don't care what is true.
You would force the whole world to be quiet?
Impossible! And each new lie—deny it?
Who in the world would want to live that way?
Let's live our lives. Let gossips have their say.   110

DORINE   It's our neighbor, Daphne. I just know it.
  They don't like us. It's obvious—they show it
  In the way they watch us—she and her mate.
  I've seen them squinting at us, through their gate.
  It's true—those whose private conduct is the worst   115
  Will mow each other down to be the first
  To weave some tale of lust, so hearts are broken
  Out of a simple kiss that's just a token
  Between friends—just friends and nothing more.
  See—those whose trysts are kept behind a door   120
  Yet everyone finds out? Well, then, they need
  New stories for the gossip mill to feed
  To all who'll listen. So they must repaint
  The deeds of others, hoping that a taint
  Will color others' lives in darker tone   125
  And, by this process, lighten up their own.
MADAME PERNELLE   Daphne and her mate are not the point.
  But when Orante says things are out of joint,
  There's a problem. She's a person who
  Prays every day and should be listened to.   130
  She condemns the mob that visits here.
DORINE   This good woman shouldn't live so near
  Those, like us, who run a bawdy house.
  I hear she lives as quiet as a mouse—
  Devout, though. Everyone applauds her zeal.   135
  She needed that when age stole her appeal.
  Her passion is policing—it's her duty.
  And compensation for her loss of beauty.
  She's a reluctant prude. And now, her art,
  Once used so well to win a lover's heart,   140
  Is gone. Her eyes, that used to flash with lust,
  Are steely from her piety. She must
  Have seen that it's too late to be a wife,
  And so she lives a plain and pious life.
  This is a strategy of old coquettes.   145
  It's how they manage once the world forgets
  Them. First, they wallow in a dark depression,
  Then see no recourse but in the profession
  Of a prude. They criticize the lives of everyone.
  They censure everything, and pardon none.   150
  It's envy. Pleasures that they are denied
  By time and age, now, they just can't abide.
MADAME PERNELLE   You do go on and on. [To ELMIRE] My dear Elmire,
  This is all your doing. It's so clear
  Because you let a servant give advice.   155
  Just be aware—I'm tired of being nice.
  It's obvious to anyone with eyes
  That what my son has done is more than wise

In welcoming this man who's so devout;
His very presence casts the devils out.   160
Or most of them—that's why I hope you hear him.
And I advise all of you to stay near him.
You need his protection and advice.
Your casual attention won't suffice.
It's heaven sent him here to fill a need,   165
To save you from yourselves—oh yes, indeed.
These visits from your friends you seem to want—
Listen to yourselves! So nonchalant!
As if no evil lurks in these events.
As if you're blind to what Satan invents.   170
And dances! What are those but food for slander!
It's to the worst desires these parties pander.
I ask you now, what purpose do they serve?
Where gossip's passed around like an hors-d'oeuvre.
A thousand cackling hens, busy with what?   175
It takes a lot of noise to cover smut.
It truly is the tower of Babylon,[4]
Where people babble on and on and on.
Ah! Case in point—there stands Monsieur Cléante,
Sniggering and eyeing me askant,   180
As if this has nothing to do with him,
And nothing that he does would God condemn.
And so, Elmire, my dear, I say farewell.
Till when? When it is a fine day in hell.
Farewell, all of you. When I pass through that door,   185
You won't have me to laugh at anymore.
Flipote! Wake up! Have you heard nothing I have said?
I'll march you home and beat you till you're dead.
March, slut, march.

1.2[5]

[DORINE, CLÉANTE]

CLÉANTE   I'm staying here. She's scary,
   That old lady—
DORINE   I know why you're wary.
   Shall I call her back to hear you say,
   "That *old* lady"? That would make her day.

---

4. That is, the biblical Tower of Babel (the Hebrew equivalent of the Akkadian Bab-ilu, or Babylon—a name explained by the similar sounding but unrelated Hebrew verb *balal*, "confuse"), described in Genesis 11.1–9; to prevent it from being constructed and reaching heaven, God scattered all the people and confused their language, creating many tongues where there had been only one.
5. In classical French drama, a new scene begins whenever a character enters or leaves the stage, even if the action continues without interruption; this convention has become known as "French scenes." Characters remaining on-stage are listed; others from the previous scene can be assumed to have exited.

CLÉANTE   She's lost her mind, she's—now we have the proof—   5
　　Head over heels in love with whom? Tartuffe.
DORINE   So here's what's worse and weird—so is her son.
　　What's more—it's obvious to everyone.
　　Before Tartuffe and he became entwined,
　　Orgon once ruled this house in his right mind.   10
　　In the troubled times,[6] he backed the prince,
　　And that took courage. We haven't seen it since.
　　He is intoxicated with Tartuffe—
　　A potion that exceeds a hundred proof.
　　It's put him in a trance, this devil's brew.   15
　　And so he worships this imposter who
　　He calls "brother" and loves more than one—
　　This charlatan—more than daughter, wife, son.
　　This charlatan hears all our master's dreams,
　　And all his secrets. Every thought, it seems,   20
　　Is poured out to Tartuffe, like he's his priest!
　　You'd think they'd see the heresy, at least.
　　Orgon caresses him, embraces him, and shows
　　More love for him than any mistress knows.
　　Come for a meal and who has the best seat?   25
　　Whose preferences determine what we eat?
　　Tartuffe consumes enough for six, is praised,
　　And to his health is every goblet raised,
　　While on his plate are piled the choicest bites.
　　Then when he belches, our master delights   30
　　In that and shouts, "God bless you!" to the beast,
　　As if Tartuffe's the reason for the feast.
　　Did I mention the quoting of each word,
　　As if it's the most brilliant thing we've heard?
　　And, oh, the miracles Tartuffe creates!   35
　　The prophecies! We write while he dictates.
　　All that's ridiculous. But what's evil
　　Is seeing the deception and upheaval
　　Of the master and everything he owns.
　　He hands him money. They're not even loans—   40
　　He's giving it away. It's gone too far.
　　To watch Tartuffe play him like a guitar!
　　And this Laurent, his man, found some lace.
　　Shredded it and threw it in my face.
　　He'd found it pressed inside *The Lives of Saints*,[7]   45
　　I thought we'd have to put him in restraints.
　　"To put the devil's finery beside

---

6. That is, during the Fronde (literally, "sling"; 1648–53), a civil war that took place while France was being ruled by a regent for Louis XIV—"the prince" whom Orgon supported—as various factions of the nobility sought to limit the growing authority of the monarchy.
7. A text (*Flos Sanctorum*, 1599–1601) by the Spanish Jesuit Pedro de Ribadeneyra, available in French translation by 1646.

The words and lives of saintly souls who died—
Is action of satanical transgression!"
And so, of course, I hurried to confession.   50

1.3

[ELMIRE, MARIANE, DAMIS, CLÉANTE, DORINE]

ELMIRE [to CLÉANTE]   Lucky you, you stayed. Yes, there was more,
And more preaching from Grandma, at the door.
My husband's coming! I didn't catch his eye.
I'll wait for him upstairs. Cléante, good-bye.
CLÉANTE   I'll see you soon. I'll wait here below,   5
Take just a second for a brief hello.
DAMIS   While you have him, say something for me?
My sister needs for Father to agree
To her marriage with Valère, as planned.
Tartuffe opposes it and will demand   10
That Father break his word, and that's not fair;
Then I can't wed the sister of Valère.
Listening only to Tartuffe's voice,
He'd break four hearts at once—
DORINE   He's here.

1.4

[ORGON, CLÉANTE, DORINE]

ORGON   Rejoice!
I'm back.
CLÉANTE   I'm glad to see you, but I'm on my way.
Just stayed to say hello.
ORGON   No more to say?
Dorine! Come back! And Cléante, why the hurry?
Indulge me for a moment. You know I worry.   5
I've been gone two days! There's news to tell.
Now don't hold back. Has everyone been well?
DORINE   Not quite. There was that headache Madame had
The day you left. Well, it got really bad.
She had a fever—   10
ORGON   And Tartuffe?
DORINE   He's fine—
Rosy-nosed and red-cheeked, drinking your wine.
ORGON   Poor man!
DORINE   And then, Madame became unable
To eat a single morsel at the table.
ORGON   Ah, and Tartuffe?
DORINE   He sat within her sight,
Not holding back, he ate with great delight,   15

A brace of partridge, and a leg of mutton.
In fact, he ate so much, he popped a button.
ORGON   Poor man!
DORINE   That night until the next sunrise,
Your poor wife couldn't even close her eyes.
What a fever! Oh, how she did suffer!   20
I don't see how that night could have been rougher.
We watched her all night long, worried and weepy.
ORGON   Ah, and Tartuffe?
DORINE   At dinner he grew sleepy.
After such a meal, it's not surprising.
He slept through the night, not once arising.   25
ORGON   Poor man!
DORINE   At last won over by our pleading,
Madame agreed to undergo a bleeding.[8]
And this, we think, has saved her from the grave.
ORGON   Ah, and Tartuffe?
DORINE   Oh, he was very brave.
To make up for the blood Madame had lost   30
Tartuffe slurped down red wine, all at your cost.
ORGON   Poor man!
DORINE   Since then, they've both been fine, although
Madame needs me. I'll go and let her know
How anxious you have been about her health,
And that you prize it more than all your wealth.   35

1.5

[ORGON, CLÉANTE]

CLÉANTE   You know that girl was laughing in your face.
I fear I'll make you angry, but in case
There is a chance you'll listen, I will try
To say that you are laughable and why.
I've never known of something so capricious   5
As letting this man do just as he wishes
In your home and to your family.
You brought him here, relieved his poverty,
And, in return—
ORGON   Now you listen to me!
You're just my brother-in-law, Cléante. Quite!   10
You don't know this man. And don't deny it!
CLÉANTE   I don't know him, yes, that may be so,
But men like him are not so rare, you know.

---

8. Bloodletting (whether by leeches or other means), for centuries a standard medical treatment
for a wide range of diseases.

ORGON   If you only could know him as I do,
    You would be his true disciple, too.   15
    The universe, your ecstasy would span.
    This is a man . . . who . . . ha! . . . well, such a man.
    Behold him. Let him teach you profound peace.
    When first we met, I felt my troubles cease.
    Yes, I was changed after I talked with him.   20
    I saw my wants and needs as just a whim!
    Everything that's written, all that's sung,
    The world, and you and me, well, it's all dung!
    Yes, it's crap! And isn't that a wonder!
    The real world—it's just some spell we're under!   25
    He's taught me to love nothing and no one!
    Mother, father, wife, daughter, son—
    They could die right now, I'd feel no pain.
CLÉANTE   What feelings you've developed, how humane.
ORGON   You just don't see him in the way I do,   30
    But if you did, you'd feel what I feel, too.
    Every day he came to church and knelt,
    And from his groans, I knew just what he felt.
    Those sounds he made from deep inside his soul,
    Were fed by piety he could not control.   35
    Of the congregation, who could ignore
    The way he humbly bowed and kissed the floor?
    And when they tried to turn away their eyes,
    His fervent prayers to heaven and deep sighs
    Made them witness his deep spiritual pain.   40
    Then something happened I can't quite explain.
    I rose to leave—he quickly went before
    To give me holy water at the door.
    He knew what I needed, so he blessed me.
    I found his acolyte, he'd so impressed me,   45
    To ask who he was and there I learned
    About his poverty and how he spurned
    The riches of this world. And when I tried
    To give him gifts, in modesty, he cried,
    "That is too much," he'd say, "A half would do."   50
    Then gave a portion back, with much ado.
    "I am not worthy. I do not deserve
    Your gifts or pity. I am here to serve
    The will of heaven, that and nothing more."
    Then takes the gift and shares it with the poor.   55
    So heaven spoke to me inside my head.
    "Just bring him home with you" is what it said
    And so I did. And ever since he came,
    My home's a happy one. I also claim
    A moral home, a house that's free of sin,   60
    Tartuffe's on watch—he won't let any in.
    His interest in my wife is reassuring,

She's innocent of course, but so alluring,
He tells me whom she sees and what she does.
He's more jealous than I ever was.   65
It's for my honor that he's so concerned.
His righteous anger's all for me, I've learned,
To the point that just the other day,
A flea annoyed him as he tried to pray,
Then he rebuked himself, as if he'd willed it—   70
His excessive anger when he killed it.

CLÉANTE   Orgon, listen. You're out of your mind.
Or you're mocking me. Or both combined.
How can you speak such nonsense without blinking?

ORGON   I smell an atheist! It's that freethinking!   75
Such nonsense is the bane of your existence.
And that explains your damnable resistance.
Ten times over, I've tried to save your soul
From your corrupted mind. That's still my goal.

CLÉANTE   You have been corrupted by your friends,   80
You know of whom I speak. Your thought depends
On people who are blind and want to spread it
Like some horrid flu, and, yes, I dread it.
I'm no atheist. I see things clearly.
And what I see is loud lip service, merely,   85
To make exhibitionists seem devout.
Forgive me, but a prayer is not a shout.
Yet those who don't adore these charlatans
Are seen as faithless heathens by your friends.
It's as if you think you'd never find   90
Reason and the sacred intertwined.
You think I'm afraid of retribution?
Heaven sees my heart and their pollution.
So we should be the slaves of sanctimony?
Monkey see, monkey do, monkey phony.   95
The true believers we should emulate
Are not the ones who groan and lay prostrate.
And yet you see no problem in the notion
Of hypocrisy as deep devotion.
You see as one the genuine and the spurious.   100
You'd extend this to your money? I'm just curious.
In your business dealings, I'd submit,
You'd not confuse the gold with counterfeit.
Men are strangely made, I'd have to say.
They're burdened with their reason, till one day,   105
They free themselves with such force that they spoil
The noblest of things for which they toil.
Because they must go to extremes. It's a flaw.
Just a word in passing, Brother-in-law.

ORGON   Oh, you are the wisest man alive, so   110
You know everything there is to know.

You are the one enlightened man, the sage.
You are Cato the Elder[9] of our age.
Next to you, all men are dumb as cows.
CLÉANTE   I'm not the wisest man, as you espouse,   115
Nor do I know—what—all there is to know?
But I do know, Orgon, that quid pro quo
Does not apply at all to "false" and "true,"
And I would never trust a person who
Cannot tell them apart. See, I revere   120
Everyone whose worship is sincere.
Nothing is more noble or more beautiful
Than fervor that is holy, not just dutiful.
So nothing is more odious to me
Than the display of specious piety   125
Which I see in every charlatan
Who tries to pass for a true holy man.
Religious passion worn as a facade
Abuses what's sacred and mocks God.
These men who take what's sacred and most holy   130
And use it as their trade, for money, solely,
With downcast looks and great affected cries,
Who suck in true believers with their lies,
Who ceaselessly will preach and then demand
"Give up the world!" and then, by sleight of hand,   135
End up sitting pretty at the court,
The best in lodging and new clothes to sport.
If you're their enemy, then heaven hates you.
That's their claim when one of them berates you.
They'll say you've sinned. You'll find yourself removed   140
And wondering if you'll be approved
For anything, at all, ever again.
Because so heinous was this fictional "sin."
When these men are angry, they're the worst,
There's no place to hide, you're really cursed.   145
They use what we call righteous as their sword,
To coldly murder in the name of the Lord.
But next to these imposters faking belief,
The devotion of the true is a relief.
Our century has put before our eyes   150
Glorious examples we can prize.
Look at Ariston, and look at Periandre,
Oronte, Alcidamas, Polydore, Clitandre:[1]
Not one points out his own morality,
Instead they speak of their mortality.   155

9. Roman statesman and author (234–149 B.C.E.), famous as a stern moralist devoted to traditional Roman ideals of honor, courage, and simplicity.
1. Made-up names.

They don't form cabals,[2] they don't have factions,
They don't censure other people's actions.
They see the flagrant pride in such correction
And know that humans can't achieve perfection.
They know this of themselves and yet their lives   160
Good faith, good works, all good, epitomize.
They don't exhibit zeal that's more intense
Than heaven shows us in its own defense.
They'd never claim a knowledge that's divine
And yet they live in virtue's own design.   165
They concentrate their hatred on the sin,
And when the sinner grieves, invite him in.
They leave to others the arrogance of speech.
Instead they practice what others only preach.
These are the men who show us how to live.   170
Their lives, the best example I can give.
These are my men, the ones whom I would follow.
Your man and his life, honestly, are hollow.
I believe you praise him quite sincerely,
I also think you'll pay for this quite dearly.   175
He's a fraud, this man whom you adore.

ORGON   Oh, you've stopped talking. Is there any more?

CLÉANTE   No.

ORGON   I am your servant, sir.

CLÉANTE   No! wait!
There's one more thing—no more debate—
I want to change the subject, if I might.   180
I heard that you said the other night,
To Valère, he'd be your son-in-law.

ORGON   I did.

CLÉANTE   And set the date?

ORGON   Yes.

CLÉANTE   Did you withdraw?

ORGON   I did.

CLÉANTE   You're putting off the wedding? Why?

ORGON   Don't know.   185

CLÉANTE   There's more?

ORGON   Perhaps.

CLÉANTE   Again I'll try:
You would break your word?

ORGON   I couldn't say.

CLÉANTE   Then, Orgon, why did you change the day?

ORGON   Who knows?

---

2. A possible allusion to the Compagnie de Saint-Sacrement, a tightly knit group of prominent French citizens known for public works as well as strict morality; they were pejoratively referred to as the *cabale*.

CLÉANTE But we need to know, don't we now?
Is there a reason you would break your vow?
ORGON That depends. 190
CLÉANTE On what? Orgon, what is it?
Valère was the reason for my visit.
ORGON Who knows? Who knows?
CLÉANTE So there's some mystery there?
ORGON Heaven knows.
CLÉANTE It does? And now, Valère—
May he know, too?
ORGON Can't say.
CLÉANTE But, dear Orgon,
We have no information to go on. 195
We need to know—
ORGON What heaven wants, I'll do.
CLÉANTE Is that your final answer? Then I'm through.
But your pledge to Valère? You'll stand by it?
ORGON Good-bye.

[ORGON *exits.*]

CLÉANTE More patience, yes, I should try it.
I let him get to me. Now I confess 200
I fear the worst for Valère's happiness.

2.1

[ORGON, MARIANE]

ORGON Mariane.
MARIANE Father.
ORGON Come. Now. Talk with me.
MARIANE Why are you looking everywhere?
ORGON To see
If everyone is minding their own business.
So, Child, I've always loved your gentleness.
MARIANE And for your love, I'm grateful, Father dear. 5
ORGON Well said. And so to prove that you're sincere,
And worthy of my love, you have the task
Of doing for me anything I ask.
MARIANE Then my obedience will be my proof.
ORGON Good. What do you think of our guest, Tartuffe? 10
MARIANE Who, me?
ORGON Yes, you. Watch what you say right now.
MARIANE Then, Father, I will say what you allow.
ORGON Wise words, Daughter. So this is what you say:
"He is a perfect man in every way;
In body and soul, I find him divine." 15
And then you say, "Please Father, make him mine."
Huh?

MARIANE Huh?

ORGON Yes?

MARIANE I heard . . .

ORGON Yes.

MARIANE What did you say?
Who is this perfect man in every way,
Whom in body and soul I find divine
And ask of you, "Please, Father, make him mine?"   20

ORGON Tartuffe.

MARIANE All that I've said, I now amend
Because you wouldn't want me to pretend.

ORGON Absolutely not—that's so misguided.
Have it be the truth, then. It's decided.

MARIANE What?! Father, you want—   25

ORGON Yes, my dear, I do—
To join in marriage my Tartuffe and you.
And since I have—

2.2

[DORINE, ORGON, MARIANE]

ORGON Dorine, I know you're there!
Any secrets in this house you don't share?

DORINE "Marriage"—I think, yes, I heard a rumor,
Someone's failed attempt at grotesque humor,
So when I heard the story, I said, "No!   5
Preposterous! Absurd! It can't be so."

ORGON Oh, you find it preposterous? And why?

DORINE It's so outrageous, it must be a lie.

ORGON Yet it's the truth and you will believe it.

DORINE Yet as a joke is how I must receive it.   10

ORGON But it's a story that will soon come true.

DORINE A fantasy!

ORGON I'm getting tired of you.
Mariane, it's not a joke—

DORINE Says he,
Laughing up his sleeve for all to see.

ORGON I'm telling you—   15

DORINE —more make-believe for fun.
It's very good—you're fooling everyone.

ORGON You have made me really angry now.

DORINE I see the awful truth across your brow.
How can a man who looks as wise as you
Be such a fool to want—   20

ORGON What can I do
About a servant with a mouth like that?
The liberties you take! Decorum you laugh at!
I'm not happy with you—

DORINE   Oh sir, don't frown.
  A smile is just a frown turned upside down.
  Be happy, sir, because you've shared your scheme,   25
  Even though it's just a crazy dream.
  Because, dear sir, your daughter is not meant
  For this zealot—she's too innocent.
  She'd be alarmed by his robust desire
  And question heaven's sanction of this fire   30
  And then the gossip! Your friends will talk a lot,
  Because you're a man of wealth and he is not.
  Could it be your reasoning has a flaw—
  Choosing a beggar for a son-in-law?
ORGON   You, shut up! If he has nothing now   35
  Admire that, as if it were his vow,
  This poverty. His property was lost
  Because he would not pay the deadly cost
  Of daily duties nibbling life away,
  Leaving him with hardly time to pray.   40
  The grandeur in his life comes from devotion
  To the eternal, thus his great emotion.
  And at those moments, I can plainly see
  What my special task has come to be:
  To end the embarrassment he feels   45
  And the sorrow he so nobly conceals
  Of the loss of his ancestral domain.
  With my money, I can end his pain.
  I'll raise him up to be, because I can,
  With my help, again, a gentleman.   50
DORINE   So he's a gentleman. Does that seem vain?
  Then what about this piety and pain?
  Those with "domains" are those of noble birth.
  A holy man's domain is not on earth.
  It seems to me a holy man of merit   55
  Wouldn't brag of what he might inherit—
  Even gifts in heaven, he won't mention.
  To live a humble life is his intention.
  Yet he wants something back? That's just ambition
  To feed his pride. Is that a holy mission?   60
  You seem upset. Is it something I said?
  I'll shut up. We'll talk of her instead.
  Look at this girl, your daughter, your own blood.
  How will her honor fare covered with mud?
  Think of his age. So from the night they're wed,   65
  Bliss, if there is any, leaves the marriage bed,
  And she'll be tied unto this elderly person.
  Her dedication to fidelity will worsen
  And soon he will sprout horns,[3] your holy man,

3. The traditional sign of the cuckold.

And no one will be happy. If I can 70
Have another word, I'd like to say
Old men and young girls are married every day,
And the young girls stray, but who's to blame
For the loss of honor and good name?
The father, who proceeds to pick a mate, 75
Blindly, though it's someone she may hate,
Bears the sins the daughter may commit,
Imperiling his soul because of it.
If you do this, I vow you'll hear the bell,
As you die, summoning you to hell. 80

ORGON You think that you can teach me how to live.
DORINE If you'd just heed the lessons that I give.
ORGON Can heaven tell me why I still endure
This woman's ramblings? Yet, of this I'm sure,
I know what's best for you—I'm your father. 85
I gave you to Valère, without a bother.
But I hear he gambles and what's more,
He thinks things that a Christian would abhor.
It's from free thinking that all evils stem.
No wonder, then, at church, I don't see him. 90
DORINE Should he race there, if he only knew
Which Mass you might attend, and be on view?
He could wait at the door with holy water.
ORGON Go away. I'm talking to my daughter.
Think, my child, he is heaven's favorite! 95
And age in marriage? It can flavor it,
A sweet comfit suffused with deep, deep pleasure.
You will be loving, faithful, and will treasure
Every single moment—two turtledoves—
Next to heaven, the only thing he loves. 100
And he will be the only one for you.
No arguments or quarrels. You'll be true,
Like two innocent children, you will thrive,
In heaven's light, thrilled to be alive.
And as a woman, surely you must know 105
Wives mold husbands, like making pies from dough.
DORINE Four and twenty cuckolds baked in a pie.
ORGON Ugh! What a thing to say!
DORINE   Oh, really, why?
He's destined to be cheated on, it's true.
You know he'd always question her virtue. 110
ORGON Quiet! Just be quiet. I command it!
DORINE I'll do just that, because you do demand it!
But your best interests—I will protect them.
ORGON Too kind of you. Be quiet and neglect them.
DORINE If I weren't fond of you— 115
ORGON   —Don't want you to
DORINE I will be fond of you in spite of you.

ORGON   Don't!
DORINE   But your honor is so dear to me,
   How can you expose yourself to mockery?
ORGON   Will you never be quiet!
DORINE   Oh, dear sir,   120
   I can't let you do this thing to her,
   It's against my conscience—
ORGON   You vicious asp!
DORINE   Sometimes the things you call me make me gasp.
   And anger, sir, is not a pious trait.
ORGON   It's your fault, girl! You make me irate!
   I am livid! Why won't you be quiet!   125
DORINE   I will. For you, I'm going to try it.
   But I'll be thinking.
ORGON   Fine. Now, Mariane,
   You have to trust—your father's a wise man.
   I have thought a lot about this mating.
   I've weighed the options—   130
DORINE   It's infuriating
   Not to be able to speak.
ORGON   And so
   I'll say this. Of up and coming men I know,
   He's not one of them, no money in the bank,
   Not handsome.
DORINE   That's the truth. Arf! Arf! Be frank.
   He's a dog!   135
ORGON   He has manly traits.
   And other gifts.
DORINE   And who will blame the fates
   For failure of this marriage made in hell?
   And whose fault will it be? Not hard to tell.
   Since everyone you know will see the truth:
   You gave away your daughter to Tartuffe.   140
   If I were in her place, I'd guarantee
   No man would live the night who dared force me
   Into a marriage that I didn't want.
   There would be war with no hope of détente.
ORGON   I asked for silence. This is what I get?   145
DORINE   You said not to talk to *you*. Did you forget?
ORGON   What do you call what you are doing now?
DORINE   Talking to myself.
ORGON   You insolent cow!
   I'll wait for you to say just one more word.
   I'm waiting . . .   150
        [ORGON *prepares to give* DORINE *a smack but each time he looks*
        over at her, she stands silent and still.]
                   Just ignore her. Look at me.
   I've chosen you a husband who would be,
   If rated, placed among the highest ranks.

[*To* DORINE]   Why don't you talk?

DORINE   Don't feel like it, thanks.

ORGON   I'm watching you.

DORINE   Do you think I'm a fool?

ORGON   I realize that you may think me cruel.   155
 But here's the thing, child, I will be obeyed,
 And this marriage, child, will not be delayed.

DORINE [*Running from* ORGON, DORINE *throws a line to* MARIANE.]
 You'll be a joke with Tartuffe as a spouse.
   [ORGON *tries to slap her but misses.*]

ORGON   What we have is a plague in our own house!
 It's her fault that I'm in the state I'm in,   160
 So furious, I might commit a sin.
 She'll drive me to murder. Or to curse.
 I need fresh air before my mood gets worse.   [ORGON *exits.*]

2.3

[DORINE, MARIANE]

DORINE   Tell me, have you lost the power of speech?
 I'm forced to play your role and it's a reach.
 How can you sit there with nothing to say
 Watching him tossing your whole life away?

MARIANE   Against my father, what am I to do?   5

DORINE   You want out of this marriage scheme, don't you?

MARIANE   Yes.

DORINE   Tell him no one can command a heart.
 That when you marry, you will have no part
 Of anyone unless he pleases you.
 And tell your father, with no more ado,   10
 That you will marry for yourself, not him,
 And that you won't obey his iron whim.
 Since he finds Tartuffe to be such a catch,
 He can marry him himself. There's a match.

MARIANE   You know that fathers have such sway   15
 Over our lives that I've nothing to say.
 I've never had the strength.

DORINE   Let's think. All right?
 Didn't Valère propose the other night?
 Do you or don't you love Valère?

MARIANE   You know the answer, Dorine—that's unfair.   20
 Just talking about it tears me apart.
 I've said a hundred times, he has my heart.
 I'm wild about him. I know. And I've told you.

DORINE   But how am I to know, for sure, that's true?

MARIANE   Because I told you. And yet you doubt it?   25
 See me blushing when I speak about it?

DORINE   So you do love him?

MARIANE   Yes, with all my might.
DORINE   He loves you just as much?
MARIANE   I think that's right.
DORINE   And it's to the altar you're both heading?
MARIANE   Yes.   30
DORINE   So what about this other wedding?
MARIANE   I'll kill myself. That's what I've decided.
DORINE   What a great solution you've provided!
     To get out of trouble, you plan to die!
     Immediately? Or sometime, by and by?
MARIANE   Oh, really, Dorine, you're not my friend,   35
     Unsympathetic—
DORINE   I'm at my wit's end,
     Talking to you whose answer is dying,
     Who, in a crisis, just gives up trying.
MARIANE   What do you want of me, then?
DORINE   Come alive!
     Love needs a resolute heart to survive.   40
MARIANE   In my love for Valère, I'm resolute.
     But the next step is his.
DORINE   And so, you're mute?
MARIANE   What can I say? It's the job of Valère,
     His duty, before I go anywhere,
     To deal with my father—   45
DORINE   —Then, you'll stay.
     "Orgon was born bizarre" is what some say.
     If there were doubts before, we have this proof—
     He is head over heels for his Tartuffe,
     And breaks off a marriage that he arranged.
     Valère's at fault if your father's deranged?   50
MARIANE   But my refusal will be seen as pride
     And, worse, contempt. And I have to hide
     My feelings for Valère, I must not show
     That I'm in love at all. If people know,
     Then all the modesty my sex is heir to   55
     Will be gone. There's more: how can I bear to
     Not be a proper daughter to my father?
DORINE   No, no, of course not. God forbid we bother
     The way the world sees you. What people see,
     What other people think of us, should be   60
     Our first concern. Besides, I see the truth:
     You really want to be Madame Tartuffe.
     What was I thinking, urging opposition
     To Monsieur Tartuffe! This proposition,
     To merge with him—he's such a catch!   65
     In fact, for you, he's just the perfect match.
     He's much respected, everywhere he goes,
     And his ruddy complexion nearly glows.
     And as his wife, imagine the delight

Of being near him, every day and night.   70
And vital? Oh, my dear, you won't want more.
MARIANE   Oh, heaven help me!
DORINE   How your soul will soar,
Savoring this marriage down to the last drop,
With such a handsome—
MARIANE   All right! You can stop!
Just help me. Please. And tell me there's a way   75
To save me. I'll do whatever you say.
DORINE   Each daughter must choose always to say yes
To what her father wants, no more and no less.
If he wants to give her an ape to marry,
Then she must do it, without a query.   80
But it's a happy fate! What is this frown?
You'll go by wagon to his little town,
Eager cousins, uncles, aunts will greet you
And will call you "sister" when they meet you,
Because you're family now. Don't look so grim.   85
You will so adore chatting with them.
Welcomed by the local high society,
You'll be expected to maintain propriety
And sit straight, or try to, in the folding chair
They offer you, and never, ever stare   90
At the wardrobe of the bailiff's wife
Because you'll see her every day for life.[4]
Let's not forget the village carnival!
Where you'll be dancing at a lavish ball
To a bagpipe orchestra of locals,   95
An organ grinder's monkey doing vocals—
And your husband—
MARIANE   —Dorine, I beg you, please,
Help me. Should I get down here on my knees?
DORINE   Can't help you.
MARIANE   Please, Dorine, I'm begging you!
DORINE   And you deserve this man.   100
MARIANE   That just not true!
DORINE   Oh yes? What changed?
MARIANE   My darling Dorine . . .
DORINE   No.
MARIANE   You can't be this mean.
I love Valère. I told you and it's true.
DORINE   Who's that? Oh. No, Tartuffe's the one for you.
MARIANE   You've always been completely on my side.   105
DORINE   No more. I sentence you to be Tartuffified!
MARIANE   It seems my fate has not the power to move you,
So I'll seek my solace and remove to

---

4. Dorine's description reflects the stereotypes associated with rural pretensions to culture.

A private place for me in my despair.
To end the misery that brought me here.   110
    [MARIANE *starts to exit.*]
DORINE   Wait! Wait! Come back! Please don't go out that door.
I'll help you. I'm not angry anymore.
MARIANE   If I am forced into this martyrdom,
You see, I'll have to die, Dorine.
DORINE   Oh come,
Give up this torment. Look at me—I swear.   115
We'll find a way. Look, here's your love, Valère.
    [DORINE *moves to the side of the stage.*]

2.4

[VALÈRE, MARIANE, DORINE]

VALÈRE   So I've just heard some news that's news to me,
And very fine news it is, do you agree?
MARIANE   What?
VALÈRE   You have plans for marriage I didn't know.
You're going to marry Tartuffe. Is this so?
MARIANE   My father has that notion, it is true.   5
VALÈRE   Madame, your father promised—
MARIANE   —me to you?
He changed his mind, announced this change to me,
Just minutes ago . . .
VALÈRE   Quite seriously?
MARIANE   It's his wish that I should marry this man.
VALÈRE   And what do you think of your father's plan?   10
MARIANE   I don't know.
VALÈRE   Honest words—better than lies.
You don't know?
MARIANE   No.
VALÈRE   No?
MARIANE   What do you advise?
VALÈRE   I advise you to . . . marry Tartuffe. Tonight.
MARIANE   You advise me to . . .
VALÈRE   Yes.
MARIANE   Really?
VALÈRE   That's right.
Consider it. It's an obvious choice.   15
MARIANE   I'll follow your suggestion and rejoice.
VALÈRE   I'm sure that you can follow it with ease.
MARIANE   Just as you gave it. It will be a breeze.
VALÈRE   Just to please you was my sole intent.
MARIANE   To please you, I'll do it and be content.   20
DORINE   I can't wait to see what happens next.
VALÈRE   And this is love to you? I am perplexed.
Was it a sham when you—

MARIANE   That's in the past
  Because you said so honestly and fast
  That I should take the one bestowed on me.   25
  I'm nothing but obedient, you see,
  So, yes, I'll take him. That's my declaration,
  Since that's your advice and expectation.
VALÈRE   I see, you're using me as an excuse,
  Any pretext, so you can cut me loose.   30
  You didn't think I'd notice—I'd be blind
  To the fact that you'd made up your mind?
MARINE   How true. Well said.
VALÈRE   And so it's plain to see,
  Your heart never felt a true love for me.
MARIANE   If you want to, you may think that is true.   35
  It's clear this thought has great appeal for you.
VALÈRE   If I want? I will, but I'm offended
  To my very soul. But your turn's ended,
  And I can win this game we're playing at:
  I've someone else in mind.   40
MARIANE   I don't doubt that.
  Your good points—
VALÈRE   Oh, let's leave them out of this.
  I've very few—in fact, I am remiss.
  I must be. Right? You've made that clear to me.
  But I know someone, hearing that I'm free,
  To make up for my loss, will eagerly consent.   45
MARIANE   The loss is not that bad. You'll be content
  With your new choice, replacement, if you will.
VALÈRE   I will. And I'll remain contented still,
  In knowing you're as happy as I am.
  A woman tells a man her love's a sham.   50
  The man's been fooled and his honor blighted.
  He can't deny his love is unrequited,
  Then he forgets this woman totally,
  And if he can't, pretends, because, you see,
  It is ignoble conduct and weak, too,   55
  Loving someone who does not love you.
MARIANE   What a fine, noble sentiment to heed.
VALÈRE   And every man upholds it as his creed.
  What? You expect me to keep on forever
  Loving you after you blithely sever   60
  The bond between us, watching as you go
  Into another's arms and not bestow
  This heart you've cast away upon someone
  Who might welcome—
MARIANE   I wish it were done.
  That's exactly what I want, you see.   65
VALÈRE   That's what you want?
MARIANE   Yes.

VALÈRE   Then let it be.
　I'll grant your wish.
MARIANE   Please do.
VALÈRE   Just don't forget,
　Whose fault it was when you, filled with regret,
　Realize that you forced me out the door.
MARIANE   True.   70
VALÈRE   You've set the example and what's more,
　I'll match you with my own hardness of heart.
　You won't see me again, if I depart.
MARIANE   That's good!
　　[VALÈRE *goes to exit, but when he gets to the door, he returns.*]
VALÈRE   What?
MARIANE   What?
VALÈRE   You said . . . ?
MARIANE   Nothing at all.
VALÈRE   Well, I'll be on my way, then.
　　[*He goes, stops.*]
　　　　　　　　　　　　　　Did you call?
MARIANE   Me? You must be dreaming.   75
VALÈRE   I'll go away.
　Good-bye, then.
MARIANE   Good-bye.
DORINE   I am here to say,
　You both are idiots! What's this about?
　I left you two alone to fight it out,
　To see how far you'd go. You're quite a pair
　In matching tit for tat—Hold on, Valère!   80
　Where are you going?
VALÈRE   What, Dorine? You spoke?
DORINE   Come here.
VALÈRE   I'm upset and will not provoke
　This lady. Do not try to change my mind.
　I'm doing what she wants.
DORINE   You are so blind.
　Just stop.   85
VALÈRE   No. It's settled.
DORINE   Oh, is that so?
MARIANE   He can't stand to look at me, I know.
　He wants to go away, so please let him.
　No, I shall leave so I can forget him.
DORINE   Where are you going?
MARIANE   Leave me alone.
DORINE   Come back here at once.   90
MARIANE   No. Even that tone
　Won't bring me. I'm not a child, you see.
VALÈRE   She's tortured by the very sight of me.
　It's better that I free her from her pain.

DORINE   What more proof do you need? You are insane!
   Now stop this nonsense! Come here both of you.   95
VALÈRE   To what purpose?
MARIANE   What are you trying to do?
DORINE   Bring you two together! And end this fight.
   It's so stupid! Yes?
VALÈRE   No. It wasn't right
   The way she spoke to me. Didn't you hear?
DORINE   Your voices are still ringing in my ear.   100
MARIANE   The way he treated me—you didn't see?
DORINE   Saw and heard it all. Now listen to me.
   The only thing she wants, Valère, is you.
   I can attest to that right now. It's true.
   And Mariane, he wants you for his wife,   105
   And only you. On that I'll stake my life.
MARIANE   He told me to be someone else's bride!
VALÈRE   She asked for my advice and I replied!
DORINE   You're both impossible. What can I do?
   Give your hand—   110
VALÈRE   What for?
DORINE   Come on, you.
   Now yours, Mariane—don't make me shout.
   Come on!
MARIANE   All right. But what is this about?
DORINE   Here. Take each other's hand and make a link.
   You love each other better than you think.
VALÈRE   Mademoiselle, this is your hand I took,   115
   You think you could give me a friendly look?
       [MARIANE *peeks at* VALÈRE *and smiles.*]
DORINE   It's true. Lovers are not completely sane.
VALÈRE   Mariane, haven't I good reason to complain?
   Be honest. Wasn't it a wicked ploy?
   To say—   120
MARIANE   You think I told you that with joy?
   And you confronted me.
DORINE   Another time.
   This marriage to Tartuffe would be a crime,
   We have to stop it.
MARIANE   So, what can we do?
   Tell us.
DORINE   All sorts of things involving you.   125
   It's all nonsense and your father's joking.
   But if you play along, say, without choking,
   And give your consent, for the time being,
   He'll take the pressure off, thereby freeing
   All of us to find a workable plan   130
   To keep you from a marriage with this man.
   Then you can find a reason every day

To postpone the wedding, in this way;
One day you're sick and that can take a week.
Another day you're better but can't speak,   135
And we all know you have to say "I do,"
Or the marriage isn't legal. And that's true.
Now bad omens—would he have his daughter
Married when she's dreamt of stagnant water,
Or broken a mirror or seen the dead?   140
He may not care and say it's in your head,
But you will be distraught in your delusion,
And require bed rest and seclusion.
I do know this—if we want to succeed,
You can't be seen together. [*To* VALÈRE] With all speed,   145
Go, and gather all your friends right now,
Have them insist that Orgon keep his vow.
Social pressure helps. Then to her brother.
All of us will work on her stepmother.
Let's go.   150
VALÈRE   Whatever happens, can you see?
    My greatest hope is in your love for me.
MARIANE   Though I don't know just what Father will do,
    I do know I belong only to you.
VALÈRE   You put my heart at ease! I swear I will . . .
DORINE   It seems that lovers' tongues are never still.   155
    Out, I tell you.
VALÈRE [*taking a step and returning*]   One last—
DORINE   No more chat!
    You go out this way, yes, and you go that.

3.1

[DAMIS, DORINE]

DAMIS   May lightning strike me dead, right here and now,
    Call me a villain, if I break this vow:
    Forces of heaven or earth won't make me sway
    From this my—
DORINE   Let's not get carried away.
    Your father only said what he intends   5
    To happen. The real event depends
    On many things and something's bound to slip,
    Between this horrid cup and his tight lip.
DAMIS   That this conceited fool Father brought here
    Has plans? Well, they'll be ended—do not fear.   10
DORINE   Now stop that! Forget him. Leave him alone.
    Leave him to your stepmother. He is prone,
    This Tartuffe, to indulge her every whim.
    So let her use her power over him.
    It does seem pretty clear he's soft on her,   15
    Pray God that's true. And if he will concur

That this wedding your father wants is bad,
That's good. But he might want it, too, the cad.
She's sent for him so she can sound him out
On this marriage you're furious about,   20
Discover what he feels and tell him clearly
If he persists that it will cost him dearly.
It seems he can't be seen while he's at prayers,
So I have my own vigil by the stairs
Where his valet says he will soon appear.   25
Do leave right now, and I'll wait for him here.

DAMIS   I'll stay to vouch for what was seen and heard.

DORINE   They must be alone.

DAMIS   I won't say a word.

DORINE   Oh, right. I know what you are like. Just go.
You'll spoil everything, believe me, I know.   30
Out!

DAMIS   I promise I won't get upset.

[DORINE *pinches* DAMIS *as she used to do when he was a child.*]
                                Ow!

DORINE   Do as I say. Get out of here right *now!*

                              3.2

                    [TARTUFFE, LAURENT, DORINE]

TARTUFFE [*noticing* DORINE]   Laurent, lock up my scourge and
    hair shirt,[5] too.
And pray that our Lord's grace will shine on you.
If anyone wants me, I've gone to share
My alms at prison with the inmates there.

DORINE   What a fake! What an imposter! What a sleaze!   5

TARTUFFE   What do you want?

DORINE   To say—

TARTUFFE [*taking a handkerchief from his pocket*]   Good heavens, please,
    Do take this handkerchief before you speak.

DORINE   What for?

TARTUFFE   Cover your bust. The flesh is weak.
Souls are forever damaged by such sights,
When sinful thoughts begin their evil flights.   10

DORINE   It seems temptation makes a meal of you—
To turn you on, a glimpse of flesh will do.
Inside your heart, a furnace must be housed.
For me, I'm not so easily aroused.
I could see you naked, head to toe—   15
Never be tempted once, and this I know.

TARTUFFE   Please! Stop! And if you're planning to resume
    This kind of talk, I'll leave the room.

-----

5. Implements to mortify his flesh (penitential practices of religious ascetics).

DORINE   If someone is to go, let it be me.
 Yes, I can't wait to leave your company.   20
 Madame is coming down from her salon,
 And wants to talk to you, if you'll hang on.
TARTUFFE   Of course. Most willingly.
DORINE [aside]   Look at him melt.
 I'm right. I always knew that's how he felt.
TARTUFFE   Is she coming soon?   25
DORINE   You want me to leave?
 Yes, here she is in person, I believe.

3.3

[ELMIRE, TARTUFFE]

TARTUFFE   Ah, may heaven in all its goodness give
 Eternal health to you each day you live,
 Bless your soul and body, and may it grant
 The prayerful wishes of this supplicant.
ELMIRE   Yes, thank you for that godly wish, and please,   5
 Let's sit down so we can talk with ease.
TARTUFFE   Are you recovered from your illness now?
ELMIRE   My fever disappeared, I don't know how.
TARTUFFE   My small prayers, I'm sure, had not the power,
 Though I was on my knees many an hour.   10
 Each fervent prayer wrenched from my simple soul
 Was made with your recovery as its goal.
ELMIRE   I find your zeal a little disconcerting.
TARTUFFE   I can't enjoy my health if you are hurting,
 Your health's true worth, I can't begin to tell.   15
 I'd give mine up, in fact, to make you well.
ELMIRE   Though you stretch Christian charity too far,
 Your thoughts are kind, however strange they are.
TARTUFFE   You merit more, that's in my humble view.
ELMIRE   I need a private space to talk to you.   20
 I think that this will do—what do you say?
TARTUFFE   Excellent choice. And this is a sweet day,
 To find myself here tête-à-tête with you,
 That I've begged heaven for this, yes, is true,
 And now it's granted to my great relief.   25
ELMIRE   Although our conversation will be brief,
 Please open up your heart and tell me all.
 You must hide nothing now, however small.
TARTUFFE   I long to show you my entire soul,
 My need for truth I can barely control.   30
 I'll take this time, also, to clear the air—
 The criticisms I have brought to bear
 Around the visits that your charms attract,
 Were never aimed at you or how you act,

But rather were my own transports of zeal,   35
Which carried me away with how I feel,
Consumed by impulses, though always pure,
Nevertheless, intense in how—
ELMIRE   I'm sure
That my salvation is your only care.
TARTUFFE [*grasping her fingertips*] Yes, you're right, and   40
    so my fervor there—
ELMIRE   Ouch! You're squeezing too hard.
TARTUFFE   —comes from this zeal . . .
I didn't mean to squeeze. How does this feel?
    [*He puts his hand on* ELMIRE'*s knee.*]
ELMIRE   Your hand—what is it doing . . . ?
TARTUFFE   So tender,
The fabric of your dress, a sweet surrender
Under my hand—   45
ELMIRE   I'm quite ticklish. Please, don't.
    [*She moves her chair back, and* TARTUFFE *moves his forward.*]
TARTUFFE   I want to touch this lace—don't fret, I won't,
It's marvelous! I so admire the trade
Of making lace. Don't tell me you're afraid.
ELMIRE   What? No. But getting back to business now,
It seems my husband plans to break a vow   50
And offer you his daughter. Is this true?
TARTUFFE   He mentioned it, but I must say to you,
The wondrous gifts that catch my zealous eye,
I see quite near in bounteous supply.
ELMIRE   Not earthly things for which you would atone.   55
TARTUFFE   My chest does not contain a heart of stone.
ELMIRE   Well, I believe your eyes follow your soul,
And your desires have heaven as their goal.
TARTUFFE   The love that to eternal beauty binds us
Doesn't stint when temporal beauty finds us.   60
Our senses can as easily be charmed
When by an earthly work we are disarmed.
You are a rare beauty, without a flaw,
And in your presence, I'm aroused with awe
But for the Author of All Nature, so,   65
My heart has ardent feelings, even though
I feared them at first, questioning their source.
Had I been ambushed by some evil force?
I felt that I must hide from this temptation:
You. My feelings threatened my salvation.   70
Yes, I found this sinful and distressing,
Until I saw your beauty as a blessing!
So now my passion never can be wrong,
And, thus, my virtue stays intact and strong.
That is how I'm here in supplication,   75
Offering my heart in celebration

Of the audacious truth that I love you,
That only you can make this wish come true,
That through your grace, my offering's received,
And accepted, and that I have achieved   80
Salvation of a sort, and by your grace,
I could be content in this low place.
It all depends on you, at your behest—
Am I to be tormented or be blest?
You are my welfare, solace, and my hope,   85
But, whatever your decision, I will cope.
Will I be happy? I'll rely on you.
If you want me to be wretched, that's fine, too.

ELMIRE   Well, what a declaration! How gallant!
But I'm surprised you want the things you want.   90
It seems your heart could use a talking to—
It's living in the chest of someone who
Proclaims to be pious—

TARTUFFE   —And so I am.
My piety's a true thing—not a sham,
But I'm no less a man, so when I find   95
Myself with you, I quickly lose my mind.
My heart is captured and, with it, my thought.
Yet since I know the cause, I'm not distraught.
Words like these from me must be alarming,
But it is your beauty that's so charming,   100
I cannot help myself, I am undone.
And I'm no angel, nor could I be one.
If my confession earns your condemnation,
Then blame your glance for the annihilation
Of my command of this: my inmost being.   105
A surrender of my soul is what you're seeing.
Your eyes blaze with more than human splendor,
And that first look had the effect to render
Powerless the bastions of my heart.
No fasting, tears or prayers, no pious art   110
Could shield my soul from your celestial gaze
Which I will worship till the End of Days.[6]
A thousand times my eyes, my sighs have told
The truth that's in my heart. Now I am bold,
Encouraged by your presence, so I say,   115
With my true voice, will this be the day
You condescend to my poor supplication,
Offered up with devout admiration,
And save my soul by granting this request:
Accept this love I've lovingly confessed?   120
Your honor has, of course, all my protection,
And you can trust my absolute discretion.

---

6. That is, the final days before human history ends and the Kingdom of God is established.

For those men that all the women die for,
Love's a game whose object is a high score.
Although they promise not to talk, they will.   125
They need to boast of their superior skill,
Receive no favors not as soon revealed,
Exposing what they vowed would be concealed.
And in the end, this love is overpriced,
When a woman's honor's sacrificed.   130
But men like me burn with a silent flame,
Our secrets safe, our loves we never name,
Because our reputations are our wealth,
When we transgress, it's with the utmost stealth.
Your honor's safe as my hand in a glove,   135
So I can offer, free from scandal, love,
And pleasure without fear of intervention.
ELMIRE   Your sophistry does not hide your intention.
In fact, you know, it makes it all too clear.
What if, through me, my husband were to hear   140
About this love for me you now confess
Which shatters the ideals you profess?
How would your friendship fare, then, I wonder?
TARTUFFE   It's your beauty cast this spell I suffer under.
I'm made of flesh, like you, like all mankind.   145
And since your soul is pure, you will be kind,
And not judge me harshly for my brashness
In speaking of my love in all its rashness.
I beg you to forgive me my offense,
I plead your perfect face as my defense.   150
ELMIRE   Some might take offense at your confession,
But I will show a definite discretion,
And keep my husband in the dark about
These sinful feelings for me that you spout.
But I want something from you in return: 155
There's a promised marriage, you will learn,
That supersedes my husband's recent plan—
The marriage of Valère and Mariane.
This marriage you will openly support,
Without a single quibble, and, in short,   160
Renounce the unjust power of a man
Who'd give his own daughter, Mariane,
To another when she's promised to Valère.
In return, my silence—

3.4

[ELMIRE, DAMIS, TARTUFFE]

DAMIS [jumping out from where he had been hiding]
                    —Hold it right there!
No, no! You're done. All this will be revealed.
I heard each word. And as I was concealed,

Something besides your infamy came clear:
Heaven in its great wisdom brought me here,   5
To witness and then give my father proof
Of the hypocrisy of his Tartuffe,
This so-called saint anointed from above,
Speaking to my father's wife of love!
ELMIRE   Damis, there is a lesson to be learned,   10
And there is my forgiveness to be earned.
I promised him. Don't make me take it back.
It's not my nature to see as an attack
Such foolishness as this, or see the need
To tell my husband of the trivial deed.   15
DAMIS   So, you have your reasons, but I have mine.
To grant this fool forgiveness? I decline.
To want to spare him is a mockery,
Because he's more than foolish, can't you see?
This fanatic in his insolent pride,   20
Brought chaos to my house, and would divide
Me and my father—unforgivable!
What's more, he's made my life unlivable,
As he undermines two true love affairs,
Mine and Valère's sister, my sister and Valère's!   25
Father must hear the truth about this man.
Heaven helped me—I must do what I can
To use this chance. I'd deserve to lose it,
If I dropped it now and didn't use it.
ELMIRE   Damis—
DAMIS   No, please, I have to follow through.
I've never felt as happy as I do
Right now. And don't try to dissuade me—
I'll have my revenge. If you forbade me,
I'd still do it, so you don't have to bother.
I'll finish this for good. Here comes my father.   35

3.5

[ORGON, DAMIS, TARTUFFE, ELMIRE]

DAMIS   Father! You have arrived. Let's celebrate!
I have a tale that I'd like to relate.
It happened here and right before my eyes,
I offer it to you—as a surprise!
For all your love, you have been repaid   5
With duplicity. You have been betrayed
By your dear friend here, whom I just surprised
Making verbal love, I quickly surmised,
To your wife. Yes, this is how he shows you
How he honors you—he thinks he knows you.   10
But as your son, I know you much better—
You demand respect down to the letter.

Madame, unflappable and so discreet,
Would keep this secret, never to repeat.
But, as your son, my feelings are too strong,   15
And to be silent is to do you wrong.
ELMIRE   One learns to spurn without being unkind,
And how to spare a husband's peace of mind.
Although I understood just what he meant,
My honor wasn't touched by this event.   20
That's how I feel. And you would have, Damis,
Said nothing, if you had listened to me.

3.6

[ORGON, DAMIS, TARTUFFE]

ORGON   Good heavens! What he said? Can it be true?
TARTUFFE   Yes, my brother, I'm wicked through and through.
The most miserable of sinners, I.
Filled with iniquity, I should just die.
Each moment of my life's so dirty, soiled,   5
Whatever I come near is quickly spoiled.
I'm nothing but a heap of filth and crime.
I'd name my sins, but we don't have the time.
And I see that heaven, to punish me,
Has mortified my soul quite publicly.   10
What punishment I get, however great,
I well deserve so I'll accept my fate.
Defend myself? I'd face my own contempt,
If I thought that were something I'd attempt.
What you've heard here, surely, you abhor,   15
So chase me like a criminal from your door.
Don't hold back your rage, please, let it flame,
For I deserve to burn, in my great shame.
ORGON [to DAMIS]   Traitor! And how dare you even try
To tarnish this man's virtue with a lie?   20
DAMIS   What? This hypocrite pretends to be contrite
And you believe him over me?
ORGON   That's spite!
And shut your mouth!
TARTUFFE   No, let him have his say.
And don't accuse him. Don't send him away.
Believe his story—why be on my side?   25
You don't know what motives I may hide.
Why give me so much loyalty and love?
Do you know what I am capable of?
My brother, you have total trust in me,
And think I'm good because of what you see?   30
No, no, by my appearance you're deceived,
And what I say you think must be believed.
Well, believe this—I have no worth at all.

The world sees me as worthy, yet I fall
Far below. Sin is so insidious.   35
[*To* DAMIS] Dear son, do treat me as perfidious,
Infamous, lost, a murderer, a thief.
Speak on, because my sins, beyond belief,
Can bring this shameful sinner to his knees,
In humble, paltry effort to appease.   40
ORGON [*to* TARTUFFE]   Brother, there is no need . . .

                            [*To* DAMIS] Will you
  relent?
DAMIS   He has seduced you!
ORGON   Can't you take a hint?
  Be quiet! [*To* TARTUFFE] Brother, please get up. [*To* DAMIS] Ingrate!
DAMIS   But father, this man
ORGON   —whom you denigrate.
DAMIS   But you should—   45
ORGON   Quiet!
DAMIS   But I saw and heard—
ORGON   I'll slap you if you say another word.
TARTUFFE   In the name of God, don't be that way.
  Brother, I'd rather suffer, come what may,
  Than have this boy receive what's meant for me.
ORGON [*to* DAMIS]   Heathen!   50
TARTUFFE   Please! I beg of you on bended knee.
ORGON [*to* DAMIS]   Wretch! See his goodness?!
DAMIS   But—
ORGON   No!
DAMIS   But—
ORGON   Be still!
  And not another word from you until
  You admit the truth. It's plain to see
  Although you thought that I would never be
  Aware and know your motives, yet I do.   55
  You all hate him. And I saw today, you,
  Wife, servants—everyone beneath my roof—
  Are trying everything to force Tartuffe
  Out of my house—this holy man, my friend.
  The more you try to banish him and end   60
  Our sacred brotherhood, the more secure
  His place is. I have never been more sure
  Of anyone. I give him as his bride
  My daughter. If that hurts the family pride,
  Then good. It needs humbling. You understand?   65
DAMIS   You're going to force her to accept his hand?
ORGON   Yes, traitor, and this evening. You know why?
  To infuriate you. Yes, I defy
  You all. I am master and you'll obey.
  And you, you ingrate, now I'll make you pay   70
  For your abuse of him—kneel on the floor,

And beg his pardon, or go out the door.
DAMIS   Me? Kneel and ask the pardon of this fraud?
ORGON   What? You refuse? Someone get me a rod!
  A stick! Something! [*To* TARTUFFE] Don't hold me.   75
  [*To* DAMIS] Here's your whack!
  Out of my house and don't ever come back!
DAMIS   Yes, I'll leave, but—
ORGON   Get out of my sight!
  I disinherit you, you traitor, you're a blight
  On this house. And you'll get nothing now
  From me, except my curse!   80

3.7

[ORGON, TARTUFFE]

ORGON   You have my vow,
  He'll never more question your honesty.
TARTUFFE [*to heaven*]   Forgive him for the pain he's given me.
  [*To* ORGON] How I suffer. If you could only see
  What I go through when they disparage me.   5
ORGON   Oh no!
TARTUFFE   The ingratitude, even in thought,
  Tortures my soul so much, it leaves me fraught
  With inner pain. My heart's stopped. I'm near death,
  I can barely speak now. Where is my breath?
ORGON [*running in tears to the door through which he chased* DAMIS]
  You demon! I held back, you little snot   10
  I should have struck you dead right on the spot!
  [*To* TARTUFFE] Get up, Brother. Don't worry anymore.
TARTUFFE   Let us end these troubles, Brother, I implore.
  For the discord I have caused, I deeply grieve,
  So for the good of all, I'll take my leave.   15
ORGON   What? Are you joking? No!
TARTUFFE   They hate me here.
  It pains me when I see them fill your ear
  With suspicions.
ORGON   But that doesn't matter.
  I don't listen.
TARTUFFE   That persistent chatter
  You now ignore, one day you'll listen to.   20
  Repetition of a lie can make it true.
ORGON   No, my brother. Never.
TARTUFFE   A man's wife
  Can so mislead his soul and ruin his life.
ORGON   No, no.
TARTUFFE   Brother, let me, by leaving here,
  Remove any cause for doubt or fear.   25
ORGON   No, no. You will stay. My soul is at stake.

TARTUFFE   Well, then, a hefty penance I must make.
  I'll mortify myself, unless . . .
ORGON   No need!
TARTUFFE   Then we will never speak of it, agreed?
  But the question of your honor still remains,   30
  And with that I'll take particular pains
  To prevent rumors. My absence, my defense—
  I'll never see your wife again, and hence—
ORGON   No. You spend every hour with her you want,
  And be seen with her. I want you to flaunt,   35
  In front of them, this friendship with my wife.
  And I know how to really turn the knife
  I'll make you my heir, my only one,
  Yes, you will be my son-in-law and son.[7]
  A good and faithful friend means more to me   40
  Than any member of my family.
  Will you accept this gift that I propose?
TARTUFFE   Whatever heaven wants I can't oppose.
ORGON   Poor man! A contract's what we need to write.
  And let all the envious burst with spite.   45

4.1

[CLÉANTE, TARTUFFE]

CLÉANTE   Yes, everyone is talking and each word
  Diminishes your glory, rest assured.
  Though your name's tainted with scandal and shame,
  I'm glad I ran across you, all the same,
  Because I need to share with you my view   5
  On this disaster clearly caused by you.
  Damis, let's say for now, was so misguided,
  He spoke before he thought. But you decided
  To just sit back and watch him be exiled
  From his own father's house. Were he a child,   10
  Then, really, would you dare to treat him so?
  Shouldn't you forgive him, not make him go?
  However, if there's vengeance in your heart,
  And you act on it, tell me what's the part
  That's Christian in that? And are you so base,   15
  You'd let a son fall from his father's grace?
  Give God your anger as an offering,
  Bring peace and forgive all for everything.
TARTUFFE   I'd do just that, if it were up to me.
  I blame him for nothing, don't you see?   20
  I've pardoned him already. That's my way.

---

7. In fact, French laws governing inheritance would have made such a change extremely difficult to accomplish.

And I'm not bitter, but have this to say:
Heaven's best interests will have been served,
When wrongdoers have got what they deserved.
In fact, if he returns here, I would leave,   25
Because God knows what people might believe.
Faking forgiveness to manipulate
My accuser, silencing the hate
He has for me could be seen as my goal,
When I would only wish to save his soul.   30
What he said to me, though unforgivable,
I give unto God to make life livable.

CLÉANTE   To this conclusion, sir, I have arrived:
Your excuses could not be more contrived.
Just how did you come by the opinion   35
Heaven's business is in your dominion,
Judging who is guilty and who is not?
Taking revenge is heaven's task, I thought.
And if you're under heaven's sovereignty,
What human verdict would you ever be   40
The least bit moved by. No, you wouldn't care—
Judging other's lives is so unfair.
Heaven seems to say "live and let live,"
And our task, I believe, is to forgive.

TARTUFFE   I said I've pardoned him. I take such pains   45
To do exactly what heaven ordains.
But after his attack on me, it's clear,
Heaven does not ordain that he live here.

CLÉANTE   Does it ordain, sir, that you nod and smile,
When taking what is not yours, all the while?   50
On this inheritance you have no claim
And yet you think it's yours. Have you no shame?

TARTUFFE   That this gift was, in any way, received
Out of self-interest, would not be believed
By anyone who knows me well. They'd say,   55
"The world's wealth, to him, holds no sway."
I am not dazzled by gold nor its glitter,
So lack of wealth has never made me bitter.
If I take this present from the father,
The source of all this folderol and bother,   60
I am saving, so everyone understands,
This wealth from falling into the wrong hands,
Waste of wealth and property's a crime,
And that is what would happen at this time.
But I would use it as part of my plan: 65
For glory of heaven, and the good of man.

CLÉANTE   Well, sir, I think these small fears that plague you,
In fact, may cause the rightful heir to sue.
Why trouble yourself, sir—couldn't you just
Let him own his property, if he must?   70

Let others say his property's misused
By him, rather than have yourself accused
Of taking it from its rightful owner.
Wouldn't a pious man be a donor
Of property? Unless there is a verse   75
Or proverb about how you fill your purse
With what's not yours, at all, in any part.
And if heaven has put into your heart
This obstacle to living with Damis,
The honorable thing, you must agree,   80
As well as, certainly, the most discreet,
Is pack your bags and, quickly, just retreat.
To have the son of the house chased away,
Because a guest objects, is a sad day.
Leaving now would show your decency,   85
Sir . . .

TARTUFFE   Yes. Well, it is half after three;
Pious duties consume this time of day,
You will excuse my hurrying away.

CLÉANTE   Ah!

4.2

[ELMIRE, MARIANE, DORINE, CLÉANTE]

DORINE   Please, come to the aid of Mariane.
She's suffering because her father's plan
To force this marriage, impossible to bear,
Has pushed her from distress into despair.
Her father's on his way here. Do your best,   5
Turn him around. Use subtlety, protest,
Whatever way will work to change his mind.

4.3

[ORGON, ELMIRE, MARIANE, CLÉANTE, DORINE]

ORGON   Ah! Here's everyone I wanted to find!
[To MARIANE] This document I have here in my hand
Will make you very happy, understand?

MARIANE   Father, in the name of heaven, I plead
To all that's good and kind in you, concede   5
Paternal power, just in this sense:
Free me from my vows of obedience.
Enforcing that inflexible law today
Will force me to confess each time I pray
My deep resentment of my obligation.   10
I know, father, that I am your creation,
That you're the one who's given life to me.
Why would you now fill it with misery?

If you destroy my hopes for the one man
I've dared to love by trying now to ban   15
Our union, then I'm kneeling to implore,
Don't give me to a man whom I abhor.
To you, Father, I make this supplication:
Don't drive me to some act of desperation,
By ruling me simply because you can.   20

ORGON [*feeling himself touched*]   Be strong! Human weakness
   shames a man!

MARIANE   Your affection for him doesn't bother me—
   Let it erupt, give him your property,
   And if that's not enough, then give him mine.
   Any claim on it, I do now decline.   25
   But in this gifting, don't give him my life.
   If I must wed, then I will be God's wife,
   In a convent, until my days are done.

ORGON   Ah! So you will be a holy, cloistered nun,
   Because your father thwarts your love affair.   30
   Get up! The more disgust you have to bear,
   The more of heaven's treasure you will earn,
   And the heaven will bless you in return.
   Through this marriage, you'll mortify your senses.
   Don't bother me with any more pretenses.   35

DORINE   But . . . !

ORGON   Quiet, you! I see you standing there.
   Don't speak a single word! don't even dare!

CLÉANTE   If you permit, I'd like to say a word . . .

ORGON   Brother, the best advice the world has heard
   Is yours—its reasoning, hard to ignore.   40
   But I refuse to hear it anymore.

ELMIRE [*to* ORGON]   And now, I wonder, have you lost your mind?
   Your love for this one man has made you blind.
   Can you stand there and say you don't believe
   A word we've said? That we're here to deceive?   45

ORGON   Excuse me—I believe in what I see.
   You, indulging my bad son, agree
   To back him up in this terrible prank,
   Accusing my dear friend of something rank.
   You should be livid if what you claim took place,   50
   And yet this look of calm is on your face.

ELMIRE   Because a man says he's in love with me,
   I'm to respond with heavy artillery?
   I laugh at these unwanted propositions.
   Mirth will quell most ardent ambitions.   55
   Why make a fuss over an indiscretion?
   My honor's safe and in my possession.
   You say I'm calm? Well, that's my constancy—
   It won't need a defense, or clemency.
   I know I'll never be a vicious prude   60

Who always seems to hear men being rude,
And then defends her honor tooth and claw,
Still snarling, even as the men withdraw.
From honor like that heaven preserve me,
If that's what you want, you don't deserve me,   65
Besides, you're the one who has been betrayed.

ORGON   I see through this trick that's being played.

ELMIRE   How can you be so dim? I am amazed
How you can hear these sins and stay unfazed.
But what if I could show you what he does?   70

ORGON   Show?

ELMIRE   Yes.

ORGON   A fiction!

ELMIRE   No, the truth because
I am quite certain I can find a way
To show you in the fullest light of day . . .

ORGON   Fairy tales!

ELMIRE   Come on, at least answer me.
I've given up expecting you to be   75
My advocate. What have you got to lose,
By hiding somewhere, anyplace you choose,
And see for yourself. And then we can
Hear what you say about your holy man.

ORGON   Then I'll say nothing because it cannot be.   80

ELMIRE   Enough. I'm tired. You'll see what you see.
I'm not a liar, though I've been accused.
The time is now and I won't be refused.
You'll be a witness. And we can stop our rants.

ORGON   All right! I call your bluff, Miss Smarty Pants.   85

ELMIRE [to DORINE]   Tell Tartuffe to come.

DORINE   Watch out. He's clever.
Men like him are caught, well, almost never.

ELMIRE   Narcissism is a great deceiver,
And he has lots of that. He's a believer
In his charisma. [To CLÉANTE and MARIANE] Leave us for a bit.   90

4.4

[ELMIRE, ORGON]

ELMIRE   See this table? Good. Get under it.

ORGON   What!

ELMIRE   You are hiding. Get under there and stay.

ORGON   Under the table?

ELMIRE: Just do as I say.
I have a plan, but for it to succeed,
You must be hidden. So are we agreed?   5
You want to know? I'm ready to divulge it.

ORGON   This fantasy of yours—I'll indulge it.
But then I want to lay this thing to rest.

ELMIRE   Oh, that'll happen. Because he'll fail the test.
  You see, I'm going to have a conversation   10
  I'd never have—just as an illustration
  Of how this hypocrite behaved with me.
  So don't be scandalized. I must be free
  To flirt. Clearly, that's what it's going to take
  To prove to you your holy man's a fake.   15
  I'm going to lead him on, to lift his mask,
  Seem to agree to anything he'll ask,
  Pretend to respond to his advances.
  It's for you I'm taking all these chances.
  I'll stop as soon as you have seen enough;   20
  I hope that comes before he calls my bluff.
  His plans for me must be circumvented,
  His passion's strong enough to be demented,
  So the moment you're convinced, you let me know
  That I've revealed the fraud I said I'd show.   25
  Stop him so I won't have a minute more
  Exposure to your friend, this lecherous boor.
  You're in control. I'm sure I'll be all right.
  And . . . here he comes—so hush, stay out of sight.

4.5

[TARTUFFE, ELMIRE, ORGON (*under the table*)]

TARTUFFE   I'm told you want to have a word with me.
ELMIRE   Yes. I have a secret but I'm not free
  To speak. Close that door, have a look around,
  We certainly do not want to be found
  The way we were just as Damis appeared.   5
  I was terrified for you and as I feared,
  He was irate. You saw how hard I tried
  To calm him down and keep him pacified.
  I was so upset; I never had the thought
  "Deny it all," which might have helped a lot,   10
  But as it turns out, we've nothing to fear,
  My husband's not upset, it would appear.
  Things are good, to heaven I defer,
  Because they're even better than they were.
  I have to say I'm quite amazed, in fact,   15
  His good opinion of you is intact.
  To clear the air and quiet every tongue,
  And to kill any gossip that's begun—
  You could've pushed me over with a feather—
  He wants us to spend all our time together!   20
  That's why, with no fear of a critical stare,
  I can be here with you or anywhere.
  Most important, I am completely free

To show my ardor for you, finally.

TARTUFFE   Ardor? This is a sudden change of tone   25
From the last time we found ourselves alone.

ELMIRE   If thinking I was turning you away
Has made you angry, all that I can say
Is that you do not know a woman's heart!
Protecting our virtue keeps us apart,   30
And makes us seem aloof, and even cold.
But cooler outside, inside the more bold.
When love overcomes us, we are ashamed,
Because we fear that we might be defamed.
We must protect our honor—not allow   35
Our love to show. I fear that even now,
In this confession, you'll think ill of me.
But now I've spoken, and I hope you see
My ardor that is there. Why would I sit
And listen to you? Why would I permit   40
Your talk of love, unless I had a notion
Just like yours, and with the same emotion?
And when Damis found us, didn't I try
To quiet him? And did you wonder why,
In speaking of Mariane's marriage deal,   45
I not only asked you, I made an appeal
That you turn it down? What was I doing?
Making sure I'd be the one you'd be wooing.

TARTUFFE   It is extremely sweet, without a doubt,
To watch your lips as loving words spill out.   50
Abundant honey there for me to drink,
But I have doubts. I cannot help but think,
"Does she tell the truth, or does she lie,
To get me to break off this marriage tie?
Is all this ardor something she could fake,   55
And just an act for her stepdaughter's sake?"
So many questions, yet I want to trust,
But need to know the truth, in fact, I must.
Pleasing you, Elmire, is my main task,
And happiness, and so I have to ask   60
To sample this deep ardor felt for me
Right here and now, in blissful ecstasy.

ELMIRE [*coughing to alert* ORGON]
You want to spend this passion instantly?
I've been opening my heart consistently,
But for you, it's not enough, this sharing.   65
Yet for a woman, it is very daring.
So why can't you be happy with a taste,
Instead of the whole meal consumed in haste?

TARTUFFE   We dare not hope, all those of us who don't
Deserve a thing. And so it is I won't   70
Be satisfied with words. I'll always doubt,
Assume my fortune's taken the wrong route

On its way to me. And that is why
I don't believe in anything till I
Have touched, partaken until satisfied.   75
ELMIRE   So suddenly, your love can't be denied.
It wants complete dominion over me,
And what it wants, it wants violently.
I know I'm flustered, I know I'm out of breath—
Your power over me could be the death   80
Of my reason. Does this seem right to you?
To use my weakness against me, just to
Conquer? No one's gallant anymore.
I invite you in. You break down the door.
TARTUFFE   If your passion for me isn't a pretense,   85
Then why deny me its best evidence?
ELMIRE   But, heaven, sir, that place that you address
So often, would judge us both if we transgress.
TARTUFFE   That's all that's in the way of my desires?
These judgments heaven makes of what transpires?   90
All you fear is heaven's bad opinion.
ELMIRE   But I am made to fear its dominion.
TARTUFFE   And I know how to exorcise these fears.
To sin is not as bad as it appears
If, and stay with me on this, one can think   95
That in some cases, heaven gives a wink
        [*It is a scoundrel speaking.*][8]
When it comes to certain needs of men
Who can remain upright but only when
There is a pure intention. So you see,
If you just let yourself be led by me,   100
You'll have no worries, and I can enjoy
You. And you, me. Because we will employ
This way of thinking—a real science
And a secret, thus, with your compliance,
Fulfilling my desires without fear,   105
Is easy now, so let it happen here.
        [ELMIRE *coughs.*]
That cough, Madame, is bad.
ELMIRE   I'm in such pain.
TARTUFFE   A piece of licorice might ease the strain.
ELMIRE [*directed to* ORGON]   This cold I have is very obstinate.
It stubbornly holds on. I can't shake it.   110
TARTUFFE   That's most annoying.
ELMIRE   More than I can say.
TARTUFFE   Let's get back to finding you a way,
Finally, to get around your scruples:
Secrecy—I'm one of its best pupils
And practitioners. Responsibility   115

---

8. This stage direction, inserted by Molière himself, supports the playwright's assertion that he took pains to demonstrate Tartuffe's true nature.

For any evil—you can put on me,
I will answer up to heaven if I must,
And give a good accounting you can trust.
There'll be no sins for which we must atone,
'Cause evil exists only when it's known.   120
Adam and Eve were public in their fall.
To sin in private is not to sin at all.

ELMIRE [*after coughing again*]   Obviously, I must give in to you,
Because, it seems, you are a person who
Refuses to believe anything I say.   125
Live testimony only can convey
The truth of passion here, no more, no less.
That it should go that far, I must confess,
Is such a pity. But I'll cross the line,
And give myself to you. I won't decline   130
Your offer, sir, to vanquish me right here.
But let me make one point extremely clear:
If there's a moral judgment to be made,
If anyone here feels the least betrayed,
Then none of that will be my fault. Instead,   135
The sin weighs twice as heavy on your head.
You forced me to this brash extremity.

TARTUFFE   Yes, yes, I will take all the sin on me.

ELMIRE   Open the door and check because I fear
My husband—just look—might be somewhere near.   140

TARTUFFE   What does it matter if he comes or goes?
The secret is, I lead him by the nose.
He's urged me to spend all my time with you.
So let him see—he won't believe it's true.

ELMIRE   Go out and look around. Indulge my whim.   145
Look everywhere and carefully for him.

4.6

[ORGON, ELMIRE]

ORGON [*coming out from under the table*]
I swear that is the most abominable man!
How will I bear this? I don't think I can.
I'm stupefied!

ELMIRE   What? Out so soon? No, no.
You can't be serious. There's more to go.
Get back under there. You can't be too sure.   5
It's never good relying on conjecture.

ORGON   That kind of wickedness comes straight from hell.

ELMIRE   You've turned against this man you know so well?
Good lord, be sure the evidence is strong
Before you are convinced. You might be wrong.
[*She steps in front of* ORGON.]

4.7

[TARTUFFE, ELMIRE, ORGON]

TARTUFFE   Yes, all is well; there's no one to be found,
   And I was thorough when I looked around.
   To my delight, my rapture, at last . . .
ORGON [*stopping him*]   Just stop a minute there! You move too fast!
   Delight and rapture? Fulfilling desire?   5
   Ah! Ah! You are a traitor and a liar!
   Some holy man you are, to wreck my life,
   Marry my daughter? Lust after my wife?
   I've had my doubts about you, but kept quiet,
   Waiting for you to slip and then deny it.   10
   Well, now it's happened and I'm so relieved,
   To stop pretending that I am deceived.
ELMIRE [*to* TARTUFFE]   I don't approve of what I've done today,
   But I needed to do it, anyway.
TARTUFFE   What? You can't think . . .   15
ORGON   No more words from you.
   Get out of here, you. . . . You and I are through.
TARTUFFE   But my intentions . . .
ORGON   You still think I'm a dunce?
   You shut your mouth and leave this house at once!
TARTUFFE   You're the one to leave, you, acting like the master.
   Now I'll make it known, the full disaster: 20
   This house belongs to me, yes, all of it,
   And I'll decide what's true, as I see fit.
   You can't entrap me with demeaning tricks,
   Yes, here's a situation you can't fix.
   Here nothing happens without my consent.   25
   You've offended heaven. You must repent.
   But I know how to really punish you.
   Those who harm me, they know not what they do.

4.8

[ELMIRE, ORGON]

ELMIRE   What was that about? I mean, the latter.
ORGON   I'm not sure, but it's no laughing matter.
ELMIRE   Why?
ORGON   I've made a mistake I now can see,
   The deed I gave him is what troubles me.
ELMIRE   The deed?   5
ORGON   And something else. I am undone.
   I think my troubles may have just begun.
ELMIRE   What else?
ORGON   You'll know it all. I have to race,
   To see if a strongbox is in its place.

5.1

[ORGON, CLÉANTE]

CLÉANTE   Where are you running to?

ORGON   Who knows.

CLÉANTE   Then wait.
    It seems to me we should deliberate,
    Meet, plan, and have some family talks.

ORGON   I can't stop thinking about the damned box
    More than anything, that's the loss I fear.   5

CLÉANTE   What about this box makes it so dear?

ORGON   I have a friend whom I felt sorry for,
    Because he chose the wrong side in the war;[9]
    Before he fled, he brought it to me,
    This locked box. He didn't leave a key.   10
    He told me it has papers, this doomed friend,
    On which his life and property depend.

CLÉANTE   Are you saying you gave the box away?

ORGON   Yes, that's true, that's what I'm trying to say.
    I was afraid that I would have to lie,   15
    If I were confronted. That is why
    I went to my betrayer and confessed
    And he, in turn, told me it would be best
    If I gave him the box, to keep, in case
    Someone were to ask me to my face   20
    About it all, and I might lie and then,
    In doing so, commit a venial sin.[1]

CLÉANTE   As far as I can see, this is a mess,
    And with a lot of damage to assess.
    This secret that you told, this deed you gave,   25
    Make the situation hard to save.
    He's holding all the cards, your holy man,
    Because you gave them to him. If you can,
    Restrain yourself a bit and stay away.
    That would be best. And do watch what you say.   30

ORGON   What? With his wicked heart and corrupt soul,
    Yet I'm to keep my rage under control?
    Yes, me who took him in, right off the street?
    Damn all holy men! They're filled with deceit!
    I now renounce them all, down to the man,   35
    And I'll treat them worse than Satan can.

CLÉANTE   Listen to yourself! You're over the top,
    Getting carried away again. Just stop.
    "Moderation." Is that a word you know?
    I think you've learned it, but then off you go.   40

9. That is, he opposed Louis in the Fronde (see 1.2.11 and note). Although Orgon supported the king, this act left him open to the charge of being a traitor to the throne—a capital offense.

1. A "pardonable" or relatively minor sin. Because Tartuffe had possession of the box, Orgon could deny that he had it without lying.

Always ignoring the strength in reason,
Flinging yourself from loyalty to treason.
Why can't you just admit that you were swayed
By the fake piety that man displayed?
But no. Rather than change your ways, you turned   45
Like that. [*Snaps fingers*] Attacking holy men who've earned
The right to stand among the true believers.
So now all holy men are base deceivers?
Instead of just admitting your delusion,
"They're all like that!" you say—brilliant conclusion.   50
Why trust reason, when you have emotion?
You've implied there is no true devotion.
Freethinkers are the ones who hold that view,
And yet, you don't agree with them, do you?
You judge a man as good without real proof.   55
Appearances can lie—witness: Tartuffe.
If your respect is something to be prized,
Don't toss it away to those disguised
In a cloak of piety and virtue.
Don't you see how deeply they can hurt you?   60
Look for simple goodness—it does exist.
And just watch for imposters in our midst,
With this in mind, try not to be unjust
To true believers, sin on the side of trust.

5.2

[DAMIS, ORGON, CLÉANTE]

DAMIS   Father, what? I can't believe it's true,
That scoundrel has the gall to threaten you?
And use the things you gave him in his case
'Gainst you? To throw you out? I'll break his face.
ORGON   My son, I'm in more pain than you can see.   5
DAMIS   I'll break both his legs. Leave it to me.
We must not bend under his insolence.
I'll finish this business, punish his offense,
I'll murder him and do it with such joy.
CLÉANTE   Damis, you're talking like a little boy.   10
Tantrums head the list of your main flaws.
We live in modern times, with things called "laws."
Murder is illegal. At least for us.

5.3

[MADAME PERNELLE, MARIANE, ELMIRE, DORINE,
DAMIS, ORGON, CLÉANTE]

MADAME PERNELLE   It's unbelievable! Preposterous!
ORGON   Believe it. I've seen it with my own eyes.
He returned kindness with deceit and lies.

I took in a man, miserable and poor,
Brought him home, gave him the key to my door,   5
I loaded him with favors every day,
To him, my daughter, I just gave away,
My house, my wealth, a locked box from a friend.
But to what depths this devil would descend.
This betrayer, this abomination,   10
Who had the gall to preach about temptation,
And know in his black heart he'd woo my wife.
Seduce her! Yes! And then to steal my life.
Using my property, which I transferred to him,
I know, I know—it was a stupid whim.   15
He wants to ruin me, chase me from my door,
He wants me as he was, abject and poor.

DORINE   Poor man!

MADAME PERNELLE   I don't believe a word, my son,
This isn't something that he could have done.

ORGON   What?   20

MADAME PERNELLE   Holy men always arouse envy.

ORGON   Mother, what are you trying to say to me?

MADAME PERNELLE   That you live rather strangely in this house;
He's hated here, especially by your spouse.

ORGON   What has this got to do with what I said?

MADAME PERNELLE   Heaven knows, I've beat into your head: 25
"In this world, virtue is mocked forever;
Envious men may die, but envy never."

ORGON   How does that apply to what's happened here?

MADAME PERNELLE   Someone made up some lies; it's all too clear.

ORGON   But I saw it myself, you understand.   30

MADAME PERNELLE   "Whoever spreads slander has a soiled hand."

ORGON   You'll make me, Mother, say something not nice.
I saw it for myself; I've told you twice.

MADAME PERNELLE   "No one can trust what gossips have to say,
Yet they'll be with us until Judgment Day."   35

ORGON   You're talking total nonsense, Mother!
I said I saw him, this man I called Brother!
I saw him with my wife, with these two eyes.
The word is "saw," past tense of "see." These "lies"
That you misnamed are just the truth.   40
I saw my wife almost beneath Tartuffe.

MADAME PERNELLE   Oh, is that all? Appearances deceive.
What we think we see, we then believe.

ORGON   I'm getting angry.

MADAME PERNELLE   False suspicions, see?
We are subject to them, occasionally,   45
Good deeds can be seen as something other.

ORGON   So I'm to see this as a good thing, Mother,
A man trying to kiss my wife?

MADAME PERNELLE   You must.
Because, to be quite certain you are just,

You should wait until you're very, very sure 50
And not rely on faulty conjecture.

ORGON   Goddammit! You would have me wait until . . . ?
And just be quiet while he has his fill,
Right before my very eyes, Mother, he'd—

MADAME PERNELLE   I can't believe that he would do this "deed" 55
Of which he's been accused. There is no way.
His soul is pure.

ORGON   I don't know what to say!
Mother!

DORINE   Just deserts, for what you put us through.
You thought we lied, now she thinks that of you.

CLÉANTE   Why are we wasting time with all of this? 60
We're standing on the edge of the abyss.
This man is dangerous! He has a plan!

DAMIS   How could he hurt us? I don't think he can.

ELMIRE   He won't get far, complaining to the law—
You'll tell the truth, and he'll have to withdraw. 65

CLÉANTE   Don't count on it; trust me, he'll find a way
To use these weapons you gave him today.
He has legal documents, and the deed.
To kick us out, just what else does he need?
And if he's doubted, there are many ways 70
To trap you in a wicked legal maze.
You give a snake his venom, nice and quick,
And after that you poke him with a stick?

ORGON   I know. But what was I supposed to do?
Emotions got the best of me, it's true. 75

CLÉANTE   If we could placate him, just for a while,
And somehow get the deed back with a smile.

ELMIRE   Had I known we had all this to lose,
I never would have gone through with my ruse.
I would've—   80

        [A knock on the door.]

ORGON   What does that man want? You go find out.
But I don't want to know what it's about.

5.4

[MONSIEUR LOYAL, MADAME PERNELLE, ORGON,
DAMIS, MARIANE, DORINE, ELMIRE, CLÉANTE]

MONSIEUR LOYAL [to DORINE]   Dear sister, hello. Please, I beg of you,
Your master is the one I must speak to.

DORINE   He's not receiving visitors today.

MONSIEUR LOYAL   I bring good news so don't send me away.
My goal in coming is not to displease; 5
I'm here to put your master's mind at ease.

DORINE   And you are . . . who?

MONSIEUR LOYAL   Just say that I have come

For his own good and with a message from
Monsieur Tartuffe.
DORINE [to ORGON]   It's a soft-spoken man,
Who says he's here to do just what he can   10
To ease your mind. Tartuffe sent him.
CLÉANTE   Let's see
What he might want.
ORGON   Oh, what's my strategy?
He's come to reconcile us, I just know.
CLÉANTE   Your strategy? Don't let your anger show,
For heaven's sake. And listen for a truce.   15
MONSIEUR LOYAL   My greetings, sir. I'm here to be of use.
ORGON   Just what I thought. His language is benign.
For the prospect of peace, a hopeful sign.
MONSIEUR LOYAL   Your family's dear to me, I hope you know.
I served your father many years ago.   20
ORGON   I humbly beg your pardon, to my shame,
I don't know you, nor do I know your name.
MONSIEUR LOYAL   My name's Loyal. I'm Norman by descent.
My job of bailiff is what pays my rent.
Thanks be to heaven, it's been forty years   25
I've done my duty free of doubts or fear.
That you invited me in, I can report,
When I serve you with this writ from the court.
ORGON   What? You're here . . .
MONSIEUR LOYAL   No upsetting outbursts, please.
It's just a warrant saying we can seize,   30
Not me, of course, but this Monsieur Tartuffe—
Your house and land as his. Here is the proof.
I have the contract here. You must vacate
These premises. Please, now, don't be irate.
Just gather up your things now, and make way   35
For this man, without hindrance or delay.
ORGON   Me? Leave my house?
MONSIEUR LOYAL   That's right, sir, out the door.
This house, at present, as I've said before,
Belongs to good Monsieur Tartuffe, you see,
He's lord and master of this property   40
By virtue of this contract I hold right here.
Is that not your signature? It's quite clear.
DAMIS   He's so rude, I do almost admire him.
MONSIEUR LOYAL   Excuse me. Is it possible to fire him?
My business is with you, a man of reason,   45
Who knows resisting would be seen as treason.
You understand that I must be permitted
To execute the orders as committed.
DAMIS   I'll execute him, Father, to be sure.
His long black nightgown won't make him secure.   50

MONSIEUR LOYAL   He's your son! I thought he was a servant.
  Control the boy. His attitude's too fervent,
  His anger is a bone of contention—
  Throw him out, or I will have to mention
  His name in this, my official report.   55
DORINE   "Loyal" is loyal only to the court.
MONSIEUR LOYAL   I have respect for all God-fearing men,
  So instantly I knew I'd come here when
  I heard your name attached to this assignment.
  I knew you'd want a bailiff with refinement.   60
  I'm here for you, just to accommodate,
  To make removal something you won't hate.
  Now, if I hadn't come, then you would find
  You got a bailiff who would be less kind.
ORGON   I'm sorry, I don't see the kindness in   65
  An eviction order.
MONSIEUR LOYAL   Let me begin:
  I'm giving you time. I won't carry out
  This order you are so upset about.
  I've come only to spend the night with you,
  With my men, who will be coming through.   70
  All ten of them, as quiet as a mouse,
  Oh, you must give me the keys to the house.
  We won't disturb you. You will have your rest—
  You need a full night's sleep—that's always best.
  There'll be no scandal, secrets won't be bared;   75
  Tomorrow morning you must be prepared,
  To pack your things, down to the smallest plate,
  And cup, and then these premises vacate.
  You'll have helpers; the men I chose are strong,
  And they'll have this house empty before long.   80
  I can't think of who would treat you better
  And still enforce the law down to the letter,
  Just later with the letter is my gift.
  So, no resistance. And there'll be no rift.
ORGON   From that which I still have, I'd give this hour,   85
  One hundred coins of gold to have the power
  To sock this bailiff with a punch as great
  As any man in this world could create.
CLÉANTE   That's enough. Let's not make it worse.
DAMIS   The nerve
  Of him. Let's see what my right fist can serve.   90
DORINE   Mister Loyal, you have a fine, broad back,
  And if I had a stick, you'd hear it crack.
MONSIEUR LOYAL   Words like that are punishable, my love—
  Be careful when a push becomes a shove.
CLÉANTE   Oh, come on, there's no reason to postpone.   95
  Just serve your writ and then leave us alone.

MONSIEUR LOYAL May heaven keep you, till we meet again!
ORGON And strangle you, and him who sent you in!

5.5

[ORGON, CLÉANTE, MARIANE, ELMIRE, MADAME
PERNELLE, DORINE, DAMIS]

ORGON Well, Mother, look at this writ. Here is proof
  Of treachery supreme by your Tartuffe.
  Don't jump to judgment—that's what you admonished.
MADAME PERNELLE I'm overwhelmed, I'm utterly astonished.
DORINE I hear you blaming him and that's just wrong.   5
  You'll see his good intentions before long.
  "Just love thy neighbor" is here on this writ,
  Between the lines, you see him saying it.
  Because men are corrupted by their wealth,
  Out of concern for your spiritual health.   10
  He's taking, with a pure motivation,
  Everything that keeps you from salvation.
ORGON Aren't you sick of hearing "Quiet!" from me?
CLÉANTE Thoughts of what to do now? And quickly?
ELMIRE Once we show the plans of that ingrate,   15
  His trickery can't get him this estate.
  As soon as they see his disloyalty,
  He'll be denied, I hope, this property.

5.6

[VALÈRE, ORGON, CLÉANTE, ELMIRE, MARIANE, *etc.*]

VALÈRE I hate to ruin your day—I have bad news.
  Danger's coming. There's no time to lose.
  A good friend, quite good, as it turns out,
  Discovered something you must know about,
  Something at the court that's happening now.   5
  That swindler—sorry, if you will allow,
  That holy faker—has gone to the king,
  Accusing you of almost everything.
  But here's the worst: he says that you have failed
  Your duty as a subject, which entailed   10
  The keeping of a strongbox so well hidden,
  That you could deny knowledge, if bidden,
  Of a traitor's whereabouts. What's more,
  That holy fraud will come right through that door,
  Accusing you. You can't do anything.   15
  He had this box and gave it to the king.
  So there's an order out for your arrest!
  And evidently, it's the king's behest,
  That Tartuffe come, so justice can be done.

CLÉANTE   Well, there it is, at last, the smoking gun.   20
  He can claim this house, at the very least.
ORGON   The man is nothing but a vicious beast.
VALÈRE   You must leave now, and I will help you hide.
  Here's ten thousand in gold. My carriage is outside.
  When a storm is bearing down on you   25
  Running is the best thing one can do.
  I have a place where both of us can stay.
ORGON   My boy, I owe you more than I can say.
  I pray to heaven that, before too long,
  I can pay you back and right the wrong   30
  I've done to you. [*To* ELMIRE] Good-bye. Take care, my dear.
CLÉANTE   We'll plan. You go while the way is still clear.

5.7

[THE EXEMPT, TARTUFFE, VALÈRE, ORGON, ELMIRE,
MARIANE, DORINE, *etc.*[2]]

TARTUFFE   Easy, just a minute, you move too fast.
  Your cowardice, dear sir, is unsurpassed.
  What I have to say is uncontested.
  Simply put, I'm having you arrested.
ORGON   You villain, you traitor, your lechery   5
  Is second only to your treachery.
  And you arrest me—that's the crowning blow.
TARTUFFE   Suffering for heaven is all I know,
  So revile me. It's all for heaven's sake.
CLÉANTE   Why does he persist when we know it's fake?   10
DAMIS   He's mocking heaven. What a loathsome beast.
TARTUFFE   Get mad—I'm not bothered in the least.
  It is my duty, what I'm doing here.
MARIANE   You really think that if you persevere
  In this lie, you'll keep your reputation?   15
TARTUFFE   My honor is safeguarded by my station,
  As I am on a mission from the king.
ORGON   You dog, have you forgotten everything?
  Who picked you up from total poverty?
TARTUFFE   I know that there were things you did for me.   20
  My duty to our monarch is what stifles
  Memory, so your past gifts are trifles.
  My obligations to him are so rife,
  That I would give up family, friends, and life.
ELMIRE   Fraud!   25
DORINE   Now there's a lie that beats everything,
  His pretended reverence for our king!

---

2. Molière himself added "etc." to the list of speaking characters. Thus Laurent and Flipote may return to the stage for this final scene.

CLÉANTE   This "duty to our monarch," as you say,
   Why didn't it come up before today?
   You had the box, you lived here for some time,
   To say the least, and yet this crime   30
   That you reported—why then did you wait?
   Orgon caught you about to desecrate
   The holy bonds of marriage with his wife.
   Suddenly, your obligations are so "rife"
   To our dear king, that you're here to turn in   35
   Your former friend and "brother" and begin
   To move into his house, a gift, but look,
   Why would you accept gifts from a crook?
TARTUFFE [to THE EXEMPT]   Save me from this whining! I have had my fill!
   Do execute your orders, if you will.   40
THE EXEMPT   I will. I've waited much too long for that.
   I had to let you have your little chat.
   It confirmed the facts our monarch knew,
   That's why, Tartuffe, I am arresting you.[3]
TARTUFFE   Who, me?   45
THE EXEMPT   Yes, you.
TARTUFFE   You're putting me in jail?
THE EXEMPT   Immediately. And there will be no bail.
   [To ORGON] You may compose yourself now, sir, because
   We're fortunate in leadership and laws.
   We have a king who sees into men's hearts,
   And cannot be deceived, so he imparts   50
   Great wisdom, and a talent for discernment,
   Thus frauds are guaranteed a quick internment.
   Our Prince of Reason sees things as they are,
   So hypocrites do not get very far.
   But saintly men and the truly devout,   55
   He cherishes and has no doubts about.
   This man could not begin to fool the king
   Who can defend himself against the sting
   Of much more subtle predators. And thus,
   When this craven pretender came to us,   60
   Demanding justice and accusing you,
   He betrayed himself. Our king could view
   The baseness lurking in his coward's heart.
   Evil like that can set a man apart,
   And so divine justice nodded her head,   65
   The king did not believe a word he said.
   It was soon confirmed, he has a crime
   For every sin, but why squander the time
   To list them or the aliases he used.
   For the king, it's enough that he abused   70

---

3. In his capacity as officer of the king, The Exempt becomes both Louis' representative and his surrogate.

Your friendship and your faith. And though we knew
Each accusation of his was untrue,
Our monarch himself, wanting to know
Just how far this imposter planned to go,
Had me wait to find this out, then pounce,   75
Arrest this criminal, quickly denounce
The man and all his lies. And now, the king
Orders delivered to you, everything
This scoundrel took, the deed, all documents,
This locked box of yours and all its contents,   80
And nullifies the contract giving away
Your property, effective today.
And finally, our monarch wants to end
Your worries about aiding your old friend
Before he went into exile because,   85
In that same way, and in spite of the laws,
You openly defended our king's right
To his throne. And you were prepared to fight.
From his heart, and because it makes good sense
That a good deed deserves a recompense,   90
He pardons you. And wanted me to add:
He remembers good longer than the bad.
DORINE   May heaven be praised!
MADAME PERNELLE   I am so relieved.
ELMIRE   A happy ending!
MARIANE   Can it be believed?
ORGON [*to* TARTUFFE]   Now then, you traitor . . .   95
CLÉANTE   Stop that, Brother, please.
You're sinking to his level. Don't appease
His expectations of mankind. His fate
Is misery. But it's never too late
To take another path, and feel remorse.
So let's wish, rather, he will change his course,   100
And turn his back upon his life of vice,
Embrace the good and know it will suffice.
We've all seen the wisdom of this great king,
Whom we should go and thank for everything.
ORGON   Yes, and well said. So come along with me,   105
To thank him for his generosity.
And then once that glorious task is done,
We'll come back here for yet another one—
I mean a wedding for which we'll prepare,
To give my daughter to the good Valère.   110

APHRA BEHN
1640?–1689

Poised between Africa and the New World, *Oroonoko* follows the heroic prince of that name into captivity, slavery, and desperate violence. The novella tantalizes us with the fiction of a narrator who personally witnesses much of Oroonoko's story, and whose close friendship with the hero makes her both sympathetic to his plight and complicit in his fate. *Oroonoko* itself is similarly ambiguous: it makes a powerful case against slavery, long before the actual birth of abolitionism, yet it also presents the prince as an exceptional victim whose enslavement is tragic only because of his exalted, aristocratic nature.

As the first professional woman writer in England, Aphra Behn gave women "the right to speak their minds," as **Virginia Woolf** put it. She wrote popular plays, longer epistolary fiction, novellas such as *Oroonoko*, and occasional poetry. Early in her career, she probably served as a spy for the English in Holland, and in later years was associated with libertines and freethinkers. Both in her personal and in her professional life she showed a pronounced disregard for convention and for the limits imposed on women's behavior in her time.

Little is known about Behn's early life, though it seems likely that her father was a barber in Canterbury. In *Oroonoko* she creates a more exalted parentage for herself, claiming to be the daughter of the "lieutenant-general of six and thirty islands, besides the continent of Surinam." This purely fictional genealogy was repeated by her first biographer and has confused readers ever since. Behn did visit the English colony of Surinam, on the northern edge of South America,

with her mother and siblings in 1663, and became involved in the political infighting there. On her return to London in 1664, she apparently married a German merchant, Johannes Behn, but the marriage did not last long, either because of his death or their separation.

In 1660, London playhouses reopened after an eighteen-year hiatus that coincided with Puritan control of England following the English Civil War. The restoration to the English throne of Charles II, an avid enthusiast of the theater, virtually guaranteed that the period later called "the Restoration" would witness a flowering of theatrical innovation and creativity. It also provided women with new opportunities to participate in the cultural life of London. For example, actresses, not actors, now routinely played female roles.

In this environment, Behn forged her writing career. It didn't hurt that her political sympathies would always lie with the king: in a time of continuing political turmoil, she supported first Charles and then James II. As political parties developed in England, she consistently sided with the more conservative Tories, who supported a strong monarchy. Her ties to the monarchy were so strong that at one point, Behn was sent by the king to Holland as a spy. Her code name during this stint in espionage was "Astrea," the Greek goddess associated with purity and renewal, one of the many names given to another exceptional early modern Englishwoman, Elizabeth I. Behn would later adopt this name in her literary pursuits whenever she needed to conceal her identity. By 1670 she had become a playwright, writing for the Duke's Company in London. Uniquely for her time, she had at least nineteen plays staged, and probably contributed to many more. In keeping with the fashion of the times, Behn wrote tragicomedies on love and political restoration, as well as city comedies full of incorrigible rakes, duped husbands, and pert heroines. The most famous of these, *The Rover* (1677), is still produced regularly.

Behn was associated with the circle of the Earl of Rochester, the most famous libertine of a libertine time. She wrote a number of explicit poems on sexual matters, which led to many accusations of indecency, both from her contemporaries and especially during the Victorian era, when her work was dismissed for its "coarseness." Yet Behn was a famous and successful writer in her own time, whose work paved the way for playwrights and novelists, both male and female, in the eighteenth century. Today, her reputation rests primarily on *Oroonoko* and her city comedies, while her wider oeuvre is increasingly read and studied.

First published in 1688, *Oroonoko* describes the triangular trade in manufactured goods, slaves, and sugar among Europe, Africa, and the Caribbean. English slave traders picked up their human cargo on the west coast of Africa, transported them to the West Indies, where those who survived the cruel passage were sold to work on the sugar plantations, and then returned to England with a cargo of sugar to complete their profitable, if brutal, trajectory. Behn's novella is partly a frame narrative: it opens in the English sugar colony of Surinam, where the first-person narrator, who identifies herself as Behn, has traveled with her father, the new governor, and her sister. There the narrator befriends the imposing slave Oroonoko, who shares his story. His fantastic narrative takes us back to an exotic West Africa of harems and vulnerable virgins, a place overcivilized in its luxury, in contrast to the supposedly innocent New World. As the tale unfolds, we learn that Oroonoko, a prince in his own land, had managed to save his beloved Imoinda from his lecherous grandfather, only to be tricked into captivity by a greedy English slave trader.

In denouncing Oroonoko's fate, the narrator insists on Oroonoko's status as a virtual European and an aristocrat, as evinced by his elegant physique and European education. These claims underscore the text's ambivalence about slavery and race. The text leaves us wondering: Is Oroonoko meant to be a representative victim, or an exalted exception? How is he different from other Africans, who, in the world of the text, can be enslaved unproblematically? As Oroonoko and Imoinda's prolonged slavery becomes unbearable to the dignified hero, he leads his fellow slaves in a revolt, bringing down upon himself the fury of the slave-owning establishment and destroying the supposed harmony that the text relates. Are Oroonoko's violent acts justified? Does the text encourage us to see his resistance as necessary but unfortunate, or instead as evidence of his ultimate savagery?

Oroonoko's first-person narrator, closely identified with the author, raises for the reader basic questions of narrative authority and omniscience: what is this narrator privy to, and what are the limits of her power? What can she and can she not do for the enslaved prince, beyond narrating his story? Ultimately, how can we read her framed and partial account of him? In its short span, Behn's novella probes the dilemmas of personal versus political morality, of the legitimacy of government in a violent colonial space, and of the true nature of heroism.

Whatever its ambiguities, *Oroonoko* resonated profoundly with opponents of slavery and was repeatedly adapted both in prose and on the stage, from Thomas Southerne's 1695 tragicomedy through several tragic versions over the course of the eighteenth century, as the abolitionist movement in England found its voice.

Oroonoko; or, The Royal Slave

The Epistle Dedicatory

To The
Right Honourable
The
Lord *MAITLAND*.[1]

* * *

My Lord, the Obligations I have to some of the Great Men of your Nation, particularly to your Lordship, gives me an Ambition of making my Acknowledg-
ments, by all the Opportunities I can; and such humble Fruits, as my Industry
produces, I lay at your Lordship's Feet. This is a true Story, of a Man Gallant
enough to merit your Protection; and, had he always been so Fortunate, he had
not made so Inglorious an end: The Royal Slave I had the Honour to know in
my Travels to the other World; and though I had none above me in that Country, yet I wanted power to preserve this Great Man. If there be any thing that
seems Romantick, I beseech your Lordship to consider, these Countries do, in
all things, so far differ from ours, that they produce unconceivable Wonders; at
least, they appear so to us, because New and Strange. What I have mention'd I
have taken care shou'd be Truth, let the Critical Reader judge as he pleases.
'Twill be no Commendation to the Book, to assure your Lordship I writ it in a
few Hours, though it may serve to Excuse some of its Faults of Connexion; for
I never rested my Pen a Moment for Thought: 'Tis purely the Merit of my Slave
that must render it worthy of the Honour it begs; and the Author of that of
Subscribing herself,

My Lord,
Your Lordship's most oblig'd
and obedient Servant,
A. BEHN.

The History of the Royal Slave

I do not pretend, in giving you the History of this *Royal Slave*, to entertain my
Reader with the Adventures of a feign'd *Hero*, whose Life and Fortunes Fancy
may manage at the Poet's Pleasure; nor in relating the Truth, design to adorn
it with any Accidents, but such as arriv'd in earnest to him: And it shall come
simply into the World, recommended by its own proper Merits, and natural
Intrigues; there being enough of Reality to support it, and to render it diverting, without the Addition of Invention.

I was my self an Eye-Witness to a great part, of what you will find here set
down; and what I cou'd not be Witness of, I receiv'd from the Mouth of the

---

1. Richard Maitland (1635–1695) held important posts in Scotland and was noted for his fine
library.

chief Actor in this History, the *Hero* himself, who gave us the whole Transactions of his Youth; and though I shall omit, for Brevity's sake, a thousand little Accidents of his Life, which, however pleasant to us, where History was scarce, and Adventures very rare; yet might prove tedious and heavy to my Reader, in a World where he finds Diversions for every Minute, new and strange: But we who were perfectly charm'd with the Character of this great Man, were curious to gather every Circumstance of his Life.

The Scene of the last part of his Adventures lies in a Colony in *America*, called *Surinam*,[2] in the *West-Indies*.

But before I give you the Story of this *Gallant Slave*, 'tis fit I tell you the manner of bringing them to these new *Colonies*; for those they make use of there, are not *Natives* of the place; for those we live with in perfect Amity, without daring to command 'em; but on the contrary, caress 'em with all the brotherly and friendly Affection in the World; trading with 'em for their Fish, Venison, Buffilo's,[3] Skins, and little Rarities; as Marmosets, a sort of *Monkey* as big as a Rat or Weasel, but of a marvellous and delicate shape, and has Face and Hands like an Humane Creature: and *Cousheries*,[4] a little Beast in the form and fashion of a Lion, as big as a Kitten; but so exactly made in all parts like that noble Beast, that it is it in *Miniature*. Then for little *Parakeetoes*, great Parrots, *Muckaws*, and a thousand other Birds and Beasts of wonderful and surprizing Forms, Shapes, and Colours. For Skins of prodigious Snakes, of which there are some threescore Yards in length; as is the Skin of one that may be seen at His Majesty's *Antiquaries*: Where are also some rare Flies,[5] of amazing Forms and Colours, presented to 'em by my self; some as big as my Fist, some less; and all of various Excellencies, such as Art cannot imitate. Then we trade for Feathers, which they order into all Shapes, make themselves little short Habits of 'em, and glorious Wreaths for their Heads, Necks, Arms and Legs, whose Tinctures are unconceivable. I had a Set of these presented to me, and I gave 'em to the King's Theatre, and it was the Dress of the *Indian Queen*,[6] infinitely admir'd by Persons of Quality; and were unimitable. Besides these, a thousand little Knacks, and Rarities in Nature, and some of Art; as their Baskets, Weapons, Aprons, &c. We dealt with 'em with Beads of all Colours, Knives, Axes, Pins and Needles; which they us'd only as Tools to drill Holes with in their Ears, Noses and Lips, where they hang a great many little things; as long Beads, bits of Tin, Brass, or Silver, beat thin; and any shining Trincket. The Beads they weave into Aprons about a quarter of an Ell long, and of the same breadth;[7] working them very prettily in Flowers of several Colours of Beads; which Apron they wear just before 'em, as *Adam* and *Eve* did the Fig-leaves; the Men wearing a long Stripe of Linen, which they deal with us for. They thread these Beads also on long Cotton-threads, and make Girdles to tie their Aprons to, which come twenty times, or more, about the Waist; and then

---

2. An English colony in the region of Guiana, on the coast of South America east of Venezuela, now Suriname. It was settled by planters from Barbados seeking more land.
3. Buffalo or wild oxen.
4. A lion-headed marmoset.
5. Butterflies. "*Antiquaries*": the new Royal Society museum.
6. A play by Robert Howard and John Dryden, set in Mexico, first performed at the Theatre Royal in 1664.
7. About one foot square. "Ell": old English measure, about forty-five inches.

cross, like a Shoulder-belt, both ways, and round their Necks, Arms and Legs. This Adornment, with their long black Hair, and the Face painted in little Specks or Flowers here and there, makes 'em a wonderful Figure to behold. Some of the Beauties which indeed are finely shap'd, as almost all are, and who have pretty Features, are very charming and novel; for they have all that is called Beauty, except the Colour, which is a reddish Yellow; or after a new Oiling, which they often use to themselves, they are of the colour of a new Brick, but smooth, soft and sleek. They are extream modest and bashful, very shy, and nice[8] of being touch'd. And though they are all thus naked, if one lives for ever among 'em, there is not to be seen an indecent Action, or Glance; and being continually us'd to see one another so unadorn'd, so like our first Parents before the Fall, it seems as if they had no Wishes; there being nothing to heighten Curiosity, but all you can see, you see at once, and every Moment see; and where there is no Novelty, there can be no Curiosity. Not but I have seen a handsom young *Indian*, dying for Love of a very beautiful young *Indian* Maid; but all his Courtship was, to fold his Arms, pursue her with his Eyes, and Sighs were all his Language: While she, as if no such Lover were present; or rather, as if she desired none such, carefully guarded her Eyes from beholding him; and never approach'd him, but she look'd down with all the blushing Modesty I have seen in the most severe and cautious of our World. And these People represented to me an absolute *Idea* of the first State of Innocence, before Man knew how to sin: And 'tis most evident and plain, that simple Nature is the most harmless, inoffensive and vertuous Mistress. 'Tis she alone, if she were permitted, that better instructs the World, than all the Inventions of Man: Religion wou'd here but destroy that Tranquillity, they possess by Ignorance; and Laws wou'd but teach 'em to know Offence, of which now they have no Notion. They once made Mourning and Fasting for the Death of the *English* Governor, who had given his Hand to come on such a Day to 'em, and neither came, nor sent; believing, when once a Man's Word was past, nothing but Death cou'd or shou'd prevent his keeping it: And when they saw he was not dead, they ask'd him, what Name they had for a Man who promis'd a thing he did not do? The Governor told them, Such a man was a *Lyar*, which was a Word of Infamy to a Gentleman. Then one of 'em reply'd, *Governor, you are a Lyar, and guilty of that Infamy.* They have a Native Justice, which knows no Fraud; and they understand no Vice, or Cunning, but when they are taught by the *White Men.* They have Plurality of Wives, which, when they grow old, they serve those that succeed 'em, who are young; but with a Servitude easie and respected; and unless they take Slaves in War, they have no other Attendants.

Those on that *Continent* where I was, had no King; but the oldest War-Captain was obey'd with great Resignation.

A War-Captain is a Man who has led them on to Battel with Conduct,[9] and Success; of whom I shall have Occasion to speak more hereafter, and of some other of their Customs and Manners, as they fall in my way.

With these People, as I said, we live in perfect Tranquillity, and good Understanding, as it behooves us to do; they knowing all the places where to seek the best Food of the Country, and the Means of getting it; and for very small and

---

8. Fastidious, careful.   9. Good leadership.

unvaluable Trifles, supply us with what 'tis impossible for us to get; for they do not only in the Wood, and over the *Sevana's*,[1] in Hunting, supply the parts of Hounds, by swiftly scouring through those almost impassable places; and by the meer Activity of their Feet, run down the nimblest Deer, and other eatable Beasts: But in the water, one wou'd think they were Gods of the Rivers, or Fellow-Citizens of the Deep; so rare an Art they have in Swimming, Diving, and almost Living in Water; by which they command the less swift Inhabitants of the Floods. And then for Shooting; what they cannot take, or reach with their Hands, they do with Arrows; and have so admirable an Aim, that they will split almost an Hair; and at any distance that an Arrow can reach, they will shoot down Oranges, and other Fruit, and only touch the Stalk with the Dart's Point, that they may not hurt the Fruit. So that they being, on all Occasions, very useful to us, we find it absolutely necessary to caress 'em as Friends, and not to treat 'em as Slaves; nor dare we do other, their Numbers so far surpassing ours in that *Continent*.

Those then whom we make use of to work in our Plantations of Sugar, are *Negro's*, *Black*-Slaves altogether; which are transported thither in this manner.

Those who want Slaves, make a Bargain with a Master, or a Captain of a Ship, and contract to pay him so much a-piece, a matter of twenty Pound a Head for as many as he agrees for, and to pay for 'em when they shall be deliver'd on such a Plantation: So that when there arrives a Ship laden with Slaves, they who have so contracted, go a-board, and receive their Number by Lot;[2] and perhaps in one Lot that may be for ten, there may happen to be three or four Men; the rest, Women and Children: Or be there more or less of either Sex, you are oblig'd to be contented with your Lot.

Coramantien,[3] a Country of *Blacks* so called, was one of those places in which they found the most advantageous Trading for these Slaves; and thither most of our great Traders in that Merchandice traffick'd; for that Nation is very war-like and brave; and having a continual Campaign, being always in Hostility with one neighbouring Prince or other, they had the fortune to take a great many Captives; for all they took in Battel, were sold as Slaves; at least, those common Men who cou'd not ransom themselves. Of these Slaves so taken, the General only has all the profit; and of these Generals, our Captains and Masters of Ships buy all their Freights.

The King of *Coramantien* was himself a Man of a Hundred and odd Years old, and had no Son, though he had many beautiful *Black*-Wives; for most certainly, there are Beauties that can charm of that Colour. In his younger Years he had had many gallant Men to his Sons, thirteen of which died in Battel, conquering when they fell; and he had only left him for his Successor, one Grand-Child, Son to one of these dead Victors; who, as soon as he cou'd bear a Bow in his Hand, and a Quiver at his Back, was sent into the Field, to be trained up by one of the oldest Generals, to War; where, from his natural Inclination to Arms, and the Occasions given him, with the good Conduct of the

---

1. I.e., savannas, tropical and subtropical grasslands.
2. Groups.
3. An English fort and slave trading station in West Africa, in what is today Ghana. Slaves shipped out of this region were mainly Fante, Ashante, and other Akan-speaking peoples, whom the English referred to as Cormantines. They were known for their beauty and dignity, and their fierceness in war.

old General, he became, at the Age of Seventeen, one of the most expert Captains, and bravest Soldiers, that ever saw the Field of *Mars*:[4] So that he was ador'd as the Wonder of all that World, and the Darling of the Soldiers. Besides, he was adorn'd with a native Beauty so transcending all those of his gloomy Race, that he strook an Awe and Reverence, even in those that knew not his Quality; as he did in me, who beheld him with Surprize and Wonder, when afterwards he arriv'd in our World.

He had scarce arriv'd at his Seventeenth Year, when fighting by his Side, the General was kill'd with an Arrow in his Eye, which the Prince *Oroonoko* (for so was this gallant *Moor*[5] call'd) very narrowly avoided; nor had he, if the General, who saw the Arrow shot, and perceiving it aim'd at the Prince, had not bow'd his Head between, on purpose to receive it in his own Body rather than it shou'd touch that of the Prince, and so saved him.

'Twas then, afflicted as *Oroonoko* was, that he was proclaim'd General in the old Man's place; and then it was, at the finishing of that War, which had continu'd for two Years, that the Prince came to Court; where he had hardly been a Month together, from the time of his fifth Year, to that of Seventeen; and 'twas amazing to imagine where it was he learn'd so much Humanity; or, to give his Accomplishments a juster Name, where 'twas he got that real Greatness of Soul, those refin'd Notions of true Honour, that absolute Generosity, and that Softness that was capable of the highest Passions of Love and Gallantry, whose Objects were almost continually fighting Men, or those mangl'd, or dead; who heard no Sounds, but those of War and Groans: Some part of it we may attribute to the Care of a *French*-Man of Wit and Learning; who finding it turn to very good Account to be a sort of Royal Tutor to this young *Black*, & perceiving him very ready, apt, and quick of Apprehension, took a great pleasure to teach him Morals, Language and Science; and was for it extreamly belov'd and valu'd by him. Another Reason was, He lov'd, when he came from War, to see all the *English* Gentlemen that traded thither; and did not only learn their Language, but that of the *Spaniards* also, with whom he traded afterwards for Slaves.

I have often seen and convers'd with this great Man, and been a Witness to many of his mighty Actions; and do assure my Reader, the most Illustrious Courts cou'd not have produc'd a braver Man, both for Greatness of Courage and Mind, a Judgment more solid, a Wit more quick, and a Conversation more sweet and diverting. He knew almost as much as if he had read much: He had heard of, and admir'd the *Romans*; he had heard of the late Civil Wars in *England*, and the deplorable Death of our great Monarch;[6] and wou'd discourse of it with all the Sense, and Abhorrence of the Injustice imaginable. He had an extream good and graceful Mien, and all the Civility of a well-bred great Man. He had nothing of Barbarity in his Nature, but in all Points address'd himself, as if his Education had been in some *European* Court.

This great and just Character of *Oroonoko* gave me an extream Curiosity to see him, especially when I knew he spoke *French* and *English*, and that I cou'd talk with him. But though I had heard so much of him, I was as greatly surpriz'd

---

4. Battlefield, after the Roman god of war.
5. Variously used in the period for Muslims or for dark-skinned peoples.

6. Charles I, tried and executed in 1649 during the civil war between Royalists and Parliamentarians.

when I saw him, as if I had heard nothing of him; so beyond all Report I found him. He came into the Room, and address'd himself to me, and some other Women, with the best Grace in the World. He was pretty tall, but of a Shape the most exact that can be fancy'd: The most famous Statuary[7] cou'd not form the Figure of a Man more admirably turn'd from Head to Foot. His Face was not of that brown, rusty Black which most of that Nation are, but a perfect Ebony, or polish'd Jett. His Eyes were the most awful that cou'd be seen, and very piercing; the White of 'em being like Snow, as were his Teeth. His Nose was rising and *Roman*, instead of *African* and flat. His Mouth, the finest shap'd that cou'd be seen; far from those great turn'd Lips, which are so natural to the rest of the *Negroes*. The whole Proportion and Air of his Face was so noble, and exactly form'd, that bating[8] his Colour there cou'd be nothing in Nature more beautiful, agreeable and handsome. There was no one Grace wanting, that bears the Standard of true Beauty: His Hair came down to his Shoulders, by the Aids of Art; which was, by pulling it out with a Quill, and keeping it comb'd; of which he took particular Care. Nor did the Perfections of his Mind come short of those of his Person; for his Discourse was admirable upon almost any Subject; and who-ever had heard him speak, wou'd have been convinc'd of their Errors, that all fine Wit is confin'd to the *White* Men, especially to those of *Christendom*; and wou'd have confess'd that *Oroonoko* was as capable even, of reigning well, and of governing as wisely, had as great a Soul, as politick[9] Maxims, and was as sensible of Power as any Prince civiliz'd in the most refin'd Schools of Humanity and Learning, or the most Illustrious Courts.

This Prince, such as I have describ'd him, whose Soul and Body were so admirably adorn'd, was (while yet he was in the Court of his Grandfather) as I said, as capable of Love, as 'twas possible for a brave and gallant Man to be; and in saying that, I have nam'd the highest Degree of Love; for sure, great Souls are most capable of that Passion.

I have already said, the old General was kill'd by the shot of an Arrow, by the Side of this Prince, in Battel; and that *Oroonoko* was made General. This old dead *Hero* had one only Daughter left of his Race; a Beauty that, to describe her truly, one need say only, she was Female to the noble Male; the beautiful *Black Venus*,[1] to our young *Mars*; as charming in her Person as he, and of delicate Vertues. I have seen an hundred *White* Men sighing after her, and making a thousand Vows at her Feet, all vain, and unsuccessful: And she was, indeed, too great for any, but a Prince of her own Nation to adore.

Oroonoko coming from the Wars, (which were now ended) after he had made his Court to his Grand-father, he thought in Honour he ought to make a Visit to *Imoinda*, the Daughter of his Foster-father, the dead General; and to make some Excuses to her, because his Preservation was the Occasion of her Father's Death; and to present her with those Slaves that had been taken in this last Battel, as the Trophies of her Father's Victories. When he came, attended by all the young Soldiers of any Merit, he was infinitely surpriz'd at the Beauty of this fair Queen of Night, whose Face and Person was so exceeding all he had ever beheld, that lovely Modesty with which she receiv'd him, that Softness in her

---

7. Sculptor.
8. Except for.
9. Prudent, shrewd.

1. Roman goddess of love; lover of Mars, the god of war.

Look, and Sighs, upon the melancholy Occasion of this Honour that was done by so great a Man as *Oroonoko*, and a Prince of whom she had heard such admirable things; the Awfulness[2] wherewith she receiv'd him, and the Sweetness of her Words and Behaviour while he stay'd, gain'd a perfect Conquest over his fierce Heart, and made him feel, the Victor cou'd be subdu'd. So that having made his first Compliments, and presented her an hundred and fifty Slaves in Fetters, he told her with his Eyes, that he was not insensible of her Charms; while *Imoinda*, who wish'd for nothing more than so glorious a Conquest, was pleas'd to believe, she understood that silent Language of new-born Love; and from that Moment, put on all her Additions to Beauty.

The Prince return'd to Court with quite another Humour than before; and though he did not speak much of the fair *Imoinda*, he had the pleasure to hear all his Followers speak of nothing but the Charms of that Maid; insomuch that, even in the Presence of the old King, they were extolling her, and heightning, if possible, the Beauties they had found in her: So that nothing else was talk'd of, no other Sound was heard in every Corner where there were Whisperers, but *Imoinda! Imoinda!*

'Twill be imagin'd *Oroonoko* stay'd not long before he made his second Visit; nor, considering his Quality, not much longer before he told her, he ador'd her. I have often heard him say, that he admir'd by what strange Inspiration he came to talk things so soft, and so passionate, who never knew Love, nor was us'd to the Conversation of Women; but (to use his own Words) he said, Most happily, some new, and till then unknown Power instructed his Heart and Tongue in the Language of Love, and at the same time, in favour of him, inspir'd *Imoinda* with a Sense of his Passion. She was touch'd with what he said, and return'd it all in such Answers as went to his very Heart, with a Pleasure unknown before: Nor did he use those Obligations[3] ill, that Love had done him; but turn'd all his happy Moments to the best advantage; and as he knew no Vice, his Flame aim'd at nothing but Honour, if such a distinction may be made in Love; and especially in that Country, where Men take to themselves as many as they can maintain; and where the only Crime and Sin with Woman is, to turn her off, to abandon her to Want, Shame and Misery: Such ill Morals are only practis'd in *Christian*-Countries, where they prefer the bare Name of Religion; and, without Vertue or Morality, think that's sufficient. But *Oroonoko* was none of those Professors; but as he had right Notions of Honour, so he made her such Propositions as were not only and barely such; but, contrary to the Custom of his Country, he made her Vows, she shou'd be the only woman he wou'd possess while he liv'd; that no Age or Wrinkles shou'd incline him to change, for her Soul wou'd be always fine, and always young; and he shou'd have an eternal *Idea* in his Mind of the Charms she now bore, and shou'd look into his Heart for that *Idea*, when he cou'd find it no longer in her Face.

After a thousand Assurances of his lasting Flame, and her eternal Empire[4] over him, she condescended to receive him for her Husband; or rather, receiv'd him, as the greatest Honour the Gods cou'd do her.

---

2. Awe, reverence.
3. Benefits.

4. Rule, power.

There is a certain Ceremony in these Cases to be observ'd, which I forgot to ask him how perform'd; but 'twas concluded on both sides, that, in Obedience to him, the Grand-father was to be first made aequainted with the Design; for they pay a most absolute Resignation[5] to the Monarch, especially when he is a Parent also.

On the other side, the old King, who had many Wives, and many Concubines, wanted not Court-Flatterers to insinuate in his Heart a thousand tender Thoughts for this young Beauty; and who represented her to his Fancy, as the most charming he had ever possess'd in all the long Race of his numerous Years. At this Character his old Heart, like an extinguish'd Brand, most apt to take Fire, felt new Sparks of Love, and began to kindle; and now grown to his second Childhood, long'd with Impatience to behold this gay thing, with whom, alas! he cou'd but innocently play. But how he shou'd be confirm'd she was this *Wonder*, before he us'd his Power to call her to Court (where Maidens never came, unless for the King's private Use) he was next to consider; and while he was so doing, he had Intelligence brought him, that *Imoinda* was most certainly Mistress to the Prince *Oroonoko*. This gave him some *Shagrien*[6] however, it gave him also an Opportunity, one Day, when the Prince was a-hunting, to wait on a Man of Quality, as his Slave and Attendant, who shou'd go and make a Present to *Imoinda*, as from the Prince; he shou'd then, unknown, see this fair Maid, and have an Opportunity to hear what Message she wou'd return the Prince for his Present; and from thence gather the state of her Heart, and degree of her Inclination. This was put in Execution, and the old Monarch saw, and burnt: He found her all he had heard, and wou'd not delay his Happiness, but found he shou'd have some Obstacle to overcome her Heart; for she express'd her Sense of the Present the Prince had sent her, in terms so sweet, so soft and pretty, with an Air of Love and Joy that cou'd not be dissembl'd; insomuch that 'twas past doubt whether she lov'd *Oroonoko* entirely. This gave the old King some Affliction: but he salv'd[7] it with this, that the Obedience the People pay their King, was not at all inferior to what they pay'd their Gods: And what Love wou'd not oblige *Imoinda* to do, Duty wou'd compel her to.

He was therefore no sooner got to his Apartment, but he sent the Royal Veil to *Imoinda*; that is, the Ceremony of Invitation: he sends the Lady, he has a Mind to honour with his Bed, a Veil, with which she is cover'd, and secur'd for the King's Use; and 'tis Death to disobey; besides, held a most impious Disobedience.

'Tis not to be imagin'd the Surprize and Grief that seiz'd this lovely Maid at this News and Sight. However, as Delays in these Cases are dangerous, and Pleading worse than Treason; trembling, and almost fainting, she was oblig'd to suffer her self to be cover'd, and led away.

They brought her thus to Court; and the King, who had caus'd a very rich Bath to be prepar'd, was led into it, where he sate under a Canopy, in State, to receive this long'd for Virgin; whom he having commanded shou'd be brought to him, they (after dis-robing her) led her to the Bath, and making fast the Doors, left her to descend. The King, without more Courtship, bad her throw

5. Deference, submission.
6. I.e., chagrin.
7. Salved: soothed or remedied a wound.

off her Mantle, and come to his Arms. But *Imoinda*, all in Tears, threw her self on the Marble, on the Brink of the Bath, and besought him to hear her. She told him, as she was a Maid, how proud of the Divine Glory she should have been of having it in her power to oblige her King: but as by the Laws, he cou'd not; and from his Royal Goodness, wou'd not take from any Man his wedded Wife: So she believ'd she shou'd be the Occasion of making him commit a great Sin, if she did not reveal her State and Condition; and tell him, she was anothers, and cou'd not be so happy to be his.

The King, enrag'd at this Delay, hastily demanded the Name of the bold Man, that had marry'd a Woman of her Degree, without his Consent. *Imoinda*, seeing his Eyes fierce, and his Hands tremble; whether with Age, or Anger, I know not; but she fancy'd the last, almost repented she had said so much, for now she fear'd the Storm wou'd fall on the Prince; she therefore said a thousand things to appease the raging of his Flame, and to prepare him to hear who it was with Calmness; but before she spoke, he imagin'd who she meant, but wou'd not seem to do so, but commanded her to lay aside her Mantle, and suffer her self to receive his Caresses; or, by his Gods, he swore, that happy Man whom she was going to name shou'd die, though it were even *Oroonoko* himself. *Therefore* (said he) *deny this Marriage, and swear thy self a Maid. That* (reply'd *Imoinda*) *by all our Powers I do; for I am not yet known to my Husband.* 'Tis enough (said the King); *'tis enough to satisfie both my Conscience, and my Heart.* And rising from his Seat, he went, and led her into the Bath; it being in vain for her to resist.

In this time the Prince, who was return'd from Hunting, went to visit his *Imoinda*, but found her gone; and not only so, but heard she had receiv'd the Royal Veil. This rais'd him to a Storm; and in his Madness, they had much ado to save him from laying violent Hands on himself. Force first prevail'd, and then Reason: They urg'd all to him, that might oppose his Rage; but nothing weigh'd so greatly with him as the King's Old Age uncapable of injuring him with *Imoinda*.[8] He wou'd give way to that Hope, because it pleas'd him most, and flatter'd best his Heart. Yet this serv'd not altogether to make him cease his different Passions, which sometimes rag'd within him, and sometimes softned into Showers. 'Twas not enough to appease him, to tell him, his Grand-father was old, and cou'd not that way injure him, while he retain'd that awful[9] Duty which the young Men are us'd there to pay to their grave Relations. He cou'd not be convinc'd he had no Cause to sigh and mourn for the Loss of a Mistress, he cou'd not with all his Strength and Courage retrieve. And he wou'd often cry, *O my Friends! were she in wall'd Cities, or confin'd from me in Fortifications of the greatest Strength; did Inchantments or Monsters detain her from me, I wou'd venture through any Hazard to free her: But here, in the Arms of a feeble old Man, my Youth, my violent Love, my Trade in Arms, and all my vast Desire of Glory, avail me nothing: Imoinda is as irrecoverably lost to me, as if she were snatch'd by the cold Arms of Death: Oh! she is never to be retriev'd. If I wou'd wait tedious Years, till Fate shou'd bow the old King to his Grave; even that wou'd not leave me Imoinda free; but still that Custom that makes it so vile a Crime for a Son to marry his Father's Wives or Mistresses, wou'd hinder my Happiness;*

---

8. The king's great age suggests he is impotent.   9. Reverent.

unless I wou'd either ignobly set an ill President[1] to my Successors, or abandon my Country, and fly with her to some unknown World, who never heard our Story.

But it was objected to him, that his Case was not the same; for *Imoinda* being his lawful Wife, by solemn Contract, 'twas he was the injur'd Man, and might, if he so pleas'd, take *Imoinda* back, the Breach of the Law being on his Grand-father's side; and that if he cou'd circumvent him, and redeem her from the *Otan*,[2] which is the Palace of the King's Women, a sort of *Seraglio*, it was both just and lawful for him so to do.

This Reasoning had some force upon him, and he shou'd have been entirely comforted, but for the Thought that she was possess'd by his Grand-father. However, he lov'd so well, that he was resolv'd to believe what most favour'd his Hope; and to endeavour to learn from *Imoinda's* own Mouth, what only she cou'd satisfie him in; whether she was robb'd of that Blessing, which was only due to his Faith and Love. But as it was very hard to get a Sight of the Women, for no Men ever enter'd into the *Otan*, but when the King went to entertain himself with some one of his Wives, or Mistresses; and 'twas Death at any other time, for any other to go in; so he knew not how to contrive to get a Sight of her.

While *Oroonoko* felt all the Agonies of Love, and suffer'd under a Torment the most painful in the World, the old King was not exempted from his share of Affliction. He was troubl'd for having been forc'd by an irresistable Passion, to rob his Son[3] of a Treasure, he knew, cou'd not but be extreamly dear to him, since she was the most beautiful that ever had been seen; and had besides, all the Sweetness and Innocence of Youth and Modesty, with a Charm of Wit surpassing all. He found that, however she was forc'd to expose her lovely Person to his wither'd Arms, she cou'd only sigh and weep there, and think of *Oroonoko*; and oftentimes cou'd not forbear speaking of him, though her Life were, by Custom, forfeited by owning her Passion. But she spoke not of a Lover only, but of a Prince dear to him, to whom she spoke; and of the Praises of a Man, who, till now, fill'd the old Man's Soul with Joy at every Recital of his Bravery, or even his Name. And 'twas this Dotage on our young *Hero*, that gave *Imoinda* a thousand Privileges to speak of him, without offending; and this Condescention in the old King, that made her take the Satisfaction of speaking of him so very often.

Besides, he many times enquir'd how the Prince bore himself; and those of whom he ask'd, being entirely Slaves to the Merits and Vertues of the Prince, still answer'd what they thought conduc'd best to his Service; which was, to make the old King fancy that the Prince had no more Interest in *Imoinda*, and had resign'd her willingly to the Pleasure of the King; that he diverted himself with his Mathematicians, his Fortifications, his Officers, and his Hunting.

This pleas'd the old Lover, who fail'd not to report these things again to *Imoinda*, that she might, by the Example of her young Lover, withdraw her Heart, and rest better contented in his Arms. But however she was forc'd to receive this unwelcome News, in all Appearance, with Unconcern, and Con-

---

1. Precedent, example.
2. *Odan* is the Fante word for house or apartment; *oda*, in Turkish, is a room in a harem or seraglio.
3. I.e., grandson.

tent, her Heart was bursting within, and she was only happy when she cou'd get alone, to vent her Griefs and Moans with Sighs and Tears.

What Reports of the Prince's Conduct were made to the King, he thought good to justifie as far as possibly he cou'd by his Actions; and when he appear'd in the Presence of the King, he shew'd a Face not at all betraying his Heart: So that in a little time the old Man, being entirely convinc'd that he was no longer a Lover of *Imoinda*, he carry'd him with him, in his Train, to the *Otan*, often to banquet with his Mistress. But as soon as he enter'd, one Day, into the Apartment of *Imoinda*, with the King, at the first Glance from her Eyes, notwithstanding all his determin'd Resolution, he was ready to sink in the place where he stood; and had certainly done so, but for the Support of *Aboan*, a young Man, who was next to him; which, with his Change of Countenance, had betray'd him, had the King chanc'd to look that way. And I have observ'd, 'tis a very great Error in those, who laugh when one says, A Negro *can change Colour*; for I have seen 'em as frequently blush, and look pale, and that as visibly as ever I saw in the most beautiful *White*. And 'tis certain that both these Changes were evident, this Day, in both these Lovers. And *Imoinda*, who saw with some Joy the Change in the Prince's Face, and found it in her own, strove to divert the King from beholding either, by a forc'd Caress, with which she met him; which was a new Wound in the Heart of the poor dying Prince. But as soon as the King was busy'd in looking on some fine thing of *Imoinda*'s making, she had time to tell the Prince with her angry, but Love-darting Eyes, that she resented his Coldness, and bemoan'd her own miserable Captivity. Nor were his Eyes silent, but answer'd hers again, as much as Eyes cou'd do, instructed by the most tender, and most passionate Heart that ever lov'd: And they spoke so well, and so effectually, as *Imoinda* no longer doubted, but she was the only Delight, and the Darling of that Soul she found pleading in 'em its Right of Love, which none was more willing to resign than she. And 'twas this powerful Language alone that in an Instant convey'd all the Thoughts of their Souls to each other; that they both found, there wanted[4] but Opportunity to make them both entirely happy. But when he saw another Door open'd by *Onahal*, a former old Wife of the King's, who now had Charge of *Imoinda*; and saw the Prospect of a Bed of State made ready, with Sweets and Flowers for the Dalliance of the King; who immediately led the trembling Victim from his Sight, into that prepar'd Repose; What Rage! what wild Frenzies seiz'd his Heart! which forcing to keep within Bounds, and to suffer without Noise, it became the more insupportable, and rent[5] his Soul with ten thousand Pains. He was forc'd to retire, to vent his Groans; where he fell down on a Carpet, and lay struggling a long time, and only breathing now and then,—O *Imoinda*! When *Onahal* had finish'd her necessary Affair within, shutting the Door, she came forth to wait, till the King call'd; and hearing some one sighing in the other Room, she pass'd on, and found the Prince in that deplorable Condition, which she thought needed her Aid: She gave him Cordials, but all in vain; till finding the nature of his Disease, by his Sighs, and naming *Imoinda*. She told him, he had not so much Cause as he imagin'd, to afflict himself; for if he knew the King so well as she did, he wou'd not lose a Moment in Jealousie, and that she was confident that *Imoinda* bore, at this Minute, part in his Affliction.

---

4. So that; wanted: lacked.   5. Tore apart.

Aboan was of the same Opinion; and both together, perswaded him to re-assume his Courage; and all sitting down on the Carpet, the Prince said so many obliging things to *Onahal*, that he half perswaded her to be of his Party. And she promis'd him, she wou'd thus far comply with his just Desires, that she wou'd let *Imoinda* know how faithful he was, what he suffer'd, and what he said.

This Discourse lasted till the King call'd, which gave *Oroonoko* a certain Satisfaction; and with the Hope *Onahal* had made him conceive, he assum'd a Look as gay as 'twas possible a Man in his Circumstances cou'd do; and presently after, he was call'd in with the rest who waited without. The King commanded Musick to be brought, and several of his young Wives and Mistresses came all together by his Command, to dance before him; where *Imoinda* perform'd her Part with an Air and Grace so passing all the rest, as her Beauty was above 'em; and receiv'd the Present, ordain'd as a Prize. The Prince was every Moment more charm'd with the new Beauties and Graces he beheld in this fair One: And while he gaz'd, and she danc'd, *Onahal* was retir'd to a Window with *Aboan*.

This *Onahal*, as I said, was one of the Cast-Mistresses of the old King; and 'twas these (now past their Beauty) that were made Guardians, or Governants[6] to the new, and the young Ones; and whose Business it was, to teach them all those wanton Arts of Love, with which they prevail'd and charm'd heretofore in their Turn; and who now treated the triumphing happy Ones with all the Severity, as to Liberty and Freedom, that was possible, in revenge of those Honours they rob them of; envying them those Satisfactions, those Gallantries and Presents, that were once made to themselves, while Youth and Beauty lasted, and which they now saw pass regardless by, and were pay'd only to the Bloomings.[7] And certainly, nothing is more afflicting to a decay'd Beauty, than to behold in it self declining Charms, that were once ador'd; and to find those Caresses paid to new Beauties, to which once she laid a Claim; to hear 'em whisper as she passes by, *That once was a delicate[8] Woman*. These abandon'd Ladies therefore endeavour to revenge all the Despights,[9] and Decays of Time, on these flourishing happy Ones. And 'twas this Severity, that gave *Oroonoko* a thousand Fears he shou'd never prevail with *Onahal*, to see *Imoinda*. But, as I said, she was now retir'd to a Window with *Aboan*.

This young Man was not only one of the best Quality, but a Man extreamly well made, and beautiful; and coming often to attend the King to the *Otan*, he had subdu'd the heart of the antiquated *Onahal*, which had not forgot how pleasant it was to be in Love: And though she had some decays in her Face, she had none in her Sense and Wit; she was there agreeable still, even to *Aboan*'s Youth, so that he took pleasure in entertaining her with Discourses of Love. He knew also, that to make his Court to these She-Favourites, was the way to be great; these being the Persons that do all Affairs and Business at Court. He had also observ'd that she had given him Glances more tender and inviting, than she had done to others of his Quality: And now, when he saw that her Favour cou'd so absolutely oblige the Prince, he fail'd not to sigh in her Ear,

---

6. Female caretakers or instructors. "Cast":
cast-off, with a pun on chaste.
7. I.e., the younger women.

8. Delightful, lovely.
9. Insults.

and to look with Eyes all soft upon her, and give her Hope that she had made some Impressions on his Heart. He found her pleas'd at this, and making a thousand Advances to him; but the Ceremony ending, and the King departing, broke up the Company for that Day, and his Conversation.

Aboan fail'd not that Night to tell the Prince of his Success, and how advantageous the Service of Onahal might be to his Amour[1] with Imoinda. The Prince was overjoy'd with this good News, and besought him, if it were possible, to caress her so, as to engage her entirely; which he cou'd not fail to do, if he comply'd with her Desires: For then (said the Prince) her Life lying at your Mercy, she must grant you the Request you make in my Behalf. Aboan understood him; and assur'd him, he would make Love so effectually[2] that he wou'd defie the most expert Mistress of the Art, to find out whether he dissembl'd it, or had it really. And 'twas with Impatience they waited the next Opportunity of going to the Otan.

The Wars came on, the Time of taking the Field approach'd, and 'twas impossible for the Prince to delay his going at the Head of his Army, to encounter the Enemy: So that every Day seem'd a tedious Year, till he saw his Imoinda; for he believ'd he cou'd not live, if he were forc'd away without being so happy. 'Twas with Impatience therefore, that he expected the next Visit the King wou'd make; and, according to his Wish, it was not long.

The Parley of the Eyes of these two Lovers had not pass'd so secretly, but an old jealous Lover cou'd spy it; or rather, he wanted not Flatterers, who told him, they observ'd it: So that the Prince was hasten'd to the Camp, and this was the last Visit he found he shou'd make to the Otan; he therefore urg'd Aboan to make the best of this last Effort, and to explain himself so to Onahal, that she, deferring her Enjoyment of her young Lover no longer, might make way for the Prince to speak to Imoinda.

The whole Affair being agreed on between the Prince and Aboan, they attended the King, as the Custom was, to the Otan; where, while the whole Company was taken up in beholding the Dancing, and antick Postures the Women Royal made, to divert the King, Onahal singl'd out Aboan, whom she found most pliable to her Wish. When she had him where she believ'd she cou'd not be heard, she sigh'd to him, and softly cry'd, Ah, Aboan! When will you be sensible of my Passion? I confess it with my Mouth, because I wou'd not give my Eyes the Lye; and you have but too much already perceiv'd they have confess'd my Flame: Nor wou'd I have you believe, that because I am the abandon'd Mistress of a King, I esteem my self altogether divested of Charms. No, Aboan; I have still a Rest of Beauty enough engaging, and have learn'd to please too well, not to be desirable. I can have Lovers still, but will have none but Aboan. Madam (reply'd the half-feigning Youth) you have already, by my Eyes, found, you can still conquer; and I believe 'tis in pity of me, you condescend to this kind Confession. But, Madam, Words are us'd to be so small a part of our Country-Courtship, that 'tis rare one can get so happy an Opportunity as to tell one's Heart; and those few Minutes we have are forc'd to be snatch'd for more certain Proofs of Love, than speaking and sighing; and such I languish for.

He spoke this with such a Tone, that she hop'd it true, and cou'd not forbear believing it; and being wholly transported with Joy, for having subdu'd the finest

1. Love (French).   2. Diligently, thoroughly.

of all the King's Subjects to her Desires, she took from her Ears two large Pearls, and commanded him to wear 'em in his. He wou'd have refus'd 'em, *crying, Madam, these are not the Proofs of your Love that I expect; 'tis Opportunity, 'tis a Lone-hour only, that can make me happy.* But forcing the Pearls into his Hand, she whisper'd softly to him, *Oh! Do not fear a Woman's Invention, when Love sets her a-thinking.* And pressing his Hand, she cry'd, *This Night you shall be happy. Come to the Gate of the Orange-Groves, behind the* Otan; *and I will be ready, about Mid-night, to receive you.* 'Twas thus agreed, and she left him, that no notice might be taken of their speaking together.

The Ladies were still dancing, and the King, laid on a Carpet, with a great deal of pleasure, was beholding them, especially *Imoinda*; who that Day appear'd more lovely than ever, being enliven'd with the good Tidings *Onahal* had brought her of the constant Passion the Prince had for her. The Prince was laid on another Carpet, at the other end of the Room, with his Eyes fix'd on the Object of his Soul; and as she turn'd, or mov'd, so did they; and she alone gave his Eyes and Soul their Motions: Nor did *Imoinda* employ her Eyes to any other Use, than in beholding with infinite Pleasure the Joy she produc'd in those of the Prince. But while she was more regarding him, than the Steps she took, she chanc'd to fall; and so near him, as that leaping with extream force from the Carpet, he caught her in his Arms as she fell; and 'twas visible to the whole Presence, the Joy wherewith he receiv'd her: He clasp'd her close to his Bosom, and quite forgot that Reverence that was due to the Mistress of a King, and that Punishment that is the Reward of a Boldness of this nature; and had not the Presence of Mind of *Imoinda* (fonder of his Safety, than her own) befriended him, in making her spring from his Arms, and fall into her Dance again, he had, at that Instant, met his Death; for the old King, jealous to the last degree, rose up in Rage, broke all the Diversion, and led *Imoinda* to her Apartment, and sent out Word to the Prince, to go immediately to the Camp; and that if he were found another Night in Court, he shou'd suffer the Death ordain'd for disobedient Offenders.

You may imagine how welcome this News was to *Oroonoko*, whose unseasonable Transport and Caress of *Imoinda* was blam'd by all Men that lov'd him; and now he perceiv'd his Fault, yet cry'd, *That for such another Moment, he wou'd be content to die.*

All the *Otan* was in disorder about this Accident; and *Onahal* was particularly concern'd, because on the Prince's Stay depended her Happiness; for she cou'd no longer expect that of *Aboan.* So that, e'er the departed, they contriv'd it so, that the Prince and he shou'd come both that Night to the Grove of the *Otan*, which was all of Oranges and Citrons; and that there they shou'd wait her Orders.

They parted thus, with Grief enough, till Night; leaving the King in possession of the lovely Maid. But nothing cou'd appease the Jealousie of the old Lover: He wou'd not be impos'd on, but wou'd have it, that *Imoinda* made a false Step on purpose to fall into *Oroonoko*'s Bosom and that all things look'd like a Design on both sides, and 'twas in vain she protested her Innocence: He was old and obstinate, and left her more than half assur'd that his Fear was true.

The King going to his Apartment, sent to know where the Prince was, and if he intended to obey his Command. The Messenger return'd, and told him, he found the Prince pensive, and altogether unpreparing for the Campaign; that he lay negligently on the Ground, and answer'd very little. This confirm'd the Jealousie of the King, and he commanded that they shou'd very narrowly and privately watch his Motions; and that he shou'd not stir from his Apartment, but one Spy or other shou'd be employ'd to watch him: So that the Hour approaching, wherein he was to go to the Citron-Grove; and taking only *Aboan* along with him, he leaves his Apartment, and was watch'd to the very Gate of the *Otan*; where he was seen to enter, and where they left him, to carry back the Tidings to the King.

Oroonoko and *Aboan* were no sooner enter'd, but *Onahal* led the Prince to the Apartment of *Imoinda*; who, not knowing any thing of her Happiness, was laid in Bed. But *Onahal* only left him in her Chamber, to make the best of his Opportunity, and took her dear *Aboan* to her own; where he shew'd the heighth of Complaisance for his Prince, when, to give him an Opportunity, he suffer'd himself to be caress'd in Bed by *Onahal*.

The Prince softly waken'd *Imoinda*, who was not a little surpriz'd with Joy to find him there; and yet she trembl'd with a thousand Fears. I believe, he omitted saying nothing to this young Maid, that might perswade her to suffer him to seize his own, and take the Rights of Love; and I believe she was not long resisting those Arms, where she so long'd to be; and having Opportunity, Night and Silence, Youth, Love and Desire, he soon prevail'd; and ravish'd in a Moment, what his old Grand-father had been endeavouring for so many Months.

'Tis not to be imagin'd the Satisfaction of these two young Lovers; nor the Vows she made him, that she remain'd a spotless Maid, till that Night; and that what she did with his Grand-father, had robb'd him of no part of her Virgin-Honour, the Gods, in Mercy and Justice, having reserv'd that for her plighted Lord, to whom of Right it belong'd. And 'tis impossible to express the Transports he suffer'd, while he listen'd to a Discourse so charming, from her lov'd Lips; and clasp'd that Body in his Arms, for whom he had so long languish'd; and nothing now afflicted him, but his suddain Departure from her; for he told her the Necessity, and his Commands; but shou'd depart satisfy'd in this, That since the old King had hitherto not been able to deprive him of those Enjoyments which only belong'd to him, he believ'd for the future he wou'd be less able to injure him; so that, abating the Scandal of the Veil, which was no otherwise so, than that she was Wife to another: He believ'd her safe, even in the Arms of the King, and innocent; yet wou'd he have ventur'd at the Conquest of the World, and have given it all, to have had her avoided that Honour of receiving the *Royal Veil*. 'Twas thus, between a thousand Caresses, that both bemoan'd the hard Fate of Youth and Beauty, so liable to that cruel Promotion: 'Twas a Glory that cou'd well have been spar'd here, though desir'd, and aim'd at by all the young Females of that Kingdom.

But while they were thus fondly employ'd, forgetting how Time ran on, and that the Dawn must conduct him far away from his only Happiness, they heard a great Noise in the *Otan*, and unusual Voices of Men; at which the Prince, starting from the Arms of the frighted *Imoinda*, ran to a little Battle-Ax he us'd to wear by his Side; and having not so much leisure, as to put on his Habit, he oppos'd himself against some who were already opening the Door; which they did with so much Violence, that *Oroonoko* was not able to defend it; but was forc'd to cry out with a commanding Voice, *Whoever ye are that have the Boldness to attempt to approach this Apartment thus rudely, know, that I, the Prince*

Oroonoko, *will revenge it with the certain Death of him that first enters: There-fore stand back, and know, this place is sacred to Love, and me this Night; to Morrow 'tis the King's.*

This he spoke with a Voice so resolv'd and assur'd, that they soon retir'd from the Door, but cry'd, *'Tis by the King's Command we are come; and being satisfy'd by thy Voice, O Prince, as much as if we had enter'd, we can report to the King the Truth of all his Fears, and leave thee to provide for thy own Safety, as thou art advis'd by thy Friends.*

At these Words they departed, and left the Prince to take a short and sad Leave of his *Imoinda*; who trusting in the strength of her Charms, believ'd she shou'd appease the Fury of a jealous King, by saying, She was surpriz'd, and that it was by force of Arms he got into her Apartment. All her Concern now was for his Life, and therefore she hasten'd him to the Camp; and with much a-do, prevail'd on him to go: Nor was it she alone that prevail'd, *Aboan* and *Onahal* both pleaded, and both assur'd him of a Lye that shou'd be well enough contriv'd to secure *Imoinda*. So that, at last, with a Heart sad as Death, dying Eyes, and sighing Soul, *Oroonoko* departed and took his way to the Camp.

It was not long after the King in Person came to the *Otan*; where beholding *Imoinda* with Rage in his Eyes, he upbraided her Wickedness and Perfidy, and threatning her Royal Lover, she fell on her Face at his Feet, bedewing the Floor with her Tears, and imploring his Pardon for a Fault which she had not with her Will committed; as *Onahal*, who was also prostrate with her, cou'd testifie: That, unknown to her, he had broke into her Apartment, and ravish'd her. She spoke this much against her Conscience; but to save her own Life, 'twas absolutely necessary she shou'd feign this Falsity. She knew it cou'd not injure the Prince, he being fled to an Army that wou'd stand by him, against any Injuries that shou'd assault him. However, this last Thought of *Imoinda*'s being ravish'd, chang'd the Measures of his Revenge; and whereas before he design'd to be himself her Executioner, he now resolv'd she shou'd not die. But as it is the greatest Crime in nature amongst 'em to touch a Woman, after hav-ing been possess'd by a Son, a Father, or a Brother; so now he look'd on *Imoinda* as a polluted thing, wholly unfit for his Embrace; nor wou'd he resign her to his Grand-son, because she had receiv'd the *Royal Veil*. He therefore removes her from the *Otan*, with *Onahal*; whom he put into safe Hands, with Order they should be both sold off, as Slaves, to another Country, either *Chris-tian*, or *Heathen*; 'twas no matter where.

This cruel Sentence, worse than Death, they implor'd, might be revers'd; but their Prayers were vain, and it was put in Execution accordingly, and that with so much Secrecy, that none, either without, or within the *Otan*, knew any thing of their Absence, or their Destiny.

The old King, nevertheless, executed this with a great deal of Reluctancy; but he believ'd he had made a very great Conquest over himself, when he had once resolv'd, and had perform'd what he resolv'd. He believ'd now, that his Love had been unjust; and that he cou'd not expect the Gods, or Captain of the Clouds (as they call the unknown Power) shou'd suffer a better Consequence from so ill a Cause. He now begins to hold *Oroonoko* excus'd; and to say, he had Reason for what he did: And now every Body cou'd assure the King, how passionately *Imoinda* was belov'd by the Prince; even those confess'd it now, who said the contrary before his Flame was abated. So that the King being old, and not able to defend himself in War, and having no Sons of all his Race[3] remaining alive, but only this, to maintain him on his Throne; and looking on this as a Man disoblig'd, first by the Rape of his Mistress, or rather, Wife; and now by depriving of him wholly of her, he fear'd, might make him desperate, and do some cruel thing, either to himself, or his old Grand-father, the Offender; he began to repent him extreamly of the Contempt he had, in his Rage, put on *Imoinda*. Besides, he consider'd he ought in Honour to have kill'd her, for this Offence, if it had been one: He ought to have had so much Value and Consideration for a Maid of her Quality, as to have nobly put her to death; and not to have sold her like a common Slave, the greatest Revenge, and the most disgraceful of any; and to which they a thousand times prefer Death, and implore it; as *Imoinda* did, but cou'd not obtain that Honour. Seeing therefore it was certain that *Oroonoko* wou'd highly resent this Affront, he thought good to make some Excuse for his Rashness to him; and to that End he sent a Messenger to the Camp, with Orders to treat with him about the Matter, to gain his Pardon, and to endeavour to mitigate his Grief; but that by no means he shou'd tell him, she was sold, but secretly put to death; for he knew he shou'd never obtain his Pardon for the other.

When the Messenger came, he found the Prince upon the point of Engaging with the Enemy; but as soon as he heard of the Arrival of the Messenger, he commanded him to his Tent, where he embrac'd him, and receiv'd him with Joy; which was soon abated, by the downcast Looks of the Messenger, who was instantly demanded the Cause by *Oroonoko*, who, impatient of Delay, ask'd a thousand Questions in a Breath; and all concerning *Imoinda*: But there needed little Return, for he cou'd almost answer himself of all he demanded, from his Sighs and Eyes. At last, the Messenger casting himself at the Prince's feet, and kissing them, with all the Submission of a Man that had something to implore which he dreaded to utter, he besought him to hear with Calmness what he had to deliver to him, and to call up all his noble and Heroick Courage, to encounter with his Words, and defend himself against the ungrateful[4] things he must relate. *Oroonoko* reply'd, with a deep Sigh, and a languishing voice,— *I am arm'd against their worst Efforts——; for I know they will tell me,* Imoinda *is no more——; and after that, you may spare the rest.* Then, commanding him to rise, he laid himself on a Carpet, under a rich Pavillion, and remain'd a good while silent, and was hardly heard to sigh. When he was come a little to himself, the Messenger ask'd him leave to deliver that part of his Embassy, which the Prince had not yet divin'd: And the Prince cry'd, *I permit thee*—. Then he told him the Affliction the old King was in, for the Rashness he had committed in his Cruelty to *Imoinda*; and how he deign'd to ask Pardon for his Offence, and to implore the Prince wou'd not suffer that Loss to touch his Heart too sensibly, which now all the Gods cou'd not restore him, but might recompence him in Glory, which he begg'd he wou'd pursue; and that Death, that common Revenger of all Injuries, wou'd soon even the Account between him, and a feeble old Man.

Oroonoko bad him return his Duty to his Lord and Master; and to assure him, there was no Account of Revenge to be adjusted between them; if there

---

3. Kin.   4. Offensive.

were, 'twas he was the Aggressor, and that Death wou'd be just, and, maugre[5] his Age, wou'd see him righted; and he was contented to leave his Share of Glory to Youths more fortunate, and worthy of that Favour from the Gods. That henceforth he wou'd never lift a Weapon, or draw a Bow; but abandon the small Remains of his Life to Sighs and Tears, and the continual Thoughts of what his Lord and Grand-father had thought good to send out of the World, with all that Youth, that Innocence, and Beauty.

After having spoken this, whatever his greatest Officers, and Men of the best Rank cou'd do, they cou'd not raise him from the Carpet, or perswade him to Action, and Resolutions of Life; but commanding all to retire, he shut himself into his Pavillion all that Day, while the Enemy was ready to engage; and won-dring at the Delay, the whole Body of the chief of the Army then address'd themselves to him, and to whom they had much a-do to get Admittance. They fell on their Faces at the Foot of his Carpet; where they lay, and besought him with earnest Prayers and Tears, to lead 'em forth to Battel, and not let the Enemy take Advantages of them; and implor'd him to have regard to his Glory, and to the World, that depended on his Courage and Conduct. But he made no other Reply to all their Supplications but this. That he had now no more Busi-ness for Glory; and for the World, it was a Trifle not worth his Care. *Go,* (continu'd he, sighing) *and divide it amongst you; and reap with Joy what you so vainly prize, and leave me to my more welcome Destiny.*

They then demanded what they shou'd do, and whom he wou'd constitute in his Room[6] that the Confusion of ambitious Youth and Power might not ruin their Order, and make them a Prey to the Enemy. He reply'd, He wou'd not give himself the Trouble—; but wish'd 'em to chuse the bravest Man amongst 'em, let his Quality or Birth be what it wou'd: *For, O my Friends!* (said he) *it is not Titles make Men brave, or good; or Birth that bestows Courage and Generosity, or makes the Owner happy. Believe this, when you behold* Oroonoko, *the most wretched, and abandon'd by Fortune, of all the Creation of the Gods.* So turning himself about, he wou'd make no more Reply to all they cou'd urge or implore.

The Army beholding their Officers return unsuccessful, with sad Faces, and ominous Looks, that presag'd no good Luck, suffer'd a thousand Fears to take Possession of their Hearts, and the Enemy to come even upon 'em, before they wou'd provide for their Safety, by any Defence; and though they were assur'd by some, who had a mind to animate 'em, that they shou'd be immediately headed by the Prince, and that in the mean time *Aboan* had Orders to com-mand as General; yet they were so dismay'd for want of that great Example of Bravery, that they cou'd make but a very feeble Resistance; and at last, down-right, fled before the Enemy, who pursu'd 'em to the very Tents, killing 'em: Nor cou'd all *Aboan*'s Courage, which that Day gain'd him immortal Glory, shame 'em into a Manly Defence of themselves. The Guards that were left behind, about the Prince's Tent, seeing the Soldiers flee before the Enemy, and scatter themselves all over the Plain, in great Disorder, made such Out-cries as rouz'd the Prince from his amorous Slumber, in which he had remain'd bury'd for two Days, without permitting any Sustenance to approach him: But, in spite of all his Resolutions, he had not the Constancy of Grief to that Degree, as to make him insensible of the Danger of his Army; and in that

---

5. Despite. Oroonoko hopes to die first.   **6.** I.e., in his place.

Instant he leap'd from his Couch, and cry'd,—*Come, if we must die, let us meet Death the noblest Way; and 'twill be more like* Oroonoko *to encounter him at an Army's Head, opposing the Torrent of a conquering Foe, than lazily, on a Couch, to wait his lingering Pleasure, and die every Moment by a thousand wrecking[7] Thoughts; or be tamely taken by an Enemy, and led a whining, Love-sick Slave, to adorn the Triumphs of* Jamoan, *that young Victor, who already is enter'd beyond the Limits I had prescrib'd him.*

While he was speaking, he suffer'd his People to dress him for the Field; and sallying out of his Pavillion, with more Life and Vigour in his Countenance than ever he shew'd, he appear'd like some Divine Power descended to save his Country from Destruction; and his People had purposely put on him all things that might make him shine with most Splendor, to strike a reverend Awe into the Beholders. He flew into the thickest of those that were pursuing his Men; and being animated with Despair, he fought as if he came on purpose to die, and did such things as will not be believ'd that Humane Strength cou'd perform; and such as soon inspir'd all the rest with new Courage, and new Order: And now it was, that they began to fight indeed; and so, as if they wou'd not be out-done, even by their ador'd *Hero*; who turning the Tide of the Victory, changing absolutely the Fate of the Day, gain'd an entire Conquest; and *Oroonoko* having the good Fortune to single out *Jamoan*, he took him Prisoner with his own Hand, having wounded him almost to death.

This *Jamoan* afterwards became very dear to him, being a Man very gallant, and of excellent Graces, and fine Parts; so that he never put him amongst the Rank of Captives, as they us'd to do, without distinction, for the common Sale, or Market; but kept him in his own Court, where he retain'd nothing of the Prisoner, but the Name, and return'd no more into his own Country, so great an Affection he took for *Oroonoko*; and by a thousand Tales and Adventures of Love and Gallantry, flatter'd[8] his Disease of Melancholy and Languishment; which I have often heard him say, had certainly kill'd him, but for the Conversation of this Prince and *Aboan*, and the *French* Governor[9] he had from his Childhood, of whom I have spoken before, and who was a Man of admirable Wit, great Ingenuity and Learning; all which he had infus'd into his young Pupil. This *French*-Man was banish'd out of his own Country, for some Heretical Notions he held; and though he was a Man of very little Religion, he had admirable Morals, and a brave Soul.

After the total Defeat of *Jamoan*'s Army, which all fled, or were left dead upon the Place, they spent some time in the Camp; *Oroonoko* chusing rather to remain a while there in his Tents, than enter into a Place, or live in a Court where he had so lately suffer'd so great a Loss. The Officers therefore, who saw and knew his Cause of Discontent, invented all sorts of Diversions and Sports, to entertain their Prince: So that what with those Amuzements abroad, and others at home, that is, within their Tents, with the Perswasions, Arguments and Care of his Friends and Servants that he more peculiarly priz'd, he wore off in time a great part of that *Shagrien*, and Torture of Despair, which the first Efforts of *Imoinda*'s Death had given him: Insomuch as having receiv'd a thousand kind Embassies from the King, and Invitations to return to Court, he

7. Racking.
8. Soothed.

9. Tutor.

obey'd, though with no little Reluctancy; and when he did so, there was a visible Change in him, and for a long time he was much more melancholy than before. But Time lessens all Extreams, and reduces 'em to *Mediums* and Unconcern; but no Motives or Beauties, though all endeavour'd it, cou'd engage him in any sort of Amour, though he had all the Invitations to it, both from his own Youth, and others Ambitions and Designs.

Oroonoko was no sooner return'd from this last Conquest, and receiv'd at Court with all the Joy and Magnificence that cou'd be express'd to a young Victor, who was not only return'd triumphant, but belov'd like a Deity, when there arriv'd in the Port an *English* Ship.

This Person[1] had often before been in these Countries, and was very well known to *Oroonoko*, with whom he had traffick'd for Slaves, and had us'd to do the same with his Predecessors.

This Commander was a Man of a finer sort of Address, and Conversation, better bred, and more engaging, than most of that sort of Men are; so that he seem'd rather never to have been bred out of a Court, than almost all his Life at Sea. This Captain therefore was always better receiv'd at Court, than most of the Traders to those Countries were; and especially by *Oroonoko*, who was more civiliz'd, according to the *European* Mode, than any other had been, and took more Delight in the *White* Nations; and, above all, Men of Parts and Wit. To this Captain he sold abundance of his Slaves; and for the Favour and Esteem he had for him, made him many Presents, and oblig'd him to stay at Court as long as possibly he cou'd. Which the Captain seem'd to take as a very great Honour done him, entertaining the Prince every Day with Globes and Maps, and Mathematical Discourses and Instruments; eating, drinking, hunting and living with him with so much Familiarity, that it was not to be doubted, but he had gain'd very greatly upon the Heart of this gallant young Man. And the Captain, in Return of all these mighty Favours, besought the Prince to honour his Vessel with his Presence, some Day or other, to Dinner, before he shou'd set Sail; which he condescended to accept, and appointed his Day. The Captain, on his part, fail'd not to have all things in a Readiness, in the most magnificent Order he cou'd possibly: And the Day being come, the Captain, in his Boat, richly adorn'd with Carpets and Velvet-Cushions, row'd to the shore to receive the Prince; with another Long-Boat, where was plac'd all his Musick and Trumpets, with which *Oroonoko* was extreamly delighted; who met him on the shore, attended by his *French* Governor, *Jamoan*, *Aboan*, and about an hundred of the noblest of the Youths of the Court: And after they had first carry'd the Prince on Board, the Boats fetch'd the rest off; where they found a very splendid Treat, with all sorts of fine Wines; and were as well entertain'd, as 'twas possible in such a place to be.

The Prince having drunk hard of Punch, and several Sorts of Wine, as did all the rest (for great Care was taken, they shou'd want nothing of that part of the Entertainment) was very merry, and in great Admiration of the Ship, for he had never been in one before; so that he was curious of beholding every place, where he decently might descend. The rest, no less curious, who were not quite overcome with Drinking, rambl'd at their pleasure *Fore* and *Aft*, as their Fancies guided 'em: So that the Captain, who had well laid his Design before,

1. The captain of the ship.

gave the Word, and seiz'd on all his Guests; they clapping great Irons suddenly on the Prince, when he was leap'd down in the Hold, to view that part of the Vessel; and locking him fast down, secur'd him. The same Treachery was us'd to all the rest; and all in one Instant, in several places of the Ship, were lash'd fast in Irons, and betray'd to Slavery. That great Design over, they set all Hands to work to hoise[2] Sail; and with as treacherous and fair a Wind, they made from the Shore with this innocent and glorious Prize, who thought of nothing less than such an Entertainment.

Some have commended this Act, as brave, in the Captain; but I will spare my sense of it, and leave it to my Reader, to judge as he pleases.

It may be easily guess'd, in what manner the Prince resented this Indignity, who may be best resembl'd to a Lion taken in a Toil[3] so he rag'd, so he struggl'd for Liberty, but all in vain; and they had so wisely manag'd his Fetters, that he cou'd not use a Hand in his Defence, to quit himself of a Life that wou'd by no Means endure Slavery; nor cou'd he move from the Place, where he was ty'd, to any solid part of the Ship, against which he might have beat his Head, and have finish'd his Disgrace that way: So that being depriv'd of all other means, he resolved to perish for want of Food: And pleased at last with that Thought, and toil'd and tired by Rage and Indignation, he laid himself down, and sullenly resolved upon dying, and refused all things that were brought him.

This did not a little vex the Captain, and the more so, because, he found almost all of 'em of the same Humour; so that the loss of so many brave Slaves, so tall and goodly to behold, wou'd have been very considerable: He therefore order'd one to go from him (for he wou'd not be seen himself) to *Oroonoko*, and to assure him he was afflicted for having rashly done so unhospitable a Deed, and which cou'd not be now remedied, since they were far from shore; but since he resented it in so high a nature, he assur'd him he wou'd revoke his Resolution, and set both him and his Friends a-shore on the next Land they shou'd touch at; and of this the Messenger gave him his Oath, provid'd he wou'd resolve to live: And *Oroonoko*, whose Honour was such as he never had violated a Word in his Life himself, much less a solemn Asseveration, believ'd in an instant what this Man said, but reply'd, He expected for a Confirmation of this, to have his shameful Fetters dismiss'd. This Demand was carried to the *Captain*, who return'd him answer, That the Offence had been so great which he had put upon the Prince, that he durst not trust him with Liberty while he remained in the Ship, for fear lest by a Valour natural to him, and a Revenge that would animate that Valour, he might commit some Outrage fatal to himself and the *King* his Master, to whom his Vessel did belong. To this *Oroonoko* replied, he would engage his Honour to behave himself in all friendly Order and Manner, and obey the Command of the *Captain*, as he was Lord of the *King*'s Vessel, and General of those Men under his Command.

This was deliver'd to the still doubting *Captain*, who could not resolve to trust a *Heathen*, he said, upon his Parole,[4] a Man that had no Sense or notion of the God that he Worshipp'd. *Oroonoko* then replied, He was very sorry to hear that the *Captain* pretended to the Knowledge and Worship of any *Gods*,

---

2. Hoist. Early accounts report the abduction of Africans who visited ships. Those of high rank were ransomed or returned to prevent the end of the slave trade.
3. Trap.
4. Word of honor.

who had taught him no better Principles, than not to Credit as he would be Credited: but they told him the Difference of their Faith occasion'd that Distrust: For the *Captain* had protested to him upon the Word of a *Christian*, and sworn in the Name of a Great *G O D*; which if he shou'd violate, he would expect eternal Torment in the World to come. *Is that all the Obligation he has to be Just to his Oath?* replied *Oroonoko. Let him know I Swear by my Honour, which to violate, wou'd not only render me contemptible and despised by all brave and honest Men, and so give my self perpetual pain, but it wou'd be eternally offending and diseasing all Mankind, harming, betraying, circumventing and outraging all Men; but Punishments hereafter are suffer'd by ones self; and the World takes no cognizances whether this God have revenged 'em, or not, 'tis done so secretly, and deferr'd so long: While the Man of no Honour, suffers every moment the scorn and contempt of the honester World, and dies every day ignominiously in his Fame, which is more valuable than Life: I speak not this to move Belief, but to shew you how you mistake, when you imagine, That he who will violate his Honour, will keep his Word with his* Gods. So turning from him with a disdainful smile, he refused to answer him, when he urg'd him to know what Answer he shou'd carry back to his *Captain*; so that he departed without saying any more.

The *Captain* pondering and consulting what to do, it was concluded that nothing but *Oroonoko*'s Liberty wou'd encourage any of the rest to eat, except the *French*-man, whom the *Captain* cou'd not pretend to keep Prisoner, but only told him he was secured because he might act something in favour of the Prince, but that he shou'd be freed as soon as they came to Land. So that they concluded it wholly necessary to free the Prince from his Irons, that he might show himself to the rest; that they might have an Eye upon him, and that they cou'd not fear a single Man.

This being resolv'd, to make the Obligation the greater, the Captain himself went to *Oroonoko*; where, after many Compliments, and Assurances of what he had already promis'd, he receiving from the Prince his *Parole*, and his Hand, for his good Behaviour, dismiss'd his Irons, and brought him to his own Cabin; where, after having treated and repos'd him a while, for he had neither eat nor slept in four Days before, he besought him to visit those obstinate People in Chains, who refus'd all manner of Sustenance, and intreated him to oblige 'em to eat, and assure 'em of their Liberty the first Opportunity.

Oroonoko, who was too generous, not to give Credit to his Words, shew'd himself to his People, who were transported with Excess of Joy at the sight of their Darling Prince; falling at his Feet, and kissing and embracing 'em; believing, as some Divine Oracle, all he assured 'em. But he besought 'em to bear their Chains with that Bravery that became those whom he had seen act so nobly in Arms; and that they cou'd not give him greater Proofs of their Love and Friendship, since 'twas all the Security the Captain (his Friend) cou'd have, against the Revenge, he said, they might possibly justly take, for the Injuries sustain'd by him. And they all, with one Accord, assur'd him, they cou'd not suffer enough, when it was for his Repose and Safety.

After this they no longer refus'd to eat, but took what was brought 'em, and were pleas'd with their Captivity, since by it they hop'd to redeem the Prince, who, all the rest of the Voyage, was treated with all the Respect due to his Birth, though nothing cou'd divert his Melancholy; and he wou'd often sigh for

Imoinda, and think this a Punishment due to his Misfortune, in having left that noble Maid behind him, that fatal Night, in the *Otan*, when he fled to the Camp.

Possess'd with a thousand Thoughts of past Joys with this fair young Person, and a thousand Griefs for her eternal Loss, he endur'd a tedious Voyage, and at last arriv'd at the Mouth of the River of *Surinam*, a Colony belonging to the King of *England*, and where they were to deliver some part of their Slaves. There the Merchants and Gentlemen of the Country going on Board, to demand those Lots of Slaves they had already agreed on; and, amongst those, the Over-seers of those Plantations where I then chanc'd to be, the Captain, who had given the Word, order'd his Men to bring up those noble Slaves in Fetters, whom I have spoken of; and having put 'em, some in one, and some in other Lots, with Women and Children (which they call *Pickaninies*), they sold 'em off, as Slaves, to several Merchants and Gentlemen; not putting any two in one Lot, because they wou'd separate 'em far from each other; not daring to trust 'em together, lest Rage and Courage shou'd put 'em upon contriving some great Action, to the Ruin of the Colony.

Oroonoko was first seiz'd on, and sold to our Over-seer, who had the first Lot, with seventeen more of all sorts and sizes, but not one of Quality with him. When he saw this, he found what they meant; for, as I said, he understood *English* pretty well; and being wholly unarm'd and defenceless, so as it was in vain to make any Resistance, he only beheld the Captain with a Look all fierce and disdainful, upbraiding him with Eyes, that forc'd Blushes on his guilty Cheeks, he only cry'd, in passing over the Side of the Ship, *Farewel, Sir: 'Tis worth my Suffering, to gain so true a Knowledge both of you, and of your Gods by whom you swear.* And desiring those that held him to forbear their pains, and telling 'em he wou'd make no Resistance, he cry'd, *Come, my Fellow-Slaves; let us descend, and see if we can meet with more Honour and Honesty in the next World we shall touch upon.* So he nimbly leap'd into the Boat, and shewing no more Concern, suffer'd himself to be row'd up the River, with his seventeen Companions.

The Gentleman that bought him was a young *Cornish* Gentleman, whose Name was *Trefry*; a Man of great Wit, and fine Learning, and was carry'd into those Parts by the Lord——— Governor,[5] to manage all his Affairs. He reflecting on the last Words of *Oroonoko* to the Captain, and beholding the Richness of his Vest,[6] no sooner came into the Boat, but he fix'd his Eyes on him; and finding something so extraordinary in his Face, his Shape and Mien, a Greatness of Look, and Haughtiness in his Air, and finding he spoke *English*, had a great mind to be enquiring into his Quality and Fortune; which, though *Oroonoko* endeavour'd to hide, by only confessing he was above the Rank of common Slaves, *Trefry* soon found he was yet something greater than he confess'd; and from that Moment began to conceive so vast an Esteem for him, that he ever after lov'd him as his dearest Brother, and shew'd him all the Civilities due to so great a Man.

Trefry was a very good Mathematician, and a Linguist; cou'd speak *French* and *Spanish*; and in the three Days they remain'd in the Boat (for so long were

5. Francis, Lord Willoughby of Parham, held a royal grant as coproprietor of Surinam. John Trefry was his plantation overseer.
6. Robe.

they going from the Ship, to the Plantation) he entertain'd *Oroonoko* so agreeably with his Art and Discourse, that he was no less pleas'd with *Trefry*, than he was with the Prince; and he thought himself, at least, fortunate in this, that since he was a Slave, as long as he wou'd suffer himself to remain so, he had a Man of so excellent Wit and Parts for a Master: So that before they had finish'd their Voyage up the River, he made no scruple of declaring to *Trefry* all his Fortunes, and most part of what I have here related, and put himself wholly into the Hands of his new Friend, whom he found resenting all the Injuries were done him, and was charm'd with all the Greatness of his Actions; which were recited with that Modesty, and delicate Sense, as wholly vanquish'd him, and subdu'd him to his Interest. And he promis'd him on his Word and Honour, he wou'd find the Means to reconduct him to his own Country again: assuring him, he had a perfect Abhorrence of so dishonourable an Action; and that he wou'd sooner have dy'd, than have been the Author of such a Perfidy. He found the Prince was very much concern'd to know what became of his Friends, and how they took their Slavery; and *Trefry* promis'd to take care about the enquiring after their Condition, and that he shou'd have an Account of 'em.

Though, as *Oroonoko* afterwards said, he had little Reason to credit the Words of a *Backearary*,[7] yet he knew not why; but he saw a kind of Sincerity, and awful Truth in the Face of *Trefry*; he saw an Honesty in his Eyes, and he found him wise and witty enough to understand Honour; for it was one of his Maxims, *A Man of Wit cou'd not be a Knave or Villain.*

In their passage up the River, they put in at several Houses for Refreshment; and ever when they landed, numbers of People wou'd flock to behold this Man; not but their Eyes were daily entertain'd with the sight of Slaves, but the Fame of *Oroonoko* was gone before him, and all People were in Admiration of his Beauty. Besides, he had a rich Habit on, in which he was taken, so different from the rest, and which the Captain cou'd not strip him of, because he was forc'd to surprize his Person in the Minute he sold him. When he found his Habit made him liable, as he thought, to be gaz'd at the more, he begg'd *Trefry* to give him something more befitting a Slave; which he did, and took off his Robes. Nevertheless, he shone through all; and his *Osenbrigs* (a sort of brown *Holland*[8] Suit he had on) cou'd not conceal the Graces of his Looks and Mien; and he had no less Admirers, than when he had his dazzling Habit on: The Royal Youth appear'd in spite of the Slave, and People cou'd not help treating him after a different manner, without designing it: As soon as they approach'd him, they venerated and esteem'd him; his Eyes insensibly commanded Respect, and his Behaviour insinuated it into every Soul. So that there was nothing talk'd of but this young and gallant Slave, even by those who yet knew not that he was a Prince.

I ought to tell you, that the *Christians* never buy any Slaves but they give 'em some Name of their own, their native ones being likely very barbarous, and hard to pronounce; so that Mr. *Trefry* gave *Oroonoko* that of *Caesar*;[9] which

---

7. Master or white person, from *backra*, an Ibo or Efik word brought to Surinam by slaves.
8. A coarse linen or cotton cloth used to clothe slaves, also called *osnaburg* after a German town where it was made.
9. Slaves often received classical names. Julius Caesar was a famous Roman general and ruler.

Name will live in that Country as long as that (scarce more) glorious one of the great *Roman*; for 'tis most evident, he wanted no part of the Personal Courage of that *Caesar*, and acted things as memorable, had they been done in some part of the World replenish'd with People, and Historians, that might have given him his due. But his Misfortune was, to fall in an obscure World, that afforded only a Female Pen to celebrate his Fame; though I doubt not but it had liv'd from others Endeavours, if the *Dutch*, who, immediately after his Time, took that Country,[1] had not kill'd, banish'd and dispers'd all those that were capable of giving the World this great Man's Life, much better than I have done. And Mr. *Trefry*, who design'd it, dy'd before he began it; and bemoan'd himself for not having undertook it in time.

For the future therefore, I must call *Oroonoko*, *Caesar*, since by that Name only he was known in our Western World, and by that Name he was receiv'd on Shore at *Parham-House*, where he was destin'd a Slave. But if the King himself (God bless him) had come a-shore, there cou'd not have been greater Expectations by all the whole Plantation, and those neighbouring ones, than was on ours at that time; and he was receiv'd more like a Governor, than a Slave. Notwithstanding, as the Custom was, they assign'd him his Portion of Land, his House, and his Business, up in the Plantation. But as it was more for Form, than any Design, to put him to his Task, he endur'd no more of the Slave but the Name, and remain'd some Days in the House, receiving all Visits that were made him, without stirring towards that part of the Plantation where the *Negroes* were.

At last, he wou'd needs go view his Land, his House, and the Business assign'd him. But he no sooner came to the Houses of the Slaves, which are like a little Town by it self, the *Negroes* all having left Work, but they all came forth to behold him, and found he was that Prince who had, at several times, sold most of 'em to these Parts; and, from a Veneration they pay to great Men, especially if they know 'em, and from the Surprize and Awe they had at the sight of him, they all cast themselves at his Feet, crying out, in their Language, *Live, O King! Long Live, O King!* And kissing his Feet, paid him even Divine Homage.

Several *English* Gentlemen were with him; and what Mr. *Trefry* had told 'em, was here confirm'd; of which he himself before had no other Witness than *Caesar* himself: But he was infinitely glad to find his Grandure confirm'd by the Adoration of all the Slaves.

Caesar troubl'd with their Over-Joy, and Over-Ceremony, besought 'em to rise, and to receive him as their Fellow-Slave; assuring them, he was no better. At which they set up with one Accord a most terrible and hidious Mourning and condoling, which he and the *English* had much a-do to appease; but at last they prevail'd with 'em, and they prepar'd all their barbarous Musick, and every one kill'd and dress'd something of his own Stock (for every Family has their Land a-part, on which, at their leisure-times they breed all eatable things); and clubbing it together, made a most magnificent Supper, inviting their *Grandee*[2] *Captain*, their *Prince*, to honour it with his Presence; which he did, and several *English* with him; where they all waited on him, some playing, others dancing

---

1. The Dutch attacked and conquered Surinam in 1667, and the British exchanged it for   New York in the treaty of Breda.
2. Eminent or noble.

before him all the time, according to the Manners of their several Nations; and with unwearied Industry, endeavouring to please and delight him.

While they sat at Meat Mr. *Trefry* told *Caesar*, that most of these young *Slaves* were undone in Love, with a fine she-*Slave*, whom they had had about Six Months on their Land; the *Prince*, who never heard the Name of *Love* without a Sigh, nor any mention of it without the Curiosity of examining further into that tale, which of all Discourses was most agreeable to him, asked, how they came to be so Unhappy, as to be all undone for one fair *Slave*? *Trefry*, who was naturally Amorous, and lov'd to talk of Love as well as any body, proceeded to tell him, they had the most charming Black that ever was beheld on their *Plantation*, about Fifteen or Sixteen Years old, as he guess'd; that, for his part, he had done nothing but Sigh for her ever since she came; and that all the white Beautys he had seen, never charm'd him so absolutely as this fine Creature had done; and that no Man, of any Nation, ever beheld her, that did not fall in Love with her; and that she had all the *Slaves* perpetually at her Feet; and the whole Country resounded with the Fame of *Clemene*, for so, said he, we have Christ'ned her: But she denys us all with such a noble Disdain, that 'tis a Miracle to see, that she, who can give such eternal Desires, shou'd herself be all Ice, and all Unconcern. She is adorn'd with the most Graceful Modesty that ever beautifyed Youth; the softest Sigher—that, if she were capable of Love, one would swear she languish'd for some absent happy Man; and so retir'd, as if she fear'd a Rape even from the God of Day,[3] or that the Breezes would steal Kisses from her delicate Mouth. Her Task of Work some sighing Lover every day makes it his Petition to perform for her, which she accepts blushing, and with reluctancy, for fear he will ask her a Look for a Recompence, which he dares not presume to hope; so great an Awe she strikes into the Hearts of her Admirers. *I do not wonder*, replied the Prince, *that* Clemene *shou'd refuse Slaves, being as you say so Beautiful, but wonder how she escapes those who can entertain her as you can do; or why, being your Slave, you do not oblige her to yield. I confess*, said *Trefry, when I have, against her will, entertain'd her with Love so long, as to be transported with my Passion; even above Decency, I have been ready to make use of those advantages of Strength and Force Nature has given me. But oh! she disarms me, with that Modesty and Weeping so tender and so moving, that I retire, and thank my Stars she overcame me.* The Company laugh'd at his Civility to a *Slave*, and *Caesar* only applauded the nobleness of his Passion and Nature; since that Slave might be Noble, or, what was better, have true Notions of Honour and Vertue in her. Thus pass'd they this Night, after having received, from the *Slaves*, all imaginable Respect and Obedience.

The next Day *Trefry* ask'd *Caesar* to walk, when the heat was allay'd, and designedly carried him by the Cottage of the *fair Slave*; and told him, she whom he spoke of last Night liv'd there retir'd. *But*, says he, *I would not wish you to approach, for, I am sure, you will be in Love as soon as you behold her.* *Caesar* assur'd him, he was proof against all the Charms of that Sex; and that if he imagin'd his Heart cou'd be so perfidious to Love again, after *Imoinda*, he believ'd he shou'd tear it from his Bosom: They had no sooner spoke, but a little shock Dog, that *Clemene* had presented[4] her, which she took great Delight

3. The sun.
4. Clemene had presented to her a long-haired

dog or poodle, associated with fashionable women.

in, ran out; and she, not knowing any body was there, ran to get it in again, and bolted out on those who were just Speaking of her: When seeing them, she wou'd have run in again; but *Trefry* caught her by the Hand, and cry'd, Clemene, *however you fly a Lover, you ought to pay some Respect to this Stranger* (pointing to *Caesar*). But she, as if she had resolv'd never to raise her Eyes to the Face of a Man again, bent 'em the more to the Earth, when he spoke, and gave the *Prince* the leisure to look the more at her. There needed no long Gazing, or Consideration, to examin who this fair Creature was; he soon saw *Imoinda* all over her; in a Minute he saw her Face, her Shape, her Air, her Modesty, and all that call'd forth his Soul with Joy at his Eyes, and left his Body destitute of almost Life; it stood without Motion, and, for a Minute, knew not that it had a Being; and, I believe, he had never come to himself, so opprest he was with over-Joy, if he had not met with this Allay,[5] that he perceiv'd *Imoinda* fall dead in the Hands of *Trefry*: this awaken'd him, and he ran to her aid, and caught her in his Arms, where, by degrees, she came to herself; and 'tis needless to tell with what transports, what extasies of Joy, they both a while beheld each other, without Speaking; then Snatcht each other to their Arms; then Gaze again, as if they still doubted whether they possess'd the Blessing: They Graspt; but when they recovered their Speech, 'tis not to be imagin'd, what tender things they exprest to each other; wondering what strange Fate had brought 'em again together. They soon inform'd each other of their Fortunes, and equally bewail'd their Fate; but, at the same time, they mutually protested, that even Fetters and Slavery were Soft and Easy; and wou'd be supported with Joy and Pleasure, while they cou'd be so happy to possess each other, and to be able to make good their Vows. *Caesar* swore he disdain'd the Empire of the World, while he cou'd behold his *Imoinda*; and she despis'd Grandure and Pomp, those Vanities of her Sex, when she cou'd Gaze on *Oroonoko*. He ador'd the very Cottage where she resided, and said, That little Inch of the World wou'd give him more Happiness than all the Universe cou'd do; and she vow'd, It was a Pallace, while adorn'd with the Presence of *Oroonoko*.

Trefry was infinitely pleas'd with this Novel,[6] and found this *Clemene* was the Fair Mistress of whom *Caesar* had before spoke; and was not a little satisfied, that Heaven was so kind to the *Prince*, as to sweeten his Misfortunes by so lucky an Accident; and leaving the Lovers to themselves, was impatient to come down to *Parham House*, (which was on the same *Plantation*) to give me an Account of what had hapned. I was as impatient to make these Lovers a Visit, having already made a Friendship with *Caesar*; and from his own Mouth learn'd what I have related, which was confirm'd by his *French*-man, who was set on Shore to seek his Fortunes; and of whom they cou'd not make a Slave, because a Christian; and he came daily to *Parham Hill* to see and pay his Respects to his Pupil *Prince*: So that concerning and intresting myself, in all that related to *Caesar*, whom I had assur'd of Liberty, as soon as the Governor arriv'd, I hasted presently to the Place where the Lovers were, and was infinitely glad to find this Beautiful young *Slave* (who had already gain'd all our Esteems, for her Modesty and be extraordinary Prettyness) to be the same I had heard *Caesar*

---

5. Intrusion.   **6.** New event.

speak so much of. One may imagine then, we paid her a treble Respect; and though from her being carv'd in fine Flowers and Birds all over her Body, we took her to be of Quality before, yet, when we knew *Clemene* was *Imoinda*, we cou'd not enough admire her.

I had forgot to tell you, that those who are Nobly born of that Country, are so delicately Cut and Rac'd all over the fore-part of the Trunk of their Bodies, that it looks as if it were Japan'd; the Works being raised like high Poynt[7] round the Edges of the Flowers: Some are only Carv'd with a little Flower, or Bird, at the Sides of the Temples, as was *Caesar* and those who are so Carv'd over the Body, resemble our Ancient *Picts*[8] that are figur'd in the Chronicles, but these Carvings are more delicate.

From that happy Day *Caesar* took *Clemene* for his Wife, to the general Joy of all People; and there was as much Magnificence as the Country wou'd afford at the Celebration of this Wedding: and in a very short time after she conceiv'd with Child; which made *Caesar* ever adore her, knowing he was the last of his Great Race. This new Accident made him more Impatient of Liberty, and he was every Day treating with *Trefry* for his and *Clemene's* Liberty; and offer'd either Gold or a vast quantity of Slaves, which shou'd be paid before they let him go, provided he cou'd have any Security that he shou'd go when his Ransom was paid: They fed him from Day to Day with Promises, and delay'd him, till the Lord Governor shou'd come; so that he began to suspect them of falshood, and that they wou'd delay him till the time of his Wives delivery, and make a Slave of that too, for all the Breed is theirs to whom the Parents belong: This Thought made him very uneasy, and his Sullenness gave them some Jealousies[9] of him; so that I was oblig'd, by some Persons, who fear'd a Mutiny (which is very Fatal sometimes in those Colonies, that abound so with Slaves, that they exceed the Whites in vast Numbers) to discourse with *Caesar*, and to give him all the Satisfaction I possibly cou'd; they knew he and *Clemene* were scarce an Hour in a Day from my Lodgings; that they eat with me, and that I oblig'd 'em in all things I was capable of: I entertain'd him with the Lives of the Romans,[1] and great Men, which charm'd him to my Company; and her, with teaching her all the pretty Works that I was Mistress of; and telling her Stories of Nuns, and endeavouring to bring her to the knowledge of the true God. But of all Discourses *Caesar* lik'd that the worst, and wou'd never be reconcil'd to our Notions of the Trinity, of which he ever made a Jest; it was a Riddle, he said, wou'd turn his Brain to conceive, and one cou'd not make him understand what Faith was. However, these Conversations fail'd not altogether so well to divert him, that he lik'd the Company of us Women much above the Men; for he cou'd not Drink; and he is but an ill Companion in that Country that cannot: So that obliging him to love us very well, we had all the Liberty of Speech with him, especially my self, whom he call'd his *Great Mistress*; and indeed my Word wou'd go a great way with him. For these Reasons, I had Opportunity to take notice to him, that he was not well pleas'd of late, as he us'd to be; was more retir'd and thoughtful; and told him, I took it Ill he shou'd

---

7. An elaborate type of lace. "Rac'd": traced, incised. "Japan'd": like lacquerwork in the Japanese style.
8. Ancient British people, named *Picti* (painted or tattooed) by the Romans.
9. Suspicions.
1. Plutarch's biographies of famous men, from the late first century.

Suspect we wou'd break our Words with him, and not permit both him and *Clemene* to return to his own Kingdom, which was not so long a way, but when he was once on his Voyage he wou'd quickly arrive there. He made me some Answers that shew'd a doubt in him, which made me ask him, what advantage it wou'd be to doubt? it would but give us a Fear of him, and possibly compel us to treat him so as I shou'd be very loath to behold: that is, it might occasion his Confinement. Perhaps this was not so Luckily spoke of me, for I perceiv'd he resented that Word, which I strove to Soften again in vain: However, he assur'd me, that whatsoever Resolutions he shou'd take, he wou'd Act nothing upon the White-People; and as for my self, and those upon that *Plantation* where he was, he wou'd sooner forfeit his eternal Liberty, and Life it self, than lift his Hand against his greatest Enemy on that Place: He besought me to suffer no Fears upon his Account, for he cou'd do nothing that Honour shou'd not dictate; but he accus'd himself for having suffer'd Slavery so long; yet he charg'd that weakness on Love alone, who was capable of making him neglect even Glory it self; and, for which, now he reproaches himself every moment of the Day. Much more to this effect he spoke, with an Air impatient enough to make me know he wou'd not be long in Bondage; and though he suffer'd only the Name of a Slave, and had nothing of the Toil and Labour of one, yet that was sufficient to render him Uneasy; and he had been too long Idle, who us'd to be always in Action, and in Arms: He had a Spirit all Rough and Fierce, and that cou'd not be tam'd to lazy Rest; and though all endeavors were us'd to exercise himself in such Actions and Sports as this World afforded, as Running, Wrastling, Pitching the Bar, Hunting and Fishing, Chasing and Killing *Tigers*[2] of a monstrous Size, which this Continent affords in abundance; and wonderful *Snakes*, such as *Alexander* is reported to have incounter'd at the River of *Amazons*,[3] and which *Caesar* took great Delight to overcome; yet these were not Actions great enough for his large Soul, which was still panting after more renown'd Action.

Before I parted that Day with him, I got, with much ado, a Promise from him to rest yet a little longer with Patience, and wait the coming of the Lord Governor, who was every Day expected on our Shore; he assur'd me he wou'd, and this Promise he desired me to know was given perfectly in Complaisance to me, in whom he had an intire Confidence.

After this, I neither thought it convenient to trust him much out of our View, nor did the Country who fear'd him; but with one accord it was advis'd to treat him Fairly, and oblige him to remain within such a compass, and that he shou'd be permitted, as seldom as cou'd be, to go up to the Plantations of the Negroes; or, if he did, to be accompany'd by some that shou'd be rather in appearance Attendants than Spys. This Care was for some time taken, and *Caesar* look'd upon it as a Mark of extraordinary Respect, and was glad his discontent had oblig'd 'em to be more observant to him; he received new assurance from the Overseer, which was confirmed to him by the Opinion of all the Gentlemen of the Country, who made their court to him. During this time that we had his Company more frequently than hitherto we had had, it may not be unpleasant to relate to you the Diversions we entertain'd him with, or rather he us.

---

2. Jaguars. "Pitching the bar": a game of distance throwing.

3. Alexander the Great supposedly encountered Amazons (and snakes) in India.

My stay was to be short in that Country, because my Father dy'd at Sea, and never arriv'd to possess the Honour was design'd him, (which was Lieutenant-General of Six and thirty Islands, besides the Continent of *Surinam*) nor the advantages he hop'd to reap by them;[4] so that though we were oblig'd to continue on our Voyage, we did not intend to stay upon the Place: Though, in a Word, I must say thus much of it, That certainly had his late Majesty, of sacred Memory, but seen and known what a vast and charming World he had been Master of in that Continent, he would never have parted so Easily with it to the *Dutch*. 'Tis a Continent whose vast Extent was never yet known, and may contain more Noble Earth than all the Universe besides; for, they say, it reaches from East to West; one Way as far as *China*, and another to *Peru*: It affords all things both for Beauty and Use; 'tis there Eternal Spring, always the very Months of *April*, *May* and *June*; the Shades are perpetual, the Trees, bearing at once all degrees of Leaves and Fruit, from blooming Buds to ripe Autumn; Groves of Oranges, Limons, Citrons, Figs, Nutmegs, and noble Aromaticks, continually bearing their Fragrancies. The Trees appearing all like Nosegays adorn'd with Flowers of different kinds; some are all White, some Purple, some Scarlet, some Blue, some Yellow; bearing, at the same time, Ripe Fruit and Blooming Young, or producing every Day new. The very Wood of all these Trees have an intrinsick Value above common Timber; for they are, when cut, of different Colours, glorious to behold; and bear a Price considerable, to inlay withal. Besides this, they yield rich Balm, and Gums; so that we make our Candles of such an Aromatick Substance, as does not only give a sufficient Light, but, as they Burn, they cast their Perfumes all about. Cedar is the common Firing, and all the Houses are built with it. The very Meat we eat, when set on the Table, if it be Native, I mean of the Country, perfumes the whole Room; especially a little Beast call'd an *Armadilly*, a thing which I can liken to nothing so well as a *Rhinoceros*; 'tis all in white Armor so joynted, that it moves as well in it, as if it had nothing on; this Beast is about the bigness of a Pig of Six Weeks old. But it were endless to give an Account of all the divers Wonderfull and Strange things that Country affords, and which we took a very great Delight to go in search of; though those adventures are oftentimes Fatal and at least Dangerous: But while we had *Caesar* in our Company on these Designs we fear'd no harm, nor suffer'd any.

As soon as I came into the Country, the best House in it was presented me, call'd *St. John's Hill*.[5] It stood on a vast Rock of white Marble, at the Foot of which the River ran a vast depth down, and not to be descended on that side; the little Waves still dashing and washing the foot of this Rock, made the softest Murmurs and Purlings in the World; and the Opposite Bank was adorn'd with such vast quantities of different Flowers eternally Blowing,[6] and every Day and Hour new, fenc'd behind 'em with lofty Trees of a Thousand rare Forms and Colours, that the Prospect was the most ravishing that fancy can create. On the Edge of this white Rock, towards the River, was a Walk or Grove of Orange and Limon Trees, about half the length of the *Mall*[7] here,

---

4. There is no record of Willoughby appointing anyone to the position of lieutenant-governor. "Continent": land joined to other lands.
5. A plantation near Willoughby's Parham Hill.
6. Blooming.
7. A fashionable park walk in London.

whose Flowery and Fruit-bearing Branches meet at the top, and hinder'd the Sun, whose Rays are very fierce there, from entering a Beam into the Grove; and the cool Air that came from the River made it not only fit to entertain People in, at all the hottest Hours of the Day, but refresh'd the sweet Blossoms, and made it always Sweet and Charming; and sure the whole Globe of the World cannot show so delightful a Place as this Grove was: Not all the Gardens of boasted *Italy* can produce a Shade to out-vie this, which Nature had joyn'd with Art to render so exceeding Fine; and 'tis a marvel to see how such vast Trees, as big as English Oaks, cou'd take footing on so solid a Rock, and in so little Earth, as cover'd that Rock; but all things by Nature there are Rare, Delightful and Wonderful. But to our Sports.

Sometimes we wou'd go surprizing,[8] and in search of young *Tigers* in their Dens, watching when the old Ones went forth to forage for Prey; and oftentimes we have been in great Danger, and have fled apace for our Lives, when surpriz'd by the Dams. But once, above all other times, we went on this Design, and *Caesar* was with us, who had no sooner stol'n a young *Tiger* from her Nest, but going off, we incounter'd the Dam, bearing a Buttock of a Cow, which he[9] had torn off with his mighty Paw, and going with it towards his *Den*; we had only found Women, *Caesar*, and an English Gentleman, Brother to *Harry Martin*,[1] the great *Oliverian*; we found there was no escaping this inrag'd and ravenous Beast. However, we Women fled as fast as we cou'd from it; but our Heels had not sav'd our Lives, if *Caesar* had not laid down his *Cub*, when he found the *Tiger* quit her Prey to make the more speed towards him; and taking Mr. *Martin*'s Sword desir'd him to stand aside, or follow the Ladies. He obey'd him, and *Caesar* met this monstrous Beast of might, size, and vast Limbs, who came with open Jaws upon him; and fixing his Awful stern Eyes full upon those of the Beast, and putting himself into a very steddy and good aiming posture of Defence, ran his Sword quite through his Breast down to his very Heart, home to the Hilt of the Sword; the dying Beast stretch'd forth her Paw, and going to grasp his Thigh, surpriz'd with Death in that very moment, did him no other harm than fixing her long Nails in his Flesh very deep, feebly wounded him, but cou'd not grasp the Flesh to tear off any. When he had done this, he hollow'd to us to return; which, after some assurance of his Victory, we did, and found him lugging out the Sword from the Bosom of the *Tiger*, who was laid in her Bloud on the Ground; he took up the *Cub*, and with an unconcern, that had nothing of the Joy or Gladness of a Victory, he came and laid the Whelp at my Feet: We all extreamly wonder'd at his Daring, and at the Bigness of the Beast, which was about the highth of an Heifer, but of mighty, great, and strong Limbs.

Another time, being in the Woods, he kill'd a *Tiger*, which had long infested that part, and born away abundance of Sheep and Oxen, and other things, that were for the support of those to whom they belong'd; abundance of People assail'd this Beast, some affirming they had shot her with several Bullets quite through the Body, at several times; and some swearing they shot her through the very Heart, and they believ'd she was a Devil rather than a Mortal thing.

---

8. Mounting sudden raids.
9. The tiger is alternatively she, he, and it.
1. Henry Martin had been one of judges who signed Charles I's death warrant. His younger brother George, a Barbados planter, moved to Surinam in 1658.

Caesar had often said, he had a mind to encounter this Monster, and spoke with several Gentlemen who had attempted her; one crying, I shot her with so many poyson'd Arrows, another with his Gun in this part of her, and another in that; so that he remarking all these Places where she was shot, fancy'd still he shou'd overcome her, by giving her another sort of a Wound than any had yet done; and one day said (at the Table) *What Trophies and Garlands, Ladies, will you make me, if I bring you home the Heart of this Ravenous Beast, that eats up all your Lambs and Pigs?* We all promis'd he shou'd be rewarded at all our Hands. So taking a Bow, which he chus'd out of a great many, he went up in the Wood, with two Gentlemen, where he imagin'd this Devourer to be; they had not past very far in it, but they heard her Voice, growling and grumbling, as if she were pleas'd with something she was doing. When they came in view, they found her muzzling in the Belly of a new ravish'd Sheep, which she had torn open; and seeing herself approach'd, she took fast hold of her Prey, with her fore Paws, and set a very fierce raging Look on *Caesar*, without offering to approach him; for fear, at the same time, of losing what she had in Possession. So that *Caesar* remain'd a good while, only taking aim, and getting an opportunity to shoot her where he design'd; 'twas some time before he cou'd accomplish it, and to wound her, and not kill her, wou'd but have enrag'd her more, and indanger'd him: He had a Quiver of Arrows at his side, so that if one fail'd he cou'd be supply'd; at last, retiring a little, he gave her opportunity to eat, for he found she was Ravenous, and fell to as soon as she saw him retire; being more eager of her Prey than of doing new Mischiefs. When he going softly to one side of her, and hiding his Person behind certain Herbage that grew high and thick, he took so good aim, that, as he intended, he shot her just into the Eye, and the Arrow was sent with so good a will, and so sure a hand, that it stuck in her Brain, and made her caper, and become mad for a moment or two; but being seconded by another Arrow, he fell dead upon the Prey: *Caesar* cut him Open with a Knife, to see where those Wounds were that had been reported to him, and why he did not Die of 'em. But I shall now relate a thing that possibly will find no Credit among Men, because 'tis a Notion commonly receiv'd with us, That nothing can receive a Wound in the Heart and Live; but when the Heart of this courageous Animal was taken out, there were Seven Bullets of Lead in it, and the Wounds seam'd up with great Scars, and she liv'd with the Bullets a great while, for it was long since they were shot: This Heart the Conqueror brought up to us, and 'twas a very great Curiosity, which all the Country came to see; and which gave *Caesar* occasion of many fine Discourses; of Accidents in War, and Strange Escapes.

At other times he wou'd go a Fishing; and discoursing on that Diversion, he found we had in that Country a very Strange Fish, call'd a *Numb Eel*,[2] (an *Eel* of which I have eaten) that while it is alive, it has a quality so Cold, that those who are Angling, though with a Line of never so great a length, with a Rod at the end of it, it shall, in the same minute the Bait is touched by this *Eel*, seize him or her that holds the Rod with benumb'dness, that shall deprive 'em of Sense, for a while; and some have fall'n into the Water, and others drop'd as dead on the Banks of the Rivers where they stood, as soon as this Fish touches the Bait. *Caesar* us'd to laugh at this, and believ'd it impossible a Man cou'd

2. Electric eel.

lose his Force at the touch of a Fish; and cou'd not understand that Philosophy,[3] that a cold Quality should be of that Nature: However, he had a great Curiosity to try whether it wou'd have the same effect on him it had on others, and often try'd, but in vain; at last, the sought for Fish came to the Bait, as he stood Angling on the Bank; and instead of throwing away the Rod, or giving it a sudden twitch out of the Water, whereby he might have caught both the *Eel*, and have dismiss'd the Rod, before it cou'd have too much Power over him; for Experiment sake, he grasp'd it but the harder, and fainting fell into the River; and being still possest of the Rod, the Tide carry'd him senseless as he was a great way, till an *Indian* Boat took him up; and perceiv'd, when they touch'd him, a Numbness seize them, and by that knew the Rod was in his Hand; which, with a Paddle (that is, a short Oar) they struck away, and snatch'd it into the Boat, *Eel* and all. If *Caesar* were almost Dead, with the effect of this Fish, he was more so with that of the Water, where he had remain'd the space of going a League; and they found they had much a-do to bring him back to Life: But, at last, they did, and brought him home, where he was in a few Hours well Recover'd and Refresh'd; and not a little Asham'd to find he shou'd be overcome by an *Eel*; and that all the People, who heard his Defiance, wou'd Laugh at him. But we cheared him up; and he, being convinc'd, we had the *Eel* at Supper; which was a quarter of an Ell about, and most delicate Meat; and was of the more Value, since it cost so Dear, as almost the Life of so gallant a Man.

About this time we were in many mortal Fears, about some Disputes the *English* had with the *Indians*; so that we cou'd scarce trust our selves, without great Numbers, to go to any *Indian* Towns, or Place, where they abode; for fear they shou'd fall upon us, as they did immediately after my coming away; and that it was in the possession of the *Dutch*, who us'd 'em not so civilly as the *English*; so that they cut in pieces all they cou'd take, getting into Houses, and hanging up the Mother, and all her Children about her; and cut a Footman, I left behind me, all in Joynts, and nail'd him to Trees.

This feud began while I was there; so that I lost half the satisfaction I propos'd, in not seeing and visiting the *Indian* Towns. But one Day, bemoaning of our Misfortunes upon this account, *Caesar* told us, we need not Fear; for if we had a mind to go, he wou'd undertake to be our Guard: Some wou'd, but most wou'd not venture; about Eighteen of us resolv'd, and took Barge; and, after Eight Days, arriv'd near an *Indian* Town: But approaching it, the Hearts of some of our Company fail'd, and they wou'd not venture on Shore; so we Poll'd who wou'd, and who wou'd not: For my part, I said, If *Caesar* wou'd, I wou'd go; he resolv'd, so did my Brother, and my Woman, a Maid of good Courage. Now none of us speaking the Language of the People, and imagining we shou'd have a half Diversion in Gazing only; and not knowing what they said, we took a Fisherman that liv'd at the Mouth of the River, who had been a long Inhabitant there, and oblig'd him to go with us: But because he was known to the *Indians*, as trading among 'em; and being, by long Living there, become a perfect *Indian* in Colour, we, who resolv'd to surprize 'em, by making 'em see something they never had seen, (that is, White People) resolv'd only my self, my Brother, and Woman shou'd go; so *Caesar*, the Fisherman, and the rest, hiding behind some thick Reeds and Flowers, that grew on the Banks, let

---

3. Principle or system.

us pass on towards the Town, which was on the Bank of the River all along. A little distant from the Houses, or Huts, we saw some Dancing, others busy'd in fetching and carrying of Water from the River: They had no sooner spy'd us, but they set up a loud Cry, that frighted us at first; we thought it had been for those that should Kill us, but it seems it was of Wonder and Amazement. They were all Naked, and we were Dress'd, so as is most comode,[4] for the hot Countries, very Glittering and Rich; so that we appear'd extreamly fine; my own Hair was cut short, and I had a Taffaty Cap, with Black Feathers, on my Head; my Brother was in a Stuff[5] Suit, with Silver Loops and Buttons, and abundance of Green Ribon; this was all infinitely surprising to them, and because we saw them stand still, till we approach'd 'em, we took Heart and advanc'd; came up to 'em, and offer'd 'em our Hands; which they took, and look'd on us round about, calling still for more Company; who came swarming out, all wondering, and crying out *Tepeeme*;[6] taking their Hair up in their Hands, and spreading it wide to those they call'd out to; as if they would say (as indeed it signify'd) *Numberless Wonders*, or not to be recounted, no more than to number the Hair of their Heads. By degrees they grew more bold, and from gazing upon us round, they touch'd us; laying their Hands upon all the Features of our Faces, feeling our Breasts and Arms, taking up one Petticoat, then wondering to see another; admiring our Shoes and Stockings, but more our Garters, which we gave 'em; and they ty'd about their Legs, being Lac'd with Silver Lace at the ends, for they much Esteem any shining things: In fine, we suffer'd 'em to survey us as they pleas'd, and we thought they wou'd never have done admiring us. When *Caesar*, and the rest, saw we were receiv'd with such wonder, they came up to us; and finding the *Indian* Trader whom they knew, (for 'tis by these Fishermen, call'd *Indian* Traders, we hold a Commerce with 'em; for they love not to go far from home, and we never go to them) when they saw him therefore they set up a new Joy; and cry'd, in their Language, *Oh! here's our* Tiguamy, *and we shall now know whether those things can speak*: So advancing to him, some of 'em gave him their Hands, and cry'd, *Amora Tiguamy*, which is as much as, *How do you*, or *Welcome Friend*; and all, with one din, began to gabble to him, and ask'd, If we had Sense, and Wit? if we cou'd talk of affairs of Life, and War, as they cou'd do? if we cou'd Hunt, Swim, and do a thousand things they use? He answer'd 'em, We cou'd. Then they invited us into their Houses, and dress'd Venison and Buffelo for us; and, going out, gathered a Leaf of a Tree, call'd a *Sarumbo* Leaf, of Six Yards long, and spread it on the Ground for a Table-Cloth; and cutting another in pieces instead of Plates, setting us on little bow *Indian* Stools, which they cut out of one intire piece of Wood, and Paint, in a sort of Japan Work: They serve every one their Mess[7] on these pieces of Leaves, and it was very good, but too high season'd with Pepper. When we had eat, my Brother, and I, took out our Flutes, and play'd to 'em, which gave 'em new Wonder; and I soon perceiv'd, by an admiration, that is natural to these People, and by the extream Ignorance and Simplicity of 'em, it were not difficult to establish any unknown or extravagant Religion among them; and to impose any Notions or Fictions upon 'em. For

---

4. Appropriate.
5. Woven fabric. "Taffaty": taffeta.
6. *Tapouimé* (a modern transcription of the word Behn transcribed as *Tepeeme*) is the word for "many" in the indigenous Galibi language.
7. Serving.

seeing a Kinsman of mine set some Paper a Fire, with a Burning-glass, a Trick they had never before seen, they were like to have Ador'd him for a God; and beg'd he wou'd give them the Characters or Figures of his Name, that they might oppose it against Winds and Storms; which he did, and they held it up in those Seasons, and fancy'd it had a Charm to conquer them; and kept it like a Holy Relique. They are very Superstitious, and call'd him the Great *Peeie*, that is, *Prophet*. They show'd us their *Indian Peeie*, a Youth of about Sixteen Years old, as handsom as Nature cou'd make a Man. They consecrate a beautiful Youth from his Infancy, and all Arts are us'd to compleat him in the finest manner, both in Beauty and Shape: He is bred to all the little Arts and cunning they are capable of; to all the Legerdemain Tricks, and Sleight of Hand, whereby he imposes upon the Rabble; and is both a Doctor in Physick and Divinity. And by these Tricks makes the Sick believe he sometimes eases their Pains; by drawing from the afflicted part little Serpents, or odd Flies, or Worms, or any Strange thing; and though they have besides undoubted good Remedies, for almost all their Diseases, they cure the Patient more by Fancy than by Medicines; and make themselves Fear'd, Lov'd, and Reverenc'd. This young *Peeie* had a very young Wife, who seeing my Brother kiss her, came running and kiss'd me; after this, they kiss'd one another, and made it a very great Jest, it being so Novel; and new Admiration and Laughing went round the Multitude, that they never will forget that Ceremony, never before us'd or known. *Caesar* had a mind to see and talk with their War *Captains*, and we were conducted to one of their Houses; where we beheld several of the great *Captains*, who had been at Councel: But so frightful a Vision it was to see 'em no Fancy can create; no such Dreams can represent so dreadful a Spectacle. For my part I took 'em for Hobgoblins, or Fiends, rather than Men; but however their Shapes appear'd, their Souls were very Humane and Noble; but some wanted their Noses, some their Lips, some both Noses and Lips, some their Ears, and others Cut through each Cheek, with long Slashes, through which their Teeth appear'd; they had other several formidable Wounds and Scars, or rather Dismemberings; they had *Comitias*, or little Aprons before 'em; and Girdles of Cotton, with their Knives naked, stuck in it; a Bow at their Backs, and a Quiver of Arrows on their Thighs; and most had Feathers on their Heads of divers Colours. They cry'd, *Amora Tigame* to us, at our entrance, and were pleas'd we said as much to 'em; they seated us, and gave us Drink of the best Sort; and wonder'd, as much as the others had done before, to see us. *Caesar* was marvelling as much at their Faces, wondering how they shou'd all be so Wounded in War; he was Impatient to know how they all came by those frightful Marks of Rage or Malice, rather than Wounds got in Noble Battel: They told us, by our Interpreter, That when any War was waging, two Men chosen out by some old *Captain*, whose Fighting was past, and who cou'd only teach the Theory of War, these two Men were to stand in Competition for the Generalship, or Great War Captain; and being brought before the old Judges, now past Labour, they are ask'd, What they dare do to shew they are worthy to lead an Army? When he, who is first ask'd, making no Reply, Cuts off his Nose, and throws it contemptably[8] on the Ground; and the other does something to himself that he thinks surpasses him, and perhaps deprives himself of Lips and an Eye; so they Slash

8. With contempt.

on till one gives out, and many have dy'd in this Debate. And 'tis by a passive Valour they shew and prove their Activity; a sort of Courage too Brutal to be applauded by our Black Hero; nevertheless he express'd his Esteem of 'em.

In this Voyage *Caesar* begot so good an understanding between the *Indians* and the *English*, that there were no more Fears, or Heart-burnings during our stay; but we had a perfect, open, and free Trade with 'em: Many things Remarkable, and worthy Reciting, we met with in this short Voyage; because *Caesar* made it his Business to search out and provide for our Entertainment, especially to please his dearly Ador'd *Imoinda*, who was a sharer in all our Adventures; we being resolv'd to make her Chains as easy as we cou'd, and to Compliment the Prince in that manner that most oblig'd him.

As we were coming up again, we met with some *Indians* of strange Aspects; that is, of a larger Size, and other sort of Features, than those of our Country: Our *Indian Slaves*, that Row'd us, ask'd 'em some Questions, but they cou'd not understand us; but shew'd us a long Cotton String, with several Knots on it;[9] and told us, they had been coming from the Mountains so many Moons as there were Knots; they were habited in Skins of a Strange Beast, and brought along with 'em Bags of Gold Dust; which, as well as they cou'd give us to understand, came streaming in little small Chanels down the high Mountains, when the Rains fell; and offer'd to be the Convoy to any Body, or Persons, that wou'd go to the Mountains. We carry'd these Men up to *Parham*, where they were kept till the Lord Governour came: And because all the Country was mad to be going on this Golden Adventure, the Governour, by his Letters, commanded (for they sent some of the Gold to him) that a Guard shou'd be set at the Mouth of the River of *Amazons*, (a River so call'd, almost as broad as the River of *Thames*) and prohibited all People from going up that River, it conducting to those Mountains of Gold.[1] But we going off for *England* before the Project was further prosecuted, and the Governour being drown'd in a Hurricane[2] either the Design dy'd, or the *Dutch* have the Advantage of it: And 'tis to be bemoan'd what his Majesty lost by losing that part of *America*.

Though this digression is a little from my Story, however since it contains some Proofs of the Curiosity and Daring of this great Man, I was content to omit nothing of his Character.

It was thus, for some time we diverted him; but now *Imoinda* began to shew she was with Child, and did nothing but Sigh and Weep for the Captivity of her Lord, her Self, and the Infant yet Unborn; and believ'd, if it were so hard to gain the Liberty of Two, 'twou'd be more difficult to get that for Three. Her Griefs were so many Darts in the great Heart of *Caesar*; and taking his Opportunity one *Sunday*, when all the Whites were overtaken in Drink, as there were abundance of several Trades, and *Slaves* for Four Years, that Inhabited among the *Negro* Houses; and *Sunday* was their Day of Debauch, (otherwise they were a sort of Spys upon Caesar); he went pretending out of Goodness to 'em, to Feast amongst 'em; and sent all his Musick, and order'd a great Treat for the whole Gang, about Three Hundred *Negros*; and about a Hundred and Fifty were able to bear Arms, such as they had, which were sufficient to do Execution

---

9. A *quipu*, used by the Incas of Peru for keeping records and accounts.
1. Spanish as well as English explorers had searched for the mythical golden city of El Dorado in Guiana.
2. Willoughby died in a storm in 1666.

with Spirits accordingly: For the *English* had none but rusty Swords, that no Strength cou'd draw from a Scabbard; except the People of particular Quality, who took care to Oyl 'em and keep 'em in good Order: The Guns also, unless here and there one, or those newly carry'd from *England*, wou'd do no good or harm; for 'tis the Nature of that Country to Rust and Eat up Iron, or any Metals, but Gold and Silver. And they are very Unexpert at the Bow, which the *Negros* and *Indians* are perfect Masters off.

Caesar, having singl'd out these Men from the Women and Children, made an Harangue to 'em of the Miseries, and Ignominies of Slavery; counting up all their Toyls and Sufferings, under such Loads, Burdens, and Drudgeries, as were fitter for Beasts than Men; Senseless Brutes, than Humane Souls. He told 'em it was not for Days, Months, or Years, but for Eternity; there was no end to be of their Misfortunes: They suffer'd not like Men who might find a Glory, and Fortitude in Oppression; but like Dogs that lov'd the Whip and Bell, and fawn'd the more they were beaten: That they had lost the Divine Quality of Men, and were become insensible Asses, fit only to bear; nay worse: and Ass, or Dog, or Horse having done his Duty, cou'd lye down in Retreat, and rise to Work again, and while he did his Duty indur'd no Stripes; but Men, Villanous, Senseless Men, such as they, Toyl'd on all the tedious Week till Black *Friday*; and then, whether they Work'd or not, whether they were Faulty or Meriting, they promiscuously, the Innocent with the Guilty, suffer'd the infamous Whip, the sordid Stripes, from their Fellow *Slaves* till their Blood trickled from all Parts of their Body; Blood, whose every drop ought to be Reveng'd with a Life of some of those Tyrants, that impose it; *And why*, said he, *my dear Friends and Fellow-sufferers, shou'd we be Slaves to an unknown People? Have they Vanquish'd us Nobly in Fight? Have they Won us in Honourable Battel? And are we, by the chance of War, become their Slaves? This wou'd not anger a Noble Heart, this wou'd not animate a Souldiers Soul; no, but we are Bought and Sold like Apes, or Monkeys, to be the Sport of Women, Fools and Cowards; and the Support of Rogues, Runagades,*[3] *that have abandon'd their own Countries, for Rapin, Murders, Thefts and Villanies: Do you not hear every Day how they upbraid each other with infamy of Life, below the Wildest Salvages; and shall we render Obedience to such a degenerate Race, who have no one Humane Vertue left, to distinguish 'em from the vilest Creatures? Will you, I say, suffer the Lash from such Hands?* They all Reply'd, with one accord, *No, no, no; Caesar has spoke like a Great Captain; like a Great King.*

After this he wou'd have proceeded, but was interrupted by a tall *Negro* of some more Quality than the rest, his Name was *Tuscan*; who Bowing at the Feet of *Caesar*, cry'd, *My Lord, we have listen'd with Joy and Attention to what you have said; and, were we only Men, wou'd follow so great a Leader through the World: But oh! consider, we are Husbands and Parents too, and have things more dear to us than Life; our Wives and Children unfit for Travel, in these unpassable Woods, Mountains and Bogs; we have not only difficult Lands to overcome, but Rivers to Wade, and Monsters to Incounter; Ravenous Beasts of Prey——.* To this, *Caesar* Reply'd, *That Honour was the First Principle in Nature, that was to be Obey'd; but as no Man wou'd pretend to that, without all the Acts of Vertue, Compassion, Charity, Love, Justice and Reason; he found it not*

---

3. Renegades.

inconsistent with that, to take an equal Care of their Wives and Children, as they wou'd of themselves; and that he did not Design, when he led them to Freedom, and Glorious Liberty, that they shou'd leave that better part of themselves to Perish by the Hand of the Tyrant's Whip: But if there were a Woman among them so degenerate from Love and Vertue to chuse Slavery before the pursuit of her Husband, and with the hazard of her Life, to share with him in his Fortunes; that such an one ought to be Abandon'd, and left as a Prey to the common Enemy.

To which they all Agreed,—and Bowed. After this, he spoke of the Impassable Woods and Rivers; and convinc'd 'em, the more Danger, the more Glory. He told them that he had heard of one *Hannibal* a great Captain, had Cut his Way through Mountains of solid Rocks; and shou'd a few Shrubs oppose them; which they cou'd Fire before 'em?[4] No, 'twas a trifling Excuse to Men resolv'd to die, or overcome. As for Bogs, they are with a little Labour fill'd and harden'd; and the Rivers cou'd be no Obstacle, since they Swam by Nature; at least by Custom, from their First Hour of their Birth: That when the Children were Weary they must carry them by turns, and the Woods and their own Industry wou'd afford them Food. To this they all assented with Joy.

Tuscan then demanded, What he wou'd do? He said, they wou'd Travel towards the Sea; Plant a New Colony, and Defend it by their Valour; and when they cou'd find a Ship, either driven by stress of Weather, or guided by Providence that way, they wou'd Seize it, and make it a Prize, till it had Transported them to their own Countries; at least, they shou'd be made Free in his Kingdom, and be Esteem'd as his Fellow-sufferers, and Men that had the Courage, and the Bravery to attempt, at least, for Liberty; and if they Dy'd in the attempt it wou'd be more brave, than to Live in perpetual Slavery.

They bow'd and kiss'd his Feet at this Resolution, and with one accord Vow'd to follow him to Death. And that Night was appointed to begin their March; they made it known to their Wives, and directed them to tie their Hamaca[5] about their Shoulder, and under their Arm like a Scarf; and to lead their Children that cou'd go, and carry those that cou'd not. The Wives, who pay an intire Obedience to their Husbands, obey'd, and stay'd for 'em, where they were appointed: The Men stay'd but to furnish themselves with what defensive Arms they cou'd get; and All met at the Rendezvous, where *Caesar* made a new incouraging Speech to 'em, and led 'em out.

But, as they cou'd not march far that Night, on Monday early, when the Overseers went to call 'em all together, to go to Work, they were extreamly surpris'd, to find not one upon the Place, but all fled with what Baggage they had. You may imagine this News was not only suddenly spread all over the *Plantation*, but soon reach'd the Neighbouring ones; and we had by Noon about Six hundred Men, they call the *Militia* of the Country, that came to assist us in the pursuit of the Fugitives: But never did one see so comical an Army march forth to War. The Men, of any fashion, wou'd not concern themselves, though it were almost the common Cause; for such Revoltings are very ill Examples, and have very fatal Consequences oftentimes in many Colonies: But they had a Respect for *Caesar*, and all hands were against the *Parhamites*, as they call'd those of *Parham Plantation*; because they did not, in the

---

4. Roman accounts relate how the Carthaginian general and his army hacked through the Alps on their way to attack Rome.
5. Hammock.

first place, love the Lord Governor; and secondly, they wou'd have it, that *Caesar* was Ill us'd, and Baffl'd with;[6] and 'tis not impossible but some of the best in the Country was of his Council in this Flight, and depriving us of all the *Slaves*; so that they of the better sort wou'd not meddle in the matter. The Deputy Governor,[7] of whom I have had no great occasion to speak, and who was the most Fawning fair-tongu'd Fellow in the World, and one that pretended the most Friendship to *Caesar*, was now the only violent Man against him; and though he had nothing, and so need fear nothing, yet talk'd and look'd bigger than any Man: He was a Fellow, whose Character is not fit to be mention'd with the worst of the *Slaves*. This Fellow wou'd lead his Army forth to meet *Caesar*, or rather to pursue him; most of their Arms were of those sort of cruel Whips they call *Cat with Nine Tayls*; some had rusty useless Guns for show; others old Basket-hilts,[8] whose Blades had never seen the Light in this Age; and others had long Staffs, and Clubs. Mr. *Trefry* went along, rather to be a Mediator than a Conqueror, in such a Battel; for he foresaw, and knew, if by fighting they put the Negroes into despair, they were a sort of sullen Fellows, that wou'd drown, or kill themselves, before they wou'd yield; and he advis'd that fair means was best: But *Byam* was one that abounded in his own Wit, and wou'd take his own Measures.

It was not hard to find these Fugitives; for as they fled they were forc'd to fire and cut the Woods before 'em, so that Night or Day they pursu'd 'em by the light they made, and by the path they had clear'd: But as soon as *Caesar* found he was pursu'd, he put himself in a Posture of Defence, placing all the Women and Children in the Rear; and himself, with *Tuscan* by his side, or next to him, all promising to Dye or Conquer. Incourag'd thus, they never stood to Parley, but fell on Pell-mell upon the *English*, and kill'd some, and wounded a good many; they having recourse to their Whips, as the best of their Weapons: And as they observ'd no Order, they perplex'd the Enemy so sorely, with Lashing 'em in the Eyes; and the Women and Children, seeing their Husbands so treated, being of fearful Cowardly Dispositions, and hearing the *English* cry out, *Yield and Live, Yield and be Pardon'd*; they all run in amongst their Husbands and Fathers, and hung about 'em, crying out, *Yield, yield; and leave* Caesar *to their Revenge*; that by degrees the Slaves abandon'd *Caesar*, and left him only *Tuscan* and his Heroick *Imoinda*; who, grown big as she was, did nevertheless press near her Lord, having a Bow, and a Quiver full of poyson'd Arrows, which she manag'd with such dexterity, that she wounded several, and shot the *Governor* into the Shoulder; of which Wound he had like to have Dy'd, but that an *Indian* Woman, his Mistress, suck'd the Wound, and cleans'd it from the Venom: But however, he stir'd not from the Place till he had Parly'd with *Caesar*, who he found was resolv'd to dye Fighting, and wou'd not be Taken; no more wou'd *Tuscan*, or *Imoinda*. But he, more thirsting after Revenge of another sort, than that of depriving him of Life, now made use of all his Art of talking, and dissembling; and besought *Caesar* to yield himself upon Terms, which he himself should propose, and should be Sacredly assented to and kept by him: He told him, It was not that he any longer fear'd him, or cou'd believe the force of Two Men, and a young Heroine, cou'd overcome all them, with all

---

6. Cheated.
7. William Byam, a Royalist exile from England
and Barbados.
8. Swords with hilt guards.

the Slaves now on their side also; but it was the vast Esteem he had for his Person; the desire he had to serve so Gallant a Man; and to hinder himself from the Reproach hereafter, of having been the occasion of the Death of a *Prince*, whose Valour and Magnanimity deserv'd the Empire of the World. He protested to him, he look'd upon this Action, as Gallant and Brave; however tending to the prejudice of his Lord and Master, who wou'd by it have lost so considerable a number of *Slaves*; that this Flight of his shou'd be look'd on as a heat of Youth, and rashness of a too forward Courage, and an unconsider'd impatience of Liberty, and no more; and that he labour'd in vain to accomplish that which they wou'd effectually perform, as soon as any Ship arriv'd that wou'd touch on his Coast. *So that if you will be pleas'd*, continued he, *to surrender your self, all imaginable Respect shall be paid you; and your Self, your Wife, and Child, if it be here born, shall depart free out of our Land.* But *Caesar* wou'd hear of no Composition,[9] though *Byam* urg'd, If he pursu'd, and went on in his Design, he wou'd inevitably Perish, either by great *Snakes*, wild Beasts, or Hunger; and he ought to have regard to his Wife, whose Condition required ease, and not the fatigues of tedious Travel; where she cou'd not be secur'd from being devoured. But *Caesar* told him, there was no Faith in the White Men, or the Gods they Ador'd; who instructed 'em in Principles so false, that honest Men cou'd not live amongst 'em; though no People profess'd so much, none perform'd so little; that he knew what he had to do, when he dealt with Men of Honour; but with them a Man ought to be eternally on his Guard, and never to Eat and Drink with *Christians* without his Weapon of Defence in his Hand; and, for his own Security, never to credit one Word they spoke. As for the rashness and inconsiderateness of his Action he wou'd confess the Governor is in the right; and that he was asham'd of what he had done, in endeavoring to make those Free, who were by Nature *Slaves*, poor wretched Rogues, fit to be us'd as *Christians* Tools; Dogs, treacherous and cowardly, fit for such Masters; and they wanted only but to be whipt into the knowledge of the *Christian Gods* to be the vilest of all creeping things; to learn to Worship such Deities as had not Power to make 'em Just, Brave, or Honest. In fine, after a thousand things of this Nature, not fit here to be recited, he told *Byam*, he had rather Dye than Live upon the same Earth with such Dogs. But *Trefry* and *Byam* pleaded and protested together so much, that *Trefry* believing the *Governor* to mean what he said; and speaking very cordially himself, generously put himself into *Caesar*'s Hands, and took him aside, and perswaded him, even with Tears, to Live, by Surrendring himself, and to name his Conditions. *Caesar* was overcome by his Wit and Reasons, and in consideration of *Imoinda*; and demanding what he desir'd, and that it shou'd be ratify'd by their Hands in Writing, because he had perceiv'd that was the common way of contract between Man and Man, amongst the Whites: All this was perform'd, and *Tuscan*'s Pardon was put in, and they Surrender to the Governor, who walked peaceably down into the *Plantation* with 'em, after giving order to bury their dead. *Caesar* was very much toyl'd with the bustle of the Day; for he had fought like a Fury, and what Mischief was done he and *Tuscan* perform'd alone; and gave their Enemies a fatal Proof that they durst do any thing, and fear'd no mortal Force.

9. Settlement.

But they were no sooner arriv'd at the Place, where all the Slaves receive their Punishments of Whipping, but they laid Hands on *Caesar* and *Tuscan*, faint with heat and toyl; and, surprising them, Bound them to two several Stakes, and Whipt them in a most deplorable and inhumane Manner, rending the very Flesh from their Bones; especially *Caesar*, who was not perceiv'd to make any Moan, or to alter his Face, only to roul his Eyes on the Faithless *Governor*, and those he believ'd Guilty, with Fierceness and Indignation; and, to compleat his Rage, he saw every one of those *Slaves*, who, but a few Days before, Ador'd him as something more than Mortal, now had a Whip to give him some Lashes, while he strove not to break his Fetters; though, if he had, it were impossible: But he pronounced a Woe and Revenge from his Eyes, that darted Fire, that 'twas at once both Awful and Terrible to behold.

When they thought they were sufficiently Reveng'd on him, they unty'd him, almost Fainting, with loss of Blood, from a thousand Wounds all over his Body; from which they had rent his Cloaths, and led him Bleeding and Naked as he was; and loaded him all over with Irons; and then rubbed his Wounds, to compleat their Cruelty, with *Indian Pepper*, which had like to have made him raving Mad; and, in this Condition, made him so fast to the Ground that he cou'd not stir, if his Pains and Wounds wou'd have given him leave. They spar'd *Imoinda*, and did not let her see this Barbarity committed towards her Lord, but carry'd her down to *Parham*, and shut her up; which was not in kindness to her, but for fear she shou'd Dye with the Sight, or Miscarry; and then they shou'd lose a young *Slave*, and perhaps the Mother.

You must know, that when the News was brought on Monday Morning, that *Caesar* had betaken himself to the Woods, and carry'd with him all the *Negroes*, we were possess'd with extream Fear, which no perswasions cou'd Dissipate, that he wou'd secure himself till Night; and then, that he wou'd come down and Cut all our Throats. This apprehension made all the Females of us fly down the River, to be secur'd; and while we were away, they acted this Cruelty: For I suppose I had Authority and Interest enough there, had I suspected any such thing, to have prevented it; but we had not gone many Leagues, but the News overtook us that *Caesar* was taken, and Whipt like a common *Slave*. We met on the River with Colonel *Martin*, a Man of great Gallantry, Wit, and Goodness, and whom I have celebrated in a Character of my New *Comedy*,[1] by his own Name, in memory of so brave a Man: He was Wise and Eloquent; and, from the fineness of his Parts, bore a great Sway over the Hearts of all the *Colony*: He was a Friend to *Caesar*, and resented this false Dealing with him very much. We carried him back to *Parham*, thinking to have made an Accommodation; when we came, the First News we heard was, that the *Governor* was Dead of a Wound *Imoinda* had given him; but it was not so well; But it seems he wou'd have the Pleasure of beholding the Revenge he took on *Caesar*; and before the cruel Ceremony was finish'd, he drop'd down; and then they perceiv'd the Wound he had on his Shoulder, was by a venom'd Arrow; which, as I said, his *Indian* Mistress heal'd, by Sucking the Wound.

We were no sooner Arriv'd, but we went up to the *Plantation* to see *Caesar*, whom we found in a very Miserable and Unexpressable Condition; and I have

1. Behn's *The Younger Brother, or The Amorous Jilt*, produced in 1696.

a Thousand times admired how he liv'd, in so much tormenting Pain. We said all things to him, that Trouble, Pitty, and Good Nature cou'd suggest; Protesting our Innocency of the Fact, and our Abhorance of such Cruelties; making a Thousand Professions of Services to him, and Begging as many Pardons for the Offenders, till we said so much, that he believ'd we had no Hand in his ill Treatment; but told us, he cou'd never Pardon *Byam*; as for *Trefry*, he confess'd he saw his Grief and Sorrow, for his Suffering, which he cou'd not hinder, but was like to have been beaten down by the very *Slaves*, for Speaking in his Defence: But for *Byam*, who was their Leader, their Head;——and shou'd, by his Justice, and Honor, have been an Example to 'em,——For him, he wish'd to Live, to take a dire Revenge of him, and said, *It had been well for him, if he had Sacrific'd me, instead of giving me the contemptable Whip.* He refus'd to Talk much, but Begging us to give him our Hands, he took 'em, and Protested never to lift up his, to do us any Harm. He had a great Respect for Colonel *Martin*, and always took his Counsel, like that of a Parent; and assur'd him, he wou'd obey him in any thing, but his Revenge on *Byam*. *Therefore*, said he, *for his own Safety, let him speedily dispatch me; for if I cou'd dispatch my self, I wou'd not, till that Justice were done to my injur'd Person, and the contempt of a Souldier: No, I wou'd not kill my self, even after a Whipping, but will be content to live with that Infamy, and be pointed at by every grinning Slave, till I have compleated my Revenge; and then you shall see that* Oroonoko *scorns to live with the Indignity that was put on* Caesar. All we cou'd do cou'd get no more Words from him; and we took care to have him put immediately into a healing Bath, to rid him of his Pepper; and order'd a Chirurgeon to anoint him with healing Balm, which he suffer'd, and in some time he began to be able to Walk and Eat; we fail'd not to visit him every Day, and, to that end, had him brought to an apartment at *Parham*.

The *Governor* was no sooner recover'd, and had heard of the menaces of *Caesar*, but he call'd his Council; who (not to disgrace them, or Burlesque the Government there) consisted of such notorious Villains as *Newgate*[2] never transported; and possibly originally were such, who understood neither the Laws of *God* or *Man*; and had no sort of Principles to make 'em worthy the Name of Men: But, at the very Council Table, wou'd Contradict and Fight with one another; and Swear so bloodily that 'twas terrible to hear, and see 'em. (Some of 'em were afterwards Hang'd, when the *Dutch* took possession of the place; others sent off in Chains.) But calling these special Rulers of the Nation together, and requiring their Counsel in this weighty Affair, they all concluded, that (Damn 'em) it might be their own Cases; and that *Caesar* ought to be made an Example to all the *Negroes*, to fright 'em from daring to threaten their Betters, their Lords and Masters; and, at this rate, no Man was safe from his own *Slaves*; and concluded, *nemine contradicente*,[3] that *Caesar* shou'd be Hang'd.

Trefry then thought it time to use his Authority; and told *Byam* his Command did not extend to his Lord's *Plantation*; and that *Parham* was as much exempt from the Law as *White-hall*,[4] and that they ought no more to touch the Servants of the Lord—— (who there represented the King's Person) than they cou'd

2. The main prison in London, from where criminals were transported to the colonies.
3. With no one disagreeing (Latin).

4. The king's palace in London. Trefry is Willoughby's deputy in Parham, Byam in the colony.

those about the King himself; and that *Parham* was a Sanctuary; and though his Lord were absent in Person, his Power was still in Being there; which he had intrusted with him, as far as the Dominions of his particular *Plantations* reach'd, and all that belong'd to it; the rest of the *Country*, as *Byam* was Lieutenant to his Lord, he might exercise his Tyrany upon. *Trefry* had others as powerful, or more, that int'rested themselves in *Caesar*'s Life, and absolutely said, He shou'd be Defended. So turning the *Governor*, and his wise Council, out of Doors, (for they sate at *Parham-house*) they set a Guard upon our Landing Place, and wou'd admit none but those we call'd Friends to us and *Caesar*.

The *Governor* having remain'd wounded at *Parham*, till his recovery was compleated, *Caesar* did not know but he was still there; and indeed, for the most part, his time was spent there; for he was one that lov'd to Live at other Peoples Expence; and if he were a Day absent, he was Ten present there; and us'd to Play, and Walk, and Hunt, and Fish, with *Caesar*. So that *Caesar* did not at all doubt, if he once recover'd Strength, but he shou'd find an opportunity of being Reveng'd on him: Though, after such a Revenge, he cou'd not hope to Live; for if he escap'd the Fury of the English *Mobile*,[5] who perhaps wou'd have been glad of the occasion to have kill'd him, he was resolv'd not to survive his Whipping; yet he had, some tender Hours, a repenting Softness, which he called his fits of Coward; wherein he struggl'd with Love for the Victory of his Heart, which took part with his charming *Imoinda* there; but, for the most part, his time was past in melancholy Thought, and black Designs; he consider'd, if he shou'd do this Deed, and Dye, either in the Attempt, or after it, he left his lovely *Imoinda* a Prey, or at best a *Slave*, to the inrag'd Multitude; his great Heart cou'd not indure that Thought. *Perhaps*, said he, *she may be first Ravished by every Brute; exposed first to their nasty Lusts, and then a shameful Death*. No; he could not Live a Moment under that Apprehension, too insupportable to be born. These were his Thoughts, and his silent Arguments with his Heart, as he told us afterwards; so that now resolving not only to kill *Byam*, but all those he thought had inrag'd him; pleasing his great Heart with the fancy'd Slaughter he shou'd make over the whole Face of the *Plantation*; he first resolv'd on a Deed, that (however Horrid it at first appear'd to us all) when we had heard his Reasons, we thought it Brave and Just: Being able to Walk, and, as he believ'd, fit for the Execution of his great Design, he beg'd *Trefry* to trust him into the Air, believing a Walk wou'd do him good; which was granted him, and taking *Imoinda* with him, as he us'd to do in his more happy and calmer Days, he led her up into a Wood, where, after (with a thousand Sighs, and long Gazing silently on her Face, while Tears gusht, in spite of him, from his Eyes) he told her his Design first of Killing her, and then his Enemies, and next himself, and the impossibility of Escaping, and therefore he told her the necessity of Dying; he found the Heroick Wife faster pleading for Death than he was to propose it, when she found his fix'd Resolution; and, on her Knees, besought him, not to leave her a Prey to his Enemies. He (griev'd to Death) yet pleased at her noble Resolution, took her up, and imbracing her, with all the Passion and Languishment of a dying Lover, drew his Knife to kill this Treasure of his Soul, this Pleasure of his Eyes; while Tears trickl'd down his

5. Mob.

Cheeks, hers were Smiling with Joy she shou'd dye by so noble a Hand, and be sent in her own Country, (for that's their Notion of the next World) by him she so tenderly Lov'd, and so truly Ador'd in this; for Wives have a respect for their Husbands equal to what any other People pay a Deity; and when a Man finds any occasion to quit his Wife, if he love her, she dyes by his Hand; if not, he sells her, or suffers some other to kill her. It being thus, you may believe the Deed was soon resolv'd on; and 'tis not to be doubted, but the Parting, the eternal Leave taking of Two such Lovers, so greatly Born, so Sensible,[6] so Beautiful, so Young, and so Fond, must be very Moving, as the Relation of it was to me afterwards.

All that Love cou'd say in such cases, being ended; and all the intermitting Irresolutions being adjusted, the Lovely, Young, and Ador'd Victim lays her self down, before the Sacrificer; while he, with a Hand resolv'd, and a Heart breaking within, gave the Fatal Stroke; first, cutting her Throat, and then severing her yet Smiling Face from that Delicate Body, pregnant as it was with Fruits of tend'rest Love. As soon as he had done, he laid the Body decently on Leaves and Flowers; of which he made a Bed, and conceal'd it under the same cover-lid of Nature; only her Face he left yet bare to look on: But when he found she was Dead, and past all Retrieve, never more to bless him with her Eyes, and soft Language; his Grief swell'd up to Rage; he Tore, he Rav'd, he Roar'd, like some Monster of the Wood, calling on the lov'd Name of *Imoinda*; a thousand times he turn'd the Fatal Knife that did the Deed, toward his own Heart, with a Resolution to go immediately after her; but dire Revenge, which now was a thousand times more fierce in his Soul than before, prevents him; and he wou'd cry out, *No; since I have sacrificed* Imoinda *to my Revenge, shall I lose that Glory which I have purchas'd so dear, as at the Price of the fairest, dearest, softest Creature that ever Nature made? No, no!* Then, at her Name, Grief wou'd get the ascendant of Rage, and he wou'd lye down by her side, and water her Face with showers of Tears, which never were wont to fall from those Eyes: And however bent he was on his intended Slaughter, he had not power to stir from the Sight of this dear Object, now more Belov'd, and more Ador'd than ever.

He remain'd in this deploring Condition for two Days, and never rose from the Ground where he had made his sad Sacrifice; at last, rousing from her side, and accusing himself with living too long, now *Imoinda* was dead; and that the Deaths of those barbarous Enemies were deferr'd too long, he resolv'd now to finish the great Work; but offering to rise, he found his Strength so decay'd, that he reel'd to and fro, like Boughs assail'd by contrary Winds; so that he was forced to lye down again, and try to summons all his Courage to his Aid; he found his Brains turn round, and his Eyes were dizzy; and Objects appear'd not the same to him they were wont to do; his Breath was short; and all his Limbs surprised with a Faintness he had never felt before: He had not Eat in two Days, which was one occasion of this Feebleness, but excess of Grief was the greatest; yet still he hop'd he shou'd recover Vigour to act his Design; and lay expecting it yet six Days longer; still mourning over the dead Idol of his Heart, and striving every Day to rise, but cou'd not.

6. Sensitive.

In all this time you may believe we were in no little affliction for *Caesar*, and his Wife; some were of Opinion he was escap'd never to return; others thought some Accident had hap'ned to him: But however, we fail'd not to send out an hundred People several ways to search for him; a Party, of about forty, went that way he took; among whom was *Tuscan*, who was perfectly reconcil'd to *Byam*; they had not go very far into the Wood, but they smelt an unusual Smell, as of a dead Body; for Stinks must be very noisom that can be distinguish'd among such a quantity of Natural Sweets, as every Inch of that Land produces. So that they concluded they shou'd find him dead, or somebody that was so; they past on towards it, as Loathsom as it was, and made such a rustling among the Leaves that lye thick on the Ground, by continual Falling, that *Caesar* heard he was approach'd; and though he had, during the space of these eight Days, endeavor'd to rise, but found he wanted Strength, yet looking up, and seeing his Pursuers, he rose, and reel'd to a Neighbouring Tree, against which he fix'd his Back; and being within a dozen Yards of those that advanc'd, and saw him, he call'd out to them, and bid them approach no nearer, if they wou'd be safe: So that they stood still, and hardly believing their Eyes, that wou'd perswade them that it was *Caesar* that spoke to 'em, so much was he alter'd, they ask'd him, What he had done with his Wife? for they smelt a Stink that almost struck them dead. He, pointing to the dead Body, sighing, cry'd, *Behold her there*; they put off the Flowers that cover'd her with their Sticks, and found she was kill'd; and cry'd out, *Oh monster! that hast murther'd thy Wife*: Then asking him, Why he did so cruel a Deed? He replied, he had no leasure to answer impertinent Questions; *You may go back*, continued he, *and tell the Faithless Governor, he may thank Fortune that I am breathing my last; and that my Arm is too feeble to obey my Heart, in what it had design'd him*: But his Tongue faultering, and trembling, he cou'd scarce end what he was saying. The *English* taking Advantage by his Weakness, cry'd, *Let us take him alive by all means*: He heard 'em; and, as if he had reviv'd from a Fainting, or a Dream, he cry'd out, *No, Gentlemen, you are deceiv'd; you will find no more Caesars to be Whipt; no more find a Faith in me: Feeble as you think me, I have Strength yet left to secure me from a second Indignity*. They swore all a-new, and he only shook his Head, and beheld them with Scorn; then they cry'd out, *Who will venture on this single Man? Will no body?* They stood all silent while *Caesar* replied, *Fatal will be the Attempt to the first Adventurer; let him assure himself*, and, at that Word, held up his Knife in a menacing Posture, *Look ye, ye faithless Crew*, said he, *'tis not Life I seek, nor am I afraid of Dying*; and, at that Word, cut a piece of Flesh from his own Throat, and threw it at 'em, *yet still I wou'd Live if I cou'd, till I had perfected my Revenge. But oh! it cannot be; I feel Life gliding from my Eyes and Heart; and, if I make not haste, I shall yet fall a Victim to the shameful Whip*. At that, he rip'd up his own Belly; and took his Bowels and pull'd 'em out, with what Strength he cou'd; while some, on their Knees imploring, besought him to hold his Hand. But when they saw him tottering, they cry'd out, *Will none venture on him?* A bold *English* cry'd, *Yes, if he were the Devil*; (taking Courage when he saw him almost Dead) and swearing a horrid Oath for his farewell to the World, he rush'd on; *Caesar*, with his Arm'd Hand met him so fairly, as stuck him to the Heart, and he fell Dead at his Feet. *Tuscan* seeing that, cry'd out, *I love thee, oh* Caesar; *and therefore will not let thee Dye, if possible*: And, running to him, took him in his Arms; but, at the same time, warding a Blow that *Caesar* made at his Bosom, he receiv'd it quite through his Arm; and *Caesar* having not the Strength to pluck the Knife forth, though he attempted it, *Tuscan* neither pull'd it out himself, nor suffer'd it to be pull'd out; but came down with it sticking in his Arm; and the reason he gave for it was, because the Air shou'd not get into the Wound: They put their Hands a-cross, and carried *Caesar* between Six of 'em, fainted as he was; and they thought Dead, or just Dying; and they brought him to *Parham*, and laid him on a Couch, and had the Chirurgeon immediately to him, who drest his Wounds, and sew'd up his Belly, and us'd means to bring him to Life, which they effected. We ran all to see him; and, if before we thought him so beautiful a Sight, he was now so alter'd, that his Face was like a Death's Head black'd over; nothing but Teeth, and Eyeholes: For some Days we suffer'd no body to speak to him, but caused Cordials to be poured down his Throat, which sustained his Life; and in six or seven Days he recover'd his Senses: For, you must know, that Wounds are almost to a Miracle cur'd in the *Indies*; unless Wounds in the Legs, which rarely ever cure.

When he was well enough to speak, we talk'd to him; and ask'd him some Questions about his Wife, and the Reasons why he kill'd her; and he then told us what I have related of that Resolution, and of his Parting; and he besought us, we would let him Dye, and was extreamly Afflicted to think it was possible he might Live; he assur'd us, if we did not Dispatch him, he wou'd prove very Fatal to a great many. We said all we cou'd to make him Live, and gave him new Assurances; but he begg'd we wou'd not think so poorly of him, or of his love to *Imoinda*, to imagine we cou'd Flatter him to Life again; but the Chirurgeon assur'd him, he cou'd not Live, and therefore he need not Fear. We were all (but *Caesar*) afflicted at this News; and the Sight was gashly;[7] his Discourse was sad; and the earthly Smell about him so strong, that I was perswaded to leave the Place for some time (being my self but Sickly, and very apt to fall into Fits of dangerous Illness upon any extraordinary Melancholy); the Servants, and *Trefry*, and the Chirurgeons, promis'd all to take what possible care they cou'd of the Life of *Caesar*; and I, taking Boat, went with other Company to Colonel *Martin*'s, about three Days Journy down the River; but I was no sooner gon, but the *Governor* taking *Trefry*, about some pretended earnest Business, a Days Journy up the River; having communicated his Design to one *Banister*,[8] a wild *Irish* Man, and one of the Council; a Fellow of absolute Barbarity, and fit to execute any Villany, but was Rich. He came up to *Parham*, and forcibly took *Caesar*, and had him carried to the same Post where he was Whip'd; and causing him to be ty'd to it, and a great Fire made before him, he told him, he shou'd Dye like a Dog, as he was. *Caesar* replied, this was the first piece of Bravery that ever *Banister* did; and he never spoke Sense till he pronounc'd that Word; and, if he wou'd keep it, he wou'd declare, in the other World, that he was the only Man, of all the Whites, that ever he heard speak Truth. And turning to the Men that bound him, he said, *My Friends, am I to Dye, or to be Whip'd? And they cry'd, Whip'd! no; you shall not*

---

7. Ghastly.
8. James Banister was the deputy governor in

1688, when Surinam was turned over to the Dutch.

escape so well: And then he replied, smiling, *A Blessing on thee*; and assur'd them, they need not tye him, for he wou'd stand fixt, like a Rock; and indure Death so as shou'd encourage them to Dye. *But if you Whip me*, said he, *be sure you tye me fast.*

He had learn'd to take Tobaco; and when he was assur'd he should Dye, he desir'd they would give him a Pipe in his Mouth, ready Lighted, which they did; and the Executioner came, and first cut off his Members[9] and threw them into the Fire; after that, with an ill-favoured Knife, they cut his Ears, and his Nose, and burn'd them; he still Smoak'd on, as if nothing had touch'd him; then they hack'd off one of his Arms, and still he bore up, and held his Pipe; but at the cutting off the other Arm, his Head sunk, and his Pipe drop'd; and he gave up the Ghost, without a Groan, or a Reproach. My Mother and Sister were by him all the while, but not suffer'd to save him; so rude and wild were the Rabble, and so inhumane were the Justices, who stood by to see the Execution, who after paid dearly enough for their Insolence. They cut *Caesar* in Quarters, and sent them to several of the chief *Plantations*: One Quarter was sent to Colonel *Martin*, who refus'd it; and swore, he had rather see the Quarters of *Banister*, and the *Governor* himself, than those of *Caesar*, on his *Plantations*; and that he cou'd govern his *Negroes* without Terrifying and Grieving them with frightful Spectacles of a mangl'd King.

Thus Dy'd this Great Man; worthy of a better Fate, and a more sublime Wit than mine to write his Praise; yet, I hope, the Reputation of my Pen is considerable enough to make his Glorious Name to survive to all Ages; with that of the Brave, the Beautiful, and the Constant *Imoinda*.

FINIS.

9. Genitals.

SOR JUANA INÉS DE LA CRUZ
1648–1695

S or [Sister] Juana, a nun from New Spain (colonial Mexico), was one of the most famous writers of her time, celebrated as the "Tenth Muse" in Europe and the Americas. She is best known for her spirited defense of women's intellectual rights in her *Response of the Poet to the Very Eminent Sor Filotea de la Cruz*. While ostensibly declaring her humility and her religious subordination in this text (note her respectful address in the very title), Sor Juana also manages to advance claims for her sex that are more far-reaching and profound than any previously offered, painting a passionate yet nuanced picture of the life of the mind that combines rhetorical precision and intense emotion. At the same time, she puts New Spain on the literary map, introducing in her writing a distinctive American sensibility.

Born illegitimate to an upper-class creole woman and a Spanish captain, Sor Juana learned to read in her grandfather's library. Despite ongoing tensions among Spaniards, creoles, and the indigenous population, Sor Juana's Mexico was a huge metropolis with a lively artistic and intellectual scene centered around the viceregal court. As a young girl, Juana served as lady-in-waiting at the court, before entering the Convent of Saint Jerome when she was eighteen. Her *Response* suggests that she became a nun in search of a safe environment in which to pursue her intellectual interests, and her religious vocation did not prevent her from writing in secular forms—lyric poetry and drama—for which she became known throughout the Spanish-speaking world. She wrote sixty-five sonnets, over sixty *romances* (ballads), and a profusion of poems in other metrical forms. She also wrote for the stage, producing everything from comedies and farces to *autos sacramentales*, religious plays that marked Catholic holidays.

Because Sor Juana's religious superiors rebuked her worldly interests, however, she struggled to continue writing secular literature without abandoning her faith. The natural disturbances and disasters that plagued Mexico City in the 1690s—a solar eclipse, storms, and famine—and the departure of some of her key supporters rekindled her religious passions and led her in 1694 to reaffirm her faith in a formal statement that she signed in her own blood with the words, "I, Sor Juana Inés de la Cruz, the worst of all." She died soon after,

while nursing the convent sick during an epidemic.

The *Response* stems directly from Sor Juana's venture into theological polemic. In 1690, she wrote a commentary on a sermon delivered forty years earlier, on the nature of Christ's love toward humanity. Her commentary, in the form of a letter, was published without her consent by the bishop of Puebla. The bishop provided the title, *Athenagoric Letter,* and also prefixed his own letter to Sor Juana, signed with the pseudonym "Filotea de la Cruz." In the letter, one "nun" advises the other to focus her attention and her talents on religious matters. In her *Response* (1691), Sor Juana nominally accepts the bishop's rebuke; the smooth surface of her elegant prose, however, conceals both rage and determination to assert her right—and that of other women—to a fully realized life of the mind.

The artistry of this piece of self-defense demonstrates Sor Juana's powers and thus constitutes part of her justification. While asserting her own unimportance, she illustrates the range of her knowledge and of her rhetorical skill. The sheer abundance of her biblical allusions and quotations from theological texts, for instance, proves that she has mastered a large body of religious material and that she has not sacrificed religious to secular study. Her elaborate protestations of deference, her vocabulary of insignificance, and her narrative of subservience all show the verbal dexterity that enables her to achieve her own rhetorical ends even as she denies her commitment to purely personal goals. No matter how often Sor Juana admits that her intellectual longings amount to a form of "vice," she embodies in her prose the energy and the vividness that they generate.

Her larger argument depends on her utter denial that intelligence or a thirst for knowledge should be attributed to only one gender. While she draws on history for evidence of female intellectual power, even more forceful is the testimony of her own experience: her account of how, deprived of books, she finds matter for intellectual inquiry everywhere—in the yolk of an egg, the spinning of a top, the reading of the Bible. If she arouses uneasiness when she implicitly equates herself, as object of persecution, with Christ, she also makes one feel directly the horror of women's official exclusion, in the past, from intellectual pursuits.

From Response of the Poet to the Very Eminent Sor Filotea de la Cruz[1]

Very eminent lady, my señora:

Neither my will nor scant health nor reasonable apprehension has delayed my response for so many days. Is it any surprise that my dull pen stumbled over two impossibilities at its first step? The first (and for me the more severe) is how to respond to your most learned, most prudent, most saintly, and most loving letter. For if the Angelic Doctor of the Schools, Saint Thomas, when questioned regarding his silence in the presence of Albertus Magnus,[2] his teacher, replied that he was silent because he could find nothing to say worthy of Albertus, with how much more reason should I be silent, not, like the saint, out of humility, but because in reality, I know nothing worthy of you. The second impossibility is how to thank you for the favor, as unwarranted as it was unexpected, of having my rough scribblings printed; a good turn so immeasurable that it surpasses the most ambitious hope and most fantastic desire, which could find no place, even as a rational concept,[3] in my thoughts; in short, it is of such magnitude that it not only cannot be reduced to the limits of words but exceeds the capacity of gratitude, as much for its dimensions as for how unforeseen it was, for as Quintilian said: *Hopes give rise to the lesser glory, benefits to the greater.*[4] So much so that they silence the beneficiary.

When the happily barren, only to be made miraculously fruitful, mother of the Baptist saw so magnificent a visitor as the Mother of the Word in her house, her understanding became clouded and her speech failed, and so

---

1. Notes in these selections include those of Edith Grossman, the translator, and Anna More, the editor of *Sor Juana Inés de la Cruz: Selected Works: A Norton Critical Edition.*
2. Albertus Magnus (ca. 1200–1280) was Saint Thomas's teacher at the University of Paris. "The Angelic Doctor": a common epithet for Saint Thomas Aquinas (ca. 1225–1274), author of the *Summa Theologica* and other works that adapted Aristotelian metaphysics to Christian theology and dogma.

3. Sor Juana uses the Spanish translation of the scholastic term *ens rationis,* or an abstract object of understanding with no real presence outside of the mind.
4. Marcus Fabius Quintilianus (35–ca. 96 C.E.), a Roman rhetorician and author of the influential *Institutio oratoria* (ca. 95 C.E.) outlining the principles of rhetoric. Throughout, Latin phrases in the text will be translated and italicized.

instead of thanks she burst into doubts and questions: *Et unde hoc mihi? From whence comes such a thing to me?*[5] The same occurred to Saul when he found himself elected and anointed king of Israel: *Am I not a son of Jemini of the least tribe of Israel, and my kindred the last among all the families of the tribe of Benjamin? Wherefore then hast thou spoken this word to me?*[6] And so say I: from whence, illustrious señora, from whence comes so great a favor to me? Am I by chance anything more than a poor nun, the most insignificant creature in the world and the least worthy of your attention? *Wherefore then speakest thou so to me? From whence comes such a thing to me?*

To the first impossibility I can respond only that I am unworthy of your eyes, and to the second I cannot respond with anything other than exclamations, not thanks, saying that I am not capable of offering you even the smallest portion of the gratitude I owe you. It is not false modesty, señora, but the candid truth of all my soul, that when the letter your eminence called *Athenagoric*[7] reached me, I burst (although this does not come easily to me) into tears of confusion, because it seemed that your favor was nothing more than a reproach from God for how poorly I meet His expectations; while He corrects others with punishments, He wants to reduce me by means of benefits. A special favor, for which I know I am in His debt, as I am for other infinite benefits from His immense kindness, but also a special mode of shaming and confusing me: for it is a more exquisite method of punishment to have me, with my knowledge, serve as the judge who sentences and condemns my own ingratitude. When I ponder this, here in solitude, I often say: *Lord may You be blessed, for You not only did not wish any other creature to judge me, and did not give me that responsibility either, but kept it for Yourself and freed me from me and the sentence I would have given myself—which, compelled by my own knowledge, could not be less than condemnation—and reserved that for Your mercy, because You love me more that I can love myself.*

Señora, forgive the digression that the power of truth demanded of me, and if I must confess the whole truth, this is also a search for havens to escape the difficulty of responding, and I almost decided to leave everything in silence, but since this is negative, although it explains a great deal with the emphasis on not explaining, it is necessary to add a brief explanation so that what one wishes the silence to say is understood; if not, the silence will say nothing, because that is its proper occupation: saying nothing. The sacred chosen vessel was carried away to the third heaven, and having seen the arcane secrets of God, the text says: *He . . . heard secret words, which it is not granted to man to utter.*[8] It does not say

5. Luke 1:43. The phrase was uttered by Elizabeth, cousin of the Virgin Mary and mother of John the Baptist, a birth considered a miracle because of Elizabeth's advanced age. In an event known as the Visitation, her pregnancy was announced when the Virgin Mary visited her cousin and the child leapt in Elizabeth's womb.
6. 1 Samuel 9:21. The response of Saul to Samuel's prophecy that he will be the first king of Israel.

7. When the Bishop Manuel Fernández de Santa Cruz published Sor Juana's critique in 1690, he titled it *Athenagoric Letter*. While for many years it was assumed that "Athenagoric" referred to "Athena," rendering the translation "Letter Worthy of Athena," it likely refers to Athenagoras, the author of an *Apologia* (177 C.E.) defending Christianity against pagan accusations.
8. 2 Corinthians 12:4.

what he saw but says that he cannot say; and so it is necessary at least to say that those things that cannot be said cannot be said, so it is understood that being silent does not mean having nothing to say, but that the great deal there is to say cannot be said in words. Saint John says that if all the miracles performed by Our Redeemer were to be written down, the entire world could not hold the books;[9] and Vieira states that the Evangelist says more in just this passage than in everything else he wrote; the Lusitanian Phoenix, speaks very well (but when does he not speak well, even when he does not speak well?),[1] because here Saint John says everything he did not say and expressed what he did not express. And I, señora, will respond only that I do not know how to respond, will only give thanks, saying I am not capable of giving thanks to you, and will say, as a brief explanation of what I leave to silence, that only with the confidence of a favored woman and the benefits of an honored one can I dare speak to your excellency. If this is foolishness, forgive it, for it is a jewel of good fortune, and in it I will provide more material for your kindness, and you will give greater form to my gratitude.

Because he stammered, Moses did not think he was worthy to speak to the Pharaoh, and afterward, finding himself so favored by God fills him with so much courage that he not only speaks to God Himself but dares ask Him for impossibilities: *Shew me thy face.*[2] And I too, señora, no longer think impossible what I wrote at the beginning, in view of how you favor me; because the person who had the letter printed without my knowledge, who gave it a title and paid for it, who honored it so greatly (since it is entirely unworthy both for its own sake and the sake of its author), what will she not do, what will she not pardon, what will she cease doing, and what will she cease pardoning? And so, under the assumption that I speak with the safe-conduct of your favors and under the protection of your kindness, and your having, like another Ahasuerus, given me the tip of the golden scepter of your affection to kiss as a sign of granting me benevolent license to speak[3] and propound in your illustrious presence, I say that I receive in my soul your most saintly admonition to turn my studies to sacred books, which although this comes in the guise of advice will have for me the substance of a precept, with the not insignificant consolation that even earlier it seems my obedience foresaw your pastoral suggestion, as well as your guidance, inferred from the subject and proofs of the same letter. I know very well that your most sage warning is not directed at it[4] but at how much you have seen of my writings on human affairs; and so what I have said is only to satisfy you with regard to the lack of application you have inferred

---

9. John 21:25.

1. António Vieira; "Lusitanian" is Portuguese, and a "phoenix" is a remarkable person. Sor Juana herself was called the "Mexican Phoenix." The citation is from his "Sermon of Our Lady of Peñafrancia" preached in 1652: "*Pergunto agora: Em que disse mais S. João: em estas duas ultimas regras ou em todo seu Evangelho?*" (I ask now: In which did Saint John say more: in these last two lines or in his entire gospel?)

2. Found in the Song of Solomon 2:14. Sor Juana combines various biblical passages to come to this conclusion. Moses's stutter is mentioned in Exodus 4:10. In Exodus 33:18, Moses says "shew me thy glory."

3. Esther 5:2. The Persian king Ahasuerus gave Esther permission to speak by holding out his golden scepter for her to touch.

4. That is, the bishop's reprimand does not refer to the contents of the *Athenagoric Letter*, which are theological.

(and rightly so) from other writings of mine. And speaking more specifically I confess, with the candor that is owed you and with the truth and clarity that in me are always natural and customary, that my not having written a great deal about sacred matters has been due not to defiance or lack of application but to an abundance of the fear and reverence owed to those sacred letters, for whose comprehension I know myself highly incapable and for whose handling I am highly unworthy; resounding always in my ears, with no small horror, is the Lord's warning and prohibition to sinners like me: *Why dost thou declare my justices, and take my covenant in thy mouth?*[5] My great father Saint Jerome confirms this question, and that even learned men are forbidden to read the Song of Solomon and even Genesis before the age of thirty (the latter because of its obscurity, the former so that impru-dent youth will not use the sweetness of those nuptial songs as an excuse to alter their meaning to carnal love), by ordering that it be the last book studied, for the same reason: *At the end one may read, without danger, the Song of Songs; for if it is read at the beginning, when one does not under-stand the epithalamium to the spiritual marriage beneath the carnal words, one may suffer harm;*[6] and Seneca says: *In the early years, faith is not bright.*[7] Then how would I dare hold it in my unworthy hands, when it is in conflict with my sex, my age, and especially, my customs? And so I confess that often this fear has removed the pen from my hand and made subjects withdraw into the same understanding from which they wished to emerge; this difficulty was not encountered in profane subjects, for a heresy against art is punished not by the Holy Office[8] but by the prudent with laughter and the critics with condemnation; and this, *just or unjust, there is no rea-son to fear it,*[9] for one can still take Communion and hear Mass and there-fore it concerns me very little or not at all; because according to the same opinion of those who cast aspersions, I have no obligation to know and no aptitude for being correct; therefore, if I err there is no blame and no dis-credit. There is no blame because I have no obligation; there is no discredit because I have no possibility of being correct, and *no one is obliged to undertake impossible things.*[1] And, truly, I have never written except reluc-tantly, when I was forced to, and only to please others; not only with no gratification but with positive repugnance, for I have never judged myself to possess the abundance of letters and intelligence demanded by the obliga-tion of one who writes; and so my usual reply to those who urge me to write, especially if the subject is sacred: "What understanding, what stud-ies, what materials, what rudimentary knowledge do I possess for this other than some superficial nonsense? Leave this for someone who under-stands it, for I wish no quarrel with the Holy Office, for I am ignorant and terrified of stating an offensive proposition or twisting the genuine signifi-

---

5. Psalm 50:16.
6. Saint Jerome, *To Laeta, Upon the Educa-tion of Her Daughter.*
7. The 1700 edition of the "Response" incor-rectly attributes this to *De beneficiis* (On Kind-ness) by Lucius Annaeus Seneca (ca. 4 B.C.E.–65 C.E.). It is from *Octavia* 1.538, a play most likely incorrectly attributed to Sen-eca, and the wording differs slightly from Sor

Juana's original.
8. The Spanish Inquisition.
9. A citation from the *Decretum*, a collection of rules and regulations of the Church, com-piled in 1140 by the Benedictine monk Gra-tian, C.11.3.1.
1. One of Boniface VIII's rules of canon law, in his *Regulae iuris* (*Sext.* V. 6).

cance of some passage. I do not study to write, much less to teach (which would be excessive pride in me), but only to see whether by studying I will be less ignorant." This is how I respond and how I feel.

Writing has never been by my own volition but at the behest of others; for I could truthfully say to them: *Ye have compelled me.*[2] A truth I will not deny (one, because it is widely known, and two, because even if used against me, God has favored me with a great love of the truth) is that ever since the first light of reason struck me, my inclination toward letters has been so strong and powerful that neither the reprimands of others—I have had many—nor my own reflections—I have engaged in more than a few—have sufficed to make me abandon this natural impulse that God placed in me: His Majesty knows why and to what end; and He knows I have asked Him to dim the light of my understanding, leaving only enough for me to obey His Law, for anything else is too much in a woman, according to some; there are even those who say it does harm. Almighty God knows too that when I did not obtain this, I attempted to bury my understanding along with my name and sacrifice it to the One who gave it to me; for no other reason did I enter a convent, although the spiritual exercises and companionship of a community were incompatible with the freedom and quiet my studious intentions demanded; the Lord knows, as does the only one in the world who had to know, that once in the community I attempted to hide my name but was not permitted to, for it was said it was a temptation; and it would have been. If I could pay you, señora, something of what I owe you, I believe I could only pay you in full by telling you this, for I have never spoken of it except to the one who had to hear it.[3] But having opened wide the doors of my heart to you, revealing its deepest secrets, I want you to find my confidence worthy of what I owe to your illustrious person and excessive favors.

I

Continuing the narration of my inclination,[4] about which I want to give you a complete account, I say that before I was three years old my mother sent an older sister of mine to learn to read in one of the primary schools for girls called *Friends*,[5] and, led by affection and mischief, I followed after her; and seeing that she was being taught a lesson, I was so set ablaze by the desire to know how to read that in the belief I was deceiving her, I told the teacher my mother wanted her to give me a lesson too. She did not believe it, because it was not believable, but to go along with the joke, she taught me. I continued to go and she continued to teach me, in earnest now, because with experience she realized the truth; and I learned to read in so short a time that I already knew how when my mother found out, for the teacher hid it from her in order to give her complete gratification and receive her reward at the same time; and I kept silent believing I would

2. 2 Corinthians 12:11.
3. I.e., her confessor.
4. In Thomist teachings, a reference to a natural instinct teleologically oriented toward a divine end. This begins the section in which

Sor Juana will describe her natural instinct to study such a divine impulse.
5. Primary schools for girls, called so after the school mistresses.

be whipped for having done this without her knowledge. The woman who taught me is still alive (may God keep her), and she can testify to this.

I remember at this time, my appetite being what is usual at that age, I abstained from eating cheese because I had heard it made people stupid, and my desire to learn was stronger in me than the desire to eat, despite this being so powerful in children. Later, when I was six or seven years old and already knew how to read and write, along with all the other skills pertaining to sewing and needlework learned by women, I heard there was a university and schools in Mexico City where sciences were studied; as soon as I heard this I began to pester my mother with insistent, inopportune pleas that she send me, dressed as a boy, to the home of some relatives she had in Mexico City, so I could study and attend classes at the university;[6] she refused, and rightly so, but I satisfied my desire by reading many different books owned by my grandfather, and there were not enough punishments and reprimands to stop me, so that when I came to Mexico City, people were surprised not so much by my intelligence as by my memory and the knowledge I possessed at an age when it seemed I had barely had enough time to learn to speak.

I began to learn Latin and believe I had fewer than twenty lessons; my seriousness was so intense that since the natural adornment of hair is so admired in women—especially in the flower of one's youth—I would cut off four to six inches, first measuring how long it was and then imposing on myself the rule that if, when it had grown back, I did not know whatever I had proposed to learn while it was growing, I would cut it again as a punishment for my stupidity. And when it grew back and I did not know what I had determined to learn, because my hair grew quickly and I learned slowly, then in fact I did cut it as punishment for my stupidity, for it did not seem right for my head to be dressed in hair when it was so bare of knowledge, which was a more desirable adornment. I entered the convent although I knew the situation had certain characteristics (I speak of secondary qualities, not formal ones) incompatible with my character, but considering the total antipathy I had toward matrimony, the convent was the least disproportionate and most honorable decision I could make to provide the certainty I desired for my salvation, and the first (and in the end the most important) obstacle to overcome was to relinquish all the minor defects in my character, such as wanting to live alone, and not wanting any obligatory occupation that would limit the freedom of my studies, or the noise of a community that would interfere with the tranquil silence of my books. These made me hesitate somewhat in my determination, until learned persons enlightened me, saying they were a temptation, which I overcame with Divine Grace and entered into the state I so unworthily am in now. I thought I would flee myself, but I, poor wretch, brought myself with me as well as this inclination, my greatest enemy (I cannot determine whether Heaven gave it to me as a gift or a punishment), for when it was dimmed or interfered with by the many spiritual exercises present in the religious life, it exploded in me like gunpowder, proof in my own person that *privation is the cause of appetite*.

---

6. During childhood, Sor Juana lived on the outskirts of Mexico City. The Royal and Pontifical University of Mexico, founded in 1551, was restricted to male students.

I returned to (no, I am wrong, for I never stopped): I mean to say I continued my studious effort (which for me was repose whenever I had time away from my obligations) to read and read some more, to study and study some more, with no teacher other than the books themselves. I learned how difficult it is to study those soulless characters without the living voice and explanations of a teacher; yet I gladly endured all this work for the sake of my love of letters. Oh, if it had only been for the sake of my love of God, which is the correct love, how meritorious it would have been! I did attempt to elevate it as much as I could and turn it to His service, because the goal to which I aspired was the study of theology, for, being Catholic, it seemed a foolish lack in me not to know everything that can be learned in this life, by natural means, about the Divine Mysteries; and being a nun and not a layperson, according to my ecclesiastical state I should profess vows to letters, and even more so, as a daughter of a Saint Jerome and a Saint Paula, for it seemed a deterioration if such learned parents produced an idiot child.[7] I proposed this to myself and it seemed correct, if it was not (and this is most likely) flattery and applause of my own inclination, its enjoyment being proposed as an obligation.

In this way I proceeded, always directing the steps of my study to the summit of sacred theology, as I have said; and to reach it, I thought it necessary to ascend by the steps of human sciences and arts, because how is one to understand the style of the queen of sciences without knowing that of the handmaidens?[8] How, without logic, was I to know the general and particular methods used in the writing of Holy Scripture? How, without rhetoric, would I understand its figures, tropes, and locutions? How, without physics, comprehend the many inherent questions concerning the nature of the animals used for sacrifices, in which so many stated subjects, as well as many others that are undeclared, are symbolized? How to know whether Saul healing at the sound of David's harp came from the virtue and natural power of music or the supernatural ability God wished to place in David?[9] How, without arithmetic, understand so many computations of years, days, months, hours, and weeks as mysterious as those in Daniel,[1] and others for whose deciphering one must know the natures, concordances, and properties of numbers? How, without geometry, can one measure the Holy Ark of the Covenant and the holy city of Jerusalem, whose mysterious measurements form a cube with all its dimensions, a marvelous proportional distribution of all its parts?[2] How, without architecture, fathom the great temple of Solomon, where God Himself was the artificer, conceiving the proportion and design, and the wise king merely the overseer who executed it;[3] where there was no base without a mystery, no column without a symbol,

---

7. Sor Juana argues that as a Hieronymite nun she should be additionally bound to study. Saint Jerome (ca. 347–420 C.E.), the founder of her order, was one of the four doctors of the Church and author of the Vulgate Bible. "Saint Paula": Jerome's student and co-patron of the Hieronymite convent in Mexico City. "Idiot": a reference to ignorance, especially of Latin.
8. Seven liberal arts, although Sor Juana adds physics (Aristotelian natural philosophy), architecture, and history to the list of grammar, logic, rhetoric, geometry, arithmetic, music, and astronomy. "Queen of sciences": theology

(sciences referring to "knowledge")
9. 1 Samuel 16:23 describes how Saul, the first king of Israel, was healed from evil spirits by the sound of the harp of David, a young soldier and future king of Israel.
1. Daniel 9:24–27.
2. Exodus 26:15–30 relates the dimensions of the Holy Ark of the Covenant, the chest that held the tablets of the Ten Commandments.
3. 1 Kings 6:2–3 relates the dimensions of the Temple of Solomon, the first temple on Mount Zion.

no cornice without an allusion, no architrave without a meaning, and so on in all its parts, so that even the smallest fillet was placed not for the service and complement of art alone but to symbolize greater things? How, without great knowledge of the rules and parts that constitute history, can the historical books[4] be understood? Those recapitulations in which what happened earlier often is placed later in the narration and seems to have occurred afterward? How, without great familiarity with both kinds of law, can one apprehend the legal books?[5] How, without great erudition, approach so many matters of profane history mentioned in Holy Scripture, so many Gentile customs, so many rites, so many ways of speaking? How, without many rules and much reading of the Holy Fathers,[6] can one grasp the obscure expression of the prophets? And without being very expert in music, how are we to understand the musical proportions and their beauty found in so many places, especially in the petition of Abraham to God on behalf of the cities,[7] that He spare them if He found fifty righteous men, and from this number he went down to forty-five, which is a *sesquinona*, going from *mi* to *re*; and from here to forty, which is a *sesquioctava*,[8] going from *re* to *ut*;[9] from here to thirty which is a *sesquitertia*, a *diatessaron*; from here to twenty, which is the *sesquialtera* proportion, a *diapente*; from here to ten, which is the dupla, a *diapason*; and since there are no other harmonic intervals, he went no further? Well, how could one understand this without music? In the Book of Job, God says: *Shalt thou be able to join together the shining stars the Pleiades, or canst thou stop the turning about of Arcturus?*[1] *Canst thou bring forth the day star in its time and make the evening star to rise upon the children of the earth?*[2] The terms, without knowledge of astronomy, would be impossible to comprehend. And not only these noble sciences, but there is no mechanical art that is not mentioned. In short, it is the book that encompasses all books, and the science that includes all sciences, which are useful for its understanding: even after learning all of them (which clearly is not easy, or even possible), another consideration demands more than all that has been said, and that is constant prayer and purity in one's life, in order to implore God for the purification of spirit and enlightenment of mind necessary for comprehending these lofty matters; if this is lacking, the rest is useless.

The Church says these words regarding the angelic doctor Saint Thomas: *When he read the most difficult passages of Holy Scripture, he combined fasting with prayer. And he would say to his companion, Brother Reginald, that all he knew was not due to study or his own labor, but that he had received it from God.*[3] And I, so distant from virtue and from letters, how was I to have the courage to write? Therefore, having attained a few elementary skills, I continually studied a

---

4. The historical books of the Old Testament (Joshua, Judges, Samuel, Kings, and Chronicles).
5. The books of the law in the Bible are the first five, or Pentateuch, (Genesis, Exodus, Numbers, Deuteronomy, Leviticus). Law was divided into civil (state) and canon (Church).
6. Patristic authorities, such as the Apostles, the Apostolic Fathers, and the Doctors of the Church (Ambrose, Augustine, Gregory I, and Jerome), whose interpretations of the Bible were considered authoritative.
7. Sodom and Gomorrah (Genesis 18:24–32).

8. A major whole tone or major second. "Sesquinona": a minor whole tone or minor second.
9. Sor Juana refers here to the intervals of classical music theory.
1. A bright star. "Pleiades": open star cluster in Taurus named after the seven daughters of the titan Atlas.
2. Job 38:31–32. "Day star": Venus. "Evening star": Mercury.
3. *Roman Breviary*, Office of the Feast of Saint Thomas Aquinas, March 7, Fifth Lesson.

variety of subjects, not having an inclination toward one in particular but toward all of them in general; as a consequence, having studied some more than others has not been by choice but because, by chance, I had access to more books about those subjects, which created the preference more than any decision of mine. And since I had no special interest that moved me, and no time limit that restricted my continuing to study one subject because of the demands of formal classes, I could study a variety of subjects or abandon some for others, although I did observe a certain order, for some I called study and others diversion, and with these I rested from the first, with the result that I have studied many subjects and know nothing, because some have interfered with my learning others. True, I say this regarding the practical aspect of those subjects that have one, because it is obvious that while one moves a pen, the compass does nothing, and while one plays the harp, the organ is silent, and so on; because since a great deal of physical practice is necessary to acquire a practical skill, the person who is divided among various exercises can never achieve perfection; but the opposite happens in formal and speculative areas, and I would like to persuade everyone with my experience that this not only does not interfere but helps, for one subject illuminates and opens a path in another by means of variations and hidden connections—placed in this universal chain by the wisdom of its Author—so that it seems they correspond and are joined with admirable unity and harmony.

* * *

I confess I find myself very far from the boundaries of wisdom and have wanted to follow it, although at a distance. Yet this has brought me closer to the fire of persecution, the crucible of torment, to the extent that some have requested that I be forbidden to study.

This once was achieved by a very saintly, very ingenuous mother superior who believed that study was a matter for the Inquisition and ordered me to stop. I obeyed (for the three months her power to command lasted) in that I did not pick up a book, but not studying at all, which is not in my power, I could not do, because although I did not study books, I studied all the things God created, and these were my letters, and my book was the entire mechanism of the universe. I saw nothing without reflecting on it, heard nothing without considering it, even the smallest material things, for there is no creature, no matter how low, in which one does not recognize *God created me*, none that does not astonish the understanding, if one considers it as one should. And so, I repeat, I looked at and admired everything; as a consequence, even the people to whom I spoke, and the things they said to me, gave rise to a thousand considerations: What is the origin of the varieties of intelligence and wit, since we are all one species? What could be the temperaments and hidden qualities that caused them? If I saw a figure, I would combine the proportion of its lines and measure it with my understanding and reduce it to other, different figures. I would walk sometimes in the front part of our dormitory (which is a very spacious room) and observe that while the lines of its two sides were parallel and the ceiling level, the eye made it seem that its lines inclined toward each other and the ceiling was lower at a distance than nearby, and from this I inferred that visual lines run straight, not parallel, but form a pyramidal shape instead. And I wondered whether this might be the reason the ancients were obliged to doubt the world was round. Because although it seems so, our sight could deceive us, showing concavities where there might not be any.

I notice everything in this manner and always have and have no control over it; in fact it tends to annoy me, for it wearies my head; I thought this, and composing verses, happened to everyone, until experience showed me the contrary; and this is so much my character or custom that I see nothing without considering it further. Two little girls were playing with a top in my presence, and no sooner did I see the movement and shape than I began, with this madness of mine, to consider the easy motion of the spherical shape and how the already transmitted impulse could last, independent of its cause, for far from the hand of the little girl, which was the motivating cause, the top still danced; not content with this, I had some flour brought in and sifted, so that as the top danced on top of it, I could learn whether the circles described by its movement were perfect or not; and I found that they were merely spiral lines that lost their circular nature as the impulse diminished. Some other girls were playing jackstraws (which is the most frivolous of children's games); I began to contemplate the figures they formed, and seeing that by chance three fell into a triangle, I began to connect one to the other, recalling that some say this was the shape of the mysterious ring of Solomon, which had distant indications and representations of the Holy Trinity, allowing him to perform countless miracles and marvels; and it is said that the harp of David had the same shape, and for that reason Saul was healed at its sound; harps in our day still have almost the same shape.

And what could I tell you, señora, about the natural secrets I have discovered when cooking? Seeing that an egg sets and fries in butter or oil but falls apart in syrup; seeing that for sugar to remain liquid it is enough to add a very small amount of water in which a quince or other bitter fruit has been placed; seeing that the yolk and the white of the same egg are so different that each can be mixed with sugar but together they cannot. I do not mean to tire you with these inconsequentialities, which I mention only to give you a complete view of my nature, and which I believe will cause you to laugh; but, señora, what can we women know but kitchen philosophies? As Lupercio Leonardo[4] so wisely said, one can philosophize very well and prepare supper. And seeing these minor details, I say that if Aristotle[5] had cooked, he would have written a great deal more. Returning to my continual cogitation, I repeat that this is so constant in me I do not need books; on one occasion, because of a serious stomach ailment, the doctors prohibited my studying; after a few days I suggested to them that it would be less harmful to allow me books, because my cogitations were so strong and vehement that they consumed more energy in a quarter of an hour than studying books did in four days; and so they were persuaded to allow me to read. And further, señora: not even my sleep was free of this continual movement of my imaginative faculty; rather, it tends to operate more freely and unencumbered, examining with greater clarity and tranquility the images of the day, arguing, and composing verses, and I could offer you a large catalogue of them and the arguments and delicate points I have formulated more successfully asleep than awake, but I put those aside in order not to weary you, for what I have said is enough for your

4. Sor Juana actually refers to Lupercio's brother, Bernardo Leonardo de Argensola, Spanish poet and satirist (1562–1631).

5. Greek philosopher (384–322 B.C.E.) who studied with Plato and wrote on logic, politics, ethics, natural science, and poetics.

intelligence and perspicacity to penetrate and see perfectly my entire nature, as well as the origin, means, and state of my studies.

If these, señora, are merits (I see them celebrated as such in men), they would not be so in me, because I act out of necessity. If they are blameworthy, for the same reason I believe I am not at fault; nonetheless, I am so wary of myself that in this or anything else I do not trust my own judgment; and so I remit the decision to your sovereign talent, submitting to whatever sentence you may impose, without contradiction or opposition, for this has been no more than a simple narration of my inclination toward letters.

III

I confess as well that since this is so true, as I have said, I needed no examples, yet the many I have read, in both divine and human letters, have not failed to help me. For I find Deborah[6] issuing laws, both military and political, and governing a people that had many learned men. I find an exceedingly wise Queen of Sheba,[7] so learned she dares to test with enigmas the wisdom of the greatest of wise men and is not rebuked for that reason; instead, because of it, she becomes judge of the unbelievers. I find numerous illustrious women: some adorned with the gift of prophecy, like Abigail; others, with the gift of persuasion, like Esther; others, with piety, like Rahab; others, with perseverance, like Hannah, mother of Samuel, and countless others possessing all kinds of gifts and virtues.[8]

If I turn to the Gentiles, I first encounter the Sibyls,[9] chosen by God to prophesy the principal mysteries of our faith, in verses so learned and elegant they enthrall our admiration. I find a woman like Minerva,[1] daughter of the foremost god Jupiter and mistress of all the knowledge of Athens, worshipped as goddess of the sciences. I find Polla Argentaria, who helped Lucan, her husband, write the great Pharsalia.[2] I find the daughter of the divine Tiresias[3] more learned than her father. I find Zenobia, queen of the Palmyrenes, as wise as she was valiant. Arete,[4] the most learned daughter of Aristippus. Nicostrata,[5] inventor of Latin characters and extremely erudite in Greek ones. Aspasia of Miletus,[6] who taught philosophy and rhetoric and was the tutor of

6. Female judge of ancient Israel, named in Judges 4–5.
7. Wealthy queen who visited King Solomon to test his wisdom and bestow gifts, as described in 1 Kings 10.
8. "Abigail": prophet who becomes the wife of King David in 1 Samuel 25. "Esther": Jewish queen of Persia (wife of Ahasuerus) who risked her life to save Jewish citizens from slaughter by the vizier Haman, as described in the Book of Esther. "Rahab": prostitute who helped the Israelites take Jericho by hiding spies in her home, as described in Joshua 2. "Hannah": mother of Samuel, conceived miraculously at an advanced age, as described in 1 Samuel 1.
9. Female prophets of the ancient world, reputed to have foretold the coming of Christianity.

1. Roman goddess of wisdom, born of the head of Jupiter.
2. Epic poem on the civil war between Caesar and Pompey.
3. In Greek mythology, a blind prophet who was transformed into a woman for seven years. His daughter was Manto, as recounted in Ovid, Metamorphoses, 6.7.
4. Said to have founded a school of philosophy (4th century B.C.E.). "Zenobia": (ca. 240–275 C.E.), queen of the Palmyrene empire in Syria, she conquered Egypt and led a revolt against Rome.
5. Legendary woman of letters said to have devised the first fifteen letters of the Latin alphabet.
6. Reputed teacher of eloquence in ancient Athens.

the philosopher Pericles. Hypatia,[7] who taught astronomy and studied for many years in Alexandria. Leontion,[8] a Greek woman who wrote arguments countering the philosopher Theophrastus, which convinced him. Jucia, Corinna, Cornelia,[9] in short, all the great number of women who deserved fame, whether as Greeks, muses, or pythonesses,[1] for all of them were simply learned women, considered and celebrated and also venerated as such in antiquity. Not to mention countless others who fill the books, for I find the Egyptian Catherine[2] studying and affecting all the wisdom of the wise men of Egypt. I find Gertrude[3] reading, writing, and teaching. And for examples closer to home, I find a most holy mother of mine, Paula,[4] learned in the Hebrew, Greek, and Latin languages and extremely skilled in interpreting Scripture. And none other than the great Saint Jerome scarcely thought himself worthy of being her chronicler, for with the lively thought and energetic exactitude he brings to his explanations, he says: *If all the members of my body were tongues, they would not suffice to publish the wisdom and virtue of Paula.*[5] The widow Blaesilla deserved the same praise, as did the illustrious virgin Eustochium, both daughters of this saint; the second, for her knowledge, was called Prodigy of the World.[6] Fabiola,[7] a Roman woman, was also extremely learned in Holy Scripture. Proba Faltonia, another Roman, wrote an elegant book, a cento of selections from Virgil, on the mysteries of our Holy Faith.[8] It is well known that our queen, Doña Isabel, the wife of Alfonso X,[9] wrote on astronomy. And many others whom I omit in order not to cite what others have said (a vice I have always despised), for in our day the great Christina Alexandra, Queen of Sweden, as learned as she is valiant and magnanimous, and the Most Honorable Ladies the Duchess of Aveiro and the Countess of Villaumbrosa[1] are all flourishing.

If the evil lies in a woman writing verses, it is clear that many have done so in a praiseworthy way; where is the evil in my being a woman? Of course I confess that I am base and despicable, but in my judgment no verse of mine has been called indecent. Moreover, I have never written anything of my own free will but only

---

7. Neoplatonist and mathematician (ca. 370–415 C.E.) in Roman Egypt.

8. Greek Epicurean philosopher (4th–3rd century B.C.E.).

9. Early Catholic saint and martyr (2nd century C.E.). "Jucia": Sor Juana may have meant Julia (Domna), an intellectual Roman empress. Corinna (active 5th century B.C.E.): ancient Greek poet, thought by some to be a contemporary of Pindar.

1. Greek priestesses.

2. Catherine of Alexandria (active 4th century C.E.), scholar and virgin saint.

3. Saint Gertrude of Helfta (1256–1302), German mystic and Benedictine theologian.

4. Saint Paula (347–404 C.E.): wealthy Roman woman who became a Desert Mother, companion of Saint Jerome, and co-patron of the Hieronymite Order.

5. The first sentence of Saint Jerome's letter to Eustochium (*Letter* 108.1).

6. Blesilla (d. 384) and Eustochium (ca. 368–420 C.E.) were daughters of Saint Paula. Blesilla died young, while Eustochium became a saint and a Desert Mother.

7. Roman noblewoman (d. 399 C.E.): who became a follower of Saint Jerome and Saint Paula.

8. Proba Faltonia (ca. 4th century C.E.): Roman Christian poet.

9. Apparently, Sor Juana commits an error. The wife of Alfonso X was Violante of Aragon, who did collaborate on Alfonso's astronomical treatises. Doña Isabel was the wife and queen of Ferdinand V.

1. An Andalusian Dominican nun. "Christina Alexandra" (1626–1689): Queen of Sweden with an interest in philosophy and science. She was a patroness of René Descartes and others. "Duchess of Aveiro" (1630–1715): a member of the Portuguese royalty and friend of the Countess of Paredes, vicereine of New Spain. Sor Juana dedicated a poem to her.

because others have entreated and ordered me to; I do not recall having written for my own pleasure except for a trifle they call *The Dream*.[2] The letter that you, my lady, so honored was written with more repugnance than anything else, because it dealt with sacred matters for which (as I have said) I have a reverent awe, and because it seemed to impugn, something for which I feel a natural aversion. And I believe that if I could have foreseen the fortunate destiny to which it was born— for, like another Moses, I abandoned it in the waters of the Nile of silence, where it was found and treated lovingly by a princess like you[3]—I believe, I repeat, that if I had thought this would happen, I would have drowned it first with the same hands from which it was born, for fear the awkward blunders of my ignorance would be seen in the light of your wisdom. In this the greatness of your kindness is revealed, for your will applauds precisely what your brilliant understanding must reject. But now that its fate has brought it to your door, so abandoned and orphaned that you even had to give it a name, I regret that along with my imperfections, it also bears the defects of haste, not only because of my continuing ill health and the countless duties my obedience imposes, and because I lack someone to help me write and feel the need for everything to be in my own hand, and because writing it went against my nature and all I wanted was to keep my promise to one I could not disobey, I did not have the time to refine it; as a consequence I failed to include entire discourses and many proofs that I had at hand but did not add in order to stop writing; and if I had known it would be printed, I would not have omitted them, if only in order to satisfy certain objections that have been raised, which I could dispatch, but I shall not be so discourteous as to place such indecent objects before the purity of your eyes, for it is enough that I offend them with my ignorance without adding the insolence of others. If they happen to fly to you (for they are so light in weight they may), then I shall do as you command; for if it does not contravene your precepts, I shall never take up the pen in my own defense, because it seems to me that one offense does not require another in response, when one recognizes error in the very place it lies hidden, for as my father Saint Jerome says, *Good discourse does not seek secrets*,[4] and Saint Ambrose: *Conceal-ment is in the nature of a guilty conscience*.[5] Nor do I consider myself refuted, for a precept of the Law says: *An accusation does not endure if not tended by the person who made it*.[6] What certainly is worth pondering is the effort it has required to make copies. A strange madness to put more effort into stripping away approval than acquiring it! I, señora, have not wanted to respond, although others have without my knowledge: it is enough that I have seen some papers,[7] among them one that I send to you because it is learned and because reading it makes up in part for the time you have wasted on what I write. If you, señora, would like me to do the opposite of what I have put forward for your judgment and opinion, at the slightest sign of what you desire my intention will cede, as it ought to; it was, as I have said, to be silent, for although Saint John Chrysostom says: *Slanderers must be refuted, and those who question taught*, I see that Saint Gregory also says: *It is no*

---

2. The poem now known as "First Dream"
3. The baby Moses was abandoned in a basket by the Nile river but was rescued by Pharaoh's daughter (Exodus 2:1–10), just as the *Athenagoric Letter* was rescued by the "princess," Sor Filotea.
4. Saint Jerome, *Letter to Gaudentius* (Letter

128.3).
5. Saint Ambrose, *On Abraham*, 1.2.4.
6. This statement has not been found in either civil or canon law.
7. Sor Juana refers to contemporary writings that attacked and defended her *Athenagoric Letter*.

less a victory to tolerate enemies than to overcome them;[8] and that patience conquers by tolerating and triumphs by suffering. And if among the Roman Gentiles it was the custom, at the height of the glory of its captains—when they entered in triumph over other nations, dressed in purple and crowned with laurel, their carriages pulled not by animals but by crowned, conquered kings, accompanied by spoils of the riches of the entire world, and the conquering army adorned with the insignias of its feats, hearing the applause of the people in their honorary titles of renown, such as Fathers of the Nation, Columns of Empire, Walls of Rome, Protectors of the Republic, and other glorious names—for a soldier, in this supreme moment of human glory and happiness, to say aloud to the conqueror, with his consent and by order of the Senate: "Remember that you are mortal; remember that you have these defects," not forgetting the most shameful, which is what occurred in the triumph of Caesar, when the lowest soldiers called out in his hearing: "Beware, Romans, we bring you the bald adulterer."[9] This was done so that in the midst of countless honors the conqueror would not become vain, the ballast of these insults would counterbalance the sails of so much praise, and the ship of good judgment would not founder in the winds of acclaim. And I say that if Gentiles did this with only the light of natural law, we who are Catholics, with the precept of loving our enemies, what would we not do to tolerate them? For my part I can assure you that at times calumny has mortified me but never done me harm, because I take for a great fool the person who, having the opportunity to gain merit, endures the great effort and loses the merit, which is like those who do not wish to accept death and in the end die; their resistance does nothing to exempt them from death, but it does take away the merit of resignation and turns what might have been a good death into one that was bad. And so, señora, I believe these things do more good than harm, and consider the effect of praise on human weakness a greater risk, for it tends to appropriate what is not ours, and we need to take great care to keep the words of the Apostle etched in our hearts: *And what hast thou that thou didst not receive? Now if thou didst receive it, why dost thou glory, as if thou hadst not received it?*[1] so they can serve as a shield that resists the sharp points of praise, which are like lances that, when not attributed to God, to Whom they belong, take our life and turn us into thieves of the honor of God and usurpers of the talents He gave us and the gifts He lent us, for which we must give a strict accounting. And so, señora, I fear praise more than calumny, because calumny, with only a simple act of patience, is transformed into benefit, while praise requires many acts of reflection and humility and knowledge of oneself to keep it from doing harm. In my case, I know and recognize that knowing this is a special favor of God, allowing me to behave in both instances according to the judgment of Saint Augustine: *One should not believe the friend who praises or the enemy who censures.* Although most of the time, given my nature, I squander what I have been given or combine it with so many defects and imperfections that I debase the good that came from Him. And so, in the little of mine that has been printed, not only

---

8. The citation paraphrases the commentary on 1 Samuel 11:13 by Gregory the Great (ca. 540–604 C.E.), *Commentarii in librum 1 Regum* (Commentaries on Book 1 of Kings) 5.1.13. The first statement is not found in the writings of the Greek Father John Chrysostom (347–407 C.E.) but rather in a text of the twelfth-century Zacharias Chrysopolitanus, *In unum ex quatuor* (In one of four), III. 127.
9. A similar line is recounted in Suetonius, *De vita Caesarum* (About the Life of the Caesars), "Divus Julius," 51.
1. Apostle: Paul. 1 Corinthians 4:7.

my name but consent for the printing has been not of my own choosing but the will of another who does not fall under my control, as in the printing of the *Athenagoric Letter*; this means that only some *Exercises of the Incarnation* and *Offerings of the Sorrows* were printed for public devotion with my approval, but without my name; I am sending copies of these to you, to give (if you agree) to our sisters the nuns of your holy community and others in the city. I am sending only one copy of the *Sorrows* because the others have been distributed and I could find no other. I wrote them years ago, solely for the devotions of my sisters, and afterward they became more widely known; their subjects are so much greater than my mediocrity and ignorance, and the only thing that helped me with them was that they dealt with our great Queen: it is notable that the iciest heart is set ablaze when one alludes to Most Holy Mary. I should like, illustrious señora, to send you works worthy of your virtue and wisdom, but as the poet said:

> *Although strength may be lacking, the will must be praised.*
> *I think the gods are satisfied with that.*[2]

If I write any other trifles, they will always seek out the sanctuary of your feet and the security of your correction, for I have no other jewel with which to pay you, and as Seneca says, whoever begins to offer benefits is obliged to continue them; in this way, your own generosity will repay you, for only in this way can I be freed in an honorable manner from my debt and avoid this warning from the same Seneca: *It is shameful to be surpassed in benefits.*[3] For it is the magnanimity of the generous creditor to give the poor debtor what is needed to satisfy the debt. This is what God gave to the world incapable of repaying Him: He gave his own Son so that He would receive a recompense worthy of Him.[4]

If the style of this letter, illustrious señora, has not been what you deserve, I beg your pardon if in the homely familiarity or lack of respect in my treating you as a veiled nun, one of my sisters, I have forgotten the distance of your most eminent person, for if I had seen you without the veil, this would not have happened; but you, with your wisdom and kindness, will supply or amend the words, and if *vos* seems incongruous, I used it because it seemed that for the reverence I owe you, *Your Reverence*[5] shows very little reverence; change it then to whatever seems honorable and what you deserve, for I have not dared to exceed the limits of your style or go past the boundary of your modesty.

Keep me in your grace and pray for divine grace for me and may the Lord grant you a large portion of it and keep you, which is my plea and my need. From this convent of our father Saint Jerome in Mexico City, on the first day of the month of March in the year 1691. I kiss your hand and am your most favored

Juana Inés de la Cruz

---

2. The poet is Ovid (*Epistulae ex Ponto* 3.4. 79–80).
3. Seneca, *De Beneficiis* (On kindness) 5.2.
4. That is, he gave the world Jesus Christ.

5. Sor Juana uses the familiar form of the second-person singular, reserved for informal and familiar relations.

VOLTAIRE
(FRANÇOIS-MARIE AROUET)
1694–1778

Imagine a writer so outspoken and so fearless that although his work landed him in prison and in exile—more than once—he never stopped writing defiantly. If he could not publish his work openly, he would have it printed secretly and smuggled across borders. If he could not circulate it by the post, he would have it hand-carried in suitcases and distributed by trusted friends. He seized freedom of speech even when it was not granted to him, and he used it to mock corrupt priests and self-regarding kings. The sheer gutsiness of Voltaire is breathtaking. In an atmosphere of stern censorship and absolute power, he managed to live to the ripe age of eighty-three, writing lively denunciations of dominant orthodoxies and powerful authorities almost every day. And his darkly comic imagination propelled him to enormous fame. He was so successful that he grew richer than many kings in Europe. His witty, light prose, and his clear and accessible style allowed him to popularize many of the revolutionary goals of the Enlightenment—human rights, the value of freedom and tolerance, the hope for progress through reasoned debate, and the urgent desire to end human suffering where we can. It is in no small part thanks to Voltaire that these ideals shape our own political landscape today.

LIFE AND TIMES

Bold, witty, and rebellious, François-Marie Arouet was a trouble to his parents as a child and became a trouble to the authorities for the rest of his life. He was born near Paris in 1694 to a middle-class family. At the age of ten he went to a boarding school run by Jesuits, where he developed an enthusiasm for literature and a passionate opposition to organized religion. His father wanted him to pursue a career in law, but he soon gave it up to write poetry and plays. So sparkling and brilliant was his conversation that he won powerful friends, but his propensity for satire also brought him enemies, and an attack on the acting head of state got him locked in the Bastille prison in Paris for almost a year. While there, he committed himself to writing, and his first play, *Oedipus*, turned into a huge success, bringing him considerable wealth and establishing his reputation.

The young writer, who was now known by his pen name, "Voltaire," spent three years in exile in England after a quarrel with a French nobleman. There he met the writers Jonathan Swift and Alexander Pope. He enjoyed the freedom from censorship and punishment allowed to writers in England, and returned to France with an even stronger sense of his right to dissent and oppose authority. His many subversive writings, called by the authorities "most dangerous to religion and civil order," earned him another spell of exile from Paris, which he spent with his longtime mistress and intellectual companion Madame du Châtelet. In 1750, Voltaire moved to Potsdam, in Prussia, where he joined the court of the young King Frederick, later to be known as Frederick the Great, who loved the arts and wanted philosophy and literature to flourish. Voltaire, like many other Enlightenment thinkers, did not see democracy as the best form of government. The masses seemed to him to impede reason, freedom, and progress (he said he would "rather obey one lion than 200 rats"). The regime he idealized was the enlightened despot—a sensitive, rational king who welcomed dissent and sought the counsel of philosophers like himself. Early on, Frederick promised to live up to that ideal, but Voltaire was soon to be disappointed. He and Frederick argued; Frederick waged violent warfare and asserted power high-handedly. Voltaire was invited to leave.

He took up residence for the rest of his life at Ferney, a town on the border between France and Switzerland, so that he could escape from France easily if necessary. It was here that he wrote the best-selling *Candide*—and a great deal more. Travelers and visitors brought suitcases filled with Voltaire's "scandal-sheets" back with them to Paris where the public eagerly gobbled them up. He repeatedly attacked religious extremism and stultifying tradition and argued for universal human rights. And he refused the traditional literary goal of immortality, casting his writing as a response to current debates and events.

Voltaire was no atheist (he once said that "if God did not exist it would be necessary to invent him"). His own religion is usually known as Deism; that is, faith in a God who created the world and then stands back, allowing nature to follow its own laws and never intervening. The Deists' signature metaphor was God as a watchmaker: the world he made was a mechanism, which then ticked away on its own. As far as human beings were concerned, God gave them reason, and then left them free to use it. Deists disagreed about whether God

had instilled human beings with a love of virtue, and whether there was an afterlife of rewards and punishments. Voltaire claimed that it was impossible for humans to know anything beyond their senses—so God's will must remain mysterious—and he believed that humans should use their senses and their reason to understand how the world works and, to the best of our ability, to make it better.

By the time of Voltaire's death, he had become a national hero. In all, he had produced enough work to fill 135 volumes, in a range of genres including tragedy, epic, philosophy, history, fiction, and journalism. In death as in life, he continued to generate scandal and division. Clergy in Paris refused to let him be buried in hallowed ground, so friends smuggled his body out of the city—propping it up on the journey like a sleeping passenger—and brought it to a monastery to be laid to rest. Later, leaders of the French Revolution, who had been inspired by Voltaire's attacks on authority and religion, had his body exhumed and reburied in Paris to huge national fanfare.

WORK

Voltaire wrote *Candide* in part as a response to a piece of news that shook him, and many of his contemporaries, badly. On November 1, 1755, a devastating earthquake hit Lisbon, in Portugal. Upwards of thirty thousand people died. Voltaire, writing almost obsessively about this tragedy in his letters, wondered how anyone could make a case for an optimistic philosophy in light of it. He worried over Alexander Pope's assertion in his *Essay on Man* that "Whatever is, is right." Could anyone really believe that this was God's will—that a just and rational God had created this world and that it was, in the words of the German philosopher Gottfried Wilhelm Leibniz, "the best of all possible worlds"? Voltaire's absurd philosopher Pangloss ("all-tongue") is a caricature of Leibniz.

Though philosophical, *Candide* is so brief and so easy to read that it was immediately popular with a wide range of readers. Voltaire deliberately opted for short, cheap, excitingly readable texts. Long works "will never make a revolution," he argued, and wrote that "if the New Testament had cost 4,200 sesterces, the Christian religion would never have taken root." Thus *Candide*'s brevity may be seen as part of its power.

It is also deliberately entertaining. Voltaire combines a lively appetite for humor with a horrifying sense of the real existence of evil. The exuberance and extravagance of the sufferings characters undergo may even prompt us to laugh: the plight of the old woman whose buttock has been cut off to make rump steak for her starving companions, the weeping of two girls whose monkey-lovers have been killed, the glum circumstances of six exiled, poverty-stricken kings. But Voltaire also manages to keep his readers off balance. Raped, cut to pieces, hanged, stabbed in the belly, the central characters of *Candide* keep coming back to life at opportune moments, as though no disaster could have permanent effects. Such reassuring fantasy at first suggests that it is all a joke, designed to ridicule an outmoded philosophical system. And yet, reality keeps intruding. An admiral really did face a firing squad and die for failing to engage an enemy ferociously enough. Those six hungry kings were actual historical figures who were dispossessed. The Lisbon earthquake was so real that it haunted Voltaire for years. And his satirical pen attacks genuine social problems as various as military discipline, class hierarchy, greed, religious extremism, slavery, and even the publishing industry. The extravagances of the story are therefore uncomfortably matched by the extravagances

of real life, and despite the comic lightness of the telling, Voltaire demands that the reader confront these horrors.

The fantastic and exaggerated nature of the events stands out against the simplicity of the narrative style. Candide is a naive traveler, like Jonathan Swift's Gulliver, who does not grasp the ironies he witnesses. He travels widely, taking in Europe, South America, and the Ottoman Empire, where Catholics, Protestants, and Muslims all emerge as cruel and hypocritical. The only exception is the mythical Eldorado, which takes place almost exactly at the half-way point of the text, where corruption, crime, malice, and poverty do not exist. Candide nonetheless insists on leaving Eldorado to find his beloved Cunégonde. Readers have often wondered about the role of this paradise in an otherwise bleak picture of human experience: does Eldorado suggest that human beings are capable of virtue, and if so, then why does Voltaire compel his protagonist to leave? Is it too stagnant, too isolated, too dull? Is it like the Garden of Eden, a paradise no longer home to fallen humanity? The fact that Candide admires Milton's *Paradise Lost* and that the novella concludes with the protagonist cultivating a garden suggests that Voltaire may have been rethinking the story of Adam and Eve in his own imaginative way.

Candide encapsulated the many problems that stoked Voltaire's anger and fed his satire: absolutism and religious bigotry, unnecessary bloodshed, restrictions on freedom of speech and religion, and the intolerable reality of human suffering. This story has always been the most famous work of its author's incalculably influential career. Voltaire inspired leaders of the American Revolution—Thomas Jefferson, Thomas Paine, and Benjamin Franklin—and helped to shape the United States Constitution. The French Revolutionaries held Voltaire up as a hero, as did generations fighting against religious intolerance. He was hotly reviled by those who wanted to maintain the authority of established churches, and some went so far as to call him the Antichrist. But in the centuries that have followed, Voltaire's ideas have become part of the common fabric of our ideals.

Candide, or Optimism[1]

translated from the German of Doctor Ralph with the additions which were found in the Doctor's pocket when he died at Minden in the Year of Our Lord 1759

CHAPTER I

How Candide Was Brought up in a Fine Castle and How He Was Driven Therefrom

There lived in Westphalia,[2] in the castle of the Baron of Thunder-Ten-Tronckh, a young man on whom nature had bestowed the perfection of gentle manners. His features admirably expressed his soul; he combined an honest mind with great simplicity of heart; and I think it was for this reason that they called him Candide. The old servants of the house suspected that he was the son of the Baron's sister by a respectable, honest gentleman of the neighborhood, whom she had refused to marry because he could prove only seventy-one quarterings,[3] the rest of his family tree having been lost in the passage of time.

The Baron was one of the most mighty lords of Westphalia, for his castle had a door and windows. His great hall was even hung with a tapestry. The dogs of his courtyard made up a hunting pack on occasion, with the stable-boys as huntsmen; the village priest was his grand almoner. They all called him "My Lord," and laughed at his stories.

The Baroness, who weighed in the neighborhood of three hundred and fifty pounds, was greatly respected for that reason, and did the honors of the house with a dignity which rendered her even more imposing. Her daughter Cunégonde,[4] aged seventeen, was a ruddy-cheeked girl, fresh, plump, and desirable. The Baron's son seemed in every way worthy of his father. The tutor Pangloss was the oracle of the household, and little Candide listened to his lectures with all the good faith of his age and character.

---

1. Translated and with notes by Robert M. Adams.
2. A province of western Germany, near Holland and the lower Rhineland. Flat, boggy, and drab, it is noted chiefly for its excellent ham. In a letter to his niece, written during his German expedition of 1750, Voltaire described the "vast, sad, sterile, detestable countryside of Westphalia."

3. Genealogical divisions of one's family tree. Seventy-one of them is a grotesque number to have, representing something over 2,000 years of uninterrupted nobility.
4. Cunégonde gets her odd name from Kunigunda (wife to Emperor Henry II) who walked barefoot and blindfolded on red-hot irons to prove her chastity; Pangloss gets his name from Greek words meaning "all-tongue."

Pangloss gave instruction in metaphysico-theologico-cosmoloonigology.[5] He proved admirably that there cannot possibly be an effect without a cause and that in this best of all possible worlds the Baron's castle was the best of all castles and his wife the best of all possible Baronesses.

—It is clear, said he, that things cannot be otherwise than they are, for since everything is made to serve an end, everything necessarily serves the best end. Observe: noses were made to support spectacles, hence we have spectacles. Legs, as anyone can plainly see, were made to be breeched, and so we have breeches. Stones were made to be shaped and to build castles with; thus My Lord has a fine castle, for the greatest Baron in the province should have the finest house; and since pigs were made to be eaten, we eat pork all year round.[6] Consequently, those who say everything is well are uttering mere stupidities; they should say everything is for the best.

Candide listened attentively and believed implicitly; for he found Miss Cunégonde exceedingly pretty, though he never had the courage to tell her so. He decided that after the happiness of being born Baron of Thunder-Ten-Tronckh, the second order of happiness was to be Miss Cunégonde; the third was seeing her every day, and the fourth was listening to Master Pangloss, the greatest philosopher in the province and consequently in the entire world.

One day, while Cunégonde was walking near the castle in the little woods that they called a park, she saw Dr. Pangloss in the underbrush; he was giving a lesson in experimental physics to her mother's maid, a very attractive and obedient brunette. As Miss Cunégonde had a natural bent for the sciences, she watched breathlessly the repeated experiments which were going on; she saw clearly the doctor's sufficient reason, observed both cause and effect, and returned to the house in a distracted and pensive frame of mind, yearning for knowledge and dreaming that she might be the sufficient reason of young Candide—who might also be hers.

As she was returning to the castle, she met Candide, and blushed; Candide blushed too. She greeted him in a faltering tone of voice; and Candide talked to her without knowing what he was saying. Next day, as everyone was rising from the dinner table, Cunégonde and Candide found themselves behind a screen; Cunégonde dropped her handkerchief, Candide picked it up; she held his hand quite innocently, he kissed her hand quite innocently with remarkable vivacity and emotion; their lips met, their eyes lit up, their knees trembled, their hands wandered. The Baron of Thunder-Ten-Tronckh passed by the screen and, taking note of this cause and this effect, drove Candide out of the castle by kicking him vigorously on the backside. Cunégonde fainted; as soon as she recovered, the Baroness slapped her face; and everything was confusion in the most beautiful and agreeable of all possible castles.

5. The "looney" buried in this burlesque word corresponds to a buried *nigaud*—"booby" in the French. Christian Wolff, disciple of Leibniz, invented and popularized the word "cosmology." The catch phrases in the following sentence, echoed by popularizers of Leibniz, make reference to the determinism of his system, its linking of cause with effect, and its optimism.
6. The argument from design supposes that everything in this world exists for a specific reason; Voltaire objects not to the argument as a whole, but to the abuse of it.

CHAPTER 2

What Happened to Candide Among the Bulgars[7]

Candide, ejected from the earthly paradise, wandered for a long time without knowing where he was going, weeping, raising his eyes to heaven, and gazing back frequently on the most beautiful of castles which contained the most beautiful of Baron's daughters. He slept without eating, in a furrow of a plowed field, while the snow drifted over him; next morning, numb with cold, he dragged himself into the neighboring village, which was called Waldberghoff-trarbk-dikdorff; he was penniless, famished, and exhausted. At the door of a tavern he paused forlornly. Two men dressed in blue[8] took note of him:

—Look, chum, said one of them, there's a likely young fellow of just about the right size.

They approached Candide and invited him very politely to dine with them.

—Gentlemen, Candide replied with charming modesty, I'm honored by your invitation, but I really don't have enough money to pay my share.

—My dear sir, said one of the blues, people of your appearance and your merit don't have to pay; aren't you five feet five inches tall?

—Yes, gentlemen, that is indeed my stature, said he, making a bow.

—Then, sir, you must be seated at once; not only will we pay your bill this time, we will never allow a man like you to be short of money; for men were made only to render one another mutual aid.

—You are quite right, said Candide; it is just as Dr. Pangloss always told me, and I see clearly that everything is for the best.

They beg him to accept a couple of crowns, he takes them, and offers an I.O.U.; they won't hear of it, and all sit down at table together.

—Don't you love dearly . . . ?

—I do indeed, says he, I dearly love Miss Cunégonde.

—No, no, says one of the gentlemen, we are asking if you don't love dearly the King of the Bulgars.

—Not in the least, says he, I never laid eyes on him.

—What's that you say? He's the most charming of kings, and we must drink his health.

—Oh, gladly, gentlemen; and he drinks.

—That will do, they tell him; you are now the bulwark, the support, the defender, the hero of the Bulgars; your fortune is made and your future assured.

Promptly they slip irons on his legs and lead him to the regiment. There they cause him to right face, left face, present arms, order arms, aim, fire, doubletime, and they give him thirty strokes of the rod. Next day he does the drill a little less awkwardly and gets only twenty strokes; the third day, they give him only ten, and he is regarded by his comrades as a prodigy.

Candide, quite thunderstruck, did not yet understand very clearly how he was a hero. One fine spring morning he took it into his head to go for a walk, stepping straight out as if it were a privilege of the human race, as of animals in general, to

---

7. Voltaire chose this name to represent the Prussian troops of Frederick the Great because he wanted to make an insinuation of pederasty against both the soldiers and their master. Cf. French *bougre*, English "bugger."

8. The recruiting officers of Frederick the Great, much feared in 18th-century Europe, wore blue uniforms. Frederick had a passion for sorting out his soldiers by size; several of his regiments would accept only six-footers.

use his legs as he chose.[9] He had scarcely covered two leagues when four other heroes, each six feet tall, overtook him, bound him, and threw him into a dungeon. At the court-martial they asked which he preferred, to be flogged thirty-six times by the entire regiment or to receive summarily a dozen bullets in the brain. In vain did he argue that the human will is free and insist that he preferred neither alternative; he had to choose; by virtue of the divine gift called "liberty" he decided to run the gauntlet thirty-six times, and actually endured two floggings. The regiment was composed of two thousand men. That made four thousand strokes, which laid open every muscle and nerve from his nape to his butt. As they were preparing for the third beating, Candide, who could endure no more, begged as a special favor that they would have the goodness to smash his head. His plea was granted; they bandaged his eyes and made him kneel down. The King of the Bulgars, passing by at this moment, was told of the culprit's crime; and as this king had a rare genius, he understood, from everything they told him of Candide, that this was a young metaphysician, extremely ignorant of the ways of the world, so he granted his royal pardon, with a generosity which will be praised in every newspaper in every age. A worthy surgeon cured Candide in three weeks with the ointments described by Dioscorides.[1] He already had a bit of skin back and was able to walk when the King of the Bulgars went to war with the King of the Abares.[2]

CHAPTER 3

How Candide Escaped from the Bulgars, and What Became of Him

Nothing could have been so fine, so brisk, so brilliant, so well-drilled as the two armies. The trumpets, the fifes, the oboes, the drums, and the cannon produced such a harmony as was never heard in hell. First the cannons battered down about six thousand men on each side; then volleys of musket fire removed from the best of worlds about nine or ten thousand rascals who were cluttering up its surface. The bayonet was a sufficient reason for the demise of several thousand others. Total casualties might well amount to thirty thousand men or so. Candide, who was trembling like a philosopher, hid himself as best he could while this heroic butchery was going on.

Finally, while the two kings in their respective camps celebrated the victory by having *Te Deums* sung, Candide undertook to do his reasoning of cause and effect somewhere else. Passing by mounds of the dead and dying, he came to a nearby village which had been burnt to the ground. It was an Abare village, which the Bulgars had burned, in strict accordance with the laws of war. Here old men, stunned from beatings, watched the last agonies of their butchered wives, who still clutched their infants to their bleeding breasts; there, disemboweled girls,

9. This episode was suggested by the experience of a Frenchman named Courtilz, who had deserted from the Prussian army and been bastinadoed for it. Voltaire intervened with Frederick to gain his release. But it also reflects the story that Wolff, Leibniz's disciple, got into trouble with Frederick's father when someone reported that his doctrine denying free will had encouraged several soldiers to desert. "The argument of the grenadier," who was said to have pleaded preestablished harmony to justify his desertion, so infuriated the king that he

had Wolff expelled from the country.
1. Dioscorides' treatise on *materia medica*, dating from the 1st century C.E., was not the most up to date.
2. A tribe of semicivilized Scythians, who might be supposed at war with the Bulgars; allegorically, the Abares are the French, who opposed the Prussians in the Seven Years' War (1756–63). According to the title page of 1761, "Doctor Ralph," the dummy author of *Candide*, himself perished at the battle of Minden (Westphalia) in 1759.

who had first satisfied the natural needs of various heroes, breathed their last; others, half-scorched in the flames, begged for their death stroke. Scattered brains and severed limbs littered the ground.

Candide fled as fast as he could to another village; this one belonged to the Bulgars, and the heroes of the Abare cause had given it the same treatment. Climbing over ruins and stumbling over corpses, Candide finally made his way out of the war area, carrying a little food in his knapsack and never ceasing to dream of Miss Cunégonde. His supplies gave out when he reached Holland; but having heard that everyone in that country was rich and a Christian, he felt confident of being treated as well as he had been in the castle of the Baron before he was kicked out for the love of Miss Cunégonde.

He asked alms of several grave personages, who all told him that if he continued to beg, he would be shut up in a house of correction and set to hard labor.

Finally he approached a man who had just been talking to a large crowd for an hour on end; the topic was charity. Looking doubtfully at him, the orator demanded:

—What are you doing here? Are you here to serve the good cause?

—There is no effect without a cause, said Candide modestly; all events are linked by the chain of necessity and arranged for the best. I had to be driven away from Miss Cunégonde, I had to run the gauntlet, I have to beg my bread until I can earn it; none of this could have happened otherwise.

—Look here, friend, said the orator, do you think the Pope is Antichrist?[3]

—I haven't considered the matter, said Candide; but whether he is or not, I'm in need of bread.

—You don't deserve any, said the other; away with you, you rascal, you rogue, never come near me as long as you live.

Meanwhile, the orator's wife had put her head out of the window, and, seeing a man who was not sure the Pope was Antichrist, emptied over his head a pot full of———Scandalous! The excesses into which women are led by religious zeal!

A man who had never been baptized, a good Anabaptist[4] named Jacques, saw this cruel and heartless treatment being inflicted on one of his fellow creatures, a featherless biped possessing a soul;[5] he took Candide home with him, washed him off, gave him bread and beer, presented him with two florins, and even undertook to give him a job in his Persian-rug factory—for these items are widely manufactured in Holland. Candide, in an ecstasy of gratitude, cried out:

—Master Pangloss was right indeed when he told me everything is for the best in this world; for I am touched by your kindness far more than by the harshness of that black-coated gentleman and his wife.

Next day, while taking a stroll about town, he met a beggar who was covered with pustules, his eyes were sunken, the end of his nose rotted off, his mouth twisted, his teeth black, he had a croaking voice and a hacking cough, and spat a tooth every time he tried to speak.

3. Voltaire is satirizing extreme Protestant sects that have sometimes seemed to make hatred of Rome the sum and substance of their creed.
4. Holland, as the home of religious liberty, had offered asylum to the Anabaptists, whose radical views on property and religious discipline had made them unpopular during the 16th century. Granted tolerance, they settled down into respectable burghers. Since this behavior confirmed some of Voltaire's major theses, he had a high opinion of contemporary Anabaptists.
5. Plato's famous minimal definition of man, which he corrected by the addition of a soul to distinguish man from a plucked chicken.

CHAPTER 4

How Candide Met His Old Philosophy Tutor, Doctor Pangloss, and What Came of It

Candide, more touched by compassion even than by horror, gave this ghastly beggar the two florins that he himself had received from his honest Anabaptist friend Jacques. The phantom stared at him, burst into tears, and fell on his neck. Candide drew back in terror.

—Alas, said one wretch to the other, don't you recognize your dear Pangloss any more?

—What are you saying? You, my dear master! you, in this horrible condition? What misfortune has befallen you? Why are you no longer in the most beautiful of castles? What has happened to Miss Cunégonde, that pearl among young ladies, that masterpiece of Nature?

—I am perishing, said Pangloss.

Candide promptly led him into the Anabaptist's stable, where he gave him a crust of bread, and when he had recovered:—Well, said he, Cunégonde?

—Dead, said the other.

Candide fainted. His friend brought him around with a bit of sour vinegar which happened to be in the stable. Candide opened his eyes.

—Cunégonde, dead! Ah, best of worlds, what's become of you now? But how did she die? It wasn't of grief at seeing me kicked out of her noble father's elegant castle?

—Not at all, said Pangloss; she was disemboweled by the Bulgar soldiers, after having been raped to the absolute limit of human endurance; they smashed the Baron's head when he tried to defend her, cut the Baroness to bits, and treated my poor pupil exactly like his sister. As for the castle, not one stone was left on another, not a shed, not a sheep, not a duck, not a tree; but we had the satisfaction of revenge, for the Abares did exactly the same thing to a nearby barony belonging to a Bulgar nobleman.

At this tale Candide fainted again; but having returned to his senses and said everything appropriate to the occasion, he asked about the cause and effect, the sufficient reason, which had reduced Pangloss to his present pitiful state.

—Alas, said he, it was love; love, the consolation of the human race, the preservative of the universe, the soul of all sensitive beings, love, gentle love.

—Unhappy man, said Candide, I too have had some experience of this love, the sovereign of hearts, the soul of our souls; and it never got me anything but a single kiss and twenty kicks in the rear. How could this lovely cause produce in you such a disgusting effect?

Pangloss replied as follows:—My dear Candide! you knew Paquette, that pretty maidservant to our august Baroness. In her arms I tasted the delights of paradise, which directly caused these torments of hell, from which I am now suffering. She was infected with the disease, and has perhaps died of it. Paquette received this present from an erudite Franciscan, who took the pains to trace it back to its source; for he had it from an elderly countess, who picked it up from a captain of cavalry, who acquired it from a marquise, who caught it from a page, who had received it from a Jesuit, who during his novitiate got it directly from one of the companions of Christopher Columbus. As for me, I shall not give it to anyone, for I am a dying man.

—Oh, Pangloss, cried Candide, that's a very strange genealogy. Isn't the devil at the root of the whole thing?

—Not at all, replied that great man; it's an indispensable part of the best of worlds, a necessary ingredient; if Columbus had not caught, on an American island, this sickness which attacks the source of generation and sometimes prevents generation entirely—which thus strikes at and defeats the greatest end of Nature herself—we should have neither chocolate nor cochineal. It must also be noted that until the present time this malady, like religious controversy, has been wholly confined to the continent of Europe. Turks, Indians, Persians, Chinese, Siamese, and Japanese know nothing of it as yet; but there is a sufficient reason for which they in turn will make its acquaintance in a couple of centuries. Meanwhile, it has made splendid progress among us, especially among those big armies of honest, well-trained mercenaries who decide the destinies of nations. You can be sure that when thirty thousand men fight a pitched battle against the same number of the enemy, there will be about twenty thousand with the pox on either side.

—Remarkable indeed, said Candide, but we must see about curing you.

—And how can I do that, said Pangloss, seeing I don't have a cent to my name? There's not a doctor in the whole world who will let your blood or give you an enema without demanding a fee. If you can't pay yourself, you must find someone to pay for you.

These last words decided Candide; he hastened to implore the help of his charitable Anabaptist, Jacques, and painted such a moving picture of his friend's wretched state that the good man did not hesitate to take in Pangloss and have him cured at his own expense. In the course of the cure, Pangloss lost only an eye and an ear. Since he wrote a fine hand and knew arithmetic, the Anabaptist made him his bookkeeper. At the end of two months, being obliged to go to Lisbon on business, he took his two philosophers on the boat with him. Pangloss still maintained that everything was for the best, but Jacques didn't agree with him.

—It must be, said he, that men have corrupted Nature, for they are not born wolves, yet that is what they become. God gave them neither twenty-four-pound cannon nor bayonets, yet they have manufactured both in order to destroy themselves. Bankruptcies have the same effect, and so does the justice which seizes the goods of bankrupts in order to prevent the creditors from getting them.[6]

—It was all indispensable, replied the one-eyed doctor, since private misfortunes make for public welfare, and therefore the more private misfortunes there are, the better everything is.

While he was reasoning, the air grew dark, the winds blew from all directions, and the vessel was attacked by a horrible tempest within sight of Lisbon harbor.

CHAPTER 5

Tempest, Shipwreck, Earthquake, and What Happened to Doctor Pangloss, Candide, and the Anabaptist, Jacques

Half of the passengers, weakened by the frightful anguish of seasickness and the distress of tossing about on stormy waters, were incapable of noticing their danger. The other half shrieked aloud and fell to their prayers, the sails were ripped to shreds, the masts snapped, the vessel opened at the seams. Everyone worked who could stir, nobody listened for orders or issued them. The Anabaptist was lending a hand in the after part of the ship when a frantic sailor struck him

---

6. Voltaire had suffered losses from various bankruptcy proceedings.

and knocked him to the deck; but just at that moment, the sailor lurched so violently that he fell head first over the side, where he hung, clutching a fragment of the broken mast. The good Jacques ran to his aid, and helped him to climb back on board, but in the process was himself thrown into the sea under the very eyes of the sailor, who allowed him to drown without even glancing at him. Candide rushed to the rail, and saw his benefactor rise for a moment to the surface, then sink forever. He wanted to dive to his rescue; but the philosopher Pangloss prevented him by proving that the bay of Lisbon had been formed expressly for this Anabaptist to drown in. While he was proving the point *a priori*, the vessel opened up and everyone perished except for Pangloss, Candide, and the brutal sailor who had caused the virtuous Anabaptist to drown; this rascal swam easily to shore, while Pangloss and Candide drifted there on a plank.

When they had recovered a bit of energy, they set out for Lisbon; they still had a little money with which they hoped to stave off hunger after escaping the storm.

Scarcely had they set foot in the town, still bewailing the loss of their benefactor, when they felt the earth quake underfoot; the sea was lashed to a froth, burst into the port, and smashed all the vessels lying at anchor there. Whirlwinds of fire and ash swirled through the streets and public squares; houses crumbled, roofs came crashing down on foundations, foundations split; thirty thousand inhabitants of every age and either sex were crushed in the ruins.[7] The sailor whistled through his teeth, and said with an oath:—There'll be something to pick up here.

—What can be the sufficient reason of this phenomenon? asked Pangloss.

—The Last Judgment is here, cried Candide.

But the sailor ran directly into the middle of the ruins, heedless of danger in his eagerness for gain; he found some money, laid violent hands on it, got drunk, and, having slept off his wine, bought the favors of the first streetwalker he could find amid the ruins of smashed houses, amid corpses and suffering victims on every hand. Pangloss however tugged at his sleeve.

—My friend, said he, this is not good form at all; your behavior falls short of that required by the universal reason; it's untimely, to say the least.

—Bloody hell, said the other, I'm a sailor, born in Batavia; I've been four times to Japan and stamped four times on the crucifix;[8] get out of here with your universal reason.

Some falling stonework had struck Candide; he lay prostrate in the street, covered with rubble, and calling to Pangloss:—For pity's sake bring me a little wine and oil; I'm dying.

—This earthquake is nothing novel, Pangloss replied; the city of Lima, in South America, underwent much the same sort of tremor, last year; same causes, same effects; there is surely a vein of sulphur under the earth's surface reaching from Lima to Lisbon.

—Nothing is more probable, said Candide; but, for God's sake, a little oil and wine.

---

7. The great Lisbon earthquake and fire occurred on November 1, 1755; between thirty and forty thousand deaths resulted.
8. The Japanese, originally receptive to foreign visitors, grew fearful that priests and proselytizers were merely advance agents of empire and expelled both the Portuguese and Spanish early in the 17th century. Only the Dutch were allowed to retain a small foothold, under humiliating conditions, of which the notion of stamping on the crucifix is symbolic. It was never what Voltaire suggests here, an actual requirement for entering the country.

—What do you mean, probable? replied the philosopher; I regard the case as proved.

Candide fainted and Pangloss brought him some water from a nearby fountain.

Next day, as they wandered amid the ruins, they found a little food which restored some of their strength. Then they fell to work like the others, bringing relief to those of the inhabitants who had escaped death. Some of the citizens whom they rescued gave them a dinner as good as was possible under the circumstances; it is true that the meal was a melancholy one, and the guests watered their bread with tears; but Pangloss consoled them by proving that things could not possibly be otherwise.

—For, said he, all this is for the best, since if there is a volcano at Lisbon, it cannot be somewhere else, since it is unthinkable that things should not be where they are, since everything is well.

A little man in black, an officer of the Inquisition,[9] who was sitting beside him, politely took up the question, and said:—It would seem that the gentleman does not believe in original sin, since if everything is for the best, man has not fallen and is not liable to eternal punishment.

—I most humbly beg pardon of your excellency, Pangloss answered, even more politely, but the fall of man and the curse of original sin entered necessarily into the best of all possible worlds.

—Then you do not believe in free will? said the officer.

—Your excellency must excuse me, said Pangloss; free will agrees very well with absolute necessity, for it was necessary that we should be free, since a will which is determined . . .

Pangloss was in the middle of his sentence, when the officer nodded significantly to the attendant who was pouring him a glass of port, or Oporto, wine.

CHAPTER 6

How They Made a Fine Auto-da-Fé to Prevent Earthquakes, and How Candide Was Whipped

After the earthquake had wiped out three quarters of Lisbon, the learned men of the land could find no more effective way of averting total destruction than to give the people a fine auto-da-fé;[1] the University of Coimbra had established that the spectacle of several persons being roasted over a slow fire with full ceremonial rites is an infallible specific against earthquakes.

In consequence, the authorities had rounded up a Biscayan convicted of marrying a woman who had stood godmother to his child, and two Portuguese who while eating a chicken had set aside a bit of bacon used for seasoning.[2] After dinner, men came with ropes to tie up Doctor Pangloss and his disciple Candide, one for talking and the other for listening with an air of approval; both were taken separately to a set of remarkably cool apartments, where the glare of the sun is

---

9. Specifically, a *familier* or *poursuivant,* an undercover agent with powers of arrest.
1. Literally, "act of faith," a public ceremony of repentance and humiliation. Such an auto-da-fé was actually held in Lisbon, June 20, 1756.

2. The Biscayan's fault lay in marrying someone within the forbidden bounds of relationship, an act of spiritual incest. The men who declined pork or bacon were understood to be crypto-Jews.

never bothersome; eight days later they were both dressed in *san-benitos* and crowned with paper mitres;[3] Candide's mitre and *san-benito* were decorated with inverted flames and with devils who had neither tails nor claws; but Pangloss's devils had both tails and claws, and his flames stood upright. Wearing these costumes, they marched in a procession, and listened to a very touching sermon, followed by a beautiful concert of plainsong. Candide was flogged in cadence to the music; the Biscayan and the two men who had avoided bacon were burned, and Pangloss was hanged, though hanging is not customary. On the same day there was another earthquake, causing frightful damage.[4]

Candide, stunned, stupefied, despairing, bleeding, trembling, said to himself:— If this is the best of all possible worlds, what are the others like? The flogging is not so bad, I was flogged by the Bulgars. But oh my dear Pangloss, greatest of philosophers, was it necessary for me to watch you being hanged, for no reason that I can see? Oh my dear Anabaptist, best of men, was it necessary that you should be drowned in the port? Oh Miss Cunégonde, pearl of young ladies, was it necessary that you should have your belly slit open?

He was being led away, barely able to stand, lectured, lashed, absolved, and blessed, when an old woman approached and said,—My son, be of good cheer and follow me.

CHAPTER 7

How an Old Woman Took Care of Candide, and How He Regained What He Loved

Candide was of very bad cheer, but he followed the old woman to a shanty; she gave him a jar of ointment to rub himself, left him food and drink; she showed him a tidy little bed; next to it was a suit of clothing.

—Eat, drink, sleep, she said; and may Our Lady of Atocha, Our Lord St. Anthony of Padua, and Our Lord St. James of Compostela watch over you. I will be back tomorrow.

Candide, still completely astonished by everything he had seen and suffered, and even more by the old woman's kindness, offered to kiss her hand.

—It's not *my* hand you should be kissing, said she. I'll be back tomorrow; rub yourself with the ointment, eat and sleep.

In spite of his many sufferings, Candide ate and slept. Next day the old woman returned bringing breakfast; she looked at his back and rubbed it herself with another ointment; she came back with lunch; and then she returned in the evening, bringing supper. Next day she repeated the same routine.

—Who are you? Candide asked continually. Who told you to be so kind to me? How can I ever repay you?

The good woman answered not a word; she returned in the evening, and without food.

—Come with me, says she, and don't speak a word.

Taking him by the hand, she walks out into the countryside with him for about a quarter of a mile; they reach an isolated house, quite surrounded by gardens

3. The cone-shaped paper cap (intended to resemble a bishop's mitre) and flowing yellow cape were customary garb for those pleading before the Inquisition.
4. In fact, the second quake occurred December 21, 1755.

and ditches. The old woman knocks at a little gate, it opens. She takes Candide up a secret stairway to a gilded room furnished with a fine brocaded sofa; there she leaves him, closes the door, disappears. Candide stood as if entranced; his life, which had seemed like a nightmare so far, was now starting to look like a delightful dream.

Soon the old woman returned; on her feeble shoulder leaned a trembling woman, of a splendid figure, glittering in diamonds, and veiled.

—Remove the veil, said the old woman to Candide.

The young man stepped timidly forward, and lifted the veil. What an event! What a surprise! Could it be Miss Cunégonde? Yes, it really was! She herself! His knees give way, speech fails him, he falls at her feet, Cunégonde collapses on the sofa. The old woman plies them with brandy, they return to their senses, they exchange words. At first they could utter only broken phrases, questions and answers at cross purposes, sighs, tears, exclamations. The old woman warned them not to make too much noise, and left them alone.

—Then it's really you, said Candide, you're alive, I've found you again in Portugal. Then you never were raped? You never had your belly ripped open, as the philosopher Pangloss assured me?

—Oh yes, said the lovely Cunégonde, but one doesn't always die of these two accidents.

—But your father and mother were murdered then?

—All too true, said Cunégonde, in tears.

—And your brother?

—Killed too.

—And why are you in Portugal? and how did you know I was here? and by what device did you have me brought to this house?

—I shall tell you everything, the lady replied; but first you must tell me what has happened to you since that first innocent kiss we exchanged and the kicking you got because of it.

Candide obeyed her with profound respect; and though he was overcome, though his voice was weak and hesitant, though he still had twinges of pain from his beating, he described as simply as possible everything that had happened to him since the time of their separation. Cunégonde lifted her eyes to heaven; she wept at the death of the good Anabaptist and at that of Pangloss; after which she told the following story to Candide, who listened to every word while he gazed on her with hungry eyes.

CHAPTER 8

Cunégonde's Story

—I was in my bed and fast asleep when heaven chose to send the Bulgars into our castle of Thunder-Ten-Tronckh. They butchered my father and brother, and hacked my mother to bits. An enormous Bulgar, six feet tall, seeing that I had swooned from horror at the scene, set about raping me; at that I recovered my senses, I screamed and scratched, bit and fought, I tried to tear the eyes out of that big Bulgar—not realizing that everything which had happened in my father's castle was a mere matter of routine. The brute then stabbed me with a knife on my left thigh, where I still bear the scar.

—What a pity! I should very much like to see it, said the simple Candide.

—You shall, said Cunégonde; but shall I go on?

—Please do, said Candide.

So she took up the thread of her tale:—A Bulgar captain appeared, he saw me covered with blood and the soldier too intent to get up. Shocked by the monster's failure to come to attention, the captain killed him on my body. He then had my wound dressed, and took me off to his quarters, as a prisoner of war. I laundered his few shirts and did his cooking; he found me attractive, I confess it, and I won't deny that he was a handsome fellow, with a smooth, white skin; apart from that, however, little wit, little philosophical training; it was evident that he had not been brought up by Doctor Pangloss. After three months, he had lost all his money and grown sick of me; so he sold me to a Jew named Don Issachar, who traded in Holland and Portugal, and who was mad after women. This Jew developed a mighty passion for my person, but he got nowhere with it; I held him off better than I had done with the Bulgar soldier; for though a person of honor may be raped once, her virtue is only strengthened by the experience. In order to keep me hidden, the Jew brought me to his country house, which you see here. Till then I had thought there was nothing on earth so beautiful as the castle of Thunder-Ten-Tronckh; I was now undeceived.

—One day the Grand Inquisitor took notice of me at mass; he ogled me a good deal, and made known that he must talk to me on a matter of secret business. I was taken to his palace; I told him of my rank; he pointed out that it was beneath my dignity to belong to an Israelite. A suggestion was then conveyed to Don Issachar that he should turn me over to My Lord the Inquisitor. Don Issachar, who is court banker and a man of standing, refused out of hand. The inquisitor threatened him with an auto-da-fé. Finally my Jew, fearing for his life, struck a bargain by which the house and I would belong to both of them as joint tenants; the Jew would get Mondays, Wednesdays, and the Sabbath, the inquisitor would get the other days of the week. That has been the arrangement for six months now. There have been quarrels; sometimes it has not been clear whether the night from Saturday to Sunday belonged to the old or the new dispensation. For my part, I have so far been able to hold both of them off; and that, I think, is why they are both still in love with me.

—Finally, in order to avert further divine punishment by earthquake, and to terrify Don Issachar, My Lord the Inquisitor chose to celebrate an auto-da-fé. He did me the honor of inviting me to attend. I had an excellent seat; the ladies were served with refreshments between the mass and the execution. To tell you the truth, I was horrified to see them burn alive those two Jews and that decent Biscayan who had married his child's godmother; but what was my surprise, my terror, my grief, when I saw, huddled in a *san-benito* and wearing a mitre, someone who looked like Pangloss! I rubbed my eyes, I watched his every move, I saw him hanged; and I fell back in a swoon. Scarcely had I come to my senses again, when I saw you stripped for the lash; that was the peak of my horror, consternation, grief, and despair. I may tell you, by the way, that your skin is even whiter and more delicate than that of my Bulgar captain. Seeing you, then, redoubled the torments which were already overwhelming me. I shrieked aloud, I wanted to call out, 'Let him go, you brutes!' but my voice died within me, and my cries would have been useless. When you had been thoroughly thrashed: 'How can it be,' I asked myself, 'that agreeable Candide and wise Pangloss have come to Lisbon, one to receive a hundred whiplashes, the other to be hanged by order of My Lord the Inquisitor, whose mistress I am? Pangloss must have deceived me cruelly when he told me that all is for the best in this world.'

—Frantic, exhausted, half out of my senses, and ready to die of weakness, I felt as if my mind were choked with the massacre of my father, my mother, my brother, with the arrogance of that ugly Bulgar soldier, with the knife slash he inflicted on me, my slavery, my cookery, my Bulgar captain, my nasty Don Issachar, my abominable inquisitor, with the hanging of Doctor Pangloss, with that great plainsong *miserere* which they sang while they flogged you—and above all, my mind was full of the kiss which I gave you behind the screen, on the day I saw you for the last time. I praised God, who had brought you back to me after so many trials. I asked my old woman to look out for you, and to bring you here as soon as she could. She did just as I asked; I have had the indescribable joy of seeing you again, hearing you and talking with you once more. But you must be frightfully hungry; I am, myself; let us begin with a dinner.

So then and there they sat down to table; and after dinner, they adjourned to that fine brocaded sofa, which has already been mentioned; and there they were when the eminent Don Issachar, one of the masters of the house, appeared. It was the day of the Sabbath; he was arriving to assert his rights and express his tender passion.

CHAPTER 9

What Happened to Cunégonde, Candide, the Grand Inquisitor, and a Jew

This Issachar was the most choleric Hebrew seen in Israel since the Babylonian captivity.

—What's this, says he, you bitch of a Christian, you're not satisfied with the Grand Inquisitor? Do I have to share you with this rascal, too?

So saying, he drew a long dagger, with which he always went armed, and, supposing his opponent defenceless, flung himself on Candide. But our good Westphalian had received from the old woman, along with his suit of clothes, a fine sword. Out it came, and though his manners were of the gentlest, in short order he laid the Israelite stiff and cold on the floor, at the feet of the lovely Cunégonde.

—Holy Virgin! she cried. What will become of me now? A man killed in my house! If the police find out, we're done for.

—If Pangloss had not been hanged, said Candide, he would give us good advice in this hour of need, for he was a great philosopher. Lacking him, let's ask the old woman.

She was a sensible body, and was just starting to give her opinion of the situation, when another little door opened. It was just one o'clock in the morning, Sunday morning. This day belonged to the inquisitor. In he came, and found the whipped Candide with a sword in his hand, a corpse at his feet, Cunégonde in terror, and an old woman giving them both good advice.

Here now is what passed through Candide's mind in this instant of time; this is how he reasoned:—If this holy man calls for help, he will certainly have me burned, and perhaps Cunégonde as well; he has already had me whipped without mercy; he is my rival; I have already killed once; why hesitate?

It was a quick, clear chain of reasoning; without giving the inquisitor time to recover from his surprise, he ran him through, and laid him beside the Jew.

—Here you've done it again, said Cunégonde; there's no hope for us now. We'll be excommunicated, our last hour has come. How is it that you, who were born so gentle, could kill in two minutes a Jew and a prelate?

—My dear girl, replied Candide, when a man is in love, jealous, and just whipped by the Inquisition, he is no longer himself.

The old woman now spoke up and said:—There are three Andalusian steeds in the stable, with their saddles and bridles; our brave Candide must get them ready: my lady has some gold coin and diamonds; let's take to horse at once, though I can only ride on one buttock; we will go to Cadiz. The weather is as fine as can be, and it is pleasant to travel in the cool of the evening.

Promptly, Candide saddled the three horses. Cunégonde, the old woman, and he covered thirty miles without a stop. While they were fleeing, the Holy Brotherhood[5] came to investigate the house; they buried the inquisitor in a fine church, and threw Issachar on the dunghill.

Candide, Cunégonde, and the old woman were already in the little town of Avacena, in the middle of the Sierra Morena; and there, as they sat in a country inn, they had this conversation.

CHAPTER 10

In Deep Distress, Candide, Cunégonde, and the Old Woman
Reach Cadiz; They Put to Sea

—Who then could have robbed me of my gold and diamonds? said Cunégonde, in tears. How shall we live? what shall we do? where shall I find other inquisitors and Jews to give me some more?

—Ah, said the old woman, I strongly suspect that reverend Franciscan friar who shared the inn with us yesterday at Badajoz. God save me from judging him unfairly! But he came into our room twice, and he left long before us.

—Alas, said Candide, the good Pangloss often proved to me that the fruits of the earth are a common heritage of all, to which each man has equal right. On these principles, the Franciscan should at least have left us enough to finish our journey. You have nothing at all, my dear Cunégonde?

—Not a maravedi, said she.

—What to do? said Candide.

—We'll sell one of the horses, said the old woman; I'll ride on the croup behind my mistress, though only on one buttock, and so we will get to Cadiz.

There was in the same inn a Benedictine prior; he bought the horse cheap. Candide, Cunégonde, and the old woman passed through Lucena, Chillas, and Lebrixa, and finally reached Cadiz. There a fleet was being fitted out and an army assembled, to reason with the Jesuit fathers in Paraguay, who were accused of fomenting among their flock a revolt against the kings of Spain and Portugal near the town of St. Sacrement.[6] Candide, having served in the Bulgar army, performed the Bulgar manual of arms before the general of the little army with such grace, swiftness, dexterity, fire, and agility, that they gave him a company of infantry to command. So here he is, a captain; and off he sails with Miss Cunégonde, the old woman, two valets, and the two Andalusian steeds which had belonged to My Lord the Grand Inquisitor of Portugal.

---

5. A semireligious order with police powers, very active in 18th-century Spain.
6. Actually, Colonia del Sacramento. Voltaire took great interest in the Jesuit role in Paraguay, which he has much oversimplified and largely misrepresented here in the interests of his satire. In 1750 they did, however, offer armed resistance to an agreement made between Spain and Portugal. They were subdued and expelled in 1769.

Throughout the crossing, they spent a great deal of time reasoning about the philosophy of poor Pangloss.

—We are destined, in the end, for another universe, said Candide; no doubt that is the one where everything is well. For in this one, it must be admitted, there is some reason to grieve over our physical and moral state.

—I love you with all my heart, said Cunégonde; but my soul is still harrowed by thoughts of what I have seen and suffered.

—All will be well, replied Candide; the sea of this new world is already better than those of Europe, calmer and with steadier winds. Surely it is the New World which is the best of all possible worlds.

—God grant it, said Cunégonde; but I have been so horribly unhappy in the world so far, that my heart is almost dead to hope.

—You pity yourselves, the old woman told them; but you have had no such misfortunes as mine.

Cunégonde nearly broke out laughing; she found the old woman comic in pretending to be more unhappy than she.

—Ah, you poor old thing, said she, unless you've been raped by two Bulgars, been stabbed twice in the belly, seen two of your castles destroyed, witnessed the murder of two of your mothers and two of your fathers, and watched two of your lovers being whipped in an auto-da-fé, I do not see how you can have had it worse than me. Besides, I was born a baroness, with seventy-two quarterings, and I have worked in a scullery.

—My lady, replied the old woman, you do not know my birth and rank; and if I showed you my rear end, you would not talk as you do, you might even speak with less assurance.

These words inspired great curiosity in Candide and Cunégonde, which the old woman satisfied with this story.

CHAPTER 11

The Old Woman's Story

—My eyes were not always bloodshot and red-rimmed, my nose did not always touch my chin, and I was not born a servant. I am in fact the daughter of Pope Urban the Tenth and the Princess of Palestrina.[7] Till the age of fourteen, I lived in a palace so splendid that all the castles of all your German barons would not have served it as a stable; a single one of my dresses was worth more than all the assembled magnificence of Westphalia. I grew in beauty, in charm, in talent, surrounded by pleasures, dignities, and glowing visions of the future. Already I was inspiring the young men to love; my breast was formed—and what a breast! white, firm, with the shape of the Venus de Medici;[8] and what eyes! what lashes, what black brows! What fire flashed from my glances and outshone the glitter of the stars, as the local poets used to tell me! The women who helped me dress and undress fell into ecstasies, whether they looked at me from in front or behind; and all the men wanted to be in their place.

---

7. Voltaire left behind a comment on this passage, a note first published in 1829: "Note the extreme discretion of the author; hitherto there has never been a pope named Urban X; he avoided attributing a bastard to a known pope. What circumspection! what an exquisite conscience!"

8. A famous Roman sculpture of Venus in marble from the 1st century B.C.E. that belonged to the Medici family in Italy; 18th-century Europeans considered it to be one of the best surviving works of art from ancient times.

—I was engaged to the ruling prince of Massa-Carrara; and what a prince he was! as handsome as I, softness and charm compounded, brilliantly witty, and madly in love with me. I loved him in return as one loves for the first time, with a devotion approaching idolatry. The wedding preparations had been made, with a splendor and magnificence never heard of before; nothing but celebrations, masks, and comic operas, uninterruptedly; and all Italy composed in my honor sonnets of which not one was even passable. I had almost attained the very peak of bliss, when an old marquise who had been the mistress of my prince invited him to her house for a cup of chocolate. He died in less than two hours, amid horrifying convulsions. But that was only a trifle. My mother, in complete despair (though less afflicted than I), wished to escape for a while the oppressive atmosphere of grief. She owned a handsome property near Gaeta.[9] We embarked on a papal galley gilded like the altar of St. Peter's in Rome. Suddenly a pirate ship from Salé swept down and boarded us. Our soldiers defended themselves as papal troops usually do; falling on their knees and throwing down their arms, they begged of the corsair absolution *in articulo mortis*.[1]

—They were promptly stripped as naked as monkeys, and so was my mother, and so were our maids of honor, and so was I too. It's a very remarkable thing, the energy these gentlemen put into stripping people. But what surprised me even more was that they stuck their fingers in a place where we women usually admit only a syringe. This ceremony seemed a bit odd to me, as foreign usages always do when one hasn't traveled. They only wanted to see if we didn't have some diamonds hidden there; and I soon learned that it's a custom of long standing among the genteel folk who swarm the seas. I learned that my lords the very religious knights of Malta never overlook this ceremony when they capture Turks, whether male or female; it's one of those international laws which have never been questioned.

—I won't try to explain how painful it is for a young princess to be carried off into slavery in Morocco with her mother. You can imagine everything we had to suffer on the pirate ship. My mother was still very beautiful; our maids of honor, our mere chambermaids, were more charming than anything one could find in all Africa. As for myself, I was ravishing, I was loveliness and grace supreme, and I was a virgin. I did not remain so for long; the flower which had been kept for the handsome prince of Massa-Carrara was plucked by the corsair captain; he was an abominable negro, who thought he was doing me a great favor. My Lady the Princess of Palestrina and I must have been strong indeed to bear what we did during our journey to Morocco. But on with my story; these are such common matters that they are not worth describing.

—Morocco was knee deep in blood when we arrived. Of the fifty sons of the emperor Muley-Ismael,[2] each had his faction, which produced in effect fifty civil wars, of blacks against blacks, of blacks against browns, halfbreeds against halfbreeds; throughout the length and breadth of the empire, nothing but one continual carnage.

—Scarcely had we stepped ashore, when some negroes of a faction hostile to my captor arrived to take charge of his plunder. After the diamonds and gold, we women were the most prized possessions. I was now witness of a struggle such as

9. About halfway between Rome and Naples.
1. Literally, when at the point of death. Absolution from a corsair in the act of murdering one is of very dubious validity.

2. Having reigned for more than fifty years, a potent and ruthless sultan of Morocco, he died in 1727 and left his kingdom in much the condition described.

you never see in the temperate climate of Europe. Northern people don't have hot blood; they don't feel the absolute fury for women which is common in Africa. Europeans seem to have milk in their veins; it is vitriol or liquid fire which pulses through these people around Mount Atlas. The fight for possession of us raged with the fury of the lions, tigers, and poisonous vipers of that land. A Moor snatched my mother by the right arm, the first mate held her by the left; a Moorish soldier grabbed one leg, one of our pirates the other. In a moment's time almost all our girls were being dragged four different ways. My captain held me behind him while with his scimitar he killed everyone who braved his fury. At last I saw all our Italian women, including my mother, torn to pieces, cut to bits, murdered by the monsters who were fighting over them. My captive companions, their captors, soldiers, sailors, blacks, browns, whites, mulattoes, and at last my captain, all were killed, and I remained half dead on a mountain of corpses. Similar scenes were occurring, as is well known, for more than three hundred leagues around, without anyone skimping on the five prayers a day decreed by Mohammed.

—With great pain, I untangled myself from this vast heap of bleeding bodies, and dragged myself under a great orange tree by a neighboring brook, where I collapsed, from terror, exhaustion, horror, despair, and hunger. Shortly, my weary mind surrendered to a sleep which was more of a swoon than a rest. I was in this state of weakness and languor, between life and death, when I felt myself touched by something which moved over my body. Opening my eyes, I saw a white man, rather attractive, who was groaning and saying under his breath: 'O che sciagura d'essere senza coglioni!'[3]

CHAPTER 12

The Old Woman's Story Continued

—Amazed and delighted to hear my native tongue, and no less surprised by what this man was saying, I told him that there were worse evils than those he was complaining of. In a few words, I described to him the horrors I had undergone, and then fainted again. He carried me to a nearby house, put me to bed, gave me something to eat, served me, flattered me, comforted me, told me he had never seen anyone so lovely, and added that he had never before regretted so much the loss of what nobody could give him back.

'I was born at Naples,' he told me, 'where they caponize two or three thousand children every year; some die of it, others acquire a voice more beautiful than any woman's, still others go on to become governors of kingdoms.[4] The operation was a great success with me, and I became court musician to the Princess of Palestrina . . .'

'Of my mother,' I exclaimed.

'Of your mother,' cried he, bursting into tears; 'then you must be the princess whom I raised till she was six, and who already gave promise of becoming as beautiful as you are now!'

'I am that very princess; my mother lies dead, not a hundred yards from here, buried under a pile of corpses.'

---

3. "Oh what a misfortune to have no testicles!"
4. The castrato Farinelli (1705–1782), origi-nally a singer, came to exercise considerable political influence on the kings of Spain, Philip V and Ferdinand VI.

—I told him my adventures, he told me his: that he had been sent by a Christian power to the King of Morocco, to conclude a treaty granting him gunpowder, cannon, and ships with which to liquidate the traders of the other Christian powers.

'My mission is concluded,' said this honest eunuch; 'I shall take ship at Ceuta and bring you back to Italy. *Ma che sciagura d'essere senza coglioni!*'

—I thanked him with tears of gratitude, and instead of returning me to Italy, he took me to Algiers and sold me to the dey of that country. Hardly had the sale taken place, when that plague which has made the rounds of Africa, Asia, and Europe broke out in full fury at Algiers. You have seen earthquakes; but tell me, young lady, have you ever had the plague?

—Never, replied the baroness.

—If you had had it, said the old woman, you would agree that it is far worse than an earthquake. It is very frequent in Africa, and I had it. Imagine, if you will, the situation of a pope's daughter, fifteen years old, who in three months' time had experienced poverty, slavery, had been raped almost every day, had seen her mother quartered, had suffered from famine and war, and who now was dying of pestilence in Algiers. As a matter of fact, I did not die; but the eunuch and the dey and nearly the entire seraglio of Algiers perished.

—When the first horrors of this ghastly plague had passed, the slaves of the dey were sold. A merchant bought me and took me to Tunis; there he sold me to another merchant, who resold me at Tripoli; from Tripoli I was sold to Alexandria, from Alexandria resold to Smyrna, from Smyrna to Constantinople. I ended by belonging to an aga of janizaries, who was shortly ordered to defend Azov against the besieging Russians.[5]

—The aga, who was a gallant soldier, took his whole seraglio with him, and established us in a little fort amid the Maeotian marshes,[6] guarded by two black eunuchs and twenty soldiers. Our side killed a prodigious number of Russians, but they paid us back nicely. Azov was put to fire and sword without respect for age or sex; only our little fort continued to resist, and the enemy determined to starve us out. The twenty janizaries had sworn never to surrender. Reduced to the last extremities of hunger, they were forced to eat our two eunuchs, lest they violate their oaths. After several more days, they decided to eat the women too.

—We had an imam,[7] very pious and sympathetic, who delivered an excellent sermon, persuading them not to kill us altogether.

'Just cut off a single rumpsteak from each of these ladies,' he said, 'and you'll have a fine meal. Then if you should need another, you can come back in a few days and have as much again; heaven will bless your charitable action, and you will be saved.'

—His eloquence was splendid, and he persuaded them. We underwent this horrible operation. The imam treated us all with the ointment that they use on newly circumcised children. We were at the point of death.

—Scarcely had the janizaries finished the meal for which we furnished the materials, when the Russians appeared in flat-bottomed boats; not a janizary escaped. The Russians paid no attention to the state we were in; but there are French physicians everywhere, and one of them, who knew his trade, took care of

5. Azov, near the mouth of the Don, was besieged by the Russians under Peter the Great in 1695–96. "Janizaries": an elite corps of the Ottoman armies.

6. The Roman name of the so-called Sea of Azov, a shallow swampy lake near the town.
7. In effect, a chaplain.

us. He cured us, and I shall remember all my life that when my wounds were healed, he made me a proposition. For the rest, he counselled us simply to have patience, assuring us that the same thing had happened in several other sieges, and that it was according to the laws of war.

—As soon as my companions could walk, we were herded off to Moscow. In the division of booty, I fell to a boyar who made me work in his garden, and gave me twenty whiplashes a day; but when he was broken on the wheel after about two years, with thirty other boyars, over some little court intrigue,[8] I seized the occasion; I ran away; I crossed all Russia; I was for a long time a chambermaid in Riga, then at Rostock, Vismara, Leipzig, Cassel, Utrecht, Leyden, The Hague, Rotterdam; I grew old in misery and shame, having only half a backside and remembering always that I was the daughter of a Pope; a hundred times I wanted to kill myself, but always I loved life more. This ridiculous weakness is perhaps one of our worst instincts; is anything more stupid than choosing to carry a burden that really one wants to cast on the ground? to hold existence in horror, and yet to cling to it? to fondle the serpent which devours us till it has eaten out our heart?

—In the countries through which I have been forced to wander, in the taverns where I have had to work, I have seen a vast number of people who hated their existence; but I never saw more than a dozen who deliberately put an end to their own misery: three negroes, four Englishmen, four Genevans, and a German professor named Robeck.[9] My last post was as servant to the Jew Don Issachar; he attached me to your service, my lovely one; and I attached myself to your destiny, till I have become more concerned with your fate than with my own. I would not even have mentioned my own misfortunes, if you had not irked me a bit, and if it weren't the custom, on shipboard, to pass the time with stories. In a word, my lady, I have had some experience of the world, I know it; why not try this diversion? Ask every passenger on this ship to tell you his story, and if you find a single one who has not often cursed the day of his birth, who has not often told himself that he is the most miserable of men, then you may throw me overboard head first.

CHAPTER 13

How Candide Was Forced to Leave the Lovely Cunégonde
and the Old Woman

Having heard out the old woman's story, the lovely Cunégonde paid her the respects which were appropriate to a person of her rank and merit. She took up the wager as well, and got all the passengers, one after another, to tell her their adventures. She and Candide had to agree that the old woman had been right.

—It's certainly too bad, said Candide, that the wise Pangloss was hanged, contrary to the custom of auto-da-fé; he would have admirable things to say of the physical evil and moral evil which cover land and sea, and I might feel within me the impulse to dare to raise several polite objections.

8. Voltaire had in mind an ineffectual conspiracy against Peter the Great known as the "revolt of the streltsy" or musketeers, which took place in 1698. Though easily put down, it provoked from the emperor a massive and atrocious program of reprisals.

9. Johann Robeck (1672–1739) published a treatise advocating suicide and showed his conviction by drowning himself at the age of sixty-seven.

As the passengers recited their stories, the boat made steady progress, and presently landed at Buenos Aires. Cunégonde, Captain Candide, and the old woman went to call on the governor, Don Fernando d'Ibaraa y Figueroa y Mascarenes y Lampourdos y Souza. This nobleman had the pride appropriate to a man with so many names. He addressed everyone with the most aristocratic disdain, pointing his nose so loftily, raising his voice so mercilessly, lording it so splendidly, and assuming so arrogant a pose, that everyone who met him wanted to kick him. He loved women to the point of fury; and Cunégonde seemed to him the most beautiful creature he had ever seen. The first thing he did was to ask directly if she were the captain's wife. His manner of asking this question disturbed Candide; he did not dare say she was his wife, because in fact she was not; he did not dare say she was his sister, because she wasn't that either; and though this polite lie was once common enough among the ancients,[1] and sometimes serves moderns very well, he was too pure of heart to tell a lie.

—Miss Cunégonde, said he, is betrothed to me, and we humbly beg your excellency to perform the ceremony for us.

Don Fernando d'Ibaraa y Figueroa y Mascarenes y Lampourdos y Souza twirled his moustache, smiled sardonically, and ordered Captain Candide to go drill his company. Candide obeyed. Left alone with My Lady Cunégonde, the governor declared his passion, and protested that he would marry her tomorrow, in church or in any other manner, as it pleased her charming self. Cunégonde asked for a quarter-hour to collect herself, consult the old woman, and make up her mind.

The old woman said to Cunégonde:—My lady, you have seventy-two quarterings and not one penny; if you wish, you may be the wife of the greatest lord in South America, who has a really handsome moustache; are you going to insist on your absolute fidelity? You have already been raped by the Bulgars; a Jew and an inquisitor have enjoyed your favors; miseries entitle one to privileges. I assure you that in your position I would make no scruple of marrying My Lord the Governor, and making the fortune of Captain Candide.

While the old woman was talking with all the prudence of age and experience, there came into the harbor a small ship bearing an alcalde and some alguazils.[2] This is what had happened.

As the old woman had very shrewdly guessed, it was a long-sleeved Franciscan who stole Cunégonde's gold and jewels in the town of Badajoz, when she and Candide were in flight. The monk tried to sell some of the gems to a jeweler, who recognized them as belonging to the Grand Inquisitor. Before he was hanged, the Franciscan confessed that he had stolen them, indicating who his victims were and where they were going. The flight of Cunégonde and Candide was already known. They were traced to Cadiz, and a vessel was hastily dispatched in pursuit of them. This vessel was now in the port of Buenos Aires. The rumor spread that an alcalde was aboard, in pursuit of the murderers of My Lord the Grand Inquisitor. The shrewd old woman saw at once what was to be done.

—You cannot escape, she told Cunégonde, and you have nothing to fear. You are not the one who killed my lord, and, besides, the governor, who is in love with you, won't let you be mistreated. Sit tight.

And then she ran straight to Candide:—Get out of town, she said, or you'll be burned within the hour.

---

1. Voltaire has in mind Abraham's adventures with Sarah (Genesis 12) and Isaac's with Rebecca (Genesis 26).

2. Police officers.

There was not a moment to lose; but how to leave Cunégonde, and where to go?

CHAPTER 14

How Candide and Cacambo Were Received by the Jesuits of Paraguay

Candide had brought from Cadiz a valet of the type one often finds in the provinces of Spain and in the colonies. He was one quarter Spanish, son of a half-breed in the Tucuman;[3] he had been choirboy, sacristan, sailor, monk, merchant, soldier, and lackey. His name was Cacambo, and he was very fond of his master because his master was a very good man. In hot haste he saddled the two Andalusian steeds.

—Hurry, master, do as the old woman says; let's get going and leave this town without a backward look.

Candide wept:—O my beloved Cunégonde! must I leave you now, just when the governor is about to marry us! Cunégonde, brought from so far, what will ever become of you?

—She'll become what she can, said Cacambo; women can always find something to do with themselves; God sees to it; let's get going.

—Where are you taking me? where are we going? what will we do without Cunégonde? said Candide.

—By Saint James of Compostela, said Cacambo, you were going to make war against the Jesuits, now we'll go make war for them. I know the roads pretty well, I'll bring you to their country, they will be delighted to have a captain who knows the Bulgar drill; you'll make a prodigious fortune. If you don't get your rights in one world, you will find them in another. And isn't it pleasant to see new things and do new things?

—Then you've already been in Paraguay? said Candide.

—Indeed I have, replied Cacambo; I was cook in the College of the Assumption, and I know the government of Los Padres[4] as I know the streets of Cadiz. It's an admirable thing, this government. The kingdom is more than three hundred leagues across; it is divided into thirty provinces. Los Padres own everything in it, and the people nothing; it's a masterpiece of reason and justice. I myself know nothing so wonderful as Los Padres, who in this hemisphere make war on the kings of Spain and Portugal, but in Europe hear their confessions; who kill Spaniards here, and in Madrid send them to heaven; that really tickles me; let's get moving, you're going to be the happiest of men. Won't Los Padres be delighted when they learn they have a captain who knows the Bulgar drill!

As soon as they reached the first barricade, Cacambo told the frontier guard that a captain wished to speak with My Lord the Commander. A Paraguayan officer ran to inform headquarters by laying the news at the feet of the commander. Candide and Cacambo were first disarmed and deprived of their Andalusian horses. They were then placed between two files of soldiers; the commander was at the end, his three-cornered hat on his head, his cassock drawn up, a sword at his side, and a pike in his hand. He nods, and twenty-four soldiers surround the newcomers. A sergeant then informs them that they must wait, that the commander

---

3. A province of Argentina, to the northwest of Buenos Aires.

4. The Jesuit fathers.

cannot talk to them, since the reverend father provincial has forbidden all Spaniards from speaking, except in his presence, and from remaining more than three hours in the country.

—And where is the reverend father provincial? says Cacambo.

—He is reviewing his troops after having said mass, the sergeant replies, and you'll only be able to kiss his spurs in three hours.

—But, says Cacambo, my master the captain, who, like me, is dying from hunger, is not Spanish at all, he is German; can't we have some breakfast while waiting for his reverence?

The sergeant promptly went off to report this speech to the commander.

—God be praised, said this worthy; since he is German, I can talk to him; bring him into my bower.

Candide was immediately led into a leafy nook surrounded by a handsome colonnade of green and gold marble and trellises amid which sported parrots, hummingbirds,[5] guinea fowl, and all the rarest species of birds. An excellent breakfast was prepared in golden vessels; and while the Paraguayans ate corn out of wooden bowls in the open fields under the glare of the sun, the reverend father commander entered into his bower.

He was a very handsome young man, with an open face, rather blonde in coloring, with ruddy complexion, arched eyebrows, liquid eyes, pink ears, bright red lips, and an air of pride, but a pride somehow different from that of a Spaniard or a Jesuit. Their confiscated weapons were restored to Candide and Cacambo, as well as their Andalusian horses; Cacambo fed them oats alongside the bower, always keeping an eye on them for fear of an ambush.

First Candide kissed the hem of the commander's cassock, then they sat down at the table.

—So you are German? said the Jesuit, speaking in that language.

—Yes, your reverence, said Candide.

As they spoke these words, both men looked at one another with great surprise, and another emotion which they could not control.

—From what part of Germany do you come? said the Jesuit.

—From the nasty province of Westphalia, said Candide; I was born in the castle of Thunder-Ten-Tronckh.

—Merciful heavens! cries the commander. Is it possible?

—What a miracle! exclaims Candide.

—Can it be you? asks the commander.

—It's impossible, says Candide.

They both fall back in their chairs, they embrace, they shed streams of tears.

—What, can it be you, reverend father! you, the brother of the lovely Cunégonde! you, who were killed by the Bulgars! you, the son of My Lord the Baron! you, a Jesuit in Paraguay! It's a mad world, indeed it is. Oh, Pangloss! Pangloss! how happy you would be, if you hadn't been hanged.

The commander dismissed his negro slaves and the Paraguayans who served his drink in crystal goblets. He thanked God and Saint Ignatius a thousand times, he clasped Candide in his arms, their faces were bathed in tears.

---

5. In this passage and several later ones, Voltaire uses in conjunction two words, both of which mean hummingbird. The French system of classifying hummingbirds, based on the work of the celebrated Buffon, distinguishes *oiseaux-mouches* with straight bills from *colibris* with curved bills. This distinction is wholly fallacious. Hummingbirds have all manner of shaped bills, and the division of species must be made on other grounds entirely.

—You would be even more astonished, even more delighted, even more beside yourself, said Candide, if I told you that My Lady Cunégonde, your sister, who you thought was disemboweled, is enjoying good health.

—Where?

—Not far from here, in the house of the governor of Buenos Aires; and to think that I came to make war on you!

Each word they spoke in this long conversation added another miracle. Their souls danced on their tongues, hung eagerly at their ears, glittered in their eyes. As they were Germans, they sat a long time at table, waiting for the reverend father provincial; and the commander spoke in these terms to his dear Candide.

CHAPTER 15

How Candide Killed the Brother of His Dear Cunégonde

—All my life long I shall remember the horrible day when I saw my father and mother murdered and my sister raped. When the Bulgars left, that adorable sister of mine was nowhere to be found; so they loaded a cart with my mother, my father, myself, two serving girls, and three little murdered boys, to carry us all off for burial in a Jesuit chapel some two leagues from our ancestral castle. A Jesuit sprinkled us with holy water; it was horribly salty, and a few drops got into my eyes; the father noticed that my lid made a little tremor; putting his hand on my heart, he felt it beat; I was rescued, and at the end of three weeks was as good as new. You know, my dear Candide, that I was a very pretty boy; I became even more so; the reverend father Croust,[6] superior of the abbey, conceived a most tender friendship for me; he accepted me as a novice, and shortly after, I was sent to Rome. The Father General had need of a resupply of young German Jesuits. The rulers of Paraguay accept as few Spanish Jesuits as they can; they prefer foreigners, whom they think they can control better. I was judged fit, by the Father General, to labor in this vineyard. So we set off, a Pole, a Tyrolean, and myself. Upon our arrival, I was honored with the posts of subdeacon and lieutenant; today I am a colonel and a priest. We are giving a vigorous reception to the King of Spain's men; I assure you they will be excommunicated as well as trounced on the battlefield. Providence has sent you to help us. But is it really true that my dear sister, Cunégonde, is in the neighborhood, with the governor of Buenos Aires?

Candide reassured him with a solemn oath that nothing could be more true. Their tears began to flow again.

The baron could not weary of embracing Candide; he called him his brother, his savior.

—Ah, my dear Candide, said he, maybe together we will be able to enter the town as conquerors, and be united with my sister Cunégonde.

—That is all I desire, said Candide; I was expecting to marry her, and I still hope to.

—You insolent dog, replied the baron, you would have the effrontery to marry my sister, who has seventy-two quarterings! It's a piece of presumption for you even to mention such a crazy project in my presence.

Candide, terrified by this speech, answered:—Most reverend father, all the quarterings in the world don't affect this case; I have rescued your sister out of

6. A Jesuit rector at Colmar with whom Voltaire had quarreled in 1754.

the arms of a Jew and an inquisitor; she has many obligations to me, she wants to marry me. Master Pangloss always taught me that men are equal; and I shall certainly marry her.

—We'll see about that, you scoundrel, said the Jesuit baron of Thunder-Ten-Tronckh; and so saying, he gave him a blow across the face with the flat of his sword. Candide immediately drew his own sword and thrust it up to the hilt in the baron's belly; but as he drew it forth all dripping, he began to weep.

—Alas, dear God! said he, I have killed my old master, my friend, my brother-in-law; I am the best man in the world, and here are three men I've killed already, and two of the three were priests.

Cacambo, who was standing guard at the entry of the bower, came running.

—We can do nothing but sell our lives dearly, said his master; someone will certainly come; we must die fighting.

Cacambo, who had been in similar scrapes before, did not lose his head; he took the Jesuit's cassock, which the commander had been wearing, and put it on Candide; he stuck the dead man's square hat on Candide's head, and forced him onto horseback. Everything was done in the wink of an eye.

—Let's ride, master; everyone will take you for a Jesuit on his way to deliver orders; and we will have passed the frontier before anyone can come after us.

Even as he was pronouncing these words, he charged off, crying in Spanish:— Way, make way for the reverend father colonel!

CHAPTER 16

What Happened to the Two Travelers with Two Girls, Two Monkeys, and the Savages Named Biglugs

Candide and his valet were over the frontier before anyone in the camp knew of the death of the German Jesuit. Foresighted Cacambo had taken care to fill his satchel with bread, chocolate, ham, fruit, and several bottles of wine. They pushed their Andalusian horses forward into unknown country, where there were no roads. Finally a broad prairie divided by several streams opened before them. Our two travelers turned their horses loose to graze; Cacambo suggested that they eat too, and promptly set the example. But Candide said:—How can you expect me to eat ham when I have killed the son of My Lord the Baron, and am now condemned never to see the lovely Cunégonde for the rest of my life? Why should I drag out my miserable days, since I must exist far from her in the depths of despair and remorse? And what will the *Journal de Trévoux*[7] say of all this?

Though he talked this way, he did not neglect the food. Night fell. The two wanderers heard a few weak cries which seemed to be voiced by women. They could not tell whether the cries expressed grief or joy; but they leaped at once to their feet, with that uneasy suspicion which one always feels in an unknown country. The outcry arose from two girls, completely naked, who were running swiftly along the edge of the meadow, pursued by two monkeys who snapped at their buttocks. Candide was moved to pity; he had learned marksmanship with the Bulgars, and could have knocked a nut off a bush without touching the leaves. He raised his Spanish rifle, fired twice, and killed the two monkeys.

---

7. A newspaper published by the Jesuit order, founded in 1701 and consistently hostile to Voltaire.

—God be praised, my dear Cacambo! I've saved these two poor creatures from great danger. Though I committed a sin in killing an inquisitor and a Jesuit, I've redeemed myself by saving the lives of two girls. Perhaps they are two ladies of rank, and this good deed may gain us special advantages in the country.

He had more to say, but his mouth shut suddenly when he saw the girls embracing the monkeys tenderly, weeping over their bodies, and filling the air with lamentations.

—I wasn't looking for quite so much generosity of spirit, said he to Cacambo; the latter replied:—You've really fixed things this time, master; you've killed the two lovers of these young ladies.

—Their lovers! Impossible! You must be joking, Cacambo; how can I believe you?

—My dear master, Cacambo replied, you're always astonished by everything. Why do you think it so strange that in some countries monkeys succeed in obtaining the good graces of women? They are one quarter human, just as I am one quarter Spanish.

—Alas, Candide replied, I do remember now hearing Master Pangloss say that such things used to happen, and that from these mixtures there arose pans, fauns, and satyrs, and that these creatures had appeared to various grand figures of antiquity; but I took all that for fables.

—You should be convinced now, said Cacambo; it's true, and you see how people make mistakes who haven't received a measure of education. But what I fear is that these girls may get us into real trouble.

These sensible reflections led Candide to leave the field and to hide in a wood. There he dined with Cacambo; and there both of them, having duly cursed the inquisitor of Portugal, the governor of Buenos Aires, and the baron, went to sleep on a bed of moss. When they woke up, they found themselves unable to move; the reason was that during the night the Biglugs,[8] natives of the country, to whom the girls had complained of them, had tied them down with cords of bark. They were surrounded by fifty naked Biglugs, armed with arrows, clubs, and stone axes. Some were boiling a caldron of water, others were preparing spits, and all cried out:—It's a Jesuit, a Jesuit! We'll be revenged and have a good meal; let's eat some Jesuit, eat some Jesuit!

—I told you, my dear master, said Cacambo sadly, I said those two girls would play us a dirty trick.

Candide, noting the caldron and spits, cried out:—We are surely going to be roasted or boiled. Ah, what would Master Pangloss say if he could see these men in a state of nature? All is for the best, I agree; but I must say it seems hard to have lost Miss Cunégonde and to be stuck on a spit by the Biglugs.

Cacambo did not lose his head.

—Don't give up hope, said he to the disconsolate Candide; I understand a little of the jargon these people speak, and I'm going to talk to them.

—Don't forget to remind them, said Candide, of the frightful inhumanity of eating their fellow men, and that Christian ethics forbid it.

—Gentlemen, said Cacambo, you have a mind to eat a Jesuit today? An excellent idea; nothing is more proper than to treat one's enemies so. Indeed, the law

8. Voltaire's name is "Oreillons," from Spanish "Orejones," a name mentioned in Garcilaso de Vega's *Historia General del Perú* (1609), on which Voltaire drew for many of the details in his picture of South America.

of nature teaches us to kill our neighbor, and that's how men behave the whole world over. Though we Europeans don't exercise our right to eat our neighbors, the reason is simply that we find it easy to get a good meal elsewhere; but you don't have our resources, and we certainly agree that it's better to eat your enemies than to let the crows and vultures have the fruit of your victory. But, gentlemen, you wouldn't want to eat your friends. You think you will be spitting a Jesuit, and it's your defender, the enemy of your enemies, whom you will be roasting. For my part, I was born in your country; the gentleman whom you see is my master, and far from being a Jesuit, he has just killed a Jesuit, the robe he is wearing was stripped from him; that's why you have taken a dislike to him. To prove that I am telling the truth, take his robe and bring it to the nearest frontier of the kingdom of Los Padres; find out for yourselves if my master didn't kill a Jesuit officer. It won't take long; if you find that I have lied, you can still eat us. But if I've told the truth, you know too well the principles of public justice, customs, and laws, not to spare our lives.

The Biglugs found this discourse perfectly reasonable; they appointed chiefs to go posthaste and find out the truth; the two messengers performed their task like men of sense, and quickly returned bringing good news. The Biglugs untied their two prisoners, treated them with great politeness, offered them girls, gave them refreshments, and led them back to the border of their state, crying joyously:— He isn't a Jesuit, he isn't a Jesuit!

Candide could not weary of exclaiming over his preservation.

—What a people! he said. What men! what customs! If I had not had the good luck to run a sword through the body of Miss Cunégonde's brother, I would have been eaten on the spot! But, after all, it seems that uncorrupted nature is good, since these folk, instead of eating me, showed me a thousand kindnesses as soon as they knew I was not a Jesuit.

CHAPTER 17

Arrival of Candide and His Servant at the Country of Eldorado, and What They Saw There

When they were out of the land of the Biglugs, Cacambo said to Candide:— You see that this hemisphere is no better than the other; take my advice, and let's get back to Europe as soon as possible.

—How to get back, asked Candide, and where to go? If I go to my own land, the Bulgars and Abares are murdering everyone in sight; if I go to Portugal, they'll burn me alive; if we stay here, we risk being skewered any day. But how can I ever leave that part of the world where Miss Cunégonde lives?

—Let's go toward Cayenne, said Cacambo, we shall find some Frenchmen there, for they go all over the world; they can help us; perhaps God will take pity on us.

To get to Cayenne was not easy; they knew more or less which way to go, but mountains, rivers, cliffs, robbers, and savages obstructed the way everywhere. Their horses died of weariness; their food was eaten; they subsisted for one whole month on wild fruits, and at last they found themselves by a little river fringed with coconut trees, which gave them both life and hope.

Cacambo, who was as full of good advice as the old woman, said to Candide:— We can go no further, we've walked ourselves out; I see an abandoned canoe on the bank, let's fill it with coconuts, get into the boat, and float with the current; a river always leads to some inhabited spot or other. If we don't find anything pleasant, at least we may find something new.

—Let's go, said Candide, and let Providence be our guide.

They floated some leagues between banks sometimes flowery, sometimes sandy, now steep, now level. The river widened steadily; finally it disappeared into a chasm of frightful rocks that rose high into the heavens. The two travelers had the audacity to float with the current into this chasm. The river, narrowly confined, drove them onward with horrible speed and a fearful roar. After twenty-four hours, they saw daylight once more; but their canoe was smashed on the snags. They had to drag themselves from rock to rock for an entire league; at last they emerged to an immense horizon, ringed with remote mountains. The countryside was tended for pleasure as well as profit; everywhere the useful was joined to the agreeable. The roads were covered, or rather decorated, with elegantly shaped carriages made of a glittering material, carrying men and women of singular beauty, and drawn by great red sheep which were faster than the finest horses of Andalusia, Tetuan, and Mequinez.

—Here now, said Candide, is a country that's better than Westphalia.

Along with Cacambo, he climbed out of the river at the first village he could see. Some children of the town, dressed in rags of gold brocade, were playing quoits at the village gate; our two men from the other world paused to watch them; their quoits were rather large, yellow, red, and green, and they glittered with a singular luster. On a whim, the travelers picked up several; they were of gold, emeralds, and rubies, and the least of them would have been the greatest ornament of the Great Mogul's throne.

—Surely, said Cacambo, these quoit players are the children of the king of the country.

The village schoolmaster appeared at that moment, to call them back to school.

—And there, said Candide, is the tutor of the royal household.

The little rascals quickly gave up their game, leaving on the ground their quoits and playthings. Candide picked them up, ran to the schoolmaster, and presented them to him humbly, giving him to understand by sign language that their royal highnesses had forgotten their gold and jewels. With a smile, the schoolmaster tossed them to the ground, glanced quickly but with great surprise at Candide's face, and went his way.

The travelers did not fail to pick up the gold, rubies, and emeralds.

—Where in the world are we? cried Candide. The children of this land must be well trained, since they are taught contempt for gold and jewels.

Cacambo was as much surprised as Candide. At last they came to the finest house of the village; it was built like a European palace. A crowd of people surrounded the door, and even more were in the entry; delightful music was heard, and a delicious aroma of cooking filled the air. Cacambo went up to the door, listened, and reported that they were talking Peruvian; that was his native language, for every reader must know that Cacambo was born in Tucuman, in a village where they talk that language exclusively.

—I'll act as interpreter, he told Candide; it's an hotel, let's go in.

Promptly two boys and two girls of the staff, dressed in cloth of gold, and wearing ribbons in their hair, invited them to sit at the host's table. The meal consisted of four soups, each one garnished with a brace of parakeets, a boiled condor which weighed two hundred pounds, two roast monkeys of an excellent flavor, three hundred birds of paradise in one dish and six hundred humming-birds in another, exquisite stews, delicious pastries, the whole thing served up in plates of what looked like rock crystal. The boys and girls of the staff poured them various beverages made from sugar cane.

The diners were for the most part merchants and travelers, all extremely polite, who questioned Cacambo with the most discreet circumspection, and answered his questions very directly.

When the meal was over, Cacambo as well as Candide supposed he could set-tle his bill handsomely by tossing onto the table two of those big pieces of gold which they had picked up; but the host and hostess burst out laughing, and for a long time nearly split their sides. Finally they subsided.

—Gentlemen, said the host, we see clearly that you're foreigners; we don't meet many of you here. Please excuse our laughing when you offered us in pay-ment a couple of pebbles from the roadside. No doubt you don't have any of our local currency, but you don't need it to eat here. All the hotels established for the promotion of commerce are maintained by the state. You have had meager enter-tainment here, for we are only a poor town; but everywhere else you will be given the sort of welcome you deserve.

Cacambo translated for Candide all the host's explanations, and Candide lis-tened to them with the same admiration and astonishment that his friend Cacambo showed in reporting them.

—What is this country, then, said they to one another, unknown to the rest of the world, and where nature itself is so different from our own? This probably is the country where everything is for the best; for it's absolutely necessary that such a country should exist somewhere. And whatever Master Pangloss said of the matter, I have often had occasion to notice that things went badly in Westphalia.

CHAPTER 18

What They Saw in the Land of Eldorado

Cacambo revealed his curiosity to the host, and the host told him:—I am an igno-rant man and content to remain so; but we have here an old man, retired from the court, who is the most knowing person in the kingdom, and the most talkative.

Thereupon he brought Cacambo to the old man's house. Candide now played second fiddle, and acted as servant to his own valet. They entered an austere little house, for the door was merely of silver and the paneling of the rooms was only gold, though so tastefully wrought that the finest paneling would not surpass it. If the truth must be told, the lobby was only decorated with rubies and emeralds; but the patterns in which they were arranged atoned for the extreme simplicity.

The old man received the two strangers on a sofa stuffed with bird-of-paradise feathers, and offered them several drinks in diamond carafes; then he satisfied their curiosity in these terms.

—I am a hundred and seventy-two years old, and I heard from my late father, who was liveryman to the king, about the astonishing revolutions in Peru which he had seen. Our land here was formerly part of the kingdom of the Incas, who rashly left it in order to conquer another part of the world, and who were ultimately destroyed by the Spaniards. The wisest princes of their house were those who had never left their native valley; they decreed, with the consent of the nation, that henceforth no inhabitant of our little kingdom should ever leave it; and this rule is what has preserved our innocence and our happiness. The Spaniards heard vague rumors about this land, they called it Eldorado;[9] and an English knight named Raleigh even came somewhere close to it about a hundred years ago; but as we are surrounded by unscalable mountains and precipices, we have managed so far to remain hidden from the rapacity of the European nations, who have an inconceivable rage for the pebbles and mud of our land, and who, in order to get some, would butcher us all to the last man.

The conversation was a long one; it turned on the form of the government, the national customs, on women, public shows, the arts. At last Candide, whose taste always ran to metaphysics, told Cacambo to ask if the country had any religion.

The old man grew a bit red.

—How's that? he said. Can you have any doubt of it? Do you suppose we are altogether thankless scoundrels?

Cacambo asked meekly what was the religion of Eldorado. The old man flushed again.

—Can there be two religions? he asked. I suppose our religion is the same as everyone's, we worship God from morning to evening.

—Then you worship a single deity? said Cacambo, who acted throughout as interpreter of the questions of Candide.

—It's obvious, said the old man, that there aren't two or three or four of them. I must say the people of your world ask very remarkable questions.

Candide could not weary of putting questions to this good old man; he wanted to know how the people of Eldorado prayed to God.

—We don't pray to him at all, said the good and respectable sage; we have nothing to ask him for, since everything we need has already been granted; we thank God continually.

Candide was interested in seeing the priests; he had Cacambo ask where they were. The old gentleman smiled.

—My friends, said he, we are all priests; the king and all the heads of household sing formal psalms of thanksgiving every morning, and five or six thousand voices accompany them.

—What! you have no monks to teach, argue, govern, intrigue, and burn at the stake everyone who disagrees with them?

—We should have to be mad, said the old man; here we are all of the same mind, and we don't understand what you're up to with your monks.

Candide was overjoyed at all these speeches, and said to himself:—This is very different from Westphalia and the castle of My Lord the Baron; if our friend Pangloss had seen Eldorado, he wouldn't have called the castle of Thunder-Ten-Tronckh the finest thing on earth; to know the world one must travel.

After this long conversation, the old gentleman ordered a carriage with six sheep made ready, and gave the two travelers twelve of his servants for their journey to the court.

—Excuse me, said he, if old age deprives me of the honor of accompanying you. The king will receive you after a style which will not altogether displease you, and you will doubtless make allowance for the customs of the country if there are any you do not like.

---

9. The myth of this land of gold somewhere in Central or South America had been widespread since the 16th century. *The Discovery of Guiana*, published in 1595, described Sir Walter Ralegh's infatuation with the myth of Eldorado and served to spread the story still further.

Candide and Cacambo climbed into the coach; the six sheep flew like the wind, and in less than four hours they reached the king's palace at the edge of the capital. The entryway was two hundred and twenty feet high and a hundred wide; it is impossible to describe all the materials of which it was made. But you can imagine how much finer it was than those pebbles and sand which we call gold and jewels.

Twenty beautiful girls of the guard detail welcomed Candide and Cacambo as they stepped from the carriage, took them to the baths, and dressed them in robes woven of hummingbird feathers; then the high officials of the crown, both male and female, led them to the royal chamber between two long lines, each of a thousand musicians, as is customary. As they approached the throne room, Cacambo asked an officer what was the proper method of greeting his majesty: if one fell to one's knees or on one's belly; if one put one's hands on one's head or on one's rear; if one licked up the dust of the earth—in a word, what was the proper form?[1]

—The ceremony, said the officer, is to embrace the king and kiss him on both cheeks.

Candide and Cacambo fell on the neck of his majesty, who received them with all the dignity imaginable, and asked them politely to dine.

In the interim, they were taken about to see the city, the public buildings rising to the clouds, the public markets and arcades, the fountains of pure water and of rose water, those of sugar cane liquors which flowed perpetually in the great plazas paved with a sort of stone which gave off odors of gilly-flower and rose petals. Candide asked to see the supreme court and the hall of parliament; they told him there was no such thing, that lawsuits were unknown. He asked if there were prisons, and was told there were not. What surprised him more, and gave him most pleasure, was the palace of sciences, in which he saw a gallery two thousand paces long, entirely filled with mathematical and physical instruments.

Having passed the whole afternoon seeing only a thousandth part of the city, they returned to the king's palace. Candide sat down to dinner with his majesty, his own valet Cacambo, and several ladies. Never was better food served, and never did a host preside more jovially than his majesty. Cacambo explained the king's witty sayings to Candide, and even when translated they still seemed witty. Of all the things which astonished Candide, this was not, in his eyes, the least astonishing.

They passed a month in this refuge. Candide never tired of saying to Cacambo:—It's true, my friend, I'll say it again, the castle where I was born does not compare with the land where we now are; but Miss Cunégonde is not here, and you doubtless have a mistress somewhere in Europe. If we stay here, we shall be just like everybody else, whereas if we go back to our own world, taking with us just a dozen sheep loaded with Eldorado pebbles, we shall be richer than all the kings put together, we shall have no more inquisitors to fear, and we shall easily be able to retake Miss Cunégonde.

This harangue pleased Cacambo; wandering is such pleasure, it gives a man such prestige at home to be able to talk of what he has seen abroad, that the two happy men resolved to be so no longer, but to take their leave of his majesty.

1. Candide's questions are probably derived from those of Gulliver on a similar occasion, in the third part of *Gulliver's Travels*.

—You are making a foolish mistake, the king told them; I know very well that my kingdom is nothing much; but when you are pretty comfortable somewhere, you had better stay there. Of course I have no right to keep strangers against their will, that sort of tyranny is not in keeping with our laws or our customs; all men are free; depart when you will, but the way out is very difficult. You cannot possibly go up the river by which you miraculously came; it runs too swiftly through its underground caves. The mountains which surround my land are ten thousand feet high, and steep as walls; each one is more than ten leagues across; the only way down is over precipices. But since you really must go, I shall order my engineers to make a machine which can carry you conveniently. When we take you over the mountains, nobody will be able to go with you, for my subjects have sworn never to leave their refuge, and they are too sensible to break their vows. Other than that, ask of me what you please.

—We only request of your majesty, Cacambo said, a few sheep loaded with provisions, some pebbles, and some of the mud of your country.

The king laughed.

—I simply can't understand, said he, the passion you Europeans have for our yellow mud; but take all you want, and much good may it do you.

He promptly gave orders to his technicians to make a machine for lifting these two extraordinary men out of his kingdom. Three thousand good physicists worked at the problem; the machine was ready in two weeks' time, and cost no more than twenty million pounds sterling, in the money of the country. Cacambo and Candide were placed in the machine; there were two great sheep, saddled and bridled to serve them as steeds when they had cleared the mountains, twenty pack sheep with provisions, thirty which carried presents consisting of the rarities of the country, and fifty loaded with gold, jewels, and diamonds. The king bade tender farewell to the two vagabonds.

It made a fine spectacle, their departure, and the ingenious way in which they were hoisted with their sheep up to the top of the mountains. The technicians bade them good-bye after bringing them to safety, and Candide had now no other desire and no other object than to go and present his sheep to Miss Cunégonde.

—We have, said he, enough to pay off the governor of Buenos Aires—if, indeed, a price can be placed on Miss Cunégonde. Let us go to Cayenne, take ship there, and then see what kingdom we can find to buy up.

CHAPTER 19

What Happened to Them at Surinam, and How Candide
Got to Know Martin

The first day was pleasant enough for our travelers. They were encouraged by the idea of possessing more treasures than Asia, Europe, and Africa could bring together. Candide, in transports, carved the name of Cunégonde on the trees. On the second day two of their sheep bogged down in a swamp and were lost with their loads; two other sheep died of fatigue a few days later; seven or eight others starved to death in a desert; still others fell, a little after, from precipices. Finally, after a hundred days' march, they had only two sheep left. Candide told Cacambo:—My friend, you see how the riches of this world are fleeting; the only solid things are virtue and the joy of seeing Miss Cunégonde again.

—I agree, said Cacambo, but we still have two sheep, laden with more treasure than the king of Spain will ever have; and I see in the distance a town which

I suspect is Surinam; it belongs to the Dutch. We are at the end of our trials and on the threshold of our happiness.

As they drew near the town, they discovered a negro stretched on the ground with only half his clothes left, that is, a pair of blue drawers; the poor fellow was also missing his left leg and his right hand.

—Good Lord, said Candide in Dutch, what are you doing in that horrible condition, my friend?

—I am waiting for my master, Mr. Vanderdendur,[2] the famous merchant, answered the negro.

—Is Mr. Vanderdendur, Candide asked, the man who treated you this way?

—Yes, sir, said the negro, that's how things are around here. Twice a year we get a pair of linen drawers to wear. If we catch a finger in the sugar mill where we work, they cut off our hand; if we try to run away, they cut off our leg: I have undergone both these experiences. This is the price of the sugar you eat in Europe. And yet, when my mother sold me for ten Patagonian crowns on the coast of Guinea, she said to me: 'My dear child, bless our witch doctors, reverence them always, they will make your life happy; you have the honor of being a slave to our white masters, and in this way you are making the fortune of your father and mother.' Alas! I don't know if I made their fortunes, but they certainly did not make mine. The dogs, monkeys, and parrots are a thousand times less unhappy than we are. The Dutch witch doctors who converted me tell me every Sunday that we are all sons of Adam, black and white alike. I am no genealogist; but if these preachers are right, we must all be remote cousins; and you must admit no one could treat his own flesh and blood in a more horrible fashion.

—Oh Pangloss! cried Candide, you had no notion of these abominations! I'm through, I must give up your optimism after all.

—What's optimism? said Cacambo.

—Alas, said Candide, it is a mania for saying things are well when one is in hell.

And he shed bitter tears as he looked at this negro, and he was still weeping as he entered Surinam.

The first thing they asked was if there was not some vessel in port which could be sent to Buenos Aires. The man they asked was a Spanish merchant who undertook to make an honest bargain with them. They arranged to meet in a café; Candide and the faithful Cacambo, with their two sheep, went there to meet with him.

Candide, who always said exactly what was in his heart, told the Spaniard of his adventures, and confessed that he wanted to recapture Miss Cunégonde.

—I shall take good care *not* to send you to Buenos Aires, said the merchant; I should be hanged, and so would you. The lovely Cunégonde is his lordship's favorite mistress.

This was a thunderstroke for Candide; he wept for a long time; finally he drew Cacambo aside.

—Here, my friend, said he, is what you must do. Each one of us has in his pockets five or six millions' worth of diamonds; you are cleverer than I; go get

2. A name perhaps intended to suggest Van-Duren, a Dutch bookseller with whom Voltaire had quarreled. In particular, the incident of gradually raising one's price recalls Van-Duren, to whom Voltaire had successively offered 1,000, 1,500, 2,000, and 3,000 florins for the return of the manuscript of Frederick the Great's *Anti-Machiavel*.

Miss Cunégonde in Buenos Aires. If the governor makes a fuss, give him a million; if that doesn't convince him, give him two millions; you never killed an inquisitor, nobody will suspect you. I'll fit out another boat and go wait for you in Venice. That is a free country, where one need have no fear either of Bulgars or Abares or Jews or inquisitors.

Cacambo approved of this wise decision. He was in despair at leaving a good master who had become a bosom friend; but the pleasure of serving him overcame the grief of leaving him. They embraced, and shed a few tears; Candide urged him not to forget the good old woman. Cacambo departed that very same day; he was a very good fellow, that Cacambo.

Candide remained for some time in Surinam, waiting for another merchant to take him to Italy, along with the two sheep which were left him. He hired servants and bought everything necessary for the long voyage; finally Mr. Vanderdendur, master of a big ship, came calling.

—How much will you charge, Candide asked this man, to take me to Venice— myself, my servants, my luggage, and those two sheep over there?

The merchant set a price of ten thousand piastres; Candide did not blink an eye.

—Oh, ho, said the prudent Vanderdendur to himself, this stranger pays out ten thousand piastres at once, he must be pretty well fixed.

Then, returning a moment later, he made known that he could not set sail under twenty thousand.

—All right, you shall have them, said Candide.

—Whew, said the merchant softly to himself, this man gives twenty thousand piastres as easily as ten.

He came back again to say he could not go to Venice for less than thirty thousand piastres.

—All right, thirty then, said Candide.

—Ah ha, said the Dutch merchant, again speaking to himself; so thirty thousand piastres mean nothing to this man; no doubt the two sheep are loaded with immense treasures; let's say no more; we'll pick up the thirty thousand piastres first, and then we'll see.

Candide sold two little diamonds, the least of which was worth more than all the money demanded by the merchant. He paid him in advance. The two sheep were taken aboard. Candide followed in a little boat, to board the vessel at its anchorage. The merchant bides his time, sets sail, and makes his escape with a favoring wind. Candide, aghast and stupefied, soon loses him from view.

—Alas, he cries, now there is a trick worthy of the old world!

He returns to shore sunk in misery; for he had lost riches enough to make the fortunes of twenty monarchs.

Now he rushes to the house of the Dutch magistrate, and, being a bit disturbed, he knocks loudly at the door; goes in, tells the story of what happened, and shouts a bit louder than is customary. The judge begins by fining him ten thousand piastres for making such a racket; then he listens patiently to the story, promises to look into the matter as soon as the merchant comes back, and charges another ten thousand piastres as the costs of the hearing.

This legal proceeding completed the despair of Candide. In fact he had experienced miseries a thousand times more painful, but the coldness of the judge, and that of the merchant who had robbed him, roused his bile and plunged him into a black melancholy. The malice of men rose up before his spirit in all its ugliness, and his mind dwelt only on gloomy thoughts. Finally, when a French vessel was ready to leave for Bordeaux, since he had no more diamond-laden sheep to transport, he took a cabin at a fair price, and made it known in the town that he would pay passage and keep, plus two thousand piastres, to any honest man who wanted to make the journey with him, on condition that this man must be the most disgusted with his own condition and the most unhappy man in the province.

This drew such a crowd of applicants as a fleet could not have held. Candide wanted to choose among the leading candidates, so he picked out about twenty who seemed companionable enough, and of whom each pretended to be more miserable than all the others. He brought them together at his inn and gave them a dinner, on condition that each would swear to tell truthfully his entire history. He would select as his companion the most truly miserable and rightly discontented man, and among the others he would distribute various gifts.

The meeting lasted till four in the morning. Candide, as he listened to all the stories, remembered what the old woman had told him on the trip to Buenos Aires, and of the wager she had made, that there was nobody on the boat who had not undergone great misfortunes. At every story that was told him, he thought of Pangloss.

—That Pangloss, he said, would be hard put to prove his system. I wish he was here. Certainly if everything goes well, it is in Eldorado and not in the rest of the world.

At last he decided in favor of a poor scholar who had worked ten years for the booksellers of Amsterdam. He decided that there was no trade in the world with which one should be more disgusted.

This scholar, who was in fact a good man, had been robbed by his wife, beaten by his son, and deserted by his daughter, who had got herself abducted by a Portuguese. He had just been fired from the little job on which he existed; and the preachers of Surinam were persecuting him because they took him for a Socinian.[3] The others, it is true, were at least as unhappy as he, but Candide hoped the scholar would prove more amusing on the voyage. All his rivals declared that Candide was doing them a great injustice, but he pacified them with a hundred piastres apiece.

CHAPTER 20

What Happened to Candide and Martin at Sea

The old scholar, whose name was Martin, now set sail with Candide for Bordeaux. Both men had seen and suffered much; and even if the vessel had been sailing from Surinam to Japan via the Cape of Good Hope, they would have been able to keep themselves amused with instances of moral evil and physical evil during the entire trip.

However, Candide had one great advantage over Martin, that he still hoped to see Miss Cunégonde again, and Martin had nothing to hope for; besides, he had gold and diamonds, and though he had lost a hundred big red sheep loaded with the greatest treasures of the earth, though he had always at his heart a memory of

---

3. A follower of Faustus and Laelius Socinus, 16th-century Polish theologians who proposed a form of "rational" Christianity that exalted the rational conscience and minimized such mysteries as the Trinity. The Socinians, by a special irony, were vigorous optimists.

the Dutch merchant's villainy, yet, when he thought of the wealth that remained in his hands, and when he talked of Cunégonde, especially just after a good dinner, he still inclined to the system of Pangloss.

—But what about you, Monsieur Martin, he asked the scholar, what do you think of all that? What is your idea of moral evil and physical evil?

—Sir, answered Martin, those priests accused me of being a Socinian, but the truth is that I am a Manichee.[4]

—You're joking, said Candide; there aren't any more Manichees in the world.

—There's me, said Martin; I don't know what to do about it, but I can't think otherwise.

—You must be possessed of the devil, said Candide.

—He's mixed up with so many things of this world, said Martin, that he may be in me as well as elsewhere; but I assure you, as I survey this globe, or globule, I think that God has abandoned it to some evil spirit—all of it except Eldorado. I have scarcely seen one town which did not wish to destroy its neighboring town, no family which did not wish to exterminate some other family. Everywhere the weak loathe the powerful, before whom they cringe, and the powerful treat them like brute cattle, to be sold for their meat and fleece. A million regimented assassins roam Europe from one end to the other, plying the trades of murder and robbery in an organized way for a living, because there is no more honest form of work for them; and in the cities which seem to enjoy peace and where the arts are flourishing, men are devoured by more envy, cares, and anxieties than a whole town experiences when it's under siege. Private griefs are worse even than public trials. In a word, I have seen so much and suffered so much, that I am a Manichee.

—Still there is some good, said Candide.

—That may be, said Martin, but I don't know it.

In the middle of this discussion, the rumble of cannon was heard. From minute to minute the noise grew louder. Everyone reached for his spyglass. At a distance of some three miles they saw two vessels fighting; the wind brought both of them so close to the French vessel that they had a pleasantly comfortable seat to watch the fight. Presently one of the vessels caught the other with a broadside so low and so square as to send it to the bottom. Candide and Martin saw clearly a hundred men on the deck of the sinking ship; they all raised their hands to heaven, uttering fearful shrieks; and in a moment everything was swallowed up.

—Well, said Martin, that is how men treat one another.

—It is true, said Candide, there's something devilish in this business.

As they chatted, he noticed something of a striking red color floating near the sunken vessel. They sent out a boat to investigate; it was one of his sheep. Candide was more joyful to recover this one sheep than he had been afflicted to lose a hundred of them, all loaded with big Eldorado diamonds.

The French captain soon learned that the captain of the victorious vessel was Spanish and that of the sunken vessel was a Dutch pirate. It was the same man who had robbed Candide. The enormous riches which this rascal had stolen were sunk beside him in the sea, and nothing was saved but a single sheep.

—You see, said Candide to Martin, crime is punished sometimes; this scoundrel of a Dutch merchant has met the fate he deserved.

---

4. Mani, a Persian sage and philosopher of the 3rd century, taught (probably under the influence of traditions stemming from Zoroaster and the worshipers of the sun god Mithra) that the earth is a field of dispute between two almost equal powers, one of light and one of darkness, both of which must be propitiated.

—Yes, said Martin; but did the passengers aboard his ship have to perish too? God punished the scoundrel, and the devil drowned the others.

Meanwhile the French and Spanish vessels continued on their journey, and Candide continued his talks with Martin. They disputed for fifteen days in a row, and at the end of that time were just as much in agreement as at the beginning. But at least they were talking, they exchanged their ideas, they consoled one another. Candide caressed his sheep.

—Since I have found you again, said he, I may well rediscover Miss Cunégonde.

CHAPTER 21

Candide and Martin Approach the Coast of France: They Reason Together

At last the coast of France came in view.

—Have you ever been in France, Monsieur Martin? asked Candide.

—Yes, said Martin, I have visited several provinces. There are some where half the inhabitants are crazy, others where they are too sly, still others where they are quite gentle and stupid, some where they venture on wit; in all of them the principal occupation is love-making, the second is slander, and the third stupid talk.

—But, Monsieur Martin, were you ever in Paris?

—Yes, I've been in Paris; it contains specimens of all these types; it is a chaos, a mob, in which everyone is seeking pleasure and where hardly anyone finds it, at least from what I have seen. I did not live there for long; as I arrived, I was robbed of everything I possessed by thieves at the fair of St. Germain; I myself was taken for a thief, and spent eight days in jail, after which I took a proofreader's job to earn enough money to return on foot to Holland. I knew the writing gang, the intriguing gang, the gang with fits and convulsions.[5] They say there are some very civilized people in that town; I'd like to think so.

—I myself have no desire to visit France, said Candide; you no doubt realize that when one has spent a month in Eldorado, there is nothing else on earth one wants to see, except Miss Cunégonde. I am going to wait for her at Venice; we will cross France simply to get to Italy; wouldn't you like to come with me?

—Gladly, said Martin; they say Venice is good only for the Venetian nobles, but that on the other hand they treat foreigners very well when they have plenty of money. I don't have any; you do, so I'll follow you anywhere.

—By the way, said Candide, do you believe the earth was originally all ocean, as they assure us in that big book belonging to the ship's captain?[6]

—I don't believe that stuff, said Martin, nor any of the dreams which people have been peddling for some time now.

—But why, then, was this world formed at all? asked Candide.

—To drive us mad, answered Martin.

—Aren't you astonished, Candide went on, at the love which those two girls showed for the monkeys in the land of the Biglugs that I told you about?

—Not at all, said Martin, I see nothing strange in these sentiments; I have seen so many extraordinary things that nothing seems extraordinary any more.

---

5. The Jansenists, a sect of strict Catholics, became notorious for spiritual ecstasies. Their public displays reached a height during the 1720s, and Voltaire described them in *Le* *Siècle de Louis XIV* (chap. 37), as well as in the article "Convulsions" in the *Philosophical Dictionary*.
6. The Bible: Genesis 1.

—Do you believe, asked Candide, that men have always massacred one another as they do today? That they have always been liars, traitors, ingrates, thieves, weaklings, sneaks, cowards, backbiters, gluttons, drunkards, misers, climbers, killers, calumniators, sensualists, fanatics, hypocrites, and fools?

—Do you believe, said Martin, that hawks have always eaten pigeons when they could get them?

—Of course, said Candide.

—Well, said Martin, if hawks have always had the same character, why do you suppose that men have changed?

—Oh, said Candide, there's a great deal of difference, because freedom of the will . . .

As they were disputing in this manner, they reached Bordeaux.

CHAPTER 22

What Happened in France to Candide and Martin

Candide paused in Bordeaux only long enough to sell a couple of Eldorado pebbles and to fit himself out with a fine two-seater carriage, for he could no longer do without his philosopher Martin; only he was very unhappy to part with his sheep, which he left to the academy of science in Bordeaux. They proposed, as the theme of that year's prize contest, the discovery of why the wool of the sheep was red; and the prize was awarded to a northern scholar[7] who demonstrated by A plus B minus C divided by Z that the sheep ought to be red and die of sheep rot.

But all the travelers with whom Candide talked in the roadside inns told him:— We are going to Paris.

This general consensus finally inspired in him too a desire to see the capital; it was not much out of his road to Venice.

He entered through the Faubourg Saint-Marceau,[8] and thought he was in the meanest village of Westphalia.

Scarcely was Candide in his hotel, when he came down with a mild illness caused by exhaustion. As he was wearing an enormous diamond ring, and people had noticed among his luggage a tremendously heavy safe, he soon found at his bedside two doctors whom he had not called, several intimate friends who never left him alone, and two pious ladies who helped to warm his broth. Martin said:— I remember that I too was ill on my first trip to Paris; I was very poor; and as I had neither friends, pious ladies, nor doctors, I got well.

However, as a result of medicines and bleedings, Candide's illness became serious. A resident of the neighborhood came to ask him politely to fill out a ticket, to be delivered to the porter of the other world.[9] Candide wanted nothing to do with it. The pious ladies assured him it was a new fashion; Candide replied that he wasn't a man of fashion. Martin wanted to throw the resident out the window.

7. Maupertuis Le Lapon, philosopher and mathematician, whom Voltaire had accused of trying to adduce mathematical proofs of the existence of God.

8. A district on the left bank, notably grubby in the 18th century. "As I entered [Paris] through the Faubourg Saint-Marceau, I saw nothing but dirty stinking little streets, ugly black houses, a general air of squalor and pov-

erty, beggars, carters, menders of clothes, sellers of herb-drinks and old hats." Jean-Jacques Rousseau, *Confessions*, Book IV.

9. In the middle of the 18th century in France, it became customary to require persons who were grievously ill to sign *billets de confession*, without which they could not be given absolution, admitted to the last sacraments, or buried in consecrated ground.

The cleric swore that without the ticket they wouldn't bury Candide. Martin swore that he would bury the cleric if he continued to be a nuisance. The quarrel grew heated; Martin took him by the shoulders and threw him bodily out the door; all of which caused a great scandal, from which developed a legal case.

Candide got better; and during his convalescence he had very good company in to dine. They played cards for money; and Candide was quite surprised that none of the aces were ever dealt to him, and Martin was not surprised at all.

Among those who did the honors of the town for Candide there was a little abbé from Perigord, one of those busy fellows, always bright, always useful, assured, obsequious, and obliging, who waylay passing strangers, tell them the scandal of the town, and offer them pleasures at any price they want to pay. This fellow first took Candide and Martin to the theatre. A new tragedy was being played. Candide found himself seated next to a group of wits. That did not keep him from shedding a few tears in the course of some perfectly played scenes. One of the commentators beside him remarked during the intermission:—You are quite mistaken to weep, this actress is very bad indeed; the actor who plays with her is even worse; and the play is even worse than the actors in it. The author knows not a word of Arabic, though the action takes place in Arabia; and besides, he is a man who doesn't believe in innate ideas. Tomorrow I will show you twenty pamphlets written against him.

—Tell me, sir, said Candide to the abbé, how many plays are there for performance in France?

—Five or six thousand, replied the other.

—That's a lot, said Candide; how many of them are any good?

—Fifteen or sixteen, was the answer.

—That's a lot, said Martin.

Candide was very pleased with an actress who took the part of Queen Elizabeth in a rather dull tragedy[1] that still gets played from time to time.

—I like this actress very much, he said to Martin, she bears a slight resemblance to Miss Cunégonde; I should like to meet her.

The abbé from Perigord offered to introduce him. Candide, raised in Germany, asked what was the protocol, how one behaved in France with queens of England.

—You must distinguish, said the abbé; in the provinces, you take them to an inn; at Paris they are respected while still attractive, and thrown on the dunghill when they are dead.[2]

—Queens on the dunghill! said Candide.

—Yes indeed, said Martin, the abbé is right; I was in Paris when Miss Monime herself[3] passed, as they say, from this life to the other; she was refused what these folk call 'the honors of burial,' that is, the right to rot with all the beggars of the district in a dirty cemetery; she was buried all alone by her troupe at the corner of the Rue de Bourgogne; this must have been very disagreeable to her, for she had a noble character.

—That was extremely rude, said Candide.

---

1. *Le Comte d'Essex* by Thomas Corneille.
2. Voltaire engaged in a long and vigorous campaign against the rule that actors and actresses could not be buried in consecrated ground. The superstition probably arose from a feeling that by assuming false identities they drained their own souls.
3. Adrienne Lecouvreur (1690–1730), so called because she made her debut as Monime in Racine's *Mithridate*. Voltaire had assisted at her secret midnight funeral and wrote an indignant poem about it.

—What do you expect? said Martin; that is how these folk are. Imagine all the contradictions, all the incompatibilities you can, and you will see them in the government, the courts, the churches, and the plays of this crazy nation.

—Is it true that they are always laughing in Paris? asked Candide.

—Yes, said the abbé, but with a kind of rage too; when people complain of things, they do so amid explosions of laughter; they even laugh as they perform the most detestable actions.

—Who was that fat swine, said Candide, who spoke so nastily about the play over which I was weeping, and the actors who gave me so much pleasure?

—He is a living illness, answered the abbé, who makes a business of slandering all the plays and books; he hates the successful ones, as eunuchs hate successful lovers; he's one of those literary snakes who live on filth and venom; he's a folliculator . . .

—What's this word *folliculator?* asked Candide.

—It's a folio filler, said the abbé, a Fréron.[4]

It was after this fashion that Candide, Martin, and the abbé from Perigord chatted on the stairway as they watched the crowd leaving the theatre.

—Although I'm in a great hurry to see Miss Cunégonde again, said Candide, I would very much like to dine with Miss Clairon,[5] for she seemed to me admirable.

The abbé was not the man to approach Miss Clairon, who saw only good company.

—She has an engagement tonight, he said; but I shall have the honor of introducing you to a lady of quality, and there you will get to know Paris as if you had lived here for years.

Candide, who was curious by nature, allowed himself to be brought to the lady's house, in the depths of the Faubourg St.-Honoré; they were playing faro;[6] twelve melancholy punters held in their hands a little sheaf of cards, blank summaries of their bad luck. Silence reigned supreme, the punters were pallid, the banker uneasy; and the lady of the house, seated beside the pitiless banker, watched with the eyes of a lynx for the various illegal redoublings and bets at long odds which the players tried to signal by folding the corners of their cards; she had them unfolded with a determination which was severe but polite, and concealed her anger lest she lose her customers. The lady caused herself to be known as the Marquise of Parolignac.[7] Her daughter, fifteen years old, sat among the punters and tipped off her mother with a wink to the sharp practices of these unhappy players when they tried to recoup their losses. The abbé from Perigord, Candide, and Martin came in; nobody arose or greeted them or looked at them; all were lost in the study of their cards.

—My Lady the Baroness of Thunder-Ten-Tronckh was more civil, thought Candide.

However, the abbé whispered in the ear of the marquise, who, half rising, honored Candide with a gracious smile and Martin with a truly noble nod; she gave a

4. A successful and popular journalist who had attacked several of Voltaire's plays, including *Tancrède*.
5. Actually Claire Leris (1723–1803). She had played the lead role in *Tancrède* and was for many years a leading figure on the Paris stage.
6. A game of cards, about which it is necessary to know only that a number of punters play against a banker or dealer. The pack is dealt out two cards at a time, and each player may bet on any card as much as he pleases. The sharp practices of the punters consist essentially of tricks for increasing their winnings without corresponding risks.
7. A *paroli* is an illegal redoubling of one's bet; her name therefore implies a title grounded in cardsharping.

seat and dealt a hand of cards to Candide, who lost fifty thousand francs in two turns; after which they had a very merry supper. Everyone was amazed that Candide was not upset over his losses; the lackeys, talking together in their usual lackey language, said:—He must be some English milord.

The supper was like most Parisian suppers: first silence, then an indistinguishable rush of words; then jokes, mostly insipid, false news, bad logic, a little politics, a great deal of malice. They even talked of new books.

—Have you seen the new novel by Dr. Gauchat, the theologian?[8] asked the abbé from Perigord.

—Oh yes, answered one of the guests; but I couldn't finish it. We have a horde of impudent scribblers nowadays, but all of them put together don't match the impudence of this Gauchat, this doctor of theology. I have been so struck by the enormous number of detestable books which are swamping us that I have taken up punting at faro.

—And the *Collected Essays* of Archdeacon T———[9] asked the abbé, what do you think of them?

—Ah, said Madame de Parolignac, what a frightful bore he is! He takes such pains to tell you what everyone knows; he discourses so learnedly on matters which aren't worth a casual remark! He plunders, and not even wittily, the wit of other people! He spoils what he plunders, he's disgusting! But he'll never disgust me again; a couple of pages of the archdeacon have been enough for me.

There was at table a man of learning and taste, who supported the marquise on this point. They talked next of tragedies; the lady asked why there were tragedies which played well enough but which were wholly unreadable. The man of taste explained very clearly how a play could have a certain interest and yet little merit otherwise; he showed succinctly that it was not enough to conduct a couple of intrigues, such as one can find in any novel, and which never fail to excite the spectator's interest; but that one must be new without being grotesque, frequently touch the sublime but never depart from the natural; that one must know the human heart and give it words; that one must be a great poet without allowing any character in the play to sound like a poet; and that one must know the language perfectly, speak it purely, and maintain a continual harmony without ever sacrificing sense to mere sound.

—Whoever, he added, does not observe all these rules may write one or two tragedies which succeed in the theatre, but he will never be ranked among the good writers; there are very few good tragedies; some are idylls in well-written, well-rhymed dialogue, others are political arguments which put the audience to sleep, or revolting pomposities; still others are the fantasies of enthusiasts, barbarous in style, incoherent in logic, full of long speeches to the gods because the author does not know how to address men, full of false maxims and emphatic commonplaces.

Candide listened attentively to this speech and conceived a high opinion of the speaker; and as the marquise had placed him by her side, he turned to ask her who was this man who spoke so well.

—He is a scholar, said the lady, who never plays cards and whom the abbé sometimes brings to my house for supper; he knows all about tragedies and

8. He had written against Voltaire, and Voltaire suspected him (wrongly) of having written the novel *L'Oracle des nouveaux philosophes*.
9. His name was Trublet, and he had said, among other disagreeable things, that Voltaire's epic poem, the *Henriade,* made him yawn and that Voltaire's genius was "the perfection of mediocrity."

books, and has himself written a tragedy that was hissed from the stage and a book, the only copy of which ever seen outside his publisher's office was dedicated to me.

—What a great man, said Candide, he's Pangloss all over.

Then, turning to him, he said:—Sir, you doubtless think everything is for the best in the physical as well as the moral universe, and that nothing could be otherwise than as it is?

—Not at all, sir, replied the scholar, I believe nothing of the sort. I find that everything goes wrong in our world; that nobody knows his place in society or his duty, what he's doing or what he ought to be doing, and that outside of mealtimes, which are cheerful and congenial enough, all the rest of the day is spent in useless quarrels, as of Jansenists against Molinists,[1] parliament-men against churchmen, literary men against literary men, courtiers against courtiers, financiers against the plebs, wives against husbands, relatives against relatives—it's one unending warfare.

Candide answered:—I have seen worse; but a wise man, who has since had the misfortune to be hanged, taught me that everything was marvelously well arranged. Troubles are just the shadows in a beautiful picture.

—Your hanged philosopher was joking, said Martin; the shadows are horrible ugly blots.

—It is human beings who make the blots, said Candide, and they can't do otherwise.

—Then it isn't their fault, said Martin.

Most of the faro players, who understood this sort of talk not at all, kept on drinking; Martin disputed with the scholar, and Candide told part of his story to the lady of the house.

After supper, the marquise brought Candide into her room and sat him down on a divan.

—Well, she said to him, are you still madly in love with Miss Cunégonde of Thunder-Ten-Tronckh?

—Yes, ma'am, replied Candide. The marquise turned upon him a tender smile.

—You answer like a young man of Westphalia, said she; a Frenchman would have told me: 'It is true that I have been in love with Miss Cunégonde; but since seeing you, madame, I fear that I love her no longer.'

—Alas, ma'am, said Candide, I will answer any way you want.

—Your passion for her, said the marquise, began when you picked up her handkerchief; I prefer that you should pick up my garter.

—Gladly, said Candide, and picked it up.

—But I also want you to put it back on, said the lady; and Candide put it on again.

—Look you now, said the lady, you are a foreigner; my Paris lovers I sometimes cause to languish for two weeks or so, but to you I surrender the very first night, because we must render the honors of the country to a young man from Westphalia.

---

1. The Jansenists (from Corneille Jansen, 1585–1638) were a relatively strict party of religious reform; the Molinists (from Luis Molina) were the party of the Jesuits. Their central issue of controversy was the relative importance of divine grace and human will to the salvation of man.

The beauty, who had seen two enormous diamonds on the two hands of her young friend, praised them so sincerely that from the fingers of Candide they passed over to the fingers of the marquise.

As he returned home with his Perigord abbé, Candide felt some remorse at having been unfaithful to Miss Cunégonde; the abbé sympathized with his grief; he had only a small share in the fifty thousand francs which Candide lost at cards, and in the proceeds of the two diamonds which had been half-given, half-extorted. His scheme was to profit, as much as he could, from the advantage of knowing Candide. He spoke at length of Cunégonde, and Candide told him that he would beg forgiveness for his beloved for his infidelity when he met her at Venice.

The Perigordian overflowed with politeness and unction, taking a tender interest in everything Candide said, everything he did, and everything he wanted to do.

—Well, sir, said he, so you have an assignation at Venice?

—Yes indeed, sir, I do, said Candide; it is absolutely imperative that I go there to find Miss Cunégonde.

And then, carried away by the pleasure of talking about his love, he recounted, as he often did, a part of his adventures with that illustrious lady of Westphalia.

—I suppose, said the abbé, that Miss Cunégonde has a fine wit and writes charming letters.

—I never received a single letter from her, said Candide; for, as you can imagine, after being driven out of the castle for love of her, I couldn't write; shortly I learned that she was dead; then I rediscovered her; then I lost her again, and I have now sent, to a place more than twenty-five hundred leagues from here, a special agent whose return I am expecting.

The abbé listened carefully, and looked a bit dreamy. He soon took his leave of the two strangers, after embracing them tenderly. Next day Candide, when he woke up, received a letter, to the following effect:

—Dear sir, my very dear lover, I have been lying sick in this town for a week, I have just learned that you are here. I would fly to your arms if I could move. I heard that you had passed through Bordeaux; that was where I left the faithful Cacambo and the old woman, who are soon to follow me here. The governor of Buenos Aires took everything, but left me your heart. Come; your presence will either return me to life or cause me to die of joy.

This charming letter, coming so unexpectedly, filled Candide with inexpressible delight, while the illness of his dear Cunégonde covered him with grief. Torn between these two feelings, he took gold and diamonds, and had himself brought, with Martin, to the hotel where Miss Cunégonde was lodging. Trembling with emotion, he enters the room; his heart thumps, his voice breaks. He tries to open the curtains of the bed, he asks to have some lights.

—Absolutely forbidden, says the serving girl; light will be the death of her.

And abruptly she pulls shut the curtain.

—My dear Cunégonde, says Candide in tears, how are you feeling? If you can't see me, won't you at least speak to me?

—She can't talk, says the servant.

But then she draws forth from the bed a plump hand, over which Candide weeps a long time, and which he fills with diamonds, meanwhile leaving a bag of gold on the chair.

Amid his transports, there arrives a bailiff followed by the abbé from Perigord and a strong-arm squad.

—These here are the suspicious foreigners? says the officer; and he has them seized and orders his bullies to drag them off to jail.

—They don't treat visitors like this in Eldorado, says Candide.

—I am more a Manichee than ever, says Martin.

—But, please sir, where are you taking us? says Candide.

—To the lowest hole in the dungeons, says the bailiff.

Martin, having regained his self-possession, decided that the lady who pretended to be Cunégonde was a cheat, the abbé from Perigord was another cheat who had imposed on Candide's innocence, and the bailiff still another cheat, of whom it would be easy to get rid.

Rather than submit to the forms of justice, Candide, enlightened by Martin's advice and eager for his own part to see the real Cunégonde again, offered the bailiff three little diamonds worth about three thousand pistoles apiece.

—Ah, my dear sir! cried the man with the ivory staff, even if you have committed every crime imaginable, you are the most honest man in the world. Three diamonds! each one worth three thousand pistoles! My dear sir! I would gladly die for you, rather than take you to jail. All foreigners get arrested here; but let me manage it; I have a brother at Dieppe in Normandy; I'll take you to him; and if you have a bit of a diamond to give him, he'll take care of you, just like me.

—And why do they arrest all foreigners? asked Candide.

The abbé from Perigord spoke up and said:—It's because a beggar from Atrebatum[2] listened to some stupidities; that made him commit a parricide, not like the one of May, 1610, but like the one of December, 1594, much on the order of several other crimes committed in other years and other months by other beggars who had listened to stupidities.

The bailiff then explained what it was all about.[3]

—Foh! what beasts! cried Candide. What! monstrous behavior of this sort from a people who sing and dance? As soon as I can, let me get out of this country, where the monkeys provoke the tigers. In my own country I've lived with bears; only in Eldorado are there proper men. In the name of God, sir bailiff, get me to Venice where I can wait for Miss Cunégonde.

—I can only get you to Lower Normandy, said the guardsman.

He had the irons removed at once, said there had been a mistake, dismissed his gang, and took Candide and Martin to Dieppe, where he left them with his brother. There was a little Dutch ship at anchor. The Norman, changed by three more diamonds into the most helpful of men, put Candide and his people aboard the vessel, which was bound for Portsmouth in England. It wasn't on the way to Venice, but Candide felt like a man just let out of hell; and he hoped to get back on the road to Venice at the first possible occasion.

2. The Latin name for the district of Artois, from which came Robert-François Damiens, who tried to stab Louis XV in 1757. The assassination failed, like that of Châtel, who tried to kill Henri IV in 1594, but unlike that of Ravaillac, who succeeded in killing him in 1610.
3. The point, in fact, is not too clear since arresting foreigners is an indirect way at best to guard against homegrown fanatics, and the position of the abbé from Perigord in the whole transaction remains confused. Has he called in the officer just to get rid of Candide? If so, why is he sardonic about the very suspicions he is trying to foster? Candide's reaction is to the notion that Frenchmen should be capable of political assassination at all; it seems excessive.

CHAPTER 23

*Candide and Martin Pass the Shores of England;
What They See There*

—Ah, Pangloss! Pangloss! Ah, Martin! Martin! Ah, my darling Cunégonde! What is this world of ours? sighed Candide on the Dutch vessel.

—Something crazy, something abominable, Martin replied.

—You have been in England; are people as crazy there as in France?

—It's a different sort of crazy, said Martin. You know that these two nations have been at war over a few acres of snow near Canada, and that they are spending on this fine struggle more than Canada itself is worth.[4] As for telling you if there are more people in one country or the other who need a strait jacket, that is a judgment too fine for my understanding; I know only that the people we are going to visit are eaten up with melancholy.

As they chatted thus, the vessel touched at Portsmouth. A multitude of people covered the shore, watching closely a rather bulky man who was kneeling, his eyes blindfolded, on the deck of a man-of-war. Four soldiers, stationed directly in front of this man, fired three bullets apiece into his brain, as peaceably as you would want; and the whole assemblage went home, in great satisfaction.[5]

—What's all this about? asked Candide. What devil is everywhere at work?

He asked who was that big man who had just been killed with so much ceremony.

—It was an admiral, they told him.

—And why kill this admiral?

—The reason, they told him, is that he didn't kill enough people; he gave battle to a French admiral, and it was found that he didn't get close enough to him.

—But, said Candide, the French admiral was just as far from the English admiral as the English admiral was from the French admiral.

—That's perfectly true, came the answer; but in this country it is useful from time to time to kill one admiral in order to encourage the others.

Candide was so stunned and shocked at what he saw and heard, that he would not even set foot ashore; he arranged with the Dutch merchant (without even caring if he was robbed, as at Surinam) to be taken forthwith to Venice.

The merchant was ready in two days; they coasted along France, they passed within sight of Lisbon, and Candide quivered. They entered the straits, crossed the Mediterranean, and finally landed at Venice.

—God be praised, said Candide, embracing Martin; here I shall recover the lovely Cunégonde. I trust Cacambo as I would myself. All is well, all goes well, all goes as well as possible.

---

4. The wars of the French and English over Canada dragged intermittently through the 18th century till the peace of Paris sealed England's conquest (1763). Voltaire thought the French should concentrate on developing Louisiana, where the Jesuit influence was less

marked.
5. Candide has witnessed the execution of Admiral John Byng, defeated off Minorca by the French fleet under Galisonnière and executed by firing squad on March 14, 1757. Voltaire had intervened to avert the execution.

CHAPTER 24

About Paquette and Brother Giroflée

As soon as he was in Venice, he had a search made for Cacambo in all the inns, all the cafés, all the stews—and found no trace of him. Every day he sent to investigate the vessels and coastal traders; no news of Cacambo.

—How's this? said he to Martin. I have had time to go from Surinam to Bordeaux, from Bordeaux to Paris, from Paris to Dieppe, from Dieppe to Portsmouth, to skirt Portugal and Spain, cross the Mediterranean, and spend several months at Venice—and the lovely Cunégonde has not come yet! In her place, I have met only that impersonator and that abbé from Perigord. Cunégonde is dead, without a doubt; and nothing remains for me too but death. Oh, it would have been better to stay in the earthly paradise of Eldorado than to return to this accursed Europe. How right you are, my dear Martin; all is but illusion and disaster.

He fell into a black melancholy, and refused to attend the fashionable operas or take part in the other diversions of the carnival season; not a single lady tempted him in the slightest. Martin told him:—You're a real simpleton if you think a half-breed valet with five or six millions in his pockets will go to the end of the world to get your mistress and bring her to Venice for you. If he finds her, he'll take her for himself; if he doesn't, he'll take another. I advise you to forget about your servant Cacambo and your mistress Cunégonde.

Martin was not very comforting. Candide's melancholy increased, and Martin never wearied of showing him that there is little virtue and little happiness on this earth, except perhaps in Eldorado, where nobody can go.

While they were discussing this important matter and still waiting for Cunégonde, Candide noticed in St. Mark's Square a young Theatine[6] monk who had given his arm to a girl. The Theatine seemed fresh, plump, and flourishing; his eyes were bright, his manner cocky, his glance brilliant, his step proud. The girl was very pretty, and singing aloud; she glanced lovingly at her Theatine, and from time to time pinched his plump cheeks.

—At least you must admit, said Candide to Martin, that these people are happy. Until now I have not found in the whole inhabited earth, except Eldorado, anything but miserable people. But this girl and this monk, I'd be willing to bet, are very happy creatures.

—I'll bet they aren't, said Martin.

—We have only to ask them to dinner, said Candide, and we'll find out if I'm wrong.

Promptly he approached them, made his compliments, and invited them to his inn for a meal of macaroni, Lombardy partridges, and caviar, washed down with wine from Montepulciano, Cyprus, and Samos, and some Lacrima Christi. The girl blushed but the Theatine accepted gladly, and the girl followed him, watching Candide with an expression of surprise and confusion, darkened by several tears. Scarcely had she entered the room when she said to Candide:—What, can it be that Master Candide no longer knows Paquette?

At these words Candide, who had not yet looked carefully at her because he was preoccupied with Cunégonde, said to her:—Ah, my poor child! so you are the one who put Doctor Pangloss in the fine fix where I last saw him.

---

6. A Catholic order founded in 1524 by Cardinal Cajetan and G. P. Caraffa, later Pope Paul IV.

—Alas, sir, I was the one, said Paquette; I see you know all about it. I heard of the horrible misfortunes which befell the whole household of My Lady the Baroness and the lovely Cunégonde. I swear to you that my own fate has been just as unhappy. I was perfectly innocent when you knew me. A Franciscan, who was my confessor, easily seduced me. The consequences were frightful; shortly after My Lord the Baron had driven you out with great kicks on the backside, I too was forced to leave the castle. If a famous doctor had not taken pity on me, I would have died. Out of gratitude, I became for some time the mistress of this doctor. His wife, who was jealous to the point of frenzy, beat me mercilessly every day; she was a gorgon. The doctor was the ugliest of men, and I the most miserable creature on earth, being continually beaten for a man I did not love. You will understand, sir, how dangerous it is for a nagging woman to be married to a doctor. This man, enraged by his wife's ways, one day gave her as a cold cure a medicine so potent that in two hours' time she died amid horrible convulsions. Her relatives brought suit against the bereaved husband; he fled the country, and I was put in prison. My innocence would never have saved me if I had not been rather pretty. The judge set me free on condition that he should become the doctor's successor. I was shortly replaced in this post by another girl, dismissed without any payment, and obliged to continue this abominable trade which you men find so pleasant and which for us is nothing but a bottomless pit of misery. I went to ply the trade in Venice. Ah, my dear sir, if you could imagine what it is like to have to caress indiscriminately an old merchant, a lawyer, a monk, a gondolier, an abbé; to be subjected to every sort of insult and outrage; to be reduced, time and again, to borrowing a skirt in order to go have it lifted by some disgusting man; to be robbed by this fellow of what one has gained from that; to be shaken down by the police, and to have before one only the prospect of a hideous old age, a hospital, and a dunghill, you will conclude that I am one of the most miserable creatures in the world.

Thus Paquette poured forth her heart to the good Candide in a hotel room, while Martin sat listening nearby. At last he said to Candide:—You see, I've already won half my bet.

Brother Giroflée[7] had remained in the dining room, and was having a drink before dinner.

—But how's this? said Candide to Paquette. You looked so happy, so joyous, when I met you; you were singing, you caressed the Theatine with such a natural air of delight; you seemed to me just as happy as you now say you are miserable.

—Ah, sir, replied Paquette, that's another one of the miseries of this business; yesterday I was robbed and beaten by an officer, and today I have to seem in good humor in order to please a monk.

Candide wanted no more; he conceded that Martin was right. They sat down to table with Paquette and the Theatine; the meal was amusing enough, and when it was over, the company spoke out among themselves with some frankness.

—Father, said Candide to the monk, you seem to me a man whom all the world might envy; the flower of health glows in your cheek, your features radiate pleasure; you have a pretty girl for your diversion, and you seem very happy with your life as a Theatine.

—Upon my word, sir, said Brother Giroflée, I wish that all the Theatines were at the bottom of the sea. A hundred times I have been tempted to set fire to my

7. His name means "carnation" and Paquette means "daisy."

convent, and go turn Turk. My parents forced me, when I was fifteen years old, to put on this detestable robe, so they could leave more money to a cursed older brother of mine, may God confound him! Jealousy, faction, and fury spring up, by natural law, within the walls of convents. It is true, I have preached a few bad sermons which earned me a little money, half of which the prior stole from me; the remainder serves to keep me in girls. But when I have to go back to the monastery at night, I'm ready to smash my head against the walls of my cell; and all my fellow monks are in the same fix.

Martin turned to Candide and said with his customary coolness:

—Well, haven't I won the whole bet?

Candide gave two thousand piastres to Paquette and a thousand to Brother Giroflée.

—I assure you, said he, that with that they will be happy.

—I don't believe so, said Martin; your piastres may make them even more unhappy than they were before.

—That may be, said Candide; but one thing comforts me, I note that people often turn up whom one never expected to see again; it may well be that, having rediscovered my red sheep and Paquette, I will also rediscover Cunégonde.

—I hope, said Martin, that she will some day make you happy; but I very much doubt it.

—You're a hard man, said Candide.

—I've lived, said Martin.

—But look at these gondoliers, said Candide; aren't they always singing?

—You don't see them at home, said Martin, with their wives and squalling children. The doge has his troubles, the gondoliers theirs. It's true that on the whole one is better off as a gondolier than as a doge; but the difference is so slight, I don't suppose it's worth the trouble of discussing.

—There's a lot of talk here, said Candide, of this Senator Pococurante,[8] who has a fine palace on the Brenta and is hospitable to foreigners. They say he is a man who has never known a moment's grief.

—I'd like to see such a rare specimen, said Martin.

Candide promptly sent to Lord Pococurante, asking permission to call on him tomorrow.

CHAPTER 25

Visit to Lord Pococurante, Venetian Nobleman

Candide and Martin took a gondola on the Brenta, and soon reached the palace of the noble Pococurante. The gardens were large and filled with beautiful marble statues; the palace was handsomely designed. The master of the house, sixty years old and very rich, received his two inquisitive visitors perfectly politely, but with very little warmth; Candide was disconcerted and Martin not at all displeased.

First two pretty and neatly dressed girls served chocolate, which they whipped to a froth. Candide could not forbear praising their beauty, their grace, their skill.

—They are pretty good creatures, said Pococurante; I sometimes have them into my bed, for I'm tired of the ladies of the town, with their stupid tricks, quarrels, jealousies, fits of ill humor and petty pride, and all the sonnets one has to make or order for them; but, after all, these two girls are starting to bore me too.

8. His name means "small care."

After lunch, Candide strolled through a long gallery, and was amazed at the beauty of the pictures. He asked who was the painter of the two finest.

—They are by Raphael, said the senator; I bought them for a lot of money, out of vanity, some years ago; people say they're the finest in Italy, but they don't please me at all; the colors have all turned brown, the figures aren't well modeled and don't stand out enough, the draperies bear no resemblance to real cloth. In a word, whatever people may say, I don't find in them a real imitation of nature. I like a picture only when I can see in it a touch of nature itself, and there are none of this sort. I have many paintings, but I no longer look at them.

As they waited for dinner, Pococurante ordered a concerto performed. Candide found the music delightful.

—That noise? said Pococurante. It may amuse you for half an hour, but if it goes on any longer, it tires everybody though no one dares to admit it. Music today is only the art of performing difficult pieces, and what is merely difficult cannot please for long. Perhaps I should prefer the opera, if they had not found ways to make it revolting and monstrous. Anyone who likes bad tragedies set to music is welcome to them; in these performances the scenes serve only to introduce, inappropriately, two or three ridiculous songs designed to show off the actress's sound box. Anyone who wants to, or who can, is welcome to swoon with pleasure at the sight of a castrate wriggling through the role of Caesar or Cato, and strutting awkwardly about the stage. For my part, I have long since given up these paltry trifles which are called the glory of modern Italy, and for which monarchs pay such ruinous prices.

Candide argued a bit, but timidly; Martin was entirely of a mind with the senator.

They sat down to dinner, and after an excellent meal adjourned to the library. Candide, seeing a copy of Homer in a splendid binding, complimented the noble lord on his good taste.

—That is an author, said he, who was the special delight of great Pangloss, the best philosopher in all Germany.

—He's no special delight of mine, said Pococurante coldly. I was once made to believe that I took pleasure in reading him; but that constant recital of fights which are all alike, those gods who are always interfering but never decisively, that Helen who is the cause of the war and then scarcely takes any part in the story, that Troy which is always under siege and never taken—all that bores me to tears. I have sometimes asked scholars if reading it bored them as much as it bores me; everyone who answered frankly told me the book dropped from his hands like lead, but that they had to have it in their libraries as a monument of antiquity, like those old rusty coins which can't be used in real trade.

Your Excellence doesn't hold the same opinion of Virgil? said Candide.

—I concede, said Pococurante, that the second, fourth, and sixth books of his *Aeneid* are fine; but as for his pious Aeneas, and strong Cloanthes, and faithful Achates, and little Ascanius, and that imbecile King Latinus, and middle-class Amata, and insipid Lavinia, I don't suppose there was ever anything so cold and unpleasant. I prefer Tasso and those sleepwalkers' stories of Ariosto.

—Dare I ask, sir, said Candide, if you don't get great enjoyment from reading Horace?

—There are some maxims there, said Pococurante, from which a man of the world can profit, and which, because they are formed into vigorous couplets, are more easily remembered; but I care very little for his trip to Brindisi, his description of a bad dinner, or his account of a quibblers' squabble between some fellow

Pupilus, whose words he says *were full of pus*, and another whose words *were full of vinegar*.[9] I feel nothing but extreme disgust at his verses against old women and witches; and I can't see what's so great in his telling his friend Maecenas that if he is raised by him to the ranks of lyric poets, he will strike the stars with his lofty forehead. Fools admire everything in a well-known author. I read only for my own pleasure; I like only what is in my style.

Candide, who had been trained never to judge for himself, was much astonished by what he heard; and Martin found Pococurante's way of thinking quite rational.

—Oh, here is a copy of Cicero, said Candide. Now this great man I suppose you're never tired of reading.

—I never read him at all, replied the Venetian. What do I care whether he pleaded for Rabirius or Cluentius? As a judge, I have my hands full of lawsuits. I might like his philosophical works better, but when I saw that he had doubts about everything, I concluded that I knew as much as he did, and that I needed no help to be ignorant.

—Ah, here are eighty volumes of collected papers from a scientific academy, cried Martin; maybe there is something good in them.

—There would be indeed, said Pococurante, if one of these silly authors had merely discovered a new way of making pins; but in all those volumes there is nothing but empty systems, not a single useful discovery.

—What a lot of stage plays I see over there, said Candide, some in Italian, some in Spanish and French.

—Yes, said the senator, three thousand of them, and not three dozen good ones. As for those collections of sermons, which all together are not worth a page of Seneca, and all these heavy volumes of theology, you may be sure I never open them, nor does anybody else.

Martin noticed some shelves full of English books.

—I suppose, said he, that a republican must delight in most of these books written in the land of liberty.

—Yes, replied Pococurante, it's a fine thing to write as you think; it is mankind's privilege. In all our Italy, people write only what they do not think; men who inhabit the land of the Caesars and Antonines dare not have an idea without the permission of a Dominican. I would rejoice in the freedom that breathes through English genius, if partisan passions did not corrupt all that is good in that precious freedom.

Candide, noting a Milton, asked if he did not consider this author a great man.

—Who? said Pococurante. That barbarian who made a long commentary on the first chapter of Genesis in ten books of crabbed verse?[1] That clumsy imitator of the Greeks, who disfigures creation itself, and while Moses represents the eternal being as creating the world with a word, has the messiah take a big compass out of a heavenly cupboard in order to design his work? You expect me to admire the man who spoiled Tasso's hell and devil? who disguises Lucifer now as a toad, now as a pigmy? who makes him rehash the same arguments a hundred times

---

9. *Satires* 1.7; Pococurante, with gentlemanly negligence, has corrupted Rupilius to Pupilus. Horace's poems against witches are *Epodes* 5.8, 12; the one about striking the stars with

his lofty forehead is *Odes* 1.1.
1. The first edition of *Paradise Lost* had ten books, which Milton later expanded to twelve.

over? who makes him argue theology? and who, taking seriously Ariosto's comic story of the invention of firearms, has the devils shooting off cannon in heaven? Neither I nor anyone else in Italy has been able to enjoy these gloomy extravagances. The marriage of Sin and Death, and the monster that Sin gives birth to, will nauseate any man whose taste is at all refined; and his long description of a hospital is good only for a gravedigger. This obscure, extravagant, and disgusting poem was despised at its birth; I treat it today as it was treated in its own country by its contemporaries. Anyhow, I say what I think, and care very little whether other people agree with me.

Candide was a little cast down by this speech; he respected Homer, and had a little affection for Milton.

—Alas, he said under his breath to Martin, I'm afraid this man will have a supreme contempt for our German poets.

—No harm in that, said Martin.

—Oh what a superior man, said Candide, still speaking softly, what a great genius this Pococurante must be! Nothing can please him.

Having thus looked over all the books, they went down into the garden. Candide praised its many beauties.

—I know nothing in such bad taste, said the master of the house; we have nothing but trifles here; tomorrow I am going to have one set out on a nobler design.

When the two visitors had taken leave of his excellency:—Well now, said Candide to Martin, you must agree that this was the happiest of all men, for he is superior to everything he possesses.

—Don't you see, said Martin, that he is disgusted with everything he possesses? Plato said, a long time ago, that the best stomachs are not those which refuse all food.

—But, said Candide, isn't there pleasure in criticizing everything, in seeing faults where other people think they see beauties?

—That is to say, Martin replied, that there's pleasure in having no pleasure?

—Oh well, said Candide, then I am the only happy man . . . or will be, when I see Miss Cunégonde again.

—It's always a good thing to have hope, said Martin.

But the days and the weeks slipped past; Cacambo did not come back, and Candide was so buried in his grief, that he did not even notice that Paquette and Brother Giroflée had neglected to come and thank him.

CHAPTER 26

About a Supper that Candide and Martin Had with Six Strangers,
and Who They Were

One evening when Candide, accompanied by Martin, was about to sit down for dinner with the strangers staying in his hotel, a man with a soot-colored face came up behind him, took him by the arm, and said:—Be ready to leave with us, don't miss out.

He turned and saw Cacambo. Only the sight of Cunégonde could have astonished and pleased him more. He nearly went mad with joy. He embraced his dear friend.

—Cunégonde is here, no doubt? Where is she? Bring me to her, let me die of joy in her presence.

—Cunégonde is not here at all, said Cacambo, she is at Constantinople.

—Good Heavens, at Constantinople! but if she were in China, I must fly there, let's go.

—We will leave after supper, said Cacambo; I can tell you no more; I am a slave, my owner is looking for me, I must go wait on him at table; mum's the word; eat your supper and be prepared.

Candide, torn between joy and grief, delighted to have seen his faithful agent again, astonished to find him a slave, full of the idea of recovering his mistress, his heart in a turmoil, his mind in a whirl, sat down to eat with Martin, who was watching all these events coolly, and with six strangers who had come to pass the carnival season at Venice.

Cacambo, who was pouring wine for one of the strangers, leaned respectfully over his master at the end of the meal, and said to him:—Sire, Your Majesty may leave when he pleases, the vessel is ready.

Having said these words, he exited. The diners looked at one another in silent amazement, when another servant, approaching his master, said to him:—Sire, Your Majesty's litter is at Padua, and the bark awaits you.

The master nodded, and the servant vanished. All the diners looked at one another again, and the general amazement redoubled. A third servant, approaching a third stranger, said to him:—Sire, take my word for it, Your Majesty must stay here no longer; I shall get everything ready.

Then he too disappeared.

Candide and Martin had no doubt, now, that it was a carnival masquerade. A fourth servant spoke to a fourth master:—Your Majesty will leave when he pleases—and went out like the others. A fifth followed suit. But the sixth servant spoke differently to the sixth stranger, who sat next to Candide. He said:—My word, sire, they'll give no more credit to Your Majesty, nor to me either; we could very well spend the night in the lockup, you and I. I've got to look out for myself, so good-bye to you.

When all the servants had left, the six strangers, Candide, and Martin remained under a pall of silence. Finally Candide broke it.

—Gentlemen, said he, here's a funny kind of joke. Why are you all royalty? I assure you that Martin and I aren't.

Cacambo's master spoke up gravely then, and said in Italian:—This is no joke, my name is Achmet the Third.[2] I was grand sultan for several years; then, as I had dethroned my brother, my nephew dethroned me. My viziers had their throats cut; I was allowed to end my days in the old seraglio. My nephew, the Grand Sultan Mahmoud, sometimes lets me travel for my health; and I have come to spend the carnival season at Venice.

A young man who sat next to Achmet spoke after him, and said:—My name is Ivan; I was once emperor of all the Russias.[3] I was dethroned while still in my cradle; my father and mother were locked up, and I was raised in prison; I sometimes have permission to travel, though always under guard, and I have come to spend the carnival season at Venice.

The third said:—I am Charles Edward, king of England;[4] my father yielded me

2. Ottoman ruler (1673–1736); he was deposed in 1730.

3. Ivan VI reigned from his birth in 1740 until 1756, then was confined in the Schlusselberg, and executed in 1764.

4. This is the Young Pretender (1720–1788), known to his supporters as Bonnie Prince Charlie. The defeat so theatrically described took place at Culloden, April 16, 1746.

his rights to the kingdom, and I fought to uphold them; but they tore out the hearts of eight hundred of my partisans, and flung them in their faces. I have been in prison; now I am going to Rome, to visit the king, my father, dethroned like me and my grandfather; and I have come to pass the carnival season at Venice.

The fourth king then spoke up, and said:—I am a king of the Poles;[5] the luck of war has deprived me of my hereditary estates; my father suffered the same losses; I submit to Providence like Sultan Achmet, Emperor Ivan, and King Charles Edward, to whom I hope heaven grants long lives; and I have come to pass the carnival season at Venice.

The fifth said:—I too am a king of the Poles;[6] I lost my kingdom twice, but Providence gave me another state, in which I have been able to do more good than all the Sarmatian kings ever managed to do on the banks of the Vistula. I too have submitted to Providence, and I have come to pass the carnival season at Venice.

It remained for the sixth monarch to speak.

—Gentlemen, said he, I am no such great lord as you, but I have in fact been a king like any other. I am Theodore; I was elected king of Corsica.[7] People used to call me *Your Majesty*, and now they barely call me *Sir*; I used to coin currency, and now I don't have a cent; I used to have two secretaries of state, and now I scarcely have a valet; I have sat on a throne, and for a long time in London I was in jail, on the straw; and I may well be treated the same way here, though I have come, like your majesties, to pass the carnival season at Venice.

The five other kings listened to his story with noble compassion. Each one of them gave twenty sequins to King Theodore, so that he might buy a suit and some shirts; Candide gave him a diamond worth two thousand sequins.

—Who in the world, said the five kings, is this private citizen who is in a position to give a hundred times as much as any of us, and who actually gives it?[8]

Just as they were rising from dinner, there arrived at the same establishment four most serene highnesses, who had also lost their kingdoms through the luck of war, and who came to spend the rest of the carnival season at Venice. But Candide never bothered even to look at these newcomers because he was only concerned to go find his dear Cunégonde at Constantinople.

CHAPTER 27

Candide's Trip to Constantinople

Faithful Cacambo had already arranged with the Turkish captain who was returning Sultan Achmet to Constantinople to make room for Candide and Martin on board. Both men boarded ship after prostrating themselves before his miserable highness. On the way, Candide said to Martin:—Six dethroned kings that we had dinner with! and yet among those six there was one on whom I had to bestow charity! Perhaps there are other princes even more unfortunate. I myself

---

5. Augustus III (1696–1763), Elector of Saxony and King of Poland, dethroned by Frederick the Great in 1756.

6. Stanislas Leczinski (1677–1766), father-in-law of Louis XV, who abdicated the throne of Poland in 1736, was made Duke of Lorraine and in that capacity befriended Voltaire.

7. Theodore von Neuhof (1690–1756), an authentic Westphalian, an adventurer and a soldier of fortune, who in 1736 was (for about

eight months) the elected king of Corsica. He spent time in an Amsterdam as well as a London debtor's prison.

8. Voltaire was very conscious of his situation as a man richer than many princes; in 1758 he had money on loan to no fewer than three highnesses, Charles Eugene, Duke of Wurtemburg; Charles Theodore, Elector Palatine; and the Duke of Saxe-Gotha.

have only lost a hundred sheep, and now I am flying to the arms of Cunégonde. My dear Martin, once again Pangloss is proved right, all is for the best.

—I hope so, said Martin.

—But, said Candide, that was a most unlikely experience we had at Venice. Nobody ever saw, or heard tell of, six dethroned kings eating together at an inn.

—It is no more extraordinary, said Martin, than most of the things that have happened to us. Kings are frequently dethroned; and as for the honor we had from dining with them, that's a trifle which doesn't deserve our notice.[9]

Scarcely was Candide on board than he fell on the neck of his former servant, his friend Cacambo.

—Well! said he, what is Cunégonde doing? Is she still a marvel of beauty? Does she still love me? How is her health? No doubt you have bought her a palace at Constantinople.

—My dear master, answered Cacambo, Cunégonde is washing dishes on the shores of the Propontis, in the house of a prince who has very few dishes to wash; she is a slave in the house of a onetime king named Ragotski,[1] to whom the Great Turk allows three crowns a day in his exile; but, what is worse than all this, she has lost all her beauty and become horribly ugly.

—Ah, beautiful or ugly, said Candide, I am an honest man, and my duty is to love her forever. But how can she be reduced to this wretched state with the five or six millions that you had?

—All right, said Cacambo, didn't I have to give two millions to Señor don Fernando d'Ibaraa y Figueroa y Mascarenes y Lampourdos y Souza, governor of Buenos Aires, for his permission to carry off Miss Cunégonde? And didn't a pirate cleverly strip us of the rest? And didn't this pirate carry us off to Cape Matapan, to Melos, Nicaria, Samos, Petra, to the Dardanelles, Marmora, Scutari? Cunégonde and the old woman are working for the prince I told you about, and I am the slave of the dethroned sultan.

—What a lot of fearful calamities linked one to the other, said Candide. But after all, I still have a few diamonds, I shall easily deliver Cunégonde. What a pity that she's become so ugly!

Then, turning toward Martin, he asked:—Who in your opinion is more to be pitied, the Emperor Achmet, the Emperor Ivan, King Charles Edward, or myself?

—I have no idea, said Martin; I would have to enter your hearts in order to tell.

—Ah, said Candide, if Pangloss were here, he would know and he would tell us.

—I can't imagine, said Martin, what scales your Pangloss would use to weigh out the miseries of men and value their griefs. All I will venture is that the earth holds millions of men who deserve our pity a hundred times more than King Charles Edward, Emperor Ivan, or Sultan Achmet.

—You may well be right, said Candide.

In a few days they arrived at the Black Sea canal. Candide began by repurchasing Cacambo at an exorbitant price; then, without losing an instant, he flung himself and his companions into a galley to go search out Cunégonde on the shores of Propontis, however ugly she might be.

There were in the chain gang two convicts who bent clumsily to the oar, and on whose bare shoulders the Levantine[2] captain delivered from time to time a few

9. Another late change adds the following question:—*What does it matter whom you dine with as long as you fare well at table?* I have omitted it, again on literary grounds.
1. Francis Leopold Rakoczy (1676–1735),

who was briefly king of Transylvania in the early 18th century. After 1720 he was interned in Turkey.
2. From the eastern Mediterranean.

lashes with a bullwhip. Candide naturally noticed them more than the other galley slaves, and out of pity came closer to them. Certain features of their disfigured faces seemed to him to bear a slight resemblance to Pangloss and to that wretched Jesuit, that baron, that brother of Miss Cunégonde. The notion stirred and saddened him. He looked at them more closely.

—To tell you the truth, he said to Cacambo, if I hadn't seen Master Pangloss hanged, and if I hadn't been so miserable as to murder the baron, I should think they were rowing in this very galley.

At the names of 'baron' and 'Pangloss' the two convicts gave a great cry, sat still on their bench, and dropped their oars. The Levantine captain came running, and the bullwhip lashes redoubled.

—Stop, stop, captain, cried Candide. I'll give you as much money as you want.

—What, can it be Candide? cried one of the convicts.

—What, can it be Candide? cried the other.

—Is this a dream? said Candide. Am I awake or asleep? Am I in this galley? Is that My Lord the Baron, whom I killed? Is that Master Pangloss, whom I saw hanged?

—It is indeed, they replied.

—What, is that the great philosopher? said Martin.

—Now, sir, Mr. Levantine Captain, said Candide, how much money do you want for the ransom of My Lord Thunder-Ten-Tronckh, one of the first barons of the empire, and Master Pangloss, the deepest metaphysician in all Germany?

—Dog of a Christian, replied the Levantine captain, since these two dogs of Christian convicts are barons and metaphysicians, which is no doubt a great honor in their country, you will give me fifty thousand sequins for them.

—You shall have them, sir, take me back to Constantinople and you shall be paid on the spot. Or no, take me to Miss Cunégonde.

The Levantine captain, at Candide's first word, had turned his bow toward the town, and he had them rowed there as swiftly as a bird cleaves the air.

A hundred times Candide embraced the baron and Pangloss.

—And how does it happen I didn't kill you, my dear baron? and my dear Pangloss, how can you be alive after being hanged? and why are you both rowing in the galleys of Turkey?

—Is it really true that my dear sister is in this country? asked the baron.

—Yes, answered Cacambo.

—And do I really see again my dear Candide? cried Pangloss.

Candide introduced Martin and Cacambo. They all embraced; they all talked at once. The galley flew, already they were back in port. A Jew was called, and Candide sold him for fifty thousand sequins a diamond worth a hundred thousand, while he protested by Abraham that he could not possibly give more for it. Candide immediately ransomed the baron and Pangloss. The latter threw himself at the feet of his liberator, and bathed them with tears; the former thanked him with a nod, and promised to repay this bit of money at the first opportunity.

—But is it really possible that my sister is in Turkey? said he.

—Nothing is more possible, replied Cacambo, since she is a dishwasher in the house of a prince of Transylvania.

At once two more Jews were called; Candide sold some more diamonds; and they all departed in another galley to the rescue of Cunégonde.

CHAPTER 28

What Happened to Candide, Cunégonde, Pangloss, Martin, &c.

—Let me beg your pardon once more, said Candide to the baron, pardon me, reverend father, for having run you through the body with my sword.

—Don't mention it, replied the baron. I was a little too hasty myself, I confess it; but since you want to know the misfortune which brought me to the galleys, I'll tell you. After being cured of my wound by the brother who was apothecary to the college, I was attacked and abducted by a Spanish raiding party; they jailed me in Buenos Aires at the time when my sister had just left. I asked to be sent to Rome, to the father general. Instead, I was named to serve as almoner in Constantinople, under the French ambassador. I had not been a week on this job when I chanced one evening on a very handsome young ichoglan.[3] The evening was hot; the young man wanted to take a swim; I seized the occasion, and went with him. I did not know that it is a capital offense for a Christian to be found naked with a young Moslem. A cadi sentenced me to receive a hundred blows with a cane on the soles of my feet, and then to be sent to the galleys. I don't suppose there was ever such a horrible miscarriage of justice. But I would like to know why my sister is in the kitchen of a Transylvanian king exiled among Turks.

—But how about you, my dear Pangloss, said Candide; how is it possible that we have met again?

—It is true, said Pangloss, that you saw me hanged; in the normal course of things, I should have been burned, but you recall that a cloudburst occurred just as they were going to roast me. So much rain fell that they despaired of lighting the fire; thus I was hanged, for lack of anything better to do with me. A surgeon bought my body, carried me off to his house, and dissected me. First he made a cross-shaped incision in me, from the navel to the clavicle. No one could have been worse hanged than I was. In fact, the executioner of the high ceremonials of the Holy Inquisition, who was a subdeacon, burned people marvelously well, but he was not in the way of hanging them. The rope was wet, and tightened badly; it caught on a knot; in short, I was still breathing. The cross-shaped incision made me scream so loudly that the surgeon fell over backwards; he thought he was dissecting the devil, fled in an agony of fear, and fell downstairs in his flight. His wife ran in, at the noise, from a nearby room; she found me stretched out on the table with my cross-shaped incision, was even more frightened than her husband, fled, and fell over him. When they had recovered a little, I heard her say to him: 'My dear, what were you thinking of, trying to dissect a heretic? Don't you know those people are always possessed of the devil? I'm going to get the priest and have him exorcised.' At these words, I shuddered, and collected my last remaining energies to cry: 'Have mercy on me!' At last the Portuguese barber[4] took courage; he sewed me up again; his wife even nursed me; in two weeks I was up and about. The barber found me a job and made me lackey to a Knight of Malta who was going to Venice; and when this master could no longer pay me, I took service under a Venetian merchant, whom I followed to Constantinople.

—One day it occurred to me to enter a mosque; no one was there but an old imam and a very attractive young worshipper who was saying her prayers. Her bosom was completely bare; and between her two breasts she had a lovely bouquet

---

3. A page to the sultan.
4. The two callings of barber and surgeon, since they both involved sharp instruments, were interchangeable in the early days of medicine.

of tulips, roses, anemones, buttercups, hyacinths, and primroses. She dropped her bouquet, I picked it up, and returned it to her with the most respectful attentions. I was so long getting it back in place that the imam grew angry, and, seeing that I was a Christian, he called the guard. They took me before the cadi, who sentenced me to receive a hundred blows with a cane on the soles of my feet, and then to be sent to the galleys. I was chained to the same galley and precisely the same bench as My Lord the Baron. There were in this galley four young fellows from Marseilles, five Neapolitan priests, and two Corfu monks, who assured us that these things happen every day. My Lord the Baron asserted that he had suffered a greater injustice than I; I, on the other hand, proposed that it was much more permissible to replace a bouquet in a bosom than to be found naked with an ichoglan. We were arguing the point continually, and getting twenty lashes a day with the bullwhip, when the chain of events within this universe brought you to our galley, and you ransomed us.

—Well, my dear Pangloss, Candide said to him, now that you have been hanged, dissected, beaten to a pulp, and sentenced to the galleys, do you still think everything is for the best in this world?

—I am still of my first opinion, replied Pangloss; for after all I am a philosopher, and it would not be right for me to recant since Leibniz could not possibly be wrong, and besides pre-established harmony is the finest notion in the world, like the plenum and subtle matter.[5]

CHAPTER 29

How Candide Found Cunégonde and the Old Woman Again

While Candide, the baron, Pangloss, Martin, and Cacambo were telling one another their stories, while they were disputing over the contingent or noncontingent events of this universe, while they were arguing over effects and causes, over moral evil and physical evil, over liberty and necessity, and over the consolations available to one in a Turkish galley, they arrived at the shores of Propontis and the house of the prince of Transylvania. The first sight to meet their eyes was Cunégonde and the old woman, who were hanging out towels on lines to dry.

The baron paled at what he saw. The tender lover Candide, seeing his lovely Cunégonde with her skin weathered, her eyes bloodshot, her breasts fallen, her cheeks seamed, her arms red and scaly, recoiled three steps in horror, and then advanced only out of politeness. She embraced Candide and her brother; everyone embraced the old woman; Candide ransomed them both.

There was a little farm in the neighborhood; the old woman suggested that Candide occupy it until some better fate should befall the group. Cunégonde did not know she was ugly, no one had told her; she reminded Candide of his promises in so firm a tone that the good Candide did not dare to refuse her. So he went to tell the baron that he was going to marry his sister.

---

5. Rigorous determinism requires that there be no empty spaces in the universe, so wherever it seems empty, one posits the existence of the "plenum." "Subtle matter" describes the soul, the mind, and all spiritual agencies— which can, therefore, be supposed subject to the influence and control of the great world machine, which is, of course, visibly material. Both are concepts needed to round out the system of optimistic determinism.

—Never will I endure, said the baron, such baseness on her part, such insolence on yours; this shame at least I will not put up with; why, my sister's children
would not be able to enter the Chapters in Germany.[6] No, my sister will never
marry anyone but a baron of the empire.

Cunégonde threw herself at his feet, and bathed them with her tears; he was
inflexible.

—You absolute idiot, Candide told him, I rescued you from the galleys, I paid
your ransom, I paid your sister's; she was washing dishes, she is ugly, I am good
enough to make her my wife, and you still presume to oppose it! If I followed my
impulses, I would kill you all over again.

—You may kill me again, said the baron, but you will not marry my sister while
I am alive.

CHAPTER 30

Conclusion

At heart, Candide had no real wish to marry Cunégonde; but the baron's extreme
impertinence decided him in favor of the marriage, and Cunégonde was so eager
for it that he could not back out. He consulted Pangloss, Martin, and the faithful
Cacambo. Pangloss drew up a fine treatise, in which he proved that the baron had
no right over his sister and that she could, according to all the laws of the empire,
marry Candide morganatically.[7] Martin said they should throw the baron into the
sea. Cacambo thought they should send him back to the Levantine captain to finish his time in the galleys, and then send him to the father general in Rome by the
first vessel. This seemed the best idea; the old woman approved, and nothing was
said to his sister; the plan was executed, at modest expense, and they had the
double pleasure of snaring a Jesuit and punishing the pride of a German baron.

It is quite natural to suppose that after so many misfortunes, Candide, married
to his mistress, and living with the philosopher Pangloss, the philosopher Martin,
the prudent Cacambo, and the old woman—having, besides, brought back so
many diamonds from the land of the ancient Incas—must have led the most
agreeable life in the world. But he was so cheated by the Jews[8] that nothing was
left but his little farm; his wife, growing every day more ugly, became sour-tempered
and insupportable; the old woman was ailing and even more ill-humored than
Cunégonde. Cacambo, who worked in the garden and went into Constantinople
to sell vegetables, was worn out with toil, and cursed his fate. Pangloss was in
despair at being unable to shine in some German university. As for Martin, he
was firmly persuaded that things are just as bad wherever you are; he endured in
patience. Candide, Martin, and Pangloss sometimes argued over metaphysics and
morals. Before the windows of the farmhouse they often watched the passage of
boats bearing effendis, pashas, and cadis into exile on Lemnos, Mytilene, and
Erzeroum; they saw other cadis, other pashas, other effendis coming, to take the

6. Knightly assemblies.
7. A morganatic marriage confers no rights on
the partner of lower rank or on the offspring.
8. Voltaire's anti-Semitism, derived from various unhappy experiences with Jewish financiers, is not the most attractive aspect of his
personality.

place of the exiles and to be exiled in their turn. They saw various heads, neatly impaled, to be set up at the Sublime Porte.[9] These sights gave fresh impetus to their discussions; and when they were not arguing, the boredom was so fierce that one day the old woman ventured to say:—I should like to know which is worse, being raped a hundred times by negro pirates, having a buttock cut off, running the gauntlet in the Bulgar army, being flogged and hanged in an auto-da-fé, being dissected and rowing in the galleys—experiencing, in a word, all the miseries through which we have passed—or else just sitting here and doing nothing?

—It's a hard question, said Candide.

These words gave rise to new reflections, and Martin in particular concluded that man was bound to live either in convulsions of misery or in the lethargy of boredom. Candide did not agree, but expressed no positive opinion. Pangloss asserted that he had always suffered horribly; but having once declared that everything was marvelously well, he continued to repeat the opinion and didn't believe a word of it.

One thing served to confirm Martin in his detestable opinions, to make Candide hesitate more than ever, and to embarrass Pangloss. It was the arrival one day at their farm of Paquette and Brother Giroflée, who were in the last stages of misery. They had quickly run through their three thousand piastres, had split up, made up, quarreled, been jailed, escaped, and finally Brother Giroflée had turned Turk. Paquette continued to ply her trade everywhere, and no longer made any money at it.

—I told you, said Martin to Candide, that your gifts would soon be squandered and would only render them more unhappy. You have spent millions of piastres, you and Cacambo, and you are no more happy than Brother Giroflée and Paquette.

—Ah ha, said Pangloss to Paquette, so destiny has brought you back in our midst, my poor girl! Do you realize you cost me the end of my nose, one eye, and an ear? And look at you now! eh! what a world it is, after all!

This new adventure caused them to philosophize more than ever.

There was in the neighborhood a very famous dervish, who was said to be the best philosopher in Turkey; they went to ask his advice. Pangloss was spokesman, and he said:—Master, we have come to ask you to tell us why such a strange animal as man was created.

—What are you getting into? answered the dervish. Is it any of your business?

—But, reverend father, said Candide, there's a horrible lot of evil on the face of the earth.

—What does it matter, said the dervish, whether there's good or evil? When his highness sends a ship to Egypt, does he worry whether the mice on board are comfortable or not?

—What shall we do then? asked Pangloss.

—Hold your tongue, said the dervish.

—I had hoped, said Pangloss, to reason a while with you concerning effects and causes, the best of possible worlds, the origin of evil, the nature of the soul, and pre-established harmony.

At these words, the dervish slammed the door in their faces.

9. The gate of the sultan's palace is often used by extension to describe his government as a whole. But it was in fact a real gate where the heads of traitors and public enemies were gruesomely exposed.

During this interview, word was spreading that at Constantinople they had just strangled two viziers of the divan,[1] as well as the mufti, and impaled several of their friends. This catastrophe made a great and general sensation for several hours. Pangloss, Candide, and Martin, as they returned to their little farm, passed a good old man who was enjoying the cool of the day at his doorstep under a grove of orange trees. Pangloss, who was as inquisitive as he was explanatory, asked the name of the mufti who had been strangled.

—I know nothing of it, said the good man, and I have never cared to know the name of a single mufti or vizier. I am completely ignorant of the episode you are discussing. I presume that in general those who meddle in public business sometimes perish miserably, and that they deserve their fate; but I never listen to the news from Constantinople; I am satisfied with sending the fruits of my garden to be sold there.

Having spoken these words, he asked the strangers into his house; his two daughters and two sons offered them various sherbets which they had made themselves, Turkish cream flavored with candied citron, orange, lemon, lime, pineapple, pistachio, and mocha coffee uncontaminated by the inferior coffee of Batavia and the East Indies. After which the two daughters of this good Moslem perfumed the beards of Candide, Pangloss, and Martin.

—You must possess, Candide said to the Turk, an enormous and splendid property?

I have only twenty acres, replied the Turk; I cultivate them with my children, and the work keeps us from three great evils, boredom, vice, and poverty.

Candide, as he walked back to his farm, meditated deeply over the words of the Turk. He said to Pangloss and Martin:—This good old man seems to have found himself a fate preferable to that of the six kings with whom we had the honor of dining.

—Great place, said Pangloss, is very perilous in the judgment of all the philosophers; for, after all, Eglon, king of the Moabites, was murdered by Ehud; Absalom was hung up by the hair and pierced with three darts; King Nadab, son of Jeroboam, was killed by Baasha; King Elah by Zimri; Ahaziah by Jehu; Athaliah by Jehoiada; and Kings Jehoiakim, Jeconiah, and Zedekiah were enslaved. You know how death came to Croesus, Astyages, Darius, Dionysius of Syracuse, Pyrrhus, Perseus, Hannibal, Jugurtha, Ariovistus, Caesar, Pompey, Nero, Otho, Vitellius, Domitian, Richard II of England, Edward II, Henry VI, Richard III, Mary Stuart, Charles I, the three Henrys of France, and the Emperor Henry IV? You know . . .

—I know also, said Candide, that we must cultivate our garden.

—You are perfectly right, said Pangloss; for when man was put into the garden of Eden, he was put there *ut operaretur eum*, so that he should work it; this proves that man was not born to take his ease.

—Let's work without speculation, said Martin; it's the only way of rendering life bearable.

The whole little group entered into this laudable scheme; each one began to exercise his talents. The little plot yielded fine crops. Cunégonde was, to tell the truth, remarkably ugly; but she became an excellent pastry cook. Paquette took up embroidery; the old woman did the laundry. Everyone, down even to Brother Giroflée, did something useful; he became a very adequate carpenter, and even an honest man; and Pangloss sometimes used to say to Candide:—All events are linked together in the best of possible worlds for, after all, if you had not been

1. Intimate advisers of the sultan.

driven from a fine castle by being kicked in the backside for love of Miss Cunégonde, if you hadn't been sent before the Inquisition, if you hadn't traveled across
America on foot, if you hadn't given a good sword thrust to the baron, if you
hadn't lost all your sheep from the good land of Eldorado, you wouldn't be sitting
here eating candied citron and pistachios.

    —That is very well put, said Candide, but we must cultivate our garden.

III

An Age of Revolutions

I f you were born in 1765, and you happened to live to a ripe old age, you would witness two dramatic revolutions. Together these revolutions would create a period of staggering upheaval unparalleled in prior human history. Whether you happened to find yourself in Texas or London or Buenos Aires, you would see daily life change for almost everyone—rich and poor, rural and urban— and the workings of governments and markets forever transformed. You would have to learn a whole new vocabulary to describe your social world: the terms "factory," "middle class," "capitalism," "industry," "journalism," "liberal," and "conservative" would come into use during your lifetime. You would learn of workers moving to cities in vast numbers. They would live in dismal conditions of filth, disease, and hunger, and at times would erupt in violent protest. You would listen to orators denouncing tyranny and demanding new rights and freedoms. You would hear about an ordinary soldier who rose to conquer most of Europe, and his name, Napoleon, would provoke either a chill of fear or a shiver of exhilaration. You would watch new constitutions take effect and new nations assert themselves. You would see the very map of the world redrawn.

Liberty Leading the People, 1830, Eugène Delacroix.

THE INDUSTRIAL REVOLUTION

The first of the two great upheavals was the industrial revolution, which began in England and then radiated outward, as other nations copied English innovations and as England's increasing commercial and military power conquered large portions of the globe. Before the 1780s economies everywhere changed only at a glacially slow pace. Most of Europe's inhabitants were peasants who worked the land which their forefathers had worked for generations before them, typically growing their own food and making their own clothes, and paying rent to their landowners in exchange for military protection. Many, including Russian serfs, were under the legal control of their landowners and thus forbidden to move from the places where they were born. But agriculture in England was different. There, large landowners rented tracts of land to tenant farmers, who then hired laborers to work for them. The farmers could get rich by finding new markets for their products, and the workers could move if they saw opportunities elsewhere. Here were the seeds of an entirely new, fast-growing capitalist economy. In the eighteenth century, English farmers started to turn into entrepreneurs, looking for faster and better ways to make profits from their lands. In order to attract investors, the nation needed to keep the economy growing, and in order to keep the economy growing, it needed to increase production and find new markets. Colonial expansion seemed like a perfect solution: England fought to acquire and control vast territories abroad, especially in North America, which would provide new land to till and new natural resources to use. Entrepreneurs also found new

An engraving depicting the interior of the Swainson & Birley Mill in Lancashire, England, ca. 1830.

markets in the colonies to buy the goods which England produced.

The great spur for this new global economy was cotton. Grown and harvested by slaves in the colonies, the raw material was shipped to English entrepreneurs, whose textile factories spun and wove the slave-picked cotton into finished cloth. They eagerly developed new technologies to keep production growing, and that meant that iron and steel industries grew too, allowing for the ever faster production of machines for manufacture and transportation. Railways expanded swiftly. Historians often date the great acceleration of the economy to the 1780s, which was the moment when English exports surpassed imports for the first time. The growth was breathtaking and unprecedented. In 1785 England imported 11 million pounds of raw cotton; by 1850 the English were importing 588 million pounds. They established trade monopolies with India and Latin America, compelling overseas consumers to buy English goods, which meant that exports grew at an astonishing rate: English mill owners had sold more than two billion yards of cotton cloth by the middle of the nineteenth century. England had become the hub of a new world economy, and other nations rushed to imitate English techniques of production. Factories sprang up everywhere.

Not everyone benefited from this extraordinary growth. The workers who moved off ancestral lands to crowd into new industrial centers labored in unregulated factories, often inhaling dust or having their limbs broken in machines. Employers looked for the cheapest labor, typically hiring women and children, and forced them to work 14- and even 16-hour days. Barely paid a subsis-

tence wage, the new urban working class made do with living conditions that were even more appalling than conditions in the factories where they worked. Cities grew at such a fast rate that urban populations quickly outpaced the availability of necessities such as adequate housing and the supply of clean water. The result was a sequence of major epidemics, including cholera and typhoid fever, which overwhelmed congested slums but hardly touched the middle and upper classes. To add to the general hardships for the poor, the economy had already begun the international cycles of boom and bust that would characterize the next two centuries. In periods of poor growth, unemployed workers literally starved. Feelings of angry discontent grew rapidly alongside the new economy.

Overseas, too, large populations began to suffer from industrialization. The huge acceleration in the English economy had absolutely depended on slavery. Six million slaves had been captured and sent from Africa to the Americas in the eighteenth century alone, many to serve the booming cotton trade. Meanwhile, India's economy plunged. Until the eighteenth century, India had had a thriving manufacturing sector that produced gorgeous textiles for export, but the new factory-made cloth from England came in at low prices and depressed the market. Many workers in India were forced back into agriculture, which deindustrialized India's economy, setting it on a slower track. Latin America, too, increasingly organized its economies of mining and agriculture around exports to England—including sugar, coffee, and silver—which made the new Latin American nations worryingly dependent on agriculture and on economic decisions made in England.

DEMOCRATIC REVOLUTIONS

As the industrial revolution was producing vast wealth, changing labor practices, molding a class of angry urban workers, rapidly expanding cities, and creating new and uneven global trade relations, a second revolution was also taking place. This revolution was political. Intent on throwing off old hierarchies that gave power to kings and compelled everyone else to act as obedient subjects, revolutionaries in North America and France argued that ordinary people should take political decision making into their own hands. This was a democratic revolution that, like the industrial revolution, had global effects, transforming expectations about basic rights and freedoms worldwide.

In North America, colonial subjects became increasingly resentful of the power of the English king, who made both political and economic decisions that favored England. In 1776 they declared independence not only from English rule but from the whole structure of the old regime, rejecting its hereditary monarchy in favor of a new elected president. They vested power in "the people," insisting that governments should derive their power only from the consent of the governed. This was a radical new foundation for politics, and it inspired many later constitutions.

In Europe, another, even more dramatic political revolution was brewing. The French monarchy had become ever more absolutist, and peasants were growing resentful of the traditional taxes and tithes they had to pay. Bad harvests in 1788 and 1789 doubled the cost of bread, but the king seemed entirely indifferent to the fate of a starving people. (When told that the peasants were calling for bread,

Queen Marie Antoinette is famous for responding, "Let them eat cake.") On July 14, 1789, a loosely organized armed mob stormed the Bastille prison—a symbol of royal power—and called for the liberation of the French people. The news spread quickly. Within a month, uprisings all across France had wrecked the traditional feudal social hierarchy and ushered in a new era. The Declaration of the Rights of Man and of the Citizen, issued by the French National Assembly in August, asserted the equality and freedom of all men and abolished all privileges based on birth. The revolutionary government insisted on ruling by reason, not by tradition. They adopted the innovative new metric system, separated church and state, abolished slavery in the French colonies, and granted equal rights to everyone, including, for the first time, Jews. The French Revolution also helped to unleash a new force in world affairs: nationalism. France was no longer a land possessed by a powerful ruling family, but stood for a self-governing and autonomous "people." In a powerful symbolic gesture, the revolutionaries renamed 1789 as "Year Zero," suggesting that nothing that had happened before the revolution mattered. They then stunned Europe by sending the king to his death in 1793, executing him with a sleek new machine intended to make killing more humane: the guillotine.

The French Revolution sent shock waves around the world. Throughout Europe and the Americas, suddenly it seemed possible that people might rise up against their oppressors, violently opposing traditional authority in the name of individual human rights. Huge divisions emerged between those who saw the revolutionaries as vicious and reckless, and those who heralded them as the open-

The siege of the Bastille, July 1789.

ing of a whole new chapter in human history.

Other European powers, fearful that revolution might spread into their territories, went to war with France in 1792, and the whole country threatened to collapse in disarray. A small group of radicals, called the Jacobins, seized control and united the nation under a strong centralized dictatorship, mobilizing the nation for war and sending all traitors—and potential traitors—to the guillotine. Their short period of leadership in 1793–94 has come to be known as the "Reign of Terror." The blood they shed sickened many observers who had once sympathized with the aims of the revolution, and the "Reign of Terror" has, ever since, been seen as a symbol of revolutionary violence taken too far.

As the new French government faltered and changed leadership, a talented young soldier who had helped the French to defeat the British at Toulon in 1793 was rising up through the ranks. Born on the remote island of Corsica, Napoleon Bonaparte had few advantages of birth or connections, but his genius for military strategy, his extraordinary ambition, and his own huge popularity allowed him to take advantage of government weakness during a wave of foreign invasions and to position himself as the new leader of France. In 1799 he installed a new dictatorship and through a vast military campaign redrew the map of Europe, bringing large parts of Spain, Germany, Austria, Italy, and Poland under French control. He crowned himself emperor in 1804. Ravenous for power, he tried

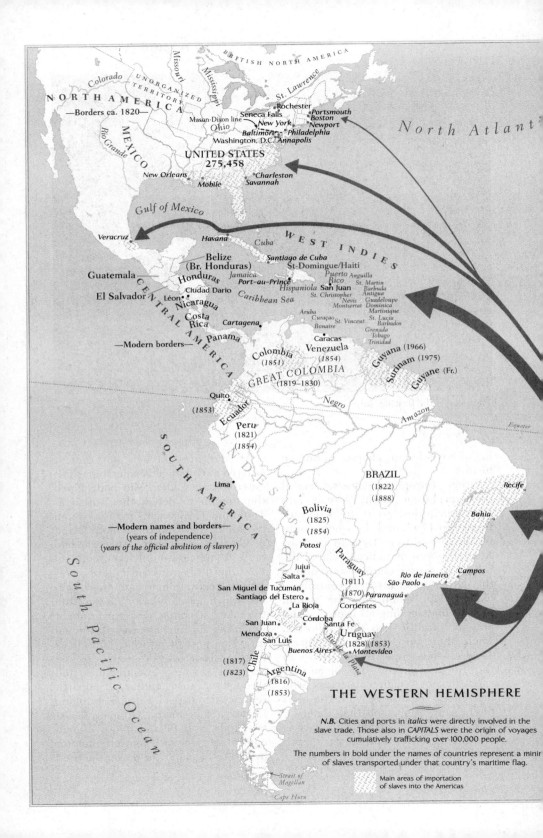

THE WESTERN HEMISPHERE

N.B. Cities and ports in *italics* were directly involved in the slave trade. Those also in *CAPITALS* were the origin of voyages cumulatively trafficking over 100,000 people.

The numbers in bold under the names of countries represent a minir of slaves transported under that country's maritime flag.

Main areas of importation of slaves into the Americas

NORTH AMERICA
—Borders ca. 1820—

UNITED STATES
275,458

UNORGANIZED TERRITORY

Colorado

Missouri

Mississippi

BRITISH NORTH AMERICA

St. Lawrence

Rochester

Portsmouth
Boston
Newport

Seneca Falls

Mason-Dixon line

New York

Ohio

Baltimore
Washington, D.C. *Philadelphia*
Annapolis

New Orleans

Mobile

Charleston
Savannah

MEXICO

Rio Grande

North Atlant'

Gulf of Mexico

Veracruz

Havana Cuba

WEST INDIES

Santiago de Cuba

St-Domingue/Haiti

Belize
(Br. Honduras)

Jamaica

Puerto Rico Anguilla

Guatemala

Honduras

Port-au-Prince

San Juan

St. Martin
Barbuda
Antigua

Ciudad Dario

Hispaniola

St. Christopher
Nevis
Montserrat

Guadeloupe
Dominica
Martinique

El Salvador

León

Nicaragua

Caribbean Sea

Aruba
Curaçao St. Vincent
Bonaire

St. Lucia
Barbados

Costa Rica

Cartagena

Grenada
Tobago
Trinidad

Panama

—Modern borders—

Colombia
(1851)

Caracas

Venezuela
(1854)

Guyana (1966)

Surinam (1975)

GREAT COLOMBIA
(1819–1830)

Guyane (Fr.)

Quito
(1853)

Negro

Amazon

Equator

Ecuador

Peru
(1821)
(1854)

Lima

Bolivia
(1825)
(1854)

BRAZIL
(1822)
(1888)

Recife

Bahia

ANDES

Potosi

—Modern names and borders—
(years of independence)
(*years of the official abolition of slavery*)

Paraguay

Jujui

(1811)

Salta

(1870) *Paranaguá*

San Miguel de Tucumán

Rio de Janeiro
São Paolo

Campos

Santiago del Estero

La Rioja

Corrientes

San Juan

Córdoba

Mendoza

Santa Fe

San Luis

Uruguay
(1828)(1853)

(1817)
(1823)

Buenos Aires

Montevideo

Chile

Argentina
(1816)
(1853)

Río de la Plata

SOUTH AMERICA

South Pacific Ocean

Strait of Magellan

Cape Horn

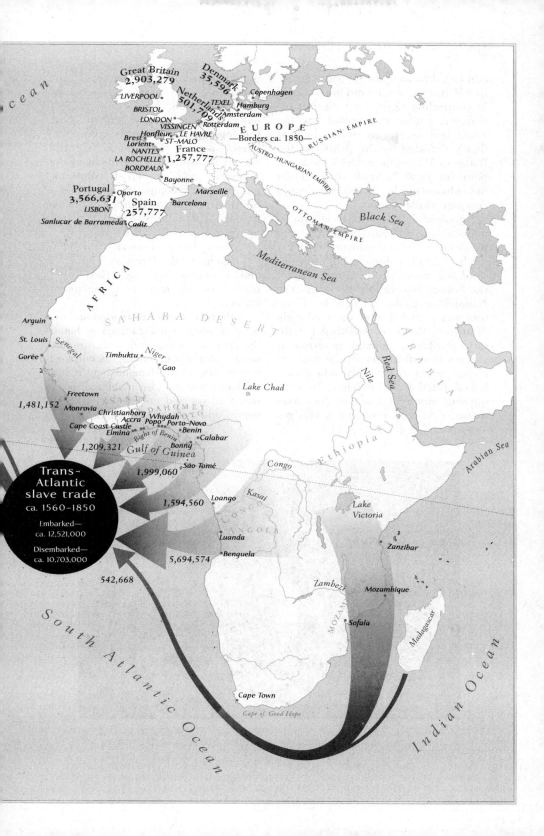

Great Britain
2,903,279
LIVERPOOL
BRISTOL
LONDON
VISSINGEN
Honfleur · LE HAVRE
Brest · ST-MALO
Lorient
NANTES
LA ROCHELLE
BORDEAUX
Bayonne
France
1,257,777

Denmark
35,596
Copenhagen
TEXEL · Hamburg
Netherlands · Amsterdam
501,709
Rotterdam

E U R O P E
—Borders ca. 1850—

RUSSIAN EMPIRE

AUSTRO-HUNGARIAN EMPIRE

OTTOMAN EMPIRE

Black Sea

Portugal
3,566,631
Oporto
LISBON
Sanlucar de Barrameda · Cadiz
Spain
257,777
Marseille
Barcelona

A F R I C A

S A H A R A   D E S E R T

Mediterranean Sea

A R A B I A

Red Sea

Nile

Arabian Sea

Arguin
St. Louis
Gorée
Senegal

Timbuktu
Niger
Gao

Lake Chad

Ethiopia

1,481,152
Freetown
Monrovia · Christianborg
Accra · Whydah
Cape Coast Castle · Popo · Porto-Novo
Elmina · Benin
1,209,321
Bight of Benin
Gulf of Guinea
Bonny · Calabar
São Tomé
1,999,060

DAHOMEY

OYO

**Trans-
Atlantic
slave trade**
ca. 1560–1850

Embarked—
ca. 12,521,000

Disembarked—
ca. 10,703,000

Loango
Kasai
Congo

Lake
Victoria

1,594,560

CONGO
ANGOLA
Luanda

Zanzibar

Benguela
5,694,574

Zambezi
Mozambique

542,668

Sofala

Madagascar

South Atlantic Ocean

Indian Ocean

Cape Town
Cape of Good Hope

and failed to conquer the vast territories of Russia, and he did not succeed in controlling Egypt for long, but his meteoric career was unlike any the world had ever seen. When he was finally defeated by the British at the Battle of Waterloo in 1815, he left a powerful myth behind: the brilliant individual who, by sheer talent, could conquer whole nations.

Napoleon left a number of crucial political legacies too. Though he ruled by dictatorship and reinstated slavery in the French colonies, he also consolidated many of the principles of the French Revolution. Known as the Napoleonic Code, his new legal system was modeled after the civil code of ancient Rome: it abolished hereditary privileges, opened government careers to individuals on the basis of ability rather than birth, and established freedom of religion. In conquering much of Europe, Napoleon managed to wipe away many vestiges of old feudal institutions across the continent. And when he occupied Spain in 1808, he destabilized its power over its colonies, opening the way for a wave of independence movements across South and Central America. Inspired by the ideals of the American and French Revolutions, groups mostly composed of *criollos*— South Americans of European ancestry—led new nations to freedom from Spanish imperial rule. By 1825 Mexico, Peru, Brazil, Bolivia, Colombia, Venezuela, Chile, Uruguay, Ecuador, and Paraguay had all taken their places on the map as independent states.

Both the industrial revolution and the political revolution continued to haunt the generations that followed. Absolute monarchies kept crumbling, as outraged people rose up to demand new rights. Exploited workers also mobilized, organizing strikes and protests against economic and political inequalities. They

Napoleon at the Battle of Waterloo, 1815, Charles Auguste Steuben. Most artists' portrayals of Napoleon, even in defeat, as here, reinforced a romanticized, heroic ideal.

began to call themselves the "proletariat" or "working class" for the first time. Each insurgency inspired other outbreaks, producing a kind of revolutionary contagion across Europe and the Americas that reached its peak in the extraordinary year of 1848, called the "Springtime of the Peoples," when revolutions broke out in France, Austria, Hungary, Switzerland, Spain, Germany, Italy, Denmark, and Romania. This was the year that Karl Marx and Friedrich Engels published the *Communist Manifesto*, which ended with the battle cry: "Workers of the world, unite!" It was in this year that the French abolished slavery for good. And it was in the same year that women's rights activists in the United States organized their first convention at Seneca Falls, New York, where, in a deliberate echo of the Declaration of Independence, they made the case "that all men and women are created equal."

LITERATURE IN THE AGE OF REVOLUTIONS

Utopian dreams have always driven political revolutionaries. In fact, there can be no revolution without acts of imagination. If the old world must be banished and a new world put in its place, what should that new world look like? The first wave of American and French revolutionaries were inspired by the work of eighteenth-century Enlightenment thinkers who envisioned a society governed by reason rather than by custom or superstition. In particular, the philosopher and novelist **Jean-Jacques Rousseau** powerfully stirred the French revolutionaries by imagining a universal emancipation from tyranny: "Man is born free," he wrote, "but everywhere is in chains." The industrial revolution, too, depended on the workings of the imagination: it was spurred by new

schemes for increasing the speed of production, for the invention of huge new machines and the creation of fast modes of communication and transportation. It was fueled, too, by dreams of unprecedented wealth.

Since imagination seemed so crucial to the making of these modern revolutions, writers and artists began to see themselves as playing an important role in the tumult of the times. Art, it seemed, could have the power to transform the world. Many writers eagerly threw themselves into the fray. In the 1790s, for example, the English poet **William Blake** boldly wore the red cap symbolizing the liberty and equality of the French Revolution, and he used his poetry to decry the corruption of church and government, as well as the poverty and enslavement of the people.

For a hundred years, the French Revolution continued to haunt literary writers. Had it ushered in a great new world based on equality and freedom, or had its violence and bloodshed produced meaningless destruction? The Anglo-Irish writer Edmund Burke called the French revolutionaries a "swinish multitude"; British poets **William Wordsworth** and Samuel Taylor Coleridge were at first caught up in the enthusiasm for the democratic ideals of the French Revolution, but the Reign of Terror horrified them and turned them into conservative voices. Charles Dickens, in his *Tale of Two Cities* (1859), exposed the terrible impoverishment of both the London poor and the French peasantry, and yet did not support the French Revolution: the sinister revolutionary Madame Defarge represents vengeful bloodshed. On the other hand, the revolutionaries continued to inspire passionate adherents. "Whatever else may be said of it," asserts a character in Victor Hugo's novel *Les Misérables*

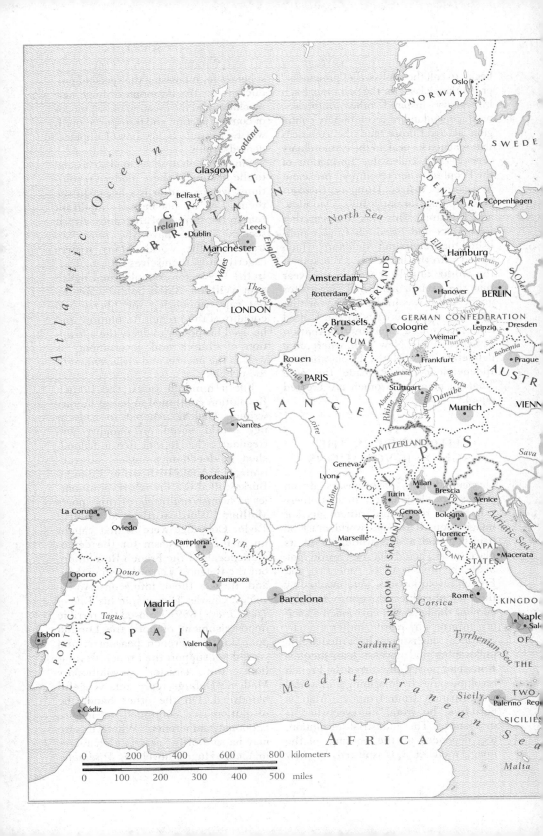

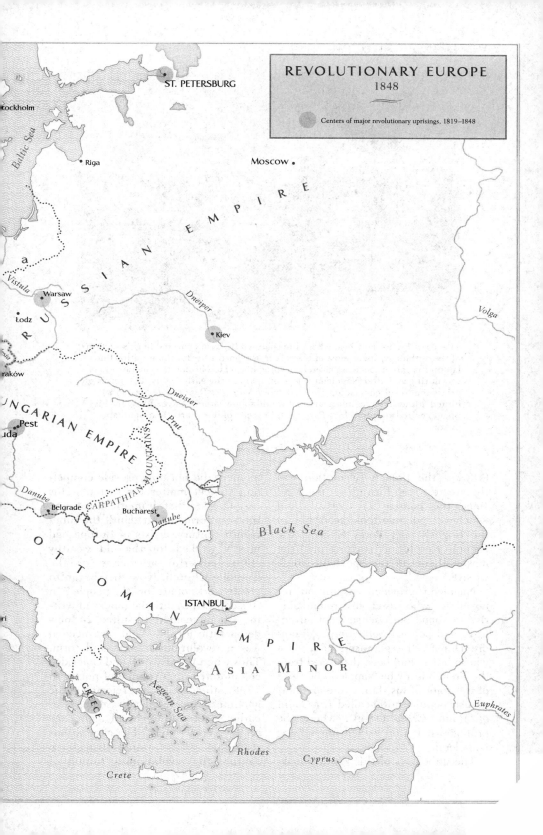

REVOLUTIONARY EUROPE
1848

Centers of major revolutionary uprisings, 1819–1848

ST. PETERSBURG

Stockholm

Baltic Sea

- Riga

Moscow •

RUSSIAN EMPIRE

Vistula

• Warsaw

• Łódź

Dneiper

• Kiev

Volga

raków

Dneister

Prut

UNGARIAN EMPIRE

Pest
uda

CARPATHIAN MOUNTAINS

Danube

Belgrade

Bucharest

Danube

Black Sea

OTTOMAN EMPIRE

ISTANBUL

ASIA MINOR

Aegean Sea

GREECE

Euphrates

Rhodes

Cyprus

Crete

The artist Francisco Goya, whose life spanned the years covered in this section of the anthology, spent most of his career as a portraitist for the wealthy. But late in his career, he also privately devoted his art to chronicling the horrors of war during and after Napoleon's siege of Spain in the early 1800s. The series of prints that resulted—called *The Disasters of War* (*Los Desastres de la Guerra*)— hinted at the stylistic upheavals that would follow later in the century. In this image, called simply *Why?* (*Por qué?*), French soldiers garrotte a Spanish prisoner.

(1862), "the French Revolution was the greatest step forward by mankind since the coming of Christ." And whichever side one took, according to the English poet Percy Shelley, the French Revolution was simply "the master theme of the epoch in which we live."

Napoleon provided inspiration for novelists, who used his remarkable rise to shape both sensational adventures and political reflections. Alexandre Dumas, the grandson of a slave whose father had been dismissed from the French army by Napoleon because of the color of his skin, wrote an enormously popular novel called *The Count of Monte Cristo* (1844), where the protagonist is imprisoned for helping Napoleon.

The upheavals of this revolutionary moment did not only provide compelling subject matter for writers. This was a period that dramatically altered the very forms of art. Until the nineteenth century, artists in Europe had mostly worked for the old wealthy elites: powerful aristocrats or the Catholic Church. Now they began to create works of art for "the people." In this context, traditional modes of writing often seemed ill-suited to new democratic ideals. What was needed was a revolution in style and form. Thus when Wordsworth and Coleridge collaborated on a volume of poetry in 1798, they outright rejected "the gaudiness and inane phraseology" of earlier poetry in favor of "language really used by men." For generations to follow, writers would struggle to capture the revolutionary tumult of the times in startling and sometimes uncomfortable new forms, insisting on experimenting, on innovating, on seeing the world afresh—and never getting buried in old routines. This impulse to revolutionize the way people saw the world was to become part of the definition of art itself. The late nineteenth-century painter Paul Gauguin maintained that every artist was "either a plagiarist or a revolutionary." And if those were the only choices, then what self-respecting artist wouldn't choose revolution?

JEAN-JACQUES ROUSSEAU
1712–1778

Jean-Jacques Rousseau played a significant role in three different revolutions: in politics, his work inspired and shaped revolutionary sentiment in the American colonies and France; in philosophy, he proposed radically unsettling ideas about human nature, justice, and progress that disrupted the dominant Enlightenment thinking of the moment and helped to spark the Romantic movement; and in literature, he invented a major new genre: the modern autobiography. The kind of life story he tells in the *Confessions* is now so familiar as to feel ordinary, recounting in detail the author's emotional life, including formative childhood experiences of desire, pain, and guilt. But in its moment this narrative broke with established conventions, erupting onto the literary scene as a shock so great that it was banned altogether. The text did not appear in full until more than a hundred years after it was written.

LIFE

As a young man, Rousseau did not seem bound for intellectual greatness. Born in the Protestant city of Geneva in 1712, the second son of a watchmaker, he spent very little time in school. Rousseau's mother died a few days after he was born, and his father, after having gotten himself involved in a violent quarrel, fled Geneva when Jean-Jacques was ten, sending his son to live with relatives. The boy did not seem adept enough to learn watchmaking, so at the age of thirteen he was apprenticed to an engraver, who turned out to be cruel and violent. Three years later, Rousseau ran away from Geneva and, craving the protection of a beautiful Catholic woman named Françoise-Louise de Warens, converted to Catholicism. Then began a period of aimless wandering, as Rousseau lived on and off with Madame de Warens, working for short periods as a domestic servant, a music teacher, a surveyor's clerk, and a tutor. Even in his thirties, he was given to idle drifting and was unable to hold down a job for long.

Despite his lack of formal schooling, the young Rousseau always read voraciously. In early childhood he developed a passionate enthusiasm for ancient Greek and Roman writers. A particular s Plutarch, who wrote morally ....ive biographies of ancient emperors and military leaders, including Julius Caesar and Alexander the Great. Rousseau was such an avid reader that while he was an apprentice he went so far as to sell his clothes in order to get his hands on books.

Madame de Warens helped the young man to pursue his intellectual interests and encouraged him to learn music. Their emotional relationship has become well known thanks to Rousseau's account of it in the *Confessions*. Rousseau called her "Mamma," while she called him "Little One." They became lovers in the period from 1733 to 1738, although, Rousseau writes, he felt considerable discomfort joining sexual longings with his love for this maternal figure. To make matters more complicated still, their household often included other men, with Rousseau at times the less favored figure in the *ménage à trois*. And yet, long after their relationship was over, he continued to speak of his lasting love for Madame de Warens and her pivotal importance in his life.

At the age of thirty, Rousseau went to Paris, where he became a personal assistant to a powerful and aristocratic family. In this period he met Denis Diderot and other important Enlightenment philosophers, and he contributed a few entries to the grand *Encyclopédie* they were compiling. At the same time that he was attracting patronage in the most refined Parisian circles, he started living with a barely literate chambermaid named Thérèse Levasseur, a relationship that lasted for three decades and finally resulted in marriage. He had five children with her—all of whom, shockingly, he insisted on leaving in a Paris orphanage.

Late in 1749 Rousseau was considering competing for an essay prize: the challenge was to write about whether advances in the arts and sciences had brought about a purification of human morals. As he was thinking about this question, he experienced a sudden flash of inspiration that would change his life. In one moment of "illumination," he said, he realized that intellectual advances had brought not moral purification but corruption, not improvement but decline. Human beings in a state of nature were compassionate and good; it was society itself that was to blame for creating inequality, greed, and aggression. He abruptly rejected the achievements that the Enlightenment philosophers were calling "progress." The essay won first prize, and it made Rousseau famous. "I dared to strip man's nature naked," he wrote, "and showed that his supposed improvement was the true fount of all his miseries."

In the years that followed, Rousseau developed these innovative ideas. In 1754 he ascribed all of the evils of human experience to property and inequality: "You are undone if you once forget that the fruits of the earth belong to us all, and the earth itself to nobody." Deciding to live the simple life that he extolled in his works, he returned to Geneva, where he converted back to Protestantism. This second conversion prompted some detractors to accuse him of insincerity and opportunism. Soon after, he made a new enemy when he published a condemnation of the French philosopher **Voltaire**. Two years later he denounced the theater as a cause of moral corruption, and inserted a personal attack on his former friend Diderot. He soon found himself isolated and labeled a traitor. From this point onward, he constantly suspected that others were conspiring against him.

Julie, or the New Heloise, Rousseau's only novel, was published in 1761. The best-selling novel of the entire eighteenth century, *Julie* extolled passionate, authentic feeling, sincere faith, and rustic nature, and it struck audiences as dramatically different from most contemporary fiction, which prized artful wit and sophistication. Readers were enthralled, and Rousseau became one of the first literary celebrities. "Women were intoxicated by both the book and its author," he boasted, "and there were hardly any, even in the highest ranks, whose conquest I might not have made if I had undertaken it."

The year after *Julie* appeared, Rousseau developed his thinking in two major philosophical works. The first, *The Social Contract*, made the radical case that legitimate government rests on the will of the people. When rulers fail to protect the populace, Rousseau argued, they break the social contract, and the people are then free to choose new rulers. Thomas Jefferson would rely on this argument when he came to write the Declaration of Independence. The second major work, *Émile*, another major best seller, was a treatise on education which argued that children should be allowed to develop according to their senses and lived experience, and should be kept from books until the age of 12. This idea inspired numerous educational programs, including Montessori schools. In *Émile*, Rousseau also made a case for "natural religion," arguing that a knowledge of God comes not from orthodox doctrine or from revelation, but from one's own observations of nature. Parliaments in both Paris and Geneva saw the book as subversive and called for it to be banned and burned, while the French government ordered Rousseau's arrest. He escaped to a Prussian town, where he asked a priest if he could take communion. His detractors were shocked: was this the man who had just condemned all established religion? Then, in 1764, an anonymous pamphlet—which turned out to have been written by Voltaire—revealed that Rousseau had abandoned all five of his children. Since the moral purpose of *Émile* was to teach readers how to raise and educate children, this latest scandal seemed to many to expose Rousseau as a thoroughgoing hypocrite. In response, he began to write a defense of himself that would shield him from public blame—a story of his own life. This was to become the *Confessions*.

Looking for refuge from scandal and capture, Rousseau fled to England to stay with the philosopher David Hume in 1766. He had become so suspicious of those around him that after a few months he became convinced that Hume was part of a large conspiracy against him, and he wrote a public letter accusing his host of persecuting him. After wandering in exile, he finally settled down in Paris in 1770. A warrant was still out for his arrest, but no one seemed eager to enforce it, and he quietly took up copying music for a living. He also finished the *Confessions*. Since he knew that he would not be permitted to publish it, he confined himself to reading portions aloud to intimate aristocratic audiences. Even these readings alarmed many of his listeners, however, who feared that their own secrets would become public in Rousseau's narrative. Former friends convinced the police to ban these events. After an intense period of despair and hopelessness, Rousseau grew comparatively serene until his death in 1778.

CENSORSHIP AND SUBVERSION IN ROUSSEAU'S FRANCE

Rousseau was not the only writer of his time to endure censorship. At the beginning of the eighteenth century, France had been ruled for decades by an absolute monarch, Louis XIV, who consolidated power so effectively that he is remembered for his stark declaration, "I am the state." Under his rule, Catholic France became the most powerful nation in Europe. It was also highly repressive, silencing criticism of the state and persecuting Protestants who lived within French borders. The king's great-grandson, Louis XV, came to the throne in 1715, a less able and decisive ruler than his predecessor. After several serious military losses, sex scandals, and spending sprees, his popularity sank, and although the government controlled all publications and ordered the death penalty for any writer who attacked religious or state authority, a lively underground book and pamphlet trade flourished. The literate population of France almost doubled between 1680 and 1780, and it included an ever greater variety of readers, including women and artisans. Printed works became cheaper and more available, and audiences began to change their habits, shifting from the conventional practice of reading a small number of works many times over to a new pattern of reading numerous works quickly, thereby gaining access to an unprecedented array of genres and points of view.

From the 1720s onward, a large network of underground printers published philosophical works outside of France in Protestant cities such as Geneva or Amsterdam and had them smuggled across the borders in oxcarts, or sewn into women's petticoats. A few publishers hid inflammatory pages inside respectable books such as Bibles. The king's advisors realized that they were losing the battle and in the 1750s became more permissive, but such an outpouring of radical publications followed that the state imposed new bans. Paradoxically, outlawing a work helped it to sell more copies, which meant that Louis XV's censorship helped to set off a vigorous public debate. For the

first time, a democratic public sphere was emerging. Literary success began to depend on a wide reading public, rather than on specific patrons. And as those beyond the elite enjoyed a growing access to such innovative works, their willingness to tolerate the conventions of the old regime would start to falter.

Among the most influential critics of authority in Rousseau's time were the Enlightenment philosophers, such as Voltaire, who forcefully attacked the Catholic Church, and the Baron de Montesquieu, who denounced despotism and the slave trade. These thinkers called for individual reason to take the place of traditional authority, and they argued that human history was progressing toward perfection by casting off old habits and fetters. This was no marginal academic argument: it threatened to rock the very foundations of the state. Rousseau's friend Denis Diderot remained under police surveillance for years and was for a time imprisoned in a dungeon for writing subversively about religion. Later, his great Enlightenment project, the *Encyclopédie*, worried those in power by promising to diffuse knowledge widely, allowing ordinary people access to unsettling new ideas about natural rights, science, and religious tolerance. In the late 1750s Enlightenment thinkers felt intensely vulnerable, and it was in these same years that Rousseau—subversive and inflammatory in his own right—began to attack them from a new angle. Exalting feeling over reason, rejecting scientific advances, and imagining a return to uncorrupted nature as the key to human happiness, Rousseau became the lightning rod for critiques of Enlightenment reason and the personification of a whole new movement that would come to be known as Romanticism. Indeed, it was Rousseau's writing that first introduced a wide audience to the values that Romantic writers and artists would enthusiastically take up in the generations to follow: an admiration for simplicity and naturalness, a pleasure in the imagination, an assertion of the importance of unique, sincere, individual experience, and, in place of reason, a celebration of the whole range of emotions, from passionate love and intense horror to patriotic loyalty and harrowing grief.

WORK

Before Rousseau's *Confessions*, European readers had sometimes encountered life stories written by aristocrats and military heroes, which recounted their heroic exploits, and they had read confessional religious works, where authors had told stories about faith and conversion. But they had never seen anything quite like a modern autobiography. For the first time, an author's intimate emotional life became the subject of his work. The *Confessions* therefore helped to revolutionize notions of what a life was and what it meant. This was a text that took the uniqueness of individual feeling more seriously than any text had done before, prizing honest self-knowledge as a new moral value. In the process, it also offered a new kind of hero: the isolated but extraordinary individual, unhappy in his solitude but brave in his resistance to social mores. Rousseau departed from convention, too, in his insistence on the importance of childhood memories as essential to the formation of adult personality. Since previous writers had generally considered children's experience inconsequential, the *Confessions* challenged the most basic expectations about what was relevant to an understanding of the self. And

then, even more strangely, the narrative focused specifically on sexual pleasures—including the pleasure of being spanked as a child—which struck many of Rousseau's first readers as embarrassingly petty. But these episodes would turn out to have a lasting impact. More than a century later, Sigmund Freud looked back on the *Confessions* as the forerunner of psychoanalysis, and into our own time, biographers, memoir writers, novelists, therapists, and talk-show hosts continue to understand childhood sexuality as a crucial shaping factor in an adult's life.

The book opens with Rousseau's own sense of his radical originality: "I am resolved on an undertaking that has no model and will have no imitator." Given this claim to being without precedent, Rousseau's title intriguingly suggests the opposite: by calling his autobiography the *Confessions*, he suggests that he is in fact modeling his own work on a famous fourth-century Christian story of spiritual conversion, **St. Augustine**'s *Confessions*. And so he invites us to consider whether or not Augustine's autobiography acts as a "model" for his own work.

This is just one of many paradoxes and contradictions that readers have noticed in Rousseau. On the one hand, for example, he casts himself as a solitary outcast. On the other hand, the *Confessions* repeatedly mentions that its author is an international celebrity, hounded by adoring fans across Europe. In another seeming paradox, Rousseau borrows from the conventionally masculine genre of the public figure's memoir, while he draws equally from the much more feminine, private, domestic style of the novel to describe his childhood and love affairs. Rousseau himself said, "I would rather be a man of paradoxes than a man of prejudices," and it is possible to see these paradoxes forming the very backbone of the work. After all, while the *Confessions* presents the private, emotional life of a unique person, it also uses this personal experience to explore larger ideas about the relationship between the individual and society—the very ideas that are also at the heart of Rousseau's philosophical works. The *Confessions* can therefore be seen to interrogate and break down conventional distinctions between private and public, unique and representative, masculine and feminine.

Many readers have been troubled by yet another tension in the text. Rousseau insists throughout that he is telling the unvarnished truth about himself, however shameful, including acts of theft and masturbation. And yet, he also says that he intends the text to vindicate him to a wide public—to show that he is, by nature, essentially good. The struggle for truth and the attempt at self-justification can seem starkly at odds. In his own time, however, Rousseau's innovative style strengthened his claims to truth telling. Most contemporary writers reveled in elaborate wit and wordplay, but Rousseau spoke frankly and powerfully in the first person, giving his readers a startling new sense of direct contact with the author. Inventing a style of prose that felt unusually plain and honest, Rousseau helped to provoke a new appetite for authenticity in life-writing. Meanwhile, his insistence on direct democracy, natural rights, the value of authentic emotion, and the perils of property ownership would win numerous followers, political, philosophical, and literary. Napoleon himself is reputed to have said that Rousseau caused the French Revolution, and added, "without the Revolution, you would not have had me."

From Confessions[1]

This is the only portrait of a man, painted exactly according to nature and in all its truth, that exists and will probably ever exist. Whoever you may be, whom destiny or my trust has made the arbiter of the fate of these notebooks, I entreat you, in the name of my misfortunes, of your compassion, and of all human kind, not to destroy a unique and useful work, which may serve as a first point of comparison in the study of man that certainly is yet to be begun, and not to take away from the honour of my memory the only sure monument to my character that has not been disfigured by my enemies. Finally, were you yourself to be one of those implacable enemies, cease to be so towards my ashes, and do not pursue your cruel injustice beyond the term both of my life and yours; so that you might do yourself the credit of having been, once at least, generous and good, when you might have been wicked and vindictive; if, that is, the evil directed at a man who has never himself done nor wanted to do any could properly bear the name of vengeance.

1. Translated by Angela Scholar.

From Part One

BOOK ONE

Intus, et in cute.[2]

I am resolved on an undertaking that has no model and will have no imitator. I want to show my fellow-men a man in all the truth of nature; and this man is to be myself.

Myself alone. I feel my heart and I know men. I am not made like any that I have seen; I venture to believe that I was not made like any that exist. If I am not more deserving, at least I am different. As to whether nature did well or ill to break the mould in which I was cast, that is something no one can judge until after they have read me.

Let the trumpet of judgement sound when it will, I will present myself with this book in my hand before the Supreme Judge. I will say boldly: 'Here is what I have done, what I have thought, what I was. I have told the good and the bad with equal frankness. I have concealed nothing that was ill, added nothing that was good, and if I have sometimes used some indifferent ornamentation, this has only ever been to fill a void occasioned by my lack of memory; I may have supposed to be true what I knew could have been so, never what I knew to be false. I have shown myself as I was, contemptible and vile when that is how I was, good, generous, sublime, when that is how I was; I have disclosed my innermost self as you alone know it to be. Assemble about me, Eternal Being, the numberless host of my fellow-men; let them hear my confessions, let them groan at my unworthiness, let them blush at my wretchedness. Let each of them, here on the steps of your throne, in turn reveal his heart with the same sincerity; and then let one of them say to you, if he dares: *I was better than that man.*'

I was born in 1712 in Geneva, the son of Isaac Rousseau and Suzanne Bernard, citizens.[3] Since an already modest family fortune to be divided between fifteen children had reduced to almost nothing my father's share of it, he was obliged to depend for his livelihood on his craft as a watchmaker, at which, indeed, he excelled. My mother, who was the daughter of M. Bernard, the minister, was wealthier; she was beautiful and she was good; and my father had not won her easily. They had loved one another almost from the day they were born; at the age of eight or nine years they were already taking walks together every evening along the Treille; by ten years they were inseparable. The sympathy, the harmony between their souls, reinforced the feelings that habit had formed. Tender and sensitive by nature, they were both of them waiting only for the moment when they would find another person of like disposition, or rather this moment was waiting for them, and each of them gave his heart to the first that opened to receive it. The destiny that had seemed to oppose their passion served only to kindle it. Unable to win his lady, the young man was consumed with grief; she counselled him to travel and to forget her. He travelled, to no avail,

---

2. "Inside and under the skin" (Latin), from Roman satirist Aulus Persius Flaccus (34–62 C.E.), referring to a man who looks back sadly on his loss of virtue.

3. Geneva, unlike its larger neighbors Savoy and France, was a republic with an elected legislature, though only a small number of adult men counted as citizens.

and returned more in love than ever. He found the woman he loved still tender and true. After such a test all that remained was for them to love one another till the end of their days; they swore to do so, and Heaven blessed the vow.

Gabriel Bernard, my mother's brother, fell in love with one of my father's sisters; but she consented to marry the brother only on condition that her brother marry the sister. Love prevailed, and the two weddings took place on the same day. And so my uncle was the husband of my aunt, and their children were my first cousins twice over. By the end of the first year a child had been born on each side; but there was to be a further separation.

My uncle Bernard was an engineer; he went away to serve in the Empire and in Hungary under Prince Eugène. He distinguished himself during the siege and the battle of Belgrade.[4] After the birth of my only brother, my father departed for Constantinople to take up a post as watchmaker to the seraglio. While he was away my mother's beauty, intelligence, and accomplishments[5] won her many admirers. M. de La Closure, the French resident in Geneva, was one of the most assiduous in his attentions. His passion must have been keenly felt; since thirty years later he still softened visibly when he spoke of her to me. My mother had more than her virtue with which to defend herself, she loved her husband tenderly; she pressed him to return; he abandoned everything and came. I was the sad fruit of this homecoming. Ten months later, I was born, weak and sickly; I cost my mother her life, and my birth was the first of my misfortunes.

I never knew how my father bore his loss; but I do know that he never got over it. He thought he could see my mother in me, without being able to forget that I had deprived him of her; he never caressed me without my sensing, from his sighs, from his urgent embraces, that a bitter regret was mingled with them, for which, however, they were the more tender. He had only to say to me: 'Let's talk about your mother, Jean-Jacques,' and I would reply: 'Very well, Father, and then we'll weep together,' and these words alone were enough to move him to tears. 'Ah!' he would sigh, 'bring her back to me, comfort me for losing her; fill the emptiness she has left in my soul. Would I love you as much if you were only my son?' Forty years after losing her he died in the arms of a second wife, but with the name of the first on his lips, and her image deep in his heart.

Such were the authors of my days. Of all the gifts bestowed on them by heaven, the only one they bequeathed to me was a tender heart; but to this they owed their happiness, just as I owe it all my misfortune.

I was born almost dying; they despaired of saving me. I already carried within me the germ of an indisposition which has worsened with the years, and which

---

4. François-Eugène, Prince of Savoy (1663–1736), led the Hungarian army to victory in the Battle of Belgrade, a famous and surprising triumph over the Turkish army in 1717.

5. These were too brilliant for her condition in life, for her father, the minister, adored her, and had taken great care over her education. She could draw and sing, she accompanied herself on the theorbo [a stringed instrument], she was well read and could write tolerable verse. Here is a little rhyme she wrote impromptu, while out walking with her sister-in-law and their children during the absence of her brother and her husband, in response to a remark that someone made to her about these latter:

These two young men, though far from here,
In many ways to us are dear;
They are our friends, our lovers;
Our husbands and our brothers,
And the fathers of these children here.
[Rousseau's note]

now allows me some occasional respite only in order that I migh~
another, more cruel, form of suffering. One of my father's sisters, an a
and virtuous young woman, took such good care of me that she saved me
is still alive as I write this, and at eighty years old cares for a husband wh is
younger than she, but ravaged by drink. I forgive you, dear Aunt, for having
preserved my life, and it grieves me that I cannot, at the end of your days, repay
you for the tender care you lavished on me at the beginning of mine. My nurse
Jacqueline, too, is still alive and in sound health. The hands that opened my
eyes at my birth may yet close them at my death.

I had feelings before I had thoughts: that is the common lot of humanity. But
I was more affected by it than others are. I have no idea what I did before the
age of five or six: I do not know how I learned to read; all I remember is what I
first read and its effect on me; this is the moment from which I date my first
uninterrupted consciousness of myself. My mother had left some romances.[6]
We began to read them after supper, my father and I. Our first intention was
simply that I should practise my reading with the help of some entertaining
books; but we soon became so engrossed in them that we spent whole nights
taking it in turns to read to one another without interruption, unable to break
off until we had finished the whole volume. Sometimes my father, hearing the
swallows at dawn, would say shamefacedly: 'We'd better go to bed now; I'm
more of a child than you are.'

By this dangerous method I acquired in a short time not only a marked facil-
ity for reading and comprehension, but also an understanding, unique in one
of my years, of the passions. I had as yet no ideas about things, but already I
knew every feeling. I had conceived nothing; I had felt everything. This rapid
succession of confused emotions did not damage my reason, since as yet I had
none; but it provided me with one of a different temper; and left me with some
bizarre and romantic notions about human life, of which experience and reflection have never quite managed to cure me.

The romances lasted us until the summer of 1719. The following winter we
found something else. Since my mother's books were exhausted, we resorted to
what we had inherited of her father's library. Fortunately it contained some good
books; and this could scarcely have been otherwise, since this library had been
collected by a man who was not only an ordained minister and even, for such
was the fashion of the day, a scholar, but also a man of taste and intelligence. Le
Sueur's *History of Church and Empire*, Bossuet's discourses on universal history, Plutarch's on famous men, Nani's *History of Venice*, Ovid's *Metamorphoses*, La Bruyère, Fontenelle's *Plurality of Worlds* and his *Dialogues of the Dead*,
and some volumes of Molière,[7] all these were moved into my father's studio,

6. Novels, often fanciful tales of adventure
and heroism.
7. The pseudonym of Jean Baptiste de Poquelin (1622–1673), French comic playwright.
Jean Le Sueur (ca. 1602–1681), French historian and Protestant minister. Jacques-Bénigne
Bossuet (1627–1704), French bishop, writer,
and orator. Plutarch (46–119), Roman histo-

rian and biographer. Giovanni Battista Nani
(1616–1678), Venetian writer, historian, and
ambassador. Ovid (43 B.C.E.–16 C.E.), Roman
poet. Jean de la Bruyère (1645–1696), French
satirist. Bernard le Bovier de Fontenelle
(1657–1757), French writer, scientist, and
philosopher.

and there, every day, I read to him while he worked. I acquired a taste for these works that was rare, perhaps unique, in one of my age. Plutarch, in particular, became my favourite author. The pleasure I took in reading and rereading him cured me in part of my passion for romances, and I soon preferred Agesilaus, Brutus, and Aristides to Orondate, Artamène, and Juba.[8] These interesting books, and the conversations they occasioned between my father and me, shaped that free, republican spirit, that proud and indomitable character, that impatience with servitude and constraint, which it has been my torment to possess all my life in circumstances not at all favourable to its development. My mind was full of Athens and Rome; I lived, as it were, in the midst of their great men; I was, besides, by birth a citizen of a republic and the son of a father whose love for his country was his greatest passion, and I was fired by his example; I thought of myself as a Greek or a Roman; I became the person whose life I was reading: when I recounted acts of constancy and fortitude that had particularly struck me, my eyes would flash and my voice grow louder. One day at table, while I was relating the story of Scaevola,[9] my family were alarmed to see me stretch out my hand and, in imitation of his great deed, place it on a hot chafing-dish.

I had a brother seven years older than I, who was learning my father's trade. The extreme affection that was lavished upon me meant that he was a little neglected, which is not something of which I can approve. His upbringing suffered in consequence. He fell into dissolute ways even before the age at which one can, properly speaking, be considered dissolute. He was placed with a new master, from whom he ran away just as he had done at home. I hardly ever saw him; I can hardly claim to have known him; but I nevertheless loved him dearly, and he loved me too, in as far as such a rascal is capable of love. I remember once when my father, in a rage, was chastising him severely, throwing myself impetuously between the two of them and flinging my arms around him. I thus protected him by taking on my own body all the blows destined for him, and I kept this up so determinedly that my father was obliged in the end to spare him, either because he was moved by my cries and my tears, or because he was afraid of hurting me more than him. My brother went from bad to worse and in the end ran off and disappeared forever. A little while later we heard that he was in Germany. He never once wrote. No more was ever heard of him; and so it was that I became an only son.

If this poor boy's upbringing was neglected, the same could not be said of his brother, for royal princes could not have been cared for more zealously than I was during my early years, idolized by everyone around me, and, which is rarer, treated always as a much-loved child and never as a spoiled one. Never once while I remained in my father's house was I allowed to roam the streets alone with the other children; never was it necessary either to discourage in me or to indulge any of those fanciful whims which are generally attributed to nature,

8. Agesilaus, Brutus, and Aristides are historical figures; Orondate and Juba are characters from novels by Gauthier de Costes, called la Calprenède (1610–1663); Artamène is the hero of a long novel by Madeleine de Scudéry (1607–1701).

9. Gaius Mucius Scaevola, a mythical Roman hero who held his right hand in a fire without showing any signs of pain.

and which are entirely the product of upbringing. I had my childish faults: ι prattled, I was greedy, I sometimes told lies. No doubt I stole fruit, sweets, things to eat; but I never, just for the fun of it, did any harm or damage, got others into trouble, or teased dumb animals. I remember on one occasion, however, peeing into the kettle belonging to one of our neighbours, Mme Clot, while she was at church. I must confess, too, that this memory still makes me laugh, for Mme Clot, although otherwise a thoroughly good person, was the grumpiest old woman I ever knew in my life. Such is the true but brief history of my childhood misdemeanours.

How could I have learnt bad ways, when I was offered nothing but examples of mildness and surrounded by the best people in the world? It was not that the people around me—my father, my aunt, my nurse, our relatives, our friends, our neighbours—obeyed me, but rather that they loved me; and I loved them in return. My whims were so little encouraged and so little opposed that it never occurred to me to have any. I am ready to swear that, until I was myself subjected to the rule of a master, I never even knew what a caprice was. When I was not reading or writing with my father, or going for walks with my nurse, I was always with my aunt, watching her at her embroidery, hearing her sing, sitting or standing at her side; and I was happy. Her good-humour, her gentleness, her agreeable features, all these have so imprinted themselves on my memory, that I can still see in my mind's eye her manner, her glance, her whole air; I still remember the affectionate little things she used to say; I could describe how she was dressed, and how she wore her hair, even to the two black curls which, after the fashion of the day, framed her temples.

I am convinced that it is to her that I owe the taste, or rather passion, for music that developed in me fully only much later. She knew a prodigious number of songs and airs, which she sang in a small, sweet voice. This excellent young woman possessed a serenity of soul that banished far from her and from everyone around her any reverie or sadness. I was so enchanted by her singing that, not only have many of her songs lingered in my memory, but, now that I have lost her, others too, totally forgotten since childhood, return to haunt me as I grow older, with a charm I cannot convey. Who would have thought that, old driveller that I am, worn out with worry and care, I should suddenly catch myself humming these little tunes in a voice already cracked and quavering, and weeping like a child? One air in particular has come back to me in full, although the words of the second verse have repeatedly resisted all my efforts to remember them, even though I dimly recall the rhymes. Here is the beginning followed by what I have been able to remember of the rest.

> Tircis,[1] I dare not stay
> Beneath the sturdy oak
> To hear your pipe's sweet play;
> Already I'm the talk
> Of all our village folk

> .   .   .   .   .   .

1. A shepherd from pastoral poetry.

> .   .   .   a shepherd's vows
> .   .   .   his repose
> .   .   .   allows
> For always the thorn lies under the rose.

What is it about this song, I wonder, that so beguiles and moves my heart? It has a capricious charm I do not understand at all; nevertheless, I am quite incapable of singing it through to the end without dissolving into tears. I have often been on the point of writing to Paris to enquire about the rest of the words, in case there should be anyone there who still knows them. But I suspect that some of the pleasure I take in recalling this little tune would fade if I knew for certain that others apart from my poor aunt Suzanne had sung it.

Such were the affections that marked my entry into life; thus there began to take shape or to manifest themselves within me this heart, at once so proud and so tender, and this character, effeminate and yet indomitable, which, continually fluctuating between weakness and courage, between laxity and virtue, has to the end divided me against myself and ensured that abstinence and enjoyment, pleasure and wisdom have all eluded me equally.

This upbringing was interrupted by an accident whose consequences have affected my life ever since. My father had a quarrel with a M. Gautier, a French captain, who had relatives in the council.[2] This Gautier, an insolent and cowardly fellow, suffered a nose-bleed and, out of revenge, accused my father of having drawn his sword on him inside the city limits. My father, threatened with imprisonment, insisted that, in accordance with the law, his accuser be taken into custody with him. Unable to obtain this, he chose to leave Geneva and to exile himself for the rest of his life rather than give way on a point where it seemed to him that both his honour and his liberty were compromised.

I remained behind under the guardianship of my uncle Bernard, who at the time was employed on the fortifications of Geneva. His eldest daughter had died, but he had a son the same age as myself. We were sent off together to Bossey to board with the minister, M. Lambercier, so that, along with some Latin, we might acquire that hotchpotch of knowledge which usually accompanies it under the name of education.

Two years spent in this village softened, somewhat, my Roman harshness and restored my childhood to me. At Geneva, where nothing was imposed on me, I had loved reading and study; it was almost my only amusement. At Bossey I was made to work, and thus grew to love the games that served as relaxation. The countryside was so new to me that I never tired of enjoying it. I came to love it with a passion that has never faded. The memory of the happy days I spent there has filled me with regret for rural life and its pleasures at every stage of my existence until the one that took me back there. M. Lambercier was a sensible man who, while not neglecting our education, did not overburden us with schoolwork. The proof that he went about this in the right way is that, in spite of my dislike of any form of compulsion, I have never remembered my hours of study with any distaste, and that, while I did not learn much from him, what I did learn, I learned without difficulty and have never forgotten.

2. The legislature of Geneva.

This simple country life bestowed on me a gift beyond price in opening up my heart to friendship. Up until then I had only known feelings that, although exalted, were imaginary. Living peaceably day after day with my cousin Bernard, I became warmly attached to him, and soon felt a more tender affection for him than I had for my brother, and one that has not been erased by time. He was a tall boy, lanky and very thin, as mild-tempered as he was feeble-bodied, and who did not take unfair advantage of the preference that, as the son of my guardian, he was shown by the whole household. We shared the same tasks, the same amusements, the same tastes; we were on our own together; we were of the same age; each of us needed a friend; so that to be separated was for both of us, so to speak, to be annihilated. Although we rarely had occasion to demonstrate our mutual attachment, it was strong, and not only could we not bear to be separated for a moment, but we could not imagine ever being able to bear it. Since we both of us responded readily to affection and were good-humoured when not crossed, we always agreed about everything. If, as the favourite of our guardians, he took precedence over me when we were with them, when we were alone the advantage was mine, and this redressed the balance between us. When he was at a loss during lessons, I whispered the answer to him; when my exercise was finished, I helped him with his, and in games, where I was the more inventive, he always followed my lead. In other words, our characters were so compatible and the friendship that united us so real, that, during the more than five years that we were virtually inseparable, whether at Bossey or in Geneva, we often, it is true, fell out, but we never needed to be separated, none of our quarrels lasted for more than a quarter of an hour, and neither of us ever once informed against the other. These remarks may seem puerile, but they nevertheless draw attention to an example that is perhaps unique among children.

The kind of life I led at Bossey suited me so well that it would have fixed my character for ever, if only it had lasted longer. It was founded on feelings that were at once tender, affectionate, and tranquil. Never, I believe, has any individual of our species possessed less natural vanity than I do. I would soar to heights of sublime feeling, but as promptly fall back into my habitual indolence. To be loved by all who came near me was my most urgent wish. I was by nature gentle, so too was my cousin; so indeed were our guardians. During two whole years I neither witnessed nor was the victim of any kind of violence. Everything fostered the tendencies that nature herself had planted in my heart. I knew no greater happiness than to see everyone content with me and with the world in general. I will never forget how, when it was my turn in chapel to recite my catechism, nothing distressed me more, if I happened to hesitate in my replies, than to see on Mlle Lambercier's face signs of anxiety and distress. I was more upset by this than by the shame of failing in public, although that, too, affected me greatly: for, not much moved by praise, I was always susceptible to shame, and I can safely say that the expectation of a reprimand from Mlle Lambercier alarmed me less than did the fear of causing her pain.

And indeed, she was not afraid, any more than was her brother, to show severity when this was necessary; but since her severity was almost always justified and never excessive, it provoked in me feelings of distress rather than of rebellion. I was more concerned about occasioning displeasure than about being chastised, for marks of disapprobation seemed more cruel to me than physical punishment. I find it embarrassing to go into greater detail, but I must. How promptly we would change our methods of dealing with the young if only the long-term effects of the one that is presently employed, always indiscriminately and often indiscreetly, could be foreseen! The lesson that may be learned from just one example of this, as common as it is pernicious, is so important that I have decided to give it.

Just as Mlle Lambercier felt for us the affection of a mother, so too she had a mother's authority, which she sometimes exerted to the point of inflicting common childhood punishments on us, when we had deserved this. For a while she restricted herself to threats of punishment which were quite new to me and which I found very frightening; but after the threat had been carried out, I discovered that it was less terrible in the event than it had been in anticipation, and, what is even more bizarre, that this punishment made me even fonder of the woman who had administered it. Indeed, it took all the sincerity of my affection for her and all my natural meekness to prevent me from seeking to merit a repetition of the same treatment; for I had found in the pain inflicted, and even in the shame that accompanied it, an element of sensuality which left me with more desire than fear at the prospect of experiencing it again from the same hand. It is true that, since without doubt some precocious sexual instinct entered into all this, the same punishment received from her brother would not have seemed to me at all pleasant. But given his temperament, this arrangement was not something that needed to be feared, so that, if I resisted the temptation to earn punishment, this was solely because I was afraid of vexing Mlle de Lambercier; for so great is the power that human kindness exercises over me, even if it has its origin in the senses, that in my heart the former will always prevail over the latter.

This second offence, which I had avoided without fearing it, duly occurred, but without involving any misdeed or at least any conscious act of will on my part, so that it was with a clear conscience that I as it were profited from it. But this second was also the last: for Mlle de Lambercier, who no doubt inferred from some sign I gave that the punishment was not achieving its aim, declared that she could not continue with it, that it exhausted her too much. Up until then we had slept in her room and sometimes, in winter, even in her bed. Two days later we were moved to another room, and I had henceforward the honour, which I would gladly have foregone, of being treated by her as a big boy.

Who would have believed that this ordinary form of childhood punishment, meted out to a boy of eight years[3] by a young woman of thirty, should have decided my tastes, my desires, my passions, my whole self, for the rest of my life, and in a direction that was precisely the opposite of what might naturally have been expected? My senses were inflamed, but at the same time my desires, confused and indeed limited by what I had already experienced, never thought of looking for anything else. My blood had burned within my veins almost from the moment of my birth, but I kept myself pure of any taint until an age when even the coldest and slowest of temperaments begins to develop. Long tormented, but without knowing why, I devoured with ardent gaze all the beauti-

---

3. Rousseau was in fact eleven years old at the time, not eight.

ful women I encountered. My imagination returned to them again and again, but only to deploy them in its own way, and to make of each of them another Mlle de Lambercier.

This bizarre taste, which persisted beyond adolescence and indeed drove me to the verge of depravity and madness, nevertheless preserved in me those very standards of upright behaviour which it might have been expected to undermine. If ever an upbringing was proper and chaste, it was certainly the one that I had received. My three aunts were not only persons of exemplary respectability, they also practised a reticence that women have long since abandoned. My father, who liked his pleasures but was gallant in the old style, never uttered, even in the presence of the women he most admired, a single word that would make a virgin blush, and the consideration that is due to children has never been more scrupulously observed than it was in my family and in front of me. M. Lambercier's household was no less strict in this regard, and indeed a very good servant was dismissed for having said something a little too free and easy in front of us. Not only had I reached adolescence before I had any clear idea about sexual union, but such confused ideas as I did have always took some odious and disgusting form. I had a horror of common prostitutes that I have never lost; I could not look at a debauchee without disdain, without dread even, so extreme was the aversion that I had felt for debauchery ever since, going to Saconnex one day along a hollow lane, I saw holes in the earth along both sides of the path and was told that this was where these people did their coupling. What I had seen dogs doing always came into my mind too when I thought of how it might be for people, and the very memory was enough to sicken me.

These prejudices, which I owed to my upbringing and which were sufficient in themselves to delay the first eruptions of a combustible temperament, were further reinforced, as I have said, by the false direction in which I had been led by the first stirrings of sensuality. I imagined only what I had experienced; in spite of a troublesome agitation in the blood, I concentrated all my desires on the kind of pleasure I already knew, without ever getting as far as that which I had been made to think of as odious, and which so closely resembled the other, although I had not the least suspicion of this. When, in the midst of my foolish fantasies, of my wild erotic flights, and of the extravagant actions to which they sometimes drove me, I resorted in imagination to the assistance of the other sex, I never dreamt that it could be put to any other use than that which I burned to make of it.

In this way, then, in spite of an ardent, lascivious, and very precocious temperament, not only did I pass beyond the age of puberty without desiring, without knowing, any sensual pleasures beyond those to which Mlle de Lambercier had quite innocently introduced me; but also, when at last the passing years had made me a man, it was again the case that what should have ruined me preserved me. The taste I had acquired as a child, instead of disappearing, became so identified with that other pleasure that I was never able to dissociate it from the desires aroused through the senses; and this vagary, in conjunction with my natural timidity, has always inhibited me in my approaches to women, because I dare not tell them everything, but nor am I able to perform everything; since my kind of pleasure, of which the other sort is only the end point, cannot be extracted by the man who desires it, nor guessed at by the woman who alone can bestow it. And so I have spent my life coveting but never declaring myself to the women I loved most. Never daring to reveal my proclivities, I have at least kept them amused with relationships that allowed my mind to dwell on them. To lie at the feet of an imperious mistress, to obey her commands, to be obliged to beg for her forgiveness, these were sweet pleasures, and the more my inflamed imagination roused my blood, the more I played the bashful lover. This way of making love does not, needless to say, result in very rapid progress, nor does it pose much threat to the virtue of the women who are its object. I have thus possessed very few, but have nevertheless achieved much pleasure in my own way, that is, through my imagination. Thus it is that my senses, conspiring with my timid nature and my romantic spirit, have kept my heart pure and my behaviour honourable, thanks to those very inclinations which, if I had been a little bolder perhaps, would have plunged me into the most brutish pleasure-seeking.

I have taken the first step, and the most painful, into the dark and miry labyrinth of my confessions. It is not what is criminal that it is the hardest to reveal, but what is laughable or shameful. But from now on I can feel certain of myself: after what I have just dared to say, nothing can stop me.

* * *

BOOK TWO

My landlady who, as I have said, had taken a liking to me, told me that she might have found a situation for me, and that a lady of quality wanted to see me. This was enough to convince me that I was at last embarked upon adventures in high places, for this was the idea I always came back to. It turned out, however, not to be as brilliant as I had imagined. I was taken to see the lady by the servant who had told her about me. She questioned me, cross-examined me, and was, apparently, satisfied, for all of a sudden I found myself in her service, not exactly as a favourite, but as a footman. I was dressed in the same colour as the other servants, except that they had a shoulder-knot which I was not given; since there was no braid on her livery, it looked very little different from any ordinary suit of clothes. Such was the unexpected fulfilment of all my high hopes!

The Comtesse de Vercellis, whose household I had entered, was a widow with no children. Her husband had been from Piedmont; as for her, I have always assumed that she came from Savoy, since I could not imagine a Piedmontese speaking French so well and with such a pure accent. She was in her middle years, distinguished in appearance, cultivated in mind, with a great love and knowledge of French literature. She wrote a great deal and always in French. Her letters had the turn of phrase and the grace, almost, of Mme de Sévigné's:[4] some of them might even have been taken for hers. My main task, not at all an unpleasant one, was to take dictation of these letters, since she was prevented by a breast cancer, which caused her much suffering, from writing them herself.

4. French writer Marie de Rabutin-Chantal, marquise de Sévigné (1626–1696), famous for her letters.

Mme de Vercellis possessed not only great intelligence but a steadfast and noble soul. I watched her during her last illness, I saw her suffer and die without betraying a moment's weakness, without making the least apparent effort to contain herself, without abandoning her woman's dignity, and without suspecting that there was any philosophy in all of this; indeed, the word 'philosophy' was not yet in vogue, and she would not have known it in the sense in which it is used today. This strength of character was so marked as to be indistinguishable, sometimes, from coldness. She always seemed to me to be as indifferent to the feelings of others as she was to her own, so that, if she performed good works among the poor and needy, she did so because this was good in itself rather than out of any true compassion. I experienced something of this indifference during the three months I was with her. It would have been natural for her to conceive a liking for a young man of some promise, who was continually in her presence, and for it to occur to her, as she felt death approach, that afterwards he would still need help and support; however, either because she did not think me worthy of any special attention, or because the people who watched over her saw to it that she thought only of them, she did nothing for me.

I well remember, however, the curiosity she showed while getting to know me. She would sometimes ask me about myself; she liked me to show her the letters I was writing to Mme de Warens, and to describe my feelings to her. But she went about discovering them in quite the wrong way, since she never revealed hers to me. My heart was eager to pour itself out, provided it felt that another was open to receive it. Cold and curt interrogation, however, with no hint either of approbation or of blame at my replies, did not inspire me with confidence. Unable to judge whether my chatter was pleasing or displeasing, I became fearful and would try, not so much to say what I felt, as to avoid saying anything that might harm me. I have since observed that this habit of coldly interrogating people whom you are trying to get to know is fairly common among women who pride themselves on their intelligence. They imagine that, by revealing nothing of their own feelings, they will the better succeed in discovering yours; what they do not realize is that they thereby deprive you of the courage to reveal them. Anyone subjected to close questioning will, for that very reason, be put on his guard, and if he suspects that, far from inspiring any real interest, he is merely being made to talk, he will either lie, say nothing, or watch his tongue even more carefully than before, preferring to be thought a fool than to be the dupe of someone's mere curiosity. It is, in short, pointless to attempt to see into the heart of another while affecting to conceal one's own.

Mme de Vercellis never said a word to me that expressed affection, pity, or benevolence. She questioned me coldly, I replied with reserve. My replies were so timid that she must have found them beneath her notice, and become bored. Towards the end she asked me no more questions and spoke to me only if she wanted me to do something for her. She judged me on the basis not so much of what I was but of what she had made me, and because she regarded me as nothing more than a footman, she prevented me from appearing to be anything else.

I think that this was my first experience of that malign play of hidden self-interest which has so often impeded me in life and which has left me with a very natural aversion towards the apparent order that produces it. Mme de Vercellis's heir, since she had no children, was a nephew, the Comte de la Roque, who was

ious in his attentions towards her. In addition, her principal servants, seeing that her end was near, were determined not to be forgotten, and all in all she was surrounded by so many over-zealous people that it was unlikely that she would find time to think of me. The head of her household was a certain M. Lorenzini, an artful man, whose wife, even more artfully, had so insinuated herself into the good graces of her mistress that she was treated by her as a friend rather than a paid servant. She had persuaded her to take on as chambermaid a niece of hers, called Mlle Pontal, a crafty little creature who gave herself the airs of a lady's maid; together, she and her aunt were so successful in ingratiating themselves with their mistress that she saw only through their eyes and acted only through their agency. I had not the good fortune to find favour with these three people; I obeyed them, but I did not serve them; I did not see why, as well as attending our common mistress, I should be a servant to her servants. I presented, moreover, something of a threat to them. They could see very well that I was not in my rightful place; they feared that Madame would see it too, and that what she might do to rectify this would diminish their own inheritance; for people of that sort are too greedy to be fair, and look upon any legacy made to others as depriving them of what is properly theirs. And so they made a concerted effort to keep me out of her sight. She liked writing letters. It was a welcome distraction for someone in her condition; they discouraged it and persuaded her doctor to oppose it on the grounds that it was too tiring for her. On the pretext that I did not understand my duties, they hired in my place two great oafs to carry her about in her chair; and in short, they were so successful in all this that, when she came to make her will, I had not even entered her room during the whole of the previous week. It is true that thereafter I entered as before, and was more assiduous in my attentions than anyone else; for the poor woman's sufferings distressed me greatly, while the constancy with which she bore them inspired admiration and affection in me; indeed I shed genuine tears in that room, unnoticed by her or by anyone else.

At last we lost her. I saw her die. In life she had been a woman of wit and good sense; in death she was a sage. I can safely say that she endeared the Catholic religion to me by the serenity of spirit with which she fulfilled its duties, without omission and without affectation. She was by nature serious, but towards the end of her illness she assumed an air of gaiety, which was too constant to be simulated, and which was as though lent her by reason itself to compensate for the gravity of her situation. It was only during her last two days that she stayed in bed, and even then she kept up a tranquil conversation with the people round about her. At last, unable to speak and already in the throes of death, she gave a great fart. 'Good,' she said, as she turned over: 'A woman who farts cannot be dead.' These were the last words she uttered.

She had bequeathed a year's wages to each of her menial servants; but, since my name did not appear on her household list, I received nothing; in spite of this, the Comte de la Roque gave me thirty francs and let me keep the new suit of clothes which, although I was wearing it, M. Lorenzini had wanted to take away from me. He even promised to try to find me a new position and gave me permission to go and see him. I went two or three times, but without managing to speak to him. Easily deterred, I did not go again. As we will soon see, this was a mistake.

If only this were all that I have to relate about my time with Mme de Vercellis! But although my situation appeared unchanged, I was not the same on leaving her house as I had been when I entered it. I took away with me the enduring memory of a crime and the intolerable burden of a remorse, with which even now, after forty years, my conscience is still weighed down, and whose bitter knowledge, far from fading, becomes more painful with the years. Who would have thought that a child's misdeed could have such cruel consequences? But it is because of these all too probable consequences that my heart is denied any consolation. I may have caused to perish, in shameful and miserable circumstances, a young woman who, amiable, honest, and deserving, was, without a doubt, worth a great deal more than I.

It is almost inevitable that the dispersal of a household should generate a certain confusion and that items should go astray. And yet, such was the loyalty of the servants and the vigilance of M. and Mme Lorenzini that nothing was missing from the inventory. All that was lost was a little ribbon, silver and rose-coloured and already quite old, which belonged to Mlle Pontal. Many other, better things had been within my reach; but I was tempted only by this ribbon, I stole it, and since I made little attempt to conceal it, I was soon found with it. They asked me where I had got it. I hesitated, stammered, and finally said, blushing, that Marion had given it to me. Marion was a young girl from the Maurienne,[5] whom Mme de Vercellis had engaged as a cook when, because she no longer entertained and had more need of nourishing soups than of delicate ragouts, she decided to dismiss her own. Not only was Marion pretty, with a freshness of complexion that is found only in the mountains, and, above all, an air of modesty and sweetness that won the heart of everyone who saw her, she was also a good girl, virtuous and totally loyal. There was thus great surprise when I named her. I was regarded as scarcely less trustworthy, and so an enquiry was thought to be necessary to establish which of us was the thief. She was summoned; a large crowd of people was present, among them the Comte de la Roque. She arrived, was shown the ribbon, and, shamelessly, I made my accusation; taken aback, she said nothing, then threw me a glance which would have disarmed the devil himself, but which my barbarous heart resisted. At length she denied the charge, firmly but calmly, remonstrated with me, urged me to recollect myself and not to bring disgrace upon an innocent girl who had never done me any harm; I persisted in my infernal wickedness, however, repeated my accusation, and asserted to her face that it was she who had given me the ribbon. The poor girl began to cry, but said no more than, 'Ah Rousseau, and I always thought you had a good character! How wretched you are making me, and yet I would not for anything be in your place.' And that was all. She continued to defend herself with steadfast simplicity but without permitting herself any attack on me. The contrast between her moderation and my decided tone worked against her. It did not seem natural to suppose that there could be such diabolical effrontery on the one hand and such angelic sweetness on the other. No formal conclusion was reached, but the presumption was in my favour. Because of the general upheaval, the matter was left there, and the Comte de la Roque, dismissing us both, contented himself with saying that the conscience of the guilty party would be certain to avenge the innocent. This was no vain prophecy, but is every day fulfilled anew.

I do not know what became of the victim of my false witness; it seems unlikely that, after this, she would easily have found another good situation.

5. A province in the kingdom of Savoy.

She had suffered an imputation to her honour that was cruel in every way. The theft was trifling; nevertheless, it was a theft and, what was worse, had been used to seduce a young boy; finally, the lie and the obstinacy with which she clung to it left nothing to be hoped for from someone who combined so many vices. I fear, too, that wretchedness and destitution were not the worst of the dangers I exposed her to. Who knows to what extremes despair and injured innocence might not, at her age, have driven her? Ah, if my remorse at having made her unhappy is intolerable, only judge how it feels to have perhaps reduced her to being worse off than myself!

At times I am so troubled by this cruel memory, and so distressed, that I lie sleepless in my bed, imagining the poor girl advancing towards me to reproach me for my crime as though I had committed it only yesterday. While I still enjoyed some tranquillity in life it tormented me less, but in these tempestuous times it deprives me of the sweetest consolation known to persecuted innocence; it brings home to me the truth of an observation I think I have made in another work, that remorse is lulled during times of good fortune and aggravated in adversity. And yet I have never been able to bring myself to unburden my heart of this confession by entrusting it to a friend. I have never, in moments of the greatest intimacy, divulged it to anyone, even to Mme de Warens. The most that I have been able to do has been to confess my responsibility for an atrocious deed, without ever saying of what exactly it consisted. This burden, then, has lain unalleviated on my conscience until this very day; and I can safely say that the desire to be in some measure relieved of it has greatly contributed to the decision I have taken to write my confessions.

I have been outspoken in the confession I have just made, and surely no one could think that I have in any way sought to mitigate the infamy of my crime. But I would not be fulfilling the purpose of this book if I did not at the same time reveal my own innermost feelings, and if I were afraid to excuse myself, even where the truth of the matter calls for it. I have never been less motivated by malice than at this cruel moment, and when I accused this unfortunate girl, it is bizarre, but it is true, that it was my fondness for her that was the cause of it. She was on my mind, and I had simply used as an excuse the first object that presented itself to me. I accused her of having done what I wanted to do, and of having given me the ribbon, because my intention had been to give it to her. When she appeared shortly afterwards I was stricken with remorse, but the presence of so many people was stronger than my repentance. It was not that I was afraid of being punished but that I was afraid of being put to shame; and I feared shame more than death, more than crime, more than anything in the world. I would have wanted the earth to swallow me up and bury me in its depths. It was shame alone, unconquerable shame, that prevailed over everything and was the cause of all my impudence; and the more criminal I became, the more my terror at having to admit it made me bold. All I could think of was the horror of being found out and of being denounced, publicly and to my face, as a thief, a liar, a slanderer. The confusion that seized my whole being robbed me of any other feeling. If I had been given time to collect myself, I would unquestionably have admitted everything. If M. de la Roque had taken me aside and had said to me: 'Don't ruin this poor girl. If you are guilty, own up to it now,' I would have thrown myself at his feet forthwith; of that I am perfectly certain. But, when what I needed was encouragement, all I received was intimidation. My age, too, was a consideration that it is only fair to take into account. I was scarcely more than a child, or rather I still was one. Real wickedness is even more criminal in a young person than in an adult, but what is merely weakness is much less so, and my offence, when it comes down to it, was little more. Thus its memory distresses me less because of any evil in the act itself than because of that which it must have caused. It has even had the good effect of preserving me for the rest of my life from any inclination towards crime, because of the terrible impression that has remained with me of the only one I ever committed, and I suspect that my aversion towards lying comes in large part from remorse at having been capable of one that was so wicked. If, as I venture to believe, such a crime can be expiated, it must surely have been so by the many misfortunes that burden my old age; by forty years of rectitude and honour in difficult circumstances; indeed, poor Marion has found so many avengers in this world that, however grave my offence against her, I am not too afraid that I will carry the guilt for it into the next. That is all that I had to say on this subject. May I be spared from ever having to speak of it again.

* * *

JOHANN WOLFGANG VON GOETHE
1749–1832

Few writers have ever surpassed Goethe in global fame and influence. He was perhaps the last European to live up to the ideal of the Renaissance man: skilled in the arts, in science, and in politics. He made groundbreaking contributions not only in all the major literary genres, but also in art criticism and the study of classical culture. He did extensive work in the fields of botany, mineralogy, comparative anatomy, and optics. And he occupied many administrative and political positions at the court of Weimar, where he was responsible for finance, the military, and mining, as well as for the Weimar Court Theatre, which he turned from an amateur theater to a professional troupe that premiered many of his own plays. Distrusting both the French Revolution, whose effects he witnessed at close hand, and growing nationalist movements in Germany and elsewhere, Goethe did not consider himself a German, but a European, and he coined the visionary notion of "world literature," eager to open Europe to the intellectual and artistic production of the non-European world.

Goethe was born into a middle-class family in Frankfurt. Despite an early interest in the arts and the theater, he followed his father's wishes and studied law. But Goethe's artistic ambitions could not be held back for long and he soon started to publish literary works. His first significant play, *Götz of Berlechingen* (1773), was shaped by his discovery of Shakespeare, whom he especially admired for being willing to violate the strict rules of drama that prevailed at the time. Yet the most important work of Goethe's early period was a novel, *The Sorrows of Young Werther*

(1774), which turned Goethe into the representative of a literary movement called *Sturm und Drang* ("storm and stress") that emphasized the expression of feelings over the strictures of literary form. Centered on subjective impressions, extreme emotions, and literary outbursts, the novel leads its tragic protagonist, who is caught in a love triangle, to his eventual suicide. *The Sorrows of Young Werther* prompted mass hysteria, also called "Werther fever," allegedly leading to several copycat suicides as well as to the marketing of Werther paraphernalia. Goethe became a European celebrity virtually overnight.

A year later, Duke Karl August of Weimar called the young writer to his elegant but provincial court, where Goethe first served as educator, but soon fulfilled more important functions and was ultimately elevated to the aristocracy. It was here, amid his extensive duties, that Goethe began his mature, more classical works: his influential novel, *Wilhelm Meister's Apprenticeship*, as well as the plays *Egmont*, *Iphigenia on Tauris*, *Torquato Tasso*, and *Faust*. He began all of these works shortly after he had arrived at Weimar, but they went through innumerable revisions, during which he slowly forged a new, less unruly and more measured style, leaving the earlier "storm and stress" behind.

Goethe was inspired by an extended voyage to Italy (1786–88), and he became the chief representative of a revival of classical forms and ideas in Germany and Europe more generally. This journey led him to revise *Faust* and other works in accordance with the classical ideal. He collected classical sculpture (he contented himself with replicas) and adapted classical stories, poetry, and drama. But the theater stood at the center of the classical revival. He worried about the training of actors, developing guidelines later published as *Rules for Actors* (1803, 1832), and intervened in all other aspects of theater production. He also insisted on introducing international playwrights, including Shakespeare, Calderón, and Goldoni, to his provincial audience. Thus, although Goethe had started the Weimar Court Theatre as a vehicle for his revival of classical drama, he opened it to a variety of dramatic styles.

In the first decades of the nineteenth century, Goethe finally completed the long-awaited first part of *Faust* (1806). While he left his mark on numerous fields and genres, *Faust* stands out as his masterpiece. He began writing it in his early twenties and continued to work on it until his death. Even more than many of his other texts, it underwent significant changes, from the first drafts in the 1770s, through the publication of the first part in 1808, to the final version of the second part, completed just before his last birthday in 1832.

For *Faust* Goethe relied on an old folk legend, a quintessentially medieval morality tale, in which an arrogant scholar gives in to the temptations of the devil, makes a famous pact to trade his soul for the use of black magic, and finally suffers in hell for his sins. In the course of his many revisions, Goethe transformed this simple material into a text that captured the spirit and desires of modernity. Although he preserved important set pieces such as the pact with the devil, what mattered to Goethe was the relation between abstract learning and sensuous experience, as well as the nature of human striving. He used the character of Faust to explore the transformative energies unleashed by modern science, philosophy, and industry.

In revising the old legend, Goethe changed its moral structure. While earlier Fausts were always lost to the devil, Goethe has Faust escape Mephistopheles' clutches at the end of *Faust II*. This decision thoroughly alters the morality play, which had punished a blaspheming protagonist as a warning to Christian audiences. Goethe still depicts Faust as a sinner, as the earlier versions had done. But now Faust's sinning has to be balanced against his irreverent and limitless thirst for knowledge, which for Goethe has great esteem. Paradoxically, the very quality that drives Faust to his pact with the devil is the one that will lead him to salvation.

Several scenes frame the play before its proper action begins. First Goethe presents a kind of curtain riser, a "Prelude in the Theater," in which a Manager, a Poet, and a Clown debate their respective visions of a theater, poised between popular entertainment and high art, a debate undoubtedly grounded in Goethe's experience as a dramatist and theater director. He then moves on to the "Prologue in Heaven," which is borrowed from the biblical book of of Job. It depicts a debate between God and Mephistopheles that ends in a wager. Mephistopheles has permission to lead Faust into temptation because God is certain that Faust's restless striving, his search for true knowledge, will eventually lead him back on the right path. Goethe then introduces the text with a "Dedication," in which he evokes the youthful world in which began this work some thirty years ago.

The main drama of *Faust I* can be divided into two parts. The first part introduces us to the medieval Doctor, who has mastered all the higher disciplines of the university—philosophy, law, medicine, and theology—but who still has not learned the inner essence of the world. Dissatisfied with this insufficient knowledge, he turns to the dangerous domains of magic and alchemy, and it is this daring that is, for Goethe, Faust's most modern attribute. Shunning inherited pieties and religious prejudices, Faust is ready to sacrifice everything to knowledge. He also longs to experience life to the fullest, and this makes him especially susceptible to the enticements of Mephistopheles, who offers him wide experience and the satisfaction of his sensual desires.

In the second part of *Faust I*, Mephistopheles tries to satisfy Faust's demands and yearnings. Although he often dismisses Mephistopheles' efforts at satisfaction as "mere spectacle," Faust nevertheless tries them all, culminating in the famous, orgiastic "Walpurgisnight" scene, a delirious meeting of all creatures of the night. None of these sensuous pleasures, however, can give Faust the kind of satisfaction he derives from the culminating event of the play: the seduction of Gretchen. It is with Gretchen that *Faust* earns its title to tragedy. Gretchen represents different pleasures from the other experiences provided by Mephistopheles. Faust genuinely falls in love with her, praising her innocence and simple religious faith. And yet he alternately neglects her and showers her with presents as he pursues, and finally achieves, his physical satisfaction, leading to a tragic end. Here the first part of *Faust* ends. These tragic events will be blissfully forgotten in the second part, which takes Faust and Mephistopheles on a wild tour through politics, science, and learning.

Not only did Goethe revise the Faust legend to rescue Faust from damnation at the end of part two, but in the first part, he shaped another, and possibly more radical, revision of the historical tale. For the real protagonist of this part is not Faust, who is alternatively pompous, idealistic, and fatuous, who does not know himself, and who manages to bring everything, including poor Gretchen, to ruin. Instead, the real protagonist is the witty, realistic, and caustic Mephistopheles. It is Mephistopheles who criticizes the medieval world of Faust, and who deflates his grandiose speeches, including his self-serving declarations of love for Gretchen. Mephistopheles is the spirit of negation, as he says of himself, but it is a negation that serves to criticize authority. Mephistopheles thus embodies the principle of critique, of questioning all kinds of inherited religious belief and orthodoxies. Since this critical spirit is central to modernity, Mephistopheles becomes the truly modern character in the play. And Goethe clandestinely turns Mephistopheles into the main protagonist. He has all the best and wittiest lines. In the theater, he simply steals the show.

Outdoing a modernized Faust with an even more modern Mephistopheles, Goethe was also daring in his use of structure and form. The play rejects the narrow rules of Aristotelian drama, constraining time and space, and instead presents a play of epic length that is composed of loosely connected scenes. *Faust* contains passages in different meters and rhyme schemes as well as in prose. It includes interludes, an allegorical dream, a satire of the university, erotic songs, and scenes of outright bacchanalia. It seeks to encompass the entirety of the modern world, aspiring to a rare totality in its hybrid form. Thus *Faust* has been considered a total work of art, a modern epic, and a strikingly new type of drama.

Faust is so startling in its dramatic innovations that Goethe himself never sought to mount even the more manageable first part in his own Weimar Court Theatre, and in fact he did not even consider it fit for the stage. When it was performed at another theater a few years before his death, he did not show much interest in the production. The much more difficult, allegorical second part has been performed even less often. Given the length of both parts taken together, few theaters have ever tried to produce the entirety of Goethe's *Faust.* In the course of the twentieth century, however, the first part attracted the most renowned theater directors, composers, and actors. French composers Hector Berlioz and Charles Gounod based operas on it, and in the twentieth century, Gertrude Stein's *Doctor Faustus Lights the Lights* is among the most modernist responses to Goethe's text. Filmmakers have turned to it again and again for inspiration, including F. W. Murnau in 1926 and Czech director Jan Švankmajer in 1994. Goethe's *Faust* has thus remained an important touchstone for two centuries of art, a testament to Goethe's ability to turn a simple medieval morality tale into a complex investigation of modernity.

Faust[1]

Prelude in the Theater

MANAGER, POET, CLOWN.

MANAGER   You two who've always stood by me
   When times were hard and the playhouse empty,
   What do you think we may hope for
   From this tour of ours through German country?
   I'd like to please the crowd here, for   5
   They're really so easy-going, so patient,
   The posts are up, the floorboards laid,
   And in they came in search of entertainment.
   Taking their seats they look around, at ease,
   Wishing to be surprised, each one,   10
   Well, I know with this audience how to please,

1. Translated by Martin Greenberg.

But I've never been in a fix like this one.
It's not to the best these good people are used,
But Lord, all the books all of them have perused.
So we need to comes up with something lively and new,   15
A piece with some meaning that amuses them too.
I don't deny what pleases me most
Are droves of people, a great host,
Trying with all their might to squeeze
Through the strait gate to our paradise,   20
When it's daylight still, not even four,
Using elbow and fist to get to the ticket seller,
Like starving men rushing the baker's door—
For the sake of a seat prepared to commit murder.
Who works on such a mixed lot such a wonder?   25
Do I need to tell you? Why, of course it's the poet,
So fall to, dear colleague, and let's see you do it!
POET   Don't talk to me about that crazy crowd,
One look at them and all my wits desert me!
Oh shield me from that shoving, shouting horde   30
That swallows you up against your will completely!
No, lead me to some quiet, remote place
Where poets know their only happiness,
Where love and dearest friends inspire and nurse
The blessed gift that is the power of verse.   35
   Oh dear, what struggles up from deep inside us,
Syllables our lips shape hesitantly
Into scenes ineffective now, and now effective,
Is drowned out in the present's hurlyburly;
Years must pass till, seen in time's perspective,   40
Its shape and soul shine forth as they are truly.
What's all flash and glitter lives a day,
The real thing's treasured by posterity.
CLOWN   Posterity! Oh that word—but let's not start a row!
If all I ever thought of was the hereafter,   45
Who'd set the audience laughing in the here and now?
To be amused, that's their hearts' desire.
Having a clown on the stage who knows what his business is
Is not to be sneezed at—it matters to know how to please.
When yours is the stuff to delight and content a whole theaterful,   50
You don't sourly mutter the public's a mob, always changeable.
What you want's a full house, the sign out saying Standing Room Only,
For the bigger the house, the better the response you can count on,
So be a good fellow and show us what drama is really.
Your imagination, let it pour out like a fountain,   55
Its marvels matched by wisdom, good sense, feeling,
By passion too—but mind you, show us some fooling!
MANAGER   But what's the first requirement? Plenty of action!
They're spectators so what they want to see is things happen.
If you've got business going on every minute   60

That catches people's attention, their roving eyes rivet,
Then you don't have to worry, they're yours, they're won over,
When the curtain comes down they'll shout "Author! Author!"
With a public so large you need an abundance to please them all
Something for everyone, that's how to seize them all,   65
The last thing you want is to be classically economical.
In the theater today only scenes and set pieces do,
The way to succeed is to serve up a stew,
You can cook it up fast, dish it out easy too.
Now tell me, what good is your artistic unity,   70
The public will only make hash of it anyway.

POET   You don't understand—all that's just hackwork,
A true artist never stoops to such stuff!
Those cheap purveyors of tawdry patchwork
For you are the measure of dramatic truth.   75

MANAGER   Go ahead, scold me, I don't mind your censure.
To do a job right you use the tools that are called for,
Remember, it's soft wood you've got to split,
Consider the people for whom you write:
One's here because he's bored, another   80
Comes stuffed from eating a seven-course dinner,
But worst are the ones who come to fill up our seats
Straight from reading the very latest news sheets.
The crowd arrives here distracted, distrait,
Thinking of this and that, not of a play,   85
The reason they come is mere curiosity,
The ladies exhibit their shoulders and finery,
Put on a great show, don't require a salary.
Oh, the dreams poets dream in their ivory tower!
Flattered, are you, to see the house full?   90
Well, take a good look at our clientele,
The half vulgar and loud, half unmoved and sour,
One's mind's on his card game after the play,
Another's on tumbling a girl in the hay.
It's for people like that you fools torture the Muses?   95
Listen to me: You'll never go wrong
If you pile it on, pile it on, and still pile it on.
Bewilder, confound them with all your variety,
The public's the public, they're a hard lot to satisfy.
But goodness, how worked up you seem to be!   100
What's wrong? Is it anguish or is it ecstasy?

POET   Go out and find yourself some other lackey!
You expect the poet, do you, frivolously,
For the sake of your blue eyes to debase
Nature's finest gift to the human race?   105
How does he teach humanity feeling,
Master the elements, every one?
I'll tell you, by the music pealing
Forth from his breast orphically,

Which then by reflux back on him returning   110
Reverberates as Nature's deep-voiced harmony.
When Nature winds life's endless thread
Indifferently on the bobbin, when
The noisy cries of her countless creatures
No music make, uproar instead,   115
Who melodizes the monotonous din
And makes all move in living measures?
Who calls each mute particular
To sing its part in the general chorus
In a glorious concord of myriad voices?   120
Who links our passions to wild tempests,
Our solemn moods to fading sunsets?
Unrolls before the feet of lovers
A lovely carpet of spring flowers?
Twines leaves which in themselves mean nothing at all   125
To crown those who have proven most worthy of all?
Assures us of Olympus, upon it assembled the gods?—
That revelation of man's powers, the poet, does!

CLOWN   Then go on and use them, your marvelous powers!
Go at your business of making verses   130
The way you go at a love adventure:
A chance encounter, you're attracted, linger,
And little by little you find yourself caught.
You're so happy, later you're not;
First you're enraptured, then it's nothing but trouble,   135
And before you know it it's a whole novel,
Write the play we want that way, you know how to do it!
Jump right into life's richness and riot,
All of us live life, few have an idea about it,
And my, how it interests wherever you scratch it!   140
Color, confusion, a wild hurlyburly,
With a glimmer of truth amid errors' obscurity,
And there you have it, exactly the right brew
To refresh everyone, make them think a bit too.
Then the best of our youth will flock here to listen,   145
Gripping their seats in anticipation.
The sensitive soul will find in your play
Food to feed his melancholy;
One thing touches one man, another another,
The end result is, all discover   150
What's in their hearts. The young are still ready
To laugh at a good thrust, let their tears flow in pity,
Warmly respond to lofty ambitions,
Cherishing still their bright dreams and illusions.
You'll never please those whose race is run,   155
For them there are no more surprises,
But the youth for whom all's just begun,
They will shower you with praises.

POET Then give me back those times again
  When I, too, was a leaf uncurled,   160
  When mists still filled the morning world,
  And song after song poured out of me
  Like a fountain flowing uninterruptedly,
  When a bud was a promised miracle,
  And I plucked the thousand flowers that filled   165
  The vales with their rich spectacle.
  The nothing I owned was more than enough,
  By fictions delighted, impelled toward truth—
  Oh give me back that unquelled ardor,
  The happiness whose depth is pain,   170
  The strength of hate, love's superpower,
  Oh give me back my youth again!
CLOWN Youth, my dear colleague, you need in the following cases:
  When the enemy's crowding you hard in the fight,
  When pretty girls in summer dresses   175
  Kiss and squeeze you with all their might,
  When running hard, you glimpse in the distance
  The wreath that rewards the fleetest foot,
  When after the madly whirling dances
  With drinking you wear the night out.   180
  But to sweep the old familiar harp strings
  Boldly yet with fine grace too,
  To make by pleasing indirections
  For the end your drama has in view—
  That's a job for you old fellows,   185
  And we respect you for your skill;
  Age doesn't make us childish, God knows,
  Just finds us the same old children still.
MANAGER We've talked enough, now let me see
  Your tardy quill produce results,   190
  Our business is to stage a play,
  Not waste the time in compliments.
  And please—don't say you're not in the mood,
  It never arrives if you hesitate timidly.
  You say you're a poet, good, very good,   195
  Let's hear it, then, your poetry.
  You know what's wanted, good strong stuff—
  To work now, work, go right at it,
  What's put off today, tomorrow's put off;
  How precious to us is every minute.   200
  A resolute spirit, acting timely,
  Seizes occasion by the short hairs,
  It won't let go but hangs on grimly,
  Once committed, it perseveres.

  You know how on our German stage   205
  We're free to try whatever we please,

So don't imagine I want you to save
Me money on paint and properties.
Hang out heaven's big and little lamps,
Scatter stars over the canvas sky,   210
Let's have fire and flood and dizzying steeps,
All sorts of birds and beasts—do the thing liberally.
And thus on a narrow platform you're able
To go all the way round Creation's great circle
At a brisk enough pace, yet deliberately as well,   215
From Heaven, through this our world, down to Hell.

Prologue in Heaven[2]

THE LORD. THE HEAVENLY HOST. *Then* MEPHISTOPHELES.[3] *The three* ARCHANGELS
advance to front.

RAPHAEL   The sun as always sounds his music
    In contest with each brother sphere,
    Marching round and around, with steps terrific,
    His appointed circle, year after year.   220
    To see him lends us angels strength,
    But what he *is*, oh who can say?
    The inconceivably great works are great
    As on the first creating day.
GABRIEL   And swift, past all conception swift,   225
    The jeweled globe spins on its axletree,
    Celestial brightness alternating
    With shuddering night's obscurity.
    Against the rock-bound littoral[4]
    The sea is backwards seething hurled,   230
    And rock and sea together hurtle
    With the eternally turning world.
MICHAEL   And tempests vying, howling, riot
    From sea to land, from land to sea,
    Linking in tremendous circuit   235
    A chain of blazing energy.
    The thunderbolt makes ready for
    The thunderclap a ruinous way—
    Yet Lord, your servants most prefer
    The stiller motions of your day.   240
ALL THREE   From seeing this we draw our strength,
    But what You *are*, oh who can say?
    And all your great works are as great
    As on the first creating day.

2. The scene is patterned on Job 1:6–12 and 2:1–6.
3. The origin of the name remains debatable. It may come from Hebrew, Persian, or Greek, with such meanings as "destroyer-liar," "no friend of Faust," and "no friend of light."
4. Near the seaside.

MEPHISTOPHELES   Lord, since you've stopped by here again, liking to know 245
    How all of us are doing, for which we're grateful,
    And since you've never made me feel *de trop*,[5]
    Well, here I am too with your other people.
    Excuse, I hope, my lack of eloquence,
    Though this whole host, I'm sure, will think I'm stupid. 250
    Coming from me, high-sounding sentiments
    Would only make you laugh—that is, provided
    Laughing is a thing Your Worship still did
    About suns and worlds I don't know beans, I only see
    How mortals find their lives pure misery. 255
    Earth's little god's shaped out of the same old clay,
    He's the same queer fish he was on the first day.
    He'd be much better off, in my opinion, without
    The bit of heavenly light you dealt him out.
    He calls it Reason, and the use he puts it to? 260
    To act more beastly than beasts ever do.
    To me he seems, if you'll pardon my saying so,
    Like a long-legged grasshopper all of whose leaping
    Only lands him back in the grass again chirping
    The tune he's always chirped. And if only he'd 265
    Stay put in the grass! But no! It's an absolute need
    With him to creep and crawl and strain and sweat
    And stick his nose in every pile of dirt.
THE LORD   Is that all you have got to say to me?
    Is that all you can do, accuse eternally? 270
    Is nothing ever right for you down there, sir?
MEPHISTOPHELES   No, nothing, Lord—all's just as bad as ever.
    I really pity humanity's myriad miseries,
    I swear I hate tormenting the poor ninnies.
THE LORD   Do you know Faust? 275
MEPHISTOPHELES   The Doctor?[6]
THE LORD   My good servant!
MEPHISTOPHELES   You[7] don't say! He serves you, I think, very queerly,
    Finds meat and drink, the fool, in nothing earthly,
    Drives madly on, there's in him such a torment,
    He himself is half aware he's crazy;
    Heaven's brightest stars he imperiously requires 280
    And from the earth its most exciting pleasures;
    All, all, the near at hand and far and wide,
    Leave your good servant quite unsatisfied.
THE LORD   If today his service shows confused, disordered,
    With my help he will see the way clear forward; 285
    When the sapling greens, the gardener can feel certain

---

5. Over the top, too much.
6. Of philosophy.
7. In the German text, Mephistopheles shifts back and forth between the informal word for "you" (*du*) and the more formal, respectful mode of address (*ihr*).

Flower and fruit will follow in due season.
MEPHISTOPHELES   Would you care to bet on that? You'll lose, I tell you,
　　If you'll give me leave to lead the fellow
　　Gently down my broad, my primrose path.　　　　　　　　290
THE LORD   As long as Faustus walks the earth
　　I shan't, I promise, interfere.
　　While still man strives, still he must err.
MEPHISTOPHELES   Well thank you, Lord—it's not the dead and gone
　　I like dealing with. By far what I prefer　　　　　　　295
　　Are round and rosy cheeks. When corpses come
　　A-knocking, sorry, Master's left the house;
　　My way of working's the cat's way with a mouse.
THE LORD   So it's agreed, you have my full consent.
　　Divert the soul of Faust from its true source　　　　　300
　　And if you're able, lead him along, Hell bent
　　With you, upon the downward course—
　　Then blush for shame to find you must admit:
　　For all his dark impulses, imperfect sight,
　　A good man always knows the way that's right.　　　　305
MEPHISTOPHELES   Of course, of course! Yet I'll seduce him from it
　　Soon enough. I'm not afraid I'll lose my bet.
　　And after I have won it,
　　You won't, I trust, begrudge me
　　My whoops of triumph, shouts of victory.　　　　　　310
　　Dust he'll eat
　　And find that he enjoys it, exactly like
　　That old aunt of mine, the famous snake.
THE LORD   There too feel free, you have carte blanche.
　　I've never hated your likes much;　　　　　　　　　315
　　I find of all the spirits of denial,
　　You jeerers not my severest trial.
　　Man's very quick to slacken in his effort,
　　What he likes best is Sunday peace and quiet;
　　So I'm glad to give him a devil—for his own good,　　　320
　　To prod and poke and incite him as a devil should.
　　[To the ANGELS] But you who are God's true and faithful progeny—
　　Delight in the world's wealth of living beauty!
　　May the force that makes all life-forms to evolve,
　　Enfold you in the dear confines of love,　　　　　　　325
　　And the fitfulness, the flux of all appearance,
　　By enduring thoughts give enduring forms to its transience.
　　　　[The Heavens close, the ARCHANGELS withdraw.]
MEPHISTOPHELES   I like to see the Old Man now and then,
　　And take good care I don't fall out with him.
　　How very decent of a Lord Celestial　　　　　　　330
　　To talk man to man with the Devil of all people.

Part I

Night

In a narrow, high-vaulted Gothic room, FAUST, *seated restlessly in an armchair at his desk.*

FAUST   I've studied, alas, philosophy,
  Law and medicine, recto and verso,[1]
  And how I regret it, theology also,
  Oh God, how hard I've slaved away,
  With what result? Poor foolish old man,   5
  I'm no whit wiser than when I began!
  I've got a Master of Arts degree,
  On top of that a Ph.D.,
  For ten long years, around and about,
  Upstairs, downstairs, in and out,   10
  I've led my students by the nose
  With what result? that nobody knows,
  Or ever shall know, the tiniest crumb!
  Which is why I feel completely undone.
    Of course I'm cleverer than these stuffed shirts,   15
  These Doctors, M.A.s, scribes and priests,
  I'm not bothered by a doubt or a scruple,
  I'm not afraid of Hell or the Devil—
  But the consequence is, my mirth's all gone.
  No longer can I fool myself   20
  I'm able to teach anyone
  How to be better, love true worth;
  I've got no money or property,
  Worldly honors or celebrity—
  A dog wouldn't put up with this life!   25
  Which is why I've turned to magic,
  Seeking to know, by ways occult,
  From ghostly mouths spells difficult,
  So I no longer need to sweat
  Painfully explaining what   30
  I don't know anything about;
  So I may penetrate the power
  That holds the universe together,
  Behold the source whence all proceeds
  And deal no more in words, words, words.   35

  O full moon, melancholy-bright,
  Friend I've watched for, many a night,
  Till your quiet-shining circle
  Appeared above my book-heaped table,

---

1. "Recto and verso": Latin terms for the front and back of a sheet of paper.

If only you might never again   40
Look down from above on my pain,
If only I might stray at will
In your mild light, high on the hill,
Haunt with spirits upland hollows,
Fade with you in dim-lit meadows,   45
And soul no longer gasping in
The stink of learning's midnight oil,
Bathe in your dews till well again!

Oh misery! Oh am I still
Stuck here in this dismal prison?   50
A musty goddamned hole in the wall
Where even the golden light of heaven
Can only weakly make its way through
The painted panes of the gothic window;
Where all about me shelves of books   55
Rise up to the vault in stacks,
Books gray with dust, worm-eaten, rotten,
With soot-stained paper for a curtain;
Where instruments, retorts and glasses
Are crammed in everywhere a space is;   60
And squeezed in somehow with these things
My family's ancient furnishings
Make complete the sad confusion—
Call this a world, this world you live in?

Can you still wonder why your heart   65
Should clench in your breast so anxiously?
Why your every impulse is stopped short
By an inexplicable misery?
Instead of the living house of Nature
God created man to dwell in,   70
About you all is dust, mold, ordure,
Bones of beasts and long dead men.

Up! Fly to the open countryside!
And do you have a better guide
Than this mysterious book inscribed   75
By Nostradamus's[2] own hand?
What better help to master the secrets
Of how the stars turn in their orbits,
From Nature learn to understand
The spirits' power to speak to spirits.   80
Sitting here and racking your brains
To puzzle out the sacred signs—

2. The Latin name of the French astrologer and physician Michel de Notredame (1503–1566).
His collection of rhymed prophecies, *The Centuries*, appeared in 1555.

What a sterile, futile business!
You hover, spirits, all around me—
Announce yourselves if you can hear me!   85
    [*He opens the book and his eye encounters the sign of
      the Macrocosm.*[3]]
The pure bliss flooding all my senses,
Seeing this! Through every nerve and vein
I feel youth's fiery, fresh spirit race again.
Was it a god marked out this sign
By which my agitated bosom's stilled,   90
By which my bleak heart's filled with joy,
By whose mysterious agency
The forces of Nature about me stand revealed?
Am *I* a god? All's bright as day!
By these pure tracings I can see,   95
At my soul's feet, great Nature unconcealed.
And the sage's words I understand them finally:
"The spirit world is not barred shut,
It's your closed mind, your dead heart!
Stand up unappalled, my scholar,   100
And bathe your breast in the rose of aurora!"
    [*He contemplates the sign.*]
How all is woven one, uniting
Each in the other, living, working!
Heavenly powers rise, descend,
Passing gold vessels from hand to hand!   105
On wings that scatter sweet-smelling blessings
Everywhere they post in earth,
And make a universal harmony sound forth!
Oh, what a show! But a show, nothing more.
How, infinite Nature, lay hold of you, where?   110
Where find your all-life-giving fountains?—breasts that sustain
The earth and the heavens which my shrunken breast
Yearns for with a feverish thirst—
You flow, overflow, must I keep on thirsting in vain?
    [*Morosely, he turns the pages of the book and comes on the sign of the*
      SPIRIT *of Earth.*[4]]
How different an effect this sign has on me!   115
O Spirit of Earth, how near, how much nearer to me!
Already fresh life-blood pours through every vein,
Already I'm aglow as if with new wine—
Now, now I possess the courage to dare
To adventure into the wide world, bear   120
Earth's ill, earth's well, and bravely battle
The howling storms, when the ship splits, not to tremble.

---

3. The great world (literal trans.); the universe as a whole. It represents the ordered, harmonious universe in its totality.

4. This figure seems to be a symbol for the energy of terrestrial nature—neither good nor bad, merely powerful.

The air grows dark overhead—
The moon's put out her light.
The oil lamp's nearly dead.   125
Vapors rise, red flashes dart
Around my head—fright,
Shuddering down from the vault,
Seizes me by the throat!
Spirit I have invoked, hovering near: 130
Reveal yourself!
Ha! How my heart beats! All of my being's
Fumbling and groping amid never felt feelings!
Appear! Oh, you must! Though it costs me my life!
    [*He seizes the book and pronounces the* SPIRIT's *mystic spell. A red flame*
    flashes, in the midst of which the SPIRIT *appears.*]

SPIRIT Who's calling?   135

FAUST (*Averting his face*)   Overpowering! Dreadful!

SPIRIT Potently you've drawn me here,
  A parched mouth sucking at my sphere.
  And now—?

FAUST   But you're unbearable!

SPIRIT You're breathless from your implorations   140
  To see my face, to hear me speak.
  I've yielded to your supplications
  And here I am.—Well, shrinking, weak,
  I find the superman! You call, I come,
  And you're struck dumb. Is yours the breast   145
  Inside of which an entire world was nursed
  Into existence, a creation
  On which you doted with mad elation,
  Puffed up to think yourself the equal
  Of us spirits, on our level?   150
  Wherever is that fellow Faust
  Who urged himself just now with all
  His strength on me, made such a fuss?
  You're Faust? The one who at my breath's
  Least touch, shudders to his depths,   155
  A thing that wriggles off, scared, a worm!

FAUST *I* shrink back from you, an airy flame?
  I'm him, yes Faust, your equal, the same.

SPIRIT In flood tides of life, in tempests of doing,
  Up and down running,   160
  The here with there joining,
  Birth with the grave,
  An eternal ocean,
  A weaving, reweaving,
  A life aglow, burning—   165
  So seated before time's humming loom,
  I weave the Godhead's living costume.

FAUST We're equals, I know! I feel so close to you, near,

You busy spirit ranging everywhere!
SPIRIT   You equal the spirit you think I am,   170
    Not me! [*Vanishes.*]
FAUST [*Deflated*]   Not you?
    Then who?
    Me, made in God's own image,
    Not even equal to you?   175
      [*A knocking*]
    Death! My famulus[5]—I know that knock.
    Finis my supremest moment—worse luck!
    That visions richer than I could have guessed
    Should be scattered by a shuffling dryasdust!
      [WAGNER *in dressing gown and nightcap, carrying a lamp.*
      FAUST *turns around impatiently.*]
WAGNER   Excuse me, sir, but that was your voice, wasn't it,   180
    I heard declaiming? A Greek tragedy,
    I'm sure. Well, that's an art that comes in handy
    Nowadays, I'd love to master it.
    People say, how often I have heard it,
    Actors could really give lessons to the clergy.   185
FAUST   Yes, so parsons can make a stage out of the pulpit—
    Something I have seen in more than one case.
WAGNER   Oh dear, to be so cooped up in one's study all day,
    Seeing the world only now and then, on holiday,
    Seeing people from far off, as if through a spyglass—   190
    How persuade them to any effect in that way?
FAUST   Unless you really feel it, no, you cannot—
    Unless the words your lips declare are heartfelt
    And by their soul-born spontaneous power,
    Seize with delight the soul of your hearer.   195
    But no! Stick in your seats, you scholars!
    Paste bits and pieces together, cook up
    A beggar's stew from others' leftovers
    Over a flame you've sweated to coax up
    From your own little heap of smoldering ashes,   200
    Filling with wonder all the jackasses,
    If that's the kind of stuff your taste favors.
    But you'll never get heart to cleave to heart
    Unless you speak from your own heart.
WAGNER   Still and all, a good delivery is what   205
    Makes the orator. I'm far behind in that art.
FAUST   Advance yourself in an honest way,
    Don't play the fool in cap and bells!
    Good sense, good understanding, they
    Are art enough, speak for themselves.   210
    When you have something serious to say,
    What need is there for hunting up

---

5. Assistant to a medieval scholar.

Fancy words, high-sounding phrases?
Your brilliant speeches, smartened up
With bits and pieces collected out   215
Of a miscellany of commonplaces
From all the languages spoken by all the races,
Are about as bracing as the foggy autumnal breeze
Swaying the last leaves on the trees.

WAGNER   Dear God, but art is long,   220
And our life—much shorter.
Often in the middle of my labor
My confidence and courage falter.
How hard it is to master all the stuff
For dealing with each and every source,   225
And before you've traveled half the course,
Poor devil, you have gone and left this life.

FAUST   Parchment, tell me—that's the sacred fount
You drink out of, to slake your eternal thirst?
The only true refreshment that exists   230
You get from where? Yourself—where all things start.

WAGNER   But sir, it's such a pleasure, isn't it,
To enter into another age's spirit,
To see what the sages before us thought
And measure how far since we've got.   235

FAUST   As far as to the stars, no doubt!
Your history, why, it's a joke;
Bygone times are a seven-sealed book.[6]
What you call an age's spirit,
What is it? Nothing but your own poor spirit   240
With the age reflected as you see it.
And it's pathetic, what's to be seen in your mirror.
One look and I head straight for the exit.
A trash can, strewn attic, junk-filled cellar,
At best a blood-and-thunder thriller   245
Improved with the most high-minded sentiments
Exactly suited for mouthing by marionettes.

WAGNER   But this great world, the human mind and heart,
They are things all want to know about.

FAUST   Yes, know as the world knows knowing!   250
Who wants to know the real truth, tell me?
Those few with vision, feeling, understanding
Who failed to stand guard, most unwisely,
Over their tongues, speaking their minds and hearts
For the mob to hear—you know what's been their fate: 255
They were crucified, burnt, torn to bits.
But we must break off, friend, it's getting late.

WAGNER   I love such serious conversation, I do!
I'd stay up all night gladly talking to you.

6. Revelation 5:1.

But sir, it's Easter Sunday in the morning   260
And perhaps I may ask you a question or two then, if you're willing?
I've studied hard, with unrelaxing zeal,
I know a lot, but I want, sir, to know all. [*Exit.*]
FAUST [*Alone*]   Such fellows keep their hopes up by forever
Busying themselves with trivialities,   265
Dig greedily in the ground for treasure
And when they turn a worm up—what ecstacies!
That banal, commonplace human accents
Should fill air just now filled with spirit voices!
Still, this one time you've earned my thanks,   270
Oh sorriest, oh shallowest of wretches!
You snatched me from the grip of a dejection
So profound, I was nearly driven off
My head. So gigantic was the apparition,
It made me feel no bigger than a dwarf—   275

Me, the image of God, certain in my belief
Soon, soon I'd behold the mirror of eternal truth,
Whose near presence I felt, already savoring
The celestial glory, stripped of my mortal clothing;
Me, higher placed than the angels, dreaming brashly   280
With the strength I possess I could flow freely,
Godlike creative, through Nature's live body—
Well, it had to be paid for: a single word
Thundered out knocked me flat, all my vain conceit curbed.
No, I can't claim we are equals, presumptuously!   285
Though I was strong enough to draw you down to me,
Holding on to you was another matter entirely.
In that exalted-humbling moment of pure delight
I felt myself at once both small and great.
And then you thrust me remorselessly back   290
Into uncertainty, which is all of humanity's fate.
Who'll tell me what to do? Not to do?
Still seek out the spirits to learn what they know?
Alas, what we do as much as what's done to us,
Obstructs the way stretching clearly before us.   295
The noblest conceptions to which our minds ever attained
Are more and more violated, oh how profaned!
When we've gained a bit of the good of this world for our prize,
Then the better's dismissed as delusion and lies;
Those radiant sentiments, once our breath of life,   300
Grow dim and expire in the madding crowd's strife.

Time was that hope and brave imagination
Boldly reached as far as to infinity,
But now misfortune piling on misfortune,
A little, confined space will satisfy.   305
It's then, heart deep, Care builds her nest,

Dithering nervously, killing joy, ruining rest,
Masking herself as this, as that concern
For house and home, for wife and children,
Fearing fire and flood, daggers and poison;   310
You shrink back in terror from imagined blows
And cry over losing what you never in fact lose.

Oh no, I'm no god, only too well do I know it!
A worm's what I am, wriggling through the dirt
And finding its nourishment in it,   315
Whom the passerby treads underfoot.

These high walls, every shelf crammed, every niche,
Dust is what shrinks them to a stifling cell,
This moth-eaten world with its all kinds of trash,
They are the reasons I feel shut up in jail.   320
And here I'll discover what it is that I lack?
Devour thousands of books so as to learn, shall I,
Mankind has always been stretched on the rack
With now and then somebody, somewhere's been happy?
You, empty skull there, smirking so, I know why—   325
What does it tell me, if not that your brain,
Whirling like mine, sought the bright sun of truth,
Only to wander, night-bewildered, in vain.
And all this apparatus, you mock me, you laugh
With your every wheel, cylinder, cog and ratchet,   330
I stood at the door, sure that you were the key,
Yet for all the bit's cunning design I couldn't unlatch it.
Mysterious even in broad daylight,
Nature lets no one part her veil,
And what she keeps hidden, out of sight,   335
All your levers and wrenches can't make her reveal.
You, ancient stuff I've left lying about,
You're here, and why?—my father[7] found you useful,
And you, old scrolls, have gathered soot
For as long as the lamp's smoked on this table.   340
Much better to have squandered the little I got
Than find myself sweating under the lot.
It's from our fathers, what we inherit,
To possess it really, we've got to earn it.
What you don't use is a dead weight,   345
What's worthwhile is what you spontaneously create.

But why do I find I must stare in that corner,
Is that bottle a magnet enchanting my sight?
Why is everything all at once brighter, clearer,
Like woods when the moon's up and floods them with light?   350

7. Later we learn that Faust's father was a doctor of medicine.

Vial, I salute you, exceptional, rare thing,
And reverently bring you down from the shelf,
Honoring in you man's craft and cunning—
Quintessence of easeful sleeping potions,
Pure distillation of subtle poisons,   355
Do your master the kindness that lies in your power!
One look at you and my agony lessens,
One touch and my feverish straining grows calmer
And my tight-stretched spirit bit by bit slackens.
The spirit's flood tide runs more and more out,   360
My way is clear, into death's immense sea,
The bright waters glitter before my feet,
A new day is dawning, new shores calling to me.

A fiery chariot, bird-winged, swoops down on me,
I am ready to follow new paths and higher,   365
Aloft into new spheres of purest activity—
An existence so exalted, so godlike a rapture,
Does the worm of a minute ago deserve it?
No matter. Never falter! Turn your back bravely
On the sunlight, sweet sunlight, of our earth forever, 370
Tear wide open those dark gates boldly
Which the whole world skulks past with averted heads.
The time has come to disprove by deeds,
Because the gods are great, man's a derision,
To cringe back no more from that black pit   375
Whose unspeakable tortures are your own invention,
To struggle toward that narrow gate
Around which all Hell flames in constant eruption,
To do it calmly, without regret;
Even at the risk of utter extinction.   380
And now let me lift this long forgotten
Crystal wine cup out of its chest.
You used to shine bright at the family feast,
Making the solemn guests' faces lighten
When you went round with each lively toast.   385
The figures artfully cut in the crystal
Which it was the duty of all at the table,
In turn, to make up rhymes about,
Then drain the cup at a single draught—
How they recall many nights of my youth!   390
But now there's no passing you on to my neighbor
Or thinking up rhymes to parade my quick wit;[8]
Here is a juice that is quick too—to intoxicate,
A brownish liquid, see, filling the beaker,

8. Faust here alludes to the drinking of toasts. The maker of a toast often produced impromptu rhymes.

Chosen by me, by me mixed together,   395
My last drink! Which now I lift up in festive greeting
To the bright new day I see dawning!
   [*He raises the cup to his lips. Bells peal, a* CHOIR *bursts into song.*]

CHORUS OF ANGELS
    Christ is arisen!
    Joy to poor mortals
    By their own baleful,   400
    Inherited, subtle
    Failings imprisoned.

FAUST   What deep-sounding burden, what tremelo strain
    Arrest the glass before I can drink?
    Does that solemn ringing already proclaim   405
    The glorious advent of Holy Week?
    Already, choirs, are you intoning
    What angels' lips sang once, a comforting chant,
    Above the sepulcher's darkness sounding,
    Certain assurance of a new covenant?   410

CHORUS OF WOMEN
    With spices and balm, we
    Prepared the body,
    Faithful ones, we
    Laid him out in the tomb,
    Clean in linen we wound him   415
    And bound up his hair,
    Oh, what do we find now?
    Christ is not here.

CHORUS OF ANGELS
    Christ is arisen!
    Blest is the man of love,   420
    He who the anguishing,
    Bitter, exacting test,
    Salvation bringing, passed.

FAUST   But why do you seek me out in the dust,
    You music of Heaven, mild and magnificent?   425
    Sound out where men and women are simple,
    Your message is clear but it leaves me indifferent,
    And where belief's lacking no miracle's possible.
    The spheres whence those glad tidings ring
    Are not for me to try and enter,   430
    Yet all's familiar from when I was young
    And back to life I feel myself sent for.
    Years ago loving Heaven's embrace
    Flew down to me in the Sabbath stillness,
    Oh, how the bells rang with such promise,   435
    And fervently praying to Jesus, what bliss!
    A yearning so sweet, not to be comprehended,
    Drove me out into green wood and field,
    In me an inner world expanded

As my cheeks ran wet from eyes tear-filled.   440
Your song gave the signal for the games we all joined in
When the springtime arrived with its gay festival,
Innocent childhood's remembered emotion
Holds me back from the last step of all—
O sound away, sound away, sweet songs of Heaven,   445
Earth claims me again, my tears well up, fall!

CHORUS OF DISCIPLES
    Only just buried,
    Ascended already.
    Who lived sublimely,
    On high rose in glory!   450
    Joy of becoming, his,
    Near to creating's bliss.
    He on the earth's hard crust
    Left us, his own, his best,
    To languish and wait—   455
    Oh, how we pity,
    Master, your fate!

CHORUS OF ANGELS
    Christ is arisen
    From the bowels of decay,
    Strike off your fetters   460
    And shout for joy,
    By good works praising him,
    By loving, upraising him.
    Feeding the least of all,
    Preaching him east and west to all,   465
    Promising bliss to all.
    You have the Master near,
    You have him here.

Outside the Town Gate

All sorts of people out walking.

SOME APPRENTICES   Where are you fellows off to?
OTHERS   To the hunters' lodge over that way.   470
FIRST BUNCH   Well, we're on our way to the old mill.
ONE APPRENTICE   The river inn—that's what I say.
SECOND APPRENTICE   But the way I don't care for at all.
OTHERS   And what about you?
THIRD APPRENTICE   I'll stick with the rest of us here.
FOURTH APPRENTICE   Let's go up to the village. There, I can promise you   475
    The best-looking girls, the best tasting beer,
    And some very good roughhousing too.
FIFTH APPRENTICE   My, but aren't you greedy!
    A third bloody nose—don't you care?
    I'll never go there, it's too scary.   480

SERVANT GIRL   No, no, I'm turning back, no, I won't stay.
ANOTHER   We're sure to find him at those poplar trees.
FIRST GIRL   Is that supposed to make me jump for joy?
   It's you he wants to walk with, wants to please,
   And you're the one he'll dance with. Fine   485
   For you. And for me what? The spring sunshine!
THE OTHER   He's not alone, I know, today. He said
   He'd bring his friend—you know, that curlyhead.
A STUDENT   Those fast-stepping girls there, look at the heft of them!
   Into action, old fellow, we're taking out after them.   490
   Beer with body, tobacco with a good rich taste,
   And red-cheeked housemaids in their Sunday best
   Are just the things to make your Hermann happiest.
A BURGHER'S DAUGHTER   Oh look over there, such fine looking boys!
   Really, I think they are simply wretches,   495
   They have their pick of the nicest girls,
   Instead they run after overweight wenches.
SECOND STUDENT [*To the first*]   Hold up, go slow! I see two more,
   And the pair of them dressed so pretty, so proper.
   But I know that one! She lives next door,   500
   And her, I can tell you, I think I could go for.
   They loiter along, eyes lowered decorously.
   After saying no twice, they'll jump at our company.
FIRST STUDENT   No, no—all that bowing and scraping, it makes me
     feel ill at ease,
   If we don't get a move on we'll lose our two birds in the bushes; 505
   The work-reddened hand that swings the broom Saturday
   On Sunday knows how to give the softest caresses.
A BURGHER   No, you can have him; our new Mayor,
   Since he took office he's been a dictator,
   All he's done is make the town poorer,   510
   Every day I get madder and madder,
   When he says a thing's so, not a peep, not a murmur
   Dare we express—and the taxes climb higher.
A BEGGAR [*Singing*]
   Good sirs and all you lovely ladies,
   Healthy in body and handsome in dress,   515
   Turn, oh turn your eyes on me, please,
   And pity the beggarman's distress!
   Must I grind the organ fruitlessly?
   Only the charitable know true joy.
   This day when the whole world dances merrily,   520
   Make it for me a harvest day.
ANOTHER BURGHER   On a Sunday or holiday nothing in all my experience
   Beats talking about war and rumors of war,
   When leagues away, in Turkey, for instance,
   Armies are wading knee deep in gore.   525
   You stand at the window, take long pulls at your schooner,
   And watch the gaily colored boats glide past,

And then at sunset go home in the best of humor
And praise God for the peace by which we're blest.

THIRD BURGHER   Yes, neighbor, yes, exactly my opinion.   530
Let them go and beat each other's brains in,
Let them turn the whole world upside down,
As long as things are just as always in our town.

OLD CRONE [*To the* BURGHERS' DAUGHTERS]
How smart we all are! And so pretty and young,
I'd like to see the man who could resist you.   535
But not so proud, my dears. Just come along,
Oh I know how to get what you want for you.

BURGHER'S DAUGHTER   Agatha, come! The awful fright!
I'm afraid of being seen with that witchwoman.
It's true that last St. Andrew's Night[1]   540
She showed me in a glass my very own one.

HER FRIEND   And mine she showed me in a crystal sphere
Looking a soldier, with swaggering friends around him,
And though I watch out everywhere,
I have no luck, I never seem to find him.   545

SOLDIERS
Castles have ramparts,
Great walls and towers,
Girls turn their noses up
At soldier-boy lovers—
We'll make both ours!   550
Boldly adventure
And rake in the pay!

Hear the shrill bugle
Summon to battle,
Forward to rapture   555
Or forward to ruin!
Oh what a struggle!
Our life—oh how stirring!
Haughty girls, high-walled castles,
We'll make them surrender!   560
Boldly adventure
And rake in the pay!
—And after, the soldiers
Go marching away.

FAUST *and* WAGNER.

FAUST   The streams put off their icy mantle   565
Under the springtime's quickening smile,
Hope's green banner flies in the valley;
White-bearded winter, old and frail,

---

1. November 29, the traditional time for young girls to consult fortune tellers about their future lovers or husbands.

Retreats back up into the mountains,
And still retreating, down he sends   570
Feeble volleys of sleet showers,
Whitening in patches new-green plains.
But the sun can bear with white no longer,
When life stirs, shaping all anew,
He wants a scene that has some color,   575
And since there's nowhere yet one flower,
Holiday crowds have got to do.
Now face about and looking down
From the hilltop back to town,
See the brightly colored crowd   580
Pouring like a spring flood
Through the gaping, gloomy arch
To bask in the sun all love so much.
They celebrate the Savior's rising,
For they themselves today are risen: 585
From airless rooms in huddled houses,
From drudgery at counters and benches,
From under cumbrous roofs and gables,
From crowded, suffocating alleys,
From the mouldering dimness of the churches,   590
They hurry to where all is brightness.
And look there, how the eager crowd
Scatters through the fields and gardens,
How over the river's length and breadth
Skiffs and sculls are busily darting,   595
And that last boat, packed near to sinking,
Already's pulled a good ways off.
Even from distant mountain slopes
Bright colored clothes wink back at us.
Now I can hear it, the village commotion,   600
Out here, you can tell, is the people's true heaven,
Young and old crying exultingly—
Here I am human, here I can be free!
WAGNER   To go for a walk with you, dear Doctor,
Is a treat for my mind as well as honoring me,   605
But by myself I'd never come near here,
For I can't abide the least vulgarity.
The fiddling, shrieking, clashing bowls,
For me are all an unbearable uproar,
All scream and shout like possessed souls   610
And call it music, call it pleasure.
PEASANTS [*Singing and dancing under the linden tree*]
    The shepherd dressed up in his best,
    Pantaloons and flowered vest,
      Oh my, how brave and handsome!
    Within the broad-leaved linden's shade   615
    Madly spun both man and maid,

Tra-la! Tra-la!
Tra-la-la-la! Tra-lay!
The fiddle bow flew and then some.
He flung himself into their midst   620
And seized a young thing round the waist,
     While saying, "Care to dance, ma'am?"
The snippy miss she tossed her head,
"You boorish shepherd boy!" she said,
     Tra-la! Tra-la!   625
     Tra-la-la-la! Tra-lay!
"Observe, do, some decorum!"
But round the circle swiftly wheeled,
To right and left the dancers whirled,
     Till all the breath flew from them.   630
They got so red, they got so warm,
They rested, panting, arm in arm,
     Tra-la! Tra-la!
     Tra-la-la-la! Tra-lay!
And breast to breast—a twosome.   635

"I'll thank you not to make so free!
We girls know well how men betray,
     What snakes lurk in your bosom!"
But still he wheedled her away—
Far off they heard the fiddle play,   640
     Tra-la! Tra-la!
     Tra-la-la-la! Tra-lay!
The screaming, uproar, bedlam!
OLD PEASANT   Professor, welcome! Oh how kind
To join us common folk today,   645
Though such a fine man, learned mind,
Not to scorn our holiday.
So please accept our best cup, sir,
Brimful with the freshest beer.
We hope that it will quench your thirst,   650
But more than that, we pray and hope
Your sum of days may be increased
By as many drops are in the cup.
FAUST   Friends, thanks for this refreshment, I
In turn wish you all health and joy.   655
     [*The people make a circle around him.*]
OLD PEASANT   Indeed it's only right that you
Should be with us this happy day,
Who when our times were hard, a true
Friend he proved in every way.
Many a one stands in his boots here   660
Whom your good father, the last minute,
Snatched from the hot grip of the fever,

That time he quelled the epidemic.[2]
And you yourself, a youngster then,
Never shrank back; every house 665
The pest went in, you did too.
Out they carried many a corpse,
But never yours. Much you went through;
Us you saved, and God saved you.

ALL   Health to our tried and trusty friend, 670
And may his kindness have no end.

FAUST   Bow down to him who dwells above
Whose love shows us how we should love.
    [*He continues on with* WAGNER.]

WAGNER   What gratification must be yours
To win such popular applause. 675
Lucky the man, thanks to his gifts,
Can count on receiving handsome emoluments!
Fathers point you out to their boys,
The fiddle stops, the dancers pause,
And as you pass between the rows 680
Of people, caps fly in the air. Why,
Next you know they'll all be on their knees
As if the host itself[3] were passing by.

FAUST   A few steps more to that rock where we'll rest
A bit, shall we, from our walk. How often 685
I would sit alone here, musing, thinking, sighing,
And torture myself with praying, fasting, crying.
So much hope I had then, such great trust—
I'd wring my hands, I'd weep, fall on my knees,
Believing God, in this way forced 690
To look below, must call a halt to the disease.
But now these people's generous praise of me
I find a mockery. If only you could see
Into my heart, you would realize
How little worthy father and son were really. 695
    My father was an upright man, a lonely,
Brooding soul who searched great Nature's processes
With a head crammed full of the most bizarre hypotheses.
Shutting himself with fellow masters up in
The vaulted confines of their vaporous Black Kitchen,[4] 700
He mixed together opposites according
To innumerable recipes. A bold Red Lion,[5]
Handsome suitor he, took for wedding

2. Pestilence or plague.
3. The Eucharist, the consecrated bread of the Sacrament.
4. Laboratory where Faust experiments with black magic and alchemy.

5. Name for the red-colored mercuric oxide which Faust here "marries" to hydrochloric acid (which he calls "White Lily") to produce "the young Queen," a medicine to be used to cure the plague.

Partner a pure White Lily, the two uniting
In a tepid bath; then being tested by fire,   705
The pair precipitately fled
From one bridal chamber to another,
Till there appeared, within the glass,
The young Queen, dazzlingly dressed
In every color of the spectrum: 710
The Sovereign Remedy—a futile nostrum.
The patients died; none stopped to inquire
How many there were who got better.[6]
   So with our infernal electuary
We killed our way across the country.   715
I poisoned, myself, by prescription, thousands,
They sickened and faded; yet I must live to see
On every side the murderers' fame emblazoned.

WAGNER   But why be so distressed, there is no reason.
If you conscientiously, with full devotion,   720
Practise all the arts your father practised,
You've done enough, done all can be expected.
A youth who is respectful of his father
Listens and learns all that he has to teach.
If he's able himself to lengthen science's reach,   725
His son in turn can reach goals even farther.

FAUST   Oh, he's a happy man who hopes
To keep from drowning in these seas of error!
What we know least we need the most,
And what we do know is no use whatever.   730
But such cheerlessness blasphemes
The quiet sweetness of this shining hour,
Look, how the sunset's level beams
Gild those cottages in their green bower,
The brightness fades, the sun makes his adieu,   735
Hurrying off to kindle new life elsewhere—
If only I had wings to rise into
The air and follow ever after!
Then I would see the whole world at my feet,
Quietly shining in the eternal sunset,   740
The peaks ablaze, the valleys gone to sleep,
And babbling into golden stream the silver runlet.
The savage mountain with its plunging cliffs
Should never balk my godlike soaring,
And there's the ocean, see, already swelling   745
Before my wondering gaze, with its sun-warmed gulfs.
But finally the bright god looks like sinking,
Whereupon a renewed urgency
Drives me on to drink his eternal light,
The day always before, behind the night,   750

6. This confusing sequence evokes a kind of medicine closely allied to magic.

The heavens overhead, below the heaving sea . . .
A lovely dream!—and meanwhile it grows dark.
Oh dear, oh dear, that our frames should lack
Wings with which to match our soaring spirit,
Yet every soul there is, no matter whose it,   755
Knows feelings that strive upwards, onwards, straining,
When high above, lost in the azure evening,
The skylark pours out his shrill rhapsody,
When over fir-clad mountain peaks
The eagle on his broad wings gyres silently,   760
And passing over prairies, over lakes,
The homeward-bound crane labors steadily.

WAGNER   Well, I've had more than one odd moment, I have,
But I have never felt those impulses you have.
Soon enough you get your fill of woods and things,   765
I don't really envy birds their wings.
How different are the pleasures of the intellect,
Sustaining one from page to page, from book to book,
And warming winter nights with dear employment
And with the consciousness your life's so lucky.   770
And goodness, when you spread out an old parchment,
Heaven's fetched straight down into your study.

FAUST   You know the one great driving force,
May you never know the other!
Two souls live in me, alas,   775
Irreconcilable with one another.
One, lusting for the world with all its might,
Grapples it close, greedy of all its pleasures,
The other rises up, up from the dirt,
Up to the blest fields where dwell our great forbears.   780

O beings of the air if you exist,
Holding sway between the heaven and earth,
Come down to me out of the golden mist
And translate me to a new, a vivid life!
Oh, if I only had a magic mantle   785
To bear me off to foreign lands, strange people,
I'd never trade it for the costliest gown
Or for a cloak however rich and royal.

WAGNER   Never call them down, the dreadful swarm
That swoop and hover through the atmosphere,   790
Bringing mankind every kind of harm
From every corner of the terrestrial sphere.
From the North they bare their razor teeth
And prick you with their arrow-pointed tongues,
From the East, sighing with parched breath,   795
They eat away your dessicated lungs.
And when from southern wastes they gust and sough.
Fire on fire on your sunk head heaping,

From the West they send for your relief
Cooling winds—then drown fields just prepared for reaping.   800
Their ears are cocked, on trickery intent,
Seem dutiful while scheming to defeat us,
Their pretense is that they are heaven sent
And lisp like angels even as they cheat us.
However, come, let's go, the world's turned gray   805
And chilly, evening mists are rising,
At nightfall it's indoors you want to be.
But why should you stand still, astonished, staring?
What can you see in the dusk to find upsetting?

FAUST   Don't you see that black dog in the stubble   810
Coursing back and forth?

WAGNER   I do. I saw that one
A while back. What about him?

FAUST   Look again.
What kind of creature is it?

WAGNER   Kind? A poodle—
Worried where his master is and always
Sniffing about to find his scent.

FAUST   Look, he's   815
Circling around us, coming near and nearer.
Unless I'm much mistaken, a wake of fire
'S streaming after him.

WAGNER   I see nothing
But a black-haired poodle. Your eyes are playing
Tricks on you, perhaps.

FAUST   I think I see   820
Him winding a magic snare, quietly,
Around our feet, a noose which he'll pull tight
In the future when the time is right.

WAGNER   He's circling us because he's timid and uncertain,
He's missed his master, come on men unknown to him.   825

FAUST   The circle's getting tighter, he's much closer!

WAGNER   You see!—a dog, and no ghost, sir.
He growls suspiciously, he hesitates,
He wags his tail, lies down and waits.
Never fear, it's all just dog behavior.   830

FAUST   Come here, doggie, come here, do!

WAGNER   A silly poodle, a poor creature,
When you stop, he stops too,
Speak to him, he'll leap and bark,
Throw something and he'll fetch it back,   835
Go after your stick right into the river.

FAUST   I guess you're right, it's just what he's been taught,
I see no sign of anything occult.

WAGNER   A dog whose conduct is so good, so clever,
Why, even a philosopher would stoop to pet him.   840

Some student trained him, he proved an apt scholar—
Sir, he deserves you should adopt him.
　　[*They enter at the Town Gate.*]

Faust's Study [I]

FAUST [*Entering with the poodle*]
　　Behind me lie the fields and meadows
　　Shrouded in the lowering dark,
　　In dread of what waits in the shadows　　　　　　　　　845
　　Our better soul now starts awake.
　　Our worser one, unruly, reckless,
　　Quietens and starts to nod;
　　In me the love of my own fellows
　　Begins to stir, and the love of God.　　　　　　　　850

　　Quiet, poodle! Stop! A dozen
　　Dogs you seem, all sniffing at the doorsill!
　　Here's my own cushion for you to doze on
　　Behind the stove—if you are gentle.
　　Just now when we came down the hillside　　　　　　855
　　You gambolled like the friendliest beast.
　　I'm glad to take you in, provide
　　Your keep—provided you're a silent guest.

　　When once again the lamp light brightens
　　With its soft glow your narrow cell,　　　　　　　　860
　　Oh in your breast how then it lightens,
　　And deeper in your heart as well.
　　Again you hear the voice of reason
　　And hope revives, it breathes afresh,
　　You long to drink the living waters,　　　　　　　　865
　　Mount upwards to our being's source.

　　You're growling, poodle! Animal squealings
　　Hardly suit the exalted feelings
　　Filling my soul to overflowing.
　　We're used to people ridiculing　　　　　　　　　　870
　　What they hardly understand,
　　Grumbling at the good and the beautiful—
　　It makes them so uncomfortable!
　　Do dogs now emulate mankind?
　　　Yet even with the best of will　　　　　　　　　875
　　I feel my new contentment fail.
　　Why must the waters cease so soon
　　And leave us thirsting once again?
　　Oh, this has happened much too often!
　　But there's an answer to it all:　　　　　　　　　880

I mean the supernatural,
I mean our hope of revelation,
Which nowhere shines so radiant
As here in the New Testament.
I'll look right now at the original[1]   885
And see if it is possible
For me to make a true translation
Into my beloved German.

    [*He opens the volume and begins.*]
"In the beginning was the Word"[2]—so goes
The text. And right off I am given pause,   890
A little help, please, someone, I'm unable
To see the *word* as first, most fundamental.
If I am filled with the true spirit
I'll find a better way to say it.
So: "In the beginning *mind* was—right?   895
Give plenty of thought to what you write,
Lest your pen prove too impetuous.
Is it mind that makes and moves the universe?
Shouldn't it be: "In the beginning
Power was," before it nothing?   900
Yet even as I write this down on paper
Something tells me don't stop there, go farther.
The Spirit's prompt in aid; now, now indeed,
I know for sure: "In the beginning was the *Deed*!"

If this cell's one we'll share, each helping.   905
Poodle, stop that barking, yelping!
You're giving me a splitting headache,
I can't put up with such a roommate.
One of us
Has got to quit the premises.   910
It goes against the grain with me
To renege on hospitality,
But there's the door, dog, leave, goodbye.

But what's that I'm seeing,
A shadow or real thing?   915
It beggars belief—
My poodle's swelled up huger than life!
He heaves up his hulk—
No dog has such bulk!
What a spook I have brought   920
In my house without thought.
He looks, with his fierce eyes and jaws,
Just like a hippopotamus—
But I've got you, you're caught!

---

1. That is, the Greek.   2. John 1:1.

For a half-hellhound like you are,   925
Solomon's Key[3] is what is called for.
SPIRITS [*Outside the door*]
      Someone is locked in there!
      No one's allowed in there!
      Like a fox hunters snared,
      Old Scratch, he shivers, scared.   930
      Be careful, watch out!
      Hover this way, now that,
      About and again about,
      And you'll soon see he's out.
      If you can help him,   935
      Don't let him sit there,
      All of us owe him
      For many a favor.
FAUST   Against such a creature my first defense,
      The Spell of the Four Elements: 940

      Let the salamander turn red,
      The undine winding flow,
      Let the sylph disappear,
      The kobold[4] go to work.

      Ignorance   945
      Of the elements,
      Their power and properties,
      Denies you all mastery
      Over the demonry.

      Up in flames fly,   950
      Salamander!
      In soft murmurings,
      Undine, die!
      Meteor bright glitter,
      Sylph!   955
      Help, help bring us,
      Incubus!
      Come out, come out, enough's enough.

None of the four
Is in the cur,   960
Calmly he lies there grinning at me;
My spells glance off him harmlessly.
—Now hear me conjure
With something stronger.

---

3. The *Clavicula Salomonis*, a standard work
used by magicians for conjuring. In many medieval legends, Solomon was noted as a great
magician.

4. A spirit of the earth. "Salamander": spirit of
fire. "Undine": spirit of water. "Sylph": spirit of
air.

Are you, grim fellow,   965
Escaped here from Hell below?
Then look at this symbol
Before which the legions
Of devils and demons
Fearfully bow.   970

How his hair bristles, how he swells up now!

Creature cast into darkness,
Can you make out its meaning?
—The never-begotten One,
Wholly ineffable One,   975
Carelessly-pierced-in-the-side One,
Whose blood in the heavens
Is everywhere streaming,

Behind the stove by me sent,
Bulging big as an elephant,   980
The entire cell filling,
Into mist himself willing—
No, no! Not through the ceiling!
At my feet fall, Master's bidding,
My threats, as you see, are hardly idle,   985
With holy fire, out I'll rout you, I will!
Wait if you wish
For my triune⁵ light's hot flash,
Wait till you force me
To use my potentest sorcery.   990
[*The mist clears, and* MEPHISTOPHELES, *dressed as a traveling student,
emerges from behind the stove.*]

MEPHISTO   Why all the racket? What's your wish, sir?
FAUST   So it's you who was the poodle!
    I have to laugh—a wandering scholar.
MEPHISTO   My greetings to you, learned doctor,
    You really had me sweating hard there.   995
FAUST   And what's your name?
MEPHISTO   Your question's trivial
    From one who finds words superficial,
    Who strives to pass beyond mere seeming
    And penetrate the heart of being.⁶
FAUST   With gentry like yourself, it's common   1000
    To find the name declares who you are
    Very plainly. I'll just mention

---

5. Perhaps the Trinity or a triangle with divergent rays.
6. Mephistopheles refers to Faust's substitution of "*Deed*" or "*Word*" in the passage from
John (see line 904).

Lord of the Flies,[7] Destroyer, Liar.
So say who you are, if you would.

MEPHISTO   A humble part of that great power   1005
Which always means evil, always does good.

FAUST   Those riddling words mean what, I'd like to know.

MEPHISTO   I am the spirit that says no, no,
Always! And how right I am! For surely
It's right that everything that comes to be   1010
Should cease to be. And so they do. Still better
Would be nothing ever was. Hence sin
And havoc and ruin—all you call evil, in sum—
For me's the element in which I swim.

FAUST   A part, you say? You look like the whole works to me.   1015

MEPHISTO   I say what's so, it isn't modesty—
Man in his world of self's a fool,
He likes to think he's all in all.
I'm part of the part which was all at first,
A part of the dark out of which light burst,   1020
Arrogant light which now usurps the air
And seeks to thrust Night from her ancient chair,
To no avail. Since light is one with all
Things bodily, making them beautiful,
Streams from them, from them is reflected,   1025
Since light by matter's manifested—
When by degrees all matter's burnt up and no more,
Why, then light shall not matter any more.

FAUST   Oh, now I understand your office:
Since you can't wreck Creation wholesale,   1030
You're going at it bit by bit, retail.

MEPHISTO   And making, I fear, little progress.
The opposite of nothing-at-all,
The *something*, this great shambling world,
In spite of how I exert myself against it,   1035
Phlegmatically endures my every onset
By earthquake, fire, tidal wave and storm:
Next day the land and sea again are calm.
And all that *stuff*, those animal and human species—
I can hardly make a dent in them.   1040
The numbers I've already buried, armies!
Yet fresh troops keep on marching up again.
That's how it is, it's enough to drive you crazy!
From air, from water, from the earth
Seeds innumerable sprout forth   1045
In dry and wet and cold and warm!
If I hadn't kept back fire for myself,
What the devil could I call my own?

FAUST   So against the goodly, never-resting,

7. An almost literal translation of the name of the Philistine deity Beelzebub.

Beneficent creative force,   1050
In impotent spite you ball your fist and
Try to arrest life's onward course?
Look around for work that's more rewarding,
You singular son of old Chaos!

MEPHISTO   Well, it's a subject for discussion—   1055
At our next meeting. Now I wish
To go. That is, with your permission.

FAUST   But why should *you* ask *me* for leave?
We've struck up an acquaintance, we two,
Drop in on me whenever you please.   1060
There's the door and there's the window,
And ever reliable, there's the chimney.

MEPHISTO   Well . . . you see . . . an obstacle
Keeps me from dropping *out*—so sorry!
That witch's foot chalked on your doorsill.   1065

FAUST   The pentagram's[8] the difficulty?
But if it's that that has you stopped,
How did you ever manage an entry?
And how should a devil like you get trapped?

MEPHISTO   Well, look close and you'll see that   1070
A corner's open: the outward pointing
Angle's lines don't quite meet.

FAUST   What a stroke of luck! I'm thinking
Now you are my prisoner.
Pure chance has put you in my power!   1075

MEPHISTO   The poodle dashed right in, saw nothing,
But now the case is the reverse;
The Devil can't get out of the house!

FAUST   There's the window, why don't you use it?

MEPHISTO   It's an iron law we devils can't flout,   1080
The way we come in we've got to go out,
We're free as to entrée but not as to exit.

FAUST   So even in Hell there's law and order!
I'm glad, for then a man might sign
A contract with you gentlemen.   1085

MEPHISTO   Whatever we promise, you get, full measure,
There's no cutting corners, no skulduggery—
But it's not a thing to be done in a hurry;
Let's save the subject for our next get-together.
And as for now, I beg you earnestly: 1090
Release me from the spell that binds me!

FAUST   Why rush off, stay a while, do.
I'd love to hear some more from you.

MEPHISTO   Let me go now, I swear I'll come back,

8. A magic five-pointed star designed to keep away evil spirits.

Then you can ask me whatever you like.   1095
FAUST   Trapping you was never my thought,
You trapped yourself, it's your own fault.
Who's nabbed the Devil must keep a tight grip,
You don't grab him again once he gives you the slip.
MEPHISTO   Oh, all right! To please you, I   1100
Will stay and keep you company,
Provided with my arts you let me
Entertain you in my own way.
FAUST   Delighted, go ahead. But please
Make sure those arts of yours amuse!   1105
MEPHISTO   You'll find, my friend, your senses in one hour
More teased and roused than all the long dull year,
The songs the fluttering spirits murmur in your ear,
The visions they unfold of sweet desire,
Oh they are more than just tricks meant to fool.   1110
By Arabian scents you'll be delighted,
Your palate tickled, never sated,
The ravishing sensations you will feel!
No preparation's needed, none,
Here we are. Let the show begin!   1115
SPIRITS   Open, you gloomy
Vaulted ceiling above him,
Let the blue ether
Look benignly in on him,
And dark cloudbanks scatter   1120
So that all is fair for him!
Starlets are glittering,
Milder suns glowing,
Angelic troops shining
In celestial beauty   1125
Hover past smiling,
Bending and bowing.
Ardent desire
Follows them yearning,
And their robes   1130
Veil the fields, veil the meadows,
Veil the arbors where lovers
In pensive surrender
Give themselves to each other
For ever and ever.   1135
Arbor on arbor!
Vines clambering and twining!
Their heavy clusters,
Poured into presses,
Pour out purple wines   1140
Which descend in dark streams
Over beds of bright stones

Down the vineyards' steep slopes
To broaden to lakes
At the foot of green hills. 1145
Birds blissfully drink there,
With beating wings sunwards soar,
Soar towards the golden isles
Shimmering hazily
On the horizon, 1150
Where we hear voices
Chorusing jubilantly,
Where we see dancers
Whirling exuberantly
Over the meadows, 1155
Here, there and everywhere.
Some climb the heights,
Some swim in the lakes,
Others float in the air—
Joying in life, all, 1160
Beneath the paradisal
Stars glowing with love
Afar in the distance.

MEPHISTO   Asleep! Well done, my every airy youngling!
Into a drowse you've sung him, never stumbling, 1165
I am in your debt for this performance.
—As for you, sir, you were never born
To keep the Prince of Darkness down!
Let sweet dream-shapes crowd round him in confusion,
Drown him in a deep sea of delusion. 1170
But from this doorsill-magic to be freed
A rat's tooth is the thing I need.
No point to conjuring long-windedly,
There's one rustling nearby, he'll soon hear me.

The lord of flies and rats and mice, 1175
Of frogs and bedbugs, worms and lice,
Commands you forth from your dark hole
To gnaw, beast, for me that doorsill
Whereon I dab this drop of oil!
—And there you are! Begin, begin! 1180
The corner that is pointing in,
That's the one that shuts me in;
One last crunch to clear my way.
Now Faustus, till we meet next—dream away!

FAUST [*Awakening*]   Deceived again, am I, by tricks, 1185
Those vanished spirits just a hoax,
A dream the Devil, nothing more,
The dog I took home just a cur?

Faust's Study [II]

FAUST, MEPHISTOPHELES.

FAUST   A knock, was that? Come in! Who is it this time?
MEPHISTO   Me.
FAUST   Come in!
MEPHISTO   You have to say it still a third time.   1190
FAUST
   All right, all right—come in!
MEPHISTO   Good, very good!
   We two shall get along, I see, just as we should.
   I've come here dressed up as a Junker[1] Why?
   To help you drive your blues away!
   In a scarlet suit, all over gold braid,   1195
   Across my shoulders a stiff silk cape,
   A gay cock's feather in my cap,
   At my side a gallant's bold blade—
   And bringing you advice that's short and sweet:
   Put fine clothes on like me, cut loose a bit,   1200
   Be free and easy, man, throw off your yoke
   And find out what real life is like.
FAUST   In any clothes, I'd feel the misery
   Of this cramped, suffocating life on earth.
   I'm too old to live for amusement only,   1205
   Too young to wish for nothing, wait for death.
   The world—what has it got to say to me?
   Renounce all that you long for, all—renounce!
   That's the truth that all pronounce
   So sagely, so interminably,   1210
   The non-stop croak, the universal chant:
   You can't have what you want, you can't!
   I awake each morning, how? Horrified,
   On the verge of tears, to confront a day
   Which at its close will not have satisfied   1215
   One smallest wish of mine, not one. Why,
   Even the hope of a bit of pleasure, some pleasantness,
   Withers in the atmosphere of mean-spirited fault-finding,
   My lively nature's quick inventiveness
   Is thwarted by cares that seem to have no ending,   1220
   And when the night draws on and all is hushed,
   I go to bed not soothed at last, but apprehensively,
   Well knowing what awaits me is not rest,
   But wild and whirling dreams that terrify me.
   The god who dwells inside my breast,   1225
   Able to stir me to my depths, so powerfully,

---

1. A noble. In the popular plays based on the Faust legend, the Devil often appeared as a monk when the play catered to a Protestant audience and as a noble squire when the audience was mainly Catholic.

The master strength of all my strengths,
Is impotent to effect a single thing outside me.
And so I find existence burdensome, wretched,
Death eagerly desired, my life hated. 1230
MEPHISTO   Yet the welcome men give death is never wholehearted.
FAUST   Happy the man, even as he conquers gloriously,
Death sets the blood-stained laurel on his brows,
Happy the man, after dancing the night through furiously,
Death finds him in a girl's arms in a drowse. 1235
If only, overwhelmed by the Spirit's power,
In raptures I had died right then and there!
MEPHISTO   And yet that very night, I seem to remember,
A fellow didn't down a drink I saw him prepare.
FAUST   Spying around, I see, is what you like to do. 1240
MEPHISTO   I don't know everything, but I know a thing or two.
FAUST   If a sweet, familiar harmony
When I was staggering, arrested me,
Beguiled what's left of childhood feeling
From a time when all was gay and smiling— 1245
Well, never again, I pronounce a curse on
All false and flattering persuasion,
All tales that cheat the soul, constrain
It to endure this house of pain.
First I curse man's mind for thinking 1250
Much too well of itself; I curse
The show of things, bedazzling, blinding,
That assails us through our every sense;
Our dreams of fame, of our name's enduring,
Oh what a sham, I curse them too; 1255
I curse as hollow all our having,
Curse wife and child, peasant and plow;
I curse Mammon[2] when he incites us
With dreams of treasure to reckless deeds,
Or plumps the cushions for our pleasure 1260
As we lie lazily at ease;
Curse comfort sucked out of the grape,
Curse love on its pinnacle of bliss,
Curse faith, so false, curse all vain hope,
And patience most of all I curse! 1265
SPIRIT CHORUS [*Invisible*]
          Pity, oh pity!
          Now you have done it—
          Spoiled
          The lovely world!
          One mighty blow 1270
          And down it falls

---

2. The Aramaic word for "riches," used in the New Testament of the Bible. Medieval writers interpreted the word as a proper noun, the name of the Devil, as representing greed.

> Smashed
> By a demigod's fist.
> We sweep the rubble
> Away into nothing,   1275
> And mourn
> All the beauty gone.
> Omnificent
> Son of the earth,
> Rebuild it,   1280
> Magnificent,
> Inside your heart,
> With a clear head and strong,
> Singing a new song.
> Come,   1285
> Make a fresh start!

MEPHISTO   Lesser ones, these are
> Of my order,
> Active be, cheerful,
> Is their sage counsel.   1290
> Out of your loneliness,
> Weak-blooded languidness,
> Their voices draw you
> Into the wide world before you.

> Stop making love to your misery,   1295
> It eats away at you like a vulture!
> Even in the meanest company
> You'd feel a man like any other.
> Not that I'm proposing to
> Put you down among the rabble.   1300
> I'm not your grandest devil, no.
> But still, throw in with me—that way, united,
> Together life's long road we'll travel,
> And my, how I would be delighted!
> I'll do your will as if my will,   1305
> Every wish of yours fulfill,
> By your leave
> Be your bond servant, be your slave.

FAUST   And in return what must I do?

MEPHISTO   There's plenty of time for that, forget it.   1310

FAUST   No, no, the Devil must have his due,
> He doesn't do things for the hell of it,
> Just to see another fellow through.
> So let's hear the terms, what the fine print is,
> Having you for a servant's a tricky business.   1315

MEPHISTO   I promise I will serve your wishes—here,
> A slave who does your bidding faithfully;
> But if we meet each other—there,
> Why, you must do the same for me.

FAUST   That "there" of yours—it doesn't scare me off;   1320
    If you pull this world down about my ears,
    Let the other one come on, who cares?
    My joys are part and parcel of this earth.
    It's under this sun that I suffer,
    And once it's goodbye, last leave taken,   1325
    Then let whatever happens happen,
    And that is that. About the hereafter
    We have had enough palaver,
    More than I want to hear, by far:
    If still we love and hate each other,   1330
    If some stand high and some stand lower,
    Et cetera, et cetera.
MEPHISTO   In that case, an agreement's easy.
    Come, dare it! Come, your signature!
    Oh, how my tricks will tickle your fancy!   1335
    I'll show you things no man has seen before.
FAUST   You poor devil, really, what have you got to offer?
    The mind of man in its sublime endeavor,
    Tell me, have you ever understood it?
    Oh yes indeed, you've bread, and when I eat it   1340
    I'm hungry still; you've yellow gold—it's flighty,
    Quicksilver-like it's gone and my purse empty;
    Games of chance no man can win at, ever;
    Girls who wind me in their arms, their lover,
    While eyeing up a fresh one over my shoulder;   1345
    There's fame, last failing of a noble nature,
    It shoots across the sky a second, then it's over.
    Oh yes, do show me fruit that rots as you try
    To pick it, trees whose leaves bud daily, daily die!
MEPHISTO   Marvels like that? For a devil, not so daunting,   1350
    I'm good for whatever you have in mind.
    —But friend, the day comes when you find
    A share of your own in life's good things,
    And peace and quiet, are what you're wanting.
FAUST   If ever you see me loll at ease,   1355
    Then it's all yours, you can have it, my life!
    If ever you fool me with flatteries
    Into feeling satisfied with myself,
    Or tempt me with visions of luxuries,
    That's it, the last day that I breathe this air,   1360
    I'll bet you!
MEPHISTO   Done! A bet!
FAUST   A bet! I swear!
    If ever I plead with the passing moment,
    "Linger a while, you are so fair!"
    Then chain me up in close confinement,   1365
    Then serving me no more's your care,
    Then let the death bell toll my finish,

Then unreluctantly I'll perish,
The clock may stop, the hands fall off,
And time for me be over with!   1370
MEPHISTO   Think twice. Forgetting's not a thing we do.
FAUST   Of course, quite right—a bet's a bet,
This isn't anything I'm rushing into.
But if I stagnate, fall into a rut,
I'm a slave, no matter who to,   1375
To this one, that one, or to you.
MEPHISTO   My service starts now—no procrastinating!—
At the dinner tonight for the just-made Ph.D.s.
But there's one thing: you know, for emergencies,
I'd like to have our arrangement down in writing.   1380
FAUST   In black and white you want it—oh the pedantry!
You've never learnt a *man's* word's your best guarantee?
It's not enough for you that I'm committed
By what I promise till the end of days?
—Yet the world's a flood sweeps all along before it,   1385
And why should I feel my word holds always?
A strange idea, but that's the way we are,
And who would want it otherwise?
That man's blessed who keeps his conscience clear,
He'll regret no sacrifice,   1390
Yet parchment signed and stamped and sealed,
Is a bogey all recoil from, scared.
The pen does in the living word,
Only sealing wax and vellum[3] count, honor must yield.
Base spirit, say what you require!   1395
Brass or marble, parchment or paper?
Shall I use a quill, a stylus, chisel?
I leave it up to you, you devil!
MEPHISTO   Why get so hot, make extravagant speeches?
Ranting away does no good.   1400
A scrap of paper takes care of the business.
And sign it with a drop of blood.
FAUST   Oh, all right. If that's what makes you happy,
I'll go along with the tomfoolery.
MEPHISTO   Blood's a very special ink, you know.   1405
FAUST   Are you afraid that I won't keep our bargain?
With every inch of me I'll strive, I'll never slacken!
So I've promised, that's what I will do.
I had ideas too big for me,
Your level's mine, that's all I'm good for.   1410
The Spirit laughed derisively,
Nature won't allow me near her.
Thinking's done with for me, I'm through,

---

3. Sealing wax is melted to close documents, and vellum is a kind of parchment used for writing.

Learning I've loathed since long ago.
—Then fling ourselves into the dance   1415
Of sensual extravagance!
Bring on your miracles, each one,
Inscrutably veiled in your sorcery!
We'll plunge into time's pell-mell run.
The vortex of activity,   1420
Where pleasure and distress,
Setbacks and success,
May come as they come, by turn-about, however;
To be always up and doing is man's nature.

MEPHISTO   No limits restrain you, do just as you like,   1425
A little taste here, a nibble, a lick,
You see something there, snatch it up on the run,
Let all that you do with gusto be done,
Only don't be bashful, wade right in.

FAUST   I told you, I'm not out to enjoy myself, have fun,   1430
I want frenzied excitements, gratifications that are painful,
Love and hatred violently mixed,
Anguish that enlivens, inspiriting trouble;
Cured of my thirst to know at last,
I'll never again shun anything distressful.   1435
From now on my wish is to undergo
All that men everywhere undergo, their whole portion,
Make mine their heights and depths, their weal and woe,
Everything human encompass in my one person,
And so enlarge myself to embrace theirs, all,   1440
And shipwreck with them when at last we shipwreck, all.

MEPHISTO   Believe me, I have chewed and chewed
At that tough meat, mankind, since long ago,
From birth to death work at it, still that food
Is indigestible as sourdough.   1445
Only a God can take in all of them,
The whole lot, for He dwells in eternal light,
While we poor devils are stuck down below
In darkness and gloom, lacking even candlelight,
And all *you* qualify for is, half day, half night.   1450

FAUST   Nevertheless I will!

MEPHISTO   All right, all right.
Still, one thing worries me.
The time allotted you is very short,
But art has always been around and shall be,
So listen, hear what is my thought: 1455
Hire a poet, learn by his instruction.
Let the good gentleman search his mind
By careful, persevering reflection,
And every noble trait he can find,
Heap on your head, his honored creation: 1460

    The lion's fierceness,
    Mild hart's swiftness,
    Italian fieriness,
    Northern steadiness.
Let him master for you the difficult feat   1465
Of combining magnanimity with deceit,
How, driven by youthful impulsiveness, unrestrained,
To fall in love as beforehand you have planned.
Such a creature—my, I'd love to know him!—
I'd call him Mr. Microcosm.   1470

FAUST What am I, then, if it can never be:
The realization of all human possibility,
That crown my soul so avidly reaches for?

MEPHISTO In the end you are—just what you are.
Wear wigs high-piled with curls, oh millions,   1475
Stick your legs in yard-high hessians,
You're still you, the one you always were.

FAUST I feel it now, how pointless my long grind
To make mine all the treasures of man's mind;
When I sit back and interrogate my soul,   1480
No new powers answer to my call;
I'm not a hair's breadth more in height,
A step nearer to the infinite.

MEPHISTO The way you see things, my dear Faust,
Is superficial—I speak frankly.   1485
If you go on repining weakly,
We'll lose our seat at life's rich feast.
Hell, man, you have hands and feet,
A headpiece and a pair of balls,
And savors from fruit fresh and sweet,   1490
That pleasure's yours, entirely yours.
If I've six studs, a sturdy span,
That horsepower's mine, my property,
My coach bowls on, ain't I the man.
Two dozen legs I've got for me!   1495
    Sir, come on, quit all that thinking,
Into the world, the pair of us!
The man who lives in his head only's
Like a donkey in the rough,
Led round and round by the bad fairies,   1500
While green grass grows a stone's throw off.

FAUST And how do we begin?

MEPHISTO   By clearing out—just leaving.
A torture chamber this place is, and that's the truth.
You call it living, to be boring
Yourself and your young men to death?   1505
Leave that to Dr. Bacon Fat next door!
Why toil and moil at threshing heaps of straw?

Anyhow, the deepest knowledge you possess
You daren't let on to before your class.
—Oh now I hear one in the passageway! 1510
FAUST   I can't see him—tell him to go away.
MEPHISTO   The poor boy's been so patient, don't be cross;
We mustn't let him leave here *désolé*.[4]
Let's have your cap and gown, Herr Doctor.
Won't I look the fine professor! 1515
      [*Changes clothes.*]
Count on me to know just what to say!
Fifteen minutes's all I need for it—
Meanwhile get ready for our little junket!

Exit FAUST.

MEPHISTO [*Wearing* FAUST's *gown*]   Despise learning, heap contempt
      on reason,
The human race's best possession, 1520
Only let the lying spirit draw you
Over into mumbo-jumbo,
Make-believe and pure illusion—
And then you're mine for sure, I have you,
No matter what we just agreed to. 1525
      Fate's given him a spirit knows no measure,
On and on it strives, relentlessly,
It soars away disdaining every pleasure,
Yet I will drag him deep into debauchery
Where all proves shallow, meaningless, 1530
I'll have him writhing, ravening, berserk;
Before his lips' insatiable greediness
I'll dangle food and drink; he'll shriek
In vain for relief from his torturing dryness!
And even if he weren't the Devil's already, 1535
He'd still be sure to perish miserably.
      [*Enter a student.*]
STUDENT   Allow me, sir, but I am a beginner
And come in quest of an adviser,
One whom all the people here
Greatly esteem, indeed revere. 1540
MEPHISTO   I thank you for your courtesy.
But I'm a man, as you can see,
Like any other. I wonder, shouldn't you look further?
STUDENT   It's you, sir, you, I want for adviser!
I came here full of youthful zeal, 1545
Eager to learn everything worthwhile.
Mother cried to see me go;
I've got an allowance, it's small, but will do.
MEPHISTO   You've come to the right place, my son.
STUDENT   But I'm ready to turn right around and run! 1550

4. Sorry (French).

It seems so sad inside these walls,
My heart misgives me. I find all's
Confined, shut in, there's nothing green,
Not even a single tree, to be seen.
I can't, on the bench in the lecture hall,   1555
Hear or see or think at all!

MEPHISTO   It's a matter of getting used to things first.
An infant starts out fighting the breast,
But soon it's feeding lustily.
Just so your appetite'll sharpen by the day   1560
The more you nurse at Wisdom's bosom.

STUDENT   I'll cling tight to her bosom, happily,
But where do I find her, by what way?

MEPHISTO   First of all, then—have you chosen
A faculty?

STUDENT   Oh well, you see,   1565
I'd like to be a learned man.
The earth below, the heavens on high—
All those things I long to understand,
All the sciences, all nature.

MEPHISTO   You've got the right idea; however,   1570
It demands close application.

STUDENT   Oh never fear, I'm in this heart and soul;
But still, a fellow gets so dull
Without time off for recreation,
In the long and lovely days of summer.   1575

MEPHISTO   Time slips away so fast you need to use it
Rationally, and not abuse it.
And for that reason I advise you:
The Principles of Logic *primo*![5]
We will drill your mind by rote,   1580
Strap it in the Spanish boot[6]
So it never shall forget
The road that's been marked out for it
And stray about incautiously,
A will-o'-the-wisp, this way, that way.   1585
Day after day you'll be taught
All you once did just like that,
Like eating and drinking, thoughtlessly,
Now needs a methodology—
Order and system: *A, B, C!*   1590
    Our thinking instrument behaves
Like a loom: every thread,
At a step on the treadle's set in motion,
Back and forth the shuttle's sped,
The strands flow too fast for the eye,   1595

5. First (Spanish).
6. The Spanish boot is an instrument of torture.

A blow of the batten and there's cloth, woven!
Now enter your philosopher, he
Proves all is just as it should be:
A being thus and *B* also,
Then *C* and *D* inevitably follow;   1600
And if there were no *A* and *B*,
There'd never be a *C* and *D*.
They're struck all of a heap, his admiring hearers,
But still, it doesn't make them weavers.
How do you study something living?   1605
Drive out the spirit, deny it being,
So there're just parts with which to deal,
Gone is what binds it all, the soul.
With lifeless pieces as the only things real,
The wonder's where's the life of the whole—   1610
Encheiresis naturae,[7] the chemists then call it,
Make fools of themselves and never know it.

STUDENT   I have trouble following what you say.

MEPHISTO   You'll get the hang of it by and by
When you learn to distinguish and classify.   1615

STUDENT   How stupid all this makes me feel;
It spins around in my head like a wheel.

MEPHISTO   Next metaphysics, a vital part
Of scholarship, its very heart.
Exert your faculties to venture   1620
Beyond the boundaries of our nature,
Gain intelligence the brain
Has difficulty taking in,
And whether it goes in or not,
There's always a big word for it.   1625
    Be very sure, your first semester,
To do things right, attend each lecture;
Five of them you'll have daily,
Be in your seat when the bell peals shrilly;
Come to class with your homework done,   1630
The sections memorized, each one,
So you are sure nothing's mistook
And nothing's said not in the book.
Still, note down all, not one word lost,
As if it came from the Holy Ghost.   1635

STUDENT   No need to say that to me twice,
They help a lot, notes do, all right.
What you've got down in black and white
Goes home with you, to a safe place.

MEPHISTO   But your faculty—you've still not told me.   1640

STUDENT   Well, I don't believe the law would hold me.

---

7. The natural process by which substances are united into a living organism—a name for an action no one understands.

MEPHISTO   I can't blame you, law is no delight.
      What's jurisprudence?—a stupid rite
      That's handed down, a kind of contagion,
      From generation to generation,   1645
      From people to people, region to region.
      Good sense is treated as nonsensical,
      Benefactions as a botheration.
      O future grandsons, how I wince for you all!
      As for the rights with which we're born—   1650
      Not a word!—as if they were unknown.
STUDENT   I hate the stuff now more than ever!
      How lucky I am to have you for adviser.
      Perhaps I'll take theology.
MEPHISTO   I shouldn't want to lead you astray,   1655
      But it's a science, if you'll allow me to say it,
      Where it's easy to lose your way.
      There's so much poison hidden in it
      It's very nearly impossible
      To tell what's toxic from what's medicinal.   1660
      Here again it's safer to choose
      One single master and echo his words dutifully—
      As a general rule, put your trust in *words*,
      They'll guide you safely past doubt and dubiety
      Into the Temple of Absolute Certainty.   1665
STUDENT   But shouldn't words convey ideas, a meaning?
MEPHISTO   Of course they should! But why overdo it?
      It's exactly when ideas are wanting,
      Words come in so handy as a substitute.
      With words we argue pro and con,   1670
      With words invent a whole system.
      Believe in words! Have faith in them!
      No jot or tittle shall pass from them.
STUDENT   Forgive me, I've another query,
      My last one and then I'll go.   1675
      Medicine, sir—what might you care to tell me
      About that study I should know?
      Three years, my God, are terribly short
      For so vast a field for the mind to survey.
      A pointer or two would provide a start   1680
      And advance one quicker on one's way.
MEPHISTO [*Aside*]   Enough of all this academic chatter,
      Back again to devilry!
      [*Aloud*] Medicine's an easy art to master.
      Up and down you study the whole world   1685
      Only so as to discover
      In the end it's all up to the Lord.
      Plough your way through all the sciences you please,
      Each learns only what he can,
      But the man who understands his opportunities,   1690

Him I call a man.
You seem a pretty strapping fellow,
Not one to hang back bashfully,
If you don't doubt yourself, I know,
Nobody else will doubt you, nobody.   1695
Above all learn your way with women
If you mean to practise medicine.
The aches and pains that torture them
From one place only, one, all stem—
Cure there, cure all. Act halfway decent   1700
And you'll find the whole sex acquiescent.
With an M.D. you enjoy great credit,
Your art, they're sure, beats others' arts;
The doctor, when he pays a visit,
For greeting reaches for those parts   1705
It takes a layman years to come at;
You feel her pulse with extra emphasis
And your arm slipping with an ardent glance
Around her slender waist,
See if it's because she's so tight-laced.   1710
STUDENT   Oh, that's much better—practical, down to earth!
MEPHISTO   All theory, my dear boy, is gray,
And green the golden tree of life.
STUDENT   I swear it seems a dream to me!
Would you permit me, sir, to impose on   1715
Your generous kindness another day
And drink still more draughts of your wisdom?
MEPHISTO   I'm glad to help you in any way.
STUDENT   I mustn't leave without presenting
You my album. Do write something   1720
In it for me, would you?
MEPHISTO   Happily.
    [*Writes and hands back the album.*]
STUDENT [*Reading*]   Eritis sicut Deus, scientes bonum et malum.[8]
    [*Closes the book reverently and exits.*]
MEPHISTO   Faithfully follow that good old verse,
That favorite line of my aunt's, the snake,
And for all your precious godlikeness   1725
You'll end up how? A nervous wreck.
        Enter FAUST.
FAUST   And now where to?
MEPHISTO   Wherever you like.
First we'll mix with little people, then with great,
The pleasure and the profit you will get
From our course—and never pay tuition for it.   1730
FAUST   But me and my long beard—we're hardly suited

---

8. A slight alteration of the serpent's words to Eve in Genesis: "Ye shall be as God, knowing good and evil" (Latin).

For the fast life. I feel myself defeated
Even before we start. I've never been
A fellow to fit in. Among other men
I feel so small, so mortified—I freeze.   1735
Oh, in the world I'm always ill at ease!
MEPHISTO   My friend, that's all soon changed, it doesn't matter;
With confidence comes *savoir-vivre*.[9]
FAUST   But how do we get out of here?
Where are your horses, groom and carriage?   1740
MEPHISTO   By air's how we make our departure,
On my cloak—you'll enjoy the voyage.
But take care, on so bold a venture,
You're sparing in the matter of luggage.
I'll heat some gas, that way we'll rise up   1745
Quickly off the face of earth;
If we're light enough we'll lift right up—
I offer my congratulations, sir, on your new life!

Auerbach's Cellar in Leipzig

Drinkers carousing.

FROSCH   Faces glum and glasses empty?
I don't call this much of a party.   1750
You fellows seem wet straw tonight
Who always used to blaze so bright.
BRANDER   It's your fault—he just sits there, hardly speaks!
Where's the horseplay, where're the dirty jokes?
FROSCH [*Emptying a glass of wine on his head*]
There! Both at once!   1755
BRANDER   O horse and swine!
FROSCH   You asked for it, so don't complain.
SIEBEL   Out in the street if you want to punch noses!
—Now take a deep breath and roar out a chorus
In praise of the grape and the jolly god Bacchus.[1]
Come, all together with a rollicking round-o!   1760
ALTMAYER   Stop, stop, man, I'm wounded, cotten, quick, someone
fetch some,
The terrible fellow has burst me an eardrum!
SIEBEL   Hear the sound rumble above in the vault?
That tells you you're hearing the true bass note.
FROSCH   That's right! Out the door, whoever don't like it!   1765
With a do-re-mi,
ALTMAYER   And a la-ti-do,
FROSCH   We will have us a concert!
[*Sings.*]

9. French for knowing how to live in polite   1. Roman god of wine.
society.

Our dear Holy Roman Empire,[2]
How does the damn thing hold together? 1770
BRANDER   Oh, but that's dreadful, and dreadfully sung,
A dreary, disgusting *political* song!
Thank the Lord when you wake each morning
You're not the one must keep the Empire running.
It's a blessing I'm grateful for 1775
To be neither Kaiser nor Chancellor.[3]
But we, too, need a chief for our group
So let's elect ourselves a pope.
To all of us here I'm sure it's well known
What a man must do to sit on that throne. 1780
FROSCH [*Singing*]
Nightingale, fly away, o'er lawn, o'er bower,
Tell her I love her ten thousand times over.
SIEBEL   Enough of that love stuff, it turns my stomach.
FROSCH   Ten thousand times, though it drives you frantic!
[*Sings.*]
Unbar the door, the night is dark! 1785
Unbar the door, my love, awake!
Bar up the door now it's daybreak.
SIEBEL   Go on, then, boast about her charms, her favor,
But I will have the latest laugh of all.
She played me false—just wait, she'll play you falser. 1790
A horned imp's what I wish her, straight from Hell,
To dawdle with her in the dust of crossroads;
And may an old goat stinking from the Brocken[4]
Bleat "Goodnight, dearie," to her, galloping homewards.
A fellow made of honest flesh and blood 1795
For a slut like that is much too good.
What kind of love note would I send that scarecrow?—
A beribboned rock tossed through her kitchen window.
BRANDER [*Banging on the table*]
Good fellows, your attention! None here will deny
I know what should be done and shouldn't at all. 1800
Now we have lovers in our company
Whom we must treat in manner suitable
To their condition, our jollity,
With a song just lately written. So mind the air
And come in on the chorus loud and clear! 1805
[*He sings.*]
A rat lived downstairs in the cellar,
Dined every day on lard and butter,
His paunch grew round as any burgher's,

---

2. Group of Central European lands ruled by Frankish and German kings from the ninth to the nineteenth centuries.

3. Head of the government. "Kaiser": German for emperor.

4. The highest mountain in northern Germany.

As round as Dr. Martin Luther's.[5]
The cook put poison down for it.   1810
Oh, how it groaned, the pangs it felt,
    As if by Cupid smitten.
CHORUS [*Loud and clear*]
    As if by Cupid smitten!

BRANDER
It rushed upstairs, it raced outdoors
And drank from every gutter,   1815
It gnawed the woodwork, scratched the floors,
Its fever burned still hotter.
In agony it hopped and squealed,
Oh, piteously the beast appealed,
    As if by Cupid smitten.   1820
CHORUS   *As if by Cupid smitten!*

BRANDER
Its torment drove it, in broad day,
Out into the kitchen,
Collapsing on the hearth, it lay
Panting hard and twitching.   1825
But that cruel Borgia[6] smiled with pleasure,
That's it, that's that rat's final seizure,
    As if by Cupid smitten.
CHORUS   *As if by Cupid smitten!*

SIEBEL   You find it funny, you coarse louts,   1830
  Oh, quite a stunt, so very cunning,
  To put down poison for poor rats!
BRANDER   You like rats, do you, find them charming?
ALTMAYER   O big of gut and bald of pate!
Losing out's subdued the oaf;   1835
What he sees in the bloated rat
'S the spitting image of himself.
    [FAUST *and* MEPHISTOPHELES *enter.*]
MEPHISTO   What your case calls for, Doctor, first,
Is some diverting company,
To teach you life affords some gaiety.   1840
For these men every night's a feast
And every day a holiday;
With little wit but lots of zest
All spin inside their little orbit
Like young cats chasing their own tails.   1845
As long as the landlord grants them credit
And they are spared a splitting headache,

---

5. Martin Luther (1483–1546), German leader of the Protestant Reformation, hence an object of distaste for Catholics.

6. Spanish and Italian family that grew powerful during the Renaissance; famous for poisoning their enemies.

They find life good, unburdened by travails.
BRANDER   They're travelers is what your Brander says,
You can tell it by their foreign ways,   1850
They've not been here, I'll bet, an hour.
FROSCH   Right, right! My Leipzig's an attraction, how I love her,
A little Paris spreading light and culture!
SIEBEL   Who might they be? What's your guess?
FROSCH   Leave it to me. I'll fill their glass,   1855
Gently extract, as you do a baby's tooth,
All there's to know about them, the whole truth.
I'd say we're dealing with nobility,
They look so proud, so dissatisfied, to me.
BRANDER   They're pitchmen at the Fair, is what I think.   1860
ALTMAYER   Maybe so.
FROSCH   Now watch me go to work.
MEPHISTO [*To* FAUST]
These dolts can't ever recognize Old Nick[7]
Even when he's got them by the neck.
FAUST   Gentlemen, good day.
SIEBEL   Thank you, the same.
[*Aside, obliquely studying* MEPHISTOPHELES]
What the hell, the fellow limps, he's lame![8]   1865
MEPHISTO   We'd like to join you, sirs, if you'll allow it.
But our landlord's wine looks so-so, I am thinking,
So the company shall make up for it.
ALTMAYER   Particular, you are, about your drinking?
FROSCH   Fresh from Dogpatch, right? From supper   1870
On cabbage soup with Goodman Clodhopper?
MEPHISTO   We couldn't stop on this trip, more's the pity!
But last time he went on so tenderly
About his Leipzig kith and kin,
And sent his very best to you, each one.   1875
        Bowing to FROSCH
ALTMAYER [*Aside to* FROSCH]
Score one for him. He's got some wit.
SIEBEL   A sly one, he is.
FROSCH   Wait, I'll fix him yet!
MEPHISTO   Unless I err, weren't we just now hearing
Some well-schooled voices joined in choral singing?
Voices, I am sure, must resonate   1880
Inside this vault to very fine effect.
FROSCH   You know music professionally, I think.
MEPHISTO   Oh no—the spirit's eager, but the voice is weak.
ALTMAYER   Give us a song!
MEPHISTO   Whatever you'd like to hear.
SIEBEL   A new one, nothing we've heard before.   1885

7. Nickname for the devil.
8. By tradition, the Devil had cloven feet, split like sheep's hooves.

MEPHISTO   Easily done. We've just come back from Spain,
    Land where the air breathes song, the rivers run wine.
       [*Sings.*]
       Once upon a time a King
         Had a flea, a big one—
FROSCH   Did you hear that? A flea, goddamn!   1890
    I'm all for fleas, myself, I am.
MEPHISTO [*Sings.*]
       Once upon a time a King
         Had a flea, a big one,
       Doted fondly on the thing
         With fatherly affection.   1895
       Calling his tailor in, he said,
         Fetch needles, thread and scissors,
       Measure the Baron up for shirts,
         Measure him, too, for trousers.
BRANDER   And make it perfectly clear to the tailor   1900
    He must measure exactly, sew perfect stitches,
    If he's fond of his head, not the least little error,
    Not a wrinkle, you hear, not one, in those breeches!
MEPHISTO
       Glowing satins, gleaming silks
         Now were the flea's attire,   1905
       Upon his chest red ribbons crossed
         And a great star shone like fire,
       In sign of his exalted post
         As the King's First Minister.
       His sisters, cousins, uncles, aunts   1910
         Enjoyed great influence too—
       The bitter torments that that Court's
         Nobility went through!
       And the Queen as well, and her lady's-maid,
         Though bitten till delirious,   1915
       Forbore to squash the fleas, afraid
         To incur the royal animus.
       But we free souls, we squash all fleas
         The instant they light on us!
CHORUS [*Loud and clear*]
       But we free souls, we squash all fleas   1920
         The instant they light on us!
FROSCH   Bravo, bravo! That was fine!
SIEBEL   May every flea's fate be the same!
BRANDER   Between finger and nail, then crack! and they're done for.
ALTMAYER   Long live freedom, long live wine!   1925
MEPHISTO   I'd gladly drink a glass in freedom's honor,
    If only your wine looked a little better.[9]

---

9. That is, not cursed.

SIEBEL   Again! You try, sir, our good humor.
MEPHISTO   I'm sure our landlord wouldn't take it kindly.
   For otherwise I'd treat this company   1930
   To wine that's wine—straight out of our own cellar.
SIEBEL   Go on, go on, let the landlord be my worry.
FROSCH   You're princes, you are, if you're able
   To put good wine upon the table;
   But a drop or two, hell, that's no trial at all,   1935
   To judge right what I need's a real mouthful.
ALTMAYER [*In an undertone*]   They're from the Rhineland,
   I would swear.
MEPHISTO   Let's have an auger,[1] please.
BRANDER   What for?
   Don't tell me you've barrels piled outside the door!   1940
ALTMAYER   There's a basket of tools—look, over there.
MEPHISTO [*Picking out an auger, to* FROSCH]
   Now gentlemen, name what you'd have, please.
FROSCH   What do you mean? We have a choice?
MEPHISTO   Whatever you wish. I will produce.
ALTMAYER [*To* FROSCH]   Licking his lips already, he is!   1945
FROSCH   Fine, fine! For me—a Rhine wine any day,
   The best stuff's from the fatherland, I say.
MEPHISTO [*Boring a hole in the table edge at* FROSCH's *place*]
   Some wax to stop the holes with, quick!
ALTMAYER   Hell, it's just a sideshow trick.
MEPHISTO [*To* BRANDER]
   And you?   1950
BRANDER   The best champagne you have, friend, please,
   With lots of sparkle, lots of fizz.
    [MEPHISTOPHELES *goes round the table boring holes at all the places,*
    which one of the drinkers stops with bungs made of wax.]
   You can't always avoid what's foreign,
   About pleasure I'm nonpartisan.
   A man who's a true German can't stand Frenchmen,   1955
   But he can stand their wine, oh yes he can!
SIEBEL [*As* MEPHISTOPHELES *reaches his place*]
   I confess your dry wines don't
   Please me, sweet is what I want.
MEPHISTO   Tokay[2] for you! Coming up shortly!
ALTMAYER   No, fellows, slow down, just look at it calmly—   1960
   The whole thing's meant to make fools of us.
MEPHISTO   Ei me! With noble guests such as you are,
   That would be going a bit far.
   Do you imagine I'd be so obtuse?
   So what's your pleasure, I'm waiting—speak.   1965
ALTMAYER   Whatever you like, just don't take all week.

1. Tool used to bore holes.   2. A sweet Hungarian wine.

MEPHISTO [*All the holes are now bored and stopped; gesturing grotesquely*]
    Grapes grow on the vine,
    Horns on the head of the goat,
    O vinestock of hard wood,
    O juice of the tender grape!   1970
    And a wooden table shall,
    When summoned, yield wine as well!
    O depths of Nature, mysterious, secret,
    Here is a miracle—if you believe it!
  Now pull the plugs, all, drink and be merry!   1975
ALL [*Drawing the bungs and the wine each drinker asked for gushing
    into his glass*]
  Sweet fountain, flowing for us only!
MEPHISTO   But take good care you don't spill any.
    [*They drink glass after glass.*]
ALL [*Singing*]
    Lovely, oh lovely, I must be dreaming!
    A party so cannabalistically cozy—
    Five hundred pigs swilling slops!   1980
MEPHISTO   The people are free! What a time they're having!
FAUST   I'd like to go now. Nincompoops!
MEPHISTO   Before we do, you must admire
    Their swinishness in all its splendor.
SIEBEL [*Spilling wine on the floor, where it bursts into flame*]
    All Hell's afire, I burn, I burn!   1985
MEPHISTO [*Conjuring the flame*]
    Peace, my own element, down, down!
    [*To the drinkers*]
    Only a pinch, for the present, of the purgatorial fire.
SIEBEL   What's going on here? For this you'll pay dear!
    You don't seem to know the kind of men you have here.
FROSCH   Once is enough for that kind of business!   1990
ALTMAYER   Throw him out on his ear, but quietly, no fuss!
SIEBEL   You've got your nerve, trying out upon us
    Stuff like that—damned hocus-pocus!
MEPHISTO   Quiet, you tub of guts!
SIEBEL   Bean pole, you!
    Now he insults us. I know what to do.   1995
BRANDER   A taste of our fists is what: one-two, one-two.
ALTMAYER [*Drawing a bung and flames shooting out at him*]
    I'm on fire, I'm on fire!
SIEBEL   It's witchcraft, no mistaking!
    Stick him, the rogue, he's free for the taking!
    [*They draw their knives and fall on* MEPHISTOPHELES.]
MEPHISTO [*Gesturing solemnly*]
    False words, false shapes
    Addle wits, muddle senses!   2000
    Let here and otherwheres
    Exchange places!

[*All stand astonished and gape at each other.*]

ALTMAYER   Where am I? What a lovely country!

FROSCH   Such vineyards! Do my eyes deceive me?

SIEBEL   And grapes you only need to reach for!   2005

BRANDER   Just look inside this green arbor!
What vines, what grapes! Cluster on cluster!
[*He seizes* SIEBEL *by the nose. The others do the same to each other, and raise their knives.*]

MEPHISTO   Unspell, illusion, eyes and ears!
—Take note the Devil's a jester, my dears!
[*He vanishes with* FAUST; *the drinkers recoil from each other.*]

SIEBEL   What's happened?

ALTMAYER   What?

FROSCH   Was that your nose?   2010

BRANDER [*To* SIEBEL]   And I'm still holding on to yours!

ALTMAYER   The shock I felt—in every limb!
Get me a chair, I'm caving in.

FROSCH   What happened? That man, and his wine—so strange!

SIEBEL   If only I could lay hands on that scoundrel,   2015
I'd give him something in exchange!

ALTMAYER   I saw him, horsed upon a barrel,
Vault straight out through the cellar door—
My feet feel leaden, so unnatural.
[*Turning toward the table.*]
Well—maybe some wine's still trickling here.   2020

SIEBEL   Lies, all lies! Deluded! Dupes!

FROSCH   I was drinking wine, I'd swear.

BRANDER   But what was it with all those grapes?

ALTMAYER   Now try and tell me, you know-it-alls,
There's no such thing as miracles!   2025

Witch's Kitchen

A low hearth, and on the fire a large cauldron. In the steam rising up from it, various figures can be glimpsed. A SHE-APE *is seated by the cauldron, skimming it to keep it from boiling over. The male with their young crouches close by, warming himself. Hanging on the walls and from the ceiling are all sorts of strange objects, the household gear of a witch.*

FAUST, MEPHISTOPHELES.

FAUST   Why, it's revolting, all this crazy witchery!
Are you telling me that I'll be born a new man
Here amid this lunatic confusion?
Is an ancient hag the doctor who will cure me?
And the mess that that beast's boiling, that's the remedy   2030
To cancel thirty years, unbow my back?
If you can do no better, the outlook's black
For me, the hopes I nursed are dead already.

Hasn't man's venturesome mind, instructed by Nature,
Discovered some sort of potent elixer? 2035
MEPHISTO   Now you're speaking sensibly!
    There is a natural way to recover your youth;
    But that's another business entirely
    And not your sort of thing, is my belief.
FAUST   No, no, come on, I want to hear it. 2040
MEPHISTO   All right. It's simple: you don't need to worry
    About money, or doctors, or necromancy.
    Go out into the fields right now, this minute,
    Start digging and hoeing, with never a stop or respite,
    Confine yourself and your thoughts to the narrowest sphere, 2045
    Eat nothing but the plainest kind of fare,
    Live with the cattle as cattle, don't think it too low
    To spread your own dung on the fields that you sow.
    So there you have it, the sane way, the healthy,
    To keep yourself young till the age of eighty! 2050
FAUST   Yes, not my sort of thing, I'm afraid,
    Humbling myself to work with a spade;
    So straitened a life would never suit me.
MEPHISTO   So it's back to the witch, my friend, are we?
FAUST   That horrible hag—no one else will do? 2055
    Why can't *you* concoct the brew?
MEPHISTO   A nice thing that, to waste the time of the Devil
    When his every moment is claimed by the business of evil!
    Please understand. Not only skill and science
    Are called for here, but also patience: 2060
    A mind must keep at it for years, very quietly,
    Only time can supply the mixture its potency.
    Such a deal of stuff goes into the process,
    All very strange, all so secret.
    The Devil, it's true, taught her how to do it. 2065
    But it's no business of his to brew it.
        [*Seeing the* APES]
    See here, those creatures, aren't they pretty!
    That one's the housemaid, that one's the flunkey.
        [*To the* APES]
    Madam is not at home, it seems?
APES
    Flew up the chimney 2070
    To dine out with friends.
MEPHISTO   And her feasting, how long does it usually take her?
APES   As long as we warm our paws by the fire.
MEPHISTO [*To* FAUST]   What do you think of these elegant folk?
FAUST   Noisome enough to make me choke. 2075
MEPHISTO   Well, just this sort of causerie
    Is what I find most pleases me.
        [*To the* APES]
    Tell me, you ugly things, oh do.

What's that you're stirring there, that brew?
APES   Beggars' soup, it's thin stuff, goes down easy.   2080
MEPHISTO   Your public's assured—they like what's wishy-washy.
HE-APE [*Sidling up to* MEPHISTOPHELES *fawningly*]
  Roll, roll the dice quick,
  And this monkey make rich,
  Have himself at last luck,
  The rich have too much.   2085
  With a few dollars and cents
  The credit I'd have for sense!
MEPHISTO   How very happy that monkey would be
 If he could buy chances in the lottery.
   [*Meanwhile the young* APES *have been rolling around a big ball
   to which they now give a push forward.*]
HE-APE
  The world, sirs, behold it!   2090
  Down goes the up side,
  Up goes the down side,
  And never a respite.
  Touch it, it'll ring,
  It's like glass, fractures easily.   2095
  When all's said and done,
  A hollow, void thing.
  See, it shines bright here,
  Here even brighter.
  —Oops, ain't I nimble!   2100
  But you, son, be careful
  And keep a safe distance,
  Or it's your last day.
  The thing's made of clay,
  A knock, and it's fragments.   2105
MEPHISTO   What is that sieve for?
HE-APE [*Taking it down*]
  If you came here to thieve,
  It would be my informer.
   [*He scampers across to the* SHE-APE *and has her look through it.*]
  Look through the sieve!
  Now say, do you know him?   2110
  Or you daren't name him?
MEPHISTO [*Approaching the fire*]   And this pot over here?
APES
  Oh, you're a dolt, sir,
  Don't know what a pot's for!
  Nor a kettle neither.   2115
MEPHISTO   What a rude creature!
HE-APE
  Here, take this duster,
  Sit down in the armchair.
   [*Presses* MEPHISTOPHELES *down in the chair.*]

FAUST [*Who meanwhile has been standing in front of a mirror,*
  going forward to peer into it from close up and then stepping back]
    What do I see? What a marvellous vision
    Shows itself in this magic glass!   2120
    Love, land me your wings, your swiftest to pass
    Through the air to the heaven she must dwell in!
    Unless I stay firmly fixed to this spot,
    If I dare to move nearer the least bit,
    Mist blurs the vision and obscures her quite.   2125
    Woman unrivaled, beauty absolute!
    Can such things be, a creature made perfectly?
    The body so indolently stretched out there
    Surely epitomizes all that is heavenly.
    Can such a marvel inhabit down here?   2130
MEPHISTO   Of course when a god's sweated six whole days
    And himself cries bravo in his works praise,
    You can be certain the results are first class.
    Look all you want now in the glass,
    But I can find you just such a prize,   2135
    And lucky the man, his bliss assured,
    Brings home such a beauty to his bed and board.
      [FAUST *continues to stare into the mirror, while* MEPHISTOPHELES,
      leaning back comfortably in the armchair and toying with the feather
      duster, talks on.]
    Here I sit like a king on a throne,
    Scepter in hand, all I'm lacking's my crown.
APES [*Who have been performing all sorts of queer, involved movements,*
  with loud cries bring MEPHISTOPHELES *a crown*]
    Here, your majesty,   2140
    If you would,
    Glue up the crown
    With sweat and blood!
    [*Their clumsy handling of the crown causes it to break apart and they*
    cavort around with the pieces.]
    Oh no, now it's broken!
    We look and we listen.   2145
    We chatter, scream curses,
    And make up our verses—
FAUST [*Still gazing raptly into the mirror*]
    Good God, how my mind reels, it's going to snap!
MEPHISTO [*Nodding toward the* APES]
    My own head's starting to spin like a top.
APES
    And if by some fluke   2150
    The words happen to suit
    Then the rhyme makes a thought!
FAUST [*As above*]   My insides burn as if on fire!
    Come on, we must get out of here.
MEPHISTO [*Keeping his seat*]   They tell the truth, these poets do.   2155

You've got to give the creatures their due.

[*The cauldron, neglected by the* SHE-APE, *starts to boil over, causing a
great tongue of flame to shoot up the chimney.* THE WITCH *comes riding
down the flame, shrieking hideously.*]

THE WITCH   It hurts, it hurts!
Monkeys, apes, incompetent brutes!
Forgetting the pot and singeing your mistress—
The servants I have! Utterly useless!   2160

[*Catching sight of* FAUST *and* MEPHISTOPHELES]

What's going on here?
Who are this pair?
What's all this about?
Sneaking in when I'm out!
Hellfire burn   2165
Them to a turn!

[*She plunges the spoon into the cauldron and scatters fire over* FAUST,
MEPHISTOPHELES *and the* APES. *The* APES *whine.*]

MEPHISTOPHELES [*Turning the duster upside down and hitting out violently
among the glasses and jars with the butt end*]

In pieces, in pieces,
Spilt soup and smashed dishes!
It's all in fun, really—
Beating time, you old carcass,   2170
To your melody.

[THE WITCH *starts back in rage and fear.*]

Can't recognize me, rattlebones, old donkey, you?
Can't recognize your lord and master?
Why I don't chop up you and your monkey crew
Into the littlest bits and pieces is a wonder!   2175
No respect at all for my red doublet?
And my cock's feather means nothing to you, beldam?
Is my face masked or can you plainly see it?
Must I tell *you* of all people who I am?

THE WITCH   Oh sir, forgive my discourteous salute!   2180
But I look in vain for your cloven foot,
And your two ravens, where are they?

MEPHISTO   All right, this time you're let off—I remember
It's been so long since we've seen each other.
Also, the world's grown so cultured today,   2185
Even the Devil's been caught up in it;
The Northern bogey has made his departure,
No horns now, no tail, to make people shiver,
And as for my hoof, though I can't do without it,
Socially it would raise too many eyebrows—   2190
So like a lot of other young fellows
I've padded my calves to try and conceal it.

THE WITCH [*Dancing with glee*]
I'm out of my mind with delight, I swear!
My lord Satan's dropped out of the air.

MEPHISTO   Woman, that name—I forbid you to use it.   2195
THE WITCH   Why not? Whyever now refuse it?
MEPHISTO   Since God knows when it belongs to mythology,
    But that's hardly improved the temper of humanity.
    The Evil One's no more, evil ones more than ever.
    Address me as Baron, that will do,   2200
    A gentleman of rank like any other,
    And if you doubt my blood is blue,
    See, here's my house's arms, the noblest ever!
        [He makes an indecent gesture.]
THE WITCH [Laughing excessively]
    Ha, ha! It's you, I see now, it's clear—
    The same old rascal you always were!   2205
MEPHISTO [To FAUST]   Observe, friend, my diplomacy
    And learn the art of witch-mastery.
THE WITCH   Gentlemen, now, what is your pleasure?
MEPHISTO   A generous glass of your famous liquor,
    But please, let it be from your oldest supply;   2210
    It doubles in strength as the years multiply.
THE WITCH   At once! Here I've got, as it happens, a bottle
    From which I myself every now and then tipple,
    And what is more, it's lost all its stink.
    I'll gladly pour you out a cup.   2215
        [Under her breath]
    But if the fellow's unprepared, the drink
    Might kill him, you know, before an hour's up.
MEPHISTO   I know the man well, he'll thrive upon it.
    I wish him the best your kitchen affords.
    Now draw your circle, say the right words,   2220
    And pour him out a brimming goblet.
        [Making bizarre gestures, THE WITCH draws a circle and sets down an
        assortment of strange objects inside it. All the glasses start to ring and the
        pots to resound, providing a kind of musical accompaniment. Last of all,
        she brings out a great tome and stands the APES in the circle to serve as a
        lectern and to hold up the torches. Then she signals FAUST to approach.]
FAUST [To MEPHISTOPHELES]
    What can I hope for here, would you tell me?
    That junk of hers, her arms waving crazily,
    All the vulgar tricks she's performing,
    Well do I know them, I don't find them amusing.   2225
MEPHISTO   Jokes, just jokes! It's not all that serious,
    Really, you're being much too difficult.
    Of course hocus-pocus! She's a sorceress—
    How else can her potion produce a result?
        [He presses FAUST inside the circle.]
THE WITCH   [Declaiming from the book, with great emphasis]
    Listen and learn!   2230
    From one make ten,
    And let two go,

And add three in,
And you are rich.
Now cancel four! 2235
From five and six,
So says the witch,
Make seven and eight—
Thus all's complete.
And nine is one 2240
And ten is none
And that's the witch's one-times-one.

FAUST   I think the old woman's throwing a fit.

MEPHISTO   We're nowhere near the end of it.
I know the book, it's all like that, 2245
The time I've wasted over it!
For a thoroughgoing paradox is what
Bemuses fools and wise men equally.
The trick's old as the hills yet it's still going strong;
With Three-in-One and One-in-Three[1] 2250
Lies are sown broadcast, truth may go hang;
Who questions professors about the claptrap they teach—
Who wants to debate and dispute with a fool?
People dutifully think, hearing floods of fine speech,
It can't be such big words mean nothing at all. 2255

THE WITCH [Continuing]
The power of science
From the whole world kept hidden!
Who don't have a thought,
To them it is given
Unbidden, unsought, 2260
It's theirs without sweat.

FAUST   Did you hear that, my God, what nonsense,
It's giving me a headache, phew!
It makes me think I'm listening to
A hundred thousand fools in chorus. 2265

MEPHISTO   Enough, enough, O excellent Sibyl![2]
Bring on the potion, fill the stoup,
Your drink won't give my friend here trouble,
He's earned his Ph.D. in many a bout.
[THE WITCH very ceremoniously pours the potion into a bowl; when FAUST
raises it to his lips, a low flame plays over it.]
Drink, now drink, no need to diddle, 2270
It'll put you into a fine glow,
When you've got a sidekick in the Devil,
Why should some fire frighten you so?
[THE WITCH breaks the circle and FAUST steps out.]
Now let's be off, you mustn't dally.

THE WITCH   I hope that little nip, sir, hits the spot! 2275

1. The Christian doctrine of the Trinity.   2. Prophetess.

MEPHISTO [*To* THE WITCH]   Madam, thanks. If I can help *you* out,
    Don't fail, upon Walpurgis Night,[3] to ask me.
THE WITCH [*To* FAUST]   Here is a song, sir, carol it now and then,
    You'll find it assists the medicine.
MEPHISTO   Come away quick! You must do as I say.   2280
    To soak up the potion body and soul,
    A man's got to sweat a bucketful.
    And after, I'll teach you the gentleman's way
    Of wasting your time expensively.
    Soon yours the delight outdelights all things—   2285
    Boy Cupid astir in you, stretching his wings.
FAUST   One more look in the mirror, let me—
    That woman was inexpressibly lovely!
MEPHISTO   No, no, soon enough, before you, vis-à-vis,
    Yours the fairest of fair women, I guarantee.   2290
    [*Aside*] With that stuff in him, old Jack will
    Soon see a Helen in every Jill.

A Street

FAUST. MARGARETE *passing by*.

FAUST   Pretty lady, here's my arm,
    Would you allow me to see you home?
MARGARETE   I'm neither pretty nor a lady,   2295
    Can find my way home quite unaided.
        [*She escapes his arm and passes by.*]
FAUST   By God, what a lovely girl,
    I've never seen her like, a pearl!
    A good girl, too, with a quick wit,
    Her manner modest and yet pert.   2300
    Those red, ripe lips and cheeks abloom
    Will haunt me till the crack of doom.
    The way she looked down, so demure,
    Had for me such allure!
    The way she cut short my come-on   2305
    Charmed me—charmed by a turn-down!
       Enter MEPHISTOPHELES.
FAUST   Get me that girl, do you hear, you must!
MEPHISTO   What girl?
FAUST   The one who just went past.
MEPHISTO   Oh, her. She's just been to confession
    To be absolved of all her sins.   2310
    I sidled near the box to listen:
    She could have spared herself her pains,
    She is the soul of innocence

---

3. May Day Eve (April 30), when witches are supposed to assemble on the Brocken, the highest peak in the Harz Mountains, which are in central Germany.

And has no reason, none at all,
To visit the confessional.   2315
Her kind is too much for me.
FAUST   She's over fourteen, isn't she?
MEPHISTO   Well, listen to him, an instant Don Juan,[1]
Demands every favor, his shyness all gone,
Conceitedly thinks it offends his honor   2320
To leave unplucked every pretty flower.
But it doesn't go so easy always.
FAUST   My dear Doctor of What's Proper,
Spare me your lectures, I beg you, please.
Let me tell it to you straight: 2325
If I don't hold that darling creature
Tight in my arms this very night,
We're through, we two, come twelve midnight.
MEPHISTO   Impossible! That's out of the question!
I require two weeks at the least   2330
To spy out a propitious occasion.
FAUST   With several hours or so, at the most,
I could seduce her handily—
Don't need the Devil to pimp for me,
MEPHISTO   You're talking like a Frenchman now.   2335
Calm down, there's no cause for vexation.
You'll find that instant gratification
Disappoints. If you allow
For compliments and billets doux,
Whisperings and rendezvous,   2340
The pleasure's felt so much more keenly.
Italian novels teach you exactly.
FAUST   I've no use for your slow-paced courting,
My appetite needs no supporting.
MEPHISTO   Please, I'm being serious.   2345
With such a pretty little miss
You mustn't be impetuous
And assault the fortress frontally.
What's called for here is strategy.
FAUST   Something of hers, do you hear, I require!   2350
Come, show me the way to the room she sleeps in,
Get me a scarf, a glove, a ribbon,
A garter with which to feed my desire!
MEPHISTO   To prove to you my earnest intention
By every means to further your passion,   2355
Not losing a minute, without delay,
I'll take you to her room today.
FAUST   I'll see her, yes? And have her?

---

1. The German reads *Hans Liederlich*, meaning a profligate because *liederlich* means "careless"
or "dissolute."

MEPHISTO   No!
  She'll be at a neighbor's—you *must* go slow!
  Meanwhile alone there, in her room,   2360
  You'll steep yourself in her perfume
  And dream of the delights to come.
FAUST   Can we start now?
MEPHISTO   Too soon! Be patient!
FAUST   Then find me a pretty thing for a present.

                                        Exit.

MEPHISTO   Presents already? The man's proving a lover!—   2365
  Now for his gift, I know there's treasure
  Buried in many an out-of-the way corner.
  Off I go to reconnoiter!

                    Evening

A small room, very neat and clean.

MARGARETE [*As she braids her hair and puts it up*]
  I'd give a lot to know, I would,
  Who the gentleman was today.   2370
  He seemed a fine man, decent, good,
  And from a noble house, I'm sure;
  It shows on him as plain as day—
  To be so bold! Who else would dare?

                                        Exit.

MEPHISTOPHELES, FAUST.

MEPHISTO   Come in now, in!—but quietly, take care.   2375
FAUST [*After a silent interval*]   Leave, please, leave me on my own.
MEPHISTO [*Sniffing around*]   Not every girl keeps things so spic and span.

                                        Exit.

FAUST   Welcome, evening's twilight gloom,
  Stealing through this holy room,
  Possess my heart, oh love's sweet anguish,   2380
  That lives in hope, in hope must languish.
  How still it's here, how happily
  It breathes good order and contentment,
  What riches in this poverty,
  What bliss there is in this confinement!   2385
      [*He flings himself into a leather armchair by the bed.*]
  Receive me as in generations past
  You received the happy and distressed.
  How often, I know, children crowded round
  This chair where their grandfather sat enthroned.
  Perhaps my darling too, a round-cheeked child,   2390
  Grateful for her Christmas present, held
  Reverentially his shrunken hand.

I feel, dear girl, where you are all is comfort,
Where you are, order, goodness all abound.
Maternally instructed by your spirit,   2395
Daily you spread the clean cloth on the table,
Sprinkle the sand on the floor so carefully—[1]
O lovely hand! Hand of a lovely angel
That's made of this home something heavenly.
And here—!
     [*He lifts a bed curtain.*]
              I tremble, frightened, with delight!   2400
Here I could linger hour after hour.
Here the dear creature, gently dreaming, slept,
Her angel substance slowly shaped by Nature.
Here warm life in her tender bosom swelled,
Here by a pure and holy weaving   2405
Of the strands, was revealed
The angelic being.

But me? What is it brought me here?
See how shaken I am, how nervous!
What do I want? Why am I so anxious?   2410
Poor Faust, I hardly know you any more.

Has this room put a spell on me?
I came here burning up with lust,
And melt with love now, helplessly.
Are we blown about by every gust?   2415

And if she came in now, this minute,
How I'd pay dear, I would, for it.
The big talker, Herr Professor,
Would dwindle to nothing, grovel before her.
MEPHISTO [*Entering*]   Hurry! I saw her, she's coming up.   2420
FAUST   Hurry indeed, I'll never come here again!
MEPHISTO   Here's a jewel box I snatched up
When I—but who cares how or when.
Put it in the closet there,
She'll jump for joy when she comes on it.   2425
It's got a number of choice things in it,
Meant for another—but I declare,
Girls are girls, they're all the same,
The only thing that matters is the game.
FAUST   Should I, I wonder?
MEPHISTO   *Should* you, you say!   2430
Do you mean to keep it for yourself?
If what you're after's treasure, pelf,
Then I have wasted my whole day,

---

1. Floors were sprinkled with sand after cleaning.

Been put to a lot of needless bother,
I hope you aren't some awful miser—   2435
After all my head-scratching, scheming, labor!
    [*He puts the box in the closet and shuts it.*]
Come on, let's go!
Our aim? Your darling's favor,
So you may do with her as you'd like to do.
And you do what? Only gape,   2440
As if going into your lecture hall,
Looming before you in human shape
Stood physics and metaphysics, ancient, stale.
Come on!

                                                 Exit.

MARGARETE [*With a lamp*] How close, oppressive it's in here.   2445
    [*She opens the window.*]
And yet outside it isn't warm.
I feel, I don't know why, so queer—
I wish Mother would come home,
I'm shivering so in every limb.
What a foolish, frightened girl I am!   2450
    [*She sings as she undresses.*]
There was a king in Thule,[2]
No truer man drank up,
To whom his mistress, dying,
Gave a golden cup.

Nothing he held dearer,   2455
And mid the feasters' cries,
Each time he drained the beaker
Tears started in his eyes.

And when death knocked, he tallied
His towns and treasure up,   2460
Yielded his heirs all gladly,
All except the cup.

In the great hall of his fathers,
In the castle by the sea,
He and his knights sat down to   2465
Their last revelry.

Up stood the old carouser,
A last time knew wine's warmth,
Then pitched his beloved beaker
Down into the gulf.   2470

2. The fabled *Ultima Thule* of Latin literature—those distant lands just beyond the reach of
every explorer. Goethe wrote the ballad in 1774; it was published in 1782 and set to music by
several composers.

He saw it fall and founder,
Deep, deep down it sank,
His eyes grew dim and never
Another drop he drank.
[*She opens the closet to put her clothes away and sees the jewel box.*]
How did this pretty box get here? 2475
I locked the closet, I'm quite sure.
Whatever's in the box? Maybe
Mother took it in pledge today.
And there's the little key on a ribbon.
I think I'd like to open it! 2480
—Look at all this, God in Heaven!
I've never seen the like of it!
Jewels! And *such* jewels, that a fine lady
Might wear on a great holiday.
How would the necklace look on me? 2485
Who is it owns these wonderful things?
 [*She puts the jewelry on and stands in front of the mirror.*]
I wish they were mine, these fine earrings!
When you put them on, you're changed completely.
What good's your pretty face, your youth,
Nice to have but little worth. 2490
Men praise you, do it half in pity,
What's on their minds is money, money,
Gold is their god, all—
Oh us poor people!

Out Walking

FAUST *strolling up and down, thinking. To him* MEPHISTOPHELES.

MEPHISTO   By true love cruelly scorned! By Hellfire fierce and fiery! 2495
  If only I could think of worse to swear by!
FAUST   What's eating you, now what's the trouble?
  Such a face I've not seen till today.
MEPHISTO   The Devil take me, that's what I would say,
  If it didn't so happen I'm the Devil. 2500
FAUST   Are you in your right mind—behaving
  Like a madman, wildly raving?
MEPHISTO   The jewels I got for Gretchen,[1] just imagine—
  Every piece a damned priest's stolen!
  The minute her mother saw them, she 2505
  Began to tremble fearfully.
  The woman has a nose! It's stuck
  Forever in her prayerbook,
  She knows right off, by the smell alone,

---

1. Diminutive of the German *Margarete*. She is called Gretchen for much of the play.

If something's sacred or profane;   2510
One whiff of the jewelry was enough
To tell her something's wrong with the stuff.
My child—she cried—and listen well to me,
All property obtained unlawfully
Does body and soul a mortal injury.   2515
These jewels we'll consecrate to the Blessed Virgin,
And for reward have showers of manna from Heaven.
Our little Margaret pouted, loath—
Why look a gift horse[2] in the mouth?
And surely the one who gave her it   2520
So generously, was hardly wicked.
Her mother sent for the priest, and he,
Seeing how the land lay,
Was mightily pleased. You've done, he said,
Just as you should, mother and maid;   2525
Who overcometh is repaid.
The Church's maw's remarkably capacious,
Gobbles up whole realms, everything precious,
Nor once suffers qualms, not even belches;
The Church alone is able to digest   2530
Goods illegitimately possessed.

FAUST   That's the way the whole world over,
From a King to a Jew, so all do ever.

MEPHISTO   So then he pockets brooches, chains and rings
As if they were the cheapest household things,   2535
And gives the women as much of a thank-you
As a body gets for a mouldy potato.
In Heaven, he says, you will receive your reward:
The women, uplifted, are reassured.

FAUST   And Gretchen?

MEPHISTO   Sits there restlessly,   2535
Her mind confused, her will uncertain,
Thinks about jewels night and day,
Even more about her unknown patron.

FAUST   I can't bear that she should suffer;
Find her new ones immediately!   2545
Poor stuff, those others, hardly suit her.

MEPHISTO   Oh yes indeed! With a snap of the fingers!

FAUST   Do what I say, march, man—how he lingers!
Insinuate yourself with her neighbor.
Damn it, devil, you move so sluggishly!   2550
Fetch Gretchen new and better jewelry!

MEPHISTO   Yes, yes, just as you wish, Your Majesty.

                                                   Exit FAUST.

---

2. Like the wooden horse in which Greek soldiers entered Troy to capture it; an emblem of
potential treachery.

A lovesick fool! To amuse his girl he'd blow up
Sun, moon, stars, the whole damned shop.

The Neighbor's House

MARTHE [*Alone*]   May God that man of mine condone!   2555
    He's done me wrong—like a bird
    Flew right off without a word
    And left me here to sleep alone.
    I never gave him cause for grief
    But loved him as a faithful wife.   2560
        [*She weeps.*]
    Suppose he's dead—oh I feel hopeless!
    If only I had an official notice.
        Enter MARGARETE.
MARGARETE   Frau Marthe!
MARTHE   Gretel, what's wrong, tell me!
MARGARETE   My knees are shaking, near collapse!
    Just now I found another box   2565
    Inside my closet. Ebony,
    And such things in it, much more splendid
    Than the first ones, I'm dumbfounded!
MARTHE   Never a word to your mother about it,
    Or the priest will have all the next minute.   2570
MARGARETE   Just look at this, and this, and this here!
MARTHE [*Decking her out in the jewels*]
    Oh, what a lucky girl you are!
MARGARETE   But I mustn't be seen in the street with such jewelry,
    And never in church. Oh, it's too cruel!
MARTHE   Come over to me whenever you're able,   2575
    Here you can wear them without any trouble,
    March back and forth in front of the mirror—
    Won't we enjoy ourselves together!
    And when it's a holiday, some such occasion,
    You can start wearing them, with discretion.   2580
    First a necklace, then a pearl earring,
    Your mother, she'll never notice anything,
    And if she does, why, we'll think of something.
MARGARETE   Who put the jewelry in my closet?
    There's something that's not right about it.   2585
        [*A knock*]
    Dear God above, can that be Mother?
MARTHE [*Peeping through the curtain*]
    Please come in!—No, it's a stranger.
        Enter MEPHISTOPHELES.
MEPHISTO   Good women, pardon, with your permission!
    I beg you to excuse the intrusion.
        [*Steps back deferentially from* MARGARETE.]
    I'm looking for Frau Marthe Schwerdtlein.   2590

MARTHE   I'm her. And what have you to say, sir?

MEPHISTO [*Under his breath to her*]
  Now I know who you are, that's enough.
  You have a lady under your roof,
  I'll go away and come back later.

MARTHE [*Aloud*]   Goodness, child, you won't believe me,   2595
  What the gentleman thinks is, you're a lady!

MARGARETE   A poor girl's what I am, no more.
  The gentleman's kind—I thank you, sir.
  These jewels don't belong to me.

MEPHISTO   Oh, it's not just the jewelry,   2600
  It's the Fräulein herself, so clear-eyed, serene.
  —So delighted I'm allowed to remain.

MARTHE   Why are you here, if you'll pardon the question.

MEPHISTO   I wish my news were pleasanter.
  Don't blame me, the messenger: 2605
  Your husband's dead, he sent his affection.

MARTHE   The good man's dead and gone, departed?
  Then I'll die too. Oh, I'm broken-hearted!

MARGARETE   Marthe dear, it's too violent, your sorrow!

MEPHISTO   Hear the sad story I've come to tell you.   2610

MARGARETE   As long as I live I'll love nobody, no!
  It would kill me with grief to lose my man so.

MEPHISTO   Joy's latter end is sorrow—and sorrow's joy.

MARTHE   Tell me how the dear man died.

MEPHISTO   He's buried in Padua, beside   2615
  The blessed saint, sweet Anthony,[1]
  In hallowed ground where he can lie
  In rest eternal, quietly.

MARTHE   And nothing else, sir, that is all?

MEPHISTO   A last request. He enjoins you solemnly: 2620
  Let three hundred masses be sung for his soul!
  As for anything else, my pocket's empty.

MARTHE   What! No jewel, nice souvenir,
  Such as every journeyman keeps in his wallet,
  And would sooner go hungry and beg than sell it?   2625

MEPHISTO   Nothing, I'm sorry to say, Madam dear.
  However—he never squandered his money,
  And he sincerely regretted his sins,
  Regretted even more he was so unlucky.

MARGARETE   Why must so many be so unhappy!   2630
  I'll pray for him often, sing requiems.

MEPHISTO   What a lovable creature, there's none dearer!
  What you should have now, right away,
  Is a good husband. It's true what I say.

---

1. Known for his care for the poor and the sick, St. Anthony of Padua is the patron saint of lost things.

MARGARETE   Oh no, it's not time yet, that must come later.   2635
MEPHISTO   If not now a husband, meanwhile a lover.
  What blessing from Heaven, which one of life's charms
  Rivals holding a dear thing like you in one's arms.
MARGARETE   With us people here it isn't the custom.
MEPHISTO   Custom or not, it's what's done and by more than some.   2640
MARTHE   Go on with your story, more's surely to come.
MEPHISTO   He lay on a bed of half-rotten straw,
  Better at least than a dunghill, and there
  He died as a Christian, knowing well
  Much remained outstanding on his bill.   2645
  "Oh how," he cried, "I hate myself!
  To abandon my trade, desert my wife!
  It kills me even to think of it,
  If only she would forgive and forget!"
MARTHE [*Weeping*]   I did, long ago! He's forgiven, the dear man.   2650
MEPHISTO   "But she's more to blame, God knows, than I am."
MARTHE   Liar! How shameless! At death's very door!
MEPHISTO   His mind wandered as the end drew near,
  If I'm anything of a connoisseur here.
  "No pleasure," he said, "no good times, nor anything nice;   2655
  First getting children, then getting them fed,
  By fed meaning lots more things than bread,
  With never a moment for having my bite in peace."
MARTHE   How could he forget my love and loyalty,
  My hard work day and night, the drudgery!   2660
MEPHISTO   He didn't forget, he remembered all tenderly.
  "When we set sail from Malta's port," he said,
  "For wife and children fervently I prayed.
  And Heaven, hearing, smiled down kindly,
  For we captured a Turkish vessel, stuffed   2665
  With the Sultan's treasure. How we rejoiced!
  Our courage being recompensed,
  I left the ship with a fatter purse
  Than ever I'd owned before in my life."
MARTHE   Treasure! Do you think he buried it?   2670
MEPHISTO   Who knows what's become of it?
  In Naples, where he wandered about,
  A pretty miss with a kind heart
  Showed the stranger such good will,
  Till the day he died he felt it still.   2675
MARTHE   The villain! Robbing his children, his wife!
  And for all our misery, dire need,
  He would never give up his scandalous life.
MEPHISTO   Well, he's been paid, the man is dead.
  If I were in your shoes, my dear,   2680
  I'd mourn him decently a year
  And meanwhile keep an eye out for another.
MARTHE   Dear God, I'm sure it won't be easy
  To find, on this earth, his successor;

So full of jokes he was, so merry!　　　　　　　　　　　　2685
But he was restless, always straying,
Loved foreign women, foreign wine,
And how he loved, drat him, dice-playing.

MEPHISTO　Oh well, I'm sure things worked out fine
If he was equally forgiving.　　　　　　　　　　　　　　　2690
With such an arrangement, why, I swear,
I'd marry you myself, my dear!

MARTHE　Oh sir, you would? You're joking, I'm sure!

MEPHISTO [*Aside*]　Time to leave! This one's an ogress,
She'd sue the Devil for breach of promise!　　　　　　　　2695
　　　[*To* GRETCHEN]
And what's your love life like, my charmer?

MARGARETE　What do you mean?

MEPHISTO [*Aside*]　　　　　　　　Oh you good girl,
All innocence! [*Aloud*] And now farewell.

MARGARETE　Farewell.

MARTHE　　　　　　　　Quick, one last matter.
If you would. I want to know　　　　　　　　　　　　　2700
If I might have some proof to show
How and when my husband died
And where the poor man now is laid?
I like to have things right and proper,
With a notice published in the paper.　　　　　　　　　　2705

MEPHISTO　Madam, yes. To attest the truth,
Two witnesses must swear an oath.
I know someone, a good man, we
Will go before the notary.
I'll introduce you to him.

MARTHE　　　　　　　　　Do.　　　　　　　　　　　2710

MEPHISTO　And she'll be here, your young friend, too?—
A very fine fellow who's been all over,
So polite to ladies, so urbane his behavior.

MARGARETE　I'd blush for shame before the gentleman.

MEPHISTO　No, not before a king or any man!　　　　　　2715

MARTHE　We'll wait for you tonight, the two of us,
Inside my garden, just behind the house.

A Street

FAUST, MEPHISTOPHELES.

FAUST　Well, speak! It's on? When will I have her?

MEPHISTO　Bravo, bravo, aren't you on fire!
Very shortly Gretchen will be all yours;　　　　　　　　　2720
This evening you will meet her at her neighbor's.
The worthy Mistress Marthe, I confess,
Needs no instruction as a procuress.

FAUST
Well done.

MEPHISTO   But something we must do for her.

FAUST   One good turn deserves another.   2725

MEPHISTO   All it is is swear an oath
  Her husband's laid out in the earth
  At Padua in consecrated ground.

FAUST   So we must make a trip there—very smart!

MEPHISTO   Sancta simplicitas![1] Whoever said that?   2730
  Just swear an oath, is all. You frowned?

FAUST   If that's the best you're able, count me out.

MEPHISTO   The saintly fellow! Turned devout.
  Declaring falsely—Heaven forbid!—
  Is something Faustus never did.   2735
  Haven't you pontificated
  About God and the world, undisconcerted,
  About man, man's mind and heart and being,
  As bold as brass, without blushing?
  Look at it closely and what's the truth?   2740
  You know as much about those things
  As you know about Herr Schwerdtlein's death.

FAUST   You always were a sophist[2] and a liar.

MEPHISTO   Indeed, indeed. If we look ahead a little further,
  To tomorrow, what do we see?   2745
  You swearing, oh so honorably,
  Your soul is Gretchen's, for ever and ever.

FAUST   My soul, and all my heart as well.

MEPHISTO   Oh noble, great!
  You'll swear undying faith and love eternal,
  Go on about desire unique and irresistable,   2750
  About longing, boundless, infinite.
  That, too, with all your loving heart.

FAUST   With all my heart! And now enough.
  What I feel, an emotion of such depth,
  Such turbulence—when I try to find   2755
  A name for it and nothing comes to mind,
  And cast about, search heaven and earth
  For words to express its transcendent worth,
  And call the fire in which I burn
  Eternal, yes, eternal, yes, undying,   2760
  Do you really mean to tell me
  That's just devil's doing, deception, lying?

MEPHISTO
  Say what you please, I'm right.

FAUST   One word more, one only,
  And then I'll save my breath. A man who is unyielding,
  Sure, absolutely, he's right, and has a tongue in his mouth—   2765
  Is right. So come, I'm sick of arguing.

---

1. Holy simplicity (Latin).   2. Philosopher.

You're right, and the reason's simple enough:
I must do what I must, can't help myself.

A Garden

MARGARETE *with* FAUST, *her arm linked with his:* MARTHE *with* MEPHISTOPHELES.
The two couples stroll up and down.

MARGARETE   You are too kind, sir, I am sure it's meant
  To spare a simple girl embarrassment.   2770
  A traveler finds whatever amusement he can,
  You've been all over, you're a gentleman—
  How can anything I say
  Interest you in any way?
FAUST   One word of yours, a single look's   2775
  Worth all the science in our books.
    [*He kisses her hand.*]
MARGARETE   No, no, sir, please, you mustn't! How could you kiss
  A hand so ugly—red and coarse?
  You can't imagine all the work I do:
  My mother must have things just so.   2780
    [*They walk on.*]
MARTHE   And you, sir, I believe you constantly travel?
MEPHISTO   Business, business! It is so demanding!
  Leaving a place you like, oh, it is dismal,
  But on you've got to go, it's just unending.
MARTHE   How fine when young and full of ginger   2785
  To roam the world, go everywhere,
  But grim days come, come even grimmer,
  When no one likes what lies in store—
  Likes crawling to his grave a lonely bachelor.
MEPHISTO   When I look at what's ahead, I tremble.   2790
MARTHE   Then think about it while you're able.
    [*They walk on.*]
MARGARETE   Yes, out of sight is out of mind.
  It's second nature with you, gallantry;
  But you have friends of every kind,
  Cleverer by far, oh much, than me.   2795
FAUST   Dear girl, believe me, what's called cleverness
  Is mostly shallowness and vanity.
MARGARETE   What do you mean?
FAUST   God, isn't it a pity
  That unspoiled innocence and simpleness
  Should never know itself and its own worth,   2800
  That meekness, lowliness, those highest gifts
  Kindly Nature endows us with—
MARGARETE   You'll think of me for a moment or two,
  I'll have hours enough to think of you.
FAUST   You're alone a good deal, are you?   2805

MARGARETE   Our family's very small, it's true,
  But still it has to be looked to.
  We have no maid, I sweep the floors, I cook and knit
  And sew, do all the errands, morning and night.
  Mother's very careful about money,   2810
  All's accounted for to the last penny.
  Not that she really needs to pinch and save,
  We can afford much more than others have.
  My father left us a good bit,
  With a small dwelling part of it,   2815
  And a garden just outside the city.
  But lately I've lived quietly.
  My brother is a soldier. My little sister died.
  The trouble that she cost me, the poor child!
  But I loved her very much, I'd gladly do   2820
  It all again.
FAUST   An angel, if at all like you.
MARGARETE   All the care of her was mine,
  And she was very fond of her sister.
  My father died before she was born,
  And Mother, well, we nearly lost her;   2825
  It took so long, oh many months, till she got better.
  It was out of the question she should nurse
  The poor little crying thing herself.
  So I nursed her, on milk and water.
  I felt she was my own daughter,   2830
  In my arms, upon my lap,
  She smiled and kicked, grew round and plump.
FAUST   The happiness it must have given you!
MARGARETE   But it was hard on me so often, too.
  Her crib stood at my bedside, near my head,   2835
  A slightest movement, cradle's creak,
  And instantly I was awake;
  I'd give her a bottle or take her into my bed.
  If still she fretted, up I'd raise,
  Walk up and down with her swaying and crooning,   2840
  And be at the washtub early the next morning.
  To market after that and getting the hearth to blaze,
  And so it went day after day, always.
  Home's not always cheerful, be it said,
  But still—how good your supper, good your bed.   2845
    [*They walk on.*]
MARTHE   It's very hard on us poor women.
  You bachelors don't listen, you're so stubborn.
MEPHISTO   What's needed are more charmers like yourself
  To bring us bachelors down from off the shelf.
MARTHE   There's never, sir, been anyone? Confess!   2850
  You've never lost your heart to one of us?
MEPHISTO   How does the proverb go? A loving wife,

And one's own hearthside, are more worth
Than all the gold that's hidden in the earth.

MARTHE   I mean, you've had no wish, yourself?   2855

MEPHISTO   Oh, everywhere I've been received politely.

MARTHE   No, what I mean is, hasn't there been somebody
    Who ever made your heart beat? Seriously?

MEPHISTO   It's never a joking matter with women, believe me.

MARTHE   Oh, you don't understand!

MEPHISTO   So sorry. Still,   2860
    I can see that you are—amiable.
            [*They walk on.*]

FAUST   You recognized me, angel, instantly
    When I came through the gate into the garden?

MARGARETE   I dropped my eyes. Didn't you see?

FAUST   And you'll forgive the liberty, you'll pardon   2865
    My swaggering up in that insulting fashion
    When you came out of the church door?

MARGARETE   I was shocked. Never before
    Had I been spoken to like that.
    I'm a good girl. Who would dare   2870
    To be so free with me, so smart?
    It seemed to me at once you thought
    There's a girl who can be bought
    On the spot. Did I look a flirt?
    Is that so, tell! Well, I'll admit   2875
    A voice spoke "Isn't he nice?" in my breast,
    And oh how vexed with myself I felt
    When I wasn't vexed with you in the least.

FAUST   Dear girl!

MARGARETE   Just wait.
            [*Picking a daisy and plucking the petals one by one*]

FAUST   What is it for, a bouquet?

MARGARETE   Only a little game of ours.

FAUST   A game, is it?   2880

MARGARETE   Never mind. I'm afraid you'll laugh at me.
            [*Murmuring to herself as she plucks the petals*]

FAUST   What are you saying!

MARGARETE [*Under her breath*]
                            Loves me—loves me not—

FAUST   Oh, what a creature, heavenly!

MARGARETE [*Continuing*]   He loves me—not—he loves me—not—
            [*Plucking the last petal and crying out delightedly*]
    He loves me!

FAUST   Dearest, yes! Yes, let the flower be   2885
    The oracle by which the truth is said.
    He loves you! Do you understand?
    He loves you! Let me take your hand.
            [*He takes her hands in his.*]

MARGARETE   I'm afraid!

FAUST   Read the look on my face,   2890
  Feel my hands gripping yours,
  They say what is the case,
  Can't ever be put in words:
  Utter surrender, and such rapture
  As must never end, must last forever!   2895
  Yes, forever! An end—it would betoken
  Utter despair! a heart forever broken!
  No—no end! No end!
      [MARGARETE *squeezes his hands, frees herself and runs away.*
      He doesn't move for a moment, thinking, then follows her.]
MARTHE   It's getting dark.
MEPHISTO   That's right. We have to go.
MARTHE   Please forgive me if I don't invite   2900
  You in. But ours is such a nasty-minded street,
  You'd think people had no more to do
  Than watch their neighbors' every coming and going.
  The gossip that goes on here, about nothing!
  But where are they, our little couple?
MEPHISTO   Flew   2905
  Up that path like butterflies.
MARTHE   He seems to like her.
MEPHISTO   And she him. Which is the way the world wags ever.

A *Summerhouse*

GRETCHEN *runs in and hides behind the door, putting her fingertips to her lips and
peeping through a crack.*

MARGARETE   Here he comes!
FAUST   You're teasing me, yes, are you?
  I've got you now! [*Kisses her.*]
MARGARETE [*Holding him around and returning the kiss*]
                          My heart! Oh, how I love you!   2910
        MEPHISTOPHELES *knocks.*
FAUST [*Stamping his foot*]
  Who's there?
MEPHISTO   A friend.
FAUST   A fiend!
MEPHISTO   We must be on our way.
MARTHE [*Coming up*]   Yes, sir, it's late.
FAUST   I'd like to walk you home.
MARGARETE   My mother, I'm afraid . . . Goodbye!
FAUST   So we must say
  Goodbye? Goodbye!
MARGARETE   I hope I'll see you soon.
                              Exit FAUST *and* MEPHISTOPHELES.

Good God, the thoughts that fill the head   2915
Of such a man, oh it's astounding!
I stand there dumbly, my face red,
And stammer yes to everything.
I don't understand. What in the world
Does he see in me, an ignorant child?   2920

Forest and Cavern

FAUST [*Alone*]   Sublime Spirit, all that I asked for, all,
You gave me. Not for nothing was it,
The face you showed me all ablaze with fire.
You gave me glorious Nature for my kingdom,
With the power to feel, to delight in her—nor as   2925
A spectator only, coolly admiring her wonders,
But letting me see deep into her bosom
As a man sees deep into a dear friend's heart.
Before me you make pass all living things,
From high to low, and teach me how to know   2930
My brother creatures in the woods, the streams, the air.
And when the shrieking storm winds make the forest
Groan, toppling the giant fir whose fall
Bears nearby branches down with it and crushes
Neighboring trees so that the hill returns   2935
A hollow thunder—oh, then you lead me to
The shelter of this cave, lay bare my being to myself,
And all the mysteries hidden in my depths
Unfold themselves and open to the day.
And when I see the moon ascend the sky,   2940
Shedding a pure, assuaging light, out
Of the walls of rock, the dripping bushes, float
The silver figures of antiquity
And temper meditation's austere joy.

That nothing perfect's ever ours, oh but   2945
I know it now. Together with the rapture
That I owe you, by which I am exalted
Nearer and still nearer to the gods, you gave me
A familiar, a creature whom already
I can't do without, though he's a cold   2950
And shameless devil who drags me down
In my own eyes and with a whisper turns
All the gifts you gave me into nothing.
The longing that I feel for that enchanting
Figure of a girl he busily blows up   2955
Into a leaping flame. And so desire
Whips me stumbling on to seize enjoyment,
And once enjoyed, I languish for desire.

Enter MEPHISTOPHELES.

MEPHISTO   Aren't you fed up with it by now,
  This mooning about? How can it still   2960
  Amuse you? You do it for a while,
  All right, but enough's enough, on to the new!
FAUST   I wish you'd more to do than criticize
  The peace I feel on one of my good days.
MEPHISTO A breather you want? Very well, I grant it;   2965
  But don't speak so, as if you really meant it.
  I wouldn't shed tears losing a companion
  Who is so mad, so rude, so sullen;
  I have my hands full every minute—
  Impossible to tell what pleases you or doesn't.   2970
FAUST   Why, that's just perfect, isn't it?
  He bores me stiff and wants praise for it.
MEPHISTO   You poor earthly creature, would
  You ever have managed at all without me?
  Whom do you have to thank for being cured   2975
  Of your mad ideas, your feverish frenzy?
  If not for me you would have disappeared
  From off the face of earth already.
  A life, you call it, to be brooding
  Owl-like in caves or toad-like feeding   2980
  On oozing moss and dripping stones?
  That's a way to spend your time?
  The old Doctor still lives in your bones.
FAUST   Try to understand, my life's renewed
  When I wander in communion with wild Nature;   2985
  But even if you could I know you would
  Begrudge me, Devil that you are, my rapture.
MEPHISTO   Oh my! Your rapture—superterrestrial!
  Sprawled on a hillside in the nocturnal dewfall,
  Penetrating intuitively the bowels of the earth,   2990
  All the six days of Creation unfolding inside yourself,
  In your arrogance enjoying I don't know what satisfaction,
  Amorously immerging with the all in its perfection,
  Nary a trace left of the child born of this earth,
  And then as finis to your deep, deep insight—   2995
    [*Making a gesture*]
  I forbid myself to say, it's not polite.
FAUST   Ugh! Oh ugly!
MEPHISTO   That's not what you care for?
  You're right, "ugh"'s right, the moral comment called for.
  Never a word, when chaste ears are about,
  Of what chaste souls can't do without.   3000
  Oh well, go on amuse yourself
  By duping now and then yourself.
  Yet you can't keep on like this any longer,
  You look done in again, almost a goner.

If you persist so, in this fashion, 3005
You'll go mad with baffled passion.
Enough, I say! Your sweetheart sits down there
And all's a dismal prison for her.
You haunt her mind continually,
She's mad about you, oh completely. 3010
At first your passion, like a freshet[1]
Swollen with melted snow, overflowing
Its peaceful banks, engulfed a soul unknowing,
But now the flood's thinned to a streamlet.
Instead of playing monarch of the wood, 3015
My opinion is the Herr Professor
Should make the silly little creature
Some return in gratitude.
For her the hours creep along,
She stands at the window watching the clouds 3020
Pass slowly over the old town walls,
"Lend me, sweet bird, your wings," is the song
She sings all day and half the night.
Sometimes she's cheerful, mostly she's downhearted,
Sometimes she cries as if brokenhearted, 3025
Then she's calm again and seems all right,
And heart-sick always.

FAUST Serpent! Snake!

MEPHISTO [*Aside*] I'll have you yet!

FAUST Away, you monster from some stinking fen! 3030
Don't mention her, the soul itself of beauty,
Don't make my half-crazed senses crave again
The sweetness of that lovely body!

MEPHISTO Then what? She thinks you've taken flight,
And I must say, the girl's half right. 3035

FAUST Far off as I may go, still she is near me,
She fills my thoughts both day and night,
I even envy the Lord's flesh the kiss
Her lips bestow upon it at the mass.[2]

MEPHISTO I understand. I've often envied *you* 3040
Her pair of roes that feed among the lilies.[3]

FAUST Pimp! I won't hear your blasphemies.

MEPHISTO Fine! Insult me! And I laugh at you.
The God that made you girls and boys
Himself was first to recognize, 3045
And practice, what's the noblest calling,
The furnishing of opportunities.
Away! A crying shame this, never linger!

---

1. Stream.
2. That is, when Margarete takes Communion, in which bread is miraculously turned to the body of Christ.

3. Compare the Song of Solomon 4:5: "Thy two breasts are like two young roes that are twins, which feed among the lilies."

> You act as if hard fate were dragging
> You to death, not to your truelove's chamber. 3050
> FAUST Heaven's out-heavened when she holds me tight,
> And though I'm warmed to life upon her breast,
> Do I ever once forget her plight?
> Am I not a fugitive, a beast,
> That's houseless, restless, purposeless, 3055
> A furious, impatient cataract
> That plunges down from rock to rock to the abyss?
> And she, her senses unawakened, a child still,
> Dwelt in her cottage on the Alpine meadow,
> Her life the same domestic ritual 3060
> Within a little world where fell no shadow.
> And I, abhorred by God,
> Was not content to batter
> Rocks to bits, I had
> To undermine her peace and overwhelm her! 3065
> This sacrifice you claimed, Hell, as your due!
> Help me, Devil, please, to shorten
> The anxious time I must go through!
> Let happen quick what has to happen!
> Let her fate fall on me, too, crushingly, 3070
> And both together perish, her and me!
> MEPHISTO All worked up again, all in a sweat!
> On your way, you fool, and comfort her.
> When dolts like you are baffled, don't know what,
> They think it's hopeless, the end near. 3075
> Long live the man who keeps on undeterred!
> I'd rate your progress as a devil pretty fair;
> But tell me, what is there that's more absurd
> Than a moping devil, mewling in despair?

Gretchen's Room

> GRETCHEN [*Alone at her spinning wheel*]
> My heart is heavy, 3080
> My peace gone,
> I'll never know any
> Peace again.
>
> For me it's death
> Where he is not, 3085
> The whole earth
> Waste, desert, rot.
>
> My poor poor head
> Is in a whirl,
> For sure I'm mad, 3090
> A poor mad girl.

My heart is heavy,
My peace gone,
I'll never know any
Peace again.   3095

I look out the window,
Walk out the door,
Him, only him,
I look for.

His bold walk,   3100
His princely person,
His smiling look,
His eyes' persuasion,

And his sweet speech—
Magicalness!   3105
His fingers' touch
And oh his kiss!

My heart is heavy,
My peace gone,
I'll never know any
Peace again.   3110

With aching breast
I strain so toward him,
Oh if I just
Could catch and hold him,   3115

And kiss him and kiss him,
Never ceasing,
Though I should die in
His arms kissing.

Marthe's Garden

MARGARETE, FAUST.

MARGARETE   Heinrich,[1] the truth—I have to insist!   3120
FAUST   As far as I'm able.
MARGARETE   Well, tell me, you must,
  About your religion—how do you feel?
  You're such a good man, kind and intelligent,
  Yet I suspect you are indifferent.
FAUST   Enough of that, my child. You know quite well   3125

---

1. That is, Faust. In the legend, Faust's name was generally Johann (John). Goethe changed it to
Heinrich (Henry).

I cherish you so very dearly,
For those I love I'd give my life up gladly,
And I never interfere with people's faith.

MARGARETE That isn't right, you've got to have belief!

FAUST You do?   3130

MARGARETE I know you think I am a dunce!
  You don't respect the sacraments.

FAUST I do respect them.

MARGARETE   Not enough to go to mass.
  And tell me when you last went to confess?
  Do you believe in God?

FAUST   Who, my dear,   3135
  Can say, I believe in God?
  Ask any priest or learned scholar
  And what you get by way of answer
  Sounds like mockery of a fool.

MARGARETE So you don't believe in God.   3140

FAUST Don't misunderstand me, lovely girl.
  Who dares name him,
  Dares affirm him,
  Dares say he believes?
    Who, feeling doubt,   3145
  Ventures to say right out,
  I don't believe?
  The All-embracing,
  All-sustaining,
  Sustains and embraces   3150
  Himself and you and me.
  Overhead the great sky arches,
  Firm lies the earth beneath our feet,
  And the friendly shining stars, don't they
  Mount aloft eternally?   3155
  Don't my eyes, seeking your eyes, meet?
  And all that is, doesn't it weigh
  On your mind and heart,
  In eternal secrecy working,
  Visibly, invisibly, about you?—   3160
  Fill heart with it to overflowing
  In an ecstasy of blissful feeling
  Which then call what you would:
  Happiness! Heart! Love! Call it God!—
  I know no name for it, nor look   3165
  For one. Feeling is all,
  Names noise and smoke
  Dimming the heavenly fire.

MARGARETE I guess what you say is all right,
  The priest speaks so, or pretty near,   3170
  Except his language isn't yours, not quite.

FAUST I speak as all speak here below,

All souls beneath bright heaven's day,
They use the language that they know,
And I use mine. Why shouldn't I?   3175
MARGARETE   It sounds fine when it's put your way,
But something's wrong, there's still a question;
The truth is, you are not a Christian.
FAUST   Now darling!
MARGARETE   I have suffered so much, I can't sleep
To see the company you keep.   3180
FAUST   Company?
MARGARETE   That man you always have with you,
I loathe him, oh how much I do
In all my life I can't remember
Anything that's made me shiver   3185
More than his face has, so horrid, hateful!
FAUST   Silly thing, don't be so fearful.
MARGARETE   His presence puts my blood into a turmoil.
I like people, most of them indeed;
But even as I long for you,   3190
I think of him with secret dread—
And he's a scoundrel, he is too!
If I'm unjust, forgive me, Lord.
FAUST   It takes all kinds to make a world.
MARGARETE   I wouldn't want to have his kind around me!   3195
His lips curl so sarcastically,
Half angrily,
When he pokes his head inside the door.
You can see there's nothing he cares for;
It's written on his face as plain as day   3200
He loves no one, we're all his enemy.
I'm so happy with your arms around me,
I'm yours, and feel so warm, so free, so easy,
But when he's here it knots up so inside me.
FAUST   You angel, you, atremble with foreboding!   3205
MARGARETE   What I feel's so strong, so overwhelming,
That let him join us anywhere
And right away I almost fear
I don't love you anymore.
And when he's near, my lips refuse to pray,   3210
Which causes me such agony.
Don't you feel the same way too?
FAUST   It's just that you dislike him so.
MARGARETE   I must go now.
FAUST   Shall we never
Pass a quiet time alone together,   3215
Breast pressed to breast, our two beings one?
MARGARETE   Oh, if I only slept alone!
I'd draw the bolt for you tonight, yes, gladly;
But my mother sleeps so lightly,

And if we were surprised by her   3220
I know I'd die right then and there.
FAUST   Angel, there's no need to worry.
Here's a vial—three drops only
In her cup will subdue nature
And lull her into pleasant slumber.   3225
MARGARETE   What would I say no
To when you ask?
It won't harm her, though
There is no risk?
FAUST   If there were,   3230
Would I suggest you give it her?
MARGARETE   Let me only look at you
And I don't know, I have to do
Your least wish.
I have gone so far already,   3235
How much farther's left for me to go?

                                                   Exit.

   Enter MEPHISTOPHELES.
MEPHISTO   The girl's a goose! I hope she's gone.
FAUST   Spying around are you, again?
MEPHISTO   I heard it all, yes, every bit of it,
How she put the Doctor through his catechism,   3240
From which he'll have, I trust, much benefit.
Does a fellow stick to the old, the true religion?—
That's what all the girls are keen to know.
If he minds there, they think, he'll mind us too.
FAUST   Monster, lacking the least comprehension   3245
How such a soul, so loving, pure,
Whose faith is all in all to her,
The sole means to obtain salvation,
Should be tormented by the fear
The one she loves is damned forever!   3250
MEPHISTO   You transcendental, hot and sensual Romeo,
See how a little skirt's got you in tow.
FAUST   You misbegotten thing of filth and fire!
MEPHISTO   And she's an expert, too, in physiognomy.
When I come in, she feels—what, she's not sure;   3255
This face I wear hides a dark mystery;
I'm a genius of some kind, a bad one,
About that she is absolutely certain,
Even the Devil, very possibly.
Now about tonight—?
FAUST   What's that to you?   3260
MEPHISTO   I get my fun out of it too.

At the Well

GRETCHEN *and* LIESCHEN *carrying pitchers.*

LIESCHEN You've heard about our Barbara, have you?
GRETCHEN No, not a word. I hardly see a soul.
LIESCHEN Sybil told me; yes, the whole thing's true.
 She's gone and done it now, the little fool.   3265
 You see what comes of being so stuck up!
GRETCHEN What comes?
LIESCHEN   Oh, it smells bad, it stinks.
 She's feeding two now when she eats and drinks.
GRETCHEN Oh dear!
LIESCHEN   Serves her right, if you ask me.
 How she kept after him, without a let-up,   3270
 Gadding about, the pair, and gallivanting
 Off to the village for the music, dancing;
 She had to be first always, everywhere,
 While he with wine and sweet cakes courted her.
 She thought her beauty echoed famously,   3275
 Accepted his gifts shamelessly,
 They kissed and fondled by the hour,
 Till it was goodbye to her little flower.
GRETCHEN The poor thing!
LIESCHEN   Poor thing, you say!
 While we two sat home spinning the whole day   3280
 And our mothers wouldn't let us out at night,
 She was where? Out—hugging her sweetheart
 On a bench or up a dark alley,
 And never found an hour passed too slowly.
 Well, now she's got to pay for it—   3285
 Shiver in church in her sinner's shift.
GRETCHEN He'll marry her. How can he not?
LIESCHEN He won't—he can.
 That one's too smart,
 He'll find a girlfriend elsewhere in a trice.   3290
 In fact he's gone.
GRETCHEN   But that's not nice!
LIESCHEN And if he does, she'll rue the day,
 The boys will snatch her bridal wreath away
 And we'll throw dirty straw down in her doorway.[1]
                                                   Exit.

GRETCHEN [*Turning to go home*]
 How full of blame I used to be, how scornful   3295
 Of any girl who got herself in trouble!

---

1. In Germany, this treatment was reserved for young women who had sexual relations before marriage.

I couldn't find words enough to express
My disgust for others' sinfulness.
Black as all their misdeeds seemed to be,
I blackened them still more, so cruelly,   3300
And still they weren't black enough for me.
I blessed myself, was smug and proud
To think I was so very good,
And who's the sinner now? Me, me, oh God!
Yet everything that brought me to it,   3305
God, was so good, oh, was so sweet!

The City Wall

In a niche in the wall, an image of the Mater Dolorosa[1] at the foot of the cross, with pots of flowers before it.

GRETCHEN [*Putting fresh flowers in the pots*]
    Look down, O
    Thou sorrow-rich Lady,
    On my need, in thy mercifulness aid me!

    With the sword in your heart,   3310
    With your infinite hurt,
    Upwards you look to your son's death.

    To the Father you gaze up.
    Send sighs upon sighs up,
    For his grief and your own sore grief.   3315

    Who's there knows
    How it gnaws
    Deep inside me, the pain?
    The heart-anguish I suffer,
    Fright, tremblings, desire?   3320
    You only know, you alone!

    Wherever I go, no matter,
    The woe, the woe I suffer
    Inside my bosom, aching!

    No sooner I'm alone   3325
    I moan, I moan, I moan,
    Mary, my heart is breaking!

    From the box outside my window,
    Dropping tears like dew,
    Leaning into the dawning,   3330
    I picked these flowers for you.

---

1. Sorrowful mother (Latin; literal trans.); that is, the Virgin Mary in mourning.

Into my bedroom early
The bright sun put his head,
Found me bolt upright sitting
Miserably on my bed.   3335

Help! Save me from shame and death!
Look down, O
Thou sorrow-rich Lady,
On my need, in thy mercifulness aid me!

Night

The street outside GRETCHEN's *door.*

VALENTINE [*A soldier,* GRETCHEN's *brother*]
Whenever at a bout the boys   3340
Would fill the tavern with the noise
Of their loud bragging, swearing Mattie,
Handsome Kate or blushing Mary
The finest girl in all the country,
Confirming what they said by drinking   3345
Many a bumper,¹ I'd say nothing,
My elbows on the table propped,
Till all their boasting at last stopped.
And then I'd stroke my beard, and smiling,
Say there was no point in quarrelling   3350
About taste; but tell me where
There was one who could compare,
A virgin who could hold a candle
To my beloved sister, Gretel?
Clink, clank, you heard the tankards rattle   3355
All around, and voices shout
He's right, he is, she gets our vote,
Among all her sex she has no equal!
Which stopped those others cold. But now—
I could tear my hair out, all,   3360
Run right up the side of the wall!
All the drunks are free to crow
Over me, to needle, sneer,
And I'm condemned to sitting there
Like a man with debts unpaid   3365
Who sweats in fear lest something's said.
I itch to smash them all, those beggars,
But still that wouldn't make them liars.

Who's sneaking up here? Who is that?
There's two! And one I bet's that rat.   3370
When I lay my hands on him

---

1. A drinking vessel filled to the top.

He won't be going home again!
    FAUST, MEPHISTOPHELES.

FAUST How through the window of the vestry, look,
  The flickering altar lamp that's always lit
  Upward throws its light, while dim and weak,   3375
  By darkness choked, a gleam dies at our feet.
  Just so all's night and gloom within my soul.
MEPHISTO But me, I'm itching like a tomcat on the prowl
  That slinks past fire ladders, hugs the wall.
  An honest devil I am, after all;   3380
  It's nothing serious, the little thievery
  I have in mind, the little lechery—
  It merely shows Walpurgis Night's already
  Spooking up and down inside me.
  Still another night of waiting, then   3385
  The glorious season's here again
  When a fellow finds out waking beats
  Sleeping life away between the sheets.
FAUST That flickering light I see, is that
  Buried treasure rising, what?   3390
MEPHISTO Very soon you'll have the pleasure
  Of lifting out a pot of treasure.
  The other day I stole a look—
  Such lovely coins, oh you're in luck!
FAUST No necklace, bracelet, some such thing   3395
  My darling can put on, a ring?
MEPHISTO I think I glimpsed a string of pearls—
  Just the thing to please the girls.
FAUST Good, good. It makes me feel unhappy
  When I turn up with my hands empty.   3400
MEPHISTO Why should you mind it if you can
  Enjoy a free visit now and then?
  Look up, how the heavens sparkle, star-full,
  Time for a song, a cunning one, artful:
  I'll sing her a ballad that's moral, proper,   3405
  So as to delude the baggage the better.
    [*Sings to the guitar.*]
      What brings you out before[2]
      Your sweet William's door,
      O Katherine, my dear,
        In morning's chill?   3410
      You pretty child, beware,
      The maid that enters there,
      Out she'll not come here
        A maiden still.

      Girls, listen, trust no one,   3415
      Or when all's said and done,

2. Lines 3407–22 are adapted by Goethe from Shakespeare's *Hamlet* 4.5.

You'll find yourselves undone
  And poor things, damned.
Of your good souls take care,
  Yield nothing though he swear,   3420
Until your finger wear
  A silver band.

VALENTINE [*Advancing*]
 Luring who here with that braying,
 Abominable rat catcher?
 The devil take that thing you're playing,   3425
 And then take you, you guitar scratcher!

MEPHISTO Smashed my guitar! Now it's no good at all.

VALENTINE And now I think I'll split your no good skull.

MEPHISTO [*To* FAUST] Hold your ground, Professor! At the ready!
 Stick close to me, I'll show you how.   3430
 Out with your pigsticker now!
 You do the thrusting, I will parry.

VALENTINE Parry that!

MEPHISTO   Why not?

VALENTINE   And this one too!

MEPHISTO Delighted, I am, oh much, to oblige you.

VALENTINE It's the Devil I think I'm fighting!—Who's grinning.   3435
 What's this? My hand is feeling feeble.

MEPHISTO [*To* FAUST] Stick him!

VALENTINE [*Falling*]   Oh!

MEPHISTO   See how the lout's turned civil.
 What's called for now is legwork. Off and running!
 In no time they will raise a hue and cry;
 I can manage sheriffs without trouble,   3440
 But not the High Judiciary.

              Exeunt.

MARTHE [*Leaning out of the window*]
 Neighbors, help!

GRETCHEN [*Leaning out of her window*]
    A light, a light!

MARTHE They curse and brawl, they scream and fight.

CROWD Here's one on the ground. He's dead.

MARTHE [*Coming out*] Where are the murderers? All fled?   3445

GRETCHEN [*Coming out*]
 Who's lying here?

CROWD   Your mother's son.

GRETCHEN My God, the misery, on and on.

VALENTINE I'm dying! Well, it's soon said, that,
 And sooner done. You women, don't
 Stand there blubbering away.   3450
 Come here, I've something I must say.
  [*All gather around him.*]
 Gretchen, look here, you're young yet,
 A green girl, not so smart about

Managing her business.
We know it, don't we, you and me,   3455
You're a whore, privately—
Go public, don't be shy, miss.
GRETCHEN   My brother! God! What wretchedness!
VALENTINE   You can leave God out of this.
What's done can't ever be undone,   3460
And as things went, so they'll go on.
You let in one at the back door,
Soon there'll be others, more and more—
A whole dozen, hot for pleasure,
And then the whole town for good measure.   3465

Shame is born in hugger-mugger,[3]
The lying-in veiled in black night,
And she is swaddled up so tight
In hopes the ugly thing will smother.
But as she thrives, grows bigger, bolder,   3470
The hussy's eager to step out,
Though she has grown no prettier.
The more she's hateful to the sight,
The more the creature seeks the light.

I look ahead and I see what?   3475
The honest people of this place
Standing back from you, you slut,
As from a plague-infected corpse.
When they look you in the face
You'll cringe with shame, pierced to the heart.   3480
In church they'll drive you from the altar,
No wearing gold chains any more,
No putting on a fine lace collar
For skipping round on the dance floor.
You'll hide in dark and dirty corners   3485
With limping cripples, lousy beggars.
God may pardon you at last,
But here on earth you stand accurst.
MARTHE   Look up to God and ask his mercy!
Don't add to all your other sins   3490
Sacrilege and blasphemy.
VALENTINE   If I could only lay my hands
On your scrawny, dried up body,
Vile panderer, repulsive bawd,
Then I might hope to find forgiveness   3495
Ten times over from the Lord!
GRETCHEN   My brother! Hell's own wretchedness!
VALENTINE   Stop your bawling, all your to-do.

3. Mess, disorder.

When you said goodbye to honor,
That is what gave me the worst blow.   3500
And now I go down in the earth,
Passing through the sleep of death,
To God—who in his life was a brave soldier.

                                        Dies.

The Cathedral

Requiem mass, organ music, singing. GRETCHEN *among a crowd of worshippers.*
Behind her an EVIL SPIRIT.

EVIL SPIRIT   How different then, Gretchen,
    It was when, all innocent,   3505
    Here at the altar
    You babbled your prayers
    From the worn little prayer book,
    Half a game playing,
    Half God adoring   3510
    In your childish heart,
    Gretchen!
    And how is it now?
    In your heart how now is it,
    What wickedness there?   3515
    Do you pray for the soul of your mother
    Who through you slept on and still on,
    Into pain and more pain?
    There at your door whose blood is it?
    —And already under your heart   3520
    A stirring, a quickening, is it,
    Affrighting you both
    With its foreboding presence?
GRETCHEN   Misery! Misery!
    To be rid of these thoughts   3525
    That go round and around in me.
    Accusing, accusing!
CHOIR   *Dies irae, dies illa*
    Solvet saeclum in favilla.[1]
        [*Organ music.*]
EVIL SPIRIT   The wrath of God grips you!   3530
    The trumpet sounds,
    The grave mounds are heaving,
    And your heart,
    From its ashen rest waking
    Into billowing flames,   3535
    Agonizingly burns!

---

1. Day of wrath, that day that dissolves the world into ashes (Latin). The choir sings a famous
mid-13th-century hymn by Thomas Celano (ca. 1200–ca. 1255).

GRETCHEN How hateful it's here!
  I feel as if stifling
  In the organ tones!
  The chanting is shrivelling   3540
  My heart into dust.
CHOIR   *Judex ergo cum sedebit,*
  Quidquid latet adparebit,
  Nil inultum remanebit.[2]
GRETCHEN How shut in I feel,   3545
  The pillars imprison me!
  The vaulting presses
  Down on me!—Air!
EVIL SPIRIT   Hide yourself, do! Sin and shame
  Never stay hidden.   3550
  Air? Light?
  Poor thing that you are!
CHOIR   *Quid sum miser tunc dicturus?*
  Quem patronum rogaturus,
  Cum vix justus sit securus?[3]   3555
EVIL SPIRIT   The blessed avert
  Their faces from you.
  Pure souls with a shudder
  Snatch their hands back from you.
  Poor thing!   3560
CHOIR   *Quid sum miser tunc dicturus?*
GRETCHEN Your smelling salts, neighbor!
    [*She swoons.*]

Walpurgis Night

The Harz Mountains, near Schierke and Elend. FAUST, MEPHISTOPHELES.

MEPHISTO What you would like now is a broomstick, right?
  Myself, give me a tough old billy goat.
  We've got a ways to go still, on this route.   3565
FAUST While legs hold up and breath comes freely,
  This knotty blackthorn's all I want.
  Hastening our journey, what's the point?
  To loiter through each winding valley,
  Then clamber up this rocky slope   3570
  Down which that stream there tumbles ceaselessly—
  That's what gives the pleasure to our tramp.
  The spring has laid her finger on the birch,
  Even the fir tree feels her touch,

---

2. When the judge shall be seated, what is hidden shall appear, nothing shall remain unavenged (Latin).

3. What shall I say in my wretchedness? To whom shall I appeal when scarcely the righteous man is safe? (Latin.)

Then mustn't our limbs feel new energy?   3575
MEPHISTO   Must they? I don't feel that way, not me.
  My season's strictly wintertime,
  I'd much prefer we went through ice and snow.
  The waning moon, making its tardy climb
  Up the sky, gives off a reddish glow   3580
  So sad and dim, at every step you run
  Into a tree or stumble on a stone.
  You won't mind my begging assistance
  Of a will-o'-the wisp[1]—and there's one no great distance,
  Shining for all he's worth, so merrily.   3585
  —Hello there, friend, we'd like your company!
  Why blaze away so uselessly, for nothing?
  Do us a favor, light up this path we're climbing.
WILL-O'-THE-WISP   I hope the deep respect I hold you in, sir,
  Will keep in check my all-too-skittish temper;   3590
  The way we go is zigzag, that's our nature.
MEPHISTO   Trying to ape mankind, poor silly flame.
  Now listen to me: fly straight, in the Devil's name,
  Or out I'll blow your feeble light immediately.
WILL-O'-THE-WISP   Yes, yes, you give the orders here, quite right;   3595
  I'll do what you require, happily,
  But don't forget, the mountain on this night
  Is mad with magic, witchcraft, sorcery,
  And if Jack-o'-Lantern is your guide,
  Don't expect more than he can provide.   3600
FAUST, MEPHISTOPHELES, WILL-O'-THE-WISP [*Singing in turn*]
     We have entered, as it seems,
     Realm of magic, realm of dreams,
     Lead us well and win such honor
     His to have, bright-shining creature,
     By whose flicker we may hasten   3605
     Forward through this wide, waste region!

     See the trees, one then another,
     Spinning past us fast and faster,
     And the cliffs impending over,
     And the jutting crags, like noses   3610
     Winds blow through with snoring noises!

     Over stones and through the heather
     Rills and runnels downwards hasten.
     Is that water splashing, listen,
     Is it singing, that soft murmur,   3615
     Is it love's sweet voice, lamenting,

1. A wavering light formed by marsh gas. In German folklore, it was thought to lead travelers to their destruction.

For the days when all was heaven?
How our hearts hoped, loving, yearning!
And like a tale, an old, familiar,
Echo once more tells it over.   3620

Whoo-oo! Owl's hoot's heard nearer,
Cry of cuckoo and of plover—
Still not nested, still awake?
Are those lizards in the brake,
Straggle-legged, big of belly?   3625
And roots winding every which way
In the rock and sand send far out
Shoots to snare and make us cry out.
Tree warts, swollen, gross excrescents,
Send their tentacles like serpents   3630
Out to catch us. And mice scamper
In great packs of every color
Through the moss and through the heather,
And the glowworms swarm around us
In dense clouds and only lead us   3635
Hither, thither, to confuse us.

Tell me, are we standing still, or
Still advancing, climbing higher?
Everything spins round us wildly,
Rocks and trees grin at us madly,   3640
And the errant lights, more of them ever,
Puff themselves up, big and bigger.

MEPHISTO   Seize hold of my coattails, quick,
   We're coming to a middling peak
   Where you'll marvel at the sight   3645
   Of Mammon's Mountain burning bright.[2]
FAUST   How strange that glow is, there, far down,
   Sad and pinkish, like the dawn.
   Its faint luminescence reaches
   Deep into the yawning gorges,   3650
   Mist rises here and streams away there,
   Penetrated by pale fire.
   Here, like a thin thread, the glitter
   Winds along, then like a fountain
   Overflowing, spills down the mountain,   3655
   And vein-like, branching all about,
   Holds in gleaming embrace the valley,
   And here, squeezed through a narrow gully,

---

2. Mammon is imagined as leading a group
of fallen angels in digging out gold and gems
from the ground of hell, presumably for Satan's
palace, as described in Milton's *Paradise Lost*
1.678 ff.

Collects into a pool apart,
Sparks fly about as if a hand   3660
Were scattering golden grains of sand,
And look there, how from base to top,
The whole cliffside is lit up.

MEPHISTO   Holiday time Lord Mammon's castle
Puts on a show that has no equal.   3665
Don't you agree? You saw it, very luckily.
I hear our guests arriving—not so quietly!

FAUST   What a gale of wind is blowing,
Buffeting my back and shoulders!

MEPHISTO   Clutch with your fingers that outcropping   3670
Or you'll fall to your death among the boulders.
The mist is making it darker than ever.
Hear how the trees are pitching and tossing!
Frightened, the owls fly up in a flutter,
The evergreen palace's pillars are creaking   3675
And cracking, boughs snapping and breaking,
As down the trunks thunder
With a shriek of roots tearing,
Piling up on each other
In a fearful disorder!   3680
And through the wreckage-strewn ravines
The hurtling storm blast howls and screams.
And hear those voices in the air,
Some far-off and others near?
That's the witches' wizard singing,   3685
Along the mountain shrilly ringing.

CHORUS OF WITCHES
    The witches ride up to the Brocken,
    Stubble's yellow, new grain green,
    The great host meets upon the peak and
    There Urian[3] mounts his throne.   3690
    So over stock and stone go stumping,
    Witches farting, billy goats stinking!

VOICE   Here comes Mother Baubo[4] now,
Riding on an old brood sow.

CHORUS
    Honor to whom honor is due!   3695
    Old Baubo to the head of the queue!
    A fat pig and a fat frau on her,
    And all the witches following after!

VOICE   How did you come?

VOICE   Ilsenstein way.
I peeked in an owl's nest, passing by.

---

3. A name for the devil.
4. In Greek mythology, the nurse of Demeter, noted for her obscenity and bestiality.

VOICE Oh, I wish you'd go to hell, all, 3700
Why such a rush, such an insane scramble?
VOICE Too fast, too fast, my bottom's skinned sore!
Oh, my wounds! Look here and here!

CHORUS OF WITCHES
Broad the way and long the road,
What a bumbling, stumbling crowd! 3705
Broomstraw scratches, pitchfork's pushed,
Mother's ripped and baby's crushed.

HALF-CHORUS OF WARLOCKS
We crawl like snails lugging their whorled shell,
The women have got a good mile's lead.
When where you're going's to the Devil, 3710
It's woman knows how to get up speed.

OTHER HALF-CHORUS
A mile or so, why should we care?
Women may get the start of us,
But for all of their forehandedness,
One jump carries a man right there. 3715

VOICE [Above] Come along with us, you down at the lake.
VOICE [From below] Is there anything better we would like?
We scrub ourselves clean as a whistle,
But it's no use, still we're infertile.

BOTH CHORUSES
The wind is still, the stars are fled, 3720
The veiled moon's glad to hide her head,
Rushing, roaring, the mad chorus
Scatters sparks by the thousands about us.

VOICE [From below] Wait, please, wait, only a minute!
VOICE [Above] A voice from that crevice, did you hear it? 3725
VOICE [From below] Take me along, don't forget me!
For three hundred years I've tried to climb
Up to the summit—all in vain.
I long for creatures who are like me.

BOTH CHORUSES
Straddle a broomstick, a pitchfork's fine too, 3730
Get up on a goat, a plain stick will do.
Who can't make it up tonight,
Forever is done for, and so good night.

HALF-WITCH [From below] I trot breathlessly, and yet
How far ahead the rest have got. 3735
No peace at all at home, and here
It's no better. Dear, oh dear!

CHORUS OF WITCHES
The unction[5] gives us hags a lift,
A bit of rag will do for a sail,

5. Magical ointment made from the fat of unborn babies that witches smear on their broomsticks.

Any tub's a fine sky boat—   3740
Don't fly now and you never will.

BOTH CHORUSES
And when we've gained the very top,
Light down, swooping, to a stop,
We'll darken the heath entirely
With all our swarming witchery.   3745
[*They alight.*]

MEPHISTO   What a crowding and shoving, rushing and clattering,
Hissing and shrieking, pushing and chattering,
Burning and sparking, stinking and shaking,
We're among witches, no mistaking!
Stick close to me or we'll lose one another.   3750
But where are you?

FAUST   Here, over here!

MEPHISTO   Already swept away so far!
I must show this mob who is master—
Out of the way of Voland the Devil,
Out of the way, you charming rabble!   3755
Doctor, hang on, we'll make a quick dash
And get ourselves out of this terrible crush—
Even for me it's too much to endure.
Yonder's a light has a strange lure,
Those bushes, I don't know why, attract me.   3760
Quick now, dive in that shrubbery!

FAUST   Spirit of Contradiction! However,
Lead the way!—He's clever, my devil:
Walpurgis Night up the Brocken we scramble
So as to do what? Hide ourselves in a corner!   3765

MEPHISTO   Look at that fire there, burning brightly,
Clubmen meeting, all seeming so sprightly;
You don't feel alone when the company's fewer.

FAUST   But I would like it better higher,
On the summit, where I make out   3770
A red glow and black smoke swirling,
Satanwards a great crowd's toiling,
And there, I haven't the least doubt,
Many a riddle at last is resolved.

MEPHISTO   And many another one revealed.   3775
Let the world rush on crazily,
We'll pass the time here cozily,
And doing what customarily's the thing done,
Inside the great world contrive us a little one.
Look there, young witches, all stark naked,   3780
And old ones wisely petticoated.
Don't sulk, be nice, if only to please me;
Plenty of fun—as for trouble, hardly.
I hear music, a damned racket!

You must learn not to mind it. 3785
No backing out now, follow me in
And find you are my debtor again.
—Now what do you think of this place, my friend?
Our eyes can hardly see to its end.
A hundred fires, in a row blinking, 3790
The people shouting, dancing, drinking,
Eating, loving, oh what a party!
Where is there anything better, show me.
FAUST   To get us admitted to the revel,
You'll appear how, as magician or devil? 3795
MEPHISTO   I travel incognito normally,
But when it comes to celebrations
A man must show his decorations.
The Garter's never been awarded me,[6]
But in these parts the split hoof's much respected. 3800
That snail there, do you see it, creeping forwards,
Its face pushing this way, that way, towards us?
Already I've been smelt out, I'm detected.
Even if deception was my aim,
Here there's no denying who I am. 3805
Come on, we'll go along from fire to fire,
The go-between me, you the cavalier.
    [Addressing figures huddled around a fire]
Old sirs, you keep apart, not very merry,
You'd please me better if you joined the party.
You ought to be carousing with the youngsters, 3810
At home we're all alone enough, we oldsters.
GENERAL   Put no trust in nations, for the people,
In spite of all you've done, are never grateful.
It's with them always as it is with women,
The young come first, and we—ignored, forgotten. 3815
MINISTER OF STATE   The world has got completely off the track.
Oh, they were men, the older generation!
When we held every high position,
That was the golden age, and no mistake.
PARVENU   We were no simpletons ourselves, we weren't, 3820
And often did so many things we shouldn't.
But everything's turned topsy-turvy now,
Just when we're foursquare with the status quo.
AUTHOR   Who wants, today, to read a book
With a modicum of sense or wit? 3825
And as for our younger folk,
I've never seen such rude conceit.
MEPHISTO [Suddenly transformed into an old man]
For Judgment Day all now are ripe and ready,

6. That is, he has no decoration of nobility, such as the Order of the Garter, the highest order of chivalry, bestowed by the king or queen of England.

Since I shan't ever again climb Brocken's top;
And considering too my wine of life is running cloudy,   3830
The world also is coming to a stop.
JUNK-DEALER WITCH   Good sirs, don't pass me unawares,
Don't miss this opportunity!
Look here, will you, at my wares,
What richness, what variety!   3835
Yet there is not a single item
Hasn't served to claim a victim,
Nowhere on earth will you find such a stall!
No dagger here but it has drunk hot blood,
No cup but from it deadly poison's flowed   3840
To waste a body once robust and hale,
No gem but has seduced a loving girl,
No sword but has betrayed an ally or a friend,
Or struck an adversary from behind.
MEPHISTO   Auntie, think about the times you live in—   3845
What's past is done. Done and gone!
The new, the latest, that's what you should deal in,
The nouveau only, turns us on.
FAUST   Oh let me not forget I'm me, me, solely!
A fair to beat all fairs this is, believe me.   3850
MEPHISTO   The scrambling mob climbs upwards, jostling, crushed,
You think you're pushing and you're being pushed.
FAUST   Who's that there?
MEPHISTO   Look at her close.
Lilith.[7]
FAUST   Lilith? What's she to us?   3855
MEPHISTO   Adam's wife, his first. Beware of her.
Her beauty's one boast is her dangerous hair.
When Lilith winds it tight around young men
She doesn't soon let go of them again.
FAUST   Look, one old witch, one young one, there they sit—   3860
They've waltzed around a lot already, I will bet!
MEPHISTO   Tonight's no night for resting but for fun,
Let's join the dance, a new one's just begun.
FAUST [*Dancing with the young witch*]
A lovely dream I dreamt one day:
I saw a green-leaved apple tree,   3865
Two apples swayed upon a stem,
So tempting! I climbed up for them.
THE PRETTY WITCH   Ever since the days of Eden
Apples have been man's desire,
How overjoyed I am to know, sir,   3870
Apples grow, too, in my garden.

7. According to rabbinical legend, Adam's first
wife; the *female* mentioned in Genesis 1:27:
"So God created man in his own image, in the
image of God created he him; male and female

created he them." After Eve was created, Lilith
became a ghost who seduced men and inflicted
evil on children.

MEPHISTO [*Dancing with the old witch*]
  A naughty dream I dreamt one day:
  I saw a tree split up the middle—
  A huge cleft, phenomenal!
  And yet it pleased me every way.   3875
THE OLD WITCH   Welcome, welcome, to you, sire,
  Cloven-footed cavalier!
  Stand to with a proper stopper,
  Unless you fear to come a cropper.
PROCTOPHANTASMIST[8]   Accursed tribe, so bold, presumptuous!   3880
  Hasn't it been proven past disputing
  Spirits all are footless, they lack standing?
  And here you're footing like the rest of us!
THE PRETTY WITCH [*Dancing*]
  What's he doing here, at our party?
FAUST [*Dancing*]
  Him? You find him everywhere, that killjoy,   3885
  We others dance, he does the criticizing,
  Every step one takes requires analyzing,
  Until it's jawed about, it hasn't yet occurred.
  He can't stand how we go forwards undeterred;
  If you keep going around in the same old circle,   3890
  As he plods year in, year out on his treadmill,
  You might be favored with his good opinion,
  Provided you most humbly beg it of him.
PROCTOPHANTASMIST   Still here, are you? It's an outrage!
  Vanish, ours is the Enlightened Age—   3895
  You devils, no respect for law and regulation,
  We've grown so wise, yet ghosts still walk in Tegel.[9]
  How long I've toiled to banish superstition,
  Yet it lives on. The whole thing is a scandal!
THE PRETTY WITCH   Stop, stop, how boring you are with your gabble!   3900
PROCTOPHANTASMIST   I tell you to your face, you ghostly freaks,
  I'll not endure this tyranny of spooks
  My spirit finds you spirits much too spiritual!
        [*They go on dancing.*]
  I see I'm getting nowhere with these devils,
  Still, it will add a chapter to my travels,   3905
  And I hope, before my sands of life run out,
  To put foul fiends and poets all to rout.
MEPHISTO   He'll go and plump himself down in a puddle—
  It solaces him for all his ghostly trouble—

8. A German coinage meaning "one who exorcises evil spirits by sitting in a pond and applying leeches to his behind" (see lines 3908–11). The figure caricatures Friedrich Nicolai (1733–1811), who opposed modern movements in German thought and literature and had parodied Goethe's *The Sorrows of Young Werther* (1774).
9. A town near Berlin where ghosts had been reported.

And purge away his ghost and all the other spirits   3910
By having leeches feed on where the M'sieur sits.[1]
    [*To* FAUST, *who has broken off dancing and withdrawn*]
What's this? You've left your partner in the lurch
As she was sweetly singing, pretty witch.
FAUST   Ugh! From her mouth a red mouse sprung
   In the middle of her song.   3915
MEPHISTO   Is that anything to fuss about?
   And anyway it wasn't gray, was it?
   To take on so, to me, seems simply rudeness
   When you are sporting with your Amaryllis.
FAUST   And then I saw—
MEPHISTO   Saw what?
FAUST   Look over there,   3920
   At that lovely child, pale-faced with fear,
   Standing by herself. How laboriously
   She pushes herself forwards, wracked by pains,
   As if her feet were shackled tight in chains.
   I must confess, it looks like Gretchen.
MEPHISTO   Let it be!   3925
   It's bad, that thing, a lifeless shape, a wraith
   No man ever wants to meet up with.
   Your blood freezes under her dead stare,
   Almost turned to stone, you are.
   Medusa,[2] did you ever hear of her?   3930
FAUST   Yes, yes, those are a corpse's eyes
   No loving hand was by to close.
   That's Gretchen's breast, which she so often
   Gave to me to rest my head on,
   That shape her dear, her lovely body,   3935
   She gave to me to enjoy freely.
MEPHISTO   It's all magic, hocus-pocus, idiot!
   Her power is, each thinks she's his own sweetheart.
FAUST   What rapture! And what suffering!
   I stand here spellbound by her look.   3940
   How strange, that bit of scarlet string
   That ornaments her lovely neck,
   No thicker than a knife blade's back.
MEPHISTO   Right you are. I see it, too.
   She's also perfectly able to   3945
   Tuck her head beneath her arm
   And stroll about. Perseus—remember him?—
   He is the one that hacked it off her.
   —Man, I'd think you'd have enough of

---

1. Nicolai claimed that he had been bothered by ghosts but had repelled them by applying leeches to his rump.

2. The Gorgon with hair of serpents whose glance turned people to stone.

The mad ideas your head is stuffed with! 3950
Come, we'll climb this hill, discover
All's as lively as inside the Prater.[3]
And unless somebody has bewitched me,
The thing I see there is a theater.
What's happening? 3955
SERVIBILIS A play, a new one, starting shortly,
Last of seven. With us here it's customary
To offer a full repertory.
The playwright's a rank amateur,
Amateurs, too, the whole company. 3960
Well, I must hurry off now, please excuse me,
I need to raise the curtain—amateurishly!
MEPHISTO How right it is that I should find you here, sirs;
The Blocksberg's just the place for amateurs.

Walpurgis Night's Dream
or
OBERON AND TITANIA'S GOLDEN WEDDING

INTERMEZZO[1]

STAGE MANAGER [To crew] Today we'll put by paint and canvas, 3965
  Mieding's[2] brave sons, all.
  Nature paints the scene for us:
  Gray steep and mist-filled vale.
HERALD For the wedding to be golden,
  Years must pass, full fifty; 3970
  But if the quarrel is made up, then
  It is golden truly.
OBERON Spirits, if you hover round,
  Appear, it's right, the hour;
  King and Queen are once more bound 3975
  Lovingly together.
PUCK[3] Here's Puck, my lord, who spins and whirls
  And cuts a merry caper,
  A hundred follow at his heels,
  Skipping to the measure. 3980
ARIEL[4] Ariel strikes up his song,
  The notes as pure as silver;
  Philistines[5] all around him throng,
  Those, too, with true culture.
OBERON Wives and husbands, learn from us 3985
  How two hearts unite:

3. A famous park in Vienna.
1. Brief interlude. Oberon and Titania are king and queen of the fairies.
2. Johann Martin Mieding (d. 1782), a master carpenter and scene builder in the Weimar theater.
3. A mischievous spirit.
4. A helpful sprite.
5. Those who disregard intellectual or artistic values.

To find connubial happiness,
Only separate.
TITANIA   If Master sulks and Mistress pouts,
Here's the remedy: 3990
Send her on a trip down south,
Him the other way.
FULL ORCHESTRA [*Fortissimo*][6]   Buzzing fly and humming gnat,
And all their consanguinity,
Frog's hoarse croak, cicada's chat   3995
Compose our symphony.
SOLO   Here I come, the bagpipes, who's
Really a soap bubble;
Hear me through my stumpy nose
Go tootle-doodle-doodle.   4000
A BUDDING IMAGINATION   A spider's foot, a green toad's gut,
Two winglets—though they hardly
Compose a living creature, yet
Make do as nonsense poetry.
A COUPLE   Short steps, smart leaps, all done neatly   4005
In the honeyed air.
I grant you foot it very featly,
We stay planted here.
AN INQUIRING TRAVELER   Can it be a fairground fraud,
The shape at which I'm looking?   4010
Oberon the handsome god
Still alive and kicking?
A PIOUS BELIEVER   I don't see claws, nor any tail,
And yet it's indisputable:
Like Greece's gods, his dishabille[7]   4015
Betrays the pagan devil.
AN ARTIST OF THE NORTH   Here everything I undertake
Is weak, is thin, is sketchy;
But I'm preparing soon to make
My Italian journey.   4020
A STICKLER FOR DECORUM   I'm here, and most unhappily,
Where all's impure, improper;
Among this riotous witchery
Only two wear powder.
A YOUNG WITCH   Powder, like a petticoat,   4025
Is right for wives with gray hair;
But I'll sit naked on my goat,
Show off my strapping figure.
A MATRON   We are too well bred by far
To bandy words about,   4030
But may you, young thing that you are,
Drop dead, and soon, cheap tart!

---

6. Italian, used as a direction in music to play   7. State of being carelessly dressed or partly
very loudly.   undressed.

THE CONDUCTOR   Mosquito's nose, gnat's proboscis,
    Mind you keep the tempo.
    Let be, you bugs, the naked miss—   4035
    On with the concerto!
A WEATHERCOCK [*Pointing one way*]
    No better company than maids
    Like these, so kind, complaisant;
    And bachelors to match, old boys,
    Agog all, all impatient!   4040
WEATHERCOCK [*Pointing the other way*]
    And if the earth don't open up
    And swallow this lewd rabble,
    Off I'll race at a great clip,
    Myself go to the Devil.
SATIRICAL EPIGRAMS [XENIEN][8]   Gadflies, we, who plant our sting   4045
    In hides highborn and bourgeois,
    In so doing honoring
    Great Satan, our dear Papa.
HENNINGS[9]   Look there at the pack of them,
    Like schoolboys jeering meanly.   4050
    Next, I'm sure, they all will claim
    It's all in fun, friends, really.
MUSAGET[1]   ["LEADER OF THE MUSES"]
    If I joined these witches here
    I'm sure I'd not repine;
    I know I'd find it easier   4055
    To lead them than the Nine.[2]
THE QUONDAM "SPIRIT OF THE AGE."[3]
    What counts is knowing the right people,
    Catch hold and we'll go places;
    Blocksberg's top holds lots, so ample,   4060
    Like Germany's Parnassus.[4]
THE INQUIRING TRAVELER   Who's that fellow who's so stiff
    And marches so majestical?
    He sniffs away for all he's worth,
    "Pursuing things Jesuitical."[5]   4065
A CRANE   An earnest fisherman I am,
    In clear and troubled waters.
    And thus you see a pious man
    Hobnobbing with devils.
A CHILD OF THIS WORLD   All occasions serve the godly   4070

---

8. Literally, polemical verses written by Goethe and Friedrich von Schiller (1759–1805). The characters here are versions of Goethe himself.
9. August Adolf von Hennings (1746–1826), publisher of *Genius of the Age*, a journal that had attacked Schiller.
1. The title of a collection of Hennings's poetry.
2. The nine muses, or Greek goddesses of art and science.

3. That is, former "Genius of the Age"; probably alludes to the journal's change of title in 1800 to *Genius of the Nineteenth Century*.
4. A mountain sacred to Apollo and the Muses; hence, figuratively, the locale of poetic excellence.
5. The Jesuits were a Catholic religious order, famous for their cunning, case-by-case arguments.

In their work. Atop
The Blocksberg, even there, they
Set up religious shop.

A DANCER   What's that booming, a new team
Of musicians coming?   4075
No, no, they're bitterns in the stream
All together drumming.

THE DANCING MASTER   How cautiously they lift their feet—
Draw back in fear of tripping!
The knock-kneed hop, they jump the stout,   4080
Heedless how they're looking.

THE FIDDLER   This riffraff's so hate-filled, each lusts
To slit the other's throat;
Orpheus with his lute tamed beasts:[6]
These march to the bagpipes' note.   4085

A DOGMATIST   I can't be rattled, no, by your
Doubts, suspicions, quibbles;
The Devil's real, he is, that's sure,
Else how would there be devils?

AN IDEALIST   The mind's creative faculty   4090
This time has gone too far;
If everything I see is me,
Daft I am for sure.

A REALIST   It's pandemonium, it's mad,
I'm floored, I am, dumbfounded!   4095
This is the first time I have stood
On ground on nothing founded.

A SUPERNATURALIST   The presence of these devils here
For me is reassuring evidence:
From the demonical I infer   4100
The angelical's existence.

A SKEPTIC   They see a flickering light and gloat,
There's treasure there, oh surely;
Devil's a word that pairs with doubt,
This is a place made for me.   4105

CONDUCTOR   Frogs in leaves, grasshoppers grass—
What damned amateurs!
Cicadas chirr, mosquitos buzz—
Call yourselves performers!

THE SMART ONES   Sans all souci[7] we are, shift   4110
About with lightning speed;
When walking on the feet is out,
We walk on the head.

THE NOT-SO-SMART ONES   At court we sat down to free dinners,
And now all doors are shut;   4115
We've worn out our dancing slippers
And must limp barefoot.

---

6. In Greek mythology, Orpheus's music was
said to have the power to quiet wild animals.

7. Without any care or unhappiness (French).

WILL-O-THE-WISPS   We're from the muddy flats, marais,[8]
    Such is our lowly origin;
    But now we shine as chevaliers   4120
    And dance in the cotillion.
A SHOOTING STAR   I shot across the sky's expanse,
    A meteor, blazing bright.
    Now fallen, I sprawl in the grass—
    Who'll help me to my feet?   4125
THE BRUISERS   Make way, make way, we're coming through,
    Trampling your lawn,
    We're spirits too, but spirits who
    Have lots of beef and brawn.
PUCK   How you tramp, so heavily,   4130
    Like infant elephants!
    Elfin Puck's stamp be today
    The heaviest of tramps.
ARIEL   Or gave you wings, our loving Nature,
    Or gave you them the Spirit,   4135
    Come, my light trace fly after,
    Up to the rose hill's summit.
ORCHESTRA [*Pianissimo*][9]
    Shrouding mists and trailing clouds
    Lighten in the dawning,
    Breeze stirs leaves, wind rattles reeds,   4140
    And all, all, gone in the morning.

An Overcast Day. A Field

FAUST *and* MEPHISTOPHELES.

FAUST   In misery! In despair! Stumbling about pitifully over the earth for
so long, and now a prisoner! A condemned criminal, shut up in a dungeon and suffering horrible torments, the poor unfortunate child!
It's come to this, to this! And not a word about it breathed to me, you   4145
treacherous, odious spirit! Stand there rolling your Devil's eyes around
in rage, oh do! Brazen it out with your intolerable presence! A prisoner! In misery, irremediable misery! Delivered up to evil spirits and the
stony-hearted justice of mankind! And meanwhile you distract me with
your insipid entertainments, keep her situation, more desperate every   4150
day, from me, and leave her to perish helplessly!
MEPHISTO   She's not the first.
FAUST   You dog, you monster! Change him, O you infinite Spirit, change
the worm back into a dog, give it back the shape it wore those evenings
when it liked to trot ahead of me and roll at the feet of some innocent   4155
wayfarer, tripping him up and leaping on him as he fell. Give it back its
favorite shape so it can crawl on its belly in the sand before me, and I
can kick it as it deserves, the abomination!—Not the first!—Such mis-

8. French for marsh or swamp.
9. Italian, direction in music to play very softly.

ery, such misery! It's inconceivable, humanly inconceivable, that more than one creature should ever have plumbed such depths of misery, $\quad$ 4160 that the first who did, writhing in her last agony under the eyes of the Eternal Forgiveness, shouldn't have expiated the guilt of all the others who came after! I am cut to the quick, pierced to the marrow, by the suffering of this one being—you grin indifferently at the fate of thousands!

MEPHISTO $\quad$ So once again we're at our wits' end, are we—reached the point $\quad$ 4165 where you fellows start feeling your brain is about to explode? Why did you ever throw in with us if you can't see the thing through? You'd like to fly, but can't stand heights. Did we force ourselves on you or you on us?

FAUST $\quad$ Don't snarl at me that way with those wolfish fangs of yours, it sickens me!—Great and glorious Spirit, Spirit who vouchsafed to $\quad$ 4170 appear to me, who knows me in my heart and soul, why did you fasten me to this scoundrel who diets on destruction, delights to hurt?

MEPHISTO $\quad$ Finished yet?

FAUST $\quad$ Save her or you'll pay for it! With a curse on you, the dreadfulest there is, for thousands of years to come! $\quad$ 4175

MEPHISTO $\quad$ I'm powerless to strike off the Great Avenger's chains or draw his bolts.—Save her indeed!—Who's the one who ruined her, I would like to know—you or me?

[FAUST *looks around wildly.*]

Looking for a thunderbolt, are you? A good thing you wretched mortals weren't given them. That's the tyrant's way of getting out of $\quad$ 4180 difficulties—strike down any innocent person who makes an objection, gets in his way.

FAUST $\quad$ Take me to where she is, you hear? She's got to be set free.

MEPHISTO $\quad$ In spite of the risk you would run? There's blood guilt on the town because of what you did. Where murder was, there the $\quad$ 4185 avenging spirits hover, waiting for the murderer to return.

FAUST $\quad$ That, from you, that too? Death and destruction, a world's worth, on your head, you monster! Take me there, I say, and set her free!

MEPHISTO $\quad$ All right, all right, I'll take you there. But hear what I can do—do you think all the powers of heaven and earth are mine? I'll $\quad$ 4190 muddle the turnkey's senses, then you seize his keys and lead her out. Only a human hand can do it. I'll keep watch. The spirit horses are ready. Off I'll carry both of you. That's what I can do.

FAUST $\quad$ Away then!

Night. Open Country

FAUST *and* MEPHISTOPHELES *going by on black horses at a furious gallop.*

FAUST $\quad$ What's that going on at the ravenstone?[1] $\quad$ 4195

MEPHISTO $\quad$ Brewing something, doing something, don't know.

FAUST $\quad$ Soaring up, swooping down, bowing, genuflecting.

MEPHISTO $\quad$ A pack of witches.

FAUST $\quad$ Strewing stuff, consecrating.

MEPHISTO $\quad$ Keep going, keep going! $\quad$ 4200

1. The block on which Gretchen will be beheaded.

A Prison

FAUST [*With a bunch of keys and carrying a lamp, at a narrow iron door*]
I shudder as I haven't for so long—
Oh, how it suffers, our humanity!
She's shut up inside these dank walls, poor thing,
And all her crime was love, the brave, the illusory.
You're hanging back from going in!   4205
You're afraid of meeting her eyes again!
In, in, your hesitation's her death, hurry!
    [*He puts the key in the lock.*]
SINGING [*From within*]
    My mother, the whore,
    She's the one slew me,
    My father, the knave,   4210
    He's the one ate me,
    My sister, wee thing,
    Heaped up my bones
    Under cold stones,
    Turned into a wood bird, I sing   4215
    Fly away, fly away!
FAUST [*Unlocking the door*]   She doesn't dream her lover's listening,
Hears her chains rattle, the straw rustling.
    [*He enters.*]
MARGARETE [*Cowering on her paillasse*][2]
They're coming, they're coming! How bitter, death, bitter!
FAUST [*Whispering*]   Hush, dear girl, hush! You'll soon be free.   4220
MARGARETE [*Groveling before him*]
If your heart's human, think how I suffer.
FAUST   You'll wake the guards. Speak quietly.
    [*Taking hold of the chains to unlock them*]
MARGARETE [*On her knees*]   Headsman, so early, it isn't right.
Have mercy on me! Too soon, too soon!
You come for me in the dead of night—   4225
Isn't it time enough at dawn?
    [*Stands up.*]
I'm still so young, too young surely—
Still I must die.
How pretty I was, that's what undid me,
He held me so close, now he's far away,   4230
My wreath pulled apart, the flowers scattered,
Don't grip me so hard! Please, won't you spare me?
What did I ever do to you?
Don't let me beg in vain for mercy.
I never before laid eyes on you.   4235
FAUST   It's unendurable, her misery!
MARGARETE   What can I do, I'm in your power,

2. Thin straw mattress (French).

Only let me nurse my baby first,
All night long I hugged the dear creature;
How mean they were, snatched it from my breast, 4240
And now they say I murdered it.
I'll never be happy, no, never again.
They sing songs about me in the street,
It's wicked of them.
There's an old fairy tale ends that way, 4245
What has it got to do with me?
FAUST [*Falling at her feet*] It's me here who loves you, me at your feet
To rescue you from this miserable fate.
MARGARETE [*Kneeling beside him*]
We'll kneel down, that's right, and pray to the saints.
Look, under those steps, 4250
Below the doorsill,
All Hell's a-boil.
The Evil One
In his horrible rage
Makes such a noise. 4255
FAUST [*Crying out*] Gretchen! Gretchen!
MARGARETE [*Listening*] That was my darling's own dear voice!
 [*She jumps up, the chains fall away.*]
I heard him call. Where can he be?
No one may stop me now, I'm free!
Into his arms I'll fly so fast, 4260
Lie on his breast at last, at last.
Gretchen, he called, from there on the sill,
Through all the howlings and gnashings of Hell,
Through the furious, devilish sneering and scorn,
I heard a dear voice, its sound so well known. 4265
FAUST It's me!
MARGARETE It's you! Oh, say it again.
 [*Catching hold of him*]
It's him! Where's the torture now, it's him!
Where's my fear of the prison, the chains they hung on me?
It's you, it's you! You've come here to save me! 4270
I'm saved!
—I see it before me, so very plain,
The street I saw you the first time on,
I see Marthe and me where we waited for you
In the sunlit garden. 4275
FAUST [*Pulling her toward the door*]
Come along, come!
MARGARETE Don't go, stay here!
I love it so being wherever you are.
 [*Caressing him*]
FAUST Hurry!
If you don't hurry
The price we will pay! 4280

MARGARETE   What? Don't know how to kiss anymore?
  Parted from me a short time only
  And quite forgotten what lips are for?
  Why am I frightened with your arms around me?
  Time was, at a word or a look from you,   4285
  Heaven herself threw her arms around me
  And you kissed me as if you'd devour me.
  Kiss me, kiss me,
  Or I'll kiss you!
     [*She embraces him.*]
  Oh the cold lips you have,   4290
  Cold and dumb.
  What's become of your love,
  All gone?
  Who stole it from me?
     [*She turns away from him.*]
FAUST   Come, follow me! Darling, be brave!   4295
  Oh, the kisses I'll give you, my love—
  Only come now, we'll slip through the door.
MARGARETE [*Turning back to him*]
  It's you, is it really? For sure?
FAUST   Yes, it's me—you must come!
MARGARETE   You strike off my chains,
  Take me into your arms.   4300
  How is it you don't shrink away from me?
  Have you any idea who you're setting free?
FAUST   Hurry, hurry! The night's almost over.
MARGARETE   I murdered my mother,
  Drowned my infant,   4305
  Weren't both of us given it—you too its parent—
  Equally? It's you, I can hardly believe it.
  Give me your hand. No, I haven't dreamt it.
  Your dear hand!—But your hand is wet!
  Wipe it off, there's blood on it!   4310
  My God, my God, what did you do?
  Put away your sword,
  I beg you to!
FAUST   What's past is done, forget it all.
  You're killing me.   4315
MARGARETE   No, live on still.
  I'll tell you how the graves should be;
  Tomorrow you must see to it.
  Give my mother the best spot,
  My brother put alongside her,   4320
  Me, put me some distance off,
  Yet not too far,
  And at my right breast put my baby,
  Nobody else shall lie beside me.
  When I used to press up close to you,   4325

How sweet it was, pure happiness,
But now I can't, it's over, all such bliss—
I feel it as an effort I must make,
That I must force myself on you,
And you, I feel, resist me, push me back.   4330
And yet it's you, with your good, kind look.
FAUST   If it's me, then come, we can't delay.
MARGARETE   Out there?
FAUST   Out there, away!
MARGARETE   If the grave's out there, death ready,
Yes, come, the two of us together,   4335
But only to the eternal place, no other.
—You're going now?
I'd go too if I could, Heinrich, believe me!
FAUST   You can! All you need is the will. Oh come!
The way is clear.   4340
MARGARETE   No, I mayn't. For me all hope is gone.
It's useless, flight. They'd keep, I'm sure,
A sharp watch out. I'd find it dreadful
To have to beg my bread of people,
Beg with a bad conscience, too;   4345
Dreadful to have to wander about
Where all is strange and new,
Only to end up getting caught.
FAUST   But I'll stick with you!
MARGARETE   Hurry! Be quick!   4350
Save your poor child—
Run! Keep to the track
That follows the brook,
Over the bridge.
Into the wood   4355
Left to the plank,
There in the pool—
Reach down, quick, catch it!
It's fighting for breath!
It's struggling still!   4360
Save it, oh, save it!
FAUST   Get hold of yourself.
One step and you're free, dear girl.
MARGARETE   If only we were well past the hill.
There on a rock Mother sits, all a-tremble—   4365
Not a sign does she make, doesn't speak.
There on a rock Mother sits, head a-wobble—
To look at her gives me a chill.
She slept so long she will never wake,
She slept so we might have our pleasure—   4370
The happy hours we spent together!
FAUST   If all my persuading is no use,
I'll have to carry you off by force.

MARGARETE   Let go, let go, how dare you compel me!
   You're gripping my arm so brutally!   4375
   I always did what you wanted, once.
FAUST   Soon day will be breaking! Darling, darling!
MARGARETE   Day? Yes, day, my last one, dawning,
   My wedding day it should have been.
   Not a word to a soul you've already been with your Gretchen.   4380
   My poor wreathe!
   All's over and done.
   We'll see one another again,
   But not to go dancing.
   The crowd presses in—not a sound, nothing,   4385
   Not the cry of a child.
   There are too many
   For square and alley
   To hold.
   The bell calls, staff's shattered,   4390
   I'm seized and I'm fettered
   And borne away, bound, to the block.
   Every neck shivers with shock
   As the sharp blade's brought down on my own.
   Dumb lies the world as the grave.   4395
FAUST   I wish I had never been born.
MEPHISTOPHELES   [Appearing outside]
   Come, come, or all's up with you, friend—
   Debating, delaying, useless jabbering!
   My horses are trembling.
   A minute or two and it's day.   4400
MARGARETE   Who's that rising up out of the ground?
   It's him, him, oh drive him away!
   It's holy here, what is he after?
   It's me he is after, me!
FAUST   Live, hear me, live!   4405
MARGARETE   It's the judgment of God! I surrender!
MEPHISTO   Die both of you, I have to leave.
MARGARETE   In your hands, our Father, oh save me!
   You angelical hosts, stand about me!
   Draw up in your ranks to protect me!   4410
   I'm afraid of you, Heinrich, afraid!
MEPHISTO   She's condemned.
VOICE [From above]
                                    She is saved!
MEPHISTO [To FAUST, peremptorily]
   Come with me!
        [He disappears with FAUST.]
VOICE [From within, dying away]
   Heinrich! Heinrich!

FREDERICK DOUGLASS

1818?–1895

There was no more important African American public figure in the nineteenth century than Frederick Douglass. Born into slavery, he could easily have remained illiterate his whole life. But with extraordinary ingenuity and perseverance, he taught himself to read, and soon turned himself into such an electrifying antislavery speaker and writer that some audiences simply could not believe that he had grown up a slave. Even skeptics found themselves won over by his charismatic personality, acerbic wit, and skillful arguments. Douglass's eloquence became a powerful weapon in the war against slavery, as he edited an influential abolitionist newspaper, stirred crowded lecture halls in the United States, Great Britain, and Ireland, and published his best-selling *Narrative of the Life of Frederick Douglass, an American Slave, Written by Himself* (1845).

LIFE

Frederick Augustus Washington Bailey was born in Talbot County in the slave state of Maryland sometime around 1818. He barely knew his mother, a slave, and never knew the identity of his father, probably a white man and perhaps his owner. At first he lived in his grandmother's cabin, and then at the age of six he went to live in the house of his owner, the chief overseer of a vast plantation belonging to one of the wealthiest men in Maryland. It was during this period, as Douglass recounts in horrifying detail in his autobiography, that he first witnessed the daily cruelty suffered by plantation slaves.

An important turning point came in 1826 when Frederick was sent to live with Hugh and Sophia Auld, relatives of his owner in Baltimore. One of the most famous episodes in the autobiography tells of the moment when Hugh Auld discovered that his wife was teaching the slave to read. He burst out angrily that literacy would make Frederick "discontented" and "unmanageable" and so "would forever unfit him to be a slave." This reprimand transformed the slave's life: "From that moment," Douglass writes, "I understood the pathway from slavery to freedom." In the seven years that he remained with the Aulds, Douglass used his best resources to learn how to read and write, discovering two texts that would significantly shape his later career: Caleb Bingham's *The Columbian Orator* (1807), and the speeches of Thomas Sheridan, an eighteenth-century Irish actor and educator. Both were guides to public speaking.

In 1833 Hugh Auld's brother, Thomas, who had become Frederick Bailey's official owner, called him back to work on his plantation. Thomas Auld was a cruel master, but he found the slave so unruly that he sent him to a harsh "slave breaker" for a year to tame him. Douglass was not tamed, however; he defied and bested this notoriously brutal master in a long physical struggle, which, he says, resolved him to break free from slavery altogether: "however long I might remain a slave in form, the day passed forever when I could be a slave in fact."

After a first abortive attempt at escape, Douglass returned to Hugh Auld in Baltimore, where he learned caulking skills in the shipyard and began to turn his weekly wages over to his master. During this period of relative independence he met and fell in love with a free black woman named Anna Murray. Then, in 1838, he managed a successful escape. In the *Narrative* he was reluctant to divulge his strategies in case publicizing them would endanger other slaves trying to escape, but much later, after slavery had ended, he told the full story. First he disguised himself as a sailor and borrowed the identification papers of a free black seaman; then he traveled by train and ferry to New York, and with the help of abolitionists, moved to New Bedford, Massachusetts. There he married Murray, changed his name, and worked odd jobs to make a living. He also began to read an abolitionist newspaper, *The Liberator*. In 1841 he met its celebrated and controversial editor, William Lloyd Garrison, who invited Douglass to work for him as a traveling lecturer, telling the story of his life and selling subscriptions to the newspaper.

This marked the beginning of Douglass's extraordinarily successful public career. From the outset, his lectures moved his audiences to laughter, tears, and rapt attention. "As a speaker, he has few equals," claimed a contemporary editor. "I would give twenty thousand dollars if I could deliver an address in that manner," said another. In a context where apologists for slavery argued that Southern slaves were contented—living comfortable lives with kindly owners—Douglass's story offered a compelling counternarrative. And yet, from the beginning, he was also accused of fabricating the facts. His oratorical elegance and skill were so striking that a few abolitionists pleaded with him to put a little more "plantation" into his speech, so that he would seem more authentic. Douglass refused.

The public lectures paved the way for the *Narrative of the Life of Frederick Douglass* in two ways. First, although Douglass's speeches regularly told of the cruelties of slaveholding, mocked hypocritical proslavery ministers, and asked Northern audiences to confront inequality and prejudice in the free states, the centerpiece of his lectures was his own life story. He had tested it out on audience after audience; he knew it had power, and he was eager to disseminate it widely. Second, given the many accusations of fraud against Douglass, he wanted to publish details about the people and places he had known as a slave, so that others could confirm the truthfulness of his account. But publishing the details also put Douglass in danger. There was always the threat that a fugitive slave would be recaptured and sent back to the South, and now his owners could recognize him from his narrative and come to claim him. Douglass left the United States for England in 1845, just a few months after the autobiography appeared.

For two years Douglass traveled through Great Britain and Ireland, lecturing to enthusiastic crowds. By 1848 the *Narrative* had gone through nine editions in England alone, and it was translated into French and German. Douglass was surprised at the relative lack of racial prejudice he encountered in Britain. Among the warmest receptions he had was from Daniel O'Connell, the leader of the struggle against British colonial rule in Ireland. In England two Quakers gave Douglass the money to buy his own freedom, and in December of 1846 he became officially a free man.

Back in the United States, Douglass broke from Garrison's organization. Garrison was a powerful voice in the antislavery cause, but he paid Douglass less than the white lecturers on his circuit and patronized him, urging him to focus only on telling the story of his own life because, Garrison suggested, a black man was not capable of analyzing slavery as a large-scale social problem. Garrison also refused to fight for the vote for African Americans. Setting up on his own, Douglass launched an antislavery newspaper called the *North Star* in Rochester, New York. This city was an important stop on the underground railroad—the secret route organized around safe houses which fugitive slaves followed to Canada. The Douglass household harbored so many runaway slaves that there were sometimes as many as eleven fugitives staying in the house at a time. But the city was less committed to full racial equality than the Douglasses had hoped: their oldest daughter, Rosetta, was not allowed to attend public school, and the private school she attended forbade her to learn with the white students. Douglass began a campaign to end segregation in the schools. In 1848 he attended the women's rights convention in Seneca Falls, and he emerged as a stalwart champion of women's suffrage. The motto of the *North Star* marked his commitment to gender as well as racial equality: "Right is of no sex," it read. "Truth is of no color."

When the Civil War broke out in 1861, Douglass led efforts to persuade Congress and President Lincoln to allow African American men to enlist in the Union Army. This struggle succeeded, and in 1863, Douglass actively recruited soldiers to fight, including his own two sons, Lewis and Charles. After the war was over, he led the campaign for black suffrage, and prevailed in 1870 with the passage of the Fifteenth Amendment to the US Constitution, which states that citizens cannot be denied the vote "on account of race, color, or previous condition of servitude."

The following years saw Douglass working tirelessly to expose and denounce discrimination and violence. He moved to Washington, DC, where he held several government offices. In 1889

he accepted the position of consul-general to Haiti and moved there, but later resigned when he was told that he was too sympathetic to Haitian interests. His wife died in 1882, and Douglass later married Helen Pitts, a white woman. After speaking at the National Council of Women, he died of a heart attack in 1895. On hearing the news of Douglass's death, the women's rights activist Elizabeth Cady Stanton remembered hearing him speak for the first time: "He stood there like an African prince, majestic in his wrath, as with wit, satire, and indignation he graphically described the bitterness of slavery. . . . Thus it was that I first saw Frederick Douglass, and wondered that any mortal man should have ever tried to subjugate a being with such talents, intensified with the love of liberty."

SLAVERY AND ABOLITION

In the southern United States in the nineteenth century, slaves worked in fields, in homes, and in mines; they built railroads and canals; they processed sugar and iron. But by far the most significant use of slave labor involved cotton production. Eli Whitney's 1793 invention of the cotton gin had accelerated the cleaning of cotton, and worldwide demand for cotton textiles—a source of cheap and lightweight clothing—had skyrocketed. But this was a crop that still needed to be handpicked in the fields. The booming cotton trade therefore demanded lots of arable land and a huge supply of labor—conditions met easily by the slave economy of the United States South. Nearly three quarters of all US slaves labored on cotton plantations, and by 1840 the southern United States produced more than half of the world's cotton. Cotton helped to drive the whole nation's economy, contributing substantially to the growth of Northern industry, shipping, and banking. It powered the global economy too. African traders used the term *americani* to refer to inexpensive cottons from the United States. And even after Britain had officially abolished slavery in its own territories, British traders imported vast quantities of cotton picked by US slaves, and British mills turned this raw material into textiles for sale around the world. About 10 percent of Britain's wealth came from the cotton trade. In 1858 US Senator James Hammond of South Carolina declared, "You dare not make war upon cotton. No power on earth dare make war upon it. Cotton is king!"

Intent on reaping as much profit as possible from their crops, plantation holders increasingly turned to the "gang system" to organize slave labor. Groups of slaves, under the command of an overseer, were forced—typically with whips, clubs, and threats—to perform a single repetitive task from the break of dawn until night. To increase efficiency, slaveholders would often rotate corn and cotton—ready at different times of the year—and use the corn to feed both slaves and animals on the plantation.

The state of Maryland, where Douglass was a slave, differed from most of the South. Maryland farms mostly grew tobacco rather than cotton, and the demand for tobacco was on the decline. Also, by the time that Frederick Douglass was born, Maryland had the highest number of free black men and women in the United States, more than half of its African American population. (By contrast, more than 99 percent of black people in Alabama, Texas, and Mississippi were slaves.) Working in the bustling city of Baltimore, surrounded by free blacks, Douglass had significantly more opportunities for escape than the plantation would have afforded.

Maryland was reputed to have a less harsh and dehumanizing slaveholder population than the "deep" South. In this respect as in many others, Douglass's *Narrative* challenged his readers'

assumptions. In general the abolitionists felt that the best weapon against slavery was a campaign to reveal its horrors as fully and as accurately as possible. They went to significant trouble to demonstrate the evils of slavery and to confirm the truth of their claims. Some former slaves on the lecture circuit corroborated their accounts of violence by baring scars on their backs to horrified audiences.

Apart from organizing lecture tours and publishing books, abolitionists also sent volleys of pamphlets by mail to Southern states. But Southerners were not the only targets. As the abolitionist movement grew in the 1830s, activists increasingly focused their attention on the indifference of white Northerners, who mostly kept quiet on the subject of slavery. Neither major political party would mention it. And even in the North, angry mobs would descend on antislavery meetings and smash their printing presses. Douglass himself had his hand broken in Indiana. Dedicating themselves to exposing slavery to a wide public, abolitionists showed just how risky—and how powerful—words could be.

WORK

While the truthfulness of Douglass's story was a central question for his contemporaries, recent readers have been more inclined to admire the literary artfulness of the *Narrative*, its metaphorical richness, rhetorical complexity, and careful construction. Douglass casts his life as a long process of self-transformation—from an object, or an animal, to a free human being with a name. The contrast between the openings of the *Narrative* and of **Rousseau's *Confessions*** is instructive. Rousseau begins by proclaiming that he differs from everyone else in his unique personality and character. Douglass, on the other hand, starts by reporting what he does *not* know of himself. He must guess his own age, he doesn't know his birthday, he has only rumor to tell him of his father's identity. Although he knows his mother, he spends virtually no time with her; she comes to him and leaves him in the dark. Most children develop their sense of who they are by precisely the clues missing in Douglass's experience: age, parentage, and such ritual occasions as birthdays. Douglass has only a generic identity: slave. Everything in Douglass's early experience denies his individuality and declares his lack of particularized identity. By the end, however, he claims a right to affirm himself: "I subscribe myself, FREDERICK DOUGLASS." The name itself is a triumph, not his father's or his mother's but the freshly bestowed name of his freedom. Each step of the way to this point— learning to read, learning to write, acquiring a name—has involved a painful self-testing, but the *word* proves for Douglass quite literally a means to salvation.

If Douglass wins himself a name and an identity by the end of the *Narrative*, the triumphant individual is not the sole focus of the story. Along the way, Douglass uses his own experience to throw light on slavery in general. The first pages in fact tell us little about the uniqueness of the author, and Douglass is careful to explain how his own circumstances are common to many slaves. He also repeatedly argues that individuals emerge out of their circumstances. He goes to some trouble to show how masters systematically *create* the slaves' mindset, deliberately starving them of intellectual or spiritual nourishment. But he makes it clear that the masters, too, are created by their conditions. Sophia Auld begins as a compassionate and generous person, but the experience of owning another human being makes her suspicious and mean-spirited. Many readers have seen the *Narrative* as fundamentally a story of

self-transformation in which the illiterate and unthinking slave is prompted to recognize the injustice of his experience and to insist on his full personhood, but Douglass reminds us many times along the way that self-transformation always involves a set of opportunities, and that under slightly different conditions, this slave might never have sought out his freedom.

There is one way that Douglass's story has disappointed recent readers. He affirms his own manhood—rejecting the bestial and objectified status of the slave—but does so at the expense of women's experience. He entirely omits descriptions of important women in his life, such as his grandmother, who raised him, and his wife-to-be. He does give graphic depictions of women slaves enduring physical violence, and he refers to the rape of slaves by masters more than once. But since his central image for slavery is a physical struggle for dominance between men, and since he depicts women mostly as lacerated bodies, Douglass's *Narrative* cannot be said to speak for all slaves.

In recounting the internal and external shifts that take him from slave to free man, Douglass's story draws on a number of other genres. As in spiritual autobiographies, the *Narrative* calls attention to moments of revelation, when the central figure undergoes a kind of conversion experience, and sees himself and his world in a fresh light. As in rags-to-riches stories, Douglass tells us how he makes a dramatic rise in social status and wealth through virtues such as perseverance, bravery, self-reliance, and determination. He draws on the sentimental novel, too, in offering us images of innocent victims whose abuses tug at our heartstrings. And the *Narrative* draws on the language of politics, economics, and religious sermons, woven together throughout the text. But perhaps most important, this autobiography belongs in the tradition of the slave narrative, which, by Douglass's time, had become a well-established genre. There had been thousands of first-person accounts of slavery published since the late eighteenth century, and slave narratives had become a major American genre. They were so popular that most American readers might never have encountered an autobiography written by anyone other than a slave. Among these many narratives, Douglass's has been widely recognized as the richest, most subtle, and most beautifully conceived, remaining worthwhile reading not only for its searing indictment of slavery, but also for its complex literary artistry.

Narrative of the Life of Frederick Douglass, An American Slave[1]

CHAPTER I

I was born in Tuckahoe, near Hillsborough, and about twelve miles from Easton, in Talbot county, Maryland. I have no accurate knowledge of my age, never having seen any authentic record containing it. By far the larger part of the slaves know as little of their ages as horses know of theirs, and it is the wish of most masters within my knowledge to keep their slaves thus ignorant. I do not remember to have ever met a slave who could tell of his birthday. They seldom come nearer to it than planting-time, harvest-time, cherry-time, spring-time, or fall-time. A want of information concerning my own was a source of unhappiness to me even during childhood. The white children could tell their ages. I could not tell why I ought to be deprived of the same privilege. I was not allowed to make any inquiries of my master concerning it. He deemed all such inquiries on the part of a slave improper and impertinent, and evidence of a restless spirit. The nearest estimate I can give makes me now between twentyseven and twenty-eight years of age. I come to this, from hearing my master say, some time during 1835, I was about seventeen years old.

My mother was named Harriet Bailey. She was the daughter of Isaac and Betsey Bailey, both colored, and quite dark. My mother was of a darker complexion than either my grandmother or grandfather.

My father was a white man. He was admitted to be such by all I ever heard speak of my parentage. The opinion was also whispered that my master was my father; but of the correctness of this opinion, I know nothing; the means of knowing was withheld from me. My mother and I were separated when I was but an infant—before I knew her as my mother. It is a common custom, in the part of Maryland from which I ran away, to part children from their mothers at a very early age. Frequently, before the child has reached its twelfth month, its mother is taken from it, and hired out on some farm a considerable distance off,

---

1. The text, printed in its entirety, is that of the first American edition, published by the Massachusetts Anti-Slavery Society in Boston in 1845.

and the child is placed under the care of an old woman, too old for field labor. For what this separation is done, I do not know, unless it be to hinder the development of the child's affection toward its mother, and to blunt and destroy the natural affection of the mother for the child. This is the inevitable result.

I never saw my mother, to know her as such, more than four or five times in my life; and each of those times was very short in duration, and at night. She was hired by a Mr. Stewart, who lived about twelve miles from my home. She made her journeys to see me in the night, travelling the whole distance on foot, after the performance of her day's work. She was a field hand, and a whipping is the penalty of not being in the field at sunrise, unless a slave has special permission from his or her master to the contrary—a permission which they seldom get, and one that gives to him that gives it the proud name of being a kind master. I do not recollect of ever seeing my mother by the light of day. She was with me in the night. She would lie down with me, and get me to sleep, but long before I waked she was gone. Very little communication ever took place between us. Death soon ended what little we could have while she lived, and with it her hardships and suffering. She died when I was about seven years old, on one of my master's farms, near Lee's Mill. I was not allowed to be present during her illness, at her death, or burial. She was gone long before I knew anything about it. Never having enjoyed, to any considerable extent, her soothing presence, her tender and watchful care, I received the tidings of her death with much the same emotions I should have probably felt at the death of a stranger.

Called thus suddenly away, she left me without the slightest intimation of who my father was. The whisper that my master was my father, may or may not be true; and, true or false, it is of but little consequence to my purpose whilst the fact remains, in all its glaring odiousness, that slaveholders have ordained, and by law established, that the children of slave women shall in all cases follow the condition of their mothers; and this is done too obviously to administer to their own lusts, and make a gratification of their wicked desires profitable as well as pleasurable; for by this cunning arrangement, the slaveholder, in cases not a few, sustains to his slaves the double relation of master and father.

I know of such cases; and it is worthy of remark that such slaves invariably suffer greater hardships, and have more to contend with, than others. They are, in the first place, a constant offence to their mistress. She is ever disposed to find fault with them; they can seldom do any thing to please her; she is never better pleased than when she sees them under the lash, especially when she suspects her husband of showing to his mulatto children favors which he withholds from his black slaves. The master is frequently compelled to sell this class of his slaves, out of deference to the feelings of his white wife; and, cruel as the deed may strike any one to be, for a man to sell his own children to human flesh-mongers, it is often the dictate of humanity for him to do so; for, unless he does this, he must not only whip them himself, but must stand by and see one white son tie up his brother, of but few shades darker complexion than himself, and ply the gory lash to his naked back; and if he lisp one word of disapproval, it is set down to his parental partiality, and only makes a bad matter worse, both for himself and the slave whom he would protect and defend.

year brings with it multitudes of this class of slaves. It was doubtless in consequence of a knowledge of this fact, that one great statesman of the south predicted the downfall of slavery by the inevitable laws of population. Whether this prophecy is ever fulfilled or not, it is nevertheless plain that a very different-looking class of people are springing up at the south, and are now held in slavery, from those originally brought to this country from Africa; and if their increase will do no other good, it will do away the force of the argument, that God cursed Ham,[2] and therefore American slavery is right. If the lineal descendants of Ham are alone to be scripturally enslaved, it is certain that slavery at the south must soon become unscriptural; for thousands are ushered into the world, annually, who, like myself, owe their existence to white fathers, and those fathers most frequently their own masters.

I have had two masters. My first master's name was Anthony. I do not remember his first name. He was generally called Captain Anthony—a title which, I presume, he acquired by sailing a craft on the Chesapeake Bay. He was not considered a rich slaveholder. He owned two or three farms, and about thirty slaves. His farms and slaves were under the care of an overseer. The overseer's name was Plummer. Mr. Plummer was a miserable drunkard, a profane swearer, and a savage monster. He always went armed with a cowskin and a heavy cudgel. I have known him to cut and slash the women's heads so horribly, that even master would be enraged at his cruelty, and would threaten to whip him if he did not mind himself. Master, however, was not a humane slaveholder. It required extraordinary barbarity on the part of an overseer to affect him. He was a cruel man, hardened by a long life of slaveholding. He would at times seem to take great pleasure in whipping a slave. I have often been awakened at the dawn of day by the most heartrending shrieks of an own aunt of mine, whom he used to tie up to a joist, and whip upon her naked back till she was literally covered with blood. No words, no tears, no prayers, from his gory victim, seemed to move his iron heart from its bloody purpose. The louder she screamed, the harder he whipped; and where the blood ran fastest, there he whipped longest. He would whip her to make her scream, and whip her to make her hush; and not until overcome by fatigue, would he cease to swing the blood-clotted cowskin. I remember the first time I ever witnessed this horrible exhibition. I was quite a child, but I well remember it. I never shall forget it whilst I remember any thing. It was the first of a long series of such outrages, of which I was doomed to be a witness and a participant. It struck me with awful force. It was the blood-stained gate, the entrance to the hell of slavery, through which I was about to pass. It was a most terrible spectacle. I wish I could commit to paper the feelings with which I beheld it.

This occurrence took place very soon after I went to live with my old master, and under the following circumstances. Aunt Hester went out one night,— where or for what I do not know,—and happened to be absent when my master desired her presence. He had ordered her not to go out evenings, and warned

2. It was widely thought that Noah cursed his second son, Ham, for mocking him; that black skin resulted from the curse; and that all black people descended from Ham. In fact, according to Genesis 9:20–27 and 10:6–14, Noah cursed not Ham but Ham's son Canaan, while Ham's son Cush was black.

her that she must never let him catch her in company with a young man, who was paying attention to her, belonging to Colonel Lloyd. The young man's name was Ned Roberts, generally called Lloyd's Ned. Why master was so careful of her, may be safely left to conjecture. She was a woman of noble form, and of graceful proportions, having very few equals, and fewer superiors, in personal appearance, among the colored or white women of our neighborhood.

Aunt Hester had not only disobeyed his orders in going out, but had been found in company with Lloyd's Ned; which circumstance, I found, from what he said while whipping her, was the chief offence. Had he been a man of pure morals himself, he might have been thought interested in protecting the innocence of my aunt; but those who knew him will not suspect him of any such virtue. Before he commenced whipping Aunt Hester, he took her into the kitchen, and stripped her from neck to waist, leaving her neck, shoulders, and back, entirely naked. He then told her to cross her hands, calling her at the same time a d—d b—h. After crossing her hands, he tied them with a strong rope, and led her to a stool under a large hook in the joist, put in for the purpose. He made her get upon the stool, and tied her hands to the hook. She now stood fair for his infernal purpose. Her arms were stretched up at their full length, so that she stood upon the ends of her toes. He then said to her, "Now, you d—d b—h, I'll learn you how to disobey my orders!" and after rolling up his sleeves, he commenced to lay on the heavy cowskin, and soon the warm, red blood (amid heart-rending shrieks from her, and horrid oaths from him) came dripping to the floor. I was so terrified and horror-stricken at the sight, that I hid myself in a closet, and dared not venture out till long after the bloody transaction was over. I expected it would be my turn next. It was all new to me. I had never seen any thing like it before. I had always lived with my grandmother on the outskirts of the plantation, where she was put to raise the children of the younger women. I had therefore been, until now, out of the way of the bloody scenes that often occurred on the plantation.

CHAPTER II

My master's family consisted of two sons, Andrew and Richard; one daughter, Lucretia, and her husband, Captain Thomas Auld. They lived in one house, upon the home plantation of Colonel Edward Lloyd. My master was Colonel Lloyd's clerk and superintendent. He was what might be called the overseer of the overseers. I spent two years of childhood on this plantation in my old master's family. It was here that I witnessed the bloody transaction recorded in the first chapter; and as I received my first impressions of slavery on this plantation, I will give some description of it, and of slavery as it there existed. The plantation is about twelve miles north of Easton, in Talbot county, and is situated on the border of Miles River. The principal products raised upon it were tobacco, corn, and wheat. These were raised in great abundance; so that, with the products of this and the other farms belonging to him, he was able to keep in almost constant employment a large sloop, in carrying them to market at Baltimore. This sloop was named *Sally Lloyd*, in honor of one of the colonel's daughters. My master's son-in-law, Captain Auld, was master of the vessel; she was otherwise manned by the colonel's own slaves. Their names were Peter,

Isaac, Rich, and Jake. These were esteemed very highly by the other slaves, and looked upon as the privileged ones of the plantation; for it was no small affair, in the eyes of the slaves, to be allowed to see Baltimore.

Colonel Lloyd kept from three to four hundred slaves on his home planta-tion, and owned a large number more on the neighboring farms belonging to him. The names of the farms nearest to the home plantation were Wye Town and New Design. "Wye Town" was under the overseership of a man named Noah Willis. New Design was under the overseership of a Mr. Townsend. The overseers of these, and all the rest of the farms, numbering over twenty, received advice and direction from the managers of the home plantation. This was the great business place. It was the seat of government for the whole twenty farms. All disputes among the overseers were settled here. If a slave was con-victed of any high misdemeanor, became unmanageable, or evinced a determi-nation to run away, he was brought immediately here, severely whipped, put on board the sloop, carried to Baltimore, and sold to Austin Woolfolk, or some other slave-trader, as a warning to the slaves remaining.

Here, too, the slaves of all the other farms received their monthly allowance of food, and their yearly clothing. The men and women slaves received, as their monthly allowance of food, eight pounds of pork, or its equivalent in fish, and one bushel of corn meal. Their yearly clothing consisted of two coarse linen shirts, one pair of linen trousers, like the shirts, one jacket, one pair of trousers for winter, made of coarse negro cloth, one pair of stockings, and one pair of shoes; the whole of which could not have cost more than seven dollars. The allowance of the slave children was given to their mothers, or the old women having the care of them. The children unable to work in the field had neither shoes, stockings, jackets, nor trousers, given to them; their clothing consisted of two coarse linen shirts per year. When these failed them, they went naked until the next allowance-day. Children from seven to ten years old, of both sexes, almost naked, might be seen at all seasons of the year.

There were no beds given the slaves, unless one coarse blanket be consid-ered such, and none but the men and women had these. This, however, is not considered a very great privation. They find less difficulty from the want of beds, than from the want of time to sleep; for when their day's work in the field is done, the most of them having their washing, mending, and cooking to do, and having few or none of the ordinary facilities for doing either of these, very many of their sleeping hours are consumed in preparing for the field the com-ing day; and when this is done, old and young, male and female, married and single, drop down side by side, on one common bed,—the cold, damp floor,— each covering himself or herself with their miserable blankets; and here they sleep till they are summoned to the field by the driver's horn. At the sound of this, all must rise, and be off to the field. There must be no halting; every one must be at his or her post; and woe betides them who hear not this morning summons to the field; for if they are not awakened by the sense of hearing, they are by the sense of feeling: no age nor sex finds any favor. Mr. Severe, the over-seer, used to stand by the door of the quarter, armed with a large hickory stick and heavy cowskin, ready to whip any one who was so unfortunate as not to hear, or, from any other cause, was prevented from being ready to start for the field at the sound of the horn.

Mr. Severe was rightly named: he was a cruel man. I have seen him whip a woman, causing the blood to run half an hour at the time; and this, too, in the midst of her crying children, pleading for their mother's release. He seemed to take pleasure in manifesting his fiendish barbarity. Added to his cruelty, he was a profane swearer. It was enough to chill the blood and stiffen the hair of an ordinary man to hear him talk. Scarce a sentence escaped him but that was commenced or concluded by some horrid oath. The field was the place to witness his cruelty and profanity. His presence made it both the field of blood and of blasphemy. From the rising till the going down of the sun, he was cursing, raving, cutting, and slashing among the slaves of the field, in the most frightful manner. His career was short. He died very soon after I went to Colonel Lloyd's; and he died as he lived, uttering, with his dying groans, bitter curses and horrid oaths. His death was regarded by the slaves as the result of a merciful providence.

Mr. Severe's place was filled by a Mr. Hopkins. He was a very different man. He was less cruel, less profane, and made less noise, than Mr. Severe. His course was characterized by no extraordinary demonstrations of cruelty. He whipped, but seemed to take no pleasure in it. He was called by the slaves a good overseer.

The home plantation of Colonel Lloyd wore the appearance of a country village. All the mechanical operations for all the farms were performed here. The shoemaking and mending, the blacksmithing, cartwrighting, coopering, weaving, and grain-grinding, were all performed by the slaves on the home plantation. The whole place wore a business-like aspect very unlike the neighboring farms. The number of houses, too, conspired to give it advantage over the neighboring farms. It was called by the slaves the *Great House Farm*. Few privileges were esteemed higher, by the slaves of the out-farms, than that of being selected to do errands at the Great House Farm. It was associated in their minds with greatness. A representative could not be prouder of his election to a seat in the American Congress, than a slave on one of the out-farms would be of his election to do errands at the Great House Farm. They regarded it as evidence of great confidence reposed in them by their overseers; and it was on this account, as well as a constant desire to be out of the field from under the driver's lash, that they esteemed it a high privilege, one worth careful living for. He was called the smartest and most trusty fellow, who had this honor conferred upon him the most frequently. The competitors for this office sought as diligently to please their overseers, as the office-seekers in the political parties seek to please and deceive the people. The same traits of character might be seen in Colonel Lloyd's slaves, as are seen in the slaves of the political parties.

The slaves selected to go to the Great House Farm, for the monthly allowance for themselves and their fellow-slaves, were peculiarly enthusiastic. While on their way, they would make the dense old woods, for miles around, reverberate with their wild songs, revealing at once the highest joy and the deepest sadness. They would compose and sing as they went along, consulting neither time nor tune. The thought that came up, came out—if not in the word, in the sound;—and as frequently in the one as in the other. They would sometimes sing the most pathetic sentiment in the most rapturous tone, and the most rapturous sentiment in the most pathetic tone. Into all of their songs they would manage to weave something of the Great House Farm. Especially would they do this, when leaving home. They would then sing most exultingly the following words:—

> "I am going away to the Great House Farm!
> O, yea! O, yea! O!"

This they would sing, as a chorus, to words which to many would seem unmeaning jargon, but which, nevertheless, were full of meaning to themselves. I have sometimes thought that the mere hearing of those songs would do more to impress some minds with the horrible character of slavery, than the reading of whole volumes of philosophy on the subject could do.

I did not, when a slave, understand the deep meaning of those rude and apparently incoherent songs. I was myself within the circle; so that I neither saw nor heard as those without might see and hear. They told a tale of woe which was then altogether beyond my feeble comprehension; they were tones loud, long, and deep; they breathed the prayer and complaint of souls boiling over with the bitterest anguish. Every tone was a testimony against slavery, and a prayer to god for deliverance from chains. The hearing of those wild notes always depressed my spirit, and filled me with ineffable sadness. I have frequently found myself in tears while hearing them. The mere recurrence to those songs, even now, afflicts me; and while I am writing these lines, an expression of feeling has already found its way down my cheek. To those songs I trace my first glimmering conception of the dehumanizing character of slavery. I can never get rid of that conception. Those songs still follow me, to deepen my hatred of slavery, and quicken my sympathies for my brethren in bonds. If any one wishes to be impressed with the soul-killing effects of slavery, let him go to Colonel Lloyd's plantation, and, on allowance-day, place himself in the deep pine woods, and there let him, in silence, analyze the sounds that shall pass through the chambers of his soul,—and if he is not thus impressed, it will only be because "there is no flesh in his obdurate heart."

I have often been utterly astonished, since I came to the north, to find persons who could speak of the singing, among slaves, as evidence of their contentment and happiness. It is impossible to conceive of a greater mistake. Slaves sing most when they are most unhappy. The songs of the slave represent the sorrows of his heart; and he is relieved by them, only as an aching heart is relieved by its tears. At least, such is my experience. I have often sung to drown my sorrow, but seldom to express my happiness. Crying for joy, and singing for joy, were alike uncommon to me while in the jaws of slavery. The singing of a man cast away upon a desolate island might be as appropriately considered as evidence of contentment and happiness, as the singing of a slave; the songs of the one and of the other are prompted by the same emotion.

CHAPTER III

Colonel Lloyd kept a large and finely cultivated garden, which afforded almost constant employment for four men, besides the chief gardener (Mr. M'Durmond). This garden was probably the greatest attraction of the place. During the summer months, people came from far and near—from Baltimore, Easton, and

Annapolis—to see it. It abounded in fruits of almost every description, from the hardy apple of the north to the delicate orange of the south. This garden was not the least source of trouble on the plantation. Its excellent fruit was quite a temptation to the hungry swarms of boys, as well as the older slaves, belonging to the colonel, few of whom had the virtue or the vice to resist it. Scarcely a day passed, during the summer, but that some slave had to take the lash for stealing fruit. The colonel had to resort to all kinds of stratagems to keep his slaves out of the garden. The last and most successful one was that of tarring his fence all around; after which, if a slave was caught with tar upon his person, it was deemed sufficient proof that he had either been into the garden, or had tried to get in. In either case, he was severely whipped by the chief gardener. This plan worked well; the slaves became as fearful of tar as of the lash. They seemed to realize the impossibility of touching *tar* without being defiled.[3]

The colonel also kept a splendid riding equipage. His stable and carriage-house presented the appearance of some of our large city livery establishments. His horses were of the finest form and noblest blood. His carriage-house contained three splendid coaches, three or four gigs, besides dearborns and barouches[4] of the most fashionable style.

This establishment was under the care of two slaves—old Barney and young Barney—father and son. To attend to this establishment was their sole work. But it was by no means an easy employment; for in nothing was Colonel Lloyd more particular than in the management of his horses. The slightest inattention to these was unpardonable, and was visited upon those, under whose care they were placed, with the severest punishment; no excuse could shield them, if the colonel only suspected any want of attention to his horses—a supposition which he frequently indulged, and one which, of course, made the office of old and young Barney a very trying one. They never knew when they were safe from punishment. They were frequently whipped when least deserving, and escaped whipping when most deserving it. Every thing depended upon the looks of the horses, and the state of Colonel Lloyd's own mind when his horses were brought to him for use. If a horse did not move fast enough, or hold his head high enough, it was owing to some fault of his keepers. It was painful to stand near the stable-door, and hear the various complaints against the keepers when a horse was taken out for use. "This horse has not had proper attention. He has not been sufficiently rubbed and curried, or he has not been properly fed; his food was too wet or too dry; he got it too soon or too late; he was too hot or too cold; he had too much hay, and not enough of grain; or he had too much grain, and not enough of hay; instead of old Barney's attending to the horse, he had very improperly left it to his son." To all these complaints, no matter how unjust, the slave must answer never a word. Colonel Lloyd could not brook any contradiction from a slave. When he spoke, a slave must stand, listen, and tremble; and such was literally the case. I have seen Colonel Lloyd make old Barney, a man between fifty and sixty years of age, uncover his bald head, kneel down upon the cold, damp ground, and receive upon his

---

3. Cf. the proverb "He who touches pitch shall be defiled."
4. Light four-wheeled carriages (*dearborns*) and carriages with a front seat for the driver and two facing back seats for couples (*barouches*).

naked and toil-worn shoulders more than thirty lashes at the time. Colonel Lloyd had three sons—Edward, Murray, and Daniel,—and three sons-in-law, Mr. Winder, Mr. Nicholson, and Mr. Lowndes. All of these lived at the Great House Farm, and enjoyed the luxury of whipping the servants when they pleased, from old Barney down to William Wilkes, the coach-driver. I have seen Winder make one of the house-servants stand off from him a suitable distance to be touched with the end of his whip, and at every stroke raise great ridges upon his back.

To describe the wealth of Colonel Lloyd would be almost equal to describing the riches of Job.[5] He kept from ten to fifteen house-servants. He was said to own a thousand slaves, and I think this estimate quite within the truth. Colonel Lloyd owned so many that he did not know them when he saw them; nor did all the slaves of the out-farms know him. It is reported of him, that, while riding along the road one day, he met a colored man, and addressed him in the usual manner of speaking to colored people on the public highways of the south: "Well, boy, whom do you belong to?" "To Colonel Lloyd," replied the slave. "Well, does the colonel treat you well?" "No, sir," was the ready reply. "What, does he work you too hard?" "Yes, sir." "Well, don't he give you enough to eat?" "Yes, sir, he gives me enough, such as it is."

The colonel, after ascertaining where the slave belonged, rode on; the man also went on about his business, not dreaming that he had been conversing with his master. He thought, said, and heard nothing more of the matter, until two or three weeks afterwards. The poor man was then informed by his overseer that, for having found fault with his master, he was now to be sold to a Georgia trader. He was immediately chained and handcuffed; and thus, without a moment's warning, he was snatched away, and forever sundered, from his family and friends, by a hand more unrelenting than death. This is the penalty of telling the truth, of telling the simple truth, in answer to a series of plain questions.

It is partly in consequence of such facts, that slaves, when inquired of as to their condition and the character of their masters, almost universally say they are contented, and that their masters are kind. The slaveholders have been known to send in spies among their slaves, to ascertain their views and feelings in regard to their condition. The frequency of this has had the effect to establish among the slaves the maxim, that a still tongue makes a wise head. They suppress the truth rather than take the consequences of telling it, and in so doing prove themselves a part of the human family. If they have any thing to say of their masters, it is generally in their masters' favor, especially when speaking to an untried man. I have been frequently asked, when a slave, if I had a kind master, and do not remember ever to have given a negative answer; nor did I, in pursuing this course, consider myself as uttering what was absolutely false; for I always measured the kindness of my master by the standard of kindness set up among slaveholders around us. Moreover, slaves are like other people, and imbibe prejudices quite common to others. They think their own better than that of others. Many, under the influence of this prejudice, think

---

5. Job 1:3: "His substance also was seven thousand sheep, and three thousand camels, and five hundred yoke of oxen, and five hun- dred she asses, and a very great household; so that this man was the greatest of all the men of the East."

their own masters are better than the masters of other slaves; and this, too, in some cases, when the very reverse is true. Indeed, it is not uncommon for slaves even to fall out and quarrel among themselves about the relative goodness of their masters, each contending for the superior goodness of his own over that of the others. At the very same time, they mutually execrate their masters when viewed separately. It was so on our plantation. When Colonel Lloyd's slaves met the slaves of Jacob Jepson, they seldom parted without a quarrel about their masters; Colonel Lloyd's slaves contending that he was the richest, and Mr. Jepson's slaves that he was the smartest, and most of a man. Colonel Lloyd's slaves would boast his ability to buy and sell Jacob Jepson. Mr. Jepson's slaves would boast his ability to whip Colonel Lloyd. These quarrels would almost always end in a fight between the parties, and those that whipped were supposed to have gained the point at issue. They seemed to think that the greatness of their masters was transferable to themselves. It was considered as being bad enough to be a slave; but to be a poor man's slave was deemed a disgrace indeed!

CHAPTER IV

Mr. Hopkins remained but a short time in the office of overseer. Why his career was so short, I do not know, but suppose he lacked the necessary severity to suit Colonel Lloyd. Mr. Hopkins was succeeded by Mr. Austin Gore, a man possessing, in an eminent degree, all those traits of character indispensable to what is called a first-rate overseer. Mr. Gore had served Colonel Lloyd, in the capacity of overseer, upon one of the out-farms, and had shown himself worthy of the high station of overseer upon the home or Great House Farm.

Mr. Gore was proud, ambitious, and persevering. He was artful, cruel, and obdurate. He was just the man for such a place, and it was just the place for such a man. It afforded scope for the full exercise of all his powers, and he seemed to be perfectly at home in it. He was one of those who could torture the slightest look, word, or gesture, on the part of the slave, into impudence, and would treat it accordingly. There must be no answering back to him; no explanation was allowed a slave, showing himself to have been wrongfully accused. Mr. Gore acted fully up to the maxim laid down by slaveholders,—"It is better that a dozen slaves suffer under the lash, than that the overseer should be convicted, in the presence of the slaves, of having been at fault." No matter how innocent a slave might be—it availed him nothing, when accused by Mr. Gore of any misdemeanor. To be accused was to be convicted, and to be convicted was to be punished; the one always following the other with immutable certainty. To escape punishment was to escape accusation; and few slaves had the fortune to do either, under the overseership of Mr. Gore. He was just proud enough to demand the most debasing homage of the slave, and quite servile enough to crouch, himself, at the feet of the master. He was ambitious enough to be contented with nothing short of the highest rank of overseers, and persevering enough to reach the height of his ambition. He was cruel enough to inflict the severest punishment, artful enough to descend to the lowest trickery, and obdurate enough to be insensible to the voice of a reproving conscience. He was, of all the overseers, the most dreaded by the slaves. His presence was painful; his eye flashed confusion; and seldom was his sharp, shrill voice heard, without producing horror and trembling in their ranks.

Mr. Gore was a grave man, and, though a young man, he indulged in no jokes, said no funny words, seldom smiled. His words were in perfect keeping with his looks, and his looks were in perfect keeping with his words. Overseers will sometimes indulge in a witty word, even with the slaves; not so with Mr. Gore. He spoke but to command, and commanded but to be obeyed; he dealt sparingly with his words, and bountifully with his whip, never using the former where the latter would answer as well. When he whipped, he seemed to do so from a sense of duty, and feared no consequences. He did nothing reluctantly, no matter how disagreeable; always at his post, never inconsistent. He never promised but to fulfil. He was, in a word, a man of the most inflexible firmness and stone-like coolness.

His savage barbarity was equalled only by the consummate coolness with which he committed the grossest and most savage deeds upon the slaves under his charge. Mr. Gore once undertook to whip one of Colonel Lloyd's slaves, by the name of Demby. He had given Demby but few stripes, when, to get rid of the scourging, he ran and plunged himself into a creek, and stood there at the depth of his shoulders, refusing to come out. Mr. Gore told him that he would give him three calls, and that, if he did not come out at the third call, he would shoot him. The first call was given. Demby made no response, but stood his ground. The second and third calls were given with the same result. Mr. Gore then, without consultation or deliberation with any one, not even giving Demby an additional call, raised his musket to his face, taking deadly aim at his standing victim, and in an instant poor Demby was no more. His mangled body sank out of sight, and blood and brains marked the water where he had stood.

A thrill of horror flashed through every soul upon the plantation, excepting Mr. Gore. He alone seemed cool and collected. He was asked by Colonel Lloyd and my old master, why he resorted to this extraordinary expedient. His reply was, (as well as I can remember,) that Demby had become unmanageable. He was setting a dangerous example to the other slaves,—one which, if suffered to pass without some such demonstration on his part, would finally lead to the total subversion of all rule and order upon the plantation. He argued that if one slave refused to be corrected, and escaped with his life, the other slaves would soon copy the example; the result of which would be, the freedom of the slaves, and the enslavement of the whites. Mr. Gore's defence was satisfactory. He was continued in his station as overseer upon the home plantation. His fame as an overseer went abroad. His horrid crime was not even submitted to judicial investigation. It was committed in the presence of slaves, and they of course could neither institute a suit, nor testify against him; and thus the guilty perpetrator of one of the bloodiest and most foul murders goes unwhipped of justice, and uncensured by the community in which he lives. Mr. Gore lived in St. Michael's, Talbot county, Maryland, when I left there; and if he is still alive, he very probably lives there now; and if so, he is now, as he was then, as highly esteemed and as much respected as though his guilty soul had not been stained with his brother's blood.

I speak advisedly when I say this,—that killing a slave, or any colored person, in Talbot county, Maryland, is not treated as a crime, either by the courts or the community. Mr. Thomas Lanman, of St. Michael's, killed two slaves, one of whom he killed with a hatchet, by knocking his brains out. He used to boast of the commission of the awful and bloody deed. I have heard him do so laughingly, saying, among other things, that he was the only benefactor of his country in the company, and that when others would do as much as he had done, we should be relieved of "the d——d niggers."

The wife of Mr. Giles Hicks, living but a short distance from where I used to live, murdered my wife's cousin, a young girl between fifteen and sixteen years of age, mangling her person in the most horrible manner, breaking her nose and breastbone with a stick, so that the poor girl expired in a few hours afterward. She was immediately buried, but had not been in her untimely grave but a few hours before she was taken up and examined by the coroner, who decided that she had come to her death by severe beating. The offence for which this girl was thus murdered was this:—She had been set that night to mind Mrs. Hicks's baby, and during the night she fell asleep, and the baby cried. She, having lost her rest for several nights previous, did not hear the crying. They were both in the room with Mrs. Hicks. Mrs. Hicks, finding the girl slow to move, jumped from her bed, seized an oak stick of wood by the fireplace, and with it broke the girl's nose and breastbone, and thus ended her life. I will not say that this most horrid murder produced no sensation in the community. It did produce sensation, but not enough to bring the murderess to punishment. There was a warrant issued for her arrest, but it was never served. Thus she escaped not only punishment, but even the pain of being arraigned before a court for her horrid crime.

Whilst I am detailing bloody deeds which took place during my stay on Colonel Lloyd's plantation, I will briefly narrate another, which occurred about the same time as the murder of Demby by Mr. Gore.

Colonel Lloyd's slaves were in the habit of spending a part of their nights and Sundays in fishing for oysters, and in this way made up the deficiency of their scanty allowance. An old man belonging to Colonel Lloyd, while thus engaged, happened to get beyond the limits of Colonel Lloyd's, and on the premises of Mr. Beal Bondly. At this trespass, Mr. Bondly took offence, and with his musket came down to the shore, and blew its deadly contents into the poor old man.

Mr. Bondly came over to see Colonel Lloyd the next day, whether to pay him for his property, or to justify himself in what he had done, I know not. At any rate, this whole fiendish transaction was soon hushed up. There was very little said about it at all, and nothing done. It was a common saying, even among little white boys, that it was worth a half-cent to kill a "nigger," and a half-cent to bury one.

CHAPTER V

As to my own treatment while I lived on Colonel Lloyd's plantation, it was very similar to that of the other slave children. I was not old enough to work in the field, and there being little else than field work to do, I had a great deal of leisure time. The most I had to do was to drive up the cows at evening, keep the fowls out of the garden, keep the front yard clean, and run off errands for my old master's daughter, Mrs. Lucretia Auld. The most of my leisure time I spent in helping Master Daniel Lloyd in finding his birds, after he had shot them. My connection with Master Daniel was of some advantage to me. He became quite attached to me, and was a sort of protector of me. He would not allow the older boys to impose upon me, and would divide his cakes with me.

I was seldom whipped by my old master, and suffered little from any thing else than hunger and cold. I suffered much from hunger, but much more from cold. In hottest summer and coldest winter, I was kept almost naked—no shoes, no stockings, no jacket, no trousers, nothing on but a coarse tow linen shirt, reaching only to my knees. I had no bed. I must have perished with cold, but that, the coldest nights, I used to steal a bag which was used for carrying corn to the mill. I would crawl into this bag, and there sleep on the cold, damp, clay floor, with my head in and feet out. My feet had been so cracked with the frost, that the pen with which I am writing might be laid in the gashes.

We were not regularly allowanced. Our food was coarse corn meal boiled. This was called *mush*. It was put into a large wooden tray or trough, and set down upon the ground. The children were then called, like so many pigs, and like so many pigs they would come and devour the mush; some with oyster-shells, others with pieces of shingle, some with naked hands, and none with spoons. He that ate fastest got most; he that was strongest secured the best place; and few left the trough satisfied.

I was probably between seven and eight years old when I left Colonel Lloyd's plantation. I left it with joy. I shall never forget the ecstasy with which I received the intelligence that my old master (Anthony) had determined to let me go to Baltimore, to live with Mr. Hugh Auld, brother to my old master's son-in-law, Captain Thomas Auld. I received this information about three days before my departure. They were three of the happiest days I ever enjoyed. I spent the most part of all these three days in the creek, washing off the plantation scurf, and preparing myself for my departure.

The pride of appearance which this would indicate was not my own. I spent the time in washing, not so much because I wished to, but because Mrs. Lucretia had told me I must get all the dead skin off my feet and knees before I could go to Baltimore; for the people in Baltimore were very cleanly, and would laugh at me if I looked dirty. Besides, she was going to give me a pair of trousers, which I should not put on unless I got all the dirt off me. The thought of owning a pair of trousers was great indeed! It was almost a sufficient motive, not only to make me take off what would be called by pig-drovers the mange, but the skin itself. I went at it in good earnest, working for the first time with the hope of reward.

The ties that ordinarily bind children to their homes were all suspended in my case. I found no severe trial in my departure. My home was charmless; it was not home to me; on parting from it, I could not feel that I was leaving any thing which I could have enjoyed by staying. My mother was dead, my grand-mother lived far off, so that I seldom saw her. I had two sisters and one brother, that lived in the same house with me; but the early separation of us from our mother had well nigh blotted the fact of our relationship from our memories. I looked for home elsewhere, and was confident of finding none which I should relish less than the one which I was leaving. If, however, I found in my new home hardship, hunger, whipping, and nakedness, I had the consolation that I should not have escaped any one of them by staying. Having already had more than a taste of them in the house of my old master, and having endured them there, I very naturally inferred my ability to endure them elsewhere, and especially at Baltimore; for I had something of the feeling about Baltimore that is expressed in the proverb, that "being hanged in England is preferable to dying a natural death in Ireland." I had the strongest desire to see Baltimore.

Cousin Tom, though not fluent in speech, had inspired me with that desire by his eloquent description of the place. I could never point out any thing at the Great House, no matter how beautiful or powerful, but that he had seen something at Baltimore far exceeding, both in beauty and strength, the object which I pointed out to him. Even the Great House itself, with all its pictures, was far inferior to many buildings in Baltimore. So strong was my desire, that I thought a gratification of it would fully compensate for whatever loss of comforts I should sustain by the exchange. I left without a regret, and with the highest hopes of future happiness.

We sailed out of Miles River for Baltimore on a Saturday morning. I remember only the day of the week, for at that time I had no knowledge of the days of the month, nor the months of the year. On setting sail, I walked aft, and gave to Colonel Lloyd's plantation what I hoped would be the last look. I then placed myself in the bows of the sloop, and there spent the remainder of the day in looking ahead, interesting myself in what was in the distance rather than in things near by or behind.

In the afternoon of that day, we reached Annapolis, the capital of the State. We stopped but a few moments, so that I had no time to go on shore. It was the first large town that I had ever seen, and though it would look small compared with some of our New England factory villages, I thought it a wonderful place for its size—more imposing even than the Great House Farm!

We arrived at Baltimore early on Sunday morning, landing at Smith's Wharf, not far from Bowley's Wharf. We had on board the sloop a large flock of sheep; and after aiding in driving them to the slaughterhouse of Mr. Curtis on Louden Slater's Hill, I was conducted by Rich, one of the hands belonging on board of the sloop, to my new home in Alliciana Street, near Mr. Gardner's ship-yard, on Fells Point.

Mr. and Mrs. Auld were both at home, and met me at the door with their little son Thomas, to take care of whom I had been given. And here I saw what I had never seen before; it was a white face beaming with the most kindly emotions; it was the face of my new mistress, Sophia Auld. I wish I could describe the rapture that flashed through my soul as I beheld it. It was a new and strange sight to me, brightening up my pathway with the light of happiness. Little Thomas was told, there was his Freddy,—and I was told to take care of little Thomas; and thus I entered upon the duties of my new home with the most cheering prospect ahead.

I look upon my departure from Colonel Lloyd's plantation as one of the most interesting events of my life. It is possible, and even quite probable, that but for the mere circumstance of being removed from that plantation to Baltimore, I should have to-day, instead of being here seated by my own table, in the enjoyment of freedom and the happiness of home, writing this Narrative, been confined in the galling chains of slavery. Going to live at Baltimore laid the foundation, and opened the gateway, to all my subsequent prosperity. I have ever regarded it as the first plain manifestation of that kind providence which has ever since attended me, and marked my life with so many favors. I regarded the selection of myself as being somewhat remarkable. There were a number of slave children that might have been sent from the plantation to Baltimore. There were those younger, those older, and those of the same age. I was chosen from among them all, and was the first, last, and only choice.

I may be deemed superstitious, and even egotistical, in regarding this event as a special interposition of divine Providence in my favor. But I should be false to the earliest sentiments of my soul, if I suppressed the opinion. I prefer to be true to myself, even at the hazard of incurring the ridicule of others, rather than to be false, and incur my own abhorrence. From my earliest recollection, I date the entertainment of a deep conviction that slavery would not always be able to hold me within its foul embrace; and in the darkest hours of my career in slavery, this living word of faith and spirit of hope departed not from me, but remained like ministering angels to cheer me through the gloom. This good spirit was from God, and to him I offer thanksgiving and praise.

CHAPTER VI

My new mistress proved to be all she appeared when I first met her at the door,—a woman of the kindest heart and finest feelings. She had never had a slave under her control previously to myself, and prior to her marriage she had been dependent upon her own industry for a living. She was by trade a weaver; and by constant application to her business, she had been in a good degree preserved from the blighting and dehumanizing effects of slavery. I was utterly astonished at her goodness. I scarcely knew how to behave towards her. She was entirely unlike any other white woman I had ever seen. I could not approach her as I was accustomed to approach other white ladies. My early instruction was all out of place. The crouching servility, usually so acceptable a quality in a slave, did not answer when manifested toward her. Her favor was not gained by it; she seemed to be disturbed by it. She did not deem it impudent or unmannerly for a slave to look her in the face. The meanest slave was put fully at ease in her presence, and none left without feeling better for having seen her. Her face was made of heavenly smiles, and her voice of tranquil music.

But, alas! this kind heart had but a short time to remain such. The fatal poison of irresponsible power was already in her hands, and soon commenced its infernal work. That cheerful eye, under the influence of slavery, soon became red with rage; that voice, made all of sweet accord, changed to one of harsh and horrid discord; and that angelic face gave place to that of a demon.

Very soon after I went to live with Mr. and Mrs. Auld, she very kindly commenced to teach me the A, B, C. After I had learned this, she assisted me in learning to spell words of three or four letters. Just at this point of my progress, Mr. Auld found out what was going on, and at once forbade Mrs. Auld to instruct me further, telling her, among other things, that it was unlawful, as well as unsafe, to teach a slave to read. To use his own words, further, he said, "If you give a nigger an inch, he will take an ell. A nigger should know nothing but to obey his master—to do as he is told to do. Learning would *spoil* the best nigger in the world. Now," said he, "if you teach that nigger (speaking of myself) how to read, there would be no keeping him. It would forever unfit him to be a slave. He would at once become unmanageable, and of no value to his master. As to himself, it could do him no good, but a great deal of harm. It would make him discontented and unhappy." These words sank deep into my heart, stirred up sentiments within that lay slumbering, and called into existence an entirely new train of thought. It was a new and special revelation, explaining dark and mysterious things, with which my youthful understanding had struggled, but struggled in vain. I now understood what had been to me a most perplexing difficulty—to wit, the white man's power to enslave the black man. It was a grand achievement, and I prized it highly. From that moment, I understood the pathway from slavery to freedom. It was just what I wanted, and I got it at a time when I the least expected it. Whilst I was saddened by the thought of losing the aid of my kind mistress, I was gladdened by the invaluable instruction which, by the merest accident, I had gained from my master. Though conscious of the difficulty of learning without a teacher, I set out with high hope, and a fixed purpose, at whatever cost of trouble, to learn how to read. The very decided manner with which he spoke, and strove to impress his wife with the evil consequences of giving me instruction, served to convince me that he was deeply sensible of the truths he was uttering. It gave me the best assurance that I might rely with the utmost confidence on the results which, he said, would flow from teaching me to read. What he most dreaded, that I most desired. What he most loved, that I most hated. That which to him was a great evil, to be carefully shunned, was to me a great good, to be diligently sought; and the argument which he so warmly urged, against my learning to read, only served to inspire me with a desire and determination to learn. In learning to read, I owe almost as much to the bitter opposition of my master, as to the kindly aid of my mistress. I acknowledge the benefit of both.

I had resided but a short time in Baltimore before I observed a marked difference, in the treatment of slaves, from that which I had witnessed in the country. A city slave is almost a freeman, compared with a slave on the plantation. He is much better fed and clothed, and enjoys privileges altogether unknown to the slave on the plantation. There is a vestige of decency, a sense of shame, that does much to curb and check those outbreaks of atrocious cruelty so commonly enacted upon the plantation. He is a desperate slaveholder, who will shock the humanity of his nonslaveholding neighbors with the cries of his lacerated slave. Few are willing to incur the odium attaching to the reputation of being a cruel master; and above all things, they would not be known as not giving a slave enough to eat. Every city slaveholder is anxious to have it known of him, that he feeds his slaves well; and it is due to them to say, that most of them do give their slaves enough to eat. There are, however, some painful exceptions to this rule. Directly opposite to us, on Philpot Street, lived Mr. Thomas Hamilton. He owned two slaves. Their names were Henrietta and Mary. Henrietta was about twenty-two years of age, Mary was about fourteen; and of all the mangled and emaciated creatures I ever looked upon, these two were the most so. His heart must be harder than stone, that could look upon these unmoved. The head, neck, and shoulders of Mary were literally cut to pieces. I have frequently felt her head, and found it nearly covered with festering sores, caused by the lash of her cruel mistress. I do not know that her master ever whipped her, but I have been an eye-witness to the cruelty of Mrs. Hamilton. I used to be in Mr. Hamilton's house nearly every day. Mrs. Hamilton used to sit in a large chair in the middle of the room, with a heavy cowskin always by her side, and scarce an hour passed during the day but was marked by the blood of one of these slaves. The girls seldom passed her without her saying, "Move faster, you *black gip!*"[6] at the same time giving

6. Cheat, swindler.

them a blow with the cowskin over the head or shoulders, often drawing the blood. She would then say, "Take that, you *black gip!*"—continuing, "If you don't move faster, I'll move you!" Added to the cruel lashings to which these slaves were subjected, they were kept nearly half-starved. They seldom knew what it was to eat a full meal. I have seen Mary contending with the pigs for the offal thrown into the street. So much was Mary kicked and cut to pieces, that she was oftener called "*pecked*" than by her name.

CHAPTER VII

I lived in Master Hugh's family about seven years. During this time, I succeeded in learning to read and write. In accomplishing this, I was compelled to resort to various stratagems. I had no regular teacher. My mistress, who had kindly commenced to instruct me, had, in compliance with the advice and direction of her husband, not only ceased to instruct, but had set her face against my being instructed by any one else. It is due, however, to my mistress to say of her, that she did not adopt this course of treatment immediately. She at first lacked the depravity indispensable to shutting me up in mental darkness. It was at least necessary for her to have some training in the exercise of irresponsible power, to make her equal to the task of treating me as though I were a brute.

My mistress was, as I have said, a kind and tender-hearted woman; and in the simplicity of her soul she commenced, when I first went to live with her, to treat me as she supposed one human being ought to treat another. In entering upon the duties of a slaveholder, she did not seem to perceive that I sustained to her the relation of a mere chattel, and that for her to treat me as a human being was not only wrong, but dangerously so. Slavery proved as injurious to her as it did to me. When I went there, she was a pious, warm, and tender-hearted woman. There was no sorrow or suffering for which she had not a tear. She had bread for the hungry, clothes for the naked, and comfort for every mourner that came within her reach. Slavery soon proved its ability to divest her of these heavenly qualities. Under its influence, the tender heart became stone, and the lamblike disposition gave way to one of tiger-like fierceness. The first step in her downward course was in her ceasing to instruct me. She now commenced to practise her husband's precepts. She finally became even more violent in her opposition than her husband himself. She was not satisfied with simply doing as well as he had commanded; she seemed anxious to do better. Nothing seemed to make her more angry than to see me with a newspaper. She seemed to think that here lay the danger. I have had her rush at me with a face made all up of fury, and snatch from me a newspaper, in a manner that fully revealed her apprehension. She was an apt woman; and a little experience soon demonstrated, to her satisfaction, that education and slavery were incompatible with each other.

From this time I was most narrowly watched. If I was in a separate room any considerable length of time, I was sure to be suspected of having a book, and was at once called to give an account of myself. All this, however, was too late. The first step had been taken. Mistress, in teaching me the alphabet, had given me the *inch*, and no precaution could prevent me from taking the *ell*.

The plan which I adopted, and the one by which I was most successful, was that of making friends of all the little white boys whom I met in the street. As many of these as I could, I converted into teachers. With their kindly aid, obtained at different times and in different places, I finally succeeded in learning to read. When I was sent of errands, I always took my book with me, and by going one part of my errand quickly, I found time to get a lesson before my return. I used also to carry bread with me, enough of which was always in the house, and to which I was always welcome; for I was much better off in this regard than many of the poor white children in our neighborhood. This bread I used to bestow upon the hungry little urchins, who, in return, would give me that more valuable bread of knowledge. I am strongly tempted to give the names of two or three of those little boys, as a testimonial of the gratitude and affection I bear them; but prudence forbids;—not that it would injure me, but it might embarrass them; for it is almost an unpardonable offence to teach slaves to read in this Christian country. It is enough to say of the dear little fellows, that they lived on Philpot Street, very near Durgin and Bailey's ship-yard. I used to talk this matter of slavery over with them. I would sometimes say to them, I wished I could be as free as they would be when they got to be men. "You will be free as soon as you are twenty-one, *but I am a slave for life!* Have not I as good a right to be free as you have?" These words used to trouble them; they would express for me the liveliest sympathy, and console me with the hope that something would occur by which I might be free.

I was now about twelve years old, and the thought of being *a slave for life* began to bear heavily upon my heart. Just about this time, I got hold of a book entitled "The Columbian Orator."[7] Every opportunity I got, I used to read this book. Among much of other interesting matter, I found in it a dialogue between a master and his slave. The slave was represented as having run away from his master three times. The dialogue represented the conversation which took place between them, when the slave was retaken the third time. In this dialogue, the whole argument in behalf of slavery was brought forward by the master, all of which was disposed of by the slave. The slave was made to say some very smart as well as impressive things in reply to his master—things which had the desired though unexpected effect; for the conversation resulted in the voluntary emancipation of the slave on the part of the master.

In the same book, I met with one of Sheridan's[8] mighty speeches on and in behalf of Catholic emancipation. These were choice documents to me. I read them over and over again with unabated interest. They gave tongue to interesting thoughts of my own soul, which had frequently flashed through my mind, and died away for want of utterance. The moral which I gained from the dialogue was the power of truth over the conscience of even a slaveholder. What I got from Sheridan was a bold denunciation of slavery, and a powerful vindication of human rights. The reading of these documents enabled me to utter my thoughts, and to meet the arguments brought forward to sustain slavery; but while they relieved me of one difficulty, they brought on another even more painful than the one of which I was relieved. The more I read, the more I was led to abhor and detest my enslavers. I could regard them in no other light

7. Caleb Bingham, *The Columbian Orator: Containing a Variety of Original and Selected Pieces: Together with Rules, Calculated to Improve Youth and Others in the Ornamental* *and Useful Art of Eloquence* (1807).
8. Thomas Sheridan (1719–1788), Irish actor, lecturer, and writer on elocution.

than a band of successful robbers, who had left their homes, and gone to Africa, and stolen us from our homes, and in a strange land reduced us to slavery. I loathed them as being the meanest as well as the most wicked of men. As I read and contemplated the subject, behold! that very discontentment which Master Hugh had predicted would follow my learning to read had already come, to torment and sting my soul to unutterable anguish. As I writhed under it, I would at times feel that learning to read had been a curse rather than a blessing. It had given me a view of my wretched condition, without the remedy. It opened my eyes to the horrible pit, but to no ladder upon which to get out. In moments of agony, I envied my fellow-slaves for their stupidity. I have often wished myself a beast. I preferred the condition of the meanest reptile to my own. Any thing, no matter what, to get rid of thinking! It was this everlasting thinking of my condition that tormented me. There was no getting rid of it. It was pressed upon me by every object within sight or hearing, animate or inanimate. The silver trump of freedom had roused my soul to eternal wakefulness. Freedom now appeared, to disappear no more forever. It was heard in every sound, and seen in every thing. It was ever present to torment me with a sense of my wretched condition. I saw nothing without seeing it, I heard nothing without hearing it, and felt nothing without feeling it. It looked from every star, it smiled in every calm, breathed in every wind, and moved in every storm.

I often found myself regretting my own existence, and wishing myself dead; and but for the hope of being free, I have no doubt but that I should have killed myself, or done something for which I should have been killed. While in this state of mind, I was eager to hear any one speak of slavery. I was a ready listener. Every little while, I could hear something about the abolitionists. It was some time before I found what the word meant. It was always used in such connections as to make it an interesting word to me. If a slave ran away and succeeded in getting clear, or if a slave killed his master, set fire to a barn, or did any thing very wrong in the mind of a slaveholder, it was spoken of as the fruit of *abolition*. Hearing the word in this connection very often, I set about learning what it meant. The dictionary afforded me little or no help. I found it was "the act of abolishing"; but then I did not know what was to be abolished. Here I was perplexed. I did not dare to ask any one about its meaning, for I was satisfied that it was something they wanted me to know very little about. After a patient waiting, I got one of our city papers, containing an account of the number of petitions from the north, praying for the abolition of slavery in the District of Columbia, and of the slave trade between the States. From this time I understood the words *abolition* and *abolitionist*, and always drew near when that word was spoken, expecting to hear something of importance to myself and fellow-slaves. The light broke in upon me by degrees. I went one day down on the wharf of Mr. Waters; and seeing two Irishmen unloading a scow of stone, I went, unasked, and helped them. When we had finished, one of them came to me and asked me if I were a slave. I told him I was. He asked, "Are ye a slave for life?" I told him that I was. The good Irishman seemed to be deeply affected by the statement. He said to the other that it was a pity so fine a little fellow as myself should be a slave for life. He said it was a shame to hold me. They both advised me to run away to the north; that I should find friends there, and that I should be free. I pretended not to be interested in what they said, and treated them as if I did not understand them; for I feared they might be treacherous. White men have been known to encourage slaves to escape, and then, to get the reward, catch them and return them to their masters. I was afraid that these seemingly good men might use me so; but I nevertheless remembered their advice, and from that time I resolved to run away. I looked forward to a time at which it would be safe for me to escape. I was too young to think of doing so immediately; besides, I wished to learn how to write, as I might have occasion to write my own pass. I consoled myself with the hope that I should one day find a good chance. Meanwhile, I would learn to write.

The idea as to how I might learn to write was suggested to me by being in Durgin and Bailey's ship-yard, and frequently seeing the ship carpenters, after hewing, and getting a piece of timber ready for use, write on the timber the name of that part of the ship for which it was intended. When a piece of timber was intended for the larboard side, it would be marked thus—"L." When a piece was for the starboard side, it would be marked thus—"S." A piece for the larboard forward, would be marked thus—"L.F." When a piece was for starboard side forward, it would be marked thus—"S.F." For larboard aft, it would be marked thus—"L.A." For starboard aft, it would be marked thus—"S.A." I soon learned the names of these letters, and for what they were intended when placed upon a piece of timber in the ship-yard. I immediately commenced copying them, and in a short time was able to make the four letters named. After that, when I met with any boy who I knew could write, I would tell him I could write as well as he. The next word would be, "I don't believe you. Let me see you try it." I would then make the letters which I had been so fortunate as to learn, and ask him to beat that. In this way I got a good many lessons in writing, which it is quite possible I should never have gotten in any other way. During this time, my copy-book was the board fence, brick wall, and pavement; my pen and ink was a lump of chalk. With these, I learned mainly how to write. I then commenced and continued copying the Italics in Webster's Spelling Book, until I could make them all without looking on the book. By this time, my little Master Thomas had gone to school, and learned how to write, and had written over a number of copy-books. These had been brought home, and shown to some of our near neighbors, and then laid aside. My mistress used to go to class meeting at the Wilk Street meetinghouse every Monday afternoon, and leave me to take care of the house. When left thus, I used to spend the time in writing in the spaces left in Master Thomas's copy-book, copying what he had written. I continued to do this until I could write a hand very similar to that of Master Thomas. Thus, after a long, tedious effort for years, I finally succeeded in learning how to write.

CHAPTER VIII

In a very short time after I went to live at Baltimore, my old master's youngest son Richard died; and in about three years and six months after his death, my old master, Captain Anthony, died, leaving only his son, Andrew, and daughter, Lucretia, to share his estate. He died while on a visit to see his daughter at Hillsborough. Cut off thus unexpectedly, he left no will as to the disposal of his property. It was therefore necessary to have a valuation of the property, that it might be equally divided between Mrs. Lucretia and Master Andrew. I was immediately sent for, to be valued with the other property. Here again my feelings rose up in detestation of slavery. I had now a new conception of my degraded condition. Prior to this, I had become, if not insensible to my lot, at least partly so. I left Baltimore with a young heart overborne with sadness, and a soul full of apprehension. I took passage with Captain Rowe, in the schooner *Wild Cat*, and, after a sail of about twenty-four hours, I found myself near the place of my birth. I had now been absent from it almost, if not quite, five years. I, however, remembered the place very well. I was only about five years old when I left it, to go and live with my old master on Colonel Lloyd's plantation; so that I was now between ten and eleven years old.

We were all ranked together at the valuation. Men and women, old and young, married and single, were ranked with horses, sheep, and swine. There were horses and men, cattle and women, pigs and children, all holding the same rank in the scale of being, and all were subjected to the same narrow examination. Silvery-headed age and sprightly youth, maids and matrons, had to undergo the same indelicate inspection. At this moment, I saw more clearly than ever the brutalizing effects of slavery upon both slave and slaveholder.

After the valuation, then came the division. I have no language to express the high excitement and deep anxiety which were felt among us poor slaves during this time. Our fate for life was now to be decided. We had no more voice in that decision than the brutes among whom we were ranked. A single word from the white men was enough—against all our wishes, prayers, and entreaties—to sunder forever the dearest friends, dearest kindred, and strongest ties known to human beings. In addition to the pain of separation, there was the horrid dread of falling into the hands of Master Andrew. He was known to us all as being a most cruel wretch,—a common drunkard, who had, by his reckless mismanagement and profligate dissipation, already wasted a large portion of his father's property. We all felt that we might as well be sold at once to the Georgia traders, as to pass into his hands; for we knew that that would be our inevitable condition,—a condition held by us all in the utmost horror and dread.

I suffered more anxiety than most of my fellow-slaves. I had known what it was to be kindly treated; they had known nothing of the kind. They had seen little or nothing of the world. They were in very deed men and women of sorrow, and acquainted with grief.[9] Their backs had been made familiar with the bloody lash, so that they had become callous; mine was yet tender; for while at Baltimore I got few whippings, and few slaves could boast of a kinder master and mistress than myself; and the thought of passing out of their hands into those of Master Andrew—a man who, but a few days before, to give me a sample of his bloody disposition, took my little brother by the throat, threw him on the ground, and with the heel of his boot stamped upon his head till the blood gushed from his nose and ears—was well calculated to make me anxious as to my fate. After he had committed this savage outrage upon my brother, he turned to me, and said that was the way he meant to serve me one of these days,—meaning, I suppose, when I came into his possession.

Thanks to a kind Providence, I fell to the portion of Mrs. Lucretia, and was sent immediately back to Baltimore, to live again in the family of Master Hugh. Their joy at my return equalled their sorrow at my departure. It was a glad day

---

9. In Isaiah 53:3, the Lord's servant is described as "a man of sorrows, and acquainted with grief."

to me. I had escaped a [fate] worse than lion's jaws. I was absent from Baltimore, for the purpose of valuation and division, just about one month, and it seemed to have been six.

Very soon after my return to Baltimore, my mistress, Lucretia, died, leaving her husband and one child, Amanda; and in a very short time after her death, Master Andrew died. Now all the property of my old master, slaves included, was in the hands of strangers,—strangers who had had nothing to do with accumulating it. Not a slave was left free. All remained slaves, from the youngest to the oldest. If any one thing in my experience, more than another, served to deepen my conviction of the infernal character of slavery, and to fill me with unutterable loathing of slaveholders, it was their base ingratitude to my poor old grandmother. She had served my old master faithfully from youth to old age. She had been the source of all his wealth; she had peopled his plantation with slaves; she had become a great grandmother in his service. She had rocked him in infancy, attended him in childhood, served him through life, and at his death wiped from his icy brow the cold death-sweat, and closed his eyes forever. She was nevertheless left a slave—a slave for life—a slave in the hands of strangers; and in their hands she saw her children, her grandchildren, and her great-grandchildren, divided, like so many sheep, without being gratified with the small privilege of a single word, as to their or her own destiny. And, to cap the climax of their base ingratitude and fiendish barbarity, my grandmother, who was now very old, having outlived my old master and all his children, having seen the beginning and end of all of them, and her present owners finding she was of but little value, her frame already racked with the pains of old age, and complete helplessness fast stealing over her once active limbs, they took her to the woods, built her a little hut, put up a little mud-chimney, and then made her welcome to the privilege of supporting herself there in perfect loneliness; thus virtually turning her out to die! If my poor old grandmother now lives, she lives to suffer in utter loneliness; she lives to remember and mourn over the loss of children, the loss of grandchildren, and the loss of great-grandchildren. They are, in the language of the slave's poet, Whittier,—

> "Gone, gone, sold and gone
> To the rice swamp dank and lone,
> Where the slave-whip ceaseless swings,
> Where the noisome insect stings,
> Where the fever-demon strews
> Poison with the falling dews,
> Where the sickly sunbeams glare
> Through the hot and misty air:—
>   Gone, gone, sold and gone
>   To the rice swamp dank and lone,
>   From Virginia hills and waters—
>   Woe is me, my stolen daughters!"[1]

1. John Greenleaf Whittier, American poet (1807–1892), wrote a large group of antislavery poems. This one is *The Farewell of a Virginia Slave Mother to her Daughters Sold into Southern Bondage.*

The hearth is desolate. The children, the unconscious children, who once sang and danced in her presence, are gone. She gropes her way, in the darkness of age, for a drink of water. Instead of the voices of her children, she hears by day the moans of the dove, and by night the screams of the hideous owl. All is gloom. The grave is at the door. And now, when weighed down by the pains and aches of old age, when the head inclines to the feet, when the beginning and ending of human existence meet, and helpless infancy and painful old age combine together—at this time, this most needful time, the time for the exercise of that tenderness and affection which children only can exercise towards a declining parent—my poor old grandmother, the devoted mother of twelve children, is left all alone, in yonder little hut, before a few dim embers. She stands—she sits—she staggers—she falls—she groans—she dies—and there are none of her children or grandchildren present, to wipe from her wrinkled brow the cold sweat of death, or to place beneath the sod her fallen remains. Will not a righteous God visit[2] for these things?

In about two years after the death of Mrs. Lucretia, Master Thomas married his second wife. Her name was Rowena Hamilton. She was the eldest daughter of Mr. William Hamilton. Master now lived in St. Michael's. Not long after his marriage, a misunderstanding took place between himself and Master Hugh; and as a means of punishing his brother, he took me from him to live with himself at St. Michael's. Here I underwent another most painful separation. It, however, was not so severe as the one I dreaded at the division of property; for, during this interval, a great change had taken place in Master Hugh and his once kind and affectionate wife. The influence of brandy upon him, and of slavery upon her, had effected a disastrous change in the characters of both; so that, as far as they were concerned, I thought I had little to lose by the change. But it was not to them that I was attached. It was to those little Baltimore boys that I felt the strongest attachment. I had received many good lessons from them, and was still receiving them, and the thought of leaving them was painful indeed. I was leaving, too, without the hope of ever being allowed to return. Master Thomas had said he would never let me return again. The barrier betwixt himself and brother he considered impassable.

I then had to regret that I did not at least make the attempt to carry out my resolution to run away; for the chances of success are tenfold greater from the city than from the country.

I sailed from Baltimore for St. Michael's in the sloop *Amanda*, Captain Edward Dodson. On my passage, I paid particular attention to the direction which the steamboats took to go to Philadelphia. I found, instead of going down, on reaching North Point they went up the bay, in a north-easterly direction. I deemed this knowledge of the utmost importance. My determination to run away was again revived. I resolved to wait only so long as the offering of a favorable opportunity. When that came, I was determined to be off.

CHAPTER IX

I have now reached a period of my life when I can give dates. I left Baltimore, and went to live with Master Thomas Auld, at St. Michael's, in March, 1832.

2. I.e., visit vengeance. Cf. Exodus 32:34: "Nevertheless, in the day when I visit I will visit their sin upon them."

It was now more than seven years since I lived with him in the family of my old master, on Colonel Lloyd's plantation. We of course were now almost entire strangers to each other. He was to me a new master, and I to him a new slave. I was ignorant of his temper and disposition; he was equally so of mine. A very short time, however, brought us into full acquaintance with each other. I was made acquainted with his wife not less than with himself. They were well matched, being equally mean and cruel. I was now, for the first time during a space of more than seven years, made to feel the painful gnawings of hunger—a something which I had not experienced before since I left Colonel Lloyd's plantation. It went hard enough with me then, when I could look back to no period at which I had enjoyed a sufficiency. It was tenfold harder after living in Master Hugh's family, where I had always had enough to eat, and of that which was good. I have said Master Thomas was a mean man. He was so. Not to give a slave enough to eat, is regarded as the most aggravated development of meanness even among slaveholders. The rule is, no matter how coarse the food, only let there be enough of it. This is the theory; and in the part of Maryland from which I came, it is the general practice,—though there are many exceptions. Master Thomas gave us enough of neither coarse nor fine food. There were four of us slaves in the kitchen—my sister Eliza, my aunt Priscilla, Henny, and myself; and we were allowed less than a half of a bushel of corn-meal per week, and very little else, either in the shape of meat or vegetables. It was not enough for us to subsist upon. We were therefore reduced to the wretched necessity of living at the expense of our neighbors. This we did by begging and stealing, whichever came handy in the time of need, the one being considered as legitimate as the other. A great many times have we poor creatures been nearly perishing with hunger, when food in abundance lay mouldering in the safe and smoke-house, and our pious mistress was aware of the fact; and yet that mistress and her husband would kneel every morning, and pray that God would bless them in basket and store!

Bad as all slaveholders are, we seldom meet one destitute of every element of character commanding respect. My master was one of this rare sort. I do not know of one single noble act ever performed by him. The leading trait in his character was meanness; and if there were any other element in his nature, it was made subject to this. He was mean; and, like most other mean men, he lacked the ability to conceal his meanness. Captain Auld was not born a slaveholder. He had been a poor man, master only of a Bay craft. He came into possession of all his slaves by marriage; and of all men, adopted slaveholders are the worst. He was cruel, but cowardly. He commanded without firmness. In the enforcement of his rules, he was at times rigid, and at times lax. At times, he spoke to his slaves with the firmness of Napoleon and the fury of a demon; at other times, he might well be mistaken for an inquirer who had lost his way. He did nothing of himself. He might have passed for a lion, but for his ears.[3] In all things noble which he attempted, his own meanness shone most conspicuous. His airs, words, and actions, were the airs, words, and actions of born slaveholders, and, being assumed, were awkward enough. He was not even a good imitator. He possessed all the disposition to deceive, but wanted the

3. A variation on Aesop's fable of the ass in a lion's skin who frightened all of the animals. The fox says: "I would have been frightened too if I had not heard you bray."

power. Having no resources within himself, he was compelled to be the copyist of many, and being such, he was forever the victim of inconsistency; and of consequence he was an object of contempt, and was held as such even by his slaves. The luxury of having slaves of his own to wait upon him was something new and unprepared for. He was a slaveholder without the ability to hold slaves. He found himself incapable of managing his slaves either by force, fear, or fraud. We seldom called him "master"; we generally called him "Captain Auld," and were hardly disposed to title him at all. I doubt not that our conduct had much to do with making him appear awkward, and of consequence fretful. Our want of reverence for him must have perplexed him greatly. He wished to have us call him master, but lacked the firmness necessary to command us to do so. His wife used to insist upon our calling him so, but to no purpose. In August, 1832, my master attended a Methodist camp-meeting held in the Bay-side, Talbot county, and there experienced religion. I indulged a faint hope that his conversion would lead him to emancipate his slaves, and that, if he did not do this, it would, at any rate, make him more kind and humane. I was disappointed in both these respects. It neither made him to be humane to his slaves, nor to emancipate them. If it had any effect on his character, it made him more cruel and hateful in all his ways; for I believe him to have been a much worse man after his conversion than before. Prior to his conversion, he relied upon his own depravity to shield and sustain him in his savage barbarity; but after his conversion, he found religious sanction and support for his slaveholding cruelty. He made the greatest pretensions to piety. His house was the house of prayer. He prayed morning, noon, and night. He very soon distinguished himself among his brethren, and was soon made a class-leader and exhorter. His activity in revivals was great, and he proved himself an instrument in the hands of the church in converting many souls. His house was the preachers' home. They used to take great pleasure in coming there to put up; for while he starved us, he stuffed them. We have had three or four preachers there at a time. The names of those who used to come most frequently while I lived there, were Mr. Storks, Mr. Ewery, Mr. Humphry, and Mr. Hickey. I have also seen Mr. George Cookman at our house. We slaves loved Mr. Cookman. We believed him to be a good man. We thought him instrumental in getting Mr. Samuel Harrison, a very rich slaveholder, to emancipate his slaves; and by some means got the impression that he was laboring to effect the emancipation of all the slaves. When he was at our house, we were sure to be called in to prayers. When the others were there, we were sometimes called in and sometimes not. Mr. Cookman took more notice of us than either of the other ministers. He could not come among us without betraying his sympathy for us, and, stupid as we were, we had the sagacity to see it.

While I lived with my master in St. Michael's, there was a white young man, a Mr. Wilson, who proposed to keep a Sabbath school for the instruction of such slaves as might be disposed to learn to read the New Testament. We met but three times, when Mr. West and Mr. Fairbanks, both class-leaders, with many others, came upon us with sticks and other missiles, drove us off, and forbade us to meet again. Thus ended our little Sabbath school in the pious town of St. Michael's.

I have said my master found religious sanction for his cruelty. As an example, I will state one of many facts going to prove the charge. I have seen him tie up a lame young woman, and whip her with a heavy cowskin upon her naked shoulders, causing the warm red blood to drip; and, in justification of the bloody deed, he would quote this passage of Scripture—"He that knoweth his master's will, and doeth it not, shall be beaten with many stripes."[4]

Master would keep this lacerated young woman tied up in this horrid situation four or five hours at a time. I have known him to tie her up early in the morning, and whip her before breakfast; leave her, go to his store, return to dinner, and whip her again, cutting her in the places already made raw with his cruel lash. The secret of master's cruelty toward "Henny" is found in the fact of her being almost helpless. When quite a child, she fell into the fire, and burned herself horribly. Her hands were so burnt that she never got the use of them. She could do very little but bear heavy burdens. She was to master a bill of expense; and as he was a mean man, she was a constant offence to him. He seemed desirous of getting the poor girl out of existence. He gave her away once to his sister; but, being a poor gift, she was not disposed to keep her. Finally, my benevolent master, to use his own words, "set her adrift to take care of herself." Here was a recently-converted man, holding on upon the mother, and at the same time turning out her helpless child, to starve and die! Master Thomas was one of the many pious slaveholders who hold slaves for the very charitable purpose of taking care of them.

My master and myself had quite a number of differences. He found me unsuitable to his purpose. My city life, he said, had had a very pernicious effect upon me. It had almost ruined me for every good purpose, and fitted me for every thing which was bad. One of my greatest faults was that of letting his horse run away, and go down to his father-in-law's farm, which was about five miles from St. Michael's. I would then have to go after it. My reason for this kind of carelessness, or carefulness, was, that I could always get something to eat when I went there. Master William Hamilton, my master's father-in-law, always gave his slaves enough to eat. I never left there hungry, no matter how great the need of my speedy return. Master Thomas at length said he would stand it no longer. I had lived with him nine months, during which time he had given me a number of severe whippings, all to no good purpose. He resolved to put me out, as he said, to be broken; and, for this purpose, he let me for one year to a man named Edward Covey. Mr. Covey was a poor man, a farm-renter. He rented the place upon which he lived, as also the hands with which he tilled it. Mr. Covey had acquired a very high reputation for breaking young slaves, and this reputation was of immense value to him. It enabled him to get his farm tilled with much less expense to himself than he could have had it done without such a reputation. Some slaveholders thought it not much loss to allow Mr. Covey to have their slaves one year, for the sake of the training to which they were subjected, without any other compensation. He could hire young help with great ease, in consequence of this reputation. Added to the natural good qualities of Mr. Covey, he was a professor of religion—a pious soul—a member and a class-leader in the Methodist church. All of this added weight to his reputation as a "nigger-breaker." I was aware of all the facts, having been made acquainted with them by a young man who had lived there. I

4. Luke 12:47.

nevertheless made the change gladly; for I was sure of getting enough to eat, which is not the smallest consideration to a hungry man.

CHAPTER X

I left Master Thomas's house, and went to live with Mr. Covey, on the 1st of January, 1833. I was now, for the first time in my life, a field hand. In my new employment, I found myself even more awkward than a country boy appeared to be in a large city. I had been at my new home but one week before Mr. Covey gave me a very severe whipping, cutting my back, causing the blood to run, and raising ridges on my flesh as large as my little finger. The details of this affair are as follows: Mr. Covey sent me, very early in the morning of one of our coldest days in the month of January, to the woods, to get a load of wood. He gave me a team of unbroken oxen. He told me which was the in-hand ox, and which the off-hand ox. He then tied the end of a large rope around the horns of the in-hand ox, and gave me the other end of it, and told me, if the oxen started to run, that I must hold on upon the rope. I had never driven oxen before, and of course I was very awkward. I, however, succeeded in getting to the edge of the woods with little difficulty; but I had got a very few rods into the woods, when the oxen took fright, and started full tilt, carrying the cart against trees, and over stumps, in the most frightful manner. I expected every moment that my brains would be dashed out against the trees. After running thus for a considerable distance, they finally upset the cart, dashing it with great force against a tree, and threw themselves into a dense thicket. How I escaped death, I do not know. There I was, entirely alone, in a thick wood, in a place new to me. My cart was upset and shattered, my oxen were entangled among the young trees, and there was none to help me. After a long spell of effort, I succeeded in getting my cart righted, my oxen disentangled, and again yoked to the cart. I now proceeded with my team to the place where I had, the day before, been chopping wood, and loaded my cart pretty heavily, thinking in this way to tame my oxen. I then proceeded on my way home. I had now consumed one half of the day. I got out of the woods safely, and now felt out of danger. I stopped my oxen to open the woods gate; and just as I did so, before I could get hold of my ox-rope, the oxen again started, rushed through the gate, catching it between the wheel and the body of the cart, tearing it to pieces, and coming within a few inches of crushing me against the gate-post. Thus twice, in one short day, I escaped death by the merest chance. On my return, I told Mr. Covey what had happened, and how it happened. He ordered me to return to the woods again immediately. I did so, and he followed on after me. Just as I got into the woods, he came up and told me to stop my cart, and that he would teach me how to trifle away my time, and break gates. He then went to a large gum-tree, and with his axe cut three large switches, and, after trimming them up neatly with his pocket-knife, he ordered me to take off my clothes. I made him no answer, but stood with my clothes on. He repeated his order. I still made him no answer, nor did I move to strip myself. Upon this he rushed at me with the fierceness of a tiger, tore off my clothes, and lashed me till he had worn out his switches, cutting me so savagely as to leave the marks visible for a long time after. This whipping was the first of a number just like it, and for similar offences.

I lived with Mr. Covey one year. During the first six months, of that year, scarce a week passed without his whipping me. I was seldom free from a sore back. My awkwardness was almost always his excuse for whipping me. We were worked fully up to the point of endurance. Long before day we were up, our horses fed, and by the first approach of day we were off to the field with our hoes and ploughing teams. Mr. Covey gave us enough to eat, but scarce time to eat it. We were often less than five minutes taking our meals. We were often in the field from the first approach of day till its last lingering ray had left us; and at saving-fodder time, midnight often caught us in the field binding blades.[5]

Covey would be out with us. The way he used to stand it was this. He would spend the most of his afternoons in bed. He would then come out fresh in the evening, ready to urge us on with his words, example, and frequently with the whip. Mr. Covey was one of the few slaveholders who could and did work with his hands. He was a hard-working man. He knew by himself just what a man or a boy could do. There was no deceiving him. His work went on in his absence almost as well as in his presence; and he had the faculty of making us feel that he was ever present with us. This he did by surprising us. He seldom approached the spot where we were at work openly, if he could do it secretly. He always aimed at taking us by surprise. Such was his cunning, that we used to call him, among ourselves, "the snake." When we were at work in the cornfield, he would sometimes crawl on his hands and knees to avoid detection, and all at once he would rise nearly in our midst, and scream out, "Ha, ha! Come, come! Dash on, dash on!" This being his mode of attack, it was never safe to stop a single minute. His comings were like a thief in the night. He appeared to us as being ever at hand. He was under every tree, behind every stump, in every bush, and at every window, on the plantation. He would sometimes mount his horse, as if bound to St. Michael's, a distance of seven miles, and in half an hour afterwards you would see him coiled up in the corner of the wood-fence, watching every motion of the slaves. He would, for this purpose, leave his horse tied up in the woods. Again, he would sometimes walk up to us, and give us orders as though he was upon the point of starting on a long journey, turn his back upon us, and make as though he was going to the house to get ready; and, before he would get half way thither, he would turn short and crawl into a fence-corner, or behind some tree, and there watch us till the going down of the sun.

Mr. Covey's *forte* consisted in his power to deceive. His life was devoted to planning and perpetrating the grossest deceptions. Every thing he possessed in the shape of learning or religion, he made conform to his disposition to deceive. He seemed to think himself equal to deceiving the Almighty. He would make a short prayer in the morning, and a long prayer at night; and, strange as it may seem, few men would at times appear more devotional than he. The exercises of his family devotions were always commenced with singing; and, as he was a very poor singer himself, the duty of raising the hymn generally came upon me. He would read his hymn, and nod at me to commence. I would at times do so; at others, I would not. My noncompliance would almost always produce much

5. Gathering cut grain into bundles or sheaves.

confusion. To show himself independent of me, he would start and stagger through with his hymn in the most discordant manner. In this state of mind, he prayed with more than ordinary spirit. Poor man! such was his disposition, and success at deceiving, I do verily believe that he sometimes deceived himself into the solemn belief, that he was a sincere worshipper of the most high God; and this, too, at a time when he may be said to have been guilty of compelling his woman slave to commit the sin of adultery. The facts in the case are these: Mr. Covey was a poor man; he was just commencing in life; he was only able to buy one slave; and, shocking as is the fact, he bought her, as he said, for a *breeder*. This woman was named Caroline. Mr. Covey bought her from Mr. Thomas Lowe, about six miles from St. Michael's. She was a large, able-bodied woman, about twenty years old. She had already given birth to one child, which proved her to be just what he wanted. After buying her, he hired a married man of Mr. Samuel Harrison, to live with him one year; and him he used to fasten up with her every night! The result was, that, at the end of the year, the miserable woman gave birth to twins. At this result Mr. Covey seemed to be highly pleased, both with the man and the wretched woman. Such was his joy, and that of his wife, that nothing they could do for Caroline during her confinement was too good, or too hard, to be done. The children were regarded as being quite an addition to his wealth.

If at any one time of my life more than another, I was made to drink the bitterest dregs of slavery, that time was during the first six months of my stay with Mr. Covey. We were worked in all weathers. It was never too hot or too cold; it could never rain, blow, hail, or snow, too hard for us to work in the field. Work, work, work, was scarcely more the order of the day than of the night. The longest days were too short for him, and the shortest nights too long for him. I was somewhat unmanageable when I first went there, but a few months of this discipline tamed me. Mr. Covey succeeded in breaking me. I was broken in body, soul, and spirit. My natural elasticity was crushed, my intellect languished, the disposition to read departed, the cheerful spark that lingered about my eye died; the dark night of slavery closed in upon me; and behold a man transformed into a brute!

Sunday was my only leisure time. I spent this in a sort of beast-like stupor, between sleep and wake, under some large tree. At times I would rise up, a flash of energetic freedom would dart through my soul, accompanied with a faint beam of hope, that flickered for a moment, and then vanished. I sank down again, mourning over my wretched condition. I was sometimes prompted to take my life, and that of Covey, but was prevented by a combination of hope and fear. My sufferings on this plantation seem now like a dream rather than a stern reality.

Our house stood within a few rods of the Chesapeake Bay, whose broad bosom was ever white with sails from every quarter of the habitable globe. Those beautiful vessels, robed in purest white, so delightful to the eye of freemen, were to me so many shrouded ghosts, to terrify and torment me with thoughts of my wretched condition. I have often, in the deep stillness of a summer's Sabbath, stood all alone upon the lofty banks of that noble bay, and traced, with saddened heart and tearful eye, the countless number of sails moving off to the mighty ocean. The sight of these always affected me powerfully. My thoughts would compel utterance; and there, with no audience but the Almighty, I would pour out my soul's complaint, in my rude way, with an apostrophe[6] to the moving multitude of ships:—

"You are loosed from your moorings, and are free; I am fast in my chains, and am a slave! You move merrily before the gentle gale, and I sadly before the bloody whip! You are freedom's swift-winged angels, that fly round the world; I am confined in bands of iron! O that I were free! O, that I were on one of your gallant decks, and under your protecting wing! Alas! betwixt me and you, the turbid waters roll. Go on, go on. O that I could also go! Could I but swim! If I could fly! O, why was I born a man, of whom to make a brute! The glad ship is gone; she hides in the dim distance. I am left in the hottest hell of unending slavery. O God, save me! God, deliver me! Let me be free! Is there any God? Why am I a slave? I will run away. I will not stand it. Get caught, or get clear, I'll try it. I had as well die with ague as the fever. I have only one life to lose. I had as well be killed running as die standing. Only think of it; one hundred miles straight north, and I am free! Try it? Yes! God helping me, I will. It cannot be that I shall live and die a slave. I will take to the water. This very bay shall bear me into freedom. The steam boats steered in a north-east course from North Point. I will do the same; and when I get to the head of the bay, I will turn my canoe adrift, and walk straight through Delaware into Pennsylvania. When I get there, I shall not be required to have a pass; I can travel without being disturbed. Let but the first opportunity offer, and, come what will, I am off. Meanwhile, I will try to bear up under the yoke. I am not the only slave in the world. Why should I fret? I can bear as much as any of them. Besides, I am but a boy, and all boys are bound to some one. It may be that my misery in slavery will only increase my happiness when I get free. There is a better day coming."

Thus I used to think, and thus I used to speak to myself; goaded almost to madness at one moment, and at the next reconciling myself to my wretched lot.

I have already intimated that my condition was much worse, during the first six months of my stay at Mr. Covey's, than in the last six. The circumstances leading to the change in Mr. Covey's course toward me form an epoch in my humble history. You have seen how a man was made a slave; you shall see how a slave was made a man. On one of the hottest days of the month of August, 1833, Bill Smith, William Hughes, a slave named Eli, and myself, were engaged in fanning wheat.[7] Hughes was clearing the fanned wheat from before the fan, Eli was turning, Smith was feeding, and I was carrying wheat to the fan. The work was simple, requiring strength rather than intellect; yet, to one entirely unused to such work, it came very hard. About three o'clock of that day, I broke down; my strength failed me; I was seized with a violent aching of the head, attended with extreme dizziness; I trembled in every limb. Finding what was coming, I nerved myself up, feeling it would never do to stop work. I stood as long as I could stagger to the hopper with grain. When I could stand no longer, I fell, and felt as if held down by an immense weight. The fan of course stopped; every one had his own work to do; and no one could do the work of the other, and have his own go on at the same time.

6. An exclamatory form of address.   7. Separating the grain from the chaff.

Mr. Covey was at the house, about one hundred yards from the treading-yard where we were fanning. On hearing the fan stop, he left immediately, and came to the spot where we were. He hastily inquired what the matter was. Bill answered that I was sick, and there was no one to bring wheat to the fan. I had by this time crawled away under the side of the post and rail-fence by which the yard was enclosed, hoping to find relief by getting out of the sun. He then asked where I was. He was told by one of the hands. He came to the spot, and, after looking at me awhile, asked me what was the matter. I told him as well as I could, for I scarce had strength to speak. He then gave me a savage kick in the side, and told me to get up. I tried to do so, but fell back in the attempt. He gave me another kick, and again told me to rise. I again tried, and succeeded in gaining my feet; but, stooping to get the tub with which I was feeding the fan, I again staggered and fell. While down in this situation, Mr. Covey took up the hickory slat with which Hughes had been striking off the half-bushel measure, and with it gave me a heavy blow upon the head, making a large wound, and the blood ran freely; and with this again told me to get up. I made no effort to comply, having now made up my mind to let him do his worst. In a short time after receiving this blow, my head grew better. Mr. Covey had now left me to my fate. At this moment I resolved, for the first time, to go to my master, enter a complaint, and ask his protection. In order to [do] this, I must that afternoon walk seven miles; and this, under the circumstances, was truly a severe undertaking. I was exceedingly feeble; made so as much by the kicks and blows which I received, as by the severe fit of sickness to which I had been subjected. I, however, watched my chance, while Covey was looking in an opposite direction, and started for St. Michael's. I succeeded in getting a considerable distance on my way to the woods, when Covey discovered me, and called after me to come back, threatening what he would do if I did not come. I disregarded both his calls and his threats, and made my way to the woods as fast as my feeble state would allow; and thinking I might be overhauled by him if I kept the road, I walked through the woods, keeping far enough from the road to avoid detection, and near enough to prevent losing my way. I had not gone far before my little strength again failed me. I could go no farther. I fell down, and lay for a considerable time. The blood was yet oozing from the wound on my head. For a time I thought I should bleed to death; and think now that I should have done so, but that the blood so matted my hair as to stop the wound. After lying there about three quarters of an hour, I nerved myself up again, and started on my way, through bogs and briers, barefooted and bareheaded, tearing my feet sometimes at nearly every step; and after a journey of about seven miles, occupying some five hours to perform it, I arrived at master's store. I then presented an appearance enough to affect any but a heart of iron. From the crown of my head to my feet, I was covered with blood. My hair was all clotted with dust and blood; my shirt was stiff with blood. My legs and feet were torn in sundry places with briers and thorns, and were also covered with blood. I suppose I looked like a man who had escaped a den of wild beasts, and barely escaped them. In this state I appeared before my master, humbly entreating him to interpose his authority for my protection. I told him all the circumstances as well as I could, and it seemed, as I spoke, at times to affect him. He would then walk the floor, and seek to justify Covey by saying he expected I deserved it. He asked me what I wanted. I told him, to let me get a new home; that as sure as I lived with Mr. Covey again, I should live with but to die with him; that Covey would surely kill me; he was in a fair way for it. Master Thomas ridiculed the idea that there was any danger of Mr. Covey's killing me, and said that he knew Mr. Covey; that he was a good man, and that he could not think of taking me from him; that, should he do so, he would lose the whole year's wages; that I belonged to Mr. Covey for one year, and that I must go back to him, come what might; and that I must not trouble him with any more stories, or that he would himself *get hold of me*. After threatening me thus, he gave me a very large dose of salts, telling me that I might remain in St. Michael's that night, (it being quite late) but that I must be off back to Mr. Covey's early in the morning; and that if I did not, he would *get hold of me*, which meant that he would whip me. I remained all night, and, according to his orders, I started off to Covey's in the morning, (Saturday morning), wearied in body and broken in spirit. I got no supper that night, or breakfast that morning. I reached Covey's about nine o'clock; and just as I was getting over the fence that divided Mrs. Kemp's fields from ours, out ran Covey with his cowskin, to give me another whipping. Before he could reach me, I succeeded in getting to the cornfield; and as the corn was very high, it afforded me the means of hiding. He seemed very angry, and searched for me a long time. My behavior was altogether unaccountable. He finally gave up the chase, thinking, I suppose, that I must come home for something to eat; he would give himself no further trouble in looking for me. I spent that day mostly in the woods, having the alternative before me,—to go home and be whipped to death, or stay in the woods and be starved to death. That night, I fell in with Sandy Jenkins, a slave with whom I was somewhat acquainted. Sandy had a free wife who lived about four miles from Mr. Covey's; and it being Saturday, he was on his way to see her. I told him my circumstances, and he very kindly invited me to go home with him. I went home with him, and talked this whole matter over, and got his advice as to what course it was best for me to pursue. I found Sandy an old adviser. He told me, with great solemnity, I must go back to Covey; but that before I went, I must go with him into another part of the woods, where there was a certain *root*, which, if I would take some of it with me, carrying it *always on my right side*, would render it impossible for Mr. Covey, or any other white man, to whip me. He said he had carried it for years; and since he had done so, he had never received a blow, and never expected to while he carried it. I at first rejected the idea, that the simple carrying of a root in my pocket would have any such effect as he had said, and was not disposed to take it; but Sandy impressed the necessity with much earnestness, telling me it could do no harm, if it did no good. To please him, I at length took the root, and, according to his direction, carried it upon my right side. This was Sunday morning. I immediately started for home; and upon entering the yard gate, out came Mr. Covey on his way to meeting. He spoke to me very kindly, bade me drive the pigs from a lot near by, and passed on towards the church. Now, this singular conduct of Mr. Covey really made me begin to think that there was something in the *root* which Sandy had given me; and had it been on any other day than Sunday, I could have attributed the conduct to no other cause than the influence of that root; and as it was, I was half inclined to think the *root* to be something more than I at first had taken it to be. All went well till Monday morning. On this morning, the virtue of the *root* was fully tested. Long before daylight, I was called to go and rub, curry, and feed, the horses. I obeyed, and was glad to obey. But whilst thus engaged, whilst in the act of throwing down some blades from the loft, Mr. Covey entered the stable with a long rope; and just as I was half out of the loft, he caught hold of my legs, and was about tying me. As soon as I found what he was up to, I gave a sudden spring, and as I did so, he holding to my legs, I was brought sprawling on the stable floor. Mr. Covey seemed now to think he had me, and could do what he pleased; but at this moment— from whence came the spirit I don't know—I resolved to fight; and, suiting my action to the resolution, I seized Covey hard by the throat; and as I did so, I rose. He held on to me, and I to him. My resistance was so entirely unexpected, that Covey seemed taken all aback. He trembled like a leaf. This gave me assurance, and I held him uneasy, causing the blood to run where I touched him with the ends of my fingers. Mr. Covey soon called out to Hughes for help. Hughes came, and, while Covey held me, attempted to tie my right hand. While he was in the act of doing so, I watched my chance, and gave him a heavy kick close under the ribs. This kick fairly sickened Hughes, so that he left me in the hands of Mr. Covey. This kick had the effect of not only weakening Hughes, but Covey also. When he saw Hughes bending over with pain, his courage quailed. He asked me if I meant to persist in my resistance. I told him I did, come what might; that he had used me like a brute for six months, and that I was determined to be used so no longer. With that, he strove to drag me to a stick that was lying just out of the stable door. He meant to knock me down. But just as he was leaning over to get the stick, I seized him with both hands by his collar, and brought him by a sudden snatch to the ground. By this time, Bill came. Covey called upon him for assistance. Bill wanted to know what he could do. Covey said, "Take hold of him, take hold of him!" Bill said his master hired him out to work, and not to help to whip me; so he left Covey and myself to fight our own battle out. We were at it for nearly two hours. Covey at length let me go, puffing and blowing at a great rate, saying that if I had not resisted, he would not have whipped me half so much. The truth was, that he had not whipped me at all. I considered him as getting entirely the worst end of the bargain; for he had drawn no blood from me, but I had from him. The whole six months afterwards, that I spent with Mr. Covey, he never laid the weight of his finger upon me in anger. He would occasionally say, he didn't want to get hold of me again. "No," thought I, "you need not; for you will come off worse than you did before."

This battle with Mr. Covey was the turning-point in my career as a slave. It rekindled the few expiring embers of freedom, and revived within me a sense of my own manhood. It recalled the departed self-confidence, and inspired me again with a determination to be free. The gratification afforded by the triumph was a full compensation for whatever else might follow, even death itself. He only can understand the deep satisfaction which I experienced, who has himself repelled by force the bloody arm of slavery. I felt as I never felt before. It was a glorious resurrection, from the tomb of slavery, to the heaven of freedom. My long-crushed spirit rose, cowardice departed, bold defiance took its place; and I now resolved that, however long I might remain a slave in form, the day had passed forever when I could be a slave in fact. I did not hesitate to let it be known of me, that the white man who expected to succeed in whipping, must also succeed in killing me.

From this time I was never again what might be called fairly whipped, though I remained a slave four years afterwards. I had several fights, but was never whipped.

It was for a long time a matter of surprise to me why Mr. Covey did not immediately have me taken by the constable to the whipping-post, and there regularly whipped for the crime of raising my hand against a white man in defence of myself. And the only explanation I can now think of does not entirely satisfy me; but such as it is, I will give it. Mr. Covey enjoyed the most unbounded reputation for being a first-rate overseer and negro-breaker. It was of considerable importance to him. That reputation was at stake; and had he sent me—a boy about sixteen years old—to the public whipping-post, his reputation would have been lost; so, to save his reputation, he suffered me to go unpunished.

My term of actual service to Mr. Edward Covey ended on Christmas day, 1833. The days between Christmas and New Year's day are allowed as holidays; and, accordingly, we were not required to perform any labor, more than to feed and take care of the stock. This time we regarded as our own, by the grace of our masters; and we therefore used or abused it nearly as we pleased. Those of us who had families at a distance, were generally allowed to spend the whole six days in their society. This time, however, was spent in various ways. The staid, sober, thinking and industrious ones of our number would employ themselves in making corn-brooms, mats, horse-collars, and baskets; and another class of us would spend the time in hunting opossums, hares, and coons. But by far the larger part engaged in such sports and merriments as playing ball, wrestling, running foot-races, fiddling, dancing, and drinking whisky; and this latter mode of spending the time was by far the most agreeable to the feelings of our masters. A slave who would work during the holidays was considered by our masters as scarcely deserving them. He was regarded as one who rejected the favor of his master. It was deemed a disgrace not to get drunk at Christmas; and he was regarded as lazy indeed, who had not provided himself with the necessary means, during the year, to get whisky enough to last him through Christmas.

From what I know of the effect of these holidays upon the slave, I believe them to be among the most effective means in the hands of the slaveholder in keeping down the spirit of insurrection. Were the slaveholders at once to abandon this practice, I have not the slightest doubt it would lead to an immediate insurrection among the slaves. These holidays serve as conductors, or safety-valves, to carry off the rebellious spirit of enslaved humanity. But for these, the slave would be forced up to the wildest desperation; and woe betide the slaveholder, the day he ventures to remove or hinder the operation of those conductors! I warn him that, in such an event, a spirit will go forth in their midst, more to be dreaded than the most appalling earthquake.

The holidays are part and parcel of the gross fraud, wrong, and inhumanity of slavery. They are professedly a custom established by the benevolence of the slaveholders; but I undertake to say, it is the result of selfishness, and one of the grossest frauds committed upon the down-trodden slave. They do not give the slaves this time because they would not like to have their work during its continuance, but because they know it would be unsafe to deprive them of it. This will be seen by the fact, that the slaveholders like to have their slaves spend those days just in such a manner as to make them as glad of their ending as of their beginning. Their object seems to be, to disgust their slaves with freedom, by plunging them into the lowest depths of dissipation. For instance, the slaveholders not only like to see the slave drink of his own accord, but will adopt various plans to make him drunk. One plan is, to make bets on their slaves, as to who can drink the most whisky without getting drunk; and in this way they succeed in getting whole multitudes to drink to excess. Thus, when the slave asks for virtuous freedom, the cunning slaveholder, knowing his ignorance, cheats him with a dose of vicious dissipation, artfully labelled with the name of liberty. The most of us used to drink it down, and the result was just what might be supposed: many of us were led to think that there was little to choose between liberty and slavery. We felt, and very properly too, that we had almost as well be slaves to man as to rum. So, when the holidays ended, we staggered up from the filth of our wallowing, took a long breath, and marched to the field,—feeling, upon the whole, rather glad to go, from what our master had deceived us into a belief was freedom, back to the arms of slavery.

I have said that this mode of treatment is a part of the whole system of fraud and inhumanity of slavery. It is so. The mode here adopted to disgust the slave with freedom, by allowing him to see only the abuse of it, is carried out in other things. For instance, a slave loves molasses; he steals some. His master, in many cases, goes off to town, and buys a large quantity; he returns, takes his whip, and commands the slave to eat the molasses, until the poor fellow is made sick at the very mention of it. The same mode is sometimes adopted to make the slaves refrain from asking for more food than their regular allowance. A slave runs through his allowance, and applies for more. His master is enraged at him; but, not willing to send him off without food, gives him more than is necessary, and compels him to eat it within a given time. Then, if he complains that he cannot eat it, he is said to be satisfied neither full nor fasting, and is whipped for being hard to please! I have an abundance of such illustrations of the same principle, drawn from my own observation, but think the cases I have cited sufficient. The practice is a very common one.

On the first of January, 1834, I left Mr. Covey, and went to live with Mr. William Freeland, who lived about three miles from St. Michael's. I soon found Mr. Freeland a very different man from Mr. Covey. Though not rich, he was what would be called an educated southern gentleman. Mr. Covey, as I have shown, was a well-trained negro-breaker and slave-driver. The former (slaveholder though he was) seemed to possess some regard for honor, some reverence for justice, and some respect for humanity. The latter seemed totally insensible to all such sentiments. Mr. Freeland had many of the faults peculiar to slaveholders, such as being very passionate and fretful; but I must do him the justice to say, that he was exceedingly free from those degrading vices to which Mr. Covey was constantly addicted. The one was open and frank, and we always knew where to find him. The other was a most artful deceiver, and could be understood only by such as were skilful enough to detect his cunningly-devised frauds. Another advantage I gained in my new master was, he made no pretensions to, or profession of, religion; and this, in my opinion, was truly a great advantage. I assert most unhesitatingly, that the religion of the south is a mere covering for the most horrid crimes,—a justifier of the most appalling barbarity,—a sanctifier of the most hateful frauds,—and a dark shelter under which the darkest, foulest, grossest, and most infernal deeds of slaveholders find the strongest protection. Were I to be again reduced to the chains of slavery, next to that enslavement, I should regard being the slave of a religious master the greatest calamity that could befall me. For of all slaveholders with whom I have ever met, religious slaveholders are the worst. I have ever found them the meanest and basest, the most cruel and cowardly, of all others. It was my unhappy lot not only to belong to a religious slaveholder, but to live in a community of such religionists. Very near Mr. Freeland lived the Rev. Daniel Weeden, and in the same neighborhood lived the Rev. Rigby Hopkins. These were members and ministers in the Reformed Methodist Church. Mr. Weeden owned, among others, a woman slave, whose name I have forgotten. This woman's back, for weeks, was kept literally raw, made so by the lash of this merciless, *religious* wretch. He used to hire hands. His maxim was, Behave well or behave ill, it is the duty of a master occasionally to whip a slave, to remind him of his master's authority. Such was his theory, and such his practice.

Mr. Hopkins was even worse than Mr. Weeden. His chief boast was his ability to manage slaves. The peculiar feature of his government was that of whipping slaves in advance of deserving it. He always managed to have one or more of his slaves to whip every Monday morning. He did this to alarm their fears, and strike terror into those who escaped. His plan was to whip for the smallest offences, to prevent the commission of large ones. Mr. Hopkins could always find some excuse for whipping a slave. It would astonish one, unaccustomed to a slaveholding life, to see with what wonderful ease a slaveholder can find things, of which to make occasion to whip a slave. A mere look, word, or motion,—a mistake, accident, or want of power,—are all matters for which a slave may be whipped at any time. Does a slave look dissatisfied? It is said, he has the devil in him, and it must be whipped out. Does he speak loudly when spoken to by his master? Then he is getting high-minded, and should be taken down a button-hole lower. Does he forget to pull off his hat at the approach of a white person? Then he is wanting in reverence, and should be whipped for it. Does he ever venture to vindicate his conduct, when censured for it? Then he is guilty of impudence,—one of the greatest crimes of which a slave can be guilty. Does he ever venture to suggest a different mode of doing things from that pointed out by his master? He is indeed presumptuous, and getting above himself; and nothing less than a flogging will do for him. Does he, while ploughing, break a plough,—or, while hoeing, break a hoe? It is owing to his carelessness, and for it a slave must always be whipped. Mr. Hopkins could always find something of this sort to justify the use of the lash, and he seldom failed to embrace such opportunities. There was not a man in the whole county, with whom the slaves who had the getting their own home, would not prefer to live, rather than with this Rev. Mr. Hopkins. And yet there was not a man any where round, who made higher professions of religion, or was more active in revivals,—more attentive to the class, love-feast, prayer and preaching meetings, or more devotional in his family,—that prayed earlier, later, louder, and longer,—than this same reverend slave-driver, Rigby Hopkins.

But to return to Mr. Freeland, and to my experience while in his employment. He, like Mr. Covey, gave us enough to eat; but, unlike Mr. Covey, he also gave us sufficient time to take our meals. He worked us hard, but always between sunrise and sunset. He required a good deal of work to be done, but gave us good tools with which to work. His farm was large, but he employed hands enough to work it, and with ease, compared with many of his neighbors. My treatment, while in his employment, was heavenly, compared with what I experienced at the hands of Mr. Edward Covey.

Mr. Freeland was himself the owner of but two slaves. Their names were Henry Harris and John Harris. The rest of his hands he hired. These consisted of myself, Sandy Jenkins,[8] and Handy Caldwell. Henry and John were quite intelligent, and in a very little while after I went there, I succeeded in creating in them a strong desire to learn how to read. This desire soon sprang up in the others also. They very soon mustered up some old spelling-books, and nothing would do but that I must keep a Sabbath school. I agreed to do so, and accordingly devoted my Sundays to teaching these my loved fellow-slaves how to read. Neither of them knew his letters when I went there. Some of the slaves of the neighboring farms found what was going on, and also availed themselves of this little opportunity to learn to read. It was understood, among all who came, that there must be as little display about it as possible. It was necessary to keep our religious masters at St. Michael's unacquainted with the fact, that, instead of spending the Sabbath in wrestling, boxing, and drinking whisky, we were trying to learn how to read the will of God; for they had much rather see us engaged in those degrading sports, than to see us behaving like intellectual, moral, and accountable beings. My blood boils as I think of the bloody manner in which Messrs. Wright Fairbanks and Garrison West, both class-leaders, in connection with many others, rushed in upon us with sticks and stones, and broke up our virtuous little Sabbath school, at St. Michael's—all calling themselves Christians! humble followers of the Lord Jesus Christ! But I am again digressing.

I held my Sabbath school at the house of a free colored man, whose name I deem it imprudent to mention; for should it be known, it might embarrass him greatly, though the crime of holding the school was committed ten years ago. I had at one time over forty scholars, and those of the right sort, ardently desiring to learn. They were of all ages, though mostly men and women. I look back to those Sundays with an amount of pleasure not to be expressed. They were great days to my soul. The work of instructing my dear fellow-slaves was the sweetest engagement with which I was ever blessed. We loved each other, and to leave them at the close of the Sabbath was a severe cross indeed. When I think that those precious souls are to-day shut up in the prison-house of slavery, my feelings overcome me, and I am almost ready to ask, "Does a righteous God govern the universe? and for what does he hold the thunders in his right hand, if not to smite the oppressor, and deliver the spoiled out of the hand of the spoiler?" These dear souls came not to Sabbath school because it was popular to do so, nor did I teach them because it was reputable to be thus engaged. Every moment they spent in that school, they were liable to be taken up, and given thirty-nine lashes. They came because they wished to learn. Their minds had been starved by their cruel masters. They had been shut up in mental dark-

---

8. This is the same man who gave me the roots to prevent my being whipped by Mr. Covey. He was "a clever soul." We used frequently to talk about the fight with Covey, and as often as we did so, he would claim my suc- cess as the result of the roots which he gave me. This superstition is very common among the more ignorant slaves. A slave seldom dies but that his death is attributed to trickery [Douglass's note].

ness. I taught them, because it was the delight of my soul to be doing something that looked like bettering the condition of my race. I kept up my school
nearly the whole year I lived with Mr. Freeland; and, beside my Sabbath school,
I devoted three evenings in the week, during the winter, to teaching the slaves
at home. And I have the happiness to know, that several of those who came to
Sabbath school learned how to read; and that one, at least, is now free through
my agency.

The year passed off smoothly. It seemed only about half as long as the year
which preceded it. I went through it without receiving a single blow. I will give
Mr. Freeland the credit of being the best master I ever had, *till I became my
own master*. For the ease with which I passed the year, I was, however, somewhat indebted to the society of my fellow-slaves. They were noble souls; they
not only possessed loving hearts, but brave ones. We were linked and inter-
linked with each other. I loved them with a love stronger than any thing I have
experienced since. It is sometimes said that we slaves do not love and confide
in each other. In answer to this assertion, I can say, I never loved any or confided in any people more than my fellow-slaves, and especially those with
whom I lived at Mr. Freeland's. I believe we would have died for each other.
We never undertook to do any thing, of any importance, without a mutual consultation. We never moved separately. We were one; and as much so by our
tempers and dispositions, as by the mutual hardships to which we were necessarily subjected by our condition as slaves.

At the close of the year 1834, Mr. Freeland again hired me of my master, for
the year 1835. But, by this time, I began to want to live *upon free land* as well
as *with Freeland*; and I was no longer content, therefore, to live with him or
any other slaveholder. I began, with the commencement of the year, to prepare
myself for a final struggle, which should decide my fate one way or the other.
My tendency was upward. I was fast approaching manhood, and year after year
had passed, and I was still a slave. These thoughts roused me—I must do
something. I therefore resolved that 1835 should not pass without witnessing
an attempt, on my part, to secure my liberty. But I was not willing to cherish
this determination alone. My fellow-slaves were dear to me. I was anxious to
have them participate with me in this, my life-giving determination. I therefore, though with great prudence, commenced early to ascertain their views
and feelings in regard to their condition, and to imbue their minds with
thoughts of freedom. I bent myself to devising ways and means for our escape,
and meanwhile strove, on all fitting occasions, to impress them with the gross
fraud and inhumanity of slavery. I went first to Henry, next to John, then to the
others. I found, in them all, warm hearts and noble spirits. They were ready to
hear, and ready to act when a feasible plan should be proposed. This was what
I wanted. I talked to them of our want of manhood, if we submitted to our
enslavement without at least one noble effort to be free. We met often, and
consulted frequently, and told our hopes and fears, recounted the difficulties,
real and imagined, which we should be called on to meet. At times we were
almost disposed to give up, and try to content ourselves with our wretched lot;
at others, we were firm and unbending in our determination to go. Whenever
we suggested any plan, there was shrinking—the odds were fearful. Our path
was beset with the greatest obstacles; and if we succeeded in gaining the end
of it, our right to be free was yet questionable—we were yet liable to be returned

to bondage. We could see no spot, this side of the ocean, where we could be free. We knew nothing about Canada. Our knowledge of the north did not extend farther than New York; and to go there, and be forever harassed with the frightful liability of being returned to slavery—with the certainty of being treated tenfold worse than before—the thought was truly a horrible one, and one which it was not easy to overcome. The case sometimes stood thus: At every gate through which we were to pass, we saw a watchman—at every ferry a guard—on every bridge a sentinel—and in every wood a patrol. We were hemmed in upon every side. Here were the difficulties, real or imagined—the good to be sought, and the evil to be shunned. On the one hand, there stood slavery, a stern reality, glaring frightfully upon us,—its robes already crimsoned with the blood of millions, and even now feasting itself greedily upon our own flesh. On the other hand, away back in the dim distance, under the flickering light of the north star, behind some craggy hill or snow-covered mountain, stood a doubtful freedom—half frozen—beckoning us to come and share its hospitality. This in itself was sometimes enough to stagger us; but when we permitted ourselves to survey the road, we were frequently appalled. Upon either side we saw grim death, assuming the most horrid shapes. Now it was starvation, causing us to eat our own flesh;—now we were contending with the waves, and were drowned;—now we were overtaken, and torn to pieces by the fangs of the terrible blood-hound. We were stung by scorpions, chased by wild beasts, bitten by snakes, and finally, after having nearly reached the desired spot,—after swimming rivers, encountering wild beasts, sleeping in the woods, suffering hunger and nakedness,—we were overtaken by our pursuers, and, in our resistance, we were shot dead upon the spot! I say, this picture sometimes appalled us, and made us

> "rather bear those ills we had,
> Than fly to others, that we knew not of."[9]

In coming to a fixed determination to run away, we did more than Patrick Henry,[1] when he resolved upon liberty or death. With us it was a doubtful liberty at most, and almost certain death if we failed. For my part, I should prefer death to hopeless bondage.

Sandy, one of our number, gave up the notion, but still encouraged us. Our company then consisted of Henry Harris, John Harris, Henry Bailey, Charles Roberts, and myself. Henry Bailey was my uncle, and belonged to my master. Charles married my aunt: he belonged to my master's father-in-law, Mr. William Hamilton.

The plan we finally concluded upon was, to get a large canoe belonging to Mr. Hamilton, and upon the Saturday night previous to Easter holidays, paddle directly up the Chesapeake Bay. On our arrival at the head of the bay, a distance of seventy or eighty miles from where we lived, it was our purpose to turn our canoe adrift, and follow the guidance of the north star till we got beyond the limits of Maryland. Our reason for taking the water route was, that

---

9. Shakespeare's *Hamlet* 3.1.81–82: "rather bear those ills we have, / Than fly to others, that we know not of."

1. American statesman and orator (1736–1799) whose most famous utterance was "Give me liberty or give me death."

we were less liable to be suspected as runaways; we hoped to be regarded as fishermen; whereas, if we should take the land route, we should be subjected to interruptions of almost every kind. Any one having a white face, and being so disposed, could stop us, and subject us to examination.

The week before our intended start, I wrote several protections, one for each of us. As well as I can remember, they were in the following words, to wit:—

> "This is to certify that I, the undersigned, have given the bearer, my servant, full liberty to go to Baltimore, and spend the Easter holidays. Written with mine own hand, &c., 1835.

> "WILLIAM HAMILTON,
> "Near St. Michael's, in Talbot county, Maryland."

We were not going to Baltimore; but, in going up the bay, we went toward Baltimore, and these protections were only intended to protect us while on the bay.

As the time drew near for our departure, our anxiety became more and more intense. It was truly a matter of life and death with us. The strength of our determination was about to be fully tested. At this time, I was very active in explaining every difficulty, removing every doubt, dispelling every fear, and inspiring all with the firmness indispensable to success in our undertaking; assuring them that half was gained the instant we made the move; we had talked long enough; we were now ready to move; if not now, we never should be; and if we did not intend to move now, we had as well fold our arms, sit down, and acknowledge ourselves fit only to be slaves. This, none of us were prepared to acknowledge. Every man stood firm; and at our last meeting, we pledged ourselves afresh, in the most solemn manner, that, at the time appointed, we would certainly start in pursuit of freedom. This was in the middle of the week, at the end of which we were to be off. We went, as usual, to our several fields of labor, but with bosoms highly agitated with thoughts of our truly hazardous undertaking. We tried to conceal our feelings as much as possible; and I think we succeeded very well.

After a painful waiting, the Saturday morning, whose night was to witness our departure, came. I hailed it with joy, bring what of sadness it might. Friday night was a sleepless one for me. I was, by common consent, at the head of the whole affair. The responsibility of success or failure lay heavily upon me. The glory of the one, and the confusion of the other, were alike mine. The first two hours of that morning were such as I never experienced before, and hope never to again. Early in the morning, we went, as usual, to the field. We were spreading manure; and all at once, while thus engaged, I was overwhelmed with an indescribable feeling, in the fulness of which I turned to Sandy, who was near by, and said, "We are betrayed!" "Well," said he, "that thought has this moment struck me." We said no more. I was never more certain of any thing.

The horn was blown as usual, and we went up from the field to the house for breakfast. I went for the form, more than for want of any thing to eat that morning. Just as I got to the house, in looking out at the lane gate, I saw four white men, with two colored men. The white men were on horseback, and the colored ones were walking behind, as if tied. I watched them a few moments till they got up to our lane gate. Here they halted, and tied the colored men to the gate-post. I was not yet certain as to what the matter was. In a few moments, in rode Mr. Hamilton, with a speed betokening great excitement. He came to the door, and inquired if Master William was in. He was told he was at the barn. Mr. Hamilton, without dismounting, rode up to the barn with extraordinary speed. In a few moments, he and Mr. Freeland returned to the house. By this time, the three constables rode up, and in great haste dismounted, tied their horses, and met Master William and Mr. Hamilton returning from the barn; and after talking awhile, they all walked up to the kitchen door. There was no one in the kitchen but myself and John. Henry and Sandy were up at the barn. Mr. Freeland put his head in at the door, and called me by name, saying, there were some gentlemen at the door who wished to see me. I stepped to the door, and inquired what they wanted. They at once seized me, and, without giving me any satisfaction, tied me—lashing my hands closely together. I insisted upon knowing what the matter was. They at length said, that they had learned I had been in a "scrape," and that I was to be examined before my master; and if their information proved false, I should not be hurt.

In a few moments, they succeeded in tying John. They then turned to Henry, who had by this time returned, and commanded him to cross his hands. "I won't!" said Henry, in a firm tone, indicating his readiness to meet the consequences of his refusal. "Won't you?" said Tom Graham, the constable. "No, I won't!" said Henry, in a still stronger tone. With this, two of the constables pulled out their shining pistols, and swore, by their Creator, that they would make him cross his hands or kill him. Each cocked his pistol, and, with fingers on the trigger, walked up to Henry, saying, at the same time, if he did not cross his hands, they would blow his damned heart out. "Shoot me, shoot me!" said Henry; "you can't kill me but once. Shoot, shoot,—and be damned! *I won't be tied!*" This he said in a tone of loud defiance; and at the same time, with a motion as quick as lightning, he with one single stroke dashed the pistols from the hand of each constable. As he did this, all hands fell upon him, and, after beating him some time, they finally overpowered him, and got him tied.

During the scuffle, I managed, I know not how, to get my pass out, and, without being discovered, put it into the fire. We were all now tied; and just as we were to leave for Easton jail, Betsy Freeland, mother of William Freeland, came to the door with her hands full of biscuits, and divided them between Henry and John. She then delivered herself of a speech, to the following effect:—addressing herself to me, she said, "*You devil! You yellow devil!* it was you that put it into the heads of Henry and John to run away. But for you, you long-legged mulatto devil! Henry nor John would never have thought of such a thing." I made no reply, and was immediately hurried off towards St. Michael's. Just a moment previous to the scuffle with Henry, Mr. Hamilton suggested the propriety of making a search for the protections which he had understood Frederick had written for himself and the rest. But, just at the moment he was about carrying his proposal into effect, his aid was needed in helping to tie Henry; and the excitement attending the scuffle caused them either to forget, or to deem it unsafe, under the circumstances, to search. So we were not yet convicted of the intention to run away.

When we got about half way to St. Michael's, while the constables having us in charge were looking ahead, Henry inquired of me what he should do with his pass. I told him to eat it with his biscuit, and own nothing; and we passed the word around, "*Own nothing*"; and "*Own nothing!*" said we all. Our confidence in each other was unshaken. We were resolved to succeed or fail together, after the calamity had befallen us as much as before. We were now prepared for any thing. We were to be dragged that morning fifteen miles behind horses, and then to be placed in the Easton jail. When we reached St. Michael's, we underwent a sort of examination. We all denied that we ever intended to run away. We did this more to bring out the evidence against us, than from any hope of getting clear of being sold; for, as I have said, we were ready for that. The fact was, we cared but little where we went, so we went together. Our greatest concern was about separation. We dreaded that more than any thing this side of death. We found the evidence against us to be the testimony of one person; our master would not tell who it was; but we came to a unanimous decision among ourselves as to who their informant was. We were sent off to the jail at Easton. When we got there, we were delivered up to the sheriff, Mr. Joseph Graham, and by him placed in jail. Henry, John, and myself, were placed in one room together—Charles, and Henry Bailey, in another. Their object in separating us was to hinder concert.

We had been in jail scarcely twenty minutes, when a swarm of slave traders, and agents for slave traders, flocked into jail to look at us, and to ascertain if we were for sale. Such a set of beings I never saw before! I felt myself surrounded by so many fiends from perdition. A band of pirates never looked more like their father, the devil. They laughed and grinned over us, saying, "Ah, my boys! we have got you, haven't we?" And after taunting us in various ways, they one by one went into an examination of us, with intent to ascertain our value. They would impudently ask us if we would not like to have them for our masters. We would make them no answer, and leave them to find out as best they could. Then they would curse and swear at us, telling us that they could take the devil out of us in a very little while, if we were only in their hands.

While in jail, we found ourselves in much more comfortable quarters than we expected when we went there. We did not get much to eat, nor that which was very good; but we had a good clean room, from the windows of which we could see what was going on in the street, which was very much better than though we had been placed in one of the dark, damp cells. Upon the whole, we got along very well, so far as the jail and its keeper were concerned. Immediately after the holidays were over, contrary to all our expectations, Mr. Hamilton and Mr. Freeland came up to Easton, and took Charles, the two Henrys, and John, out of jail, and carried them home, leaving me alone. I regarded this separation as a final one. It caused me more pain than any thing else in the whole transaction. I was ready for any thing rather than separation. I supposed that they had consulted together, and had decided that, as I was the whole cause of the intention of the others to run away, it was hard to make the innocent suffer with the guilty; and that they had, therefore, concluded to take the others home, and sell me, as a warning to the others that remained. It is due to the noble Henry to say, he seemed almost as reluctant at leaving the prison as at leaving home to come to the prison. But we knew we should, in all probability, be separated, if we were sold; and since he was in their hands, he concluded to go peaceably home.

I was now left to my fate. I was all alone, and within the walls of a stone prison. But a few days before, and I was full of hope. I expected to have been safe in a land of freedom; but now I was covered with gloom, sunk down to the utmost despair. I thought the possibility of freedom was gone. I was kept in this way about one week, at the end of which, Captain Auld, my master, to my surprise and utter astonishment, came up, and took me out, with the intention of sending me, with a gentleman of his acquaintance, into Alabama. But, from some cause or other, he did not send me to Alabama, but concluded to send me back to Baltimore, to live again with his brother Hugh, and to learn a trade.

Thus, after an absence of three years and one month, I was once more permitted to return to my old home at Baltimore. My master sent me away, because there existed against me a very great prejudice in the community, and he feared I might be killed.

In a few weeks after I went to Baltimore, Master Hugh hired me to Mr. William Gardner, an extensive ship-builder, on Fell's Point. I was put there to learn how to calk. It, however, proved a very unfavorable place for the accomplishment of this object. Mr. Gardner was engaged that spring in building two large man-of-war brigs, professedly for the Mexican government. The vessels were to be launched in the July of that year, and in failure thereof, Mr. Gardner was to lose a considerable sum; so that when I entered, all was hurry. There was no time to learn any thing. Every man had to do that which he knew how to do. In entering the shipyard, my orders from Mr. Gardner were, to do whatever the carpenters commanded me to do. This was placing me at the beck and call of about seventy-five men. I was to regard all these as masters. Their word was to be my law. My situation was a most trying one. At times I needed a dozen pair of hands. I was called a dozen ways in the space of a single minute. Three or four voices would strike my ear at the same moment. It was—"Fred., come help me to cant this timber here."—"Fred., come carry this timber yonder."—"Fred., bring that roller here."—"Fred., go get a fresh can of water."—"Fred., come help saw off the end of this timber."—"Fred., go quick, and get the crowbar."—"Fred., hold on the end of this fall."—"Fred., go to the blacksmith's shop, and get a new punch."—"Hurra,[2] Fred.! run and bring me a cold chisel."—"I say, Fred., bear a hand, and get up a fire as quick as lightning under that steambox."—"Halloo, nigger! come, turn this grindstone."—"Come, come! move, move! and bowse[3] this timber forward."—"I say, darky, blast your eyes, why don't you heat up some pitch?"—"Halloo! halloo! halloo!" (Three voices at the same time.) "Come here!—Go there!—Hold on where you are! Damn you, if you move, I'll knock your brains out!"

This was my school for eight months, and I might have remained there longer, but for a most horrid fight I had with four of the white apprentices, in which my left eye was nearly knocked out, and I was horribly mangled in other respects. The facts in the case were these: Until a very little while after I went there, white and black ship-carpenters worked side by side, and no one seemed to see any impropriety in it. All hands seemed to be very well satisfied. Many of the black carpenters were freemen. Things seemed to be going on very well. All at once, the white carpenters knocked off, and said they would not work

2. Hurry.

3. Lift or haul (usually with the help of block and tackle).

with free colored workmen. Their reason for this, as alleged, was, that if free colored carpenters were encouraged, they would soon take the trade into their own hands, and poor white men would be thrown out of employment. They therefore felt called upon at once to put a stop to it. And, taking advantage of Mr. Gardner's necessities, they broke off, swearing they would work no longer, unless he would discharge his black carpenters. Now, though this did not extend to me in form, it did reach me in fact. My fellow-apprentices very soon began to feel it degrading to them to work with me. They began to put on airs, and talk about the "niggers" taking the country, saying we all ought to be killed; and, being encouraged by the journeymen, they commenced making my condition as hard as they could, by hectoring me around, and sometimes striking me. I, of course, kept the vow I made after the fight with Mr. Covey, and struck back again, regardless of consequences; and while I kept them from combining, I succeeded very well; for I could whip the whole of them, taking them separately. They, however, at length combined, and came upon me, armed with sticks, stones, and heavy handspikes. One came in front with a half brick. There was one at each side of me, and one behind me. While I was attending to those in front, and on either side, the one behind ran up with the handspike, and struck me a heavy blow upon the head. It stunned me. I fell, and with this they all ran upon me, and fell to beating me with their fists. I let them lay on for a while, gathering strength. In an instant, I gave a sudden surge, and rose to my hands and knees. Just as I did that, one of their number gave me, with his heavy boot, a powerful kick in the left eye. My eyeball seemed to have burst. When they saw my eye closed, and badly swollen, they left me. With this I seized the handspike, and for a time pursued them. But here the carpenters interfered, and I thought I might as well give it up. It was impossible to stand my hand against so many. All this took place in sight of not less than fifty white ship-carpenters, and not one interposed a friendly word; but some cried, "Kill the damned nigger! Kill him! kill him! He struck a white person." I found my only chance for life was in flight. I succeeded in getting away without an additional blow, and barely so; for to strike a white man is death by Lynch law,—and that was the law in Mr. Gardner's ship-yard; nor is there much of any other out of Mr. Gardner's ship-yard.

I went directly home, and told the story of my wrongs to Master Hugh; and I am happy to say of him, irreligious as he was, his conduct was heavenly, compared with that of his brother Thomas under similar circumstances. He listened attentively to my narration of the circumstances leading to the savage outrage, and gave many proofs of his strong indignation of it. The heart of my once overkind mistress was again melted into pity. My puffed-out eye and blood-covered face moved her to tears. She took a chair by me, washed the blood from my face, and, with a mother's tenderness, bound up my head, covering the wounded eye with a lean piece of fresh beef. It was almost compensation for my suffering to witness, once more, a manifestation of kindness from this, my once affectionate old mistress. Master Hugh was very much enraged. He gave expression to his feelings by pouring out curses upon the heads of those who did the deed. As soon as I got a little the better of my bruises, he took me with him to Esquire Watson's, on Bond Street, to see what could be done about the matter. Mr. Watson inquired who saw the assault committed. Master Hugh told him it was done in Mr. Gardner's ship-yard, at midday, where there were a large company of men at work. "As to that," he said, "the deed was done, and there was no question as to who did it." His answer was, he could do nothing in the case, unless some white man would come forward and testify. He could issue no warrant on my word. If I had been killed in the presence of a thousand colored people, their testimony combined would have been insufficient to have arrested one of the murderers. Master Hugh, for once, was compelled to say this state of things was too bad. Of course, it was impossible to get any white man to volunteer his testimony in my behalf, and against the white young men. Even those who may have sympathized with me were not prepared to do this. It required a degree of courage unknown to them to do so; for just at that time, the slightest manifestation of humanity toward a colored person was denounced as abolitionism, and that name subjected its bearer to frightful liabilities. The watchwords of the bloody-minded in that region, and in those days, were, "Damn the abolitionists!" and "Damn the niggers!" There was nothing done, and probably nothing would have been done if I had been killed. Such was, and such remains, the state of things in the Christian city of Baltimore.

Master Hugh, finding he could get no redress, refused to let me go back again to Mr. Gardner. He kept me himself, and his wife dressed my wound till I was again restored to health. He then took me into the ship-yard of which he was foreman, in the employment of Mr. Walter Price. There I was immediately set to calking, and very soon learned the art of using my mallet and irons. In the course of one year from the time I left Mr. Gardner's, I was able to command the highest wages given to the most experienced calkers. I was now of some importance to my master. I was bringing him from six to seven dollars per week. I sometimes brought him nine dollars per week: my wages were a dollar and a half a day. After learning how to calk, I sought my own employment, made my own contracts, and collected the money which I earned. My pathway became much more smooth than before; my condition was now much more comfortable. When I could get no calking to do, I did nothing. During these leisure times, those old notions about freedom would steal over me again. When in Mr. Gardner's employment, I was kept in such a perpetual whirl of excitement, I could think of nothing, scarcely, but my life; and in thinking of my life, I almost forgot my liberty. I have observed this in my experience of slavery,—that whenever my condition was improved, instead of its increasing my contentment, it only increased my desire to be free, and set me to thinking of plans to gain my freedom. I have found that, to make a contented slave, it is necessary to make a thoughtless one. It is necessary to darken his moral and mental vision, and, as far as possible, to annihilate the power of reason. He must be made to feel that slavery is right; and he can be brought to that only when he ceases to be a man.

I was now getting, as I have said, one dollar and fifty cents per day. I contracted for it; I earned it; it was paid to me; it was rightfully my own; yet, upon each returning Saturday night, I was compelled to deliver every cent of that money to Master Hugh. And why? Not because he earned it,—not because he had any hand in earning it,—not because I owed it to him,—nor because he possessed the slightest shadow of a right to it; but solely because he had the power to compel me to give it up. The right of the grim-visaged pirate upon the high seas is exactly the same.

CHAPTER XI

I now come to that part of my life during which I planned, and finally succeeded in making, my escape from slavery. But before narrating any of the peculiar circumstances, I deem it proper to make known my intention not to state all the facts connected with the transaction. My reasons for pursuing this course may be understood from the following: First, were I to give a minute statement of all the facts, it is not only possible, but quite probable, that others would thereby be involved in the most embarrassing difficulties. Secondly, such a statement would most undoubtedly induce greater vigilance on the part of slaveholders than has existed heretofore among them; which would, of course, be the means of guarding a door whereby some dear brother bondman might escape his galling chains. I deeply regret the necessity that impels me to suppress any thing of importance connected with my experience in slavery. It would afford me great pleasure indeed, as well as materially add to the interest of my narrative, were I at liberty to gratify a curiosity, which I know exists in the minds of many, by an accurate statement of all the facts pertaining to my most fortunate escape. But I must deprive myself of this pleasure, and the curious of the gratification which such a statement would afford. I would allow myself to suffer under the greatest imputations which evil-minded men might suggest, rather than exculpate myself, and thereby run the hazard of closing the slightest avenue by which a brother slave might clear himself of the chains and fetters of slavery.

I have never approved of the very public manner in which some of our western friends have conducted what they call the *underground railroad*,[4] but which, I think, by their open declarations, has been made most emphatically the *upperground railroad*. I honor those good men and women for their noble daring, and applaud them for willingly subjecting themselves to bloody persecution, by openly avowing their participation in the escape of slaves. I, however, can see very little good resulting from such a course, either to themselves or the slaves escaping; while, upon the other hand, I see and feel assured that those open declarations are a positive evil to the slaves remaining, who are seeking to escape. They do nothing towards enlightening the slave, whilst they do much towards enlightening the master. They stimulate him to greater watchfulness, and enhance his power to capture his slave. We owe something to the slaves south of the line[5] as well as to those north of it; and in aiding the latter on their way to freedom, we should be careful to do nothing which would be likely to hinder the former from escaping from slavery. I would keep the merciless slaveholder profoundly ignorant of the means of flight adopted by the slave. I would leave him to imagine himself surrounded by myriads of invisible tormentors, ever ready to snatch from his infernal grasp his trembling prey. Let him be left to feel his way in the dark; let darkness commensurate with his crime hover over him; and let him feel that at every step he takes, in pursuit of the flying bondman, he is running the frightful risk of having his hot brains dashed out by an invisible agency. Let us render the tyrant no aid; let us

4. A system set up by opponents of slavery to help fugitive slaves from the South escape to free states and to Canada.

5. The Mason-Dixon Line, the boundary between Pennsylvania and Maryland and between slave and free states.

not hold the light by which he can trace the footprints of our flying brother. But enough of this. I will now proceed to the statement of those facts, connected with my escape, for which I am alone responsible, and for which no one can be made to suffer but myself.

In the early part of the year 1838, I became quite restless. I could see no reason why I should, at the end of each week, pour the reward of my toil into the purse of my master. When I carried to him my weekly wages, he would, after counting the money, look me in the face with a robber-like fierceness, and ask, "Is this all?" He was satisfied with nothing less than the last cent. He would, however, when I made him six dollars, sometimes give me six cents, to encourage me. It had the opposite effect. I regarded it as a sort of admission of my right to the whole. The fact that he gave me any part of my wages was proof, to my mind, that he believed me entitled to the whole of them. I always felt worse for having received any thing; for I feared that the giving me a few cents would ease his conscience, and make him feel himself to be a pretty honorable sort of robber. My discontent grew upon me. I was ever on the look-out for means of escape; and, finding no direct means, I determined to try to hire my time, with a view of getting money with which to make my escape. In the spring of 1838, when Master Thomas came to Baltimore to purchase his spring goods, I got an opportunity, and applied to him to allow me to hire my time. He unhesitatingly refused my request, and told me this was another stratagem by which to escape. He told me I could go nowhere but that he could get me; and that, in the event of my running away, he should spare no pains in his efforts to catch me. He exhorted me to content myself, and be obedient. He told me, if I would be happy, I must lay out no plans for the future. He said, if I behaved myself properly, he would take care of me. Indeed, he advised me to complete thoughtlessness of the future, and taught me to depend solely upon him for happiness. He seemed to see fully the pressing necessity of setting aside my intellectual nature, in order to [insure] contentment in slavery. But in spite of him, and even in spite of myself, I continued to think, and to think about the injustice of my enslavement, and the means of escape.

About two months after this, I applied to Master Hugh for the privilege of hiring my time. He was not acquainted with the fact that I had applied to Master Thomas, and had been refused. He too, at first, seemed disposed to refuse; but, after some reflection, he granted me the privilege, and proposed the following terms: I was to be allowed all my time, make all contracts with those for whom I worked, and find my own employment; and, in return for this liberty, I was to pay him three dollars at the end of each week; find myself in calking tools, and in board and clothing. My board was two dollars and a half per week. This, with the wear and tear of clothing and calking tools, made my regular expenses about six dollars per week. This amount I was compelled to make up, or relinquish the privilege of hiring my time. Rain or shine, work or no work, at the end of each week the money must be forthcoming, or I must give up my privilege. This arrangement, it will be perceived, was decidedly in my master's favor. It relieved him of all need of looking after me. His money was sure. He received all the benefits of slave-holding without its evils; while I endured all the evils of a slave, and suffered all the care and anxiety of a freeman. I found it a hard bargain. But, hard as it was, I thought it better than the old mode of getting along. It was a step towards freedom to be allowed to bear the responsibilities of a freeman, and I was determined to hold on upon it. I bent myself to the work of making money.

I was ready to work at night as well as day, and by the most untiring persever-ance and industry, I made enough to meet my expenses, and lay up a little money every week. I went on thus from May till August. Master Hugh then refused to allow me to hire my time longer. The ground for his refusal was a failure on my part, one Saturday night, to pay him for my week's time. This failure was occa-sioned by my attending a camp meeting about ten miles from Baltimore. During the week, I had entered into an engagement with a number of young friends to start from Baltimore to the camp ground early Saturday evening; and being detained by my employer, I was unable to get down to Master Hugh's without disappointing the company. I knew that Master Hugh was in no special need of the money that night. I therefore decided to go to camp meeting, and upon my return pay him the three dollars. I staid at the camp meeting one day longer than I intended when I left. But as soon as I returned, I called upon him to pay him what he considered his due. I found him very angry; he could scarce restrain his wrath. He said he had a great mind to give me a severe whipping. He wished to know how I dared go out of the city without asking his permission. I told him I hired my time, and while I paid him the price which he asked for it, I did not know that I was bound to ask him when and where I should go. This reply trou-bled him, and, after reflecting a few moments, he turned to me, and said I should hire my time no longer; that the next thing he should know of, I would be run-ning away. Upon the same plea, he told me to bring my tools and clothing home forthwith. I did so; but instead of seeking work, as I had been accustomed to do previously to hiring my time, I spent the whole week without the performance of a single stroke of work. I did this in retaliation. Saturday night, he called upon me as usual for my week's wages. I told him I had no wages; I had done no work that week. Here we were upon the point of coming to blows. He raved, and swore his determination to get hold of me. I did not allow myself a single word; but was resolved, if he laid the weight of his hand upon me, it should be blow for blow. He did not strike me, but told me that he would find me in constant employment in future. I thought the matter over during the next day, Sunday, and finally resolved upon the third day of September, as the day upon which I would make a second attempt to secure my freedom. I now had three weeks dur-ing which to prepare for my journey. Early on Monday morning, before Master Hugh had time to make any engagement for me, I went out and got employment of Mr. Butler, at his ship-yard near the draw-bridge, upon what is called the City Block, thus making it unnecessary for him to seek employment for me. At the end of the week, I brought him between eight and nine dollars. He seemed very well pleased, and asked me why I did not do the same the week before. He little knew what my plans were. My object in working steadily was to remove any sus-picion he might entertain of my intent to run away; and in this I succeeded admirably. I suppose he thought I was never better satisfied with my condition than at the very time during which I was planning my escape. The second week passed, and again I carried him my full wages; and so well pleased was he, that he gave me twenty-five cents, (quite a large sum for a slaveholder to give a slave,) and bade me to make a good use of it. I told him I would.

Things went on without very smoothly indeed, but within there was trouble. It is impossible for me to describe my feelings as the time of my contemplated start drew near. I had a number of warm-hearted friends in Baltimore,—friends that I loved almost as I did my life,—and the thought of being separated from them forever was painful beyond expression. It is my opinion that thousands would escape from slavery, who now remain, but for the strong cords of affection that bind them to their friends. The thought of leaving my friends was decidedly the most painful thought with which I had to contend. The love of them was my tender point, and shook my decision more than all things else. Besides the pain of separation, the dread and apprehension of a failure exceeded what I had experienced at my first attempt. The appalling defeat I then sustained returned to torment me. I felt assured that, if I failed in this attempt, my case would be a hopeless one—it would seal my fate as a slave forever. I could not hope to get off with any thing less than the severest punishment, and being placed beyond the means of escape. It required no very vivid imagination to depict the most frightful scenes through which I should have to pass, in case I failed. The wretchedness of slavery, and the blessedness of freedom, were perpetually before me. It was life and death with me. But I remained firm, and, according to my resolution, on the third day of September, 1838, I left my chains, and succeeded in reaching New York without the slightest interruption of any kind. How I did so,— what means I adopted,— what direction I travelled, and by what mode of conveyance,—I must leave unexplained, for the reasons before mentioned.

I have been frequently asked how I felt when I found myself in a free State. I have never been able to answer the question with any satisfaction to myself. It was a moment of the highest excitement I ever experienced. I suppose I felt as one may imagine the unarmed mariner to feel when he is rescued by a friendly man-of-war from the pursuit of a pirate. In writing to a dear friend, immediately after my arrival at New York, I said I felt like one who had escaped a den of hungry lions. This state of mind, however, very soon subsided; and I was again seized with a feeling of great insecurity and loneliness. I was yet liable to be taken back, and subjected to all the tortures of slavery. This in itself was enough to damp the ardor of my enthusiasm. But the loneliness overcame me. There I was in the midst of thousands, and yet a perfect stranger; without home and without friends, in the midst of thousands of my own brethren— children of a common Father, and yet I dared not to unfold to any one of them my sad condition. I was afraid to speak to any one for fear of speaking to the wrong one, and thereby falling into the hands of money-loving kidnappers, whose business it was to lie in wait for the panting fugitive, as the ferocious beasts of the forest lie in wait for their prey. The motto which I adopted when I started from slavery was this—"Trust no man!" I saw in every white man an enemy, and in almost every colored man cause for distrust. It was a most painful situation; and, to understand it, one must needs experience it, or imagine himself in similar circumstances. Let him be a fugitive slave in a strange land— a land given up to be the hunting-ground for slaveholders—whose inhabitants are legalized kidnappers—where he is every moment subjected to the terrible liability of being seized upon by his fellow-men, as the hideous crocodile seizes upon his prey!—I say, let him place himself in my situation—without home or friends—without money or credit—wanting shelter, and no one to give it— wanting bread, and no money to buy it,—and at the same time let him feel that he is pursued by merciless men-hunters, and in total darkness as to what to do, where to go, or where to stay,—perfectly helpless both as to the means of defence and means of escape,—in the midst of plenty, yet suffering the terrible gnawings of hunger,—in the midst of houses, yet having no home,—among fellow-men, yet feeling as if in the midst of wild beasts, whose greediness to swallow up the trembling and half-famished fugitive is only equalled by that with which the monsters of the deep swallow up the helpless fish upon which they subsist,—I say, let him be placed in this most trying situation,—the situation in which I was placed,—then, and not till then, will he fully appreciate the hardships of, and know how to sympathize with, the toil-worn and whip-scarred fugitive slave.

Thank Heaven, I remained but a short time in this distressed situation. I was relieved from it by the humane hand of Mr. DAVID RUGGLES,[6] whose vigilance, kindness, and perseverance, I shall never forget. I am glad of an opportunity to express, as far as words can, the love and gratitude I bear him. Mr. Ruggles is now afflicted with blindness, and is himself in need of the same kind offices which he was once so forward in the performance of toward others. I had been in New York but a few days, when Mr. Ruggles sought me out, and very kindly took me to his boarding-house at the corner of Church and Lespenard Streets. Mr. Ruggles was then very deeply engaged in the memorable *Darg* case, as well as attending to a number of other fugitive slaves, devising ways and means for their successful escape; and, though watched and hemmed in on almost every side, he seemed to be more than a match for his enemies. Very soon after I went to Mr. Ruggles, he wished to know of me where I wanted to go; as he deemed it unsafe for me to remain in New York. I told him I was a calker, and should like to go where I could get work. I thought of going to Canada; but he decided against it, and in favor of my going to New Bedford, thinking I should be able to get work there at my trade. At this time, Anna,[7] my intended wife, came on; for I wrote to her immediately after my arrival at New York, (notwithstanding my homeless, houseless, and helpless condition,) informing her of my successful flight, and wishing her to come on forthwith. In a few days after her arrival, Mr. Ruggles called in the Rev. J. W. C. Pennington, who, in the presence of Mr. Ruggles, Mrs. Michaels, and two or three others, performed the marriage ceremony, and gave us a certificate, of which the following is an exact copy:—

"THIS may certify, that I joined together in holy matrimony Frederick Johnson[8] and Anna Murray, as man and wife, in the presence of Mr. David Ruggles and Mrs. Michaels.

"JAMES W. C. PENNINGTON.
"*New York, Sept.* 15, 1838."

Upon receiving this certificate, and a five-dollar bill from Mr. Ruggles, I shouldered one part of our baggage, and Anna took up the other, and we set out forthwith to take passage on board of the steamboat *John W. Richmond* for Newport, on our way to New Bedford. Mr. Ruggles gave me a letter to a Mr. Shaw in Newport, and told me, in case my money did not serve me to New Bedford, to stop in Newport and obtain further assistance; but upon our arrival at Newport, we were so anxious to get to a place of safety, that, notwithstanding we lacked the necessary money to pay our fare, we decided to take seats in the stage, and promise to pay when we got to New Bedford. We were encouraged to

6. A black abolitionist (1810–1849), at this time living in New York, who helped many slaves to escape.

7. She was free [Douglass's note].
8. I had changed my name from Frederick *Bailey* to that of *Johnson* [Douglass's note].

do this by two excellent gentlemen, residents of New Bedford, whose names I afterward ascertained to be Joseph Ricketson and William C. Taber. They seemed at once to understand our circumstances, and gave us such assurance of their friendliness as put us fully at ease in their presence. It was good indeed to meet with such friends, at such a time. Upon reaching New Bedford, we were directed to the house of Mr. Nathan Johnson, by whom we were kindly received, and hospitably provided for. Both Mr. and Mrs. Johnson took a deep and lively interest in our welfare. They proved themselves quite worthy of the name of abolitionists. When the stage-driver found us unable to pay our fare, he held on upon our baggage as security for the debt. I had but to mention the fact to Mr. Johnson, and he forthwith advanced the money.

We now began to feel a degree of safety, and to prepare ourselves for the duties and responsibilities of a life of freedom. On the morning after our arrival at New Bedford, while at the breakfast-table, the question arose as to what name I should be called by. The name given me by my mother was, "Frederick Augustus Washington Bailey." I, however, had dispensed with the two middle names long before I left Maryland so that I was generally known by the name of "Frederick Bailey." I started from Baltimore bearing the name of "Stanley." When I got to New York, I again changed my name to "Frederick Johnson," and thought that would be the last change. But when I got to New Bedford, I found it necessary again to change my name. The reason of this necessity was, that there were so many Johnsons in New Bedford, it was already quite difficult to distinguish between them. I gave Mr. Johnson the privilege of choosing me a name, but told him he must not take from me the name of "Frederick." I must hold on to that, to preserve a sense of my identity. Mr. Johnson had just been reading the "Lady of the Lake,"[9] and at once suggested that my name be "Douglass." From that time until now I have been called "Frederick Douglass"; and as I am more widely known by that name than by either of the others, I shall continue to use it as my own.

I was quite disappointed at the general appearance of things in New Bedford. The impression which I had received respecting the character and condition of the people of the north, I found to be singularly erroneous. I had very strangely supposed, while in slavery, that few of the comforts, and scarcely any of the luxuries, of life were enjoyed at the north, compared with what were enjoyed by the slaveholders of the south. I probably came to this conclusion from the fact that northern people owned no slaves. I supposed that they were about upon a level with the non-slaveholding population of the south. I knew *they* were exceedingly poor, and I had been accustomed to regard their poverty as the necessary consequence of their being non-slaveholders. I had somehow imbibed the opinion that, in the absence of slaves, there could be no wealth, and very little refinement. And upon coming to the north, I expected to meet with a rough, hard-handed, and uncultivated population, living in the most Spartan-like simplicity, knowing nothing of the ease, luxury, pomp, and grandeur of southern slaveholders. Such being my conjectures, any one acquainted with the appearance of New Bedford may very readily infer how palpably I must have seen my mistake.

In the afternoon of the day when I reached New Bedford, I visited the wharves, to take a view of the shipping. Here I found myself surrounded with the strongest

---

9. A narrative poem by Sir Walter Scott (1810) about the fortunes of the Douglas clan in Scotland.

proofs of wealth. Lying at the wharves, and riding in the stream, I saw many ships of the finest model, in the best order, and of the largest size. Upon the right and left, I was walled in by granite warehouses of the widest dimensions, stowed to their utmost capacity with the necessaries and comforts of life. Added to this, almost every body seemed to be at work, but noiselessly so, compared with what I had been accustomed to in Baltimore. There were no loud songs heard from those engaged in loading and unloading ships. I heard no deep oaths or horrid curses on the laborer. I saw no whipping of men; but all seemed to go smoothly on. Every man appeared to understand his work, and went at it with a sober, yet cheerful earnestness, which betokened the deep interest which he felt in what he was doing, as well as a sense of his own dignity as a man. To me this looked exceedingly strange. From the wharves I strolled around and over the town, gazing with wonder and admiration at the splendid churches, beautiful dwellings, and finely-cultivated gardens; evincing an amount of wealth, comfort, taste, and refinement, such as I had never seen in any part of slaveholding Maryland.

Every thing looked clean, new, and beautiful. I saw few or no dilapidated houses, with poverty-stricken inmates; no half-naked children and barefooted women, such as I had been accustomed to see in Hillsborough, Easton, St. Michael's, and Baltimore. The people looked more able, stronger, healthier, and happier, than those of Maryland. I was for once made glad by a view of extreme wealth, without being saddened by seeing extreme poverty. But the most astonishing as well as the most interesting thing to me was the condition of the colored people, a great many of whom, like myself, had escaped thither as a refuge from the hunters of men. I found many, who had not been seven years out of their chains, living in finer houses, and evidently enjoying more of the comforts of life, than the average of slave-holders in Maryland. I will venture to assert that my friend Mr. Nathan Johnson (of whom I can say with a grateful heart, "I was hungry, and he gave me meat; I was thirsty, and he gave me drink; I was a stranger, and he took me in")[1] lived in a neater house; dined at a better table; took, paid for, and read, more newspapers; better understood the moral, religious, and political character of the nation,—than nine tenths of the slave-holders in Talbot county Maryland. Yet Mr. Johnson was a working man. His hands were hardened by toil, and not his alone, but those also of Mrs. Johnson. I found the colored people much more spirited than I had supposed they would be. I found among them a determination to protect each other from the blood-thirsty kidnapper, at all hazards. Soon after my arrival, I was told of a circumstance which illustrated their spirit. A colored man and a fugitive slave were on unfriendly terms. The former was heard to threaten the latter with informing his master of his whereabouts. Straightway a meeting was called among the colored people, under the stereotyped notice, "Business of importance!" The betrayer was invited to attend. The people came at the appointed hour, and organized the meeting by appointing a very religious old gentleman as president, who, I believe, made a prayer, after which he addressed the meeting as follows: *"Friends, we have got him here, and I would recommend that you young men just take him outside the door, and kill him!"* With this, a number of them bolted at him; but they were intercepted by some more timid than themselves, and the

1. Matthew 25:35: "For I was an hungered, and ye gave me meat: I was thirsty, and ye gave me drink: I was a stranger, and ye took me in."

betrayer escaped their vengeance, and has not been seen in New Bedford since. I believe there have been no more such threats, and should there be hereafter, I doubt not that death would be the consequence.

I found employment, the third day after my arrival, in stowing a sloop with a load of oil. It was new, dirty, and hard work for me; but I went at it with a glad heart and a willing hand. I was now my own master. It was a happy moment, the rapture of which can be understood only by those who have been slaves. It was the first work, the reward of which was to be entirely my own. There was no Master Hugh standing ready, the moment I earned the money, to rob me of it. I worked that day with a pleasure I had never before experienced. I was at work for myself and newly-married wife. It was to me the starting-point of a new existence. When I got through with that job, I went in pursuit of a job of calking; but such was the strength of prejudice against color, among the white calkers, that they refused to work with me, and of course I could get no employment.[2] Finding my trade of no immediate benefit, I threw off my calking habiliments, and prepared myself to do any kind of work I could get to do. Mr. Johnson kindly let me have his woodhorse and saw, and I very soon found myself a plenty of work. There was no work too hard—none too dirty. I was ready to saw wood, shovel coal, carry the hod, sweep the chimney, or roll oil casks,—all of which I did for nearly three years in New Bedford, before I became known to the anti-slavery world.

In about four months after I went to New Bedford there came a young man to me, and inquired if I did not wish to take the "Liberator."[3] I told him I did; but, just having made my escape from slavery, I remarked that I was unable to pay for it then. I, however, finally became a subscriber to it. The paper came, and I read it from week to week with such feelings as it would be quite idle for me to attempt to describe. The paper became my meat and my drink. My soul was set all on fire. Its sympathy for my brethren in bonds—its scathing denunciations of slaveholders—its faithful exposures of slavery—and its powerful attacks upon the upholders of the institution—sent a thrill of joy through my soul, such as I had never felt before!

I had not long been a reader of the "Liberator," before I got a pretty correct idea of the principles, measures and spirit of the anti-slavery reform. I took right hold of the cause. I could do but little; but what I could, I did with a joyful heart, and never felt happier than when in an anti-slavery meeting. I seldom had much to say at the meetings, because what I wanted to say was said so much better by others. But, while attending an anti-slavery convention at Nantucket, on the 11th of August, 1841, I felt strongly moved to speak, and was at the same time much urged to do so by Mr. William C. Coffin, a gentleman who had heard me speak in the colored people's meeting at New Bedford. It was a severe cross, and I took it up reluctantly. The truth was, I felt myself a slave, and the idea of speaking to white people weighed me down. I spoke but a few moments, when I felt a degree of freedom, and said what I desired with considerable ease. From that time until now, I have been engaged in pleading the cause of my brethren—with what success, and with what devotion, I leave those acquainted with my labors to decide.

---

2. I am told that colored persons can now get employment at calking in New Bedford—a result of antislavery effort [Douglass's note].

3. William Lloyd Garrison's antislavery newspaper, which began publication in 1831.

APPENDIX

I find, since reading over the foregoing Narrative, that I have, in several instances, spoken in such a tone and manner, respecting religion, as may possibly lead those unacquainted with my religious views to suppose me an opponent of all religion. To remove the liability of such misapprehension, I deem it proper to append the following brief explanation. What I have said respecting and against religion, I mean strictly to apply to the *slaveholding religion* of this land, and with no possible reference to Christianity proper; for, between the Christianity of this land, and the Christianity of Christ, I recognize the widest possible difference—so wide, that to receive the one as good, pure, and holy, is of necessity to reject the other as bad, corrupt, and wicked. To be the friend of the one, is of necessity to be the enemy of the other. I love the pure, peaceable, and impartial Christianity of Christ: I therefore hate the corrupt, slaveholding, women-whipping, cradle-plundering, partial and hypocritical Christianity of this land. Indeed, I can see no reason, but the most deceitful one, for calling the religion of this land Christianity. I look upon it as the climax of all misnomers, the boldest of all frauds, and the grossest of all libels. Never was there a clearer case of "stealing the livery of the court of heaven to serve the devil in." I am filled with unutterable loathing when I contemplate the religious pomp and show, together with the horrible inconsistencies, which every where surround me. We have men-stealers for ministers, women-whippers for missionaries, and cradle-plunderers for church members. The man who wields the blood-clotted cowskin during the week fills the pulpit on Sunday, and claims to be a minister of the meek and lowly Jesus. The man who robs me of my earnings at the end of each week meets me as a class-leader on Sunday morning, to show me the way of life, and the path of salvation. He who sells my sister, for purposes of prostitution, stands forth as the pious advocate of purity. He who proclaims it a religious duty to read the Bible denies me the right of learning to read the name of the God who made me. He who is the religious advocate of marriage robs whole millions of its sacred influence, and leaves them to the ravages of wholesale pollution. The warm defender of the sacredness of the family relation is the same that scatters whole families,—sundering husbands and wives, parents and children, sisters and brothers,—leaving the hut vacant, and the hearth desolate. We see the thief preaching against theft, and the adulterer against adultery. We have men sold to build churches, women sold to support the gospel, and babes sold to purchase Bibles for the *poor heathen! all for the glory of God and the good of souls!* The slave auctioneer's bell and the church-going bell chime in with each other, and the bitter cries of the heart-broken slave are drowned in the religious shouts of his pious master. Revivals of religion and revivals in the slave-trade go hand in hand together. The slave prison and the church stand near each other. The clanking of fetters and the rattling of chains in the prison, and the pious psalm and solemn prayer in the church, may be heard at the same time. The dealers in the bodies and souls of men erect their stand in the presence of the pulpit, and they mutually help each other. The dealer gives his blood-stained gold to support the pulpit, and the pulpit, in return, covers his infernal business with the garb of Christianity. Here we have religion and robbery the allies of each other—devils dressed in angels' robes, and hell presenting the semblance of paradise.

> "Just God! and these are they,
>   Who minister at thine altar, God of right!

Men who their hands, with prayer and blessing, lay
    On Israel's ark of light.

"What! preach, and kidnap men?
    Give thanks, and rob thy own afflicted poor?
Talk of thy glorious liberty, and then
    Bolt hard the captive's door?

"What! servants of thy own
    Merciful Son, who came to seek and save
The homeless and the outcast, fettering down
    The tasked and plundered slave!

"Pilate and Herod friends!
    Chief priests and rulers, as of old, combine!
Just God and holy! is that church which lends
    Strength to the spoiler thine?"

The Christianity of America is a Christianity, of whose votaries it may be as truly said, as it was of the ancient scribes and Pharisees, "They bind heavy burdens, and grievous to be borne, and lay them on men's shoulders, but they themselves will not move them with one of their fingers. All their works they do for to be seen of men.—— They love the uppermost rooms at feasts, and the chief seats in the synagogues, ... and to be called of men, Rabbi, Rabbi.——But woe unto you, scribes and Pharisees, hypocrites! for ye neither go in yourselves, neither suffer ye them that are entering to go in. Ye devour widows' houses, and for a pretence make long prayers; therefore ye shall receive the greater damnation. Ye compass sea and land to make one proselyte, and when he is made, ye make him twofold more the child of hell than yourselves.——Woe unto you, scribes and Pharisees, hypocrites! for ye pay tithe of mint, and anise, and cumin, and have omitted the weightier matters of the law, judgment, mercy, and faith; these ought ye to have done, and not to leave the other undone. Ye blind guides! which strain at a gnat, and swallow a camel. Woe unto you, scribes and Pharisees, hypocrites! for ye make clean the outside of the cup and of the platter; but within, they are full of extortion and excess.——Woe unto you, scribes and Pharisees, hypocrites! for ye are like unto whited sepulchres, which indeed appear beautiful outward, but are within full of dead men's bones, and of all uncleanness. Even so ye also outwardly appear righteous unto men, but within ye are full of hypocrisy and iniquity."[4]

    Dark and terrible as is this picture, I hold it to be strictly true of the overwhelming mass of professed Christians in America. They strain at a gnat, and swallow a camel. Could anything be more true of our churches? They would be shocked at the proposition of fellowshipping a *sheep*-stealer; and at the same time they hug to their communion a *man*-stealer, and brand me with being an infidel, if I find fault with them for it. They attend with Pharisaical strictness to the outward forms of religion, and at the same time neglect the weightier matters of the law, judgment, mercy, and faith. They are always ready to sacrifice, but seldom to show mercy. They are they who are represented as professing to love God whom they have not seen, whilst they hate their brother whom they have seen. They love

4. Matthew 23.

the heathen on the other side of the globe. They can pray for him, pay money to have the Bible put into his hand, and missionaries to instruct him; while they despise and totally neglect the heathen at their own doors.

Such is, very briefly, my view of the religion of this land; and to avoid any misunderstanding, growing out of the use of general terms, I mean, by the religion of this land, that which is revealed in the words, deeds, and actions, of those bodies, north and south, calling themselves Christian churches, and yet in union with slaveholders. It is against religion, as presented by these bodies, that I have felt it my duty to testify.

I conclude these remarks by copying the following portrait of the religion of the south, (which is, by communion and fellowship, the religion of the north) which I soberly affirm is "true to the life," and without caricature or the slightest exaggeration. It is said to have been drawn, several years before the present anti-slavery agitation began, by a northern Methodist preacher, who, while residing at the south, had an opportunity to see slaveholding morals, manners, and piety, with his own eyes. "Shall I not visit for these things? saith the Lord. Shall not my soul be avenged on such a nation as this?"[5]

"*A Parody.*

"Come, saints and sinners, hear me tell
How pious priests whip Jack and Nell,
And women buy and children sell,
And preach all sinners down to hell,
  And sing of heavenly union.

"They'll bleat and baa, dona[6] like goats,
Gorge down black sheep, and strain at motes,
Array their backs in fine black coats,
Then seize their negroes by their throats,
  And choke, for heavenly union.

"They'll church you if you sip a dram,
And damn you if you steal a lamb;
Yet rob old Tony, Doll, and Sam,
Of human rights, and bread and ham;
  Kidnapper's heavenly union.

"They'll loudly talk of Christ's reward,
And bind his image with a cord,
And scold, and swing the lash abhorred,
And sell their brother in the Lord
  To handcuffed heavenly union.

"They'll read and sing a sacred song,
And make a prayer both loud and long,
And teach the right and do the wrong,
Hailing the brother, sister throng,
  With words of heavenly union.

"We wonder how such saints can sing,

5. Jeremiah 5:9.
6. Believed to be a printer's error in the original edition for "go on" or "go n-a-a-ah."

Or praise the Lord upon the wing,
Who roar, and scold, and whip, and sting,
And to their slaves and mammon cling,
  In guilty conscience union.

"They'll raise tobacco, corn, and rye,
And drive, and thieve, and cheat, and lie,
And lay up treasures in the sky,
By making switch and cowskin fly,
  In hope of heavenly union.

"They'll crack old Tony on the skull,
And preach and roar like Bashan bull,
Or braying ass, of mischief full,
Then seize old Jacob by the wool,
  And pull for heavenly union.

"A roaring, ranting, sleek man-thief,
Who lived on mutton, veal, and beef,
Yet never would afford relief
To needy, sable sons of grief,
  Was big with heavenly union.

"'Love not the world,' the preacher said,
And winked his eye, and shook his head;
He seized on Tom, and Dick, and Ned,
Cut short their meat, and clothes, and bread,
  Yet still loved heavenly union.

"Another preacher whining spoke
Of One whose heart for sinners broke:
He tied old Nanny to an oak,
And drew the blood at every stroke,
  And prayed for heavenly union.

"Two others oped their iron jaws,
And waved their children-stealing paws;
There sat their children in gewgaws;
By stinting negroes' backs and maws,
  They kept up heavenly union.

"All good from Jack another takes,
And entertains their flirts and rakes,
Who dress as sleek as glossy snakes,
And cram their mouths with sweetened cakes;
  And this goes down for union."

Sincerely and earnestly hoping that this little book may do something toward throwing light on the American slave system, and hastening the glad day of deliverance to the millions of my brethren in bonds—faithfully relying upon the power of truth, love, and justice, for success in my humble efforts—and solemnly pledging my self anew to the sacred cause,—I subscribe myself,

FREDERICK DOUGLASS.

Lynn, Mass., April 28, 1845.

WILLIAM BLAKE
1757–1827

William Blake condemned authority of all kinds. He cast priests and kings as responsible for exploiting the poor, repressing sexuality, and stifling art, and he admired the devil himself for his disobedience. "I must Create a System or be enslaved by another Man's," claims one of his characters. But the rebellious Blake also harbored profound religious beliefs, developing his own unorthodox visions of divine love, justice, and creativity. When asked if he believed in the divinity of Jesus Christ, he is reported to have said, "*He is the only God,*" and then added: "And so am I and so are you." Some of his contemporaries hailed him as a saint: one legend has it that on his deathbed he burst out in songs of joy. To many others, he seemed a pitiable madman. Only a few admirers in his own time acclaimed him as the creative visionary he would appear to later generations.

LIFE

Born in 1757 in London, Blake was the third of six children. His father kept a hosiery shop, and both parents were lower-middle-class Londoners, radical in their politics and unorthodox in their religion. He grew up among small tradesmen and artisans, who typically took pride in their skilled labor and had a tradition of political radicalism that pitted them against the aristocratic elite. At the age of ten, Blake started drawing school, and at fourteen he was apprenticed to an engraver who taught him complex techniques of engraving and printmaking. He had no formal education beyond drawing school, but he read widely, including history, philosophy, classical literature, the Bible, Shakespeare, Milton, and other English poets, and he began writing poetry himself at around the age of thirteen. From childhood onward he repeatedly saw visions. "I write when commanded by the spirits," he once said, "and the moment I have written I see the words fly about the room in all directions." After exhibiting engravings and watercolors at the prestigious Royal Academy of Arts in 1779, Blake went to work as an engraver for Joseph Johnson, a bookseller and publisher who associated with the most influential radical thinkers of the Enlightenment period.

At the age of 25 Blake married Catherine Boucher, an illiterate daughter of a small farmer, whom he taught to read and write. By all accounts, their married life was a happy one, if occasionally tempestuous, and Catherine actively helped William in his work. The couple had no children.

In the late 1780s Blake developed a revolutionary new technique which he called "illuminated printing." Conventional print shops at the time separated the printing of images and words, integrating them only in the final stage of book production. Blake's method, by contrast, involved combining visual and written materials. He drew and wrote directly on the same copper plate, which then formed the basis for print reproductions. This process allowed Blake to adopt a much more spontaneous multimedia artistic practice than was usual, and ensured that the end product was entirely his own: he was at once the writer, the illustrator, and the printer. In characteristically visionary fashion, Blake explained that the spirit of his dead brother Robert had come to teach him this new technique.

Excited by the radical energies unleashed by the French Revolution in 1789, Blake threw himself into his creative endeavors and produced many of his greatest works in the following few years. *Songs of Innocence* in 1789 marked the beginnings of Blake's innovations. Frustrated with the poetry of his contemporaries, he looked backward to ancient ballads and sixteenth- and seventeenth-century English poetry for models. But he also took his work into some startlingly new poetic directions, including experimental rhythms, prophecies, themes of madness and jealousy, and the beginnings of a grand cosmological history. He wrote directly about politics while also pursuing his growing interest in myths and symbols.

One day in 1803 a soldier came into the Blakes' garden uttering threats and curses; Blake physically pushed him out. Because he had supposedly assaulted a soldier, the artist went on trial for sedition, or inciting rebellion, then punishable by hanging. In the end, he was acquitted, but the experience drove him further into isolation than ever. He spent the rest of his life poor and obscure. In his final years, a group of young painters recognized Blake's innovations in visual art, hailing him as a genius and an inspiration. He began to feel less angry and isolated, and his last few years were probably his happiest. But although he had finally won admiration as a visual artist, it was only long after his death in 1827 that Blake's extraordinary inventiveness as a poet would be understood and acclaimed.

TIMES

Blake was not alone in wanting to see tyrannical and corrupt authorities toppled, but he was often seen as eccentric even among revolutionaries. He rejected the Enlightenment insistence on cold rationality, mechanical science, and individual rights, envisioning a more spiritual, imaginative, and collective future. He wrote, "God is not a mathematical diagram." His famous poem "Mock On, Mock On, **Voltaire, Rousseau**" expresses his sense of the dangers of Enlightenment philosophy.

Blake put a much greater emphasis on economic inequality than most English supporters of the French Revolution. While many of his Enlightenment contemporaries argued for legal rights and political representation, Blake fiercely condemned the vast economic gulf between rich and poor. This was a moment when working conditions were changing dramatically: factories were springing up in urban centers, drawing vast numbers of laborers from the rural countryside, and machines were beginning to replace traditional craftsmanship. Blake angrily denounced a society willing to thrust workers into "dark Satanic Mills." Chimney sweeps, notorious as emblems of child labor, endured particularly severe hardships. Typically, these boys started working around the age of five, and by the time they had grown too large to climb chimneys, at twelve or thirteen, their bodies had been deformed and broken, rendered incapable of further work. In "The Chimney Sweeper," Blake expressed horror at the life of the laboring child who worked in darkness, inhaled soot and smoke, and had to endure burns, bruises, and debilitating illnesses.

It was not an easy time to speak out against injustice. The 1790s saw a wave of repressive laws that clamped down on dissenting expression in Britain. Public speakers, inflamed by the French Revolution, were trying to whip up antimonarchical sentiment and crowds were actively protesting—even at one point attacking the king's carriage. The British government responded harshly, suspending habeas corpus (the right not to be detained indefinitely without trial), banning most meetings larger than fifty people, and prosecuting "wicked and seditious writing." In 1793 France declared war on England, and the two nations were at war almost continuously until 1815. The wars intensified popular unrest, and revolutionary sympathizers were forced underground. Blake's former employer, Joseph Johnson, landed in jail for nine months for publishing an antiwar pamphlet. During this time, Blake's explicit engagements with poverty, slavery, and revolution gave way to more cryptic, biblical, and mythological themes.

But it would also be a mistake to imagine too strict a separation between Blake's politics and his religion. British law had long denied civil liberties to those who did not belong to the Church of England, and many Protestants, such as Methodists, Baptists, and Presbyterians—called Dissenters—had a robust tradition of resistance to official power. They wove together their religious beliefs with their political opposition. Blake was no exception. He was drawn to the mystical, charitable Swedenborg Church of the New Jerusalem, though he later criticized and rejected its doctrines. The 1780s and '90s saw a rise in evangelical and millenarian enthusiasm, and many Dissenters took the French Revolution to be the sign of a coming apocalypse. Blake repeatedly treated politics in terms of biblical models, and he, like many of his dissenting contemporaries, understood political revolutions as a violent purifying process that would bring about prophecies foretold in the Bible. In Blake's *Jerusalem*, one character asks, "Are not Religion & Politics the same thing? Brotherhood is Religion." Although Blake can seem eccentric among his rationalist Enlightenment contemporaries, then, his fusion of radical political beliefs and unorthodox, mystical spirituality was not entirely unusual among Dissenters in London.

WORK

Blake called for an open, accessible, democratic poetry and claimed that chil-

dren were often the best readers of his work. His poems typically reject regular rhythms and conventional images in favor of unorthodox forms and unusually plain, forceful language. But he also opted for complicated systems of allegorical images and symbols, and in his stories characters often meld into others, change names, and appear and disappear in new guises. Not surprisingly, then, Blake's meanings remain a subject of fierce debate after two centuries. Many readers protest that much of his work is impenetrable and obscure— precisely the opposite of what Blake himself seems to have intended. And yet this debate might not have surprised or bothered Blake, since deliberate oppositions are often at the very heart of his work. He moves back and forth between innocence and experience, mystical vision and wry irony, joyful optimism and bleak prophecy, visual art and poetry.

In *Songs of Innocence*, Blake explores in simple language what it would be like to perceive the world through the eyes of a child. This means rendering familiar ideas radically unfamiliar. For instance, if we are accustomed to living in a culture that associates darkness with evil, then what does it feel like to be a dark-skinned child? His later *Songs of Experience* (1794) offers a set of companion pieces that return to the same subject matter from a more knowing perspective. Blake juxtaposes the two sets of poems, inviting us to think about the different ways that an innocent child and an experienced adult might understand God, love, and justice. There are echoes and recurrences within as well as across these two groups of poems, and perhaps this is not surprising: after all, Blake's major occupation throughout his life involved making copies—as an engraver, printmaker, and printer—and he seems to have been at least as interested in ideas of doubling and repetition as he was in uniqueness and originality. But he also complicates many of these echoes. In the famous "Tyger," for example, he rhymes "symmetry" and "eye"—a sight rhyme or pairing that might look like a rhyme but does not sound like one. He also unsettles conventional distinctions: the usual lines dividing human and divine states dissolve, for example, and the child leads the poet, rather than the other way around. These apparently simple but highly complex poems have remained Blake's most famous and beloved works.

SONGS OF INNOCENCE AND OF EXPERIENCE
SHEWING THE TWO CONTRARY STATES OF THE HUMAN SOUL

From Songs of Innocence[1]

Introduction

Piping down the valleys wild
Piping songs of pleasant glee
On a cloud I saw a child,
And he laughing said to me,

"Pipe a song about a Lamb";   5
So I piped with merry chear;
"Piper pipe that song again"—
So I piped, he wept to hear.

"Drop thy pipe thy happy pipe
Sing thy songs of happy chear";   10
So I sung the same again
While he wept with joy to hear.

"Piper sit thee down and write
In a book that all may read"—
So he vanished from my sight.   15
And I plucked a hollow reed,

And I made a rural pen,
And I stained the water clear,
And I wrote my happy songs
Every child may joy to hear.   20

The Lamb

Little Lamb, who made thee?
Dost thou know who made thee?
Gave thee life & bid thee feed,

1. The text for all of Blake's works is edited by David V. Erdman and Harold Bloom. *Songs of Innocence* (1789) was later combined with *Songs of Experience* (1794), and the poems were etched and accompanied by Blake's illustrations, the process accomplished by copper engravings stamped on paper, then colored by hand.

By the stream & o'er the mead;
Gave thee clothing of delight,   5
Softest clothing wooly bright;
Gave thee such a tender voice,
Making all the vales rejoice!
   Little Lamb who made thee?
   Dost thou know who made thee?   10

   Little Lamb I'll tell thee,
   Little Lamb I'll tell thee!
He is callèd by thy name,
For he calls himself a Lamb:
He is meek & he is mild,   15
He became a little child:
I a child & thou a lamb,
We are callèd by his name.[1]
   Little Lamb God bless thee.
   Little Lamb God bless thee.   20

The Little Black Boy

My mother bore me in the southern wild,
And I am black, but O! my soul is white;
White as an angel is the English child:
But I am black as if bereaved of light.

My mother taught me underneath a tree,   5
And sitting down before the heat of day,
She took me on her lap and kissèd me,
And pointing to the east, began to say:

"Look on the rising sun: there God does live,
And gives his light, and gives his heat away;   10
And flowers and trees and beasts and men receive
Comfort in morning, joy in the noon day.

"And we are put on earth a little space,
That we may learn to bear the beams of love,
And these black bodies and this sun-burnt face   15
Is but a cloud, and like a shady grove.

"For when our souls have learned the heat to bear,
The cloud will vanish; we shall hear his voice,
Saying: 'Come out from the grove, my love & care,
And round my golden tent like lambs rejoice.'"   20

Thus did my mother say, and kissèd me;
And thus I say to little English boy:
When I from black and he from white cloud free,
And round the tent of God like lambs we joy,

---

1. I.e., Christians use the name of Christ to designate themselves.

I'll shade him from the heat till he can bear   25
To lean in joy upon our father's knee;
And then I'll stand and stroke his silver hair,
And be like him, and he will then love me.

Holy Thursday[1]

'Twas on a Holy Thursday, their innocent faces clean,
The children walking two & two, in red & blue & green,[2]
Grey headed beadles[3] walked before with wands as white as snow,
Till into the high dome of Paul's they like Thames' waters flow.

O what a multitude they seemed, these flowers of London town!   5
Seated in companies they sit with radiance all their own.
The hum of multitudes was there, but multitudes of lambs,
Thousands of little boys & girls raising their innocent hands.

Now like a mighty wind they raise to heaven the voice of song,
Or like harmonious thunderings the seats of heaven among.   10
Beneath them sit the agèd men, wise guardians[4] of the poor;
Then cherish pity, lest you drive an angel from your door.[5]

The Chimney Sweeper

When my mother died I was very young,
And my father sold me[1] while yet my tongue
Could scarcely cry " 'weep![2] 'weep! 'weep! 'weep!"
So your chimneys I sweep & in soot I sleep.

There's little Tom Dacre, who cried when his head   5
That curled like a lamb's back, was shaved, so I said,
"Hush, Tom! never mind it, for when your head's bare,
You know that the soot cannot spoil your white hair."

And so he was quiet, & that very night,
As Tom was a-sleeping he had such a sight!   10
That thousands of sweepers, Dick, Joe, Ned, & Jack,
Were all of them locked up in coffins of black;

1. Ascension Day, forty days after Easter, when children from charity schools were marched to St. Paul's Cathedral.
2. Each school had its own distinctive uniform.
3. Ushers and minor functionaries, whose job was to maintain order.
4. The governors of the charity schools.
5. See Hebrews 13:2: "Be not forgetful to entertain strangers: for thereby some have entertained angels unawares."

1. It was common practice in Blake's day for fathers to sell, or indenture, their children to become chimney sweeps. The average age at which such children began working was six or seven; they were generally employed for seven years, until they were too big to ascend the chimneys.
2. The child's lisping effort to say "sweep," as he walks the streets looking for work.

And by came an Angel who had a bright key,
And he opened the coffins & set them all free;
Then down a green plain, leaping, laughing they run,   15
And wash in a river and shine in the Sun;

Then naked[3] & white, all their bags left behind,
They rise upon clouds, and sport in the wind.
And the Angel told Tom, if he'd be a good boy,
He'd have God for his father & never want joy.   20

And so Tom awoke; and we rose in the dark
And got with our bags & our brushes to work.
Tho' the morning was cold, Tom was happy & warm;
So if all do their duty, they need not fear harm.

From Songs of Experience

Introduction

Hear the voice of the Bard!
Who Present, Past, & Future sees;
    Whose ears have heard
    The Holy Word
That walked among the ancient trees;[1]   5

Calling the lapsèd Soul
And weeping in the evening dew;[2]
    That might control
    The starry pole,
And fallen, fallen light renew!   10

"O Earth, O Earth, return!
Arise from out the dewy grass;
    Night is worn,
    And the morn
Rises from the slumberous mass.   15

"Turn away no more;
Why wilt thou turn away?
    The starry floor
    The watery shore
Is given thee till the break of day."   20

3. They climbed up the chimneys naked.
1. Genesis 3:8: "And [Adam and Eve] heard the voice of the Lord God walking in the garden in the cool of the day."
2. Blake's ambiguous use of pronouns makes for interpretative difficulties. It would seem that *The Holy Word* (Jehovah, a name for God in the Old Testament of the Bible) calls *the lapsèd Soul*, and weeps—not the Bard.

Earth's Answer

Earth raised up her head,
From the darkness dread & drear.
Her light fled:
Stony dread!
And her locks covered with grey despair.   5

"Prisoned on watery shore
Starry Jealousy does keep my den,
Cold and hoar
Weeping o'er
I hear the Father[1] of the ancient men.   10

"Selfish father of men,
Cruel, jealous, selfish fear!
Can delight
Chained in night
The virgins of youth and morning bear?   15

"Does spring hide its joy
When buds and blossoms grow?
Does the sower
Sow by night,
Or the plowman in darkness plow?   20

"Break this heavy chain
That does freeze my bones around;
Selfish! vain!
Eternal bane!
That free Love with bondage bound."   25

The Tyger

Tyger! Tyger! burning bright
In the forests of the night,
What immortal hand or eye
Could frame thy fearful symmetry?

In what distant deeps or skies   5
Burnt the fire of thine eyes?
On what wings dare he aspire?
What the hand dare seize the fire?

---

1. In Blake's later prophetic works, one of the four Zoas, representing the four chief faculties of humankind, is Urizen. In general, he stands for the orthodox conception of the Divine Creator, sometimes Jehovah in the Old Testament, often the God conceived by Newton and Locke—in all instances a tyrant associated with excessive rationalism and sexual repression, and the opponent of the imagination and creativity. This may be "the Holy Word" in line 4 of "Introduction" (p. 537).

And what shoulder, & what art,
Could twist the sinews of thy heart?   10
And when thy heart began to beat,
What dread hand? & what dread feet?

What the hammer? what the chain?
In what furnace was thy brain?
What the anvil? what dread grasp   15
Dare its deadly terrors clasp?

When the stars threw down their spears,
And watered heaven with their tears,
Did he smile his work to see?
Did he who made the Lamb make thee?   20

Tyger! Tyger! burning bright
In the forests of the night,
What immortal hand or eye
Dare frame thy fearful symmetry?

The Sick Rose

O Rose, thou art sick.
The invisible worm
That flies in the night
In the howling storm

Has found out thy bed   5
Of crimson joy,
And his dark secret love
Does thy life destroy.

London

I wander thro' each chartered[1] street,
Near where the chartered Thames does flow,
And mark in every face I meet
Marks of weakness, marks of woe.

In every cry of every Man,   5
In every Infant's cry of fear,
In every voice, in every ban,
The mind-forged manacles I hear:

1. Hired (literally). Blake implies that the streets and the river are controlled by commercial interests.

How the Chimney-sweeper's cry
Every blackening Church appalls;[2]   10
And the hapless Soldier's sigh
Runs in blood down Palace walls.

But most thro' midnight streets I hear
How the youthful Harlot's curse
Blasts the new-born Infant's tear,[3]   15
And blights with plagues the Marriage hearse.

The Chimney Sweeper

A little black thing among the snow
Crying "'weep, 'weep," in notes of woe!
"Where are thy father & mother? say?"
"They are both gone up to the church to pray.

"Because I was happy upon the heath,   5
And smiled among the winter's snow;
They clothèd me in the clothes of death,
And taught me to sing the notes of woe.

"And because I am happy, & dance & sing,
They think they have done me no injury,   10
And are gone to praise God & his Priest & King,
Who make up a heaven of our misery."

Mock On, Mock On, Voltaire, Rousseau

Mock on, Mock on, Voltaire, Rousseau;
Mock on, Mock on, 'tis all in vain.
You throw the sand against the wind,
And the wind blows it back again.

And every sand becomes a Gem   5
Reflected in the beams divine;
Blown back, they blind the mocking Eye,
But still in Israel's paths they shine.

The Atoms of Democritus[1]
And Newton's Particles of light[2]   10
Are sands upon the Red sea shore,
Where Israel's tents do shine so bright.

2. Makes white (literally), punning also on *appall* (to dismay) and *pall* (the cloth covering a corpse or bier).
3. The harlot infects the parents with venereal disease, and thus the infant is inflicted with neonatal blindness.

1. Greek philosopher (460?–362? B.C.E.), who advanced a theory that all things are merely patterns of atoms.
2. Sir Isaac Newton's (1642–1727) corpuscular theory of light. For Blake, both men were condemned as materialists.

And Did Those Feet

And did those feet[1] in ancient time
Walk upon England's mountains green?
And was the holy Lamb of God
On England's pleasant pastures seen?

And did the Countenance Divine   5
Shine forth upon our clouded hills?
And was Jerusalem builded here,
Among those dark Satanic Mills?[2]

Bring me my Bow of burning gold:
Bring me my Arrows of desire: 10
Bring me my Spear: O clouds unfold!
Bring me my Chariot of fire!

I will not cease from Mental Fight,
Nor shall my Sword sleep in my hand,
Till we have built Jerusalem   15
In England's green & pleasant Land.

1. A reference to an ancient legend that Jesus came to England with Joseph of Arimathea.
2. Possibly industrial England, but for Blake *mills* also meant 18th-century arid, mechanistic philosophy.

WILLIAM WORDSWORTH
1770–1850

After William Wordsworth, English poetry would never be the same again. The sense that poets should convey intensely personal, individual expression, which now feels like the ordinary stuff of poetry, can be traced to Wordsworth's deliberate rejection of his eighteenth-century precursors. He turned readers' attention away from classical models and Gothic supernatural stories to everyday emotion and imagination, championing the spontaneity of authentic feeling. Like **Jean-Jacques Rousseau**, Wordsworth approached children's experience as crucial and determinative, in defiance of many of his contemporaries, who considered childhood trivial. And he chose to focus on common people—often poor and marginal figures such as elderly farmers and vagrant beggars. Just as important, Wordsworth also launched a new set of stylistic values for poetry, jettisoning "the gaudiness and inane phraseology" of contemporary poets in favor of a language that would feel direct, authentic, and plain. And finally, Wordsworth committed himself in surprising new ways to honoring the natural world as a benevolent nurturer and guide, and many have credited him with launching an ecological consciousness that continues to inspire environmentalists today.

LIFE

William Wordsworth was born in the small town of Cockermouth, in England's wild and rugged Lake District, in 1770. As a boy he was sent to a grammar school in the countryside, where he learned Greek and Latin and committed large portions of Shakespeare and Milton to memory. After his father's death in 1783, he began to feel restless and unsettled. While at Cambridge University, he failed to apply himself to his studies. "I am doomed to be an idler thro' my whole life," he wrote.

Wordsworth's perspective on the world took a turn in the summer of 1790, when he and a friend set off for a walking tour of France and the Alps. It was a critical moment in French history: the country was "mad with joy in consequence of the revolution," as Wordsworth put it. He also had a love affair with a Frenchwoman named Annette Vallon and had a child with her. He returned to England in 1793, meaning to make some money so that he could marry Vallon, but Britain went to war with France, and Wordsworth was not permitted to cross back for a decade.

The following few years were the most difficult of Wordsworth's life. He had no source of income, and his revolutionary sympathies made him an outsider in England. He moved to London and for a time became a disciple of the anarchist William Godwin, who favored the abolition of marriage and all forms of government. In 1795 Wordsworth began a formative friendship with another young radical poet, Samuel Taylor Coleridge. So close did Wordsworth and Coleridge become that they deliberately moved to within walking distance of one another in rural Somerset. There they entertained revolutionary thinkers and were suspected of being spies: "a mischievous gang of disaffected Englishmen," reported a government agent, "a Sett of violent Democrats." In fact, however, both Wordsworth and Coleridge were horrified by the bloody turn the revolution in France had taken, and they soon began to lose faith in radical politics. Loving the beauty of the countryside and each other's company, the two poets started to work together on a different kind of revolutionary ideal: the production of a new kind of poetry. Together, in 1798, they published a collection of poems called *Lyrical Ballads*. It contained works that would count among their best loved, including Wordsworth's "Tintern Abbey" and "We Are Seven," and Coleridge's "Rime of the Ancient Mariner." They published the first edition anonymously. ("Wordsworth's name is nothing," Coleridge explained, and "to a large number of persons mine *stinks*.")

This book succeeded in accomplishing a revolution in English poetry. Radically democratic, it focused on subject matter conventionally ignored by poets—the lives of lowly people, such as the very poor, the insane, children, shepherds, and tinkers. This new subject matter, Wordsworth wrote, demanded a simple and unaffected language, like the prose spoken by ordinary people. Thus *Lyrical Ballads* prized not only humble and simple subjects but also the poet's own internal state of mind, a focus that would become ever more important to Wordsworth's work. In 1801 he included a new preface, which has become as well known as his poetry. Here he put forward his revolutionary new ideas: "I have proposed to myself to imitate, and, as far as is possible, to adopt the very language of men," he wrote. Famously, he defined poetry as "the spontaneous overflow of powerful feelings," explaining that it comes from "emotion recollected in tranquility."

Critics were not prepared for this innovative volume, and Wordsworth's poetry garnered almost entirely hostile reviews. One critic wrote, "Than the volumes now before us we never saw any thing better calculated to excite disgust and anger in a lover of poetry. The drivelling nonsense of some of Mr. Wordsworth's poems is insufferable, and it is equally insufferable that such nonsense should have been written by a man capable, as he is, of writing well."

Wordsworth was appalled by Napoleon's rise to power across Europe, and his political views turned increasingly conservative. In the following years, Wordsworth became very much part of the conservative establishment. He was appointed distributor of stamps, collecting taxes on government documents, a civil service job that seemed to many contemporary radicals to represent a betrayal of his earlier commitment to the artist's independence. In 1818 he campaigned for the Tories—the conservative party—in local elections.

Wordsworth died on April 23, traditionally thought to be Shakespeare's birth- and death-day, in 1850.

WORK

Since Wordsworth's style is often purposefully simple, his poetry can seem deceptively uncomplicated. For many readers, its pleasures lie in the philosophical questions it poses. "Tintern Abbey" asks what makes a self a self: how do we become what we are? "We Are Seven" interrogates the abstraction of death and asks whether the dead may be considered part of the human community. And the "Ode on Intimations of Immortality" considers the immortality of the soul, using Plato's ideas as a touchstone.

But the poems also reward close attention to their language. Even the most seemingly straightforward Wordsworthian lines often yield more questions than answers. Consider, for example, the title of the poem "Lines Composed a Few Miles above Tintern Abbey, on Revisiting the Banks of the Wye during a Tour, July 13, 1798." Why such a curiously long and descriptive title, going to such trouble to mark the place and date of composition? The poem itself, surprisingly, says nothing at all about the ruined abbey. Some readers have noted that Wordsworth is careful to use the title to note his position "above" the landscape; others have remarked on the date, which commemorates the anniversary of the day *before* the French Revolution started, hinting that Wordsworth's explorations of memory and selfhood in this poem are bound up with his ambivalence about the revolution. In another example, the central tension of "We Are Seven" turns on the definition of one of the simplest and most common words in the English language—"we." The poem explores the idea that two different uses of an ordinary pronoun reveal radically dissimilar ways of seeing the world. How is it, Wordsworth's poetry insistently asks, that complex conceptions of faith, nature, selfhood, community, and knowledge are revealed in the most commonplace language that we use?

Wordsworth is famous for his plain style and his philosophical explorations, but he is also notable for his ease in moving among poetic forms and genres. While "Tintern Abbey" is composed in the regular and highly traditional English form of iambic pentameter, "Ode on Intimations of Immortality" is strikingly irregular, with both lines and stanzas varying widely in length. Wordsworth borrows here from an English tradition of deliberately irregular odes in which the poet meditates on a problem or object in changing rhythms. Since both "Tintern Abbey" and the "Ode" are about time and memory, it is intriguing that Wordsworth should choose such different forms for the two poems.

The other genre represented here is the sonnet, a form that had languished for a couple of centuries but became popular again in the late eighteenth century. Wordsworth was among many Romantic poets—among them, numerous women—who brought the sonnet back to prominence. He wrote a poem called "Scorn not the Sonnet," which reminds the reader of the sonnet's illustrious history, begun by the Italian poet Petrarch and later taken up by Shakespeare and Milton. Wordsworth was clearly self-conscious about his place in this poetic tradition. The two examples included here, "Composed upon West- minster Bridge" and "The World Is Too Much with Us," steer clear of the sonnet's traditional focus on romantic love, meditating instead on the specific conditions of modern, industrial, and urban society, thus pointedly bringing this traditional poetic form into the present. In re-imagining the sonnet, then, as in his innovative ideas about democracy, poetic style, nature, childhood, and the importance of individual experience, Wordsworth is a quintessentially modern poet.

We Are Seven

——A simple Child,
That lightly draws its breath,
And feels its life in every limb,
What should it know of death?

I met a little cottage Girl: 5
She was eight years old, she said;
Her hair was thick with many a curl
That clustered round her head.

She had a rustic, woodland air,
And she was wildly clad: 10
Her eyes were fair, and very fair;
—Her beauty made me glad.

"Sisters and brothers, little Maid,
How many may you be?"
"How many? Seven in all," she said,   15
And wondering looked at me.

"And where are they? I pray you tell."
She answered, "Seven are we;
And two of us at Conway[1] dwell,
And two are gone to sea.   20

"Two of us in the church-yard lie,
My sister and my brother;
And, in the church-yard cottage, I
Dwell near them with my mother."

"You say that two at Conway dwell,   25
And two are gone to sea,
Yet ye are seven! I pray you tell,
Sweet Maid, how this may be."

1. Port town in Wales.

Then did the little Maid reply,
"Seven boys and girls are we;   30
Two of us in the church-yard lie,
Beneath the church-yard tree."

"You run about, my little Maid,
Your limbs they are alive;
If two are in the church-yard laid,   35
Then ye are only five."

"Their graves are green, they may be seen,"
The little Maid replied,
"Twelve steps or more from my mother's door,
And they are side by side.   40

"My stockings there I often knit,
My kerchief there I hem;
And there upon the ground I sit,
And sing a song to them.

"And often after sun-set, Sir,   45
When it is light and fair,
I take my little porringer,[2]
And eat my supper there.

"The first that died was sister Jane;
In bed she moaning lay,   50
Till God released her of her pain;
And then she went away.

"So in the church-yard she was laid;
And, when the grass was dry,
Together round her grave we played,   55
My brother John and I.

"And when the ground was white with snow,
And I could run and slide,
My brother John was forced to go,
And he lies by her side."   60

"How many are you, then," said I,
"If they two are in heaven?"
Quick was the little Maid's reply,
"O Master! we are seven."

"But they are dead; those two are dead!   65
Their spirits are in heaven!"
'Twas throwing words away; for still
The little Maid would have her will,
And said, "Nay, we are seven!"

2. A bowl or dish.

Lines Composed a Few Miles above Tintern Abbey

On Revisiting the Banks of the Wye During a Tour, July 13, 1798

Five years have past; five summers, with the length
Of five long winters! and again I hear
These waters, rolling from their mountain-springs
With a soft inland murmur.—Once again
Do I behold these steep and lofty cliffs,   5
That on a wild secluded scene impress
Thoughts of more deep seclusion; and connect
The landscape with the quiet of the sky.
The day is come when I again repose
Here, under this dark sycamore, and view   10
These plots of cottage-ground, these orchard-tufts,
Which at this season, with their unripe fruits,
Are clad in one green hue, and lose themselves
'Mid groves and copses. Once again I see
These hedge-rows, hardly hedge-rows, little lines   15
Of sportive wood run wild: these pastoral farms,
Green to the very door; and wreaths of smoke
Sent up, in silence, from among the trees!
With some uncertain notice, as might seem
Of vagrant dwellers in the houseless woods,   20
Or of some Hermit's cave, where by his fire
The Hermit sits alone.

                      These beauteous forms,
Through a long absence, have not been to me
As is a landscape to a blind man's eye:
But oft, in lonely rooms, and 'mid the din   25
Of towns and cities, I have owed to them,
In hours of weariness, sensations sweet,
Felt in the blood, and felt along the heart;
And passing even into my purer mind,
With tranquil restoration:—feelings too   30
Of unremembered pleasure: such, perhaps,
As have no slight or trivial influence
On that best portion of a good man's life,
His little, nameless, unremembered, acts
Of kindness and of love. Nor less, I trust,   35
To them I may have owed another gift,
Of aspect more sublime; that blessèd mood,
In which the burthen of the mystery,
In which the heavy and the weary weight
Of all this unintelligible world,   40
Is lightened:—that serene and blessèd mood,
In which the affections gently lead us on,—
Until, the breath of this corporeal frame
And even the motion of our human blood
Almost suspended, we are laid asleep   45

In body, and become a living soul:
While with an eye made quiet by the power
Of harmony, and the deep power of joy,
We see into the life of things.

                    If this
Be but a vain belief, yet, oh! how oft—   50
In darkness and amid the many shapes
Of joyless daylight; when the fretful stir
Unprofitable, and the fever of the world,
Have hung upon the beatings of my heart—
How oft, in spirit, have I turned to thee,   55
O sylvan Wye! thou wanderer thro' the woods,
How often has my spirit turned to thee!

   And now, with gleams of half-extinguished thought,
With many recognitions dim and faint,
And somewhat of a sad perplexity,   60
The picture of the mind revives again:
While here I stand, not only with the sense
Of present pleasure, but with pleasing thoughts
That in this moment there is life and food
For future years. And so I dare to hope,   65
Though changed, no doubt, from what I was when first
I came among these hills; when like a roe
I bounded o'er the mountains, by the sides
Of the deep rivers, and the lonely streams,
Wherever nature led: more like a man   70
Flying from something that he dreads, than one
Who sought the thing he loved. For nature then
(The coarser pleasures of my boyish days,
And their glad animal movements all gone by)
To me was all in all.—I cannot paint   75
What then I was. The sounding cataract
Haunted me like a passion: the tall rock,
The mountain, and the deep and gloomy wood,
Their colours and their forms, were then to me
An appetite; a feeling and a love,   80
That had no need of a remoter charm,
By thought supplied, nor any interest
Unborrowed from the eye.—That time is past,
And all its aching joys are now no more,
And all its dizzy raptures. Not for this   85
Faint I, nor mourn nor murmur; other gifts
Have followed; for such loss, I would believe,
Abundant recompense. For I have learned
To look on nature, not as in the hour
Of thoughtless youth; but hearing oftentimes   90
The still, sad music of humanity,
Nor harsh nor grating, though of ample power
To chasten and subdue. And I have felt

A presence that disturbs me with the joy
Of elevated thoughts; a sense sublime   95
Of something far more deeply interfused,
Whose dwelling is the light of setting suns,
And the round ocean and the living air,
And the blue sky, and in the mind of man:
A motion and a spirit, that impels   100
All thinking things, all objects of all thought,
And rolls through all things. Therefore am I still
A lover of the meadows and the woods,
And mountains; and of all that we behold
From this green earth; of all the mighty world   105
Of eye, and ear,—both what they half create,
And what perceive; well pleased to recognise
In nature and the language of the sense,
The anchor of my purest thoughts, the nurse,
The guide, the guardian of my heart, and soul   110
Of all my moral being.

            Nor perchance,
If I were not thus taught, should I the more
Suffer my genial[1] spirits to decay:
For thou art with me here upon the banks
Of this fair river; thou my dearest Friend,   115
My dear, dear Friend; and in thy voice I catch
The language of my former heart, and read
My former pleasures in the shooting lights
Of thy wild eyes. Oh! yet a little while
May I behold in thee what I was once,   120
My dear, dear Sister! and this prayer I make,
Knowing that Nature never did betray
The heart that loved her; 'tis her privilege,
Through all the years of this our life, to lead
From joy to joy: for she can so inform   125
The mind that is within us, so impress
With quietness and beauty, and so feed
With lofty thoughts, that neither evil tongues,
Rash judgments, nor the sneers of selfish men,
Nor greetings where no kindness is, nor all   130
The dreary intercourse of daily life,
Shall e'er prevail against us, or disturb
Our cheerful faith, that all which we behold
Is full of blessings. Therefore let the moon
Shine on thee in thy solitary walk;   135
And let the misty mountain-winds be free
To blow against thee: and, in after years,
When these wild ecstasies shall be matured
Into a sober pleasure; when thy mind
Shall be a mansion for all lovely forms,   140
Thy memory be as a dwelling-place

---

1. Generative, creative.

For all sweet sounds and harmonies; oh! then,
If solitude, or fear, or pain, or grief
Should be thy portion, with what healing thoughts
Of tender joy wilt thou remember me,   145
And these my exhortations! Nor, perchance—
If I should be where I no more can hear
Thy voice, nor catch from thy wild eyes these gleams
Of past existence—wilt thou then forget
That on the banks of this delightful stream   150
We stood together; and that I, so long
A worshipper of Nature, hither came
Unwearied in that service; rather say
With warmer love—oh! with far deeper zeal
Of holier love. Nor wilt thou then forget   155
That after many wanderings, many years
Of absence, these steep woods and lofty cliffs,
And this green pastoral landscape, were to me
More dear, both for themselves and for thy sake!

Ode on Intimations of Immortality

From Recollections of Early Childhood

> The Child is father of the Man:
> And I could wish my days to be
> Bound each to each by natural piety.

I

There was a time when meadow, grove, and stream,
The earth, and every common sight,
    To me did seem
    Apparelled in celestial light,
The glory and the freshness of a dream.   5
It is not now as it hath been of yore;—
    Turn wheresoe'er I may,
    By night or day,
The things which I have seen I now can see no more.

II

    The Rainbow comes and goes,   10
    And lovely is the Rose;
    The Moon doth with delight
Look round her when the heavens are bare,
    Waters on a starry night
    Are beautiful and fair;   15
    The sunshine is a glorious birth;
    But yet I know, where'er I go,
That there hath passed away a glory from the earth.

III

Now, while the birds thus sing a joyous song,
  And while the young lambs bound   20
    As to the tabor's sound,
To me alone there came a thought of grief:
A timely utterance gave that thought relief,
  And I again am strong:
The cataracts blow their trumpets from the steep;   25
No more shall grief of mine the season wrong;
I hear the Echoes through the mountains throng,
The Winds come to me from the fields of sleep,
  And all the earth is gay;
    Land and sea   30
  Give themselves up to jollity,
    And with the heart of May
  Doth every Beast keep holiday;—
    Thou Child of Joy,
Shout round me, let me hear thy shouts, thou happy   35
  Shepherd-boy!

IV

Ye blessèd Creatures, I have heard the call
  Ye to each other make; I see
The heavens laugh with you in your jubilee;
  My heart is at your festival,   40
    My head hath its coronal,
The fulness of your bliss, I feel—I feel it all.
    Oh evil day! if I were sullen
    While Earth herself is adorning,
      This sweet May-morning,   45
    And the Children are culling
      On every side,
    In a thousand valleys far and wide,
    Fresh flowers; while the sun shines warm,
And the Babe leaps up on his Mother's arm:—   50
    I hear, I hear, with joy I hear!
    —But there's a Tree, of many, one,
A single Field which I have looked upon,
Both of them speak of something that is gone:
    The Pansy at my feet   55
    Doth the same tale repeat:
Whither is fled the visionary gleam?
Where is it now, the glory and the dream?

V

Our birth is but a sleep and a forgetting:
The Soul that rises with us, our life's Star,   60
    Hath had elsewhere its setting,

And cometh from afar:
    Not in entire forgetfulness,
    And not in utter nakedness,
But trailing clouds of glory do we come   65
    From God, who is our home:
Heaven lies about us in our infancy!
Shades of the prison-house begin to close
    Upon the growing Boy,
But He beholds the light, and whence it flows,   70
    He sees it in his joy;
The Youth, who daily farther from the east
    Must travel, still is Nature's Priest,
    And by the vision splendid
    Is on his way attended;   75
At length the Man perceives it die away,
And fade into the light of common day.

VI

Earth fills her lap with pleasures of her own;
Yearnings she hath in her own natural kind,
And, even with something of a Mother's mind,
    And no unworthy aim,   80
    The homely Nurse doth all she can
To make her Foster-child, her Inmate, Man,
    Forget the glories he hath known,
And that imperial palace whence he came.   85

VII

Behold the Child among his new-born blisses,
A six years' Darling of a pigmy size!
See, where 'mid work of his own hand he lies,
Fretted by sallies of his mother's kisses,
With light upon him from his father's eyes!   90
See, at his feet, some little plan or chart,
Some fragment from his dream of human life,
Shaped by himself with newly-learnèd art;
    A wedding or a festival,
    A mourning or a funeral;   95
      And this hath now his heart,
    And unto this he frames his song:
      Then will he fit his tongue
To dialogues of business, love, or strife;
    But it will not be long   100
    Ere this be thrown aside,
    And with new joy and pride
The little Actor cons another part;
Filling from time to time his "humorous stage"
With all the Persons, down to palsied Age,   105
That Life brings with her in her equipage;

As if his whole vocation
Were endless imitation.

VIII

Thou, whose exterior semblance doth belie
    Thy Soul's immensity;   110
Thou best Philosopher, who yet dost keep
Thy heritage, thou Eye among the blind,
That, deaf and silent, read'st the eternal deep,
Haunted for ever by the eternal mind,—
    Mighty Prophet! Seer blest!   115
    On whom those truths do rest,
Which we are toiling all our lives to find,
In darkness lost, the darkness of the grave;
Thou, over whom thy Immortality
Broods like the Day, a Master o'er a Slave,   120
A Presence which is not to be put by;
    [To whom the grave
Is but a lonely bed without the sense or sight
    Of day or the warm light,
A place of thought where we in waiting lie;][1]   125
Thou little Child, yet glorious in the might
Of heaven-born freedom on thy being's height,
Why with such earnest pains dost thou provoke
The years to bring the inevitable yoke,
Thus blindly with thy blessedness at strife?   130
Full soon thy Soul shall have her earthly freight,
And custom lie upon thee with a weight,
Heavy as frost, and deep almost as life!

IX

    O joy! that in our embers
    Is something that doth live,   135
    That nature yet remembers
    What was so fugitive!
The thought of our past years in me doth breed
Perpetual benediction: not indeed
For that which is most worthy to be blest;   140
Delight and liberty, the simple creed
Of Childhood, whether busy or at rest,
With new-fledged hope still fluttering in his breast—
    Not for these I raise
    The song of thanks and praise;   145
But for those obstinate questionings

1. The lines within brackets were included in the 1807 and 1815 editions of Wordsworth's poems but omitted in the 1820 and subsequent editions, as a result of Coleridge's severe censure of them.

Of sense and outward things,
    Fallings from us, vanishings;
    Blank misgivings of a Creature
Moving about in worlds not realized,   150
High instincts before which our mortal Nature
Did tremble like a guilty Thing surprised:
    But for those first affections,
    Those shadowy recollections,
   Which, be they what they may,   155
Are yet the fountain-light of all our day,
Are yet a master-light of all our seeing;
  Uphold us, cherish, and have power to make
Our noisy years seem moments in the being
Of the eternal Silence: truths that wake,   160
     To perish never;
Which neither listlessness, nor mad endeavour,
    Nor Man nor Boy,
Nor all that is at enmity with joy,
Can utterly abolish or destroy!   165
  Hence in a season of calm weather
    Though inland far we be,
Our Souls have sight of that immortal sea
    Which brought us hither,
  Can in a moment travel thither,   170
And see the Children sport upon the shore,
And hear the mighty waters rolling evermore.

X

Then sing, ye Birds, sing, sing a joyous song!
    And let the young Lambs bound
    As to the tabor's sound!   175
We in thought will join your throng,
    Ye that pipe and ye that play,
    Ye that through your hearts to-day
    Feel the gladness of the May!
What though the radiance which was once so bright   180
Be now for ever taken from my sight,
  Though nothing can bring back the hour
Of splendour in the grass, of glory in the flower;
    We will grieve not, rather find
    Strength in what remains behind;   185
    In the primal sympathy
    Which having been must ever be;
    In the soothing thoughts that spring
    Out of human suffering;
    In the faith that looks through death,   190
In years that bring the philosophic mind.

XI

And O, ye Fountains, Meadows, Hills, and Groves,
Forebode not any severing of our loves!
Yet in my heart of hearts I feel your might;
I only have relinquished one delight   195
To live beneath your more habitual sway.
I love the Brooks which down their channels fret,
Even more than when I tripped lightly as they;
The innocent brightness of a new-born Day
　　　　　Is lovely yet;   200
The Clouds that gather round the setting sun
Do take a sober colouring from an eye
That hath kept watch o'er man's mortality;
Another race hath been, and other palms are won.
Thanks to the human heart by which we live,   205
Thanks to its tenderness, its joys, and fears,
To me the meanest flower that blows can give
Thoughts that do often lie too deep for tears.

Composed upon Westminster Bridge,
September 3, 1802

Earth has not anything to show more fair:
Dull would he be of soul who could pass by
A sight so touching in its majesty;
This City now doth, like a garment, wear
The beauty of the morning; silent, bare,   5
Ships, towers, domes, theatres, and temples lie
Open unto the fields, and to the sky;
All bright and glittering in the smokeless air.
Never did sun more beautifully steep
In his first splendour, valley, rock, or hill;   10
Ne'er saw I, never felt, a calm so deep!
The river glideth at his own sweet will:
Dear God! the very houses seem asleep;
And all that mighty heart is lying still!

The World Is Too Much with Us

The world is too much with us; late and soon,
Getting and spending, we lay waste our powers:
Little we see in Nature that is ours;
We have given our hearts away, a sordid boon![1]
This Sea that bares her bosom to the moon,   5

1. Gift. "Sordid": refers to the act of giving the heart away.

The winds that will be howling at all hours,
And are up-gathered now like sleeping flowers;
For this, for everything, we are out of tune;
It moves us not.—Great God! I'd rather be
A Pagan suckled in a creed outworn;   10
So might I, standing on this pleasant lea,
Have glimpses that would make me less forlorn;
Have sight of Proteus[2] rising from the sea;
Or hear old Triton[3] blow his wreathèd horn.

2. An old man of the sea who, in the *Odyssey*, could assume a variety of shapes.

3. A sea deity, usually represented as blowing on a conch shell.

CHARLES BAUDELAIRE
1821–1867

Crowds and prostitutes, boredom and hypocrisy, garbage and cheap perfume: from these ugly materials, Charles Baudelaire crafted such shocking, painful, and exquisite poetry that he became the most widely read French poet around the globe. Haunted by a vision of human nature as fallen and corrupt, he was drawn to explore his own weaknesses and transgressions, as well as the sins of society. Lust, hatred, laziness, a disabling self-awareness, a horror of death and decay, and above all an all-encompassing *ennui*—a kind of disgusted, existential boredom—consumed the poet. But it is not only this anguished worldview that makes Baudelaire so significant: for many thinkers who followed, he opened the way to understanding what it means to be modern, to live in the exciting, disorienting, technologically changing, often hideous world of the industrialized city. And for writers, what is so extraordinary about Baudelaire is that he examined the unsettling shocks of modernity through perfectly controlled and beautiful art forms.

LIFE

Born in Paris in 1821, Baudelaire quickly became a rebellious youth. His elderly father died when he was six, and his mother married a stern military man whom the young Baudelaire came to detest. In his late teens, he was expelled from boarding school and sent away on a boat to India to remove him from bad influences. He jumped ship on the African island of Mauritius, then slowly wended his way home without ever reaching India. Back in Paris, he began to consort with artists, bohemians, and prostitutes in the famous Latin Quarter. By his early twenties, he had contracted syphilis and had started to spend his father's inheritance with alarming speed, buying up gorgeous furniture, dandyish clothing, and costly paintings. In 1842 he fell passionately in love with a woman named Jeanne Duval, an actress of African descent, who lived with him on and off for most of his adult life. To his family, he seemed to be going nowhere. His mother was disturbed at his spending habits and obtained a court order to control his finances. Humiliated, Baudelaire remained for the rest of his life dependent on an allowance dispensed by the family lawyer.

In 1845 he published a work of art criticism that established his reputation as a writer, and he would go on to write important reviews of painting and photography, championing the most daring contemporary art. In the 1850s he reviewed and translated the works of American writer Edgar Allan Poe, who shared his dedication to beauty, his fascination with death, and his passion for perfectly crafted writing. Only in 1857, at the age of thirty-six, did his first slim volume of poetry appear. With its horrifyingly evocative images of lust, duplicity, and decay, *The Flowers of Evil* was fully intended to scandalize its readers. It succeeded. French authorities seized the book and fined the writer, making Baudelaire famous—but more reviled than admired. Ever more ill and in debt, Baudelaire spent his last years in distress. He added new poems to *The Flowers of Evil* and began to write some experimental works that would come to be known as *Paris Spleen*. He died in 1867, leaving behind few admirers. At the graveside, in the pouring rain, accompanied by a few stragglers, only one close friend predicted that Baudelaire would someday be recognized as a "poet of genius."

BAUDELAIRE'S PARIS

Most French poets of the first half of the nineteenth century were drawn to the beauties of the natural world: to mountains, lakes, and flowers. Baudelaire was different. "I find myself incapable of feeling moved by vegetation," he wrote. Instead, he observed the social life of the city.

At the time, Paris was an exciting and disorienting place. It grew rapidly over the first few decades of the nineteenth century, as new industries drew peasants from the impoverished countryside in search of work. Competing for badly paid jobs, the urban poor were visible everywhere, many of them sick from factory smoke, or reduced to beggary and prostitution. Also visible in the city, however, were the glossy carriages and flamboyant dresses of the rich. Commentators often remarked that on a single stroll through the city one might find ragpickers searching through street refuse for scraps to sell, as well as glittering new shopping arcades offering seductive, mass-produced commodities for wealthy consumers. Everything in this modern world, it seemed, could be bought and sold.

During the 1850s the streets of Paris underwent a huge transformation, as the government razed winding old alleyways and installed clean, wide boulevards in their place. These smooth streets radiated outward to allow easy access to the city center from many directions. The poor were evicted and moved in large numbers to the suburbs, while gleaming new apartment houses, street cafes, shops, and theaters rose up quickly. In this new urban milieu, one encountered vast numbers of strangers. Dramatically unlike village life, the city typically felt both crowded and lonely, both stimulating and alienating. Baudelaire used the term *flâneur*—meaning "saunterer"—to refer to those who wandered alone and detached through urban streets to experience the city's fleeting spectacles. Many of the first *flâneurs* were writers who found a new kind of inspiration in this fragmented experience. And so the bustling commercial city became an important literary theme, supplanting rural beauty for self-consciously "modern" writers in the decades to follow.

WORK

It is difficult to grasp just how shocking Baudelaire's work must have seemed to his contemporaries. French poets before him typically worked in what was called the "noble style," which was formal and elevated, deliberately remote from everyday speech. Poets were not supposed to refer to ordinary objects (even the word "nose" was forbidden as prosaic). We can only imagine, then, how outrageous Baudelaire's deliberately brutal wording—"pissing hogwash" or "lecherous whore"—must have seemed. And not only did he offer up explicit, often coarse, images of the body, but his contemporaries were horrified to find him willing to connect sexual desire to the horrors of sadism and putrefaction, as we see in his poem "A Carcass."

And yet it would be misleading to see Baudelaire as rejecting beauty: he luxuriated in gorgeous, lavish, and exotic images, and crafted passages of lyrical magnificence. Unlike some of his other rebellious-poet contemporaries—such as Walt Whitman, born just two years before him—Baudelaire loved strictly traditional metrical forms and rhyme schemes. And so it is worth exploring the ways that the poet associates the shockingly foul with the traditionally lovely. Even the very title of his volume, *The Flowers of Evil*, sig-nals the juxtaposition of beauty with corruption.

Always attracted by dissonance and contrast, Baudelaire is famous for his irony—his willingness to undermine one perspective with another more-knowing, cynical point of view. Many of his works explore both lived experience and the desire to stand skeptically apart from that experience. In the process, Baudelaire's poetic speakers often emerge as self-divided, torn between beautiful ideals and what he called "spleen," a thoroughgoing disgust with life. (The ancient Greeks had believed that sadness originated with fluids of the spleen.)

Late in his life, Baudelaire experimented with "prose poems"—then highly innovative and, according to many of his contemporaries, confusingly paradoxical. Dissolving the distinction between poetry and prose, these brief pieces lack the line breaks associated with poetry, but they feel like lyric, capturing brief moments of experience in compressed and meditative passages. For Baudelaire, this kind of writing was momentous: he claimed to dream of "the miracle of a poetic prose, musical, without rhythm and without rhyme, supple enough and rugged enough to adapt itself to the lyrical impulses of the soul."

From The Flowers of Evil

To the Reader[1]

Infatuation, sadism, lust, avarice
possess our souls and drain the body's force;
we spoonfeed our adorable remorse,
like whores or beggars nourishing their lice.

Our sins are mulish, our confessions lies;   5
we play to the grandstand with our promises,

---

1. Translated by Robert Lowell. The translation pays primary attention to the insistent rhythm of the original poetic language and keeps the *abba* rhyme scheme.

we pray for tears to wash our filthiness,
importantly pissing hogwash through our styes.

The devil, watching by our sickbeds, hissed
old smut and folk-songs to our soul, until   10
the soft and precious metal of our will
boiled off in vapor for this scientist.

Each day his flattery[2] makes us eat a toad,
and each step forward is a step to hell,
unmoved, though previous corpses and their smell   15
asphyxiate our progress on this road.

Like the poor lush who cannot satisfy,
we try to force our sex with counterfeits,
die drooling on the deliquescent tits,
mouthing the rotten orange we suck dry.   20

Gangs of demons are boozing in our brain—
ranked, swarming, like a million warrior-ants,[3]
they drown and choke the cistern of our wants;
each time we breathe, we tear our lungs with pain.

If poison, arson, sex, narcotics, knives   25
have not yet ruined us and stitched their quick,
loud patterns on the canvas of our lives,
it is because our souls are still too sick.[4]

Among the vermin, jackals, panthers, lice,
gorillas and tarantulas that suck   30
and snatch and scratch and defecate and fuck
in the disorderly circus of our vice,

there's one more ugly and abortive birth.
It makes no gestures, never beats its breast,
yet it would murder for a moment's rest,[5]   35
and willingly annihilate the earth.

It's BOREDOM. Tears have glued its eyes together.
You know it well, my Reader. This obscene
beast chain-smokes yawning for the guillotine—
you—hypocrite Reader—my double—my brother!   40

2. The devil is literally described as a puppet   4. Literally, not bold enough.
master controlling our strings.   5. Literally, swallow the world in a yawn.
3. Literally, intestinal worms.

Correspondences[1]

Nature is a temple whose living colonnades
Breathe forth a mystic speech in fitful sighs;
Man wanders among symbols in those glades
Where all things watch him with familiar eyes.

Like dwindling echoes gathered far away   5
Into a deep and thronging unison
Huge as the night or as the light of day,
All scents and sounds and colors meet as one.

Perfumes there are as sweet as the oboe's sound,
Green as the prairies, fresh as a child's caress,[2]   10
—And there are others, rich, corrupt, profound[3]

And of an infinite pervasiveness,
Like myrrh, or musk, or amber,[4] that excite
The ecstasies of sense, the soul's delight.

Her Hair[1]

O fleece, that down the neck waves to the nape!
O curls! O perfume nonchalant and rare!
O ecstasy! To fill this alcove[2] shape
With memories that in these tresses sleep,
I would shake them like pennons in the air!   5

Languorous Asia, burning Africa,
And a far world, defunct almost, absent,
Within your aromatic forest stay!
As other souls on music drift away,
Mine, o my love! still floats upon your scent.   10

I shall go there where, full of sap, both tree
And man swoon in the heat of southern climes;
Strong tresses, be the swell that carries me!
I dream upon your sea of ebony
Of dazzling sails, of oarsmen, masts and flames: 15

A sun-drenched and reverberating port,
Where I imbibe color and sound and scent;

---

1. Translated by Richard Wilbur. The translation keeps the intricate melody of the sonnet's original rhyme scheme.
2. Literally, flesh.
3. Literally, triumphant.
4. Or ambergris, a substance secreted by whales.

Ambergris and musk (a secretion of the male musk deer) are used in making perfume.
1. Translated by Doreen Bell. The translation emulates the French original's challenging *abaab* rhyme pattern.
2. Bedroom.

Where vessels, gliding through the gold and moire,
Open their vast arms as they leave the shore
To clasp the pure and shimmering firmament.   20

I'll plunge my head, enamored of its pleasure,
In this black ocean where the other hides;
My subtle spirit then will know a measure
Of fertile idleness and fragrant leisure,
Lulled by the infinite rhythm of its tides!   25

Pavilion, of blue-shadowed tresses spun,
You give me back the azure from afar;
And where the twisted locks are fringed with down
Lurk mingled odors I grow drunk upon
Of oil of coconut, of musk and tar.   30

A long time! always! my hand in your hair
Will sow the stars of sapphire, pearl, ruby,
That you be never deaf to my desire,
My oasis and gourd whence I aspire
To drink deep of the wine of memory![3]   35

A Carcass[1]

Remember, my love, the item you saw
    That beautiful morning in June:
By a bend in the path a carcass reclined
    On a bed sown with pebbles and stones;

Her legs were spread out like a lecherous whore,   5
    Sweating out poisonous fumes,
Who opened in slick invitational style
    Her stinking and festering womb.

The sun on this rottenness focused its rays
    To cook the cadaver till done,   10
And render to Nature a hundredfold gift
    Of all she'd united in one.

And the sky cast an eye on this marvelous meat
    As over the flowers in bloom.

3. The last two lines are a question: "Are you not . . . ?"
1. Translated by James McGowan with special attention to imagery. The alternation of long and short lines in English emulates the French meter's rhythmic swing between twelve- and eight-syllable lines in an *abab* rhyme scheme.

The stench was so wretched that there on the grass   15
    You nearly collapsed in a swoon.

The flies buzzed and droned on these bowels of filth
    Where an army of maggots arose,
Which flowed like a liquid and thickening stream
    On the animate rags of her clothes.   20

And it rose and it fell, and pulsed like a wave,
    Rushing and bubbling with health.
One could say that this carcass, blown with vague breath,
    Lived in increasing itself.

And this whole teeming world made a musical sound   25
    Like babbling brooks and the breeze,
Or the grain that a man with a winnowing-fan
    Turns with a rhythmical ease.

The shapes wore away as if only a dream
    Like a sketch that is left on the page   30
Which the artist forgot and can only complete
    On the canvas, with memory's aid.

From back in the rocks, a pitiful bitch
    Eyed us with angry distaste,
Awaiting the moment to snatch from the bones   35
    The morsel she'd dropped in her haste.

—And you, in your turn, will be rotten as this:
    Horrible, filthy, undone,
Oh sun of my nature and star of my eyes,
    My passion, my angel[2] in one!   40

Yes, such will you be, oh regent of grace,
    After the rites have been read,
Under the weeds, under blossoming grass
    As you molder with bones of the dead.

Ah then, oh my beauty, explain to the worms   45
    Who cherish your body so fine,
That I am the keeper for corpses of love
    Of the form, and the essence divine![3]

2. Series of conventional Petrarchan images that idealize the beloved.
3. "Any form created by man is immortal. For form is independent of matter..." (from Baudelaire's journal *My Heart Laid Bare* 80).

Invitation to the Voyage[1]

My child, my sister, dream
How sweet all things would seem
Were we in that kind land to live together,
And there love slow and long,
There love and die among   5
Those scenes that image you, that sumptuous weather.
Drowned suns that glimmer there
Through cloud-disheveled air
Move me with such a mystery as appears
Within those other skies   10
Of your treacherous eyes
When I behold them shining through their tears.

There, there is nothing else but grace and measure,
Richness, quietness, and pleasure.

Furniture that wears   15
The lustre of the years
Softly would glow within our glowing chamber,
Flowers of rarest bloom
Proffering their perfume
Mixed with the vague fragrances of amber;   20
Gold ceilings would there be,
Mirrors deep as the sea,
The walls all in an Eastern splendor hung—
Nothing but should address
The soul's loneliness,   25
Speaking her sweet and secret native tongue.

There, there is nothing else but grace and measure,
Richness, quietness, and pleasure.

See, sheltered from the swells
There in the still canals   30
Those drowsy ships that dream of sailing forth;
It is to satisfy
Your least desire, they ply
Hither through all the waters of the earth.
The sun at close of day   35
Clothes the fields of hay,
Then the canals, at last the town entire
In hyacinth and gold:
Slowly the land is rolled
Sleepward under a sea of gentle fire.   40

---

1. Translated by Richard Wilbur. The translation maintains both the rhyme scheme and the rocking motion of the original meter, which follows an unusual pattern of two five-syllable lines followed by one seven-syllable line, and a seven-syllable couplet as refrain.

There, there is nothing else but grace and measure,
Richness, quietness, and pleasure.

Song of Autumn I[1]

Soon we shall plunge into the chilly fogs;
Farewell, swift light! our summers are too short!
I hear already the mournful fall of logs
Re-echoing from the pavement of the court.

All of winter will gather in my soul: 5
Hate, anger, horror, chills, the hard forced work;
And, like the sun in his hell by the north pole,
My heart will be only a red and frozen block.

I shudder, hearing every log that falls;
No scaffold could be built with hollower sounds.   10
My spirit is like a tower whose crumbling walls
The tireless battering-ram brings to the ground.

It seems to me, lulled by monotonous shocks,
As if they were hastily nailing a coffin today.
For whom?—Yesterday was summer. Now autumn knocks.   15
That mysterious sound is like someone's going away.

Spleen LXXVIII[1]

Old Pluvius,[2] month of rains, in peevish mood
Pours from his urn chill winter's sodden gloom
On corpses fading in the near graveyard,
On foggy suburbs pours life's tedium.

My cat seeks out a litter on the stones,   5
Her mangy body turning without rest.
An ancient poet's soul in monotones
Whines in the rain-spouts like a chilblained ghost.

A great bell mourns, a wet log wrapped in smoke
Sings in falsetto to the wheezing clock,   10
While from a rankly perfumed deck of cards
(A dropsical old crone's fatal bequest)

1. Translated by C. F. MacIntyre to follow the original rhyme pattern.
1. Translated by Kenneth O. Hanson, with emphasis on the imagery. The French original uses identical *abab* rhymes in the two quatrains and shifts to *ccd, eed* in the tercets.
2. "The rainy time" (Latin, literal trans.); a period extending from January 20 to February 18 as the fifth month of the French Revolutionary calendar.

The Queen of Spades, the dapper Jack of Hearts
Speak darkly of dead loves, how they were lost.

Spleen LXXIX[1]

I have more memories than if I had lived a thousand years.

Even a bureau crammed with souvenirs,
Old bills, love letters, photographs, receipts,
Court depositions, locks of hair in plaits,
Hides fewer secrets than my brain could yield.   5
It's like a tomb, a corpse-filled Potter's Field,[2]
A pyramid where the dead lie down by scores.
I am a graveyard that the moon abhors:
Like guilty qualms, the worms burrow and nest
Thickly in bodies that I loved the best.   10
I'm a stale boudoir where old-fashioned clothes
Lie scattered among wilted fern and rose,
Where only the Boucher girls[3] in pale pastels
Can breathe the uncorked scents and faded smells.

Nothing can equal those days for endlessness   15
When in the winter's blizzardy caress
Indifference expanding to Ennui[4]
Takes on the feel of Immortality.
O living matter, henceforth you're no more
Than a cold stone encompassed by vague fear   20
And by the desert, and the mist and sun;
An ancient Sphinx ignored by everyone,
Left off the map, whose bitter irony
Is to sing as the sun sets in that dry sea.[5]

Spleen LXXXI[1]

When the low heavy sky weighs like a lid
Upon the spirit aching for the light
And all the wide horizon's line is hid
By a black day sadder than any night;

---

1. Translated by Anthony Hecht. The translation follows the original rhymed couplets, except for one technical impossibility: Baudelaire's repetition (in a poem about monotony) of an identical rhyme for eight lines (lines 11–18, the sound of long *a*).
2. A general term describing the common cemetery for those buried at public expense.
3. François Boucher (1703–1770), court painter for Louis XV of France, drew many pictures of young women clothed and nude.
4. Melancholy, paralyzing boredom.
5. Baudelaire combines two references to ancient Egypt, the Sphinx and the legendary statue of Memnon at Thebes, which was supposed to sing at sunset.
1. Translated by Sir John Squire in accord with the original rhyme scheme.

When the changed earth is but a dungeon dank 5
Where batlike Hope goes blindly fluttering
And, striking wall and roof and mouldered plank,
Bruises his tender head and timid wing;

When like grim prison bars stretch down the thin,
Straight, rigid pillars of the endless rain, 10
And the dumb throngs of infamous spiders spin
Their meshes in the caverns of the brain,

Suddenly, bells leap forth into the air,
Hurling a hideous uproar to the sky
As 'twere a band of homeless spirits who fare 15
Through the strange heavens, wailing stubbornly.

And hearses, without drum or instrument,
File slowly through my soul; crushed, sorrowful,
Weeps Hope, and Grief, fierce and omnipotent,
Plants his black banner on my drooping skull. 20

The Voyage[1]

To Maxime du Camp[2]

I

The child, in love with prints and maps,
Holds the whole world in his vast appetite.
How large the earth is under the lamplight!
But in the eyes of memory, how the world is cramped!

We set out one morning, brain afire, 5
Hearts fat with rancor and bitter desires,
Moving along to the rhythm of wind and waves,
Lull the inner infinite on the finite of seas:

Some are glad, glad to leave a degraded home;
Others, happy to shake off the horror of their hearts, 10
Still others, astrologers drowned in the eyes of woman—
Oh the perfumes of Circe,[3] the power and the pig!—

To escape conversion to the Beast, get drunk
On space and light and the flames of skies;

1. Translated by Charles Henri Ford. The French poem is written in the traditional twelve-syllable (alexandrine) line with an *abab* rhyme scheme.
2. A wry dedication to the progress-oriented author of *Modern Songs* (1855), which began "I was born a traveler."
3. In Homer's *Odyssey*, an island sorceress who changed visitors into beasts. Odysseus's men were transformed into pigs.

The tongue of the sun and the ice that bites   15
Slowly erase the mark of the Kiss.

But the true voyagers are those who leave
Only to be going; hearts nimble as balloons,
They never diverge from luck's black sun,
And with or without reason, cry, Let's be gone!   20

Desire to them is nothing but clouds,
They dream, as a draftee dreams of the cannon,
Of vast sensualities, changing, unknown,
Whose name the spirit has never pronounced!

II

We imitate—horrible!—the top and ball   25
In their waltz and bounce; even in sleep
We're turned and tormented by Curiosity,
Who, like a mad Angel, lashes the stars.

Peculiar fortune that changes its goal,
And being nowhere, is anywhere at all!   30
And Man, who is never untwisted from hope,
Scrambling like a madman to get some rest!

The soul's a three-master seeking Icaria;[4]
A voice on deck calls: "Wake up there!"
A voice from the mast-head, vehement, wild: 35
"Love . . . fame . . . happiness!" We're on the rocks!

Every island that the lookout hails
Becomes the Eldorado[5] foretold by Fortune;
Then Imagination embarks on its orgy
But runs aground in the brightness of morning.   40

Poor little lover of visionary fields!
Should he be put in irons, dumped in the sea,
This drunken sailor, discoverer of Americas,
Mirage that makes the gulf more bitter?

So the old vagabond, shuffling in mud,   45
Dreams, nose hoisted, of a shining paradise,
His charmed eye lighting on Capua's[6] coast
At every candle aglow in a hovel.

---

4. Greek island in the Aegean Sea named after the mythological Icarus, who, escaping from prison using wings made by his father, Daedalus, plunged into nearby waters and drowned when the wings gave way. His name was associated with utopian flights, as in Étienne Cabet's novel about a utopian community, *Voyage to Icaria* (1840). "Three-master": a ship.
5. Fabled country of gold and abundance.
6. City on the Volturno River in southern Italy, famous for its luxury and sensuality.

III

Astounding voyagers! what noble stories
We read in your eyes, deeper than seas;   50
Show us those caskets, filled with rich memories,
Marvelous jewels, hewn from stars and aether.

Yes, we would travel, without sail or steam!
Gladden a little our jail's desolation,
Sail over our minds, stretched like a canvas,   55
All your memories, framed with gold horizons.

Tell us, what have you seen?

IV

                    "We have seen stars
And tides; we have seen sands, too,
And, despite shocks and unforeseen disasters,
We were often bored, just as we are here.   60

The glory of sun on a violet sea,
The glory of cities in the setting sun,
Kindled our hearts with torment and longing
To plunge into the sky's magnetic reflections.

Neither the rich cities nor sublime landscapes,   65
Ever possessed that mysterious attraction
Of Change and Chance having fun with the clouds.
And always Desire kept us anxious!

—Enjoyment adds force to Appetite!
Desire, old tree nurtured by pleasure,   70
Although your dear bark thicken and harden,
Your branches throb to hold the sun closer!

Great tree, will you outgrow the cypress?
Still we have gathered carefully
Some sketches for your hungry album,   75
Brothers, for whom all things from far away

Are precious! We've bowed down to idols;
To thrones encrusted with luminous rocks;
To figured palaces whose magic pomp
Would ruin your bankers with a ruinous dream;   80

To costumes that intoxicate the eye,
To women whose teeth and nails are dyed,
To clever jugglers, fondled by the snake."[7]

---

7. Snake charmers. The images in this stanza evoke India.

V

And then, and what more?

VI

"O childish minds!

Not to forget the principal thing,   85
We saw everywhere, without looking for it,
From top to toe of the deadly scale,
The tedious drama of undying sin:

Woman, low slave, vain and stupid,
Without laughter self-loving, and without disgust,   90
Man, greedy despot, lewd, hard and covetous,
Slave of the slave, rivulet in the sewer;

The hangman exulting, the martyr sobbing;
Festivals that season and perfume the blood;[8]
The poison of power unnerving the tyrant,   95
The masses in love with the brutalizing whip;

Many religions, very like our own,
All climbing to heaven; and Holiness,
Like a delicate wallower in a feather bed,
Seeking sensation from hair shirts and nails.   100

Jabbering humanity, drunk with its genius,
As crazy now as it was in the past,
Crying to God in its raging agony:
'O master, fellow creature, I curse thee forever!'

And then the least stupid, brave lovers of Lunacy,   105
Fleeing the gross herd that Destiny pens in,
Finding release in the vast dreams of opium!
—Such is the story, the whole world over."

VII

Bitter knowledge that traveling brings!
The globe, monotonous and small, today,   110
Yesterday, tomorrow, always, throws us our image:
An oasis of horror in a desert of boredom!

Should we go? Or stay? If you can stay, stay;
But go if you must. Some run, some hide
To outwit Time, the enemy so vigilant and   115
Baleful. And many, alas, must run forever

---

8. Literally, "Festivals seasoned and perfumed by blood."

Like the wandering Jew[9] and the twelve apostles,
Who could not escape his relentless net[1]
By ship or by wheel; while others knew how
To destroy him without leaving home.   120

When finally he places his foot on our spine,
May we be able to hope and cry, Forward!
As in days gone by when we left for China,
Eyes fixed on the distance, hair in the wind,

With heart as light as a young libertine's   125
We'll embark on the sea of deepening shadows.
Do you hear those mournful, enchanting voices[2]
That sing: "Come this way, if you would taste

The perfumed Lotus. Here you may pick
Miraculous fruits for which the heart hungers.   130
Come and drink deep of this strange,
Soft afternoon that never ends?"

Knowing his voice, we visualize the phantom—
It is our Pylades there, his arms outstretched.
While she whose knees we used to kiss cries out,   135
"For strength of heart, swim back to your Electra!"[3]

VIII

O Death, old captain, it is time! weigh anchor!
This country confounds us; hoist sail and away!
If the sky and sea are black as ink,
Our hearts, as you know them, burst with blinding rays.   140

Pour us your poison, that last consoling draft!
For we long, so the fire burns in the brain,
To sound the abyss, Hell or Heaven, what matter?
In the depths of the Unknown, we'll discover the New!

9. According to medieval legend, a Jew who mocked Christ on his way to the cross and was condemned to wander unceasingly until Judgment Day.
1. These three stanzas describe Time (ultimately Death) as a Roman gladiator, the *retiarius*, who used a net to trap his opponent.

2. The voices of the dead, luring the sailor to the Lotus-land of ease and forgetfulness.
3. In Greek mythology, Orestes and Pylades were close friends ready to sacrifice their lives for each other. Electra was Orestes' faithful sister, who saved him from the Furies.

EMILY DICKINSON
1830–1886

In the 1880s, visitors to Amherst, Massachusetts, gossiped about the strange woman, dressed only in white gowns, who never left her father's house—except once, it was rumored, "to see a new church, when she crept out by night, and viewed it by moonlight." Neighbors and friends knew that this woman wrote, but she published only ten poems during her lifetime, and even those appeared anonymously. She begged those closest to her to burn her papers after her death. They refused, instead startling audiences by publishing Emily Dickinson's unusual lyrics, with their passionate intensity, broken meter, slant rhymes, and unconventional dashes and capitalizations. From the moment that they first appeared, these poems have been beloved by both readers and critics. Dickinson's works can seem, on the one hand, like childlike and accessible meditations on such universal themes as death, faith, and nature, and on the other hand, like highly artful, philosophically demanding, and radically innovative experiments in lyric form. It is with this unlikely combination of innocence and sophistication that the mysterious Dickinson has become one of the best-known of American poets.

LIFE

Born to a prominent Amherst family— her father was elected to Congress— Dickinson attended Amherst Academy and later, for a year, the Mount Holyoke Female Seminary. Conflicted and ambivalent about Christian orthodoxy even as a child, she resisted the Puritan attitudes that surrounded her, especially at school. "Christ is calling everyone here," she wrote, "and I am standing alone in rebellion." This sense of isolation would only deepen. From early in her twenties, she confined herself almost entirely to her family home, leading the life of a recluse with her tyrannical father and absent-minded mother. She did have close attachments to her brother and sister, and she developed a few close friendships, though she pursued these mainly through correspondence. Some of her works reflect on the pain of unrequited love and erotic desire, and biographers have speculated about Dickinson's passions, but no scholar has been able to determine indisputably the name of the one—or ones—she loved.

Dickinson began writing verse seriously in the 1850s, putting groups of her poems together in fascicles (booklets of pages bound together by hand). In these works she seldom remarked on the burning issues of the day, from slavery and women's rights to the violence of the Civil War. Concerned with domestic matters and the torments of the soul, she can seem excruciatingly inward-looking. But her literary life was expansive. She wrote more than a thousand letters, linking herself to the outside world more readily by mail than by face-to-face contact. Dickinson also read widely. Shakespeare was a major touchstone (she once asked: "why is any other book needed?"), and she named John Keats, Elizabeth Barrett Browning, Robert Browning, and Charlotte Brontë as among her foremost inspirations.

In 1862, after seeing an article with advice for aspiring writers by Thomas Wentworth Higginson, Dickinson wrote to solicit his opinion of her poems. He was both enthusiastic and shocked, warning her away from publishing such unconventional work. Their friendship continued to the end of Dickinson's life. After her death, Dickinson's sister Lavinia was surprised to discover almost two thousand poems stashed away in a box, and she began the difficult task of trying to figure out how to edit and organize these works for publication, a process that has puzzled and divided editors ever since. Higginson was one of the first to publish volumes of Dickinson's poetry, editing the work to make it seem as conventional as he could.

WORK

With singular conviction and independence, Dickinson produced poetry unlike anyone else of her time. Her works are noteworthy, first of all, for their brevity and compression, throwing readers immediately into the thick of the poem, eschewing any preparation. And while she draws on familiar poetic themes— nature, death, love, and faith—she pushes her explorations of feeling to their most extreme intensity, and her images persistently unsettle expectation. Nature can turn out to be revolting, as when a bird devours a worm; the grandest subjects can turn ordinary, as when death appears as an everyday conveyance; and the human body can be estranged from itself, turned into a corpse, a gun, or a tomb.

Dickinson's use of meter is as striking as her imagery. She relies most heavily on popular metrical patterns associated with Protestant hymns, such as common meter (quatrains that begin with one line of eight syllables followed by a line of six syllables, repeated to form an 8/6/8/6 pattern).

But while she depends on the hymnal, she also breaks with it. Sometimes she speeds up or slows down its familiar rhythms; and sometimes she even interrupts them altogether. For example, she introduces dashes that cluster syllables together in a way that interrupts the feeling of a smooth rhythm (as in the first line of one of her most famous poems, "I heard a Fly buzz— when I died"); or she changes meter suddenly (as in "I like to see it lap the Miles," a poem that opens and closes with common-meter quatrains but swerves into a different pattern altogether in the third stanza). Dickinson's rhymes also play with traditional patterns. In "A Bird came down the Walk," for example, she offers us a couple of perfect rhymes (saw/raw, Grass/pass). But in the same poem she gives us two slant rhymes (Crumb/home, seam/ swim), and in the middle, where one expects a rhyme, she presents sounds that share a rough resemblance but do not rhyme at all (around/Head).

Perhaps most strikingly experimental of all is Dickinson's use of punctuation. Her dramatic dashes are famous, and the manuscripts suggest that they are even more innovative than they look on the printed page. In her own handwriting, Dickinson's dashes are of varying lengths, and sometimes turn up or down (a few are completely vertical). These marks do not always work the same way: sometimes her dashes draw thoughts together; at other times they separate them. And finally, while Dickinson capitalizes many important proper nouns, such as Soul and Beauty, she also opts to capitalize some unexpected words: Onset, for example, or Buckets.

That Dickinson never published these outrageously unconventional and demanding poems might not surprise us. Higginson had led her to believe that the world would not appreciate them, and the few of her poems that did appear in print in her lifetime were heavily edited to conform to unadventurous tastes. "Publication—is the Auction / Of the Mind of Man," she wrote, disgusted by the idea of selling what she cared for most. And so she withdrew to what she called the "freedom" of her narrow room to create great poetry for herself alone.

258

There's a certain Slant of light,
Winter Afternoons—
That oppresses, like the Heft
Of Cathedral Tunes—

Heavenly Hurt, it gives us—   5
We can find no scar,
But internal difference,
Where the Meanings, are—

None may teach it—Any—
'Tis the Seal Despair—   10
An imperial affliction
Sent us of the Air—

When it comes, the Landscape listens—
Shadows—hold their breath—
When it goes, 'tis like the Distance   15
On the look of Death—

303

The Soul selects her own Society—
Then—shuts the Door—
To her divine Majority—
Present no more—

Unmoved—she notes the Chariots—pausing   5
At her low Gate—
Unmoved—an Emperor be kneeling
Upon her Mat—

I've known her—from an ample nation—
Choose One—   10
Then—close the Valves of her attention—
Like Stone—

435

Much Madness is divinest Sense—
To a discerning Eye—
Much Sense—the starkest Madness—
'Tis the Majority
In this, as All, prevail—   5
Assent—and you are sane—
Demur—you're straightway dangerous—
And handled with a Chain—

465

I heard a Fly buzz—when I died—
The Stillness in the Room
Was like the Stillness in the Air—
Between the Heaves of Storm—

The Eyes around—had wrung them dry—   5
And Breaths were gathering firm
For that last Onset—when the King
Be witnessed—in the Room—

I willed my Keepsakes—Signed away
What portion of me be   10
Assignable—and then it was
There interposed a Fly—

With Blue—uncertain stumbling Buzz—
Between the light—and me—
And then the Windows failed—and then   15
I could not see to see—

712

Because I could not stop for Death—
He kindly stopped for me—
The Carriage held but just Ourselves—
And Immortality.

We slowly drove—He knew no haste   5
And I had put away
My labor and my leisure too,
For His Civility—

We passed the School, where Children strove
At Recess—in the Ring—   10
We passed the Fields of Gazing Grain—
We passed the Setting Sun—

Or rather—He passed Us—
The Dews drew quivering and chill—
For only Gossamer, my Gown—   15
My Tippet—only Tulle[1]—

We paused before a House that seemed
A Swelling of the Ground—
The Roof was scarcely visible—
The Cornice—in the Ground—   20

Since then—'tis Centuries—and yet
Feels shorter than the Day
I first surmised the Horses' Heads
Were toward Eternity—

754

My Life had stood—a Loaded Gun—
In Corners—till a Day
The Owner passed—identified—
And carried Me away—

And now We roam in Sovereign Woods—   5
And now We hunt the Doe—
And every time I speak for Him—
The Mountains straight reply—
And do I smile, such cordial light
Upon the Valley glow—   10
It is as a Vesuvian face[1]
Had let its pleasure through—

And when at Night—Our good Day done—
I guard My Master's Head—
'Tis better than the Eider-Duck's   15
Deep Pillow—to have shared—

To foe of His—I'm deadly foe—
None stir the second time—
On whom I lay a Yellow Eye—
Or an emphatic Thumb—   20

Though I than He—may longer live
He longer must—than I—
For I have but the power to kill,
Without—the power to die—

1. Fine, silken netting. "Tippet": a scarf.
1. A face glowing with light like that from an erupting volcano.

1129

Tell all the Truth but tell it slant—
Success in Circuit lies
Too bright for our infirm Delight
The Truth's superb surprise

As Lightning to the Children eased   5
With explanation kind
The Truth must dazzle gradually
Or every man be blind—

Bourne 1218

IV

At the Crossroads of Empire

Many a ruler has dreamed of acquiring a great empire. The first challenge is to subjugate neighboring peoples and then, as one grows rich and powerful from those conquests, to vanquish ever-more-distant peoples and lands. And yet maintaining an empire turns out to be a grueling task. Crossing vast distances is difficult enough, but keeping control of far-off places requires canny and forceful administration. The subjugated peoples may well rise up, and they have some advantages: they know the local terrain, and they may be able to rally substantial popular support for resistance to foreign domination. Meanwhile, imperial troops and administrators can easily grow weary of spending their lives far from home, in places where local people resent them. Their families back home may not benefit much, if at all, from the new imperial possessions, and popular enthusiasm for conquest at home may dwindle, as people begrudge the cost in lives and taxes that it takes to maintain an empire. Emperors need to persuade their own subjects to value the mission of empire, which means that they must invoke a sense of urgent or high purpose. For this, rulers depend in part on the use of words, on rousing rhetoric to muster broad support for their dreams of conquest. Thus,

The Amar Singh Gate of the Agra Fort, India; picture taken by British photographer Samuel Bourne in 1865.

577

writers can play a crucial role in the making and keeping of empires.

Of course, many a subjugated people has also dreamed of throwing out foreign invaders. The humiliation of being conquered is often the primary source of their discontent. But foreign empires not only inflict armies from far away, they also typically impose their language, their laws, and their religion. New imperial administrators disrupt long-standing ways of life with imported rules; they exploit local resources, including the people themselves; and they assert the superiority of the conquering state, insisting on wiping away values and traditions they see as backward or primitive in favor of their own ways of life. The occupied people may well feel outraged to the point of violence and begin to rally support for rebellion against the foreign invaders. This support is often easy enough to rouse at the beginning, but it can get difficult if the conquered people begin to believe that the conquering power is too strong or too advanced to unseat. Perhaps, after a few generations of intermarriage between the conquerors and the conquered, it becomes difficult to wrench the two peoples apart. Hence those who wish to fight off the bonds of empire feel the need for writers just as the mighty emperors do: they crave stirring words to capture the value of native customs and beliefs under threat and to build up the people's determination to struggle against the empire—knowing full well that any resistance may entail horrific sacrifices.

A great deal of our experience of the world today is a consequence of the dominance of European empires in the nineteenth century. Our feelings of global interconnectedness as well as our sense of the deep economic inequalities that divide the developed world from developing nations are effects of Europe's imperial reach. Britain and France became the world's major superpowers then, centers of vast empires that stretched across the globe. These empires had emerged out of fierce economic competition among European nations going back several centuries. Hoping to profit from new natural resources and new markets, England, France, Spain, Holland, and Portugal had sent ships both eastward and westward, trying to establish monopolies on trade relations with Turkey, Russia, India, and China, and establishing colonies in North and South America. European consumers developed a growing appetite for products from these distant places, goods such as tea, coffee, sugar, furs, cotton, silver, tobacco, rubber, silk, spices, and opium. The profits reaped by European companies soared. The slave trade played a crucial role in this new economy: traders would buy slaves in Africa and sell them to plantation owners in the United States, Brazil, and the Caribbean. Slave traders would then use the profits to buy products of slave labor, such as tobacco and sugar, which they would transport to Europe to sell to eager customers there.

Since all of Europe coveted the same valuable markets, tensions rose among European nations, frequently erupting into outright war. In the eighteenth century, France lost a series of wars with Britain, which frustrated its dreams of controlling North America, the Caribbean, and India. France then looked elsewhere. Long interested in opening up trade with Vietnam, the French army invaded in the 1850s and took control. They industrialized the Vietnamese economy, investing in railroads and factories, and made huge profits from Vietnamese rubber, coal, and sugar. But few Vietnamese people benefited: under French rule, poverty, disease, and starvation became commonplace.

Conflicts among European empires redrew the maps of whole continents. When Napoleon invaded Spain and put his brother on the throne there, he destabilized monarchical authority so profoundly that emboldened Latin

A colonial French family in Vietnam with a machine gun, ca. 1900.

Americans were able to win wars of independence from Spanish rule. Many of these struggles were aided by Britain, which was eager to limit Spanish economic and political power. In the 1880s, European powers that had held various territories on the African coast began to compete for power inland, dividing up Africa into spheres of control. The diverse territories of South Africa prompted the Boer Wars, battles between the British army and Dutch settlers. In west central Africa, Great Britain, Germany, France, and Portugal vied for territory. By the turn of the century, 90 percent of the African continent was under European control. Around this time, the United States and Japan also began to build empires, entering into the competition with European states. In 1898, the United States intervened in Cuba and the Philippines, sparking the Spanish–American War and beginning its new role as another powerful imperial player on the world stage.

Until the nineteenth century, European nations had been unashamed to admit that their imperial missions were above all about profits. But if the Europeans traveled to distant lands for economic reasons, they often stayed for political ones. Over the course of the nineteenth century, the rhetoric of racial difference deepened, as Europeans saw themselves less and less as economic actors and more and more as liberators and civilizers of less "advanced" races. Advocates of colonialism often argued that empires existed not for the benefit of the conquerors but for the sake of the conquered "primitive" peoples, who were believed incapable of self-government but who could, with European guidance, eventually become civilized. Global empires had filled European coffers, but this the Europeans often conveniently forgot, speaking of themselves instead as responsible world leaders, reluctantly taking up what Rudyard Kipling famously called "the white man's burden."

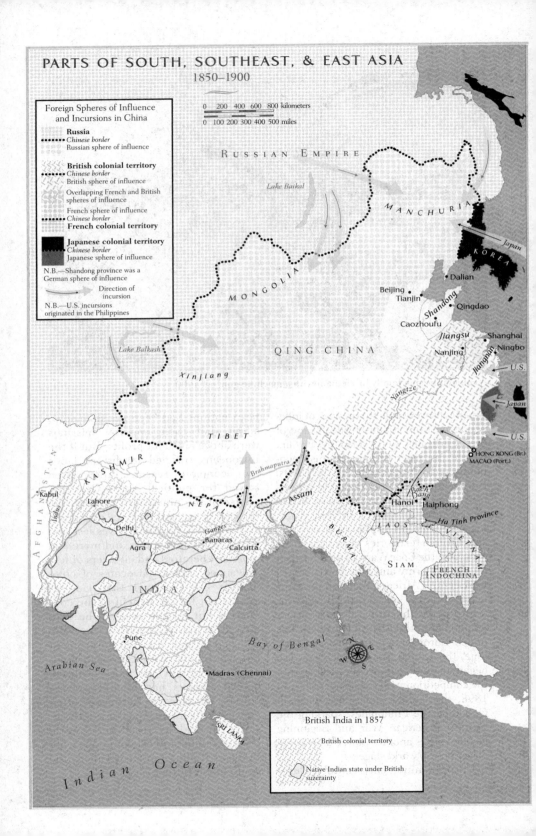

PARTS OF SOUTH, SOUTHEAST, & EAST ASIA
1850–1900

Foreign Spheres of Influence
and Incursions in China

Russia
••••• *Chinese border*
Russian sphere of influence

British colonial territory
••••• *Chinese border*
British sphere of influence

Overlapping French and British
spheres of influence

French sphere of influence
••••• *Chinese border*
French colonial territory

Japanese colonial territory
Chinese border
Japanese sphere of influence

N.B.—Shandong province was a
German sphere of influence

→ Direction of
incursion

N.B.—U.S. incursions
originated in the Philippines

0 200 400 600 800 kilometers
0 100 200 300 400 500 miles

RUSSIAN EMPIRE

Lake Baikal

MANCHURIA

Japan

KOREA

MONGOLIA

• Dalian

Beijing •
Tianjin •

Shandong

Qingdao

Caozhoufu •

Jiangsu

Shanghai •

QING CHINA

Nanjing •

Ningbo •

Jiangxi

— U.S.

Lake Balkash

Xinjiang

Yangtze

Japan

— U.S.

TIBET

○ HONG KONG (Br.)
● MACAO (Port.)

KASHMIR

Brahmaputra

NEPAL Assam

Red River

AFGHANISTAN

Kabul •

Lahore •

Hanoi • Haiphong •

Delhi •

Ganges

BURMA

LAOS

Ha Tinh Province

Agra •

Banaras •
Calcutta •

VIETNAM

INDIA

SIAM

FRENCH
INDOCHINA

Pune •

Bay of Bengal

N
W   E
S

Arabian Sea

• Madras (Chennai)

British India in 1857

British colonial territory

SRI LANKA

Native Indian state under British
suzerainty

Indian Ocean

But while Europeans often claimed to be motivated by a high-minded responsibility to spread reason and progress, reports of atrocities made it clear that the zeal to civilize was often a mask for brutal exploitation. King Leopold II of Belgium sent explorers to the Congo Free State, for example, under the guise of a scientific and charitable association, but in fact intending to subdue the Congolese through economic and military force. Eager to profit from the rubber trade, Leopold's agents enslaved Congolese workers and brutally tortured and mutilated them, often leaving them to starve. As much as half the population—ten million people—died under Leopold's regime. Around the globe, the violence and exploitation of European empires fostered resentment and out-and-out insurrection. A major blow to British imperialism, for example, came in 1857 when Indian soldiers rebelled against the British army. The British violently suppressed the rebellion, resorting to brutality that left lasting scars. Indian subjects began to feel a profound mistrust of the British that would fuel increasingly insistent movements for independence.

Writers in South and East Asia in the nineteenth century faced particularly daunting challenges. Struggling to define their own linguistic and literary roles in relation to long-standing local and imperial traditions, they also got caught up in new collisions between vast empires. For many centuries China had been the great unchallenged superpower in East Asia, and the Islamic Mughal Empire successfully ruled India, but in the eighteenth and nineteenth centuries the expanding European empires headed eastward and began to establish significant power in Asia. Britain, which managed to conquer a full quarter of the world's population, building the largest empire in human history, had taken over from the Mughals in India and by the middle of the nineteenth century had made inroads into China.

Meanwhile, France, Russia, Portugal, the Netherlands, and Japan claimed land and trading rights in different places across Asia, leading to hostility with one another and with Britain and China.

What was it like to write at the crossroads of contending empires? The writers collected in this section reveal a complex variety of attitudes, all of them profoundly ambivalent. Vietnam's **Nguyễn Du** cherished a deep love and respect for the intellectual traditions of imperial China, which had ruled Vietnam for many centuries and remained a menacing neighbor. But Nguyễn Du resisted the easy assumption of Chinese superiority: he deliberately chose to write in vernacular Vietnamese, crafting a new heroic epic for his nation in the language of the people. A generation later in India, the poet **Ghalib** belonged to the Muslim ruling elite and wrote in two different imperial languages—Persian, the official court language imported from afar, and Urdu, an Indian idiom that reflected his particular hybrid Indo-Muslim culture. When Indian princes and soldiers rose up in an unsuccessful revolt against the British in 1857, Ghalib's court patronage ended and the poet struggled to make a living as he refused to show the mandatory deference to the British Empire. **Rabrindranath Tagore** was born into a prominent Calcutta family that had amassed a fortune through trade in British India. When he embarked on his literary career, he wrote in Bengali but translated many of his works into English, the language of his colonial masters. Once he had risen to fame, he traveled the world and identified as a cosmopolitan and a proponent of world literature, but when Great Britain offered him a knighthood in 1919, he rejected it out of protest over colonial violence.

These three writers remained torn between loyalty to local traditions and respect or even admiration for a

A photograph of men in a Chinese opium den, ca. 1900.

conquering imperial power. All of them had to negotiate between two or more languages and power structures. But their responses were strikingly varied. And so together they give a rich sense of the multiple ways that bitterness, inspiration, and responsibility combine to create the complex experience of writing at the crossroads of powerful empires.

NGUYỄN DU
1765–1820

Memorized by illiterate farmers, consulted by lovers, esteemed by learned scholars, and popular with readers of all classes, *The Tale of Kiều* has no rival in Vietnamese literature. Many Vietnamese people can recite the whole narrative by heart—more than 3,000 lines of poetry—and some use the text to divine the future. This story of a young woman buffeted by fate—forced into prostitution and slavery—has come to stand for a nation that has been repeatedly attacked by foreign invaders and oppressed by tyrants. But it is also a gripping love story whose talented and heroic protagonist lives on in the memory long after we have finished reading. And it is a work of literary genius that displays the richness of Vietnamese linguistic and cultural traditions while addressing themes—lust, loyalty, sacrifice, corruption, faith, and justice—that extend beyond any single nation.

LIFE AND TIMES

China ruled Vietnam for over a thousand years (111 B.C.E.–939 C.E.). Periodically, Vietnamese rebels tried to unseat Chinese rule until the tenth century, when Vietnamese leaders defeated the Chinese in the famous Battle of Bạch Đàng River, thus ending a millennium of Chinese domination and asserting independence. Buddhism and Confucianism remained the dominant religious traditions, along with Taoism, and these merged to become a distinctively Vietnamese religion. Classical Chinese remained the nation's official language for many hundreds of years, a period in which Vietnam was wracked by civil war and continued to repel threats of invasion by Chinese armies, often successfully adopting tactics of guerilla warfare.

Nguyễn Du was born in 1766 to a learned and powerful family in the Nghệ Tĩnh province in northern Vietnam. He was well educated. His father had been prime minister under the Lê dynasty, but his father's high rank was hardly an advantage in late-eighteenth-century Vietnam, as the Lê rulers came under attack by the Tây Sơn, a unified peasant uprising that brought the nation together and drove out Chinese and Siamese invaders. Since Nguyễn Du's family had been loyal to the old Lê dynasty, the poet spent the first thirty years of his life struggling to survive the tumult of the Tây Sơn revolution, remaining poor and obscure. In 1802, however, he reluctantly pledged his loyalty to a new ruler, Gia Long, who had suppressed the Tây Sơn revolution and established a national capital in central Vietnam. So began an era of relative peace and national unity.

The writer felt suspicious of Gia Long, who seemed to him an illegitimate ruler, and *The Tale of Kiều* suggests that he may even have felt some admiration for the peasant revolution, since his own glorious war hero, Tu-Hai, is possibly modeled on the rebel Tây Sơn leader. It is well known, too, that Nguyễn Du wrote his great poem while oppressed with a sense of great loss and disenchantment, his family's longstanding loyalty to the Lê dynasty having given way to pretensions of loyalty to an upstart regime. Nguyễn Du's heroine, Kiều, battered by fate and forced to prostitute herself, has long been a folk symbol of what it means to suffer injustice and struggle to survive, but she may also stand for Nguyễn Du's own discontent, resentment, and shame at having betrayed his own convictions to play the part of a faithful official in order to protect himself and his family.

Under the new regime, Nguyễn Du was highly regarded as a poet, but was granted only official positions that had no real power. He became ambassador to China in 1813, for example, but this post was by custom reserved for scholars who had a wide knowledge of Chinese poetry and were not expected to exert any political control. It was on one of his diplomatic visits to China that Nguyễn Du may have come across his inspiration for *The Tale of Kiều*—a prose narrative called *The Tale of Jin, Yun, and Qiao*, written in Chinese, probably in the seventeenth century. Nguyễn Du also wrote other poems, some of them in Chinese style, though none reached the stature of his great verse novel. He died in 1820.

The Tale of Kiều continued to resonate as a symbol of Vietnam's troubled history well after its first publication. When France invaded Vietnam in 1862, some Vietnamese leaders who collaborated with the foreign invaders saw themselves, like Kiều, as victims of circumstance who must bow to fate. They were cast as traitors by others, who claimed they resembled Scholar Mã—a greedy pimp in the story—rather than his innocent prey.

French missionaries had been in Vietnam since the sixteenth century, and the French, eager especially for new markets for their own products, had long been interested in opening up trade with Vietnam. For the first half of the nineteenth century, Vietnamese leaders remained divided: should they ban foreign trade and the Christian religion, or should they welcome wealth and influence from overseas? Emperors leaned one way and then the other until the late 1850s when the French army invaded, intent on establishing an empire that could compete with the British in Asia. By the end of the nineteenth century, the French colony of Indochina had grown to include all of Vietnam as well as Laos and Cambodia. French companies made huge profits from Vietnamese rubber, coal, and sugar, while poverty, disease, and starvation became commonplace for the indigenous people. As late as 1939, 80 percent of the population was still illiterate. Numerous anti-French resistance movements took shape, none of them successful until the Second World War, when Imperial Japan occupied Vietnam and temporarily expelled the French.

Vietnam would remain a battleground for competing world powers through most of the rest of the twentieth century. The struggle for control of Vietnam by China, the Soviet Union, and the United States reinforced the idea that the nation was, like Kiều, cursed by fate to suffer at the hands of others, and those who were forced to flee Vietnam have often turned to the story as solace meant for sufferers and survivors.

WORK

The Tale of Kiều is widely considered one of the greatest achievements of Vietnamese literature. For the first time, the Vietnamese language was on display in all of the diversity of its rhythms, moods, and expressions. And for its contemporaries, the text triumphantly broke the tradition of dominance by classical Chinese in favor of a gorgeous and distinguished vernacular.

Some of the poem's power lies in Nguyễn Du's rich blending of folk traditions and scholarly knowledge. On the one hand, the text owes a great deal to popular oral songs and poetry. Its metrical regularity of alternating lines of six and eight syllables is derived from folk ballads, and one reason for the lasting popularity of the poem is that its quintessentially oral rhyming patterns make it easy to memorize. This meter also differs markedly from the patterns of classical Chinese poetry, which favor odd numbers of syllables (often five and seven). The poem thus transforms traditional oral patterns into highly crafted written form, but retains enough of the feeling of a popular ballad that it is easily reincorporated back into a predominantly oral culture, learned and loved by people who do not have access to literacy.

On the other hand, Kiều is a remarkable storehouse of classical Chinese learning, including over a hundred quotations from the **Classics of Poetry** and other Confucian texts, over a hundred references to Chinese poetry and fiction, and two dozen mentions of Buddhist or Daoist texts. Analogous in some ways to the role of ancient Greece in nineteenth-century Western Europe, classical Chinese tradition was a rich philosophical and literary resource for Vietnamese thinkers. Both Buddhism and Confucianism were dominant religious traditions in Vietnam, with Chinese religious texts exerting a powerful influence. And even nine centuries after Vietnamese independence, classical Chinese remained both the language of official business and the prevailing language of literature. It was in this context that we can recognize what a remarkable achievement it was for Nguyễn Du to take the vernacular language of folktales and ordinary people and transform it into the consummately literary language of *The Tale of Kiều*.

Admirers of the poem have often noted that Nguyễn Du weaves Chinese allusions gracefully into the text without their seeming dreary or pedantic. And for those who recognize the references to Chinese tradition, such allusions lend a depth to the poem. For example, the poet represents his war hero Từ Hải as both a powerful soldier and a lover of music: "Plying his oar, he roved the streams and lakes / with sword and lute upon his shoulders slung" (lines 2173–74). The combination of martial bravery and aesthetic sensitivity communicates itself to any reader, but those who grasp the reference will know that Nguyễn Du is also alluding to Huang Chao, the ninth-century Chinese warlord who rebelled against the Tang court and established himself as emperor for two short years, helping to bring about the demise of the Tang dynasty.

It is intriguing that Nguyễn Du chose a female protagonist for his great poem. In doing so, he drew on his Chinese model, but he also followed in the footsteps of other male Vietnamese writers, who often chose heroines to explore life's struggles. Some have speculated that the focus on central female characters might be a ploy, in a context of strict political censorship, to distract political leaders from potentially subversive political messages: that is, by putting rebellious ideas in the mouth of a relatively powerless character who is clearly distant from the author's own life and experience, the writer could gain a measure of freedom. It was also true that Vietnam adopted a far more liberal set of norms for women than did neighboring China. For many centuries, women had nearly equal rights in matters of marriage and inheritance, and two sisters, the legendary "Trưng queens," had even successfully rebelled against the Chinese Han Empire for a few years during the first century C.E.

At the same time, Confucianism was influential throughout Vietnam and dictated a subordinate role for women. It is possible that oppressed women seemed like ideal vehicles for male Vietnamese writers feeling frustrated at their subjection to unjust political leaders who insisted on strict obedience, in keeping with Confucian principles.

And indeed, some scholars suggest that *The Tale of Kiều* offers a rebellious response to both Confucian and Buddhist ideas. The text certainly draws on Buddhist thinking, including the notion that past, present, and future existences are interwoven, but it seems to reject the idea that living for passion will necessarily result in sorrow and punishment. Instead, the story rewards individual acts in the name of love, and it imagines a woman who remains pure and good despite many lovers—a terrible breach of Confucian principles. Kiều's decision to meet her young lover privately in his room would have seemed unthinkable to Confucian believers, and the story celebrates the worst of Confucian transgressions—rebellion—when it lavishes adoring attention on Từ Hải, a hero so noble and brave, in Nguyễn Du's narrative, that even his enemies are in awe of him. Từ Hải actively redresses injustices rather than passively bowing to fate, and seems much more like a stirring folk hero than a proper follower of the Buddha or of Confucius.

The complexity of moral decision making in *The Tale of Kiều* is clearly part of the story's lasting power. For example, Nguyễn Du does not offer Kiều's agonizing choice between loyalty to her family, who have raised and nurtured her, and loyalty to the young man she loves passionately, as a matter of clear or straightforward judgment. Kiều must reason her way through it, with compelling arguments made on both sides. Similarly, when a victorious Từ Hải compels all of those who have wronged Kiều to come before her and receive justice, Kiều surprises onlookers by forgiving Miss Hoạn, who has tormented and enslaved her. This wrongdoer has acted out of jealousy, Kiều concludes, responding to passionate feeling and expressing a genuine remorse. Given the text's thought-provoking engagement with ethical questions, it is perhaps not surpris-ing that readers have turned to *The Tale of Kiều* not only for the richness of its language, for the fascinating possiblities of its political messages, or for its exciting plot and vivid characters, but also for guidance in the struggle to figure out how to live in the face of suffering and cruelty, divided loyalties and intoxicating love.

From The Tale of Kiều[1]

I

A hundred years—in this life span on earth
talent and destiny are apt to feud.
You must go through a play of ebb and flow
and watch such things as make you sick at heart.
Is it so strange that losses balance gains?   5
Blue Heaven's wont to strike a rose[2] from spite.

By lamplight turn these scented leaves and read
a tale of love recorded in old books.
Under the Jiajing reign when Ming held sway,
all lived at peace—both capitals stood strong.[3]   10
There was a burgher in the clan of Vương,
a man of modest wealth and middle rank.
He had a last-born son, Vương Quan—his hope
to carry on a line of learned folk.
Two daughters, beauties both, had come before: 15
Thúy Kiều was oldest, younger was Thúy Vân.
Bodies like slim plum branches, snow-pure souls:
each her own self, each perfect in her way.
In quiet grace Vân was beyond compare:
her face a moon, her eyebrows two full curves;   20
her smile a flower, her voice the song of jade;
her hair the sheen of clouds, her skin white snow.
Yet Kiều possessed a keener, deeper charm,
surpassing Vân in talents and in looks.
Her eyes were autumn streams, her brows spring hills.   25
Flowers grudged her glamour, willows her fresh hue.
A glance or two from her, and kingdoms rocked!
Supreme in looks, she had few peers in gifts.
By Heaven blessed with wit, she knew all skills:
she could write verse and paint, could sing and chant.   30
Of music she had mastered all five tones,

1. Translated by Huynh Sanh Thông.
2. From the Vietnamese "má hồng," an expression referring to beautiful women.
3. There were two capitals of China during the Ming dynasty (1368–1644)—Beijing in the north and Nanjing in the south. "Jiaqing": name given to the reign of Chinese emperor Shizong (r. 1522–66).

and played the lute far better than Ai Zhang.[4]
She had composed a song called *Cruel Fate*
to mourn all women in soul-rending strains.
A paragon of grace for womanhood,   35
she neared that time when maidens pinned their hair.[5]
She calmly lived behind drawn shades and drapes,
as wooers swarmed, unheeded, by the wall.

　　Swift swallows and spring days were shuttling by—
of ninety radiant ones three score had fled.   40
Young grass spread all its green to heaven's rim;
some blossoms marked pear branches with white dots.
Now came the Feast of Light[6] in the third month
with graveyard rites and junkets on the green.
As merry pilgrims flocked from near and far,   45
the sisters and their brother went for a stroll.
　　Fine men and beauteous women on parade:
a crush of clothes, a rush of wheels and steeds.
Folks clambered burial knolls to strew and burn
sham gold or paper coins, and ashes swirled.   50
　　Now, as the sun was dipping toward the west,
the youngsters started homeward, hand in hand.
With leisured steps they walked along a brook,
admiring here and there a pretty view.
The rivulet, babbling, curled and wound its course   55
under a bridge that spanned it farther down.
Beside the road a mound of earth loomed up
where withered weeds, half yellow and half green.
　　Kiều asked: "Now that the Feast of Light is on,
why is no incense burning for this grave?"   60
Vương Quan told her this tale from first to last:
"She was a famous singer once, Đam Tiên.
Renowned for looks and talents in her day,
she lacked not lovers jostling at her door.
But fate makes roses fragile—in mid-spring   65
off broke the flower that breathed forth heaven's scents.
From overseas a stranger came to woo
and win a girl whose name spread far and wide.
But when the lover's boat sailed into port,
he found the pin had snapped, the vase had crashed.[7]   70
A death-still silence filled the void, her room;
all tracks of horse or wheels had blurred to moss.
He wept, full of a grief no words could tell:
'Harsh is the fate that has kept us apart!
Since in this life we are not meant to meet,   75

---

4. The most famous lute player in China during the Han dynasty (206 B.C.E.–265 C.E.).
"Five tones": traditional Chinese music follows a five-tone (pentatonic) system.
5. An old Chinese custom held that when
girls were fifteen and ready for marriage, they

would pin up their hair.
6. Chinese spring festival when people tend
the graves of the dead and make offerings to
them.
7. Chinese metaphors for the death of a wife
or lover.

let me pledge you my troth for our next life.'
He purchased both a coffin and a hearse
and rested her in dust beneath this mound,
among the grass and flowers. For many moons,
who's come to tend a grave that no one claims?"   80
   A well of pity lay within Kiều's heart:
as soon as she had heard her tears burst forth.
"How sorrowful is women's lot!" she cried.
"We all partake of woe, our common fate.
Creator, why are you so mean and cruel,   85
blighting green days and fading rose-fresh cheeks?
Alive, she played the wife to all the world,
alas, to end down there without a man!
Where are they now who shared in her embrace?
Where are they now who lusted for her charms?   90
Since no one else gives her a glance, a thought,
I'll light some incense candles while I'm here.
I'll mark our chance encounter on the road—
perhaps, down by the Yellow Springs,[8] she'll know."
   She prayed in mumbled tones, then she knelt down   95
to make a few low bows before the tomb.
Dusk gathered on a patch of wilted weeds—
reed tassels swayed as gently blew the breeze.
She pulled a pin out of her hair and graved
four lines of stop-short verse[9] on a tree's bark.   100
Deeper and deeper sank her soul in trance—
all hushed, she tarried there and would not leave.
The cloud on her fair face grew darker yet,
as sorrow ebbed or flowed, tears dropped or streamed.
   Vân said: "My sister, you should be laughed at,   105
lavishing tears on one long dead and gone!"
"Since ages out of mind," retorted Kiều,
"harsh fate has cursed all women, sparing none.
As I see her lie there, it hurts to think
what will become of me in later days."   110
   "A fine speech you just made!" protested Quan.
"It jars the ears to hear you speak of her
and mean yourself. Dank air hangs heavy here—
day's failing, and there's still a long way home."
   Kiều said: "When one who shines in talent dies,   115
the body passes on, the soul remains.
In her, perhaps, I've found a kindred heart:
let's wait and soon enough she may appear."
   Before they could respond to what Kiều said,
a whirlwind rose from nowhere, raged and raved.   120
It blustered, strewing buds and shaking trees
and scattering whiffs of perfume in the air.
They strode along the path the whirlwind took

8. The underworld.
9. Compact poetic form of four lines developed by poets in Tang-dynasty China (618–907).

and plainly saw fresh footprints on the moss.
They stared at one another, terror-struck.   125
"You've heard the prayer of my pure faith!" Kiều cried.
"As kindred hearts, we've joined each other here—
transcending life and death, soul sisters meet."
    Đam Tiên had cared to manifest herself;
to what she'd written Kiều now added thanks.   130
A poet's feelings, rife with anguish, flowed:
she carved an old-style poem[1] on the tree.

    To leave or stay—they all were wavering still
when nearby rang the sound of harness bells.
They saw a youthful scholar come their way   135
astride a colt he rode with slackened rein.
He carried poems packing half his bag,
and tagging at his heels were some page boys.
His frisky horse's coat was dyed with snow.
His gown blent tints of grass and pale blue sky.   140
He spied them from afar, at once alit
and walked toward them to pay them his respects.
His figured slippers trod the green—the field
now sparkled like some jade-and-ruby grove.
Young Vương stepped forth and greeted him he knew   145
while two shy maidens hid behind the flowers.
    He came from somewhere not so far away,
Kim Trọng, a scion of the noblest stock.
Born into wealth and talent, he'd received
his wit from heaven, a scholar's trade from men.   150
Manner and mien set him above the crowd:
he studied books indoors, lived high abroad.
Since birth he'd always called this region home—
he and young Vương were classmates at their school.
    His neighbors' fame had spread and reached his ear: 155
two beauties locked in their Bronze Sparrow Tower![2]
But, as if hills and streams had barred the way,
he had long sighed and dreamt of them, in vain.
How lucky, in this season of new leaves,
to roam about and find his yearned-for flowers!   160
He caught a fleeting glimpse of both afar:
spring orchid, autumn mum—a gorgeous pair!
    Beautiful girl and talented young man—
what stirred their hearts their eyes still dared not say.
They hovered, rapture-bound, 'tween wake and dream;   165
they could not stay, nor would they soon depart.
The dusk of sunset prompted thoughts of gloom—
he left, and longingly she watched him go.
Below a stream flowed clear, and by the bridge
a twilit willow rustled threads of silk.   170

1. Ancient poetic form with a five-word meter.
2. In the Three Kingdoms period of Chinese
history (220–280), the heroic leader Cao Cao
tried to capture two beautiful sisters from his
enemies and lock them in his palace, the
Bronze Sparrow Tower, but was defeated by a
young commander named Zhou Yu.

When Kiều got back behind her flowered drapes,
the sun had set, the curfew gong had rung.
Outside the window, squinting, peeped the moon—
gold spilled on waves, trees shadowed all the yard.
East drooped a red camellia, toward the next house: 175
as dewdrops fell, the spring branch bent and bowed.
   Alone, in silence, she beheld the moon,
her heart a raveled coil of hopes and fears.
"Lower than that no person could be brought!
It's just a bauble then, the glittering life.   180
And who is he? Why did we chance to meet?
Does fate intend some tie between us two?"
Her bosom heaved in turmoil—she poured forth
a wondrous lyric fraught with all she felt.
   The moonlight through the blinds was falling slant.   185
Leaning against the window, she drowsed off.
Now out of nowhere there appeared a girl
of worldly glamour joined to virgin grace:
face washed with dewdrops, body clad in snow,
and hovering feet, two golden lotus blooms.[3]   190
   With joy Kiều hailed the stranger, asking her:
"Did you stray here from that Peach Blossom Spring?"[4]
"We two are sister souls," the other said.
"Have you forgotten? We just met today!
My cold abode lies west of here, out there,   195
above a running brook, below a bridge.
By pity moved, you stooped to notice me
and strew on me poetic pearls and gems.
I showed them to our League Chief[5] and was told
your name is marked in the Book of the Damned.   200
We both reap what we sowed in our past lives:
of the same League, we ride the selfsame boat.
Well, ten new subjects our League Chief just set;
again please work your magic with a brush."
   Kiều did as asked and wrote—with nymphic grace   205
her hand dashed off ten lyrics at one stroke.
Đam Tiên read them and marveled to herself:
"Rich-wrought embroidery from a heart of gold!
Included in the Book of Sorrow Songs,[6]
they'll yield the palm to none but win first prize."   210
   The caller crossed the doorsill, turned to leave,
but Kiều would hold her back and talk some more.
A sudden gust of wind disturbed the blinds,
and Kiều awakened, knowing she had dreamed.
She looked, but nowhere could she see the girl,   215
though hints of perfume lingered here and there.

---

3. Bound feet, traditionally considered beautiful for women in China, but not a custom adopted in Vietnam.
4. Legendary paradise, once found by a fisherman and then lost again forever, described by the Chinese poet Tao Qian (365–427).
5. Chief of the League of Sorrow, a group of beautiful and talented women who are doomed.
6. Collection of poetry and songs written by members of the League of Sorrow.

Alone with her dilemma in deep night,
she viewed the road ahead and dread seized her.
A rose afloat, a water fern adrift:
such was the lot her future held in store. 220
Her inmost feelings surged, wave after wave—
again and yet again she broke and cried.
 Kiều's sobs sent echoes through the phoenix drapes.
Aroused, her mother asked: "What troubles you
that you still stir and fret at dead of night, 225
your cheeks like some pear blossoms drenched with rain?"
Kiều said: "You once bore me, you've brought me up,
a double debt I've not repaid one whit.
Today, while strolling, I found Đam Tiên's grave,
then in a dream she just revealed herself. 230
She told me how by fate I'm doomed to grief,
delivered themes on which I wrote some songs.
As I interpret what the dream portends,
my life in days ahead won't come to much!"
Her mother said: "Are dreams and vapors grounds 235
whereon to build a tale of woe? Just think!"
 Kiều tried to heed such words of sound advice,
but soon her tears welled up and flowed again.
Outside the window chirped an oriole—
over the wall a catkin flew next door. 240
The tilting moonlight lay aslant the porch—
she stayed alone, alone with her own grief.

 How strange, the race of lovers! Try as you will,
you can't unsnarl their hearts' entangled threads.
Since Kim was back inside his book-lined walls, 245
he could not drive her from his haunted mind.
He drained the cup of gloom: it filled anew—
one day without her seemed three autumns long.
Silk curtains veiled her windows like dense clouds,
and toward the rose within he'd dream his way. 250
The moon kept waning, oil kept burning low,
his face yearned for her face, his heart her heart.
The study-room turned icy, metal-cold—
brushes lay dry, lute strings hung loose on frets.
Xiang bamboo blinds[7] stirred rustling in the wind— 255
incense roused longing, tea lacked love's sweet taste.
If fate did not mean them to join as mates,
why had the temptress come and teased his eyes?
Forlorn, he missed the scene, he missed the girl:
he rushed back where by chance the two had met. 260
A tract of land with grasses lush and green,
with waters crystal-clear: he saw naught else.
The breeze at twilight stirred a mood of grief—
the reeds waved back and forth as if to taunt.

---

7. According to legend, when the Emperor Shun died, his wives Ehuang and Nüying wept so
heavily that their tears stained this species of bamboo.

A lover's mind is full of her he loves: 265
he walked straight on and made toward her Blue Bridge.[8]
  Fast gate, high wall: no stream for his red leaf,
no passage for his bluebird bearing word.[9]
A willow dropped its curtain of silk threads—
perched on a branch, an oriole chirped jeers. 270
All doors were shut, all bolts were locked in place.
A threshold strewn with flowers—where was she?
  He lingered, standing there as time passed by,
then to the rear he strolled—he saw a house.
Its owner, traveling heathen climes for trade, 275
was still away—left vacant were the rooms.
  Young Kim, as student, came to rent the house—
he brought his lute, his books, and settled in.
He lacked for nothing—trees and rocks, a porch
inscribed in vivid gold: "Kingfisher View."[1] 280
The porch's name made him exult inside:
"It must be Heaven's will that we should meet!"
He left his window open just a crack
and daily glanced his eyes toward that east wall.
Nearby both spring and grotto stayed tight shut: 285
he failed to see the nymph flit in and out.
  Since he left home to dwell at this strange lodge,
twice on its rounds the moon had come and gone.
Now, on a balmy day, across the wall,
he glimpsed a lissome form beneath peach trees. 290
He dropped the lute, smoothed down his gown, rushed out:
her scent was wafting still—of her no trace.
  As he paced round the wall, his eye espied
a golden hairpin caught on a peach branch.
He reached for it and took it home. He thought: 295
"It left a woman's chamber and came here.
This jewel must be hers. Why, fate binds us—
if not, could it have fallen in my hands?"
Now sleepless, he admired and stroked the pin
still faintly redolent of sandalwood. 300
  At dawn when mists had cleared, he found the girl
peering along the wall with puzzled eyes.
The student had been lurking there in wait—
across the wall he spoke to test her heart:
"From nowhere I have found this hairpin here: 305
I would send back the pearl, but where's Hepu?"[2]
  Now from the other side Kiều's voice was heard:
"I thank him who won't keep a jewel found.

8. The place where a man will meet the woman
he will marry, an expression that comes from a
Chinese legend about a man who encounters
an immortal nymph near a blue bridge and marries her, becoming immortal himself.
9. In Chinese Daoist literature, the bluebird
brings messages of love; the red leaf is a symbol of love determined by fate.

1. Kiều's other name, Thuy, means kingfisher.
2. The Chinese city of Hepu was famous for
its pearls, but when too many people fished for
pearls, the supply threatened to disappear;
thus a prudent ruler regulated the fisheries. A
"pearl going back to Hepu" is an expression
that means that something is being returned to
its proper place.

A pin's worth little, but it means so much
that in your scale what's right weighs more than gold."   310
   He said: "We come and go in these same parts—
we're neighbors, not two strangers, not at all!
I owe this moment to some scent you dropped,
but countless torments I've endured till now.
So long I've waited for just this one day!   315
Stay on and let me ask your private thoughts."
   He hurried off and fetched some things from home:
gold bracelets in a pair, a scarf of silk.
By ladder he could climb across the wall:
she was the one he'd met that day, no doubt!   320
Ashamed, the girl maintained a shy reserve:
while he gazed at her face, she hung her head.
   He said: "We chanced to meet—and ever since
I have in secret yearned and pined for you.
My slender frame has wasted—who'd have thought   325
that I could linger on to see this day?
For months I dreamt my goddess in the clouds:
lovelorn, I hugged my post, prepared to drown.[3]
But you are here—I beg to ask one thing:
will on a leaf of grass the mirror shine?"[4]   330
   She faltered—after some demur she said:
"Our ways are snow-pure, plain as turnip greens.
When comes the time for love, the marriage bond,
my parents' wish will tie it or will not.
You deign to care for me, but I'm too young   335
to know what's right and dare not give my word."
   He said: "It blows one day and rains the next—
how often does chance favor us in spring?
If you ignore and scorn my desperate love,
you'll hurt me—yet what will it profit you?   340
Let's pledge our troth with something—once that's done,
I'll plan our wedding through a go-between.
Should Heaven disappoint my fondest hopes,
I'll throw away a life in vernal bloom.
If to a lover's plea you shut your heart,   345
I'll have pursued you all in vain, for naught!"
   All hushed, she drank in words whose music lulled—
love stirred the autumn calm of her fair eyes.
She said: "Although our friendship's still quite new,
how can my heart resist your heart's behest?   350
To your kind bosom you have taken me—
I'll etch your word, our troth, in stone and bronze."
   Her words untied a knot within his breast—
to her he passed gold bracelets and red scarf.
"Henceforth I'm bound to you for life," he said.   355

---

3. Having arranged a meeting with his beloved under a bridge, a young man named Wei Sheng waited for her so long that he eventually drowned, as he held onto a pillar.

4. The leaf of grass here is an image of someone worthless; elsewhere in the poem water plants are metaphors for women destined to wander.

"Call these small gifts a token of my love."
In hand she had a sunflower-figured fan:[5]
she traded it that instant for her pin.
    They had just sworn an oath to seal their pact
when from the backyard voices came, abuzz.   360
Both fled—in flurries leaves and flowers fell,
and he regained his study, she her room.

    The stone and gold had touched—and from that time,
their love grew deeper, more distraught their minds.
The Xiang, the stream of longing tears, ran low: 365
he waited at the spring, she at the mouth.[6]
The wall rose like a snow-capped mountain range,
and words of love could not go back and forth.
    As windswept days and moonlit nights wheeled round,
red dimmed, green deepened—spring was past and gone.   370
A birthday feast fell due in Mother's clan:
with their two younger children, both old folks
in gay attire left home to journey forth
presenting their best wishes and a gift.
    A hushed, deserted house—she stayed alone: 375
a chance to see him on this day, she thought.
She set out fare in season, treats galore,
then toward the wall she bent her nimble steps.
She sent a soft-voiced call across the flowers:
he was already there awaiting her.   380
    He said: "Your heart cares not for what I feel—
so long you've let love's fire burn to cold ash.
Sorrow and yearning I have felt by turns,
and half my head of hair frost's tinged with gray."
She said: "Wind's held me up, rain's kept me back—   385
I've hurt your feelings much against my wish.
I'm home alone today—I've come out here
to make amends repaying love for love."
    She slid around the rock garden and reached
a fresh-barred passage at the wall's far end.   390
She rolled up sleeves, unlocked the fairy cave[7]
and cleared through clouds the path to Paradise!
    Face gazed at face to glow with purest joy.
Fond greetings they exchanged. Then, side by side,
they walked together toward his study-room   395
while mingling words of love and vows of troth.
    Brush rack and tube for poems on his desk—
above, there hung a sketch of pale green pines.
Frost-bitten and wind-battered, they looked real;

5. In the Confucian tradition, the sunflower stands for feminine submission and fidelity; the fan is a symbol of femininity across East Asia.
6. According to an old Chinese song, "He stays at the source of the Xiang. / She stays at the mouth of the Xiang. / Unseeing, both yearn for each other. / Both drink the water of the Xiang."
7. Legendary cave that leads to paradise.

the more she gazed, the more they sprang to life.   400
"It's something I dashed off just now," he said.
"Please write your comments, lending it some worth."
Her nymphic hand moved like a lashing storm
and penned some quatrains right atop the pines.
"Your magic conjures gems and pearls!" he cried.   405
"Could Ban and Xie[8] have measured up to this?
If I did not earn merit in past lives,
could I be blessed with you, my treasure, now?"
    She said: "I've dared to peek and read your face:
you shall wear jade or cross the Golden Gate.[9]   410
But I deem my own lot a mayfly's wing:
will Heaven square things out and round things off?
Back in my childish years, I still recall,
a seer observed my features—he foretold,
'All charms and splendors from within burst forth: 415
she'll live an artist's life, a life of woe.'
I look at you, then on myself look back:
how could good luck, ill luck conjoin and thrive?"
    He said: "That we have met means fate binds us.
Man's will has often vanquished Heaven's whim.   420
But should the knot which ties us fall apart,
I'll keep my troth and sacrifice my life."
They bared and shared all secrets of their souls—
spring feelings quivered hearts, spring wine turned heads.
    A happy day is shorter than a span: 425
the western hills had swallowed up the sun.
With none at home, she could no longer stay:
she left him, rushing back to her own room.

    News of her folks she learned when she reached home:
her feasting parents would not soon be back.   430
She dropped silk curtains at the entrance door,
then crossed the garden in dark night, alone.
The moon through branches cast shapes bright or dark—
through curtains glimmered flickers of a lamp.
    The student at his desk had nodded off,   435
reclining half awake and half asleep.
The girl's soft footsteps woke him from his drowse:
the moon was setting as she hovered near.
He wondered—was this Wuxia the fairy hill,[1]
where he was dreaming now a spring night's dream?   440
    "Along a lonesome, darkened path," she said,
"for love of you I found my way to you.
Now we stand face to face—but who can tell
we shan't wake up and learn it was a dream?"

---

8. Famous Chinese women scholars: Ban Zhao (ca. 45–116) and Xie Daoyun (4th century).
9. Only highly ranked court ministers could pass through the Golden Portal. Officials who were also scholars typically wore jade emblems to indicate their high position.
1. Where the goddess of love lives.

He bowed and welcomed her, then he replaced   445
the candle and refilled the incense urn.
Both wrote a pledge of troth, and with a knife
they cut in two a lock of her long hair.
The stark bright moon was gazing from the skies
as with one voice both mouths pronounced the oath.   450
Their hearts' recesses they explored and probed,
etching their vow of union in their bones.
    Both sipped a nectar wine from cups of jade—
silks breathed their scents, the mirror glassed their selves.
"The breeze blows cool, the moon shines clear," he said,   455
"but in my heart still burns a thirst unquenched.
The pestle's yet to pound on the Blue Bridge—
I fear my bold request might give offense."
She said: "By the red leaf, the crimson thread,[2]
we're bound for life—our oath proves mutual faith.   460
Of love make not a sport, a dalliance,
and what would I begrudge you otherwise?"
He said: "You've won wide fame as lutanist:
like Zhong Ziqi I've longed to hear you play."[3]
"It's no great art, my luting," answered she,   465
"but if you so command, I must submit."
In the back porch there hung his moon-shaped lute:
he hastened to present it in both hands,
at eyebrow's height. "My petty skill," she cried,
"is causing you more bother than it's worth!"   470
    By turns she touched the strings, both high and low,
to tune all four to five tones, then she played.
An air, *The Battlefield of Han and Chu*,[4]
made one hear bronze and iron clash and clang.
The Sima tune, *A Phoenix Seeks His Mate*,[5]   475
sounded so sad, the moan of grief itself.
Here was Ji Kang's famed masterpiece, *Guangling*[6]—
was it a stream that flowed, a cloud that roamed?
Crossing the Border-gate—here was Zhaojun,
half lonesome for her lord, half sick for home.[7]   480
Clear notes like cries of egrets flying past:
dark tones like torrents tumbling in mid-course.
Andantes languid as a wafting breeze:
allegros rushing like a pouring rain.

2. The Wedlock God ties two people together in marriage with a red thread.
3. According to Confucian tradition, Zhong Ziqi always appreciated and understood the lute playing of his friend Bo Ya. When he died Bo Ya smashed his lute.
4. Liu Bang (256–195 B.C.E.) defeated Xiang Yu of the state of Chu and went on to found the Han dynasty.
5. Song played on a lute by the writer Sima Xiangru (179–117 B.C.E.) to win the heart of a young woman, who married him against her family's wishes.
6. Ji Kang (223–262) was a famous Chinese musician and music theorist who was best known for a song called *Guangling*.
7. The Emperor Han Yuandi sent his concubine Zhaojun as a gift to the leader of the Xiongnu tribes, who wanted a Chinese wife.

The lamp now flared, now dimmed—and there he sat 485
hovering between sheer rapture and deep gloom.
He'd hug his knees or he'd hang down his head—
he'd feel his entrails wrenching, knit his brows.
"Indeed, a master's touch," he said at last,
"but it betrays such bitterness within! 490
Why do you choose to play those plaintive strains
which grieve your heart and sorrow other souls?"
"I'm settled in my nature," she replied.
"Who knows why Heaven makes one sad or gay?
But I shall mark your golden words, their truth, 495
and by degrees my temper may yet mend."
   A fragrant rose, she sparkled in full bloom,
bemused his eyes, and kindled his desire.
When waves of lust had seemed to sweep him off,
his wooing turned to wanton liberties. 500
   She said: "Treat not our love as just a game—
please stay away from me and let me speak.
What is a mere peach blossom that one should
fence off the garden, thwart the bluebird's quest?
But you've named me your bride—to serve her man, 505
she must place chastity above all else.
They play in mulberry groves along the Pu,[8]
but who would care for wenches of that ilk?
Are we to snatch the moment, pluck the fruit,
and in one sole day wreck a lifelong trust? 510
Let's ponder those love stories old and new—
what well-matched pair could equal Cui and Zhang?[9]
Yet passion's storms did topple stone and bronze:
she cloyed her lover humoring all his whims.
As wing to wing and limb to limb they lay, 515
contempt already lurked beside their hearts.
Under the western roof the two burned out
the incense of their vow, and love turned shame.
If I don't cast the shuttle in defense,[1]
we'll later blush for it—who'll bear the guilt? 520
Why force your wish on your shy flower so soon?
While I'm alive, you'll sometime get your due."
   The voice of sober reason gained his ear,
and tenfold his regard for her increased.
As silver paled along the caves, they heard 525
an urgent call from outside his front gate.
She ran back toward her chamber while young Kim
rushed out and crossed the yard where peaches bloomed.

---

8. The mulberry groves along the Pu River were traditional places for lovers' secret meetings.
9. Famous lovers in Chinese literature; they appear in "The Story of Yingying" by the Tang writer Yuan Zhen (779–831).
1. According to legend, a girl working at a loom threw the shuttle at an unwelcome suitor and broke his teeth.

II

The brush wood gate unbolted, there came in
a houseboy with a missive fresh from home.   530
It said Kim's uncle while abroad had died,
whose poor remains were now to be brought back.
To far Liaoyang, beyond the hills and streams,[2]
he'd go and lead the cortege, Father bade.
    What he'd just learned astounded Kim—at once   535
he hurried to her house and broke the news.
In full detail he told her how a death,
striking his clan, would send him far away:
"We've scarcely seen each other—now we part.
We've had no chance to tie the marriage tie.   540
But it's still there, the moon that we swore by:
not face to face, we shall stay heart to heart.
A day will last three winters far from you:
my tangled knot of grief won't soon unknit.
Care for yourself, my gold, my jade, that I,   545
at the world's ends, may know some peace of mind."
    She heard him speak, her feelings in a snarl.
With broken words, she uttered what she thought:
"Why does he hate us so who spins silk threads?[3]
Before we've joined in joy we part in grief.   550
Together we did swear a sacred oath:
my hair shall gray and wither, not my love.
What matter if I must wait months and years?
I'll think of my wayfaring man and grieve.
We've pledged to wed our hearts—I'll never leave   555
and play my lute aboard another's boat.[4]
As long as hills and streams endure, come back,
remembering her who is with you today."
    They lingered hand in hand and could not part,
but now the sun stood plumb above the roof.   560
Step by slow step he tore himself away—
at each farewell their tears would fall in streams.
Horse saddled and bags tied in haste, he left:
they split their grief in half and parted ways.
    Strange landscapes met his mournful eyes—on trees   565
cuckoos galore, at heaven's edge some geese.
Grieve for him who must bear through wind and rain
a heart more loaded down with love each day.

    There she remained, her back against the porch,
her feelings snarled like raveled skeins of silk.   570
Through window bars she gazed at mists beyond—
a washed-out rose, a willow gaunt and pale.
    Distraught, she tarried walking back and forth

2. Province in Manchuria, now in northeast
China.
3. The Wedlock God.

4. To play a lute aboard another man's boat is
an expression meaning that a woman betrays
her lover, leaving him for someone else.

when from the birthday feast her folks returned.
Before they could trade news of health and such,   575
in burst a mob of bailiffs on all sides.
    With cudgels under arm and swords in hand,
those fiends and monsters rushed around, berserk.
They cangued[5] them both, the old man, his young son—
one cruel rope trussed two dear beings up.   580
Then, like bluebottles buzzing through the house,
they smashed workbaskets, shattered looms to bits.
They grabbed all jewels, fineries, personal things,
scooping the household clean to fill greed's bag.
    From nowhere woe had struck—who'd caused it all?   585
Who'd somehow set the snare and sprung the trap?
Upon inquiry it was later learned
some knave who sold raw silk had brought a charge.
Fear gripped the household—cries of innocence
shook up the earth, injustice dimmed the clouds.   590
All day they groveled, begged, and prayed—deaf ears
would hear no plea, harsh hands would spare no blow.
A rope hung each from girders, by his heels—
rocks would have broken, let alone mere men.
Their faces spoke sheer pain and fright—this wrong   595
could they appeal to Heaven far away?
Lawmen behaved that day as is their wont,
wreaking dire havoc just for money's sake.

    By what means could she save her flesh and blood?
When evil strikes, you bow to circumstance.   600
As you must weigh and choose between your love
and filial duty, which will turn the scale?
She put aside all vows of love and troth—
a child first pays the debts of birth and care.
Resolved on what to do, she said: "Hands off—   605
I'll sell myself and Father I'll redeem."
    There was an elderly scrivener surnamed Chung,
a bureaucrat who somehow had a heart.
He witnessed how a daughter proved her love
and felt some secret pity for her plight.   610
Planning to pave this way and clear that path,
he reckoned they would need three hundred liang.
He'd have her kinsmen freed for now, bade her
provide the sum within two days or three.
    Pity the child, so young and so naive—   615
misfortune, like a storm, swooped down on her.
To part from Kim meant sorrow, death in life—
would she still care for life, much less for love?
A raindrop does not brood on its poor fate:
a leaf of grass repays three months of spring.   620
    Matchmakers were advised of her intent—
brisk rumor spread the tidings near and far.

---

5. Forced them to wear a cangue, a heavy wooden collar worn by criminals as punishment.

There lived a woman in that neighborhood,
who brought a suitor, one from out of town.
When asked, he gave his name as Scholar Mã   625
and claimed his home to be "Lin-ching, near here."
Past forty, far beyond the bloom of youth,
he wore a smooth-shaved face and smart attire.
Master and men behind came bustling in—
the marriage broker ushered him upstairs.   630
He grabbed the best of seats and sat in state
while went the broker bidding Kiều come out.
    Crushed by her kinsfolk's woe and her own grief,
she crossed the sill, tears flowing at each step.
She felt the chill of winds and dews, ashamed   635
to look at flowers or see her mirrored face.
The broker smoothed her hair and stroked her hand,
coaxing a wilted mum, a gaunt plum branch.
    He pondered looks, gauged skills—he made her play
the moon-shaped lute, write verses on a fan.   640
Of her lush charms he relished each and all:
well pleased, he set to bargaining a deal.
    He said: "For jade I've come to this Blue Bridge:
tell me how much the bridal gift will cost."
The broker said: "She's worth her weight in gold!   645
But in distress they'll look to your big heart."
They haggled hard and long, then struck a deal:
the price for her, four hundred and some liang.
All was smooth paddling once they gave their word—
as pledges they swapped horoscopic cards   650
and set the day when, full paid for, she'd wed.
When cash is ready, what cannot be fixed?
Old Chung was asked to help—at his request,
old Vương could on probation go back home.
    Pity the father facing his young child.   655
Looking at her, he bled and died within:
"You raise a daughter wishing she might find
a fitting match, might wed a worthy mate.
O Heaven, why inflict such woes on us?
Who slandered us to tear our home apart?   660
I would not mind the ax for these old bones,
but how can I endure my child's ordeal?
Death now or later happens only once—
I'd rather pass away than suffer so."
    After he'd said those words he shed more tears   665
and made to knock his head against a wall.
They rushed to stop him, then she softly spoke
and with some words of comfort calmed him down:
"What is she worth, a stripling of a girl
who's not repaid one whit a daughter's debts?   670
Ying once shamed me, petitioning the throne—

could I fall short of Li who sold herself?[6]
As it grows old, the cedar is a tree
that singly shoulders up so many boughs.
If moved by love you won't let go of me.   675
I fear a storm will blow and blast our home.
You'd better sacrifice just me—one flower
will turn to shreds, but green will stay the leaves.
Whatever lot befalls me I accept—
think me a blossom nipped when budding green.   680
Let no wild notions run around your head
or you shall wreck our home and hurt yourself."
Words of good sense sank smoothly in his ear—
they stared at one another, pouring tears.

    Outside, that Scholar Mã appeared again—   685
they signed the contract, silver then changed hands.
A wanton god, the Old Man of the Moon,[7]
at random tying couples with his threads!
When money's held in hand it's no great trick
swaying men's hearts and turning black to white.   690
Old Chung did all he could and gave all help:
gifts once presented, charges were dismissed.

*   *   *

    How to express her grief while on the tower
a watchman tolled and tolled the hours of night?

    A carriage, flower-decked, arrived outside
with flutes and lutes to bid dear kin part ways.   780
She grieved to go, they grieved to stay behind:
tears soaked stone steps as parting tugged their hearts.

    Across a twilit sky dragged sullen clouds—
grasses and branches drooped, all drenched with dew.
He led her to an inn and left her there   785
within four walls, a maiden in her spring.
The girl felt torn between dire dread and shame—
she'd sadly brood, her heart would ache and ache.
A rose divine lay fallen in vile hands,
once kept from sun or rain for someone's sake.   790
"If only I had known I'd sink so low,
I should have let my true love pluck my bud.
Because I fenced it well from the east wind,[8]
I failed him then and make him suffer now.
When we're to meet again, what will be left   795
of my poor body here to give much hope?
If I indeed was born to float and drift,

---

6. Li Ji, the heroine of a Tang story, sold herself as a sacrifice to a snake demon to save her
parents.

7. A name for the god of marriage.
8. The east wind blows in the springtime and
is supposed to bring love.

how can a woman live with such a fate?"
   Upon the table lay a knife at hand—
she grabbed it, hid it wrapped inside her scarf:
"Yes, if and when the flood should reach my feet,
this knife may later help decide my life."   800
   The autumn night wore on, hour after hour—
alone, she mused, half wakeful, half asleep.
She did not know that Scholar Mã, the rogue,   805
had always patronized the haunts of lust.
The rake had hit a run of blackest luck:
in whoredom our whoremaster sought his bread.
   Now, in a brothel, languished one Dame Tú
whose wealth of charms was taxed by creeping age.   810
Mere hazard, undesigned, can bring things off:
sawdust and bitter melon⁹ met and merged.
They pooled resources, opening a shop
to sell their painted dolls all through the year.
Country and town they scoured for "concubines"   815
whom they would teach the trade of play and love.
   With Heaven lies your fortune, good or ill,
and woe will pick you if you're marked for woe.
Pity a small, frail bit of womankind,
a flower sold to board a peddler's boat.   820
She now was caught in all his bag of tricks:
a paltry bridal gift, some slapdash rites.
   He crowed within: "The flag has come to hand!¹
I view rare jade—it stirs my heart of gold!
The kingdom's queen of beauty! Heaven's scent!   825
One smile of hers is worth pure gold—it's true.
When she gets there, to pluck the maiden bud,
princes and gentlefolk will push and shove.
She'll bring at least three hundred liang, about
what I have paid—net profit after that.   830
A morsel dangles at my mouth—what God
serves up I crave, yet money hate to lose.
A heavenly peach within a mortal's grasp:
I'll bend the branch, pick it, and quench my thirst.
How many flower-fanciers on earth   835
can really tell one flower from the next?
Juice from pomegranate skin and cockscomb blood
will heal it up and lend the virgin look.
In dim half-light some yokel will be fooled:
she'll fetch that much, and not one penny less.   840
If my old broad finds out and makes a scene,
I'll take it like a man, down on my knees!
Besides, it's still a long, long way from home:
if I don't touch her, later she'll suspect."

9. Vietnamese expression meaning two con
artists who are well-matched.
1. Reference to the Vietnamese proverb

"Whoever holds the flag waves it," meaning
that those who hold power are free to use it as
they please.

Oh, shame! A pure camellia had to let   845
the bee explore and probe all ins and outs.
A storm of lust broke forth—it would not spare
the flawless jade, respect the pristine scent.
All this spring night was one bad dream—she woke
to lie alone beneath the nuptial torch.   850
Her tears of silent grief poured down like rain—
she hated him, she loathed herself as much:
"What breed is he, a creature foul and vile?
My body's now a blot on womanhood.
What hope is left to cherish after this?   855
A life that's come to this is life no more."
   By turns she cursed her fate, she moaned her lot.
She grabbed the knife and thought to kill herself.
She mulled it over: "If I were alone,
it wouldn't matter—I've two loved ones, though.   860
If trouble should develop afterwards,
an inquest might ensue and work their doom.
Perhaps my plight will ease with passing time.
Sooner or later, I'm to die just once."
   While she kept tossing reasons back and forth,   865
a rooster shrilly crowed outside the wall.
The watchtower horn soon blared through morning mists,
so Mã gave orders, making haste to leave.
Oh, how it rends the heart, the parting hour,
when horse begins to trot and wheels to jolt!   870
   Ten miles beyond the city, at a post,
the father gave a feast to bid farewell.
While host and guests were making cheer outside,
mother and Kiều were huddling now indoors.
   As they gazed at each other through hot tears,   875
Kiều whispered all her doubts in mother's ear:
"I'm just a girl, so helpless, to my shame—
when could I ever pay a daughter's debts?
Lost here where water's mud and dust's soil-free,[2]
I'll leave with you my heart from now, for life.   880
To judge by what I've noticed these past days,
I fear a scoundrel's hands are holding me.
When we got there, he left me all alone.
He tarried coming in, but out he dashed.
He halts and stammers often when he talks.   885
His men make light of him, treat him with scorn.
He lacks the ease and grace of gentlefolk,
seeming just like some merchant on close watch.
What else to say? Your daughter's doomed to live
on foreign land and sleep in alien soil."   890
At all those words, Dame Vương let out a shriek
that would pierce heaven, crying for redress.
   Before they had drunk dry the parting cup,

2. Chinese expression implying that society corrupts the innocent.

Mã rushed outside and urged the coach to leave.
Mourning his daughter in his heavy heart,   895
old Vương stood by the saddle begging Mã:
"Because fate struck her family, this frail girl
is now reduced to serving you as slave.
Henceforth, beyond the sea, at heaven's edge,
she'll live lone days with strangers, rain or shine.   900
On you, her lofty oak, she will depend,
a vine you'll shelter from cold frosts and snows."
Whereat the bridegroom said: "Our feet are bound
by that mysterious thread of crimson silk.
The sun's my witness—if I should break faith,   905
may all the demons strike me with their swords!"
    By stormwinds hurtled under rolling clouds,
the coach roared off in swirls of ocher dust.
Wiping their tears, they followed with their eyes:
on that horizon, day and night, they'd gaze.   910

III

    She traveled far, far into the unknown.
Bridges stark white with frost, woods dark with clouds.
Reeds huddling close while blew the cold north wind:
an autumn sky for her and her alone.
A road that stretched far off in hushed, still night: 915
she saw the moon, felt shame at her love vows.
Fall woods—green tiers all interlaid with red:
bird cries reminded her of her old folks.
She crossed unheard-of streams, climbed nameless hills—
the moon waxed full again: Linzi[3] was reached.   920
    The carriage stopped before an entrance gate—
a woman, parting curtains, stalked right out.
One noticed at first glance her pallid skin—
what did she feed upon to gain such bulk?
With wanton cheer she met them by the coach—   925
Kiều, at her bidding, meekly stepped indoors.
    On one side, there sat girls with penciled brows,
and on the other four or five gay blades.
Between, an altar all rigged out: above,
the image of that god with hoary brows.   930
In bawdyhouses old tradition bids
them worship him as patron of their trade,
offer him flowers, burn incense day and night.
When some jinxed gal drew too few customers,
in front of him she'd doff her shirt and skirt,   935
then light some incense candles mumbling prayer.
She'd take all faded flowers to line her mat,
and bees would swarm a-buzzing all around!
    Bewildered, unaware of what it was,
Kiều just knelt down as told—the bawd then prayed: 940

3. City in China's Shandong province.

"May fortune bless this house and business thrive
on nights of mirth, on days of revelry!
May all men fall in love with her and come
flocking like orioles and swallow-birds!
Let billets-doux and messages pour in! 945
Let clients throng both doorways, front and back!"
Strange sounds that made no sense to Kiều's stunned ears,
and that whole scene struck her as all amiss.
    Once she'd paid homage to her household god,
Dame Tú installed herself upon a couch. 950
She ordered: "Kneel and bow before your aunt,
then go and kowtow to your uncle there."
    "By fortune banished from my home," said Kiều,
"I hugged my humble lot as concubine.
A swallow's somehow turned an oriole:[4] 955
what's my real status I'm too young to know.
With bridal presents, wedding rites, and all,
we did share bed and board, as man and wife.
But now it seems the roles and ranks have changed:
may I beg you to make it clear for me?" 960
    The woman heard the tale and learned the truth—
her devils, fiends, and demons all broke loose:
"What happened is as plain as day to see!
She caught my man alive for her own use!
I sent him for some lass to bring back here 965
and put to work as hostess, earn our bread.
But that false-hearted knave, that beastly rogue
had his damn itch—he played and messed with her.
Now that the cloth has lost all starch and glaze,
there goes to hell the money I put up! 970
You little strumpet, they sold you to me,
and in my house you go by my house rules.
When that old lecher tried his dirty trick,
why did you listen? Slap his face, instead!
Why did you just lie there and take it all? 975
The merest chit, do you already rut?
I must teach you how I lay down the law."
She grabbed a whip, about to pounce and lash.
    "Heaven and earth bear witness!" Kiều cried out.
"My life I threw away when I left home. 980
What now remains of it to have and hold?"
At once she pulled the knife out of her sleeve—
O horror, she found heart to kill herself!
The bawd stood watching, helpless, as Kiều stabbed.
    Alas, were all such perfect gifts and charms 985
to leave this earth, dissevered by a knife?
The girl's misfortune soon got noised abroad—
a crowd came pouring in and packed the house.
While she was lying there in slumber's lap,

4. Scholars often interpret this line as a veiled reference to the new Vietnamese dynasty, which Nguyễn Du felt had usurped the old Lê dynasty's rule.

the bawd just stared and shook, her wits scared off.   990
Then Kiều was carried out to the west porch—
someone nursed her, a doctor was called in.
    Her ties to earth were not yet sundered, though—
asleep, Kiều sensed a girl was standing by.
And whispered she: "Your karma's still undone: 995
how could you shirk your debt of grief to life?
You're still to bear the fortune of a rose:
you wish to quit, but Heaven won't allow.
Live and fulfill your destiny, frail reed:
on the Qiantang[5] we two shall meet again."   1000
    With balms and salves applied all through the day,
Kiều slowly wakened from her deathlike swoon.
Dame Tú was waiting by the patient's bed
to coax her into line with chosen words:
"How many lives can anybody claim?   1005
You are a rosebud—spring has scarcely sprung.
Something has gone awry—how could I force
your sterling virtue into games of love?
But since you've strayed and ended here, lock up
your chamber waiting for your nuptial day.   1010
While you still have your body you have all—
you'll make a perfect match with some young heir.
Why visit havoc on a blameless head?
Why lose your life and hurt me? What's the good?"
    The earnest plea she murmured in Kiều's ear   1015
sounded like logic, sorting right from wrong.
Besides, there was the message of her dream:
in human fortune Heaven takes a hand.
If she died now and left her debt unpaid,
she'd pay with interest in some future life.   1020

                    *   *   *

Summary   Imprisoned and sorrowful, Kiều is urged to escape by a man who declares his love and wants her to escape with him. Kiều starts off, only to find that the man has tricked her and disappeared. She is recaptured and forced to work as a prostitute in the brothel. A scholar's son, Thúc, falls in love with her. They live together for a year. But he is already married, and his first wife, Miss Hoan, has heard of his infidelity. She arranges to drug and kidnap Kiều, forcing her to work in her house as a slave. Kiều begs Miss Hoan to allow her to renounce the world and devote her life to Buddhist piety. She takes refuge with a nun named Giác Duyên, who puts her in the care of a neighbor. The neighbor turns out to be another villain: she forces Kiều to marry a man who again sells her into prostitution.

5. River in China's Zhejiang province.

From V

    Cool breeze, clear moon—her nights were going round   2165
when from the far frontier a guest turned up.
A tiger's beard, a swallow's jaw, and brows
as thick as silkworms—he stood broad and tall.
A towering hero, he outfought all foes
with club or fist and knew all arts of war.   2170
Between the earth and heaven he lived free:
he was Từ Hải, a native of Yuedong.[6]
Plying his oar, he roved the streams and lakes
with sword and lute upon his shoulders slung.
    In town for fun, he heard loud praise of Kiều—   2175
love for a woman bent a hero's will.
He brought his calling card to her boudoir—
thus eyes met eyes and heart encountered heart.
    "Two kindred souls have joined," Từ said to Kiều.
"We're not those giddy fools who play at love.   2180
For long I've heard them rave about your charms,
but none's won favor yet in your clear eyes.
How often have you lucked upon a *man*?
Why bother with caged birds or fish in pots?"
    She said: "My lord, you're overpraising me.   2185
For who am I to slight this man or that?
Within I crave the touchstone for the gold—
but whom can I turn to and give my heart?
As for all those who come and go through here,
am I allowed to sift real gold from brass?"   2190
    "What lovely words you utter!" Từ exclaimed.
"They call to mind the tale of Prince Pingyuan.[7]
Come here and take a good, close look at me
to see if I deserve a bit of trust."
    "It's large, your heart," she said. "One of these days,   2195
Jinyang[8] shall see a dragon in the clouds.
If you care for this weed, this lowly flower,
tomorrow may I count on your good grace?"
    Well pleased, he nodded saying with a laugh:
"Through life how many know what moves one's soul?   2200
Those eyes be praised that, keen and worldly-wise,
can see the hero hid in common dust!
Your words prove you discern me from the rest—
we'll sit together when I sit on high."
Two minds at one, two hearts in unison—   2205
unbidden, love will seek those meant for love.
    Now he approached a go-between—through her
he paid some hundred liang for Kiều's release.
They picked a quiet spot, built their love nest:

6. Now Guangdong, a province in southern China.
7. Tang poem about Prince Pingyuan, famous for his hospitality and generous protection.
8. The place where the rebel leader Li Yuan, founder of the Tang dynasty, took over the throne in the year 618.

a sumptuous bed and curtains decked with gods.   2210
The hero chose a phoenix as his mate:
the beauty found a dragon for her mount.⁹
    A year half gone—their love was burning bright,
but now he heard the call of all four winds.
He gazed afar on sea and heaven, then   2215
he leapt into the saddle with his sword.
    "A woman's place is near her man," she said.
"If go you must, I beg to go with you."
"We read each other's hearts, don't we?" Từ said.
"Yet you act like some vulgar woman—why?   2220
When I can lead a hundred thousand men,
when drumbeats shake the earth and banners throw
thick shadows on the road, when all the world
admires this hero, then I'll take you home.
There's nowhere I belong. If you're to come,   2225
you'll hinder me—I know not where I'll go.
Have patience—just wait here for me a while:
I shall be back no later than a year."
This said, he tore himself away and left—
wind-winged, the eagle soared to hunt the skies.   2230
    Alone beside the window where grew plums,
she passed long nights within fast-bolted doors.
The courtyard moss bore no more marks of shoes—
the weeds ran wild, but gaunt the willow grew.
She peered through space to glimpse the elms back home   2235
and, riding clouds, her fancy would fly there.
For her old parents how it ached, her heart!
Had time allayed their sorrow at their loss?
With more than ten years gone, if still alive,
they must have skin with scales and hair like frost.   2240
Oh, how she pined and mourned for her old love—
cut from her mind, it clung on to her heart.
If her young sister had retied the knot,
she must be cuddling children in both arms.
An exile's yearning thoughts of her far land   2245
entwined and interwove with other cares.
    After the eagle vanished into space,
she kept her eyes fast set on heaven's edge.
In silence she was waiting, night and day,
when through the region roared the flames of war.   2250
Gray phantoms, fumes of slaughter leapt the skies
as sharks roved streams and armored men prowled roads.
Her friends and neighbors all exhorted her
to flee and somewhere stay out of harm's reach.
But she replied: "I once gave him my word—   2255
though danger threatens, I shall not break faith."
    Perplexed, she was still wavering when, outside,
she now saw flags and heard the clang of gongs.

_____

9. Expression referring to marrying a worthy husband.

Armor-clad troops had come and ringed the house—
in chorus they all asked, "Where is our queen?"   2260
Ten officers, in two rows, laid down their arms,
took off their coats, and kowtowed on the ground.
Ladies-in-waiting followed, telling her:
"By order we'll escort you to our lord."
     The phoenix-coach held ready for a queen   2265
her glittering diadem, her sparkling robe.
They hoisted flags, beat drums, and off they marched—
musicians led the way, maids closed the rear.
A herald rushed ahead—the Southern Court
called all to its headquarters with the drum.   2270
     On ramparts banners waved and cannons boomed—
Lord Từ rode out to meet her at the gate.
Turbaned and sashed, he looked unlike himself,
but he still had the hero's face of old.
     He laughed and said: "When fish and water meet,   2275
it's love! Remember what you told me once?
To spot a hero took a heroine—
well, now, have I fulfilled your fondest hopes?"
She said: "I'm just a humble clinging vine
that by good luck may flourish in your shade.   2280
It's only now we see it all come true,
yet from the first I felt it in my bones."
Eyes locked and laughing, hand in hand they walked
to their own niche where they could pour their hearts.
     They gave a feast rewarding all their troops—   2285
the wardrums thumped, the battle marches throbbed.
Triumph proved fair amends for hardships past,
and day by day their love bloomed forth afresh.

     At camp, together in an idle hour,
they talked about those squalid days gone by.   2290
In turn Kiều spoke of Wuxi and Linzi,[1]
where they'd betrayed her, where they'd cherished her:
"My life's now eased of burdens it once bore.
But wrongs or favors I've not yet repaid."
     Lord Từ gave ear to her complete account,   2295
then like a thunderblast his anger burst.
He mustered men, named captains—he bade them
rush off with flags unfurled and race the stars.
Red banners would show all his troops the way:
one wing bound for Wuxi, one for Linzi.   2300
Those traitors who of old had wrought Kiều's woes
would be tracked down, dragged back to stand due trial.
A herald was dispatched to take such steps
as would protect the clan of Thúc from harm.
The woman chamberlain, the nun Giác Duyên   2305
would both be asked to come as honored guests.

---

1. Places where Kiều has been ill-treated.

Kiều briefed all soldiers, swearing them to act:
all, outraged, vowed to execute her will.
Awesome is Heaven's law of recompense—
one haul and all were caught, brought back to camp.   2310
    Wielding big swords or brandishing long spears,
the guardsmen stood arrayed in rank and file.
All pomp and pageantry on ready view—
the grounds lay thick with weapons, dark with flags.
    Under a tent erected in the midst,   2315
Lord Từ and his fair lady took their seats.
No sooner had the drumroll died away
than guards checked names, led captives to the gate.
"Whether they used you well or ill," he said,
"pronounce yourself upon their just deserts."   2320
She said: "I'll borrow your almighty power
to pay such dues as gratitude deems fit.
I'll render good, then make return for ill."
Lord Từ replied, "Consider your own wish."
    A swordsman fetched young Thúc—face soaked with sweat   2325
like indigo, frame shaking like a leaf.
Kiều said: "What I owe you weighs like the hills.
Remember me, your erstwhile Linzi mate?
A morning star weds not an evening star,[2]
but how could I deny my debt to you?   2330
Brocade, a hundred bolts, a thousand pounds
of silver—with my heartfelt thanks take this.
Your wife, though, is a fiend in woman's guise—
this time, the thief has met the shrewd old gal!
Inside the cup the ant shan't crawl for long: 2335
her deep-laid scheme shall reap its fit reward."
    Meanwhile Thúc's face was quite a sight to see,
for sweat was dripping fast from it like rain.
His breast was bursting with both joy and fear:
fear for himself and joy for Kiều's own sake.   2340
    Next came the chamberlain, the elder nun:
to seats of honor they were promptly led.
Kiều clasped their hands, then off she took her veil:
"Flower the slave, Pure Spring, and I are one!
I yet recall how I once tripped and fell—   2345
a hill of gold could not repay your love.
A thousand liang is meager wages, for
no gold can match the washerwoman's heart!"[3]
Both women stared at Kiều in stunned surprise,
all torn between awed dread and sheer delight.   2350
She said: "Don't leave your seats as yet—stay on
and watch how I will take my sweet revenge."

2. Two stars that never see one another, like
lovers or brothers who are separated or at
odds.
3. In the 3rd century B.C.E., an old washerwoman gave a bowl of rice to a poor fisherman
named Xin; later he became one of the emper-
or's highest generals and repaid the washerwoman with gold.

Captains were bid to turn their prisoners in,
submitting proofs of crimes to be perused.
Under the flags swords were unsheathed and raised—   2355
the major culprit's name was called: Miss Hoan.
  Kiều greeted her as soon as she appeared:
"Your ladyship has deigned to come today!
Before or now, a woman of your stamp
is seldom found, one with your heart of steel.   2360
A woman, though, should wield a gentle hand—
more cruelties she sows, more woes she reaps."
  The lady's wits and spirits all took flight—
under the tent she bowed her head and cried:
"I have a woman's mind, a petty soul,   2365
and jealousy's a trait all humans share.
But please recall I let you tend the shrine,
and when you fled I stopped pursuing you.
I felt esteem for you in my own heart—
what woman, though, would gladly share her man?   2370
I'm sorry I strewed thorns along your path—
may I beseech your mercy on my fate?"
  In praise Kiều cried: "To tell the truth, you boast
a matchless wit, you know just what to say.
You have your luck to thank that I'll spare you,   2375
for if I strike I'll look a small, mean soul.
You show a contrite spirit, as you should."
She gave an order setting free Miss Hoan,
who gratefully fell prostrate on the ground.
Now a long string of captives crossed the gate.   2380
  Kiều said: "High Heaven towers over all!
It's not my law that ill be paid with ill."
Before their judge, Bạc Hạnh, Dame Bạc came first,
then Hawk and Hound, these followed by Sở Khanh,
and last, not least, Dame Tú and Scholar Mã[4]—   2385
guilty as charged, how could they go scot-free?
The executioner now received the word:
mete out such pains as fit each broken oath.
Blood flowed in streams while flesh was hacked to bits—
the scene struck terror into every soul.   2390
With Heaven rest all matters here below:
harm people and they'll harm you in their turn.
Perfidious humans who do fiendish deeds
shall suffer, crying quarter all in vain.
All soldiers, crowded on the grounds, could watch   2395
the scourage divine deal justice in broad day.
  When Kiều had paid due wages to them all,
Giác Duyên soon begged to take her leave—Kiều said:
"Once in a thousand years! Is that the most
the best of friends may ever hope to meet?   2400

---

4. All of the characters who have mistreated Kiều in the story, including those who have betrayed her and sold her into prostitution.

Two wanderers will part ways—where shall I find
the crane, the cloud that roams the wilds and heights?"
    "But it will not be long," the nun replied.
"Our paths will cross again within five years.
As I remember, on my pilgrim's way,   2405
I chanced upon a prophetess, Tam Hop.
She forecast you and I would meet this year,
then yet another time five twelvemonths hence.
Indeed, her prophecy's not missed the mark,
once proven true, it shall prove true again.   2410
Our friendship still has many days ahead.
Why worry? Karma still binds us two fast."
    Kiều said: "Yes, destiny can be foreseen:
what she predicts shall doubtless come to pass.
Should you encounter her along your road,   2415
please bid her tell my fortune yet ahead."
Gladly the nun agreed to that request,
then said goodbye and left for other parts.
    Since she'd paid good for good or ill for ill,
her soul's deep sea of wrongs soon ebbed away.   2420
She knelt before Lord Từ to say her thanks:
"Could this frail reed once hope to live this day?
For me your lightning brought the wicked low
and cast a load of sorrows off my soul.
I've etched your favors in my heart, my bones—   2425
my life itself could not discharge such debts."
    Từ answered: "Down the ages have great men
so often found that mate, that sister soul?
And does a man live up to his proud name
If he confronts a wrong and winks at it?   2430
Besides, it was a family matter, too!
Need you bow low and offer me your thanks?
But you still have your parents—I regret
that you should dwell in Yue and they in Qin.
May you rejoin them both beneath one roof   2435
and see their faces—then, I'll rest at ease."
At his command, all gathered, spread the boards
to celebrate the just redress of wrongs.
    Bamboos split fast; tiles slip, soon fall apart:
his martial might now thundered far and wide.   2440
In his own corner he installed his court
for peace or war and cut the realm in two.
Time after time he stormed across the land
and trampled down five strongholds in the South.
He fought and honed his sword on wind and dust,   2445
scorning those racks for coats, those sacks for rice.[5]
He stalked and swaggered through his border fief,
with no less stature than a prince, a king.

---

5. Expression referring to men whose only concerns are their desires and appetites.

Who dared oppose his flag, dispute his sway?
For five years, by the sea, he reigned sole lord.   2450

    There was an eminent province governor,
Lord Hó Tôn Hiền, who plied a statesman's craft.
The emperor sent him off with special powers
to quell revolt and rule the borderland.
    He knew Từ Hải would prove a gallant foe—   2455
but then, in all his plans, Kiều had a voice.
He camped his troops and feigned to seek a truce,
sending an envoy with rich gifts for Từ.
For Kiều some presents, too: two waiting maids,
a thousand pounds of finest jade and gold.   2460
    When his headquarters got the plea for peace,
Lord Từ himself felt gnawing doubts and thought:
"My own two hands have built this realm—at will,
I've roamed the sea of Chu, the streams of Wu.
If I turn up at court, bound hand and foot,   2465
what will become of me, surrendered man?
Why let them swaddle me in robes and skirts?
Why play a duke so as to cringe and crawl?
Had I not better rule my march domain?
For what can they all do against my might?   2470
At pleasure I stir heaven and shake earth—
I come and go, I bow my head to none."
    But trust in people moved Kiều's guileless heart:
sweet words and lavish gifts could make her yield.
"A fern that floats on water," she now thought,   2475
"I've wandered long enough, endured enough.
Let's swear allegiance to the emperor's throne—
we'll travel far up fortune's royal road.
Public and private ends will both be met,
and soon I may arrange to go back home.   2480
A lord's own consort, head erect, I'll walk
and make my parents glow with pride and joy.
Then, both the state above, my home below,
I'll have well served as liege and daughter both.
Is that not better than to float and drift,   2485
a skiff the waves and waters hurl about?"
    When they discussed the wisest course to take,
she sought to win him over to her views.
"The emperor's munificence," she would say,
"has showered on the world like drenching rain.   2490
His virtues and good works have kept the peace,
placing each subject deeply in his debt.
Since you rose up in arms, dead men's white bones
have piled head-high along the Wayward Stream.[6]
Why should you leave an ill repute behind?   2495

---

6. The Wuding River, which twists and turns.

For ages who has ever praised Huang Chao?[7]
Why not accept high post and princely purse?
Is there some surer avenue to success?"
    Her words struck home: he listened giving ground.
He dropped all schemes for war and sued for peace.   2500
The envoy he received with pomp and rites—
he pledged to lay down arms, disband his troops.
    Trusting the truce they'd sworn below the walls,
Lord Từ let flags hang loose, watch-drums go dead.
He slackened all defense—imperial spies   2505
observed his camp and learned of its true state.
Lord Hồ conceived a ruse to snatch this chance:
behind a screen of gifts he'd poise his troops.
The flying flag of friendship led the van,
with gifts in front and weapons hid behind.   2510
    Lord Từ suspected nothing, caught off guard—
in cap and gown, he waited at the gate.
Afield, Lord Hồ now gave the secret cue:
flags on all sides unfurled and guns fired off.
    The fiercest tiger, taken unawares,   2515
will lick the dust and meet an abject end.
Now doomed, Từ fought his one last fight on earth
to show them all a soldier's dauntless heart.
When his brave soul left him to join the gods,
he still stood on his feet amidst his foes.   2520
His body, firm as rock and hard as bronze,
who in the whole wide world could shake or move?
    Imperial troops rushed forward giving chase—
death vapors choked the skies: who could resist?
All battlements tumbled down, inside and out—   2525
some fleeing men found Kiều and led her there.
As stones and arrows flew and whizzed around,
Từ stood there still, transfixed, beneath the skies.
    "You had stout heart and clever mind," she cried,
"but you took my advice and came to this!   2530
How can I bear to look you in the face?
I'd rather die with you on this same day."
Her pent-up grief gushed forth in floods of tears—
she flung herself head first upon the ground.
Oh, strange affinity of two wronged souls!   2535
As she collapsed, he too fell down with her.
    Some government soldiers now were walking past—
sorry, they picked her up, helped her revive.
To their headquarters they delivered her—
Lord Hồ caught sight of her and kindly spoke: 2540
"Defenseless, fragile woman that you are,
you've been war-tossed and suffered grievous blows.
Our plans, laid down at Court, won this campaign,

---

7. Rebel who proclaimed himself emperor in 881 but was defeated a few years later, disastrously weakening the Tang dynasty.

but you did help—you talked the traitor round.
Now all is well that has come off so well—   2545
I'll leave you free to choose your own reward."
   Her bitter tears poured forth, a flow of pearls—
she heaved with sobs, unburdening her breast:
"A hero was my Từ—he went his way
beneath the skies, he roamed the open seas.   2550
I talked, he listened overtrusting me—
the victor laid down arms to serve at court!
He hoped to gain the world for man and wife—
alas, he came to nothing in a trice.
Five years he roved between the sky and sea,   2555
then dropped his body on the field like trash.
Now you suggest I ask for my reward—
the more you praise my act, the more I grieve.
I judge myself a culprit, nothing less—
that's why I tried to end my futile life.   2560
Please give me just a paltry patch of earth
to cover him I love in life and death."
Her plea moved him—the lord had Từ's remains
wrapped up in grass and buried by the stream.

*   *   *

Summary   Lord Hó decrees that Kiều must be married to a tribal chief. During the wedding procession, she throws herself into a river, and her body drifts along until it is found by Giác Duyên, the nun who saved her earlier. Meanwhile, Kiều's first love, Kim, has found Kiều's father, mother, and siblings.

From VI

Kim sent his card and bade Thúc visit him.
He asked his guest to settle dubious points: 2915
"Where is Kiều's husband now? And what's his name?"
   Thúc answered: "Caught in those wild times of strife,
I probed and asked some questions while at camp.
The chieftain's name was Hái, his surname Từ—
he won all battles, overwhelmed all foes.   2920
He chanced to meet her while he was in Tai—
genius and beauty wed, a natural course.
For many years he stormed about the world:
his thunder made earth quake and heaven quail!
He garrisoned his army in the East—   2925
since then, all signs and clues of him are lost."
   Kim heard and knew the story root and branch—
anguish and dread played havoc with his heart:
"Alas for my poor leaf, a toy of winds!
When could she ever shake the world's foul dust?   2930
As flows the stream, the flower's swept along—
I grieve her wave-tossed life, detached from mine.
From all our broken pledges I still keep
a bit of incense there, and here this lute.

Its soul has fled the strings—will incense there   2935
give us its fire and fragrance in this life?
While she's now wandering, rootless, far from home,
how can I wallow in soft ease and wealth?"
His seal of office he'd as soon resign—
then he would cross all streams and scale all heights,   2940
then he would venture onto fields of war
and risk his life to look for his lost love.
But heaven showed no track, the sea no trail—
where could he seek the bird or find the fish?
    While he was pausing, waiting for some news,   2945
who knows how often cycled sun and rain?
Now from the throne, on rainbow-tinted sheets,
arrived decrees that clearly ordered thus:
Kim should assume new office in Nanbing,
Vương was transferred to functions at Fuyang.[8]   2950
In haste they purchased horse and carriage, then
both families left together for their posts.
The news broke out: The rebels had been crushed—
waves stilled, fires quenched in Fujian and Zhejiang.[9]
Informed, Kim thereupon requested Vương   2955
to help him look for Kiều along the way.
When they both reached Hangzhou,[1] they could obtain
precise and proven facts about her fate.
This they were told: "One day, the fight was joined.
Từ, ambushed, fell a martyr on the field.   2960
Kiều's signal service earned her no reward:
by force they made her wed a tribal chief.
She drowned that body fine as jade, as pearl:
the Qiantang river has become her grave."
    Ah, torn asunder not to meet again!   2965
They all were thriving—she had died foul death.

    To rest her soul, they set her tablet up,
installed an altar on the riverbank.
The tide cast wave on silver-crested wave:
gazing, all pictured how the bird had dropped.   2970
Deep love, a sea of griefs—so strange a fate!
Where had it strayed, the bird's disconsolate soul?[2]
    How queerly fortune's wheel will turn and spin!
Giác Duyên now somehow happened by the spot.
She saw the tablet, read the written name.   2975
She cried, astonished: "Who are you, my friends?
Are you perchance some kith or kin of hers?
But she's alive! Why all these mourning rites?"

8. City in Zhejiang province.   daughter of an emperor drowned, her soul
9. Provinces on the coast of southeast China. turned into a bird that dropped stones into the
1. A major city in Zhejiang province.   sea in a struggle to fill it all up.
2. According to a Chinese legend, when the

They heard the news and nearly fell with shock.
All mobbed her, talked away, asked this and that: 2980
"Her husband here, her parents over there,
and there her sister, brother, and his wife.
From truthful sources we heard of her death,
but now you tell us this amazing news!"
"Karma drew us together," said the nun, 2985
"first at Linzi, and next by the Qiantang.
When she would drown her beauteous body there,
I stood at hand and brought her safe to shore.
She's made her home within the Bodhi gate—
our grass-roofed cloister's not too far from here. 2990
At Buddha's feet calm days go round and round,
but her mind's eye still fastens on her home."
At what was heard all faces glowed and beamed:
could any bliss on earth exceed this joy?
The leaf had left its grove—since that dark day, 2995
they'd vainly searched all streams and scanned all clouds.
The rose had fallen, its sweet scent had failed:
they might see her in afterworlds, not here.
She'd gone the way of night, they dwelt with day—
now, back from those Nine Springs,[3] she walked on earth! 3000
All knelt and bowed their thanks to old Giác Duyên,
then in a group they followed on her heels.
They cut and cleared their way through reed and rush,
their loving hearts half doubting yet her word.
By twists and turns they edged along the shore, 3005
pushed past that jungle, reached the Buddha's shrine.
In a loud voice, the nun Giác Duyên called Kiều,
and from an inner room she hurried out.
She glanced and saw her folks—they all were here:
Father looked still quite strong, and Mother spry: 3010
both sister Vân and brother Quan grown up:
and over there was Kim, her love of yore.
Could she believe this moment, what it seemed?
Was she now dreaming open-eyed, awake?
Tear-pearls dropped one by one and damped her smock— 3015
she felt such joy and grief, such grief and joy.
She cast herself upon her mother's knees
and, weeping, told of all she had endured:
"Since I set out to wander through strange lands,
a wave-tossed fern, some fifteen years have passed. 3020
I sought to end it in the river's mud—
who could have hoped to see you all on earth?"
The parents held her hands, admired her face:
that face had not much changed since she left home.
The moon, the flower, lashed by wind and rain 3025
for all that time, had lost some of its glow.
What scale could ever weigh their happiness?

3. The underworld.

Present and past, so much they talked about!
The two young ones kept asking this or that
while Kim looked on, his sorrow turned to joy.   3030
Before the Buddha's altar all knelt down
and for Kiều's resurrection offered thanks.
    At once they ordered sedans decked with flowers—
old Vương bade Kiều be carried home with them.
"I'm nothing but a fallen flower," she said.   3035
"I drank of gall and wormwood half my life.
I thought to die on waves beneath the clouds—
how could my heart nurse hopes to see this day?
Yet I've survived and met you all again,
and slaked the thirst that long has parched my soul.   3040
This cloister's now my refuge in the wilds—
to live with grass and trees befits my age.
I'm used to salt and greens in Dhyana⁴ fare:
I've grown to love the drab of Dhyana garb.
Within my heart the fire of lust is quenched—   3045
why should I roll again in worldly dust?
What good is that, a purpose half achieved?
To nunhood vowed, I'll stay here till the end.
I owe to her who saved me sea-deep debts—
how can I cut my bonds with her and leave?"   3050
    Old Vương exclaimed: "Other times, other tides!
Even a saint must bow to circumstance.
You worship gods and Buddhas—who'll discharge
a daughter's duties, keep a lover's vows?
High Heaven saved your life—we'll build a shrine   3055
and have our Reverend come, live there near us."
Heeding her father's word, Kiều had to yield:
she took her leave of cloister and old nun.
    The group returned to Kim's own yamen where,
for their reunion, they all held a feast.   3060
After mum wine instilled a mellow mood,
Vân rose and begged to air a thought or two:
"It's Heaven's own design that lovers meet,
so Kim and Kiều did meet and swear their troth.
Then, over peaceful earth wild billows swept,   3065
and in my sister's place I wedded him.
Amber and mustard seed, lodestone and pin!⁵
Besides, 'when blood is split, the gut turns soft.'⁶
Day after day, we hoped and prayed for Kiều
with so much love and grief these fifteen years.   3070
But now the mirror cracked is whole again:
wise Heaven's put her back where she belongs.
She still loves him and, luckily, still has him—

4. The Buddhist practice of meditation.
5. Expression referring to objects that are
irresistibly drawn to one another, as people are
in marriage.

6. Vietnamese expression meaning that when
one member of a family is in pain, all the rest
suffer, too.

still shines the same old moon both once swore by.
The tree still bears some three or seven plums,   3075
the peach stays fresh—it's time to tie the knot!"[7]
    Kiều brushed her sister's speech aside and said:
"Why now retell a tale of long ago?
We once did pledge our troth, but since those days,
my life has been exposed to wind and rain.   3080
I'd die of shame discussing what's now past—
let those things flow downstream and out to sea!"
    "A curious way to put it!" Kim cut in.
"Whatever you may feel, your oath remains.
A vow of troth is witnessed by the world,   3085
by earth below and heaven far above.
Though things may change and stars may shift their course,
sworn pledges must be kept in life or death.
Does fate, which brought you back, oppose our love?
We two are one—why split us in two halves?"   3090
    "A home where love and concord reign," Kiều said,
"whose heart won't yearn for it? But I believe
that to her man a bride should bring the scent
of a close bud, the shape of a full moon.
It's priceless, chastity—by nuptial torch,   3095
am I to blush for what I'll offer you?
Misfortune struck me—since that day the flower
fell prey to bees and butterflies, ate shame.
For so long lashed by rain and swept by wind,
a flower's bound to fade, a moon to wane.   3100
My cheeks were once two roses—what's now left?
My life is done—how can it be remade?
How dare I, boldfaced, soil with worldly filth
the homespun costume of a virtuous wife?
You bear a constant love for me, I know—   3105
but where to hide my shame by bridal light?
From this day on I'll shut my chamber door:
though I will take no vows, I'll live a nun.
If you still care for what we both once felt,
let's turn it into friendship—let's be friends.   3110
Why speak of marriage with its red silk thread?
It pains my heart and further stains my life."
    "How skilled you are in spinning words!" Kim said.
"You have your reasons—others have their own.
Among those duties falling to her lot,   3115
a woman's chastity means many things.
For there are times of ease and times of stress:
in crisis, must one rigid rule apply?
True daughter, you upheld a woman's role:
what dust or dirt could ever sully you?   3120
Heaven grants us this hour: now from our gate
all mists have cleared; on high, clouds roll away.

7. Allusion to ancient Chinese poetry, suggesting that Kiều is not too old to marry.

The faded flower's blooming forth afresh,
the waning moon shines more than at its full.
What is there left to doubt? Why treat me like   3125
another Xiao, a passerby ignored?"[8]
    He argued, pleaded, begged—she heard him through.
Her parents also settled on his plans.
Outtalked, she could no longer disagree:
she hung her head and yielded, stifling sighs.   3130
    They held a wedding-feast—bright candles lit
all flowers, set aglow the red silk rug.
Before their elders groom and bride bowed low—
all rites observed, they now were man and wife.
    In their own room they traded toasts, still shy   3135
of their new bond, yet moved by their old love.
Since he, a lotus sprout,[9] first met with her,
a fresh peach bud, fifteen full years had fled.
To fall in love, to part, to reunite—
both felt mixed grief and joy as rose the moon.   3140
    The hour was late—the curtain dropped its fringe:
under the light gleamed her peach-blossom cheeks.
Two lovers met again—out of the past,
a bee, a flower constant in their love.
    "I've made my peace with my own fate," she said.   3145
"What can this cast-off body be good for?
I thought of your devotion to our past—
to please you, I went through those wedding rites.
But how ashamed I felt in my own heart,
lending a brazen front to all that show!   3150
Don't go beyond the outward marks of love—
perhaps, I might then look you in the face.
But if you want to get what they all want,
glean scent from dirt, or pluck a wilting flower,
then we'll flaunt filth, put on a foul display,   3155
and only hate, not love, will then remain.
When you make love and I feel only shame,
then rank betrayal's better than such love.
If you must give your clan a rightful heir,
you have my sister—there's no need for me.   3160
What little chastity I may have saved,
am I to fling it under trampling feet?
More tender feelings pour from both our hearts—
why toy and crumple up a faded flower?"
    "An oath bound us together," he replied.   3165
"We split, like fish to sea and bird to sky.
Through your long exile how I grieved for you!
Breaking your troth, you must have suffered so.

---

8. Xiao, a man who lived during the Tang dynasty, was married to a woman named Luzhu; when a high-ranking official took Luzhu as his concubine, she refused to acknowledge her husband when she passed him in the street.
9. In Chinese poetry the lotus often symbolizes love.

We loved each other, risked our lives, braved death—
now we two meet again, still deep in love.   3170
The willow in mid-spring still has green leaves—
I thought you still attached to human love.
But no more dust stains your clear mirror now:
your vow can't but increase my high regard.
If I long searched the sea for my lost pin,[1]   3175
it was true love, not lust, that urged me on.
We're back together now, beneath one roof:
to live in concord, need two share one bed?"
        Kiều pinned her hair and straightened up her gown,
then knelt to touch her head in gratitude: 3180
"If ever my soiled body's cleansed of stains,
I'll thank a gentleman, a noble soul.
The words you spoke came from a kindred heart:
no truer empathy between two souls.
A home, a refuge—what won't you give me?   3185
My honor lives again as of tonight."
        Their hands unclasped, then clasped and clasped again—
now he esteemed her, loved her all the more.
They lit another candle up, refilled
the incense urn, then drank to their new joy.   3190
His old desire for her came flooding back—
he softly asked about her luting skill.
"Those strings of silk entangled me," she said,
"in sundry woes which haven't ceased till now.
Alas, what's done regrets cannot undo—   3195
but I'll obey your wish just one more time."
        Her elfin fingers danced and swept the strings—
sweet strains made waves with curls of scentwood smoke.
Who sang this hymn to life and peace on earth?
Was it a butterfly or Master Zhuang?[2]   3200
And who poured forth this rhapsody of love?
The king of Shu or just a cuckoo-bird?[3]
Clear notes like pearls dropped in a moon-lit bay.
Warm notes like crystals of new Lantian jade.[4]
        His ears drank in all five tones of the scale—   3205
all sounds which stirred his heart and thrilled his soul.
"Whose hand is playing that old tune?" he asked.
"What sounded once so sad now sounds so gay!
It's from within that joy or sorrow comes—
have bitter days now set and sweet ones dawned?"   3210
"This pleasant little pastime," answered she,
"once earned me grief and woe for many years.

1. Vietnamese equivalent of searching for a
needle in a haystack.
2. The Daoist master Zhuang Zhou, who does
not know whether he is really a man dreaming
of being a butterfly or a butterfly dreaming of
being a man.
3. Wangdi, the king of Shu, turned into a
cuckoo when he was found to be having an
affair with his minister's wife.
4. In Shaanxi, Mount Lantian (meaning "blue
field") is famous for its jade.

For you my lute just sang its one last song—
henceforth, I'll roll its strings and play no more."
    The secrets of their hearts were flowing still   3215
when cocks crowed up the morning in the east.
Kim spoke, told all about their private pact.
All marveled at her wish and lauded her—
a woman of high mind, not some coquette
who'd with her favors skip from man to man.   3220
    Of love and friendship they fulfilled both claims—
they shared no bed but joys of lute and verse.
Now they sipped wine, now played a game of chess,
admiring flowers, waiting for the moon.
Their wishes all came true since fate so willed,   3225
and of two lovers marriage made two friends.
    As pledged, they built a temple on a hill,
then sent a trusted man to fetch the nun.
When he got there, he found doors shut and barred—
he saw a weed-grown rooftop, moss-filled cracks.   3230
She'd gone to gather simples, he was told:
the cloud had flown, the crane had fled—but where?
For old times' sake, Kiều kept the temple lit,
its incense candles burning night and day.
    The twice-blessed home enjoyed both weal and wealth.   3235
Kim climbed the office ladder year by year.
Vân gave him many heirs: a stooping tree,
a yardful of sophoras and cassia shrubs.[5]
In rank or riches who could rival them?
Their garden throve, won glory for all times.   3240

    This we have learned: with Heaven rest all things.
Heaven appoints each human to a place.
If doomed to roll in dust, we'll roll in dust;
we'll sit on high when destined for high seats.
Does Heaven ever favor anyone,   3245
bestowing both rare talent and good luck?
In talent take no overweening pride,
for talent and disaster form a pair.[6]
Our karma we must carry as our lot—
let's stop decrying Heaven's whims and quirks.   3250
Inside ourselves there lies the root of good:
the heart outweighs all talents on this earth.

    May these crude words, culled one by one and strung,
beguile an hour or two of your long night.

---

5. Plants symbolizing sons who will become officials and scholars.

6. The words for "talent" and "disaster" rhyme in both Chinese and Vietnamese.

GHALIB

1797–1869

Ghalib is probably the most frequently quoted poet of the nineteenth and twentieth centuries in India
and Pakistan, where tens of millions of
people know some of his Urdu poems by
heart. His popularity, which has only
grown since his death nearly a century
and a half ago, is especially remarkable
given the complexity of his work. Despite
the fact that he is a difficult poet, his
phrases, images, and ideas have become
part of the common speech of Urdu and
Hindi, which are closely interrelated languages. He wrote haunting love poems
in a style that still seems contemporary,
and his words and emotions are on the
lips of lovers young and old everywhere
on the subcontinent.

LIFE AND TIMES

India in the nineteenth century passed
from one vast imperial power to another.
The Mughal Empire, which at its height
commanded 100 million people, had
once boasted great wealth and military
might. Babur (1483–1530), the first
Mughal emperor, had brought with him
rich traditions of Persian art and literature as well as his Islamic faith to create
a new dynasty that would rule over the
Hindu majority in India for three centuries. His grandson, the great Emperor
Akbar, established a well-organized
bureaucracy and permitted multiple
religions to flourish, allowing Hindus to
serve as generals and administrators.

The British arrived in India during
Akbar's reign. As Indian tea, cotton, silk,
spices, and opium flowed into Britain,
consumers there developed a growing
appetite for Indian products. The profits

of British companies soared. The French
and the Dutch competed for the same
goods, and tensions rose between European contenders for the Indian market.
These hostilities would last until 1757,
when the British defeated the French in
battle and seized control of European
trade with the entire subcontinent.

While the Europeans struggled for
Indian markets, Akbar and his successors expanded the territory under
Mughal control, bringing almost the
entire Indian peninsula into the hands
of the Mughals by the late seventeenth
century. Their grand capital was Delhi,
where they gathered the works of skilled
artists in luxurious palaces. The majestic
Taj Mahal, built in 1648 as the mausoleum for the favorite wife of Mughal
emperor Shah Jahan, captures the sump-
tuousness and grandeur of this period
in Indian history. To European visitors,
the enviably powerful Mughal Empire
seemed home to untold riches.

In the seventeenth century, Emperor
Aurangzeb, a devout Muslim who dismounted from his horse in the thick of
battle to recite his evening prayers,
pushed to expand the empire and
succeeded—but only by stretching his
resources to the point of collapse. Some
Hindu kingdoms continued to resist
Mughal control, and by the middle of
the eighteenth century they had helped
to weaken the empire. Attacks on Delhi
by the Hindu Marathas, as well as foreign invaders from Persia and Afghanistan, further exhausted the regime.

As the Mughal Empire weakened, the
British East India Company gradually
assumed more and more military and
administrative power. In 1804, the East

India Company officially took control of India. At first, the British tended to leave local leaders in place rather than getting involved in direct administration; they did not try to convert Indians to Christianity. Over the course of the nineteenth century, however, the nature of British control over India underwent a major shift. A new generation of British career men, feeling superior to the Indians, began a campaign to impose their own moral, linguistic, and cultural traditions on India. Christian missionaries arrived in ever larger numbers, and increasingly the British back home were whipped into an enthusiasm for advancing the "backward" peoples of India. Ironically, it was partly thanks to British imperialism that the Indians could be seen as backward in the first place. India had once had a thriving economy based on beautiful textiles—in 1700 it had been the leading exporter of woven cloth—but Britain's cheap factory-made textiles and its demand for raw materials from India had forced many workers back into a peasant-based rural economy.

Born in Agra in December 1797, Asadullah Khan—later known by his literary pseudonym, Ghalib ("Conqueror" in Persian and Urdu)—was a descendant of Turkish military settlers in north India. His grandfather as well as his father and an uncle, who ranked as minor nobles in the Muslim ruling class of the nineteenth century, served in the Mughal emperor's army. After his father died, when he was five, and his uncle, who then supported the extended family, died only three years later, Ghalib was raised mostly among his mother's relatives. When he was thirteen, his family (then in financial decline) arranged his marriage to an eleven-year-old girl from a wealthier segment of the nobility. In 1810 he moved to Delhi, where the young couple lived in comfortable circumstances with support from her family, a dependence that was to continue for the rest of his life. The young poet, who had begun to write

Urdu verse and prose at seven and in Persian by the age of nine, matured rapidly in the next few years, completing a significant portion of his oeuvre of Urdu poetry by 1816, when he was nineteen.

However, in 1822, partly in response to widespread incomprehension and criticism of his early poetry, Ghalib stopped writing verse in Urdu and switched to Persian as his only poetic medium—a practice he adhered to until 1850. Persian had been the premier literary language of Muslim society across Asia for much of the preceding seven or eight hundred years; and, since the end of the sixteenth century, it had also been the official imperial language of the subcontinent under the Mughals. By the 1840s Ghalib had produced a large body of poetry and prose in Persian, and he had become a prominent Indian authority on the language and its literature.

Despite his renown, much of Ghalib's adult life was marked by bitter disappointments. He spent most of the 1820s unsuccessfully seeking an aristocratic patron near Delhi; in 1827–30, he tried in vain to secure a British pension in Calcutta; and in 1842 he failed to get a position as Persian instructor at Delhi College, a new British-Indian institution. Ghalib's public humiliations reached a peak in 1847, when he was arrested for gambling in his home and imprisoned for three months. His personal and family life also proved to be deeply unhappy during this period. He and his wife had seven children, but none survived beyond the age of fifteen months, a cycle of tragedies that contributed to the couple's emotional alienation from each other. In the 1840s Ghalib adopted his wife's adult nephew 'Arif as his son, but the untimely deaths of both 'Arif and his wife from tuberculosis in 1852 only added to the poet's sorrows. Ghalib's elegy for 'Arif—included here as "It was essential"—remains one of his most famous poems today, a memorable mourning of human mortality and a celebration of family life and familial love.

And yet his deepest emotional relationship—one that haunted him for more than forty years after its tragic end—may have been with a low-caste Hindu courtesan who died very young and whose loss he mourned publicly at her funeral and in his letters and poetry.

The year 1850 brought significant changes to the poet's literary and professional life, and alleviated his financial circumstances to some extent. Emperor Bahadur Shah Zafar—who proved to be the last in the long line of Mughal rulers on Delhi's throne—commissioned Ghalib to write a history of the dynasty in Persian; and, four years later, the emperor finally appointed him as royal tutor and court poet. At Zafar's urging, Ghalib also resumed writing poetry and prose in Urdu, the "mixed" language (combining Hindi syntax and Persian vocabulary) that was the first language of north-Indian Muslims. In the 1850s and 1860s Ghalib became the most sought-after master of Urdu and Persian poetry among Muslim as well as Hindu writers, developing a rich and voluminous correspondence in Urdu with more than four hundred friends and admirers of various faiths across the subcontinent.

The events of 1857, however, transformed Ghalib's life and his beloved city of Delhi irreversibly. The "Mutiny" (now often called the First Indian War of Independence from British rule) started that summer and quickly overtook the Mughal capital, where large-scale violence ravaged all segments of Muslim and Hindu society over several months, first with the arrival of large contingents of Indian soldiers rebelling against the British colonial army, and subsequently with British retaliation. After crushing the uprising and arresting and deporting the emperor, the British administration and British militias summarily executed some 3,000 citizens of Delhi and razed the most densely populated part of the city (now known as Old Delhi), exiling its inhabitants to the surrounding countryside. Several hundreds of Ghalib's fellow-courtiers, friends, acquaintances, and neighbors—Hindu, Muslim, and Sikh—lost their lives, families, homes, or property; and for many months he lived in fear for his own life and the safety of his family. In 1858 he published *Dastanbuy*, his personal account of these events, which asserted his political innocence in the Mughal court's complicity with the rebels.

Ghalib survived the catastrophe of 1857 by a dozen years, but as a broken and lonely man. He wrote some of his best late poems in Urdu in the 1850s and early 1860s, but old age, deteriorating eyesight and hearing, and long illness increasingly confined him to his dilapidated home in Delhi; much of this is foreshadowed in his first poem in our selection, "Now Go and Live in a Place." Despite his personal difficulties, however, he kept up a vivid and generous correspondence with younger poets and admirers, including the close Hindu friends who preserved his works. These letters became a celebrated part of his oeuvre in his own lifetime, when, in 1868, they were collected and published as *Urdu-i-mu'alla*.

Looking back from our own times, Ghalib's life and poetry seem to represent the Indian subcontinent's transition from tradition to modernity in all its many-sided complexity. He was the last major poet to be trained in the traditional disciplines (language, poetics, philosophy, and theology), and to work only in inherited forms, even as Indian society engaged fully with Western-style modernity. He was the first—and last—traditional writer to publish his work in the print medium in his own lifetime (which he did around its midpoint), and to experience at first hand the extraordinary transformation that print culture brings to long-standing cultures of manuscript circulation, by fundamentally changing the nature of authorship, the author-audience connection, and literary reputation itself. He also underwent this experience by positioning himself quite uniquely in the shadowy space between tradition and modernity. While most of his contemporaries confronted the British presence in India from the perspective of a traditional "Hindu" or "Muslim" identity, Ghalib explicitly located himself in a prior synthesis of Muslim and Hindu cultures (or a hybrid Indo-Islamic civilization) that was open to a productive interaction with European culture. His life and career thus give us a glimpse into the unusual "triangle" of Muslim, Hindu, and European cultures intersecting in unprecedented proximity in the turmoil of nineteenth-century India.

WORK

Ghalib composed his poetry entirely in the inherited verse forms and genres of Persian and Urdu, both influenced heavily by Arabic traditions and the literary conventions of Islam. His favorite form in both Persian and Urdu was the *ghazal*, but he also wrote the equivalents of odes, panegyrics, satires, epigrams, epithalamiums, verse-epistles, prayers, and chronograms. The *ghazal*, invented in classical Arabic but widely practiced throughout the past millennium in Persian and Urdu, among other languages, is technically one of the most demanding metrical forms in world poetry. A *ghazal* consists of a sequence of couplets—most often between five and twelve in number—in a single meter; and each couplet is end-stopped, hence representing one complete poetic thought. All the couplets in a *ghazal* have to be connected to each other by end-rhyme; the rhyme, however, has to occur at the end of each couplet, not in an isolated word but in an entire phrase. This "rhyming phrase" has two required parts: a final word or set of words that is repeated in each couplet, and hence serves as a refrain; and a word preceding the refrain that rhymes with the corresponding word in each of the other couplets. The rhyming phrase in a *ghazal*

thus consists of a "monorhyme" followed by a refrain. The following metrical translation of two separate couplets from an Urdu *ghazal* by Ghalib captures this pattern in English, with the repeated word "good" at the end of each couplet defining the refrain, and "more" and "restore" representing the monorhyme that precedes it.

> The beauty of the moon, its sheer
>   beauty when it's full, is good—
> And yet, compared to it, her beauty
>   dazzles like the sun, is more than
>   good.

> When my face lights up merely
>   because she has looked at me,
> She thinks, mistakenly, the patient's
>   on the mend, restored for good.

The stringent rules of the *ghazal* also require that the opening couplet contain this rhyme-and-repetition pattern in both its lines (rather than only in the second one), thus defining the paradigm strongly; and that the closing couplet contain the poet's literary pseudonym, thus embedding the author's signature in the *ghazal* itself. This complicated structure leaves the poet free to make each couplet an entire miniature poem that is thematically and rhetorically independent of the other couplets. At the same time, it challenges him to create a thematic continuity against impossible prosodic odds. In the history of the *ghazal* across Arabic, Persian, and Urdu, Ghalib stands out as an astonishing craftsman who could construct continuous poetic arguments within the strictest constraints of meter, repetition, and rhyme, without sacrificing wit, emotional integrity, intellectual rigor, and range of experience. Among the examples included in our selection, his versatility with the *ghazal* is especially evident in "I've made my home next door to you," "It was essential," and "My tongue begs for the power of speech."

The poems below display Ghalib's

imaginative range and depth in several genres in Urdu. The three poems just mentioned, together with "Now go and live in a place," are translations of complete *ghazal*s, and they capture the recursive structure of the form as closely as possible in metrical English, while retaining the semantic richness of the originals. Of these, "I've made my home next door to you" is represented in two parallel translations, one rendering the *ghazal* as a "secular" piece (a lover's plea and complaint), and the other highlighting the same text as a "sacred" poem (about love between God and human beings); the original conveys both meanings simultaneously, which is impossible to achieve in a single English version. In contrast, "Where's the foothold" is a translation of a complete poem that is composed as a single unrhymed couplet, but is nevertheless classified among Ghalib's *ghazal*s in Urdu. The separate selection of couplets offers self-contained verses taken from a dozen different *ghazal*s, each presenting a complete and independent poetic thought with epigrammatic force. The final piece, "Petition: My Salary," is an excerpt from one of Ghalib's miscellaneous poems, addressed to Emperor Bahadur Shah Zafar, who was formally his literary student as well as his royal employer; in this unusual verse epistle, he sought to improve his working conditions and salary as court poet. Most of the poems here contain "Ghalib" as the poet's signature, and hence they may belong to the latter half of his career; the exception is the prayer "My tongue begs for the power of speech," which refers to him as "Asad," the pseudonym he used often as a young man.

Ghalib's value as a poet also rests on his larger cultural position. In the predominantly Sunni Muslim community of nineteenth-century Delhi, he professed to be a Shi'a; in the midst of organized Sunni Islam, with its mosques, public prayers and rituals, and powerful clerics, he adopted a radical and subversive Sufism in private, as evident from "I've made my home next door to You." He did not practice the five daily prayers or the weekly Friday prayer, did not fast during the month of Ramadan, and did not undertake the pilgrimage to Mecca; at the same time, he conspicuously violated the taboo against alcohol—among the "sins committed" that he mentions in the third piece in our selection of couplets. Moreover, as the fifth couplet in that selection shows, he openly advocated a complete reconciliation between Islam and Hinduism, arguing for a secular merger in shared ways of everyday life. Ghalib was also a universal humanist before his time, as the sixth couplet indicates: in his view, being fully human was more essential than, and prior to, being either Muslim or Hindu, believer or infidel. He actively sympathized with, acted for, and spoke out on behalf of the poor and the dispossessed, and he was doggedly committed to freedom of thought and speech, always speaking his mind tactfully yet forcefully, regardless of his interlocutor's status or power. At the same time, his contemporaries valued him immensely for his personal kindness and generosity: he had a remarkable gift for friendship, and he conducted himself with wit, humor, and dignity even with his enemies. We see all these qualities vividly at work in his extraordinary prayer "My tongue begs for the power of speech," which remained unpublished in his lifetime, perhaps because of its subversively modern message.

Ghalib was one of the last figures in a seven-century tradition of Persian writing in India; while his Persian prose was a model for a few later writers, his Persian poetry (about 11,000 verses) has had little effect on later poets in India or Pakistan, and none on poets in Iran. In contrast, his Urdu prose (in his letters) and especially his Urdu poetry have deeply influenced writers and readers in every generation after him. His *ghazal*s have perpetuated this traditional form among

Indian, Pakistani, and diasporic Urdu writers down to the present; and, just as importantly, they have spread the *ghazal* tradition among other contemporary Indian languages, such as Punjabi, Hindi, and Marathi. Since the international commemoration of the centenary of Ghalib's death in 1969, dozens of American, British, and Irish poets—from Adrienne Rich to Paul Muldoon—have cultivated the Ghalib-style *ghazal* in English. Since the mid-twentieth century, in India as well as Pakistan, Ghalib's *ghazal*s have been set to music and performed, live and in recordings, by many popular singers, and his life and work have been the subjects of several films and a television serial. A century and a half after his death, Ghalib remains a living presence in the two countries that have inherited his poetic legacy.

[Now go and live in a place][1]

Now go and live in a place where no one lives—
no one who fathoms your verse, no one who shares your speech.

Build yourself a house, as if without a wall or gate—
no neighbour to keep you company, no watchman to keep you safe.

If you fall ill, no one to nurse you there—   5
and if you die, no one to mourn you there.

[Be merciful and send for me]

Be merciful and send for me,
anytime you please—
   I'm not some moment
that has passed
   and can't come back again.   5

Why do I complain
about my rival's power[2]
   as though I were a weakling?
My cause isn't so lost
   it can't be taken up again.   10

I just can't lay my hands
on poison, darling,
   and even if I could,
I couldn't swallow it—
   because I've made a vow   15

that we two shall be one again.

1. All the poems in this selection are translated by Vinay Dharwadker.
2. The woman addressed in this poem may be a courtesan, and one of her other suitors would then be the speaker's rival. Like other Muslim aristocrats in 19th-century India, Ghalib frequently visited courtesans, especially in his youth and early adulthood.

[Where's the foothold]

Where's the foothold, Lord,
for desire's second step?

I found this barren world—
this wilderness of possibilities—

to be an imprint   5
of just the first step.

[I've made my home next door to you]

1. The secular version

I've made my home next door to you, without being asked,
    without a word being said—
you still can't find my whereabouts without my help,
    without a word being said.

She says to me: "Since you don't have   5
    the power of words, how can you tell
what's in someone else's heart—
    without a word being said?"

I've work to do with her—I have to make it work—
    though no one in the world   10
can even speak her name without the word
    "tormentor" having to be said.

There's nothing in my heart, or else,
    even if my life were on the line,
I wouldn't hold my tongue,   15
    I wouldn't leave a thing unsaid.

I won't stop worshipping the one I love—
    that idol of an infidel[3]—
even though the world won't let me go
    without the phrase "You infidel!" being said.   20

Ghalib, don't press your case on her
    again and again and again.
Your state's completely evident to her—
    without a word being said.

---

3. Following Sufi mystical tradition, Ghalib often represents the beloved woman in his *ghazals* as an "infidel," someone who has not submitted to the true faith (Islam), and who is also sexually unfaithful or incapable of fidelity. The image is provocative because it suggests that she may not be a Muslim, which is why the speaker himself is accused of being disloyal to his religion. Ghalib may be referring here to the low-caste Hindu courtesan with whom he fell in love as a young man, and whose early tragic death he mourned throughout much of his adult life.

2. The sacred version

I've made my home next door to You, without being asked,
  without a word being said—
You still can't find my whereabouts without my help,
  without a word being said.

He says to me: "Since you don't have   5
  the power of words, how can you tell
what's in someone else's heart—
  without a word being said?"

I've work to do with Him—I have to make it work—
  though no one in the world   10
can even speak His Name without the word
  "Tormentor" having to be said.[4]

There's nothing in my heart, or else,
  even if my life were on the line,
I wouldn't hold my tongue,   15
  I wouldn't leave a thing unsaid.

I won't stop worshipping the One I love—
  that Idol of an Infidel—
even though the world won't let me go
  without the phrase "You infidel!" being said.[5]   20

Ghalib, don't press your case on Him
  again and again and again.
Your state's completely evident to Him—
  without a word being said.

Couplets

1

Ghalib, it's no use
forcing your way with love:
  it's a form of fire
that doesn't catch when lit
and doesn't die when doused.

2

I have hopes,
I have hopes of faithfulness

---

4. In Sufi poetry in Persian and Urdu, God
is often portrayed as a Beloved who torments
worshipers, much as a beloved woman may
torment a suitor in order to deepen his emotional dependence on her.

5. From the perspective of orthodox Islam,
this characterization is theologically provocative; it suggests that God himself is not "faithful" to the faith that focuses on him.

from her—
              she
who doesn't have a clue
what faithfulness might be.

                    3

Dear God:
if there are punishments
for sins committed,

there also ought to be
rewards
for sins craved

but not committed.

                    4

What I have
isn't a case of love
but madness—

I grant you that.

But then it's true—
your reputation rests
upon the fact that it was you

who drove me mad.

                    5

We're monotheists,
we believe in the unity of God.[6]
For them, our message is:
Abandon your rituals![7]

But when communities
have cancelled their differences
and mingled and merged,
they've already converged

upon a common faith.[8]

---

6. The "we" in this verse refers to the fraternity of Muslims; Ghalib here repeats Islam's central claim that it believes in one God and in his absolute unity.
7. "They" and "them" refer to Hindus; Ghalib here alludes to the standard Muslim position that Hinduism valorizes many gods, the worship of idols, and numerous rituals.

8. This is Ghalib's famous argument for a "secularization" of both Islam and Hinduism, in which the two communities, after living with each other for centuries, have already created a shared way of life in practice, and hence ought not to be ideologically pitted against each other anymore.

6

Just this
    that it's so hard
to make each task
look easy.

So too
    it isn't simple
for humans
to be human.[9]

7

There are other poets
in the world
who're also very good:

but Ghalib's style
of saying things, they say,
is something else.

8

Tonight, somewhere,
    you're sleeping by the side
of another lover, a stranger:
    otherwise, what reason would you have
for visiting my dreams
    and smiling your half-smile?

9

I've been
set free
from the prison of love
a hundred times—

but what can I do
if the heart itself
proves to be
an enemy of freedom?

10

Pulling
that image
from my memory—

9. The last word in this verse translates *insān* in the Urdu original, which points explicitly to Ghalib's emphasis on *insāniyat*, literally "humanism" as well as "the set of qualities that render a creature fully human." Like his much younger contemporary Rabindranath Tagore, Ghalib was a proponent of a "universal humanism."

of your finger
imprinted with designs
in henna[1]—

was exactly like
pulling a fingernail
from my flesh.

11

If no one but You
    is manifest,
if nothing but You
    exists, O Lord,
then what's this great commotion
    all about?

12

The news was hot—
that Ghalib would self-destruct,
and all his parts
would go flying!
I, too, went to see the show—
but the promised mayhem
never materialized.

[It was essential]

Elegy for his wife's nephew and adopted son, 'Arif[2]

It was essential
that you wait for me
    for a few more days.
Why did you leave alone—
now wait alone
    for a few more days.

If your gravestone hasn't
worn it down for me,
    my head will soon be dust—

5

---

1. Among Muslims as well as Hindus in India, henna is used as a cosmetic, both routinely and for brides at weddings. Dry henna leaves are crushed and mixed into a paste, which is applied in designs or patterns on the skin, especially the forearms, palms and hands, and soles and feet.

2. 'Arif was a young adult when Ghalib and his wife formally adopted him, but both the young man and Ghalib's wife died prematurely due to ill health. This *ghazal*, Ghalib's famous elegy for 'Arif, also celebrates family life and domesticity.

for I'll be rubbing my brow   10
upon your threshold
    for a few more days.

You arrived yesterday—
and, now, today you say,
    "I'm leaving."   15
I agree that staying forever
isn't good—but stay with us
    for a few more days.

As you depart you say,
"We'll meet once more   20
    on Doomsday."[3]
How great—
that doom will have its day
    on one more day.

Yes, oh yes,   25
O wise and ancient sky,
    'Arif was young—
what would have gone so wrong
if he hadn't died
    for a few more days?   30

You were the moon
of the fourteenth night,
    the full moon of my home[4]—
why didn't that remain
the picture of my household   35
    for a few more days?

You weren't so uptight
about the give-and-take of life—
    couldn't Death have been
bribed and dissuaded   40
from pressing His case
    for a few more days?

Fine, you hated me,
and fought with Nayyir[5]—
    but you didn't even stay   45
to watch, with pleasure,
your children's boisterous games
    for a few more days.

---

3. The day specified in the Qur'an on which
the world will end, and on which Allah will call
the living and the dead to Judgment.
4. Each month on the Muslim lunar calendar
in India begins with the new moon; the full
moon thus appears on the fourteenth night of
the month. In Urdu *ghazals*, the full moon is a
multifaceted image of beauty, happiness, and
blessedness.
5. A relative of Ghalib's who lived in his
neighborhood in Ballimaran, Old Delhi; for
'Arif, Nayyir was one of the "elders" in the
extended family to be treated with respect and
affection.

Our time together didn't pass
through every sort of circumstance,   50
    to seal enduring bonds—
dead before your time,
you should have passed the time with us
    for a few more days.

Those of you around me   55
are fools to ask,
    "Ghalib, why are you still living?"
It's my destiny
to continue to wish for death
    for a few more days.   60

[My tongue begs for the power of speech]⁶

My tongue begs
for the power of speech
    that is Your gift to us;
for silence gets
its style of representation   5
    from Your gift to us.

The melancholic weeping
of those who live with disappointment
    is Your gift to us;
daybreak's smothered lamp   10
and autumn's wilted bloom
    are Your gifts to us.

The blossoming of wonder
at the sights we see
    is tough Love's gift: 15
the henna on the feet of death,⁷
the blood of slaughter's victims
    are Your gifts to us.

The predawn hour's concupiscence,
the contrivance of effects   20
    that follow later—
the flood of tears,
the colours of grief—
    are all Your gifts to us.

---

6. One of Ghalib's most technically skilled, thematically complex, and powerful *ghazals*, which he did not publish in his lifetime and which was discovered in the 1970s among his papers. Written with an almost entirely Persian vocabulary and syntax, linguistically and poetically it lies on the thin line separating Ghalib's Urdu and Persian verse. An intensely personal prayer, it is the poet's most direct and sustained conversation with, and tribute to, God.

7. Henna is a traditional cosmetic in India; this image suggests the death of a young woman, perhaps a bride, in the prime of her life.

Garden after garden   25
multiplies the mirrors
    that fill desire's lap;
the hope that flowers there,
immersed in spring's displays,
    is Your gift to us.   30

Devotion is the veil[8]
that keeps our hubris hidden,
    held in check;
the brow that scrapes the ground,
the square prayer mat,[9]   35
    are Your gifts to us.

Our farce-like search for mercy,
our secretive retreat
    behind a festival's facade—
the firmness of our courage,   40
our sorrow at the tests we fail—
    are all Your gifts to us.

Asad, in the season of roses,
in an arbour that enchants us
    with its overarching latticework,   45
the winding walk, the bracing easterly,
the flowerbed in bloom
    are all Your gifts to us.

Petition: My Salary

The conclusion of a petition in verse,
addressed to Bahadur Shah Zafar, the last Mughal emperor,
with its famous final lines[1]

My master and my pupil! . . .
My salary, agreed upon,
is paid to me
in the strangest way.
The custom is   5
to consecrate the dead
once in six months—
that's the basis

---

8. Islam enjoins women always to remain behind a veil outside the *zenana*, the "women's quarters" in a home; theologically, God is "veiled" from human eyes, as is any form of true piety or "devotion" to God.
9. One of the "pillars" of Islam is the set of five prayers that a Muslim must offer at prescribed times every day, facing in the direction of the Ka'aba in Mecca; since the prayers must be performed, in part, while kneeling on the ground, most Muslims use a personal mat for the purpose.
1. Emperor Bahadur Shah, who wrote verse under the pen name "Zafar," appointed Ghalib as his court poet and poetry teacher in 1854. This poem is a formal petition in verse addressed to the emperor.

on which the world runs.
But if you look at me,   10
you'll see that I am
a prisoner of life, not death—
and six-monthly paydays[2]
fall only twice a year.
All I do each month   15
is take out a debt,
with wrangles over interest
repeated endlessly—
my money-lender has become
a partner   20
in one-third of my earnings.
Today, the world
has no one like me—
a poet of worth
who speaks beautifully.   25
If you wish to hear
an epic of war,
my tongue's a sharp sword;
if you convene an assembly,
my pen's a cloud   30
that rains down pearls.
It's a violation of etiquette
not to praise poetry,
it's an act of violence
not to love me.   35
I'm your slave
and I wander naked,
I'm your servant
and all I eat is debt.
Let my salary be paid   40
month by month,
let my life
cease to be a burden.
And now I conclude
my discourse   45
of prayer and supplication—
my business isn't poetry.
May you live
safe and sound
for a thousand years,   50
may the days
in every year
be fifty thousand.[3]

---

2. Ghalib was paid his salary twice a year, rather than once a month; he compares this biannual schedule to the customary practice, among Muslims in India, of remembering the dead twice a year.
3. The final sentence of this poem, its con-cluding verse, has become the most wide-spread benediction or blessing in Urdu and Hindi in northern Indian society and is used especially on birthdays, at partings or depar-tures, and at life-cycle ceremonies.

RABINDRANATH TAGORE

1861–1941

Rabindranath Tagore, the first Asian to receive the Nobel Prize, won the award in 1913 for literature, specifically for his contribution to poetry. But, by the end of his career in 1941, Tagore had become an international influence not only with his poetry but also with his novels, novellas, short stories, plays, and essays; and his continuing, broader impact on the modern world has been as much due to his other artistic work as a musician, painter, and performer, as to his activism as an educator, political thinker, and cosmopolitan intellectual. The challenge he poses for readers today is to understand how he interwove these roles into a remarkably productive career, and how he combined his diverse talents into coherent individual works.

LIFE AND TIMES

Tagore was born in Calcutta in 1861, into one of India's most famous families. His grandfather, Dwarkanath Tagore, amassed a great fortune in agriculture, mining, banking, and trade in British India, and helped establish such major institutions in the city as Hindu College (known as Presidency College today), Calcutta Medical College, the National Library, and the Agricultural and Horticultural Society of India. Dwarkanath also cofounded the Brahmo Sabha, an influential association dedicated to far-reaching reforms of Hindu religious and social life, which Rabindranath's father, Debendranath, expanded and renamed as the Brahmo Samaj. Growing up in an exceptionally talented family and a stimulating cultural environment, almost all of Debendranath's fourteen surviving children—of whom Rabindranath was the youngest—became notable writers, artists, intellectuals, and civil servants in a late-colonial India that was shaped by this legacy of reformist activism.

Tagore was educated in several schools in Calcutta but rebelled against formal education so strongly that, after the age of fourteen, he was trained by tutors at home in history, science, mathematics, literature, and art, as well as in Bengali, Sanskrit, and English. He spent 1878–80 in England, first in Brighton and then in London, but returned to India after failing to complete a law degree at University College. Back in Calcutta, he published his first book of poems in Bengali in 1880; two years later, his family arranged his marriage to Mrinalini Devi, with whom he had three daughters and two sons. What followed proved to be one of the most fertile periods in his artistic career: between 1891 and 1895 he wrote forty-two short stories, single-handedly establishing this modern genre in India, besides inventing what we now recognize as Indian realism and aesthetic modernism.

A reformist and activist in education, Tagore founded a school at Shantiniketan, about a hundred miles northwest of Calcutta, in 1901; twenty years later, he launched a college called Vishwa Bharati at the same site, which became Vishwa Bharati University in 1951 (a decade after his death), an unconventional "open-air" teaching and research institution that continues to serve as an international model for alternative education in the arts and humanities today. Tagore's two elder daughters were married in 1901, but the next few years brought several tragedies to the family: his wife died in 1902, his middle daughter the following year, his father in 1905, and his younger son two years later. Despite this emotional devastation, Tagore remained productive and innovative during the first decade of the twentieth century, publishing several important works, including the novel *Chokher Bali* (*A Speck of Sand in the Eye*, 1903), and a book of poems, *Gitanjali* (*An Offering of Songs*, 1910), which was the primary citation by the Noble Prize Committee in 1913.

After the award, Tagore's range of activities and influence became truly global, as he visited some thirty countries, including Russia, China, Japan, Vietnam, Argentina, the United States, Iran, Iraq, Bulgaria, Germany, and Sweden. He lectured on the most pressing issues of the time, speaking out in *Nationalism* (1917), a pioneering early-twentieth-century critique of this phenomenon, and he became a moral and political authority in the international arena. In 1919 he rejected the British knighthood bestowed on him a few years earlier, in protest against the British massacre of Indians at a peaceful rally in Jallianwalla Bagh, Amritsar. Even though his health deteriorated in the late 1930s, he continued to write poems and stories until the final months of his life.

Although Tagore's career as a writer was full, it was only one part of his creative life. Over several decades he also wrote more than 2,200 songs and set them to music; unique in style, they constitute an entire genre of modern South Asian music, known as *Rabindra-sangit*. India and Bangladesh would both use songs written and set to music by Tagore for their national anthems. In 1928 he also took up drawing and painting, and produced a large number of artworks in the last dozen years of his life, mostly in graphite, pen and ink, wash, and watercolor; his visual art has been exhibited in several major cities around the world. Moreover, he wrote or composed more than sixty-five works for the stage, including short and long plays as well as operatic works and dance-dramas, and Tagore himself performed in them in India as well as during his visits to Europe.

Tagore's influence on modern life and literature has been as multifarious and far-reaching as his output in many media. In his own time, he became a notable representative of universal humanism, especially of a "spiritual" version of it; seventy years after his death, he continues to be celebrated as a model of cosmopolitanism. Tagore has left a lasting impression in many unexpected places around the world. Modern education in the Czech Republic, for example, still carries the impact of his pedagogic experiments in the arts and humanities. The main waterfront in the beautiful resort town of Balatonfured, Hungary, is called the Tagore Promenade; dozens of artists gather there regularly to paint in the open air. The Abbey Theater in Dublin staged Tagore's play *The Post Office* (1912); James Joyce watched a performance during one of his rare visits to his native city, and he modeled the twin characters Shem and Shaun in *Finneganns Wake* (1939) on the central character in the play.

WORK

Tagore was fluent in Bengali and English, but he wrote almost all his literary works originally in Bengali. In the second half of his six-decade-long career he translated and supervised the translation of most of his work into English; he also wrote numerous book reviews, articles, and public lectures directly in English, and carried on an extensive English correspondence with many associates around the world. He described himself as first and foremost a poet; his language in his verse as well as his prose was always lyrical. The hallmark of his prose style was its poetic and musical quality: it was infused with the rhythms and melodic sounds of spoken Bengali, as well as with the figures of speech and thought that we normally associate with poetry.

Tagore was not a systematic thinker, and he was rarely successful in explaining his ideas and philosophical positions at length in expository prose; but his insights and intuitions ran deep, and he was able to express them in imaginative structures of startling originality. He was equally at home in song, narrative, and drama; many of his poems, tales, and plays display an effortless organic unity, as though they "came to him" fully formed, without needing any conscious artistry or intervention on his part. One of the unusual aspects of Tagore's work is that each of the genres in which he wrote serves a different artistic function, and all the genres together complement each other imaginatively.

Our selection here consists of two short stories, and like many of Tagore's shorter pieces of fiction, they are realistic in style, organization, and effect. The first, "Punishment" (1892), is set in the Bengal countryside (probably in what is now west-central Bangladesh) in the late nineteenth century. It is told crisply from the perspective of a narrator whose omniscience and veracity play crucial roles in the story; and its theme is the administration of justice, in this case in the British colonial justice system. "Punishment," in fact, is the first modern short story in world literature about the legal phenomenon that lawyers and judges call "the Rashomon effect." Named after the famous Japanese art film *Rashomon* (1950), directed by Akira Kurosawa, this is a universal phenomenon: whenever there are two or more eyewitnesses to an event or a crime, even their most truthful accounts of what happened differ fundamentally from

each other. When a judge or a jury has to decide a case solely on the basis of eyewitness accounts, without material evidence to clinch the matter, there is no purely rational way to choose between equally reliable but conflicting eyewitness testimonies given under oath. In Tagore's story, written nearly seventy years before the movie, the problem of conflicting testimony goes much deeper: for different reasons, the various eyewitnesses produce dishonest as well as truthful accounts of a spontaneous murder. When the colonial judge (an Englishman) assesses the witnesses' stories, he has no means of separating the truth from the fabrications, even though the murderer confesses fully in court. The judge then arrives at a decision that is blatantly biased (by class and gender), bringing the story to its famous surprise ending. The narrative combines social realism with psychological realism to confront the troubling questions of what constitutes justice under such circumstances and how we might solve this most intractable of problems.

The second story, "Kabuliwala" (1894), seeks to dismantle the social distinction between biological and surrogate parenthood, and it represents love—rather than biology—as the only validation of fatherhood. The central puzzle in the story appears at the beginning, where the little girl Mini asks the first-person narrator what his relationship with her mother is; what he is unable to explain to her is that her biological father, his younger brother, died in her infancy, leaving her mother a widow; and that, following Hindu custom, he as the elder brother has assumed the role of surrogate husband and father. Given the strictures in conventional Hindu society against widows, the alternative would have been to segregate the girl's mother, deprive her of the normal comforts of home and family life, and leave her to raise the child in stigmatizing conditions. The story famously extends this validation of surrogate parenthood, paternal love, and the rehabilitation of widows within the framework of the extended family by bringing in a second, symbolic father figure: Rahmat, the "traveling salesman" from Kabul, Afghanistan, who comes to Calcutta every winter to sell dry fruit as well as luxury items such as hand-embroidered woolen shawls. A Pathan by ethnicity and a Muslim by religion, Rahmat leaves behind a young family in Kabul during his wanderings; he intensely misses his own daughters, and cultivates a deeply affectionate relationship—based predominantly on wonderful storytelling skills—with Mini. Despite the early suspicions of Mini's mother, and despite even the fact that Rahmat, in an unfortunate moment of rage, subsequently commits a serious crime in the neighborhood, the narrator of the story recognizes him as an innocent and affectionate father figure for Mini, and allows him to meet her even on her wedding day, after his release from prison. Like "Punishment," this story mixes psychological realism with social realism, but does so in order to explore the treatment of women in the Hindu society of colonial Bengal, as well as the related phenomena of fatherhood, paternal love, and surrogate parenthood.

Both these stories are drawn from Tagore's early work, and both represent his writing in the realistic mode. His poetry, novelistic fiction, and plays take us in other directions, but his short stories remain among his most memorable pieces. Tagore is not a writer who fits into the usual model of linear development in which the later writing supersedes the earlier on the grounds of maturity. Since he attempts rather different kinds of effects in different genres, his output in any one genre frequently brings together his best qualities, regardless of chronology. "Punishment" and "Kabuliwala" already display the skills for which Tagore is most celebrated: vivid and diverse characters who come alive in a few brushstrokes and invite our deeper sympathies; evolving human situations that refuse to stand still; problems and dilemmas that turn up in many different times, places, and guises; and insights into the larger rhythms and patterns of life that fully engage our emotions and reveal a great deal about ourselves.

Punishment[1]

I

When the brothers Dukhiram Rui and Chidam Rui went out in the morning with their heavy farm-knives, to work in the fields, their wives would quarrel and shout. But the people nearby were as used to the uproar as they were to other customary, natural sounds. When they heard the shrill screams of the women, they would say, "They're at it again"—that is, what was happening was only to be expected: it was not a violation of Nature's rules. When the sun rises at dawn, no one asks why; and whenever the two wives in this *kuri*-caste[2] household let fly at each other, no one was at all curious to investigate the cause.

Of course this wrangling and disturbance affected the husbands more than the neighbours, but they did not count it a major nuisance. It was as if

1. Translated by William Radice.
2. In Bengal, a low caste originally of bird catchers, but by the 19th century, general laborers.

they were riding together along life's road in a cart whose rattling, clattering, unsprung wheels were inseparable from the journey. Indeed, days when there was no noise, when everything was uncannily silent, carried a greater threat of unpredictable doom.

The day on which our story begins was like this. When the brothers returned home at dusk, exhausted by their work, they found the house eerily quiet. Outside, too, it was extremely sultry. There had been a sharp shower in the afternoon, and clouds were still massing. There was not a breath of wind. Weeds and scrub round the house had shot up after the rain: the heavy scent of damp vegetation, from these and from the waterlogged jute-fields, formed a solid wall all around. Frogs croaked from the milkman's pond behind the house, and the buzz of crickets filled the leaden sky.

Not far off the swollen Padma[3] looked flat and sinister under the mounting clouds. It had flooded most of the grain-fields, and had come close to the houses. Here and there, roots of mango and jackfruit trees on the slipping bank stuck up out of the water, like helpless hands clawing at the air for a last fingerhold.

That day, Dukhiram and Chidam had been working near the zamindar's office. On a sandbank opposite, paddy[4] had ripened. The paddy needed to be cut before the sandbank was washed away, but the village people were busy either in their own fields or in cutting jute: so a messenger came from the office and forcibly engaged the two brothers. As the office roof was leaking in places, they also had to mend that and make some new wickerwork panels: it had taken them all day. They couldn't come home for lunch; they just had a snack from the office. At times they were soaked by the rain; they were not paid normal labourers' wages; indeed, they were paid mainly in insults and sneers.

When the two brothers returned at dusk, wading through mud and water, they found the younger wife, Chandara, stretched on the ground with her sari[5] spread out. Like the sky, she had wept buckets in the afternoon, but had now given way to sultry exhaustion. The elder wife, Radha, sat on the verandah sullenly: her eighteen-month son had been crying, but when the brothers came in they saw him lying naked in a corner of the yard, asleep.

Dukhiram, famished, said gruffly, "Give me my food."

Like a spark on a sack of gunpowder, the elder wife exploded, shrieking out, "Where is there food? Did you give me anything to cook? Must I earn money myself to buy it?"

After a whole day of toil and humiliation, to return—raging with hunger—to a dark, joyless, foodless house, to be met by Radha's sarcasm, especially her final jibe, was suddenly unendurable. "What?" he roared, like a furious tiger, and then, without thinking, plunged his knife into her head. Radha collapsed into her sister-in-law's lap, and in minutes she was dead.

"What have you done?" screamed Chandara, her clothes soaked with blood. Chidam pressed his hand over her mouth. Dukhiram, throwing aside the knife, fell to his knees with his head in his hands, stunned. The little boy woke up and started to wail in terror.

Outside there was complete quiet. The herd-boys were returning with the cattle. Those who had been cutting paddy on the far sandbanks were crossing

---

3. A major river in what is now Bangladesh.
4. The rice crop. "Zamindar": landlord.

5. A long strip of cloth draped around the body; Indian women's traditional clothing.

back in groups in a small boat—with a couple of bundles of paddy on their heads as payment. Everyone was heading for home.

Ramlochan Chakravarti, pillar of the village, had been to the post office with a letter, and was now back in his house, placidly smoking. Suddenly he remembered that his sub-tenant Dukhiram was very behind with his rent: he had promised to pay some today. Deciding that the brothers must be home by now, he threw his chadar[6] over his shoulders, took his umbrella, and stepped out.

As he entered the Ruis' house, he felt uneasy. There was no lamp alight. On the dark verandah, the dim shapes of three or four people could be seen. In a corner of the verandah there were fitful, muffled sobs: the little boy was trying to cry for his mother, but was stopped each time by Chidam.

"Dukhi," said Ramlochan nervously, "are you there?"

Dukhiram had been sitting like a statue for a long time; now, on hearing his name, he burst into tears like a helpless child.

Chidam quickly came down from the verandah into the yard, to meet Ramlochan. "Have the women been quarelling again?" Ramlochan asked. "I heard them yelling all day."

Chidam, all this time, had been unable to think what to do. Various impossible stories occurred to him. All he had decided was that later that night he would move the body somewhere. He had never expected Ramlochan to come. He could think of no swift reply. "Yes," he stumbled, "today they were quarrelling terribly."

"But why is Dukhi crying so?" asked Ramlochan, stepping towards the verandah.

Seeing no way out now, Chidam blurted, "In their quarrel, *Chotobau* struck at *Barobau's*[7] head with a farm-knife."

When immediate danger threatens, it is hard to think of other dangers. Chidam's only thought was to escape from the terrible truth—he forgot that a lie can be even more terrible. A reply to Ramlochan's question had come instantly to mind, and he had blurted it out.

"Good grief," said Ramlochan in horror. "What are you saying? Is she dead?"

"She's dead," said Chidam, clasping Ramlochan's feet.

Ramlochan was trapped. "*Rām, Rām*,"[8] he thought, "what a mess I've got into this evening. What if I have to be a witness in court?" Chidam was still clinging to his feet, saying, "*Thākur*,[9] how can I save my wife?"

Ramlochan was the village's chief source of advice on legal matters. Reflecting further he said, "I think I know a way. Run to the police station: say that your brother Dukhi returned in the evening wanting his food, and because it wasn't ready he struck his wife on the head with his knife. I'm sure that if you say that, she'll get off."

Chidam felt a sickening dryness in his throat. He stood up and said, "*Thākur*, if I lose my wife I can get another, but if my brother is hanged, how can I replace him?" In laying the blame on his wife, he had not seen it that way. He

---

6. In Bengal, a sheet of cloth draped around the shoulders, usually worn by men but sometimes by women.
7. "Elder Daughter-in-Law"; members of a family address each other by kinship terms. *Chotobau*: "Younger Daughter-in-Law."

8. God's name, repeated to express great emotion.
9. "Master" or "lord," term of address for gods and upper-class (*brāhmaṇa*) men. *Tagore* is an anglicized form of *Thākur*.

had spoken without thought; now, imperceptibly, logic and awareness were returning to his mind.

Ramlochan appreciated his logic. "Then say what actually happened," he said. "You can't protect yourself on all sides."

He had soon, after leaving, spread it round the village that Chandara Rui had, in a quarrel with her sister-in-law, split her head open with a farm-knife. Police charged into the village like a river in flood. Both the guilty and the innocent were equally afraid.

II

Chidam decided he would have to stick to the path he had chalked out for himself. The story he had given to Ramlochan Chakravarti had gone all round the village; who knew what would happen if another story was circulated? But he realized that if he kept to the story he would have to wrap it in five more stories if his wife was to be saved.

Chidam asked Chandara to take the blame on to herself. She was dumbfounded. He reassured her: "Don't worry—if you do what I tell you, you'll be quite safe." But whatever his words, his throat was dry and his face was pale.

Chandara was not more than seventeen or eighteen. She was buxom, well-rounded, compact and sturdy—so trim in her movements that in walking, turning, bending or climbing there was no awkwardness at all. She was like a brand-new boat: neat and shapely, gliding with ease, not a loose joint anywhere. Everything amused and intrigued her; she loved to gossip; her bright, restless, deep black eyes missed nothing as she walked to the *ghāt*,[1] pitcher on her hip, parting her veil slightly with her finger.

The elder wife had been her exact opposite: unkempt, sloppy and slovenly. She was utterly disorganized in her dress, housework, and the care of her child. She never had any proper work in hand, yet never seemed to have time for anything. The younger wife usually refrained from comment, for at the mildest barb Radha would rage and stamp and let fly at her, disturbing everyone around.

Each wife was matched by her husband to an extraordinary degree. Dukhiram was a huge man—his bones were immense, his nose was squat, in his eyes and expression he seemed not to understand the world very well, yet he never questioned it either. He was innocent yet fearsome: a rare combination of power and helplessness. Chidam, however, seemed to have been carefully carved from shiny black rock. There was not an inch of excess fat on him, not a wrinkle or dimple anywhere. Each limb was a perfect blend of strength and finesse. Whether jumping from a riverbank, or punting[2] a boat, or climbing up bamboo-shoots for sticks, he showed complete dexterity, effortless grace. His long black hair was combed with oil back from his brow and down to his shoulders—he took great care over his dress and appearance. Although he was not unresponsive to the beauty of other women in the village, and was keen to make himself charming in their eyes, his real love was for his young wife. They quarrelled sometimes, but there was mutual respect too: neither could defeat the other. There was a further reason why the bond between them was firm:

1. Steps leading down to a pond or river; meeting place, especially for women, who go there to get water or to wash clothes. 2. Propelling a boat with a long pole.

Chidam felt that a wife as nimble and sharp as Chandara could not be wholly trusted, and Chandara felt that all eyes were on her husband—that if she didn't bind him tightly to her she might one day lose him.

A little before the events in this story, however, they had a major row. Chandara had noticed that when her husband's work took him away for two days or more, he brought no extra earnings. Finding this ominous, she also began to overstep the mark. She would hang around by the *ghāt*, or wander about talking rather too much about Kashi Majumdar's middle son.

Something now seemed to poison Chidam's life. He could not settle his attention on his work. One day his sister-in-law rounded on him: she shook her finger and said in the name of her dead father, "That girl runs before the storm. How can I restrain her? Who knows what ruin she will bring?"

Chandara came out of the next room and said sweetly, "What's the matter, *Didi*?"[3] and a fierce quarrel broke out between them.

Chidam glared at his wife and said, "If I ever hear that you've been to the *ghāt* on your own, I'll break every bone in your body."

"The bones will mend again," said Chandara, starting to leave. Chidam sprang at her, grabbed her by the hair, dragged her back to the room and locked her in.

When he returned from work that evening he found that the room was empty. Chandara had fled three villages away, to her maternal uncle's house. With great difficulty Chidam persuaded her to return, but he had to surrender to her. It was as hard to restrain his wife as to hold a handful of mercury; she always slipped through his fingers. He did not have to use force any more, but there was no peace in the house. Ever-fearful love for his elusive young wife wracked him with intense pain. He even once or twice wondered if it would be better if she were dead: at least he would get some peace then. Human beings can hate each other more than death.

It was at this time that the crisis hit the house.

When her husband asked her to admit to the murder, Chandara stared at him, stunned; her black eyes burnt him like fire. Then she shrank back, as if to escape his devilish clutches. She turned her heart and soul away from him. "You've nothing to fear," said Chidam. He taught her repeatedly what she should say to the police and the magistrate. Chandara paid no attention—sat like a wooden statue whenever he spoke.

Dukhiram relied on Chidam for everything. When he told him to lay the blame on Chandara, Dukhiram said, "But what will happen to her?" "I'll save her," said Chidam. His burly brother was content with that.

III

This was what he instructed his wife to say: "The elder wife was about to attack me with the vegetable-slicer. I picked up a farm-knife to stop her, and it somehow cut into her." This was all Ramlochan's invention. He had generously supplied Chidam with the proofs and embroidery that the story would require.

---

3. "Elder Sister," respectful form of address for Bengali women.

The police came to investigate. The villagers were sure now that Chandara had murdered her sister-in-law, and all the witnesses confirmed this. When the police questioned Chandara, she said, "Yes, I killed her."

"Why did you kill her?"

"I couldn't stand her anymore."

"Was there a brawl between you?"

"No."

"Did she attack you first?"

"No."

"Did she ill-treat you?"

"No."

Everyone was amazed at these replies, and Chidam was completely thrown off balance. "She's not telling the truth," he said. "The elder wife first—"

The inspector silenced him sharply. He continued according to the rules of cross-examination and repeatedly received the same reply: Chandara would not accept that she had been attacked in any way by her sister-in-law. Such an obstinate girl was never seen! She seemed absolutely bent on going to the gallows; nothing would stop her. Such fierce, passionate pride! In her thoughts, Chandara was saying to her husband, "I shall give my youth to the gallows instead of to you. My final ties in this life will be with them."

Chandara was arrested, and left her home for ever, by the paths she knew so well, past the festival carriage, the market-place, the *ghāt*, the Majumdars' house, the post office, the school—an ordinary, harmless, flirtatious, fun-loving village wife; leaving a shameful impression on all the people she knew. A bevy of boys followed her, and the women of the village, her friends and companions—some of them peering through their veils, some from their doorsteps, some from behind trees—watched the police leading her away and shuddered with embarrassment, fear and contempt.

To the Deputy Magistrate, Chandara again confessed her guilt, claiming no ill-treatment from her sister-in-law at the time of the murder. But when Chidam was called to the witness-box he broke down completely, weeping, clasping his hands and saying, "I swear to you, sir, my wife is innocent." The magistrate sternly told him to control himself, and began to question him. Bit by bit the true story came out.

The magistrate did not believe him, because the chief, most trustworthy, most educated witness—Ramlochan Chakravarti—said: "I appeared on the scene a little after the murder. Chidam confessed everything to me and clung to my feet saying, 'Tell me how I can save my wife.' I did not say anything one way or the other. Then Chidam said, 'If I say that my elder brother killed his wife in a fit of fury because his food wasn't ready, then she'll get off.' I said, 'Be careful, you rogue: don't say a single false word in court—there's no worse offence than that.'" Ramlochan had previously prepared lots of stories that would save Chandara, but when he found that she herself was bending her neck to receive the noose, he decided, "Why take the risk of giving false evidence now? I'd better say what little I know." So Ramlochan said what he knew—or rather said a little more than he knew.

The Deputy Magistrate committed the case to a sessions trial.[4] Meanwhile in fields, houses, markets and bazaars, the sad or happy affairs of the world

---

4. A trial that is settled through a special *sessions* court in one continuous sitting.

carried on; and just as in previous years, torrential monsoon rains fell on to the new rice-crop.

Police, defendant and witnesses were all in court. In the civil court opposite hordes of people were waiting for their cases. A Calcutta lawyer had come on a suit about the sharing of a pond behind a kitchen; the plaintiff had thirty-nine witnesses. Hundreds of people were anxiously waiting for hair-splitting judgements, certain that nothing, at present, was more important. Chidam stared out of the window at the constant throng, and it seemed like a dream. A koel-bird[5] was hooting from a huge banyan tree in the compound: no courts or cases in *his* world!

Chandara said to the judge, "Sir, how many times must I go on saying the same thing?"

The judge explained, "Do you know the penalty for the crime you have confessed?"

"No," said Chandara.

"It is death by the hanging."

"Then please give it to me, sir," said Chandara. "Do what you like—I can't take any more."

When her husband was called to the court, she turned away. "Look at the witness," said the judge, "and say who he is."

"He is my husband," said Chandara, covering her face with her hands.

"Does he not love you?"

"He loves me greatly."

"Do you not love him?"

"I love him greatly."

When Chidam was questioned, he said, "I killed her."

"Why?"

"I wanted my food and my sister-in-law didn't give it to me."

When Dukhiram came to give evidence, he fainted. When he had come round again, he answered, "Sir, I killed her."

"Why?"

"I wanted a meal and she didn't give it to me."

After extensive cross-examination of various other witnesses, the judge concluded that the brothers had confessed to the crime in order to save the younger wife from the shame of the noose. But Chandara had, from the police investigation right through to the sessions trial, said the same thing repeatedly—she had not budged an inch from her story. Two barristers did their utmost to save her from the death-sentence, but in the end were defeated by her.

Who, on that auspicious night when, at a very young age, a dusky, diminutive, round-faced girl had left her childhood dolls in her father's house and come to her in-laws' house, could have imagined these events? Her father, on his deathbed, had happily reflected that at least he had made proper arrangements for his daughter's future.

In gaol,[6] just before the hanging, a kindly Civil Surgeon asked Chandara, "Do you want to see anyone?"

"I'd like to see my mother," she replied.

"Your husband wants to see you," said the doctor. "Shall I call him?"

"To hell with him,"[7] said Chandara.

5. Common Indian songbird.
6. Jail.

7. "Death to him" (literal trans.); an expression usually uttered in jest.

Kabuliwala[1]

My five-year-old daughter Mini cannot stop chattering for even a moment. From the time she came into this world, it took her hardly a year to acquire the gift of language, and thereafter she has not wasted a single moment of her waking hours in silence. Her mother scolds her sometimes to stop her from talking, but I cannot do that. Mini holding her peace is such an unnatural sight that I cannot bear it for long; so her conversations with me proceed with a great deal of vigour.

One morning, I had just started on the seventeenth chapter of my novel when Mini came in and started off. 'Baba, Ramdayal the doorman calls a crow a *kauwa* instead of a *kak*.[2] He doesn't know a thing, does he?'

Before I could explain to her about the diversity of languages in this world, she was off on another tack. 'You know, Baba,[3] Bhola was saying that an elephant pours water from the sky with his trunk and that's how we get rain.[4] What rubbish he talks day and night!'

She didn't wait for my opinion on the matter, but came up suddenly with, 'Baba, who's Ma to you?'

My sister-in-law, I said to myself;[5] but aloud I said, 'Mini, go and play with Bhola. I have work to do.'

Whereupon she flopped down close to my feet and, tapping her knees and clapping her hands, started a game of knick-knack, chanting *Agdumbagdum*.[6] Meanwhile, in my seventeenth chapter, Pratapsingh was leaping with Kanchanmala on a dark night from his high prison window down to the river below.

My room faces the street. Mini suddenly stopped her game, sped across to the window and started yelling, 'Kabuliwala, Kabuliwala!'

A tall, turbanned[7] Afghan pedlar in a dirty costume, with a sack over his shoulder and a few boxes of grapes in his hands, was making his way down the street. What came over my dear daughter I do not know, but she started calling out to him frantically. Now we'll have another nuisance walking in, sack and all, thought I. There goes my seventeenth chapter.

But as soon as the Kabuliwala looked up smilingly and started towards us, Mini turned tail and ran off into the house: not a sign of her could be seen. She was somehow possessed of a blind belief that if one searched the Kabuli's sack, one would find a couple of humanlings like her concealed in it.

---

1. Translated by Madhuchhanda Karlekar.
2. *Kauwa* is the Hindi word for "crow," whereas *kak* is the word for it in Bengali. Mini, whose mother tongue is Bengali, is too young at this moment in the story to know that the doorman, Ramdayal, is a Hindi speaker, not a Bengali.
3. "Baba" is Mini's word for her father, equivalent to the English "Dad."
4. Bhola, a servant in the household, has told Mini a simplified version of an ancient Indian myth, according to which Airavat, the divine elephant of Lord Indra (the principal god of the Vedic pantheon), is responsible for rain on earth.
5. Here the narrator reveals to the reader (but not to Mini) that he is, most likely, the elder brother of the deceased husband of Mini's mother. In orthodox Hinduism, a widow loses all her privileges with respect to "normal family life"; to prevent that from happening, a brother-in-law may assume the role of surrogate husband or guardian, and that of surrogate father to the widow's children.
6. A nonsense-rhyme that playfully mimics the meaningless sounds of a magic spell.
7. Traditional headgear for Indian men, a turban is a long scarf wrapped around the head, worn (instead of a hat) for protection from the elements, to designate social status, and for ceremonial purposes.

In the meantime, the Kabuliwala had walked in with a smile and a big salaam. Although Pratapsingh and Kanchanmala's fate was in jeopardy, I could not very well have called this man in and then turned him away without buying anything.

So I bought some of his stuff, and then we got talking of this and that. We chatted about Abdur Rahman and the Frontier Policy[8] of the Russians and the English.

Finally, as he got up to leave, he asked, 'Babu, where did your little girl go?'

I thought I ought to break Mini's irrational fear, so I called for her to come and meet him. She came and hung close to me, keeping a wary eye on the Kabuliwala and his sack. He brought out some raisins and dried apricots from his sack and held them out to her. She would not touch them, but clung to my knee and looked at him with redoubled suspicion. That's how the first meeting went.

A few days later, I was going out one morning on some work when I saw my girl perched on a bench beside the front door, chattering away without a stop, while the Kabuliwala sat at her feet, listening with a smile and expressing his own opinion now and then in broken Bengali. Mini in her five years of existence had never found such a patient audience, except for her father. I noticed that the train of her little sari[9] had been tucked into her waist and filled with raisins and nuts. 'Why have you given her all that?' I asked the man. 'You mustn't any more.' I took out an eight-anna bit and handed it to him. He accepted it without demur and put it into his sack.

When I came back, I found that half-rupee had set off a full-scale row.

Mini's mother was holding out a shiny coin and questioning her sternly, 'Where did you get this?'

'The Kabuliwala gave it to me,' said Mini.

'Why did you take it from him?' asked her mother.

'I didn't ask for it, he gave it to me of his own,' said Mini, close to tears.

I stepped in at this point and rescued her from impending danger.

What I gathered was that this was not the second time she had met the Kabuliwala. He had been coming almost every day, bribing her with his goodies, and had already won quite a large space in her greedy little heart.

I noticed that these two friends shared a few stock jokes between them. For instance, the minute she saw Rahamat[1] my girl would laugh and ask him, 'Kabuliwala, Kabuliwala, what have you got in your sack?' And Rahamat would answer with a big smile and an unnecessary nasal in the first syllable, 'Hanti!'[2]

In other words, the subtle point of his joke was that his sack contained a Nellyphant. It was not very subtle really, but it seemed to amuse them both

---

8. Abdur Rahman Khan was the Amir (ruler) of Afghanistan from 1880 to 1901, immediately after the Second Anglo-Afghan War. Under Abdur Rahman, Afghanistan was a separate state, geographically sandwiched between the northwestern end of the British-Indian empire and Tsarist Russia. "Frontier Policy" refers to the triangular politics of the region around the close of the nineteenth century, characterized as "the Great Game" in Rudyard Kipling's novel *Kim* (1901).

9. A long strip of cloth draped around the body; Indian women's traditional clothing.

1. His name indicates that Rahamat, the Kabuliwala ("the man from Kabul"), is a Muslim; the narrator and his family are Hindus.

2. "Hanti" is Rahamat's mispronunciation of the Hindi word *hathi*, "elephant."

immensely. And I too enjoyed the simple laughter of that elderly man and the little girl filling the autumn morning.

There was another routine exchange the two of them went through. Rahamat would tell Mini in his halting Bengali, 'Khonkhi,[3] you must never go to your in-laws' house.'

Bengali girls are usually taught from childhood about the in-laws' house they must go to. But we, being a little more modern, had not filled our daughter's head with that sort of talk. Mini did not quite catch the significance of Rahamat's words; but as not to reply would go against her nature, she asked him back, 'Will you go to your in-laws?'

Rahamat would shake his big fist and say, 'I'll beat up my father-in-law!'

And Mini, imagining the plight of that unknown creature called a father-in-law, would go into gales of laughter.

It was early autumn: the season when, in olden times, kings would march out on conquest. I myself have never been anywhere outside Calcutta; probably that is why my mind constantly travels across the world. Within my own home, I feel like an eternal outsider, longing continually for the big world. The minute I hear the name of some foreign country, off I go on my imaginary travels; and so too when I meet someone from a foreign land. I imagine some little cottage far across the rivers, seas and forests, where one can live a joyous life of freedom.

Yet am I so much a vegetable, anchored by my root, that the thought of actually venturing out of my little corner unnerves me. For this reason, sitting at my table every morning and talking to the Kabuliwala served me in lieu of travel. The Kabuli talked of his homeland in broken Bengali, and I pictured it all in my mind's eye: tall, impassable mountains on either side, burnt red with heat, and a caravan moving along the narrow desert track between them; turbanned traders and other travellers, some on camel-back, others on foot, some with spears in hand, others holding old-fashioned flintlock rifles.

Mini's mother is a very timid sort of person. If she hears a sound outside, she imagines that every drunken man in the world is charging towards our house. After all these years (not very many really), she is still not convinced that the world is not crawling with all kinds of horrors—thieves, robbers, drunks, snakes, tigers, malaria, caterpillars, cockroaches and British soldiers.

Hence she could not trust Rahamat the Kabuliwala either. She told me over and over again to keep a close watch on him. When I tried to laugh off her doubts, she asked me a series of pertinent questions. Are children never kidnapped? Is there or is there not a slave trade in Afghanistan? Is it quite impossible for a hulking big Kabuli to steal a little child?

I had to admit it was not impossible, but unbelievable. Not everyone has the same strength of conviction, however, so my wife remained as suspicious as ever. Still, I could not very well stop Rahamat, for no fault of his own, from visiting our home.

Rahamat would visit his native land every year in the middle of Magh.[4] Being a money-lender, he had a very busy time collecting all his dues from various

---

3. Rahamat's mispronunciation of *khuki*, a common term of endearment for a young girl in Bengali.

4. Late winter month in the Bengali calendar.

people before he left. He trudged from house to house all day, but he still found time to look Mini up. It really seemed as if they were hatching a conspiracy. If he could not come in the morning, he certainly would in the evening. Seeing that big man sitting in a dark corner in his baggy clothes, with all his various bags and sacks, made one apprehensive. But when Mini came running up so happily to meet him with her usual 'Kabuliwala, Kabuliwala,' and the two friends of unmatched years shared their simple old jokes together, it gladdened one's heart.

One morning, I was busy correcting proofs in my little room. The winter on its way out had thrown a sudden chill over the past few days, making everyone shiver. A little strip of sunlight had forced itself through the window and fallen under my table; I was enjoying its warmth upon my feet. It must have been around eight o'clock. The early risers with muffled heads had finished their morning walks and returned home. Just then I heard a deep voice coming from the street outside.

I looked out and saw two policemen approaching with our Rahamat bound in ropes between them. Behind them walked a long line of curious street urchins. There was blood on Rahamat's clothes, and one of the policemen was holding a blood-stained knife. I rushed out, stopped the policemen and asked what it was all about.

Partly from the policemen and partly from Rahamat, I learnt that one of our neighbours owed Rahamat money for a Rampuri shawl[5] he had bought. The man had told lies, denied the debt, and started an argument, in the midst of which Rahamat had pulled out a knife and stabbed him.

Rahamat was still hurling filthy abuse at the liar when Mini came skipping out of the house with her 'Kabuliwala, Kabuliwala!'

Rahamat's face instantly relaxed into a happy smile. As he had no sack on his shoulder that day, the usual exchange regarding its contents could not take place. So Mini asked him straight off, 'Will you go to your in-laws' house?'

'That's just where I'm going,' Rahamat answered with a laugh.

He saw that Mini did not find this answer funny, so he held out his hands and added, 'I would have beaten up my father-in-law, but what can I do? My hands are tied.'

Charged with causing grievous harm, Rahamat was sentenced to several years in prison.

We almost forgot about him. Year after year, as we went about our daily business in the safety of our home, never once did we think of how that freedom-loving man from the mountains was spending his time in prison.

As for Mini's flighty little heart, her own father cannot deny its shameful conduct. She forgot her old friend quite easily, and found a new one in Nabi the groom. Gradually, as she grew older, girlfriends took the place of men: so much so that she was hardly ever seen in her father's study. We were practically not on talking terms anymore.

---

5. An expensive, hand-embroidered woolen wrap made in Rampur, now in Uttar Pradesh, India, near the Nepal border. Between the late 18th and mid-20th century, Rampur was a Shi'a Muslim kingdom ruled by descendants of Afghan Rohilla ethnicity, and it became a center for handicrafts such as the Rampuri cap and the Rampuri knife.

Years went by. It was autumn again. Mini was going to be married. A match had been arranged, and the wedding day fixed during the Puja vacation. Along with Durga of Mount Kailas, my Mini too would leave her father's house in darkness and set off for her husband's home.[6]

It was a beautiful day. The rain-washed autumn sunshine was like pure gold. Even the mouldy brickwork of the houses huddled along our old Calcutta lane looked lovely as they basked in the golden haze.

The wedding shehnai had been playing since dawn. Each note of the music seemed to be playing tearfully in my own rib-cage. The piercing Bhairavi raga[7] intensified the pain of the impending farewell, spilling it across the world outside like the autumn sunlight. My Mini was to be married that day.

The house was in commotion from the early morning, with people milling around. Down in the courtyard, bamboo poles had been fixed and an awning set up. From every room in the house, one heard the tinkle of chandeliers being fitted up, with endless yelling and shouting of orders.

I was sitting in my study looking through the bills, when all of a sudden Rahamat appeared.

I did not recognise him at first. He did not have his sack, nor his long hair, nor that robust look of old. I finally placed him by his smile.

'Ah, Rahamat, how long have you been back?' I said.

'I came out of prison last evening,' he replied.

His words jarred on my ears. I had never seen a murderer in flesh and blood, but my heart shrank at the sight of this man. I wanted him to go away that very minute and not spoil the auspicious day.

'There's a ceremony in the house today, and I'm very busy. You had better go now,' I told him.

He got up when he heard this and prepared to leave right away; but he stopped half-way and asked, 'Can't I see Khonkhi for just a short while?'

He must have thought that Mini would remain exactly as before: that she would come running up with her usual 'Kabuliwala, Kabuliwala!' and share their familiar jokes. He had even brought a box of grapes, and some nuts and raisins in a paper packet—no doubt begged from a fellow Kabuli, since he no longer had his own sack of wares.

'I told you there's a ceremony in the house,' I said again. 'You can't meet anyone else today.'

He seemed a little upset. He stood up without a word, looked steadily at me for a while, said 'Salaam,[8] Babu,' and left.

6. Durga is the fearsome form of the goddess Pārvatī, Lord Śiva's consort; she is worshipped widely in Bengal as a "mother goddess," in preference to the male gods in the Hindu pantheon. The annual festival called Durga Puja ("Worship of Durga") is celebrated over six days in September or October on the lunar calendar; Durga is associated with Mount Kailash (in the Himalayas) which, in Hindu mythology, is her and Śiva's "heavenly abode" on earth.
7. The *shehnai*, a double-reed conical oboe, is played at Hindu weddings; its music is associated with purity and sanctity. In Indian classical music, a *rāga* ("musical mode") is a tonal structure with a framework of progressions and melodic and rhythmic patterns; any particular composition is set to a specific *rāga*. Compositions in the Bhairavi *rāga* are prized for their emotion-charged melodies, sung or played at dawn or early in the morning.
8. *Salaam*, from the Arabic and corresponding to the Hebrew *shalom*, is a common greeting and expression at parting in northern India. *Babu* is a masculine honorific term, used to address social superiors.

I felt sorry for him. I was thinking of calling him back when I saw him returning on his own.

'I'd brought these grapes, raisins and nuts for Khonkhi. Will you give them to her, please?' he said.

I was about to pay him for them when he suddenly caught hold of my hand and said, 'You're a very kind man. I'll always remember you, but please don't pay me for these. Babu, just as you have a daughter, I too have a daughter at home. I remember her face when I bring these things for Khonkhi. I don't come here to trade.'

With that he plunged a hand into his big loose shirt and brought out a soiled piece of paper from near his breast. He unfolded it very carefully with both hands and laid it on my table.

I saw the black imprint of a little hand on that paper: not a photograph, nor a painting, just a rough print of a little hand made from burnt charcoal smeared on the palm. He brought back this little memento of his daughter with him every year, held it close to his big lonely heart as he roamed the streets of Calcutta, as if the touch of her little soft hand brought some comfort to his great pining heart.

My eyes were moist as I examined that scrap of paper. I forgot that he was just a dry-fruit vendor from Kabul, and I a well-born Bengali gentleman. I knew then that he and I were really just the same. He was a father, and so was I. The rough print of his little mountain-dwelling Parvati's[9] hand reminded me of my own Mini. I sent for her that very minute. The women were very reluctant to let her out, but I paid no heed. She came out, dressed in her red silk sari and bridal make-up, and stood shyly at the door.

Rahamat was quite taken aback when he saw her. He did not know how to pick up the thread of their old friendship. Finally he laughed and said, 'Are you going to your in-laws, Khonkhi?'

Mini now knew what 'in-laws' meant. She could not answer him back as before, but blushed and turned her face away. I recalled the day she had met the Kabuliwala for the first time, and my heart ached.

After Mini had left, Rahamat gave a deep sigh and sat down on the floor. It struck him suddenly that his daughter too would have grown as old. He would have to make friends with her again: she would not be the same girl he had left behind. Who knows how she had fared in these eight years? The shehnai played on in the mellow morning sunshine, and Rahamat, sitting in a narrow city lane, saw visions of the barren Afghan mountains.

I took out a banknote from my purse and handed it to him. 'Go home to your daughter, Rahamat,' I said. 'Have a happy reunion, and may your joy bring good fortune to my Mini.'

By gifting him that money, I had to cut down on a few frills for the wedding. The electric lights were not as dazzling as we had planned, and the big band had to be cancelled. The women were most upset; but to me the ceremony was the brighter for being bathed in a great beneficent light.

---

9. In Hinduism, the goddess Pārvatī is Lord Śiva's consort; she is the daughter of the Himalayas (mythologized as an old man), and dwells with her husband in the mountains. Here the narrator sympathetically imagines Rahamat's daughter as a little "goddess" in the Kabul Valley, among the Hindu Kush mountains, just west of the Himalayas.

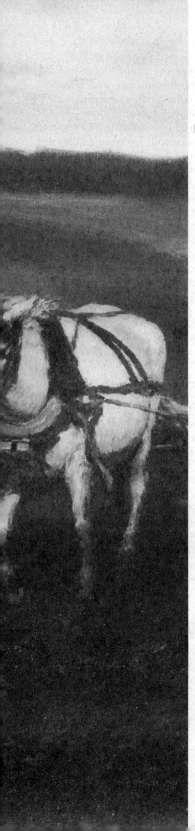

V

Realism across the Globe

As the world grew closer together in the nineteenth century, thanks to rapidly expanding empires and new methods of transportation and communication, including the steamship and the telegraph, literary movements were able to spread fast, too. Writers could find inspiration in texts composed across the world; they could nurture new ideas at home that then spread quickly outward; and they could readily mix and fuse traditions that came from different continents. "World literature" as a globally interconnected phenomenon became a reality in this period. Symbolism, for example—the poetic movement launched by **Charles Baudelaire** in Paris—had an impact as far away as Nicaragua and Japan, and the *ghazal*, an Arabic poetic form used for many centuries in India and Persia, inspired imitators in nineteenth-century Europe, including **Johann Wolfgang von Goethe**, who made it a popular poetic form in Germany, and Thomas Hardy in Britain.

One of the most powerfully influential global artistic movements in the nineteenth century was realism. It began in Britain and France, hotbeds of industrial and political revolution, but it soon spread worldwide. And yet realism in literature did not always arise in response to European influences.

Leo Tolstoy Ploughing a Field, 1882, by Ilya Yefimovich Repin.

It would be a mistake to see Joaquim Maria Machado de Assis in Brazil, **Rabindranath Tagore** in India, and Rebecca Harding Davis in the United States as mere imitators of the European model: they invented techniques, subjects, and plots, they altered conventions, and they experimented with styles to generate realisms all their own.

Despite its rich variety, realist writing around the world tended to share some crucial aims and characteristics. In the nineteenth century many artists felt a new urgency to tell the unvarnished truth about the world, to observe social life unsentimentally, and to convey it as objectively as possible. To be sure, the struggle to give a realistic representation of the world—sometimes called verisimilitude or mimesis—was nothing new. But while artists for many generations had been aiming at truth in their representations of the world, the nineteenth century ushered in a new realist philosophy, shocking new subject matter, and a specific new constellation of literary techniques.

The revolutionary overturning of old regimes and hierarchies, the rise of democracy and the middle class, and the industrial revolution—which created smoky, grimy cities teeming with an impoverished working class—had already inspired writers to throw off old literary forms and conventions. In Europe and the Americas, the Romantic poets (described in detail in this volume) had sought to liberate literature from the grip of traditional courtly manners and traditions to focus instead on nature as a model of freedom and beauty. For them, the natural environment offered an antidote to the artifices and injustices of human societies. Realist writers, by and large, lost faith in this ideal: nature no longer seemed to provide a plausible alternative. Now all that was left of reality was what you could see with your naked eyes: gritty, ugly industries; the power of money; starving, broken workers; social hierarchies; dirt, decay, and disease. The realists thus shocked their audiences by representing characters who for centuries had been considered too low and coarse for art: ragged orphans and exhausted workers, washerwomen and prostitutes, drunks and thieves. They routinely chose the city over the coun-

The Stonebreakers, 1848, by Gustave Courbet. A realist masterpiece that was destroyed in the Allied bombing of Dresden during World War II, this painting now exists only in reproductions and photographs.

tryside for their settings. And they were willing to lavish their descriptive attention on squalid surroundings—sickening slums, smoggy factories, dusty barrooms. Gone was the equation of art with beauty: visual art and literature could now be deliberately, powerfully hideous.

The realists were not only concerned with the unfortunate, however. In throwing off the ideals associated with earlier art forms, realist artists often threw their energies into representing the commonplace—the mundane experience of ordinary people. They wanted to capture the world as it was, and that meant describing plausible individuals in recognizable circumstances. Realism is as closely associated with middle-class characters, then, as it is with the poor, and many of the most famous realist writers of the nineteenth century—including Honoré de Balzac, Charles Dickens, and **Fyodor Dostoyevsky**—wrote fiction that deliberately cut across different classes, showing encounters between rich and poor in an attempt to give a realistic picture of a whole society.

While some realist writers tried to capture entire nations and social classes, others focused intensively on a few individuals. Some put their emphasis on internal, psychological reality, others on the shaping force of external circumstances. Usually those who stuck to the small scale implied larger social relationships, and they used individual characters to represent whole groups, but their fictions do feel more local and intimate than the vast and sprawling novels of the period—*Bleak House* or *War and Peace*—that contain many characters and strive to represent a whole nation. These differences were in part philosophical, revolving around the question of what it is possible to know. What *is* reality? Can we rely on our senses, or do we need to turn to facts and statistics, the-

ories about hidden causes and social structures? Can we see reality from a single, individual perspective, or do we need to take a bird's-eye view?

The realists did not always agree about what constituted reality or how best to capture it in words or paint, but in general they resisted symbols and allegories, sentimentality and sensationalism, otherworldly ideals and timeless values in favor of the literal, the specific, and observable—the social world as it appeared in the here and the now. They tended to focus on the immediate, material causes of social misery and looked to scientists and social thinkers for solutions, rather than aspiring to transcendent or beautiful ideals. Though frequently the writers themselves were religious, realism was typically a secular project that put its emphasis on empirical experience—what we can know through our senses—rather than on providential explanations. Many realist writers were influenced by currents in science, and a later offshoot of realism, called naturalism, turned to the evolutionary science of Charles Darwin for a brutal explanatory model: human beings would only survive to the extent that they could adapt to their social environments; those who proved unfit would die.

Realist writers introduced a whole new range of formal techniques that transformed the literary landscape. Most wrote novels or short stories, though realist drama changed the history of theater in the late nineteenth century. The novel had the advantage of being relatively formless: it could be long or short; it could include many central characters or a single protagonist; it could be told in the first person or the third person; it could focus on domestic settings or foreign travel; and it could entwine many stories or follow a single main path. Unlike more traditional and compact forms, such as the sonnet or *ghazal*, it could swallow up

Reading by Lamplight, 1858, by James Abbott McNeill Whistler.

other kinds of writing—letters, dialogue, description, history, biography, satire, even poetry—without being bound by the rules of any of those particular forms itself. In Europe, the novel was a new genre in the eighteenth century—hence its name "novel"—and its flexibility as a form allowed it to adapt to many different kinds of philosophies and social circumstances. Often written and read by more women than men, novels were a popular form that did not acquire a serious, highbrow status until the beginning of the twentieth century.

The novel and drama suited the aims of realism in some very specific ways. Prose is of course prosaic—suited to capturing ordinariness and even ugliness. Realist writers often opted for plain, unstylized diction and usually tried to convey the many ways of speaking that characterized the social groups they represented, including dialect speech. Prose and drama lend themselves much better to this linguistic variety than does poetry, with its strict forms and connotations of artful beauty. Fiction also lends itself well to movement between action and description: it can pause the plot to include highly detailed depictions of the characters and their environments. For writers wanting to capture the whole social world in a style that seemed objective, the omniscient third-person narrator provided the perfect, impersonal perspective. Other writers opted for first-person narrators, guided only by their own senses and experience as they try to make sense of the world. Fiction can accommodate both of these perspectives easily, and some realist novels even move back and forth between the narrator's bird's-eye view and the characters' more restricted knowledge.

The elements of both character and plot raised particular challenges and opportunities for realist writers. Some realists tried to present uniquely individual characters, conveying some of the complexity of real people in the world; others felt that the truth lay instead in types, and they used individual characters to represent whole social groups—the outraged worker, the subjugated wife, the social climber. As for plot, realist writers often tried to steer clear of sensational events and neat endings, which jeopardized the goal of unvarnished truth telling, but they also wanted to keep their readers absorbed. One solution was to put characters in believable social situations where they faced ethical dilemmas. The dramatic interest of the plot then lay in having the character make a difficult choice. Should the heroine choose respectable poverty or agree to a luxurious but disreputable life as a kept woman? Should the hero climb the social ladder at the expense of an innocent victim?

One of the advantages of dramatizing ethical predicaments is that these allowed fiction to engage the question of moral action in the new social environments of the nineteenth century. Can individuals have an impact on unjust social relationships? What responsibility does each of us have toward others in a city, a nation, or a densely interconnected world? For many realists, the purpose of describing the social world in great detail—with a particular emphasis on poverty and injustice—was to prompt readers to try to change that world.

With its emphasis on ordinary language, new social circumstances, and plausible human predicaments, realism transformed the literary landscape across the globe, inviting writers everywhere to try to capture the troubled, painful, struggling worlds of their own experience. And the mark these writers left remains palpable everywhere today, as realism continues to exert a powerful cultural force, still part of the daily fare of television, fiction, drama, and film around the world. Realism is nothing if not a capacious, roomy genre—able to move across borders and oceans, and as it moves, to take up new social relationships, new styles, new perspectives, and new resolutions.

FYODOR DOSTOYEVSKY

1821–1881

At seven o'clock on a bitter winter morning in 1849, a young man, meagerly dressed and shivering, went to meet his death. He had been convicted of circulating subversive writings that attacked both the Russian Orthodox Church and the tsar. Led to a platform surrounded by a crowd, he looked out over a cart filled with coffins. He heard his name and faced a firing squad. A priest administered his last rites and pressed him to confess. His cap was pulled over his face. Then, just as the firing squad took aim, a carriage screeched to a halt, and a messenger leapt out, shouting, "Long live the tsar! The good tsar!" Fyodor Dostoyevsky had been allowed to live. Astonished and thankful, he pledged his lifelong loyalty to the tsar. Drawing on this and other experiences from his eventful life, he would go on to write some of the most gripping fiction of the nineteenth century, works characterized by dramatic extremes of authority and subjection. Intense and unforgettable, Dostoyevsky's characters are often, like their author, wracked by violence, guilt, obsession, and addiction.

LIFE

Fyodor Dostoyevsky was born in 1821, the son of a doctor in Moscow. He was the second of six children. The family lived next to a hospital for poor people, which also housed a morgue. Their father was stern and efficient, their mother compassionate, and both were devout members of the Russian Orthodox Church. The children were encouraged to read widely, and Fyodor became an admirer of such writers as **William Shakespeare**, Pierre Corneille, **Johann Wolfgang von Goethe**, and Charles Dickens.

In 1837 Dostoyevsky's beloved mother died, and his father sent him to be educated at the military Academy for Engineers in St. Petersburg. On the way there, he witnessed an act of violence that later became a famous scene in *Crime and Punishment*, one of his best-known novels. A government courier, after throwing back a few shots of vodka, jumped into a carriage and started beating the peasant driver mercilessly. The driver, in turn, began to thrash his horses. Dostoyevsky retained a lifelong fascination with what he considered the basic human desire to subdue those weaker than oneself. After his mother's death, his father withdrew and became violent, drinking excessively, talking aloud to his dead wife, and beating his servants. In 1839 he was mysteriously murdered on his own estate, probably by his serfs.

Once Dostoyevsky had finished his engineering courses, he worked at a government job, which he found as "tiresome as potatoes." He lived beyond his means, gambling and eating in expensive restaurants. Soon he quit his job to write *Poor Folk*, his first novel, which turned out to be a great success, especially with political radicals. In the revolutionary year 1848, he took up with a group of subversive St. Petersburg socialists and atheists. A spy who had infiltrated the group informed on them, leading to Dostoyevsky's arrest and death sentence.

After being pardoned at the last moment by the tsar, the writer was exiled to hard labor in remote Siberia. For four years he marched with shackles on his legs, moving snow and firing bricks. "Every minute," he wrote later, "weighed upon my soul like a stone." The only book he was allowed was the New Testament, and he was not permitted to write letters or receive them. Dostoyevsky's thinking and writing would be transformed by the experience: in Siberia, he found renewed faith in the Orthodox Christianity of his childhood and artistic inspiration in the religious and folk traditions of the poorest Russian people.

Dostoyevsky served out the next four years of his sentence as a soldier in the small town of Semipalatinsk, where he fell in love for the first time with a married woman. In 1857, after her husband died, they were married. Then began a period of restlessness. The marriage was not a success. The couple traveled to Western Europe, where they were poor and unhappy. Ill with epilepsy and subject to increasingly serious episodes of the disease, Dostoyevsky gambled compulsively, squandering all of the money he had begged relatives to give him. As Dostoyevsky and his wife grew ever more estranged and her health declined from tuberculosis, he fell in love with another woman who disappointed him and then left him.

It was in 1864, during the lowest point of his bitter wandering, that he composed *Notes from Underground*. Soon after this his wife died, and he began work on the manuscript that would become *Crime and Punishment*, a novel about a young man named Raskolnikov who believes that he is superior to the ordinary run of humanity and therefore not subject to the usual moral laws. He kills two women with an axe and is consumed both with guilt and with the terror of being caught. Dostoyevsky burned the first draft of this novel and then rewrote it from scratch. All the while, he was miserably poor, forced to plead with acquaintances for money and to sell everything he owned, including most of his clothes.

The next phase of the writer's life proved slightly more stable. He married a much younger woman with good business sense who managed his publications and their finances better than he had done on his own, though he remained in debt until the last year of his life. They had four children. The last, Alyosha, died from epilepsy at the age of three, and Dostoyevsky, heartbroken, blamed himself for having passed on the disease. His final novel, *The Brothers Karamazov*, features not only the murder of a father but also a saintly son named Alyosha. This novel proved extremely popular, hailed by fellow writer **Leo Tolstoy** as the best of the century. A life packed with dramatic incidents and great suffering came to an end soon after. At the time of his death in 1881, Dostoyevsky was acclaimed as one of the greatest Russian writers of all time. Thirty thousand people attended his funeral.

TIMES

By the middle of the nineteenth century, Russians had a long tradition of ambivalence toward Western Europe. On the one hand, Russia had been instituting Western-inspired reforms since the late seventeenth century, borrowing ideas about military organization, industry, law, and culture from France, Britain, and Germany. Most high-born Russians spoke French almost as a native language. On the other hand, the Russians had proudly fought off the invasion of Napoleon's French troops in 1812, and some saw European influences as weakening and corrupting Russian traditions. Tsar Nicholas I, who ruled the Russian empire from 1825 to 1855, instituted a policy he called Official Nationalism. He believed in exerting absolute power himself, and he imposed a regime of strict suppression, punishing dissenters, censoring subversive publications, and demanding allegiance to the Russian nation. He also insisted that everyone at court speak Russian. Nicholas I was followed by a very different kind of leader, Tsar Alexander II, who looked to the West for reformist ideas. His most sweeping reform was the abolition of serfdom—the possession of peasants by landowners, a system very much like slavery. He also introduced trial by jury and modest forms of representative government. His relatively liberal administration came to an end when he was assassinated in 1881.

Russian thinkers in this period tended to divide themselves into two broad camps. The first, called the Westernizers, favored European-style modernizations. Many of these were moderate liberals who defended gradual progress toward rights and freedoms, welcoming Alexander II's reforms, but others were more radical and utopian, imagining that only a thoroughgoing revolution would bring about the change Russia needed. Both liberals and radicals believed that the Western European Enlightenment, with its emphasis on reason and on universal rights, offered the best model for Russia's future.

Other Russians resisted this whole-hearted embrace of Western Enlightenment values. Most of these, known as Slavophiles, envisioned all of the Slavic peoples uniting around a unique set of spiritual and cultural traditions, including a shared loyalty to the Orthodox Church. Dostoyevsky, after his brief flirtation with European radicalism, helped to bring into being a movement called "Native Soil" conservatism. He imagined all of Russia, rich and poor, joined in a new national union that would be spiritually superior to all of Western Europe. Somewhat ambivalent about the Orthodox Church, he was always drawn to the image of Christ as a loving figure of universal reconciliation and self-sacrifice who could regenerate the nation. He saw the Russian peasantry as a repository of great spiritual wealth, and he felt that intellectuals must now return to their native soil to create a new bond with the vast mass of the people through *sobornost*, or spiritual oneness.

These "native soil" views sometimes come as a surprise to readers of Dostoyevsky's fiction, since he delves so compellingly into the minds of dogmatic atheists and violent killers that it seems he must in some way have shared their perspective. But part of what makes Dostoyevsky remarkable is his capacity to see from multiple, often conflicting viewpoints, and perhaps this is not surprising, given the extraordinary range of his experiences: his pious childhood, his fraternizing with socialists and atheists, his incarceration in a Siberian prison with murderous convicts and devout peasants, his humiliating poverty, his addiction to gambling, and his misery in love.

WORK

From the outset, *Notes from Underground* poses questions about what kind of human one should be. The narrator begins, "I am a sick man. . . . I am a spiteful man. I am a most unpleasant man." But if this character is sick, then what does it mean to be healthy? If he is spiteful and unpleasant, are others good and generous? Or, as the underground man suggests at times, are we all actually versions of him, and is humanity therefore sick, spiteful, and unpleasant? In the first few pages, the narrator compares himself to an insect, a mouse, a monkey, a slave, a peasant, and a civilized European. Later he mocks those who see humans as musical instruments—mechanical devices. But

FYODOR DOSTOYEVSKY | 663

if we are not bugs, animals, machines, slaves, or civilized people, then what is the proper model for thinking about what it means to be human?

Dostoyevsky does not give us a character who can answer any of these questions to our satisfaction. Constantly contradicting himself, he calls himself a "paradoxicalist," taking pleasure in spitefulness and pride in pain. One of the most tortuous aspects of the narrator's experience is his acute self-awareness. He is horrified at being seen by others and then more troubled still by the idea that he may not be seen. And he cannot escape his obsessive self-consciousness even when alone, since he is always watching and judging himself and imagining himself through the eyes of others. Indeed, although he is painfully lonely, he is never truly free of the social world. We see him always in dialogue, constantly responding to another's views, anticipating someone else's response, even when that someone else is himself.

The "underground man" moves back and forth between casting his intense self-awareness as unique and seeing it as representative of all humanity. But Dostoyevsky also hints at a third possibility: that his antihero is a particular social type, a representative of a specifically *modern* condition. The "underground man" is a new kind of rootless urban intellectual, bombarded with fashionably progressive ideas about science, who cannot reason his way to any kind of satisfying conclusion. *Notes from Underground* is packed with references to contemporary ideas. For example, the socialist utopian novel *What Is to Be Done?*, published in 1863 (just a year prior to *Notes from Underground*), with its vision of an intrinsically good human nature governed by scientific laws, is one of the central targets of Dostoyevsky's biting critique, as is Charles Darwin's theory of evolution, first translated into Russian in 1864. The narrator also mocks an 1863 con-

troversy over N. N. Ge's painting *The Last Supper*, which offered a startling realism, showing Jesus recumbent and thoughtful instead of upright and authoritative, and presenting his disciples as scared and puzzled. This attention to up-to-date ideas was no accident: Dostoyevsky saw his own time as a "thunderous epoch permeated with so many colossal, astounding, and rapidly shifting actual events" that he could not imagine writing historical fiction, such as Leo Tolstoy's hugely popular *War and Peace*, which was set in 1812. *Notes from Underground*, then, may be less about the human condition in general than about the specific dilemma of being an educated man in modern, urban Russia.

Dostoyevsky captures this troubled mindset through a carefully crafted and complex work of literature. It is split into two quite distinct parts: in the first section we hear about the narrator from his own perspective in the present, and in the second we move backwards in time to see him through his encounters with others. The genre of *Notes from Underground* has long puzzled readers. It certainly draws on the tradition of the confession, as the narrator makes a declaration of guilt to an implied audience. And yet religious confessions require feelings of repentance, whereas Dostoyevsky's narrator defends himself and resists expressions of contrition. Is this novel, as some readers have believed, a parody of a confession? In many ways, the narrator is most like **Jean-Jacques Rousseau**, whose secular *Confessions* was the first text to explore the intimate psychological life of the author, including petty experiences of guilt and shame. And yet *Notes from Underground* is hardly a straightforward autobiography. The text's split structure does not follow a chronological arc. Instead, it gives us a picture of the narrator in two different pieces, first present and then past.

On first reading, this text may seem to

meander with the narrator's tortured perceptions, but in fact it is tightly organized. After the long first section, in which he is entirely alone, we see him engaging with a sequence of other people, each of whom is lower on the social ladder than the one before. First, he becomes obsessed with a stranger—a military officer who is socially superior to him and snubs him by failing to recognize his existence. Next he meets with a group of his peers, schoolmates who refuse to take him seriously as an equal. In the final section we see him try to assert his superiority over two others: his dignified servant Apollon and the compassionate, self-sacrificing prostitute Liza.

However extreme and contradictory his characters, Dostoyevsky laid claim to a specific version of realism in his fiction. "They call me a psychologist," he said, but "it's not true. I'm merely a realist in a higher sense, that is to say I describe all the depths of the human soul." Reaching low, into the depths of the soul, as a way of achieving a "higher realism," his literature is nothing if

not paradoxical. But Dostoyevsky's brilliance lies precisely in its capacity to fold together extremes—it is in the poorest prostitute that one finds the greatest spiritual wealth, and in the cruelest spite that a man can experience pleasure. Not surprisingly, then, Dostoyevsky's realism did not involve attention to the humdrum, as did the work of other realists, but offered up extremes of emotion and violence. "What most people regard as fantastic and exceptional is sometimes for me the very essence of reality," he wrote. "Everyday trivialities and a conventional view of them, in my opinion, not only fall short of realism but are even contrary to it."

Dostoyevsky influenced an astonishing array of writers and thinkers. From **Franz Kafka** and William Faulkner to **Gabriel García Márquez** and Ralph Ellison, some of the most imaginative minds of the following century acknowledged him as an inspiration. Perhaps the most unexpected of these was Albert Einstein. "Dostoevsky," he wrote, "gives me more than any scientist."

Notes from Underground[1]

I

Underground[2]

I

I am a sick man. . . .[3] I am a spiteful man. I am a most unpleasant man. I think my liver is diseased. Then again, I don't know a thing about my illness; I'm not even sure what hurts. I'm not being treated and never have been, though I respect both medicine and doctors. Besides, I'm extremely superstitious—well

1. Translated by Michael Katz.
2. Both the author of these notes and the *Notes* themselves are fictitious, of course. Nevertheless, people like the author of these notes not only may, but actually must exist in our society, considering the general circumstances under which our society was formed. I wanted to bring before the public with more prominence than usual one of the characters of the recent past. He's a representative of the current generation. In the excerpt entitled "Underground" this person introduces himself and his views, and, as it were, wants to explain the reasons why he appeared and why he had to appear in our midst. The following excerpt [*Apropos of Wet Snow*] contains the actual "notes" of this person about several events in his life [Dostoyevsky's note].
3. The ellipses are Dostoyevsky's and do not indicate omissions from the text.

at least enough to respect medicine. (I'm sufficiently educated not to be super-stitious; but I am, anyway.) No, gentlemen, it's out of spite that I don't wish to be treated. Now then, that's something you probably won't understand. Well, I do. Of course, I won't really be able to explain to you precisely who will be hurt by my spite in this case; I know perfectly well that I can't possibly "get even" with doctors by refusing their treatment; I know better than anyone that all this is going to hurt me alone, and no one else. Even so, if I refuse to be treated, it's out of spite. My liver hurts? Good, let it hurt even more!

I've been living this way for some time—about twenty years. I'm forty now. I used to be in the civil service. But no more. I was a nasty official. I was rude and took pleasure in it. After all, since I didn't accept bribes, at least I had to reward myself in some way. (That's a poor joke, but I won't cross it out. I wrote it thinking that it would be very witty; but now, having realized that I merely wanted to show off disgracefully, I'll make a point of not crossing it out!) When petitioners used to approach my desk for information, I'd gnash my teeth and feel unending pleasure if I succeeded in causing someone dis-tress. I almost always succeeded. For the most part they were all timid peo-ple: naturally, since they were petitioners. But among the dandies there was a certain officer whom I particularly couldn't bear. He simply refused to be humble, and he clanged his saber in a loathsome manner. I waged war with him over that saber for about a year and a half. At last I prevailed. He stopped clanging. All this, however, happened a long time ago, during my youth. But do you know, gentlemen, what the main component of my spite really was? Why, the whole point, the most disgusting thing, was the fact that I was shamefully aware at every moment, even at the moment of my greatest bitter-ness, that not only was I not a spiteful man, I was not even an embittered one, and that I was merely scaring sparrows to no effect and consoling myself by doing so. I was foaming at the mouth—but just bring me some trinket to play with, just serve me a nice cup of tea with sugar, and I'd probably have calmed down. My heart might even have been touched, although I'd probably have gnashed my teeth out of shame and then suffered from insomnia for several months afterward. That's just my usual way.

I was lying about myself just now when I said that I was a nasty official. I lied out of spite. I was merely having some fun at the expense of both the petitioners and that officer, but I could never really become spiteful. At all times I was aware of a great many elements in me that were just the opposite of that. I felt how they swarmed inside me, these contradictory elements. I knew that they had been swarming inside me my whole life and were begging to be let out; but I wouldn't let them out, I wouldn't, I deliberately wouldn't let them out. They tormented me to the point of shame; they drove me to convulsions and—and finally I got fed up with them, oh how fed up! Perhaps it seems to you, gentlemen, that I'm repenting about something, that I'm ask-ing your forgiveness for something? I'm sure that's how it seems to you. . . . But really, I can assure you, I don't care if that's how it seems. . . .

Not only couldn't I become spiteful, I couldn't become anything at all: nei-ther spiteful nor good, neither a scoundrel nor an honest man, neither a hero nor an insect. Now I live out my days in my corner, taunting myself with the spiteful and entirely useless consolation that an intelligent man cannot seri-ously become anything and that only a fool can become something. Yes, sir, an intelligent man in the nineteenth century must be, is morally obliged to be, principally a characterless creature; a man possessing character, a man of action, is fundamentally a limited creature. That's my conviction at the age of forty. I'm forty now; and, after all, forty is an entire lifetime; why it's extreme old age. It's rude to live past forty, it's indecent, immoral! Who lives more than forty years? Answer sincerely, honestly. I'll tell you who: only fools and rascals. I'll tell those old men that right to their faces, all those venerable old men, all those silver-haired and sweet-smelling old men! I'll say it to the whole world right to its face! I have a right to say it because I myself will live to sixty. I'll make it to seventy! Even to eighty! . . . Wait! Let me catch my breath. . . .

You probably think, gentlemen, that I want to amuse you. You're wrong about that, too. I'm not at all the cheerful fellow I seem to be, or that I may seem to be; however, if you're irritated by all this talk (and I can already sense that you are irritated), and if you decide to ask me just who I really am, then I'll tell you: I'm a collegiate assessor. I worked in order to have something to eat (but only for that reason); and last year, when a distant relative of mine left me six thousand rubles in his will, I retired immediately and settled down in this corner. I used to live in this corner before, but now I've settled down in it. My room is nasty, squalid, on the outskirts of town. My servant is an old peasant woman, spiteful out of stupidity; besides, she has a foul smell. I'm told that the Petersburg climate is becoming bad for my health, and that it's very expensive to live in Petersburg with my meager resources. I know all that; I know it better than all those wise and experienced advisers and admonishers. But I shall remain in Petersburg; I shall not leave Petersburg! I shall not leave here because . . . Oh, what difference does it really make whether I leave Petersburg or not?

Now, then, what can a decent man talk about with the greatest pleasure?

Answer: about himself.

Well, then, I too will talk about myself.

II

Now I would like to tell you, gentlemen, whether or not you want to hear it, why it is that I couldn't even become an insect. I'll tell you solemnly that I wished to become an insect many times. But not even that wish was granted. I swear to you, gentlemen, that being overly conscious is a disease, a genuine, full-fledged disease. Ordinary human consciousness would be more than sufficient for everyday human needs—that is, even half or a quarter of the amount of consciousness that's available to a cultured man in our unfortunate nineteenth century, especially to one who has the particular misfortune of living in St. Petersburg, the most abstract and premeditated city in the whole world.[4] (Cities can be either premeditated or unpremeditated.) It would have been entirely sufficient, for example, to have the consciousness with which all so-called spontaneous people and men of action are endowed. I'll bet that you think I'm writing all this to show off, to make fun of these men of action, that I'm clanging my saber just like that officer did to show off in bad taste. But, gentlemen, who could possibly be proud of his illnesses and want to show them off?

---

4. St. Petersburg was conceived of as an imposing city; plans called for regular streets, broad avenues, and spacious squares.

But what am I saying? Everyone does that; people do take pride in their illnesses, and I, perhaps, more than anyone else. Let's not argue; my objection is absurd. Nevertheless, I remain firmly convinced that not only is being overly conscious a disease, but so is being conscious at all. I insist on it. But let's leave that alone for a moment. Tell me this: why was it, as if on purpose, at the very moment, indeed, at the precise moment that I was most capable of becoming conscious of the subtleties of everything that was "beautiful and sublime,"[5] as we used to say at one time, that I didn't become conscious, and instead did such unseemly things, things that . . . well, in short, probably everyone does, but it seemed as if they occurred to me deliberately at the precise moment when I was most conscious that they shouldn't be done at all? The more conscious I was of what was good, of everything "beautiful and sublime," the more deeply I sank into the morass and the more capable I was of becoming entirely bogged down in it. But the main thing is that all this didn't seem to be occurring accidentally; rather, it was as if it all had to be so. It was as if this were my most normal condition, not an illness or an affliction at all, so that finally I even lost the desire to struggle against it. It ended when I almost came to believe (perhaps I really did believe) that this might really have been my normal condition. But at first, in the beginning, what agonies I suffered during that struggle! I didn't believe that others were experiencing the same thing; therefore, I kept it a secret about myself all my life. I was ashamed (perhaps I still am even now); I reached the point where I felt some secret, abnormal, despicable little pleasure in returning home to my little corner on some disgusting Petersburg night, acutely aware that once again I'd committed some revolting act that day, that what had been done could not be undone, and I used to gnaw and gnaw at myself inwardly, secretly, nagging away, consuming myself until finally the bitterness turned into some kind of shameful, accursed sweetness and at last into genuine, earnest pleasure! Yes, into pleasure, real pleasure! I absolutely mean that. . . . That's why I first began to speak out, because I want to know for certain whether other people share this same pleasure. Let me explain: the pleasure resulted precisely from the overly acute consciousness of one's own humiliation; from the feeling that one had reached the limit; that it was disgusting, but couldn't be otherwise; you had no other choice—you could never become a different person; and that even if there were still time and faith enough for you to change into something else, most likely you wouldn't even want to change, and if you did, you wouldn't have done anything, perhaps because there really was nothing for you to change into. But the main thing and the final point is that all of this was taking place according to normal and fundamental laws of overly acute consciousness and of the inertia which results directly from these laws; consequently, not only couldn't one change, one simply couldn't do anything at all. Hence it follows, for example, as a result of this overly acute consciousness, that one is absolutely right in being a scoundrel, as if this were some consolation to the scoundrel. But enough of this. . . . Oh, my,

---

5. This phrase originated in Edmund Burke's *Philosophical Inquiry into the Origin of Our Ideas of the Sublime and Beautiful* (1756) and was repeated in Immanuel Kant's *Observations* *on the Feeling of the Beautiful and the Sublime* (1756). It became a cliché in the writings of Russian critics during the 1830s.

I've gone on rather a long time, but have I really explained anything? How can I explain this pleasure? But I will explain it! I shall see it through to the end! That's why I've taken up my pen. . . ,

For example, I'm terribly proud. I'm as mistrustful and as sensitive as a hunchback or a dwarf; but, in truth, I've experienced some moments when, if someone had slapped my face, I might even have been grateful for it. I'm being serious. I probably would have been able to derive a peculiar sort of pleasure from it—the pleasure of despair, naturally, but the most intense pleasures occur in despair, especially when you're very acutely aware of the hopelessness of your own predicament. As for a slap in the face—why, here the consciousness of being beaten to a pulp would overwhelm you. The main thing is, no matter how I try, it still turns out that I'm always the first to be blamed for everything and, what's even worse, I'm always the innocent victim, so to speak, according to the laws of nature. Therefore, in the first place, I'm guilty inasmuch as I'm smarter than everyone around me. (I've always considered myself smarter than everyone around me, and sometimes, believe me, I've been ashamed of it. At the least, all my life I've looked away and never could look people straight in the eye.) Finally, I'm to blame because even if there were any magnanimity in me, it would only have caused more suffering as a result of my being aware of its utter uselessness. After all, I probably wouldn't have been able to make use of that magnanimity: neither to forgive, as the offender, perhaps, had slapped me in accordance with the laws of nature, and there's no way to forgive the laws of nature; nor to forget, because even if there were any laws of nature, it's offensive nonetheless. Finally, even if I wanted to be entirely unmagnanimous, and had wanted to take revenge on the offender, I couldn't be revenged on anyone for anything because, most likely, I would never have decided to do anything, even if I could have. Why not? I'd like to say a few words about that separately.

III

Let's consider people who know how to take revenge and how to stand up for themselves in general. How, for example, do they do it? Let's suppose that they're seized by an impulse to take revenge—then for a while nothing else remains in their entire being except for that impulse. Such an individual simply rushes toward his goal like an enraged bull with lowered horns; only a wall can stop him. (By the way, when actually faced with a wall such individuals, that is, spontaneous people and men of action, genuinely give up. For them a wall doesn't constitute the evasion that it does for those of us who think and consequently do nothing; it's not an excuse to turn aside from the path, a pretext in which a person like me usually doesn't believe, but one for which he's always extremely grateful. No, they give up in all sincerity. For them the wall possesses some kind of soothing, morally decisive and definitive meaning, perhaps even something mystical . . . But more about the wall later.) Well, then, I consider such a spontaneous individual to be a genuine, normal person, just as tender mother nature wished to see him when she lovingly gave birth to him on earth. I'm green with envy at such a man. He's stupid, I won't argue with you about that; but perhaps a normal man is supposed to be stupid—how do we know? Perhaps it's even very beautiful. And I'm all the more convinced of the suspicion, so to speak, that if, for example, one were to take the antithesis of a normal man—that is, a man of overly acute consciousness, who emerged, of course, not from the bosom of nature, but from a laboratory test tube (this is almost mysticism, gentlemen, but I suspect that it's the case), then this test tube man sometimes gives up so completely in the face of his antithesis that he himself, with his overly acute consciousness, honestly considers himself not as a person, but a mouse. It may be an acutely conscious mouse, but a mouse nonetheless, while the other one is a person and consequently, . . . and so on and so forth. But the main thing is that he, he himself, considers himself to be a mouse; nobody asks him to do so, and that's the important point. Now let's take a look at this mouse in action. Let's assume, for instance, that it feels offended (it almost always feels offended), and that it also wishes to be revenged. It may even contain more accumulated malice than *l'homme de la nature et de la vérité*.[6] The mean, nasty, little desire to pay the offender back with evil may indeed rankle in it even more despicably than in *l'homme de la nature et de la vérité*, because *l'homme de la nature et de la vérité*, with his innate stupidity, considers his revenge nothing more than justice, pure and simple; but the mouse, as a result of its overly acute consciousness, rejects the idea of justice. Finally, we come to the act itself, to the very act of revenge. In addition to its original nastiness, the mouse has already managed to pile up all sorts of other nastiness around itself in the form of hesitations and doubts; so many unresolved questions have emerged from that one single question, that some kind of fatal blow is concocted unwillingly, some kind of stinking mess consisting of doubts, anxieties and, finally, spittle showered upon it by the spontaneous men of action who stand by solemnly as judges and arbiters, roaring with laughter until their sides split. Of course, the only thing left to do is dismiss it with a wave of its paw and a smile of assumed contempt which it doesn't even believe in, and creep ignominiously back into its mousehole. There, in its disgusting, stinking underground, our offended, crushed, and ridiculed mouse immediately plunges into cold, malicious, and, above all, everlasting spitefulness. For forty years on end it will recall its insult down to the last, most shameful detail; and each time it will add more shameful details of its own, spitefully teasing and irritating itself with its own fantasy. It will become ashamed of that fantasy, but it will still remember it, rehearse it again and again, fabricating all sorts of incredible stories about itself under the pretext that they too could have happened; it won't forgive a thing. Perhaps it will even begin to take revenge, but only in little bits and pieces, in trivial ways, from behind the stove, incognito, not believing in its right to be revenged, nor in the success of its own revenge, and knowing in advance that from all its attempts to take revenge, it will suffer a hundred times more than the object of its vengeance, who might not even feel a thing. On its deathbed it will recall everything all over again, with interest compounded over all those years and. . . . But it's precisely in that cold, abominable state of half-despair and half-belief, in that conscious burial of itself alive in the underground for forty years because of

6. "The man of nature and truth" (French). The basic idea is borrowed from Jean-Jacques Rousseau's *Confessions* (1782–89), namely, that human beings in a state of nature are honest and direct and that they are corrupted only by civilization.

its pain, in that powerfully created, yet partly dubious hopelessness of its own predicament, in all that venom of unfulfilled desire turned inward, in all that fever of vacillation, of resolutions adopted once and for all and followed a moment later by repentance—herein precisely lies the essence of that strange enjoyment I was talking about earlier. It's so subtle, sometimes so difficult to analyze, that even slightly limited people, or those who simply have strong nerves, won't understand anything about it. "Perhaps," you'll add with a smirk, "even those who've never received a slap in the face won't understand," and by so doing you'll be hinting to me ever so politely that perhaps during my life I too have received such a slap in the face and that therefore I'm speaking as an expert. I'll bet that's what you're thinking. Well, rest assured, gentlemen, I've never received such a slap, although it's really all the same to me what you think about it. Perhaps I may even regret the fact that I've given so few slaps during my lifetime. But that's enough, not another word about this subject which you find so extremely interesting.

I'll proceed calmly about people with strong nerves who don't understand certain refinements of pleasure. For example, although under particular circumstances these gentlemen may bellow like bulls as loudly as possible, and although, let's suppose, this behavior bestows on them the greatest honor, yet, as I've already said, when confronted with impossibility, they submit immediately. Impossibility—does that mean a stone wall? What kind of stone wall? Why, of course, the laws of nature, the conclusions of natural science and mathematics. As soon as they prove to you, for example, that it's from a monkey you're descended,[7] there's no reason to make faces; just accept it as it is. As soon as they prove to you that in truth one drop of your own fat is dearer to you than the lives of one hundred thousand of your fellow creatures and that this will finally put an end to all the so-called virtues, obligations, and other such similar ravings and prejudices, just accept that too; there's nothing more to do, since two times two is a fact of mathematics. Just you try to object.

"For goodness sake," they'll shout at you, "it's impossible to protest: it's two times two makes four! Nature doesn't ask for your opinion; it doesn't care about your desires or whether you like or dislike its laws. You're obliged to accept it as it is, and consequently, all its conclusions. A wall, you see, is a wall . . . etc. etc." Good Lord, what do I care about the laws of nature and arithmetic when for some reason I dislike all these laws and I dislike the fact that two times two makes four? Of course, I won't break through that wall with my head if I really don't have the strength to do so, nor will I reconcile myself to it just because I'm faced with such a stone wall and lack the strength.

As though such a stone wall actually offered some consolation and contained some real word of conciliation, for the sole reason that it means two times two makes four. Oh, absurdity of absurdities! How much better it is to understand it all, to be aware of everything, all the impossibilities and stone walls; not to be reconciled with any of those impossibilities or stone walls if it so disgusts you; to reach, by using the most inevitable logical combinations, the most revolting conclusions on the eternal theme that you are somehow or other to blame even for that stone wall, even though it's absolutely clear once

7. A reference to the theory of evolution by natural selection developed by Charles Darwin (1809–1882). A book on the subject was translated into Russian in 1864.

again that you're in no way to blame, and, as a result of all this, while silently and impotently gnashing your teeth, you sink voluptuously into inertia, musing on the fact that, as it turns out, there's no one to be angry with; that an object cannot be found, and perhaps never will be; that there's been a substitution, some sleight of hand, a bit of cheating, and that it's all a mess—you can't tell who's who or what's what; but in spite of all these uncertainties and sleights-of-hand, it hurts you just the same, and the more you don't know, the more it hurts!

IV

"Ha, ha, ha! Why, you'll be finding enjoyment in a toothache next!" you cry out with a laugh.

"Well, what of it? There is some enjoyment even in a toothache," I reply. I've had a toothache for a whole month; I know what's what. In this instance, of course, people don't rage in silence; they moan. But these moans are insincere; they're malicious, and malice is the whole point. These moans express the sufferer's enjoyment; if he didn't enjoy it, he would never have begun to moan. This is a good example, gentlemen, and I'll develop it. In the first place, these moans express all the aimlessness of the pain which consciousness finds so humiliating, the whole system of natural laws about which you really don't give a damn, but as a result of which you're suffering nonetheless, while nature isn't. They express the consciousness that while there's no real enemy to be identified, the pain exists nonetheless; the awareness that, in spite of all possible Wagenheims,[8] you're still a complete slave to your teeth; that if someone so wishes, your teeth will stop aching, but that if he doesn't so wish, they'll go on aching for three more months; and finally, that if you still disagree and protest, all there's left to do for consolation is flagellate yourself or beat your fist against the wall as hard as you can, and absolutely nothing else. Well, then, it's these bloody insults, these jeers coming from nowhere, that finally generate enjoyment that can sometimes reach the highest degree of voluptuousness. I beseech you, gentlemen, to listen to the moans of an educated man of the nineteenth century who's suffering from a toothache, especially on the second or third day of his distress, when he begins to moan in a very different way than he did on the first day, that is, not simply because his tooth aches; not the way some coarse peasant moans, but as a man affected by progress and European civilization, a man "who's renounced both the soil and the common people," as they say nowadays. His moans become somehow nasty, despicably spiteful, and they go on for days and nights. Yet he himself knows that his moans do him no good; he knows better than anyone else that he's merely irritating himself and others in vain; he knows that the audience for whom he's trying so hard, and his whole family, have now begun to listen to him with loathing; they don't believe him for a second, and they realize full well that he could moan in a different, much simpler way, without all the flourishes and affectation, and that he's only indulging himself out of spite and malice. Well, it's precisely in this

8. The *General Address Book of St. Petersburg* listed eight dentists named Wagenheim; contemporary readers would have recognized the name from signs throughout the city.

awareness and shame that the voluptuousness resides. "It seems I'm disturbing you, tearing at your heart, preventing anyone in the house from getting
any sleep. Well, then, you won't sleep; you too must be aware at all times that
I have a toothache. I'm no longer the hero I wanted to pass for earlier, but
simply a nasty little man, a rogue. So be it! I'm delighted that you've seen
through me. Does it make you feel bad to hear my wretched little moans?
Well, then, feel bad. Now let me add an even nastier flourish. . . ." You still
don't understand, gentlemen? No, it's clear that one has to develop further
and become even more conscious in order to understand all the nuances of
this voluptuousness! Are you laughing? I'm delighted. Of course my jokes are
in bad taste, gentlemen; they're uneven, contradictory, and lacking in self-
assurance. But that's because I have no respect for myself. Can a man possessing consciousness ever really respect himself?

V

Well, and is it possible, is it really possible for a man to respect himself if he
even presumes to find enjoyment in the feeling of his own humiliation? I'm
not saying this out of any feigned repentance. In general I could never bear
to say: "I'm sorry, Daddy, and I won't do it again," not because I was incapable
of saying it, but, on the contrary, perhaps precisely because I was all too
capable, and how! As if on purpose it would happen that I'd get myself into
some sort of mess for which I was not to blame in any way whatsoever. That
was the most repulsive part of it. What's more, I'd feel touched deep in my
soul; I'd repent and shed tears, deceiving even myself of course, though not
feigning in the least. It seemed that my heart was somehow playing dirty
tricks on me. . . . Here one couldn't even blame the laws of nature, although
it was these very laws that continually hurt me during my entire life. It's disgusting to recall all this, and it was disgusting even then. Of course, a moment
or so later I would realize in anger that it was all lies, lies, revolting, made-up
lies, that is, all that repentance, all that tenderness, all those vows to mend
my ways. But you'll ask why I mauled and tortured myself in that way? The
answer is because it was so very boring to sit idly by with my arms folded; so
I'd get into trouble. That's the way it was. Observe yourselves better, gentlemen; then you'll understand that it's true. I used to think up adventures for
myself, inventing a life so that at least I could live. How many times did it
happen, well, let's say, for example, that I took offense, deliberately, for no
reason at all? All the while I knew there was no reason for it; I put on airs
nonetheless, and would take it so far that finally I really did feel offended. I've
been drawn into such silly tricks all my life, so that finally I lost control over
myself. Another time, even twice, I tried hard to fall in love. I even suffered,
gentlemen, I can assure you. In the depths of my soul I really didn't believe
that I was suffering; there was a stir of mockery, but suffer I did, and in
a genuine, normal way at that; I was jealous, I was beside myself with
anger. . . . And all as a result of boredom, gentlemen, sheer boredom; I was
overcome by inertia. You see, the direct, legitimate, immediate result of consciousness is inertia, that is, the conscious sitting idly by with one's arms
folded. I've referred to this before. I repeat, I repeat emphatically: all spontaneous men and men of action are so active precisely because they're stupid

and limited. How can one explain this? Here's how: as a result of their limitations they mistake immediate and secondary causes for primary ones, and thus they're convinced more quickly and easily than other people that they've located an indisputable basis for action, and this puts them at ease; that's the main point. For, in order to begin to act, one must first be absolutely at ease, with no lingering doubts whatsoever. Well, how can I, for example, ever feel at ease? Where are the primary causes I can rely upon, where's the foundation? Where shall I find it? I exercise myself in thinking, and consequently, with me every primary cause drags in another, an even more primary one, and so on to infinity. This is precisely the essence of all consciousness and thought. And here again, it must be the laws of nature. What's the final result? Why, the very same thing. Remember: I was talking about revenge before. (You probably didn't follow.) I said: a man takes revenge because he finds justice in it. That means, he's found a primary cause, a foundation: namely, justice. Therefore, he's completely at ease, and, as a result, he takes revenge peacefully and successfully, convinced that he's performing an honest and just deed. But I don't see any justice here at all, nor do I find any virtue in it whatever; consequently, if I begin to take revenge, it's only out of spite. Of course, spite could overcome everything, all my doubts, and therefore could successfully serve instead of a primary cause precisely because it's not a cause at all. But what do I do if I don't even feel spite (that's where I began before)? After all, as a result of those damned laws of consciousness, my spite is subject to chemical disintegration. You look—and the object vanishes, the arguments evaporate, a guilty party can't be identified, the offense ceases to be one and becomes a matter of fate, something like a toothache for which no one's to blame, and, as a consequence, there remains only the same recourse: that is, to bash the wall even harder. So you throw up your hands because you haven't found a primary cause. Just try to let yourself be carried away blindly by your feelings, without reflection, without a primary cause, suppressing consciousness even for a moment; hate or love, anything, just in order not to sit idly by with your arms folded. The day after tomorrow at the very latest, you'll begin to despise yourself for having deceived yourself knowingly. The result: a soap bubble and inertia. Oh, gentlemen, perhaps I consider myself to be an intelligent man simply because for my whole life I haven't been able to begin or finish anything. All right, suppose I am a babbler, a harmless, annoying babbler, like the rest of us. But then what is to be done[9] if the direct and single vocation of every intelligent man consists in babbling, that is, in deliberately talking in endless circles?

VI

Oh, if only I did nothing simply as a result of laziness. Lord, how I'd respect myself then. I'd respect myself precisely because at least I'd be capable of being lazy; at least I'd possess one more or less positive trait of which I could

9. Reference to a then-new novel by Nikolai Chernyshevsky (1828–1889) called *What Is to Be Done?* (1863). Dostoyevsky disliked the main idea of the novel, which was that Russians could be freed from the delusions of tra- dition and faith by scientific knowledge and could build a rational new nation; *Notes from Underground* is in part a response to Cherny-shevsky.

be certain. Question: who am I? Answer: a sluggard. Why, it would have been very pleasant to hear that said about oneself. It would mean that I'd been positively identified; it would mean that there was something to be said about me. "A sluggard!" Why, that's a calling and a vocation, a whole career! Don't joke, it's true. Then, by rights I'd be a member of the very best club and would occupy myself exclusively by being able to respect myself continually. I knew a gentleman who prided himself all his life on being a connoisseur of Lafite.[1] He considered it his positive virtue and never doubted himself. He died not merely with a clean conscience, but with a triumphant one, and he was absolutely correct. I should have chosen a career for myself too: I would have been a sluggard and a glutton, not an ordinary one, but one who, for example, sympathized with everything beautiful and sublime. How do you like that? I've dreamt about it for a long time. The "beautiful and sublime" have been a real pain in the neck during my forty years, but then it's been *my* forty years, whereas then—oh, then it would have been otherwise! I would've found myself a suitable activity at once— namely, drinking to everything beautiful and sublime. I would have seized upon every opportunity first to shed a tear into my glass and then drink to everything beautiful and sublime. Then I would have turned everything into the beautiful and sublime; I would have sought out the beautiful and sublime in the nastiest, most indisputable trash. I would have become as tearful as a wet sponge. An artist, for example, has painted a portrait of Ge.[2] At once I drink to the artist who painted that portrait of Ge because I love everything beautiful and sublime. An author has written the words, "Just as you please,"[3] at once I drink to "Just as you please," because I love everything "beautiful and sublime." I'd demand respect for myself in doing this, I'd persecute anyone who didn't pay me any respect. I'd live peacefully and die triumphantly—why, it's charming, perfectly charming! And what a belly I'd have grown by then, what a triple chin I'd have acquired, what a red nose I'd have developed—so that just looking at me any passerby would have said, "Now that's a real plus! That's something really positive!" Say what you like, gentlemen, it's extremely pleasant to hear such comments in our negative age.

VII

But these are all golden dreams. Oh, tell me who was first to announce, first to proclaim that man does nasty things simply because he doesn't know his own true interest; and that if he were to be enlightened, if his eyes were to be opened to his true, normal interests, he would stop doing nasty things at once and would immediately become good and noble, because, being so enlightened and understanding his real advantage, he would realize that his own advantage really did lie in the good; and that it's well known that there's not a single man capable of acting knowingly against his own interest; conse-

---

1. A variety of red wine from Médoc in France.
2. N. N. Ge (1831–1894), Russian artist who rebelled against official styles in favor of a new realism in art; just before *Notes from Underground* appeared, Ge's *Last Supper* (1863) provoked considerable controversy in St. Petersburg because the painter had refused the conventional imagery of Jesus seated at a long table and instead showed him reclined and meditative, with his disciples confused and frightened.
3. An attack on the writer M. E. Saltykov-Shchedrin, who published a sympathetic review of Ge's painting titled *Just As You Please*.

quently, he would, so to speak, begin to do good out of necessity. Oh, the child! Oh, the pure, innocent babe! Well, in the first place, when was it during all these millennia, that man has ever acted only in his own self interest? What does one do with the millions of facts bearing witness to the one fact that people knowingly, that is, possessing full knowledge of their own true interests, have relegated them to the background and have rushed down a different path, that of risk and chance, compelled by no one and nothing, but merely as if they didn't want to follow the beaten track, and so they stubbornly, willfully forged another way, a difficult and absurd one, searching for it almost in the darkness? Why, then, this means that stubbornness and willfulness were really more pleasing to them than any kind of advantage. . . . Advantage! What is advantage? Will you take it upon yourself to define with absolute precision what constitutes man's advantage? And what if it turns out that man's advantage sometimes not only may, but even must in certain circumstances, consist precisely in his desiring something harmful to himself instead of something advantageous? And if this is so, if this can ever occur, then the whole theory falls to pieces. What do you think, can such a thing happen? You're laughing; laugh, gentlemen, but answer me: have man's advantages ever been calculated with absolute certainty? Aren't there some which don't fit, can't be made to fit into any classification? Why, as far as I know, you gentlemen have derived your list of human advantages from averages of statistical data and from scientific-economic formulas. But your advantages are prosperity, wealth, freedom, peace, and so on and so forth; so that a man who, for example, expressly and knowingly acts in opposition to this whole list, would be, in your opinion, and in mine, too, of course, either an obscurantist or a complete madman, wouldn't he? But now here's what's astonishing: why is it that when all these statisticians, sages, and lovers of humanity enumerate man's advantages, they invariably leave one out? They don't even take it into consideration in the form in which it should be considered, although the entire calculation depends upon it. There would be no great harm in considering it, this advantage, and adding it to the list. But the whole point is that this particular advantage doesn't fit into any classification and can't be found on any list. I have a friend, for instance. . . . But gentlemen! Why, he's your friend, too! In fact, he's everyone's friend! When he's preparing to do something, this gentleman straight away explains to you eloquently and clearly just how he must act according to the laws of nature and truth. And that's not all: with excitement and passion he'll tell you all about genuine, normal human interests; with scorn he'll reproach the shortsighted fools who understand neither their own advantage nor the real meaning of virtue; and then—exactly a quarter of an hour later, without any sudden outside cause, but precisely because of something internal that's stronger than all his interests—he does a complete about-face; that is, he does something which clearly contradicts what he's been saying: it goes against the laws of reason and his own advantage, in a word, against everything. . . . I warn you that my friend is a collective personage; therefore it's rather difficult to blame only him. That's just it, gentlemen; in fact, isn't there something dearer to every man than his own best advantage, or (so as not to violate the rules of logic) isn't there one more advantageous advantage (exactly the one omitted, the one we mentioned before), which is more important and more advantageous than all others and, on behalf of which, a man will, if necessary, go against all laws, that is, against reason, honor, peace, and prosperity—in a word, against all those splendid and useful things, merely in order to attain this fundamental, most advantageous advantage which is dearer to him than everything else?

"Well, it's advantage all the same," you say, interrupting me. Be so kind as to allow me to explain further; besides, the point is not my pun, but the fact that this advantage is remarkable precisely because it destroys all our classifications and constantly demolishes all systems devised by lovers of humanity for the happiness of mankind. In a word, it interferes with everything. But, before I name this advantage, I want to compromise myself personally; therefore I boldly declare that all these splendid systems, all these theories to explain to mankind its real, normal interests so that, by necessarily striving to achieve them, it would immediately become good and noble—are, for the time being, in my opinion, nothing more than logical exercises! Yes, sir, logical exercises! Why, even to maintain a theory of mankind's regeneration through a system of its own advantages, why, in my opinion, that's almost the same as . . . well, claiming, for instance, following Buckle,[4] that man has become kinder as a result of civilization; consequently, he's becoming less bloodthirsty and less inclined to war. Why, logically it all even seems to follow. But man is so partial to systems and abstract conclusions that he's ready to distort the truth intentionally, ready to deny everything that he himself has ever seen and heard, merely in order to justify his own logic. That's why I take this example, because it's such a glaring one. Just look around: rivers of blood are being spilt, and in the most cheerful way, as if it were champagne. Take this entire nineteenth century of ours during which even Buckle lived. Take Napoleon—both the great and the present one.[5] Take North America—that eternal union.[6] Take, finally, that ridiculous Schleswig-Holstein[7]. . . . What is it that civilization makes kinder in us? Civilization merely promotes a wider variety of sensations in man and . . . absolutely nothing else. And through the development of this variety man may even reach the point where he takes pleasure in spilling blood. Why, that's even happened to him already. Haven't you noticed that the most refined bloodshedders are almost always the most civilized gentlemen to whom all these Attila the Huns and Stenka Razins[8] are scarcely fit to hold a candle; and if they're not as conspicuous as Attila and Stenka Razin, it's precisely because they're too common and have become too familiar to us. At least if man hasn't become more bloodthirsty as a result of civilization, surely he's become bloodthirsty in a nastier, more repulsive way than before. Previously man saw justice in bloodshed and exterminated whomever he wished with a clear conscience; whereas now, though we con-

---

4. In his *History of Civilization in England* (1857–61), Henry Thomas Buckle (1821–1862) argued that the development of civilization necessarily leads to the cessation of war. Russia had recently been involved in fierce fighting in the Crimea (1853–56).
5. The French emperors Napoleon I (1769–1821) and his nephew Napoleon III (1808–1873), both of whom engaged in numerous wars, though on vastly different scales.

6. The United States was in the middle of its Civil War (1861–65).
7. The German duchies of Schleswig and Holstein, held by Denmark since 1773, were reunited with Prussia after a brief war in 1864.
8. Cossack leader (d. 1671) who organized a peasant rebellion in Russia. Attila (406?–453 C.E.), king of the Huns, who conducted devastating wars against the Roman emperors.

sider bloodshed to be abominable, we nevertheless engage in this abomination even more than before. Which is worse? Decide for yourselves. They say that Cleopatra (forgive an example from Roman history) loved to stick gold pins into the breasts of her slave girls and take pleasure in their screams and writhing. You'll say that this took place, relatively speaking, in barbaric times; that these are barbaric times too, because (also comparatively speaking), gold pins are used even now; that even now, although man has learned on occasion to see more clearly than in barbaric times, *he's still far from having learned* how to act in accordance with the dictates of reason and science. Nevertheless, you're still absolutely convinced that he will learn how to do so, as soon as he gets rid of some bad, old habits and as soon as common sense and science have completely re-educated human nature and have turned it in the proper direction. You're convinced that then man will voluntarily stop committing blunders, and that he will, so to speak, never willingly set his own will in opposition to his own normal interests. More than that: then, you say, science itself will teach man (though, in my opinion, that's already a luxury) that in fact he possesses neither a will nor any whim of his own, that he never did, and that he himself is nothing more than a kind of piano key or an organ stop;[9] that, moreover, there still exist laws of nature, so that everything he's done has been not in accordance with his own desire, but in and of itself, according to the laws of nature. Consequently, we need only discover these laws of nature, and man will no longer have to answer for his own actions and will find it extremely easy to live. All human actions, it goes without saying, will then be tabulated according to these laws, mathematically, like tables of logarithms up to 108,000, and will be entered on a schedule; or even better, certain edifying works will be published, like our contemporary encyclopedic dictionaries, in which everything will be accurately calculated and specified so that there'll be no more actions or adventures left on earth.

At that time, it's still you speaking, new economic relations will be established, all ready-made, also calculated with mathematical precision, so that all possible questions will disappear in a single instant, simply because all possible answers will have been provided. Then the crystal palace[1] will be built. And then . . . Well, in a word, those will be our halcyon days. Of course, there's no way to guarantee (now this is me talking) that it won't be, for instance, terribly boring then (because there won't be anything left to do, once everything has been calculated according to tables); on the other hand, everything will be extremely rational. Of course, what don't people think up out of boredom! Why, even gold pins get stuck into other people out of boredom, but that wouldn't matter. What's really bad (this is me talking again) is that for all I know, people might even be grateful for those gold pins. For man is stupid, phenomenally stupid. That is, although he's not really stupid at all, he's really so ungrateful that it's hard to find another being quite like him. Why,

9. A reference to the last discourse of the French philosopher Denis Diderot (1713–1784) in the *Conversation of D'Alembert and Diderot* (1769).
1. An allusion to the crystal palace described in Vera Pavlovna's fourth dream in Cherny-shevsky's *What Is to Be Done?* and to the actual building designed by Sir Joseph Paxton, erected for the Great Exhibition in London in 1851 and at that time admired as the newest wonder of architecture; Dostoevsky described it in *Winter Notes on Summer Impressions* (1863).

I, for example, wouldn't be surprised in the least, if, suddenly, for no reason at all, in the midst of this future, universal rationalism, some gentleman with an offensive, rather, a retrograde and derisive expression on his face were to stand up, put his hands on his hips, and declare to us all: "How about it, gentlemen, what if we knock over all this rationalism with one swift kick for the sole purpose of sending all these logarithms to hell, so that once again we can live according to our own stupid will!" But that wouldn't matter either; what's so annoying is that he would undoubtedly find some followers; such is the way man is made. And all because of the most foolish reason, which, it seems, is hardly worth mentioning: namely, that man, always and everywhere, whoever he is, has preferred to act as he wished, and not at all as reason and advantage have dictated; one might even desire something opposed to one's own advantage, and sometimes (this is now my idea) one *positively must do so*. One's very own free, unfettered desire, one's own whim, no matter how wild, one's own fantasy, even though sometimes roused to the point of madness—all this constitutes precisely that previously omitted, most advantageous advantage which isn't included under any classification and because of which all systems and theories are constantly smashed to smithereens. Where did these sages ever get the idea that man needs any normal, virtuous desire? How did they ever imagine that man needs any kind of rational, advantageous desire? Man needs only one thing— his own *independent* desire, whatever that independence might cost and wherever it might lead. And as far as desire goes, the devil only knows. . . .

VIII

"Ha, ha, ha! But in reality even this desire, if I may say so, doesn't exist!" you interrupt me with a laugh. "Why science has already managed to dissect man so now we know that desire and so-called free choice are nothing more than . . ."

Wait, gentlemen, I myself wanted to begin like that. I must confess that even I got frightened. I was just about to declare that the devil only knows what desire depends on and perhaps we should be grateful for that, but then I remembered about science and I . . . stopped short. But now you've gone and brought it up. Well, after all, what if someday they really do discover the formula for all our desires and whims, that is, the thing that governs them, precise laws that produce them, how exactly they're applied, where they lead in each and every case, and so on and so forth, that is, the genuine mathematical formula—why, then all at once man might stop desiring, yes, indeed, he probably would. Who would want to desire according to some table? And that's not all: he would immediately be transformed from a person into an organ stop or something of that sort; because what is man without desire, without will, and without wishes if not a stop in an organ pipe? What do you think? Let's consider the probabilities—can this really happen or not?

"Hmmm . . . ," you decide, "our desires are mistaken for the most part because of an erroneous view of our own advantage. Consequently, we sometimes desire pure rubbish because, in our own stupidity, we consider it the easiest way to achieve some previously assumed advantage. Well, and when all this has been analyzed, calculated on paper (that's entirely possible, since it's repugnant and senseless to assume in advance that man will never come to understand the laws of nature) then, of course, all so-called desires will no longer exist. For if someday desires are completely reconciled with reason, we'll follow reason instead of desire simply because it would be impossible, for example, while retaining one's reason, to *desire* rubbish, and thus knowingly oppose one's reason, and desire something harmful to oneself. . . . And, since all desires and reasons can really be tabulated, since someday the laws of our so-called free choice are sure to be discovered, then, all joking aside, it may be possible to establish something like a table, so that we could actually desire according to it. If, for example, someday they calculate and demonstrate to me that I made a rude gesture because I couldn't possibly refrain from it, that I had to make precisely that gesture, well, in that case, what sort of *free choice* would there be, especially if I'm a learned man and have completed a course of study somewhere? Why, then I'd be able to calculate in advance my entire life for the next thirty years; in a word, if such a table were to be drawn up, there'd be nothing left for us to do; we'd simply have to accept it. In general, we should be repeating endlessly to ourselves that at such a time and in such circumstances nature certainly won't ask our opinion; that we must accept it as is, and not as we fantasize it, and that if we really aspire to prepare a table, a schedule, and, well . . . well, even a laboratory test tube, there's nothing to be done—one must even accept the test tube! If not, it'll be accepted even without you. . . ."

Yes, but that's just where I hit a snag! Gentlemen, you'll excuse me for all this philosophizing; it's a result of my forty years in the underground! Allow me to fantasize. Don't you see: reason is a fine thing, gentlemen, there's no doubt about it, but it's only reason, and it satisfies only man's rational faculty, whereas desire is a manifestation of all life, that is, of all human life, which includes both reason, as well as all of life's itches and scratches. And although in this manifestation life often turns out to be fairly worthless, it's life all the same, and not merely the extraction of square roots. Why, take me, for instance; I quite naturally want to live in order to satisfy all my faculties of life, not merely my rational faculty, that is, some one-twentieth of all my faculties. What does reason know? Reason knows only what it's managed to learn. (Some things it may never learn; while this offers no comfort, why not admit it openly?) But human nature acts as a whole, with all that it contains, consciously and unconsciously; and although it may tell lies, it's still alive. I suspect, gentlemen, that you're looking at me with compassion; you repeat that an enlightened and cultured man, in a word, man as he will be in the future, cannot knowingly desire something disadvantageous to himself, and that this is pure mathematics. I agree with you: it really is mathematics. But I repeat for the one-hundredth time, there is one case, only one, when a man may intentionally, consciously desire even something harmful to himself, something stupid, even very stupid, namely: in order *to have the right* to desire something even very stupid and not be bound by an obligation to desire only what's smart. After all, this very stupid thing, one's own whim, gentlemen, may in fact be the most advantageous thing on earth for people like me, especially in certain cases. In particular, it may be more advantageous than any other advantage, even in a case where it causes obvious harm and contradicts the most sensible conclusions of reason about advantage—because in any case it preserves for us what's most important and precious, that is, our personality and our individuality. There are some people who maintain that in fact this is more precious to man than anything else; of course, desire can, if it so chooses, coincide with reason, especially if it doesn't abuse this option, and chooses to coincide in moderation; this is useful and sometimes even commendable. But very often, even most of the time, desire absolutely and stubbornly disagrees with reason and . . . and . . . and, do you know, sometimes this is also useful and even very commendable? Let's assume, gentlemen, that man isn't stupid. (And really, this can't possibly be said about him at all, if only because if he's stupid, then who on earth is smart?) But even if he's not stupid, he is, nevertheless, monstrously ungrateful. Phenomenally ungrateful. I even believe that the best definition of man is this: a creature who walks on two legs and is ungrateful. But that's still not all; that's still not his main defect. His main defect is his perpetual misbehavior, perpetual from the time of the Great Flood to the Schleswig-Holstein period of human destiny. Misbehavior, and consequently, imprudence; for it's long been known that imprudence results from nothing else but misbehavior. Just cast a glance at the history of mankind; well, what do you see? Is it majestic? Well, perhaps it's majestic; why, the Colossus of Rhodes,[2] for example— that alone is worth something! Not without reason did Mr Anaevsky[3] report that some people consider it to be the product of human hands, while others maintain that it was created by nature itself. Is it colorful? Well, perhaps it's also colorful; just consider the dress uniforms, both military and civilian, of all nations at all times—why, that alone is worth something, and if you include everyday uniforms, it'll make your eyes bulge; not one historian will be able to sort it all out. Is it monotonous? Well, perhaps it's monotonous, too: men fight and fight; now they're fighting; they fought first and they fought last—you'll agree that it's really much too monotonous. In short, anything can be said about world history, anything that might occur to the most disordered imagination. There's only one thing that can't possibly be said about it—that it's rational. You'll choke on the word. Yet here's just the sort of thing you'll encounter all the time: why, in life you're constantly running up against people who are so well-behaved and so rational, such wise men and lovers of humanity who set themselves the lifelong goal of behaving as morally and rationally as possible, so to speak, to be a beacon for their nearest and dearest, simply in order to prove that it's really possible to live one's life in a moral and rational way. And so what? It's a well-known fact that many of these lovers of humanity, sooner or later, by the end of their lives, have betrayed themselves: they've pulled off some caper, sometimes even quite an indecent one. Now I ask you: what can one expect from man as a creature endowed with such strange qualities? Why, shower him with all sorts of earthly blessings, submerge him in happiness over his head so that only little bubbles appear on the surface of this happiness, as if on water, give him such economic prosperity that he'll have absolutely nothing left to do except sleep, eat gingerbread, and worry about the continuation of world history—even then, out of pure ingratitude, sheer perversity, he'll commit some repulsive act. He'll even risk losing his gingerbread, and will intentionally desire the most wicked rubbish, the most uneconomical absurdity, simply in order to inject his own pernicious fantastic element into all this positive rationality. He wants to hold onto those most fantastic dreams, his

2. A large bronze statue of the Greek sun god, Helios, built between 292 and 280 B.C.E. in the harbor of Rhodes (an island in the Aegean Sea) and considered one of the Seven Won-

ders of the Ancient World.
3. A. E. Anaevsky was a critic whose articles were frequently ridiculed in literary polemics of the period.

own indecent stupidity solely for the purpose of assuring himself (as if it were necessary) that men are still men and not piano keys, and that even if the laws of nature play upon them with their own hands, they're still threatened by being overplayed until they won't possibly desire anything more than a schedule. But that's not all: even if man really turned out to be a piano key, even if this could be demonstrated to him by natural science and pure mathematics, even then he still won't become reasonable; he'll intentionally do something to the contrary, simply out of ingratitude, merely to have his own way. If he lacks the means, he'll cause destruction and chaos, he'll devise all kinds of suffering and have his own way! He'll leash a curse upon the world; and, since man alone can do so (it's his privilege and the thing that most distinguishes him from other animals), perhaps only through this curse will he achieve his goal, that is, become really convinced that he's a man and not a piano key! If you say that one can also calculate all this according to a table, this chaos and darkness, these curses, so that the mere possibility of calculating it all in advance would stop everything and that reason alone would prevail—in that case man would go insane deliberately in order not to have reason, but to have his own way! I believe this, I vouch for it, because, after all, the whole of man's work seems to consist only in proving to himself constantly that he's a man and not an organ stop! Even if he has to lose his own skin, he'll prove it; even if he has to become a troglodyte, he'll prove it. And after that, how can one not sin, how can one not praise the fact that all this hasn't yet come to pass and that desire still depends on the devil knows what . . . ?

You'll shout at me (if you still choose to favor me with your shouts) that no one's really depriving me of my will; that they're merely attempting to arrange things so that my will, by its own free choice, will coincide with my normal interests, with the laws of nature, and with arithmetic.

But gentlemen, what sort of free choice will there be when it comes down to tables and arithmetic, when all that's left is two times two makes four? Two times two makes four even without my will. Is that what you call free choice?

IX

Gentlemen, I'm joking of course, and I myself know that it's not a very good joke; but, after all, you can't take everything as a joke. Perhaps I'm gnashing my teeth while I joke. I'm tormented by questions, gentlemen; answer them for me. Now, for example, you want to cure man of his old habits and improve his will according to the demands of science and common sense. But how do you know not only whether it's possible, but even if it's *necessary* to remake him in this way? Why do you conclude that human desire *must* undoubtedly be improved? In short, how do you know that such improvement will really be to man's advantage? And, to be perfectly frank, why are you so *absolutely* convinced that not to oppose man's real, normal advantage guaranteed by the conclusions of reason and arithmetic is really always to man's advantage and constitutes a law for all humanity? After all, this is still only an assumption of yours. Let's suppose that it's a law of logic, but perhaps not a law of humanity. Perhaps, gentlemen, you're wondering if I'm insane? Allow me to explain. I agree that man is primarily a creative animal, destined to strive consciously toward a goal and to engage in the art of engineering, that, is, externally and incessantly building new roads for himself *wherever they lead*. But sometimes he may want to swerve aside precisely because he's *compelled* to build these roads, and perhaps also because, no matter how stupid the spontaneous man of action may generally be, nevertheless it sometimes occurs to him that the road, as it turns out, almost always leads *somewhere or other*, and that the main thing isn't so much where it goes, but the fact that it does, and that the well-behaved child, disregarding the art of engineering, shouldn't yield to pernicious idleness which, as is well known, constitutes the mother of all vices. Man loves to create and build roads; that's indisputable. But why is he also so passionately fond of destruction and chaos? Now, then, tell me. But I myself want to say a few words about this separately. Perhaps the reason that he's so fond of destruction and chaos (after all, it's indisputable that he sometimes really loves it, and that's a fact) is that he himself has an instinctive fear of achieving his goal and completing the project under construction? How do you know if perhaps he loves his building only from afar, but not from close up; perhaps he only likes building it, but not living in it, leaving it afterward *aux animaux domestiques*,[4] such as ants or sheep, or so on and so forth. Now ants have altogether different tastes. They have one astonishing structure of a similar type, forever indestructible—the anthill.

The worthy ants began with the anthill, and most likely, they will end with the anthill, which does great credit to their perseverance and steadfastness. But man is a frivolous and unseemly creature and perhaps, like a chess player, he loves only the process of achieving his goal, and not the goal itself. And, who knows (one can't vouch for it), perhaps the only goal on earth toward which mankind is striving consists merely in this incessant process of achieving or to put it another way, in life itself, and not particularly in the goal which, of course, must always be none other than two times two makes four, that is, a formula; after all, two times two makes four is no longer life, gentlemen, but the beginning of death. At least man has always been somewhat afraid of this two times two makes four, and I'm afraid of it now, too. Let's suppose that the only thing man does is search for this two times two makes four; he sails across oceans, sacrifices his own life in the quest; but to seek it out and find it—really and truly, he's very frightened. After all, he feels that as soon as he finds it, there'll be nothing left to search for. Workers, after finishing work, at least receive their wages, go off to a tavern, and then wind up at a police station—now that's a full week's occupation. But where will man go? At any rate a certain awkwardness can be observed each time he approaches the achievement of similar goals. He loves the process, but he's not so fond of the achievement, and that, of course is terribly amusing. In short, man is made in a comical way; obviously there's some sort of catch in all this. But two times two makes four is an insufferable thing, nevertheless. Two times two makes four—why, in my opinion, it's mere insolence. Two times two makes four stands there brazenly with its hands on its hips, blocking your path and spitting at you. I agree that two times two makes four is a splendid thing; but if we're going to lavish praise, then two times two makes five is sometimes also a very charming little thing.

And why are you so firmly, so triumphantly convinced that only the normal and positive—in short, only well-being is advantageous to man? Doesn't reason ever make mistakes about advantage? After all, perhaps man likes something

4. "To domestic animals" (French).

other than well-being? Perhaps he loves suffering just as much? Perhaps suffering is just as advantageous to him as well-being? Man sometimes loves suffering terribly, to the point of passion, and that's a fact. There's no reason to study world history on this point; if indeed you're a man and have lived at all, just ask yourself. As far as my own personal opinion is concerned, to love only well-being is somehow even indecent. Whether good or bad, it's sometimes also very pleasant to demolish something. After all, I'm not standing up for suffering here, nor for well-being, either. I'm standing up for . . . my own whim and for its being guaranteed to me whenever necessary. For instance, suffering is not permitted in vaudevilles,[5] that I know. It's also inconceivable in the crystal palace; suffering is doubt and negation. What sort of crystal palace would it be if any doubt were allowed? Yet, I'm convinced that man will never renounce real suffering, that is, destruction and chaos. After all, suffering is the sole cause of consciousness. Although I stated earlier that in my opinion consciousness is man's greatest misfortune, still I know that man loves it and would not exchange it for any other sort of satisfaction. Consciousness, for example, is infinitely higher than two times two. Of course, after two times two, there's nothing left, not merely nothing to do, but nothing to learn. Then the only thing possible will be to plug up your five senses and plunge into contemplation. Well, even if you reach the same result with consciousness, that is, having nothing left to do, at least you'll be able to flog yourself from time to time, and that will liven things up a bit. Although it may be reactionary, it's still better than nothing.

X[6]

You believe in the crystal palace, eternally indestructible, that is, one at which you can never stick out your tongue furtively nor make a rude gesture, even with your fist hidden away. Well, perhaps I'm so afraid of this building precisely because it's made of crystal and it's eternally indestructible, and because it won't be possible to stick one's tongue out even furtively.

Don't you see: if it were a chicken coop instead of a palace, and if it should rain, then perhaps I could crawl into it so as not to get drenched; but I would still not mistake a chicken coop for a palace out of gratitude, just because it sheltered me from the rain. You're laughing, you're even saying that in this case there's no difference between a chicken coop and a mansion. Yes, I reply, if the only reason for living is to keep from getting drenched.

But what if I've taken it into my head that this is not the only reason for living, and, that if one is to live at all, one might as well live in a mansion? Such is my wish, my desire. You'll expunge it from me only when you've changed my desires. Well, then, change them, tempt me with something else, give me some other ideal. In the meantime, I still won't mistake a chicken coop for a palace. But let's say that the crystal palace is a hoax, that according to the laws of nature it shouldn't exist, and that I've invented it only out of my own stupidity, as a result of certain antiquated, irrational habits of my generation. But what do I care if it doesn't exist? What difference does it make if it exists only

---

5. A dramatic genre, popular on the Russian stage, consisting of scenes from contemporary life acted with a satirical twist, often in racy dialogue.

6. This chapter was badly mutilated by the censor, as Dostoyevsky makes clear in the letter to his brother Mikhail, dated March 26, 1864.

in my own desires, or, to be more precise, if it exists as long as my desires exist? Perhaps you're laughing again? Laugh, if you wish; I'll resist all your laughter and I still won't say I'm satiated if I'm really hungry; I know all the same that I won't accept a compromise, an infinitely recurring zero, just because it exists according to the laws of nature and it *really* does exist. I won't accept as the crown of my desires a large building with tenements for poor tenants to be rented for a thousand years and, just in case, with the name of the dentist Wagenheim on the sign. Destroy my desires, eradicate my ideals, show me something better and I'll follow you. You may say, perhaps, that it's not worth getting involved; but, in that case, I'll say the same thing in reply. We're having a serious discussion; if you don't grant me your attention, I won't grovel for it. I still have my underground.

And, as long as I'm still alive and feel desire—may my arm wither away before it contributes even one little brick to that building! Never mind that I myself have just rejected the crystal palace for the sole reason that it won't be possible to tease it by sticking out one's tongue at it. I didn't say that because I'm so fond of sticking out my tongue. Perhaps the only reason I got angry is that among all your buildings there's still not a single one where you don't feel compelled to stick out your tongue. On the contrary, I'd let my tongue be cut off out of sheer gratitude, if only things could be so arranged that I'd no longer want to stick it out. What do I care if things can't be so arranged and if I must settle for some tenements? Why was I made with such desires? Can it be that I was made this way only in order to reach the conclusion that my entire way of being is merely a fraud? Can this be the whole purpose? I don't believe it.

By the way, do you know what? I'm convinced that we underground men should be kept in check. Although capable of sitting around quietly in the underground for some forty years, once he emerges into the light of day and bursts into speech, he talks on and on and on. . . .

XI

The final result, gentlemen, is that it's better to do nothing! Conscious inertia is better! And so, long live the underground! Even though I said that I envy the normal man to the point of exasperation, I still wouldn't want to be him under the circumstances in which I see him (although I still won't keep from envying him. No, no, in any case the underground is more advantageous!) At least there one can . . . Hey, but I'm lying once again! I'm lying because I know myself as surely as two times two, that it isn't really the underground that's better, but something different, altogether different, something that I long for, but I'll never be able to find! To hell with the underground! Why, here's what would be better: if I myself were to believe even a fraction of everything I've written. I swear to you, gentlemen, that I don't believe one word, not one little word of all that I've scribbled. That is, I do believe it, perhaps, but at the very same time, I don't know why, I feel and suspect that I'm lying like a trooper.

"Then why did you write all this?" you ask me.

"What if I'd shut you up in the underground for forty years with nothing to do and then came back forty years later to see what had become of you? Can a man really be left alone for forty years with nothing to do?"

"Isn't it disgraceful, isn't it humiliating!" you might say, shaking your head in contempt. "You long for life, but you try to solve life's problems by means of a logical tangle. How importunate, how insolent your outbursts, and how frightened you are at the same time! You talk rubbish, but you're constantly afraid of them and make apologies. You maintain that you fear nothing, but at the same time you try to ingratiate yourself with us. You assure us that you're gnashing your teeth, yet at the same time you try to be witty and amuse us. You know that your witticisms are not very clever, but apparently you're pleased by their literary merit. Perhaps you really have suffered, but you don't even respect your own suffering. There's some truth in you, too, but no chastity; out of the pettiest vanity you bring your truth out into the open, into the market-place, and you shame it. . . . You really want to say something, but you conceal your final word out of fear because you lack the resolve to utter it; you have only cowardly impudence. You boast about your consciousness, but you merely vac-illate, because even though your mind is working, your heart has been black-ened by depravity, and without a pure heart, there can be no full, genuine consciousness. And how importunate you are; how you force yourself upon others; you behave in such an affected manner. Lies, lies, lies!"

Of course, it was I who just invented all these words for you. That, too, comes from the underground. For forty years in a row I've been listening to all your words through a crack. I've invented them myself, since that's all that's occurred to me. It's no wonder that I've learned it all by heart and that it's taken on such a literary form. . . .

But can you really be so gullible as to imagine that I'll print all this and give it to you to read? And here's another problem I have: why do I keep call-ing you "gentlemen"? Why do I address you as if you really were my readers? Confessions such as the one I plan to set forth here aren't published and given to other people to read. Anyway, I don't possess sufficient fortitude, nor do I consider it necessary to do so. But don't you see, a certain notion has come into my mind, and I wish to realize it at any cost. Here's the point.

Every man has within his own reminiscences certain things he doesn't reveal to anyone, except, perhaps, to his friends. There are also some that he won't reveal even to his friends, only to himself perhaps, and even then, in secret. Finally, there are some which a man is afraid to reveal even to himself; every decent man has accumulated a fair number of such things. In fact, it can even be said that the more decent the man, the more of these things he's accumu-lated. Anyway, only recently I myself decided to recall some of my earlier adventures; up to now I've always avoided them, even with a certain anxiety. But having decided not only to recall them, but even to write them down, now is when I wish to try an experiment: is it possible to be absolutely honest even with one's own self and not to fear the whole truth? Incidentally, I'll mention that Heine maintains that faithful autobiographies are almost impossible, and that a man is sure to lie about himself.[7] In Heine's opinion, Rousseau, for example, undoubtedly told untruths about himself in his confession and even lied intentionally, out of vanity. I'm convinced that Heine is correct; I under-stand perfectly well that sometimes it's possible out of vanity alone to impute

---

7. A reference to the work *On Germany* (1853–54) by the German poet Heinrich Heine (1797–1856), in which on the very first page Heine speaks of Rousseau as lying and inventing disgraceful incidents about himself for his *Confessions*.

all sorts of crimes to oneself, and I can even understand what sort of vanity that might be. But Heine was making judgments about a person who confessed to the public. I, however, am writing for myself alone and declare once and for all that if I write as if I were addressing readers, that's only for show, because it's easier for me to write that way. It's a form, simply a form; I shall never have any readers. I've already stated that. . . . I don't want to be restricted in any way by editing my notes. I won't attempt to introduce any order or system. I'll write down whatever comes to mind.

Well, now, for example, someone might seize upon my words and ask me, if you really aren't counting on any readers, why do you make such compacts with yourself, and on paper no less; that is, if you're not going to introduce any order or system, if you're going to write down whatever comes to mind, etc., etc.? Why do you go on explaining? Why do you keep apologizing?

"Well, imagine that," I reply.

This, by the way, contains an entire psychology. Perhaps it's just that I'm a coward. Or perhaps it's that I imagine an audience before me on purpose, so that I behave more decently when I'm writing things down. There may be a thousand reasons.

But here's something else: why is it that I want to write? If it's not for the public, then why can't I simply recall it all in my own mind and not commit it to paper?

Quite so; but somehow it appears more dignified on paper. There's something more impressive about it; I'll be a better judge of myself; the style will be improved. Besides, perhaps I'll actually experience some relief from the process of writing it all down. Today, for example, I'm particularly oppressed by one very old memory from my distant past. It came to me vividly several days ago and since then it's stayed with me, like an annoying musical motif that doesn't want to leave you alone. And yet you must get rid of it. I have hundreds of such memories; but at times a single one emerges from those hundreds and oppresses me. For some reason I believe that if I write it down I can get rid of it. Why not try?

Lastly, I'm bored, and I never do anything. Writing things down actually seems like work. They say that work makes a man become good and honest. Well, at least there's chance.

It's snowing today, an almost wet, yellow, dull snow. It was snowing yesterday too, a few days ago as well. I think it was apropos of the wet snow that I recalled this episode and now it doesn't want to leave me alone. And so, let it be a tale apropos of wet snow.

II

Apropos of Wet Snow

When from the darkness of delusion
I saved your fallen soul
With ardent words of conviction,
And, full of profound torment,
Wringing your hands, you cursed
The vice that had ensnared you;

When, punishing by recollection
Your forgetful conscience,
You told me the tale
Of all that had happened before,
And, suddenly, covering your face,
Full of shame and horror,
You tearfully resolved,
Indignant, shaken . . .
Etc., etc., etc.
From the poetry of N. A. Nekrasov[8]

I

At that time I was only twenty-four years old. Even then my life was gloomy, disordered, and solitary to the point of savagery. I didn't associate with anyone; I even avoided talking, and I retreated further and further into my corner. At work in the office I even tried not to look at anyone; I was aware not only that my colleagues considered me eccentric, but that they always seemed to regard me with a kind of loathing. Sometimes I wondered why it was that no one else thinks that others regard him with loathing. One of our office-workers had a repulsive pock-marked face which even appeared somewhat villainous. It seemed to me that with such a disreputable face I'd never have dared look at anyone. Another man had a uniform so worn that there was a foul smell emanating from him. Yet, neither of these two gentlemen was embarrassed— neither because of his clothes, nor his face, nor in any moral way. Neither one imagined that other people regarded him with loathing; and if either had so imagined, it wouldn't have mattered at all, as long as their supervisor chose not to view him that way. It's perfectly clear to me now, because of my unlimited vanity and the great demands I accordingly made on myself, that I frequently regarded myself with a furious dissatisfaction verging on loathing; as a result, I intentionally ascribed my own view to everyone else. For example, I despised my own face; I considered it hideous, and I even suspected that there was something repulsive in its expression. Therefore, every time I arrived at work, I took pains to behave as independently as possible, so that I couldn't be suspected of any malice, and I tried to assume as noble an expression as possible. "It may not be a handsome face," I thought, "but let it be noble, expressive, and above all, extremely *intelligent*." But I was agonizingly certain that my face couldn't possibly express all these virtues. Worst of all, I considered it positively stupid. I'd have been reconciled if it had looked intelligent. In fact, I'd even have agreed to have it appear repulsive, on the condition that at the same time people would find my face terribly intelligent.

Of course, I hated all my fellow office-workers from the first to the last and despised every one of them; yet, at the same time it was as if I were afraid of them. Sometimes it happened that I would even regard them as superior to me. At this time these changes would suddenly occur: first I would despise them, then I would regard them as superior to me. A cultured and decent

8. A Russian poet and editor of radical sympathies (1821–1878). The poem quoted dates from 1845 and is untitled. It ends with the lines "And enter my house bold and free / To become its full mistress!"

man cannot be vain without making unlimited demands on himself and without hating himself, at times to the point of contempt. But, whether hating them or regarding them as superior, I almost always lowered my eyes when meeting anyone. I even conducted experiments: could I endure someone's gaze? I'd always be the first to lower my eyes. This infuriated me to the point of madness. I slavishly worshipped the conventional in everything external. I embraced the common practice and feared any eccentricity with all my soul. But how could I sustain it? I was morbidly refined, as befits any cultured man of our time. All others resembled one another as sheep in a flock. Perhaps I was the only one in the whole office who constantly thought of himself as a coward and a slave; and I thought so precisely because I was so cultured. But not only did I think so, it actually was so: I was a coward and a slave. I say this without any embarrassment. Every decent man of our time is and must be a coward and a slave. This is his normal condition. I'm deeply convinced of it. This is how he's made and what he's meant to be. And not only at the present time, as the result of some accidental circumstance, but in general at all times, a decent man must be a coward and a slave. This is a law of nature for all decent men on earth. If one of them should happen to be brave about something or other, we shouldn't be comforted or distracted: he'll still lose his nerve about something else. That's the single and eternal way out. Only asses and their mongrels are brave, and even then, only until they come up against a wall. It's not worthwhile paying them any attention because they really don't mean anything at all.

There was one more circumstance tormenting me at that time: no one was like me, and I wasn't like anyone else. "I'm alone," I mused, "and they are *everyone*"; and I sank deep into thought.

From all this it's clear that I was still just a boy.

The exact opposite would also occur. Sometimes I would find it repulsive to go to the office: it reached the point where I would often return home from work ill. Then suddenly, for no good reason at all, a flash of skepticism and indifference would set in (everything came to me in flashes); I would laugh at my own intolerance and fastidiousness, and reproach myself for my *romanticism*. Sometimes I didn't even want to talk to anyone; at other times it reached a point where I not only started talking, but I even thought about striking up a friendship with others. All my fastidiousness would suddenly disappear for no good reason at all. Who knows? Perhaps I never really had any, and it was all affected, borrowed from books. I still haven't answered this question, even up to now. And once I really did become friends with others; I began to visit their houses, play préférence,[9] drink vodka, talk about promotions. . . . But allow me to digress.

We Russians, generally speaking, have never had any of those stupid, transcendent German romantics, or even worse, French romantics, on whom nothing produces any effect whatever: the earth might tremble beneath them, all of France might perish on the barricades, but they remain the same, not even changing for decency's sake; they go on singing their transcendent songs, so to speak, to their dying day, because they're such fools. We here on Russian soil have no fools. It's a well-known fact; that's precisely what distinguishes us from

9. A card game for three players.

foreigners. Consequently, transcendent natures cannot be found among us in their pure form. That's the result of our "positive" publicists and critics of that period, who hunted for the Kostanzhouglo and the Uncle Pyotr Ivanoviches,[1] foolishly mistaking them for our ideal and slandering our own romantics, considering them to be the same kind of transcendents as one finds in Germany or France. On the contrary, the characteristics of our romantics are absolutely and directly opposed to the transcendent Europeans; not one of those European standards can apply here. (Allow me to use the word "romantic"—it's an old-fashioned little word, well-respected and deserving, familiar to everyone.) The characteristics of our romantics are to understand everything, *to see everything, often to see it much more clearly than our most positive minds*; not to be reconciled with anyone or anything, but, at the same time, not to balk at anything; to circumvent everything, to yield on every point, to treat everyone diplomatically; never to lose sight of some useful, practical goal (an apartment at government expense, a nice pension, a decoration)—to keep an eye on that goal through all his excesses and his volumes of lyrical verse, and, at the same time, to preserve intact the "beautiful and sublime" to the end of their lives; and, incidentally, to preserve themselves as well, wrapped up in cotton like precious jewelry, if only, for example, for the sake of that same "beautiful and sublime." Our romantic has a very broad nature and is the biggest rogue of all, I can assure you of that . . . even by my own experience. Of course, all this is true if the romantic is smart. But what am I saying? A romantic is always smart; I merely wanted to observe that although we've had some romantic fools, they really don't count at all, simply because while still in their prime they would degenerate completely into Germans, and, in order to preserve their precious jewels more comfortably, they'd settle over there, either in Weimar or in the Black Forest. For instance, I genuinely despised my official position and refrained from throwing it over merely out of necessity, because I myself sat there working and received good money for doing it. And, as a result, please note, I still refrained from throwing it over. Our romantic would sooner lose his mind (which, by the way, very rarely occurs) than give it up, if he didn't have another job in mind; nor is he ever kicked out, unless he's hauled off to the insane asylum as the "King of Spain,"[2] and only if he's gone completely mad. Then again, it's really only the weaklings and towheads who go mad in our country. An enormous number of romantics later rise to significant rank. What extraordinary versatility! And what a capacity for the most contradictory sensations! I used to be consoled by these thoughts back then, and still am even nowadays. That's why there are so many "broad natures" among us, people who never lose their ideals, no matter how low they fall; even though they never lift a finger for the sake of their ideals, even though they're outrageous villains and thieves, nevertheless they respect their original ideals to the point of tears and are extremely honest men at heart. Yes, only among us Russians can the most

---

1. A character in Ivan Goncharov's novel *A Common Story* (1847); a high bureaucrat, a factory owner who teaches lessons of sobriety and good sense to the romantic hero, Alexander Aduyev. Konstanzhouglo is the ideal efficient landowner in the second part of Nikolai Gogol's novel *Dead Souls* (1852).

2. An allusion to the hero of Gogol's short story "Diary of a Madman" (1835). Poprishchin, a low-ranking civil servant, sees his aspirations crushed by the enormous bureaucracy. He ends by going insane and imagining himself to be king of Spain.

outrageous scoundrel be absolutely, even sublimely honest at heart, while at the same time never ceasing to be a scoundrel. I repeat, nearly always do our romantics turn out to be very efficient rascals (I use the word "rascal" affectionately); they suddenly manifest such a sense of reality and positive knowledge that their astonished superiors and the general public can only click their tongues at them in amazement.

Their versatility is really astounding; God only knows what it will turn into, how it will develop under subsequent conditions, and what it holds for us in the future. The material is not all that bad! I'm not saying this out of some ridiculous patriotism or jingoism. However, I'm sure that once again you think I'm joking. But who knows? Perhaps it's quite the contrary, that is, you're convinced that this is what I really think. In any case, gentlemen, I'll consider that both of these opinions constitute an honor and a particular pleasure. And do forgive me for this digression.

Naturally, I didn't sustain any friendships with my colleagues, and soon I severed all relations after quarreling with them; and, because of my youthful inexperience at the same time, I even stopped greeting them, as if I'd cut them off entirely. That, however, happened to me only once. On the whole, I was always alone.

At home I spent most of my time reading. I tried to stifle all that was constantly seething within me with external sensations. And of all external sensations available, only reading was possible for me. Of course, reading helped a great deal—it agitated, delighted, and tormented me. But at times it was terribly boring. I still longed to be active; and suddenly I sank into dark, subterranean, loathsome depravity—more precisely, petty vice. My nasty little passions were sharp and painful as a result of my constant, morbid irritability. I experienced hysterical fits accompanied by tears and convulsions. Besides reading, I had nowhere else to go—that is, there was nothing to respect in my surroundings, nothing to attract me. In addition, I was overwhelmed by depression; I possessed a hysterical craving for contradictions and contrasts; and, as a result, I plunged into depravity. I haven't said all this to justify myself. . . . But, no, I'm lying. I did want to justify myself. It's for myself, gentlemen, that I include this little observation. I don't want to lie. I've given my word.

I indulged in depravity all alone, at night, furtively, timidly, sordidly, with a feeling of shame that never left me even in my most loathsome moments and drove me at such times to the point of profanity. Even then I was carrying around the underground in my soul. I was terribly afraid of being seen, met, recognized. I visited all sorts of dismal places.

Once, passing by some wretched little tavern late at night, I saw through a lighted window some gentlemen fighting with billiard cues; one of them was thrown out the window. At some other time I would have been disgusted; but just then I was overcome by such a mood that I envied the gentleman who'd been tossed out; I envied him so much that I even walked into the tavern and entered the billiard room. "Perhaps," I thought, "I'll get into a fight, and they'll throw me out the window, too."

I wasn't drunk, but what could I do—after all, depression can drive a man to this kind of hysteria. But nothing came of it. It turned out that I was incapable of being tossed out the window; I left without getting into a fight.

As soon as I set foot inside, some officer put me in my place.

I was standing next to the billiard table inadvertently blocking his way as he wanted to get by; he took hold of me by the shoulders and without a word of warning or explanation, moved me from where I was standing to another place, and he went past as if he hadn't even noticed me. I could have forgiven even a beating, but I could never forgive his moving me out of the way and entirely failing to notice me.

The devil knows what I would have given for a genuine, ordinary quarrel, a decent one, a more *literary* one, so to speak. But I'd been treated as if I were a fly. The officer was about six feet tall, while I'm small and scrawny. The quarrel, however, was in my hands; all I had to do was protest, and of course they would've thrown me out the window. But I reconsidered and preferred . . . to withdraw resentfully.

I left the tavern confused and upset and went straight home; the next night I continued my petty vice more timidly, more furtively, more gloomily than before, as if I had tears in my eyes—but I continued nonetheless. Don't conclude, however, that I retreated from that officer as a result of any cowardice; I've never been a coward at heart, although I've constantly acted like one in deed, but—wait before you laugh—I can explain this. I can explain anything, you may rest assured.

Oh, if only this officer had been the kind who'd have agreed to fight a duel! But no, he was precisely one of those types (alas, long gone) who preferred to act with their billiard cues or, like Gogol's Lieutenant Pirogov,[3] by appealing to the authorities. They didn't fight duels; in any case, they'd have considered fighting a duel with someone like me, a lowly civilian, to be indecent. In general, they considered duels to be somehow inconceivable, free-thinking, French, while they themselves, especially if they happened to be six feet tall, offended other people rather frequently.

In this case I retreated not out of any cowardice, but because of my unlimited vanity. I wasn't afraid of his height, nor did I think I'd receive a painful beating and get thrown out the window. In fact, I'd have had sufficient physical courage; it was moral fortitude I lacked. I was afraid that everyone present— from the insolent billiard marker to the foul-smelling, pimply little clerks with greasy collars who used to hang about—wouldn't understand and would laugh when I started to protest and speak to them in literary Russian. Because, to this very day, it's still impossible for us to speak about a point of honor, that is, not about honor itself, but a point of honor (*point d'honneur*), except in literary language. One can't even refer to a "point of honor" in everyday language. I was fully convinced (a sense of reality, in spite of all my romanticism!) that they would all simply split their sides laughing, and that the officer, instead of giving me a simple beating, that is, an inoffensive one, would certainly apply his knee to my back and drive me around the billiard table; only then perhaps would he have the mercy to throw me out the window. Naturally, this wretched story of mine couldn't possibly end with this alone. Afterward I used to meet this officer frequently on the street and I observed him very carefully. I don't know

3. One of two main characters in Gogol's short story "Nevsky Prospect" (1835). A shallow and self-satisfied officer, he mistakes the wife of a German artisan for a woman of easy virtue and receives a sound thrashing. He decides to lodge an official complaint but, after consuming a cream-filled pastry, thinks better of it.

whether he ever recognized me. Probably not; I reached that conclusion from various observations. As for me, I stared at him with malice and hatred, and continued to do so for several years! My malice increased and became stronger over time. At first I began to make discreet inquiries about him. This was difficult for me to do, since I had so few acquaintances. But once, as I was following him at a distance as though tied to him, someone called to him on the street: that's how I learned his name. Another time I followed him back to his own apartment and for a ten-kopeck piece learned from the doorman where and how he lived, on what floor, with whom, etc.—in a word, all that could be learned from a doorman. One morning, although I never engaged in literary activities, it suddenly occurred to me to draft a description of this officer as a kind of exposé, a caricature, in the form of a tale. I wrote it with great pleasure. I exposed him; I even slandered him. At first I altered his name only slightly, so that it could be easily recognized; but then, upon careful reflection, I changed it. Then I sent the tale off to *Notes of the Fatherland*.[4] But such exposés were no longer in fashion, and they didn't publish my tale. I was very annoyed by that. At times I simply choked on my spite. Finally, I resolved to challenge my opponent to a duel. I composed a beautiful, charming letter to him, imploring him to apologize to me; in case he refused, I hinted rather strongly at a duel. The letter was composed in such a way that if that officer had possessed even the smallest understanding of the "beautiful and sublime," he would have come running, thrown his arms around me, and offered his friendship. That would have been splendid! We would have led such a wonderful life! Such a life! He would have shielded me with his rank; I would have ennobled him with my culture, and, well, with my ideas. Who knows what might have come of it! Imagine it, two years had already passed since he'd insulted me; my challenge was the most ridiculous anachronism, in spite of all the cleverness of my letter in explaining and disguising that fact. But, thank God (to this day I thank the Almighty with tears in my eyes), I didn't send that letter. A shiver runs up and down my spine when I think what might have happened if I had. Then suddenly . . . suddenly, I got my revenge in the simplest manner, a stroke of genius! A brilliant idea suddenly occurred to me. Sometimes on holidays I used to stroll along Nevsky Prospect at about four o'clock in the afternoon, usually on the sunny side. That is, I didn't really stroll; rather, I experienced innumerable torments, humiliations, and bilious attacks. But that's undoubtedly just what I needed. I darted in and out like a fish among the strollers, constantly stepping aside before generals, cavalry officers, hussars, and young ladies. At those moments I used to experience painful spasms in my heart and a burning sensation in my back merely at the thought of my dismal apparel as well as the wretchedness and vulgarity of my darting little figure. This was sheer torture, uninterrupted and unbearable humiliation at the thought, which soon became an incessant and immediate sensation, that I was a fly in the eyes of society, a disgusting, obscene fly—smarter than the rest, more cultured, even nobler—all that goes without saying, but a fly, nonetheless, who incessantly steps aside, insulted and injured by everyone. For what reason did I inflict this torment on myself? Why did I stroll along Nevsky Prospect? I don't know. But something simply *drew* me there at every opportunity.

Then I began to experience surges of that pleasure about which I've already

4. A radical literary and political journal published in St. Petersburg from 1839 to 1867.

spoken in the first chapter. After the incident with the officer I was drawn there even more strongly; I used to encounter him along Nevsky most often, and it was there that I could admire him. He would also go there, mostly on holidays. He, too, would give way before generals and individuals of superior rank; he, too, would spin like a top among them. But he would simply trample people like me, or even those slightly superior; he would walk directly toward them, as if there were empty space ahead of him; and under no circumstance would he ever step aside. I revelled in my malice as I observed him, and . . . bitterly stepped aside before him every time. I was tortured by the fact that even on the street I found it impossible to stand on an equal footing with him. "Why is it you're always first to step aside?" I badgered myself in insane hysteria, at times waking up at three in the morning. "Why always you and not he? After all, there's no law about it; it isn't written down anywhere. Let it be equal, as it usually is when people of breeding meet: he steps aside halfway and you halfway, and you pass by showing each other mutual respect." But that was never the case, and I continued to step aside, while he didn't even notice that I was yielding to him. Then a most astounding idea suddenly dawned on me. "What if," I thought, "what if I were to meet him and . . . not step aside? Deliberately not step aside, even if it meant bumping into him: how would that be?" This bold idea gradually took such a hold that it afforded me no peace. I dreamt about it incessantly, horribly, and even went to Nevsky more frequently so that I could imagine more clearly how I would do it. I was in ecstasy. The scheme was becoming more and more possible and even probable to me. "Of course, I wouldn't really collide with him," I thought, already feeling more generous toward him in my joy, "but I simply won't turn aside. I'll bump into him, not very painfully, but just so, shoulder to shoulder, as much as decency allows. I'll bump into him the same amount as he bumps into me." At last I made up my mind completely. But the preparations took a very long time. First, in order to look as presentable as possible during the execution of my scheme, I had to worry about my clothes. "In any case, what if, for example, it should occasion a public scandal? (And the public there was *superflu*:[5] a countess, Princess D., and the entire literary world.) It was essential to be well-dressed; that inspires respect and in a certain sense will place us immediately on an equal footing in the eyes of high society." With that goal in mind I requested my salary in advance, and I purchased a pair of black gloves and a decent hat at Churkin's store. Black gloves seemed to me more dignified, more *bon ton*[6] than the lemon-colored ones I'd considered at first. "That would be too glaring, as if the person wanted to be noticed"; so I didn't buy the lemon-colored ones. I'd already procured a fine shirt with white bone cufflinks; but my overcoat constituted a major obstacle. In and of itself it was not too bad at all; it kept me warm; but it was quilted and had a raccoon collar, the epitome of bad taste. At all costs I had to replace the collar with a beaver one, just like on an officer's coat. For this purpose I began to frequent the Shopping Arcade; and, after several attempts, I turned up some cheap German beaver. Although these German beavers wear out very quickly and soon begin to look shabby, at first, when they're brand new, they look very fine indeed; after all, I only needed it for a single occasion. I asked the price: it was still expensive. After considerable reflection I resolved to sell my raccoon collar. I decided to request

5. "Excessively refined" (French).   6. "In good taste" (French).

a loan for the remaining amount—a rather significant sum for me—from Anton Antonych Setochkin, my office chief, a modest man, but a serious and solid one, who never lent money to anyone, but to whom, upon entering the civil service, I'd once been specially recommended by an important person who'd secured the position for me. I suffered terribly. It seemed monstrous and shameful to ask Anton Antonych for money. I didn't sleep for two or three nights in a row; in general I wasn't getting much sleep those days, and I always had a fever. I would have either a vague sinking feeling in my heart, or else my heart would suddenly begin to thump, thump, thump! . . . At first Anton Antonych was surprised, then he frowned, thought it over, and finally gave me the loan, after securing from me a note authorizing him to deduct the sum from my salary two weeks later. In this way everything was finally ready; the splendid beaver reigned in place of the mangy raccoon, and I gradually began to get down to business. It was impossible to set about it all at once, in a foolhardy way; one had to proceed in this matter very carefully, step by step. But I confess that after many attempts I was ready to despair: we didn't bump into each other, no matter what! No matter how I prepared, no matter how determined I was—it seems that we're just about to bump, when I look up—and once again I've stepped aside while he's gone by without even noticing me. I even used to pray as I approached him that God would grant me determination. One time I'd fully resolved to do it, but the result was that I merely stumbled and fell at his feet because, at the very last moment, only a few inches away from him, I lost my nerve. He stepped over me very calmly, and I bounced to one side like a rubber ball. That night I lay ill with a fever once again and was delirious. Then, everything suddenly ended in the best possible way. The night before I decided once and for all not to go through with my pernicious scheme and to give it all up without success; with that in mind I went to Nevsky Prospect for one last time simply in order to see how I'd abandon the whole thing. Suddenly, three paces away from my enemy, I made up my mind unexpectedly; I closed my eyes and—we bumped into each other forcefully, shoulder to shoulder! I didn't yield an inch and walked by him on a completely equal footing! He didn't even turn around to look at me and pretended that he hadn't even noticed; but he was merely pretending, I'm convinced of that. To this very day I'm convinced of that! Naturally, I got the worst of it; he was stronger, but that wasn't the point. The point was that I'd achieved my goal, I'd maintained my dignity, I hadn't yielded one step, and I'd publicly placed myself on an equal social footing with him. I returned home feeling completely avenged for everything. I was ecstatic. I rejoiced and sang Italian arias. Of course, I won't describe what happened to me three days later; if you've read the first part entitled "Underground," you can guess for yourself. The officer was later transferred somewhere else; I haven't seen him for some fourteen years. I wonder what he's doing nowadays, that dear friend of mine! Whom is he trampling underfoot?

II

But when this phase of my nice, little dissipation ended I felt terribly nauseated. Remorse set in; I tried to drive it away because it was too disgusting. Little by little, however, I got used to that, too. I got used to it all; that is, it wasn't that I got used to it, rather, I somehow voluntarily consented to endure it. But I had a way out that reconciled everything—to escape into "all that was beautiful and sublime," in my dreams, of course. I was a terrible dreamer; I dreamt for three months in a row, tucked away in my little corner. And well you may believe that in those moments I was not at all like the gentleman who, in his faint-hearted anxiety, had sewn a German beaver onto the collar of his old overcoat. I suddenly became a hero. If my six-foot-tall lieutenant had come to see me then, I'd never have admitted him. I couldn't even conceive of him at that time. It's hard to describe now what my dreams consisted of then, and how I could've been so satisfied with them, but I was. Besides, even now I can take pride in them at certain times. My dreams were particularly sweet and vivid after my little debauchery; they were filled with remorse and tears, curses and ecstasy. There were moments of such positive intoxication, such happiness, that I felt not even the slightest trace of mockery within me, really and truly. It was all faith, hope and love. That's just it: at the time I believed blindly that by some kind of miracle, some external circumstance, everything would suddenly open up and expand; a vista of appropriate activity would suddenly appear— beneficent, beautiful, and most of all, *ready-made* (what precisely, I never knew, but, most of all, it had to be ready-made), and that I would suddenly step forth into God's world, almost riding on a white horse and wearing a laurel wreath. I couldn't conceive of a secondary role; and that's precisely why in reality I very quietly took on the lowest one. Either a hero or dirt—there was no middle ground. That was my ruin because in the dirt I consoled myself knowing that at other times I was a hero, and that the hero covered himself with dirt; that is to say, an ordinary man would be ashamed to wallow in filth, but a hero is too noble to become defiled; consequently, he can wallow. It's remarkable that these surges of everything "beautiful and sublime" occurred even during my petty depravity, and precisely when I'd sunk to the lowest depths. They occurred in separate spurts, as if to remind me of themselves; however, they failed to banish my depravity by their appearance. On the contrary, they seemed to add spice to it by means of contrast; they came in just the right amount to serve as a tasty sauce. This sauce consisted of contradictions, suffering, and agonizing internal analysis; all of these torments and trifles lent a certain piquancy, even some meaning to my depravity—in a word, they completely fulfilled the function of a tasty sauce. Nor was all this even lacking in a measure of profundity. Besides, I would never have consented to the simple, tasteless, spontaneous little debauchery of an ordinary clerk and have endured all that filth! How could it have attracted me then and lured me into the street late at night? No, sir, I had a noble loophole for everything. . . .

But how much love, oh Lord, how much love I experienced at times in those dreams of mine, in those "escapes into everything beautiful and sublime." Even though it was fantastic love, even though it was never directed at anything human, there was still so much love that afterward, in reality, I no longer felt any impulse to direct it: that would have been an unnecessary luxury. However, everything always ended in a most satisfactory way by a lazy and intoxicating transition into art, that is, into beautiful forms of being, ready-made, largely borrowed from poets and novelists, and adapted to serve every possible need. For instance, I would triumph over everyone; naturally, everyone else grovelled in the dust and was voluntarily impelled to acknowledge my superiority, while I would forgive them all for everything. Or else, being a famous poet and chamberlain, I would fall in love; I'd receive an enormous fortune and would immediately sacrifice it all for the benefit of humanity, at the same time confessing before all peoples my own infamies, which, needless to say, were not simple infamies, but contained a great amount of "the beautiful and sublime," something in the style of Manfred.[7] Everyone would weep and kiss me (otherwise what idiots they would have been), while I went about barefoot and hungry preaching new ideas and defeating all the reactionaries of Austerlitz.[8] Then a march would be played, a general amnesty declared, and the Pope would agree to leave Rome and go to Brazil;[9] a ball would be hosted for all of Italy at the Villa Borghese on the shores of Lake Como,[1] since Lake Como would have been moved to Rome for this very occasion; then there would be a scene in the bushes, etc., etc.—as if you didn't know. You'll say that it's tasteless and repugnant to drag all this out into the open after all the raptures and tears to which I've confessed. But why is it so repugnant? Do you really think I'm ashamed of all this or that it's any more stupid than anything in your own lives, gentlemen? Besides, you can rest assured that some of it was not at all badly composed. . . . Not everything occurred on the shores of Lake Como. But you're right; in fact, it is tasteless and repugnant. And the most repugnant thing of all is that now I've begun to justify myself before you. And even more repugnant is that now I've made that observation. But enough, otherwise there'll be no end to it: each thing will be more repugnant than the last. . . .

I was never able to dream for more than three months in a row, and I began to feel an irresistible urge to plunge into society. To me plunging into society meant paying a visit to my office chief, Anton Antonych Setochkin. He's the only lasting acquaintance I've made during my lifetime; I too now marvel at this circumstance. But even then I would visit him only when my dreams had reached such a degree of happiness that it was absolutely essential for me to embrace people and all humanity at once; for that reason I needed to have at least one person on hand who actually existed. However, one could only call upon Anton Antonych on Tuesdays (his receiving day); consequently, I always had to adjust the urge to embrace all humanity so that it occurred on Tuesday. This Anton Antonych lived near Five Corners,[2] on the fourth floor, in four small, low-ceilinged rooms, each smaller than the last, all very frugal and yellowish in appearance. He lived with his two daughters and an aunt who used to serve tea. The daughters, one thirteen, the other fourteen, had little snub noses. I was very embarrassed by them because they used to whisper all the time and giggle to each other. The host usually sat in his study on a leather couch in front of a table together with some gray-haired guest, a civil servant either from our office or another one. I never saw more than two or three guests there, and they

7. The romantic hero of Byron's poetic tragedy *Manfred* (1817), a lonely, defiant figure whose past conceals some mysterious crime.
8. The site of Napoleon's great victory in December 1805 over the combined armies of the Russian tsar Alexander I and the Austrian emperor Francis II.
9. Napoleon announced his annexation of the Papal States to France in 1809 and was promptly excommunicated by Pope Pius VII.

The pope was imprisoned and forced to sign a new concordat, but in 1814 he returned to Rome in triumph.
1. Located in the foothills of the Italian Alps in Lombardy. Villa Borghese was the elegant summer palace built by Scipione Cardinal Borghese outside the Porta del Popolo in Rome.
2. A well-known landmark in St. Petersburg.

were always the same ones. They talked about excise taxes, debates in the Senate, salaries, promotions, His Excellency and how to please him, and so on and so forth. I had the patience to sit there like a fool next to these people for four hours or so; I listened without daring to say a word to them or even knowing what to talk about. I sat there in a stupor; several times I broke into a sweat; I felt numbed by paralysis; but it was good and useful. Upon returning home I would postpone for some time my desire to embrace all humanity.

I had one other sort of acquaintance, however, named Simonov, a former schoolmate of mine. In fact, I had a number of schoolmates in Petersburg, but I didn't associate with them, and I'd even stopped greeting them along the street. I might even have transferred into a different department at the office so as not to be with them and to cut myself off from my hated childhood once and for all. Curses on that school and those horrible years of penal servitude. In short, I broke with my schoolmates as soon as I was released. There remained only two or three people whom I would greet upon encountering them. One was Simonov, who hadn't distinguished himself in school in any way; he was even-tempered and quiet, but I detected in him a certain independence of character, even honesty. I don't even think that he was all that limited. At one time he and I experienced some rather bright moments, but they didn't last very long and somehow were suddenly clouded over. Evidently he was burdened by these recollections, and seemed in constant fear that I would lapse into that former mode. I suspect that he found me repulsive, but not being absolutely sure, I used to visit him nonetheless.

So once, on a Thursday, unable to endure my solitude, and knowing that on that day Anton Antonych's door was locked, I remembered Simonov. As I climbed the stairs to his apartment on the fourth floor, I was thinking how burdensome this man found my presence and that my going to see him was rather useless. But since it always turned out, as if on purpose, that such reflections would impel me to put myself even further into an ambiguous situation, I went right in. It had been almost a year since I'd last seen Simonov.

III

I found two more of my former schoolmates there with him. Apparently they were discussing some important matter. None of them paid any attention to me when I entered, which was strange since I hadn't seen them for several years. Evidently they considered me some sort of ordinary house fly. They hadn't even treated me like that when we were in school together, although they'd all hated me. Of course, I understood that they must despise me now for my failure in the service and for the fact that I'd sunk so low, was badly dressed, and so on, which, in their eyes, constituted proof of my ineptitude and insignificance. But I still hadn't expected such a degree of contempt. Simonov was even surprised by my visit. All this disconcerted me; I sat down in some distress and began to listen to what they were saying.

The discussion was serious, even heated, and concerned a farewell dinner which these gentlemen wanted to organize jointly as early as the following day for their friend Zverkov, an army officer who was heading for a distant province. Monsieur Zverkov had also been my schoolmate all along. I'd begun to hate him especially in the upper grades. In the lower grades he was merely an attractive, lively lad whom everyone liked. However, I'd hated him in the lower grades, too, precisely because he was such an attractive, lively lad. He was perpetually a poor student and had gotten worse as time went on; he managed to graduate, however, because he had influential connections. During his last year at school he'd come into an inheritance of some two hundred serfs, and, since almost all the rest of us were poor, he'd even begun to brag. He was an extremely uncouth fellow, but a nice lad nonetheless, even when he was bragging. In spite of our superficial, fantastic, and high-flown notions of honor and pride, all of us, except for a very few, would fawn upon Zverkov, the more so the more he bragged. They didn't fawn for any advantage; they fawned simply because he was a man endowed by nature with gifts. Moreover, we'd somehow come to regard Zverkov as a cunning fellow and an expert on good manners. This latter point particularly infuriated me. I hated the shrill, self-confident tone of his voice, his adoration for his own witticisms, which were terribly stupid in spite of his bold tongue; I hated his handsome, stupid face (for which, however, I'd gladly have exchanged my own intelligent one), and the impudent bearing typical of officers during the 1840s. I hated the way he talked about his future successes with women. (He'd decided not to get involved with them yet, since he still hadn't received his officer's epaulettes; he awaited those epaulettes impatiently.) And he talked about all the duels he'd have to fight. I remember how once, although I was usually very taciturn, I suddenly clashed with Zverkov when, during our free time, he was discussing future exploits with his friends; getting a bit carried away with the game like a little puppy playing in the sun, he suddenly declared that not a single girl in his village would escape his attention—that it was his *droit de seigneur*,[3] and that if the peasants even dared protest, he'd have them all flogged, those bearded rascals; and he'd double their quit-rent.[4] Our louts applauded, but I attacked him—not out of any pity for the poor girls or their fathers, but simply because everyone else was applauding such a little insect. I got the better of him that time, but Zverkov, although stupid, was also cheerful and impudent. Therefore he laughed it off to such an extent that, in fact, I really didn't get the better of him. The laugh remained on his side. Later he got the better of me several times, but without malice, just so, in jest, in passing, in fun. I was filled with spite and hatred, but I didn't respond. After graduation he took a few steps toward me; I didn't object strongly because I found it flattering; but soon we came to a natural parting of the ways. Afterward I heard about his barrack-room successes as a lieutenant and about his *binges*. Then there were other rumors—about his *successes* in the service. He no longer bowed to me on the street; I suspected that he was afraid to compromise himself by acknowledging such an insignificant person as myself. I also saw him in the theater once, in the third tier, already sporting an officer's gold braids. He was fawning and grovelling before the daughters of some aged general. In those three years he'd let himself go, although he was still as handsome and agile as before; he sagged somehow and had begun to put on weight; it was clear that by the age of thirty he'd be totally

---

3. "Lord's privilege" (French); the feudal lord's right to spend the first night with the bride of a newly married serf.
4. The annual sum paid in cash or produce by

serfs to landowners for the right to farm their land in feudal Russia, as opposed to the *corvée*, a certain amount of labor owed.

flabby. So it was for this Zverkov, who was finally ready to depart, that our schoolmates were organizing a farewell dinner. They'd kept up during these three years, although I'm sure that inwardly they didn't consider themselves on an equal footing with him.

One of Simonov's two guests was Ferfichkin, a Russified German, a short man with a face like a monkey, a fool who made fun of everybody, my bitterest enemy from the lower grades—a despicable, impudent show-off who affected the most ticklish sense of ambition, although, of course, he was a coward at heart. He was one of Zverkov's admirers and played up to him for his own reasons, frequently borrowing money from him. Simonov's other guest, Trudolyubov, was insignificant, a military man, tall, with a cold demeanor, rather honest, who worshipped success of any kind and was capable of talking only about promotions. He was a distant relative of Zverkov's, and that, silly to say, lent him some importance among us. He'd always regarded me as a nonentity; he treated me not altogether politely, but tolerably.

"Well, if each of us contributes seven rubles," said Trudolyubov, "with three of us that makes twenty-one altogether—we can have a good dinner. Of course, Zverkov won't have to pay."

"Naturally," Simonov agreed, "since we're inviting him."

"Do you really think," Ferfichkin broke in arrogantly and excitedly, just like an insolent lackey bragging about his master-the-general's medals, "do you really think Zverkov will let us pay for everything? He'll accept out of decency, but then he'll order *half a dozen bottles* on his own."

"What will the four of us do with half a dozen bottles?" asked Trudolyubov, only taking note of the number.

"So then, three of us plus Zverkov makes four, twenty-one rubles, in the Hôtel de Paris, tomorrow at five o'clock," concluded Simonov definitively, since he'd been chosen to make the arrangements.

"Why only twenty-one?" I asked in trepidation, even, apparently, somewhat offended. "If you count me in, you'll have twenty-eight rubles instead of twenty-one."

It seemed to me that to include myself so suddenly and unexpectedly would appear as quite a splendid gesture and that they'd all be smitten at once and regard me with respect.

"Do you really want to come, too?" Simonov inquired with displeasure, managing somehow to avoid looking at me. He knew me inside out.

It was infuriating that he knew me inside out.

"And why not? After all, I was his schoolmate, too, and I must admit that I even feel a bit offended that you've left me out," I continued, just about to boil over again.

"And how were we supposed to find you?" Ferfichkin interjected rudely.

"You never got along very well with Zverkov," added Trudolyubov frowning. But I'd already latched on and wouldn't let go.

"I think no one has a right to judge that," I objected in a trembling voice, as if God knows what had happened. "Perhaps that's precisely why I want to take part now, since we didn't get along so well before."

"Well, who can figure you out . . . such lofty sentiments . . . ," Trudolyubov said with an ironic smile.

"We'll put your name down," Simonov decided, turning to me. "Tomorrow at five o'clock at the Hôtel de Paris. Don't make any mistakes."

"What about the money?" Ferfichkin started to say in an undertone to Simonov while nodding at me, but he broke off because Simonov looked embarrassed.

"That'll do," Trudolyubov said getting up. "If he really wants to come so much, let him."

"But this is our own circle of friends," Ferfichkin grumbled, also picking up his hat. "It's not an official gathering. Perhaps we really don't want you at all. . . ."

They left. Ferfichkin didn't even say goodbye to me as he went out; Trudolyubov barely nodded without looking at me. Simonov, with whom I was left alone, was irritated and perplexed, and he regarded me in a strange way. He neither sat down nor invited me to.

"Hmmm . . . yes . . . , so, tomorrow. Will you contribute your share of the money now? I'm asking just to know for sure," he muttered in embarrassment.

I flared up; but in doing so, I remembered that I'd owed Simonov fifteen rubles for a very long time, which debt, moreover, I'd forgotten, but had also never repaid.

"You must agree, Simonov, that I couldn't have known when I came here . . . oh, what a nuisance, but I've forgotten. . . ."

He broke off and began to pace around the room in even greater irritation. As he paced, he began to walk on his heels and stomp more loudly.

"I'm not detaining you, am I?" I asked after a few moments of silence.

"Oh, no!" he replied with a start. "That is, in fact, yes. You see, I still have to stop by at . . . It's not very far from here . . . ," he added in an apologetic way with some embarrassment.

"Oh, good heavens! Why didn't you say so?" I exclaimed, seizing my cap; moreover I did so with a surprisingly familiar air, coming from God knows where.

"But it's really not far . . . only a few steps away . . . ," Simonov repeated, accompanying me into the hallway with a bustling air which didn't suit him well at all. "So, then, tomorrow at five o'clock sharp!" he shouted to me on the stairs. He was very pleased that I was leaving. However, I was furious.

"What possessed me, what on earth possessed me to interfere?" I gnashed my teeth as I walked along the street. "And for such a scoundrel, a pig like Zverkov! Naturally, I shouldn't go. Of course, to hell with them. Am I bound to go, or what? Tomorrow I'll inform Simonov by post. . . ."

But the real reason I was so furious was that I was sure I'd go. I'd go on purpose. The more tactless, the more indecent it was for me to go, the more certain I'd be to do it.

There was even a definite impediment to my going: I didn't have any money. All I had was nine rubles. But of those, I had to hand over seven the next day to my servant Apollon for his monthly wages; he lived in and received seven rubles for his meals.

Considering Apollon's character it was impossible not to pay him. But more about that rascal, that plague of mine, later.

In any case, I knew that I wouldn't pay him his wages and that I'd definitely go.

That night I had the most hideous dreams. No wonder: all evening I was burdened with recollections of my years of penal servitude at school and I couldn't get rid of them. I'd been sent off to that school by distant relatives on whom I was dependent and about whom I've heard nothing since. They dispatched me, a lonely boy, crushed by their reproaches, already introspective, taciturn, and regarding everything around him savagely. My schoolmates received me with spiteful and pitiless jibes because I wasn't like any of them. But I couldn't tolerate their jibes; I couldn't possibly get along with them as easily as they got along with each other. I hated them all at once and took refuge from everyone in fearful, wounded and excessive pride. Their crudeness irritated me. Cynically they mocked my face and my awkward build; yet, what stupid faces they all had! Facial expressions at our school somehow degenerated and became particularly stupid. Many attractive lads had come to us, but in a few years they too were repulsive to look at. When I was only sixteen I wondered about them gloomily; even then I was astounded by the pettiness of their thoughts and the stupidity of their studies, games and conversations. They failed to understand essential things and took no interest in important, weighty subjects, so that I couldn't help considering them beneath me. It wasn't my wounded vanity that drove me to it; and, for God's sake, don't repeat any of those nauseating and hackneyed clichés, such as, "I was merely a dreamer, whereas they already understood life." They didn't understand a thing, not one thing about life, and I swear, that's what annoyed me most about them. On the contrary, they accepted the most obvious, glaring reality in a fantastically stupid way, and even then they'd begun to worship nothing but success. Everything that was just, but oppressed and humiliated, they ridiculed hard-heartedly and shamelessly. They mistook rank for intelligence; at the age of sixteen they were already talking about occupying comfortable little niches. Of course, much of this was due to their stupidity and the poor examples that had constantly surrounded them in their childhood and youth. They were monstrously depraved. Naturally, even this was more superficial, more affected cynicism; of course, their youth and a certain freshness shone through their depravity; but even this freshness was unattractive and manifested itself in a kind of rakishness. I hated them terribly, although, perhaps, I was even worse than they were. They returned the feeling and didn't conceal their loathing for me. But I no longer wanted their affection; on the contrary, I constantly longed for their humiliation. In order to avoid their jibes, I began to study as hard as I could on purpose and made my way to the top of the class. That impressed them. In addition, they all began to realize that I'd read certain books which they could never read and that I understood certain things (not included in our special course) about which they'd never even heard. They regarded this with savagery and sarcasm, but they submitted morally, all the more since even the teachers paid me some attention on this account. Their jibes ceased, but their hostility remained, and relations between us became cold and strained. In the end I myself couldn't stand it: as the years went by, my need for people, for friends, increased. I made several attempts to get closer to some of them; but these attempts always turned out to be unnatural and ended of their own accord. Once I even had a friend of sorts. But I was already a despot at heart; I wanted to exercise unlimited power over his soul; I wanted to instill in him contempt for his surroundings; and I demanded from him a disdainful and definitive break with those surroundings. I frightened him with my passionate friendship, and I reduced him to tears and convulsions. He was a naive and giving soul, but as soon as he'd surrendered himself to me totally, I began to despise him and reject him immediately—as if I only needed to achieve a victory over him, merely to subjugate him. But I was unable to conquer them all; my one friend was not at all like them, but rather a rare exception. The first thing I did upon leaving school was abandon the special job in the civil service for which I'd been trained, in order to sever all ties, break with my past, cover it over with dust. . . . The devil only knows why, after all that, I'd dragged myself over to see this Simonov! . . .

Early the next morning I roused myself from bed, jumped up in anxiety, just as if everything was about to start happening all at once. But I believed that some radical change in my life was imminent and was sure to occur that very day. Perhaps because I wasn't used to it, but all my life, at any external event, albeit a trivial one, it always seemed that some sort of radical change would occur. I went off to work as usual, but returned home two hours earlier in order to prepare. The most important thing, I thought, was not to arrive there first, or else they'd all think I was too eager. But there were thousands of most important things, and they all reduced me to the point of impotence. I polished my boots once again with my own hands. Apollon wouldn't polish them twice in one day for anything in the world; he considered it indecent. So I polished them myself, after stealing the brushes from the hallway so that he wouldn't notice and then despise me for it afterward. Next I carefully examined my clothes and found that everything was old, shabby, and worn out. I'd become too slovenly. My uniform was in better shape, but I couldn't go to dinner in a uniform. Worst of all, there was an enormous yellow stain on the knee of my trousers. I had an inkling that the spot alone would rob me of nine-tenths of my dignity. I also knew that it was unseemly for me to think that. "But this isn't the time for thinking. Reality is now looming," I thought, and my heart sank. I also knew perfectly well at that time, that I was monstrously exaggerating all these facts. But what could be done? I was no longer able to control myself, and was shaking with fever. In despair I imagined how haughtily and coldly that "scoundrel" Zverkov would greet me; with what dull and totally relentless contempt that dullard Trudolyubov would regard me; how nastily and impudently that insect Ferfichkin would giggle at me in order to win Zverkov's approval; how well Simonov would understand all this and how he'd despise me for my wretched vanity and cowardice; and worst of all, how petty all this would be, not *literary*, but commonplace. Of course, it would have been better not to go at all. But that was no longer possible; once I began to feel drawn to something, I plunged right in, head first. I'd have reproached myself for the rest of my life: "So, you retreated, you retreated before reality, you retreated!" On the contrary, I desperately wanted to prove to all this "rabble" that I really wasn't the coward I imagined myself to be. But that's not all: in the strongest paroxysm of cowardly fever I dreamt of gaining the upper hand, of conquering them, of carrying them away, compelling them to love me—if only "for the nobility of my thought and my indisputable wit." They would abandon Zverkov; he'd sit by in silence and embarassment, and I'd crush him. Afterward, perhaps, I'd be reconciled with Zverkov and drink to our *friendship*, but what was most spiteful and insulting for me was that I knew even then, I knew completely and for sure, that I didn't need any of this at all; that in fact I really didn't want to crush them, conquer them, or attract them, and that if I could have ever achieved all that, I'd be the first to say that it wasn't worth a damn. Oh, how I prayed to God that this day would pass quickly! With inexpressible anxiety I approached the window, opened the transom,[5] and peered out into the murky mist of the thickly falling wet snow. . . .

At last my worthless old wall clock sputtered out five o'clock. I grabbed my hat, and, trying not to look at Apollon—who'd been waiting since early morning to receive his wages, but didn't want to be the first one to mention it out of pride—I slipped out the door past him and intentionally hired a smart cab with my last half-ruble in order to arrive at the Hôtel de Paris in style.

IV

I knew since the day before that I'd be the first one to arrive. But it was no longer a question of who was first.

Not only was no one else there, but I even had difficulty finding our room. The table hadn't even been set. What did it all mean? After many inquiries I finally learned from the waiters that dinner had been ordered for closer to six o'clock, instead of five. This was also confirmed in the buffet. It was too embarrassing to ask any more questions. It was still only twenty-five minutes past five. If they'd changed the time, they should have let me know; that's what the city mail was for. They shouldn't have subjected me to such "shame" in my own eyes and . . . and, at least not in front of the waiters. I sat down. A waiter began to set the table. I felt even more ashamed in his presence. Toward six o'clock candles were brought into the room in addition to the lighted lamps already there, yet it hadn't occurred to the waiters to bring them in as soon as I'd arrived. In the next room two gloomy customers, angry-looking and silent, were dining at separate tables. In one of the distant rooms there was a great deal of noise, even shouting. One could hear the laughter of a whole crowd of people, including nasty little squeals in French—there were ladies present at that dinner. In short, it was disgusting. Rarely had I passed a more unpleasant hour, so that when they all arrived together precisely at six o'clock, I was initially overjoyed to see them, as if they were my liberators, and I almost forgot that I was supposed to appear offended.

Zverkov, obviously the leader, entered ahead of the rest. Both he and they were laughing; but, upon seeing me, Zverkov drew himself up, approached me unhurriedly, bowed slightly from the waist almost coquettishly, and extended his hand politely, but not too, with a kind of careful civility, almost as if he were a general both offering his hand, but also guarding against something. I'd imagined, on the contrary, that as soon as he entered he'd burst into his former, shrill laughter with occasional squeals, and that he'd immediately launch into his stale jokes and witticisms. I'd been preparing for them since the previous evening; but in no way did I expect such condescension, such courtesy characteristic of a general. Could it be that he now considered himself so immeasurably superior to me in all respects? If he'd merely wanted to offend me by this superior attitude, it wouldn't have been so bad, I thought; I'd manage to pay him back somehow. But what if, without any desire to offend, the notion had crept into his dumb sheep's brain that he

---

5. A small hinged pane in the window of a Russian house, used for ventilation especially during the winter when the main part of the window is sealed.

really was immeasurably superior to me and that he could only treat me in a patronizing way? From this possibility alone I began to gasp for air.

"Have you been waiting long?" Trudolyubov asked.

"I arrived at five o'clock sharp, just as I was told yesterday," I answered loudly and with irritation presaging an imminent explosion.

"Didn't you let him know that we changed the time?" Trudolyubov asked, turning to Simonov.

"No, I didn't. I forgot," he replied, but without any regret; then, not even apologizing to me, he went off to order the hors d'oeuvres.

"So you've been here for a whole hour, you poor fellow!" Zverkov cried sarcastically, because according to his notions, this must really have been terribly amusing. That scoundrel Ferfichkin chimed in after him with nasty, ringing laughter that sounded like a dog's yapping. My situation seemed very amusing and awkward to him, too.

"It's not the least bit funny!" I shouted at Ferfichkin, getting more and more irritated. "The others are to blame, not me. They neglected to inform me. It's, it's, it's . . . simply preposterous."

"It's not only preposterous, it's more than that," muttered Trudolyubov, naively interceding on my behalf. "You're being too kind. It's pure rudeness. Of course, it wasn't intentional. And how could Simonov have . . . hmm!"

"If a trick like that had been played on me," said Ferfichkin, "I'd . . ."

"Oh, you'd have ordered yourself something to eat," interrupted Zverkov, "or simply asked to have dinner served without waiting for the rest of us."

"You'll agree that I could've done that without asking anyone's permission," I snapped. "If I did wait, it was only because . . ."

"Let's be seated, gentlemen," cried Simonov upon entering. "Everything's ready. I can vouch for the champagne; it's excellently chilled. . . . Moreover, I didn't know where your apartment was, so how could I find you?" he said turning to me suddenly, but once again not looking directly at me. Obviously he was holding something against me. I suspect he got to thinking after what had happened yesterday.

Everyone sat down; I did, too. The table was round. Trudolyubov sat on my left, Simonov, on my right. Zverkov sat across; Ferfichkin, next to him, between Trudolyubov and him.

"Tell-l-l me now, are you . . . in a government department?" Zverkov continued to attend to me. Seeing that I was embarrassed, he imagined in earnest that he had to be nice to me, encouraging me to speak. "Does he want me to throw a bottle at his head, or what?" I thought in a rage. Unaccustomed as I was to all this, I was unnaturally quick to take offense.

"In such and such an office," I replied abruptly, looking at my plate.

"And . . . is it p-p-profitable? Tell-l-l me, what ma-a-de you decide to leave your previous position?"

"What ma-a-a-de me leave my previous position was simply that I wanted to," I dragged my words out three times longer than he did, hardly able to control myself. Ferfichkin snorted. Simonov looked at me ironically; Trudolyubov stopped eating and began to stare at me with curiosity.

Zverkov was jarred, but didn't want to show it.

"Well-l, and how is the support?"

"What support?"

"I mean, the s-salary?"

"Why are you cross-examining me?"

However, I told him right away what my salary was. I blushed terribly.

"That's not very much," Zverkov observed pompously.

"No, sir, it's not enough to dine in café-restaurants!" added Ferfichkin insolently.

"In my opinion, it's really very little," Trudolyubov observed in earnest.

"And how thin you've grown, how you've changed . . . since . . . ," Zverkov added, with a touch of venom now, and with a kind of impudent sympathy, examining me and my apparel.

"Stop embarrassing him," Ferfichkin cried with a giggle.

"My dear sir, I'll have you know that I'm not embarrassed," I broke in at last. "Listen! I'm dining in this 'café-restaurant' at my own expense, my own, not anyone else's; note that, Monsieur Ferfichkin."

"Wha-at? And who isn't dining at his own expense? You seem to be . . ." Ferfichkin seized hold of my words, turned as red as a lobster, and looked me straight in the eye with fury.

"Just so-o," I replied, feeling that I'd gone a bit too far, "and I suggest that it would be much better if we engaged in more intelligent conversation."

"It seems that you're determined to display your intelligence."

"Don't worry, that would be quite unnecessary here."

"What's all this cackling, my dear sir? Huh? Have you taken leave of your senses in that *duh*-partment of yours?"

"Enough, gentlemen, enough," cried Zverkov authoritatively.

"How stupid this is!" muttered Simonov.

"Really, it is stupid. We're gathered here in a congenial group to have a farewell dinner for our good friend, while you're still settling old scores," Trudolyubov said, rudely addressing only me. "You forced yourself upon us yesterday; don't disturb the general harmony now. . . ."

"Enough, enough," cried Zverkov. "Stop it, gentlemen, this'll never do. Let me tell you instead how I very nearly got married a few days ago . . ."

There followed some scandalous, libelous anecdote about how this gentleman very nearly got married a few days ago. There wasn't one word about marriage, however; instead, generals, colonels, and even gentlemen of the bed chamber figured prominently in the story, while Zverkov played the leading role among them all. Approving laughter followed; Ferfichkin even squealed.

Everyone had abandoned me by now, and I sat there completely crushed and humiliated.

"Good Lord, what kind of company is this for me?" I wondered. "And what a fool I've made of myself in front of them all! But I let Ferfichkin go too far. These numbskulls think they're doing me an honor by allowing me to sit with them at their table, when they don't understand that it's I who's done them the honor, and not the reverse. 'How thin I've grown! What clothes!' Oh, these damned trousers! Zverkov's already noticed the yellow spot on my knee. . . . What's the use? Right now, this very moment, I should stand up, take my hat, and simply leave without saying a single word. . . . Out of contempt! And tomorrow—I'll even be ready for a duel. Scoundrels! It's not the seven rubles I care about. But they may think that . . . To hell with it! I don't care about the seven rubles. I'm leaving at once! . . ."

Of course, I stayed.

In my misery I drank Lafite and sherry by the glassful. Being unaccustomed to it, I got drunk very quickly; the more intoxicated I became, the greater my annoyance. Suddenly I felt like offending them all in the most impudent manner—and then I'd leave. To seize the moment and show them all who I really was—let them say: even though he's ridiculous, he's clever . . . and . . . and . . . in short, to hell with them!

I surveyed them all arrogantly with my dazed eyes. But they seemed to have forgotten all about me. *They* were noisy, boisterous and merry. Zverkov kept on talking. I began to listen. He was talking about some magnificent lady whom he'd finally driven to make a declaration of love. (Of course, he was lying like a trooper.) He said that he'd been assisted in this matter particularly by a certain princeling, the hussar Kolya, who possessed some three thousand serfs.

"And yet, this same Kolya who has three thousand serfs hasn't even come to see you off," I said, breaking into the conversation suddenly. For a moment silence fell.

"You're drunk already," Trudolyubov said, finally deigning to notice me, and glancing contemptuously in my direction. Zverkov examined me in silence as if I were an insect. I lowered my eyes. Simonov quickly began to pour champagne.

Trudolyubov raised his glass, followed by everyone but me.

"To your health and to a good journey!" he cried to Zverkov. "To old times, gentlemen, and to our future, hurrah!"

Everyone drank up and pressed around to exchange kisses with Zverkov. I didn't budge; my full glass stood before me untouched.

"Aren't you going to drink?" Trudolyubov roared at me, having lost his patience and turning to me menacingly.

"I wish to make my own speech, all by myself . . . and then I'll drink, Mr. Trudolyubov."

"Nasty shrew!" Simonov muttered.

I sat up in my chair, feverishly seized hold of my glass, and prepared for something extraordinary, although I didn't know quite what I'd say.

"*Silence!*" cried Ferfichkin. "And now for some real intelligence!" Zverkov waited very gravely, aware of what was coming.

"Mr. Lieutenant Zverkov," I began, "you must know that I detest phrases, phrasemongers, and corsetted waists. . . . That's the first point; the second will follow."

Everyone stirred uncomfortably.

"The second point: I hate obscene stories and the men who tell them.[6] I especially hate the men who tell them!"

"The third point: I love truth, sincerity and honesty," I continued almost automatically, because I was beginning to become numb with horror, not knowing how I could be speaking this way. . . . "I love thought, Monsieur Zverkov. I love genuine comradery, on an equal footing, but not . . . hmmm . . . I love . . . But, after all, why not? I too will drink to your health, Monsieur

---

6. A phrase borrowed from the inveterate liar Nozdryov, one of the provincial landowners in the first volume of Gogol's *Dead Souls* (1842).

Zverkov. Seduce those Circassian[7] maidens, shoot the enemies of the fatherland, and . . . and . . . To your health, Monsieur Zverkov!"

Zverkov rose from his chair, bowed, and said: "I'm most grateful."

He was terribly offended and had even turned pale.

"To hell with him," Trudolyubov roared, banging his fist down on the table.

"No, sir, people should be whacked in the face for saying such things!" squealed Ferfichkin.

"We ought to throw him out!" muttered Simonov.

"Not a word, gentlemen, not a move!" Zverkov cried triumphantly, putting a stop to this universal indignation. "I'm grateful to you all, but I can show him myself how much I value his words."

"Mr. Ferfichkin, tomorrow you'll give me satisfaction for the words you've just uttered!" I said loudly, turning to Ferfichkin with dignity.

"Do you mean a duel? Very well," he replied, but I must have looked so ridiculous as I issued my challenge, it must have seemed so out of keeping with my entire appearance, that everyone, including Ferfichkin, collapsed into laughter.

"Yes, of course, throw him out! Why, he's quite drunk already," Trudolyubov declared in disgust.

"I shall never forgive myself for letting him join us," Simonov muttered again.

"Now's the time to throw a bottle at the lot of them," I thought. So I grabbed a bottle and . . . poured myself another full glass.

". . . No, it's better to sit it out to the very end!" I went on thinking. "You'd be glad, gentlemen, if I left. But nothing doing! I'll stay here deliberately and keep on drinking to the very end, as a sign that I accord you no importance whatsoever. I'll sit here and drink because this is a tavern, and I've paid good money to get in. I'll sit here and drink because I consider you to be so many pawns, nonexistent pawns. I'll sit here and drink . . . and sing too, if I want to, yes, sir, I'll sing because I have the right to . . . sing . . . hmm."

But I didn't sing. I just tried not to look at any of them; I assumed the most carefree poses and waited impatiently until they would be the first to speak to me. But, alas, they did not. How much, how very much I longed to be reconciled with them at that moment! The clock struck eight, then nine. They moved from the table to the sofa. Zverkov sprawled on the couch, placing one foot on the round table. They brought the wine over, too. He really had ordered three bottles at his own expense. Naturally, he didn't invite me to join them. Everyone surrounded him on the sofa. They listened to him almost with reverence. It was obvious they liked him. "What for? What for?" I wondered to myself. From time to time they were moved to drunken ecstasy and exchanged kisses. They talked about the Caucasus,[8] the nature of true passion, card games, profitable positions in the service; they talked about the income of a certain hussar Podkharzhevsky, whom none of them knew personally, and they rejoiced that his income was so large; they talked about the unusual

7. Women from the region between the Black Sea and the Caspian Sea, famous for their beauty and much in demand as concubines in the Ottoman Empire.

8. Region in which various peoples opposed Russian rule, and thus a constant source of trouble for the Russian Empire.

beauty and charm of Princess D., whom none of them had ever seen; finally, they arrived at the question of Shakespeare's immortality.

I smiled contemptuously and paced up and down the other side of the room, directly behind the sofa, along the wall from the table to the stove and back again. I wanted to show them with all my might that I could get along without them; meanwhile, I deliberately stomped my boots, thumping my heels. But all this was in vain. *They* paid me no attention. I had the forbearance to pace like that, right in front of them, from eight o'clock until eleven, in the very same place, from the table to the stove and from the stove back to the table. "I'm pacing just as I please, and no one can stop me." A waiter who came into the room paused several times to look at me; my head was spinning from all those turns; there were moments when it seemed that I was delirious. During those three hours I broke out in a sweat three times and then dried out. At times I was pierced to the heart with a most profound, venomous thought: ten years would pass, twenty, forty; and still, even after forty years, I'd remember with loathing and humiliation these filthiest, most absurd, and horrendous moments of my entire life. It was impossible to humiliate myself more shamelessly or more willingly, and I fully understood that, fully; nevertheless, I continued to pace from the table to the stove and back again. "Oh, if you only knew what thoughts and feelings I'm capable of, and how cultured I really am!" I thought at moments, mentally addressing the sofa where my enemies were seated. But my enemies behaved as if I weren't even in the room. Once, and only once, they turned to me, precisely when Zverkov started in about Shakespeare, and I suddenly burst into contemptuous laughter. I snorted so affectedly and repulsively that they broke off their conversation immediately and stared at me in silence for about two minutes, in earnest, without laughing, as I paced up and down, from the table to the stove, while *I paid not the slightest bit of attention to them*. But nothing came of it; they didn't speak to me. A few moments later they abandoned me again. The clock struck eleven.

"Gentlemen," exclaimed Zverkov, getting up from the sofa, "Now let's all go to *that place*."[9]

"Of course, of course!" the others replied.

I turned abruptly to Zverkov. I was so exhausted, so broken, that I'd have slit my own throat to be done with all this! I was feverish; my hair, which had been soaked through with sweat, had dried and now stuck to my forehead and temples.

"Zverkov, I ask your forgiveness," I said harshly and decisively. "Ferfichkin, yours too, and everyone's, everyone's. I've insulted you all!"

"Aha! So a duel isn't really your sort of thing!" hissed Ferfichkin venomously.

His remark was like a painful stab to my heart.

"No, I'm not afraid of a duel, Ferfichkin! I'm ready to fight with you tomorrow, even after we're reconciled. I even insist upon it, and you can't refuse me. I want to prove that I'm not afraid of a duel. You'll shoot first, and I'll fire into the air."

"He's amusing himself," Simonov observed.

9. I.e., a brothel.

"He's simply taken leave of his senses!" Trudolyubov added.

"Allow us to pass; why are you blocking our way? . . . Well, what is it you want?" Zverkov asked contemptuously. They were all flushed, their eyes glazed. They'd drunk a great deal.

"I ask for your friendship, Zverkov, I've insulted you, but . . ."

"Insulted me? You? In-sul-ted me? My dear sir, I want you to know that never, under any circumstances, could you possibly insult *me*!"

"And that's enough from you. Out of the way!" Trudolyubov added. "Let's go."

"Olympia is mine, gentlemen, that's agreed!" cried Zverkov.

"We won't argue, we won't," they replied, laughing.

I stood there as if spat on. The party left the room noisily, and Trudolyubov struck up a stupid song. Simonov remained behind for a brief moment to tip the waiters. All of a sudden I went up to him.

"Simonov! Give me six rubles," I said decisively and desperately.

He looked at me in extreme amazement with his dulled eyes. He was drunk, too.

"Are you really going *to that place* with us?"

"Yes!"

"I have no money!" he snapped; then he laughed contemptuously and headed out of the room.

I grabbed hold of his overcoat. It was a nightmare.

"Simonov! I know that you have some money. Why do you refuse me? Am I really such a scoundrel? Beware of refusing me: if you only knew, if you only knew why I'm asking. Everything depends on it, my entire future, all my plans. . . ."

Simonov took out the money and almost threw it at me.

"Take it, if you have no shame!" he said mercilessly, then ran out to catch up with the others.

I remained behind for a minute. The disorder, the leftovers, a broken glass on the floor, spilled wine, cigarette butts, drunkenness and delirium in my head, agonizing torment in my heart; and finally, a waiter who'd seen and heard everything and who was now looking at me with curiosity.

"*To that place!*" I cried. "Either they'll all fall on their knees, embracing me, begging for my friendship, or . . . or else, I'll give Zverkov a slap in the face."

V

"So here it is, here it is at last, a confrontation with reality," I muttered, rushing headlong down the stairs. "This is no longer the Pope leaving Rome and going to Brazil; this is no ball on the shores of Lake Como!"

"You're a scoundrel," the thought flashed through my mind, "if you laugh at that now."

"So what!" I cried in reply. "Everything is lost now, anyway!"

There was no sign of them, but it didn't matter. I knew where they were going.

At the entrance stood a solitary, late-night cabby in a coarse peasant coat powdered with wet, seemingly warm snow that was still falling. It was steamy and stuffy outside. The little shaggy piebald nag was also dusted with snow and was coughing; I remember that very well. I headed for the rough-hewn sledge; but as soon as I raised one foot to get in, the recollection of how Simonov had just given me six rubles hit me with such force that I tumbled into the sledge like a sack.

"No! There's a lot I have to do to make up for that!" I cried. "But make up for it I will or else I'll perish on the spot this very night. Let's go!" We set off. There was an entire whirlwind spinning around inside my head.

"They won't fall on their knees to beg for my friendship. That's a mirage, an indecent mirage, disgusting, romantic, and fantastic; it's just like the ball on the shores of Lake Como. Consequently, I *must* give Zverkov a slap in the face! I am obligated to do it. And so, it's all decided; I'm rushing there to give him a slap in the face."

"Hurry up!"

The cabby tugged at the reins.

"As soon as I go in, I'll slap him. Should I say a few words first before I slap him in the face? No! I'll simply go in and slap him. They'll all be sitting there in the drawing room; he'll be on the sofa with Olympia. That damned Olympia! She once ridiculed my face and refused me. I'll drag Olympia around by the hair and Zverkov by the ears. No, better grab one ear and lead him around the room like that. Perhaps they'll begin to beat me, and then they'll throw me out. That's even likely. So what? I'll still have slapped him first; the initiative will be mine. According to the laws of honor, that's all that matters. He'll be branded, and nothing can wipe away that slap except a duel.[1] He'll have to fight. So just let them beat me now! Let them, the ingrates! Trudolyubov will hit me hardest, he's so strong. Ferfichkin will sneak up alongside and will undoubtedly grab my hair, I'm sure he will. But let them, let them. That's why I've come. At last these blockheads will be forced to grasp the tragedy in all this! As they drag me to the door, I'll tell them that they really aren't even worth the tip of my little finger!"

"Hurry up, driver, hurry up!" I shouted to the cabby.

He was rather startled and cracked his whip. I'd shouted very savagely.

"We'll fight at daybreak, and that's settled. I'm through with the department. Ferfichkin recently said duh-partment, instead of department. But where will I get pistols? What nonsense! I'll take my salary in advance and buy them. And powder? Bullets? That's what the second will attend to. And how will I manage to do all this by daybreak? And where will I find a second? I have no acquaintances. . . ."

"Nonsense!" I shouted, whipping myself up into even more of a frenzy, "Nonsense!"

"The first person I meet on the street will have to act as my second, just as he would pull a drowning man from the water. The most extraordinary possibilities have to be allowed for. Even if tomorrow I were to ask the director himself to act as my second, he too would have to agree merely out of a sense of chivalry, and he would keep it a secret! Anton Antonych . . ."

The fact of the matter was that at that very moment I was more clearly and vividly aware than anyone else on earth of the disgusting absurdity of my intentions and the whole opposite side of the coin, but . . .

---

1. Duels as a means of resolving points of honor were officially discouraged but still fairly common.

"Hurry up, driver, hurry, you rascal, hurry up!"

"Hey, sir!" that son of the earth replied.

A sudden chill came over me.

"Wouldn't it be better . . . wouldn't it be better . . . to go straight home right now? Oh, my God! Why, why did I invite myself to that dinner yesterday? But no, it's impossible. And my pacing for three hours from the table to the stove? No, they, and no one else will have to pay me back for that pacing! They must wipe out that disgrace!"

"Hurry up!"

"What if they turn me over to the police? They wouldn't dare! They'd be afraid of a scandal. And what if Zverkov refuses the duel out of contempt? That's even likely; but I'll show them. . . . I'll rush to the posting station when he's supposed to leave tomorrow; I'll grab hold of his leg, tear off his overcoat just as he's about to climb into the carriage. I'll fasten my teeth on his arm and bite him. 'Look, everyone, see what a desperate man can be driven to!' Let him hit me on the head while others hit me from behind. I'll shout to the whole crowd, 'Behold, here's a young puppy who's going off to charm Circassian maidens with my spit on his face!'"

"Naturally, it'll all be over after that. The department will banish me from the face of the earth. They'll arrest me, try me, drive me out of the service, send me to prison; ship me off to Siberia for resettlement. Never mind! Fifteen years later when they let me out of jail, a beggar in rags, I'll drag myself off to see him. I'll find him in some provincial town. He'll be married and happy. He'll have a grown daughter. . . . I'll say, 'Look, you monster, look at my sunken cheeks and my rags. I've lost everything—career, happiness, art, science, a *beloved woman*—all because of you. Here are the pistols. I came here to load my pistol, and . . . and I forgive you.' Then I'll fire into the air, and he'll never hear another word from me again. . . ."

I was actually about to cry, even though I knew for a fact at that very moment that all this was straight out of Silvio and Lermontov's *Masquerade*.[2] Suddenly I felt terribly ashamed, so ashamed that I stopped the horse, climbed out of the sledge, and stood there amidst the snow in the middle of the street. The driver looked at me in amazement and sighed.

What was I to do? I couldn't go there—that was absurd; and I couldn't drop the whole thing, because then it would seem like . . . Oh, Lord! How could I drop it? After such insults!

"No!" I cried, throwing myself back into the sledge. "It's predestined; it's fate! Drive on, hurry up, *to that place!*"

In my impatience, I struck the driver on the neck with my fist.

"What's the matter with you? Why are you hitting me?" cried the poor little peasant, whipping his nag so that she began to kick up her hind legs.

Wet snow was falling in big flakes; I unbuttoned my coat, not caring about the snow. I forgot about everything else because now, having finally resolved on the slap, *I felt with horror that it was imminent* and that *nothing on earth could possibly stop it*. Lonely street lamps shone gloomily in the snowy mist

<hr />

2. A drama by Mikhail Lermontov (1835) about romantic conventions of love and honor. Silvio is the protagonist of Alexander Pushkin's short story "The Shot" (1830), about a man dedicated to revenge. Both works conclude with bizarre twists.

like torches at a funeral. Snow got in under my overcoat, my jacket, and my necktie, and melted there. I didn't button up; after all, everything was lost, anyway. At last we arrived. I jumped out, almost beside myself, ran up the stairs, and began to pound at the door with my hands and feet. My legs, especially my knees, felt terribly weak. The door opened rather quickly; it was as if they knew I was coming. (In fact, Simonov had warned them that there might be someone else, since at this place one had to give notice and in general take precautions. It was one of those "fashionable shops" of the period that have now been eliminated by the police. During the day it really was a shop; but in the evening men with recommendations were able to visit as guests.) I walked rapidly through the darkened shop into a familiar drawing-room where there was only one small lit candle, and I stopped in dismay: there was no one there.

"Where are they?" I asked.

Naturally, by now they'd all dispersed. . . .

Before me stood a person with a stupid smile, the madam herself, who knew me slightly. In a moment a door opened, and another person came in.

Without paying much attention to anything, I walked around the room, and, apparently, was talking to myself. It was as if I'd been delivered from death, and I felt it joyously in my whole being. I'd have given him the slap, certainly, I'd certainly have given him the slap. But now they weren't here and . . . everything had vanished, everything had changed! . . . I looked around. I still couldn't take it all in. I glanced up mechanically at the girl who'd come in: before me there flashed a fresh, young, slightly pale face with straight dark brows and a serious, seemingly astonished look. I liked that immediately; I would have hated her if she'd been smiling. I began to look at her more carefully, as though with some effort: I'd still not managed to collect my thoughts. There was something simple and kind in her face, but somehow it was strangely serious. I was sure that she was at a disadvantage as a result, and that none of those fools had even noticed her. She couldn't be called a beauty, however, even though she was tall, strong, and well built. She was dressed very simply. Something despicable took hold of me; I went up to her. . . .

I happened to glance into a mirror. My overwrought face appeared extremely repulsive: it was pale, spiteful and mean; and my hair was dishevelled. "It doesn't matter. I'm glad," I thought. "In fact, I'm even delighted that I'll seem so repulsive to her; that pleases me. . . ."

VI

Somewhere behind a partition a clock was wheezing as if under some strong pressure, as though someone were strangling it. After this unnaturally prolonged wheezing there followed a thin, nasty, somehow unexpectedly hurried chime, as if someone had suddenly leapt forward. It struck two. I recovered, although I really hadn't been asleep, only lying there half-conscious.

It was almost totally dark in the narrow, cramped, low-ceilinged room, which was crammed with an enormous wardrobe and cluttered with cartons, rags, and all sorts of old clothes. The candle burning on the table at one end of the room flickered faintly from time to time, and almost went out completely. In a few moments total darkness would set in.

It didn't take long for me to come to my senses; all at once, without any effort, everything returned to me, as though it had been lying in ambush ready to pounce on me again. Even in my unconscious state some point had constantly remained in my memory, never to be forgotten, around which my sleepy visions had gloomily revolved. But it was a strange thing: everything that had happened to me that day now seemed, upon awakening, to have occurred in the distant past, as if I'd long since left it all behind.

My mind was in a daze. It was as though something were hanging over me, provoking, agitating, and disturbing me. Misery and bile were welling inside me, seeking an outlet. Suddenly I noticed beside me two wide-open eyes, examining me curiously and persistently. The gaze was coldly detached, sullen, as if belonging to a total stranger. I found it oppressive.

A dismal thought was conceived in my brain and spread throughout my whole body like a nasty sensation, such as one feels upon entering a damp, mouldy underground cellar. It was somehow unnatural that only now these two eyes had decided to examine me. I also recalled that during the course of the last two hours I hadn't said one word to this creature, and that I had considered it quite unnecessary; that had even given me pleasure for some reason. Now I'd suddenly realized starkly how absurd, how revolting as a spider, was the idea of debauchery, which, without love, crudely and shamelessly begins precisely at the point where genuine love is consummated. We looked at each other in this way for some time, but she didn't lower her gaze before mine, nor did she alter her stare, so that finally, for some reason, I felt very uneasy.

"What's your name?" I asked abruptly, to put an end to it quickly.

"Liza," she replied, almost in a whisper, but somehow in a very unfriendly way; and she turned her eyes away.

I remained silent.

"The weather today . . . snow . . . foul!" I observed, almost to myself, drearily placing one arm behind my head and staring at the ceiling.

She didn't answer. The whole thing was obscene.

"Are you from around here?" I asked her a moment later, almost angrily, turning my head slightly toward her.

"No."

"Where are you from?"

"Riga," she answered unwillingly.

"German?"

"No, Russian."

"Have you been here long?"

"Where?"

"In this house."

"Two weeks." She spoke more and more curtly. The candle had gone out completely; I could no longer see her face.

"Are your mother and father still living?"

"Yes . . . no . . . they are."

"Where are they?"

"There . . . in Riga."

"Who are they?"

"Just . . ."

"Just what? What do they do?"

"Tradespeople."

"Have you always lived with them?"

"Yes."

"How old are you?"

"Twenty."

"Why did you leave them?"

"Just because . . ."

That "just because" meant: leave me alone, it makes me sick. We fell silent.

Only God knows why, but I didn't leave. I too started to feel sick and more depressed. Images of the previous day began to come to mind all on their own, without my willing it, in a disordered way. I suddenly recalled a scene that I'd witnessed on the street that morning as I was anxiously hurrying to work. "Today some people were carrying a coffin and nearly dropped it," I suddenly said aloud, having no desire whatever to begin a conversation, but just so, almost accidentally.

"A coffin?"

"Yes, in the Haymarket; they were carrying it up from an underground cellar."

"From a cellar?"

"Not a cellar, but from a basement . . . well, you know . . . from downstairs . . . from a house of ill repute . . . There was such filth all around. . . . Eggshells, garbage . . . it smelled foul . . . it was disgusting."

Silence.

"A nasty day to be buried!" I began again to break the silence.

"Why nasty?"

"Snow, slush . . ." (I yawned.)

"It doesn't matter," she said suddenly after a brief silence.

"No, it's foul. . . ." (I yawned again.) "The grave diggers must have been cursing because they were getting wet out there in the snow. And there must have been water in the grave."

"Why water in the grave?" she asked with some curiosity, but she spoke even more rudely and curtly than before. Something suddenly began to goad me on.

"Naturally, water on the bottom, six inches or so. You can't ever dig a dry grave at Volkovo cemetery."

"Why not?"

"What do you mean, why not? The place is waterlogged. It's all swamp. So they bury them right in the water. I've seen it myself . . . many times. . . ."

(I'd never seen it, and I'd never been to Volkovo cemetery, but I'd heard about it from other people.)

"Doesn't it matter to you if you die?"

"Why should I die?" she replied, as though defending herself.

"Well, someday you'll die; you'll die just like that woman did this morning. She was a . . . she was also a young girl . . . she died of consumption."

"The wench should have died in the hospital. . . ." (She knows all about it, I thought, and she even said "wench" instead of "girl.")

"She owed money to her madam," I retorted, more and more goaded on by the argument. "She worked right up to the end, even though she had consumption. The cabbies standing around were chatting with the soldiers, telling them all about it. Her former acquaintances, most likely. They were all laughing. They were planning to drink to her memory at the tavern." (I invented a great deal of this.)

Silence, deep silence. She didn't even stir.

"Do you think it would be better to die in a hospital?"

"Isn't it just the same? . . . Besides, why should I die?" she added irritably.

"If not now, then later?"

"Well, then later . . ."

"That's what you think! Now you're young and pretty and fresh—that's your value. But after a year of this life, you won't be like that any more; you'll fade."

"In a year?"

"In any case, after a year your price will be lower," I continued, gloating. "You'll move out of here into a worse place, into some other house. And a year later, into a third, each worse and worse, and seven years from now you'll end up in a cellar on the Haymarket. Even that won't be so bad. The real trouble will come when you get some disease, let's say a weakness in the chest . . . or you catch cold or something. In this kind of life it's no laughing matter to get sick. It takes hold of you and may never let go. And so, you die."

"Well, then, I'll die," she answered now quite angrily and stirred quickly.

"That'll be a pity."

"For what?"

"A pity to lose a life."

Silence.

"Did you have a sweetheart? Huh?"

"What's it to you?"

"Oh, I'm not interrogating you. What do I care? Why are you angry? Of course, you may have had your own troubles. What's it to me? Just the same, I'm sorry."

"For whom?"

"I'm sorry for you."

"No need . . . ," she whispered barely audibly and stirred once again.

That provoked me at once. What! I was being so gentle with her, while she . . .

"Well, and what do you think? Are you on the right path then?"

"I don't think anything."

"That's just the trouble—you don't think. Wake up, while there's still time. And there is time. You're still young and pretty; you could fall in love, get married, be happy.[3] . . ."

"Not all married women are happy," she snapped in her former, rude manner.

"Not all, of course, but it's still better than this. A lot better. You can even live without happiness as long as there's love. Even in sorrow life can be good; it's good to be alive, no matter how you live. But what's there besides . . . stench? Phew!"

I turned away in disgust; I was no longer coldly philosophizing. I began to feel what I was saying and grew excited. I'd been longing to expound these cherished *little ideas* that I'd been nurturing in my corner. Something had suddenly caught fire in me, some kind of goal had "manifested itself" before me.

"Pay no attention to the fact that I'm here. I'm no model for you. I may be even worse than you are. Moreover, I was drunk when I came here." I hastened nonetheless to justify myself. "Besides, a man is no example to a woman. It's a different thing altogether; even though I degrade and defile myself, I'm still no one's slave; if I want to leave, I just get up and go. I shake

---

3. A popular theme treated by Gogol, Chernyshevsky, and Nekrasov, among others. Typically, an innocent and idealistic young man attempts to rehabilitate a prostitute or "fallen" woman.

it all off and I'm a different man. But you must realize right from the start that you're a slave. Yes, a slave! You give away everything, all your freedom. Later, if you want to break this chain, you won't be able to; it'll bind you ever more tightly. That's the kind of evil chain it is. I know. I won't say anything else; you might not even understand me. But tell me this, aren't you already in debt to your madam? There, you see!" I added, even though she hadn't answered, but had merely remained silent; but she was listening with all her might. "There's your chain! You'll never buy yourself out. That's the way it's done. It's just like selling your soul to the devil. . . .

"And besides . . . I may be just as unfortunate, how do you know, and I may be wallowing in mud on purpose, also out of misery. After all, people drink out of misery. Well, I came here out of misery. Now, tell me, what's so good about this place? Here you and I were . . . intimate . . . just a little while ago, and all that time we didn't say one word to each other; afterward you began to examine me like a wild creature, and I did the same. Is that the way people love? Is that how one person is supposed to encounter another? It's a disgrace, that's what it is!"

"Yes!" she agreed with me sharply and hastily. The haste of her answer surprised even me. It meant that perhaps the very same idea was flitting through her head while she'd been examining me earlier. It meant that she too was capable of some thought. . . . "Devil take it; this is odd, this *kinship*," I thought, almost rubbing my hands together. "Surely I can handle such a young soul."

It was the sport that attracted me most of all.

She turned her face closer to mine, and in the darkness it seemed that she propped her head up on her arm. Perhaps she was examining me. I felt sorry that I couldn't see her eyes. I heard her breathing deeply.

"Why did you come here?" I began with some authority.

"Just so . . ."

"But think how nice it would be living in your father's house! There you'd be warm and free; you'd have a nest of your own."

"And what if it's worse than that?"

"I must establish the right tone," flashed through my mind. "I won't get far with sentimentality."

However, that merely flashed through my mind. I swear that she really did interest me. Besides, I was somewhat exhausted and provoked. After all, artifice goes along so easily with feeling.

"Who can say?" I hastened to reply. "All sorts of things can happen. Why, I was sure that someone had wronged you and was more to blame than you are. After all, I know nothing of your life story, but a girl like you doesn't wind up in this sort of place on her own accord. . . ."

"What kind of a girl am I?" she whispered hardly audibly; but I heard it.

"What the hell! Now I'm flattering her. That's disgusting! But, perhaps it's a good thing. . . ." She remained silent.

"You see, Liza, I'll tell you about myself. If I'd had a family when I was growing up, I wouldn't be the person I am now. I think about this often. After all, no matter how bad it is in your own family—it's still your own father and mother, and not enemies or strangers. Even if they show you their love only once a year, you still know that you're at home. I grew up without a family; that must be why I turned out the way I did—so unfeeling."

I waited again.

"She might not understand," I thought. "Besides, it's absurd—all this moralizing."

"If I were a father and had a daughter, I think that I'd have loved her more than my sons, really," I began indirectly, talking about something else in order to distract her. I confess that I was blushing.

"Why's that?"

Ah, so she's listening!

"Just because. I don't know why, Liza. You see, I knew a father who was a stern, strict man, but he would kneel before his daughter and kiss her hands and feet; he couldn't get enough of her, really. She'd go dancing at a party, and he'd stand in one spot for five hours, never taking his eyes off her. He was crazy about her; I can understand that. At night she'd be tired and fall asleep, but he'd wake up, go in to kiss her, and make the sign of the cross over her while she slept. He used to wear a dirty old jacket and was stingy with every-one else, but would spend his last kopeck on her, buying her expensive pres-ents; it afforded him great joy if she liked his presents. A father always loves his daughters more than their mother does. Some girls have a very nice time living at home. I think that I wouldn't even have let my daughter get married."

"Why not?" she asked with a barely perceptible smile.

"I'd be jealous, so help me God. Why, how could she kiss someone else? How could she love a stranger more than her own father? It's even painful to think about it. Of course, it's all nonsense; naturally, everyone finally comes to his senses. But I think that before I'd let her marry, I'd have tortured myself with worry. I'd have found fault with all her suitors. Nevertheless, I'd have ended up by allowing her to marry whomever she loved. After all, the one she loves always seems the worst of all to the father. That's how it is. That causes a lot of trouble in many families."

"Some are glad to sell their daughters, rather than let them marry honor-ably," she said suddenly.

Aha, so that's it!

"That happens, Liza, in those wretched families where there's neither God nor love," I retorted heatedly. "And where there's no love, there's also no good sense. There are such families, it's true, but I'm not talking about them. Obviously, from the way you talk, you didn't see much kindness in your own family. You must be very unfortunate. Hmm . . . But all this results primarily from poverty."

"And is it any better among the gentry? Honest folk live decently even in poverty."

"Hmmm . . . Yes. Perhaps. There's something else, Liza. Man only likes to count his troubles; he doesn't calculate his happiness. If he figured as he should, he'd see that everyone gets his share. So, let's say that all goes well in a particular family; it enjoys God's blessing, the husband turns out to be a good man, he loves you, cherishes you, and never leaves you. Life is good in that family. Sometimes, even though there's a measure of sorrow, life's still good. Where isn't there sorrow? If you choose to get married, *you'll find out for yourself*. Consider even the first years of a marriage to the one you love: what happiness, what pure bliss there can be sometimes! Almost without exception. At first even quarrels with your husband turn out well. For some women, the more they love their husbands, the more they pick fights with them. It's true; I once knew a woman like that. 'That's how it is,' she'd say. 'I love you very much and I'm tormenting you out of love, so that you'll feel it.' Did you know that one can torment a person intentionally out of love? It's mostly women who do that. Then she thinks to herself, 'I'll love him so much afterward, I'll be so affectionate, it's no sin to torment him a little now.' At home everyone would rejoice over you, and it would be so pleasant, cheerful, serene, and honorable. . . . Some other women are very jealous. If her husband goes away, I knew one like that, she can't stand it; she jumps up at night and goes off on the sly to see. Is he there? Is he in that house? Is he with that one? Now that's bad. Even she herself knows that it's bad; her heart sinks and she suffers because she really loves him. It's all out of love. And how nice it is to make up after a quarrel, to admit one's guilt or forgive him! How nice it is for both of them, how good they both feel at once, just as if they'd met again, married again, and begun their love all over again. No one, no one at all has to know what goes on between a husband and wife, if they love each other. However their quarrel ends, they should never call in either one of their mothers to act as judge or to hear complaints about the other one. They must act as their own judges. Love is God's mystery and should be hidden from other people's eyes, no matter what happens. This makes it holier, much better. They respect each other more, and a great deal is based on this respect. And, if there's been love, if they got married out of love, why should love disappear? Can't it be sustained? It rarely happens that it can't be sustained. If the husband turns out to be a kind and honest man, how can the love disappear? The first phase of married love will pass, that's true, but it's followed by an even better kind of love. Souls are joined together and all their concerns are managed in common; there'll be no secrets from one another. When children arrive, each and every stage, even a very difficult one, will seem happy, as long as there's both love and courage. Even work is cheerful; even when you deny yourself bread for your children's sake, you're still happy. After all, they'll love you for it afterward; you're really saving for your own future. Your children will grow up, and you'll feel that you're a model for them, a support. Even after you die, they'll carry your thoughts and feelings all during their life. They'll take on your image and likeness, since they received it from you. Consequently, it's a great obligation. How can a mother and father keep from growing closer? They say it's difficult to raise children. Who says that? It's heavenly joy! Do you love little children, Liza? I love them dearly. You know— a rosy little boy, suckling at your breast; what husband's heart could turn against his wife seeing her sitting there holding his child? The chubby, rosy little baby sprawls and snuggles; his little hands and feet are plump; his little nails are clean and tiny, so tiny it's even funny to see them; his little eyes look as if he already understood everything. As he suckles, he tugs at your breast playfully with his little hand. When the father approaches, the child lets go of the breast, bends way back, looks at his father, and laughs—as if God only knows how funny it is—and then takes to suckling again. Afterward, when he starts cutting teeth, he'll sometimes bite his mother's breast; looking at her sideways his little eyes seem to say, 'See, I bit you!' Isn't this pure bliss— the three of them, husband, wife, and child, all together? You can forgive a great deal for such moments. No, Liza, I think you must first learn how to live by yourself, and only afterward blame others."

"It's by means of images," I thought to myself, "just such images that I can get to you," although I was speaking with considerable feeling, I swear it; and all at once I blushed. "And what if she suddenly bursts out laughing—where will I hide then?" That thought drove me into a rage. By the end of my speech I'd really become excited, and now my pride was suffering somehow. The silence lasted for a while. I even considered shaking her.

"Somehow you . . ." she began suddenly and then stopped.

But I understood everything already: something was trembling in her voice now, not shrill, rude or unyielding as before, but something soft and timid, so timid that I suddenly was rather ashamed to watch her and felt guilty.

"What?" I asked with tender curiosity.

"Well, you . . ."

"What?"

"You somehow . . . it sounds just like a book," she said, and once again something which was noticeably sarcastic was suddenly heard in her voice.

Her remark wounded me dreadfully. That's not what I'd expected.

Yet, I didn't understand that she was intentionally disguising her feelings with sarcasm; that was usually the last resort of people who are timid and chaste of heart, whose souls have been coarsely and impudently invaded; and who, until the last moment, refuse to yield out of pride and are afraid to express their own feelings to you. I should've guessed it from the timidity with which on several occasions she tried to be sarcastic, until she finally managed to express it. But I hadn't guessed, and a malicious impulse took hold of me.

"Just you wait," I thought.

VII

"That's enough, Liza. What do books have to do with it, when this disgusts me as an outsider? And not only as an outsider. All this has awakened in my heart . . . Can it be, can it really be that you don't find it repulsive here? No, clearly habit means a great deal. The devil only knows what habit can do to a person. But do you seriously think that you'll never grow old, that you'll always be pretty, and that they'll keep you on here forever and ever? I'm not even talking about the filth. . . . Besides, I want to say this about your present life: even though you're still young, good-looking, nice, with soul and feelings, do you know, that when I came to a little while ago, I was immediately disgusted to be here with you! Why, a man has to be drunk to wind up here. But if you were in a different place, living as nice people do, I might not only chase after you, I might actually fall in love with you. I'd rejoice at a look from you, let alone a word; I'd wait for you at the gate and kneel down before you; I'd think of you as my betrothed and even consider that an honor. I wouldn't dare have any impure thoughts about you. But here, I know that I need only whistle, and you, whether you want to or not, will come to me, and that I don't have to do your bidding, whereas you have to do mine. The lowliest peasant may hire himself out as a laborer, but he doesn't make a complete slave of himself; he knows that it's only for a limited term. But what's your term? Just think about it. What are you giving up here? What are you enslaving? Why, you're enslaving your soul, something you don't really own, together with your body! You're giving away your love to be defiled by any drunkard! Love! After all, that's all there is! It's a precious jewel, a maiden's treasure, that's what it is! Why, to earn that love a man might be ready to offer up his own soul, to face death. But what's your love worth now? You've been bought, all of you; and why should anyone strive for your love, when you offer everything even without it? Why, there's no greater insult for a girl, don't you understand? Now, I've heard that they console you foolish girls, they allow you to see your own lovers here. But that's merely child's play, deception, making fun of you, while you believe it. And do you really think he loves you, that lover of yours? I don't believe it. How can he, if he knows that you can be called away from him at any moment? He'd have to be depraved after all that. Does he possess even one drop of respect for you? What do you have in common with him? He's laughing at you and stealing from you at the same time—so much for his love. It's not too bad, as long as he doesn't beat you. But perhaps he does. Go on, ask him, if you have such a lover, whether he'll ever marry you. Why, he'll burst out laughing right in your face, if he doesn't spit at you or smack you. He himself may be worth no more than a few lousy kopecks. And for what, do you think, did you ruin your whole life here? For the coffee they give you to drink, or for the plentiful supply of food? Why do you think they feed you so well? Another girl, an honest one, would choke on every bite, because she'd know why she was being fed so well. You're in debt here, you'll be in debt, and will remain so until the end, until such time comes as the customers begin to spurn you. And that time will come very soon; don't count on your youth. Why, here youth flies by like a stagecoach. They'll kick you out. And they'll not merely kick you out, but for a long time before that they'll pester you, reproach you, and abuse you—as if you hadn't ruined your health for the madam, hadn't given up your youth and your soul for her in vain, but rather, as if you'd ruined her, ravaged her, and robbed her. And don't expect any support. Your friends will also attack you to curry her favor, because they're all in bondage here and have long since lost both conscience and pity. They've become despicable, and there's nothing on earth more despicable, more repulsive, or more insulting than their abuse. You'll lose everything here, everything, without exception—your health, youth, beauty, and hope—and at the age of twenty-two you'll look as if you were thirty-five, and even that won't be too awful if you're not ill. Thank God for that. Why, you probably think that you're not even working, that it's all play! But there's no harder work or more onerous task than this one in the whole world and there never has been. I'd think that one's heart alone would be worn out by crying. Yet you dare not utter one word, not one syllable; when they drive you out, you leave as if you were the guilty one. You'll move to another place, then to a third, then somewhere else, and finally you'll wind up in the Haymarket. And there they'll start beating you for no good reason at all; it's a local custom; the clients there don't know how to be nice without beating you. You don't think it's so disgusting there? Maybe you should go and have a look sometime, and see it with your own eyes. Once, at New Year's, I saw a woman in a doorway. Her own kind had pushed her outside as a joke, to freeze her for a little while because she was wailing too much; they shut the door behind her. At nine o'clock in the morning she was already dead drunk, dishevelled, half-naked, and all beaten up. Her face was powdered, but her eyes were bruised; blood was streaming from her nose and mouth; a certain cabby had just fixed her up. She was sitting on a stone step, holding a piece of salted fish in her hand; she was howling, wailing something about her 'fate,' and slapping the fish against the stone step. Cabbies and drunken soldiers had gathered around the steps and were taunting her. Don't you think you'll wind up the same way? I wouldn't want to believe it myself, but how do you know, perhaps eight or ten years ago this same girl, the one with the salted fish, arrived here from somewhere or other, all fresh like a little cherub, innocent, and pure; she knew no evil and blushed at every word. Perhaps she was just like you—proud, easily offended, unlike all the rest; she looked like a queen and knew that total happiness awaited the man who would love her and whom she would also love. Do you see how it all ended? What if at the very moment she was slapping the fish against that filthy step, dead drunk and dishevelled, what if, even at that very moment she'd recalled her earlier, chaste years in her father's house when she was still going to school, and when her neighbor's son used to wait for her along the path and assure her that he'd love her all his life and devote himself entirely to her, and when they vowed to love one another forever and get married as soon as they grew up! No, Liza, you'd be lucky, very lucky, if you died quickly from consumption somewhere in a corner, in a cellar, like that other girl. In a hospital, you say? All right—they'll take you off, but what if the madam still requires your services? Consumption is quite a disease—it's not like dying from a fever. A person continues to hope right up until the last minute and declares that he's in good health. He consoles himself. Now that's useful for your madam. Don't worry, that's the way it is. You've sold your soul; besides, you owe her money—that means you don't dare say a thing. And while you're dying, they'll all abandon you, turn away from you—because there's nothing left to get from you. They'll even reproach you for taking up space for no good reason and for taking so long to die. You won't even be able to ask for something to drink, without their hurling abuse at you: 'When will you croak, you old bitch? You keep on moaning and don't let us get any sleep— and you drive our customers away.' That's for sure; I've overheard such words myself. And as you're breathing your last, they'll shove you into the filthiest corner of the cellar—into darkness and dampness; lying there alone, what will you think about then? After you die, some stranger will lay you out hurriedly, grumbling all the while, impatiently—no one will bless you, no one will sigh over you; they'll merely want to get rid of you as quickly as possible. They'll buy you a wooden trough and carry you out as they did that poor woman I saw today; then they'll go off to a tavern and drink to your memory. There'll be slush, filth, and wet snow in your grave—why bother for the likes of you? 'Let her down, Vanyukha; after all, it's her fate to go down with her legs up, that's the sort of girl she was. Pull up on that rope, you rascal!' 'It's okay like that.' 'How's it okay? See, it's lying on its side. Was she a human being or not? Oh, never mind, cover it up.' They won't want to spend much time arguing over you. They'll cover your coffin quickly with wet, blue clay and then go off to the tavern. . . . That'll be the end of your memory on earth; for other women, children will visit their graves, fathers, husbands—but for you—no tears, no sighs; no remembrances. No one, absolutely no one in the whole world, will ever come to visit you; your name will disappear from the face of the earth, just as if you'd never been born and had never existed. Mud and filth, no matter how you pound on the lid of your coffin at night when other corpses arise: 'Let me out, kind people, let me live on earth for a little while! I lived, but I didn't really see life; my life went down the drain; they drank it away in a tavern at the Haymarket; let me out, kind people, let me live in the world once again!'"

I was so carried away by my own pathos that I began to feel a lump forming in my throat, and . . . I suddenly stopped, rose up in fright, and, leaning over apprehensively, I began to listen carefully as my own heart pounded. There was cause for dismay.

For a while I felt that I'd turned her soul inside out and had broken her heart; the more I became convinced of this, the more I strived to reach my goal as quickly and forcefully as possible. It was the sport, the sport that attracted me; but it wasn't only the sport. . . .

I knew that I was speaking clumsily, artificially, even bookishly; in short, I didn't know how to speak except "like a book." But that didn't bother me, for I knew, I had a premonition, that I would be understood and that this bookishness itself might even help things along. But now, having achieved this effect, I suddenly lost all my nerve. No, never, never before had I witnessed such despair! She was lying there, her face pressed deep into a pillow she was clutching with her hands. Her heart was bursting. Her young body was shuddering as if she were having convulsions. Suppressed sobs shook her breast, tore her apart, and suddenly burst forth in cries and moans. Then she pressed her face even deeper into the pillow: she didn't want anyone, not one living soul, to hear her anguish and her tears. She bit the pillow; she bit her hand until it bled (I noticed that afterward); or else, thrusting her fingers into her dishevelled hair, she became rigid with the strain, holding her breath and clenching her teeth. I was about to say something, to ask her to calm down; but I felt that I didn't dare. Suddenly, all in a kind of chill, almost in a panic, I groped hurriedly to get out of there as quickly as possible. It was dark: no matter how I tried, I couldn't end it quickly. Suddenly I felt a box of matches and a candlestick with a whole unused candle. As soon as the room was lit up, Liza started suddenly, sat up, and looked at me almost senselessly, with a distorted face and a half-crazy smile. I sat down next to her and took her hands; she came to and threw herself at me, wanting to embrace me, yet not daring to. Then she quietly lowered her head before me.

"Liza, my friend, I shouldn't have . . . you must forgive me," I began, but she squeezed my hands so tightly in her fingers that I realized I was saying the wrong thing and stopped.

"Here's my address, Liza. Come to see me."

"I will," she whispered resolutely, still not lifting her head.

"I'm going now, good-bye . . . until we meet again."

I stood up; she did, too, and suddenly blushed all over, shuddered, seized a shawl lying on a chair, threw it over her shoulders, and wrapped herself up to her chin. After doing this, she smiled again somewhat painfully, blushed, and looked at me strangely. I felt awful. I hastened to leave, to get away.

"Wait," she said suddenly as we were standing in the hallway near the door, and she stopped me by putting her hand on my overcoat. She quickly put the candle down and ran off; obviously she'd remembered something or wanted to show me something. As she left she was blushing all over, her eyes were gleaming, and a smile had appeared on her lips—what on earth did it all mean? I waited against my own will; she returned a moment later with a glance that seemed to beg forgiveness for something. All in all it was no longer the same face or the same glance as before—sullen, distrustful, obstinate. Now her glance was imploring, soft, and, at the same time, trusting, affectionate, and timid. That's how children look at people whom they love very much, or when they're asking for something. Her eyes were light hazel, lovely, full of life, as capable of expressing love as brooding hatred.

Without any explanation, as if I were some kind of higher being who was supposed to know everything, she held a piece of paper out toward me. At that moment her whole face was shining with a most naive, almost childlike triumph. I unfolded the paper. It was a letter to her from some medical student containing a high-flown, flowery, but very respectful declaration of love. I don't remember the exact words now, but I can well recall the genuine emotion that can't be feigned shining through that high style. When I'd finished reading the letter, I met her ardent, curious, and childishly impatient gaze. She'd fixed her eyes on my face and was waiting eagerly to see what I'd say. In a few words, hurriedly, but with some joy and pride, she explained that she'd once been at a dance somewhere, in a private house, at the home of some "very, very good people, *family people*, where they *knew nothing*, nothing at all," because she'd arrived at this place only recently and was just . . . well, she hadn't quite decided whether she'd stay here and she'd certainly leave as soon as she'd paid off her debt. . . . Well, and this student was there; he danced with her all evening and talked to her. It turned out he was from Riga; he'd known her as a child, they'd played together, but that had been a long time ago; he was acquainted with her parents—but he knew nothing, absolutely nothing *about this place* and he didn't even suspect it! And so, the very next day, after the dance, (only some three days ago), he'd sent her this letter through the friend with whom she'd gone to the party . . . and . . . well, that's the whole story."

She lowered her sparkling eyes somewhat bashfully after she finished speaking.

The poor little thing, she'd saved this student's letter as a treasure and had run to fetch this one treasure of hers, not wanting me to leave without knowing that she too was the object of sincere, honest love, and that someone exists who had spoken to her respectfully. Probably that letter was fated to lie in her box without results. But that didn't matter; I'm sure that she'll guard it as a treasure her whole life, as her pride and vindication; and now, at a moment like this, she remembered it and brought it out to exult naively before me, to raise herself in my eyes, so that I could see it for myself and could also think well of her. I didn't say a thing; I shook her hand and left. I really wanted to get away. . . . I walked all the way home in spite of the fact that wet snow was still falling in large flakes. I was exhausted, oppressed, and perplexed. But the truth was already glimmering behind that perplexity. The ugly truth!

VIII

It was some time, however, before I agreed to acknowledge that truth. I awoke the next morning after a few hours of deep, leaden sleep. Instantly recalling the events of the previous day, even I was astonished at my *sentimentality* with Liza last night, at all of yesterday's "horror and pity." "Why, it's an attack of old woman's nervous hysteria, phew!" I decided. "And why on earth did I force my address on her? What if she comes? Then again, let her come, it doesn't make any difference. . . ." But *obviously* that was not the main, most important matter: I had to make haste and rescue at all costs my reputation in the eyes of Zverkov and Simonov. That was my main task. I even forgot all about Liza in the concerns of that morning.

First of all I had to repay last night's debt to Simonov immediately. I resolved on desperate means: I would borrow the sum of fifteen rubles from Anton Antonych. As luck would have it, he was in a splendid mood that morning and gave me the money at once, at my first request. I was so delighted that I signed a promissory note with a somewhat dashing air, and told him *casually* that on the previous evening "I'd been living it up with some friends at the Hôtel de Paris. We were holding a farewell dinner for a comrade, one might even say, a childhood friend, and, you know—he's a great carouser, very spoiled—well, naturally; he comes from a good family, has considerable wealth and a brilliant career; he's witty and charming, and has affairs with certain ladies, you understand. We drank up an extra 'half-dozen bottles' and . . ." There was nothing to it; I said all this very easily, casually, and complacently.

Upon arriving home I wrote to Simonov at once.

To this very day I recall with admiration the truly gentlemanly, good-natured, candid tone of my letter. Cleverly and nobly, and, above all, without unnecessary words, I blamed myself for everything. I justified myself, "if only I could be allowed to justify myself," by saying that, being so totally unaccustomed to wine, I'd gotten drunk with the first glass, which (supposedly) I'd consumed even before their arrival, as I waited for them in the Hôtel de Paris between the hours of five and six o'clock. In particular, I begged for Simonov's pardon; I asked him to convey my apology to all the others, especially to Zverkov, whom, "I recall, as if in a dream," it seems, I'd insulted. I added that I'd have called upon each of them, but was suffering from a bad headache, and, worst of all, I was ashamed. I was particularly satisfied by the "certain lightness," almost casualness (though, still very proper), unexpectedly reflected in my style; better than all possible arguments, it conveyed to them at once that I regarded "all of last night's unpleasantness" in a rather detached way, and that I was not at all, not in the least struck down on the spot as you, gentlemen, probably suspect. On the contrary, I regard this all serenely, as any self-respecting gentleman would. The true story, as they say, is no reproach to an honest young man.

"Why, there's even a hint of aristocratic playfulness in it," I thought admiringly as I reread my note. "And it's all because I'm such a cultured and educated man! Others in my place wouldn't know how to extricate themselves, but I've gotten out of it, and I'm having a good time once again, all because I'm an 'educated and cultured man of our time.' It may even be true that the whole thing occurred as a result of that wine yesterday. Hmmm . . . well, no, it wasn't really the wine. And I didn't have anything to drink between five and six o'clock when I was waiting for them. I lied to Simonov; it was a bold-faced lie—yet I'm not ashamed of it even now. . . ."

But, to hell with it, anyway! The main thing is, I got out of it.

I put six rubles in the letter, sealed it up, and asked Apollon to take it to Simonov. When he heard that there was money in it, Apollon became more respectful and agreed to deliver it. Toward evening I went out for a stroll. My head was still aching and spinning from the events of the day before. But as evening approached and twilight deepened, my impressions changed and became more confused, as did my thoughts. Something hadn't yet died within me, deep within my heart and conscience; it didn't want to die, and it expressed itself as burning anguish. I jostled my way along the more populous, commercial streets, along Meshchanskaya, Sadovaya, near the Yusupov Garden. I particularly liked to stroll along these streets at twilight, just as they became most crowded with all sorts of pedestrians, merchants, and tradesmen, with faces preoccupied to the point of hostility, on their way home from a hard day's work. It was precisely the cheap bustle that I liked, the crass prosaic quality. But this time all that street bustle irritated me even more. I couldn't get a hold of myself or puzzle out what was wrong. Something was rising, rising up in my soul continually, painfully, and didn't want to settle down. I returned home completely distraught. It was just as if some crime were weighing on my soul.

I was constantly tormented by the thought that Liza might come to see me. It was strange, but from all of yesterday's recollections, the one of her tormented me most, somehow separately from all the others. I'd managed to forget the rest by evening, to shrug everything off, and I still remained completely satisfied with my letter to Simonov. But in regard to Liza, I was not at all satisfied. It was as though I were tormented by her alone. "What if she comes?" I thought continually. "Well, so what? It doesn't matter. Let her come. Hmm. The only unpleasant thing is that she'll see, for instance, how I live. Yesterday I appeared before her such a . . . hero . . . but now, hmm! Besides, it's revolting that I've sunk so low. The squalor of my apartment. And I dared go to dinner last night wearing such clothes! And that oilcloth sofa of mine with its stuffing hanging out! And my dressing gown that doesn't quite cover me! What rags! . . . She'll see it all—and she'll see Apollon. That swine will surely insult her. He'll pick on her, just to be rude to me. Of course, I'll be frightened, as usual. I'll begin to fawn before her, wrap myself up in my dressing gown. I'll start to smile and tell lies. Ugh, the indecency! And that's not even the worst part! There's something even more important, nastier, meaner! Yes, meaner! Once again, I'll put on that dishonest, deceitful mask! . . ."

When I reached this thought, I simply flared up.

"Why deceitful? How deceitful? Yesterday I spoke sincerely. I recall that there was genuine feeling in me, too. I was trying no less than to arouse noble feelings in her . . . and if she wept, that's a good thing; it will have a beneficial effect. . . ."

But I still couldn't calm down.

All that evening, even after I returned home, even after nine o'clock, when by my calculations Liza could no longer have come, her image continued to haunt me, and, what's most important, she always appeared in one and the same form. Of all that had occurred yesterday, it was one moment in particular which stood out most vividly: that was when I lit up the room with a match and saw her pale, distorted face with its tormented gaze. What a pitiful, unnatural, distorted smile she'd had at that moment! But little did I know then that even fifteen years later I'd still picture Liza to myself with that same pitiful, distorted, and unnecessary smile which she'd had at that moment.

The next day I was once again prepared to dismiss all this business as nonsense, as the result of overstimulated nerves; but most of all, as exaggeration. I was well aware of this weakness of mine and sometimes was even afraid of it; "I exaggerate everything, that's my problem," I kept repeating to myself hour after hour. And yet, "yet, Liza may still come, all the same"; that was the refrain which concluded my reflections. I was so distressed that I sometimes became furious. "She'll come! She'll definitely come!" If not today, then tomorrow, she'll seek me out! That's just like the damned romanticism of all these *pure hearts*! Oh, the squalor, the stupidity, the narrowness of these "filthy, sentimental souls!' How could all this not be understood, how on earth could it not be understood? . . ." But at this point I would stop myself, even in the midst of great confusion.

"And how few, how very few words were needed," I thought in passing, "how little idyllic sentiment (what's more, the sentiment was artificial, bookish, composed) was necessary to turn a whole human soul according to my wishes at once. That's innocence for you! That's virgin soil!"

At times the thought occurred that I might go to her myself "to tell her everything," and to beg her not to come to me. But at this thought such venom arose in me that it seemed I'd have crushed that "damned" Liza if she'd suddenly turned up next to me. I'd have insulted her, spat at her, struck her, and chased her away!

One day passed, however, then a second, and a third; she still hadn't come, and I began to calm down. I felt particularly reassured and relaxed after nine o'clock in the evening, and even began to daydream sweetly at times. For instance, I'd save Liza, precisely because she'd come to me, and I'd talk to her. . . . I'd develop her mind, educate her. At last I'd notice that she loved me, loved me passionately. I'd pretend I didn't understand. (For that matter, I didn't know why I'd pretend; most likely just for the effect.) At last, all embarrassed, beautiful, trembling, and sobbing, she'd throw herself at my feet and declare that I was her saviour and she loved me more than anything in the world. I'd be surprised, but . . . "Liza," I'd say, "Do you really think that I haven't noticed your love? I've seen everything. I guessed, but dared not be first to make a claim on your heart because I had such influence over you, and because I was afraid you might deliberately force yourself to respond to my love out of gratitude, that you might forcibly evoke within yourself a feeling that didn't really exist. No, I didn't want that because it would be . . . despotism. . . . It would be indelicate (well, in short, here I launched on some European, George Sandian,[4] inexplicably lofty subtleties . . .). But now, now—you're mine, you're my creation, you're pure and lovely, you're my beautiful wife."

> And enter my house bold and free
> To become its full mistress![5]

"Then we'd begin to live happily together, travel abroad, etc., etc." In short, it began to seem crude even to me, and I ended it all by sticking my tongue out at myself.

"Besides, they won't let her out of there, the 'bitch,'" I thought. "After all,

---

4. George Sand was the pseudonym of the French woman novelist Aurore Dudevant (1804–1876), famous also as a promoter of feminism.

5. The last lines of the poem by Nekrasov used as the epigraph of Part II of this story (see pp. 686–687).

it seems unlikely that they'd release them for strolls, especially in the evening (for some reason I was convinced that she had to report there every evening, precisely at seven o'clock). Moreover, she said that she'd yet to become completely enslaved there, and that she still had certain rights; that means, hmm. Devil take it, she'll come, she's bound to come!"

It was a good thing I was distracted at the time by Apollon's rudeness. He made me lose all patience. He was the bane of my existence, a punishment inflicted on me by Providence. We'd been squabbling constantly for several years now and I hated him. My God, how I hated him! I think that I never hated anyone in my whole life as much as I hated him, especially at those times. He was an elderly, dignified man who worked part-time as a tailor. But for some unknown reason he despised me, even beyond all measure, and looked down upon me intolerably. However, he looked down on everyone. You need only glance at that flaxen, slicked-down hair, at that single lock brushed over his forehead and greased with vegetable oil, at his strong mouth, always drawn up in the shape of the letter V,[6] and you felt that you were standing before a creature who never doubted himself. He was a pedant of the highest order, the greatest one I'd ever met on earth; in addition he possessed a sense of self-esteem appropriate perhaps only to Alexander the Great, King of Macedonia. He was in love with every one of his buttons, every one of his fingernails—absolutely in love, and he looked it! He treated me quite despotically, spoke to me exceedingly little, and, if he happened to look at me, cast a steady, majestically self-assured, and constantly mocking glance that sometimes infuriated me. He carried out his tasks as if he were doing me the greatest of favors. Moreover, he did almost nothing at all for me; nor did he assume that he was obliged to do anything. There could be no doubt that he considered me the greatest fool on earth, and, that if he "kept me on," it was only because he could receive his wages from me every month. He agreed to "do nothing" for seven rubles a month. I'll be forgiven many of my sins because of him. Sometimes my hatred reached such a point that his gait alone would throw me into convulsions. But the most repulsive thing about him was his lisping. His tongue was a bit larger than normal or something of the sort; as a result, he constantly lisped and hissed. Apparently, he was terribly proud of it, imagining that it endowed him with enormous dignity. He spoke slowly, in measured tones, with his hands behind his back and his eyes fixed on the ground. It particularly infuriated me when he used to read the Psalter to himself behind his partition. I endured many battles on account of it. He was terribly fond of reading during the evening in a slow, even singsong voice, as if chanting over the dead. It's curious, but that's how he ended up: now he hires himself out to recite the Psalter over the dead; in addition, he exterminates rats and makes shoe polish. But at that time I couldn't get rid of him; it was as if he were chemically linked to my own existence. Besides, he'd never have agreed to leave for anything. It was impossible for me to live in a furnished room: my own apartment was my private residence, my shell, my case, where I hid from all humanity. Apollon, the devil only knows why, seemed to belong to this apartment, and for seven long years I couldn't get rid of him.

6. The last letter of the old Russian alphabet, triangular in shape.

It was impossible, for example, to delay paying him his wages for even two or three days. He'd make such a fuss that I wouldn't know where to hide. But in those days I was so embittered by everyone that I decided, heaven knows why or for what reason, to *punish* Apollon by not paying him his wages for two whole weeks. I'd been planning to do this for some time now, about two years, simply in order to teach him that he had no right to put on such airs around me, and that if I chose to, I could always withhold his wages. I resolved to say nothing to him about it and even remain silent on purpose, to conquer his pride and force him to be the first one to mention it. Then I would pull all seven rubles out of a drawer and show him that I actually had the money and had intentionally set it aside, but that "I didn't want to, didn't want to, simply didn't want to pay him his wages, and that I didn't want to simply because *that's what I wanted*," because such was "my will as his master," because he was disrespectful and because he was rude. But, if he were to ask respectfully, then I might relent and pay him; if not, he might have to wait another two weeks, or three, or even a whole month. . . .

But, no matter how angry I was, he still won. I couldn't even hold out for four days. He began as he always did, because there had already been several such cases (and, let me add, I knew all this beforehand; I knew his vile tactics by heart), to wit: he would begin by fixing an extremely severe gaze on me. He would keep it up for several minutes in a row, especially when meeting me or accompanying me outside of the house. If, for example, I held out and pretended not to notice these stares, then he, maintaining his silence as before, would proceed to further tortures. Suddenly, for no reason at all, he'd enter my room quietly and slowly, while I was pacing or reading; he'd stop at the door, place one hand behind his back, thrust one foot forward, and fix his gaze on me, no longer merely severe, but now utterly contemptuous. If I were suddenly to ask him what he wanted, he wouldn't answer at all. He'd continue to stare at me reproachfully for several more seconds; then, compressing his lips in a particular way and assuming a very meaningful air, he'd turn slowly on the spot and slowly withdraw to his own room. Two hours later he'd emerge again and suddenly appear before me in the same way. It's happened sometimes that in my fury I hadn't even asked what he wanted, but simply raised my head sharply and imperiously, and begun to stare reproachfully back at him. We would stare at each other thus for some two minutes or more; at last he'd turn slowly and self-importantly, and withdraw for another few hours.

If all this failed to bring me back to my senses and I continued to rebel, he'd suddenly begin to sigh while staring at me. He'd sigh heavily and deeply, as if trying to measure with each sigh the depth of my moral decline. Naturally, it would end with his complete victory: I'd rage and shout, but I was always forced to do just as he wished on the main point of dispute.

This time his usual maneuvers of "severe stares" had scarcely begun when I lost my temper at once and lashed out at him in a rage. I was irritated enough even without that.

"Wait!" I shouted in a frenzy, as he was slowly and silently turning with one hand behind his back, about to withdraw to his own room. "Wait! Come back, come back, I tell you!" I must have bellowed so unnaturally that he turned around and even began to scrutinize me with a certain amazement.

He continued, however, not to utter one word, and that was what infuriated me most of all.

"How dare you come in here without asking permission and stare at me? Answer me!"

But after regarding me serenely for half a minute, he started to turn around again.

"Wait!" I roared, rushing up to him. "Don't move! There! Now answer me: why do you come in here to stare?"

"If you've got any orders for me now, it's my job to do 'em," he replied after another pause, lisping softly and deliberately, raising his eyebrows, and calmly shifting his head from one side to the other—what's more, he did all this with horrifying composure.

"That's not it! That's not what I'm asking you about, you executioner!" I shouted, shaking with rage. "I'll tell you myself, you executioner, why you came in here. You know that I haven't paid you your wages, but you're so proud that you don't want to bow down and ask me for them. That's why you came in here to punish me and torment me with your stupid stares, and you don't even sus-s-pect, you torturer, how stupid it all is, how stupid, stupid, stupid, stupid!"

He would have turned around silently once again, but I grabbed hold of him.

"Listen," I shouted to him. "Here's the money, you see! Here it is! (I pulled it out of a drawer.) All seven rubles. But you won't get it, you won't until you come to me respectfully, with your head bowed, to ask my forgiveness. Do you hear?"

"That can't be!" he replied with some kind of unnatural self-confidence.

"It will be!" I shrieked. "I give you my word of honor, it will be!"

"I have nothing to ask your forgiveness for," he said as if he hadn't even noticed my shrieks, "because it was you who called me an 'executioner,' and I can always go lodge a complaint against you at the police station."

"Go! Lodge a complaint!" I roared. "Go at once, this minute, this very second! You're still an executioner! Executioner! Executioner!" But he only looked at me, then turned and, no longer heeding my shouts, calmly withdrew to his own room without looking back.

"If it hadn't been for Liza, none of this would have happened!" I thought to myself. Then, after waiting a minute, pompously and solemnly, but with my heart pounding heavily and forcefully, I went in to see him behind the screen.

"Apollon!" I said softly and deliberately, though gasping for breath, "go at once, without delay to fetch the police supervisor!"

He'd already seated himself at his table, put on his eyeglasses, and picked up something to sew. But, upon hearing my order, he suddenly snorted with laughter.

"At once! Go this very moment! Go, go, or you can't imagine what will happen to you!"

"You're really not in your right mind," he replied, not even lifting his head, lisping just as slowly, and continuing to thread his needle. "Who's ever heard of a man being sent to fetch a policeman against himself? And as for trying to frighten me, you're only wasting your time, because nothing will happen to me."

"Go," I screeched, seizing him by the shoulder. I felt that I might strike him at any moment.

I never even heard the door from the hallway suddenly open at that very moment, quietly and slowly, and that someone walked in, stopped, and began to examine us in bewilderment. I glanced up, almost died from shame, and ran back into my own room. There, clutching my hair with both hands, I leaned my head against the wall and froze in that position.

Two minutes later I heard Apollon's deliberate footsteps.

"There's *some woman* asking for you," he said, staring at me with particular severity; then he stood aside and let her in—it was Liza. He didn't want to leave, and he scrutinized us mockingly.

"Get out, get out!" I commanded him all flustered. At that moment my clock strained, wheezed, and struck seven.

IX

> And enter my house bold and free,
> To become its full mistress!
> From the same poem.[7]

I stood before her, crushed, humiliated, abominably ashamed; I think I was smiling as I tried with all my might to wrap myself up in my tattered, quilted dressing gown—exactly as I'd imagined this scene the other day during a fit of depression. Apollon, after standing over us for a few minutes, left, but that didn't make things any easier for me. Worst of all was that she suddenly became embarrassed too, more than I'd ever expected. At the sight of me, of course.

"Sit down," I said mechanically and moved a chair up to the table for her, while I sat on the sofa. She immediately and obediently sat down, staring at me wide-eyed, and, obviously, expecting something from me at once. This naive expectation infuriated me, but I restrained myself.

She should have tried not to notice anything, as if everything were just as it should be, but she . . . And I vaguely felt that she'd have to pay dearly *for everything*.

"You've found me in an awkward situation, Liza," I began, stammering and realizing that this was precisely the wrong way to begin.

"No, no, don't imagine anything!" I cried, seeing that she'd suddenly blushed. "I'm not ashamed of my poverty. . . . On the contrary, I regard it with pride. I'm poor, but noble. . . . One can be poor and noble," I muttered. "But . . . would you like some tea?"

"No . . . ," she started to say.

"Wait!"

I jumped up and ran to Apollon. I had to get away somehow.

"Apollon," I whispered in feverish haste, tossing down the seven rubles which had been in my fist the whole time, "here are your wages. There, you see, I've given them to you. But now you must rescue me: bring us some tea and a dozen rusks from the tavern at once. If you don't go, you'll make me a very miserable

---

7. I.e., from the poem quoted on pp. 686–687 and 726.

man. You have no idea who this woman is. . . . This means—everything! You may think she's . . . But you've no idea at all who this woman really is!"

Apollon, who'd already sat down to work and had put his glasses on again, at first glanced sideways in silence at the money without abandoning his needle; then, paying no attention to me and making no reply, he continued to fuss with the needle he was still trying to thread. I waited there for about three minutes standing before him with my arms folded *à la Napoleon*.[8] My temples were soaked in sweat. I was pale, I felt that myself. But, thank God, he must have taken pity just looking at me. After finishing with the thread, he stood up slowly from his place, slowly pushed back his chair, slowly took off his glasses, slowly counted the money and finally, after inquiring over his shoulder whether he should get a whole pot, slowly walked out of the room. As I was returning to Liza, it occurred to me: shouldn't I run away just as I was, in my shabby dressing gown, no matter where, and let come what may.

I sat down again. She looked at me uneasily. We sat in silence for several minutes.

"I'll kill him." I shouted suddenly, striking the table so hard with my fist that ink splashed out of the inkwell.

"Oh, what are you saying?" she exclaimed, startled.

"I'll kill him, I'll kill him!" I shrieked, striking the table in an absolute frenzy, but understanding full well at the same time how stupid it was to be in such a frenzy.

"You don't understand, Liza, what this executioner is doing to me. He's my executioner. . . . He's just gone out for some rusks; he . . ."

And suddenly I burst into tears. It was a nervous attack. I felt so ashamed amidst my sobs, but I couldn't help it. She got frightened.

"What's the matter? What's wrong with you?" she cried, fussing around me.

"Water, give me some water, over there!" I muttered in a faint voice, realizing full well, however, that I could've done both without the water and without the faint voice. But I was *putting on an act*, as it's called, in order to maintain decorum, although my nervous attack was genuine.

She gave me some water while looking at me like a lost soul. At that very moment Apollon brought in the tea. It suddenly seemed that this ordinary and prosaic tea was horribly inappropriate and trivial after everything that had happened, and I blushed. Liza stared at Apollon with considerable alarm. He left without looking at us.

"Liza, do you despise me?" I asked, looking her straight in the eye, trembling with impatience to find out what she thought.

She was embarrassed and didn't know what to say.

"Have some tea," I said angrily. I was angry at myself, but she was the one who'd have to pay, naturally. A terrible anger against her suddenly welled up in my heart; I think I could've killed her. To take revenge I swore inwardly not to say one more word to her during the rest of her visit. "She's the cause of it all," I thought.

Our silence continued for about five minutes. The tea stood on the table; we didn't touch it. It reached the point of my not wanting to drink on pur-

8. In the style of Napoleon.

pose, to make it even more difficult for her; it would be awkward for her to begin alone. Several times she glanced at me in sad perplexity. I stubbornly remained silent. I was the main sufferer, of course, because I was fully aware of the despicable meanness of my own spiteful stupidity; yet, at the same time, I couldn't restrain myself.

"I want to . . . get away from . . . that place . . . once and for all," she began just to break the silence somehow; but, poor girl, that was just the thing she shouldn't have said at that moment, stupid enough as it was to such a person as me, stupid as I was. My own heart even ached with pity for her tactlessness and unnecessary straightforwardness. But something hideous immediately suppressed all my pity; it provoked me even further. Let the whole world go to hell. Another five minutes passed.

"Have I disturbed you?" she began timidly, barely audibly, and started to get up.

But as soon as I saw this first glimpse of injured dignity, I began to shake with rage and immediately exploded.

"Why did you come here? Tell me why, please," I began, gasping and neglecting the logical order of my words. I wanted to say it all at once, without pausing for breath; I didn't even worry about how to begin.

"Why did you come here? Answer me! Answer!" I cried, hardly aware of what I was saying. "I'll tell you, my dear woman, why you came here. You came here because I spoke some *words of pity* to you that time. Now you've softened, and want to hear more 'words of pity.' Well, you should know that I was laughing at you then. And I'm laughing at you now. Why are you trembling? Yes, I was laughing at you! I'd been insulted, just prior to that, at dinner, by those men who arrived just before me that evening. I came intending to thrash one of them, the officer; but I didn't succeed; I couldn't find him; I had to avenge my insult on someone, to get my own back; you turned up and I took my anger out at you, and I laughed at you. I'd been humiliated, and I wanted to humiliate someone else; I'd been treated like a rag, and I wanted to exert some power. . . . That's what it was; you thought that I'd come there on purpose to save you, right? Is that what you thought? Is that it?"

I knew that she might get confused and might not grasp all the details, but I also knew that she'd understand the essence of it very well. That's just what happened. She turned white as a sheet; she wanted to say something. Her lips were painfully twisted, but she collapsed onto a chair just as if she'd been struck down with an ax. Subsequently she listened to me with her mouth gaping, her eyes wide open, shaking with awful fear. It was the cynicism, the cynicism of my words that crushed her. . . .

"To save you!" I continued, jumping up from my chair and rushing up and down the room in front of her, "to save you from what? Why, I may be even worse than you are. When I recited that sermon to you, why didn't you throw it back in my face? You should have said to me, 'Why did you come here? To preach morality or what?' Power, it was the power I needed then, I craved the sport, I wanted to reduce you to tears, humiliation, hysteria—that's what I needed then! But I couldn't have endured it myself, because I'm such a wretch. I got scared. The devil only knows why I foolishly gave you my address. Afterward, even before I got home, I cursed you like nothing on earth on account of that address. I hated you already because I'd lied to you then, because it was all playing with words, dreaming in my own mind. But, do you know what I really want now? For you to get lost, that's what! I need some peace. Why, I'd sell the whole world for a kopeck if people would only stop bothering me. Should the world go to hell, or should I go without my tea? I say, let the world go to hell as long as I can always have my tea. Did you know that or not? And I know perfectly well that I'm a scoundrel, a bastard, an egotist, and a sluggard. I've been shaking from fear for the last three days wondering whether you'd ever come. Do you know what disturbed me most of all these last three days? The fact that I'd appeared to you then as such a hero, and that now you'd suddenly see me in this torn dressing gown, dilapidated and revolting. I said before that I wasn't ashamed of my poverty; well, you should know that I am ashamed, I'm ashamed of it more than anything, more afraid of it than anything, more than if I were a thief, because I'm so vain; it's as if the skin's been stripped away from my body so that even wafts of air cause pain. By now surely even you've guessed that I'll never forgive you for having come upon me in this dressing gown as I was attacking Apollon like a vicious dog. Your saviour, your former hero, behaving like a mangy, shaggy mongrel, attacking his own lackey, while that lackey stood there laughing at me! Nor will I ever forgive you for those tears which, like an embarrassed old woman, I couldn't hold back before you. And I'll never forgive *you* for all that I'm confessing now. Yes—you, you alone must pay for everything because you turned up like this, because I'm a scoundrel, because I'm the nastiest, most ridiculous, pettiest, stupidest, most envious worm of all those living on earth who're no better than me in any way, but who, the devil knows why, never get embarrassed, while all my life I have to endure insults from every louse—that's my fate. What do I care that you don't understand any of this? What do I care, what do I care about you and whether or not you perish there? Why, don't you realize how much I'll hate you now after having said all this with your being here listening to me? After all, a man can only talk like this once in his whole life, and then only in hysteria! . . . What more do you want? Why, after all this, are you still hanging around here tormenting me? Why don't you leave?"

But at this point a very strange thing suddenly occurred.

I'd become so accustomed to inventing and imagining everything according to books, and picturing everything on earth to myself just as I'd conceived of it in my dreams, that at first I couldn't even comprehend the meaning of this strange occurrence. But here's what happened: Liza, insulted and crushed by me, understood much more than I'd imagined. She understood out of all this what a woman always understands first of all, if she sincerely loves—namely, that I myself was unhappy.

The frightened and insulted expression on her face was replaced at first by grieved amazement. When I began to call myself a scoundrel and a bastard, and my tears had begun to flow (I'd pronounced this whole tirade in tears), her whole face was convulsed by a spasm. She wanted to get up and stop me; when I'd finished, she paid no attention to my shouting, "Why are you here? Why don't you leave?" She only noticed that it must have been very painful for me to utter all this. Besides, she was so defenseless, the poor girl. She considered herself immeasurably beneath me. How could she get angry or take offense? Suddenly she jumped up from the chair with a kind of uncontrollable impulse, and yearning toward me, but being too timid and not daring to stir from her place, she extended her arms in my direction. . . . At this moment my heart leapt inside me, too. Then suddenly she threw herself at me, put her arms around my neck, and burst into tears. I, too, couldn't restrain myself and sobbed as I'd never done before.

"They won't let me . . . I can't be . . . good!" I barely managed to say; then I went over to the sofa, fell upon it face down, and sobbed in genuine hysterics for a quarter of an hour. She knelt down, embraced me, and remained motionless in that position.

But the trouble was that my hysterics had to end sometime. And so (after all, I'm writing the whole loathsome truth), lying there on the sofa and pressing my face firmly into that nasty leather cushion of mine, I began to sense gradually, distantly, involuntarily, but irresistibly, that it would be awkward for me to raise my head and look Liza straight in the eye. What was I ashamed of? I don't know, but I was ashamed. It also occurred to my overwrought brain that now our roles were completely reversed; now she was the heroine, and I was the same sort of humiliated and oppressed creature she'd been in front of me that evening—only four days ago. . . . And all this came to me during those few minutes as I lay face down on the sofa!

My God! Was it possible that I envied her?

I don't know; to this very day I still can't decide. But then, of course, I was even less able to understand it. After all, I couldn't live without exercising power and tyrannizing over another person. . . . But . . . but, then, you really can't explain a thing by reason; consequently, it's useless to try.

However, I regained control of myself and raised my head; I had to sooner or later. . . . And so, I'm convinced to this day that it was precisely because I felt too ashamed to look at her, that another feeling was suddenly kindled and burst into flame in my heart—the feeling of domination and possession. My eyes gleamed with passion; I pressed her hands tightly. How I hated her and felt drawn to her simultaneously! One feeling intensified the other. It was almost like revenge! . . . At first there was a look of something resembling bewilderment, or even fear, on her face, but only for a brief moment. She embraced me warmly and rapturously.

X

A quarter of an hour later I was rushing back and forth across the room in furious impatience, constantly approaching the screen to peer at Liza through the crack. She was sitting on the floor, her head leaning against the bed, and she must have been crying. But she didn't leave, and that's what irritated me. By this time she knew absolutely everything. I'd insulted her once and for all, but . . . there's nothing more to be said. She guessed that my outburst of passion was merely revenge, a new humiliation for her, and that to my former, almost aimless, hatred there was added now a *personal, envious* hatred of her. . . . However, I don't think that she understood all this explicitly; on the other hand, she fully understood that I was a despicable man, and, most important, that I was incapable of loving her.

I know that I'll be told this is incredible—that it's impossible to be as spiteful and stupid as I am; you may even add that it was impossible not to return, or at least to appreciate, this love. But why is this so incredible? In the first place, I could no longer love because, I repeat, for me love meant tyrannizing and demonstrating my moral superiority. All my life I could never even conceive of any other kind of love, and I've now reached the point that I some-times think that love consists precisely in a voluntary gift by the beloved person of the right to tyrannize over him. Even in my underground dreams I couldn't conceive of love in any way other than a struggle. It always began with hatred and ended with moral subjugation; afterward, I could never imagine what to do with the subjugated object. And what's so incredible about that, since I'd previously managed to corrupt myself morally; I'd already become unaccustomed to "real life," and only a short while ago had taken it into my head to reproach her and shame her for having come to hear "words of pity" from me. But I never could've guessed that she'd come not to hear words of pity at all, but to love me, because it's in that kind of love that a woman finds her resurrection, all her salvation from whatever kind of ruin, and her rebirth, as it can't appear in any other form. However, I didn't hate her so much as I rushed around the room and peered through the crack behind the screen. I merely found it unbearably painful that she was still there. I wanted her to disappear. I longed for "peace and quiet"; I wanted to remain alone in my underground. "Real life" oppressed me—so unfamiliar was it—that I even found it hard to breathe.

But several minutes passed, and she still didn't stir, as if she were oblivious. I was shameless enough to tap gently on the screen to remind her. . . . She started suddenly, jumped up, and hurried to find her shawl, hat, and coat, as if she wanted to escape from me. . . . Two minutes later she slowly emerged from behind the screen and looked at me sadly. I smiled spitefully; it was forced, however, for *appearance's sake only*; and I turned away from her look.

"Good-bye," she said, going toward the door.

Suddenly I ran up to her, grabbed her hand, opened it, put something in . . . and closed it again. Then I turned away at once and bolted to the other corner, so that at least I wouldn't be able to see. . . .

I was just about to lie—to write that I'd done all this accidentally, without knowing what I was doing, in complete confusion, out of foolishness. But I don't want to lie; therefore I'll say straight out, that I opened her hand and placed something in it . . . out of spite. It occurred to me to do this while I was rushing back and forth across the room and she was sitting there behind the screen. But here's what I can say for sure: although I did this cruel thing deliberately, it was not from my heart, but from my stupid head. This cruelty of mine was so artificial, cerebral, intentionally invented, *bookish*, that I couldn't stand it myself even for one minute—at first I bolted to the corner so as not to see, and then, out of shame and in despair, I rushed out after Liza. I opened the door into the hallway and listened. "Liza! Liza!" I called down the stairs, but timidly, in a soft voice.

There was no answer; I thought I could hear her footsteps at the bottom of the stairs.

"Liza!" I cried more loudly.

No answer. But at that moment I heard down below the sound of the tight outer glass door opening heavily with a creak and then closing again tightly. The sound rose up the stairs.

She'd gone. I returned to my room deep in thought. I felt horribly oppressed.

I stood by the table near the chair where she'd been sitting and stared senselessly into space. A minute or so passed, then I suddenly started: right before me on the chair I saw . . . in a word, I saw the crumpled blue five-ruble note, the very one I'd thrust into her hand a few moments before. It was the same one; it couldn't be any other; I had none other in my apartment. So she'd managed to toss it down on the table when I'd bolted to the other corner.

So what? I might have expected her to do that. Might have expected it? No. I was such an egotist, in fact, I so lacked respect for other people, that I couldn't even conceive that she'd ever do that. I couldn't stand it. A moment later, like a madman, I hurried to get dressed. I threw on whatever I happened to find, and rushed headlong after her. She couldn't have gone more than two hundred paces when I ran out on the street.

It was quiet; it was snowing heavily, and the snow was falling almost perpendicularly, blanketing the sidewalk and the deserted street. There were no passers-by; no sound could be heard. The street lights were flickering dismally and vainly. I ran about two hundred paces to the crossroads and stopped.

"Where did she go? And why am I running after her? Why? To fall down before her, sob with remorse, kiss her feet, and beg her forgiveness! That's just what I wanted. My heart was being torn apart; never, never will I recall that moment with indifference. But—why?" I wondered. "Won't I grow to hate her, perhaps as soon as tomorrow, precisely because I'm kissing her feet today? Will I ever be able to make her happy? Haven't I found out once again today, for the hundredth time, what I'm really worth? Won't I torment her?"

I stood in the snow, peering into the murky mist, and thought about all this.

"And wouldn't it be better, wouldn't it," I fantasized once I was home again, stifling the stabbing pain in my heart with such fantasies, "wouldn't it be better if she were to carry away the insult with her forever? Such an insult—after all, is purification; it's the most caustic and painful form of consciousness. Tomorrow I would have defiled her soul and wearied her heart. But now that insult will never die within her; no matter how abominable the filth that awaits her, that insult will elevate and purify her . . . by hatred . . . hmm . . . perhaps by forgiveness as well. But will that make it any easier for her?"

And now, in fact, I'll pose an idle question of my own. Which is better: cheap happiness or sublime suffering? Well, come on, which is better?

These were my thoughts as I sat home that evening, barely alive with the anguish in my soul. I'd never before endured so much suffering and remorse; but could there exist even the slightest doubt that when I went rushing out of my apartment, I'd turn back again after going only halfway? I never met Liza afterward, and I never heard anything more about her. I'll also add that for a long time I remained satisfied with my theory about the use of insults and hatred, in spite of the fact that I myself almost fell ill from anguish at the time.

Even now, after so many years, all this comes back to me as *very unpleasant*. A great deal that comes back to me now is very unpleasant, but . . . perhaps I should end these *Notes* here? I think that I made a mistake in beginning to write them. At least, I was ashamed all the time I was writing this *tale*: consequently, it's not really literature, but corrective punishment. After all, to tell you long stories about how, for example, I ruined my life through moral decay in my corner, by the lack of appropriate surroundings, by isolation from any living beings, and by futile malice in the underground—so help me God, that's not very interesting. A novel needs a hero, whereas here all the traits of an anti-hero have been assembled *deliberately*; but the most important thing is that all this produces an extremely unpleasant impression because we've all become estranged from life, we're all cripples, every one of us, more or less. We've become so estranged that at times we feel some kind of revulsion for genuine "real life," and therefore we can't bear to be reminded of it. Why, we've reached a point where we almost regard "real life" as hard work, as a job, and we've all agreed in private that it's really better in books. And why do we sometimes fuss, indulge in whims, and make demands? We don't know ourselves. It'd be even worse if all our whimsical desires were fulfilled. Go on, try it. Give us, for example, a little more independence; untie the hands of any one of us, broaden our sphere of activity, relax the controls, and . . . I can assure you, we'll immediately ask to have the controls reinstated. I know that you may get angry at me for saying this, you may shout and stamp your feet: "Speak for yourself," you'll say, "and for your own miseries in the underground, but don't you dare say *all of us.*'" If you'll allow me, gentlemen; after all, I'm not trying to justify myself by saying *all of us*. What concerns me in particular, is that in my life I've only taken to an extreme that which you haven't even dared to take halfway; what's more, you've mistaken your cowardice for good sense; and, in so deceiving yourself, you've consoled yourself. So, in fact, I may even be "more alive" than you are. Just take a closer look! Why, we don't even know where this "real life" lives nowadays, what it really is, and what it's called. Leave us alone without books and we'll get confused and lose our way at once—we won't know what to join, what to hold on to, what to love or what to hate, what to respect or what to despise. We're even oppressed by being men—men with real bodies and blood of *our very own*. We're ashamed of it; we consider it a disgrace and we strive to become some kind of impossible "general-human-beings." We're stillborn; for some time now we haven't been conceived by living fathers; we like it more and more. We're developing a taste for it. Soon we'll conceive of a way to be born from ideas. But enough; I don't want to write any more "from Underground. . . ."

However, the "notes" of this paradoxalist don't end here. He couldn't resist and kept on writing. But it also seems to us that we might as well stop here.

GUSTAVE FLAUBERT

1821–1880

Living mostly as a hermit in a small country town, Gustave Flaubert threw himself into the making of art. He saw literature as a realm superior to the "stupidity" and "mediocrity" of lived experience. He labored over every sentence he wrote, sometimes taking as much as a week to complete a paragraph, determined to perfect the style of each phrase. He did travel, spending months at a time in Paris and taking journeys to North Africa, Syria, Turkey, and Italy. He was even in Paris to witness the revolution of 1848, as workers rose up against the monarchy and demanded the vote. But Flaubert's greatest excitement lay in the tormented process of writing: "I get drunk on ink as others do on wine," he wrote. "I love my work with a frenetic and perverted love, as the ascetic loves the hair shirt that scratches his belly."

LIFE

Gustave Flaubert was the son of a chief surgeon in the provincial French town of Rouen. When he was fourteen, he developed an unrequited passion for an older married woman. A few years later he went to Paris to study law, which he hated. Anxious and unhappy, he failed his exams and suffered a sudden nervous breakdown, which sent him back to his family home in the small town of Croisset near Rouen, where he would stay for most of his life with his mother. It was there that he began to write seriously.

In 1846, on a visit to Paris, he met the beautiful Louise Colet, a professional writer who lived and worked among bohemian artists. This was Flaubert's only serious love affair, though it would take place mostly by correspondence—for him reality never lived up to the imagination—and he treated her coldly. Otherwise, he frequented prostitutes and had some fleeting sexual relationships with men. His mother declared that his "passion for sentences" had "dried up" his heart.

Flaubert's works did not make it easily into the world. In 1849 he asked his two closest friends to read a draft of his first novel, *The Temptation of Saint Anthony.* "We think you should throw it in the fire and never speak of it again," they advised. He put it aside and labored for five years on his masterpiece, *Madame Bovary* (1857). He said he wanted to write "a book about nothing," one held together by the "internal force of its style" alone. The

protagonist he developed for this was a doctor's wife who longs to lead a romantic life like that of the heroines she encounters in books. She seeks out grand love affairs but is doomed to a narrow middle-class life among mediocrities in the provinces. Though sales of *Madame Bovary* were strong, critics denounced it as repugnant, consumed with the ugly banality of everyday life and offering nothing uplifting or consoling. One critic famously charged that Flaubert wielded his pen as a surgeon wields a scalpel. The novel was so shocking in its distanced and ironic treatment of adultery that Flaubert was tried for "offending public morals and religion." Although he was acquitted, *Madame Bovary* maintained its reputation as an immoral book for decades. Now it is viewed as one of the great works of nineteenth-century realism— perhaps the greatest. In 1869 Flaubert published *Sentimental Education*, a novel about the generation that lived through the revolutions of 1848. It flopped with the public, and the reviewers at the time sneered, although it has been enormously influential and highly regarded since.

Flaubert returned to *The Temptation of Saint Anthony* late in life, burying his manuscript in the ground temporarily when the Prussians invaded Normandy in 1870. In a period of despondency, when he was struggling financially and grieving over the loss of his mother and several close friends, he wrote *Three Tales* (1877), which included *A Simple Heart.* As Flaubert's body succumbed to syphilis, he told his niece, "Sometimes I think I'm liquefying like an old Camembert cheese." He died from a brain hemorrhage in 1880.

WORK

"It's no easy business to be simple," Flaubert said, pointing us to the great paradox at the center of *A Simple*

A late Ming Dynasty (ca. seventeenth century) ink-on-paper illustration of Dushi Huang, one of the "Yama" kings of the ten courts of the underworld. The concept of layers and courts of hell appears to have arisen from a blending of ideas from Daoism, Buddhism, and Chinese folk religion. In this image, Dushi Huang appears as a divine record-keeper

An image of the Chŏngyangsa temple, which is nestled in the Diamond Mountain Range in today's North Korea, painted on a fan by Chŏng Sŏn (1676–1759). Known for his stunning depictions of Korean locales and landscapes, Chŏng's paintings were also widely appreciated in China. Fans were popular everyday objects in early-modern Asia and were often decorated with delicate ink paintings and calligraphy. And yet

The Peddler. A seventeenth-century painting by an unidentified French artist of a street

quite

The Indian plant being withered
Growes in ye morne cut downe ere night
Showes thy decay all flesh is v clay
Thus thinke

The pipe of clay being lily white
Showes thou art but a mortall wight
Euen such gon wth a touch
Thus thinke. then drinke Tobacco

The smoke ascends on high
Showes yt all is but vanity
A world off stuffe gon wth a puffe
Thus thinke

The pipe being foule w{thin}
And the soule defild wth sin
to be purgd wth fire it doth require
Thus

Bees th' ashes left behind
still to put thee in mind
that vnto dust returne y{u} must
Thus thinke then drinke
Tobacco.

As literacy spread and flourished in Europe, more people kept "commonplace books"—
journals in which one could record quotations from books one had read or compose one's
own work. These pages from a mid-seventeenth-century commonplace book contain texts
by two different hands; one text is a poem about tobacco.

Captain Lemuel Gulliver, of
Redriff Ætat. suæ 58.

TRAVELS

INTO SEVERAL

Remote Nations

OF THE

WORLD.

In FOUR PARTS.

By LEMUEL GULLIVER,
First a SURGEON, and then a CAP-
TAIN of several SHIPS.

VOL. I.

LONDON:

Printed for BENJ. MOTTE, at the
Middle Temple-Gate in Fleet-street.
MDCCXXVI.

Frontispiece and title page of *Travels Into Several Remote Nations of the World. In Four Parts. By Lemuel Gulliver, First a Surgeon, and then a Captain of Several Ships,* later known as *Gulliver's Travels,* by Jonathan Swift. Especially in its early history in English, much prose fiction was presented in a nonfiction guise, as a memoir or, as here, a travel journal of a real person.

Daytime in the Gay Quarters (ca. 1739), a woodblock color print by Okumura Masanobu (1686–1764), a prolific Japanese print designer, painter, and publisher. The geisha in the foreground is about to use a brush to render calligraphy on paper.

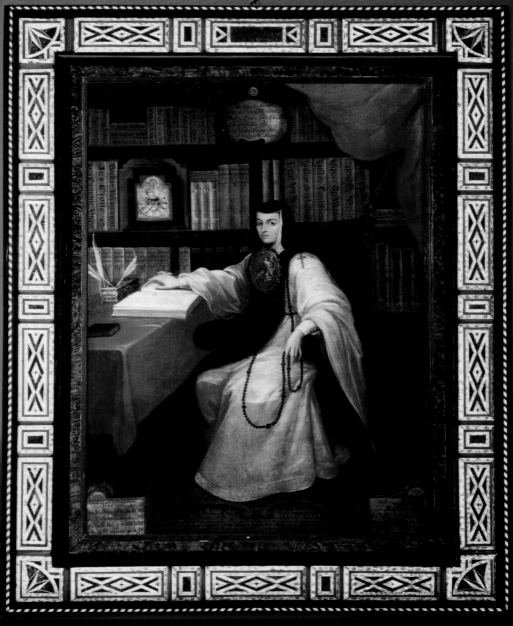

A posthumous portrait, by Miguel Cabrera (1695–1768), of Sor Juana Inés de la Cruz (1648–1695), a pioneering writer and thinker in New Spain. Sor Juana is revered as a major figure in Mexican literature, and as a brave and eloquent advocate of formal

This medallion, designed in 1787 by the English potter and ceramicist Josiah Wedgwood (1730–1795), features an inscription, "Am I not a man and a brother?" that became one of the most recognizable mottoes of the abolitionist movement. The medallion became a wildly popular fashion accessory among people sympathetic to the abolitionist cause, and thus raised public awareness of the issue.

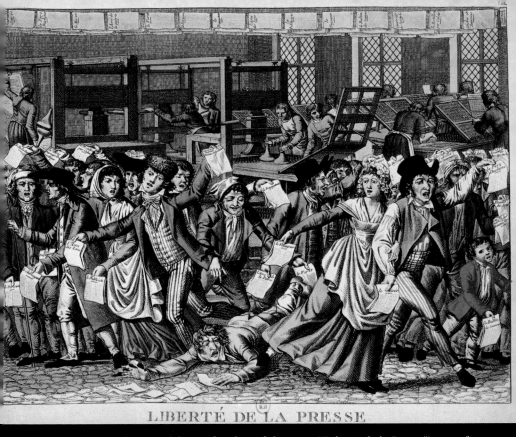

LIBERTÉ DE LA PRESSE

This French colored print celebrates freedom of the press ("Liberté de la Presse"), one of the principles of popular sovereignty declared in the *Declaration of the Rights of Man and of the Citizen* (1793), the core document of the French Revolution.

This 1820 oil painting by Dutch artist Johannes Jelgerhuis (1770–1836) of the bookshop of Pieter Meijer Warnars in Amsterdam provides a wonderfully detailed portrait of early nineteenth-century middle-class book selling.

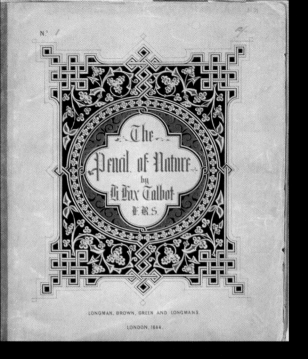

The Pencil of Nature, assembled and published in 1844 by William Henry Fox Talbot (1800–1877), was the first commercially available book illustrated with photographs. Shown here are the cover of the first issue (it was published in six installments) and one of the "plates" inside that issue: Fox's 1841 photograph "Bust of Patroclus."

During the nineteenth century, inventors raced to improve the speed and output of printing technologies. Richard Hoe, an American inventor, pushed the technology significantly forward with his design in 1847 of the lithographic rotary press. The version of Hoe's printing machine pictured here was used to produce *The Daily Telegraph* newspaper in

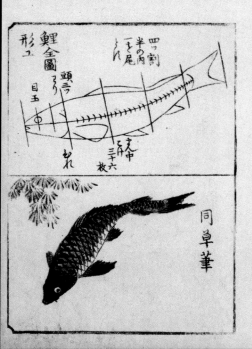

Sketches of swimming carp from *A Picture Book Miscellany* (1849), a book by the Japanese ukiyo-e artist Utagawa Hiroshige (1797–1858) that displays his commitment to realistic renderings of subjects from nature.

SKETCHES IN JAPAN BY OUR SPECIAL ARTIST: THE STORYTELLER (A DAILY SCENE) IN YOKOHAMA.

A street scene from 1861 in Yokohoma, Japan, shows a storyteller (center, seated on small stage) accompanying himself with a stringed instrument.

The world's first commercially produced typewriter: the Hansen Writing Ball designed by Rasmus Malling-Hansen (1835–1890), minister and principal at the Danish Royal Institute for the Deaf. First designed in 1865 and improved over the next fifteen years, Hansen's machine would eventually be overshadowed by late nineteenth-century typewriters that allowed one to see the result on paper as one typed (rather than operating 'blind,' as with the writing ball).

A photograph of Queen Victoria (1819–1901) in July 1893 accompanied by her Indian "Munshi" (personal secretary and attendant), Abdul Karim, who was one of her closest confidants during the final fifteen years of her reign. The queen was an early adopter of the typewriter, which she used for her official correspondence.

Futurism, a modernist movement centered in Italy in the early twentieth century, focused on the technologies and dynamism of modern life. This photograph (*Dattilografa*, 1913) by Anton Giulio Bragaglia (1890–1960) captures the spirit of the futurist movement perfectly, portraying writing as an energetic and technology-enhanced activity.

The Reader (Woman in Grey), 1920, an oil painting by the twentieth-century's most

Soviet propaganda poster, 1921. The text reads, "From the gloom to the light; from battle to books; from grief to happiness."

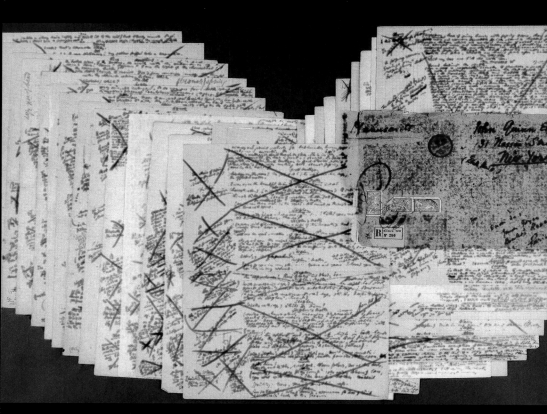

Manuscript pages—heavily marked with corrections and additions—from the "Circe" chapter of James Joyce's novel *Ulysses* (1922).

Portrait of Virginia Woolf (1882–1941) taken in 1902, and a page from Woolf's draft notebook for her novel *Mrs. Dalloway* (1925). Surveying the history of literature and finding so few women, Woolf had this to say in *A Room of One's Own* (1929): "I would venture to guess that Anon, who wrote so many poems without signing them, was often a woman."

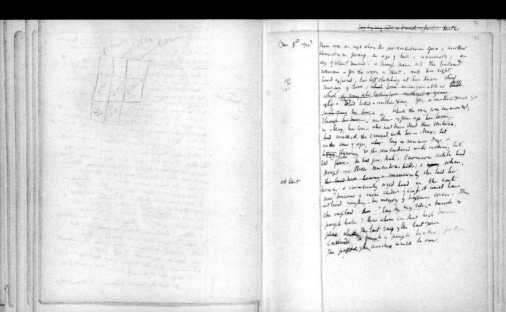

The Nigerian author Chinua Achebe (born 1930), photographed in 1960 holding two editions of his book *Things Fall Apart* (1958), which would become the most widely read and respected African novel in English.

THE
WASTE LAND

By
T. S. ELIOT

Winner of The Dial's 1922 Award.

This prize of two thousand dollars is given annually to a young American writer in recognition of his service to letters.

The Waste Land

T.S. ELIOT

Poem The full published text of The Waste Land (1922)	**Performance** A specially filmed performance of the entire poem by Fiona Shaw
Perspectives Commentary on the poem and on Eliot from a range of interesting people	**Readings** Hear the poem spoken aloud by different voices including Eliot himself
Notes Annotations and references explaining the text of the poem	**Manuscript** A facsimile of Eliot's original manuscript with hand-written edits by Ezra Pound
Tips How to get the best from this electronic edition of The Waste Land	**Gallery** A selection of photographs and images related to the poem

CREDITS   SETTINGS

The cover of the first American edition of T. S. Eliot's modernist masterpiece, *The Waste Land*, published in 1922, and the opening menu of an ebook/app version of the poem, released in 2011. Clearly, the new media and technologies of the twenty-first century will change the way we read and experience poetry, drama, fiction, and other writing. But in what ways? How quickly?

Heart. On the one hand, this is a straightforward tale of a relatively uneventful life: there is nothing complex or convoluted about the prose, about the chronology of events, or about the protagonist's experience. On the other hand, the sophisticated Flaubert invites us to see the world from the perspective of a naïve, exploited, illiterate servant woman whose last great love is a stuffed parrot, and allows us to understand her viewpoint as serious and sad rather than absurd or contemptible. The contemporary British novelist Julian Barnes, in a novel called *Flaubert's Parrot*, puts it this way: "Imagine the technical difficulty of writing a story in which a badly stuffed bird with a ridiculous name ends up standing for one third of the Trinity, and in which the intention is neither satirical, sentimental nor blasphemous. Imagine further telling the story from the point of view of an ignorant old woman without making it sound derogatory or coy." If we remember that Flaubert labored over every single sentence, suffering the "torments of style," we can read the simplicity he represents here as the result of a complex and careful artistic process.

Three elements of the story's highly refined technique are worth noticing. First of all, its economy: Flaubert distills his protagonist's experience into brief, clipped sentences. No word is wasted, and often it is tiny details that carry rich significance. For example, when the narrator tells us that Félicité's nephew keeps her "amused by telling her stories full of nautical jargon," he suggests that she cherishes precisely what she cannot understand—a language of her nephew's that is foreign to her. Second, Flaubert is famous for the impersonality or objectivity of his narrative style: he never intrudes his own feelings or opinions, maintaining a deliberate detachment. He wrote that "the author in his work should be like God in the universe—present everywhere and visible nowhere." Finally, it is worth paying attention to the story's structure: Félicité's experience follows the same pattern again and again—she falls in love and experiences a short period of happiness; this is followed by some kind of parting or death and a long spell of grief. But each time she falls in love with a new object, and the sequence of beloved objects is itself intriguing: first it is a lover, then the little girl in her care, then her nephew, then an elderly neighbor, then a live parrot, and finally the same parrot, stuffed. If on the one hand Flaubert seems to suggest a decline from human to animal to dead thing, on the other hand he suggests an ascent, as Félicité moves from erotic love to a wider, more charitable love and finally to a kind of mystical and heavenly adoration.

The parrot's role in the text goes beyond Félicité's love for it. As an animal from overseas brought to the town by an outsider-bureaucrat, it is above all a strange and foreign thing. Yet parrots learn to repeat human phrases, and so it becomes a strange echo of the social world it inhabits. First it learns Félicité's own expressions of respect and humility: "Your servant, sir!" and "Hail Mary!" Later it imitates Madame Aubain, and when the doorbell rings, it screams out "Félicité! The door, the door!" And yet it refuses to obey the rules of class and decorum itself, mocking the corrupt Boulais with screeches of laughter and leaving its droppings everywhere. At once symbolizing the stupidity and rote clichés of human life and acting as a focus for sincere love and spiritual veneration, the parrot remains one of Flaubert's most startling and fascinating figures.

Félicité too emerges as more complex than she may at first appear. On the one hand, Flaubert uses her to explore the psychology of servitude: what makes a person willingly accept the monotony and humiliation of spending a lifetime serving the needs of callous and thoughtless others? Intellectually, she is certainly simple: she has so little power of abstract thought that she cannot understand how a map works, and her understanding of religious doctrine is limited indeed. Compared to an animal herself, she bears numerous interesting relations to animals in the text. On the other hand, Flaubert allows her simplicity to feel powerful and moving and even sometimes surprising. For example, Félicité experiences an intense identification with Virginie at the moment of her first communion, and then disappointment with her own experience of taking communion the following day. She herself cannot interpret this difference, but Flaubert implies that sincere feeling may take place by way of concrete realities— people and objects—rather than abstractions. Indeed, Félicité endows not only animals but her cherished collection of things with meaning and value. And along the way, although she is cheated, exploited, discounted, and misguided, she reaches moments of heroism and even sublimity.

Flaubert wrote the story at a moment when he himself was thinking back over his life with sadness. Félicité's life is set in the very places that had been his own haunts in childhood: all of the place names are real, and many of the farms and beach scenes evoke specific spots the writer remembered with fondness. Flaubert's early readers assumed that the detached writer must feel scorn for his simple heroine, but he declared otherwise: *A Simple Heart* is "not at all ironic, as you suppose, but on the contrary very serious and very sad. I want to arouse people's pity, to make sensitive souls weep, since I am one myself."

A Simple Heart[1]

I

For half a century the women of Pont-l'Évêque[2] envied Mme Aubain her maidservant Félicité.

In return for a hundred francs a year she did all the cooking and the housework, the sewing, the washing, and the ironing. She could bridle a horse, fatten poultry, and churn butter, and she remained faithful to her mistress, who was by no means an easy person to get on with.

Mme Aubain had married a young fellow who was good-looking but badly-off, and who died at the beginning of 1809, leaving her with two small children and a pile of debts. She then sold all her property except for the farms of Toucques and Geffosses, which together brought in five thousand francs a year at the most, and left her house at Saint-Melaine for one behind the covered market which was cheaper to run and had belonged to her family.

This house had a slate roof and stood between an alley-way and a lane leading down to the river. Inside there were differences in level which were the cause of many a stumble. A narrow entrance-hall separated the kitchen

1. Translated by Robert Baldick.   2. Town in the rural French province of Normandy.

from the parlour, where Mme Aubain sat all day long in a wicker easy-chair by the window. Eight mahogany chairs were lined up against the white-painted wainscoting, and under the barometer stood an old piano loaded with a pyramid of boxes and cartons. On either side of the chimney-piece, which was carved out of yellow marble in the Louis Quinze style, there was a tapestry-covered arm-chair, and in the middle was a clock designed to look like a temple of Vesta.[3] The whole room smelt a little musty, as the floor was on a lower level than the garden.

On the first floor was 'Madame's' bedroom—very spacious, with a patterned wallpaper of pale flowers and a portrait of 'Monsieur' dressed in what had once been the height of fashion. It opened into a smaller room in which there were two cots, without mattresses. Then came the drawing-room, which was always shut up and full of furniture covered with dustsheets. Next there was a passage leading to the study, where books and papers filled the shelves of a book-case in three sections built round a big writing-table of dark wood. The two end panels were hidden under pen-and-ink drawings, landscapes in gouache, and etchings by Audran,[4] souvenirs of better days and bygone luxury. On the second floor a dormer window gave light to Félicité's room, which looked out over the fields.

Every day Félicité got up at dawn, so as not to miss Mass, and worked until evening without stopping. Then, once dinner was over, the plates and dishes put away, and the door bolted, she piled ashes on the log fire and went to sleep in front of the hearth, with her rosary in her hands. Nobody could be more stubborn when it came to haggling over prices, and as for cleanliness, the shine on her saucepans was the despair of all the other servants. Being of a thrifty nature, she ate slowly, picking up from the table the crumbs from her loaf of bread—a twelve-pound loaf which was baked specially for her and lasted her twenty days.

All the year round she wore a kerchief of printed calico fastened behind with a pin, a bonnet which covered her hair, grey stockings, a red skirt, and over her jacket a bibbed apron such as hospital nurses wear.

Her face was thin and her voice was sharp. At twenty-five she was often taken for forty; once she reached fifty, she stopped looking any age in particular. Always silent and upright and deliberate in her movements, she looked like a wooden doll driven by clock-work.

2

Like everyone else, she had had her love-story.

Her father, a mason, had been killed when he fell off some scaffolding. Then her mother died, and when her sisters went their separate ways, a farmer took her in, sending her, small as she was, to look after the cows out in the fields. She went about in rags, shivering with cold, used to lie flat on the ground to

---

3. The ancient temple of Vesta, Roman goddess of the hearth, is a round building with a conical roof supported by columns. "Louis Quinze style": ornate furniture style dating from the 18th century.
4. Claude Audran III (1658–1734), French painter, sculptor, engraver, and decorator.

drink water out of the ponds, would be beaten for no reason at all, and was finally turned out of the house for stealing thirty sous,[5] a theft of which she was innocent. She found work at another farm, looking after the poultry, and as she was liked by her employers the other servants were jealous of her.

One August evening—she was eighteen at the time—they took her off to the fête[6] at Colleville. From the start she was dazed and bewildered by the noise of the fiddles, the lamps in the trees, the medley of gaily coloured dresses, the gold crosses and lace, and the throng of people jigging up and down. She was standing shyly on one side when a smart young fellow, who had been leaning on the shaft of a cart, smoking his pipe, came up and asked her to dance. He treated her to cider, coffee, girdle-cake, and a silk neckerchief, and imagining that she knew what he was after, offered to see her home. At the edge of a field of oats, he pushed her roughly to the ground. Thoroughly frightened, she started screaming for help. He took to his heels.

Another night, on the road to Beaumont, she tried to get past a big, slow-moving waggon loaded with hay, and as she was squeezing by she recognized Théodore.

He greeted her quite calmly, saying that she must forgive him for the way he had behaved to her, as 'it was the drink that did it.'

She did not know what to say in reply and felt like running off.

Straight away he began talking about the crops and the notabilities of the commune, saying that his father had left Colleville for the farm at Les Écots, so that they were now neighbours.

'Ah!' she said.

He added that his family wanted to see him settled but that he was in no hurry and was waiting to find a wife to suit his fancy. She lowered her head. Then he asked her if she was thinking of getting married. She answered with a smile that it was mean of him to make fun of her.

'But I'm not making fun of you!' he said. 'I swear I'm not!'

He put his left arm round her waist, and she walked on supported by his embrace. Soon they slowed down. There was a gentle breeze blowing, the stars were shining, the huge load of hay was swaying about in front of them, and the four horses were raising clouds of dust as they shambled along. Then, without being told, they turned off to the right. He kissed her once more and she disappeared into the darkness.

The following week Théodore got her to grant him several rendezvous.

They would meet at the bottom of a farm-yard, behind a wall, under a solitary tree. She was not ignorant of life as young ladies are, for the animals had taught her a great deal; but her reason and an instinctive sense of honour prevented her from giving way. The resistance she put up inflamed Théodore's passion to such an extent that in order to satisfy it (or perhaps out of sheer naivety) he proposed to her. At first she refused to believe him, but he swore that he was serious.

Soon afterwards he had a disturbing piece of news to tell her: the year before, his parents had paid a man to do his military service for him, but now

---

5. About the price of a good dinner. **6.** "Festival" (French).

he might be called up again any day, and the idea of going into the army frightened him. In Félicité's eyes this cowardice of his appeared to be a proof of his affection, and she loved him all the more for it. Every night she would steal out to meet him, and every night Théodore would plague her with his worries and entreaties.

In the end he said that he was going to the Prefecture himself to make inquiries, and that he would come and tell her how matters stood the following Sunday, between eleven and midnight.

At the appointed hour she hurried to meet her sweetheart, but found one of his friends waiting for her instead.

He told her that she would not see Théodore again. To make sure of avoiding conscription, he had married a very rich old woman, Mme Lehoussais of Toucques.

Her reaction was an outburst of frenzied grief. She threw herself on the ground, screaming and calling on God, and lay moaning all alone in the open until sunrise. Then she went back to the farm and announced her intention of leaving. At the end of the month, when she had received her wages, she wrapped her small belongings up in a kerchief and made her way to Pont-l'Évêque.

In front of the inn there, she sought information from a woman in a widow's bonnet, who, as it happened, was looking for a cook. The girl did not know much about cooking, but she seemed so willing and expected so little that finally Mme Aubain ended up by saying: 'Very well, I will take you on.'

A quarter of an hour later Félicité was installed in her house.

At first she lived there in a kind of fearful awe caused by 'the style of the house' and by the memory of 'Monsieur' brooding over everything. Paul and Virginie, the boy aged seven and the girl barely four, seemed to her to be made of some precious substance. She used to carry them about pick-a-back,[7] and when Mme Aubain told her not to keep on kissing them she was cut to the quick. All the same, she was happy now, for her pleasant surroundings had dispelled her grief.

On Thursdays, a few regular visitors came in to play Boston,[8] and Félicité got the cards and the footwarmers ready beforehand. They always arrived punctually at eight, and left before the clock struck eleven.

Every Monday morning the second-hand dealer who lived down the alley put all his junk out on the pavement. Then the hum of voices began to fill the town, mingled with the neighing of horses, the bleating of lambs, the grunting of pigs, and the rattle of carts in the streets.

About midday, when the market was in full swing, a tall old peasant with a hooked nose and his cap on the back of his head would appear at the door. This was Robelin, the farmer from Geffosses. A little later, and Liébard, the farmer from Toucques, would arrive—a short, fat, red-faced fellow in a grey jacket and leather gaiters fitted with spurs.

Both men had hens or cheeses they wanted to sell to 'Madame.' But Félicité was up to all their tricks and invariably outwitted them, so that they went away full of respect for her.

7. Piggy-back.   8. A card game.

From time to time Mme Aubain had a visit from an uncle of hers, the Marquis de Grémanville, who had been ruined by loose living and was now living at Falaise on his last remaining scrap of property. He always turned up at lunch-time, accompanied by a hideous poodle which dirtied all the furniture with its paws. However hard he tried to behave like a gentleman, even going so far as to raise his hat every time he mentioned 'my late father,' the force of habit was usually too much for him, for he would start pouring himself one glass after another and telling bawdy stories. Félicité used to push him gently out of the house, saying politely: 'You've had quite enough, Monsieur de Grémanville. See you another time!' and shutting the door on him.

She used to open it with pleasure to M. Bourais, who was a retired solicitor. His white tie and his bald head, his frilled shirt-front and his ample brown frock-coat, the way he had of rounding his arm to take a pinch of snuff, and indeed everything about him made an overwhelming impression on her such as we feel when we meet some outstanding personality.

As he looked after 'Madame's' property, he used to shut himself up with her for hours in 'Monsieur's' study. He lived in dread of compromising his reputation, had a tremendous respect for the Bench, and laid claim to some knowledge of Latin.

To give the children a little painless instruction, he made them a present of a geography book with illustrations. These represented scenes in different parts of the world, such as cannibals wearing feather head-dresses, a monkey carrying off a young lady, Bedouins in the desert, a whale being harpooned, and so on.

Paul explained these pictures to Félicité, and that indeed was all the education she ever had. As for the children, they were taught by Guyot, a poor devil employed at the Town Hall, who was famous for his beautiful handwriting, and who had a habit of sharpening his penknife on his boots.

When the weather was fine the whole household used to set off early for a day at the Geffosses farm.

The farm-yard there was on a slope, with the house in the middle; and the sea, in the distance, looked like a streak of grey. Félicité would take some slices of cold meat out of her basket, and they would have their lunch in a room adjoining the dairy. It was all that remained of a country house which had fallen into ruin, and the wallpaper hung in shreds, fluttering in the draught. Mme Aubain used to sit with bowed head, absorbed in her memories, so that the children were afraid to talk. 'Why don't you run along and play?' she would say, and away they went.

Paul climbed up into the barn, caught birds, played ducks and drakes on the pond, or banged with a stick on the great casks, which sounded just like drums.

Virginie fed the rabbits, or scampered off to pick cornflowers, showing her little embroidered knickers as she ran.

One autumn evening they came home through the fields. The moon, which was in its first quarter, lit up part of the sky, and there was some mist floating like a scarf over the winding Toucques. The cattle, lying out in the middle of the pasture, looked peacefully at the four people walking by. In the third field a few got up and made a half circle in front of them.

'Don't be frightened!' said Félicité, and crooning softly, she stroked the back of the nearest animal. It turned about and the others did the same. But while they were crossing the next field they suddenly heard a dreadful bellowing. It came from a bull which had been hidden by the mist, and which now came towards the two women.

Mme Aubain started to run.

'No! No!' said Félicité. 'Not so fast!'

All the same they quickened their pace, hearing behind them a sound of heavy breathing which came nearer and nearer. The bull's hooves thudded like hammers on the turf, and they realized that it had broken into a gallop. Turning round, Félicité tore up some clods of earth and flung them at its eyes. It lowered its muzzle and thrust its horns forward, trembling with rage and bellowing horribly.

By now Mme Aubain had got to the end of the field with her two children and was frantically looking for a way over the high bank. Félicité was still backing away from the bull, hurling clods of turf which blinded it, and shouting: 'Hurry! Hurry!'

Mme Aubain got down into the ditch, pushed first Virginie and then Paul up the other side, fell once or twice trying to climb the bank, and finally managed it with a valiant effort.

The bull had driven Félicité back against a gate, and its slaver was spurting into her face. In another second it would have gored her, but she just had time to slip between two of the bars, and the great beast halted in amazement.

This adventure was talked about at Pont-l'Évêque for a good many years, but Félicité never prided herself in the least on what she had done, as it never occurred to her that she had done anything heroic.

Virginie claimed all her attention, for the fright had affected the little girl's nerves, and M. Poupart, the doctor, recommended sea-bathing at Trouville.

In those days the resort had few visitors. Mme Aubain made inquiries, consulted Bourais, and got everything ready as though for a long journey.

Her luggage went off in Liébard's cart the day before she left. The next morning he brought along two horses, one of which had a woman's saddle with a velvet back, while the other carried a cloak rolled up to make a kind of seat on its crupper. Mme Aubain sat on this, with Liébard in front. Félicité looked after Virginie on the other horse, and Paul mounted M. Lechaptois's donkey, which he had lent them on condition they took great care of it.

The road was so bad that it took two hours to travel the five miles to Toucques. The horses sank into the mud up to their pasterns and had to jerk their hind-quarters to get out; often they stumbled in the ruts, or else they had to jump. In some places, Liébard's mare came to a sudden stop, and while he waited patiently for her to move off again, he talked about the people whose properties bordered the road, adding moral reflexions to each story. For instance, in the middle of Toucques, as they were passing underneath some windows set in a mass of nasturtiums, he shrugged his shoulders and said:

'There's a Madame Lehoussais lives here. Now instead of taking a young man, she . . .'

Félicité did not hear the rest, for the horses had broken into a trot and the donkey was galloping along. All three turned down a bridle-path, a gate swung open, a couple of boys appeared, and everyone dismounted in front of a manure-heap right outside the farm-house door.

Old Mother Liébard welcomed her mistress with every appearance of pleasure. She served up a sirloin of beef for lunch, with tripe and black pudding, a fricassee of chicken, sparkling cider, a fruit tart and brandy-plums, garnishing the whole meal with compliments to Madame, who seemed to be enjoying better health, to Mademoiselle, who had turned into a 'proper little beauty,' and to Monsieur Paul, who had 'filled out a lot.' Nor did she forget their deceased grandparents, whom the Liébards had known personally, having been in the family's service for several generations.

Like its occupants, the farm had an air of antiquity. The ceiling-beams were worm-eaten, the walls black with smoke, and the window-panes grey with dust. There was an oak dresser laden with all sorts of odds and ends— jugs, plates, pewter bowls, wolf-traps, sheep-shears, and an enormous syringe which amused the children. In the three yards outside there was not a single tree without either mushrooms at its base or mistletoe in its branches. Several had been blown down and had taken root again at the middle; all of them were bent under the weight of their apples. The thatched roofs, which looked like brown velvet and varied in thickness, weathered the fiercest winds, but the cart-shed was tumbling down. Mme Aubain said that she would have it seen to, and ordered the animals to be reharnessed.

It took them another half-hour to reach Trouville. The little caravan dismounted to make their way along the Écores, a cliff jutting right out over the boats moored below; and three minutes later they got to the end of the quay and entered the courtyard of the Golden Lamb, the inn kept by Mère David.

After the first few days Virginie felt stronger, as a result of the change of air and the sea-bathing. Not having a costume, she went into the water in her chemise and her maid dressed her afterwards in a customs officer's hut which was used by the bathers.

In the afternoons they took the donkey and went off beyond the Roches-Noires,[9] in the direction of Hennequeville. To begin with, the path went uphill between gentle slopes like the lawns in a park, and then came out on a plateau where pastureland and ploughed fields alternated. On either side there were holly-bushes standing out from the tangle of brambles, and here and there a big dead tree spread its zigzag branches against the blue sky.

They almost always rested in the same field, with Deauville on their left, Le Havre on their right, and the open sea in front. The water glittered in the sunshine, smooth as a mirror, and so still that the murmur it made was scarcely audible; unseen sparrows could be heard twittering, and the sky covered the whole scene with its huge canopy. Mme Aubain sat doing her needlework, Virginie plaited rushes beside her, Félicité gathered lavender, and Paul, feeling profoundly bored, longed to get up and go.

Sometimes they crossed the Toucques in a boat and hunted for shells. When the tide went out, sea-urchins, ormers, and jelly-fish were left behind; and the children scampered around, snatching at the foam-flakes carried on the wind.

9. "Black rocks," visible on the Normandy coast at low tide.

The sleepy waves, breaking on the sand, spread themselves out along the shore. The beach stretched as far as the eye could see, bounded on the land side by the dunes which separated it from the Marais, a broad meadow in the shape of an arena. When they came back that way, Trouville, on the distant hillside, grew bigger at every step, and with its medley of oddly assorted houses seemed to blossom out in gay disorder.

On exceptionally hot days they stayed in their room. The sun shone in dazzling bars of light between the slats of the blind. There was not a sound to be heard in the village, and not a soul to be seen down in the street. Everything seemed more peaceful in the prevailing silence. In the distance caulkers were hammering away at the boats, and the smell of tar was wafted along by a sluggish breeze.

The principal amusement consisted in watching the fishing-boats come in. As soon as they had passed the buoys, they started tacking. With their canvas partly lowered and their foresails blown out like balloons they glided through the splashing waves as far as the middle of the harbour, where they suddenly dropped anchor. Then each boat came alongside the quay, and the crew threw ashore their catch of quivering fish. A line of carts stood waiting, and women in cotton bonnets rushed forward to take the baskets and kiss their men.

One day one of these women spoke to Félicité, who came back to the inn soon after in a state of great excitement. She explained that she had found one of her sisters—and Nastasie Barette, now Leroux, made her appearance, with a baby at her breast, another child holding her right hand, and on her left a little sailor-boy, his arms akimbo and his cap over one ear.

Mme Aubain sent her off after a quarter of an hour. From then on they were forever hanging round the kitchen or loitering about when the family went for a walk, though the husband kept out of sight.

Félicité became quite attached to them. She bought them a blanket, several shirts, and a stove; and it was clear that they were bent on getting all they could out of her.

This weakness of hers annoyed Mme Aubain, who in any event disliked the familiar way in which the nephew spoke to Paul. And so, as Virginie had started coughing and the good weather was over, she decided to go back to Pont-l'Évêque.

M. Bourais advised her on the choice of a school; Caen[1] was considered the best, so it was there that Paul was sent. He said good-bye bravely, feeling really rather pleased to be going to a place where he would have friends of his own.

Mme Aubain resigned herself to the loss of her son, knowing that it was unavoidable. Virginie soon got used to it. Félicité missed the din he used to make, but she was given something new to do which served as a distraction: from Christmas onwards she had to take the little girl to catechism every day.

3

After genuflecting at the door, she walked up the centre aisle under the nave, opened the door of Mme Aubain's pew, sat down, and started looking about her.

1. A cathedral school.

The choir stalls were all occupied, with the boys on the right and the girls on the left, while the curé[2] stood by the lectern. In one of the stained-glass windows in the apse the Holy Ghost looked down on the Virgin; another window showed her kneeling before the Infant Jesus; and behind the tabernacle there was a wood-carving of St. Michael slaying the dragon.[3]

The priest began with a brief outline of sacred history. Listening to him, Félicité saw in imagination the Garden of Eden, the Flood, the Tower of Babel, cities burning, peoples dying, and idols being overthrown; and this dazzling vision left her with a great respect for the Almighty and profound fear of His wrath.

Then she wept as she listened to the story of the Passion.[4] Why had they crucified Him, when He loved children, fed the multitudes, healed the blind, and had chosen out of humility to be born among the poor, on the litter of a stable? The sowing of the seed, the reaping of the harvest, the pressing of the grapes—all those familiar things of which the Gospels speak had their place in her life. God had sanctified them in passing, so that she loved the lambs more tenderly for love of the Lamb of God, and the doves for the sake of the Holy Ghost.

She found it difficult, however, to imagine what the Holy Ghost looked like, for it was not just a bird but a fire as well, and sometimes a breath.[5] She wondered whether that was its light she had seen flitting about the edge of the marshes at night, whether that was its breath she had felt driving the clouds across the sky, whether that was its voice she had heard in the sweet music of the bells. And she sat in silent adoration, delighting in the coolness of the walls and the quiet of the church.

Of dogma she neither understood nor even tried to understand anything. The curé discoursed, the children repeated their lesson, and she finally dropped off to sleep, waking up suddenly at the sound of their sabots[6] clattering across the flagstones as they left the church.

It was in this manner, simply by hearing it expounded, that she learnt her catechism, for her religious education had been neglected in her youth. From then on she copied all Virginie's observances, fasting when she did and going to confession with her. On the feast of Corpus Christi the two of them made an altar of repose together.[7]

The preparations for Virginie's first communion caused her great anxiety. She worried over her shoes, her rosary, her missal, and her gloves. And how she trembled as she helped Mme Aubain to dress the child!

All through the Mass her heart was in her mouth. One side of the choir was hidden from her by M. Bourais, but directly opposite her she could see the flock of maidens, looking like a field of snow with their white crowns perched on top of their veils; and she recognized her little darling from a distance by

2. "Priest" (French).
3. Satan, depicted as a dragon in the Book of Revelation, is cast out of heaven by St. Michael.
4. The crucifixion and death of Christ.
5. The Holy Spirit appears as both fire and breath (or wind) in the Bible.

6. Heavy wooden shoes.
7. The resting-place for the Eucharist during the Tridduum, the holiest three days of the Christian year. "Corpus Christi": "Body of Christ" (Latin), a liturgical celebration of Christ's gift of himself, in the form of bread and wine, during the mass.

her dainty neck and her rapt attitude. The bell tinkled.[8] Every head bowed low, and there was a silence. Then, to the thunderous accompaniment of the organ, choir and congregation joined in singing the *Agnus Dei*.[9] Next the boys' procession began, and after that the girls got up from their seats. Slowly, their hands joined in prayer, they went towards the brightly lit altar, knelt on the first step, received the Host one by one, and went back to their places in the same order. When it was Virginie's turn, Félicité leant forward to see her, and in one of those imaginative flights born of real affection, it seemed to her that she herself was in the child's place. Virginie's face became her own, Virginie's dress clothed her, Virginie's heart was beating in her breast; and as she closed her eyes and opened her mouth, she almost fainted away.

Early next morning she went to the sacristy and asked M. le Curé to give her communion. She received the sacrament with all due reverence, but did not feel the same rapture as she had the day before.

Mme Aubain wanted her daughter to possess every accomplishment, and since Guyot could not teach her English or music, she decided to send her as a boarder to the Ursuline[1] Convent at Honfleur.

Virginie raised no objection, but Félicité went about sighing at Madame's lack of feeling. Then she thought that perhaps her mistress was right: such matters, after all, lay outside her province.

Finally the day arrived when an old waggonette stopped at their door, and a nun got down from it who had come to fetch Mademoiselle. Félicité hoisted the luggage up on top, gave the driver some parting instructions, and put six pots of jam, a dozen pears, and a bunch of violets in the boot.

At the last moment Virginie burst into a fit of sobbing. She threw her arms round her mother, who kissed her on the forehead, saying: 'Come now, be brave, be brave.' The step was pulled up and the carriage drove away.

Then Mme Aubain broke down, and that evening all her friends, M. and Mme Lormeau, Mme Lechaptois, the Rochefeuille sisters, M. de Houppeville, and Bourais, came in to console her.

To begin with she missed her daughter badly. But she had a letter from her three times a week, wrote back on the other days, walked round her garden, did a little reading, and thus contrived to fill the empty hours.

As for Félicité, she went into Virginie's room every morning from sheer force of habit and looked round it. It upset her not having to brush the child's hair any more, tie her bootlaces, or tuck her up in bed; and she missed seeing her sweet face all the time and holding her hand when they went out together. For want of something to do, she tried making lace, but her fingers were too clumsy and broke the threads. She could not settle to anything, lost her sleep, and, to use her own words, was 'eaten up inside.'

To 'occupy her mind,' she asked if her nephew Victor might come and see her, and permission was granted.

He used to arrive after Mass on Sunday, his cheeks flushed, his chest bare, and smelling of the countryside through which he had come. She laid a place

---

8. The bell marks the moment of transubstantiation during the mass.
9. "Lamb of God" (Latin); a plea for God's mercy.

1. Catholic religious order concerned with the education of girls.

for him straight away, opposite hers, and they had lunch together. Eating as little as possible herself, in order to save the expense, she stuffed him so full of food that he fell asleep after the meal. When the first bell for vespers rang, she woke him up, brushed his trousers, tied his tie, and set off for church, leaning on his arm with all a mother's pride.

His parents always told him to get something out of her—a packet of brown sugar perhaps, some soap, or a little brandy, sometimes even money. He brought her his clothes to be mended, and she did the work gladly, thankful for anything that would force him to come again.

In August his father took him on a coasting trip. The children's holidays were just beginning, and it cheered her up to have them home again. But Paul was turning capricious and Virginie was getting too old to be addressed familiarly—a state of affairs which put a barrier of constraint between them.

Victor went to Morlaix, Dunkirk, and Brighton in turn, and brought her a present after each trip. The first time it was a box covered with shells, the second a coffee cup, the third a big gingerbread man. He was growing quite handsome, with his trim figure, his little moustache, his frank open eyes, and the little leather cap that he wore on the back of his head like a pilot. He kept her amused by telling her stories full of nautical jargon.

One Monday—it was the fourteenth of July 1819,[2] a date she never forgot—Victor told her that he had signed on for an ocean voyage, and that on the Wednesday night he would be taking the Honfleur packet to join his schooner, which was due to sail shortly from Le Havre. He might be away, he said, for two years.

The prospect of such a long absence made Félicité extremely unhappy, and she felt she must bid him godspeed once more. So on the Wednesday evening, when Madame's dinner was over, she put on her clogs and swiftly covered the ten miles between Pont-l'Évêque and Honfleur.

When she arrived at the Calvary[3] she turned right instead of left, got lost in the shipyards, and had to retrace her steps. Some people she spoke to advised her to hurry. She went right round the harbour, which was full of boats, constantly tripping over moorings. Then the ground fell away, rays of light crisscrossed in front of her, and for a moment she thought she was going mad, for she could see horses up in the sky.

On the quayside more horses were neighing, frightened by the sea. A derrick was hoisting them into the air and dropping them into one of the boats, which was already crowded with passengers elbowing their way between barrels of cider, baskets of cheese, and sacks of grain. Hens were cackling and the captain swearing, while a cabin-boy stood leaning on the cats-head, completely indifferent to it all. Félicité, who had not recognized him, shouted: 'Victor!' and he raised his head. She rushed forward, but at that very moment the gangway was pulled ashore.

The packet moved out of the harbour with women singing as they hauled

---

2. The national holiday called Bastille Day, which commemorates the start of the French Revolution.

3. Public crucifix.

it along, its ribs creaking and heavy waves lashing its bows. The sail swung round, hiding everyone on board from view, and against the silvery, moonlit sea the boat appeared as a dark shape that grew ever fainter, until at last it vanished in the distance.

As Félicité was passing the Calvary, she felt a longing to commend to God's mercy all that she held most dear; and she stood there praying for a long time, her face bathed in tears, her eyes fixed upon the clouds. The town was asleep, except for the customs officers walking up and down. Water was pouring ceaselessly through the holes in the sluice-gate, making as much noise as a torrent. The clocks struck two.

The convent parlour would not be open before daybreak, and Madame would be annoyed if she were late; so, although she would have liked to give a kiss to the other child, she set off for home. The maids at the inn were just waking up as she got to Pont-l'Évêque.

So the poor lad was going to be tossed by the waves for months on end! His previous voyages had caused her no alarm. People came back from England and Brittany; but America, the Colonies, the Islands, were all so far away, somewhere at the other end of the world.

From then on Félicité thought of nothing but her nephew. On sunny days she hoped he was not too thirsty, and when there was a storm she was afraid he would be struck by lightning. Listening to the wind howling in the chimney or blowing slates off the roof, she saw him being buffeted by the very same storm, perched on the top of a broken mast, with his whole body bent backwards under a sheet of foam; or again—and these were reminiscences of the illustrated geography-book—he was being eaten by savages, captured by monkeys in a forest, or dying on a desert shore. But she never spoke of her worries.

Mme Aubain had worries of her own about her daughter. The good nuns said that she was an affectionate child, but very delicate. The slightest emotion upset her, and she had to give up playing the piano.

Her mother insisted on regular letters from the convent. One morning when the postman had not called, she lost patience and walked up and down the room, between her chair and the window. It was really extraordinary! Four days without any news!

Thinking her own example would comfort her, Félicité said:

'I've been six months, Madame, without news.'

'News of whom?'

The servant answered gently:

'Why—of my nephew.'

'Oh, your nephew!' And Mme Aubain started pacing up and down again, with a shrug of her shoulders that seemed to say: 'I wasn't thinking of him—and indeed, why should I? Who cares about a young, good-for-nothing cabin-boy? Whereas my daughter—why, just think!'

Although she had been brought up the hard way, Félicité was indignant with Madame, but she soon forgot. It struck her as perfectly natural to lose one's head where the little girl was concerned. For her, the two children were of equal importance; they were linked together in her heart by a single bond, and their destinies should be the same.

The chemist[4] told her that Victor's ship had arrived at Havana: he had seen this piece of information in a newspaper.

Because of its association with cigars, she imagined Havana as a place where nobody did anything but smoke, and pictured Victor walking about among crowds of Negroes in a cloud of tobacco-smoke. Was it possible, she wondered, 'in case of need' to come back by land? And how far was it from Pont-l'Évêque? To find out she asked M. Bourais.

He reached for his atlas, and launched forth into an explanation of latitudes and longitudes, smiling like the pedant he was at Félicité's bewilderment. Finally he pointed with his pencil at a minute black dot inside a ragged oval patch, saying:

'There it is.'

She bent over the map, but the network of coloured lines meant nothing to her and only tired her eyes. So when Bourais asked her to tell him what was puzzling her, she begged him to show her the house where Victor was living. He threw up his hands, sneezed, and roared with laughter, delighted to come across such simplicity. And Félicité—whose intelligence was so limited that she probably expected to see an actual portrait of her nephew—could not make out why he was laughing.

It was a fortnight later that Liébard came into the kitchen at market-time, as he usually did, and handed her a letter from her brother-in-law. As neither of them could read, she turned to her mistress for help.

Mme Aubain, who was counting the stitches in her knitting, put it down and unsealed the letter. She gave a start, and, looking hard at Félicité, said quietly:

'They have some bad news for you . . . Your nephew . . .'

He was dead. That was all the letter had to say.

Félicité dropped on to a chair, leaning her head against the wall and closing her eyelids, which suddenly turned pink. Then, with her head bowed, her hands dangling, and her eyes set, she kept repeating:

'Poor little lad! Poor little lad!'

Liébard looked at her and sighed. Mme Aubain was trembling slightly. She suggested that she should go and see her sister at Trouville, but Félicité shook her head to indicate that there was no need for that.

There was a silence. Old Liébard thought it advisable to go.

Then Félicité said:

'It doesn't matter a bit, not to them it doesn't.'

Her head fell forward again, and from time to time she unconsciously picked up the knitting needles lying on the worktable.

Some women went past carrying a tray full of dripping linen.

Catching sight of them through the window, she remembered her own washing; she had passed the lye through it the day before and today it needed rinsing. So she left the room.

Her board and tub were on the bank of the Toucques. She threw a pile of chemises down by the water's edge, rolled up her sleeves, and picked up her battledore. The lusty blows she gave with it could be heard in all the neighbouring gardens.

4. Pharmacist.

The fields were empty, the river rippling in the wind; at the bottom long weeds were waving to and fro, like the hair of corpses floating in the water. She held back her grief, and was very brave until the evening; but in her room she gave way to it completely, lying on her mattress with her face buried in the pillow and her fists pressed against her temples.

Long afterwards she learnt the circumstances of Victor's death from the captain of his ship. He had gone down with yellow fever, and they had bled him too much at the hospital. Four doctors had held him at once. He had died straight away, and the chief doctor had said:

'Good! There goes another!'

His parents had always treated him cruelly. She preferred not to see them again, and they made no advances, either because they had forgotten about her or out of the callousness of the poor.

Meanwhile Virginie was growing weaker. Difficulty in breathing, fits of coughing, protracted bouts of fever, and mottled patches on the cheekbones all indicated some deep-seated complaint. M. Poupart had advised a stay in Provence. Mme Aubain decided to follow this suggestion, and, if it had not been for the weather at Pont-l'Évêque, she would have brought her daughter home at once.

She arranged with a jobmaster[5] to drive her out to the convent every Tuesday. There was a terrace in the garden, overlooking the Seine, and there Virginie, leaning on her mother's arm, walked up and down over the fallen vine-leaves. Sometimes, while she was looking at the sails in the distance, or at the long stretch of horizon from the Château de Tancarville to the lighthouses of Le Havre, the sun would break through the clouds and make her blink. Afterwards they would rest in the arbour. Her mother had secured a little cask of excellent Malaga,[6] and, laughing at the idea of getting tipsy, Virginie used to drink a thimbleful, but no more.

Her strength revived. Autumn slipped by, and Félicité assured Mme Aubain that there was nothing to fear. But one evening, coming back from some errand in the neighbourhood, she found M. Poupart's gig standing at the door. He was in the hall, and Mme Aubain was tying on her bonnet.

'Give me my foot warmer, purse, gloves. Quickly now!'

Virginie had pneumonia and was perhaps past recovery.

'Not yet!' said the doctor; and the two of them got into the carriage with snow-flakes swirling around them. Night was falling and it was very cold.

Félicité rushed into the church to light a candle, and then ran after the gig. She caught up with it an hour later, jumped lightly up behind, and hung on to the fringe. But then a thought struck her: the courtyard had not been locked up, and burglars might get in. So she jumped down again.

At dawn the next day she went to the doctor's. He had come home and gone out again on his rounds. Then she waited at the inn, thinking that somebody who was a stranger to the district might call there with a letter. Finally, when it was twilight, she got into the coach for Lisieux.

---

5. One who loans horses and carriages.   6. A Spanish dessert wine.

The convent was at the bottom of a steep lane. When she was half-way down the hill, she heard a strange sound which she recognized as a death-bell tolling.

'It's for somebody else,' she thought, as she banged the door-knocker hard.

After a few minutes she heard the sound of shuffling feet, the door opened a little way, and a nun appeared.

The good sister said with an air of compunction that 'she had just passed away.' At that moment the bell of Saint-Léonard was tolled more vigorously than ever.

Félicité went up to the second floor. From the doorway of the room she could see Virginie lying on her back, her hands clasped together, her mouth open, her head tilted back under a black crucifix that leant over her, her face whiter than the curtains that hung motionless on either side. Mme Aubain was clinging to the foot of the bed and sobbing desperately. The Mother Superior stood on the right. Three candlesticks on the chest of drawers added touches of red to the scene, and fog was whitening the windows. Some nuns led Mme Aubain away.

For two nights Félicité never left the dead girl. She said the same prayers over and over again, sprinkled holy water on the sheets, then sat down again to watch. At the end of her first vigil, she noticed that the child's face had gone yellow, the lips were turning blue, the nose looked sharper, and the eyes were sunken. She kissed them several times, and would not have been particularly surprised if Virginie had opened them again: to minds like hers the supernatural is a simple matter. She laid her out, wrapped her in a shroud, put her in her coffin, placed a wreath on her, and spread out her hair. It was fair and amazingly long for her age. Félicité cut off a big lock, half of which she slipped into her bosom, resolving never to part with it.

The body was brought back to Pont-l'Évêque at the request of Mme Aubain, who followed the hearse in a closed carriage.

After the Requiem Mass, it took another three-quarters of an hour to reach the cemetery. Paul walked in front, sobbing. Then came M. Bourais, and after him the principal inhabitants of the town, the women all wearing long black veils, and Félicité. She was thinking about her nephew; and since she had been unable to pay him these last honours, she felt an added grief, just as if they were burying him with Virginie.

Mme Aubain's despair passed all bounds. First of all she rebelled against God, considering it unfair of Him to have taken her daughter from her—for she had never done any harm, and her conscience was quite clear. But was it? She ought to have taken Virginie to the south; other doctors would have saved her life. She blamed herself, wished she could have joined her daughter, and cried out in anguish in her dreams. One dream in particular obsessed her. Her husband, dressed like a sailor, came back from a long voyage, and told her amid tears that he had been ordered to take Virginie away—whereupon they put their heads together to discover somewhere to hide her.

One day she came in from the garden utterly distraught. A few minutes earlier—and she pointed to the spot—father and daughter had appeared to her, doing nothing, but simply looking at her.

For several months she stayed in her room in a kind of stupor. Félicité scolded her gently telling her that she must take care of herself for her son's sake, and also in remembrance of 'her.'

'Her?' repeated Mme Aubain, as if she were waking from a sleep. 'Oh, yes, of course! You don't forget her, do you!' This was an allusion to the cemetery, where she herself was strictly forbidden to go.

Félicité went there every day. She would set out on the stroke of four, going past the houses, up the hill, and through the gate, until she came to Virginie's grave. There was a little column of pink marble with a tablet at its base, and a tiny garden enclosed by chains. The beds were hidden under a carpet of flowers. She watered their leaves and changed the sand, going down on her knees to fork the ground thoroughly. The result was that when Mme Aubain was able to come here, she experienced a feeling of relief, a kind of consolation.

Then the years slipped by, each one like the last, with nothing to vary the rhythm of the great festivals: Easter, the Assumption, All Saints' Day.[7] Domestic events marked dates that later served as points of reference. Thus in 1825 a couple of glaziers whitewashed the hall; in 1827 a piece of the roof fell into the courtyard and nearly killed a man; and in the summer of 1828 it was Madame's turn to provide the bread for consecration. About this time Bourais went away in a mysterious fashion; and one by one the old acquaintances disappeared: Guyot, Liébard, Mme Lechaptois, Robelin, and Uncle Grémanville, who had been paralysed for a long time.

One night the driver of the mail-coach brought Pont-l'Évêque news of the July Revolution.[8] A few days later a new sub-prefect[9] was appointed. This was the Baron de Larsonnière, who had been a consul in America, and who brought with him, besides his wife, his sister-in-law and three young ladies who were almost grown-up. They were to be seen on their lawn, dressed in loose-fitting smocks; and they had a Negro servant and a parrot. They paid a call on Mme Aubain, who made a point of returning it. As soon as Félicité saw them coming, she would run and tell her mistress. But only one thing could really awaken her interest, and that was her son's letters.

He seemed to be incapable of following any career and spent all his time in taverns. She paid his debts, but he contracted new ones, and the sighs Mme Aubain heaved as she knitted by the window reached Félicité at her spinning-wheel in the kitchen.

The two women used to walk up and down together beside the espalier, forever talking of Virginie and debating whether such and such a thing would have appealed to her, or what she would have said on such and such an occasion.

All her little belongings were in a cupboard in the children's bedroom. Mme Aubain went through them as seldom as possible. One summer day she resigned herself to doing so, and the moths were sent fluttering out of the cupboard.

Virginie's frocks hung in a row underneath a shelf containing three dolls, a few hoops, a set of toy furniture, and the wash-basin she had used. Besides the frocks, they took out her petticoats, her stockings and her handkerchiefs, and spread them out on the two beds before folding them up again.

---

7. Catholic holy days that mark the arrival of souls into heaven.
8. The July Revolution of 1830 toppled the French king Charles X and established a new constitutional monarchy.
9. Government official responsible for a region.

The sunlight streamed in on these pathetic objects, bringing out the stains and showing up the creases made by the child's movements. The air was warm, the sky was blue, a blackbird was singing, and everything seemed to be utterly at peace.

They found a little chestnut-coloured hat, made of plush with a long nap; but the moths had ruined it. Félicité asked if she might have it. The two women looked at each other and their eyes filled with tears. Then the mistress opened her arms, the maid threw herself into them, and they clasped each other in a warm embrace, satisfying their grief in a kiss which made them equal.

It was the first time that such a thing had happened, for Mme Aubain was not of a demonstrative nature. Félicité was as grateful as if she had received a great favour, and henceforth loved her mistress with dog-like devotion and religious veneration.

Her heart grew softer as time went by.

When she heard the drums of a regiment coming down the street she stood at the door with a jug of cider and offered the soldiers a drink. She looked after the people who went down with cholera. She watched over the Polish refugees,[1] and one of them actually expressed a desire to marry her. But they fell out, for when she came back from the Angelus[2] one morning, she found that he had got into her kitchen and was calmly eating an oil-and-vinegar salad.

After the Poles it was Père Colmiche, an old man who was said to have committed fearful atrocities in '93.[3] He lived by the river in a ruined pig-sty. The boys of the town used to peer at him through the cracks in the walls, and threw pebbles at him which landed on the litter where he lay, constantly shaken by fits of coughing. His hair was extremely long, his eyelids inflamed, and on one arm there was a swelling bigger than his head. Félicité brought him some linen, tried to clean out his filthy hovel, and even wondered if she could install him in the wash-house without annoying Madame. When the tumour had burst, she changed his dressings every day, brought him some cake now and then, and put him out in the sun on a truss of hay. The poor old fellow would thank her in a faint whisper, slavering and trembling all the while, fearful of losing her and stretching his hands out as soon as he saw her moving away.

He died, and she had a Mass said for the repose of his soul.

That same day a great piece of good fortune came her way. Just as she was serving dinner, Mme de Larsonnière's Negro appeared carrying the parrot in its cage, complete with perch, chain, and padlock. The Baroness had written a note informing Mme Aubain that her husband had been promoted to a Prefecture and they were leaving that evening; she begged her to accept the parrot as a keepsake and a token of her regard.

This bird had engrossed Félicité's thoughts for a long time, for it came from America, and that word reminded her of Victor. So she had asked the Negro all about it, and once she had even gone so far as to say:

'How pleased Madame would be if it were hers!'

---

1. After the July Revolution, a spirit of revolt spread throughout Europe, prompting Poles and other Europeans to seek refuge in France.
2. A daily prayer to the Virgin Mary.

3. I.e., 1793, the height of the Reign of Terror during the French Revolution when thousands of people were guillotined.

The Negro had repeated this remark to his mistress, who, unable to take the parrot with her, was glad to get rid of it in this way.

4

His name was Loulou. His body was green, the tips of his wings were pink, his poll blue, and his breast golden.

Unfortunately he had a tiresome mania for biting his perch, and also used to pull his feathers out, scatter his droppings everywhere, and upset his bath water. He annoyed Mme Aubain, and so she gave him to Félicité for good.

Félicité started training him, and soon he could say: 'Nice boy! Your servant, sir! Hail, Mary!' He was put near the door, and several people who spoke to him said how strange it was that he did not answer to the name of Jacquot, as all parrots were called Jacquot.[4] They likened him to a turkey or a block of wood, and every sneer cut Félicité to the quick. How odd, she thought, that Loulou should be so stubborn, refusing to talk whenever anyone looked at him!

For all that, he liked having people around him, because on Sundays, while the Rochefeuille sisters, M. Houppeville and some new friends—the apothecary Onfroy, M. Varin, and Captain Mathieu—were having their game of cards, he would beat on the window-panes with his wings and make such a din that it was impossible to hear oneself speak.

Bourais's face obviously struck him as terribly funny, for as soon as he saw it he was seized with uncontrollable laughter. His shrieks rang round the courtyard, the echo repeated them, and the neighbours came to their windows and started laughing too. To avoid being seen by the bird, M. Bourais used to creep along by the wall, hiding his face behind his hat, until he got to the river, and then come into the house from the garden. The looks he gave the parrot were far from tender.

Loulou had once been cuffed by the butcher's boy for poking his head into his basket; and since then he was always trying to give him a nip through his shirt. Fabu threatened to wring his neck, although he was not a cruel fellow, in spite of his tattooed arms and bushy whiskers. On the contrary, he rather liked the parrot, so much so indeed that in a spirit of jovial camaraderie he tried to teach him a few swear-words. Félicité, alarmed at this development, put the bird in the kitchen. His little chain was removed and he was allowed to wander all over the house.

Coming downstairs, he used to rest the curved part of his beak on each step and then raise first his right foot, then his left; and Félicité was afraid that this sort of gymnastic performance would make him giddy. He fell ill and could neither talk nor eat for there was a swelling under his tongue such as hens sometimes have. She cured him by pulling this pellicule out with her finger-nails. One day M. Paul was silly enough to blow the smoke of his cigar at him; another time Mme Lormeau started teasing him with the end of her parasol, and he caught hold of the ferrule with his beak. Finally he got lost.

Félicité had put him down on the grass in the fresh air, and left him there for a minute. When she came back, the parrot had gone. First of all she looked for him in the bushes, by the river and on the rooftops, paying no attention to

---

4. A species of parrot native to the island of St. Lucia in the West Indies.

her mistress's shouts of: 'Be careful, now! You must be mad!' Next she went over all the gardens in Pont-l'Évêque, stopping passersby and asking them: 'You don't happen to have seen my parrot by any chance?' Those who did not know him already were given a description of the bird. Suddenly she thought she could make out something green flying about behind the mills at the foot of the hill. But up on the hill there was nothing to be seen. A pedlar told her that he had come upon the parrot a short time before in Mère Simon's shop at Saint-Melaine. She ran all the way there, but no one knew what she was talking about. Finally she came back home, worn out, her shoes falling to pieces, and death in her heart. She was sitting beside Madame on the garden-seat and telling her what she had been doing, when she felt something light drop on her shoulder. It was Loulou! What he had been up to, no one could discover: perhaps he had just gone for a little walk round the town.

Félicité was slow to recover from this fright, and indeed never really got over it.

As the result of a chill she had an attack of quinsy,[5] and soon after that her ears were affected. Three years later she was deaf, and she spoke at the top of her voice, even in church. Although her sins could have been proclaimed over the length and breadth of the diocese without dishonour to her or offence to others, M. le Curé thought it advisable to hear her confession in the sacristy.

Imaginary buzzings in the head added to her troubles. Often her mistress would say: 'Heavens, how stupid you are!' and she would reply: 'Yes, Madame,' at the same time looking all around her for something.

The little circle of her ideas grew narrower and narrower, and the pealing of bells and the lowing of cattle went out of her life. Every living thing moved about in a ghostly silence. Only one sound reached her ears now, and that was the voice of the parrot.

As if to amuse her, he would reproduce the click-clack of the turn-spit, the shrill call of a man selling fish, and the noise of the saw at the joiner's across the way; and when the bell rang he would imitate Mme Aubain's 'Félicité ! The door, the door !'

They held conversations with each other, he repeating *ad nauseam* the three phrases in his repertory, she replying with words which were just as disconnected but which came from the heart. In her isolation, Loulou was almost a son or a lover to her. He used to climb up her fingers, peck at her lips, and hang on to her shawl; and as she bent over him, wagging her head from side to side as nurses do, the great wings of her bonnet and the wings of the bird quivered in unison.

When clouds banked up in the sky and there was a rumbling of thunder, he would utter piercing cries, no doubt remembering the sudden downpours in his native forests. The sound of the rain falling roused him to frenzy. He would flap excitedly around, shoot up to the ceiling, knocking everything over, and fly out of the window to splash about in the garden. But he would soon come back to perch on one of the firedogs, hopping about to dry his feathers and showing tail and beak in turn.

5. Tonsillitis.

One morning in the terrible winter of 1837, when she had put him in front of the fire because of the cold she found him dead in the middle of his cage, hanging head down with his claws caught in the bars. He had probably died of a stroke, but she thought he had been poisoned with parsley,[6] and despite the absence of any proof, her suspicions fell on Fabu.

She wept so much that her mistress said to her: 'Why don't you have him stuffed?'

Félicité asked the chemist's advice, remembering that he had always been kind to the parrot. He wrote to Le Havre, and a man called Fellacher agreed to do the job. As parcels sometimes went astray on the mail-coach, she decided to take the parrot as far as Honfleur herself.

On either side of the road stretched an endless succession of apple-trees, all stripped of their leaves, and there was ice in the ditches. Dogs were barking around the farms; and Félicité, with her hands tucked under her mantlet, her little black sabots and her basket, walked briskly along the middle of the road.

She crossed the forest, passed Le Haut-Chêne, and got as far as Saint-Gatien.

Behind her, in a cloud of dust, and gathering speed as the horses galloped downhill, a mail-coach swept along like a whirlwind. When he saw this woman making no attempt to get out of the way, the driver poked his head out above the hood, and he and the postilion shouted at her. His four horses could not be held in and galloped faster, the two leaders touching her as they went by. With a jerk of the reins the driver threw them to one side, and then, in a fury, he raised his long whip and gave her such a lash, from head to waist, that she fell flat on her back.

The first thing she did on regaining consciousness was to open her basket. Fortunately nothing had happened to Loulou. She felt her right cheek burning, and when she touched it her hand turned red; it was bleeding.

She sat down on a heap of stones and dabbed her face with her handkerchief. Then she ate a crust of bread which she had taken the precaution of putting in her basket, and tried to forget her wound by looking at the bird.

As she reached the top of the hill at Ecquemauville, she saw the lights of Honfleur twinkling in the darkness like a host of stars, and the shadowy expanse of the sea beyond. Then a sudden feeling of faintness made her stop; and the misery of her childhood, the disappointment of her first love, the departure of her nephew, and the death of Virginie all came back to her at once like the waves of a rising tide, and, welling up in her throat, choked her.

When she got to the boat she insisted on speaking to the captain, and without telling him what was in her parcel, asked him to take good care of it.

Fellacher kept the parrot a long time. Every week he promised it for the next; after six months he announced that a box had been sent off, and nothing more was heard of it. It looked as though Loulou would never come back, and Félicité told herself: 'They've stolen him for sure!'

At last he arrived—looking quite magnificent, perched on a branch screwed into a mahogany base, one foot in the air, his head cocked to one side, and biting a nut which the taxidermist, out of a love of the grandiose, had gilded.

---

6. Fool's Parsley, a poisonous plant resembling parsley in appearance.

Félicité shut him up in her room.

This place, to which few people were ever admitted, contained such a quantity of religious bric-à-brac and miscellaneous oddments that it looked like a cross between a chapel and a bazaar.

A big wardrobe prevented the door from opening properly. Opposite the window that overlooked the garden was a little round one looking on to the courtyard. There was a table beside the bed, with a water-jug, a couple of combs, and a block of blue soap in a chipped plate. On the walls there were rosaries, medals, several pictures of the Virgin, and a holy-water stoup made out of a coconut. On the chest of drawers, which was draped with a cloth just like an altar, was the shell box Victor had given her, and also a watering-can and a ball, some copy-books, the illustrated geography book, and a pair of ankle-boots. And on the nail supporting the looking-glass, fastened by its ribbons, hung the little plush hat.

Félicité carried this form of veneration to such lengths that she even kept one of Monsieur's frock-coats. All the old rubbish Mme Aubain had no more use for, she carried off to her room. That was how there came to be artificial flowers along the edge of the chest of drawers, and a portrait of the Comte d'Artois[7] in the window-recess.

With the aid of a wall-bracket, Loulou was installed on a chimney-breast that jutted out into the room. Every morning when she awoke, she saw him in the light of the dawn, and then she remembered the old days, and the smallest details of insignificant actions, not in sorrow but in absolute tranquillity.

Having no intercourse with anyone, she lived in the torpid state of a sleep-walker. The Corpus Christi processions roused her from this condition, for she would go round the neighbours collecting candlesticks and mats to decorate the altar of repose which they used to set up in the street.

In church she was forever gazing at the Holy Ghost, and one day she noticed that it had something of the parrot about it. This resemblance struck her as even more obvious in a colour-print depicting the baptism of Our Lord. With its red wings and its emerald-green body, it was the very image of Loulou.

She bought the print and hung it in the place of the Comte d'Artois, so that she could include them both in a single glance. They were linked together in her mind, the parrot being sanctified by this connexion with the Holy Ghost, which itself acquired new life and meaning in her eyes. God the Father could not have chosen a dove as a means of expressing Himself, since doves cannot talk, but rather one of Loulou's ancestors. And although Félicité used to say her prayers with her eyes on the picture, from time to time she would turn slightly towards the bird.

She wanted to join the Children of Mary,[8] but Mme Aubain dissuaded her from doing so.

An important event now loomed up—Paul's wedding.

After starting as a lawyer's clerk, he had been in business, in the Customs, and in Inland Revenue, and had even begun trying to get into the Department

---

7. Charles Philippe, Comte d' Artois (1757–1836), reigned as King Charles X from 1824 until 1830, when he was overthrown in the July Revolution.

8. Society of laywomen who pledge to imitate the Virgin Mary.

of Woods and Forests, when, at the age of thirty-six, by some heaven-sent inspiration, he suddenly discovered his real vocation—in the Wills and Probate Department. There he proved so capable that one of the auditors had offered him his daughter in marriage and promised to use his influence on his behalf.

Paul, grown serious-minded, brought her to see his mother. She criticized the way things were done at Pont-l'Évêque, put on airs, and hurt Félicité's feelings. Mme Aubain was relieved to see her go.

The following week came news of M. Bourais's death in an inn in Lower Brittany. Rumours that he had committed suicide were confirmed, and doubts arose as to his honesty. Mme Aubain went over her accounts and was soon conversant with the full catalogue of his misdeeds—embezzlement of interest, secret sales of timber, forged receipts, etc. Besides all this, he was the father of an illegitimate child, and had had 'relations with a person at Dozulé.'

These infamies upset Mme Aubain greatly. In March 1853 she was afflicted with a pain in the chest; her tongue seemed to be covered with a film; leeches failed to make her breathing any easier; and on the ninth evening of her illness she died. She had just reached the age of seventy-two.

She was thought to be younger because of her brown hair, worn in bandeaux round her pale, pock-marked face. There were few friends to mourn her, for she had a haughty manner which put people off. Yet Félicité wept for her as servants rarely weep for their masters. That Madame should die before her upset her ideas, seemed to be contrary to the order of things, monstrous and unthinkable.

Ten days later—the time it took to travel hot-foot from Besançon—the heirs arrived. The daughter-in-law ransacked every drawer, picked out some pieces of furniture and sold the rest; and then back they went to the Wills and Probate Department.

Madame's arm-chair, her pedestal table, her foot warmer, and the eight chairs had all gone. Yellow squares in the centre of the wall-panels showed where the pictures had hung. They had carried off the two cots with their mattresses, and no trace remained in the cupboard of all Virginie's things. Félicité climbed the stairs to her room, numbed with sadness.

The next day there was a notice on the door, and the apothecary shouted in her ear that the house was up for sale.

She swayed on her feet, and was obliged to sit down.

What distressed her most of all was the idea of leaving her room, which was so suitable for poor Loulou. Fixing an anguished look on him as she appealed to the Holy Ghost, she contracted the idolatrous habit of kneeling in front of the parrot to say her prayers. Sometimes the sun, as it came through the little window, caught his glass eye, so that it shot out a great luminous ray which sent her into ecstasies.

She had a pension of three hundred and eighty francs a year which her mistress had left her. The garden kept her in vegetables. As for clothes, she had enough to last her till the end of her days, and she saved on lighting by going to bed as soon as darkness fell.

She went out as little as possible, to avoid the second-hand dealer's shop, where some of the old furniture was on display. Ever since her fit of giddiness, she had been dragging one leg; and as her strength was failing, Mère Simon, whose grocery business had come to grief, came in every morning to chop wood and pump water for her.

Her eyes grew weaker. The shutters were not opened any more. Years went by, and nobody rented the house and nobody bought it.

For fear of being evicted, Félicité never asked for any repairs to be done. The laths in the roof rotted, and all through one winter her bolster was wet. After Easter she began spitting blood.

When this happened Mère Simon called in a doctor. Félicité wanted to know what was the matter with her, but she was so deaf that only one word reached her: 'Pneumonia.' It was a word she knew, and she answered gently: 'Ah! like Madame,' thinking it natural that she should follow in her mistress's footsteps.

The time to set up the altars of repose was drawing near.

The first altar was always at the foot of the hill, the second in front of the post office, the third about half-way up the street. There was some argument as to the siting of this one, and finally the women of the parish picked on Mme Aubain's courtyard.

The fever and the tightness of the chest grew worse. Félicité fretted over not doing anything for the altar. If only she could have put something on it! Then she thought of the parrot. The neighbours protested that it would not be seemly, but the curé gave his permission, and this made her so happy that she begged him to accept Loulou, the only thing of value she possessed, when she died.

From Tuesday to Saturday, the eve of Corpus Christi, she coughed more and more frequently. In the evening her face looked pinched and drawn, her lips stuck to her gums, and she started vomiting. At dawn the next day, feeling very low, she sent for a priest.

Three good women stood by her while she was given extreme unction. Then she said that she had to speak to Fabu.

He arrived in his Sunday best, very ill at ease in this funereal atmosphere.

'Forgive me,' she said, making an effort to stretch out her arm. 'I thought it was you who had killed him.'

What could she mean by such nonsense? To think that she had suspected a man like him of murder! He got very indignant and was obviously going to make a scene.

'Can't you see,' they said, 'that she isn't in her right mind any more?'

From time to time Félicité would start talking to shadows. The women went away. Mère Simon had her lunch.

A little later she picked Loulou up and held him out to Félicité, saying: 'Come now, say good-bye to him.'

Although the parrot was not a corpse, the worms were eating him up. One of his wings was broken, and the stuffing was coming out of his stomach. But she was blind by now, and she kissed him on the forehead and pressed him against her cheek. Mère Simon took him away from her to put him on the altar.

5

The scents of summer came up from the meadows; there was a buzzing of flies; the sun was glittering in the river and warming the slates of the roof. Mère Simon had come back into the room and was gently nodding off to sleep.

The noise of church bells woke her up; the congregation was coming out from vespers. Félicité's delirium abated. Thinking of the procession, she could see it as clearly as if she had been following it.

All the school-children, the choristers, and the firemen were walking along the pavements, while advancing up the middle of the street came the church officer armed with his halberd, the beadle carrying a great cross, the schoolmaster keeping an eye on the boys, and the nun fussing over her little girls—three of the prettiest, looking like curly-headed angels, were throwing rose-petals into the air. Then came the deacon, with both arms outstretched, conducting the band, and a couple of censer-bearers who turned round at every step to face the Holy Sacrament, which the curé, wearing his splendid chasuble, was carrying under a canopy of poppy-red velvet held aloft by four churchwardens. A crowd of people surged along behind, between the white cloths covering the walls of the houses, and eventually they got to the bottom of the hill.

A cold sweat moistened Félicité's temples. Mère Simon sponged it up with a cloth, telling herself that one day she would have to go the same way.

The hum of the crowd increased in volume, was very loud for a moment, then faded away.

A fusillade shook the window-panes. It was the postilions saluting the monstrance. Félicité rolled her eyes and said as loud as she could: 'Is he all right?'—worrying about the parrot.

She entered into her death-agony. Her breath, coming ever faster, with a rattling sound, made her sides heave. Bubbles of froth appeared at the corners of her mouth, and her whole body trembled.

Soon the booming of the ophicleides,[9] the clear voices of the children, and the deep voices of the men could be heard near at hand. Now and then everything was quiet, and the tramping of feet, deadened by a carpet of flowers, sounded like a flock moving across pasture-land.

The clergy appeared in the courtyard. Mère Simon climbed on to a chair to reach the little round window, from which she had a full view of the altar below.

It was hung with green garlands and adorned with a flounce in English needle-point lace. In the middle was a little frame containing some relics, there were two orange-trees at the corners, and all the way along stood silver candlesticks and china vases holding sunflowers, lilies, peonies, foxgloves, and bunches of hydrangea. This pyramid of bright colours stretched from the first floor right down to the carpet which was spread out over the pavement. Some rare objects caught the eye: a silver-gilt sugar-basin wreathed in violets, some pendants of Alençon gems gleaming on a bed of moss, and two Chinese screens with landscape decorations. Loulou, hidden under roses, showed nothing but his blue poll, which looked like a plaque of lapis lazuli.

The churchwardens, the choristers, and the children lined up along the three sides of the courtyard. The priest went slowly up the steps and placed his great shining gold sun[1] on the lace altar cloth. Everyone knelt down. There

9. Bugles.
1. Used in Catholic services, the vessel called a "monstrance" resembles a sun.

was a deep silence. And the censers, swinging at full tilt, slid up and down their chains.

A blue cloud of incense was wafted up into Félicité's room. She opened her nostrils wide and breathed it in with a mystical, sensuous fervour. Then she closed her eyes. Her lips smiled. Her heart-beats grew slower and slower, each a little fainter and gentler, like a fountain running dry, an echo fading away. And as she breathed her last, she thought she could see, in the opening heavens, a gigantic parrot hovering above her head.

LEO TOLSTOY

1828–1910

A gambler, womanizer, and aristocrat of the highest rank, Count Leo Tolstoy was also a vegetarian, pacifist, and anarchist, and a passionate advocate for the Russian peasantry. He was world-famous for his wisdom on the subject of marriage, but suffered through a remarkably stormy marriage himself. He became widely known as a moral and religious sage, but was excommunicated from the Russian Orthodox Church. He produced some of the century's best fiction but came to believe that novels were immoral. And yet this heap of contradictions should not be seen as the mark of a hypocrite. Tolstoy was always fully conscious of the disparity between his ideals and his life. "Blame *me*," he wrote, "and not the path I tread." This painful self-division reflects his intense, lifelong struggle to find the best way to live in the world—how to respond to the pressures of guilt and pleasure, authority and money, sex and war. And it suggests the source of one of his great talents as a writer: the capacity to represent a vast, various, and conflicting array of desires and ideals.

LIFE

Born in 1828, Tolstoy was the fourth of five children. Both of his parents belonged to the highest class of Russian society—aristocrats who had access to the tsar and the tsar's court. And yet Tolstoy never took advantage of his high birth to pursue a grand career as a diplomat or courtier. Having lost his mother at the age of two and his father at nine, he spent his youth in relative isolation. Much of his long life was passed on the family estate, Yasnaya Polyana, about 130 miles from Moscow, in the company of his close family members and his serfs—Russian peasants who were the property of aristocratic landowners, much like slaves.

Despite the fact that he was an orphan and moved from one guardian to another, Tolstoy looked back on his childhood as idyllic. He was close to his siblings, and together they imagined a perfect society based on the ideal of universal love. At the age of fourteen Tolstoy started to visit brothels, which prompted terrible bouts of remorse and self-revulsion. After his first experience, he claimed to have stood next to the bed and wept. A few years later he started to write in a diary, which he then kept compulsively for the rest of his life. This daily writing often furnished material for his fiction, as well as developing his skills and habits as a writer. Here, he would explore questions about how to act and what to believe, wondering about the purpose and meaning of life. He would also repeatedly make vows to give up his dalliances with women, and just as often break his promise. Thus began a chronicle of sex and shame, played out in countless affairs with women, almost all of them members of the peasant class.

Intending to take up a diplomatic career, Tolstoy went to the provincial university at Kazan to study Arabic, Turko-Tartar, French, and German. He later switched to law, a course of study open only to the highest-ranking aristocrats. But this too he dropped in 1847 when he inherited the family estate, a large sum of money, and the ownership of over three hundred serfs. This sudden inheritance allowed him to drift aimlessly for a while, moving in aristocratic circles in the cities of St. Petersburg and Moscow, where he spent night after night at gambling tables.

Tolstoy's life changed radically in 1851 when he followed his older brother Nikolay, a soldier, to the mountains of the Caucasus, where the Russian army was protecting the hotly contested boundary between Russia and the Ottoman and Persian empires. It was here, observing military life and conflict, that Tolstoy began publishing his work. He decided to join the army and to serve in the war between Russia and Britain in Crimea. There he witnessed appalling devastation, incompetence, and confusion. He also gambled away his fortune, observed the heat of battle and the pettiness of military life, and became a literary sensation with his detailed descriptions of the war in *Sebastopol Sketches* (1854). He began to be known in literary circles as an emerging genius, and in government circles as a potentially dangerous critic.

Although he had been an indifferent student, Tolstoy was a great reader, and from adolescence he passionately admired the French Romantic **Jean-Jacques Rousseau**, who argued against the artificiality of social manners and institutions in favor of the simplicity of life in and through nature. Tolstoy read widely in European and American literature, from **Johann Wolfgang von Goethe** to Harriet Beecher Stowe. One of his greatest influences was the English novelist Charles Dickens, who was highly popular in Russia. Tolstoy would often read a Dickens novel when he needed a catalyst to begin writing himself.

At the age of thirty-four, Tolstoy, now a famous writer, married Sofya Andreyevna Bers, an eighteen-year-old, upper-class St. Petersburg girl. A day after he proposed, he offered his fiancée the chance to read his diaries, which recorded, among other things, twenty years of sexual activity with prostitutes, gypsies, and serfs. "I forgive you," she said to him after reading it, "but it's dreadful." From the beginning, both Tolstoys wrote constantly about one another in their diaries, and read each other's accounts, leading to many jealous battles—and perhaps the most documented marriage in history. Over their long and tumultuous life together, Sofya bore thirteen children, made four handwritten copies of the 1,500-page *War and Peace*, and did her best to protect her husband's literary property.

By his mid-thirties, Tolstoy had run afoul of the Russian government. As a local justice of the peace, he had made eccentric and radical decisions, taking the side of serfs against his fellow landowners, and he had founded an experimental school for peasant children at Yasnaya Polyana based on new theories of education emerging out of France, Belgium, Germany, and England. Instead of cramming children with information, Tolstoy argued, it made sense for education to draw on their own experience. This seemed dangerously foreign, and his writing seemed unsettling, too. The tsar, concerned about threats to his life and his regime, had a team of censors who excised paragraphs from a number of Tolstoy's early short stories. In 1862 the police made a raid on his house. They found little evidence of subversive writings or activity, but the search infuriated Tolstoy, whose antigovernment sentiment increased as he grew older. Arguing that governments always relied on violence, he became a vocal anarchist and pacifist, advocating civil disobedience rather than submission to the state.

Tolstoy's two greatest works, *War and Peace* (1865–69) and *Anna Karenina* (1875–77), were hugely popular and established him as the greatest novelist of the Russian experience. *War and Peace* was an epic that recounted Napoleon's invasion of Russia in 1812, a huge swarming story of a nation's resistance to a foreign power. Tolstoy unsettles the myth of Napoleon as one of the world's greatest heroes, interpreting history instead as a struggle of anonymous collective forces; events are the consequences of waves of irrational communal feeling. *Anna Karenina* is a moving story of marriage and adultery that juxtaposes characters who are searching for meaning and fulfillment. Its hero, Levin, ends a painful struggle with the promise of salvation,

adopting the ideal of a simple life in which we should "remember God." So bound up with national pride were these two works that they survived successive waves of censorship. In fact, the repressive Russian government was so fearful of making a martyr out of the much-beloved novelist that they left Tolstoy almost entirely alone, even while they imprisoned and executed a vast number of his fellow writers for subversive antitsarist sentiment. As Tolstoy became an increasingly outspoken critic of the state, his own fiction protected him.

After he published *Anna Karenina* Tolstoy underwent an acute personal and spiritual crisis, thrown into such despair by the pointlessness of existence that he considered suicide (a despair shared by some of the characters in the novel). Then he had a conversion experience that set him on a new path. After exploring and rejecting the Russian Orthodox Church, he began to pursue his own search for God. It was the peasants who seemed to Tolstoy to know how to live best, and in the late 1870s he started to try to live a peasant life, dressing like them, eating peasant food, and even making his own shoes. Rereading the Gospels closely, he founded his own religion. This involved rejecting any idea of an afterlife and following the model of Jesus's life as closely as possible, giving away wealth and rejecting all forms of violence. Tolstoy's first work of fiction after his conversion was *The Death of Ivan Ilyich* in 1886.

The last decades of his life saw Tolstoy writing mostly religious and philosophical treatises. By the 1880s the writer was arguing in favor of complete sexual abstinence. He condemned literature and singled out Shakespeare as particularly bad. He became an outspoken vegetarian. At one point, an elderly relative visiting Yasnaya Polyana asked that meat be served to her; when she came to the table, she discovered a meat cleaver at her place and a live chicken tied to her chair. In his later years, many followers saw Tolstoy as a wise prophet and made long journeys to Yasnaya Polyana from distant places to meet the great man. They often reported that he seemed larger than life—saintly and heroic.

At Tolstoy's death in 1910 students rioted, anarchists were rounded up by the police, and thousands of people followed his coffin. Seven years later, when Russia erupted in political turmoil, some saw the first tide of communism as a "Tolstoyan revolution." But Tolstoy left another kind of political legacy as well. So influential was his notion of nonviolent resistance for a young Indian man named Mohandas Gandhi that he called his first political base "Tolstoy farm."

TIMES

In the century leading up to Tolstoy's birth, Russian society was divided into three major groups: the aristocracy, which was small in number but exerted all of the nation's political power; town merchants, who had fixed duties and privileges; and serfs, who made up the vast majority of the population but had no power at all. The aristocrats were the only Russians who could attend universities, hold civil service positions, and remain exempt from taxation. Meanwhile, serfs had neither freedom nor authority: one tsar after another reduced serfs' rights, and by the middle of the eighteenth century, serfs were forbidden to travel and had the legal status of personal property, exactly like slaves. When Tolstoy was young, 23 million Russians were privately owned serfs.

This drastically lopsided political and social system was clearly unstable, and anxious tsars struggled to stave off outright revolution. Alexander II emancipated the serfs in 1861 for purely pragmatic reasons: "It is better to abolish serfdom from above," he explained, "than to wait for the time when it will begin to abolish itself from below." The emancipation did not put an end to social unrest, however. By 1880 there had been six attempts to kill the tsar by anarchists and nihilists. Alexander increased his secret police force, imposed severe censorship, and promised political reforms. In 1881 an assassin succeeded in killing him, and he was succeeded by his son, Alexander III, who rejected his father's reform efforts in favor of harsh and repressive measures, including even tighter censorship and persecution of non-Orthodox minorities, especially Jews. Most writers were persecuted—thrown in jail or kept under house arrest. In this context, it is astonishing that Tolstoy managed to remain free, especially given his sharp and vocal criticism of both church and state.

In Russian intellectual circles, one urgent question constantly reemerged in the nineteenth century: should Russia follow the lead of a modernizing Western Europe in terms of culture, politics, and industry, or should the nation instead reach for models drawn from its own religious and national history, developing its own distinctive heritage? On the one side, the so-called Westernizers, based largely in St. Petersburg, argued for liberal democracy, religious freedom, and the emancipation of the serfs. They spoke French, and often felt ashamed of Russian backwardness. On the other side, the Moscow-based Slavophiles resisted rationalism and technological innovation, embraced the Russian Orthodox Church, and typically favored bringing together all Slavic peoples under the Russian tsar. Tolstoy belonged to neither camp—or to both. While he favored European models of education and rejected the Orthodox Church, he also prized the Russian peasantry as a source of national renewal and meaning.

WORK

Tolstoy's great novels *War and Peace* and *Anna Karenina* told vast and sweeping realist stories of life in nineteenth-century Russia, filled with vivid depictions of aristocratic pursuits, military battles, and the complexities of love and marriage. Later he turned to a different kind of writing, producing impassioned and often didactic stories and nonfiction essays in favor of spiritual principles. *The Death of Ivan Ilyich*, the story included here, falls midway between these two phases of his career. As the first piece of fiction written after the writer's conversion, it has seemed to many readers to combine Tolstoy's earlier, richly realistic representations of contemporary life with his later turn to religious ideals.

There may be a biographical source for this novella. In 1856—thirty years before he began writing it—Tolstoy's brother Dmitry had died of tuberculosis in the arms of a prostitute. Revolted by his brother's emaciated body and the smell of illness, Tolstoy felt remarkably little concern for Dmitry and selfishly rushed back to St. Petersburg to enjoy his growing literary fame. This experience—Dmitry's death, his own indifference, and his resulting guilt—seems to have provided the writer with the contrasting perspectives he explores in *The Death of Ivan Ilyich*.

This is the story of an average man of the prosperous middle class who faces the unbearable fact that he is soon going to die. Tolstoy is famous for peppering his prose with startlingly opinionated, intrusive judgments, and among the most famous of these is the narrator's assessment of his protagonist's life at the opening of chapter II: "Ivan Ilyich's life had been the most simple and most ordinary and therefore most terrible."

The relationship between terror and ordinariness here appears straightforward and categorical, but the story then asks us to think about how we respond to such blunt claims of truth. Ivan Ilyich himself knows that everyone must die—"Caius is a man, men are mortal, therefore Caius is mortal"—but he rebels against applying this to himself: "he was not Caius, not an abstract man, but a creature quite, quite separate from all others." What, Tolstoy asks us, is the relationship between abstract, universal truths and our intensely felt personal experience?

Ordinary social life, it seems, allows us to avoid this question, as characters immerse themselves in card games, interior decorating, career advancement, financial dealings, and the desire to "live pleasantly." Ivan Ilyich, whose first symptoms of illness appear when he tries to hang his curtains properly, comes to see his family, friends, and doctors as false and deceitful. Gerasim, the peasant, represents the only appealing alternative described in the narrative.

Tolstoy experiments with perspective, choosing to begin the story at its chronological endpoint, as the news of Ivan Ilyich's death comes to his acquaintances. For them it appears as an interruption of ordinary life, and we see the event through their uncomfortable eyes. It is only after this introduction that the narrator switches to Ivan Ilyich's perspective. In the first draft, two characters, Peter Ivanovich and Ivan Ilyich, told the story in the first person. Later Tolstoy shifted to a third-person omniscient narrator, who filters our experience through these two characters.

Tolstoy not only multiplies perspectives, he also multiplies metaphors: dying is like being "thrust into a narrow, deep black sack"; it is also like a "stone falling downwards," like flying, and "like the sensation one sometimes experiences in a railway carriage when one thinks one is going backwards while one is really going forwards." Death emerges variously as nothingness, a black hole, a judge (like the character himself), and perhaps most memorably, as "*It.*" In Russian this pronoun is feminine and thus closer to the English "*She.*" As death slowly comes to the protagonist, language itself begins to break down. In the final chapter, he starts screaming, "I won't," but this becomes simply "Oh! Oh! Oh!"—a sound that lasts for three solid days. In his final moments of illumination, the protagonist tries to ask his son to "forgive" him but says only "forgo." As Ivan Ilyich's viewpoint develops and changes, the story narrows in time and space; the focus tightens, his range of movements contracts, the chapters get shorter, and the time of the events shrinks.

Guy de Maupassant, a French writer whom Tolstoy admired, read *The Death of Ivan Ilyich* late in his own life, and said, sadly: "I realize that everything I have done now was to no purpose, and that my ten volumes are worthless."

The Death of Ivan Ilyich[1]

I

During a break in the hearing of the Melvinsky case, the members of the court and the prosecutor met in Ivan Yegorovich Shebek's room in the big law courts building and began talking about the famous Krasovsky case. Fyodor Vasilyevich became heated, contending that it didn't come under their jurisdiction; Ivan Yegorovich held his ground; while Pyotr Ivanovich, not having joined in the argument at the beginning, took no part in it and was looking through the *Gazette*, which had just been delivered.

"Gentlemen!" he said. "Ivan Ilyich has died."

"He hasn't!"

"Look, read this," he said to Fyodor Vasilyevich, handing him a fresh copy which still smelled of ink.

Within a black border was printed: "Praskovya Fyodorovna Golovina with deep sorrow informs family and friends of the passing of her beloved spouse Ivan Ilyich Golovin, member of the Court of Justice, which took place on the 4th of February of this year 1882. The funeral will be on Friday at 1 p.m."

Ivan Ilyich was a colleague of the gentlemen meeting there and they all liked him. He had been ill for several weeks; people were saying his illness was incurable. His position had been kept for him, but there had been conjectures that, in the event of his death, Alekseyev might be appointed to his position, and either Vinnikov or Shtabel to Alekseyev's. So on hearing of Ivan Ilyich's death the first thought of each of the gentlemen meeting in the room was of the significance the death might have for the transfer or promotion of the members themselves or their friends.

Now I will probably get Shtabel's or Vinnikov's position, thought Fyodor Vasilyevich. *It was promised to me long ago and this promotion means a raise of eight hundred rubles, plus a private office.*

1. Translated by Peter Carson.

Now I must ask about the transfer of my brother-in-law from Kaluga, thought Pyotr Ivanovich. *My wife will be very pleased. Now she won't be able to say that I've never done anything for her family.*

"I thought he wouldn't leave his bed," Pyotr Ivanovich said aloud. "Such a pity."

"What was actually wrong with him?"

"The doctors couldn't make a diagnosis. That is, they did, but different ones. When I saw him the last time, I thought he would recover."

"And I didn't go and see him after the holidays. I kept meaning to."

"Did he have any money?"

"I think his wife had a very small income. But next to nothing."

"Yes, we'll have to go and see her. They lived a terribly long way off."

"That is, a long way from you. Everything's a long way from you."

"He just can't forgive me for living on the other side of the river," said Pyotr Ivanovich, smiling at Shebek. And they started talking about distances in the city, and went back into the courtroom.

Apart from the thoughts the death brought each of them about the possible moves and changes at work that might follow, the actual fact of the death of a close acquaintance evoked, as always, in all who learned of it a complacent feeling that it was "he who had died, not I."

So—he's dead; but here I am still, each thought or felt. At this point his closer acquaintances, the so-called friends of Ivan Ilyich, involuntarily thought that they now needed to carry out the very tedious requirements of etiquette and go to the requiem service and pay a visit of condolence to the widow.

Closest of all were Fyodor Vasilyevich and Pyotr Ivanovich.

Pyotr Ivanovich was a friend from law school and considered himself under an obligation to Ivan Ilyich.

Having given his wife over dinner the news of Ivan Ilyich's death and his thoughts about the possibility of his brother-in-law's transfer to their district, Pyotr Ivanovich didn't lie down to have a rest but put on a formal tailcoat and drove to Ivan Ilyich's.

At the entrance to Ivan Ilyich's apartment stood a carriage and two cabs. Downstairs in the hall by the coatrack, leaning against the wall, was the brocade-covered lid of the coffin with tassels and a gold braid that had been cleaned with powder. Two ladies in black were taking off their fur coats. One of them, Ivan Ilyich's sister, he knew; the other was an unknown lady. Pyotr Ivanovich's colleague Schwarz was coming downstairs and, seeing from the top step who had come in, he winked at him as if to say, "Ivan Ilyich has made a silly mess of things; you and I have done things differently."

Schwarz's face with his English side-whiskers and his whole thin figure in a tailcoat as usual had an elegant solemnity, and this solemnity, which was always at odds with Schwarz's playful character, was especially piquant here. So Pyotr Ivanovich thought.

Pyotr Ivanovich let the ladies go in front of him and slowly followed them up the stairs. Schwarz didn't come down but stayed at the top. Pyotr Ivanovich understood why: he obviously wanted to arrange where they should play *vint*[2] today. The ladies went up the stairs to the widow but Schwarz, with a serious

---

2. A Russian card game, similar to whist and bridge.

set to his strong lips and a playful look, indicated by a twitch of his eyebrows that Pyotr Ivanovich should go to the right, into the room where the corpse lay.

Pyotr Ivanovich went in, feeling, as is always the case, at a loss as to what he should do there. One thing he did know was that in these circumstances it never does any harm to cross oneself. He wasn't altogether sure whether one should also bow and so he chose a middle course: entering the room, he started to cross himself and made a kind of slight bow. Insofar as the movements of his head and hands would allow, he looked round the room at the same time. Two young men, probably nephews, one of them a gymnasium[3] pupil, were crossing themselves as they left the room. An old woman stood motionless, and a lady with oddly arched eyebrows was saying something to her in a whisper. A church lector[4] in a frock coat with a vigorous and decisive way to him was reading something out loudly with an expression that permitted no contradiction; the peasant manservant Gerasim, stepping lightly in front of Pyotr Ivanovich, scattered something on the ground. Seeing that, Pyotr Ivanovich at once sensed the faint smell of a decomposing body. On his last visit to Ivan Ilyich he had seen this peasant in the study; he carried out the duties of a sick-nurse, and Ivan Ilyich was especially fond of him. Pyotr Ivanovich kept crossing himself and bowing slightly in an intermediate direction between the coffin, the lector, and the icons on a table in the corner. Then, when he thought the movement of crossing himself with his hand had gone on for too long, he stopped and started to examine the dead man.

The dead man lay, as dead men always do, especially heavily, his stiffened limbs sunk in the padded lining of the coffin with his head bent back forever on the pillow, and, as always with dead men, his yellow waxen forehead sticking out, showing bald patches on his hollow temples, his nose protruding as if it pressed on his upper lip. He had greatly changed, had become even thinner since Pyotr Ivanovich had seen him, but like all dead men, his face was handsomer, above all more imposing than when he was alive. On his face was an expression that said what had to be done had been done, and done properly. This expression also held a reproach or reminder to the living. Pyotr Ivanovich found this reminder inappropriate—or at the least one not applying to himself. This gave Pyotr Ivanovich an unpleasant feeling, and so he hurriedly crossed himself once more and turned, too hurriedly he thought, and not in accordance with propriety, and went to the door. Schwarz was waiting for him in the next room, his legs wide apart and both hands playing behind his back with his top hat. One look at Schwarz's playful, neat, and elegant figure refreshed Pyotr Ivanovich. Pyotr Ivanovich felt that Schwarz stood above all this and didn't allow himself to give in to depressing thoughts. The very way he looked stated the following: the fact of Ivan Ilyich's requiem cannot serve as a sufficient reason to consider the order of the courts disrupted; in other words, nothing can stop us unsealing and shuffling a pack of cards this evening while the manservant puts out four fresh candles; in general there are no grounds for assuming that this fact can prevent us from spending a pleasant evening, even today. He said this in a whisper to Pyotr Ivanovich as he came in, proposing they meet for

3. School for preparing students to enter university.
4. High position in the minor orders of the Eastern Orthodox Church, responsible for reading from scripture during services.

a game at Fyodor Vasilyevich's. But apparently Pyotr Ivanovich was not fated to play *vint* this evening. Praskovya Fyodorovna, a short, plump woman who broadened from the shoulders down in spite of all her efforts to achieve the opposite, was dressed all in black with her head covered in lace and with oddly arched eyebrows like the lady standing by the coffin. She came out of her rooms with the other ladies, and taking them to the door where the dead man lay, said:

"Now there'll be the requiem; do go in."

Schwarz stopped, making a vague bow—clearly neither accepting nor rejecting this proposal. Praskovya Fyodorovna, recognizing Pyotr Ivanovich, sighed, went right up to him, took him by the hand, and said:

"I know that you were a true friend of Ivan Ilyich . . ." and looked at him, waiting for an action on his part that corresponded to these words.

Pyotr Ivanovich knew that just as in that room one had had to cross oneself, so here one must press the hand, sigh, and say, "Believe me!" And that's what he did. And having done it he felt that the desired result had been obtained: he was moved and she was moved.

"Come while they haven't started in there; I need to talk to you," said the widow. "Give me your hand."

Pyotr Ivanovich gave his hand and they went off into the inner rooms, past Schwarz who winked sadly at Pyotr Ivanovich. "There's your *vint* gone! Don't take it out on us; we'll find another partner. Maybe you can cut in once you've gotten free," said his playful look.

Pyotr Ivanovich sighed even more deeply and sadly, and Praskovya Fyodorovna gratefully pressed his hand. They went into her dimly lit drawing room hung with pink cretonne[5] and sat down by a table, she on a sofa and Pyotr Ivanovich on a low pouf built on springs that awkwardly gave way as he sat down. (Praskovya Fyodorovna was going to warn him to sit on another chair but found such a warning inappropriate for the situation and changed her mind.) As he sat down on the pouf, Pyotr Ivanovich remembered how Ivan Ilyich had arranged this drawing room and consulted him about this very pink cretonne with green leaves. On her way to sit down on the sofa, as she passed the table (the whole drawing room was full of furniture and knick-knacks), the widow caught the lace of her black mantilla on the carving of the table. Pyotr Ivanovich got up to unhook her, and the sprung pouf now released below began to sway and push at him. The widow started to unhook the lace herself and Pyotr Ivanovich sat down again, quelling the rebellious pouf underneath him. But the widow hadn't unhooked it all, and Pyotr Ivanovich again got up and the pouf again rebelled and even made a noise. When all this was over she took out a clean cambric handkerchief and began to cry. Pyotr Ivanovich felt chilled by the episode of the lace and the battle with the pouf and sat frowning. This awkward situation was interrupted by Sokolov, Ivan Ilyich's butler, reporting that the place in the cemetery Praskovya Fyodorovna had selected would cost two hundred rubles. She stopped crying and, looking at Pyotr Ivanovich with the air of a victim, said in French[6] that

---

5. Heavy upholstery fabric, often printed with a fancy or gaudy pattern.
6. It was common for members of the upper classes in Russia in the 19th century to speak French to one another.

she was suffering greatly. Pyotr Ivanovich made a silent sign expressing a firm conviction that it couldn't be otherwise.

"Do smoke, please," she said in a gracious and, at the same time, broken voice and talked to Sokolov about the matter of the price of the place in the cemetery. Pyotr Ivanovich smoked and heard her asking very detailed questions about the different prices of plots and deciding on the one that should be bought. When that was done, she went on to give instructions about the singers. Sokolov went out.

"I do everything myself," she said to Pyotr Ivanovich, moving some albums lying on the table to one side. Noticing that his ash was posing a threat to the table, she speedily pushed an ashtray towards Pyotr Ivanovich and said, "I find it a pretence to state that because of grief I can't deal with practical matters. On the contrary, if there is something that can . . . not console . . . but distract me, then it's bothering about him." She again took out her handkerchief as if she were going to cry, and suddenly, as if pulling herself together, she shook herself and began to speak quietly:

"However, I have to talk to you about something."

Pyotr Ivanovich bowed, not letting the pouf release its springs, which had at once started to move underneath him.

"He suffered terribly in the last days."

"Did he suffer very much?" Pyotr Ivanovich asked.

"Oh. Terribly! At the end he never stopped screaming, not for minutes, for hours. For three whole days he screamed without drawing breath. It was unbearable. I can't understand how I bore it; one could hear it from three doors away. Oh, what I've been through!"

"And was he really conscious?" Pyotr Ivanovich asked.

"Yes," she whispered, "till the final moment. He said goodbye to us a quarter of an hour before he died and asked as well for Volodya to be taken out."

The thought of the sufferings of a man he had known so well, first as a cheerful lad, a schoolboy, then as an adult colleague, suddenly horrified Pyotr Ivanovich in spite of his unpleasant consciousness of his own and this woman's pretense. He saw again that forehead, the nose pressing on the lip, and he became fearful for himself.

Three days of terrible suffering and death. That can happen to me too, now, any minute, he thought, and for a moment he became frightened. But right away, he didn't know how, there came to his aid the ordinary thought that this had happened to Ivan Ilyich and not to him; and this ought not and could not happen to him; that in thinking like this he was giving in to gloomy thoughts, which one shouldn't, as had been clear from Schwarz's face. And having reached this conclusion, Pyotr Ivanovich was reassured and started to ask with interest about the details of Ivan Ilyich's end, as if death were an adventure peculiar to Ivan Ilyich but absolutely not to himself.

After some talk about the details of the truly terrible physical sufferings which Ivan Ilyich had undergone (details that Pyotr Ivanovich learned only by way of the effect that Ivan Ilyich's torment had had on Praskovya Fyodorovna's nerves), the widow apparently found it necessary to move on to business.

"Ah, Pyotr Ivanovich, it's so hard, so terribly hard." And she again started to cry.

Pyotr Ivanovich sighed and waited for her to blow her nose. When she had blown her nose, he said:

"Believe me . . ." and again she talked away and unburdened herself of what was clearly her main business with him—how on her husband's death she could get money from the treasury. She gave the appearance of asking Pyotr Ivanovich for advice about the pension, but he saw that she already knew down to the smallest details even what he didn't know—everything that one could extract from the public purse on this death—but that she wanted to learn if one couldn't somehow extract a bit more money. Pyotr Ivanovich tried to think of a way, but, having thought a little and out of politeness abusing the government for its meanness, he said that he thought one couldn't get more. Then she sighed and clearly began to think of a way to get rid of her visitor. He understood this, put out his cigarette, got up, shook her hand, and went into the hall.

In the dining room with the clock that Ivan Ilyich had been so pleased to buy in a junk shop, Pyotr Ivanovich met the priest and also a few acquaintances who had come to the requiem, and he saw a beautiful young lady he knew, Ivan Ilyich's daughter. She was all in black. That made her very slender waist seem even more so. She had a somber, decisive, almost angry expression. She bowed to Pyotr Ivanovich as if he had done something wrong. Behind the daughter, with a similarly offended expression, stood a rich young man whom Pyotr Ivanovich knew, an examining magistrate who he'd heard was her fiancé. He glumly bowed to them and was about to go on into the room where the dead man lay when from under the stairs there appeared the figure of the son, a gymnasium student, who looked terribly like Ivan Ilyich. He was a little Ivan Ilyich just as Pyotr Ivanovich remembered him at law school. His eyes were tearstained and had the look that the eyes of boys with impure thoughts have at the age of thirteen or fourteen. When he recognized Pyotr Ivanovich the boy began to scowl sullenly and shamefacedly. Pyotr Ivanovich nodded to him and went into the dead man's room. The requiem began—candles, groans, incense, tears, sobs. Pyotr Ivanovich stood frowning, looking at the feet in front of him. He didn't look once at the dead man and right until the end didn't give in to any depressing influences. He was one of the first to leave. There was no one in the hall. Gerasim, the peasant manservant, darted out of the dead man's study, rummaged with his strong hands among all the fur coats to find Pyotr Ivanovich's, and gave it to him.

"So, Gerasim my friend," said Pyotr Ivanovich in order to say something. "It's sad, isn't it?"

"It's God's will. We'll all be there," said Gerasim, showing his white, regular, peasant's teeth, and like a man in the full swing of intensive work, briskly opened the door, called the coachman, helped Pyotr Ivanovich in, and jumped back to the steps as if trying to think what else he might do.

It was particularly pleasant for Pyotr Ivanovich to breathe the fresh air after the smells of incense, the dead body, and the carbolic acid.[7]

"Where to, sir?" asked the coachman.

"It's not late. So I'll still drop in at Fyodor Vasilyevich's."

---

7. Phenol, used as a disinfectant.

And off Pyotr Ivanovich went. And indeed he found his friends finishing the first rubber;[8] it was easy for him to cut in as a fifth.

II

Ivan Ilyich's past life had been very simple and ordinary and very awful.

Ivan Ilyich had died at the age of forty-five, a member of the Court of Justice. He was the son of a St. Petersburg civil servant who had in various ministries and departments the kind of career that brings people to a position in which, although it is quite clear that they are incapable of performing any meaningful job, they still by reason of their long past service and seniority cannot be dismissed; so they receive invented, fictitious positions and thousands of rubles, from six to ten thousand, which are not fictitious, with which they live on to a ripe old age.

Such was Privy Councillor Ilya Yefimovich Golovin, the superfluous member of various superfluous institutions.

He had three sons, Ivan Ilyich being the second. The eldest had the same kind of career as his father, only in a different ministry, and he was already approaching the age at which salary starts increasing automatically. The third son was a failure. Wherever he had been in various positions he had made a mess of things and he was now working in the railways. Both his father and his brothers, and especially their wives, not only didn't like to see him but didn't even mention his existence unless absolutely compelled to do so. Their sister was married to Baron Gref, the same kind of St. Petersburg civil servant as his father-in-law. Ivan Ilyich was *le phénix de la famille*,[9] as they said. He wasn't as cold and precise as the eldest or as hopeless as the youngest. He was somewhere between them—a clever, lively, pleasant, and decent man. He had been educated with his younger brother in the law school. The younger one didn't finish and was expelled from the fifth class. Ivan Ilyich completed the course with good marks. In law school he was already what he would later be during his entire life: a capable, cheerful, good-natured, and sociable man, but one who strictly did what he considered his duty, and he considered his duty to be everything that it was considered to be by his superiors. Neither as a boy nor afterward as a grown man did he seek to ingratiate himself, but there was in him from a young age the characteristic of being drawn to people of high station like a fly toward the light; he adopted their habits and their views on life and established friendly relations with them. All the passions of childhood and youth went by without leaving much of a trace in him; he gave in both to sensuality and to vanity, and—toward the end, in the senior classes—to liberalism,[1] but always within the defined limits that his sense accurately indicated to him as correct.

At law school he had done things that previously had seemed to him quite vile and had filled him with self-disgust while he did them; but later, seeing these things were done by people in high positions and were not thought by them to be bad, he didn't quite think of them as good but completely forgot them and wasn't at all troubled by memories of them.

8. A round of a card game.
9. "The phoenix of the family" (French). The word *phoenix* is used here to mean "rare bird,"
"prodigy."
1. Here meaning libertinism, wild sexual behavior.

Having left law school in the tenth class and received money from his father for fitting himself out, Ivan Ilyich ordered clothes at Sharmer's, hung on his watch chain a medallion with the inscription *respice finem*, took his leave of the princely patron of the school and his tutor, dined with his schoolmates at Donon's,[2] and, equipped with a new and fashionable trunk, linen, clothes, shaving and toilet things, and traveling rug ordered and bought from the very best shops, he went off to a provincial city to the post of assistant to the governor for special projects, which his father had procured for him.

In the provincial city Ivan Ilyich at once established for himself the kind of easy and pleasant position he had had at law school. He worked, made his career, and at the same time amused himself in a pleasant and seemly way; from time to time he went around the district towns on a mission from his chief. He behaved to both superiors and inferiors with dignity and he carried out the responsibilities he had been given, mainly for the affairs of religious dissenters,[3] with an exactness and incorruptible honesty of which he could not but be proud.

In his work, despite his youth and liking for frivolous amusement, he was exceptionally reserved, formal, and even severe; but in society he was often playful and witty and always good-humored, well-behaved and *bon enfant*,[4] as his chief and his chief's wife, with whom he was one of the family, used to say of him.

There was also in the provincial city an affair with one of the ladies who attached herself to the smart lawyer; there was a little dressmaker; there were drinking sessions with visiting aides-de-camp and trips to a remote street after supper; there was also some fawning deference to his chief and even to his chief's wife, but all this wore such a high tone of probity that it couldn't be described in bad words; all this could only go under the rubric of the French expression *il faut que jeunesse se passe*.[5] Everything took place with clean hands, in clean shirts, with French words, and, most importantly, in the highest society, consequently with the approval of people in high position.

Ivan Ilyich worked in this way for five years, and then there came changes in his official life. New legal bodies were founded; new men were needed.

And Ivan Ilyich was this new man.

Ivan Ilyich was offered the position of examining magistrate and he accepted it, despite the fact that this position was in another province and he had to abandon the relationships he had established and establish new ones. His friends saw Ivan Ilyich off: they took a group photograph, they presented him with a silver cigarette case, and off he went to his new position.

As an examining magistrate Ivan Ilyich was just as *comme il faut*,[6] well-behaved, capable of separating his official duties from his private life and of inspiring general respect as he had been as a special projects officer. The actual work of a magistrate had much more interest and attraction for him

2. One of St. Petersburg's better restaurants. "Sharmer's": a fashionable St. Petersburg tailor. "*Respice finem*": "regard the end" (a Latin motto).
3. The Old Believers, a large group of Russians (about 25 million in 1900), members of a sect that originated in a break with the Orthodox Church in the 17th century; they were subject to many legal restrictions.
4. A nice boy (French).
5. "Youth must have its fling" [translators' note].
6. Literally, "as one must" (French); proper.

than his previous work. In his previous position it had been pleasant to walk with a light step in his Sharmer uniform past trembling petitioners and envious officials waiting to be seen, straight into his chief's room to sit down with him over a cup of tea with a cigarette. But there were few people who depended directly on his say-so—only district police officers and religious schismatics when he was sent on missions—and he liked to treat such people dependent on him politely, almost as comrades; he liked to let them feel that here he was, someone who could crush them, treating them in a simple and friendly way. There were only a few such people then. Now, as an examining magistrate, Ivan Ilyich felt that all of them, all without exception, even the most important, self-satisfied people, were in his hands, and that he only had to write certain words on headed paper and this or that important, self-satisfied man would be brought to him as a defendant or a witness, and if he wouldn't let him sit down, would have to stand before him and answer his questions. Ivan Ilyich never abused this power of his—on the contrary he tried to use it lightly—but the consciousness of this power and the possibility of using it lightly constituted for him the chief interest and attraction of his new job. In the work itself, in the actual investigations, Ivan Ilyich very quickly mastered a way of setting aside all circumstances that didn't relate to the investigation and expressing the most complicated case in a terminology in which the case only appeared on paper in its externals and his personal view was completely excluded, and most importantly all requisite formality was observed. This work was something new. And he was one of the first people who worked out the practical application of the statutes of 1864.[7]

Moving to a new city to the post of examining magistrate, Ivan Ilyich made new acquaintances and connections, positioned himself afresh, and adopted a slightly different tone. He positioned himself at a certain respectable distance from the governing authorities, but chose the best circle of the lawyers and nobles who lived in the city and adopted a tone of slight dissatisfaction with government, moderate liberalism, and enlightened civic-mindedness. Moreover, without changing the elegance of his dress, in his new job Ivan Ilyich stopped shaving his chin and let his beard grow freely.

Ivan Ilyich's life turned out very pleasantly in the new city as well: the society that took a critical view of the governor was good and friendly; his salary was larger; and a not inconsiderable pleasure was added to his life by *vint*, which Ivan Ilyich started to play, having an ability to play cards cheerfully, quick-wittedly, and very shrewdly so that generally he won.

After two years working in the new city Ivan Ilyich met his future wife. Praskovya Fyodorovna Mikhel was the most attractive, cleverest, most brilliant girl of the group in which Ivan Ilyich moved. Among the other amusements and relaxations from the labors of a magistrate Ivan Ilyich developed a playful, easy relationship with Praskovya Fyodorovna.

While he had been a special assignments official Ivan Ilyich used to dance as a matter of course; as an examining magistrate he now danced only on special occasions. He danced now in the sense that although he was a part of

---

7. The emancipation of the serfs in 1861 was followed by a thorough all-round reform of judicial proceedings [translators' note].

the new institutions and in the fifth grade,[8] when it came to dancing, then he could show that in this field he could do things better than others. So from time to time at the end of an evening he used to dance with Praskovya Fyodorovna, and it was during these dances in particular that he conquered her. She fell in love with him. Ivan Ilyich didn't have a clear, defined intention of marrying, but when the girl fell in love with him, he asked himself a question. "Actually, why not get married?" he said to himself.

Miss Praskovya Fyodorovna was from a good noble family, was not bad-looking, and had a bit of money. Ivan Ilyich could aspire to a more brilliant match, but this too was a good match. Ivan Ilyich had his salary; she, he hoped, would have as much again. The family connection was good; she was a sweet, pretty, and absolutely decent woman. To say that Ivan Ilyich married because he fell in love with his bride and found in her sympathy for his views on life would have been as unjust as to say that he married because people in his social circle approved of the match. Ivan Ilyich married because of both considerations: he was doing something pleasant for himself in acquiring such a wife, and at the same time he was doing something his superiors thought a right thing to do.

And so Ivan Ilyich married.

The actual process of marriage and the first period of married life, with its conjugal caresses, new furniture, new china, and new linen, went very well until his wife's pregnancy, so that Ivan Ilyich was beginning to think that marriage not only would not destroy the character of an easy, pleasant, cheerful life, one wholly decorous and approved of by society, which Ivan Ilyich thought the true quality of life, but would enhance it further. But then from the first months of his wife's pregnancy something new appeared, something unexpected, unpleasant, oppressive, and indecorous that one couldn't expect and from which one couldn't escape.

His wife for no reason, so Ivan Ilyich thought, as he said to himself, began *de gaieté de coeur*[9] to destroy the pleasant tenor and decorum of life. She was jealous of him without any cause, demanded attentions to herself from him, found fault with everything, and made crude and unpleasant scenes.

At first Ivan Ilyich had hoped to be freed from the unpleasantness of this situation by the same easy and decorous attitude to life which had rescued him before—he tried to ignore his wife's state of mind and continued to live pleasantly and decorously as before: he invited friends home for a game of cards; he tried to go out to his club or see his friends. But on one occasion his wife started to abuse him rudely with such energy and continued to abuse him so persistently every time he didn't fulfill her demands, clearly having made a firm decision not to stop until he would submit—that is, sit at home and be miserable like her—that Ivan Ilyich was horrified. He understood that married life—at any rate with his wife—does not always make for the pleasures and decorum of life but on the contrary often destroys them, and therefore it was essential to protect himself from this destruction. And Ivan Ilyich began to seek the means for this. His official work was one thing that impressed Praskovya Fyodorovna, and Ivan

8. That is, the government service sector of the Table of Ranks; the fifth grade was reserved for high-ranking civil servants.

9. Literally, "from gaiety of heart" (French); that is, from sheer impulsiveness.

Ilyich through his official work and the duties that arose out of it began to fight his wife, securing his own independent world.

A child was born. There were attempts at feeding and various failures in this, along with the real and imaginary illnesses of child and mother. Sympathy for all this was demanded from Ivan Ilyich but he could understand nothing of it. So the requirement of Ivan Ilyich to fence in a world for himself outside of the family became all the more pressing.

As his wife became more irritable and demanding, so Ivan Ilyich moved the center of gravity of his life more and more into his official work. He came to like his work more and became more ambitious than he had been before.

Very soon, not more than a year after their marriage, Ivan Ilyich understood that married life, which offers certain conveniences, in reality is a very complicated and difficult business with which, in order to do one's duty—that is, to lead a decorous life that is approved of by society—one has to develop a defined relationship as one does with one's work.

And Ivan Ilyich did develop for himself such a relationship with married life. He required of family life only those conveniences it could give him, of dinner at home, a mistress of the house, a bed, and most importantly, that decorum of external appearances which were defined by public opinion. For the rest he looked for cheerfulness and pleasure, and if he found them was very grateful; if he met rejection and querulousness, he at once went off into the separate world of official work that he had fenced in for himself and found pleasure there.

Ivan Ilyich was valued as a good official and in three years he was made assistant prosecutor. His new responsibilities, their importance, the ability to bring anyone to trial and send him to prison, the public nature of his speeches, the success Ivan Ilyich had in this work—all of this tied him even more closely to his official work.

More children came. His wife became more and more querulous and angry, but the relationship Ivan Ilyich had developed with domestic life had made him almost impervious to her querulousness.

After seven years of working in one city Ivan Ilyich was promoted to the position of prosecutor in a different province. They moved; they now had little money and his wife didn't like the place to which they had moved. Though his salary was more than it had been, life cost more; also two children died, and so family life became even more unpleasant for Ivan Ilyich.

Praskovya Fyodorovna blamed her husband for all the misfortunes that befell them in their new home. Most subjects of conversation between husband and wife, particularly the education of the children, led to questions that recalled past disputes, and quarrels were ready to break out at every minute. There remained only rare periods of tenderness that came to the married couple but did not last long. These were islands on which they landed for a while but then again sailed off into the sea of hidden animosity which expressed itself in their alienation from each other. This alienation might have distressed Ivan Ilyich if he had thought that it should not be like this, but he now recognized this situation not just as normal but as the actual goal of his family life. His object was to free himself more and more from these unpleasant things and to give them a character of innocuous decorum; he achieved it by spending less and less time with his family and when he was forced to do it, he tried to protect his situation by the presence of outsiders. The important thing was that Ivan

Ilyich had his official work. For him all the interest of life was concentrated in that official world, and this interest absorbed him. The consciousness of his power, of his ability to bring down anyone he chose to, his importance, even in externals when he entered the court and at meetings with subordinates, his mastery of conducting the work—all this made him feel glad, and together with talking to his friends, with dinners and *vint*, it filled up his life. So overall Ivan Ilyich's life continued to go on as he thought that it should: pleasantly and with decorum.

So he lived for another seven years. His elder daughter was now sixteen, another child had died, and there only remained a boy at the gymnasium, a subject of dissension. Ivan Ilyich had wanted to send him to law school but to spite him Praskovya Fyodorovna had sent the boy to the gymnasium. The daughter was taught at home and had grown into a good-looking girl; the boy too wasn't bad at his studies.

III

That was Ivan Ilyich's life for seventeen years after his marriage. He was now a senior prosecutor, having refused various promotions in the expectation of a more desirable position, when something very unpleasant happened which completely destroyed the tranquility of his life. Ivan Ilyich was expecting the position of president of the tribunal in a university town, but somehow Hoppe overtook him and got the place. Ivan Ilyich was angry, started to make accusations, and quarreled with him and his closest superiors; they cooled towards him and passed him over for the next appointment.

That was in 1880. That year was the hardest in Ivan Ilyich's life. In that year his salary wasn't sufficient for living; everyone forgot him, and what appeared to him to be the greatest, the cruelest injustice toward him was found by others to be something completely ordinary. Even his father didn't see it as his duty to help him. He felt everyone had abandoned him, considering his situation on a 3,500-ruble[1] salary quite normal and even fortunate. He alone knew that with his consciousness of the injustices done to him, his wife's constant nagging, and the debts he was beginning to run, living above his means—he alone knew that his situation was far from normal.

In the summer of that year, to ease his finances he took some leave and went with his wife to spend the summer at Praskovya Fyodorovna's brother's home.

In the country, without his work, Ivan Ilyich for the first time felt not just boredom but unbearable depression, felt that he could not live like that and that he absolutely had to take some decisive action.

Having spent a sleepless night pacing the terrace, Ivan Ilyich decided to go to Petersburg to make a petition and, in order to punish *them*, those who could not appreciate him, to transfer to another ministry.

The next day, in spite of all the attempts of his wife and brother-in-law to dissuade him, he traveled to Petersburg.

He went for one thing: to obtain a five-thousand-ruble[2] salary. He was no longer holding out for any particular ministry or direction or type of work. He

---

1. The equivalent of nearly $100,000 in today's U.S. currency.

2. The equivalent of over $140,000, in today's U.S. currency.

just needed a position, a position on five thousand rubles, in government, in banking, in the railways, in the Empress Maria's Foundations,[3] even in customs, but he absolutely had to have five thousand rubles and he absolutely had to leave the ministry where they couldn't appreciate him.

And now this trip of Ivan Ilyich's was crowned with amazing, unexpected success. In Kursk he was joined in a first-class carriage by F. S. Ilyin, someone he knew, who told him about a telegram the governor of Kursk had just received that announced a reorganization to take place in the ministry: Pyotr Ivanovich's position was going to be taken by Ivan Semyonovich.

The planned upheaval, apart from its significance for Russia, had a particular significance for Ivan Ilyich: by promoting a new face, Pyotr Petrovich, and of course Zakhar Ivanovich, his classmate and friend, it was highly propitious for him.

In Moscow the news was confirmed. And when he reached Petersburg, Ivan Ilyich found Zakhar Ivanovich and got the promise of a sure place in his old ministry of justice.

After a week he telegraphed his wife: *Zakhar has Miller's place stop*[4] *I receive position at next report.*

Thanks to this change of personnel Ivan Ilyich got this position in his old ministry, which placed him two ranks above his old colleagues as well as a salary of 5,000 rubles and 3,500 for removal expenses. All his anger against his former enemies and the entire ministry was forgotten, and Ivan Ilyich was altogether happy.

Ivan Ilyich returned to the country more cheerful and content than he had ever been. Praskovya Fyodorovna cheered up too and a truce was established between them. Ivan Ilyich told her how in Petersburg everyone had feted him, how all his old enemies had been shamed and were now crawling before him, how he was envied for his position, and especially how highly he was regarded by everyone in Petersburg.

Praskovya Fyodorovna listened to all this and appeared to believe it, and she didn't contradict him in anything but just made plans for their new life in the city to which they were moving. And Ivan Ilyich joyfully saw that these plans were his plans, that the plans were tallying, and that his life which had faltered was again taking on its true and natural character of cheerful pleasantness and decorum.

Ivan Ilyich had come just for a short time. On September 10 he had to take up the new job and furthermore he needed time to settle in their new home, to move everything from the provincial city, and to buy and order many more things; in a word, to settle as had been decided in his own mind and almost exactly as had been decided in that of Praskovya Fyodorovna.

And now, when everything had worked out so well and he and his wife were agreed about their goals (and furthermore weren't living much together), they got on harmoniously as they hadn't done since the first years of married life. Ivan Ilyich thought of taking his family away with him immediately but the insistence of his brother-in-law and his wife, who had suddenly become

3. Reference to the charitable organization founded by the Empress Maria, wife of Paul I, late in the 18th century.

4. Indicating a period (full stop) in a telegram.

particularly friendly and familial towards Ivan Ilyich and his family, resulted in Ivan Ilyich going away alone.

Ivan Ilyich left, and the cheerful state of mind brought about by his success and the harmony with his wife, one reinforcing the other, stayed with him the whole time. A delightful apartment was found, the very one husband and wife had been dreaming of. High, spacious, old-fashioned reception rooms; a comfortable, imposing study; rooms for his wife and daughter; a schoolroom for his son—everything as if devised purposely for them. Ivan Ilyich set about arranging it himself: he chose wallpaper, he bought more furniture (antiques in particular whose style he found particularly *comme il faut*), he had things upholstered, and it all grew and grew and approached the ideal he had composed for himself. Even when he had half arranged things, his arrangements exceeded his expectation. He understood the *comme il faut* look, elegant without vulgarity, which everything would take on once it was ready. As he went to sleep he imagined to himself how the reception room would be. Looking at the drawing room, which wasn't yet finished, he could already see the fireplace, the screen, the whatnot and the little chairs disposed about the room, the plates and saucers on the walls, and the bronzes all standing in their places. He was pleased by the thought that he would surprise Pasha and Lizanka, his wife and daughter, who also had a taste for this. They were certainly not expecting this. He was particularly successful in finding old things and buying them cheaply; they gave everything a particularly aristocratic air. In his letters he deliberately described everything in less attractive terms than the reality to surprise them. All this absorbed him so much that even his new job absorbed him less than he had expected—though he loved his work. During sittings of the court he had moments of absent-mindedness; he started thinking about whether the curtain pelmets[5] should be straight or curved. He was so absorbed by this that he often did things himself; he even moved the furniture about and rehung the curtains himself. Once he got up on a ladder to show a slow-witted decorator how he wanted the drapes hung; he missed his footing and fell, but being a strong and agile man he held his balance and only knocked his side on the handle of the window frame. The bruise was painful but soon disappeared. During all this time Ivan Ilyich felt particularly well and cheerful. He wrote, "I feel I'm fifteen years younger." He thought the work would be finished in September but it dragged on till mid-October. But the apartment was delightful—it wasn't just he who said this but everyone who saw it said so to him.

In actual fact it was the same as the houses of all people who are not so rich but want to be like the rich and so are only like one another: brocade, ebony, flowers, carpets, and bronzes, everything dark and shiny—everything that all people of a certain type do to be like all people of a certain type. And what he had was so like that that one couldn't even notice it, but to him it all looked somehow special. When he met his family at the railway station and took them to his apartment, all finished and lit up, and a manservant in a white tie opened the door into the flower-decked hall, and they went into the drawing room and study, he was very happy, he took them everywhere, drank

---

5. Fabric borders above windows, used to hide curtain fittings.

in their praise, and beamed with pleasure. That evening, when over tea Praskovya Fyodorovna asked him among other things how he had fallen, he laughed and in front of them showed how he had gone flying and frightened the decorator.

"It's lucky I am a gymnast. Someone else might have been killed but I only knocked myself a bit here; when you touch it—it hurts, but it'll pass; it's just a bruise."

And they started to live in the new home which, as always, once they had settled in properly, turned out to have one room too few, with the new income which, as always, turned out to be too little (only not by very much—five hundred rubles). And life was very good. Especially good at first when all was not yet done and more still had to be done: things to be bought, ordered, moved, adjusted. Although there were some disagreements between husband and wife, they were both so pleased and there was so much to do that everything was finished without serious quarrels. When there was nothing left to do, it became a bit more boring and something seemed lacking, but now friendships were made and habits established and life filled up.

After spending the morning in court Ivan Ilyich returned for dinner, and at first his mood was good, although it suffered a little, specifically because of their home. (Every stain on a tablecloth or brocade or broken curtain cord irritated him; he had put so much work into the arrangement that every disruption of it was painful to him.) But in general Ivan Ilyich's life went on just as in his view life should flow: easily, pleasantly, and decorously. He rose at nine, drank his coffee, read the newspapers, then put on his uniform and drove to the court. There the harness in which he worked was already molded for him and he slipped into it right away: petitioners, chancery inquiries, the chancery itself, public and executive sittings of the court. In all of these one had to know how to exclude anything raw and vital, which always destroys the even flow of official work: one couldn't admit any human relationships except official ones; the occasion for a relationship had to be solely official and so had the relationship itself. For example, a man would come in and want to find out something. Outside his official role Ivan Ilyich could not have any relationship with him; but if this man had a relationship with him as a member of the court—one that could be expressed on headed paper—then within the bounds of this relationship Ivan Ilyich would do everything, absolutely everything he could, and in doing this would observe the semblance of friendly relations, that is, courtesy. As soon as the official relationship was ended, so was any other. This ability to separate out the official side without combining it with his real life Ivan Ilyich possessed in the highest degree, and by his talents and long practice he had developed it to such a point that he even sometimes, like a virtuoso, would allow himself as if in jest to combine personal and official relationships. He would allow himself this because he always felt in himself the power to split off the official again when necessary and to reject the personal. Ivan Ilyich handled this work of his not just easily, agreeably, and decorously but even with the mastery of a virtuoso. Between cases he would smoke, drink tea, chat a bit about politics, a bit about generalities, a bit about cards, and most of all about official appointments. And he would return home tired but with the feeling of a virtuoso who had given a lucid performance of his part, one of the first violins in the orchestra. At home mother and daughter would go out somewhere or someone came to see them; his son was at the gymnasium, preparing his lessons with tutors and diligently studying the things they teach in a gymnasium. Everything was good. After dinner, if there were no guests, Ivan Ilyich would sometimes read a book about which people were talking a lot, and in the evenings he would sit down to his work, that is, read his papers, consult the law, examine testimony, and check it against the law. All this he found neither boring nor amusing. It was boring if he could be playing *vint*; but if there was no *vint*—then all the same this was better than sitting by himself or with his wife. Ivan Ilyich's pleasures were little dinners to which he would invite ladies and gentlemen who were important in terms of worldly position and spending his time with them: that was just like the usual way such people spend their time, just as his drawing room was like all drawing rooms.

Once they even had an evening party, with dancing. And Ivan Ilyich felt cheerful and everything was good, except he had a big quarrel with his wife over the cakes and sweets: Praskovya Fyodorovna had her own plan, but Ivan Ilyich insisted on getting everything from an expensive confectioner and the quarrel was because there were cakes left over and the confectioner's bill came to forty-five rubles.[6] The quarrel was a big and unpleasant one to such a point that Praskovya Fyodorovna called him "an idiot and a misery," and he took his head in his hands and in a fit of temper said something about divorce. But the actual party was enjoyable. The very best society was there and Ivan Ilyich danced with Princess Trufonova, sister of the famous founder of the Goodbye Sorrow Society. His official pleasures were pleasures of pride; his social pleasures were pleasures of vanity; but Ivan Ilyich's real pleasures were the pleasures of playing *vint*. He admitted that after all the various unhappy events in his life the pleasure that burnt like a candle above all others was to sit down at *vint* with good players and partners who didn't shout, definitely in a four (when you're five it's really annoying to have to stand out, although you pretend you very much like it), and to have an intelligent, serious game (when the cards are right), and then to have supper and drink a glass of wine. After *vint*, especially after a little win (a big win was unpleasant), Ivan Ilyich went to bed in an especially good mood.

That's how they lived. They formed around them a group of the best society, important people went to them and young people, too.

Husband, wife, and daughter were agreed in their views of their circle of acquaintances, and without any formal understanding they dropped and were rid of all sorts of shabby little friends and relatives who used to drop in to see them, spouting endearments into the drawing room with Japanese plates hanging on the wall. Soon these shabby little friends stopped dropping in and the Golovins were left with just the very best society. Young men paid court to Lizanka and Petrishchev, an examining magistrate, the son of Dmitry Ivanovich Petrishchev and sole heir to his property, began to pay so much attention to her that Ivan Ilyich even talked about it to Praskovya Fyodorovna. Shouldn't they bring them together in a troika ride or organize some theatricals? That's how they lived. And everything went on like that, without any change, and everything was very good.

---

6. The equivalent of over $1,200 in today's U.S. currency.

IV

They were all in good health. One couldn't call poor health the fact that Ivan Ilyich sometimes said he had an odd taste in his mouth and something felt uncomfortable on the left side of his stomach.

But it happened that this discomfort started to grow and to become not quite pain but the consciousness of a constant heaviness in his side accompanied by a bad mood. This bad mood, which got worse and worse, began to spoil the pleasant course of the easy and decorous life that had been established in the Golovin house. Husband and wife began to quarrel more and more often, and soon the ease and pleasantness disappeared and only decorum was preserved, with difficulty. Again scenes became more frequent. Again there remained just some islands of calm, and only a few of those, on which husband and wife could meet without an outburst.

And Praskovya Fyodorovna now said, not without cause, that her husband had a difficult character. With her natural habit of exaggeration she said he had always had this dreadful character, and that one needed her good nature to stand it for twenty years. It was true that the quarrels now started with him. His fault-finding always began just before dinner and often when he was starting to eat, over the soup. He would remark that one of the dishes was damaged, or the food wasn't right, or his son had his elbow on the table, or it was his daughter's hairstyle. And he blamed Praskovya Fyodorovna for everything. At first Praskovya Fyodorovna answered back and was rude to him, but a couple of times at the beginning of dinner he flew into such a rage that she understood this was a morbid condition brought on by the intake of food, so she controlled herself and didn't answer back but ate her dinner quickly. Praskovya Fyodorovna regarded her self-control as greatly to her own credit. Having decided that her husband had a dreadful character and that he had created the unhappiness of her life, she started to feel sorry for herself. And the more she felt sorry for herself, the more she hated her husband. She began to wish that he would die, but she couldn't wish for that because then there would be no salary. And that irritated her even more. She considered herself terribly unhappy precisely because even his death could not rescue her and she became irritated; she concealed it and her concealed irritation increased his own irritation.

After one scene, in which Ivan Ilyich was particularly unfair, and after which in explaining himself he said he was indeed prone to irritability but that it came from his illness, she said to him that if he was ill then he must get treatment, and demanded from him that he see a famous doctor.

He went. Everything was as he had expected; everything happened as it always does. The waiting and the doctor's assumed pompousness, something familiar to him that he knew from himself in court, and the tapping and the auscultation[7] and the questions requiring predetermined and clearly unnecessary answers, and the meaningful air suggesting that you just submit to us, we'll fix everything—we know, we have no doubts about how to fix everything, in the very same way for any man you choose. Everything was precisely as in court. Just as he in court put on an air towards the

---

7. Listening to internal organs, as with a stethoscope.

accused, so in precisely the same way the famous doctor put on an air towards him.

The doctor said: such and such shows that you have such and such inside; but if that isn't confirmed by examining such and such, then one must assume you have such and such. If one does assume such and such, then . . . and so forth. Only one question was important to Ivan Ilyich: was his condition dangerous or not? But the doctor ignored this inappropriate question. From the doctor's point of view the question was pointless and wasn't the one under discussion; it was only a question of assessing various possibilities—a floating kidney, chronic catarrh, or an infection of the appendix. It wasn't a question of Ivan Ilyich's life but an argument between a floating kidney and the appendix. And before Ivan Ilyich's eyes the doctor resolved the argument brilliantly in favor of the floating kidney, with the reservation that an examination of his urine could provide new evidence and then the case would be looked at again. All this was very precisely what Ivan Ilyich himself had done a thousand times with defendants and as brilliantly. The doctor did his summing-up just as brilliantly, triumphantly, even cheerfully, looking at the defendant over his glasses. From the doctor's summing-up Ivan Ilyich drew the conclusion that things were bad, that it didn't matter much to the doctor or probably to anyone else, but that for him things were bad. And Ivan Ilyich was painfully struck by this conclusion that aroused in him a feeling of great self-pity and of great anger toward this doctor who was indifferent to such an important question.

But he didn't say anything and got up, put the money on the desk, and said with a sigh:

"Probably we patients often put inappropriate questions to you. In general terms, is this a dangerous illness or not?"

The doctor gave him one stern look through his glasses as if to say: Accused, if you will not stay within the boundaries of the questions that are put to you, then I will be compelled to give instructions for your removal from the courtroom.

"I have already told you what I consider necessary and proper," said the doctor. "An examination will show the rest." And the doctor bowed.

Ivan Ilyich slowly went out, despondently got into the sleigh, and went home. For the whole journey he ceaselessly went over everything the doctor had said, trying to turn those confused, unclear, scientific words into simple language and to read in them an answer to the question: Am I in a bad way, or a very bad way, or aren't things yet so bad? And he thought that the sense of everything the doctor had said was that he was in a very bad way. Everything in the streets looked sad to Ivan Ilyich. The cab drivers were sad, the houses were sad, the passersby, the shops. This pain, this dull nagging pain that didn't stop for a single second, combined with the doctor's unclear pronouncements acquired another more serious meaning. Ivan Ilyich listened to his pain with a new heavy feeling.

He arrived home and started to tell his wife. His wife listened but in the middle of his account his daughter came in wearing a hat: she and her mother were going out. She sat down for a moment to listen to this boring stuff but she couldn't stand it for long, and her mother didn't listen to the end.

"Now I'm very pleased," his wife said. "So mind you take your medicine properly. Give me the prescription, I'll send Gerasim to the chemist's." And she went to dress.

While she was in the room he was barely able to breathe and he sighed heavily when she went out.

"Well then," he said. "Perhaps it's not so bad."

He began to take the medicines and to follow the doctor's directions, which changed after the urine examination. But it was the case now that there had been some kind of confusion in the examination and in what followed from it. It was impossible to get through to the doctor himself, but it turned out that what was happening was not what the doctor had told him. Either he had forgotten or he had lied or he had concealed something from Ivan Ilyich.

But Ivan Ilyich still started to follow the directions precisely and in doing so at first found some comfort.

From the time he visited the doctor Ivan Ilyich's chief occupations became the precise following of the doctor's directions about hygiene and the monitoring of his pain and all his bodily functions. Ivan Ilyich's chief interests became human illness and human health. When others talked in front of him about people who were ill or had died or had gotten better, and in particular about any illness that resembled his own, he would listen, trying to conceal his agitation, ask questions, and apply what was said to his own illness.

The pain got no less but Ivan Ilyich made an effort to force himself to think he was better. And he could deceive himself as long as nothing disturbed him. But as soon as there was some unpleasantness with his wife or something went wrong at work or he had bad cards at *vint*, he at once felt the full force of his illness. In the past he had endured things going wrong in the expectation that *I'll soon put things right, I'll overcome, I'll be successful, I'll get a grand slam.* Now anything that went wrong brought him down and cast him into despair. He would say to himself, "I was just starting to get better and the medicine was already beginning to work, and along comes this cursed accident or unpleasantness. . . ." And he was angry with the accident or with the people who were causing him unpleasantnesses and killing him, and he felt that this anger was killing him but he couldn't restrain himself. One might have thought it would have been clear to him that this anger against circumstances and people made his illness worse, and that therefore he shouldn't pay any attention to unpleasant incidents, but his reasoning was quite the reverse: He said he needed calm; he watched out for anything that might breach that calm and at the smallest breach he got angry. His condition was made worse by the fact that he consulted medical books and doctors. His deterioration progressed so evenly that comparing one day with another he could deceive himself—there was little difference. But when he consulted doctors, he thought he was getting worse and that very quickly. And in spite of that he constantly consulted doctors.

That month he went to see another celebrity doctor; this other celebrity doctor said almost the same as the first but put the questions differently. And consulting this celebrity doctor only deepened Ivan Ilyich's doubt and terror. A friend of a friend—a very good doctor—diagnosed his illness quite differently, and in spite of promising recovery, his questions and assumptions confused Ivan Ilyich even more and increased his doubts. A homeopath diagnosed his illness again quite differently and gave him some medicine, and Ivan Ilyich took it in secret from everyone for about a week. But after a week, feeling no relief and having lost confidence both in the previous treatments and in this one, he fell into greater despair. On one occasion a lady he knew was talking about the healing powers of icons.[8] Ivan Ilyich found himself listening carefully and believing the reality of this. This incident frightened him. "Have I really become so feeble-minded?" he said to himself. "What rubbish! It's all nonsense. I mustn't give in to hypochondria, but having chosen one doctor I must firmly stick to his treatment. That's what I'll do. Now it's settled. I'm not going to think and I'm going to follow the treatment strictly till the summer. Then there'll be something to show. Let's now have an end to all this wavering!" It was easy to say that but impossible to put it into action. The pain in his side wore him down; it seemed to keep getting worse; it became constant; the taste in his mouth became stronger; he thought a disgusting smell was coming from his mouth; and his appetite and strength were going. He couldn't deceive himself: something terrible, new, and important was happening in him, something more important than anything that had happened to Ivan Ilyich in his life. And only he knew about this; all those around him either didn't understand or didn't want to understand and thought that everything in the world was going on as before. That was what tormented Ivan Ilyich most of all. He could see that his household—chiefly his wife and daughter who were in the full swing of visits and parties—understood nothing, and they were vexed that he was so gloomy and demanding, as if he were guilty in that. Although they tried to conceal it, he saw that he was a burden to them, but that his wife had evolved a particular attitude to his illness and adhered to that irrespective of what he said and did. Her attitude was like this:

"You know," she would say to friends, "Ivan Ilyich can't strictly follow a prescribed treatment, as most good people can. Today he'll take his drops and eat what he's been told to and go to bed in good time, but tomorrow if I don't look properly, he'll suddenly forget to take them and eat oysters (which are forbidden him) and sit down to *vint* till one in the morning."

"When did I do that?" Ivan Ilyich would say crossly. "Once at Pyotr Ivanovich's."

"Yesterday with Shebek."

"I just couldn't sleep from the pain . . ."

"Well, whatever it was from, like that you won't get better and you make us miserable."

Praskovya Fyodorovna's public attitude to her husband's illness, which she expressed to others and to him, was that this illness was Ivan Ilyich's own fault and that the whole illness was a new unpleasantness he was bringing down on his wife. Ivan Ilyich felt that this came out in her involuntarily, but that didn't make it any easier for him.

In court Ivan Ilyich noticed or thought he noticed the same strange attitude to him: now he would think that people were scrutinizing him like a man whose position was soon going to be vacant; now all of a sudden his friends would start to joke in an amicable way about his hypochondria, as if this thing, this awful, terrible, unheard-of thing that had grown in him and was ceaselessly gnawing at him and irrepressibly dragging him somewhere, were the most pleasant subject for a joke. He was especially irritated by Schwarz with his playfulness and energy and *comme il faut* ways, all of which reminded Ivan Ilyich of himself ten years back.

---

8. Paintings of religious images, commonly used for devotional purposes in the Russian Orthodox Church.

Friends came to make up a game; they sat down. They dealt, bending the new cards; he put diamonds next to diamonds, seven of them. His partner bid no trumps—and held two diamonds. What could be better? Things were cheerful and bright—they had a grand slam. And suddenly Ivan Ilyich felt that gnawing pain, that taste in the mouth, and there seemed to him to be something absurd in the fact that he could rejoice in a grand slam.

He looked at Mikhail Mikhaylovich, his partner, rapping his powerful hand on the table and politely and condescendingly refraining from scooping up the tricks but pushing the cards toward Ivan Ilyich to give him the pleasure of picking them up without straining himself and stretching out his arm. "Does he think I'm so weak I can't stretch out my arm?" Ivan Ilyich thought. He forgot about trumps and trumped his partner, losing the grand slam by three tricks— and what was really dreadful was that he saw how Mikhail Mikhaylovich was suffering, but he didn't care. And it was dreadful to think just why he didn't care.

They all saw he was feeling bad and said to him, "We can stop if you are tired. You must rest." Rest? No, he wasn't tired at all, and they finished the rubber. They were all gloomy and silent. Ivan Ilyich felt he had brought down this gloom upon them and he couldn't dispel it. They had supper and went their ways, and Ivan Ilyich was left alone with the knowledge that his life had been poisoned for him, that it was poisoning the lives of others, and that this poison wasn't losing its power but was penetrating his whole being more and more.

And with this knowledge, with the physical pain, and with the terror, he had to get into bed and often be unable to sleep from the pain the greater part of the night. And the next morning he had to get up again, dress, go to court, talk, write, or if he didn't go to court he had to stay at home with those twenty-four hours of the day, each one of which was a torment. And he had to live like that on the brink of the abyss, all alone, without a single person who could understand and take pity on him.

V

A month went by like that and then another. Before the new year his brother-in-law came to the city and stayed with them. Ivan Ilyich was in court. Praskovya Fyodorovna had gone out shopping. When Ivan Ilyich went into his study he found his brother-in-law, a healthy, full-blooded fellow, unpacking his suitcase himself. He raised his head when he heard Ivan Ilyich's footsteps and looked at him for a second in silence. That look revealed everything to Ivan Ilyich. His brother-in-law opened his mouth to say "oh" and stopped himself. That movement confirmed everything.

"So, I've changed, haven't I?"

"Yes . . . there is a change."

And however much afterwards Ivan Ilyich turned the conversation with his brother-in-law to his appearance, his brother-in-law said nothing. Praskovya Fyodorovna arrived, his brother-in-law went out to her. Ivan Ilyich locked his door and started to examine himself in the mirror—face-on, then from the side. He took up a photograph of himself with his wife and compared the image with the one he saw in the mirror. The change was huge. Then he bared his arms to the elbow, looked, rolled his sleeves down again, and sat on an ottoman, and his mood became darker than night.

"You mustn't, you mustn't," he said to himself; he jumped up, went to the desk, opened a case file, and began to read it, but he couldn't. He unlocked the door and went into the salon. The drawing-room door was shut. He tiptoed to it and began to listen.

"No, you're exaggerating," said Praskovya Fyodorovna.

"Exaggerating? You don't see—he's a dead man, look at his eyes. There's no light in them. What's the matter with him?"

"Nobody knows. Nikolayev [that was the second doctor] said something, but I don't know what. Leshchetitsky [that was the celebrated doctor] said the opposite . . ."

Ivan Ilyich moved away, went to his room, lay down, and started to think: *A kidney, a floating kidney.* He remembered everything the doctor had told him—how it had become detached and was floating. And with an effort of the imagination he tried to understand his kidney and to halt it and strengthen it; so little was needed for that, he thought. *No, I'll go again to Pyotr Ivanovich.* (That was the friend who had a friend who was a doctor.) He rang, gave orders for the horse to be harnessed, and got ready to leave.

"Where are you off to, *Jean?*"[9] his wife said, using a particularly sad and unusually kind expression.

This unusual kindness angered him. He looked at her morosely.

"I have to go to Pyotr Ivanovich."

He went to his friend who had a friend who was a doctor. He found him at home and had a long conversation with him.

When he considered both the anatomical and physiological details of what, in the doctor's opinion, had been happening inside him, he understood everything.

There was something, a little something in the appendix. All that might be put right. Stimulate the activity of one organ, weaken the activity of another; the something would be absorbed and everything would be put right. He got back a little late for dinner, talked cheerfully for a bit, but for a long time he couldn't go to his room to work. Finally he went into his study and at once sat down to work. He read his cases and worked, but the consciousness that he had set something aside—an important and intimate matter which he would take up once his work was over—did not leave him. When he had finished his cases, he remembered that this intimate matter was his thinking about his appendix. But he didn't indulge it; he went to the drawing room for tea. There were guests, including the examining magistrate, his daughter's intended; they talked and played the piano and sang. Ivan Ilyich spent the evening, as Praskovya Fyodorovna noticed, more cheerfully than he had spent others, but he didn't forget for one minute that he had set aside some important thinking about his appendix. At eleven o'clock he said goodnight and went to his room. Since he had become ill he slept in a little room next to his study. He went in, undressed, and picked up a novel of Zola's,[1] which he didn't read.

---

9. French for Ivan (in English, John).
1. Émile Zola (1840–1902), French novelist, author of the Rougon-Macquart novels (*Nana*,

Germinal, etc.). Tolstoy condemned Zola for his naturalistic theories and considered his novels crude.

He began thinking instead. The desired cure of the appendix took place in his imagination. Matter was absorbed, matter was expelled, and normal activity was restored. "Yes, that's how it all is," he said to himself. "Only nature needs a little help." He remembered his medicine, sat up, took it, watching for the beneficial effects of the medicine and the removal of the pain. "Just take it regularly and avoid unhealthy influences; I already feel a bit better, much better." He started to feel his side—it wasn't painful to the touch. "Yes, I can't feel it; I'm really much better now." He put out the candle and lay on his side. "The appendix is getting better; things are being absorbed." Suddenly he felt the familiar old dull nagging pain, the persistent, quiet, serious pain. The familiar nastiness in his mouth. His heart began to pump, his head turned. "My God, my God!" he said. "It's here again, it's here again and it's never going to stop." And suddenly his case presented itself to him from a different perspective. "Appendix! Kidney!" he said to himself. "It's not a case of the appendix or of the kidney, but of life . . . and death. Yes, I had life and now it's passing, passing, and I can't hold it back. That's it. Why deceive oneself? Isn't it obvious to everyone but myself that I am dying, and it's only a question of the number of weeks, days—maybe now. There was light and now there's darkness. I was here but now I'm going there! Where?" A chill came over him, his breathing stopped. He could only hear the beating of his heart.

"I won't exist, so what will exist? Nothing will exist. So where will I be when I don't exist? Is this really death? No, I don't want it." He got up quickly, tried to light a candle, groped with shaking hands, dropped the candle and candlestick on the floor, and slumped back again onto the pillow. "Why? Nothing matters," he said to himself, looking into the darkness with open eyes. "Death. Yes, death. And none of them knows and they don't want to know and they have no pity for me. They're enjoying themselves." Outside the door he could hear the distant noise of music and singing. "They don't care but they too will die. Fools. It'll come to me first, to them later; they too will have the same. But they're having fun, the beasts!" Anger choked him. And he felt painful, unbearable misery. "It cannot be that we're all doomed to this terrible fear." He raised himself.

"Something's not right; I must calm down, I must think over everything from the outset." And he began to think. "Yes, the start of my illness. I knocked my side, and I stayed just the same that day and the next; it ached a bit, then more, then the doctors, then depression, despair, the doctors again; and I kept getting nearer and nearer to the abyss. Less strength. Nearer and nearer. And now I've wasted away, there's no light in my eyes. And death, and I think about my appendix. I think of how to mend my appendix, but this is death. Is it really death?" Again horror came over him; he bent down, tried to find the matches, and banged his elbow on the nighttable. It got in his way and hurt him; he got angry with it; in his irritation he banged his elbow harder and knocked the nighttable over. And in his despair he fell back, gasping for breath, expecting death to come now.

Now the guests were leaving. Praskovya Fyodorovna was seeing them out. She heard something fall and came in.

"What's the matter with you?"

"Nothing. I knocked it over by mistake."

She went out and brought back a candle. He lay breathing heavily and very fast, like a man who has run a mile, looking at her with motionless eyes.

"What's the matter with you, *Jean?*"

"Nothing. I . . . knocked . . . it . . . over." (*What should I say? She won't understand*, he thought.)

Indeed she didn't. She picked the table up, lit a candle for him, and quickly went out; she had to see a guest out.

When she returned, he was lying in the same position, on his back, looking up.

"How are you feeling? Is it worse?"

"Yes, it is."

She shook her head and sat down.

"You know, *Jean*, I am wondering whether we shouldn't ask Leshchetitsky to the house."

That meant asking the celebrated doctor regardless of cost. He smiled venomously and said, "No." She sat for a while, then went over to him and kissed him on the forehead.

When she kissed him he hated her with all his might and made an effort not to push her away.

"Good night. With God's help you'll go to sleep."

"Yes."

VI

Ivan Ilyich saw that he was dying and was in constant despair.

Ivan Ilyich knew in the very depths of his soul that he was dying but not only could he not get accustomed to this, he simply didn't understand it; he just couldn't understand it.

All his life the example of a syllogism he had studied in Kiesewetter's[2] logic—"Caius is a man, men are mortal, therefore Caius is mortal"—had seemed to him to be true only in relation to Caius but in no way to himself. There was Caius the man, man in general, and it was quite justified, but he wasn't Caius and he wasn't man in general, and he had always been something quite, quite special apart from all other beings; he was Vanya,[3] with Mama, with Papa, with Mitya and Volodya, with his toys and the coachman, with Nyanya, then with Katenka, with all the joys, sorrows, passions of childhood, boyhood, youth. Did Caius know the smell of the striped leather ball Vanya loved so much? Did Caius kiss his mother's hand like that and did the silken folds of Caius's mother's dress rustle like that for him? Was Caius in love like that? Could Caius chair a session like that?

And Caius is indeed mortal and it's right that he should die, but for me, Vanya, Ivan Ilyich, with all my feelings and thoughts—for me it's quite different. And it cannot be that I should die. It would be too horrible.

That's what he felt.

"If I had to die like Caius, then I would know it, an inner voice would be telling me, but nothing like that happened in me, and I and all my friends—we understood that things weren't at all like with Caius. But now there's this!" he said to himself. "It can't be. It can't be, but it is. How has this happened? How can one understand it?"

---

2. Karl Kiesewetter (1766–1819) was a German popularizer of Kant's philosophy. His *Outline of Logic According to Kantian Principles* (1796) was widely used in Russian adaptations as a schoolbook.

3. Diminutive, familiar form of Ivan.

And he couldn't understand it and tried to banish this thought as false, inaccurate, morbid, and to replace it with other true and healthy thoughts. But this thought, and not just the thought but reality as it were came and stopped in front of him.

And in the place of this thought he called up others in turn in the hope of finding support in them. He tried to return to his previous ways of thought, which had concealed the thought of death from him. But—strangely—everything which previously had concealed and covered up and obliterated the awareness of death now could no longer produce this result. Ivan Ilyich now spent most of his time attempting to restore his previous ways of feeling that had concealed death. Now he would say to himself, "I'll take up some work, that's what I live by." And he went to court, banishing all his doubts; he talked to friends and sat down, absentmindedly looking over the crowd of people with a pensive look as he used to and supporting both wasted hands on the arms of his oak chair; leaning over toward a friend as usual, moving the papers of a case, whispering together, and then suddenly raising his eyes and sitting up straight, he would pronounce the particular words and open the case. But suddenly in the middle of it, the pain in his side, ignoring the stages of the case's development, began its own gnawing work. Ivan Ilyich listened and tried not to think about it, but it kept on. It came and stood right in front of him and looked at him, and he became petrified; the fire in his eyes died down, and he again began to ask himself, "Is it alone the truth?" And his friends and staff saw with surprise and dismay that he, such a brilliant, subtle judge, was getting confused and making mistakes. He would give himself a shake, make an effort to recover himself, and somehow or other bring the session to an end, and he would return home with the depressing awareness that his work as a judge couldn't hide from him as it used to what he wanted it to hide; that with his work as a judge he couldn't be rid of It. And what was worst of all was that It was distracting him not to make him do anything but only for him to look at It, right in the eye, look at it and without doing anything endure inexpressible sufferings.

And to rescue himself from this condition, Ivan Ilyich looked for relief—for new screens—and new screens appeared and for a short time seemed to offer him salvation, but very soon they again not so much collapsed as let the light through, as if It penetrated everything and nothing could hide it.

Latterly he would go into the drawing room he had arranged—the drawing room where he had fallen—how venomously comic it was to think of it—for the arrangement of which he had sacrificed his life, for he knew that his illness had started with that injury; he would go in and see that something had made a scratch on a polished table. He would look for the cause and find it in the bronze ornament of an album that had become bent at the edge. He would pick up the album, an expensive one he had lovingly compiled, and be cross at the carelessness of his daughter and her friends—things were torn and the photographs bent. He would carefully set things to rights and bend the decoration back again.

He then would have the thought of moving this whole *établissement*[4] of albums over into another corner by the flowers. He would call the manservant; either his daughter or his wife would come to his help; they would disagree,

4. Arrangement (French).

contradict him; he would argue, get angry, but everything would be all right because he didn't remember It, couldn't see It.

And then his wife would say when he himself was moving something, "Let the servants do it, you'll hurt yourself again," and suddenly It would flash through the screens; he would see It flash just for a moment, and he still would hope It would disappear, but without wanting to he would pay attention to his side—the same thing would still be sitting there, still aching, and he couldn't forget it, and It would be looking at him quite openly from behind the flowers. Why?

It's true, it was here on these curtains that I lost my life as if in an assault. Did I really? How terrible and how stupid! It can't be so! It can't be, but it is.

He would go into his study, lie down, and be left alone with It. Face-to-face with It, but nothing to be done with It. Just look at It and turn cold.

VII

How it happened in the third month of Ivan Ilyich's illness is impossible to say because it happened step by step, imperceptibly, but it did happen that his wife and his daughter and his son and the servants and his friends and the doctors and, above all, he himself knew that all interest others had in him lay solely in whether he would soon, at last, vacate his place, free the living from the constraint brought about by his presence, and be liberated himself from his sufferings.

He slept less and less; they gave him opium and started to inject morphine. But that gave him no relief. The dull pangs he felt in his half-somnolent state at first gave him relief as being something new, but then they became as agonizing as outright pain or even more so.

They prepared special food to the doctors' prescriptions, but this food he found more and more tasteless, more and more disgusting.

Special contrivances had to be made for excretion, and every time this was a torment for him. A torment because of the uncleanliness, the loss of decorum, and the odor, from the consciousness that another person had to take part in this.

But some comfort for Ivan Ilyich did come out of this unpleasant business. Gerasim, the manservant, always came to take things out for him.

Gerasim was a clean, fresh young peasant who had filled out on city food. He was always cheerful and sunny. At first Ivan Ilyich was embarrassed by seeing this man, always dressed in his clean, traditional clothes, having to do this repulsive job.

Once getting up from the pan and lacking the strength to pull up his trousers, he collapsed into an easy chair and looked with horror at his feeble bare thighs with their sharply defined muscles.

Gerasim came in with firm, light steps in his heavy boots, giving off a pleasant smell of tar from the boots and of fresh winter air; he had on a clean hessian[5] apron and a clean cotton shirt, the sleeves rolled up over his strong, young, bare arms; without looking at Ivan Ilyich, he went to the vessel, obviously masking the joy in living shining out from his face so as not to hurt the sick man.

"Gerasim," Ivan Ilyich said weakly.

---

5. Coarse, strong fabric made from hemp.

Gerasim started, obviously scared he had made some mistake, and with a quick movement turned toward the sick man his fresh, kind, simple, young face, which was just beginning to grow a beard.

"Do you need something, sir?"

"I think this must be unpleasant for you. You must forgive me. I can't manage."

"No, sir." Gerasim's eyes were shining and he showed his young white teeth. "What's a little trouble? You've got an illness."

And with strong, dexterous hands he did his usual job and went out, treading lightly. And in five minutes, treading just as lightly, he came back. Ivan Ilyich was still sitting there like that in the armchair.

"Gerasim," he said when Gerasim had put down the clean, rinsed vessel, "please, come here and help me." Gerasim came. "Lift me up. It's difficult by myself and I've sent Dmitry away."

Gerasim came over to him; he put his strong arms around him and, gently and deftly, the same way he walked, lifted and supported him; he pulled up his trousers with one hand and was going to sit him down. But Ivan Ilyich asked Gerasim to take him to the sofa. Effortlessly and with next to no pressure, Gerasim led him, almost carrying him, to the sofa and sat him down.

"Thank you. How easily, how well . . . you do everything."

Gerasim again smiled and was about to go out. But Ivan Ilyich felt so good with him around that he didn't want to let him go.

"Now. Please move this chair over to me. No, that one, underneath my legs. I feel better when my legs are higher."

Gerasim brought the chair, placed it without making any noise, lowering it in one movement to the floor, and lifted Ivan Ilyich's legs onto the chair; Ivan Ilyich thought he felt better the moment Gerasim raised up his legs.

"I feel better when my legs are higher," Ivan Ilyich said. "Put that cushion under me."

Gerasim did that. Again he lifted his legs up and put the cushion into position. Again Ivan Ilyich felt better when Gerasim held his legs up. When he lowered them, he thought he felt worse.

"Gerasim," he said to him, "are you busy now?"

"No sir, not at all," said Gerasim, who had learned from the townsfolk how to talk to the gentry.

"What do you still have to do?"

"What is there to do? I've done everything; I've just got to chop the wood for tomorrow."

"So hold my legs up a bit higher, can you do that?"

"Of course I can." Gerasim lifted up his legs and Ivan Ilyich thought that in this position he felt absolutely no pain.

"But what about the wood?"

"Don't worry, sir. We'll manage."

Ivan Ilyich told Gerasim to sit down and hold up his legs, and he talked to him. And—strange to say—he thought he felt better while Gerasim held up his legs.

From that day Ivan Ilyich started sometimes to call Gerasim in to him and made him hold up his legs on his shoulders, and he liked to talk to him. Gerasim did this easily, willingly, simply, and with a goodness of heart that touched Ivan

Ilyich. In all other people Ivan Ilyich was offended by health, strength, high spirits; only Gerasim's strength and high spirits didn't depress but calmed Ivan Ilyich.

Ivan Ilyich's chief torment was the lie—that lie, for some reason recognized by everyone, that he was only ill but not dying, and that he only needed rest and treatment and then there would be some very good outcome. But he knew that whatever they did, there would be no outcome except even more painful suffering and death. And he was tormented by this lie; he was tormented by their unwillingness to acknowledge what everyone knew and he knew, by their wanting to lie to him about his terrible situation, by their wanting him to and making him take part in that lie himself. The lie, this lie being perpetrated above him on the eve of his death, the lie which could only bring down this terrible solemn act of his death to the level of all their visits and curtains and sturgeon for dinner . . . was horribly painful for Ivan Ilyich. And, strangely, many times when they were performing their tricks above him, he was within a hair's breadth of crying out to them, "Stop lying; you know and I know that I am dying; so at least stop lying." But he never had the strength to do it. The terrible, horrific act of his dying, he saw, had been brought down by all those surrounding him to the level of a casual unpleasantness, some breach of decorum (as one treats a man who, entering a drawing room, emits a bad smell); brought down by that very "decorum" he had served his whole life, he saw that no one had pity for him because no one even wanted to understand his situation. Only Gerasim understood his situation and felt pity for him. And so Ivan Ilyich only felt comfortable with Gerasim. He felt comfortable when Gerasim held up his legs, sometimes for whole nights without a break, and wouldn't go off to bed, saying, "Please, sir, don't worry, Ivan Ilyich, I'll still get plenty of sleep"; or when he would suddenly add, going over to the familiar "thou," "You're sick, so why shouldn't I do something for you?" Gerasim was the only one not to lie; everything showed he was the only one who understood what the matter was and didn't think it necessary to hide it, and simply felt pity for his wasted, feeble master. He even once said directly when Ivan Ilyich was dismissing him:

"We'll all die. So why not take a little trouble?" He said this, conveying by it that he wasn't bothered by the work precisely because he was doing it for a dying man and hoped that in his time someone would do this work for him.

Apart from this lie, or as a consequence of it, what was most painful for Ivan Ilyich was that no one had pity on him as he wanted them to have pity; at some moments after prolonged sufferings Ivan Ilyich wanted most of all, however much he felt ashamed to admit it, for someone to have pity on him like a sick child. He wanted them to caress him, to kiss him, to cry over him as one caresses and comforts children. He knew he was an important legal official, that he had a graying beard and that therefore this was impossible, but he still wanted it. And in his relations with Gerasim there was something close to that, and therefore his relations with Gerasim comforted him. Ivan Ilyich would want to cry, would want them to caress him and cry over him; then in would come his friend, the lawyer Shebek, and instead of crying and caresses Ivan Ilyich would assume a serious, stern, pensive expression and out of inertia would give his opinion on the meaning of a verdict of the court of appeal and stubbornly insist on it. This lie all around him and inside him more than anything poisoned the last days of Ivan Ilyich's life.

VIII

It was morning. It was morning only because Gerasim had gone out and Pyotr the manservant came in, put out the candles, opened one curtain, and started quietly to tidy up. Whether it was morning or evening, Friday or Sunday, was immaterial, it was all one and the same: the gnawing, agonizing pain that didn't abate for a moment; the consciousness of life departing without hope but still not yet departed; the same terrible, hateful death advancing, which was the only reality, and always the same lie. What did days, weeks, and times of day matter here?

"Would you like some tea?"

He has to have order; masters should drink tea in the mornings, he thought and only said:

"No."

"Would you like to move to the sofa?"

He has to tidy the chamber, and I'm in the way; I am dirt, disorder, he thought and only said:

"No, leave me be."

The manservant did some more things. Ivan Ilyich stretched out his hand. Pyotr came up to serve.

"What do you want?"

"My watch."

Pyotr got the watch, which was lying right there, and handed it to him.

"Half past eight. Have they got up?"

"No, sir. Vasily Ivanovich"—that was his son—"has gone to the gymnasium, but Praskovya Fyodorovna gave orders to wake her if you asked for her. Shall I?"

"No, don't." *Shall I try some tea?* he thought. "Yes, tea . . . bring it."

Pyotr went to the door. Ivan Ilyich felt terrified of being left alone. *How can I detain him? Yes, my medicine.* "Pyotr, give me my medicine." *Why not, maybe the medicine will still help.* He took the spoon and drank. *No, it won't help. It's all nonsense and a sham*, he decided as soon as he sensed the familiar sickly, hopeless taste. *No, I can't believe in it anymore. But the pain, why the pain, if it would just go down even for a minute.* And he groaned. Pyotr turned round again. "No, go away. Bring me some tea."

Pyotr went out. Left alone, Ivan Ilyich groaned not so much from the pain, however frightful it was, as from anguish. "Always the same, always these endless days and nights. If only it could be soon. What could be soon? Death, darkness. No, no. Anything is better than death!"

When Pyotr came in with the tea on a tray, Ivan Ilyich looked distractedly at him for a long time, not taking in who and what he was. Pyotr was embarrassed by this stare. And when Pyotr was embarrassed, Ivan Ilyich came to himself.

"Yes," he said, "tea . . . good, put it down. Only help me wash and give me a clean shirt."

And Ivan Ilyich began to wash. Stopping to rest, he washed his hands, his face, cleaned his teeth, began to brush his hair, and looked in the mirror. He felt frightened, especially frightened by the way his hair stuck flat to his forehead.

When his shirt was being changed, he knew that he would be even more frightened if he looked at his body, and so he didn't look at himself. But now it was all done. He put on a dressing gown, covered himself with a blanket, and sat in an armchair to have his tea. For one minute he felt refreshed, but as soon as he began to drink the tea, again the same taste, the same pain. With an effort he finished the tea and lay down, stretching out his legs. He lay down and sent Pyotr away.

Always the same. There'd be a small flash of hope, then a sea of despair would surge, and always pain, always pain, always despair, and always the same. It was horribly depressing being alone; he wanted to ask for someone but he knew in advance that with others there it would be even worse. "If only I could have morphine again—and lose consciousness. I'll tell him, the doctor, to think of something else. Like this it's impossible, impossible."

An hour, a couple of hours would go by like that. But now there's a bell in the hall. Maybe it's the doctor. It is; it's the doctor, fresh, bright, plump, cheerful, his expression saying, "You've gotten frightened of something there but now we'll fix all that for you." The doctor knows that this expression isn't appropriate here, but he has assumed it once and for all and he can't take it off, like a man who has put on a tailcoat in the morning and is paying visits.

The doctor rubs his hands briskly and reassuringly.

"I'm cold. There's a cracking frost. Let me warm myself up," he says, his expression being as if one just had to wait a little for him to warm himself, and when he had, then he would set everything to rights.

"So, how are we?"

Ivan Ilyich feels the doctor wants to say, "How are things?" but feels one can't talk like that, and he says, "How did you spend the night?"

Ivan Ilyich looks at the doctor, his expression asking, "Will you really never be ashamed of telling lies?" But the doctor doesn't want to understand the question.

And Ivan Ilyich says:

"Just as dreadfully. The pain isn't going, it isn't going away. If I could just have something!"

"Yes, you patients are always like that. Well, sir, now I've warmed up, even our very particular Praskovya Fyodorovna wouldn't have anything to say against my temperature. So, sir, good morning." And the doctor shakes his hand.

And, dropping all his earlier playfulness, the doctor begins to examine the patient with a serious expression, takes pulse and temperature, and then begin the tappings and auscultations.

Ivan Ilyich knows firmly and without any doubt that all this is nonsense, an empty fraud, but when the doctor on his knees stretches over him, applying his ear first higher, then lower, and performs over him various gymnastic exercises, Ivan Ilyich succumbs to all this as he used to succumb to lawyers' speeches when he knew very well that they were lying and why they were lying.

The doctor, kneeling on the sofa, was still tapping something when there was a rustling at the door of Praskovya Fyodorovna's silk dress, and they could hear her scolding Pyotr for not informing her of the doctor's arrival.

She comes in, kisses her husband, and at once starts to make it clear that she has got up long ago and that it's because of a misunderstanding that she wasn't there when the doctor came.

Ivan Ilyich looks at her, examines her closely, and holds against her the whiteness and plumpness and cleanliness of her arms and neck, the gloss of her hair and the shine of her eyes that are so full of life. He hates her with his whole soul. And her touch makes him suffer from a surge of hatred towards her.

Her attitude to him and to his illness is always the same. Just as the doctor has developed for himself an attitude toward his patients which he hasn't been able to put aside, so has she developed a simple attitude towards him—he isn't doing something he should be doing, and it's his fault, and she lovingly scolds him for this—and she hasn't yet managed to put this attitude toward him aside.

"He just doesn't listen. He doesn't take his medicine when he should. And above all—he lies in a position that has to be bad for him—with his legs up." She described how he makes Gerasim hold his legs.

The doctor smiled a smile of amiable scorn, as if saying, "What can one do? Sometimes these patients dream up such silly things; but one can forgive them."

When the examination was over the doctor looked at his watch, and then Praskovya Fyodorovna announced to Ivan Ilyich that whatever he might want, today she had asked in a famous doctor and he and Mikhail Danilovich (that was the usual doctor's name) would examine him together and discuss the case.

"So please don't go against this. I'm doing this for myself," she said ironically, letting him understand that she did everything for him and just by her saying this he was given no right to refuse her. He said nothing and frowned. He felt that the lies surrounding him had become so tangled that it was difficult now to see anything clearly.

Everything she did for him she did only for herself, and she told him so, as if that was something so unlikely that he had to understand it in the opposite sense.

Indeed the famous doctor did arrive at half past eleven. Again there started the auscultations and serious conversations, both in front of Ivan Ilyich and in another room, about his kidney and appendix, and questions and answers delivered with such a serious air that again, instead of the real question about life and death which now was the only one that confronted him, there came a question about his kidney and appendix, which were doing something not quite as they should be and which Mikhail Danilovich and the celebrity doctor would get to grips with right away and make them correct themselves.

The famous doctor said his goodbyes with a serious expression, but one that hadn't given up hope. And to the timid question Ivan Ilyich put to him, raising eyes that were shining with fear and hope—is there any possibility of recovery?—he answered that though one couldn't guarantee it, there was a possibility. The look of hope with which Ivan Ilyich said goodbye to the doctor was so pitiful that, when she saw it, Praskovya Fyodorovna burst into tears as she went through the study doors to give the famous doctor his fee.

The rise in his spirits brought about by the doctor's encouragement didn't last long. Again it was the same room, the same pictures, curtains, wallpaper, medicine bottles, and his same hurting, suffering body. And Ivan Ilyich started to groan; they gave him an injection and he lost consciousness.

When he came to, it was beginning to get dark; they brought in his dinner. With some effort he took some broth; and again all those same things and again night was coming on.

After dinner at seven o'clock Praskovya Fyodorovna came into his room dressed for an evening out, her breasts large and lifted and traces of powder on her face. That morning she had reminded him that they were going to the theater. Sarah Bernhardt[6] was visiting and they had a box which Ivan Ilyich had insisted they take. Now he had forgotten that, and her clothes outraged him. But he concealed his outrage when he remembered that he himself had insisted they get a box and go because it was a cultural treat for their children.

Praskovya Fyodorovna came in pleased with herself but also with a kind of guilty feeling. She sat down, asked about his health—as he could see, just for the sake of asking rather than to learn, knowing that there was nothing to learn—and began to say what she needed to: that she wouldn't have gone out for anything but the box was taken and Hélène was going and their daughter and Petrishchev (the examining magistrate, their daughter's fiancé), and it was impossible to let them go alone. But it would be so much more agreeable for her to sit with him. He must just do what the doctor had ordered without her.

"Yes, and Fyodor Petrovich—the fiancé—wanted to come in. Can he? Liza, too."

"Let them come in."

His daughter came in all dressed up with her young body bared, that body which made him suffer so. But she was flaunting it. Strong, healthy, clearly in love and angry at the illness, suffering, and death that stood in the way of her happiness.

Fyodor Petrovich came too, in a tailcoat, his hair curled à la Capoul,[7] his long sinewy neck encased in a white collar, with a huge white shirtfront and with powerful thighs squeezed into narrow black trousers, with one white glove pulled onto his hand and an opera hat.

After him the schoolboy crept in inconspicuously in a new school uniform, poor fellow, wearing white gloves and with terrible dark patches under his eyes, the meaning of which Ivan Ilyich knew.

His son always made him feel sorry for him. And the look he gave him was terrible, full of sympathy and fear. Apart from Gerasim, only Vasya understood him and felt pity for him, so Ivan Ilyich thought.

They all sat down, asked again about his health. A silence fell. Liza asked her mother about the opera glasses. There ensued an argument between mother and daughter about who had put them where. It felt unpleasant.

Fyodor Petrovich asked Ivan Ilyich if he had seen Sarah Bernhardt. At first Ivan Ilyich didn't understand what he was being asked and then said:

"No, but have you?"

"Yes, in *Adrienne Lecouvreur*."[8]

Praskovya Fyodorovna said that she was particularly good in something or other. Their daughter disagreed. There began a conversation about the elegance and realism of her acting—that conversation which is always exactly the same.

In the middle of the conversation Fyodor Petrovich looked at Ivan Ilyich and fell silent. The others looked and fell silent. Ivan Ilyich looked straight

---

6. Stage name of French actress Rosine Bernard (1844–1923), famed for romantic and tragic roles.
7. That is, worn in tight curls in the manner of famed French tenor Victor Capoul (1839–1924).

8. A play (1849) by the French dramatist Eugène Scribe (1791–1861), in which the heroine was a famous actress of the 18th century. Tolstoy considered Scribe, who wrote over 400 plays, a shoddy, commercial playwright.

ahead with shining eyes, clearly becoming angry with them. This had to be put right, but it was quite impossible to put right. Somehow this silence had to be broken. No one had the resolve, and they all became frightened that somehow the decorous lie would collapse and the true state of things would become obvious to all. Liza was the first to take the resolve. She broke the silence. She wanted to hide what they were all feeling, but she said it wrong.

"So, *if we are going to go*, it's time," she said, looking at her watch, a present from her father, and she gave a barely perceptible smile to the young man, which meant something known to them alone, and got up, her dress rustling.

They all got up, said goodbye, and went off.

When they had gone out, Ivan Ilyich thought he felt better: the lie wasn't there—it had gone out with them—but the pain remained. The same constant pain, the same constant fear made nothing more difficult, nothing easier. Everything was worse.

Again minute followed minute, hour followed hour; it was always the same and there was still no end and the inevitable end became more terrifying.

"Yes, send me Gerasim," he said in reply to a question Pyotr asked.

IX

His wife came back late at night. She walked on tiptoe but he heard her; he opened his eyes and quickly shut them again. She wanted to send Gerasim away and sit with him herself. He opened his eyes and said:

"No. Go away."

"Are you in a lot of pain?"

"It doesn't matter."

"Take some opium."

He agreed and drank. She went out.

Till three o'clock he was in a tormented stupor. He thought that in some way they were pushing him and his pain into a narrow, deep, black sack; they kept pushing further but they couldn't push them right in. And this terrible business for him was crowned by his suffering. And he was both struggling and wanting to drop right down, both fighting against it and assisting. And suddenly he was free and fell and came to. The same Gerasim was still sitting on the bed at his feet, dozing quietly, patiently. And Ivan Ilyich was lying there, having lifted his emaciated legs in their socks onto Gerasim's shoulders; there was the same candle with its shade and the same unceasing pain.

"Go, Gerasim," he whispered.

"It doesn't matter, sir, I'll sit a bit longer."

"No, go."

He removed his legs and lay on his side on top of his arm, and he began to feel sorry for himself. He waited for Gerasim to go out into the next room and he couldn't control himself anymore, and he burst into tears like a child. He wept for his helplessness, for his horrible loneliness, for people's cruelty, for God's cruelty, for God's absence.

"Why have you done all this? Why have you brought me here? Why, why do you torment me so horribly?"

He didn't expect an answer, but he also wept because there wasn't and couldn't be an answer. The pain increased again but he didn't move or call anyone. He said to himself, "More, go on, beat me! But why? What have I done to you, why?"

Then he calmed down; he not only stopped weeping, he stopped breathing and became all attention, as if he were listening not to a voice speaking in sounds but to the voice of his soul, to the train of thoughts rising within him.

"What do you want?" was the first clear idea capable of being expressed in words that he heard. "What do you want? What do you want?" he repeated to himself. "What? Not to suffer. To live," he answered.

And again he became absorbed with such intense attention that even the pain did not distract him.

"To live? To live how?" asked the voice of his soul.

"Yes, to live, as I lived before: well and pleasantly."

"As you lived before, well, pleasantly?" asked the voice. And he began to go over in his imagination the best moments of his pleasant life. But—strange to relate—all these best moments of a pleasant life now seemed quite different from what they had seemed then. All of them—except for his first memories of childhood. There in childhood was something so truly pleasant with which he could live, if it returned. But the person who had experienced those pleasant things no longer existed: it was like a memory of something else.

As soon as the process began which had resulted in Ivan Ilyich, the man of today, all the things which had seemed joys melted away before his eyes and were changed into something worthless and often vile.

And the further from childhood, the nearer to the present, the more worthless and dubious were the joys. That began with law school. There was still something there truly good: there was gaiety, there was friendship, there were hopes. But in the senior classes these good moments were already less frequent. After that, at the time of his first period of service with the governor, again good moments appeared: there were memories of love for a woman. After that all this became confused and there was even less of what was good. Further on there was still less good, and the further he went the less there was.

Marriage . . . so casually entered, and disillusionment, and the smell that came from his wife's mouth, and sensuality, hypocrisy! And that deadly work of his and those worries about money, and on for a year, and two, and ten, and twenty—and always the same. And the further he went, the more deadly it became. "As if I were walking downhill at a regular pace, imagining I was walking uphill. That's how it was. In the eyes of the world I was walking uphill, and to just that extent life was slipping away from under me . . . And now it's time, to die!

"So what is this? Why? It can't be. It can't be that life was so meaningless and vile. But if it was indeed so meaningless and vile, then why die and die suffering? Something is wrong.

"Maybe I have lived not as I should have"—the thought suddenly came into his head. "But how so when I did everything in the proper way?" he said to himself, and immediately rejected this solution of the whole riddle of life as something wholly impossible.

"What do you want now? To live? To live how? To live as you lived in court when the court officer pronounces, 'The court is opening!' The court is opening, opening, the court," he repeated to himself. "Here's the court! But I'm not guilty!" he shouted angrily. "For what?" And he stopped weeping and, turning his face to the wall, he began to think of just the one thing: why all this horror, for what?

But however much he thought, he found no answer. And when there came to him the thought, as it often did, that all this was happening because he had lived wrongly, he at once remembered all the correctness of his life and rejected this strange thought.

X

Two more weeks went by. Ivan Ilyich didn't get up from the sofa anymore. He didn't want to lie in bed and instead lay on the sofa. And, lying almost all the time with his face to the wall, he suffered in his loneliness all those same insoluble sufferings and in his loneliness thought the same insoluble thoughts. What is this? Is it really true that this is death? And a voice within answered: Yes, it's true. Why these torments? And the voice answered: That's the way it is; there is no why. Apart from that there was nothing more.

From the very start of his illness, when Ivan Ilyich went to the doctor for the first time, his life was divided into two diametrically opposed moods, which alternated with each other: on the one hand despair and the expectation of an incomprehensible and horrible death, on the other hope and the absorbed observation of the activity of his body. Now he had before his eyes just a kidney or appendix which for a time had deviated from the performance of its duties; now there was just incomprehensible, horrible death from which it was impossible to escape in any way.

From the very beginning of his illness these two moods alternated with each other; but the more the illness progressed, the more fantastic and questionable became thoughts about his kidney and the more real the consciousness of approaching death.

He only had to remember what he had been three months previously and what he was now—to remember how he had been walking downhill at a regular pace—for all possibility of hope to crumble.

In the recent loneliness in which he found himself, lying with his face to the back of the sofa, loneliness in the midst of a crowded city and his numerous acquaintances and family—loneliness that could not be more absolute anywhere, either at the bottom of the sea or underneath the earth—in his recent terrible loneliness Ivan Ilyich lived only by his imagination in the past. One after another pictures of his past presented themselves to him. It always began with the closest in time and went back to the most remote, to his childhood, and rested there. If Ivan Ilyich thought of the stewed prunes he was offered to eat now, he remembered the moist, wrinkled French prunes of his childhood, their particular taste and the flow of saliva when he got to the stone, and alongside this memory of taste there arose a whole row of memories of that time: his *nyanya*, his brother, his toys. "You mustn't think of that. . . . It's too painful," Ivan Ilyich said to himself, and was again transported into the present. A button on the back of the sofa and the creases in its morocco leather. "Morocco is expensive and wears badly; there was a quarrel because of it. But it was different leather and a different row when we ripped our father's briefcase and were punished, but Mama brought us some pies." And again he stopped in his childhood and again it was painful for Ivan Ilyich, and he tried to push it away and think of something else.

And here again, together with this train of memories, another train of memories went through his mind—of how his illness had intensified and grown. It was the same; the further back he went, the more life there was. There was more good in life and more of life itself. And the two merged together. *As my torments kept getting worse and worse, so the whole of life became worse and worse*, he thought. One bright spot, there, at the start of his life, and after that everything blacker and blacker, and everything quicker and quicker. *In inverse ratio to the square of the distance from death*, thought Ivan Ilyich. And an image of a stone flying downward with increasing speed became fixed in his mind. Life, a sequence of increasing sufferings, flies quicker and quicker to the end, to the most terrible suffering of all. *I am flying* . . . He shivered, moved, tried to resist, but he now knew that resistance was impossible, and again, with eyes that were tired of looking but which couldn't help looking at what was in front of him, he gazed at the back of the sofa and waited—waited for that terrible fall, the crash, and annihilation. "I can't resist," he said to himself. "But if I could just understand why. That too I can't. I might be able to explain it if I said I had lived not as I should have. But it's impossible to admit that," he said to himself, remembering all the lawfulness, the correctness, and the decorum of his life. "It's impossible to admit that now," he said to himself, grimacing with his lips, as if anyone could see this smile of his and be deceived by it. "There's no explanation! Torment, death. . . . Why?"

XI

Two weeks went by like that. In those weeks an event took place that had been desired by Ivan Ilyich and his wife: Petrishchev made a formal proposal. It happened in the evening. The next day Praskovya Fyodorovna went in to her husband, wondering how to announce Fyodor Petrovich's proposal to him, but that very night Ivan Ilyich had taken a turn for the worse. Praskovya Fyodorovna found him on the same sofa, but in a new position. He was lying on his back, groaning and looking ahead with a fixed gaze.

She started talking about medicines. He turned his eyes to her. She didn't finish what she had begun to say; there was so much anger expressed in those eyes, aimed directly at her.

"For Christ's sake, let me die in peace," he said.

She was about to go, but at that moment his daughter came in and went up to say good morning. He looked at his daughter as he had at his wife and to her questions about his health he drily said to her that he would soon liberate them all from himself. They both said nothing, sat briefly, and went out.

"What can we be blamed for?" Liza said to her mother. "As if we'd done this! I'm sorry for Papa, but why must he torment us?"

The doctor came at the usual time. Ivan Ilyich answered him "yes, no," not taking his angry eyes from him, and finally said:

"You know that you won't be of any help, so leave me."

"We can relieve the suffering," the doctor said.

"You can't do that either; leave me."

The doctor went out into the drawing room and informed Praskovya Fyodorovna that things were very bad and that there was only one resource—opium, to relieve the suffering, which must be terrible.

The doctor said that Ivan Ilyich's physical sufferings were terrible, and that was true; but even more terrible than his physical sufferings were his mental sufferings, and there was his chief torment.

His mental sufferings lay in the fact that that night, as he looked at Gerasim's sleepy, good-natured face with its high cheekbones, there suddenly had entered his head the thought: *But what if in actual fact all my life, my conscious life, has been "wrong"?*

It occurred to him that the notion that had previously seemed to him a complete impossibility—that he had not lived his life as he should have done—could be the truth. It occurred to him that his barely noticeable attempts at struggling against what was considered good by those in high positions above him, those barely noticeable attempts which he had immediately rejected, could be genuine, and everything else wrong. His work and the structure of his life and his family and his social and professional interests—all that could be wrong. He tried to defend all that to himself. And suddenly he felt the fragility of what he was defending. And there was nothing to defend.

"But if this is so," he said to himself, "and I am leaving life with the realization that I have lost everything I was given and that it's impossible to put right, then what?" He lay on his back and started to go over his whole life afresh. When in the morning he saw the manservant, then his wife, then his daughter, then the doctor—every one of their movements, every one of their words confirmed for him the terrible truth that had been disclosed to him in the night. He saw in them himself, everything by which he had lived, and saw clearly that all this was wrong, all this was a terrible, huge fraud concealing both life and death. This realization increased, increased tenfold his physical sufferings. He groaned and tossed about and pulled at the clothes on him. He felt suffocated and crushed. And he hated them for that.

They gave him a big dose of opium; he lost consciousness, but at dinnertime the same began again. He drove them all away from him and tossed about from side to side.

His wife came to him and said:

"*Jean,* my dear, do this for me. It can't do any harm, but it often helps. So, it's nothing. And people in good health often . . ."

He opened his eyes wide.

"What? Take communion? Why? There's no need to! But then . . ."

She started crying.

"Yes, my dear? I'll call for our man, he's so sweet."

"Fine, very well," he said.

When the priest came and took his confession, he was calmed; he felt a kind of relief from his doubts and, as a consequence of that, from his sufferings, and a moment of hope came to him. He again began to think of his appendix and the possibility of curing it. He received communion with tears in his eyes.

When, after communion, he was put to bed, for a moment he felt comfortable and hope for life appeared again. He began to think of the operation being suggested to him. "To live, I want to live," he said to himself. His wife came to congratulate him on taking communion; she said the usual words and added:

"You feel better, don't you?"

Without looking at her he said, "Yes."

Her clothes, her body, the expression of her face, the sound of her voice—everything said to him one thing: "Wrong. Everything by which you have lived and are living is a lie, a fraud, concealing life and death from you." And as soon as he thought that, hatred rose up in him, and together with hatred agonizing physical suffering, and with those sufferings an awareness of the end, nearby and unavoidable. Something new happened: his breath started to strain and come in spurts and be squeezed out.

His expression when he said "yes" was terrible. Having said that yes, he looked her straight in the eye and with unusual strength for his weakness turned himself facedown and cried:

"Go away, go away, leave me!"

XII

From that minute began three days of unceasing screams that were so horrible one couldn't hear them from two doors away without feeling horror. The minute he answered his wife, he understood that he was lost, that there was no return, that the end had come, the very end, but the doubt still wasn't resolved; it still remained doubt.

"Oh! Oh! Oh!" he cried out in various tones. He began to cry out, "I don't want to, no!" and went on like that crying out the letter O.

For the whole three days, during which time did not exist for him, he tossed about in the black sack into which he was being pushed by an invisible, insurmountable force. He struggled as a man condemned to death struggles in the arms of the executioner, knowing he cannot save himself; and with every minute he felt that for all his efforts at struggling he was coming nearer and nearer to what filled him with horror. He felt that his agony lay both in being pushed into that black hole and even more in being unable to get into it. He was prevented from climbing in by his declaration that his life had been good. This justification of his life caught on something and stopped him from going forward, and that distressed him most of all.

Suddenly some kind of force struck him in the chest and on the side; his breath was constricted even more; he collapsed into the hole and there at the bottom of the hole some light was showing. There happened to him what he used to experience in a railway carriage when you think you are going forward but are going backward and suddenly realize your true direction.

"Yes, everything was wrong," he said to himself, "but it doesn't matter. I can, I can do what is right. But what is right?" he asked himself, and at once fell silent.

It was the end of the third day, an hour before his death. At that very moment the gymnasium schoolboy quietly slipped into his father's room and approached his bed. The dying man was still crying out despairingly and waving his arms about. One of his hands hit the schoolboy's head. The schoolboy took it, pressed it to his lips, and wept.

At that very moment Ivan Ilyich fell through and saw a light, and it was revealed to him that his life had been wrong but that it was still possible to mend things. He asked himself, "What is right?" and fell silent, listening. Now he felt someone was kissing his hand. He opened his eyes and looked at his son. He felt sorry for him. His wife came to him. He looked at her. She looked at him, mouth open and tears on her nose and cheeks that she hadn't wiped away. He felt sorry for her.

"Yes, I make them unhappy," he thought. "They are sorry for me, but it'll be better for them when I die." He wanted to say that but didn't have the strength to utter it. "However, why say things? One must act," he thought. With a look to his wife he pointed to his son and said:

"Take him away . . . sorry for him . . . and for you . . ." He wanted to add "forgive" but said "give," and not having the strength to correct himself, waved his hand, knowing that He who needed to understand would understand.

And suddenly it became clear to him that what had been oppressing him and not coming to an end—now everything was coming to an end at once, on two sides, on ten sides, on every side. He was sorry for them, he must make it so they had no pain. Free them and free himself from these sufferings. "So good and so simple," he thought. "And the pain?" he asked himself. "Where's it gone? Well, where are you, pain?"

He began to listen.

"There it is. So—let the pain be. And death? Where is it?"

He searched for his old habitual fear of death and didn't find it. Where was death? What death? There was no fear, because there was no death.

Instead of death there was light.

"So that's it!" he suddenly said aloud. "Such joy!"

For him all this took place in a moment, and the significance of this moment didn't change. For those there his death agony lasted two hours more. Something bubbled in his chest; his emaciated body shivered. Then the gurgling and wheezing became less and less frequent.

"It is finished!" someone said above him.

He heard these words and repeated them in his heart. "Death is finished," he said to himself. "It is no more."

He breathed in, stopped halfway, stretched himself, and died.

HENRIK IBSEN

1828–1906

Writing in an era when drama had become a second-rate occupation, with most gifted writers turning instead to novels or poetry, Henrik Ibsen restored prestige and relevance to the theater. Over the course of the nineteenth century, the invention of new theatrical machinery and techniques had turned theater into spectacle. Theater producers spent their time and money on special effects, dazzling audiences with lighting, horses, or even nautical battles in addition to, of course, trying to sign the latest acting stars. One might compare nineteenth-century theater with present-day Hollywood and its focus on blockbuster action movies packed with special effects and star actors. Ibsen showed Europe that theater could be more than just spectacle, that it could be an art form addressing the most serious moral and social questions of the time. The theatergoing public was first shocked, and later thrilled, to have controversial themes presented on the stage, and to have them presented not through special effects but through carefully drawn characters and well-constructed dramatic situations. Honing his dramatic technique over half a century, Ibsen almost single-handedly brought a new seriousness to the theater, and he has been regarded as the originator of modern drama ever since.

Ibsen achieved his unparalleled success against all odds. He was born in Skien, a small town in Norway, far removed from the cultural centers of Europe, and he spoke Norwegian, a marginal language unlikely to launch a European career in literature. When Ibsen left his provincial home at the age of fifteen, he was apprenticed to a chemist. Only at the age of twenty-two was he able to free himself from his apprenticeship—and from a liaison with a maid that had resulted in an illegitimate child—and move to the capital, Christiania (now Oslo), to study for the university entrance exam. During this time his first play was performed. After a few years spent learning the craft, he assumed positions of greater responsibility—as artistic director and dramaturge—at theaters in Bergen and Christiania.

Ibsen at first learned from the standard dramatic form of the time, the so-called well-made play. Popularized by the French playwrights Victorien Sardou and Augustine-Eugène Scribe, the well-made play revolved around complicated plots and well-timed confrontations. Immensely popular with audiences, well-made plays excelled at fast-moving action, intrigues, alliances, and sudden revelations.

But Ibsen would soon turn against these sensational formulas. In two plays, *Brand* (1866) and *Peer Gynt* (1867), Ibsen startlingly rejected not only the well-made play, but the theater as such. He wrote these works as "dramatic poems," plays that were not supposed to be performed but were written exclusively to be read. All the rules that governed conventional stage action could thus be circumvented entirely. Drawing on literary models such as **Goethe's** *Faust* and Byron's *Don Juan, Peer Gynt* freely mixes fantasy and reality, conjuring mountain trolls, mad German philosophers, and the devil himself. The play established Ibsen as a writer of European significance.

And so Europe, rather than Norway, became Ibsen's home: he would spend the next twenty-seven years on the continent, mostly in Italy and Germany, before moving back to Norway at the age of sixty-three. After *Brand* and *Peer Gynt* had secured his Europe-wide reputation, he changed course and started writing for the stage once more, but in an entirely different style. He gave up on Norway's past and chose to write, once and for all, about the world he knew best: the contemporary Norwegian middle class. His singular purpose was to lay bare the ugly reality behind the façade of middle-class respectability, to expose the lies of bourgeois characters and indeed of bourgeois society as a whole. The five plays of this period, *The Pillars of Society* (1877), *A Doll's House* (1879), *Ghosts* (1881), *Enemy of the People* (1882), and *The Wild Duck* (1884), made Ibsen notorious throughout Europe and established him as an author of shock, confrontation, and revolt.

The main reason why these plays caused such consternation and excitement is that they introduced realism to the theater. Realism had already been established in the novel, but not in drama. In these realist plays, Ibsen wrote in ordinary language and devoted his drama to undoing deceit and pretense, to unveiling hidden motives and past misdeeds so that the truth would shine forth on the stage. Realism, for Ibsen, meant creating a theater of emotional and moral truth, where audiences could understand both the subjective experience and the objective conditions of modern life.

After becoming notorious with his realist plays, Ibsen changed course once more. He had been trying to write modern versions of Greek tragedy for a long while, but it was only in the last phase of his career that he managed to give definite shape to the tragedy of modern middle-class life. Of these plays *Hedda Gabler* (1890) is the most compelling and famous. It is set in the same bourgeois milieu as his realist plays, but is no longer directed towards social deceptions and pretense. Instead it is interested in the bourgeois characters themselves, presenting them in all their complexity, with the hidden yearnings and fantasies that take them outside of the constricted worlds in which they live.

Hedda Gabler is a play about the daughter of a general who marries Tesman, an aspiring scholar waiting for his university post. As the play begins, we see almost immediately that the marriage is unequal and unsettled. Tesman is eager to start his new life and he is clearly proud of his trophy wife. Hedda, by contrast, is dismissive of his affectionate tone and also his values. She snubs him, is impatient, abruptly changes the topic of conversation, and sulks. There is a clear class difference between them. As the daughter of a general, Hedda is used to an upper-middle-class life. Tesman, by contrast, is lower middle class, with all the difference in habit and taste that entails. The collision between Hedda's and Tesman's respective classes, expectations, and attitudes centers on the bourgeois home. Gradually we learn that Hedda only married Tesman and convinced him to get the house out of boredom, feeling that no other options were available to her. But now she finds herself trapped: trapped in her marriage and trapped in the house.

Far from merely a setting for the characters, the house and its furnishings emerge as the main object of Hedda's scorn. The play revolves around furniture and what it represents: class and taste. Hedda despises those objects associated with Tesman and his class, and she admires the remnants of her former life. Tesman's scholarly study is also a set of objects: the handicrafts of the Middle Ages. For Ibsen tangible things become pawns in larger struggles between classes and wills.

Hedda Gabler, bored and without a function except to bear children—a thought she rejects with horror—manipulates every single character in the play, from Tesman and his aunt to Løvborg and his companion, her old school friend, Mrs. Elvsted. She gets them to do her bidding through force, lies, flattery, and utter ruthlessness. As the play progresses, we find her destroying careers and lives without blinking an eye. Hedda sees plotting as an end in itself and for this reason she is often seen as a modern version of Medea or Lady Macbeth.

The main victim of Hedda's plotting is Tesman's rival, Løvborg, who has written nothing less than a book about the future (after completing one about the history of civilization). Ibsen again here focuses on an object, Løvborg's sole manuscript, which becomes a central plot device, a stage prop that drives the action forward. Ibsen had learned from the well-made play how to weave objects and characters into suspenseful plots. But these props are rich in meaning too, throwing light on characters and themes, multifaceted devices that develop a life of their own.

Hedda Gabler may be a manipulator, but she is a manipulator with a vision. She is driven by her hunger for a more fulfilling, ideal, and beautiful life. She fantasizes about acts of heroism and beauty, and she tries to bring about such acts by directing the people around her the way a director assigns roles to actors. She shares her desire for a

'ith many tragic characters
ater plays, characters who
..not get rid of the chains that bind
them to their houses, their objects, their
habits, their class, and their past. Ibsen's attitude towards his characters' desire for beauty tends to be ambivalent.
On the one hand, he sympathizes with
them, even with the cold-hearted Hedda
Gabler. On the other hand, his plays
show that the single-minded desire to
achieve an ideal life leads to destruction. Hedda Gabler's vision is an escape
fantasy, the stuff of historical and idealist plays of the kind Ibsen had written in
his youth. Ibsen saw both: the intense
longing to live a life of ideals as well as
the destructive effects of that idealism.

Since his own time, Ibsen's work has
inspired important actors and directors
worldwide. In England, George Bernard
Shaw and the writer William Archer led
what some have called the Ibsen campaign, turning the Norwegian playwright into the central figure in modern
British drama, and the influential Russian director Konstantin Stanislavsky,
whose Moscow Art Theater promoted
an acting style based on authentic
emotional responses, drew on Ibsen's
drama. His later plays, including *Hedda*

Gabler, have attracted a different set of
directors, less interested in naturalism
and truth telling than in symbolism
and poetry. Film directors drawn to
surrealism and suggestive stagecraft,
such as Ingmar Bergman, continue to be
attracted first and foremost to Ibsen's
late plays.

Ibsen's influential career is full of
enigmas and contradictions. He began
with historical dramas, looking to the
past, and yet he would become the
herald of modern drama. He rejected
the dramatic techniques of standard
nineteenth-century drama, but he also
managed to transform them into something that seemed new, shocking, and
modern to his audience. He received
the most attention for his realist plays
but later turned realism itself in a more
poetic and symbolist direction. In the
end, he created a dramatic oeuvre of
unparalleled variety and complexity,
and this versatility has allowed him to
become one of the most popular dramatists of all time. Today, he ranks second only to Shakespeare as the world's
most-performed playwright. Shocking
and novel when it was first presented
to audiences, Ibsen's work has also stood
the test of time.

Hedda Gabler[1]

CHARACTERS

GEORGE TESMAN, *research fellow in
cultural history*
HEDDA TESMAN, *his wife*
MISS JULIANE TESMAN, *his aunt*

MRS. ELEVSTED
JUDGE BRACK
EILERT LØVBORG
BERTA, *the maid to the Tesmans*

The action takes place in the fashionable west side of Christiania, Norway's capital.

---

1. Translated by Rick Davis and Brian Johnston.

Act 1

A large, pleasantly and tastefully furnished drawing room, decorated in somber tones. In the rear wall is a wide doorway with the curtains pulled back. This doorway leads into a smaller room decorated in the same style. In the right wall of the drawing room is a folding door leading into the hall. In the opposite wall, a glass door, also with its curtains pulled back. Outside, through the windows, part of a covered veranda can be seen, along with trees in their autumn colors. In the foreground, an oval table surrounded by chairs. Downstage, near the right wall, is a broad, dark porcelain stove, a high-backed armchair, a footstool with cushions and two stools. Up in the right-hand corner, a corner-sofa and a small round table. Downstage, on the left side, a little distance from the wall, a sofa. Beyond the glass door, a piano. On both sides of the upstage doorway stand shelves displaying terra cotta and majolica objects. By the back wall of the inner room, a sofa, a table and a couple of chairs can be seen. Above the sofa hangs the portrait of a handsome elderly man in a general's uniform. Above the table, a hanging lamp with an opalescent glass shade. There are many flowers arranged in vases and glasses all around the drawing room. More flowers lie on the tables. The floors of both rooms are covered with thick rugs.

Morning light. The sun shines in through the glass door.

[MISS JULIE TESMAN, with hat and parasol, comes in from the hall, followed by BERTA, who carries a bouquet wrapped in paper. MISS TESMAN is a kindly, seemingly good-natured lady of about sixty-five, neatly but simply dressed in a grey visiting outfit. BERTA is a housemaid, getting on in years, with a homely and somewhat rustic appearance.]

MISS TESMAN [Stops just inside the doorway, listens, and speaks softly.] Well— I believe they're just now getting up!

BERTA [Also softly.] That's what I said, Miss. Just think—the steamer got in so late last night, and then—Lord, the young mistress wanted so much unpacked before she could settle down.

MISS TESMAN Well, well. Let them have a good night's sleep at least. But— they'll have some fresh morning air when they come down. [She crosses to the glass door and throws it wide open.]

BERTA [By the table, perplexed, holding the bouquet.] Hmm. Bless me if I can find a spot for these. I think I'd better put them down here, Miss. [Puts the bouquet down on the front of the piano.]

MISS TESMAN So, Berta dear, now you have a new mistress. As God's my witness, giving you up was a heavy blow.

BERTA And me, Miss—what can I say? I've been in yours and Miss Rina's service for so many blessed years—

MISS TESMAN We must bear it patiently, Berta. Truly, there's no other way. You know George has to have you in the house with him—he simply has to. You've looked after him since he was a little boy.

BERTA Yes, but Miss—I keep worrying about her, lying there at home—so completely helpless, poor thing. And that new girl! She'll never learn how to take care of sick people.

MISS TESMAN   Oh, I'll teach her how soon enough. And I'll be doing most of the work myself, you know. Don't you worry about my sister, Berta dear.

BERTA   Yes, but there's something else, Miss. I'm so afraid I won't satisfy the new mistress—

MISS TESMAN   Ffft—Good Lord—there might be a thing or two at first—

BERTA   Because she's so particular about things—

MISS TESMAN   Well, what do you expect? General Gabler's daughter—the way she lived in the general's day! Do you remember how she would go out riding with her father? In that long black outfit, with the feather in her hat?

BERTA   Oh, yes—I remember that all right. But I never thought she'd make a match with our Mr. Tesman.

MISS TESMAN   Neither did I. But—while I'm thinking about it, don't call George "Mister Tesman" any more. Now it's "Doctor Tesman."

BERTA   Yes—that's what the young mistress said as soon as they came in last night. So it's true?

MISS TESMAN   Yes, it's really true. Think of it, Berta—they've made him a doctor. While he was away, you understand. I didn't know a thing about it, until he told me himself, down at the pier.

BERTA   Well, he's so smart he could be anything he wanted to be. But I never thought he'd take up curing people too!

MISS TESMAN   No, no, no. He's not that kind of doctor. [*Nods significantly.*] As far as that goes, you might have to start calling him something even grander soon.

BERTA   Oh no! What could that be?

MISS TESMAN   [*Smiling.*] Hmm—wouldn't you like to know? [*Emotionally.*] Oh, dear God . . . if our sainted Joseph could look up from his grave and see what's become of his little boy. [*She looks around.*] But, Berta—what's this now? Why have you taken all the slipcovers off the furniture?

BERTA   The mistress told me to. She said she can't stand covers on chairs.

MISS TESMAN   But are they going to use this for their everyday living room?

BERTA   Yes, they will. At least she will. He—the doctor—he didn't say anything.

> [GEORGE TESMAN *enters, humming, from the right of the inner room, carry-ing an open, empty suitcase. He is a youthful-looking man of thirty-three, of medium height, with an open, round, and cheerful face, blond hair and beard. He wears glasses and is dressed in comfortable, somewhat disheveled clothes.*]

MISS TESMAN   Good morning, good morning, George!

TESMAN   Aunt Julie! Dear Aunt Julie! [*Goes over and shakes her hand.*] All the way here—so early in the day! Hm!

MISS TESMAN   Yes, you know me—I just had to peek in on you a little.

TESMAN   And after a short night's sleep at that!

MISS TESMAN   Oh, that's nothing at all to me.

TESMAN   So—you got home all right from the pier, hm?

MISS TESMAN   Yes, as it turned out, thanks be to God. The Judge was kind enough to see me right to the door.

TESMAN We felt so bad that we couldn't take you in the carriage—but you saw how many trunks and boxes Hedda had to bring.

MISS TESMAN Yes, it was amazing.

BERTA [*To* TESMAN.] Perhaps I should go in and ask the mistress if there's anything I can help her with.

TESMAN No, thank you, Berta. You don't have to do that. If she needs you, she'll ring—that's what she said.

BERTA [*Going out to right.*] Very well.

TESMAN Ah—but—Berta—take this suitcase with you.

BERTA [*Takes the case.*] I'll put it in the attic.

TESMAN Just imagine, Auntie. I'd stuffed that whole suitcase with notes—just notes! The things I managed to collect in those archives—really incredible! Ancient, remarkable things that no one had any inkling of.

MISS TESMAN Ah yes—you certainly haven't wasted any time on your honeymoon.

TESMAN Yes—I can really say that's true. But, Auntie, take off your hat—Here, let's see. Let me undo that ribbon, hm?

MISS TESMAN [*While he does so.*] Ah, dear God—this is just what it was like when you were home with us.

TESMAN [*Examining the hat as he holds it.*] My, my—isn't this a fine, elegant hat you've got for yourself.

MISS TESMAN I bought it for Hedda's sake.

TESMAN For Hedda's—hm?

MISS TESMAN Yes, so Hedda won't feel ashamed of me if we go out for a walk together.

TESMAN [*Patting her cheek.*] You think of everything, Auntie Julie, don't you? [*Putting her hat on a chair by the table.*] And now—let's just settle down here on the sofa until Hedda comes. [*They sit. She puts her parasol down near the sofa.*]

MISS TESMAN [*Takes both his hands and gazes at him.*] What a blessing to have you here, bright as day, right before my eyes again, George. Sainted Joseph's own boy!

TESMAN For me too. To see you again, Aunt Julie—who've been both father and mother to me.

MISS TESMAN Yes, I know you'll always have a soft spot for your old aunts.

TESMAN But no improvement at all with Rina, hm?

MISS TESMAN Oh dear no—and none to be expected poor thing. She lies there just as she has all these years. But I pray that Our Lord lets me keep her just a little longer. Otherwise I don't know what I'd do with my life, George. Especially now, you know—when I don't have you to take care of any more.

TESMAN [*Patting her on the back.*] There. There. There.

MISS TESMAN Oh—just to think that you've become a married man, George. And that you're the one who carried off Hedda Gabler! Beautiful Hedda Gabler. Imagine—with all her suitors.

TESMAN [*Hums a little and smiles complacently.*] Yes, I believe I have quite a few friends in town who envy me, hm?

MISS TESMAN And then—you got to take such a long honeymoon—more than five—almost six months . . .

TESMAN Yes, but it was also part of my research, you know. All those archives I had to wade through—and all the books I had to read!

MISS TESMAN I suppose you're right. [*Confidentially and more quietly.*] But listen, George—isn't there something—something extra you want to tell me?

TESMAN About the trip?

MISS TESMAN Yes.

TESMAN No—I can't think of anything I didn't mention in my letters. I was given my doctorate—but I told you that yesterday.

MISS TESMAN So you did. But I mean—whether you might have any—any kind of—prospects—?

TESMAN Prospects?

MISS TESMAN Good Lord, George—I'm your old aunt.

TESMAN Well of course I have prospects.

MISS TESMAN Aha!

TESMAN I have excellent prospects of becoming a professor one of these days. But Aunt Julie dear, you already know that.

MISS TESMAN [*With a little laugh.*] You're right, I do. [*Changing the subject.*] But about your trip. It must have cost a lot.

TESMAN Well, thank God, that huge fellowship paid for a good part of it.

MISS TESMAN But how did you make it last for the both of you?

TESMAN That's the tricky part, isn't it?

MISS TESMAN And on top of that, when you're travelling with a lady! That's always going to cost you more, or so I've heard.

TESMAN You're right—it was a bit more costly. But Hedda just had to have that trip, Auntie. She really had to. There was no choice.

MISS TESMAN Well, I suppose not. These days a honeymoon trip is essential, it seems. But now tell me—have you had a good look around the house?

TESMAN Absolutely! I've been up since dawn.

MISS TESMAN And what do you think about all of it?

TESMAN It's splendid! Only I can't think of what we'll do with those two empty rooms between the back parlor and Hedda's bedroom.

MISS TESMAN [*Lightly laughing.*] My dear George—when the time comes, you'll think of what to do with them.

TESMAN Oh, of course—as I add to my library, hm?

MISS TESMAN That's right, my boy—of course I was thinking about your library.

TESMAN Most of all I'm just so happy for Hedda. Before we got engaged she'd always say how she couldn't imagine living anywhere but here—in Prime Minister Falk's house.

MISS TESMAN Yes—imagine. And then it came up for sale just after you left for your trip.

TESMAN Aunt Julie, we really had luck on our side, hm?

MISS TESMAN But the expense, George. This will all be costly for you.

TESMAN [*Looks at her disconcertedly.*] Yes. It might be. It might be, Auntie.

MISS TESMAN Ah, God only knows.

TESMAN How much, do you think? Approximately. Hm?

MISS TESMAN I can't possibly tell before all the bills are in.

TESMAN Luckily Judge Brack lined up favorable terms for me—he wrote as much to Hedda.

MISS TESMAN That's right—don't you ever worry about that, my boy. All this furniture, and the carpets? I put up the security for it.

TESMAN Security? You? Dear Auntie Julie, what kind of security could you give?

MISS TESMAN I took out a mortgage on our annuity.

TESMAN What? On your—and Aunt Rina's annuity!

MISS TESMAN I couldn't think of any other way.

TESMAN [*Standing in front of her.*] Have you gone completely out of your mind, Auntie? That annuity is all you and Aunt Rina have to live on.

MISS TESMAN Now, now, take it easy. It's just a formality, you understand. Judge Brack said so. He was good enough to arrange it all for me. Just a formality, he said.

TESMAN That could very well be, but all the same . . .

MISS TESMAN You'll be earning your own living now, after all. And, good Lord, so what if we do have to open the purse a little, spend a little bit at first? That would only make us happy.

TESMAN Auntie . . . you never get tired of sacrificing yourself for me.

MISS TESMAN [*Rises and lays her hands on his shoulders.*] What joy do I have in the world, my dearest boy, other than smoothing out the path for you? You, without a father or mother to take care of you . . . but we've reached our destination, my dear. Maybe things looked black from time to time. But, praise God, George, you've come out on top!

TESMAN Yes, it's really amazing how everything has gone according to plan.

MISS TESMAN And those who were against you—those who would have blocked your way—they're at the bottom of the pit. They've fallen, George. And the most dangerous one, he fell the farthest. Now he just lies there where he fell, the poor sinner.

TESMAN Have you heard anything about Eilert—since I went away, I mean?

MISS TESMAN Nothing, except they say he published a new book.

TESMAN What? Eilert Løvborg? Just recently, hm?

MISS TESMAN That's what they say. God only knows how there could be anything to it. But when *your* book comes out—now that will be something else again, won't it, George? What's it going to be about?

TESMAN It will deal with the Domestic Craftsmanship Practices of Medieval Brabant.[2]

MISS TESMAN Just think—you can write about that kind of thing too.

TESMAN However, it might be quite a while before that book is ready. I've got all these incredible collections that have to be put in order first.

MISS TESMAN Ordering and collecting—you're certainly good at that. You're not the son of sainted Joseph for nothing.

TESMAN And I'm so eager to get going. Especially now that I've got my own snug house and home to work in.

MISS TESMAN And most of all, now that you've got her—your heart's desire, dear, dear George!

---

2. In the Middle Ages, Brabant was a duchy located in parts of what are now Belgium and the Netherlands.

TESMAN [*Embracing her.*] Yes, Auntie Julie! Hedda . . . that's the most beautiful thing of all! [*Looking toward the doorway.*] I think that's her, hm?

> [HEDDA *comes in from the left side of the inner room. She is a lady of twenty-nine. Her face and figure are aristocratic and elegant. Her complexion is pale. Her eyes are steel-grey, cold and clear. Her hair is an attractive medium brown but not particularly full. She is wearing a tasteful, somewhat loose-fitting morning gown.*]

MISS TESMAN [*Going to meet* HEDDA.] Good morning, Hedda, my dear. Good morning.

HEDDA [*Extending her hand.*] Good morning, Miss Tesman, my dear. You're here so early. How nice of you.

MISS TESMAN [*Looking somewhat embarrassed.*] Well now, how did the young mistress sleep in her new home?

HEDDA Fine thanks. Well enough.

TESMAN [*Laughing.*] Well enough! That's a good one, Hedda. You were sleeping like a log when I got up.

HEDDA Yes, lucky for me. But of course you have to get used to anything new, Miss Tesman. A little at a time. [*Looks toward the window.*] Uch! Look at that. The maid opened the door. I'm drowning in all this sunlight.

MISS TESMAN [*Going to the door.*] Well then, let's close it.

HEDDA No, no, don't do that. Tesman my dear, just close the curtains. That gives a gentler light.

TESMAN [*By the door.*] All right, all right. Now then, Hedda. You've got both fresh air and sunlight.

HEDDA Yes, fresh air. That's what I need with all these flowers all over the place. But Miss Tesman, won't you sit down?

MISS TESMAN No, but thank you. Now that I know everything's all right here, I've got to see about getting home again. Home to that poor dear who's lying there in pain.

TESMAN Be sure to give her my respects, won't you? And tell her I'll stop by and look in on her later today.

MISS TESMAN Yes, yes I'll certainly do that. But would you believe it, George? [*She rustles around in the pocket of her skirt.*] I almost forgot. Here, I brought something for you.

TESMAN And what might that be, Auntie, hm?

MISS TESMAN [*Brings out a flat package wrapped in newspaper and hands it to him.*] Here you are, my dear boy.

TESMAN [*Opening it.*] Oh my Lord. You kept them for me, Aunt Julie. Hedda, isn't this touching, hm?

HEDDA Well, what is it?

TESMAN My old house slippers. My slippers.

HEDDA Oh yes, I remember how often you talked about them on our trip.

TESMAN Yes, well, I really missed them. [*Goes over to her.*] Now you can see them for yourself, Hedda.

HEDDA [*Moves over to the stove.*] Oh, no thanks. I don't really care to.

TESMAN [*Following after her.*] Just think, Aunt Rina lying there embroidering for me, sick as she was. Oh, you couldn't possibly believe how many memories are tangled up in these slippers.

HEDDA [*By the table.*]   Not for me.

MISS TESMAN   Hedda's quite right about that, George.

TESMAN   Yes, but now that she's in the family I thought—

HEDDA   That maid won't last, Tesman.

MISS TESMAN   Berta—?

TESMAN   What makes you say that, hm?

HEDDA [*Pointing.*]   Look, she's left her old hat lying there on that chair.

TESMAN [*Terrified, dropping the slippers on the floor.*]   Hedda—!

HEDDA   What if someone came in and saw that.

TESMAN   But Hedda—that's Aunt Julie's hat.

HEDDA   Really?

MISS TESMAN [*Taking the hat.*]   Yes, it really is. And for that matter it's not so old either, my dear little Hedda.

HEDDA   Oh, I really didn't get a good look at it, Miss Tesman.

MISS TESMAN [*Tying the hat on her head.*]   Actually I've never worn it before today—and the good Lord knows that's true.

TESMAN   And an elegant hat it is too. Really magnificent.

MISS TESMAN [*She looks around.*]   Oh that's as may be, George. My parasol? Ah, here it is. [*She takes it.*] That's mine too. [*She mutters.*] Not Berta's.

TESMAN   A new hat and a new parasol. Just think, Hedda.

HEDDA   Very charming, very attractive.

TESMAN   That's true, hm? But Auntie, take a good look at Hedda before you go. Look at how charming and attractive she is.

MISS TESMAN   Oh my dear, that's nothing new. Hedda's been lovely all her life. [*She nods and goes across to the right.*]

TESMAN [*Following her.*]   Yes, but have you noticed how she's blossomed, how well she's filled out on our trip?

HEDDA   Oh, leave it alone!

MISS TESMAN [*Stops and turns.*]   Filled out?

TESMAN   Yes, Aunt Julie. You can't see it so well right now in that gown— but I, who have a little better opportunity to—

HEDDA [*By the glass door impatiently.*]   Oh you don't have the opportunity for anything.

TESMAN   It was that mountain air down in the Tyrol.

HEDDA [*Curtly interrupting.*]   I'm the same as when I left.

TESMAN   You keep saying that. But it's true, isn't it Auntie?

MISS TESMAN [*Folding her hands and gazing at* HEDDA.]   Lovely . . . lovely . . . lovely. That's Hedda. [*She goes over to her and with both her hands takes her head, bends it down, kisses her hair.*]   God bless and keep Hedda Tesman for George's sake.

HEDDA [*Gently freeing herself.*]   Ah—! Let me out!

MISS TESMAN [*With quiet emotion.*]   I'll come look in on you two every single day.

TESMAN   Yes, Auntie, do that, won't you, hm?

MISS TESMAN   Good-bye, good-bye.

> [*She goes out through the hall door.* TESMAN *follows her out. The door remains half open.* TESMAN *is heard repeating his greetings to Aunt Rina and his thanks for the slippers. While this is happening,* HEDDA *walks around the*

room raising her arms and clenching her fists as if in a rage. Then she draws the curtains back from the door, stands there and looks out. After a short time, TESMAN *comes in and closes the door behind him.*]

TESMAN [*Picking up the slippers from the floor.*] What are you looking at, Hedda?

HEDDA [*Calm and controlled again.*] Just the leaves. So yellow and so withered.

TESMAN [*Wrapping up the slippers and placing them on the table.*] Yes, well—we're into September now.

HEDDA [*Once more uneasy.*] Yes—It's already—already September.

TESMAN Didn't you think Aunt Julie was acting strange just now, almost formal? What do you suppose got into her?

HEDDA I really don't know her. Isn't that the way she usually is?

TESMAN No, not like today.

HEDDA [*Leaving the glass door.*] Do you think she was upset by the hat business?

TESMAN Not really. Maybe a little, for just a moment—

HEDDA But where did she get her manners, flinging her hat around any way she likes here in the drawing room. People just don't act that way.

TESMAN Well, I'm sure she won't do it again.

HEDDA Anyway, I'll smooth everything over with her soon enough.

TESMAN Yes, Hedda, if you would do that.

HEDDA When you visit them later today, invite her here for the evening.

TESMAN Yes, that's just what I'll do. And there's one more thing you can do that would really make her happy.

HEDDA Well?

TESMAN If you just bring yourself to call her Aunt Julie, for my sake, Hedda, hm?

HEDDA Tesman, for God's sake, don't ask me to do that. I've told you that before. I'll try to call her Aunt once in a while and that's enough.

TESMAN Oh well, I just thought that now that you're part of the family . . .

HEDDA Hmm. I don't know—[*She crosses upstage to the doorway.*]

TESMAN [*After a pause.*] Is something the matter, Hedda?

HEDDA I was just looking at my old piano. It really doesn't go with these other things.

TESMAN As soon as my salary starts coming in, we'll see about trading it in for a new one.

HEDDA Oh, no, don't trade it in. I could never let it go. We'll leave it in the back room instead. And then we'll get a new one to put in here. I mean, as soon as we get the chance.

TESMAN [*A little dejectedly.*] Yes, I suppose we could do that.

HEDDA [*Taking the bouquet from the piano.*] These flowers weren't here when we got in last night.

TESMAN I suppose Aunt Julie brought them.

HEDDA [*Looks into the bouquet.*] Here's a card. [*Takes it out and reads.*] "Will call again later today." Guess who it's from.

TESMAN Who is it, hm?

HEDDA It says Mrs. Elvsted.

TESMAN   Really. Mrs. Elvsted. She used to be Miss Rysing.

HEDDA   Yes, that's the one. She had all that irritating hair she'd always be fussing with. An old flame of yours, I've heard.

TESMAN [*Laughs.*]   Oh, not for long and before I knew you, Hedda. And she's here in town. How about that.

HEDDA   Strange that she should come visiting us. I hardly know her except from school.

TESMAN   Yes, and of course I haven't seen her since—well God knows how long. How could she stand it holed up out there so far from everything, hm?

HEDDA [*Reflects a moment and then suddenly speaks.*]   Just a minute, Tesman. Doesn't he live out that way, Eilert Løvborg, I mean?

TESMAN   Yes, right up in that area.

[BERTA *comes in from the hallway.*]

BERTA   Ma'am, she's back again. The lady who came by with the flowers an hour ago. [*Pointing.*] Those you've got in your hand, Ma'am.

HEDDA   Is she then? Please ask her to come in.

[BERTA *opens the door for* MRS. ELVSTED *and then leaves.* MRS. ELVSTED *is slender with soft, pretty features. Her eyes are light blue, large, round and slightly protruding. Her expression is one of alarm and question. Her hair is remarkably light, almost a white gold and exceptionally rich and full. She is a couple of years younger than* HEDDA. *Her costume is a dark visiting dress, tasteful but not of the latest fashion.*]

HEDDA [*Goes to meet her in a friendly manner.*]   Hello my dear Mrs. Elvsted. So delightful to see you again.

MRS. ELVSTED [*Nervous, trying to control herself.*]   Yes, it's been so long since we've seen each other.

TESMAN [*Shakes her hand.*]   And we could say the same, hm?

HEDDA   Thank you for the lovely flowers.

MRS. ELVSTED   I would have come yesterday right away but I heard you were on a trip—

TESMAN   So you've just come into town, hm?

MRS. ELVSTED   Yesterday around noon. I was absolutely desperate when I heard you weren't home.

HEDDA   Desperate, why?

TESMAN   My dear Miss Rysing—I mean Mrs. Elvsted.

HEDDA   There isn't some sort of trouble—?

MRS. ELVSTED   Yes there is—and I don't know another living soul to turn to here in town.

HEDDA [*Sets the flowers down on the table.*]   All right then, let's sit down here on the sofa.

MRS. ELVSTED   Oh no, I'm too upset to sit down.

HEDDA   No you're not. Come over here. [*She draws* MRS. ELVSTED *to the sofa and sits beside her.*]

TESMAN   Well, and now Mrs.—

HEDDA   Did something happen up at your place?

MRS. ELVSTED   Yes—That's it—well, not exactly—Oh, I don't want you to misunderstand me—

HEDDA Well then the best thing is just to tell it straight out, Mrs. Elvsted—why?

TESMAN That's why you came here, hm?

MRS. ELVSTED Yes, of course. So I'd better tell you, if you don't already know, that Eilert Løvborg is in town.

HEDDA Løvborg?

TESMAN Eilert Løvborg's back again? Just think, Hedda.

HEDDA Good Lord, Tesman, I can hear.

MRS. ELVSTED He's been back now for about a week. The whole week alone here where he can fall in with all kinds of bad company. This town's a dangerous place for him.

HEDDA But my dear Mrs. Elvsted, how does this involve you?

MRS. ELVSTED [*With a scared expression, speaking quickly.*] He was the children's tutor.

HEDDA Your children?

MRS. ELVSTED My husband's. I don't have any.

HEDDA The stepchildren then?

MRS. ELVSTED Yes.

TESMAN [*Somewhat awkwardly.*] But was he sufficiently—I don't know how to say this—sufficiently regular in his habits to be trusted with that kind of job, hm?

MRS. ELVSTED For the past two years no one could say anything against him.

TESMAN Really, nothing. Just think, Hedda.

HEDDA I hear.

MRS. ELVSTED Nothing at all, I assure you. Not in any way. But even so, now that I know he's here in the city alone and with money in his pocket I'm deathly afraid for him.

TESMAN But why isn't he up there with you and your husband, hm?

MRS. ELVSTED When the book came out he was too excited to stay up there with us.

TESMAN Yes, that's right. Aunt Julie said he'd come out with a new book.

MRS. ELVSTED Yes, a major new book on the progress of civilization—in its entirety I mean. That was two weeks ago. And it's been selling wonderfully. Everyone's reading it. It's created a huge sensation—why?

TESMAN All that really? Must be something he had lying around from his better days.

MRS. ELVSTED From before, you mean?

TESMAN Yes.

MRS. ELVSTED No, he wrote the whole thing while he was up there living with us. Just in the last year.

TESMAN That's wonderful to hear, Hedda. Just think!

MRS. ELVSTED Yes, if only it continues.

HEDDA Have you met him here in town?

MRS. ELVSTED No, not yet. I had a terrible time hunting down his address but this morning I finally found it.

HEDDA [*Looks searchingly.*] I can't help thinking this is a little odd on your husband's part.

MRS. ELVSTED [*Starts nervously.*]   My husband—What?

HEDDA   That he'd send you to town on this errand. That he didn't come himself to look for his friend.

MRS. ELVSTED   Oh no, no, no. My husband doesn't have time for that. And anyway I had to do some shopping too.

HEDDA [*Smiling slightly.*]   Oh well, that's different then.

MRS. ELVSTED [*Gets up quickly, ill at ease.*]   And now I beg you, Mr. Tesman, please be kind to Eilert Løvborg if he comes here—and I'm sure he will. You were such good friends in the old days. You have interests in common. The same area of research, as far as I can tell.

TESMAN   Yes, that used to be the case anyway.

MRS. ELVSTED   Yes, that's why I'm asking you—from the bottom of my heart to be sure to—that you'll—that you'll keep a watchful eye on him. Oh, Mr. Tesman, will you do that—will you promise me that?

TESMAN   Yes, with all my heart, Mrs. Rysing.

HEDDA   Elvsted.

TESMAN   I'll do anything in my power for Eilert. You can be sure of it.

MRS. ELVSTED   Oh, that is so kind of you. [*She presses his hands.*] Many, many thanks. [*Frightened.*] Because my husband thinks so highly of him.

HEDDA [*Rising.*]   You should write to him, Tesman. He might not come to you on his own.

TESMAN   Yes, that's the way to do it, Hedda, hm?

HEDDA   And the sooner the better. Right now, I think.

MRS. ELVSTED [*Beseechingly.*]   Yes, if you only could.

TESMAN   I'll write to him this moment. Do you have his address, Mrs. Elvsted?

MRS. ELVSTED   Yes. [*She takes a small slip of paper from her pocket and hands it to him.*] Here it is.

TESMAN   Good, good. I'll go write him—[*Looks around just a minute.*]—Where are my slippers? Ah, here they are. [*Takes the packet and is about to leave.*]

HEDDA   Make sure your note is very friendly—nice and long too.

TESMAN   Yes, you can count on me.

MRS. ELVSTED   But please don't say a word about my asking you to do it.

TESMAN   Oh, that goes without saying.

   [TESMAN *leaves to the right through the rear room.*]

HEDDA [*Goes over to* MRS. ELVSTED, *smiles and speaks softly.*]   There, now we've killed two birds with one stone.

MRS. ELVSTED   What do you mean?

HEDDA   Didn't you see that I wanted him out of the way?

MRS. ELVSTED   Yes, to write the letter—

HEDDA   So I could talk to you alone.

MRS. ELVSTED [*Confused.*]   About this thing?

HEDDA   Yes, exactly, about this thing.

MRS. ELVSTED [*Apprehensively.*]   But there's nothing more to it, Mrs. Tesman, really there isn't.

HEDDA   Ah, but there is indeed. There's a great deal more. I can see that much. Come here, let's sit down together. Have a real heart-to-heart talk.

   [*She forces* MRS. ELVSTED *into the armchair by the stove and sits down herself on one of the small stools.*]

MRS. ELVSTED [*Nervously looking at her watch.*]   Mrs. Tesman, I was just thinking of leaving.

HEDDA   Now you can't be in such a hurry, can you? Talk to me a little bit about how things are at home.

MRS. ELVSTED   Oh, that's the last thing I want to talk about.

HEDDA   But to me? Good Lord, we went to the same school.

MRS. ELVSTED   Yes, but you were one class ahead of me. Oh, I was so afraid of you then.

HEDDA   Afraid of me?

MRS. ELVSTED   Horribly afraid. Whenever we'd meet on the stairs you always used to pull my hair.

HEDDA   No, did I do that?

MRS. ELVSTED   Yes, you did—and once you said you'd burn it off.

HEDDA   Oh, just silly talk, you know.

MRS. ELVSTED   Yes, but I was so stupid in those days and anyway since then we've gotten to be so distant from each other. Our circles have just been totally different.

HEDDA   Well let's see if we can get closer again. Listen now, I know we were good friends in school. We used to call each other by our first names.

MRS. ELVSTED   No, no, I think you're mistaken.

HEDDA   I certainly am not. I remember it perfectly and so we have to be perfectly open with each other just like in the old days. [*Moves the stool closer.*] There now. [*Kisses her cheek.*] Now you must call me Hedda.

MRS. ELVSTED [*Pressing and patting her hands.*]   Oh, you're being so friendly to me. I'm just not used to that.

HEDDA   There, there, there. I'll stop being so formal with you and I'll call you my dear Thora.

MRS. ELVSTED   My name is Thea.

HEDDA   That's right, of course, I meant Thea. [*Looks at her compassionately.*] So you're not used to friendship, Thea, in your own home?

MRS. ELVSTED   If I only had a home, but I don't. I've never had one.

HEDDA [*Glances at her.*]   I suspected it might be something like that.

MRS. ELVSTED [*Staring helplessly before her.*]   Yes, yes, yes.

HEDDA   I can't exactly remember now, but didn't you go up to Sheriff Elvsted's as a housekeeper?

MRS. ELVSTED   Actually I was supposed to be a governess but his wife—at that time—she was an invalid, mostly bedridden, so I had to take care of the house too.

HEDDA   So in the end you became mistress of your own house.

MRS. ELVSTED [*Heavily.*]   Yes, that's what I became.

HEDDA   Let me see. How long has that been?

MRS. ELVSTED   Since I was married?

HEDDA   Yes.

MRS. ELVSTED   Five years now.

HEDDA   That's right, it must be about that.

MRS. ELVSTED   Oh these five years—! Or the last two or three anyway—! Ah, Mrs. Tesman, if you could just imagine.

HEDDA [*Slaps her lightly on the hand.*]   Mrs. Tesman; really, Thea.

MRS. ELVSTED   No, no, of course, I'll try to remember. Anyway, Hedda, if you could only imagine.

HEDDA [*Casually.*]   It seems to me that Eilert Løvborg's been living up there for about three years, hasn't he?

MRS. ELVSTED [*Looks uncertainly at her.*]   Eilert Løvborg? Yes, that's about right.

HEDDA   Did you know him from before—from here in town?

MRS. ELVSTED   Hardly at all. I mean his name of course.

HEDDA   But up there he'd come to visit you at the house?

MRS. ELVSTED   Yes, every day. He'd read to the children. I couldn't manage everything myself, you see.

HEDDA   No, of course not. And what about your husband? His work must take him out of the house quite a bit.

MRS. ELVSTED   Yes, as you might imagine. He's the sheriff so he has to go traveling around the whole district.

HEDDA [*Leaning against the arm of the chair.*]   Thea, my poor sweet Thea— You've got to tell me everything just the way it is.

MRS. ELVSTED   All right, but you've got to ask the questions.

HEDDA   So, Thea, what's your husband really like? I mean, you know, to be with? Is he good to you?

MRS. ELVSTED [*Evasively.*]   He thinks he does everything for the best.

HEDDA   I just think he's a little too old for you. He's twenty years older, isn't he?

MRS. ELVSTED [*Irritatedly.*]   There's that too. There's a lot of things. I just can't stand being with him. We don't have a single thought in common, not a single thing in the world, he and I.

HEDDA   But doesn't he care for you at all in his own way?

MRS. ELVSTED   I can't tell what he feels. I think I'm just useful to him, and it doesn't cost very much to keep me. I'm very inexpensive.

HEDDA   That's a mistake.

MRS. ELVSTED [*Shaking her head.*]   Can't be any other way, not with him. He only cares about himself and maybe about the children a little.

HEDDA   And also for Eilert Løvborg, Thea.

MRS. ELVSTED [*Stares at her.*]   For Eilert Løvborg? Why do you think that?

HEDDA   Well, my dear, he sent you all the way into town to look for him. [*Smiling almost imperceptibly.*] And besides, you said so yourself, to Tesman.

MRS. ELVSTED [*With a nervous shudder.*]   Oh yes, I suppose I did. No, I'd better just tell you the whole thing. It's bound to come to light sooner or later anyway.

HEDDA   But my dear Thea.

MRS. ELVSTED   All right, short and sweet. My husband doesn't know that I'm gone.

HEDDA   What, your husband doesn't know?

MRS. ELVSTED   Of course not. Anyway he's not at home. He was out traveling. I just couldn't stand it any longer, Hedda, it was impossible. I would have been so completely alone up there.

HEDDA   Well, then what?

MRS. ELVSTED   Then I packed some of my things, just the necessities, all in secret, and I left the house.

HEDDA   Just like that?

MRS. ELVSTED   Yes, and I took the train to town.

HEDDA   Oh, my good, dear Thea. You dared to do that!

MRS. ELVSTED   [*Gets up and walks across the floor.*]   Well, what else could I do?

HEDDA   What do you think your husband will say when you go home again?

MRS. ELVSTED   [*By the table looking at her.*]   Up there to him?

HEDDA   Of course, of course.

MRS. ELVSTED   I'm never going back up there.

HEDDA   [*Gets up and goes closer to her.*]   So you've really done it? You've really run away from everything?

MRS. ELVSTED   Yes, I couldn't think of anything else to do.

HEDDA   But you did it—so openly.

MRS. ELVSTED   Oh, you can't keep something like that a secret anyway.

HEDDA   Well, what do you think people will say about you, Thea?

MRS. ELVSTED   They'll say whatever they want, God knows. [*She sits tired and depressed on the sofa.*] But I only did what I had to do.

HEDDA   [*After a brief pause.*]   So what will you do with yourself now?

MRS. ELVSTED   I don't know yet. All I know is that I've got to live here where Eilert Løvborg lives if I'm going to live at all.

HEDDA   [*Moves a chair closer from the table, sits beside her and strokes her hands.*]   Thea, my dear, how did it come about, this—bond between you and Eilert Løvborg?

MRS. ELVSTED   Oh, it just happened, little by little. I started to have a kind of power over him.

HEDDA   Really?

MRS. ELVSTED   He gave up his old ways—and not because I begged him to. I never dared do that. But he started to notice that those kinds of things upset me, so he gave them up.

HEDDA   [*Concealing an involuntary, derisive smile.*]   So you rehabilitated him, as they say. You, little Thea.

MRS. ELVSTED   That's what he said, anyway. And for his part he's made a real human being out of me. Taught me to think, to understand all sorts of things.

HEDDA   So he read to you too, did he?

MRS. ELVSTED   No, not exactly, but he talked to me. Talked without stopping about all sorts of great things. And then there was that wonderful time when I shared in his work, when I helped him.

HEDDA   You got to do that?

MRS. ELVSTED   Yes. Whenever he wrote anything, we had to agree on it first.

HEDDA   Like two good comrades.

MRS. ELVSTED   [*Eagerly.*]   Yes, comrades. Imagine, Hedda, that's what he called it too. I should feel so happy, but I can't yet because I don't know how long it will last.

HEDDA   Are you that unsure of him?

MRS. ELVSTED   [*Dejectedly.*]   There's the shadow of a woman between Eilert Løvborg and me.

HEDDA [*Stares intently at her.*] Who could that be?

MRS. ELVSTED I don't know. Someone from his past. Someone he's never really been able to forget.

HEDDA What has he told you about all this?

MRS. ELVSTED He's only talked about it once and very vaguely.

HEDDA Yes, what did he say?

MRS. ELVSTED He said that when they broke up she was going to shoot him with a pistol.

HEDDA [*Calm and controlled.*] That's nonsense, people just don't act that way here.

MRS. ELVSTED No they don't—so I think it's got to be that red-haired singer that he once—

HEDDA Yes, that could well be.

MRS. ELVSTED Because I remember they used to say about her that she went around with loaded pistols.

HEDDA Well, then it's her, of course.

MRS. ELVSTED [*Wringing her hands.*] Yes, but Hedda, just think, I hear this singer is in town again. Oh, I'm so afraid.

HEDDA [*Glancing toward the back room.*] Shh, here comes Tesman. [*She gets up and whispers.*] Now, Thea, all of this is strictly between you and me.

MRS. ELVSTED [*Jumping up.*] Oh yes, yes, for God's sake!

[GEORGE TESMAN, *a letter in his hand, comes in from the right side of the inner room.*]

TESMAN There now, the epistle is prepared.

HEDDA Well done—but Mrs. Elvsted's got to leave now, I think. Just a minute, I'll follow you as far as the garden gate.

TESMAN Hedda dear, do you think Berta could see to this?

HEDDA [*Takes the letter.*] I'll instruct her.

[BERTA *comes in from the hall.*]

BERTA Judge Brack is here. Says he'd like to pay his respects.

HEDDA Yes, ask the Judge to be so good as to come in, and then—listen here now—Put this letter in the mailbox.

BERTA [*Takes the letter.*] Yes, ma'am.

[*She opens the door for* JUDGE BRACK *and then goes out.* JUDGE BRACK *is forty-five years old, short, well built and moves easily. He has a round face and an aristocratic profile. His short hair is still almost black. His eyes are lively and ironic. He has thick eyebrows and a thick moustache, trimmed square at the ends. He is wearing outdoor clothing, elegant, but a little too young in style. He has a monocle in one eye. Now and then he lets it drop.*]

BRACK [*Bows with his hat in his hand.*] Does one dare to call so early?

HEDDA One does dare.

TESMAN [*Shakes his hand.*] You're welcome any time. Judge Brack, Mrs. Rysing. [HEDDA *sighs.*]

BRACK [*Bows.*] Aha, delighted.

HEDDA [*Looks at him laughing.*] Nice to see you by daylight for a change, Judge.

BRACK Do I look different?

HEDDA Yes, younger.

BRACK   You're too kind.

TESMAN   Well, how about Hedda, hm? Doesn't she look fine? Hasn't she filled out?

HEDDA   Stop it now. You should be thanking Judge Brack for all of his hard work—

BRACK   Nonsense. It was my pleasure.

HEDDA   There's a loyal soul. But here's my friend burning to get away. Excuse me, Judge, I'll be right back.

[*Mutual good-byes.* MRS. ELVSTED *and* HEDDA *leave by the hall door.*]

BRACK   Well, now, your wife's satisfied, more or less?

TESMAN   Oh yes, we can't thank you enough. I gather there might be a little more rearrangement here and there and one or two things still missing. A couple of small things yet to be procured.

BRACK   Is that so?

TESMAN   But nothing for you to worry about. Hedda said that she'd look for everything herself. Let's sit down.

BRACK   Thanks. Just for a minute. [*Sits by the table.*] Now, my dear Tesman, there's something we need to talk about.

TESMAN   Oh yes, ah, I understand. [*Sits down.*] Time for a new topic. Time for the serious part of the celebration, hm?

BRACK   Oh, I wouldn't worry too much about the finances just yet— although I must tell you that it would have been better if we'd managed things a little more frugally.

TESMAN   But there was no way to do that. You know Hedda, Judge, you know her well. I couldn't possibly ask her to live in a middle-class house.

BRACK   No, that's precisely the problem.

TESMAN   And luckily it can't be too long before I get my appointment.[3]

BRACK   Well, you know, these things often drag on and on.

TESMAN   Have you heard anything further, hm?

BRACK   Nothing certain. [*Changing the subject.*] But there is one thing. I've got a piece of news for you.

TESMAN   Well?

BRACK   Your old friend Eilert Løvborg's back in town.

TESMAN   I already know.

BRACK   Oh, how did you find out?

TESMAN   She told me, that lady who just left with Hedda.

BRACK   Oh, I see. I didn't quite get her name.

TESMAN   Mrs. Elvsted.

BRACK   Ah yes, the sheriff's wife. Yes, he's been staying up there with them.

TESMAN   And I'm so glad to hear that he's become a responsible person again.

BRACK   Yes, one is given to understand that.

TESMAN   And he's come out with a new book, hm?

BRACK   He has indeed.

TESMAN   And it's caused quite a sensation.

BRACK   It's caused an extraordinary sensation.

---

3. Tesman expects to be appointed to a professorship. These positions were much less numerous and more socially prominent than their contemporary American counterparts.

TESMAN   Just think, isn't that wonderful to hear. With all his remarkable talents, I was absolutely certain he was down for good.

BRACK   That was certainly the general opinion.

TESMAN   But I can't imagine what he'll do with himself now. What will he live on, hm?

[*During these last words,* HEDDA *has entered from the hallway.*]

HEDDA [*To* BRACK, *laughing a little scornfully.*]   Tesman is constantly going around worrying about what to live on.

TESMAN   My Lord, we're talking about Eilert Løvborg, dear.

HEDDA [*Looking quickly at him.*]   Oh yes? [*Sits down in the armchair by the stove and asks casually.*] What's the matter with him?

TESMAN   Well, he must have spent his inheritance a long time ago, and he can't really write a new book every year, hm? So I was just asking what was going to become of him.

BRACK   Perhaps I can enlighten you on that score.

TESMAN   Oh?

BRACK   You might remember that he has some relatives with more than a little influence.

TESMAN   Unfortunately they've pretty much washed their hands of him.

BRACK   In the old days they thought of him as the family's great shining hope.

TESMAN   Yes, in the old days, possibly, but he took care of that himself.

HEDDA   Who knows? [*Smiles slightly.*] Up at the Elvsteds' he's been the target of a reclamation project.

BRACK   And there's this new book.

TESMAN   Well, God willing, they'll help him out some way or another. I've just written to him, Hedda, asking him to come over this evening.

BRACK   But my dear Tesman, you're coming to my stag party[4] this evening. You promised me on the pier last night.

HEDDA   Had you forgotten, Tesman?

TESMAN   Yes, to be perfectly honest, I had.

BRACK   For that matter, you can be sure he won't come.

TESMAN   Why do you say that, hm?

BRACK [*Somewhat hesitantly getting up and leaning his hands on the back of his chair.*]   My dear Tesman, you too, Mrs. Tesman, in good conscience I can't let you go on living in ignorance of something like this.

TESMAN   Something about Eilert, hm?

BRACK   About both of you.

TESMAN   My dear Judge, tell me what it is.

BRACK   You ought to prepare yourself for the fact that your appointment might not come through as quickly as you expect.

TESMAN [*Jumps up in alarm.*]   Has something held it up?

BRACK   The appointment might just possibly be subject to a competition.

TESMAN   A competition! Just think of that, Hedda!

HEDDA [*Leans further back in her chair.*]   Ah yes—yes.

TESMAN   But who on earth would it—surely not with—?

BRACK   Yes, precisely, with Eilert Løvborg.

---

4. A party for men only, whether single or married.

TESMAN [*Clasping his hands together.*] No, no, this is absolutely unthinkable, absolutely unthinkable, hm?

BRACK Hmm—well, we might just have to learn to get used to it.

TESMAN No, but Judge Brack, that would be incredibly inconsiderate. [*Waving his arms.*] Because—well—just look, I'm a married man. We went and got married on this very prospect, Hedda and I. Went and got ourselves heavily into debt. Borrowed money from Aunt Julie too. I mean, good Lord, I was as much as promised the position, hm?

BRACK Now, now, you'll almost certainly get it but first there'll have to be a contest.

HEDDA [*Motionless in the armchair.*] Just think, Tesman, it will be a sort of match.

TESMAN But Hedda, my dear, how can you be so calm about this?

HEDDA Oh I'm not, not at all. I can't wait for the final score.

BRACK In any case, Mrs. Tesman, it's a good thing that you know how matters stand. I mean, before you embark on any more of these little purchases I hear you're threatening to make.

HEDDA What's that got to do with this?

BRACK Well, well, that's another matter. Good-bye. [*To* TESMAN.] I'll come by for you when I take my afternoon walk.

TESMAN Oh yes, yes, forgive me—I don't know if I'm coming or going.

HEDDA [*Reclining, stretching out her hand.*] Good-bye, Judge, and do come again.

BRACK Many thanks. Good-bye, good-bye.

TESMAN [*Following him to the door.*] Good-bye, Judge. You'll have to excuse me.

[JUDGE BRACK *goes out through the hallway door.*]

TESMAN [*Pacing about the floor.*] We should never let ourselves get lost in a wonderland, Hedda, hm?

HEDDA [*Looking at him and smiling.*] Do you do that?

TESMAN Yes, well, it can't be denied. It was like living in wonderland to go and get married and set up housekeeping on nothing more than prospects.

HEDDA You may be right about that.

TESMAN Well, at least we have our home, Hedda, our wonderful home. The home both of us dreamt about, that both of us craved, I could almost say, hm?

HEDDA [*Rises slowly and wearily.*] The agreement was that we would live in society, that we would entertain.

TESMAN Yes, good Lord, I was so looking forward to that. Just think, to see you as a hostess in our own circle. Hm. Well, well, well, for the time being at least we'll just have to make do with each other, Hedda. We'll have Aunt Julie here now and then. Oh you, you should have such a completely different—

HEDDA To begin with, I suppose I can't have the liveried footmen.[5]

TESMAN Ah no, unfortunately not. No footmen. We can't even think about that right now.

---

5. Uniformed servants.

HEDDA   And the horse!

TESMAN   [*Horrified.*]   The horse.

HEDDA   I suppose I mustn't think about that any more.

TESMAN   No, God help us, you can see that for yourself.

HEDDA   [*Walking across the floor.*]   Well, at least I've got one thing to amuse myself with.

TESMAN   [*Beaming with pleasure.*]   Ah, thank God for that, and what is that, Hedda?

HEDDA   [*In the center doorway looking at him with veiled scorn.*]   My pistols, George.

TESMAN   [*Alarmed.*]   Pistols?

HEDDA   [*With cold eyes.*]   General Gabler's pistols.
   [*She goes through the inner room and out to the left.*]

TESMAN   [*Running to the center doorway and shouting after her.*]   No, for the love of God, Hedda, dearest, don't touch those dangerous things. For my sake, Hedda, hm?

Act 2

The TESMANS' *rooms as in the first act except that the piano has been moved out and an elegant little writing table with a bookshelf has been put in its place. Next to the sofa a smaller table has been placed. Most of the bouquets have been removed.* MRS. ELVSTED's *bouquet stands on the larger table in the foreground. It is afternoon.*

[HEDDA, *dressed to receive visitors, is alone in the room. She stands by the open glass door loading a pistol. The matching pistol lies in an open pistol case on the writing table.*]

HEDDA   [*Looking down into the garden and calling.*]   Hello again, Judge.

BRACK   [*Is heard some distance below.*]   Likewise, Mrs. Tesman.

HEDDA   [*Raises the pistol and aims.*]   Now, Judge Brack, I am going to shoot you.

BRACK   [*Shouting from below.*]   No, no, no. Don't stand there aiming at me like that.

HEDDA   That's what you get for coming up the back way. [*She shoots.*]

BRACK   Are you out of your mind?

HEDDA   Oh, good Lord, did I hit you?

BRACK   [*Still outside.*]   Stop this nonsense.

HEDDA   Then come on in, Judge.
   [JUDGE BRACK, *dressed for a bachelor party, comes in through the glass doors. He carries a light overcoat over his arm.*]

BRACK   In the devil's name, are you still playing this game? What were you shooting at?

HEDDA   Oh, I just stand here and shoot at the sky.

BRACK   [*Gently taking the pistol out of her hands.*]   With your permission, ma'am? [*Looks at it.*] Ah, this one. I know it well. [*Looks around.*] And where do we keep the case? I see, here it is. [*Puts the pistol inside and shuts the case.*] All right, we're through with these little games for today.

HEDDA   Then what in God's name am I to do with myself?

BRACK   No visitors?

HEDDA [*Closes the glass door.*]   Not a single one. Our circle is still in the country.

BRACK   Tesman's not home either, I suppose.

HEDDA [*At the writing table, locks the pistol case in the drawer.*]   No, as soon as he finished eating he was off to the aunts. He wasn't expecting you so early.

BRACK   Hmm, I never thought of that. Stupid of me.

HEDDA [*Turns her head, looks at him.*]   Why stupid?

BRACK   Then I would have come a little earlier.

HEDDA [*Going across the floor.*]   Then you wouldn't have found anyone here at all. I've been in my dressing room since lunch.

BRACK   Isn't there even one little crack in the door wide enough for a negotiation?

HEDDA   Now that's something you forgot to provide for.

BRACK   That was also stupid of me.

HEDDA   So we'll just have to flop down here and wait. Tesman won't be home any time soon.

BRACK   Well, well, Lord knows I can be patient.

[HEDDA *sits in the corner of the sofa.* BRACK *lays his overcoat over the back of the nearest chair and sits down, keeps his hat in his hand. Short silence. They look at each other.*]

HEDDA   So?

BRACK [*In the same tone.*]   So?

HEDDA   I asked first.

BRACK [*Leaning a little forward.*]   Yes, why don't we allow ourselves a cozy little chat, Mrs. Hedda.

HEDDA [*Leaning further back in the sofa.*]   Doesn't it feel like an eternity since we last talked together? A few words last night and this morning, but I don't count them.

BRACK   Like this, between ourselves, just the two of us?

HEDDA   Well, yes, more or less.

BRACK   I wished you were back home every single day.

HEDDA   The whole time I was wishing the same thing.

BRACK   You, really, Mrs. Hedda? Here I thought you were having a wonderful time on your trip.

HEDDA   Oh yes, you can just imagine.

BRACK   But that's what Tesman always wrote.

HEDDA   Yes, him! He thinks it's the greatest thing in the world to go scratching around in libraries. He loves sitting and copying out old parchments or whatever they are.

BRACK [*Somewhat maliciously.*]   Well, that's his calling in the world, at least in part.

HEDDA   Yes, so it is, and no doubt it's—but for me, oh dear Judge, I've been so desperately bored.

BRACK [*Sympathetically.*]   Do you really mean that? You're serious?

HEDDA   Yes, you can imagine it for yourself. Six whole months never meeting with a soul who knew the slightest thing about our circle. No one we could talk with about our kinds of things.

BRACK Ah no, I'd agree with you there. That would be a loss.

HEDDA Then what was most unbearable of all.

BRACK Yes?

HEDDA To be together forever and always—with one and the same person.

BRACK [*Nodding agreement.*] Early and late, yes, night and day, every waking and sleeping hour.

HEDDA That's it, forever and always.

BRACK Yes, all right, but with our excellent Tesman I would have imagined
that you might—

HEDDA Tesman is—a specialist, dear Judge.

BRACK Undeniably.

HEDDA And specialists aren't so much fun to travel with. Not for the long
run anyway.

BRACK Not even the specialist that one loves?

HEDDA Uch, don't use that syrupy word.

BRACK [*Startled.*] Mrs. Hedda.

HEDDA [*Half laughing, half bitterly.*] Well, give it a try for yourself. Hearing about the history of civilization every hour of the day.

BRACK Forever and always.

HEDDA Yes, yes, yes. And then his particular interest, domestic crafts in
the Middle Ages. Uch, the most revolting thing of all.

BRACK [*Looks at her curiously.*] But, tell me now, I don't quite understand
how—hmmm.

HEDDA That we're together? George Tesman and I, you mean?

BRACK Well, yes. That's a good way of putting it.

HEDDA Good Lord, do you think it's so remarkable?

BRACK I think—yes and no, Mrs. Hedda.

HEDDA I'd danced myself out, dear Judge. My time was up. [*Shudders
slightly.*] Uch, no, I'm not going to say that or even think it.

BRACK You certainly have no reason to think it.

HEDDA Ah, reasons—[*Looks watchfully at him.*] And George Tesman?
Well, he'd certainly be called a most acceptable man in every way.

BRACK Acceptable and solid, God knows.

HEDDA And I can't find anything about him that's actually ridiculous, can
you?

BRACK Ridiculous? No—I wouldn't quite say that.

HEDDA Hmm. Well, he's a very diligent archivist anyway. Some day he
might do something interesting with all of it. Who knows.

BRACK [*Looking at her uncertainly.*] I thought you believed, like everyone
else, that he'd turn out to be a great man.

HEDDA [*With a weary expression.*] Yes, I did. And then when he went
around constantly begging with all his strength, begging for permission
to let him take care of me, well, I didn't see why I shouldn't take him up
on it.

BRACK Ah well, from that point of view . . .

HEDDA It was a great deal more than any of my other admirers were offering.

BRACK [*Laughing.*] Well, of course I can't answer for all the others, but
as far as I'm concerned you know very well that I've always maintained
a certain respect for the marriage bond, that is, in an abstract kind of
way, Mrs. Hedda.

HEDDA [*Playfully.*]   Oh, I never had any hopes for you.

BRACK   All I ask is an intimate circle of good friends, friends I can be of service to in any way necessary. Places where I am allowed to come and go as a trusted friend.

HEDDA   Of the man of the house, you mean.

BRACK [*Bowing.*]   No, to be honest, of the lady. Of the man as well, you understand, because you know that kind of—how should I put this— that kind of triangular arrangement is really a magnificent convenience for everyone concerned.

HEDDA   Yes, you can't imagine how many times I longed for a third person on that trip. Ach, huddled together alone in a railway compartment.

BRACK   Fortunately, the wedding trip is over now.

HEDDA [*Shaking her head.*]   Oh no, it's a very long trip. It's nowhere near over. I've only come to a little stopover on the line.

BRACK   Then you should jump out, stretch your legs a little, Mrs. Hedda.

HEDDA   I'd never jump out.

BRACK   Really?

HEDDA   No, because there's always someone at the stop who—

BRACK [*Laughing.*]   Who's looking at your legs, you mean?

HEDDA   Yes, exactly.

BRACK   Yes, but for heaven's sake.

HEDDA [*With a disdainful gesture.*]   I don't hold with that sort of thing. I'd rather remain sitting, just like I am now, a couple alone. On a train.

BRACK   But what if a third man climbed into the compartment with the couple?

HEDDA   Ah yes. Now that's quite different.

BRACK   An understanding friend, a proven friend—

HEDDA   Who can be entertaining on all kinds of topics—

BRACK   And not a specialist in any way!

HEDDA [*With an audible sigh.*]   Yes, that would be a relief.

BRACK [*Hears the front door open and glances toward it.*]   The triangle is complete.

HEDDA [*Half audibly.*]   And there goes the train.

[GEORGE TESMAN *in a gray walking suit and with a soft felt hat comes in from the hallway. He is carrying a large stack of unbound books under his arm and in his pockets.*]

TESMAN [*Goes to the table by the corner sofa.*]   Phew—hot work lugging all these here. [*Puts the books down.*] Would you believe I'm actually sweating, Hedda? And you're already here, Judge, hm. Berta didn't mention anything about that.

BRACK [*Getting up.*]   I came up through the garden.

HEDDA   What are all those books you've got there?

TESMAN [*Stands leafing through them.*]   All the new works by my fellow specialists. I've absolutely got to have them.

HEDDA   By your fellow specialists.

BRACK   Ah, the specialists, Mrs. Tesman. [BRACK *and* HEDDA *exchange a knowing smile.*]

HEDDA   You need even more of these specialized works?

TESMAN   Oh, yes, my dear Hedda, you can never have too many of these. You have to keep up with what's being written and published.

HEDDA   Yes, you certainly must do that.

TESMAN   [*Searches among the books.*] And look here, I've got Eilert Løvborg's new book too. [*Holds it out.*] Maybe you'd like to look at it, Hedda, hm?

HEDDA   No thanks—or maybe later.

TESMAN   I skimmed it a little on the way.

HEDDA   And what's your opinion as a specialist?

TESMAN   I think the argument's remarkably thorough. He never wrote like this before. [*Collects the books together.*] Now I've got to get all these inside. Oh, it's going to be such fun to cut the pages.[6] Then I'll go and change. [*To* BRACK.] We don't have to leave right away, hm?

BRACK   No, not at all. No hurry at all.

TESMAN   Good, I'll take my time then. [*Leaves with the books but stands in the doorway and turns.*] Oh, Hedda, by the way, Aunt Julie won't be coming over this evening.

HEDDA   Really? Because of that hat business?

TESMAN   Not at all. How could you think that of Aunt Julie? No, it's just that Aunt Rina is very ill.

HEDDA   She always is.

TESMAN   Yes, but today she's gotten quite a bit worse.

HEDDA   Well, then it's only right that the other one should stay at home with her. I'll just have to make the best of it.

TESMAN   My dear, you just can't believe how glad Aunt Julie was, in spite of everything, at how healthy and rounded out you looked after the trip.

HEDDA [*Half audibly getting up.*]   Oh, these eternal aunts.

TESMAN   Hm?

HEDDA [*Goes over to the glass door.*]   Nothing.

TESMAN   Oh, all right. [*He goes out through the rear room and to the right.*]

BRACK   What were you saying about a hat?

HEDDA   Oh, just a little run-in with Miss Tesman this morning. She'd put her hat down there on that chair [*Looks at him smiling.*] and I pretended I thought it was the maid's.

BRACK [*Shaking his head.*]   My dear Mrs. Hedda, how could you do such a thing to that harmless old lady.

HEDDA [*Nervously walking across the floor.*]   Oh, you know—these things just come over me like that and I can't resist them. [*Flings herself into the armchair by the stove.*] I can't explain it, even to myself.

BRACK [*Behind the armchair.*]   You're not really happy—that's the heart of it.

HEDDA [*Staring in front of her.*]   And why should I be happy? Maybe you can tell me.

BRACK   Yes. Among other things, be happy you've got the home that you've always longed for.

HEDDA [*Looks up at him and laughs.*]   You also believe that myth?

BRACK   There's nothing to it?

HEDDA   Yes, heavens, there's something to it.

---

6. Books used to be sold with the pages folded but uncut; one had to cut the pages to read the book.

BRACK So?

HEDDA And here's what it is. I used George Tesman to walk me home from parties last summer.

BRACK Yes, regrettably I had to go another way.

HEDDA Oh yes, you certainly were going a different way last summer.

BRACK [*Laughs.*] Shame on you, Mrs. Hedda. So you and Tesman . . .

HEDDA So we walked past here one evening and Tesman, the poor thing, was twisting and turning in his agony because he didn't have the slightest idea what to talk about and I felt sorry that such a learned man—

BRACK [*Smiling skeptically.*] You did . . .

HEDDA Yes, if you will, I did, and so just to help him out of his torment I said, without really thinking about it, that this was the house I would love to live in.

BRACK That was all?

HEDDA For that evening.

BRACK But afterward?

HEDDA Yes, dear Judge, my thoughtlessness has had its consequences.

BRACK Unfortunately, our thoughtlessness often does, Mrs. Hedda.

HEDDA Thanks, I'm sure. But it so happens that George Tesman and I found our common ground in this passion for Prime Minister Falk's villa. And after that it all followed. The engagement, the marriage, the honeymoon and everything else. Yes, yes, Judge, I almost said: you make your bed, you have to lie in it.

BRACK That's priceless. Essentially what you're telling me is you didn't care about any of this here.

HEDDA God knows I didn't.

BRACK What about now, now that we've made it into a lovely home for you?

HEDDA Ach, I feel an air of lavender and dried roses in every room—or maybe Aunt Julie brought that in with her.

BRACK [*Laughing.*] No, I think that's probably a relic of the eminent prime minister's late wife.

HEDDA Yes, that's it, there's something deathly about it. It reminds me of a corsage the day after the ball. [*Folds her hands at the back of her neck, leans back in her chair and gazes at him.*] Oh, my dear Judge, you can't imagine how I'm going to bore myself out here.

BRACK What if life suddenly should offer you some purpose or other, something to live for? What about that, Mrs. Hedda?

HEDDA A purpose? Something really tempting for me?

BRACK Preferably something like that, of course.

HEDDA God knows what sort of purpose that would be. I often wonder if— [*Breaks off.*] No, that wouldn't work out either.

BRACK Who knows. Let me hear.

HEDDA If I could get Tesman to go into politics, I mean.

BRACK [*Laughing.*] Tesman? No, you have to see that politics, anything like that, is not for him. Not in his line at all.

HEDDA No, I can see that. But what if I could get him to try just the same?

BRACK Yes, but why should he do that if he's not up to it? Why would you want him to?

HEDDA Because I'm bored, do you hear me? [*After a pause.*] So you don't think there's any way that Tesman could become a cabinet minister?

BRACK Hmm, you see my dear Mrs. Hedda, that requires a certain amount of wealth in the first place.

HEDDA [*Rises impatiently.*] Yes, that's it, this shabby little world I've ended up in. [*Crosses the floor.*] That's what makes life so contemptible, so completely ridiculous. That's just what it is.

BRACK I think the problem's somewhere else.

HEDDA Where's that?

BRACK You've never had to live through anything that really shakes you up.

HEDDA Anything serious, you mean.

BRACK Yes, you could call it that. Perhaps now, though, it's on its way.

HEDDA [*Tosses her head.*] You mean that competition for that stupid professorship? That's Tesman's business. I'm not going to waste a single thought on it.

BRACK No, forget about that. But when you find yourself facing what one calls in elegant language a profound and solemn calling—[*Smiling.*] a new calling, my dear little Mrs. Hedda.

HEDDA [*Angry.*] Quiet. You'll never see anything like that.

BRACK [*Gently.*] We'll talk about it again in a year's time, at the very latest.

HEDDA [*Curtly.*] I don't have any talent for that, Judge. I don't want anything to do with that kind of calling.

BRACK Why shouldn't you, like most other women, have an innate talent for a vocation that—

HEDDA [*Over by the glass door.*] Oh, please be quiet. I often think I only have one talent, one talent in the world.

BRACK [*Approaching.*] And what is that may I ask?

HEDDA [*Standing, staring out.*] Boring the life right out of me. Now you know. [*Turns, glances toward the inner room and laughs.*] Perfect timing; here comes the professor.

BRACK [*Warning softly.*] Now, now, now, Mrs. Hedda.

[GEORGE TESMAN, *in evening dress, carrying his gloves and hat, comes in from the right of the rear room.*]

TESMAN Hedda, no message from Eilert Løvborg?

HEDDA No.

BRACK Do you really think he'll come?

TESMAN Yes, I'm almost certain he will. What you told us this morning was just idle gossip.

BRACK Oh?

TESMAN Yes, at least Aunt Julie said she couldn't possibly believe that he would stand in my way anymore. Just think.

BRACK So, then everything's all right.

TESMAN [*Puts his hat with his gloves inside on a chair to the right.*] Yes, but I'd like to wait for him as long as I can.

BRACK We have plenty of time. No one's coming to my place until seven or even half past.

TESMAN Meanwhile, we can keep Hedda company and see what happens, hm?

HEDDA [*Sets* BRACK's *overcoat and hat on the corner sofa.*] At the very worst, Mr. Løvborg can stay here with me.

BRACK [*Offering to take his things.*]   At the worst, Mrs. Tesman, what do you mean?

HEDDA   If he won't go out with you and Tesman.

TESMAN [*Looking at her uncertainly.*]   But, Hedda dear, do you think that would be quite right, him staying here with you? Remember, Aunt Julie can't come.

HEDDA   No, but Mrs. Elvsted will be coming and the three of us can have a cup of tea together.

TESMAN   Yes, that's all right then.

BRACK [*Smiling.*]   And I might add, that would be the best plan for him.

HEDDA   Why so?

BRACK   Good Lord, Mrs. Tesman, you've had enough to say about my little bachelor parties in the past. Don't you agree they should be open only to men of the highest principle?

HEDDA   That's just what Mr. Løvborg is now, a reclaimed sinner.

[BERTA *comes in from the hall doorway.*]

BERTA   Madam, there's a gentleman who wishes to—

HEDDA   Yes, please, show him in.

TESMAN [*Softly.*]   It's got to be him. Just think.

[EILERT LØVBORG *enters from the hallway. He is slim and lean, the same age as* TESMAN, *but he looks older and somewhat haggard. His hair and beard are dark brown. His face is longish, pale, with patches of red over the cheekbones. He is dressed in an elegant suit, black, quite new dark gloves and top hat. He stops just inside the doorway and bows hastily. He seems somewhat embarrassed.*]

TESMAN [*Goes to him and shakes his hands.*]   Oh my dear Eilert, we meet again at long last.

LØVBORG [*Speaks in a low voice.*]   Thanks for the letter, George. [*Approaches* HEDDA.] May I shake your hand also, Mrs. Tesman?

HEDDA [*Takes his hand.*]   Welcome, Mr. Løvborg. [*With a gesture.*] I don't know if you two gentlemen—

LØVBORG [*Bowing.*]   Judge Brack, I believe.

BRACK [*Similarly.*]   Indeed. It's been quite a few years—

TESMAN [*To* LØVBORG, *his hands on his shoulders.*]   And now Eilert, make yourself completely at home. Right, Hedda? I hear you're going to settle down here in town, hm?

LØVBORG   Yes, I will.

TESMAN   Well, that's only sensible. Listen, I got your new book. I haven't really had time to read it yet.

LØVBORG   You can save yourself the trouble.

TESMAN   What do you mean?

LØVBORG   There's not much to it.

TESMAN   How can you say that?

BRACK   But everyone's been praising it so highly.

LØVBORG   Exactly as I intended—so I wrote the sort of book that everyone can agree with.

BRACK   Very clever.

TESMAN   Yes, but my dear Eilert.

LØVBORG   Because I want to reestablish my position, begin again.

TESMAN [*A little downcast.*]   Yes, I suppose you'd want to, hm.

LØVBORG [*Smiling, putting down his hat and pulling a package wrapped in paper from his coat pocket.*]   But when this comes out, George Tesman—this is what you should read. It's the real thing. I've put my whole self into it.

TESMAN   Oh yes? What's it about?

LØVBORG   It's the sequel.

TESMAN   Sequel to what?

LØVBORG   To my book.

TESMAN   The new one?

LØVBORG   Of course.

TESMAN   But my dear Eilert, that one takes us right to the present day.

LØVBORG   So it does—and this one takes us into the future.

TESMAN   The future. Good Lord! We don't know anything about that.

LØVBORG   No, we don't—but there are still one or two things to say about it, just the same. [*Opens the packages.*] Here, you'll see.

TESMAN   That's not your handwriting, is it?

LØVBORG   I dictated it. [*Turns the pages.*] It's written in two sections. The first is about the cultural forces which will shape the future, and this other section [*Turning the pages.*] is about the future course of civilization.

TESMAN   Extraordinary. It would never occur to me to write about something like that.

HEDDA [*By the glass door, drumming on the pane.*]   Hmm, no, no.

LØVBORG [*Puts the papers back in the packet and sets it on the table.*]   I brought it along because I thought I might read some of it to you tonight.

TESMAN   Ah, that was very kind of you, Eilert, but this evening [*Looks at* BRACK.] I'm not sure it can be arranged—

LØVBORG   Some other time then, there's no hurry.

BRACK   I should tell you, Mr. Løvborg, we're having a little party at my place this evening, mostly for Tesman, you understand—

LØVBORG [*Looking for his hat.*]   Aha, well then I'll—

BRACK   No, listen, why don't you join us?

LØVBORG [*Briefly but firmly.*]   No, that I can't do, but many thanks just the same.

BRACK   Oh come now, you certainly can do that. We'll be a small, select circle and I guarantee we'll be "lively," as Mrs. Hed—Mrs. Tesman would say.

LØVBORG   No doubt, but even so—

BRACK   And then you could bring your manuscript along and read it to Tesman at my place. I've got plenty of rooms.

TESMAN   Think about that, Eilert. You could do that, hm?

HEDDA [*Intervening.*]   Now, my dear, Mr. Løvborg simply doesn't want to. I'm quite sure Mr. Løvborg would rather settle down here and have supper with me.

LØVBORG [*Staring at her.*]   With you, Mrs. Tesman?

HEDDA   And with Mrs. Elvsted.

LØVBORG   Ah—[*Casually.*] I saw her this morning very briefly.

HEDDA   Oh did you? Well, she's coming here; so you might almost say it's essential that you stay here, Mr. Løvborg. Otherwise she'll have no one to see her home.

LØVBORG That's true. Yes, Mrs. Tesman, many thanks. I'll stay.

HEDDA I'll go and have a word with the maid.

[*She goes over to the hall door and rings.* BERTA *enters.* HEDDA *speaks quietly to her and points toward the rear room.* BERTA *nods and goes out again.*]

TESMAN [*At the same time to* LØVBORG.] Listen, Eilert, your lecture—Is it about this new subject? About the future?

LØVBORG Yes.

TESMAN Because I heard down at the bookstore that you'd be giving a lecture series here this fall.

LØVBORG I plan to. Please don't hold it against me.

TESMAN No, God forbid, but—?

LØVBORG I can easily see how this might make things awkward.

TESMAN [*Dejectedly.*] Oh, for my part, I can't expect you to—

LØVBORG But I'll wait until you get your appointment.

TESMAN You will? Yes but—yes but—you won't be competing then?

LØVBORG No. I only want to conquer you in the marketplace of ideas.

TESMAN But, good Lord, Aunt Julie was right after all. Oh yes, yes, I was quite sure of it. Hedda, imagine, my dear—Eilert Løvborg won't stand in our way.

HEDDA [*Curtly.*] Our way? Leave me out of it.

[*She goes up toward the rear room where* BERTA *is placing a tray with decanters and glasses on the table.* HEDDA *nods approvingly, comes forward again.* BERTA *goes out.*]

TESMAN [*Meanwhile.*] So, Judge Brack, what do you say about all this?

BRACK Well now, I say that honor and victory, hmm—they have a powerful appeal—

TESMAN Yes, yes, I suppose they do but all the same—

HEDDA [*Looking at* TESMAN *with a cold smile.*] You look like you've been struck by lightning.

TESMAN Yes, that's about it—or something like that, I think—

BRACK That was quite a thunderstorm that passed over us, Mrs. Tesman.

HEDDA [*Pointing toward the rear room.*] Won't you gentlemen go in there and have a glass of punch?

BRACK [*Looking at his watch.*] For the road? Yes, not a bad idea.

TESMAN Wonderful, Hedda, wonderful! And I'm in such a fantastic mood now.

HEDDA You too, Mr. Løvborg, if you please.

LØVBORG [*Dismissively.*] No, thank you, not for me.

BRACK Good Lord, cold punch isn't exactly poison, you know.

LØVBORG Maybe not for everybody.

HEDDA Then I'll keep Mr. Løvborg company in the meantime.

TESMAN Yes, yes, Hedda dear, you do that.

[TESMAN *and* BRACK *go into the rear room, sit down and drink punch, smoking cigarettes and talking animatedly during the following.* EILERT LØVBORG *remains standing by the stove and* HEDDA *goes to the writing table.*]

HEDDA [*In a slightly raised voice.*] Now, if you like, I'll show you some photographs. Tesman and I—we took a trip to the Tyrol on the way home.

[*She comes over with an album and lays it on the table by the sofa, seating herself in the farthest corner.* EILERT LØVBORG *comes closer, stooping and* looking at her. Then he takes a chair and sits on her left side with his back to the rear room.]

HEDDA [*Opening the album.*] Do you see these mountains, Mr. Løvborg? That's the Ortler group. Tesman's written a little caption. Here. "The Ortler group near Meran."[7]

LØVBORG [*Who has not taken his eyes off her from the beginning, says softly and slowly.*] Hedda Gabler.

HEDDA [*Glances quickly at him.*] Shh, now.

LØVBORG [*Repeating softly.*] Hedda Gabler.

HEDDA [*Staring at the album.*] Yes, so I was once, when we knew each other.

LØVBORG And from now—for the rest of my life—do I have to teach myself never to say Hedda Gabler?

HEDDA [*Turning the pages.*] Yes, you have to. And I think you'd better start practicing now. The sooner the better, I'd say.

LØVBORG [*In a resentful voice.*] Hedda Gabler married—and then—with George Tesman.

HEDDA That's how it goes.

LØVBORG Ah, Hedda, Hedda—how could you have thrown yourself away like that?

HEDDA [*Looks sharply at him.*] What? Now stop that.

LØVBORG Stop what, what do you mean?

HEDDA Calling me Hedda and[8]—

[TESMAN *comes in and goes toward the sofa.*]

HEDDA [*Hears him approaching and says casually.*] And this one here, Mr. Løvborg, this was taken from the Ampezzo Valley. Would you just look at these mountain peaks. [*Looks warmly up at* TESMAN.] George, dear, what were these extraordinary mountains called?

TESMAN Let me see. Ah, yes, those are the Dolomites.

HEDDA Of course. Those, Mr. Løvborg, are the Dolomites.

TESMAN Hedda, dear, I just wanted to ask you if we should bring some punch in here, for you at least.

HEDDA Yes, thank you my dear. And a few pastries perhaps.

TESMAN Any cigarettes?

HEDDA No.

TESMAN Good.

[*He goes into the rear room and off to the right.* BRACK *remains sitting, from time to time keeping his eye on* HEDDA *and* LØVBORG.]

LØVBORG [*Quietly, as before.*] Then answer me, Hedda—how could you go and do such a thing?

HEDDA [*Apparently absorbed in the album.*] If you keep talking to me that way, I just won't speak to you.

7. I.e., Merano, a city in the Austrian Tyrol, since 1918 a city in Italy. The scenic features mentioned here and later are tourist attractions. The Ortler group and the Dolomites are Alpine mountain ranges. The Ampezzo Valley lies beyond the Dolomites to the east. The Brenner Pass is a major route through the Alps to Austria.

8. This line is interpolated in an attempt to suggest the difference between the informal *du* (thee or thou) and the formal *de* (you) in the Norwegian text. Løvborg has just addressed Hedda in the informal manner and she is warning him not to [translators' note].

LØVBORG Not even when we're alone together?

HEDDA No. You can think whatever you want but you can't talk about it.

LØVBORG Ah, I see. It offends your love for George Tesman.

HEDDA [*Glances at him and smiles.*] Love? Don't be absurd.

LØVBORG Not love then either?

HEDDA But even so—nothing unfaithful. I will not allow it.

LØVBORG Answer me just one thing—

HEDDA Shh.

[TESMAN, *with a tray, enters from the rear room.*]

TESMAN Here we are, here come the treats. [*He places the tray on the table.*]

HEDDA Why are you serving us yourself?

TESMAN [*Filling the glasses.*] I have such a good time waiting on you, Hedda.

HEDDA But now you've gone and poured two drinks and Mr. Løvborg definitely does not want—

TESMAN No, but Mrs. Elvsted's coming soon.

HEDDA Yes, that's right, Mrs. Elvsted.

TESMAN Did you forget about her?

HEDDA We were just sitting here so completely wrapped up in these. [*Shows him a picture.*] Do you remember this little village?

TESMAN Yes, that's the one below the Brenner Pass. We spent the night there—

HEDDA —and ran into all those lively summer visitors.

TESMAN Ah yes, that was it. Imagine—if you could have been with us, Eilert, just think. [*He goes in again and sits with* BRACK.]

LØVBORG Just answer me one thing—

HEDDA Yes?

LØVBORG In our relationship—wasn't there any love there either? No trace? Not a glimmer of love in any of it?

HEDDA I wonder if there really was. For me it was like we were two good comrades, two really good, faithful friends. [*Smiling.*] I remember you were particularly frank and open.

LØVBORG That's how you wanted it.

HEDDA When I look back on it, there was something really beautiful—something fascinating, something brave about this secret comradeship, this secret intimacy that no living soul had any idea about.

LØVBORG Yes, Hedda, that's true isn't it? That was it. When I'd come to your father's in the afternoon—and the General would sit in the window reading his newspaper with his back toward the room—

HEDDA And us on the corner sofa.

LØVBORG Always with the same illustrated magazine in front of us.

HEDDA Instead of an album, yes.

LØVBORG Yes, Hedda—and when I made all those confessions to you—telling you things about myself that no one else knew in those days. Sat there and told you how I'd lost whole days and nights in drunken frenzy, frenzy that would last for days on end. Ah, Hedda—what kind of power was in you that drew these confessions out of me?

HEDDA You think it was a power in me?

LØVBORG   Yes. I can't account for it in any other way. And you'd ask me all those ambiguous leading questions—

HEDDA   Which you understood implicitly—

LØVBORG   How did you sit there and question me so fearlessly?

HEDDA   Ambiguously?

LØVBORG   Yes, but fearlessly all the same. Questioning me about—About things like that.

HEDDA   And how could you answer them, Mr. Løvborg?

LØVBORG   Yes, yes. That's just what I don't understand anymore. But now tell me, Hedda, wasn't it love underneath it all? Wasn't that part of it? You wanted to purify me, to cleanse me—when I'd seek you out to make my confessions. Wasn't that it?

HEDDA   No, no, not exactly.

LØVBORG   Then what drove you?

HEDDA   Do you find it so hard to explain that a young girl—when it becomes possible—in secret—

LØVBORG   Yes?

HEDDA   That she wants a glimpse of a world that—

LØVBORG   That—

HEDDA   That is not permitted to her.

LØVBORG   So that was it.

HEDDA   That too, that too—I almost believe it.

LØVBORG   Comrades in a quest for life. So why couldn't it go on?

HEDDA   That was your own fault.

LØVBORG   You broke it off.

HEDDA   Yes, when it looked like reality threatened to spoil the situation. Shame on you, Eilert Løvborg, how could you do violence to your comrade in arms?

LØVBORG   [*Clenching his hands together.*]   Well, why didn't you do it for real? Why didn't you shoot me dead right then and there like you threatened to?

HEDDA   Oh, I'm much too afraid of scandal.

LØVBORG   Yes, Hedda, underneath it all, you're a coward.

HEDDA   A terrible coward. [*Changes her tone.*] Lucky for you. And now you've got plenty of consolation up there at the Elvsteds'.

LØVBORG   I know what Thea's confided to you.

HEDDA   And no doubt you've confided to her about us.

LØVBORG   Not one word. She's too stupid to understand things like this.

HEDDA   Stupid?

LØVBORG   In things like this she's stupid.

HEDDA   And I'm a coward. [*Leans closer to him without looking him in the eyes and says softly.*] Now I'll confide something to you.

LØVBORG   [*In suspense.*]   What?

HEDDA   My not daring to shoot you—

LØVBORG   Yes?!

HEDDA   —that wasn't my worst cowardice that evening.

LØVBORG   [*Stares at her a moment, understands and whispers passionately.*] Ah, Hedda Gabler, now I see the hidden reason why we're such comrades. This craving for life in you—

HEDDA [*Quietly, with a sharp glance at him.*]   Watch out, don't believe anything of the sort.

[*It starts to get dark. The hall door is opened by* BERTA.]

HEDDA [*Clapping the album shut and crying out with a smile.*]   Ah, finally. Thea, darling, do come in.

[MRS. ELVSTED *enters from the hall. She is in evening dress. The door is closed after her.*]

HEDDA [*On the sofa, stretching out her arms.*]   Thea, my sweet, you can't imagine how I've been expecting you.

[MRS. ELVSTED, *in passing, exchanges a greeting with the gentlemen in the inner room, crosses to the table, shakes* HEDDA's *hand.* EILERT LØVBORG *has risen. He and* MRS. ELVSTED *greet each other with a single nod.*]

MRS. ELVSTED   Perhaps I should go in and have a word with your husband.

HEDDA   Not at all. Let them sit there. They'll be on their way soon.

MRS. ELVSTED   They're leaving?

HEDDA   Yes, they're going out on a little binge.

MRS. ELVSTED [*Quickly to* LØVBORG.]   You're not?

LØVBORG   No.

HEDDA   Mr. Løvborg . . . he'll stay here with us.

MRS. ELVSTED [*Takes a chair and sits down beside him.*]   It's so nice to be here.

HEDDA   No, you don't, little Thea, not there. Come right over here next to me. I want to be in the middle between you.

MRS. ELVSTED   All right, whatever you like. [*She goes around the table and sits on the sofa to the right of* HEDDA. LØVBORG *takes his chair again.*]

LØVBORG [*After a brief pause, to* HEDDA.]   Isn't she lovely to look at?

HEDDA [*Gently stroking her hair.*]   Only to look at?

LØVBORG   Yes. We're true comrades, the two of us. We trust each other completely and that's why we can sit here and talk so openly and boldly together.

HEDDA   With no ambiguity, Mr. Løvborg.

LØVBORG   Well—

MRS. ELVSTED [*Softly, clinging to* HEDDA.]   Oh, Hedda, I'm so lucky. Just think, he says I've inspired him too.

HEDDA [*Regards her with a smile.*]   No, dear, does he say that?

LØVBORG   And she has the courage to take action, Mrs. Tesman.

MRS. ELVSTED   Oh God, me, courage?

LØVBORG   Tremendous courage when it comes to comradeship.

HEDDA   Yes, courage—yes! That's the crucial thing.

LØVBORG   Why is that, do you suppose?

HEDDA   Because then—maybe—life has a chance to be lived. [*Suddenly changing her tone.*] But now, my dearest Thea. Why don't you treat yourself to a nice cold glass of punch?

MRS. ELVSTED   No thank you, I never drink anything like that.

HEDDA   Then for you, Mr. Løvborg.

LØVBORG   No thank you, not for me either.

MRS. ELVSTED   No, not for him either.

HEDDA [*Looking steadily at him.*]   But if I insisted.

LØVBORG   Doesn't matter.

HEDDA [*Laughing.*]   Then I have absolutely no power over you? Ah, poor me.

LØVBORG   Not in that area.

HEDDA   But seriously now, I really think you should, for your own sake.

MRS. ELVSTED   No, Hedda—

LØVBORG   Why is that?

HEDDA   Or to be more precise, for others' sakes.

LØVBORG   Oh?

HEDDA   Because otherwise people might get the idea that you don't, deep down inside, feel really bold, really sure of yourself.

LØVBORG   Oh, from now on people can think whatever they like.

MRS. ELVSTED   Yes, that's right, isn't it.

HEDDA   I saw it so clearly with Judge Brack a few minutes ago.

LØVBORG   What did you see?

HEDDA   That condescending little smile when you didn't dare join them at the table.

LØVBORG   Didn't dare? I'd just rather stay here and talk with you, of course.

MRS. ELVSTED   That's only reasonable, Hedda.

HEDDA   How was the Judge supposed to know that? I saw how he smiled and shot a glance at Tesman when you didn't dare join them in their silly little party.

LØVBORG   Didn't dare. You're saying I don't dare.

HEDDA   Oh, I'm not. But that's how Judge Brack sees it.

LØVBORG   Well let him.

HEDDA   So you won't join them?

LØVBORG   I'm staying here with you and Thea.

MRS. ELVSTED   Yes, Hedda, you can be sure he is.

HEDDA [*Smiling and nodding approvingly to* LØVBORG.]   What a strong foundation you've got. Principles to last a lifetime. That's what a man ought to have. [*Turns to* MRS. ELVSTED.] See now, wasn't that what I told you when you came here this morning in such a panic—

LØVBORG [*Startled.*]   Panic?

MRS. ELVSTED [*Terrified.*]   Hedda, Hedda, no.

HEDDA   Just see for yourself. No reason at all to come running here in mortal terror. [*Changing her tone.*] There, now all three of us can be quite jolly.

LØVBORG [*Shocked.*]   What does this mean, Mrs. Tesman?

MRS. ELVSTED   Oh God, oh God, Hedda. What are you doing? What are you saying?

HEDDA   Keep calm now. That disgusting Judge is sitting there watching you.

LØVBORG   In mortal terror on my account?

MRS. ELVSTED [*Quietly wailing.*]   Oh, Hedda—

LØVBORG [*Looks at her steadily for a moment; his face is drawn.*]   So that, then, was how my brave, bold comrade trusted me.

MRS. ELVSTED [*Pleading.*]   Oh, my dearest friend, listen to me—

LØVBORG [*Takes one of the glasses of punch, raises it and says in a low, hoarse voice.*]   Your health, Thea. [*Empties the glass, takes another.*]

MRS. ELVSTED [*Softly.*]   Oh Hedda, Hedda—how could you want this to happen?

HEDDA   Want it? I want this? Are you mad?

LØVBORG   And your health too, Mrs. Tesman. Thanks for the truth. Long
may it live. [*He drinks and goes to refill the glass.*]

HEDDA [*Placing her hand on his arm.*]   That's enough for now. Remember,
you're going to the party.

MRS. ELVSTED   No, no, no.

HEDDA   Shh. They're watching us.

LØVBORG [*Putting down the glass.*]   Thea, be honest with me now.

MRS. ELVSTED   Yes.

LØVBORG   Was your husband told that you came here to look for me?

MRS. ELVSTED [*Wringing her hands.*]   Oh, Hedda, listen to what he's asking me!

LØVBORG   Did he arrange for you to come to town to spy on me? Maybe
he put you up to it himself. Aha, that's it. He needed me back in the
office again. Or did he just miss me at the card table?

MRS. ELVSTED [*Softly moaning.*]   Oh, Løvborg, Løvborg—

LØVBORG [*Grabs a glass intending to fill it.*]   Skøal to the old Sheriff too.

HEDDA [*Preventing him.*]   No more now. Remember, you're going out to
read to Tesman.

LØVBORG [*Calmly putting down his glass.*]   Thea, that was stupid of me.
What I did just now. Taking it like that I mean. Don't be angry with me,
my dear, dear comrade. You'll see. Both of you and everyone else will see
that even though I once was fallen—now I've raised myself up again,
with your help, Thea.

MRS. ELVSTED [*Radiant with joy.*]   Oh God be praised.

[*Meanwhile* BRACK *has been looking at his watch. He and* TESMAN *get up
and come into the drawing room.*]

BRACK [*Taking his hat and overcoat.*]   Well, Mrs. Tesman, our time is up.

HEDDA   Yes, it must be.

LØVBORG [*Rising.*]   Mine too.

MRS. ELVSTED [*Quietly pleading.*]   Løvborg, don't do it.

HEDDA [*Pinching her arm.*]   They can hear you.

MRS. ELVSTED [*Crying out faintly.*]   Ow.

LØVBORG [*To* BRACK.]   You were kind enough to ask me along.

BRACK   So you're coming after all.

LØVBORG   Yes, thanks.

BRACK   I'm delighted.

LØVBORG [*Putting the manuscript packet in his pocket and saying to* TESMAN.]
I'd really like you to look at one or two things before I send it off.

TESMAN   Just think, that will be splendid. But, Hedda dear, how will you
get Mrs. Elvsted home?

HEDDA   Oh, there's always a way out.

LØVBORG [*Looking at the ladies.*]   Mrs. Elvsted? Well, of course, I'll come
back for her. [*Coming closer.*] Around ten o'clock, Mrs. Tesman, will
that do?

HEDDA   Yes, that will be fine.

TESMAN   Well, everything's all right then; but don't expect me that early,
Hedda.

HEDDA   No dear, you stay just as long—as long as you like.

MRS. ELVSTED [*With suppressed anxiety.*] Mr. Løvborg—I'll stay here until you come.

LØVBORG [*His hat in his hand.*] That's understood.

BRACK All aboard then, the party train's pulling out. Gentlemen, I trust it will be a lively trip, as a certain lovely lady suggested.

HEDDA Ah yes, if only that lovely lady could be there—invisible, of course.

BRACK Why invisible?

HEDDA To hear a little of your liveliness, Judge, uncensored.

BRACK [*Laughing.*] Not recommended for the lovely lady.

TESMAN [*Also laughing.*] You really are the limit, Hedda. Think of it.

BRACK Well, well, my ladies. Good night. Good night.

LØVBORG [*Bowing as he leaves.*] Until ten o'clock, then.

> [BRACK, LØVBORG *and* TESMAN *leave through the hall door. At the same time* BERTA *comes in from the rear room with a lighted lamp which she places on the drawing room table, going out the way she came in.*]

MRS. ELVSTED [*Has gotten up and wanders uneasily about the room.*] Oh, Hedda, where is all this going?

HEDDA Ten o'clock—then he'll appear. I see him before me with vine leaves in his hair,[9] burning bright and bold.

MRS. ELVSTED Yes, if only it could be like that.

HEDDA And then you'll see—then he'll have power over himself again. Then he'll be a free man for the rest of his days.

MRS. ELVSTED Oh God yes—if only he'd come back just the way you see him.

HEDDA He'll come back just that way and no other. [*Gets up and comes closer.*] You can doubt him as much as you like. I believe in him. And so we'll see—

MRS. ELVSTED There's something behind this, something else you're trying to do.

HEDDA Yes, there is. Just once in my life I want to help shape someone's destiny.

MRS. ELVSTED Don't you do that already?

HEDDA I don't and I never have.

MRS. ELVSTED Not even your husband?

HEDDA Oh yes, that was a real bargain. Oh, if you could only understand how destitute I am while you get to be so rich. [*She passionately throws her arms around her.*] I think I'll burn your hair off after all.

MRS. ELVSTED Let me go, let me go. I'm afraid of you.

BERTA [*In the doorway.*] Tea is ready in the dining room, Madam.

HEDDA Good. We're on our way.

MRS. ELVSTED No, no, no! I'd rather go home alone! Right now!

HEDDA Nonsense! First you're going to have some tea, you little bubble-head, and then—at ten o'clock—Eilert Løvborg—with vine leaves in his hair! [*She pulls* MRS. ELVSTED *toward the doorway almost by force.*]

---

9. Like Bacchus, the Greek god of wine, and his followers.

Act 3

The room at the TESMANS'. *The curtains are drawn across the center door-way and also across the glass door. The lamp covered with a shade burns low on the table. In the stove, with its door standing open, there has been a fire that is almost burned out.*

[MRS. ELVSTED, *wrapped in a large shawl and with her feet on a footstool, sits sunk back in an armchair.* HEDDA, *fully dressed, lies sleeping on the sofa with a rug over her.*]

MRS. ELVSTED [*After a pause suddenly straightens herself in the chair and listens intently. Then she sinks back wearily and moans softly.*] STILL NOT BACK . . . OH GOD, OH GOD . . . STILL NOT BACK.

[BERTA *enters tiptoeing carefully through the hall doorway; she has a letter in her hand.*]

MRS. ELVSTED   Ah—did someone come?

BERTA   Yes, a girl came by just now with this letter.

MRS. ELVSTED [*Quickly stretching out her hand.*]   A letter? Let me have it.

BERTA   No ma'am, it's for the doctor.

MRS. ELVSTED   Oh.

BERTA   It was Miss Tesman's maid who brought it. I'll put it on the table here.

MRS. ELVSTED   Yes, do that.

BERTA [*Puts down the letter.*]   I'd better put out the lamp; it's starting to smoke.

MRS. ELVSTED   Yes, put it out. It'll be light soon anyway.

BERTA [*Putting out the light.*]   Oh, ma'am, it's already light.

MRS. ELVSTED   So, morning and still not back—!

BERTA   Oh, dear Lord—I knew all along it would go like this.

MRS. ELVSTED   You knew?

BERTA   Yes, when I saw a certain person was back in town. And then when he went off with them—oh we'd heard plenty about that gentleman.

MRS. ELVSTED   Don't speak so loud, you'll wake your mistress.

BERTA [*Looks over to the sofa and sighs.*]   No, dear Lord—let her sleep, poor thing. Shouldn't I build the stove up a little more?

MRS. ELVSTED   Not for me, thanks.

BERTA   Well, well then. [*She goes out quietly through the hall doorway.*]

HEDDA [*Awakened by the closing door, looks up.*]   What's that?

MRS. ELVSTED   Only the maid.

HEDDA [*Looking around.*]   In here—! Oh, now I remember. [*Straightens up, stretches sitting on the sofa and rubs her eyes.*] What time is it, Thea?

MRS. ELVSTED [*Looks at her watch.*]   It's after seven.

HEDDA   What time did Tesman get in?

MRS. ELVSTED   He hasn't.

HEDDA   Still?

MRS. ELVSTED [*Getting up.*]   No one's come back.

HEDDA   And we sat here waiting and watching until almost four.

MRS. ELVSTED [*Wringing her hands.*]   Waiting for him!

HEDDA [*Yawning and speaking with her hand over her mouth.*] Oh yes— we could have saved ourselves the trouble.

MRS. ELVSTED Did you finally manage to sleep?

HEDDA Yes, I think I slept quite well. Did you?

MRS. ELVSTED Not a wink. I couldn't, Hedda. It was just impossible for me.

HEDDA [*Gets up and goes over to her.*] Now, now, now. There's nothing to worry about. I know perfectly well how it all turned out.

MRS. ELVSTED Yes, what do you think? Can you tell me?

HEDDA Well, of course they dragged it out dreadfully up at Judge Brack's.

MRS. ELVSTED Oh God yes—that must be true. But all the same—

HEDDA And then you see, Tesman didn't want to come home and create a fuss by ringing the bell in the middle of the night. [*Laughing.*] He probably didn't want to show himself either right after a wild party like that.

MRS. ELVSTED For goodness sake—where would he have gone?

HEDDA Well, naturally, he went over to his aunts' and laid himself down to sleep there. They still have his old room standing ready for him.

MRS. ELVSTED No, he's not with them. A letter just came for him from Miss Tesman. It's over there.

HEDDA Oh? [*Looks at the inscription.*] Yes, that's Aunt Julie's hand all right. So then, he's still over at Judge Brack's and Eilert Løvborg—he's sitting—reading aloud with vine leaves in his hair.

MRS. ELVSTED Oh, Hedda, you don't even believe what you're saying.

HEDDA You are such a little noodlehead, Thea.

MRS. ELVSTED Yes, unfortunately I probably am.

HEDDA And you look like you're dead on your feet.

MRS. ELVSTED Yes, I am. Dead on my feet.

HEDDA And so now you're going to do what I tell you. You'll go into my room and lie down on my bed.

MRS. ELVSTED Oh no, no—I couldn't get to sleep anyway.

HEDDA Yes, you certainly will.

MRS. ELVSTED But your husband's bound to be home any time now and I've got to find out right away—

HEDDA I'll tell you as soon as he comes.

MRS. ELVSTED Promise me that, Hedda?

HEDDA Yes, that you can count on. Now just go in and sleep for a while.

MRS. ELVSTED Thanks. At least I'll give it a try. [*She goes in through the back room.*]

[HEDDA *goes over to the glass door and draws back the curtains. Full daylight floods the room. She then takes a small hand mirror from the writing table, looks in it and arranges her hair. Then she goes to the hall door and presses the bell. Soon after* BERTA *enters the doorway.*]

BERTA Did Madam want something?

HEDDA Yes, build up the stove a little bit. I'm freezing in here.

BERTA Lord, in no time at all it'll be warm in here. [*She rakes the embers and puts a log inside. She stands and listens.*] There's the front doorbell, Madam.

HEDDA So, go answer it. I'll take care of the stove myself.

BERTA It'll be burning soon enough. [*She goes out through the hall door.*]

[HEDDA *kneels on the footstool and puts more logs into the stove. After a brief moment,* GEORGE TESMAN *comes in from the hall. He looks weary and rather serious. He creeps on tiptoes toward the doorway and is about to slip through the curtains.*]

HEDDA [*By the stove, without looking up.*] Good morning.

TESMAN [*Turning around.*] Hedda. [*Comes nearer.*] What in the world— Up so early, hm?

HEDDA Yes, up quite early today.

TESMAN And here I was so sure you'd still be in bed. Just think, Hedda.

HEDDA Not so loud. Mrs. Elvsted's lying down in my room.

TESMAN Has Mrs. Elvsted been here all night?

HEDDA Yes. No one came to pick her up.

TESMAN No, no, they couldn't have.

HEDDA [*Shuts the door of the stove and gets up.*] So, did you have a jolly time at the Judge's?

TESMAN Were you worried about me?

HEDDA No, that would never occur to me. I asked if you had a good time.

TESMAN Yes, I really did, for once, in a manner of speaking—Mostly in the beginning, I'd say. We'd arrived an hour early. How about that? And Brack had so much to get ready. But then Eilert read to me.

HEDDA [*Sits at the right of the table.*] So, tell me.

TESMAN Hedda, you can't imagine what this new work will be like. It's one of the most brilliant things ever written, no doubt about it. Think of that.

HEDDA Yes, yes, but that's not what I'm interested in.

TESMAN But I have to confess something, Hedda. After he read—something horrible came over me.

HEDDA Something horrible?

TESMAN I sat there envying Eilert for being able to write like that. Think of it, Hedda.

HEDDA Yes, yes, I'm thinking.

TESMAN And then, that whole time, knowing that he—even with all the incredible powers at his command—is still beyond redemption.

HEDDA You mean he's got more of life's courage in him than the others?

TESMAN No, for heaven sakes—he just has no control over his pleasures.

HEDDA And what happened then—at the end?

TESMAN Well, Hedda, I guess you'd have to say it was a bacchanal.

HEDDA Did he have vine leaves in his hair?

TESMAN Vine leaves? No, I didn't see anything like that. But he did make a long wild speech for the woman who had inspired him in his work. Yes—that's how he put it.

HEDDA Did he name her?

TESMAN No, he didn't, but I can only guess that it must be Mrs. Elvsted. Wouldn't you say?

HEDDA Hmm—where did you leave him?

TESMAN On the way back. Most of our group broke up at the same time and Brack came along with us to get a little fresh air. And you see, we agreed to follow Eilert home because—well—he was so far gone.

HEDDA He must have been.

TESMAN   But here's the strangest part, Hedda! Or maybe I should say the saddest. I'm almost ashamed for Eilert's sake—to tell you—

HEDDA   So?

TESMAN   There we were walking along, you see, and I happened to drop back a bit, just for a couple of minutes, you understand.

HEDDA   Yes, yes, good Lord but—

TESMAN   And then when I was hurrying to catch up—can you guess what I found in the gutter, hm?

HEDDA   How can I possibly guess?

TESMAN   Don't ever tell a soul, Hedda. Do you hear? Promise me that for Eilert's sake. [*Pulls a package out of his coat pocket.*] Just think—this is what I found.

HEDDA   That's the package he had with him here yesterday, isn't it?

TESMAN   That's it. His precious, irreplaceable manuscript—all of it. And he's lost it—without even noticing it. Oh just think, Hedda—the pity of it—

HEDDA   Well, why didn't you give it back to him right away?

TESMAN   Oh, I didn't dare do that—The condition he was in—

HEDDA   You didn't tell any of the others that you found it either?

TESMAN   Absolutely not. I couldn't, you see, for Eilert's sake.

HEDDA   So nobody knows you have Eilert's manuscript? Nobody at all?

TESMAN   No. And they mustn't find out either.

HEDDA   What did you talk to him about later?

TESMAN   I didn't get a chance to talk to him any more. We got to the city limits, and he and a couple of the others went a different direction. Just think—

HEDDA   Aha, they must have followed him home then.

TESMAN   Yes, I suppose so. Brack also went his way.

HEDDA   And, in the meantime, what became of the bacchanal?

TESMAN   Well, I and some of the others followed one of the revelers up to his place and had morning coffee with him—or maybe we should call it morning-after coffee, hm? Now, I'll rest a bit—and as soon as I think Eilert has managed to sleep it off, poor man, then I've got to go over to him with this.

HEDDA   [*Reaching out for the envelope.*]   No, don't give it back. Not yet, I mean. Let me read it first.

TESMAN   Oh no.

HEDDA   Oh, for God's sake.

TESMAN   I don't dare do that.

HEDDA   You don't dare?

TESMAN   No, you can imagine how completely desperate he'll be when he wakes up and realizes he can't find the manuscript. He's got no copy of it. He said so himself.

HEDDA   [*Looks searchingly at him.*]   Couldn't it be written again?

TESMAN   No, I don't believe that could ever be done because the inspiration—you see—

HEDDA   Yes, yes—That's the thing, isn't it? [*Casually.*] But, oh yes—there's a letter here for you.

TESMAN   No, think of that.

HEDDA [*Hands it to him.*]   It came early this morning.

TESMAN   From Aunt Julie, Hedda. What can it be? [*Puts the manuscript on the other stool, opens the letter and jumps up.*] Oh Hedda—poor Aunt Rina's almost breathing her last.

HEDDA   It's only what's expected.

TESMAN   And if I want to see her one more time, I've got to hurry. I'll charge over there right away.

HEDDA [*Suppressing a smile.*]   You'll charge?

TESMAN   Oh, Hedda dearest—if you could just bring yourself to follow me. Just think.

HEDDA [*Rises and says wearily and dismissively.*]   No, no. Don't ask me to do anything like that. I won't look at sickness and death. Let me stay free from everything ugly.

TESMAN   Oh, good Lord, then—[*Darting around.*] My hat—? My overcoat—? Ah, in the hall—Oh, I hope I'm not too late, Hedda, hm?

HEDDA   Then charge right over—
   [BERTA *appears in the hallway.*]

BERTA   Judge Brack is outside.

HEDDA   Ask him to come in.

TESMAN   At a time like this! No, I can't possibly deal with him now.

HEDDA   But I can. [*To* BERTA.] Ask the Judge in.
   [BERTA *goes out.*]

HEDDA [*In a whisper.*]   The package, Tesman. [*She snatches it off the stool.*]

TESMAN   Yes, give it to me.

HEDDA   No, I'll hide it until you get back.
   [*She goes over to the writing table and sticks the package in the bookcase.* TESMAN *stands flustered, and can't get his gloves on.* BRACK *enters through the hall doorway.*]

HEDDA [*Nodding to him.*]   Well, you're an early bird.

BRACK   Yes, wouldn't you say. [*To* TESMAN.] You're going out?

TESMAN   Yes, I've got to go over to my aunt's. Just think, the poor dear is dying.

BRACK   Good Lord, is she really? Then don't let me hold you up for even a moment, at a time like this—

TESMAN   Yes, I really must run—Good-bye. Good-bye. [*He hurries through the hall doorway.*]

HEDDA [*Approaches.*]   So, things were livelier than usual at your place last night, Judge.

BRACK   Oh yes, so much so that I haven't even been able to change clothes, Mrs. Hedda.

HEDDA   You too.

BRACK   As you see. But, what has Tesman been telling you about last night's adventures?

HEDDA   Oh, just some boring things. He went someplace to drink coffee.

BRACK   I've already looked into the coffee party. Eilert Løvborg wasn't part of that group, I presume.

HEDDA   No, they followed him home before that.

BRACK   Tesman too?

HEDDA   No, but a couple of others, he said.

BRACK [*Smiles.*]   George Tesman is a very naïve soul, Mrs. Hedda.

HEDDA   God knows, he is. But is there something more behind this?

BRACK   I'd have to say so.

HEDDA   Well then, Judge, let's be seated. Then you can speak freely. [*She sits to the left side of the table,* BRACK *at the long side near her.*] Well, then—

BRACK   I had certain reasons for keeping track of my guests—or, more precisely, some of my guests' movements last night.

HEDDA   For example, Eilert Løvborg?

BRACK   Yes, indeed.

HEDDA   Now I'm hungry for more.

BRACK   Do you know where he and a couple of the others spent the rest of the night, Mrs. Hedda?

HEDDA   Why don't you tell me, if it can be told.

BRACK   Oh, it's certainly worth the telling. It appears that they found their way into a particularly animated soirée.[1]

HEDDA   A lively one?

BRACK   The liveliest.

HEDDA   Tell me more, Judge.

BRACK   Løvborg had received an invitation earlier—I knew all about that. But he declined because, as you know, he's made himself into a new man.

HEDDA   Up at the Elvsteds', yes. But he went just the same?

BRACK   Well, you see, Mrs. Hedda—unfortunately, the spirit really seized him at my place last evening.

HEDDA   Yes, I hear he was quite inspired.

BRACK   Inspired to a rather powerful degree. And so, he started to reconsider, I assume, because we men, alas, are not always so true to our principles as we ought to be.

HEDDA   Present company excepted, Judge Brack. So, Løvborg—?

BRACK   Short and sweet—He ended up at the salon of a certain Miss Diana.

HEDDA   Miss Diana?

BRACK   Yes, it was Miss Diana's soirée for a select circle of ladies and their admirers.

HEDDA   Is she a redhead?

BRACK   Exactly.

HEDDA   A sort of a—singer?

BRACK   Oh, yes—She's also that. And a mighty huntress—of men, Mrs. Hedda. You must have heard of her. Eilert Løvborg was one of her most strenuous admirers—in his better days.

HEDDA   And how did all this end?

BRACK   Apparently less amicably than it began. Miss Diana, after giving him the warmest of welcomes, soon turned to assault and battery.

HEDDA   Against Løvborg?

BRACK   Oh, yes. He accused her, or one of her ladies, of robbing him. He insisted that his pocketbook was missing, along with some other things. In short, he seems to have created a dreadful spectacle.

1. "Evening party" (French).

HEDDA   And what did that lead to?

BRACK   A regular brawl between both the men and the women. Luckily the police finally got there.

HEDDA   The police too?

BRACK   Yes. It's going to be quite a costly little romp for Eilert Løvborg. What a madman.

HEDDA   Well!

BRACK   Apparently, he resisted arrest. It seems he struck one of the officers on the ear, and ripped his uniform to shreds, so he had to go to the police station.

HEDDA   How do you know all this?

BRACK   From the police themselves.

HEDDA   [*Gazing before her.*]   So, that's how it ended? He had no vine leaves in his hair.

BRACK   Vine leaves, Mrs. Hedda?

HEDDA   [*Changing her tone.*]   Tell me now, Judge, why do you go around snooping and spying on Eilert Løvborg?

BRACK   For starters, I'm not a completely disinterested party—especially if the hearing uncovers the fact that he came straight from my place.

HEDDA   There's going to be a hearing?

BRACK   You can count on it. Be that as it may, however—My real concern was my duty as a friend of the house to inform you and Tesman of Løvborg's nocturnal adventures.

HEDDA   Why, Judge Brack?

BRACK   Well, I have an active suspicion that he'll try to use you as a kind of screen.

HEDDA   Oh! What makes you think that?

BRACK   Good God—we're not that blind, Mrs. Hedda. Wait and see. This Mrs. Elvsted—she won't be in such a hurry to leave town again.

HEDDA   If there's anything going on between those two, there's plenty of places they can meet.

BRACK   Not one single home. Every respectable house will be closed to Eilert Løvborg from now on.

HEDDA   And mine should be too—Is that what you're saying?

BRACK   Yes. I have to admit it would be more than painful for me if this man secured a foothold here. If this—utterly superfluous—and intrusive individual—were to force himself into—

HEDDA   Into the triangle?

BRACK   Precisely! It would leave me without a home.

HEDDA   [*Looks smilingly at him.*]   I see—The one cock of the walk—That's your goal.

BRACK   [*Slowly nodding and dropping his voice.*]   Yes, that's my goal. And it's a goal that I'll fight for—with every means at my disposal.

HEDDA   [*Her smile fading.*]   You're really a dangerous man, aren't you—when push comes to shove.

BRACK   You think so?

HEDDA   Yes, I'm starting to. And that's all right—just as long as you don't have any kind of hold on me.

BRACK   [*Laughing ambiguously.*]   Yes, Mrs. Hedda—you might be right about that. Of course, then, who knows whether I might not find some way or other—

HEDDA Now listen, Judge Brack! That sounds like you're threatening me.

BRACK [*Gets up.*] Oh, far from it. A triangle, you see—is best fortified by free defenders.

HEDDA I think so too.

BRACK Well, I've had my say so I should be getting back. Good-bye, Mrs. Hedda. [*He goes toward the glass doors.*]

HEDDA Out through the garden?

BRACK Yes, it's shorter for me.

HEDDA And then, it's also the back way.

BRACK That's true. I have nothing against back ways. Sometimes they can be very piquant.

HEDDA When there's sharpshooting.

BRACK [*In the doorway, laughing at her.*] Oh, no—you never shoot your tame cocks.

HEDDA [*Also laughing.*] Oh, no, especially when there's only one—
    [*Laughing and nodding they take their farewells. He leaves. She closes the door after him.* HEDDA *stands for a while, serious, looking out. Then she goes and peers through the curtains in the back wall. She goes to the writing table, takes* LØVBORG's *package from the bookcase, and is about to leaf through it.* BERTA's *voice, raised in indignation, is heard out in the hall.* HEDDA *turns and listens. She quickly locks the package in the drawer and sets the key on the writing table.* EILERT LØVBORG, *wearing his overcoat and carrying his hat, bursts through the hall doorway. He looks somewhat confused and excited.*]

LØVBORG [*Turned toward the hallway.*] And I'm telling you, I've got to go in! And that's that! [*He closes the door, sees* HEDDA, *controls himself immediately, and bows.*]

HEDDA [*By the writing table.*] Well, Mr. Løvborg, it's pretty late to be calling for Thea.

LØVBORG Or a little early to be calling on you. I apologize.

HEDDA How do you know that she's still here?

LØVBORG I went to where she was staying. They told me she'd been out all night.

HEDDA [*Goes to the table.*] Did you notice anything special when they told you that?

LØVBORG [*Looks inquiringly at her.*] Notice anything?

HEDDA I mean—did they seem to have any thought on the subject—one way or the other?

LØVBORG [*Suddenly understanding.*] Oh, of course, it's true. I'm dragging her down with me. Still, I didn't notice anything. Tesman isn't up yet, I suppose?

HEDDA No, I don't think so.

LØVBORG When did he get home?

HEDDA Very late.

LØVBORG Did he tell you anything?

HEDDA Yes. I heard Judge Brack's was very lively.

LØVBORG Nothing else?

HEDDA No, I don't think so. I was terribly tired, though—
  [MRS. ELVSTED *comes in through the curtains at the back.*]
MRS. ELVSTED [*Runs toward him.*] Oh, Løvborg—at last!
LØVBORG Yes, at last, and too late.
MRS. ELVSTED [*Looking anxiously at him.*] What's too late?
LØVBORG Everything's too late. I'm finished.
MRS. ELVSTED Oh no, no—Don't say that!
LØVBORG You'll say it too, when you've heard—
MRS. ELVSTED I won't listen—
HEDDA Shall I leave you two alone?
LØVBORG No, stay—You too, I beg you.
MRS. ELVSTED But I won't listen to anything you tell me.
LØVBORG I don't want to talk about last night.
MRS. ELVSTED What is it, then?
LØVBORG We've got to go our separate ways.
MRS. ELVSTED Separate!
HEDDA [*Involuntarily.*] I knew it!
LØVBORG Because I have no more use for you, Thea.
MRS. ELVSTED You can stand there and say that! No more use for me!
  Can't I help you now, like I did before? Won't we go on working together?
LØVBORG I don't plan to work any more.
MRS. ELVSTED [*Desperately.*] Then what do I have to live for?
LØVBORG Just try to live your life as if you'd never known me.
MRS. ELVSTED I can't do that.
LØVBORG Try, Thea. Try, if you can. Go back home.
MRS. ELVSTED [*Defiantly.*] Where you are, that's where I want to be. I won't
  let myself be just driven off like this. I want to stay at your side—be with
  you when the book comes out.
HEDDA [*Half aloud, tensely.*] Ah, the book—Yes.
LØVBORG [*Looking at her.*] Mine and Thea's, because that's what it is.
MRS. ELVSTED Yes, that's what I feel it is. That's why I have a right to be
  with you when it comes out. I want to see you covered in honor and glory
  again, and the joy. I want to share that with you too.
LØVBORG Thea—our book's never coming out.
HEDDA Ah!
MRS. ELVSTED Never coming out?
LØVBORG It can't ever come out.
MRS. ELVSTED [*In anxious foreboding.*] Løvborg, what have you done with
  the manuscript?
HEDDA [*Looking intently at him.*] Yes, the manuscript—?
MRS. ELVSTED What have you—?
LØVBORG Oh, Thea, don't ask me that.
MRS. ELVSTED Yes, yes, I've got to know. I have the right to know.
LØVBORG The manuscript—all right then, the manuscript—I've ripped it
  up into a thousand pieces.
MRS. ELVSTED [*Screams.*] Oh no, no!
HEDDA [*Involuntarily.*] But that's just not—!
LØVBORG [*Looking at her.*] Not true, you think?

HEDDA [*Controls herself.*]   All right then. Of course it is, if you say so. It sounds so ridiculous.

LØVBORG   But it's true, just the same.

MRS. ELVSTED [*Wringing her hands.*]   Oh God—oh God, Hedda. Torn his own work to pieces.

LØVBORG   I've torn my own life to pieces. I might as well tear up my life's work too—

MRS. ELVSTED   And you did that last night!

LØVBORG   Yes. Do you hear me? A thousand pieces. Scattered them all over the fjord.[2] Way out where there's pure salt water. Let them drift in it. Drift with the current in the wind. Then, after a while, they'll sink. Deeper and deeper. Like me, Thea.

MRS. ELVSTED   You know, Løvborg, all this with the book—? For the rest of my life, it will be just like you'd killed a little child.

LØVBORG   You're right. Like murdering a child.

MRS. ELVSTED   But then, how could you—! That child was partly mine, too.

HEDDA [*Almost inaudibly.*]   Ah, the child—

MRS. ELVSTED [*Sighs heavily.*]   So it's finished? All right, Hedda, now I'm going.

HEDDA   You're not going back?

MRS. ELVSTED   Oh, I don't know what I'm going to do. I can't see anything out in front of me. [*She goes out through the hall doorway.*]

HEDDA [*Standing a while, waiting.*]   Don't you want to see her home, Mr. Løvborg?

LØVBORG   Through the streets? So that people can get a good look at us together?

HEDDA   I don't know what else happened to you last night but if it's so completely beyond redemption—

LØVBORG   It won't stop there. I know that much. And I can't bring myself to live that kind of life again either. Not again. Once I had the courage to live life to the fullest, to break every rule. But she's taken that out of me.

HEDDA [*Staring straight ahead.*]   That sweet little fool has gotten hold of a human destiny. [*Looks at him.*] And you're so heartless to her.

LØVBORG   Don't call it heartless.

HEDDA   To go and destroy the thing that has filled her soul for this whole long, long time. You don't call that heartless?

LØVBORG   I can tell you the truth, Hedda.

HEDDA   The truth?

LØVBORG   First, promise me—Give me your word that Thea will never find out what I'm about to confide to you.

HEDDA   You have my word.

LØVBORG   Good. Then I'll tell you—What I stood here and described—It wasn't true.

HEDDA   About the manuscript?

LØVBORG   Yes. I haven't ripped it up. I didn't throw it in the fjord, either.

---

2. "Inlet of the sea" (Norwegian).

HEDDA   No, well—so—Where is it?

LØVBORG   I've destroyed it just the same. Utterly and completely, Hedda!

HEDDA   I don't understand any of this.

LØVBORG   Thea said that what I'd done seemed to her like murdering a child.

HEDDA   Yes, she did.

LØVBORG   But killing his child—that's not the worst thing a father can do to it.

HEDDA   Not the worst?

LØVBORG   No. And the worst—that is what I wanted to spare Thea from hearing.

HEDDA   And what is the worst?

LØVBORG   Imagine, Hedda, a man—in the very early hours of the morning— after a wild night of debauchery, came home to the mother of his child and said, "Listen—I've been here and there to this place and that place, and I had our child with me in this place and that place. And the child got away from me. Just got away. The devil knows whose hands it's fallen into, who's got a hold of it."

HEDDA   Well—when you get right down to it—it's only a book—

LØVBORG   All of Thea's soul was in that book.

HEDDA   Yes, I can see that.

LØVBORG   And so, you must also see that there's no future for her and me.

HEDDA   So, what will your road be now?

LØVBORG   None. Only to see to it that I put an end to it all. The sooner the better.

HEDDA   [Comes a step closer.]   Eilert Løvborg—Listen to me now—Can you see to it that—that when you do it, you bathe it in beauty?

LØVBORG   In beauty? [Smiles.] With vine leaves in my hair, as you used to imagine?

HEDDA   Ah, no. No vine leaves—I don't believe in them any longer. But in beauty, yes! For once! Good-bye. You've got to go now. And don't come here any more.

LØVBORG   Good-bye, Mrs. Tesman. And give my regards to George Tesman. [He is about to leave.]

HEDDA   No, wait! Take a souvenir to remember me by.
[She goes over to the writing table, opens the drawer and the pistol case. She returns to LØVBORG with one of the pistols.]

LØVBORG   [Looks at her.]   That's the souvenir?

HEDDA   [Nodding slowly.]   Do you recognize it? It was aimed at you once.

LØVBORG   You should have used it then.

HEDDA   Here, you use it now.

LØVBORG   [Puts the pistol in his breast pocket.]   Thanks.

HEDDA   In beauty, Eilert Løvborg. Promise me that.

LØVBORG   Good-bye, Hedda Gabler. [He goes out the hall doorway.]
[HEDDA listens a moment at the door. Afterward, she goes to the writing table and takes out the package with the manuscript, looks inside the wrapper, pulls some of the pages half out and looks at them. She then takes it all over to the armchair by the stove and sits down. She has the package in her lap. Soon after she opens the stove door and then opens the package.]

HEDDA [*Throws one of the sheets into the fire and whispers to herself.*]   Now, I'm burning your child, Thea—You with your curly hair. [*Throws a few more sheets into the fire.*] Your child and Eilert Løvborg's. [*Throws in the rest.*] Now I'm burning—burning the child.

Act 4

The same room at the TESMANS'. *It is evening. The drawing room is in darkness. The rear room is lit with a hanging lamp over the table. The curtains are drawn across the glass door.*

[HEDDA, *dressed in black, wanders up and down in the darkened room. Then she goes into the rear room, and over to the left side. Some chords are heard from the piano. Then she emerges again, and goes into the drawing room.* BERTA *comes in from the right of the rear room, with a lighted lamp, which she places on the table in front of the sofa, in the salon. Her eyes show signs of crying, and she has black ribbons on her cap. She goes quietly and carefully to the right.* HEDDA *goes over to the glass door, draws the curtains aside a little, and stares out into the darkness. Soon after,* MISS TESMAN *enters from the hallway dressed in black with a hat and a veil.* HEDDA *goes over to her and shakes her hand.*]

MISS TESMAN   Yes, here I am, Hedda—in mourning black. My poor sister's struggle is over at last.

HEDDA   As you can see, I've already heard. Tesman sent me a note.

MISS TESMAN   Yes, he promised he would but I thought I should bring the news myself. This news of death into this house of life.

HEDDA   That was very kind of you.

MISS TESMAN   Ah, Rina shouldn't have left us right now. Hedda's house is no place for sorrow at a time like this.

HEDDA [*Changing the subject.*]   She died peacefully, Miss Tesman?

MISS TESMAN   Yes, so gently—Such a peaceful release. And she was happy beyond words that she got to see George once more and could say a proper good-bye to him. Is it possible he's not home yet?

HEDDA   No. He wrote saying I shouldn't expect him too early. But, please sit down.

MISS TESMAN   No, thank you, my dear—blessed Hedda. I'd like to, but I have so little time. She'll be dressed and arranged the best that I can. She'll look really splendid when she goes to her grave.

HEDDA   Can I help you with anything?

MISS TESMAN   Oh, don't even think about it. These kinds of things aren't for Hedda Tesman's hands or her thoughts either. Not at this time. No, no.

HEDDA   Ah—thoughts—Now they're not so easy to master—

MISS TESMAN [*Continuing.*]   Yes, dear God, that's how this world goes. Over at my house we'll be sewing a linen shroud for Aunt Rina, and here there will be sewing too, but of a whole different kind, praise God.

   [GEORGE TESMAN *enters through a hall door.*]

HEDDA   Well, it's good you're finally here.

TESMAN   You here, Aunt Julie, with Hedda. Just think.

MISS TESMAN   I was just about to go, my dear boy. Well. Did you manage to finish everything you promised to?

TESMAN   No, I'm afraid I've forgotten half of it. I have to run over there tomorrow again. Today my brain is just so confused. I can't keep hold of two thoughts in a row.

MISS TESMAN   George, my dear, you mustn't take it like that.

TESMAN   Oh? How should I take it, do you think?

MISS TESMAN   You must be joyful in your sorrow. You must be glad for what has happened, just as I am.

TESMAN   Ah, yes. You're thinking of Aunt Rina.

HEDDA   You'll be lonely now, Miss Tesman.

MISS TESMAN   For the first few days, yes. But that won't last long, I hope. Our sainted Rina's little room won't stand empty. That much I know.

TESMAN   Really? Who'll be moving in there, hm?

MISS TESMAN   Oh, there's always some poor invalid or other who needs care and attention, unfortunately.

HEDDA   You'd really take on a cross like that again?

MISS TESMAN   Cross? God forgive you child. It's not a cross for me.

HEDDA   But a complete stranger—

MISS TESMAN   It's easy to make friends with sick people. And I so badly need someone to live for. Well, God be praised and thanked—there'll be a thing or two to keep an old aunt busy here in this house soon enough.

HEDDA   Oh, please don't think about us.

TESMAN   Yes. The three of us could be quite cozy here if only—

HEDDA   If only—?

TESMAN   [*Uneasily.*] Oh, it's nothing. Everything'll be fine. Let's hope, hm?

MISS TESMAN   Well, well, you two have plenty to talk about, I'm sure. [*Smiling.*] And Hedda may have something to tell you, George. Now it's home to Rina. [*Turning in the doorway.*] Dear Lord, isn't it strange to think about. Now Rina's both with me and our sainted Joseph.

TESMAN   Yes, just think, Aunt Julie, hm?

[MISS TESMAN *leaves through the hall door.*]

HEDDA   [*Follows* TESMAN *with cold, searching eyes.*] I think all this has hit you harder than your aunt.

TESMAN   Oh, it's not just this death. It's Eilert I'm worried about.

HEDDA   [*Quickly.*] Any news?

TESMAN   I wanted to run to him this afternoon and tell him that his manuscript was safe—in good hands.

HEDDA   Oh? Did you find him?

TESMAN   No, he wasn't home. But later I met Mrs. Elvsted, and she told me he'd been here early this morning.

HEDDA   Yes, just after you left.

TESMAN   And apparently he said that he'd ripped the manuscript up into a thousand pieces, hm?

HEDDA   That's what he said.

TESMAN   But, good God, he must have been absolutely crazy. So you didn't dare give it back to him, Hedda?

HEDDA No, he didn't get it back.

TESMAN But, you told him we had it?

HEDDA No. [*Quickly.*] Did you tell Mrs. Elvsted?

TESMAN No, I didn't want to. But you should have told him. What would happen if in his desperation he went and did something to himself? Let me have the manuscript, Hedda. I'll run it over to him right away. Where did you put it?

HEDDA [*Cold and impassively leaning on the armchair.*] I don't have it any more.

TESMAN Don't have it! What in the world do you mean?

HEDDA I burned it up—every page.

TESMAN [*Leaps up in terror.*] Burned? Burned? Eilert's manuscript!

HEDDA Don't shout like that. The maid will hear you.

TESMAN Burned! But good God—! No, no, no—That's absolutely impossible.

HEDDA Yes, but all the same it's true.

TESMAN Do you have any idea what you've done, Hedda? That's—that's criminal appropriation of lost property. Think about that. Yes, just ask Judge Brack, then you'll see.

HEDDA Then it's probably wise for you not to talk about it, isn't it? To the Judge or anyone else.

TESMAN How could you have gone and done something so appalling? What came over you? Answer me that, Hedda, hm?

HEDDA [*Suppressing an almost imperceptible smile.*] I did it for your sake, George.

TESMAN My sake?

HEDDA Remember you came home this morning and talked about how he had read to you?

TESMAN Yes, yes.

HEDDA You confessed that you envied him.

TESMAN Good God, I didn't mean it literally.

HEDDA Nevertheless, I couldn't stand the idea that someone would over shadow you.

TESMAN [*Exclaiming between doubt and joy.*] Hedda—Oh, is this true?—What you're saying?—Yes, but. Yes, but. I never noticed that you loved me this way before. Think of that!

HEDDA Well, you need to know—that at a time like this—[*Violently breaking off.*] No, no—go and ask your Aunt Julie. She'll provide all the details.

TESMAN Oh, I almost think I understand you, Hedda. [*Clasps his hands together.*] No, good God—Can it be, hm?

HEDDA Don't shout like that. The maid can hear you.

TESMAN [*Laughing in extraordinary joy.*] The maid! Oh, Hedda, you are priceless. The maid—why it's—why it's Berta. I'll go tell Berta myself.

HEDDA [*Clenching her hands as if frantic.*] Oh, I'm dying—Dying of all this.

TESMAN All what, Hedda, what?

HEDDA [*Coldly controlled again.*] All this—absurdity—George.

TESMAN Absurdity? I'm so incredibly happy. Even so, maybe I shouldn't say anything to Berta.

HEDDA Oh yes, go ahead. Why not?

TESMAN   No, no. Not right now. But Aunt Julie, yes, absolutely. And then, you're calling me George. Just think. Oh, Aunt Julie will be so happy— so happy.

HEDDA   When she hears I've burned Eilert Løvborg's manuscript for your sake?

TESMAN   No, no, you're right. All this with the manuscript. No. Of course, nobody can find out about that. But, Hedda—you're burning for me— Aunt Julie really must share in that. But I wonder—all this—I wonder if it's typical with young wives, hm?

HEDDA   You'd better ask Aunt Julie about that too.

TESMAN   Oh yes, I certainly will when I get the chance. [*Looking uneasy and thoughtful again.*] No, but, oh no, the manuscript. Good Lord, it's awful to think about poor Eilert, just the same.

[MRS. ELVSTED, *dressed as for her first visit with hat and coat, enters through the hall door.*]

MRS. ELVSTED   [*Greets them hurriedly and speaks in agitation.*]   Oh, Hedda, don't be offended that I've come back again.

HEDDA   What happened to you, Thea?

TESMAN   Something about Eilert Løvborg?

MRS. ELVSTED   Oh yes, I'm terrified that he's had an accident.

HEDDA   [*Grips her arm.*]   Ah, do you think so?

TESMAN   Good Lord, where did you get that idea, Mrs. Elvsted?

MRS. ELVSTED   I heard them talking at the boarding house—just as I came in. There are the most incredible rumors about him going around town today.

TESMAN   Oh yes, imagine, I heard them too. And still I can swear he went straight home to sleep. Just think.

HEDDA   So—What were they saying at the boarding house?

MRS. ELVSTED   Oh, I couldn't get any details, either because they didn't know or—or they saw me and stopped talking. And I didn't dare ask.

TESMAN   [*Uneasily pacing the floor.*]   Let's just hope—you misunderstood.

MRS. ELVSTED   No, I'm sure they were talking about him. Then I heard them say something about the hospital—

TESMAN   Hospital?

HEDDA   No—That's impossible.

MRS. ELVSTED   I'm deathly afraid for him, so I went up to his lodgings and asked about him there.

HEDDA   You dared to do that?

MRS. ELVSTED   What else should I have done? I couldn't stand the uncertainty any longer.

TESMAN   You didn't find him there either, hm?

MRS. ELVSTED   No. And the people there didn't know anything at all. They said he hadn't been home since yesterday afternoon.

TESMAN   Yesterday? How could they say that?

MRS. ELVSTED   It could only mean one thing—Something terrible's happened to him.

TESMAN   You know, Hedda—What if I were to go into town and ask around at different places—?

HEDDA   No! You stay out of this.

[JUDGE BRACK, *carrying his hat, enters through the hall door, which* BERTA *opens and closes after him. He looks serious and bows in silence.*]

TESMAN   Oh, here you are, Judge, hm?

BRACK   Yes, it was essential for me to see you this evening.

TESMAN   I see you got the message from Aunt Julie.

BRACK   Yes, that too.

TESMAN   Isn't it sad, hm?

BRACK   Well, my dear Tesman, that depends on how you look at it.

TESMAN   [*Looks at him uneasily.*]   Has anything else happened?

BRACK   Yes, it has.

HEDDA   [*Tensely.*]   Something sad, Judge Brack?

BRACK   Once again, it depends on how you look at it, Mrs. Tesman.

MRS. ELVSTED   [*In an uncontrollable outburst.*]   It's Eilert Løvborg.

BRACK   [*Looks briefly at her.*]   How did you guess, Mrs. Elvsted? Do you already know something—?

MRS. ELVSTED   [*Confused.*]   No, no, I don't know anything but—

TESMAN   Well, for God's sake, tell us what it is.

BRACK   [*Shrugging his shoulders.*]   Well then—I'm sorry to tell you—that Eilert Løvborg has been taken to the hospital. He is dying.

MRS. ELVSTED   [*Crying out.*]   Oh God, oh God.

TESMAN   Dying?

HEDDA   [*Involuntarily.*]   So quickly—?

MRS. ELVSTED   [*Wailing.*]   And we were quarrelling when we parted, Hedda.

HEDDA   [*Whispers.*]   Now, Thea—Thea.

MRS. ELVSTED   [*Not noticing her.*]   I'm going to him. I've got to see him alive.

BRACK   It would do you no good, Mrs. Elvsted. No visitors are allowed.

MRS. ELVSTED   At least tell me what happened. What—?

TESMAN   Yes, because he certainly wouldn't have tried to—hm?

HEDDA   Yes, I'm sure that's what he did.

TESMAN   Hedda. How can you—

BRACK   [*Who is watching her all the time.*]   Unfortunately, Mrs. Tesman, you've guessed right.

MRS. ELVSTED   Oh, how awful.

TESMAN   To himself, too. Think of it.

HEDDA   Shot himself!

BRACK   Right again, Mrs. Tesman.

MRS. ELVSTED   [*Tries to compose herself.*]   When did this happen, Mr. Brack?

BRACK   Just this afternoon, between three and four.

TESMAN   Oh, my God—Where did he do it, hm?

BRACK   [*Slightly uncertain.*]   Where? Oh, I suppose at his lodgings.

MRS. ELVSTED   No, that can't be. I was there between six and seven.

BRACK   Well then, some other place. I don't know precisely. All I know is that he was found—he'd shot himself—in the chest.

MRS. ELVSTED   Oh, how awful to think that he should die like that.

HEDDA   [*To* BRACK.]   In the chest?

BRACK   Yes, like I said.

HEDDA   Not through the temple?

BRACK   The chest, Mrs. Tesman.

HEDDA   Well, well. The chest is also good.

BRACK   What was that, Mrs. Tesman?

HEDDA [*Evasively.*]   Oh, nothing—nothing.

TESMAN   And the wound is fatal, hm?

BRACK   The wound is absolutely fatal. In fact, it's probably already over.

MRS. ELVSTED   Yes, yes, I can feel it. It's over. It's all over. Oh, Hedda—!

TESMAN   Tell me, how did you find out about all this?

BRACK [*Curtly.*]   From a police officer. One I spoke with.

HEDDA [*Raising her voice.*]   Finally—an action.

TESMAN   God help us, Hedda, what are you saying?

HEDDA   I'm saying that here, in this—there is beauty.

BRACK   Uhm, Mrs. Tesman.

TESMAN   Beauty! No, don't even think it.

MRS. ELVSTED   Oh, Hedda. How can you talk about beauty?

HEDDA   Eilert Løvborg has come to terms with himself. He's had the courage to do what had to be done.

MRS. ELVSTED   No, don't ever believe it was anything like that. What he did, he did in a moment of madness.

TESMAN   It was desperation.

MRS. ELVSTED   Yes, madness. Just like when he tore his book in pieces.

BRACK [*Startled.*]   The book. You mean his manuscript? Did he tear it up?

MRS. ELVSTED   Yes, last night.

TESMAN [*Whispering softly.*]   Oh, Hedda, we'll never get out from under all this.

BRACK   Hmm, that's very odd.

TESMAN [*Pacing the floor.*]   To think that Eilert Løvborg should leave the world this way. And then not to leave behind the work that would have made his name immortal.

MRS. ELVSTED   Oh, what if it could be put together again.

TESMAN   Yes—just think—what if it could? I don't know what I wouldn't give—

MRS. ELVSTED   Maybe it can, Mr. Tesman.

TESMAN   What do you mean?

MRS. ELVSTED [*Searching in the pocket of her skirt.*]   See this? I saved all the notes he dictated from.

HEDDA [*A step closer.*]   Ah.

TESMAN   You saved them, Mrs. Elvsted, hm?

MRS. ELVSTED   Yes, they're all here. I brought them with me when I came to town, and here they've been. Tucked away in my pocket—

TESMAN   Oh, let me see them.

MRS. ELVSTED [*Gives him a bundle of small papers.*]   But they're all mixed up, completely out of order.

TESMAN   Just think. What if we could sort them out. Perhaps if the two of us helped each other.

MRS. ELVSTED   Oh yes. Let's at least give it a try—

TESMAN   It will happen. It must happen. I'll give my whole life to this.

HEDDA   You, George, your life?

TESMAN   Yes, or, anyway, all the time I have. Every spare minute. My own research will just have to be put aside. Hedda—you understand, don't you, hm? I owe this to Eilert's memory.

HEDDA   Maybe so.

TESMAN   Now, my dear Mrs. Elvsted, let's pull ourselves together. God knows there's no point brooding about what's happened. We've got to try to find some peace of mind so that—

MRS. ELVSTED   Yes, yes, Mr. Tesman. I'll do my best.

TESMAN   Well. So, come along then. We've got to get started on these notes right away. Where should we sit? Here? No. In the back room. Excuse us, Judge. Come with me, Mrs. Elvsted.

MRS. ELVSTED   Oh God—if only it can be done.

[TESMAN *and* MRS. ELVSTED *go into the rear room. She takes her hat and coat off. Both sit at the table under the hanging lamp and immerse themselves in eager examination of the papers.* HEDDA *goes across to the stove and sits in the armchair. Soon after,* BRACK *goes over to her.*]

HEDDA   [*Softly.*]   Ah, Judge—This act of Eilert Løvborg's—there's a sense of liberation in it.

BRACK   Liberation, Mrs. Hedda? Yes, I guess it's a liberation for him, all right.

HEDDA   I mean, for me. It's a liberation for me to know that in this world an act of such courage, done in full, free will, is possible. Something bathed in a bright shaft of sudden beauty.

BRACK   [*Smiles.*]   Hmm—Dear Mrs. Hedda—

HEDDA   Oh, I know what you're going to say, because you're a kind of specialist too, after all, just like—Ah well.

BRACK   [*Looking steadily at her.*]   Eilert Løvborg meant more to you than you might admit—even to yourself. Or am I wrong?

HEDDA   I don't answer questions like that. All I know is that Eilert Løvborg had the courage to live life his own way, and now—his last great act—bathed in beauty. He—had the will to break away from the banquet of life—so soon.

BRACK   It pains me, Mrs. Hedda—but I'm forced to shatter this pretty illusion of yours.

HEDDA   Illusion?

BRACK   Which would have been taken away from you soon enough.

HEDDA   And what's that?

BRACK   He didn't shoot himself—so freely.

HEDDA   Not freely?

BRACK   No. This whole Eilert Løvborg business didn't come off exactly the way I described it.

HEDDA   [*In suspense.*]   Are you hiding something? What is it?

BRACK   I employed a few euphemisms for poor Mrs. Elvsted's sake.

HEDDA   Such as—?

BRACK   First, of course, he's already dead.

HEDDA   At the hospital?

BRACK   Yes. And without regaining consciousness.

HEDDA What else?

BRACK The incident took place somewhere other than his room.

HEDDA That's insignificant.

BRACK Not completely. I have to tell you—Eilert Løvborg was found shot in—Miss Diana's boudoir.

HEDDA [*About to jump up but sinks back again.*] That's impossible, Judge. He can't have gone there again today.

BRACK He was there this afternoon. He came to demand the return of something that he said they'd taken from him. He talked crazily about a lost child.

HEDDA Ah, so that's why—

BRACK I thought maybe he was referring to his manuscript but I hear he'd already destroyed that himself so I guess it was his pocketbook.

HEDDA Possibly. So—that's where he was found.

BRACK Right there, with a discharged pistol in his coat pocket, and a fatal bullet wound.

HEDDA In the chest, yes?

BRACK No—lower down.

HEDDA [*Looks up at him with an expression of revulsion.*] That too! Oh absurdity—! It hangs like a curse over everything I so much as touch.

BRACK There's still one more thing, Mrs. Hedda. Also in the ugly category.

HEDDA And what is that?

BRACK The pistol he had with him—

HEDDA [*Breathless.*] Well, what about it?

BRACK He must have stolen it.

HEDDA [*Jumping up.*] Stolen? That's not true. He didn't.

BRACK There's no other explanation possible. He must have stolen it— Shh.

[TESMAN *and* MRS. ELVSTED *have gotten up from the table in the rear room and come into the living room.*]

TESMAN [*With papers in both hands.*] Hedda, my dear—I can hardly see anything in there under that lamp. Just think—

HEDDA I'm thinking.

TESMAN Do you think you might let us sit a while at your desk, hm?

HEDDA Oh, gladly. [*Quickly.*] No, wait. Let me just clean it up a bit first.

TESMAN Oh, not necessary, Hedda. There's plenty of room.

HEDDA No, no, I'll just straighten it up, I'm telling you. I'll just move these things here under the piano for a while.

[*She has pulled an object covered with sheet music out of the bookcase. She adds a few more sheets and carries the whole pile out to the left of the rear room.* TESMAN *puts the papers on the desk and brings over the lamp from the corner table. He and* MRS. ELVSTED *sit and continue their work.*]

HEDDA Well, Thea, my sweet. Are things moving along with the memorial?

MRS. ELVSTED [*Looks up at her dejectedly.*] Oh, God—It's going to be so difficult to find the order in all of this.

TESMAN But it must be done. There's simply no other choice. And finding the order in other people's papers—that's precisely what I'm meant for.

[HEDDA *goes over to the stove and sits on one of the stools.* BRACK *stands over her, leaning over the armchair.*]

HEDDA [*Whispers.*] What were you saying about the pistol?

BRACK [*Softly.*] That he must have stolen it.

HEDDA Why stolen exactly?

BRACK Because there shouldn't be any other way to explain it, Mrs. Hedda.

HEDDA I see.

BRACK [*Looks briefly at her.*] Eilert Løvborg was here this morning, am I correct?

HEDDA Yes.

BRACK Were you alone with him?

HEDDA Yes, for a while.

BRACK You didn't leave the room at all while he was here?

HEDDA No.

BRACK Think again. Weren't you out of the room, even for one moment?

HEDDA Yes. Perhaps. Just for a moment—out in the hallway.

BRACK And where was your pistol case at that time?

HEDDA I put it under the—

BRACK Well, Mrs. Hedda—

HEDDA It was over there on the writing table.

BRACK Have you looked since then to see if both pistols are there?

HEDDA No.

BRACK It's not necessary. I saw the pistol Løvborg had, and I recognized it immediately from yesterday, and from before as well.

HEDDA Have you got it?

BRACK No, the police have it.

HEDDA What will the police do with that pistol?

BRACK Try to track down its owner.

HEDDA Do you think they can do that?

BRACK [*Bends over her and whispers.*] No, Hedda Gabler, not as long as I keep quiet.

HEDDA [*Looking fearfully at him.*] And what if you don't keep quiet—then what?

BRACK Then the way out is to claim that the pistol was stolen.

HEDDA I'd rather die.

BRACK [*Smiling.*] People make those threats but they don't act on them.

HEDDA [*Without answering.*] So—let's say the pistol is not stolen and the owner is found out? What happens then?

BRACK Well, Hedda—then there'll be a scandal.

HEDDA A scandal?

BRACK Oh, yes, a scandal. Just what you're so desperately afraid of. You'd have to appear in court, naturally. You and Miss Diana. She'd have to detail how it all occurred. Whether it was an accident or a homicide. Was he trying to draw the pistol to threaten her? Is that when the gun went off? Did she snatch it out of his hands to shoot him, and then put the pistol back in his pocket? That would be thoroughly in character for her. She's a feisty little thing, that Miss Diana.

HEDDA But all this ugliness has got nothing to do with me.

BRACK   No. But you would have to answer one question. Why did you give the pistol to Eilert Løvborg? And what conclusions would people draw from the fact that you gave it to him?

HEDDA [*Lowers her head.*]   That's true. I didn't think of that.

BRACK   Well. Fortunately you have nothing to worry about as long as I keep quiet.

HEDDA [*Looking up at him.*]   So I'm in your power now, Judge. You have a hold over me from now on.

BRACK [*Whispering more softly.*]   Dearest Hedda—Believe me—I won't abuse my position.

HEDDA   But in your power. Totally subject to your demands—And your will. Not free. Not free at all. [*She gets up silently.*] No, that's one thought I just can't stand. Never!

BRACK [*Looks mockingly at her.*]   One can usually learn to live with the inevitable.

HEDDA [*Returning his look.*]   Maybe so. [*She goes over to the writing table, suppressing an involuntary smile and imitating* TESMAN's *intonation.*] Well, George, this is going to work out, hm?

TESMAN   Oh, Lord knows, dear. Anyway, at this rate, it's going to be months of work.

HEDDA [*As before.*]   No, just think. [*Runs her fingers lightly through* MRS. ELVSTED's *hair.*] Doesn't it seem strange, Thea. Here you are, sitting together with Tesman—just like you used to sit with Eilert Løvborg.

MRS. ELVSTED   Oh, God, if only I could inspire your husband too.

HEDDA   Oh, that will come—in time.

TESMAN   Yes, you know what, Hedda—I really think I'm beginning to feel something like that. But why don't you go over and sit with Judge Brack some more.

HEDDA   Can't you two find any use for me here?

TESMAN   No, nothing in the world. [*Turning his head.*] From now on, my dear Judge, you'll have to be kind enough to keep Hedda company.

BRACK [*With a glance at* HEDDA.]   That will be an infinite pleasure for me.

HEDDA   Thanks, but I'm tired tonight. I'll go in there and lie down on the sofa for a while.

TESMAN   Yes, do that, Hedda, hm?

[HEDDA *goes into the rear room and draws the curtains after her. Short pause. Suddenly she is heard to play a wild dance melody on the piano.*]

MRS. ELVSTED [*Jumping up from her chair.*]   Oh—what's that?

TESMAN [*Running to the doorway.*]   Oh, Hedda, my dear—Don't play dance music tonight. Just think of poor Aunt Rina and of Eilert Løvborg too.

HEDDA [*Putting her head out from between the curtains.*]   And Aunt Julie and all the rest of them too. From now on I shall be quiet. [*She closes the curtains again.*]

TESMAN [*At the writing table.*]   This can't be making her very happy—Seeing us at this melancholy work. You know what, Mrs. Elvsted—You're going to move in with Aunt Julie. Then I can come over in the evening, and we can sit and work there, hm?

MRS. ELVSTED   Yes, maybe that would be the best—

HEDDA [*From the rear room.*] I can hear you perfectly well, Tesman. So, how am I supposed to get through the evenings out here?

TESMAN [*Leafing through the papers.*] Oh, I'm sure Judge Brack will be good enough to call on you.

BRACK [*In the armchair, shouts merrily.*] I'd be delighted, Mrs. Tesman. Every evening. Oh, we're going to have some good times together, the two of us.

HEDDA [*Loudly and clearly.*] Yes, that's what you're hoping for, isn't it, Judge? You, the one and only cock of the walk—

[*A shot is heard within.* TESMAN, MRS. ELVSTED *and* BRACK *all jump to their feet.*]

TESMAN Oh, she's playing around with those pistols again.

[*He pulls the curtains aside and runs in.* MRS. ELVSTED *follows.* HEDDA *is stretched out lifeless on the sofa. Confusion and cries.* BERTA *comes running in from the right.*]

[*Shrieking to* BRACK.] Shot herself! Shot herself in the temple! Just think!

BRACK [*Half prostrate in the armchair.*] But God have mercy—People just don't act that way!

END OF PLAY

ANTON CHEKHOV
1860–1904

Anton Chekhov visited the literary giant **Leo Tolstoy** late in the great novelist's life. Tolstoy embraced him warmly, and said: "I can't stand your plays. **Shakespeare**'s are terrible, but yours are worse!" Tolstoy particularly objected that the dramas lacked purpose. "Where does one get to with your heroes?" he asked the young dramatist. "From the sofa to the privy and from the privy back to the sofa?" The ever-modest Chekhov was apparently amused, finding it hard to take offense at a judgment that likened him to Shakespeare. And perhaps he was pleased, too, that Tolstoy's perplexity got at the very heart of Chekhov's innovative writing, which both puzzled and startled his early audiences by refusing grand actions and melodramatic plots: no deaths, no great love affairs, no shocking revelations. Tolstoy was looking for heroes, and Chekhov refuses to give us any, typically offering a constellation of characters, each of whom—even the most minor—can lay claim to a separate life and perspective. Aged servants and bumbling tutors have as much to say as aristocrats and beauties. His works are like life, Chekhov said, "just as complex and just as simple."

LIFE

Anton Chekhov was born in the thriving Russian seaport town of Taganrog in 1860. His grandfather had been a serf who eventually saved enough money to purchase his freedom. Chekhov himself never forgot how narrowly he had escaped being born into serfdom, and he struggled his whole life against feelings of subservience and inferiority. Chekhov's father owned a grimy and decrepit grocery store and forced his children to work there. A tyrannical man, he had outbursts of temper, beat his children, insulted his wife, and held fervent religious beliefs. When Chekhov was sixteen, his father went bankrupt and slunk off to Moscow to escape his debtors, where his family soon joined him. They left only Anton behind in Taganrog to fend for himself. Survival was difficult. His parents insisted that he send them money, so he sold the family furniture and lived with relatives, begging them for small sums.

In 1879, Chekhov won a scholarship to study medicine at Moscow University. In Moscow he found his family poverty-stricken and gloomy, his two older brothers spending what money they earned on drinking and women. Anton took financial responsibility for all of them, writing humorous stories for magazines to make money while studying medicine. He was so prolific that by the age of 26, he had published over 400 short pieces in popular magazines, as well as two books of stories.

During this period, Chekhov developed two techniques as a writer that would serve him for the rest of his life. First, his medical training taught him to pay close attention to details; readers have long praised his skill as an objective observer of subtle signs and gestures.

Second, his work as a humor writer demanded brevity; he wrote frequently for a magazine called *Splinters*, which had a strict limit of 100 words, and so forced the young writer to express his ideas within tight constraints. Once when friend found him condensing a story by Tolstoy, he explained that he frequently did this kind of exercise to practice conciseness.

In his third year of medical school, Chekhov began writing for more serious literary magazines. He was launched on two careers, managing to work as both a physician and a writer until he died. "Medicine is my lawful wife," he once said; "Writing is my mistress." His medical practice was draining, since he often treated poor patients for nothing and was called out to visit the sick in the middle of the night. Alarmingly, he started showing symptoms of tuberculosis in 1884.

Chekhov's first full-length play, *Ivanov*, went on stage in 1887. The production was a disaster: none of the actors had learned their lines, and one was clearly drunk on stage. Chekhov later dismissed his early plays as conventional and frivolous. It would be another decade before his drama would be treated as seriously as his short fiction, which was making him famous. He won the prestigious Pushkin Prize for his short stories in 1888.

Surprising everyone who knew him, Chekhov decided to write a report about Sakhalin, a penal colony off the coast of Siberia that was notorious for its appalling conditions. What he found was worse even than he had imagined: a "perfect hell," as he described it. Chained to wheelbarrows, flogged, starved, sometimes even raped and murdered, the prisoners endured a life of daily horror. The women survived mostly by prostitution. Since the Russian government had never collected much information about the prisoners and their families, Chekhov decided to perform a full census of the island himself. This was a massive task, and the writer took notes on the brutal conditions as he moved, offering his medical services to sick prisoners. When he returned, he lobbied for reform of Sakhalin, especially for the island's children, and in 1894 published a long and detailed book on the colony, filled with statistics and shocking truths. The press praised the book, the public was scandalized by the conditions in Sakhalin, and the government began to undertake reforms.

In the 1890s Chekhov finally turned his hand to writing drama again, and this time the plays he wrote were radically experimental, casting off the conventions of sensational melodrama that had dominated Russian theater and ushering in a new style that stressed ensembles rather than heroes and moods rather than actions. The first of these dramas, *The Seagull*, had such a disastrous opening that Chekhov vowed never to write another play. But this failure marked the beginning of a new era in Russian drama. In 1897, a theater opened in Moscow insisting on naturalistic, modern styles, and its great director, Konstantin Stanislavsky, saw *The Seagull* as the ideal play to mark this innovation. His new production astonished its first audiences. When the curtain fell on the first act, there was total silence. The hush went on for so long that one actress began to sob. But then the audience burst into wild applause. The actors were too stunned to take their bow. What followed were rave reviews and packed houses. Stanislavky's production of *The Seagull* was hailed as "one of the greatest events in the history of Russian theater and one of the greatest new developments in the history of world drama." The Moscow Art Theatre took the seagull as its emblem, and it staged all of Chekhov's late dramatic works.

The Moscow Art Theatre launched a new phase in Chekhov's personal life as well. He fell in love with one of the actresses in *The Seagull*, Olga Knipper, and married her in 1901, at the age of 41. They moved to Yalta, where they hoped that his health would improve. It did not. Chekhov died of tuberculosis in 1904.

TIMES

Huge social inequalities, fast-paced economic change, and rising political instability produced the pervasive anxiety that characterized Russia at the end of the nineteenth century. The country had begun a phase of rapid industrialization— about a century later than most of Western Europe—and saw a dramatic rise in the production of coal, steel, iron, oil, textiles, and beet sugar after 1850. Its population exploded from 50 million in 1860 to about 100 million in 1900. Russian cities grew quickly, and the railroad expanded dramatically. Tsar Alexander II officially abolished serfdom in 1860, diminishing the traditional influence of landowners, while business and bureaucratic sectors grew and employed ever larger numbers. Newly rich merchants and professionals began to buy property from the old aristocracy.

This profound shift in wealth and power brought a sense of impending crisis. Social groups that had new access to wealth and education frequently expressed anger at the autocratic tsarist regime, and voices across the class spectrum criticized the government for allowing the poor to suffer. Anarchists and other revolutionary groups assassinated numerous high-ranking officials, including Tsar Alexander II himself in 1881. The government tried to crack down on social turmoil with widespread arrests. Writers and intellectuals lived in constant fear that they would be thrown into prison, and their work was subject to frequent censorship. Chekhov was among the writers who signed a petition for freedom of the press, which brought him under the surveillance of the tsar's secret police. The end of the century witnessed massive demonstrations against tsarist authority, with students often acting as the leading agitators. In 1901, the Russian minister of education tried to draft 200 student leaders into the army. In *The Cherry Orchard*, the perpetual student Trofimov would have evoked these dissidents for contemporary audiences, and in fact the censors forced Chekhov to revise his character's most inflammatory speeches.

In the final years of Chekhov's life, Russian society was turning ever more volatile. Tsar Nicholas II was a weak-willed leader, inclined to bow to the dictates of reactionary ministers. Russian liberals clamored for constitutional reforms, while increasingly visible socialists responded to widespread crop failures, cholera epidemics, and grinding rural poverty by demanding outright revolution. In 1904, mounting tensions between Japan and Russia exploded into war. The very day that Chekhov died, July 15, 1904, a homemade bomb thrown by a socialist revolutionary killed the minister of the interior in his carriage. A year later, the Imperial Guard killed a thousand peaceful demonstrators, who had been singing patriotic songs and hymns. "Bloody Sunday," as this event came to be called, inflamed antimonarchical sentiment, launched the Russian Revolution of 1905, and heralded the ultimate end of tsarism. In 1917 the Bolshevik-led revolution would bring about a wholly new kind of social organization—the communist state.

Writers and artists working in this atmosphere of violence and instability hotly debated the proper role of the arts. Should art act as provocative political opposition, offering criticism of the status quo and images of a better future? Should it instead glorify the nation, prompting patriotism and loyalty? Or should art retain a fierce independence from politics, dedicated to purely aesthetic aims and aspirations? Chekhov had friends who propounded all of these positions, but he managed to elude them all. Throughout his career, for example, Chekhov stood up for oppressed and marginalized groups, but his stories and plays often steered clear of strong political and moral messages. From the 1930s onward, Chekhov became a favorite among Soviet leaders, who saw him as a proponent of communist ideals and insisted that his plays be produced across the USSR. Meanwhile, in the West, his work was taken to stand for individualism—and against Soviet collectivism. Throughout the twentieth century, Chekhov remained widely popular around the world—and exceptionally difficult to categorize.

WORK

Chekhov made a lasting mark on two major genres, short fiction and drama. When twenty-five famous short-story writers in our own time were asked to name the authors who had had the greatest influence on their art, ten of them—including Eudora Welty, Nadine Gordimer, and Raymond Carver—named Chekhov, more than any other writer. (Tied for second place, with five votes each, were Henry James and **James Joyce**.) Chekhov's special aptitude—and what makes him seem especially modern—is his reliance on small, delicate details in place of sensational actions or sudden plot twists. The driving force of his narratives is often not external events at all but mental processes that are subtle and unsettling: unexpected emotions, ambivalent desires, and gradually dawning recognitions.

Vladimir Nabokov called "The Lady with the Dog" (our selection below) "one of the greatest stories ever written." Contradictory impulses propel the two main characters from the beginning: the jaded philanderer Gurov scorns women and yet craves their company, while the bored young woman he casually seduces at a seaside resort deceives a husband she condemns as a "flunky" but is then rocked by waves of remorse. Gurov thinks of the affair as a passing thrill, but later, in the woman's absence, he is surprised to discover that he has actually fallen in love with her. Chekhov invites us to recognize this as a major crisis in Gurov's life—his old life becomes unbearable—but it does not interrupt the narrative as a sudden turning point. Instead, the crisis unfolds as a series of fleeting, quiet moments of painful perception. Chekhov does not judge his characters' adultery, as most of his contemporaries would have done, but hints at the value of their transformation, as both are slowly estranged from their earlier selves. And in characteristically Chekhovian fashion, he does not end with a clear or comforting resolution but with a fragile, fleeting, inconclusive moment of genuine intimacy.

The Lady with the Dog[1]

I

People were telling one another that a newcomer had been seen on the promenade—a lady with a dog. Dmitri Dmitrich Gurov had been a fortnight in Yalta,[2] and was accustomed to its ways, and he, too, had begun to take an interest in fresh arrivals. From his seat in Vernet's outdoor café, he caught sight of a young woman in a toque, passing along the promenade; she was fair and not very tall; after her trotted a white Pomeranian.

Later he encountered her in the municipal park and in the square several times a day. She was always alone, wearing the same toque, and the Pomeranian always trotted at her side. Nobody knew who she was, and people referred to her simply as "the lady with the dog."

"If she's here without her husband, and without any friends," thought Gurov, "it wouldn't be a bad idea to make her acquaintance."

He was not yet forty but had a twelve-year-old daughter and two sons in high school. He had been talked into marrying in his second year at college, and his wife now looked nearly twice as old as he did. She was a tall woman with dark eyebrows, erect, dignified, imposing, and, as she said of herself, a "thinker." She was a great reader, omitted the "hard sign"[3] at the end of words in her letters, and called her husband "Dimitry" instead of Dmitry; and though he secretly considered her shallow, narrow-minded, and dowdy, he stood in awe of her, and disliked being at home. He had first begun deceiving her long ago and he was now constantly unfaithful to her, and this was no doubt why he spoke slightingly of women, to whom he referred as *the lower race*.

He considered that the ample lessons he had received from bitter experience entitled him to call them whatever he liked, but without this "lower race" he could not have existed a single day. He was bored and ill-at-ease in the company of men, with whom he was always cold and reserved, but felt quite at

1. Translated by Ivy Litvinov.
2. A fashionable seaside resort in the Crimea.
3. Certain progressive intellectuals, anticipating the reform of the Russian alphabet, omitted the hard sign after consonants in writing; here, however, it is an affectation.

home among women, and knew exactly what to say to them, and how to behave; he could even be silent in their company without feeling the slightest awkwardness. There was an elusive charm in his appearance and disposition which attracted women and caught their sympathies. He knew this and was himself attracted to them by some invisible force.

Repeated and bitter experience had taught him that every fresh intimacy, while at first introducing such pleasant variety into everyday life, and offering itself as a charming, light adventure, inevitably developed, among decent people (especially in Moscow, where they are so irresolute and slow to move), into a problem of excessive complication leading to an intolerably irksome situation. But every time he encountered an attractive woman he forgot all about this experience, the desire for life surged up in him, and everything suddenly seemed simple and amusing.

One evening, then, while he was dining at the restaurant in the park, the lady in the toque came strolling up and took a seat at a neighboring table. Her expression, gait, dress, coiffure, all told him that she was from the upper classes, that she was married, that she was in Yalta for the first time, alone and bored. . . . The accounts of the laxity of morals among visitors to Yalta are greatly exaggerated, and he paid no heed to them, knowing that for the most part they were invented by people who would gladly have transgressed themselves, had they known how to set about it. But when the lady sat down at a neighboring table a few yards away from him, these stories of easy conquests, of excursions to the mountains, came back to him, and the seductive idea of a brisk transitory liaison, an affair with a woman whose very name he did not know, suddenly took possession of his mind.

He snapped his fingers at the Pomeranian and, when it trotted up to him, shook his forefinger at it. The Pomeranian growled. Gurov shook his finger again.

The lady glanced at him and instantly lowered her eyes.

"He doesn't bite," she said, and blushed.

"May I give him a bone?" he asked, and on her nod of consent added in friendly tones: "Have you been long in Yalta?"

"About five days."

"And I am dragging out my second week here."

Neither spoke for a few minutes.

"The days pass quickly, and yet one is so bored here," she said, not looking at him.

"It's the thing to say it's boring here. People never complain of boredom in godforsaken holes like Belyev or Zhizdra, but when they get here it's: 'Oh, the dullness! Oh, the dust!' You'd think they'd come from Granada[4] to say the least."

She laughed. Then they both went on eating in silence, like complete strangers. But after dinner they left the restaurant together, and embarked upon the light, jesting talk of people free and contented, for whom it is all the same where they go, or what they talk about. They strolled along, remarking on the strange light over the sea. The water was a warm, tender purple, the moonlight

---

4. A famous medieval city in Spain, once capital of the Moorish kingdom of Granada and now a tourist center known for its art and architecture. Belyev and Zhizdra are small provincial towns.

lay on its surface in a golden strip. They said how close it was, after the hot day. Gurov told her he was from Moscow, that he was really a philologist, but worked in a bank; that he had at one time trained himself to sing in a private opera company, but had given up the idea; that he owned two houses in Moscow. . . . And from her he learned that she had grown up in Petersburg,[5] but had gotten married in the town of S., where she had been living two years, that she would stay another month in Yalta, and that perhaps her husband, who also needed a rest, would join her. She was quite unable to explain whether her husband was a member of the province council, or on the board of the zemstvo,[6] and was greatly amused at herself for this. Further, Gurov learned that her name was Anna Sergeyevna.

Back in his own room he thought about her, and felt sure he would meet her the next day. It was inevitable. As he went to bed he reminded himself that only a very short time ago she had been a schoolgirl, like his own daughter, learning her lessons, he remembered how much there was of shyness and constraint in her laughter, in her way of conversing with a stranger—it was probably the first time in her life that she found herself alone, and in a situation in which men could follow her and watch her, and speak to her, all the time with a secret aim she could not fail to divine. He recalled her slender, delicate neck, her fine gray eyes.

"And yet there's something pathetic about her," he thought to himself as he fell asleep.

II

A week had passed since the beginning of their acquaintance. It was a holiday. Indoors it was stuffy, but the dust rose in clouds out of doors, and people's hats blew off. It was a parching day and Gurov kept going to the outdoor café for fruit drinks and ices to offer Anna Sergeyevna. The heat was overpowering.

In the evening, when the wind had dropped, they walked to the pier to see the steamer come in. There were a great many people strolling about the landing-place; some, bunches of flowers in their hands, were meeting friends. Two peculiarities of the smart Yalta crowd stood out distinctly—the elderly ladies all tried to dress very youthfully, and there seemed to be an inordinate number of generals about.

Owing to the roughness of the sea the steamer arrived late, after the sun had gone down, and it had to maneuver for some time before it could get alongside the pier. Anna Sergeyevna scanned the steamer and passengers through her lorgnette,[7] as if looking for someone she knew, and when she turned to Gurov her eyes were glistening. She talked a great deal, firing off abrupt questions and forgetting immediately what it was she had wanted to know. Then she lost her lorgnette in the crush.

The smart crowd began dispersing, features could no longer be made out, the wind had quite dropped, and Gurov and Anna Sergeyevna stood there as if waiting for someone else to come off the steamer. Anna Sergeyevna had fallen silent, every now and then smelling her flowers, but not looking at Gurov.

---

5. St. Petersburg, the former capital of Russia: an important port and cultural center.

6. District administration.

7. Small eyeglasses on a short handle.

"It's turned out a fine evening," he said. "What shall we do? We might go for a drive."

She made no reply.

He looked steadily at her and suddenly took her in his arms and kissed her lips, and the fragrance and dampness of the flowers closed round him, but the next moment he looked behind him in alarm—had anyone seen them?

"Let's go to your room," he murmured.

And they walked off together, very quickly.

Her room was stuffy and smelt of some scent she had bought in the Japanese shop.[8] Gurov looked at her, thinking to himself: "How full of strange encounters life is!" He could remember carefree, good-natured women who were exhilarated by love-making and grateful to him for the happiness he gave them, however short-lived; and there had been others—his wife among them—whose caresses were insincere, affected, hysterical, mixed up with a great deal of quite unnecessary talk, and whose expression seemed to say that all this was not just lovemaking or passion, but something much more significant; then there had been two or three beautiful, cold women, over whose features flitted a predatory expression, betraying a determination to wring from life more than it could give, women no longer in their first youth, capricious, irrational, despotic, brainless, and when Gurov had cooled to these, their beauty aroused in him nothing but repulsion, and the lace trimming on their underclothes reminded him of fish-scales.

But here the timidity and awkwardness of youth and inexperience were still apparent; and there was a feeling of embarrassment in the atmosphere, as if someone had just knocked at the door. Anna Sergeyevna, "the lady with the dog," seemed to regard the affair as something very special, very serious, as if she had become a fallen woman, an attitude he found odd and disconcerting. Her features lengthened and drooped, and her long hair hung mournfully on either side of her face. She assumed a pose of dismal meditation, like a repentant sinner in some classical painting.[9]

"It isn't right," she said. "You will never respect me anymore."

On the table was a watermelon. Gurov cut himself a slice from it and began slowly eating it. At least half an hour passed in silence.

Anna Sergeyevna was very touching, revealing the purity of a decent, naïve woman who had seen very little of life. The solitary candle burning on the table scarcely lit up her face, but it was obvious that her heart was heavy.

"Why should I stop respecting you?" asked Gurov. "You don't know what you're saying."

"May God forgive me!" she exclaimed, and her eyes filled with tears. "It's terrible."

"No need to seek to justify yourself."

"How can I justify myself? I'm a wicked, fallen woman, I despise myself and have not the least thought of self-justification. It isn't my husband I have deceived, it's myself. And not only now, I have been deceiving myself for ever so long. My husband is no doubt an honest, worthy man, but he's a flunky. I

8. Probably a tourist shop with imported goods.
9. A famous painting of Mary Magdalen (see Luke 7:36–50) by the French classical artist Georges de la Tour (1593–1652) shows her seated at a table meditating, her face and long hair illuminated by a candle.

don't know what it is he does at his office, but I know he's a flunky. I was only twenty when I married him, and I was devoured by curiosity, I wanted something higher. I told myself that there must be a different kind of life I wanted to live, to live. . . . I was burning with curiosity . . . you'll never understand that, but I swear to God I could no longer control myself, nothing could hold me back, I told my husband I was ill, and I came here. . . . And I started going about like one possessed, like a madwoman . . . and now I have become an ordinary, worthless woman, and everyone has the right to despise me."

Gurov listened to her, bored to death. The naïve accents, the remorse, all was so unexpected, so out of place. But for the tears in her eyes, she might have been jesting or play-acting.

"I don't understand," he said gently. "What is it you want?"

She hid her face against his breast and pressed closer to him.

"Do believe me, I implore you to believe me," she said. "I love all that is honest and pure in life, vice is revolting to me, I don't know what I'm doing. The common people say they are snared by the Devil. And now I can say that I have been snared by the Devil, too."

"Come, come," he murmured.

He gazed into her fixed, terrified eyes, kissed her, and soothed her with gentle affectionate words, and gradually she calmed down and regained her cheerfulness. Soon they were laughing together again.

When, a little later, they went out, there was not a soul on the promenade, the town and its cypresses looked dead, but the sea was still roaring as it dashed against the beach. A solitary fishing-boat tossed on the waves, its lamp blinking sleepily.

They found a carriage and drove to Oreanda.[1]

"I discovered your name in the hall, just now," said Gurov, "written up on the board. Von Diederitz. Is your husband a German?"

"No. His grandfather was, I think, but he belongs to the Orthodox Church himself."

When they got out of the carriage at Oreanda they sat down on a bench not far from the church, and looked down at the sea, without talking. Yalta could be dimly discerned through the morning mist, and white clouds rested motionless on the summits of the mountains. Not a leaf stirred, the grasshoppers chirruped, and the monotonous hollow roar of the sea came up to them, speaking of peace, of the eternal sleep lying in wait for us all. The sea had roared like this long before there was any Yalta or Oreanda, it was roaring now, and it would go on roaring, just as indifferently and hollowly, when we had passed away. And it may be that in this continuity, this utter indifference of life and death, lies the secret of our ultimate salvation, of the stream of life on our planet, and of its never-ceasing movement towards perfection.

Side by side with a young woman, who looked so exquisite in the early light, soothed and enchanted by the sight of all this magical beauty—sea, mountains, clouds and the vast expanse of the sky—Gurov told himself that, when you came to think of it, everything in the world is beautiful really, everything but our own thoughts and actions, when we lose sight of the higher aims of life, and of our dignity as human beings.

1. A hotel and beach compound near Yalta; the whole area is known as the Ukrainian Riviera.

Someone approached them—a watchman, probably—looked at them and went away. And there was something mysterious and beautiful even in this. The steamer from Feodosia[2] could be seen coming towards the pier, lit up by the dawn, its lamps out.

"There's dew on the grass," said Anna Sergeyevna, breaking the silence.

"Yes. Time to go home."

They went back to the town.

After this they met every day at noon on the promenade, lunching and dining together, going for walks, and admiring the sea. She complained of sleeplessness, of palpitations, asked the same questions over and over again, alternately surrendering to jealousy and the fear that he did not really respect her. And often, when there was nobody in sight in the square or the park, he would draw her to him and kiss her passionately. The utter idleness, these kisses in broad daylight, accompanied by furtive glances and the fear of discovery, the heat, the smell of the sea, and the idle, smart, well-fed people continually crossing their field of vision, seemed to have given him a new lease of life. He told Anna Sergeyevna she was beautiful and seductive, made love to her with impetuous passion, and never left her side, while she was always pensive, always trying to force from him the admission that he did not respect her, that he did not love her a bit, and considered her just an ordinary woman. Almost every night they drove out of town, to Oreanda, the waterfall, or some other beauty-spot. And these excursions were invariably a success, each contributing fresh impressions of majestic beauty.

All this time they kept expecting her husband to arrive. But a letter came in which he told his wife that he was having trouble with his eyes, and implored her to come home as soon as possible. Anna Sergeyevna made hasty preparations for leaving.

"It's a good thing I'm going," she said to Gurov. "It's the intervention of fate."

She left Yalta in a carriage, and he went with her as far as the railway station. The drive took nearly a whole day. When she got into the express train, after the second bell had been rung, she said:

"Let me have one more look at you. . . . One last look. That's right."

She did not weep, but was mournful, and seemed ill, the muscles of her cheeks twitching.

"I shall think of you . . . I shall think of you all the time," she said. "God bless you! Think kindly of me. We are parting forever, it must be so, because we ought never to have met. Good-bye—God bless you."

The train steamed rapidly out of the station, its lights soon disappearing, and a minute later even the sound it made was silenced, as if everything were conspiring to bring this sweet oblivion, this madness, to an end as quickly as possible. And Gurov, standing alone on the platform and gazing into the dark distance, listened to the shrilling of the grasshoppers and the humming of the telegraph wires, with a feeling that he had only just awakened. And he told himself that this had been just one more of the many adventures in his life, and that it, too, was over, leaving nothing but a memory. . . . He was moved and sad, and felt a slight remorse. After all, this young woman whom he would never

2. A coastal town seventy miles northeast of Yalta.

again see had not been really happy with him. He had been friendly and affectionate with her, but in his whole behaviour, in the tones of his voice, in his very caresses, there had been a shade of irony, the insulting indulgence of the fortunate male, who was, moreover, almost twice her age. She had insisted in calling him good, remarkable, high-minded. Evidently he had appeared to her different from his real self, in a word he had involuntarily deceived her. . . .

There was an autumnal feeling in the air, and the evening was chilly.

"It's time for me to be going north, too," thought Gurov, as he walked away from the platform. "High time!"

III

When he got back to Moscow it was beginning to look like winter; the stoves were heated every day, and it was still dark when the children got up to go to school and drank their tea, so that the nurse had to light the lamp for a short time. Frost had set in. When the first snow falls, and one goes for one's first sleigh-ride, it is pleasant to see the white ground, the white roofs; one breathes freely and lightly, and remembers the days of one's youth. The ancient lime-trees and birches, white with hoarfrost, have a good-natured look, they are closer to the heart than cypresses and palms, and beneath their branches one is no longer haunted by the memory of mountains and the sea.

Gurov had always lived in Moscow, and he returned to Moscow on a fine frosty day, and when he put on his fur-lined overcoat and thick gloves, and sauntered down Petrovka Street, and when, on Saturday evening, he heard the church bells ringing, his recent journey and the places he had visited lost their charm for him. He became gradually immersed in Moscow life, reading with avidity three newspapers a day, while declaring he never read Moscow newspapers on principle. Once more he was caught up in a whirl of restaurants, clubs, banquets, and celebrations, once more he glowed with the flattering consciousness that well-known lawyers and actors came to his house, that he played cards in the Medical Club opposite a professor. He could once again eat a whole serving of Moscow Fish Stew served in a pan.

He had believed that in a month's time Anna Sergeyevna would be nothing but a vague memory, and that hereafter, with her wistful smile, she would only occasionally appear to him in dreams, like others before her. But the month was now well over and winter was in full swing, and all was as clear in his memory as if he had parted with Anna Sergeyevna only the day before. And his recollections grew ever more insistent. When the voices of his children at their lessons reached him in his study through the evening stillness, when he heard a song, or the sounds of a music-box in a restaurant, when the wind howled in the chimney, it all came back to him: early morning on the pier, the misty mountains, the steamer from Feodosia, the kisses. He would pace up and down his room for a long time, smiling at his memories, and then memory turned into dreaming, and what had happened mingled in his imagination with what was going to happen. Anna Sergeyevna did not come to him in his dreams, she accompanied him everywhere, like his shadow, following him everywhere he went. When he closed his eyes, she seemed to stand before him in the flesh, still lovelier, younger, tenderer than she had really been, and looking back, he saw himself, too, as better than he had been in Yalta. In the evenings she looked out at him from the bookshelves, the fireplace, the corner, he could hear her breathing, the sweet rustle of her skirts. In the streets he followed women with his eyes, to see if there were any like her. . . .

He began to feel an overwhelming desire to share his memories with someone. But he could not speak of his love at home, and outside his home who was there for him to confide in? Not the tenants living in his house, and certainly not his colleagues at the bank. And what was there to tell? Was it love that he had felt? Had there been anything exquisite, poetic, anything instructive or even amusing about his relations with Anna Sergeyevna? He had to content himself with uttering vague generalizations about love and women, and nobody guessed what he meant, though his wife's dark eyebrows twitched as she said:

"The role of a coxcomb doesn't suit you a bit, Dimitry."

One evening, leaving the Medical Club with one of his card-partners, a government official, he could not refrain from remarking:

"If you only knew what a charming woman I met in Yalta!"

The official got into his sleigh, and just before driving off, turned and called out:

"Dmitry Dmitrich!"

"Yes?"

"You were quite right, you know—the sturgeon was just a *leetle* off."

These words, in themselves so commonplace, for some reason infuriated Gurov, seemed to him humiliating, gross. What savage manners, what people! What wasted evenings, what tedious, empty days! Frantic card-playing, gluttony, drunkenness, perpetual talk always about the same thing. The greater part of one's time and energy went on business that was no use to anyone, and on discussing the same thing over and over again, and there was nothing to show for it all but a stunted, earth-bound existence and a round of trivialities, and there was nowhere to escape to, you might as well be in a madhouse or a convict settlement.

Gurov lay awake all night, raging, and went about the whole of the next day with a headache. He slept badly on the succeeding nights, too, sitting up in bed, thinking, or pacing the floor of his room. He was sick of his children, sick of the bank, felt not the slightest desire to go anywhere or talk about anything.

When the Christmas holidays came, he packed his things, telling his wife he had to go to Petersburg in the interests of a certain young man, and set off for the town of S. To what end? He hardly knew himself. He only knew that he must see Anna Sergeyevna, must speak to her, arrange a meeting, if possible.

He arrived at S. in the morning and engaged the best suite in the hotel, which had a carpet of gray military frieze, and a dusty ink-pot on the table, surmounted by a headless rider, holding his hat in his raised hand. The hall porter told him what he wanted to know: von Diederitz had a house of his own in Staro-Goncharnaya Street. It wasn't far from the hotel, he lived on a grand scale, luxuriously, kept carriage-horses, the whole town knew him. The hall porter pronounced the name "Drideritz."

Gurov strolled over to Staro-Goncharnaya Street and discovered the house. In front of it was a long gray fence with inverted nails hammered into the tops of the palings.

"A fence like that is enough to make anyone want to run away," thought Gurov, looking at the windows of the house and the fence.

He reasoned that since it was a holiday, Anna's husband would probably be at home. In any case it would be tactless to embarrass her by calling at the house. And a note might fall into the hands of the husband, and bring about catastrophe. The best thing would be to wait about on the chance of seeing her. And he walked up and down the street, hovering in the vicinity of the fence, watching for his chance. A beggar entered the gate, only to be attacked by dogs, then, an hour later, the faint, vague sounds of a piano reached his ears. That would be Anna Sergeyevna playing. Suddenly the front door opened and an old woman came out, followed by a familiar white Pomeranian. Gurov tried to call to it, but his heart beat violently, and in his agitation he could not remember its name.

He walked on, hating the gray fence more and more, and now ready to tell himself irately that Anna Sergeyevna had forgotten him, had already, perhaps, found distraction in another—what could be more natural in a young woman who had to look at this accursed fence from morning to night? He went back to his hotel and sat on the sofa in his suite for some time, not knowing what to do, then he ordered dinner, and after dinner, had a long sleep.

"What a foolish, restless business," he thought, waking up and looking towards the dark windowpanes. It was evening by now. "Well, I've had my sleep out. And what am I to do in the night?"

He sat up in bed, covered by the cheap gray quilt, which reminded him of a hospital blanket, and in his vexation he fell to taunting himself.

"You and your lady with a dog . . . there's adventure for you! See what you get for your pains."

On his arrival at the station that morning he had noticed a poster announcing in enormous letters the first performance at the local theatre of *The Geisha*.[3] Remembering this; he got up and made for the theatre.

"It's highly probable that she goes to first nights," he told himself.

The theatre was full. It was a typical provincial theatre, with a mist collecting over the chandeliers, and the crowd in the gallery fidgeting noisily. In the first row of the stalls the local dandies stood waiting for the curtain to go up, their hands clasped behind them. There, in the front seat of the governor's box, sat the governor's daughter, wearing a boa, the governor himself hiding modestly behind the drapes, so that only his hands were visible. The curtain stirred, the orchestra took a long time tuning up their instruments. Gurov's eyes roamed eagerly over the audience as they filed in and occupied their seats.

Anna Sergeyevna came in, too. She seated herself in the third row of the stalls, and when Gurov's glance fell on her, his heart seemed to stop, and he knew in a flash that the whole world contained no one nearer or dearer to him, no one more important to his happiness. This little woman, lost in the provincial crowd, in no way remarkable, holding a silly lorgnette in her hand, now filled his whole life, was his grief, his joy, all that he desired. Lulled by the sounds coming from the wretched orchestra, with its feeble, amateurish violinists, he thought how beautiful she was . . . thought and dreamed. . . .

---

3. An operetta (1896) by the English composer Sidney Jones.

Anna Sergeyevna was accompanied by a tall, round-shouldered young man with small whiskers, who nodded at every step before taking the seat beside her and seemed to be continually bowing to someone. This must be her husband, whom, in a fit of bitterness, at Yalta, she had called a "flunky." And there really was something of a lackey's servility in his lanky figure, his sidewhiskers, and the little bald spot on the top of his head. And he smiled sweetly, and the badge of some scientific society gleaming in his buttonhole was like the number on a footman's livery.

The husband went out to smoke in the first interval, and she was left alone in her seat. Gurov, who had taken a seat in the stalls, went up to her and said in a trembling voice, with a forced smile: "How d'you do?"

She glanced up at him and turned pale, then looked at him again in alarm, unable to believe her eyes, squeezing her fan and lorgnette in one hand, evidently struggling to overcome a feeling of faintness. Neither of them said a word. She sat there, and he stood beside her, disconcerted by her embarrassment, and not daring to sit down. The violins and flutes sang out as they were tuned, and there was a tense sensation in the atmosphere, as if they were being watched from all the boxes. At last she got up and moved rapidly towards one of the exits. He followed her and they wandered aimlessly along corridors, up and down stairs; figures flashed by in the uniforms of legal officials, high-school teachers and civil servants, all wearing badges; ladies, coats hanging from pegs flashed by; there was a sharp draft, bringing with it an odor of cigarette butts. And Gurov, whose heart was beating violently, thought:

"What on earth are all these people, this orchestra for? . . ."

The next minute he suddenly remembered how, after seeing Anna Sergeyevna off that evening at the station, he had told himself that all was over, and they would never meet again. And how far away the end seemed to be now!

She stopped on a dark narrow staircase over which was a notice bearing the inscription "To the upper circle."[4]

"How you frightened me!" she said, breathing heavily, still pale and half-stunned. "Oh, how you frightened me! I'm almost dead! Why did you come? Oh, why?"

"But, Anna," he said, in low, hasty tones. "But, Anna. . . . Try to understand . . . do try. . . ."

She cast him a glance of fear, entreaty, love, and then gazed at him steadily, as if to fix his features firmly in her memory.

"I've been so unhappy," she continued, taking no notice of his words. "I could think of nothing but you the whole time, I lived on the thoughts of you. I tried to forget—why, oh, why did you come?"

On the landing above them were two schoolboys, smoking and looking down, but Gurov did not care, and, drawing Anna Sergeyevna towards him, began kissing her face, her lips, her hands.

"What are you doing, oh, what are you doing?" she said in horror, drawing back. "We have both gone mad. Go away this very night, this moment. . . . By all that is sacred, I implore you. . . . Somebody is coming."

Someone was ascending the stairs.

---

4. The stalls or back rows; a medium-priced area behind the orchestra seats on the main floor.

"You must go away," went on Anna Sergeyevna in a whisper. "D'you hear me, Dmitry Dmitrich? I'll come to you in Moscow. I have never been happy, I am unhappy now, and I shall never be happy—never! Do not make me suffer still more! I will come to you in Moscow, I swear it! And now we must part! My dear one, my kind one, my darling, we must part."

She pressed his hand and hurried down the stairs, looking back at him continually, and her eyes showed that she was in truth unhappy. Gurov stood where he was for a short time, listening, and when all was quiet, went to look for his coat, and left the theatre.

IV

And Anna Sergeyevna began going to Moscow to see him. Every two or three months she left the town of S., telling her husband that she was going to consult a specialist on female diseases, and her husband believed her and did not believe her. In Moscow she always stayed at the Slavyanski Bazaar,[5] sending a man in a red cap to Gurov the moment she arrived. Gurov went to her, and no one in Moscow knew anything about it.

One winter morning he went to see her as usual (the messenger had been to him the evening before, but had not found him at home). His daughter was with him, for her school was on the way and he thought he might as well see her to it.

"It is forty degrees," said Gurov to his daughter, "and yet it is snowing. You see it is only above freezing close to the ground, the temperature in the upper layers of the atmosphere is quite different."

"Why doesn't it ever thunder in winter, Papa?"

He explained this, too. As he was speaking, he kept reminding himself that he was going to a rendezvous and that not a living soul knew about it, or, probably, ever would. He led a double life—one in public, in the sight of all whom it concerned, full of conventional truth and conventional deception, exactly like the lives of his friends and acquaintances, and another which flowed in secret. And, owing to some strange, possibly quite accidental chain of circumstances, everything that was important, interesting, essential, everything about which he was sincere and never deceived himself, everything that composed the kernel of his life, went on in secret, while everything that was false in him, everything that composed the husk in which he hid himself and the truth which was in him—his work at the bank, discussions at the club, his "lower race," his attendance at anniversary celebrations with his wife—was on the surface. He began to judge others by himself, no longer believing what he saw, and always assuming that the real, the only interesting life of every individual goes on as under cover of night, secretly. Every individual existence revolves around mystery, and perhaps that is the chief reason that all cultivated individuals insisted so strongly on the respect due to personal secrets.

After leaving his daughter at the door of her school Gurov set off for the Slavyanski Bazaar. Taking off his overcoat in the lobby, he went upstairs and

5. A luxurious hotel in Moscow.

knocked softly on the door. Anna Sergeyevna, wearing the gray dress he liked most, exhausted by her journey and by suspense, had been expecting him since the evening before. She was pale and looked at him without smiling, but was in his arms almost before he was fairly in the room. Their kiss was lingering, prolonged, as if they had not met for years.

"Well, how are you?" he asked. "Anything new?"

"Wait, I'll tell you in a minute. . . . I can't. . . ."

She could not speak, because she was crying. Turning away, she held her handkerchief to her eyes.

"I'll wait till she's had her cry out," he thought, and sank into a chair.

He rang for tea, and a little later, while he was drinking it, she was still standing there, her face to the window. She wept from emotion, from her bitter consciousness of the sadness of their life; they could only see one another in secret, hiding from people, as if they were thieves. Was not their life a broken one?

"Don't cry," he said.

It was quite obvious to him that this love of theirs would not soon come to an end, and that no one could say when this end would be. Anna Sergeyevna loved him ever more fondly, worshipped him, and there would have been no point in telling her that one day it must end. Indeed, she would not have believed him.

He moved over and took her by the shoulders, intending to fondle her with light words, but suddenly he caught sight of himself in the looking-glass.

His hair was already beginning to turn gray. It struck him as strange that he should have aged so much in the last few years. The shoulders on which his hands lay were warm and quivering. He felt a pity for this life, still so warm and exquisite, but probably soon to fade and droop like his own. Why did she love him so? Women had always believed him different from what he really was, had loved in him not himself but the man their imagination pictured him, a man they had sought for eagerly all their lives. And afterwards when they discovered their mistake, they went on loving him just the same. And not one of them had ever been happy with him. Time had passed, he had met one woman after another, become intimate with each, parted with each, but had never loved. There had been all sorts of things between them, but never love.

And only now, when he was gray-haired, had he fallen in love properly, thoroughly, for the first time in his life.

He and Anna Sergeyevna loved one another as people who are very close and intimate, as husband and wife, as dear friends love one another. It seemed to them that fate had intended them for one another, and they could not understand why she should have a husband, and he a wife. They were like two migrating birds, the male and the female, who had been caught and put into separate cages. They forgave one another all that they were ashamed of in the past and in the present, and felt that this love of theirs had changed them both.

Formerly, in moments of melancholy, he had consoled himself by the first argument that came into his head, but now arguments were nothing to him, he felt profound pity, desired to be sincere, tender.

"Stop crying, my dearest," he said. "You've had your cry, now stop. . . . Now let us have a talk, let us try and think what we are to do."

Then they discussed their situation for a long time, trying to think how they could get rid of the necessity for hiding, deception, living in different towns, being so long without meeting. How were they to shake off these intolerable fetters?

"How? How?" he repeated, clutching his head. "How?"

And it seemed to them that they were within an inch of arriving at a decision, and that then a new, beautiful life would begin. And they both realized that the end was still far, far away, and that the hardest, the most complicated part was only just beginning.

VI

Modernity
and Modernism,
1900–1945

At the beginning of the twentieth century, the world was interconnected as never before. New means of transportation, such as the steamship, the railroad, the automobile, and the airplane, allowed people in the industrialized West to cover vast distances quickly. Other technologies, such as the telegraph and the telephone, allowed them to communicate instantaneously. In the decades to come, such inventions, powered either by electricity or by the internal combustion engine, along with improvements in agriculture, nutrition, public health, and medical care, would foster remarkable growth in human health and material prosperity. Infant mortality declined and world population more than tripled, from under two billion to around six billion. In unprecedented numbers, people were living in large cities; correspondingly, the experience of urban life is one of the major themes of twentieth-century literature. Together, these vast transformations in human experience can be characterized as *modernization*.

Yet the technological advances that undeniably improved human life led, as well, to the production of weapons that were increasingly effective, and therefore increasingly destructive. As distant parts of the globe grew closer through trade, immigration,

Books! (1925), a promotional poster by the Russian artist Alexander Rodchenko (1891–1956).

885

and communications, they often came into deadly conflict. Indeed, the twentieth century was the bloodiest in human history: as many as 200 million died in wars, revolutions, genocides, and related famines. In response to the century's horrors, the old dream of a unified, peaceful world became ever more appealing; and to many, in the splendid light of new technologies and optimistic ideas of progress, it even seemed achievable as never before. Frequently, those who sought to end war looked to supranational bodies, such as the League of Nations, the United Nations, the European Community (later the European Union), the Organization of American States, and the Organization for African Unity, as the future guarantors of "peaceful coexistence," a term that gained currency during the Cold War to refer to the arms race between the United States and the Soviet Union.

MODERNITY AND CONFLICT IN WORLD HISTORY, 1900–1945

As Europe and North America became industrialized over the course of the nineteenth century, they extended their political power to cover most of the globe. By 1900, after centuries of European expansion, there were no longer, in the words of **Joseph Conrad**'s **Heart of Darkness**, any "blank spaces" on the map. Within a few years, explorers would even reach the North and South Poles. At the 1884 Berlin Conference, the European powers had carved up Africa among themselves; they also controlled most of southern Asia. The remaining independent nations in the Americas and the antipodes maintained close ties with their former colonial masters—Britain, Spain, France, Portugal, and the Netherlands. The small kingdom of Belgium and the recently unified nations of Germany and Italy

A caricature of Cecil John Rhodes, perhaps the most famous supporter of British colonialism and imperialism in the late nineteenth century, here straddling the continent of Africa. The wires in his hands are telegraph cables. The cartoon was drawn soon after Rhodes announced his intention to connect Cape Town, South Africa, with Cairo, Egypt, by telegraph and rail.

sought to acquire overseas empires of their own. The British Empire was still at its zenith, and since Britain retained colonial possessions in all parts of the world, it was known as "the empire on which the sun never sets."

Yet as the twentieth century advanced, the sun did set on the British Empire—and on every other European empire as well. During the first half of the century, the world system that the European powers dominated experienced massive crises in the forms of two world wars, the Russian Revolution, the Great Depression, and the Holocaust. These upheavals became central concerns for the literature of the period and contributed to a rethinking of traditional literary forms and techniques.

The First World War (1914–18) took place mainly in Europe; it was the most mechanized war to date and killed some 15 million people. Much of the

A large parade in support of women's suffrage, Manhattan, 1913.

war on the Western Front (in Belgium and France) was characterized by stalemate, as each side ferociously defended entrenched positions with machine guns, resulting in massive battles over tiny slices of territory, as at Ypres, Vimy Ridge, and Verdun. It was only after the United States joined the war, in 1917, that the Allies (France, Britain and its colonies, Italy, and the United States) gained the initiative and were able to repel Germany.

In the East, Germany and Austria-Hungary drove deep into Russian territory. Russia's near-defeat contributed to the revolution of 1917, in which the Bolsheviks under V. I. Lenin sought to establish a communist "dictatorship of the proletariat," with a tiny vanguard of party members taking power in the name of the working classes. During the succeeding decades, forced collectivization of agriculture and enterprise (which led to widespread famine), as well as purges of people considered enemies of the Communist Party (especially under Lenin's successor, Joseph Stalin), caused tens of millions of deaths, both in Russia and in other former territories of the Russian Empire, such as the Ukraine. (They were united under the communist regime of the Soviet Union.) The communist movement, initially supportive of some literary experiments, increasingly restricted the scope of acceptable artistic expression in the countries where it gained control. In response, a dissident literature developed, published abroad or in informal, private editions that could circulate without being censored. Writers such as **Anna Akhmatova** and Alexander Solzhenitsyn had to work within these constraints.

The Treaty of Versailles (1919) formalized the end of the war, and of four great empires—the German, Austro-Hungarian, Russian, and Ottoman—dividing most of Central and Eastern Europe into a multitude of smaller nations (some of which would later be reabsorbed by the resurgent Soviet Union and Nazi Germany). The treaty also founded the first of the great interna-

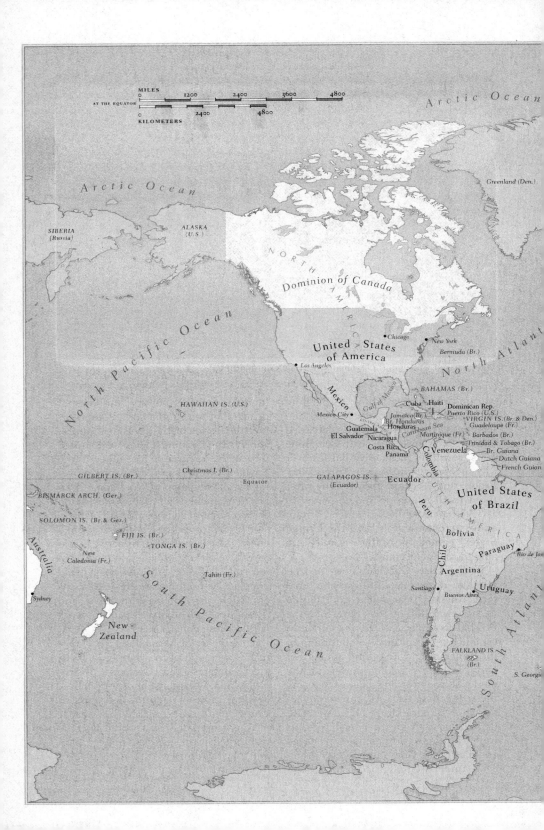

MILES
1200   2400   3600   4800
AT THE EQUATOR
KILOMETERS
2400   4800

Arctic Ocean

Arctic Ocean

SIBERIA
(Russia)

ALASKA
(U.S.)

Greenland (Den.)

NORTH AMERICA

Dominion of Canada

North Pacific Ocean

United States
of America

Chicago   New York

Bermuda (Br.)

Los Angeles

North Atlantic

HAWAIIAN IS. (U.S.)

Mexico

BAHAMAS (Br.)

Gulf of Mexico

Cuba   Haiti   Dominican Rep.
Puerto Rico (U.S.)

Mexico City   Jamaica (Br.)   VIRGIN IS. (Br. & Den.)
Br. Honduras   Guadeloupe (Fr.)
Guatemala   Honduras   Martinique (Fr.)   Barbados (Br.)
El Salvador   Nicaragua   Caribbean Sea   Trinidad & Tobago (Br.)
Costa Rica   Venezuela   Br. Guiana
Panama   Colombia   Dutch Guiana
French Guiana

GILBERT IS. (Br.)   Christmas I. (Br.)
Equator   GALAPAGOS IS.   Ecuador
(Ecuador)

BISMARCK ARCH. (Ger.)

SOUTH AMERICA

United States
of Brazil

SOLOMON IS. (Br. & Ger.)

FIJI IS. (Br.)

Bolivia

Australia

New
Caledonia (Fr.)

TONGA IS. (Br.)

Peru

Paraguay

Rio de Ja

Tahiti (Fr.)

Chile

Argentina

Sydney

Santiago   Buenos Aires   Uruguay

South Pacific Ocean

New
Zealand

South Atlantic

FALKLAND IS.
(Br.)

S. Georgi

THE WORLD
1913

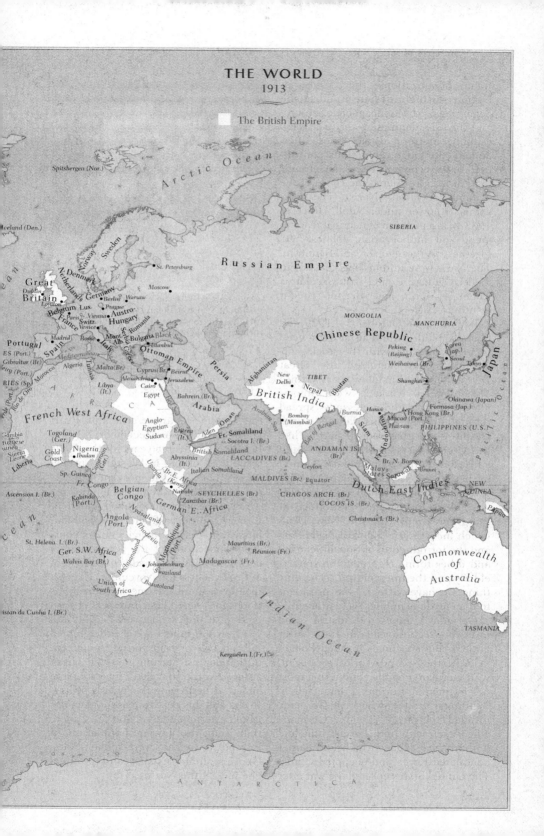

The British Empire

Spitsbergen (Nor.)

Arctic Ocean

Iceland (Den.)

SIBERIA

Russian Empire

St. Petersburg

Sweden

Norway

Moscow

MONGOLIA

MANCHURIA

Denmark

Great
Britain

Dublin
London

Netherlands
Belgium Lux. Germany Berlin Warsaw

Prague

Paris Austro-
Switz. Vienna Hungary

France

Venice Romania

Chinese Republic

Peking
(Beijing)

Korea
(Jap.)

Seoul

Weihaiwei (Br.)

Japan

Tokyo

Portugal

Madrid

Spain

Rome Italy

Bulgaria

Istanbul

Black Sea

Serbia Greece

Ottoman Empire

Shanghai

Okinawa (Japan)

ES (Port.)

Gibraltar (Br.)

(Port.)

Morocco

Algeria

Tunisia

Malta (Br.)

Cyprus (Br.)

Beirut

Jerusalem

Persia

Afghanistan

New
Delhi

TIBET

Nepal Bhutan

Formosa (Jap.)

Macao Hong Kong (Br.)

BIES (Sp.)

Rio de Oro (Port.)

Libya
(It.)

Alexandria
Cairo

Egypt

Bahrein (Br.)

Arabia

Oman

British India

Bombay
(Mumbai)

Burma

Hanoi

Hainan

PHILIPPINES (U.S.)

AFRICA

French West Africa

Anglo-
Egyptian
Sudan

Eritrea
(It.)

Aden

Fr. Somaliland

Socotra I. (Br.)

Arabian Sea

Bay of Bengal

Siam

Pacific Ocean

Gambia

tuguese

uinea

Sierra
Leone

Togoland
(Ger.)

Nigeria

Gold
Coast

Ibadan

Cameroon (Ger.)

British Somaliland

Abyssinia

LACCADIVES (Br.)

Italian Somaliland

Ceylon

ANDAMAN IS.
(Br.)

Indochina

Malay States

Br. N. Borneo

Sarawak

Dutch East Indies

Brunei

NEW
GUINEA

Liberia

Sp. Guinea

Fr. Congo

Uganda

Br. E. Africa
(Kenya)

Nairobi

MALDIVES (Br.)

Equator

Papua

Ascension I. (Br.)

Kabinda
(Port.)

Belgian
Congo

German E. Africa

Zanzibar (Br.)

SEYCHELLES (Br.)

CHAGOS ARCH. (Br.)

COCOS IS. (Br.)

Angola
(Port.)

Nyasaland

Rhodesia

Mozambique (Port.)

Christmas I. (Br.)

Commonwealth
of
Australia

St. Helena I. (Br.)

Ger. S.W. Africa

Walvis Bay (Br.)

Bechuanaland

Johannesburg

Swaziland

Basutoland

Union of
South Africa

Mauritius (Br.)

Réunion (Fr.)

Madagascar (Fr.)

Indian Ocean

TASMANIA

istan da Cunha I. (Br.)

Kerguélen I. (Fr.)

ANTARCTICA

tional organizations, the League of Nations—which, despite its idealistic beginnings, proved incapable of enforcing the demilitarization of Germany. Making matters worse, the Allies' demand for huge reparations contributed to the economic chaos in Germany that, in turn, furthered the cause of the National Socialists (Nazis). The party came to power under Adolf Hitler in 1933 with a program of national rearmament and authoritarian politics held together by the glue of anti-Semitism. The Nazis were unremittingly hostile to modern literature, and writers such as Thomas Mann and Bertolt Brecht went into exile.

Beginning on October 24, 1929, the liberal capitalist world also experienced financial disaster, with the stock market crash that heralded the Great Depression. Within a few years, a third of American workers were unemployed; hunger and joblessness spread throughout the industrialized world. Despite fears that radical parties like the Communists or the Nazis would emerge from the economic devastation in the United States, Franklin D. Roosevelt (president from 1933 to 1945) was able to reverse the worst effects of the Depression with the New Deal, which included public works spending and the introduction of Social Security and other forms of protection for the elderly and the unemployed. "The only thing we have to fear," the president told an anxious public, "is fear itself."

Germany annexed Austria and invaded Czechoslovakia in 1938. After Hitler's military forces invaded Poland in 1939, the Second World War began, with Germany rapidly conquering most of continental Europe. France fell in 1940, and the following year Germany invaded the Soviet Union. Germany allied itself with both Fascist Italy and authoritarian Japan, which had earlier conquered Korea and occupied China. The United States entered the war after

In November 1940, the Nazis closed off a portion of Warsaw, Poland, and designated it a Jewish ghetto—essentially condemning 400,000 people to an urban prison. Predictably, nearly 100,000 of the people in the ghetto died of disease and starvation over the next year and a half. Among those trapped behind the wall were these two children, begging for food.

the surprise Japanese attack on Pearl Harbor, Hawaii, on December 7, 1941. It took almost three years for the Allies to find a foothold in Western Europe; during that time, the most intense battles took place in the Soviet Union.

Once Germany controlled much of Eastern Europe, Hitler, who had enforced anti-Semitic policies and encouraged persecution of the Jews on such occasions as *Kristallnacht,* or the Night of Broken Glass (on November 9, 1938), took even more extreme measures. His troops massacred large numbers of Jews (and also Poles) between 1939 and 1941, while others were either forced into ghettos or transported to concentration camps. Starting in 1941, Hitler authorized the so-called Final Solution, aimed at destroying the Jewish people. In the end, his death squads and camps would exterminate 6 million Jews (more than half the Jewish population of Europe), as well as several million Poles, Gypsies, homosexuals, and political enemies of the Nazis.

The war in Europe ended when the Soviets entered Berlin in May 1945; Hitler had committed suicide the previous month. Fighting still raged in the Pacific, and the United States dropped atomic bombs on Hiroshima and on Nagasaki, obliterating those Japanese cities and starting the nuclear age. The cessation of the global hostilities, which had resulted in some 60 million deaths, took place on August 14, 1945. The return to peacetime brought much relief, but also the sense that a new era of conflict was at hand. The wartime British prime minister Winston Churchill spoke of an "iron curtain" that had "descended across the Continent." The aftermath of the Second World War led quickly to the Cold War, in which most nations aligned themselves with either the capitalist West or the communist East.

MODERNISM IN WORLD LITERATURE

Writers around the world responded to these cataclysmic events with an unprecedented wave of literary experimentation, known collectively as *modernism*, which linked the political crises with a crisis of representation—a sense that the old ways of portraying the human experience were no longer adequate. The modernists therefore broke away from such conventions as standard plots, verse forms, narrative techniques, and the boundaries of genre. They often grouped themselves in avant-garde movements with names like futurism, Dadaism, and surrealism, seeing their literary experiments in the context of a broader search for a type of society to replace the broken prewar consensus.

The modernist crisis of representation also reflected a broader "crisis of reason" that had begun in Europe in the late nineteenth century, as radical thinkers challenged the ability of human reason

to understand the world. In the wake of Charles Darwin's discovery of the process of natural selection, human beings could no longer be so easily distinguished from the other animals; the animal nature of human existence was a crucial concept to three thinkers from the nineteenth century who wielded significant influence in the twentieth. Karl Marx saw the struggle between social classes for control of the means of economic production as the motor force of history; his thought inspired the communist revolutions in Russia and China during the twentieth century and also the more moderate Socialist and Communist Parties of Western Europe. Friedrich Nietzsche attacked both a belief in God and the conviction that humans are fundamentally rational. His emphasis on the variety of perspectives from which we shape our notions of truth would have a substantial affect on both modernists and postmodernists. Sigmund Freud published the first major work of psychoanalysis, *The Interpretation of Dreams*, in 1900. His exploration of the unconscious, the power of sexual and destructive instincts, the shaping force of early childhood, and the Oedipal conflict between fathers and sons led many writers to reimagine the wellsprings of family interactions. More specifically, Freud's stress on the hidden, or "latent," meanings contained in dreams, jokes, and slips of the tongue lent itself to creative wordplay.

While philosophers and psychologists were examining the dynamics of the human mind, scientists found that the natural world does not necessarily function in the way it appears to. The most famous of the scientific discoveries of the early twentieth century was Albert Einstein's theory of relativity (Special Theory, 1905; General Theory, 1915). Other discoveries around the turn of the century, such as radioactivity, X-rays, and quantum theory, presented

Although Pablo Picasso's *Guernica* (1937) memorializes a historical event—the bombing of Guernica, in the Basque region of Spain, in April 1937, during the Spanish Civil War—the painting stresses the psychological horror, rather than the physical appearance, of the event.

counterintuitive understandings of the physical universe that conflicted with classical Newtonian physics and even with common sense.

Modernism began in Europe and can be traced both to these new currents of thought and to the experimental literature of the late nineteenth century, including the Symbolist poets and the realist novelists. Like such Symbolists as **Charles Baudelaire** and Stéphane Mallarmé, the modernist poets held a high conception of the power and significance of poetry. In their works, they often drew on Symbolist techniques, such as ambiguous and esoteric meanings. **T. S. Eliot's** ***The Waste Land*** (1922) responded to the prevalent sense of devastation after the First World War and was seen at the time as the high-water mark of modernism in the English language.

Modernist fiction followed the realists, especially **Gustave Flaubert**, in attempting to portray life "as it is" by using precise language. Modernists found, however, that in depicting characters, settings, and events with directness and without sentiment, they discovered mysteries that lay beyond language. The great modern novelists, including Conrad, Marcel Proust, Mann,

James Joyce, and **Virginia Woolf**, all started out by writing realistic works in the manner of Flaubert or **Leo Tolstoy**. The great difference, which became more apparent as the modernists reached maturity, was that the realists tended to balance their attention between the objective, outside world and the inner world of their characters, whereas the modernists shifted the balance toward interiority. Thus, rather than offer objective descriptions of the outside world, they increasingly focused on the more limited perspective of an individual, often idiosyncratic, character. In this approach they were following the lead of another great nineteenth-century precursor, **Fyodor Dostoyevsky**.

It would be too simple to say that the modernists did away with the omniscient narrator. They might retain a narrator who seemed to be observing the characters and events with an objective, all-knowing eye, but the authors counterbalanced such narrators with storytellers like Conrad's Marlow or Proust's Marcel, who were themselves characters in the stories they related and whose reliability might therefore be in doubt. Joyce's story "**The Dead**," with its narrator who sees into the mind of the protagonist Gabriel Conroy, could easily belong to the nineteenth century, but Joyce later pioneered the move toward a deeper interiority in two novels, *A Portrait of the Artist as a Young Man* (1916) and *Ulysses* (1922)—the latter is, in fact, the most famous and influential of all modernist novels. The new method, called "the stream of consciousness," was well described by another of its great practitioners, Woolf, when she wrote: "Let us record the atoms as they fall upon the mind in the order in which they fall, let us trace the pattern, however disconnected and incoherent in appearance, which each sight or incident scores upon the consciousness."

A similar, possibly even farther-reaching transformation took place in the theater. Just as novelists questioned the role of an omniscient narrator, dramatists challenged the separation of the audience from the action of the play—specifically, the tradition of the "fourth wall." According to this concept, developed in realist and naturalist theater of the nineteenth century, the actors on stage went about their business as if they did not know that an audience was watching them. In different ways, the major modernist playwrights, represented in this section by **Luigi Pirandello**, broke down the fourth wall. Pirandello introduced a playful "meta-theater," calling attention to the fictionality of his works by having his characters debate the nature of drama. In Brecht's Epic Theater, audience members were encouraged not to identify with the characters and be carried away by the drama but to think critically about the actions they were witnessing. The German writer's notion of an "estrangement effect" that would shock audiences out of their complacency was linked closely to broader modernist theories in which the task of art was to break through our habitual assumptions to make the world appear strange and new.

Many of these modernist experiments took place on the level of form; but modernism also entailed a change in the content of literature, specifically in the inclusion of previously taboo subject matter (especially sexuality), as well as greater attention to shifting social roles (often relating to the impact of feminism). Woolf was famous both as a novelist and as an essayist on feminist issues. Her work *A Room of One's Own* makes the case for women's writing and, more broadly, for women's admission into traditionally male professions and institutions of learning, which were gradually becoming more open to women during the first decades of the century. Feminism had won a major victory with the achievement of women's suffrage in 1918 in Britain; the United States would guarantee all women the vote in 1920. Conrad's novel *Heart of Darkness* criticizes the actions of European imperialists in Africa, although he seems to make an exception for the British Empire. Joyce addresses the political situation of Ireland in the midst of its quest for independence from Britain. **Franz Kafka**'s work has been seen as a commentary on the status of the Jews in a hostile world.

Modernist experimentation persisted in various forms throughout the century. Somewhat younger than the European novelists represented here, **Jorge Luis Borges** wrote short pieces that present alternative universes; in "**The Garden of Forking Paths**," the fictional universe he creates starts out as a commentary on a work of history. Whereas Pirandello's play with theatricality came to be known as "metatheater," Borges's games with the border between fact and fiction have been called "metafiction" or even "metahistory." Borges is also representative of the mobility of writers in the twentieth century: educated mostly in Europe, he returned home to Argentina and formed a bridge between European modernism and the significant expansion of Latin

American fiction in the second half of the century.

Asian writers followed European and American developments with interest and typically responded in one of three ways. Some embraced modern Western themes and styles; others, while drawing on nineteenth-century European realist forms, tended to blend them with more traditional Asian subject matter or linguistic styles. A substantial number of Asian writers embraced communist or socialist politics and a related style of politically engaged fiction. Often, a single writer would combine more than one of these responses.

In other parts of the world, nationalist movements against colonization were gathering force and would result in a wave of independence after the Second World War. The African American writer and activist W. E. B. Du Bois had said early in the century that "the problem of the Twentieth Century is the problem of the color line." Literature played a major role both in the articulation of this challenge and in the attempts to solve it.

These developments pointed the way to a postwar and postcolonial literature that often rejected the formal experiments of the modernist generation and sought a more direct engagement with the pressing political issues of the day, such as decolonization, civil rights, and economic empowerment. The Holocaust also presented a distinct challenge to writers who sought to record the unspeakable: some took a straightforward, documentary style, while others turned to a minimalist, almost mystical language. While Europe, after 1945, set about rebuilding the cities destroyed in the war, much of the rest of the world entered a period of decolonization, establishing nation-states on the basis of the principles (democracy, equality) that the Allies had defended during the war and that they now had to acknowledge as the basis for their colonies' self-determination. The postwar world would inspire both avant-garde literary movements and a return to more traditional forms, but the literature of the twentieth century had been decisively marked by the experiments of the modernists, who created a diverse, remarkable range of masterpieces during a period of continual social crisis.

JOSEPH CONRAD

1857–1924

Born in Polish Ukraine, learning English at twenty-one, and then serving as a sailor for sixteen years, Joseph Conrad nonetheless became a prolific, innovative writer of English fiction. Works like *Heart of Darkness* and *Lord Jim* have influenced novelists throughout the twentieth century, because of Conrad's ability to evoke the feel and color of distant places as well as the complexity of human responses to moral crisis. Conrad's sense of separation and exile, his yearning for the kinship and solidarity of humanity, permeates these works, along with the despairing vision of a universe in which even the most ardent idealist finds no ultimate meaning or moral value.

He was born Jozef Teodor Konrad Korzeniowski on December 3, 1857, the only child of Polish patriots who were involved in resistance to Russian rule. (He changed his name to the more English-sounding Conrad for the publication of his first novel, in 1895.) Their country had been partitioned through most of the nineteenth century among Russia, Prussia, and Austria. The town where Conrad was born, now part of Ukraine, had traditionally been ruled by the Polish aristocracy, and Conrad's family bore a coat of arms. When his father was condemned for conspiracy in 1862, the family went into exile in northern Russia, where Conrad's mother died three years later from tuberculosis. Conrad's father, a poet and a translator, supported the small family by translating **Shakespeare** and Victor Hugo; Conrad himself read English novels by William Makepeace Thackeray,

Walter Scott, and Charles Dickens in Polish and in French translation. When his father, too, succumbed to tuberculosis in 1869, the eleven-year-old orphan went to live with his maternal uncle, Tadeusz Bobrowski, who sent him to school in Cracow (in Austrian-ruled Poland) and Switzerland. Bobrowski supported his orphaned nephew both financially and emotionally, and, when Conrad asked to fulfill a long-standing dream of going to sea, he gave him an annual allowance (which Conrad consistently overspent) and helped him find a berth in the merchant marine. The decision to go to sea reflected the gallant and romantic aspirations of a child who had often been frail and sickly; it also marked a permanent departure from the nation that his parents had fought and, as Conrad saw it, died for.

During the next few years, he worked on French ships, traveling to the West Indies and participating in various activities—some of which, such as smuggling, were probably illegal—that would play a role in his novels of the sea. He also lost money at the casino in Monte Carlo, may have had an unhappy romance, and attempted suicide. Many events of these years are known only through the fictionalized versions Conrad used in short stories written years later. After signing onto a British ship in 1878 to avoid conscription by the French or the Russians (he had just turned twenty-one), Conrad visited England for the first time, speaking the language only haltingly. He served for sixteen years on British merchant ships, earning his Master's Certificate in 1886 (the same year that he became a British subject) and learning English fast and well. During this period, he made trips to the Far East and India that would provide material for his fiction throughout his writing career, including major works like *The Nigger of the "Narcissus"* (1897) and *Typhoon* (1903). When he married in 1896, he turned his back on the sea as a profession and, buoyed by the publication of his first novel, *Almayer's Folly* (1895), chose writing as his new career. His early novels, including *An Outcast of the Islands* (1896), established his initial literary reputation as an exotic storyteller and novelist of adventure at sea.

Among the many voyages that furnished material for his fiction, one stands out as the most emotional and intense: the trip up the Congo River that Conrad made in 1890, straight into the heart of King Leopold II's privately owned Congo Free State. Like many nineteenth-century explorers, Conrad was fascinated by the mystery of this "dark" (because uncharted by Europeans) continent, and he persuaded a relative to find him a job as pilot on a Belgian merchant steamer. The steamer that Conrad was supposed to pilot had been damaged, and while he waited for a replacement, his supervisors shifted him to another where he could help out and learn about the river. The boat traveled upstream to collect a seriously ill trader, Georges Antoine Klein (who died on the return trip), and Conrad, after speaking with Klein and observing the inhuman conditions imposed by slave labor and the ruthless search for ivory, returned seriously ill and traumatized by his journey. The experience marked Conrad both physically and mentally. After a few years, he began to write about it with a moral rage that emerged openly at first and subsequently in more complex, ironic form. *An Outpost of Progress*, a harshly satirical story of two murderous incompetents in a jungle trading post, was published in 1897, and Conrad wrote *Heart of Darkness* two years later;

it appeared in *Blackwood's Magazine* in 1899 and in the volume *"Youth" and Other Stories* in 1902.

Along with *Lord Jim* (1900) and *Nostromo* (1904), this volume established him as one of the leading novelists of the day. He became friendly with other writers such as Henry James, Stephen Crane, H. G. Wells, John Galsworthy, and Ford Madox Ford. Yet he preferred a quiet life in the country to the attractions of literary London. From 1898 he lived on Pent Farm in Kent, near James, Wells, and Crane. He found writing difficult, often suffering from insomnia and physical ailments while trying to complete a novel (one biographer remarks that each of his later novels "cost him a tooth"). His novels from this period, *The Secret Agent* (1907) and *Under Western Eyes* (1911), revolve around political conflicts, but Conrad usually refrained from taking sides in politics—his interest lay in the effect that espionage and intrigue have on individual character. He hated autocratic rule but opposed revolution and was skeptical of social reform movements. His two abiding political commitments were to his adoptive homeland, England, and to the cause of Polish independence; he traveled to Poland on the eve of the First World War, returning with difficulty to England once war broke out. Although he had struggled financially throughout his writing life, Conrad had his first popular success with *Chance* (1913), which is now less highly regarded than his other works. His later works returned, typically with a more optimistic tone, to the Eastern settings with which he began. They have not received much appreciation from critics, although *The Shadow Line* (1917) recaptures some of the earlier works' appreciation of the moment of crisis in a youthful life.

HEART OF DARKNESS

Although the subject matter of *Heart of Darkness* is clearly one of the reasons for its continued influence, equally important is Conrad's introduction of many literary techniques that would be central to modern fiction. In the preface to *The Nigger of the "Narcissus,"* Conrad describes the task of the writer as "before all, to make you *see*," and his works stress the visual perception of reality. His technique of registering the way that a scene appears to an individual before explaining the scene's contents has been described as "delayed decoding"; it is an element of his literary impressionism, his emphasis on how the mind processes the information that the senses provide. In *Heart of Darkness*, Conrad records first the impressions that an event makes on Marlow and only later Marlow's arrival at an explanation of the event. The reader must continually decide when to accept Marlow's account as accurate and when to treat it as ironic and unreliable. Marlow describes his experiences in Africa from a position of experience, having contemplated the episode for many years, but the reader, like the narrator, may question some aspects of Marlow's story as self-justification. Conrad also uses symbolism in a distinctly modern way. As he later wrote, "a work of art is very seldom limited to one exclusive meaning and not necessarily tending to a definite conclusion. And this for the reason that the nearer it approaches art, the more it acquires a symbolic character." Frequently, Marlow's story seems to carry symbolic overtones that are not easily extracted from the story as a simple kernel of wisdom. This symbolic character has its exemplar in the primary narrator's comment that "the yarns of seamen have a direct simplicity, the whole meaning of which lies within the shell of a cracked nut. . . . [But to Marlow,] the meaning of an episode was not inside like a kernel but outside, enveloping the tale which brought it out only as a glow brings out a haze." *Heart of Darkness* does not reveal its meaning in digestible morsels, like the kernel of a nut. Rather, its meanings evade the interpreter; they are larger than the story itself. The story's hazy atmosphere, rich symbolic suggestiveness, and complex narrative structure have all appealed to later readers and writers. Although it was published at the end of the nineteenth century, *Heart of Darkness* became one of the most influential works of the twentieth century. It greatly influenced Nobel Prize winners **T. S. Eliot,** William Faulkner, and **Gabriel García Márquez**. In the second half of the century, the novella was seen as so relevant to the aftermath of imperialism that the filmmaker Francis Ford Coppola used it as the basis of his film about the Vietnam War, *Apocalypse Now*.

The "darkness" of the title exemplifies this symbolism. Although it is both a conventional metaphor for obscurity and evil and a cliché referring to Africa and the "unenlightened" state of its indigenous population, the story leaves it unclear where the heart of darkness is located: in the "uncivilized" jungle or in the hearts of the European imperialists. Leopold II of Belgium, who owned the trading company that effectively was the Congo Free State, gained a free hand in the area after calling an international conference in 1876 "to open to civilization the only part of our globe where Christianity has not penetrated and to pierce the darkness which envelops the entire population." Leopold had pledged to end the slave trade in central Africa, but his rule continued slavery under another guise, extracting forced labor for infrastructure projects, such as road building, that were poorly managed. Throughout the novella, Conrad plays on images of darkness and savagery and complicates any simple opposition by associating moral darkness—the evil that lurks within humans and underlies their predatory idealism—with a white exterior, beginning with the town (Brussels) that serves as the Belgian firm's headquarters and that Marlow describes as a "whited sepulchre."

Still, it is not surprising that later critics and writers, most notably the Nigerian novelist and essayist **Chinua Achebe**, would criticize *Heart of Darkness* for its racist portrayal of Africans. Marlow's words and behavior—indeed, the selectivity of his narrative—can be as distant and cruelly patronizing as those of any European colonialist. Yet he also recognizes his "kinship" with the Africans and often sees them as morally superior to the Europeans; Marlow's quiet critique of imperialism has inspired many postcolonial writers. For the most part, however, the Africans in his story constitute the background for the strange figure of Kurtz, the charismatic, once idealistic, now totally corrupt trader who becomes the destination of Marlow's journey. Marlow's strange bond with this maddened soul stems initially from a desire to see a man whom others have described to him as a universal genius—an "emissary of pity, and science, and progress" and part of the "gang of virtue." In time, though, it becomes a horrified fascination with someone who has explored moral extremes to their furthest end. Kurtz's famous judgment on what he has lived and seen—"The horror! The horror!"—speaks at once to personal despair, to the political realities of imperialism, and to a broader sense of the human condition.

Heart of Darkness

1

The *Nellie*, a cruising yawl,[1] swung to her anchor without a flutter of the sails, and was at rest. The flood had made, the wind was nearly calm, and being bound down the river, the only thing for it was to come to[2] and wait for the turn of the tide.

The sea-reach of the Thames stretched before us like the beginning of an interminable waterway. In the offing[3] the sea and the sky were welded together without a joint, and in the luminous space the tanned sails of the barges drifting up with the tide seemed to stand still in red clusters of canvas sharply peaked, with gleams of varnished sprits. A haze rested on the low shores that ran out to sea in vanishing flatness. The air was dark above Gravesend,[4] and farther back still seemed condensed into a mournful gloom, brooding motionless over the biggest, and the greatest, town on earth.

The Director of Companies was our captain and our host. We four affectionately watched his back as he stood in the bows looking to seaward. On the whole river there was nothing that looked half so nautical. He resembled a pilot, which to a seaman is trustworthiness personified. It was difficult to realise his work was not out there in the luminous estuary, but behind him, within the brooding gloom.

1. A two-masted boat.
2. To come to a standstill in a fixed position.
3. The part of the sea distant but visible from the shore.
4. A port on the Thames River, and the last major town in the estuary.

Between us there was, as I have already said somewhere, the bond of the sea.[5] Besides holding our hearts together through long periods of separation, it had the effect of making us tolerant of each other's yarns—and even convictions. The Lawyer—the best of old fellows—had, because of his many years and many virtues, the only cushion on deck, and was lying on the only rug. The Accountant had brought out already a box of dominoes, and was toying architecturally with the bones. Marlow sat cross-legged right aft, leaning against the mizzenmast.[6] He had sunken cheeks, a yellow complexion, a straight back, an ascetic aspect, and, with his arms dropped, the palms of hands outwards, resembled an idol. The Director, satisfied the anchor had good hold, made his way aft and sat down amongst us. We exchanged a few words lazily. Afterwards there was silence on board the yacht. For some reason or other we did not begin that game of dominoes. We felt meditative, and fit for nothing but placid staring. The day was ending in a serenity of still and exquisite brilliance. The water shone pacifically; the sky, without a speck, was a benign immensity of unstained light; the very mist on the Essex marshes was like a gauzy and radiant fabric, hung from the wooded rises inland, and draping the low shores in diaphanous folds. Only the gloom to the west, brooding over the upper reaches, became more sombre every minute, as if angered by the approach of the sun.

And at last, in its curved and imperceptible fall, the sun sank low, and from glowing white changed to a dull red without rays and without heat, as if about to go out suddenly, stricken to death by the touch of that gloom brooding over a crowd of men.

Forthwith a change came over the waters, and the serenity became less brilliant but more profound. The old river in its broad reach rested unruffled at the decline of day, after ages of good service done to the race that peopled its banks, spread out in the tranquil dignity of a waterway leading to the uttermost ends of the earth. We looked at the venerable stream not in the vivid flush of a short day that comes and departs for ever, but in the august light of abiding memories. And indeed nothing is easier for a man who has, as the phrase goes, "followed the sea" with reverence and affection, than to evoke the great spirit of the past upon the lower reaches of the Thames. The tidal current runs to and fro in its unceasing service, crowded with memories of men and ships it has borne to the rest of home or to the battles of the sea. It had known and served all the men of whom the nation is proud, from Sir Francis Drake to Sir John Franklin, knights all, titled and untitled—the great knights-errant of the sea. It had borne all the ships whose names are like jewels flashing in the night of time, from the *Golden Hind* returning with her round flanks full of treasure, to be visited by the Queen's Highness and thus pass out of the gigantic tale, to the *Erebus* and *Terror*,[7] bound on other conquests—and that never returned. It had known the ships and the men. They had sailed from Deptford, from Green-

---

5. "The bond of the sea" appears in "Youth," Conrad's first story to feature Marlow. "Youth" and *Heart of Darkness* were first published in book form as part of the same volume, with "Youth" immediately preceding *Heart of Darkness*.
6. The mast aft (to the rear) of the mainmast on any ship with two or more masts.

7. The *Erebus* and the *Terror* were ships commanded by Arctic explorer Sir John Franklin (1786–1847) and lost in an attempt to find a passage from the Atlantic Ocean to the Pacific. *Golden Hind*: the ship in which Elizabethan explorer Sir Francis Drake (1540–1596) sailed around the world.

wich, from Erith—the adventurers and the settlers; kings' ships and the ships of men on 'Change; captains, admirals, the dark "interlopers"[8] of the Eastern trade, and the commissioned "generals" of East India fleets. Hunters for gold or pursuers of fame, they all had gone out on that stream, bearing the sword, and often the torch, messengers of the might within the land, bearers of a spark from the sacred fire.[9] What greatness had not floated on the ebb of that river into the mystery of an unknown earth! . . . The dreams of men, the seed of commonwealths, the germs of empires.

The sun set; the dusk fell on the stream, and lights began to appear along the shore. The Chapman lighthouse, a three-legged thing erect on a mudflat, shone strongly. Lights of ships moved in the fairway[1]—a great stir of lights going up and going down. And farther west on the upper reaches the place of the monstrous town[2] was still marked ominously on the sky, a brooding gloom in sunshine, a lurid glare under the stars.

"And this also," said Marlow suddenly, "has been one of the dark places of the earth."

He was the only man of us who still "followed the sea." The worst that could be said of him was that he did not represent his class. He was a seaman, but he was a wanderer too, while most seamen lead, if one may so express it, a sedentary life. Their minds are of the stay-at-home order, and their home is always with them—the ship; and so is their country—the sea. One ship is very much like another, and the sea is always the same. In the immutability of their surroundings the foreign shores, the foreign faces, the changing immensity of life, glide past, veiled not by a sense of mystery but by a slightly disdainful ignorance; for there is nothing mysterious to a seaman unless it be the sea itself, which is the mistress of his existence and as inscrutable as Destiny. For the rest, after his hours of work, a casual stroll or a casual spree on shore suffices to unfold for him the secret of a whole continent, and generally he finds the secret not worth knowing. The yarns of seamen have a direct simplicity, the whole meaning of which lies within the shell of a cracked nut. But Marlow was not typical (if his propensity to spin yarns be excepted), and to him the meaning of an episode was not inside like a kernel but outside, enveloping the tale which brought it out only as a glow brings out a haze, in the likeness of one of these misty halos that sometimes are made visible by the spectral illumination of moonshine.

His remark did not seem at all surprising. It was just like Marlow. It was accepted in silence. No one took the trouble to grunt even; and presently he said, very slow:

"I was thinking of very old times, when the Romans first came here, nineteen hundred years ago[3]—the other day. . . . Light came out of this river since—you

---

8. Private ships intruding on the East India Company's legal trade monopoly. "Deptford, Greenwich, Erith": ports on the Thames between London and Gravesend. "'Change": the stock exchange.
9. An allusion to the myth of Prometheus, who stole fire from the gods to give to humankind; by extension, refers to civilization, human ingenuity, and adventurousness.

1. A navigable passage in a river between rocks or sandbanks; the usual route into or out of a port.
2. I.e., London.
3. Romans first invaded England under Julius Caesar, in 55 and 54 B.C.E. These attempts were unsuccessful; in 43 C.E. a lengthy and effective conquest began.

say Knights? Yes; but it is like a running blaze on a plain, like a flash of lightning in the clouds. We live in the flicker—may it last as long as the old earth keeps rolling! But darkness was here yesterday. Imagine the feelings of a commander of a fine—what d'ye call 'em?—trireme[4] in the Mediterranean, ordered suddenly to the north; run overland across the Gauls[5] in a hurry; put in charge of one of these craft the legionaries[6]—a wonderful lot of handy men they must have been too—used to build, apparently by the hundred, in a month or two, if we may believe what we read. Imagine him here—the very end of the world, a sea the colour of lead, a sky the colour of smoke, a kind of ship about as rigid as a concertina[7]—and going up this river with stores, or orders, or what you like. Sandbanks, marshes, forests, savages—precious little to eat fit for a civilised man, nothing but Thames water to drink. No Falernian wine[8] here, no going ashore. Here and there a military camp lost in a wilderness, like a needle in a bundle of hay—cold, fog, tempests, disease, exile, and death—death skulking in the air, in the water, in the bush. They must have been dying like flies here. Oh yes—he did it. Did it very well, too, no doubt, and without thinking much about it either, except afterwards to brag of what he had gone through in his time, perhaps. They were men enough to face the darkness. And perhaps he was cheered by keeping his eye on a chance of promotion to the fleet at Ravenna[9] by and by, if he had good friends in Rome and survived the awful climate. Or think of a decent young citizen in a toga—perhaps too much dice, you know—coming out here in the train of some prefect, or tax-gatherer, or trader, even, to mend his fortunes. Land in a swamp, march through the woods, and in some inland post feel the savagery, the utter savagery, had closed round him—all that mysterious life of the wilderness that stirs in the forest, in the jungles, in the hearts of wild men. There's no initiation either into such mysteries. He has to live in the midst of the incomprehensible, which is also detestable. And it has a fascination, too, that goes to work upon him. The fascination of the abomination—you know. Imagine the growing regrets, the longing to escape, the powerless disgust, the surrender, the hate."

He paused.

"Mind," he began again, lifting one arm from the elbow, the palm of the hand outwards, so that, with his legs folded before him, he had the pose of a Buddha preaching in European clothes and without a lotus-flower[1]—"Mind, none of us would feel exactly like this. What saves us is efficiency—the devotion to efficiency. But these chaps were not much account, really. They were no colonists; their administration was merely a squeeze, and nothing more, I suspect. They were conquerors, and for that you want only brute force— nothing to boast of, when you have it, since your strength is just an accident arising from the weakness of others. They grabbed what they could get for the sake of what was to be got. It was just robbery with violence, aggravated murder

---

4. A Roman galley with three banks of oars.
5. Name used by the Romans to refer to the three regions of what is now France.
6. The members of a legion, a unit of Roman infantrymen.
7. An instrument resembling an accordion, with a bellows and buttons on either end: hence, not rigid at all.

8. Wine from a famous wine-making district in southern Italy.
9. Once a major Roman port on the Adriatic Sea.
1. Siddhartha Gautama, founder of Buddhism, is traditionally portrayed seated cross-legged on a lotus flower.

on a great scale, and men going at it blind—as is very proper for those who tackle a darkness. The conquest of the earth, which mostly means the taking it away from those who have a different complexion or slightly flatter noses than ourselves, is not a pretty thing when you look into it too much. What redeems it is the idea only. An idea at the back of it; not a sentimental pretence but an idea; and an unselfish belief in the idea—something you can set up, and bow down before, and offer a sacrifice to. . . ."

He broke off. Flames glided in the river, small green flames, red flames, white flames, pursuing, overtaking, joining, crossing each other—then separating slowly or hastily. The traffic of the great city went on in the deepening night upon the sleepless river. We looked on, waiting patiently—there was nothing else to do till the end of the flood; but it was only after a long silence, when he said, in a hesitating voice, "I suppose you fellows remember I did once turn fresh-water sailor for a bit," that we knew we were fated, before the ebb began to run,[2] to hear about one of Marlow's inconclusive experiences.

"I don't want to bother you much with what happened to me personally," he began, showing in this remark the weakness of many tellers of tales who seem so often unaware of what their audience would best like to hear; "yet to understand the effect of it on me you ought to know how I got out there, what I saw, how I went up that river to the place where I first met the poor chap. It was the farthest point of navigation and the culminating point of my experience. It seemed somehow to throw a kind of light on everything about me—and into my thoughts. It was sombre enough too—and pitiful—not extraordinary in any way—not very clear either. No, not very clear. And yet it seemed to throw a kind of light.

"I had then, as you remember, just returned to London after a lot of Indian Ocean, Pacific, China Seas—a regular dose of the East—six years or so, and I was loafing about, hindering you fellows in your work and invading your homes, just as though I had got a heavenly mission to civilise you. It was very fine for a time, but after a bit I did get tired of resting. Then I began to look for a ship—I should think the hardest work on earth. But the ships wouldn't even look at me. And I got tired of that game too.

"Now when I was a little chap I had a passion for maps. I would look for hours at South America, or Africa, or Australia, and lose myself in all the glories of exploration. At that time there were many blank spaces[3] on the earth, and when I saw one that looked particularly inviting on a map (but they all look that) I would put my finger on it and say, When I grow up I will go there. The North Pole was one of these places, I remember. Well, I haven't been there yet, and shall not try now. The glamour's off. Other places were scattered about the Equator, and in every sort of latitude all over the two hemispheres. I have been in some of them, and . . . well, we won't talk about that. But there was one yet—the biggest, the most blank, so to speak—that I had a hankering after.

"True, by this time it was not a blank space any more. It had got filled since my boyhood with rivers and lakes and names. It had ceased to be a blank space of delightful mystery—a white patch for a boy to dream gloriously over. It had become a place of darkness. But there was in it one river especially, a mighty

---

2. "Flood" and "ebb": the rise and fall of the tide in the river.

3. I.e., regions unexplored by Europeans at the time and hence left blank on European maps.

big river,[4] that you could see on the map, resembling an immense snake uncoiled, with its head in the sea, its body at rest curving afar over a vast country, and its tail lost in the depths of the land. And as I looked at the map of it in a shop-window, it fascinated me as a snake would a bird—a silly little bird. Then I remembered there was a big concern, a Company for trade on that river. Dash it all! I thought to myself, they can't trade without using some kind of craft on that lot of fresh water—steamboats![5] Why shouldn't I try to get charge of one? I went on along Fleet Street,[6] but could not shake off the idea. The snake had charmed me.

"You understand it was a Continental concern, that Trading Society;[7] but I have a lot of relations living on the Continent, because it's cheap and not so nasty as it looks, they say.

"I am sorry to own I began to worry them. This was already a fresh departure for me. I was not used to get things that way, you know. I always went my own road and on my own legs where I had a mind to go. I wouldn't have believed it of myself; but, then—you see—I felt somehow I must get there by hook or by crook. So I worried them. The men said, 'My dear fellow,' and did nothing. Then—would you believe it?—I tried the women. I, Charlie Marlow, set the women to work—to get a job. Heavens! Well, you see, the notion drove me. I had an aunt, a dear enthusiastic soul. She wrote: 'It will be delightful. I am ready to do anything, anything for you. It is a glorious idea. I know the wife of a very high personage in the Administration, and also a man who has lots of influence with,' etc. etc. She was determined to make no end of fuss to get me appointed skipper of a river steamboat, if such was my fancy.

"I got my appointment—of course; and I got it very quick. It appears the Company had received news that one of their captains had been killed in a scuffle with the natives. This was my chance, and it made me the more anxious to go. It was only months and months afterwards, when I made the attempt to recover what was left of the body, that I heard the original quarrel arose from a misunderstanding about some hens. Yes, two black hens. Fresleven—that was the fellow's name, a Dane—thought himself wronged somehow in the bargain, so he went ashore and started to hammer the chief of the village with a stick. Oh, it didn't surprise me in the least to hear this, and at the same time to be told that Fresleven was the gentlest, quietest creature that ever walked on two legs. No doubt he was; but he had been a couple of years already out there engaged in the noble cause, you know, and he probably felt the need at last of asserting his self-respect in some way. Therefore he whacked the old nigger mercilessly, while a big crowd of his people watched him, thunderstruck, till some man—I was told the chief's son—in desperation at hearing the old chap yell, made a tentative jab with a spear at the white man—and of course it went quite easy between the shoulder-blades. Then the whole population cleared into the forest, expecting all kinds of calamities to happen, while, on the other hand, the steamer Fresleven commanded left also in a bad panic, in charge of

4. The Congo River.
5. Flat-bottomed steamboats were essential for navigating the shallow waters of the Congo.
6. A major street in central London, famous as a publishing center.

7. The trading company—specifically, a Belgian company that operated ships on the Congo River in the protectorate of King Leopold II of Belgium.

the engineer, I believe. Afterwards nobody seemed to trouble much about Fresleven's remains, till I got out and stepped into his shoes. I couldn't let it rest, though; but when an opportunity offered at last to meet my predecessor, the grass growing through his ribs was tall enough to hide his bones. They were all there. The supernatural being had not been touched after he fell. And the village was deserted, the huts gaped black, rotting, all askew within the fallen enclosures. A calamity had come to it, sure enough. The people had vanished. Mad terror had scattered them, men, women, and children, through the bush, and they had never returned. What became of the hens I don't know either. I should think the cause of progress got them, anyhow. However, through this glorious affair I got my appontment, before I had fairly begun to hope for it.

"I flew around like mad to get ready, and before forty-eight hours I was crossing the Channel to show myself to my employers, and sign the contract. In a very few hours I arrived in a city that always makes me think of a whited sepulchre.[8] Prejudice no doubt. I had no difficulty in finding the Company's offices. It was the biggest thing in the town, and everybody I met was full of it. They were going to run an overseas empire, and make no end of coin by trade.

"A narrow and deserted street in deep shadow, high houses, innumerable windows with venetian blinds, a dead silence, grass sprouting between the stones, imposing carriage archways right and left, immense double doors standing ponderously ajar. I slipped through one of these cracks, went up a swept and ungarnished staircase, as arid as a desert, and opened the first door I came to. Two women, one fat and the other slim, sat on straw-bottomed chairs, knitting black wool.[9] The slim one got up and walked straight at me—still knitting with downcast eyes—and only just as I began to think of getting out of her way, as you would for a somnambulist, stood still, and looked up. Her dress was as plain as an umbrella-cover, and she turned round without a word and preceded me into a waiting-room. I gave my name, and looked about. Deal table in the middle, plain chairs all round the walls, on one end a large shining map, marked with all the colours of a rainbow. There was a vast amount of red— good to see at any time, because one knows that some real work is done in there, a deuce of a lot of blue, a little green, smears of orange, and, on the East Coast, a purple patch, to show where the jolly pioneers of progress drink the jolly lager-beer.[1] However, I wasn't going into any of these. I was going into the yellow. Dead in the centre. And the river was there—fascinating—deadly—like a snake. Ough! A door opened, a white-haired secretarial head, but wearing a compassionate expression, appeared, and a skinny forefinger beckoned me into

---

8. The city is based on Brussels. "Whited sepulchre": a biblical allusion, Matthew 23:27: "Woe unto you, scribes and Pharisees, hypocrites! for ye are like unto whited sepulchres, which indeed appear beautiful outward, but are within full of dead men's bones, and of all uncleanness."
9. The knitters allude to at least two sources: in Charles Dickens's *Tale of Two Cities*, the villainous Madame Defarge knits the names of those she condemns to die. In Greek mythology, the Fates were usually three women spin-

ning, measuring, and cutting the thread of life.
1. The map shows territories claimed by European nations in the aftermath of the Berlin Conference of 1884–85: red is England, Conrad's adopted nation; blue territories belonged to France; and purple, Germany. Although color schemes varied, in the map Marlow is looking at, orange presumably refers to Portugal and green to Italy, which also had holdings in Africa. Yellow stands for the Congo Free State, controlled by King Leopold II.

the sanctuary. Its light was dim, and a heavy writing desk squatted in the middle. From behind that structure came out an impression of pale plumpness in a frockcoat. The great man himself. He was five feet six, I should judge, and had his grip on the handle-end of ever so many millions. He shook hands, I fancy, murmured vaguely, was satisfied with my French. *Bon voyage.*[2]

"In about forty-five seconds I found myself again in the waiting-room with the compassionate secretary, who, full of desolation and sympathy, made me sign some document. I believe I undertook amongst other things not to disclose any trade secrets. Well, I am not going to.

"I began to feel slightly uneasy. You know I am not used to such ceremonies, and there was something ominous in the atmosphere. It was just as though I had been let into some conspiracy—I don't know—something not quite right; and I was glad to get out. In the outer room the two women knitted black wool feverishly. People were arriving, and the younger one was walking back and forth introducing them. The old one sat on her chair. Her flat cloth slippers were propped up on a foot-warmer, and a cat reposed on her lap. She wore a starched white affair on her head, had a wart on one cheek, and silver-rimmed spectacles hung on the tip of her nose. She glanced at me above the glasses. The swift and indifferent placidity of that look troubled me. Two youths with foolish and cheery countenances were being piloted over, and she threw at them the same quick glance of unconcerned wisdom. She seemed to know all about them and about me too. An eerie feeling came over me. She seemed uncanny and fateful. Often far away there I thought of these two, guarding the door of Darkness, knitting black wool as for a warm pall, one introducing, introducing continuously to the unknown, the other scrutinising the cheery and foolish faces with unconcerned old eyes. *Ave!* Old knitter of black wool. *Morituri te salutant.*[3] Not many of those she looked at ever saw her again—not half, by a long way.

"There was yet a visit to the doctor. 'A simple formality,' assured me the secretary, with an air of taking an immense part in all my sorrows. Accordingly a young chap wearing his hat over the left eyebrow, some clerk I suppose—there must have been clerks in the business, though the house was as still as a house in a city of the dead—came from somewhere upstairs, and led me forth. He was shabby and careless, with ink-stains on the sleeves of his jacket, and his cravat was large and billowy, under a chin shaped like the toe of an old boot. It was a little too early for the doctor, so I proposed a drink, and thereupon he developed a vein of joviality. As we sat over our vermuths[4] he glorified the Company's business, and by and by I expressed casually my surprise at him not going out there. He became very cool and collected all at once. 'I am not such a fool as I look, quoth Plato to his disciples,' he said sententiously, emptied his glass with great resolution, and we rose.

"The old doctor felt my pulse, evidently thinking of something else the while. 'Good, good for there,' he mumbled, and then with a certain eagerness asked me whether I would let him measure my head. Rather surprised, I said Yes, when he produced a thing like callipers and got the dimensions back and front

---

2. "Have a good trip" (French).
3. "Those who are about to die salute you" (Latin): the greeting of gladiators to the Roman emperor before beginning combat in the arena.

4. Vermuth, now known as vermouth, is wine fortified with alcohol and, usually, additional flavors.

and every way, taking notes carefully. He was an unshaven little man in a threadbare coat like a gaberdine, with his feet in slippers, and I thought him a harmless fool. 'I always ask leave, in the interests of science, to measure the crania of those going out there,'[5] he said. 'And when they come back too?' I asked. 'Oh, I never see them,' he remarked; 'and, moreover, the changes take place inside, you know.' He smiled, as if at some quiet joke. 'So you are going out there. Famous. Interesting too.' He gave me a searching glance, and made another note. 'Ever any madness in your family?' he asked, in a matter-of-fact tone. I felt very annoyed. 'Is that question in the interests of science too?' 'It would be,' he said, without taking notice of my irritation, 'interesting for science to watch the mental changes of individuals, on the spot, but . . .' 'Are you an alienist?' I interrupted. 'Every doctor should be—a little,' answered that original[6] imperturbably. 'I have a little theory which you Messieurs who go out there must help me to prove. This is my share in the advantages my country shall reap from the possession of such a magnificent dependency. The mere wealth I leave to others. Pardon my questions, but you are the first Englishman coming under my observation . . .' I hastened to assure him I was not in the least typical. 'If I were,' said I, 'I wouldn't be talking like this with you.' 'What you say is rather profound, and probably erroneous,' he said, with a laugh. 'Avoid irritation more than exposure to the sun. Adieu. How do you English say, eh? Good-bye. Ah! Good-bye. Adieu. In the tropics one must before everything keep calm.' . . . He lifted a warning forefinger. . . . '*Du calme, du calme. Adieu.*'[7]

"One thing more remained to do—say good-bye to my excellent aunt. I found her triumphant. I had a cup of tea—the last decent cup of tea for many days— and in a room that most soothingly looked just as you would expect a lady's drawing-room to look, we had a long quiet chat by the fireside. In the course of these confidences it became quite plain to me I had been represented to the wife of the high dignitary, and goodness knows to how many more people besides, as an exceptional and gifted creature—a piece of good fortune for the Company—a man you don't get hold of every day. Good heavens! and I was going to take charge of a two-penny-halfpenny river-steamboat with a penny whistle attached! It appeared, however, I was also one of the Workers, with a capital—you know. Something like an emissary of light, something like a lower sort of apostle. There had been a lot of such rot let loose in print and talk just about that time,[8] and the excellent woman, living right in the rush of all that humbug, got carried off her feet. She talked about 'weaning those ignorant millions from their horrid ways,' till, upon my word, she made me quite uncomfortable. I ventured to hint that the Company was run for profit.

"'You forget, dear Charlie, that the labourer is worthy of his hire,'[9] she said brightly. It's queer how out of touch with truth women are. They live in a world of their own, and there had never been anything like it, and never can be. It is

---

5. The doctor may practice some form of phrenology, a pseudoscience holding that personality traits could be determined by the shape and size of the skull.
6. Unusual or eccentric person. "Alienist": early term for a psychiatrist.
7. "Calm, calm. Goodbye" (French).
8. Initially, Leopold II was viewed as a philanthropist—bringing missionaries to pagans and, it was thought, using Belgian military forces to rescue the native people from homegrown slave traders.
9. The aunt quotes Luke 10:7, one of Christ's instructions to his disciples as they depart to proselytize: to make themselves welcome in the homes they visit.

too beautiful altogether, and if they were to set it up it would go to pieces before the first sunset. Some confounded fact we men have been living contentedly with ever since the day of creation would start up and knock the whole thing over.

"After this I got embraced, told to wear flannel, be sure to write often, and so on—and I left. In the street—I don't know why—a queer feeling came to me that I was an impostor. Odd thing that I, who used to clear out for any part of the world at twenty-four hours' notice, with less thought than most men give to the crossing of a street, had a moment—I won't say of hesitation, but of startled pause, before this commonplace affair. The best way I can explain it to you is by saying that, for a second or two, I felt as though, instead of going to the centre of a continent, I were about to set off for the centre of the earth.[1]

"I left in a French steamer, and she called in every blamed port they have out there, for, as far as I could see, the sole purpose of landing soldiers and custom-house officers.[2] I watched the coast. Watching a coast as it slips by the ship is like thinking about an enigma. There it is before you—smiling, frowning, inviting, grand, mean, insipid, or savage, and always mute with an air of whispering, Come and find out. This one was almost featureless, as if still in the making, with an aspect of monotonous grimness. The edge of a colossal jungle, so dark green as to be almost black, fringed with white surf, ran straight, like a ruled line, far, far away along a blue sea whose glitter was blurred by a creeping mist. The sun was fierce, the land seemed to glisten and drip with steam. Here and there greyish-whitish specks showed up clustered inside the white surf, with a flag flying above them perhaps—settlements some centuries old, and still no bigger than pin-heads on the untouched expanse of their background. We pounded along, stopped, landed soldiers; went on, landed custom-house clerks to levy toll in what looked like a God-forsaken wilderness, with a tin shed and a flag-pole lost in it; landed more soldiers—to take care of the custom-house clerks presumably. Some, I heard, got drowned in the surf; but whether they did or not, nobody seemed particularly to care. They were just flung out there, and on we went. Every day the coast looked the same, as though we had not moved; but we passed various places—trading places—with names like Gran' Bassam, Little Popo;[3] names that seemed to belong to some sordid farce acted in front of a sinister back-cloth. The idleness of a passenger, my isolation amongst all these men with whom I had no point of contact, the oily and languid sea, the uniform sombreness of the coast, seemed to keep me away from the truth of things, within the toil of a mournful and senseless delusion. The voice of the surf heard now and then was a positive pleasure, like the speech of a brother. It was something natural, that had its reason, that had a meaning. Now and then a boat from the shore gave one a momentary contact with reality. It was paddled by black fellows. You could see from afar the white of their eyeballs glistening. They shouted, sang; their bodies streamed with perspiration; they had faces like grotesque masks—these chaps; but they had bone, muscle, a wild vitality, an intense energy of movement, that was as

1. Jules Verne's science fiction novel *Journey to the Center of the Earth* (1864) featured characters encountering prehistoric animals of greater age in successive layers of the earth.
2. Colonial officials.

3. The former name of Aného, a coastal city in Togo, then under German control. "Gran' Bassam": Grand-Bassam, a city in Côte d'Ivoire, was then a French colony and a major seaport.

natural and true as the surf along their coast. They wanted no excuse for being there. They were a great comfort to look at. For a time I would feel I belonged still to a world of straightforward facts; but the feeling would not last long. Something would turn up to scare it away. Once, I remember, we came upon a man-of-war anchored off the coast. There wasn't even a shed there, and she was shelling the bush. It appears the French had one of their wars going on thereabouts. Her ensign dropped limp like a rag; the muzzles of the long six-inch guns stuck out all over the low hull; the greasy, slimy swell swung her up lazily and let her down, swaying her thin masts. In the empty immensity of earth, sky, and water, there she was, incomprehensible, firing into a continent. Pop, would go one of the six-inch guns; a small flame would dart and vanish, a little white smoke would disappear, a tiny projectile would give a feeble screech—and nothing happened. Nothing could happen. There was a touch of insanity in the proceeding, a sense of lugubrious drollery in the sight; and it was not dissipated by somebody on board assuring me earnestly there was a camp of natives—he called them enemies!—hidden out of sight somewhere.

"We gave her her letters (I heard the men in that lonely ship were dying of fever at the rate of three a day) and went on. We called at some more places with farcical names, where the merry dance of death and trade goes on in a still and earthy atmosphere as of an overheated catacomb; all along the formless coast bordered by dangerous surf, as if Nature herself had tried to ward off intruders; in and out of rivers, streams of death in life, whose banks were rotting into mud, whose waters, thickened into slime, invaded the contorted mangroves, that seemed to writhe at us in the extremity of an impotent despair. Nowhere did we stop long enough to get a particularised impression, but the general sense of vague and oppressive wonder grew upon me. It was like a weary pilgrimage amongst hints for nightmares.

"It was upward of thirty days before I saw the mouth of the big river. We anchored off the seat of the government.[4] But my work would not begin till some two hundred miles farther on. So as soon as I could I made a start for a place thirty miles higher up.

"I had my passage on a little sea-going steamer. Her captain was a Swede, and knowing me for a seaman, invited me on the bridge. He was a young man, lean, fair, and morose, with lanky hair and a shuffling gait. As we left the miserable little wharf, he tossed his head contemptuously at the shore. 'Been living there?' he asked. I said, 'Yes.' 'Fine lot these government chaps—are they not?' he went on, speaking English with great precision and considerable bitterness. 'It is funny what some people will do for a few francs a month. I wonder what becomes of that kind when it goes up country?' I said to him I expected to see that soon. 'So-o-o!' he exclaimed. He shuffled athwart, keeping one eye ahead vigilantly. 'Don't be too sure,' he continued. 'The other day I took up a man who hanged himself on the road. He was a Swede, too.' 'Hanged himself! Why, in God's name?' I cried. He kept on looking out watchfully. 'Who knows? The sun too much for him, or the country perhaps.'

"At last we opened a reach.[5] A rocky cliff appeared, mounds of turned-up earth by the shore, houses on a hill, others with iron roofs, amongst a waste of

---

4. The capital of the Congo Free State was Boma, a port at the mouth of the Congo. **5.** Found an open, visible stretch of river.

excavations, or hanging to the declivity. A continuous noise of the rapids above hovered over this scene of inhabited devastation. A lot of people, mostly black and naked, moved about like ants. A jetty projected into the river. A blinding sunlight drowned all this at times in a sudden recrudescence of glare. 'There's your Company's station,' said the Swede, pointing to three wooden barrack-like structures on the rocky slope. 'I will send your things up. Four boxes did you say? So. Farewell.'

"I came upon a boiler[6] wallowing in the grass, then found a path leading up the hill. It turned aside for the boulders, and also for an undersized railway truck lying there on its back with its wheels in the air. One was off. The thing looked as dead as the carcass of some animal. I came upon more pieces of decaying machinery, a stack of rusty nails. To the left a clump of trees made a shady spot, where dark things seemed to stir feebly. I blinked, the path was steep. A horn tooted to the right, and I saw the black people run. A heavy and dull detonation shook the ground, a puff of smoke came out of the cliff, and that was all. No change appeared on the face of the rock. They were building a railway. The cliff was not in the way or anything; but this objectless blasting was all the work going on.

"A slight clinking behind me made me turn my head. Six black men advanced in a file, toiling up the path. They walked erect and slow, balancing small baskets full of earth on their heads, and the clink kept time with their footsteps. Black rags were wound round their loins, and the short ends behind waggled to and fro like tails. I could see every rib, the joints of their limbs were like knots in a rope; each had an iron collar on his neck, and all were connected together with a chain whose bights[7] swung between them, rhythmically clinking. Another report from the cliff made me think suddenly of that ship of war I had seen firing into a continent. It was the same kind of ominous voice; but these men could by no stretch of imagination be called enemies. They were called criminals, and the outraged law, like the bursting shells, had come to them, an insoluble mystery from the sea. All their meagre breasts panted together, the violently dilated nostrils quivered, the eyes stared stonily uphill. They passed me within six inches, without a glance, with that complete, deathlike indifference of unhappy savages. Behind this raw matter one of the reclaimed, the product of the new forces at work, strolled despondently, carrying a rifle by its middle. He had a uniform jacket with one button off, and seeing a white man on the path, hoisted his weapon to his shoulder with alacrity. This was simple prudence, white men being so much alike at a distance that he could not tell who I might be. He was speedily reassured, and with a large, white, rascally grin, and a glance at his charge, seemed to take me into partnership in his exalted trust. After all, I also was a part of the great cause of these high and just proceedings.

"Instead of going up, I turned and descended to the left. My idea was to let that chain-gang get out of sight before I climbed the hill. You know I am not particularly tender; I've had to strike and to fend off. I've had to resist and to attack sometimes—that's only one way of resisting—without counting the exact cost, according to the demands of such sort of life as I had blundered into. I've seen the devil of violence, and the devil of greed, and the devil of hot desire; but, by all the stars! these were strong, lusty, red-eyed devils, that

---

6. A machine for converting water into steam.   7. The dangling excess of chain.

swayed and drove men—men, I tell you. But as I stood on this hillside, I foresaw that in the blinding sunshine of that land I would become acquainted with a flabby, pretending, weak-eyed devil of a rapacious and pitiless folly. How insidious he could be, too, I was only to find out several months later and a thousand miles farther. For a moment I stood appalled, as though by a warning. Finally I descended the hill, obliquely, towards the trees I had seen.

"I avoided a vast artificial hole somebody had been digging on the slope, the purpose of which I found it impossible to divine. It wasn't a quarry or a sandpit, anyhow. It was just a hole. It might have been connected with the philanthropic desire of giving the criminals something to do. I don't know. Then I nearly fell into a very narrow ravine, almost no more than a scar in the hillside. I discovered that a lot of imported drainage-pipes for the settlement had been tumbled in there. There wasn't one that was not broken. It was a wanton smash-up. At last I got under the trees. My purpose was to stroll into the shade for a moment; but no sooner within than it seemed to me I had stepped into the gloomy circle of some Inferno.[8] The rapids were near, and an uninterrupted, uniform, headlong, rushing noise filled the mournful stillness of the grove, where not a breath stirred, not a leaf moved, with a mysterious sound—as though the tearing pace of the launched earth had suddenly become audible.

"Black shapes crouched, lay, sat between the trees, leaning against the trunks, clinging to the earth, half coming out, half effaced within the dim light, in all the attitudes of pain, abandonment, and despair. Another mine[9] on the cliff went off, followed by a slight shudder of the soil under my feet. The work was going on. The work! And this was the place where some of the helpers had withdrawn to die.

"They were dying slowly—it was very clear. They were not enemies, they were not criminals, they were nothing earthly now—nothing but black shadows of disease and starvation, lying confusedly in the greenish gloom. Brought from all the recesses of the coast in all the legality of time contracts, lost in uncongenial surroundings, fed on unfamiliar food, they sickened, became inefficient, and were then allowed to crawl away and rest.[1] These moribund shapes were free as air—and nearly as thin. I began to distinguish the gleam of eyes under the trees. Then, glancing down, I saw a face near my hand. The black bones reclined at full length with one shoulder against the tree, and slowly the eyelids rose and the sunken eyes looked up at me, enormous and vacant, a kind of blind, white flicker in the depths of the orbs, which died out slowly. The man seemed young—almost a boy—but you know with them it's hard to tell. I found nothing else to do but to offer him one of my good Swede's ship's biscuits I had in my pocket. The fingers closed slowly on it and held—there was no other movement and no other glance. He had tied a bit of white worsted[2] round his neck—Why? Where did he get it? Was it a badge—an ornament—a charm—a propitiatory act? Was there any idea at all connected with it? It looked startling round his black neck, this bit of white thread from beyond the seas.

---

8. Hell, often of fire. The term is associated with the portrayal of hell in the *Inferno*, the first section of the *Divine Comedy*, by Dante Alighieri (ca. 1265–1321).
9. Explosive charge.

1. The workers and porters who provided the infrastructure of the Congo Free State were often conscripts: overworked, underfed, and beaten, they died in enormous numbers.
2. Wool fabric.

"Near the same tree two more bundles of acute angles sat with their legs drawn up. One, with his chin propped on his knees, stared at nothing, in an intolerable and appalling manner: his brother phantom rested its forehead, as if overcome with a great weariness; and all about others were scattered in every pose of contorted collapse, as in some picture of a massacre or a pestilence. While I stood horror-struck, one of these creatures rose to his hands and knees, and went off on all-fours towards the river to drink. He lapped out of his hand, then sat up in the sunlight, crossing his shins in front of him, and after a time let his woolly head fall on his breastbone.

"I didn't want any more loitering in the shade, and I made haste towards the station. When near the buildings I met a white man, in such an unexpected elegance of get-up that in the first moment I took him for a sort of vision. I saw a high starched collar, white cuffs, a light alpaca[3] jacket, snowy trousers, a clear necktie, and varnished boots. No hat. Hair parted, brushed, oiled, under a green-lined parasol held in a big white hand. He was amazing, and had a penholder behind his ear.

"I shook hands with this miracle, and I learned he was the Company's chief accountant, and that all the book-keeping was done at this station. He had come out for a moment, he said, 'to get a breath of fresh air.' The expression sounded wonderfully odd, with its suggestion of sedentary desk-life. I wouldn't have mentioned the fellow to you at all, only it was from his lips that I first heard the name of the man who is so indissolubly connected with the memories of that time. Moreover, I respected the fellow. Yes; I respected his collars, his vast cuffs, his brushed hair. His appearance was certainly that of a hairdresser's dummy; but in the great demoralisation of the land he kept up his appearance. That's backbone. His starched collars and got-up shirt-fronts were achievements of character. He had been out nearly three years; and, later, I could not help asking him how he managed to sport such linen. He had just the faintest blush, and said modestly, 'I've been teaching one of the native women about the station. It was difficult. She had a distaste for the work.' Thus this man had verily accomplished something. And he was devoted to his books, which were in apple-pie order.

"Everything else in the station was in a muddle,—heads, things, buildings. Strings of dusty niggers with splay feet arrived and departed; a stream of manufactured goods, rubbishy cottons, beads, and brass-wire sent into the depths of darkness, and in return came a precious trickle of ivory.[4]

"I had to wait in the station for ten days—an eternity. I lived in a hut in the yard, but to be out of the chaos I would sometimes get into the accountant's office. It was built of horizontal planks, and so badly put together that, as he bent over his high desk, he was barred from neck to heels with narrow strips of sunlight. There was no need to open the big shutter to see. It was hot there too; big flies buzzed fiendishly, and did not sting, but stabbed. I sat generally on the floor, while, of faultless appearance (and even slightly scented), perching on a high stool, he wrote, he wrote. Sometimes he stood up for exercise.

3. An expensive fine wool that comes from a South American animal of the same name.
4. Congolese were not allowed currency, and the enormous disparity between the value of goods returning from the Congo and the value of goods being sent there eventually gave activists the first hint of the forced labor conditions that would turn public opinion against Leopold.

When a truckle-bed[5] with a sick man (some invalided agent from up country) was put in there, he exhibited a gentle annoyance. 'The groans of this sick person' he said, 'distract my attention. And without that it is extremely difficult to guard against clerical errors in this climate.'

"One day he remarked, without lifting his head, 'In the interior you will no doubt meet Mr Kurtz.' On my asking who Mr Kurtz was, he said he was a first-class agent; and seeing my disappointment at this information, he added slowly, laying down his pen, 'He is a very remarkable person.' Further questions elicited from him that Mr Kurtz was at present in charge of a trading-post, a very important one, in the true ivory-country, at 'the very bottom of there. Sends in as much ivory as all the others put together . . .' He began to write again. The sick man was too ill to groan. The flies buzzed in a great peace.

"Suddenly there was a growing murmur of voices and a great tramping of feet. A caravan had come in. A violent babble of uncouth sounds burst out on the other side of the planks. All the carriers were speaking together, and in the midst of the uproar the lamentable voice of the chief agent was heard 'giving it up' tearfully for the twentieth time that day. . . . He rose slowly. 'What a frightful row,' he said. He crossed the room gently to look at the sick man, and returning, said to me, 'He does not hear.' 'What! Dead?' I asked, startled. 'No, not yet,' he answered, with great composure. Then, alluding with a toss of the head to the tumult in the station-yard, 'When one has got to make correct entries, one comes to hate those savages—hate them to the death.' He remained thoughtful for a moment. 'When you see Mr Kurtz,' he went on, 'tell him from me that everything here'—he glanced at the desk—'is very satisfactory. I don't like to write to him—with those messengers of ours you never know who may get hold of your letter—at that Central Station.' He stared at me for a moment with his mild, bulging eyes. 'Oh, he will go far, very far,' he began again. 'He will be a somebody in the Administration before long. They, above—the Council in Europe, you know—mean him to be.'

"He turned to his work. The noise outside had ceased, and presently in going out I stopped at the door. In the steady buzz of flies the homeward-bound agent was lying flushed and insensible; the other, bent over his books, was making correct entries of perfectly correct transactions; and fifty feet below the doorstep I could see the still tree-tops of the grove of death.

"Next day I left that station at last, with a caravan of sixty men, for a two-hundred-mile tramp.

"No use telling you much about that. Paths, paths, everywhere; a stamped-in network of paths spreading over the empty land, through long grass, through burnt grass, through thickets, down and up chilly ravines, up and down stony hills ablaze with heat; and a solitude, a solitude, nobody, not a hut. The population had cleared out a long time ago. Well, if a lot of mysterious niggers armed with all kinds of fearful weapons suddenly took to travelling on the road between Deal and Gravesend,[6] catching the yokels right and left to carry heavy loads for them, I fancy every farm and cottage thereabouts would get empty very soon. Only here the dwellings were gone too. Still, I passed through several abandoned

5. I.e., trundle bed, a low portable bed that is on castors and that may be slid under a higher bed when not being used.

6. Deal, like Gravesend, is a coastal town in southeastern England.

villages. There's something pathetically childish in the ruins of grass walls. Day after day, with the stamp and shuffle of sixty pair of bare feet behind me, each pair under a 60-lb. load. Camp, cook, sleep, strike camp, march. Now and then a carrier dead in harness, at rest in the long grass near the path, with an empty water-gourd and his long staff lying by his side. A great silence around and above. Perhaps on some quiet night the tremor of far-off drums, sinking, swelling, a tremor vast, faint; a sound weird, appealing, suggestive, and wild—and perhaps with as profound a meaning as the sound of bells in a Christian country. Once a white man in an unbuttoned uniform, camping on the path with an armed escort of lank Zanzibaris,[7] very hospitable and festive—not to say drunk. Was looking after the upkeep of the road, he declared. Can't say I saw any road or any upkeep, unless the body of a middle-aged negro, with a bullet-hole in the forehead, upon which I absolutely stumbled three miles farther on, may be considered as a permanent improvement. I had a white companion too, not a bad chap, but rather too fleshy and with the exasperating habit of fainting on the hot hillsides, miles away from the least bit of shade and water. Annoying, you know, to hold your own coat like a parasol over a man's head while he is coming-to. I couldn't help asking him once what he meant by coming there at all. 'To make money, of course. What do you think?' he said scornfully. Then he got fever, and had to be carried in a hammock slung under a pole. As he weighed sixteen stone[8] I had no end of rows with the carriers. They jibbed, ran away, sneaked off with their loads in the night—quite a mutiny. So, one evening, I made a speech in English with gestures, not one of which was lost to the sixty pairs of eyes before me, and the next morning I started the hammock off in front all right. An hour afterwards I came upon the whole concern wrecked in a bush—man, hammock, groans, blankets, horrors. The heavy pole had skinned his poor nose. He was very anxious for me to kill somebody, but there wasn't the shadow of a carrier near. I remembered the old doctor—'It would be interesting for science to watch the mental changes of individuals, on the spot.' I felt I was becoming scientifically interesting. However, all that is to no purpose. On the fifteenth day I came in sight of the big river again, and hobbled into the Central Station. It was on a back water surrounded by scrub and forest, with a pretty border of smelly mud on one side, and on the three others enclosed by a crazy fence of rushes. A neglected gap was all the gate it had, and the first glance at the place was enough to let you see the flabby devil was running that show. White men with long staves in their hands appeared languidly from amongst the buildings, strolling up to take a look at me, and then retired out of sight somewhere. One of them, a stout, excitable chap with black moustaches, informed me with great volubility and many digressions, as soon as I told him who I was, that my steamer was at the bottom of the river. I was thunderstruck. What, how, why? Oh, it was 'all right.' The 'manager himself' was there. All quite correct. 'Everybody had behaved splendidly! splendidly!'—'You must,' he said in agitation, 'go and see the general manager at once. He is waiting!'

"I did not see the real significance of that wreck at once. I fancy I see it now, but I am not sure—not at all. Certainly the affair was too stupid—when I think of it—to be altogether natural. Still . . . But at the moment it presented itself

---

7. Mercenary soldiers from the island of Zan-   8. I.e., 224 pounds (1 stone equals 14 pounds).
zibar, off the east African coast.

simply as a confounded nuisance. The steamer was sunk. They had started two days before in a sudden hurry up the river with the manager on board, in charge of some volunteer skipper, and before they had been out three hours they tore the bottom out of her on stones, and she sank near the south bank. I asked myself what I was to do there, now my boat was lost. As a matter of fact, I had plenty to do in fishing my command out of the river. I had to set about it the very next day. That, and the repairs when I brought the pieces to the station, took some months.

"My first interview with the manager was curious. He did not ask me to sit down after my twenty-mile walk that morning. He was commonplace in complexion, in feature, in manners, and in voice. He was of middle size and of ordinary build. His eyes, of the usual blue, were perhaps remarkably cold, and he certainly could make his glance fall on one as trenchant and heavy as an axe. But even at these times the rest of his person seemed to disclaim the intention. Otherwise there was only an indefinable, faint expression of his lips, something stealthy—a smile—not a smile—I remember it, but I can't explain. It was unconscious, this smile was, though just after he had said something it got intensified for an instant. It came at the end of his speeches like a seal applied on the words to make the meaning of the commonest phrase appear absolutely inscrutable. He was a common trader, from his youth up employed in these parts—nothing more. He was obeyed, yet he inspired neither love nor fear, nor even respect. He inspired uneasiness. That was it! Uneasiness. Not a definite mistrust—just uneasiness—nothing more. You have no idea how effective such a . . . a . . . faculty can be. He had no genius for organising, for initiative, or for order even. That was evident in such things as the deplorable state of the station. He had no learning, and no intelligence. His position had come to him—why? Perhaps because he was never ill . . . He had served three terms of three years out there . . . Because triumphant health in the general rout of constitutions is a kind of power in itself. When he went home on leave he rioted on a large scale—pompously. Jack ashore[9]—with a difference—in externals only. This one could gather from his casual talk. He originated nothing, he could keep the routine going—that's all. But he was great. He was great by this little thing that it was impossible to tell what could control such a man. He never gave that secret away. Perhaps there was nothing within him. Such a suspicion made one pause—for out there there were no external checks. Once when various tropical diseases had laid low almost every 'agent' in the station, he was heard to say, 'Men who come out here should have no entrails.' He sealed the utterance with that smile of his, as though it had been a door opening into a darkness he had in his keeping. You fancied you had seen things—but the seal was on. When annoyed at meal-times by the constant quarrels of the white men about precedence, he ordered an immense round table[1] to be made, for which a special house had to be built. This was the station's mess-room. Where he sat was the first place—the rest were nowhere. One felt this to be his unalterable conviction. He was neither civil nor uncivil. He was quiet. He allowed his 'boy'—an overfed young negro from the coast—to treat the white men, under his very eyes, with provoking insolence.

9. The carousing of seamen ("Jack Tar") on shore leave was proverbial.
1. King Arthur, legendary ruler of England, seated his knights at a round table so that none would take precedence over any of the others.

"He began to speak as soon as he saw me. I had been very long on the road. He could not wait. Had to start without me. The up-river stations had to be relieved. There had been so many delays already that he did not know who was dead and who was alive, and how they got on—and so on, and so on. He paid no attention to my explanations, and, playing with a stick of sealing-wax, repeated several times that the situation was 'very grave, very grave.' There were rumours that a very important station was in jeopardy, and its chief, Mr Kurtz, was ill. Hoped it was not true. Mr Kurtz was . . . I felt weary and irritable. Hang Kurtz, I thought. I interrupted him by saying I had heard of Mr Kurtz on the coast. 'Ah! So they talk of him down there,' he murmured to himself. Then he began again, assuring me Mr Kurtz was the best agent he had, an exceptional man, of the greatest importance to the Company; therefore I could understand his anxiety. He was, he said, 'very, very uneasy.' Certainly he fidgeted on his chair a good deal, exclaimed, 'Ah, Mr Kurtz!' broke the stick of sealing-wax and seemed dumbfounded by the accident. Next thing he wanted to know 'how long it would take to' . . . I interrupted him again. Being hungry, you know, and kept on my feet too, I was getting savage. 'How can I tell?' I said, 'I haven't even seen the wreck yet—some months, no doubt.' All this talk seemed to me so futile. 'Some months,' he said. 'Well, let us say three months before we can make a start. Yes. That ought to do the affair.' I flung out of his hut (he lived all alone in a clay hut with a sort of verandah) muttering to myself my opinion of him. He was a chattering idiot. Afterwards I took it back when it was borne in upon me startlingly with what extreme nicety he had estimated the time requisite for the 'affair.'

"I went to work the next day, turning, so to speak, my back on that station. In that way only it seemed to me I could keep my hold on the redeeming facts of life. Still, one must look about sometimes; and then I saw this station, these men strolling aimlessly about in the sunshine of the yard. I asked myself sometimes what it all meant. They wandered here and there with their absurd long staves in their hands, like a lot of faithless pilgrims bewitched inside a rotten fence. The word 'ivory' rang in the air, was whispered, was sighed. You would think they were praying to it. A taint of imbecile rapacity blew through it all, like a whiff from some corpse. By Jove! I've never seen anything so unreal in my life. And outside, the silent wilderness surrounding this cleared speck on the earth struck me as something great and invincible, like evil or truth, waiting patiently for the passing away of this fantastic invasion.

"Oh, these months! Well, never mind. Various things happened. One evening a grass shed full of calico, cotton prints, beads, and I don't know what else, burst into a blaze so suddenly that you would have thought the earth had opened to let an avenging fire consume all that trash. I was smoking my pipe quietly by my dismantled steamer, and saw them all cutting capers[2] in the light, with their arms lifted high, when the stout man with moustaches came tearing down to the river, a tin pail in his hand, assured me that everybody was 'behaving splendidly, splendidly,' dipped about a quart of water and tore back again. I noticed there was a hole in the bottom of his pail.

"I strolled up. There was no hurry. You see the thing had gone off like a box of matches. It had been hopeless from the very first. The flame had leaped high,

2. Jumping, dancing.

driven everybody back, lighted up everything—and collapsed. The shed was already a heap of embers glowing fiercely. A nigger was being beaten near by. They said he had caused the fire in some way; be that as it may, he was screeching most horribly. I saw him, later, for several days, sitting in a bit of shade looking very sick and trying to recover himself: afterwards he arose and went out—and the wilderness without a sound took him into its bosom again. As I approached the glow from the dark I found myself at the back of two men, talking. I heard the name of Kurtz pronounced, then the words, 'take advantage of this unfortunate accident.' One of the men was the manager. I wished him a good evening. 'Did you ever see anything like it—eh? it is incredible,' he said, and walked off. The other man remained. He was a first-class agent, young, gentlemanly, a bit reserved, with a forked little beard and a hooked nose. He was standoffish with the other agents, and they on their side said he was the manager's spy upon them. As to me, I had hardly ever spoken to him before. We got into talk, and by and by we strolled away from the hissing ruins. Then he asked me to his room, which was in the main building of the station. He struck a match, and I perceived that this young aristocrat had not only a silver-mounted dressing-case but also a whole candle all to himself. Just at that time the manager was the only man supposed to have any right to candles. Native mats covered the clay walls; a collection of spears, assegais,[3] shields, knives, was hung up in trophies. The business entrusted to this fellow was the making of bricks—so I had been informed; but there wasn't a fragment of a brick anywhere in the station, and he had been there more than a year—waiting. It seems he could not make bricks without something, I don't know what—straw maybe. Anyway, it could not be found there, and as it was not likely to be sent from Europe, it did not appear clear to me what he was waiting for. An act of special creation[4] perhaps. However, they were all waiting—all the sixteen or twenty pilgrims of them—for something; and upon my word it did not seem an uncongenial occupation, from the way they took it, though the only thing that ever came to them was disease—as far as I could see. They beguiled the time by backbiting and intriguing against each other in a foolish kind of way. There was an air of plotting about that station, but nothing came of it, of course. It was as unreal as everything else—as the philanthropic pretence of the whole concern, as their talk, as their government, as their show of work. The only real feeling was a desire to get appointed to a trading-post where ivory was to be had, so that they could earn percentages. They intrigued and slandered and hated each other only on that account—but as to effectually lifting a little finger—oh no. By heavens! there is something after all in the world allowing one man to steal a horse while another must not look at a halter. Steal a horse straight out. Very well. He has done it. Perhaps he can ride. But there is a way of looking at a halter that would provoke the most charitable of saints into a kick.

"I had no idea why he wanted to be sociable, but as we chatted in there it suddenly occurred to me the fellow was trying to get at something—in fact, pumping me. He alluded constantly to Europe, to the people I was supposed to know there—putting leading questions as to my acquaintances in the sepulchral city,

---

3. Slender hardwood javelins used as weapons.
4. The religious doctrine of "special creation" referred to a literal interpretation of Genesis in which the universe came into being by instant divine decree.

and so on. His little eyes glittered like mica[5] discs—with curiosity—though he tried to keep up a bit of superciliousness. At first I was astonished, but very soon I became awfully curious to see what he would find out from me. I couldn't possibly imagine what I had in me to make it worth his while. It was very pretty to see how he baffled himself, for in truth my body was full only of chills, and my head had nothing in it but that wretched steamboat business. It was evident he took me for a perfectly shameless prevaricator. At last he got angry, and, to conceal a movement of furious annoyance, he yawned. I rose. Then I noticed a small sketch in oils, on a panel, representing a woman, draped and blindfolded, carrying a lighted torch.[6] The background was sombre—almost black. The movement of the woman was stately, and the effect of the torchlight on the face was sinister.

"It arrested me, and he stood by civilly, holding an empty half-pint champagne bottle (medical comforts) with the candle stuck in it. To my question he said Mr Kurtz had painted this—in this very station more than a year ago—while waiting for means to go to his trading-post. 'Tell me, pray,' said I, 'who is this Mr Kurtz?'

"'The chief of the Inner Station,' he answered in a short tone, looking away. 'Much obliged,' I said, laughing. 'And you are the brickmaker of the Central Station. Every one knows that.' He was silent for a while. 'He is a prodigy,' he said at last. 'He is an emissary of pity, and science, and progress, and devil knows what else. We want,' he began to declaim suddenly, 'for the guidance of the cause entrusted to us by Europe, so to speak, higher intelligence, wide sympathies, a singleness of purpose.' 'Who says that?' I asked. 'Lots of them,' he replied. 'Some even write that; and so *he* comes here, a special being, as you ought to know.' 'Why ought I to know?' I interrupted, really surprised. He paid no attention. 'Yes. To-day he is chief of the best station, next year he will be assistant-manager, two years more and . . . but I daresay you know what he will be in two years' time. You are of the new gang—the gang of virtue. The same people who sent him specially also recommended you. Oh, don't say no. I've my own eyes to trust.' Light dawned upon me. My dear aunt's influential acquaintances were producing an unexpected effect upon that young man. I nearly burst into a laugh. 'Do you read the Company's confidential correspondence?' I asked. He hadn't a word to say. It was great fun. 'When Mr Kurtz,' I continued severely, 'is General Manager, you won't have the opportunity.'

"He blew the candle out suddenly, and we went outside. The moon had risen. Black figures strolled about listlessly, pouring water on the glow, whence proceeded a sound of hissing; steam ascended in the moonlight; the beaten nigger groaned somewhere. 'What a row the brute makes!' said the indefatigable man with the moustaches, appearing near us. 'Serve him right. Transgression—punishment—bang! Pitiless, pitiless. That's the only way. This will prevent all conflagrations for the future. I was just telling the manager . . .' He noticed my companion, and became crestfallen all at once. 'Not in bed yet,' he said, with a kind of servile heartiness; 'it's so natural. Ha! Danger—agitation.' He vanished. I went on to the river-side, and the other followed me. I heard a scathing murmur

---

5. A mineral silicate that separates into glittering layers.
6. Justice was traditionally portrayed as a blind-

folded woman, although usually bearing scales and a sword rather than a torch.

at my ear, 'Heap of muffs[7]—go to.' The pilgrims could be seen in knots gesticu-lating, discussing. Several had still their staves in their hands. I verily believe they took these sticks to bed with them. Beyond the fence the forest stood up spectrally in the moonlight, and through the dim stir, through the faint sounds of that lamentable courtyard, the silence of the land went home to one's very heart—its mystery, its greatness, the amazing reality of its concealed life. The hurt nigger moaned feebly somewhere near by, and then fetched a deep sigh that made me mend my pace away from there. I felt a hand introducing itself under my arm. 'My dear sir,' said the fellow, 'I don't want to be misunderstood, and especially by you, who will see Mr Kurtz long before I can have that pleasure. I wouldn't like him to get a false idea of my disposition. . . .'

"I let him run on, this papier-mâché Mephistopheles,[8] and it seemed to me that if I tried I could poke my forefinger through him, and would find nothing inside but a little loose dirt, maybe. He, don't you see, had been planning to be assistant-manager by and by under the present man, and I could see that the coming of that Kurtz had upset them both not a little. He talked precipitately, and I did not try to stop him. I had my shoulders against the wreck of my steamer, hauled up on the slope like a carcass of some big river animal. The smell of mud, of primeval mud, by Jove! was in my nostrils, the high stillness of primeval forest was before my eyes; there were shiny patches on the black creek. The moon had spread over everything a thin layer of silver—over the rank grass, over the mud, upon the wall of matted vegetation standing higher than the wall of a temple, over the great river I could see through a sombre gap glittering, glittering, as it flowed broadly by without a murmur. All this was great, expectant, mute, while the man jabbered about himself. I wondered whether the stillness on the face of the immensity looking at us two were meant as an appeal or as a menace. What were we who had strayed in here? Could we handle that dumb thing, or would it handle us? I felt how big, how confoundedly big, was that thing that couldn't talk and perhaps was deaf as well. What was in there? I could see a little ivory coming out from there, and I had heard Mr Kurtz was in there. I had heard enough about it too—God knows! Yet somehow it didn't bring any image with it—no more than if I had been told an angel or a fiend was in there. I believed it in the same way one of you might believe there are inhabitants in the planet Mars. I knew once a Scotch sail-maker who was certain, dead sure, there were people in Mars.[9] If you asked him for some idea how they looked and behaved, he would get shy and mutter something about 'walking on all-fours.' If you as much as smiled, he would—though a man of sixty—offer to fight you. I would not have gone so far as to fight for Kurtz, but I went for him near enough to a lie. You know I hate, detest, and can't bear a lie, not because I am straighter than the rest of us, but simply because it appals me. There is a taint of death, a flavour of mortality in lies—which is exactly what I hate and detest in the world—what I want to for-get. It makes me miserable and sick, like biting something rotten would do.

---

7. A "muff" is a foolish, stupid, feeble, or incompetent person, especially in matters of physical skill.
8. A devil, associated with the legend of Faust, who sells his soul to Mephistopheles; in exchange, the devil is to do his bidding on earth.

"Papier-mâché": method of constructing (e.g., masks, props, ornaments) using paper and glue; suggestive of fragility, pretension, illusoriness.
9. H. G. Wells's *The War of the Worlds*, about an invasion of Earth by aliens from Mars, was first serialized in 1897.

Temperament, I suppose. Well, I went near enough to it by letting the young fool there believe anything he liked to imagine as to my influence in Europe. I became in an instant as much of a pretence as the rest of the bewitched pilgrims. This simply because I had a notion it somehow would be of help to that Kurtz whom at the time I did not see—you understand. He was just a word for me. I did not see the man in the name any more than you do. Do you see him? Do you see the story? Do you see anything? It seems to me I am trying to tell you a dream—making a vain attempt, because no relation of a dream can convey the dream-sensation, that commingling of absurdity, surprise, and bewilderment in a tremor of struggling revolt, that notion of being captured by the incredible which is of the very essence of dreams. . . ."

He was silent for a while.

". . . No, it is impossible; it is impossible to convey the life-sensation of any given epoch of one's existence—that which makes its truth, its meaning—its subtle and penetrating essence. It is impossible. We live, as we dream—alone. . . ."

He paused again as if reflecting, then added:

"Of course in this you fellows see more than I could then. You see me, whom you know. . . ."

It had become so pitch dark that we listeners could hardly see one another. For a long time already he, sitting apart, had been no more to us than a voice. There was not a word from anybody. The others might have been asleep, but I was awake. I listened, I listened on the watch for the sentence, for the word, that would give me the clue to the faint uneasiness inspired by this narrative that seemed to shape itself without human lips in the heavy night-air of the river.

". . . Yes—I let him run on," Marlow began again, "and think what he pleased about the powers that were behind me. I did! And there was nothing behind me! There was nothing but that wretched, old, mangled steamboat I was leaning against, while he talked fluently about 'the necessity for every man to get on.' 'And when one comes out here, you conceive, it is not to gaze at the moon.' Mr Kurtz was a 'universal genius,' but even a genius would find it easier to work with 'adequate tools—intelligent men.' He did not make bricks—why, there was a physical impossibility in the way—as I was well aware; and if he did secretarial work for the manager, it was because 'no sensible man rejects wantonly the confidence of his superiors.' Did I see it? I saw it. What more did I want? What I really wanted was rivets, by heaven! Rivets. To get on with the work—to stop the hole. Rivets I wanted. There were cases of them down at the coast—cases—piled up—burst—split! You kicked a loose rivet at every second step in that station yard on the hillside. Rivets had rolled into the grove of death. You could fill your pockets with rivets for the trouble of stooping down—and there wasn't one rivet to be found where it was wanted. We had plates that would do, but nothing to fasten them with. And every week the messenger, a lone negro, letter-bag on shoulder and staff in hand, left our station for the coast. And several times a week a coast caravan came in with trade goods—ghastly glazed calico that made you shudder only to look at it, glass beads value about a penny a quart, confounded spotted cotton handkerchiefs. And no rivets. Three carriers could have brought all that was wanted to set that steamboat afloat.

"He was becoming confidential now, but I fancy my unresponsive attitude must have exasperated him at last, for he judged it necessary to inform me he feared neither God nor devil, let alone any mere man. I said I could see that very well, but what I wanted was a certain quantity of rivets—and rivets were what really Mr Kurtz wanted, if he had only known it. Now letters went to the coast every week. . . . 'My dear sir,' he cried, 'I write from dictation.' I demanded rivets. There was a way—for an intelligent man. He changed his manner; became very cold, and suddenly began to talk about a hippopotamus; wondered whether sleeping on board the steamer (I stuck to my salvage night and day) I wasn't disturbed. There was an old hippo that had the bad habit of getting out on the bank and roaming at night over the station grounds. The pilgrims used to turn out in a body and empty every rifle they could lay hands on at him. Some even had sat up o' nights for him. All this energy was wasted, though. 'That animal has a charmed life,' he said; 'but you can say this only of brutes in this country. No man—you apprehend me?—no man here bears a charmed life.' He stood there for a moment in the moonlight with his delicate hooked nose set a little askew, and his mica eyes glittering without a wink, then, with a curt Good-night, he strode off. I could see he was disturbed and considerably puzzled, which made me feel more hopeful than I had been for days. It was a great comfort to turn from that chap to my influential friend, the battered, twisted, ruined, tinpot steamboat. I clambered on board. She rang under my feet like an empty Huntley & Palmer biscuit-tin[1] kicked along a gutter; she was nothing so solid in make, and rather less pretty in shape, but I had expended enough hard work on her to make me love her. No influential friend would have served me better. She had given me a chance to come out a bit—to find out what I could do. No, I don't like work. I had rather laze about and think of all the fine things that can be done. I don't like work—no man does—but I like what is in the work—the chance to find yourself. Your own reality—for yourself, not for others—what no other man can ever know. They can only see the mere show, and never can tell what it really means.

"I was not surprised to see somebody sitting aft, on the deck, with his legs dangling over the mud. You see I rather chummed with the few mechanics there were in that station, whom the other pilgrims naturally despised—on account of their imperfect manners, I suppose. This was the foreman—a boiler-maker by trade—a good worker. He was a lank, bony, yellow-faced man, with big intense eyes. His aspect was worried, and his head was as bald as the palm of my hand; but his hair in falling seemed to have stuck to his chin, and had prospered in the new locality, for his beard hung down to his waist. He was a widower with six young children (he had left them in charge of a sister of his to come out there), and the passion of his life was pigeon-flying. He was an enthusiast and a connoisseur. He would rave about pigeons. After work hours he used to sometimes come over from his hut for a talk about his children and his pigeons; at work, when he had to crawl in the mud under the bottom of the steamboat, he would tie up that beard of his in a kind of white serviette[2] he brought for the purpose. It had loops to go over his ears. In the evening he

---

1. Huntley & Palmer biscuits were made in Reading, England, and exported throughout the British Empire; they came in a variety of collectible tins.
2. Table napkin (French).

could be seen squatted on the bank rinsing that wrapper in the creek with great care, then spreading it solemnly on a bush to dry.

"I slapped him on the back and shouted 'We shall have rivets!' He scrambled to his feet exclaiming 'No! Rivets!' as though he couldn't believe his ears. Then in a low voice, 'You . . . eh?' I don't know why we behaved like lunatics. I put my finger to the side of my nose and nodded mysteriously. 'Good for you!' he cried, snapped his fingers above his head, lifting one foot. I tried a jig. We capered on the iron deck. A frightful clatter came out of that hulk, and the virgin forest on the other bank of the creek sent it back in a thundering roll upon the sleeping station. It must have made some of the pilgrims sit up in their hovels. A dark figure obscured the lighted doorway of the manager's hut, vanished, then, a second or so after, the doorway itself vanished too. We stopped, and the silence driven away by the stamping of our feet flowed back again from the recesses of the land. The great wall of vegetation, an exuberant and entangled mass of trunks, branches, leaves, boughs, festoons, motionless in the moonlight, was like a rioting invasion of soundless life, a rolling wave of plants, piled up, crested, ready to topple over the creek, to sweep every little man of us out of his little existence. And it moved not. A deadened burst of mighty splashes and snorts reached us from afar, as though an ichthyosaurus[3] had been taking a bath of glitter in the great river. 'After all,' said the boiler-maker in a reasonable tone, 'why shouldn't we get the rivets?' Why not, indeed! I did not know of any reason why we shouldn't. 'They'll come in three weeks,' I said confidently.

"But they didn't. Instead of rivets there came an invasion, an infliction, a visitation. It came in sections during the next three weeks, each section headed by a donkey carrying a white man in new clothes and tan shoes, bowing from that elevation right and left to the impressed pilgrims. A quarrelsome band of footsore sulky niggers trod on the heels of the donkey; a lot of tents, camp-stools, tin boxes, white cases, brown bales would be shot down in the court-yard, and the air of mystery would deepen a little over the muddle of the station. Five such instalments came, with their absurd air of disorderly flight with the loot of innumerable outfit shops and provision stores, that, one would think, they were lugging, after a raid, into the wilderness for equitable division. It was an inextricable mess of things decent in themselves but that human folly made look like the spoils of thieving.

"This devoted band called itself the Eldorado[4] Exploring Expedition, and I believe they were sworn to secrecy. Their talk, however, was the talk of sordid buccaneers: it was reckless without hardihood, greedy without audacity, and cruel without courage; there was not an atom of foresight or of serious intention in the whole batch of them, and they did not seem aware these things are wanted for the work of the world. To tear treasure out of the bowels of the land was their desire, with no more moral purpose at the back of it than there is in burglars breaking into a safe. Who paid the expenses of the noble enterprise I don't know; but the uncle of our manager was leader of that lot.

"In exterior he resembled a butcher in a poor neighbourhood, and his eyes had a look of sleepy cunning. He carried his fat paunch with ostentation on his

---

3. An extinct prehistoric marine reptile resembling a fish or a dolphin.
4. *El Dorado* (literally, "the gilded one," Span-

ish); the mythical land of gold sought by the Spanish conquistadors in South America.

short legs, and during the time his gang infested the station spoke to no one but his nephew. You could see these two roaming about all day long with their heads close together in an everlasting confab.[5]

"I had given up worrying myself about the rivets. One's capacity for that kind of folly is more limited than you would suppose. I said Hang!—and let things slide. I had plenty of time for meditation, and now and then I would give some thought to Kurtz. I wasn't very interested in him. No. Still, I was curious to see whether this man, who had come out equipped with moral ideas of some sort, would climb to the top after all, and how he would set about his work when there."

2

"One evening as I was lying flat on the deck of my steamboat, I heard voices approaching—and there were the nephew and the uncle strolling along the bank. I laid my head on my arm again, and had nearly lost myself in a doze, when somebody said in my ear, as it were: 'I am as harmless as a little child, but I don't like to be dictated to. Am I the manager—or am I not? I was ordered to send him there. It's incredible.' . . . I became aware that the two were standing on the shore alongside the forepart of the steamboat, just below my head. I did not move; it did not occur to me to move: I was sleepy. 'It *is* unpleasant,' grunted the uncle. 'He has asked the Administration to be sent there,' said the other, 'with the idea of showing what he could do; and I was instructed accordingly. Look at the influence that man must have. Is it not frightful?' They both agreed it was frightful, then made several bizarre remarks: 'Make rain and fine weather—one man—the Council—by the nose'—bits of absurd sentences that got the better of my drowsiness, so that I had pretty near the whole of my wits about me when the uncle said, 'The climate may do away with this difficulty for you. Is he alone there?' 'Yes,' answered the manager; 'he sent his assistant down the river with a note to me in these terms: "Clear this poor devil out of the country, and don't bother sending more of that sort. I had rather be alone than have the kind of men you can dispose of with me." It was more than a year ago. Can you imagine such impudence?' 'Anything since then?' asked the other hoarsely. 'Ivory,' jerked the nephew; 'lots of it—prime sort—lots—most annoying, from him.' 'And with that?' questioned the heavy rumble. 'Invoice,' was the reply fired out, so to speak. Then silence. They had been talking about Kurtz.

"I was broad awake by this time, but, lying perfectly at ease, remained still, having no inducement to change my position. 'How did that ivory come all this way?' growled the elder man, who seemed very vexed. The other explained that it had come with a fleet of canoes in charge of an English half-caste[6] clerk Kurtz had with him; that Kurtz had apparently intended to return himself, the station being by that time bare of goods and stores, but after coming three hundred miles, had suddenly decided to go back, which he started to do alone in a small dugout with four paddlers, leaving the half-caste to continue down the river with the ivory. The two fellows there seemed astounded at anybody attempting such a thing. They were at a loss for an adequate motive. As for me, I seemed to see Kurtz for the first time. It was a distinct glimpse: the dugout, four paddling

5. Conversation.   6. Of mixed race.

savages, and the lone white man turning his back suddenly on the headquarters, on relief, on thoughts of home—perhaps; setting his face towards the depths of the wilderness, towards his empty and desolate station. I did not know the motive. Perhaps he was just simply a fine fellow who stuck to his work for its own sake. His name, you understand, had not been pronounced once. He was 'that man.' The half-caste, who, as far as I could see, had conducted a difficult trip with great prudence and pluck, was invariably alluded to as 'that scoundrel.' The 'scoundrel' had reported that the 'man' had been very ill—had recovered imperfectly. . . . The two below me moved away then a few paces, and strolled back and forth at some little distance. I heard: 'Military post—doctor—two hundred miles—quite alone now—unavoidable delays—nine months—no news—strange rumours.' They approached again, just as the manager was saying, 'No one, as far as I know, unless a species of wandering trader—a pestilential fellow, snapping ivory from the natives.' Who was it they were talking about now? I gathered in snatches that this was some man supposed to be in Kurtz's district, and of whom the manager did not approve. 'We will not be free from unfair competition till one of these fellows is hanged for an example,' he said. 'Certainly,' grunted the other; 'get him hanged! Why not? Anything—anything can be done in this country. That's what I say; nobody here, you understand, *here*, can endanger your position. And why? You stand the climate—you outlast them all. The danger is in Europe; but there before I left I took care to—' They moved off and whispered, then their voices rose again. 'The extraordinary series of delays is not my fault. I did my possible.' The fat man sighed, 'Very sad.' 'And the pestiferous absurdity of his talk,' continued the other; 'he bothered me enough when he was here. "Each station should be like a beacon on the road towards better things, a centre for trade of course, but also for humanising, improving, instructing." Conceive you[7]—that ass! And he wants to be manager! No, it's—' Here he got choked by excessive indignation, and I lifted my head the least bit. I was surprised to see how near they were—right under me. I could have spat upon their hats. They were looking on the ground, absorbed in thought. The manager was switching his leg with a slender twig: his sagacious relative lifted his head. 'You have been well since you came out this time?' he asked. The other gave a start. 'Who? I? Oh! Like a charm—like a charm. But the rest—oh, my goodness! All sick. They die so quick, too, that I haven't the time to send them out of the country—it's incredible!' 'H'm. Just so,' grunted the uncle. 'Ah! my boy, trust to this—I say, trust to this.' I saw him extend his short flipper of an arm for a gesture that took in the forest, the creek, the mud, the river—seemed to beckon with a dishonouring flourish before the sunlit face of the land a treacherous appeal to the lurking death, to the hidden evil, to the profound darkness of its heart. It was so startling that I leaped to my feet and looked back at the edge of the forest, as though I had expected an answer of some sort to that black display of confidence. You know the foolish notions that come to one sometimes. The high stillness confronted these two figures with its ominous patience, waiting for the passing away of a fantastic invasion.

"They swore aloud together—out of sheer fright, I believe—then, pretending not to know anything of my existence, turned back to the station. The sun was

---

7. "Just imagine." This phrase, like "I did my possible" (I did the best I could), above, and others throughout the novel, is a literal translation of the French spoken by Belgian traders.

low; and leaning forward side by side, they seemed to be tugging painfully uphill their two ridiculous shadows of unequal length, that trailed behind them slowly over the tall grass without bending a single blade.

"In a few days the Eldorado Expedition went into the patient wilderness, that closed upon it as the sea closes over a diver. Long afterwards the news came that all the donkeys were dead. I know nothing as to the fate of the less valuable animals.[8] They, no doubt, like the rest of us, found what they deserved. I did not inquire. I was then rather excited at the prospect of meeting Kurtz very soon. When I say very soon I mean it comparatively. It was just two months from the day we left the creek when we came to the bank below Kurtz's station.

"Going up that river was like travelling back to the earliest beginnings of the world, when vegetation rioted on the earth and the big trees were kings. An empty stream, a great silence, an impenetrable forest. The air was warm, thick, heavy, sluggish. There was no joy in the brilliance of sunshine. The long stretches of the waterway ran on, deserted, into the gloom of overshadowed distances. On silvery sandbanks hippos and alligators sunned themselves side by side. The broadening waters flowed through a mob of wooded islands; you lost your way on that river as you would in a desert, and butted all day long against shoals, trying to find the channel, till you thought yourself bewitched and cut off for ever from everything you had known once—somewhere—far away—in another existence perhaps. There were moments when one's past came back to one, as it will sometimes when you have not a moment to spare to yourself; but it came in the shape of an unrestful and noisy dream, remembered with wonder amongst the overwhelming realities of this strange world of plants, and water, and silence. And this stillness of life did not in the least resemble a peace. It was the stillness of an implacable force brooding over an inscrutable intention. It looked at you with a vengeful aspect. I got used to it afterwards; I did not see it any more; I had no time. I had to keep guessing at the channel; I had to discern, mostly by inspiration, the signs of hidden banks; I watched for sunken stones; I was learning to clap my teeth smartly before my heart flew out, when I shaved by a fluke some infernal sly old snag[9] that would have ripped the life out of the tin-pot steamboat and drowned all the pilgrims; I had to keep a look-out for the signs of dead wood we could cut up in the night for next day's steaming. When you have to attend to things of that sort, to the mere incidents of the surface, the reality—the reality, I tell you—fades. The inner truth is hidden—luckily, luckily. But I felt it all the same; I felt often its mysterious stillness watching me at my monkey tricks, just as it watches you fellows performing on your respective tight-ropes for—what is it? half a crown[1] a tumble—"

"Try to be civil, Marlow," growled a voice, and I knew there was at least one listener awake besides myself.

"I beg your pardon. I forgot the heartache which makes up the rest of the price. And indeed what does the price matter, if the trick be well done? You do your tricks very well. And I didn't do badly either, since I managed not to sink that steamboat on my first trip. It's a wonder to me yet. Imagine a blindfolded

8. I.e., humans.
9. A large branch or tree trunk embedded in the river bottom with one end pointing up.
1. British denomination of coin, equal to 2 shillings and 6 pence, or an eighth of a pound. Not much money: at the time, the value of a London cab fare or a generous tip.

man set to drive a van over a bad road. I sweated and shivered over that business considerably, I can tell you. After all, for a seaman, to scrape the bottom of the thing that's supposed to float all the time under his care is the unpardonable sin. No one may know of it, but you never forget the thump—eh? A blow on the very heart. You remember it, you dream of it, you wake up at night and think of it—years after—and go hot and cold all over. I don't pretend to say that steamboat floated all the time. More than once she had to wade for a bit, with twenty cannibals splashing around and pushing. We had enlisted some of these chaps on the way for a crew. Fine fellows—cannibals—in their place. They were men one could work with, and I am grateful to them. And, after all, they did not eat each other before my face: they had brought along a provision of hippo-meat which went rotten, and made the mystery of the wilderness stink in my nostrils. Phoo! I can sniff it now. I had the manager on board and three or four pilgrims with their staves—all complete. Sometimes we came upon a station close by the bank, clinging to the skirts of the unknown, and the white men rushing out of a tumble-down hovel, with great gestures of joy and surprise and welcome, seemed very strange—had the appearance of being held there captive by a spell. The word 'ivory' would ring in the air for a while—and on we went again into the silence, along empty reaches, round the still bends, between the high walls of our winding way, reverberating in hollow claps the ponderous beat of the stern-wheel.[2] Trees, trees, millions of trees, massive, immense, running up high; and at their foot, hugging the bank against the stream, crept the little begrimed steamboat, like a sluggish beetle crawling on the floor of a lofty portico. It made you feel very small, very lost, and yet it was not altogether depressing, that feeling. After all, if you were small, the grimy beetle crawled on—which was just what you wanted it to do. Where the pilgrims imagined it crawled to I don't know. To some place where they expected to get something, I bet! For me it crawled towards Kurtz—exclusively; but when the steam-pipes started leaking we crawled very slow. The reaches opened before us and closed behind, as if the forest had stepped leisurely across the water to bar the way for our return. We penetrated deeper and deeper into the heart of darkness. It was very quiet there. At night sometimes the roll of drums behind the curtain of trees would run up the river and remain sustained faintly, as if hovering in the air high over our heads, till the first break of day. Whether it meant war, peace, or prayer we could not tell. The dawns were heralded by the descent of a chill stillness; the woodcutters slept, their fires burned low; the snapping of a twig would make you start. We were wanderers on a prehistoric earth, on an earth that wore the aspect of an unknown planet. We could have fancied ourselves the first of men taking possession of an accursed inheritance, to be subdued at the cost of profound anguish and of excessive toil. But suddenly, as we struggled round a bend, there would be a glimpse of rush walls, of peaked grass-roofs, a burst of yells, a whirl of black limbs, a mass of hands clapping, of feet stamping, of bodies swaying, of eyes rolling, under the droop of heavy and motionless foliage. The steamer toiled along slowly on the edge of a black and incomprehensible frenzy. The prehistoric man was cursing us, praying to us, welcoming us—who could tell? We were cut off from the

2. The paddle wheel at the rear of the boat; the main source of propulsion on a steamboat.

comprehension of our surroundings; we glided past like phantoms, wondering and secretly appalled, as sane men would be before an enthusiastic outbreak in a madhouse. We could not understand because we were too far and could not remember, because we were travelling in the night of first ages, of those ages that are gone, leaving hardly a sign—and no memories.

"The earth seemed unearthly. We are accustomed to look upon the shackled form of a conquered monster, but there—there you could look at a thing monstrous and free. It was unearthly, and the men were—No, they were not inhuman. Well, you know, that was the worst of it—this suspicion of their not being inhuman. It would come slowly to one. They howled and leaped, and spun, and made horrid faces; but what thrilled you was just the thought of their humanity—like yours—the thought of your remote kinship with this wild and passionate uproar. Ugly. Yes, it was ugly enough; but if you were man enough you would admit to yourself that there was in you just the faintest trace of a response to the terrible frankness of that noise, a dim suspicion of there being a meaning in it which you—you so remote from the night of first ages—could comprehend. And why not? The mind of man is capable of anything—because everything is in it, all the past as well as all the future. What was there after all? Joy, fear, sorrow, devotion, valour, rage—who can tell?—but truth—truth stripped of its cloak of time. Let the fool gape and shudder—the man knows, and can look on without a wink. But he must at least be as much of a man as these on the shore. He must meet that truth with his own true stuff—with his own inborn strength. Principles? Principles won't do. Acquisitions, clothes, pretty rags—rags that would fly off at the first good shake. No; you want a deliberate belief. An appeal to me in this fiendish row—is there? Very well; I hear; I admit, but I have a voice too, and for good or evil mine is the speech that cannot be silenced. Of course, a fool, what with sheer fright and fine sentiments, is always safe. Who's that grunting? You wonder I didn't go ashore for a howl and a dance? Well, no—I didn't. Fine sentiments, you say? Fine sentiments be hanged! I had no time. I had to mess about with white-lead[3] and strips of woollen blanket helping to put bandages on those leaky steam-pipes—I tell you. I had to watch the steering, and circumvent those snags, and get the tin-pot along by hook or by crook. There was surface-truth enough in these things to save a wiser man. And between whiles I had to look after the savage who was fireman. He was an improved specimen; he could fire up a vertical boiler.[4] He was there below me, and, upon my word, to look at him was as edifying as seeing a dog in a parody of breeches and a feather hat, walking on his hind legs. A few months of training had done for that really fine chap. He squinted at the steam-gauge and at the water-gauge with an evident effort of intrepidity—and he had filed teeth too, the poor devil, and the wool of his pate shaved into queer patterns, and three ornamental scars on each of his cheeks. He ought to have been clapping his hands and stamping his feet on the bank, instead of which he was hard at work, a thrall to strange witchcraft, full of improving knowledge. He was useful because he had been instructed; and what he knew was this—that should the water in that transparent thing disappear, the evil spirit inside the boiler would get angry through the greatness of

---

3. Lead compound often used in white paint for caulking seams and waterproofing timber.

4. A simple and easily fired narrow boiler.

his thirst, and take a terrible vengeance. So he sweated and fired up and watched the glass fearfully (with an impromptu charm, made of rags, tied to his arm, and a piece of polished bone, as big as a watch, stuck flatways through his lower lip), while the wooded banks slipped past us slowly, the short noise was left behind, the interminable miles of silence—and we crept on, towards Kurtz. But the snags were thick, the water was treacherous and shallow, the boiler seemed indeed to have a sulky devil in it, and thus neither that fireman nor I had any time to peer into our creepy thoughts.

"Some fifty miles below the Inner Station we came upon a hut of reeds, an inclined and melancholy pole, with the unrecognisable tatters of what had been a flag of some sort flying from it, and a neatly stacked wood-pile. This was unexpected. We came to the bank, and on the stack of firewood found a flat piece of board with some faded pencil-writing on it. When deciphered it said: 'Wood for you. Hurry up. Approach cautiously.' There was a signature, but it was illegible—not Kurtz—a much longer word. Hurry up. Where? Up the river? 'Approach cautiously.' We had not done so. But the warning could not have been meant for the place where it could be only found after approach. Something was wrong above. But what—and how much? That was the question. We commented adversely upon the imbecility of that telegraphic style.[5] The bush around said nothing, and would not let us look very far, either. A torn curtain of red twill hung in the doorway of the hut, and flapped sadly in our faces. The dwelling was dismantled; but we could see a white man had lived there not very long ago. There remained a rude table—a plank on two posts; a heap of rubbish reposed in a dark corner, and by the door I picked up a book. It had lost its covers, and the pages had been thumbed into a state of extremely dirty softness; but the back had been lovingly stitched afresh with white cotton thread, which looked clean yet. It was an extraordinary find. Its title was, *An Inquiry into some Points of Seamanship*, by a man Towser, Towson—some such name—Master in His Majesty's Navy.[6] The matter looked dreary reading enough, with illustrative diagrams and repulsive tables of figures, and the copy was sixty years old. I handled this amazing antiquity with the greatest possible tenderness, lest it should dissolve in my hands. Within, Towson or Towser was inquiring earnestly into the breaking strain of ships' chains and tackle, and other such matters. Not a very enthralling book; but at the first glance you could see there a singleness of intention, an honest concern for the right way of going to work, which made these humble pages, thought out so many years ago, luminous with another than a professional light. The simple old sailor, with his talk of chains and purchases,[7] made me forget the jungle and the pilgrims in a delicious sensation of having come upon something unmistakably real. Such a book being there was wonderful enough; but still more astounding were the notes pencilled in the margin, and plainly referring to the text. I couldn't believe my eyes! They were in cipher! Yes, it looked like cipher. Fancy a man lugging with him a book of that description into this nowhere and studying it—and making notes—in cipher at that! It was an extravagant mystery.

---

5. Using as few words as possible, as in a telegram.
6. I.e., the British Navy.
7. Nautical terms. "Chains": contrivances for fastening ropes supporting the mast to the deck and the sides of a ship. "Purchases": devices for applying or increasing force: pulleys, windlasses, etc.

"I had been dimly aware for some time of a worrying noise, and when I lifted my eyes I saw the wood-pile was gone, and the manager, aided by all the pilgrims, was shouting at me from the river-side. I slipped the book into my pocket. I assure you to leave off reading was like tearing myself away from the shelter of an old and solid friendship.

"I started the lame engine ahead. 'It must be this miserable trader—this intruder,' exclaimed the manager, looking back malevolently at the place we had left. 'He must be English,' I said. 'It will not save him from getting into trouble if he is not careful,' muttered the manager darkly. I observed with assumed innocence that no man was safe from trouble in this world.

"The current was more rapid now, the steamer seemed at her last gasp, the stern-wheel flopped languidly, and I caught myself listening on tiptoe for the next beat of the float,[8] for in sober truth I expected the wretched thing to give up every moment. It was like watching the last flickers of a life. But still we crawled. Sometimes I would pick out a tree a little way head to measure our progress towards Kurtz by, but I lost it invariably before we got abreast. To keep the eyes so long on one thing was too much for human patience. The manager displayed a beautiful resignation. I fretted and fumed and took to arguing with myself whether or no I would talk openly with Kurtz; but before I could come to any conclusion it occurred to me that my speech or my silence, indeed any action of mine, would be a mere futility. What did it matter what any one knew or ignored? What did it matter who was manager? One gets sometimes such a flash of insight. The essentials of this affair lay deep under the surface, beyond my reach, and beyond my power of meddling.

"Towards the evening of the second day we judged ourselves about eight miles from Kurtz's station. I wanted to push on; but the manager looked grave, and told me the navigation up there was so dangerous that it would be advisable, the sun being very low already, to wait where we were till next morning. Moreover, he pointed out that if the warning to approach cautiously were to be followed, we must approach in daylight—not at dusk, or in the dark. This was sensible enough. Eight miles meant nearly three hours' steaming for us, and I could also see suspicious ripples at the upper end of the reach. Nevertheless, I was annoyed beyond expression at the delay, and most unreasonably too, since one night more could not matter much after so many months. As we had plenty of wood, and caution was the word, I brought up in the middle of the stream. The reach was narrow, straight, with high sides like a railway cutting. The dusk came gliding into it long before the sun had set. The current ran smooth and swift, but a dumb immobility sat on the banks. The living trees, lashed together by the creepers and every living bush of the undergrowth, might have been changed into stone, even to the slenderest twig, to the lightest leaf. It was not sleep—it seemed unnatural, like a state of trance. Not the faintest sound of any kind could be heard. You looked on amazed, and began to suspect yourself of being deaf—then the night came suddenly, and struck you blind as well. About three in the morning some large fish leaped, and the loud splash made me jump as though a gun had been fired. When the sun rose there was a white fog, very warm and clammy, and more blinding than the night. It did not shift or drive; it was just there, standing all round you like something

8. The sound of the paddle ("paddle float") as it hits the water.

solid. At eight or nine, perhaps, it lifted as a shutter lifts. We had a glimpse of the towering multitude of trees, of the immense matted jungle, with the blazing little ball of the sun hanging over it—all perfectly still—and then the white shutter came down again, smoothly, as if sliding in greased grooves. I ordered the chain, which we had begun to heave in, to be paid out again. Before it stopped running with a muffled rattle, a cry, a very loud cry, as of infinite desolation, soared slowly in the opaque air. It ceased. A complaining clamour, modulated in savage discords, filled our ears. The sheer unexpectedness of it made my hair stir under my cap. I don't know how it struck the others: to me it seemed as though the mist itself had screamed, so suddenly, and apparently from all sides at once, did this tumultuous and mournful uproar arise. It culminated in a hurried outbreak of almost intolerably excessive shrieking, which stopped short, leaving us stiffened in a variety of silly attitudes, and obstinately listening to the nearly as appalling and excessive silence. 'Good God! What is the meaning—?' stammered at my elbow one of the pilgrims—a little fat man, with sandy hair and red whiskers, who wore side-spring boots, and pink pyjamas tucked into his socks. Two others remained open-mouthed a whole minute, then dashed into the little cabin, to rush out incontinently and stand darting scared glances, with Winchesters[9] at 'ready' in their hands. What we could see was just the steamer we were on, her outlines blurred as though she had been on the point of dissolving, and a misty strip of water, perhaps two feet broad, around her—and that was all. The rest of the world was nowhere, as far as our eyes and ears were concerned. Just nowhere. Gone, disappeared; swept off without leaving a whisper or a shadow behind.

"I went forward, and ordered the chain to be hauled in short, so as to be ready to trip the anchor and move the steamboat at once if necessary. 'Will they attack?' whispered an awed voice. 'We will all be butchered in this fog,' murmured another. The faces twitched with the strain, the hands trembled slightly, the eyes forgot to wink. It was very curious to see the contrast of expressions of the white men and of the black fellows of our crew, who were as much strangers to that part of the river as we, though their homes were only eight hundred miles away. The whites, of course greatly discomposed, had besides a curious look of being painfully shocked by such an outrageous row. The others had an alert, naturally interested expression; but their faces were essentially quiet, even those of the one or two who grinned as they hauled at the chain. Several exchanged short, grunting phrases, which seemed to settle the matter to their satisfaction. Their headman, a young, broad-chested black, severely draped in dark-blue fringed cloths, with fierce nostrils and his hair all done up artfully in oily ringlets, stood near me. 'Aha!' I said, just for good fellowship's sake. 'Catch 'im,' he snapped, with a bloodshot widening of his eyes and a flash of sharp teeth—'catch 'im. Give 'im to us.' 'To you, eh?' I asked; 'what would you do with them?' 'Eat 'im!' he said curtly, and, leaning his elbow on the rail, looked out into the fog in a dignified and profoundly pensive attitude. I would no doubt have been properly horrified, had it not occurred to me that he and his chaps must be very hungry: that they must have been growing increasingly hungry for at least this month past. They had been engaged for six months (I don't think a

9. Lever-action repeating rifles.

single one of them had any clear idea of time, as we at the end of countless ages have. They still belonged to the beginnings of time—had no inherited experience to teach them, as it were), and of course, as long as there was a piece of paper written over in accordance with some farcical law or other made down the river, it didn't enter anybody's head to trouble how they would live. Certainly they had brought with them some rotten hippo-meat, which couldn't have lasted very long, anyway, even if the pilgrims hadn't, in the midst of a shocking hullabaloo, thrown a considerable quantity of it overboard. It looked like a high-handed proceeding; but it was really a case of legitimate self-defence. You can't breathe dead hippo waking, sleeping, and eating, and at the same time keep your precarious grip on existence. Besides that, they had given them every week three pieces of brass wire, each about nine inches long; and the theory was they were to buy their provisions with that currency in river-side villages. You can see how *that* worked. There were either no villages, or the people were hostile, or the director, who like the rest of us fed out of tins, with an occasional old he-goat thrown in, didn't want to stop the steamer for some more or less recondite reasons. So, unless they swallowed the wire itself, or made loops of it to snare the fishes with, I don't see what good their extravagant salary could be to them. I must say it was paid with a regularity worthy of a large and honourable trading company. For the rest, the only thing to eat—though it didn't look eatable in the least—I saw in their possession was a few lumps of some stuff like half-cooked dough, of a dirty lavender colour, they kept wrapped in leaves, and now and then swallowed a piece of, but so small that it seemed done more for the look of the thing than for any serious purpose of sustenance. Why in the name of all the gnawing devils of hunger they didn't go for us—they were thirty to five—and have a good tuck-in for once, amazes me now when I think of it. They were big powerful men, with not much capacity to weigh the consequences, with courage, with strength, even yet, though their skins were no longer glossy and their muscles no longer hard. And I saw that something restraining, one of those human secrets that baffle probability, had come into play there. I looked at them with a swift quickening of interest—not because it occurred to me I might be eaten by them before very long, though I own to you that just then I perceived—in a new light, as it were—how unwholesome the pilgrims looked, and I hoped, yes, I positively hoped, that my aspect was not so—what shall I say?—so—unappetising: a touch of fantastic vanity which fitted well with the dream-sensation that pervaded all my days at that time. Perhaps I had a little fever too. One can't live with one's finger everlastingly on one's pulse. I had often 'a little fever,' or a little touch of other things—the playful paw-strokes of the wilderness, the preliminary trifling before the more serious onslaught which came in due course. Yes; I looked at them as you would on any human being, with a curiosity of their impulses, motives, capacities, weaknesses, when brought to the test of an inexorable physical necessity. Restraint! What possible restraint? Was it superstition, disgust, patience, fear—or some kind of primitive honour? No fear can stand up to hunger, no patience can wear it out, disgust simply does not exist where hunger is; and as to superstition, beliefs, and what you may call principles, they are less than chaff in a breeze. Don't you know the devilry of lingering starvation, its exasperating torment, its black thoughts, its sombre and brooding ferocity? Well, I do. It takes a man all his inborn strength to fight hunger properly. It's really easier to face bereavement, dishonour, and the perdition of one's soul—than this kind of prolonged hunger. Sad, but true. And these chaps too had no earthly reason for any kind of scruple. Restraint! I would just as soon have expected restraint from a hyena prowling amongst the corpses of a battlefield. But there was the fact facing me—the fact dazzling, to be seen, like the foam on the depths of the sea, like a ripple on an unfathomable enigma, a mystery greater—when I thought of it—than the curious, inexplicable note of desperate grief in this savage clamour that had swept by us on the river-bank, behind the blind whiteness of the fog.

"Two pilgrims were quarrelling in hurried whispers as to which bank. 'Left.' 'No, no; how can you? Right, right, of course.' 'It is very serious,' said the manager's voice behind me; 'I would be desolated if anything should happen to Mr. Kurtz before we came up.' I looked at him, and had not the slightest doubt he was sincere. He was just the kind of man who would wish to preserve appearances. That was his restraint. But when he muttered something about going on at once, I did not even take the trouble to answer him. I knew, and he knew, that it was impossible. Were we to let go our hold of the bottom, we would be absolutely in the air—in space. We wouldn't be able to tell where we were going to—whether up or down stream, or across—till we fetched against one bank or the other—and then we wouldn't know at first which it was. Of course I made no move. I had no mind for a smashup. You couldn't imagine a more deadly place for a shipwreck. Whether drowned at once or not, we were sure to perish speedily in one way or another. 'I authorise you to take all the risks,' he said, after a short silence. 'I refuse to take any,' I said shortly; which was just the answer he expected, though its tone might have surprised him. 'Well, I must defer to your judgment. You are captain,' he said, with marked civility. I turned my shoulder to him in sign of my appreciation, and looked into the fog. How long would it last? It was the most hopeless look-out. The approach to this Kurtz grubbing for ivory in the wretched bush was beset by as many dangers as though he had been an enchanted princess sleeping in a fabulous castle. 'Will they attack, do you think?' asked the manager, in a confidential tone.

"I did not think they would attack, for several obvious reasons. The thick fog was one. If they left the bank in their canoes they would get lost in it, as we would be if we attempted to move. Still, I had also judged the jungle of both banks quite impenetrable—and yet eyes were in it, eyes that had seen us. The river-side bushes were certainly very thick; but the undergrowth behind was evidently penetrable. However, during the short lift I had seen no canoes anywhere in the reach—certainly not abreast of the steamer. But what made the idea of attack inconceivable to me was the nature of the noise—of the cries we had heard. They had not the fierce character boding of immediate hostile intention. Unexpected, wild, and violent as they had been, they had given me an irresistible impression of sorrow. The glimpse of the steamboat had for some reason filled those savages with unrestrained grief. The danger, if any, I expounded, was from our proximity to a great human passion let loose. Even extreme grief may ultimately vent itself in violence—but more generally takes the form of apathy. . . .

"You should have seen the pilgrims stare! They had no heart to grin, or even to revile me; but I believe they thought me gone mad—with fright, maybe. I delivered a regular lecture. My dear boys, it was no good bothering. Keep a look-out? Well, you may guess I watched the fog for the signs of lifting as a cat watches a mouse; but for anything else our eyes were of no more use to us than if we had been buried miles deep in a heap of cottonwool. It felt like it too—choking, warm, stifling. Besides, all I said, though it sounded extravagant, was absolutely true to fact. What we afterwards alluded to as an attack was really an attempt at repulse. The action was very far from being aggressive—it was not even defensive, in the usual sense: it was undertaken under the stress of desperation, and in its essence was purely protective.

"It developed itself, I should say, two hours after the fog lifted, and its commencement was at a spot, roughly speaking, about a mile and a half below Kurtz's station. We had just floundered and flopped round a bend, when I saw an islet, a mere grassy hummock of bright green, in the middle of the stream. It was the only thing of the kind; but as we opened the reach more, I perceived it was the head of a long sandbank, or rather of a chain of shallow patches stretching down the middle of the river. They were discoloured, just awash, and the whole lot was seen just under the water, exactly as a man's backbone is seen running down the middle of his back under the skin. Now, as far as I did see, I could go to the right or to the left of this. I didn't know either channel, of course. The banks looked pretty well alike, the depth appeared the same; but as I had been informed the station was on the west side, I naturally headed for the western passage.

"No sooner had we fairly entered it than I became aware it was much narrower than I had supposed. To the left of us there was the long uninterrupted shoal, and to the right a high steep bank heavily overgrown with bushes. Above the bush the trees stood in serried ranks. The twigs overhung the current thickly, and from distance to distance a large limb of some tree projected rigidly over the stream. It was then well on in the afternoon, the face of the forest was gloomy, and a broad strip of shadow had already fallen on the water. In this shadow we steamed up—very slowly, as you may imagine. I sheered her well inshore—the water being deepest near the bank, as the sounding-pole[1] informed me.

"One of my hungry and forbearing friends was sounding in the bows just below me. This steamboat was exactly like a decked scow.[2] On the deck there were two little teak-wood houses, with doors and windows. The boiler was in the fore-end, and the machinery right astern. Over the whole there was a light roof, supported on stanchions. The funnel projected through that roof, and in front of the funnel a small cabin built of light planks served for a pilot-house. It contained a couch, two camp-stools, a loaded Martini-Henry[3] leaning in one corner, a tiny table, and the steering-wheel. It had a wide door in front and a broad shutter at each side. All these were always thrown open, of course. I spent my days perched up there on the extreme fore-end of that roof, before the door. At night I slept, or tried to, on the couch. An athletic black belonging to some coast tribe, and educated by my poor predecessor, was the helmsman. He sported a pair of brass earrings, wore a blue cloth wrapper from the waist to the

1. A pole with measurements, stuck in the water until it hits bottom, to determine the depth of a shallow body of water. "Sheered her well inshore": i.e., steered so as to be going upriver while close to the bank.

2. A large, flat-bottomed boat for cargo; in this case, with the addition of a deck.

3. A lever-action rifle taking an especially powerful charge; standard British service weapon of the time.

ankles, and thought all the world of himself. He was the most unstable kind of fool I had ever seen. He steered with no end of a swagger while you were by; but if he lost sight of you, he became instantly the prey of an abject funk, and would let that cripple of a steamboat get the upper hand of him in a minute.

"I was looking down at the sounding-pole, and feeling much annoyed to see at each try a little more of it stick out of that river, when I saw my poleman give up the business suddenly, and stretch himself flat on the deck, without even taking the trouble to haul his pole in. He kept hold on it though, and it trailed in the water. At the same time the fireman, whom I could also see below me, sat down abruptly before his furnace and ducked his head. I was amazed. Then I had to look at the river mighty quick, because there was a snag in the fairway. Sticks, little sticks, were flying about—thick; they were whizzing before my nose, dropping below me, striking behind me against my pilot-house. All this time the river, the shore, the woods, were very quiet—perfectly quiet. I could only hear the heavy splashing thump of the stern-wheel and the patter of these things. We cleared the snag clumsily. Arrows, by Jove! We were being shot at! I stepped in quickly to close the shutter on the land-side. That fool-helmsman, his hands on the spokes, was lifting his knees high, stamping his feet, champing his mouth, like a reined-in horse. Confound him! And we were staggering within ten feet of the bank. I had to lean right out to swing the heavy shutter, and I saw a face amongst the leaves on the level with my own, looking at me very fierce and steady; and then suddenly, as though a veil had been removed from my eyes, I made out, deep in the tangled gloom, naked breasts, arms, legs, glaring eyes— the bush was swarming with human limbs in movement, glistening, of bronze colour. The twigs shook, swayed, and rustled, the arrows flew out of them, and then the shutter came to. 'Steer her straight,' I said to the helmsman. He held his head rigid, face forward; but his eyes rolled, he kept on lifting and setting down his feet gently, his mouth foamed a little. 'Keep quiet!' I said in a fury. I might just as well have ordered a tree not to sway in the wind. I darted out. Below me there was a great scuffle of feet on the iron deck; confused exclamations; a voice screamed, 'Can you turn back?' I caught sight of a V-shaped ripple on the water ahead. What? Another snag! A fusillade[4] burst out under my feet. The pilgrims had opened with their Winchesters, and were simply squirting lead into that bush. A deuce of a lot of smoke came up and drove slowly forward. I swore at it. Now I couldn't see the ripple or the snag either. I stood in the doorway, peering, and the arrows came in swarms. They might have been poisoned, but they looked as though they wouldn't kill a cat. The bush began to howl. Our wood-cutters raised a warlike whoop; the report of a rifle just at my back deafened me. I glanced over my shoulder, and the pilot-house was yet full of noise and smoke when I made a dash at the wheel. The fool-nigger had dropped everything, to throw the shutter open and let off that Martini-Henry. He stood before the wide opening, glaring, and I yelled at him to come back, while I straightened the sudden twist out of that steamboat. There was no room to turn even if I had wanted to, the snag was somewhere very near ahead in that confounded smoke, there was no time to lose, so I just crowded her into the bank— right into the bank, where I knew the water was deep.

4. The simultaneous discharge of many firearms.

"We tore slowly along the overhanging bushes in a whirl of broken twigs and flying leaves. The fusillade below stopped short, as I had foreseen it would when the squirts got empty. I threw my head back to a glinting whizz that traversed the pilot-house, in at one shutter-hole and out at the other. Looking past that mad helmsman, who was shaking the empty rifle and yelling at the shore, I saw vague forms of men running bent double, leaping, gliding, distinct, incomplete, evanescent. Something big appeared in the air before the shutter, the rifle went overboard, and the man stepped back swiftly, looked at me over his shoulder in an extraordinary, profound, familiar manner, and fell upon my feet. The side of his head hit the wheel twice, and the end of what appeared a long cane clattered round and knocked over a little camp-stool. It looked as though after wrenching that thing from somebody ashore he had lost his balance in the effort. The thin smoke had blown away, we were clear of the snag, and looking ahead I could see that in another hundred yards or so I would be free to sheer off, away from the bank; but my feet felt so very warm and wet that I had to look down. The man had rolled on his back and stared straight up at me; both his hands clutched that cane. It was the shaft of a spear that, either thrown or lunged through the opening, had caught him in the side just below the ribs; the blade had gone in out of sight, after making a frightful gash; my shoes were full; a pool of blood lay very still, gleaming dark-red under the wheel; his eyes shone with an amazing lustre. The fusillade burst out again. He looked at me anxiously, gripping the spear like something precious, with an air of being afraid I would try to take it away from him. I had to make an effort to free my eyes from his gaze and attend to the steering. With one hand I felt above my head for the line of the steam whistle, and jerked out screech after screech hurriedly. The tumult of angry and warlike yells was checked instantly, and then from the depths of the woods went out such a tremulous and prolonged wail of mournful fear and utter despair as may be imagined to follow the flight of the last hope from the earth. There was a great commotion in the bush; the shower of arrows stopped, a few dropping shots rang out sharply—then silence, in which the languid beat of the stern-wheel came plainly to my ears. I put the helm hard a-starboard at the moment when the pilgrim in pink pyjamas, very hot and agitated, appeared in the doorway. 'The manager sends me—' he began in an official tone, and stopped short. 'Good God!' he said, glaring at the wounded man.

"We two whites stood over him, and his lustrous and inquiring glance enveloped us both. I declare it looked as though he would presently put to us some question in an understandable language; but he died without uttering a sound, without moving a limb, without twitching a muscle. Only in the very last moment, as though in response to some sign we could not see, to some whisper we could not hear, he frowned heavily, and that frown gave to his black death-mask an inconceivably sombre, brooding, and menacing expression. The lustre of inquiring glance faded swiftly into vacant glassiness. 'Can you steer?' I asked the agent eagerly. He looked very dubious; but I made a grab at his arm, and he understood at once I meant him to steer whether or no. To tell you the truth, I was morbidly anxious to change my shoes and socks. 'He is dead,' murmured the fellow, immensely impressed. 'No doubt about it,' said I, tugging like mad at the shoelaces. 'And by the way, I suppose Mr Kurtz is dead as well by this time.'

"For the moment that was the dominant thought. There was a sense of extreme disappointment, as though I had found out I had been striving after something altogether without a substance. I couldn't have been more disgusted if I had travelled all this way for the sole purpose of talking with Mr Kurtz. Talking with . . . I flung one shoe overboard, and became aware that that was exactly what I had been looking forward to—a talk with Kurtz. I made the strange discovery that I had never imagined him as doing, you know, but as discoursing. I didn't say to myself, 'Now I will never see him,' or 'Now I will never shake him by the hand,' but, 'Now I will never hear him.' The man presented himself as a voice. Not of course that I did not connect him with some sort of action. Hadn't I been told in all the tones of jealousy and admiration that he had collected, bartered, swindled, or stolen more ivory than all the other agents together? That was not the point. The point was in his being a gifted creature, and that of all his gifts the one that stood out pre-eminently, that carried with it a sense of real presence, was his ability to talk, his words— the gift of expression, the bewildering, the illuminating, the most exalted and the most contemptible, the pulsating stream of light, or the deceitful flow from the heart of an impenetrable darkness.

"The other shoe went flying unto the devil-god of that river. I thought, By Jove! it's all over. We are too late; he has vanished—the gift has vanished, by means of some spear, arrow, or club. I will never hear that chap speak after all—and my sorrow had a startling extravagance of emotion, even such as I had noticed in the howling sorrow of these savages in the bush. I couldn't have felt more of lonely desolation somehow, had I been robbed of a belief or had missed my destiny in life. . . . Why do you sigh in this beastly way, somebody? Absurd? Well, absurd. Good Lord! mustn't a man ever—Here, give me some tobacco." . . .

There was a pause of profound stillness, then a match flared, and Marlow's lean face appeared, worn, hollow, with downward folds and dropped eyelids, with an aspect of concentrated attention; and as he took vigorous draws at his pipe, it seemed to retreat and advance out of the night in the regular flicker of the tiny flame. The match went out.

"Absurd!" he cried. "This is the worst of trying to tell . . . Here you all are, each moored with two good addresses, like a hulk with two anchors, a butcher round one corner, a policeman round another, excellent appetites, and temperature normal—you hear—normal from year's end to year's end. And you say, Absurd! Absurd be—exploded! Absurd! My dear boys, what can you expect from a man who out of sheer nervousness had just flung overboard a pair of new shoes? Now I think of it, it is amazing I did not shed tears. I am, upon the whole, proud of my fortitude. I was cut to the quick at the idea of having lost the inestimable privilege of listening to the gifted Kurtz. Of course I was wrong. The privilege was waiting for me. Oh yes, I heard more than enough. And I was right, too. A voice. He was very little more than a voice. And I heard—him— it—this voice—other voices—all of them were so little more than voices—and the memory of that time itself lingers around me, impalpable, like a dying vibration of one immense jabber, silly, atrocious, sordid, savage, or simply mean, without any kind of sense. Voices, voices—even the girl herself—now—"

He was silent for a long time.

"I laid the ghost of his gifts at last with a lie," he began suddenly. "Girl! What? Did I mention a girl? Oh, she is out of it—completely. They—the women I mean—are out of it—should be out of it. We must help them to stay in that beautiful world of their own, lest ours gets worse. Oh, she had to be out of it. You should have heard the disinterred body of Mr Kurtz saying, 'My Intended.' You would have perceived directly then how completely she was out of it. And the lofty frontal bone of Mr Kurtz! They say the hair goes on growing sometimes, but this—ah—specimen was impressively bald. The wilderness had patted him on the head, and, behold, it was like a ball—an ivory ball; it had caressed him, and—lo!—he had withered; it had taken him, loved him, embraced him, got into his veins, consumed his flesh, and sealed his soul to its own by the inconceivable ceremonies of some devilish initiation. He was its spoiled and pampered favourite. Ivory? I should think so. Heaps of it, stacks of it. The old mud shanty was bursting with it. You would think there was not a single tusk left either above or below the ground in the whole country. 'Mostly fossil,' the manager had remarked disparagingly. It was no more fossil than I am; but they call it fossil when it is dug up. It appears these niggers do bury the tusks sometimes—but evidently they couldn't bury this parcel deep enough to save the gifted Mr Kurtz from his fate. We filled the steamboat with it, and had to pile a lot on the deck. Thus he could see and enjoy as long as he could see, because the appreciation of this favour had remained with him to the last. You should have heard him say, 'My ivory.' Oh yes, I heard him. 'My Intended, my ivory, my station, my river, my—' everything belonged to him. It made me hold my breath in expectation of hearing the wilderness burst into a prodigious peal of laughter that would shake the fixed stars in their places. Everything belonged to him—but that was a trifle. The thing was to know what he belonged to, how many powers of darkness claimed him for their own. That was the reflection that made you creepy all over. It was impossible—it was not good for one either—trying to imagine. He had taken a high seat amongst the devils of the land—I mean literally. You can't understand. How could you?—with solid pavement under your feet, surrounded by kind neighbours ready to cheer you or to fall on you, stepping delicately between the butcher and the policeman, in the holy terror of scandal and gallows and lunatic asylums—how can you imagine what particular region of the first ages a man's untrammelled feet may take him into by the way of solitude—utter solitude without a policeman—by the way of silence—utter silence, where no warning voice of a kind neighbour can be heard whispering of public opinion? These little things make all the great difference. When they are gone you must fall back upon your own innate strength, upon your own capacity for faithfulness. Of course you may be too much of a fool to go wrong—too dull even to know you are being assaulted by the powers of darkness. I take it, no fool ever made a bargain for his soul with the devil: the fool is too much of a fool, or the devil too much of a devil—I don't know which. Or you may be such a thunderingly exalted creature as to be altogether deaf and blind to anything but heavenly sights and sounds. Then the earth for you is only a standing place—and whether to be like this is your loss or your gain I won't pretend to say. But most of us are neither one nor the other. The earth for us is a place to live in, where we must put up with sights, with sounds, with smells, too, by Jove!—breathe dead hippo, so to speak, and not be contaminated. And there, don't you see? your strength comes in, the faith in your ability for the digging of unostentatious holes to bury the stuff in—your power of devotion, not to yourself, but to an obscure, back-breaking business. And that's difficult enough. Mind, I am not trying to excuse or even explain—I am trying to account to myself for—for—Mr Kurtz—for the shade of Mr Kurtz. This initiated wraith[5] from the back of Nowhere honoured me with its amazing confidence before it vanished altogether. This was because it could speak English to me. The original Kurtz had been educated partly in England, and—as he was good enough to say himself—his sympathies were in the right place. His mother was half-English, his father was half-French. All Europe contributed to the making of Kurtz; and by and by I learned that, most appropriately, the International Society for the Suppression of Savage Customs[6] had entrusted him with the making of a report, for its future guidance. And he had written it too. I've seen it. I've read it. It was eloquent, vibrating with eloquence, but too high-strung, I think. Seventeen pages of close writing he had found time for! But this must have been before his—let us say—nerves went wrong, and caused him to preside at certain midnight dances ending with unspeakable rites, which—as far as I reluctantly gathered from what I heard at various times—were offered up to him—do you understand?—to Mr Kurtz himself. But it was a beautiful piece of writing. The opening paragraph, however, in the light of later information, strikes me now as ominous. He began with the argument that we whites, from the point of development we had arrived at, 'must necessarily appear to them [savages] in the nature of supernatural beings—we approach them with the might as of a deity,' and so on, and so on. 'By the simple exercise of our will we can exert a power for good practically unbounded,' etc. etc. From that point he soared and took me with him. The peroration was magnificent, though difficult to remember, you know. It gave me the notion of an exotic Immensity ruled by an august Benevolence. It made me tingle with enthusiasm. This was the unbounded power of eloquence—of words—of burning noble words. There were no practical hints to interrupt the magic current of phrases, unless a kind of note at the foot of the last page, scrawled evidently much later, in an unsteady hand, may be regarded as the exposition of a method. It was very simple, and at the end of that moving appeal to every altruistic sentiment it blazed at you, luminous and terrifying, like a flash of lightning in a serene sky: 'Exterminate all the brutes!' The curious part was that he had apparently forgotten all about that valuable postscriptum, because, later on, when he in a sense came to himself, he repeatedly entreated me to take good care of 'my pamphlet' (he called it), as it was sure to have in the future a good influence upon his career. I had full information about all these things, and, besides, as it turned out, I was to have the care of his memory. I've done enough for it to give me the indisputable right to lay it, if I choose, for an everlasting rest in the dust-bin of progress, amongst all the sweepings and, figuratively speaking, all the dead cats of civilisation. But then, you see, I can't choose. He won't be forgotten. Whatever he was, he was not common. He had the power to charm or frighten rudimentary souls into an aggravated witchdance in his honour; he could also fill the small souls of the pilgrims with bitter misgivings: he had one devoted friend at least, and he had conquered one soul in the world that was neither rudimentary nor tainted with

5. Either the spectral or immaterial appearance of a living being, often viewed as a portent of that person's death, or simply a ghost.
6. This society is fictional, but in 1889–90 the international Anti-Slavery Conference at Brussels in effect granted Leopold control of the Congo trade, ostensibly in return for his help in eliminating African slavers.

self-seeking. No; I can't forget him, though I am not prepared to affirm the fellow was exactly worth the life we lost in getting to him. I missed my late helmsman awfully—I missed him even while his body was still lying in the pilot-house. Perhaps you will think it passing strange this regret for a savage who was no more account than a grain of sand in a black Sahara. Well, don't you see, he had done something, he had steered; for months I had him at my back—a help—an instrument. It was a kind of partnership. He steered for me—I had to look after him, I worried about his deficiencies, and thus a subtle bond had been created, of which I only became aware when it was suddenly broken. And the intimate profundity of that look he gave me when he received his hurt remains to this day in my memory—like a claim of distant kinship affirmed in a supreme moment.

"Poor fool! If he had only left that shutter alone. He had no restraint, no restraint—just like Kurtz—a tree swayed by the wind. As soon as I had put on a dry pair of slippers, I dragged him out, after first jerking the spear out of his side, which operation I confess I performed with my eyes shut tight. His heels leaped together over the little doorstep; his shoulders were pressed to my breast; I hugged him from behind desperately. Oh! he was heavy, heavy; heavier than any man on earth, I should imagine. Then without more ado I tipped him overboard. The current snatched him as though he had been a wisp of grass, and I saw the body roll over twice before I lost sight of it for ever. All the pilgrims and the manager were then congregated on the awning-deck about the pilot-house, chattering at each other like a flock of excited magpies, and there was a scandalised murmur at my heartless promptitude. What they wanted to keep that body hanging about for I can't guess. Embalm it, maybe. But I had also heard another, and a very ominous, murmur on the deck below. My friends the wood-cutters were likewise scandalised, and with a better show of reason—though I admit that the reason itself was quite inadmissible. Oh, quite! I had made up my mind that if my late helmsman was to be eaten, the fishes alone should have him. He had been a very second-rate helmsman while alive, but now he was dead he might have become a first-class temptation, and possibly cause some startling trouble. Besides, I was anxious to take the wheel, the man in pink pyjamas showing himself a hopeless duffer at the business.

"This I did directly the simple funeral was over. We were going half-speed, keeping right in the middle of the stream, and I listened to the talk about me. They had given up Kurtz, they had given up the station; Kurtz was dead, and the station had been burnt—and so on—and so on. The red-haired pilgrim was beside himself with the thought that at least this poor Kurtz had been properly revenged. 'Say! We must have made a glorious slaughter of them in the bush. Eh? What do you think? Say?' He positively danced, the bloodthirsty little gingery beggar.[7] And he had nearly fainted when he saw the wounded man! I could not help saying, 'You made a glorious lot of smoke, anyhow.' I had seen, from the way the tops of the bushes rustled and flew, that almost all the shots had gone too high. You can't hit anything unless you take aim and fire from the shoulder; but these chaps fired from the hip with their eyes shut. The retreat, I maintained—and I was right—was caused by the screeching of the steam-whistle. Upon this they forgot Kurtz, and began to howl at me with indignant protests.

7. Red-haired rascal (British slang).

"The manager stood by the wheel murmuring confidentially about the necessity of getting well away down the river before dark at all events, when I saw in the distance a clearing on the river-side and the outlines of some sort of building. 'What's this?' I asked. He clapped his hands in wonder. 'The station!' he cried. I edged in at once, still going half-speed.

"Through my glasses I saw the slope of a hill interspersed with rare trees and perfectly free from undergrowth. A long decaying building on the summit was half buried in the high grass; the large holes in the peaked roof gaped black from afar; the jungle and the woods made a background. There was no enclosure or fence of any kind; but there had been one apparently, for near the house half a dozen slim posts remained in a row, roughly trimmed, and with their upper ends ornamented with round carved balls. The rails, or whatever there had been between, had disappeared. Of course the forest surrounded all that. The river-bank was clear, and on the water side I saw a white man under a hat like a cart-wheel beckoning persistently with his whole arm. Examining the edge of the forest above and below, I was almost certain I could see movements—human forms gliding here and there. I steamed past prudently, then stopped the engines and let her drift down. The man on the shore began to shout, urging us to land. 'We have been attacked,' screamed the manager. 'I know—I know. It's all right,' yelled back the other, as cheerful as you please. 'Come along. It's all right. I am glad.'

"His aspect reminded me of something I had seen—something funny I had seen somewhere. As I manœuvred to get alongside, I was asking myself, 'What does this fellow look like?' Suddenly I got it. He looked like a harlequin. His clothes had been made of some stuff that was brown holland[8] probably, but it was covered with patches all over, with bright patches, blue, red, and yellow—patches on the back, patches on the front, patches on elbows, on knees; coloured binding round his jacket, scarlet edging at the bottom of his trousers; and the sunshine made him look extremely gay and wonderfully neat withal, because you could see how beautifully all this patching had been done. A beardless, boyish face, very fair, no features to speak of, nose peeling, little blue eyes, smiles and frowns chasing each other over that open countenance like sunshine and shadow on a wind-swept plain. 'Look out, captain!' he cried; 'there's a snag lodged in here last night.' What! Another snag? I confess I swore shamefully. I had nearly holed my cripple, to finish off that charming trip. The harlequin on the bank turned his little pug nose up to me. 'You English?' he asked, all smiles. 'Are you?' I shouted from the wheel. The smiles vanished, and he shook his head as if sorry for my disappointment. Then he brightened up. 'Never mind!' he cried encouragingly. 'Are we in time?' I asked. 'He is up there,' he replied, with a toss of the head up the hill, and becoming gloomy all of a sudden. His face was like the autumn sky, overcast one moment and bright the next.

"When the manager, escorted by the pilgrims, all of them armed to the teeth, had gone to the house, this chap came on board. 'I say, I don't like this. These natives are in the bush,' I said. He assured me earnestly it was all right. 'They are simple people,' he added; 'well, I am glad you came. It took me all my time to keep them off.' 'But you said it was all right,' I cried. 'Oh, they meant no

---

8. Unbleached linen fabric. "Harlequin": a traditional clown figure known by his multicolored costume.

harm,' he said; and as I stared he corrected himself, 'Not exactly.' Then vivaciously, 'My faith, your pilot-house wants a clean up!' In the next breath he advised me to keep enough steam on the boiler to blow the whistle in case of any trouble. 'One good screech will do more for you than all your rifles. They are simple people,' he repeated. He rattled away at such a rate he quite overwhelmed me. He seemed to be trying to make up for lots of silence, and actually hinted, laughing, that such was the case. 'Don't you talk with Mr Kurtz?' I said. 'You don't talk with that man—you listen to him,' he exclaimed with severe exaltation. 'But now—' He waved his arm, and in the twinkling of an eye was in the uttermost depths of despondency. In a moment he came up again with a jump, possessed himself of both my hands, shook them continuously, while he gabbled: 'Brother sailor . . . honour . . . pleasure . . . delight . . . introduce myself . . . Russian . . . son of an arch-priest . . . Government of Tambov[9] . . . What? Tobacco! English tobacco; the excellent English tobacco! Now, that's brotherly. Smoke? Where's a sailor that does not smoke?'

"The pipe soothed him, and gradually I made out he had run away from school, had gone to sea in a Russian ship; ran away again; served some time in English ships; was now reconciled with the arch-priest. He made a point of that. 'But when one is young one must see things, gather experience, ideas; enlarge the mind.' 'Here!' I interrupted. 'You can never tell! Here I met Mr Kurtz,' he said, youthfully solemn and reproachful. I held my tongue after that. It appears he had persuaded a Dutch trading-house on the coast to fit him out with stores and goods, and had started for the interior with a light heart, and no more idea of what would happen to him than a baby. He had been wandering about that river for nearly two years alone, cut off from everybody and everything. 'I am not so young as I look. I am twenty-five,' he said. 'At first old Van Shuyten would tell me to go to the devil,' he narrated with keen enjoyment; 'but I stuck to him, and talked and talked, till at last he got afraid I would talk the hind-leg off his favourite dog, so he gave me some cheap things and a few guns, and told me he hoped he would never see my face again. Good old Dutchman, Van Shuyten. I sent him one small lot of ivory a year ago, so that he can't call me a little thief when I get back. I hope he got it. And for the rest I don't care. I had some wood stacked for you. That was my old house. Did you see?'

"I gave him Towson's book. He made as though he would kiss me, but restrained himself. 'The only book I had left, and I thought I had lost it,' he said, looking at it ecstatically. 'So many accidents happen to a man going about alone, you know. Canoes get upset sometimes—and sometimes you've got to clear out so quick when the people get angry.' He thumbed the pages. 'You made notes in Russian?' I asked. He nodded. 'I thought they were written in cipher,' I said. He laughed, then became serious. 'I had lots of trouble to keep these people off,' he said. 'Did they want to kill you?' I asked. 'Oh no!' he cried, and checked himself. 'Why did they attack us?' I pursued. He hesitated, then said shamefacedly, 'They don't want him to go.' 'Don't they?' I said curiously. He nodded a nod full of mystery and wisdom. 'I tell you,' he cried, 'this man has enlarged my mind.' He opened his arms wide, staring at me with his little blue eyes that were perfectly round."

9. A province in Russia, south of Moscow, a cultural center.

3

"I looked at him, lost in astonishment. There he was before me, in motley,[1] as though he had absconded from a troupe of mimes, enthusiastic, fabulous. His very existence was improbable, inexplicable, and altogether bewildering. He was an insoluble problem. It was inconceivable how he had existed, how he had succeeded in getting so far, how he had managed to remain—why he did not instantly disappear. 'I went a little farther,' he said, 'then still a little farther—till I had gone so far that I don't know how I'll ever get back. Never mind. Plenty time. I can manage. You take Kurtz away quick—quick—I tell you.' The glamour of youth enveloped his particoloured rags, his destitution, his loneliness, the essential desolation of his futile wanderings. For months— for years—his life hadn't been worth a day's purchase; and there he was gallantly, thoughtlessly alive, to all appearance indestructible solely by the virtue of his few years and of his unreflecting audacity. I was seduced into something like admiration—like envy. Glamour urged him on, glamour kept him unscathed. He surely wanted nothing from the wilderness but space to breathe in and to push on through. His need was to exist, and to move onwards at the greatest possible risk, and with a maximum of privation. If the absolutely pure, uncalculating, unpractical spirit of adventure had ever ruled a human being, it ruled this be-patched youth. I almost envied him the possession of this modest and clear flame. It seemed to have consumed all thought of self so completely, that, even while he was talking to you, you forgot that it was he—the man before your eyes—who had gone through these things. I did not envy him his devotion to Kurtz, though. He had not meditated over it. It came to him, and he accepted it with a sort of eager fatalism. I must say that to me it appeared about the most dangerous thing in every way he had come upon so far.

"They had come together unavoidably, like two ships becalmed near each other, and lay rubbing sides at last. I suppose Kurtz wanted an audience, because on a certain occasion, when encamped in the forest, they had talked all night, or more probably Kurtz had talked. 'We talked of everything,' he said, quite transported at the recollection. 'I forgot there was such a thing as sleep. The night did not seem to last an hour. Everything! Everything! . . . Of love too.' 'Ah, he talked to you of love!' I said, much amused. 'It isn't what you think,' he cried, almost passionately. 'It was in general. He made me see things—things.'

"He threw his arms up. We were on deck at the time, and the head-man of my wood-cutters, lounging near by, turned upon him his heavy and glittering eyes. I looked around, and I don't know why, but I assure you that never, never before, did this land, this river, this jungle, the very arch of this blazing sky, appear to me so hopeless and so dark, so impenetrable to human thought, so pitiless to human weakness. 'And, ever since, you have been with him, of course?' I said.

"On the contrary. It appears their intercourse had been very much broken by various causes. He had, as he informed me proudly, managed to nurse Kurtz through two illnesses (he alluded to it as you would to some risky feat), but as a rule Kurtz wandered alone, far in the depths of the forest. 'Very often coming to this station, I had to wait days and days before he would turn up,' he said. 'Ah, it was worth waiting for!—sometimes.' 'What was he doing? exploring or what?'

---

1. Like a jester, who wore a distinctive multicolored costume.

I asked. 'Oh yes, of course'; he had discovered lots of villages, a lake too—he did not know exactly in what direction; it was dangerous to inquire too much—but mostly his expeditions had been for ivory. 'But he had no goods to trade with by that time,' I objected. 'There's a good lot of cartridges left even yet,' he answered, looking away. 'To speak plainly, he raided the country,'[2] I said. He nodded. 'Not alone, surely!' He muttered something about the villages round that lake. 'Kurtz got the tribe to follow him, did he?' I suggested. He fidgeted a little. 'They adored[3] him,' he said. The tone of these words was so extraordinary that I looked at him searchingly. It was curious to see his mingled eagerness and reluctance to speak of Kurtz. The man filled his life, occupied his thoughts, swayed his emotions. 'What can you expect?' he burst out; 'he came to them with thunder and lightning, you know—and they had never seen anything like it—and very terrible. He could be very terrible. You can't judge Mr Kurtz as you would an ordinary man. No, no, no! Now—just to give you an idea—I don't mind telling you, he wanted to shoot me too one day—but I don't judge him.' 'Shoot you!' I cried. 'What for?' 'Well, I had a small lot of ivory the chief of that village near my house gave me. You see I used to shoot game for them. Well, he wanted it, and wouldn't hear reason. He declared he would shoot me unless I gave him the ivory and then cleared out of the country, because he could do so, and had a fancy for it, and there was nothing on earth to prevent him killing whom he jolly well pleased. And it was true too. I gave him the ivory. What did I care! But I didn't clear out. No, no. I couldn't leave him. I had to be careful, of course, till we got friendly again for a time. He had his second illness then. Afterwards I had to keep out of the way; but I didn't mind. He was living for the most part in those villages on the lake. When he came down to the river, some-times he would take to me, and sometimes it was better for me to be careful. This man suffered too much. He hated all this, and somehow he couldn't get away. When I had a chance I begged him to try and leave while there was time; I offered to go back with him. And he would say yes, and then he would remain; go off on another ivory hunt; disappear for weeks; forget himself amongst these people—forget himself—you know.' 'Why! he's mad,' I said. He protested indignantly. Mr Kurtz couldn't be mad. If I had heard him talk, only two days ago, I wouldn't dare hint at such a thing. . . . I had taken up my binoculars while we talked, and was looking at the shore, sweeping the limit of the forest at each side and at the back of the house. The consciousness of there being people in that bush, so silent, so quiet—as silent and quiet as the ruined house on the hill—made me uneasy. There was no sign on the face of nature of this amazing tale that was not so much told as suggested to me in desolate exclamations, completed by shrugs, in interrupted phrases, in hints ending in deep sighs. The woods were unmoved, like a mask—heavy, like the closed door of a prison—they looked with their air of hidden knowledge, of patient expectation, of unap-proachable silence. The Russian was explaining to me that it was only lately that Mr Kurtz had come down to the river, bringing along with him all the fighting men of that lake tribe. He had been absent for several months—getting himself adored, I suppose—and had come down unexpectedly, with the intention to all appearance of making a raid either across the river or down stream. Evidently

<hr />

2. Raids for ivory were a common practice, with little or no attempt to compensate natives for the stolen goods.
3. Literally, worshipped as a deity.

the appetite for more ivory had got the better of the—what shall I say?—less material aspirations. However, he had got much worse suddenly. 'I heard he was lying helpless, and so I came up—took my chance,' said the Russian. 'Oh, he is bad, very bad.' I directed my glass to the house. There were no signs of life, but there was the ruined roof, the long mud wall peeping above the grass, with three little square window-holes, no two of the same size; all this brought within reach of my hand, as it were. And then I made a brusque movement, and one of the remaining posts of that vanished fence leaped up in the field of my glass. You remember I told you I had been struck at the distance by certain attempts at ornamentation, rather remarkable in the ruinous aspect of the place. Now I had suddenly a nearer view, and its first result was to make me throw my head back as if before a blow. Then I went carefully from post to post with my glass, and I saw my mistake. These round knobs were not ornamental but symbolic; they were expressive and puzzling, striking and disturbing—food for thought and also for the vultures if there had been any looking down from the sky; but at all events for such ants as were industrious enough to ascend the pole. They would have been even more impressive, those heads on the stakes, if their faces had not been turned to the house. Only one, the first I had made out, was facing my way. I was not so shocked as you may think. The start back I had given was really nothing but a movement of surprise. I had expected to see a knob of wood there, you know. I returned deliberately to the first I had seen—and there it was, black, dried, sunken, with closed eyelids—a head that seemed to sleep at the top of that pole, and, with the shrunken dry lips showing a narrow white line of the teeth, was smiling too, smiling continuously at some endless and jocose dream of that eternal slumber.

"I am not disclosing any trade secrets. In fact the manager said afterwards that Mr Kurtz's methods[4] had ruined the district. I have no opinion on that point, but I want you clearly to understand that there was nothing exactly profitable in these heads being there. They only show that Mr Kurtz lacked restraint in the gratification of his various lusts, that there was something wanting in him—some small matter which, when the pressing need arose, could not be found under his magnificent eloquence. Whether he knew of this deficiency himself I can't say. I think the knowledge came to him at last—only at the very last. But the wilderness had found him out early, and had taken on him a terrible vengeance for the fantastic invasion. I think it had whispered to him things about himself which he did not know, things of which he had no conception till he took counsel with this great solitude—and the whisper had proved irresistibly fascinating. It echoed loudly within him because he was hollow at the core. . . . I put down the glass, and the head that had appeared near enough to be spoken to seemed at once to have leaped away from me into inaccessible distance.

"The admirer of Mr Kurtz was a bit crestfallen. In a hurried, indistinct voice he began to assure me he had not dared to take these—say, symbols—down. He was not afraid of the natives; they would not stir till Mr Kurtz gave the word. His ascendancy was extraordinary. The camps of these people surrounded the place, and the chiefs came every day to see him. They would crawl . . . 'I don't

4. Perhaps an allusion to *Hamlet*, where Polonius comments on Hamlet's apparent insanity, "Though this be madness, yet there is method in 't."

want to know anything of the ceremonies used when approaching Mr Kurtz,' I shouted. Curious, this feeling that came over me that such details would be more intolerable than those heads drying on the stakes under Mr Kurtz's windows. After all, that was only a savage sight, while I seemed at one bound to have been transported into some lightless region of subtle horrors, where pure, uncomplicated savagery was a positive relief, being something that had a right to exist—obviously—in the sunshine. The young man looked at me with surprise. I suppose it did not occur to him that Mr Kurtz was no idol of mine. He forgot I hadn't heard any of these splendid monologues on, what was it? on love, justice, conduct of life—or what not. If it had come to crawling before Mr Kurtz, he crawled as much as the veriest savage of them all. I had no idea of the conditions, he said: these heads were the heads of rebels. I shocked him excessively by laughing. Rebels! What would be the next definition I was to hear? There had been enemies, criminals, workers—and these were rebels. Those rebellious heads looked very subdued to me on their sticks. 'You don't know how such a life tries a man like Kurtz,' cried Kurtz's last disciple. 'Well, and you?' I said. 'I! I! I am a simple man. I have no great thoughts. I want nothing from anybody. How can you compare me to . . .?' His feelings were too much for speech, and suddenly he broke down. 'I don't understand,' he groaned. 'I've been doing my best to keep him alive, and that's enough. I had no hand in all this. I have no abilities. There hasn't been a drop of medicine or a mouthful of invalid food for months here. He was shamefully abandoned. A man like this, with such ideas. Shamefully! Shamefully! I—I—haven't slept for the last ten nights. . . .'

"His voice lost itself in the calm of the evening. The long shadows of the forest had slipped down hill while we talked, had gone far beyond the ruined hovel, beyond the symbolic row of stakes. All this was in the gloom, while we down there were yet in the sunshine, and the stretch of the river abreast of the clearing glittered in a still and dazzling splendour, with a murky and overshadowed bend above and below. Not a living soul was seen on the shore. The bushes did not rustle.

"Suddenly round the corner of the house a group of men appeared, as though they had come up from the ground. They waded waist-deep in the grass, in a compact body, bearing an improvised stretcher in their midst. Instantly, in the emptiness of the landscape, a cry arose whose shrillness pierced the still air like a sharp arrow flying straight to the very heart of the land; and, as if by enchantment, streams of human beings—of naked human beings—with spears in their hands, with bows, with shields, with wild glances and savage movements, were poured into the clearing by the darkfaced and pensive forest. The bushes shook, the grass swayed for a time, and then everything stood still in attentive immobility.

"'Now, if he does not say the right thing to them we are all done for,' said the Russian at my elbow. The knot of men with the stretcher had stopped too, halfway to the steamer, as if petrified. I saw the man on the stretcher sit up, lank and with an uplifted arm, above the shoulders of the bearers. 'Let us hope that the man who can talk so well of love in general will find some particular reason to spare us this time,' I said. I resented bitterly the absurd danger of our situation, as if to be at the mercy of that atrocious phantom had been a dishonouring necessity. I could not hear a sound, but through my glasses I saw the thin arm extended commandingly, the lower jaw moving, the eyes of that apparition shining darkly far in its bony head that nodded with grotesque jerks. Kurtz—Kurtz—that means 'short' in German—don't it? Well, the name was as true as everything else in his life—and death. He looked at least seven feet long. His covering had fallen off, and his body emerged from it pitiful and appalling as from a winding-sheet. I could see the cage of his ribs all astir, the bones of his arm waving. It was as though an animated image of death carved out of old ivory had been shaking its hand with menaces at a motionless crowd of men made of dark and glittering bronze. I saw him open his mouth wide—it gave him a weirdly voracious aspect, as though he had wanted to swallow all the air, all the earth, all the men before him. A deep voice reached me faintly. He must have been shouting. He fell back suddenly. The stretcher shook as the bearers staggered forward again, and almost at the same time I noticed that the crowd of savages was vanishing without any perceptible movement of retreat, as if the forest that had ejected these beings so suddenly had drawn them in again as the breath is drawn in a long aspiration.

"Some of the pilgrims behind the stretcher carried his arms—two shotguns, a heavy rifle, and a light revolver-carbine[5]—the thunderbolts of that pitiful Jupiter.[6] The manager bent over him murmuring as he walked beside his head. They laid him down in one of the little cabins—just a room for a bedplace and a camp-stool or two, you know. We had brought his belated correspondence, and a lot of torn envelopes and open letters littered his bed. His hand roamed feebly amongst these papers. I was struck by the fire of his eyes and the composed languor of his expression. It was not so much the exhaustion of disease. He did not seem in pain. This shadow looked satiated and calm, as though for the moment it had had its fill of all the emotions.

"He rustled one of the letters, and looking straight in my face said, 'I am glad.' Somebody had been writing to him about me. These special recommendations were turning up again. The volume of tone he emitted without effort, almost without the trouble of moving his lips, amazed me. A voice! a voice! It was grave, profound, vibrating, while the man did not seem capable of a whisper. However, he had enough strength in him—factitious[7] no doubt—to very nearly make an end of us, as you shall hear directly.

"The manager appeared silently in the doorway; I stepped out at once and he drew the curtain after me. The Russian, eyed curiously by the pilgrims, was staring at the shore. I followed the direction of his glance.

"Dark human shapes could be made out in the distance, flitting indistinctly against the gloomy border of the forest, and near the river two bronze figures, leaning on tall spears, stood in the sunlight under fantastic head-dresses of spotted skins, warlike and still in statuesque repose. And from right to left along the lighted shore moved a wild and gorgeous apparition of a woman.

"She walked with measured steps, draped in striped and fringed cloths, treading the earth proudly, with a slight jingle and flash of barbarous ornaments. She carried her head high; her hair was done in the shape of a helmet; she had brass leggings to the knee,[8] brass wire gauntlets to the elbow, a crimson spot on her

---

5. A rifle with a revolving clip.
6. The Roman god of the sky, ruler over the other gods.

7. Not natural; got up for a particular purpose; artificial.
8. From the ankle to the knee.

tawny cheek, innumerable necklaces of glass beads on her neck; bizarre things, charms, gifts of witch-men, that hung about her, glittered and trembled at every step. She must have had the value of several elephant tusks upon her. She was savage and superb, wild-eyed and magnificent; there was something ominous and stately in her deliberate progress. And in the hush that had fallen suddenly upon the whole sorrowful land, the immense wilderness, the colossal body of the fecund and mysterious life seemed to look at her, pensive, as though it had been looking at the image of its own tenebrous[9] and passionate soul.

"She came abreast of the steamer, stood still, and faced us. Her long shadow fell to the water's edge. Her face had a tragic and fierce aspect of wild sorrow and of dumb pain mingled with the fear of some struggling, half-shaped resolve. She stood looking at us without a stir, and like the wilderness itself, with an air of brooding over an inscrutable purpose. A whole minute passed, and then she made a step forward. There was a low jingle, a glint of yellow metal, a sway of fringed draperies, and she stopped as if her heart had failed her. The young fellow by my side growled. The pilgrims murmured at my back. She looked at us all as if her life had depended upon the unswerving steadiness of her glance. Suddenly she opened her bared arms and threw them up rigid above her head, as though in an uncontrollable desire to touch the sky, and at the same time the swift shadows darted out on the earth, swept around on the river, gathering the steamer into a shadowy embrace. A formidable silence hung over the scene.

"She turned away slowly, walked on, following the bank, and passed into the bushes to the left. Once only her eyes gleamed back at us in the dusk of the thickets before she disappeared.

"'If she had offered to come aboard I really think I would have tried to shoot her,' said the man of patches nervously. 'I had been risking my life every day for the last fortnight to keep her out of the house. She got in one day and kicked up a row about those miserable rags I picked up in the storeroom to mend my clothes with. I wasn't decent. At least it must have been that, for she talked like a fury to Kurtz for an hour, pointing at me now and then. I don't understand the dialect of this tribe. Luckily for me, I fancy Kurtz felt too ill that day to care, or there would have been mischief. I don't understand. . . . No—it's too much for me. Ah, well, it's all over now.'

"At this moment I heard Kurtz's deep voice behind the curtain: 'Save me!—save the ivory, you mean. Don't tell me. Save _me_! Why, I've had to save you. You are interrupting my plans now. Sick! Sick! Not so sick as you would like to believe. Never mind. I'll carry my ideas out yet—I will return. I'll show you what can be done. You with your little peddling notions—you are interfering with me. I will return. I . . .'

"The manager came out. He did me the honour to take me under the arm and lead me aside. 'He is very low, very low,' he said. He considered it necessary to sigh, but neglected to be consistently sorrowful. 'We have done all we could for him—haven't we? But there is no disguising the fact, Mr Kurtz has done more harm than good to the Company. He did not see the time was not ripe for vigorous action. Cautiously, cautiously—that's my principle. We must be cautious yet. The district is closed to us for a time. Deplorable! Upon the whole, the trade will suffer. I don't deny there is a remarkable quantity of ivory—mostly

9. Full of darkness or shadows; obscure; gloomy.

fossil. We must save it, at all events—but look how precarious the position is—and why? Because the method is unsound.' 'Do you,' said I, looking at the shore, 'call it "unsound method"?' 'Without doubt,' he exclaimed hotly, 'Don't you?' . . . 'No method at all,' I murmured after a while. 'Exactly,' he exulted. 'I anticipated this. Shows a complete want of judgment. It is my duty to point it out in the proper quarter.' 'Oh,' said I, 'that fellow—what's his name?—the brickmaker, will make a readable report for you.' He appeared confounded for a moment. It seemed to me I had never breathed an atmosphere so vile, and I turned mentally to Kurtz for relief—positively for relief. 'Nevertheless, I think Mr Kurtz is a remarkable man,' I said with emphasis. He started, dropped on me a cold heavy glance, said very quietly, 'He *was*,' and turned his back on me. My hour of favour was over; I found myself lumped along with Kurtz as a partisan of methods for which the time was not ripe: I was unsound! Ah! but it was something to have at least a choice of nightmares.

"I had turned to the wilderness really, not to Mr Kurtz, who, I was ready to admit, was as good as buried. And for a moment it seemed to me as if I also were buried in a vast grave full of unspeakable secrets. I felt an intolerable weight oppressing my breast, the smell of the damp earth, the unseen presence of victorious corruption, the darkness of an impenetrable night. . . . The Russian tapped me on the shoulder. I heard him mumbling and stammering something about 'brother seaman—couldn't conceal—knowledge of matters that would affect Mr Kurtz's reputation.' I waited. For him evidently Mr Kurtz was not in his grave; I suspect that for him Mr Kurtz was one of the immortals. 'Well!' said I at last, 'speak out. As it happens, I am Mr Kurtz's friend—in a way.'

"He stated with a good deal of formality that had we not been 'of the same profession,' he would have kept the matter to himself without regard to consequences. He suspected 'there was an active ill-will towards him on the part of these white men that—' 'You are right,' I said, remembering a certain conversation I had overheard. 'The manager thinks you ought to be hanged.' He showed a concern at this intelligence which amused me at first. 'I had better get out of the way quietly,' he said earnestly. 'I can do no more for Kurtz now, and they would soon find some excuse. What's to stop them? There's a military post three hundred miles from here.' 'Well, upon my word,' said I, 'perhaps you had better go if you have any friends amongst the savages near by.' 'Plenty,' he said. 'They are simple people—and I want nothing, you know.' He stood biting his lip, then: 'I don't want any harm to happen to these whites here, but of course I was thinking of Mr Kurtz's reputation—but you are a brother seaman and—' 'All right,' said I, after a time. 'Mr Kurtz's reputation is safe with me.' I did not know how truly I spoke.

"He informed me, lowering his voice, that it was Kurtz who had ordered the attack to be made on the steamer. 'He hated sometimes the idea of being taken away—and then again . . . But I don't understand these matters. I am a simple man. He thought it would scare you away—that you would give it up, thinking him dead. I could not stop him. Oh, I had an awful time of it this last month.' 'Very well,' I said. 'He is all right now.' 'Ye-e-es,' he muttered, not very convinced apparently. 'Thanks,' said I; 'I shall keep my eyes open.' 'But quiet—eh?' he urged anxiously. 'It would be awful for his reputation if anybody here—' I promised a complete discretion with great gravity. 'I have a canoe and three black fellows waiting not very far. I am off. Could you give me a few Martini-Henry cartridges?' I could, and did, with proper secrecy. He helped himself, with a wink at me, to a handful of my tobacco. 'Between sailors—you know—good English tobacco.' At the door of the pilot-house he turned round—'I say, haven't you a pair of shoes you could spare?' He raised one leg. 'Look.' The soles were tied with knotted strings sandal-wise under his bare feet. I rooted out an old pair, at which he looked with admiration before tucking it under his left arm. One of his pockets (bright red) was bulging with cartridges, from the other (dark blue) peeped 'Towson's Inquiry,' etc. etc. He seemed to think himself excellently well equipped for a renewed encounter with the wilderness. 'Ah! I'll never, never meet such a man again. You ought to have heard him recite poetry—his own too it was, he told me. Poetry!' He rolled his eyes at the recollection of these delights. 'Oh, he enlarged my mind!' 'Good-bye,' said I. He shook hands and vanished in the night. Sometimes I ask myself whether I had ever really seen him—whether it was possible to meet such a phenomenon! . . .

"When I woke up shortly after midnight his warning came to my mind with its hint of danger that seemed, in the starred darkness, real enough to make me get up for the purpose of having a look round. On the hill a big fire burned, illuminating fitfully a crooked corner of the station-house. One of the agents with a picket of a few of our blacks, armed for the purpose, was keeping guard over the ivory; but deep within the forest, red gleams that wavered, that seemed to sink and rise from the ground amongst confused columnar shapes of intense blackness, showed the exact position of the camp where Mr Kurtz's adorers were keeping their uneasy vigil. The monotonous beating of a big drum filled the air with muffled shocks and a lingering vibration. A steady droning sound of many men chanting each to himself some weird incantation came out from the black, flat wall of the woods as the humming of bees comes out of a hive, and had a strange narcotic effect upon my half-awake senses. I believe I dozed off leaning over the rail, till an abrupt burst of yells, an overwhelming outbreak of a pent-up and mysterious frenzy, woke me up in a bewildered wonder. It was cut short all at once, and the low droning went on with an effect of audible and soothing silence. I glanced casually into the little cabin. A light was burning within, but Mr Kurtz was not there.

"I think I would have raised an outcry if I had believed my eyes. But I didn't believe them at first—the thing seemed so impossible. The fact is I was completely unnerved by a sheer blank fright, pure abstract terror, unconnected with any distinct shape of physical danger. What made this emotion so overpowering was—how shall I define it?—the moral shock I received, as if something altogether monstrous, intolerable to thought and odious to the soul, had been thrust upon me unexpectedly. This lasted of course the merest fraction of a second, and then the usual sense of commonplace, deadly danger, the possibility of a sudden onslaught and massacre, or something of the kind, which I saw impending, was positively welcome and composing. It pacified me, in fact, so much, that I did not raise an alarm.

"There was an agent buttoned up inside an ulster[1] and sleeping on a chair on deck within three feet of me. The yells had not awakened him; he snored very slightly; I left him to his slumbers and leaped ashore. I did not betray Mr Kurtz—it was ordered I should never betray him—it was written I should be loyal to the

---

1. A long, loose overcoat, often with a belt.

nightmare of my choice. I was anxious to deal with this shadow by myself alone—and to this day I don't know why I was so jealous of sharing with any one the peculiar blackness of that experience.

"As soon as I got on the bank I saw a trail—a broad trail through the grass. I remember the exultation with which I said to myself, 'He can't walk—he is crawling on all-fours—I've got him.' The grass was wet with dew. I strode rapidly with clenched fists. I fancy I had some vague notion of falling upon him and giving him a drubbing. I don't know. I had some imbecile thoughts. The knitting old woman with the cat obtruded herself upon my memory as a most improper person to be sitting at the other end of such an affair. I saw a row of pilgrims squirting lead in the air out of Winchesters held to the hip. I thought I would never get back to the steamer, and imagined myself living alone and unarmed in the woods to an advanced age. Such silly things—you know. And I remember I confounded the beat of the drum with the beating of my heart, and was pleased at its calm regularity.

"I kept to the track though—then stopped to listen. The night was very clear; a dark blue space, sparkling with dew and starlight, in which black things stood very still. I thought I could see a kind of motion ahead of me. I was strangely cocksure of everything that night. I actually left the track and ran in a wide semicircle (I verily believe chuckling to myself) so as to get in front of that stir, of that motion I had seen—if indeed I had seen anything. I was circumventing Kurtz as though it had been a boyish game.

"I came upon him, and, if he had not heard me coming, I would have fallen over him too, but he got up in time. He rose, unsteady, long, pale, indistinct, like a vapour exhaled by the earth, and swayed slightly, misty and silent before me; while at my back the fires loomed between the trees, and the murmur of many voices issued from the forest. I had cut him off cleverly; but when actually confronting him I seemed to come to my senses, I saw the danger in its right proportion. It was by no means over yet. Suppose he began to shout? Though he could hardly stand, there was still plenty of vigour in his voice. 'Go away—hide yourself,' he said, in that profound tone. It was very awful. I glanced back. We were within thirty yards of the nearest fire. A black figure stood up, strode on long black legs, waving long black arms, across the glow. It had horns—antelope horns, I think—on its head. Some sorcerer, some witch-man no doubt: it looked fiend-like enough. 'Do you know what you are doing?' I whispered. 'Perfectly,' he answered, raising his voice for that single word: it sounded to me far off and yet loud, like a hail through a speaking-trumpet. If he makes a row we are lost, I thought to myself. This clearly was not a case for fisticuffs, even apart from the very natural aversion I had to beat that Shadow— this wandering and tormented thing. 'You will be lost,' I said—'utterly lost.' One gets sometimes such a flash of inspiration, you know. I did say the right thing, though indeed he could not have been more irretrievably lost than he was at this very moment, when the foundations of our intimacy were being laid—to endure—to endure—even to the end—even beyond.

"'I had immense plans,' he muttered irresolutely. 'Yes,' said I; 'but if you try to shout I'll smash your head with—' There was not a stick or a stone near. 'I will throttle you for good,' I corrected myself. 'I was on the threshold of great things,' he pleaded, in a voice of longing, with a wistfulness of tone that made my blood run cold. 'And now for this stupid scoundrel—' 'Your success in

Europe is assured in any case,' I affirmed steadily. I did not want to have the throttling of him, you understand—and indeed it would have been very little use for any practical purpose. I tried to break the spell—the heavy, mute spell of the wilderness—that seemed to draw him to its pitiless breast by the awakening of forgotten and brutal instincts, by the memory of gratified and monstrous passions. This alone, I was convinced, had driven him out to the edge of the forest, to the bush, towards the gleam of fires, the throb of drums, the drone of weird incantations; this alone had beguiled his unlawful soul beyond the bounds of permitted aspirations. And, don't you see, the terror of the position was not in being knocked on the head—though I had a very lively sense of that danger too—but in this, that I had to deal with a being to whom I could not appeal in the name of anything high or low. I had, even like the niggers, to invoke him—himself—his own exalted and incredible degradation. There was nothing either above or below him, and I knew it. He had kicked himself loose of the earth. Confound the man! he had kicked the very earth to pieces. He was alone, and I before him did not know whether I stood on the ground or floated in the air. I've been telling you what we said—repeating the phrases we pronounced—but what's the good? They were common everyday words—the familiar, vague sounds exchanged on every waking day of life. But what of that? They had behind them, to my mind, the terrific suggestiveness of words heard in dreams, of phrases spoken in nightmares. Soul! If anybody had ever struggled with a soul, I am the man. And I wasn't arguing with a lunatic either. Believe me or not, his intelligence was perfectly clear—concentrated, it is true, upon himself with horrible intensity, yet clear; and therein was my only chance—barring, of course, the killing him there and then, which wasn't so good, on account of unavoidable noise. But his soul was mad. Being alone in the wilderness, it had looked within itself, and, by heavens! I tell you, it had gone mad. I had—for my sins, I suppose, to go through the ordeal of looking into it myself. No eloquence could have been so withering to one's belief in mankind as his final burst of sincerity. He struggled with himself too. I saw it—I heard it. I saw the inconceivable mystery of a soul that knew no restraint, no faith, and no fear, yet struggling blindly with itself. I kept my head pretty well; but when I had him at last stretched on the couch, I wiped my forehead, while my legs shook under me as though I had carried half a ton on my back down that hill. And yet I had only supported him, his bony arm clasped round my neck—and he was not much heavier than a child.

"When next day we left at noon, the crowd, of whose presence behind the curtain of trees I had been acutely conscious all the time, flowed out of the woods again, filled the clearing, covered the slope with a mass of naked, breathing, quivering, bronze bodies. I steamed up a bit, then swung downstream, and two thousand eyes followed the evolutions of the splashing, thumping, fierce river-demon beating the water with its terrible tail and breathing black smoke into the air. In front of the first rank, along the river, three men, plastered with bright red earth from head to foot, strutted to and fro restlessly. When we came abreast again, they faced the river, stamped their feet, nodded their horned heads, swayed their scarlet bodies; they shook towards the fierce river-demon a bunch of black feathers, a mangy skin with a pendent tail—something that looked like a dried gourd; they shouted periodically together strings of amazing words that resembled no sounds of human language; and the deep murmurs of the crowd, interrupted suddenly, were like the responses of some satanic litany.

"We had carried Kurtz into the pilot-house: there was more air there. Lying on the couch, he stared through the open shutter. There was an eddy in the mass of human bodies, and the woman with helmeted head and tawny cheeks rushed out to the very brink of the stream. She put out her hands, shouted something, and all that wild mob took up the shout in a roaring chorus of articulated, rapid, breathless utterance.

"'Do you understand this?' I asked.

"He kept on looking out past me with fiery, longing eyes, with a mingled expression of wistfulness and hate. He made no answer, but I saw a smile, a smile of indefinable meaning, appear on his colourless lips that a moment after twitched convulsively. 'Do I not?' he said slowly, gasping, as if the words had been torn out of him by a supernatural power.

"I pulled the string of the whistle, and I did this because I saw the pilgrims on deck getting out their rifles with an air of anticipating a jolly lark. At the sudden screech there was a movement of abject terror through that wedged mass of bodies. 'Don't! don't you frighten them away,' cried someone on deck disconsolately. I pulled the string time after time. They broke and ran, they leaped, they crouched, they swerved, they dodged the flying terror of the sound. The three red chaps had fallen flat, face down on the shore, as though they had been shot dead. Only the barbarous and superb woman did not so much as flinch, and stretched tragically her bare arms after us over the sombre and glittering river.

"And then that imbecile crowd down on the deck started their little fun, and I could see nothing more for smoke.

"The brown current ran swiftly out of the heart of darkness, bearing us down towards the sea with twice the speed of our upward progress; and Kurtz's life was running swiftly too, ebbing, ebbing out of his heart into the sea of inexorable time. The manager was very placid, he had no vital anxieties now, he took us both in with a comprehensive and satisfied glance: the 'affair' had come off as well as could be wished. I saw the time approaching when I would be left alone of the party of 'unsound method.' The pilgrims looked upon me with disfavour. I was, so to speak, numbered with the dead. It is strange how I accepted this unforeseen partnership, this choice of nightmares forced upon me in the tenebrous land invaded by these mean and greedy phantoms.

"Kurtz discoursed. A voice! a voice! It rang deep to the very last. It survived his strength to hide in the magnificent folds of eloquence the barren darkness of his heart. Oh, he struggled! he struggled! The wastes of his weary brain were haunted by shadowy images now—images of wealth and fame revolving obsequiously round his unextinguishable gift of noble and lofty expression. My Intended, my station, my career, my ideas—these were the subjects for the occasional utterances of elevated sentiments. The shade of the original Kurtz frequented the bedside of the hollow sham, whose fate it was to be buried presently in the mould of primeval earth. But both the diabolic love and the unearthly hate of the mysteries it had penetrated fought for the possession of that soul satiated with primitive emotions, avid of lying fame, of sham distinction, of all the appearances of success and power.

"Sometimes he was contemptibly childish. He desired to have kings meet him at railway stations on his return from some ghastly Nowhere, where he intended to accomplish great things. 'You show them you have in you something that is really profitable, and then there will be no limits to the recognition of your ability,' he would say. 'Of course you must take care of the motives—right motives—always.' The long reaches that were like one and the same reach, monotonous bends that were exactly alike, slipped past the steamer with their multitude of secular[2] trees looking patiently after this grimy fragment of another world, the forerunner of change, of conquest, of trade, of massacres, of blessings. I looked ahead—piloting. 'Close the shutter,' said Kurtz suddenly one day; 'I can't bear to look at this.' I did so. There was a silence. 'Oh, but I will wring your heart yet!' he cried at the invisible wilderness.

"We broke down—as I had expected—and had to lie up for repairs at the head of an island. This delay was the first thing that shook Kurtz's confidence. One morning he gave me a packet of papers and a photograph—the lot tied together with a shoe-string. 'Keep this for me,' he said. 'This noxious fool' (meaning the manager) 'is capable of prying into my boxes when I am not looking.' In the afternoon I saw him. He was lying on his back with closed eyes, and I withdrew quietly, but I heard him mutter, 'Live rightly, die, die . . .' I listened. There was nothing more. Was he rehearsing some speech in his sleep, or was it a fragment of a phrase from some newspaper article? He had been writing for the papers and meant to do so again, 'for the furthering of my ideas. It's a duty.'

"His was an impenetrable darkness. I looked at him as you peer down at a man who is lying at the bottom of a precipice where the sun never shines. But I had not much time to give him, because I was helping the engine-driver to take to pieces the leaky cylinders, to straighten a bent connecting-rod, and in other such matters. I lived in an infernal mess of rust, filings, nuts, bolts, spanners, hammers, ratchet-drills—things I abominate, because I don't get on with them. I tended the little forge we fortunately had aboard; I toiled wearily in a wretched scrap-heap—unless I had the shakes too bad to stand.

"One evening coming in with a candle I was startled to hear him say a little tremulously, 'I am lying here in the dark waiting for death.' The light was within a foot of his eyes. I forced myself to murmur, 'Oh, nonsense!' and stood over him as if transfixed.

"Anything approaching the change that came over his features I have never seen before, and hope never to see again. Oh, I wasn't touched. I was fascinated. It was as though a veil had been rent. I saw on that ivory face the expression of sombre pride, of ruthless power, of craven terror—of an intense and hopeless despair. Did he live his life again in every detail of desire, temptation, and surrender during that supreme moment of complete knowledge? He cried in a whisper at some image, at some vision—he cried out twice, a cry that was no more than a breath:

"'The horror! The horror!'

"I blew the candle out and left the cabin. The pilgrims were dining in the mess-room, and I took my place opposite the manager, who lifted his eyes to give me a questioning glance, which I successfully ignored. He leaned back,

2. Centuries old (from *séculaire*, French).

serene, with that peculiar smile of his sealing the unexpressed depths of his meanness. A continuous shower of small flies streamed upon the lamp, upon the cloth, upon our hands and faces. Suddenly the manager's boy put his insolent black head in the doorway, and said in a tone of scathing contempt:

"'Mistah Kurtz—he dead.'

"All the pilgrims rushed out to see. I remained, and went on with my dinner. I believe I was considered brutally callous. However, I did not eat much. There was a lamp in there—light, don't you know—and outside it was so beastly, beastly dark. I went no more near the remarkable man who had pronounced a judgement upon the adventures of his soul on this earth. The voice was gone. What else had been there? But I am of course aware that next day the pilgrims buried something in a muddy hole.

"And then they very nearly buried me.

"However, as you see, I did not go to join Kurtz there and then. I did not. I remained to dream the nightmare out to the end, and to show my loyalty to Kurtz once more. Destiny. My destiny! Droll thing life is—that mysterious arrangement of merciless logic for a futile purpose. The most you can hope from it is some knowledge of yourself—that comes too late—a crop of unextinguishable regrets. I have wrestled with death. It is the most unexciting contest you can imagine. It takes place in an impalpable greyness, with nothing underfoot, with nothing around, without spectators, without clamour, without glory, without the great desire of victory, without the great fear of defeat, in a sickly atmosphere of tepid scepticism, without much belief in your own right, and still less in that of your adversary. If such is the form of ultimate wisdom, then life is a greater riddle than some of us think it to be. I was within a hair's-breadth of the last opportunity for pronouncement, and I found with humiliation that probably I would have nothing to say. This is the reason why I affirm that Kurtz was a remarkable man. He had something to say. He said it. Since I had peeped over the edge myself, I understand better the meaning of his stare, that could not see the flame of the candle, but was wide enough to embrace the whole universe, piercing enough to penetrate all the hearts that beat in the darkness. He had summed up—he had judged. 'The horror!' He was a remarkable man. After all, this was the expression of some sort of belief; it had candour, it had conviction, it had a vibrating note of revolt in its whisper, it had the appalling face of a glimpsed truth—the strange commingling of desire and hate. And it is not my own extremity I remember best—a vision of greyness without form filled with physical pain, and a careless contempt for the evanescence of all things— even of this pain itself. No! It is his extremity that I seem to have lived through. True, he had made that last stride, he had stepped over the edge, while I had been permitted to draw back my hesitating foot. And perhaps in this is the whole difference; perhaps all the wisdom, and all truth, and all sincerity, are just compressed into that inappreciable moment of time in which we step over the threshold of the invisible. Perhaps! I like to think my summing-up would not have been a word of careless contempt. Better his cry—much better. It was an affirmation, a moral victory paid for by innumerable defeats, by abominable terrors, by abominable satisfactions. But it was a victory! That is why I have remained loyal to Kurtz to the last, and even beyond, when a long time after I heard once more, not his own voice, but the echo of his magnificent eloquence thrown to me from a soul as translucently pure as a cliff of crystal.

"No, they did not bury me, though there is a period of time which I remember mistily, with a shuddering wonder, like a passage through some inconceivable world that had no hope in it and no desire. I found myself back in the sepulchral city resenting the sight of people hurrying through the streets to filch a little money from each other, to devour their infamous cookery, to gulp their unwholesome beer, to dream their insignificant and silly dreams. They trespassed upon my thoughts. They were intruders whose knowledge of life was to me an irritating pretence, because I felt so sure they could not possibly know the things I knew. Their bearing, which was simply the bearing of commonplace individuals going about their business in the assurance of perfect safety, was offensive to me like the outrageous flauntings of folly in the face of a danger it is unable to comprehend. I had no particular desire to enlighten them, but I had some difficulty in restraining myself from laughing in their faces, so full of stupid importance. I daresay I was not very well at that time. I tottered about the streets—there were various affairs to settle—grinning bitterly at perfectly respectable persons. I admit my behaviour was inexcusable, but then my temperature was seldom normal in these days. My dear aunt's endeavours to 'nurse up my strength' seemed altogether beside the mark. It was not my strength that wanted nursing, it was my imagination that wanted soothing. I kept the bundle of papers given me by Kurtz, not knowing exactly what to do with it. His mother had died lately, watched over, as I was told, by his Intended. A clean-shaven man, with an official manner and wearing gold-rimmed spectacles, called on me one day and made inquiries, at first circuitous, afterwards suavely pressing, about what he was pleased to denominate certain 'documents.' I was not surprised, because I had had two rows with the manager on the subject out there. I had refused to give up the smallest scrap out of that package, and I took the same attitude with the spectacled man. He became darkly menacing at last, and with much heat argued that the Company had the right to every bit of information about its 'territories.' And, said he, 'Mr Kurtz's knowledge of unexplored regions must have been necessarily extensive and peculiar—owing to his great abilities and to the deplorable circumstances in which he had been placed: therefore—' I assured him Mr Kurtz's knowledge, however extensive, did not bear upon the problems of commerce or administration. He invoked then the name of science. 'It would be an incalculable loss if,' etc. etc. I offered him the report on the 'Suppression of Savage Customs,' with the postscriptum torn off. He took it up eagerly, but ended by sniffing at it with an air of contempt. 'This is not what we had a right to expect,' he remarked. 'Expect nothing else,' I said. 'There are only private letters.' He withdrew upon some threat of legal proceedings, and I saw him no more; but another fellow, calling himself Kurtz's cousin, appeared two days later, and was anxious to hear all the details about his dear relative's last moments. Incidentally he gave me to understand that Kurtz had been essentially a great musician. 'There was the making of an immense success,' said the man, who was an organist, I believe, with lank grey hair flowing over a greasy coat-collar. I had no reason to doubt his statement; and to this day I am unable to say what was Kurtz's profession, whether he ever had any—which was the greatest of his talents. I had taken him for a painter who wrote for the papers, or else for a journalist who could paint—but even the cousin (who took snuff during the interview) could not tell me what he had been—exactly. He was a universal genius—on that point I agreed with the old chap, who thereupon blew his nose noisily into a large cotton handkerchief and withdrew in senile agitation, bearing off some family letters and memoranda without importance. Ultimately a journalist anxious to know something of the fate of his 'dear colleague' turned up. This visitor informed me Kurtz's proper sphere ought to have been politics 'on the popular side.' He had furry straight eyebrows, bristly hair cropped short, an eyeglass on a broad ribbon, and, becoming expansive, confessed his opinion that Kurtz really couldn't write a bit—'but heavens! how that man could talk! He electrified large meetings. He had faith—don't you see?—he had the faith. He could get himself to believe anything—anything. He would have been a splendid leader of an extreme party.' 'What party?' I asked. 'Any party,' answered the other. 'He was an—an—extremist.' Did I not think so? I assented. Did I know, he asked, with a sudden flash of curiosity, 'what it was that had induced him to go out there?' 'Yes,' said I, and forthwith handed him the famous Report for publication, if he thought fit. He glanced through it hurriedly, mumbling all the time, judged 'it would do,' and took himself off with this plunder.

"Thus I was left at last with a slim packet of letters and the girl's portrait. She struck me as beautiful—I mean she had a beautiful expression. I know that the sunlight can be made to lie too, yet one felt that no manipulation of light and pose could have conveyed the delicate shade of truthfulness upon those features. She seemed ready to listen without mental reservation, without suspicion, without a thought for herself. I concluded I would go and give her back her portrait and those letters myself. Curiosity? Yes; and also some other feeling perhaps. All that had been Kurtz's had passed out of my hands: his soul, his body, his station, his plans, his ivory, his career. There remained only his memory and his Intended—and I wanted to give that up too to the past, in a way—to surrender personally all that remained of him with me to that oblivion which is the last word of our common fate. I don't defend myself. I had no clear perception of what it was I really wanted. Perhaps it was an impulse of unconscious loyalty, or the fulfilment of one of those ironic necessities that lurk in the facts of human existence. I don't know. I can't tell. But I went.

"I thought his memory was like the other memories of the dead that accumulate in every man's life—a vague impress on the brain of shadows that had fallen on it in their swift and final passage; but before the high and ponderous door, between the tall houses of a street as still and decorous as a well-kept alley in a cemetery, I had a vision of him on the stretcher, opening his mouth voraciously, as if to devour all the earth with all its mankind. He lived then before me; he lived as much as he had ever lived—a shadow insatiable of splendid appearances, of frightful realities; a shadow darker than the shadow of the night, and draped nobly in the folds of a gorgeous eloquence. The vision seemed to enter the house with me—the stretcher, the phantom-bearers, the wild crowd of obedient worshippers, the gloom of the forests, the glitter of the reach between the murky bends, the beat of the drum, regular and muffled like the beating of a heart—the heart of a conquering darkness. It was a moment of triumph for the wilderness, an invading and vengeful rush which, it seemed to me, I would have to keep back alone for the salvation of another soul. And the memory of what I had heard him say afar there, with the horned shapes stirring at my back, in the glow of fires, within the patient woods, those broken phrases came back to me, were heard again in their ominous and terrifying simplicity. I remembered his abject pleading, his abject threats, the colossal scale of his vile desires, the meanness, the torment, the tempestuous anguish of his soul. And later on I seemed to see his collected languid manner, when he said one day, 'This lot of ivory now is really mine. The Company did not pay for it. I collected it myself at a very great personal risk. I am afraid they will try to claim it as theirs though. H'm. It is a difficult case. What do you think I ought to do—resist? Eh? I want no more than justice.' . . . He wanted no more than justice—no more than justice. I rang the bell before a mahogany door on the first floor, and while I waited he seemed to stare at me out of the glossy panel— stare with that wide and immense stare embracing, condemning, loathing all the universe. I seemed to hear the whispered cry, 'The horror! The horror!'

"The dusk was falling. I had to wait in a lofty drawing room with three long windows from floor to ceiling that were like three luminous and bedraped columns. The bent gilt legs and backs of the furniture shone in indistinct curves. The tall marble fireplace had a cold and monumental whiteness. A grand piano stood massively in a corner; with dark gleams on the flat surfaces like a sombre and polished sarcophagus. A high door opened—closed. I rose.

"She came forward, all in black, with a pale head, floating towards me in the dusk. She was in mourning. It was more than a year since his death, more than a year since the news came; she seemed as though she would remember and mourn for ever. She took both my hands in hers and murmured, 'I had heard you were coming.' I noticed she was not very young—I mean not girlish. She had a mature capacity for fidelity, for belief, for suffering. The room seemed to have grown darker, as if all the sad light of the cloudy evening had taken refuge on her forehead. This fair hair, this pale visage, this pure brow, seemed surrounded by an ashy halo from which the dark eyes looked out at me. Their glance was guileless, profound, confident, and trustful. She carried her sorrowful head as though she were proud of that sorrow, as though she would say, I—I alone know how to mourn for him as he deserves. But while we were still shaking hands, such a look of awful desolation came upon her face that I perceived she was one of those creatures that are not the playthings of Time. For her he had died only yesterday. And, by Jove! the impression was so powerful that for me too he seemed to have died only yesterday—nay, this very minute. I saw her and him in the same instant of time—his death and her sorrow—I saw her sorrow in the very moment of his death. Do you understand? I saw them together—I heard them together. She had said, with a deep catch of the breath, 'I have survived'; while my strained ears seemed to hear distinctly, mingled with her tone of despairing regret, the summing-up whisper of his eternal condemnation. I asked myself what I was doing there, with a sensation of panic in my heart as though I had blundered into a place of cruel and absurd mysteries not fit for a human being to behold. She motioned me to a chair. We sat down. I laid the packet gently on the little table, and she put her hand over it. . . . 'You knew him well,' she murmured, after a moment of mourning silence.

"'Intimacy grows quickly out there,' I said. 'I knew him as well as it is possible for one man to know another.'

"'And you admired him,' she said. 'It was impossible to know him and not to admire him. Was it?'

"'He was a remarkable man,' I said unsteadily. Then before the appealing fixity of her gaze, that seemed to watch for more words on my lips, I went on, 'It was impossible not to—'

"'Love him,' she finished eagerly, silencing me into an appalled dumbness. 'How true! how true! But when you think that no one knew him so well as I! I had all his noble confidence. I knew him best.'

"'You knew him best,' I repeated. And perhaps she did. But with every word spoken the room was growing darker, and only her forehead, smooth and white, remained illumined by the unextinguishable light of belief and love.

"'You were his friend,' she went on. 'His friend,' she repeated, a little louder. 'You must have been, if he had given you this, and sent you to me. I feel I can speak to you—and oh! I must speak. I want you—you who have heard his last words—to know I have been worthy of him. . . . It is not pride. . . . Yes! I am proud to know I understood him better than any one on earth—he told me so himself. And since his mother died I have had no one—no one—to—to—'

"I listened. The darkness deepened. I was not even sure whether he had given me the right bundle. I rather suspect he wanted me to take care of another batch of his papers which, after his death, I saw the manager examining under the lamp. And the girl talked, easing her pain in the certitude of my sympathy; she talked as thirsty men drink. I had heard that her engagement with Kurtz had been disapproved by her people. He wasn't rich enough or something. And indeed I don't know whether he had not been a pauper all his life. He had given me some reason to infer that it was his impatience of comparative poverty that drove him out there.

"'. . . Who was not his friend who had heard him speak once?' she was saying. 'He drew men towards him by what was best in them.' She looked at me with intensity. 'It is the gift of the great,' she went on, and the sound of her low voice seemed to have the accompaniment of all the other sounds, full of mystery, desolation, and sorrow, I had ever heard—the ripple of the river, the soughing[3] of the trees swayed by the wind, the murmurs of the crowds, the faint ring of incomprehensible words cried from afar, the whisper of a voice speaking from beyond the threshold of an eternal darkness. 'But you have heard him! You know!' she cried.

"'Yes, I know,' I said with something like despair in my heart, but bowing my head before the faith that was in her, before that great and saving illusion that shone with an unearthly glow in the darkness, in the triumphant darkness from which I could not have defended her—from which I could not even defend myself.

"'What a loss to me—to us!'—she corrected herself with beautiful generosity; then added in a murmur, 'To the world.' By the last gleams of twilight I could see the glitter of her eyes, full of tears—of tears that would not fall.

"'I have been very happy—very fortunate—very proud,' she went on. 'Too fortunate. Too happy for a little while. And now I am unhappy for—for life.'

"She stood up; her fair hair seemed to catch all the remaining light in a glimmer of gold. I rose too.

---

3. A rushing or murmuring sound.

"'And of all this,' she went on mournfully, 'of all his promise, and of all his greatness, of his generous mind, of his noble heart, nothing remains—nothing but a memory. You and I—'

"'We shall always remember him,' I said hastily.

"'No!' she cried. 'It is impossible that all this should be lost—that such a life should be sacrificed to leave nothing—but sorrow. You know what vast plans he had. I knew of them too—I could not perhaps understand—but others knew of them. Something must remain. His words, at least, have not died.'

"'His words will remain,' I said.

"'And his example,' she whispered to herself. 'Men looked up to him—his goodness shone in every act. His example—'

"'True,' I said; 'his example too. Yes, his example. I forgot that.'

"'But I do not. I cannot—I cannot believe—not yet. I cannot believe that I shall never see him again, that nobody will see him again, never, never, never.'

"She put out her arms as if after a retreating figure, stretching them back and with clasped pale hands across the fading and narrow sheen of the window. Never see him! I saw him clearly enough then. I shall see this eloquent phantom as long as I live, and I shall see her too, a tragic and familiar Shade, resembling in this gesture another one, tragic also, and bedecked with powerless charms, stretching bare brown arms over the glitter of the infernal stream, the stream of darkness. She said suddenly very low, 'He died as he lived.'

"'His end,' said I, with dull anger stirring in me, 'was in every way worthy of his life.'

"'And I was not with him,' she murmured. My anger subsided before a feeling of infinite pity.

"'Everything that could be done—' I mumbled.

"'Ah, but I believed in him more than any one on earth—more than his own mother, more than—himself. He needed me! Me! I would have treasured every sigh, every word, every sign, every glance.'

"I felt like a chill grip on my chest. 'Don't,' I said, in a muffled voice.

"'Forgive me. I—I—have mourned so long in silence—in silence. . . . You were with him—to the last? I think of his loneliness. Nobody near to understand him as I would have understood. Perhaps no one to hear. . . .'

"'To the very end,' I said shakily. 'I heard his very last words. . . .' I stopped in a fright.

"'Repeat them,' she murmured in a heart-broken tone. 'I want—I want—something—something—to—to live with.'

"I was on the point of crying at her, 'Don't you hear them?' The dusk was repeating them in a persistent whisper all around us, in a whisper that seemed to swell menacingly like the first whisper of a rising wind. 'The horror! The horror!'

"'His last word—to live with,' she insisted. 'Don't you understand I loved him—I loved him—I loved him!'

"I pulled myself together and spoke slowly.

"'The last word he pronounced was—your name.'

"I heard a light sigh and then my heart stood still, stopped dead short by an exulting and terrible cry, by the cry of inconceivable triumph and of unspeakable pain. 'I knew it—I was sure!' . . . She knew. She was sure. I heard her weeping; she had hidden her face in her hands. It seemed to me that the house would collapse before I could escape, that the heavens would fall upon my head. But nothing happened. The heavens do not fall for such a trifle. Would they have fallen, I wonder, if I had rendered Kurtz that justice which was his due? Hadn't he said he wanted only justice? But I couldn't. I could not tell her. It would have been too dark—too dark altogether. . . ."

Marlow ceased, and sat apart, indistinct and silent, in the pose of a meditating Buddha. Nobody moved for a time. "We have lost the first of the ebb," said the Director suddenly. I raised my head. The offing was barred by a black bank of clouds, and the tranquil waterway leading to the uttermost ends of the earth flowed sombre under an overcast sky—seemed to lead into the heart of an immense darkness.

1899

JAMES JOYCE
1882–1941

More than any other writer of the twentieth century, James Joyce shaped modern literature. His experiments with narrative form helped to define the major literary movements of the century, from modernism to postmodernism. By developing methods of tracing individual consciousness, Joyce, along with Marcel Proust and **Virginia Woolf**, helped us to understand the functioning of the human mind. Equally capable of realistic portrayal of urban life in Dublin and playful deformations of the English language, Joyce expanded the possibilities of the novel—as a record of intimate human experiences, as a massive encyclopedia of human culture, and as a funhouse mirror that shows the world a transformed image of itself.

Joyce left Ireland as a young man but made his native country the subject of all his works. Born in Dublin on February 2, 1882, to May Murray and John Stanislaus Joyce, he was given the impressive name James Augustine Aloysius Joyce; he was the eldest surviving child of what would soon be a large family (ten children plus three who died in infancy). His father held a well-paid and undemanding post in the civil service, and the family was comfortable until 1891, when his job was eliminated. John received a small pension and declined to take up more demanding work elsewhere. The Joyce family moved steadily down the social and economic scale, and life became difficult under the improvident guidance of a man whom Joyce later portrayed as "a drinker, a good fellow, a storyteller, somebody's secretary, something in a distillery, a tax-gatherer, a bankrupt, and at present a praiser of his own past."

Joyce attended the well-known Catholic preparatory school of Clongowes Wood College from the ages of six to nine, leaving when his family could no longer afford the tuition. Two years later, he was admitted as a scholarship student to Belvedere College in Dublin. Both were Jesuit schools and provided a rigorous Catholic training against which Joyce violently rebelled but which he never forgot. In Belvedere College, shaken by a dramatic hell-fire sermon shortly after his first experience with sex, he even seriously considered becoming a priest; in the end, the life of the senses and his sense of vocation as an artist won out. After graduating from Belvedere in 1898, Joyce entered another Catholic institution—University College, Dublin—where he rejected Irish tradition and looked abroad for new values. Teaching himself Norwegian in order to read **Henrik Ibsen** in the original, he criticized the writers of the Irish Literary Renaissance as provincial and showed no interest in joining their ranks. His first published piece was an essay on Ibsen, to which the great playwright responded in a brief note of thanks. Like Stephen Dedalus, the hero, of his autobiographical novel, *A Portrait of the Artist as a Young Man* (1916), Joyce decided (in 1902) to escape the stifling conventions of his native country and leave for the Continent.

This trip did not last long. He studied medicine briefly, then for six months supported himself in Paris by giving English lessons, but when his mother became seriously ill, he was called home. After her death, he taught school for a time in Dublin and then returned to the Continent with Nora Barnacle, a country woman from western Ireland with whom he had two children and whom he married (after twenty-seven years of cohabitation) in 1931. The young couple moved to Trieste, where Joyce taught English in a Berlitz school and started writing both the short stories collected as *Dubliners* (1914) and an early version, partially published as *Stephen Hero* in 1944, of *A Portrait of the Artist as a Young Man*. He also wrote some mostly forgettable poetry and a play, *Exiles* (1918), that he had trouble getting produced. The couple remained poor for much of Joyce's life and relied on grants from the British government and gifts from wealthy patrons to allow Joyce to complete his literary projects. Joyce made a few brief business trips to Dublin, but, after 1912, never returned to the city.

When the First World War broke out, the Joyces moved to neutral Zurich, then after the war to Paris, where Joyce completed his most famous work, *Ulysses* (1922). In Paris he briefly met the other great novelist of the day, Marcel Proust, but claimed never to have read his work. He did, however, attend Proust's funeral. By now, Joyce was a celebrity and developed a circle of literary friends who supported and publicized his work. Throughout his life Joyce was a heavy drinker, and his conversation was legendary. His eyesight deteriorated as he devoted himself to the project he called *Work in Progress* (completed as *Finnegans Wake* in 1939). He sometimes relied on others, including the young Irish writer Samuel Beckett, to take dictation. These years were blighted by the mental illness of Joyce's daughter, Lucia, who ended up institutionalized for most of her life. The Joyces remained in Paris until the German occupation during the Second World War, when Joyce and his wife returned to Zurich, where Joyce died in 1941 after an operation for a perforated ulcer.

From *Dubliners* to *Ulysses* and *Finnegans Wake*, Joyce developed ways of exploring the lives and dreams of characters, including his youthful self, from the parochial Dublin society he had fled. Each of the major works presents innovative literary approaches that were to have a substantial impact on later writers. *A Portrait of the Artist as a Young Man* introduced into English the technique of stream of consciousness, as a means of capturing thoughts and emotions. Because it suggests the seemingly arbitrary manner in which thoughts and feelings often arise and then dissipate, stream-of-conscious writing may sound illogical or confusing; nevertheless it can indeed be convincing, since it gives the reader apparent access to the workings of a character's mind. The author's aim in employing the technique is to achieve a deeper understanding of human experience by displaying subconscious associations along with conscious thoughts. *Portrait* is based on Joyce's life until 1902, but the novel is clearly not a conventional autobiography and the reader recognizes in the first pages a radical experiment in fictional language. The novel's sophisticated symbolism and stress on dramatic dialogue hint at the radical break with narrative tradition that Joyce was preparing in *Ulysses*.

While introducing a host of stylistic devices to English, including an expanded form of stream of consciousness, a complex set of mythic parallels, and a series of literary parodies, *Ulysses* also provided one of the most celebrated instances of modern literary censorship. Its serial publication in the New York *Little Review* (from 1918 to 1920) was halted by the U.S. Post Office after a complaint, from the New York Society for the Prevention of Vice, that the work was obscene. The novel was outlawed and all available copies were actually burned in England and in America, until a 1933 decision by Judge Woolsey in federal district court lifted the ban in the United States. Although Joyce's descriptions have lost none of their pungency, it is hard to imagine a reader who would not be struck by another element—the density and mythic scope of this complex, symbolic, and linguistically innovative novel. Openly referring to an ancient predecessor, the **Odyssey** of **Homer** ("Ulysses" is the Latin name for the hero Odysseus), *Ulysses* structures numerous episodes to suggest parallels with the Greek epic, and transforms the twenty-year Homeric journey home into the daylong wanderings through Dublin of an unheroic advertising man, Leopold Bloom, and a rebellious young teacher and writer from *Portrait*, Stephen Dedalus. **T. S. Eliot** saw Joyce's use of ancient myth to explore modern life as "a way of controlling, of ordering, of giving a shape and significance to the immense panorama of futility and anarchy which is contemporary history." The first half of *Ulysses* uses stream-of-consciousness technique to explore Bloom's and Stephen's thoughts through the course of the day. By the second half of the novel, however, a number of intrusive and parodic narrators intervene in the action; Joyce's games with language and representation in this section were prime influences on postmodernism.

After the publication of *Ulysses*, Joyce spent the next seventeen years writing an even more complex work: *Finnegans Wake* (1939). Despite the title, a reference to a balled in which the bricklayer Tim Finnegan is brought back to life at his wake when somebody spills whiskey on him, the novel is the multivoiced, multidimensional dream of Humphrey Chimpden Earwicker. *Finnegans Wake* expands on the encyclopedic series of literary and cultural references underlying *Ulysses*, in language that has been even more radically broken apart and reassembled than that of *Ulysses*. Digressing exuberantly in all directions at once, with complex puns and hybrid words that mix languages, *Finnegans Wake* is—in spite of its cosmic symbolism—a game of language and reference by an artist "hoppy on akkant of his joyicity."

"THE DEAD"

These influential literary experiments had their roots in Joyce's command of more traditional narrative technique. "The Dead," presented here, was the last and greatest story in Joyce's first published volume, *Dubliners*. The collection as a whole sketches aspects of life in the Irish capital as Joyce knew it, in which the parochialism, piety, and repressive conventions of life are shown stifling artistic and psychological development. Whether it is the young boy who arrives too late at the fair in "Araby," the poor-aunt laundress of "Clay," or the frustrated writer Gabriel Conroy of "The Dead," the characters in *Dubliners* dream of a better life against a dismal, impoverishing background whose cumulative effect is of despair. The style of *Dubliners* is more realistic than in Joyce's later fiction, but he already employs a structure of symbolic meanings and revelatory moments he called "epiphanies." Joyce wrote to his publisher that the collection would be "a chapter of the moral history of my country," and he further explained that he had chosen Dublin because it was the "centre of paralysis" in Ireland—a city of blunted hopes and lost dreams: desperately poor, with large slums and more people than jobs, it stagnated in political, religious, and cultural divisions that color the lives of the characters in the stories. The book is arranged, Joyce noted, in an order that represents four aspects of life in the city: "childhood, adolescence, maturity and public life." Individual stories focus on one or a few characters, who may dream of a better life but are eventually frustrated by, or sink voluntarily back into, their shabby reality. Stories often end with a moment of special insight (epiphany), evident to the reader but not always to the protagonist, that puts events into sharp and illuminating perspective.

Several aspects of "The Dead" recall—and transmute—elements in Joyce's life. As in other stories, the neighborhood setting is familiar from his youth. The real-life models for Miss Kate and Miss Julia were indeed music teachers. Mr. Bartell D'Arcy evokes a contemporary tenor who performed under a similar name. The figure of Gabriel Conroy—who writes reviews for local journals, dislikes Irish nationalism, and prefers European culture—physically resembles

Joyce—a lesser Joyce who might never have had the courage to leave home for Europe. The tale that Gretta tells Gabriel at the end of the story echoes Nora's experience.

"The Dead" is divided into three parts, chronicling the stages of the Misses Morkan's party and also the stages by which Gabriel Conroy moves from the rather pompous, insecure, and externally oriented figure of the beginning to a man who has been forced to reassess himself and human relationships at the end. The party is an annual dinner dance that takes place after the New Year, probably on January 6, the Catholic Feast of the Epiphany (which many have connected with Gabriel's personal epiphany at the end of the story). A jovial occasion, it brings together friends and acquaintances for an evening of music, dancing, sumptuous food, and a formal after-dinner speech that Gabriel delivers. The undercurrents are not always harmonious, however, for small anxieties and personal frictions crop up that both create a realistic picture and suggest tensions in contemporary Irish society: nationalism, religion, poverty, and class differences. Gabriel has a position to maintain, and he is determined to live up to his responsibilities: he is at once cultured speaker and intellectual, carver and master of ceremonies, and the man whom the Misses Morkan expect to take care of occasional problems like alcoholic guests. He is a complex character, both a writer of real imagination and a narcissistic figure who is so used to focusing on himself that he has drawn apart from other people.

Joyce's method in "The Dead" relies heavily on free indirect discourse, the presentation of a character's thoughts (without quotation marks) by the narrator. Joyce drew this style partly from **Flaubert**—in *Portrait*, Stephen Dedalus quotes Flaubert's idea of the artist who "like the God of the creation, remains within or behind or beyond or above his handiwork, invisible, refined out of existence, indifferent, paring his fingernails." Joyce's later development of stream of consciousness would allow the character's thoughts to be presented directly to the reader, sometimes without the intervention of a narrator, but in "The Dead" the narrator unobtrusively filters Gabriel's thoughts for us, allowing us to sympathize with Gabriel in his insecurity but also inviting us to judge him in his complacency.

The Dead

Lily, the caretaker's daughter, was literally run off her feet. Hardly had she brought one gentleman into the little pantry behind the office on the ground floor and helped him off with his overcoat than the wheezy hall-door bell clanged again and she had to scamper along the bare hallway to let in another guest. It was well for her she had not to attend to the ladies also. But Miss Kate and Miss Julia had thought of that and had converted the bathroom upstairs into a ladies' dressing-room. Miss Kate and Miss Julia were there, gossiping and laughing and fussing, walking after each other to the head of the stairs, peering down over the banisters and calling down to Lily to ask her who had come.

It was always a great affair, the Misses Morkan's annual dance. Everybody who knew them came to it, members of the family, old friends of the family, the members of Julia's choir, any of Kate's pupils that were grown up enough and even some of Mary Jane's pupils too. Never once had it fallen flat. For years and years it had gone off in splendid style as long as anyone could remember; ever since Kate and Julia, after the death of their brother Pat, had left the house in Stoney Batter and taken Mary Jane, their only niece, to live with them in the dark gaunt house on Usher's Island,[1] the upper part of which they had rented from Mr. Fulham, the cornfactor[2] on the ground floor. That was a good thirty years ago if it was a day. Mary Jane, who was then a little girl in short clothes, was now the main prop of the household for she had the organ[3] in Haddington Road. She had been through the Academy[4] and gave a pupils' concert every year in the upper room of the Antient Concert Rooms. Many of her pupils belonged to better-class families on the Kingstown and Dalkey line.[5] Old as they were, her aunts also did their share. Julia, though she was quite grey, was still the leading soprano in Adam and Eve's, and Kate, being too feeble to go about much, gave music lessons to beginners on the old square[6] piano in the back room. Lily, the caretaker's daughter, did housemaid's work for them. Though their life was modest they believed in eating well; the best of everything: diamond-bone sirloins, three-shilling tea and the best bottled stout.[7] But Lily seldom made a mistake in the orders so that she got on well with her three mistresses. They were fussy, that was all. But the only thing they would not stand was back answers.

1. Not an island, but an area in western Dublin on the south bank of the River Liffey. Stoney Batter is a street of small shops and a few houses in Dublin.
2. Dealer in grain.
3. I.e., earned money by playing the organ at church.

4. The Royal Academy of Music.
5. Railway to a fashionable section of Dublin.
6. I.e., upright. "Adam and Eve's": popular name (taken from a nearby inn) for a Dublin Catholic church.
7. Strong beer.

Of course they had good reason to be fussy on such a night. And then it was long after ten o'clock and yet there was no sign of Gabriel and his wife. Besides they were dreadfully afraid that Freddy Malins might turn up screwed.[8] They would not wish for worlds that any of Mary Jane's pupils should see him under the influence; and when he was like that it was sometimes very hard to manage him. Freddy Malins always came late but they wondered what could be keeping Gabriel: and that was what brought them every two minutes to the banisters to ask Lily had Gabriel or Freddy come.

—O, Mr. Conroy, said Lily to Gabriel when she opened the door for him, Miss Kate and Miss Julia thought you were never coming. Good-night, Mrs. Conroy.

—I'll engage they did, said Gabriel, but they forgot that my wife here takes three mortal hours to dress herself.

He stood on the mat, scraping the snow from his goloshes, while Lily led his wife to the foot of the stairs and called out:

—Miss Kate, here's Mrs. Conroy.

Kate and Julia came toddling down the dark stairs at once. Both of them kissed Gabriel's wife, said she must be perished alive and asked was Gabriel with her.

—Here I am as right as the mail,[9] Aunt Kate! Go on up. I'll follow, called out Gabriel from the dark.

He continued scraping his feet vigorously while the three women went upstairs, laughing, to the ladies' dressing-room. A light fringe of snow lay like a cape on the shoulders of his overcoat and like toecaps on the toes of his goloshes: and, as the buttons of his overcoat slipped with a squeaking noise through the snow-stiffened frieze, a cold fragrant air from out-of-doors escaped from crevices and folds.

—Is it snowing again, Mr. Conroy? asked Lily.

She had preceded him into the pantry to help him off with his overcoat. Gabriel smiled at the three syllables she had given his surname and glanced at her. She was a slim, growing girl, pale in complexion and with hay-coloured hair. The gas in the pantry made her look still paler. Gabriel had known her when she was a child and used to sit on the lowest step nursing a rag doll.

—Yes, Lily, he answered, and I think we're in for a night of it.

He looked up at the pantry ceiling, which was shaking with the stamping and shuffling of feet on the floor above, listened for a moment to the piano and then glanced at the girl, who was folding his overcoat carefully at the end of a shelf.

—Tell me, Lily, he said in a friendly tone, do you still go to school?

—O no, sir, she answered. I'm done schooling this year and more.

—O, then, said Gabriel gaily, I suppose we'll be going to your wedding one of these fine days with your young man, eh?

The girl glanced back at him over her shoulder and said with great bitterness:

—The men that is now is only all palaver[1] and what they can get out of you.

Gabriel coloured as if he felt he had made a mistake and, without looking at her, kicked off his goloshes and flicked actively with his muffler at his patent-leather shoes.

8. Drunk.
9. Reliable as mail delivery.

1. Fancy talk.

He was a stout tallish young man. The high colour of his cheeks pushed upwards even to his forehead where it scattered itself in a few formless patches of pale red; and on his hairless face there scintillated restlessly the polished lenses and the bright gilt rims of the glasses which screened his delicate and restless eyes. His glossy black hair was parted in the middle and brushed in a long curve behind his ears where it curled slightly beneath the groove left by his hat.

When he had flicked lustre into his shoes he stood up and pulled his waist-coat down more tightly on his plump body. Then he took a coin rapidly from his pocket.

—O Lily, he said, thrusting it into her hands, it's Christmastime, isn't it? Just . . . here's a little. . . .

He walked rapidly towards the door.

—O no, sir! cried the girl, following him. Really, sir, I wouldn't take it.

—Christmas-time! Christmas-time! said Gabriel, almost trotting to the stairs and waving his hand to her in deprecation.

The girl, seeing that he had gained the stairs, called out after him:

—Well, thank you, sir.

He waited outside the drawing-room door until the waltz should finish, listening to the skirts that swept against it and to the shuffling of feet. He was still discomposed by the girl's bitter and sudden retort. It had cast a gloom over him which he tried to dispel by arranging his cuffs and the bows of his tie. Then he took from his waistcoat pocket a little paper and glanced at the headings he had made for his speech. He was undecided about the lines from Robert Browning[2] for he feared they would be above the heads of his hearers. Some quotation that they could recognise from Shakespeare or from the Melodies[3] would be better. The indelicate clacking of the men's heels and the shuffling of their soles reminded him that their grade of culture differed from his. He would only make himself ridiculous by quoting poetry to them which they could not understand. They would think that he was airing his superior education. He would fail with them just as he had failed with the girl in the pantry. He had taken up a wrong tone. His whole speech was a mistake from first to last, an utter failure.

Just then his aunts and his wife came out of the ladies' dressing-room. His aunts were two small plainly dressed old women. Aunt Julia was an inch or so the taller. Her hair, drawn low over the tops of her ears, was grey; and grey also, with darker shadows, was her large flaccid face. Though she was stout in build and stood erect her slow eyes and parted lips gave her the appearance of a woman who did not know where she was or where she was going. Aunt Kate was more vivacious. Her face, healthier than her sister's, was all puckers and creases, like a shrivelled red apple, and her hair, braided in the same old-fashioned way, had not lost its ripe nut colour.

They both kissed Gabriel frankly. He was their favourite nephew, the son of their dead elder sister, Ellen, who had married T. J. Conroy of the Port and Docks.[4]

---

2. English poet (1812–1889) who had a contemporary reputation for obscurity.
3. Thomas Moore's (1779–1852) immensely popular *Irish Melodies*, a collection of poems with many set to old Irish melodies.
4. The Dublin Port and Docks Board, which regulated customs and shipping.

—Gretta tells me you're not going to take a cab back to Monkstown[5] tonight, Gabriel, said Aunt Kate.

—No, said Gabriel, turning to his wife, we had quite enough of that last year, hadn't we? Don't you remember, Aunt Kate, what a cold Gretta got out of it? Cab windows rattling all the way, and the east wind blowing in after we passed Merrion.[6] Very jolly it was. Gretta caught a dreadful cold.

Aunt Kate frowned severely and nodded her head at every word.

—Quite right, Gabriel, quite right, she said. You can't be too careful.

—But as for Gretta there, said Gabriel, she'd walk home in the snow if she were let.

Mrs. Conroy laughed.

—Don't mind him, Aunt Kate, she said. He's really an awful bother, what with green shades for Tom's eyes at night and making him do the dumb-bells, and forcing Eva to eat the stirabout.[7] The poor child! And she simply hates the sight of it! . . . O, but you'll never guess what he makes me wear now!

She broke out into a peal of laughter and glanced at her husband, whose admiring and happy eyes had been wandering from her dress to her face and hair. The two aunts laughed heartily too, for Gabriel's solicitude was a standing joke with them.

—Goloshes! said Mrs. Conroy. That's the latest. Whenever it's wet underfoot I must put on my goloshes. To-night even he wanted me to put them on, but I wouldn't. The next thing he'll buy me will be a diving suit.

Gabriel laughed nervously and patted his tie reassuringly while Aunt Kate nearly doubled herself, so heartily did she enjoy the joke. The smile soon faded from Aunt Julia's face and her mirthless eyes were directed towards her nephew's face. After a pause she asked:

—And what are goloshes, Gabriel?

—Goloshes, Julia! exclaimed her sister. Goodness me, don't you know what goloshes are? You wear them over your . . . over your boots, Gretta, isn't it?

—Yes, said Mrs. Conroy. Guttapercha[8] things. We both have a pair now. Gabriel says everyone wears them on the continent.

—O, on the continent, murmured Aunt Julia, nodding her head slowly.

Gabriel knitted his brows and said, as if he were slightly angered:

—It's nothing very wonderful but Gretta thinks it very funny because she says the word reminds her of Christy Minstrels.[9]

—But tell me, Gabriel, said Aunt Kate, with brisk tact. Of course, you've seen about the room. Gretta was saying . . .

—O, the room is all right, replied Gabriel. I've taken one in the Gresham.[1]

—To be sure, said Aunt Kate, by far the best thing to do. And the children, Gretta, you're not anxious about them?

—O, for one night, said Mrs. Conroy. Besides, Bessie will look after them.

—To be sure, said Aunt Kate again. What a comfort it is to have a girl like that, one you can depend on! There's that Lily, I'm sure I don't know what has come over her lately. She's not the girl she was at all.

5. Well-to-do suburb of Dublin.
6. Village on Dublin Bay.
7. Porridge.
8. A rubberlike substance.

9. "Goloshes" sounds like "golly shoes," which reminds Gretta of the Christy Minstrels, a popular blackface minstrel show.
1. Fashionable hotel in central Dublin.

Gabriel was about to ask his aunt some questions on this point but she broke off suddenly to gaze after her sister who had wandered down the stairs and was craning her neck over the banisters.

—Now, I ask you, she said, almost testily, where is Julia going? Julia! Julia! Where are you going?

Julia, who had gone halfway down one flight, came back and announced blandly:

—Here's Freddy.

At the same moment a clapping of hands and a final flourish of the pianist told that the waltz had ended. The drawing-room door was opened from within and some couples came out. Aunt Kate drew Gabriel aside hurriedly and whispered into his ear:

—Slip down, Gabriel, like a good fellow and see if he's all right, and don't let him up if he's screwed. I'm sure he's screwed. I'm sure he is.

Gabriel went to the stairs and listened over the banisters. He could hear two persons talking in the pantry. Then he recognised Freddy Malins' laugh. He went down the stairs noisily.

—It's such a relief, said Aunt Kate to Mrs. Conroy, that Gabriel is here. I always feel easier in my mind when he's here. . . . Julia, there's Miss Daly and Miss Power will take some refreshment. Thanks for your beautiful waltz, Miss Daly. It made lovely time.

A tall wizen-faced man, with a stiff grizzled moustache and swarthy skin, who was passing out with his partner said:

—And may we have some refreshment, too, Miss Morkan?

—Julia, said Aunt Kate summarily, and here's Mr. Browne and Miss Furlong. Take them in, Julia, with Miss Daly and Miss Power.

—I'm the man for the ladies, said Mr. Browne, pursing his lips until his moustache bristled and smiling in all his wrinkles. You know, Miss Morkan, the reason they are so fond of me is—

He did not finish his sentence, but, seeing that Aunt Kate was out of earshot, at once led the three young ladies into the back room. The middle of the room was occupied by two square tables placed end to end, and on these Aunt Julia and the caretaker were straightening and smoothing a large cloth. On the sideboard were arrayed dishes and plates, and glasses and bundles of knives and forks and spoons. The top of the closed square piano served also as a sideboard for viands and sweets. At a smaller sideboard in one corner two young men were standing, drinking hop-bitters.[2]

Mr. Browne led his charges thither and invited them all, in jest, to some ladies' punch, hot, strong and sweet. As they said they never took anything strong he opened three bottles of lemonade for them. Then he asked one of the young men to move aside, and, taking hold of the decanter, filled out for himself a goodly measure of whiskey. The young men eyed him respectfully while he took a trial sip.

—God help me, he said, smiling, it's the doctor's orders.

His wizened face broke into a broader smile, and the three young ladies laughed in musical echo to his pleasantry, swaying their bodies to and fro, with nervous jerks of their shoulders. The boldest said:

2. Unfermented beer.

—O, now, Mr. Browne, I'm sure the doctor never ordered anything of the kind.

Mr. Browne took another sip of his whiskey and said, with sidling mimicry:

—Well, you see, I'm like the famous Mrs. Cassidy, who is reported to have said: *Now, Mary Grimes, if I don't take it, make me take it, for I feel I want it.*

His hot face had leaned forward a little too confidentially and he had assumed a very low Dublin accent so that the young ladies, with one instinct, received his speech in silence. Miss Furlong, who was one of Mary Jane's pupils, asked Miss Daly what was the name of the pretty waltz she had played; and Mr. Browne, seeing that he was ignored, turned promptly to the two young men who were more appreciative.

A red-faced young woman, dressed in pansy,[3] came into the room, excitedly clapping her hands and crying:

—Quadrilles![4] Quadrilles!

Close on her heels came Aunt Kate, crying:

—Two gentlemen and three ladies, Mary Jane!

—O, here's Mr. Bergin and Mr. Kerrigan, said Mary Jane. Mr. Kerrigan, will you take Miss Power? Miss Furlong, may I get you a partner, Mr. Bergin. O, that'll just do now.

—Three ladies, Mary Jane, said Aunt Kate.

The two young gentlemen asked the ladies if they might have the pleasure, and Mary Jane turned to Miss Daly.

—O, Miss Daly, you're really awfully good, after playing for the last two dances, but really we're so short of ladies to-night.

—I don't mind in the least, Miss Morkan.

—But I've a nice partner for you, Mr. Bartell D'Arcy, the tenor. I'll get him to sing later on. All Dublin is raving about him.

—Lovely voice, lovely voice! said Aunt Kate.

As the piano had twice begun the prelude to the first figure Mary Jane led her recruits quickly from the room. They had hardly gone when Aunt Julia wandered slowly into the room, looking behind her at something.

—What is the matter, Julia? asked Aunt Kate anxiously. Who is it?

Julia, who was carrying in a column of table-napkins, turned to her sister and said, simply, as if the question had surprised her:

—It's only Freddy, Kate, and Gabriel with him.

In fact right behind her Gabriel could be seen piloting Freddy Malins across the landing. The latter, a young man of forty, was of Gabriel's size and build, with very round shoulders. His face was fleshy and pallid, touched with colour only at the thick hanging lobes of his ears and at the wide wings of his nose. He had coarse features, a blunt nose, a convex and receding brow, tumid and protruded lips. His heavy-lidded eyes and the disorder of his scanty hair made him look sleepy. He was laughing heartily in a high key at a story which he had been telling Gabriel on the stairs and at the same time rubbing the knuckles of his left fist backwards and forwards into his left eye.

—Good-evening, Freddy, said Aunt Julia.

3. Violet.   4. An intricate square dance for four couples.

Freddy Malins bade the Misses Morkan good-evening in what seemed an offhand fashion by reason of the habitual catch in his voice and then, seeing that Mr. Browne was grinning at him from the sideboard, crossed the room on rather shaky legs and began to repeat in an undertone the story he had just told to Gabriel.

—He's not so bad, is he? said Aunt Kate to Gabriel.

Gabriel's brows were dark but he raised them quickly and answered:

—O no, hardly noticeable.

—Now, isn't he a terrible fellow! she said. And his poor mother made him take the pledge on New Year's Eve. But come on, Gabriel, into the drawing-room.

Before leaving the room with Gabriel she signalled to Mr. Browne by frowning and shaking her forefinger in warning to and fro. Mr. Browne nodded in answer and, when she had gone, said to Freddy Malins:

—Now, then, Teddy, I'm going to fill you out a good glass of lemonade just to buck you up.

Freddy Malins, who was nearing the climax of his story, waved the offer aside impatiently but Mr. Browne, having first called Freddy Malins' attention to a disarray in his dress,[5] filled out and handed him a full glass of lemonade. Freddy Malins' left hand accepted the glass mechanically, his right hand being engaged in the mechanical readjustment of his dress. Mr. Browne, whose face was once more wrinkling with mirth, poured out for himself a glass of whisky while Freddy Malins exploded, before he had well reached the climax of his story, in a kink of high-pitched bronchitic laughter and, setting down his untasted and overflowing glass, began to rub the knuckles of his left fist backwards and forwards into his left eye, repeating words of his last phrase as well as his fit of laughter would allow him.

Gabriel could not listen while Mary Jane was playing her Academy piece, full of runs and difficult passages, to the hushed drawing-room. He liked music but the piece she was playing had no melody for him and he doubted whether it had any melody for the other listeners, though they had begged Mary Jane to play something. Four young men, who had come from the refreshment-room to stand in the doorway at the sound of the piano, had gone away quietly in couples after a few minutes. The only persons who seemed to follow the music were Mary Jane herself, her hands racing along the key-board or lifted from it at the pauses like those of a priestess in momentary imprecation, and Aunt Kate standing at her elbow to turn the page.

Gabriel's eyes, irritated by the floor, which glittered with beeswax under the heavy chandelier, wandered to the wall above the piano. A picture of the balcony scene in *Romeo and Juliet* hung there and beside it was a picture of the two murdered princes[6] in the Tower which Aunt Julia had worked in red, blue and brown wools when she was a girl. Probably in the school they had gone to as girls that kind of work had been taught, for one year his mother had worked for him as a birthday present a waistcoat of purple tabinet,[7] with little foxes'

---

5. That his fly was open.
6. According to Shakespeare's *Richard III*, the young heirs to the British throne were murdered in the Tower of London by order of

their uncle, King Richard III. Balcony scene: Shakespeare's *Romeo and Juliet* 2.2.
7. A damasklike fabric.

heads upon it, lined with brown satin and having round mulberry buttons. It was strange that his mother had had no musical talent though Aunt Kate used to call her the brains carrier of the Morkan family. Both she and Julia had always seemed a little proud of their serious and matronly sister. Her photograph stood before the pierglass.[8] She held an open book on her knees and was pointing out something in it to Constantine who, dressed in a man-o'-war suit,[9] lay at her feet. It was she who had chosen the names for her sons for she was very sensible of the dignity of family life. Thanks to her, Constantine was now senior curate in Balbriggan and, thanks to her, Gabriel himself had taken his degree in the Royal University. A shadow passed over his face as he remembered her sullen opposition to his marriage. Some slighting phrases she had used still rankled in his memory; she had once spoken of Gretta as being country cute[1] and that was not true of Gretta at all. It was Gretta who had nursed her during all her last long illness in their house at Monkstown.

He knew that Mary Jane must be near the end of her piece for she was playing again the opening melody with runs of scales after every bar and while he waited for the end the resentment died down in his heart. The piece ended with a trill of octaves in the treble and a final deep octave in the bass. Great applause greeted Mary Jane as, blushing and rolling up her music nervously, she escaped from the room. The most vigorous clapping came from the four young men in the doorway who had gone away to the refreshment-room at the beginning of the piece but had come back when the piano had stopped.

Lancers were arranged. Gabriel found himself partnered with Miss Ivors. She was a frank-mannered talkative young lady, with a freckled face and prominent brown eyes. She did not wear a low-cut bodice and the large brooch which was fixed in the front of her collar bore on it an Irish device.

When they had taken their places she said abruptly:

—I have a crow to pluck[2] with you.

—With me? said Gabriel.

She nodded her head gravely.

—What is it? asked Gabriel, smiling at her solemn manner.

—Who is G. C.? answered Miss Ivors, turning her eyes upon him.

Gabriel coloured and was about to knit his brows, as if he did not understand, when she said bluntly:

—O, innocent Amy! I have found out that you write for *The Daily Express*.[3] Now, aren't you ashamed of yourself?

—Why should I be ashamed of myself? asked Gabriel, blinking his eyes and trying to smile.

—Well, I'm ashamed of you, said Miss Ivors frankly. To say you'd write for a rag like that. I didn't think you were a West Briton.[4]

A look of perplexity appeared on Gabriel's face. It was true that he wrote a literary column every Wednesday in *The Daily Express*, for which he was paid fifteen shillings. But that did not make him a West Briton surely. The books he received for review were almost more welcome than the paltry cheque. He

---

8. A large mirror.
9. A sailor suit.
1. Unintelligent (not acute).
2. A bone to pick; an argument.

3. Conservative Dublin newspaper opposed to Irish independence.
4. An Irishman who supports union with Britain (an insult).

loved to feel the covers and turn over the pages of newly printed books. Nearly every day when his teaching in the college was ended he used to wander down the quays to the second-hand booksellers, to Hickey's on Bachelor's Walk, to Webb's or Massey's on Aston's Quay, or to O'Clohissey's in the by-street. He did not know how to meet her charge. He wanted to say that literature was above politics. But they were friends of many years' standing and their careers had been parallel, first at the University and then as teachers: he could not risk a grandiose phrase with her. He continued blinking his eyes and trying to smile and murmured lamely that he saw nothing political in writing reviews of books.

When their turn to cross[5] had come he was still perplexed and inattentive. Miss Ivors promptly took his hand in a warm grasp and said in a soft friendly tone:

—Of course, I was only joking. Come, we cross now.

When they were together again she spoke of the University question,[6] and Gabriel felt more at ease. A friend of hers had shown her his review of Browning's poems. That was how she had found out the secret: but she liked the review immensely. Then she said suddenly:

—O, Mr. Conroy, will you come for an excursion to the Aran Isles[7] this summer? We're going to stay there a whole month. It will be splendid out in the Atlantic. You ought to come. Mr. Clancy is coming, and Mr. Kilkelly and Kathleen Kearney. It would be splendid for Gretta too if she'd come. She's from Connacht,[8] isn't she?

—Her people are, said Gabriel shortly.

—But you will come, won't you? said Miss Ivors, laying her warm hand eagerly on his arm.

—The fact is, said Gabriel, I have already arranged to go—

—Go where? asked Miss Ivors.

—Well, you know, every year I go for a cycling tour with some fellows and so—

—But where? asked Miss Ivors.

—Well, we usually go to France or Belgium or perhaps Germany, said Gabriel awkwardly.

—And why do you go to France and Belgium, said Miss Ivors, instead of visiting your own land?

—Well, said Gabriel, it's partly to keep in touch with the languages and partly for a change.

—And haven't you your own language to keep in touch with—Irish? asked Miss Ivors.

—Well, said Gabriel, if it comes to that, you know, Irish is not my language.

Their neighbours had turned to listen to the cross-examination. Gabriel glanced right and left nervously and tried to keep his good humour under the ordeal which was making a blush invade his forehead.

5. A step in the square dance.
6. Controversy over the establishment of Irish Catholic universities to rival the dominant Protestant tradition of Oxford and Cambridge in England, and Trinity College in Dublin.

7. Off the west coast of Ireland, idealized by the nationalists as an example of unspoiled Irish culture and language.
8. The westernmost province of Ireland.

—And haven't you your own land to visit, continued Miss Ivors, that you know nothing of, your own people, and your own country?

—O, to tell you the truth, retorted Gabriel suddenly, I'm sick of my own country, sick of it!

—Why? asked Miss Ivors.

Gabriel did not answer for his retort had heated him.

—Why? repeated Miss Ivors.

They had to go visiting together[9] and, as he had not answered her, Miss Ivors said warmly:

—Of course, you've no answer.

Gabriel tried to cover his agitation by taking part in the dance with great energy. He avoided her eyes for he had seen a sour expression on her face. But when they met in the long chain[1] he was surprised to feel his hand firmly pressed. She looked at him from under her brows for a moment quizzically until he smiled. Then, just as the chain was about to start again, she stood on tiptoe and whispered into his ear:

—West Briton!

When the lancers were over Gabriel went away to a remote corner of the room where Freddy Malins' mother was sitting. She was a stout feeble old woman with white hair. Her voice had a catch in it like her son's and she stuttered slightly. She had been told that Freddy had come and that he was nearly all right. Gabriel asked her whether she had had a good crossing. She lived with her married daughter in Glasgow and came to Dublin on a visit once a year. She answered placidly that she had had a beautiful crossing and that the captain had been most attentive to her. She spoke also of the beautiful house her daughter kept in Glasgow, and of all the nice friends they had there. While her tongue rambled on Gabriel tried to banish from his mind all memory of the unpleasant incident with Miss Ivors. Of course the girl or woman, or whatever she was, was an enthusiast but there was a time for all things. Perhaps he ought not to have answered her like that. But she had no right to call him a West Briton before people, even in joke. She had tried to make him ridiculous before people, heckling him and staring at him with her rabbit's eyes.

He saw his wife making her way towards him through the waltzing couples. When she reached him she said into his ear:

—Gabriel, Aunt Kate wants to know won't you carve the goose as usual. Miss Daly will carve the ham and I'll do the pudding.

—All right, said Gabriel.

—She's sending in the younger ones first as soon as this waltz is over so that we'll have the table to ourselves.

—Were you dancing? asked Gabriel.

—Of course I was. Didn't you see me? What words had you with Molly Ivors?

—No words. Why? Did she say so?

—Something like that. I'm trying to get that Mr. D'Arcy to sing. He's full of conceit, I think.

---

9. A square-dance step. 1. Another square-dance step.

—There were no words, said Gabriel moodily, only she wanted me to go for a trip to the west of Ireland and I said I wouldn't.

His wife clasped her hands excitedly and gave a little jump.

—O, do go, Gabriel, she cried. I'd love to see Galway again.

—You can go if you like, said Gabriel coldly.

She looked at him for a moment, then turned to Mrs. Malins and said:

—There's a nice husband for you, Mrs. Malins.

While she was threading her way back across the room Mrs. Malins, without adverting to the interruption, went on to tell Gabriel what beautiful places there were in Scotland and beautiful scenery. Her son-in-law brought them every year to the lakes and they used to go fishing. Her son-in-law was a splendid fisher. One day he caught a fish, a beautiful big big fish, and the man in the hotel boiled it for their dinner.

Gabriel hardly heard what she said. Now that supper was coming near he began to think again about his speech and about the quotation. When he saw Freddy Malins coming across the room to visit his mother Gabriel left the chair free for him and retired into the embrasure[2] of the window. The room had already cleared and from the back room came the clatter of plates and knives. Those who still remained in the drawing-room seemed tired of dancing and were conversing quietly in little groups. Gabriel's warm trembling fingers tapped the cold pane of the window. How cool it must be outside! How pleasant it would be to walk out alone, first along by the river and then through the park! The snow would be lying on the branches of the trees and forming a bright cap on the top of the Wellington Monument.[3] How much more pleasant it would be there than at the supper-table!

He ran over the headings of his speech: Irish hospitality, sad memories, the Three Graces, Paris,[4] the quotation from Browning. He repeated to himself a phrase he had written in his review: *One feels that one is listening to a thought-tormented music*. Miss Ivors had praised the review. Was she sincere? Had she really any life of her own behind all her propagandism? There had never been any ill-feeling between them until that night. It unnerved him to think that she would be at the supper-table, looking up at him while he spoke with her critical quizzing eyes. Perhaps she would not be sorry to see him fail in his speech. An idea came into his mind and gave him courage. He would say, alluding to Aunt Kate and Aunt Julia: *Ladies and Gentlemen, the generation which is now on the wane among us may have had its faults but for my part I think it had certain qualities of hospitality, of humour, of humanity, which the new and very serious and hypereducated generation that is growing up around us seems to me to lack*. Very good: that was one for Miss Ivors. What did he care that his aunts were only two ignorant old women?

A murmur in the room attracted his attention. Mr. Browne was advancing from the door, gallantly escorting Aunt Julia, who leaned upon his arm, smiling and hanging her head. An irregular musketry of applause escorted her also as

2. Window nook.
3. A tall obelisk in Phoenix Park, celebrating the Duke of Wellington (1769–1852), an Anglo-Irish statesman and general, who served as British prime minister and commander-in-chief of the army.
4. The Trojan prince of Homer's *Iliad*. "Three Graces": daughters of Zeus and Eurynome in Greek mythology; they embodied (and bestowed) charm.

far as the piano and then, as Mary Jane seated herself on the stool, and Aunt Julia, no longer smiling, half turned so as to pitch her voice fairly into the room, gradually ceased. Gabriel recognized the prelude. It was that of an old song of Aunt Julia's—*Arrayed for the Bridal*.[5] Her voice, strong and clear in tone, attacked with great spirit the runs which embellish the air and though she sang very rapidly she did not miss even the smallest of the grace notes. To follow the voice, without looking at the singer's face, was to feel and share the excitement of swift and secure flight. Gabriel applauded loudly with all the others at the close of the song and loud applause was borne in from the invisible supper-table. It sounded so genuine that a little colour struggled into Aunt Julia's face as she bent to replace in the music-stand the old leather-bound song-book that had her initials on the cover. Freddy Malins, who had listened with his head perched sideways to hear her better, was still applauding when everyone else had ceased and talking animatedly to his mother who nodded her head gravely and slowly in acquiescence. At last, when he could clap no more, he stood up suddenly and hurried across the room to Aunt Julia whose hand he seized and held in both his hands, shaking it when words failed him or the catch in his voice proved too much for him.

—I was just telling my mother, he said, I never heard you sing so well, never. No, I never heard your voice so good as it is to-night. Now! Would you believe that now? That's the truth. Upon my word and honour that's the truth. I never heard your voice sound so fresh and so . . . so clear and fresh, never.

Aunt Julia smiled broadly and murmured something about compliments as she released her hand from his grasp. Mr. Browne extended his open hand towards her and said to those who were near him in the manner of a showman introducing a prodigy to an audience:

—Miss Julia Morkan, my latest discovery!

—He was laughing very heartily at this himself when Freddy Malins turned to him and said:

—Well, Browne, if you're serious you might make a worse discovery. All I can say is I never heard her sing half so well as long as I am coming here. And that's the honest truth.

—Neither did I, said Mr. Browne. I think her voice has greatly improved.

Aunt Julia shrugged her shoulders and said with meek pride:

—Thirty years ago I hadn't a bad voice as voices go.

—I often told Julia, said Aunt Kate emphatically, that she was simply thrown away in that choir. But she never would be said by me.

She turned as if to appeal to the good sense of the others against a refractory child while Aunt Julia gazed in front of her, a vague smile of reminiscence playing on her face.

—No, continued Aunt Kate, she wouldn't be said or led by anyone, slaving there in that choir night and day, night and day. Six o'clock on Christmas morning! And all for what?

—Well, isn't it for the honour of God, Aunt Kate? asked Mary Jane, twisting round on the piano-stool and smiling.

Aunt Kate turned fiercely on her niece and said:

5. An English lyric by George Linley; from the first act of Vincenzo Bellini's 1835 opera *I Puritani* (The Puritans).

—I know all about the honour of God, Mary Jane, but I think it's not at all honourable for the pope to turn out the women out of the choirs that have slaved there all their lives and put little whipper-snappers of boys over their heads.[6] I suppose it is for the good of the Church if the pope does it. But it's not just, Mary Jane, and it's not right.

She had worked herself into a passion and would have continued in defence of her sister for it was a sore subject with her but Mary Jane, seeing that all the dancers had come back, intervened pacifically:

—Now, Aunt Kate, you're giving scandal to Mr. Browne who is of the other persuasion.

Aunt Kate turned to Mr. Browne, who was grinning at this allusion to his religion, and said hastily:

—O, I don't question the pope's being right. I'm only a stupid old woman and I wouldn't presume to do such a thing. But there's such a thing as common everyday politeness and gratitude. And if I were in Julia's place I'd tell that Father Healy straight up to his face . . .

—And besides, Aunt Kate, said Mary Jane, we really are all hungry and when we are hungry we are all very quarrelsome.

—And when we are thirsty we are also quarrelsome, added Mr. Browne.

—So that we had better go to supper, said Mary Jane, and finish the discussion afterwards.

On the landing outside the drawing-room Gabriel found his wife and Mary Jane trying to persuade Miss Ivors to stay for supper. But Miss Ivors, who had put on her hat and was buttoning her cloak, would not stay. She did not feel in the least hungry and she had already overstayed her time.

—But only for ten minutes, Molly, said Mrs. Conroy. That won't delay you.

—To take a pick itself, said Mary Jane, after all your dancing.

—I really couldn't, said Miss Ivors.

—I am afraid you didn't enjoy yourself at all, said Mary Jane hopelessly.

—Ever so much, I assure you, said Miss Ivors, but you really must let me run off now.

—But how can you get home? asked Mrs. Conroy.

—O, it's only two steps up the quay.

Gabriel hesitated a moment and said:

—If you will allow me, Miss Ivors, I'll see you home if you really are obliged to go.

But Miss Ivors broke away from them.

—I won't hear of it, she cried. For goodness sake go in to your suppers and don't mind me. I'm quite well able to take care of myself.

—Well, you're the comical girl, Molly, said Mrs. Conroy frankly.

—*Beannacht libh*,[7] cried Miss Ivors, with a laugh, as she ran down the staircase.

Mary Jane gazed after her, a moody puzzled expression on her face, while Mrs. Conroy leaned over the banisters to listen for the hall-door. Gabriel asked himself was he the cause of her abrupt departure. But she did not seem to be in ill humour: she had gone away laughing. He stared blankly down the staircase.

6. In 1903, Pope Pius X decreed that all church singers be male.   7. Farewell: blessings on you (Irish).

At that moment Aunt Kate came toddling out of the supper-room, almost wringing her hands in despair.

—Where is Gabriel? she cried. Where on earth is Gabriel? There's everyone waiting in there, stage to let, and nobody to carve the goose!

—Here I am, Aunt Kate! cried Gabriel, with sudden animation, ready to carve a flock of geese, if necessary.

A fat brown goose lay at one end of the table and at the other end, on a bed of creased paper strewn with sprigs of parsley, lay a great ham, stripped of its outer skin and peppered over with crust crumbs, a neat paper frill round its shin and beside this was a round of spiced beef. Between these rival ends ran parallel lines of side-dishes: two little minsters[8] of jelly, red and yellow; a shallow dish full of blocks of blancmange and red jam, a large green leaf-shaped dish with a stalk-shaped handle, on which lay bunches of purple raisins and peeled almonds, a companion dish on which lay a solid rectangle of Smyrna figs, a dish of custard topped with grated nutmeg, a small bowl full of chocolates and sweets wrapped in gold and silver papers and a glass vase in which stood some tall celery stalks. In the center of the table there stood, as sentries to a fruit-stand which upheld a pyramid of oranges and American apples, two squat old-fashioned decanters of cut glass, one containing port and the other dark sherry. On the closed square piano a pudding in a huge yellow dish lay in waiting and behind it were three squads of bottles of stout and ale and minerals,[9] drawn up according to the colours of their uniforms, the first two black, with brown and red labels, the third and smallest squad white, with transverse green sashes.

Gabriel took his seat boldly at the head of the table and, having looked to the edge of the carver, plunged his fork firmly into the goose. He felt quite at ease now for he was an expert carver and liked nothing better than to find himself at the head of a well-laden table.

—Miss Furlong, what shall I send you? he asked. A wing or a slice of the breast?

—Just a small slice of the breast.

—Miss Higgins, what for you?

—O, anything at all, Mr. Conroy.

While Gabriel and Miss Daly exchanged plates of goose and plates of ham and spiced beef Lily went from guest to guest with a dish of hot floury potatoes wrapped in a white napkin. This was Mary Jane's idea and she had also suggested apple sauce for the goose but Aunt Kate had said that plain roast goose without apple sauce had always been good enough for her and she hoped she might never eat worse. Mary Jane waited on her pupils and saw that they got the best slices and Aunt Kate and Aunt Julia opened and carried across from the piano bottles of stout and ale for the gentlemen and bottles of minerals for the ladies. There was a great deal of confusion and laughter and noise, the noise of orders and counter-orders, of knives and forks, of corks and glass-stoppers. Gabriel began to carve second helpings as soon as he had finished the first round without serving himself. Everyone protested loudly so that he compromised by taking a long draught of stout for he had found the carving hot

8. Confectioneries shaped to look like cathedrals.

9. Carbonated drinks.

work. Mary Jane settled down quietly to her supper but Aunt Kate and Aunt Julia were still toddling round the table, walking on each other's heels, getting in each other's way and giving each other unheeded orders. Mr. Browne begged of them to sit down and eat their suppers and so did Gabriel but they said there was time enough so that, at last, Freddy Malins stood up and, capturing Aunt Kate, plumped her down on her chair amid general laughter.

When everyone had been well served Gabriel said, smiling:

—Now, if anyone wants a little more of what vulgar people call stuffing let him or her speak.

A chorus of voices invited him to begin his own supper and Lily came forward with three potatoes which she had reserved for him.

—Very well, said Gabriel amiably, as he took another preparatory draught, kindly forget my existence, ladies and gentlemen, for a few minutes.

He sat to his supper and took no part in the conversation with which the table covered Lily's removal of the plates. The subject of talk was the opera company which was then at the Theatre Royal. Mr. Bartell D'Arcy, the tenor, a dark-complexioned young man with a smart moustache, praised very highly the leading contralto of the company but Miss Furlong thought she had a rather vulgar style of production. Freddy Malins said there was a negro chieftain[1] singing in the second part of the Gaiety pantomime who had one of the finest tenor voices he had ever heard.

—Have you heard him? he asked Mr. Bartell D'Arcy across the table.

—No, answered Mr. Bartell D'Arcy carelessly.

—Because, Freddy Malins explained, now I'd be curious to hear your opinion of him. I think he has a grand voice.

—It takes Teddy to find out the really good things, said Mr. Browne familiarly to the table.

—And why couldn't he have a voice too? asked Freddy Malins sharply. Is it because he's only a black?

Nobody answered this question and Mary Jane led the table back to the legitimate opera. One of her pupils had given her a pass for *Mignon*.[2] Of course it was very fine, she said, but it made her think of poor Georgina Burns. Mr. Browne could go back farther still, to the old Italian companies that used to come to Dublin—Tietjens, Ilma de Murzka, Campanini, the great Trebelli, Giuglini, Ravelli, Aramburo.[3] Those were the days, he said, when there was something like singing to be heard in Dublin. He told too of how the top gallery of the old Royal used to be packed night after night, of how one night an Italian tenor had sung five encores to *Let Me Like a Soldier Fall*,[4] introducing a high C every time, and of how the gallery boys would sometimes in their enthusiasm unyoke the horses from the carriage of some great *prima donna* and pull her themselves through the streets to her hotel. Why did they never play the grand old operas now, he asked, *Dinorah, Lucrezia Borgia?*[5] Because they could not get the voices to sing them: that was why.

---

1. Actually, a blackface performer.
2. Popular French opera (1866) by Ambroise Thomas.
3. Famous opera singers.

4. From William V. Wallace's romantic light opera *Maritana* (1845).
5. Operas by Giacomo Meyerbeer (1859) and Gaetano Donizetti (1833), respectively.

—O, well, said Mr. Bartell D'Arcy, I presume there are as good singers today as there were then.

—Where are they? asked Mr. Browne defiantly.

—In London, Paris, Milan, said Mr. Bartell D'Arcy warmly. I suppose Caruso,[6] for example, is quite as good, if not better than any of the men you have mentioned.

—Maybe so, said Mr. Browne. But I may tell you I doubt it strongly.

—O, I'd give anything to hear Caruso sing, said Mary Jane.

—For me, said Aunt Kate, who had been picking a bone, there was only one tenor. To please me, I mean. But I suppose none of you ever heard of him.

—Who was he, Miss Morkan? asked Mr. Bartell D'Arcy politely.

—His name, said Aunt Kate, was Parkinson. I heard him when he was in his prime and I think he had then the purest tenor voice that was ever put into a man's throat.

—Strange, said Mr. Bartell D'Arcy. I never even heard of him.

—Yes, yes, Miss Morkan is right, said Mr. Browne. I remember hearing of old Parkinson but he's too far back for me.

—A beautiful pure sweet mellow English tenor, said Aunt Kate with enthusiasm.

Gabriel having finished, the huge pudding was transferred to the table. The clatter of forks and spoons began again. Gabriel's wife served out spoonfuls of the pudding and passed the plates down the table. Midway down they were held up by Mary Jane, who replenished them with raspberry or orange jelly or with blancmange and jam. The pudding was of Aunt Julia's making and she received praises for it from all quarters. She herself said that it was not quite brown enough.

—Well, I hope, Miss Morkan, said Mr. Browne, that I'm brown enough for you because, you know, I'm all brown.

All the gentlemen, except Gabriel, ate some of the pudding out of compliment to Aunt Julia. As Gabriel never ate sweets the celery had been left for him. Freddy Malins also took a stalk of celery and ate it with his pudding. He had been told that celery was a capital thing for the blood and he was just then under doctor's care. Mrs. Malins, who had been silent all through the supper, said that her son was going down to Mount Melleray[7] in a week or so. The table then spoke of Mount Melleray, how bracing the air was down there, how hospitable the monks were and how they never asked for a penny-piece from their guests.

—And do you mean to say, asked Mr. Browne incredulously, that a chap can go down there and put up there as if it were a hotel and live on the fat of the land and then come away without paying a farthing?

—O, most people give some donation to the monastery when they leave, said Mary Jane.

—I wish we had an institution like that in our Church, said Mr. Browne candidly.

He was astonished to hear that the monks never spoke, got up at two in the morning and slept in their coffins.[8] He asked what they did it for.

---

6. Enrico Caruso (1873–1921).
7. A Trappist abbey whose hospitality included the treatment of wealthy alcoholics.
8. The coffin story is a popular fiction.

—That's the rule of the order, said Aunt Kate firmly.

—Yes, but why? asked Mr. Browne.

Aunt Kate repeated that it was the rule, that was all. Mr. Browne still seemed not to understand. Freddy Malins explained to him, as best he could, that the monks were trying to make up for the sins committed by all the sinners in the outside world. The explanation was not very clear for Mr. Browne grinned and said:

—I like that idea very much but wouldn't a comfortable spring bed do them as well as a coffin?

—The coffin, said Mary Jane, is to remind them of their last end.

As the subject had grown lugubrious it was buried in a silence of the table during which Mrs. Malins could be heard saying to her neighbour in an indistinct undertone:

—They are very good men, the monks, very pious men.

The raisins and almonds and figs and apples and oranges and chocolates and sweets were now passed about the table and Aunt Julia invited all the guests to have either port or sherry. At first Mr. Bartell D'Arcy refused to take either but one of his neighbours nudged him and whispered something to him upon which he allowed his glass to be filled. Gradually as the last glasses were being filled the conversation ceased. A pause followed, broken only by the noise of the wine and by unsettlings of chairs. The Misses Morkan, all three, looked down at the tablecloth. Someone coughed once or twice and then a few gentlemen patted the table gently as a signal for silence. The silence came and Gabriel pushed back his chair and stood up.

The patting at once grew louder in encouragement and then ceased altogether. Gabriel leaned his ten trembling fingers on the tablecloth and smiled nervously at the company. Meeting a row of upturned faces he raised his eyes to the chandelier. The piano was playing a waltz tune and he could hear the skirts sweeping against the drawing-room door. People, perhaps, were standing in the snow on the quay outside, gazing up at the lighted windows and listening to the waltz music. The air was pure there. In the distance lay the park where the trees were weighted with snow. The Wellington Monument wore a gleaming cap of snow that flashed westward over the white field of Fifteen Acres.[9]

He began:

—Ladies and Gentlemen.

—It has fallen to my lot this evening, as in years past, to perform a very pleasing task but a task for which I am afraid my poor powers as a speaker are all too inadequate.

—No, no! said Mr. Browne.

—But, however that may be, I can only ask you to-night to take the will for the deed and to lend me your attention for a few moments while I endeavour to express to you in words what my feelings are on this occasion.

—Ladies and Gentlemen. It is not the first time that we have gathered together under this hospitable roof, around this hospitable board. It is not the first time that we have been the recipients—or perhaps, I had better say, the victims—of the hospitality of certain good ladies.

9. A section of Phoenix Park used for British military reviews.

He made a circle in the air with his arm and paused. Everyone laughed or smiled at Aunt Kate and Aunt Julia and Mary Jane who all turned crimson with pleasure. Gabriel went on more boldly:

—I feel more strongly with every recurring year that our country has no tradition which does it so much honour and which it should guard so jealously as that of its hospitality. It is a tradition that is unique as far as my experience goes (and I have visited not a few places abroad) among the modern nations. Some would say, perhaps, that with us it is rather a failing than anything to be boasted of. But granted even that, it is, to my mind, a princely failing, and one that I trust will long be cultivated among us. Of one thing, at least, I am sure. As long as this one roof shelters the good ladies aforesaid—and I wish from my heart it may do so for many and many a long year to come—the tradition of genuine warm-hearted courteous Irish hospitality, which our forefathers have handed down to us and which we in turn must hand down to our descendants, is still alive among us.

A hearty murmur of assent ran around the table. It shot through Gabriel's mind that Miss Ivors was not there and that she had gone away discourteously: and he said with confidence in himself:

—Ladies and Gentlemen.

—A new generation is growing up in our midst, a generation actuated by new ideas and new principles. It is serious and enthusiastic for these new ideas and its enthusiasm, even when it is misdirected, is, I believe, in the main sincere. But we are living in a skeptical and, if I may use the phrase, a thought-tormented age: and sometimes I fear that this new generation, educated or hypereducated as it is, will lack those qualities of humanity, of hospitality, of kindly humour which belonged to an older day. Listening tonight to the names of all those great singers of the past it seemed to me, I must confess, that we were living in a less spacious age. Those days might, without exaggeration, be called spacious days: and if they are gone beyond recall let us hope, at least, that in gatherings such as this we shall still speak of them with pride and affection, still cherish in our hearts the memory of those dead and gone great ones whose fame the world will not willingly let die.

—Hear, hear! said Mr. Browne loudly.

—But yet, continued Gabriel, his voice falling into a softer inflection, there are always in gatherings such as this sadder thoughts that will recur to our minds: thoughts of the past, of youth, of changes, of absent faces that we miss here tonight. Our path through life is strewn with many such sad memories: and were we to brood upon them always we could not find the heart to go on bravely with our work among the living. We have all of us living duties and living affections which claim, and rightly claim, our strenuous endeavours.

—Therefore, I will not linger on the past. I will not let any gloomy moralising intrude upon us here to-night. Here we are gathered together for a brief moment from the bustle and rush of our everyday routine. We are met here as friends, in the spirit of good-fellowship, as colleagues, also to a certain extent, in the true spirit of *camaraderie*, and as the guests of—what shall I call them?— the Three Graces of the Dublin musical world.

The table burst into applause and laughter at this sally. Aunt Julia vainly asked each of her neighbours in turn to tell her what Gabriel had said.

—He says we are the Three Graces, Aunt Julia, said Mary Jane.

Aunt Julia did not understand but she looked up, smiling, at Gabriel, who continued in the same vein:

—Ladies and Gentlemen.

—I will not attempt to play to-night the part that Paris played on another occasion.[1] I will not attempt to choose between them. The task would be an invidious one and one beyond my poor powers. For when I view them in turn, whether it be our chief hostess herself, whose good heart, whose too good heart, has become a byword with all who know her, or her sister, who seems to be gifted with perennial youth and whose singing must have been a surprise and a revelation to us all to-night, or, last but not least, when I consider our youngest hostess, talented, cheerful, hard-working and the best of nieces, I confess, Ladies and Gentlemen, that I do not know to which of them I should award the prize.

Gabriel glanced down at his aunts and, seeing the large smile on Aunt Julia's face and the tears which had risen to Aunt Kate's eyes, hastened to his close. He raised his glass of port gallantly, while every member of the company fingered a glass expectantly, and said loudly:

—Let us toast them all three together. Let us drink to their health, wealth, long life, happiness and prosperity and may they long continue to hold the proud and self-won position which they hold in their profession and the position of honour and affection which they hold in our hearts.

All the guests stood up, glass in hand, and, turning towards the three seated ladies, sang in unison, with Mr. Browne as leader:

For they are jolly gay fellows,
For they are jolly gay fellows,
For they are jolly gay fellows,
Which nobody can deny.

Aunt Kate was making frank use of her handkerchief and even Aunt Julia seemed moved. Freddy Malins beat time with his pudding-fork and the singers turned towards one another, as if in melodious conference, while they sang, with emphasis:

Unless he tells a lie,
Unless he tells a lie,

Then, turning once more towards their hostesses, they sang:

For they are jolly gay fellows,
For they are jolly gay fellows,
For they are jolly gay fellows,
Which nobody can deny.

The acclamation which followed was taken up beyond the door of the supper-room by many of the other guests and renewed time after time, Freddy Malins acting as officer with his fork on high.

---

1. Paris was required to judge a beauty contest between the Greek goddesses Hera, Athena, and Aphrodite; see p. 973, n. 4.

The piercing morning air came into the hall where they were standing so that Aunt Kate said:

—Close the door, somebody. Mrs. Malins will get her death of cold.

—Browne is out there, Aunt Kate, said Mary Jane.

—Browne is everywhere, said Aunt Kate, lowering her voice.

Mary Jane laughed at her tone.

—Really, she said archly, he is very attentive.

—He has been laid on here like the gas, said Aunt Kate in the same tone, all during the Christmas.

She laughed herself this time good-humouredly and then added quickly:

—But tell him to come in, Mary Jane, and close the door. I hope to goodness he didn't hear me.

At that moment the hall-door was opened and Mr. Browne came in from the doorstep, laughing as if his heart would break. He was dressed in a long green overcoat with mock astrakhan[2] cuffs and collar and wore on his head an oval fur cap. He pointed down the snow-covered quay from where the sound of shrill prolonged whistling was borne in.

—Teddy will have all the cabs in Dublin out, he said.

Gabriel advanced from the little pantry behind the office, struggling into his overcoat and, looking round the hall, said:

—Gretta not down yet?

—She's getting on her things, Gabriel, said Aunt Kate.

—Who's playing up there? asked Gabriel.

—Nobody. They're all gone.

—O no, Aunt Kate, said Mary Jane. Bartell D'Arcy and Miss O'Callaghan aren't gone yet.

—Someone is strumming at the piano, anyhow, said Gabriel.

Mary Jane glanced at Gabriel and Mr. Browne and said with a shiver:

—It makes me feel cold to look at you two gentlemen muffled up like that. I wouldn't like to face your journey home at this hour.

—I'd like nothing better this minute, said Mr. Browne stoutly, than a rattling fine walk in the country or a fast drive with a good spanking goer between the shafts.

—We used to have a very good horse and trap at home, said Aunt Julia sadly.

—The never-to-be-forgotten Johnny, said Mary Jane, laughing.

Aunt Kate and Gabriel laughed too.

—Why, what was wonderful about Johnny? asked Mr. Browne.

—The late lamented Patrick Morkan, our grandfather, that is, explained Gabriel, commonly known in his later years as the old gentleman, was a glue-boiler.

—O, now, Gabriel, said Aunt Kate, laughing, he had a starch mill.

—Well, glue or starch, said Gabriel, the old gentleman had a horse by the name of Johnny. And Johnny used to work in the old gentleman's mill, walking round and round in order to drive the mill. That was all very well; but now comes the tragic part about Johnny. One fine day the old gentleman thought he'd like to drive out with the quality[3] to a military review in the park.

2. Tight, curly-haired lambswool.   3. Social eliter.

—The Lord have mercy on his soul, said Aunt Kate compassionately.

—Amen, said Gabriel. So the old gentleman, as I said, harnessed Johnny and put on his very best tall hat and his very best stock collar and drove out in grand style from his ancestral mansion somewhere near Back Lane,[4] I think.

Everyone laughed, even Mrs. Malins, at Gabriel's manner and Aunt Kate said:

—O now, Gabriel, he didn't live in Back Lane, really. Only the mill was there.

—Out from the mansion of his forefathers, continued Gabriel, he drove with Johnny. And everything went on beautifully until Johnny came in sight of King Billy's[5] statue: and whether he fell in love with the horse King Billy sits on or whether he thought he was back again in the mill, anyhow he began to walk round the statue.

Gabriel paced in a circle round the hall in his goloshes amid the laughter of the others.

—Round and round he went, said Gabriel, and the old gentleman, who was a very pompous old gentleman, was highly indignant. *Go on, sir! What do you mean, sir? Johnny! Johnny! Most extraordinary conduct! Can't understand the horse!*

The peals of laughter which followed Gabriel's imitation of the incident were interrupted by a resounding knock at the hall-door. Mary Jane ran to open it and let in Freddy Malins. Freddy Malins, with his hat well back on his head and his shoulders humped with cold, was puffing and steaming after his exertions.

—I could only get one cab, he said.

—O, we'll find another along the quay, said Gabriel.

—Yes, said Aunt Kate. Better not keep Mrs. Malins standing in the draught.

Mrs. Malins was helped down the front steps by her son and Mr. Browne and, after many manœuvres, hoisted into the cab. Freddy Malins clambered in after her and spent a long time settling her on the seat, Mr. Browne helping him with advice. At last she was settled comfortably and Freddy Malins invited Mr. Browne into the cab. There was a good deal of confused talk, and then Mr. Browne got into the cab. The cabman settled his rug over his knees, and bent down for the address. The confusion grew greater and the cabman was directed differently by Freddy Malins and Mr. Browne, each of whom had his head out through a window of the cab. The difficulty was to know where to drop Mr. Browne along the route and Aunt Kate, Aunt Julia and Mary Jane helped the discussion from the doorstep with cross-directions and contradictions and abundance of laughter. As for Freddy Malins he was speechless with laughter. He popped his head in and out of the window every moment, to the great danger of his hat, and told his mother how the discussion was progressing till at last Mr. Browne shouted to the bewildered cabman above the din of everybody's laughter:

—Do you know Trinity College?

—Yes, sir, said the cabman.

—Well, drive bang up against Trinity College gates, said Mr. Browne, and then we'll tell you where to go. You understand now?

4. A shabby street in a run-down area of Dublin.
5. William III, king of England from 1689 to 1702, defeated the Irish nationalists at the Battle of the Boyne.

—Yes, sir, said the cabman.

—Make like a bird for Trinity College.

—Right, sir, cried the cabman.

The horse was whipped up and the cab rattled off along the quay amid a chorus of laughter and adieus.

Gabriel had not gone to the door with the others. He was in a dark part of the hall gazing up the staircase. A woman was standing near the top of the first flight, in the shadow also. He could not see her face but he could see the terracotta and salmonpink panels of her skirt which the shadow made appear black and white. It was his wife. She was leaning on the banisters, listening to something. Gabriel was surprised at her stillness and strained his ear to listen also. But he could hear little save the noise of laughter and dispute on the front steps, a few chords struck on the piano and a few notes of a man's voice singing.

He stood still in the gloom of the hall, trying to catch the air that the voice was singing and gazing up at his wife. There was grace and mystery in her attitude as if she were a symbol of something. He asked himself what is a woman standing on the stairs in the shadow, listening to distant music, a symbol of. If he were a painter he would paint her in that attitude. Her blue felt hat would show off the bronze of her hair against the darkness and the dark panels of her skirt would show off the light ones. *Distant Music* he would call the picture if he were a painter.

The hall-door was closed; and Aunt Kate, Aunt Julia and Mary Jane came down the hall, still laughing.

—Well, isn't Freddy terrible? said Mary Jane. He's really terrible.

Gabriel said nothing but pointed up the stairs towards where his wife was standing. Now that the hall-door was closed the voice and the piano could be heard more clearly. Gabriel held up his hand for them to be silent. The song seemed to be in the old Irish tonality[6] and the singer seemed uncertain both of his words and of his voice. The voice, made plaintive by distance and by the singer's hoarseness, faintly illuminated the cadence of the air with words expressing grief:

> *O, the rain falls on my heavy locks*
> *And the dew wets my skin,*
> *My babe lies cold*[7] . . .

—O, exclaimed Mary Jane. It's Bartell D'Arcy singing and he wouldn't sing all the night. O, I'll get him to sing a song before he goes.

—O do, Mary Jane, said Aunt Kate.

Mary Jane brushed past the others and ran to the staircase but before she reached it the singing stopped and the piano was closed abruptly.

—O, what a pity! she cried. Is he coming down, Gretta?

Gabriel heard his wife answer yes and saw her come down towards them. A few steps behind her were Mr. Bartell D'Arcy and Miss O'Callaghan.

6. Based on five (and later seven) tones rather than the modern eight-tone scale.
7. From "The Lass of Aughrim," a ballad about a peasant girl seduced by a lord; when she brings her baby to the castle door, the lord's mother imitates his voice and sends her away. Mother and child are drowned at sea, and the repentant lord curses his mother.

—O, Mr. D'Arcy, cried Mary Jane, it's downright mean of you to break off like that when we were all in raptures listening to you.

—I have been at him all the evening, said Miss O'Callaghan, and Mrs. Conroy too and he told us he had a dreadful cold and couldn't sing.

—O, Mr. D'Arcy, said Aunt Kate, now that was a great fib to tell.

—Can't you see that I'm as hoarse as a crow? said Mr. D'Arcy roughly.

He went into the pantry hastily and put on his overcoat. The others, taken aback by his rude speech, could find nothing to say. Aunt Kate wrinkled her brows and made signs to the others to drop the subject. Mr. D'Arcy stood swathing his neck carefully and frowning.

—It's the weather, said Aunt Julia, after a pause.

—Yes, everybody has colds, said Aunt Kate readily, everybody.

—They say, said Mary Jane, we haven't had snow like it for thirty years; and I read this morning in the newspapers that the snow is general all over Ireland.

—I love the look of snow, said Aunt Julia sadly.

—So do I, said Miss O'Callaghan. I think Christmas is never really Christmas unless we have the snow on the ground.

—But poor Mr. D'Arcy doesn't like the snow, said Aunt Kate, smiling.

Mr. D'Arcy came from the pantry, fully swathed and buttoned, and in a repentant tone told them the history of his cold. Everyone gave him advice and said it was a great pity and urged him to be very careful of his throat in the night air. Gabriel watched his wife who did not join in the conversation. She was standing right under the dusty fanlight and the flame of the gas lit up the rich bronze of her hair which he had seen her drying at the fire a few days before. She was in the same attitude and seemed unaware of the talk about her. At last she turned towards them and Gabriel saw that there was colour on her cheeks and that her eyes were shining. A sudden tide of joy went leaping out of his heart.

—Mr. D'Arcy, she said, what is the name of that song you were singing?

—It's called *The Lass of Aughrim*, said Mr. D'Arcy, but I couldn't remember it properly. Why? Do you know it?

—*The Lass of Aughrim*, she repeated. I couldn't think of the name.

—It's a very nice air, said Mary Jane. I'm sorry you were not in voice to-night.

—Now, Mary Jane, said Aunt Kate, don't annoy Mr. D'Arcy. I won't have him annoyed.

Seeing that all were ready to start she shepherded them to the door where good-night was said:

—Well, good-night, Aunt Kate, and thanks for the pleasant evening.

—Good-night, Gabriel. Good-night, Gretta!

—Good-night, Aunt Kate, and thanks ever so much. Good-night, Aunt Julia.

—O, good-night, Gretta, I didn't see you.

—Good-night, Mr. D'Arcy. Good-night, Miss O'Callaghan.

—Good-night, Miss Morkan.

—Good-night, again.

—Good-night, all. Safe home.

—Good-night. Good-night.

The morning was still dark. A dull yellow light brooded over the houses and the river; and the sky seemed to be descending. It was slushy underfoot; and only streaks and patches of snow lay on the roofs, on the parapets of the quay and on the area railings. The lamps were still burning redly in the murky air and, across the river, the palace of the Four Courts[8] stood out menacingly against the heavy sky.

She was walking on before him with Mr. Bartell D'Arcy, her shoes in a brown parcel tucked under one arm and her hands holding her skirt up from the slush. She had no longer any grace of attitude but Gabriel's eyes were still bright with happiness. The blood went bounding along his veins; and the thoughts went rioting through his brain, proud, joyful, tender, valorous.

She was walking on before him so lightly and so erect that he longed to run after her noiselessly, catch her by the shoulders and say something foolish and affectionate into her ear. She seemed to him so frail that he longed to defend her against something and then to be alone with her. Moments of their secret life together burst like stars upon his memory. A heliotrope envelope was lying beside his breakfast-cup and he was caressing it with his hand. Birds were twittering in the ivy and the sunny web of the curtain was shimmering along the floor: he could not eat for happiness. They were standing on the crowded platform and he was placing a ticket inside the warm palm of her glove. He was standing with her in the cold, looking in through a grated window at a man making bottles in a roaring furnace. It was very cold. Her face, fragrant in the cold air, was quite close to his; and suddenly she called out to the man at the furnace:

—Is the fire hot, sir?

But the man could not hear her with the noise of the furnace. It was just as well. He might have answered rudely.

A wave of yet more tender joy escaped from his heart and went coursing in warm flood along his arteries. Like the tender fires of stars moments of their life together, that no one knew of or would ever know of, broke upon and illumined his memory. He longed to recall to her those moments, to make her forget the years of their dull existence together and remember only their moments of ecstasy. For the years, he felt, had not quenched his soul or hers. Their children, his writing, her household cares had not quenched all their souls' tender fire. In one letter that he had written to her then he had said: *Why is it that words like these seem to me so dull and cold? Is it because there is no word tender enough to be your name?*

Like distant music these words that he had written years before were borne towards him from the past. He longed to be alone with her. When the others had gone away, when he and she were in their room in the hotel, then they would be alone together. He would call her softly:

—Gretta!

Perhaps she would not hear at once: she would be undressing. Then something in his voice would strike her. She would turn and look at him.

At the corner of Winetavern Street they met a cab. He was glad of its rattling noise as it saved him from conversation. She was looking out of the window and seemed tired. The others spoke only a few words, pointing out some building or street. The horse galloped along wearily under the murky morning sky, dragging his old rattling box after his heels, and Gabriel was again in a cab with her, galloping to catch the boat, galloping to their honeymoon.

---

8. The Irish law courts building.

As the cab drove across O'Connell Bridge Miss O'Callaghan said:

—They say you never cross O'Connell Bridge without seeing a white horse.

—I see a white man this time, said Gabriel.

—Where? asked Mr. Bartell D'Arcy.

Gabriel pointed to the statue,[9] on which lay patches of snow. Then he nodded familiarly to it and waved his hand.

—Good-night, Dan, he said gaily.

When the cab drew up before the hotel Gabriel jumped out and, in spite of Mr. Bartell D'Arcy's protest, paid the driver. He gave the man a shilling over his fare. The man saluted and said:

—A prosperous New Year to you, sir.

—The same to you, said Gabriel cordially.

She leaned for a moment on his arm in getting out of the cab and while standing at the curbstone, bidding the others good-night. She leaned lightly on his arm, as lightly as when she had danced with him a few hours before. He had felt proud and happy then, happy that she was his, proud of her grace and wifely carriage. But now, after the kindling again of so many memories, the first touch of her body, musical and strange and perfumed, sent through him a keen pang of lust. Under cover of her silence he pressed her arm closely to his side; and, as they stood at the hotel door, he felt that they had escaped from their lives and duties, escaped from home and friends and run away together with wild and radiant hearts to a new adventure.

An old man was dozing in a great hooded chair in the hall. He lit a candle in the office and went before them to the stairs. They followed him in silence, their feet falling in soft thuds on the thickly carpeted stairs. She mounted the stairs behind the porter, her head bowed in the ascent, her frail shoulders curved as with a burden, her skirt girt tightly about her. He could have flung his arms about her hips and held her still for his arms were trembling with desire to seize her and only the stress of his nails against the palms of his hands held the wild impulse of his body in check. The porter halted on the stairs to settle his guttering candle. They halted too on the steps below him. In the silence Gabriel could hear the falling of the molten wax into the tray and the thumping of his own heart against his ribs.

The porter led them along a corridor and opened a door. Then he set his unstable candle down on a toilet-table and asked at what hour they were to be called in the morning.

—Eight, said Gabriel.

The porter pointed to the tap of the electric-light and began a muttered apology but Gabriel cut him short.

—We don't want any light. We have light enough from the street. And I say, he added, pointing to the candle, you might remove that handsome article, like a good man.

The porter took up his candle again, but slowly for he was surprised by such a novel idea. Then he mumbled good-night and went out. Gabriel shot the lock to.

9. Of Daniel O'Connell (1775–1847), called "The Liberator" by the Irish independence movement.

A ghostly light from the street lamp lay in a long shaft from one window to the door. Gabriel threw his overcoat and hat on a couch and crossed the room towards the window. He looked down into the street in order that his emotion might calm a little. Then he turned and leaned against a chest of drawers with his back to the light. She had taken off her hat and cloak and was standing before a large swinging mirror, unhooking her waist.[1] Gabriel paused for a few moments, watching her, and then said:

—Gretta!

She turned away from the mirror slowly and walked along the shaft of light towards him. Her face looked so serious and weary that the words would not pass Gabriel's lips. No, it was not the moment yet.

—You looked tired, he said.

—I am a little, she answered.

—You don't feel ill or weak?

—No, tired: that's all.

She went on to the window and stood there, looking out. Gabriel waited again and then, fearing that diffidence was about to conquer him, he said abruptly:

—By the way, Gretta!

—What is it?

—You know that poor fellow Malins? he said quickly.

—Yes. What about him?

—Well, poor fellow, he's a decent sort of chap after all, continued Gabriel in a false voice. He gave me back that sovereign I lent him and I didn't expect it really. It's a pity he wouldn't keep away from that Browne, because he's not a bad fellow at heart.

He was trembling now with annoyance. Why did she seem so abstracted? He did not know how he could begin. Was she annoyed, too, about something? If she would only turn to him or come to him of her own accord! To take her as she was would be brutal. No, he must see some ardour in her eyes first. He longed to be master of her strange mood.

—When did you lend him the pound? she asked, after a pause.

Gabriel strove to restrain himself from breaking out into brutal language about the sottish Malins and his pound. He longed to cry to her from his soul, to crush her body against his, to overmaster her. But he said:

—O, at Christmas, when he opened that little Christmas-card shop in Henry Street.

He was in such a fever of rage and desire that he did not hear her come from the window. She stood before him for an instant, looking at him strangely. Then, suddenly raising herself on tiptoe and resting her hands lightly on his shoulders, she kissed him.

—You are a very generous person, Gabriel, she said.

Gabriel, trembling with delight at her sudden kiss and at the quaintness of her phrase, put his hands on her hair and began smoothing it back, scarcely touching it with his fingers. The washing had made it fine and brilliant. His heart was brimming over with happiness. Just when he was wishing for it she had come to him of her own accord. Perhaps her thoughts had been running with his. Perhaps she had felt the impetuous desire that was in him and then

---

1. I.e., loosening her waistband.

the yielding mood had come upon her. Now that she had fallen to him so easily he wondered why he had been so diffident.

He stood, holding her head between his hands. Then, slipping one arm swiftly about her body and drawing her towards him, he said softly:

—Gretta dear, what are you thinking about?

She did not answer nor yield wholly to his arm. He said again, softly:

—Tell me what it is, Gretta. I think I know what is the matter. Do I know?

She did not answer at once. Then she said in an outburst of tears:

—O, I am thinking about that song, *The Lass of Aughrim.*

She broke loose from him and ran to the bed and, throwing her arms across the bed-rail, hid her face. Gabriel stood stock-still for a moment in astonishment and then followed her. As he passed in the way of the cheval-glass he caught sight of himself in full length, his broad, well-filled shirt-front, the face whose expression always puzzled him when he saw it in a mirror and his glimmering gilt-rimmed eyeglasses. He halted a few paces from her and said:

—What about the song? Why does that make you cry?

She raised her head from her arms and dried her eyes with the back of her hand like a child. A kinder note than he had intended went into his voice.

—Why, Gretta? he asked.

—I am thinking about a person long ago who used to sing that song.

—And who was the person long ago? asked Gabriel, smiling.

—It was a person I used to know in Galway when I was living with my grandmother, she said.

The smile passed away from Gabriel's face. A dull anger began to gather again at the back of his mind and the dull fires of his lust began to glow angrily in his veins.

—Someone you were in love with? he asked ironically.

—It was a young boy I used to know, she answered, named Michael Furey. He used to sing that song, *The Lass of Aughrim.* He was very delicate.

Gabriel was silent. He did not wish her to think that he was interested in this delicate boy.

—I can see him so plainly, she said after a moment. Such eyes as he had: big dark eyes! And such an expression in them—an expression!

—O then, you were in love with him? said Gabriel.

—I used to go out walking with him,[2] she said, when I was in Galway. A thought flew across Gabriel's mind.

—Perhaps that was why you wanted to go to Galway with that Ivors girl? he said coldly.

She looked at him and asked in surprise:

—What for?

Her eyes made Gabriel feel awkward. He shrugged his shoulders and said:

—How do I know? To see him perhaps.

She looked away from him along the shaft of light towards the window in silence.

—He is dead, she said at length. He died when he was only seventeen. Isn't it a terrible thing to die so young as that?

—What was he? asked Gabriel, still ironically.

2. I.e., she dated him.

—He was in the gasworks,[3] she said.

Gabriel felt humiliated by the failure of his irony and by the evocation of this figure from the dead, a boy in the gasworks. While he had been full of memories of their secret life together, full of tenderness and joy and desire, she had been comparing him in her mind with another. A shameful consciousness of his own person assailed him. He saw himself as a ludicrous figure, acting as a pennyboy[4] for his aunts, a nervous well-meaning sentimentalist, orating to vulgarians and idealising his own clownish lusts, the pitiable fatuous fellow he had caught a glimpse of in the mirror. Instinctively he turned his back more to the light lest she might see the shame that burned upon his forehead.

He tried to keep up his tone of cold interrogation but his voice when he spoke was humble and indifferent.

—I suppose you were in love with this Michael Furey, Gretta, he said.

—I was great[5] with him at that time, she said.

Her voice was veiled and sad. Gabriel, feeling now how vain it would be to try to lead her whither he had purposed, caressed one of her hands and said, also sadly:

—And what did he die of so young, Gretta? Consumption, was it?

—I think he died for me, she answered.

A vague terror seized Gabriel at this answer as if, at that hour when he had hoped to triumph, some impalpable and vindictive being was coming against him, gathering forces against him in its vague world. But he shook himself free of it with an effort of reason and continued to caress her hand. He did not question her again for he felt that she would tell him of herself. Her hand was warm and moist: it did not respond to his touch but he continued to caress it just as he had caressed her first letter to him that spring morning.

—It was in the winter, she said, about the beginning of the winter when I was going to leave my grandmother's and come up here to the convent. And he was ill at the time in his lodgings in Galway and wouldn't be let out and his people in Oughterard[6] were written to. He was in decline, they said, or something like that. I never knew rightly.

She paused for a moment and sighed.

—Poor fellow, she said. He was very fond of me and he was such a gentle boy. We used to go out together, walking, you know, Gabriel, like the way they do in the country. He was going to study singing only for his health. He had a very good voice, poor Michael Furey.

—Well; and then? asked Gabriel.

—And then when it came to the time for me to leave Galway and come up to the convent he was much worse and I wouldn't be let see him so I wrote a letter saying I was going up to Dublin and would be back in the summer and hoping he would be better then.

She paused for a moment to get her voice under control and then went on:

—Then the night before I left I was in my grandmother's house in Nun's Island,[7] packing up, and I heard gravel thrown up against the window. The window was so wet I couldn't see so I ran downstairs as I was and slipped out

3. A utilities plant that manufactured coal gas. Working there was an unhealthy occupation.
4. Errand boy.
5. Close friends.

6. A small village in western Ireland.
7. An island in the western city of Galway, on which is located the Convent of Poor Clares.

the back into the garden and there was the poor fellow at the end of the garden, shivering.

—And did you not tell him to go back? asked Gabriel.

—I implored of him to go home at once and told him he would get his death in the rain. But he said he did not want to live. I can see his eyes as well as well! He was standing at the end of the wall where there was a tree.

—And did he go home? asked Gabriel.

—Yes, he went home. And when I was only a week in the convent he died and he was buried in Oughterard where his people came from. O, the day I heard that, that he was dead!

She stopped, choking with sobs, and, overcome by emotion, flung herself face downward on the bed, sobbing in the quilt. Gabriel held her hand for a moment longer, irresolutely, and then, shy of intruding on her grief, let it fall gently and walked quietly to the window.

She was fast asleep.

Gabriel, leaning on his elbow, looked for a few moments unresentfully on her tangled hair and half-open mouth, listening to her deep-drawn breath. So she had that romance in her life: a man had died for her sake. It hardly pained him now to think how poor a part he, her husband, had played in her life. He watched her while she slept as though he and she had never lived together as man and wife. His curious eyes rested long upon her face and on her hair: and, as he thought of what she must have been then, in that time of her first girlish beauty, a strange friendly pity for her entered his soul. He did not like to say even to himself that her face was no longer beautiful but he knew that it was no longer the face for which Michael Furey had braved death.

Perhaps she had not told him all the story. His eyes moved to the chair over which she had thrown some of her clothes. A petticoat string dangled to the floor. One boot stood upright, its limp upper fallen down: the fellow of it lay upon its side. He wondered at his riot of emotions of an hour before. From what had it proceeded? From his aunt's supper, from his own foolish speech, from the wine and dancing, the merrymaking when saying goodnight in the hall, the pleasure of the walk along the river in the snow. Poor Aunt Julia! She, too, would soon be a shade with the shade of Patrick Morkan and his horse. He had caught that haggard look upon her face for a moment when she was singing *Arrayed for the Bridal*. Soon, perhaps, he would be sitting in that same drawing-room, dressed in black, his silk hat on his knees. The blinds would be drawn down and Aunt Kate would be sitting beside him, crying and blowing her nose and telling him how Julia had died. He would cast about in his mind for some words that might console her, and would find only lame and useless ones. Yes, yes: that would happen very soon.

The air of the room chilled his shoulders. He stretched himself cautiously along under the sheets and lay down beside his wife. One by one they were all becoming shades. Better pass boldly into that other world, in the full glory of some passion, than fade and wither dismally with age. He thought of how she who lay beside him had locked in her heart for so many years that image of her lover's eyes when he had told her that he did not wish to live.

Generous tears filled Gabriel's eyes. He had never felt like that himself towards any woman but he knew that such a feeling must be love. The tears gathered more thickly in his eyes and in the partial darkness he imagined he saw the form of a young man standing under a dripping tree. Other forms were near. His soul had approached that region where dwell the vast hosts of the dead. He was conscious of, but could not apprehend, their wayward and flickering existence. His own identity was fading out into a grey impalpable world: the solid world itself which these dead had one time reared and lived in was dissolving and dwindling.

A few light taps upon the pane made him turn to the window. It had begun to snow again. He watched sleepily the flakes, silver and dark, falling obliquely against the lamplight. The time had come for him to set out on his journey westward. Yes, the newspapers were right: snow was general all over Ireland. It was falling on every part of the dark central plain, on the treeless hills, falling softly upon the Bog of Allen and, farther westward, softly falling into the dark mutinous Shannon[8] waves. It was falling, too, upon every part of the lonely churchyard on the hill where Michael Furey lay buried. It lay thickly drifted on the crooked crosses and headstones, on the spears of the little gate, on the barren thorns. His soul swooned slowly as he heard the snow falling faintly through the universe and faintly falling, like the descent of their last end, upon all the living and the dead.

1914

---

8. An estuary of the Shannon River, west-southwest of Dublin. The Bog of Allen is southwest of Dublin.

FRANZ KAFKA
1883–1924

Franz Kafka's stories and novels contain such nightmarish scenarios that the word *Kafkaesque* has been coined to describe the most unpleasant and bizarre aspects of modern life, especially when it comes to bureaucracy. Despite the bleakness of the world he depicted, Kafka was in fact a highly amusing writer who, when reading his work to friends, would sometimes leave them laughing out loud. A master of dark humor and an artist of unique vision, Kafka captures perfectly the anxiety and absurdity of contemporary urban society.

Born in Prague, a majority Catholic, Czech-speaking city in the Austro-Hungarian Empire, to a nonobservant Jewish, German-speaking family, Kafka trained as a lawyer and went to work for an insurance company, while still living at home with his parents. He began writing in his twenties and published his first short prose works in 1908. Around the same time, he developed a renewed interest in Judaism, which he had mostly ignored as a child. Although he was an attractive and popular person—in this respect not much like his character Gregor Samsa—he was never quite satisfied with his relationships with women or with his family. He was engaged three times, twice to the same woman, and broke off all three engagements. Kafka had a difficult relationship with his father, a self-made man who could not take his son's writing seriously. Having learned from friends about the psychoanalytic theories of Sigmund Freud, Kafka recognized the oedipal tension in aspects of his family life and expressed uneasiness with authority, especially parental authority, in his fiction. He also kept extensive diaries about his dissatisfaction with his personal and work life and, in his late thirties, wrote a long letter to his father harshly criticizing his upbringing.

Most of Kafka's writing published during his life consisted of short stories, parables, and two novellas, including The Metamorphosis, the selection here, which were released in six slim volumes. Kafka did not believe himself to be a successful author, although he had won a prestigious literary award, the Fontane Prize of the City of Berlin, for one of his early stories, "The Stoker." He wrote three long novels, The Trial, The Castle, and Amerika, but completed none of them. In despair, he asked his friend and executor, Max Brod, to have them all burned at his death. Brod disobeyed Kafka's instructions and instead had the three novels published posthumously. Apparently reflecting the guilt their author experienced over his relations with women, and his failure to get married, the three novels are haunted by regret and a sense of culpability, although the source of the characters' disquiet can never be identified with certainty.

Unlike some of his characters—resentful employees of large bureaucracies—Kafka was a successful senior executive who handled an array of business matters. Nonetheless, he was unhappy with his day job and blamed the hours he spent at work for his inability to complete the novels: in his mind, he was a failure both in life and in art. After developing tuberculosis in his mid-thirties, Kafka quit his job, at age thirty-nine, in 1922. He published a number of stories, collected in The Hunger Artist, and traveled extensively, spending a year in Berlin; but as his health deteriorated, he eventually moved to a sanatorium outside Vienna, where he died. Once Brod released the novels and unfinished stories, the author's fame grew quickly. During the Great Depression and the political crises of the 1930s, Kafka became popular in the English-speaking world. Readers viewed his work as demonstrating the anxiety and isolation of modern life, particularly the problem of living in alienation from God, a major theme of existentialist philosophers after World War II. More recently, however, critics have emphasized Kafka's humor and the social contexts of his work, including his experiences in his native Prague.

Until the middle of the nineteenth century, Jews had been excluded from most aspects of Austro-Hungarian society. Kafka and his family felt a strong affinity for the emperor, who represented for them German high culture and whose family had emancipated the Jews. The old city of Prague, with its narrow streets, crowded apartment houses, Gothic cathedral, and huge medieval castle, was cosmopolitan for a small town. After 1918, Czechoslovakia became an independent republic, and Czech replaced German as the official language. Kafka was able to adapt—he knew Czech well—and in fact was one of the few "German" business executives who were retained after Czech independence. And yet he felt himself to be an outsider—a German-speaking Jew among Czech-speaking Christians. This feeling was no doubt reinforced by a resurgent anti-Semitism that coincided with the rise of Czech nationalism and that threatened the Jews' relatively recent emancipation. (Kafka didn't live to see the final confirmation of his sense of alienation and isolation, but his three sisters would later die in Nazi concentration camps.) In his thirties, Kafka studied Hebrew and Yiddish and became interested in the Yiddish theater; the Jewish Enlightenment of his friend Martin Buber (Austrian philosopher, 1878–1965); Jewish folklore; and the philosophical writings of Søren Kierkegaard (1813–1855). Kafka's work seldom discusses Judaism directly, but the sense of exclusion and persecution that underlies much of his writing may spring in part from his experience of anti-Semitism; certainly his interest in interpretation and the nature of language owes much to his understanding of Jewish thought.

THE METAMORPHOSIS

Written in 1912 and published in 1915, *The Metamorphosis*, Kafka's longest work published in his lifetime, was, as well, his most famous work released before his death. It is a consummate narrative: from the moment Gregor Samsa wakes up to find himself transformed into a "monstrous insect," the reader asks, "What happens next?" Although the events seem dreamlike, the narrator assures us "it was no dream," no nightmarish fantasy in which Gregor temporarily identified himself with other downtrodden vermin of society. Instead, this grotesque transformation is permanent, a single, unshakable fact that renders almost comic his family's calculations and attempts to adjust. Indeed, the events of the story are described in great detail, often with an emphasis on the kind of concrete, vivid imagery that plays a prominent role in dreams and in Freud's interpretations of them: the father's fist, the bug's blood, the sister's violin playing.

When the novella begins, Gregor seems to be simply a man in a bug suit, but as the tale progresses, his thinking becomes increasingly buglike, and he loses touch with the people around him. A major theme of the work is the mean-

ing of humanity, and Gregor experiences a sense of exclusion from what Kafka calls the "circle of humankind." As the author relays the protagonist's thoughts, the reader gets the impression that Gregor considers himself to be put upon: he has taken a job he dislikes in order to pay off his parents' debt. Yet even before his transformation, he felt that his family misunderstood him. Once he becomes a bug, he loses the power of speech: although he continues to think, he cannot express his thoughts. Thus, when he turns into a despised species, the lack of communication Gregor perceived as a man becomes an actuality.

"The terror of art," said Kafka in a conversation about *The Metamorphosis*, is that "the dream reveals the reality." This dream, which in the novella becomes Gregor's reality, sheds light on the intolerable nature of his former existence. Another aspect of his professional life is its mechanical rigidity, personal rivalries, and threatening suspicion of any deviation from the norm. Gregor himself is part of this world, as he shows when he fawns on the chief clerk and tries to manipulate him by criticizing their boss.

More disturbing is the transformation that takes place in Gregor's family, where the expected love and support turn into shamed resignation and animal resentment now that Gregor has let the family down. Mother and sister are ineffectual, and their sympathy is slowly replaced by disgust. Gregor's father quickly reassumes his position of authority and beats the vermin back into his room: first with the newspaper and chief clerk's cane, and later with a barrage of apples from the family table. Gregor eventually becomes an "it" for whom the family feels no affection. Even before his transformation, Gregor seems to have lost all purpose in life except earning money to repay his parents' debts.

These frustrated desires contribute to the central conflict: whether Gregor can ever emerge from his bedroom and become part of the family again. The slapstick-like comedy of Gregor's attempts to use his insect body underlines the sense of frustration and exclusion. This, indeed, may lie at the heart of the novella's appeal; perhaps everyone has, occasionally, felt like an outsider. Gregor's metamorphosis, though, makes him an alien of a literal sort. His attitude at times reflects the sullenness of an unhappy teenager; at other times, he seems more like a terminal patient who fears placing an undue burden on his family. The theme of transformation goes back to Ovid's *Metamorphoses*, in which frustrated sexual desire often plays a role in turning people into plants or animals. The dark humor and uncanniness of Kafka's work links it to fantastic works by authors such as Edgar Allan Poe (American, 1809–1849) and Heinrich Wilhelm Kleist (German, 1771–1811) and to the analysis of the psyche conducted, during Kafka's lifetime, by Sigmund Freud. Without directly blaming Gregor, Kafka sometimes seems to hint that his transformation results in part from the protagonist's desire to escape from human interaction.

Kafka exposes both the pathos and the humor of the situation, and for this reason the story retains its attraction today. He has been recognized as an important influence by a range of modern writers, including Samuel Beckett, Harold Pinter (English playwright, 1930–2008), and many Latin Americans, including **Jorge Luis Borges** and **Gabriel García Márquez**. Kafka was one of the great storytellers of modern life, capable of revealing the lonely emptiness of even a busy life in a crowded city apartment.

The Metamorphosis[1]

I

When Gregor Samsa woke one morning from troubled dreams, he found himself transformed right there in his bed into some sort of monstrous insect.[2] He was lying on his back—which was hard, like a carapace—and when he raised his head a little he saw his curved brown belly segmented by rigid arches atop which the blanket, already slipping, was just barely managing to cling. His many legs, pitifully thin compared to the rest of him, waved helplessly before his eyes.

"What in the world has happened to me?" he thought. It was no dream. His room, a proper human room, if admittedly rather too small, lay peacefully between the four familiar walls. Above the table, where an unpacked collection of cloth samples was arranged (Samsa was a traveling salesman), hung the picture he had recently clipped from a glossy magazine and placed in an attractive gilt frame. This picture showed a lady in a fur hat and fur boa who sat erect, holding out to the viewer a heavy fur muff in which her entire forearm had vanished.

Gregor's gaze then shifted to the window, where the bleak weather—raindrops could be heard striking the metal sill—made him feel quite melan-

1. Translated by Susan Bernofsky.
2. Kafka uses the adjective *ungeheuer* (monstrous) and the noun *Ungeziefer* (in Old High German, an unclean animal unfit for sacrifice). In his *Essays on Literature*, Russian novelist (and entomologist) Vladimir Nabokov identifies the insect simply as a "big beetle" about three feet long.

choly. "What if I just go back to sleep for a little while and forget all this foolishness," he thought, but this proved utterly impossible, for it was his habit to sleep on his right side, and in his present state he was unable to assume this position. No matter how forcefully he thrust himself onto his side, he kept rolling back. Perhaps a hundred times he attempted it, closing his eyes so as not to have to see those struggling legs, and relented only when he began to feel a faint dull ache in his side, unlike anything he'd ever felt before.

"Good Lord," he thought, "what an exhausting profession I've chosen. Day in and day out on the road. Work like this is far more unsettling than business conducted at home, and then I have the agony of traveling itself to contend with: worrying about train connections, the irregular, unpalatable meals, and human intercourse that is constantly changing, never developing the least constancy or warmth. Devil take it all!" He felt a faint itch high up on his belly; still on his back, he laboriously edged himself over to the bedpost so he could raise his head more easily; identified the site of the itch: a cluster of tiny white dots he was unable to judge; and wanted to probe the spot with a leg, but drew it back again at once, for the touch sent cold shivers rippling through him.

He slid back into his earlier position. "All this early rising," he thought, "it's enough to make one soft in the head. Human beings need their sleep. Other traveling salesmen live like harem girls. When I go back to the boardinghouse, for example, to copy out the morning's commissions: why, these gentlemen may still be sitting at breakfast. I'd like to see my boss's face if I tried that some time; he'd can me on the spot. Although who knows, maybe that would be the best thing for me. If I didn't have to hold back for my parents' sake, I'd have given notice long ago—I'd have marched right up to him and given him a piece of my mind. He'd have fallen right off his desk! And what an odd custom that is: perching high up atop one's elevated desk and from this considerable height addressing one's employee down below, especially as the latter is obliged to stand quite close because his boss is hard of hearing. Well, all hope is not yet lost; as soon as I've saved up enough money to pay back what my parents owe him—another five or six years ought to be enough—I'll most definitely do just that. This will be the great parting of ways. For the time being, though, I've got to get up, my train leaves at five."

And he glanced over at the alarm clock ticking away atop the wardrobe. "Heavenly Father!" he thought. It was half past six, and the clock's hands kept shifting calmly forward, in fact the half-hour had already passed, it was getting on toward six forty-five. Could the alarm have failed to ring? Even from the bed one could see it was properly set for four o'clock; it must have rung. Yes, but was it possible to sleep tranquilly through this furniture-shaking racket? Well, his sleep hadn't been exactly tranquil, but no doubt that's why it had been so sound. But what should he do now? The next train was at seven o'clock; to catch it, he would have to rush like a madman, and his sample case wasn't even packed yet, and he himself felt far from agile or alert. And even if he managed to catch this train, his boss was certain to unleash a thunderstorm of invective upon his head, for the clerk who met the five o'clock train had no doubt long since reported Gregor's absence. This clerk was the boss's underling, a creature devoid of backbone and wit. What if he called in sick? But that would be mortifying and also suspicious, since Gregor had never once been ill in all his five years of service. No doubt his boss would come calling with the company doctor, would reproach Gregor's parents for their son's laziness, silencing all objections by referring them to this doctor, in whose opinion there existed only healthy individuals unwilling to work. And would the doctor be so terribly wrong in this instance? Aside from a mild drowsiness that was certainly superfluous after so many hours of sleep, Gregor felt perfectly fine; in fact, he was ravenous.

While he was considering these matters with the greatest possible speed, yet still without managing to make up his mind to leave the bed (the clock was just striking a quarter to seven), a timid knock came at the door at the head of his bed. "Gregor," the voice called—it was his mother—"it's a quarter to seven. Didn't you want to catch your train?" That gentle voice! Gregor flinched when he heard his own in response: it was unmistakably his old voice, but now it had been infiltrated as if from below by a tortured peeping sound that was impossible to suppress—leaving each word intact, comprehensible, but only for an instant before so completely annihilating it as it continued to reverberate that a person could not tell for sure whether his ears were deceiving him. Gregor had meant to give a proper response explaining everything, but under the circumstances he limited himself to saying, "Yes, thank you, Mother, I'm just getting up." Because of the wooden door, the change in Gregor's voice appeared not to be noticeable from the other side, for his mother was reassured by his response and shuffled off. But their brief conversation had alerted the other family members that Gregor was unexpectedly still at home, and already his father was knocking at one of the room's side doors, softly, but with his fist: "Gregor, Gregor," he called. "What's the problem?" And after a short while he repeated his question in a deeper register: "Gregor! Gregor!" Meanwhile, at the other side door came his sister's faint lament: "Gregor? Are you unwell? Do you need anything?" "Just a second," Gregor answered in both directions at once, making an effort, by enunciating as clearly as possible and inserting long pauses between the individual words, to remove anything conspicuous from his voice. And in fact his father returned to his breakfast, but his sister whispered: "Gregor, open the door, I implore you." But Gregor had no intention of opening the door; he praised the cautious habit he had acquired while traveling of locking all his doors at night, even at home.

First he would get up calmly and undisturbed, he would get dressed and above all have breakfast, and only then would he consider his next steps, for all these supine contemplations, he suddenly realized, would yield no useful results. He recalled often having felt mild aches and pains in bed, caused perhaps by lying in an awkward position, and this pain had then proven to be a figment of his imagination the moment he got up; he was curious to see how this morning's imaginings would gradually fade. The change in his voice was nothing more than the harbinger of a proper head cold, an occupational hazard among traveling salesmen; this he doubted not in the least.

It was simple enough to rid himself of the blanket; he needed only puff himself up a bit, and it fell right off. But the rest proved difficult, not least because he was so exceedingly wide. He would have needed arms and hands to prop himself up; but instead all he had were these many little legs, variously in motion, that he was unable to control. If he tried to bend one leg, it would be the first to straighten; and when he finally succeeded in getting one leg to do his bidding, all the others went flailing about in an unnerving frenzy. "Enough of this lying about uselessly in bed," Gregor said to himself.

At first he tried to maneuver the lower part of his body out of the bed, but this lower part—which, by the way, he had not yet seen and couldn't properly imagine—proved too unwieldy; it all went so slowly; and when at last, half-mad with impatience, he thrust himself recklessly forward with all his strength, it was in the wrong direction, and he slammed against the lower bedpost; the throbbing pain he felt instructed him that for now at least the lower part of his body was perhaps the most sensitive.

So he decided to try leading instead with his upper body and carefully twisted his head toward the edge of the bed. This was easily accomplished, and in the end, despite his width and weight, the mass of his body slowly followed the turning of his head. But once his head was dangling in midair outside the bed, he was afraid to keep shifting forward like this, since if eventually he had to let himself fall in this position, it would be practically a miracle if his head escaped injury. And right now he had to keep his wits about him at all costs, even if it meant staying where he was.

But when, sighing after redoubled efforts, he found himself lying there as before, watching his little legs engaged in their struggles, perhaps more flail-ingly now, and seeing no possible way to bring calm or order to this chaos, he told himself once more that he could not possibly remain lying here any longer and that the most sensible thing would be to sacrifice anything and everything as long as there remained even the slightest hope of liberating himself from the bed. Simultaneously, though, he continued to remind himself that calm consideration—indeed, the calmest consideration—was far preferable to reso-lutions seized on in despair. At such moments he fixed his eyes as sharply as possible on the window, but regrettably the view of the morning fog, which veiled even the far side of the narrow street, offered little by way of optimism and good spirits. "Seven o'clock already," he said to himself as the clock struck once more, "already seven and still such dense fog." And for a little while he lay there quietly, his breathing shallow, in the expectation, perhaps, that this per-fect silence might possibly restore the real and ordinary state of things.

Then he said to himself: "Before it strikes a quarter past seven, I must abso-lutely have gotten myself completely out of bed. Besides, by then someone will have come from the office to inquire after me, as the office opens before seven." And he now set himself to rocking his body out of the bed as evenly as possible along his entire length. If he allowed himself to fall from the bed like this, his head—which he intended to lift up cleanly as he fell—would in all likelihood remain unharmed. His back seemed to be hard; surely it would sustain no damage as he fell to the rug. His greatest concern was what to do about the loud crash that would clearly result, no doubt calling forth not ter-ror perhaps but certainly alarm behind each door. Nonetheless it would have to be ventured.

By the time Gregor was already protruding halfway out of bed—this new method was more a game than a struggle, all he had to do was keep rocking sideways a little at a time—it occurred to him how simple things would be if only someone came to his aid. Two strong individuals—he was thinking of his father and the maidservant—would suffice; all they'd have to do was slip their arms beneath his curved back to scoop him out of bed, then crouch down with their burden and wait patiently for him to flip himself over onto the floor, where he hoped those tiny legs of his would take on some meaning. But even aside from the fact that the doors were locked, should he really call for help? Despite his distress, he couldn't help smiling at the thought.

Already he'd reached the point where the vigorous rocking motion was making it almost impossible for him to keep his balance, and soon he would have to make up his mind and take the plunge, for a quarter after seven was only five minutes away—when the front doorbell rang. "It's someone from the office," he said to himself and nearly froze while his little legs went on scrabbling all the more frenetically. For a moment all was still. "They won't answer," Gregor said to himself, caught up in some deluded hope. But then of course, as always, the maid strode resolutely to the door and opened it.

Gregor needed only hear the visitor's first words of greeting to know who it was: the general manager himself. Why oh why was Gregor condemned to serve in a firm where even the most negligible falling short was enough to arouse the greatest possible suspicion? Was every last one of the firm's employees a scoundrel, was there not a single loyal, devoted soul among them who would be driven mad by pangs of conscience should he fail to make the best possible use of even just a few morning hours for his employer's benefit, such that his guilt would render him virtually incapable of rising from his bed? Would it really not have sufficed to send an apprentice to inquire—if indeed such inquiries were necessary at all—did the general manager have to come in person, and was it necessary to demonstrate to the entire innocent family that the investigation of this suspicious matter could be entrusted only to the general manager's sharp intellect? And more because of the agitation aroused in Gregor by this train of thought than because of some proper resolution on his part, he swung himself out of bed with all his might. There was a loud thud, you couldn't really call it a crash. The rug cushioned the impact a little, and since his back was more elastic than he'd thought, the resulting sound was muffled and not so obvious. But he hadn't managed to hold his head up carefully enough and had bumped it; he turned it this way and that, pressing it against the rug in his vexation and pain.

"Something just fell in there," the general manager now said in the room on the left. Gregor tried to imagine whether anything like what he was now experiencing could ever befall the general manager; the possibility must certainly be admitted. But as if brusquely dismissing the question, the manager now took a few purposeful steps in the next room, making his patent leather boots creak. From the room on the right came the whisper of Gregor's sister informing him: "Gregor, the general manager is here." "I know," Gregor murmured; but he didn't dare raise his voice high enough for his sister to hear.

"Gregor," his father now said from the room on the left, "the general manager has come to inquire why you failed to depart by the early train. We don't know what to tell him. Besides, he'd like to have a word with you in person. So please open the door. I'm sure he'll be kind enough not to take offense at the untidiness of your room." "Good morning, Herr Samsa," the general manager now cried out in a friendly tone. "He isn't well," Gregor's mother said to the general manager while his father was still having his say beside the door, "not well at all, take my word for it, sir. Why else would Gregor miss his train! The office is the only thing that boy ever thinks of. It really bothers me that he never goes out in the evening; he's been back in the city an entire week now, but he's spent every last evening at home. He just sits at the table with us, quietly reading the newspaper, or else studies the timetables. Even just doing woodworking projects seems to entertain him. He carved a little picture frame, for example, did it in two or three evenings with his fretsaw; you'll be amazed how pretty it is; it's hanging there in his room; you'll see it in a minute when Gregor opens the door. Oh, and I'm so glad you paid us a visit, sir; on our own we'd never have managed to persuade Gregor to open up; he's so stubborn; and surely he isn't well, even though he denied it this morning." "Be . . . right . . . there," Gregor said, not moving, so as not to miss a single word of their conversation. "No other explanation, madam, is conceivable to me," the general manager said. "Let us hope it is nothing grave. Though on the other hand I would note that, as businessmen— fortunately or unfortunately, as one will—we are very often obliged to suppress indispositions out of consideration for the firm." "So are you ready to let the general manager in?" Gregor's impatient father asked, knocking again at the door. "No," Gregor responded. In the left-hand room horrified silence, while in the room on the right Gregor's sister began to sob.

Why didn't his sister go to join the others? She must have just gotten out of bed and not yet begun to dress. And why was she crying? Because he wasn't getting up and opening his door to the general manager, because he was in danger of losing his position, and because his boss would then start hounding his parents once more over their ancient debt? For the time being, all such worries were assuredly unnecessary. Gregor was still here, and abandoning his family was the farthest thing from his thoughts. At the moment, to be sure, he was lying on the rug, and no one familiar with his current state would seriously expect him to let the general manager in. But surely he wouldn't be sent packing just like that because of so trivial an act of discourtesy, for which it would be simple enough to find an appropriate excuse later on. And it seemed to Gregor it would be far more sensible to just leave him in peace rather than disturbing him with all this weeping and cajoling. But the others were distressed by the uncertainty of it all; their behavior was understandable.

"Herr Samsa," the general manager now called out, raising his voice. "What has come over you? You barricade yourself in your room, you reply to queries only with yes and no, you cause your parents onerous, unnecessary worries, and you are neglecting—let me permit myself to note—your professional responsibilities in a truly unprecedented manner. I speak here in the name of your parents as well as your employer and in all seriousness must ask you for a clear and immediate explanation. I am astonished, utterly astonished. I have always known you as a calm, sensible person, and now it seems you've begun to permit yourself the most whimsical extravagances. To be sure, the boss did suggest one possible explanation for your absence this morning—it concerns the cash payments recently entrusted to your care—and truthfully, I all but gave him my word of honor that this explanation could not be correct. But confronted here with your incomprehensible obstinacy, I find myself losing any desire I might have had to come to your defense. And your position is anything but secure. It was originally my intention to discuss all this with you in a private conversation, but since you compel me to waste my time here, I do not know why your esteemed parents should not hear of it as well. In short: your productivity of late has been highly unsatisfactory; admittedly this is not the best season for drumming up business, we do acknowledge this; but a season in which no business at all is drummed up is something that does not, and indeed may not exist, Herr Samsa."

"But sir," Gregor cried out, beside himself and forgetting all else in his agitation, "I shall open the door at once, this very instant. A slight indisposition, a fit of dizziness kept me from getting up. Even now I'm still in bed. But already I am feeling very much refreshed. Here, I'm getting up. Just a moment's patience! It's a bit more difficult than I thought. But already I'm feeling quite fine. How odd, the way such a thing can suddenly come over one. Yesterday evening I felt perfectly all right, my parents can attest to this, or rather: I did in fact feel a mild foreboding yesterday evening already. Surely it was noticeable to anyone looking at me. Why didn't I send word to the office? But we always just assume we'll be able to overcome these illnesses without staying home. Sir! Do be gentle with my parents. The allegations you make are unfounded, and no one has ever mentioned anything of the sort to me. Perhaps you haven't yet looked over the most recent commissions I sent in. In any case, I'll be back on the road in time for the eight o'clock train; these additional hours of rest have fortified me. Please do not allow me to detain you any longer, sir; I shall be at the office myself in no time; do be so good as to say I'm on my way and give my regards to the boss."

And while Gregor was hastily blurting out all of this, scarcely knowing what he said, he edged closer to the wardrobe with minimal effort, no doubt thanks to the practice he had already acquired while still in bed, and now he did his best to haul himself upright. Indeed, he really did want to open the door, to show himself and speak with the general manager; he was eager to learn what the others, who were so anxious to see him, would say when they finally laid eyes on him. If they recoiled in horror, Gregor could surrender all responsibility and rest easy. But if they accepted it all calmly, that meant he too had no reason to get himself worked up, and if he hurried, he could still make it to the station by eight. At first he couldn't get a grip on the wardrobe's smooth surface, but finally he gave a great heave and found himself standing upright; he no longer paid any heed to the pain in his lower body, ache as it might. Now he let himself drop against the back of a nearby chair, clinging to its edges with his little legs. And having thus attained control over himself, he fell silent, for now he could listen to the general manager.

"Did you understand a single word?" the manager was asking Gregor's parents. "Surely he isn't trying to make fools of us?" "For heaven's sake," Gregor's mother cried, already weeping, "he might be gravely ill, and here we are tormenting him. Grete! Grete!" she cried out. "Mother?" Gregor's sister called from the other side. They were communicating through Gregor's room. "You must go for the doctor at once. Gregor is ill. Quick, fetch the doctor. Did you hear him speaking just now?" "That was an animal's voice," the general manager said, speaking in noticeably subdued tones compared to the cries of Gregor's mother. "Anna! Anna!" the father shouted into the kitchen through the vestibule, clapping his hands. "Run and fetch a locksmith, hurry!" And already the two girls were racing through the vestibule, their skirts rustling (how had Gregor's sister possibly gotten dressed so quickly?), and flung open the front door. There was no sound of the door closing again; no doubt they had left it standing open, as one sees with apartments in which a great calamity has occurred.

But Gregor was far less troubled now. Even though the others were no longer able to understand his words—though they had seemed to him clear enough, clearer than in the past, perhaps because his ear had grown accustomed to their sound—they were now convinced that things were not right with him and were prepared to offer help. The confidence and conviction with which these first arrangements had been made comforted him. He felt drawn once more into the circle of humankind and was expecting both the doctor and the locksmith—without properly differentiating between the two—to perform magnificent, astounding feats. So as to have as intelligible a voice as possible for the crucial discussions that lay ahead, he cleared his throat a little, making an effort to do this as discreetly as possible, since even this sound might differ from human throat-clearing, which he no longer trusted himself to judge. In the next room, meanwhile, all was quiet. Perhaps his parents sat whispering at the table with the general manager, or perhaps all of them were leaning against the door, listening.

Gregor slowly pushed himself over to the door using the armchair, then let go and allowed himself to fall against the door, propping himself upright—the pads of his little legs turned out to be slightly sticky—and there he rested briefly from his exertions. Then he set about turning the key in the lock using his mouth. Unfortunately it seemed he had no real teeth—so how was he supposed to grasp the key?—but his jaws turned out to be surprisingly strong; and with their help he actually succeeded in causing the key to move, paying no heed to the fact that he was no doubt injuring himself in the process, for a brown fluid ran out of his mouth and down the key, dripping onto the floor. "Listen to that," the general manager said in the next room, "he's turning the key in the lock." Gregor found these words most encouraging; but all of them should have been cheering him on, including his father and mother: "Come on, Gregor!" they should have shouted, "just keep at it, keep working on that lock!" And now, imagining all of them following his efforts with great suspense, he bit down on the key uncomprehendingly, with all the force he could muster. With each revolution of the key, he danced about the lock, holding himself upright using only his mouth and, as needed, either clinging to the key or using the entire weight of his body to press it down. The brighter sound of the lock finally springing open positively revived him. Sighing in relief, he said to himself: "I guess I didn't need the locksmith after all," and he laid his head upon the handle of the door to press it open.

But he remained hidden from view as the door swung toward him, even after it was wide open. To be seen, he had to work his way slowly around one of the wings of the double door, a delicate operation if he wanted to avoid plopping down awkwardly on his back before he'd even entered the room. He was still occupied with this difficult maneuver and had no leisure to attend to anything else when he heard the general manager utter a loud "Oh!"—it sounded like wind howling—and now he saw him too, saw how the general manager, who was standing closest to the door, pressed his hand to his open mouth, slowly retreating, as though being driven back by an invisible, steady force. Gregor's mother—who despite the general manager's presence stood with her hair still undone from the night, wildly bristling—first looked over at his father, her hands clasped, then took two steps in Gregor's direction before falling down in the midst of all her billowing skirts, her face vanishing completely where it sank to her bosom. Gregor's father clenched his fist with a hostile grimace, as if he intended to thrust Gregor back into his room, then glanced uncertainly about the living room, shaded his eyes with his hands, and wept until his mighty chest shook.

Gregor made no move to enter the room, instead he leaned from the inside against the wing of the door that was bolted fast, so that only half his body and the head inclined sideways above it could be seen as he peered across at the others. Meanwhile it had grown much lighter out; on the far side of the street, a section of the infinitely long, dark gray building opposite—a hospital—came into view with its regular windows punched into the facade; rain was still falling, but only in large drops that were separately visible and seemed to have been hurled one by one to the ground. An inordinate number of breakfast dishes crowded the table, for Gregor's father considered breakfast the most important meal of the day and would drag it out for hours reading various newspapers. Straight ahead, on the opposite wall, hung a photograph of Gregor from his time in the military, showing him as a second lieutenant whose carefree smile as he rested his hand on his dagger commanded respect for his bearing and his uniform. The door to the vestibule was open, and since the front door was open as well, one could see all the way out to the landing and the head of the stairs leading down.

"Well," Gregor said, quite conscious of the fact that he was the only one who had retained his composure, "I shall get dressed at once, pack up my samples and be on my way. As for the rest of you, are you prepared to let me do so? You can see, sir"—he said, addressing the general manager—"I am not obstinate, nor a shirker; traveling is burdensome, but without it I could not live. Where are you going now, sir? To the office? Yes? Will you report all these things truthfully? A person can be incapable of working at the moment, but this is precisely the right time to recall his earlier accomplishments and consider that he will later, once the hindrance has been overcome, work all the more industriously and with greater focus. I am so dreadfully indebted to the boss, surely you're aware of this. On the other hand, I have my parents and sister to think of. Truly I'm in a bind, but I shall work my way out of it. Don't make things more difficult for me than they already are. Take my side at the office! No one loves us drummers,[3] I know. Everyone thinks the salesmen rake in a king's ransom while enjoying life's pleasures. And there's never any particular cause to reconsider this prejudice. But you, sir, have a far better grasp of the general circumstances than the rest of the staff, better even—if I may speak confidentially—than the boss himself, who in his role as businessman can easily err in his opinion to an employee's disadvantage. And you no doubt know quite well that a drummer, who spends almost the entire year away from the office, can easily become the victim of gossip, happenstance and groundless complaints against which he cannot possibly defend himself, as he usually never even learns of them, or only when he has completed one of his journeys, exhausted, and then back at home is forced to observe the dire physical effects of causes that can no longer be identified. Please, sir, do not leave without saying something to show you agree with me at least to some small extent!"

But the general manager had already turned away as soon as Gregor began to speak, and merely glanced back at him over a hunched shoulder, his mouth contorted. And during Gregor's speech he did not stand still for a moment but instead continued to retreat—not letting Gregor out of his sight—in the direction of the door, but only gradually, as though it were secretly prohibited to exit this room. Already he was in the vestibule, and to judge by the abrupt motion

3. Traveling salesmen.

with which he withdrew his foot from the living room for the last time, one might have supposed he'd just burned it. Having reached the vestibule, however, he stretched out his right hand, gesturing broadly in the direction of the stairs, as if some all but supernatural salvation awaited him there.

Gregor realized he could not possibly allow the general manager to depart in his present frame of mind if his own position at the firm was not to be put in the gravest jeopardy. His parents didn't fully comprehend his situation: over these long years they had formed the conviction that Gregor was provided for in this office for life, and besides they were so preoccupied with their present worries that they were bereft of all foresight. But Gregor had this foresight. The general manager would have to be detained, reasoned with, convinced and finally won over; after all, Gregor's future and that of his family depended on it. If only his sister were here! She was clever; she had already begun to weep while Gregor was still lying quietly on his back. And surely the general manager, ever the ladies' man, would have let himself be assuaged by her; she would have closed the front door of the apartment and talked him out of his fear in the vestibule. But his sister was not there, so Gregor himself would have to act. And without stopping to consider that he was not yet familiar with his current abilities with respect to locomotion, nor even taking into account the fact that this last speech of his had quite possibly—indeed probably—eluded comprehension, he let go of the door; forced his way through the opening; meant to walk over to where the general manager, already out on the landing, was foolishly clutching at the banister with both hands; but right away, groping in vain for something to catch hold of, he fell with a faint shriek upon his many little legs. No sooner had this occurred than he felt—for the first time all morning—a sense of physical well-being; his legs had solid ground beneath them; they obeyed his will perfectly, as he noted to his delight; they even strove to bear him wherever he wished; and already it seemed to him he would soon be delivered from all his sufferings. But as he lay there on the floor directly in front of his mother and not far from her, swaying with mobility held in check, she suddenly leapt up—rapt as she had appeared within her own contemplations—leapt high up into the air, her arms thrust wide, fingers spread, crying out: "Help me, for God's sake, help!" her head cocked at an angle, as if to see Gregor better, but then, contradicting this, she senselessly retreated; but she had forgotten the table set for breakfast just behind her; sat down hurriedly upon it as soon as she reached it, as if absent-mindedly; and didn't seem to notice that the big overturned coffeepot beside her was pouring a thick stream of coffee on the rug.

"Mother, Mother," Gregor said softly, gazing up at her. For a moment he had forgotten all about the general manager; on the other hand, he could not restrain himself, when he beheld this flowing coffee, from snapping his jaws several times. At this, the mother gave another shriek and fled from the table into the arms of Gregor's father as he rushed to her aid. But Gregor had no time for his parents now; the general manager was already on the stairs; his chin propped on the banister, he looked back on the scene one last time. Gregor was just preparing to dash after him to be sure of catching up with him; but the manager must have sensed something, for he leapt down several steps at once and vanished; and the cry of horror he gave as he fled resounded through the stairwell. Unfortunately the manager's flight now appeared to utterly discombobulate Gregor's father, who up till then had been relatively composed, for instead of running after the manager himself or at least not hindering Gregor in his own pursuit, he seized the manager's walking stick in one hand—it had been left lying on an armchair along with his overcoat and hat—with the other took up a large newspaper from the table, and set about driving Gregor back into his room with a great stamping of feet, brandishing both newspaper and stick. All Gregor's entreaties were in vain, nor were they even understood, for as submissively as he might swivel his head, his father only stamped his feet all the more ferociously. Across the room, his mother had flung open a window despite the chilly weather, and, leaning out, she pressed her face into her hands far outside the window frame. Between street and stair-well, a powerful draft arose, the window curtains flew into the air, the newspapers on the table rustled, and a few pages scudded across the floor. Inexorably Gregor's father drove him backward, uttering hissing sounds like a wild man. But Gregor had no practice at all in reverse locomotion, and his progress was very slow. If only he'd been permitted to turn around, he'd have been back in his room at once, but he was afraid of provoking his father's fury with this time-consuming maneuver, and at any moment a fatal blow from the stick in his father's hand might come crashing down on his back or head. In the end, though, he had no alternative: horrified, he realized he was incapable of con-trolling his direction; and so he began, with constant anxious glances back at his father, to turn around as quickly as he could, which in fact was rather slowly. Perhaps his father discerned his good intentions, for he did not hinder him in this operation but instead even guided his rotation here and there from a distance, using the tip of his stick. If only his father were not making that unbearable hissing noise! It made Gregor lose his head completely. He had already turned almost all the way around when—still with this hissing in his ear—he became confused and started turning back in the wrong direction. But when finally he succeeded in positioning his head in front of the doorway, it turned out that his body was too wide to fit through the opening. And of course in his father's current state it could not possibly have occurred to him to open the door's other wing to create an adequate passage. He was fixated on the notion that Gregor must disappear into his room as quickly as possible. Never would he have tolerated the complicated preparations necessary for Gregor to prop himself up so as possibly to pass through the door in an upright position. Instead, as though there were no obstacle at all, he now drove Gregor before him, raising a great din: what Gregor heard at his back no longer resembled the voice of merely a single father; it was do or die, and Gregor thrust himself—come what would—into the doorway. One side of his body tilted up, rising at an angle as he pressed forward, scraping his one flank raw and leaving ugly stains behind on the white door, and soon he was wedged tight, unable to move on his own; on one side, his little legs dangled trembling in midair, while on the other they were crushed painfully beneath him—then his father adminis-tered a powerful shove from behind, a genuinely liberating thrust that sent him flying, bleeding profusely, into the far reaches of his room. The door was banged shut with the stick, and then at last all was still.

II

Only as dusk was falling did Gregor wake from his heavy, faintlike sleep. He prob-ably wouldn't have slept much longer even without a disturbance, for he felt suf-ficiently rested and restored, but it seemed to him he had been woken by a fleeting step and the careful shutting of the door to the vestibule. The pallid gleam of the electric streetlamps touched the ceiling here and there and the upper edges of the furniture, but down where Gregor lay, all was dark. Slowly, groping awkwardly with his feelers, which he was only now learning to appreciate, he dragged himself toward the door, wanting to see what had happened. His left side felt like one long unpleasantly contracting scar, and he was forced to limp outright on his two rows of legs. One of these diminutive legs, incidentally, had suffered grievous injuries in the course of the morning's events—it was almost miraculous only one had been injured—and now trailed lifelessly behind him.

Not until he reached the door did he realize what in fact had lured him there: it was the smell of something edible. There stood a bowl filled with sweet milk in which little pieces of white bread were floating. He almost laughed with delight, for his hunger was now even more powerful than in the morning, and right away he dunked his head in the milk almost up to his eyes. But he quickly drew it out again in disappointment; it wasn't just that eating was difficult thanks to his tender left side—and he couldn't eat at all without his entire body becoming gaspingly involved—but beyond that: even though milk had always been his favorite drink, which is no doubt why his sister had brought him some, now it didn't taste good to him at all, indeed it was almost with revulsion that he turned away from the bowl and crept back to the center of the room.

In the living room, as Gregor saw through the crack, the gas had been lit, but while usually at this hour his father liked to read aloud from the afternoon paper to Gregor's mother and sometimes his sister as well in a dramatic voice, now there was not a sound to be heard. Well, perhaps this customary reading aloud that his sister had often told and written him about had recently fallen out of practice. But even in the other rooms everything was so still, even though the apartment was surely not empty. "What a quiet life my family has been leading," Gregor said to himself, and as he gazed fixedly into the darkness before him, he felt great pride at having been able to give his parents and sister a life like this in such a beautiful apartment. But what if all this tranquility, all this prosperity and contentment were now coming to a horrific end? So as not to get lost in such contemplations, Gregor set himself in motion, crawling back and forth across the room.

Once in the course of this long evening one of the side doors was opened a tiny crack and then quickly shut again, and once the other one; someone must have felt an urge to enter and then been overcome by misgivings. Gregor now stationed himself just in front of the living room door, determined to somehow coax the hesitant visitor inside or at least find out who it was; but the door did not open again, and Gregor waited in vain. Before, when all the doors were locked, everyone kept trying to come in, and now that he had opened the one door and the others had apparently been opened during the day, no one came, and the keys were sticking in their locks from the outside.

It was late at night by the time the light in the living room went out, and now it was easy to ascertain that Gregor's parents and sister had remained awake all this time, for all three of them could clearly be heard departing on tiptoe. Now it was unlikely anyone would come into Gregor's room before morning; so he had plenty of time to ponder how best to reorder his life. But this high open room in which he was forced to lie flat on the floor distressed him, without his being able to determine the cause—after all, it was his room, which he had been living in for five years now—and with a half-unconscious motion, and not without a twinge of shame, he scurried beneath the settee, where even though his back was a bit cramped and he could no longer raise his head, he at once felt right at home, his only regret being that his body was too wide across to be accommodated entirely beneath this piece of furniture.

Here he remained the entire night, which he spent by turns dozing—though he was woken again and again by his hunger—and mulling over his worries and indistinct hopes, which however all led to the conclusion that, for the time being, he should behave calmly and, by employing patience and the utmost consideration, assist his family in enduring the inconveniences his current state inevitably forced him to impose on them.

Early the next morning already, so early it was almost still night, Gregor had the opportunity to test the strength of these resolutions he had made, for from the vestibule his sister, almost completely clothed, opened his door and cast an anxious glance into the room. She didn't immediately spot him, but when she noticed him beneath the settee—well, goodness, he had to be somewhere, it's not as if he might have flown away—the sight so alarmed her that, unable to control herself, she slammed the door from the outside. But as if regretting this conduct, she opened it again at once and came in, walking on tiptoe as though she were entering the room of a gravely ill patient or even a stranger. Gregor, having slid his head to just beneath the edge of the settee, observed her. Would she see that he had left the milk standing, and not because of a lack of hunger, and would she bring him some other food more to his liking? If she failed to do so of her own accord, he would sooner starve than call this to her attention, though in fact he felt a nearly monstrous urge to scoot out from beneath the settee, throw himself at his sister's feet, and beg her for something good to eat. But his sister immediately remarked with surprise that the bowl was still full, with just a little of its milk spilled on the floor around it, and she picked it up right away—not with her bare hands, to be sure, but with a rag—and carried it out of the room. Gregor was exceptionally curious to see what she would bring in its stead and mulled over various possibilities. But never would he have been able to predict what his sister in her kindness proceeded to do. To gauge his tastes, she brought him an entire assortment of foodstuffs, all spread out on an old newspaper. There were old, half-rotten vegetables; bones from the family supper the night before caked in a congealed white sauce; a few raisins and almonds; a piece of cheese Gregor had declared inedible two days before; a dry piece of bread; a slice of buttered bread; and a slice of bread with butter and salt. In addition, she placed beside this feast the bowl that apparently had been reserved for Gregor once and for all; it was now filled with water. And out of delicacy, since she knew Gregor would not eat in front of her, she quickly withdrew and even turned the key in the lock so that Gregor would understand he could make himself at home. Gregor's little legs whirred as he now went to take his meal. His wounds, incidentally, seemed to have healed entirely in the meantime, for he no longer felt the least impairment; this was astonishing, for more than a month ago he had cut his finger just a tiny bit with a knife, and this wound had still been painful enough just the day before yesterday. "Might I be less fastidious than before?" he thought, already sucking greedily at the cheese, to which he'd found himself immediately, inexorably drawn, more than to any of the other items. Quickly, his eyes shedding tears of gratification, he devoured in swift succession: the cheese, the vegetables, and the sauce; the fresh food, by contrast, did not taste good to him, in fact he could not even stand the smell of it and so dragged the things he wished to eat a little to one side. He had long since finished everything and was just lying indolently where he was when his sister slowly turned the key in the lock as a signal for him to withdraw. At once he gave a start, though he'd been on the point of nodding off, and he hurried back under the settee. But it cost him a great deal of willpower to remain there even for the short period of time his sister spent in the room, for the hearty meal he'd enjoyed had caused his abdomen to swell, and he could scarcely breathe in his confinement. In between little attacks of suffocation, he peered out with slightly bulging eyes as his sister, oblivious, used a broom to sweep up not only the remains of his meal but also the food he hadn't even touched, as if these items too were no longer fit for consumption, then she hastily dumped everything in a bucket that she covered with a wooden lid before carrying it all out of the room again. She had scarcely turned her back when Gregor hauled himself out from under the settee, stretching and puffing up his body.

This was how Gregor now received his food each day, once in the morning, when his parents and the maid were still asleep, and the second time after everyone had eaten lunch, for his parents would always nap a little afterward, and his sister would send the maid out on some errand or other. Surely they didn't want Gregor to starve either, but perhaps it would have been too much for them to experience his meals through more than hearsay, or perhaps his sister wanted to spare them even this modest sorrow, for Lord knows they were suffering enough.

Gregor never learned on what pretext the doctor and locksmith had been sent away that first morning, for since he himself could not be understood, it occurred to no one, not even his sister, that he could understand the others, so when his sister came to his room, he had to be content merely with hearing the sighs she heaved now and then and her words of supplication addressed to the saints. Only later, when she had started to grow accustomed to all of this— though of course it was impossible to become fully accustomed to circumstances like these—would Gregor sometimes catch a remark that was meant in a friendly way or could be interpreted as such. "He tucked right in today," she would say when Gregor had found the food she left him particularly tasty, while in the opposite case, which gradually began to occur more and more often, she was in the habit of saying almost mournfully: "This time he didn't touch a thing."

But while no news reached Gregor directly, he sometimes was able to overhear this and that from the rooms to either side of his, and whenever he heard voices, he would immediately run over to the door in question and press his entire body against it. Especially in the early days there was rarely a conversation that did not somehow, if only indirectly, refer to him. For two days, every mealtime was spent deliberating how the family should now comport itself; but even between meals this same discussion continued, for at least two members of the household were present at all times, since apparently no one wanted to remain at home alone, and of course leaving the apartment unattended was out of the question. What's more, the maid had fallen on her knees before Gregor's mother that very first day—it was not entirely clear what and how much she knew of what had occurred—begging to be released from the family's service, and when she took her leave a quarter of an hour later, she tearfully thanked them for dismissing her, as though this were the greatest benefaction she had experienced at their hands, and without anyone asking this of her, she swore a solemn oath never to reveal anything at all to anyone.

Now Gregor's sister was forced to do the cooking in concert with his mother; to be sure, not much effort was involved, as no one did much eating. Again and again Gregor would hear one of them pressing the others to eat—always in vain, and never with any other response than "Thank you, I've had all I want," or similar words. Perhaps they didn't drink anything either. Often Gregor's sister would ask her father if he wouldn't like a beer, affectionately offering to fetch it herself, and when he did not respond, she would say, wishing to relieve him of all scruples, that she could send the porter's wife for it as well, but then the father would utter a great "No," and no one spoke of it any longer.

Already in the course of the first day, Gregor's father explained the family's finances and prospects not only to Gregor's mother but to his sister as well. Now and then he would get up from the table and, from his small Wertheim safe,[4] which he had salvaged when his business collapsed five years before, extract some receipt or memorandum book. One could hear him opening the complicated lock and then bolting it shut again after removing the desired item. These explanations on his father's part included the first bits of heartening news Gregor had heard since his captivity began. He had been under the impression that his father had retained nothing at all of his former firm's holdings, or at least his father had never said anything to the contrary, and admittedly Gregor himself had never asked him about this. At the time, his only concern had been to do everything in his power to let the family forget, as quickly as possible, the mercantile catastrophe that had plunged all of them into a state of utter hopelessness. And so he had set to work with particular zeal and risen almost overnight from petty clerk to salesman, in which capacity of course he had a quite different earning potential, and his professional accomplishments, in the form of commissions, were immediately transformed into cash that could be plunked down on the table at home, before the eyes of his astonished, delighted family. Those had been lovely times, and never since had they been repeated, at least not with such glory, although Gregor later earned so much money that he was in a position to cover the expenses for the entire family, which he then did. All had grown accustomed to this arrangement, not just the family but Gregor as well: they gratefully accepted the money, and he was happy to provide it, but the exchange no longer felt particularly warm. Only Gregor's sister had remained close to him all this time, and it was his secret plan to send her off to study at the Conservatory next year (unlike Gregor, she dearly loved music and could play the violin quite movingly), despite the considerable costs this would no doubt entail, money that could surely be brought in by other means. Often during the brief periods of time Gregor spent in town, the Conservatory would come up in his conversations with his sister, but only ever as a lovely dream whose realization was unthinkable, and their parents did not like to hear it mentioned even in this innocuous way; but Gregor was thinking the matter over with great determination and intended to make a formal announcement on Christmas Eve.

Thoughts like these, utterly futile in his current state, passed through his head as he stood pressed against the door, eavesdropping. Sometimes general exhaustion made it impossible for him to go on listening, and he would carelessly let his

4. Safe manufactured by the German firm Wertheim, founded in 1852 and still in operation today.

head bump against the door, but then he would immediately hold his head still again, for even the faint sound this produced had been heard in the next room, causing everyone to fall silent. "I wonder what he's getting up to now," his father would say after a while, apparently facing the door, and only then would the interrupted conversation resume.

Gregor now learned, and learned quite well (his father tended to repeat himself in his explanations, in part because it had been so long since he'd last concerned himself with such matters, in part because Gregor's mother did not always understand everything the first time), that despite all their misfortunes, a small nest egg—really only a tiny one—still remained to them from before, and had even grown a little thanks to the untouched interest that had accumulated meanwhile. In addition, the money Gregor had brought home each month—he only ever kept a few gulden[5] for himself—had not yet been entirely used up and had grown into a small capital. Behind his door, Gregor nodded eagerly, delighted at this unexpected prudence and thrift. To be sure, he might have used this surplus to pay off more of his father's debts with his boss, and the day on which he would have been able to divest himself of his post would no longer have been nearly so far off, but as things stood, his father's arrangements were no doubt for the best.

Now this money was by no means sufficient to allow the family to live off the interest or anything of that sort; it might possibly have been enough to sustain the family for a year, two at most, but that's all there was. So in fact it was the kind of sum one really shouldn't touch, one to be set aside in case of emergency; the money to live on would have to be earned. Gregor's father was admittedly in good health, but he was old and hadn't worked in a full five years, and in any case he was supposed to avoid overtaxing himself; in those five years—the first holiday in his strenuous and yet unsuccessful life—he had put on a lot of weight and now lumbered as he walked. And was Gregor's old mother now supposed to hold down a job, despite her asthma and the fact that it was already an exertion for her to cross from one end of the apartment to the other, for which reason she spent every second day gasping for breath on the sofa beside the open window? And was his sister to go out working, this child of seventeen whose lifestyle no one would begrudge her: dressing nicely, sleeping late, helping out around the house, taking part in a few modest entertainments, and above all, playing the violin? Whenever the family came to speak of the necessity of someone earning money, Gregor would let go of the door and throw himself down upon the cool leather sofa beside it, burning with shame and sorrow.

Often he would lie there the entire long night, not sleeping for a moment, just scrabbling for hours against the leather. Or, not shunning the great effort it cost him to push an armchair over to the window, he would climb up the sill and, propped in the armchair, lean against the window, apparently lost in some sort of reverie of how liberating he'd always found it to gaze outside. For in truth he saw even the objects that were quite near at hand less and less clearly as the days progressed; the hospital across the way whose all too constant sight he had earlier reviled was now no longer even visible to him, and if he had not known perfectly well that he was a resident of Charlottenstrasse, a quiet but perfectly urban street, he might have imagined he was gazing out his window onto a desert in which the gray sky and the gray earth were indistinguishably

5. Guilders, a unit of currency, worth somewhat less than a dollar.

conjoined. His attentive sister only had to see the armchair standing beside the window twice before she started pushing it back to its place there each time she tidied his room; indeed she even began leaving the window's inner sash open.

If only Gregor had been able to speak to his sister and thank her for all she was compelled to do for him, he would have found her ministrations easier to bear; as it was, he suffered beneath them. His sister, to be sure, did all she could to obscure the awkwardness of the situation, and the more time passed, the better she succeeded, of course, but Gregor came to see it all more and more clearly. Even the way she made her entrance jangled his nerves. The moment she came in, without even pausing to shut the door—although she always took such pains to shield the others from the sight of Gregor's room—she would race straight away to the window and fling it open with hasty hands as though she were on the point of suffocating, then remain standing there, however cold it might be, gulping in the air. All this racing and racket was inflicted on Gregor twice a day; he would be trembling beneath the settee, painfully aware that she would no doubt have willingly spared him this disruption if it were possible for her to endure being in the same room as Gregor with the window closed.

Once—it must have been a month since Gregor's metamorphosis, so there was no particular call for his sister to be startled by his appearance—she came into his room a little earlier than usual and discovered him, motionless and propped upright as if for horrific effect, gazing out the window. Gregor would not have found it surprising if she had chosen not to enter, since his position prevented her from opening the window right away, but she didn't just not enter: she started in alarm and shut the door; a stranger might have thought Gregor had been lying in wait, meaning to bite her. Gregor naturally went and hid himself away beneath the settee, but he had to wait there until noon before his sister returned, and she seemed far more agitated than usual. From this he understood that his appearance was still unbearable to her and would remain so, and that she no doubt had to struggle to force herself not to run away at the sight of even the small part of his body that protruded from beneath the settee. In order to spare her even this sight, one day he carried the bedsheet over to the settee on his back—this labor cost him four hours—and arranged it in such a way that he was now completely covered, so that his sister would not be able to see him even if she bent down. If she considered the sheet unnecessary, she could have removed it, since it was clear enough that it could not possibly be considered a pleasure for Gregor to shut himself off so completely, but she left the sheet where it was, and Gregor even thought he glimpsed a grateful look when at one point he carefully lifted the sheet just a little with his head to see how his sister liked the new arrangement.

During the first fortnight, Gregor's parents could not bring themselves to enter his room, and often he heard them expressing their heartfelt appreciation of his sister's labors, whereas earlier they had often been annoyed with her, since she had seemed to them a rather useless girl. But now both of them, father and mother alike, would often be waiting just outside Gregor's door while his sister tidied up his room, and as soon as she emerged, she had to give a full report on what things looked like in the room, what Gregor had eaten, how he had behaved this time, and whether perhaps any modest improvement could be seen. His mother, incidentally, had wanted to visit him relatively soon, but his father and sister held her back, appealing at first to her sense of reason as Gregor listened attentively, wholeheartedly approving. Later, though, she had to be held back by force, and when she then cried out: "Let me go to Gregor, he is my unhappy son! Can't you understand that I must go to him?" then Gregor thought it would perhaps be good for his mother to visit him, not every day of course, but perhaps once a week; after all, she had a far better grasp of things than his sister, who despite her courage was still a child and, when it came right down to it, had perhaps only taken on this difficult task out of childish frivolity.

Gregor's wish to see his mother was soon fulfilled. During the day, Gregor avoided showing himself at the window, if only out of consideration for his parents, but there wasn't much crawling he could do in the few square meters of space the floor provided, lying still was already difficult for him to endure during the night, eating had soon ceased to give him even the slightest pleasure, and so to divert himself he took up the habit of crawling back and forth across the walls and ceiling. He particularly liked hanging from the ceiling high above the room; it was completely different from lying on the floor; one could breathe more freely there; a gentle swaying motion rocked the body; and in the almost happy absentmindedness Gregor experienced, it might happen, to his own astonishment, that he would let go and crash to the floor. But now, of course, he had his body far better under control than before, and even as great a fall as this did him no harm. His sister immediately noticed the new entertainment Gregor had devised for himself—his peregrinations left behind sticky trails here and there—and she got it into her head to make it possible for Gregor to range as widely as possible by removing the furniture that impeded his movement, above all the wardrobe and desk. But she wasn't able to do so on her own; she didn't dare ask her father for help; the maid most certainly would not have helped her, for this girl of sixteen or so, though she had courageously remained in the household after the departure of the former cook, had at the same time requested the privilege of keeping the kitchen locked at all times and only opening the door upon particular request; and so the sister had no choice but to summon her mother one day when her father was out. The mother arrived with exclamations of feverish joy but fell silent at the door to Gregor's room. At first, of course, Gregor's sister checked to confirm that all in the room was as it should be; only then did she allow her mother to enter. With the utmost haste, Gregor had tugged the sheet down lower and in looser folds so that it really did look as if a bedsheet just happened to have been tossed over the settee. He also refrained from peering out from beneath the sheet this time; for the moment, he would resign himself to not seeing his mother and just be glad she had come. "It's all right, come in, you won't see him," Gregor's sister said, apparently leading her mother by the hand. Gregor now heard the sounds of these two weak women grappling with this in fact quite heavy old wardrobe, with his sister laying claim to the bulk of the work, not listening to the admonitions of her mother, who was afraid she would overtax herself. It took a very long time. After perhaps a quarter of an hour's labor, Gregor's mother said they should leave the wardrobe where it was after all; in the first place, it was too heavy—they would not finish before Gregor's father came home, and by leaving the wardrobe in the middle of the room, they would prevent Gregor from moving around at all—and secondly, it wasn't even clear they were doing him a favor by taking away the furniture. To her, it seemed the opposite was true: the sight of the empty wall positively oppressed her heart; and why should Gregor not experience this same sentiment, since after all he was long accustomed to having this furniture around him—wouldn't he feel abandoned in an emptied-out room? "And is it not as if," his mother concluded in a low voice—in fact, she had been whispering all along, as though she wished to avoid letting Gregor, whose exact whereabouts she did not know, hear so much as the sound of her voice, for she was convinced he could not understand her words—"and is it not as if by removing the furniture we would be showing that we are giving up all hope of a cure and are ruthlessly abandoning him to his own devices? I think it would be best if we try to keep the room in precisely the same state it was in before, so that when Gregor returns to us he will find everything unchanged, which will make it that much easier for him to forget all that has happened in the meantime."

Hearing his mother's words, Gregor realized that the absence of all direct human address, combined with the monotony of life in his family's midst, must have muddled his understanding over the course of these two months, for he could not otherwise explain to himself how he could seriously have wished to have his room emptied out. Did he really want to have this warm room, comfortably furnished with family heirlooms, transformed into a cave or den—in which, to be sure, he would be able to crawl about unhindered in every direction, but at the price of simultaneously swiftly and completely forgetting his human past? He was already on the verge of forgetting, and only his mother's voice, which he had gone so long now without hearing, had shaken him awake. Nothing should be removed; everything must remain; he was unwilling to forego the good influence this furniture had on his condition; and if the furniture got in the way of his practicing this mindless crawling about, this was by no means to his detriment, in fact, it was a great advantage.

Unfortunately his sister was of a different opinion; she had developed the habit—not entirely without cause, to be sure—of presenting herself as the holder of particular expertise when discussing Gregor with her parents, and so now too her mother's counsel was reason enough for her to insist on the removal not only of the wardrobe and desk, as she had originally been intending, but of every last bit of the room's furnishings, with the exception of the indispensable settee. Naturally, it was not simply childish defiance and the hard-won self-assurance she had so unexpectedly acquired in recent weeks that dictated this demand; she had, in fact, observed that Gregor needed a great deal of space to crawl around in, while as far as anyone could see, he made no use whatever of the furniture. But perhaps the fanciful imagination of a girl of her age played a role as well, a sensibility always seeking its own gratification, and one which Grete now allowed to persuade her to render Gregor's situation even more horrific than before, so as to be able to do even more for him than she had hitherto. For a room in which Gregor held sole dominion over empty walls was a place where no one other than Grete would ever dare to set foot.

And so she held fast to her resolve despite the protests of her mother, who appeared troubled to the point of indecision even by the room in its present state; she soon fell silent and helped Gregor's sister remove the wardrobe as best she could. Well, the wardrobe was something Gregor could do without if need be, but the desk would certainly have to stay. And no sooner had the women left the room with the cabinet, groaning as they pressed against its weight, than Gregor poked out his head from beneath the settee to see how he might, cautiously and as considerately as possible, intervene. But unfortunately his mother was the first to return while Grete was still in the next room, clasping the wardrobe in her arms and tipping it back and forth on her own—without, of course, moving it from the spot. But Gregor's mother was unaccustomed to his appearance, it might have made her ill to catch a glimpse of him, and so Gregor in alarm withdrew as fast as he could to the far end of the settee, but it was too late to prevent the front edge of the bedsheet from stirring a little. This was enough to attract his mother's notice. Startled, she froze for a moment, then went back to where Grete was.

Although Gregor kept telling himself that nothing extraordinary was happening, just a few sticks of furniture being shifted about, he was soon forced to admit that all this coming and going on the part of the women, their little exclamations, the furniture scraping against the floor, had the combined effect of a tumultuous hubbub intensifying all around him, and no matter how tightly he drew his head and legs in and pressed his body against the floor, he soon was forced to consider that he would not be able to endure this much longer. They were clearing out his room; taking from him all that was dear to him; they had already borne away the cabinet in which lay his fretsaw and other tools; and now they were prying loose the desk that had dug itself firmly into the floorboards, this desk at which he had written his homework assignments as a student at the commercial academy, and as a secondary and even primary school pupil—truly there was no time left to explore the good intentions of these two women, whose existence, by the way, he had almost forgotten, for their exhaustion was now making them labor in silence, and one heard only their heavy footsteps.

And so he burst out of hiding—the women in the next room were just leaning on the desk to catch their breath—changing direction four times as he raced about, for he really didn't know what to save first, but then his eyes lit on the picture of the lady clad all in furs, conspicuous now on the otherwise empty wall, and quickly he made his way up to it and pressed himself against the glass, which adhered to him, pleasantly cool against his hot belly. At least this picture, which Gregor's body now covered up completely, was absolutely certain not to be taken away from him. He swiveled his head toward the living room door to observe the women as they returned.

They hadn't permitted themselves much rest at all and were already on their way back; Grete had slung one arm about her mother and was nearly carrying her. "So what should we take next?" Grete said, looking around. Then her eyes met those of Gregor where he clung to the wall. It was no doubt only because of her mother's presence that she kept her composure; bowing her face toward her mother to prevent her from glancing about, she said—hastily and trembling, to be sure—"Let's go back to the living room for a moment, shall we?" Grete's intentions were perfectly clear to Gregor: she meant to bring their mother to safety and then chase him from the wall. Well, let her try! He sat there on his picture and would not give it up. He'd sooner leap right in her face.

But Grete's words succeeded in unsettling her mother even more: taking one step to the side, she saw the huge brown blotch on the flowered wallpaper, and before she was even able to realize that what she saw there was Gregor, she cried out in a hoarse, shrieking voice, "Oh God, oh God!" and fell back upon the settee, her arms spread wide as though she were giving up everything, and lay there without moving. "Gregor!" his sister shouted, raising her fist with a threatening glower. It was the first time she had addressed him directly since his metamorphosis. She ran into the next room to fetch some sort of essence that could be used to awaken her mother from her faint; Gregor wanted to help as well—there would be time enough to save the picture later—but he stuck fast to the glass and had to tear himself away by force; he too then ran into the next room as if he might offer his sister advice of some sort, like in the old days; but then could only stand idly behind her as she rummaged among various little bottles, and scared her out of her wits when she turned around; one bottle flew to the floor and shattered; a shard of glass scratched Gregor's face, and some sort of corrosive medicine engulfed him; without further delay, Grete took up as many bottles as she could hold and ran with them to her mother, slamming the door behind her with her foot. Gregor was now cut off from his mother, who was possibly on the brink of death, for which he himself was to blame; he could not open the door if he didn't want to drive away his sister, who had to stay there with his mother; there was nothing for him to do but wait; and tormented by his worries and self-reproach, he began to crawl about, crawling over everything, walls, furniture, the ceiling, and finally in his despair, as the entire room began to spin around him, he fell smack in the middle of the big table.

A short while passed. Gregor lay there, spent, and around him all was still, possibly a good sign. Then the bell rang. The maid was naturally locked up in her kitchen and so Grete had to open the door. Their father was back. "What happened?" were his first words; the look on Grete's face had no doubt revealed all. Grete's voice as she responded was muffled, apparently she was pressing her face against his chest: "Mother fainted, but she's better already. Gregor has broken out." "That's just what I expected," the father said. "I kept telling you, but you women refused to listen." To Gregor it was clear his father had misinterpreted Grete's all too brief pronouncement to assume him guilty of some act of violence. So it behooved Gregor to try to pacify his father, as he was lacking both the time and means to enlighten him. With this in mind, he fled to the door of his room and pressed himself against it, so that the moment his father came into the living room from the vestibule he would see that Gregor had every intention of returning at once to his room, that it was unnecessary to drive him back inside, and that one had merely to open the door, and he would disappear at once.

But his father was in no mood to take note of subtleties. "Ah!" he exclaimed upon entering, in a tone of voice suggesting he was at once furious and glad. Gregor pulled his head back from the door and turned it toward his father. He had truly not expected to see his father looking as he looked now standing before him; though to be sure the novelty of crawling about had distracted him recently from paying as much attention as before to the goings-on in the rest of the apartment, and really he ought to have been prepared to find a changed set of circumstances. Even so, even so: was this still his father? The same man who used to lie wearily entombed in his bed when Gregor set off on a business trip; who would greet him on the evening of his return sitting in an armchair in his nightshirt; who, incapable of rising, would merely raise his arms to signify his delight, and on the rare walks they still shared, a few Sundays each year and on major holidays, would trudge between Gregor and his mother, who themselves were already walking rather slowly, moving even a bit slower than they, bundled up in his old overcoat, always with his gingerly advancing cane and almost invariably coming to a halt and collecting his companions around him whenever he had something to say? Now he was standing properly erect; dressed in a smart blue uniform with gold buttons of the sort worn by porters in banking establishments; above the jacket's tall, stiff collar his powerful double chin unfurled; beneath bushy eyebrows, his black eyes peered out acutely and attentively; his once disheveled white hair had been painstakingly combed and parted until it gleamed. He tossed his cap, to which a gold monogram was affixed, probably that of a bank, across the entire room in a wide arc to land on the settee, then advanced grim-faced upon Gregor with the tips of his long uniform jacket flung back and his hands in his trouser pockets. He himself probably had no idea what he intended to do; at any rate, he raised up each foot unusually high, and Gregor marveled at the gigantic dimensions of his bootsoles. But he did not lose any time over them, having learned on the very first day of his new life that his father considered only the utmost severity appropriate for him. And so he fled from his father, hesitating whenever his father stopped short, and then rushing forward again as soon as he stirred. They circled the room several times in this manner without anything decisive occurring, and indeed, given the slow speed at which this interaction was taking place, without its even having the appearance of a chase. For this reason Gregor remained at floor level for the time being, especially as he feared his father might consider it particular wickedness on his part if he were to take refuge on the walls or ceiling. To be sure, he was forced to realize he would not be able to keep up even this pace for long, since each time his father took a step, he himself had to execute any number of motions. A shortness of breath began to set in—even in his earlier life his lungs had been none too reliable. As he now lurched along, reserving all his strength for this continued flight, his eyes barely open (and not thinking, in his stupefaction, that there might be other ways of saving himself than running across the floor, indeed he had almost forgotten he also had the walls at his disposal, though here, to be sure, they were obstructed by delicately carved furniture full of jagged, pointy edges), all at once something flew to the rug beside him, casually flung, and rolled across his path. It was an apple; and already a second one came flying after it; in horror, Gregor stopped in his tracks; there was no point continuing to run now that his father had decided to bombard him. He had filled his pockets from the fruit bowl on the sideboard and now was tossing apple after apple in Gregor's direction, for the moment not even bothering to take particular aim. The petite red apples rolled around the floor as if electrified, knocking into each other. One lightly lobbed apple grazed Gregor's back and slid off again harmlessly. But it was immediately followed by another that embedded itself in his back. Gregor tried to drag himself forward, as if this sudden shocking pain might vanish with a change of place; but he felt nailed to the spot and collapsed there, his legs splaying out, all his senses in a state of utter bewilderment. He caught only a last glimpse of the door to his room flying open, his shrieking sister, and his mother running out of the room before her wearing only a chemise, for his sister had undressed the unconscious woman to let her breathe more freely, then he saw his mother rush to his father's side, her unfastened skirts slipping one by one from about her waist as she ran, saw her stumble across these skirts as she threw herself at his father and, embracing him, in perfect union with him—but now Gregor's vision began to fail him—she clasped her hands at the back of his father's head and pleaded with him to spare Gregor's life.

III

The grievous wound Gregor had received, which plagued him for over a month— the apple remained lodged there in his flesh, a visible memento, since no one dared to remove it—seemed to have reminded even his father that Gregor, despite his current lamentable, repulsive form, was a member of the family who should not be treated like an enemy, for family duty dictated that the others swallow down the disgust he aroused in them and show him tolerance, only tolerance.

And even though this wound cost Gregor some of his mobility, probably for good, and for the time being he required many, many minutes to hobble across his room like an old invalid—crawling up the walls was out of the question now—he was compensated for this worsening of his condition by what seemed to him a perfectly adequate substitute: as evening approached, the door to the living room, on which he would start keeping a sharp eye an hour or two before-hand, would always be opened so as to permit him, lying in his own dark room and invisible from the living room, to watch the entire family sitting at the brightly lit table and listen to their conversations now, as it were, in an officially sanctioned capacity and thus quite differently than before.

To be sure, these were no longer the animated conversations of earlier times that Gregor used to think back on with a certain longing from various cramped hotel rooms when it was time to throw himself, exhausted, into the damp bedding. Now everything was fairly quiet. Gregor's father would fall asleep in his armchair soon after supper; his mother and sister would admonish one another to silence; his mother, bent far over beneath the light, would be sewing ladies' underthings for a dress shop; his sister, who had taken a job as a salesgirl, was studying stenography and French in the evenings so as possibly to move to a better position later on. Sometimes Gregor's father would wake up and, as if unaware he had been sleeping, would say to Gregor's mother: "How long you've been sewing again today!" and then go right back to sleep, which would prompt Gregor's mother and sister to exchange weary smiles.

In a peculiar form of stubbornness, Gregor's father refused to take off his porter's uniform even at home; and while his nightshirt hung uselessly on its hook, he would slumber where he sat, fully clothed, as though he remained ready for service at all times and even here was awaiting his supervisor's call. As a result, his uniform, which had not been new to start with, soon forfeited much of its cleanliness, despite the care lavished on it by mother and sister, and Gregor would sometimes gaze for an entire evening at this stain-covered jacket resplendent with gold buttons, always highly polished, in which the old man slept in considerable discomfort but nonetheless soundly.

The moment the clock struck ten, Gregor's mother would attempt to rouse his father with a few hushed words and then persuade him to go to bed, for he would get no proper sleep sitting here, and sleep was something Gregor's father—who had to report for duty at six in the morning—desperately needed. But in keeping with the stubbornness that had taken hold of him when he started working as a porter, he always insisted on continuing to sit there at the table, even though he kept falling asleep, and then it was only with the greatest effort that he could be persuaded to exchange armchair for bed. Gregor's mother and sister could persist in their little admonishments as doggedly as they liked; for a quarter of an hour, he would just shake his head slowly, his eyes closed, without getting up. Gregor's mother would pluck at his sleeve, whispering cajoling words in his ear, and his sister would set aside her studies to come to her mother's aid, but to no avail. Gregor's father only settled deeper into his armchair. Only when the women gripped him beneath the arms would he open his eyes, looking by turns at mother and sister and saying: "What sort of life is this? Is this the peace and quiet of my old age?" Then, supported by the two women, he would rise, laboriously, as though he himself were receiving the brunt of this burden, and allow the women to escort him to the doorway, where he would shoo them away and continue on his own, while Gregor's mother hastily threw down her sewing and his sister her pen so they could run after him to offer further assistance. The household was ever further reduced; the maid was now let go after all; a bony giant of a charwoman with white hair flapping about her head came by in the morning and evening to perform the heaviest labors; everything else was handled by Gregor's mother along with all her sewing. It even came to pass that several pieces of jewelry that had been in the family—jewels Gregor's mother and sister had delighted in wearing at entertainments and festivities—were sold, as Gregor would learn in the evening when the price each piece had brought would be discussed. But their greatest lament was always that they were unable to leave this apartment, which was far too large for their current circumstances, since no one could imagine how Gregor might be moved. But Gregor understood that it was not only out of consideration for him that a move was being ruled out, since he could easily enough have been transported in a crate of appropriate size with a few air holes; the main thing keeping the family from moving to a new apartment was their complete sense of hopelessness and the thought that they had been struck with a misfortune such as no one else in their entire circle of relations and friends had ever experienced. They were fulfilling to the utmost the demands the world makes on the poor: Gregor's father fetched breakfast for the petty employees at the bank, his mother sacrificed herself for the underclothes of strangers, his sister ran back and forth behind the shop counter at her customers' behest, but this was all the strength they had. And the wound in Gregor's back would begin to ache anew when mother and sister, having brought his father to bed, would now return and, leaving their work where it lay, huddle close beside one another pressing their cheeks together; when Gregor's mother, gesturing toward his room, would say: "Shut the door now, Grete"; and when Gregor was left in the dark again while next door the two women intermingled their tears or else sat there tearless, staring down at the table.

Gregor spent his nights and days almost entirely without sleeping. Sometimes he thought about taking the family's affairs in hand again, just as he used to, the next time his door was opened; once more his boss and the general manager would appear before his mind's eye after all this time, the clerks and apprentices, the dull-witted hired man, two or three friends from other firms, a chambermaid from a provincial hotel (a sweet, fleeting specter), the shopgirl from a haberdashery whom he had courted earnestly but too slowly—all of these now appeared to him, interspersed with strangers or people already forgotten, but instead of coming to his aid and that of his family, every last one of them was unapproachable, and he was glad when they disappeared. At other times he would be not at all in a frame of mind to look after his family; instead he was filled with rage at how poorly he was attended to, and although he could not imagine anything he would have liked to eat, he plotted how he might gain access to the pantry so as to help himself to what—despite his total absence of hunger—was his due. Without bothering to consider how she might give Gregor particular pleasure, his sister would quickly thrust some randomly chosen foodstuff into his room with her foot on her way to work in the morning or at midday, only to sweep it out again at night with a quick swipe of the broom, paying no heed if the food had been only barely nibbled at or—as was most often the case now—not touched at all. Setting Gregor's room to rights, a task she now saved for the evenings, could not possibly have been done any more perfunctorily. Great streaks of dirt extended across the walls, with balls of dust and rubbish lying scattered about. At first when Gregor's sister came into his room he would position himself in corners particularly indicative of this problem—to reproach her, as it were, by his presence there. But he could just as well have spent entire weeks sitting there without any improvement on his sister's part; after all, she saw the dirt as plainly as he did, but had made up her mind to leave it be. At the same time, with a sensitivity that was new in her, one that had now taken hold of the family as a whole, she was on her guard to make sure the task of tidying Gregor's room was reserved for her. Once Gregor's mother had subjected his room to a thorough scrubbing, which she accomplished only after using up several buckets of water—admittedly, all this moisture was itself an affront to Gregor, who lay stretched out, bitter and immobile, upon the settee—but his mother did not escape punishment. For no sooner had his sister remarked the change in Gregor's room that evening than she ran into the living room, grievously insulted, and ignoring her mother's imploringly raised hands, set to weeping so violently that her parents—naturally her father was startled out of his chair—at first stood by helpless and astonished; until they too began to stir; on the right, Gregor's father reproached his mother for not having left the cleaning of Gregor's room to his sister; while on the left he shouted at Gregor's sister, threatening that she would never again be permitted to clean Gregor's room; while his mother attempted to drag his father, now so agitated he hardly recognized himself, into the bedroom; Gregor's sister, shaking with sobs, pummeled the table with her tiny fists; and Gregor hissed loudly in fury because it had occurred to no one to shut the door of his room to spare him this sight and commotion.

But even if Gregor's sister, who was exhausted by her professional work, had wearied of caring for Gregor as she'd previously done, there was absolutely no need for his mother to fill her shoes, and Gregor needn't have suffered neglect. For now the charwoman was here. This old widow—who had seen and survived the worst in her long life with the help of her sturdy bones—felt no particular repugnance toward Gregor. Without being at all inquisitive, she had once chanced to open the door to his room and, seeing Gregor, who had begun to run back and forth although no one was chasing him, she stood there staring in astonishment, her hands clasped across her lap. Ever since, she never failed to open the door a crack for a moment every morning and evening to look in on him. At the beginning she would call him over to her, saying things that were probably intended to sound friendly, like "Hey, over here, you old dung beetle!" or "Just look at the old dung beetle!" Thus addressed, Gregor gave no reply but instead remained where he was, immobile, as if the door had never been opened. If only this charwoman, instead of being allowed to disturb him uselessly at whim, had been given instructions to clean his room daily! Once, early in the morning—a heavy rain, perhaps already a portent of the coming spring, was beating against the windowpanes—Gregor became so infuriated when the charwoman started up again with her quips that he turned on her as if to attack, if admittedly slowly and decrepitly. But instead of being frightened, the charwoman just picked up a chair that was standing beside the door and held it high in the air; and as she stood there, her mouth gaping wide, her intention was clear: not to close her mouth again until the chair in her hand had come crashing down upon Gregor's back. "Aha, so that's as far as it goes?" she asked as Gregor turned around again, and she placed the chair calmly back in its corner.

Gregor now ate almost nothing at all. Only if he happened by chance to wander past the food that had been prepared for him might he playfully take a bite of something into his mouth, where he would hold it for hours and then usually spit it out again later. At first he thought it was his sorrow at the state of his room that prevented him from eating, but in fact he had resigned himself very quickly to the changes there. Everyone had gotten into the habit of using his room to store things there was no space for in other parts of the apartment, and now there were many such things, since one room of the apartment had been rented out to three lodgers. These solemn gentlemen—all three of them were bearded, as Gregor once noted, peering through the crack of the door—were scrupulously intent on having everything tidy, not just in their room but also, since they were now paying rent here, in the entire household, particularly the kitchen. They could not bear the presence of unnecessary, much less dirty items. Moreover, they had brought most of their own furnishings with them. For this reason, many things had become superfluous, things that could not be sold but were still too valuable to throw out. All of this found its way into Gregor's room. As did the ash box and the garbage pail from the kitchen. The charwoman, always in a great hurry, would simply fling any unserviceable item into Gregor's room; mercifully, Gregor generally saw only the object in question and the hand that held it. The charwoman may have intended at some point, when she had occasion or a free minute, to come collect these things, or else throw all of them out at once, but as it was they remained wherever they first landed, except when Gregor made his way through the refuse, stirring it around—at first out of necessity, since there was no room left for him to crawl about, but later with ever-increasing pleasure, though after these wanderings, which left him mortally exhausted and sad, he would spend hours without moving.

Since the lodgers sometimes also took their supper at home in the shared living room, the living room door remained shut on some evenings, but Gregor was happy to forgo having the door open; in fact, even when it was open, he sometimes failed to take advantage of it and instead, unbeknownst to his family, would remain lying in the darkest corner of his room. Once, however, the charwoman had left the door to the living room slightly ajar, and ajar it remained even when the lodgers came in that evening and struck a light. They sat down at the head of the table where in earlier times Gregor had sat with his father and mother, unfolded the napkins and took up their knives and forks. At once Gregor's mother appeared in the doorway with a serving dish filled with meat, and right behind her came his sister bearing a plate piled high with potatoes. A heavy vapor rose from the steaming food. The lodgers bent over the dishes that had been placed before them, as though wishing to inspect them before beginning their meal, and in fact the one who sat in the middle and appeared to be an authority figure to the other two cut off a piece of meat right there on the platter to check whether it was tender enough and didn't have to be sent back to the kitchen. He was satisfied, and Gregor's mother and sister, who had been watching nervously, now smiled with relief.

The family members themselves ate in the kitchen. Nonetheless Gregor's father visited the living room on his way to the kitchen and with a single bow, cap in hand, took a tour around the table. The lodgers all rose from their seats and mumbled into their beards. Left alone again, they ate in almost perfect silence. It struck Gregor as peculiar that amid all the various sounds of this meal, one could also make out their champing teeth, as if to demonstrate to Gregor that a person needs teeth to eat and that even the most splendid jaws, if toothless, can accomplish nothing at all. "I'm hungry," Gregor said sorrowfully to himself, "but not for these things. Just look how these lodgers take their nourishment while I am wasting away!"

On this very evening—Gregor couldn't remember having heard the violin once in all this time—the sound of it was heard coming from the kitchen. The lodgers had already finished their evening meal, the one in the middle had pulled out a newspaper, giving each of the others a page, and now the three of them were reading, leaning back in their chairs and smoking. When the violin began to play, their interest was piqued, they got up from their chairs and tiptoed over to the doorway leading to the vestibule, where they stood in a tight cluster. The sounds of this activity must have traveled to the kitchen, for Gregor's father now called out: "Are the gentlemen disturbed by this playing? It can be silenced at once." "On the contrary," said the one in the middle, "would the young lady care to join us and play here in the living room, where it is much more comfortable and pleasant?" "Why, of course," Gregor's father exclaimed, as though he were the violinist. The gentlemen went back into the room and waited. Soon Gregor's father arrived with the music stand, his mother with the sheet music and his sister with the violin. His sister calmly prepared to play; his parents, who never rented out rooms in earlier days and therefore were treating these lodgers with exaggerated deference, did not even dare to sit in their own armchairs; his father leaned against the door, his right hand tucked between two buttons of his closed livery jacket; his mother, meanwhile, was offered an armchair by one of the lodgers, and since she left the chair where he had happened to place it, she sat off to one side in a corner.

Gregor's sister began to play; on either side, his father and mother attentively followed each movement of her hands. Attracted by her playing, Gregor had ventured a bit further than usual and was already sticking his head into the living room. It scarcely surprised him that he had become so inconsiderate of the others; earlier on, his considerateness had been a source of pride. And he had all the more reason to keep himself hidden away now: thanks to the dust that lay everywhere in his room and would swirl up at the slightest motion, he too was covered in dust; he dragged around threads, hair and food scraps clinging to his back and sides; his general indifference was far too great now for him to keep up with a habit he'd once practiced several times a day: flipping over so as to scrub his back against the rug. And despite his condition, he did not hesitate now to continue his advance a little way out onto the immaculate floor of the living room.

To be sure, no one paid him the slightest heed. The family was completely absorbed in the violin playing; the lodgers, on the other hand, having at first positioned themselves, hands in their trouser pockets, much too close behind his sister's music stand, so that they could all look at the sheet music, which surely must have distracted her, soon withdrew to the window, conversing in an undertone, and remained there, anxiously observed by Gregor's father. It appeared more than clear they had been disappointed in their expectation of hearing beautiful or entertaining violin music and now, tired of the whole performance, were continuing to tolerate this disturbance of their peace only out of politeness. Particularly the way in which all of them were blowing the smoke of their cigars high into the air from their noses and mouths suggested extreme agitation. And yet his sister's playing was so lovely. Her face was tilted to one side; searchingly, sadly, her eyes followed the lines of notes. Gregor crept a bit farther forward and ducked his head down close to the floor so as perhaps to catch her eye. Was he a beast, that music so moved him? He felt as if he were being shown the way to that unknown nourishment he craved. He was determined to creep all the way up to his sister, to pluck at her skirt and in this way indicate to her that she should come to his room with her violin, for no one here was rewarding her playing as he meant to reward her. He would not allow her to leave his room ever again, at least as long as he was alive; his horrific figure would, for the first time ever, be useful to him; he would be at all the doors of his room at once, growling at his attackers; but his sister should remain with him not by force but of her own free will; she should sit beside him on the settee, bend down, the better to hear, and he would confess to her that he'd had the firm intention of sending her to the Conservatory and that if the disaster had not disrupted his plans, he would have made a general announcement last Christmas—Christmas had passed now, hadn't it?—without letting himself be swayed by objections of any sort. After this declaration, his sister would be moved to the point of tears, and Gregor would raise himself to the height of her armpit and kiss her throat, which, now that she went to the office every day, she wore free of ribbon or collar.

"Herr Samsa!" the gentleman in the middle shouted at Gregor's father, and without wasting a single word, pointed his finger at Gregor, who was slowly advancing. The violin fell silent, the middle lodger at first just smiled and shook his head, turning toward his friends, then looked again at Gregor. Gregor's father apparently found the task of driving Gregor back into his room less urgent than that of calming the lodgers, despite the fact that they did not appear particularly worked up and seemed to be finding Gregor more entertaining than the music. He hurried over to them and tried with outspread arms to herd them back into their room, at the same time using his body to shield Gregor from their view. And now they did in fact become a little angry, though it was no longer clear whether this was on account of Gregor's father's behavior or the realization dawning on them that without their knowledge they had been sharing their home with a roommate of this sort. They demanded explanations of Gregor's father; now it was their turn to throw their arms into the air; they plucked uneasily at their beards and only slowly withdrew in the direction of their room. Meanwhile Gregor's sister, who had been standing there at a loss since her playing had been so unexpectedly interrupted—she still held violin and bow in her carelessly dangling hands, looking over at the notes as though she were continuing to play—all at once pulled herself together, laid her instrument in the lap of her mother, who still sat there in her armchair, her lungs heaving as she fought for breath, and ran into the next room, toward which the lodgers were now moving somewhat more quickly as Gregor's father urged them on. One saw how, beneath his sister's practiced hands, the beds' blankets and pillows flew into the air and into orderliness. Even before the lodgers reached the room, she had finished making up the beds and slipped out. Gregor's father appeared to be once more so firmly in the grip of his own stubbornness that he forgot the basic respect that, after all, he owed his tenants. He kept up his pressing and urging until, already standing in the doorway, the middle lodger thunderously stamped his foot, causing Gregor's father to stop short. "I hereby declare," he said, raising his hand and seeking out Gregor's mother and sister too as he glanced about, "that in consideration of the reprehensible circumstances prevailing in this apartment and family"—and here he spat on the floor without forethought—"I give notice on my room effective immediately. It goes without saying that I will not pay a penny for the days I have spent here; on the contrary, I shall consider whether or not to pursue you with—please believe me—easily justifiable claims." He fell silent and went on looking straight before him expectantly. And indeed his two friends at once chimed in with the words, "We too give notice effective immediately." Hereupon he seized the door handle and with a great crash slammed the door.

Gregor's father staggered to his armchair with groping hands and let himself fall into it; it looked as though he was stretching out for his customary evening nap, but the violent nodding of his anchorless head showed that he was absolutely not sleeping. Gregor had gone on lying quietly on the spot where the lodgers had espied him. His disappointment at the failure of his plan and perhaps also the weakness caused by starvation rendered him incapable of moving. With a certain definitiveness he sensed, terrified, that everything was about to collapse all around him, and so he waited. Not even the violin startled him when it fell from his mother's lap beneath her trembling fingers, giving off a note that echoed in the air.

"Dear parents," his sister said, striking the table by way of preamble, "things cannot go on like this. Even if you two perhaps do not realize it, I most certainly do. I am unwilling to utter my brother's name before this creature, and therefore will say only: we have to try to get rid of it. We have done everything humanly possible to care for it and show it tolerance, I don't think anyone would reproach us on this account."

"She is right a thousand times over," Gregor's father murmured under his breath. His mother, still incapable of breathing freely, began to cough dully into her lifted hand, a lunatic expression in her eyes.

Gregor's sister hurried over to her mother and held her forehead. Her words seemed to have given her father an idea, for he now sat up straight, playing with his uniform cap between the plates left behind on the table from the lodgers' supper and glancing over from time to time at a quiet Gregor.

"We have to try to get rid of it," his sister said, addressing her words exclusively to Gregor's father this time, for his mother was coughing too hard to hear anything. "It'll be the death of you two, I can see it now. When people have to work as hard as all of us have been doing, it just isn't possible to endure these endless torments at home. I cannot bear it anymore either." And she burst into sobs, weeping so forcefully that her tears flowed down upon her mother's face, from which the girl wiped them with a mechanical gesture.

"Child," her father said sympathetically and with noticeable compassion, "but what can we do?"

Gregor's sister just shrugged her shoulders as a sign of the helplessness that had come over her while she was weeping, in contrast to the confidence she'd displayed a moment before.

"If he understood us," Gregor's father said, half-questioning; his sister, still caught up in her weeping, shook one hand vehemently as a sign of how unthinkable she found this.

"If he understood us," his father repeated, closing his eyes to absorb her conviction that this was utterly out of the question, "then it might be possible to come to an agreement with him. But as things stand—"

"It has to go," Gregor's sister cried out, "that's the only way, Father. You just have to try to let go of the notion that this thing is Gregor. The real disaster is that we believed this for so long. But how could it be Gregor? If it were Gregor, it would have realized a long time ago that it just isn't possible for human beings to live beside such a creature, and it would have gone away on its own. We still would have been lacking a brother but we would have been able to go on living and honoring his memory. But now we have this beast tormenting us; it drives away our lodgers and apparently intends to take over the entire apartment and have us sleep in the gutter. Just look, Father," she suddenly shrieked, "he's starting again!" And in a fright that Gregor found bewildering, she now went so far as to leave her mother behind, launching herself from her chair as if she would rather sacrifice her mother than remain in Gregor's proximity, and ran to take cover behind her father who, agitated by the way she was carrying on, rose from his own chair and half-raised his arms as if to shield her.

But Gregor was far from wanting to frighten anyone, above all his sister. All he'd done was start to turn around to make his way back to his room, and admittedly this operation would have been hard not to notice, since in his current injured state he was obliged to use his head to help with this difficult maneuver; he kept raising it up and then thumping it against the floor. Pausing, he glanced around. His good intentions seemed to have been recognized; it had been only a momentary fright. Now all of them gazed at him sadly and in silence. His mother lay in her armchair, her extended legs pressed together, barely able to keep her eyes open in her exhaustion; his father and sister sat side by side, and his sister had draped one hand across her father's neck.

"Perhaps I'll be allowed to turn around now," Gregor thought and resumed his labors. He could not entirely suppress the wheezing this exertion produced, and now and then he had to rest. Otherwise no one was harassing him, he had been left to attend to matters on his own. When he had completed this rotation, he immediately made straight for the door to his room. He was astonished at how great a distance separated him from his destination, and he didn't understand how, weak as he was, he had been able to traverse the same distance just a little while before almost without noticing. Steadfastly concentrating only on crawling as quickly as possible, he scarcely paid any heed to the fact that not a word, not a cry came from his family to disturb him. Only when he was already in the doorway did he turn his head—not all the way around, as he felt his neck growing stiff, but even so he was able to see that all was unchanged behind him, except that his sister had risen to her feet. The last thing he saw was a glimpse of his mother, who had now fallen entirely asleep.

No sooner was he in his room again than the door was hastily pressed shut, locked and bolted. The sudden commotion at his back gave him such a frightful start that his little legs gave way beneath him. It was his sister who had hurried thus. She had already been standing there upright and waiting, then pounced so lightfootedly Gregor didn't hear her approach, and she cried out, "Finally!" to her parents as she turned the key in the lock.

"And now?" Gregor wondered, looking around in the dark. He soon made the discovery that he was no longer capable of moving at all. He wasn't surprised at this; on the contrary, it struck him as unnatural that he had actually until now been able to support himself on those thin little legs. As for the rest, he felt relatively at ease. Admittedly his entire body was racked with pain, but it seemed to him as if it was gradually becoming weaker and weaker and in the end would fade away altogether. Already he could scarcely feel the rotting apple in his back, nor the inflamed area surrounding it, both now enveloped in soft dust. He thought back on his family with tenderness and love. His opinion that he must by all means disappear was possibly even more emphatic than that of his sister. He remained in this state of empty, peaceful reflection until the clock-tower struck the third hour of morning. He watched as everything began to lighten outside his window. Then his head sank all the way to the floor without volition and from his nostrils his last breath faintly streamed.

When the charwoman arrived early the next morning, slamming the doors so loudly in her strength and haste—often as she'd been asked to avoid this—that sleep was out of the question anywhere in the apartment after her arrival, her usual cursory visit to Gregor's room revealed at first nothing out of the ordinary. She thought he was lying there so motionless on purpose, feigning indignation; she considered him perfectly capable of rational thought. Since she happened to be holding the long broom in her hand, she tried tickling Gregor with it from the doorway. When even this had no effect, she grew vexed and began to poke Gregor a little, and only when she had actually shifted him from the spot where he lay with no resistance at all were her suspicions roused. When soon thereafter the facts of the matter became clear to her, she gawked in surprise, gave a low whistle, then without further delay flung open the door of the bedroom and in a loud voice shouted into the darkness: "Come have a look, it's gone and croaked—just lying there, dead as a doornail!"

The Samsa couple shot upright in their marital bed and first had to struggle to recover from their shock at the charwoman's conduct before they were able to grasp her words. But then Herr and Frau Samsa hurriedly got out of bed, one on either side, Herr Samsa threw the blanket about his shoulders while Frau Samsa emerged wearing only her nightdress; in this state, they entered Gregor's room. Meanwhile the door to the living room, where Grete had been sleeping since the lodgers' arrival, had opened as well; she was fully dressed, as though she had not slept at all, as even the pallor of her cheeks seemed to prove. "Dead?" Frau Samsa asked, looking questioningly up at the charwoman, although she herself was free to investigate and, indeed, could see how things stood even without investigation. "I should say so," the charwoman said, and by way of proof, pushed Gregor's corpse quite some way to the side with her broom. Frau Samsa made a gesture as though she wanted to hold back the broom but didn't. "Well," Herr Samsa said, "now we can thank God." He crossed himself, and the three women followed his example. Grete, who did not take her eyes off the corpse for a moment, said: "Just look how skinny he was. He went such a long time without eating anything at all. All the food that went into his room would come out again just as before." And indeed Gregor's body was completely flat and dry, which hadn't really been noticeable until now when he was no longer raised up on those little legs and nothing else remained to distract the gaze.

"Grete, come sit with us for a bit," Frau Samsa said with a melancholy smile, and Grete, glancing back at the corpse, followed her parents into their bedroom. The charwoman shut the door and opened the window wide. Despite the early morning, the crisp air was already tempered by a certain mildness: after all, it was already the end of March.

The three lodgers now emerged from their room and looked about in aston-ishment for their breakfast; they had been forgotten. "Where's breakfast?" the one in the middle asked the charwoman peevishly. But she just put a finger to her lips and then quickly, without a word, beckoned the lodgers into Gregor's room. They did as she bade them and with their hands in the pockets of their slightly threadbare little jackets, they surrounded Gregor's corpse in the room that had meanwhile become quite bright.

Then the bedroom door opened, and Herr Samsa appeared wearing his liv-ery, with his wife on one arm, his daughter on the other. All three looked as if they'd been weeping; Grete kept pressing her face against her father's arm.

"Leave my home at once!" Herr Samsa said, pointing at the door without let-ting go of the womenfolk. "What do you mean?" the gentleman in the middle inquired, dumbfounded, and gave a saccharine smile. The two others held their hands at their backs and kept rubbing them together uninterruptedly, as if in gleeful expectation of a fight that was certain to be decided in their favor. "I mean exactly what I say," Herr Samsa replied, now advancing on the lodger flanked by his two companions. The lodger just stood there at first, looking at the ground, as if things were just rearranging themselves in his head into a new order. "So we'll be leaving," he said then, looking up at Herr Samsa as if this new humility that had suddenly come over him required him to petition for the approval of even this decision. Herr Samsa merely nodded curtly in his direction a few times, goggle-eyed. At this, the gentleman did, in fact, make haste to stride back out to the vestibule, where his two friends had been listening attentively for some moments, their hands at rest, and now they practically hopped and skipped in their hurry to follow, as if worried Herr Samsa might somehow precede them into the vestibule, cutting off their line of communication with their leader.

In the vestibule, all three of them took their hats from the coat rack, withdrew their walking sticks from the cane stand, made a silent bow and left the apart-ment. Displaying what soon proved to be an utterly unfounded mistrustfulness, Herr Samsa stepped out onto the landing with the two women; leaning against the banister, they watched as the three gentlemen descended the long staircase, moving slowly but at a steady pace and disappearing on each floor at a certain bend of the stairwell only to appear again a few moments later; the farther down they went, the more the Samsa family's interest in them faded, and when a butcher's apprentice came toward and then passed them on his way up, proudly bearing his tray upon his head, Herr Samsa and the women abandoned the ban-ister, and all of them returned, seemingly relieved, to their apartment.

They decided to spend the day resting and to go out for a stroll; they had not only earned this respite from their work, but were desperately in need of it. And so they all sat down at the table and wrote three letters of excuse: Herr Samsa to his supervisor, Frau Samsa to her employer, and Grete to her superior. While they were writing, the charwoman came in to say she was leaving, as her morn-ing's work was completed. The three scribes at first merely nodded without looking up, and only when the charwoman failed to go on her way did they glance up in annoyance. "Well?" Herr Samsa asked. The charwoman stood smiling in the doorway as if she had some splendid good fortune to announce to the family but would not do so until she was properly questioned. The nearly vertical little ostrich feathers on her hat, which had annoyed Herr Samsa for as long as she had been in the family's service, bobbed gently in all directions. "So what is it you want?" she was asked now by Frau Samsa, the member of the family for whom the charwoman still had the most respect. "Well," the charwoman replied, her own good-natured laughter making it impossible at first for her to go on speaking, "there's no need for you to go worrying about how to get rid of that mess in there. It's already taken care of." Frau Samsa and Grete bent down over their letters as if they meant to go on writing; Herr Samsa, who saw that the charwoman was about to start describing everything in detail, summarily silenced her with an outstretched hand. And since she was not permitted to say what she wished, she suddenly remembered the great hurry she was in, and so with an insulted air she cried, "So long, everyone," turned wildly on her heel, and with the most excruciating slamming of doors left the apartment.

"Tonight she'll be let go," Herr Samsa said, but received an answer neither from his wife nor his daughter, for the charwoman seemed to have disturbed the equanimity they had only just attained. They rose from their seats, went to the window, and remained there with their arms about each other. Herr Samsa turned in his chair to look at them and observed them quietly for a little while. Then he cried out: "So come here already. Let these old matters rest. And show a little consideration for me as well." At once the women obeyed, hurried over to him, caressed him and quickly finished their letters.

Then all three of them left the apartment together, something they had not done for months, and took the electric tram all the way to the open countryside at the edge of town. The car in which they sat all alone was entirely suffused with warm sunlight. Cozily leaning back in their seats, they discussed their future prospects, and on closer investigation it appeared that these prospects were not bad at all, for all three of their positions—something they had never before properly discussed—were in fact quite advantageous and above all offered promising opportunities for advancement. The greatest immediate improvement in their situation, of course, would be easily achieved by moving to a new apartment; they now wished to take a smaller and cheaper but more convenient and above all more practical flat than their current one, which had been picked out for them by Gregor. As they were conversing in this way, Herr and Frau Samsa were struck almost as one while observing their daughter, who was growing ever more vivacious, by the thought that despite all the torments that had made her cheeks grow pale, she had recently blossomed into a beautiful, voluptuous girl. Growing quieter now and communicating with one another almost unconsciously by an exchange of glances, they thought about how it would soon be time to find her a good husband. And when they arrived at their destination, it seemed to them almost a confirmation of their new dreams and good intentions when their daughter swiftly sprang to her feet and stretched her young body.

1915

LU XUN

1881–1936

•

Modern China has produced many talented writers, with the usual division of critical opinion concerning them. There is, however, almost universal agreement on one authentic genius: Lu Xun (also Romanized Lu Hsün), the pen name of Zhou Shuren. Few writers of fiction have gained so much fame for such a small oeuvre. His reputation rests mostly on twenty-five stories released between 1918 and 1926, gathered into two collections: *Cheering from the Sidelines* and *Wondering Where to Turn.* In addition to his fiction, he published a collection of prose poems, *Wild Grass*, and a number of literary and political essays. His small body of stories offers a bleak portrayal of a culture that, despite its failures, continues to capture the modern Chinese imagination. Whether the older culture had indeed failed is less important here than Lu Xun's powerful representation of it and the deep chord of response that his work has touched in Chinese readers. Lu Xun was a controlled ironist and a craftsman whose narrative skill far exceeded that of most of his contemporaries; yet beneath his stylistic mastery the reader senses the depth of his anger at traditional culture.

Born into a Shaoxing family of Confucian scholar-officials, Lu Xun had a traditional education and became a classical scholar of considerable erudition, as well as a writer of poetry in the classical language. Sometimes he displays this learning in his fiction, where it is always undercut with irony. He grew up at a time when the traditional education system, based on the Confu-

cian classics, was giving way, to the approval of Lu Xun and others, to a more modern one; and after the early death of his father in 1896, he joined the many young Chinese intellectuals of the era in traveling abroad for higher education—first in Tokyo, then in Sendai, where he attended a Japanese medical school. (Because it was successfully modernizing a traditional culture, Japan attracted young Chinese intellectuals who wished the same for their own society.) During the period of his studies, the Russians and Japanese were at war in the former Chinese territory of Manchuria. In a famous anecdote describing his decision to become a writer, Lu Xun tells of seeing a classroom slide of a Chinese prisoner about to be decapitated as a Russian spy. What shocked the young medical student was the apathetic crowd of Chinese onlookers, gathered around to watch the execution. At that moment, he decided that what truly needed healing were not their bodies but their dulled spirits.

Returning to Tokyo, Lu Xun founded a journal in which he published literary essays and Western works of fiction in translation. In 1909, financial difficulties drove him back to China, where he worked as a teacher in Hangzhou and his native Shaoxing. With the arrival of the Republican Revolution of 1911, which overthrew the Qing, or Manchu, dynasty, he joined the ministry of education, moving north to Beijing, where he also taught at various universities. The Republican government was soon at the mercy of the powerful armies competing for regional power; during this period, perhaps for self-protection, Lu Xun devoted himself to traditional scholarship. One might have expected this revolutionary to write, as Lu Xun did, a groundbreaking work of scholarship, the first history of Chinese fiction; but he also produced an erudite textual study of the third-century writer Xi Kang, which is still used.

On May 4, 1919, a massive student strike forced the Chinese government not to sign the Versailles Peace Treaty, which would have given Japan effective control over the province of Shandong. The date gave its name to the May Fourth Movement, led by a group of young intellectuals who advocated the use of vernacular Chinese in all writing and the repudiation of classical Chinese literature. Though Lu Xun himself was not an active participant in the political side of the May Fourth Movement, it was during this period (1918–26) that he wrote all but one of his short stories. In the final decade of his life, he became a political activist and put his satirical talents at the service of the left, becoming one of the favorite writers of the Communist Party leader Mao Zedong.

"Diary of a Madman" (1918), Lu Xun's earliest story in modern Chinese, opens with a preface in mannered classical Chinese, giving an account of the discovery of the diary. Such ironic use of classical Chinese to suggest a falsely polite world of social appearances had been common in traditional Chinese fiction. Usually its presence suggested, however, the alternative possibility, of immediate, direct, and genuine language, a language of the heart that shows up the language of society. Here, the diary that follows the preface is indeed immediate, direct, and genuine, but it is also deluded and twisted. The diarist becomes increasingly convinced that everyone around him wants to eat him; after observing this growing circle of cannibals in the present, the diarist then turns to examine old texts, where he discovers that the history of the culture has been one of secret cannibalism. Beneath society's false politeness, the veneer of such decorous forms as the voice in the preface, he detects a brutality lurking, a hunger to assimilate others, to "eat men."

As the diary progresses, it becomes increasingly clear that the diarist, who sees himself as a potential victim, recapitulates the flaws and dangers of the society he describes, assimilating everyone around him into his fixed view of the world. His reading of ancient texts to discover evidence of cannibalism, with its distorting discovery of "secret meanings" that only serve to confirm beliefs already held, works in part as a parody of traditional Confucian scholarship. His is a world closed in on itself, one that survives by feeding on itself and its young. Yet the story opens itself to other interpretations: some see the madman as understanding the truth to which everyone else in the tale is blind, while others have noted that the madman's possible cannibalism undermines his apparent vision and that in any case his account is suspect because he is awaiting appointment to an official position.

Diary of a Madman[1]

There was once a pair of male siblings whose actual names I beg your indulgence to withhold. Suffice it to say that we three were boon companions during our school years. Subsequently, circumstances contrived to rend us asunder so that we were gradually bereft of knowledge regarding each other's activities.

1. Translated by and with notes adapted from William A. Lyell.

Not too long ago, however, I chanced to hear that one of them had been hard afflicted with a dread disease. I obtained this intelligence at a time when I happened to be returning to my native haunts and, hence, made so bold as to detour somewhat from my normal course in order to visit them. I encountered but one of the siblings. He apprised me that it had been his younger brother who had suffered the dire illness. By now, however, he had long since become sound and fit again; in fact he had already repaired to other parts to await a substantive official appointment.[2]

The elder brother apologized for having needlessly put me to the inconvenience of this visitation, and concluding his disquisition with a hearty smile, showed me two volumes of diaries which, he assured me, would reveal the nature of his brother's disorder during those fearful days.

As to the lapsus calami[3] *that occur in the course of the diaries, I have altered not a word. Nonetheless, I have changed all the names, despite the fact that their publication would be of no great consequence since they are all humble villagers unknown to the world at large.*

Recorded this 2nd day in the 7th year of the Republic.[4]

I

Moonlight's really nice tonight. Haven't seen it in over thirty years. Seeing it today, I feel like a new man. I know now that I've been completely out of things for the last three decades or more. But I've still got to be *very* careful. Otherwise, how do you explain those dirty looks the Zhao family's dog gave me?

I've got good reason for my fears.

2

No moonlight at all tonight—something's not quite right. When I made my way out the front gate this morning—ever so carefully—there was something funny about the way the Venerable Old Zhao looked at me: seemed as though he was afraid of me and yet, at the same time, looked as though he had it in for me. There were seven or eight other people who had their heads together whispering about me. They were afraid I'd see them too! All up and down the street people acted the same way. The meanest looking one of all spread his lips out wide and actually *smiled* at me! A shiver ran from the top of my head clear down to the tips of my toes, for I realized that meant they already had their henchmen well deployed, and were ready to strike.

But I wasn't going to let that intimidate *me*. I kept right on walking. There was a group of children up ahead and they were talking about me too. The expressions in their eyes were just like the Venerable Old Zhao's, and their faces were iron gray. I wondered what grudge the children had against me that

---

2. When there were too many officials for the number of offices to be filled, a man might well be appointed to an office that was already occupied. The new appointee would go to his post and wait until the office was vacated. Sometimes there would be a number of such appointees waiting their turns.

3. "The fall of the reed [writing instrument]" (Latin, literal trans.); hence, lapses in writing.
4. The Qing dynasty was overthrown and the Republic of China was established in 1911; thus it is April 2, 1918. The introduction is written in classical Chinese, whereas the diary entries that follow are all in the colloquial language.

they were acting this way too. I couldn't contain myself any longer and shouted, "Tell me, tell me!" But they just ran away.

Let's see now, what grudge can there be between me and the Venerable Old Zhao, or the people on the street for that matter? The only thing I can think of is that twenty years ago I trampled the account books kept by Mr. Antiquity, and he was hopping mad about it too. Though the Venerable Old Zhao doesn't know him, he must have gotten wind of it somehow. Probably decided to right the injustice I had done Mr. Antiquity by getting all those people on the street to gang up on me. But the children? Back then they hadn't even come into the world yet. Why should they have given me those funny looks today? Seemed as though they were afraid of me and yet, at the same time, looked as though they would like to do me some harm. That really frightens me. Bewilders me. Hurts me.

I have it! Their fathers and mothers have *taught* them to be like that!

3

I can never get to sleep at night. You really have to study something before you can understand it.

Take all those people: some have worn the cangue on the district magistrate's order, some have had their faces slapped by the gentry, some have had their wives ravished by yamen[5] clerks, some have had their dads and moms dunned to death by creditors; and yet, right at the time when all those terrible things were taking place, the expressions on their faces were never as frightened, or as savage, as the ones they wore yesterday.

Strangest of all was that woman on the street. She slapped her son and said: "Damn it all, you've got me so riled up I could take a good bite right out of your hide!" She was talking to him, but she was looking at me! I tried, but couldn't conceal a shudder of fright. That's when that ghastly crew of people, with their green faces and protruding fangs, began to roar with laughter. Old Fifth Chen[6] ran up, took me firmly in tow, and dragged me away.

When we got back, the people at home all pretended not to know me. The expressions in their eyes were just like all the others too. After he got me into the study, Old Fifth Chen bolted the door from the outside—just the way you would pen up a chicken or a duck! That made figuring out what was at the bottom of it all harder than ever.

A few days back one of our tenant farmers came in from Wolf Cub Village to report a famine. Told my elder brother the villagers had all ganged up on a "bad" man and beaten him to death. Even gouged out his heart and liver. Fried them up and ate them to bolster their own courage! When I tried to horn in on the conversation, Elder Brother and the tenant farmer both gave me sinister looks. I realized for the first time today that the expression in their eyes was just the same as what I saw in those people on the street.

---

5. Local government offices. The petty clerks who worked in them were notorious for relying on their proximity to power to bully and abuse the common people. "Cangue": a split board, hinged at one end and locked at the other; holes were cut out to accommodate the prisoner's neck and wrists.
6. People were often referred to by their hierarchical position within their extended family.

As I think of it now, a shiver's running from the top of my head clear down to the tips of my toes.

If they're capable of eating people, then who's to say they won't eat *me*?

Don't you see? That woman's words about "taking a good bite," and the laughter of that ghastly crew with their green faces and protruding fangs, and the words of our tenant farmer a few days back—it's perfectly clear to me now that all that talk and all that laughter were really a set of secret signals. Those words were poison! That laughter, a knife! Their teeth are bared and waiting—white and razor sharp! Those people are cannibals!

As I see it myself, though I'm not what you'd call an evil man, still, ever since I trampled the Antiquity family's account books, it's hard to say *what* they'll do. They seem to have something in mind, but I can't begin to guess what. What's more, as soon as they turn against someone, they'll *say* he's evil anyway. I can still remember how it was when Elder Brother was teaching me composition.[7] No matter how good a man was, if I could find a few things wrong with him he would approvingly underline my words; on the other hand, if I made a few allowances for a bad man, he'd say I was "an extraordinary student, an absolute genius." When all is said and done, how can I possibly guess what people like *that* have in mind, especially when they're getting ready for a cannibals' feast?

You have to *really* go into something before you can understand it. I seemed to remember, though not too clearly, that from ancient times on people have often been eaten, and so I started leafing through a history book to look it up. There were no dates in this history, but scrawled this way and that across every page were the words BENEVOLENCE, RIGHTEOUSNESS, and MORALITY. Since I couldn't get to sleep anyway, I read that history very carefully for most of the night, and finally I began to make out what was written *between* the lines; the whole volume was filled with a single phrase: EAT PEOPLE!

The words written in the history book, the things the tenant farmer said—all of it began to stare at me with hideous eyes, began to snarl and growl at me from behind bared teeth!

Why sure, *I'm* a person too, and they want to eat *me*!

4

In the morning I sat in the study for a while, calm and collected. Old Fifth Chen brought in some food—vegetables and a steamed fish. The fish's eyes were white and hard. Its mouth was wide open, just like the mouths of those people who wanted to eat human flesh. After I'd taken a few bites, the meat felt so smooth and slippery in my mouth that I couldn't tell whether it was fish or human flesh. I vomited.

"Old Fifth," I said, "tell Elder Brother that it's absolutely stifling in here and that I'd like to take a walk in the garden." He left without answering, but sure enough, after a while the door opened. I didn't even budge—just sat there waiting to see what they'd do to me. I *knew* that they wouldn't be willing to set me loose.

Just as I expected! Elder Brother came in with an old man in tow and walked slowly toward me. There was a savage glint in the old man's eyes. He was afraid I'd

---

7. That is, to compose essays in the classical style.

see it and kept his head tilted toward the floor while stealing sidewise glances at me over the temples of his glasses. "You seem to be fine today," said Elder Brother.

"You bet!" I replied.

"I've asked Dr. He to come and examine your pulse today."

"He's welcome!" I said. But don't think for one moment that I didn't know the old geezer was an executioner in disguise! Taking my pulse was nothing but a ruse; he wanted to feel my flesh and decide if I was fat enough to butcher yet. He'd probably even get a share of the meat for his troubles. I wasn't a *bit* afraid. Even though I don't eat human flesh, I still have a lot more courage than those who do. I thrust both hands out to see how the old buzzard would make his move. Sitting down, he closed his eyes and felt my pulse[8] for a good long while. Then he froze. Just sat there without moving a muscle for another good long while. Finally he opened his spooky eyes and said: "Don't let your thoughts run away with you. Just convalesce in peace and quiet for a few days and you'll be all right."

Don't let my thoughts run away with me? Convalesce in peace and quiet? If I convalesce till I'm good and fat, they get more to eat, but what do *I* get out of it? How can I possibly be *all right*? What a bunch! All they think about is eating human flesh, and then they go sneaking around, thinking up every which way they can to camouflage their real intentions. They were comical enough to crack *anybody* up. I couldn't hold it in any longer and let out a good loud laugh. Now *that* really felt good. I knew in my heart of hearts that my laughter was *packed* with courage and righteousness. And do you know what? They were so completely subdued by it that the old man and my elder brother both went pale!

But the more *courage* I had, the more that made them want to eat me so that they could get a little of it for free. The old man walked out. Before he had taken many steps, he lowered his head and told Elder Brother, "To be eaten as soon as possible!" He nodded understandingly. So, Elder Brother, you're in it too! Although that discovery seemed unforeseen, it really wasn't, either. My own elder brother had thrown in with the very people who wanted to eat me!

My elder brother is a cannibal!

I'm brother to a cannibal.

Even though I'm to be the victim of cannibalism, I'm *brother* to a cannibal all the same!

5

During the past few days I've taken a step back in my thinking. Supposing that old man wasn't an executioner in disguise but really was a doctor—well, he'd still be a cannibal just the same. In *Medicinal . . . something or other* by Li Shizhen,[9] the grandfather of the doctor's trade, it says quite clearly that human flesh can be eaten, so how can that old man say that *he's* not a cannibal too?

And as for my own elder brother, I'm not being the least bit unfair to him. When he was explaining the classics to me, he said with his very own tongue that it was all right to *exchange children and eat them*. And then there was another time when he happened to start in on an evil man and said that not

---

8. In Chinese medicine, the pulse is taken at both wrists.
9. Lived from 1518 to 1593. *Taxonomy of*

Medicinal Herbs, a gigantic work, was the most important pharmacopoeia in traditional China.

only should the man be killed, but his *flesh should be eaten* and *his skin used as a sleeping mat*[1] as well.

When our tenant farmer came in from Wolf Cub Village a few days back and talked about eating a man's heart and liver, Elder Brother didn't seem to see anything out of the way in that either—just kept nodding his head. You can tell from that alone that his present way of thinking is every bit as malicious as it was when I was a child. If it's all right to exchange *children* and eat them, then *anyone* can be exchanged, anyone can be eaten. Back then I just took what he said as explanation of the classics and let it go at that, but now I realize that while he was explaining, the grease of human flesh was smeared all over his lips, and what's more, his mind was filled with plans for further cannibalism.

6

Pitch black out. Can't tell if it's day or night. The Zhao family's dog has started barking again.

Savage as a lion, timid as a rabbit, crafty as a fox . . .

7

I'm on to the way they operate. They'll never be willing to come straight out and kill me. Besides, they wouldn't dare. They'd be afraid of all the bad luck it might bring down on them if they did. And so, they've gotten everyone into cahoots with them and have set traps all over the place so that I'll do *myself* in. When I think back on the looks of those men and women on the streets a few days ago, coupled with the things my elder brother's been up to recently, I can figure out eight or nine tenths of it. From their point of view, the best thing of all would be for me to take off my belt, fasten it around a beam, and hang myself. They wouldn't be guilty of murder, and yet they'd still get everything they're after. Why, they'd be so beside themselves with joy, they'd sob with laughter. Or if they couldn't get me to do that, maybe they could torment me until I died of fright and worry. Even though I'd come out a bit leaner that way, they'd still nod their heads in approval.

Their kind only know how to eat dead meat. I remember reading in a book somewhere about something called the *hai-yi-na*.[2] Its general appearance is said to be hideous, and the expression in its eyes particularly ugly and malicious. Often eats carrion, too. Even chews the bones to a pulp and swallows them down. Just thinking about it's enough to frighten a man.

1. Both italicized expressions are from the *Zuozhuan* (Zuo commentary to the *Spring and Summer Annals*, a historical work that dates from the 3rd century B.C.E.). In 448 B.C.E., an officer who was exhorting his own side not to surrender is recorded as having said, "When the army of Chu besieged the capital of Song [in 603 B.C.E.], the people exchanged their children and ate them, and used the bones for fuel; and still they would not submit to a covenant at the foot of their walls. For us who have sustained no great loss, to do so is to cast our state away" (translated by James Legge, 5.817). It is also recorded that in 551 B.C.E. an officer boasting of his own prowess before his ruler pointed to two men whom his ruler considered brave and said, "As to those two, they are like beasts, whose flesh I will eat, and then sleep upon their skins" (Legge 5.492).
2. Three Chinese characters are used here for phonetic value only; that is, *hai yi na* is a transliteration into Chinese of the English word *hyena*.

The *hai-yi-na* is kin to the wolf. The wolf's a relative of the dog, and just a few days ago the Zhao family dog gave me a funny look. It's easy to see that he's in on it too. How did that old man expect to fool *me* by staring at the floor?

My elder brother's the most pathetic of the whole lot. Since he's a human being too, how can he manage to be so totally without qualms, and what's more, even gang up with them to eat me? Could it be that he's been used to this sort of thing all along and sees nothing wrong with it? Or could it be that he's lost all conscience and just goes ahead and does it even though he knows it's wrong?

If I'm going to curse cannibals, I'll have to start with him. And if I'm going to *convert* cannibals, I'll have to start with him too.

8

Actually, by now even they should long since have understood the truth of this . . .

Someone came in. Couldn't have been more than twenty or so. I wasn't able to make out what he looked like too clearly, but he was all smiles. He nodded at me. His smile didn't look like the real thing either. And so I asked him, "Is this business of eating people right?"

He just kept right on smiling and said, "Except perhaps in a famine year, how could anyone get eaten?" I knew right off that he was one of them—one of those monsters who devour people!

At that point my own courage increased a hundredfold and I asked him, "Is it right?"

"Why are you talking about this kind of thing anyway? You really know how to . . . uh . . . how to pull a fellow's leg. Nice weather we're having."

"The weather *is* nice. There's a nice moon out, too, but I *still* want to know if it's right."

He seemed quite put out with me and began to mumble, "It's not—"

"Not right? Then how come they're still eating people?"

"No one's eating anyone."

"No one's *eating* anyone? They're eating people in Wolf Cub Village this very minute. And it's written in all the books, too, written in bright red blood!"

His expression changed and his face went gray like a slab of iron. His eyes started out from their sockets as he said, "Maybe they are, but it's always been that way, it's—"

"Just because it's always been that way, does that make it *right*?"

"I'm not going to discuss such things with you. If you insist on talking about that, then *you're* the one who's in the wrong!"

I leaped from my chair, opened my eyes, and looked around—but the fellow was nowhere to be seen. He was far younger than my elder brother, and yet he was actually one of them. It must be because his mom and dad taught him to be that way. And he's probably already passed it on to his own son. No wonder that even the children give me murderous looks.

9

They want to eat others and at the same time they're afraid that other people are going to eat them. That's why they're always watching each other with such suspicious looks in their eyes.

But all they'd have to do is give up that way of thinking, and then they could travel about, work, eat, and sleep in perfect security. Think how happy they'd feel! It's only a threshold, a pass. But what do they do instead? What is it that these fathers, sons, brothers, husbands, wives, friends, teachers, students, enemies, and even people who don't know each other *really* do? Why they all join together to hold each other back, and talk each other out of it!

That's it! They'd rather *die* than take that one little step.

10

I went to see Elder Brother bright and early. He was standing in the courtyard looking at the sky. I went up behind him so as to cut him off from the door back into the house. In the calmest and friendliest of tones, I said, "Elder Brother, there's something I'd like to tell you."

"Go right ahead." He immediately turned and nodded his head.

"It's only a few words, really, but it's hard to get them out. Elder Brother, way back in the beginning, it's probably the case that primitive peoples *all* ate some human flesh. But later on, because their ways of thinking changed, some gave up the practice and tried their level best to improve themselves; they kept on changing until they became human beings, *real* human beings. But the others didn't; they just kept right on with their cannibalism and stayed at that primitive level.

"You have the same sort of thing with evolution[3] in the animal world. Some reptiles, for instance, changed into fish, and then they evolved into birds, then into apes, and then into human beings. But the others didn't want to improve themselves and just kept right on being reptiles down to this very day.

"Think how ashamed those primitive men who have remained cannibals must feel when they stand before *real* human beings. They must feel even more ashamed than reptiles do when confronted with their brethren who have evolved into apes.

"There's an old story from ancient times about Yi Ya boiling his son and serving him up to Jie Zhou.[4] But if the truth be known, people have *always* practiced cannibalism, all the way from the time when Pan Gu separated heaven and earth down to Yi Ya's son, down to Xu Xilin,[5] and on down to the man they killed in Wolf Cub Village. And just last year when they executed a criminal in town, there was even someone with T.B. who dunked a steamed bread roll in his blood and then licked it off.

3. Charles Darwin's (1809–1892) theory of evolution was immensely important to Chinese intellectuals during Lu's lifetime and the common coin of much discourse.
4. An early philosophical text, *Guan Zi*, reports that the famous cook Yi Ya boiled his son and served him to his ruler, Duke Huan of Qi (685–643 B.C.E.), because the meat of a human infant was one of the few delicacies the duke had never tasted. Ji and Zhou were the last evil rulers of the Sang (1776–1122 B.C.E.) and Zhou (1122–221 B.C.E.) dynasties. The madman has mixed up some facts here.
5. From Lu's hometown, Shaoxing (1873–1907). After studies in Japan, he returned to China and served as head of the Anhui Police Academy. When a high Qing official, En Ming, participated in a graduation ceremony at the academy, Xu assassinated him, hoping that this would touch off the revolution. After the assassination, he and some of his students at the academy occupied the police armory and managed, for a while, to hold off En Ming's troops. When Xu was finally captured, En Ming's personal body guards dug out his heart and liver and ate them. Pan Gu (literally, "Coiled-up Antiquity") was born out of an egg. As he stood up, he separated heaven and earth. The world as we know it was formed from his body.

"When they decided to eat me, by yourself, of course, you couldn't do much to prevent it, but why did you have to go and *join* them? Cannibals are capable of anything! If they're capable of eating me, then they're capable of eating *you* too! Even within their own group, they think nothing of devouring each other. And yet all they'd have to do is turn back—*change*—and then everything would be fine. Even though people may say, 'It's always been like this,' we can still do our best to improve. And we can start today!

"You're going to tell me it can't be done! Elder Brother, I think you're very likely to say that. When that tenant wanted to reduce his rent the day before yesterday, wasn't it you who said it couldn't be done?"

At first he just stood there with a cold smile, but then his eyes took on a murderous gleam. (I had exposed their innermost secrets.) His whole face had gone pale. Some people were standing outside the front gate. The Venerable Old Zhao and his dog were among them. Stealthily peering this way and that, they began to crowd through the open gate. Some I couldn't make out too well—their faces seemed covered with cloth. Some looked the same as ever—smiling green faces with protruding fangs. I could tell at a glance that they all belonged to the same gang, that they were all cannibals. But at the same time I also realized that they didn't all think the same way. Some thought *it's always been like this* and that they really should eat human flesh. Others knew they shouldn't but went right on doing it anyway, always on the lookout for fear someone might give them away. And since that's exactly what I had just done, I knew they must be furious. But they were all *smiling* at me—cold little smiles!

At this point Elder Brother suddenly took on an ugly look and barked, "Get out of here! All of you! What's so funny about a madman?"

Now I'm on to *another* of their tricks: not only are they unwilling to change, but they're already setting me up for their next cannibalistic feast by labeling me a "madman." That way, they'll be able to eat me without getting into the slightest trouble. Some people will even be grateful to them. Wasn't that the very trick used in the case that the tenant reported? Everybody ganged up on a "bad" man and ate him. It's the same old thing.

Old Fifth Chen came in and made straight for me, looking mad as could be. But he wasn't going to shut *me* up! I was going to tell that bunch of cannibals off, and no two ways about it!

"You can change! You can change from the bottom of your hearts! You ought to know that in the future they're not going to allow cannibalism in the world anymore. If you don't change, you're going to devour each other anyway. And even if a lot of you *are* left, a real human being's going to come along and eradicate the lot of you, just like a hunter getting rid of wolves—or reptiles!"

Old Fifth Chen chased them all out. I don't know where Elder Brother disappeared to. Old Fifth talked me into going back to my room.

It was pitch black inside. The beams and rafters started trembling overhead. They shook for a bit, and then they started getting bigger and bigger. They piled themselves up into a great heap on top of my body!

The weight was incredibly heavy and I couldn't even budge—they were trying to kill me! But I knew their weight was an illusion, and I struggled out from under them, my body bathed in sweat. I was still going to have my say. "Change this minute! Change from the bottom of your hearts! You ought to know that in the future they're not going to allow cannibals in the world anymore . . ."

II

The sun doesn't come out. The door doesn't open. It's two meals a day.

I picked up my chopsticks and that got me thinking about Elder Brother. I realized that the reason for my younger sister's death lay entirely with him. I can see her now—such a lovable and helpless little thing, only five at the time. Mother couldn't stop crying, but *he* urged her to stop, probably because he'd eaten sister's flesh himself and hearing mother cry over her like that shamed him! But if he's still capable of feeling shame, then maybe . . .

Younger Sister was eaten by Elder Brother. I have no way of knowing whether Mother knew about it or not.

I think she *did* know, but while she was crying she didn't say anything about it. She probably thought it was all right, too. I can remember once when I was four or five, I was sitting out in the courtyard taking in a cool breeze when Elder Brother told me that when parents are ill, a son, in order to be counted as a really good person, should slice off a piece of his own flesh, boil it, and let them eat it.[6] At the time Mother didn't come out and say there was anything wrong with that. But if it was all right to eat one piece, then there certainly wouldn't be anything wrong with her eating the whole body. And yet when I think back to the way she cried and cried that day, it's enough to break my heart. It's all strange—very, very strange.

12

Can't think about it anymore. I just realized today that I too have muddled around for a good many years in a place where they've been continually eating people for four thousand years. Younger Sister happened to die at just the time when Elder Brother was in charge of the house. Who's to say he didn't slip some of her meat into the food we ate?

Who's to say I didn't eat a few pieces of my younger sister's flesh without knowing it? And now it's my turn . . .

Although I wasn't aware of it in the beginning, now that I *know* I'm someone with four thousand years' experience of cannibalism behind me, how hard it is to look real human beings in the eye!

13

Maybe there are some children around who still haven't eaten human flesh. Save the children . . .

1918

---

6. In traditional literature, stories about such gruesome acts of filial piety were not unusual.

LUIGI PIRANDELLO

1867–1936

"Who am I?" and "What is real?" are the persistent questions that underlie Luigi Pirandello's novels, short stories, and plays. Sometimes in a playful mood, sometimes more anxiously, Pirandello toys with these questions but refuses to answer them definitively. In fact, the term *Pirandellismo*, or "Pirandellism"—coined from the author's name—has come to stand in for the idea that there are as many truths as there are points of view. Yet Pirandello treats such weighty philosophical issues with a combination of humor and pathos that makes them highly entertaining.

Pirandello's great fame came late in life, as a result of his experimental dramas, but he had been an active writer for decades. Born in Girgenti (now Agrigento), Sicily, on June 28, 1867, Pirandello was the son of a sulfur merchant who intended his son to follow him into business. Pirandello preferred language and literature. After studying in Palermo and at the University of Rome, he traveled to the University of Bonn, where he received a doctorate in romance philology with a dissertation on the dialect of his hometown. Soon after completing his doctorate, Pirandello agreed to an arranged marriage with the daughter of a rich sulfur merchant, although he had never met her. They lived for ten years in Rome, where he wrote poetry and short stories, until flooding of the sulfur mines destroyed the fortunes of both families, and he was suddenly forced to earn a living. To add to their misfortune, his wife developed a jealous paranoia that grew so severe she had to be committed to an insane asylum in 1919; she remained institutionalized until her death four decades later.

Pirandello's early work included short stories and novellas written under the influence of the narrative style *verismo* (realism or naturalism) that he found exemplified in the work of the Sicilian writer Giovanni Verga (1840–1922). Pirandello wrote hundreds of stories of all lengths. He is recognized—in his clarity, realism, and psychological acuteness (often including a taste for the grotesque)—as an Italian master of the story form. His anthology of 1922, *A Year's Worth of Stories*, remains hugely popular in Italy. Not until he was in his fifties, however, did Pirandello write the more experimental plays, such as *Six Characters in Search of an Author* (1921) and *Henry IV* (1922), that established him as a major dramatist.

Despite the intellectualism of his plays, in politics Pirandello favored the irrational appeal of a strong leader. He was drawn to the fascist dictator Benito Mussolini and supported his regime at key moments—for example, in the wake of the murder by fascists of a socialist member of Parliament, Giacomo Matteotti. As Pirandello's fame spread, he directed his own company (Il Teatro d'Arte di Roma) with support from Mussolini's government and toured Europe with his plays. In 1934 he received the Nobel Prize in Literature. His later plays, featuring fantastic and grotesque elements, did not achieve the wide popularity of their predecessors.

Pirandello's plays turn the trappings of the theater itself—the stage, the producer, the author, the actors—into the material for comedy and invention. In their manipulation of ambiguous appearances and tragicomic effects, these plays foreshadow the absurdist theater of Samuel Beckett and others. Above all, they insist that "real" life is that which changes from moment to moment, exhibiting a fluidity that renders difficult and perhaps impossible any single formulation of either character or situation. Pirandello's playful treatment of the theatrical enterprise has been dubbed "metatheater," or theater about theater.

SIX CHARACTERS IN SEARCH OF AN AUTHOR

Six Characters in Search of an Author, the selection below, combines the elements of "metatheater" in an extraordinary self-reflexive style. At the beginning of the play, the Technician's interrupted hammering suggests that the audience has chanced on a rehearsal—of still another play by Pirandello—instead of coming to an actual performance. Concurrently, Pirandello's stage dialogue pokes fun at his reputation for obscurity. Just as the Actors are apparently set to rehearse *The Game of Role Playing*, six unexpected persons come down the aisle seeking an author: they are Characters from an unwritten novel who demand to be given dramatic existence. The play *Six Characters* is continually in the process of being composed: composed as the interwoven double plot we see on stage, composed by the Prompter writing a script in shorthand for the Actors to reproduce, and composed as the inner drama of the Characters finally achieves its rightful existence as a work of art.

The play's initial absurdity emerges when the six fictional Characters arrive with their claim to be "truer and more real" than the "real" Actors who seek to impersonate them. (Of course, to the audience all the figures onstage are equally real—or unreal.) Each Charac-

ter represents a particular identity created by the author. Pirandello later had the Characters wear masks to distinguish them from the Actors—not the conventional masks of ancient Greek drama or of the Japanese Noh theater that identify the characters' roles, nor the ceremonial masks, representing spirits in African ritual, that temporarily invest the wearer with the spirit's identity and authority. Instead, they are a theatrical device, a symbol and visual reminder of each Character's unchanging being. The six Characters are incapable of developing outside their roles and are condemned, in their search for existence, painfully to reenact their essential roles.

Conversely, the fictional Characters have more stable personalities than "real" people, including the Actors, who are still "no one," incomplete, open to change and misinterpretation. Characters can claim to be "someone" because their natures have been decided once and for all. Yet further complications attend this contrast between fictional characters and real actors: for instance, the Characters feel the urge to play their own roles and are disturbed at the prospect of having the Actors misrepresent them. All human beings, asserts Pirandello, whether fictional or real, are subject to being misunderstood; we even misunderstand ourselves when we think our identities are constant in all situations. We always have "the illusion of being always one thing for all men," says the Father, but "It's not true!"

Pirandello does not hold his audience's attention simply by uttering grand philosophical truths, however. *Six Characters* hums with suspense and discovery, from the moment that the Characters interrupt the rehearsal with its complaining Actors and Stage Manager. The story that the Characters tell about themselves hints of melodrama and family scandal, like attention-grabbing headlines from a sensationalist newspaper. Indeed, Pirandello plays with the risqué element by focusing on the Characters' repeated attempts to portray one emotionally fraught scene. Eventually, the pathos of this play within the play comes to overwhelm the more philosophical metatheatrical frame.

Six Characters in Search of an Author underwent an interesting evolution to become the play that we see today. First performed in 1921 in Rome, where its unsettling plot and characters scandalized a traditionalist audience, it was reshaped in more radical form after the remarkable performance produced by Georges Pitoëff in 1923. Pirandello, who came to Paris wary of Pitoëff's innovations (for instance, he had the Characters arrive in a green-lit stage elevator), was soon convinced that the Russian director's stagecraft enhanced the original text. Pitoëff used his knowledge of technical effects to accentuate the relationship of appearance and reality: he extended the stage with several steps leading down to the auditorium (a break from the conventional "fourth wall" concept, in which the actors on stage proceed as if unaware of the audience); underscored the play within a play with rehearsal effects, showing the Technician hammering and the Director arranging suitable props and lighting; he emphasized the division between Characters and Actors by separating the groups on stage and dressing all the Characters (except the Little Girl) in black. Pirandello welcomed these changes and expanded on many of

them. To distinguish the Characters even further from the Actors, he proposed contrasting clothing in addition to masks, black for the former and pale for the latter. Most striking, however, is his transformation of Pitoëff's steps into an actual bridge between the world of the stage and the auditorium, a strategy that allows the Actors (and Characters) to come and go in the "real world" of the audience.

In breaking down comfortable illusions of compartmentalized, stable reality, Pirandello revolutionized European stage techniques. In place of the nineteenth century's "well-made play"— with its neatly constructed plot that boxes real life into a conventional beginning, middle, and end, and its safely inaccessible characters on the other side of the footlights—he offers unpredictable plots and ambiguous roles. It is not easy to know the truth about others, he suggests, or to make ourselves known behind the "mask" that each of us wears.

Readers might enjoy testing the enduring liveliness of Pirandello's dialogue by rehearsing their own selection of scenes—or perhaps by relocating them in a contemporary setting. According to the director Robert Brustein, whose 1988 production of *Six Characters in Search of an Author* set the action in New York and replaced Madam Pace with a pimp, "Pirandello both encourages and stimulates a pluralism in theater because there can be dozens, hundreds, thousands of productions of *Six Characters*, and every one of them is going to be different."

Six Characters in Search of an Author[1]

CHARACTERS OF THE PLAY-IN-THE-MAKING

The FATHER
The MOTHER
The SON, *aged 22*
The STEPDAUGHTER, *18*

The BOY, *14*
The LITTLE GIRL, *4*
   (*these two last do not speak*)
Then, called into being: MADAM PACE

ACTORS IN THE COMPANY

The DIRECTOR (*direttore-capocomico*)
LEADING LADY
LEADING MAN
SECOND ACTRESS
INGENUE
JUVENILE LEAD
Other actors and actresses

STAGE MANAGER
PROMPTER
PROPERTY MAN
TECHNICIAN
Director's SECRETARY
STAGE DOOR MAN
STAGE CREW

THE PLACE: *The stage of a playhouse.*

When the audience arrives in the theater, the curtain is raised; and the stage, as normally in the daytime, is without wings or scenery and almost completely dark and empty. From the beginning we are to receive the impression of an unrehearsed performance.

Two stairways, left and right respectively, connect the stage with the auditorium.

Onstage the dome of the prompter's box has been placed on one side of the box itself. On the other side, at the front of the stage, a small table and an armchair with its back to the audience, for the DIRETTORE-CAPOCOMICO [DIRECTOR].

Two other small tables of different sizes with several chairs around them have also been placed at the front of the stage, ready as needed for the rehearsal. Other chairs here and there, left and right, for the actors, and at the back, a piano, on one side and almost hidden.

As soon as the houselights dim, the TECHNICIAN is seen entering at the door onstage. He is wearing a blue shirt, and a tool bag hangs from his belt. From a corner at the back he takes several stage braces, then arranges them on the floor downstage, and kneels down to hammer some nails in. At the sound of the hammering, the STAGE MANAGER comes running from the door that leads to the dressing rooms.

STAGE MANAGER   Oh! What are you doing?

TECHNICIAN   What am I doing? Hammering.

---

1. Translated by Eric Bentley. In the Italian editions, Pirandello notes that he did not divide the play into formal acts or scenes. The translator has marked the divisions for clarity, however, according to the stage directions.

STAGE MANAGER   At this hour? [*He looks at the clock.*] It's ten-thirty already. The Director will be here any moment. For the rehearsal.

TECHNICIAN   I gotta have time to work, too, see.

STAGE MANAGER   You will have. But not now.

TECHNICIAN   When?

STAGE MANAGER   Not during rehearsal hours. Now move along, take all this stuff away, and let me set the stage for the second act of, um, *The Game of Role Playing.*[2]

[*Muttering, grumbling, the* TECHNICIAN *picks up the stage braces and goes away. Meanwhile, from the door onstage, the actors of the company start coming in, both men and women, one at a time at first, then in twos, at random, nine or ten of them, the number one would expect as the cast in rehearsals of Pirandello's play* The Game of Role Playing, *which is the order of the day. They enter, greet the* STAGE MANAGER *and each other, all saying good-morning to all. Several go to their dressing rooms. Others, among them the* PROMPTER, *who has a copy of the script rolled up under his arm, stay onstage, waiting for the* DIRECTOR *to begin the rehearsal. Meanwhile, either seated in conversational groups, or standing, they exchange a few words among themselves. One lights a cigarette, one complains about the part he has been assigned, one reads aloud to his companions items of news from a theater journal. It would be well if both the Actresses and the Actors wore rather gay and brightly colored clothes and if this first improvised scene* (scena a soggetto) *combined vivacity with naturalness. At a certain point, one of the actors can sit down at the piano and strike up a dance tune. The younger actors and actresses start dancing.*]

STAGE MANAGER   [*clapping his hands to call them to order*]   All right, that's enough of that. The Director's here.

[*The noise and the dancing stop at once. The Actors turn and look toward the auditorium from the door of which the* DIRECTOR *is now seen coming. A bowler hat on his head, a walking stick under his arm, and a big cigar in his mouth, he walks down the aisle and, greeted by the Actors, goes onstage by one of the two stairways. The* SECRETARY *hands him his mail: several newspapers and a script in a wrapper.*]

DIRECTOR   Letters?

SECRETARY   None. That's all the mail there is.

DIRECTOR   [*handing him the script*]   Take this to my room. [*Then, looking around and addressing himself to the* STAGE MANAGER]   We can't see each other in here. Want to give us a little light?

STAGE MANAGER   OK.

[*He goes to give the order, and shortly afterward, the whole left side of the stage where the Actors are is lit by a vivid white light. Meanwhile, the* PROMPTER *has taken up his position in his box. He uses a small lamp and has the script open in front of him.*]

DIRECTOR   [*clapping his hands*]   Very well, let's start. [*To the* STAGE MANAGER]   Someone missing?

---

2. *Il Giuoco delle Parti* (1918), a stage adaptation of Pirandello's own novella. The hero, Leone Gala, pretends to ignore his wife Silia's infidelity until the end, when he takes revenge by tricking her lover, Guido Venanzi, into taking his place in a fatal duel she had engineered to get rid of her husband.

STAGE MANAGER   The Leading Lady.

DIRECTOR   As usual! [*He looks at the clock.*] We're ten minutes late already. Fine her for that, would you, please? Then she'll learn to be on time.

[*He has not completed his rebuke when the voice of the* LEADING LADY *is heard from the back of the auditorium.*]

LEADING LADY   No, no, for heaven's sake! I'm here! I'm here! [*She is dressed all in white with a big, impudent hat on her head and a cute little dog in her arms. She runs down the aisle and climbs one of the sets of stairs in great haste.*]

DIRECTOR   You've sworn an oath always to keep people waiting.

LEADING LADY   You must excuse me. Just couldn't find a taxi. But you haven't even begun, I see. And I'm not on right away. [*Then, calling the* STAGE MANAGER *by name, and handing the little dog over to him*] Would you please shut him in my dressing room?

DIRECTOR [*grumbling*]   And the little dog to boot! As if there weren't enough dogs around here. [*He claps his hands again and turns to the* PROMPTER.] Now then, the second act of *The Game of Role Playing*. [*As he sits down in his armchair*] Quiet, gentlemen. Who's onstage?

[*The Actresses and Actors clear the front of the stage and go and sit on one side, except for the three who will start the rehearsal and the* LEADING LADY *who, disregarding the* DIRECTOR's *request, sits herself down at one of the two small tables.*]

DIRECTOR [*to the* LEADING LADY]   You're in this scene, are you?

LEADING LADY   Me? No, no.

DIRECTOR [*irritated*]   Then how about getting up, for Heaven's sake?

[*The* LEADING LADY *rises and goes and sits beside the other Actors who have already gone to one side.*]

DIRECTOR [*to the* PROMPTER]   Start, start.

PROMPTER [*reading from the script*]   "In the house of Leone Gala. A strange room, combined study and dining room."

DIRECTOR [*turning to the* STAGE MANAGER]   We'll use the red room.

STAGE MANAGER [*making a note on a piece of paper*]   Red room. Very good.

PROMPTER [*continuing to read from the script*]   "The table is set and the desk has books and papers on it. Shelves with books on them, and cupboards with lavish tableware. Door in the rear through which one goes to Leone's bedroom. Side door on the left through which one goes to the kitchen. The main entrance is on the right."

DIRECTOR [*rising and pointing*]   All right, now listen carefully. That's the main door. This is the way to the kitchen. [*Addressing himself to the Actor playing the part of Socrates*[3]] You will come on and go out on this side. [*To the* STAGE MANAGER] The compass at the back. And curtains. [*He sits down again.*]

STAGE MANAGER [*making a note*]   Very good.

---

3. Nickname given to Gala's servant, Filippo, in *The Game of Role Playing*, the play they are rehearsing.

PROMPTER [*reading as before*] "Scene One. Leone Gala, Guido Venanzi, Filippo called Socrates." [*To the* DIRECTOR] Am I supposed to read the stage directions, too?

DIRECTOR Yes, yes, yes! I've told you that a hundred times!

PROMPTER [*reading as before*] "At the rise of the curtain, Leone Gala, wearing a chef's hat and apron, is intent on beating an egg in a saucepan with a wooden spoon. Filippo, also dressed as a cook, is beating another egg. Guido Venanzi, seated, is listening."

LEADING ACTOR [*to the* DIRECTOR] Excuse me, but do I really have to wear a chef's hat?

DIRECTOR [*annoyed by this observation*] I should say so! It's in the script. [*And he points at it.*]

LEADING ACTOR But it's ridiculous, if I may say so.

DIRECTOR [*leaping to his feet, furious*] "Ridiculous, ridiculous!" What do you want me to do? We never get a good play from France any more,[4] so we're reduced to producing plays by Pirandello, a fine man and all that, but neither the actors, the critics, nor the audience are ever happy with his plays, and if you ask me, he does it all on purpose. [*The Actors laugh. And now he rises and coming over to the* LEADING ACTOR *shouts.*] A cook's hat, yes, my dear man! And you beat eggs. And you think you have nothing more on your hands than the beating of eggs? Guess again. You symbolize the shell of those eggs. [*The Actors resume their laughing, and start making ironical comments among themselves.*] Silence! And pay attention while I explain. [*Again addressing himself to the* LEADING ACTOR] Yes, the shell: that is to say, the empty *form* of reason without the *content* of instinct, which is blind. You are reason, and your wife is instinct in the game of role playing. You play the part assigned you, and you're your own puppet—of your own free will.[5] Understand?

LEADING ACTOR [*extending his arms, palms upward*] Me? No.

DIRECTOR [*returning to his place*] Nor do I. Let's go on. Wait and see what I do with the ending. [*In a confidential tone*] I suggest you face three-quarters front. Otherwise, what with the abstruseness of the dialogue, and an audience that can't hear you, good-bye play! [*Again clapping*] Now, again, order! Let's go.

PROMPTER Excuse me, sir, may I put the top back on the prompter's box? There's rather a draft.

DIRECTOR Yes, yes, do that.

[*The* STAGE DOOR MAN *has entered the auditorium in the meanwhile, his braided cap on his head. Proceeding down the aisle, he goes up onstage to announce to the* DIRECTOR *the arrival of the Six Characters, who have also entered the auditorium, and have started following him at a certain distance, a little lost and perplexed, looking around them.*]

---

4. The Director refers to the realistic, tightly constructed plays (often French) that were internationally popular in the late 19th century and a staple of Italian theaters at the beginning of the 20th.

5. Leone Gala is a rationalist and an aesthete—the opposite of his impulsive, passionate wife, Silia. By masking his feelings and constantly playing the role of gourmet cook, he chooses his own role and thus becomes his own "puppet."

Whoever is going to try and translate this play into scenic terms must take all possible measures not to let these Six Characters get confused with the Actors of the Company. Placing both groups correctly, in accordance with the stage directions, once the Six are onstage, will certainly help, as will lighting the two groups in contrasting colors. But the most suitable and effective means to be suggested here is the use of special masks for the Characters: masks specially made of material which doesn't go limp when sweaty and yet masks which are not too heavy for the Actors wearing them, cut out and worked over so they leave eyes, nostrils, and mouth free. This will also bring out the inner significance of the play. The Characters in fact should not be presented as ghosts but as created realities, unchanging constructs of the imagination, and therefore more solidly real than the Actors with their fluid naturalness. The masks will help to give the impression of figures constructed by art, each one unchangeably fixed in the expression of its own fundamental sentiment, thus:

remorse in the case of the FATHER; *revenge in the case of the* STEPDAUGHTER; *disdain in the case of the* SON; *grief in the case of the* MOTHER, *who should have wax tears fixed in the rings under her eyes and on her cheeks, as with the sculpted and painted images of the* mater dolorosa[6] *in church. Their clothes should be of special material and design, without extravagance, with rigid, full folds like a statue, in short not suggesting a material you might buy at any store in town, cut out and tailored at any dressmaker's.*

The FATHER *is a man of about fifty, hair thin at the temples, but not bald, thick mustache coiled round a still youthful mouth that is often open in an uncertain, pointless smile. Pale, most notably on his broad forehead: blue eyes, oval, very clear and piercing; dark jacket and light trousers: at times gentle and smooth, at times he has hard, harsh outbursts.*

The MOTHER *seems scared and crushed by an intolerable weight of shame and self-abasement. Wearing a thick black crepe widow's veil, she is modestly dressed in black, and when she lifts the veil, the face does not show signs of suffering, and yet seems made of wax. Her eyes are always on the ground.*

The STEPDAUGHTER, *eighteen, is impudent, almost insolent. Very beautiful, and also in mourning, but mourning of a showy elegance. She shows contempt for the timid, afflicted, almost humiliated manner of her little brother, rather a mess of a* BOY, *fourteen, also dressed in black, but a lively tenderness for her little sister, a* LITTLE GIRL *of around four, dressed in white with a black silk sash round her waist.*

The SON, *twenty-two, tall, almost rigid with contained disdain for the* FATHER *and supercilious indifference toward the* MOTHER, *wears a mauve topcoat and a long green scarf wound round his neck.]*

STAGE DOOR MAN [*beret in hand*]   Excuse me, your honor.

DIRECTOR [*rudely jumping on him*]   What is it now?

STAGE DOOR MAN [*timidly*]   There are some people here asking for you.

[*The* DIRECTOR *and the Actors turn in astonishment to look down into the auditorium.*]

DIRECTOR [*furious again*]   But I'm rehearsing here! And you know perfectly well no one can come in during rehearsal! [*Turning again toward the house*] Who are these people? What do they want?

---

6. Mother of Sorrows (Latin), a traditional representation of Mary, mother of Jesus.

THE FATHER [*stepping forward, followed by the others, to one of the two little stairways to the stage*]   We're here in search of an author.

DIRECTOR [*half angry, half astounded*]   An author? What author?

FATHER   Any author, sir.

DIRECTOR   There's no author here at all. It's not a new play we're rehearsing.

STEPDAUGHTER [*very vivaciously as she rushes up the stairs*]   Then so much the better, sir! *We* can be your new play!

ONE OF THE ACTORS [*among the racy comments and laughs of the others*]   Did you hear that?

FATHER [*following the* STEPDAUGHTER *onstage*]   Certainly, but if the author's not here . . . [*To the* DIRECTOR] Unless *you'd* like to be the author?

[*The* MOTHER, *holding the* LITTLE GIRL *by the hand, and the* BOY *climb the first steps of the stairway and remain there waiting. The* SON *stays morosely below.*]

DIRECTOR   Is this your idea of a joke?

FATHER   Heavens, no! Oh, sir, on the contrary: we bring you a painful drama.

STEPDAUGHTER   We can make your fortune for you.

DIRECTOR   Do me a favor, and leave. We have no time to waste on madmen.

FATHER [*wounded, smoothly*]   Oh, sir, you surely know that life is full of infinite absurdities which, brazenly enough, do not need to appear probable, because they're true.

DIRECTOR   What in God's name are you saying?

FATHER   I'm saying it can actually be considered madness, sir, to force oneself to do the opposite: that is, to give probability to things so they will seem true. But permit me to observe that, if this is madness, it is also the *raison d'être*[7] of your profession.

[*The Actors become agitated and indignant.*]

DIRECTOR [*rising and looking him over*]   It is, is it? It seems to you an affair for madmen, our profession?

FATHER   Well, to make something seem true which is not true . . . without any need, sir: just for fun . . . Isn't it your job to give life onstage to creatures of fantasy?

DIRECTOR [*immediately, making himself spokesman for the growing indignation of his Actors*]   Let me tell you something, my good sir. The actor's profession is a very noble one. If, as things go nowadays, our new playwrights give us nothing but stupid plays, with puppets in them instead of men, it is our boast, I'd have you know, to have given life—on these very boards—to immortal works of art.

[*Satisfied, the Actors approve and applaud their* DIRECTOR.]

FATHER [*interrupting and bearing down hard*]   Exactly! That's just it. You have created living beings—*more* alive than those that breathe and wear clothes! Less real, perhaps; but more true! We agree completely!

[*The Actors look at each other, astounded.*]

DIRECTOR   What? You were saying just now . . .

---

7. Reason for being (French).

FATHER   No, no, don't misunderstand me. You shouted that you hadn't time to waste on madmen. So I wanted to tell you that no one knows better than you that Nature employs the human imagination to carry her work of creation on to a higher plane!

DIRECTOR   All right, all right. But what are you getting at, exactly?

FATHER   Nothing, sir. I only wanted to show that one may be born to this life in many modes, in many forms: as tree, as rock, water or butterfly . . . or woman. And that . . . characters are born too.

DIRECTOR   [*his amazement ironically feigned*]   And you—with these companions of yours—were born a character?

FATHER   Right, sir. And alive, as you see.

[*The* DIRECTOR *and the Actors burst out laughing as at a joke.*]

FATHER [*wounded*]   I'm sorry to hear you laugh, because, I repeat, we carry a painful drama within us, as you all might deduce from the sight of that lady there, veiled in black.

[*As he says this, he gives his hand to the* MOTHER *to help her up the last steps and, still holding her by the hand, he leads her with a certain tragic solemnity to the other side of the stage, which is suddenly bathed in fantastic light. The* LITTLE GIRL *and the* BOY *follow the* MOTHER; *then the* SON, *who stands on one side at the back; then the* STEPDAUGHTER *who also detaches herself from the others—downstage and leaning against the proscenium arch. At first astonished at this development, then overcome with admiration, the Actors now burst into applause as at a show performed for their benefit.*]

DIRECTOR [*bowled over at first, then indignant*]   Oh, stop this! Silence please! [*Then, turning to the Characters*] And you, leave! Get out of here! [*To the* STAGE MANAGER] For God's sake, get them out!

STAGE MANAGER [*stepping forward but then stopping, as if held back by a strange dismay*]   Go! Go!

FATHER [*to the* DIRECTOR]   No, look, we, um—

DIRECTOR [*shouting*]   I tell you we've got to work!

LEADING MAN   It's not right to fool around like this . . .

FATHER [*resolute, stepping forward*]   I'm amazed at your incredulity! You're accustomed to seeing the created characters of an author spring to life, aren't you, right here on this stage, the one confronting the other? Perhaps the trouble is there's no script *there* [*Pointing to the* PROMPTER's *box*] with us in it?

STEPDAUGHTER [*going right up to the* DIRECTOR, *smiling, coquettish*]   Believe me, we really are six characters, sir. Very interesting ones at that. But lost. Adrift.

FATHER [*brushing her aside*]   Very well: lost, adrift. [*Going right on*] In the sense, that is, that the author who created us, made us live, did not wish, or simply and materially was not able, to place us in the world of art.[8] And that was a real crime, sir, because whoever has the luck to be born a living character can also laugh at death. He will never die! The man will die, the writer, the instrument of creation; the creature will never die! And to have

---

8. In the 1925 preface to *Six Characters*, Pirandello explains that these characters came to him first as characters for a novel that he later abandoned. Haunted by their half-realized personalities, he decided to use the situation in a play.

eternal life it doesn't even take extraordinary gifts, nor the performance of miracles. Who was Sancho Panza? Who was Don Abbondio?[9] But they live forever because, as live germs, they have the luck to find a fertile matrix, an imagination which knew how to raise and nourish them, make them live through all eternity!

DIRECTOR   That's all well and good. But what do you people want here?

FATHER   We want to live, sir.

DIRECTOR [*ironically*]   Through all eternity?

FATHER   No, sir. But for a moment at least. In you.

AN ACTOR   Well, well, well!

LEADING LADY   They want to live in us.

JUVENILE LEAD [*pointing to the* STEPDAUGHTER]   Well, I've no objection, so long as I get that one.

FATHER   Now look, look. The play is still in the making. [*To the* DIRECTOR] But if you wish, and your actors wish, we can make it right away. Acting in concert.

LEADING MAN [*annoyed*]   Concert? We don't put on concerts! We do plays, dramas, comedies!

FATHER   Very good. That's why we came.

DIRECTOR   Well, where's the script?

FATHER   Inside us, sir. [*The Actors laugh.*] The drama is inside us. It *is* us. And we're impatient to perform it. According to the dictates of the passion within us.

STEPDAUGHTER [*scornful, with treacherous grace, deliberate impudence*]   My passion—if you only knew, sir! My passion—for him! [*She points to the* FATHER *and makes as if to embrace him but then breaks into a strident laugh.*]

FATHER [*an angry interjection*]   You keep out of this now. And please don't laugh that way!

STEPDAUGHTER   No? Then, ladies and gentlemen, permit me. A two months' orphan, I shall dance and sing for you all. Watch how! [*She mischievously starts to sing "Beware of Chu Chin Chow" by Dave Stamper, reduced to fox-trot or slow one-step by Francis Salabert: the first verse, accompanied by a step or two of dancing.*[1] *While she sings and dances, the Actors, especially the young ones, as if drawn by some strange fascination, move toward her and half raise their hands as if to take hold of her. She runs away and when the Actors burst into applause she just stands there, remote, abstracted, while the* DIRECTOR *protests.*]

ACTORS and ACTRESSES [*laughing and clapping*]   Brava! Fine! Splendid!

DIRECTOR [*annoyed*]   Silence! What do you think this is, a night spot? [*Taking the* FATHER *a step or two to one side, with a certain amount of consternation*] Tell me something. Is she crazy?

FATHER   Crazy? Of course not. It's much worse than that.

---

9. A rural priest in Alessandro Manzoni's novel *I Promessi sposi* (*The Betrothed*, 1825–27). Sancho Panza was Don Quixote's servant in Cervantes' novel *Don Quixote* (1605–15).

1. "Chu-Chin-Chow" was a contemporary popular song from the Ziegfeld Follies of 1917.

STEPDAUGHTER [*running over at once to the* DIRECTOR] Worse! Worse! Not crazy but worse! Just listen: I'll play it for you right now, this drama, and at a certain point you'll see me—when this dear little thing—[*She takes the* LITTLE GIRL *who is beside the* MOTHER *by the hand and leads her to the* DIRECTOR.]—isn't she darling? [*Takes her in her arms and kisses her.*] Sweetie! Sweetie! [*Puts her down again and adds with almost involuntary emotion.*] Well, when God suddenly takes this little sweetheart away from her poor mother, and that idiot there—[*Thrusting the* BOY *forward, rudely seizing him by a sleeve*] does the stupidest of things, like the nitwit that he is, [*With a shove she drives him back toward the* MOTHER] then you will see me take to my heels. Yes, ladies and gentlemen, take to my heels! I can hardly wait for that moment. For after what happened between him and me—[*She points to the* FATHER *with a horrible wink.*] something very intimate, you understand—I can't stay in such company any longer, witnessing the anguish of our mother on account of that fool there—[*She points to the* SON.] Just look at him, look at him!—how indifferent, how frozen, because he is the legitimate son, that's what he is, full of contempt for me, for him [*the* BOY], and for that little creature [*the* LITTLE GIRL], because we three are bastards, d'you see? Bastards. [*Goes to the* MOTHER *and embraces her.*] And this poor mother, the common mother of us all, he—well, he doesn't want to acknowledge her as *his* mother too, and he looks down on her, that's what he does, looks on her as only the mother of us three bastards, the wretch! [*She says this rapidly in a state of extreme excitement. Her voice swells to the word: "bastards!" and descends again to the final "wretch," almost spitting it out.*]

MOTHER [*to the* DIRECTOR, *with infinite anguish*] In the name of these two small children, sir, I implore you . . . [*She grows faint and sways.*] Oh, heavens . . .

FATHER [*rushing over to support her with almost all the Actors, who are astonished and scared*] Please! Please, a chair, a chair for this poor widow!

ACTORS [*rushing over*] —Is it true then?—She's *really* fainting?

DIRECTOR A chair!

[*One of the Actors proffers a chair. The others stand around, ready to help. The* MOTHER, *seated, tries to stop the* FATHER *from lifting the veil that hides her face.*]

FATHER [*to the* DIRECTOR] Look at her, look at her . . .

MOTHER Heavens, no, stop it!

FATHER Let them see you. [*He lifts her veil.*]

MOTHER [*rising and covering her face with her hands, desperate*] Oh, sir, please stop this man from carrying out his plan. It's horrible for me!

DIRECTOR [*surprised, stunned*] I don't know where we're at! What's this all about? [*To the* FATHER] Is this your wife?

FATHER [*at once*] Yes, sir, my wife.

DIRECTOR Then how is she a widow, if you're alive?

[*The Actors relieve their astonishment in a loud burst of laughter.*]

FATHER [*wounded, with bitter resentment*] Don't laugh! Don't laugh like that! Please! Just that is her drama, sir. She had another man. Another man who should be here!

MOTHER [*with a shout*]   No! No!

STEPDAUGHTER   He had the good luck to die. Two months ago, as I told you. We're still in mourning as you see.

FATHER   But he's absent, you see, not just because he's dead. He's absent— take a look at her, sir, and you will understand at once!—Her drama wasn't in the love of two men for whom she was incapable of feeling anything— except maybe a little gratitude [not to me, but to him]—She is not a woman, she is a mother!—And her drama—a powerful one, very powerful—is in fact all in those four children which she bore to her two men.

MOTHER   *My* men? Have you the gall to say I wanted two men? It was him, sir. He forced the other man on me. Compelled—yes, compelled—me to go off with him!

STEPDAUGHTER [*cutting in, roused*]   It's not true!

MOTHER [*astounded*]   How d'you mean, not true?

STEPDAUGHTER   It's not true! It's not true!

MOTHER   And what can you know about it?

STEPDAUGHTER   It's not true. [*To the* DIRECTOR] Don't believe it. Know why she says it? For his sake. [*Pointing to the* SON] His indifference tortures her, destroys her. She wants him to believe that, if she abandoned him when he was two, it was because he [*the* FATHER] compelled her to.

MOTHER [*with violence*]   He did compel me, he did compel me, as God is my witness! [*To the* DIRECTOR] Ask him if that isn't true. [*Her husband*] Make him tell him. [*The* SON] She couldn't know anything about it.

STEPDAUGHTER   With my father, while he lived, I know you were always happy and content. Deny it if you can.

MOTHER   I don't deny it, I don't . . .

STEPDAUGHTER   He loved you, he cared for you! [*To the* BOY, *with rage*] Isn't that so? Say it! Why don't you speak, you dope?

MOTHER   Leave the poor boy alone. Why d'you want to make me out ungrateful, daughter? I have no wish to offend your father! I told him [*the* FATHER] I didn't abandon my son and my home for my own pleasure. It wasn't my fault.

FATHER   That's true, sir. It was mine.

   [*Pause.*]

LEADING MAN [*to his companions*]   What a show!

LEADING LADY   And *they* put it on—for us.

JUVENILE LEAD   Quite a change!

DIRECTOR [*who is now beginning to get very interested*]   Let's listen to this, let's listen! [*And saying this, he goes down one of the stairways into the auditorium, and stands in front of the stage, as if to receive a spectator's impression of the show.*]

SON [*without moving from his position, cold, quiet, ironic*]   Oh yes, you can now listen to the philosophy lecture. He will tell you about the Demon of Experiment.

FATHER   You are a cynical idiot, as I've told you a hundred times. [*To the* DIRECTOR, *now in the auditorium*] He mocks me, sir, on account of that phrase I found to excuse myself with.

SON [*contemptuously*] Phrases!

FATHER Phrases! Phrases! As if they were not a comfort to everyone: in the face of some unexplained fact, in the face of an evil that eats into us, to find a word that says nothing but at least quiets us down!

STEPDAUGHTER Quiets our guilt feelings too. That above all.

FATHER Our guilt feelings? Not so. I have never quieted my guilt feelings with words alone.

STEPDAUGHTER It took a little money as well, didn't it, it took a little dough! The hundred lire[2] he was going to pay me, ladies and gentlemen!

[*Movement of horror among the Actors.*]

SON [*with contempt toward the* STEPDAUGHTER] That's filthy.

STEPDAUGHTER Filthy? The dough was there. In a small pale blue envelope on the mahogany table in the room behind the shop. Madam Pace's [*she pronounces it "Pah-chay"*] shop. One of those Madams who lure us poor girls from good families into their *ateliers* under the pretext of selling *Robes et Manteaux.*[3]

SON And with those hundred lire he was going to pay she has bought the right to tyrannize over us all. Only it so happens—I'd have you know—that he never actually incurred the debt.

STEPDAUGHTER Oh, oh, but we were really going to it, I assure you! [*She bursts out laughing.*]

MOTHER [*rising in protest*] Shame, daughter! Shame!

STEPDAUGHTER [*quickly*] Shame? It's my revenge! I am frantic, sir, frantic to live it, live that scene! The room . . . here's the shop window with the coats in it; there's the bed-sofa; the mirror; a screen; and in front of the window the little mahogany table with the hundred lire in the pale blue envelope. I can see it. I could take it. But you men should turn away now: I'm almost naked. I don't blush anymore. It's he that blushes now. [*Points to the* FATHER.] But I assure you he was very pale, very pale, at that moment. [*To the* DIRECTOR] You must believe me, sir.

DIRECTOR You lost me some time ago.

FATHER Of course! Getting it thrown at you like that! Restore a little order, sir, and let *me* speak. And never mind this ferocious girl. She's trying to heap opprobrium on me by withholding the relevant explanations!

STEPDAUGHTER This is no place for long-winded narratives!

FATHER I said—explanations.

STEPDAUGHTER Oh, certainly. Those that suit your turn.

[*At this point, the* DIRECTOR *returns to the stage to restore order.*]

FATHER But that's the whole root of the evil. Words. Each of us has, inside him, a world of things—to everyone, his world of things. And how can we understand each other, sir, if, in the words I speak, I put the sense and value of things as they are inside me, whereas the man who hears them inevitably receives them in the sense and with the value they have for him,

---

2. About $40 in today's U.S. currency.
3. The implication is that Madam Pace (Italian for "peace") runs a call-girl operation under the guise of selling fashionable *Robes et Manteaux*, or dressing gowns and coats (French). "*Ateliers*": workshops (French).

the sense and value of the world inside him? We think we understand each other but we never do. Consider: the compassion, all the compassion I feel for this woman [*the* MOTHER] has been received by her as the most ferocious of cruelties!

MOTHER   You ran me out of the house.

FATHER   Hear that? Ran her out. It *seemed to her* that I ran her out.

MOTHER   You can talk; I can't . . . But, look, sir, after he married me . . . and who knows why he did? I was poor, of humble birth . . .

FATHER   And that's why I married you for your . . . humility. I loved you for it, believing . . . [*He breaks off, seeing her gestured denials; seeing the impossibility of making himself understood by her, he opens his arms wide in a gesture of despair, and turns to the* DIRECTOR.] See that? She says No. It's scarifying, isn't it, sir, scarifying, this deafness of hers, this mental deafness! She has a heart, oh yes, where her children are concerned! But she's deaf, deaf in the brain, deaf, sir, to the point of desperation!

STEPDAUGHTER [*to the* DIRECTOR]   All right, but now make him tell you what his intelligence has ever done for us.

FATHER   If we could only foresee all the evil that can result from the good we believe we're doing!

[*At this point, the* LEADING LADY, *who has been on hot coals seeing the* LEADING MAN *flirt with the* STEPDAUGHTER, *steps forward and asks of the* DIRECTOR:]

LEADING LADY   Excuse me, is the rehearsal continuing?

DIRECTOR   Yes, of course! But let me listen a moment.

JUVENILE LEAD   This is something quite new.

INGENUE   Very interesting!

LEADING LADY   If that sort of thing interests you. [*And she darts a look at the* LEADING MAN.]

DIRECTOR [*to the* FATHER]   But you must give us *clear* explanations. [*He goes and sits down.*]

FATHER   Right. Yes. Listen. There was a man working for me. A poor man. As my secretary. Very devoted to me. Understood *her* [*the* MOTHER] very well. There was mutual understanding between them. Nothing wrong in it. They thought no harm at all. Nothing off-color about it. No, no, he knew his place, as she did. They didn't do anything wrong. Didn't even think it.

STEPDAUGHTER   So he thought it *for* them. And did it.

FATHER   It's not true! I wanted to do them some good. And myself too, oh yes, I admit. I'd got to this point, sir: I couldn't say a word to either of them but they would exchange a significant look. The one would consult the eyes of the other, asking how what I had said should be taken, if they didn't want to put me in a rage. That sufficed, you will understand, to keep me continually in a rage, in a state of unbearable exasperation.

DIRECTOR   Excuse me, why didn't you fire him, this secretary?

FATHER   Good question! That's what I did do, sir. But then I had to see that poor woman remain in my house, a lost soul. Like an animal without a master that one takes pity on and carries home.

MOTHER   No, no, it's—

FATHER [*at once, turning to her to get it in first*]   Your son? Right?

MOTHER   He'd already snatched my son from me.

FATHER   But not from cruelty. Just so he'd grow up strong and healthy. In touch with the soil.

STEPDAUGHTER [*pointing at the latter, ironic*]   And just look at him!

FATHER [*at once*]   Uh? Is it also my fault if he then grew up this way? I sent him to a wet nurse, sir, in the country, a peasant woman. I didn't find her [*the* MOTHER] strong enough, despite her humble origin. I'd married her for similar reasons, as I said. All nonsense maybe, but there we are. I always had these confounded aspirations toward a certain solidity, toward what is morally sound. [*Here the* STEPDAUGHTER *bursts out laughing.*] Make her stop that! It's unbearable!

DIRECTOR   Stop it. I can't hear, for Heaven's sake!

[*Suddenly, again, as the* DIRECTOR *rebukes her, she is withdrawn and remote, her laughter cut off in the middle. The* DIRECTOR *goes down again from the stage to get an impression of the scene.*]

FATHER   I couldn't bear to be with that woman anymore. [*Points to the* MOTHER] Not so much, believe me, because she irritated me, and even made me feel physically ill, as because of the pain—a veritable anguish—that I felt on her account.

MOTHER   And he sent me away!

FATHER.   Well provided for. And to that man. Yes, sir. So she could be free of me.

MOTHER   And so *he* could be free.

FATHER   That, too. I admit it. And much evil resulted. But I intended good. And more for her than for me, I swear it! [*He folds his arms across his chest. Then, suddenly, turning to the* MOTHER] I never lost sight of you, never lost sight of you till, from one day to the next, unbeknown to me, he carried you off to another town. He noticed I was interested in her, you see, but that was silly, because my interest was absolutely pure, absolutely without ulterior motive. The interest I took in her new family, as it grew up, had an unbelievable tenderness to it. Even she should bear witness to that! [*He points to the* STEPDAUGHTER.]

STEPDAUGHTER   Oh, very much so! I was a little sweetie. Pigtails over my shoulders. Panties coming down a little bit below my skirt. A little sweetie. He would see me coming out of school, at the gate. He would come and see me as I grew up . . .

FATHER   This is outrageous. You're betraying me!

STEPDAUGHTER   I'm not! What do you mean?

FATHER   Outrageous. Outrageous. [*Immediately, still excited, he continues in a tone of explanation, to the* DIRECTOR.] My house, sir, when she had left it, at once seemed empty. [*Points to the* MOTHER.] She was an incubus. But she filled my house for me. Left alone, I wandered through these rooms like a fly without a head. This fellow here [*the* SON] was raised away from home. Somehow, when he got back, he didn't seem mine anymore. Without a mother between me and him, he grew up on his own, apart, without any relationship to me, emotional or intellectual. And then—strange, sir, but true—first I grew curious, then I was gradually attracted toward *her* family, which I had brought into being. The thought of *this* family began to fill the void around me. I had to—really had to—believe she was at peace, absorbed in the simplest cares of life, lucky to be away and far removed from the complicated torments of my spirit. And to have proof of this, I would go and see that little girl at the school gate.

STEPDAUGHTER   Correct! He followed me home, smiled at me and, when I was home, waved to me, like this! I would open my eyes wide and look at him suspiciously. I didn't know who it was. I told mother. And she guessed right away it was him. [*The* MOTHER *nods.*] At first she didn't want to send me back to school for several days. When I did go, I saw him again at the gate—the clown!—with a brown paper bag in his hand. He came up to me, caressed me, and took from the bag a lovely big Florentine straw hat with a ring of little May roses round it—for me!

DIRECTOR   You're making too long a story of this.

SON [*contemptuously*]   Story is right! Fiction! Literature!

FATHER   Literature? This is life, sir. Passion!

DIRECTOR   Maybe! But not actable!

FATHER   I agree. This is all preliminary. I wouldn't *want* you to act it. As you see, in fact, she [*the* STEPDAUGHTER] is no longer that little girl with pigtails—

STEPDAUGHTER   —and the panties showing below her skirt!

FATHER   The drama comes now, sir. Novel, complex—

STEPDAUGHTER [*gloomy, fierce, steps forward*]   —What my father's death meant for us was—

FATHER [*not giving her time to continue*]   —poverty, sir. They returned, unbeknownst to me. She's so thickheaded. [*Pointing to the* MOTHER] It's true she can hardly write herself, but she could have had her daughter write, or her son, telling me they were in need!

MOTHER   But, sir, how could I have guessed he felt the way he did?

FATHER   Which is just where you always went wrong. You could never guess how I felt about anything!

MOTHER   After so many years of separation, with all that had happened . . .

FATHER   And is it my fault if that fellow carried you off as he did? [*Turning to the* DIRECTOR] From one day to the next, as I say. He'd found some job someplace. I couldn't even trace them. Necessarily, then, my interest dwindled, with the years. The drama breaks out, sir, unforeseen and violent, at their return. When I, alas, was impelled by the misery of my still-living flesh . . . Oh, and what misery that is for a man who is alone, who has not wanted to form debasing relationships, not yet old enough to do without a woman, and no longer young enough to go and look for one without shame! Misery? It's horror, horror, because no woman can give him love anymore.— Knowing this, one should go without! Well, sir, on the outside, when other people are watching, each man is clothed in dignity: but, on the inside, he knows what unconfessable things are going on within him. One gives way, gives way to temptation, to rise again, right afterward, of course, in a great hurry to put our dignity together again, complete, solid, a stone on a grave that hides and buries from our eyes every sign of our shame and even the very memory of it! It's like that with everybody. Only the courage to say it is lacking—to say certain things.

STEPDAUGHTER   The courage to do them, though—everybody's got that.

FATHER   Everybody. But in secret. That's why it takes more courage to say them. A man only has to say them and it's all over: he's labeled a cynic. But, sir, he isn't! He's just like everybody else. Better! He's better because he's not afraid to reveal, by the light of intelligence, the red stain of shame, there, in the human beast, which closes its eyes to it. Woman—yes, woman—what is she like, actually? She looks at us, inviting, tantalizing. You take hold of her. She's no sooner in your arms than she shuts her eyes. It is the sign of her submission. The sign with which she tells the man: Blind yourself for I am blind.

STEPDAUGHTER   How about when she no longer keeps them shut? When she no longer feels the need to hide the red stain of shame from herself by closing her eyes, and instead, her eyes now dry and impassive, sees the shame of the man, who has blinded himself even without love? They make me vomit, all those intellectual elaborations, this philosophy that begins by revealing the beast and then goes on to excuse it and save its soul . . . I can't bear to hear about it! Because when a man feels obliged to *reduce* life this way, reduce it all to "the beast," throwing overboard every vestige of the truly human, every aspiration after chastity, all feelings of purity, of the ideal, of duties, of modesty, of shame, then nothing is more contemptible, more nauseating than his wretched guilt feelings! Crocodile tears!

DIRECTOR   Let's get to the facts, to the facts! This is just discussion.

FATHER   Very well. But a fact is like a sack. When it's empty, it won't stand up. To make it stand up you must first pour into it the reasons and feelings by which it exists. I couldn't know that—when that man died and they returned here in poverty—she went out to work as a dressmaker to support the children, nor that the person she went to work for was that . . . that Madam Pace!

STEPDAUGHTER   A high-class dressmaker, if you'd all like to know! To all appearances, she serves fine ladies, but then she arranges things so that the fine ladies serve *her* . . . without prejudice to ladies not so fine!

MOTHER   Believe me, sir, I never had the slightest suspicion that that old witch hired me because she had her eye on my daughter . . .

STEPDAUGHTER   Poor mama! Do you know, sir, what the woman did when I brought her my mother's work? She would point out to me the material she'd ruined by giving it to my mother to sew. And she deducted for that, she deducted. And so, you understand, *I* paid, while that poor creature thought she was making sacrifices for me and those two by sewing, even at night, Madam Pace's material!

[*Indignant movements and exclamations from the Actors.*]

DIRECTOR [*without pause*]   And there, one day, you met—

STEPDAUGHTER [*pointing to the* FATHER]   —him, him, yes sir! An old client! Now there's a scene for you to put on! Superb!

FATHER   Interrupted by her—the mother—

STEPDAUGHTER [*without pause, treacherously*]   —almost in time!—

FATHER [*shouting*]   No, no, *in* time! Because, luckily, I recognized the girl in time. And I took them all back, sir, into my home. Now try to visualize my situation and hers, the one confronting the other—she as you see her now, myself unable to look her in the face anymore.

STEPDAUGHTER   It's too absurd! But—afterward—was it possible for me to be a modest little miss, virtuous and well-bred, in accordance with those confounded aspirations toward a certain solidity, toward what is morally sound?

FATHER   And therein lies the drama, sir, as far as I'm concerned: in my awareness that each of us thinks of himself as *one* but that, well, it's not true, each of us is many, oh so many, sir, according to the possibilities of being that are in us. We are one thing for this person, another for that! Already *two* utterly different things! And with it all, the illusion of being always one thing for all men, and always this one thing in every single action. It's not true! Not true! We realize as much when, by some unfortunate chance, in one or another of our acts, we find ourselves suspended, hooked. We see, I mean, that we are not wholly in that act, and that therefore it would be abominably unjust to judge us by that act alone, to hold us suspended, hooked, in the pillory, our whole life long, as if our life were summed up in that act! Now do you understand this girl's treachery? She surprised me in a place, in an act, in which she should never have had to know me—I couldn't be that way for her. And she wants to give me a reality such as I could never had expected I would have to assume for her, the reality of a fleeting moment, a shameful one, in my life! This, sir, this is what I feel most strongly. And you will see that the drama will derive tremendous value from this. But now add the situation of the others! His . . . [*He points to the* SON.]

SON [*shrugging contemptuously*]   Leave me out of this! It's none of my business.

FATHER   What? None of your business?

SON   None. And I *want* to be left out. I wasn't made to be one of you, and you know it.

STEPDAUGHTER   We're common, aren't we?—And he's so refined.—But from time to time I give him a hard, contemptuous look, and he looks down at the ground. You may have noticed that, sir. He looks down at the ground. For he knows the wrong he's done me.

SON [*hardly looking at her*]   Me?

STEPDAUGHTER   You! You! I'm on the streets because of you! [*A movement of horror from the Actors*] Did you or did you not, by your attitude, deny us—I won't say the intimacy of home but even the hospitality which puts guests at their ease? We were the intruders, coming to invade the kingdom of your legitimacy! I'd like to have you see, sir, certain little scenes between just him and me! He says I tyrannized over them all. But it was entirely because of his attitude that I started to exploit the situation he calls filthy, a situation which had brought me into his home with my mother, who is also *his* mother, *as its mistress!*

SON [*coming slowly forward*]   They can't lose, sir, three against one, an easy game. But figure to yourself a son, sitting quietly at home, who one fine day sees a young woman arrive, an impudent type with her nose in the air, asking for his father, with whom she has heaven knows what business; and then he sees her return, in the same style, accompanied by that little girl over there; and finally he sees her treat his father—who can say why?—in a very ambiguous and cool manner, demanding money, in a tone that takes for granted that he *has* to give it, has to, is obligated—

FATHER   —but I *am* obligated: it's for your mother!

SON   How would I know? When, sir, [*To the* DIRECTOR] have I ever seen her? When have I ever heard her spoken of? One day I see her arrive with her [*the* STEPDAUGHTER], with that boy, with that little girl. They say to me: "It's your mother too, know that?" I manage to figure out from her carryings-on [*Pointing at the* STEPDAUGHTER] why they arrived in our home from one day to the next . . . What I'm feeling and experiencing I can't put into words, and wouldn't want to. I wouldn't want to confess it, even to myself. It cannot therefore result in any action on my part. You can see that. Believe me, sir, I'm a character that, dramatically speaking, remains unrealized. I'm out of place in their company. So please leave me out of it all!

FATHER   What? But it's just because you're so—

SON [*in violent exasperation*]   —I'm so what? How would *you* know? When did you ever care about me?

FATHER   Touché! Touché![4] But isn't even that a dramatic situation? This withdrawnness of yours, so cruel to me, and to your mother who, on her return home is seeing you almost for the first time, a grown man she doesn't recognize, though she knows you're her son . . . [*Pointing out the* MOTHER *to the* DIRECTOR] Just look at her, she's crying.

STEPDAUGHTER [*angrily, stamping her foot*]   Like the fool she is!

FATHER [*pointing her out to the* DIRECTOR]   And she can't abide him, you know. [*Again referring to the* SON]—He says it's none of his business. The truth is he's almost the pivot of the action. Look at that little boy, clinging to his mother all the time, scared, humiliated . . . It's all because of *him* [*the* SON]. Perhaps the most painful situation of all is that little boy's: he feels alien, more than all the others, and the poor little thing is so mortified, so anguished at being taken into our home—out of charity, as it were . . . [*Confidentially*] He's just like his father: humble, doesn't say anything . . .

DIRECTOR   He won't fit anyway. You've no idea what a nuisance children are onstage.

FATHER   But he wouldn't be a nuisance for long. Nor would the little girl, no, she's the first to go . . .

DIRECTOR   Very good, yes! The whole thing interests me very much indeed. I have a hunch, a definite hunch, that there's material here for a fine play!

STEPDAUGHTER [*trying to inject herself*]   With a character like me in it!

FATHER [*pushing her to one side in his anxiety to know what the* DIRECTOR *will decide*]   You be quiet!

DIRECTOR [*going right on, ignoring the interruption*]   Yes, it's new stuff . . .

---

4. Literally, "touched" (French), a term in fencing to acknowledge a hit by an opponent; here used ironically.

FATHER   Very new!

DIRECTOR   You had some gall, though, to come and throw it at me this way . . .

FATHER   Well, you see, sir, born as we are to the stage . . .

DIRECTOR   You're amateurs, are you?

FATHER   No. I say: "born to the stage" because . . .

DIRECTOR   Oh, come on, you must have done some acting!

FATHER   No, no, sir, only as every man acts the part assigned to him—by himself or others—in this life. In me you see passion itself, which—in almost all people, as it rises—invariably becomes a bit theatrical . . .

DIRECTOR   Well, never mind! Never mind about that!—You see, my dear sir, without the author . . . I could direct you to an author . . .

FATHER   No, no, look: you be the author!

DIRECTOR   Me? What are you talking about?

FATHER   Yes, you. You. Why not?

DIRECTOR   Because I've never been an author, that's why not!

FATHER   Couldn't you be one now, hm? There's nothing to it. Everyone's doing it. And your job is made all the easier by the fact that you have us—here—alive—right in front of your nose!

DIRECTOR   It wouldn't be enough.

FATHER   Not enough? Seeing us live our own drama . . .

DIRECTOR   I know, but you always need someone to write it!

FATHER   No. Just someone to take it down, maybe, since you have us here—in action—scene by scene. It'll be enough if we piece together a rough sketch for you, then you can rehearse it.

DIRECTOR   [*tempted, goes up onstage again*] Well, I'm almost, almost tempted . . . Just for kicks . . . We could actually rehearse . . .

FATHER   Of course you could! What scenes you'll see emerge! I can list them for you right away.

DIRECTOR   I'm tempted . . . I'm tempted . . . Let's give it a try . . . Come to my office. [*Turns to the Actors.*] Take a break, will you? But don't go away. We'll be back in fifteen or twenty minutes. [*To the* FATHER] Let's see what we can do . . . Maybe we can get something very extraordinary out of all this . . .

FATHER   We certainly can. Wouldn't it be better to take *them* along? [*He points to the Characters.*]

DIRECTOR   Yes, let them all come. [*Starts going off, then comes back to address the Actors.*] Now don't forget. Everyone on time. Fifteen minutes.

[DIRECTOR *and Six Characters cross the stage and disappear. The Actors stay there and look at one another in amazement.*]

LEADING MAN   Is he serious? What's he going to do?

JUVENILE   This is outright insanity.

A THIRD ACTOR   We have to improvise a drama right off the bat?

JUVENILE LEAD   That's right. Like Commedia dell'Arte.[5]

LEADING LADY   Well, if he thinks *I'm* going to lend myself to that sort of thing . . .

INGENUE   Count me out.

---

5. A form of popular theater beginning in 16th-century Italy; the actors improvised dialogue according to basic comic or dramatic plots and in response to the audience's reaction.

A FOURTH ACTOR [*alluding to the Characters*] I'd like to know who those people are.

THE THIRD ACTOR Who would they be? Madmen or crooks!

JUVENILE LEAD And he's going to pay attention to them?

INGENUE Carried away by vanity! Wants to be an author now . . .

LEADING MAN It's out of this world. If this is what the theater is coming to, my friends . . .

A FIFTH ACTOR I think it's rather fun.

THE THIRD ACTOR Well! We shall see. We shall see. [*And chatting thus among themselves, the Actors leave the stage, some using the little door at the back, others returning to their dressing rooms.*]

The curtain remains raised. The performance is interrupted by a twenty-minute intermission.

Bells ring. The performance is resumed.

[*From dressing rooms, from the door, and also from the house, the Actors, the* STAGE MANAGER, *the* TECHNICIAN, *the* PROMPTER, *the* PROPERTY MAN *return to the stage; at the same time the* DIRECTOR *and the Six Characters emerge from the office.*

As soon as the house lights are out, the stage lighting is as before.]

DIRECTOR Let's go, everybody! Is everyone here? Quiet! We're beginning. [*Calls the* TECHNICIAN *by name.*]

TECHNICIAN Here!

DIRECTOR Set the stage for the parlor scene. Two wings and a backdrop with a door in it will do, quickly please!

[*The* TECHNICIAN *at once runs to do the job, and does it while the* DIRECTOR *works things out with the* STAGE MANAGER, *the* PROPERTY MAN, *the* PROMPTER, *and the Actors. This indication of a set consists of two wings, a drop with a door in it, all in pink and gold stripes.*]

DIRECTOR [*to the* PROPERTY MAN] See if we have some sort of bed-sofa in the prop room.

PROPERTY MAN Yes, sir, there's the green one.

STEPDAUGHTER No, no, not green! It was yellow, flowered, plush, and very big. Extremely comfortable.

PROPERTY MAN Well, we have nothing like that.

DIRECTOR But it doesn't matter. Bring the one you have.

STEPDAUGHTER Doesn't matter? Madam Pace's famous chaise longue!

DIRECTOR This is just for rehearsal. Please don't meddle! [*To the* STAGE MANAGER] See if we have a display case—long and rather narrow.

STEPDAUGHTER The table, the little mahogany table for the pale blue envelope!

STAGE MANAGER [*to the* DIRECTOR] There's the small one. Gilded.

DIRECTOR All right. Get that one.

FATHER A large mirror.

STEPDAUGHTER And the screen. A screen, please, or what'll I do?

STAGE MANAGER Yes, ma'am, we have lots of screens, don't worry.

DIRECTOR [*to the* STEPDAUGHTER] A few coat hangers?

STEPDAUGHTER A great many, yes.

DIRECTOR [*to the* STAGE MANAGER]   See how many we've got, and have them brought on.

STAGE MANAGER   Right, sir, I'll see to it.

[*The* STAGE MANAGER *also hurries to do his job and while the* DIRECTOR *goes on talking with the* PROMPTER *and then with the Characters and the Actors, has the furniture carried on by stagehands and arranges it as he thinks fit.*]

DIRECTOR [*to the* PROMPTER]   Meanwhile you can get into position. Look: this is the outline of the scenes, act by act. [*He gives him several sheets of paper.*] You'll have to be a bit of a virtuoso today.

PROMPTER   Shorthand?

DIRECTOR [*pleasantly surprised*]   Oh, good! You know shorthand?

PROMPTER   I may not know prompting, but shorthand . . . [*Turning to a stagehand*] Get me some paper from my room—quite a lot—all you can find!

[*The stagehand runs off and returns a little later with a wad of paper which he gives to the* PROMPTER.]

DIRECTOR [*going right on, to the* PROMPTER]   Follow the scenes line by line as we play them, and try to pin down the speeches, at least the most important ones. [*Then, turning to the Actors*] Clear the stage please, everyone! Yes, come over to this side and pay close attention. [*He indicates the left.*]

LEADING LADY   Excuse me but—

DIRECTOR [*forestalling*]   There'll be no improvising, don't fret.

LEADING MAN   Then what are we to do?

DIRECTOR   Nothing. For now, just stop, look, and listen. Afterward you'll be given written parts. Right now we'll rehearse. As best we can. With them doing the rehearsing for us. [*He points to the Characters.*]

FATHER [*amid all the confusion onstage, as if he'd fallen from the clouds*] We're rehearsing? How d'you mean?

DIRECTOR   Yes, for them. You rehearse for them. [*Indicates the Actors.*]

FATHER   But if we are the characters . . .

DIRECTOR   All right, you're characters, but, my dear sir, characters don't perform here, actors perform here. The characters are there, in the script [*He points to the* PROMPTER's *box.*]—when there *is* a script!

FATHER   Exactly! Since there isn't, and you gentlemen have the luck to have them right here, alive in front of you, those characters . . .

DIRECTOR   Oh, great! Want to do it all yourselves? Appear before the public, do the acting yourselves?

FATHER   Of course. Just as we are.

DIRECTOR [*ironically*]   I'll bet you'd put on a splendid show!

LEADING MAN   Then what's the use of staying?

DIRECTOR [*without irony, to the Characters*]   Don't run away with the idea that you can act! That's laughable . . . [*And in fact the Actors laugh.*] Hear that? They're laughing. [*Coming back to the point*] I was forgetting. I must cast the show. It's quite easy. It casts itself. [*To the* SECOND ACTRESS] You, ma'am, will play the Mother. [*To the* FATHER] You'll have to find her a name.

FATHER   Amalia, sir.

DIRECTOR   But that's this lady's real name. We wouldn't want to call her by her real name!

FATHER   Why not? If that is her name . . . But of course, if it's to be this lady . . . [*He indicates the* SECOND ACTRESS *with a vague gesture.*] To me *she* [*the* MOTHER] is Amalia. But suit yourself . . . [*He is getting more and more confused.*] I don't know what to tell you . . . I'm beginning to . . . oh, I don't know . . . to find my own words ringing false, they sound different somehow.

DIRECTOR   Don't bother about that, just don't bother about it. We can always find the right sound. As for the name, if you say Amalia, Amalia it shall be; or we'll find another. For now, we'll designate the characters thus: [*To the* JUVENILE LEAD] You're the Son. [*To the* LEADING LADY] You, ma'am, are of course the Stepdaughter.

STEPDAUGHTER [*excitedly*]   What, what? That one there is me? [*She bursts out laughing.*]

DIRECTOR [*mad*]   What is there to laugh at?

LEADING LADY [*aroused*]   No one has ever dared laugh at me! I insist on respect—or I quit!

STEPDAUGHTER   But, excuse me, I'm not laughing at you.

DIRECTOR [*to the* STEPDAUGHTER]   You should consider yourself honored to be played by . . .

LEADING LADY [*without pause, contemptuously*]   —"That one there!"

STEPDAUGHTER   But I wasn't speaking of you, believe me. I was speaking of me. I don't see me in you, that's all. I don't know why . . . I guess you're just not like me!

FATHER   That's it, exactly, my dear sir! What is *expressed* in us . . .

DIRECTOR   Expression, expression! You think that's your business? Not at all!

FATHER   Well, but what *we* express . . .

DIRECTOR   But you don't. You don't express. You provide us with raw material. The actors give it body and face, voice and gesture. They've given expression to much loftier material, let me tell you. Yours is on such a small scale that, if it stands up onstage at all, the credit, believe me, should all go to my actors.

FATHER   I don't dare contradict you, sir, but it's terribly painful for us who are as you see us—with these bodies, these faces—

DIRECTOR [*cutting in, out of patience*]   —that's where makeup comes in, my dear sir, for whatever concerns the face, the remedy is makeup!

FATHER   Yes. But the voice, gesture—

DIRECTOR   Oh, for Heaven's sake! You can't exist here! Here the actor acts you, and that's that!

FATHER   I understand, sir. But now perhaps I begin to guess also why our author who saw us, alive as we are, did not want to put us onstage. I don't want to offend your actors. God forbid! But I feel that seeing myself acted . . . I don't know by whom . . .

LEADING MAN [*rising with dignity and coming over, followed by the gay young Actresses who laugh*]   By me, if you've no objection.

FATHER [*humble, smooth*]   I'm very honored, sir. [*He bows.*] But however much art and willpower the gentleman puts into absorbing me into himself . . . [*He is bewildered now.*]

LEADING MAN   Finish. Finish.

[*The Actresses laugh.*]

FATHER   Well, the performance he will give, even forcing himself with makeup to resemble me, well, with that figure [*All the Actors laugh.*] he can hardly play me as I am. I shall rather be—even apart from the face—what he interprets me to be, as he feels I am—if he feels I am anything—and not as I feel myself inside myself. And it seems to me that whoever is called upon to judge us should take this into account.

DIRECTOR   So now you're thinking of what the critics will say? And I was still listening! Let the critics say what they want. We will concentrate on putting on your play! [*He walks away a little, and looks around.*] Come on, come on. Is the set ready? [*To the Actors and the Characters*] Don't clutter up the stage, I want to be able to see! [*He goes down from the stage.*] Let's not lose any more time! [*To the* STEPDAUGHTER] Does the set seem pretty good to you?

STEPDAUGHTER   Oh! But I can't recognize it!

DIRECTOR   Oh my God, don't tell me we should reconstruct Madam Pace's back room for you! [*To the* FATHER] Didn't you say a parlor with flowered wallpaper?

FATHER   Yes, sir. White.

DIRECTOR   It's not white. Stripes. But it doesn't matter. As for furniture we're in pretty good shape. That little table—bring it forward a bit! [*Stagehands do this. To the* PROPERTY MAN] Meanwhile you get an envelope, possibly a light blue one, and give it to the gentleman. [*Indicating the* FATHER]

PROPERTY MAN   A letter envelope?

DIRECTOR and FATHER   Yes, a letter envelope.

PROPERTY MAN   I'll be right back.

[*He exits.*]

DIRECTOR   Come on, come on. It's the young lady's scene first. [*The* LEADING LADY *comes forward.*] No, no, wait. I said the young lady. [*Indicating the* STEPDAUGHTER] You will just watch—

STEPDAUGHTER [*adding, without pause*]   —watch me live it!

LEADING LADY [*resenting this*]   I'll know how to live it, too, don't worry, once I put myself in the role!

DIRECTOR [*raising his hands to his head*]   Please! No more chatter! Now, scene one. The Young Lady with Madam Pace. Oh, and how about this Madam Pace? [*Bewildered, looking around him, he climbs back onstage.*]

FATHER   She isn't with us, sir.

DIRECTOR   Then what do we do?

FATHER   But she's alive. She's alive too.

DIRECTOR   Fine. But where?

FATHER   I'll tell you. [*Turning to the Actresses*] If you ladies will do me the favor of giving me your hats for a moment.

THE ACTRESSES [*surprised a little, laughing a little, in chorus*]   —What?—Our hats?—What does he say?—Why?—Oh, dear!

DIRECTOR   What are you going to do with the ladies' hats?

[*The Actors laugh.*]

FATHER   Oh, nothing. Just put them on these coathooks for a minute. And would some of you be so kind as to take your coats off too?

ACTORS [*as before*]   Their coats too?—And then?—He's nuts!

AN ACTRESS OR TWO [*as above*]   —But why?—Just the coats?

FATHER   Just so they can be hung there for a moment. Do me this favor. Will
you?

ACTRESSES [*taking their hats off, and one or two of them their coats, too, continuing to laugh, and going to hang the hats here and there on the coathooks*]
—Well, why not?—There!—This is getting to be really funny!—Are we to
put them on display?

FATHER   Exactly! That's just right, ma'am: on display!

DIRECTOR   May one inquire *why* you are doing this?

FATHER   Yes, sir. If we set the stage better, who knows but she may come to
us, drawn by the objects of her trade . . . [*Inviting them to look toward the
entrance at the back*] Look! Look!

[*The entrance at the back opens, and* MADAM PACE *walks a few paces downstage, a hag of enormous fatness with a pompous wig of carrot-colored wool
and a fiery red rose on one side of it,* à l'espagnole,[6] *heavily made up, dressed
with gauche elegance in garish red silk, a feathered fan in one hand and the
other hand raised to hold a lighted cigarette between two fingers. At the sight
of this apparition, the* DIRECTOR *and the Actors at once dash off the stage with
a yell of terror, rushing down the stairs and making as if to flee up the aisle.
The* STEPDAUGHTER, *on the other hand runs to* MADAM PACE—*deferentially, as
to her boss.*]

STEPDAUGHTER [*running to her*]   Here she is, here she is!

FATHER [*beaming*]   It's she! What did I tell you? Here she is!

DIRECTOR [*overcoming his first astonishment, and incensed now*]   What tricks
are these?

[*The next four speeches are more or less simultaneous.*]

LEADING MAN   What goes on around here?

JUVENILE LEAD   Where on earth did she come from?

INGENUE   They must have been holding her in reserve.

LEADING LADY   Hocus pocus! Hocus pocus!

FATHER [*dominating these protests*]   Excuse me, though! Why, actually, would
you want to destroy this prodigy in the name of vulgar truth, this miracle of
a reality that is born of the stage itself—called into being by the stage,
drawn here by the stage, and shaped by the stage—and which has more
right to live on the stage than you have because it is much truer? Which of
you actresses will later re-create Madam Pace? This lady *is* Madam Pace.
You must admit that the actress who re-creates her will be less true than
this lady—who is Madam Pace. Look: my daughter recognized her, and
went right over to her. Stand and watch the scene!

[*Hesitantly, the* DIRECTOR *and the Actors climb back onstage. But the scene
between the* STEPDAUGHTER *and* MADAM PACE *has begun during the protest
of the Actors and the* FATHER's *answer: sotto voce,[7] very quietly, in short
naturally—as would never be possible on a stage. When, called to order by
the* FATHER, *the Actors turn again to watch, they hear* MADAM PACE, *who
has just placed her hand under the* STEPDAUGHTER's *chin in order to raise
her head, talk unintelligibly. After trying to hear for a moment, they just
give up.*]

6. In the Spanish manner.   7. In a low voice (Italian).

DIRECTOR Well?

LEADING MAN What's she saying?

LEADING LADY One can't hear a thing.

JUVENILE LEAD Louder!

STEPDAUGHTER [*leaving* MADAM PACE, *who smiles a priceless smile, and walking down toward the Actors*] Louder, huh? How d'you mean: louder? These aren't things that can be said louder. *I* was able to say them loudly—to shame him [*Indicating the* FATHER]—that was my revenge. For Madam, it's different, my friends: it would mean—jail.

DIRECTOR Oh my God! It's like that, is it? But, my dear young lady, in the theater one must be heard. And even we couldn't hear you, right here on the stage. How about an audience out front? There's a scene to be done. And anyway you *can* speak loudly—it's just between yourselves, we won't be standing here listening like now. Pretend you're alone. In a room. The back room of the shop. No one can hear you. [*The* STEPDAUGHTER *charmingly and with a mischievous smile tells him No with a repeated movement of the finger.*] Why not?

STEPDAUGHTER [*sotto voce, mysteriously*] There's someone who'll hear if she [MADAM PACE] speaks loudly.

DIRECTOR [*in consternation*] Is someone else going to pop up now?

[*The Actors make as if to quit the stage again.*]

FATHER No, no, sir. She means me. I'm to be there—behind the door—waiting. And Madam knows. So if you'll excuse me. I must be ready for my entrance. [*He starts to move.*]

DIRECTOR [*stopping him*] No, wait. We must respect the exigencies of the theater. Before you get ready—

STEPDAUGHTER [*interrupting him*] Let's get on with it! I tell you I'm dying with desire to live it, to live that scene! If he's ready, I'm more than ready!

DIRECTOR [*shouting*] But first we have to get that scene out of you and her! [*Indicating* MADAM PACE] Do you follow me?

STEPDAUGHTER Oh dear, oh dear, she was telling me things you already know—that my mother's work had been badly done once again, the material is ruined, and I'm going to have to bear with her if I want her to go on helping us in our misery.

MADAM PACE [*coming forward with a great air of importance*] Sí, sí, señor, porque yo[8] no want profit. No advantage, no.

DIRECTOR [*almost scared*] What, what? She talks like *that*?!

[*All the Actors loudly burst out laughing.*]

STEPDAUGHTER [*also laughing*] Yes, sir, she talks like that—halfway between Spanish and English—very funny, isn't it?

MADAM PACE Now that is not good manners, no, that you laugh at me! Yo hablo[9] the English as good I can, señor!

DIRECTOR And it *is* good! Yes! Do talk that way, ma'am! It's a surefire effect! There couldn't be anything better to, um, soften the crudity of the situation! Do talk that way! It's fine!

---

8. Yes, yes, Mister, because I (broken Spanish). 9. I speak (Spanish).

STEPDAUGHTER   Fine! Of course! To have certain propositions put to you in a lingo like that. Surefire, isn't it? Because, sir, it seems almost a joke. When I hear there's "an old señor" who wants to "have good time conmigo," I start to laugh—don't I, Madam Pace?

MADAM PACE   Old, viejo, no. Viejito—leetle beet old, sí, darling? Better like that: if he no give you fun, he bring you prudencia.[1]

MOTHER [*jumping up, to the stupefaction and consternation of all the Actors, who had been taking no notice of her, and who now respond to her shouts with a start and, smiling, try to restrain her, because she has grabbed* MADAM PACE's *wig and thrown it on the floor*]   Witch! Witch! Murderess! My daughter!

STEPDAUGHTER [*running over to restrain her* MOTHER]   No, no, mama, no, please!

FATHER [*running over too at the same time*]   Calm down, calm down! Sit here.

MOTHER   Then send that woman away!

STEPDAUGHTER [*to the* DIRECTOR, *who also has run over*]   It's not possible, not possible that my mother should be here!

FATHER [*also to the* DIRECTOR]   They can't be together. That's why, you see, the woman wasn't with us when we came. Their being together would spoil it, you understand.

DIRECTOR   It doesn't matter, doesn't matter at all. This is just a preliminary sketch. Everything helps. However confusing the elements, I'll piece them together somehow. [*Turning to the* MOTHER *and sitting her down again in her place*]   Come along, come along, ma'am, calm down: sit down again.

STEPDAUGHTER [*who meanwhile has moved center stage again. Turning to* MADAM PACE]   All right, let's go!

MADAM PACE   Ah, no! No thank you! Yo aquí no do nada[2] with your mother present.

STEPDAUGHTER   Oh, come on! Bring in that old señor who wants to have good time conmigo! [*Turning imperiously to all the others*]   Yes, we've got to have it, this scene!—Come on, let's go! [*To* MADAM PACE]   You may leave.

MADAM PACE   Ah sí, I go, I go, go seguramente[3] . . . [*She makes her exit furiously, putting her wig back on, and looking haughtily at the Actors who applaud mockingly.*]

STEPDAUGHTER [*to the* FATHER]   And you can make your entrance. No need to go out and come in again. Come here. Pretend, you're already in. Right. Now I'm here with bowed head, modest, huh? Let's go! Speak up! With a different voice, the voice of someone just in off the street: "Hello, miss."

DIRECTOR [*by this time out front again*]   Now look: are you directing this, or am I? [*To the* FATHER *who looks undecided and perplexed.*]   Do it, yes. Go to the back. Don't leave the stage, though. And then come forward.

[*The* FATHER *does it, almost dismayed. Very pale; but already clothed in the reality of his created life, he smiles as he approaches from the back, as if still*

---

1. Discretion (Spanish). *Viejo*: old man (Spanish). *Viejito*: little old man (Spanish).

2. Here I don't do anything (broken Spanish).

3. Certainly (Spanish).

alien to the drama which will break upon him. The Actors now pay attention to the scene which is beginning.]

DIRECTOR [*softly, in haste, to the* PROMPTER *in the box*] And you, be ready now, ready to write!

THE SCENE

FATHER [*coming forward, with a different voice*] Hello, miss.

STEPDAUGHTER [*with bowed head and contained disgust*] Hello.

FATHER [*scrutinizing her under her hat which almost hides her face and noting that she is very young, exclaims, almost to himself, a little out of complaisance and a little out of fear of compromising himself in a risky adventure*] Oh . . . —Well, I was thinking, it wouldn't be the first time, hm? The first time you came here.

STEPDAUGHTER [*as above*] No, sir.

FATHER You've been here other times? [*And when the* STEPDAUGHTER *nods*] More than once? [*He waits a moment for her to answer, then again scrutinizes her under her hat; smiles; then says*] Well then, hm . . . it shouldn't any longer be so . . . May I take this hat off for you?

STEPDAUGHTER [*without pause, to forestall him, not now containing her disgust*] No, sir, I will take it off! [*And she does so in haste, convulsed.*]

[*The* MOTHER, *watching the scene with the* SON *and with the two others, smaller and more her own, who are close to her all the time, forming a group at the opposite side of the stage from the Actors, is on tenterhooks as she follows the words and actions of* FATHER *and* STEPDAUGHTER *with varied expression: grief, disdain, anxiety, horror, now hiding her face, now emitting a moan.*]

MOTHER Oh God! My God!

FATHER [*is momentarily turned to stone by the moaning; then he reassumes the previous tone*] Now give it to me: I'll hang it up for you. [*He takes the hat from her hands.*] But I could wish for a little hat worthier of such a dear, lovely little head! Would you like to help me choose one? From the many Madam has?—You wouldn't?

INGENUE [*interrupting*] Oh now, come on, those are *our* hats!

DIRECTOR [*without pause, very angry*] Silence, for Heaven's sake, don't try to be funny!—This is the stage. [*Turning back to the* STEPDAUGHTER] Would you begin again, please?

STEPDAUGHTER [*beginning again*] No, thank you, sir.

FATHER Oh, come on now, don't say no. Accept one from me. To please me . . . There are some lovely ones you know. And we would make Madam happy. Why else does she put them on display?

STEPDAUGHTER No, no, sir, look: I wouldn't even be able to wear it.

FATHER You mean because of what the family would think when they saw you come home with a new hat on? Think nothing of it. Know how to handle that? What to tell them at home?

STEPDAUGHTER [*breaking out, at the end of her rope*] But that's not why, sir. I couldn't wear it because I'm . . . as you see me. You might surely have noticed! [*Points to her black attire.*]

FATHER In mourning, yes. Excuse me. It's true: I do see it. I beg your pardon. I'm absolutely mortified, believe me.

STEPDAUGHTER [*forcing herself and plucking up courage to conquer her contempt and nausea*]   Enough! Enough! It's for me to thank you, it is not for you to be mortified or afflicted. Please pay no more attention to what I said. Even for me, you understand . . . [*She forces herself to smile and adds*] I need to forget I am dressed like this.

DIRECTOR [*interrupting, addressing himself to the* PROMPTER *in his box, and going up onstage again*]   Wait! Wait! Don't write. Leave that last sentence out, leave it out! [*Turning to the* FATHER *and* STEPDAUGHTER] It's going very well indeed. [*Then to the* FATHER *alone*] This is where you go into the part we prepared. [*To the Actors*] Enchanting, that little hat scene, don't you agree?

STEPDAUGHTER   Oh, but the best is just coming. Why aren't we continuing?

DIRECTOR   Patience one moment. [*Again addressing himself to the Actors*] Needs rather delicate handling, of course . . .

LEADING MAN   —With a certain *ease*—

LEADING LADY   Obviously. But there's nothing to it. [*To the* LEADING MAN] We can rehearse it at once, can't we?

LEADING MAN   As far as I'm . . . Very well, I'll go out and make my entrance. [*And he does go out by the back door, ready to reenter.*]

DIRECTOR [*to the* LEADING LADY]   And so, look, your scene with that Madam Pace is over. I'll write it up later. You are standing . . . Hey, where are you going?

LEADING LADY   Wait. I'm putting my hat back on . . . [*She does so, taking the hat from the hook.*]

DIRECTOR   Oh yes, good.—Now, you're standing here with your head bowed.

STEPDAUGHTER [*amused*]   But she's not wearing black!

LEADING LADY   *I shall* wear black! And I'll carry it better than you!

DIRECTOR [*to the* STEPDAUGHTER]   Keep quiet, please! Just watch. You can learn something. [*Claps his hands.*] Get going, get going! The entrance! [*And he goes back out front to get an impression of the stage.*]

[*The door at the back opens, and the* LEADING MAN *comes forward, with the relaxed, waggish manner of an elderly Don Juan.[4] From the first speeches, the performance of the scene by the Actors is quite a different thing, without, however, having any element of parody in it—rather, it seems corrected, set to rights. Naturally, the* STEPDAUGHTER *and the* FATHER, *being quite unable to recognize themselves in this* LEADING LADY *and* LEADING MAN *but hearing them speak their own words, express in various ways, now with gestures, now with smiles, now with open protests, their surprise, their wonderment, their suffering, etc., as will be seen forthwith.*

The PROMPTER'S *voice is clearly heard from the box.*]

LEADING MAN   Hello, miss.

FATHER [*without pause, unable to contain himself*]   No, no!

[*The* STEPDAUGHTER, *seeing how the* LEADING MAN *makes his entrance, has burst out laughing.*]

DIRECTOR [*coming from the proscenium, furious*]   Silence here! And stop that laughing at once! We can't go ahead till it stops.

---

4. Stereotypical Spanish lover.

STEPDAUGHTER [*coming from the proscenium*]   How can I help it? This lady [*the* LEADING LADY] just stands there. If she's supposed to be me, let me tell you that if anyone said hello to me in that manner and that tone of voice, I'd burst out laughing just as I actually did!

FATHER [*coming forward a little too*]   That's right . . . the manner, the tone . . .

DIRECTOR   Manner! Tone! Stand to one side now, and let me see the rehearsal.

LEADING MAN [*coming forward*]   If I'm to play an old man entering a house of ill—

DIRECTOR   Oh, pay no attention, please. Just begin again. It was going fine. [*Waiting for the Actor to resume*] Now then . . .

LEADING MAN   Hello, miss.

LEADING LADY   Hello.

LEADING MAN [*re-creating the* FATHER's *gesture of scrutinizing her under her hat, but then expressing very distinctly first the complaisance and then the fear*]   Oh . . . Well . . . I was thinking it wouldn't be the first time, I hope . . .

FATHER [*unable to help correcting him*]   Not "I hope." "Would it?" "Would it?"

DIRECTOR   He says: "would it?" A question.

LEADING MAN [*pointing to the* PROMPTER]   I heard: "I hope."

DIRECTOR   Same thing! "Would it." Or: "I hope." Continue, continue.—Now, maybe a bit less affected . . . Look, I'll do it for you. Watch me . . . [*Returns to the stage, then repeats the bit since the entrance*]—Hello, miss.

LEADING LADY   Hello.

DIRECTOR   Oh, well . . . I was thinking . . . [*Turning to the* LEADING MAN *to have him note how he has looked at the* LEADING LADY *under her hat*] Surprise . . . fear and complaisance. [*Then, going on, and turning to the* LEADING LADY] It wouldn't be the first time, would it? The first time you came here. [*Again turning to the* LEADING MAN *with an inquiring look*] Clear? [*To the* LEADING LADY] Then you say: No, sir. [*Back to the* LEADING MAN] How shall I put it? Plasticity! [*Goes back out front.*]

LEADING LADY   No, sir.

LEADING MAN   You came here other times? More than once?

DIRECTOR   No, no, wait. [*Indicating the* LEADING LADY] First let her nod. "You came here other times?"

[*The* LEADING LADY *raises her head a little, closes her eyes painfully as if in disgust, then nods twice at the word "Down" from the* DIRECTOR.]

STEPDAUGHTER [*involuntarily*]   Oh, my God! [*And she at once puts her hand on her mouth to keep the laughter in.*]

DIRECTOR [*turning round*]   What is it?

STEPDAUGHTER [*without pause*]   Nothing, nothing.

DIRECTOR [*to the* LEADING MAN   That's your cue. Go straight on.

LEADING MAN   More than once? Well then, hm . . . it shouldn't any longer be so . . . May I take this little hat off for you?

[*The* LEADING MAN *says this last speech in such a tone and accompanies it with such a gesture that the* STEPDAUGHTER, *her hands on her mouth, much as she wants to hold herself in, cannot contain her laughter, which comes bursting out through her fingers irresistibly and very loud.*]

LEADING LADY [*returning to her place, enraged*]   Now look, I'm not going to be made a clown of by that person!

LEADING MAN   Nor am I. Let's stop.

DIRECTOR [*to the* STEPDAUGHTER, *roaring*]   Stop it! Stop it!

STEPDAUGHTER   Yes, yes. Forgive me, forgive me . . .

DIRECTOR   You have no manners! You're presumptuous! So there!

FATHER [*seeking to intervene*]   That's true, yes, that's true, sir, but forgive . . .

DIRECTOR [*onstage again*]   Forgive nothing! It's disgusting!

FATHER   Yes, sir. But believe me, it has such a strange effect—

DIRECTOR   Strange? Strange? What's strange about it?

FATHER   I admire your actors, sir, I really admire them, this gentleman [LEADING MAN] and that lady [LEADING LADY] but assuredly . . . well, they're not us . . .

DIRECTOR   So what? How *could* they be you, if they're the actors?

FATHER   Exactly, the actors! And they play our parts well, both of them. But of course, to us, they seem something else—that tries to be the same but simply isn't!

DIRECTOR   How d'you mean: isn't? What is it then?

FATHER   Something that . . . becomes theirs. And stops being ours.

DIRECTOR   Necessarily! I explained that to you!

FATHER   Yes. I understand, I do under—

DIRECTOR   Then that will be enough! [*Turning to the Actors*] We'll be rehearsing by ourselves as we usually do. Rehearsing with authors present has always been hell, in my experience. There's no satisfying them. [*Turning to the* FATHER *and the* STEPDAUGHTER] Come along then. Let's resume. And let's hope you find it possible not to laugh this time.

STEPDAUGHTER   Oh, no, I won't be laughing this time around. My big moment comes up now. Don't worry!

DIRECTOR   Very well, when she says: "Please pay no more attention to what I said . . . Even for me—you understand . . ." [*Turning to the* FATHER] You'll have to cut right in with: "I understand, oh yes, I understand . . ." and ask her right away—

STEPDAUGHTER [*interrupting*]   Oh? Ask me what?

DIRECTOR   —why she is in mourning.

STEPDAUGHTER   No, no, look: when I told him I needed to forget I was dressed like this, do you know what his answer was? "Oh, good! Then let's take that little dress right off, shall we?"

DIRECTOR   Great! Terrific! It'll knock 'em right out of their seats!

STEPDAUGHTER   But it's the truth.

DIRECTOR   Truth, is it? Well, well, well. This is the theater! Our motto is: truth up to a certain point!

STEPDAUGHTER   Then what would you propose?

DIRECTOR   You'll see. You'll see it. Just leave me alone.

STEPDAUGHTER   Certainly not. From my nausea—from all the reasons one more cruel than another why I am what I am, why I am "that one there"— you'd like to cook up some romantic, sentimental concoction, wouldn't you? He asks me why I'm in mourning, and I tell him, through my tears, that Papa died two months ago! No, my dear sir! He has to say what he did say: "Then let's take that little dress right off, shall we?" And I, with my two-months mourning in my heart, went back there—you see? behind that screen—and—my fingers quivering with shame, with loathing—I took off my dress, took off my corset . . .

DIRECTOR [*running his hands through his hair*] Good God, what are you saying?

STEPDAUGHTER [*shouting frantically*] The truth, sir, the truth!

DIRECTOR Well, yes, of course, that must be the truth . . . and I quite understand your horror, young lady. Would you try to understand that all that is impossible *on the stage*?

STEPDAUGHTER Impossible? Then, thanks very much, I'm leaving.

DIRECTOR No, no, look . . .

STEPDAUGHTER I'm leaving, I'm leaving! You went in that room, you two, didn't you, and figured out "what is possible on the stage"? Thanks very much. I see it all. He wants to skip to the point where he can act out his [*Exaggerating*] spiritual travail! But I want to play *my* drama. Mine!

DIRECTOR [*annoyed, and shrugging haughtily*] Oh well, *your* drama. This is not just your drama, if I may say so. How about the drama of the others? His drama [*the* FATHER], hers [*the* MOTHER]? We can't let one character hog the limelight, just taking the whole stage over, and overshadowing all the others! Everything must be placed within the frame of one harmonious picture! We must perform only what is performable! I know as well as you do that each of us has a whole life of his own inside him and would like to bring it all out. But the difficult thing is this: to bring out only as much as is needed—in relation to the others—and in this to *imply* all the rest, *suggest* what remains inside! Oh, it would be nice if every character could come down to the footlights and tell the audience just what is brewing inside him—in a fine monologue or, if you will, a lecture! [*Good-natured, conciliatory*] Miss, you will have to *contain yourself*. And it will be in your interest. It could make a bad impression—let me warn you—this tearing fury, this desperate disgust—since, if I may say so, you confessed having been with others at Madam Pace's—before him—more than once!

STEPDAUGHTER [*lowering her head, pausing to recollect, a deeper note in her voice*] It's true. But to me the others are also *him*, all of them equally!

DIRECTOR [*not getting it*] The others? How d'you mean?

STEPDAUGHTER People "go wrong." And wrong follows on the heels of wrong. Who is responsible, if not whoever it was who first brought them down? Isn't that always the case? And for me that is him. Even before I was born. Look at him, and see if it isn't so.

DIRECTOR Very good. And if he has so much to feel guilty about, can't you appreciate how it must weigh him down? So let's at least permit him to act it out.

STEPDAUGHTER And how, may I ask, how could he act out all that "noble" guilt, all those so "moral" torments, if you propose to spare him the horror of one day finding in his arms—after having bade her take off the black clothes that marked her recent loss—a woman now, and already gone wrong—that little girl, sir, that little girl whom he used to go watch coming out of school?

[*She says these last words in a voice trembling with emotion. The* MOTHER, *hearing her say this, overcome with uncontrollable anguish, which comes out first in suffocated moans and subsequently bursts out in bitter weeping. The emotion takes hold of everyone. Long pause.*]

STEPDAUGHTER [*as soon as the* MOTHER *gives signs of calming down, somber, determined*]   We're just among ourselves now. Still unknown to the public. Tomorrow you will make of us the show you have in mind. You will put it together in your way. But would you like to really see—our drama? Have it explode—the real thing?

DIRECTOR   Of course. Nothing I'd like better. And I'll use as much of it as I possibly can!

STEPDAUGHTER   Very well. Have this Mother here go out.

MOTHER [*ceasing to weep, with a loud cry*]   No, no! Don't allow this, don't allow it!

DIRECTOR   I only want to take a look, ma'am.

MOTHER   I can't, I just can't!

DIRECTOR   But if it's already happened? Excuse me but I just don't get it.

MOTHER   No, no, it's happening now. It's always happening. My torment is not a pretense! I am alive and present—always, in every moment of my torment—it keeps renewing itself, it too is alive and always present. But those two little ones over there—have you heard them speak? They cannot speak, sir, not anymore! They still keep clinging to me—to keep my torment alive and present. For themselves they don't exist, don't exist any longer. And she [*the* STEPDAUGHTER], she just fled, ran away from me, she's lost, lost . . . If I see her before me now, it's for the same reason: to renew the torment, keep it always alive and present forever—the torment I've suffered on her account too—forever!

FATHER [*solemn*]   The eternal moment, sir, as I told you. She [*the* STEP-DAUGHTER] is here to catch me, fix me, hold me there in the pillory, hanging there forever, hooked, in that single fleeting shameful moment of my life! She cannot give it up. And, actually, sir, *you* cannot spare me.

DIRECTOR   But I didn't say I wouldn't use that. On the contrary, it will be the nucleus of the whole first act. To the point where she [*the* MOTHER] surprises you.

FATHER   Yes, exactly. Because that is the sentence passed upon me: all our passion which has to culminate in her [*the* MOTHER's] final cry!

STEPDAUGHTER   It still rings in my ears. It's driven me out of my mind, that cry!—You can present me as you wish, sir, it doesn't matter. Even dressed. As long as at least my arms—just my arms—are bare. Because it was like this. [*She goes to the* FATHER *and rests her head on his chest.*] I was standing like this with my head on his chest and my arms round his neck like this. Then I saw something throbbing right here on my arm. A vein. Then, as if it was just this living vein that disgusted me, I jammed my eyes shut, like this, d'you see? and buried my head on his chest. [*Turning to the* MOTHER] Scream, scream, mama! [*Buries her head on the* FATHER's *chest and with her shoulders raised as if to avoid hearing the scream she adds in a voice stifled with torment.*] Scream as you screamed then!

MOTHER [*rushing forward to part them*] No! My daughter! My daughter! [*Having pulled her from him*] Brute! Brute! It's my daughter, don't you see—my daughter!

DIRECTOR [*the outburst having sent him reeling to the footlights, while the Actors show dismay*] Fine! Splendid! And now: curtain, curtain!

FATHER [*running to him, convulsed*] Right! Yes! Because that, sir, is how it actually was!

DIRECTOR [*in admiration and conviction*] Yes, yes, of course! Curtain! Curtain!

> [*Hearing this repeated cry of the* DIRECTOR, *the* TECHNICIAN *lets down the curtain, trapping the* DIRECTOR *and the* FATHER *between curtain and footlights.*]

DIRECTOR [*looking up, with raised arms*] What an idiot! I say Curtain, meaning that's how the act should end, and they let down the actual curtain! [*He lifts a corner of the curtain so he can get back onstage. To the* FATHER] Yes, yes, fine, splendid! Absolutely surefire! Has to end that way. I can vouch for the first act. [*Goes behind the curtain with the* FATHER.]

> [*When the curtain rises we see that the stagehands have struck that first "indication of a set," and have put onstage in its stead a small garden fountain. On one side of the stage, the Actors are sitting in a row, and on the other are the Characters. The* DIRECTOR *is standing in the middle of the stage, in the act of meditating with one hand, fist clenched, on his mouth.*]

DIRECTOR [*shrugging after a short pause*] Yes, well then, let's get to the second act. Just leave it to me as we agreed beforehand and everything will be all right.

STEPDAUGHTER Our entrance into his house [*the* FATHER] in spite of him [*the* SON].

DIRECTOR [*losing patience*] Very well. But leave it all to me, I say.

STEPDAUGHTER In spite of him. Just let that be clear.

MOTHER [*shaking her head from her corner*] For all the good that's come out of it . . .

STEPDAUGHTER [*turning quickly on her*] It doesn't matter. The more damage to us, the more guilt feelings for him.

DIRECTOR [*still out of patience*] I understand, I understand. All this will be taken into account, especially at the beginning. Rest assured.

MOTHER [*supplicatingly*] Do make them understand, I beg you, sir, for my conscience's sake, for I tried in every possible way—

STEPDAUGHTER [*continuing her* MOTHER's *speech, contemptuously*] To placate me, to advise me not to give him trouble. [*To the* DIRECTOR] Do what she wants, do it because it's true. I enjoy the whole thing very much because, look: the more she plays the suppliant and tries to gain entrance into his heart, the more he holds himself aloof: he's an absentee! How I relish this!

DIRECTOR We want to get going—on the second act, don't we?

STEPDAUGHTER I won't say another word. But to play it all in the garden, as you want to, won't be possible.

DIRECTOR Why won't it be possible?

STEPDAUGHTER Because he [*the* SON] stays shut up in his room, on his own. Then again we need the house for the part about this poor bewildered little boy, as I told you.

DIRECTOR Quite right. But on the other hand, we can't change the scenery in view of the audience three or four times in one act, nor can we stick up signs—

LEADING MAN They used to at one time . . .

DIRECTOR Yes, when the audiences were about as mature as that little girl.

LEADING LADY They got the illusion more easily.

FATHER [*suddenly, rising*] The illusion, please don't say illusion! Don't use that word! It's especially cruel to us.

DIRECTOR [*astonished*] And why, if I may ask?

FATHER Oh yes, cruel, cruel! You should understand that.

DIRECTOR What word would you have us use anyway? The illusion of creating here for our spectators—

LEADING MAN   —By our performance—

DIRECTOR   —the illusion of a reality.

FATHER I understand, sir, but perhaps you do not understand us. Because, you see, for you and for your actors all this—quite rightly—is a game—

LEADING LADY [*indignantly interrupting*] Game! We are not children, sir. We act in earnest.

FATHER I don't deny it. I just mean the game of your art which, as this gentleman rightly says, must provide a perfect illusion of reality.

DIRECTOR Yes, exactly.

FATHER But consider this. We [*He quickly indicates himself and the other five Characters.*], we have no reality outside this illusion.

DIRECTOR [*astonished, looking at his Actors who remain bewildered and lost*] And that means?

FATHER [*after observing them briefly, with a pale smile*] Just that, ladies and gentlemen. How should we have any other reality? What for you is an illusion, to be created, is for us our unique reality. [*Short pause. He takes several short steps toward the* DIRECTOR, *and adds*] But not for us alone, of course. Think a moment. [*He looks into his eyes.*] Can you tell me who you are? [*And he stands there pointing his first finger at him.*]

DIRECTOR [*upset, with a half-smile*] How do you mean, who I am? I am I.

FATHER And if I told you that wasn't true because you are me?

DIRECTOR I would reply that you are out of your mind. [*The Actors laugh.*]

FATHER You are right to laugh: because this is a game. [*To the* DIRECTOR] And you can object that it's only in a game that that gentleman there [LEADING MAN], who is himself, must be me, who am *myself*. I've caught you in a trap, do you see that?

   [*Actors start laughing again.*]

DIRECTOR [*annoyed*] You said all this before. Why repeat it?

FATHER I won't—I didn't intend to say that. I'm inviting you to emerge from this game. [*He looks at the* LEADING LADY *as if to forestall what she might say.*] This game of art which you are accustomed to play here with your actors. Let me again ask quite seriously: Who are you?

DIRECTOR [*turning to the Actors, amazed and at the same time irritated*]   The gall of this fellow! Calls himself a character and comes here to ask me who I am!

FATHER [*dignified, but not haughty*]   A character, sir, can always ask a man who he is. Because a character really has his own life, marked with his own characteristics, by virtue of which he is always someone. Whereas, a man— I'm not speaking of you now—*a man* can be no one.

DIRECTOR   Oh sure. But you are asking me! And I am the manager, understand?

FATHER [*quite softly with mellifluous modesty*]   Only in order to know, sir, if you as you now are see yourself . . . for example, at a distance in time. Do you see the man you once were, with all the illusions you had then, with everything, inside you and outside, as it seemed then—as it was then for you?—Well sir, thinking back to those illusions which you don't have anymore, to all those things which no longer seem to be what at one time they were for you, don't you feel, not just the boards of this stage, but the very earth beneath slipping away from you? For will not all that you feel yourself to be now, your whole reality of today, as it is now, inevitably seem an illusion tomorrow?

DIRECTOR [*who has not followed exactly, but has been staggered by the plausibilities of the argument*]   Well, well, what do you want to prove?

FATHER   Oh nothing, sir. I just wanted to make you see that if *we* [*pointing again at himself and the other Characters*] have no reality outside of illusion, it would be well if you should distrust your reality because, though you breathe it and touch it today, it is destined like that of yesterday to stand revealed to you tomorrow as illusion.

DIRECTOR [*deciding to mock him*]   Oh splendid! And you'll be telling me next that you and this play that you have come to perform for me are truer and more real than I am.

FATHER [*quite seriously*]   There can be no doubt of that, sir.

DIRECTOR   Really?

FATHER   I thought you had understood that from the start.

DIRECTOR   More real than me?

FATHER   If your reality can change overnight . . .

DIRECTOR   Of course it can, it changes all the time, like everyone else's.

FATHER [*with a cry*]   But ours does not, sir. You see, that is the difference. It does not change, it cannot ever change or be otherwise because it is already fixed, it is what is, just that, forever—a terrible thing, sir!—an immutable reality. You should shudder to come near us.

DIRECTOR [*suddenly struck by a new idea, he steps in front of the* FATHER]   I should like to know, however, when anyone ever saw a character get out of his part and set about expounding and explicating it, delivering lectures on it. Can you tell me? I have never seen anything like that.

FATHER   You have never seen it, sir, because authors generally hide the travail of their creations. When characters are alive and turn up, living, before their author, all that author does is follow the words and gestures which they propose to him. He has to want them to be as they themselves want to be. Woe betide him if he doesn't! When a character is born, he at once acquires such an independence, even of his own author, that the whole world can imagine him in innumerable situations other than those the author thought to place him in. At times he acquires a meaning that the author never dreamt of giving him.

DIRECTOR   Certainly, I know that.

FATHER   Then why all this astonishment at us? Imagine what a misfortune it is for a character such as I described to you—given life in the imagination of an author who then wished to deny him life—and tell me frankly: isn't such a character, given life and left without life, isn't he right to set about doing just what we are doing now as we stand here before you, after having done just the same—for a very long time, believe me—before *him,* trying to persuade him, trying to push him . . . I would appear before him sometimes, sometimes she [*looks at* STEPDAUGHTER] would go to him, sometimes that poor mother . . .

STEPDAUGHTER   [*coming forward as if in a trance*]   It's true. I too went there, sir, to tempt him, many times, in the melancholy of that study of his, at the twilight hour, when he would sit stretched out in his armchair, unable to make up his mind to switch the light on, and letting the evening shadows invade the room, knowing that these shadows were alive with us and that we were coming to tempt him . . . [*As if she saw herself still in that study and felt only annoyance at the presence of all of these Actors*] Oh, if only you would all go away! Leave us alone! My mother there with her son—I with this little girl—the boy there always alone—then I with him [*the* FATHER]—then I by myself, I by myself . . . in those shadows. [*Suddenly she jumps up as if she wished to take hold of herself in the vision she has of herself lighting up the shadows and alive.*] Ah, my life! What scenes, what scenes we went there to propose to him: I, I tempted him more than the others.

FATHER   Right, but perhaps that was the trouble: you insisted too much. You thought you could seduce him.

STEPDAUGHTER   Nonsense. He wanted me that way. [*She comes up to the* DIRECTOR *to tell him as in confidence.*] If you ask me, sir, it was because he was so depressed, or because he despised the theater the public knows and wants . . .

DIRECTOR   Let's continue. Let's continue, for heaven's sake. Enough theories, I'd like some facts. Give me some facts.

STEPDAUGHTER   It seems to me that we have already given you more facts than you can handle—with our entry into his [*the* FATHER's] house! You said you couldn't change the scene every five minutes or start hanging signs.

DIRECTOR   Nor can we, of course not, we have to combine the scenes and group them in one simultaneous close-knit action. Not your idea at all. You'd like to see your brother come home from school and wander through the house like a ghost, hiding behind the doors, and brooding on a plan which—how did you put it—?

STEPDAUGHTER   —shrivels him up, sir, completely shrivels him up, sir.

DIRECTOR   "Shrivels!" What a word! All right then: his growth was stunted except for his eyes. Is that what you said?

STEPDAUGHTER   Yes, sir. Just look at him. [*She points him out next to the* MOTHER.]

DIRECTOR   Good girl. And then at the same time you want this little girl to be playing in the garden, dead to the world. Now, the boy in the house, the girl in the garden, is that possible?

STEPDAUGHTER   Happy in the sunshine! Yes, that is my only reward, her pleasure, her joy in that garden! After the misery, the squalor of a horrible room
where we slept, all four of us, she with me: just think, of the horror of my
contaminated body next to hers! She held me tight, oh so tight with her
loving innocent little arms! In the garden she would run and take my hand
as soon as she saw me. She did not see the big flowers, she ran around
looking for the teeny ones and wanted to show them to me, oh the joy of it!
   [*Saying this and tortured by the memory she breaks into prolonged desperate
   sobbing, dropping her head onto her arms which are spread out on the work
   table. Everyone is overcome by her emotion. The* DIRECTOR *goes to her almost
   paternally and says to comfort her*]

DIRECTOR   We'll do the garden. We'll do the garden, don't worry, and you'll
be very happy about it. We'll bring all the scenes together in the garden.
[*Calling a* STAGEHAND *by name*] Hey, drop me a couple of trees, will you,
two small cypress trees, here in front of the fountain.
   [*Two small cypress trees are seen descending from the flies. A* STAGEHAND *runs
   on to secure them with nails and a couple of braces.*]

DIRECTOR [*to the* STEPDAUGHTER]   Something to go on with anyway. Gives us
an idea. [*Again calling the* STAGEHAND *by name*] Hey, give me a bit of sky.

STAGEHAND [*from above*]   What?

DIRECTOR   Bit of sky, a backcloth, to go behind that fountain. [*A white
backdrop is seen descending from the flies.*] Not white, I said sky. It doesn't
matter, leave it, I'll take care of it. [*Shouting*] Hey, Electrician, put these
lights out. Let's have a bit of atmosphere, lunar atmosphere, blue background, and give me a blue spot on that backcloth. That's right. That's
enough. [*At his command a mysterious lunar scene is created which
induces the Actors to talk and move as they would on an evening in the
garden beneath the moon.*] [*To* STEPDAUGHTER] You see? And now instead
of hiding behind doors in the house the boy could move around here in
the garden and hide behind trees. But it will be difficult, you know, to
find a little girl to play the scene where she shows you the flowers. [*Turning to the* BOY] Come down this way a bit. Let's see how this can be
worked out. [*And when the* BOY *doesn't move*] Come on, come on. [*Then
dragging him forward he tries to make him hold his head up but it falls
down again every time.*] Oh dear, another problem, this boy . . . What *is*
it? . . . My God, he'll have to say something . . . [*He goes up to him, puts
a hand on his shoulder and leads him behind one of the tree drops.*] Come
on. Come on. Let me see. You can hide a bit here . . . Like this . . . You
can stick your head out a bit to look . . . [*He goes to one side to see the
effect. The* BOY *has scarcely run through the actions when the Actors are
deeply affected; and they remain quite overwhelmed.*] Ah! Fine! Splendid!
[*He turns again to the* STEPDAUGHTER.] If the little girl surprises him looking out and runs over to him, don't you think she might drag a few words
out of him too?

STEPDAUGHTER [*jumping to her feet*]   Don't expect him to speak while *he's*
here. [*She points to the* SON.] You have to send *him* away first.

SON [*going resolutely toward one of the two stairways*]   Suits me. Glad to go.
Nothing I want more.

DIRECTOR [*immediately calling him*]   No. Where are you going? Wait.

[*The* MOTHER *rises, deeply moved, in anguish at the thought that he is really going. She instinctively raises her arms as if to halt him, yet without moving away from her position.*]

SON [*arriving at the footlights, where the* DIRECTOR *stops him*]   I have absolutely nothing to do here. So let me go please. Just let me go.

DIRECTOR   How do you mean, you have nothing to do?

STEPDAUGHTER [*placidly, with irony*]   Don't hold him! He won't go.

FATHER   He has to play the terrible scene in the garden with his mother.

SON [*unhesitating, resolute, proud*]   I play nothing. I said so from the start. [*To the* DIRECTOR] Let me go.

STEPDAUGHTER [*running to the* DIRECTOR *to get him to lower his arms so that he is no longer holding the* SON *back*]   Let him go. [*Then turning to the* SON *as soon as the* DIRECTOR *has let him go*] Very well, go. [*The* SON *is all set to move toward the stairs but, as if held by some occult power, he cannot go down the steps. While the Actors are both astounded and deeply troubled, he moves slowly across the footlights straight to the other stairway. But having arrived there he remains poised for the descent but unable to descend. The* STEPDAUGHTER, *who has followed him with her eyes in an attitude of defiance, bursts out laughing.*] He can't, you see. He can't. He has to stay here, has to. Bound by a chain, indissolubly. But if I who do take flight, sir, when that happens which has to happen, and precisely because of the hatred I feel for him, precisely so as not to see him again—very well, if *I* am still here and can bear the sight of him and his company—you can imagine whether *he* can go away. He who really must, must remain here with that fine father of his and that mother there who no longer has any other children. [*Turning again to the* MOTHER] Come on, Mother, come on. [*Turning again to the* DIRECTOR *and pointing to the* MOTHER] Look, she got up to hold him back. [*To the* MOTHER, *as if exerting a magical power over her*] Come. Come . . . [*Then to the* DIRECTOR] You can imagine how little she wants to display her love in front of your actors. But so great is her desire to get at him that—look, you see—she is even prepared to live her scene.

[*In fact the* MOTHER *has approached and no sooner has the* STEPDAUGHTER *spoken her last words than she spreads her arms to signify consent.*]

SON [*without pause*]   But *I* am not, *I* am not. If I cannot go I will stay here, but I repeat: I will play nothing.

FATHER [*to the* DIRECTOR, *enraged*]   You can force him, sir.

SON   No one can force me.

FATHER   I will force you.

STEPDAUGHTER   Wait, wait. First the little girl must be at the fountain. [*She runs to take the* LITTLE GIRL, *drops on her knees in front of her, takes her little face in her hands.*] My poor little darling, you look bewildered with those lovely big eyes of yours. Who knows where you think you are? We are on a stage, my dear. What is a stage? It is a place where you play at being serious, a place for playacting, where we will now playact. But seriously! For real! You too . . . [*She embraces her, presses her to her bosom, and rocks her a little.*] Oh, little darling, little darling, what an ugly play you will enact! What a horrible thing has been planned for you, the garden, the fountain . . . All pretense, of course, that's the trouble, my sweet, everything is make-believe here, but perhaps for you, my child, a make-believe fountain is nicer than a real one for playing in, hmm? It will be a game for the others, but not for you, alas, because you are real, my darling, and are actually playing in a fountain that is real, beautiful, big, green with many bamboo plants reflected in it and giving it shade. Many, many ducklings can swim in it, breaking the shade to bits. You want to take hold of one of these ducklings . . . [*With a shout that fills everyone with dismay*] No! No, my Rosetta! Your mother is not looking after you because of that beast of a son. A thousand devils are loose in my head . . . and he . . . [*She leaves the* LITTLE GIRL *and turns with her usual hostility to the* BOY.] And what are you doing here, always looking like a beggar child? It will be your fault too if this little girl drowns—with all your standing around like that. As if I hadn't paid for everybody when I got you all into this house. [*Grabbing one of his arms to force him to take a hand out of his pocket*] What have you got there? What are you hiding? Let's see this hand. [*Tears his hand out of his pocket, and to the horror of everyone discovers that it holds a small revolver. She looks at it for a moment as if satisfied and then says*] Ah! Where did you get that and how? [*And as the* BOY *in his confusion, with his eyes staring and vacant all the time, does not answer her*] Idiot, if I were you I wouldn't have killed myself, I would have killed one of those two—or both of them—the father and the son! [*She hides him behind the small cypress tree from which he had been looking out, and she takes the* LITTLE GIRL *and hides her in the fountain, having her lie down in it in such a way as to be quite hidden. Finally, the* STEPDAUGHTER *goes down on her knees with her face in her hands, which are resting on the rim of the fountain.*]

DIRECTOR   Splendid! [*Turning to the* SON] And at the same time . . .

SON [*with contempt*]   And at the same time, nothing. It is not true, sir. There was never any scene between me and her. [*He points to the* MOTHER.] Let her tell you herself how it was.

[*Meanwhile the* SECOND ACTRESS *and the* JUVENILE LEAD *have detached themselves from the group of Actors. The former has started to observe the* MOTHER, *who is opposite her, very closely. And the other has started to observe the* SON. *Both are planning how they will re-create the roles.*]

MOTHER   Yes, it is true, sir. I had gone to his room.

SON   My room, did you hear that? Not the garden.

DIRECTOR   That is of no importance. We have to rearrange the action, I told you that.

SON [*noticing that the* JUVENILE LEAD *is observing him*]   What do *you* want?

JUVENILE LEAD   Nothing. I am observing you.

SON [*turning to the other side where the* SECOND ACTRESS *is*]   Ah, and here we have you to re-create the role, eh? [*He points to the* MOTHER.]

DIRECTOR   Exactly, exactly. You should be grateful, it seems to me, for the attention they are giving you.

SON   Oh yes, thank you. But you still haven't understood that you cannot do this drama. We are not inside you, not in the least, and your actors are looking at us from the outside. Do you think it's possible for us to live before a mirror which, not content to freeze us in the fixed image it provides of our expression, also throws back at us an unrecognizable grimace purporting to be ourselves?

FATHER   That is true. That is true. You must see that.

DIRECTOR [*to the* JUVENILE LEAD *and the* SECOND ACTRESS] Very well, get away from here.

SON No good. I won't cooperate.

DIRECTOR Just be quiet a minute and let me hear your mother. [*To the* MOTHER] Well? You went into his room?

MOTHER Yes sir, into his room. I was at the end of my tether. I wanted to pour out all of the anguish which was oppressing me. But as soon as he saw me come in—

SON —There was no scene. I went away. I went away so there would be no scene. Because I have never made scenes, never, understand?

MOTHER That's true. That's how it was. Yes.

DIRECTOR But now there's got to be a scene between you and him. It is indispensable.

MOTHER As for me, sir, I am ready. If only you could find some way to have me speak to him for one moment, to have me say what is in my heart.

FATHER [*going right up to the* SON, *very violent*] You will do it! For your mother! For your mother!

SON [*more decisively than ever*] I will do nothing!

FATHER [*grabbing him by the chest and shaking him*] By God, you will obey! Can't you hear how she is talking to you? Aren't you her son?

SON [*grabbing his* FATHER] No! No! Once and for all let's have done with it!

[*General agitation. The* MOTHER, *terrified, tries to get between them to separate them.*]

MOTHER [*as before*] Please, please!

FATHER [*without letting go of the* SON] You must obey, you must obey!

SON [*wrestling with his* FATHER *and in the end throwing him to the ground beside the little stairway, to the horror of everyone*] What's this frenzy that's taken hold of you? To show your shame and ours to everyone? Have you no restraint? I won't cooperate, I won't cooperate! And that is how I interpret the wishes of the man who did not choose to put us onstage.

DIRECTOR But you came here.

SON [*pointing to his* FATHER] He came here—not me!

DIRECTOR But aren't you here too?

SON It was he who wanted to come, dragging the rest of us with him, and then getting together with you to plot not only what really happened, but also—as if that did not suffice—*what did not happen.*

DIRECTOR Then tell me. Tell me what did happen. Just tell me. You came out of your room without saying a thing?

SON [*after a moment of hesitation*] Without saying a thing. In order not to make a scene.

DIRECTOR [*driving him on*] Very well, and then, what did you do then?

SON [*while everyone looks on in anguished attention, he moves a few steps on the front part of the stage*] Nothing . . . crossing the garden . . . [*He stops, gloomy, withdrawn.*]

DIRECTOR [*always driving him on to speak, impressed by his reticence*] Very well, crossing the garden?

SON [*desperate, hiding his face with one arm*] Why do you want to make me say it, sir? It is horrible.

[*The* MOTHER *trembles all over, and stifles groans, looking toward the fountain.*]

DIRECTOR [*softly, noticing this look of hers, turning to the* SON, *with growing apprehension*]   The little girl?

SON [*looking out into the auditorium*]   Over there—in the fountain . . .

FATHER [*on the ground, pointing compassionately toward the* MOTHER]   And she followed him, sir.

DIRECTOR [*to the* SON, *anxiously*]   And then you . . .

SON [*slowly, looking straight ahead all the time*]   I ran out. I started to fish her out . . . but all of a sudden I stopped. Behind those trees I saw something that froze me: the boy, the boy was standing there, quite still. There was madness in the eyes. He was looking at his drowned sister in the fountain. [*The* STEPDAUGHTER, *who has been bent over the fountain, hiding the* LITTLE GIRL, *is sobbing desperately, like an echo from the bottom. Pause.*] I started to approach and then . . .

[*From behind the trees where the* BOY *has been hiding, a revolver shot rings out.*]

MOTHER [*running up with a tormented shout, accompanied by the* SON *and all the Actors in a general tumult*]   Son! My son! [*And then amid the hubbub and the disconnected shouts of the others*] Help! Help!

DIRECTOR [*amid the shouting, trying to clear a space while the* BOY *is lifted by his head and feet and carried away behind the backcloth*]   Is he wounded, is he wounded, really?

[*Everyone except the* DIRECTOR *and the* FATHER, *who has remained on the ground beside the steps, has disappeared behind the backcloth which has served for a sky, where they can still be heard for a while whispering anxiously. Then from one side and the other of this curtain, the Actors come back onstage.*]

LEADING LADY [*reentering from the right, very much upset*]   He's dead! Poor boy! He's dead! What a terrible thing!

LEADING MAN [*reentering from the left, laughing*]   How do you mean, dead? Fiction, fiction, one doesn't believe such things.

OTHER ACTORS [*on the right*]   Fiction? Reality! Reality! He is dead!

OTHER ACTORS [*on the left*]   No! Fiction! Fiction!

FATHER [*rising, and crying out to them*]   Fiction indeed! Reality, reality, gentlemen, reality! [*Desperate, he too disappears at the back.*]

DIRECTOR [*at the end of his rope*]   Fiction! Reality! To hell with all of you! Lights, lights, lights![5] [*At a single stroke the whole stage and auditorium is flooded with very bright light. The* DIRECTOR *breathes again, as if freed from an incubus, and they all look each other in the eyes, bewildered and lost.*] Things like this don't happen to me, they've made me lose a whole day. [*He looks at his watch.*] Go, you can all go. What could we do now anyway? It is too late to pick up the rehearsal where we left off. See you this evening. [*As soon as the Actors have gone he talks to the* ELECTRICIAN *by name.*] Hey, Electrician, lights out. [*He has hardly said the words when the theater is plunged for a moment into complete darkness.*] Hey, for God's sake, leave me at least one light! I like to see where I am going!

5. I.e., house lights as well as onstage working lights.

[*Immediately, from behind the backcloth, as if the wrong switch had been pulled, a green light comes on which projects the silhouettes, clear-cut and large, of the Characters, minus the* BOY *and the* LITTLE GIRL. *Seeing the silhouettes, the* DIRECTOR, *terrified, rushes from the stage. At the same time the light behind the backcloth goes out and the stage is again lit in nocturnal blue as before.*

Slowly, from the right side of the curtain, the SON *comes forward first, followed by the* MOTHER *with her arms stretched out toward him; then from the left side, the* FATHER. *They stop in the middle of the stage and stay there as if in a trance. Last of all from the right, the* STEPDAUGHTER *comes out and runs toward the two stairways. She stops on the first step, to look for a moment at the other three, and then breaks into a harsh laugh before throwing herself down the steps; she runs down the aisle between the rows of seats; she stops one more time and again laughs, looking at the three who are still onstage; she disappears from the auditorium, and from the lobby her laughter is still heard. Shortly thereafter the curtain falls.*]

VIRGINIA WOOLF
1882–1941

Virginia Woolf was one of the great modern novelists, known for her precise evocations of states of mind—or of mind and body, since she refused to separate the two. She was an ardent feminist who explored—directly in her essays and indirectly in her novels and short stories—the situation of women in society, the construction of gender identity, and the predicament of the woman writer.

Born Adeline Virginia Stephen on January 25, 1882, she was one of the four children of the eminent Victorian editor and historian Leslie Stephen and his wife, Julia, both of whom also had children from earlier marriages. The family actively pursued intellectual and artistic interests, and Julia was admired and sketched by some of the most famous Pre-Raphaelite artists. Following the customs of the day, only the sons, Adrian and Thoby, were sent to boarding school and university; Virginia and her sister, Vanessa (the painter Vanessa Bell), were instructed at home by their parents and depended for further education on their father's immense library. Woolf bitterly resented this unequal treatment and the systematic discouragement of women's intellectual development that it implied.

After her mother's death in 1895, Woolf was expected to take over the supervision of the household, which she did until her father's death in 1904. She worried that women in literary families like hers were expected to write memoirs of their fathers or to edit their correspondence. Woolf did in fact write a memoir of her father, but she later noted that if he had not died when she was relatively young, she never would have become an author. Of fragile physical health after an attack of whooping cough when she was six, Woolf suffered psychological breakdowns after the death of each parent and was frequently hospitalized, especially after a number of suicide attempts. During her lifetime Woolf consulted at least twelve doctors and, consequently, experienced firsthand the developments in medicine for treating the mentally ill, from the Victorian era to the shell shock of the First World War.

Woolf moved to central London with her sister and brother Adrian after their father's death and took a house in the Bloomsbury district. It was a time of shifting social and cultural mores, of which Woolf later claimed: "on or about December, 1910, human character changed." She and her sister, though unmarried, lived with several men (some of them openly homosexual), challenging the social conventions that respectable unmarried women were expected to follow. She and her friends soon became the focus of what was later called the Bloomsbury Group, a gathering of writers, artists, and intellectuals impatient with conservative Edwardian society who met regularly to discuss ideas and to promote a freer view of culture. This eclectic group included the novelist E. M. Forster, the historian Lytton Strachey, the economist John Maynard Keynes, and the art critics Clive Bell (who married Vanessa) and Roger Fry (who introduced the group to the work of French painters Édouard Manet and Paul Cézanne).

Woolf was not yet writing fiction but contributed reviews to the *Times Literary Supplement*, taught literature and composition at Morley College (an institution with a volunteer faculty that provided educational opportunities for workers), and participated in the adult suffrage movement and a feminist group. In 1912 she married Leonard Woolf, who encouraged her to write and with whom she founded the Hogarth Press in 1917. One of the most respected of the small literary presses, it published works by such major authors as **T. S. Eliot**, Katherine Mansfield, Strachey, Forster, Maxim Gorky, and John Middleton Murry, as well as Woolf's own novels and translations of Sigmund Freud's most significant output. Over the next two decades she produced her best-known work while coping with frequent bouts of physical and mental illness. Already depressed during World War II and exhausted after the completion of her final novel, *Between the Acts* (1941), Woolf sensed the approach of a serious attack of psychosis and the confinement it would entail: in such situations, she was obliged to "rest" and forbidden to read or write. In March 1941 she drowned herself in a river close to her Sussex home.

Woolf is admired for her poetic evocations of the way we think and feel. Like Proust and **Joyce**, she brings to life the concrete, sensuous details of everyday experience; like them, she explores the structures of consciousness. Championing modern fiction as an alternative to the realism of the preceding generation, she proposed a more subjective and, therefore, more accurate account of experience. Her focus was not so much on the object under observation as on the observers' perception of it: "Let us record the atoms as they fall upon the mind in the order in which they fall, let us trace the pattern, however disconnected and incoherent in appearance, which sight or incident scores upon the consciousness." Such writing, undertaken with a woman's creative vision, would open avenues for literature. Although she was dismayed by what she saw as Joyce's vulgarity, she recognized him as one of the few living writers who achieved the successful rendering of stream of consciousness.

Woolf's writing has been compared with modern painting in its emphasis on the abstract arrangement of perspectives to suggest networks of meaning. After two relatively traditional novels, she developed a more flexible approach that manipulated fictional structure. The unfolding plot gave way to an organization by juxtaposed points of view; the experience of "real," or chronological, time was partially displaced by a mind ranging ambiguously among its memories; and an intricate pattern of symbolic themes connected otherwise unrelated characters. These techniques made unfamiliar demands on the reader's ability to synthesize and re-create a complete picture. In *Jacob's Room* (1922), an understanding of the hero must be assembled from a series of partial points of view. In *The Waves* (1931), the multiple perspectives of several characters soliloquizing on their relationship to the dead Percival are broken by ten interludes that together construct an additional, interacting perspective as they describe the passage of a single day from dawn to dusk. Woolf's novels may expand or telescope the passage of time: *Mrs. Dalloway* (1925) seems to focus on Clarissa Dalloway's preparations for a party that evening, but at the same time calls up—at different times, and according to different contexts—her entire life, from childhood to her present age of fifty. Woolf also concerned herself with the question of women's equality with men in marriage, and she brilliantly evoked the inequality in her parents' marriage in her novel *To the Lighthouse* (1927).

A ROOM OF ONE'S OWN

One of Woolf's major themes is society's different attitudes toward men and toward women. The work presented here, *A Room of One's Own* (1929), examines the history of literature written by women and offers an impassioned plea that women writers be given conditions equal to those available for men: specifically, the privacy of a room in which to write and economic independence. (At the time Woolf wrote, it was unusual for women to have money of their own or to be able to devote themselves to a career.) *A Room of One's Own* does not conform to any fixed form. At once lecture and essay, autobiography and fiction, it originated in a pair of lectures on women and fiction that the author gave at Newnham and Girton Colleges (for women) at Cambridge University in 1928. Woolf warns her audience that, instead of defining either women or fiction, she will use "all the liberties and licenses of a novelist" to approach the matter obliquely and leave her auditors to sort out the truth from the "lies [that] will flow from my lips." She will, she claims, retrace the days (that is, the narrator's days) preceding her visit, and lay bare the thought processes leading up to the lecture itself.

The lecture (or, in its written form, Chapter 1), continues as a meditative ramble through various parts of Oxbridge (an informal verbal linking of *Oxford* and *Cambridge* universities) and London. It includes the famous, and apparently true, anecdote in which Woolf is warned off the university lawn and forbidden entrance to the library because she is a woman, as well as a vivid description of the differences between the food and the living quarters for women and those for men at Oxbridge. By the end of her visit, frustrated, furious, and puzzled, she decides that the subject needs research—and London's British Museum, at least, is open to all.

In Chapter 2 the narrator heads for the British Museum to locate a comprehensive definition of femininity. To her surprise and mounting anger, she discovers that the thousands of books on the subject written by men all define women as inferior animals, useful but somewhat alien in nature. Moreover, those very definitions have become prescriptions for generations of young women who learn to see themselves and their place in life accordingly. Raised in poverty and dependence, such women have neither the material means nor the self-confidence to write seriously or to become anything other than the Victorian "Angel in the House." What they require, asserts the narrator, is the self-sufficiency brought by an annual income of five hundred pounds. (Woolf had recently inherited such a sum.)

Chapter 3 pursues similar themes, adding to the five hundred pounds the need for "a room of one's own" and the privacy necessary to follow out an idea. Moving to history and focusing on the Elizabethan Age, after a discouraging inspection of the well-known *History of England* by George Macaulay Trevelyan (1876–1962), Woolf evokes the career of the "wonderfully gifted" Judith Shakespeare, William's imaginary sister (his actual sister was named Joan). Judith has the same literary and dramatic ambitions as her brother, and she too finds her way to London, but she is blocked at each turn by her identity as a woman. Woolf does not belittle William Shakespeare with this contrast; instead, her narrator remarks meaningfully that his work reveals an "incandescent, unimpeded mind."

The bleak portrayals in these chapters are lightened by satirical wit and humor, often conveyed by calculated historical distortion. Woolf uses her novelist's license to subvert and criticize the patriarchal message she describes. The Reading Room of the British Museum, august repository of masculine knowledge about women, is seen as a (bald-foreheaded) dome crowned with the names of famous men. The narrator's scholarly-seeming list of feminine characteristics is not only amusingly biased but contradictory and incoherent; it implies that the "masculine" passion for lists and documentation is not the best way to learn about human nature. Professor von X.'s portrait is an open caricature linked to suggestions that his scientific disdain hides repressed fear and anger. *A Room of One's Own* is still famous for its vivid, scathing, and occasionally humorous portrayal of women as objects of male definition and disapproval. Its model of a feminine literary history and its hypothesis of a separate feminine consciousness and manner of writing had substantial influence on writers and literary theory in the latter half of the twentieth century.

From A Room of One's Own[1]

CHAPTER I

But, you may say, we asked you to speak about women and fiction—what has that got to do with a room of one's own? I will try to explain. When you asked me to speak about women and fiction I sat down on the banks of a river and began to wonder what the words meant. They might mean simply a few remarks about Fanny Burney; a few more about Jane Austen; a tribute to the Brontës and a sketch of Haworth Parsonage under snow; some witticisms if

1. This essay is based upon two papers read to the Arts Society at Newnham and the Odtaa at Girton in October 1928. The papers were too long to be read in full, and have since been altered and expanded [Woolf's note]. Newn-

ham and Girton are women's colleges at Cambridge University, and Odtaa ("One damn thing after another") is the acronym of a literary society. Woolf's talk was entitled *Women and Fiction*.

possible about Miss Mitford; a respectful allusion to George Eliot; a reference to Mrs. Gaskell[2] and one would have done. But at second sight the words seemed not so simple. The title women and fiction might mean, and you may have meant it to mean, women and what they are like; or it might mean women and the fiction that they write; or it might mean women and the fiction that is written about them; or it might mean that somehow all three are inextricably mixed together and you want me to consider them in that light. But when I began to consider the subject in this last way, which seemed the most interesting, I soon saw that it had one fatal drawback. I should never be able to come to a conclusion. I should never be able to fulfil what is, I understand, the first duty of a lecturer—to hand you after an hour's discourse a nugget of pure truth to wrap up between the pages of your notebooks and keep on the mantelpiece for ever. All I could do was to offer you an opinion upon one minor point—a woman must have money and a room of her own if she is to write fiction; and that, as you will see, leaves the great problem of the true nature of woman and the true nature of fiction unsolved. I have shirked the duty of coming to a conclusion upon these two questions—women and fiction remain, so far as I am concerned, unsolved problems. But in order to make some amends I am going to do what I can to show you how I arrived at this opinion about the room and the money. I am going to develop in your presence as fully and freely as I can the train of thought which led me to think this. Perhaps if I lay bare the ideas, the prejudices, that lie behind this statement you will find that they have some bearing upon women and some upon fiction. At any rate, when a subject is highly controversial—and any question about sex is that—one cannot hope to tell the truth. One can only show how one came to hold whatever opinion one does hold. One can only give one's audience the chance of drawing their own conclusions as they observe the limitations, the prejudices, the idiosyncrasies of the speaker. Fiction here is likely to contain more truth than fact. Therefore I propose, making use of all the liberties and licences of a novelist, to tell you the story of the two days that preceded my coming here—how, bowed down by the weight of the subject which you have laid upon my shoulders, I pondered it, and made it work in and out of my daily life. I need not say that what I am about to describe has no existence; Oxbridge[3] is an invention; so is Fernham; "I" is only a convenient term for somebody who has no real being. Lies will flow from my lips, but there may perhaps be some truth mixed up with them; it is for you to seek out this truth and to decide whether any part of it is worth keeping. If not, you will of course throw the whole of it into the wastepaper basket and forget all about it.

Here then was I (call me Mary Beton, Mary Seton, Mary Carmichael or by any name you please—it is not a matter of any importance) sitting on the banks of a river a week or two ago in fine October weather, lost in thought. That collar I have

---

2. English novelist Elizabeth Gaskell (1810–1865) was the author of *Cranford* (1853). British writers: Fanny (Frances) Burney (1752–1840), author of *Evelina* (1778); Jane Austen (1775–1817), author of *Pride and Prejudice* (1813); the three Brontë sisters, who were raised in the Yorkshire parsonage of Haworth—Charlotte (1816–1855), author of *Jane Eyre* (1847); Emily (1818–1848), author of *Wuthering Heights* (1847); and Anne (1820–1849), author of *Agnes Grey* (1847); Mary Russell Mitford (1787–1855), author of the blank-verse tragedy *Rienzi* (1828); George Eliot (pen name of Mary Ann Evans; 1819–1880), author of *Middlemarch* (1871–72).

3. A fictional university combining the names of Oxford and Cambridge.

spoken of, women and fiction, the need of coming to some conclusion on a subject that raises all sorts of prejudices and passions, bowed my head to the ground. To the right and left bushes of some sort, golden and crimson, glowed with the colour, even it seemed burnt with the heat, of fire. On the further bank the willows wept in perpetual lamentation, their hair about their shoulders. The river reflected whatever it chose of sky and bridge and burning tree, and when the undergraduate had oared his boat through the reflections they closed again, completely, as if he had never been. There one might have sat the clock round lost in thought. Thought—to call it by a prouder name than it deserved—had let its line down into the stream. It swayed, minute after minute, hither and thither among the reflections and the weeds, letting the water lift it and sink it, until—you know the little tug—the sudden conglomeration of an idea at the end of one's line: and then the cautious hauling of it in, and the careful laying of it out? Alas, laid on the grass how small, how insignificant this thought of mine looked; the sort of fish that a good fisherman puts back into the water so that it may grow fatter and be one day worth cooking and eating. I will not trouble you with that thought now, though if you look carefully you may find it for yourselves in the course of what I am going to say.

But however small it was, it had, nevertheless, the mysterious property of its kind—put back into the mind, it became at once very exciting, and important; and as it darted and sank, and flashed hither and thither, set up such a wash and tumult of ideas that it was impossible to sit still. It was thus that I found myself walking with extreme rapidity across a grass plot. Instantly a man's figure rose to intercept me. Nor did I at first understand that the gesticulations of a curious-looking object, in a cut-away coat and evening shirt, were aimed at me. His face expressed horror and indignation. Instinct rather than reason came to my help; he was a Beadle;[4] I was a woman. This was the turf; there was the path. Only the Fellows and Scholars are allowed here; the gravel is the place for me. Such thoughts were the work of a moment. As I regained the path the arms of the Beadle sank, his face assumed its usual repose, and though turf is better walking than gravel, no very great harm was done. The only charge I could bring against the Fellows and Scholars of whatever the college might happen to be was that in protection of their turf, which has been rolled for 300 years in succession, they had sent my little fish into hiding.

What idea it had been that had sent me so audaciously trespassing I could not now remember. The spirit of peace descended like a cloud from heaven, for if the spirit of peace dwells anywhere, it is in the courts and quadrangles of Oxbridge on a fine October morning. Strolling through those colleges past those ancient halls the roughness of the present seemed smoothed away; the body seemed contained in a miraculous glass cabinet through which no sound could penetrate, and the mind, freed from any contact with facts (unless one trespassed on the turf again), was at liberty to settle down upon whatever meditation was in harmony with the moment. As chance would have it, some stray memory of some old essay about revisiting Oxbridge in the long vacation brought Charles Lamb to mind—Saint Charles, said Thackeray,[5] putting a letter of Lamb's to his forehead.

---

4. A lower-ranked university officer, assistant to authority.
5. I.e., William Makepeace Thackeray (1811–1863), whose novels include *Vanity Fair* (1847–1848) and *The History of Henry Esmond, Esq.*

(1852). Charles Lamb (1775–1834): English essayist and letter writer, author of *Essays of Elia* (1823), which contains *Oxford in the Vacation*, mentioned in Woolf's text.

Indeed, among all the dead (I give you my thoughts as they came to me), Lamb is one of the most congenial; one to whom one would have liked to say, Tell me then how you wrote your essays? For his essays are superior even to Max Beerbohm's,[6] I thought, with all their perfection, because of that wild flash of imagination, that lightning crack of genius in the middle of them which leaves them flawed and imperfect, but starred with poetry. Lamb then came to Oxbridge perhaps a hundred years ago. Certainly he wrote an essay—the name escapes me—about the manuscript of one of Milton's poems which he saw here. It was *Lycidas* perhaps, and Lamb wrote how it shocked him to think it possible that any word in *Lycidas* could have been different from what it is. To think of Milton changing the words in that poem seemed to him a sort of sacrilege. This led me to remember what I could of *Lycidas* and to amuse myself with guessing which word it could have been that Milton had altered, and why. It then occurred to me that the very manuscript itself which Lamb had looked at was only a few hundred yards away, so that one could follow Lamb's footsteps across the quadrangle to that famous library[7] where the treasure is kept. Moreover, I recollected, as I put this plan into execution, it is in this famous library that the manuscript of Thackeray's *Esmond* is also preserved. The critics often say that *Esmond* is Thackeray's most perfect novel. But the affectation of the style, with its imitation of the eighteenth century, hampers one, so far as I remember; unless indeed the eighteenth-century style was natural to Thackeray—a fact that one might prove by looking at the manuscript and seeing whether the alterations were for the benefit of the style or of the sense. But then one would have to decide what is style and what is meaning, a question which—but here I was actually at the door which leads into the library itself. I must have opened it, for instantly there issued, like a guardian angel barring the way with a flutter of black gown instead of white wings, a deprecating, silvery, kindly gentleman, who regretted in a low voice as he waved me back that ladies are only admitted to the library if accompanied by a Fellow of the College or furnished with a letter of introduction.

That a famous library has been cursed by a woman is a matter of complete indifference to a famous library. Venerable and calm, with all its treasures safe locked within its breast, it sleeps complacently and will, so far as I am concerned, so sleep for ever. Never will I wake those echoes, never will I ask for that hospitality again, I vowed as I descended the steps in anger. Still an hour remained before luncheon, and what was one to do? Stroll on the meadows? sit by the river? Certainly it was a lovely autumn morning; the leaves were fluttering red to the ground; there was no great hardship in doing either. But the sound of music reached my ear. Some service or celebration was going forward. The organ complained magnificently as I passed the chapel door. Even the sorrow of Christianity sounded in that serene air more like the recollection of sorrow than sorrow itself; even the groanings of the ancient organ seemed lapped in peace. I had no wish to enter had I the right, and this time the verger might have stopped me, demanding perhaps my baptismal certificate, or a letter of introduction from the Dean. But the outside of these magnificent buildings is often as beautiful as the inside. Moreover, it was amusing enough to watch the congregation assembling, coming in and going out again, busying themselves at the door of the chapel like bees at the

6. English caricaturist and writer (1872–1956).
7. Trinity College Library, in Cambridge, designed by Sir Christopher Wren and built from 1676 to 1684.

mouth of a hive. Many were in cap and gown; some had tufts of fur on their shoulders; others were wheeled in bath-chairs; others, though not past middle age, seemed creased and crushed into shapes so singular that one was reminded of those giant crabs and crayfish who heave with difficulty across the sand of an aquarium. As I leant against the wall the University indeed seemed a sanctuary in which are preserved rare types which would soon be obsolete if left to fight for existence on the pavement of the Strand.[8] Old stories of old deans and old dons came back to mind, but before I had summoned up courage to whistle—it used to be said that at the sound of a whistle old Professor —— instantly broke into a gallop—the venerable congregation had gone inside. The outside of the chapel remained. As you know, its high domes and pinnacles can be seen, like a sailing-ship always voyaging never arriving, lit up at night and visible for miles, far away across the hills. Once, presumably, this quadrangle with its smooth lawns, its massive buildings, and the chapel itself was marsh too, where the grasses waved and the swine rootled. Teams of horses and oxen, I thought, must have hauled the stone in wagons from far countries, and then with infinite labour the grey blocks in whose shade I was now standing were poised in order one on top of another, and then the painters brought their glass for the windows, and the masons were busy for centuries[9] up on that roof with putty and cement, spade and trowel. Every Saturday somebody must have poured gold and silver out of a leathern purse into their ancient fists, for they had their beer and skittles presumably of an evening. An unending stream of gold and silver, I thought, must have flowed into this court perpetually to keep the stones coming and the masons working; to level, to ditch, to dig and to drain. But it was then the age of faith, and money was poured liberally to set these stones on a deep foundation, and when the stones were raised, still more money was poured in from the coffers of kings and queens and great nobles to ensure that hymns should be sung here and scholars taught. Lands were granted; tithes were paid. And when the age of faith was over and the age of reason had come, still the same flow of gold and silver went on; fellowships were founded; lectureships endowed; only the gold and silver flowed now, not from the coffers of the king, but from the chests of merchants and manufacturers, from the purses of men who had made, say, a fortune from industry, and returned, in their wills, a bounteous share of it to endow more chairs, more lectureships, more fellowships in the university where they had learnt their craft. Hence the libraries and laboratories; the observatories; the splendid equipment of costly and delicate instruments which now stands on glass shelves, where centuries ago the grasses waved and the swine rootled. Certainly, as I strolled round the court, the foundation of gold and silver seemed deep enough; the pavement laid solidly over the wild grasses. Men with trays on their heads went busily from staircase to staircase. Gaudy blossoms flowered in window-boxes. The strains of the gramophone blared out from the rooms within. It was impossible not to reflect—the reflection whatever it may have been was cut short. The clock struck. It was time to find one's way to luncheon.

It is a curious fact that novelists have a way of making us believe that luncheon parties are invariably memorable for something very witty that was said, or for

8. One of the busiest streets in London, the main artery between the city and the West End.
9. Just over one century: King's College Chapel at Cambridge was built from 1446 to 1547. The college guidebook attributes its superb craftsmanship to the work of four master masons: Reginald Ely, John Wolrich, Simon Clerk, and John Wastell.

something very wise that was done. But they seldom spare a word for what was eaten. It is part of the novelist's convention not to mention soup and salmon and ducklings, as if soup and salmon and ducklings were of no importance whatsoever, as if nobody ever smoked a cigar or drank a glass of wine. Here, however, I shall take the liberty to defy that convention and to tell you that the lunch on this occasion began with soles, sunk in a deep dish, over which the college cook had spread a counterpane of the whitest cream, save that it was branded here and there with brown spots like the spots on the flanks of a doe. After that came the partridges, but if this suggests a couple of bald, brown birds on a plate you are mistaken. The partridges, many and various, came with all their retinue of sauces and salads, the sharp and the sweet, each in its order; their potatoes, thin as coins but not so hard; their sprouts, foliated as rosebuds but more succulent. And no sooner had the roast and its retinue been done with than the silent serving-man, the Beadle himself perhaps in a milder manifestation, set before us, wreathed in napkins, a confection which rose all sugar from the waves. To call it pudding and so relate it to rice and tapioca would be an insult. Meanwhile the wineglasses had flushed yellow and flushed crimson; had been emptied; had been filled. And thus by degrees was lit, halfway down the spine, which is the seat of the soul, not that hard little electric light which we call brilliance, as it pops in and out upon our lips, but the more profound, subtle and subterranean glow, which is the rich yellow flame of rational intercourse. No need to hurry. No need to sparkle. No need to be anybody but oneself. We are all going to heaven and Vandyck[1] is of the company—in other words, how good life seemed, how sweet its rewards, how trivial this grudge or that grievance, how admirable friendship and the society of one's kind, as, lighting a good cigarette, one sunk among the cushions in the window-seat.

If by good luck there had been an ash-tray handy, if one had not knocked the ash out of the window in default, if things had been a little different from what they were, one would not have seen, presumably, a cat without a tail. The sight of that abrupt and truncated animal padding softly across the quadrangle changed by some fluke of the subconscious intelligence the emotional light for me. It was as if some one had let fall a shade. Perhaps the excellent hock was relinquishing its hold. Certainly, as I watched the Manx cat pause in the middle of the lawn as if it too questioned the universe, something seemed lacking, something seemed different. But what was lacking, what was different, I asked myself, listening to the talk. And to answer that question I had to think myself out of the room, back into the past, before the war indeed, and to set before my eyes the model of another luncheon party held in rooms not very far distant from these; but different. Everything was different. Meanwhile the talk went on among the guests, who were many and young, some of this sex, some of that; it went on swimmingly, it went on agreeably, freely, amusingly. And as it went on I set it against the background of that other talk, and as I matched the two together I had no doubt that one was the descendant, the legitimate heir of the other. Nothing was changed; nothing was different save only—here I listened with all my ears not entirely to what was being said, but to the murmur or current behind it. Yes, that was it—the change was there. Before the war at a luncheon party like this people

---

1. The Flemish portrait painter Sir Anthony Van Dyck (1599–1641), who was appointed court painter by Charles I of England in 1632 and painted many portraits of the royal family and the nobility.

would have said precisely the same things but they would have sounded different, because in those days they were accompanied by a sort of humming noise, not articulate, but musical, exciting, which changed the value of the words themselves. Could one set that humming noise to words? Perhaps with the help of the poets one could. A book lay beside me and, opening it, I turned casually enough to Tennyson.[2] And here I found Tennyson was singing:

> There has fallen a splendid tear
>   From the passion-flower at the gate.
> She is coming, my dove, my dear;
>   She is coming, my life, my fate;
> The red rose cries, "She is near, she is near";
>   And the white rose weeps, "She is late";
> The larkspur listens, "I hear, I hear";
>   And the lily whispers, "I wait."

Was that what men hummed at luncheon parties before the war? And the women?

> My heart is like a singing bird
>   Whose nest is in a water'd shoot;
> My heart is like an apple tree
>   Whose boughs are bent with thick-set fruit;
> My heart is like a rainbow shell
>   That paddles in a halcyon sea;
> My heart is gladder than all these
>   Because my love is come to me.[3]

Was that what women hummed at luncheon parties before the war?

There was something so ludicrous in thinking of people humming such things even under their breath at luncheon parties before the war that I burst out laughing, and had to explain my laughter by pointing at the Manx cat, who did look a little absurd, poor beast, without a tail, in the middle of the lawn. Was he really born so, or had he lost his tail in an accident? The tailless cat, though some are said to exist in the Isle of Man, is rarer than one thinks. It is a queer animal, quaint rather than beautiful. It is strange what a difference a tail makes—you know the sort of things one says as a lunch party breaks up and people are finding their coats and hats.

This one, thanks to the hospitality of the host, had lasted far into the afternoon. The beautiful October day was fading and the leaves were falling from the trees in the avenue as I walked through it. Gate after gate seemed to close with gentle finality behind me. Innumerable beadles were fitting innumerable keys into well-oiled locks; the treasure-house was being made secure for another night. After the avenue one comes out upon a road—I forget its name—which leads you, if you take the right turning, along to Fernham. But there was plenty of time. Dinner was not till half-past seven. One could almost do without dinner after such a luncheon. It is strange how a scrap of poetry works in the mind and makes the legs move in time to it along the road. Those words

2. Alfred, Lord Tennyson (1809–1892); a passage from his long poem *Maud* (1855) follows.

3. The first stanza of "A Birthd⸗ poem by Christina Rossetti (1830–

> *There has fallen a splendid tear*
> *From the passion-flower at the gate.*
> *She is coming, my dove, my dear—*

sang in my blood as I stepped quickly along towards Headingley.[4] And then, switching off into the other measure, I sang, where the waters are churned up by the weir:

> *My heart is like a singing bird*
> *Whose nest is in a water'd shoot;*
> *My heart is like an apple tree . . .*

What poets, I cried aloud, as one does in the dusk, what poets they were!

In a sort of jealousy, I suppose, for our own age, silly and absurd though these comparisons are, I went on to wonder if honestly one could name two living poets now as great as Tennyson and Christina Rossetti were then. Obviously it is impossible, I thought, looking into those foaming waters, to compare them. The very reason why the poetry excites one to such abandonment, such rapture, is that it celebrates some feeling that one used to have (at luncheon parties before the war perhaps), so that one responds easily, familiarly, without troubling to check the feeling, or to compare it with any that one has now. But the living poets express a feeling that is actually being made and torn out of us at the moment. One does not recognize it in the first place; often for some reason one fears it; one watches it with keenness and compares it jealously and suspiciously with the old feeling that one knew. Hence the difficulty of modern poetry; and it is because of this difficulty that one cannot remember more than two consecutive lines of any good modern poet. For this reason—that my memory failed me—the argument flagged for want of material. But why, I continued, moving on towards Headingley, have we stopped humming under our breath at luncheon parties? Why has Alfred ceased to sing

> *She is coming, my dove, my dear?*

Why has Christina ceased to respond

> *My heart is gladder than all these*
> *Because my love is come to me?*

Shall we lay the blame on the war? When the guns fired in August 1914, did the faces of men and women show so plain in each other's eyes that romance was killed? Certainly it was a shock (to women in particular with their illusions about education, and so on) to see the faces of our rulers in the light of the shell-fire. So ugly they looked—German, English, French—so stupid. But lay the blame where one will, on whom one will, the illusion which inspired Tennyson and Christina Rossetti to sing so passionately about the coming of their loves is far rarer now than then. One has only to read, to look, to listen, to remember. But why say "blame"? Why, if it was an illusion, not praise the catastrophe, whatever it was, that destroyed illusion and put truth in its place? For truth . . . those dots mark the spot where, in search of truth, I missed the

4. In Leeds (Yorkshire).

turning up to Fernham. Yes indeed, which was truth and which was illusion, I asked myself. What was the truth about these houses, for example, dim and festive now with their red windows in the dusk, but raw and red and squalid, with their sweets and their boot-laces, at nine o'clock in the morning? And the willows and the river and the gardens that run down to the river, vague now with the mist stealing over them, but gold and red in the sunlight—which was the truth, which was the illusion about them? I spare you the twists and turns of my cogitations, for no conclusion was found on the road to Headingley, and I ask you to suppose that I soon found out my mistake about the turning and retraced my steps to Fernham.

As I have said already that it was an October day, I dare not forfeit your respect and imperil the fair name of fiction by changing the season and describing lilacs hanging over garden walls, crocuses, tulips and other flowers of spring. Fiction must stick to facts, and the truer the facts the better the fiction—so we are told. Therefore it was still autumn and the leaves were still yellow and falling, if anything, a little faster than before, because it was now evening (seven twenty-three to be precise) and a breeze (from the southwest to be exact) had risen. But for all that there was something odd at work:

> My heart is like a singing bird
> Whose nest is in a water'd shoot;
> My heart is like an apple tree
> Whose boughs are bent with thick-set fruit—

perhaps the words of Christina Rossetti were partly responsible for the folly of the fancy—it was nothing of course but a fancy—that the lilac was shaking its flowers over the garden walls, and the brimstone butterflies were scudding hither and thither, and the dust of the pollen was in the air. A wind blew, from what quarter I know not, but it lifted the half-grown leaves so that there was a flash of silver grey in the air. It was the time between the lights when colours undergo their intensification and purples and golds burn in window-panes like the beat of an excitable heart; when for some reason the beauty of the world revealed and yet soon to perish (here I pushed into the garden, for, unwisely, the door was left open and no beadles seemed about), the beauty of the world which is so soon to perish, has two edges, one of laughter, one of anguish, cutting the heart asunder. The gardens of Fernham lay before me in the spring twilight, wild and open, and in the long grass, sprinkled and carelessly flung, were daffodils and bluebells, not orderly perhaps at the best of times, and now wind-blown and waving as they tugged at their roots. The windows of the building, curved like ships' windows among generous waves of red brick, changed from lemon to silver under the flight of the quick spring clouds. Somebody was in a hammock, somebody, but in this light they were phantoms only, half guessed, half seen, raced across the grass—would no one stop her?—and then on the terrace, as if popping out to breathe the air, to glance at the garden, came a bent figure, formidable yet humble, with her great forehead and her shabby dress—could it be the famous scholar, could it be J—— H—— herself?[5]

5. Jane Harrison (1850–1928), English classical scholar, fellow, and lecturer at Newnham College, and author of *Prolegomena to the Study* *of Greek Religion* (1903) and *Ancient Art and Ritual* (1913).

All was dim, yet intense too, as if the scarf which the dusk had flung over the garden were torn asunder by star or sword—the flash of some terrible reality leaping, as its way is, out of the heart of the spring. For youth——

Here was my soup. Dinner was being served in the great dining-hall. Far from being spring it was in fact an evening in October. Everybody was assembled in the big dining-room. Dinner was ready. Here was the soup. It was a plain gravy soup. There was nothing to stir the fancy in that. One could have seen through the transparent liquid any pattern that there might have been on the plate itself. But there was no pattern. The plate was plain. Next came beef with its attendant greens and potatoes—a homely trinity, suggesting the rumps of cattle in a muddy market, and sprouts curled and yellowed at the edge, and bargaining and cheapening, and women with string bags on Monday morning. There was no reason to complain of human nature's daily food, seeing that the supply was sufficient and coal-miners doubtless were sitting down to less. Prunes and custard followed. And if any one complains that prunes, even when mitigated by custard, are an uncharitable vegetable (fruit they are not), stringy as a miser's heart and exuding a fluid such as might run in misers' veins who have denied themselves wine and warmth for eighty years and yet not given to the poor, he should reflect that there are people whose charity embraces even the prune. Biscuits and cheese came next, and here the water-jug was liberally passed round, for it is the nature of biscuits to be dry, and these were biscuits to the core. That was all. The meal was over. Everybody scraped their chairs back; the swing-doors swung violently to and fro; soon the hall was emptied of every sign of food and made ready no doubt for breakfast next morning. Down corridors and up staircases the youth of England went banging and singing. And was it for a guest, a stranger (for I had no more right here in Fernham than in Trinity or Somerville or Girton or Newnham or Christchurch), to say, "The dinner was not good," or to say (we were now, Mary Seton and I, in her sitting-room), "Could we not have dined up here alone?" for if I had said anything of the kind I should have been prying and searching into the secret economies of a house which to the stranger wears so fine a front of gaiety and courage. No, one could say nothing of the sort. Indeed, conversation for a moment flagged. The human frame being what it is, heart, body and brain all mixed together, and not contained in separate compartments as they will be no doubt in another million years, a good dinner is of great importance to good talk. One cannot think well, love well, sleep well, if one has not dined well. The lamp in the spine does not light on beef and prunes. We are all *probably* going to heaven, and Vandyck is, we *hope*, to meet us round the next corner—that is the dubious and qualifying state of mind that beef and prunes at the end of the day's work breed between them. Happily my friend, who taught science, had a cupboard where there was a squat bottle and little glasses—(but there should have been sole and partridge to begin with)—so that we were able to draw up to the fire and repair some of the damages of the day's living. In a minute or so we were slipping freely in and out among all those objects of curiosity and interest which form in the mind in the absence of a particular person, and are naturally to be discussed on coming together again—how somebody has married, another has not; one thinks this, another that; one has improved out of all knowledge, the other most amazingly gone to the bad—with all those speculations upon human nature and the character of the amazing world we live in which spring naturally from such beginnings. While these things were being said, however, I became shamefacedly aware of a current setting in of its own accord and carrying everything forward to an end of its own. One might be talking of Spain or Portugal, of book or racehorse, but the real interest of whatever was said was none of those things, but a scene of masons on a high roof some five centuries ago. Kings and nobles brought treasure in huge sacks and poured it under the earth. This scene was for ever coming alive in my mind and placing itself by another of lean cows and a muddy market and withered greens and the stringy hearts of old men—these two pictures, disjointed and disconnected and nonsensical as they were, were for ever coming together and combating each other and had me entirely at their mercy. The best course, unless the whole talk was to be distorted, was to expose what was in my mind to the air, when with good luck it would fade and crumble like the head of the dead king when they opened the coffin at Windsor.[6] Briefly, then, I told Miss Seton about the masons who had been all those years on the roof of the chapel, and about the kings and queens and nobles bearing sacks of gold and silver on their shoulders, which they shovelled into the earth; and then how the great financial magnates of our own time came and laid cheques and bonds, I suppose, where the others had laid ingots and rough lumps of gold. All that lies beneath the colleges down there, I said; but this college, where we are now sitting, what lies beneath its gallant red brick and the wild unkempt grasses of the garden? What force is behind the plain china off which we dined, and (here it popped out of my mouth before I could stop it) the beef, the custard and the prunes?

Well, said Mary Seton, about the year 1860—Oh, but you know the story, she said, bored, I suppose, by the recital. And she told me—rooms were hired. Committees met. Envelopes were addressed. Circulars were drawn up. Meetings were held; letters were read out; so-and-so has promised so much; on the contrary, Mr. —— won't give a penny. The *Saturday Review* has been very rude. How can we raise a fund to pay for offices? Shall we hold a bazaar? Can't we find a pretty girl to sit in the front row? Let us look up what John Stuart Mill said on the subject. Can any one persuade the editor of the —— to print a letter? Can we get Lady —— to sign it? Lady —— is out of town. That was the way it was done, presumably, sixty years ago, and it was a prodigious effort, and a great deal of time was spent on it. And it was only after a long struggle and with the utmost difficulty that they got thirty thousand pounds together.[7] So obviously we cannot have wine and partridges and servants carrying tin dishes on their heads, she said. We cannot have sofas and separate rooms. "The amenities," she said, quoting from some book or other, "will have to wait."[8]

At the thought of all those women working year after year and finding it hard to get two thousand pounds together, and as much as they could do to get thirty thousand pounds, we burst out in scorn at the reprehensible poverty of our sex.

6. At the royal residence of Windsor Castle, nine English kings are buried in two chapels serving as royal mausoleums.
7. "We are told that we ought to ask for £30,000 at least. . . . It is not a large sum, considering that there is to be but one college of this sort for Great Britain, Ireland and the Colonies, and considering how easy it is to raise immense sums for boys' schools. But considering how few people really wish women to be educated, it is a good deal."—Lady Stephen, *Life of Miss Emily Davies* [Woolf's note].
8. "Every penny which could be scraped together was set aside for building, and the amenities had to be postponed."—R. Strachey, *The Cause* [Woolf's note].

What had our mothers been doing then that they had no wealth to leave us? Powdering their noses? Looking in at shop windows? Flaunting in the sun at Monte Carlo? There were some photographs on the mantel-piece. Mary's mother—if that was her picture—may have been a wastrel in her spare time (she had thirteen children by a minister of the church), but if so her gay and dissipated life had left too few traces of its pleasures on her face. She was a homely body; an old lady in a plaid shawl which was fastened by a large cameo; and she sat in a basket-chair, encouraging a spaniel to look at the camera, with the amused, yet strained expression of one who is sure that the dog will move directly the bulb is pressed. Now if she had gone into business; had become a manufacturer of artificial silk or a magnate on the Stock Exchange; if she had left two or three hundred thousand pounds to Fernham, we could have been sitting at our ease tonight and the subject of our talk might have been archaeology, botany, anthropology, physics, the nature of the atom, mathematics, astronomy, relativity, geography. If only Mrs Seton and her mother and her mother before her had learnt the great art of making money and had left their money, like their fathers and their grandfathers before them, to found fellowships and lectureships and prizes and scholarships appropriated to the use of their own sex, we might have dined very tolerably up here alone off a bird and a bottle of wine; we might have looked forward without undue confidence to a pleasant and honourable lifetime spent in the shelter of one of the liberally endowed professions. We might have been exploring or writing; mooning about the venerable places of the earth; sitting contemplative on the steps of the Parthenon, or going at ten to an office and coming home comfortably at half-past four to write a little poetry. Only, if Mrs Seton and her like had gone into business at the age of fifteen, there would have been—that was the snag in the argument—no Mary. What, I asked, did Mary think of that? There between the curtains was the October night, calm and lovely, with a star or two caught in the yellowing trees. Was she ready to resign her share of it and her memories (for they had been a happy family, though a large one) of games and quarrels up in Scotland, which she is never tired of praising for the fineness of its air and the quality of its cakes, in order that Fernham might have been endowed with fifty thousand pounds or so by a stroke of the pen? For, to endow a college would necessitate the suppression of families altogether. Making a fortune and bearing thirteen children—no human being could stand it. Consider the facts, we said. First there are nine months before the baby is born. Then the baby is born. Then there are three or four months spent in feeding the baby. After the baby is fed there are certainly five years spent in playing with the baby. You cannot, it seems, let children run about the streets. People who have seen them running wild in Russia say that the sight is not a pleasant one. People say, too, that human nature takes its shape in the years between one and five. If Mrs Seton, I said, had been making money, what sort of memories would you have had of games and quarrels? What would you have known of Scotland, and its fine air and cakes and all the rest of it? But it is useless to ask these questions, because you would never have come into existence at all. Moreover, it is equally useless to ask what might have happened if Mrs Seton and her mother and her mother before her had amassed great wealth and laid it under the foundations of college and library, because, in the first place, to earn money was impossible for them, and in the second, had it been possible, the law denied them the right to possess what money they earned. It is only for the last forty-eight years that Mrs Seton has had a penny of her own. For all the centuries before that it would have been her husband's property—a thought which, perhaps, may have had its share in keeping Mrs Seton and her mothers off the Stock Exchange. Every penny I earn, they may have said, will be taken from me and disposed of according to my husband's wisdom—perhaps to found a scholarship or to endow a fellowship in Balliol or Kings,[9] so that to earn money, even if I could earn money, is not a matter that interests me very greatly. I had better leave it to my husband.

At any rate, whether or not the blame rested on the old lady who was looking at the spaniel, there could be no doubt that for some reason or other our mothers had mismanaged their affairs very gravely. Not a penny could be spared for "amenities"; for partridges and wine, beadles and turf, books and cigars, libraries and leisure. To raise bare walls out of the bare earth was the utmost they could do.

So we talked standing at the window and looking, as so many thousands look every night, down on the domes and towers of the famous city beneath us. It was very beautiful, very mysterious in the autumn moonlight. The old stone looked very white and venerable. One thought of all the books that were assembled down there; of the pictures of old prelates and worthies hanging in the panelled rooms; of the painted windows that would be throwing strange globes and crescents on the pavement; of the tablets and memorials and inscriptions; of the fountains and the grass; of the quiet rooms looking across the quiet quadrangles. And (pardon me the thought) I thought, too, of the admirable smoke and drink and the deep armchairs and the pleasant carpets: of the urbanity, the geniality, the dignity which are the offspring of luxury and privacy and space. Certainly our mothers had not provided us with anything comparable to all this—our mothers who found it difficult to scrape together thirty thousand pounds, our mothers who bore thirteen children to ministers of religion at St Andrews.[1]

So I went back to my inn, and as I walked through the dark streets I pondered this and that, as one does at the end of the day's work. I pondered why it was that Mrs Seton had no money to leave us; and what effect poverty has on the mind; and what effect wealth has on the mind; and I thought of the queer old gentlemen I had seen that morning with tufts of fur upon their shoulders; and I remembered how if one whistled one of them ran; and I thought of the organ booming in the chapel and of the shut doors of the library; and I thought how unpleasant it is to be locked out; and I thought how it is worse perhaps to be locked in; and, thinking of the safety and prosperity of the one sex and of the poverty and insecurity of the other and of the effect of tradition and of the lack of tradition upon the mind of a writer, I thought at last that it was time to roll up the crumpled skin of the day, with its arguments and its impressions and its anger and its laughter, and cast it into the hedge. A thousand stars were flashing across the blue wastes of the sky. One seemed alone with an inscrutable society. All human beings were laid asleep—prone, horizontal, dumb.

9. I.e., King's College, Cambridge. "Balliol": Balliol College, Oxford.
1. Probably St. Andrew's in Holborn, an old London church rebuilt under the famous architect Sir Christopher Wren during 1683–95.

Nobody seemed stirring in the streets of Oxbridge. Even the door of the hotel sprang open at the touch of an invisible hand—not a boots was sitting up to light me to bed, it was so late.

CHAPTER 2

The scene, if I may ask you to follow me, was now changed. The leaves were still falling, but in London now, not Oxbridge; and I must ask you to imagine a room, like many thousands, with a window looking across people's hats and vans and motor-cars to other windows, and on the table inside the room a blank sheet of paper on which was written in large letters WOMEN AND FICTION, but no more. The inevitable sequel to lunching and dining at Oxbridge seemed, unfortunately, to be a visit to the British Museum. One must strain off what was personal and accidental in all these impressions and so reach the pure fluid, the essential oil of truth. For that visit to Oxbridge and the luncheon and the dinner had started a swarm of questions. Why did men drink wine and women water? Why was one sex so prosperous and the other so poor? What effect has poverty on fiction? What conditions are necessary for the creation of works of art?—a thousand questions at once suggested themselves. But one needed answers, not questions; and an answer was only to be had by consulting the learned and the unprejudiced, who have removed themselves above the strife of tongue and the confusion of body and issued the result of their reasoning and research in books which are to be found in the British Museum. If truth is not to be found on the shelves of the British Museum, where, I asked myself, picking up a notebook and a pencil, is truth?

Thus provided, thus confident and enquiring, I set out in the pursuit of truth. The day, though not actually wet, was dismal, and the streets in the neighborhood of the Museum were full of open coal-holes, down which sacks were showering; four-wheeled cabs were drawing up and depositing on the pavement corded boxes containing, presumably, the entire wardrobe of some Swiss or Italian family seeking fortune or refuge or some other desirable commodity which is to be found in the boarding-houses of Bloomsbury[2] in the winter. The usual hoarse-voiced men paraded the streets with plants on barrows. Some shouted; others sang. London was like a workshop. London was like a machine. We were all being shot backwards and forwards on this plain foundation to make some pattern. The British Museum was another department of the factory. The swing-doors swung open; and there one stood under the vast dome, as if one were a thought in the huge bald forehead which is so splendidly encircled by a band of famous names.[3] One went to the counter; one took a slip of paper; one opened a volume of the catalogue, and . . . . . the five dots here indicate five separate minutes of stupefaction, wonder and bewilderment. Have you any notion how many books are written about women in the course of one year? Have you any notion how many are written by men?

---

2. A residential and academic borough in London, site of the British Museum and various educational institutions.
3. The names of famous men, including Chaucer, Spenser, Shakespeare, Milton, Pope, Wordsworth, Byron, Carlyle, and Tennyson, are painted in a circle around the dome of the Reading Room at the British Museum.

Are you aware that you are, perhaps, the most discussed animal in the universe? Here had I come with a notebook and a pencil proposing to spend a morning reading, supposing that at the end of the morning I should have transferred the truth to my notebook. But I should need to be a herd of elephants, I thought, and a wilderness of spiders, desperately referring to the animals that are reputed longest lived and most multitudinously eyed, to cope with all this. I should need claws of steel and beak of brass even to penetrate the husk. How shall I ever find the grains of truth embedded in all this mass of paper, I asked myself, and in despair began running my eye up and down the long list of titles. Even the names of the books gave me food for thought. Sex and its nature might well attract doctors and biologists; but what was surprising and difficult of explanation was the fact that sex—woman, that is to say—also attracts agreeable essayists, light-fingered novelists, young men who have taken the M.A. degree; men who have taken no degree; men who have no apparent qualification save that they are not women. Some of these books were, on the face of it, frivolous and facetious; but many, on the other hand, were serious and prophetic, moral and hortatory. Merely to read the titles suggested innumerable schoolmasters, innumerable clergymen mounting their platforms and pulpits and holding forth with a loquacity which far exceeded the hour usually allotted to such discourse on this one subject. It was a most strange phenomenon; and apparently—here I consulted the letter M—one confined to male sex. Women do not write books about men—a fact that I could not help welcoming with relief, for if I had first to read all that men have written about women, then all that women have written about men, the aloe that flowers once in a hundred years would flower twice before I could set pen to paper. So, making a perfectly arbitrary choice of a dozen volumes or so, I sent my slips of paper to lie in the wire tray, and waited in my stall, among the other seekers for the essential oil of truth.

What could be the reason, then, of this curious disparity, I wondered, drawing cart-wheels on the slips of paper provided by the British taxpayer for other purposes. Why are women, judging from this catalogue, so much more interesting to men than men are to women? A very curious fact it seemed, and my mind wandered to picture the lives of men who spend their time in writing books about women; whether they were old or young, married or unmarried, red-nosed or humpbacked—anyhow, it was flattering, vaguely, to feel oneself the object of such attention, provided that it was not entirely bestowed by the crippled and the infirm—so I pondered until all such frivolous thoughts were ended by an avalanche of books sliding down on to the desk in front of me. Now the trouble began. The student who has been trained in research at Oxbridge has no doubt some method of shepherding his question past all distractions till it runs into its answer as a sheep runs into its pen. The student by my side, for instance, who was copying assiduously from a scientific manual was, I felt sure, extracting pure nuggets of the essential ore every ten minutes or so. His little grunts of satisfaction indicated so much. But if, unfortunately, one has had no training in a university, the question far from being shepherded to its pen flies like a frightened flock hither and thither, helter-skelter, pursued by a whole pack of hounds. Professors, schoolmasters, sociologists, clergymen, novelists, essayists, journalists, men who had no qualification save that they were not women, chased my simple and single question—Why are women poor?—until it became fifty questions; until the fifty questions leapt frantically into mid-stream and were carried away. Every page in my notebook was scribbled over with notes. To show the state of mind I was in, I will read you a few of them, explaining that the page was headed quite simply, WOMEN AND POVERTY, in block letters; but what followed was something like this:

> Condition in Middle Ages of,
> Habits in the Fiji Islands of,
> Worshipped as goddesses by,
> Weaker in moral sense than,
> Idealism of,
> Greater conscientiousness of,
> South Sea Islanders, age of puberty among,
> Attractiveness of,
> Offered as sacrifice to,
> Small size of brain of,
> Profounder sub-consciousness of,
> Less hair on the body of,
> Mental, moral and physical inferiority of,
> Love of children of,
> Greater length of life of,
> Weaker muscles of,
> Strength of affections of,
> Vanity of,
> Higher education of,
> Shakespeare's opinion of,
> Lord Birkenhead's opinion of,
> Dean Inge's opinion of,
> La Bruyère's opinion of,
> Dr. Johnson's opinion of,
> Mr. Oscar Browning's[4] opinion of, . . .

Here I drew breath and added, indeed, in the margin, Why does Samuel Butler[5] say, "Wise men never say what they think of women"? Wise men never say anything else apparently. But, I continued, leaning back in my chair and looking at the vast dome in which I was a single but by now somewhat harassed thought, what is so unfortunate is that wise men never think the same thing about women. Here is Pope:[6]

---

4. A schoolmaster and later fellow of King's College, Cambridge (1837–1923); anecdotes about his strong opinions (see p. 391) were published in a 1927 biography. The first earl of Birkenhead, F. E. Smith (1872–1930), a conservative politician who opposed women's suffrage and praised the domestic "true functions of womanhood." William Ralph Inge (1860–1954), dean of St. Paul's Cathedral in London and a religious writer. Jean de La Bruyère (1645–1696), French moralist and author of

satirical *Characters* (1688), imitating the Greek writer Theophrastus. Samuel Johnson (1709–1784), author of moral essays and of the famous *A Dictionary of the English Language* (1747).
5. Satirical author (1835–1902) who wrote *Erewhon* (1872) and *The Way of All Flesh* (1903); his *Notebooks* are the source of this statement.
6. Alexander Pope (1688–1744), translator of Homer and author of *An Essay on Man* (1733–34) and the satirical *The Rape of the Lock* (1712–14).

Most women have no character at all.

And here is La Bruyère:

> Les femmes sont extrêmes; elles sont meilleures ou pires que les hommes—[7]

a direct contradiction by keen observers who were contemporary. Are they capable of education or incapable? Napoleon thought them incapable.[8] Dr. Johnson thought the opposite.[9] Have they souls or have they not souls? Some savages say they have none. Others, on the contrary, maintain that women are half divine and worship them on that account.[1] Some sages hold that they are shallower in the brain; others that they are deeper in the consciousness. Goethe honoured them; Mussolini[2] despises them. Wherever one looked men thought about women and thought differently. It was impossible to make head or tail of it all, I decided, glancing with envy at the reader next door who was making the neatest abstracts, headed often with an A or a B or a C, while my own notebook rioted with the wildest scribble of contradictory jottings. It was distressing, it was bewildering, it was humiliating. Truth had run through my fingers. Every drop had escaped.

I could not possibly go home, I reflected, and add as a serious contribution to the study of women and fiction that women have less hair on their bodies than men, or that the age of puberty among the South Sea Islanders[3] is nine—or is it ninety?—even the handwriting had become in its distraction indecipherable. It was disgraceful to have nothing more weighty or respectable to show after a whole morning's work. And if I could not grasp the truth about W. (as for brevity's sake I had come to call her) in the past, why bother about W. in the future? It seemed pure waste of time to consult all those gentlemen who specialise in woman and her effect on whatever it may be—politics, children, wages, morality—numerous and learned as they are. One might as well leave their books unopened.

But while I pondered I had unconsciously, in my listlessness, in my desperation, been drawing a picture where I should, like my neighbour, have been writing a conclusion. I had been drawing a face, a figure. It was the face and

---

7. Women are extreme; they are better or worse than men (French).

8. Napoleon wrote: "What we ask of education is not that girls should think, but that they should believe. The weakness of women's brains, the instability of their ideas, the place they will fill in society, their need for perpetual resignation, and for an easy and generous type of charity—all this can only be met by religion" (notes written on May 15, 1807, concerning the establishment of a girl's school at Écouen).

9. "'Men know that women are an overmatch for them, and therefore they choose the weakest or the most ignorant. If they did not think so, they never could be afraid of women knowing as much as themselves.'. . . In justice to the sex, I think it but candid to acknowledge that, in a subsequent conversation, he told me that he was serious in what he said."—BOSWELL, *The Journal of a Tour to the Hebrides* [Woolf's note].

1. "The ancient Germans believed that there was something holy in women, and accordingly consulted them as oracles."—FRAZER, *Golden Bough* [Woolf's note].

2. Benito Mussolini (1883–1945), fascist dictator of Italy between 1922 and 1943. Johann Wolfgang von Goethe (1749–1832), German author of *Faust*. "The eternal feminine draws us along" is the last line of *Faust*, Part 2.

3. The native peoples of the islands in the south-central Pacific Ocean were the subject of several anthropological studies in the early 20th century, including Margaret Mead's widely read *Coming of Age in Samoa* (1928).

the figure of Professor von X. engaged in writing his monumental work entitled *The Mental, Moral, and Physical Inferiority of the Female Sex*.[4] He was not
in my picture a man attractive to women. He was heavily built; he had a great
jowl; to balance that he had very small eyes; he was very red in the face. His
expression suggested that he was labouring under some emotion that made
him jab his pen on the paper as if he were killing some noxious insect as he
wrote, but even when he had killed it that did not satisfy him; he must go on
killing it; and even so, some cause for anger and irritation remained. Could it
be his wife, I asked, looking at my picture. Was she in love with a cavalry officer? Was the cavalry officer slim and elegant and dressed in astrachan?[5] Had
he been laughed at, to adopt the Freudian theory, in his cradle by a pretty girl?
For even in his cradle the professor, I thought, could not have been an attractive child. Whatever the reason, the professor was made to look very angry and
very ugly in my sketch, as he wrote his great book upon the mental, moral and
physical inferiority of women. Drawing pictures was an idle way of finishing
an unprofitable morning's work. Yet it is in our idleness, in our dreams, that
the submerged truth sometimes comes to the top. A very elementary exercise
in psychology, not to be dignified by the name of psycho-analysis, showed me,
on looking at my notebook, that the sketch of the angry professor had been
made in anger. Anger had snatched my pencil while I dreamt. But what was
anger doing there? Interest, confusion, amusement, boredom—all these emotions I could trace and name as they succeeded each other throughout the
morning. Had anger, the black snake, been lurking among them? Yes, said
the sketch, anger had. It referred me unmistakably to the one book, to the
one phrase, which had roused the demon; it was the professor's statement
about the mental, moral and physical inferiority of women. My heart had
leapt. My cheeks had burnt. I had flushed with anger. There was nothing specially remarkable, however foolish, in that. One does not like to be told that
one is naturally the inferior of a little man—I looked at the student next me—
who breathes hard, wears a ready-made tie, and has not shaved this fortnight.
One has certain foolish vanities. It is only human nature, I reflected, and
began drawing cart-wheels and circles over the angry professor's face till he
looked like a burning bush or a flaming comet—anyhow, an apparition without human semblance or significance. The professor was nothing now but a
faggot burning on the top of Hampstead Heath.[6] Soon my own anger was
explained and done with; but curiosity remained. How explain the anger of the
professors? Why were they angry? For when it came to analysing the impression left by these books there was always an element of heat. This heat took
many forms; it showed itself in satire, in sentiment, in curiosity, in reproba-
tion. But there was another element which was often present and could not
immediately be identified. Anger, I called it. But it was anger that had gone
underground and mixed itself with all kinds of other emotions. To judge from
its odd effects, it was anger disguised and complex, not anger simple and open.

---

4. A fictional portrait, probably based on Otto
Weininger's *Sex and Character* (1906), that
distinguished between male (productive and
moral) and female (negative and amoral)
characteristics.
5. Curly lambskin.
6. A public open space in the village of Hampstead, in London. Faggot: a bundle of sticks.

Whatever the reason, all these books,[7] I thought, surveying the pile on the desk, are worthless for my purposes. They were worthless scientifically, that is to say, though humanly they were full of instruction, interest, boredom, and very queer facts about the habits of the Fiji Islanders. They had been written in the red light of emotion and not in the white light of truth. Therefore they must be returned to the central desk and restored each to his own cell in the enormous honeycomb. All that I had retrieved from that morning's work had been the one fact of anger. The professors—I lumped them together thus—were angry. But why, I asked myself, having returned the books, why, I repeated, standing under the colonnade among the pigeons and the prehistoric canoes, why are they angry? And, asking myself this question, I strolled off to find a place for luncheon. What is the real nature of what I call for the moment their anger? I asked. Here was a puzzle that would last all the time that it takes to be served with food in a small restaurant somewhere near the British Museum. Some previous luncher had left the lunch edition of the evening paper on a chair, and, waiting to be served, I began idly reading the headlines. A ribbon of very large letters ran across the page. Somebody had made a big score in South Africa. Lesser ribbons announced that Sir Austen Chamberlain was at Geneva.[8] A meat axe with human hair on it had been found in a cellar. Mr. Justice —— commented in the Divorce Courts upon the Shamelessness of Women. Sprinkled about the paper were other pieces of news. A film actress had been lowered from a peak in California and hung suspended in mid-air. The weather was going to be foggy. The most transient visitor to this planet, I thought, who picked up this paper could not fail to be aware, even from this scattered testimony, that England is under the rule of a patriarchy. Nobody in their senses could fail to detect the dominance of the professor. His was the power and the money and the influence. He was the proprietor of the paper and its editor and sub-editor. He was the Foreign Secretary and the Judge. He was the cricketer; he owned the race-horses and the yachts. He was the director of the company that pays two hundred per cent to its shareholders. He left millions to charities and colleges that were ruled by himself. He suspended the film actress in mid-air. He will decide if the hair on the meat axe is human; he it is who will acquit or convict the murderer, and hang him, or let him go free. With the exception of the fog he seemed to control everything. Yet he was angry. I knew that he was angry by this token. When I read what he wrote about women I thought, not of what he was saying, but of himself. When an arguer argues dispassionately he thinks only of the argument; and the reader cannot help thinking of the argument too. If he had written dispassionately about women, had used indisputable proofs to establish his argument and had shown no trace of wishing that the result should be one thing rather than another, one would not have been angry either. One would have accepted the fact, as one accepts the fact that a pea is green or a canary yellow. So be it, I should have said. But I had been angry because he was

---

7. E.g., *Fijian Society, or the Sociology and Psychology of the Fijians* (1921), by Reverend W. Deane, principal of a teachers' training college in Ndávuilévu, Fiji; and *The Hill Tribes of Fiji* (1922), by A. B. Brewster, a colonial functionary, mixed facts with interpretation. Reverend Deane remarks that "the amount of sexual immorality and promiscuous intercourse during the past forty years is appalling." Fiji is an island in the South Pacific (see n. 3, p. 1101).
8. The site of the League of Nations. Chamberlain was the British foreign secretary between 1924 and 1929.

angry. Yet it seemed absurd, I thought, turning over the evening paper, that a man with all this power should be angry. Or is anger, I wondered, somehow, the familiar, the attendant sprite on power? Rich people, for example, are often angry because they suspect that the poor want to seize their wealth. The professors, or patriarchs, as it might be more accurate to call them, might be angry for that reason partly, but partly for one that lies a little less obviously on the surface. Possibly they were not "angry" at all; often, indeed, they were admiring, devoted, exemplary in the relations of private life. Possibly when the professor insisted a little too emphatically upon the inferiority of women, he was concerned not with their inferiority, but with his own superiority. That was what he was protecting rather hot-headedly and with too much emphasis, because it was a jewel to him of the rarest price. Life for both sexes—and I looked at them, shouldering their way along the pavement—is arduous, difficult, a perpetual struggle. It calls for gigantic courage and strength. More than anything, perhaps, creatures of illusion as we are, it calls for confidence in oneself. Without self-confidence we are as babes in the cradle. And how can we generate this imponderable quality, which is yet so invaluable, most quickly? By thinking that other people are inferior to oneself. By feeling that one has some innate superiority—it may be wealth, or rank, a straight nose, or the portrait of a grandfather by Romney[9]—for there is no end to the pathetic devices of the human imagination—over other people. Hence the enormous importance to a patriarch who has to conquer, who has to rule, of feeling that great numbers of people, half the human race indeed, are by nature inferior to himself. It must indeed be one of the chief sources of his power. But let me turn the light of this observation on to real life, I thought. Does it help to explain some of those psychological puzzles that one notes in the margin of daily life? Does it explain my astonishment the other day when Z, most humane, most modest of men, taking up some book by Rebecca West[1] and reading a passage in it, exclaimed, "The arrant feminist! She says that men are snobs!" The exclamation, to me so surprising—for why was Miss West an arrant feminist for making a possibly true if uncomplimentary statement about the other sex?—was not merely the cry of wounded vanity; it was a protest against some infringement of his power to believe in himself. Women have served all these centuries as looking-glasses possessing the magic and delicious power of reflecting the figure of man at twice its natural size. Without that power probably the earth would still be swamp and jungle. The glories of all our wars would be unknown. We should still be scratching the outlines of deer on the remains of mutton bones and bartering flints for sheepskins or whatever simple ornament took our unsophisticated taste. Supermen[2] and Fingers of Destiny would never have existed. The Czar and the Kaiser would never have worn their crowns or lost them. Whatever may be their use in civilized societies, mirrors are essential to all violent and heroic action. That is why Napoleon and Mussolini both insist so emphatically upon the inferiority of women, for if they were not inferior, they would cease to enlarge. That serves to

9. George Romney (1734–1802), portrait painter of 18th-century British society.
1. Pseudonym of Cicely Isabel Andrews (1892–1983), British novelist and journalist.
2. Fascist politicians, such as Adolf Hitler (1889–1945) in Germany and Mussolini (1883–1945) in Italy, rationalized their aggressive policies by exploiting and distorting Friedrich Nietzsche's (1844–1900) concept of the *Übermensch*, or superior being (in *Thus Spake Zarathustra*, 1883–85).

explain in part the necessity that women so often are to men. And it serves to explain how restless they are under her criticism; how impossible it is for her to say to them this book is bad, this picture is feeble, or whatever it may be, without giving far more pain and rousing far more anger than a man would do who gave the same criticism. For if she begins to tell the truth, the figure in the looking-glass shrinks; his fitness for life is diminished. How is he to go on giving judgment, civilising natives, making laws, writing books, dressing up and speechifying at banquets, unless he can see himself at breakfast and at dinner at least twice the size he really is? So I reflected, crumbling my bread and stirring my coffee and now and again looking at the people in the street. The looking-glass vision is of supreme importance because it charges the vitality; it stimulates the nervous system. Take it away and man may die, like the drug fiend deprived of his cocaine. Under the spell of that illusion, I thought, looking out of the window, half the people on the pavement are striding to work. They put on their hats and coats in the morning under its agreeable rays. They start the day confident, braced, believing themselves desired at Miss Smith's tea party; they say to themselves as they go into the room, I am the superior of half the people here, and it is thus that they speak with that self-confidence, that self-assurance, which have had such profound consequences in public life and lead to such curious notes in the margin of the private mind.

But these contributions to the dangerous and fascinating subject of the psychology of the other sex—it is one, I hope, that you will investigate when you have five hundred a year of your own—were interrupted by the necessity of paying the bill. It came to five shillings and ninepence. I gave the waiter a ten-shilling note and he went to bring me change. There was another ten-shilling note in my purse; I noticed it, because it is a fact that still takes my breath away—the power of my purse to breed ten-shilling notes automatically. I open it and there they are. Society gives me chicken and coffee, bed and lodging, in return for a certain number of pieces of paper which were left me by an aunt, for no other reason than that I share her name.

My aunt, Mary Beton, I must tell you, died by a fall from her horse when she was riding out to take the air in Bombay. The news of my legacy reached me one night about the same time that the act was passed that gave votes to women.[3] A solicitor's letter fell into the post-box and when I opened it I found that she had left me five hundred pounds[4] a year for ever. Of the two—the vote and the money—the money, I own, seemed infinitely the more important. Before that I had made my living by cadging odd jobs from newspapers, by reporting a donkey show here or a wedding there; I had earned a few pounds by addressing envelopes, reading to old ladies, making artificial flowers, teaching the alphabet to small children in a kindergarten. Such were the chief occupations that were open to women before 1918. I need not, I am afraid, describe in any detail the hardness of the work, for you know perhaps women who have done it; nor the difficulty of living on the money when it was earned, for you may have tried. But what still remains with me as a worse infliction than either was the poison of fear and bitterness which those days bred in me. To begin with, always to be doing work that one did not wish to do, and to do it like a

---

3. Women were given the vote in 1918; the voting age for women was lowered from thirty to twenty-one in 1928.

4. Roughly $30,000 today.

slave, flattering and fawning, not always necessarily perhaps, but it seemed necessary and the stakes were too great to run risks; and then the thought of that one gift which it was death to hide[5]—a small one but dear to the possessor—perishing and with it myself, my soul—all this became like a rust eating away the bloom of the spring, destroying the tree at its heart. However, as I say, my aunt died; and whenever I change a ten-shilling note a little of that rust and corrosion is rubbed off; fear and bitterness go. Indeed, I thought, slipping the silver into my purse, it is remarkable, remembering the bitterness of those days, what a change of temper a fixed income will bring about. No force in the world can take from me my five hundred pounds. Food, house and clothing are mine for ever. Therefore not merely do effort and labour cease, but also hatred and bitterness. I need not hate any man; he cannot hurt me. I need not flatter any man; he has nothing to give me. So imperceptibly I found myself adopting a new attitude towards the other half of the human race. It was absurd to blame any class or any sex, as a whole. Great bodies of people are never responsible for what they do. They are driven by instincts which are not within their control. They too, the patriarchs, the professors, had endless difficulties, terrible drawbacks to contend with. Their education had been in some ways as faulty as my own. It had bred in them defects as great. True, they had money and power, but only at the cost of harbouring in their breasts an eagle, a vulture, for ever tearing the liver out and plucking at the lungs—the instinct for possession, the rage for acquisition which drives them to desire other people's fields and goods perpetually; to make frontiers and flags; battleships and poison gas; to offer up their own lives and their children's lives. Walk through the Admiralty Arch[6] (I had reached that monument), or any other avenue given up to trophies and cannon, and reflect upon the kind of glory celebrated there. Or watch in the spring sunshine the stockbroker and the great barrister going indoors to make money and more money and more money when it is a fact that five hundred pounds a year will keep one alive in the sunshine. These are unpleasant instincts to harbour, I reflected. They are bred of the conditions of life; of the lack of civilisation, I thought, looking at the statue of the Duke of Cambridge,[7] and in particular at the feathers in his cocked hat, with a fixity that they have scarcely ever received before. And, as I realised these drawbacks, by degrees fear and bitterness modified themselves into pity and toleration; and then in a year or two, pity and toleration went, and the greatest release of all came, which is freedom to think of things in themselves. That building, for example, do I like it or not? Is that picture beautiful or not? Is that in my opinion a good book or a bad? Indeed my aunt's legacy unveiled the sky to me, and substituted for the large and imposing figure of a gentleman, which Milton recommended for my perpetual adoration, a view of the open sky.

So thinking, so speculating, I found my way back to my house by the river. Lamps were being lit and an indescribable change had come over London since

---

5. From "When I Consider How My Light Is Spent" by John Milton (1608–1673): "And that one talent which is death to hide, / Lodged with me useless."
6. A triple arch in Trafalgar Square (London)
at the entrance to the Mall, erected in 1910.
7. An equestrian statue of the second duke of Cambridge (1819–1904), cousin of Queen Victoria, in the full dress uniform of a field marshal.

the morning hour. It was as if the great machine after labouring all day had made with our help a few yards of something very exciting and beautiful—a fiery fabric flashing with red eyes, a tawny monster roaring with hot breath. Even the wind seemed flung like a flag as it lashed the houses and rattled the hoardings.

In my little street, however, domesticity prevailed. The house painter was descending his ladder; the nursemaid was wheeling the perambulator carefully in and out back to nursery tea; the coal-heaver was folding his empty sacks on top of each other; the woman who keeps the green-grocer's shop was adding up the day's takings with her hands in red mittens. But so engrossed was I with the problem you have laid upon my shoulders that I could not see even these usual sights without referring them to one centre. I thought how much harder it is now than it must have been even a century ago to say which of these employments is the higher, the more necessary. Is it better to be a coal-heaver or a nursemaid; is the charwoman who has brought up eight children of less value to the world than the barrister who has made a hundred thousand pounds? It is useless to ask such questions; for nobody can answer them. Not only do the comparative values of charwomen and lawyers rise and fall from decade to decade, but we have no rods with which to measure them even as they are at the moment. I had been foolish to ask my professor to furnish me with "indisputable proofs" of this or that in his argument about women. Even if one could state the value of any one gift at the moment, those values will change; in a century's time very possibly they will have changed completely. Moreover, in a hundred years, I thought, reaching my own doorstep, women will have ceased to be the protected sex. Logically they will take part in all the activities and exertions that were once denied them. The nursemaid will heave coal. The shop-woman will drive an engine. All assumptions founded on the facts observed when women were the protected sex will have disappeared—as, for example (here a squad of soldiers marched down the street), that women and clergymen and gardeners live longer than other people. Remove that protection, expose them to the same exertions and activities, make them soldiers and sailors and engine-drivers and dock labourers, and will not women die off so much younger, so much quicker, than men that one will say, "I saw a woman today," as one used to say, "I saw an aeroplane." Anything may happen when womanhood has ceased to be a protected occupation, I thought, opening the door. But what bearing has all this upon the subject of my paper, Women and Fiction? I asked, going indoors.

CHAPTER 3

It was disappointing not to have brought back in the evening some important statement, some authentic fact. Women are poorer than men because—this or that. Perhaps now it would be better to give up seeking for the truth, and receiving on one's head an avalanche of opinion hot as lava, discoloured as dish-water. It would be better to draw the curtains; to shut out distractions; to light the lamp; to narrow the enquiry and to ask the historian, who records not opinions but facts, to describe under what conditions women lived, not throughout the ages, but in England, say in the time of Elizabeth.[8]

8. Queen of England from 1558 to 1603.

For it is a perennial puzzle why no woman wrote a word of that extraordinary literature when every other man, it seemed, was capable of song or sonnet. What were the conditions in which women lived, I asked myself; for fiction, imaginative work that is, is not dropped like a pebble upon the ground, as science may be; fiction is like a spider's web, attached ever so lightly perhaps, but still attached to life at all four corners. Often the attachment is scarcely perceptible; Shakespeare's plays, for instance, seem to hang there complete by themselves. But when the web is pulled askew, hooked up at the edge, torn in the middle, one remembers that these webs are not spun in mid-air by incorporeal creatures, but are the work of suffering human beings, and are attached to grossly material things, like health and money and the houses we live in.

I went, therefore, to the shelf where the histories stand and took down one of the latest, Professor Trevelyan's *History of England*.[9] Once more I looked up Women, found "position of," and turned to the pages indicated. "Wife-beating," I read, "was a recognised right of man, and was practised without shame by high as well as low. . . . Similarly," the historian goes on, "the daughter who refused to marry the gentleman of her parents' choice was liable to be locked up, beaten and flung about the room, without any shock being inflicted on public opinion. Marriage was not an affair of personal affection, but of family avarice, particularly in the 'chivalrous' upper classes. . . . Betrothal often took place while one or both of the parties was in the cradle, and marriage when they were scarcely out of the nurses' charge." That was about 1470, soon after Chaucer's[1] time. The next reference to the position of women is some two hundred years later, in the time of the Stuarts.[2] "It was still the exception for women of the upper and middle class to choose their own husbands, and when the husband had been assigned, he was lord and master, so far at least as law and custom could make him. Yet even so," Professor Trevelyan concludes, "neither Shakespeare's women nor those of authentic seventeenth-century memoirs, like the Verneys and the Hutchinsons,[3] seem wanting in personality and character." Certainly, if we consider it, Cleopatra must have had a way with her; Lady Macbeth,[4] one would suppose, had a will of her own; Rosalind, one might conclude, was an attractive girl. Professor Trevelyan is speaking no more than the truth when he remarks that Shakespeare's women do not seem wanting in personality and character. Not being a historian, one might go even further and say that women have burnt like beacons in all the works of all the poets from the beginning of time—Clytemnestra, Antigone, Cleopatra, Lady Macbeth, Phèdre, Cressida, Rosalind, Desdemona, the Duchess of Malfi,[5]

---

9. Published in London in 1926. References are to pages 260–61 and, later, to pages 436–37.
1. Geoffrey Chaucer (1340?–1400), author of *The Canterbury Tales* (1390–1400).
2. The British royal house from 1603 to 1714 (except for the Commonwealth interregnum of 1649–60).
3. F. P. Verney compiled *The Memoirs of the Verney Family during the Seventeenth Century* (1892–1899), and Lucy Hutchinson recounted her husband's life in *Memoirs of the Life of Colonel Hutchinson* (1806).

4. Heroine of Shakespeare's *Macbeth*. Cleopatra (69–30 B.C.E.), queen of Egypt and heroine of Shakespeare's *Antony and Cleopatra*.
5. Doomed heroine of John Webster's *The Duchess of Malfi* (ca. 1613). Clytemnestra is the heroine of Aeschylus's *Agamemnon* (458 B.C.E.). Antigone is the eponymous heroine of a 442 B.C.E. play by Sophocles. Phèdre is the heroine of Jean Racine's *Phèdre* (1677). Cressida, Rosalind, and Desdemona are heroines of Shakespeare's *Troilus and Cressida*, *As You Like It*, and *Othello*, respectively.

among the dramatists; then among the prose writers: Millamant, Clarissa, Becky Sharp, Anna Karenina, Emma Bovary, Madame de Guermantes[6]—the names flock to mind, nor do they recall women "lacking in personality and character." Indeed, if woman had no existence save in the fiction written by men, one would imagine her a person of the utmost importance; very various; heroic and mean; splendid and sordid; infinitely beautiful and hideous in the extreme; as great as a man, some think even greater.[7] But this is woman in fiction. In fact, as Professor Trevelyan points out, she was locked up, beaten and flung about the room.

A very queer, composite being thus emerges. Imaginatively she is of the highest importance; practically she is completely insignificant. She pervades poetry from cover to cover; she is all but absent from history. She dominates the lives of kings and conquerors in fiction; in fact she was the slave of any boy whose parents forced a ring upon her finger. Some of the most inspired words, some of the most profound thoughts in literature fall from her lips; in real life she could hardly read, could scarcely spell, and was the property of her husband.

It was certainly an odd monster that one made up by reading the historians first and the poets afterwards—a worm winged like an eagle; the spirit of life and beauty in a kitchen chopping up suet. But these monsters, however amusing to the imagination, have no existence in fact. What one must do to bring her to life was to think poetically and prosaically at one and the same moment, thus keeping in touch with fact—that she is Mrs. Martin, aged thirty-six, dressed in blue, wearing a black hat and brown shoes; but not losing sight of fiction either—that she is a vessel in which all sorts of spirits and forces are coursing and flashing perpetually. The moment, however, that one tries this method with the Elizabethan woman, one branch of illumination fails; one is held up by the scarcity of facts. One knows nothing detailed, nothing perfectly true and substantial about her. History scarcely mentions her. And I turned to Professor Trevelyan again to see what history meant to him. I found by looking at his chapter headings that it meant—

"The Manor Court and the Methods of Open-field Agriculture . . . The Cistercians and Sheep-farming . . . The Crusades . . . The University . . . The

---

6. A character in Marcel Proust's *Remembrance of Things Past* (*The Guermantes Way*, 1920–21). Millamant is the heroine of William Congreve's satirical comedy *The Way of the World* (1700). Clarissa is the eponymous heroine of Samuel Richardson's seven-volume epistolary novel (1747–48). Becky Sharp appears in William Thackeray's *Vanity Fair* (1847–48). Anna Karenina is the title character in a Leo Tolstoy novel (1875–77). Emma Bovary is the heroine of Gustave Flaubert's *Madame Bovary* (1856).

7. "It remains a strange and almost inexplicable fact that in Athena's city, where women were kept in almost Oriental suppression as odalisques or drudges, the stage should yet have produced figures like Clytemnestra and Cassandra, Atossa and Antigone, Phèdre and Medea, and all the other heroines who dominate play after play of the 'misogynist' Eurip-

ides. But the paradox of this world where in real life a respectable woman could hardly show her face alone in the street, and yet on the stage woman equals or surpasses man, has never been satisfactorily explained. In modern tragedy the same predominance exists. At all events, a very cursory survey of Shakespeare's work (similarly with Webster, though not with Marlowe or Jonson) suffices to reveal how this dominance, this initiative of women, persists from Rosalind to Lady Macbeth. So too in Racine; six of his tragedies bear their heroines' names; and what male characters of his shall we set against Hermione and Andromaque, Bérénice and Roxane, Phèdre and Athalie? So again with Ibsen; what men shall we match with Solveig and Nora, Hedda and Hilda Wangel and Rebecca West?"—F. L. Lucas, *Tragedy*, pp. 114–15 [Woolf's note].

House of Commons . . . The Hundred Years' War . . . The Wars of the Roses . . . The Renaissance Scholars . . . The Dissolution of the Monasteries . . . Agrarian and Religious Strife . . . The Origin of English Sea-power . . . The Armada . . ." and so on. Occasionally an individual woman is mentioned, an Elizabeth, or a Mary; a queen or a great lady. But by no possible means could middle-class women with nothing but brains and character at their command have taken part in any one of the great movements which, brought together, constitute the historian's view of the past. Nor shall we find her in any collection of anecdotes. Aubrey[8] hardly mentions her. She never writes her own life and scarcely keeps a diary; there are only a handful of her letters in existence. She left no plays or poems by which we can judge her. What one wants, I thought—and why does not some brilliant student at Newnham or Girton[9] supply it?—is a mass of information; at what age did she marry; how many children had she as a rule; what was her house like; had she a room to herself; did she do the cooking; would she be likely to have a servant? All these facts lie somewhere, presumably, in parish registers and account books; the life of the average Elizabethan woman must be scattered about somewhere, could one collect it and make a book of it. It would be ambitious beyond my daring, I thought, looking about the shelves for books that were not there, to suggest to the students of those famous colleges that they should re-write history, though I own that it often seems a little queer as it is, unreal, lop-sided; but why should they not add a supplement to history? calling it, of course, by some inconspicuous name so that women might figure there without impropriety? For one often catches a glimpse of them in the lives of the great, whisking away into the background, concealing, I sometimes think, a wink, a laugh, perhaps a tear. And, after all, we have lives enough of Jane Austen; it scarcely seems necessary to consider again the influence of the tragedies of Joanna Baillie[1] upon the poetry of Edgar Allan Poe; as for myself, I should not mind if the homes and haunts of Mary Russell Mitford were closed to the public for a century at least. But what I find deplorable, I continued, looking about the bookshelves again, is that nothing is known about women before the eighteenth century. I have no model in my mind to turn about this way and that. Here am I asking why women did not write poetry in the Elizabethan age, and I am not sure how they were educated; whether they were taught to write; whether they had sitting-rooms to themselves; how many women had children before they were twenty-one; what, in short, they did from eight in the morning till eight at night. They had no money evidently; according to Professor Trevelyan they were married whether they liked it or not before they were out of the nursery, at fifteen or sixteen very likely. It would have been extremely odd, even upon this showing, had one of them suddenly written the plays of Shakespeare, I concluded, and I thought of that old gentleman, who is dead now, but was a bishop, I think, who declared that it was impossible for any woman, past, present, or to come, to have the genius of Shakespeare. He wrote to the papers

8. John Aubrey (1626–1697), author of *Brief Lives*, which includes sketches of his famous contemporaries.
9. Woolf delivered her lectures at Newnham and Girton Colleges for women, part of Cambridge University since 1880 and 1873, respectively.
1. Joanna Baillie (1762–1851) was a poet and dramatist whose *Plays on the Passions* (1798–1812) were famous in her day.

about it. He also told a lady who applied to him for information that cats do not as a matter of fact go to heaven, though they have, he added, souls of a sort. How much thinking those old gentlemen used to save one! How the borders of ignorance shrank back at their approach! Cats do not go to heaven. Women cannot write the plays of Shakespeare.

Be that as it may, I could not help thinking, as I looked at the works of Shakespeare on the shelf, that the bishop was right at least in this; it would have been impossible, completely and entirely, for any woman to have written the plays of Shakespeare in the age of Shakespeare. Let me imagine, since facts are so hard to come by, what would have happened had Shakespeare had a wonderfully gifted sister, called Judith,[2] let us say. Shakespeare himself went, very probably—his mother was an heiress—to the grammar school, where he may have learnt Latin—Ovid, Virgil and Horace[3]—and the elements of grammar and logic. He was, it is well known, a wild boy who poached rabbits, perhaps shot a deer, and had, rather sooner than he should have done, to marry a woman in the neighbourhood, who bore him a child rather quicker than was right. That escapade sent him to seek his fortune in London. He had, it seemed, a taste for the theatre; he began by holding horses at the stage door. Very soon he got work in the theatre, became a successful actor, and lived at the hub of the universe, meeting everybody, knowing everybody, practising his art on the boards, exercising his wits in the streets, and even getting access to the palace of the queen. Meanwhile his extraordinarily gifted sister, let us suppose, remained at home. She was as adventurous, as imaginative, as agog to see the world as he was. But she was not sent to school. She had no chance of learning grammar and logic, let alone of reading Horace and Virgil. She picked up a book now and then, one of her brother's perhaps, and read a few pages. But then her parents came in and told her to mend the stockings or mind the stew and not moon about with books and papers. They would have spoken sharply but kindly, for they were substantial people who knew the conditions of life for a woman and loved their daughter—indeed, more likely than not she was the apple of her father's eye. Perhaps she scribbled some pages up in an apple loft on the sly, but was careful to hide them or set fire to them. Soon, however, before she was out of her teens, she was to be betrothed to the son of a neighbouring wool-stapler.[4] She cried out that marriage was hateful to her, and for that she was severely beaten by her father. Then he ceased to scold her. He begged her instead not to hurt him, not to shame him in this matter of her marriage. He would give her a chain of beads or a fine petticoat, he said; and there were tears in his eyes. How could she disobey him? How could she break his heart? The force of her own gift alone drove her to it. She made up a small parcel of her belongings, let herself down by a rope one summer's night and took the road to London. She was not seventeen. The birds that sang in the hedge were not more musical than she was. She had the quickest fancy, a gift like her brother's, for the tune of words. Like him, she had a taste for the theatre. She stood at the stage door; she wanted to act, she said. Men laughed in her face.

---

2. The name of Shakespeare's younger daughter.
3. Roman authors. Publius Ovidius Naso (43 B.C.E.–17 C.E.), author of the *Metamorphoses*. Publius Vergilius Maro (70–19 B.C.E.), author of the *Aeneid*. Quintus Horatius Flaccus (65–8 B.C.E.), author of *Odes* and satires.
4. A dealer in woolen goods, which were a "staple" or established type of merchandise.

The manager—a fat, loose-lipped man—guffawed. He bellowed something about poodles dancing and women acting—no woman, he said, could possibly be an actress. He hinted—you can imagine what. She could get no training in her craft. Could she even seek her dinner in a tavern or roam the streets at midnight? Yet her genius was for fiction and lusted to feed abundantly upon the lives of men and women and the study of their ways. At last—for she was very young, oddly like Shakespeare the poet in her face, with the same grey eyes and rounded brows—at last Nick Greene[5] the actor-manager took pity on her; she found herself with child by that gentleman and so—who shall measure the heat and violence of the poet's heart when caught and tangled in a woman's body?—killed herself one winter's night and lies buried at some cross-roads where the omnibuses now stop outside the Elephant and Castle.[6]

That, more or less, is how the story would run, I think, if a woman in Shakespeare's day had had Shakespeare's genius. But for my part, I agree with the deceased bishop, if such he was—it is unthinkable that any woman in Shakespeare's day should have had Shakespeare's genius. For genius like Shakespeare's is not born among labouring, uneducated, servile people. It was not born in England among the Saxons and the Britons. It is not born today among the working classes. How, then, could it have been born among women whose work began, according to Professor Trevelyan, almost before they were out of the nursery, who were forced to it by their parents and held to it by all the power of law and custom? Yet genius of a sort must have existed among women as it must have existed among the working classes. Now and again an Emily Brontë or a Robert Burns[7] blazes out and proves its presence. But certainly it never got itself on to paper. When, however, one reads of a witch being ducked, of a woman possessed by devils, of a wise woman selling herbs, or even of a very remarkable man who had a mother, then I think we are on the track of a lost novelist, a suppressed poet, of some mute and inglorious[8] Jane Austen, some Emily Brontë who dashed her brains out on the moor or mopped and mowed about the highways crazed with the torture that her gift had put her to. Indeed, I would venture to guess that Anon, who wrote so many poems without signing them, was often a woman. It was a woman Edward Fitzgerald,[9] I think, suggested who made the ballads and the folk-songs, crooning them to her children, beguiling her spinning with them, or the length of the winter's night.

This may be true or it may be false—who can say?—but what is true in it, so it seemed to me, reviewing the story of Shakespeare's sister as I had made it, is that any woman born with a great gift in the sixteenth century would certainly have gone crazed, shot herself, or ended her days in some lonely cottage outside the village, half witch, half wizard, feared and mocked at. For it needs little skill in psychology to be sure that a highly gifted girl who had tried to use her gift for poetry would have been so thwarted and hindered by other people, so tortured and pulled asunder by her own contrary instincts, that she must have lost her health and sanity to a certainty. No girl could have walked to London and stood

5. A fictional character based on Shakespeare's contemporary Robert Greene (1558–1592) and appearing in Woolf's *Orlando*.
6. A popular London pub. "Cross-roads": suicides were commonly buried at crossroads.
7. Scottish poet (1759–1796).

8. A reference to Thomas Gray's line in *Elegy Written in a Country Churchyard* (1751): "Some mute inglorious Milton here may rest."
9. British author (1809–1883), known for his translation from the Persian of *The Rubáiyát of Omar Khayyám* (1859).

at a stage door and forced her way into the presence of actor-managers without doing herself a violence and suffering an anguish which may have been irrational—for chastity may be a fetish invented by certain societies for unknown reasons—but were none the less inevitable. Chastity had then, it has even now, a religious importance in a woman's life, and has so wrapped itself round with nerves and instincts that to cut it free and bring it to the light of day demands courage of the rarest. To have lived a free life in London in the sixteenth century would have meant for a woman who was poet and playwright a nervous stress and dilemma which might well have killed her. Had she survived, whatever she had written would have been twisted and deformed, issuing from a strained and morbid imagination. And undoubtedly, I thought, looking at the shelf where there are no plays by women, her work would have gone unsigned. That refuge she would have sought certainly. It was the relic of the sense of chastity that dictated anonymity to women even so late as the nineteenth century. Currer Bell, George Eliot, George Sand,[1] all the victims of inner strife as their writings prove, sought ineffectively to veil themselves by using the name of a man. Thus they did homage to the convention, which if not implanted by the other sex was liberally encouraged by them (the chief glory of a woman is not to be talked of, said Pericles,[2] himself a much-talked-of man), that publicity in women is detestable. Anonymity runs in their blood. The desire to be veiled still possesses them. They are not even now as concerned about the health of their fame as men are, and, speaking generally, will pass a tombstone or a signpost without feeling an irresistible desire to cut their names on it, as Alf, Bert or Chas. must do in obedience to their instinct, which murmurs if it sees a fine woman go by, or even a dog, Ce chien est à moi.[3] And, of course, it may not be a dog, I thought, remembering Parliament Square, the Sièges Allée[4] and other avenues; it may be a piece of land or a man with curly black hair. It is one of the great advantages of being a woman that one can pass even a very fine negress without wishing to make an Englishwoman of her.

That woman, then, who was born with a gift of poetry in the sixteenth century, was an unhappy woman, a woman at strife against herself. All the conditions of her life, all her own instincts, were hostile to the state of mind which is needed to set free whatever is in the brain. But what is the state of mind that is most propitious to the act of creation, I asked. Can one come by any notion of the state that furthers and makes possible that strange activity? Here I opened the volume containing the Tragedies of Shakespeare. What was Shakespeare's state of mind, for instance, when he wrote *Lear* and *Antony and Cleopatra*? It was certainly the state of mind most favourable to poetry that there has ever existed. But Shakespeare himself said nothing about it. We only know casually and by chance that he "never blotted a line."[5] Nothing indeed was ever said by the artist himself about his state of mind until the eighteenth century perhaps.

1. Pseudonyms of Charlotte Brontë, Mary Ann Evans (1819–1880), and Lucile-Aurore Dupin (1804–1876), author of *Lélia* (1833), respectively.
2. From the Greek leader Pericles' funeral oration (431 B.C.E.) as reported in Thucydides' history of the Peloponnesian War (2.35–46).
3. This dog is mine (French); from the philosopher Blaise Pascal's *Thoughts* (1657–58). He uses an anecdote about poor children to illustrate what he considers a universal impulse to assert property claims.
4. An avenue in Berlin containing statues of Hohenzollern rulers. Parliament Square is in London next to the Houses of Parliament and Westminster Abbey.
5. Ben Jonson's (1572–1637) description of Shakespeare.

Rousseau[6] perhaps began it. At any rate, by the nineteenth century self-consciousness had developed so far that it was the habit for men of letters to describe their minds in confessions and autobiographies. Their lives also were written, and their letters were printed after their deaths. Thus, though we do not know what Shakespeare went through when he wrote *Lear*, we do know what Carlyle went through when he wrote the *French Revolution*; what Flaubert went through when he wrote *Madame Bovary*; what Keats[7] was going through when he tried to write poetry against the coming of death and the indifference of the world.

And one gathers from this enormous modern literature of confession and self-analysis that to write a work of genius is almost always a feat of prodigious difficulty. Everything is against the likelihood that it will come from the writer's mind whole and entire. Generally material circumstances are against it. Dogs will bark; people will interrupt; money must be made; health will break down. Further, accentuating all these difficulties and making them harder to bear is the world's notorious indifference. It does not ask people to write poems and novels and histories; it does not need them. It does not care whether Flaubert finds the right word or whether Carlyle scrupulously verifies this or that fact. Naturally, it will not pay for what it does not want. And so the writer, Keats, Flaubert, Carlyle, suffers, especially in the creative years of youth, every form of distraction and discouragement. A curse, a cry of agony, rises from those books of analysis and confession. "Mighty poets in their misery dead"[8]—that is the burden of their song. If anything comes through in spite of all this, it is a miracle, and probably no book is born entire and uncrippled as it was conceived.

But for women, I thought, looking at the empty shelves, these difficulties were infinitely more formidable. In the first place, to have a room of her own, let alone a quiet room or a sound-proof room, was out of the question, unless her parents were exceptionally rich or very noble, even up to the beginning of the nineteenth century. Since her pin money, which depended on the good will of her father, was only enough to keep her clothed, she was debarred from such alleviations as came even to Keats or Tennyson or Carlyle, all poor men, from a walking tour, a little journey to France, from the separate lodging which, even if it were miserable enough, sheltered them from the claims and tyrannies of their families. Such material difficulties were formidable; but much worse were the immaterial. The indifference of the world which Keats and Flaubert and other men of genius have found so hard to bear was in her case not indifference but hostility. The world did not say to her as it said to them, Write if you choose; it makes no difference to me. The world said with a guffaw, Write? What's the good of your writing? Here the psychologists of Newnham and Girton might come to our help, I thought, looking again at the blank spaces on the shelves. For surely it is time that the effect of discouragement upon the mind of the artist should be measured, as I have seen a dairy company measure the effect of ordinary milk and Grade A milk upon the body of the rat. They set two rats in cages side by side, and of the two one was furtive, timid and small, and the other was glossy, bold and big. Now what food do we feed women as artists upon? I asked, remembering, I suppose, that din-

6. Jean-Jacques Rousseau (1712–1778), French author of the *Confessions* (1781).
7. John Keats (1795–1821), British poet. Thomas Carlyle (1795–1881), essayist and historian, translator of Goethe and author of *The French Revolution* (1837).
8. From Wordsworth's "Resolution and Independence" (1807).

ner of prunes and custard. To answer that question I had only to open the evening paper and to read that Lord Birkenhead is of opinion—but really I am not going to trouble to copy out Lord Birkenhead's opinion upon the writing of women. What Dean Inge says I will leave in peace. The Harley Street specialist may be allowed to rouse the echoes of Harley Street[9] with his vociferations without raising a hair on my head. I will quote, however, Mr. Oscar Browning, because Mr. Oscar Browning was a great figure in Cambridge at one time, and used to examine the students at Girton and Newnham. Mr. Oscar Browning was wont to declare "that the impression left on his mind, after looking over any set of examination papers, was that, irrespective of the marks he might give, the best woman was intellectually the inferior of the worst man." After saying that Mr. Browning went back to his rooms—and it is this sequel that endears him and makes him a human figure of some bulk and majesty—he went back to his rooms and found a stable-boy lying on the sofa—"a mere skeleton, his cheeks were cavernous and sallow, his teeth were black, and he did not appear to have the full use of his limbs. . . .'That's Arthur' [said Mr. Browning]. 'He's a dear boy really and most high-minded.'" The two pictures always seem to me to complete each other. And happily in this age of biography the two pictures often do complete each other, so that we are able to interpret the opinions of great men not only by what they say, but by what they do.

But though this is possible now, such opinions coming from the lips of important people must have been formidable enough even fifty years ago. Let us suppose that a father from the highest motives did not wish his daughter to leave home and become writer, painter or scholar. "See what Mr. Oscar Browning says," he would say; and there was not only Mr. Oscar Browning; there was the *Saturday Review*; there was Mr. Greg[1]—the "essentials of a woman's being," said Mr. Greg emphatically, "are that *they are supported by, and they minister to, men*"—there was an enormous body of masculine opinion to the effect that nothing could be expected of women intellectually. Even if her father did not read out loud these opinions, any girl could read them for herself; and the reading, even in the nineteenth century, must have lowered her vitality, and told profoundly upon her work. There would always have been that assertion—you cannot do this, you are incapable of doing that—to protest against, to overcome. Probably for a novelist this germ is no longer of much effect; for there have been women novelists of merit. But for painters it must still have some sting in it; and for musicians, I imagine, is even now active and poisonous in the extreme. The woman composer stands where the actress stood in the time of Shakespeare. Nick Greene, I thought, remembering the story I had made about Shakespeare's sister, said that a woman acting put him in mind of a dog dancing. Johnson repeated the phrase two hundred years later of women preaching. And here, I said, opening a book about music, we have the very words used again in this year of grace, 1928, of women who try to write music. "Of Mlle. Germaine Tailleferre one can only repeat Dr. Johnson's dictum concerning a woman preacher, transposed into terms of music. 'Sir, a woman's composing is like a dog's walking

---

9. A London street known for its many prominent physicians' offices.

1. William Rathbone Greg (1809–1891), cited from a *Saturday Review* essay entitled "Why Are Women Redundant?" (1873).

on his hind legs. It is not done well, but you are surprised to find it done at all.'"[2]
So accurately does history repeat itself.

Thus, I concluded, shutting Mr. Oscar Browning's life and pushing away the rest, it is fairly evident that even in the nineteenth century a woman was not encouraged to be an artist. On the contrary, she was snubbed, slapped, lectured and exhorted. Her mind must have been strained and her vitality lowered by the need of opposing this, of disproving that. For here again we come within range of that very interesting and obscure masculine complex which has had so much influence upon the woman's movement; that deep-seated desire, not so much that *she* shall be inferior as that *he* shall be superior, which plants him wherever one looks, not only in front of the arts, but barring the way to politics too, even when the risk to himself seems infinitesimal and the suppliant humble and devoted. Even Lady Bessborough,[3] I remembered, with all her passion for politics, must humbly bow herself and write to Lord Granville Leveson-Gower: ". . . notwithstanding all my violence in politics and talking so much on that subject, I perfectly agree with you that no woman has any business to meddle with that or any other serious business, farther than giving her opinion (if she is ask'd)." And so she goes on to spend her enthusiasm where it meets with no obstacle whatsoever upon that immensely important subject, Lord Granville's maiden speech in the House of Commons. The spectacle is certainly a strange one, I thought. The history of men's opposition to women's emancipation is more interesting perhaps than the story of that emancipation itself. An amusing book might be made of it if some young student at Girton or Newnham would collect examples and deduce a theory—but she would need thick gloves on her hands, and bars to protect her of solid gold.

But what is amusing now, I recollected, shutting Lady Bessborough, had to be taken in desperate earnest once. Opinions that one now pastes in a book labelled cock-a-doodle-dum and keeps for reading to select audiences on summer nights once drew tears, I can assure you. Among your grandmothers and great-grandmothers there were many that wept their eyes out. Florence Nightingale shrieked aloud in her agony.[4] Moreover, it is all very well for you, who have got yourselves to college and enjoy sitting-rooms—or is it only bed-sitting-rooms?—of your own to say that genius should disregard such opinions; that genius should be above caring what is said of it. Unfortunately, it is precisely the men or women of genius who mind most what is said of them. Remember Keats. Remember the words he had cut on his tombstone.[5] Think of Tennyson; think—but I need hardly multiply instances of the undeniable, if very unfortunate, fact that it is the nature of the artist to mind excessively what is said about him. Literature is strewn with the wreckage of men who have minded beyond reason the opinions of others.

2. *A Survey of Contemporary Music*, Cecil Gray, p. 246 [Woolf's note]. The statement is originally found in James Boswell's *Life of Johnson* (1791).
3. Henrietta, Countess of Bessborough (1761–1821), who corresponded with Lord Granville George Leveson-Gower (1815–1891), British foreign secretary in William Gladstone's administrations and after him the leader of the Liberal Party.
4. See *Cassandra*, by Florence Nightingale, printed in *The Cause*, by R. Strachey [Woolf's note]. Nightingale (1820–1910) was an English nurse and founder of nursing as a profession for women.
5. "Here lies one whose name was writ in water."

And this susceptibility of theirs is doubly unfortunate, I thought, returning again to my original enquiry into what state of mind is most propitious for creative work, because the mind of an artist, in order to achieve the prodigious effort of freeing whole and entire the work that is in him, must be incandescent, like Shakespeare's mind, I conjectured, looking at the book which lay open at *Antony and Cleopatra*. There must be no obstacle in it, no foreign matter unconsumed.

For though we say that we know nothing about Shakespeare's state of mind, even as we say that, we are saying something about Shakespeare's state of mind. The reason perhaps why we know so little of Shakespeare—compared with Donne or Ben Jonson or Milton—is that his grudges and spites and antipathies are hidden from us. We are not held up by some "revelation" which reminds us of the writer. All desire to protest, to preach, to proclaim an injury, to pay off a score, to make the world the witness of some hardship or grievance was fired out of him and consumed. Therefore his poetry flows from him free and unimpeded. If ever a human being got his work expressed completely, it was Shakespeare. If ever a mind was incandescent, unimpeded, I thought, turning again to the bookcase, it was Shakespeare's mind.

1929

JORGE LUIS BORGES
1899–1986

In the briefest of short stories, Jorge Luis Borges created convincing fictional worlds: alternate universes that obey their own laws of time and causation and shed light on the peculiarities of our own world. Borges's favorite symbol of these imaginary settings was the labyrinth, and readers the world over have enjoyed being lost in the mazes Borges built from his thought experiments. To read one of Borges's stories is to enter a new reality, imagined with great concreteness as an extension of our own world yet bearing distinctive features of the universes of fantasy and science fiction.

Born in Buenos Aires, Argentina, on August 24, 1899, Borges grew up in a large house whose library and garden were to form an essential part of his imagination. His father, who was half-English, was an unsuccessful lawyer with philosophical and literary interests; he spent much of his son's childhood working on a novel that he eventually published in middle age. Borges's mother also had literary ambitions; she translated works by William Faulkner, **Franz Kafka**, and D. H. Lawrence into Spanish. Her family, which the young Borges idealized, included Argentine patriots who had fought for independence from Spain and in the civil wars of the nineteenth century. At home Borges spoke English with his father, his paternal grandmother, and his tutor. He read widely in English as well as Spanish; his first publication was a Spanish translation of a children's story by Oscar Wilde, which a Buenos Aires newspaper published when he was only nine years old. Later he would translate works by Walt Whitman, **James Joyce**, and others. He remained close to his mother all his life and lived with her until her death, when she was ninety-nine and he was seventy-five.

Borges's father suffered from eye troubles and traveled to Europe with his family in 1914 for an operation. The family was caught in Geneva at the outbreak of World War I. Borges attended secondary school in Switzerland, learning French, German, and Latin. After the war the family moved to Spain, where he associated with a group of young experimental poets known as the Ultraists. When he returned to his homeland in 1921, Borges founded the Argentinian Ultraists, and befriended and collaborated with other intellectuals and artists, including the philosopher Macedonio Fernandez and a younger writer, Adolfo Bioy Casares.

Around the time of his father's death, in 1938, Borges got his first job, as a librarian in a small municipal library. His workplace served as the basis for one of the first, and most famous, of his stories, partly inspired by **Kafka**, "The Library of Babel." Taking the format of an academic essay, it tells of an endless library whose mazelike, interlocking galleries contain not only all books ever written but all possible combinations of letters. Although the library is infinite, the books, many of them meaningless, are shelved at random and therefore useless.

Early in the twentieth century, Argentina was among the wealthiest Latin American countries, but it suffered during the Great Depression and the years of Juan Perón's military dictatorship that followed. Borges openly opposed the Perón regime and its fascist tendencies, making his political views plain in his speeches and nonliterary writings, some of which circulated privately and were not published until after his death. His political leanings did not go unno-

ticed. When Perón became president in 1946, his government removed Borges from the librarian's post that he had held since 1938 and offered him a job as a chicken inspector. Borges refused the position and instead began teaching English and North American literature at the University of Buenos Aires. Having inherited weak eyes from his father, Borges suffered from increasingly poor vision in middle age; despite undergoing eight operations, he was forced eventually to dictate his work and to rely on his prodigious memory.

After the fall of Perón's regime in 1955, Borges was given the prestigious post of director of the National Library—in the same year that he became almost totally blind. When Perón's party returned to power, Borges opposed him, eventually supporting the military coup that overthrew the Peronists in 1976. His failure to recognize the autocratic character of the military government was a misjudgment that tarnished his image in his final years. Until his death, Borges lived in his beloved Buenos Aires, the city he had celebrated in his first volume of poetry.

The Garden of Forking Paths (1941), his first major collection, introduced Borges to a wider public as an idealist writer whose short stories subordinate character, scene, plot, and narration to a central concept, which is often a philosophical premise. Borges uses these ideas not didactically but as the starting point of fantastic elaborations that entertain and perplex readers—much like a challenging game or puzzle. In the immense labyrinth, or "garden of forking paths," that is Borges's world, images of mazes and infinite mirroring, of cyclical repetition and recall, leave the reader in a sort of hall of mirrors, unsure of what is reality and what is illusion. In *Borges and I* the author commented on the parallel existence of two Borgeses: the one who exists in his work (the one his readers know) and the warm, living identity felt by the man who sets pen to paper. "Little by little, I am giving over everything to him. . . . I do not know which one of us has written this page." Borges elaborated this notion by spinning out fictional identities and alternate realities. Disdaining the "psychological fakery" of realistic novels (the "draggy novel of characters"), he preferred art that calls attention to its own artificiality. He wrote many of his stories in the style of encyclopedia entries or historical essays, as in "The Garden of Forking Paths." Borges was fond, too, of detective stories (and wrote several of them), in which the search for an elusive explanation, the pursuit of intricately planted clues, matters more than the characters' recognizability. The author contrives an art of puzzles and discovery.

"The Garden of Forking Paths," the first selection below, begins as a simple spy story purporting to reveal the hidden truth about a German bombing raid during World War I. Borges alludes to documented facts: the geographic setting of the town of Albert and the Ancre River; a famous Chinese novel that serves as Ts'ui Pên's proposed model; the *History of the World War (1914–1918)* published by B. H. Liddell Hart in 1934. Official history is undermined on the first page, however, both by the recently discovered confession of Dr. Yu Tsun and by his editor's suspiciously defensive footnote, which calls into question the work we are about to read. Although Borges presents the story as a historical document, he warns his readers that it contains interpretive traps. In fact, the story is far from simple—it is a complex labyrinth in which the reader may easily be misled.

Borges executes his detective story with the carefully planted clues traditional to the genre, such as the need to convey the name of a bombing target and the presence of a single bullet in a revolver. Yet halfway through, what started as a conventional spy story takes on bizarre spatial and temporal dimensions. Coincidences—those chance relationships that might well have had different outcomes—introduce the idea of forking paths, or choice between two routes, for history. By inventing an ancient Chinese text modeled on a labyrinth, Borges portrays the universe as a series of alternative versions of experience. An infinite number of worlds opens up—but only one is embodied in this particular story: Yu Tsun faces a dilemma that places his personal loyalties at odds with his military duty. Both the personal and the philosophical ramifications of this choice are at the center of Borges's story.

Just as the "forking paths" present alternative versions of experience, so too has Borges's reputation and influence led in various directions. Perceived by outsiders as a major Argentine writer and a forerunner of the magical realism of successive Latin American generations, he is seen by many Latin Americans as a primarily European writer, a precursor to postmodernism. A favorite of literary intellectuals, he has influenced the development of science fiction. In the labyrinth of contemporary literature, Borges's fictions open up many paths for later writers.

In "The Library of Babel," also published in 1941, Borges seems to have envisioned the development of the information age. The narrator, in the style of an essayist, describes a library that is infinite and coextensive with the fictional universe of the story. The books, each of the same length, arranged on shelves in chambers of identical size and layout, contain "all that it is given to express, in all languages," as well as a great deal of nonsense. Although the number of possible combinations is not infinite, the library itself is infinite because it repeats itself continuously, thus creating a sort of order out of the vast disorder of books both meaningful and meaningless. Much of the story presents itself as a history of theories and beliefs held by residents of this universal library: the Vindicators who search for the one book that will vindicate their existence, the Inquisitors who try to catalogue the library's contents, the Purifiers who destroy meaningless books. To the narrator, "it does not seem unlikely that on some shelf of the universe there lies a total book," one that would explain all the mysteries of the universe. Having spent his whole life in search of it, however, his simple prayer is that someone someday may find this book.

The name Babel comes from the Bible, where it is the location of a tower created by humans who seek to rival God and ascend to heaven. In the Bible, God creates multiple languages to ensure that the builders of the tower cannot under-stand each other and therefore cannot complete their tower. This biblical story is said to explain the origin of multiple human languages. Borges's Library of Babel has become an irresistible meta-phor for the internet, which was invented half a century after the story was written. Borges describes both a world with a seemingly inexhaustible store of information, much of which is unreli-able, and also the challenges of finding what one really needs within it. But even if the internet had never been invented, Borges's story would stand as a medita-tion on the infinity of space and time, the complexities of language, and the limita-tions of human understanding.

The Garden of Forking Paths[1]

On page 22 of Liddell Hart's *History of World War I* you will read that an attack against the Serre-Montauban line by thirteen British divisions (supported by 1,400 artillery pieces), planned for the 24th of July, 1916, had to be postponed until the morning of the 29th. The torrential rains, Captain Liddell Hart comments, caused this delay, an insignificant one, to be sure.

The following statement, dictated, reread and signed by Dr. Yu Tsun, former professor of English at the *Hochschule* at Tsingtao,[2] throws an unsuspected light over the whole affair. The first two pages of the document are missing.

". . . and I hung up the receiver. Immediately afterwards, I recognized the voice that had answered in German. It was that of Captain Richard Madden. Madden's presence in Viktor Runeberg's apartment meant the end of our anxi-eties and—but this seemed, *or should have seemed,* very secondary to me—also the end of our lives. It meant that Runeberg had been arrested or murdered.[3] Before the sun set on that day, I would encounter the same fate. Madden was implacable. Or rather, he was obliged to be so. An Irishman at the service of England, a man accused of laxity and perhaps of treason, how could he fail to seize and be thankful for such a miraculous opportunity: the discovery, cap-ture, maybe even the death of two agents of the German Reich?[4] I went up to my room; absurdly I locked the door and threw myself on my back on the nar-row iron cot. Through the window I saw the familiar roofs and the cloud-shaded six o'clock sun. It seemed incredible to me that that day without premonitions or symbols should be the one of my inexorable death. In spite of my dead father, in spite of having been a child in a symmetrical garden of Hai

1. Translated by Donald A. Yates.
2. Or Ch'ing-tao; a major port in east China, part of territory leased to (and developed by) Germany in 1898. "Hochschule": university (German).
3. "A hypothesis both hateful and odd. The Prussian spy Hans Rabener, alias Viktor Rune-berg, attacked with drawn automatic the bearer of the warrant for his arrest, Captain Richard Madden. The latter, in self-defense, inflicted the wound which brought about Runeberg's death [Editor's note]." This entire note is by Borges as "Editor."
4. Empire (German).

Feng, was I—now—going to die? Then I reflected that everything happens to a man precisely, precisely *now*. Centuries of centuries and only in the present do things happen; countless men in the air, on the face of the earth and the sea, and all that really is happening is happening to me . . . The almost intolerable recollection of Madden's horselike face banished these wanderings. In the midst of my hatred and terror (it means nothing to me now to speak of terror, now that I have mocked Richard Madden, now that I have mocked Richard Madden, now that my throat yearns for the noose) it occurred to me that that tumultuous and doubtless happy warrior did not suspect that I possessed the Secret. The name of the exact location of the new British artillery park on the River Ancre. A bird streaked across the gray sky and blindly I translated it into an airplane and that airplane into many (against the French sky) annihilating the artillery station with vertical bombs. If only my mouth, before a bullet shattered it, could cry out that secret name so it could be heard in Germany . . . My human voice was very weak. How might I make it carry to the ear of the Chief? To the ear of that sick and hateful man who knew nothing of Runeberg and me save that we were in Staffordshire[5] and who was waiting in vain for our report in his arid office in Berlin, endlessly examining newspapers . . . I said out loud: *I must flee.* I sat up noiselessly, in a useless perfection of silence, as if Madden were already lying in wait for me. Something—perhaps the mere vain ostentation of proving my resources were nil—made me look through my pockets. I found what I knew I would find. The American watch, the nickel chain and the square coin, the key ring with the incriminating useless keys to Runeberg's apartment, the notebook, a letter which I resolved to destroy immediately (and which I did not destroy), a crown, two shillings and a few pence, the red and blue pencil, the handkerchief, the revolver with one bullet. Absurdly, I took it in my hand and weighed it in order to inspire courage within myself. Vaguely I thought that a pistol report can be heard at a great distance. In ten minutes my plan was perfected. The telephone book listed the name of the only person capable of transmitting the message; he lived in a suburb of Fenton,[6] less than a half hour's train ride away.

I am a cowardly man. I say it now, now that I have carried to its end a plan whose perilous nature no one can deny. I know its execution was terrible. I didn't do it for Germany, no. I care nothing for a barbarous country which imposed upon me the abjection of being a spy. Besides, I know of a man from England—a modest man—who for me is no less great than Goethe.[7] I talked with him for scarcely an hour, but during that hour he was Goethe . . . I did it because I sensed that the Chief somehow feared people of my race—for the innumerable ancestors who merge within me. I wanted to prove to him that a yellow man could save his armies. Besides, I had to flee from Captain Madden. His hands and his voice could call at my door at any moment. I dressed silently, bade farewell to myself in the mirror, went downstairs, scrutinized the peaceful street and went out. The station was not far from my home, but I judged it wise to take a cab. I argued that in this way I ran less risk of being recognized; the fact is that in the deserted street I felt myself visible and vulnerable, infinitely so. I remember that I told the cab driver to stop a short distance before the main entrance. I got out with voluntary, almost painful slowness; I was going to the

---

5. County in west-central England.
6. In Lincolnshire, a county in east England.
7. Johann Wolfgang von Goethe (1749–

1832), German poet, novelist, and dramatist; author of *Faust*; often taken as representing the peak of German cultural achievement.

village of Ashgrove but I bought a ticket for a more distant station. The train left within a very few minutes, at eight-fifty. I hurried; the next one would leave at nine-thirty. There was hardly a soul on the platform. I went through the coaches; I remember a few farmers, a woman dressed in mourning, a young boy who was reading with fervor the *Annals* of Tacitus,[8] a wounded and happy soldier. The coaches jerked forward at last. A man whom I recognized ran in vain to the end of the platform. It was Captain Richard Madden. Shattered, trembling, I shrank into the far corner of the seat, away from the dreaded window.

From this broken state I passed into an almost abject felicity. I told myself that the duel had already begun and that I had won the first encounter by frustrating, even if for forty minutes, even if by a stroke of fate, the attack of my adversary. I argued that this slightest of victories foreshadowed a total victory. I argued (no less fallaciously) that my cowardly felicity proved that I was a man capable of carrying out the adventure successfully. From this weakness I took strength that did not abandon me. I foresee that man will resign himself each day to more atrocious undertakings; soon there will be no one but warriors and brigands; I give them this counsel: *The author of an atrocious undertaking ought to imagine that he has already accomplished it, ought to impose upon himself a future as irrevocable as the past.* Thus I proceeded as my eyes of a man already dead registered the elapsing of that day, which was perhaps the last, and the diffusion of the night. The train ran gently along, amid ash trees. It stopped, almost in the middle of the fields. No one announced the name of the station. "Ashgrove?" I asked a few lads on the platform. "Ashgrove," they replied. I got off.

A lamp enlightened the platform but the faces of the boys were in shadow. One questioned me, "Are you going to Dr. Stephen Albert's house?" Without waiting for my answer, another said, "The house is a long way from here, but you won't get lost if you take this road to the left and at every crossroads turn again to your left." I tossed them a coin (my last), descended a few stone steps and started down the solitary road. It went downhill, slowly. It was of elemental earth; overhead the branches were tangled; the low, full moon seemed to accompany me.

For an instant, I thought that Richard Madden in some way had penetrated my desperate plan. Very quickly, I understood that that was impossible. The instructions to turn always to the left reminded me that such was the common procedure for discovering the central point of certain labyrinths. I have some understanding of labyrinths: not for nothing am I the great grandson of that Ts'ui Pên who was governor of Yunnan and who renounced worldly power in order to write a novel that might be even more populous than the *Hung Lu Meng*[9] and to construct a labyrinth in which all men would become lost. Thirteen years he dedicated to these heterogeneous tasks, but the hand of a stranger murdered him—and his novel was incoherent and no one found the labyrinth. Beneath English trees I meditated on that lost maze: I imagined it inviolate and perfect at the secret crest of a mountain; I imagined it erased by rice fields or beneath the water; I imagined it infinite, no longer composed of octagonal kiosks and returning paths, but of rivers and provinces and kingdoms . . . I thought of a labyrinth of labyrinths, of one sinuous spreading labyrinth that would encompass the past and the future and in some way involve the stars.

---

8. Cornelius Tacitus (55–117), Roman historian whose *Annals* give a vivid picture of the decadence and corruption of the Roman Empire under Tiberius, Claudius, and Nero.

9. *The Dream of the Red Chamber* (1791) by Ts'ao Hsüeh-ch'in; the most famous Chinese novel, a love story and panorama of Chinese family life involving more than 430 characters.

Absorbed in these illusory images, I forgot my destiny of one pursued. I felt myself to be, for an unknown period of time, an abstract perceiver of the world. The vague, living countryside, the moon, the remains of the day worked on me, as well as the slope of the road which eliminated any possibility of weariness. The afternoon was intimate, infinite. The road descended and forked among the now confused meadows. A high-pitched, almost syllabic music approached and receded in the shifting of the wind, dimmed by leaves and distance. I thought that a man can be an enemy of other men, of the moments of other men, but not of a country: not of fireflies, words, gardens, streams of water, sunsets. Thus I arrived before a tall, rusty gate. Between the iron bars I made out a poplar grove and a pavilion. I understood suddenly two things, the first trivial, the second almost unbelievable: the music came from the pavilion, and the music was Chinese. For precisely that reason I had openly accepted it without paying it any heed. I do not remember whether there was a bell or whether I knocked with my hand. The sparkling of the music continued.

From the rear of the house within a lantern approached: a lantern that the trees sometimes striped and sometimes eclipsed, a paper lantern that had the form of a drum and the color of the moon. A tall man bore it. I didn't see his face for the light blinded me. He opened the door and said slowly, in my own language: "I see that the pious Hsi P'êng persists in correcting my solitude. You no doubt wish to see the garden?"

I recognized the name of one of our consuls and I replied, disconcerted, "The garden?"

"The garden of forking paths."

Something stirred in my memory and I uttered with incomprehensible certainty, "The garden of my ancestor Ts'ui Pên."

"Your ancestor? Your illustrious ancestor? Come in."

The damp path zigzagged like those of my childhood. We came to a library of Eastern and Western books. I recognized bound in yellow silk several volumes of the Lost Encyclopedia, edited by the Third Emperor of the Luminous Dynasty but never printed.[1] The record on the phonograph revolved next to a bronze phoenix. I also recall a *famille rose*[2] vase and another, many centuries older, of that shade of blue which our craftsmen copied from the potters of Persia . . .

Stephen Albert observed me with a smile. He was, as I have said, very tall, sharp-featured, with gray eyes and a gray beard. He told me that he had been a missionary in Tientsin "before aspiring to become a Sinologist."

We sat down—I on a long, low divan, he with his back to the window and a tall circular clock. I calculated that my pursuer, Richard Madden, could not arrive for at least an hour. My irrevocable determination could wait.

"An astounding fate, that of Ts'ui Pên," Stephen Albert said. "Governor of his native province, learned in astronomy, in astrology and in the tireless interpretation of the canonical books, chess player, famous poet and calligrapher—he abandoned all this in order to compose a book and a maze. He renounced the pleasures of both tyranny and justice, of his populous couch, of his banquets and

1. The Yung-lo emperor of the Ming ("bright") dynasty commissioned a massive encyclopedia between 1403 and 1408. A single copy of the 11,095 manuscript volumes was made in the mid-1500s; the original was later destroyed, and only 370 volumes of the copy remain today.

2. Pink family (French); refers to a Chinese decorative enamel ranging in color from an opaque pink to purplish rose. *Famille rose* pottery was at its best during the reign of Yung Chên (1723–35).

even of erudition—all to close himself up for thirteen years in the Pavilion of the Limpid Solitude. When he died, his heirs found nothing save chaotic manuscripts. His family, as you may be aware, wished to condemn them to the fire; but his executor—a Taoist or Buddhist monk—insisted on their publication."

"We descendants of Ts'ui Pên," I replied, "continue to curse that monk. Their publication was senseless. The book is an indeterminate heap of contradictory drafts. I examined it once: in the third chapter the hero dies, in the fourth he is alive. As for the other undertaking of Ts'ui Pên, his labyrinth . . ."

"Here is Ts'ui Pên's labyrinth," he said, indicating a tall lacquered desk.

"An ivory labyrinth!" I exclaimed. "A minimum labyrinth."

"A labyrinth of symbols," he corrected. "An invisible labyrinth of time. To me, a barbarous Englishman, has been entrusted the revelation of this diaphanous mystery. After more than a hundred years, the details are irretrievable; but it is not hard to conjecture what happened. Ts'ui Pên must have said once: *I am withdrawing to write a book.* And another time: *I am withdrawing to construct a labyrinth.* Every one imagined two works; to no one did it occur that the book and the maze were one and the same thing. The Pavilion of the Limpid Solitude stood in the center of a garden that was perhaps intricate; that circumstance could have suggested to the heirs a physical labyrinth. Ts'ui Pên died; no one in the vast territories that were his came upon the labyrinth; the confusion of the novel suggested to me that *it* was the maze. Two circumstances gave me the correct solution of the problem. One: the curious legend that Ts'ui Pên had planned to create a labyrinth which would be strictly infinite. The other: a fragment of a letter I discovered."

Albert rose. He turned his back on me for a moment; he opened a drawer of the black and gold desk. He faced me and in his hands he held a sheet of paper that had once been crimson, but was now pink and tenuous and cross-sectioned. The fame of Ts'ui Pên as a calligrapher had been justly won. I read, uncomprehendingly and with fervor, these words written with a minute brush by a man of my blood: *I leave to the various futures (not to all) my garden of forking paths.* Wordlessly, I returned the sheet. Albert continued:

"Before unearthing this letter, I had questioned myself about the ways in which a book can be infinite. I could think of nothing other than a cyclic volume, a circular one. A book whose last page was identical with the first, a book which had the possibility of continuing indefinitely. I remembered too that night which is at the middle of the Thousand and One Nights when Scheherazade[3] (through a magical oversight of the copyist) begins to relate word for word the story of the Thousand and One Nights, establishing the risk of coming once again to the night when she must repeat it, and thus on to infinity. I imagined as well a Platonic, hereditary work, transmitted from father to son, in which each new individual adds a chapter or corrects with pious care the pages of his elders. These conjectures diverted me; but none seemed to correspond, not even remotely, to the contradictory chapters of Ts'ui Pên. In the midst of this perplexity, I received from Oxford the manuscript you have examined. I lingered, naturally, on the sentence: *I leave to the various futures (not to all) my garden of forking paths.* Almost instantly, I understood: 'The garden of forking paths' was the chaotic novel; the phrase 'the various futures (not to all)' suggested to me the forking in time, not in space. A broad rereading of the work confirmed the theory. In all

3. The narrator of the collection also known as the *Arabian Nights*, a thousand and one tales supposedly told by Scheherazade to her husband, Shahrayar, king of Samarkand, to postpone her execution.

fictional works, each time a man is confronted with several alternatives, he chooses one and eliminates the others; in the fiction of Ts'ui Pên, he chooses—simultaneously—all of them. *He creates*, in this way, diverse futures, diverse times which themselves also proliferate and fork. Here, then, is the explanation of the novel's contradictions. Fang, let us say, has a secret; a stranger calls at his door; Fang resolves to kill him. Naturally, there are several possible outcomes: Fang can kill the intruder, the intruder can kill Fang, they both can escape, they both can die, and so forth. In the work of Ts'ui Pên, all possible outcomes occur; each one is the point of departure for other forkings. Sometimes, the paths of this labyrinth converge: for example, you arrive at this house, but in one of the possible pasts you are my enemy, in another, my friend. If you will resign yourself to my incurable pronunciation, we shall read a few pages."

His face, within the vivid circle of the lamplight, was unquestionably that of an old man, but with something unalterable about it, even immortal. He read with slow precision two versions of the same epic chapter. In the first, an army marches to a battle across a lonely mountain; the horror of the rocks and shadows makes the men undervalue their lives and they gain an easy victory. In the second, the same army traverses a palace where a great festival is taking place; the resplendent battle seems to them a continuation of the celebration and they win the victory. I listened with proper veneration to these ancient narratives, perhaps less admirable in themselves than the fact that they had been created by my blood and were being restored to me by a man of a remote empire, in the course of a desperate adventure, on a Western isle. I remember the last words, repeated in each version like a secret commandment: *Thus fought the heroes, tranquil their admirable hearts, violent their swords, resigned to kill and to die.*

From that moment on, I felt about me and within my dark body an invisible, intangible swarming. Not the swarming of the divergent, parallel and finally coalescent armies, but a more inaccessible, more intimate agitation that they in some manner prefigured. Stephen Albert continued:

"I don't believe that your illustrious ancestor played idly with these variations. I don't consider it credible that he would sacrifice thirteen years to the infinite execution of a rhetorical experiment. In your country, the novel is a subsidiary form of literature; in Ts'ui Pên's time it was a despicable form. Ts'ui Pên was a brilliant novelist, but he was also a man of letters who doubtless did not consider himself a mere novelist. The testimony of his contemporaries proclaims—and his life fully confirms—his metaphysical and mystical interests. Philosophic controversy usurps a good part of the novel. I know that of all problems, none disturbed him so greatly nor worked upon him so much as the abysmal problem of time. Now then, the latter is the only problem that does not figure in the pages of the *Garden*. He does not even use the word that signifies *time*. How do you explain this voluntary omission?"

I proposed several solutions—all unsatisfactory. We discussed them. Finally, Stephen Albert said to me:

"In a riddle whose answer is chess, what is the only prohibited word?"

I thought a moment and replied, "The word *chess*."

"Precisely," said Albert. "*The Garden of Forking Paths* is an enormous riddle, or parable, whose theme is time; this recondite cause prohibits its mention. To omit a word always, to resort to inept metaphors and obvious periphrases, is perhaps the most emphatic way of stressing it. That is the tortuous method preferred, in each of the meanderings of his indefatigable novel, by the oblique Ts'ui Pên. I have compared hundreds of manuscripts, I have corrected the errors that the negligence of the copyists has introduced, I have guessed the plan of this chaos, I have re-established—I believe I have re-established—the primordial organization, I have translated the entire work: it is clear to me that not once does he employ the word 'time.' The explanation is obvious: *The Garden of Forking Paths* is an incomplete, but not false, image of the universe as Ts'ui Pên conceived it. In contrast to Newton and Schopenhauer,[4] your ancestor did not believe in a uniform, absolute time. He believed in an infinite series of times, in a growing, dizzying net of divergent, convergent and parallel times. This network of times which approached one another, forked, broke off, or were unaware of one another for centuries, embraces *all* possibilities of time. We do not exist in the majority of these times; in some you exist, and not I; in others I, and not you; in others, both of us. In the present one, which a favorable fate has granted me, you have arrived at my house; in another, while crossing the garden, you found me dead; in still another, I utter these same words, but I am a mistake, a ghost."

"In every one," I pronounced, not without a tremble to my voice, "I am grateful to you and revere you for your re-creation of the garden of Ts'ui Pên."

"Not in all," he murmured with a smile. "Time forks perpetually toward innumerable futures. In one of them I am your enemy."

Once again I felt the swarming sensation of which I have spoken. It seemed to me that the humid garden that surrounded the house was infinitely saturated with invisible persons. Those persons were Albert and I, secret, busy and multiform in other dimensions of time. I raised my eyes and the tenuous nightmare dissolved. In the yellow and black garden there was only one man; but this man was as strong as a statue . . . this man was approaching along the path and he was Captain Richard Madden.

"The future already exists," I replied, "but I am your friend. Could I see the letter again?"

Albert rose. Standing tall, he opened the drawer of the tall desk; for the moment his back was to me. I had readied the revolver. I fired with extreme caution. Albert fell uncomplainingly, immediately. I swear his death was instantaneous—a lightning stroke.

The rest is unreal, insignificant. Madden broke in, arrested me. I have been condemned to the gallows. I have won out abominably; I have communicated to Berlin the secret name of the city they must attack. They bombed it yesterday; I read it in the same papers that offered to England the mystery of the learned Sinologist Stephen Albert who was murdered by a stranger, one Yu Tsun. The Chief had deciphered this mystery. He knew my problem was to indicate (through the uproar of the war) the city called Albert, and that I had found no other means to do so than to kill a man of that name. He does not know (no one can know) my innumerable contrition and weariness.

For Victoria Ocampo

1941

4. Arthur Schopenhauer (1788–1860), German philosopher whose concept of will proceeded from a concept of the self as enduring through time. In *Seven Conversations with Jorge Luis Borges*, Borges also comments on Schopen- hauer's interest in the "oneiric [dreamlike] essence of life." Isaac Newton (1642–1727), English mathematician and philosopher best known for his formulation of laws of gravitation and motion.

The Library of Babel[1]

By this art you may contemplate the variation of the 23 letters . . .
The Anatomy of Melancholy,[2] part 2, sect. II, mem. IV

The universe (which others call the Library) is composed of an indefinite and perhaps infinite number of hexagonal galleries, with vast air shafts between, surrounded by very low railings. From any of the hexagons one can see, interminably, the upper and lower floors. The distribution of the galleries is invariable. Twenty shelves, five long shelves per side, cover all the sides except two; their height, which is the distance from floor to ceiling, scarcely exceeds that of a normal bookcase. One of the free sides leads to a narrow hallway which opens onto another gallery, identical to the first and to all the rest. To the left and right of the hallway there are two very small closets. In the first, one may sleep standing up; in the other, satisfy one's fecal necessities. Also through here passes a spiral stairway, which sinks abysmally and soars upwards to remote distances. In the hallway there is a mirror which faithfully duplicates all appearances. Men usually infer from this mirror that the Library is not infinite (if it really were, why this illusory duplication?); I prefer to dream that its polished surfaces represent and promise the infinite . . . Light is provided by some spherical fruit which bear the name of lamps. There are two, transversally placed, in each hexagon. The light they emit is insufficient, incessant.

Like all men of the Library, I have traveled in my youth; I have wandered in search of a book, perhaps the catalogue of catalogues; now that my eyes can hardly decipher what I write, I am preparing to die just a few leagues from the hexagon in which I was born. Once I am dead, there will be no lack of pious hands to throw me over the railing; my grave will be the fathomless air; my body will sink endlessly and decay and dissolve in the wind generated by the fall, which is infinite. I say that the Library is unending. The idealists argue that the hexagonal rooms are a necessary form of absolute space or, at least, of our intuition of space. They reason that a triangular or pentagonal room is inconceivable. (The mystics claim that their ecstasy reveals to them a circular chamber containing a great circular book, whose spine is continuous and which follows the complete circle of the walls; but their testimony is suspect; their words, obscure. This cyclical book is God.) Let it suffice now for me to repeat the classic dictum: *The Library is a sphere whose exact center is any one of its hexagons and whose circumference is inaccessible.*

There are five shelves for each of the hexagon's walls; each shelf contains thirty-five books of uniform format; each book is of four hundred and ten pages; each page, of forty lines, each line, of some eighty letters which are black in color. There are also letters on the spine of each book; these letters do not indicate or prefigure what the pages will say. I know that this incoherence at one time seemed mysterious. Before summarizing the solution (whose discovery, in spite of its tragic projections, is perhaps the capital fact in history) I wish to recall a few axioms.

---

1. Translated by James E. Irby. "Babel": in Genesis 11, city whose inhabitants tried to build a tower that would reach heaven. God is said to have created multiple languages in order to prevent the inhabitants of Babel from understanding each other and completing their tower.
2. Philosophical work (1638) by English scholar Robert Burton (1577–1640).

First: The Library exists *ab aeterno*.[3] This truth, whose immediate corollary is the future eternity of the world, cannot be placed in doubt by any reasonable mind. Man, the imperfect librarian, may be the product of chance or of malevolent demiurgi;[4] the universe, with its elegant endowment of shelves, of enigmatical volumes, of inexhaustible stairways for the traveler and latrines for the seated librarian, can only be the work of a god. To perceive the distance between the divine and the human, it is enough to compare these crude wavering symbols which my fallible hand scrawls on the cover of a book, with the organic letters inside: punctual, delicate, perfectly black, inimitably symmetrical.

Second: *The orthographical symbols are twenty-five in number*.[5] This finding made it possible, three hundred years ago, to formulate a general theory of the Library and solve satisfactorily the problem which no conjecture had deciphered: the formless and chaotic nature of almost all the books. One which my father saw in a hexagon on circuit fifteen ninety-four was made up of the letters MCV, perversely repeated from the first line to the last. Another (very much consulted in this area) is a mere labyrinth of letters, but the next-to-last page says *Oh time thy pyramids*. This much is already known: for every sensible line of straightforward statement, there are leagues of senseless cacophonies, verbal jumbles and incoherences. (I know of an uncouth region whose librarians repudiate the vain and superstitious custom of finding a meaning in books and equate it with that of finding a meaning in dreams or in the chaotic lines of one's palm . . . They admit that the inventors of this writing imitated the twenty-five natural symbols, but maintain that this application is accidental and that the books signify nothing in themselves. This dictum, we shall see, is not entirely fallacious.)

For a long time it was believed that these impenetrable books corresponded to past or remote languages. It is true that the most ancient men, the first librarians, used a language quite different from the one we now speak; it is true that a few miles to the right the tongue is dialectal and that ninety floors farther up, it is incomprehensible. All this, I repeat, is true, but four hundred and ten pages of inalterable MCV's cannot correspond to any language, no matter how dialectal or rudimentary it may be. Some insinuated that each letter could influence the following one and that the value of MCV in the third line of page 71 was not the one the same series may have in another position on another page, but this vague thesis did not prevail. Others thought of cryptographs; generally, this conjecture has been accepted, though not in the sense in which it was formulated by its originators.

Five hundred years ago, the chief of an upper hexagon[6] came upon a book as confusing as the others, but which had nearly two pages of homogeneous lines. He showed his find to a wandering decoder who told him the lines were written in Portuguese; others said they were Yiddish. Within a century, the language was established: a Samoyedic Lithuanian dialect of Guarani,[7] with classical

---

3. From the beginning of time (Latin).
4. Heavenly beings said in some Gnostic religions to have created the universe.
5. The original manuscript does not contain digits or capital letters. The punctuation has been limited to the comma and the period. These two signs, the space and the twenty-two letters of the alphabet are the twenty-five symbols considered sufficient by this unknown author [Borges's note].

6. Before, there was a man for every three hexagons. Suicide and pulmonary diseases have destroyed that proportion. A memory of unspeakable melancholy: at times I have traveled for many nights through corridors and along polished stairways without finding a single librarian [Borges's note].
7. A native South American language. "Samoyedic": from a language group native to northern Eurasia. (There is, of course, no such dialect.)

Arabian inflections. The content was also deciphered: some notions of combinative analysis, illustrated with examples of variation with unlimited repetition. These examples made it possible for a librarian of genius to discover the fundamental law of the Library. This thinker observed that all the books, no matter how diverse they might be, are made up of the same elements: the space, the period, the comma, the twenty-two letters of the alphabet. He also alleged a fact which travelers have confirmed: *In the vast Library there are no two identical books.* From these two incontrovertible premises he deduced that the Library is total and that its shelves register all the possible combinations of the twenty-odd orthographical symbols (a number which, though extremely vast, is not infinite): in other words, all that it is given to express, in all languages. Everything: the minutely detailed history of the future, the archangels' autobiographies, the faithful catalogue of the Library, thousands and thousands of false catalogues, the demonstration of the fallacy of those catalogues, the demonstration of the fallacy of the true catalogue, the Gnostic gospel of Basilides,[8] the commentary on that gospel, the commentary on the commentary on that gospel, the true story of your death, the translation of every book in all languages, the interpolations of every book in all books.

When it was proclaimed that the Library contained all books, the first impression was one of extravagant happiness. All men felt themselves to be the masters of an intact and secret treasure. There was no personal or world problem whose eloquent solution did not exist in some hexagon. The universe was justified, the universe suddenly usurped the unlimited dimensions of hope. At that time a great deal was said about the Vindications: books of apology and prophecy which vindicated for all time the acts of every man in the universe and retained prodigious arcana for his future. Thousands of the greedy abandoned their sweet native hexagons and rushed up the stairways, urged on by the vain intention of finding their Vindication. These pilgrims disputed in the narrow corridors, proffered dark curses, strangled each other on the divine stairways, flung the deceptive books into the air shafts, met their death cast down in a similar fashion by the inhabitants of remote regions. Others went mad . . . The Vindications exist (I have seen two which refer to persons of the future, to persons who perhaps are not imaginary) but the searchers did not remember that the possibility of a man's finding his Vindication, or some treacherous variation thereof, can be computed as zero.

At that time it was also hoped that a clarification of humanity's basic mysteries—the origin of the Library and of time—might be found. It is verisimilar that these grave mysteries could be explained in words: if the language of philosophers is not sufficient, the multiform Library will have produced the unprecedented language required, with its vocabularies and grammars. For four centuries now men have exhausted the hexagons . . . There are official searchers, *inquisitors.* I have seen them in the performance of their function: they always arrive extremely tired from their journeys; they speak of a broken stairway which almost killed them; they talk with the librarian of galleries and stairs; sometimes they pick up the nearest volume and leaf through it, looking for infamous words. Obviously, no one expects to discover anything.

As was natural, this inordinate hope was followed by an excessive depression. The certitude that some shelf in some hexagon held precious books and that these precious books were inaccessible, seemed almost intolerable. A blasphemous

---

8. A religious leader in Alexandria, Egypt, in the second century C.E.

sect suggested that the searches should cease and that all men should juggle letters and symbols until they constructed, by an improbable gift of chance, these
canonical books. The authorities were obliged to issue severe orders. The sect
disappeared, but in my childhood I have seen old men who, for long periods of
time, would hide in the latrines with some metal disks in a forbidden dice cup
and feebly mimic the divine disorder.

Others, inversely, believed that it was fundamental to eliminate useless works.
They invaded the hexagons, showed credentials which were not always false,
leafed through a volume with displeasure and condemned whole shelves: their
hygienic, ascetic furor caused the senseless perdition of millions of books. Their
name is execrated, but those who deplore the "treasures" destroyed by this frenzy
neglect two notable facts. One: the Library is so enormous that any reduction of
human origin is infinitesimal. The other: every copy is unique, irreplaceable, but
(since the Library is total) there are always several hundred thousand imperfect
facsimiles: works which differ only in a letter or a comma. Counter to general
opinion, I venture to suppose that the consequences of the Purifiers' depreda-
tions have been exaggerated by the horror these fanatics produced. They were
urged on by the delirium of trying to reach the books in the Crimson Hexagon:
books whose format is smaller than usual, all-powerful, illustrated and magical.

We also know of another superstition of that time: that of the Man of the
Book. On some shelf in some hexagon (men reasoned) there must exist a book
which is the formula and perfect compendium *of all the rest*: some librarian has
gone through it and he is analogous to a god. In the language of this zone vestiges of this remote functionary's cult still persist. Many wandered in search of
Him. For a century they exhausted in vain the most varied areas. How could one
locate the venerated and secret hexagon which housed Him? Someone proposed
a regressive method: To locate book A, consult first a book B which indicates A's
position; to locate book B, consult first a book C, and so on to infinity . . . In
adventures such as these, I have squandered and wasted my years. It does not
seem unlikely to me that there is a total book on some shelf of the universe;[9] I
pray to the unknown gods that a man—just one, even though it were thousands
of years ago!—may have examined and read it. If honor and wisdom and happiness are not for me, let them be for others. Let heaven exist, though my place be
in hell. Let me be outraged and annihilated, but for one instant, in one being, let
Your enormous Library be justified. The impious maintain that nonsense is normal in the Library and that the reasonable (and even humble and pure coherence) is an almost miraculous exception. They speak (I know) of the "feverish
Library whose chance volumes are constantly in danger of changing into others
and affirm, negate and confuse everything like a delirious divinity." These words,
which not only denounce the disorder but exemplify it as well, notoriously prove
their authors' abominable taste and desperate ignorance. In truth, the Library
includes all verbal structures, all variations permitted by the twenty-five orthographical symbols, but not a single example of absolute nonsense. It is useless to
observe that the best volume of the many hexagons under my administration is
entitled *The Combed Thunderclap* and another *The Plaster Cramp* and another

---

9. I repeat: it suffices that a book be possible
for it to exist. Only the impossible is excluded.
For example: no book can be a ladder,
although no doubt there are books which discuss and negate and demonstrate this possibility and others whose structure corresponds to
that of a ladder [Borges's note].

Axaxaxas mlö. These phrases, at first glance incoherent, can no doubt be justified in a cryptographical or allegorical manner; such a justification is verbal and, *ex hypothesi,*[1] already figures in the Library. I cannot combine some characters

dhcmrlchtdj

which the divine Library has not foreseen and which in one of its secret tongues do not contain a terrible meaning. No one can articulate a syllable which is not filled with tenderness and fear, which is not, in one of these languages, the powerful name of a god. To speak is to fall into tautology. This wordy and useless epistle already exists in one of the thirty volumes of the five shelves of one of the innumerable hexagons—and its refutation as well. (An *n* number of possible languages use the same vocabulary; in some of them, the symbol *library* allows the correct definition *a ubiquitous and lasting system of hexagonal galleries,* but *library* is *bread* or *pyramid* or anything else, and these seven words which define it have another value. You who read me, are You sure of understanding my language?)

The methodical task of writing distracts me from the present state of men. The certitude that everything has been written negates us or turns us into phantoms. I know of districts in which the young men prostrate themselves before books and kiss their pages in a barbarous manner, but they do not know how to decipher a single letter. Epidemics, heretical conflicts, peregrinations which inevitably degenerate into banditry, have decimated the population. I believe I have mentioned the suicides, more and more frequent with the years. Perhaps my old age and fearfulness deceive me, but I suspect that the human species—the unique species—is about to be extinguished, but the Library will endure: illuminated, solitary, infinite, perfectly motionless, equipped with precious volumes, useless, incorruptible, secret.

I have just written the word "infinite." I have not interpolated this adjective out of rhetorical habit; I say that it is not illogical to think that the world is infinite. Those who judge it to be limited postulate that in remote places the corridors and stairways and hexagons can conceivably come to an end—which is absurd. Those who imagine it to be without limit forget that the possible number of books does have such a limit. I venture to suggest this solution to the ancient problem: *The Library is unlimited and cyclical.* If an eternal traveler were to cross it in any direction, after centuries he would see that the same volumes were repeated in the same disorder (which, thus repeated, would be an order: the Order). My solitude is gladdened by this elegant hope.[2]

---

1. According to the assumptions of the theory (Latin).

2. Letizia Álvarez de Toledo has observed that this vast Library is useless: rigorously speaking, *a single volume* would be sufficient, a volume of ordinary format, printed in nine or ten point type, containing an infinite number of infinitely thin leaves. (In the early seventeenth century, Cavalieri said that all solid bodies are the superimposition of an infinite num-

ber of planes.) The handling of this silky vade mecum would not be convenient: each apparent page would unfold into other analogous ones; the inconceivable middle page would have no reverse [Borges's note]. "Letizia Álvarez de Toledo": Argentine writer, socialite, and contemporary of Borges. "Cavalieri": Bonaventura Cavalieri, Italian mathematician (1598–1647). "Vade mecum": literally, "go with me" (Latin), a handbook or guidebook.

WILLIAM BUTLER YEATS

1865–1939

The twentieth century's greatest English-language poet, William Butler Yeats became a major voice of modern, independent Ireland. His captivating imagery and his fusion of history and vision continue to stir readers around the world, and many of his poetic phrases have entered the language. Yeats created a private mythology that helped him come to terms with personal and cultural pain and allowed him to explain—as symptoms of Western civilization's declining spiral—the plight of Irish society and the chaos in Europe in the period surrounding the First World War.

The eldest of four children born to John Butler and Susan Pollexfen Yeats, William came from a middle-class Protestant family. His father, a cosmopolitan Irishman who had turned from law to painting and whose inherited fortune had mostly evaporated, gave his son an unconventional education at home. J. B. Yeats was an argumentative religious skeptic who alternately terrorized his son and fostered the boy's interest in poetry and the visual arts, inspiring rebellion against scientific rationalism and belief in the superiority of art. His mother's ties to her home in County Sligo, where Yeats spent many summers and school holidays with his wealthy grandparents, introduced him to the beauties of the Irish countryside and to the folklore and supernatural legends that appear throughout his work. Living alternately in Ireland and England for much of his youth, Yeats became part of literary society in both countries and—though an Irish nationalist—rejected any narrowly patriotic point of view. Before he turned fully to literature in 1886, Yeats attended art school and had planned to become an artist. (His brother Jack became a well-known painter.) Yeats's early works show the influence of the Pre-Raphaelite school in art and in literature. Pre-Raphaelitism called for a return to the sensuous representation and concrete details found in Italian painting before Raphael (1483–1520); Pre-Raphaelite poetry evoked a realm of luminous supernatural beauty in allusive, erotic imagery. Yeats combined the Pre-Raphaelite fascination with the medieval with his exploration of Irish legend: in 1889 he published an archaically styled poem describing a traveler in fairyland ("The Wanderings of Oisin") that established his reputation and won the praise of the designer and writer William Morris. The musical style of Yeats's Pre-Raphaelite period is evident in one of his most popular poems, "The Lake Isle of Innisfree" (1890), with its hidden "bee-loud glade" where "peace comes dropping slow" and evening, after the "purple glow" of noon, is "full of the linnet's wings."

In 1887, Yeats's family moved to London, where the writer pursued his interest in mystical philosophy by studying theosophy under its Russian interpreter, Madame Blavatsky. She claimed mystical knowledge from Tibetan monks and preached the doctrine of the Universal Oversoul, individual spiritual evolution through cycles of reincarnation, and the world as a conflict of opposing forces. Yeats was taken with the grandeur of her cosmology, although he inconveniently wished to test it by experiment and analysis and, in 1890, was expelled from the Theosophical Society. He found a more congenial literary model in the works of **William Blake**, which he coedited in 1893 with F. J. Ellis. The appeal that mysticism had for Yeats later waned but never disappeared; traces may be seen in the introduction he wrote in 1913 for *Gitanjali*, a collection of poems by the Indian author **Rabindranath Tagore**, the preeminent figure in modern Bengali literature.

Several anthologies of Irish folk and fairy tales and a book describing Irish traditions (*The Celtic Twilight*, 1893) demonstrated a corresponding interest in Irish national identity. In 1896 he had met Lady Augusta Gregory, a nationalist who invited him to spend summers at Coole Park, her country house in Galway, and who worked closely with him (and later J. M. Synge) in founding the Irish National Theater (later the Abbey Theater). Along with other participants in the Irish literary renaissance, Yeats aimed to create "a national literature that made Ireland beautiful in the memory . . . freed from provincialism by an exacting criticism." To this end, he wrote *Cathleen ni Houlihan* (1902), a play in which the title character personified Ireland; it became immensely popular with the nationalists. Yeats also established literary societies, promoted and reviewed Irish books, and lectured and wrote about the need for Irish community. Gradually Yeats became embittered by the barriers he believed nationalism was erecting around the free expression of Irish culture. He was outraged at the attacks on Synge's *Playboy of the Western World* (1907) for its supposed derogatory picture of Irish culture, and he commented scathingly in *Poems Written in Discouragement* (1913; reprinted in *Responsibilities*, 1914) on the inability of the middle class to appreciate art or literature.

Except for summers at Coole Park, Yeats in his middle age was spending more time in England than in Ireland. He began *Autobiographies* in 1914 and wrote symbolic plays intended for small audiences on the model of the Japanese Noh theater. His works of this period display a change in tone—a precision and epigrammatic quality that reflects partly his disappointment with Irish nationalism and partly the tastes in poetry promulgated by his friend Ezra Pound and by **T. S. Eliot**. Although Yeats had claimed in a poem just before the First World War that "Romantic Ireland's dead and gone," he found himself drawn again to politics as a subject for poetry and as an arena for action. Shocked by the aftermath of the Easter 1916 uprising against British rule, when sixteen leaders were shot for treason, Yeats wrote that, through their sacrifice, "a terrible beauty is born." The revolutionary figures whom Yeats had known in life took their place in a mythic framework within which he interpreted human history. In the subsequent Anglo-Irish War (1919–21) and Irish Civil War (1922–23), great violence, as Yeats had prophesied, attended the birth of the Irish nation-state. In the Irish Free State, Yeats became a senator from 1922 to 1928, Nobel Prize laureate in 1924, and a "sixty-year-old smiling public man," in the words of "Among School Children" (1926). Much of his best poetry was still to come.

Yeats's marriage in 1917 to Georgie Hyde-Lees provided him with much-needed stability. Intrigued by his wife's experiments with automatic writing (jotting down whatever comes to mind, without correction or rational intent), he viewed them as glimpses into a cosmic order; he gradually evolved his interpretation into a symbolic scheme. He explained the system in *A Vision* (1926): the wheel of history takes 26,000 years to turn; and inside the wheel, civilizations evolve in roughly

2,000-year gyres, spirals expanding outward until they collapse at the onset of a new gyre, which reverses the direction of the old. Within the system human personalities fall into various types, and both gyres and types relate to the phases of the moon. Yeats's later poems in *The Tower* (1928), *The Winding Stair* (1933), and *Last Poems* (1939) are set in the context of this system. His enthusiasms for mythical systems sometimes led him astray, notably when he flirted with the Irish Blue Shirts, a para-fascist movement in the 1930s. Throughout his life, he affected an aristocratic disdain for the rough-and-tumble of democratic politics; by the end of his life, he had abandoned practical politics and devoted himself to the reality of personal experience inside a mystic view of history. The final poem in his posthumous *Last Poems*, "Politics," suggests that events in Russia, Italy, and Spain (communism, fascism, and the impending Second World War) held less interest for the poet than a girl standing nearby: "maybe what they say is true / Of war and war's alarms / But O that I were young again / And held her in my arms."

For many readers Yeats's "masterful images" (in the words of another late poem, "The Circus Animals' Desertion," 1939) define his work. From his early use of symbols as metaphors for personal emotions, to the cosmology of his last work, Yeats created a poetry whose power derives from the interweaving of sharp-edged images. Symbols such as the Tower, Byzantium, Helen of Troy, the sun and the moon, birds of prey, the blind man, and the fool recur frequently and draw their meaning not from connections established inside the poem (as is true for the French symbolists) but from an underlying myth based on occult tradition, Irish folklore, history, and Yeats's private experience. Even readers unacquainted with his mythic system will respond to images that express a

situation or state of mind—for example, golden Byzantium for intellect, art, wisdom—all that "body" cannot supply.

When Yeats adopted a political tone, he did so with an element of meditative distance. His celebration of the abortive nationalist uprisings in "Easter 1916" (1916), for example, is from a universal, aesthetic point of view: "A terrible beauty is born" in the self-sacrifice that leads even a "drunken, vainglorious lout" to be "transformed utterly" by martyrdom. Yeats recognized that the Easter Rebellion, led by radicals whose politics and violence he disapproved, had altered not just the political situation in Ireland but its spiritual state as well.

His early poetry made substantial use of public, straightforward symbols, such as the rose for Ireland. Later on, Yeats employed symbols in a more indirect, allusive way. For example, in "The Second Coming" (1921), the "gyre," or spiral unfolding of history, is represented by the falcon's spiral flight. The sphinxlike beast slouching blank-eyed toward Bethlehem is an enigmatic but terrifying image. Yeats believed that contemporary society was witnessing a transformation similar to that of the fall of Troy or the birth of Christ: "twenty centuries of stony sleep" since Christ's birth are again to be "vexed to nightmare by a rocking cradle," the poem declares; he asks what sort of savior or Antichrist will announce the impending age. This poem demonstrates how Yeats, a master of English meter and rhyme, evolved a loose poetic line with only hints of rhyme. The fourteen lines of the second stanza can be read as an unconventional sonnet.

In form a more conventional sonnet, "Leda and the Swan" (1924) is an erotic retelling of a mythical rape. But it also foreshadows the Trojan War—brute force mirroring brute force. Yeats called the poem's subject "a violent annunciation": as the event that conceives Helen of Troy, Zeus's transformation into a swan and rape of Leda embodies a moment of world-historical change. Once again Yeats draws parallels between the upheavals of history and the catastrophic events of ancient narratives. The poem combines the Shakespearean sonnet in its first two quatrains (the eight lines rhyming *ababcdcd*) with the Petrarchan form in the sestet (the final six lines rhyming *defdef*).

In the two poems on the legendary city of Byzantium, "Sailing to Byzantium" (1926) and "Byzantium" (1930), Yeats admires an artistic civilization that "could answer all my questions" but that was, in fact, only a moment in history. Byzantine art, with its stylized perspectives and mosaics assembled from colored bits of stone, represents the opposite of the tendency of Western art to imitate nature, and it provides a kind of escape for the poet. The idea in "Sailing to Byzantium" of an inhuman, metallic, abstract beauty that art separates "out of nature" expresses a mystic, symbolist quest for an invulnerable world distinct from the ravages of time. This world is to be found in an idealized Byzantium, where the poet's body will be transmuted into artifice. By the time of the second of these poems, the possibility of achieving such a separation seems problematic: the speaker recognizes, on the one hand, that artistic images remain close to the living, suffering world—"the dolphin's mire and blood"—and, on the other hand, that such images have a life independent of the people who would merge with them—"Those images that yet / Fresh images beget."

At the close of "Among School Children," the sixty-year-old "public man" compensates for the passing of youth by dreaming of pure "Presences" that never fade. This poem, like "Sailing to Byzantium," is written in a complex, courtly stanza form, ottava rima (eight lines rhyming *abababcc*), which Yeats often uses for philosophical reflection. He often adopts, as well, the persona of the old man for whom the perspectives of age, idealized beauty, and history are ways to keep human agony at a distance.

Yet the world is still there, tragedies still abound, and Yeats's poetry remains aware of the physical and emotional roots from which the words spring. Whatever the wished-for distance, his poems are full of passionate feelings, erotic desire and disappointment, delight in beauty, horror at civil war and anarchy, dismay at degradation and change.

Easter 1916[1]

I have met them at close of day
Coming with vivid faces
From counter or desk among grey
Eighteenth-century houses.
I have passed with a nod of the head   5
Or polite meaningless words,
Or have lingered awhile and said
Polite meaningless words,
And thought before I had done
Of a mocking tale or a gibe   10
To please a companion

1. On Easter Sunday 1916, Irish nationalists began an unsuccessful rebellion against British rule, which lasted throughout the week and ended in the surrender and execution of its leaders.

Around the fire at the club,
Being certain that they and I
But lived where motley is worn:
All changed, changed utterly: 15
A terrible beauty is born.
That woman's[2] days were spent
In ignorant good-will,
Her nights in argument
Until her voice grew shrill.   20
What voice more sweet than hers
When, young and beautiful,
She rode to harriers?
This man had kept a school
And rode our wingèd horse;   25
This other his helper and friend[3]
Was coming into his force;
He might have won fame in the end,
So sensitive his nature seemed,
So daring and sweet his thought.   30
This other man[4] I had dreamed
A drunken, vainglorious lout.
He had done most bitter wrong
To some who are near my heart,
Yet I number him in the song;   35
He, too, has resigned his part
In the casual comedy;
He, too, has been changed in his turn,
Transformed utterly:
A terrible beauty is born.   40

Hearts with one purpose alone
Through summer and winter seem
Enchanted to a stone
To trouble the living stream.
The horse that comes from the road,   45
The rider, the birds that range
From cloud to tumbling cloud,
Minute by minute they change;
A shadow of cloud on the stream
Changes minute by minute;   50
A horse-hoof slides on the brim,
And a horse plashes within it;
The long-legged moor-hens dive,
And hens to moor-cocks call;
Minute by minute they live: 55
The stone's in the midst of all.

2. Constance Gore-Booth (1868–1927), later Countess Markiewicz, an ardent nationalist.
3. Patrick Pearse (1879–1916) and his friend Thomas MacDonagh (1878–1916), both schoolmasters and leaders of the rebellion and both executed by the British. As a Gaelic poet, Pearse symbolically rode the winged horse of the Muses, Pegasus.
4. Major John MacBride (1865–1916), who had married and separated from Maud Gonne (1866–1953), Yeats's great love.

Too long a sacrifice
Can make a stone of the heart.
O when may it suffice?
That is Heaven's part, our part   60
To murmur name upon name,
As a mother names her child
When sleep at last has come
On limbs that had run wild.
What is it but nightfall?   65
No, no, not night but death;
Was it needless death after all?
For England may keep faith
For all that is done and said.
We know their dream; enough   70
To know they dreamed and are dead;
And what if excess of love
Bewildered them till they died?
I write it out in a verse—
MacDonagh and MacBride   75
And Connolly[5] and Pearse
Now and in time to be,
Wherever green is worn,
Are changed, changed utterly:
A terrible beauty is born.   80

1916

The Second Coming[1]

Turning and turning in the widening gyre[2]
The falcon cannot hear the falconer;
Things fall apart; the centre cannot hold;
Mere anarchy is loosed upon the world,
The blood-dimmed tide is loosed, and everywhere   5
The ceremony of innocence is drowned;
The best lack all conviction, while the worst
Are full of passionate intensity.

Surely some revelation is at hand;
Surely the Second Coming is at hand.   10
The Second Coming! Hardly are those words out
When a vast image out of *Spiritus Mundi*[3]
Troubles my sight: somewhere in sands of the desert
A shape with lion body and the head of a man
A gaze blank and pitiless as the sun,   15

5. James Connolly (1870–1916), labor leader and nationalist executed by the British.
1. The Second Coming of Christ, believed by Christians to herald the end of the world, is transformed here into the prediction of a birth initiating an era and terminating the two-thousand-year cycle of Christianity.

2. The cone pattern of the falcon's flight and of historical cycles, in Yeats's vision.
3. World-soul (Latin) or, as *Anima Mundi* in Yeats's *Per Amica Silentia Lunae*, a "great memory" containing archetypal images; recalls C. G. Jung's collective unconscious.

Is moving its slow thighs, while all about it
Reel shadows of the indignant desert birds.
The darkness drops again; but now I know
That twenty centuries of stony sleep
Were vexed to nightmare by a rocking cradle,   20
And what rough beast, its hour come round at last,
Slouches towards Bethlehem to be born?

                                                            1921

Leda and the Swan[1]

A sudden blow: the great wings beating still
Above the staggering girl, her thighs caressed
By the dark webs, her nape caught in his bill,
He holds her helpless breast upon his breast.

How can those terrified vague fingers push   5
The feathered glory from her loosening thighs?
And how can body, laid in that white rush,
But feel the strange heart beating where it lies?

A shudder in the loins engenders there
The broken wall, the burning roof and tower   10
And Agamemnon dead.[2]
                          Being so caught up,
So mastered by the brute blood of the air,
Did she put on his knowledge with his power
Before the indifferent beak could let her drop?

                                                            1924

Sailing to Byzantium[1]

I

That is no country for old men. The young
In one another's arms, birds in the trees
—Those dying generations—at their song,
The salmon-falls, the mackerel-crowded seas,
Fish, flesh, or fowl, commend all summer long   5
Whatever is begotten, born, and dies.
Caught in the sensual music all neglect
Monuments of unageing intellect.

1. Zeus, ruler of the Greek gods, took the form of a swan to rape the mortal Leda; she gave birth to Helen of Troy, whose beauty caused the Trojan War.
2. The ruins of Troy and the death of Agamemnon, the Greek leader, whose sacrifice of his daughter Iphigenia to win the gods' favor caused his wife, Clytemnestra (also a daughter of Leda), to assassinate him on his return.
1. The ancient name for modern Istanbul, the capital of the Eastern Roman Empire, which represented for Yeats (who had seen Byzantine mosaics in Italy) a highly stylized and perfectly integrated artistic world where "religious, aesthetic, and practical life were one."

2

An aged man is but a paltry thing,
A tattered coat upon a stick, unless   10
Soul clap its hands and sing, and louder sing
For every tatter in its mortal dress,
Nor is there singing school but studying
Monuments of its own magnificence;
And therefore I have sailed the seas and come   15
To the holy city of Byzantium.

3

O sages standing in God's holy fire
As in the gold mosaic of a wall,
Come from the holy fire, perne in a gyre,[2]
And be the singing-masters of my soul.   20
Consume my heart away; sick with desire
And fastened to a dying animal
It knows not what it is; and gather me
Into the artifice of eternity.

4

Once out of nature I shall never take   25
My bodily form from any natural thing,
But such a form as Grecian goldsmiths make
Of hammered gold and gold enamelling
To keep a drowsy Emperor awake;
Or set upon a golden bough to sing   30
To lords and ladies of Byzantium
Of what is past, or passing, or to come.

1926

Among School Children

I

I walk through the long schoolroom questioning;
A kind old nun in a white hood replies;
The children learn to cipher and to sing,
To study reading-books and history,
To cut and sew, be neat in everything   5
In the best modern way—the children's eyes
In momentary wonder stare upon
A sixty-year-old smiling public man.[1]

2. I.e., come spinning down in a spiral. "Perne": a spool or bobbin. "Gyre": the cone pattern of the falcon's flight and of historical cycles, in Yeats's vision.
1. Yeats was elected senator of the Irish Free State in 1922.

2

I dream of a Ledaean[2] body, bent
Above a sinking fire, a tale that she   10
Told of a harsh reproof, or trivial event
That changed some childish day to tragedy—
Told, and it seemed that our two natures blent
Into a sphere from youthful sympathy,
Or else, to alter Plato's parable,   15
Into the yolk and white of the one shell.[3]

3

And thinking of that fit of grief or rage
I look upon one child or t'other there
And wonder if she stood so at that age—
For even daughters of the swan can share   20
Something of every paddler's heritage—
And had that color upon cheek or hair,
And thereupon my heart is driven wild:
She stands before me as a living child.

4

Her present image floats into the mind—   25
Did Quattrocento finger fashion it
Hollow of cheek[4] as though it drank the wind
And took a mess of shadows for its meat?
And I though never of Ledaean kind
Had pretty plumage once—enough of that,   30
Better to smile on all that smile, and show
There is a comfortable kind of old scarecrow.

5

What youthful mother, a shape upon her lap
Honey of generation had betrayed,
And that must sleep, shriek, struggle to escape   35
As recollection or the drug decide,[5]
Would think her son, did she but see that shape
With sixty or more winters on its head,
A compensation for the pang of his birth,
Or the uncertainty of his setting forth?   40

2. Beautiful as Leda or as her daughter, Helen of Troy.
3. In Plato's *Symposium*, Socrates explains love by telling how the gods split human beings into two halves—like halves of an egg—so that each half seeks its opposite throughout life. Yeats compares the two parts to the yolk and white of an egg.
4. Italian painters of the 15th century (the Quattrocento), such as Botticelli (1444–1510), were known for their delicate figures.
5. Yeats's note to this poem recalls the Greek scholar Porphyry (ca. 234–305), who associates "honey" with "the pleasure arising from copulation" that engenders children; the poet further describes honey as a drug that destroys the child's "'recollection' of pre-natal freedom."

6

Plato thought nature but a spume that plays
Upon a ghostly paradigm of things;
Solider Aristotle played the taws
Upon the bottom of a king of kings;
World-famous golden-thighed Pythagoras[6]   45
Fingered upon a fiddle-stick or strings
What a star sang and careless Muses heard:
Old clothes upon old sticks to scare a bird.

7

Both nuns and mothers worship images,
But those the candles light are not as those   50
That animate a mother's reveries,
But keep a marble or a bronze repose.
And yet they too break hearts—O Presences
That passion, piety, or affection knows,
And that all heavenly glory symbolize—   55
O self-born mockers of man's enterprise;

8

Labor is blossoming or dancing where
The body is not bruised to pleasure soul,
Nor beauty born out of its own despair,
Nor blear-eyed wisdom out of midnight oil.   60
O chestnut tree, great-rooted blossomer,
Are you the leaf, the blossom, or the bole?
O body swayed to music, O brightening glance,
How can we know the dancer from the dance?

1926

Byzantium[1]

The unpurged images of day recede;
The Emperor's drunken soldiery are abed;
Night resonance recedes, night-walkers' song
After great cathedral gong;
A starlit or a moonlit dome[2] disdains   5

6. Greek philosophers. Plato (427–337 B.C.E.) believed that nature was a series of illusionistic reflections or appearances cast by abstract "forms" that were the true realities. Aristotle (384–322 B.C.E.), more pragmatic, was Alexander the Great's tutor and spanked him with the "taws" (leather straps). Pythagoras (582–407 B.C.E.), a demigod to his disciples and thought to have a golden thigh bone, pondered the relationship between music, mathematics, and the stars.
1. The holy city of "Sailing to Byzantium"
(p. 1138), seen here as it resists and transforms the blood and mire of human life into its own transcendent world of art.
2. According to Yeats's system in A Vision (1925), the first "starlit" phase in which the moon does not shine and the fifteenth, opposing phase of the full moon represent complete objectivity (potential being) and complete subjectivity (the achievement of complete beauty). In between these absolute phases lie the evolving "mere complexities" of human life.

All that man is,
All mere complexities,
The fury and the mire of human veins.

Before me floats an image, man or shade,
Shade more than man, more image than a shade;   10
For Hades' bobbin bound in mummy-cloth
May unwind the winding path;[3]
A mouth that has no moisture and no breath
Breathless mouths may summon;
I hail the superhuman;   15
I call it death-in-life and life-in-death.

Miracle, bird or golden handiwork,
More miracle than bird or handiwork,
Planted on the starlit golden bough,
Can like the cocks of Hades crow,[4]   20
Or, by the moon embittered, scorn aloud
In glory of changeless metal
Common bird or petal
And all complexities of mire or blood.

At midnight on the Emperor's pavement flit   25
Flames that no faggot feeds, nor steel has lit,
Nor storm disturbs, flames begotten of flame,
Where blood-begotten spirits come
And all complexities of fury leave,
Dying into a dance,   30
An agony of trance,
An agony of flame that cannot singe a sleeve.

Astraddle on the dolphin's[5] mire and blood,
Spirit after spirit! The smithies break the flood,
The golden smithies of the Emperor!   35
Marbles of the dancing floor
Break bitter furies of complexity,
Those images that yet
Fresh images beget,
That dolphin-torn, that gong-tormented sea.   40

1930

---

3. Unwinding the spool of fate that leads from mortal death to the superhuman. "Hades": the realm of the dead in Greek mythology.
4. To mark the transition from death to the dawn of new life.
5. A dolphin rescued the famous singer Arion by carrying him on his back over the sea. Dolphins were associated with Apollo, Greek god of music and prophecy, and in ancient art they are often shown escorting the souls of the dead to the Isles of the Blessed. Here, the dolphin is also flesh and blood, a part of life.

RAINER MARIA RILKE

1875–1926

In his intensely personal quest to understand the "great mysteries" of the universe, Rilke asks questions that we ordinarily think of as religious. Whether his gaze turns toward earth, which he describes with extraordinary clarity and affection, or toward a higher realm whose enigmas remain to be deciphered, he seeks a comprehensive vision of cosmic unity. Rilke's sharply focused yet visionary lyricism made him the best-known and most influential German poet of the twentieth century.

Born in Prague on December 4, 1875, to German-speaking parents who separated when he was nine, Rilke had an unhappy childhood. His mother dressed him as a girl to compensate for the earlier loss of a baby daughter; as a teenager he was sent to military academies, where he was lonely and miserable. After a year in business school, he worked in his uncle's law firm and studied at the University of Prague. His heart was already set on a literary career, however, and between his work and his studies, he stole enough time to publish two books of poetry and write plays, stories, and reviews. In 1897 he moved to Munich and fell in love with the married psychoanalyst Lou Andreas-Salomé, who would be an influence on him throughout his life. Accompanying Andreas-Salomé and her husband to Russia in 1899, Rilke met **Leo Tolstoy** and Boris Pasternak and—swayed by Russian mysticism and the Russian landscape—wrote some of his first successful poems.

Rilke met his future wife, the sculptor Clara Westhoff, when the two were living in the artists' colony Worpswede, in northern Germany; they soon separated, and Rilke moved to Paris to begin a book on the sculptor Auguste Rodin. In Rodin, who became his friend, the German poet found a dedication to the technical demands of his craft; an intense concentration on visible, tangible objects; and, above all, a belief in art as an essentially religious activity. In Paris Rilke was also struck by the poetry of **Charles Baudelaire**. Although he wrote in distress to Lou Andreas-Salomé, complaining of nightmares and a sense of failure, it is at this time (and with her encouragement) that Rilke launched his major work. The anguished, semiautobiographical spiritual confessions of *The Notebook of Malte Laurids Brigge* (1910) date from this period, as do *New Poems* (1907–8), in which the writer develops a symbolic vision focused on objects.

When a patron, Princess Marie von Thurn und Taxis-Hohenlohe, proposed that he stay by himself in her castle at Duino, near Trieste, during the winter of 1911–12, Rilke found the quiet and isolation that he needed as a writer. Walking on the rocks above the sea and puzzling over his answer to a bothersome business letter, Rilke seemed to hear in the roar of the wind the first lines of an elegy: "Who, if I cried out, would hear me among the angels' / hierarchies?" (An elegy is a mournful lyric poem, usually a lament for loss.) By February he had written two elegies, and when he left Duino Castle in May, he had conceived the cycle and written fragments of four other elegies, which would eventually be published in the sequence of ten poems called the *Duino Elegies* (1923).

Drafted into the German army during

the First World War, Rilke spent his days drawing precise vertical and horizontal lines on paper for the War Archives Office in Vienna. Released from military service in 1916, he produced few poems and feared that he would never be able to complete the Duino sequence. In 1922, however, a friend's purchase of the tiny Château de Muzot in Switzerland gave him a peaceful place to retire to and write. Not only did he complete the *Duino Elegies* in Muzot, he also wrote—as a memorial for the young daughter of a friend—a two-part sequence of fifty-five sonnets, *Sonnets to Orpheus* (1922). Affirming the essential unity of life and death, Rilke closed his two complementary sequences ("the little rust-colored sail of the Sonnets and the Elegies' gigantic white canvas") and wrote little—chiefly poems in French—over the next few years. Increasingly ill with leukemia, he died on December 29, 1926, as the result of an infection that developed after he pricked himself while cutting roses in his garden for a friend.

The five selections from *New Poems* (1907–8) printed here demonstrate Rilke's visual imagination of his "thing-poems" (*Dinggedichte*). *New Poems* emphasizes physical reality, the absolute otherness and "thing-like" nature of what is observed—be it fountain, panther, flower, human being, or the "Archaic Torso of Apollo," which is presented here in both English and German to give readers a sense of Rilke's original language. A letter to Andreas-Salomé describes the poet's sense that ancient art objects take on a peculiar luster once they are detached from history and are

seen as "things" in and for themselves: "No subject matter is attached to them, no irrelevant voice interrupts the silence of their concentrated reality . . . no history casts a shadow over their naked clarity—: they *are*. That is all . . . one day one of them reveals itself to you, and shines like a first star." Such "things" are not dead or inanimate but supremely alive, filled with a strange vitality before the poet's glance: the charged sexuality of the marble torso, the caged panther padding around his prison, and the metamorphosis of the Spanish dancer. Faced with a physical presence that transcends words, the viewer is challenged on an existential level. The "archaic torso of Apollo" is not a living being but an ancient Greek sculpture on display in the Louvre Museum in Paris. This headless marble is truly a "thing": a lifeless, even defaced chunk of stone. Yet such is the perfection of its luminous sensuality—derived, the speaker suggests, from the brilliant gaze of its missing head and "ripening" eyes—that it seems alive, and an inner radiance bursts starlike from the marble. The torso puts to shame the observer's puny existence, demanding: "You must change your life."

In his poetry Rilke is haunted by the incompleteness of human experience and by the passage of time. His response is to turn to art to draw objects into a "human" world, infusing them with ideas, emotions, and value. The poet's role, according to Rilke, is to observe with renewed sensitivity "this fleeting world, which in some strange way / keeps calling to us," and to bear witness, by means of language, to the transfiguration of its materiality through human emotions.

From NEW POEMS[1]

Archaic Torso of Apollo[2]

We did not know his legendary head[3]
in which the eyeballs ripened. But
his torso still glows like a candelabrum
in which his gaze only turned low,

holds and gleams. Else could not the curve   5
of the breast blind you, nor in the slight turn
of the loins could a smile be running
to that middle, which carried procreation.

Else would this stone be standing maimed and short
under the shoulders' translucent plunge   10
nor flimmering like the fell of beasts of prey

nor breaking out of all its contours
like a star: for there is no place
that does not see you. You must change your life.

Archaïscher Torso Apollos

Wir kannten nicht sein unerhörtes Haupt,
darin die Augenäpfel reiften. Aber
sein Torso glüht noch wie ein Kandelaber,
in dem sein Schauen, nur zurückgeschraubt,

sich hält und glänzt. Sonst könnte nicht der Bug   5
der Brust dich blenden, und im leisen Drehen
der Lenden könnte nicht ein Lächeln gehen
zu jener Mitte, die die Zeugung trug.

Sonst stünde dieser Stein entstellt und kurz
unter der Schultern durchsichtigem Sturz   10
und flimmerte nicht so wie Raubtierfelle

1. All Rilke selections are translated by M. D. Herter Norton.
2. The first poem in the second volume of Rilke's *New Poems* (1908), which were dedicated "to my good friend, Auguste Rodin" (the French sculptor [1840–1917] whose secretary Rilke was for a brief period and on whom he wrote two monographs, in 1903 and 1907). The poem itself was inspired by an ancient Greek statue discovered at Miletus (a Greek colony on the coast of Asia Minor) that was called simply the *Torso of a Youth from Miletus*; since the god Apollo was an ideal of youthful male beauty, his name was often associated with such statues.
3. In a torso, the head and limbs are missing.

und bräche nicht aus allen seinen Rändern
aus wie ein Stern: denn da ist keine Stelle,
die dich nicht sieht. Du musst dein Leben ändern.

The Panther

jardin des plantes,[1] *paris*

His vision from the passing of the bars
is grown so weary that it holds no more.
To him it seems there are a thousand bars
and behind a thousand bars no world.

The padding gait of flexibly strong strides,   5
that in the very smallest circle turns,
is like a dance of strength around a center
in which stupefied a great will stands.

Only sometimes the curtain of the pupil
soundlessly parts—. Then an image enters,   10
goes through the tensioned stillness of the limbs—
and in the heart ceases to be.

The Swan

This toiling to go through something yet
undone, heavily and as though in bonds,
is like the ungainly gait of the swan.

And dying, this no longer grasping
of that ground on which we daily stand,   5
like his anxious letting-himself-down—:

into the waters, which receive him smoothly
and which, as though happy and bygone,
draw back underneath him, flow on flow;
while he, infinitely still and sure,   10
ever more maturely and more royally
and more serenely deigns to draw along.

---

1. A zoo in Paris. Rilke also admired, at Rodin's studio, the plaster cast of an ancient statue of a
panther.

Spanish Dancer[1]

As in one's hand a sulphur match, whitely,
before it comes aflame, to every side
darts twitching tongues—: within the circle
of close watchers hasty, bright and hot
her round dance begins twitching to spread itself.   5

And suddenly it is altogether flame.

With her glance she sets alight her hair
and all at once with daring art
whirls her whole dress within this conflagration,
out of which her naked arms upstretch   10
like startled snakes awake and rattling.[2]

And then: as though the fire were tightening round her,
she gathers it all in one and casts it off
very haughtily, with imperious gesture
and watches: it lies there raging on the ground   15
and still flames and will not give in—.
Yet conquering, sure and with a sweet
greeting smile she lifts her countenance
and stamps it out with little sturdy feet.

1907

1. The dance described in the poem is the fla-
menco (from *flamear*, "to flame").
2. The dancer accompanies herself with the
rhythmic clicking of castanets (worn on the
fingers).

T. S. ELIOT
1888–1965

Thomas Stearns Eliot had a unique role in defining modernist taste and style. As a poet and as a literary critic, he rejected the narrative, moralizing, frequently "noble" style of late Victorian poetry, instead employing highly focused, startling images and an elliptical, ironic voice that has had enormous impact on modern poetry throughout the world.

Readers in far-flung regions who know nothing of Eliot's other works are likely to be familiar with *The Waste Land* (1922), a literary-historical landmark representing the cultural crisis in Europe after the First World War. Although Eliot did not consider himself a generational icon, his challenging, quirky, memorable poetry is indissolubly linked with the spiritual and intellectual crises of modernism.

Two countries, England and the United States, claim Eliot as part of their national literature. Although Eliot was born in St. Louis, the Eliots were a distinguished New England family; Eliot's grandfather had gone west to found Washington University in St. Louis. Eliot attended Harvard (where his father's cousin was president of the university) for his undergraduate and graduate education. There he found literary models that would feed his work in future years: the poetry of **Dante** and John Donne, and the plays of Elizabethan and Jacobean dramatists. In 1908, Eliot read Arthur Symons's *The Symbolist Movement in Literature* and became acquainted with the French Symbolist poets, whose richly allusive images—and highly self-conscious, ironic, and craftsmanlike technique—he would adopt as his own. He began writing poetry while still in college and published his first major work, "The Love Song of J. Alfred Prufrock," in *Poetry* magazine in 1915.

At twenty-two he left for Europe to study at Oxford and the Sorbonne; the outbreak of the First World War prevented him from returning to Harvard, where he intended to continue graduate study in philosophy. Nonetheless, he completed a doctoral dissertation on the philosopher F. H. Bradley, whose examination of private consciousness became a theme of Eliot's later essays and poems. Settling in England, Eliot married, taught briefly, and worked for several years in the foreign department of Lloyd's Bank. Unhappy in his marriage and under pressure in his job at the bank, Eliot suffered from writer's block and then had a breakdown soon after the First World War. He wrote most of *The Waste Land* while recovering in a sanatorium in Lausanne, Switzerland. It was immediately hailed as one of the most important poems of the modernist movement and an expression of the postwar sense of social crisis. Already well known for his essays, collected in *The Sacred Wood* (1920), and his editorial work for the literary journals *The Egoist* and *The Criterion*, Eliot left Lloyd's for a position with the publishing firm Faber & Faber.

Raised an American Unitarian, Eliot joined the Church of England in 1927 and became a naturalized British subject the same year. He continued to write poetry and also turned to drama, composing a verse play on the death of the English St. Thomas à Becket (*Murder in the Cathedral*, 1935) as well as more conventional stage plays, *The Family Reunion* (1939), which recasts the Orestes story from Greek tragedy, and *The Cocktail Party* (1949), a drawing-room comedy that explores the search for salvation. During this time, Eliot became increasingly conservative in his political attitudes; the anti-Semitic remarks in his speeches and poems from this period have tarnished his reputation. By the time he received the Nobel Prize in Literature, in 1948, however, Eliot was recognized as a major contemporary writer in English. For such an influential poet, his output was relatively small; but in addition to writing some of the greatest verse of the twentieth century and essays that shaped literary opinion, he nurtured many younger writers as a director at Faber & Faber. Despite his social, political, and religious conservatism, Eliot ushered in the revolution in literary form known as modernism.

The selection here includes two of Eliot's major poems from different phases of his career. "The Love Song of J. Alfred Prufrock" displays the evocative yet confounding images, abrupt shifts in focus, and combination of human sympathy and ironic wit that would attract and puzzle readers of his later works. Clearly Prufrock's dramatic monologue aims to startle readers—by bidding them, in the opening lines, to imagine the evening spread out "like a patient etherised upon a table," and by shifting focus abruptly among metaphysical questions, drawing-room chatter, imaginary landscapes, and literary and biblical allusions. Tones of high seriousness jar against banal and even singsong speech: "I grow old . . . I grow old . . . / I shall wear the bottoms of my trousers rolled." The stanzas of "Prufrock" are individual scenes, each with a stylistic coherence (for example, the third stanza's yellow fog as a cat). Together, they create a symbolic landscape that unfolds in the narrator's mind as a combination of factual observation and subjective feelings. In its discontinuity, its precise yet evocative imagery, its mixture of romantic and everyday reference, and its formal and conversational speech, as well as in the complex and ironic self-consciousness of its very unheroic hero, "The Love Song of J. Alfred Prufrock" anticipates the modernist traits typical of Eliot's larger corpus. Also anticipating Eliot's later work are the theme of spiritual void and the disoriented protagonist helpless to cope with a crisis that is as much the face of modern Western culture as of his personal tragedy.

Eliot dedicated *The Waste Land*, the next selection, to his friend, fellow poet, and editor Ezra Pound, with a quotation from Dante that praises the "better craftsman." Quotations from, or allusions to, a vast range of sources—including **Shakespeare**, Dante, **Charles Baudelaire**, Richard Wagner, **Ovid**, **St. Augustine**, Buddhist sermons, folk songs, and the anthropologists Jessie Weston and James Frazer—punctuate this lengthy work, to which Eliot added explanatory notes when it appeared in book form. A poem that depicts society in a time of cultural and spiritual crisis, *The Waste Land* juxtaposes images of the fragmentation of modern experience, on the one hand, and references (some in foreign languages) to a more

stable heritage, on the other. The classical prophet Tiresias is contrasted to the contemporary charlatan Madame Sosostris; the celebrated lovers Antony and Cleopatra, to a real estate agent's clerk who mechanically seduces a bored typist at the end of her workday; Buddhist sermons and the religious visions of St. Augustine, to a sterile world of rock and dust where "one can neither stand nor lie nor sit." Throughout the poem runs a series of oblique allusions to the legend of a knight passing trials in a Chapel Perilous and healing a Fisher King by asking the right questions about the Holy Grail and the Holy Lance. The implication is that the modern wasteland might be redeemed if its inhabitants learned to answer (or perhaps to ask) the appropriate questions. These and other references that Eliot integrates into the poem constitute, the speaker says, "fragments I have shored against my ruins"—pieces of a puzzle whose resolution might bring "shantih," or the peace that passeth understanding but that remains enigmatically out of reach, as the poem's final lines in a mosaic of foreign languages suggest.

The groundbreaking technical innovation in *The Waste Land* is the deliberate use of fragmentation and discontinuity. Eliot pointedly refused to provide transitional passages or narrative thread, relying on the reader to construct a pattern whose implications would make sense as a whole. The writer's approach represents a direct attack on the conventional experience of the written word; the poem undercuts readers' expectations of linearity by inserting unexplained literary references, sudden shifts in scene or perspective, interpolations of foreign language, and changes of verbal register from lofty diction to slang. Eliot's refusal to fulfill traditional expectations serves several functions: it contributes to the poem's picture of cultural disintegration; it allows Eliot to exploit the Symbolist or allusive powers of language, since the diction rather than the narrative content must carry the burden of meaning; and by drawing attention to itself as a technique, it exemplifies modernist self-reflexive, or self-conscious, style.

Eliot's early essays on literature and literary history helped to bring about a different understanding of poetry, which afterward was no longer seen as the expression of personal feeling but as a carefully made aesthetic object. Yet much of Eliot's impact was not merely formal but spiritual and philosophical. The search for meaning that pervades his work created a lasting picture of the barrenness of modern culture and of the search for alternatives. But while many later poets rejected Eliot's religious beliefs, they found inspiration in his expression of the dilemmas facing an anxious and infinitely vulnerable modern soul.

The Love Song of J. Alfred Prufrock

S'io credessi che mia risposta fosse
a persona che mai tornasse al mondo,
questa fiamma staria senza più scosse.
Ma per ciò che giammai di questo fondo
non tornò vivo alcun, s'i'odo il vero,
senza tema d'infamia ti rispondo.[1]

Let us go then, you and I,
When the evening is spread out against the sky
Like a patient etherised upon a table;
Let us go, through certain half-deserted streets,
The muttering retreats   5
Of restless nights in one-night cheap hotels
And sawdust restaurants with oyster-shells:
Streets that follow like a tedious argument
Of insidious intent
To lead you to an overwhelming question . . .   10
Oh, do not ask, "What is it?"
Let us go and make our visit.

In the room the women come and go
Talking of Michelangelo.[2]

The yellow fog that rubs its back upon the window-panes,   15
The yellow smoke that rubs its muzzle on the window-panes
Licked its tongue into the corners of the evening,
Lingered upon the pools that stand in drains,
Let fall upon its back the soot that falls from chimneys,
Slipped by the terrace, made a sudden leap,   20

1. From Dante's *Inferno* 27.61–66, in which the false counselor Guido da Montefeltro, enveloped in flame, explains that he would never reveal his past if he thought the traveler could report it: "If I thought my reply were meant for one / who ever could return into the world, / this flame would stir no more; and yet, since none— / if what I hear is true—ever returned / alive from this abyss, then without fear / of facing infamy, I answer you."
2. Michelangelo Buonarroti (1475–1564), famous Italian Renaissance sculptor, painter, architect, and poet; here, merely a topic of fashionable conversation.

And seeing that it was a soft October night,
Curled once about the house, and fell asleep.

   And indeed there will be time[3]
For the yellow smoke that slides along the street,
Rubbing its back upon the window-panes;   25
There will be time, there will be time
To prepare a face to meet the faces that you meet;
There will be time to murder and create,
And time for all the works and days of hands[4]
That lift and drop a question on your plate;   30
Time for you and time for me,
And time yet for a hundred indecisions,
And for a hundred visions and revisions,
Before the taking of a toast and tea.

   In the room the women come and go   35
Talking of Michelangelo.

   And indeed there will be time
To wonder, "Do I dare?" and, "Do I dare?"
Time to turn back and descend the stair,
With a bald spot in the middle of my hair—   40
(They will say: "How his hair is growing thin!")
My morning coat, my collar mounting firmly to the chin,
My necktie rich and modest, but asserted by a simple pin—
(They will say: "But how his arms and legs are thin!")
Do I dare   45
Disturb the universe?
In a minute there is time
For decisions and revisions which a minute will reverse.

   For I have known them all already, known them all—
Have known the evenings, mornings, afternoons,   50
I have measured out my life with coffee spoons;
I know the voices dying with a dying fall[5]
Beneath the music from a farther room.
   So how should I presume?

   And I have known the eyes already, known them all—   55
The eyes that fix you in a formulated phrase,
And when I am formulated, sprawling on a pin,
When I am pinned and wriggling on the wall,
Then how should I begin
To spit out all the butt-ends of my days and ways?   60
   And how should I presume?

3. Echo of a love poem by Andrew Marvell (1621–1678), *To His Coy Mistress*: "Had we but world enough and time."
4. An implied contrast with the more productive agricultural labor of hands in the *Works and Days* of the Greek poet Hesiod (8th century B.C.E.).
5. Recalls Duke Orsino's description of a musical phrase in Shakespeare's *Twelfth Night* (1.1.4): "It has a dying fall."

And I have known the arms already, known them all—
Arms that are braceleted and white and bare
(But in the lamplight, downed with light brown hair!)
Is it perfume from a dress   65
That makes me so digress?
Arms that lie along a table, or wrap about a shawl.
  And should I then presume?
  And how should I begin?

    • • •

Shall I say, I have gone at dusk through narrow streets   70
And watched the smoke that rises from the pipes
Of lonely men in shirt-sleeves, leaning out of windows? . . .

I should have been a pair of ragged claws
Scuttling across the floors of silent seas.

    • • •

 And the afternoon, the evening, sleeps so peacefully!   75
Smoothed by long fingers,
Asleep . . . tired . . . or it malingers,
Stretched on the floor, here beside you and me.
Should I, after tea and cakes and ices,
Have the strength to force the moment to its crisis?   80
But though I have wept and fasted, wept and prayed,
Though I have seen my head (grown slightly bald) brought in
  upon a platter,
I am no prophet[6]—and here's no great matter;
I have seen the moment of my greatness flicker,
And I have seen the eternal Footman hold my coat, and snicker,   85
And in short, I was afraid.

 And would it have been worth it, after all,
After the cups, the marmalade, the tea,
Among the porcelain, among some talk of you and me,
Would it have been worth while,   90
To have bitten off the matter with a smile,
To have squeezed the universe into a ball
To roll it toward some overwhelming question,[7]
To say: "I am Lazarus, come from the dead,[8]
Come back to tell you all, I shall tell you all"—   95
If one, settling a pillow by her head,
  Should say: "That is not what I meant at all.
  That is not it, at all."

---

6. Salome obtained the head of the prophet
John the Baptist on a platter as a reward for
dancing before the tetrarch Herod (Matthew
14:3–11).
7. Another echo of Marvell's "To His Coy Mistress," when the lover suggests rolling "all our
strength and all / our sweetness up into one
ball" to send against the "iron gates of life."
8. The story of Lazarus, raised from the dead,
is told in John 11:1–44.

And would it have been worth it, after all,
Would it have been worth while,   100
After the sunsets and the dooryards and the sprinkled streets,
After the novels, after the teacups, after the skirts that trail along
    the floor—
And this, and so much more?—
It is impossible to say just what I mean!
But as if a magic lantern[9] threw the nerves in patterns on a screen: 105
Would it have been worth while
If one, settling a pillow or throwing off a shawl,
And turning toward the window, should say:
    "That is not it at all,
    That is not what I meant, at all."   110

                        •   •   •

        No! I am not Prince Hamlet, nor was meant to be;
Am an attendant lord, one that will do
To swell a progress,[1] start a scene or two,
Advise the prince; no doubt, an easy tool,
Deferential, glad to be of use,   115
Politic, cautious, and meticulous;
Full of high sentence, but a bit obtuse;
At times, indeed, almost ridiculous—
Almost, at times, the Fool.

        I grow old . . . I grow old . . .   120
I shall wear the bottoms of my trousers rolled.

        Shall I part my hair behind? Do I dare to eat a peach?
I shall wear white flannel trousers, and walk upon the beach.
I have heard the mermaids singing, each to each.

        I do not think that they will sing to me.   125

        I have seen them riding seaward on the waves
Combing the white hair of the waves blown back
When the wind blows the water white and black.

        We have lingered in the chambers of the sea
By sea-girls wreathed with seaweed red and brown   130
Till human voices wake us, and we drown.

                                                                   1915

9. A slide projector.
1. A procession of attendants accompanying a

king or nobleman across the stage, as in Elizabethan drama.

The Waste Land[1]

"Nam Sibyllam quidem Cumis ego ipse oculis meis vidi in ampulla pendere, et cum illi pueri dicerent: Σίβυλλα τί θέλεισ; respondebat illa: ἀποθανεῖν θέλω."[2]

For Ezra Pound
il miglior fabbro.[3]

1. The Burial of the Dead[4]

April is the cruellest month, breeding
Lilacs out of the dead land, mixing
Memory and desire, stirring
Dull roots with spring rain.
Winter kept us warm, covering   5
Earth in forgetful snow, feeding
A little life with dried tubers.
Summer surprised us, coming over the Starnbergersee[5]
With a shower of rain; we stopped in the colonnade,
And went on in sunlight, into the Hofgarten,[6]   10
And drank coffee, and talked for an hour.
Bin gar keine Russin, stamm' aus Litauen, echt deutsch.[7]
And when we were children, staying at the arch-duke's,
My cousin's, he took me out on a sled,
And I was frightened. He said, Marie,   15
Marie, hold on tight. And down we went.[8]
In the mountains, there you feel free.
I read, much of the night, and go south in the winter.

What are the roots that clutch, what branches grow
Out of this stony rubbish? Son of man,[9]   20
You cannot say, or guess, for you know only

1. Eliot provided footnotes for *The Waste Land* when it was first published in book form; these notes are included here. A general note at the beginning referred readers to the religious symbolism described in Jessie L. Weston's study of the Grail legend, *From Ritual to Romance* (1920), and to fertility myths and vegetation ceremonies (especially those involving Adonis, Attis, and Osiris) as described in the *The Golden Bough* (1890–1918) by the anthropologist Sir James Frazer.
2. Lines from Petronius's *Satyricon* (ca. 60 C.E.) describing the Sibyl, a prophetess shriveled with age and suspended in a bottle. "For indeed I myself have seen with my own eyes the Sibyl at Cumae, hanging in a bottle, and when those boys would say to her: 'Sibyl, what do you want?' she would reply: 'I want to die.'"

3. The dedication to Pound, who suggested cuts and changes in the first manuscript of *The Waste Land*, borrows words used by Guido Guinizelli to describe his predecessor, the Provençal poet Arnaut Daniel, in Dante's *Purgatorio* (26.117): he is "the better craftsman."
4. From the burial service of the Anglican Church.
5. A lake near Munich.
6. A public park.
7. "I am certainly no Russian, I come from Lithuania and am pure German." German settlers in Lithuania considered themselves superior to the Baltic natives.
8. Lines 8–16 recall *My Past*, the memoirs of Countess Marie Larisch.
9. "Cf. Ezekiel II, i" [Eliot's note]. The passage reads "Son of man, stand upon thy feet, and I will speak unto thee."

A heap of broken images, where the sun beats,
And the dead tree gives no shelter, the cricket no relief,[1]
And the dry stone no sound of water. Only
There is shadow under this red rock,   25
(Come in under the shadow of this red rock),
And I will show you something different from either
Your shadow at morning striding behind you
Or your shadow at evening rising to meet you;
I will show you fear in a handful of dust.   30
          Frisch weht der Wind
          Der Heimat zu
          Mein Irisch Kind,
          Wo weilest du?[2]
"You gave me hyacinths first a year ago;   35
"They called me the hyacinth girl."
—Yet when we came back, late, from the hyacinth garden,
Your arms full, and your hair wet, I could not
Speak, and my eyes failed, I was neither
Living nor dead, and I knew nothing,   40
Looking into the heart of light, the silence.
Oed' und leer das Meer.[3]

    Madame Sosostris,[4] famous clairvoyante,
Had a bad cold, nevertheless
Is known to be the wisest woman in Europe,   45
With a wicked pack of cards.[5] Here, said she,
Is your card, the drowned Phoenician Sailor,
(Those are pearls that were his eyes.[6] Look!)
Here is Belladonna, the Lady of the Rocks,

1. "Cf. Ecclesiastes XII, v" [Eliot's note]. "Also when they shall be afraid of that which is high, and fears shall be in the way, . . . the grasshopper shall be a burden, and desire shall fail."
2. "V. *Tristan und Isolde*, I, verses 5–8" [Eliot's note]. A sailor in Richard Wagner's opera sings, "The wind blows fresh / Towards the homeland / My Irish child / Where are you waiting?" (German)
3. "Id. III, verse 24" [Eliot's note]. "Barren and empty is the sea" (German) is the erroneous report the dying Tristan hears as he waits for Isolde's ship in the third act of Wagner's opera.
4. A fortune-teller with an assumed Egyptian name, possibly suggested by a similar figure in a novel by Aldous Huxley (*Crome Yellow*, 1921).
5. "I am not familiar with the exact constitution of the Tarot pack of cards, from which I have obviously departed to suit my own convenience. The Hanged Man, a member of the traditional pack, fits my purpose in two ways: because he is associated in my mind with the Hanged God of Frazer, and because I associate him with the hooded figure in the passage of the disciples to Emmaus in Part V. The Phoenician Sailor and the Merchant appear later; also the 'crowds of people,' and Death by Water is executed in Part IV. The Man with Three Staves (an authentic member of the Tarot pack) I associate, quite arbitrarily, with the Fisher King himself" [Eliot's note]. Tarot cards are used for telling fortunes; the four suits (cup, lance, sword, and coin) are life symbols related to the Grail legend; and, as Eliot suggests, various figures on the cards are associated with different characters and situations in *The Waste Land*. For example, the "drowned Phoenician Sailor" (line 47) recurs in the merchant from Smyrna (III) and Phlebas the Phoenician (IV). "Belladonna" (line 49)—a poison, hallucinogen, medicine, and cosmetic (in Italian, "beautiful lady"); also an echo of Leonardo da Vinci's painting of the Virgin, *Madonna of the Rocks*—heralds the neurotic society woman amid her jewels and perfumes (II). "The Wheel" (line 51) is the wheel of fortune. "The Hanged Man" (line 55) becomes the sacrificed fertility god whose death ensures resurrection and new life for his people.
6. A line from Ariel's song in Shakespeare's *The Tempest* (1.2.398), which describes the transformation of a drowned man.

The lady of situations.   50
Here is the man with three staves, and here the Wheel,
And here is the one-eyed merchant, and this card,
Which is blank, is something he carries on his back,
Which I am forbidden to see. I do not find
The Hanged Man. Fear death by water.   55
I see crowds of people, walking round in a ring.
Thank you. If you see dear Mrs. Equitone,
Tell her I bring the horoscope myself:
One must be so careful these days.

Unreal City,[7]   60
Under the brown fog of a winter dawn,
A crowd flowed over London Bridge, so many,
I had not thought death had undone so many.[8]
Sighs, short and infrequent, were exhaled,[9]
And each man fixed his eyes before his feet.   65
Flowed up the hill and down King William Street,
To where Saint Mary Woolnoth kept the hours
With a dead sound on the final stroke of nine.[1]
There I saw one I knew, and stopped him, crying: "Stetson!
"You who were with me in the ships at Mylae![2]   70
"That corpse you planted last year in your garden,
"Has it begun to sprout? Will it bloom this year?
"Or has the sudden frost disturbed its bed?
"Oh keep the Dog far hence, that's friend to men,[3]
"Or with his nails he'll dig it up again!   75
"You! hypocrite lecteur!—mon semblable,—mon frère!"[4]

7. "Cf. Baudelaire: 'Fourmillante cité, cité pleine de rêves, / Où le spectre en plein jour raccroche le passant'" [Eliot's note]. "Swarming city, city full of dreams, / Where the specter in broad daylight accosts the passerby"; a description of Paris from "The Seven Old Men" in *The Flowers of Evil* (1857).

8. "Cf. *Inferno* III, 55–57: 'si lunga tratta / di gente, ch'io non avrei mai creduto / che morte tanta n' avesse disfatta'" [Eliot's note]. "Behind that banner trailed so long a file / of people—I should never have believed / that death could have unmade so many souls"; not only is Dante amazed at the number of people who have died but he is also describing a crowd of people who were neither good nor bad—non-entities denied even the entrance to hell.

9. "Cf. *Inferno* IV, 25–27: 'Quivi, secondo che per ascoltare, / non avea pianto, ma' che di sospiri, / che l'aura eterna facevan tremare'" [Eliot's note]. "Here, so far as I could tell by listening, there was no weeping but so many sighs that they caused the everlasting air to tremble"; the first circle of hell, or limbo, contained the souls of virtuous people who lived before Christ or had not been baptized.

1. "A phenomenon which I have often noticed" [Eliot's note]. The church is in the financial district of London, where King William Street is also located.

2. An "average" modern name (with business associations) linked to the ancient battle of Mylae (260 B.C.E.), where Rome was victorious over its commercial rival, Carthage.

3. "Cf. the Dirge in Webster's *White Devil*" [Eliot's note]. The dirge, or song of lamentation, sung by Cornelia in John Webster's play (1625), asks to "keep the wolf far thence, that's foe to men," so that the wolf's nails may not dig up the bodies of her murdered relatives. Eliot's reversal of dog for wolf, and friend for foe, domesticates the grotesque scene; it may also foreshadow rebirth since (according to Weston's book) the rise of the Dog Star, Sirius, announced the flooding of the Nile and the consequent return of fertility to Egyptian soil.

4. "V. Baudelaire, Preface to *Fleurs du Mal*" [Eliot's note]. Baudelaire's poem preface, titled "To the Reader," ended "hypocrite Reader—my double—my brother!" The poet challenges the reader to recognize that both are caught up in the worst sin of all—the moral wasteland of *ennui* ("boredom") as lack of will, the refusal to care one way or the other.

II. A Game of Chess[5]

The Chair she sat in, like a burnished throne,[6]
Glowed on the marble, where the glass
Held up by standards wrought with fruited vines
From which a golden Cupidon peeped out   80
(Another hid his eyes behind his wing)
Doubled the flames of sevenbranched candelabra
Reflecting light upon the table as
The glitter of her jewels rose to meet it,
From satin cases poured in rich profusion.   85
In vials of ivory and coloured glass
Unstoppered, lurked her strange synthetic perfumes,
Unguent, powdered, or liquid—troubled, confused
And drowned the sense in odours; stirred by the air
That freshened from the window, these ascended   90
In fattening the prolonged candle-flames,
Flung their smoke into the laquearia,[7]
Stirring the pattern on the coffered ceiling.
Huge sea-wood fed with copper
Burned green and orange, framed by the coloured stone,   95
In which sad light a carvèd dolphin swam.
Above the antique mantel was displayed
As though a window gave upon the sylvan scene[8]
The change of Philomel,[9] by the barbarous king
So rudely forced; yet there the nightingale[1]   100
Filled all the desert with inviolable voice
And still she cried, and still the world pursues,
"Jug Jug"[2] to dirty ears.
And other withered stumps of time
Were told upon the walls; staring forms   105
Leaned out, leaning, hushing the room enclosed.
Footsteps shuffled on the stair.
Under the firelight, under the brush, her hair

5. Reference to a play, *A Game of Chess* (1627) by Thomas Middleton (1580–1627); see n. 5, p. 1158. Part II juxtaposes two scenes of modern sterility: an initial setting of wealthy boredom, neurosis, and lack of communication, and a pub scene in which similar concerns of appearance, sexual attraction, and thwarted childbirth are brought out more visibly, and in more vulgar language.
6. "Cf. *Antony and Cleopatra*, II, ii, 1.190" [Eliot's note]. A paler version of Cleopatra's splendor as she met her future lover, Antony: "The barge she sat in, like a burnished throne, / Burned on the water."
7. "Laquearia. V. *Aeneid*, 1, 726: dependent lychni laquearibus aureis incensi, et noctem flammis funalia vincunt" [Eliot's note]. "Glowing lamps hang from the gold-paneled ceiling,

and the torches conquer night with their flames"; the banquet setting of another classical love scene, in which Dido is inspired with a fatal passion for Aeneas.
8. "Sylvan scene. V. Milton, *Paradise Lost*, IV, 140" [Eliot's note]. Eden as first seen by Satan.
9. "V. Ovid, *Metamorphoses*, VI, Philomela" [Eliot's note]. Philomela was raped by her brother-in-law, King Tereus, who cut out her tongue so that she could not tell her sister, Procne. Later Procne is changed into a swallow and Philomela into a nightingale to save them from the king's rage after they have revenged themselves by killing his son.
1. "Cf. Part III, 1.204" [Eliot's note].
2. Represents the nightingale's song in Elizabethan poetry.

Spread out in fiery points
Glowed into words, then would be savagely still.   110

   'My nerves are bad to-night. Yes, bad. Stay with me.
'Speak to me. Why do you never speak. Speak.
  'What are you thinking of? What thinking? What?
'I never know what you are thinking. Think.'

   I think we are in rats' alley[3]   115
Where the dead men lost their bones.

'What is that noise?'
                    The wind under the door.[4]
'What is that noise now? What is the wind doing?'
                    Nothing again nothing.   120
                    'Do
'You know nothing? Do you see nothing? Do you remember
'Nothing?'

   I remember
Those are pearls that were his eyes.   125
'Are you alive, or not? Is there nothing in your head?'
                                        But

O O O O that Shakespeherian Rag—
It's so elegant
So intelligent   130
'What shall I do now? What shall I do?'
'I shall rush out as I am, and walk the street
'With my hair down, so. What shall we do to-morrow?
'What shall we ever do?'
                    The hot water at ten.   135
And if it rains, a closed car at four.
And we shall play a game of chess,[5]
Pressing lidless eyes and waiting for a knock upon the door.

   When Lil's husband got demobbed,[6] I said—
I didn't mince my words, I said to her myself,   140
HURRY UP PLEASE ITS TIME[7]
Now Albert's coming back, make yourself a bit smart.
He'll want to know what you done with that money he gave you
To get yourself some teeth. He did, I was there.
You have them all out, Lil, and get a nice set,   145
He said, I swear, I can't bear to look at you.
And no more can't I, I said, and think of poor Albert,

---

3. "Cf. Part III, 1.195" [Eliot's note].
4. "Cf. Webster: 'Is the wind in that door
still?'" [Eliot's note]. From *The Devil's Law
Case* (1623), 3.2.162, with the implied meaning "is there still breath in him?"
5. "Cf. the game of chess in Middleton's
Women Beware Women" [Eliot's note]. In this

scene, a woman is seduced in a series of strategic steps that parallel the moves of a chess
game, which is occupying her mother-in-law
at the same time.
6. Demobilized, discharged from the army.
7. The British bartender's warning that the
pub is about to close.

He's been in the army four years, he wants a good time,
And if you don't give it him, there's others will, I said.
Oh is there, she said. Something o' that, I said.   150
Then I'll know who to thank, she said, and give me a straight look.
HURRY UP PLEASE ITS TIME
If you don't like it you can get on with it, I said.
Others can pick and choose if you can't.
But if Albert makes off, it won't be for lack of telling.   155
You ought to be ashamed, I said, to look so antique.
(And her only thirty-one.)
I can't help it, she said, pulling a long face,
It's them pills I took, to bring it off, she said.
(She's had five already, and nearly died of young George.)   160
The chemist[8] said it would be all right, but I've never been the same.
You are a proper fool, I said.
Well, if Albert won't leave you alone, there it is, I said,
What you get married for if you don't want children?
HURRY UP PLEASE ITS TIME   165
Well, that Sunday Albert was home, they had a hot gammon,[9]
And they asked me in to dinner, to get the beauty of it hot—
HURRY UP PLEASE ITS TIME
HURRY UP PLEASE ITS TIME
Goonight Bill. Goonight Lou. Goonight May. Goonight.   170
Ta ta. Goonight. Goonight.
Good night, ladies, good night, sweet ladies, good night, good night.[1]

III. The Fire Sermon[2]

The river's tent is broken: the last fingers of leaf
Clutch and sink into the wet bank. The wind
Crosses the brown land, unheard. The nymphs are departed.   175
Sweet Thames, run softly, till I end my song.[3]
The river bears no empty bottles, sandwich papers,
Silk handkerchiefs, cardboard boxes, cigarette ends
Or other testimony of summer nights. The nymphs are departed.
And their friends, the loitering heirs of city directors;   180
Departed, have left no addresses.
By the waters of Leman I sat down and wept[4] . . .
Sweet Thames, run softly till I end my song,

8. The druggist, who gave her pills to cause a miscarriage.
9. Ham.
1. The popular song for a party's end ("Good Night, Ladies") shifts into Ophelia's last words in *Hamlet* (4.5.72) as she goes off to drown herself.
2. Reference to the Buddha's Fire Sermon (see n. 2, p. 1164), in which he denounced the fiery lusts and passions of earthly experience. "All things are on fire . . . with the fire of passion . . . of hatred . . . of infatuation." Part III describes the degeneration of even these pas-

sions in the sterile decadence of the modern Waste Land.
3. "V. Spenser, *Prothalamion*" [Eliot's note]. The line is the refrain of a marriage song by the Elizabethan poet Edmund Spenser (1552?–1599) and evokes a river of unpolluted pastoral beauty.
4. In Psalms 137.1, the exiled Hebrews sit by the rivers of Babylon and weep for their lost homeland. "Waters of Leman": Lake Geneva (where Eliot wrote much of *The Waste Land*). A "leman" is a mistress or lover.

Sweet Thames, run softly, for I speak not loud or long.
But at my back in a cold blast I hear[5]   185
The rattle of the bones, and chuckle spread from ear to ear.

A rat crept softly through the vegetation
Dragging its slimy belly on the bank
While I was fishing in the dull canal
On a winter evening round behind the gashouse   190
Musing upon the king my brother's wreck
And on the king my father's death before him.[6]
White bodies naked on the low damp ground
And bones cast in a little low dry garret,
Rattled by the rat's foot only, year to year.   195
But at my back from time to time I hear[7]
The sound of horns and motors, which shall bring[8]
Sweeney to Mrs. Porter in the spring.
O the moon shone bright on Mrs. Porter[9]
And on her daughter   200
They wash their feet in soda water
Et O ces voix d'enfants, chantant dans la coupole![1]

Twit twit twit
Jug jug jug jug jug jug
So rudely forc'd.   205
Tereu[2]

Unreal City
Under the brown fog of a winter noon
Mr. Eugenides, the Smyrna merchant
Unshaven, with a pocket full of currants   210
C.i.f. London: documents at sight,[3]

---

5. Distorted echo of Andrew Marvell's (1621–1678) poem "To His Coy Mistress." "But at my back I always hear / Time's wingèd chariot hurrying near."
6. "Cf. *The Tempest* I.ii" [Eliot's note]. Ferdinand, the king's son, believing his father drowned and mourning his death, hears in the air a song containing the line that Eliot quotes earlier at lines 48 and 125.
7. "Cf. Marvell, 'To His Coy Mistress'." [Eliot's note].
8. "Cf. Day, *Parliament of Bees*: 'When of the sudden, listening, you shall hear, / A noise of horns and hunting, which shall bring / Actaeon to Diana in the spring, / Where all shall see her naked skin'" [Eliot's note]. The young hunter Actaeon was changed into a stag, hunted down, and killed when he came upon the goddess Diana bathing. Sweeney is in no such danger from his visit to Mrs. Porter.
9. "I do not know the origin of the ballad from which these lines are taken: it was reported to me from Sydney, Australia" [Eliot's note]. A song popular among Allied troops during World War I. One version continues lines 199–201 as follows: "And so they oughter / To keep them clean."
1. "V. Verlaine, *Parsifal*" [Eliot's note]. "And O these children's voices, singing in the dome!" (French); the last lines of a sonnet by Paul Verlaine (1844–1896), which ambiguously celebrates the Grail hero's chaste restraint. In Richard Wagner's opera, Parsifal's feet are washed to purify him before entering the presence of the Grail.
2. Tereus, who raped Philomela (see line 99); also the nightingale's song.
3. "The currants were quoted at a price 'carriage and insurance free to London'; and the Bill of Lading etc. were to be handed to the buyer upon payment of the sight draft" [Eliot's note].

Asked me in demotic French
To luncheon at the Cannon Street Hotel
Followed by a weekend at the Metropole.[4]

At the violet hour, when the eyes and back   215
Turn upward from the desk, when the human engine waits
Like a taxi throbbing waiting,
I Tiresias,[5] though blind, throbbing between two lives,
Old man with wrinkled female breasts, can see
At the violet hour, the evening hour that strives   220
Homeward, and brings the sailor home from sea,[6]
The typist home at teatime, clears her breakfast, lights
Her stove, and lays out food in tins.
Out of the window perilously spread
Her drying combinations touched by the sun's last rays,   225
On the divan are piled (at night her bed)
Stockings, slippers, camisoles, and stays.
I Tiresias, old man with wrinkled dugs
Perceived the scene, and foretold the rest—
I too awaited the expected guest.   230
He, the young man carbuncular, arrives,
A small house agent's clerk, with one bold stare,
One of the low on whom assurance sits
As a silk hat on a Bradford[7] millionaire.
The time is now propitious, as he guesses,   235
The meal is ended, she is bored and tired,
Endeavours to engage her in caresses
Which still are unreproved, if undesired.
Flushed and decided, he assaults at once;
Exploring hands encounter no defence;   240
His vanity requires no response,
And makes a welcome of indifference.
(And I Tiresias have foresuffered all
Enacted on this same divan or bed;
I who have sat by Thebes below the wall   245

4. Smyrna is an ancient Phoenician seaport, and early Smyrna merchants spread the Eastern fertility cults. In contrast, their descendant Mr. Eugenides ("Well-born") invites the poet to lunch in a large commercial hotel and a weekend at a seaside resort in Brighton.
5. "Tiresias, although a mere spectator and not indeed a 'character,' is yet the most important personage in the poem, uniting all the rest. Just as the one-eyed merchant, seller of currants, melts into the Phoenician Sailor, and the latter is not wholly distinct from Ferdinand Prince of Naples, so all the women are one woman, and the two sexes meet in Tiresias. What Tiresias *sees*, in fact, is the substance of the poem. The whole passage from Ovid is one of great anthropological interest" [Eliot's note]. The passage then quoted from Ovid's *Metamorphoses* (3.320–38) describes how Tiresias spent seven years of his life as a woman and thus experienced love from the point of view of both sexes. Blinded by Juno, he was recompensed by Jove with the gift of prophecy.
6. "This may or may not appear as exact as Sappho's lines, but I had in mind the 'longshore' or 'dory' fisherman, who returns at nightfall" [Eliot's note]. The Greek poet Sappho's poem describes how the evening star brings home those whom dawn has sent abroad; there is also an echo of Robert Louis Stevenson's (1850–1894) *Requiem* 1.221: "Home is the sailor, home from the sea."
7. A manufacturing town in Yorkshire that prospered greatly during World War I.

And walked among the lowest of the dead.)[8]
Bestows one final patronising kiss,
And gropes his way, finding the stairs unlit . . .

She turns and looks a moment in the glass,
Hardly aware of her departed lover;   250
Her brain allows one half-formed thought to pass:
'Well now that's done: and I'm glad it's over.'
When lovely woman stoops to folly and[9]
Paces about her room again, alone,
She smoothes her hair with automatic hand,   255
And puts a record on the gramophone.

     'This music crept by me upon the waters'[1]
And along the Strand, up Queen Victoria Street.
O City city,[2] I can sometimes hear
Beside a public bar in Lower Thames Street,   260
The pleasant whining of a mandoline
And a clatter and a chatter from within
Where fishmen lounge at noon: where the walls
Of Magnus Martyr[3] hold
Inexplicable splendour of Ionian white and gold.   265

               The river sweats[4]
               Oil and tar
               The barges drift
               With the turning tide
               Red sails   270
               Wide
               To leeward, swing on the heavy spar.
               The barges wash
               Drifting logs
               Down Greenwich reach   275
               Past the Isle of Dogs.[5]

---

8. Tiresias prophesied in the marketplace at Thebes for many years before dying and continuing to prophesy in Hades.

9. "V. Goldsmith, the song in *The Vicar of Wakefield*" [Eliot's note]. "When lovely woman stoops to folly / And finds too late that men betray / What charm can soothe her melancholy, / What art can wash her guilt away?" Oliver Goldsmith (ca. 1730–1774), *The Vicar of Wakefield* (1766).

1. "V. *The Tempest*, as above" [Eliot's note, referring to line 191]. Spoken by Ferdinand as he hears Ariel sing of his father's transformation by the sea, his eyes turning to pearls, his bones to coral, and everything else he formerly was into "something rich and strange."

2. A double invocation: the city of London and the City as London's central financial district (see lines 60 and 207). See also lines 375–76,

the great cities of Western civilization.

3. "The interior of St. Magnus Martyr is to my mind one of the finest among Wren's interiors. See *The Proposed Demolition of Nineteen City Churches*: (P. S. King & Son, Ltd)" [Eliot's note]. The architect was Christopher Wren (1632–1723), and the church is located just below London Bridge on Lower Thames Street.

4. "The Song of the (three) Thames-daughters begins here. From line 292 to 306 inclusive they speak in turn. V. *Götterdämmerung* III.i.: the Rhine-daughters" [Eliot's note]. In Wagner's opera *The Twilight of the Gods* (1876), the three Rhine-maidens mourn the loss of their gold, which gave the river its sparkling beauty; lines 277–78 here echo the Rhine-maidens' refrain.

5. A peninsula opposite Greenwich on the Thames.

Weialala leia
Wallala leialala

Elizabeth and Leicester[6]
Beating oars   280
The stern was formed
A gilded shell
Red and gold
The brisk swell
Rippled both shores   285
Southwest wind
Carried down stream
The peal of bells
White towers
     Weialala leia   290
     Wallala leialala

'Trams and dusty trees.
Highbury bore me. Richmond and Kew
Undid me.[7] By Richmond I raised my knees
Supine on the floor of a narrow canoe.'   295
'My feet are at Moorgate,[8] and my heart
Under my feet. After the event
He wept. He promised "a new start."
I made no comment. What should I resent?'

'On Margate Sands.[9]   300
I can connect
Nothing with nothing.
The broken fingernails of dirty hands.
My people humble people who expect
Nothing.'   305
     la la

To Carthage then I came[1]

---

6. "V. Froude, *Elizabeth*, vol. I, ch. iv, letter of De Quadra to Philip of Spain: 'In the afternoon we were in a barge, watching the games on the river. (The queen) was alone with Lord Robert and myself on the poop, when they began to talk nonsense, and went so far that Lord Robert at last said, as I was on the spot there was no reason why they should not be married if the queen pleased" [Eliot's note]. Sir Robert Dudley (1532–1588), the earl of Leicester, was a favorite of Queen Elizabeth and at one point hoped to marry her.
7. "Cf. *Purgatorio*, V, 133: 'Ricorditi di me, che son la Pia; / Siena mi fe', disfecemi Maremma'"

[Eliot's note]. La Pia, in Purgatory, recalls her seduction: "Remember me, who am La Pia. / Siena made me, Maremma undid me." Eliot's parody substitutes Highbury (a London suburb) and Richmond and Kew, popular excursion points on the Thames.
8. A London slum.
9. A seaside resort on the Thames.
1. "V. St. Augustine's *Confessions*: 'to Carthage then I came, where a cauldron of unholy loves sang all about mine ears'" [Eliot's note]. The youthful Augustine is described. Carthage is also the scene of Dido's faithful love for Aeneas, referred to in line 92.

Burning burning burning burning[2]
O Lord Thou pluckest me out[3]
O Lord Thou pluckest   310

burning

IV. Death by Water

Phlebas the Phoenician, a fortnight dead,
Forgot the cry of gulls, and the deep sea swell
And the profit and loss.
     A current under sea   315
Picked his bones in whispers. As he rose and fell
He passed the stages of his age and youth
Entering the whirlpool.
     Gentile or Jew
O you who turn the wheel and look to windward,   320
Consider Phlebas, who was once handsome and tall as you.

V. What the Thunder Said[4]

After the torchlight red on sweaty faces
After the frosty silence in the gardens
After the agony in stony places
The shouting and the crying   325
Prison and palace and reverberation
Of thunder of spring over distant mountains
He who was living is now dead[5]
We who were living are now dying
With a little patience   330

Here is no water but only rock
Rock and no water and the sandy road
The road winding above among the mountains
Which are mountains of rock without water
If there were water we should stop and drink   335

---

2. "The complete text of the Buddha's Fire Sermon (which corresponds in importance to the Sermon on the Mount) from which these words are taken, will be found translated in the late Henry Clarke Warren's *Buddhism in Translation* (Harvard Oriental Studies). Mr. Warren was one of the great pioneers of Buddhist studies in the Occident" [Eliot's note]. The Sermon on the Mount is in Matthew 5–7.
3. "From St. Augustine's *Confessions* again. The collocation of these two representatives of eastern and western asceticism, as the culmination of this part of the poem is not an accident" [Eliot's note]. See also Zechariah 3.2, where the high priest Joshua is described as a "brand plucked out of the fire."

4. "In the first part of Part V three themes are employed: the journey to Emmaus, the approach to the Chapel Perilous (see Miss Weston's book) and the present decay of eastern Europe" [Eliot's note]. On their journey to Emmaus (Luke: 24:13–34), Jesus's disciples were joined by a stranger who later revealed himself to be the crucified and resurrected Christ. The *thunder* of the title is a divine voice in the Hindu *Upanishads* (see n. 3, p. 1166).
5. Allusions to stages in Christ's Passion: the betrayal, prayer in the garden of Gethsemane, imprisonment, trial, crucifixion, and burial. Despair reigns, for this is death before the Resurrection.

Amongst the rock one cannot stop or think
Sweat is dry and feet are in the sand
If there were only water amongst the rock
Dead mountain mouth of carious teeth that cannot spit
Here one can neither stand nor lie nor sit   340
There is not even silence in the mountains
But dry sterile thunder without rain
There is not even solitude in the mountains
But red sullen faces sneer and snarl
From doors of mudcracked houses   345
                              If there were water
    And no rock
    If there were rock
    And also water
    And water   350
    A spring
    A pool among the rock
    If there were the sound of water only
    Not the cicada⁶
    And dry grass singing   355
    But sound of water over a rock
    Where the hermit-thrush⁷ sings in the pine trees
    Drip drop drip drop drop drop drop
    But there is no water

    Who is the third who walks always beside you?   360
When I count, there are only you and I together⁸
But when I look ahead up the white road
There is always another one walking beside you
Gliding wrapt in a brown mantle, hooded
I do not know whether a man or a woman   365
—But who is that on the other side of you?

    What is that sound high in the air⁹
Murmur of maternal lamentation
Who are those hooded hordes swarming
Over endless plains, stumbling in cracked earth   370
Ringed by the flat horizon only
What is the city over the mountains
Cracks and reforms and bursts in the violet air

6. Grasshopper or cricket; see line 23.
7. "The hermit-thrush which I have heard in Quebec Province. . . . Its 'water-dripping song' is justly celebrated" [Eliot's note].
8. "The following lines were stimulated by the account of one of the Antarctic expeditions (I forget which, but I think one of Shackleton's): it was related that the party of explorers, at the extremity of their strength, had the constant delusion that there was *one more member* than could actually be counted" [Eliot's note]. See also n. 4, p. 1164.

9. Eliot's note to lines 367–77 refers to Hermann Hesse's *Blick ins Chaos* (Glimpse into Chaos) and a passage that reads, translated, "Already half of Europe, already at least half of Eastern Europe is on the way to Chaos, drives drunk in holy madness on the edge of the abyss and sings at the same time, sings drunk and hymn-like, as Dimitri Karamazov sang [in Dostoyevsky's *The Brothers Karamazov*]. The offended bourgeois laughs at the songs; the saint and the seer hear them with tears."

Falling towers
Jerusalem Athens Alexandria   375
Vienna London
Unreal

    A woman drew her long black hair out tight
And fiddled whisper music on those strings
And bats with baby faces in the violet light   380
Whistled, and beat their wings
And crawled head downward down a blackened wall
And upside down in air were towers
Tolling reminiscent bells, that kept the hours
And voices singing out of empty cisterns and exhausted wells.   385

    In this decayed hole among the mountains
In the faint moonlight, the grass is singing
Over the tumbled graves, about the chapel
There is the empty chapel, only the wind's home.
It has no windows, and the door swings,   390
Dry bones can harm no one.
Only a cock stood on the rooftree
Co co rico co co rico[1]
In a flash of lightning. Then a damp gust
Bringing rain   395

    Ganga was sunken, and the limp leaves
Waited for rain, while the black clouds
Gathered far distant, over Himavant.[2]
The jungle crouched, humped in silence.
Then spoke the thunder   400
DA
Datta: what have we given?[3]
My friend, blood shaking my heart
The awful daring of a moment's surrender
Which an age of prudence can never retract   405
By this, and this only, we have existed
Which is not to be found in our obituaries
Or in memories draped by the beneficent spider[4]
Or under seals broken by the lean solicitor
In our empty rooms   410
DA

1. European version of the cock's crow: *cock-a-doodle-doo*. The cock crowed in Matthew 26:34 and 74, after Peter had denied Jesus three times.
2. A mountain in the Himalayas. "Ganga": the river Ganges in India.
3. "'Datta, dayadhvam, damyata' (Give, sympathise, control). The fable of the meaning of the Thunder is found in the *Brihadaranyaka*—Upanishad 5,1" [Eliot's note]. In the fable, the word DA, spoken by the supreme being Prajapati, is interpreted as *Datta* ("to give alms"),

Dayadhvam ("to sympathize or have compassion"), and *Damyata* ("to have self-control") by gods, human beings, and demons respectively. The conclusion is that when the thunder booms DA DA DA, Prajapati is commanding that all three virtues be practiced simultaneously.
4. "Cf. Webster, *The White Devil*, V, vi: '. . . they'll remarry / Ere the worm pierce your winding-sheet, ere the spider / Make a thin curtain for your epitaphs'" [Eliot's note].

Dayadhvam:[5] I have heard the key
Turn in the door once and turn once only
We think of the key, each in his prison
Thinking of the key, each confirms a prison   415
Only at nightfall, aethereal rumours
Revive for a moment a broken Coriolanus[6]
DA
Damyata: The boat responded
Gaily, to the hand expert with sail and oar   420
The sea was calm, your heart would have responded
Gaily, when invited, beating obedient
To controlling hands
                         I sat upon the shore
Fishing,[7] with the arid plain behind me   425
Shall I at least set my lands in order?
London Bridge is falling down falling down falling down

Poi s'ascose nel foco che gli affina[8]
Quando fiam uti chelidon[9]—O swallow swallow
Le Prince d'Aquitaine à la tour abolie[1]   430
These fragments I have shored against my ruins
Why then Ile fit you. Hieronymo's mad againe.[2]
Datta. Dayadhvam. Damyata.
           Shantih   shantih   shantih[3]

1922

---

5. Eliot's note on the command "to sympathize" or reach outside the self cites two descriptions of helpless isolation. The first comes from Dante's *Inferno* 33.46: as Ugolino, imprisoned in a tower with his children to die of starvation, says, "And I heard below the door of the horrible tower being locked up." The second is a modern description by the English philosopher F. H. Bradley (1846–1924) of the inevitably self-enclosed or private nature of consciousness: "My external sensations are no less private to myself than are my thoughts or my feelings. In either case my experience falls within my own circle, a circle closed on the outside; and, with all its elements alike, every sphere is opaque to the others which surround it. . . . In brief, regarded as an existence which appears in a soul, the whole world for each is peculiar and private to that soul" (*Appearance and Reality*).
6. A proud Roman patrician who was exiled and led an army against his homeland. In Shakespeare's play, both his grandeur and his downfall come from a desire to be ruled only by himself.
7. "V. Weston: *From Ritual to Romance*; chapter on the Fisher King" [Eliot's note].
8. Eliot's note quotes a passage in the *Purgatorio* in which Arnaut Daniel (see n. 3, p. 1154) asks Dante to remember his pain. The line cited here, "then he, too, hid himself in the fire that makes those spirits ready to go higher" (*Purgatorio* 26.148), shows Daniel departing in fire which—in Purgatory—exists as a purifying rather than a destructive element.
9. "V. *Pervigilium Veneris*. Cf. Philomela in Parts II and III" [Eliot's note]. "When shall I be as a swallow?" A line from the *Vigil of Venus*, an anonymous late Latin poem, that asks for the gift of song; here associated with Philomela as a swallow, not the nightingale of lines 99–103 and 203–06.
1. "V. Gerard de Nerval, Sonnet *El Desdichado*" [Eliot's note]. The Spanish title means "The Disinherited One," and the sonnet is a monologue describing the speaker as a melancholy, ill-starred dreamer: "the Prince of Aquitaine in his ruined tower."
2. "V. Kyd's *Spanish Tragedy*" [Eliot's note]. Thomas Kyd's revenge play (1594) is subtitled *Hieronymo's Mad Againe*. The protagonist "fits" his son's murderers into appropriate roles in a court entertainment so that they may all be killed.
3. "Shantih. Repeated as here, a formal ending to an Upanishad. 'The Peace which passeth understanding' is our equivalent to this word" [Eliot's note]. The *Upanishads* comment on the sacred Hindu scriptures, the *Vedas*.

ANNA AKHMATOVA
1889–1966

One of the great Russian poets of the twentieth century, Anna Akhmatova expresses herself in an intensely personal, poetic voice, whether as lover, wife, and mother or as a national poet commemorating the mute agony of millions. From the subjective romantic lyrics of her earliest work to the communal mourning of *Requiem*, she conveys universal themes in terms of individual experience, and historical events through the filter of fear, love, hope, and pain. Yet what most distinguishes her work is the way these basic emotions arise from the historical traumas of Akhmatova's native land.

Born Anna Andreevna Gorenko, in a suburb of the Black Sea port of Odessa, she was the daughter of a maritime engineer and an independent woman of revolutionary sympathies. She took the pen name Akhmatova (accented on the second syllable) from her maternal great-grandmother, who was of Tatar descent. Anna attended the local school at Tsarskoe Selo, near St. Petersburg, but completed her degree in Kiev. In 1907 she briefly studied law at the Kiev College for Women before moving to St. Petersburg to study literature. In Tsarskoe Selo, Akhmatova met Nikolai Gumilyov, whom she married in 1910. Gumilyov helped organize the Poets Guild, which became the core of a small new literary movement. Acmeism rejected the romantic, quasi-religious aims of Russian symbolism and valued clarity, concreteness, and closeness to the things of this earth. The Symbolist–Acmeist debate went on inside a lively literary and social life, while the three main figures of the movement—Akhmatova, Gumilyov, and Osip Mandelstam—gained a reputation as important poets.

Although Akhmatova and Gumilyov divorced, his arrest and execution for counterrevolutionary activities in 1921 put her status into question. After 1922 she was no longer allowed to publish and was forced into the withdrawal from public activity that Russians call "internal emigration." Officially forgotten, she was not forgotten in fact; in the schools, students who would never hear her name mentioned in class copied out her poems by hand and circulated them secretly. Relying for her living on a meager, irregular pension, Akhmatova prepared essays on the life and works of the Russian author Aleksandr Pushkin (1799–1837) and wrote poems that would not appear until much later. Stalin's "Great Purge" of 1935–38 sent millions of people to prison camps and made the 1930s a time of terror and uncertainty for everyone.

Akhmatova's friend Osip Mandelstam was exiled to Voronezh in 1934 and then sent to a prison camp in 1938, where he died that year. In 1935 her partner, the art critic Nikolai Punin, was arrested briefly and her son Lev Gumilyov, then twenty-three, was imprisoned, an event that inspired the first poems of the cycle that would become *Requiem*. Lev was ultimately imprisoned for a total of fourteen years as the government sought a way to punish his mother for what it perceived as her disloyalty to the regime. Composing *Requiem* was a risky act carried out over several years, and Akhmatova and her friend Lidia Chukovskaya memorized the stanzas in order to preserve the poem in the absence of written copy.

During the Second World War, Akhmatova's interest in larger musical forms motivated her to develop cycles of poems instead of her accustomed individual lyrics. She also began work on *Poem Without a Hero*, a long, complex verse narrative in three parts that sums up many of her earlier themes: love, death, creativity, the unity of European culture, and the suffering of her people. The poet was allowed a partial return to public life, addressing women on the radio during the siege of Leningrad (St. Petersburg) in 1941 and writing patriotic lyrics such as the famous *Courage* (published in *Pravda* in 1942), which rallied the Russian people to defend their homeland (and their national language) from enslavement. Her son was briefly released to serve in the military before being imprisoned again after the war.

Despite her patriotic activities, Akhmatova was subject to vicious official attacks after the war. Because she was considered too independent and cosmopolitan to be tolerated by the authorities, Akhmatova's books were suppressed. Her works did not fit the government-approved model of literature: they were too "individualistic" and were not "socially useful." After the death of Joseph Stalin, in 1953, however, her collected poems—including poems of the war years and unknown texts written during the periods of enforced silence—brought the range of her work to public attention. *Requiem* was first published "without her consent" in Munich in 1963 (not until 1987 was the complete text published in the Soviet Union). Her death, in 1966, signaled the end of an era in modern Russian poetry, for she was the last of the famous "quartet" that also included Mandelstam, Marina Tsvetaeva, and Boris Pasternak.

Requiem (1940), presented here, is a lyrical cycle, a series of poems written on a theme, but it is also a short epic narrative. The story it tells is acutely personal, even autobiographical, but like an epic it transcends personal significance and describes (as in *The Song of Roland*) a moment in the history of a nation. Akhmatova, who had seen her husband and son arrested and her friends die in prison camps, was only one of millions who had suffered similar losses in the purges of the 1930s. "Instead of a Preface," "Dedication," "Prologue," and two epilogues to *Requiem* constitute a framework examining this image of a common fate, while the core group of numbered poems develops a subjective picture and stages an individual drama. The "Dedication" and "Prologue" establish the context for the poem as a whole: the mass arrests in the 1930s after the assassination on December 1, 1934, of Sergei Kirov, the top Communist Party official in Leningrad. In the inner poems, Akhmatova blends her individual personal losses—husband, son, and friends—to create a single focus: the figure of a mother grieving for her condemned son. The speaker identifies herself with the crowd of women with whom she waited for seventeen months outside the Kresty ("Crosses") prison in Leningrad; at dawn each day they would all arrive, hoping to be allowed to pass their loved ones a parcel or a letter, and fearing that the prisoners would be sentenced to death or exile to the prison camps of Siberia. Instead of experiencing a natural life—one in which "for someone the sunset luxuriates"—these women and the prisoners are forced into a suspended, uncertain existence where all values are inverted and the city itself has become merely the setting for its prisons.

The "I" of the speaker throughout remains anonymous, in spite of the fact that Akhmatova describes her personal emotions in the central poems; her identity is that of a sorrowing mother, and she is distinguished from her fellow sufferers only by the poetic gift that makes her the "exhausted mouth, / Through which a hundred million scream." *Requiem* is at once both public and private: a picture of individual grief linked to the country's disaster, and a vision of community suffering that extends beyond contemporary national tragedy into medieval Russian history and Greek mythology. The poem consistently figures the martyrdom of the Soviet people in religious terms, from the recurrent mention of crosses and Crucifixion to the culminating image of maternal suffering in Mary, the mother of Christ.

With the numbered poems, Akhmatova recounts the growing anguish of a mother as her son is arrested and sentenced to death. The speaker has described her partner's arrest at dawn, in the midst of the family. Her son is arrested later, and in the rest of the poem she relives her numb incomprehension as she struggles against the increasing likelihood that he will be condemned to death. After the sentence is passed, the mother can speak of his execution only in oblique terms, by shifting the image of death onto the plane of the Crucifixion and God's will. It is a tragedy that cannot be comprehended or beheld directly, just as, she suggests, at the Crucifixion "No one glanced and no one would have dared" to look at the grieving Mary.

In the two epilogues, the grieving speaker returns from religious transcendence to Earth and current history. Here she takes on a composite identity, seeing herself not as an isolated sufferer but as the women whose fate she has shared. It is their memory she perpetuates by writing *Requiem*, and it is in their memory that she herself lives on. No longer the victim of purely personal tragedy, she has become a bronze statue commemorating a community of suffering—a figure shaped by circumstances into a monument of public and private grief.

Requiem[1]

1935–1940

No, not under the vault of alien skies,[2]
And not under the shelter of alien wings—
I was with my people then,
There, where my people, unfortunately, were.

1961

Instead of a Preface

In the terrible years of the Yezhov terror,[3] I spent seventeen months in the prison lines of Leningrad. Once, someone "recognized" me. Then a woman with bluish lips standing behind me, who, of course, had never heard me called by name before, woke up from the stupor to which every one had succumbed and whispered in my ear (everyone spoke in whispers there):

"Can you describe this?"

And I answered: "Yes, I can."

---

1. Translated by Judith Hemschemeyer.
2. A phrase borrowed from *Message to Siberia* by the Russian poet Aleksandr Pushkin

(1799–1837).
3. In 1937–38, mass arrests were carried out by the secret police, headed by Nikolai Yezhov.

Then something that looked like a smile passed over what had once been her face.

April 1, 1957
Leningrad[4]

Dedication

Mountains bow down to this grief,
Mighty rivers cease to flow,
But the prison gates hold firm,
And behind them are the "prisoners' burrows"
And mortal woe.   5
For someone a fresh breeze blows,
For someone the sunset luxuriates—
We[5] wouldn't know, we are those who everywhere
Hear only the rasp of the hateful key
And the soldiers' heavy tread.   10
We rose as if for an early service,
Trudged through the savaged capital
And met there, more lifeless than the dead;
The sun is lower and the Neva[6] mistier,
But hope keeps singing from afar.   15
The verdict . . . And her tears gush forth,
Already she is cut off from the rest,
As if they painfully wrenched life from her heart,
As if they brutally knocked her flat,
But she goes on . . . Staggering . . . Alone . . .   20
Where now are my chance friends
Of those two diabolical years?
What do they imagine is in Siberia's storms,[7]
What appears to them dimly in the circle of the moon?
I am sending my farewell greeting to them.   25

March 1940

Prologue

That was when the ones who smiled
Were the dead, glad to be at rest.
And like a useless appendage, Leningrad
Swung from its prisons.
And when, senseless from torment,   5
Regiments of convicts marched,

---

4. The prose preface was written after her son had been released from prison and it was possible to think of editing the poem for publication.
5. The women waiting in line before the prison gates.
6. The large river that flows through St. Petersburg.
7. Victims of the purges who were not executed were condemned to prison camps in Siberia. Their wives were allowed to accompany them into exile, although they had to live in towns at a distance from the camps.

And the short songs of farewell
Were sung by locomotive whistles.
The stars of death stood above us
And innocent Russia writhed   10
Under bloody boots
And under the tires of the Black Marias.[8]

I

They led you away at dawn,
I followed you, like a mourner,
In the dark front room the children were crying,[9]
By the icon shelf the candle was dying.
On your lips was the icon's chill.[1]   5
The deathly sweat on your brow . . . Unforgettable!—
I will be like the wives of the Streltsy,[2]
Howling under the Kremlin towers.

1935

II

Quietly flows the quiet Don,[3]
Yellow moon slips into a home.

He slips in with cap askew,
He sees a shadow, yellow moon.

This woman is ill,   5
This woman is alone,
Husband in the grave,[4] son in prison,
Say a prayer for me.

III

No, it is not I, it is somebody else who is suffering.
I would not have been able to bear what happened,
Let them shroud it in black,
And let them carry off the lanterns . . .

                                                        Night.   5

1940

---

8. Police cars for conveying those arrested.
9. Akhmatova's third husband, the art historian
Nikolai Punin, was arrested at dawn while the
children (his daughter and her cousin) cried.
1. The icon—a small religious painting—was
set on a shelf before which a candle was kept
lit. Punin had kissed the icon before being
taken away.
2. Elite troops organized by Ivan the Terrible

around 1550. They rebelled and were executed by Peter the Great in 1698. Pleading in
vain, their wives and mothers saw the men
killed under the towers of the Kremlin.
3. The great Russian river, often celebrated in
folk songs. This poem is modeled on a simple,
rhythmic, short folk song known as a *chastuska*.
4. Akhmatova's first husband, the poet Nikolai Gumilyov, was shot in 1921.

IV

You should have been shown, you mocker,
Minion of all your friends,
Gay little sinner of Tsarskoye Selo,[5]
What would happen in your life—
How three-hundredth in line, with a parcel,   5
You would stand by the Kresty prison,

Your tempestuous tears
Burning through the New Year's ice.
Over there the prison poplar bends,
And there's no sound—and over there how many   10
Innocent lives are ending now . . .

V

For seventeen months I've been crying out,
Calling you home.
I flung myself at the hangman's[6] feet,
You are my son and my horror.
Everything is confused forever,   5
And it's not clear to me
Who is a beast now, who is a man,
And how long before the execution.
And there are only dusty flowers,
And the chinking of the censer, and tracks   10
From somewhere to nowhere.
And staring me straight in the eyes,
And threatening impending death,
Is an enormous star.[7]

1939

VI

The light weeks will take flight,
I won't comprehend what happened.
Just as the white nights[8]
Stared at you, dear son, in prison

So they are staring again,   5
With the burning eyes of a hawk,
Talking about your lofty cross,
And about death.

1939

5. Akhmatova recalls her early, carefree, and privileged life in Tsarskoe Selo, outside St. Petersburg.
6. Stalin's. Akhmatova wrote a letter to him pleading for the release of her son.
7. The star, the censer, the foliage, and the confusion between beast and man recall apocalyptic passages in the Book of Revelation (8:5, 7, 10–11 and 9:7–10).
8. In St. Petersburg, because it is so far north, the nights around the summer solstice are never totally dark.

VII

THE SENTENCE

And the stone word fell
On my still-living breast.
Never mind, I was ready.
I will manage somehow.

Today I have so much to do: 5
I must kill memory once and for all,
I must turn my soul to stone,
I must learn to live again—

Unless . . . Summer's ardent rustling
Is like a festival outside my window.   10
For a long time I've foreseen this
Brilliant day, deserted house.

June 22, 1939[9]
Fountain House

VIII

TO DEATH

You will come in any case—so why not now?
I am waiting for you—I can't stand much more.
I've put out the light and opened the door
For you, so simple and miraculous.
So come in any form you please,   5
Burst in as a gas shell
Or, like a gangster, steal in with a length of pipe,
Or poison me with typhus fumes.
Or be that fairy tale you've dreamed up,[1]
So sickeningly familiar to everyone—   10
In which I glimpse the top of a pale blue cap[2]
And the house attendant white with fear.
Now it doesn't matter anymore. The Yenisey[3] swirls,
The North Star shines.
And the final horror dims   15
The blue luster of beloved eyes.

August 19, 1939
Fountain House

---

9. The date that her son was sentenced to labor camp.
1. A denunciation to the police for imaginary crimes, common during the purges as people hastened to protect themselves by accusing their neighbors.
2. The NKVD (secret police) wore blue caps.
3. A river in Siberia along which there were many prison camps.

IX

Now madness half shadows
My soul with its wing,
And makes it drunk with fiery wine
And beckons toward the black ravine.

And I've finally realized   5
That I must give in,
Overhearing myself
Raving as if it were somebody else.

And it does not allow me to take
Anything of mine with me   10
(No matter how I plead with it,
No matter how I supplicate):

Not the terrible eyes of my son—
Suffering turned to stone,
Not the day of the terror,   15
Not the hour I met with him in prison,

Not the sweet coolness of his hands,
Not the trembling shadow of the lindens,
Not the far-off, fragile sound—
Of the final words of consolation.   20

May 4, 1940
Fountain House

X

CRUCIFIXION

*"Do not weep for Me, Mother,
I am in the grave."*

1

A choir of angels sang the praises of that momentous hour,
And the heavens dissolved in fire.
To his Father He said: "Why hast Thou forsaken me!"[4]
And to his Mother: "Oh, do not weep for Me . . ."[5]

1940
Fountain House

---

4. Jesus's last words from the Cross (Matthew 27:46).
5. These words and the epigraph refer to a line from the Russian Orthodox prayer sung at services on Easter Saturday: "Weep not for Me, Mother, when you look upon the grave." Jesus is comforting Mary with the promise of his resurrection.

2

Mary Magdalene beat her breast and sobbed,
The beloved disciple[6] turned to stone,
But where the silent Mother stood, there
No one glanced and no one would have dared.

1943
Tashkent

Epilogue I

I learned how faces fall,
How terror darts from under eyelids,
How suffering traces lines
Of stiff cuneiform on cheeks,
How locks of ashen-blonde or black   5
Turn silver suddenly,
Smiles fade on submissive lips
And fear trembles in a dry laugh.
And I pray not for myself alone,
But for all those who stood there with me   10
In cruel cold, and in July's heat,
At that blind, red wall.

Epilogue II

Once more the day of remembrance[7] draws near.
I see, I hear, I feel you:

The one they almost had to drag at the end,
And the one who tramps her native land no more,

And the one who, tossing her beautiful head,   5
Said: "Coming here's like coming home."

I'd like to name them all by name,
But the list[8] has been confiscated and is nowhere to be found.

I have woven a wide mantle for them
From their meager, overheard words.   10

I will remember them always and everywhere,
I will never forget them no matter what comes.

And if they gag my exhausted mouth
Through which a hundred million scream,

---

6. The apostle John.
7. In the Russian Orthodox Church, a memorial service is held on the anniversary of a death.
8. Of prisoners.

Then may the people remember me   15
On the eve of my remembrance day.

And if ever in this country
They decide to erect a monument to me,

I consent to that honor
Under these conditions—that it stand   20

Neither by the sea, where I was born:
My last tie with the sea is broken,

Nor in the tsar's garden near the cherished pine stump,[9]
Where an inconsolable shade[1] looks for me,

But here, where I stood for three hundred hours,   25
And where they never unbolted the doors for me.

This, lest in blissful death
I forget the rumbling of the Black Marias,

Forget how that detested door slammed shut
And an old woman howled like a wounded animal.   30

And may the melting snow stream like tears
From my motionless lids of bronze,

And a prison dove coo in the distance,
And the ships of the Neva sail calmly on.

March 1940

                                                                1963

9. The gardens and park surrounding the summer palace in Tsarskoe Selo. Akhmatova writes elsewhere of the stump of a favorite tree in the gardens and of the poet Pushkin, whom she describes as walking in the park.
1. A ghost; probably the restless spirit of Akhmatova's executed husband, Gumilyov, who had courted her in Tsarskoe Selo.

PABLO NERUDA

1904–1973

The son of a railroad worker and a schoolteacher, with both Spanish and Indian ancestry, the Nobel Prize winner Pablo Neruda became Latin America's most important twentieth-century poet, as well as an advocate for social justice and a leading cultural figure on the communist left. He wrote in a variety of styles (lyrical, polemic, objective, and prophetic) on an array of subjects (love, daily life, the natural world, political oppression), evoking the most elemental levels of human emotion and experience. In the second half of his life, moved especially by the Spanish Civil War, Neruda adopted the role of public poet, putting his writing at the service of the people.

The writer was born Neftalí Ricardo Reyes y Basoalto, on July 12, 1904, in the small town of Parral, in southern Chile. His mother died a month after his birth. Two years later his father moved to Temuco, where he remarried and where Neruda had his early schooling. Temuco was a frontier town, and the boy's father, who disapproved of aesthetic pursuits, did not encourage his love of literature. Neruda was fortunate to find a mentor in the poet Gabriela Mistral, the principal of the girls' school at Temuco, who would herself win the Nobel Prize in Literature in 1945. To encourage the young writer, Mistral loaned him books. He began publishing his poetry at age thirteen. Seeking a pen name that would not be tied to the provinces, he chose the surname of a Czech writer, Jan Neruda, and the given name Pablo, which some critics have associated with Saint Paul the apostle.

After working and studying in poverty in Chile's capital, Santiago, from 1921 to 1927, Neruda was appointed the nation's consul to Rangoon, Burma (now Myanmar). He would serve in Ceylon (now Sri Lanka), Java (in Indonesia), and Singapore, and then, after 1933, in Buenos Aires, Barcelona, Madrid, Paris, and Mexico City. During his residence in Spain, Neruda, influenced by his friends the poets Federico García Lorca, Rafael Alberti, and Miguel Hernández, assumed a more activist political stance. In 1936, civil war broke out in Spain between the Republic and the forces of General Francisco Franco. Franco's fascist guards dragged Neruda's friend Lorca out of a friend's house; he was presumably shot, but his body was never recovered. (Neruda recalls the event in the poem "I'm Explaining a Few Things.") From that point on, Neruda would be a public poet, dedicating his voice to social issues rather than to private feelings and addressing a larger community.

Neruda returned to Chile in 1943, and, within two years, was elected to the Senate, as a representative of the Communist Party. When he criticized Chile's president in a speech on the Senate floor, Neruda's house was attacked, the government ordered his arrest, and he was forced to flee the country. Though he was celebrated internationally, with official honors from Latin America, the Soviet Union, Europe, India, and China, Neruda nonetheless could not return to Chile until 1952. He retained his close association with the Communist Party and even wrote a poem in praise of the Soviet dictator Joseph Stalin.

In 1970, Neruda ran for president of

Chile as the communist candidate, but he withdrew in favor of the socialist Salvador Allende, who won the election and appointed Neruda ambassador to Paris. In 1971, Neruda received the Nobel Prize for Literature; the following year he returned to his home in Isla Negra, gravely ill with cancer. The news at home was not good: political tensions were mounting, and Neruda watched television coverage of the rising unrest. On September 11, 1973, President Allende was assassinated in a military coup led by General Augusto Pinochet. Neruda died twelve days later. It was at Neruda's funeral that the first public demonstration against Pinochet's military government took place—a fitting tribute to Chile's national poet and representative of the people.

The selections presented here begin with Neruda's beautiful and popular early love poem "Tonight I Can Write . . ." (1924), which makes use of couplets, repetition, and chiasmus (rhetorical inversion) to explore the speaker's evolving consciousness of a love affair. While maintaining the lyrical and personal tone of his earlier poetry, "Walking Around" demonstrates Neruda's turn toward public subject matter—here expressed not in the political terms of his later work but as a description of urban life and the sufferings of the poor. In "I'm Explaining a Few Things" (1936), however, Neruda engages explicitly with politics, and his repeated exhortation, "Come and see the blood in the streets!" illustrates the speaker's intention to address his audience directly and to dedicate his voice to public issues rather than private feelings.

Canto General (1950) celebrates both Latin American identity and humanity at large. It also recreates the continent's history—anchored, for Neruda, especially after a spiritual experience he had in 1943, in the lost Inca city of Macchu Picchu, in Peru. (The usual spelling is "Machu Picchu," but Neruda uses "Macchu" throughout.) On climbing to the city's stone ruins in October of that year, the poet had an almost mystical vision showing the past linked with natural forces and the progress of humanity—a vision he described two years later in the crucial second canto of *Canto General: The Heights of Macchu Picchu*, published as a separate poem in 1946 and only later integrated into the larger work. Its twelve sections (also called cantos) are divided into two broad movements that express several philosophical attitudes and represent a turning point in the poet's thought. Throughout the first five cantos, the speaker struggles with a sense of loss and alienation; but, starting with Canto VI, as he depicts his ascent to Macchu Picchu, he comes to an understanding of a suffering human community that now gives meaning to his hitherto solitary existence. The portion printed here, the second half of *The Heights of Macchu Picchu*, begins with the speaker's invocation of the abandoned city, after climbing to its perch on a precipice in the Andes. He addresses the city as a "mother of stone"—the mother of the Latin American people—and bears witness to a lost civilization. Canto IX consists of a sequence of extraordinary metaphors that portray the city in fused images of nature and daily life—images of the passage of time and of intuited connections that transcend chronology. In Cantos X through XII, the speaker imagines the experience of the people who interest him most: the laborers who built Macchu Picchu and knew hunger and fatigue. Though they are long dead, he senses their voices and memories entering his flesh and blood, as both he and they are reborn in a unity of the people.

The final work here, "Ode to the Tomato" (1954), shows Neruda shifting his poetic style once again, employing an unadorned expression to focus on everyday subject matter. His *Elemental Odes*

(1954) examines such ordinary topics as fire, rain, bread, clothes, bees, and tomatoes. The new simplicity stemmed from Neruda's commitment to his role as public poet; he felt a responsibility to write for a broader audience, he said, including those who were just learning to read. "We must go back to what is simply human," he said; the joyous "Ode to the Tomato" responds to this need.

Tonight I Can Write . . .[1]

Tonight I can write the saddest lines.

Write, for example, 'The night is shattered
and the blue stars shiver in the distance.'

The night wind revolves in the sky and sings.

Tonight I can write the saddest lines.   5
I loved her, and sometimes she loved me too.

Through nights like this one I held her in my arms.
I kissed her again and again under the endless sky.

She loved me, sometimes I loved her too.
How could one not have loved her great still eyes.   10

Tonight I can write the saddest lines.
To think that I do not have her. To feel that I have lost her.

To hear the immense night, still more immense without her.
And the verse falls to the soul like dew to the pasture.

What does it matter that my love could not keep her.   15
The night is shattered and she is not with me.

This is all. In the distance someone is singing. In the distance.
My soul is not satisfied that it has lost her.

My sight searches for her as though to go to her.
My heart looks for her, and she is not with me.   20

The same night whitening the same trees.
We, of that time, are no longer the same.

I no longer love her, that's certain, but how I loved her.
My voice tried to find the wind to touch her hearing.

---

1. Translated by W. S. Merwin.

Another's. She will be another's. Like my kisses before.   25
Her voice. Her bright body. Her infinite eyes.

I no longer love her, that's certain, but maybe I love her.
Love is so short, forgetting is so long.

Because through nights like this one I held her in my arms
my soul is not satisfied that it has lost her.   30

Though this be the last pain that she makes me suffer
and these the last verses that I write for her.

                                                              1924

Walking Around[1]

It happens that I am tired of being a man.
It happens that I go into the tailors' shops and the movies
all shrivelled up, impenetrable, like a felt swan
navigating on a water of origin and ash.

The smell of barber shops makes me sob out loud.   5
I want nothing but the repose either of stones or of wool,
I want to see no more establishments, no more gardens,
nor merchandise, nor glasses, nor elevators.

It happens that I am tired of my feet and my nails
and my hair and my shadow.   10
It happens that I am tired of being a man.

Just the same it would be delicious
to scare a notary with a cut lily
or knock a nun stone dead with one blow of an ear.

It would be beautiful   15
to go through the streets with a green knife
shouting until I died of cold.

I do not want to go on being a root in the dark,
hesitating, stretched out, shivering with dreams,
downwards, in the wet tripe of the earth,   20
soaking it up and thinking, eating every day.

I do not want to be the inheritor of so many misfortunes.
I do not want to continue as a root and as a tomb,
as a solitary tunnel, as a cellar full of corpses,
stiff with cold, dying with pain.   25

---

1. Translated by W. S. Merwin.

For this reason Monday burns like oil
at the sight of me arriving with my jail-face,
and it howls in passing like a wounded wheel,
and its footsteps towards nightfall are filled with hot blood.

And it shoves me along to certain corners, to certain damp houses,   30
to hospitals where the bones come out of the windows,
to certain cobblers' shops smelling of vinegar,
to streets horrendous as crevices.

There are birds the colour of sulphur, and horrible intestines
hanging from the doors of the houses which I hate,   35
there are forgotten sets of teeth in a coffee-pot,
there are mirrors
which should have wept with shame and horror,
there are umbrellas all over the place, and poisons, and navels.

I stride along with calm, with eyes, with shoes,   40
with fury, with forgetfulness,
I pass, I cross offices and stores full of orthopaedic appliances,
and courtyards hung with clothes on wires,
underpants, towels and shirts which weep
slow dirty tears.   45

1933

I'm Explaining a Few Things[1]

You are going to ask: and where are the lilacs?
and the poppy-petalled metaphysics?
and the rain repeatedly spattering
its words and drilling them full
of apertures and birds?   5

I'll tell you all the news.

I lived in a suburb,
a suburb of Madrid,[2] with bells,
and clocks, and trees.

From there you could look out   10
over Castile's[3] dry face:
a leather ocean.
                    My house was called
the house of flowers, because in every cranny

1. Translated by Nathaniel Tarn.   3. Spain.
2. The capital of Spain.

geraniums burst: it was
a good-looking house   15
with its dogs and children.
                         Remember, Raúl?
Eh, Rafael?
           Federico,[4] do you remember
from under the ground
my balconies on which
the light of June drowned flowers in your mouth?
                              Brother, my brother!   20

Everything
loud with big voices, the salt of merchandises,
pile-ups of palpitating bread,
the stalls of my suburb of Argüelles with its statue
like a drained inkwell in a swirl of hake:[5]   25
oil flowed into spoons,
a deep baying
of feet and hands swelled in the streets,
metres, litres, the sharp
measure of life,
                    stacked-up fish,   30
the texture of roofs with a cold sun in which
the weather vane falters,
the fine, frenzied ivory of potatoes,
wave on wave of tomatoes rolling down to the sea.

And one morning all that was burning,   35
one morning the bonfires
leapt out of the earth
devouring human beings—
and from then on fire,
gunpowder from then on,   40
and from then on blood.
Bandits with planes and Moors,
bandits with finger-rings and duchesses,
bandits with black friars[6] spattering blessings
came through the sky to kill children   45
and the blood of children ran through the streets
without fuss, like children's blood.

Jackals that the jackals would despise,
stones that the dry thistle would bite on and spit out,
vipers that the vipers would abominate!   50

---

4. I.e., the poet Federico García Lorca, who was murdered by the Fascists on August 19, 1936. "Rafael": his friend, the poet Rafael Alberti.
5. A fish similar to the cod. "Argüelles": a busy shopping area in Madrid, near the university.
6. "Finger-rings," "duchesses," "friars" imply a collusion of the wealthy, the aristocracy, and the church to suppress the people. "Bandits": Neruda lists categories of invaders. "Moors": probably an analogy between the early Muslim invaders of Spain and German and Italian pilots who bombed the village of Guernica in April 1937.

Face to face with you I have seen the blood
of Spain tower like a tide
to drown you in one wave
of pride and knives!

Treacherous   55
generals:
see my dead house,
look at broken Spain:
from every house burning metal flows
instead of flowers,   60
from every socket of Spain
Spain emerges
and from every dead child a rifle with eyes,
and from every crime bullets are born
which will one day find   65
the bull's eye of your hearts.

And you will ask: why doesn't his poetry
speak of dreams and leaves
and the great volcanoes of his native land?

Come and see the blood in the streets.   70
Come and see
the blood in the streets.
Come and see the blood
in the streets!

                                                                    1936

General Song (Canto General)[1]

From Canto II. The Heights of Macchu Picchu[2]

VI

And so I scaled the ladder of the earth
amid the atrocious maze of lost jungles
up to you, Macchu Picchu.
High citadel of terraced stones,
at long last the dwelling of him whom the earth   5
did not conceal in its slumbering vestments.
In you, as in two parallel lines,
the cradle of lightning and man
was rocked in a wind of thorns.

1. Translated by Jack Schmitt.
2. Ancient city of the Incas, situated on a remote precipice in the Andes mountains of
Peru; the city escaped the Spanish invaders
and was rediscovered in 1911. The Inca empire
flourished in the 14th century and was destroyed by Francisco Pizarro in 1532.

Mother of stone, sea spray of the condors.   10

Towering reef of the human dawn.

Spade lost in the primal sand.

This was the dwelling, this is the site:
here the full kernels of corn rose
and fell again like red hailstones.
Here the golden fiber emerged from the vicuña[3]   15
to clothe love, tombs, mothers,
the king, prayers, warriors.

Here man's feet rested at night
beside the eagle's feet, in the high gory   20
retreats, and at dawn
they trod the rarefied mist with feet of thunder
and touched lands and stones
until they recognized them in the night or in death.

I behold vestments and hands,   25
the vestige of water in the sonorous void,
the wall tempered by the touch of a face
that beheld with my eyes the earthen lamps,
that oiled with my hands the vanished
wood: because everything—clothing, skin, vessels,   30
words, wine, bread—
is gone, fallen to earth.

And the air flowed with orange-blossom
fingers over all the sleeping:
a thousand years of air, months, weeks of air,   35
of blue wind, of iron cordillera,[4]
like gentle hurricanes of footsteps
polishing the solitary precinct of stone.

VII

O remains of a single abyss, shadows of one gorge—
the deep one—the real, most searing death
attained the scale
of your magnitude,
and from the quarried stones,   5
from the spires,
from the terraced aqueducts
you tumbled as in autumn

---

3. A llama-like animal, found in the Andes,   **4.** Mountain range.
that has a fine soft fleece.

to a single death.
Today the empty air no longer weeps, 10
no longer knows your feet of clay,
has now forgotten your pitchers that filtered the sky
when the lightning's knives emptied it,
and the powerful tree was eaten away
by the mist and felled by the wind. 15
It sustained a hand that fell suddenly
from the heights to the end of time.
You are no more, spider hands, fragile
filaments, spun web:
all that you were has fallen: customs, frayed 20
syllables, masks of dazzling light.
But a permanence of stone and word:
the citadel was raised like a chalice in the hands
of all, the living, the dead, the silent, sustained
by so much death, a wall, from so much life a stroke 25
of stone petals: the permanent rose, the dwelling:
this Andean reef of glacial colonies.

When the clay-colored hand
turned to clay, when the little eyelids closed,
filled with rough walls, brimming with castles, 30
and when the entire man was trapped in his hole,
exactitude remained hoisted aloft:
this high site of the human dawn:
the highest vessel that has contained silence:
a life of stone after so many lives. 35

VIII

Rise up with me, American[5] love.

Kiss the secret stones with me.
The torrential silver of the Urubamba[6]
makes the pollen fly to its yellow cup.
It spans the void of the grapevine,
the petrous plant, the hard wreath 5
upon the silence of the highland casket.
Come, minuscule life, between the wings
of the earth, while—crystal and cold, pounded air
extracting assailed emeralds—
O, wild water, you run down from the snow. 10

Love, love, even the abrupt night,
from the sonorous Andean flint

---

5. For Neruda (and for many Latin Americans), *America* refers to Latin America; North America is called "Saxon America."

6. The river flowing through the valley below Macchu Picchu, called Wilkamayu by the Indians.

to the dawn's red knees,
contemplates the snow's blind child.   15

O, sonorous threaded Wilkamayu,
when you beat your lineal thunder
to a white froth, like wounded snow,
when your precipitous storm
sings and batters, awakening the sky,   20
what language do you bring to the ear recently
wrenched from your Andean froth?

Who seized the cold's lightning
and left it shackled in the heights,
dispersed in its glacial tears,   25
smitten in its swift swords,
hammering its embattled stamens,
borne on its warrior's bed,
startled in its rocky end?

What are your tormented sparks saying?   30
Did your secret insurgent lightning
once journey charged with words?
Who keeps on shattering frozen syllables,
black languages, golden banners,
deep mouths, muffled cries,   35
in your slender arterial waters?

Who keeps on cutting floral eyelids
that come to gaze from the earth?
Who hurls down the dead clusters
that fell in your cascade hands   40
to strip the night stripped
in the coal of geology?

Who flings the branch down from its bonds?
Who once again entombs farewells?

Love, love, never touch the brink   45
or worship the sunken head:
let time attain its stature
in its salon of shattered headsprings,
and, between the swift water and the walls,
gather the air from the gorge,   50
the parallel sheets of the wind,
the cordilleras' blind canal,
the harsh greeting of the dew,
and, rise up, flower by flower, through the dense growth,
treading the hurtling serpent.   55

In the steep zone—forest and stone,
mist of green stars, radiant jungle—

Mantur explodes like a blinding lake
or a new layer of silence.

Come to my very heart, to my dawn,   60
up to the crowned solitudes.
The dead kingdom is still alive.

And over the Sundial the sanguinary shadow
of the condor[7] crosses like a black ship.

IX

Sidereal eagle, vineyard of mist.
Lost bastion, blind scimitar.
Spangled waistband, solemn bread.
Torrential stairway, immense eyelid.
Triangular tunic, stone pollen.   5
Granite lamp, stone bread.
Mineral serpent, stone rose.
Entombed ship, stone headspring.
Moonhorse, stone light.
Equinoctial square, stone vapor.   10
Ultimate geometry, stone book.
Tympanum fashioned amid the squalls.
Madrepore[8] of sunken time.
Rampart tempered by fingers.
Ceiling assailed by feathers.   15
Mirror bouquets, stormy foundations.
Thrones toppled by the vine.
Regime of the enraged claw.
Hurricane sustained on the slopes.
Immobile cataract of turquoise.   20
Patriarchal bell of the sleeping.
Hitching ring of the tamed snows.
Iron recumbent upon its statues.
Inaccessible dark tempest.
Puma hands, bloodstained rock.   25
Towering sombrero, snowy dispute.
Night raised on fingers and roots.
Window of the mists, hardened dove.
Nocturnal plant, statue of thunder.
Essential cordillera, searoof.   30
Architecture of lost eagles.
Skyrope, heavenly bee.

7. The heights of Macchu Picchu and the
smaller Huayna Picchu were said to form the
shape of a condor, a large vulturelike bird seen
as the messenger of humanity. "Sundial": the
intihuatana, or "hitching post of the sun," a
large altar carved directly out of the granite;
its shape and position served to predict the
date of the winter solstice and other periods of
importance to agriculture.
8. Coral.

Bloody level, man-made star.
Mineral bubble, quartz moon.
Andean serpent, brow of amaranth.[9]   35
Cupola of silence, pure land.
Seabride, tree of cathedrals.
Cluster of salt, black-winged cherry tree.
Snow-capped teeth, cold thunderbolt.
Scored moon, menacing stone.   40
Headdresses of the cold, action of the air.
Volcano of hands, obscure cataract.
Silver wave, pointer of time.

X

Stone upon stone, and man, where was he?
Air upon air, and man, where was he?
Time upon time, and man, where was he?
Were you too a broken shard
of inconclusive man, of empty raptor,   5
who on the streets today, on the trails,
on the dead autumn leaves, keeps
tearing away at the heart right up to the grave?
Poor hand, foot, poor life . . .
Did the days of light   10
unraveled in you, like raindrops
on the banners of a feast day,
give petal by petal of their dark food
to the empty mouth?
                       Hunger, coral of mankind,
hunger, secret plant, woodcutters' stump,   15
hunger, did the edge of your reef rise up
to these high suspended towers?

I want to know, salt of the roads,
show me the spoon—architecture, let me
scratch at the stamens of stone with a little stick,   20
ascend the rungs of the air up to the void,
scrape the innards until I touch mankind.

Macchu Picchu, did you put
stone upon stone and, at the base, tatters?
Coal upon coal and, at the bottom, tears?   25
Fire in gold and, within it, the trembling
drop of red blood?
Bring me back the slave that you buried!
Shake from the earth the hard bread
of the poor wretch, show me   30

---

9. An annual plant with flowers and highly nutritious edible seeds.

the slave's clothing and his window.
Tell me how he slept when he lived.
Tell me if his sleep was
harsh, gaping, like a black chasm
worn by fatigue upon the wall.   35
The wall, the wall! If upon his sleep
each layer of stone weighed down, and if he fell beneath it
as beneath a moon, with his dream!
Ancient America, sunken bride,
your fingers too,   40
on leaving the jungle for the high void of the gods,
beneath the nuptial standards of light and decorum,
mingling with the thunder of drums and spears,
your fingers, your fingers too,
which the abstract rose, the cold line, and   45
the crimson breast of the new grain transferred
to the fabric of radiant substance, to the hard cavities—
did you, entombed America, did you too store in the depths
of your bitter intestine, like an eagle, hunger?

XI

Through the hazy splendor,
through the stone night, let me plunge my hand,
and let the aged heart of the forsaken beat in me
like a bird captive for a thousand years!
Let me forget, today, this joy, which is greater than the sea,   5
because man is greater than the sea and its islands,
and we must fall into him as into a well to emerge from the bottom
with a bouquet of secret water and sunken truths.
Let me forget, great stone, the powerful proportion,
the transcendent measure, the honeycombed stones,   10
and from the square let me today run
my hand over the hypotenuse of rough blood and sackcloth.
When, like a horseshoe of red elytra,[1] the frenzied condor
beats my temples in the order of its flight,
and the hurricane of cruel feathers sweeps the somber dust   15
from the diagonal steps, I do not see the swift brute,
I do not see the blind cycle of its claws,
I see the man of old, the servant, asleep in the fields,
I see a body, a thousand bodies, a man, a thousand women,
black with rain and night, beneath the black squall,   20
with the heavy stone of the statue:
Juan Stonecutter, son of Wiracocha[2]
Juan Coldeater, son of a green star,
Juan Barefoot, grandson of turquoise,
rise up to be born with me, my brother.   25

1. An insect's wing cases.
2. Inca rain god who taught the arts of civilization to humanity.

XII

Rise up to be born with me, my brother.

Give me your hand from the deep
zone of your disseminated sorrow.
You'll not return from the bottom of the rocks.
You'll not return from subterranean time.   5
Your stiff voice will not return.
Your drilled eyes will not return.
Behold me from the depths of the earth,
laborer, weaver, silent herdsman:
tamer of the tutelary guanacos:[3]   10
mason of the defied scaffold:
bearer of the Andean tears:
jeweler with your fingers crushed:
tiller trembling in the seed:
potter spilt in your clay: 15
bring to the cup of this new life, brothers,
all your timeless buried sorrows.
Show me your blood and your furrow,
tell me: I was punished here,
because the jewel did not shine or the earth   20
did not surrender the gemstone or kernel on time:
show me the stone on which you fell
and the wood on which you were crucified,
strike the old flintstones,
the old lamps, the whips sticking   25
throughout the centuries to your wounds
and the war clubs glistening red.
I've come to speak through your dead mouths.
Throughout the earth join all
the silent scattered lips   30
and from the depths speak to me all night long,
as if I were anchored with you,
tell me everything, chain by chain,
link by link, and step by step,
sharpen the knives that you've kept,   35
put them in my breast and in my hand,
like a river of yellow lightning,
like a river of buried jaguars,
and let me weep hours, days, years,
blind ages, stellar centuries.   40

Give me silence, water, hope.

Give me struggle, iron, volcanoes.

---

3. Reddish-brown grazing animals related to the llama.

Cling to my body like magnets.

Hasten to my veins and to my mouth.

Speak through my words and my blood.   45

1950

Ode to the Tomato[1]

The street
drowns in tomatoes:
noon,
summer,
light   5
breaks
in two
tomato
halves,
and the streets   10
run
with juice.
In December[2]
the tomato
cuts loose,   15
invades
kitchens,
takes over lunches,
settles
at rest   20
on sideboards,
with the glasses,
butter dishes,
blue salt-cellars.
It has   25
its own radiance,
a goodly majesty.
Too bad we must
assassinate:
a knife   30
plunges
into its living pulp,
red
viscera,
a fresh,   35

---

1. Translated by Nathaniel Tarn.   2. Summer in Chile.

deep,
inexhaustible
sun
floods the salads
of Chile,   40
beds cheerfully
with the blonde onion,
and to celebrate
oil
the filial essence   45
of the olive tree
lets itself fall
over its gaping hemispheres,
the pimento
adds   50
its fragrance,
salt its magnetism—
we have the day's
wedding:
parsley   55
flaunts
its little flags,
potatoes
thump to a boil,
the roasts   60
beat
down the door
with their aromas:
it's time!
let's go!   65
and upon
the table,
belted by summer,
tomatoes,
stars of the earth,   70
stars multiplied
and fertile
show off
their convolutions,
canals   75
and plenitudes
and the abundance
boneless,
without husk,
or scale or thorn,   80
grant us
the festival
of ardent colour
and all-embracing freshness.

1954

VII

Postwar and Postcolonial Literature, 1945–68

I n the middle of the twentieth century, the two superpowers, the United States and the Soviet Union, having emerged from the bloody, or "hot," wars of the previous decades, found themselves locked in a Cold War: their most powerful weapons, though fired only in tests, would be capable of annihilating the planet. The two sides—the North Atlantic Treaty Organization, representing Western Europe and North America, and the Warsaw Pact, uniting the military forces of Soviet-dominated Eastern Europe—divided most of the globe into spheres of influence. By 1949, with the success of the Communist Revolution in China, led by Mao Zedong, almost half of the world's population lived under communism. The competing blocs, as they were called, understood that if either one launched a nuclear attack, the enemy would retaliate, an unstable balance known as "mutually assured destruction" (producing an ironic acronym).

To avoid planetary disaster, the two sides fought wars by proxy, notably in Korea (1950–53) and Vietnam (1955–75). Within the communist world, the purges and mass imprisonments initiated by the Soviet dictator Joseph Stalin were selectively

A photograph from October 1947 by Margaret Bourke-White (American, 1904–1971) of a refugee camp in Delhi. The picture was taken a month before British-ruled India was partitioned into two nations, India and Pakistan.

repudiated, after Stalin's death in 1953, by his successor, Nikita Khrushchev. The bloody suppression of the Hungarian revolt against communism in 1956, however, showed the limits of de-Stalinization. Stalin's techniques spread, moreover, to Mao's China. The forced collectivization of the Great Leap Forward (1958–59) led to a famine that caused an estimated twenty million deaths, while the Cultural Revolution, which began in 1966 and lasted until Mao's death in 1976, attacked intellectuals and the middle classes, resulting in the destruction of most of the country's functioning institutions.

While the communist world was undergoing radical transformations, the colonial powers of Western Europe, facing pressure from nationalist movements among their subject peoples, began to relinquish direct political control of their colonies. The process of decolonization, often accompanied by conflicts over redrawn borders, became a major topic for a generation of writers who, though born in the formerly colonized nations, were likely to have been educated in Europe and who sought to give voice to the concerns of their recently independent nations. The initial stages of postcolonial development were frequently marked by internal conflicts, civil wars, and dictatorships, and by jockeying to align newly independent nations with either the United States or the Soviet Union (or to find an alternative, "nonaligned" path). It was also in these years, however, that the basis was laid for the prosperity of what was then known as the "third world" (in contrast to the liberal capitalist democracies of the developed first world and the rapidly industrializing second world of communist regimes). In particular, the Green Revolution of the 1960s and 1970s improved agricultural methods in the developing world and made it possible to feed a rapidly expanding population, while smallpox was eliminated and other serious illnesses, such as tuberculosis, malaria, and plague, were brought under control. Still, in the poorer countries of Africa and South Asia, it was common for as much as half the population to live in poverty.

In Western Europe, the postwar period saw rapid rebuilding and further industrialization, even as thinkers and writers struggled to comprehend the enormity of the Holocaust. The young Polish journalist **Tadeusz Borowski** shocked his compatriots with his account of life in the Nazi concentration camps, while the Romanian-born Jew Paul Celan, writing in German, turned his experiences in the camps into austere and beautiful poetry. In the wake of the Nazi occupation of France (1940–44), the theme of choice became critical to a generation of authors who had had to decide between allegiance to the collaborationist Vichy state or to the Resistance movement. **Albert Camus**, who had worked for the Resistance, develops the theme of choice in his account of a schoolteacher's experiences in Algeria in "**The Guest**." In different ways, these writers turned to a stripped-down literary style and thus away from the exuberant modernism of the earlier part of the century.

Partly because it had been incorporated into the French state (unlike British colonies, which tended to be governed locally), Algeria became one of the bloodiest colonial battlefields until its eventual independence in 1962. Elsewhere, decolonization occurred more rapidly. In the immediate aftermath of the war, faced with nationalist pressures in the colonies and with the moral bankruptcy of any claims to racial superiority, many colonial powers began granting independence.

The Algerian writer Albert Camus (1913–1960), on the balcony of his Paris publisher's office in 1955.

At midnight on August 14, 1947, Britain divided its territorial possessions in South Asia into two states, India and Pakistan. The partition took place along religious (or "communal") lines between Hindus and Muslims, but there remained many Muslims in India and Hindus in Pakistan. During the weeks before and after independence, large populations were transferred and an untold number were killed in communal violence—the subject of **Salman Rushdie**'s *Midnight's Children*. The following year, under a United Nations mandate, Britain left most of its former territories in Palestine in the hands of the new Jewish state, Israel. Its Arab neighbors attacked the new country and, during a series of short wars from 1948 to 1968, Israel expanded its national boundaries, at the same time occupying territories inhabited by Arab Palestinians.

Elsewhere in the Middle East and North Africa, a series of military coups created dictatorships, sometimes focused on the Pan-Arabist movement for Muslim unity, at other times oriented more toward socialism. It was in this context that Arabic writers such as **Naguib Mahfouz** combined traditional literary language with the European form of the novel to chronicle the transformations of their cultures. Sub-Saharan Africa also experienced a series of civil wars and dictatorships, as well as ongoing minority rule by the white settler communities in South Africa and Rhodesia, which **Doris Lessing** describes. Despite Africa's hardships, it developed a remarkable literature, typically in the languages of the former colonial powers, represented here by **Chinua Achebe**, **Wole Soyinka**, and **Chimamanda Ngozi Adichie**. Although they sometimes took inspiration from the celebration of African identity typical of the earlier French-speaking writers of the Négritude movement, these anglophone authors typically explore village life as it has been transformed by contact with Europeans and then by the process of establishing independence.

In the United States, too, racial

Egyptian premier Gamal Abdel Nasser Hussein (right) and the prime minister of the Sudan, Ismail Al Azhari, clasp hands among a crowd of supporters in Egypt in July 1954. Nasser, a central figure in the Egyptian revolution of 1952, which overthrew the monarchy of Egypt and Sudan, became Egypt's president in 1956.

segregation and the disenfranchisement of African Americans were challenged in the civil rights movement, whose landmarks included the Supreme Court decision *Brown v. Board of Education* of 1954, which ended public school segregation, and the Civil Rights Acts of 1964, which banned segregation in public accommodations and outlawed discriminatory voter registration. **James Baldwin** explores the challenges that African Americans faced in the North during and after the Second World War.

The postwar period also witnessed the increasing globalization of literature and the media, and writers frequently adapted certain genres, especially the short story and the novel but drama and lyric poetry as well, to local conditions. For example, authors might use the language of a traditional literature (Classical Chinese, Standard Arabic, and biblical Hebrew) to pro-

duce a colloquial, contemporary short story. In other cases, writers transformed a historically European genre by introducing elements of local customs and storytelling techniques (examples include magic realism in Latin America; the postcolonial African novel). More broadly, the encounters between indigenous societies and widely accepted literary forms caused writers to rethink the defining characteristics of their homeland; many authors valued hybrid qualities that tended to dismantle claims to cultural uniqueness or homogeneity.

Much of the writing of the postwar period engages in the movement toward "neorealism"—a return to political and social issues, in contrast to the interiority and linguistic inventiveness of the modernists. While sometimes drawing on modernist techniques such as the representation of individual consciousness and intense irony, the realists tended to use the chronological plot, omniscient narrator, and objective description typical of nineteenth-century European works. Such preferences apply equally to postcolonial writers eager to portray the history of their nations and to Western authors grappling with social issues such as civil rights, immigration, and gender relations. There are some notable exceptions, however, to the reinvigorated realism of postwar literature. Many politically oriented writers, such as Mahfouz and Solzhenitsyn, wove allegory into their seeming realism, sometimes conveying hidden political messages in apparently straightforward narratives, at other times using allegory openly as a way of commenting on current events. At the same time, writers of all nationalities continued to use language wittily, finding expressiveness in the sounds and unexpected meanings of words.

Writers of this era introduced many of the characteristics associated with postmodernism, although the term itself became widespread only in the later decades of the twentieth century. Like the modernists before them, they called attention to their use of language and choice of literary form. They differ from the earlier group in their sense of the limits of literature's ability to find meaning in the world; an acute consciousness of the instability of language and of its potential to carry multiple meanings; and a particular concern with the boundary between fiction and reality—what is sometimes called "metafiction" or "metatheater." Although they did not think of themselves as postmodernists, these authors were conscious of succeeding the modernists **Joyce**, **Woolf**, and **Kafka**, and of seeking the possibilities for literary experiment even if they no longer believed that such efforts could reveal the ultimate meaningfulness of life.

TADEUSZ BOROWSKI

1922–1951

Incarcerated in the extermination camps of Auschwitz-Birkenau, Dautmergen, and Dachau-Allach between the ages of twenty and twenty-two, a tormented suicide by gas at twenty-eight, Tadeusz Borowski wrote stories of life in the camps that have made him the foremost writer of what is called the "literature of atrocity." His fiction is still read for its powerful evocation of the death camps, for its analysis of human relationships under pressure, and for its agonizing portrayal of individuals forced to choose between physical or spiritual survival.

Tadeusz Borowski was born on November 12, 1922, to Polish Catholic parents in Żytomierz, a Soviet-controlled city with Polish, Ukrainian, Jewish, and Russian residents. When he was three years old, his father was sent to a labor camp in Siberia as a suspected dissident. Four years later, his mother was deported as well, and

Tadeusz was separated from his twelve-year-old brother. Tadeusz was raised by an aunt and educated in a Soviet school until a prisoner exchange in 1932 brought his father home; his mother's release in 1934 reunited the family. Money was scarce, however, and the boy was sent away to a Franciscan boarding school where he could be educated inexpensively. Later he commented that he had never had a family life: "Either my father was sitting in Murmansk or my mother was in Siberia, or I was in a boarding school, on my own, or in a camp." The Second World War began when he was sixteen, and—since the Nazis did not permit higher education for Poles—Borowski continued his studies at Warsaw University via illegal underground classes. Unlike his fellow students, he refused to join political groups and did not become involved in the Resistance; he wanted merely to write poetry and continue his literary studies. Polish publications were illegal, however, and his first poetry collection, *Wherever the Earth* (1942)—run off in 165 copies on a clandestine mimeograph machine—was enough to condemn him. *Wherever the Earth* prefigures the bleak perspective of the concentration camp stories: prophesying the end of the human race, it sees the world as a gigantic labor camp and the sky as a "low, steel lid" or "a factory ceiling" (an oppressive image that he may have adapted from **Baudelaire's "Spleen LXXXI"**). In late February 1943, Borowski and his fiancée, Maria Rundo, were arrested; they were sent to Auschwitz two months later. In the meantime, Borowski was able to see, from his cell window, both the Jewish uprising in the Warsaw ghetto and the ghetto's fiery destruction by Nazi soldiers.

On arriving in Auschwitz, Borowski was put to hard labor with the other prisoners. After a bout with pneumonia, he survived by taking a position as an orderly in the Auschwitz hospital—which was not just a clinic but a place where doctors used prisoners as experimental subjects. Rundo had been sent to the women's barracks at the same camp, and he wrote daily letters that were smuggled to her. He got to see her when he was sent to the women's camp to pick up the corpses of infants, and later when he was assigned to repair roofs in the women's camp. Borowski wrote about his camp experiences immediately after the war, when he was living in Munich with two other former Auschwitz prisoners, Janusz Nel Siedlecki and Krystyn Olszewski. The three men were transferred from Dachau-Allach to the Freimann repatriation camp, outside Munich, which they soon left when the Polish artist and publisher Anatol Girs located them and found them jobs. Sharing an apartment in Munich, they published their slightly fictionalized memoirs, including Borowski's "This Way for the Gas, Ladies and Gentlemen," in the 1946 collection *We Were in Auschwitz*. On his return to Poland, Borowski's searing talent was recognized and he became a prominent writer. He married Maria Rundo and was courted by Poland's Stalinist government. At the government's urging, he wrote journalism and weekly stories that followed communist political lines and employed a newly strident tone. The Cold War had begun, and Borowski was persuaded that he had joined a popular revolution that would prevent more horrors like Auschwitz. He went so far as to do intelligence work in Berlin for the Polish secret police in 1949. The revelation of Soviet prison camps, however, as well as the spectacle of political purges in Poland, gradually disillusioned him: once more, he was part of a concentration-camp system and complicit with the oppressors. Although he and his wife had a newborn daughter, he committed suicide by gas on July 1, 1951.

Narrated in an impersonal tone by one of the prisoners, "This Way for the Gas, Ladies and Gentlemen" describes the extermination camp of Birkenau, the largest of three concentration camps at Auschwitz (Polish: *Oświęcim*), an en-closed world of hierarchical authority and desperate struggles to survive. Food, shoes, shirts, underwear: this vital currency of the camp is obtained when prisoners are stripped of their belongings as they arrive in railway cattle cars. The story follows the narrator's first trip to the railroad station with the labor battalion "Canada." The trip will salvage goods from three trains bringing fifteen thousand Polish Jews, former inhabitants of the cities Sosnowiec and Będzin. By the end of the day, most of the travelers will be burning in the crematorium, and the camp will live for a few more days on the loot from "a good, rich transport."

Borowski suggests from the beginning the systematic dehumanization of the camps: prisoners are equated with lice, and they mill around by the naked thousands in blocked-off sections. The same gas is used in exterminating lice and humans—who will later be equated with sick horses (the converted stables retain their old signs), lumber and concrete trucked in from the railroad station, and insects whose jaws work away at moldy pieces of bread. Constantly supervised, subject to arbitrary rules and punishment, malnourished and pushed to exhaustion, their identities reduced to numerals tattooed on their arms, the prisoners live in the shadow of a hierarchical authority that is to be both feared and placated. Paradoxically, their common vulnerability leads to alienation and rage at their fellow victims rather than at the executioners. The Nazis have foreseen everything, explains the narrator's friend Henri, including the fact that weakness needs to vent itself on the weaker. The only way to cope is to distance oneself from what is happening, to become a cog in the machine so that one does not actually experience the events—to suspend, for the moment, one's humanity.

The story's brutal realism and matter-of-fact tone convey as no passionate oratory could the mind-numbing horror of a situation in which systematic slaughter was the background for everyday life. The narrator, Tadeusz, is modeled partly on Borowski, but he is also a composite figure; he has become another part of the concentration-camp system, a survivor. He has a job in the system; assists the Kapos, or senior prisoners who organize the camp; and carries a burden of guilt that his adopted impersonal attitude cannot quite suppress. Borowski's stories shocked their postwar audience with their uncompromising honesty: here were no saintly victims and demonic executioners, but rather human beings— human beings—going about the business of extermination or, reduced to near-animal level, cooperating in the destruction of themselves and others. It is a picture that sorely tests any belief in civilization, common humanity, or divine providence; Borowski's bleak outlook questions everything and does not pretend to offer encouragement.

The narrator's dispassionate tone, as he describes senseless cruelty and mass murder, individual scenes of desperation, or the eccentric emotions of people about to die, continues to shock many readers. Borowski is certainly describing a world of antiheroes, those who survive by accommodating themselves to things as they are and avoiding acts of heroism. Borowski wrote this story after the Nazi defeat, but for its duration the picture is one of a spiritual desolation that not only illustrates a shameful moment in modern history but raises questions about what it means to be civilized, or even human.

This Way for the Gas, Ladies and Gentlemen[1]

All of us[2] walk around naked. The delousing is finally over, and our striped suits are back from the tanks of Cyclone B[3] solution, an efficient killer of lice in clothing and of men in gas chambers. Only the inmates in the blocks cut off from ours by the 'Spanish goats'[4] still have nothing to wear. But all the same, all of us walk around naked: the heat is unbearable. The camp has been sealed off tight. Not a single prisoner, not one solitary louse, can sneak through the gate. The labour Kommandos have stopped working. All day, thousands of naked men shuffle up and down the roads, cluster around the squares, or lie against the walls and on top of the roofs. We have been sleeping on plain boards, since our mattresses and blankets are still being disinfected. From the rear blockhouses we have a view of the F.K.L.—*Frauen Konzentration Lager*;[5] there too the delousing is in full swing. Twenty-eight thousand women have been stripped naked and driven out of the barracks. Now they swarm around the large yard between the blockhouses.

The heat rises, the hours are endless. We are without even our usual diversion: the wide roads leading to the crematoria are empty. For several days now, no new transports have come in. Part of 'Canada'[6] has been liquidated and detailed to a labour Kommando—one of the very toughest—at Harmenz.[7] For there exists in the camp a special brand of justice based on envy: when the rich and mighty fall, their friends see to it that they fall to the very bottom. And Canada, our Canada, which smells not of maple forests but of French perfume, has amassed great fortunes in diamonds and currency from all over Europe.

Several of us sit on the top bunk, our legs dangling over the edge. We slice the neat loaves of crisp, crunchy bread. It is a bit coarse to the taste, the kind that stays fresh for days. Sent all the way from Warsaw[8]—only a week ago my mother held this white loaf in her hands . . . dear Lord, dear Lord . . .

We unwrap the bacon, the onion, we open a can of evaporated milk. Henri, the fat Frenchman, dreams aloud of the French wine brought by the transports from Strasbourg, Paris, Marseille[9] . . . Sweat streams down his body.

'Listen, *mon ami*,[1] next time we go up on the loading ramp, I'll bring you real champagne. You haven't tried it before, eh?'

'No. But you'll never be able to smuggle it through the gate, so stop teasing. Why not try and "organize" some shoes for me instead—you know, the perforated kind, with a double sole,[2] and what about that shirt you promised me long ago?'

---

1. Translated by Barbara Vedder.
2. Inmates in Auschwitz 11, or Birkenau, the largest of the Nazi extermination camps, established in October 1941 near the town of Birkenau, Poland. Its death toll is usually estimated between 1 million and 2.5 million people.
3. Gas used in extermination camps.
4. Crossed wooden beams wrapped in barbed wire.
5. Women's concentration camp (German).
6. The name given to the camp stores (as well as prisoners working there) where valuables and clothing taken from prisoners were sorted for dispatch to Germany. Like the nation of Canada, the store symbolized wealth and prosperity to the camp inmates.
7. One of the subcamps outside Birkenau itself.
8. Capital of Poland; most of its Jewish residents were executed by the Nazis.
9. A large French port on the Mediterranean Sea. Strasbourg is a city in northeast France.
1. My friend (French).
2. A Hungarian style.

'*Patience, patience.* When the new transports come, I'll bring all you want. We'll be going on the ramp again!'

'And what if there aren't any more "cremo"[3] transports?' I say spitefully. 'Can't you see how much easier life is becoming around here: no limit on packages, no more beatings? You even write letters home . . . One hears all kind of talk, and, dammit, they'll run out of people!'

'Stop talking nonsense.' Henri's serious fat face moves rhythmically, his mouth is full of sardines. We have been friends for a long time, but I do not even know his last name. 'Stop talking nonsense,' he repeats, swallowing with effort. 'They can't run out of people, or we'll starve to death in this blasted camp. All of us live on what they bring.'

'All? We have our packages . . .'

'Sure, you and your friend, and ten other friends of yours. Some of you Poles get packages. But what about us, and the Jews, and the Russkis? And what if we had no food, no "organization" from the transports, do you think you'd be eating those packages of yours in peace? We wouldn't let you!'

'You would, you'd starve to death like the Greeks. Around here, whoever has grub, has power.'

'Anyway, you have enough, we have enough, so why argue?'

Right, why argue? They have enough, I have enough, we eat together and we sleep on the same bunks. Henri slices the bread, he makes a tomato salad. It tastes good with the commissary mustard.

Below us, naked, sweat-drenched men crowd the narrow barracks aisles or lie packed in eights and tens in the lower bunks. Their nude, withered bodies stink of sweat and excrement; their cheeks are hollow. Directly beneath me, in the bottom bunk, lies a rabbi. He has covered his head[4] with a piece of rag torn off a blanket and reads from a Hebrew prayer book (there is no shortage of this type of literature at the camp), wailing loudly, monotonously.

'Can't somebody shut him up? He's been raving as if he'd caught God himself by the feet.'

'I don't feel like moving. Let him rave. They'll take him to the oven that much sooner.'

'Religion is the opium of the people,'[5] Henri, who is a Communist and a *rentier*,[6] says sententiously. 'If they didn't believe in God and eternal life, they'd have smashed the crematoria long ago.'

'Why haven't you done it then?'

The question is rhetorical; the Frenchman ignores it.

'Idiot,' he says simply, and stuffs a tomato in his mouth.

Just as we finish our snack, there is a sudden commotion at the door. The Muslims[7] scurry in fright to the safety of their bunks, a messenger runs into the Block Elder's shack. The Elder,[8] his face solemn, steps out at once.

'Canada! *Antreten!*[9] But fast! There's a transport coming!'

---

3. The crematorium.
4. Jews are expected to keep their heads covered while at prayer.
5. A quotation from the German political philosopher Karl Marx (1818–1883).
6. Someone with unearned income, a stock-holder (French).
7. Camp nickname for people who had given up, considered the camp pariahs.
8. A Kapo, or senior prisoner in charge of a group of prisoners.
9. Report (German).

'Great God!' yells Henri, jumping off the bunk. He swallows the rest of his tomato, snatches his coat, screams '*Raus*'[1] at the men below, and in a flash is at the door. We can hear a scramble in the other bunks. Canada is leaving for the ramp.

'Henri, the shoes!' I call after him.

'*Keine Angst!*'[2] he shouts back, already outside.

I proceed to put away the food. I tie a piece of rope around the suitcase where the onions and the tomatoes from my father's garden in Warsaw mingle with Portuguese sardines, bacon from Lublin (that's from my brother), and authentic sweetmeats from Salonica.[3] I tie it all up, pull on my trousers, and slide off the bunk.

'*Platz!*'[4] I yell, pushing my way through the Greeks. They step aside. At the door I bump into Henri.

'*Was ist los?*'[5]

'Want to come with us on the ramp?'

'Sure, why not?'

'Come along then, grab your coat! We're short of a few men. I've already told the Kapo,' and he shoves me out of the barracks door.

We line up. Someone has marked down our numbers, someone up ahead yells, 'March, march,' and now we are running towards the gate, accompanied by the shouts of a multilingual throng that is already being pushed back to the barracks. Not everybody is lucky enough to be going on the ramp . . . We have almost reached the gate. *Links, zwei, drei, vier! Mützen ab!*[6] Erect, arms stretched stiffly along our hips, we march past the gate briskly, smartly, almost gracefully. A sleepy S.S.[7] man with a large pad in his hand checks us off, waving us ahead in groups of five.

'*Hundert!*'[8] he calls after we have all passed.

'*Stimmt!*'[9] comes a hoarse answer from out front.

We march fast, almost at a run. There are guards all around, young men with automatics. We pass camp II B, then some deserted barracks and a clump of unfamiliar green—apple and pear trees. We cross the circle of watchtowers and, running, burst on to the highway. We have arrived. Just a few more yards. There, surrounded by trees, is the ramp.

A cheerful little station, very much like any other provincial railway stop: a small square framed by tall chestnuts and paved with yellow gravel. Not far off, beside the road, squats a tiny wooden shed, uglier and more flimsy than the ugliest and flimsiest railway shack; farther along lie stacks of old rails, heaps of

1. Outside (German).
2. Don't panic (German).
3. Major port city in northeast Greece. Lublin is a city in eastern Poland.
4. Make room (German).
5. What's the matter? (German).
6. Left, two, three, four! Caps off! (German).
7. Abbreviation for *Schutzstaffel* (Protective Echelon, German), the Nazi police system that began as Hitler's private guard and grew, by 1939, to a 250,000-member military and political organization that administered all state security functions. The SS was divided into numerous bureaucratic units, one of which, the Death's Head Battalions, managed the concentration camps. Selected for physical perfection and (Aryan) racial purity, SS members wore black or gray-green uniforms decorated with silver insignia.
8. A hundred! (German).
9. Right! (German).

wooden beams, barracks parts, bricks, paving stones. This is where they load freight for Birkenau: supplies for the construction of the camp, and people for the gas chambers. Trucks drive around, load up lumber, cement, people—a regular daily routine.

And now the guards are being posted along the rails, across the beams, in the green shade of the Silesian chestnuts,[1] to form a tight circle around the ramp. They wipe the sweat from their faces and sip out of their canteens. It is unbearably hot; the sun stands motionless at its zenith.

'Fall out!'

We sit down in the narrow streaks of shade along the stacked rails. The hungry Greeks (several of them managed to come along, God only knows how) rummage underneath the rails. One of them finds some pieces of mildewed bread, another a few half-rotten sardines. They eat.

'*Schweinedreck*,'[2] spits a young, tall guard with corn-coloured hair and dreamy blue eyes. 'For God's sake, any minute you'll have so much food to stuff down your guts, you'll bust!' He adjusts his gun, wipes his face with a handkerchief.

'Hey you, fatso!' His boot lightly touches Henri's shoulder. '*Pass mal auf*,[3] want a drink?'

'Sure, but I haven't got any marks,' replies the Frenchman with a professional air.

'*Schade*, too bad.'

'Come, come, Herr[4] Posten, isn't my word good enough any more? Haven't we done business before? How much?'

'One hundred. *Gemacht*?'[5]

'*Gemacht.*'

We drink the water, lukewarm and tasteless. It will be paid for by the people who have not yet arrived.

'Now you be careful,' says Henri, turning to me. He tosses away the empty bottle. It strikes the rails and bursts into tiny fragments. 'Don't take any money, they might be checking. Anyway, who the hell needs money? You've got enough to eat. Don't take suits, either, or they'll think you're planning to escape. Just get a shirt, silk only, with a collar. And a vest. And if you find something to drink, don't bother calling me. I know how to shift for myself, but you watch your step or they'll let you have it.'

'Do they beat you up here?'

'Naturally. You've got to have eyes in your ass. *Arschaugen*.'[6]

Around us sit the Greeks, their jaws working greedily, like huge human insects. They munch on stale lumps of bread. They are restless, wondering what will happen next. The sight of the large beams and the stacks of rails has them worried. They dislike carrying heavy loads.

'*Was wir arbeiten?*'[7] they ask.

---

1. Probably local chestnuts. Silesia, in central Europe, was partitioned among Poland, Czechoslovakia, and Germany after World War I; Germany occupied Polish Silesia in 1939.
2. Dirty pigs (German).
3. See here (German).
4. Mister (German).
5. Done? (German).
6. Eyes on your ass (German; literal trans.).
7. What are we working on? (German).

'Niks. Transport kommen, alles Krematorium, compris?'[8]

'Alles verstehen,' they answer in crematorium Esperanto.[9] All is well—they will not have to move the heavy rails or carry the beams.

In the meantime, the ramp has become increasingly alive with activity, increasingly noisy. The crews are being divided into those who will open and unload the arriving cattle cars and those who will be posted by the wooden steps. They receive instructions on how to proceed most efficiently. Motor cycles drive up, delivering S.S. officers, bemedalled, glittering with brass, beefy men with highly polished boots and shiny, brutal faces. Some have brought their briefcases, others hold thin, flexible whips. This gives them an air of military readiness and agility. They walk in and out of the commissary—for the miserable little shack by the road serves as their commissary, where in the summertime they drink mineral water, Sudetenquelle,[1] and where in winter they can warm up with a glass of hot wine. They greet each other in the state-approved way, raising an arm Roman fashion, then shake hands cordially, exchange warm smiles, discuss mail from home, their children, their families. Some stroll majestically on the ramp. The silver squares on their collars glitter, the gravel crunches under their boots, their bamboo whips snap impatiently.

We lie against the rails in the narrow streaks of shade, breathe unevenly, occasionally exchange a few words in our various tongues, and gaze listlessly at the majestic men in green uniforms, at the green trees, and at the church steeple of a distant village.

'The transport is coming,' somebody says. We spring to our feet, all eyes turn in one direction. Around the bend, one after another, the cattle cars begin rolling in. The train backs into the station, a conductor leans out, waves his hand, blows a whistle. The locomotive whistles back with a shrieking noise, puffs, the train rolls slowly alongside the ramp. In the tiny barred windows appear pale, wilted, exhausted human faces, terror-stricken women with tangled hair, unshaven men. They gaze at the station in silence. And then, suddenly, there is a stir inside the cars and a pounding against the wooden boards.

'Water! Air!'—weary, desperate cries.

Heads push through the windows, mouths gasp frantically for air. They draw a few breaths, then disappear; others come in their place, then also disappear. The cries and moans grow louder.

A man in a green uniform covered with more glitter than any of the others jerks his head impatiently, his lips twist in annoyance. He inhales deeply, then with a rapid gesture throws his cigarette away and signals to the guard. The guard removes the automatic from his shoulder, aims, sends a series of shots along the train. All is quiet now. Meanwhile, the trucks have arrived, steps are being drawn up, and the Canada men stand ready at their posts by the train doors. The S.S. officer with the briefcase raises his hand.

---

8. Nothing. Transport coming, everything crematorium, understood? (German; *compris* is French).

9. An artificial language, created in 1887 by L. L. Zamenhof, to simplify communication between nationalities. "*Alles verstehen*": Everything understood.

1. Water from the Sudetenland or Sudeten Mountains; a narrow strip of land on the northern and western borders of the Czech Republic. The Sudeten was annexed by Hitler in 1938.

'Whoever takes gold, or anything at all besides food, will be shot for stealing Reich property. Understand? *Verstanden?*'

'*Jawohl!*'[2] we answer eagerly.

'*Also los!*[3] Begin!'

The bolts crack, the doors fall open. A wave of fresh air rushes inside the train. People . . . inhumanly crammed, buried under incredible heaps of luggage, suitcases, trunks, packages, crates, bundles of every description (everything that had been their past and was to start their future). Monstrously squeezed together, they have fainted from heat, suffocated, crushed one another. Now they push towards the opened doors, breathing like fish cast out on the sand.

'Attention! Out, and take your luggage with you! Take out everything. Pile all your stuff near the exits. Yes, your coats too. It is summer. March to the left. Understand?'

'Sir, what's going to happen to us?' They jump from the train on to the gravel, anxious, worn-out.

'Where are you people from?'

'Sosnowiec-Będzin.[4] Sir, what's going to happen to us?' They repeat the question stubbornly, gazing into our tired eyes.

'I don't know. I don't understand Polish.'

It is the camp law: people going to their death must be deceived to the very end. This is the only permissible form of charity. The heat is tremendous. The sun hangs directly over our heads, the white, hot sky quivers, the air vibrates, an occasional breeze feels like a sizzling blast from a furnace. Our lips are parched, the mouth fills with the salty taste of blood, the body is weak and heavy from lying in the sun. Water!

A huge, multicoloured wave of people loaded down with luggage pours from the train like a blind, mad river trying to find a new bed. But before they have a chance to recover, before they can draw a breath of fresh air and look at the sky, bundles are snatched from their hands, coats ripped off their backs, their purses and umbrellas taken away.

'But please, sir, it's for the sun, I cannot . . .'

'*Verboten!*'[5] one of us barks through clenched teeth. There is an S.S. man standing behind your back, calm, efficient, watchful.

'*Meine Herrschaften,*[6] this way, ladies and gentlemen, try not to throw your things around, please. Show some goodwill,' he says courteously, his restless hands playing with the slender whip.

'Of course, of course,' they answer as they pass, and now they walk alongside the train somewhat more cheerfully. A woman reaches down quickly to pick up her handbag. The whip flies, the woman screams, stumbles, and falls under the feet of the surging crowd. Behind her, a child cries in a thin little voice 'Mamele!'—a very small girl with tangled black curls.

---

2. Yes! (German). "*Verstanden*": understand? (German).
3. Then get going! (German).
4. Two cities in Katowice province (southern Poland). Będzin was also the site of a concen-

tration camp, and more than ten thousand of its inhabitants were exterminated.
5. Forbidden (German).
6. Gentlemen (German).

The heaps grow. Suitcases, bundles, blankets, coats, handbags that open as they fall, spilling coins, gold, watches; mountains of bread pile up at the exits, heaps of marmalade, jams, masses of meat, sausages; sugar spills on the gravel. Trucks, loaded with people, start up with a deafening roar and drive off amidst the wailing and screaming of the women separated from their children, and the stupefied silence of the men left behind. They are the ones who had been ordered to step to the right—the healthy and the young who will go to the camp. In the end, they too will not escape death, but first they must work.

Trucks leave and return, without interruption, as on a monstrous conveyor belt. A Red Cross van drives back and forth, back and forth, incessantly: it transports the gas that will kill these people. The enormous cross on the hood, red as blood, seems to dissolve in the sun.

The Canada men at the trucks cannot stop for a single moment, even to catch their breath. They shove the people up the steps, pack them in tightly, sixty per truck, more or less. Near by stands a young, cleanshaven 'gentleman', an S.S. officer with a notebook in his hand. For each departing truck he enters a mark; sixteen gone means one thousand people, more or less. The gentleman is calm, precise. No truck can leave without a signal from him, or a mark in his notebook: *Ordnung muss sein.*[7] The marks swell into thousands, the thousands into whole transports, which afterwards we shall simply call 'from Salonica', 'from Strasbourg', 'from Rotterdam.'[8] This one will be called 'Sosnowiec-Będzin'. The new prisoners from Sosnowiec-Będzin will receive serial numbers 131–2—thousand, of course, though afterwards we shall simply say 131–2, for short.

The transports swell into weeks, months, years. When the war is over, they will count up the marks in their notebooks—all four and a half million of them. The bloodiest battle of the war, the greatest victory of the strong, united Germany. *Ein Reich, ein Volk, ein Führer*[9]—and four crematoria.

The train has been emptied. A thin, pock-marked S.S. man peers inside, shakes his head in disgust and motions to our group, pointing his finger at the door.

'*Rein.*[1] Clean it up!'

We climb inside. In the corners amid human excrement and abandoned wrist-watches lie squashed, trampled infants, naked little monsters with enormous heads and bloated bellies. We carry them out like chickens, holding several in each hand.

'Don't take them to the trucks, pass them on to the women,' says the S.S. man, lighting a cigarette. His cigarette lighter is not working properly; he examines it carefully.

'Take them, for God's sake!' I explode as the women rush from me in horror, covering their eyes.

The name of God sounds strangely pointless, since the women and the infants will go on the trucks, every one of them without exception. We all know what this means, and we look at each other with hate and horror.

---

7. Order in everything (German).
8. Large port city in the Netherlands.
9. One State, One People, One Leader! (the

slogan of Nazi Germany).
1. Clean (German).

'What, you don't want to take them?' asks the pockmarked S.S. man with a note of surprise and reproach in his voice, and reaches for his revolver.

'You mustn't shoot, I'll carry them.' A tall, grey-haired woman takes the little corpses out of my hands and for an instant gazes straight into my eyes.

'My poor boy,' she whispers and smiles at me. Then she walks away, staggering along the path. I lean against the side of the train. I am terribly tired. Someone pulls at my sleeve.

'*En avant*,[2] to the rails, come on!'

I look up, but the face swims before my eyes, dissolves, huge and transparent, melts into the motionless trees and the sea of people . . . I blink rapidly: Henri.

'Listen, Henri, are we good people?'

'That's stupid. Why do you ask?'

'You see, my friend, you see, I don't know why, but I am furious, simply furious with these people—furious because I must be here because of them. I feel no pity. I am not sorry they're going to the gas chamber. Damn them all! I could throw myself at them, beat them with my fists. It must be pathological, I just can't understand . . .'

'Ah, on the contrary, it is natural, predictable, calculated. The ramp exhausts you, you rebel—and the easiest way to relieve your hate is to turn against someone weaker. Why, I'd even call it healthy. It's simple logic, *compris?*' He props himself up comfortably against the heap of rails. 'Look at the Greeks, they know how to make the best of it! They stuff their bellies with anything they find. One of them has just devoured a full jar of marmalade.'

'Pigs! Tomorrow half of them will die of the shits.'

'Pigs? You've been hungry.'

'Pigs!' I repeat furiously. I close my eyes. The air is filled with ghastly cries, the earth trembles beneath me, I can feel sticky moisture on my eyelids. My throat is completely dry.

The morbid procession streams on and on—trucks growl like mad dogs. I shut my eyes tight, but I can still see corpses dragged from the train, trampled infants, cripples piled on top of the dead, wave after wave . . . freight cars roll in, the heaps of clothing, suitcases and bundles grow, people climb out, look at the sun, take a few breaths, beg for water, get into the trucks, drive away. And again freight cars roll in, again people . . . The scenes become confused in my mind—I am not sure if all of this is actually happening, or if I am dreaming. There is a humming inside my head; I feel that I must vomit.

Henri tugs at my arm.

'Don't sleep, we're off to load up the loot.'

All the people are gone. In the distance, the last few trucks roll along the road in clouds of dust, the train has left, several S.S. officers promenade up and down the ramp. The silver glitters on their collars. Their boots shine, their red, beefy faces shine. Among them there is a woman—only now I realize she has been here all along—withered, flat-chested, bony, her thin, colourless hair pulled back and tied in a 'Nordic'[3] knot; her hands are in the pockets of her

2. Forward (French).
3. A northern (especially Scandinavian) style   encouraged by the Nazis to establish an image of Teutonic racial purity.

wide skirt. With a rat-like, resolute smile glued on her thin lips she sniffs around the corners of the ramp. She detests feminine beauty with the hatred of a woman who is herself repulsive, and knows it. Yes, I have seen her many times before and I know her well: she is the commandant of the F.K.L. She has come to look over the new crop of women, for some of them, instead of going on the trucks, will go on foot—to the concentration camp. There our boys, the barbers from Zauna,[4] will shave their heads and will have a good laugh at their 'outside world' modesty.

We proceed to load the loot. We lift huge trunks, heave them on to the trucks. There they are arranged in stacks, packed tightly. Occasionally somebody slashes one open with a knife, for pleasure or in search of vodka and perfume. One of the crates falls open; suits, shirts, books drop out on the ground . . . I pick up a small, heavy package. I unwrap it—gold, about two handfuls, bracelets, rings, brooches, diamonds . . .

'*Gib hier*,'[5] an S.S. man says calmly, holding up his briefcase already full of gold and colourful foreign currency. He locks the case, hands it to an officer, takes another, an empty one, and stands by the next truck, waiting. The gold will go to the Reich.[6]

It is hot, terribly hot. Our throats are dry, each word hurts. Anything for a sip of water! Faster, faster, so that it is over, so that we may rest. At last we are done, all the trucks have gone. Now we swiftly clean up the remaining dirt: there must be 'no trace left of the *Schweinerei*'. But just as the last truck disappears behind the trees and we walk, finally, to rest in the shade, a shrill whistle sounds around the bend. Slowly, terribly slowly, a train rolls in, the engine whistles back with a deafening shriek. Again weary, pale faces at the windows, flat as though cut out of paper, with huge, feverishly burning eyes. Already trucks are pulling up, already the composed gentleman with the notebook is at his post, and the S.S. men emerge from the commissary carrying briefcases for the gold and money. We unseal the train doors.

It is impossible to control oneself any longer. Brutally we tear suitcases from their hands, impatiently pull off their coats. Go on, go on, vanish! They go, they vanish. Men, women, children. Some of them know.

Here is a woman—she walks quickly, but tries to appear calm. A small child with a pink cherub's face runs after her and, unable to keep up, stretches out his little arms and cries: 'Mama! Mama!'

'Pick up your child, woman!'

'It's not mine, sir, not mine!' she shouts hysterically and runs on, covering her face with her hands. She wants to hide, she wants to reach those who will not ride the trucks, those who will go on foot, those who will stay alive. She is young, healthy, good-looking, she wants to live.

But the child runs after her, wailing loudly: 'Mama, mama, don't leave me!'

'It's not mine, not mine, no!'

Andrei, a sailor from Sevastopol,[7] grabs hold of her. His eyes are glassy from vodka and the heat. With one powerful blow he knocks her off her feet, then,

---

4. The "sauna" barracks, in front of Canada, where prisoners were bathed, shaved, and deloused.
5. Give it to me (German).

6. The German state.
7. A Soviet (now, Ukrainian) port on the Black Sea.

as she falls, takes her by the hair and pulls her up again. His face twitches with rage.

'Ah, you bloody Jewess! So you're running from your own child! I'll show you, you whore!' His huge hand chokes her, he lifts her in the air and heaves her on to the truck like a heavy sack of grain.

'Here! And take this with you, bitch!' and he throws the child at her feet.

'*Gut gemacht*, good work. That's the way to deal with degenerate mothers,' says the S.S. man standing at the foot of the truck. '*Gut, gut, Russki*.'[8]

'Shut your mouth,' growls Andrei through clenched teeth, and walks away. From under a pile of rags he pulls out a canteen, unscrews the cork, takes a few deep swallows, passes it to me. The strong vodka burns the throat. My head swims, my legs are shaky, again I feel like throwing up.

And suddenly, above the teeming crowd pushing forward like a river driven by an unseen power, a girl appears. She descends lightly from the train, hops on to the gravel, looks around inquiringly, as if somewhat surprised. Her soft, blonde hair has fallen on her shoulders in a torrent, she throws it back impatiently. With a natural gesture she runs her hands down her blouse, casually straightens her skirt. She stands like this for an instant, gazing at the crowd, then turns and with a gliding look examines our faces, as though searching for someone. Unknowingly, I continue to stare at her, until our eyes meet.

'Listen, tell me, where are they taking us?'

I look at her without saying a word. Here, standing before me, is a girl, a girl with enchanting blonde hair, with beautiful breasts, wearing a little cotton blouse, a girl with a wise, mature look in her eyes. Here she stands, gazing straight into my face, waiting. And over there is the gas chamber: communal death, disgusting and ugly. And over in the other direction is the concentration camp: the shaved head, the heavy Soviet trousers in sweltering heat, the sickening, stale odour of dirty, damp female bodies, the animal hunger, the inhuman labour, and later the same gas chamber, only an even more hideous, more terrible death . . .

Why did she bring it? I think to myself, noticing a lovely gold watch on her delicate wrist. They'll take it away from her anyway.

'Listen, tell me,' she repeats.

I remain silent. Her lips tighten.

'I know,' she says with a shade of proud contempt in her voice, tossing her head. She walks off resolutely in the direction of the trucks. Someone tries to stop her; she boldly pushes him aside and runs up the steps. In the distance I can only catch a glimpse of her blonde hair flying in the breeze.

I go back inside the train; I carry out dead infants; I unload luggage. I touch corpses, but I cannot overcome the mounting, uncontrollable terror. I try to escape from the corpses, but they are everywhere: lined up on the gravel, on the cement edge of the ramp, inside the cattle cars. Babies, hideous naked women, men twisted by convulsions. I run off as far as I can go, but immediately a whip slashes across my back. Out of the corner of my eye I see an S.S. man, swearing profusely. I stagger forward and run, lose myself in the Canada group. Now, at last, I can once more rest against the stack of rails. The sun has leaned low over the horizon and illuminates the ramp with a reddish glow; the

8. Good, good, Russky (German). "*Gut gemacht*": well done (German).

shadows of the trees have become elongated, ghostlike. In the silence that settles over nature at this time of day, the human cries seem to rise all the way to the sky.

Only from this distance does one have a full view of the inferno on the teeming ramp. I see a pair of human beings who have fallen to the ground locked in a last desperate embrace. The man has dug his fingers into the woman's flesh and has caught her clothing with his teeth. She screams hysterically, swears, cries, until at last a large boot comes down over her throat and she is silent. They are pulled apart and dragged like cattle to the truck. I see four Canada men lugging a corpse: a huge, swollen female corpse. Cursing, dripping wet from the strain, they kick out of their way some stray children who have been running all over the ramp, howling like dogs. The men pick them up by the collars, heads, arms, and toss them inside the trucks, on top of the heaps. The four men have trouble lifting the fat corpse on to the car, they call others for help, and all together they hoist up the mound of meat. Big, swollen, puffed-up corpses are being collected from all over the ramp; on top of them are piled the invalids, the smothered, the sick, the unconscious. The heap seethes, howls, groans. The driver starts the motor, the truck begins rolling.

'Halt! Halt!' an S.S. man yells after them. 'Stop, damn you.'

They are dragging to the truck an old man wearing tails and a band around his arm. His head knocks against the gravel and pavement; he moans and wails in an uninterrupted monotone: '*Ich will mit dem Herrn Kommandanten sprechen*[9]— I wish to speak with the commandant . . .' With senile stubbornness he keeps repeating these words all the way. Thrown on the truck, trampled by others, choked, he still wails: '*Ich will mit dem . . .*'

'Look here, old man!' a young S.S. man calls, laughing jovially. 'In half an hour you'll be talking with the top commandant! Only don't forget to greet him with a *Heil Hitler!*'

Several other men are carrying a small girl with only one leg. They hold her by the arms and the one leg. Tears are running down her face and she whispers faintly: 'Sir, it hurts, it hurts . . .' They throw her on the truck on top of the corpses. She will burn alive along with them.

The evening has come, cool and clear. The stars are out. We lie against the rails. It is incredibly quiet. Anaemic bulbs hang from the top of the high lamp-posts; beyond the circle of light stretches an impenetrable darkness. Just one step, and a man could vanish for ever. But the guards are watching, their automatics ready.

'Did you get the shoes?' asks Henri.

'No.'

'Why?'

'My God, man, I am finished, absolutely finished!'

'So soon? After only two transports? Just look at me, I . . . since Christmas, at least a million people have passed through my hands. The worst of all are the transports from around Paris—one is always bumping into friends.'

'And what do you say to them?'

'That first they will have a bath, and later we'll meet at the camp. What would you say?'

---

9. I want to speak with the commandant (German).

I do not answer. We drink coffee with vodka; somebody opens a tin of cocoa and mixes it with sugar. We scoop it up by the handful, the cocoa sticks to the lips. Again coffee, again vodka.

'Henri, what are we waiting for?'

'There'll be another transport.'

'I'm not going to unload it! I can't take any more.'

'So, it's got you down? Canada is nice, eh?' Henri grins indulgently and disappears into the darkness. In a moment he is back again.

'All right. Just sit here quietly and don't let an S.S. man see you. I'll try to find you your shoes.'

'Just leave me alone. Never mind the shoes.' I want to sleep. It is very late.

Another whistle, another transport. Freight cars emerge out of the darkness, pass under the lamp-posts, and again vanish in the night. The ramp is small, but the circle of lights is smaller. The unloading will have to be done gradually. Somewhere the trucks are growling. They back up against the steps, black, ghostlike, their searchlights flash across the trees. *Wasser! Luft!*[1] The same all over again, like a late showing of the same film: a volley of shots, the train falls silent. Only this time a little girl pushes herself halfway through the small window and, losing her balance, falls out on to the gravel. Stunned, she lies still for a moment, then stands up and begins walking around in a circle, faster and faster, waving her rigid arms in the air, breathing loudly and spasmodically, whining in a faint voice. Her mind has given way in the inferno inside the train. The whining is hard on the nerves: an S.S. man approaches calmly, his heavy boot strikes between her shoulders. She falls. Holding her down with his foot, he draws his revolver, fires once, then again. She remains face down, kicking the gravel with her feet, until she stiffens. They proceed to unseal the train.

I am back on the ramp, standing by the doors. A warm, sickening smell gushes from inside. The mountain of people filling the car almost halfway up to the ceiling is motionless, horribly tangled, but still steaming.

'*Ausladen!*[2] comes the command. An S.S. man steps out from the darkness. Across his chest hangs a portable searchlight. He throws a stream of light inside.

'Why are you standing about like sheep? Start unloading!' His whip flies and falls across our backs. I seize a corpse by the hand; the fingers close tightly around mine. I pull back with a shriek and stagger away. My heart pounds, jumps up to my throat. I can no longer control the nausea. Hunched under the train I begin to vomit. Then, like a drunk, I weave over to the stack of rails.

I lie against the cool, kind metal and dream about returning to the camp, about my bunk, on which there is no mattress, about sleep among comrades who are not going to the gas tonight. Suddenly I see the camp as a haven of peace. It is true, others may be dying, but one is somehow still alive, one has enough food, enough strength to work . . .

The lights on the ramp flicker with a spectral glow, the wave of people—feverish, agitated, stupefied people—flows on and on, endlessly. They think that now they will have to face a new life in the camp, and they prepare themselves emotionally for the hard struggle ahead. They do not know that in just a few moments they will die, that the gold, money, and diamonds which they

1. Water! Air! (German).
2. Unload! (German).

have so prudently hidden in their clothing and on their bodies are now useless to them. Experienced professionals will probe into every recess of their flesh, will pull the gold from under the tongue and the diamonds from the uterus and the colon. They will rip out gold teeth. In tightly sealed crates they will ship them to Berlin.[3]

The S.S. men's black figures move about, dignified, businesslike. The gentleman with the notebook puts down his final marks, rounds out the figures: fifteen thousand.

Many, very many, trucks have been driven to the crematoria today.

It is almost over. The dead are being cleared off the ramp and piled into the last truck. The Canada men, weighed down under a load of bread, marmalade and sugar, and smelling of perfume and fresh linen, line up to go. For several days the entire camp will live off this transport. For several days the entire camp will talk about 'Sosnowiec-Będzin'. 'Sosnowiec-Będzin' was a good, rich transport.

The stars are already beginning to pale as we walk back to the camp. The sky grows translucent and opens high above our heads—it is getting light.

Great columns of smoke rise from the crematoria and merge up above into a huge black river which very slowly floats across the sky over Birkenau and disappears beyond the forests in the direction of Trzebinia.[4] The 'Sosnowiec-Będzin' transport is already burning.

We pass a heavily armed S.S. detachment on its way to change guard. The men march briskly, in step, shoulder to shoulder, one mass, one will.

'*Und morgen die ganze Welt* . . .'[5] they sing at the top of their lungs.

'*Rechts ran!*[6] To the right march!' snaps a command from up front. We move out of their way.

1946

---

3. The capital of Germany.
4. A town west of Auschwitz, near Krakow.
5. And tomorrow the whole world (German): the last line of the Nazi song "The Rotten Bones Are Shaking," written by Hans Baumann. The previous line reads "for today Germany belongs to us."
6. To the right, get going! (German).

DORIS LESSING

1919–2013

Conflicts between cultures, between values within a culture, and even between elements of a personality, are fundamental themes in Doris Lessing's work—as is the struggle to integrate these entities into a higher, unified order. The recipient of the 2007 Nobel Prize in Literature, Lessing has spent her life in the midst of such conflicts. A witness to harsh colonial policies toward native subjects in Rhodesia as well as to the sexual and feminist revolutions in Europe, she has used her writing to interrogate both the psychology of the self and the larger relations between the personal and the political.

Lessing was born Doris May Tayler in October 1919 in Persia (now Iran). Her parents were British: her mother was a nurse, and her father a clerk in the Imperial Bank of Persia who had been crippled in World War I; his horrific memories of combat would seep into his daughter's recollections of childhood. In 1925 the family moved to the British colony of Rhodesia (now Zimbabwe), where the colonial government was offering economic incentives to encourage the immigration of white settlers. For ten shillings an acre, the family bought three thousand acres of farmland in Mashonaland, a section of Southern Rhodesia that once had been the home of the Matabele tribe but from which the government had evicted most of the native population. The farm never prospered. Lessing attended a convent school until she was fourteen, but she considered herself largely self-educated, from her avid reading of the classics of European and American literature. Above all, she loved the nineteenth-century novel; realists such as Stendhal, **Tolstoy**, and **Dostoevsky** impressed her, she later said, with "the warmth, the compassion, the humanity, the love of people" that gave impetus and passion to their social criticism. Gradually Lessing became aware of the racial injustice in Southern Rhodesia, and of the fact that she was, as she later put it, "a member of the white minority pitted against a black majority that was abominably treated and still is."

Social awareness is a defining theme of her early work, especially her first novel, *The Grass Is Singing* (1949), and the collection *African Stories* (1964). Arguing that "literature should be committed" to political issues, Lessing was herself politically active in Rhodesia, as well as a member of the British Communist Party from 1952 until 1956, the year of the Soviet intervention in Hungary. Her activism and socially oriented writing made their mark, and in 1956 she was declared a prohibited alien in both Southern Rhodesia and South Africa.

While still in Rhodesia, Lessing worked in several office jobs in Salisbury and made two unsuccessful marriages. (Lessing is the name of her second husband.) In 1949 she moved to England with the son from her second marriage and took a gamble on a literary career: "I was working in a lawyer's office at the time, and I remember walking in and saying to my boss, 'I'm giving up my job and writing a novel.' He very properly laughed, and I indignantly walked home and wrote *The*

Grass Is Singing." The novel was a surprising and immediate success, and she was able, from that point, to make a profession of writing. Her next project was the five-volume series, *Children of Violence* (1952–69): the portrait of an era, after the form of the nineteenth-century bildungsroman, or "education novel," *Children of Violence* follows the life of a symbolically named heroine, Martha Quest, while exploring social and moral issues including race relations, the conflict between autonomy and socialization, and the hopes and frustrations of political idealism.

Lessing's most famous novel, *The Golden Notebook* (1962), makes a sharp break with the linear narrative style that *Children of Violence* shares with the bildungsroman tradition. In this work, too, a female protagonist (Anna Wulf) struggles to build a unified identity from the multiple, fragmented elements that constitute her personality; yet the exploratory process by which she pursues this goal takes her story beyond the confines of chronological narrative. Although the book is framed by a conventional short novel called *Free Women*, the governing structure is a series of different-colored notebooks that Anna uses to record the distinct versions of her experience: black for Africa, red for politics, yellow for a fictionalized rendering of herself as a character named Ella, and blue for a factual diary. By analyzing her life from these varying perspectives, Anna learns to understand and reconcile her contradictions—to write, ultimately, the "Golden Notebook," which is "all of me in one book."

During the 1970s and early 1980s, Lessing embarked on a series of science-fiction novels, which she termed "inner-space fiction," extending her interest in psychology and consciousness into speculative and quasi-mystical regions of the imagination. She then shifted to realistic stories that carry a sharp satiric or symbolic twist, such as *The Good Ter-*

rorist (1985), a satire in which a group of naïve British terrorists try to create a homey atmosphere in an empty house in London while carrying out bombing raids. She also published collections of essays and interviews that address politics, life, and art in a nonfiction voice. In presenting Lessing with the Nobel Prize in 2007, the committee praised her as an epic poet of "the female experience, who with scepticism, fire and visionary power has subjected a divided civilisation to scrutiny."

"The Old Chief Mshlanga" is one of Lessing's earliest African stories, written during the period, from 1950 to 1958, when she wrote most of her fiction set on that continent. The collection in which the story first appeared, *This Was the Old Chief's Country* (1951), together with *The Grass Is Singing* and *Five* (1953), a group of novellas set in Africa, established Lessing as an important interpreter of the colonial experience in contemporary Africa. The long act of dispossession that underlies "The Old Chief Mshlanga" began with the economic infiltration of the country by white settlers, under the leadership of the Chartered Company, a private firm that ruled the land under a British charter. Company policies soon formalized segregation by dividing land into tracts categorized as "alienated" (owned by white settlers) or "unalienated" (occupied by natives). The Land Apportionment Act of 1930 confirmed this arrangement by dividing the territory into areas called Native and European. In the story the figure of the Old Chief bridges the earlier dispensation, an era fifty years before, when his people owned the country, and the new, when they can be forcibly relocated to a Reserve after disagreeing with a white settler. Yet the Old Chief is not the protagonist here: significantly, his story comes into the foreground only some distance in, when it intrudes on the consciousness of a young white girl. The "vein of richness" that his tribe represents makes itself known only gradually. By the narrative's end, the tribe has disappeared altogether; the girl visits their village to find it disintegrating into the landscape.

Yet in spite of her remark that "there was nothing there," the girl's intimate description of the lush landscape shows that her encounter, however brief, with its former inhabitants has opened her eyes to an African presence that initially she had not been able to see. Nonetheless, the gain is one-sided: even her altered perceptions can bring her no closer to the members of the tribe, only throw light on the ground they occupied. For the Old Chief, there is no advantage: he and his people have disappeared into a symbolic essence, a "richness" that the settlers derive from the land they take over. Lessing's observant young girl has been changed by her encounter with the Old Chief, but the awakening is a bleak one that endows her with a sense of loss and responsibility. Perhaps, one day, she will write about it.

The Old Chief Mshlanga

They were good, the years of ranging the bush over her father's farm which, like every white farm, was largely unused, broken only occasionally by small patches of cultivation. In between, nothing but trees, the long sparse grass, thorn and cactus and gully, grass and outcrop and thorn. And a jutting piece of rock which had been thrust up from the warm soil of Africa unimaginable eras of time ago, washed into hollows and whorls by sun and wind that had travelled so many thousands of miles of space and bush, would hold the weight of a small girl whose eyes were sightless for anything but a pale willowed river, a pale gleaming castle—a small girl singing: "Out flew the web and floated wide, the mirror cracked from side to side . . ."[1]

Pushing her way through the green aisles of the mealie[2] stalks, the leaves arching like cathedrals veined with sunlight far overhead, with the packed red earth underfoot, a fine lace of red starred witchweed would summon up a black bent figure croaking premonitions: the Northern witch, bred of cold Northern forests, would stand before her among the mealie fields, and it was the mealie fields that faded and fled, leaving her among the gnarled roots of an oak, snow falling thick and soft and white, the woodcutter's fire glowing red welcome through crowding tree trunks.

A white child, opening its eyes curiously on a sun-suffused landscape, a gaunt and violent landscape, might be supposed to accept it as her own, to make the msasa trees and the thorn trees as familiars, to feel her blood running free and responsive to the swing of the seasons.

This child could not see a msasa tree,[3] or the thorn, for what they were. Her books held tales of alien fairies, her rivers ran slow and peaceful, and she knew the shape of the leaves of an ash or an oak, the names of the little creatures that lived in English streams, when the words "the veld"[4] meant strangeness, though she could remember nothing else.

1. The child is reciting lines 114–15 of Tennyson's "The Lady of Shalott."
2. Maize; corn.
3. A large tree of central Africa, notable for the vivid colorings (pink through copper) of its spring foliage and for the fragrance of its white flowers.
4. Unenclosed country, open grassland.

Because of this, for many years, it was the veld that seemed unreal; the sun was a foreign sun, and the wind spoke a strange language.

The black people on the farm were as remote as the trees and the rocks. They were an amorphous black mass, mingling and thinning and massing like tadpoles, faceless, who existed merely to serve, to say "Yes, Baas,"[5] take their money and go. They changed season by season, moving from one farm to the next, according to their outlandish needs, which one did not have to understand, coming from perhaps hundreds of miles north or east, passing on after a few months—where? Perhaps even as far away as the fabled gold mines of Johannesburg,[6] where the pay was so much better than the few shillings a month and the double handful of mealie meal twice a day which they earned in that part of Africa.

The child was taught to take them for granted: the servants in the house would come running a hundred yards to pick up a book if she dropped it. She was called "Nkosikaas"—Chieftainess, even by the black children her own age.

Later, when the farm grew too small to hold her curiosity, she carried a gun in the crook of her arm and wandered miles a day, from *vlei* to *vlei*, from *kopje*[7] to *kopje*, accompanied by two dogs: the dogs and the gun were an armour against fear. Because of them she never felt fear.

If a native came into sight along the kaffir[8] paths half a mile away, the dogs would flush him up a tree as if he were a bird. If he expostulated (in his uncouth language which was by itself ridiculous) that was cheek. If one was in a good mood, it could be a matter for laughter. Otherwise one passed on, hardly glancing at the angry man in the tree.

On the rare occasions when white children met together they could amuse themselves by hailing a passing native in order to make a buffoon of him; they could set the dogs on him and watch him run; they could tease a small black child as if he were a puppy—save that they would not throw stones and sticks at a dog without a sense of guilt.

Later still, certain questions presented themselves in the child's mind; and because the answers were not easy to accept, they were silenced by an even greater arrogance of manner.

It was even impossible to think of the black people who worked about the house as friends, for if she talked to one of them, her mother would come running anxiously: "Come away; you mustn't talk to natives."

It was this instilled consciousness of danger, of something unpleasant, that made it easy to laugh out loud, crudely, if a servant made a mistake in his English or if he failed to understand an order—there is a certain kind of laughter that is fear, afraid of itself.

One evening, when I was about fourteen, I was walking down the side of a mealie field that had been newly ploughed, so that the great red clods showed fresh and tumbling to the vlei beyond, like a choppy red sea; it was that hushed

5. Boss.
6. The largest city in the Union (now Republic) of South Africa.
7. A small hill (Afrikaans). "Vlei": a shallow pool or swamp (Afrikaans).
8. Black African; usually used disparagingly.

and listening hour, when the birds send long sad calls from tree to tree, and all the colours of earth and sky and leaf are deep and golden. I had my rifle in the curve of my arm, and the dogs were at my heels.

In front of me, perhaps a couple of hundred yards away, a group of three Africans came into sight around the side of a big antheap. I whistled the dogs close in to my skirts and let the gun swing in my hand, and advanced, waiting for them to move aside, off the path, in respect for my passing. But they came on steadily, and the dogs looked up at me for the command to chase. I was angry. It was "cheek"[9] for a native not to stand off a path, the moment he caught sight of you.

In front walked an old man, stooping his weight on to a stick, his hair grizzled white, a dark red blanket slung over his shoulders like a cloak. Behind him came two young men, carrying bundles of pots, assegais,[1] hatchets.

The group was not a usual one. They were not natives seeking work. These had an air of dignity, of quietly following their own purpose. It was the dignity that checked my tongue. I walked quietly on, talking softly to the growling dogs, till I was ten paces away. Then the old man stopped, drawing his blanket close.

"Morning, Nkosikaas," he said, using the customary greeting for any time of the day.

"Good morning," I said. "Where are you going?" My voice was a little truculent.

The old man spoke in his own language, then one of the young men stepped forward politely and said in careful English: "My Chief travels to see his brothers beyond the river."

A Chief! I thought, understanding the pride that made the old man stand before me like an equal—more than an equal, for he showed courtesy, and I showed none.

The old man spoke again, wearing dignity like an inherited garment, still standing ten paces off, flanked by his entourage, not looking at me (that would have been rude) but directing his eyes somewhere over my head at the trees.

"You are the little Nkosikaas from the farm of Baas Jordan?"

"That's right," I said.

"Perhaps your father does not remember," said the interpreter for the old man, "but there was an affair with some goats. I remember seeing you when you were . . ." The young man held his hand at knee level and smiled.

We all smiled.

"What is your name?" I asked.

"This is Chief Mshlanga," said the young man.

"I will tell my father that I met you," I said.

The old man said: "My greetings to your father, little Nkosikaas."

"Good morning," I said politely, finding the politeness difficult, from lack of use.

"Morning, little Nkosikaas," said the old man, and stood aside to let me pass.

I went by, my gun hanging awkwardly, the dogs sniffing and growling, cheated of their favourite game of chasing natives like animals.

9. Impudence.
1. Spears.

Not long afterwards I read in an old explorer's book the phrase: "Chief Mshlanga's country." It went like this: "Our destination was Chief Mshlanga's country, to the north of the river; and it was our desire to ask his permission to prospect for gold in his territory."

The phrase "ask his permission" was so extraordinary to a white child, brought up to consider all natives as things to use, that it revived those questions, which could not be suppressed: they fermented slowly in my mind.

On another occasion one of those old prospectors who still move over Africa looking for neglected reefs, with their hammers and tents, and pans for sifting gold from crushed rock, came to the farm and, in talking of the old days, used that phrase again: "This was the Old Chief's country," he said. "It stretched from those mountains over there way back to the river, hundreds of miles of country." That was his name for our district: "The Old Chief's Country"; he did not use our name for it—a new phrase which held no implication of usurped ownership.

As I read more books about the time when this part of Africa was opened up, not much more than fifty years before, I found Old Chief Mshlanga had been a famous man, known to all the explorers and prospectors. But then he had been young; or maybe it was his father or uncle they spoke of—I never found out.

During that year I met him several times in the part of the farm that was traversed by natives moving over the country. I learned that the path up the side of the big red field where the birds sang was the recognized highway for migrants. Perhaps I even haunted it in the hope of meeting him: being greeted by him, the exchange of courtesies, seemed to answer the questions that troubled me.

Soon I carried a gun in a different spirit; I used it for shooting food and not to give me confidence. And now the dogs learned better manners. When I saw a native approaching, we offered and took greetings; and slowly that other landscape in my mind faded, and my feet struck directly on the African soil, and I saw the shapes of tree and hill clearly, and the black people moved back, as it were, out of my life: it was as if I stood aside to watch a slow intimate dance of landscape and men, a very old dance, whose steps I could not learn.

But I thought: this is my heritage, too; I was bred here; it is my country as well as the black man's country; and there is plenty of room for all of us, without elbowing each other off the pavements and roads.

It seemed it was only necessary to let free that respect I felt when I was talking with old Chief Mshlanga, to let both black and white people meet gently, with tolerance for each other's differences: it seemed quite easy.

Then, one day, something new happened. Working in our house as servants were always three natives: cook, houseboy, garden boy. They used to change as the farm natives changed: staying for a few months, then moving on to a new job, or back home to their kraals.[2] They were thought of as "good" or "bad" natives; which meant: how did they behave as servants? Were they lazy, efficient, obedient, or disrespectful? If the family felt good-humoured, the phrase was:

2. Native villages: collections of huts surrounding a central space.

"What can you expect from raw black savages?" If we were angry, we said: "These damned niggers, we would be much better off without them."

One day, a white policeman was on his rounds of the district, and he said laughingly: "Did you know you have an important man in your kitchen?"

"What!" exclaimed my mother sharply. "What do you mean?"

"A Chief's son." The policeman seemed amused. "He'll boss the tribe when the old man dies."

"He'd better not put on a Chief's son act with me," said my mother.

When the policeman left, we looked with different eyes at our cook: he was a good worker, but he drank too much at week-ends—that was how we knew him.

He was a tall youth, with very black skin, like black polished metal, his tightly growing black hair parted white man's fashion at one side, with a metal comb from the store stuck into it; very polite, very distant, very quick to obey an order. Now that it had been pointed out, we said: "Of course, you can see. Blood always tells."

My mother became strict with him now she knew about his birth and prospects. Sometimes, when she lost her temper, she would say: "You aren't the Chief yet, you know." And he would answer her very quietly, his eyes on the ground: "Yes, Nkosikaas."

One afternoon he asked for a whole day off, instead of the customary half-day, to go home next Sunday.

"How can you go home in one day?"

"It will take me half an hour on my bicycle," he explained.

I watched the direction he took; and the next day I went off to look for this kraal; I understood he must be Chief Mshlanga's successor: there was no other kraal near enough our farm.

Beyond our boundaries on that side the country was new to me. I followed unfamiliar paths past *kopjes* that till now had been part of the jagged horizon, hazed with distance. This was Government land, which had never been cultivated by white men; at first I could not understand why it was that it appeared, in merely crossing the boundary, I had entered a completely fresh type of landscape. It was a wide green valley, where a small river sparkled, and vivid water-birds darted over the rushes. The grass was thick and soft to my calves, the trees stood tall and shapely.

I was used to our farm, whose hundreds of acres of harsh eroded soil bore trees that had been cut for the mine furnaces and had grown thin and twisted, where the cattle had dragged the grass flat, leaving innumerable criss-crossing trails that deepened each season into gullies, under the force of the rains.

This country had been left untouched, save for prospectors whose picks had struck a few sparks from the surface of the rocks as they wandered by; and for migrant natives whose passing had left, perhaps, a charred patch on the trunk of a tree where their evening fire had nestled.

It was very silent: a hot morning with pigeons cooing throatily, the midday shadows lying dense and thick with clear yellow spaces of sunlight between and in all that wide green park-like valley, not a human soul but myself.

I was listening to the quick regular tapping of a woodpecker when slowly a chill feeling seemed to grow up from the small of my back to my shoulders, in a constricting spasm like a shudder, and at the roots of my hair a tingling sensation began and ran down over the surface of my flesh, leaving me goose-fleshed and cold, though I was damp with sweat. Fever? I thought; then uneasily, turned to look over my shoulder; and realized suddenly that this was fear. It was extraordinary, even humiliating. It was a new fear. For all the years I had walked by myself over this country I had never known a moment's uneasiness; in the beginning because I had been supported by a gun and the dogs, then because I had learnt an easy friendliness for the Africans I might encounter.

I had read of this feeling, how the bigness and silence of Africa, under the ancient sun, grows dense and takes shape in the mind, till even the birds seem to call menacingly, and a deadly spirit comes out of the trees and the rocks. You move warily, as if your very passing disturbs something old and evil, something dark and big and angry that might suddenly rear and strike from behind. You look at groves of entwined trees, and picture the animals that might be lurking there; you look at the river running slowly, dropping from level to level through the *vlei*, spreading into pools where at night the bucks come to drink, and the crocodiles rise and drag them by their soft noses into underwater caves. Fear possessed me. I found I was turning round and round, because of that shapeless menace behind me that might reach out and take me; I kept glancing at the files of *kopjes* which, seen from a different angle, seemed to change with every step so that even known landmarks, like a big mountain that had sentinelled my world since I first became conscious of it, showed an unfamiliar sunlit valley among its foothills. I did not know where I was. I was lost. Panic seized me. I found I was spinning round and round, staring anxiously at this tree and that, peering up at the sun which appeared to have moved into an eastern slant, shedding the sad yellow light of sunset. Hours must have passed! I looked at my watch and found that this state of meaningless terror had lasted perhaps ten minutes.

The point was that it was meaningless. I was not ten miles from home: I had only to take my way back along the valley to find myself at the fence; away among the foothills of the *kopjes* gleamed the roof of a neighbour's house, and a couple of hours' walking would reach it. This was the sort of fear that contracts the flesh of a dog at night and sets him howling at the full moon. It had nothing to do with what I thought or felt; and I was more disturbed by the fact that I could become its victim than of the physical sensation itself: I walked steadily on, quietened, in a divided mind, watching my own pricking nerves and apprehensive glances from side to side with a disgusted amusement. Deliberately I set myself to think of this village I was seeking, and what I should do when I entered it—if I could find it, which was doubtful, since I was walking aimlessly and it might be anywhere in the hundreds of thousands of acres of bush that stretched about me. With my mind on that village, I realized that a new sensation was added to the fear: loneliness. Now such a terror of isolation invaded me that I could hardly walk; and if it were not that I came over the crest of a small rise and saw a village below me, I should have turned and gone home. It was a cluster of thatched huts in a clearing among trees. There were neat patches of mealies and pumpkins and millet, and cattle grazed under some trees at a distance. Fowls scratched among the huts, dogs lay sleeping on the grass, and goats friezed a *kopje* that jutted up beyond a tributary of the river lying like an enclosing arm around the village.

As I came close I saw the huts were lovingly decorated with patterns of yellow and red and ochre mud on the walls; and the thatch was tied in place with plaits of straw.

This was not at all like our farm compound, a dirty and neglected place, a temporary home for migrants who had no roots in it.

And now I did not know what to do next. I called a small black boy, who was sitting on a lot playing a stringed gourd, quite naked except for the strings of blue beads round his neck, and said: "Tell the Chief I am here." The child stuck his thumb in his mouth and stared shyly back at me.

For minutes I shifted my feet on the edge of what seemed a deserted village, till at last the child scuttled off, and then some women came. They were draped in bright cloths, with brass glinting in their ears and on their arms. They also stared, silently; then turned to chatter among themselves.

I said again: "Can I see Chief Mshlanga?" I saw they caught the name; they did not understand what I wanted. I did not understand myself.

At last I walked through them and came past the huts and saw a clearing under a big shady tree, where a dozen old men sat crosslegged on the ground, talking. Chief Mshlanga was leaning back against the tree, holding a gourd in his hand, from which he had been drinking. When he saw me, not a muscle of his face moved, and I could see he was not pleased: perhaps he was afflicted with my own shyness, due to being unable to find the right forms of courtesy for the occasion. To meet me, on our own farm, was one thing; but I should not have come here. What had I expected? I could not join them socially: the thing was unheard of. Bad enough that I, a white girl, should be walking the veld alone as a white man might: and in this part of the bush where only Government officials had the right to move.

Again I stood, smiling foolishly, while behind me stood the groups of brightly clad, chattering women, their faces alert with curiosity and interest, and in front of me sat the old men, with old lined faces, their eyes guarded, aloof. It was a village of ancients and children and women. Even the two young men who kneeled beside the Chief were not those I had seen with him previously: the young men were all away working on the white men's farms and mines, and the Chief must depend on relatives who were temporarily on holiday for his attendants.

"The small white Nkosikaas is far from home," remarked the old man at last.

"Yes," I agreed, "it is far." I wanted to say: "I have come to pay you a friendly visit, Chief Mshlanga." I could not say it. I might now be feeling an urgent helpless desire to get to know these men and women as people, to be accepted by them as a friend, but the truth was I had set out in a spirit of curiosity: I had wanted to see the village that one day our cook, the reserved and obedient young man who got drunk on Sundays, would one day rule over.

"The child of Nkosi Jordan is welcome," said Chief Mshlanga.

"Thank you," I said, and could think of nothing more to say. There was a silence, while the flies rose and began to buzz around my head; and the wind shook a little in the thick green tree that spread its branches over the old men.

"Good morning," I said at last. "I have to return now to my home."

"Morning, little Nkosikaas," said Chief Mshlanga.

I walked away from the indifferent village, over the rise past the staring amber-eyed goats, down through the tall stately trees into the great rich green valley where the river meandered and the pigeons cooed tales of plenty and the woodpecker tapped softly.

The fear had gone; the loneliness had set into stiff-necked stoicism; there was now a queer hostility in the landscape, a cold, hard, sullen indomitability that walked with me, as strong as a wall, as intangible as smoke; it seemed to say to me: you walk here as a destroyer. I went slowly homewards, with an empty heart: I had learned that if one cannot call a country to heel like a dog, neither can one dismiss the past with a smile in an easy gush of feeling, saying: I could not help it, I am also a victim.

I only saw Chief Mshlanga once again.

One night my father's big red land was trampled down by small sharp hooves, and it was discovered that the culprits were goats from Chief Mshalanga's kraal. This had happened once before, years ago.

My father confiscated all the goats. Then he sent a message to the old Chief that if he wanted them he would have to pay for the damage.

He arrived at our house at the time of sunset one evening, looking very old and bent now, walking stiffly under his regally-draped blanket, leaning on a big stick. My father sat himself down in his big chair below the steps of the house; the old man squatted carefully on the ground before him, flanked by his two young men.

The palaver was long and painful, because of the bad English of the young man who interpreted, and because my father could not speak dialect, but only kitchen kaffir.

From my father's point of view, at least two hundred pounds' worth of damage had been done to the crop. He knew he could not get the money from the old man. He felt he was entitled to keep the goats. As for the old Chief, he kept repeating angrily: "Twenty goats! My people cannot lose twenty goats! We are not rich, like the Nkosi Jordan, to lose twenty goats at once."

My father did not think of himself as rich, but rather as very poor. He spoke quickly and angrily in return, saying that the damage done meant a great deal to him, and that he was entitled to the goats.

At last it grew so heated that the cook, the Chief's son, was called from the kitchen to be interpreter, and now my father spoke fluently in English, and our cook translated rapidly so that the old man could understand how very angry my father was. The young man spoke without emotion, in a mechanical way, his eyes lowered, but showing how he felt his position by a hostile uncomfortable set of the shoulders.

It was now in the late sunset, the sky a welter of colours, the birds singing their last songs, and the cattle, lowing peacefully, moving past us towards their sheds for the night. It was the hour when Africa is most beautiful; and here was this pathetic, ugly scene, doing no one any good.

At last my father stated finally: "I'm not going to argue about it. I am keeping the goats."

The old Chief flashed back in his own language: "That means that my people will go hungry when the dry season comes."

"Go to the police, then," said my father, and looked triumphant.

There was, of course, no more to be said.

The old man sat silent, his head bent, his hands dangling helplessly over his withered knees. Then he rose, the young men helping him, and he stood facing my father. He spoke once again, very stiffly; and turned away and went home to his village.

"What did he say?" asked my father of the young man, who laughed uncomfortably and would not meet his eyes.

"What did he say?" insisted my father.

Our cook stood straight and silent, his brows knotted together. Then he spoke. "My father says: All this land, this land you call yours, is his land, and belongs to our people."

Having made this statement, he walked off into the bush after his father, and we did not see him again.

Our next cook was a migrant from Nyasaland, with no expectations of greatness.

Next time the policeman came on his rounds he was told this story. He remarked: "That kraal has no right to be there; it should have been moved long ago. I don't know why no one has done anything about it. I'll have a chat with the Native Commissioner next week. I'm going over for tennis on Sunday, anyway."

Some time later we heard that Chief Mshlanga and his people had been moved two hundred miles east, to a proper Native Reserve; the Government land was going to be opened up for white settlement soon.

I went to see the village again, about a year afterwards. There was nothing there. Mounds of red mud, where the huts had been, had long swathes of rotting thatch over them, veined with the red galleries of the white ants. The pumpkin vines rioted everywhere, over the bushes, up the lower branches of trees so that the great golden balls rolled underfoot and dangled overhead: it was a festival of pumpkins. The bushes were crowding up, the new grass sprang vivid green.

The settler lucky enough to be allotted the lush warm valley (if he chose to cultivate this particular section) would find, suddenly, in the middle of a mealie field, the plants were growing fifteen feet tall, the weight of the cobs dragging at the stalks, and wonder what unsuspected vein of richness he had struck.

1951

JAMES BALDWIN

1924–1987

A leading African American novelist, James Baldwin was one of the great prose stylists of the twentieth century. He is best known for his remarkable essays that, in poetic rhetoric drawing on both the classics of English literature and the tones of biblical prophecy, combine personal reflection with a wider view of social justice. An icon of the civil rights movement, Baldwin nonetheless felt considerably alienated both from black culture and from white liberal society. He lived much of his life abroad but continually affirmed his American identity as a "native son."

Baldwin grew up in his "father's house"—that is, in the Harlem home of his stepfather, David Baldwin, a preacher whom his mother married when James was two. David Baldwin, a preacher in small black churches, reacted with suspicion when a white teacher, Orilla Miller, took James to plays, including Orson Welles's all-black production of Shakespeare's *Macbeth*. (The elder Baldwin did not approve of theater.) David Baldwin's mother, who had been born in slavery, lived with the family in Harlem. Although his acquaintance with secular literature strained his relationship to the church, James remained affiliated with various churches over the years and preached sermons as a young man.

As the United States mobilized for the Second World War, Baldwin found a job in a defense plant in New Jersey— and hated both the job and the place, where he had his first serious experiences of racial discrimination. When his stepfather died, in 1943, he was expected to move back home and take care of his mother and siblings. Instead, Baldwin moved to Greenwich Village, in lower Manhattan, to pursue his career as a writer. Here he met older writers, including Richard Wright. "Writing was an act of love," Baldwin would later say, "an attempt to be loved." While living in the Village, he became aware of his homosexuality.

After the war Baldwin left New York for Paris, following in the paths of a generation of famous American writers before him. Of this self-imposed expatriation, he later wrote, "In my own case, I think my exile saved my life." In the years that followed, Baldwin wrote and then suffered writer's block; he was arrested on a false charge of theft; he tried to commit suicide; and he succeeded in finishing *Go Tell It on the Mountain* (1953), his first published novel, an autobiographical story of a deeply religious young man who ultimately leaves the church. For the rest of his life, Baldwin divided his time between New York, Paris, Switzerland, and Turkey. Amid constant interpersonal turmoil (and additional suicide attempts), his literary career was now on the rise: in 1955, *Notes of a Native Son*, a collection of essays that cemented his public voice, was released; a year later, *Giovanni's Room*, a novel about a white American in Paris struggling with his homosexuality, appeared. Despite difficulties in finding a publisher, the work increased Baldwin's fame. Encouraged by the rise of the civil rights movement, he renewed his political engagement; with *The Fire Next Time* (1963), in which he commented on race and American history, he became an international figure.

Like other leading African Americans of the civil rights era, Baldwin was unhappy with the radicalization of movements with which he had been associated. Although he had known the Black Nationalist leader Malcolm X and met Elijah Muhammad of the Nation of Islam, their successors in such groups as the Black Panthers tended to think of Baldwin as a darling of white liberals who was more concerned with cosmopolitan life in Paris than with the plight of ordinary African Americans. Baldwin's generally optimistic, liberal views led him to exhort his readers to work together for change: "If we—and now I mean the relatively conscious whites and the relatively conscious blacks, who must, like lovers, insist on, or create, the consciousness of the others—do not falter in our duty now, we may be able, handful that we are, to end the racial nightmare, and achieve our country, and change the history of the world." In his later years, Baldwin's primary home was a farmhouse in Saint-Paul-de-Vence, a town in southern France, but he continued traveling in the United States, writing essays, and teaching in several colleges. He died in Saint-Paul in 1987.

Baldwin begins "Notes of a Native Son," the essay printed here, with the conjunction of two profound events in his personal life: the death of his father (actually his stepfather) and the birth of his father's youngest child. These personal rites of passage are, however, quickly placed in the context of broader social and political events—namely, the race riots that shook Detroit in June 1943. The protests, in which nearly three dozen people died, were a shocking episode in a series of conflicts between blacks and whites in the wake of the Great Migration between the two world wars. African Americans were leaving the segregated South in search of greater freedom, and work, in northern industrial cities, where they were not always welcomed. Baldwin's father had likewise moved to New York from New Orleans not long before the boy's birth, and Baldwin describes the racial tensions of wartime New York and New Jersey. The juxtaposition of experiences of great personal significance with momentous public events becomes a central issue in the essay.

While it offers a profound meditation on a relationship between a son and a father who was both physically and mentally ill, the essay explains how both men's encounters with racial discrimination contributed to the conflicts in their private lives. Baldwin represents the relationship, and his evolving consciousness of his place in the family and in American society, with subtlety and nuance. Baldwin's style—direct but meditative, confessional but aware of the broader context—gives this classic work its status as one of the most memorable personal meditations published in the twentieth century.

Notes of a Native Son[1]

On the 29th of July, in 1943, my father died. On the same day, a few hours later, his last child was born. Over a month before this, while all our energies were concentrated in waiting for these events, there had been, in Detroit, one of the bloodiest race riots of the century.[2] A few hours after my father's funeral, while he lay in state in the undertaker's chapel, a race riot broke out

1. The title alludes to Richard Wright's novel *Native Son* (1940).
2. Three days of rioting in June 1943, in which 25 African Americans and 9 whites were killed.

in Harlem. On the morning of the 3rd of August, we drove my father to the graveyard through a wilderness of smashed plate glass.

The day of my father's funeral had also been my nineteenth birthday. As we drove him to the graveyard, the spoils of injustice, anarchy, discontent, and hatred were all around us. It seemed to me that God himself had devised, to mark my father's end, the most sustained and brutally dissonant of codas. And it seemed to me, too, that the violence which rose all about us as my father left the world had been devised as a corrective for the pride of his eldest son. I had declined to believe in that apocalypse which had been central to my father's vision; very well, life seemed to be saying, here is something that will certainly pass for an apocalypse until the real thing comes along. I had inclined to be contemptuous of my father for the conditions of his life, for the conditions of our lives. When his life had ended I began to wonder about that life and also, in a new way, to be apprehensive about my own.

I had not known my father very well. We had got on badly, partly because we shared, in our different fashions, the vice of stubborn pride. When he was dead I realized that I had hardly ever spoken to him. When he had been dead a long time I began to wish I had. It seems to be typical of life in America, where opportunities, real and fancied, are thicker than anywhere else on the globe, that the second generation has no time to talk to the first. No one, including my father, seems to have known exactly how old he was, but his mother had been born during slavery. He was of the first generation of free men. He, along with thousands of other Negroes, came North after 1919 and I was part of that generation which had never seen the landscape of what Negroes sometimes call the Old Country.[3]

He had been born in New Orleans and had been a quite young man there during the time that Louis Armstrong,[4] a boy, was running errands for the dives and honky-tonks of what was always presented to me as one of the most wicked of cities—to this day, whenever I think of New Orleans, I also helplessly think of Sodom and Gomorrah.[5] My father never mentioned Louis Armstrong, except to forbid us to play his records; but there was a picture of him on our wall for a long time. One of my father's strong-willed female relatives had placed it there and forbade my father to take it down. He never did, but he eventually maneuvered her out of the house and when, some years later, she was in trouble and near death, he refused to do anything to help her.

He was, I think, very handsome. I gather this from photographs and from my own memories of him, dressed in his Sunday best and on his way to preach a sermon somewhere, when I was little. Handsome, proud, and ingrown, "like a toe-nail," somebody said. But he looked to me, as I grew older, like pictures I had seen of African tribal chieftains: he really should have been naked, with war-paint on and barbaric mementos, standing among spears. He could be chilling in the pulpit and indescribably cruel in his personal life and he was certainly the most bitter man I have ever met; yet it must be said that there was something else in him, buried in him, which lent him his tremendous power and, even, a rather crushing charm. It had something to do with his blackness,

3. The South. Over a million African Americans left the South for the Midwest and the Northeast after the First World War (1914–18).

4. Armstrong (1901–1971), jazz trumpeter, cornetist, and singer.
5. Biblical cities destroyed by God for their wickedness. See Genesis 18–19.

I think—he was very black—with his blackness and his beauty, and with the fact that he knew that he was black but did not know that he was beautiful. He claimed to be proud of his blackness but it had also been the cause of much humiliation and it had fixed bleak boundaries to his life. He was not a young man when we were growing up and he had already suffered many kinds of ruin; in his outrageously demanding and protective way he loved his children, who were black like him and menaced, like him; and all these things sometimes showed in his face when he tried, never to my knowledge with any success, to establish contact with any of us. When he took one of his children on his knee to play, the child always became fretful and began to cry; when he tried to help one of us with our homework the absolutely unabating tension which emanated from him caused our minds and our tongues to become paralyzed, so that he, scarcely knowing why, flew into a rage and the child, not knowing why, was punished. If it ever entered his head to bring a surprise home for his children, it was, almost unfailingly, the wrong surprise and even the big watermelons he often brought home on his back in the summertime led to the most appalling scenes. I do not remember, in all those years, that one of his children was ever glad to see him come home. From what I was able to gather of his early life, it seemed that this inability to establish contact with other people had always marked him and had been one of the things which had driven him out of New Orleans. There was something in him, therefore, groping and tentative, which was never expressed and which was buried with him. One saw it most clearly when he was facing new people and hoping to impress them. But he never did, not for long. We went from church to smaller and more improbable church, he found himself in less and less demand as a minister, and by the time he died none of his friends had come to see him for a long time. He had lived and died in an intolerable bitterness of spirit and it frightened me, as we drove him to the graveyard through those unquiet, ruined streets, to see how powerful and overflowing this bitterness could be and to realize that this bitterness now was mine.

When he died I had been away from home for a little over a year. In that year I had had time to become aware of the meaning of all my father's bitter warnings, had discovered the secret of his proudly pursed lips and rigid carriage: I had discovered the weight of white people in the world. I saw that this had been for my ancestors and now would be for me an awful thing to live with and that the bitterness which had helped to kill my father could also kill me.

He had been ill a long time—in the mind, as we now realized, reliving instances of his fantastic intransigence in the new light of his affliction and endeavoring to feel a sorrow for him which never, quite, came true. We had not known that he was being eaten up by paranoia, and the discovery that his cruelty, to our bodies and our minds, had been one of the symptoms of his illness was not, then, enough to enable us to forgive him. The younger children felt, quite simply, relief that he would not be coming home anymore. My mother's observation that it was he, after all, who had kept them alive all these years meant nothing because the problems of keeping children alive are not real for children. The older children felt, with my father gone, that they could invite their friends to the house without fear that their friends would be insulted or, as had sometimes happened with me, being told that their friends were in league with the devil and intended to rob our family of everything we owned. (I didn't fail to wonder, and it made me hate him, what on earth we owned that anybody else would want.)

His illness was beyond all hope of healing before anyone realized that he was ill. He had always been so strange and had lived, like a prophet, in such unimaginably close communion with the Lord that his long silences which were punctuated by moans and hallelujahs and snatches of old songs while he sat at the living-room window never seemed odd to us. It was not until he refused to eat because, he said, his family was trying to poison him that my mother was forced to accept as a fact what had, until then, been only an unwilling suspicion. When he was committed, it was discovered that he had tuberculosis and, as it turned out, the disease of his mind allowed the disease of his body to destroy him. For the doctors could not force him to eat, either, and, though he was fed intravenously, it was clear from the beginning that there was no hope for him.

In my mind's eye I could see him, sitting at the window, locked up in his terrors; hating and fearing every living soul including his children who had betrayed him, too, by reaching towards the world which had despised him. There were nine of us. I began to wonder what it could have felt like for such a man to have had nine children whom he could barely feed. He used to make little jokes about our poverty, which never, of course, seemed very funny to us; they could not have seemed very funny to him, either, or else our all too feeble response to them would never have caused such rages. He spent great energy and achieved, to our chagrin, no small amount of success in keeping us away from the people who surrounded us, people who had all-night rent parties[6] to which we listened when we should have been sleeping, people who cursed and drank and flashed razor blades on Lenox Avenue.[7] He could not understand why, if they had so much energy to spare, they could not use it to make their lives better. He treated almost everybody on our block with a most uncharitable asperity and neither they, nor, of course, their children were slow to reciprocate.

The only white people who came to our house were welfare workers and bill collectors. It was almost always my mother who dealt with them, for my father's temper, which was at the mercy of his pride, was never to be trusted. It was clear that he felt their very presence in his home to be a violation: this was conveyed by his carriage, almost ludicrously stiff, and by his voice, harsh and vindictively polite. When I was around nine or ten I wrote a play which was directed by a young, white schoolteacher, a woman, who then took an interest in me, and gave me books to read and, in order to corroborate my theatrical bent, decided to take me to see what she somewhat tactlessly referred to as "real" plays. Theater-going was forbidden in our house, but, with the really cruel intuitiveness of a child, I suspected that the color of this woman's skin would carry the day for me. When, at school, she suggested taking me to the theater, I did not, as I might have done if she had been a Negro, find a way of discouraging her, but agreed that she should pick me up at my house one evening. I then, very cleverly, left all the rest to my mother, who suggested to my

---

6. Parties at which money was collected from the guests to help cover tenants' rent; normally, the parties included hired bands; during

Prohibition (1920–33), bootlegged alcohol was served.

7. Major north–south thoroughfare in Harlem.

father, as I knew she would, that it would not be very nice to let such a kind woman make the trip for nothing. Also, since it was a schoolteacher, I imagine that my mother countered the idea of sin with the idea of "education," which word, even with my father, carried a kind of bitter weight.

Before the teacher came my father took me aside to ask *why* she was coming, what *interest* she could possibly have in our house, in a boy like me. I said I didn't know but I, too, suggested that it had something to do with education. And I understood that my father was waiting for me to say something—I didn't quite know what; perhaps that I wanted his protection against this teacher and her "education." I said none of these things and the teacher came and we went out. It was clear, during the brief interview in our living room, that my father was agreeing very much against his will and that he would have refused permission if he had dared. The fact that he did not dare caused me to despise him: I had no way of knowing that he was facing in that living room a wholly unprecedented and frightening situation.

Later, when my father had been laid off from his job, this woman became very important to us. She was really a very sweet and generous woman and went to a great deal of trouble to be of help to us, particularly during one awful winter. My mother called her by the highest name she knew: she said she was a "christian." My father could scarcely disagree but during the four or five years of our relatively close association he never trusted her and was always trying to surprise in her open, Midwestern face the genuine, cunningly hidden, and hideous motivation. In later years, particularly when it began to be clear that this "education" of mine was going to lead me to perdition, he became more explicit and warned me that my white friends in high school were not really my friends and that I would see, when I was older, how white people would do anything to keep a Negro down. Some of them could be nice, he admitted, but none of them were to be trusted and most of them were not even nice. The best thing was to have as little to do with them as possible. I did not feel this way and I was certain, in my innocence, that I never would.

But the year which preceded my father's death had made a great change in my life. I had been living in New Jersey, working in defense plants, working and living among southerners, white and black. I knew about the south, of course, and about how southerners treated Negroes and how they expected them to behave, but it had never entered my mind that anyone would look at me and expect *me* to behave that way. I learned in New Jersey that to be a Negro meant, precisely, that one was never looked at but was simply at the mercy of the reflexes the color of one's skin caused in other people. I acted in New Jersey as I had always acted, that is as though I thought a great deal of myself—I had to *act* that way— with results that were, simply, unbelievable. I had scarcely arrived before I had earned the enmity, which was extraordinarily ingenious, of all my superiors and nearly all my co-workers. In the beginning, to make matters worse, I simply did not know what was happening. I did not know what I had done, and I shortly began to wonder what *anyone* could possibly do, to bring about such unanimous, active, and unbearably vocal hostility. I knew about jim-crow[8] but I had never experienced it. I went to the same self-service restaurant three times and

---

8. System of laws and customs enforcing segregation of blacks and whites in southern states; some aspects of Jim Crow were also in force in northern states, including New Jersey.

stood with all the Princeton boys before the counter, waiting for a hamburger and coffee; it was always an extraordinarily long time before anything was set before me; but it was not until the fourth visit that I learned that, in fact, nothing had ever been set before me: I had simply picked something up. Negroes were not served there, I was told, and they had been waiting for me to realize that I was always the only Negro present. Once I was told this, I determined to go there all the time. But now they were ready for me and, though some dreadful scenes were subsequently enacted in that restaurant, I never ate there again.

It was the same story all over New Jersey, in bars, bowling alleys, diners, places to live. I was always being forced to leave, silently, or with mutual imprecations. I very shortly became notorious and children giggled behind me when I passed and their elders whispered or shouted—they really believed that I was mad. And it did begin to work on my mind, of course; I began to be afraid to go anywhere and to compensate for this I went places to which I really should not have gone and where, God knows, I had no desire to be. My reputation in town naturally enhanced my reputation at work and my working day became one long series of acrobatics designed to keep me out of trouble. I cannot say that these acrobatics succeeded. It began to seem that the machinery of the organization I worked for was turning over, day and night, with but one aim: to eject me. I was fired once, and contrived, with the aid of a friend from New York, to get back on the payroll; was fired again, and bounced back again. It took a while to fire me for the third time, but the third time took. There were no loopholes anywhere. There was not even any way of getting back inside the gates.

That year in New Jersey lives in my mind as though it were the year during which, having an unsuspected predilection for it, I first contracted some dread, chronic disease, the unfailing symptom of which is a kind of blind fever, a pounding in the skull and fire in the bowels. Once this disease is contracted, one can never be really carefree again, for the fever, without an instant's warning, can recur at any moment. It can wreck more important things than race relations. There is not a Negro alive who does not have this rage in his blood—one has the choice, merely, of living with it consciously or surrendering to it. As for me, this fever has recurred in me, and does, and will until the day I die.

My last night in New Jersey, a white friend from New York took me to the nearest big town, Trenton, to go to the movies and have a few drinks. As it turned out, he also saved me from, at the very least, a violent whipping. Almost every detail of that night stands out very clearly in my memory. I even remember the name of the movie we saw because its title impressed me as being so patly ironical. It was a movie about the German occupation of France, starring Maureen O'Hara and Charles Laughton and called *This Land Is Mine*. I remember the name of the diner we walked into when the movie ended: it was the "American Diner." When we walked in the counterman asked what we wanted and I remember answering with the casual sharpness which had become my habit: "We want a hamburger and a cup of coffee, what do you think we want?" I do not know why, after a year of such rebuffs, I so completely failed to anticipate his answer, which was, of course, "We don't serve Negroes here." This reply failed to discompose me, at least for the moment. I made some sardonic comment about the name of the diner and we walked out into the streets.

This was the time of what was called the "brown-out," when the lights in all American cities were very dim. When we re-entered the streets something happened to me which had the force of an optical illusion, or a nightmare. The streets were very crowded and I was facing north. People were moving in every direction but it seemed to me, in that instant, that all of the people I could see, and many more than that, were moving toward me, against me, and that everyone was white. I remember how their faces gleamed. And I felt, like a physical sensation, a *click* at the nape of my neck as though some interior string connecting my head to my body had been cut. I began to walk. I heard my friend call after me, but I ignored him. Heaven only knows what was going on in his mind, but he had the good sense not to touch me—I don't know what would have happened if he had—and to keep me in sight. I don't know what was going on in my mind, either; I certainly had no conscious plan. I wanted to do something to crush these white faces, which were crushing me. I walked for perhaps a block or two until I came to an enormous, glittering, and fashionable restaurant in which I knew not even the intercession of the Virgin would cause me to be served. I pushed through the doors and took the first vacant seat I saw, at a table for two, and waited.

I do not know how long I waited and I rather wonder, until today, what I could possibly have looked like. Whatever I looked like, I frightened the waitress who shortly appeared, and the moment she appeared all of my fury flowed towards her. I hated her for her white face, and for her great, astounded, frightened eyes. I felt that if she found a black man so frightening I would make her fright worth-while.

She did not ask me what I wanted, but repeated, as though she had learned it somewhere, "We don't serve Negroes here." She did not say it with the blunt, derisive hostility to which I had grown so accustomed, but, rather, with a note of apology in her voice, and fear. This made me colder and more murderous than ever. I felt I had to do something with my hands. I wanted her to come close enough for me to get her neck between my hands.

So I pretended not to have understood her, hoping to draw her closer. And she did step a very short step closer, with her pencil poised incongruously over her pad, and repeated the formula: ". . . don't serve Negroes here."

Somehow, with the repetition of that phrase, which was already ringing in my head like a thousand bells of a nightmare, I realized that she would never come any closer and that I would have to strike from a distance. There was nothing on the table but an ordinary watermug half full of water, and I picked this up and hurled it with all my strength at her. She ducked and it missed her and shattered against the mirror behind the bar. And, with that sound, my frozen blood abruptly thawed, I returned from wherever I had been, I *saw*, for the first time, the restaurant, the people with their mouths open, already, as it seemed to me, rising as one man, and I realized what I had done, and where I was, and I was frightened. I rose and began running for the door. A round, potbellied man grabbed me by the nape of the neck just as I reached the doors and began to beat me about the face. I kicked him and got loose and ran into the streets. My friend whispered, "*Run!*" and I ran.

My friend stayed outside the restaurant long enough to misdirect my pursuers and the police, who arrived, he told me, at once. I do not know what I said to him when he came to my room that night. I could not have said much. I felt, in the oddest, most awful way, that I had somehow betrayed him. I lived it over and over and over again, the way one relives an automobile accident after it has happened and one finds oneself alone and safe. I could not get over two facts, both equally difficult for the imagination to grasp, and one was that I could have been murdered. But the other was that I had been ready to commit murder. I saw nothing very clearly but I did see this: that my life, my *real* life, was in danger, and not from anything other people might do but from the hatred I carried in my own heart.

II

I had returned home around the second week in June—in great haste because it seemed that my father's death and my mother's confinement were both but a matter of hours. In the case of my mother, it soon became clear that she had simply made a miscalculation. This had always been her tendency and I don't believe that a single one of us arrived in the world, or has since arrived anywhere else, on time. But none of us dawdled so intolerably about the business of being born as did my baby sister. We sometimes amused ourselves, during those endless, stifling weeks, by picturing the baby sitting within in the safe, warm dark, bitterly regretting the necessity of becoming a part of our chaos and stubbornly putting it off as long as possible. I understood her perfectly and congratulated her on showing such good sense so soon. Death, however, sat as purposefully at my father's bedside as life stirred within my mother's womb and it was harder to understand why he so lingered in that long shadow. It seemed that he had bent, and for a long time, too, all of his energies towards dying. Now death was ready for him but my father held back.

All of Harlem, indeed, seemed to be infected by waiting. I had never before known it to be so violently still. Racial tensions throughout this country were exacerbated during the early years of the war,[9] partly because the labor market brought together hundreds of thousands of ill-prepared people and partly because Negro soldiers, regardless of where they were born, received their military training in the south. What happened in defense plants and army camps had repercussions, naturally, in every Negro ghetto. The situation in Harlem had grown bad enough for clergymen, policemen, educators, politicians, and social workers to assert in one breath that there was no "crime wave" and to offer, in the very next breath, suggestions as to how to combat it. These suggestions always seemed to involve playgrounds, despite the fact that racial skirmishes were occurring in the playgrounds, too. Playground or not, crime wave or not, the Harlem police force had been augmented in March, and the unrest grew—perhaps, in fact, partly as a result of the ghetto's instinctive hatred of policemen. Perhaps the most revealing news item, out of the steady parade of reports of muggings, stabbings, shootings, assaults, gang wars, and accusations of police brutality, is the item concerning six Negro girls who set upon a white girl in the subway because, as they all too accurately put it, she was stepping on their toes. Indeed she was, all over the nation.

9. The Second World War (1939–45), which the United States entered on December 8, 1941.

I had never before been so aware of policemen, on foot, on horseback, on corners, everywhere, always two by two. Nor had I ever been so aware of small knots of people. They were on stoops and on corners and in doorways, and what was striking about them, I think, was that they did not seem to be talking. Never, when I passed these groups, did the usual sound of a curse or a laugh ring out and neither did there seem to be any hum of gossip. There was certainly, on the other hand, occurring between them communication extraordinarily intense. Another thing that was striking was the unexpected diversity of the people who made up these groups. Usually, for example, one would see a group of sharpies standing on the street corner, jiving the passing chicks;[1] or a group of older men, usually, for some reason, in the vicinity of a barber shop, discussing baseball scores, or the numbers,[2] or making rather chilling observations about women they had known. Women, in a general way, tended to be seen less often together—unless they were church women, or very young girls, or prostitutes met together for an unprofessional instant. But that summer I saw the strangest combinations: large, respectable, churchly matrons standing on the stoops or the corners with their hair tied up, together with a girl in sleazy satin whose face bore the marks of gin and the razor, or heavy-set, abrupt, no-nonsense older men, in company with the most disreputable and fanatical "race" men,[3] or these same "race" men with the sharpies, or these sharpies with the churchly women. Seventh Day Adventists and Methodists and Spiritualists seemed to be hobnobbing with Holyrollers[4] and they were all, alike, entangled with the most flagrant disbelievers; something heavy in their stance seemed to indicate that they had all, incredibly, seen a common vision, and on each face there seemed to be the same strange, bitter shadow.

The churchly women and the matter-of-fact, no-nonsense men had children in the Army. The sleazy girls they talked to had lovers there, the sharpies and the "race" men had friends and brothers there. It would have demanded an unquestioning patriotism, happily as uncommon in this country as it is undesirable, for these people not to have been disturbed by the bitter letters they received, by the newspaper stories they read, not to have been enraged by the posters, then to be found all over New York, which described the Japanese as "yellow-bellied Japs." It was only the "race" men, to be sure, who spoke ceaselessly of being revenged—how this vengeance was to be exacted was not clear—for the indignities and dangers suffered by Negro boys in uniform; but everybody felt a directionless, hopeless bitterness, as well as that panic which can scarcely be suppressed when one knows that a human being one loves is beyond one's reach, and in danger. This helplessness and this gnawing uneasiness does something, at length, to even the toughest mind. Perhaps the best way to sum all this up is to say that the people I knew felt, mainly, a peculiar kind of relief when they knew that their boys were being shipped out of the south, to do battle overseas. It was, perhaps, like feeling that the most dangerous part of a dangerous journey had been passed and that now, even if death should come, it would come with honor and without the complicity of their countrymen. Such a death would be, in short, a fact with which one could hope to live.

1. Talking nonsense with the girls passing by. "Sharpies": tricksters or con men.
2. An illegal lottery.
3. Men who emphasized the importance of

African American pride and mutual support.
4. Pentecostalists, who emphasized prophecy, healing, and speaking in tongues.

It was on the 28th of July, which I believe was a Wednesday, that I visited my father for the first time during his illness and for the last time in his life. The moment I saw him I knew why I had put off this visit so long. I had told my mother that I did not want to see him because I hated him. But this was not true. It was only that I *had* hated him and I wanted to hold on to this hatred. I did not want to look on him as a ruin: it was not a ruin I had hated. I imagine that one of the reasons people cling to their hates so stubbornly is because they sense, once hate is gone, that they will be forced to deal with pain.

We traveled out to him, his older sister and myself, to what seemed to be the very end of a very Long Island. It was hot and dusty and we wrangled, my aunt and I, all the way out, over the fact that I had recently begun to smoke and, as she said, to give myself airs. But I knew that she wrangled with me because she could not bear to face the fact of her brother's dying. Neither could I endure the reality of her despair, her unstated bafflement as to what had happened to her brother's life, and her own. So we wrangled and I smoked and from time to time she fell into a heavy reverie. Covertly, I watched her face, which was the face of an old woman; it had fallen in, the eyes were sunken and lightless; soon she would be dying, too.

In my childhood—it had not been so long ago—I had thought her beautiful. She had been quick-witted and quick-moving and very generous with all the children and each of her visits had been an event. At one time one of my brothers and myself had thought of running away to live with her. Now she could no longer produce out of her handbag some unexpected and yet familiar delight. She made me feel pity and revulsion and fear. It was awful to realize that she no longer caused me to feel affection. The closer we came to the hospital the more querulous she became and at the same time, naturally, grew more dependent on me. Between pity and guilt and fear I began to feel that there was another me trapped in my skull like a jack-in-the-box who might escape my control at any moment and fill the air with screaming.

She began to cry the moment we entered the room and she saw him lying there, all shriveled and still, like a little black monkey. The great, gleaming apparatus which fed him and would have compelled him to be still even if he had been able to move brought to mind, not beneficence, but torture; the tubes entering his arm made me think of pictures I had seen when a child, of Gulliver,[5] tied down by the pygmies on that island. My aunt wept and wept, there was a whistling sound in my father's throat; nothing was said; he could not speak. I wanted to take his hand, to say something. But I do not know what I could have said, even if he could have heard me. He was not really in that room with us, he had at last really embarked on his journey; and though my aunt told me that he said he was going to meet Jesus, I did not hear anything except that whistling in his throat. The doctor came back and we left, into that unbearable train again, and home. In the morning came the telegram saying that he was dead. Then the house was suddenly full of relatives, friends, hysteria, and confusion and I quickly left my mother and the children to the care of those impressive women, who, in Negro communities at least, automatically appear at times of bereavement armed with lotions, proverbs, and patience,

---

5. The hero of *Gulliver's Travels* (1726) by the English-Irish writer Jonathan Swift (1667–1745); Gulliver is washed ashore on Lilliput, an island inhabited by tiny people who tie him down with cords while he is sleeping.

and an ability to cook. I went downtown. By the time I returned, later the same day, my mother had been carried to the hospital and the baby had been born.

III

For my father's funeral I had nothing black to wear and this posed a nagging problem all day long. It was one of those problems, simple, or impossible of solution, to which the mind insanely clings in order to avoid the mind's real trouble. I spent most of that day at the downtown apartment of a girl I knew, celebrating my birthday with whiskey and wondering what to wear that night. When planning a birthday celebration one naturally does not expect that it will be up against competition from a funeral and this girl had anticipated taking me out that night, for a big dinner and a night club afterwards. Sometime during the course of that long day we decided that we would go out anyway, when my father's funeral service was over. I imagine I decided it, since, as the funeral hour approached, it became clearer and clearer to me that I would not know what to do with myself when it was over. The girl, stifling her very lively concern as to the possible effects of the whiskey on one of my father's chief mourners, concentrated on being conciliatory and practically helpful. She found a black shirt for me somewhere and ironed it and, dressed in the darkest pants and jacket I owned, and slightly drunk, I made my way to my father's funeral.

The chapel was full, but not packed, and very quiet. There were, mainly, my father's relatives, and his children, and here and there I saw faces I had not seen since childhood, the faces of my father's one-time friends. They were very dark and solemn now, seeming somehow to suggest that they had known all along that something like this would happen. Chief among the mourners was my aunt, who had quarreled with my father all his life; by which I do not mean to suggest that her mourning was insincere or that she had not loved him. I suppose that she was one of the few people in the world who had, and their incessant quarreling proved precisely the strength of the tie that bound them. The only other person in the world, as far as I knew, whose relationship to my father rivaled my aunt's in depth was my mother, who was not there.

It seemed to me, of course, that it was a very long funeral. But it was, if anything, a rather shorter funeral than most, nor, since there were no overwhelming, uncontrollable expressions of grief, could it be called—if I dare to use the word—successful. The minister who preached my father's funeral sermon was one of the few my father had still been seeing as he neared his end. He presented to us in his sermon a man whom none of us had ever seen—a man thoughtful, patient, and forbearing, a Christian inspiration to all who knew him, and a model for his children. And no doubt the children, in their disturbed and guilty state, were almost ready to believe this; he had been remote enough to be anything and, anyway, the shock of the incontrovertible, that it was really our father lying up there in that casket, prepared the mind for anything. His sister moaned and this grief-stricken moaning was taken as corroboration. The other faces held a dark, non-committal thoughtfulness. This was not the man they had known, but they had scarcely expected to be confronted with *him*; this was, in a sense deeper than questions of fact, the man they had not known, and the man they had not known may have been the real one. The real man, whoever he had been, had suffered and now he was dead: this was all that was sure and all that mattered now. Every man in the chapel hoped that when his hour came he, too, would be eulogized, which is to say forgiven, and that all of his lapses, greeds, errors, and strayings from the truth would be invested with coherence and looked upon with charity. This was perhaps the last thing human beings could give each other and it was what they demanded, after all, of the Lord. Only the Lord saw the midnight tears, only He was present when one of His children, moaning and wringing hands, paced up and down the room. When one slapped one's child in anger the recoil in the heart reverberated through heaven and became part of the pain of the universe. And when the children were hungry and sullen and distrustful and one watched them, daily, growing wilder, and further away, and running headlong into danger, it was the Lord who knew what the charged heart endured as the strap was laid to the backside; the Lord alone who knew what one *would* have said if one had had, like the Lord, the gift of the living word. It was the Lord who knew of the impossibility every parent in that room faced: how to prepare the child for the day when the child would be despised and how to *create* in the child—by what means?—a stronger antidote to this poison than one had found for oneself. The avenues, side streets, bars, billiard halls, hospitals, police stations, and even the playgrounds of Harlem—not to mention the houses of correction, the jails, and the morgue—testified to the potency of the poison while remaining silent as to the efficacy of whatever antidote, irresistibly raising the question of whether or not such an antidote existed; raising, which was worse, the question of whether or not an antidote was desirable; perhaps poison should be fought with poison. With these several schisms in the mind and with more terrors in the heart than could be named, it was better not to judge the man who had gone down under an impossible burden. It was better to remember: *Thou knowest this man's fall; but thou knowest not his wrassling.*[6]

While the preacher talked and I watched the children—years of changing their diapers, scrubbing them, slapping them, taking them to school, and scolding them had had the perhaps inevitable result of making me love them, though I am not sure I knew this then—my mind was busily breaking out with a rash of disconnected impressions. Snatches of popular songs, indecent jokes, bits of books I had read, movie sequences, faces, voices, political issues—I thought I was going mad; all these impressions suspended, as it were, in the solution of the faint nausea produced in me by the heat and liquor. For a moment I had the impression that my alcoholic breath, inefficiently disguised with chewing gum, filled the entire chapel. Then someone began singing one of my father's favorite songs and, abruptly, I was with him, sitting on his knee, in the hot, enormous, crowded church which was the first church we attended. It was the Abyssinia Baptist Church on 138th Street.[7] We had not gone there long. With this image, a host of others came. I had forgotten, in the rage of my growing up, how proud my father had been of me when I was little. Apparently, I had had a voice and my father had liked to show me off before the members of the church. I had forgotten what he had looked like when he was pleased but now I remembered that he had always been grinning with pleasure when my solos ended. I even remembered certain expressions on his face when he

6. From the English author John Donne (1572–1631), *Biathanatos* (1608), a defense of suicide. "Wrassling": wrestling.

7. A famous African American church in Harlem.

teased my mother—had he loved her? I would never know. And when had it all begun to change? For now it seemed that he had not always been cruel. I remembered being taken for a haircut and scraping my knee on the footrest of the barber's chair and I remembered my father's face as he soothed my crying and applied the stinging iodine. Then I remembered our fights, fights which had been of the worst possible kind because my technique had been silence.

I remembered the one time in all our life together when we had really spoken to each other.

It was on a Sunday and it must have been shortly before I left home. We were walking, just the two of us, in our usual silence, to or from church. I was in high school and had been doing a lot of writing and I was, at about this time, the editor of the high school magazine. But I had also been a Young Minister and had been preaching from the pulpit. Lately, I had been taking fewer engagements and preached as rarely as possible. It was said in the church, quite truthfully, that I was "cooling off."

My father asked me abruptly, "You'd rather write than preach, wouldn't you?"

I was astonished at his question—because it was a real question. I answered, "Yes."

That was all we said. It was awful to remember that that was all we had *ever* said.

The casket now was opened and the mourners were being led up the aisle to look for the last time on the deceased. The assumption was that the family was too overcome with grief to be allowed to make this journey alone and I watched while my aunt was led to the casket and, muffled in black, and shaking, led back to her seat. I disapproved of forcing the children to look on their dead father, considering that the shock of his death, or, more truthfully, the shock of death as a reality, was already a little more than a child could bear, but my judgment in this matter had been overruled and there they were, bewildered and frightened and very small, being led, one by one, to the casket. But there is also something very gallant about children at such moments. It has something to do with their silence and gravity and with the fact that one cannot help them. Their legs, somehow, seem *exposed*, so that it is at once incredible and terribly clear that their legs are all they have to hold them up.

I had not wanted to go to the casket myself and I certainly had not wished to be led there, but there was no way of avoiding either of these forms. One of the deacons led me up and I looked on my father's face. I cannot say that it looked like him at all. His blackness had been equivocated by powder and there was no suggestion in that casket of what his power had or could have been. He was simply an old man dead, and it was hard to believe that he had ever given any-one either joy or pain. Yet, his life filled that room. Further up the avenue his wife was holding his newborn child. Life and death so close together, and love and hatred, and right and wrong, said something to me which I did not want to hear concerning man, concerning the life of man.

After the funeral, while I was downtown desperately celebrating my birthday, a Negro soldier, in the lobby of the Hotel Braddock,[8] got into a fight with a white policeman over a Negro girl. Negro girls, white policemen, in or out of

8. Hotel at Eighth Avenue and 126th Street in Harlem.

uniform, and Negro males—in or out of uniform—were part of the furniture of the lobby of the Hotel Braddock and this was certainly not the first time such an incident had occurred. It was destined, however, to receive an unprecedented publicity, for the fight between the policeman and the soldier ended with the shooting of the soldier. Rumor, flowing immediately to the streets outside, stated that the soldier had been shot in the back, an instantaneous and revealing invention, and that the soldier had died protecting a Negro woman. The facts were somewhat different—for example, the soldier had not been shot in the back, and was not dead, and the girl seems to have been as dubious a symbol of womanhood as her white counterpart in Georgia usually is,[9] but no one was interested in the facts. They preferred the invention because this invention expressed and corroborated their hates and fears so perfectly. It is just as well to remember that people are always doing this. Perhaps many of those legends, including Christianity, to which the world clings began their conquest of the world with just some such concerted surrender to distortion. The effect, in Harlem, of this particular legend was like the effect of a lit match in a tin of gasoline. The mob gathered before the doors of the Hotel Braddock simply began to swell and to spread in every direction, and Harlem exploded.

The mob did not cross the ghetto lines. It would have been easy, for example, to have gone over Morningside Park on the west side or to have crossed the Grand Central railroad tracks at 125th Street on the east side, to wreak havoc in white neighborhoods. The mob seems to have been mainly interested in something more potent and real than the white face, that is, in white power, and the principal damage done during the riot of the summer of 1943 was to white business establishments in Harlem. It might have been a far bloodier story, of course, if, at the hour the riot began, these establishments had still been open. From the Hotel Braddock the mob fanned out, east and west along 125th Street, and for the entire length of Lenox, Seventh, and Eighth avenues. Along each of these avenues, and along each major side street—116th, 125th, 135th, and so on—bars, stores, pawnshops, restaurants, even little luncheonettes had been smashed open and entered and looted—looted, it might be added, with more haste than efficiency. The shelves really looked as though a bomb had struck them. Cans of beans and soup and dog food, along with toilet paper, corn flakes, sardines and milk tumbled every which way, and abandoned cash registers and cases of beer leaned crazily out of the splintered windows and were strewn along the avenues. Sheets, blankets, and clothing of every description formed a kind of path, as though people had dropped them while running. I truly had not realized that Harlem *had* so many stores until I saw them all smashed open; the first time the word *wealth* ever entered my mind in relation to Harlem was when I saw it scattered in the streets. But one's first, incongruous impression of plenty was countered immediately by an impression of waste. None of this was doing anybody any good. It would have been better to have left the plate glass as it had been and the goods lying in the stores.

It would have been better, but it would also have been intolerable, for Harlem had needed something to smash. To smash something is the ghetto's chronic need. Most of the time it is the members of the ghetto who smash each

---

9. Baldwin here refers to the origins of many lynchings in the South: allegations that black men had insulted white women.

other, and themselves. But as long as the ghetto walls are standing there will always come a moment when these outlets do not work. That summer, for example, it was not enough to get into a fight on Lenox Avenue, or curse out one's cronies in the barber shops. If ever, indeed, the violence which fills Harlem's churches, pool halls, and bars erupts outward in a more direct fashion, Harlem and its citizens are likely to vanish in an apocalyptic flood. That this is not likely to happen is due to a great many reasons, most hidden and powerful among them the Negro's real relation to the white American. This relation prohibits, simply, anything as uncomplicated and satisfactory as pure hatred. In order really to hate white people, one has to blot so much out of the mind—and the heart—that this hatred itself becomes an exhausting and self-destructive pose. But this does not mean, on the other hand, that love comes easily: the white world is too powerful, too complacent, too ready with gratuitous humiliation, and, above all, too ignorant and too innocent for that. One is absolutely forced to make perpetual qualifications and one's own reactions are always canceling each other out. It is this, really, which has driven so many people mad, both white and black. One is always in the position of having to decide between amputation and gangrene. Amputation is swift but time may prove that the amputation was not necessary—or one may delay the amputation too long. Gangrene is slow, but it is impossible to be sure that one is reading one's symptoms right. The idea of going through life as a cripple is more than one can bear, and equally unbearable is the risk of swelling up slowly, in agony, with poison. And the trouble, finally, is that the risks are real even if the choices do not exist.

"But as for me and my house," my father had said, "we will serve the Lord." I wondered, as we drove him to his resting place, what this line had meant for him. I had heard him preach it many times. I had preached it once myself, proudly giving it an interpretation different from my father's. Now the whole thing came back to me, as though my father and I were on our way to Sunday school and I were memorizing the golden text: *And if it seem evil unto you to serve the Lord, choose you this day whom you will serve; whether the gods which your fathers served that were on the other side of the flood, or the gods of the Amorites, in whose land ye dwell: but as for me and my house, we will serve the Lord.*[1] I suspected in these familiar lines a meaning which had never been there for me before. All of my father's texts and songs, which I had decided were meaningless, were arranged before me at his death like empty bottles, waiting to hold the meaning which life would give them for me. This was his legacy: nothing is ever escaped. That bleakly memorable morning I hated the unbelievable streets and the Negroes and whites who had, equally, made them that way. But I knew that it was folly, as my father would have said, this bitterness was folly. It was necessary to hold on to the things that mattered. The dead man mattered, the new life mattered; blackness and whiteness did not matter; to believe that they did was to acquiesce in one's own destruction. Hatred, which could destroy so much, never failed to destroy the man who hated and this was an immutable law.

It began to seem that one would have to hold in the mind forever two ideas which seemed to be in opposition. The first idea was acceptance, the

---

1. Joshua 24:15.

acceptance, totally without rancor, of life as it is, and men as they are: in the light of this idea, it goes without saying that injustice is a commonplace. But this did not mean that one could be complacent, for the second idea was of equal power: that one must never, in one's own life, accept these injustices as commonplace but must fight them with all one's strength. This fight begins, however, in the heart and it now had been laid to my charge to keep my own heart free of hatred and despair. This intimation made my heart heavy and, now that my father was irrecoverable, I wished that he had been beside me so that I could have searched his face for the answers which only the future would give me now.

1955

ALBERT CAMUS
1913–1960

From his childhood among the most disadvantaged in Algiers to his later roles as journalist, Resistance fighter in World War II, iconic literary figure, and winner of the Nobel Prize in Literature, in 1957, Albert Camus was intensely aware of the basic levels of human existence and of the struggles of the poor and the oppressed. "I can understand only in human terms," he said. "I understand the things I touch, things that offer me resistance." He describes the raw experience of life that human beings share, the humble but ineradicable bond between them. Camus kept a sympathetic yet critical eye on the tensions of his day: observing the Soviet Union from afar, and the bloody battles for Algerian independence up-close, led him to examine the way people can respond to oppressive systems without themselves becoming oppressors.

Camus was born on November 7, 1913, into a "world of poverty and light" in Mondavi, Algeria, then a colony of France. He was the second son in a poor family of mixed Alsatian and Spanish descent, and his father died in an early battle of the First World War. Camus's mother was illiterate; an untreated childhood illness had left her deaf and with a speech impediment. The two boys lived together with their mother, uncle, and grandmother in a two-room apartment in the working-class section of the capital city, Algiers. Camus and his brother, Lucien, were raised by their strict grandmother while their mother worked as a cleaning woman to support the family. Images of the Mediterranean landscape, with the sensual appeal of sea and blazing sun, recur throughout his work, as does a profound compassion for those who—like his mother—labor unrecognized and in silence.

A passionate athlete as well as a scholarship recipient, Camus completed his secondary education and enrolled as a philosophy student at the University of Algiers before contracting, at seventeen, the tuberculosis that corroded his health and made him aware of the body's vulnerability to disease and death. Camus eventually finished his degree, but in the meantime his illness had provided a metaphor for the personal and natural events that oppose and limit human fulfillment and happiness: elements he was later to term the "plague," which infects bodies, minds, cities, and society. (*The Plague* is the title of his second novel.)

Camus lived and worked as a journalist and essayist. Then, as later, however, his work extended well beyond journalism. He founded a collective theater, Le Théâtre du Travail (The Labor Theater), for which he wrote and adapted a number of plays. The theater fascinated Camus, possibly because it involved groups of people and spontaneous interaction between actors and audience. Sponsored by the Communist Party, the Labor Theater was designed for the working people, with performances on the docks in Algiers. Like many intellectuals of his day, Camus joined the Communist Party, but he withdrew after a year to protest its opposition to Algerian nationalism. He eventually left the Labor Theater too and, with a group of young Algerians associated with the publishing house Charlot, organized the politically independent Team Theater (Théâtre de l'Équipe). In 1940 he moved to France after his political commentary, including a famous report on administrative mismanagement during a famine among the Berbers (tribal peoples in North Africa), so outraged the Algerian government that his newspaper was suspended and he himself refused a work permit.

Soon after leaving Algeria, Camus published his first and most famous novel, *The Stranger* (1942), the play *Caligula* (1944), and a lengthy essay defining his concept of the "absurd" hero, *The Myth of Sisyphus* (1942). During World War II, Camus worked in Paris as a reader for the publishing firm of Gallimard, a post that he kept until his death, in 1960. At the same time, he took part in the French Resistance and helped edit the underground journal *Combat*. His friendship with the existentialist philosopher Jean-Paul Sartre began in 1944; after the war he and Sartre were internationally known as uncompromising analysts of the modern conscience. Camus's second novel, *The Plague* (1947), portrays an epidemic in a quarantined city, Oran, Algeria, to symbolize the spread of evil during World War II ("the feeling of suffocation from which we all suffered, and the atmosphere of threat and exile") and to show the struggle against physical and spiritual death in its many forms. He continued, as well, to write plays (*Cross Purposes*, 1944; *The Just Assassins*, 1949). Not content to express his views symbolically in fiction, Camus also spoke out in philosophical essays and political statements. His independent mind and rejection of doctrinaire positions brought him attacks from both the left and the right.

Unlike many intellectuals of his day, Camus did not place a higher value on ideology than on its practical effects: when word emerged about Stalinist labor camps, for instance, he criticized the Soviets rather than defend the communist ideal, as many of his friends did. Camus's open anti-communism led to a spectacular break with Sartre, whose magazine, *Les Temps Modernes* (Modern Times), condemned Camus's book-length essay *The Rebel* (1951); the personal and public dispute between the old friends may have been unavoidable. In the bitter struggle over Algeria, Camus supported the claims of French colonists, including his own family, and therefore opposed Algerian independence, while at the same time attacking the violence of the French colonial regime. Camus did not live to witness the end of the Algerian conflict, which led to independence in 1962. After being awarded the Nobel Prize in 1957, he died in a car accident in 1960. His death at the height of his powers contributed to his posthumous fame as an analyst of the tragic elements of the human condition.

Camus is often linked with Sartre as an existentialist writer, and indeed—as novelist, playwright, and essayist—he is widely known for his analysis of two issues fundamental to existentialism: its distinctive assessment of the human condition and its search for authentic beliefs and values. Yet Camus rejected doctrinaire labels, and Sartre himself suggested that Camus was better placed in the tradition of French moralist writers, such as Michel de Montaigne and René Pascal, who observed human behavior within an implied ethical context that had its own standards of good and evil.

A consummate artist as well as a moralist, Camus was well aware of both the opportunities and the illusions of his craft. When he received the Nobel Prize, his acceptance speech emphasized the artificial but necessary "human" order that art imposes on the chaos of immediate experience. Artists are important as *creators*, because they shape a human perspective, allow understanding in human terms, and therefore provide a basis for action. By stressing the gap between art and reality, Camus provides a link between two poles of human understanding. His works juxtapose realistic detail and a philosophical, almost mythical dimension. The symbolism of his titles, from *The Stranger* to the last collection of stories, *Exile and the Kingdom* (1957), indicates the status of outsider, and the feeling of alienation in the world, while suggesting a search for the realm of human solidarity and agency.

The two terms around which Camus's thinking and writing revolve are the nouns *the absurd* and *revolt*. Camus's wartime output established his reputation as a philosopher of the absurd: the impossibility of "making sense" of a world that has no discernible sense. How to live in such an enviroment nevertheless becomes the main object of his philosophical and literary work. *Revolt*, for Camus, is more ethical than political, a rejection of the conventional and the inauthentic, but also an embrace of a shared humanity. Because the impulse to rebel is a basis for social tolerance and has no patience for master plans that prescribe patterns of thought or action, *revolt* actually opposes revolutionary nihilism.

In the story presented here, "The Guest" (1957), taken from *Exile and the Kingdom*, Camus returns to the landscape of his native Algeria. The colonial context is crucial in this story, not only to explain the real threat of guerrilla reprisal (Camus may be recalling the actual killing of rural schoolteachers in 1954) but to establish the dimensions of a political situation in which the government, police, educational system, and economic welfare of Algeria are all controlled by France. As in the works of **Doris Lessing**, **Naguib Mahfouz**, **Chinua Achebe**, and **Wole Soyinka**, the colonial (or newly postcolonial) setting generates a charged atmosphere. The beginning of the story illustrates how French colonial education emphasizes French rather than local concerns: the schoolteacher's geography lesson outlines the four main rivers of France. The Arab is led along like an animal behind the gendarme Balducci, who rides a horse (here too, Camus may be recalling a humiliation reported two decades before and used as a way to inspire Algerian nationalists). Within this specific context, however, Camus concentrates on wider issues: freedom, brotherhood, responsibility, and the ambiguity of actions along with the inevitability of choice.

The remote desert landscape establishes a complete physical and moral isolation for the story's events. "No one, in this desert, . . . mattered," and the schoolteacher and his guest must each decide, independently, what to do. When Balducci invades Daru's monastic solitude and tells him that he must deliver the Arab to prison, Daru is outraged to be given involvement in, and indeed responsibility for, another's fate. Cursing both the system that tries to force him into complicity and the Arab who has not had enough sense to get away, Daru tries, in every way possible, to avoid taking a stand. Yet he finds himself confronted with the essential human demand for hospitality, which creates burdens and links between guest and host. The choice that Daru must make leads to a further necessary choice by the Arab prisoner. As possible titles for this story, Camus considered "Cain" and "The Law" before settling on "The Guest": the title word, *l'hôte*, means both "guest" and "host" in French. Joined in their fundamental humanity, both guest and host are obliged to shoulder the ambiguous, and potentially fatal, burden of freedom.

The Guest[1]

The schoolmaster was watching the two men climb toward him. One was on horseback, the other on foot. They had not yet tackled the abrupt rise leading to the schoolhouse built on the hillside. They were toiling onward, making slow progress in the snow, among the stones, on the vast expanse of the high, deserted plateau. From time to time the horse stumbled. Without hearing anything yet, he could see the breath issuing from the horse's nostrils. One of the men, at least, knew the region. They were following the trail although it had disappeared days ago under a layer of dirty white snow. The schoolmaster calculated that it would take them half an hour to get onto the hill. It was cold; he went back into the school to get a sweater.

He crossed the empty, frigid classroom. On the blackboard the four rivers of France,[2] drawn with four different colored chalks, had been flowing toward their estuaries for the past three days. Snow had suddenly fallen in mid-October after eight months of drought without the transition of rain, and the twenty pupils, more or less, who lived in the villages scattered over the plateau had stopped coming. With fair weather they would return. Daru now heated only the single room that was his lodging, adjoining the classroom and giving also onto the plateau to the east. Like the class windows, his window looked to the south too. On that side the school was a few kilometers from the point where the plateau began to slope toward the south. In clear weather could be seen the purple mass of the mountain range where the gap opened onto the desert.

Somewhat warmed, Daru returned to the window from which he had first seen the two men. They were no longer visible. Hence they must have tackled the rise. The sky was not so dark, for the snow had stopped falling during the night. The morning had opened with a dirty light which had scarcely become brighter as the ceiling of clouds lifted. At two in the afternoon it seemed as if the day were merely beginning. But still this was better than those three days when the thick snow was falling amidst unbroken darkness with little gusts of wind that rattled the double door of the classroom. Then Daru had spent long hours in his room, leaving it only to go to the shed and feed the chickens or get some coal. Fortunately the delivery truck from Tadjid, the nearest village to the north, had brought his supplies two days before the blizzard. It would return in forty-eight hours.

1. Translated by Justin O'Brien.
2. The Seine, Loire, Rhone, and Gironde rivers. French geography was taught in the French colonies.

Besides, he had enough to resist a siege, for the little room was cluttered with bags of wheat that the administration left as a stock to distribute to those of his pupils whose families had suffered from the drought. Actually they had all been victims because they were all poor. Every day Daru would distribute a ration to the children. They had missed it, he knew, during these bad days. Possibly one of the fathers or big brothers would come this afternoon and he could supply them with grain. It was just a matter of carrying them over to the next harvest. Now shiploads of wheat were arriving from France and the worst was over. But it would be hard to forget that poverty, that army of ragged ghosts wandering in the sunlight, the plateaus burned to a cinder month after month, the earth shriveled up little by little, literally scorched, every stone bursting into dust under one's foot. The sheep had died then by thousands and even a few men, here and there, sometimes without anyone's knowing.

In contrast with such poverty, he who lived almost like a monk in his remote schoolhouse, nonetheless satisfied with the little he had and with the rough life, had felt like a lord with his whitewashed walls, his narrow couch, his unpainted shelves, his well, and his weekly provision of water and food. And suddenly this snow, without warning, without the foretaste of rain. This is the way the region was, cruel to live in, even without men—who didn't help matters either. But Daru had been born here. Everywhere else, he felt exiled.

He stepped out onto the terrace in front of the schoolhouse. The two men were now halfway up the slope. He recognized the horseman as Balducci, the old gendarme he had known for a long time. Balducci was holding on the end of a rope an Arab who was walking behind him with hands bound and head lowered. The gendarme waved a greeting to which Daru did not reply, lost as he was in contemplation of the Arab dressed in a faded blue jellaba, his feet in sandals but covered with socks of heavy raw wool, his head surmounted by a narrow, short *chèche*.[3] They were approaching. Balducci was holding back his horse in order not to hurt the Arab, and the group was advancing slowly.

Within earshot, Balducci shouted: "One hour to do the three kilometers from El Ameur!" Daru did not answer. Short and square in his thick sweater, he watched them climb. Not once had the Arab raised his head. "Hello," said Daru when they got up onto the terrace. "Come in and warm up." Balducci painfully got down from his horse without letting go the rope. From under his bristling mustache he smiled at the schoolmaster. His little dark eyes, deep-set under a tanned forehead, and his mouth surrounded with wrinkles made him look attentive and studious. Daru took the bridle, led the horse to the shed, and came back to the two men, who were now waiting for him in the school. He led them into his room. "I am going to heat up the classroom," he said. "We'll be more comfortable there." When he entered the room again, Balducci was on the couch. He had undone the rope tying him to the Arab, who had squatted near the stove. His hands still bound, the *chèche* pushed back on his head, he was looking toward the window. At first Daru noticed only his huge lips, fat, smooth, almost Negroid; yet his nose was straight, his eyes were dark and full of fever. The *chèche* revealed an obstinate forehead and, under the weathered skin now rather discolored by the cold, the whole face had a restless

---

3. Scarf; here, wound as a turban around the head. "Jellaba": a long hooded robe worn by Arabs in North Africa.

and rebellious look that struck Daru when the Arab, turning his face toward him, looked him straight in the eyes. "Go into the other room," said the schoolmaster, "and I'll make you some mint tea." "Thanks," Balducci said. "What a chore! How I long for retirement." And addressing his prisoner in Arabic: "Come on, you." The Arab got up and, slowly, holding his bound wrists in front of him, went into the classroom.

With the tea, Daru brought a chair. But Balducci was already enthroned on the nearest pupil's desk and the Arab had squatted against the teacher's platform facing the stove, which stood between the desk and the window. When he held out the glass of tea to the prisoner, Daru hesitated at the sight of his bound hands. "He might perhaps be untied." "Sure," said Balducci. "That was for the trip." He started to get to his feet. But Daru, setting the glass on the floor, had knelt beside the Arab. Without saying anything, the Arab watched him with his feverish eyes. Once his hands were free, he rubbed his swollen wrists against each other, took the glass of tea, and sucked up the burning liquid in swift little sips.

"Good," said Daru. "And where are you headed?"

Balducci withdrew his mustache from the tea. "Here, son."

"Odd pupils! And you're spending the night?"

"No. I'm going back to El Ameur. And you will deliver this fellow to Tinguit. He is expected at police headquarters."

Balducci was looking at Daru with a friendly little smile.

"What's this story?" asked the schoolmaster. "Are you pulling my leg?"

"No, son. Those are the orders."

"The orders? I'm not . . ." Daru hesitated, not wanting to hurt the old Corsican.[4] "I mean, that's not my job."

"What! What's the meaning of that? In wartime people do all kinds of jobs."

"Then I'll wait for the declaration of war!"

Balducci nodded.

"O.K. But the orders exist and they concern you too. Things are brewing, it appears. There is talk of a forthcoming revolt. We are mobilized, in a way."

Daru still had his obstinate look.

"Listen, son," Balducci said. "I like you and you must understand. There's only a dozen of us at El Ameur to patrol throughout the whole territory of a small department[5] and I must get back in a hurry. I was told to hand this guy over to you and return without delay. He couldn't be kept there. His village was beginning to stir; they wanted to take him back. You must take him to Tinguit tomorrow before the day is over. Twenty kilometers shouldn't faze a husky fellow like you. After that, all will be over. You'll come back to your pupils and your comfortable life."

Behind the wall the horse could be heard snorting and pawing the earth. Daru was looking out the window. Decidedly, the weather was clearing and the light was increasing over the snowy plateau. When all the snow was melted, the sun would take over again and once more would burn the fields of stone. For days, still, the unchanging sky would shed its dry light on the solitary expanse where nothing had any connection with man.

---

4. Balducci is a native of Corsica, a French island north of Sardinia.

5. French administrative and territorial division; like a county.

"After all," he said, turning around toward Balducci, "what did he do?" And, before the gendarme had opened his mouth, he asked: "Does he speak French?"

"No, not a word. We had been looking for him for a month, but they were hiding him. He killed his cousin."

"Is he against us?"[6]

"I don't think so. But you can never be sure."

"Why did he kill?"

"A family squabble, I think. One owed the other grain, it seems. It's not at all clear. In short, he killed his cousin with a billhook. You know, like a sheep, *kreezk!*"

Balducci made the gesture of drawing a blade across his throat and the Arab, his attention attracted, watched him with a sort of anxiety. Daru felt a sudden wrath against the man, against all men with their rotten spite, their tireless hates, their blood lust.

But the kettle was singing on the stove. He served Balducci more tea, hesitated, then served the Arab again, who, a second time, drank avidly. His raised arms made the jellaba fall open and the schoolmaster saw his thin, muscular chest.

"Thanks, kid," Balducci said. "And now, I'm off."

He got up and went toward the Arab, taking a small rope from his pocket.

"What are you doing?" Daru asked dryly.

Balducci, disconcerted, showed him the rope.

"Don't bother."

The old gendarme hesitated. "It's up to you. Of course, you are armed?"

"I have my shotgun."

"Where?"

"In the trunk."

"You ought to have it near your bed."

"Why? I have nothing to fear."

"You're crazy, son. If there's an uprising, no one is safe, we're all in the same boat."

"I'll defend myself. I'll have time to see them coming."

Balducci began to laugh, then suddenly the mustache covered the white teeth.

"You'll have time? O.K. That's just what I was saying. You have always been a little cracked. That's why I like you, my son was like that."

At the same time he took out his revolver and put it on the desk.

"Keep it; I don't need two weapons from here to El Ameur."

The revolver shone against the black paint of the table. When the gendarme turned toward him, the schoolmaster caught the smell of leather and horseflesh.

"Listen, Balducci," Daru said suddenly, "every bit of this disgusts me, and first of all your fellow here. But I won't hand him over. Fight, yes, if I have to. But not that."

The old gendarme stood in front of him and looked at him severely.

"You're being a fool," he said slowly. "I don't like it either. You don't get used to putting a rope on a man even after years of it, and you're even ashamed— yes, ashamed. But you can't let them have their way."

---

6. I.e., against the French colonial government.

"I won't hand him over," Daru said again.

"It's an order, son, and I repeat it."

"That's right. Repeat to them what I've said to you: I won't hand him over."

Balducci made a visible effort to reflect. He looked at the Arab and at Daru. At last he decided.

"No, I won't tell them anything. If you want to drop us, go ahead; I'll not denounce you. I have an order to deliver the prisoner and I'm doing so. And now you'll just sign this paper for me."

"There's no need. I'll not deny that you left him with me."

"Don't be mean with me. I know you'll tell the truth. You're from hereabouts and you are a man. But you must sign, that's the rule."

Daru opened his drawer, took out a little square bottle of purple ink, the red wooden penholder with the "sergeant-major" pen he used for making models of penmanship, and signed. The gendarme carefully folded the paper and put it into his wallet. Then he moved toward the door.

"I'll see you off," Daru said.

"No," said Balducci. "There's no use being polite. You insulted me."

He looked at the Arab, motionless in the same spot, sniffed peevishly, and turned away toward the door. "Good-by, son," he said. The door shut behind him. Balducci appeared suddenly outside the window and then disappeared. His footsteps were muffled by the snow. The horse stirred on the other side of the wall and several chickens fluttered in fright. A moment later Balducci reappeared outside the window leading the horse by the bridle. He walked toward the little rise without turning around and disappeared from sight with the horse following him. A big stone could be heard bouncing down. Daru walked back toward the prisoner, who, without stirring, never took his eyes off him. "Wait," the schoolmaster said in Arabic and went toward the bedroom. As he was going through the door, he had a second thought, went to the desk, took the revolver, and stuck it in his pocket. Then, without looking back, he went into his room.

For some time he lay on his couch watching the sky gradually close over, listening to the silence. It was this silence that had seemed painful to him during the first days here, after the war. He had requested a post in the little town at the base of the foothills separating the upper plateaus from the desert. There, rocky walls, green and black to the north, pink and lavender to the south, marked the frontier of eternal summer. He had been named to a post farther north, on the plateau itself. In the beginning, the solitude and the silence had been hard for him on these wastelands peopled only by stones. Occasionally, furrows suggested cultivation, but they had been dug to uncover a certain kind of stone good for building. The only plowing here was to harvest rocks. Elsewhere a thin layer of soil accumulated in the hollows would be scraped out to enrich paltry village gardens. This is the way it was: bare rock covered three quarters of the region. Towns sprang up, flourished, then disappeared; men came by, loved one another or fought bitterly, then died. No one in this desert, neither he nor his guest, mattered. And yet, outside this desert neither of them, Daru knew, could have really lived.

When he got up, no noise came from the classroom. He was amazed at the unmixed joy he derived from the mere thought that the Arab might have fled and that he would be alone with no decision to make. But the prisoner was there. He had merely stretched out between the stove and the desk. With eyes open, he was staring at the ceiling. In that position, his thick lips were particularly noticeable, giving him a pouting look. "Come," said Daru. The Arab got up and followed him. In the bedroom, the schoolmaster pointed to a chair near the table under the window. The Arab sat down without taking his eyes off Daru.

"Are you hungry?"

"Yes," the prisoner said.

Daru set the table for two. He took flour and oil, shaped a cake in a frying-pan, and lighted the little stove that functioned on bottled gas. While the cake was cooking, he went out to the shed to get cheese, eggs, dates, and condensed milk. When the cake was done he set it on the window sill to cool, heated some condensed milk diluted with water, and beat up the eggs into an omelette. In one of his motions he knocked against the revolver stuck in his right pocket. He set the bowl down, went into the classroom, and put the revolver in his desk drawer. When he came back to the room, night was falling. He put on the light and served the Arab. "Eat," he said. The Arab took a piece of the cake, lifted it eagerly to his mouth, and stopped short.

"And you?" he asked.

"After you. I'll eat too."

The thick lips opened slightly. The Arab hesitated, then bit into the cake determinedly.

The meal over, the Arab looked at the schoolmaster. "Are you the judge?"

"No, I'm simply keeping you until tomorrow."

"Why do you eat with me?"

"I'm hungry."

The Arab fell silent. Daru got up and went out. He brought back a folding bed from the shed, set it up between the table and the stove, perpendicular to his own bed. From a large suitcase which, upright in a corner, served as a shelf for papers, he took two blankets and arranged them on the camp bed. Then he stopped, felt useless, and sat down on his bed. There was nothing more to do or to get ready. He had to look at this man. He looked at him, therefore, trying to imagine his face bursting with rage. He couldn't do so. He could see nothing but the dark yet shining eyes and the animal mouth.

"Why did you kill him?" he asked in a voice whose hostile tone surprised him.

The Arab looked away.

"He ran away. I ran after him."

He raised his eyes to Daru again and they were full of a sort of woeful interrogation. "Now what will they do to me?"

"Are you afraid?"

He stiffened, turning his eyes away.

"Are you sorry?"

The Arab stared at him openmouthed. Obviously he did not understand. Daru's annoyance was growing. At the same time he felt awkward and self-conscious with his big body wedged between the two beds.

"Lie down there," he said impatiently. "That's your bed."

The Arab didn't move. He called to Daru:

"Tell me!"

The schoolmaster looked at him.

"Is the gendarme coming back tomorrow?"

"I don't know."

"Are you coming with us?"

"I don't know. Why?"

The prisoner got up and stretched out on top of the blankets, his feet toward the window. The light from the electric bulb shone straight into his eyes and he closed them at once.

"Why?" Daru repeated, standing beside the bed.

The Arab opened his eyes under the blinding light and looked at him, trying not to blink.

"Come with us," he said.

In the middle of the night, Daru was still not asleep. He had gone to bed after undressing completely; he generally slept naked. But when he suddenly realized that he had nothing on, he hesitated. He felt vulnerable and the temptation came to him to put his clothes back on. Then he shrugged his shoulders; after all, he wasn't a child and, if need be, he could break his adversary in two. From his bed he could observe him, lying on his back, still motionless with his eyes closed under the harsh light. When Daru turned out the light, the darkness seemed to coagulate all of a sudden. Little by little, the night came back to life in the window where the starless sky was stirring gently. The schoolmaster soon made out the body lying at his feet. The Arab still did not move, but his eyes seemed open. A faint wind was prowling around the schoolhouse. Perhaps it would drive away the clouds and the sun would reappear.

During the night the wind increased. The hens fluttered a little and then were silent. The Arab turned over on his side with his back to Daru, who thought he heard him moan. Then he listened for his guest's breathing, become heavier and more regular. He listened to that breath so close to him and mused without being able to go to sleep. In this room where he had been sleeping alone for a year, this presence bothered him. But it bothered him also by imposing on him a sort of brotherhood he knew well but refused to accept in the present circumstances. Men who share the same rooms, soldiers or prisoners, develop a strange alliance as if, having cast off their armor with their clothing, they fraternized every evening, over and above their differences, in the ancient community of dream and fatigue. But Daru shook himself; he didn't like such musings, and it was essential to sleep.

A little later, however, when the Arab stirred slightly, the schoolmaster was still not asleep. When the prisoner made a second move, he stiffened, on the alert. The Arab was lifting himself slowly on his arms with almost the motion of a sleepwalker. Seated upright in bed, he waited motionless without turning his head toward Daru, as if he were listening attentively. Daru did not stir; it had just occurred to him that the revolver was still in the drawer of his desk. It was better to act at once. Yet he continued to observe the prisoner, who, with the same slithery motion, put his feet on the ground, waited again, then began to stand up slowly. Daru was about to call out to him when the Arab began to walk, in a quite natural but extraordinarily silent way. He was heading toward the door at the end of the room that opened into the shed. He lifted the latch with precaution and went out, pushing the door behind him but without shutting it. Daru had not stirred. "He is running away," he merely thought. "Good riddance!" Yet he listened attentively. The hens were not fluttering; the guest must be on the plateau. A faint sound of water reached him, and he didn't know what it was until the Arab again stood framed in the doorway, closed the door carefully, and came back to bed without a sound. Then Daru turned his back on him and fell asleep. Still later he seemed, from the depths of his sleep, to hear furtive steps around the schoolhouse. "I'm dreaming! I'm dreaming!" he repeated to himself. And he went on sleeping.

When he awoke, the sky was clear; the loose window let in a cold, pure air. The Arab was asleep, hunched up under the blankets now, his mouth open, utterly relaxed. But when Daru shook him, he started dreadfully, staring at Daru with wild eyes as if he had never seen him and such a frightened expression that the schoolmaster stepped back. "Don't be afraid. It's me. You must eat." The Arab nodded his head and said yes. Calm had returned to his face, but his expression was vacant and listless.

The coffee was ready. They drank it seated together on the folding bed as they munched their pieces of the cake. Then Daru led the Arab under the shed and showed him the faucet where he washed. He went back into the room, folded the blankets and the bed, made his own bed and put the room in order. Then he went through the classroom and out onto the terrace. The sun was already rising in the blue sky; a soft, bright light was bathing the deserted plateau. On the ridge the snow was melting in spots. The stones were about to reappear. Crouched on the edge of the plateau, the schoolmaster looked at the deserted expanse. He thought of Balducci. He had hurt him, for he had sent him off in a way as if he didn't want to be associated with him. He could still hear the gendarme's farewell and, without knowing why, he felt strangely empty and vulnerable. At that moment, from the other side of the schoolhouse, the prisoner coughed. Daru listened to him almost despite himself and then, furious, threw a pebble that whistled through the air before sinking into the snow. That man's stupid crime revolted him, but to hand him over was contrary to honor. Merely thinking of it made him smart with humiliation. And he cursed at one and the same time his own people who had sent him this Arab and the Arab too who had dared to kill and not managed to get away. Daru got up, walked in a circle on the terrace, waited motionless, and then went back into the schoolhouse.

The Arab, leaning over the cement floor of the shed, was washing his teeth with two fingers. Daru looked at him and said: "Come." He went back into the room ahead of the prisoner. He slipped a hunting-jacket on over his sweater and put on walking-shoes. Standing, he waited until the Arab had put on his chèche and sandals. They went into the classroom and the schoolmaster pointed to the exit, saying: "Go ahead." The fellow didn't budge. "I'm coming," said Daru. The Arab went out. Daru went back into the room and made a package of pieces of rusk, dates, and sugar. In the classroom, before going out, he hesitated a second in front of his desk, then crossed the threshold and locked the door. "That's the way," he said. He started toward the east, followed by the prisoner. But, a short distance from the schoolhouse, he thought he heard a slight sound behind them. He retraced his steps and examined the surroundings of the house, there was no one there. The Arab watched him without seeming to understand. "Come on," said Daru.

They walked for an hour and rested beside a sharp peak of limestone. The snow was melting faster and faster and the sun was drinking up the puddles at once, rapidly cleaning the plateau, which gradually dried and vibrated like the air itself. When they resumed walking, the ground rang under their feet. From time to time a bird rent the space in front of them with a joyful cry. Daru breathed in deeply the fresh morning light. He felt a sort of rapture before the vast familiar expanse, now almost entirely yellow under its dome of blue sky. They walked an hour more, descending toward the south. They reached a level height made up of crumbly rocks. From there on, the plateau sloped down, eastward, toward a low plain where there were a few spindly trees and, to the south, toward outcroppings of rock that gave the landscape a chaotic look.

Daru surveyed the two directions. There was nothing but the sky on the horizon. Not a man could be seen. He turned toward the Arab, who was looking at him blankly. Daru held out the package to him. "Take it," he said. "There are dates, bread, and sugar. You can hold out for two days. Here are a thousand francs too." The Arab took the package and the money but kept his full hands at chest level as if he didn't know what to do with what was being given him. "Now look," the schoolmaster said as he pointed in the direction of the east, "there's the way to Tinguit. You have a two-hour walk. At Tinguit you'll find the administration and the police. They are expecting you." The Arab looked toward the east, still holding the package and the money against his chest. Daru took his elbow and turned him rather roughly toward the south. At the foot of the height on which they stood could be seen a faint path. "That's the trail across the plateau. In a day's walk from here you'll find pasturelands and the first nomads. They'll take you in and shelter you according to their law." The Arab had now turned toward Daru and a sort of panic was visible in his expression. "Listen," he said. Daru shook his head: "No, be quiet. Now I'm leaving you." He turned his back on him, took two long steps in the direction of the school, looked hesitantly at the motionless Arab, and started off again. For a few minutes he heard nothing but his own step resounding on the cold ground and did not turn his head. A moment later, however, he turned around. The Arab was still there on the edge of the hill, his arms hanging now, and he was looking at the schoolmaster. Daru felt something rise in his throat. But he swore with impatience, waved vaguely, and started off again. He had already gone some distance when he again stopped and looked. There was no longer anyone on the hill.

Daru hesitated. The sun was now rather high in the sky and was beginning to beat down on his head. The schoolmaster retraced his steps, at first somewhat uncertainly, then with decision. When he reached the little hill, he was bathed in sweat. He climbed it as fast as he could and stopped, out of breath, at the top. The rock-fields to the south stood out sharply against the blue sky, but on the plain to the east a steamy heat was already rising. And in that slight haze, Daru, with heavy heart, made out the Arab walking slowly on the road to prison.

A little later, standing before the window of the classroom, the schoolmaster was watching the clear light bathing the whole surface of the plateau, but he hardly saw it. Behind him on the blackboard, among the winding French rivers, sprawled the clumsily chalked-up words he had just read: "You handed over our brother. You will pay for this." Daru looked at the sky, the plateau, and, beyond, the invisible lands stretching all the way to the sea. In this vast landscape he had loved so much, he was alone.

1957

CHINUA ACHEBE

1930–2013

The best-known African writer today is the Nigerian Chinua Achebe, whose first novel, *Things Fall Apart,* exploded the colonialist image of Africans as childlike people living in a primitive society. Achebe's novels, stories, poetry, and essays have made him a respected and prophetic figure in Africa and the West. In Western countries, where he has traveled, taught, and lectured widely, he is admired as a major writer who has given a new direction to the English-language novel. Achebe helped to create the African postcolonial novel with its themes and characters; he also developed a complex narrative voice that questions cultural assumptions with a subtle irony and compassion born from bicultural experience.

Achebe was born in Ogidi, an Igbo-speaking town of Eastern Nigeria, on November 16, 1930. He was the fifth of six children in the family of Isaiah Okafor Achebe, a teacher for the Church Missionary Society, and his wife, Janet. Achebe's parents christened him Albert after Prince Albert, husband of Queen Victoria. Two cultures coexisted in Ogidi: on the one hand, African social customs and traditional religion; on the other, British colonial authority and Christianity. Instead of being torn between the two, Achebe found himself curious about both ways of life and fascinated with the dual perspective that came from living "at the crossroads of cultures."

He attended church schools in Ogidi, where instruction was carried out in English. Achebe read the various books in his father's library, most of them primers or church related, but he also listened eagerly to his mother and sister when they told traditional Igbo stories. Entering a prestigious secondary school in Umuahia, he immediately took advantage of its well-stocked library. Achebe later recalled that when he read books about Africa, he tended to identify with the white narrators rather than the black inhabitants: "I did not see myself as an African in those books. I took sides with the white men against the savages." After graduating in 1948, Achebe entered University College, Ibadan, on a scholarship to study medicine. In the following year he changed to a program in liberal arts that combined English, history, and religious studies. Research in the last two fields deepened his knowledge of Nigerian history and culture; the assigned literary texts, however, brought into sharp focus the distorted image of African culture offered by British colonial literature. Reading Joyce Cary's *Mister Johnson* (1939), a novel recommended for its depiction of life in Nigeria, he was shocked to find Nigerians described as violent savages with passionate instincts and simple minds: "and so I thought if this was famous, then perhaps someone ought to try and look at this from the inside." While at the university, Achebe rejected his British name in favor of his indigenous name Chinua, which abbreviates *Chinualumogu,* or "My spirit come fight for me."

Achebe began writing while at the university, contributing articles and sketches to several campus papers and publishing four stories in the *University Herald,* a magazine whose editor he became in his third year. His first novel, *Things Fall Apart* (1958), was a conscious attempt to counteract the distortions of English literature about Africa by describing the richness and complexity of traditional African society before the colonial and missionary invasion. It was important, Achebe said, to "teach my readers that their past—with all its imperfections—was not one long night of savagery from which the first Europeans acting on God's behalf delivered them." The novel was recognized immediately as an extraordinary work of literature in English. It also became the first classic work of modern African fiction, translated into nine languages, and Achebe became, for many readers and writers, the teacher of a whole generation. His later novels continue to examine the individual and cultural dilemmas of Nigerian society, although their background varies from the traditional religious society of *Arrow of God* (1964) to thinly disguised accounts of contemporary political strife.

Achebe worked as a radio journalist for the Nigerian Broadcasting Service, ultimately rising to the position of director of external services in charge of the Voice of Nigeria. The radio position was more than a merely administrative post, for Achebe and his colleagues were creating a sense of shared national identity through the broadcasting of national news and information about Nigerian culture. Since the end of the Second World War, Nigeria had been torn by intellectual and political rivalries that overlaid the common struggle for independence (achieved in 1960). The three major ethnolinguistic groups—Yoruba, Hausa-Fulani, and Igbo—were increasingly locked in economic and political competition at the same time they were fighting to erase the vestiges of British colonial rule. These problems eventually boiled over in the Nigerian Civil War (1967–70).

It is hard to overestimate the influence of Nigerian politics on Achebe's life after 1966. In January a military coup d'état led by young Igbo officers overthrew the government; six months later a second coup led by non-Igbo officers took power. Ethnic strife intensified: thousands of Igbos were killed and driven out of the north. Soldiers were sent to find Achebe in Lagos; his wife and young children fled by boat to Eastern Nigeria, where after a dangerous and roundabout journey, Achebe joined them, taking up the post of senior research fellow at the University of Nigeria, Nsukka. In May 1967 the eastern region, mainly populated by Igbo-speakers, seceded as the new nation of Biafra. From then until the defeat of Biafra in January 1970, a bloody civil war was waged with high civilian casualties and widespread starvation. Achebe traveled in Europe, North America, and Africa to win support for Biafra, proclaiming that "no government, black or white, has the right to stigmatize and destroy groups of its own citizens without undermining the basis of its own existence." A group of his poems about the war won the Commonwealth Poetry Prize in 1972, the same year that he published a volume of short stories, *Girls at War*, and left Nigeria to take up a three-year position at the University of Massachusetts at Amherst. Returning to Nsukka as professor of literature in 1976, Achebe continued to participate in his country's political life. Badly hurt in a car accident in 1990, Achebe slowly recovered and returned to writing and teaching at Bard College in Annandale-on-Hudson, New York, where he stayed for most of the following two decades. Later, he taught at Brown University in Providence, Rhode Island. Among many other novels and memoirs, he published the essay collection *Education of a British Protected Child* (2009). Achebe died in Boston in 2013.

Chinua Achebe's writings emphasize an author's social responsibility. He draws frequent contrasts between the European "art for art's sake" tradition and the African belief in the indivisibility of art and society. His favorite example is the Owerri Igbo custom of *mbari*, a communal art project in which villagers selected by the priest of the earth goddess Ala live in a forest clearing for a year or more, working under the direction of master artists to prepare a temple of images in the goddess's honor. This creative communal enterprise and its culminating festival are diametrically opposed, the writer says, to the European custom of secluding art objects in museums or private collections. Instead, *mbari* celebrates art as a cultural process, affirming that "art belongs to all and is a 'function' of society." Achebe's own practice as novelist, poet, essayist, founder and editor of two journals, lecturer, and active representative of African letters exemplifies this commitment to the community.

"Chike's School Days" (1960), published in the year of Nigerian independence, tells the story of a child with a dual inheritance like Achebe's own. Like Achebe himself, the boy has three names: the Christian John, the familiar Chike, and the more formal African name Obiajulu, meaning "the mind at last is at rest." Yet if Chike is the answer to his parents' prayers for a son, he is also about to enter a transformative experience in a Christian school, where he will master the English language.

Achebe's literary language is an English skillfully blended with Igbo vocabulary, proverbs, images, and speech patterns to create a voice embodying the linguistic pluralism of modern African experience. By including Standard English, Igbo, and pidgin in different contexts, Achebe demonstrates the existence of a diverse society that is otherwise concealed behind language barriers. He thereby acknowledges that his primary African audience is composed of younger, schooled readers who are relatively fluent in English, readers like Chike. Chike's story, however, focuses less on the school days of the title than on his background. Chike's education turns out to be the product of his paternal grandmother's conversion to Christianity, and of his father's marriage (following his own new Christian convictions) to an outcaste woman, an *Osu* (a member of the traditional Igbo slave caste). Thus a seemingly simple tale about a boy going to school turns out to be a story of historical change as it affects three generations. Chike's love of English, while it separates him from his neighbors, suggests the potential for a love of literature. Elsewhere, Achebe wrote that literature is important because it liberates the human imagination; it "begins as an adventure in self-discovery and ends in wisdom and human conscience."

Chike's School Days

Sarah's last child was a boy, and his birth brought great joy to the house of his father, Amos. The child received three names at his baptism—John, Chike, Obiajulu. The last name means "the mind at last is at rest."[1] Anyone hearing this name knew at once that its owner was either an only child or an only son. Chike was an only son. His parents had had five daughters before him.

Like his sisters Chike was brought up "in the ways of the white man," which meant the opposite of traditional. Amos had many years before bought a tiny bell with which he summoned his family to prayers and hymn-singing first thing in the morning and last thing at night. This was one of the ways of the white man. Sarah taught her children not to eat in their neighbours' houses

---

1. In the Igbo or Ibo language.

because "they offered their food to idols." And thus she set herself against the age-old custom which regarded children as the common responsibility of all so that, no matter what the relationship between parents, their children played together and shared their food.

One day a neighbour offered a piece of yam to Chike, who was only four years old. The boy shook his head haughtily and said, "We don't eat heathen food." The neighbour was full of rage, but she controlled herself and only muttered under her breath that even an *Osu*[2] was full of pride nowadays, thanks to the white man.

And she was right. In the past an *Osu* could not raise his shaggy head in the presence of the free-born. He was a slave to one of the many gods of the clan. He was a thing set apart, not to be venerated but to be despised and almost spat on. He could not marry a free-born, and he could not take any of the titles of his clan. When he died, he was buried by his kind in the Bad Bush.

Now all that had changed, or had begun to change. So that an *Osu* child could even look down his nose at a free-born, and talk about heathen food! The white man had indeed accomplished many things.

Chike's father was not originally an *Osu*, but had gone and married an *Osu* woman in the name of Christianity. It was unheard of for a man to make himself *Osu* in that way, with his eyes wide open. But then Amos was nothing if not mad. The new religion had gone to his head. It was like palm-wine. Some people drank it and remained sensible. Others lost every sense in their stomach.

The only person who supported Amos in his mad marriage venture was Mr. Brown, the white missionary, who lived in a thatch-roofed, red-earth-walled parsonage and was highly respected by the people, not because of his sermons, but because of a dispensary he ran in one of his rooms. Amos had emerged from Mr. Brown's parsonage greatly fortified. A few days later he told his widowed mother, who had recently been converted to Christianity and had taken the name of Elizabeth. The shock nearly killed her. When she recovered, she went down on her knees and begged Amos not to do this thing. But he would not hear; his ears had been nailed up. At last, in desperation, Elizabeth went to consult the diviner.

This diviner was a man of great power and wisdom. As he sat on the floor of his hut beating a tortoise shell, a coating of white chalk round his eyes, he saw not only the present, but also what had been and what was to be. He was called "the man of the four eyes." As soon as old Elizabeth appeared, he cast his stringed cowries[3] and told her what she had come to see him about. "Your son has joined the white man's religion. And you too in your old age when you should know better. And do you wonder that he is stricken with insanity? Those who gather ant-infested faggots must be prepared for the visit of lizards." He cast his cowries a number of times and wrote with a finger on a bowl of sand, and all the while his *nwifulu*,[4] a talking calabash, chatted to itself. "Shut up!" he roared, and it immediately held its peace. The diviner then muttered a few incantations and rattled off a breathless reel of proverbs that followed one another like the cowries in his magic string.

At last he pronounced the cure. The ancestors were angry and must be appeased with a goat. Old Elizabeth performed the rites, but her son remained

---

2. An untouchable, the lowest caste in the Igbo class system.
3. Snail shells used as currency and, here, in fortune-telling.
4. A pipe made of a gourd.

insane and married an *Osu* girl whose name was Sarah. Old Elizabeth renounced her new religion and returned to the faith of her people.

We have wandered from our main story. But it is important to know how Chike's father became an *Osu*, because even today when everything is upside down, such a story is very rare. But now to return to Chike who refused heathen food at the tender age of four years, or maybe five.

Two years later he went to the village school. His right hand could now reach across his head to his left ear, which proved that he was old enough to tackle the mysteries of the white man's learning. He was very happy about his new slate and pencil, and especially about his school uniform of white shirt and brown khaki shorts. But as the first day of the new term approached, his young mind dwelt on the many stories about teachers and their canes. And he remembered the song his elder sisters sang, a song that had a somewhat disquieting refrain:

> *Onye nkuzi ewelu itali piagbusie umuaka.*[5]

One of the ways an emphasis is laid in Ibo is by exaggeration, so that the teacher in the refrain might not actually have flogged the children to death. But there was no doubt he did flog them. And Chike thought very much about it.

Being so young, Chike was sent to what was called the "religious class" where they sang, and sometimes danced, the catechism. He loved the sound of words and he loved rhythm. During the catechism lesson the class formed a ring to dance the teacher's question. "Who was Caesar?"[6] he might ask, and the song would burst forth with much stamping of feet.

> *Siza bu eze Rome*
> *Onye nachi enu uwa dum.*[7]

It did not matter to their dancing that in the twentieth century Caesar was no longer ruler of the whole world.

And sometimes they even sang in English. Chike was very fond of "Ten Green Bottles." They had been taught the words but they only remembered the first and the last lines. The middle was hummed and hie-ed and mumbled:

> *Ten grin botr angin on dar war,*
> *Ten grin botr angin on dar war,*
> *Hm hm hm hm hm*
> *Hm, hm hm hm hm hm,*
> *An ten grin botr angin on dar war.*[8]

In this way the first year passed. Chike was promoted to the "Infant School," where work of a more serious nature was undertaken.

We need not follow him through the Infant School. It would make a full story in itself. But it was no different from the story of other children. In the Primary

---

5. "The teacher took a whip and flogged the pupils mercilessly" (Ibo).
6. Julius Caesar (100–44 B.C.E.), Roman general and political leader whose near-monopoly on power in the late days of the Roman Republic led to the creation of the Roman Empire.
7. "Caesar was the chief of Rome, / the ruler of the whole world" (Ibo).
8. A British children's song, "Ten green bottles hanging on the wall," as pronounced by African children who are learning English.

School, however, his individual character began to show. He developed a strong hatred for arithmetic. But he loved stories and songs. And he liked particularly the sound of English words, even when they conveyed no meaning at all. Some of them simply filled him with elation. "Periwinkle" was such a word. He had now forgotten how he learned it or exactly what it was. He had a vague private meaning for it and it was something to do with fairyland. "Constellation" was another.

Chike's teacher was fond of long words. He was said to be a very learned man. His favourite pastime was copying out jaw-breaking words from his *Chambers' Etymological Dictionary*. Only the other day he had raised applause from his class by demolishing a boy's excuse for lateness with unanswerable erudition. He had said: "Procrastination is a lazy man's apology." The teacher's erudition showed itself in every subject he taught. His nature study lessons were memorable. Chike would always remember the lesson on the methods of seed dispersal. According to teacher, there were five methods: by man, by animals, by water, by wind, and by explosive mechanism. Even those pupils who forgot all the other methods remembered "explosive mechanism."

Chike was naturally impressed by teacher's explosive vocabulary. But the fairyland quality which words had for him was of a different kind. The first sentences in his *New Method Reader* were simple enough and yet they filled him with a vague exultation: "Once there was a wizard. He lived in Africa. He went to China to get a lamp." Chike read it over and over again at home and then made a song of it. It was a meaningless song. "Periwinkles" got into it, and also "Damascus." But it was like a window through which he saw in the distance a strange, magical new world. And he was happy.

1960

NAGUIB MAHFOUZ
1911–2006

The first Arabic novelist to win the Nobel Prize, Naguib Mahfouz traced the roots of his work to the civilization of the ancient Egyptians, over five thousand years ago. Past and present combine in his novels and stories, as he explores the destiny of his people and their often traumatic adjustment to industrial society. To chronicle the rapidly changing culture, Mahfouz adapts the techniques of nineteenth-century European realism and combines them with a mystical outlook and a command of both the literary resources of classical Arabic and the idioms of contemporary speech.

Without Mahfouz, it is said, the turbulent history of twentieth-century Egypt would never be known. Indeed, he lived through almost a century of transition and documented the successive stages of social and political life from the time the country cast off foreign rule and became a postcolonial society. Mahfouz was born in Cairo on December 11, 1911, the youngest of seven children in the family of a civil servant. The family moved from its home in the old Jamaliya district to the suburbs of Cairo when Mahfouz was a young boy. He attended government schools and the University of Cairo, graduating in 1934 with a degree in philosophy. These were not quiet years: Egypt, officially under Ottoman rule, had been occupied by the British since 1883 and was declared a British protectorate at the start of the First World War, in 1914. Mahfouz grew up in the midst of the struggle for national independence that culminated in a violent uprising against the British in 1919 and the negotiation of a constitutional monarchy in 1923. The consistent focus on Egyptian cultural identity that permeates his work may well have its roots in this turbulent period.

While at the university, Mahfouz befriended the socialist and Darwinian thinker Salama Musa and began to write articles for Musa's journal *Al-Majalla al-Jadida* (*The Modern Magazine*). In 1938 he published his first collection of stories, *Whispers of Madness*, and in 1939 the first of three historical novels set in ancient Egypt. At that time he planned to write a set of forty books on the model of the historical romances written by the British novelist Sir Walter Scott (1771–1832). These first novels contained allegories of modern politics, and readers easily recognized the criticism of the reigning King Farouk in *Radubis* (1943) and the analogy in *The Struggle for Thebes* (1944) between the ancient Egyptian battle to expel Hyksos usurpers and twentieth-century rebellions against foreign rule. In 1945, Mahfouz shifted decisively to the realistic novel and a portrayal of modern society. He focused on the social and spiritual dilemmas of the middle class in Cairo, documenting in vivid detail the life of an urban society that represented Egypt.

The major work of this period, and Mahfouz's masterwork in many eyes, is *The Cairo Trilogy* (1956–57), three volumes depicting the experience of three generations of a Cairo family between 1918 and 1944. Into this story Mahfouz wove a social history of Egypt after the First World War. Mahfouz has been called the "Balzac of Egypt"—a comparison to the French novelist and panoramic chronicler of society Honoré de Balzac (1799–1850)—and he was well acquainted with the nineteenth-century realists. Traditional Arabic literature has many forms of narrative, but the novel is not one of them; Arabic writers like Mahfouz adapted the Western form to their own needs. He made use of familiar nineteenth-century strategies such as a chronological plot, unified characters, the inclusion of documentary information and realistic details, a panoramic view of society including a strong moral and humanistic perspective, and a picture of urban middle-class life. Mahfouz's achievement was recognized in the State Prize for literature in 1956, but he temporarily ceased to write after finishing the *Trilogy* in 1952.

In that year, an officers' coup headed by Gamal Abdel Nasser overthrew the monarchy and instituted a republic that promised democratic reforms, and Mahfouz described the changes in Egyptian society that resulted. Although the author was at first optimistic about the new order, he soon recognized that few improvements had occurred in the lives of the general population. When he started publishing again in 1959, Mahfouz's works included open criticism of the Nasser regime. Three years after *The Cairo Trilogy* brought him international praise, Mahfouz shocked many readers with a new book, *Children of Gebelawi*. An allegory of religious history, *Children of Gebelawi* scandalized orthodox believers by its personification of God and its depiction of the prophets chiefly as social reformers rather than as religious figures. The book was banned throughout the Arab world except in Lebanon, and the Jordan League of Writers attacked Mahfouz as a "delinquent man" whose novels were "plagued with sex and drugs." From this point on, Mahfouz tended to add an element of political or social allegory and subjective mysticism to his literary realism.

Although he had become the best-known writer in the Arab world, his works read by millions, Mahfouz was unable to make a living from his books. Copyright protection was minimal, and without such safeguards, even best-selling authors received only small sums for their books. Until he began writing for motion pictures in the 1960s, he supported himself and his family through various positions in governmental ministries and as a contributing editor for the leading newspaper, *Al-Ahram* (*The Pyramids*). Attached to the Ministry of Culture in 1954, he adapted novels for film and television and later became director-general of the governmental Cinema Organization, overseeing production and also, controversially, censorship. Eventually more than thirty of his stories and novels were made into films. After his retirement from the civil service in 1971, Mahfouz continued to publish articles and short stories in *Al-Ahram*, where most of his novels appeared in serialized form before being issued as paperbacks. When he received the Nobel Prize in Literature, in 1988, at the age of seventy-six, he was still contributing a weekly column, "Point of View," to *Al-Ahram*. Despite his fame, Mahfouz's books were censored and banned in many Arab nations; in his own country, he faced attacks from Islamic fundamentalists. Sheikh Omar Abdel-Rahman (later convicted in the first bombing of the World Trade Center, in New York, in 1993) condemned his work publicly and made death threats against Mahfouz in the early 1990s. In 1994, Mahfouz was stabbed

in the neck by an assailant who fled the scene. Although the writer recovered from the attack, he lost most of his sight in old age and became reclusive. He died in Cairo at the age of ninety-four.

"Zaabalawi," the selection here, is a story from Mahfouz's second collection, *God's World* (1963). It contains many of the author's predominant themes and draws on an Islamic mystical tradition whose comprehensive tolerance is far from (and often opposed by) the rigid beliefs of contemporary Muslim fundamentalists. Written two years after *Children of Gebelawi*, it echoes the earlier work's religious symbolism in the mysterious character of Zaabalawi himself. It also demonstrates Mahfouz's shift from an "objective," realistic style toward one emphasizing subjective, mystical awareness. The perceptions of individual characters—here, the narrator—dominate many of his short stories. Mahfouz's later works would include adaptations of folk narratives like the *Arabian Nights*, and there is an element of the folktale in this story, as it draws on Arabic culture and comments, from a broader, often prophetic perspective, on the contemporary scene. Yet this story is also a social document: the narrator's quest for Zaabalawi brings him before various representatives of modern Egyptian society inside a realistically described Cairo. "Zaabalawi," therefore, takes on the character of a social and metaphysical allegory. Its terminally ill narrator seeks to be cured in a quest that implies not only physical healing but religious salvation as well. He has exhausted the resources of medical science and, in desperation, seeks out a holy man whose name he recalls from childhood tales.

Although he is never fully identified, Zaabalawi seems to stand for a spiritual principle of some sort. Zaabalawi's former acquaintances, whom the narrator interviews, form an allegorical portrait of Egyptian society. The bureaucrats who depend on reason, technology, and businesslike efficiency seem least capable of encountering Zaabalawi, while the artists have a closer relationship with him, even if they cannot quickly find him. As the narrator's quest proceeds, he is continually surprised by the difficulty in locating this mystical figure. The story, which combines concreteness with mysticism, the spirit of nineteenth-century realism with that of the *Arabian Nights*, suggests that magic is still possible, even in twentieth-century industrial Cairo.

Zaabalawi[1]

Finally I became convinced that I had to find Sheikh[2] Zaabalawi.

The first time I had heard of his name had been in a song:

> Oh what's become of the world, Zaabalawi?
> They've turned it upside down and taken away its taste.

It had been a popular song in my childhood, and one day it had occurred to me to demand of my father, in the way children have of asking endless questions:

"Who is Zaabalawi?"

He had looked at me hesitantly as though doubting my ability to understand the answer. However, he had replied, "May his blessing descend upon you, he's a true saint of God, a remover of worries and troubles. Were it not for him I would have died miserably—"

In the years that followed, I heard my father many a time sing the praises of this good saint and speak of the miracles he performed. The days passed and brought with them many illnesses, for each one of which I was able, without too much trouble and at a cost I could afford, to find a cure, until I became afflicted with that illness for which no one possesses a remedy. When I had tried everything in vain and was overcome by despair, I remembered by chance what I had heard in my childhood: Why, I asked myself, should I not seek out Sheikh Zaabalawi? I recollected my father saying that he had made his acquaintance in Khan Gaafar[3] at the house of Sheikh Qamar, one of those sheikhs who practiced law in the religious courts, and so I took myself off to his house. Wishing to make sure that he was still living there, I made inquiries of a vendor of beans whom I found in the lower part of the house.

"Sheikh Qamar!" he said, looking at me in amazement. "He left the quarter ages ago. They say he's now living in Garden City and has his office in al-Azhar Square."[4]

I looked up the office address in the telephone book and immediately set off to the Chamber of Commerce Building, where it was located. On asking to see Sheikh Qamar, I was ushered into a room just as a beautiful woman with a most intoxicating perfume was leaving it. The man received me with a smile

---

1. Translated by Denys Johnson-Davies.
2. A title of respect (originally "old man"), often indicating rulership.
3. Gaafar Market, an area of shops.
4. An area of Cairo close to the famous mosque and university of al-Azhar.

and motioned me toward a fine leather-upholstered chair. Despite the thick soles of my shoes, my feet were conscious of the lushness of the costly carpet. The man wore a lounge suit and was smoking a cigar; his manner of sitting was that of someone well satisfied both with himself and with his worldly possessions. The look of warm welcome he gave me left no doubt in my mind that he thought me a prospective client, and I felt acutely embarrassed at encroaching upon his valuable time.

"Welcome!" he said, prompting me to speak.

"I am the son of your old friend Sheikh Ali al-Tatawi," I answered so as to put an end to my equivocal position.

A certain languor was apparent in the glance he cast at me; the languor was not total in that he had not as yet lost all hope in me.

"God rest his soul," he said. "He was a fine man."

The very pain that had driven me to go there now prevailed upon me to stay.

"He told me," I continued, "of a devout saint named Zaabalawi whom he met at Your Honor's. I am in need of him, sir, if he be still in the land of the living."

The languor became firmly entrenched in his eyes, and it would have come as no surprise if he had shown the door to both me and my father's memory.

"That," he said in the tone of one who has made up his mind to terminate the conversation, "was a very long time ago and I scarcely recall him now."

Rising to my feet so as to put his mind at rest regarding my intention of going, I asked, "Was he really a saint?"

"We used to regard him as a man of miracles."

"And where could I find him today?" I asked, making another move toward the door.

"To the best of my knowledge he was living in the Birgawi Residence in al-Azhar," and he applied himself to some papers on his desk with a resolute movement that indicated he would not open his mouth again. I bowed my head in thanks, apologized several times for disturbing him, and left the office, my head so buzzing with embarrassment that I was oblivious to all sounds around me.

I went to the Birgawi Residence, which was situated in a thickly populated quarter. I found that time had so eaten at the building that nothing was left of it save an antiquated façade and a courtyard that, despite being supposedly in the charge of a caretaker, was being used as a rubbish dump. A small, insignificant fellow, a mere prologue to a man, was using the covered entrance as a place for the sale of old books on theology and mysticism.

When I asked him about Zaabalawi, he peered at me through narrow, inflamed eyes and said in amazement, "Zaabalawi! Good heavens, what a time ago that was! Certainly he used to live in this house when it was habitable. Many were the times he would sit with me talking of bygone days, and I would be blessed by his holy presence. Where, though, is Zaabalawi today?"

He shrugged his shoulders sorrowfully and soon left me, to attend to an approaching customer. I proceeded to make inquiries of many shopkeepers in the district. While I found that a large number of them had never even heard of Zaabalawi, some, though recalling nostalgically the pleasant times they had spent with him, were ignorant of his present whereabouts, while others openly made fun of him, labeled him a charlatan, and advised me to put myself in the hands of a doctor—as though I had not already done so. I therefore had no alternative but to return disconsolately home.

With the passing of days like motes in the air, my pains grew so severe that I was sure I would not be able to hold out much longer. Once again I fell to wondering about Zaabalawi and clutching at the hope his venerable name stirred within me. Then it occurred to me to seek the help of the local sheikh of the district; in fact, I was surprised I had not thought of this to begin with. His office was in the nature of a small shop, except that it contained a desk and a telephone, and I found him sitting at his desk, wearing a jacket over his striped galabeya.[5] As he did not interrupt his conversation with a man sitting beside him, I stood waiting till the man had gone. The sheikh then looked up at me coldly. I told myself that I should win him over by the usual methods, and it was not long before I had him cheerfully inviting me to sit down.

"I'm in need of Sheikh Zaabalawi," I answered his inquiry as to the purpose of my visit.

He gazed at me with the same astonishment as that shown by those I had previously encountered.

"At least," he said, giving me a smile that revealed his gold teeth, "he is still alive. The devil of it is, though, he has no fixed abode. You might well bump into him as you go out of here, on the other hand you might spend days and months in fruitless searching."

"Even you can't find him!"

"Even I! He's a baffling man, but I thank the Lord that he's still alive!"

He gazed at me intently, and murmured, "It seems your condition is serious."

"Very."

"May God come to your aid! But why don't you go about it systematically?" He spread out a sheet of paper on the desk and drew on it with unexpected speed and skill until he had made a full plan of the district, showing all the various quarters, lanes, alleyways, and squares. He looked at it admiringly and said, "These are dwelling-houses, here is the Quarter of the Perfumers, here the Quarter of the Coppersmiths, the Mouski,[6] the police and fire stations. The drawing is your best guide. Look carefully in the cafés, the places where the dervishes perform their rites, the mosques and prayer-rooms, and the Green Gate,[7] for he may well be concealed among the beggars and be indistinguishable from them. Actually, I myself haven't seen him for years, having been somewhat preoccupied with the cares of the world, and was only brought back by your inquiry to those most exquisite times of my youth."

I gazed at the map in bewilderment. The telephone rang, and he took up the receiver.

"Take it," he told me, generously. "We're at your service."

Folding up the map, I left and wandered off through the quarter, from square to street to alleyway, making inquiries of everyone I felt was familiar with the place. At last the owner of a small establishment for ironing clothes told me, "Go to the calligrapher[8] Hassanein in Umm al-Ghulam—they were friends."

I went to Umm al-Ghulam,[9] where I found old Hassanein working in a deep, narrow shop full of signboards and jars of color. A strange smell, a mixture of

---

5. The traditional Arabic robe, over which this modernized district officer wears a European jacket.

6. The central bazaar.

7. A medieval gate in Cairo.

8. One who practices the art of decorative lettering (literally "beautiful writing"), which is respected as a fine art in Arabic and Asian cultures.

9. A street in Cairo.

glue and perfume, permeated its every corner. Old Hassanein was squatting on a sheepskin rug in front of a board propped against the wall; in the middle of it he had inscribed the word "Allah"[1] in silver lettering. He was engrossed in embellishing the letters with prodigious care. I stood behind him, fearful of disturbing him or breaking the inspiration that flowed to his masterly hand. When my concern at not interrupting him had lasted some time, he suddenly inquired with unaffected gentleness, "Yes?"

Realizing that he was aware of my presence, I introduced myself. "I've been told that Sheikh Zaabalawi is your friend; I'm looking for him," I said.

His hand came to a stop. He scrutinized me in astonishment. "Zaabalawi! God be praised!" he said with a sigh.

"He *is* a friend of yours, isn't he?" I asked eagerly.

"He was, once upon a time. A real man of mystery: he'd visit you so often that people would imagine he was your nearest and dearest, then would disappear as though he'd never existed. Yet saints are not to be blamed."

The spark of hope went out with the suddenness of a lamp snuffed by a power-cut.

"He was so constantly with me," said the man, "that I felt him to be a part of everything I drew. But where is he today?"

"Perhaps he is still alive?"

"He's alive, without a doubt. . . . He had impeccable taste, and it was due to him that I made my most beautiful drawings."

"God knows," I said, in a voice almost stifled by the dead ashes of hope, "how dire my need for him is, and no one knows better than you[2] of the ailments in respect of which he is sought."

"Yes, yes. May God restore you to health. He is, in truth, as is said of him, a man, and more. . . ."

Smiling broadly, he added, "And his face possesses an unforgettable beauty. But where is he?"

Reluctantly I rose to my feet, shook hands, and left. I continued wandering eastward and westward through the quarter, inquiring about Zaabalawi from everyone who, by reason of age or experience, I felt might be likely to help me. Eventually I was informed by a vendor of lupine[3] that he had met him a short while ago at the house of Sheikh Gad, the well-known composer. I went to the musician's house in Tabakshiyya,[4] where I found him in a room tastefully furnished in the old style, its walls redolent with history. He was seated on a divan, his famous lute beside him, concealing within itself the most beautiful melodies of our age, while somewhere from within the house came the sound of pestle and mortar and the clamor of children. I immediately greeted him and introduced myself, and was put at my ease by the unaffected way in which he received me. He did not ask, either in words or gesture, what had brought me, and I did not feel that he even harbored any such curiosity. Amazed at his understanding and kindness, which boded well, I said, "O Sheikh Gad, I am an admirer of yours, having long been enchanted by the renderings of your songs."

"Thank you," he said with a smile.

1. God (Arabic).
2. One of the calligrapher's major tasks is to write religious documents and prayers to Allah.
3. Beans.
4. A quarter named for the straw trays made and sold there.

"Please excuse my disturbing you," I continued timidly, "but I was told that Zaabalawi was your friend, and I am in urgent need of him."

"Zaabalawi!" he said, frowning in concentration. "You need him? God be with you, for who knows, O Zaabalawi, where you are."

"Doesn't he visit you?" I asked eagerly.

"He visited me some time ago. He might well come right now; on the other hand I mightn't see him till death!"

I gave an audible sigh and asked, "What made him like that?"

The musician took up his lute. "Such are saints or they would not be saints," he said, laughing.

"Do those who need him suffer as I do?"

"Such suffering is part of the cure!"

He took up the plectrum and began plucking soft strains from the strings. Lost in thought, I followed his movements. Then, as though addressing myself, I said, "So my visit has been in vain."

He smiled, laying his cheek against the side of the lute. "God forgive you," he said, "for saying such a thing of a visit that has caused me to know you and you me!"

I was much embarrassed and said apologetically, "Please forgive me; my feelings of defeat made me forget my manners."

"Do not give in to defeat. This extraordinary man brings fatigue to all who seek him. It was easy enough with him in the old days when his place of abode was known. Today, though, the world has changed, and after having enjoyed a position attained only by potentates, he is now pursued by the police on a charge of false pretenses. It is therefore no longer an easy matter to reach him, but have patience and be sure that you will do so."

He raised his head from the lute and skillfully fingered the opening bars of a melody. Then he sang:

I make lavish mention, even though I blame myself, of those I love,
For the stories of the beloved are my wine.[5]

With a heart that was weary and listless, I followed the beauty of the melody and the singing.

"I composed the music to this poem in a single night," he told me when he had finished. "I remember that it was the eve of the Lesser Bairam.[6] Zaabalawi was my guest for the whole of that night, and the poem was of his choosing. He would sit for a while just where you are, then would get up and play with my children as though he were one of them. Whenever I was overcome by weariness or my inspiration failed me, he would punch me playfully in the chest and joke with me, and I would bubble over with melodies, and thus I continued working till I finished the most beautiful piece I have ever composed."

"Does he know anything about music?"

---

5. From a poem by the medieval mystic poet Ibn al-Farid, who represents spiritual ecstasy as a kind of drunkenness.

6. A major Islamic holiday, celebrated for three days to end the month's fasting during Ramadan.

"He is the epitome of things musical. He has an extremely beautiful speaking voice, and you have only to hear him to want to burst into song and to be inspired to creativity. . . ."

"How was it that he cured those diseases before which men are powerless?"

"That is his secret. Maybe you will learn it when you meet him."

But when would that meeting occur? We relapsed into silence, and the hubbub of children once more filled the room.

Again the sheikh began to sing. He went on repeating the words "and I have a memory of her" in different and beautiful variations until the very walls danced in ecstasy. I expressed my wholehearted admiration, and he gave me a smile of thanks. I then got up and asked permission to leave, and he accompanied me to the front door. As I shook him by the hand, he said, "I hear that nowadays he frequents the house of Hagg Wanas al-Damanhouri. Do you know him?"

I shook my head, though a modicum of renewed hope crept into my heart.

"He is a man of private means," the sheikh told me, "who from time to time visits Cairo, putting up at some hotel or other. Every evening, though, he spends at the Negma Bar in Alfi Street."

I waited for nightfall and went to the Negma Bar. I asked a waiter about Hagg Wanas, and he pointed to a corner that was semisecluded because of its position behind a large pillar with mirrors on all four sides. There I saw a man seated alone at a table with two bottles in front of him, one empty, the other two-thirds empty. There were no snacks or food to be seen, and I was sure that I was in the presence of a hardened drinker. He was wearing a loosely flowing silk galabeya and a carefully wound turban; his legs were stretched out toward the base of the pillar, and as he gazed into the mirror in rapt contentment, the sides of his face, rounded and handsome despite the fact that he was approaching old age, were flushed with wine. I approached quietly till I stood but a few feet away from him. He did not turn toward me or give any indication that he was aware of my presence.

"Good evening, Mr. Wanas," I greeted him cordially.

He turned toward me abruptly, as though my voice had roused him from slumber, and glared at me in disapproval. I was about to explain what had brought me to him when he interrupted in an almost imperative tone of voice that was none the less not devoid of an extraordinary gentleness, "First, please sit down, and, second, please get drunk!"

I opened my mouth to make my excuses but, stopping up his ears with his fingers, he said, "Not a word till you do what I say."

I realized I was in the presence of a capricious drunkard and told myself that I should at least humor him a bit. "Would you permit me to ask one question?" I said with a smile, sitting down.

Without removing his hands from his ears he indicated the bottle. "When engaged in a drinking bout like this, I do not allow any conversation between myself and another unless, like me, he is drunk, otherwise all propriety is lost and mutual comprehension is rendered impossible."

I made a sign indicating that I did not drink.

"That's your lookout," he said offhandedly. "And that's my condition!"

He filled me a glass, which I meekly took and drank. No sooner had the wine settled in my stomach than it seemed to ignite. I waited patiently till I had grown used to its ferocity, and said, "It's very strong, and I think the time has come for me to ask you about—"

Once again, however, he put his fingers in his ears. "I shan't listen to you until you're drunk!"

He filled up my glass for the second time. I glanced at it in trepidation; then, overcoming my inherent objection, I drank it down at a gulp. No sooner had the wine come to rest inside me than I lost all willpower. With the third glass, I lost my memory, and with the fourth the future vanished. The world turned round about me and I forgot why I had gone there. The man leaned toward me attentively, but I saw him—saw everything—as a mere meaningless series of colored planes. I don't know how long it was before my head sank down onto the arm of the chair and I plunged into deep sleep. During it, I had a beautiful dream the like of which I had never experienced. I dreamed that I was in an immense garden surrounded on all sides by luxuriant trees, and the sky was nothing but stars seen between the entwined branches, all enfolded in an atmosphere like that of sunset or a sky overcast with cloud. I was lying on a small hummock of jasmine petals, more of which fell upon me like rain, while the lucent spray of a fountain unceasingly sprinkled the crown of my head and my temples. I was in a state of deep contentedness, of ecstatic serenity. An orchestra of warbling and cooing played in my ear. There was an extraordinary sense of harmony between me and my inner self, and between the two of us and the world, everything being in its rightful place, without discord or distortion. In the whole world there was no single reason for speech or movement, for the universe moved in a rapture of ecstasy. This lasted but a short while. When I opened my eyes, consciousness struck at me like a policeman's fist and I saw Wanas al-Damanhouri regarding me with concern. Only a few drowsy customers were left in the bar.

"You have slept deeply," said my companion. "You were obviously hungry for sleep."

I rested my heavy head in the palms of my hands. When I took them away in astonishment and looked down at them, I found that they glistened with drops of water.

"My head's wet," I protested.

"Yes, my friend tried to rouse you," he answered quietly.

"Somebody saw me in this state?"

"Don't worry, he is a good man. Have you not heard of Sheikh Zaabalawi?"

"Zaabalawi!" I exclaimed, jumping to my feet.

"Yes," he answered in surprise. "What's wrong?"

"Where is he?"

"I don't know where he is now. He was here and then he left."

I was about to run off in pursuit but found I was more exhausted than I had imagined. Collapsed over the table, I cried out in despair, "My sole reason for coming to you was to meet him! Help me to catch up with him or send someone after him."

The man called a vendor of prawns and asked him to seek out the sheikh and bring him back. Then he turned to me. "I didn't realize you were afflicted. I'm very sorry. . . ."

"You wouldn't let me speak," I said irritably.

"What a pity! He was sitting on this chair beside you the whole time. He was playing with a string of jasmine petals he had around his neck, a gift from one of his admirers, then, taking pity on you, he began to sprinkle some water on your head to bring you around."

"Does he meet you here every night?" I asked, my eyes not leaving the doorway through which the vendor of prawns had left.

"He was with me tonight, last night and the night before that, but before that I hadn't seen him for a month."

"Perhaps he will come tomorrow," I answered with a sigh.

"Perhaps."

"I am willing to give him any money he wants."

Wanas answered sympathetically, "The strange thing is that he is not open to such temptations, yet he will cure you if you meet him."

"Without charge?"

"Merely on sensing that you love him."

The vendor of prawns returned, having failed in his mission.

I recovered some of my energy and left the bar, albeit unsteadily. At every street corner I called out "Zaabalawi!" in the vague hope that I would be rewarded with an answering shout. The street boys turned contemptuous eyes on me till I sought refuge in the first available taxi.

The following evening I stayed up with Wanas al-Damanhouri till dawn, but the sheikh did not put in an appearance. Wanas informed me that he would be going away to the country and would not be returning to Cairo until he had sold the cotton crop.

I must wait, I told myself; I must train myself to be patient. Let me content myself with having made certain of the existence of Zaabalawi, and even of his affection for me, which encourages me to think that he will be prepared to cure me if a meeting takes place between us.

Sometimes, however, the long delay wearied me. I would become beset by despair and would try to persuade myself to dismiss him from my mind completely. How many weary people in this life know him not or regard him as a mere myth! Why, then, should I torture myself about him in this way?

No sooner, however, did my pains force themselves upon me than I would again begin to think about him, asking myself when I would be fortunate enough to meet him. The fact that I ceased to have any news of Wanas and was told he had gone to live abroad did not deflect me from my purpose; the truth of the matter was that I had become fully convinced that I had to find Zaabalawi.

Yes, I have to find Zaabalawi.

1963

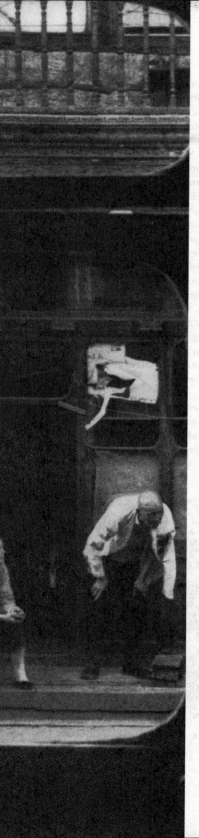

VIII

Contemporary World Literature

Certain years in world history stand out in the blaze of a revolution that transforms world politics: 1789 for the French Revolution, 1848 for a series of European revolutions, 1917 for the Russian Revolution. More recently, 1968, a year of student rebellion in Prague, Paris, Mexico City, and elsewhere, seemed at the time to be such a milestone. Challenges to traditional authority shook the 1960s. The subsequent changes to Western culture have shaped all that came after—especially in literature, where the intimate relations among men and women and the tensions between public responsibility and private desire play a central role. Meanwhile, the vision of a post-communist world that was glimpsed in Prague in the spring of 1968 found its realization in the dismantling of communist regimes in Eastern Europe in 1989 and the dissolution of the Soviet Union in 1991. The crushing of the Prague Spring led immediately to a period of pessimism and "normalization" (that is, a return to repressive practices) that restricted social movements. The only successful effort to thwart normalization was the Polish trade union Solidarity, which, however, was trampled by the imposition of martial law in 1981.

In the West, especially in the United States, the

A 1965 photograph by Marc Riboud of a street in Beijing as seen from inside an antique dealer's shop.

focus of protest was the Vietnam War—a conflict the Americans had taken over from the French—in which over half a million (mostly drafted) Americans had failed to defeat a guerrilla insurgency. Communist North Vietnam, backed by the Soviet Union (and for a time by China), eventually reached Saigon, the capital of South Vietnam, in 1975, and unified the country the following year. There were a number of other minor proxy wars between the superpowers during the 1970s and 1980s, but this was the period of détente, or relaxation of hostility, when the Soviet premier Leonid Brezhnev and American presidents including Richard Nixon and Jimmy Carter sought to defuse Cold War tensions and signed a number of treaties on arms control and human rights. Détente, eclipsed by the Soviet invasion of Afghanistan in 1979, was followed by a period of rearmament under President Ronald Reagan, which culminated, surprisingly, in the disarmament agreement with Russian premier Mikhail Gorbachev at Reykjavik, Iceland, in 1986. Seeking to transform the moribund economy and society he had inherited from his communist predecessors, Gorbachev introduced the principles of glasnost (or openness) and perestroika (or restructuring), intending to make the Soviet system more flexible and accountable. In the end, however, the restructuring went much further than Gorbachev had intended, resulting in the demise of the Communist Party of the Soviet Union and the dissolution of both the Warsaw Pact military alliance and the Soviet Union itself.

If 1968 marks the high point of the protest movements that would transform contemporary society, 1989 is an equally memorable year, during which the nations of Eastern Europe rebelled against—and finally overthrew—communist regimes, and the wall that had separated East and West Berlin fell. Also in 1989, the first steps were taken to dismantle the system of apartheid, or racial segregation and white minority rule in South Africa (white minority rule had ended in Zimbabwe, formerly Rhodesia, in 1980). That same year thousands of Chinese

Young men in Ho Chi Minh City (formerly Saigon, the capital of South Vietnam), in 1975, after "Liberation Day."

students mounted an unsuccessful rebellion against the communist government of the People's Republic of China; this brief uprising ended with a massacre in Tiananmen Square, in Beijing, the historic center of Chinese politics.

During the 1990s, as the Soviet Union disintegrated and as China moved closer to a capitalist economy, many hoped that humanity's bloodiest century would end with something like the accomplishment of world peace that had been such a bright dream at its beginning. The dictatorships of Latin America, supported by the United States as a bulwark against communism, gave way to democratically elected governments. Peace agreements in Northern Ireland and between Israel and Palestine seemed to confirm such promises. Another date, September 11, 2001, undermined such hopes: on that day, terrorists claiming to act in the name of Islam hijacked four airplanes and flew into the World Trade Center, in New York, and the Pentagon, near Washington, D.C. (one of the planes was forced, by the passengers, to crash in a remote field in Pennsylvania). The wars of the twenty-first century, which began in the aftermath of the terrorist attacks, have chilled the hope that ours would be a uniquely peaceful age. Likewise, the expectation that industrialization would lead inevitably to a more secular world has proved mistaken. Communal violence continues in India, and the Arab-Israeli conflict and Islamic fundamentalism have intensified during the first decades of the twenty-first century, while in much of the world outside Europe, religion is resurgent.

During the past half century or so, even if dreams of world peace have often appeared illusory, great improvement in the living standards of much of the world's still-expanding population has occurred. The years since World War II have been an era of globalization in investment, knowledge, politics, and cul-

Supporters of antiapartheid activist Nelson Mandela gather outside the Victor Verster prison in Cape Town, South Africa, demanding his freedom. After twenty-seven years of confinement, Mandela was finally released in 1990. In 1994 he became South Africa's first black president.

ture. The information revolution, made possible first by satellite television and then by ever-more-sophisticated computers and the Internet, has unified distant parts of the globe more rapidly than did the telegraph and telephone at the beginning of the twentieth century. Today, a world connected by telecommunications responds more quickly than ever before to news about politics, markets, and even sporting events. It is also a world of increased migration, in which the movements of people from poorer to richer nations have created immense cultural hybridity while sometimes producing tensions in the host countries. A diverse literature chronicles the experiences of political refugees and immigrants, both documented and undocumented. The political upheavals of

ARCTIC OCEAN

Spitsbergen (Nor.)

Greenland (Den.)

Iceland

Sweden
Finland

Norway

Leningrad (St. Petersbu

NORTH AMERICA

Canada

Moscow

Union

P E

Northern
Ireland

United
Kingdom

Denmark

East
Germany
Berlin

Warsaw

Dublin

London

Netherlands
West Germany

Belgium

Prague
Czechoslovakia

Ireland

Paris

Austria
Vienna
Hungary

Romania

France

Switz.

Yugoslavia

Chicago

New York

Portugal

Madrid
Spain

Venice
Italy
Rome

Bulgaria

Albania
Greece

Istanbul
Turkey

United States
of America

Los Angeles

NORTH ATLANTIC OCEAN

Beirut
Syria
Lebanon

disp
bord

Israel
Jerusalem
Jordan

Iraq

Isr

Mexico

Morocco

W. Sahara

Tunisia

Mediterranean Sea

Alexandria
Cairo

Egypt

Kuw

Bahrain

Cuba

Haiti
Dominican Rep.

Algeria

Libya

Saudi Arabia

Mexico City

VIRGIN IS. (Br. & U.S.)

Antigua

AFRICA

Eritrea

Yemen

Sou Yeme

Guatemala

Jamaica

Belize

Honduras

Martinique (Fr.)
St. Lucia

Mauritania

Mali

Niger

Chad

El Salvador

Nicaragua

Trinidad & Tobago

Senegal

Burkina
Faso

Sudan

Costa Rica

Panama

Venezuela

Guyana

Gambia

Guinea-Bissau

Nigeria

Ethiopia

Colombia

Surinam

French Guiana

Guinea

Ivory
Coast

Ghana

Ibadan

Central African Rep.

Somalia

GALAPAGOS IS.
(Ecuador)

Ecuador

Equator

Sierra
Leone

Liberia

Benin
Togo

Cameroon

Uganda

Kenya

Equatorial Guinea

Congo

Rwanda
Burundi

Nairobi

Peru

Brazil

SOUTH AMERICA

Gabon

Zaire

Tanzania

SEYCHE

SOUTH PACIFIC OCEAN

Bolivia

Rio de Janeiro

Angola

Zambia

Malawi

Paraguay

Namibia

Zimbabwe

Mozambique

Botswana

Madaga

Chile

Uruguay

SOUTH ATLANTIC OCEAN

Johannesburg

South Africa

Swaziland

Santiago

Buenos Aires

Lesotho

Argentina

FALKLAND IS.
(Br.)

MILES

0   1200   2400   3600   4800

AT THE EQUATOR

0   2400   4800

KILOMETERS

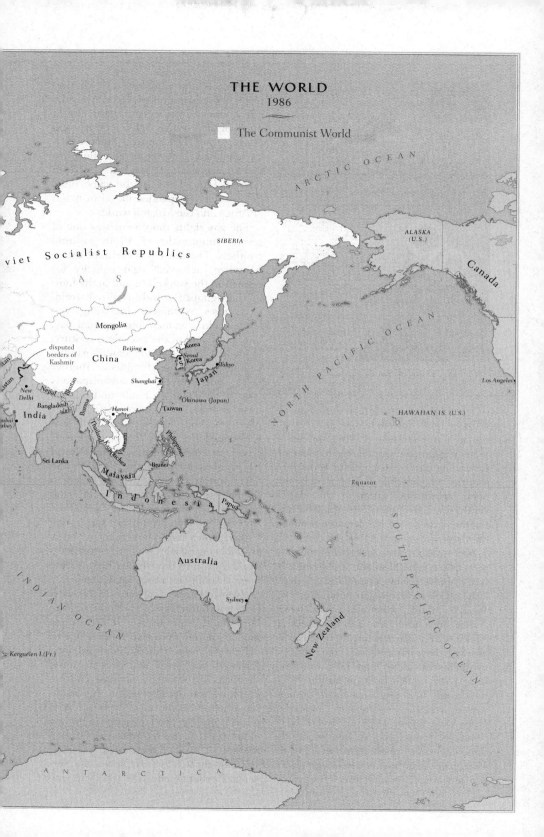

THE WORLD
1986

The Communist World

ARCTIC OCEAN

SIBERIA

ALASKA
(U.S.)

Canada

...viet Socialist Republics

A S I

Mongolia

disputed
borders of
Kashmir

China

Beijing

Korea

Seoul
Korea

Tokyo

Japan

Shanghai

Okinawa (Japan)

New
Delhi

Nepal

Bhutan

Burma

Taiwan

Bangladesh

Hanoi

India

Laos

...bai
...bay)

Thailand Kampuchea

Sri Lanka

Malaysia

Philippines

Brunei

I n d o n e s i a

Papua

NORTH PACIFIC OCEAN

Los Angeles

HAWAIIAN IS. (U.S.)

Equator

SOUTH PACIFIC OCEAN

Australia

Sydney

INDIAN OCEAN

New Zealand

Kerguelen I.(Fr.)

A N T A R C T I C A

Speechless, 1996, by Shirin Neshat.

the twentieth century created millions of refugees and entrenched conflicts that remain unresolved. Within nations, many migrants left rural areas to move to expanding cities. In search of economic security, meanwhile, immigrants left poorer countries, often in the global south, for the developed world. The immigrant experience has become a major theme of writers in this era.

Illness, too, travels faster than before; even as the general state of public health has improved, new epidemics, particularly AIDS, have ravaged populations in the West and much more broadly in Africa. In Europe and North America, AIDS at first affected mostly homosexuals. The decimation of gay communities by the disease led to more militant forms of activism, which built on antidiscrimination efforts dating back to the Stonewall uprising. A popular gay bar in the Greenwich Village neighborhood of New York City, Stonewall had been frequently targeted by the police. One evening in June 1969, patrons and their supporters resisted arrest, igniting the struggle for

acceptance and equality. Yet another result of the gay rights movement was the introduction of same-sex marriages in much of the West, as well as in Brazil and South Africa. Tension over homosexuality remained, however: it is a theme in the writings of the Dominican American novelist Junot Díaz. At the same time, homosexuality remained illegal in much of Africa and the Muslim world.

The gay rights movement was one of several outgrowths of 1960s cultural conflicts. The most successful of these, feminism, achieved legal equality for women in the workplace and in the family throughout the industrialized world. Challenges remained, including violence against women and unequal pay, but by the end of the twentieth century, many successful young career women claimed to be "post-feminist." Another factor enabling these transformations was the availability of safe and reliable birth control, which allowed for family planning (the contraceptive pill was introduced in 1960). Works by writers as diverse as **Leslie Marmon Silko, Nawal El Saadawi, Hanan Al Shaykh** and **Chimamanda Ngozi Adichie** touch on the changes in the status of women and in social norms governing sexuality. Abortion remained controversial in the United States and Ireland but was widely available elsewhere, except Latin America, Africa, and the Middle East, where homosexuality also remained illegal.

Even relatively conservative regions were not untouched by the youth culture born in the 1960s, broadcast by the mass media, and emphasizing the breaking of old taboos and the liberation of sexuality. Although the great writers were often skeptical of the appeal of mass culture, literature too participated in the breaking of taboos. Almost a century ago, **Virginia Woolf** spoke of a change in human character that the modernist generation registered: "All human relations have shifted—those between masters and servants, husbands and wives, parents and children." The literature of the last century has continually reimagined these perpetually shifting relations, and the theme of generational conflict or cultural transmission across the generations plays a prominent role in much contemporary literature.

The literature of the late twentieth century, presented here along with a few works from the twenty-first century, has responded in manifold ways to the period's unprecedented historical transformations. While the cultural hybridity that attends the movement of peoples and the sharing of information sometimes inspires literary innovations, it can also sharpen nostalgia for tradition and the past. Increasingly, writers are conscious of having an audience beyond their nation or region and even beyond their language. Writers with a global readership may feel both responsibility for representing their own people to the world and the need to accommodate their style of writing to the demands of the international marketplace. Indeed, Nobel Prize winners such as **Orhan Pamuk** have often been accused in their homelands of speaking primarily to an international audience. Writers thus find themselves striving to defend and honor the spirit and culture of historically marginalized groups while reaching out to a more elite international audience.

As in the immediate postwar period, many writers seeking to address the need for social change and the elimination of political inequality turn to traditional literary realism or to political allegory. A literary movement emerging in the 1960s, magic realism draws both on the realist tradition of the historical novel and on the inspiration of modernists such as **Franz Kafka**, who depicted his nightmarish worlds in lifelike detail. In various ways, novelists such as **Gabriel García Marquéz** and **Salman Rushdie** combine realistic historical narration with fanciful folktales in which individuals and societies seem to be transformed by distinctly nonrealistic events—a character who can fly, perhaps, or a mystical link among people born on the night of Indian independence. The juxtaposition emphasizes the coexistence of modern notions of causality and traditional, prescientific belief in the unexplainable and thus has had its greatest impact in zones of uneven economic development, where educated writers have incorporated the folk wisdom of their rural, sometimes illiterate communities.

The magic realists are sometimes described as a postmodernist. In common with an earlier generation inspired by the modernists, postmodernists often question the boundary between fiction and history. While treating historical events, writers such as Orhan Pamuk may call attention to the fictionality of their reconstruction of those events—encouraging the reader to keep in mind that stories are the creations of writers who may, by the very act of narration, distort historical reality. These authors tend to present an oblique account of atrocities, whether involving colonization, genocide, or political repression. Both in magic realism and in postmodernism, stories may seem whimsical or fantastical even when they are playing for deadly serious stakes.

The twenty-first century began with reminders of the interconnectedness of a global society linked by industrial capitalism and communications technology but divided by religion and politics. While war, terrorism, and poverty are events that divide us, the greatest world literature suggests, as it always has, what unites us.

DEREK WALCOTT
1930–2017

A cosmopolitan poet from a small Caribbean island, a West Indian of mixed African and European ancestry, Derek Walcott depicted the hybridity of Caribbean culture while drawing on the traditions of English literature. In contemplating the violent uprising in Kenya against British colonialism, he wrote in an early poem, "A Far Cry from Africa" (1956), of his dual inheritance: "I who am poisoned with the blood of both / Where shall I turn, divided to the vein?" Yet if he treated his mixed blood as poison, he also made it a source of strength in his verse, which draws on the rhythms and idioms of Caribbean speech to enliven what he called, in the same poem, "the English tongue I love."

Derek Walcott was born, along with his twin brother, Roderick, on January 23, 1930, in Castries, the capital of the island of St. Lucia, then a British colony. (It had been occupied alternately by the French and the British since the seventeenth century and would not gain its independence from Britain until 1979.) Shortly after their first birthday, the boys' father, who was a government functionary and a talented artist, suddenly died, and the two boys were brought up by their mother, a schoolteacher who later became headmistress of the Methodist elementary school where they began their education. Both inherited their father's creative gift, Derek primarily in language, Roderick in the pictorial arts, and they remained intellectual and artistic companions until Roderick's death, in 1999. Their mother provided an environment in which their talents could be nurtured,

an essential factor in Walcott's development as a poet.

Walcott acquired, early on, a sense of his singularity from the fact that he was of mixed ancestry in a predominantly black society (both his grandfathers were white, his grandmothers black). He was also a Protestant and member of the educated middle class in a peasant, Catholic community. Moreover, although he was brought up to speak Standard English as his first language, his exposure to the local French creole reinforced his sense of his ambiguous relation to the communal life around him. Far from unsettling Walcott, these factors of personal history became a source of strength and fascination. He began to write poetry in high school and published his first works as a teenager.

After high school education at St. Mary's College, Walcott studied at the University of West Indies in Jamaica, where he came to understand the Caribbean as a region unified by a common experience and a common historical legacy. His literary studies familiarized him with the great works of Western literature and particularly with the modern English poets **T. S. Eliot, W. B. Yeats**, and W. H. Auden. After his graduation, in 1953, Walcott taught school for a while in Kingston, while doing occasional work in journalism, before moving to Port of Spain, Trinidad, where he became a feature writer for a major local newspaper, the *Sunday Guardian*. In 1957, he was awarded a Rockefeller Fellowship to study theater at New York University. His encounter with the problems of race during his American sojourn gave further definition to his self-awareness as a West Indian; the experience confirmed for him the inescapable connection between race and history with which black people in the New World have to contend. On his return two years later to Port of Spain, he founded the Trinidad Theatre Workshop, to which he devoted his energies for nearly two decades. He was eager to bring the technical knowledge associated with the theater and stagecraft to the West Indies. He became well-known for his plays before he gained a following for his poetry, which won an international audience after the publication of his collection *In a Green Night* (1962) in England. Alienated by the Black Power revolts of the 1970s in Trinidad, Walcott resigned from the Trinidad Theatre Workshop and, after winning a MacArthur Fellowship ("genius" grant) in 1981, began teaching regularly at Boston University. He divided his time between the United States and St. Lucia until his death in 2017. He was awarded the Nobel Prize in Literature in 1992.

All Walcott's poetry flows into his mature masterpiece *Omeros* (1990), which is best grasped as the imaginative summation of human history as seen from his Caribbean perspective. Its retrospective vision assumes an emotional value for the poet for whom, as he said, "Art is History's nostalgia." In an expansive recollection of his previous themes, *Omeros* sums up the West Indian experience through the adventures of Achille, a humble St. Lucian fisherman, whose travels take him to the compass points of the West Indian consciousness. **Homer's** great epics, the *Iliad* and the *Odyssey*, serve as explicit references for the work, and the figure of Homer himself, in his modern

Greek rendering of "Omeros," is evoked in a key passage of the poem in which he is represented as the quintessential exile. Moreover, Walcott's use of the blind poet in the character of Seven Seas, modeled on Demodokos in Homer's *Odyssey*, reinforces the importance of this Greek frame of reference. The poem employs some of the standard tropes of the classical epic, such as descent into the underworld and conflict and contest.

Despite these connections, *Omeros* is not a mere rehash of Homer. Although the poem contains stretches of narration, they do not build up to a dramatic progression of events such as we find in a conventional epic. The rivalry between Achille and another local fisherman, Hector, over Helen (who is hardly idealized in the poem and remains, for all her beauty, an ordinary village woman) is presented as part of a strictly local history that features other characters such as the white settler couple, Major Plunkett and his wife, Maud, as well as minor characters who move in and out of the narrative. Thus the poem does not develop a linear plot, but represents, rather, a vast kaleidoscope, a series of episodes that are woven around its protagonist.

Walcott's epic explores the African element in Caribbean life and the theme of collective memory and its relation to identity. *Omeros* reconnects with Africa by emphasizing the continuing tie of the West Indians to the continent of their forbears yet helps its West Indian audience take cultural repossession of their island home. *Omeros* registers both the Afro-Caribbean quest for an established sense of place and of community and, at the same time, the compulsion to move toward the wider horizon of world literature.

OMEROS

From Book One

From *Chapter I*

II

Achille looked up at the hole[1] the laurel had left.
He saw the hole silently healing with the foam
of a cloud like a breaker. Then he saw the swift[2]

crossing the cloud-surf, a small thing, far from its home,
confused by the waves of blue hills. A thorn vine gripped   5
his heel. He tugged it free. Around him, other ships

were shaping from the saw. With his cutlass he made
a swift sign of the cross, his thumb touching his lips
while the height rang with axes. He swayed back the blade,

and hacked the limbs from the dead god,[3] knot after knot,   10
wrenching the severed veins from the trunk as he prayed:
"Tree! You can be a canoe! Or else you cannot!"

The bearded elders endured the decimation
of their tribe without uttering a syllable
of the language they had uttered as one nation,[4]   15

the speech taught their saplings: from the towering babble
of the cedar to green vowels of *bois-campêche*.
The *bois-flot* held its tongue with the *laurier-cannelle*,[5]

the red-skinned logwood endured the thorns in its flesh,
while the Aruacs' patois[6] crackled in the smell   20
of a resinous bonfire that turned the leaves brown

with curling tongues, then ash, and their language was lost.
Like barbarians striding columns they have brought down,
the fishermen shouted. The gods were down at last.

Like pygmies they hacked the trunks of wrinkled giants   25
for paddles and oars. They were working with the same
concentration as an army of fire-ants.[7]

---

1. The opening stanza describes the ritual fell-
ing of a laurel tree from which a dugout canoe
is to be made. This refers to the hole in the
ground where the tree had stood. The section
that follows describes the making of the canoe.
2. A small, plainly colored bird, related to the
swallow, that serves as a guide to the wandering hero.
3. The laurel tree, venerated as nature.

4. The flora as part of the total living environment.
5. *Bois-campêche, bois-flot, laurier-cannelle:*
French for logwood, timber, and laurel, respectively.
6. Dialect. "Aruacs": the original inhabitants
of the Caribbean; also Arawaks.
7. Omnivorous ants with powerful stingers in
their tails.

But vexed by the smoke for defaming their forest,
blow-darts of mosquitoes kept needling Achille's trunk.
He frotted white rum on both forearms that, at least,   30

those that he flattened to asterisks would die drunk.
They went for his eyes. They circled them with attacks
that made him weep blindly. Then the host retreated

to high bamboo like the archers of Aruacs
running from the muskets of cracking logs,[8] routed   35
by the fire's banner and the remorseless axe

hacking the branches. The men bound the big logs first
with new hemp[9] and, like ants, trundled them to a cliff
to plunge through tall nettles.[1] The logs gathered that thirst

for the sea which their own vined bodies were born with.   40
Now the trunks in eagerness to become canoes
ploughed into breakers of bushes, making raw holes

of boulders, feeling not death inside them, but use—
to roof the sea, to be hulls. Then, on the beach, coals[2]
were set in their hollows that were chipped with an adze.   45

A flat-bed truck had carried their rope-bound bodies.
The charcoals, smouldering, cored the dugouts for days
till heat widened the wood enough for ribbed gunwales.[3]

Under his tapping chisel Achille felt their hollows
exhaling to touch the sea, lunging towards the haze   50
of bird-printed islets, the beaks of their parted bows.

Then everything fit. The pirogues[4] crouched on the sand
like hounds with sprigs in their teeth. The priest
sprinkled them with a bell, then he made the swift's sign.[5]

When he smiled at Achille's canoe, *In God We Troust,*[6]   55
Achille said: "Leave it! Is God' spelling and mine."
After Mass one sunrise the canoes entered the troughs[7]

of the surpliced[8] shallows, and their nodding prows
agreed with the waves to forget their lives as trees;
one would serve Hector and another, Achilles.   60

8. Log houses from which white men shot at
the Aruacs.
9. The vine is excellent for making ropes.
1. A plant that stings.
2. They are used to fire the hollowed-out logs.
3. That is, the heat expanded the wood so
that metal strips could be inserted to reinforce
the sides of the boat.

4. French for dugout canoes.
5. The swift's wings are shaped like a cross.
6. The boat's name. The phrase "In God We
Trust" is found on American money.
7. Sea channels.
8. The canoes make a lacelike pattern on the
water, resembling the surplice worn by Catholic priests at Mass.

From Book Seven

From *Chapter LXIV*

I

I sang[1] of quiet Achille, Afolabe's son,
who never ascended in an elevator,
who had no passport, since the horizon needs none,

never begged nor borrowed, was nobody's waiter,
whose end, when it comes, will be a death by water   5
(which is not for this book, which will remain unknown

and unread by him). I sang the only slaughter
that brought him delight, and that from necessity—
of fish, sang the channels of his back[2] in the sun.

I sang our wide country, the Caribbean Sea.   10
Who hated shoes, whose soles were as cracked as a stone,
who was gentle with ropes, who had one suit alone,

whom no man dared insult and who insulted no one,
whose grin was a white breaker cresting, but whose frown
was a growing thunderhead, whose fist of iron   15

would do me a greater honour if it held on
to my casket's oarlocks[3] than mine lifting his own
when both anchors are lowered in the one island,

but now the idyll dies, the goblet is broken,
and rainwater trickles down the brown cheek of a jar   20
from the clay of Choiseul. So much left unspoken

by my chirping nib![4] And my earth-door lies ajar.
I lie wrapped in a flour-sack sail. The clods thud
on my rope-lowered canoe. Rasping shovels scrape

a dry rain of dirt on its hold, but turn your head   25
when the sea-almond rattles or the rust-leaved grape
from the shells of my unpharaonic pyramid[5]

towards paper shredded by the wind and scattered
like white gulls that separate their names from the foam
and nod to a fisherman[6] with his khaki dog   30

1. The invocation, usually placed at the beginning of an epic poem, is here put at the end
and expressed in the past tense.
2. The ripples of muscles, denoting strength.
The human frame represented as a furrowed
landscape.

3. At the poet's own funeral.
4. The point of a pen dipped in ink often
makes a rasping noise on the paper.
5. Modest, without the monumental grandeur
of Egypt's pyramids.
6. I.e., Philoctete.

that skitters from the wave-crash, then frown at his form
for one swift second. In its earth-trough, my pirogue
with its brass-handled oarlocks is sailing. Not from

but with them, with Hector, with Maud[7] in the rhythm
of her beds[8] trowelled over, with a swirling log   35
lifting its mossed head from the swell; let the deep hymn

of the Caribbean continue my epilogue;
may waves remove their shawls as my mourners walk home
to their rusted villages, good shoes in one hand,

passing a boy who walked through the ignorant foam,   40
and saw a sail going out or else coming in,
and watched asterisks of rain[9] puckering the sand.

* * *

1990

---

7. The wife of an English colonial officer, Major Plunkett, whose adventures, intertwined with the life of the St. Lucians, are narrated in earlier passages of the poem. "Hector": rival of Achille who was killed in a car accident.

8. A reference to the flowerbeds tended by Maud. The image evokes her final resting place in the earth.
9. Which is life-giving.

SEAMUS HEANEY
1939–2013

Having reached his maturity as a poet during the sectarian violence known as the Troubles in his native Northern Ireland, Seamus Heaney developed a keen awareness of the poet's relationship to history and conflict. A student of the Irish language and of Anglo-Saxon (Old English), he has drawn on the resources of both in reinventing modern English poetry. His verse, alive to historical resonances, explores the ethical commitments of the poet in a world of enduring conflicts.

Born to a Catholic family on a farm in County Derry, Northern Ireland, Heaney was the eldest of nine children. He attended the nearby Anahorish School and then St. Columb's College, a Catholic boarding school in Derry, Northern Ireland's second city, before enrolling in Queen's University, Belfast, where he studied English language and literature. In addition to Anglo-Saxon, he learned Irish and Latin. After briefly teaching middle school, Heaney returned to Queen's in 1966 as an instructor in English literature. In the same year, his first major volume of poems, *Death of a Naturalist,* was released. During the following several years, as tensions heightened in Northern Ireland, Heaney addressed political concerns in his poetry, although often in an indirect fashion that was sometimes criticized for its lack of explicit commitment. In 1972, in a move that was seen at the time as indicating sympathies with the Nationalist cause (unification with the Republic of Ireland), Heaney moved to Dublin. He taught college there for several years, then, as his reputation as a poet grew, began an association with Harvard University, where he would teach part-time for a quarter of a century. He also taught at Oxford University, and in 1995, he received the Nobel Prize in Literature.

The late 1960s were a period of intense violence in Northern Ireland, a majority Protestant region that had remained part of the United Kingdom when the rest of Ireland gained its independence. Some members of the substantial Catholic population of Northern Ireland supported the illegal Irish Republican Army, which used violence to promote unification with the Irish Republic (the "Nationalist" position). Catholics often faced hostility and discrimination from Protestant groups, notably the paramilitary Ulster Volunteer Force, that favored continued union with Britain (the "Unionists"). British police and military forces were generally perceived as supporting the Unionists, particularly in the Bloody Sunday massacre of 1972, when thirteen unarmed Catholic protesters were killed by British army forces. The cycle of violence by the IRA, the UVF, and British forces continued until the Good Friday agreement of 1998, which ushered in a period of disarmament and power sharing by Nationalist and Unionist politicians.

The Northern Irish landscape of Heaney's youth plays a central role in his poetry. Regularly placed by Heaney at the beginning of collections of his poetry, "Digging" (1964) announces his poetic vocation by comparing the poet's pen to the shovels wielded by Heaney's father and grandfather, both farmers, and also to a gun. Heaney the poet will use a pen to make his mark. Although not following a strict form, the poem generally has four heavy accents per line and caesuras (pauses in the middle of a line); its rhythm and use of alliteration and assonance (repetition of vowel sounds) echo those of Old English poetry.

Heaney was interested in the sounds of words, and many of his poems draw on the significance and pronunciation of place-names. He frequently used words of Anglo-Saxon origin, which he associated with the land. His telling choice of diction can be observed in "The Tollund Man" (1972), one of the first of Heaney's poems about the bog people, an ancient folk, related to the Irish, whose bodies were preserved in the wetlands of Jutland, Denmark. In this poem and in "Punishment" (1975), the speaker contemplates the bodies of victims of sacrificial slaughter in the Iron Age society, hinting that such primitive violence is not all that different from the Troubles of Northern Ireland.

Heaney was attentive to the formal qualities of his verse, whether in loose blank verse (unrhymed iambic pentameter) or in his characteristic short quatrains (four-line stanzas). Although seldom making use of rhyme, these quatrains recall ballad forms associated with folk tradition, while in other poems (like "The Tollund Man" and "Punishment") they create a melancholy, meditative mood. Preferring relatively formal poetry rather than experimental verse, Heaney drew heavily on the literary tradition, including **Dante**, **T. S. Eliot**, and the medieval epic *Beowulf,* which he translated into modern English. His work is distinguished by its concreteness and descriptive precision.

Digging

Between my finger and my thumb
The squat pen rests; snug as a gun.

Under my window, a clean rasping sound
When the spade sinks into gravelly ground:
My father, digging. I look down   5

Till his straining rump among the flowerbeds
Bends low, comes up twenty years away
Stooping in rhythm through potato drills
Where he was digging.

The coarse boot nestled on the lug, the shaft   10
Against the inside knee was levered firmly.
He rooted out tall tops, buried the bright edge deep
To scatter new potatoes that we picked,
Loving their cool hardness in our hands.

By God, the old man could handle a spade.   15
Just like his old man.

My grandfather cut more turf in a day
Than any other man on Toner's bog.[1]
Once I carried him milk in a bottle
Corked sloppily with paper. He straightened up   20
To drink it, then fell to right away
Nicking and slicing neatly, heaving sods
Over his shoulder, going down and down
For the good turf. Digging.

The cold smell of potato mould, the squelch and slap   25
Of soggy peat, the curt cuts of an edge
Through living roots awaken in my head.
But I've no spade to follow men like them.

Between my finger and my thumb
The squat pen rests.   30
I'll dig with it.

                                                                      1964

---

1. The boy belongs to a man named Toner. The speaker's father cuts turf for a fire.

The Tollund Man[1]

I

Some day I will go to Aarhus[2]
To see his peat-brown head,
The mild pods of his eyelids,
His pointed skin cap.

In the flat country nearby   5
Where they dug him out,
His last gruel of winter seeds
Caked in his stomach,

Naked except for
The cap, noose and girdle,   10
I will stand a long time.
Bridegroom to the goddess,

She tightened her torc[3] on him
And opened her fen,
Those dark juices working   15
Him to a saint's kept body,

Trove of the turf-cutters'
Honeycombed workings.
Now his stained face
Reposes at Aarhus.   20

II

I could risk blasphemy,
Consecrate the cauldron bog
Our holy ground and pray
Him to make germinate

The scattered, ambushed   25
Flesh of labourers,
Stockinged corpses
Laid out in the farmyards,

Tell-tale skin and teeth
Flecking the sleepers   30
Of four young brothers,[4] trailed
For miles along the lines.

---

1. The corpse of a man killed in the 4th century B.C.E, probably a sacrificial victim, preserved in a bog in Jutland, Denmark. Heaney had seen photographs of the Tollund Man and associated Denmark's bogs with those of Northern Ireland.
2. A town in Jutland (the Tollund Man is actually displayed in nearby Silkeborg).
3. An ancient style of metal necklace.
4. The speaker compares the Tollund Man to four Irish nationalist brothers killed by the Protestant Ulster Constabulary Force (forerunner of the Ulster Volunteer Force), in the early 1920s, in Northern Ireland.

III

Something of his sad freedom
As he rode the tumbril
Should come to me, driving,   35
Saying the names

Tollund, Grauballe, Nebelgard,⁵
Watching the pointing hands
Of country people,
Not knowing their tongue.   40

Out there in Jutland
In the old man-killing parishes
I will feel lost,
Unhappy and at home.

1972

Punishment¹

I can feel the tug
of the halter at the nape
of her neck, the wind
on her naked front.

It blows her nipples   5
to amber beads,
it shakes the frail rigging
of her ribs.

I can see her drowned
body in the bog,   10
the weighing stone,
the floating rods and boughs.

Under which at first
she was a barked sapling
that is dug up   15
oak-bone, brain-firkin:²

her shaved head
like a stubble of black corn,
her blindfold a soiled bandage,
her noose a ring   20

to store
the memories of love.

---

5. Other places in Jutland where bog bodies had been found.
1. The speaker contemplates the body, pre-served in a bog, of a young woman in ancient Scandinavia, drowned for adultery.
2. Refers to a head covering on the dead body.

Little adulteress,
before they punished you

you were flaxen-haired,   25
undernourished, and your
tar-black face was beautiful.
My poor scapegoat,

I almost love you
but would have cast, I know,   30
the stones of silence.
I am the artful voyeur

of your brain's exposed
and darkened combs,
your muscles' webbing   35
and all your numbered bones:

I who have stood dumb
when your betraying sisters,
cauled in tar,
wept by the railings,   40

who would connive
in civilized outrage
yet understand the exact
and tribal, intimate revenge.

                                                          1975

GABRIEL GARCÍA MÁRQUEZ
1928–2014

The best-known novelist of the Latin American "Boom" of the 1960s and 1970s, Gabriel García Márquez embodied, in his work, the mixture of fantasy and actuality known as "magic realism." Again and again García Márquez returned to certain themes: the contrast between dreamlike experiences and everyday reality; the enchanted or inexplicable aspect of fictional creation; and the solitude of individuals in societies that can never quite incorporate them. His fiction, which contains mythic dimensions that are often rooted in local folklore, reimagines regional tales to explore broader social and psychological conflicts. Even those works based in historical fact transform the characters and events into a fictional universe with its own set of laws.

García Márquez was born on March 6, 1928, in the small town of Aracataca, in the "banana zone" of Colombia. The first of twelve children, he was raised by his maternal grandparents until 1936, when his grandfather died. As an adult, he would attribute his love of fantasy to his grandmother, who told him fantastical tales whenever she wanted to shush his incessant questions. His grandfather, meanwhile, passed on a marked interest in politics, having fought on the Liberal side of a civil war early in the century. After receiving his undergraduate degree as a scholarship student at the National Colegio in Zipaquirá, García Márquez studied law at the University of Bogotá in 1947. It was there, he later claimed, that he read Kafka's *The Metamorphosis,* in a Spanish translation by Jorge Luis Borges. "Shit," he said to himself after reading the first sentence, "that's just the way my grandmother talked!" The next day he wrote "The Third Resignation," the Kafkaesque tale of a man in his coffin who continued to grow (and retain consciousness) for seventeen years after his death. It was the first of his works to be published. García Márquez found in Kafka the mobile balance of nonrealistic events and realistic detail that—combined with his grandmother's quixotic stories and his grandfather's political concerns—would become the genre known as magic realism. In this mode the narrator treats the subjective beliefs and experiences of the characters, often derived from folklore and supernatural beliefs, as if they were real, even when (to a scientifically minded observer) they seem impossible. Some

of García Márquez's early novels also reflected the influence of William Faulkner, whom he later described as "my master"—in particular, Faulkner's representation of subjective experience through stream-of-consciousness technique and the southern writer's depiction of an underdeveloped geographical region beset by a long history of conflict.

In 1950, García Márquez abandoned his legal studies for journalism. As a correspondent for various Latin American newspapers, he traveled to Paris and later to Eastern Europe, Venezuela, Cuba, and New York. After writing several novels, short stories, and film scripts, he gained international fame for his novel *One Hundred Years of Solitude.* Published in 1967, it chronicles the rise and fall of the fortunes of the Buendía family in a mythical town called Macondo (based on the author's hometown of Aracataca). A global best seller, it was soon translated into multiple languages and received prizes in Italy and France. When it was published in English, in 1970, American critics praised it as one of the best books of the year, and it has since become a monument of world literature.

The author's later work was preoccupied with contemporary events, especially the prevalence of dictatorship in Latin American societies. As García Márquez continued to publish successful novels, he also became an advocate for social justice, speaking out for revolutionary governments in Latin America and organizing assistance for political prisoners. There were even rumors of a plot, backed by the Colombian government, to assassinate García Márquez because of his antigovernment activities; in 1981 he sought asylum in Mexico. In his later years, he lived primarily in Mexico City, although he spent time in Colombia and Europe as well.

The story printed here, "Death Constant Beyond Love" (1970), dates from the author's later, more politically active period. It has a political background, although its protagonist, Senator Onésimo Sánchez, appears chiefly through the lens of his struggles with the existential problem of death. García Márquez presents an essentially satirical portrait of Sánchez, a corrupt politician who accepts bribes and stays in power by helping the local property owners avoid reform. His electoral train is a traveling circus with carnival wagons, fireworks, a ready-made audience of hired Indians, and a cardboard village with imitation brick houses and a painted ocean liner to represent the (shallow) promise of prosperity. Among the citizenry, Sánchez uses carefully placed gifts to encourage support and a feeling of dependence.

Yet the spectacle of the senator's campaign for office, and even the sordid background of poverty and corruption that enables it, fade into insignificance before the broader themes of life and death. Forty-two, happily married, and in full control, as a powerful politician in mid-career, of the lives of himself and others, he is made suddenly to feel—when told that he will be dead "forever" by next Christmas—helpless, vulnerable, and alone. Theoretically he knows that death is inevitable and that the course of nature cannot be defeated. He has read Marcus Aurelius (121–180 C.E.) and refers to the Stoic philosopher's *Meditations*, which criticizes the delusions of those "who have

tenaciously stuck to life" and recommends the cheerful acceptance of natural order, including death.

In this crisis the senator is reduced to basic, instinctual existence, drawing him deeper into García Márquez's recurrent themes of solitude, love, and death. The beautiful Laura provides an opportunity for him to submerge his fear of death in erotic passion. This choice means scandal and the destruction of his political career, but by now Onésimo Sánchez has felt the emptiness of his earlier activities—and has given them up for the hopeless struggle to cheat death. "Death Constant Beyond Love" reverses the ambitious claim of a famous sonnet by the Spanish Golden Age writer Quevedo (1580–1645), according to which there is "Love Constant Beyond Death." Such love is an illusion, for it is death, beyond everything else, that awaits us.

Gabriel García Márquez received the Nobel Prize in Literature in 1982. In his acceptance speech he drew connections between his novels and the sufferings of the peoples of Latin America through dictatorship and civil war. Voicing hope for an end to the nuclear arms race, the writer spoke of a "new and sweeping utopia of life, where no one will be able to decide for others how they die, where love will prove true and happiness be possible, and where the races condemned to one hundred years of solitude will have, at last and forever, a second opportunity on earth."

Death Constant beyond Love[1]

Senator Onésimo Sánchez had six months and eleven days to go before his death when he found the woman of his life. He met her in Rosal del Virrey,[2] an illusory village which by night was the furtive wharf for smugglers' ships, and on the other hand, in broad daylight looked like the most useless inlet on the desert, facing a sea that was arid and without direction and so far from everything no one would have suspected that someone capable of changing the destiny of anyone lived there. Even its name was a kind of joke, because the only rose in that village was being worn by Senator Onésimo Sánchez himself on the same afternoon when he met Laura Farina.

It was an unavoidable stop in the electoral campaign he made every four years. The carnival wagons had arrived in the morning. Then came the trucks with the rented Indians[3] who were carried into the towns in order to enlarge the crowds at public ceremonies. A short time before eleven o'clock, along with the music and rockets and jeeps of the retinue, the ministerial automobile, the color of strawberry soda, arrived. Senator Onésimo Sánchez was placid and weatherless inside the air-conditioned car, but as soon as he opened the door he was shaken by a gust of fire and his shirt of pure silk was soaked in a kind of light-colored soup and he felt many years older and more alone than ever. In real life he had just turned forty-two, had been graduated from Göttingen[4] with honors as a metallurgical engineer, and was an avid reader, although without much reward, of badly translated Latin classics. He was married to a radiant German woman who had given him five children and they were all happy in their home, he the happiest of all until they told him, three months before, that he would be dead forever by next Christmas.

While the preparations for the public rally were being completed, the senator managed to have an hour alone in the house they had set aside for him to rest in. Before he lay down he put in a glass of drinking water the rose he had kept alive all across the desert, lunched on the diet cereals that he took with him so as to avoid the repeated portions of fried goat that were waiting for him during the rest of the day, and he took several analgesic pills before the time prescribed so that he would have the remedy ahead of the pain. Then he put the electric fan close to the hammock and stretched out naked for fifteen minutes in the shadow of the rose, making a great effort at mental distraction so as not to think about death while he dozed. Except for the doctors, no one knew that he had been sentenced to a fixed term, for he had decided to endure his secret all alone, with no change in his life, not because of pride but out of shame.[5]

He felt in full control of his will when he appeared in public again at three in the afternoon, rested and clean, wearing a pair of coarse linen slacks and a floral shirt, and with his soul sustained by the anti-pain pills. Nevertheless, the erosion of death was much more pernicious than he had supposed, for as he

---

1. Translated by Gregory Rabassa.
2. The Rosebush of the Viceroy (governor).
3. People descended from the original inhabitants of the continent; generally poorer and less privileged than those descended from Spanish or Portuguese colonists.

4. A well-known German university.
5. "Death is such as generation is, a mystery of nature . . . altogether not a thing of which any man should be ashamed" (Marcus Aurelius, *Meditations* 4.5).

went up onto the platform he felt a strange disdain for those who were fighting for the good luck to shake his hand, and he didn't feel sorry as he had at other times for the groups of barefoot Indians who could scarcely bear the hot salt-peter coals of the sterile little square. He silenced the applause with a wave of his hand, almost with rage, and he began to speak without gestures, his eyes fixed on the sea, which was sighing with heat. His measured, deep voice had the quality of calm water, but the speech that had been memorized and ground out so many times had not occurred to him in the nature of telling the truth, but, rather, as the opposite of a fatalistic pronouncement by Marcus Aurelius in the fourth book of his *Meditations.*

"We are here for the purpose of defeating nature," he began, against all his convictions. "We will no longer be foundlings in our own country, orphans of God in a realm of thirst and bad climate, exiles in our own land. We will be different people, ladies and gentlemen, we will be a great and happy people."

There was a pattern to his circus. As he spoke his aides threw clusters of paper birds into the air and the artificial creatures took on life, flew about the platform of planks, and went out to sea. At the same time, other men took some prop trees with felt leaves out of the wagons and planted them in the saltpeter soil behind the crowd. They finished by setting up a cardboard façade with make-believe houses of red brick that had glass windows, and with it they covered the miserable real-life shacks.

The senator prolonged his speech with two quotations in Latin in order to give the farce more time. He promised rainmaking machines, portable breed-ers for table animals, the oils of happiness which would make vegetables grow in the saltpeter and clumps of pansies in the window boxes. When he saw that his fictional world was all set up, he pointed to it. "That's the way it will be for us, ladies and gentlemen," he shouted. "Look! That's the way it will be for us."

The audience turned around. An ocean liner made of painted paper was passing behind the houses and it was taller than the tallest houses in the artifi-cial city. Only the senator himself noticed that since it had been set up and taken down and carried from one place to another the superimposed cardboard town had been eaten away by the terrible climate and that it was almost as poor and dusty as Rosal del Virrey.

For the first time in twelve years, Nelson Farina didn't go to greet the sena-tor. He listened to the speech from his hammock amidst the remains of his siesta, under the cool bower of a house of unplaned boards which he had built with the same pharmacist's hands with which he had drawn and quartered his first wife. He had escaped from Devil's Island[6] and appeared in Rosal del Virrey on a ship loaded with innocent macaws, with a beautiful and blasphemous black woman he had found in Paramaribo[7] and by whom he had a daughter. The woman died of natural causes a short while later and she didn't suffer the fate of the other, whose pieces had fertilized her own cauliflower patch, but was buried whole and with her Dutch name in the local cemetery. The daugh-ter had inherited her color and her figure along with her father's yellow and astonished eyes, and he had good reason to imagine that he was rearing the most beautiful woman in the world.

6. A former French penal colony off the coast of French Guiana in northern South America.

7. Capital of Suriname (formerly Dutch Gui-ana) and a large port.

Ever since he had met Senator Onésimo Sánchez during his first electoral campaign, Nelson Farina had begged for his help in getting a false identity card which would place him beyond the reach of the law. The senator, in a friendly but firm way, had refused. Nelson Farina never gave up, and for several years, every time he found the chance, he would repeat his request with a different recourse. But this time he stayed in his hammock, condemned to rot alive in that burning den of buccaneers. When he heard the final applause, he lifted his head, and looking over the boards of the fence, he saw the back side of the farce: the props for the buildings, the framework of the trees, the hidden illusionists who were pushing the ocean liner along. He spat without rancor.

"*Merde,*" he said. "*C'est le Blacamán de la politique.*"[8]

After the speech, as was customary, the senator took a walk through the streets of the town in the midst of the music and the rockets and was besieged by the townspeople, who told him their troubles. The senator listened to them good-naturedly and he always found some way to console everybody without having to do them any difficult favors. A woman up on the roof of a house with her six youngest children managed to make herself heard over the uproar and the fireworks.

"I'm not asking for much, Senator," she said. "Just a donkey to haul water from Hanged Man's Well."

The senator noticed the six thin children. "What became of your husband?" he asked.

"He went to find his fortune on the island of Aruba,"[9] the woman answered good-humoredly, "and what he found was a foreign woman, the kind that put diamonds on their teeth."

The answer brought on a roar of laughter.

"All right," the senator decided, "you'll get your donkey."

A short while later an aide of his brought a good pack donkey to the woman's house and on the rump it had a campaign slogan written in indelible paint so that no one would ever forget that it was a gift from the senator.

Along the short stretch of street he made other, smaller gestures, and he even gave a spoonful of medicine to a sick man who had had his bed brought to the door of his house so he could see him pass. At the last corner, through the boards of the fence, he saw Nelson Farina in his hammock, looking ashen and gloomy, but nonetheless the senator greeted him, with no show of affection.

"Hello, how are you?"

Nelson Farina turned in his hammock and soaked him in the sad amber of his look.

"*Moi, vous savez,*"[1] he said.

His daughter came out into the yard when she heard the greeting. She was wearing a cheap, faded Guajiro Indian[2] robe, her head was decorated with

8. Shit. He's the Blacamán of politics (French). Blacamán is a charlatan and huckster who appears in several of García Márquez's stories, including "Blacamán the Good, Vendor of Miracles."
9. Off the coast of Venezuela, famous as a tourist resort.
1. "Oh well, as for me, you know" (French).

2. Inhabitant of the rural Guajira Peninsula of northern Colombia. The figure of Laura Farina is thus connected with the rustic poor, with earthy reality (*farina* means "flour"), and with erotic inspiration. (*Laura* was the beloved celebrated by the Italian Renaissance poet Francis Petrarch, 1304–1374.)

colored bows, and her face was painted as protection against the sun, but even in that state of disrepair it was possible to imagine that there had never been another so beautiful in the whole world. The senator was left breathless. "I'll be damned!" he breathed in surprise. "The Lord does the craziest things!"

That night Nelson Farina dressed his daughter up in her best clothes and sent her to the senator. Two guards armed with rifles who were nodding from the heat in the borrowed house ordered her to wait on the only chair in the vestibule.

The senator was in the next room meeting with the important people of Rosal del Virrey, whom he had gathered together in order to sing for them the truths he had left out of his speeches. They looked so much like all the ones he always met in all the towns in the desert that even the senator himself was sick and tired of that perpetual nightly session. His shirt was soaked with sweat and he was trying to dry it on his body with the hot breeze from an electric fan that was buzzing like a horse fly in the heavy heat of the room.

"We, of course, can't eat paper birds," he said. "You and I know that the day there are trees and flowers in this heap of goat dung, the day there are shad[3] instead of worms in the water holes, that day neither you nor I will have anything to do here, do I make myself clear?"

No one answered. While he was speaking, the senator had torn a sheet off the calendar and fashioned a paper butterfly out of it with his hands. He tossed it with no particular aim into the air current coming from the fan and the butterfly flew about the room and then went out through the half-open door. The senator went on speaking with a control aided by the complicity of death.

"Therefore," he said, "I don't have to repeat to you what you already know too well: that my reelection is a better piece of business for you than it is for me, because I'm fed up with stagnant water and Indian sweat, while you people, on the other hand, make your living from it."

Laura Farina saw the paper butterfly come out. Only she saw it because the guards in the vestibule had fallen asleep on the steps, hugging their rifles. After a few turns, the large lithographed butterfly unfolded completely, flattened against the wall, and remained stuck there. Laura Farina tried to pull it off with her nails. One of the guards, who woke up with the applause from the next room, noticed her vain attempt.

"It won't come off," he said sleepily. "It's painted on the wall."

Laura Farina sat down again when the men began to come out of the meeting. The senator stood in the doorway of the room with his hand on the latch, and he only noticed Laura Farina when the vestibule was empty.

"What are you doing here?"

"*C'est de la part de mon père*,"[4] she said.

The senator understood. He scrutinized the sleeping guards, then he scrutinized Laura Farina, whose unusual beauty was even more demanding than his pain, and he resolved then that death had made his decision for him.

"Come in," he told her.

Laura Farina was struck dumb standing in the doorway to the room: thousands of bank notes were floating in the air, flapping like the butterfly. But the senator turned off the fan and the bills were left without air and alighted on the objects in the room.

"You see," he said, smiling, "even shit can fly."

3. A kind of fish.   4. "My father sent me" (French).

Laura Farina sat down on a schoolboy's stool. Her skin was smooth and firm, with the same color and the same solar density as crude oil, her hair was the mane of a young mare, and her huge eyes were brighter than the light. The senator followed the thread of her look and finally found the rose, which had been tarnished by the saltpeter.

"It's a rose," he said.

"Yes," she said with a trace of perplexity. "I learned what they were in Riohacha."[5]

The senator sat down on an army cot, talking about roses as he unbuttoned his shirt. On the side where he imagined his heart to be inside his chest he had a corsair's tattoo of a heart pierced by an arrow. He threw the soaked shirt to the floor and asked Laura Farina to help him off with his boots.

She knelt down facing the cot. The senator continued to scrutinize her, thoughtfully, and while he was untying the laces he wondered which one of them would end up with the bad luck of that encounter.

"You're just a child," he said.

"Don't you believe it," she said. "I'll be nineteen in April."

The senator became interested.

"What day?"

"The eleventh," she said.

The senator felt better. "We're both Aries,"[6] he said. And smiling, he added: "It's the sign of solitude."

Laura Farina wasn't paying attention because she didn't know what to do with the boots. The senator, for his part, didn't know what to do with Laura Farina, because he wasn't used to sudden love affairs and, besides, he knew that the one at hand had its origins in indignity. Just to have some time to think, he held Laura Farina tightly between his knees, embraced her about the waist, and lay down on his back on the cot. Then he realized that she was naked under her dress, for her body gave off the dark fragrance of an animal of the woods, but her heart was frightened and her skin disturbed by a glacial sweat.

"No one loves us," he sighed.

Laura Farina tried to say something, but there was only enough air for her to breathe. He laid her down beside him to help her, he put out the light and the room was in the shadow of the rose. She abandoned herself to the mercies of her fate. The senator caressed her slowly, seeking her with his hand, barely touching her, but where he expected to find her, he came across something iron that was in the way.

"What have you got there?"

"A padlock,"[7] she said.

"What in hell!" the senator said furiously and asked what he knew only too well. "Where's the key?"

Laura Farina gave a breath of relief.

"My papa has it," she answered. "He told me to tell you to send one of your people to get it and to send along with him a written promise that you'll straighten out his situation."

---

5. A port on the Guajira Peninsula.
6. Sign in the zodiac; people born between March 21 and April 19 are said to be under the sign of Aries.

7. She is wearing a chastity belt, a medieval device worn by women to prevent sexual intercourse.

The senator grew tense. "Frog[8] bastard," he murmured indignantly. Then he closed his eyes in order to relax and he met himself in the darkness. *Remember, he remembered, that whether it's you or someone else, it won't be long before you'll be dead and it won't be long before your name won't even be left.*[9]

He waited for the shudder to pass.

"Tell me one thing," he asked then. "What have you heard about me?"

"Do you want the honest-to-God truth?"

"The honest-to-God truth."

"Well," Laura Farina ventured, "they say you're worse than the rest because you're different."

The senator didn't get upset. He remained silent for a long time with his eyes closed, and when he opened them again he seemed to have returned from his most hidden instincts.

"Oh, what the hell," he decided. "Tell your son of a bitch of a father that I'll straighten out his situation."

"If you want, I can go get the key myself," Laura Farina said.

The senator held her back.

"Forget about the key," he said, "and sleep awhile with me. It's good to be with someone when you're so alone."

Then she laid his head on her shoulder with her eyes fixed on the rose. The senator held her about the waist, sank his face into woods-animal armpit, and gave in to terror. Six months and eleven days later he would die in that same position, debased and repudiated because of the public scandal with Laura Farina and weeping with rage at dying without her.

1970

8. Epithet for "French."
9. A direct translation of a sentence from Marcus Aurelius's *Meditations* (4.6).

LESLIE MARMON SILKO
born 1948

Novelist, poet, memoirist, and writer of short fiction, Leslie Marmon Silko can comfortably alternate between prose and poetry within the confines of a single work, in a manner reminiscent of traditional Native American storytellers. For all its seriousness and lyricism, Silko's work is marked by a touch of irreverence. Well acquainted with the proverbial trickster Coyote, Silko has demonstrated her own wit and versatility as a narrator of Coyote tales. But storytelling is a game with serious ends. "I will tell you something about stories," warns an unnamed voice in one of her novels: "They aren't just entertainment. Don't be fooled."

Silko was born in Albuquerque but grew up in Laguna Pueblo, New Mexico. "I am of mixed-breed ancestry," she has written, "but what I know is Laguna. This place I am from is everything I am as a writer and human being." A Keresan-speaking district, Laguna Pueblo is an old Native community that whites first joined in the mid-nineteenth century when two government employees from Ohio, Walter and Robert Marmon, arrived as surveyors and set down roots. The brothers wrote a constitution for Laguna modeled after the U.S. Constitution; each served a term as governor of the pueblo, an office that no non-Native had held before. They also married Laguna women: Robert Marmon is the great-grandfather of Leslie Marmon Silko. Silko attended Laguna Day School until fifth grade, when she was transferred to Manzano Day School, a small private academy in Albuquerque. Between 1964 and 1969, she studied English at the University of New Mexico, married while still in college, and gave birth to the older of her two sons, Cazimir Silko. During these years she published her first story, "Tony's Story," a provocative tale of witchery.

Following graduation, Silko stayed on at the university and taught courses in creative writing and oral literature. She studied for a time in the university's American Indian Law Program, with the intention of working in the legal area of Native land claims. In 1971, however, a National Endowment for the Arts Discovery Grant changed Silko's mind about law school, and she quit to devote herself to writing. Seven of her stories, including "Yellow Woman," were published in 1974 in a collection edited by Kenneth Rosen—*The Man to Send Rain Clouds: Contemporary Stories by American Indians*. The novel *Ceremony*, her first large-scale work, appeared in 1977. An enormously complex novel that appeared just after the Vietnam War, *Ceremony* follows a Second World War veteran of mixed ancestry through his struggle for healing. Widely hailed, the novel propelled its author to the front of the growing ranks of indigenous

writers in the United States. On the strength of *Ceremony*, Silko was awarded a MacArthur Fellowship (known as the "genius grant") in 1981.

Although much of Silko's work emphasizes the healing of conflicts—between white and Native Americans, between the human and natural worlds, between warring aspects of the self—some of her novels also reveal a more aggressive and despairing tone. Such a novel is *Almanac of the Dead* (1991), which turns a merciless eye on an America that drugs, prostitution, torture, organized crime, and forms of sexual violence have corrupted and deformed. On the map that opens the book read the stern lines: "The Indian Wars have never ended in the Americas. Native Americans acknowledge no borders; they seek nothing less than the return of all tribal lands." Formerly a professor at the University of Arizona, Silko continues to live and write in Tucson.

The story presented here, "Yellow Woman," is one of Silko's shortest and earliest pieces, that has, all the same, come to occupy a still-growing place in the canon of short fiction. Often reprinted, it became the subject of a volume of critical essays published in 1993. In traditional Laguna lore, Yellow Woman is either the heroine or a minor character in a wide range of tales. In her earliest incarnations, she might possibly have been a corn spirit—occasionally, Yellow Woman is named together with her three sisters, Blue Woman, Red Woman, and White Woman, thus completing the four colors of corn—but in Laguna lore she eventually became a kind of Everywoman. A traditional Laguna prayer song, recited at the naming ceremony for a newborn daughter, begins, "Yellow Woman is born, Yellow Woman is born." In narrative lore Yellow Woman most frequently appears in tales of abduction, where she is said to have been captured by a strange man at a stream while she is fetching water. Her captor, who carries her off to another world, is sometimes a kachina, or ancestral spirit; and when at last she returns to her home, she is imbued with power that proves of value for her people. In Silko's version of the tale, traditional elements remain constantly in the foreground. Yet whether the central figures in the story are human or supernatural remains unclear; the story's ambiguity is the source of its fascination. Thus Silko draws on Native tradition to make a major contribution to contemporary American fiction.

Yellow Woman

My thigh clung to his with dampness, and I watched the sun rising up through the tamaracks and willows. The small brown water birds came to the river and hopped across the mud, leaving brown scratches in the alkali-white crust. They bathed in the river silently. I could hear the water, almost at our feet where the narrow fast channel bubbled and washed green ragged moss and fern leaves. I looked at him beside me, rolled in the red blanket on the white river sand. I cleaned the sand out of the cracks between my toes, squinting because the sun was above the willow trees. I looked at him for the last time, sleeping on the white river sand.

I felt hungry and followed the river south the way we had come the afternoon before, following our footprints that were already blurred by lizard tracks and bug trails. The horses were still lying down, and the black one whinnied when he saw me but he did not get up—maybe it was because the corral was made out of thick cedar branches and the horses had not yet felt the sun like I had. I tried to look beyond the pale red mesas to the pueblo. I knew it was there, even if I could not see it, on the sandrock hill above the river, the same river that moved past me now and had reflected the moon last night.

The horse felt warm underneath me. He shook his head and pawed the sand. The bay whinnied and leaned against the gate trying to follow, and I remembered him asleep in the red blanket beside the river. I slid off the horse and tied him close to the other horse, I walked north with the river again, and the white sand broke loose in footprints over footprints.

"Wake up."

He moved in the blanket and turned his face to me with his eyes still closed. I knelt down to touch him.

"I'm leaving."

He smiled now, eyes still closed. "You are coming with me, remember?" He sat up now with his bare dark chest and belly in the sun.

"Where?"

"To my place."

"And will I come back?"

He pulled his pants on. I walked away from him, feeling him behind me and smelling the willows.

"Yellow Woman," he said.

I turned to face him. "Who are you?" I asked.

He laughed and knelt on the low, sandy bank, washing his face in the river. "Last night you guessed my name, and you knew why I had come."

I stared past him at the shallow moving water and tried to remember the night, but I could only see the moon in the water and remember his warmth around me.

"But I only said that you were him and that I was Yellow Woman—I'm not really her—I have my own name and I come from the pueblo on the other side of the mesa. Your name is Silva and you are a stranger I met by the river yesterday afternoon."

He laughed softly. "What happened yesterday has nothing to do with what you will do today, Yellow Woman."

"I know—that's what I'm saying—the old stories about the ka'tsina[1] spirit and Yellow Woman can't mean us."

My old grandpa liked to tell those stories best. There is one about Badger and Coyote who went hunting and were gone all day, and when the sun was going down they found a house. There was a girl living there alone, and she had light hair and eyes and she told them that they could sleep with her. Coyote wanted to be with her all night so he sent Badger into a prairie-dog hole, telling him he thought he saw something in it. As soon as Badger crawled in, Coyote blocked up the entrance with rocks and hurried back to Yellow Woman.

"Come here," he said gently.

He touched my neck and I moved close to him to feel his breathing and to hear his heart. I was wondering if Yellow Woman had known who she was—if she knew that she would become part of the stories. Maybe she'd had another name that her husband and relatives called her so that only the ka'tsina from the north and the storytellers would know her as Yellow Woman. But I didn't go on; I felt him all around me, pushing me down into the white river sand.

Yellow Woman went away with the spirit from the north and lived with him and his relatives. She was gone for a long time, but then one day she came back and she brought twin boys.

"Do you know the story?"

"What story?" He smiled and pulled me close to him as he said this. I was afraid lying there on the red blanket. All I could know was the way he felt, warm, damp, his body beside me. This is the way it happens in the stories, I was thinking, with no thought beyond the moment she meets the ka'tsina spirit and they go.

"I don't have to go. What they tell in stories was real only then, back in time immemorial, like they say."

He stood up and pointed at my clothes tangled in the blanket. "Let's go," he said.

I walked beside him, breathing hard because he walked fast, his hand around my wrist. I had stopped trying to pull away from him, because his hand felt cool and the sun was high, drying the river bed into alkali. I will see someone, eventually I will see someone, and then I will be certain that he is only a man—some man from nearby—and I will be sure that I am not Yellow Woman. Because she is from out of time past and I live now and I've been to school and there are highways and pickup trucks that Yellow Woman never saw.

It was an easy ride north on horseback. I watched the change from the cottonwood trees along the river to the junipers that brushed past us in the foothills,

---

1. Kachina, an ancestral spirit.

and finally there were only piñons, and when I looked up at the rim of the mountain plateau I could see pine trees growing on the edge. Once I stopped to look down, but the pale sandstone had disappeared and the river was gone and the dark lava hills were all around. He touched my hand, not speaking, but always singing softly a mountain song and looking into my eyes.

I felt hungry and wondered what they were doing at home now—my mother, my grandmother, my husband, and the baby. Cooking breakfast, saying, "Where did she go?—maybe kidnapped." And Al going to the tribal police with the details: "She went walking along the river."

The house was made with black lava rock and red mud. It was high above the spreading miles of arroyos and long mesas. I smelled a mountain smell of pitch and buck brush. I stood there beside the black horse, looking down on the small, dim country we had passed, and I shivered.

"Yellow Woman, come inside where it's warm."

He lit a fire in the stove. It was an old stove with a round belly and an enamel coffeepot on top. There was only the stove, some faded Navajo blankets, and a bedroll and cardboard box. The floor was made of smooth adobe plaster, and there was one small window facing east. He pointed at the box.

"There's some potatoes and the frying pan." He sat on the floor with his arms around his knees pulling them close to his chest and he watched me fry the potatoes. I didn't mind him watching me because he was always watching me—he had been watching me since I came upon him sitting on the river bank trimming leaves from a willow twig with his knife. We ate from the pan and he wiped the grease from his fingers on his Levi's.

"Have you brought women here before?" He smiled and kept chewing, so I said, "Do you always use the same tricks?"

"What tricks?" He looked at me like he didn't understand.

"The story about being a ka'tsina from the mountains. The story about Yellow Woman."

Silva was silent; his face was calm.

"I don't believe it. Those stories couldn't happen now," I said.

He shook his head and said softly, "But someday they will talk about us, and they will say, 'Those two lived long ago when things like that happened.' "

He stood up and went out. I ate the rest of the potatoes and thought about things—about the noise the stove was making and the sound of the mountain wind outside. I remembered yesterday and the day before, and then I went outside.

I walked past the corral to the edge where the narrow trail cut through the black rim rock. I was standing in the sky with nothing around me but the wind that came down from the blue mountain peak behind me. I could see faint mountain images in the distance miles across the vast spread of mesas and valleys and plains. I wondered who was over there to feel the mountain wind on those sheer blue edges—who walks on the pine needles in those blue mountains.

"Can you see the pueblo?" Silva was standing behind me.

I shook my head. "We're too far away."

"From here I can see the world." He stepped out on the edge. "The Navajo reservation begins over there." He pointed to the east. "The Pueblo boundaries are over here." He looked below us to the south, where the narrow trail seemed to come from. "The Texans have their ranches over there, starting with that valley, the Concho Valley. The Mexicans run some cattle over there too."

"Do you ever work for them?"

"I steal from them," Silva answered. The sun was dropping behind us and the shadows were filling the land below. I turned away from the edge that dropped forever into the valleys below.

"I'm cold," I said, "I'm going inside." I started wondering about this man who could speak the Pueblo language so well but who lived on a mountain and rustled cattle. I decided that this man Silva must be Navajo, because Pueblo men didn't do things like that.

"You must be a Navajo."

Silva shook his head gently. "Little Yellow Woman," he said, "you never give up, do you? I have told you who I am. The Navajo people know me, too." He knelt down and unrolled the bedroll and spread the extra blankets out on a piece of canvas. The sun was down, and the only light in the house came from outside—the dim orange light from sundown.

I stood there and waited for him to crawl under the blankets.

"What are you waiting for?" he said, and I lay down beside him. He undressed me slowly like the night before beside the river—kissing my face gently and running his hands up and down my belly and legs. He took off my pants and then he laughed.

"Why are you laughing?"

"You are breathing so hard."

I pulled away from him and turned my back to him.

He pulled me around and pinned me down with his arms and chest. "You don't understand, do you, little Yellow Woman? You will do what I want."

And again he was all around me with his skin slippery against mine, and I was afraid because I understood that his strength could hurt me. I lay underneath him and I knew that he could destroy me. But later, while he slept beside me, I touched his face and I had a feeling—the kind of feeling for him that overcame me that morning along the river. I kissed him on the forehead and he reached out for me.

When I woke up in the morning he was gone. It gave me a strange feeling because for a long time I sat there on the blankets and looked around the little house for some object of his—some proof that he had been there or maybe that he was coming back. Only the blankets and the cardboard box remained. The .30-30 that had been leaning in the corner was gone, and so was the knife I had used the night before. He was gone, and I had my chance to go now. But first I had to eat, because I knew it would be a long walk home.

I found some dried apricots in the cardboard box, and I sat down on a rock at the edge of the plateau rim. There was no wind and the sun warmed me. I was surrounded by silence. I drowsed with apricots in my mouth, and I didn't believe that there were highways or railroads or cattle to steal.

When I woke up, I stared down at my feet in the black mountain dirt. Little black ants were swarming over the pine needles around my foot. They must have smelled the apricots. I thought about my family far below me. They would be wondering about me, because this had never happened to me before. The tribal police would file a report. But if old Grandpa weren't dead he would tell them what happened—he would laugh and say, "Stolen by a ka'tsina, a mountain spirit. She'll come home—they usually do." There are enough of them to handle things. My mother and grandmother will raise the baby like they raised me. Al will find someone else, and they will go on like before, except that there will be a story about the day I disappeared while I was walking along the river. Silva had come for me; he said he had. I did not decide to go. I just went. Moonflowers blossom in the sand hills before dawn, just as I followed him. That's what I was thinking as I wandered along the trail through the pine trees.

It was noon when I got back. When I saw the stone house I remembered that I had meant to go home. But that didn't seem important any more, maybe because there were little blue flowers growing in the meadow behind the stone house and the gray squirrels were playing in the pines next to the house. The horses were standing in the corral, and there was a beef carcass hanging on the shady side of a big pine in front of the house. Flies buzzed around the clotted blood that hung from the carcass. Silva was washing his hands in a bucket full of water. He must have heard me coming because he spoke to me without turning to face me.

"I've been waiting for you."

"I went walking in the big pine trees."

I looked into the bucket full of bloody water with brown-and-white animal hairs floating in it. Silva stood there letting his hand drip, examining me intently.

"Are you coming with me?"

"Where?" I asked him.

"To sell the meat in Marquez."

"If you're sure it's O.K."

"I wouldn't ask you if it wasn't," he answered.

He sloshed the water around in the bucket before he dumped it out and set the bucket upside down near the door. I followed him to the corral and watched him saddle the horses. Even beside the horses he looked tall, and I asked him again if he wasn't Navajo. He didn't say anything; he just shook his head and kept cinching up the saddle.

"But Navajos are tall."

"Get on the horse," he said, "and let's go."

The last thing he did before we started down the steep trail was to grab the .30-30 from the corner. He slid the rifle into the scabbard that hung from his saddle.

"Do they ever try to catch you?" I asked.

"They don't know who I am."

"Then why did you bring the rifle?"

"Because we are going to Marquez where the Mexicans live."

The trail leveled out on a narrow ridge that was steep on both sides like an animal spine. On one side I could see where the trail went around the rocky gray hills and disappeared into the southeast where the pale sandrock mesas stood in the distance near my home. On the other side was a trail that went west, and as I looked far into the distance I thought I saw the little town. But

Silva said no, that I was looking in the wrong place, that I just thought I saw houses. After that I quit looking off into the distance; it was hot and the wild-flowers were closing up their deep-yellow petals. Only the waxy cactus flowers bloomed in the bright sun, and I saw every color that a cactus blossom can be; the white ones and the red ones were still buds, but the purple and the yellow were blossoms, open full and the most beautiful of all.

Silva saw him before I did. The white man was riding a big gray horse, coming up the trail towards us. He was traveling fast and the gray horse's feet sent rocks rolling off the trail into the dry tumbleweeds. Silva motioned for me to stop and we watched the white man. He didn't see us right away, but finally his horse whinnied at our horses and he stopped. He looked at us briefly before he lapped the gray horse across the three hundred yards that separated us. He stopped his horse in front of Silva, and his young fat face was shad-owed by the brim of his hat. He didn't look mad, but his small, pale eyes moved from the blood-soaked gunny sacks hanging from my saddle to Silva's face and then back to my face.

"Where did you get the fresh meat?" the white man asked.

"I've been hunting," Silva said, and when he shifted his weight in the saddle the leather creaked.

"The hell you have, Indian. You've been rustling cattle. We've been looking for the thief for a long time."

The rancher was fat, and sweat began to soak through his white cowboy shirt and the wet cloth stuck to the thick rolls of belly fat. He almost seemed to be panting from the exertion of talking, and he smelled rancid, maybe because Silva scared him.

Silva turned to me and smiled. "Go back up the mountain, Yellow Woman."

The white man got angry when he heard Silva speak in a language he couldn't understand. "Don't try anything, Indian. Just keep riding to Marquez. We'll call the state police from there."

The rancher must have been unarmed because he was very frightened and if he had a gun he would have pulled it out then. I turned my horse around and the rancher yelled, "Stop!" I looked at Silva for an instant and there was something ancient and dark—something I could feel in my stomach—in his eyes, and when I glanced at his hand I saw his finger on the trigger of the .30-30 that was still in the saddle scabbard. I slapped my horse across the flank and the sacks of raw meat swung against my knees as the horse leaped up the trail. It was hard to keep my balance, and once I thought I felt the saddle slip-ping backward; it was because of this that I could not look back.

I didn't stop until I reached the ridge where the trail forked. The horse was breathing deep gasps and there was a dark film of sweat on its neck. I looked down in the direction I had come from, but I couldn't see the place. I waited. The wind came up and pushed warm air past me. I looked up at the sky, pale blue and full of thin clouds and fading vapor trails left by jets.

I think four shots were fired—I remember hearing four hollow explosions that reminded me of deer hunting. There could have been more shots after that, but I couldn't have heard them because my horse was running again and the loose rocks were making too much noise as they scattered around his feet.

Horses have a hard time running downhill, but I went that way instead of uphill to the mountain because I thought it was safer. I felt better with the horse running southeast past the round gray hills that were covered with cedar trees and black lava rock. When I got to the plain in the distance I could see the dark green patches of tamaracks that grew along the river; and beyond the river I could see the beginning of the pale sandrock mesas. I stopped the horse and looked back to see if anyone was coming; then I got off the horse and turned the horse around, wondering if it would go back to its corral under the pines on the mountain. It looked back at me for a moment and then plucked a mouthful of green tumbleweeds before it trotted back up the trail with its ears pointed forward, carrying its head daintily to one side to avoid stepping on the dragging reins. When the horse disappeared over the last hill, the gunny sacks full of meat were still swinging and bouncing.

I walked toward the river on a wood-hauler's road that I knew would eventually lead to the paved road. I was thinking about waiting beside the road for someone to drive by, but by the time I got to the pavement I had decided it wasn't very far to walk if I followed the river back the way Silva and I had come.

The river water tasted good, and I sat in the shade under a cluster of silvery willows. I thought about Silva, and I felt sad at leaving him; still, there was something strange about him, and I tried to figure it out all the way back home.

I came back to the place on the river bank where he had been sitting the first time I saw him. The green willow leaves that he had trimmed from the branch were still lying there, wilted in the sand. I saw the leaves and I wanted to go back to him—to kiss him and to touch him—but the mountains were too far away now. And I told myself, because I believe it, he will come back sometime and be waiting again by the river.

I followed the path up from the river into the village. The sun was getting low, and I could smell supper cooking when I got to the screen door of my house. I could hear their voices inside—my mother was telling my grandmother how to fix the Jell-O and my husband, Al, was playing with the baby. I decided to tell them that some Navajo had kidnaped me, but I was sorry that old Grandpa wasn't alive to hear my story because it was the Yellow Woman stories he liked to tell best.

1974

WOLE SOYINKA

born 1934

A political activist as well as a playwright, Wole Soyinka portrays modern Africa in transition, capturing the transformations in life, sensibility, and thought that have taken place as Western modernity impinges on indigenous customs. But Soyinka shows, as well, the tensions within the Yoruba world, its own struggle for modernity. To move beyond a simple division between Western and Yoruba traditions, Soyinka draws on both Yoruba and Greek myths, weaving them into a poetic system. It is perhaps his reliance on this frame of reference that has allowed Soyinka to turn the violence of British colonialism into the material for compelling novels and plays, which combine satire and myth with a meditation on the most fundamental human and historical conflicts of the twentieth century.

Soyinka's sense of Africa as a divided culture owes much to his personal background. He was born on July 13, 1934, in Abeokuta, western Nigeria, the second child in a family that had ties to the traditional Yoruba ruling class as well as to the educated elite that arose from Christian missionary activity; his father was a Christian clergyman. Soyinka has written extensively about his childhood and the growth of the Yoruba intelligentsia, whose nationalist aspirations and modernizing zeal have been largely responsible for the making of present-day Nigeria.

Soyinka began his education at the parsonage school at Aké, where his father was headmaster. He later attended Government College, an elite English-style boarding school at Ibadan, some sixty miles north of his native city. After two years at the newly founded University College, Ibadan, Soyinka entered the University of Leeds, in England, to study English literature; he had a particular interest in **Shakespeare**. After graduating, Soyinka evaluated new plays for the Royal Court Theatre in London, an influential institution that produced innovative works by Samuel Beckett, John Osborne, and Arnold Wesker. Soyinka was also influenced by the verse drama of **T. S. Eliot** and the "theatre of ideas" of George Bernard Shaw and Bertolt Brecht. From these sources and his knowledge of Yoruba culture, the writer developed a type of performance that combines dialogue in verse and prose with mime and song, a version of the "total theater" that has intrigued modernist and postmodernist playwrights elsewhere in the West. Soyinka's first plays were performed at the University Arts Theatre at Ibadan, where he returned in 1960 (the year of Nigerian independence) with the intention of researching traditional West African drama. He later taught at the universities of Ife and Lagos.

In writing plays for his recently independent nation, Soyinka was motivated by his conception of the creative artist as one who must serve as a public agent of moral insight and renewal. He thus incorporated Yoruba folktales, performance styles, and even religious practices into his English-language dramas. Soyinka founded the Orisun Theatre, a semiprofessional company that he trained and directed in a wide range of plays. His own works were already appearing in print, helping to establish his reputation beyond Nigeria. His first novel, *The Interpreters* (1965), portrayed a group of young Nigerian intellectuals seeking to give purpose to their lives and to chart a moral course for their society.

During these turbulent postindependence years, Soyinka became involved in Nigerian politics. Arrested in 1965 for broadcasting a message critical of rigged elections and accused of storming a government radio station, Soyinka was acquitted at his trial for lack of evidence. Civil war broke out in Nigeria in 1967, and Soyinka was arrested again for his efforts at reconciliation with the rebel regime of Biafra; he was held without trial until October 1969. His prison experience gave urgency to his moral concerns. As he writes in *The Man Died* (1972), a moving account of his detention and a searing indictment of the military regime, "The man dies in all who keep silent in the face of tyranny." These years of crisis and war account for the somber mood that runs through Soyinka's subsequent plays. In 1971, the author went into exile, living mostly in England until it was safe to return home to Nigeria, where he continued his teaching and writing. Awarded the Nobel Prize for Literature in 1986, he devoted his acceptance speech to condemning apartheid, the system of racial segregation and minority rule in South Africa. During the 1990s he was sentenced to death in absentia under the government of dictator Sani Abacha; again he went into exile. Soyinka has remained a prominent critic of dictatorships in Nigeria and elsewhere in Africa; in the years following the terrorist attacks of September 11, 2001, he has spoken against both Islamic fundamentalism and racial profiling. Since his homeland's return to democracy, in 1999, Soyinka has divided his time between Nigeria and the United States, where he has held a number of professorships.

Death and the King's Horseman (1975) is based on an actual event: a British colonial officer's intervention to prevent the ritual suicide, following the death of the king of Oyo, of his "horseman," a minor chief whose privileges were conditional on his accompanying the king to the afterworld. The officer does not realize the dire consequences his intervention will have for the village and, most important, for the King's Horseman's son, who is also the officer's protégé. In depicting historical figures, Soyinka shifts the focus from the story's symbolic and ethnographic interest to the concrete response of human beings to death.

The opening scene offers a view of Yoruba society. The market setting, with its fusion of economic, social, and religious life, projects the people's belief system in festive tones. Elesin, the King's Horseman destined to die, prepares to accept his burden joyously. Although the opening scene seems to display the original coherence of the Yoruba world, it hints at its latent tensions. Essential for this effect is the presence of the oral tradition, for much of the language the characters exchange, especially that between Elesin and his praise singer, derives from familiar forms of oral poetry, proverbs, and lineage praise names (*oriki orile*) that situate the individual within a network of social relations and obligations.

The intensity of this scene contrasts with the deliberate flatness of the second, when the ignorance of the British colonial officers becomes the object of satire and, in fact, the British colonial system is depicted as offensive and violent. Pilkings, the colonial official, for example, wears traditional Yoruba dress, which is reserved for specific ritual uses, as costume for a masked ball. When he learns of the impending suicide of the King's Horseman and seeks to prevent it, the colonial and indigenous worlds collide. Yet Soyinka insists that the play should not be reduced to a simple conflict between two cultures. And indeed, the play spends considerable energy bridging this gulf: for instance, Soyinka shows that both cultures have a tradition of honorable suicide and that both have rituals involving masked dancing. Mediating figures such as Mrs. Pilkings and Olunde, the son of the King's Horseman, offer more nuanced perspectives on the central conflict, which nevertheless cannot yield to an easy solution. This impasse reflects the challenges of Soyinka's attempt to negotiate, in his work, the competing claims of Yoruba tradition and Western theater, as he seeks to help shape a Nigerian culture that would draw on native traditions without barricading them from the wider world.

The different forms of ceremony, ritual, and dance that make up this complex play are mirrored and reinforced by its unusual language and poetry. Certain Yoruba songs are rendered in poetic English. The idiom of the non-British characters is informed by the syntax, expressions, proverbs, and metaphors of Yoruba. The result is a multilayered English that draws on the Yoruba world, its flora, fauna, social structure, and cosmology, for comparison and insight. The play contrasts and intermingles languages, cultures, characters, and forms of theater and performance.

Such juxtaposing is perhaps the most important innovation of *Death and the King's Horseman*. The play certainly shows the violence that occurs at a moment of contact between British and Yoruba ways of life. By revealing the tensions within each society, however, Soyinka avoids blaming the conflicts arising under colonialism on each side's ignorance, and often intolerance, of the other. Yoruba culture, for Soyinka, is never simple, authentic, or monolithic. Rather, for Soyinka, it has itself undergone a process of modernization; it therefore is compatible with the international, cosmopolitan world represented by the son of the King's Horseman. At the same time, Soyinka points to the traditionalist, even ritualistic, aspects of British life. This way, both the Yoruba people and the British are divided between tradition and modernization— even if Soyinka never lets us forget that it was the British who sought to interrupt and dismiss Yoruba traditions, not the other way around.

Death and the King's Horseman is Soyinka's masterpiece. In it the verbal resourcefulness and mastery of theatrical effects evident in his earlier plays unite to produce a work whose evocative power ensures its appeal as both a model of connection to an indigenous tradition and an exploration of a universal human dilemma.

Death and the King's Horseman

Cast

PRAISE-SINGER	BRIDE
ELESIN, *Horseman of the King*	H.R.H. THE PRINCE
IYALOJA, *"Mother" of the market*	THE RESIDENT
SIMON PILKINGS, *District Officer*	AIDE-DE-CAMP
JANE PILKINGS, *his wife*	OLUNDE, *eldest son of Elesin*
SERJEANT AMUSA	DRUMMERS, WOMEN, YOUNG GIRLS,
JOSEPH, *houseboy to the Pilkingses*	DANCERS *at the Ball*

Scene One

A passage through a market in its closing stages. The stalls are being emptied, mats folded. A few WOMEN *pass through on their way home, loaded with baskets. On a cloth-stand, bolts of cloth are taken down, display pieces folded and piled on a tray.*

ELESIN *oba enters along a passage before the market, pursued by his* DRUMMERS *and* PRAISE-SINGERS. *He is a man of enormous vitality, speaks, dances and sings with that infectious enjoyment of life which accompanies all his actions.*

PRAISE-SINGER: Elesin o! Elesin Oba! Howu![1] What tryst is this the cockerel goes to keep with such haste that he must leave his tail behind?

ELESIN: [*Slows down a bit, laughing.*] A tryst where the cockerel needs no adornment.

PRAISE-SINGER: O-oh, you hear that my companions? That's the way the world goes. Because the man approaches a brand new bride he forgets the long faithful mother of his children.

ELESIN: When the horse sniffs the stable does he not strain at the bridle? The market is the long-suffering home of my spirit and the women are packing up to go. That Esu[2]-harrassed day slipped into the stewpot while we feasted. We ate it up with the rest of the meat. I have neglected my women.

PRAISE-SINGER: We know all that. Still it's no reason for shedding your tail on this day of all days. I know the women will cover you in damask and *alari*[3] but when the wind blows cold from behind, that's when the fowl knows his true friends.

ELESIN: Olohun-iyo![4]

PRAISE-SINGER: Are you sure there will be one like me on the other side?

ELESIN: Olohun-iyo!

PRAISE-SINGER: Far be it for me to belittle the dwellers of that place but, a man is either born to his art or he isn't. And I don't know for certain that you'll meet my father, so who is going to sing these deeds in accents that will pierce the deafness of the ancient ones. I have prepared my going—just tell me: Olohun-iyo, I need you on this journey and I shall be behind you.

ELESIN: You're like a jealous wife. Stay close to me, but only on this side. My fame, my honour are legacies to the living; stay behind and let the world sip its honey from your lips.

PRAISE-SINGER: Your name will be like the sweet berry a child places under his tongue to sweeten the passage of food. The world will never spit it out.

ELESIN: Come then. This market is my roost. When I come among the women I am a chicken with a hundred mothers. I become a monarch whose palace is built with tenderness and beauty.

PRAISE-SINGER: They love to spoil you but beware. The hands of women also weaken the unwary.

ELESIN: This night I'll lay my head upon their lap and go to sleep. This night I'll touch feet with their feet in a dance that is no longer of this earth. But the smell of their flesh, their sweat, the smell of indigo[5] on their cloth, this is the last air I wish to breathe as I go to meet my great forebears.

PRAISE-SINGER: In their time the world was never tilted from its groove, it shall not be in yours.

ELESIN: The gods have said No.

1. An exclamation of surprise.
2. The god of fate in the Yoruba pantheon: also a trickster figure.
3. A rich woven cloth, brightly coloured

[Author's note].
4. "Sweet voice": affectionate nickname for the praise-singer.
5. A deep blue dye.

PRAISE-SINGER: In their time the great wars came and went, the little wars came and went; the white slavers came and went, they took away the heart of our race, they bore away the mind and muscle of our race. The city fell and was rebuilt; the city fell and our people trudged through mountain and forest to find a new home but—Elesin Oba do you hear me?

ELESIN: I hear your voice Olohun-iyo.

PRAISE-SINGER: Our world was never wrenched from its true course.

ELESIN: The gods have said No.

PRAISE-SINGER: There is only one home to the life of a river-mussel; there is only one home to the life of a tortoise; there is only one shell to the soul of man; there is only one world to the spirit of our race. If that world leaves its course and smashes on boulders of the great void, whose world will give us shelter?

ELESIN: It did not in the time of my forebears, it shall not in mine.

PRAISE-SINGER: The cockerel must not be seen without his feathers.

ELESIN: Nor will the Not-I bird be much longer without his nest.

PRAISE-SINGER: [*Stopped in his lyric stride.*] The Not-I bird, Elesin?

ELESIN: I said, the Not-I bird.

PRAISE-SINGER: All respect to our elders but, is there really such a bird?

ELESIN: What! Could it be that he failed to knock on your door?

PRAISE-SINGER: [*Smiling.*] Elesin's riddles are not merely the nut in the kernel that breaks human teeth; he also buries the kernel in hot embers and dares a man's fingers to draw it out.

ELESIN: I am sure he called on you, Olohun-iyo. Did you hide in the loft and push out the servant to tell him you were out?

[ELESIN *executes a brief, half-taunting dance. The* DRUMMER *moves in and draws a rhythm out of his steps.* ELESIN *dances towards the market-place as he chants the story of the Not-I bird, his voice changing dexterously to mimic his characters. He performs like a born raconteur,[6] infecting his retinue with his humour and energy. More* WOMEN *arrive during his recital, including* IYALOJA.]

    Death came calling
    Who does not know his rasp of reeds?
    A twilight whisper in the leaves before
    The great araba[7] falls? Did you hear it?
    Not I! swears the farmer. He snaps
    His fingers round his head,[8] abandons
    A hard-worn harvest and begins
    A rapid dialogue with his legs.

    "Not I," shouts the fearless hunter, "but—
    It's getting dark, and this night-lamp
    Has leaked out all its oil. I think
    It's best to go home and resume my hunt
    Another day." But now he pauses, suddenly
    Lets out a wail: "Oh foolish mouth, calling
    Down a curse on your own head! Your lamp

---

6. A storyteller.   8. The gesture for warding off evil.
7. A tall and majestic tropical tree.

Has leaked out all its oil, has it?"
Forwards or backwards now he dare not move.
To search for leaves and make etutu[9]
On that spot? Or race home to the safety
Of his hearth? Ten market-days have passed
My friends, and still he's rooted there
Rigid as the plinth of Orayan[1]

The mouth of the courtesan barely
Opened wide enough to take a ha'penny *robo*[2]
When she wailed: "Not I." All dressed she was
To call upon my friend the Chief Tax Officer.
But now she sends her go between instead:
"Tell him I'm ill: my period[3] has come suddenly
But not—I hope—my time."

Why is the pupil crying?
His hapless head was made to taste
The knuckles of my friend the Mallam:[4]
"If you were then reciting the Koran
Would you have ears for idle noises
Darkening the trees, you child of ill omen?"
He shuts down school before its time
Runs home and rings himself with amulets.
And take my good kinsman Ifawomi.[5]
His hands were like a carver's, strong
And true. I saw them
Tremble like wet wings of a fowl.
One day he cast his time-smoothed opele[6]
Across the divination board. And all because
The suppliant looked him in the eye and asked,
"Did you hear that whisper in the leaves?"
"Not I," was his reply; "perhaps I'm growing deaf—
Good-day." And Ifa spoke no more that day
The priest locked fast his doors,
Sealed up his leaking roof—but wait!
This sudden care was not for Fawomi
But for Osenyin,[7] a courier-bird of Ifa's
Heart of wisdom. I did not know a kite
Was hovering in the sky
And Ifa now a twittering chicken in
The brood of Fawomi the Mother Hen.[8]

---

9. Rites of propitiation, often involving a sacrifice.
1. The mythical founder of Ife, the sacred city of the Yoruba people. "Plinth": a tall stone column planted into the earth at Ife, reputed to have been the staff of Orayan.
2. A delicacy made from crushed melon seeds, fried in tiny balls [author's note].
3. That is, she is menstruating.
4. A teacher in a koranic school.

5. A name (later shortened to Fawomi) that designates a devotee of Ifa, the god of divination, referred to further in the passage.
6. A string of beads used in Ifa divination [Author's note].
7. The tutelary deity of Yoruba traditional healers.
8. That is, reduced in status, humiliated. Even a god as powerful as Ifa can be cowed by death.

Ah, but I must not forget my evening
Courier from the abundant palm, whose groan
Became Not I, as he constipated down
A wayside bush. He wonders if Elegbara[9]
Has tricked his buttocks to discharge
Against a sacred grove. Hear him
Mutter spells to ward off penalties
For an abomination he did not intend.
If any here
Stumbles on a gourd of wine, fermenting
Near the road, and nearby hears a stream
Of spells issuing from a crouching form.
Brother to a *sigidi*,[1] bring home my wine,
Tell my tapper I have ejected
Fear from home and farm. Assure him,
All is well.

PRAISE-SINGER: In your time we do not doubt the peace of farmstead and
home, the peace of road and hearth, we do not doubt the peace of the forest.

ELESIN: There was fear in the forest too.
Not-I was lately heard even in the lair
Of beasts. The hyena cackled loud. Not I,
The civet twitched his fiery tail and glared:
Not I. Not-I became the answering name
Of the restless bird,[2] that little one
Whom Death found nesting in the leaves
When whisper of his coming ran
Before him on the wind. Not-I
Has long abandoned home. This same dawn
I heard him twitter in the gods' abode.
Ah, companions of this living world
What a thing this is, that even those
We call immortal
Should fear to die.

IYALOJA: But you, husband of multitudes?

ELESIN: I, when that Not-I bird perched
Upon my roof, bade him seek his nest again.
Safe, without care or fear. I unrolled
My welcome mat for him to see. Not-I
Flew happily away, you'll hear his voice
No more in this lifetime—You all know
What I am.

PRAISE-SINGER: That rock which turns its open lodes
Into the path of lightning. A gay
Thoroughbred whose stride disdains
To falter though an adder[3] reared
Suddenly in his path.

9. Another name for Esu.
1. A malevolent spirit.
2. Most likely the canary, which, when caged,

is constantly making short, rapid movements.
3. Or puff-adder, an extremely poisonous
snake.

ELESIN: My rein is loosened.
I am master of my Fate. When the hour comes
Watch me dance along the narrowing path
Glazed by the soles of my great precursors.
My soul is eager. I shall not turn aside.

WOMEN: You will not delay?

ELESIN: Where the storm pleases, and when, it directs
The giants of the forest. When friendship summons
Is when the true comrade goes.

WOMEN: Nothing will hold you back?

ELESIN: Nothing. What! Has no one told you yet
I go to keep my friend and master company.
Who says the mouth does not believe in
"No, I have chewed all that before?" I say I have.
The world is not a constant honey-pot.
Where I found little I made do with little.
Where there was plenty I gorged myself.
My master's hands and mine have always
Dipped together and, home or sacred feast,
The bowl was beaten bronze, the meats
So succulent our teeth accused us of neglect.
We shared the choicest of the season's
Harvest of yams. How my friend would read
Desire in my eyes before I knew the cause—
However rare, however precious, it was mine.

WOMEN: The town, the very land was yours.

ELESIN: The world was mine. Our joint hands
Raised housepots[4] of trust that withstood
The siege of envy and the termites of time.
But the twilight hour brings bats and rodents—
Shall I yield them cause to foul the rafters?

PRAISE-SINGER: Elesin Oba! Are you not that man who
Looked out of doors that stormy day
The god of luck[5] limped by, drenched
To the very lice that held
His rags together? You took pity upon
His sores and wished him fortune.
Fortune was footloose this dawn, he replied,
Till you trapped him in a heartfelt wish
That now returns to you. Elesin Oba!
I say you are that man who
Chanced upon the calabash of honour
You thought it was palm wine[6] and
Drained its contents to the final drop.

---

4. Used for storing the household's water.
5. Esu, who is represented as lame.
6. The sweet sap of the palm oil tree, which ferments naturally to become a potent drink. "Calabash": container made from the fruit of a vine.

ELESIN: Life has an end. A life that will outlive
Fame and friendship begs another name.
What elder takes his tongue to his plate,
Licks it clean of every crumb?[7] He will encounter
Silence when he calls on children to fulfill
The smallest errand! Life is honour.
It ends when honour ends.

WOMEN: We know you for a man of honour.

ELESIN: Stop! Enough of that!

WOMEN: [*Puzzled, they whisper among themselves, turning mostly to* IYALOJA.]
What is it? Did we say something to give offence? Have we slighted him in some way?

ELESIN: Enough of that sound I say. Let me hear no more in that vein. I've heard enough.

IYALOJA: We must have said something wrong. [*Comes forward a little.*] Elesin Oba, we ask forgiveness before you speak.

ELESIN: I am bitterly offended.

IYALOJA: Our unworthiness has betrayed us. All we can do is ask your forgiveness. Correct us like a kind father.

ELESIN: This day of all days . . .

IYALOJA: It does not bear thinking. If we offend you now we have mortified the gods. We offend heaven itself. Father of us all, tell us where we went astray. [*She kneels, the other* WOMEN *follow.*]

ELESIN: Are you not ashamed? Even a tear-veiled
Eye preserves its function of sight.
Because my mind was raised to horizons
Even the boldest man lowers his gaze
In thinking of, must my body here
Be taken for a vagrant's?

IYALOJA: Horseman of the King, I am more baffled than ever.

PRAISE-SINGER: The strictest father unbends his brow when the child is penitent, Elesin. When time is short, we do not spend it prolonging the riddle. Their shoulders are bowed with the weight of fear lest they have marred your day beyond repair. Speak now in plain words and let us pursue the ailment to the home of remedies.

ELESIN: Words are cheap. "We know you for
A man of honour." Well tell me, is this how
A man of honour should be seen?
Are these not the same clothes in which
I came among you a full half-hour ago?
[*He roars with laughter and the* WOMEN, *relieved, rise and rush into stalls to fetch rich clothes.*]

WOMEN: The gods are kind. A fault soon remedied is soon forgiven. Elesin Oba, even as we match our words with deed, let your heart forgive us completely.

ELESIN: You who are breath and giver of my being
How shall I dare refuse you forgiveness
Even if the offence was real.

---

7. Elders are expected to deny themselves for the young.

IYALOJA: [*Dancing round him. Sings.*]
               He forgives us. He forgives us.
               What a fearful thing it is when
               The voyager sets forth
               But a curse remains behind.

WOMEN: For a while we truly feared
               Our hands had wrenched the world adrift
               In emptiness.

IYALOJA: Richly, richly, robe him richly
               The cloth of honour is alari
               Sanyan[8] is the band of friendship
               Boa-skin makes slippers of esteem.

WOMEN: For a while we truly feared
               Our hands had wrenched the world adrift
               In emptiness.

PRAISE-SINGER: He who must, must voyage forth
               The world will not roll backwards
               It is he who must, with one
               Great gesture overtake the world.

WOMEN: For a while we truly feared
               Our hands had wrenched the world
               In emptiness.

PRAISE-SINGER: The gourd[9] you bear is not for shirking.
               The gourd is not for setting down
               At the first crossroad or wayside grove.
               Only one river may know its contents.

WOMEN: We shall all meet at the great market
               We shall all meet at the great market
               He who goes early takes the best bargains
               But we shall meet, and resume our banter.

               [ELESIN *stands resplendent in rich clothes, cap, shawl, etc. His sash is of a
               bright red alari cloth. The* WOMEN *dance round him. Suddenly, his atten-
               tion is caught by an object off-stage.*]

ELESIN: The world I know is good.

WOMEN: We know you'll leave it so.

ELESIN: The world I know is the bounty
               Of hives after bees have swarmed.
               No goodness teems with such open hands
               Even in the dreams of deities.

WOMEN: And we know you'll leave it so.

ELESIN: I was born to keep it so. A hive
               Is never known to wander. An anthill
               Does not desert its roots. We cannot see
               The still great womb of the world—
               No man beholds his mother's womb—
               Yet who denies it's there? Coiled

---

8. Richly decorated woven cloth.   9. Used for carrying water.

To the navel of the world is that
Endless cord that links us all
To the great origin. If I lose my way
The trailing cord will bring me to the roots.

WOMEN: The world is in your hands.

[*The earlier distraction, a beautiful young girl, comes along the passage
through which* ELESIN *first made his entry.*]

ELESIN: I embrace it. And let me tell you, women—
I like this farewell that the world designed,
Unless my eyes deceive me, unless
We are already parted, the world and I,
And all that breeds desire is lodged
Among our tireless ancestors. Tell me friends,
Am I still earthed in that beloved market
Of my youth? Or could it be my will
Has outleapt the conscious act and I have come
Among the great departed?

PRAISE-SINGER: Elesin Oba why do your eyes roll like a bush-rat who sees his
fate like his father's spirit, mirrored in the eye of a snake? And all those
questions! You're standing on the same earth you've always stood upon.
This voice you hear is mine, Oluhun-iyo, not that of an acolyte in heaven.

ELESIN: How can that be? In all my life
As Horseman of the King, the juiciest
Fruit on every tree was mine. I saw,
I touched, I wooed, rarely was the answer No.
The honour of my place, the veneration I
Received in the eye of man or woman
Prospered my suit and
Played havoc with my sleeping hours.
And they tell me my eyes were a hawk
In perpetual hunger. Split an iroko tree[1]
In two, hide a woman's beauty in its heartwood
And seal it up again—Elesin, journeying by,
Would make his camp beside that tree
Of all the shades in the forest.

PRAISE-SINGER: Who would deny your reputation, snake-on-the-loose in dark
passages of the market! Bed-bug who wages war on the mat and receives
the thanks of the vanquished! When caught with his bride's own sister he
protested—but I was only prostrating myself to her as becomes a grateful in-law.
Hunter who carries his powder-horn on the hips and fires crouching or standing! Warrior who never makes that excuse of the whining coward—but how can
I go to battle without my trousers?—trouserless or shirtless it's all one to him.
Oka[2]-rearing-from-a-camouflage-of-leaves, before he strikes the victim is
already prone! Once they told me, Howu, a stallion does not feed on the grass
beneath him; he replied, true, but surely he can roll on it!

---

1. A tropical hardwood tree: it is a large tree
with abundant foliage.

2. The python, a huge snake that swallows its
victims whole.

WOMEN: Ba-a-a-ba O!³

PRAISE-SINGER: Ah, but listen yet. You know there is the leaf-nibbling grub and there is the cola-chewing beetle; the leaf-nibbling grub lives on the leaf, the cola-chewing beetle lives in the colanut. Don't we know what our man feeds on when we find him cocooned in a woman's wrapper?

ELESIN: Enough, enough, you all have cause
      To know me well. But, if you say this earth
      Is still the same as gave birth to those songs,
      Tell me who was that goddess through whose lips
      I saw the ivory pebbles of Oya's⁴ river-bed.
      Iyaloja, who is she? I saw her enter
      Your stall; all your daughters I know well.
      No, not even Ogun⁵-of-the-farm toiling
      Dawn till dusk on his tuber patch
      Not even Ogun with the finest hoe he ever
      Forged at the anvil could have shaped
      That rise of buttocks, not though he had
      The richest earth between his fingers.
      Her wrapper was no disguise
      For thighs whose ripples shamed the river's
      Coils around the hills of Ilesi.⁶ Her eyes
      Were new-laid eggs glowing in the dark.
      Her skin . . .

IYALOJA: Elesin Oba . . .

ELESIN: What! Where do you all say I am?

IYALOJA: Still among the living.

ELESIN: And that radiance which so suddenly
      Lit up this market I could boast
      I knew so well?

IYALOJA: Has one step already in her husband's home. She is betrothed.

ELESIN: [*Irritated.*] Why do you tell me that?
      [IYALOJA *falls silent. The* WOMEN *shuffle uneasily.*]

IYALOJA: Not because we dare give you offence Elesin. Today is your day and the whole world is yours. Still, even those who leave town to make a new dwelling elsewhere like to be remembered by what they leave behind.

ELESIN: Who does not seek to be remembered?
      Memory is Master of Death, the chink
      In his armour of conceit. I shall leave
      That which makes my going the sheerest
      Dream of an afternoon. Should voyagers
      Not travel light? Let the considerate traveller
      Shed, of his excessive load, all
      That may benefit the living.

WOMEN: [*Relieved.*] Ah Elesin Oba, we knew you for a man of honour.

ELESIN: Then honour me. I deserve a bed of honour to lie upon.

3. A form of salute to an elder male.
4. A Yoruba goddess said to live in the River Niger.

5. The Yoruba god of iron and of war (equivalent in some ways to Mars).
6. A town.

IYALOJA: The best is yours. We know you for a man of honour. You are not one who eats and leaves nothing on his plate for children. Did you not say it yourself? Not one who blights the happiness of others for a moment's pleasure.

ELESIN: Who speaks of pleasure? O women, listen!
Pleasure palls. Our acts should have meaning.
The sap of the plantain[7] never dries.
You have seen the young shoot swelling
Even as the parent stalk begins to wither.
Women, let my going be likened to
The twilight hour of the plantain.

WOMEN: What does he mean Iyaloja? This language is the language of our elders, we do not fully grasp it.

IYALOJA: I dare not understand you yet Elesin.

ELESIN: All you who stand before the spirit that dares
The opening of the last door of passage,
Dare to rid my going of regrets! My wish
Transcends the blotting out of thought
In one mere moment's tremor of the senses.
Do me credit. And do me honour.
I am girded for the route beyond
Burdens of waste and longing.
Then let me travel light. Let
Seed that will not serve the stomach
On the way remain behind. Let it take root
In the earth of my choice, in this earth
I leave behind.

IYALOJA: [*Turns to* WOMEN.] The voice I hear is already touched by the waiting fingers of our departed. I dare not refuse.

WOMAN: But Iyaloja . . .

IYALOJA: The matter is no longer in our hands.

WOMAN: But she is betrothed to your own son. Tell him.

IYALOJA: My son's wish is mine. I did the asking for him, the loss can be remedied. But who will remedy the blight of closed hands on the day when all should be openness and light? Tell him, you say! You wish that I burden him with knowledge that will sour his wish and lay regrets on the last moments of his mind. You pray to him who is your intercessor to the world—don't set this world adrift in your own time; would you rather it was my hand whose sacrilege wrenched it loose?

WOMAN: Not many men will brave the curse of a dispossessed husband.

IYALOJA: Only the curses of the departed are to be feared. The claims of one whose foot is on the threshold of their abode surpasses even the claims of blood. It is impiety even to place hindrances in their ways.

ELESIN: What do my mothers[8] say? Shall I step
Burdened into the unknown?

---

7. A plant related to the banana. It constantly regenerates itself from its young shoots ("suckers").   8. Here, a term of affection.

IYALOJA: Not we, but the very earth says No. The sap in the plantain does not
dry. Let grain that will not feed the voyager at his passage drop here and
take root as he steps beyond this earth and us. Oh you who fill the home
from hearth to threshold with the voices of children, you who now bestride
the hidden gulf and pause to draw the right foot across and into the resting-
home of the great forebears, it is good that your loins be drained into the
earth we know, that your last strength be ploughed back into the womb that
gave you being.

PRAISE-SINGER: Iyaloja, mother of multitudes in the teeming market of the
world, how your wisdom transfigures you!

IYALOJA: [*Smiling broadly, completely reconciled.*] Elesin, even at the narrow
end of the passage I know you will look back and sigh a last regret for the
flesh that flashed past your spirit in flight. You always had a restless eye.
Your choice has my blessing. [*To the* WOMEN.] Take the good news to our
daughter and make her ready. [*Some* WOMEN *go off.*]

ELESIN: Your eyes were clouded at first.

IYALOJA: Not for long. It is those who stand at the gateway of the great
change to whose cry we must pay heed. And then, think of this—it makes
the mind tremble. The fruit of such a union is rare. It will be neither of this
world nor of the next. Nor of the one behind us. As if the timelessness of
the ancestor world and the unborn have joined spirits to wring an issue of
the elusive being of passage . . . Elesin!

ELESIN: I am here. What is it?

IYALOJA: Did you hear all I said just now?

ELESIN: Yes.

IYALOJA: The living must eat and drink. When the moment comes, don't turn
the food to rodents' droppings in their mouth. Don't let them taste the
ashes of the world when they step out at dawn to breathe the morning dew.

ELESIN: This doubt is unworthy of you Iyaloja.

IYALOJA: Eating the awusa nut is not so difficult as drinking water afterwards.[9]

ELESIN: The waters of the bitter stream are honey to a man
Whose tongue has savoured all.

IYALOJA: No one knows when the ants desert their home; they leave the
mound intact. The swallow is never seen to peck holes in its nest when it is
time to move with the season. There are always throngs of humanity behind
the leave-taker. The rain should not come through the roof for them, the
wind must not blow through the walls at night.

ELESIN: I refuse to take offence.

IYALOJA: You wish to travel light. Well, the earth is yours. But be sure the
seed you leave in it attracts no curse.

ELESIN: You really mistake my person Iyaloja.

IYALOJA: I said nothing. Now we must go prepare your bridal chamber. Then
these same hands will lay your shrouds.

ELESIN: [*Exasperated.*] Must you be so blunt? [*Recovers.*] Well, weave your
shrouds, but let the fingers of my bride seal my eyelids with earth and wash
my body.

---

9. The awasa nut eaten alone has a pleasant taste, but it turns bitter in the mouth if water is
drunk just after.

IYALOJA: Prepare yourself Elesin.

> [*She gets up to leave. At that moment the* WOMEN *return, leading the bride.* ELESIN's *face glows with pleasure. He flicks the sleeves of his agbada*[1] *with renewed confidence and steps forward to meet the group. As the girl kneels before* IYALOJA, *lights fade out on the scene.*]

Scene Two

The verandah of the District Officer's bungalow. A tango is playing from an old hand-cranked gramophone and, glimpsed through the wide windows and doors which open onto the forestage verandah, are the shapes of SIMON PILKINGS *and his wife,* JANE, *tangoing in and out of shadows in the living room. They are wearing what is immediately apparent as some form of fancy-dress. The dance goes on for some moments and then the figure of a "Native Administration" policeman emerges and climbs up the steps onto the verandah. He peeps through and observes the dancing couple, reacting with what is obviously a long-standing bewilderment. He stiffens suddenly, his expression changes to one of disbelief and horror. In his excitement he upsets a flower-pot and attracts the attention of the couple. They stop dancing.*

PILKINGS: Is there anyone out there?

JANE: I'll turn off the gramophone.

PILKINGS: [*Approaching the verandah.*] I'm sure I heard something fall over. [*The* CONSTABLE *retreats slowly, open-mouthed as* PILKINGS *approaches the verandah.*] Oh it's you Amusa. Why didn't you just knock instead of knocking things over?

AMUSA: [*Stammers badly and points a shaky finger at his dress.*] Mista Pirinkin . . . Mista Pirinkin . . .

PILKINGS: What is the matter with you?

JANE: [*Emerging.*] Who is it dear? Oh, Amusa . . .

PILKINGS: Yes it's Amusa, and acting most strangely.

AMUSA: [*His attention now transferred to* MRS. PILKINGS.] Mammadam[2] . . . you too!

PILKINGS: What the hell is the matter with you man!

JANE: Your costume darling. Our fancy dress.

PILKINGS: Oh hell, I'd forgotten all about that. [*Lifts the face mask over his head showing his face. His wife follows suit.*]

JANE: I think you've shocked his big pagan heart bless him.

PILKINGS: Nonsense, he's a Moslem. Come on Amusa, you don't believe in all that nonsense do you? I thought you were a good Moslem.

AMUSA: Mista Pirinkin, I beg you sir, what you think you do with that dress? It belong to dead cult, not for human being.

PILKINGS: Oh Amusa, what a let down you are. I swear by you at the club you know—thank God for Amusa, he doesn't believe in any mumbo-jumbo. And now look at you!

AMUSA: Mista Pirinkin, I beg you, take it off. Is not good for man like you to touch that cloth.

---

1. A long flowing robe. 2. A confused stammer of the word "madam."

PILKINGS: Well, I've got it on. And what's more Jane and I have bet on it we're taking first prize at the ball. Now, if you can just pull yourself together and tell me what you wanted to see me about . . .

AMUSA: Sir, I cannot talk this matter to you in that dress. I no fit.

PILKINGS: What's that rubbish again?

JANE: He is dead earnest too Simon. I think you'll have to handle this delicately.

PILKINGS: Delicately my . . . ! Look here Amusa, I think this little joke has gone far enough hm? Let's have some sense. You seem to forget that you are a police officer in the service of His Majesty's Government. I order you to report your business at once or face disciplinary action.

AMUSA: Sir, it is a matter of death. How can man talk against death to person in uniform of death? Is like talking against government to person in uniform of police. Please sir, I go and come back.

PILKINGS: [Roars.] Now! [AMUSA switches his gaze to the ceiling suddenly, remains mute.]

JANE: Oh Amusa, what is there to be scared of in the costume? You saw it confiscated last month from those egungun³ men who were creating trouble in town. You helped arrest the cult leaders yourself—if the juju⁴ didn't harm you at the time how could it possibly harm you now? And merely by looking at it?

AMUSA: [Without looking down.] Madam, I arrest the ringleaders who make trouble but me I no touch egungun. That egungun inself,⁵ I no touch. And I no abuse 'am. I arrest ringleader but I treat egungun with respect.

PILKINGS: It's hopeless. We'll merely end up missing the best part of the ball. When they get this way there is nothing you can do. It's simply hammering against a brick wall. Write your report or whatever it is on that pad Amusa and take yourself out of here. Come on Jane. We only upset his delicate sensibilities by remaining here.

[AMUSA waits for them to leave, then writes in the notebook, somewhat laboriously. Drumming from the direction of the town wells up. AMUSA listens, makes a movement as if he wants to recall pilkings but changes his mind. Completes his note and goes. A few moments later PILKINGS emerges, picks up the pad and reads.]

Jane!

JANE: [From the bedroom.] Coming darling. Nearly ready.

PILKINGS: Never mind being ready, just listen to this.

JANE: What is it?

PILKINGS: Amusa's report. Listen. "I have to report that it come to my information that one prominent chief, namely, the Elesin Oba, is to commit death tonight as a result of native custom. Because this is criminal offence I await further instruction at charge office. Sergeant Amusa."

[JANE comes out onto the verandah while he is reading.]

JANE: Did I hear you say commit death?

PILKINGS: Obviously he means murder.

JANE: You mean a ritual murder?

---

3. Ancestral masks.
4. Charms and the occult power they possess.

5. Itself (pidgin English).

PILKINGS: Must be. You think you've stamped it all out but it's always lurking under the surface somewhere.

JANE: Oh. Does it mean we are not getting to the ball at all?

PILKINGS: No-o. I'll have the man arrested. Everyone remotely involved. In any case there may be nothing to it. Just rumours.

JANE: Really? I thought you found Amusa's rumours generally reliable.

PILKINGS: That's true enough. But who knows what may have been giving him the scare lately. Look at his conduct tonight.

JANE: [*Laughing.*] You have to admit he had his own peculiar logic. [*Deepens her voice.*] How can man talk against death to person in uniform of death? [*Laughs.*] Anyway, you can't go into the police station dressed like that.

PILKINGS: I'll send Joseph with instructions. Damn it, what a confounded nuisance!

JANE: But don't you think you should talk first to the man, Simon?

PILKINGS: Do you want to go to the ball or not?

JANE: Darling, why are you getting rattled? I was only trying to be intelligent. It seems hardly fair just to lock up a man—and a chief at that—simply on the er . . . what is the legal word again? uncorroborated word of a sergeant.

PILKINGS: Well, that's easily decided. Joseph!

JOSEPH: [*From within.*] Yes master.

PILKINGS: You're quite right of course, I am getting rattled. Probably the effect of those bloody drums. Do you hear how they go on and on?

JANE: I wondered when you'd notice. Do you suppose it has something to do with this affair?

PILKINGS: Who knows? They always find an excuse for making a noise . . . [*Thoughtfully.*] Even so . . .

JANE: Yes Simon?

PILKINGS: It's different Jane. I don't think I've heard this particular— sound—before. Something unsettling about it.

JANE: I thought all bush drumming sounded the same.

PILKINGS: Don't tease me now Jane. This may be serious.

JANE: I'm sorry. [*Gets up and throws her arms around his neck. Kisses him. The houseboy enters, retreats and knocks.*]

PILKINGS: [*Wearily.*] Oh, come in Joseph! I don't know where you pick up all these elephantine notions of tact. Come over here.

JOSEPH: Sir?

PILKINGS: Joseph, are you a Christian or not?

JOSEPH: Yessir.

PILKINGS: Does seeing me in this outfit bother you?

JOSEPH: No sir, it has no power.

PILKINGS: Thank God for some sanity at last. Now Joseph, answer me on the honour of a Christian—what is supposed to be going on in town tonight?

JOSEPH: Tonight sir? You mean the chief who is going to kill himself?

PILKINGS: What?

JANE: What do you mean, kill himself?

PILKINGS: You do mean he is going to kill somebody don't you?

JOSEPH: No master. He will not kill anybody and no one will kill him. He will simply die.

JANE: But why Joseph?

JOSEPH: It is native law and custom. The King die last month. Tonight is his burial. But before they can bury him, the Elesin must die so as to accompany him to heaven.

PILKINGS: I seem to be fated to clash more often with that man than with any of the other chiefs.

JOSEPH: He is the King's Chief Horseman.

PILKINGS: [*In a resigned way.*] I know.

JANE: Simon, what's the matter?

PILKINGS: It would have to be him!

JANE: Who is he?

PILKINGS: Don't you remember? He's that chief with whom I had a scrap some three or four years ago. I helped his son get to a medical school in England, remember? He fought tooth and nail to prevent it.

JANE: Oh now I remember. He was that very sensitive young man. What was his name again?

PILKINGS: Olunde.[6] Haven't replied to his last letter come to think of it. The old pagan wanted him to stay and carry on some family tradition or the other. Honestly I couldn't understand the fuss he made. I literally had to help the boy escape from close confinement and load him onto the next boat. A most intelligent boy, really bright.

JANE: I rather thought he was much too sensitive you know. The kind of person you feel should be a poet munching rose petals in Bloomsbury.[7]

PILKINGS: Well, he's going to make a first-class doctor. His mind is set on that. And as long as he wants my help he is welcome to it.

JANE: [*After a pause.*] Simon.

PILKINGS: Yes?

JANE: This boy, he was the eldest son wasn't he?

PILKINGS: I'm not sure. Who could tell with that old ram?

JANE: Do you know, Joseph?

JOSEPH: Oh yes madam. He was the eldest son. That's why Elesin cursed master good and proper. The eldest son is not supposed to travel away from the land.

JANE: [*Giggling.*] Is that true Simon? Did he really curse you good and proper?

PILKINGS: By all accounts I should be dead by now.

JOSEPH: Oh no, master is white man. And good Christian. Black man juju can't touch master.

JANE: If he was his eldest, it means that he would be the Elesin to the next king. It's a family thing isn't it Joseph?

JOSEPH: Yes madam. And if this Elesin had died before the King, his eldest son must take his place.

JANE: That would explain why the old chief was so mad you took the boy away.

PILKINGS: Well it makes me all the more happy I did.

---

6. "My lord or deliverer has come"; a contraction of Olumide.
7. An area in central London associated with a brilliant group of writers in the years between the world wars; Virginia Woolf was the principal figure among them.

JANE: I wonder if he knew.

PILKINGS: Who? Oh, you mean Olunde?

JANE: Yes. Was that why he was so determined to get away? I wouldn't stay if I knew I was trapped in such a horrible custom.

PILKINGS: [*Thoughtfully.*] No, I don't think he knew. At least he gave no indication. But you couldn't really tell with him. He was rather close you know, quite unlike most of them. Didn't give much away, not even to me.

JANE: Aren't they all rather close, Simon?

PILKINGS: These natives here? Good gracious. They'll open their mouths and yap with you about their family secrets before you can stop them. Only the other day . . .

JANE: But Simon, do they really give anything away? I mean, anything that really counts. This affair for instance, we didn't know they still practised that custom did we?

PILKINGS: Ye-e-es, I suppose you're right there. Sly, devious bastards.

JOSEPH: [*Stiffly.*] Can I go now master? I have to clean the kitchen.

PILKINGS: What? Oh, you can go. Forgot you were still here.
[JOSEPH goes.]

JANE: Simon, you really must watch your language. Bastard isn't just a simple swear-word in these parts, you know.

PILKINGS: Look, just when did you become a social anthropologist, that's what I'd like to know.

JANE: I'm not claiming to know anything. I just happen to have overheard quarrels among the servants. That's how I know they consider it a smear.

PILKINGS: I thought the extended family system took care of all that. Elastic family, no bastards.

JANE: [*Shrugs.*] Have it your own way.
[*Awkward silence. The drumming increases in volume.* JANE *gets up suddenly, restless.*]
That drumming Simon, do you think it might really be connected with this ritual? It's been going on all evening.

PILKINGS: Let's ask our native guide. Joseph! Just a minute Joseph. [JOSEPH *re-enters.*] What's the drumming about?

JOSEPH: I don't know master.

PILKINGS: What do you mean you don't know? It's only two years since your conversion. Don't tell me all that holy water nonsense also wiped out your tribal memory.

JOSEPH: [*Visibly shocked.*] Master!

JANE: Now you've done it.

PILKINGS: What have I done now?

JANE: Never mind. Listen Joseph, just tell me this. Is that drumming connected with dying or anything of that nature?

JOSEPH: Madam, this is what I am trying to say: I am not sure. It sounds like the death of a great chief and then, it sounds like the wedding of a great chief. It really mix me up.

PILKINGS: Oh get back to the kitchen. A fat lot of help you are.

JOSEPH: Yes master. [*Goes.*]

JANE: Simon . . .

PILKINGS: All right, all right. I'm in no mood for preaching.

JANE: It isn't my preaching you have to worry about, it's the preaching of the missionaries who preceded you here. When they make converts they really convert them. Calling holy water nonsense to our Joseph is really like insulting the Virgin Mary before a Roman Catholic. He's going to hand in his notice tomorrow you mark my word.

PILKINGS: Now you're being ridiculous.

JANE: Am I? What are you willing to bet that tomorrow we are going to be without a steward-boy? Did you see his face?

PILKINGS: I am more concerned about whether or not we will be one native chief short by tomorrow. Christ! Just listen to those drums. [*He strides up and down, undecided.*]

JANE: [*Getting up.*] I'll change and make up some supper.

PILKINGS: What's that?

JANE: Simon, it's obvious we have to miss this ball.

PILKINGS: Nonsense. It's the first bit of real fun the European club has managed to organise for over a year, I'm damned if I'm going to miss it. And it is a rather special occasion. Doesn't happen every day.

JANE: You know this business has to be stopped Simon. And you are the only man who can do it.

PILKINGS: I don't have to stop anything. If they want to throw themselves off the top of a cliff or poison themselves for the sake of some barbaric custom what is that to me? If it were ritual murder or something like that I'd be duty-bound to do something. I can't keep an eye on all the potential suicides in this province. And as for that man—believe me it's good riddance.

JANE: [*Laughs.*] I know you better than that Simon. You are going to have to do something to stop it—after you've finished blustering.

PILKINGS: [*Shouts after her.*] And suppose after all it's only a wedding? I'd look a proper fool if I interrupted a chief on his honeymoon, wouldn't I? [*Resumes his angry stride, slows down.*] Ah well, who can tell what those chiefs actually do on their honeymoon anyway? [*He takes up the pad and scribbles rapidly on it.*] Joseph! Joseph! Joseph! [*Some moments later* JOSEPH *puts in a sulky appearance.*] Did you hear me call you? Why the hell didn't you answer?

JOSEPH: I didn't hear master.

PILKINGS: You didn't hear me! How come you are here then?

JOSEPH: [*Stubbornly.*] I didn't hear master.

PILKINGS: [*Controls himself with an effort.*] We'll talk about it in the morning. I want you to take this note directly to Sergeant Amusa. You'll find him at the charge office. Get on your bicycle and race there with it. I expect you back in twenty minutes exactly. Twenty minutes, is that clear?

JOSEPH: Yes master [*Going.*]

PILKINGS: Oh er . . . Joseph.

JOSEPH: Yes master?

PILKINGS: [*Between gritted teeth.*] Er . . . forget what I said just now. The holy water is not nonsense. *I* was talking nonsense.

JOSEPH: Yes master [*Goes.*]

JANE: [*Pokes her head round the door.*] Have you found him?

PILKINGS: Found who?

JANE: Joseph. Weren't you shouting for him?

PILKINGS: Oh yes, he turned up finally.

JANE: You sounded desperate. What was it all about?

PILKINGS: Oh nothing. I just wanted to apologise to him. Assure him that the holy water isn't really nonsense.

JANE: Oh? And how did he take it?

PILKINGS: Who the hell gives a damn! I had a sudden vision of our Very Reverend Macfarlane[8] drafting another letter of complaint to the Resident about my unchristian language towards his parishioners.

JANE: Oh I think he's given up on you by now.

PILKINGS: Don't be too sure. And anyway, I wanted to make sure Joseph didn't "lose" my note on the way. He looked sufficiently full of the holy crusade to do some such thing.

JANE: If you've finished exaggerating, come and have something to eat.

PILKINGS: No, put it all away. We can still get to the ball.

JANE: Simon . . .

PILKINGS: Get your costume back on. Nothing to worry about. I've instructed Amusa to arrest the man and lock him up.

JANE: But that station is hardly secure Simon. He'll soon get his friends to help him escape.

PILKINGS: A-ah, that's where I have out-thought you. I'm not having him put in the station cell. Amusa will bring him right here and lock him up in my study. And he'll stay with him till we get back. No one will dare come here to incite him to anything.

JANE: How clever of you darling. I'll get ready.

PILKINGS: Hey.

JANE: Yes darling.

PILKINGS: I have a surprise for you. I was going to keep it until we actually got to the ball.

JANE: What is it?

PILKINGS: You know the Prince is on a tour of the colonies don't you? Well, he docked in the capital only this morning but he is already at the Residency. He is going to grace the ball with his presence later tonight.

JANE: Simon! Not really.

PILKINGS: Yes he is. He's been invited to give away the prizes and he has agreed. You must admit old Engleton is the best Club Secretary we ever had. Quick off the mark that lad.

JANE: But how thrilling.

PILKINGS: The other provincials are going to be damned envious.

JANE: I wonder what he'll come as.

PILKINGS: Oh I don't know. As a coat-of-arms perhaps. Anyway it won't be anything to touch this.

JANE: Well that's lucky. If we are to be presented I won't have to start looking for a pair of gloves. It's all sewn on.[9]

---

8. Irish priests were predominant in Catholic missionary activity in Nigeria.

9. The masquerade costume is designed to cover the entire body of the wearer, to conceal his or her identity.

PILKINGS: [*Laughing.*] Quite right. Trust a woman to think of that. Come on, let's get going.

JANE: [*Rushing off.*] Won't be a second. [*Stops.*] Now I see why you've been so edgy all evening. I thought you weren't handling this affair with your usual brilliance—to begin with, that is.

PILKINGS: [*His mood is much improved.*] Shut up woman and get your things on.

JANE: All right boss, coming.

[PILKINGS *suddenly begins to hum the tango to which they were dancing before. Starts to execute a few practice steps. Lights fade.*]

Scene Three

A swelling, agitated hum of WOMEN's *voices rises immediately in the background. The lights come on and we see the frontage of a converted cloth stall in the market. The floor leading up to the entrance is covered in rich velvets and woven cloth. The* WOMEN *come on stage, borne backwards by the determined progress of* SERJEANT, AMUSA *and his two constables who already have their batons out and use them as a pressure against the* WOMEN. *At the edge of the cloth-covered floor however the* WOMEN *take a determined stand and block all further progress of the men. They begin to tease them mercilessly.*

AMUSA: I am tell you women for last time to commot my road.[1] I am here on official business.

WOMAN: Official business you white man's eunuch? Official business is taking place where you want to go and it's a business you wouldn't understand.

WOMAN: [*Makes a quick tug at the constable's baton.*] That doesn't fool anyone you know. It's the one you carry under your government knickers that counts. [*She bends low as if to peep under the baggy shorts. The embarrassed constable quickly puts his knees together. The* WOMEN *roar.*]

WOMAN: You mean there is nothing there at all?

WOMAN: Oh there was something. You know that handbell which the whiteman uses to summon his servants . . . ?

AMUSA: [*He manages to preserve some dignity throughout.*] I hope you women know that interfering with officer in execution of his duty is criminal offence.

WOMAN: Interfere? He says we're interfering with him. You foolish man we're telling you there's nothing to interfere with.

AMUSA: I am order you now to clear the road.

WOMAN: What road? The one your father built?

WOMAN: You are a policeman not so? Then you know what they call trespassing in court. Or—[*pointing to the cloth-lined steps*]—do you think that kind of road is built for every kind of feet.

WOMAN: Go back and tell the white man who sent you to come himself.

AMUSA: If I go I will come back with reinforcement. And we will all return carrying weapons.

1. Get out of my way.

WOMAN: Oh, now I understand. Before they can put on those knickers the white man first cuts off their weapons.

WOMAN: What a cheek! You mean you come here to show power to women and you don't even have a weapon.

AMUSA: [*Shouting above the laughter.*] For the last time I warn you women to clear the road.

WOMAN: To where?

AMUSA: To that hut. I know he dey dere.

WOMAN: Who?

AMUSA: The chief who call himself Elesin Oba.

WOMAN: You ignorant man. It is not he who calls himself Elesin Oba, it is his blood that says it. As it called out to his father before him and will to his son after him. And that is in spite of everything your white man can do.

WOMAN: Is it not the same ocean that washes this land and the white man's land? Tell your white man he can hide our son away as long as he likes. When the time comes for him, the same ocean will bring him back.

AMUSA: The government say dat kin' ting[2] must stop.

WOMAN: Who will stop it? You? Tonight our husband and father will prove himself greater than the laws of strangers.

AMUSA: I tell you nobody go prove anything tonight or anytime. Is ignorant and criminal to prove dat kin' prove.

IYALOJA: [*Entering from the hut. She is accompanied by a group of young girls who have been attending the* BRIDE.] What is it Amusa? Why do you come here to disturb the happiness of others.

AMUSA: Madame Iyaloja, I glad you come. You know me, I no like trouble but duty is duty. I am here to arrest Elesin for criminal intent. Tell these women to stop obstructing me in the performance of my duty.

IYALOJA: And you? What gives you the right to obstruct our leader of men in the performance of his duty.

AMUSA: What kin' duty be dat one Iyaloja.

IYALOJA: What kin' duty? What kin' duty does a man have to his new bride?

AMUSA: [*Bewildered, looks at the women and at the entrance to the hut.*] Iyaloja, is it wedding you call dis kin' ting?

IYALOJA: You have wives haven't you? Whatever the white man has done to you he hasn't stopped you having wives. And if he has, at least he is married. If you don't know what a marriage is, go and ask him to tell you.

AMUSA: This no to wedding.[3]

IYALOJA: And ask him at the same time what he would have done if anyone had come to disturb him on his wedding night.

AMUSA: Iyaloja, I say dis no to wedding.

IYALOJA: You want to look inside the bridal chamber? You want to see for yourself how a man cuts the virgin knot?

AMUSA: Madam . . .

WOMAN: Perhaps his wives are still waiting for him to learn.

AMUSA: Iyaloja, make you tell dese women make den no insult me again. If I hear dat kin' insult once more . . .

---

2. That kind of thing.   3. This is not a wedding.

GIRL: [*Pushing her way through.*] You will do what?

GIRL: He's out of his mind. It's our mothers you're talking to, do you know that? Not to any illiterate villager you can bully and terrorise. How dare you intrude here anyway?

GIRL: What a cheek, what impertinence!

GIRL: You've treated them too gently. Now let them see what it is to tamper with the mothers of this market.

GIRL: Your betters dare not enter the market when the women say no!

GIRL: Haven't you learnt that yet, you jester in khaki and starch?

IYALOJA: Daughters . . .

GIRL: No no Iyaloja, leave us to deal with him. He no longer knows his mother, we'll teach him.

[*With a sudden movement they snatch the batons of the two constables. They begin to hem them in.*]

GIRL: What next? We have your batons? What next? What are you going to do?

[*With equally swift movements they knock off their hats.*]

GIRL: Move if you dare. We have your hats, what will you do about it? Didn't the white man teach you to take off your hats before women?

IYALOJA: It's a wedding night. It's a night of joy for us. Peace . . .

GIRL: Not for him. Who asked him here?

GIRL: Does he dare go to the Residency without an invitation?

GIRL: Not even where the servants eat the left-overs.

GIRLS: [*In turn. In an "English" accent.*] Well well it's Mister Amusa. Were you invited? [*Play acting to one another. The older* WOMEN *encourage them with their titters.*]

—Your invitation card please?

—Who are you? Have we been introduced?

—And who did you say you were?

—Sorry, I didn't quite catch your name.

—May I take your hat?

—If you insist. May I take yours? [*Exchanging the* POLICEMEN's *hats.*]

—How very kind of you.

—Not at all. Won't you sit down?

—After you.

—Oh no.

—I insist.

—You're most gracious.

—And how do you find the place?

—The natives are all right.

—Friendly?

—Tractable.

—Not a teeny-weeny bit restless?

—Well, a teeny-weeny bit restless.

—One might, even say, difficult?

—Indeed one might be tempted to say, difficult.

—But you do manage to cope?

—Yes indeed I do. I have a rather faithful ox called Amusa.

—He's loyal?

—Absolutely.
—Lay down his life for you what?
—Without a moment's thought.
—Had one like that once. Trust him with my life.
—Mostly of course they are liars.
—Never known a native to tell the truth.
—Does it get rather close around here?
—It's mild for this time of the year.
—But the rains may still come.
—They are late this year aren't they?
—They are keeping African time.[4]
—Ha ha ha ha
—Ha ha ha ha
—The humidity is what gets me.
—It used to be whisky
—Ha ha ha ha
—Ha ha ha ha
—What's your handicap old chap?
—Is there racing by golly?
—Splendid golf course, you'll like it.
—I'm beginning to like it already.
—And a European club, exclusive.
—You've kept the flag flying.
—We do our best for the old country.
—It's a pleasure to serve.
—Another whisky old chap?
—You are indeed too too kind.
—Not at all sir. Where is that boy? [*With a sudden bellow.*] Sergeant!

AMUSA: [*Snaps to attention.*] Yessir!
　　　　　[*The women collapse with laughter.*]
GIRL:　Take your men out of here.
AMUSA: [*Realising the trick, he rages from loss of face.*] I'm give you warning . . .
GIRL:　All right then. Off with his knickers! [*They surge slowly forward.*]
IYALOJA:　Daughters, please.
AMUSA: [*Squaring himself for defence.*] The first woman wey touch me . . .
IYALOJA:　My children, I beg of you . . .
GIRL:　Then tell him to leave this market. This is the home of our mothers.
　　We don't want the eater of white left-overs at the feast their hands have
　　prepared.
IYALOJA:　You heard them Amusa. You had better go.
GIRL:　Now!
AMUSA: [*Commencing his retreat.*] We dey go now, but make you no say we
　　no warn you.[5]
GIRLS:　Now!

---

4. A standard colonial prejudice was that Africans lack a sense of time.

5. Don't say that we didn't warn you.

GIRL: Before we read the riot act—you should know all about that.

AMUSA: Make we go. [*They depart, more precipitately.*]

[*The* WOMEN *strike their palms across in the gesture of wonder.*]

WOMEN: Do they teach you all that at school?

WOMAN: And to think I nearly kept Apinke[6] away from the place.

WOMAN: Did you hear them? Did you see how they mimicked the white man?

WOMAN: The voices exactly. Hey, there are wonders in this world!

IYALOJA: Well, our elders have said it: Dada[7] may be weak, but he has a younger sibling who is truly fearless.

WOMAN: The next time the white man shows his face in this market I will set Wuraola[8] on his tail.

[*A* WOMAN *bursts into song and dance of euphoria—"Tani l'awa o l'ogbeja? Kayi! A l'ogbeja. Omo Kekere l'ogbeja."*[9] *The rest of the* WOMEN *join in, some placing the girls on their back like infants, others dancing round them. The dance becomes general, mounting in excitement.* ELESIN *appears, in wrapper only. In his hands a white velvet cloth folded loosely as if it held some delicate object. He cries out.*]

ELESIN: Oh you mothers of beautiful brides! [*The dancing stops. They turn and see him, and the object in his hands.* IYALOJA *approaches and gently takes the cloth from him.*] Take it. It is no mere virgin stain, but the union of life and the seeds of passage. My vital flow, the last from this flesh is intermingled with the promise of future life. All is prepared. Listen! [*A steady drum beat from the distance.*] Yes. It is nearly time. The King's dog has been killed. The King's favourite horse is about to follow his master. My brother chiefs know their task and perform it well. [*He listens again.*]

[*The* BRIDE *emerges, stands shyly by the door. He turns to her.*]

Our marriage is not yet wholly fulfilled. When earth and passage wed, the consummation is complete only when there are grains of earth on the eyelids of passage. Stay by me till then. My faithful drummers, do me your last service. This is where I have chosen to do my leave-taking, in this heart of life, this hive which contains the swarm of the world in its small compass. This is where I have known love and laughter away from the palace. Even the richest food cloys when eaten days on end; in the market, nothing ever cloys. Listen. [*They listen to the drums.*] They have begun to seek out the heart of the King's favourite horse. Soon it will ride in its bolt of raffia[1] with the dog at its feet. Together they will ride on the shoulders of the King's grooms through the pulse centres of the town. They know it is here I shall await them. I have told them. [*His eyes appear to cloud. He passes his hand over them as if to clear his sight. He gives a faint smile.*] It promises well; just then I felt my spirit's eagerness. The kite makes for wide spaces and the wind creeps up behind its tail; can the kite say less than—thank you, the quicker the better? But wait a while my spirit. Wait. Wait for the coming of

---

6. "One Who Is Equally Cherished by All"; the name of one of the girls.
7. A child born with tangled hair.
8. "Dear as Gold"; a woman's name.
9. Who says we haven't a defender? Silence!

We have our defenders. Little children are our champions [Author's translation].
1. The stem of this shrub is used for the decorative skirt worn in many African dances.

the courier of the King. Do you know friends, the horse is born to this one destiny, to bear the burden that is man upon its back. Except for this night, this night alone when the spotless stallion will ride in triumph on the back of man. In the time of my father I witnessed the strange sight. Perhaps tonight also I shall see it for the last time. If they arrive before the drums beat for me, I shall tell him to let the Alafin[2] know I follow swiftly. If they come after the drums have sounded, why then, all is well for I have gone ahead. Our spirits shall fall in step along the great passage. [*He listens to the drums. He seems again to be falling into a state of semi-hypnosis; his eyes scan the sky but it is in a kind of daze. His voice is a little breathless.*] The moon has fed, a glow from its full stomach fills the sky and air, but I cannot tell where is that gateway through which I must pass. My faithful friends, let our feet touch together this last time, lead me into the other market with sounds that cover my skin with down yet make my limbs strike earth like a thoroughbred. Dear mothers, let me dance into the passage even as I have lived beneath your roofs. [*He comes down progressively among them. They make way for him, the* DRUMMERS *playing. His dance is one of solemn, regal motions, each gesture of the body is made with a solemn finality. The* WOMEN *join him, their steps a somewhat more fluid version of his. Beneath the* PRAISE-SINGER's *exhortations the* WOMEN *dirge "Ale le le, awo mi lo."*]

PRAISE-SINGER: Elesin Alafin, can you hear my voice?

ELESIN: Faintly, my friend, faintly.

PRAISE-SINGER: Elesin Alafin, can you hear my call?

ELESIN: Faintly my king, faintly.

PRAISE-SINGER: Is your memory sound Elesin?
        Shall my voice be a blade of grass and
        Tickle the armpit of the past?

ELESIN: My memory needs no prodding but
        What do you wish to say to me?

PRAISE-SINGER: Only what has been spoken. Only what concerns
        The dying wish of the father of all.

ELESIN: It is buried like seed-yam in my mind
        This is the season of quick rains, the harvest
        Is this moment due for gathering.

PRAISE-SINGER: If you cannot come, I said, swear
        You'll tell my favourite horse. I shall
        Ride on through the gates alone.

ELESIN: Elesin's message will be read
        Only when his loyal heart no longer beats.

PRAISE-SINGER: If you cannot come Elesin, tell my dog.
        I cannot stay the keeper too long
        At the gate.

ELESIN: A dog does not outrun the hand
        That feeds it meat. A horse that throws its rider
        Slows down to a stop. Elesin Alafin
        Trusts no beasts with messages between
        A king and his companion.

---

2. "Owner of the Palace" (literal trans.); the title of the king of Oyo.

PRAISE-SINGER: If you get lost my dog will track
    The hidden path to me.
ELESIN: The seven-way crossroads confuses
    Only the stranger. The Horseman of the King
    Was born in the recesses of the house.
PRAISE-SINGER: I know the wickedness of men. If there is
    Weight on the loose end of your sash, such weight
    As no mere man can shift; if your sash is earthed
    By evil minds who mean to part us at the last . . .
ELESIN: My sash is of the deep purple *alari*;
    It is no tethering-rope. The elephant
    Trails no tethering-rope; that king
    Is not yet crowned who will peg an elephant—
    Not even you my friend and King
PRAISE-SINGER: And yet this fear will not depart from me
    The darkness of this new abode is deep—
    Will your human eyes suffice?
ELESIN: In a night which falls before our eyes
    However deep, we do not miss our way.
PRAISE-SINGER: Shall I now not acknowledge I have stood
    Where wonders met their end? The elephant deserves
    Better than that we say "I have caught
    A glimpse of something."[3] If we see the tamer
    Of the forest let us say plainly, we have seen
    An elephant.
ELESIN: [*His voice is drowsy.*]
    I have freed myself of earth and now
    It's getting dark. Strange voices guide my feet.
PRAISE-SINGER: The river is never so high that the eyes
    Of a fish are covered. The night is not so dark
    That the albino fails to find his way.[4] A child
    Returning homewards craves no leading by the hand.
    Gracefully does the mask[5] regain his grove at the end of the
        day . . .
    Gracefully. Gracefully does the mask dance
    Homeward at the end of the day, gracefully . . .
    [ELESIN's *trance appears to be deepening, his steps heavier.*]
IYALOJA: It is the death of war that kills the valiant,
    Death of water is how the swimmer goes
    It is the death of markets that kills the trader
    And death of indecision takes the idle away
    The trade of the cutlass blunts its edge
    And the beautiful die the death of beauty.
    It takes an Elesin to die the death of death . . .
    Only Elesin . . . dies the unknowable death of death . . .

---

3. A Yoruba saying, meaning that an outstanding person or deed must be granted proper recognition.

4. Many albinos have poor eyesight.
5. Of the *egungun* masquerade.

> Gracefully, gracefully does the horseman regain
> The stables at the end of day, gracefully . . .

PRAISE-SINGER: How shall I tell what my eyes have seen? The Horseman gallops on before the courier, how shall I tell what my eyes have seen? He says a dog may be confused by new scents of beings he never dreamt of, so he must precede the dog to heaven. He says a horse may stumble on strange boulders and be lamed, so he races on before the horse to heaven. It is best, he says, to trust no messenger who may falter at the outer gate, oh how shall I tell what my ears have heard? But do you hear me still Elesin, do you hear your faithful one?

> [ELESIN *in his motions appears to feel for a direction of sound, subtly, but he only sinks deeper into his trance dance.*]

Elesin Alafin, I no longer sense your flesh. The drums are changing now but you have gone far ahead of the world. It is not yet noon in heaven; let those who claim it is begin their own journey home. So why must you rush like an impatient bride: why do you race to desert your Olohun-iyo?

> [ELESIN *is now sunk fully deep in his trance, there is no longer sign of any awareness of his surroundings.*]

Does the deep voice of *gbedu*[6] cover you then, like the passage of royal elephants? Those drums that brook no rivals, have they blocked the passage to your ears that my voice passes into wind, a mere leaf floating in the night? Is your flesh lightened Elesin, is that lump of earth I slid between your slippers to keep you longer slowly sifting from your feet? Are the drums on the other side now tuning skin to skin with ours in *osugbo*?[7] Are there sounds there I cannot hear, do footsteps surround you which pound the earth like *gbedu*, roll like thunder round the dome of the world? Is the darkness gathering in your head Elesin? Is there now a streak of light at the end of the passage, a light I dare not look upon? Does it reveal whose voices we often heard, whose touches we often felt, whose wisdoms come suddenly into the mind when the wisest have shaken their heads and murmured: It cannot be done? Elesin Alafin, don't think I do not know why your lips are heavy, why your limbs are drowsy as palm oil in the cold of harmattan.[8] I would call you back but when the elephant heads for the jungle, the tail is too small a handhold for the hunter that would pull him back. The sun that heads for the sea no longer heeds the prayers of the farmer. When the river begins to taste the salt of the ocean, we no longer know what deity to call on, the river-god or Olokun.[9] No arrow flies back to the string, the child does not return through the same passage that gave it birth. Elesin Oba, can you hear me at all? Your eyelids are glazed like a courtesan's, is it that you see the dark groom and master of life? And will you see my father? Will you tell him that I stayed with you to the last? Will my voice ring in your ears awhile, will you remember Olohun-iyo even if the music on the other side surpasses his mortal craft? But will they know you over there? Have they eyes to gauge

---

6. Drums. Their deep resonance is caused by the hardwood from which they are made.
7. The secret executive cult of the Yoruba; its meeting place [Author's note].
8. A sharp, dry wind from the Sahara that blows over western Africa in December. The wind brings dust and noticeably cools the air. Palm oil congeals in cold weather and is thus said to sleep. Compare the American "slow as molasses in January."
9. Goddess of the sea.

your worth, have they the heart to love you, will they know what thorough-bred prances towards them in caparisons[1] of honour? If they do not Elesin, if any there cuts your yam with a small knife, or pours you wine in a small calabash, turn back and return to welcoming hands. If the world were not greater than the wishes of Olohun-iyo, I would not let you go . . .

> [*He appears to break down.* ELESIN *dances on, completely in a trance. The dirge wells up louder and stronger.* ELESIN'*s dance does not lose its elasticity but his gestures become, if possible, even more weighty. Lights fade slowly on the scene.*]

Scene Four

A Masque. The front side of the stage is part of a wide corridor around the great hall of the Residency extending beyond vision into the rear and wings. It is redolent of the tawdry decadence of a far-flung but key imperial frontier. The couples in a variety of fancy-dress are ranged around the walls, gazing in the same direction. The guest-of-honour is about to make an appearance. A portion of the local police brass band with its white conductor is just visible. At last, the entrance of royalty. The band plays "Rule Britannia," badly, beginning long before he is visible. The couples bow and curtsey as he passes by them. Both he and his companions are dressed in seventeenth-century European costume. Following behind are the RESIDENT *and his partner similarly attired. As they gain the end of the hall where the orchestra dais begins the music comes to an end. The* PRINCE *bows to the guests. The band strikes up a Viennese waltz and the* PRINCE *formally opens the floor. Several bars later the* RESIDENT *and his companion follow suit. Others follow in appropriate pecking order. The orchestra's waltz rendition is not of the highest musical standard.*

Some time later the PRINCE *dances again into view and is settled into a corner by the* RESIDENT *who then proceeds to select couples as they dance past for introduction, sometimes threading his way through the dancers to tap the lucky couple on the shoulder. Desperate efforts from many to ensure that they are recognised in spite of perhaps, their costume. The ritual of introductions soon takes in* PILKINGS *and his wife. The* PRINCE *is quite fascinated by their costume and they demonstrate the adaptations they have made to it, pulling down the mask to demonstrate how the egungun normally appears, then showing the various press-button controls they have innovated for the face flaps, the sleeves, etc. They demonstrate the dance steps and the guttural sounds made by the egungun, harass other dancers in the hall,* MRS. PILKINGS *playing the "restrainer"[2] to* PILKINGS' *manic darts. Everyone is highly entertained, the Royal Party especially who lead the applause.*

At this point a liveried footman comes in with a note on a salver and is intercepted almost absent-mindedly by the RESIDENT *who takes the note and reads it. After polite coughs he succeeds in excusing the* PILKINGS *from the* PRINCE *and takes them aside. The* PRINCE *considerately offers the* RESIDENT'*s wife his hand and dancing is resumed.*

On their way out the RESIDENT *gives an order to his* AIDE-DE-CAMP. *They come into the side corridor where the* RESIDENT *hands the note to* PILKINGS.

---

1. Rich ceremonial cloth draped over the saddle of a horse.
2. Masqueraders sometimes become possessed and go berserk; ropes are, therefore, tied to their waists and held by "restrainers."

RESIDENT: As you see it says "emergency" on the outside. I took the liberty of opening it because His Highness was obviously enjoying the entertainment. I didn't want to interrupt unless really necessary.

PILKINGS: Yes, yes of course, sir.

RESIDENT: Is it really as bad as it says? What's it all about?

PILKINGS: Some strange custom they have, sir. It seems because the King is dead some important chief has to commit suicide.

RESIDENT: The King? Isn't it the same one who died nearly a month ago?

PILKINGS: Yes, sir.

RESIDENT: Haven't they buried him yet?

PILKINGS: They take their time about these things, sir. The pre-burial ceremonies last nearly thirty days. It seems tonight is the final night.

RESIDENT: But what has it got to do with the market women? Why are they rioting? We've waived that troublesome tax haven't we?

PILKINGS: We don't quite know that they are exactly rioting yet, sir. Sergeant Amusa is sometimes prone to exaggerations.

RESIDENT: He sounds desperate enough. That comes out even in his rather quaint grammar. Where is the man anyway? I asked my aide-de-camp to bring him here.

PILKINGS: They are probably looking in the wrong verandah. I'll fetch him myself.

RESIDENT: No no you stay here. Let your wife go and look for them. Do you mind my dear . . . ?

JANE: Certainly not, your Excellency. [Goes.]

RESIDENT: You should have kept me informed, Pilkings. You realise how disastrous it would have been if things had erupted while His Highness was here.

PILKINGS: I wasn't aware of the whole business until tonight, sir.

RESIDENT: Nose to the ground Pilkings, nose to the ground. If we all let these little things slip past us where would the empire be eh? Tell me that. Where would we all be?

PILKINGS: [Low voice.] Sleeping peacefully at home I bet.

RESIDENT: What did you say, Pilkings?

PILKINGS: It won't happen again, sir.

RESIDENT: It mustn't, Pilkings. It mustn't. Where is that damned sergeant? I ought to get back to His Highness as quickly as possible and offer him some plausible explanation for my rather abrupt conduct. Can you think of one, Pilkings?

PILKINGS: You could tell him the truth, sir.

RESIDENT: I could? No no no no Pilkings, that would never do. What! Go and tell him there is a riot just two miles away from him? This is supposed to be a secure colony of His Majesty, Pilkings.

PILKINGS: Yes, sir.

RESIDENT: Ah, there they are. No, these are not our native police. Are these the ring-leaders of the riot?

PILKINGS: Sir, these are my police officers.

RESIDENT: Oh, I beg your pardon officers. You do look a little . . . I say, isn't there something missing in their uniform? I think they used to have some rather colourful sashes. If I remember rightly I recommended them myself in my young days in the service. A bit of colour always appeals to the natives, yes, I remember putting that in my report. Well well well, where are we? Make your report man.

PILKINGS: [*Moves close to* AMUSA, *between his teeth.*] And let's have no more superstitious nonsense from you Amusa or I'll throw you in the guardroom for a month and feed you pork![3]

RESIDENT: What's that? What has pork to do with it?

PILKINGS: Sir, I was just warning him to be brief. I'm sure you are most anxious to hear his report.

RESIDENT: Yes yes yes of course. Come on man, speak up. Hey, didn't we give them some colourful fez[4] hats with all those wavy things, yes, pink tassells . . .

PILKINGS: Sir, I think if he was permitted to make his report we might find that he lost his hat in the riot.

RESIDENT: Ah yes indeed. I'd better tell His Highness that. Lost his hat in the riot, ha ha. He'll probably say well, as long as he didn't lose his head. [*Chuckles to himself.*] Don't forget to send me a report first thing in the morning young Pilkings.

PILKINGS: No, sir.

RESIDENT: And whatever you do, don't let things get out of hand. Keep a cool head and—nose to the ground Pilkings. [*Wanders off in the general direction of the hall.*]

PILKINGS: Yes, sir.

AIDE-DE-CAMP: Would you be needing me, sir?

PILKINGS: No thanks, Bob. I think His Excellency's need of you is greater than ours.

AIDE-DE-CAMP: We have a detachment of soldiers from the capital, sir. They accompanied His Highness up here.

PILKINGS: I doubt if it will come to that but, thanks, I'll bear it in mind. Oh, could you send an orderly with my cloak.

AIDE-DE-CAMP: Very good, sir. [*Goes.*]

PILKINGS: Now, sergeant.

AMUSA: Sir . . . [*Makes an effort, stops dead. Eyes to the ceiling.*]

PILKINGS: Oh, not again.

AMUSA: I cannot against death to dead cult. This dress get power of dead.

PILKINGS: All right, let's go. You are relieved of all further duty Amusa. Report to me first thing in the morning.

JANE: Shall I come, Simon?

PILKINGS: No, there's no need for that. If I can get back later I will. Otherwise get Bob to bring you home.

JANE: Be careful Simon . . . I mean, be clever.

PILKINGS: Sure I will. You two, come with me. [*As he turns to go, the clock in the Residency begins to chime.* PILKINGS *looks at his watch then turns, horror-stricken, to stare at his wife. The same thought clearly occurs to her. He swallows hard. An orderly brings his cloak.*] It's midnight. I had no idea it was that late.

---

3. Muslims are prohibited from eating pork.
4. Red caps worn by African officials in the colonial service.

JANE: But surely . . . they don't count the hours the way we do. The moon, or something . . .

PILKINGS: I am . . . not so sure.

[*He turns and breaks into a sudden run. The two constables follow, also at a run.* AMUSA, *who has kept his eyes on the ceiling throughout waits until the last of the footsteps has faded out of hearing. He salutes suddenly, but without once looking in the direction of the* WOMAN.]

AMUSA: Goodnight, madam.

JANE: Oh. [*She hesitates.*] Amusa . . . [*He goes off without seeming to have heard.*] Poor Simon . . . [*A figure emerges from the shadows, a young black man dressed in a sober western suit. He peeps into the hall, trying to make out the figures of the dancers.*]

Who is that?

OLUNDE: [*Emerges into the light.*] I didn't mean to startle you madam. I am looking for the District Officer.

JANE: Wait a minute . . . don't I know you? Yes, you are Olunde, the young man who . . .

OLUNDE: Mrs. Pilkings! How fortunate. I came here to look for your husband.

JANE: Olunde! Let's look at you. What a fine young man you've become. Grand but solemn. Good God, when did you return? Simon never said a word. But you do look well Olunde. Really!

OLUNDE: You are . . . well, you look quite well yourself Mrs. Pilkings. From what little I can see of you.

JANE: Oh, this. It's caused quite a stir I assure you, and not all of it very pleasant. You are not shocked I hope?

OLUNDE: Why should I be? But don't you find it rather hot in there? Your skin must find it difficult to breathe.

JANE: Well, it is a little hot I must confess, but it's all in a good cause.

OLUNDE: What cause Mrs. Pilkings?

JANE: All this. The ball. And His Highness being here in person and all that.

OLUNDE: [*Mildly.*] And that is the good cause for which you desecrate an ancestral mask?

JANE: Oh, so you are shocked after all. How disappointing.

OLUNDE: No I am not shocked, Mrs. Pilkings. You forget that I have now spent four years among your people. I discovered that you have no respect for what you do not understand.

JANE: Oh. So you've returned with a chip on your shoulder. That's a pity Olunde. I am sorry.

[*An uncomfortable silence follows.*]

I take it then that you did not find your stay in England altogether edifying.

OLUNDE: I don't say that. I found your people quite admirable in many ways, their conduct and courage in this war[5] for instance.

JANE: Ah yes, the war. Here of course it is all rather remote. From time to time we have a black-out drill just to remind us that there is a war on. And the rare convoy passes through on its way somewhere or on manoeuvres.

---

5. That is, World War II.

Mind you there is the occasional bit of excitement like that ship that was blown up in the harbour.[6]

OLUNDE: Here? Do you mean through enemy action?

JANE: Oh no, the war hasn't come that close. The captain did it himself. I don't quite understand it really. Simon tried to explain. The ship had to be blown up because it had become dangerous to the other ships, even to the city itself. Hundreds of the coastal population would have died.

OLUNDE: Maybe it was loaded with ammunition and had caught fire. Or some of those lethal gases they've been experimenting on.

JANE: Something like that. The captain blew himself up with it. Deliberately. Simon said someone had to remain on board to light the fuse.

OLUNDE: It must have been a very short fuse.

JANE: [Shrugs.] I don't know much about it. Only that there was no other way to save lives. No time to devise anything else. The captain took the decision and carried it out.

OLUNDE: Yes . . . I quite believe it. I met men like that in England.

JANE: Oh just look at me! Fancy welcoming you back with such morbid news. Stale too. It was at least six months ago.

OLUNDE: I don't find it morbid at all. I find it rather inspiring. It is an affirmative commentary on life.

JANE: What is?

OLUNDE: That captain's self-sacrifice.

JANE: Nonsense. Life should never be thrown deliberately away.

OLUNDE: And the innocent people around the harbour?

JANE: Oh, how does one know? The whole thing was probably exaggerated anyway.

OLUNDE: That was a risk the captain couldn't take. But please Mrs. Pilkings, do you think you could find your husband for me? I have to talk to him.

JANE: Simon? [As she recollects for the first time the full significance of OLUNDE's presence.] Simon is . . . there is a little problem in town. He was sent for. But . . . when did you arrive? Does Simon know you're here?

OLUNDE: [Suddenly earnest.] I need your help Mrs. Pilkings. I've always found you somewhat more understanding than your husband. Please find him for me and when you do, you must help me talk to him.

JANE: I'm afraid I don't quite . . . follow you. Have you seen my husband already?

OLUNDE: I went to your house. Your houseboy told me you were here. [He smiles.] He even told me how I would recognise you and Mr. Pilkings.

JANE: Then you must know what my husband is trying to do for you.

OLUNDE: For me?

JANE: For you. For your people. And to think he didn't even know you were coming back! But how do you happen to be here? Only this evening we were talking about you. We thought you were still four thousand miles away.

OLUNDE: I was sent a cable.

---

6. A reference to an incident that occurred in Lagos, the capital of Nigeria, in 1944.

JANE: A cable? Who did? Simon? The business of your father didn't begin till tonight.

OLUNDE: A relation sent it weeks ago, and it said nothing about my father. All it said was, Our King is dead. But I knew I had to return home at once so as to bury my father. I understood that.

JANE: Well, thank God you don't have to go through that agony. Simon is going to stop it.

OLUNDE: That's why I want to see him. He's wasting his time. And since he has been so helpful to me I don't want him to incur the enmity of our people. Especially over nothing.

JANE: [Sits down open-mouthed.] You . . . you Olunde!

OLUNDE: Mrs. Pilkings, I came home to bury my father. As soon as I heard the news I booked my passage home. In fact we were fortunate. We travelled in the same convoy as your Prince, so we had excellent protection.

JANE: But you don't think your father is also entitled to whatever protection is available to him?

OLUNDE: How can I make you understand? He *has* protection. No one can undertake what he does tonight without the deepest protection the mind can conceive. What can you offer him in place of his peace of mind, in place of the honour and veneration of his own people? What would you think of your Prince if he refused to accept the risk of losing his life on this voyage? This . . . showing the flag tour of colonial possessions.

JANE: I see. So it isn't just medicine you studied in England.

OLUNDE: Yet another error into which your people fall. You believe that everything which appears to make sense was learnt from you.

JANE: Not so fast Olunde. You have learnt to argue I can tell that, but I never said you made sense. However clearly you try to put it, it is still a barbaric custom. It is even worse—it's feudal! The king dies and a chieftan must be buried with him. How feudalistic can you get!

OLUNDE: [Waves his hand towards the background. The PRINCE is dancing past again—to a different step—and all the guests are bowing and curtseying as he passes.] And this? Even in the midst of a devastating war, look at that. What name would you give to that?

JANE: Therapy, British style. The preservation of sanity in the midst of chaos.

OLUNDE: Others would call it decadence. However, it doesn't really interest me. You white races know how to survive; I've seen proof of that. By all logical and natural laws this war should end with all the white races wiping out one another, wiping out their so-called civilisation for all time and reverting to a state of primitivism the like of which has so far only existed in your imagination when you thought of us. I thought all that at the beginning. Then I slowly realised that your greatest art is the art of survival. But at least have the humility to let others survive in their own way.

JANE: Through ritual suicide?

OLUNDE: Is that worse than mass suicide? Mrs. Pilkings, what do you call what those young men are sent to do by their generals in this war? Of course you have also mastered the art of calling things by names which don't remotely describe them.

JANE: You talk! You people with your long-winded, roundabout way of making conversation.

OLUNDE: Mrs. Pilkings, whatever we do, we never suggest that a thing is the opposite of what it really is. In your newsreels I heard defeats, thorough, murderous defeats described as strategic victories. No wait, it wasn't just on your newsreels. Don't forget I was attached to hospitals all the time. Hordes of your wounded passed through those wards. I spoke to them. I spent long evenings by their bedsides while they spoke terrible truths of the realities of that war. I know now how history is made.

JANE: But surely, in a war of this nature, for the morale of the nation you must expect . . .

OLUNDE: That a disaster beyond human reckoning be spoken of as a triumph? No, I mean, is there no mourning in the home of the bereaved that such blasphemy is permitted?

JANE: [After a moment's pause.] Perhaps I can understand you now. The time we picked for you was not really one for seeing us at our best.

OLUNDE: Don't think it was just the war. Before that even started I had plenty of time to study your people. I saw nothing, finally, that gave you the right to pass judgement on other peoples and their ways. Nothing at all.

JANE: [Hesitantly.] Was it the . . . colour thing? I know there is some discrimination.

OLUNDE: Don't make it so simple, Mrs. Pilkings. You make it sound as if when I left, I took nothing at all with me.

JANE: Yes . . . and to tell the truth, only this evening, Simon and I agreed that we never really knew what you left with.

OLUNDE: Neither did I. But I found out over there. I am grateful to your country for that. And I will never give it up.

JANE: Olunde, please . . . promise me something. Whatever you do, don't throw away what you have started to do. You want to be a doctor. My husband and I believe you will make an excellent one, sympathetic and competent. Don't let anything make you throw away your training.

OLUNDE: [Genuinely surprised.] Of course not. What a strange idea. I intend to return and complete my training. Once the burial of my father is over.

JANE: Oh, please . . . !

OLUNDE: Listen! Come outside. You can't hear anything against that music.

JANE: What is it?

OLUNDE: The drums. Can you hear the drums? Listen.

[The drums come over, still distant but more distinct. There is a change of rhythm, it rises to a crescendo and then, suddenly, it is cut off. After a silence, a new beat begins, slow and resonant.]

There it's all over.

JANE: You mean he's . . .

OLUNDE: Yes, Mrs. Pilkings, my father is dead. His will power has always been enormous; I know he is dead.

JANE: [Screams.] How can you be so callous! So unfeeling! You announce your father's own death like a surgeon looking down on some strange . . . stranger's body! You're just a savage like all the rest.

AIDE-DE-CAMP: [Rushing out.] Mrs. Pilkings. Mrs. Pilkings. [She breaks down, sobbing.] Are you all right, Mrs. Pilkings?

OLUNDE: She'll be all right. [Turns to go.]

AIDE-DE-CAMP: Who are you? And who the hell asked your opinion?

OLUNDE: You're quite right, nobody. [*Going.*]

AIDE-DE-CAMP: What the hell! Did you hear me ask you who you were?

OLUNDE: I have business to attend to.

AIDE-DE-CAMP: I'll give you business in a moment you impudent nigger. Answer my question!

OLUNDE: I have a funeral to arrange. Excuse me. [*Going.*]

AIDE-DE-CAMP: I said stop! Orderly!

JANE: No, no, don't do that. I'm all right. And for heaven's sake don't act so foolishly. He's a family friend.

AIDE-DE-CAMP: Well he'd better learn to answer civil questions when he's asked them. These natives put a suit on and they get high opinions of themselves.

OLUNDE: Can I go now?

JANE: No no don't go. I must talk to you. I'm sorry about what I said.

OLUNDE: It's nothing, Mrs. Pilkings. And I'm really anxious to go. I couldn't see my father before, it's forbidden for me, his heir and successor to set eyes on him from the moment of the king's death. But now . . . I would like to touch his body while it is still warm.

JANE: You will. I promise I shan't keep you long. Only, I couldn't possibly let you go like that. Bob, please excuse us.

AIDE-DE-CAMP: If you're sure . . .

JANE: Of course I'm sure. Something happened to upset me just then, but I'm all right now. Really.

[*The* AIDE DE CAMP *goes, somewhat reluctantly.*]

OLUNDE: I mustn't stay long.

JANE: Please, I promise not to keep you. It's just that . . . oh you saw yourself what happens to one in this place. The Resident's man thought he was being helpful, that's the way we all react. But I can't go in among that crowd just now and if I stay by myself somebody will come looking for me. Please, just say something for a few moments and then you can go. Just so I can recover myself.

OLUNDE: What do you want me to say?

JANE: Your calm acceptance for instance, can you explain that? It was so unnatural. I don't understand that at all. I feel a need to understand all I can.

OLUNDE: But you explained it yourself. My medical training perhaps. I have seen death too often. And the soldiers who returned from the front, they died on our hands all the time.

JANE: No. It has to be more than that. I feel it has to do with the many things we don't really grasp about your people. At least you can explain.

OLUNDE: All these things are part of it. And anyway, my father has been dead in my mind for nearly a month. Ever since I learnt of the King's death. I've lived with my bereavement so long now that I cannot think of him alive. On that journey on the boat, I kept my mind on my duties as the one who must perform the rites over his body. I went through it all again and again in my mind as he himself had taught me. I didn't want to do anything wrong, something which might jeopardise the welfare of my people.

JANE: But he had disowned you. When you left he swore publicly you were no longer his son.

OLUNDE: I told you, he was a man of tremendous will. Sometimes that's another way of saying stubborn. But among our people, you don't disown a child just like that. Even if I had died before him I would still be buried like his eldest son. But it's time for me to go.

JANE: Thank you. I feel calmer. Don't let me keep you from your duties.

OLUNDE: Goodnight, Mrs. Pilkings.

JANE: Welcome home.

[*She holds out her hand. As he takes it footsteps are heard approaching the drive. A short while later a woman's sobbing is also heard.*]

PILKINGS: [*Off.*] Keep them here till I get back. [*He strides into view, reacts at the sight of* OLUNDE *but turns to his wife.*] Thank goodness you're still here.

JANE: Simon, what happened?

PILKINGS: Later Jane, please. Is Bob still here?

JANE: Yes, I think so. I'm sure he must be.

PILKINGS: Try and get him out here as quickly as you can. Tell him it's urgent.

JANE: Of course. Oh Simon, you remember . . .

PILKINGS: Yes yes. I can see who it is. Get Bob out here. [*She runs off.*] At first I thought I was seeing a ghost.

OLUNDE: Mr. Pilkings, I appreciate what you tried to do. I want you to believe that. I can tell you it would have been a terrible calamity if you'd succeeded.

PILKINGS: [*Opens his mouth several times, shuts it.*] You . . . said what?

OLUNDE: A calamity for us, the entire people.

PILKINGS: [*Sighs.*] I see. Hm.

OLUNDE: And now I must go. I must see him before he turns cold.

PILKINGS: Oh ah . . . em . . . but this is a shock to see you. I mean er thinking all this while you were in England and thanking God for that.

OLUNDE: I came on the mail boat. We travelled in the Prince's convoy.

PILKINGS: Ah yes, a ah, hm . . . er well . . .

OLUNDE: Goodnight. I can see you are shocked by the whole business. But you must know by now there are things you cannot understand—or help.

PILKINGS: Yes. Just a minute. There are armed policemen that way and they have instructions to let no one pass. I suggest you wait a little. I'll er . . . give you an escort.

OLUNDE: That's very kind of you. But do you think it could be quickly arranged.

PILKINGS: Of course. In fact, yes, what I'll do is send Bob over with some men to the er . . . place. You can go with them. Here he comes now. Excuse me a minute.

AIDE-DE-CAMP: Anything wrong sir?

PILKINGS: [*Takes him to one side.*] Listen Bob, that cellar in the disused annex of the Residency, you know, where the slaves were stored before being taken down to the coast . . .

AIDE-DE-CAMP: Oh yes, we use it as a storeroom for broken furniture.

PILKINGS: But it's still got the bars on it?

AIDE-DE-CAMP: Oh yes, they are quite intact.

PILKINGS: Get the keys please. I'll explain later. And I want a strong guard over the Residency tonight.

AIDE-DE-CAMP: We have that already. The detachment from the coast . . .

PILKINGS: No, I don't want them at the gates of the Residency. I want you to deploy them at the bottom of the hill, a long way from the main hall so they can deal with any situation long before the sound carries to the house.

AIDE-DE-CAMP: Yes of course.

PILKINGS: I don't want His Highness alarmed.

AIDE-DE-CAMP: You think the riot will spread here?

PILKINGS: It's unlikely but I don't want to take a chance. I made them believe I was going to lock the man up in my house, which was what I had planned to do in the first place. They are probably assailing it by now. I took a roundabout route here so I don't think there is any danger at all. At least not before dawn. Nobody is to leave the premises of course—the native employees I mean. They'll soon smell something is up and they can't keep their mouths shut.

AIDE-DE-CAMP: I'll give instructions at once.

PILKINGS: I'll take the prisoner down myself. Two policemen will stay with him throughout the night. Inside the cell.

AIDE-DE-CAMP: Right sir. [*Salutes and goes off at the double.*]

PILKINGS: Jane. Bob is coming back in a moment with a detachment. Until he gets back please stay with Olunde. [*He makes an extra warning gesture with his eyes.*]

OLUNDE: Please, Mr. Pilkings . . .

PILKINGS: I hate to be stuffy old son, but we have a crisis on our hands. It has to do with your father's affair if you must know. And it happens also at a time when we have His Highness here. I am responsible for security so you'll simply have to do as I say. I hope that's understood.
[*Marches off quickly, in the direction from which he made his first appearance.*]

OLUNDE: What's going on? All this can't be just because he failed to stop my father killing himself.

JANE: I honestly don't know. Could it have sparked off a riot?

OLUNDE: No. If he'd succeeded that would be more likely to start the riot. Perhaps there were other factors involved. Was there a chieftancy dispute?

JANE: None that I know of.

ELESIN: [*An animal bellow from off.*] Leave me alone! Is it not enough that you have covered me in shame! White man, take your hand from my body!
[OLUNDE *stands frozen to the spot.* JANE *understanding at last, tries to move him.*]

JANE: Let's go in. It's getting chilly out here.

PILKINGS: [*Off.*] Carry him.

ELESIN: Give me back the name you have taken away from me you ghost from the land of the nameless!

PILKINGS: Carry him! I can't have a disturbance here. Quickly! stuff up his mouth.

JANE: Oh God! Let's go in. Please Olunde.
[OLUNDE *does not move.*]

ELESIN: Take your albino's hand from me you . . .
[*Sounds of a struggle. His voice chokes as he is gagged.*]

OLUNDE: [*Quietly.*] That was my father's voice.

JANE: Oh you poor orphan, what have you come home to?

[*There is a sudden explosion of rage from off-stage and powerful steps come running up the drive.*]

PILKINGS: You bloody fools, after him!

[*Immediately* ELESIN, *in handcuffs, comes pounding in the direction of* JANE *and* OLUNDE, *followed some moments afterwards by* PILKINGS *and the constables.* ELESIN, *confronted by the seeming statue of his son, stops dead.* OLUNDE *stares above his head into the distance. The constables try to grab him.* JANE *screams at them.*]

JANE: Leave him alone! Simon, tell them to leave him alone.

PILKINGS: All right, stand aside you. [*Shrugs.*] Maybe just as well. It might help to calm him down.

[*For several moments they hold the same position.* ELESIN *moves a step forward, almost as if he's still in doubt.*]

ELESIN: Olunde? [*He moves his head, inspecting him from side to side.*] Olunde! [*He collapses slowly at* OLUNDE's *feet.*] Oh son, don't let the sight of your father turn you blind!

OLUNDE: [*He moves for the first time since he heard his voice, brings his head slowly down to look on him.*] I have no father, eater of left-overs.

[*He walks slowly down the way his father had run. Light fades out on elesin, sobbing into the ground.*]

Scene Five

A wide iron barred gate stretches almost the whole width of the cell in which ELESIN *is imprisoned. His wrists are encased in thick iron bracelets, chained together; he stands against the bars, looking out. Seated on the ground to one side on the outside is his recent* BRIDE, *her eyes bent perpetually to the ground. Figures of the two guards can be seen deeper inside the cell, alert to every movement* ELESIN *makes.* PILKINGS *now in a police officer's uniform enters noiselessly, observes him a while. Then he coughs ostentatiously and approaches. Leans against the bars near a corner, his back to* ELE-SIN. *He is obviously trying to fall in mood with him. Some moments' silence.*

PILKINGS: You seem fascinated by the moon.

ELESIN: [*After a pause.*] Yes, ghostly one. Your twin-brother up there engages my thoughts.

PILKINGS: It is a beautiful night.

ELESIN: Is that so?

PILKINGS: The light on the leaves, the peace of the night . . .

ELESIN: The night is not at peace, District Officer.

PILKINGS: No? I would have said it was. You know, quiet . . .

ELESIN: And does quiet mean peace for you?

PILKINGS: Well, nearly the same thing. Naturally there is a subtle difference . . .

ELESIN: The night is not at peace, ghostly one. The world is not at peace. You have shattered the peace of the world for ever. There is no sleep in the world tonight.

PILKINGS: It is still a good bargain if the world should lose one night's sleep as the price of saving a man's life.

ELESIN: You did not save my life, District Officer. You destroyed it.

PILKINGS: Now come on . . .

ELESIN: And not merely my life but the lives of many. The end of the night's work is not over. Neither this year nor the next will see it. If I wished you well, I would pray that you do not stay long enough on our land to see the disaster you have brought upon us.

PILKINGS: Well, I did my duty as I saw it. I have no regrets.

ELESIN: No. The Regrets of life always come later.

[*Some moments' pause.*]

You are waiting for dawn, white man. I hear you saying to yourself: only so many hours until dawn and then the danger is over. All I must do is to keep him alive tonight. You don't quite understand it all but you know that tonight is when what ought to be must be brought about. I shall ease your mind even more, ghostly one. It is not an entire night but a moment of the night, and that moment is past. The moon was my messenger and guide. When it reached a certain gateway in the sky, it touched that moment for which my whole life has been spent in blessings. Even I do not know the gateway. I have stood here and scanned the sky for a glimpse of that door but, I cannot see it. Human eyes are useless for a search of this nature. But in the house of *osugbo*, those who keep watch through the spirit recognised the moment, they sent word to me through the voice of our sacred drums to prepare myself. I heard them and I shed all thoughts of earth. I began to follow the moon to the abode of the gods . . . servant of the white king, that was when you entered my chosen place of departure on feet of desecration.

PILKINGS: I'm sorry, but we all see our duty differently.

ELESIN: I no longer blame you. You stole from me my first-born, sent him to your country so you could turn him into something in your own image. Did you plan it all beforehand? There are moments when it seems part of a larger plan. He who must follow my footsteps is taken from me, sent across the ocean. Then, in my turn, I am stopped from fulfilling my destiny. Did you think it all out before, this plan to push our world from its course and sever the cord that links us to the great origin?

PILKINGS: You don't really believe that. Anyway, if that was my intention with your son, I appear to have failed.

ELESIN: You did not fail in the main, ghostly one. We know the roof covers the rafters, the cloth covers blemishes; who would have known that the white skin covered our future, preventing us from seeing the death our enemies had prepared for us. The world is set adrift and its inhabitants are lost. Around them, there is nothing but emptiness.

PILKINGS: Your son does not take so gloomy a view.

ELESIN: Are you dreaming now, white man? Were you not present at my reunion of shame? Did you not see when the world reversed itself and the father fell before his son, asking forgiveness?

PILKINGS: That was in the heat of the moment. I spoke to him and . . . if you want to know, he wishes he could cut out his tongue for uttering the words he did.

ELESIN: No. What he said must never be unsaid. The contempt of my own son rescued something of my shame at your hands. You have stopped me in my duty but I know now that I did give birth to a son. Once I mistrusted him for seeking the companionship of those my spirit knew as enemies of our race. Now I understand. One should seek to obtain the secrets of his enemies. He will avenge my shame, white one. His spirit will destroy you and yours.

PILKINGS: That kind of talk is hardly called for. If you don't want my consolation . . .

ELESIN: No white man, I do not want your consolation.

PILKINGS: As you wish. Your son anyway, sends his consolation. He asks your forgiveness. When I asked him not to despise you his reply was: I cannot judge him, and if I cannot judge him, I cannot despise him. He wants to come to you and say goodbye and to receive your blessing.

ELESIN: Goodbye? Is he returning to your land?

PILKINGS: Don't you think that's the most sensible thing for him to do? I advised him to leave at once, before dawn, and he agrees that is the right course of action.

ELESIN: Yes, it is best. And even if I did not think so, I have lost the father's place of honour. My voice is broken.

PILKINGS: Your son honours you. If he didn't he would not ask your blessing.

ELESIN: No. Even a thoroughbred is not without pity for the turf he strikes with his hoof. When is he coming?

PILKINGS: As soon as the town is a little quieter. I advised it.

ELESIN: Yes, white man, I am sure you advised it. You advise all our lives although on the authority of what gods, I do not know.

PILKINGS: [*Opens his mouth to reply, then appears to change his mind. Turns to go. Hesitates and stops again.*] Before I leave you, may I ask just one thing of you?

ELESIN: I am listening.

PILKINGS: I wish to ask you to search the quiet of your heart and tell me—do you not find great contradictions in the wisdom of your own race?

ELESIN: Make yourself clear, white one.

PILKINGS: I have lived among you long enough to learn a saying or two. One came to my mind tonight when I stepped into the market and saw what was going on. You were surrounded by those who egged you on with song and praises. I thought, are these not the same people who say: the elder grimly approaches heaven and you ask him to bear your greetings yonder; do you really think he makes the journey willingly? After that, I did not hesitate.

[*A pause.* ELESIN *sighs. Before he can speak a sound of running feet is heard.*]

JANE: [*Off.*] Simon! Simon!

PILKINGS: What on earth . . . ! [*Runs off.*]

[ELESIN *turns to his new wife, gazes on her for some moments.*]

ELESIN: My young bride, did you hear the ghostly one? You sit and sob in your silent heart but say nothing to all this. First I blamed the white man, then I blamed my gods for deserting me. Now I feel I want to blame you for the mystery of the sapping of my will. But blame is a strange peace offering for a man to bring a world he has deeply wronged, and to its innocent dwellers. Oh little mother, I have taken countless women in my life but you were more than a desire of the flesh. I needed you as the abyss across which my body must be drawn, I filled it with earth and dropped my seed in it at the moment of preparedness for my crossing. You were the final gift of the living to their emissary to the land of the ancestors, and perhaps your warmth and youth brought new insights of this world to me and turned my feet leaden on this side of the abyss. For I confess to you, daughter, my weakness came not merely from the abomination of the white man who came violently into my fading presence, there was also a weight of longing on my earth-held limbs. I would have shaken it off, already my foot had begun to lift but then, the white ghost entered and all was defiled.

[*Approaching voices of* PILKINGS *and his wife.*]

JANE: Oh Simon, you will let her in won't you?

PILKINGS: I really wish you'd stop interfering.

[*They come into view.* JANE *is in a dressing gown.* PILKINGS *is holding a note to which he refers from time to time.*]

JANE: Good gracious, I didn't initiate this. I was sleeping quietly, or trying to anyway, when the servant brought it. It's not my fault if one can't sleep undisturbed even in the Residency.

PILKINGS: He'd have done the same thing if we were sleeping at home so don't sidetrack the issue. He knows he can get round you or he wouldn't send you the petition in the first place.

JANE: Be fair Simon. After all he was thinking of your own interests. He is grateful you know, you seem to forget that. He feels he owes you something.

PILKINGS: I just wish they'd leave this man alone tonight, that's all.

JANE: Trust him Simon. He's pledged his word it will all go peacefully.

PILKINGS: Yes, and that's the other thing. I don't like being threatened.

JANE: Threatened? [*Takes the note.*] I didn't spot any threat.

PILKINGS: It's there. Veiled, but it's there. The only way to prevent serious rioting tomorrow—what a cheek!

JANE: I don't think he's threatening you Simon.

PILKINGS: He's picked up the idiom all right. Wouldn't surprise me if he's been mixing with commies or anarchists over there. The phrasing sounds too good to be true. Damn! If only the Prince hadn't picked this time for his visit.

JANE: Well, even so Simon, what have you got to lose? You don't want a riot on your hands, not with the Prince here.

PILKINGS: [*Going up to* ELESIN.] Let's see what he has to say. Chief Elesin, there is yet another person who wants to see you. As she is not a next-of-kin I don't really feel obliged to let her in. But your son sent a note with her, so it's up to you.

ELESIN: I know who that must be. So she found out your hiding place. Well, it was not difficult. My stench of shame is so strong, it requires no hunter's dog to follow it.

PILKINGS: If you don't want to see her, just say so and I'll send her packing.

ELESIN: Why should I not want to see her? Let her come. I have no more holes in my rag of shame. All is laid bare.

PILKINGS: I'll bring her in. [*Goes off.*]

JANE: [*Hesitates, then goes to* ELESIN.] Please, try and understand. Everything my husband did was for the best.

ELESIN: [*He gives her a long strange stare, as if he is trying to understand who she is.*] You are the wife of the District Officer?

JANE: Yes. My name, is Jane.

ELESIN: That is my wife sitting down there. You notice how still and silent she sits? My business is with your husband.

[PILKINGS *returns with* IYALOJA.]

PILKINGS: Here she is. Now first I want your word of honour that you will try nothing foolish.

ELESIN: Honour? White one, did you say you wanted my word of honour?

PILKINGS: I know you to be an honourable man. Give me your word of honour you will receive nothing from her.

ELESIN: But I am sure you have searched her clothing as you would never dare touch your own mother. And there are these two lizards[7] of yours who roll their eyes even when I scratch.

PILKINGS: And I shall be sitting on that tree trunk watching even how you blink. Just the same I want your word that you will not let her pass anything to you.

ELESIN: You have my honour already. It is locked up in that desk in which you will put away your report of this night's events. Even the honour of my people you have taken already; it is tied together with those papers of treachery[8] which make you masters in this land.

PILKINGS: All right. I am trying to make things easy but if you must bring in politics we'll have to do it the hard way. Madam, I want you to remain along this line and move no nearer to the cell door. Guards! [*They spring to attention.*] If she moves beyond this point, blow your whistle. Come on Jane. [*They go off.*]

IYALOJA: How boldly the lizard struts before the pigeon when it was the eagle itself he promised us he would confront.

ELESIN: I don't ask you to take pity on me Iyaloja. You have a message for me or you would not have come. Even if it is the curses of the world, I shall listen.

IYALOJA: You made so bold with the servant of the white king who took your side against death. I must tell your brother chiefs when I return how bravely you waged war against him. Especially with words.

ELESIN: I more than deserve your scorn.

IYALOJA: [*With sudden anger.*] I warned you, if you must leave a seed behind, be sure it is not tainted with the curses of the world. Who are you to open a new life when you dared not open the door to a new existence? I say who are you to make so bold? [*The* BRIDE *sobs and* IYALOJA *notices her. Her contempt noticeably increases as she turns back to* ELESIN.] Oh you self-vaunted stem of the plantain, how hollow it all proves. The pith is gone in the parent stem, so how will it prove with the new shoot? How will it go with that earth that bears it? Who are you to bring this abomination on us!

ELESIN: My powers deserted me. My charms, my spells, even my voice lacked strength when I made to summon the powers that would lead me over the last measure of earth into the land of the fleshless. You saw it, Iyaloja. You

---

7. That is, the guards.
8. The treaties of annexation forced by the

British on African traditional rulers, who often did not understand their implications.

saw me struggle to retrieve my will from the power of the stranger whose shadow fell across the doorway and left me floundering and blundering in a maze I had never before encountered. My senses were numbed when the touch of cold iron came upon my wrists. I could do nothing to save myself.

IYALOJA: You have betrayed us. We fed you sweetmeats such as we hoped awaited you on the other side. But you said No, I must eat the world's left-overs. We said you were the hunter who brought the quarry down; to you belonged the vital portions of the game. No, you said, I am the hunter's dog and I shall eat the entrails of the game and the faeces of the hunter. We said you were the hunter returning home in triumph, a slain buffalo pressing down on his neck; you said wait, I first must turn up this cricket hole with my toes. We said yours was the doorway at which we first spy the tapper when he comes down from the tree, yours was the blessing of the twilight wine, the purl[9] that brings night spirits out of doors to steal their portion before the light of day. We said yours was the body of wine whose burden shakes the tapper like a sudden gust on his perch. You said, No, I am content to lick the dregs from each calabash when the drinkers are done. We said, the dew on earth's surface was for you to wash your feet along the slopes of honour. You said No, I shall step in the vomit of cats and the droppings of mice; I shall fight them for the left-overs of the world.

ELESIN: Enough Iyaloja, enough.

IYALOJA: We called you leader and oh, how you led us on. What we have no intention of eating should not be held to the nose.[1]

ELESIN: Enough, enough. My shame is heavy enough.

IYALOJA: Wait. I came with a burden.

ELESIN: You have more than discharged it.

IYALOJA: I wish I could pity you.

ELESIN: I need neither pity nor the pity of the world. I need understanding. Even I need to understand. You were present at my defeat. You were part of the beginnings. You brought about the renewal of my tie to earth, you helped in the binding of the cord.

IYALOJA: I gave you warning. The river which fills up before our eyes does not sweep us away in its flood.

ELESIN: What were warnings beside the moist contact of living earth between my fingers? What were warnings beside the renewal of famished embers lodged eternally in the heart of man. But even that, even if it overwhelmed one with a thousandfold temptations to linger a little while, a man could overcome it. It is when the alien hand pollutes the source of will, when a stranger's force of violence shatters the mind's calm resolution, this is when a man is made to commit the awful treachery of relief, commit in his thought the unspeakable blasphemy of seeing the hand of the gods in this alien rupture of his world. I know it was this thought that killed me, sapped my powers and turned me into an infant in the hands of unnamable strangers. I made to utter my spells anew but my tongue merely rattled in my mouth. I fingered hidden charms and the contact was damp; there was

9. The frothy head of the palm wine. "Tapper": one who climbs to the very top of the palm tree for its wine. The profession is a highly specialized one. "Cricket hole": hunting crickets is a favorite game of Yoruba boys.
1. Considered uncouth by Yorubas.

no spark left to sever the life-strings that should stretch from every finger-tip. My will was squelched in the spittle of an alien race, and all because I had committed this blasphemy of thought—that there might be the hand of the gods in a stranger's intervention.

IYALOJA: Explain it how you will, I hope it brings you peace of mind. The bush rat fled his rightful cause, reached the market and set up a lamenta-tion. "Please save me!"—are these fitting words to hear from an ancestral mask? "There's a wild beast at my heels" is not becoming language from a hunter.

ELESIN: May the world forgive me.

IYALOJA: I came with a burden I said. It approaches the gates which are so well guarded by those jackals whose spittle will from this day be on your food and drink. But first, tell me, you who were once Elesin Oba, tell me, you who know so well the cycle of the plantain: is it the parent shoot which withers to give sap to the younger or, does your wisdom see it running the other way?

ELESIN: I don't see your meaning Iyaloja?

IYALOJA: Did I ask you for a meaning? I asked a question. Whose trunk with-ers to give sap to the other? The parent shoot or the younger?

ELESIN: The parent.

IYALOJA: Ah. So you do know that. There are sights in this world which say different Elesin. There are some who choose to reverse the cycle of our being. Oh you emptied bark that the world once saluted for a pith-laden being, shall I tell you what the gods have claimed of you?

[*In her agitation she steps beyond the line indicated by* PILKINGS *and the air is rent by piercing whistles. The two guards also leap forward and place safe-guarding hands on* ELESIN. IYALOJA *stops, astonished.* PILKINGS *comes rac-ing in, followed by* JANE.]

PILKINGS: What is it? Did they try something?

GUARD: She stepped beyond the line.

ELESIN: [*In a broken voice.*] Let her alone. She meant no harm.

IYALOJA: Oh Elesin, see what you've become. Once you had no need to open your mouth in explanation because evil-smelling goats, itchy of hand and foot had lost their senses. And it was a brave man indeed who dared lay hands on you because Iyaloja stepped from one side of the earth onto another. Now look at the spectacle of your life. I grieve for you.

PILKINGS: I think you'd better leave. I doubt you have done him much good by coming here. I shall make sure you are not allowed to see him again. In any case we are moving him to a different place before dawn, so don't bother to come back.

IYALOJA: We foresaw that. Hence the burden I trudged here to lay beside your gates.

PILKINGS: What was that you said?

IYALOJA: Didn't our son explain? Ask that one. He knows what it is. At least we hope the man we once knew as Elesin remembers the lesser oaths he need not break.

PILKINGS: Do you know what she is talking about?

ELESIN: Go to the gates, ghostly one. Whatever you find there, bring it to me.

IYALOJA: Not yet. It drags behind me on the slow, weary feet of women. Slow as it is Elesin, it has long overtaken you. It rides ahead of your laggard will.

PILKINGS: What is she saying now? Christ! Must your people forever speak in riddles?

ELESIN: It will come white man, it will come. Tell your men at the gates to let it through.

PILKINGS: [*Dubiously.*] I'll have to see what it is.

IYALOJA: You will. [*Passionately.*] But this is one oath he cannot shirk. White one, you have a king here, a visitor from your land. We know of his presence here. Tell me, were he to die would you leave his spirit roaming restlessly on the surface of earth? Would you bury him here among those you consider less than human? In your land have you no ceremonies of the dead?

PILKINGS: Yes. But we don't make our chiefs commit suicide to keep him company.

IYALOJA: Child, I have not come to help your understanding. [*Points to* ELESIN.] This is the man whose weakened understanding holds us in bondage to you. But ask him if you wish. He knows the meaning of a king's passage; he was not born yesterday. He knows the peril to the race when our dead father, who goes as intermediary, waits and waits and knows he is betrayed. He knows when the narrow gate was opened and he knows it will not stay for laggards who drag their feet in dung and vomit, whose lips are reeking of the left-overs of lesser men. He knows he has condemned our king to wander in the void of evil with beings who are enemies of life.

PILKINGS: Yes er . . . but look here . . .

IYALOJA: What we ask is little enough. Let him release our King so he can ride on homewards alone. The messenger is on his way on the backs of women. Let him send word through the heart that is folded up within the bolt. It is the least of all his oaths, it is the easiest fulfilled.

[*The* AIDE-DE-CAMP *runs in.*]

PILKINGS: Bob?

AIDE-DE-CAMP: Sir, there's a group of women chanting up the hill.

PILKINGS: [*Rounding on* IYALOJA.] If you people want trouble . . .

JANE: Simon, I think that's what Olunde referred to in his letter.

PILKINGS: He knows damned well I can't have a crowd here! Damn it, I explained the delicacy of my position to him. I think it's about time I got him out of town. Bob, send a car and two or three soldiers to bring him in. I think the sooner he takes his leave of his father and gets out the better.

IYALOJA: Save your labour white one. If it is the father of your prisoner you want, Olunde, he who until this night we knew as Elesin's son, he comes soon himself to take his leave. He has sent the women ahead, so let them in.

[PILKINGS *remains undecided.*]

AIDE-DE-CAMP: What do we do about the invasion? We can still stop them far from here.

PILKINGS: What do they look like?

AIDE-DE-CAMP: They're not many. And they seem quite peaceful.

PILKINGS: No men?

AIDE-DE-CAMP: Mm, two or three at the most.

JANE: Honestly, Simon, I'd trust Olunde. I don't think he'll deceive you about their intentions.

PILKINGS: He'd better not. All right then, let them in Bob. Warn them to control themselves. Then hurry Olunde here. Make sure he brings his baggage because I'm not returning him into town.

AIDE-DE-CAMP: Very good, sir. [*Goes.*]

PILKINGS: [*To* IYALOJA.] I hope you understand that if anything goes wrong it will be on your head. My men have orders to shoot at the first sign of trouble.

IYALOJA: To prevent one death you will actually make other deaths? Ah, great is the wisdom of the white race. But have no fear. Your Prince will sleep peacefully. So at long last will ours. We will disturb you no further, servant of the white king. Just let Elesin fulfil his oath and we will retire home and pay homage to our King.

JANE: I believe her Simon, don't you?

PILKINGS: Maybe.

ELESIN: Have no fear ghostly one. I have a message to send my King and then you have nothing more to fear.

IYALOJA: Olunde would have done it. The chiefs asked him to speak the words but he said no, not while you lived.

ELESIN: Even from the depths to which my spirit has sunk, I find some joy that this little has been left to me.

[*The* WOMEN *enter, intoning the dirge "Ale le le" and swaying from side to side. On their shoulders is borne a longish object roughly like a cylindrical bolt, covered in cloth. They set it down on the spot where* IYALOJA *had stood earlier, and form a semi-circle round it. The* PRAISE-SINGER *and* DRUMMER *stand on the inside of the semi-circle but the drum is not used at all. The* DRUMMER *intones under the* PRAISE-SINGER's *invocations.*]

PILKINGS: [*As they enter.*] What is *that*?

IYALOJA: The burden you have made white one, but we bring it in peace.

PILKINGS: I said *what* is it?

ELESIN: White man, you must let me out. I have a duty to perform.

PILKINGS: I most certainly will not.

ELESIN: There lies the courier of my King. Let me out so I can perform what is demanded of me.

PILKINGS: You'll do what you need to do from inside there or not at all. I've gone as far as I intend to with this business.

ELESIN: The worshipper who lights a candle in your church to bear a message to his god bows his head and speaks in a whisper to the flame. Have I not seen it ghostly one? His voice does not ring out to the world. Mine are no words for anyone's ears. They are not words even for the bearers of this load. They are words I must speak secretly, even as my father whispered them in my ears and I in the ears of my first-born. I cannot shout them to the wind and the open night sky.

JANE: Simon . . .

PILKINGS: Don't interfere. Please!

IYALOJA: They have slain the favourite horse of the king and slain his dog. They have borne them from pulse to pulse centre of the land receiving prayers for their king. But the rider has chosen to stay behind. Is it too much to ask that he speak his heart to heart of the waiting courier? [PILKINGS *turns his back on her.*] So be it. Elesin Oba, you see how even the mere leavings are denied you. [*She gestures to the* PRAISE-SINGER.]

PRAISE-SINGER: Elesin Oba! I call you by that name only this last time. Remember when I said, if you cannot come, tell my horse. [*Pause*.] What? I cannot hear you? I said, if you cannot come, whisper in the ears of my horse. Is your tongue severed from the roots? Elesin? I can hear no response. I said, if there are boulders you cannot climb, mount my horse's back, this spotless black stallion, he'll bring you over them. [*Pauses*.] Elesin Oba, once you had a tongue that darted like a drummer's stick. I said, if you get lost my dog will track a path to me. My memory fails me but I think you replied: My feet have found the path, Alafin.

> [*The dirge rises and falls.*]

I said at the last, if evil hands hold you back, just tell my horse there is weight on the hem of your smock. I dare not wait too long.

> [*The dirge rises and falls.*]

There lies the swiftest ever messenger of a king, so set me free with the errand of your heart. There lie the head and heart of the favourite of the gods, whisper in his ears. Oh my companion, if you had followed when you should, we would not say that the horse preceded its rider. If you had followed when it was time, we would not say the dog has raced beyond and left his master behind. If you had raised your will to cut the thread of life at the summons of the drums, we would not say your mere shadow fell across the gateway and took its owner's place at the banquet. But the hunter, laden with slain buffalo, stayed to root in the cricket's hole with his toes. What now is left? If there is a dearth of bats, the pigeon must serve us for the offering.[2] Speak the words over your shadow which must now serve in your place.

ELESIN: I cannot approach. Take off the cloth. I shall speak my message from heart to heart of silence.

IYALOJA: [*Moves forward and removes the covering.*] Your courier Elesin, cast your eyes on the favoured companion of the King.

> [*Rolled up in the mat, his head and feet showing at either end, is the body of* OLUNDE.]

There lies the honour of your household and of our race. Because he could not bear to let honour fly out of doors, he stopped it with his life. The son has proved the father Elesin, and there is nothing left in your mouth to gnash but infant gums.

PRAISE-SINGER: Elesin, we placed the reins of the world in your hands yet you watched it plunge over the edge of the bitter precipice. You sat with folded arms while evil strangers tilted the world from its course and crashed it beyond the edge of emptiness—you muttered, there is little that one man can do, you left us floundering in a blind future. Your heir has taken the burden on himself. What the end will be, we are not gods to tell. But this young shoot has poured its sap into the parent stalk, and we know this is not the way of life. Our world is tumbling in the void of strangers, Elesin.

> [ELESIN *has stood rock-still, his knuckles taut on the bars, his eyes glued to the body of his son. The stillness seizes and paralyses everyone, including* PILKINGS *who has turned to look. Suddenly* ELESIN *flings one arm round his neck, once, and with the loop of the chain, strangles himself in a swift,*

---

2. Sacrifice.

*decisive pull. The guards rush forward to stop him but they are only in time
to let his body down.* PILKINGS *has leapt to the door at the same time and
struggles with the lock. He rushes within, fumbles with the handcuffs and
unlocks them, raises the body to a sitting position while he tries to give resus-
citation. The* WOMEN *continue their dirge, unmoved by the sudden event.*]

IYALOJA: Why do you strain yourself? Why do you labour at tasks for which
no one, not even the man lying there would give you thanks? He is gone at
last into the passage but oh, how late it all is. His son will feast on the meat
and throw him bones. The passage is clogged with droppings from the
King's stallion; he will arrive all stained in dung.

PILKINGS: [*In a tired voice.*] Was this what you wanted?

IYALOJA: No child, it is what you brought to be, you who play with strangers'
lives, who even usurp the vestments of our dead, yet believe that the stain
of death will not cling to you. The gods demanded only the old expired
plantain but you cut down the sap-laden shoot to feed your pride. There is
your board, filled to overflowing. Feast on it. [*She screams at him suddenly,
seeing that* PILKINGS *is about to close* ELESIN's *staring eyes.*] Let him alone!
However sunk he was in debt he is no pauper's carrion abandoned on the
road. Since when have strangers donned clothes of indigo[3] before the
bereaved cries out his loss?

[*She turns to the* BRIDE *who has remained motionless throughout.*]
Child.

[*The girl takes up a little earth, walks calmly into the cell and closes* ELESIN's
eyes. She then pours some earth over each eyelid and comes out again.]

Now forget the dead, forget even the living. Turn your mind only to the
unborn.

[*She goes off, accompanied by the* BRIDE. *The dirge rises in volume and the*
WOMEN *continue their sway. Lights fade to a black-out.*]

1975

3. Worn for mourning.

NAWAL EL SAADAWI
born 1931

In her autobiography *A Daughter of
Isis* (1999), the Egyptian novelist
Nawal El Saadawi writes that she realized early in her life how gender discrimination limits the opportunities of
women in the Arab-Islamic world: "I
had been born a female in a world that
wanted only males." Her acute awareness of the damaging impact of this
burden and her sense of solidarity with
women around the world have sustained her abundant output—novels,

short stories, autobiography, essays, and addresses as well as scientific treatises and sociological studies—in an active career that has spanned some sixty years.

Nawal El Saadawi was born in 1931 in Kafir Tahla, a small village on the banks of the Nile, into a well-to-do middle-class family with strong connections to the ruling elite of the country. Her mother descended from the traditional aristocracy; her father, a government functionary, had been active in the Egyptian Revolution of 1919. Both parents saw to it that their nine children all received a university education. Nawal El Saadawi herself studied medicine at the University of Cairo and participated in student protests against the British occupation. She also began writing short articles about her childhood for Egyptian newspapers. After her graduation in 1955, she practiced as a psychiatrist before being appointed to the Ministry of Health, where she rose to become director of public health. She was dismissed from her post in 1972, however, after the publication of her book *Woman and Sex*, which aroused the displeasure of the Egyptian authorities for its frank treatment of a subject that was considered taboo. Among other things, the book criticized the practice of female circumcision, or genital mutilation. This was the beginning of her long struggle for the right of expression and of her crusade for female emancipation in Egypt and the Arab world.

After losing her government position, El Saadawi devoted herself to research on women; she also worked for a year with the United Nations as an advisor on women's development in the Middle East and Africa. In 1981 she was imprisoned for three months during the campaign of repression against intellectuals by the Sadat regime, an experience that inspired El Saadawi's novel *The Fall of the Imam* (1987). On her release, in 1982, she founded the Arab Women's Solidarity Association (AWSA), a nongovernmental organization dedicated to informed discussion of women's issues. The association was dissolved by the government in 1991 and its assets confiscated. El Saadawi sued the government, but, despite support from a distinguished panel of lawyers, she could not prevail against the forces ranged against her. Because she had also incurred the wrath of Islamic fundamentalists and ran a real risk of being assassinated, she went into exile in the United States in 1992, returning to Egypt in 1999. She joined the opposition to the government in 2011 and became a symbol for the young people who crowded Tahrir Square, the hub of the uprising that unseated Egypt's president Hosni Mubarak. She remains well-known in Egypt for her political activism as well as her writing.

Internationally, El Saadawi is probably best known for her novel *Woman at Point Zero* (1979), an account of a female prisoner condemned to death for killing a pimp. The main character had come to the city and become a prostitute in order to escape a forced marriage and the constricted existence it promised. The psychological and moral dilemmas highlighted by El Saadawi's works and the simplicity of her narrative style allow her to explore customs and religious beliefs as they affect women in her society, especially women whose freedom has been taken from them by government institutions. In their bleak depiction of the female predicament, her novels seek to document, albeit in fictional form, the vicissitudes in the lives of Egyptian women, denied fulfillment by forces beyond their control.

The short story "In Camera," taken from the collection entitled *Death of an Ex-Minister* (1980), is a representative sample of her work. The story criticizes the social system and state machinery in a fictional kingdom, which might be any dictatorial regime. Its political theme is developed through the narrative of the trial and the irreverent portrayal of the king and the agents of the state. The story's emphasis, however, is firmly on the ordeal of the female protagonist, on trial for an act of defiance against the system. Her physical violation and mental agony are reconstructed through the series of flashbacks that shape the story's atmosphere. As El Saadawi explores both the protagonist's perspective and that of her parents during the trial, the writer shows both the private and the public dimensions of the unfolding tragedy.

For El Saadawi, writing about the inner workings of female consciousness is an effort to break the silence that surrounds the culture of abuse and repression of which women are often victims. Her work is politically engaged; she calls on her readers not just to sympathize with her characters but to undertake political action in order to meet the moral challenges of a repressive society.

In Camera[1]

The first thing she felt was a blinding light. She saw nothing. The light was painful, even though her eyes were still shut. The cold air hit her face and bare neck, crept down to her chest and stomach and then fell lower to the weeping wound, where it turned into a sharp blow. She put one hand over her eyes to protect them from the light, whilst with the other she covered her neck, clenching her thighs against the sudden pain. Her lips too were clenched tight against a pain the like of which her body had never known, like the sting of a needle in her eyes and breasts and armpits and lower abdomen. From sleeping so long while standing and standing so long while sleeping, she no longer knew what position her body was in, whether vertical or horizontal, dangling in the air by her feet or standing on her head in water.

The moment they sat her down and she felt the seat on which she was sitting with the palms of her hands, the muscles of her face relaxed and resumed their human form. A shudder of sudden and intense pleasure shook her from inside when her body took up a sitting position on the wooden seat and her lips curled into a feeble smile as she said to herself: Now I know what pleasure it is to sit!

The light was still strong and her eyes still could not see, but her eyes were beginning to catch the sound of voices and murmurings. She lifted her hand off her eyes and gradually began to open them. Blurred human silhouettes moved before her on some elevated construction. She suddenly felt frightened, for human forms frightened her more than any others. Those long, rapid and agile bodies, legs inside trousers and feet inside shoes. Everything had been done in the dark with the utmost speed and agility. She could not cry or scream. Her tongue, her eyes, her mouth, her nose, all the parts of her body, were constrained. Her body was no longer hers but was like that of a small calf struck by the heels of boots. A rough stick entered between her thighs to tear at her insides. Then she was kicked into a dark corner where she remained curled up until the following day. By the third day, she still had not returned to normal but remained like a small animal incapable of uttering the simple words: My God! She said to herself: Do animals, like humans, know of the existence of something called God?

1. Translated by Shirley Eber. "In camera": the judicial term for "closed session." The oppressive atmosphere of the trial scene is immediately conveyed by the title.

Her eyes began to make out bodies sitting on that elevated place, above each head a body, smooth heads without hair, in the light as red as monkeys' rumps. They must all be males, for however old a woman grew, her head could never look like a monkey's rump. She strained to see more clearly. In the centre was a fat man wearing something like a black robe, his mouth open; in his hand something like a hammer. It reminded her of the village magician, when her eyes and those of all the other children had been mesmerized by the hand which turned a stick into a snake or into fire. The hammer squirmed in his hand like a viper and in her ears a sharp voice resounded: The Court! To herself she said: He must be the judge. It was the first time in her life she'd seen a judge or been inside a court. She'd heard the word 'court' for the first time as a child. She'd heard her aunt tell her mother: The judge did not believe me and told me to strip so he could see where I'd been beaten. I told him that I would not strip in front of a strange man, so he rejected my claim and ordered me to return to my husband. Her aunt had cried and at that time she had not understood why the judge had told her aunt to strip. I wonder if the judge will ask me to strip and what he will say when he sees that wound, she said to herself.

Gradually, her eyes were growing used to the light. She began to see the judge's face more clearly. His face was as red as his head, his eyes as round and bulging as a frog's, moving slowly here and there, his nose as curved as a hawk's beak, beneath it a yellow moustache as thick as a bundle of dry grass, which quivered above the opening of a mouth as taut as wire and permanently gaping like a mousetrap.

She did not understand why his mouth stayed open. Was he talking all the time or breathing through it? His shiny bald head moved continually with a nodding movement. It moved upwards a little and then backwards, entering into something pointed; then it moved downwards and forwards, so that his chin entered his neck opening. She could not yet see what was behind him, but when he raised his head and moved it backwards, she saw it enter something pointed which looked like the cap of a shoe. She focused her vision and saw that it really was a shoe, drawn on the wall above the judge's head. Above the shoe she saw taut legs inside a pair of trousers of expensive leather or leopard skin or snakeskin and a jacket, also taut, over a pair of shoulders. Above the shoulders appeared the face she'd seen thousands of times in the papers, eyes staring into space filled with more stupidity than simplicity, the nose as straight as though evened out by a hammer, the mouth pursed to betray that artificial sincerity which all rulers and kings master when they sit before a camera. Although his mouth was pinched in arrogance and sincerity, his cheeks were slack, beneath them a cynical and comical smile containing chronic corruption and childish petulance.

She had been a child in primary school the first time she saw a picture of the king. The face was fleshy, the eyes narrow, the lips thin and clenched in impudent arrogance. She recalled her father's voice saying: he was decadent and adulterous. But they were all the same. When they stood in front of a camera, they thought they were god.

Although she could still feel her body sitting on the wooden seat, she began to have doubts. How could they allow her to sit all this time? Sitting like this was so very relaxing. She could sit, leaving her body in a sitting position, and enjoy that astounding ability which humans have. For the first time she understood that the human body differed from that of an animal in one important way—sitting. No animal could sit the way she could. If it did, what would it do with its four legs? She remembered a scene that had made her laugh as a child, of a calf which had tried to sit on its backside and had ended up on its back. Her lips curled in a futile attempt to open her mouth and say something or smile. But her mouth remained stuck, like a horizontal line splitting the lower part of her face into two. Could she open her mouth a little to spit? But her throat, her mouth, her neck, her chest, everything, was dry, all except for that gaping wound between her thighs.

She pressed her legs together tighter to close off the wound and the pain and to enjoy the pleasure of sitting on a seat. She could have stayed in that position for ever, or until she died, had she not suddenly heard a voice calling her name: Leila Al-Fargani.

Her numbed senses awoke and her ears pricked up to the sound of that strange name: Leila Al-Fargani. As though it wasn't her name. She hadn't heard it for ages. It was the name of a young woman named Leila, a young woman who had worn young woman's clothes, had seen the sun and walked on two feet like other human beings. She had been that woman a very long time ago, but since then she hadn't worn a young woman's clothes nor seen the sun nor walked on two feet. For a long time she'd been a small animal inside a dark and remote cave and when they addressed her, they only used animal names.

Her eyes were still trying to see clearly. The judge's head had grown clearer and moved more, but it was still either inside the cap of the shoe whenever he raised it or was inside his collar whenever he lowered it. The picture hanging behind him had also become clearer. The shiny pointed shoes, the suit as tight as a horseman's, the face held taut on the outside by artificial muscles full of composure and stupidity, on the inside depraved and contentious.

The power of her sight was no longer as it had been, but she could still see ugliness clearly. She saw the deformed face and remembered her father's words: They only reach the seat of power, my girl, when they are morally deformed and internally corrupt.

And what inner corruption! She had seen their real corruption for herself. She wished at that moment they would give her pen and paper so that she could draw that corruption. But would her fingers still be capable of holding a pen or of moving it across a piece of paper? Would she still have at least two fingers which could hold a pen? What could she do if they cut off one of those two fingers? Could she hold a pen with one finger? Could a person walk on one leg? It was one of those questions her father used to repeat. But she hated the questions of the impotent and said to herself: I will split the finger and press the pen into it, just as Isis split the leg of Osiris.[2] She remembered that old story, still saw the split leg pouring with blood. What a long nightmare she was living! How she wanted her mother's hand to shake her so she could open her

---

2. Isis and Osiris were a royal couple in Egyptian mythology. In the celebrated story of the couple, Isis wandered the land in search of the body of her murdered husband (who was also her brother), whose body had been thrown into the Nile in a golden casket. She recovered the body, into which she was able to breathe life and from which she conceived a son. However, the body was discovered by his murderer, who tore it into pieces, leaving Isis to collect the limbs and other parts, into which she again breathed life. Osiris soon died again and descended into the underworld, where he reigned over the dead.

eyes and wake up. She used to be so happy when, as a child, she opened her eyes and realized that the monster which had tried to rip her body to pieces was nothing but a dream, or a nightmare as her mother used to call it. Each time she had opened her eyes, she was very happy to discover that the monster had vanished, that it was only a dream. But now she opened her eyes and the monster did not go away. She opened her eyes and the monster stayed on her body. Her terror was so great that she closed her eyes again to sleep, to make believe that it was a nightmare. But she opened her eyes and knew it was no dream. And she remembered everything.

The first thing she remembered was her mother's scream in the silence of the night. She was sleeping in her mother's arms, like a child of six even though she was an adult and in her twenties. But her mother had said: You'll sleep in my arms so that even if they come in the middle of the night, I will know it and I'll hold on to you with all my might and if they take you they'll have to take me as well.

Nothing was as painful to her as seeing her mother's face move further and further away until it disappeared. Her face, her eyes, her hair, were so pale. She would rather have died than see her mother's face so haggard. To herself she said: Can you forgive me, Mother, for causing you so much pain? Her mother always used to say to her: What's politics got to do with you? You're not a man. Girls of your age think only about marriage. She hadn't replied when her mother had said: Politics is a dirty game which only ineffectual men play.

The voices had now become clearer. The picture also looked clearer, even though the fog was still thick. Was it winter and the hall roofless, or was it summer and they were smoking in a windowless room? She could see another man sitting not far from the judge. His head, like the judge's, was smooth and red but, unlike the judge's, it was not completely under the shoe. He was sitting to one side and above his head hung another picture in which there was something like a flag or a small multicoloured banner. And for the first time, her ears made out some intelligible sentences:

Imagine, ladies and gentlemen. This student, who is not yet twenty years old, refers to Him, whom God protect to lead this noble nation all his life, as 'stupid'.

The word 'stupid' fell like a stone in a sea of awesome silence, making a sound like the crash of a rock in water or the blow of a hand against something solid, like a slap or the clap of one hand against another.

Was someone clapping? She pricked up her ears to catch the sound. Was it applause? Or a burst of laughter, like a cackle? Then that terrifying silence pervaded the courtroom once again, a long silence in which she could hear the beating of her heart. The sound of laughter or of applause echoed in her ears. She asked herself who could be applauding at so serious a moment as when the mighty one was being described as stupid, and aloud too.

Her body was still stuck to the wooden seat, clinging on to it, frightened it would suddenly be taken away. The wound in her lower abdomen was still weeping. But she was able to move her head and half opened her eyes to search for the source of that applause. Suddenly she discovered that the hall was full of heads crammed together in rows, all of them undoubtedly human. Some of the heads appeared to have a lot of hair, as if they were those of women or girls. Some of them were small, as if those of children. One head seemed to be like that of her younger sister. Her body trembled for a moment on the seat as her eyes searched around. Had she come alone or with her father and mother? Were they looking at her now? How did she look? Could they recognize her face or her body?

She turned her head to look. Although her vision had grown weak, she could just make out her mother. She could pick out her mother's face from among thousands of faces even with her eyes closed. Could her mother really be here in the hall? Her heartbeats grew audible and anxiety grew inside her. Anxiety often gripped her and she felt that something terrible had happened to her mother. One night, fear had overcome her when she was curled up like a small animal and she'd told herself: She must have died and I will not see her when I get out. But the following day, she had seen her mother when she came to visit. She'd come, safe and sound. She was happy and said: Don't die, Mother, before I get out and can make up for all the pain I've caused you.

The sound was now clear in her ears. It wasn't just one clap but a whole series of them. The heads in the hall were moving here and there. The judge was still sitting, his smooth head beneath the shoe. The hammer in his hand was moving impatiently, banging rapidly on the wooden table. But the clapping did not stop. The judge rose to his feet so that his head was in the centre of the stomach in the picture. His lower lip trembled as he shouted out words of rebuke which she couldn't hear in all the uproar.

Then silence descended for a period. She was still trying to see, her hands by her side holding on to the seat, clinging on to it, pressing it as if she wanted to confirm that it was really beneath her or that she was really sitting on it. She knew she was awake and not asleep with her eyes closed. Before, when she opened her eyes, the monster would disappear and she'd be happy that it was only a dream. But now she was no longer capable of being happy and had become frightened of opening her eyes.

The noise in the hall had died down and the heads moved as they had done before. All except one head. It was neither smooth nor red. It was covered in a thick mop of white hair and was fixed and immobile. The eyes also did not move and were open, dry and fixed on that small body piled on top of the wooden seat. Her hands were clasped over her chest, her heart under her hand beating fast, her breath panting as if she were running to the end of the track and could no longer breathe. Her voice broke as she said to herself: My God! Her eyes turn in my direction but she doesn't see me. What have they done to her eyes? Or is she fighting sleep? God of Heaven and Earth, how could you let them do all that? How, my daughter, did you stand so much pain? How did I stand it together with you? I always felt that you, my daughter, were capable of anything, of moving mountains or of crumbling rocks, even though your body is small and weak like mine. But when your tiny feet used to kick the walls of my stomach, I'd say to myself: God, what strength and power there is inside my body? Your movements were strong while you were still a foetus and shook me from inside, like a volcano shakes the earth. And yet I knew that you were as small as I was, your bones as delicate as your father's, as tall and slim as your grandmother, your feet as large as the feet of prophets.[3] When I gave birth to you, your grandmother

3. The passage conjures up an image of devoted pupils sitting at the feet of the prophets.

pursed her lips in sorrow and said: A girl and ugly too! A double catastrophe! I tensed my stomach muscles to close off my womb to the pain and the blood and, breathing with difficulty, for your birth had been hard and I suffered as though I'd given birth to a mountain, I said to her: She's more precious to me than the whole world! I held you to my breast and slept deeply. Can I, my daughter, again enjoy another moment of deep sleep whilst you are inside me or at least near to me so that I can reach out to touch you? Or whilst you are in your room next to mine so that I can tiptoe in to see you whilst you sleep? The blanket always used to fall off you as you slept, so I'd lift it and cover you. Anxiety would waken me every night and make me creep into your room. What was that anxiety and at what moment did it happen? Was it the moment the cover fell off your body? I could always feel you, even if you had gone away and were out of my sight. Even if they were to bury you under the earth or build a solid wall of mud or iron around you, I would still feel a draught of air on your body as though it were on mine. I sometimes wonder whether I ever really gave birth to you or if you are still inside me. How else could I feel the air when it touches you and hunger when it grips you. Your pain is mine, like fire burning in my breast and stomach. God of Heaven and Earth, how did your body and mine stand it? But I couldn't have stood it were it not for the joy of you being my daughter, of having given birth to you. And you can raise your head high above the mountains of filth. For three thousand and twenty-five hours (I've counted them one by one), they left you with the vomit and pus and the weeping wound in your stomach. I remember the look in your eyes when you told me, the bars between us: If only the weeping were red blood. But it's not red. It's white and has the smell of death. What was it I said to you that day? I don't know, but I said something. I said that the smell becomes normal when we get used to it and live with it every day. I could not look into your emaciated face, but I heard you say: It's not a smell, mother, like other smells which enter through the nose or mouth. It's more like liquid air or steam turned to viscid[4] water or molten lead flowing into every opening of the body. I don't know, mother, if it is burning hot or icy cold. I clasped my hands to my breast, then grasped your slender hand through the bars, saying: When heat became like cold, my daughter, then everything is bearable. But as soon as I left you, I felt my heart swell and swell until it filled my chest and pressed on my lungs so I could no longer breathe. I felt I was choking and tilted my head skywards to force air into my lungs. But the sky that day was void of air and the sun over my head was molten lead like the fire of hell. The eyes of the guards stung me and their uncouth voices piled up inside me. If the earth had transformed into the face of one of them, I'd have spat and spat and spat on it until my throat and chest dried up. Yes, my daughter, brace the muscles of your back and raise your head and turn it in my direction, for I'm sitting near you. You may have heard them when they applauded you. Did you hear them? I saw you move your head towards us. Did you see us? Me and your father and little sister? We all applauded with them. Did you see us?

Her eyes were still trying to penetrate the thick fog. The judge was still standing, his head smooth and red, his lower lip trembling with rapid words. To his right and to his left, she saw smooth red heads begin to move away from that

4. Sticky.

elevated table. The judge's head and the others vanished, although the picture on the wall remained where it was. The face and the eyes were the same as they had been, but now one eye appeared to her to be smaller, as though half-closed or winking at her, that common gesture that a man makes to a woman when he wants to flirt with her. Her body trembled in surprise. Was it possible that he was winking at her? Was it possible for his eyes in the picture to move? Could objects move? Or was she sick and hallucinating? She felt the seat under her palm and raised her hand to touch her body. A fierce heat emanated from it, like a searing flame, a fire within her chest. She wanted to open her mouth and say: Please, a glass of water. But her lips were stuck together, a horizontal line as taut as wire. Her eyes too were stuck on the picture, while the eye in the picture continued to wink at her. Why was it winking at her? Was it flirting with her? She had only discovered that winking was a form of greeting when, two years previously, she'd seen a file of foreign tourists walking in the street. She'd been on her way to the university. Whenever she looked at the faces of one of the men or women, an eye would suddenly wink at her strangely. She had been shocked and hadn't understood how a woman could flirt with her in such a way. Only later had she understood that it was an American form of greeting.

The podium was still empty, without the judge and the smooth heads around him. Silence prevailed. The heads in the hall were still close together in rows and her eyes still roamed in search of a mop of white hair, a pair of black eyes which she could see with eyes closed. But there were so many heads close together she could only see a mound of black and white, circles or squares or oblongs. Her nose began to move as if she were sniffing, for she knew her mother's smell and could distinguish it from thousands of others. It was the smell of milk when she was a child at the breast or the smell of the morning when it rises or the night when it sleeps or the rain on wet earth or the sun above the bed or hot soup in a bowl. She said to herself: Is it possible that you're not here, Mother? And Father, have you come?

The fog before her eyes was still thick. Her head continued to move in the direction of the rows of crammed heads. The black and white circles were interlocked in tireless movement. Only one circle of black hair was immobile above a wide brown forehead, two firm eyes in a pale slender face and a small body piled on to a chair behind bars. His large gaunt hands gripped his knees, pressing on them from the pain. But the moment he heard the applause, he took his hands off his knees and brought them together to clap. His hands did not return to his knees, the pain in his legs no longer tangible. His heart beat loudly in time to his clapping which shook his slender body on the seat. His eyes began to scour the faces and eyes, and his lips parted a little as though he were about to shout: I'm her father, I'm Al-Fargani who fathered her and whose name she bears. My God, how all the pain in my body vanished in one go with the burst of applause. What if I were to stand up now and reveal my identity to them? This moment is unique and I must not lose it. Men like us live and die for one moment such as this, for others to recognize us, to applaud us, for us to become heroes with eyes looking at us and fingers pointing at us. I have suffered the pain and torture with her, day after day, hour after hour, and now I have the right to enjoy some of the reward and share in her heroism.

He shifted his body slightly on his seat as if he were about to stand up. But he remained seated, though his head still moved. His eyes glanced from face to face, as if he wanted someone to recognize him. The angry voice of the judge and the sharp rapid blows of his hammer on the table broke into the applause. Presently the judge and those with him withdrew to the conference chambers. Silence again descended on the hall, a long and awesome silence, during which some faint whispers reached his ears: They'll cook up the case in the conference chamber . . . That's common practice . . . Justice and law don't exist here . . . In a while they'll declare the public hearing closed . . . She must be a heroine to have stayed alive until now . . . Imagine that young girl who is sitting in the dock causing the government so much alarm . . . Do you know how they tortured her? Ten men raped her, one after the other. They trampled on her honour and on her father's honour. Her poor father! Do you know him! They say he's ill in bed. Maybe he can't face people after his honour was violated!

At that moment he raised his hands to cover his ears so as not to hear, to press on his head so that it sunk into his chest, pushing it more and more to merge his body into the seat or underneath it or under the ground. He wanted to vanish so that no one would see or know him. His name was not Al-Fargani, not Assharqawi, not Azziftawi, not anything. He had neither name nor existence. What is left of a man whose honour is violated? He had told her bitterly: Politics, my girl, is not for women and girls. But she had not listened to him. If she had been a man, he would not be suffering now the way he was. None of those dogs would have been able to violate his honour and dignity. Death was preferable for him and for her now.[5]

Silence still reigned over the hall. The judge and his entourage had not yet reappeared. Her eyes kept trying to see, searching out one face amongst the faces, for eyes she recognized, for a mop of white hair the colour of children's milk. But all she could see were black and white circles and squares intermingled and constantly moving. Is it possible you're not here, Mother? Is Father still ill? Her nose too continued to move here and there, searching for a familiar smell, the smell of a warm breast full of milk, the smell of the sun and of drizzle on grass. But her nose was unable to pick up the smell. All it could pick up was the smell of her body crumpled on the seat and the weeping wound between her thighs. It was a smell of pus and blood and the putrid stench of the breath and sweat of ten men, the marks of whose nails were still on her body, with their uncouth voices, their saliva and the sound of their snorting. One of them, lying on top of her, had said: This is the way we torture you women—by depriving you of the most valuable thing you possess. Her body under him was as cold as a corpse but she had managed to open her mouth and say to him: You fool! The most valuable thing I possess is not between my legs. You're all stupid. And the most stupid among you is the one who leads you.

She craned her neck to raise her head and penetrate the fog with her weak eyes. The many heads were still crammed together and her eyes still strained. If only she could have seen her mother for a moment, or her father or little sister, she would have told them something strange. She would have told them

---

5. According to the Arab-Islamic code of honor, decreed and upheld by men.

that they had stopped using that method of torture when they discovered that it didn't torture her. They began to search for other methods.

In the conference chamber next to the hall, the judge and his aides were meeting, deliberating the case. What should they do now that the public had applauded the accused? The judge began to face accusations in his turn:

—We're not accusing you, Your Honour, but you did embarrass us all. As the saying goes: 'The road to hell is paved with good intentions'! You did what you thought was right, but you only managed to make things worse. How could you say, Your Honour, about Him, whom God protect to lead this noble nation all his life, that he is stupid?

—God forbid, sir! I didn't say that, I said that *she* said he was stupid.

—Don't you know the saying, 'What the ear doesn't hear, the heart doesn't grieve over'? You declared in public that he's stupid.

—I didn't say it, sir. I merely repeated what the accused said to make the accusation stick. That's precisely what my job is.

—Yes, that's your job, Your Honour. We know that. But you should have been smarter and wiser than that.

—I don't understand.

—Didn't you hear how the people applauded her?

—Is that my fault?

—Don't you know why they applauded?

—No, I don't.

—Because you said in public what is said in private and it was more like confirming a fact than proving an accusation.

—What else could I have done, sir?

—You could have said that she cursed the mighty one without saying exactly *what* she said.

—And if I'd been asked what kind of curse it was?

—Nobody would have asked you. And besides, you volunteered the answer before anyone asked, as though you'd seized the opportunity to say aloud and in her words, what you yourself wanted to say or perhaps what you do say to yourself in secret.

—Me? How can you accuse me in this way? I was simply performing my duty as I should. Nobody can accuse me of anything. Perhaps I was foolish, but you cannot accuse me of bad faith.

—But foolishness can sometimes be worse than bad faith. You must know that foolishness is the worst label you can stick on a man. And as far as he's concerned, better that he be a swindler, a liar, a miser, a trickster, even a thief or a traitor, rather than foolish. Foolishness means that he doesn't think, that he's mindless, that he's an animal. That's the worst thing you can call an ordinary man. And all the more so if he's a ruler. You don't know rulers, Your Honour, but I know them well. Each of them fancies his brain to be better than any other man's. And it's not just a matter of fantasy, but of blind belief, like the belief in God. For the sake of this illusion, he can kill thousands.[6]

—I didn't know that, sir. How can I get out of this predicament?

---

6. An overt critique of the murderous inclinations fostered by religious fanaticism.

—I don't know why you began with the description 'stupid', Your Honour. If you'd read everything she said, you'd have found that she used other less ugly terms to describe him.

—Such as what, sir? Please, use your experience to help me choose some of them. I don't want to leave here accused, after coming in this morning to raise an accusation.

—Such descriptions cannot be voiced in public. The session must be closed. Even a less ugly description will find an echo in the heart of the people if openly declared. That's what closed sessions are for, Your Honour. Many matters escape you and it seems you have little experience in law.

A few minutes later, utter silence descended on the hall. The courtroom was completely emptied. As for her, they took her back to where she'd been before.

1980

SALMAN RUSHDIE
born 1947

Salman Rushdie, whose extended family lives in India as well as Pakistan, published his fourth novel, *The Satanic Verses*, in England in September 1988. On Valentine's Day 1989, Ayatollah Ruholla Khomeini, then the leader of Shi'a Muslims in Iran, issued a *fatwa*, or religious decree, urging Muslims around the world to murder Rushdie for his acts of blasphemy against Islam in writing the novel. With typical irony, Rushdie called the *fatwa* an unusually harsh "book review." The incident sparked off a global controversy about freedom of expression, modernity, and "Islam versus the West," and Rushdie had to live underground for a decade, with maximum security provided by the British secret service. For many readers ever since, the international fallout from *The Satanic Verses* has been a public measure of its literary value, and a confirmation of Rushdie's status as the world's most important living writer.

Rushdie was born into a wealthy Muslim business family in Bombay in 1947, a few weeks before the end of British colonial rule and the partition of the subcontinent into the two new nations of India and Pakistan. After early education in the city, Rushdie attended boarding school in England and received his undergraduate and master's degrees from the University of Cambridge, where he studied Islamic history. He worked in advertising in London for several years, and wrote his first book—a science-fiction novel—on the side. With the publication of *Midnight's Children* (1980) and its immense literary and commercial success, however, Rushdie was able to turn to writing full time, contributing to periodicals throughout the anglophone world in the 1980s while producing his next two novels, *Shame* (1983) and *The Satanic Verses*.

During his retreat from public view for a dozen years after the Ayatollah Khomeini's *fatwa*, Rushdie's "normal" life was seriously interrupted—two of his first three marriages ended—but seemingly the experience did not affect his creativity. In fact, the voluminous, multifarious criticism of his work and the continued threat to his life strengthened his resolve to imagine, write, and speak his mind as freely as possible. Among his important works published during this period were *The Moor's Last Sigh* (1995), the surreal saga of an Indian family of Jewish Portuguese descent, with connections to the last Muslim ruler of Moorish Spain in the fifteenth century, and *The Ground Beneath Her Feet* (1999), a novel about a love triangle interwoven with the Greek myth of Orpheus and Eurydice. Around the end of the millennium, Rushdie eased back into public life by moving to the United States, teaching at various universities as a writer-in-residence, and reading from his work and speaking to large audiences. His more recent novels—such as *Shalimar the Clown* (2005) and *The Enchantress of Florence* (2008)—and a book for children, *Luka and the Fire of Life* (2010), have not won as much acclaim as his early work. Rushdie's preeminence among his contemporaries was affirmed when the Booker Prize was awarded to *Midnight's Children* in 1981; the novel's enduring achievement was confirmed by special Booker awards, in 1993 and 2008. As a naturalized British citizen, Rushdie was knighted in 2007; toward the end of the decade, he began to spend time in London again, helping his third (former) wife to raise their son.

Rushdie has frequently described himself as a "historian of ideas," and many of his novels are "novels of ideas" rather than narratives centered on plot or character. He is not a realistic writer; he is the foremost practitioner in English of magic realism. Invented before the middle of the twentieth century by Latin American fiction writers, who popularized the genre in the 1950s and 1960s, magic realism is a mode or style in which "reality" is permeated by supernatural forces, miraculous events, larger-than-life presences, and extraordinary characters who may possess magical powers. In his works of magic realism, Rushdie creates characters, objects, and occurrences that break the rules of everyday logic and causality: a person may be present in two places at once, for example, or a human being may travel in time, or live for centuries. Rushdie's goal is to bring the reader closer to reality, which has its rational or rationally explicable features (as described by science) but is also irrational, unpredictable, and bizarre. If magic realism gives Rushdie's work its dimension of fantasy, his fascination with ideas gives it the quality of abstraction. Many of his characters are allegorical, or personifications of ideas: Saleem Sinai, the protagonist of *Midnight's Children*, for instance, is an embodiment of "the idea of India," with his large nose shaped like the country's peninsula on a map, and his physique threatening to break up into 580 million pieces, as many as India's population at the time of writing. In *The Satanic Verses*, a voice asks one of the novel's characters: "What kind of idea are you?" Unlike realistically represented characters, Rushdie's have inner conflicts not of emotions or passions but of ideas.

Rushdie builds his narratives around conflicting ideas and fantastic characters and events with wit and playfulness, and with precise attention to the sensuous details of everyday life. A significant element of his disorienting realism comes from the use of newspaper reports of current events and historical accounts. *Midnight's Children* and *Shame*, for example, draw extensively on the journalistic record on contemporary India and Pakistan, respectively; much of *The Satanic Verses*, *The Moor's Last Sigh*, and *The Enchantress of Florence* relies on readers' historical knowledge of diverse regions of the world, from Arabia in the seventh century, and Spain and Portugal between the eighth and fifteenth centuries, to Italy in the high Renaissance. These shifts in place and time stem from Rushdie's interest in large-scale flux and transformation in human societies: he is the foremost writer of our times on migration, immigrant communities, diasporas, and cultural mixing, or hybridity.

"The Perforated Sheet," the selection below, reads like a self-contained short story but is actually an excerpt, prepared by Rushdie himself, from the first two chapters of *Midnight's Children*, with a few connecting lines not found in the novel. It introduces us to Saleem Sinai, the protagonist and narrator, and to the story of his life and origins, which constitutes the novel's Protean narrative. Saleem is born at midnight, between August 14 and 15, 1947, the moment at which India and Pakistan became separate nations; as a "child" of that historic hour, he finds that his destiny is entwined with India's fate as a nation, so that his life unfolds as a precise parallel to the country's collective history thereafter. In "The Perforated Sheet" we encounter the beginning of that story as Saleem sees it: the time, almost half a century before his birth, when his grandfather returns from Europe with a medical degree; sets up a practice in his hometown of Srinagar, Kashmir; and meets the woman who is destined to become his wife, thereby launching the cascade of events that will culminate, two generations later, in Saleem's momentous arrival.

In the novel itself, every important event in the history of the Sinai family, from Saleem's grandparents onward, is a funny, farcical echo of every major event in the history of the Indian subcontinent. Thus Saleem's birth coincides with the birth of the nation of India. And, since the twin nations of India and Pakistan (which represent the religions of Hinduism and Islam, respectively) are born at the same moment, the birth of Saleem (a Muslim boy) coincides, as well, with the birth of his hateful "nemesis," Shiva (a Hindu boy). Saleem and Shiva's lives, from infancy to adulthood, then replicate the simultaneous histories of India/Hinduism and Pakistan/Islam. This comical story is complicated by the fact that a poor Christian nurse at the hospital where Saleem and Shiva are born (to different mothers) switches the babies, as an act of impersonal class revenge on their well-to-do parents. Saleem, who grows up in the Sinai family believing that he is a Muslim, is actually the biological son of a Hindu mother, and the reverse is true of Shiva.

A further fictional complication then ensues. During the first hour after the fateful midnight of August 14–15, 1947, exactly 1,001 children are born in India and Pakistan, and all of them—including Saleem and Shiva—possess magical powers. They are, as it were, the Chosen Ones; they are all "Midnight's Children" (hence the novel's title), they can telepathically connect with one another, and their individual destinies are intertwined with their nations' and each other's destinies, down to the last detail. Saleem grows up with an inexplicable "buzzing" in his head, and discovers that it is the buzz of the voices of hundreds of other Midnight's Children, with whom he can communicate directly. The culmination of the narrative is that everything that happens on the Indian subcontinent after 1947 has only one objective: to destroy these gifted children. "The Perforated Sheet" is thus the beginning of a story that is at once comic and tragic, on an epic scale.

The Perforated Sheet[1]

I was born in the city of Bombay . . . once upon a time. No, that won't do, there's no getting away from the date: I was born in Doctor Narlikar's Nursing Home on August 15th, 1947.[2] And the time? The time matters, too. Well then: at night. No, it's important to be more . . . On the stroke of midnight, as a matter of fact. Clock-hands joined palms in respectful greeting as I came. Oh, spell it out, spell it out: at the precise instant of India's arrival at independence, I tumbled forth into the world. There were gasps. And, outside the window, fireworks and crowds. A few seconds later, my father broke his big toe; but his accident was a mere trifle when set beside what had befallen me in that benighted moment, because thanks to the occult tyrannies of those blandly saluting clocks I had been mysteriously handcuffed to history, my destinies indissolubly chained to those of my country. For the next three decades, there was to be no escape. Soothsayers had prophesied me, newspapers celebrated my arrival, politicos ratified my authenticity. I was left entirely without a say in the matter. I, Saleem Sinai, later variously called Snotnose, Stainface, Baldy, Sniffer, Buddha and even Piece-of-the-Moon, had become heavily embroiled in Fate—at the best of times a dangerous sort of involvement. And I couldn't even wipe my own nose at the time.

Now, however, time (having no further use for me) is running out. I will soon be thirty-one years old. Perhaps. If my crumbling, over-used body permits. But I have no hope of saving my life, nor can I count on having even a thousand nights and a night. I must work fast, faster than Scheherazade,[3] if I am to end up meaning—yes, meaning—something. I admit it: above all things, I fear absurdity.

And there are so many stories to tell, too many, such an excess of intertwined lives events miracles places rumours, so dense a commingling of the improbable and the mundane! I have been a swallower of lives; and to know me, just the one of me, you'll have to swallow the lot as well. Consumed multitudes are jostling and shoving inside me; and guided only by the memory of a large white bedsheet with a roughly circular hole some seven inches in diameter cut into the centre, clutching at the dream of that holey, mutilated square of linen, which is my talisman, my open-sesame, I must commence the business of remaking my life from the point at which it really began, some thirty-two years before anything as obvious, as *present*, as my clock-ridden crime-stained birth.

(The sheet, incidentally, is stained too, with three drops of old, faded redness. As the Quran tells us: *Recite, in the name of the Lord thy Creator, who created Man from clots of blood.*)

One Kashmiri morning in the early spring of 1915, my grandfather Aadam Aziz[4] hit his nose against a frost-hardened tussock of earth while attempting to pray. Three drops of blood plopped out of his left nostril, hardened instantly in the

---

1. Excerpted by the author from the first two chapters of *Midnight's Children*, with connecting material not in the original novel.
2. The date is that of India's official independence from British colonial rule.
3. Shahrazad, the narrator in the *Arabian*

Nights, who, night after night, tells stories to Prince Shahrayar, the kingdom's ruler, in order to defer, perhaps indefinitely, her execution.
4. A Muslim name; "Aadam" is the Arabic equivalent of Adam.

brittle air and lay before his eyes on the prayer-mat, transformed into rubies. Lurching back until he knelt with his head once more upright, he found that the tears which had sprung to his eyes had solidified, too; and at that moment, as he brushed diamonds contemptuously from his lashes, he resolved never again to kiss earth for any god or man. This decision, however, made a hole in him, a vacancy in a vital inner chamber, leaving him vulnerable to women and history. Unaware of this at first, despite his recently completed medical training, he stood up, rolled the prayer-mat into a thick cheroot, and holding it under his right arm surveyed the valley through clear, diamond-free eyes.

The world was new again. After a winter's gestation in its eggshell of ice, the valley had beaked its way out into the open, moist and yellow. The new grass bided its time underground: the mountains were retreating to their hill-stations for the warm season. (In the winter, when the valley shrank under the ice, the mountains closed in and snarled like angry jaws around the city on the lake.)

In those days the radio mast had not been built and the temple of Sankara Acharya, a little black blister on a khaki hill, still dominated the streets and lake of Srinagar.[5] In those days there was no army camp at the lakeside, no endless snakes of camouflaged trucks and jeeps clogged the narrow mountain roads, no soldiers hid behind the crests of the mountains past Baramulla and Gulmarg.[6] In those days travellers were not shot as spies if they took photographs of bridges, and apart from the Englishmen's houseboats on the lake, the valley had hardly changed since the Mughal Empire,[7] for all its springtime renewals; but my grandfather's eyes—which were, like the rest of him, twenty-five years old—saw things differently . . . and his nose had started to itch.

To reveal the secret of my grandfather's altered vision: he had spent five years, five springs, away from home. (The tussock of earth, crucial though its presence was as it crouched under a chance wrinkle of the prayer-mat, was at bottom no more than a catalyst.) Now, returning, he saw through travelled eyes. Instead of the beauty of the tiny valley circled by giant teeth, he noticed the narrowness, the proximity of the horizon; and felt sad, to be at home and feel so utterly enclosed. He also felt—inexplicably—as though the old place resented his educated, stethoscoped return. Beneath the winter ice, it had been coldly neutral, but now there was no doubt; the years in Germany had returned him to a hostile environment. Many years later, when the hole inside him had been clogged up with hate, and he came to sacrifice himself at the shrine of the black stone god in the temple on the hill, he would try and recall his childhood springs in Paradise,[8] the way it was before travel and tussocks and army tanks messed everything up.

---

5. The main city in the Valley of Kashmir, now in the northernmost state of India, Srinagar is set on Lake Dal. In the late classical period (ca. 8th to 11th centuries), Kashmir was a Hindu kingdom famous for its patronage of learning and the arts; Shankara Acharya (ca. 8th century) was the period's most influential Hindu philosopher and theologian.
6. Situated close to the western edge of Kashmir, Baramulla is the second-largest city in the region, after Srinagar. Gulmarg is a famous ski resort near Baramulla.
7. The subcontinent's largest and wealthiest empire, the Mughal Empire lasted from 1526 to 1858. "Mughal" is a variation on "Mongol"; the Mughals were descended matrilineally from the Mongolian conqueror Genghis Khan (late 12th–early 13th centuries).
8. The Mughal emperor Jahangir (ruled 1600–1625) called Kashmir "Paradise," and the epithet has been popular ever since.

On the morning when the valley, gloved in a prayer-mat,[9] punched him on the nose, he had been trying, absurdly, to pretend that nothing had changed. So he had risen in the bitter cold of four-fifteen, washed himself in the prescribed fashion, dressed and put on his father's astrakhan cap; after which he had carried the rolled cheroot of the prayer-mat into the small lakeside garden in front of their old dark house and unrolled it over the waiting tussock. The ground felt deceptively soft under his feet and made him simultaneously uncertain and unwary. 'In the Name of God, the Compassionate, the Merciful . . .'—the exordium, spoken with hands joined before him like a book, comforted a part of him, made another, larger part feel uneasy— '. . . Praise be to Allah, Lord of the Creation . . .'[1]—but now Heidelberg invaded his head; here was Ingrid, briefly his Ingrid, her face scorning him for this Mecca-turned parroting; here, their friends Oskar and Ilse Lubin the anarchists, mocking his prayer with their anti-ideologies—'. . . The Compassionate, the Merciful. King of the Last Judgment! . . .'—Heidelberg, in which, along with medicine and politics, he learned that India—like radium—had been 'discovered' by the Europeans; even Oskar was filled with admiration for Vasco da Gama,[2] and this was what finally separated Aadam Aziz from his friends, this belief of theirs that he was somehow the invention of their ancestors—'. . . You alone we worship, and to You alone we pray for help . . .'—so here he was, despite their presence in his head, attempting to re-unite himself with an earlier self which ignored their influence but knew everything it ought to have known, about submission for example, about what he was doing now, as his hands, guided by old memories, fluttered upwards, thumbs pressed to ears, fingers spread, as he sank to his knees—'. . . Guide us to the straight path. The path of those whom You have favoured . . .' But it was no good, he was caught in a strange middle ground, trapped between belief and disbelief, and this was only a charade after all—'. . . Not of those who have incurred Your wrath. Nor of those who have gone astray.' My grandfather bent his forehead towards the earth. Forward he bent, and the earth, prayer-mat-covered, curved up towards him. And now it was the tussock's time. At one and the same time a rebuke from Ilse-Oskar-Ingrid-Heidelberg as well as valley-and-God, it smote him upon the point of the nose. Three drops fell. There were rubies and diamonds. And my grandfather, lurching upright, made a resolve. Stood. Rolled cheroot. Stared across the lake. And was knocked forever into that middle place, unable to worship a God in whose existence he could not wholly disbelieve. Permanent alteration: a hole.

The lake was no longer frozen over. The thaw had come rapidly, as usual; many of the small boats, the shikaras,[3] had been caught napping, which was also normal. But while these sluggards slept on, on dry land, snoring peacefully beside their owners, the oldest boat was up at the crack as old folk often are,

---

9. As prescribed for Muslims, Aadam Aziz prays five times a day, kneeling on his prayer mat; his injury occurs during one of his prayers.
1. Aadam Aziz's words of prayer are from the Qur'an, and invoke Allah, the one and only true God in Islam.
2. Vasco da Gama (ca. 1460–1524), Portu-

guese explorer and first European to navigate the sea route from Europe, around Africa, to India, in 1498.
3. A "shikara" is a distinctive, long rowboat used on Lake Dal, similar to a British double skiff used on the Thames. It transports people and goods around Srinagar.

and was therefore the first craft to move across the unfrozen lake. Tai's shikara . . . this, too, was customary.

Watch how the old boatman,[4] Tai, makes good time through the misty water, standing stooped over at the back of his craft! How his oar, a wooden heart on a yellow stick, drives jerkily through the weeds! In these parts he's considered very odd because he rows standing up . . . among other reasons. Tai, bringing an urgent summons to Doctor Aziz, is about to set history in motion . . . while Aadam, looking down into the water, recalls what Tai taught him years ago: 'The ice is always waiting, Aadam baba,[5] just under the water's skin.' Aadam's eyes are a clear blue, the astonishing blue of mountain sky, which has a habit of dripping into the pupils of Kashmiri men; they have not forgotten how to look. They see—there! like the skeleton of a ghost, just beneath the surface of Lake Dal!—the delicate tracery, the intricate crisscross of colourless lines, the cold waiting veins of the future. His German years, which have blurred so much else, haven't deprived him of the gift of seeing. Tai's gift. He looks up, sees the approaching V of Tai's boat, waves a greeting. Tai's arm rises—but this is a command. 'Wait!' My grandfather waits; and during this hiatus, as he experiences the last peace of his life, a muddy, ominous sort of peace, I had better get round to describing him.

Keeping out of my voice the natural envy of the ugly man for the strikingly impressive, I record that Doctor Aziz was a tall man. Pressed flat against a wall of his family home, he measured twenty-five bricks (a brick for each year of his life), or just over six foot two. A strong man also. His beard was thick and red— and annoyed his mother, who said only Hajis, men who had made the pilgrimage to Mecca, should grow red beards. His hair, however, was rather darker. His sky-eyes you know about. Ingrid had said, 'They went mad with the colours when they made your face.' But the central feature of my grandfather's anatomy was neither colour nor height, neither strength of arm nor straightness of back. There it was, reflected in the water, undulating like a mad plantain in the centre of his face . . . Aadam Aziz, waiting for Tai, watches his rippling nose. It would have dominated less dramatic faces than his easily; even on him, it is what one sees first and remembers longest. 'A cyranose,' Ilse Lubin said, and Oskar added, 'A proboscissimus.' Ingrid announced, 'You could cross a river on that nose.' (Its bridge was wide.)

My grandfather's nose: nostrils flaring, curvaceous as dancers. Between them swells the nose's triumphal arch, first up and out, then down and under, sweeping in to his upper lip with a superb and at present red-tipped flick. An easy nose to hit a tussock with. I wish to place on record my gratitude to this mighty organ—if not for it, who would ever have believed me to be truly my mother's son, my grandfather's grandson?—this colossal apparatus which was to be my birthright, too. Doctor Aziz's nose—comparable only to the trunk of the elephant-headed god Ganesh—established incontrovertibly his right to be a patriarch. It was Tai who taught him that, too. When young Aadam was barely past puberty the dilapidated boatman said, 'That's a nose to start a family

---

4. Tai operates a ferry boat on Lake Dal in Srinagar.
5. In Hindu and Urdu, "baba" is a term of respect (for a social superior) as well as of affec-

tion (for a child, an adult, or an old person); here Tai, an old man, uses it in both senses at once.

on, my princeling. There'd be no mistaking whose brood they were. Mughal Emperors would have given their right hands for noses like that one. There are dynasties waiting inside it,'—and here Tai lapsed into coarseness—'like snot.'

Nobody could remember when Tai had been young. He had been plying this same boat, standing in the same hunched position, across the Dal and Nageen Lakes . . . forever. As far as anyone knew. He lived somewhere in the insanitary bowels of the old wooden-house quarter and his wife grew lotus roots and other curious vegetables on one of the many 'floating gardens' lilting on the surface of the spring and summer water. Tai himself cheerily admitted he had no idea of his age. Neither did his wife—he was, she said, already leathery when they married. His face was a sculpture of wind on water: ripples made of hide. He had two golden teeth and no others. In the town, he had few friends. Few boatmen or traders invited him to share a hookah when he floated past the shikara moorings or one of the lakes' many ramshackle, waterside provision-stores and tea-shops.

The general opinion of Tai had been voiced long ago by Aadam Aziz's father the gemstone merchant: 'His brain fell out with his teeth.' It was an impression the boatman fostered by his chatter, which was fantastic, grandiloquent and ceaseless, and as often as not addressed only to himself. Sound carries over water, and the lake people giggled at his monologues; but with undertones of awe, and even fear. Awe, because the old halfwit knew the lakes and hills better than any of his detractors; fear, because of his claim to an antiquity so immense it defied numbering, and moreover hung so lightly round his chicken's neck that it hadn't prevented him from winning a highly desirable wife and fathering four sons upon her . . . and a few more, the story went, on other lakeside wives. The young bucks at the shikara moorings were convinced he had a pile of money hidden away somewhere—a hoard, perhaps, of priceless golden teeth, rattling in a sack like walnuts. And, as a child, Aadam Aziz had loved him.

He made his living as a simple ferryman, despite all the rumours of wealth, taking hay and goats and vegetables and wood across the lakes for cash; people, too. When he was running his taxi-service he erected a pavilion in the centre of the shikara, a gay affair of flowered-patterned curtains and canopy, with cushions to match; and deodorised his boat with incense. The sight of Tai's shikara approaching, curtains flying, had always been for Doctor Aziz one of the defining images of the coming of spring. Soon the English sahibs would arrive and Tai would ferry them to the Shalimar Gardens and the King's Spring, chattering and pointy and stooped, a quirky, enduring familiar spirit of the valley.[6] A watery Caliban, rather too fond of cheap Kashmiri brandy.

The Boy Aadam, my grandfather-to-be, fell in love with the boatman Tai precisely because of the endless verbiage which made others think him cracked. It was magical talk, words pouring from him like fools' money, past his two gold teeth, laced with hiccups and brandy, soaring up to the most remote Himalayas[7] of the past, then swooping shrewdly on some present detail, Aadam's nose for instance, to vivisect its meaning like a mouse. This friendship had

---

6. The Shalimar Gardens are the modern form of the Mughal-style rose garden first laid near Srinagar for Emperor Jahangir in 1619.

7. The western end of the Himalayas, the world's highest mountain range, wraps around the north of Kashmir.

plunged Aadam into hot water with great regularity. (Boiling water. Literally. While his mother said. 'We'll kill that boatman's bugs if it kills you.') But still the old soliloquist would dawdle in his boat at the garden's lakeside toes and Aziz would sit at his feet until voices summoned him indoors to be lectured on Tai's filthiness and warned about the pillaging armies of germs his mother envisaged leaping from that hospitably ancient body on to her son's starched white loose-pajamas. But always Aadam returned to the water's edge to scan the mists for the ragged reprobate's hunched-up frame steering its magical boat through the enchanted waters of the morning.

'But how old are you really, Taiji?'[8] (Doctor Aziz, adult, red-bearded, slanting towards the future, remembers the day he asked the unaskable question.) For an instant, silence, noisier than a waterfall. The monologue, interrupted. Slap of oar in water. He was riding in the shikara with Tai, squatting amongst goats, on a pile of straw, in full knowledge of the stick and bathtub waiting for him at home. He had come for stories—and with one question had silenced the storyteller.

'No, tell, Taiji, how old, *truly?*' And now a brandy bottle, materialising from nowhere: cheap liquor from the folds of the great warm chugha-coat.[9] Then a shudder, a belch, a glare. Glint of gold. And—at last!—speech. 'How old? You ask how old, you little wet-head, you nosey . . .' Tai pointed at the mountains. 'So old, nakkoo!' Aadam, the nakkoo, the nosey one, followed his pointing finger. 'I have watched the mountains being born; I have seen Emperors die. Listen. Listen, nakkoo[1] . . .'—the brandy bottle again, followed by brandy-voice, and words more intoxicating than booze—'. . . I saw that Isa, that Christ, when he came to Kashmir.[2] Smile, smile, it is your history I am keeping in my head. Once it was set down in old lost books. Once I knew where there was a grave with pierced feet carved on the tombstone, which bled once a year. Even my memory is going now; but I know, although I can't read.' Illiteracy, dismissed with a flourish; literature crumbled beneath the rage of his sweeping hand. Which sweeps again to chugha-pocket, to brandy bottle, to lips chapped with cold. Tai always had woman's lips. 'Nakkoo, listen, listen. I have seen plenty. Yara,[3] you should've seen that Isa when he came, beard down to his balls, bald as an egg on his head. He was old and fagged-out but he knew his manners. "You first, Taiji," he'd say, and "Please to sit"; always a respectful tongue, he never called me crackpot, never called me *tu* either. Always *aap*.[4] Polite, see? And what an appetite! Such a hunger, I would catch my ears in fright. Saint or devil, I swear he could eat a whole kid in one go. And so what? I told him, eat, fill your hole, a man comes to Kashmir to enjoy life, or to end it, or both. His work was finished. He just came up here to live it up a little.' Mesmerised by

8. In Hindi and Urdu, the main languages of northern India, the suffix "-ji" is an honorific added to names and epithets, to address elders and superiors. Aadam Aziz addresses the "lowly" boatman as "Taiji" out of respect for the latter's age.
9. "Chuga" or "choga," the Persian word for a loose, cassocklike garment for Muslim men.
1. "Nakkoo," literally "nosy" in Hindi and Urdu, is Tai's playful epithet for the large-nosed Aadam Aziz.

2. An apocryphal legend in the Muslim and Hindu worlds is that at the end of his life, as recorded in the Bible, Jesus Christ left Jerusalem, living out his last days in Kashmir.
3. "Yara" is the common Urdu term of endearment for friend, buddy, loved one, or close companion.
4. In Hindi and Urdu, *tu* is the intimate or familiar form of "you," whereas *aap* is the formal, respectful form of the pronoun.

this brandied portrait of a bald, gluttonous Christ, Aziz listened, later repeating every word to the consternation of his parents, who dealt in stones and had no time for 'gas.'

'Oh, you don't believe?'—licking his sore lips with a grin, knowing it to be the reverse of the truth; 'Your attention is wandering?'—again, he knew how furiously Aziz was hanging on his words. 'Maybe the straw is pricking your behind, hey? Oh, I'm so sorry, babaji, not to provide for you silk cushions with gold brocade-work—cushions such as the Emperor Jehangir[5] sat upon! You think the Emperor Jehangir as a gardener only, no doubt,' Tai accused my grandfather, 'because he built Shalimar. Stupid! What do you know? His name meant Encompasser of the Earth. Is that a gardener's name? God knows what they teach you boys these days. Whereas I' . . . puffing up a little here . . . 'I knew his precise weight, to the tola! Ask me how many maunds, how many seers! When he was happy he got heavier and in Kashmir he was heaviest of all. I used to carry his litter . . . no, no, look, you don't believe again, that big cucumber in your face is waggling like the little one in your pajamas! So, come on, come on, ask me questions! Give examination! Ask how many times the leather thongs wound round the handles of the litter—the answer is thirty-one. Ask me what was the Emperor's dying word—I tell you it was "Kashmir." He had bad breath and a good heart. Who do you think I am? Some common ignorant lying pie-dog? Go, get out of the boat now, your nose makes it too heavy to row; also your father is waiting to beat my gas out of you, and your mother to boil off your skin.'

Despite beating and boiling, Aadam Aziz floated with Tai in his shikara, again and again, amid goats hay flowers furniture lotus-roots, though never with the English sahibs,[6] and heard again and again the miraculous answers to that single terrifying question: 'But Taiji, how old are you, *honestly*?'

From Tai, Aadam learned the secrets of the lake—where you could swim without being pulled down by weeds; the eleven varieties of water-snake; where the frogs spawned; how to cook a lotus-root; and where the three English women had drowned a few years back. 'There is a tribe of feringhee women who come to this water to drown,' Tai said. 'Sometimes they know it, sometimes they don't, but I know the minute I smell them. They hide under the water from God knows what or who—but they can't hide from me, baba!' Tai's laugh, emerging to infect Aadam—a huge, booming laugh that seemed macabre when it crashed out of that old, withered body, but which was so natural in my giant grandfather that nobody knew, in later times, that it wasn't really his. And, also from Tai, my grandfather heard about noses.

Tai tapped his left nostril. 'You know what this is, nakkoo? It's the place where the outside world meets the world inside you. If they don't get on, you feel it here. Then you rub your nose with embarrassment to make the itch go away. A nose like that, little idiot, is a great gift. I say: trust it. When it warns you, look out or you'll be finished. Follow your nose and you'll go far.' He cleared his throat; his eyes rolled away into the mountains of the past. Aziz

---

5. The fourth ruler in the Mughal dynasty, on the throne from 1600 to 1625.
6. "Sahib" is the Anglicized form of the Persian *saheb*, a respectful term of address for a rich or powerful man, a ruler or administrator, or a superior; it became the common epithet for British colonial administrators in India.

settled back on the straw. 'I knew one officer once—in the army of that Iskandar the Great. Never mind his name. He had a vegetable just like yours hanging between his eyes. When the army halted near Gandhara,[7] he fell in love with some local floozy. At once his nose itched like crazy. He scratched it, but that was useless. He inhaled vapours from crushed boiled eucalyptus leaves. Still no good, baba! The itching sent him wild; but the damn fool dug in his heels and stayed with his little witch when the army went home. He became— what?—a stupid thing, neither this nor that, a half-and-halfer with a nagging wife and an itch in the nose, and in the end he pushed his sword into his stomach. What do you think of that?'

Doctor Aziz in 1915, whom rubies and diamonds have turned into a half-and-halfer, remembers this story as Tai enters hailing distance. His nose is itching still. He scratches, shrugs, tosses his head; and then Tai shouts.

'Ohé! Doctor Sahib! Ghani the landowner's daughter is sick.'

. . . The young Doctor has entered the throes of a most unhippocratic excitement at the boatman's cry, and shouts, 'I'm coming just now! Just let me bring my things!' The shikara's prow touches the garden's hem. Aadam is rushing indoors, prayer-mat rolled like a cheroot under one arm, blue eyes blinking in the sudden interior gloom; he has placed the cheroot on a high shelf on top of stacked copies of *Vorwärts* and Lenin's *What Is to Be Done?*[8] and other pamphlets, dusty echoes of his half-faded German life; he is pulling out, from under his bed, a second-hand leather case which his mother called his 'doctori-attaché,'[9] and as he swings it and himself upwards and runs from the room, the word HEIDELBERG is briefly visible, burned into the leather on the bottom of the bag. A landowner's daughter is good news indeed to a doctor with a career to make, even if she is ill. No: *because* she is ill.

. . . Slap of oar in water. Plop of spittle in lake. Tai clears his throat and mutters angrily, 'A fine business. A wet-head nakkoo child goes away before he's learned one damn thing and he comes back a big doctor sahib with a big bag full of foreign machines, and he's still as silly as an owl. I swear: a too bad business.'

. . . 'Big shot,' Tai is spitting into the lake, 'big bag, big shot. Pah! We haven't got enough bags at home that you must bring back that thing made of a pig's skin that makes one unclean just by looking at it? And inside, God knows what all.' Doctor Aziz, seated amongst flowery curtains and the smell of incense, has his thoughts wrenched away from the patient waiting across the lake. Tai's bitter monologue breaks into his consciousness, creating a sense of dull shock, a smell like a casualty ward overpowering the incense . . . the old man is clearly furious about something, possessed by an incomprehensible rage that appears to be directed at his erstwhile acolyte, or, more precisely and oddly, at his bag. Doctor Aziz attempts to make small talk . . . 'Your wife is well? Do they still talk

7. "Iskandar" or "Sikandar" is the Indian equivalent of "Alexander" the Great, whose army reached the subcontinent in 327 B.C.E. The farthest north Alexander went was to Gandhara, the region now around Peshawar and the Swat Valley in northwest Pakistan. When he turned back, Alexander left behind a Greek colony in Gandhara, which flourished there for several centuries as the eastern out-post of his empire.
8. Vladimir Lenin's small book, first published in 1902, quickly became a classic of socialist and communist theory and polemics, outlining a program that culminated in the Bolshevik Revolution of 1917 in Russia.
9. "Doctori-attaché" is an Indianized term for a doctor's satchel or attache case.

about your bag of golden teeth?' . . . tries to remake an old friendship; but Tai is in full flight now, a stream of invective pouring out of him. The Heidelberg bag quakes under the torrent of abuse. 'Sistersleeping pigskin bag[1] from Abroad full of foreigners' tricks. Big-shot bag. Now if a man breaks an arm that bag will not let the bone-setter bind it in leaves. Now a man must let his wife lie beside that bag and watch knives come and cut her open. A fine business, what these foreigners put in our young men's heads. I swear: it is a too-bad thing. That bag should fry in Hell with the testicles of the ungodly.'

. . . 'Do you still pickle water-snakes in brandy to give you virility, Taiji? Do you still like to eat lotus-root without any spices?' Hesitant questions, brushed aside by the torrent of Tai's fury. Doctor Aziz begins to diagnose. To the ferryman, the bag represents Abroad; it is the alien thing, the invader, progress. And yes, it has indeed taken possession of the young Doctor's mind: and yes, it contains knives, and cures for cholera and malaria and smallpox; and yes, it sits between doctor and boatman, and has made them antagonists. Doctor Aziz begins to fight, against sadness, and against Tai's anger, which is beginning to infect him, to become his own, which erupts only rarely, but comes, when it does come, unheralded in a roar from his deepest places, laying waste everything in sight; and then vanishes, leaving him wondering why everyone is so upset . . . They are approaching Ghani's house. A bearer[2] awaits the shikara, standing with clasped hands on a little wooden jetty. Aziz fixes his mind on the job in hand.

The bearer holds the shikara steady as Aadam Aziz climbs out, bag in hand. And now, at last, Tai speaks directly to my grandfather. Scorn in his face, Tai asks, 'Tell me this, Doctor Sahib: have you got in that bag made of dead pigs one of those machines that foreign doctors use to smell with?' Aadam shakes his head, not understanding. Tai's voice gathers new layers of disgust. 'You know, sir, a thing like an elephant's trunk.' Aziz, seeing what he means, replies: 'A stethoscope? Naturally.' Tai pushes the shikara off from the jetty. Spits. Begins to row away. 'I knew it,' he says. 'You will use such a machine now, instead of your own big nose.'

My grandfather does not trouble to explain that a stethoscope is more like a pair of ears than a nose. He is stifling his own irritation, the resentful anger of a cast-off child; and besides, there is a patient waiting.

The house was opulent but badly lit. Ghani was a widower and the servants clearly took advantage. There were cobwebs in corners and layers of dust on ledges. They walked down a long corridor; one of the doors was ajar and through it Aziz saw a room in a state of violent disorder. This glimpse, connected with a glint of light in Ghani's dark glasses, suddenly informed Aziz that the land-owner was blind. This aggravated his sense of unease . . . They halted outside a thick teak door. Ghani said, 'Wait here two moments,' and went into the room behind the door.

In later years, Doctor Aadam Aziz swore that during those two moments of solitude in the gloomy spidery corridors of the landowner's mansion he was

---

1. Muslims and Semitic people consider the pig a polluting animal; a pigskin bag is therefore a proscribed object in this context. "Sistersleeping" is the narrator's playful variation on the most common curse word in Hindi and Urdu.
2. Common British-Indian colonial-era term for a servant, helper, or waiter.

gripped by an almost uncontrollable desire to turn and run away as fast as his legs would carry him. Unnerved by the enigma of the blind art-lover, his insides filled with tiny scrabbling insects as a result of the insidious venom of Tai's mutterings, his nostrils itching to the point of convincing him that he had somehow contracted venereal disease, he felt his feet begin slowly, as though encased in boots of lead, to turn; felt blood pounding in his temples; and was seized by so powerful a sensation of standing upon a point of no return that he very nearly wet his German woollen trousers. He began, without knowing it, to blush furiously; and at this point a woman with the biceps of a wrestler appeared, beckoning him to follow her into the room. The state of her sari[3] told him that she was a servant; but she was not servile. 'You look green as a fish,' she said. 'You young doctors. You come into a strange house and your liver turns to jelly. Come, Doctor Sahib, they are waiting for you.' Clutching his bag a fraction too tightly, he followed her through the dark teak door.

. . . Into a spacious bedchamber that was as ill-lit as the rest of the house; although here there were shafts of dusty sunlight seeping in through a fanlight high on one wall. These fusty rays illuminated a scene as remarkable as anything the Doctor had ever witnessed: a tableau of such surpassing strangeness that his feet began to twitch towards the door once again. Two more women, also built like professional wrestlers, stood stiffly in the light, each holding one corner of an enormous white bedsheet, their arms raised high above their heads so that the sheet hung between them like a curtain.[4] Mr Ghani welled up out of the murk surrounding the sunlit sheet and permitted the nonplussed Aadam to stare stupidly at the peculiar tableau for perhaps half a minute, at the end of which, and before a word had been spoken, the Doctor made a discovery:

In the very centre of the sheet, a hole had been cut, a crude circle about seven inches in diameter.

'Close the door, ayah.' Ghani instructed the first of the lady wrestlers, and then, turning to Aziz, became confidential. 'This town contains many good-for-nothings who have on occasion tried to climb into my daughter's room. She needs,' he nodded at the three musclebound women, 'protectors.'

Aziz was still looking at the perforated sheet. Ghani said, 'All right, come on, you will examine my Naseem right now. *Pronto.*'

My grandfather peered around the room. 'But where is she, Ghani Sahib?' he blurted out finally. The lady wrestlers adopted supercilious expressions and, it seemed to him, tightened their musculatures, just in case he intended to try something fancy.

'Ah, I see your confusion,' Ghani said, his poisonous smile broadening. 'You Europe-returned chappies forget certain things. Doctor Sahib, my daughter is a decent girl, it goes without saying. She does not flaunt her body under the noses of strange men. You will understand that you cannot be permitted to see her, no, not in any circumstances; accordingly I have required her to be positioned behind that sheet. She stands there, like a good girl.'

---

3. The sari, a full-body wrap, is the most common attire for adult Hindu women.
4. Muslim women are required to be fully veiled in the presence of men not belonging to their families or intimate social circles. In this part of the novel, the bedsheet serving as a "curtain" between patient and doctor becomes an elaborate, comical proxy for the traditional Muslim veil.

A frantic note had crept into Doctor Aziz's voice. 'Ghani Sahib, tell me how I am to examine her without looking at her?' Ghani smiled on.

'You will kindly specify which portion of my daughter it is necessary to inspect. I will then issue her with my instructions to place the required segment against that hole which you see there. And so, in this fashion the thing may be achieved.'

'But what, in any event, does the lady complain of?'—my grandfather, despairingly. To which Mr Ghani, his eyes rising upwards in their sockets, his smile twisting into a grimace of grief, replied: 'The poor child! She has a terrible, a too dreadful stomach-ache.'

'In that case,' Doctor Aziz said with some restraint, 'will she show me her stomach, please.'

My grandfather's premonitions in the corridor were not without foundation. In the succeeding months and years, he fell under what I can only describe as the sorcerer's spell of that enormous—and as yet unstained—perforated cloth.

In those years, you see, the landowner's daughter Naseem Ghani contracted a quite extraordinary number of minor illnesses, and each time a shikara-wallah was dispatched to summon the tall young Doctor Sahib with the big nose who was making such a reputation for himself in the valley. Aadam Aziz's visits to the bedroom with the shaft of sunlight and the three lady wrestlers became weekly events; and on each occasion he was vouchsafed a glimpse, through the mutilated sheet, of a different seven-inch circle of the young woman's body. Her initial stomach-ache was succeeded by a very slightly twisted right ankle, an ingrowing toenail on the big toe of the left foot, a tiny cut on the lower left calf. 'Tetanus is a killer, Doctor Sahib,' the landowner said. 'My Naseem must not die for a scratch.' There was the matter of her stiff right knee, which the Doctor was obliged to manipulate through the hole in the sheet . . . and after a time the illnesses leapt upwards, avoiding certain unmentionable zones, and began to proliferate around her upper half. She suffered from something mysterious which her father called Finger Rot, which made the skin flake off her hands; from weakness of the wrist-bones, for which Aadam prescribed calcium tablets; and from attacks of constipation, for which he gave her a course of laxatives, since there was no question of being permitted to administer an enema. She had fevers and she also had sub-normal temperatures. At these times his thermometer would be placed under her armpit and he would hum and haw about the relative inefficiency of the method. In the opposite armpit she once developed a slight case of tineachloris and he dusted her with yellow powder; after this treatment—which required him to rub the powder in, gently but firmly, although the soft secret body began to shake and quiver and he heard helpless laughter coming through the sheet, because Naseem Ghani was very ticklish—the itching went away, but Naseem soon found a new set of complaints. She waxed anaemic in the summer and bronchial in the winter. ('Her tubes are most delicate,' Ghani explained, 'like little flutes.') Far away the Great War moved from crisis to crisis, while in the cobwebbed house Doctor Aziz was also engaged in a total war against his sectioned patient's inexhaustible complaints. And, in all those war years, Naseem never repeated an illness. 'Which only shows,' Ghani told him, 'that you are a good doctor. When you cure, she is cured for good. But alas!'—he struck his forehead—'She pines for her late mother, poor baby, and her body suffers. She is a too loving child.'

So gradually Doctor Aziz came to have a picture of Naseem in his mind, a badly-fitting collage of her severally-inspected parts. This phantasm of a partitioned woman began to haunt him, and not only in his dreams. Glued together by his imagination, she accompanied him on all his rounds, she moved into the front room of his mind, so that waking and sleeping he could feel in his fingertips the softness of her ticklish skin or the perfect tiny wrists or the beauty of the ankles; he could smell her scent of lavender and chambeli; he could hear her voice and her helpless laughter of a little girl; but she was headless, because he had never seen her face.

By 1918, Aadam Aziz had come to live for his regular trips across the lake. And now his eagerness became even more intense, because it became clear that, after three years, the landowner and his daughter had become willing to lower certain barriers. Now, for the first time, Ghani said, 'A lump in the right chest. Is it worrying, Doctor? Look. Look well.' And there, framed in the hole, was a perfectly-formed and lyrically lovely . . . 'I must touch it,' Aziz said, fighting with his voice. Ghani slapped him on the back. 'Touch, touch!' he cried. 'The hands of the healer! The curing touch, eh, Doctor?' And Aziz reached out a hand . . . 'Forgive me for asking; but is it the lady's time of the month?' . . . Little secret smiles appearing on the faces of the lady wrestlers. Ghani, nodding affably: 'Yes. Don't be so embarrassed, old chap. We are family and doctor now.' And Aziz, 'Then don't worry. The lumps will go when the time ends.' . . . And the next time, 'A pulled muscle in the back of her thigh, Doctor Sahib. Such pain!' And there, in the sheet, weakening the eyes of Aadam Aziz, hung a superbly rounded and impossible buttock . . . And now Aziz: 'Is it permitted that . . .' Whereupon a word from Ghani; an obedient reply from behind the sheet; a drawstring pulled; and pajamas fall from the celestial rump, which swells wondrously through the hole. Aadam Aziz forces himself into a medical frame of mind . . . reaches out . . . feels. And swears to himself, in amazement, that he sees the bottom reddening in a shy, but compliant blush.

That evening, Aadam contemplated the blush. Did the magic of the sheet work on both sides of the hole? Excitedly, he envisaged his headless Naseem tingling beneath the scrutiny of his eyes, his thermometer, his stethoscope, his fingers, and trying to build a picture in her mind of *him*. She was at a disadvantage, of course, having seen nothing but his hands . . . Aadam began to hope with an illicit desperation for Naseem Ghani to develop a migraine or graze her unseen chin, so they could look each other in the face. He knew how unprofessional his feelings were; but did nothing to stifle them. There was not much he could do. They had acquired a life of their own. In short: my grandfather had fallen in love, and had come to think of the perforated sheet as something sacred and magical, because through it he had seen the things which had filled up the hole inside him which had been created when he had been hit on the nose by a tussock and insulted by the boatman Tai.

On the day the World War ended, Naseem developed the longed-for headache. Such historical coincidences have littered, and perhaps befouled, my family's existence in the world.

He hardly dared to look at what was framed in the hole in the sheet. Maybe she was hideous; perhaps that explained all this performance . . . he looked.

And saw a soft face that was not at all ugly, a cushioned setting for her glittering, gemstone eyes, which were brown with flecks of gold: tiger's-eyes. Doctor Aziz's fall was complete. And Naseem burst out, 'But Doctor, my God, what a *nose!*' Ghani, angrily, 'Daughter, mind your . . .' But patient and doctor were laughing together, and Aziz was saying, 'Yes, yes, it is a remarkable specimen. They tell me there are dynasties waiting in it . . .' And he bit his tongue because he had been about to add, '. . . like snot.'

And Ghani, who had stood blindly beside the sheet for three long years, smiling and smiling and smiling, began once again to smile his secret smile, which was mirrored in the lips of the wrestlers.

1980

JAMAICA KINCAID
born 1949

Born and raised among an extended family of "poor, ordinary people," "banana and citrus-fruit farmers, fishermen, carpenters and obeah women," Jamaica Kincaid rose from humble beginnings to become a successful contemporary writer, well known for her books and magazine articles about the immigrant experience. These works often convey a sense of immediacy through Kincaid's use of first-person narration or imagined dialogue.

Born Elaine Cynthia Potter Richardson in Antigua, a small island in the Caribbean, Kincaid grew up in the island's capital city of St. Johns. Part of the British Leeward Island chain, Antigua was a colony of Britain throughout the writer's childhood and adolescence; it gained political independence in 1981 and now belongs to the British Commonwealth. Kincaid's mother was a homemaker, and her stepfather worked as a carpenter (her biological father, a taxi driver, showed no interest in his children). Though Kincaid and her brothers were raised as Methodists,

her mother and grandmother also practiced obeah, West Indian voodoo. Kincaid learned from them how to protect herself against the evil eye, how to appease local spirits, how to use herbs to conjure and heal—a familiarity with the supernatural that she later incorporated into her fiction.

At school, Kincaid was a quick student, taking a special interest in history and botany. Although her family had high aspirations for her three brothers and intended them to enter the professions, because Kincaid was a girl, they placed no value on her gifts: "No one expected anything from me at all," she later said. Her teachers often treated her eagerness in the classroom as a disciplinary problem. At thirteen, when Kincaid was about to take university qualifying examinations, her stepfather fell ill, forcing her to leave school and help raise her siblings. Angry and dispirited, she withdrew into books. Later she said that her passion for reading "saved her life." The island's colonial status meant that the local libraries and bookstores carried almost exclusively British literature, mainly of the nineteenth century. The lack of access to more recent works, or to the West Indian literary canon to which Kincaid would contribute so prominent a voice, prevented her at first from seeing art as more than an escape: "I thought writing was something that people just didn't do anymore, that went out of fashion, like the bustle."

Still, she chafed against her colonial upbringing and looked for ways to enter a wider world. At the age of seventeen she accepted a job as a nanny in the United States, and for four years lived with families in the New York City borough of Manhattan and in suburban Scarsdale. She earned a general equivalency diploma and briefly attended a college in New Hampshire before deciding she was too old. Back in Manhattan, and now determined to write, she started freelancing for magazines and weekly newspapers, including the *Village Voice*. It was during this period that she changed her name. Jamaica refers to the West Indies; Kincaid, to an unfinished novel by the playwright George Bernard Shaw. She explained that the alteration allowed her to evade her family, who opposed her writing, as well as her broader colonial inheritance: the new name was "a way for me to do things without being the same person who couldn't do them—the same person who had all these weights."

Kincaid's first collection of short stories, *At the Bottom of the River*, appeared in 1983. An autobiographical novel, *Annie John*, followed in 1985; her second and third novels also draw on her own and her family's experiences in Antigua. She has continued to publish books and magazine articles and has won many prestigious awards, including the 2000 French Prix Femina Etranger. In recent years the author has turned her attention to nature writing and to botanical studies of the landscape. Throughout her career, though, Kincaid has retained a strong commitment to issues of identity, colonialism, and the color line. In *A Small Place*, written following Kincaid's first visit to Antigua since her youth, she criticizes what she sees as the island's complicity in its exploitation, carried over from the colonial past.

The story selected here, "Girl" (1978), was the first piece of fiction that Kincaid published. It consists of a single, winding sentence; the speaker is a mother giving instructions to her daughter on the rules and rites of womanhood. (The daughter's replies break into the narration in two passages, both printed in italics.) The setting is Antigua, although this point is never explicitly stated and can only be inferred from the story's details. Some of the instructions refer to folk medicine and obeah; for example, the warning against throwing stones at blackbirds, which might be malicious spirits in disguise. As the speaker discusses with equal matter-of-factness such topics as keeping house, enduring a cruel husband, and aborting unwanted pregnancies, a picture emerges of the harshness of countless women's lives, not just in this setting but throughout history and across the globe. During the lecture, the mother stresses how important it is for a young woman to maintain a sense of sexual propriety: the woman warns her daughter repeatedly that she will look like a "slut" if she does not behave properly. The edict against squatting to play marbles suggests that the listener has not left childhood entirely, but the early reference to washing "your little cloths" indicates that she has reached puberty and that the time when these instructions will come into use is not far off.

Girl

Wash the white clothes on Monday and put them on the stone heap; wash the color clothes on Tuesday and put them on the clothesline to dry; don't walk bare-head in the hot sun; cook pumpkin fritters in very hot sweet oil; soak your little cloths[1] right after you take them off; when buying cotton to make yourself a nice blouse, be sure that it doesn't have gum on it, because that way it won't hold up well after a wash; soak salt fish overnight before you cook it; is it true that you sing benna[2] in Sunday school?; always eat your food in such a way that it won't turn someone else's stomach; on Sundays try to walk like a lady and not like the slut you are so bent on becoming; don't sing benna in Sunday school; you mustn't speak to wharf-rat boys, not even to give directions; don't eat fruits on the street—flies will follow you; *but I don't sing benna on Sundays at all and never in Sunday school*; this is how to sew on a button; this is how to make a buttonhole for the button you have just sewed on; this is how to hem a dress when you see the hem coming down and so to prevent yourself from looking like the slut I know you are so bent on becoming; this is how you iron your father's khaki shirt so that it doesn't have a crease; this is how you iron your father's khaki pants so that they don't have a crease; this is how you grow okra—far from the house, because okra tree harbors red ants; when you are growing dasheen,[3] make sure it gets plenty of water or else it makes your throat itch when you are eating it; this is how you sweep a corner; this is how you sweep a whole house; this is how you sweep a yard; this is how you smile to someone you don't like too much; this is how you smile to someone you don't like at all; this is how you smile to someone you like completely; this is how you set a table for tea; this is how you set a table for dinner; this is how you set a table for dinner with an important guest; this is how you set a table for lunch; this is how you set a table for breakfast; this is how to behave in the presence of men who don't know you very well, and this way they won't recognize immediately the slut I have warned you against becoming; be sure to wash every day, even if it is with your own spit; don't squat down to play marbles—you are not a boy, you know; don't pick people's flowers—you might catch something; don't throw stones at blackbirds, because it might not be a blackbird at all; this is how to make a bread pudding; this is how to make dou-kona;[4] this is how to make pepper pot;[5] this is how to make a good medicine for a cold; this is how to make a good medicine to throw away a child before it even becomes a child; this is how to catch a fish; this is how to throw back a fish you don't like, and that way something bad won't fall on you; this is how to bully a man; this is how a man bullies you; this is how to love a man, and if this doesn't work there are other ways, and if they don't work don't feel too bad about giving up; this is how to spit up in the air if you feel like it, and this is how to move quick so that it doesn't fall on you; this is how to make ends meet; always squeeze bread to make sure it's fresh; *but what if the baker won't let me feel the bread?*; you mean to say that after all you are really going to be the kind of woman who the baker won't let near the bread?

1978

---

1. Pads for menstruation.
2. Improvised Antiguan folk song with African roots.
3. A type of taro, a root vegetable.
4. A pudding made of plantains.
5. A spicy stew.

HANAN AL-SHAYKH
born 1945

Lebanese writer Hanan Al-Shaykh explores the conflicts between tradition and modernity as they affect women in the Arab world. Her feminist critique of Arab culture shares much with that of **Nawal El Saadawi**, but Al-Shaykh's fiction is more intimate, focused less on government oppression and more on the daily choices women must make to assert their freedom in a social system that often constrains them. By examining life through the innocent perspectives of girls and young women, the author provides social commentary while concentrating on the human dimensions of the issues raised.

Born in southern Lebanon, Hanan Al-Shaykh was raised in Beirut by her strict Shiite family. Later, Al-Shaykh would recall that her family's traditional religious practices seemed out of place in the cosmopolitan capital: "we lived in a street full of Beirutis. We were from the south, we always felt like outsiders. The whole street thought my father was mad: he wore a shawl on his head and would wash the stairs of the whole building." Her father, a conservative merchant, and her mother, an illiterate homemaker, divorced when she was young, and Al-Shaykh began to write short stories in part as an act of rebellion against the restrictive influences of her father and brothers.

Al-Shaykh attended a traditional Muslim girls' primary school and, later, the more cosmopolitan Ahliyyah School and the American College for Girls in Cairo. After graduating, she worked as a journalist for the magazine *al-Hasna* (*Beautiful Woman*) and for the journal *al-Nahar* (*The Day*), which published her earliest short stories. Her first novel, *Suicide of a Dead Man* (1970), relates a teenage girl's affair with a middle-aged man but, surprisingly, from the man's point of view. It brought comparisons to the work of **Naguib Mahfouz**, particularly for its faithful representation of the spoken language. As Al-Shaykh later explained, "My generation of Arab writers adopted a language between the classical and the spoken dialect. The dialogue is, at times, even colloquial and thus much closer to the way people really speak."

During the Lebanese Civil War (1975–90), Al-Shaykh left the country to live in London and in Saudi Arabia, where she wrote *The Story of Zahra* (1980). She released the novel at her own expense, as no publisher in Lebanon would accept the manuscript, but it became her first international success. The protagonist of the story, Zahra, is a young woman mired in the oppressive and misogynistic milieu of war-torn Lebanon. Trapped in a loveless marriage, she falls in love with a sniper, who at some point turns on her as one of his political targets. Al-Shaykh's later novels likewise focus on the life experiences of Arab women, especially during the civil war. *Only in London* (2000) was her first novel set in Europe, although the main figures in it are Middle Eastern immigrants. She has written two experimental plays, performed by the Hampstead Theatre in London. Her frank treatment of such topics as abortion, adultery, homosexuality, prostitution, rape, and transvestism has made her work controversial in the Arab world. She has lived in London since 1983.

The story presented here, "The Women's Swimming Pool" (1982), although it addresses none of these controversial subjects, nonetheless concerns the breaking of taboos. The narrator, accustomed to having to cover her head and wear long-sleeve clothes in the fierce heat of southern Lebanese tobacco fields, wants to visit the sea and to bathe in a swimming pool that her friend has seen in Beirut. With great sensitivity Al-Shaykh portrays the innocent perspective of the narrator, an orphan who simply wants to go swimming but who, because of social customs barring women from displaying their bodies, has never had access to a swimming pool. Her grandmother, hoping to fulfill the little girl's wishes, takes her on a long bus ride from their home village, but she is as bewildered as her granddaughter by the metropolis of Beirut. The girl and the old woman have a close, loving relationship, but, as the story progresses, the narrator sees her grandmother, and indeed the customs of her village, in a new light. Although the narrator says little about her adult life, this recollection of childhood seems to mark a turning point, setting the girl on the path to become the woman who writes stories of liberation and separating her from the grandmother she loves but does not want to emulate.

The Women's Swimming Pool[1]

I am in the tent for threading the tobacco, amidst the mounds of tobacco plants and the skewers. Cross-legged, I breathe in the green odor, threading one leaf after another. I find myself dreaming and growing thirsty and dreaming. I open the magazine: I devour the words and surreptitiously gaze at the pictures. I am exasperated at being in the tent, then my exasperation turns to sadness.

Thirsty, I rise to my feet. I hear Abu Ghalib say, "Where are you off to, little lady?" I make my way to my grandmother, saying, "I'm thirsty." I go out. I make my way to the cistern, stumbling in the sandy ground. I see the greenish-blue water. I stretch out my hand to its still surface, hot from the harsh sun. I stretch out my hand and wipe it across my brow and face and neck, across my chest. Before being able to savor its relative coldness, I hear my name and see my grandmother standing in her black dress at the doorway of the tent. Aloud I express the wish that someone else had called to me. We have become like an orange and its navel: my grandmother has welded me so close to her that the village girls no longer dare to make friends with me, perhaps for fear of rupturing this close union.

I returned to the tent, growing thirsty and dreaming, with the sea ever in my mind. What were its waters like? What color would they be now? If only this week would pass in a flash, for I had at last persuaded my grandmother to go down to Beirut and the sea, after my friend Sumayya had sworn that the swimming pool she'd been at had been for women only.

My grandmother sat on the edge of a jagged slab of stone, leaning on my arm. Her hand was hot and rough. She sighed as she chased away a fly.

1. Translated from the Arabic by Denys Johnson-Davies.

What is my grandmother gazing at? There was nothing in front of us but the asphalt road, which, despite the sun's rays, gave off no light, and the white marble tombs that stretched along the high mountainside, while the houses of upper Nabatieh[2] looked like deserted Crusader castles, their alleyways empty, their windows of iron. Our house likewise seemed to be groaning in its solitude, shaded by the fig tree. The washing line stirs with the wind above the tomb of my grandfather, the celebrated religious scholar, in the courtyard of the house. What is my grandmother staring at? Or does someone who is waiting not stare?

Turning her face toward me, she said, "Child, what will we do if the bus doesn't come?" Her face, engraved in my mind, seemed overcast, also her half-closed eyes and the blue tattoo mark on her chin.[3] I didn't answer her for fear I'd cry if I talked. This time I averted my gaze from the white tombs; moving my foot away from my grandmother's leg clothed in thick black stockings, I began to walk about, my gaze directed to the other side where lay the extensive fields of green tobacco, towering and gently swaying, their leaves glinting under the sun, leaves that were imprinted on my brain, their marks still showing on my hands.

My gaze reached out behind the thousands of plants, then beyond them, moving away till it arrived at the tent where the tobacco was threaded. I came up close to my grandmother, who was still sitting in her place, still gazing in front of her. As I drew close to her, I heard her give a sigh. A sprinkling of sweat lay on the pouches under her eyes. "Child, what do you want with the sea? Don't you know that the sea puts a spell on people?" I didn't answer her: I was worried that the morning would pass, that noonday would pass, and that I wouldn't see the green bus come to a stop by the stone my grandmother sat on, to take us to the sea, to Beirut. Again I heard my grandmother mumbling. "That devil Sumayya . . ." I pleaded with her to stop, and my thoughts rose up and left the stone upon which my grandmother sat, the rough road, left everything. I went back to my dreams, to the sea.

The sea had always been my obsession, ever since I had seen it for the first time inside a colored ball; with its blue color it was like a magic lantern, wide open, the surface of its water unrippled unless you tilted the piece of glass, with its small shells and white specks like snow. When I first became aware of things, this ball, which I had found in the parlor, was the sole thing that animated and amused me. The more I gazed at it, the cooler I felt its waters to be, and the more they invited me to bathe in them; they knew that I had been born amidst dust and mud and the stench of tobacco.

If only the green bus would come along—and I shifted my bag from one hand to the other. I heard my grandmother wail, "Child, bring up a stone and sit down. Put down the bag and don't worry." My distress increased, and I was no longer able to stop it turning into tears that flowed freely down my face, veiling it from the road. I stretched up to wipe them with my sleeve; in this heat I still had to wear that dress with long sleeves, that head covering over my braids,[4] despite the hot wind that set the tobacco plants and the sparse poplars

---

2. A town in southern Lebanon.
3. Shia Islam allows tattooing, a cultural practice that preceded the introduction of Islam and that is prohibited by Sunni Islam.

Blue tattoos on the face and hands are a marker for a generation of aging women.
4. Islamic custom requires girls and women to keep their hair, arms, and legs covered.

swaying. Thank God I had resisted her and refused to wear my stockings. I gave a deep sigh as I heard the bus's horn from afar. Fearful and anxious, I shouted at my grandmother as I helped her to her feet, turning round to make sure that my bag was still in my hand and my grandmother's hand in the other. The bus came to a stop and the conductor helped my grandmother on. When I saw myself alongside her and the stone on its own, I tightened my grip on my bag in which lay Sumayya's bathing costume, a sleeveless dress, and my money.

I noticed as the bus slowly made its way along the road that my anxiety was still there, that it was in fact increasing: Why didn't the bus pass by all these trees and fallow land like lightning? Why was it crawling along? My anxiety was still there and increased till it predominated over my other sensations, my nausea and curiosity.

How would we find our way to the sea? Would we see it as soon as we arrived in Beirut? Was it at the other end of it? Would the bus stop in the district of Zeytouna,[5] at the door of the women's swimming pool? Why, I wondered, was it called Zeytouna?—were there olive trees there? I leaned toward my grandmother and her silent face and long nose that almost met up with her mouth. Thinking that I wanted a piece of cane sugar, she put her hand to her bosom to take out a small twist of cloth. Impatiently I asked her if she was sure that Maryam at-Taweela knew Zeytouna, to which she answered, her mouth sucking at the cane sugar and making a noise with her tongue, "God will look after everything." Then she broke the silence by saying. "All this trouble is that devil Sumayya's fault—it was she who told you she'd seen with her own eyes the swimming pool just for women and not for men." "Yes, Grandma," I answered her. She said, "Swear by your mother's grave." I thought to myself absently: "Why only my mother's grave? What about my father? Or did she only acknowledge her daughter's death . . .?" "By my mother's grave, it's for women." She inclined her head and still munching the cane sugar and making a noise with her tongue, she said, "If any man were to see you, you'd be done for, and so would your mother and father and your grandfather, the religious scholar— and I'd be done for more than anyone because it's I who agreed to this and helped you."

I would have liked to say to her, "They've all gone, they've all died, so what do we have to be afraid of?" But I knew what she meant: that she was frightened they wouldn't go to heaven.

I began to sweat, and my heart again contracted as Beirut came into view with its lofty buildings, car horns, the bared arms of the women, the girls' hair, the tight trousers they were wearing. People were sitting on chairs in the middle of the pavement, eating and drinking; the trams; the roasting chickens revolving on spits. Ah, these dresses for sale in the windows, would anyone be found actually to wear them? I see a Japanese man, the first-ever member of the yellow races outside of books; the Martyrs' monument; Riad Solh Square.[6] I was wringing wet with sweat and my heart pounded—it was as though I regretted having come to Beirut, perhaps because I was accompanied by my

5. A cosmopolitan district of Lebanon; the name means "olive."
6. One of the main squares in Beirut's com-
mercial district; the Martyrs' monument commemorates Lebanese nationalists who opposed Ottoman rule in the early 20th century.

grandmother. It was soon all too evident that we were outsiders to the capital. We began walking after my grandmother had asked the bus driver the where-abouts of the district of Khandaq al-Ghamiq[7] where Maryam at-Taweela lived. Once again my body absorbed all the sweat and allowed my heart to flee its cage. I find myself treading on a pavement on which for long years I have dreamed of walking; I hear sounds that have been engraved on my imagination; and everything I see I have seen in daydreams at school or in the tobacco-threading tent. Perhaps I shouldn't say that I was regretting it, for after this I would never forget Beirut. We begin walking and losing our way in a Beirut that never ends, that leads nowhere. We begin asking and walking and losing our way, and my going to the sea seems an impossibility; the sea is fleeing from me. My grandmother comes to a stop and leans against a lamppost, or against the litter bin attached to it, and against my shoulders, and puffs and blows. I have the feeling that we shall never find Maryam at-Taweela's house. A man we had stopped to ask the way walks with us. When we knock at the door and no one opens to us, I become convinced that my bathing in the sea is no longer possible. The sweat pours off me, my throat contracts. A woman's voice brings me back to my senses as I drown in a lake of anxiety, sadness, and fear; then it drowns me once again. It was not Maryam at-Taweela but her neighbor who is asking us to wait at her place. We go down the steps to the neighbor's outdoor stone bench, and my grandmother sits down by the door but gets to her feet again when the woman entreats her to sit in the cane chair. Then she asks to be excused while she finishes washing down the steps. While she is cursing the heat of Beirut in the summer, I notice the tin containers lined up side by side containing red and green peppers. We have a long wait, and I begin to weep inwardly as I stare at the containers.

I wouldn't be seeing the sea today, perhaps not for years, but the thought of its waters would not leave me, would not be erased from my dreams. I must persuade my grandmother to come to Beirut with Sumayya. Perhaps I should not have mentioned the swimming pool in front of her. I wouldn't be seeing the sea today—and once again I sank back into a lake of doubt and fear and sadness. A woman's voice again brought me back to my senses: it was Maryam at-Taweela, who had stretched out her long neck and had kissed me, while she asked my grandmother: 'She's the child of your late daughter, isn't she?'—and she swore by the Imam[8] that we must have lunch with her, doing so before we had protested, feeling perhaps that I would do so. When she stood up and took the primus stove from under her bed and brought out potatoes and tomatoes and bits of meat, I had feelings of nausea, then of frustration. I nudged my grandmother, who leant over and whispered "What is it, dear?" at which Maryam at-Taweela turned and asked "What does your granddaughter want—to go to the bathroom?" My mouth went quite dry and my tears were all stored up waiting for a signal from my heartbeats to fall. My grandmother said with embarrassment, "She wants to go to the sea, to the women's swimming pool—that devil Sumayya put it into her head." To my amazement Maryam at-Taweela said loudly, "And why not? Right now Ali Mousa, our neighbor, will be coming and he'll take you, he's got a car"—and

7. A well-to-do neighborhood in West Beirut.
8. The Imam Ali (ca. 600–661), cousin and son-in-law of the prophet Muhammad and founder of the Shi'a branch of Islam.

Maryam at-Taweela began peeling the potatoes at a low table in the middle of the room and my grandmother asked, "Where's Ali Mousa from? Where does he live?"

I can't wait, I shan't eat, I shan't drink. I want to go now, now. I remained seated, crying inwardly because I was born in the South, because there's no escape for me from the South, and I go on rubbing my fingers and gnawing at my nails. Again I begin to sweat: I shan't eat, I shan't drink, I shan't reply to Maryam at-Taweela. It was as though I was taking vengeance on my grandmother for some wrong she did not know about. My patience vanished. I stood up and said to my grandmother before I should burst out sobbing, "Come along, Grandma, get up, and let's go." I helped her to her feet, and Maryam at-Taweela asked in bewilderment what had suddenly come over me. I went on dragging my grandmother out to the street so that I might stop the first taxi.

Only moments passed before the driver shut off his engine and said, "Zeytouna." I looked about me but saw no sea. As I gave him a lira I asked him, "Where's the women's swimming pool?" He shrugged his shoulders. We got out of the car with difficulty, as was always the case with my grandmother. To my astonishment the driver returned, stretching out his head in concern at us. "Jump in," he said, and we got in. He took us round and round, stopping once at a petrol station and then by a newspaper seller, asking about the women's swimming pool and nobody knowing where it was. Once again he dropped us in the middle of Zeytouna Street.

Then, behind the hotels and the beautiful buildings and the date palms, I saw the sea. It was like a blue line of quicksilver: it was as though pieces of silver paper were resting on it. The sea that was in front of me was more beautiful than it had been in the glass ball. I didn't know how to get close to it, how to touch it. Cement lay between us. We began inquiring about the whereabouts of the swimming pool, but no one knew. The sea remains without waves, a blue line. I feel frustrated. Perhaps this swimming pool is some secret known only to the girls of the South. I began asking every person I saw. I tried to choke back my tears; I let go of my grandmother's hand as though wishing to reproach her, to punish her for having insisted on accompanying me instead of Sumayya. Poor me. Poor Grandma. Poor Beirut. Had my dreams come to an end in the middle of the street? I clasp my bag and my grandmother's hand, with the sea in front of me, separating her from me. My stubbornness and vexation impel me to ask and go on asking. I approached a man leaning against a bus, and to my surprise he pointed to an opening between two shops. I hurried back to my grandmother, who was supporting herself against a lamppost, to tell her I'd found it. When I saw with what difficulty she attempted to walk, I asked her to wait for me while I made sure. I went through the opening but didn't see the sea. All I saw was a fat woman with bare shoulders sitting behind a table. Hesitating, I stood and looked at her, not daring to step forward. My enthusiasm had vanished, taking with it my courage. "Yes," said the woman. I came forward and asked her, "Is the women's swimming pool here?" She nodded her head and said, "The entrance fee is a lira." I asked her if it was possible for my grandmother to wait for me here and she stared at me and said, "Of course." There was contempt in the way she looked at me: Was it my southern accent or my long-sleeved dress? I had disregarded my grandmother and had taken off my head shawl and hidden it in my bag. I handed her a lira and could hear the sounds of women and children—and still I did not see the sea. At the end of the portico were steps; which I was certain led to the roofed-in sea. The important thing was that I'd arrived, that I would be tasting the salty spray of its waters. I wouldn't be seeing the waves; never mind, I'd be bathing in its waters.

I found myself saying to the woman, or rather to myself because no sound issued from my throat, "I'll bring my grandmother." Going out through the opening and still clasping my bag to my chest, I saw my grandmother standing and looking up at the sky. I called to her, but she was reciting to herself under her breath as she continued to look upward: she was praying, right there in the street, praying on the pavement at the door of the swimming pool. She had spread out a paper bag and had stretched out her hands to the sky. I walked off in another direction and stopped looking at her. I would have liked to persuade myself that she had nothing to do with me, that I didn't know her. How, though? She's my grandmother whom I've dragged with my entreaties from the tobacco-threading tent, from the jagged slab of stone, from the winds of the South; I have crammed her into the bus and been lost with her in the streets as we searched for Maryam at-Taweela's house. And now here were the two of us standing at the door of the swimming pool, and she, having heard the call to prayers,[9] had prostrated herself in prayer. She was destroying what lay in my bag, blocking the road between me and the sea. I felt sorry for her, for her knees that knelt on the cruelly hard pavement, for her tattooed hands that lay on the dirt. I looked at her again and saw the passers-by staring at her. For the first time her black dress looked shabby to me. I felt how far removed we were from these passers-by, from this street, this city, this sea. I approached her, and she again put her weight on my hand.

1982

---

9. The Islamic call to prayer, heard five times a day in Muslim countries but ignored by secular residents of some large cities like Beirut.

MO YAN
born 1955

M o Yan burst onto China's literary scene in 1986 with the publication of his novel *Red Sorghum*, which won high critical praise and was subsequently made into a film directed by Zhang Yimou. Since then he has published a host of novels and short stories, many of which have been translated into English by Howard Goldblatt, his longtime collaborator (the selection here was translated by Janice Wickeri). Much of Mo Yan's fiction is set in his native Gaomi County, in Shandong province—a real place, albeit one that Mo Yan's fictions enhance and transform almost into myth. Rich language and creative description are hallmarks of his style, which serves to create a mythic and surreal world that at once romanticizes and mourns the past. In 2012, Mo Yan was awarded the Nobel Prize for Literature.

Many critics describe Mo Yan's work as exemplary of the literary movement called "Roots Seeking." This movement arose in the 1980s, one of many waves of response in China to the collective experience of swift modernization in the preceding decades. The optimistic narratives of revolutionary progress that had buoyed the nation through the middle part of the century had declined by this period, giving way to fresh anxieties over China's eroding cultural identity as well as its continuing technological and economic lag behind the West. The writers of the Roots movement, most of them young men, sought to turn from grand models of the future and instead to look for Chinese selfhood in the intimate, local, and rooted places around them: in the rural past, in family lines,

in small-h history. These sources, they argued, are the strongest materials for building a cultural identity on which a modern China can rise.

The Roots school tends to favor a decidedly masculine aesthetic, celebrating raw potency, toughness, and bravado, a tone that some feminist critics have challenged. The novelist Can Xue has criticized Mo Yan for what she regards as his excessive celebration of virility and masculinity, presenting a biting parody of his school's worst excesses: "His hometown is in the country where his ancestors were bandits. The village raises so many dogs to bite strangers that no outsiders can go in. It is a special village situated on top of a mountain which is covered by clouds and fog all year round. The village consists of eight hundred strong men and bewitching women with bound feet."

The story selected here, "The Old Gun" (written in 1985), is in many respects a typical Roots text, since it portrays a younger generation trying to reconnect with its ancestors. Narrated in the third person, the story revolves around a boy and his relation to his dead father through the trope of the "old gun." The story is typical of the movement, too, in its masculine emphases, narrating a young male's relationship with the spirit of a lost, primitive, masculine past. The boy has been in a sense emasculated, a condition that (as critics have noted) offers a metaphor for the general unmanning of the Chinese people by their Confucian and Maoist pasts. His desire to perform a difficult and symbolically charged act, namely firing a gun, represents compensation for wrongs done to him in the past, but it also represents the larger desire for control, vitality, and power. In the end, after the narration of the events surrounding his low estate, he manages to fire the gun in a violent explosion. Like much of Mo Yan's fiction, the story expresses a desire for a world lost, a world that possessed a vitality that the present lacks. That the protagonist's victory is a pyrrhic one, leading to ultimate failure, reflects the mood of pessimism and despondency that pervades so much of the work of this school. There is a sense of fatality to the quest these writers portray, as though it were a final test of resolve, or as though from a suspicion that the search for paradise entails the search for something lost.

The story narrates the boy's attempt to kill wild ducks in some local sorghum fields, which have transformed, almost magically, into primitive swampland. As is typical for Mo Yan, the most important aspect of the work is the richness and suggestiveness of the descriptive language. The language creates an almost mythical world of wild ducks, flooding waters, waving sorghum stalks, kaleidoscopic colors as the sun slants across the landscape—an untamed natural world, for feeding, hunting, and killing. As the boy prepares to fire his gun, we learn that part of his index finger is missing. The boy's observations and reflections are presented in free indirect discourse, a realist technique in which the narrator reports the thoughts of the character in the third person.

Through flashbacks, the story shows how the boy lost his finger, and how his father and grandfather died. The narrative returns periodically to the present, where the boy ruminates as he prowls through the sorghum fields, having defied his mother and taken down the gun to go hunting. Part of his motivation is simple hunger—he reflects that he hasn't eaten meat for what feels like ages—but more than that, he is overcome by the desire to kill, to attain explosive power, to connect with his paternal lineage, to recover a missing part of himself that he feels the gun represents. The narrative carefully builds a picture of the boy's mind and thoughts as he approaches a crisis in his existence.

The Old Gun[1]

As he swung the gun down from his right shoulder with his index-finger-less right hand, he was caught in a ray of golden sunlight. The sun was sinking rapidly in a smooth shallow arc; fragmentary sounds like those of a receding tide rippled from the fields, along with an air of desolation by turns pronounced and faint. Gingerly he placed the gun on the ground among the patches of coin-shaped moss, feeling a sense of distress as he saw how damp the earth was. The long-barrelled, home-made musket, its butt mahogany, lay unevenly on the soggy ground; beside it the evening sun picked out a fallen sorghum ear on which a great cluster of delicate, tender golden shoots had sprouted, casting discolouring shadows onto the black gun-barrel and deep-red butt. He took the powder-horn from around his waist, at the same time slipping off his black jacket to reveal a raw-boned torso. He wrapped the gun and the powder-horn in the jacket and lay them on the ground, then took three paces forward. Bending

---

1. Translated from Chinese by Duncan Hewitt.

down, he stretched out his sun-drenched arms and dragged out one sheaf from among the great clump of sorghum stalks.

The autumn floods had been heavy and the land, water-logged for thousands of hectares, looked like an ocean. In the water the sorghum held high its crimson heads; whole platoons of rats scurried across them as nimbly as birds in flight. By harvest time the water was at chest height, and the people waded in and took the ears of sorghum away on rafts. Red-finned carp and black-backed grass carp appeared from nowhere to dart about among the green aerial roots of the sorghum stalks. Now and again an emerald green kingfisher shot into the water, then shot back out with a tiny glistening fish in its beak. In August the flood waters gradually subsided, revealing roads covered in mud. On the low-lying land the water remained, forming pools of all shapes and sizes. The cut sorghum stalks could not be hauled away; they were dragged out of the water and stacked on the road or on the higher ground around the edges of the pools. A glorious sunlight shone on the low-lying plains. For miles around there was hardly a village; the pools sparkled; the clumps of sorghum stood like clusters of blockhouses.

Silhouetted against the bright warm sun and a big expanse of water, he dragged aside sheaf after sheaf of sorghum, piling them up at the edge of the pool until he had made a square hide half a man's height. Then he picked up the gun, jumped into the hide and sat down. His head came just level with the top of the hide. From outside he was invisible, but through the holes he had left he could clearly see the pool and the sand-bar which rose in its middle like a solitary island; he could see the rosy sky and the brown earth, too. The sky seemed very low; the sun's rays daubed the surface of the water a deep red. The pool stretched away into the hazy dusk, sparkling brilliantly, darts of radiance dancing around its edge like a ring of warm eyelashes. On the sand-bar in the pool, by now a pale shade of blue, clumps of yellow reeds stood solemnly upright. The sand-bar itself, surrounded by flickering light, seemed gently adrift. The hazier the surroundings grew, the brighter the water gleamed, and the more pronounced the impression that the sand-bar was drifting—he felt that it was floating towards him, floating nearer, until it was only a few steps away and he could have jumped onto it. They still hadn't arrived on the sand-bar; he gazed uneasily at the sky once more, thinking, it's about time, they ought to be here by now.

He had no idea where they came from. That day the workers had spent the whole afternoon shifting sorghum stalks. When the team leader said time to down tools, the men headed for home by the dozen, their long shadows swaying as they went. He had rushed over here to relieve himself when suddenly he caught sight of them. It was as though he had been punched in the chest—his heart faltered for a moment before it resumed beating. His eyes were dazzled by the great flock of wild ducks landing on the sand-bar. Every night for two weeks he hid among the sorghum sheafs watching them; he observed that they always arrived, cawing loudly, at around this time of the evening, as if they had come flying from beyond the sky. Before landing they would circle elegantly above the pool, like a great grey-green cloud now unfurling, now rolling back . . . When they descended onto the sand-bar, their wings beating the air, he was beside himself with excitement. Never before had he come across so many wild ducks on such a small piece of land, never . . .

They still weren't here—by now they really should have been. They weren't here *yet* . . . or they weren't coming? He was feeling anxious, even began to suspect that what he had seen before had been just an illusion—all along he had never quite believed there could really be such a large flock of wild ducks in this place. He had often heard the old people in the village telling tales of heavenly ducks, but the ducks in the stories were always pure white, and this flock of wild ducks was not. The ones with pretty green feathers on their heads and necks, a white ring round their throats and wings like blue mirrors— weren't they drakes? Those with golden-brown bodies, dappled with dark brown markings—weren't they females? They certainly weren't heavenly ducks, for they left little green and brown feathers all over the sand-bar. He felt greatly reassured at the sight of these feathers. He sat down, picked up his jacket and shook it open, revealing the gun and the shiny powder-horn. The gun lay peacefully on top of the sorghum stalks, its body gleaming dark-red, almost the colour of rust. In the past red rust had covered it several times and had eaten away at the metal, leaving it pocked and pitted. Now, though, there was no rust—he had sandpapered it all away. The gun lay there twisted like a hibernating snake; at any moment, he felt, it might wake up, fly into the air and start thrashing the sorghum stalks with its steel tail. When he stretched out his hand to touch the gun, his first sensation was an iciness in his fingertips, and the chill spread to his chest and made him shiver for a long while. The sun was sinking faster now, its shape altering all the while, flattening out and distorting, like a semi-fluid sphere hitting a smooth steel surface. Its underside was a flat line, its curved surfaces under extreme tension; at last they burst and the bubbling icy red liquid meandered away in every direction. A trance-like calm descended on the pool as the crimson liquid seeped down, turning its depths into a thick red broth, while the surface remained crystal clear and blindingly bright. Suddenly, he caught sight of a gold-hooped dragonfly suspended from a tall, withered blade of grass, its bulging eyes like purple gems, turning now to the left, now to the right, refracting light as they did so.

He reached for the gun and laid it across his legs, its body stretching out behind him along the right-angle of his thighs and belly; the barrel peeped out from beneath his chin at the pale grey southern sky. He opened the lid of the powder-horn, then pulled from his pocket a long, thin measuring cylinder which he filled with gunpowder. He poured this measure into the gun barrel, the smooth sound it made as it fell echoed from the muzzle. He then took a pinch of iron shot from a small iron box and tipped it into the muzzle of the gun; from inside the barrel there came a clatter. Now he pulled out a long rod from below the barrel and tamped down the mixture of gunpowder and shot with its uneven head. He moved as gingerly as if he were scratching a drowsy tiger's itch, nerve-ends tingling, heart pounding. As soon as he had put the third measure of gunpowder and the third handful of shot into the barrel, an icy cold clutched him; beads of cold sweat broke out on his forehead. His hands were trembling as he took out the cotton-wool stopper he had prepared for the purpose and plugged the mouth of the gun. He felt starving, his whole body limp. He snapped a piece of grass from the ground, rubbed the mud from it, put it into his mouth and began to chew on it, but this only made his hunger worse . . .

Just then, though, he heard the whistle of wings beating the air above the water-flats. He had to hurry and complete his final task of preparation: attaching the percussion cap. He pulled back the protruding head of the hammer, revealing a nipple-shaped protuberance connected to the gun barrel. There was a round groove in the top of the protuberance with a tiny hole in its centre.

With great care he tore away several layers of paper from around the golden percussion cap, then fitted it into this groove. The percussion cap contained yellow gunpowder; as soon as the hammer struck it, this would explode, igniting the powder in the barrel and sending a fiery snake leaping from the muzzle, slender at first, then bigger until finally the gun looked like an iron broom. This gun had hung on the pitch-black gable in their house for so long that he had learned the mystery of its workings as if by revelation. Two days before, when he took it down and rubbed it clean of the rust which pocked its surface, he was actually completely at ease with it.

The wild ducks were here. At first they circled a hundred metres up in the air, wings beating. They dived and climbed, merged, then scattered again, hurtling down from all directions to skim across the sparkling surface of the reddened water. He got to his knees, holding his breath, eyes glued to the circle upon circle of purple radiance. Gently he edged the barrel of the gun through the gap in the sorghum stalks, heart pounding crazily. The wild ducks were still whirling around in circles of ever-changing size; it was almost as if the water-flats were spinning with them. Several times, some of the green-feathered drakes almost flew straight into the muzzle of his gun; he caught a glimpse of their pale green beaks and the gleam of cunning in their black eyes. The sun had grown wider and flatter still, turning black around the edges, its centre still like molten iron, crackling and spitting sparks.

The ducks suddenly started calling, the "quack quack quack" of the drakes merging with the "quack quack quack" of the females in a great cacophony. He knew they were about to land—after observing them minutely for a dozen days now he knew they always cried out just before they landed. It was only a few moments since their silhouettes had first appeared in the sky, but already he felt as if an extremely long time had passed; the violent cramps in his stomach reminded him again of his hunger. At last the ducks descended, only extending their purple legs and stretching their wings out flat when they were almost on the ground. Their snowy tails fluffed out like feathery fans, they hit the ground at such speed that the momentum made them stagger a couple of paces. Suddenly the mud was no longer brown: countless suns shimmered in the ducks' brilliant plumage as the entire flock waddled to and fro, carrying the sunlight with it.

Stealthily he raised the gun, rested the butt on his shoulder, and trained the muzzle on the increasingly dense pack of ducks. Another piece had vanished from the sun, which looked distorted, bizarre. Some of the wild ducks had settled on the ground, some were standing, some flew a little way then landed again. It's time, he thought, I should open fire, but he didn't do it. As he ran his hand over the trigger he suddenly realized his great disadvantage, recalling with a sense of pain his index finger: two of the joints were missing, the last one alone remained, a gnarled tree stump squatting between his thumb and his middle finger.

He was only six years old when his mother came back from his father's funeral, dressed in mourning—a long white cotton gown with a hempen cord tied around the waist, her hair flowing loose. Her eyelids were so swollen they were transparent, her eyes merely narrow slits from which her tear-stained, darkling gaze flashed out. She called out his name: "Dasuo, come here." He approached her with trepidation. She grabbed hold of his hand and gulped twice, craning her neck as though trying to swallow something hard. "Dasuo, your dad's died, do you realize that?" she said. He nodded, and heard her carry on, "Your dad's died. When you die you can never come back to life, do you realize that?" He gazed perplexedly at her, nodding energetically all the while. "You know how your dad died?" she asked. "He was shot with this gun; this gun was handed down from your grandmother. You're never to touch it: I'm going to hang it on the wall; you're going to look at it every day. And when you look at it you should think of your father, and study hard so you can live a decent life and bring a bit of credit to your ancestors." He wasn't sure how well he understood his mum's words, but he carried on nodding energetically.

And so the gun hung in their house on the gable, which was stained black and shiny by the smoke of decades. Every day he saw it. Later, when he went up from first to second grade, his mum hung a paraffin lamp on the gable every evening to give him enough light to study by. Whenever he saw the black characters in the books his head started spinning, and he couldn't help thinking of the gun and the story behind it. The wind off the desolate plain seeped through the lattice window, buffeting the flames in the oil lamp; the flames looked like the head of a writing brush, with wisps of black smoke shimmering at its tip. Though he appeared intent on his books, he was always aware of the spirit of the gun; he even seemed to hear it clicking. He felt like you do when you see a snake—wanting to look but scared at the same time. The gun hung there, barrel pointing down, butt upwards, a gloomy black glow emanating from its body. The powder-horn hung alongside, tangled up with it, its slender waist resting against the hammer. It was red-gold in colour, its big end facing downwards, its small end upwards. How high the gun and the powder-horn hung, how beautiful they looked hanging there—an ancient gun and an ancient powder-horn hanging on an ancient gable, tormenting his soul.

One evening he climbed up on a high stool and took the gun and the powder-horn down. Holding them up to the lamp-light, he inspected them carefully; the leaden weight of the gun in his hands brought him an acute sense of grief. Just at this moment, his mum walked in from the other room. She was not yet forty, but her hair was already grey, and she said: "Dasuo, what are you doing?" He just stood there blankly, the gun in one hand and the powder-horn in the other. "Where did you come in your class exams?" she asked him. "Second from bottom," he replied. "You good-for-nothing! Hang that gun back up!" He replied stubbornly, "No, I want to go and kill . . ." His mum slapped him round the face and said, "Hang it up. The only thing you're going to do is get on with your studies, and don't you forget it." He hung the gun on the wall. His mum went over to the stove, picked up a chopper and told him calmly, "Hold out your index finger." He stretched it out obediently. She pressed the finger onto the edge of the *kang*;[2] he began to squirm with fear. "Don't move," she told him. "Now remember this, you're never to touch that gun again." She raised the chopper . . . it fell in a flash of cold steel, a violent jolt surged from his fingertips up to his shoulders, his vertebrae arched with the strain. Blood oozed slowly from the severed finger. His mother was weeping as she staunched the wound with a handful of lime . . .

As he looked at the stub of his finger with its single joint, his nose began to twitch. How many days had he gone without meat now? Couldn't remember

2. A type of bed found in northern China that is heated with fire from below.

exactly; but he could distinctly remember all the meat he had eaten in the past. He seemed never to have eaten his fill of meat. The first time he caught sight of those plump wild ducks, meat was the first thing he thought of. The next thing he thought of was the gun—he had come out in goose-pimples all over as he recalled how his mum had chopped off his finger at the joint because of it. But in the end, yesterday afternoon, he had taken the gun down. Its body was covered in dust, as thick as a coin, and it was enmeshed from top to bottom in a tangle of spider's webs. The leather strap, chewed through by insects, snapped as soon as he touched it. There was still a lot of gunpowder in the horn—when he poured it out to dry he discovered a golden percussion cap. He picked up this single percussion cap, hands trembling with excitement. The first thing that came into his mind was his father: he felt how lucky he was, for where would you get one of these percussion caps nowadays? . . . I haven't got any money, even if I had some I still wouldn't be able to get a meat coupon;[3] I'm thick, even if I wasn't I still wouldn't get a chance to go to school, and anyway what use would it be? Looking at the stump of his finger, he tried to console himself. His mum had only chopped off the tip, but afterwards the wound had turned septic and he had lost another section—hence its present state. As he thought of all these things, he became filled with hatred for this flock of wild ducks with all their fine feathers. I'm going to kill you, kill the lot of you if it's the last thing I do! Then I'll eat you, chew your bones to a pulp and swallow them down. He imagined how crispy and aromatic their bones must be. He stretched his middle finger into the trigger guard.

Still he didn't pull the trigger. This was because another gaggle of wild ducks was swirling down from the sky in another spinning cloud of colour. There was a great commotion among the ducks on the sand-bar. Some stamped their feet, some took off; it was hard to tell whether they were expressing welcome or anger towards their fellows. He gazed irritably at the flurry of birds and gently withdrew the gun. The sun had grown pointed like a sweet potato, its rays now dark green and brilliant purple. The ducks' activity startled the gold-hooped dragonfly into flight. It skimmed low across the surface of the water and came to rest on his hide, its six legs clamped fast to a sorghum leaf, its long golden-hooped tail dangling down. He saw the two bright beads of light in its eyes. The flock of wild ducks was gradually regrouping and growing calmer. On the water's surface, shattered by their claws, concentric ripples spread out, creating new ripples where they collided.

The two flocks of ducks had merged into one. If I had a big net, he thought, and suddenly flung it over them . . . but he knew he had no net, just a gun. Gingerly he removed the percussion cap, pulled out the cotton wool stopper, and poured three more measures of gunpowder and three more measures of shot into the muzzle . . . Once more he took aim at the ducks, his heart filled with a primitive blood-lust . . . Such a huge flock of ducks, such a slender gun barrel . . . He edged stealthily back once more and poured another two cylinders of gunpowder into the muzzle, then plugged it again. The barrel was almost full now, and when he lifted the gun up he felt how heavy it was. His trembling middle finger pressed on the trigger—at the split second of firing he closed his eyes.

3. A ration coupon required for purchasing basic items in Communist China under Mao Zedong (ruled 1949–76).

The head of the hammer struck the golden percussion cap with a click, but no shot rang out. The rings on the water's surface seemed to be slowly contracting; the purple vapour which hung between heaven and earth was denser than ever, the red glow fading fast, the brightness of the water's surface undiminished but gradually assuming a deeper hue. Clustered together, the ducks looked so solid, beautiful, warm, their soft, clean plumage dazzling. Their cunning eyes seemed to be staring disdainfully at the muzzle of his gun, as if in mockery of his impotence. He took out the percussion cap, glancing at the mark left on the firing plate by the hammer. A warm breath of putrid air wafted over from the flock of ducks; their bodies gave off a soft, smooth sound as they rubbed against each other. He replaced the percussion cap, not believing that this could really have happened. Dad, Granny, hadn't it fired for them at the first attempt? It was ten or more years since his dad died, but his story was still common currency in the village. He could dimly recall a very tall man with a pitted face and yellow whiskers.

His dad's story had been so widely repeated that it had already taken on the status of a legend among the villagers: he had only to close his eyes for it to unfold in all its detail. It began on the grey dirt road to the fields, with his dad setting out with a throng of hard-headed peasants to sow the sorghum, a heavy wooden seed-drill across his shoulders. The road was lined with mulberry trees, their out-stretched leaves as big as copper coins. Birds were chattering; the grass along the roadside was very green. The water in the ditches lay deep, patches of frogspawn shimmered on the pale yellow reeds. Dad was panting noisily under the weight of the seed-drill, when a bicycle suddenly shot out of nowhere and crashed sidelong into him. He staggered a few paces but didn't fall over, unlike the bicycle which did. Dad flung down his seed-drill, picked up the bicycle, then picked up its rider. The latter was a short-arsed individual; as soon as he tried to walk his knee-joints began cracking. Dad greeted him respectfully, Officer Liu.

Officer Liu said: Have you gone blind, you dog?

Dad said: Yes, the dog is blind, don't be angry sir.

Liu: You dare to insult me? You sonofabitch bastard!

Dad: Officer, it was you who bumped into me.

Liu: Up yours!

Dad: Don't swear, sir, it was you who bumped into me.

Liu: x x x x.

Dad: You're being unreasonable, sir. Even in the old society there were honest officials who listened to reason.

Liu: What, are you saying the New Society[4] is worse than the old society?

Dad: I never said that.

Liu: Counter-revolutionary! Renegade! I'll blow you away! Officer Liu pulled a Mauser[5] from his waistband and pointed the gaping black muzzle at dad's chest.

Dad: I haven't done anything to deserve the death penalty.

Liu: Near as damn it you have.

Dad: Go on then, shoot me.

Liu: I didn't bring any bullets.

Dad: Fuck off then!

4. Communist society, officially egalitarian.   5. A German-made pistol.

Liu: Maybe I can't shoot you, but there's nothing to stop me beating you up.

Officer Liu leapt at Dad like an arrow, knees cracking, and stabbed straight at the bridge of his nose with the long barrel of the pistol. Black blood began to trickle slowly from Dad's nostrils. The peasants pulled him away, and some of the older ones tried to placate Officer Liu. Officer Liu said angrily: I'll let you off this once. Dad was standing to one side, wiping away the blood with his fingers; he lifted them up and inspected them carefully. Liu said: That'll teach you some respect.

Dad: My friends, you all saw it, you'll be my witnesses—He wiped his face vigorously a couple of times, it was covered in blood—Old Liu, fuck your ancestors to the eighth generation.

As Dad stomped towards him, Old Liu raised his gun, and shouted: Come any nearer and I'll shoot. Dad said: You won't get a peep out of that gun. Dad seized Old Liu's wrist, wrested the gun away from him and flung it viciously into the ditch, sending spray flying high into the air. Clasping Old Liu by the scruff of the neck, he shook him backwards and forwards for a moment, then took aim at his buttocks and gave them a gentle kick. Officer Liu plunged head-first into the ditch, buttocks skywards; his head lodged in the sludge and his legs splashed noisily in the water. The crowd of onlookers turned pale; some edged away, others rushed down into the ditch to drag the officer out. One old man said to Dad: Quick, nephew, run for it! Dad said: Fourth uncle, we'll meet again on the road to the yellow springs.[6] And he strode off towards home.

Officer Liu was extracted by the locals, weeping and wailing like a baby. He begged the crowd to find his gun for him, and at least a dozen of them went down into the ditch. Their searching hands stirred up plenty of mud, but they couldn't find the gun.

Dad felt among the dust on the beam and pulled down a long oil-paper sack, from which he withdrew a long, twisted gun. His eyes were glistening with tears. You mean we've still got a gun in the house? Mum asked him in astonishment. Dad said: Haven't you heard how my mum shot my dad? This was the gun she used. Mum was wide-eyed with fear. Get rid of it quick, she said. Dad said: No. Mum said: What are you going to do? Dad said: Kill someone. He now took down a powder-horn with a narrow waist, and a tin box, and deftly filled the gun with powder and shot. Dad said: Make sure that Dasuo studies hard. Make sure that he looks at this gun every day, just looks, mind, you're not to let him touch it. Have you got that? Mum said: Are you crazy? Dad pointed the gun at her: Get back!

Dad walked into the pear-orchard. The blossom on the trees was like a layer of snow. He hung the gun from a tree, muzzle downwards, and tied a thin piece of string to the hammer. Then he lay on his back on the ground and put the muzzle into his mouth. Eyes wide, he gazed at the golden bees and gave a sharp tug on the string. Pear blossom swirled down like snowflakes. A few bees fell to the ground, dead.[7]

He pulled the trigger again, but still there was no report. He sat down, disheartened. The sun lay across the horizon like a doughnut, its colour the same deep-

---

6. The underworld, where souls go after the body dies.

7. There is a long tradition in China of suicide as a form of political protest.

fried golden brown. The pool had shrunk even smaller, the fringes of the plain grew even hazier, the white half-moon was already visible. In the distance, on a clump of reeds, insects sparkled with a green light. The ducks tucked their beaks under their wings and gazed mockingly at him. They were so close to him, getting even closer now as the sky grew darker. His stomach protested bitterly; countless roast ducks, dripping with oil, flashed before his eyes. He pulled the trigger again and again, until the percussion cap was knocked out of shape by the hammer and embedded itself inextricably in the groove. He slumped disconsolately against the hide, like an animal which had just been filleted; the sorghum stalks cracked beneath him. The wild ducks paid not the slightest heed to the noise; they were silent, motionless, a heap of dappled cobble-stones. The sun disappeared, taking with it all the reds and greens, all shades of colour, leaving a world returned to its original state of grey and white. The crickets and cicadas beat their wings, their chirring merging into a constant drone. On the verge of tears, he stared up at the alfalfa-coloured vault of the sky, casting a sidelong glance, filled with hatred, at the gun. Was this decrepit old gun really the same one? Could such a foul-looking old wreck really have such an extraordinary history?

But when Wang Laoka started telling his tales of the old days, it really was as if they were unfolding before the villagers' eyes, and so everyone young and old loved to listen to him talking. Wang Laoka told them:

In the days of the Republic[8] none of the three counties controlled these parts—there were more bandits round here than hairs on a cow's back; men, women, they'd all turn violent at the drop of a hat, they'd kill a man as calmly as slicing a melon. Have you heard the story of Dasuo here's granny? Well, Dasuo's grandad was a compulsive gambler who lived off Dasuo's granny—that little woman was tough, she built up a home from nothing, all by herself, and that ain't easy for a woman. She sweated her guts out for three years and managed to buy a few dozen hectares of land, even a couple of horses. And what a beauty she was, Dasuo's granny, people called her "the queen of the eight villages". Lovely pointed bound feet she had, a fringe like a curtain of black silk.[9] To protect her house and home she swapped a stone and two pecks of grain for a gun. Now this gun had a long, long barrel and a mahogany butt, and they say that in the dead of night the hammer used to start clicking. She used to sling that gun across her back and ride off into the fields on her big horse to hunt foxes. A dead-shot she was—always shot 'em right up the arse. But then she got sick, a terrible thing, she was in a fever for seven whole weeks of seven whole days. Dasuo's grandad saw his chance—off he went roistering with whores and gambling to his heart's content: he lost all their land, even lost those two fine steeds. When the winner came to collect the horses, Dasuo's granny was lying on the *kang*, gasping for breath. Dasuo's dad was just a lad of five or six then, and when he saw that some people were trying to lead their horses away, he yelled: Mum, someone's taking the horses! The second she heard this, Dasuo's granny rolled straight off the *kang*, grabbed the gun from the wall, and dragged herself painfully into the courtyard. And what right have you to take out the horses, pray? she shouted. The two fellers leading the horses knew that this woman took no prisoners, so they said: Your man lost

8. The Republic of China (1912–49), before the Communist revolution.
9. Until the early 20th century, the Chinese bound the feet of young girls so that they would not grow to full size; the practice caused severe deformity.

these horses to our boss, lady. She said: Since that's the case, might I trouble you two brothers to bring my man to see me, there's something I'd like to say to him. Dasuo's grandad—his name was Santao—was so afraid of his wife he was skulking outside the door, too scared to come in. But when he heard her shouting he knew it was too late to chicken out. He plucked up courage, did his best to look tough, marched into the courtyard, thrust out his chest and said: Hot today, isn't it. Dasuo's granny smiled and said: You lost the horses, didn't you? Santao said: Sure did. She said: So, you lost the horses, what are you going to lose next? Santao said: I'm going to lose you. She said: Good old Santao. Fate must bring enemies together, it was really my luck to marry you. You've lost my horses, lost my land, forty-nine days I've been lying here sick and you haven't so much as brought me a bowl of water. And now you think you can lose me—I reckon I'd rather lose you first. On this day next year, Santao, I'll bring the child to your grave and burn paper money for you . . . The words were hardly out of her mouth when there was a great boom; the courtyard filled with a red flash . . . and his grandad was dead . . .

When he heard this story his dad was still alive. He asked his dad where the gun was, but his dad screamed furiously at him: You get the hell out of here.

The half-moon was becoming brighter, fireflies flitted unhurriedly, tracing a series of green-tinted arcs across his face. The pool had assumed a sombre, dim, steely-grey hue, but the sky was not yet completely black—he could still make out the pale green eyes of the gold-hooped dragonflies. The chirring of the insects came in bursts, each close on the heels of the last. The damp air congealed and wafted heavenwards. He wasn't watching the flock of ducks any more, he was thinking only about eating duck, again feeling the sharp contractions in his stomach. The image of the hunter with dead ducks slung all around his body became superimposed on the image of the woman warrior on horseback, her gun slung over her shoulder; at last they merged with that of the decent man under a covering of pear blossoms.

The sun had finally gone out. All that remained was a strip of fading golden warmth on the western horizon. The tip of the half-moon was rising in the south-west, scattering a tender feeling as soft as water. Mist rose from the pool like so many clumps of vegetation, the wild ducks shimmered in and out of sight through the gaps in the mist, and the splashing of big fish echoed from the water. He stood up, as if drunk or in a trance, and flexed his stiff, numb joints. He strapped on the powder-horn, slung the gun over his shoulder and strode out of the hide. Why doesn't anything happen when I pull the trigger? He swung the gun down, cradled it in his arms and stared at it. It shimmered with a blue glow in the moonlight. Why don't you fire? he thought. He cocked the hammer and casually pulled the trigger.

The low, rumbling explosion rolled in waves across the autumn fields and a ball of red light lit up the water-flats and the wild ducks. Shreds of iron and shards of wood hurtled through the air; the ducks took off in startled flight. He toppled slowly to the ground, trying with all his strength to open his eyes. He seemed to see the ducks floating down around him like rocks, falling onto his body, piling up into a great mound, pressing down on him so that it became difficult to breathe.

1985

ORHAN PAMUK
born 1952

Orhan Pamuk's life and work are closely bound up with Istanbul, a historic city at the border between East and West. Pamuk described looking out his window and seeing both the Asian and the European portions of the city, separated by the Bosphorus strait. Of his attachment to Istanbul, Pamuk has written: "Conrad, Nabokov, and Naipaul— these are writers known for having managed to migrate between languages, cultures, countries, continents, even civilizations. Their imaginations were fed by exile, a nourishment drawn not through roots but through rootlessness. My imagination, however, requires that I stay in the same city, on the same street, in the same house, gazing at the same view. Istanbul's fate is my fate." Combining Turkish and European influences, Pamuk's work re-creates the city of his childhood in realistic detail colored by the transformative power of memory and imagination.

Born in Istanbul to a wealthy, secularized Muslim family whose fortune had recently declined, Pamuk grew up in Westernized surroundings. Educated at the elite Robert College, he considered becoming a painter or an architect, but after three years at the Istanbul Technical University, he decided instead to become a writer and studied journalism at Istanbul University. His first novel, *Cevdet Bey ve Ogullari* (*Cevdet Bey and His Sons*, 1982), offered a partly autobiographical panorama spanning three generations of a Turkish family. The more realistic tone of his early works gave way to greater experimentation in a series of novels set in Istanbul, often involving multiple narrators,

doppelgängers, and mysterious coincidences and containing commentary on Turkish history. Some of these works have been described as postmodernist for their play with the relationship between history and fiction, reality and imagination. After winning a number of Turkish literary prizes, Pamuk's work began to be translated into foreign languages, and he received international acclaim, culminating in the Nobel Prize in 2006. His views on Turkish history have sometimes been controversial, especially in his criticisms of the Armenian genocide, conducted by the Turkish government during the First World War, and the later killings of Turkish Kurds. Many in Turkey deny both events, and right-wing nationalists charged Pamuk in court with "insulting Turkish-ness." Pamuk's books were burned by angry crowds, but the charges were later dropped. While continuing to live mostly in Istanbul, Pamuk has also taught abroad, notably at Columbia University in New York.

Pamuk has often considered his work to be at the crossroads of the West and Islam, Europe and the Middle East. In his Nobel lecture, he spoke of a suitcase bequeathed to him that was full of his father's youthful attempts at writing (composed mainly in Paris):

As for my place in the world—in life, as in literature, my basic feeling was that I was "not in the centre." In the centre of the world, there was a life richer and more exciting than our own, and with all of Istanbul, all of Turkey, I was outside it. . . . My father's library was evidence of this. At one end, there were Istanbul's books—our literature, our local world, in all its beloved detail—and at the other end were the books from this other, Western, world, to which our own bore no resemblance, to which our lack of resemblance gave us both pain and hope. To write, to read, was like leaving one world to find consolation in the other world's otherness, the strange and the wondrous.

"To Look Out the Window" (1999) returns to the theme of East and West, as the narrator recalls his boyhood in Istanbul and his father's departure for Paris. Pamuk has written that the story "is so autobiographical that the hero's name might well have been Orhan." (Pamuk's brother, however, was not as cruel as the brother in the story.) The story also involves a return to the realistic, autobiographical writing of Pamuk's early work, although the way that the experience is filtered through

memory and longing, and the emphasis on the naive viewpoint of the child, evoke the modernism of Marcel Proust. Like Proust, Pamuk is able to call up the emotions of childhood, including the child's incomprehension in the face of adult conflicts and the child's not always innocent response to this bewilderment.

Pamuk writes in the tradition of the great modernists, attentive to the finer points of the individual consciousness faced with a hostile or incomprehensible world. Yet what is perhaps most distinctive about Pamuk is his awareness of the way such consciousness is shaped by the movements of history. The author's re-creations of Turkish and Ottoman history, sometimes playful and sometimes terrifying, have occasionally caused him to be described as a postmodernist. Such labels ultimately tell us little about Pamuk's main contribution to world literature: his rich and vivid imagination.

To Look Out the Window[1]

I

If there's nothing to watch and no stories to listen to, life can get tedious. When I was a child, boredom was something we fought off by listening to the radio or looking out the window into neighboring apartments or at people passing in the street below. In those days, in 1958, there was still no television in Turkey. But we didn't like to admit it: We talked about television optimistically, just as we did the Hollywood adventure films that took four or five years to reach Istanbul's film theaters, saying it "had yet to arrive."

Looking out the window was such an important pastime that when television did finally come to Turkey, people acted the same way in front of their sets as they had in front of their windows. When my father, my uncles, and my grandmother watched television, they would argue without looking at one another, pausing now and again to report on what they'd just seen, just as they did while gazing out the window.

"If if keeps snowing like this, it's going to stick," my aunt would say, looking at the snowflakes swirling past.

---

1. Translated by Maureen Freely.

"That man who sells *helva* is back on the Nişantaşi[2] corner!" I would say, peering from the other window, which looked out over the avenue with the streetcar lines.

On Sundays, we'd go upstairs with my uncles and aunts and everyone else who lived in the downstairs apartments to have lunch with my grandmother. As I stood at the window, waiting for the food to arrive, I'd be so happy to be there with my mother, my father, my aunts, and my uncles that everything before me seemed to glow with the pale light of the crystal chandelier hanging over the long dining table. My grandmother's sitting room was dark, as were the downstairs sitting rooms, but to me it always seemed darker. Maybe this was because of the tulle curtains and the heavy drapes that hung at either side of the never-opened balcony doors, casting fearsome shadows. Or maybe it was the screens inlaid with mother-of-pearl, the massive tables, the chests, and the baby grand piano, with all those framed photographs on top, or the general clutter of this airless room that always smelled of dust.

The meal was over, and my uncle was smoking in one of the dark adjoining rooms. "I have a ticket to a football match, but I'm not going," he'd say. "Your father is going to take you instead."

"Daddy, take us to the football match!" my older brother would cry from the other room.

"The children could use some fresh air," my mother would call from the sitting room.

"Then you take them out," my father said to my mother.

"I'm going to my mother's," my mother replied.

"We don't want to go to Granny's," said my brother.

"You can have the car," said my uncle.

"Please, Daddy!" said my brother.

There was a long, strange silence. It was as if everyone in the room was thinking certain thoughts about my mother, and as if my father could tell what those thoughts were.

"So you're giving me your car, are you?" my father asked my uncle.

Later, when we had gone downstairs, while my mother was helping us put on our pullovers and our thick checked woolen socks, my father paced up and down the corridor, smoking a cigarette. My uncle had parked his "elegant, cream colored" '52 Dodge in front of the Teşvikiye Mosque. My father allowed both of us to sit in the front seat and managed to get the motor started with one turn of the key.

There was no line at the stadium. "This ticket for the two of them," said my father to the man at the turnstile. "One is eight, and the other is ten." As we went through, we were afraid to look into the man's eyes. There were lots of empty seats in the stands, and we sat down at once.

The two teams had already come out to the muddy field, and I enjoyed watching the players run up and down in their dazzling white shorts to warm up. "Look, that's Little Mehmet," said my brother, pointing to one of them. "He's just come from the junior team."

"We know."

The match began, and for a long time we didn't speak. A while later my thoughts wandered from the match to other things. Why did footballers all

---

2. An elegant neighborhood in central Istanbul. "Helva": a sweet made of sesame seeds (or similar nuts), popular throughout the Middle East, Eastern Europe, and South Asia.

wear the same strip when their names were all different? I imagined that there were no longer players running up and down the field, just names. Their shorts were getting dirtier and dirtier. A while later, I watched a ship with an interesting smokestack passing slowly down the Bosphorus,[3] just behind the bleachers. No one had scored by halftime, and my father bought us each a cone of chickpeas and a cheese pita.

"Daddy, I can't finish this," I said, showing him what was left in my hand.

"Put it over there," he said. "No one will see you."

We got up and moved around to warm up, just like everyone else. Like our father, we had shoved our hands into the pockets of our woolen trousers and turned away from the field to look at the people sitting behind us, when someone in the crowd called out to my father. My father brought his hand to his ear, to indicate that he couldn't hear a thing with all the noise.

"I can't come," he said, as he pointed in our direction. "I have my children with me."

The man in the crowd was wearing a purple scarf. He fought his way to our row, pushing the seatbacks and shoving quite a few people to reach us.

"Are these your boys?" he asked, after he had embraced my father. "They're so big. I can hardly believe it."

My father said nothing.

"So when did these children appear?" said the man, looking at us admiringly. "Did you get married as soon as you finished school?"

"Yes," said my father, without looking him in his face. They spoke for a while longer. The man with the purple scarf turned to my brother and me and put an unshelled American peanut into each of our palms. When he left, my father sat down in his seat and for a long time said nothing.

Not long after the two teams had returned to the field in fresh shorts, my father said, "Come on, let's go home. You're getting cold."

"I'm not getting cold," said my brother.

"Yes, you are," said my father. "And Ali's cold. Come on, let's get going."

As we were making our way past the others in our row, jostling against knees and sometimes stepping on feet, we stepped on the cheese pita I'd left on the ground. As we walked down the stairs, we heard the referee blowing his whistle to signal the start of the second half.

"Were you getting cold?" my brother asked. "Why didn't you say you weren't cold?" I stayed quiet. "Idiot," said my brother.

"You can listen to the second half on the radio at home," said my father.

"This match is not on the radio," my brother said.

"Quiet, now," said my father. "I'm taking you through Taksim on our way back."

We stayed quiet. Driving across the square, my father stopped the car just before we got to the off-track betting shop—just as we'd guessed. "Don't open the door for anyone," he said. "I'll be back in a moment."

He got out of the car. Before he had a chance to lock the car from the outside, we'd pressed down on the buttons and locked it from the inside. But my father didn't go into the betting shop; he ran over to the other side of the cobblestone street. There was a shop over there that was decorated with posters of

---

3. The strait that bisects Istanbul, traditionally the border between Asia and Europe. The story takes place on the European side of the city.

ships, big plastic airplanes, and sunny landscapes, and it was even open on Sundays, and that's where he went.

"Where did Daddy go?"

"Are we going to play upstairs or downstairs when we get home?" my brother asked.

When my father got back, my brother was playing with the accelerator. We drove back to Nişantaşı and parked again in front of the mosque. "Why don't I buy you something!" said my father. "But please, don't ask for that Famous People series again."

"Oh, please, Daddy!" we pleaded.

When we got to Alaaddin's shop, my father bought us each ten packs of chewing gum from the Famous People series. We went into our building; I was so excited by the time we got into the lift that I thought I might wet my pants. It was warm inside and my mother wasn't back yet. We ripped open the chewing gum, throwing the wrappers on the floor. The result:

I got two Field Marshal Fevzi Çakmaks; one each of Charlie Chaplin, the wrestler Hamit Kaplan, Gandhi, Mozart, and De Gaulle; two Atatürks, and one Greta Garbo—number 21—which my brother didn't have yet. With these I now had 173 pictures of Famous People, but I still needed another 27 to complete the series. My brother got four Field Marshal Fevzi Çakmaks, five Atatürks, and one Edison.[4] We tossed the chewing gum into our mouths and began to read the writing on the backs of the cards.

Field Marshal Fevzi Çakmak
General in the War of Independence
(1876–1950)

MAMBO SWEETS CHEWING GUM, INC
A leather soccer ball will be awarded to the lucky person who collects all 100 famous people.

My brother was holding his stack of 165 cards. "Do you want to play Tops or Bottoms?"

"No."

"Would you give me your Greta Garbo for my twelve Fevzi Çakmaks?" he asked. "Then you'll have one hundred and eighty-four cards."

"No."

4. Thomas Alva Edison (1847–1931), American inventor. The cards include internationally famous figures from history and popular culture as well as many Turks whose fame was more local. Fevzi Çakmak (1876–1950), Turkish general in the War of Independence (1919–23), fought against the occupying Allied forces after the First World War (1914–18). Charlie Chaplin, British-American movie star (1889–1977). Hamit Kaplan, Turkish world champion Olympic wrestler (1934–1976). Mahondas K. (Mahatma) Gandhi (1869–1948), leader of the movement for Indian independence and philosopher of nonviolence. Wolfgang Amadeus Mozart (1756–1791), Austrian classical composer. Charles de Gaulle (1890–1970), wartime leader of Free French forces and later president of France. Mustafa Kemal Atatürk (1881–1938), leader of the movement for Turkish independence and first president of Turkey. Greta Garbo (1905–1990), Swedish movie star.

"But now you have two Greta Garbos."

I said nothing.

"When they do our inoculations at school tomorrow, it's really going to hurt," he said. "Don't expect me to take care of you, okay?"

"I wouldn't anyway."

We ate supper in silence. When *World of Sports* came on the radio, we found out that the match had been a draw, 2–2, and then our mother came into our room to put us to bed. My brother started getting his bag ready for school, and I ran into the sitting room. My father was at the window, staring down at the street.

"Daddy, I don't want to go to school tomorrow."

"Now how can you say that?"

"They're giving us those inoculations tomorrow. I come down with a fever, and then I can hardly breathe. Ask Mummy."

He looked at me, saying nothing. I raced over to the drawer and got out a pen and a piece of paper.

"Does your mother know about this?" he asked, putting the paper down on the volume of Kierkegaard[5] that he was always reading but never managed to finish. "You're going to school, but you won't have that injection," he said. "That's what I'll write."

He signed his name. I blew on the ink and then folded up the paper and put it in my pocket. Running back to the bedroom, I slipped it into my bag, and then I climbed up onto my bed and began to bounce on it.

"Calm down," said my mother. "It's time to go to sleep."

2

I was at school, and it was just after lunch. The whole class was lined up two by two, and we were going back to that stinking cafeteria to have our inoculations. Some children were crying; others were waiting in nervous anticipation. When a whiff of iodine floated up the stairs, my heart began to race. I stepped out of line and went over to the teacher standing at the head of the stairs. The whole class passed us noisily.

"Yes?" said the teacher. "What is it?"

I took out the piece of paper my father had signed and gave it to the teacher. She read it with a frown. "Your father's not a doctor, you know," she said. She paused to think. "Go upstairs. Wait in Room Two-A."

There were six or seven children in 2-A who like me had been excused. One was staring in terror out the window. Cries of panic came floating down the corridor; a fat boy with glasses was munching on pumpkin seeds and reading a Kinova comic book. The door opened and in came thin, gaunt Deputy Headmaster Seyfi Bey.

"Probably some of you are genuinely ill, and if you are, we won't take you downstairs," he said. "But I have this to say to those of you who've lied to get excused. One day you will grow up, serve our country, and maybe even die for it. Today it's just an injection you're running away from—but if you try something like this when you grow up, and if you don't have a genuine excuse, you'll be guilty of treason. Shame on you!"

---

5. Søren Kierkegaard, Danish philosopher (1813–1855), forerunner of existentialism.

There was a long silence. I looked at Atatürk's picture, and tears came to my eyes.

Later, we slipped unnoticed back to our classrooms. The children who'd had their inoculations started coming back: Some had their sleeves rolled up, some had tears in their eyes, some scuffled in with very long faces.

"Children living close by can go home," said the teacher. "Children with no one to pick them up must wait until the last bell. Don't punch one another on the arm! Tomorrow there's no school."

Everyone started shouting. Some were holding their arms as they left the building; others stopped to show the janitor, Hilmi Efendi, the iodine tracks on their arms.

When I got out to the street, I slung my bag over my shoulder and began to run. A horse cart had blocked traffic in front of Karabet's butcher shop, so I weaved between the cars to get to our building on the other side. I ran past Hayri's fabric shop and Salih's florist shop. Our janitor, Hazim Efendi, let me in.

"What are you doing here all alone at this hour?" he asked.

"They gave us our inoculations today. They let us out early."

"Where's your brother? Did you come back alone?"

"I crossed the streetcar lines by myself. Tomorrow we have the day off."

"Your mother's out," he said. "Go up to your grandmother's."

"I'm ill," I said. "I want to go to our house. Open the door for me."

He took a key off the wall and we got into the lift. By the time we had reached our floor, his cigarette had filled the whole cage with smoke that burned my eyes. He opened our door. "Don't play with the electrical sockets," he said, as he pulled the door closed.

There was no one at home, but I still shouted out, "Is anyone here, anyone home? Isn't there anyone home?" I threw down my bag, opened up my brother's drawer, and began to look at the film ticket collection he'd never shown me. Then I had a good long look at the pictures of football matches that he'd cut out of newspapers and glued into a book. I could tell from the footsteps that it wasn't my mother coming in now, it was my father. I put my brother's tickets and his scrapbook back where they belonged, carefully, so he wouldn't know I'd been looking at them.

My father was in his bedroom; he'd opened up his wardrobe and was looking inside.

"You're home already, are you?"

"No, I'm in Paris," I said, the way they did at school.

"Didn't you go to school today?"

"Today they gave us our inoculations."

"Isn't your brother here?" he asked. "All right then, go to your room and show me how quiet you can be."

I did as he asked. I pressed my forehead against the window and looked outside. From the sounds coming from the hallway I could tell that my father had taken one of the suitcases out of the cupboard there. He went back into his room and began to take his jackets and his trousers out of the wardrobe; I could tell from the rattling of the hangers. He began to open and close the drawers where he kept his shirts, his socks, and his underpants. I listened to him put them all into the suitcase. He went into the bathroom and came out again. He snapped the suitcase latches shut and turned the lock. He came to join me in my room.

"So what have you been up to in here?"

"I've been looking out the window."

"Come here, let's look out the window together."

He took me on his lap, and for a long time we looked out the window together. The tips of the tall cypress tree that stood between us and the apartment building opposite began to sway in the wind. I liked the way my father smelled.

"I'm going far away," he said. He kissed me. "Don't tell your mother. I'll tell her myself later."

"Are you going by plane?"

"Yes," he said, "to Paris. Don't tell this to anyone either." He took a huge two-and-a-half-lira coin from his pocket and gave it to me, and then he kissed me again. "And don't say you saw me here."

I put the money right into my pocket. When my father had lifted me from his lap and picked up his suitcase, I said, "Don't go, Daddy." He kissed me one more time, and then he left.

I watched him from the window. He walked straight to Alaaddin's store, and then he stopped a passing taxi. Before he got in, he looked up at our apartment one more time and waved. I waved back, and he took off.

I looked at the empty avenue for a long, long time. A streetcar passed, and then the water seller's horse cart. I rang the bell and called Hazim Efendi.

"Did you ring the bell?" he said, when he got to the door. "Don't play with the bell."

"Take this two-and-a-half-lira coin," I said, "go to Alaaddin's shop, and buy me ten chewing gums from the Famous People series. Don't forget to bring back the fifty kuruş change."

"Did your father give you this money?" he asked. "Let's hope your mother doesn't get angry."

I said nothing, and he left. I stood at the window and watched him go into Alaaddin's shop. He came out a little later. On his way back, he ran into the janitor from the Marmara Apartments across the way, and they stopped to chat.

When he came back, he gave me the change. I immediately ripped open the chewing gum: three more Fevzi Çakmaks, one Atatürk, and one each of Leonardo da Vinci and Süleyman the Magnificent, Churchill, General Franco,[6] and one more number 21, the Greta Garbo that my brother still didn't have. So now I had 183 pictures in all. But to complete the full set of 100, I still needed 26 more.

I was admiring my first 91, which showed the plane in which Lindbergh had crossed the Atlantic,[7] when I heard a key in the door. My mother! I quickly gathered up the gum wrappers that I had thrown on the floor and put them in the bin.

---

6. Francisco Franco (1892–1975), Spanish general and fascist dictator. Leonardo da Vinci, Renaissance artist and inventor (1452–1519). Süleyman the Magnificent, sultan of the Ottoman Empire (1494–1566). Winston Churchill (1874–1965), British wartime prime minister.

7. Charles Lindbergh (1902–1974), American pilot, first to fly nonstop across the Atlantic Ocean.

"We had our inoculations today, so I came home early," I said. "Typhoid, typhus, tetanus."

"Where's your brother?"

"His class hadn't had their inoculations yet," I said. "They sent us home. I crossed the avenue all by myself."

"Does your arm hurt?"

I said nothing. A little later, my brother came home. His arm was hurting. He lay down on his bed, resting on his other arm, and looked miserable as he fell asleep. It was very dark out by the time he woke up. "Mummy, it hurts a lot," he said.

"You might have a fever later on," my mother said, as she was ironing in the other room. "Ali, is your arm hurting too? Lie down, keep still."

We went to bed and kept still. After sleeping for a little my brother woke up and began to read the sports page, and then he told me it was because of me that we'd left the match early yesterday, and because we'd left early our team had missed four goals.

"Even if we hadn't left, we might not have made those goals," I said.

"What?"

After dozing a little longer, my brother offered me six Fevzi Çakmaks, four Atatürks, and three other cards I already had in exchange for one Greta Garbo, and I turned him down.

"Shall we play Tops or Bottoms?" he asked me.

"Okay, let's play."

You press the whole stack between the palms of your hands. You ask, "Tops or Bottoms?" If he says Bottoms, you look at the bottom picture, let's say number 68, Rita Hayworth.[8] Now let's say it's number 18, Dante the Poet, on top. If it is, then Bottoms wins and you give him the picture you like the least, the one you already have the most of. Field Marshal Fevzi Çakmak pictures passed back and forth between us until it was evening and time for supper.

"One of you go upstairs and take a look," said my mother. "Maybe your father's come back."

We both went upstairs. My uncle was sitting, smoking, with my grandmother; my father wasn't there. We listened to the news on the radio, we read the sports page. When my grandmother sat down to eat, we went downstairs.

"What kept you?" said my mother. "You didn't eat anything up there, did you? Why don't I give you your lentil soup now. You can eat it very slowly until your father gets home."

"Isn't there any toasted bread?" my brother asked.

While we were silently eating our soup, our mother watched us. From the way she held her head and the way her eyes darted away from us, I knew she was listening for the lift. When we finished our soup, she asked, "Would you like some more?" She glanced into the pot. "Why don't I have mine before it gets cold," she said. But instead she went to the window and looked down at Nişantaşi Square; she stood there looking for some time. Then she turned around, came back to the table, and began to eat her soup. My brother and I were discussing yesterday's match.

"Be quiet! Isn't that the lift?"

8. American movie star and sex symbol (1918–1987).

We fell quiet and listened carefully. It wasn't the lift. A streetcar broke the silence, shaking the table, the glasses, the pitcher, and the water inside it. When we were eating our oranges, we all definitely heard the lift. It came closer and closer, but it didn't stop at our floor; it went right up to my grandmother's. "It went all the way up," said my mother.

After we had finished eating, my mother said, "Take your plates to the kitchen. Leave your father's plate where it is." We cleared the table. My father's clean plate sat alone on the empty table for a long time.

My mother went over to the window that looked down at the police station; she stood there looking for a long time. Then suddenly she made up her mind. Gathering up my father's knife and fork and empty plate, she took them into the kitchen. "I'm going upstairs to your grandmother's," she said. "Please don't get into a fight while I'm gone."

My brother and I went back to our game of Tops or Bottoms.

"Tops," I said, for the first time.

He revealed the top card: number 34, Koca Yusuf, the world-famous wrestler. He pulled out the card from the bottom of the stack: number 50, Atatürk. "You lose. Give me a card."

We played for a long time and he kept on winning. Soon he had taken nineteen of my twenty Fevzi Çakmaks and two of my Atatürks.

"I'm not playing anymore," I said, getting angry. "I'm going upstairs. To Mummy."

"Mummy will get angry."

"Coward! Are you afraid of being home all alone?"

My grandmother's door was open as usual. Supper was over. Bekir, the cook, was washing the dishes; my uncle and my grandmother were sitting across from each other. My mother was at the window looking down on Nişantaşi Square.

"Come," she said, still looking out the window. I moved straight into the empty space that seemed to be reserved just for me. Leaning against her, I too looked down at Nişantaşi Square. My mother put her hand on my head and gently stroked my hair.

"Your father came home early this afternoon, I hear. You saw him."

"Yes."

"He took his suitcase and left. Hazim Efendi saw him."

"Yes."

"Did he tell you where he was going, darling?"

"No," I said. "He gave me two and a half lira."

Down in the street, everything—the dark stores along the avenue, the car lights, the little empty space in the middle where the traffic policemen stood, the wet cobblestones, the letters on the advertising boards that hung from the trees—everything was lonely and sad. It began to rain, and my mother passed her fingers slowly through my hair.

That was when I noticed that the radio that sat between my grandmother's chair and my uncle's—the radio that was always on—was silent. A chill passed through me.

"Don't stand there like that, my girl," my grandmother said then.

My brother had come upstairs.

"Go to the kitchen, you two," said my uncle. "Bekir!" he called. "Make these boys a ball; they can play football in the hallway."

In the kitchen, Bekir had finished the dishes. "Sit down over there," he said. He went out to the glass-enclosed balcony that my grandmother had turned into a greenhouse and brought back a pile of newspapers that he began to crumple into a ball. When it was as big as a fist, he asked, "Is this good enough?"

"Wrap a few more sheets around it," said my brother.

While Bekir was wrapping a few more sheets of newsprint around the ball, I looked through the doorway to watch my mother, my grandmother, and my uncle on the other side. With a rope he took from a drawer, Bekir bound the paper ball until it was as round as it could be. To soften its sharp edges, he wiped it lightly with a damp rag and then he compressed it again. My brother couldn't resist touching it.

"Wow. It's hard as a rock."

"Put your finger down there for me." My brother carefully placed his finger on the spot where the last knot was to be tied. Bekir tied the knot and the ball was done. He tossed it into the air and we began to kick it around.

"Play in the hallway," said Bekir. "If you play in here, you'll break something."

For a long time we gave our game everything we had. I was pretending to be Lefter from Fenerbahçe, and I twisted and turned like he did. Whenever I did a wall pass, I ran into my brother's bad arm. He hit me, too, but it didn't hurt. We were both perspiring, the ball was falling to pieces, and I was winning five to three when I hit his bad arm very hard. He threw himself down on the floor and began to cry.

"When my arm gets better I'm going to kill you!" he said, as he lay there.

He was angry because he'd lost. I left the hallway for the sitting room; my grandmother, my mother, and my uncle had all gone into the study. My grandmother was dialing the phone.

"Hello, my girl," she said then, in the same voice she used when she called my mother the same thing. "Is that Yeşilköy Airport? Listen, my girl, we want to make an inquiry about a passenger who flew out to Europe earlier today." She gave my father's name and twisted the phone cord around her finger while she waited. "Bring me my cigarettes," she said then to my uncle. When my uncle had left the room, she took the receiver away from her ear.

"Please, my girl, tell us," my grandmother said to my mother. "You would know. Is there another woman?"

I couldn't hear my mother's answer. My grandmother was looking at her as if she hadn't said a thing. Then the person at the other end of the line said something and she got angry. "They're not going to tell us," she said, when my uncle returned with a cigarette and an ashtray.

My mother saw my uncle looking at me, and that was when she noticed I was there. Taking me by the arm, she pulled me back into the hallway. When she'd felt my back and the nape of my neck, she saw how much I'd perspired, but she didn't get angry at me.

"Mummy, my arm hurts," said my brother.

"You two go downstairs now, I'll put you both to bed."

Downstairs on our floor, the three of us were silent for a long time. Before I went to bed I padded into the kitchen in my pajamas for a glass of water, and then I went into the sitting room. My mother was smoking in front of the window, and at first she didn't hear me.

"You'll catch cold in those bare feet," she said. "Is your brother in bed?"

"He's asleep. Mummy, I'm going to tell you something." I waited for my mother to make room for me at the window. When she had opened up that sweet space for me, I sidled into it. "Daddy went to Paris," I said. "And you know what suitcase he took?"

She said nothing. In the silence of the night, we watched the rainy street for a very long time.

3

My other grandmother's house was next to Şişli Mosque[9] and the end of the streetcar line. Now the square is full of minibus and municipal bus stops, and high ugly buildings and department stores plastered with signs, and offices whose workers spill out onto the pavements at lunchtime and look like ants, but in those days it was at the edge of the European city. It took us fifteen minutes to walk from our house to the wide cobblestone square, and as we walked hand in hand with my mother under the linden and mulberry trees, we felt as if we had come to the countryside.

My other grandmother lived in a four-story stone and concrete house that looked like a matchbox turned on its side; it faced Istanbul to the west and in the back the mulberry groves in the hills. After her husband died and her three daughters were married, my grandmother had taken to living in a single room of this house, which was crammed with wardrobes, tables, trays, pianos, and other furniture. My aunt would cook her food and bring it over or pack it in a metal container and have her driver deliver it for her. It wasn't just that my grandmother would not leave her room to go two flights down to the kitchen to cook; she didn't even go into the other rooms of the house, which were covered with a thick blanket of dust and silky cobwebs. Like her own mother, who had spent her last years alone in a great wooden mansion, my grandmother had succumbed to a mysterious solitary disease and would not even permit a caretaker or a daily cleaner.

When we went to visit her, my mother would press down on the bell for a very long time and pound on the iron door, until my grandmother would at last open the rusty iron shutters on the second-floor window overlooking the mosque and peer down on us, and because she didn't trust her eyes—she could no longer see very far—she would ask us to wave at her.

"Come out of the doorway so your grandmother can see you, children," said my mother. Coming out into the middle of the pavement with us, she waved and cried, "Mother dear, it's me and the children; it's us, can you hear us?"

We understood from her sweet smile that she had recognized us. At once she drew back from the window, went into her room, took out the large key she kept under her pillow, and, after wrapping it in newsprint, threw it down. My brother and I pushed and shoved each other, struggling to catch it.

My brother's arm was still hurting, and that slowed him down, so I got to the key first, and I gave it to my mother. With some effort, my mother man-

---

9. A mosque in the European part of Istanbul.

aged to unlock the great iron door. The door slowly yielded as the three of us pushed against it, and out from the darkness came that smell I would never come across again: decay, mold, dust, age, and stagnant air. On the coat rack right next to the door—to make the frequent robbers think there was a man in the house—my grandmother had left my grandfather's felt hat and his fur-collared coat, and in the corner were the boots that always scared me so.

A little later, at the end of two straight flights of wooden stairs, far, far away, standing in a white light, we saw our grandmother. She looked like a ghost, standing perfectly still in the shadows with her cane, lit only by the light filtering through the frosted Art Deco[1] doors.

As she walked up the creaking stairs, my mother said nothing to my grandmother. (Sometimes she would say, "How are you, darling Mother?" or "Mother dear, I've missed you; it's very cold out, dear Mother!") When I reached the top of the stairs, I kissed my grandmother's hand, trying not to look at her face, or the huge mole on her wrist. But still we were frightened by the lone tooth in her mouth, her long chin, and the whiskers on her face, so once we were in the room we huddled next to our mother. My grandmother went back to the bed, where she spent most of the day in her long nightgown and her woolen vest, and she smiled at us, giving us a look that said, All right, now entertain me.

"Your stove isn't working so well, Mother," said my mother. She took the poker and stirred the coals.

My grandmother waited for a while, and then she said, "Leave the stove alone now. Give me some news. What's going on in the world?"

"Nothing at all," said my mother, sitting at our side.

"You have nothing to tell me at all?"

"Nothing at all, Mother dear."

After a short silence, my grandmother asked, "Haven't you seen anyone?"

"You know that already, Mother dear."

"For God's sake, have you no news?"

There was a silence.

"Grandmother, we had our inoculations at school," I said.

"Is that so?" said my grandmother, opening up her large blue eyes as if she were surprised. "Did it hurt?"

"My arm still hurts," said my brother.

"Oh, dear," said my grandmother with a smile.

There was another long silence. My brother and I got up and looked out the window at the hills in the distance, the mulberry trees, and the empty old chicken coop in the back garden.

"Don't you have any stories for me at all?" pleaded my grandmother. "You go up to see the mother-in-law. Doesn't anyone else?"

"Dilruba Hanim came yesterday afternoon," said my mother. "They played bezique with the children's grandmother."

In a rejoicing voice, our grandmother then said what we'd expected: "That's the palace lady!"

We knew she was talking not about one of the cream-colored palaces we read so much about in fairy tales and newspapers in those years but about Dolmabahçe

---

1. Decorative style, originating in Western Europe in the early 20th century.

Palace;[2] it was only much later I realized that my grandmother looked down on Dilruba Hanim—who had come from the last sultan's harem—because she had been a concubine before marrying a businessman, and that she also looked down on my grandmother for having befriended this woman.[3] Then they moved to another subject that they discussed every time my mother visited: Once a week, my grandmother would go to Beyoğlu to lunch alone at a famous and expensive restaurant called Aptullah Efendi, and afterward she would complain at great length about everything she'd eaten. She opened the third ready-made topic by asking us this question: "Children, does your other grandmother make you eat parsley?"

We answered with one voice, saying what our mother told us to say. "No, Grandmother, she doesn't."

As always, our grandmother told us how she'd seen a cat peeing on parsley in a garden, and how it was highly likely that the same parsley had ended up barely washed in some idiot's food, and how she was still arguing about this with the greengrocers of Şişli and Nişantaşi.

"Mother dear," said my mother, "the children are getting bored; they want to take a look at the other rooms. I'm going to open up the room next door."

My grandmother locked all the rooms in the house from the outside, to keep any thief who might enter through a window from reaching any other room in the house. My mother opened up the large cold room that looked out on the avenue with the streetcar line, and for a moment she stood there with us, looking at the armchairs and the divans under their dust covers, the rusty, dusty lamps, trays, and chairs, the bundles of old newspaper; at the worn saddle and the drooping handlebars of the creaky girl's bicycle listing in the corner. But she did not take anything out of the trunk to show us, as she had done on happier days. ("Your mother used to wear these sandals when she was little, children; look at your aunt's school uniform, children; would you like to see your mother's childhood piggy bank, children?")

"If you get cold, come and tell me," she said, and then she left.

My brother and I ran to the window to look at the mosque and the streetcar in the square. Then we read about old football matches in the newspapers. "I'm bored," I said. "Do you want to play Tops or Bottoms?"

"The defeated wrestler still wants to fight," said my brother, without looking up from his newspaper. "I'm reading the paper."

We'd played again that morning, and my brother had won again.

"Please."

"I have one condition: If I win, you have to give me two pictures, and if you win, I only give you one."

"No, one."

"Then I'm not playing," said my brother. "As you can see, I'm reading the paper."

He held the paper just like the English detective in a black-and-white film we'd seen recently at the Angel Theater. After looking out the window a little

2. 19th-century palace where the sultans kept their harems.
3. The children's maternal grandmother looks down at Dilruba Hanim for being a former concubine; she also looks down on the children's paternal grandmother for befriending Dilruba Hanim.

longer, I agreed to my brother's conditions. We took our Famous People cards from our pockets and began to play. First I won, but then I lost seventeen more cards.

"When we play this way, I always lose," I said. "I'm not playing anymore unless we go back to the old rules."

"Okay," said my brother, still imitating that detective. "I wanted to read those newspapers anyway."

For a while I looked out the window. I carefully counted my pictures: I had 121 left. When my father left the day before, I'd had 183! But I didn't want to think about it. I had agreed to my brother's conditions.

In the beginning, I'd been winning, but then he started winning again. Hiding his joy, he didn't smile when he took my cards and added them to his pack.

"If you want, we can play by some other rules," he said, a while later. "Whoever wins takes one card. If I win, I can choose which card I take from you. Because I don't have any of some of them, and you never give me those."

Thinking I would win, I agreed. I don't know how it happened. Three times in a row I lost my high card to his, and before I knew it I had lost both my Greta Garbos (21) and my only King Faruk (78). I wanted to take them all back at once, so the game got bigger: This was how a great many other cards I had and he didn't— Einstein (63), Rumi (3), Sarkis Nazaryan, the founder of Mambo Chewing Gum– Candied Fruit Company (100), and Cleopatra (51)[4]—passed over to him in only two rounds.

I couldn't even swallow. Because I was afraid I might cry, I ran to the window and looked outside: How beautiful everything had seemed only five minutes earlier—the streetcar approaching the terminus, the apartment buildings visible in the distance through the branches that were losing their leaves, the dog lying on the cobblestones, scratching himself so lazily! If only time had stopped. If only we could go back five squares as we did when we played Horse Race Dice. I was never playing Tops or Bottoms with my brother again.

"Shall we play again?" I said, without taking my forehead off the windowpane.

"I'm not playing," said my brother. "You'll only cry."

"Cevat, I promise. I won't cry," I insisted, as I went to his side. "But we have to play the way we did at the beginning, by the old rules."

"I'm going to read my paper."

"Okay," I said. I shuffled my thinner-than-ever stack. "With the old rules. Tops or Bottoms?"

"No crying," he said. "Okay, high."

I won and he gave me one of his Field Marshal Fevzi Çakmaks. I wouldn't take it. "Can you please give me seventy-eight, King Faruk?"

"No," he said. "That isn't what we agreed."

We played two more rounds, and I lost. If only I hadn't played that third round: When I gave him my 49, Napoleon,[5] my hand was shaking.

"I'm not playing anymore," said my brother.

---

4. Egyptian queen (69–30 B.C.E.). Faruk (1920–1965), king of Egypt. Albert Einstein (1879–1955), German-Swiss-American founder of modern physics. Rumi (1207–1273), Persian poet.
5. French emperor Napoleon Bonaparte (1769–1821).

I pleaded. We played two more rounds, and instead of giving him the pictures he asked for, I threw all the cards I had left at his head and into the air: the cards I had been collecting for two and a half months, thinking about each and every one of them every single day, hiding them and nervously accumulating them with care—number 28, Mae West, and 82, Jules Verne; 7, Mehmet the Conqueror, and 70, Queen Elizabeth; 41, Celal Salik the columnist, and 42, Voltaire[6]—they went flying through the air to scatter all over the floor.

If only I was in a completely different place, in a completely different life. Before I went back into my grandmother's room, I crept quietly down the creaky stairs, thinking about a distant relative who had worked in insurance and committed suicide. My father's mother had told me that suicides stayed in a dark place underground and never went to Heaven. When I'd gone a long way down the stairs, I stopped to stand in the darkness. I turned around and went upstairs and sat on the last step, next to my grandmother's room.

"I'm not well off like your mother-in-law," I heard my grandmother say. "You are going to look after your children and wait."

"But please, Mother dear, I beg you. I want to come back here with the children," my mother said.

"You can't live here with two children, not with all this dust and ghosts and thieves," said my grandmother.

"Mother dear," said my mother, "don't you remember how happily we lived here, just the two of us, after my sisters got married and my father passed away?"

"My lovely Mebrure, all you did all day was to leaf through old issues of your father's *Illustrations*."

"If I lit the big stove downstairs, this house would be cosy and warm in the space of two days."

"I told you not to marry him, didn't I?" said my grandmother.

"If I bring in a maid, it will only take us two days to get rid of all this dust," said my mother.

"I'm not letting any of those thieving maids into this house," said my grandmother. "Anyway, it would take six months to sweep out all this dust and cobwebs. By then your errant husband will be back home again."

"Is that your last word, Mother dear?" my mother asked.

"Mebrure, my lovely girl, if you came here with your two children what would we live on, the four of us?"

"Mother dear, how many times have I asked you—pleaded with you—to sell the lots in Bebek before they're expropriated?"

"I'm not going to the deeds office to give those dirty men my signature and my picture."

"Mother dear, please don't say this: My older sister and I brought a notary right to your door," said my mother, raising her voice.

6. Pen name of François-Marie Arouet (1694–1778), French Enlightenment philosopher. Mae West, American actress and sex symbol (1893–1980). Jules Verne, French novelist (1828–1905), author of *Twenty Thousand Leagues Under the Sea*. Mehmet the Conqueror, sultan (1432–1481) who conquered Constantinople (modern Istanbul) in 1453, establishing the Ottoman Empire. Elizabeth I, queen of England (1533–1603), long-reigning monarch celebrated in Renaissance literature. Celal Salik, Turkish journalist much admired by Orhan Pamuk.

"I've never trusted that notary," said my grandmother. "You can see from his face that he's a swindler. Maybe he isn't even a notary. And don't shout at me like that."

"All right, then, Mother dear, I won't!" said my mother. She called into the room for us. "Children, children, come on now, gather up your things; we're leaving."

"Slow down!" said my grandmother. "We haven't even said two words."

"You don't want us, Mother dear," my mother whispered

"Take this, let the children have some Turkish delight."[7]

"They shouldn't eat it before lunch," said my mother, and as she left the room she passed behind me to enter the room opposite. "Who threw these pictures all over the floor? Pick them up at once. And you help him," she said to my brother.

As we silently gathered the pictures, my mother lifted the lids of the old trunks and looked at the dresses from her childhood, her ballet costumes, the boxes. The dust underneath the black skeleton of the pedal sewing machine filled my nostrils, making my eyes water, filling my nose.

As we washed our hands in the little lavatory, my grandmother pleaded in a soft voice. "Mebrure dear, you take this teapot; you love it so much, you have a right to," she said. "My grandfather brought it for my dear mother when he was the governor of Damascus.[8] It came all the way from China. Please take it."

"Mother dear, from now on I don't want anything from you," my mother said. "And put that into your cupboard or you'll break it. Come, children, kiss your grandmother's hand."

"My little Mebrure, my lovely daughter, please don't be angry at your poor mother," said my grandmother, as she let us kiss her hand. "Please don't leave me here without any visitors, without anyone."

We raced down the stairs, and when the three of us had pushed open the heavy metal door, we were greeted by brilliant sunlight as we breathed in the clean air.

"Shut the door firmly behind you!" cried my grandmother. "Mebrure, you'll come to see me again this week, won't you?"

As we walked hand in hand with my mother, no one spoke. We listened in silence as the other passengers coughed and waited for the streetcar to leave. When finally we began to move, my brother and I moved to the next row, saying we wanted to watch the conductor, and began to play Tops or Bottoms. First I lost some cards, then I won a few back. When I upped the ante, he happily agreed, and I quickly began to lose again. When we had reached the Osmanbey[9] stop, my brother said, "In exchange for all the pictures you have left, here is this Fifteen you want so much."

I played and lost. Without letting him see, I removed two cards from the stack before handing it to my brother. I went to the back row to sit with my mother. I wasn't crying. I looked sadly out the window as the streetcar moaned and slowly gathered speed, and I watched them pass us by, all those people and places that are gone forever: the little sewing shops, the bakeries, the pudding shops with their awnings, the Tan cinema where we saw those films about

7. A nut-based sweet.
8. Capital of Syria, ruled by the Ottoman

Empire until 1918.
9. District in the European part of Istanbul.

ancient Rome, the children standing along the wall next to the front selling used comics, the barber with the sharp scissors who scared me so, and the half-naked neighborhood madman, always standing in the barbershop door.

We got off at Harbiye. As we walked toward home, my brother's satisfied silence was driving me mad. I took out the Lindbergh, which I'd hidden in my pocket.

This was his first sight of it. "Ninety-one: Lindbergh!" he read in admiration. "With the plane he flew across the Atlantic! Where did you find this?"

"I didn't have my injection yesterday," I said. "I went home early, and I saw Daddy before he left. Daddy bought it for me."

"Then half is mine," he said. "In fact, when we played that last game, the deal was you'd give me all the pictures you had left." He tried to grab the picture from my hand, but he couldn't manage it. He caught my wrist, and he twisted it so badly that I kicked his leg. We laid into each other.

"Stop!" said my mother. "Stop! We're in the middle of the street!"

We stopped. A man in a suit and a woman wearing a hat passed us. I felt ashamed for having fought in the street. My brother took two steps and fell to the ground. "It hurts so much," he said, holding his leg.

"Stand up," whispered my mother. "Come on now, stand up. Everyone's watching."

My brother stood up and began to hop down the road like a wounded soldier in a film. I was afraid he was really hurt, but I was still glad to see him that way. After we had walked for some time in silence, he said, "Just you see what happens when we get home. Mummy, Ali didn't have his injection yesterday."

"I did too, Mummy!"

"Be quiet!" my mother shouted.

We were now just across from our house. We waited for the streetcar coming up from Maçka[1] to pass before we crossed the street. After it came a truck, a clattering Beşiktaş[2] bus spewing great clouds of exhaust, and, in the opposite direction, a light violet De Soto.[3] That was when I saw my uncle looking down at the street from the window. He didn't see me; he was staring at the passing cars. For a long time, I watched him.

The road had long since cleared. I turned to my mother, wondering why she had not yet taken our hands and crossed us over to the other side, and saw that she was silently crying.

1999

---

1. District in central Istanbul.
2. District in the European part of Istanbul.

3. A model produced by the Chrysler Motor Company (1928–61).

CHIMAMANDA NGOZI ADICHIE
born 1977

A leading contemporary novelist, Chimamanda Ngozi Adichie ranges over the historical and modern experiences of Nigerians, especially Nigerian women, from before colonization through the Biafran War of the 1960s to contemporary immigrant communities in Britain and the United States. Her acute observations of contemporary life and deep sense of history have made her work timeless, even as she has become a famous spokesperson for feminism. Her novels have been adapted as films, and her lectures on race and gender are widely admired; one of them was sampled by the artist Beyoncé in her song "Flawless."

A member of the Igbo people of southern Nigeria, Adichie was born in 1977, after the defeat of the Igbo independence movement in the Biafran War, also known as the Nigerian Civil War (1967–70). She was strongly influenced by the historical legacy of the war, in which several of her family members died, and it seems to have shaped her understanding of the ways that private life can be transformed by political events. Born in Enugu, in southern Nigeria, the fifth of six children, Adichie grew up mostly in Nsukka, where her parents worked at the University of Nigeria. Her father was a professor of statistics while her mother served as the university's first female registrar. Adichie began her studies in medicine there but later studied at a number of universities in the United States. She graduated from Eastern Connecticut State University and received master's degrees in writ-

ing from Johns Hopkins University and in African Studies from Yale. She was awarded the MacArthur Fellowship (informally known as the "genius grant") in 2008 and currently spends time in both Nigeria and the United States. She has one daughter.

As a young girl, Adichie discovered the writings of **Chinua Achebe**, who had previously taught at the university where her parents worked and who had by that time achieved worldwide fame for his portrayals of the colonization of Nigeria. (Her family even lived in a house once inhabited by the renowned writer.) Adichie has credited the influence of Achebe's work in helping her to imagine what it would be like to be an African writer. As a child, Adichie read British and American books voraciously. When she began writing her own stories, her characters had blue eyes and white skin, ate apples, played in the snow, and talked about the weather. Adichie notes that she herself was black, ate mangoes, had never seen snow, and never heard talk of the weather, as on the equator it stays more or less the same. Reading Achebe's work convinced her that Africans could be the subject of fiction, although her approach to African history was distinctively shaped by her perspective as a woman and a feminist.

Her first novel, *Purple Hibiscus* (2003), opens with a reference to Achebe's novel *Things Fall Apart* (1958) and goes on to describe the effects of Nigeria's postcolonial history on a well-to-do Igbo family. The novel juxtaposes the power of the abusive father in the family with that of African dictators. Adichie uses the relatively small canvas of private family life to portray the sweeping historical changes affecting Nigeria in the late twentieth century, especially the dictatorship of General Sani Abacha from 1993 to 1998. More broadly, she chronicles the move from the traditional mores of the countryside to the more impersonal interactions of life in Africa's growing cities.

Adichie's work is distinguished by her strong sense of historical empathy. In her second novel, *Half of a Yellow Sun* (2006), for example, while recounting the horrors of the Biafran War, she describes the suffering of a rape victim but also explores the life story of one of her attackers. In 1967, massacres in northern Nigeria of the southeastern Igbo resulted in the people of southeastern Nigeria seceding to form Biafra, their own nation. Nigeria invaded Biafra, and more than 1 million people lost their lives in the conflict. Adichie's novel describes the effects of the war on two middle-class female twins, their male partners, and one of their servants (the houseboy Ugwu). They endure violent air raids, invading Nigerian soldiers, and economic deprivation: their worlds turn upside down, and they must change as a result. Adichie's poignant and nuanced portrayal of human relationships during the ravages of war makes this a particularly powerful novel.

Her third novel, *Americanah* (2013), the most autobiographical of her works to date, shifts focus to describe the experiences of a young Nigerian woman who has come to the United States to study. Her life is contrasted with that of her boyfriend who moves to England and eventually becomes an undocumented immigrant. Adichie's vivid characterizations and shifting geographical focus create a moving portrait of both the Nigerian diaspora and American society in the age of President Barack Obama. It is also the funniest of Adichie's nov-

els. Although she writes frequently on political issues, she seldom takes simple or straightforward political positions; rather, she tends to see the complexity of social issues as they intersect with questions of personal identity.

Adichie has also written incisive essays on such subjects as Nigerian and American politics. Her prose style is clear, direct, and can be deceptively simple, as under the surface she often explores deep and troubling tensions and conflicts, whether social or familial. Her works have won a number of honors, including the O. Henry Prize, the Commonwealth Writers' Prize for Best First Book, and the National Book Critics Circle Award.

The story presented here, "The Headstrong Historian," comes from her collection of short stories, *The Thing Around Your Neck* (2009). This work returns to her earlier inspiration by the novels of Chinua Achebe. The story begins in nineteenth-century western Africa during the "scramble for Africa," in which colonial powers sought influence on the continent. Written from a woman's perspective and thus showing a different side of the events chronicled by Achebe in *Things Fall Apart* and his other writings, "The Headstrong Historian" describes how an Igbo woman of the late nineteenth century negotiates native marriage practices, the competing demands of missionaries from the Catholic and Anglican churches, and the education of her son. (Several of the characters have the same names as characters in Achebe's *Things Fall Apart*, and the study *The Pacification of the Primitive Tribes of Southern Nigeria*, mentioned in the story, was invented by Achebe in his fiction.) The story displays Adichie's characteristic empathy as she imagines how Nwamgba, a woman raised in a traditional culture, tries to understand and succeed in a world that is being transformed by European colonialism. She sends her son to a missionary school in hopes that acquiring English will allow him to reclaim land that once belonged to his father. But her son eventually becomes almost a foreigner to her, no longer following traditional customs and moving far away. Ultimately, though, she develops a close relationship with her granddaughter Afamefuna, or Grace. The character Grace, who is introduced in the last pages of the story, shares the given name of Adichie's mother, Grace Ifeoma.

Although it is difficult to tell how much of the story is closely based on family history and how much is literary invention, Adichie has found an effective way to link Africa's pre-colonial and colonial history to its contemporary reality. At least in an imaginative sense, Nwamgba is the author's great-grandmother, and the writing of the story becomes a link to a living but distant past. This ability to use the everyday details of modern life to telescope two centuries of African history marks out Adichie's work as great historical writing that also has tremendous contemporary relevance.

The Headstrong Historian

Many years after her husband died, Nwamgba still closed her eyes from time to time to relive his nightly visits to her hut and the mornings after, when she would walk to the stream humming a song, thinking of the smoky scent of him, the firmness of his weight, those secrets she shared with herself, and feeling as if she were surrounded by light. Other memories of Obierika remained clear— his stubby fingers curled around his flute when he played in the evenings, his delight when she set down his bowls of food, his sweaty back when he returned with baskets filled with fresh clay for her pottery. From the moment she first saw him at a wrestling match, both of them staring and staring at each other, both of them too young, her waist not yet wearing the menstruation cloth, she had believed with a quiet stubbornness that her chi[1] and his chi had destined their marriage, and so when he came to her father a few years later bringing pots of palm wine and accompanied by his relatives, she told her mother that this was the man she would marry. Her mother was aghast. Did Nwambga not know that Obierika was an only child, that his late father had been an only child whose wives had lost pregnancies and buried babies? Perhaps somebody in their family had committed the taboo of selling a girl into slavery and the earth god Ani was visiting misfortune on them. Nwamgba ignored her mother. She went into her father's obi[2] and told him she would run away from any other man's house if she was not allowed to marry Obierika. Her father found her exhausting, this sharp-tongued, headstrong daughter who had once wrestled her brother to the ground. (After which her father had warned everybody not to let the news leave the compound that the girl had thrown a boy.) He, too, was concerned about the infertility in Obierika's family, but it was not a bad family: Obierika's late father had taken the ozo[3] title; Obierika was already giving out his seed yams to sharecroppers.

1. In Igbo cultural practice, individuals have *chi*, or spiritual beings, which are parallel to their physical beings.

2. Central building in an Igbo family compound.
3. Title of highest distinction in Igbo society.

Nwamgba would not do badly if she married him. Besides, it was better that he let her go with the man she chose, to save himself years of trouble when she would keep returning home after confrontations with in-laws. And so he gave his blessing and she smiled and called him by his praise name.

To pay her bride price, Obierika came with two maternal cousins, Okafo and Okoye, who were like brothers to him. Nwamgba loathed them at first sight. She saw a grasping envy in their eyes that afternoon as they drank palm wine in her father's obi, and in the following years, years in which Obierika took titles and widened his compound and sold his yams to strangers from afar, she saw their envy blacken. But she tolerated them, because they mattered to Obierika, because he pretended not to notice that they didn't work but came to him for yams and chickens, because he wanted to imagine that he had brothers. It was they who urged him, after her third miscarriage, to marry another wife. Obierika told them he would give it some thought but when he and Nwamgba were alone in her hut at night, he told her that he was sure they would have a home full of children, and that he would not marry another wife until they were old, so that they would have somebody to care for them. She thought this strange of him, a prosperous man with only one wife, and she worried more than he did about their childlessness, about the songs that people sang, melodious mean-spirited words: *She has sold her womb. She has eaten his penis. He plays his flute and hands over his wealth to her.*

Once, at a moonlight gathering, the square full of women telling stories and learning new dances, a group of girls saw Nwamgba and began to sing, their aggressive breasts pointing at her. She stopped and asked whether they would mind singing a little louder so that she could hear the words and then show them who was the greater of two tortoises.[4] They stopped singing. She enjoyed their fear, the way they backed away from her, but it was then that she decided to find a wife for Obierika herself.

Nwamgba liked going to the Oyi stream, untying her wrapper from her waist and walking down the slope to the silvery rush of water that burst out from a rock. The waters of Oyi were fresher than those of the other stream, Ogalanya, or perhaps it was simply that she felt comforted by the shrine of the Oyi goddess, tucked away in a corner; as a child she had learned that Oyi was the protector of women, the reason women were not to be sold into slavery. Her closest friend, Ayaju, was already at the stream, and as Nwamgba helped her raise her pot to her head, she asked Ayaju who might be a good second wife for Obierika.

She and Ayaju had grown up together and married men from the same clan. The difference between them, though, was that Ayaju was of slave descent; her father had been brought as a slave after a war. Ayaju did not care for her husband, Okenwa, who she said resembled and smelled like a rat, but her marriage prospects had been limited; no man from a freeborn family would have come for her hand. Ayaju's long-limbed, quick-moving body spoke of her many trading journeys; she had traveled even beyond Onicha.[5] It was she who had first brought tales of the strange customs of the Igala and Edo traders, she who first told of the

---

4. The tortoise is a symbol of wisdom in folk-tales told by the Igbo people.

5. Major port city on the Niger River.

white-skinned men who arrived in Onicha with mirrors and fabrics and the biggest guns the people of those parts had ever seen. This cosmopolitanism earned her respect, and she was the only person of slave descent who talked loudly at the Women's Council, the only person who had answers for everything.

And so she promptly suggested, for Obierika's second wife, the young girl from the Okonkwo family; the girl had beautiful wide hips and was respectful, nothing like the young girls of today with their heads full of nonsense. As they walked home from the stream, Ayaju said that perhaps Nwamgba should do what other women in her situation did—take a lover and get pregnant in order to continue Obierika's lineage. Nwamgba's retort was sharp, because she did not like Ayaju's tone, which suggested that Obierika was impotent, and as if in response to her thoughts she felt a furious stab in her back and knew that she was pregnant again, but she said nothing, because she knew, too, that she would lose the baby again.

Her miscarriage happened a few weeks later, lumpy blood running down her legs. Obierika comforted her and suggested they go to the famous oracle, Kisa, as soon as she was well enough for the half day's journey. After the *dibia*[6] had consulted the oracle, Nwamgba cringed at the thought of sacrificing a whole cow; Obierika certainly had greedy ancestors. But they did the ritual cleansings and the sacrifices, and when she suggested he go and see the Okonkwo family about their daughter, he delayed and delayed until another sharp pain spliced her back; and months later, she was lying on a pile of freshly washed banana leaves behind her hut, straining and pushing until the baby slipped out.

They named him Anikwenwa: the earth god Ani had finally granted a child. He was dark and solidly built and had Obierika's happy curiosity. Obierika took him to pick medicinal herbs, to collect clay for Nwamgba's pottery, to twist yam vines at the farm. Obierika's cousins Okafo and Okoye visited too often. They marveled at how well Anikwenwa played the flute, how quickly he was learning poetry and wrestling moves from his father, but Nwamgba saw the glowing malevolence that their smiles could not hide. She feared for her child and her husband, and when Obierika died—a man who had been hearty and laughing and drinking palm wine moments before he slumped—she knew that they had killed him with medicine. She clung to his corpse until a neighbor slapped her to make her let go; she lay in the cold ash for days; she tore at the patterns shaved into her hair.[7] Obierika's death left her with an unending despair. She thought often of the woman who, after her tenth successive child died, had gone to her backyard and hanged herself on a kola tree. But she would not do it, because of Anikwenwa.

Later, she wished she had insisted that his cousins drink Obierika's *mmili ozu*[8] before the oracle. She had witnessed this once, when a wealthy man died and his family insisted his rival drink his *mmili ozu*. Nwamgba had watched the unmarried woman take a cupped leaf full of water, touch it to the dead man's body, all the time speaking solemnly, and give the leaf-cup to the accused man. He drank. Everyone watched to make sure he swallowed, a grave silence in the air because they knew that if he was guilty he would die. He died days later, and his family

6. Doctor and priest (Igbo).
7. Igbo mourning customs.
8. Literally "corpse water"; an Igbo cultural practice for determining responsibility for a person's death.

lowered their heads in shame and Nwamgba felt strangely shaken by it all. She should have insisted on this with Obierika's cousins, but she had been blinded by grief and now Obierika was buried and it was too late.

His cousins, during the funeral, took his ivory tusk, claiming that the trappings of titles went to brothers and not to sons. It was when they emptied his barn of yams and led away the adult goats in his pen that she confronted them, shouting, and when they brushed her aside, she waited until evening and then walked around the clan singing about their wickedness, the abominations they were heaping on the land by cheating a widow, until the elders asked them to leave her alone. She complained to the Women's Council, and twenty women went at night to Okafo and Okoye's home, brandishing pestles, warning them to leave Nwamgba alone. Members of Obierika's age grade, too, told them to leave her alone. But Nwamgba knew those grasping cousins would never really stop. She dreamed of killing them. She certainly could—those weaklings who had spent their lives scrounging off Obierika instead of working—but of course she would be banished and there would be nobody to care for her son. So she took Anikwenwa on long walks, telling him that the land from that palm tree to that plantain tree was theirs, that his grandfather had passed it on to his father. She told him the same things over and over, even though he looked bored and bewildered, and she did not let him go and play at moonlight unless she was watching.

Ayaju came back from a trading journey with another story: the women in Onicha were complaining about the white men. They had welcomed the white men's trading station, but now the white men wanted to tell them how to trade, and when the elders of Agueke, a clan of Onicha, refused to place their thumbs on a paper, the white men came at night with their normal-men helpers and razed the village. There was nothing left. Nwamgba did not understand. What sort of guns did these white men have? Ayaju laughed and said their guns were nothing like the rusty thing her own husband owned. Some white men were visiting different clans, asking parents to send their children to school, and she had decided to send Azuka, the son who was laziest on the farm, because although she was respected and wealthy, she was still of slave descent, her sons still barred from taking titles. She wanted Azuka to learn the ways of these foreigners, since people ruled over others not because they were better people but because they had better guns; after all, her own father would not have been brought as a slave if his clan had been as well armed as Nwamgba's clan. As Nwamgba listened to her friend, she dreamed of killing Obierika's cousins with the white men's guns.

The day that the white men visited her clan, Nwamgba left the pot she was about to put in her oven, took Anikwenwa and her girl apprentices, and hurried to the square. She was at first disappointed by the ordinariness of the two white men; they were harmless-looking, the color of albinos, with frail and slender limbs. Their companions were normal men, but there was something foreign about them, too, and only one spoke a strangely accented Igbo. He said that he was from Elele;[9] the other normal men were from Sierra Leone, and the white men from France, far across the sea. They were all of the Holy Ghost Congregation;[1] they had arrived in Onicha in 1885 and were building their school and

---

church there. Nwamgba was first to ask a question: Had they brought their guns by any chance, the ones used to destroy the people of Agueke, and could she see one? The man said unhappily that it was the soldiers of the British government and merchants of the Royal Niger Company[2] who destroyed villages; they, instead, brought good news. He spoke about their god, who had come to the world to die, and who had a son but no wife, and who was three but also one. Many of the people around Nwamgba laughed loudly. Some walked away, because they had imagined that the white man was full of wisdom. Others stayed and offered cool bowls of water.

Weeks later, Ayaju brought another story: the white men had set up a courthouse in Onicha where they judged disputes. They had indeed come to stay. For the first time, Nwamgba doubted her friend. Surely the people of Onicha had their own courts. The clan next to Nwamgba's, for example, held its courts only during the new yam festival, so that people's rancor grew while they awaited justice. A stupid system, Nwamgba thought, but surely everyone had one. Ayaju laughed and told Nwamgba again that people ruled others when they had better guns. Her son was already learning about these foreign ways, and perhaps Anikwenwa should, too. Nwamgba refused. It was unthinkable that her only son, her single eye, should be given to the white men, never mind how superior their guns might be.

Three events, in the following years, caused Nwamgba to change her mind. The first was that Obierika's cousins took over a large piece of land and told the elders that they were farming it for her, a woman who had emasculated their dead brother and now refused to remarry even though suitors were coming and her breasts were still round. The elders sided with them. The second was that Ayaju told a story of two people who took a land case to the white men's court; the first man was lying but could speak the white men's language, while the second man, the rightful owner of the land, could not, and so he lost his case, was beaten and locked up and ordered to give up his land. The third was the story of the boy Iroegbunam, who had gone missing many years ago and then suddenly reappeared, a grown man, his widowed mother mute with shock at his story: a neighbor, whom his father often shouted down at age-grade meetings, had abducted him when his mother was at the market and taken him to the Aro slave dealers, who looked him over and complained that the wound on his leg would reduce his price. Then he and some others were tied together by the hands, forming a long human column, and he was hit with a stick and asked to walk faster. There was only one woman among them. She shouted herself hoarse, telling the abductors that they were heartless, that her spirit would torment them and their children, that she knew she was to be sold to the white man, and did they not know that the white man's slavery was very different, that people were treated like goats, taken on large ships a long way and eventually eaten? Iroegbunam walked and walked and walked, his feet bloodied, his body numb, with a little water poured into his mouth from time to time, until all he could remember later was the smell of dust. Finally they stopped at a coastal clan, where a man spoke a nearly incomprehensible Igbo, but Iroegbunam made out enough to understand that another man, who

2. 19th-century British mercantile company.

was to sell the abductees to the white people on the ship, had gone up to bargain with the white people but had himself been kidnapped. There were loud arguments, scuffling; some of the abductees yanked at the ropes and Iroegbunam passed out. He awoke to find a white man rubbing his feet with oil, and at first he was terrified, certain that he was being prepared for the white man's meal. But this was a different kind of white man, a missionary who bought slaves only to free them, and he took Iroegbunam to live with him and trained him to be a Christian missionary.

Iroegbunam's story haunted Nwamgba, because this, she was sure, was the way Obierika's cousins were likely to get rid of her son. Killing him was too dangerous, the risk of misfortunes from the oracle too high, but they would be able to sell him as long as they had strong medicine to protect themselves. She was struck, too, by how Iroegbunam lapsed into the white man's language from time to time. It sounded nasal and disgusting. Nwamgba had no desire to speak such a thing herself, but she was suddenly determined that Anikwenwa would speak it well enough to go to the white men's court with Obierika's cousins and defeat them and take control of what was his. And so, shortly after Iroegbunam's return, she told Ayaju that she wanted to take her son to school.

They went first to the Anglican mission. The classroom had more girls than boys—a few curious boys wandered in with their catapults[3] and then wandered out. The students sat with slates on their laps while the teacher stood in front of them, holding a big cane, telling them a story about a man who transformed a bowl of water into wine. Nwamgba was impressed by the teacher's spectacles, and she thought that the man in the story must have had fairly powerful medicine to be able to transform water into wine. But when the girls were separated and a woman teacher came to teach them how to sew, Nwamgba found this silly; in her clan girls learned to make pottery and a man sewed cloth. What dissuaded her completely about the school, however, was that the instruction was done in Igbo. Nwamgba asked the first teacher why. He said that of course the students were taught English—he held up the English primer— but children learned best in their own language, and the children in the white men's land were taught in their own language, too. Nwamgba turned to leave. The teacher stood in her way and told her that the Catholic missionaries were harsh and did not have the best interests of the natives at heart. Nwamgba was amused by these foreigners, who did not seem to know that one must, in front of strangers, pretend to have unity. But she had come in search of English, and so she walked past him and went to the Catholic mission.

Father Shanahan told her that Anikwenwa would have to take an English name, because it was not possible to be baptized with a heathen name. She agreed easily. His name was Anikwenwa as far as she was concerned; if they wanted to name him something she could not pronounce before teaching him their language, she did not mind at all. All that mattered was that he learn enough of the language to fight his father's cousins. Father Shanahan looked at Anikwenwa, a dark-skinned, well-muscled child, and guessed that he was about twelve, although he found it difficult to estimate the ages of these people; sometimes a mere boy would look like a man, nothing like in Eastern Africa, where he had previously worked and

3. I.e., slingshots.

where the natives tended to be slender, less confusingly muscular. As he poured some water on the boy's head, he said, "Michael, I baptize you in the name of the Father and of the Son and of the Holy Spirit."

He gave the boy a singlet and a pair of shorts, because the people of the living God did not walk around naked, and he tried to preach to the boy's mother, but she looked at him as if he were a child who did not know any better. There was something troublingly assertive about her, something he had seen in many women here; there was much potential to be harnessed if their wildness could be tamed. This Nwamgba would make a marvelous missionary among the women. He watched her leave. There was a grace in her straight back, and she, unlike others, had not spent too much time going round and round in her speech. It infuriated him, their overlong talk and circuitous proverbs, their never getting to the point, but he was determined to excel here; it was the reason he had joined the Holy Ghost Congregation, whose special vocation was the redemption of black heathens.

Nwamgba was alarmed by how indiscriminately the missionaries flogged students—for being late, for being lazy, for being slow, for being idle. And once, as Anikwenwa told her, Father Lutz had put metal cuffs around a girl's wrists to teach her a lesson about lying, all the time saying in Igbo—for Father Lutz spoke a broken brand of Igbo—that native parents pampered their children too much, that teaching the Gospel also meant teaching proper discipline. The first weekend Anikwenwa came home, Nwamgba saw angry welts on his back. She tightened her wrapper on her waist and went to the school. She told the teacher that she would gouge out the eyes of everyone at the mission if they ever did that to him again. She knew that Anikwenwa did not want to go to school, and she told him that it was only for a year or two, so that he would learn English, and although the mission people told her not to come so often, she insistently came every weekend to take him home. Anikwenwa always took off his clothes even before they left the mission compound. He disliked the shorts and shirt that made him sweat, the fabric that was itchy around his armpits. He disliked, too, being in the same class as old men and missing out on wrestling contests.

Perhaps it was because he began to notice the admiring glances his clothes brought in the clan but Anikwenwa's attitude to school slowly changed. Nwamgba first noticed this when some of the other boys with whom he swept the village square complained that he no longer did his share because he was at school, and Anikwenwa said something in English, something sharp-sounding, which shut them up and filled Nwamgba with an indulgent pride. Her pride turned to a vague worry when she noticed that the curiosity in his eyes had diminished. There was a new ponderousness in him, as if he had suddenly found himself bearing the weight of a too-heavy world. He stared at things for too long. He stopped eating her food, because, he said, it was sacrificed to idols. He told her to tie her wrapper around her chest instead of her waist, because her nakedness was sinful. She looked at him, amused by his earnestness, but worried nonetheless, and asked why he had only just begun to notice her nakedness.

When it was time for his *ima mmuo* ceremony,[4] he said he would not participate, because it was a heathen custom for boys to be initiated into the world of

4. Rite of passage through which Igbo boys become men by joining with ancestral spirits.

spirits, a custom that Father Shanahan had said would have to stop. Nwamgba roughly yanked his ear and told him that a foreign albino could not determine when their customs would change, so until the clan itself decided that the initiation would stop, he would participate or else he would tell her whether he was her son or the white man's son. Anikwenwa reluctantly agreed, but as he was taken away with a group of boys, she noticed that he lacked their excitement. His sadness saddened her. She felt her son slipping away from her, and yet she was proud that he was learning so much, that he could become a court interpreter or a letter writer, and that with Father Lutz's help he had brought home some papers that showed that their lands belonged to him and his mother. Her proudest moment was when he went to his father's cousins Okafo and Okoye and asked for his father's ivory tusk back. And they gave it to him.

Nwamgba knew that her son now inhabited a mental space that was foreign to her. He told her that he was going to Lagos to learn how to be a teacher, and even as she screamed—How can you leave me? Who will bury me when I die?—she knew he would go. She did not see him for many years, years during which his father's cousin Okafo died. She often consulted the oracle to ask whether Anikwenwa was still alive; the *dibia* admonished her and sent her away, because of course he was alive. At last Anikwenwa returned, in the year that the clan banned all dogs after a dog killed a member of the Mmangala age grade, the age grade to which Anikwenwa would have belonged if he had not said that such things were devilish.

Nwamgba said nothing when he announced that he had been appointed catechist at the new mission. She was sharpening her *aguba*[5] on the palm of her hand, about to shave patterns in the hair of a little girl, and she continued to do so—*flick-flick-flick*—while Anikwenwa talked about winning souls in their clan. The plate of breadfruit seeds she had offered him was untouched—he no longer ate anything at all of hers—and she looked at him, this man wearing trousers, and a rosary around his neck, and wondered whether she had meddled with his destiny. Was this what his chi had ordained for him, this life in which he was like a person diligently acting a bizarre pantomime?

The day that he told her about the woman he would marry, she was not surprised. He did not do it as it was done, did not consult people to ask about the bride's family, but simply said that somebody at the mission had seen a suitable young woman from Ifite Ukpo[6] and the suitable young woman would be taken to the Sisters of the Holy Rosary[7] in Onicha to learn how to be a good Christian wife. Nwamgba was sick with malaria on that day, lying on her mud bed, rubbing her aching joints, and she asked Anikwenwa the young woman's name. Anikwenwa said it was Agnes. Nwamgba asked for the young woman's real name. Anikwenwa cleared his throat and said she had been called Mgbeke before she became a Christian, and Nwamgba asked whether Mgbeke would at least do the confession ceremony even if Anikwenwa would not follow the other marriage rites of their clan. He shook his head furiously and told her that the confession made by a woman before marriage, in which she, surrounded by female relatives, swore that no man had touched her since her husband had declared his interest, was sinful, because Christian wives should not have been touched *at all*.

5. Razor (Igbo).
6. Town in Nigeria about 10 miles northeast of Onicha.
7. Roman Catholic order of missionary nuns.

The marriage ceremony in church was laughably strange, but Nwamgba bore it silently and told herself that she would die soon and join Obierika and be free of a world that increasingly made no sense. She was determined to dislike her son's wife, but Mgbeke was difficult to dislike; she was small-waisted and gentle, eager to please the man to whom she was married, eager to please everyone, quick to cry, apologetic about things over which she had no control. And so, instead, Nwamgba pitied her. Mgbeke often visited Nwamgba in tears, saying that Anikwenwa had refused to eat dinner because he was upset with her or that Anikwenwa had banned her from going to a friend's Anglican wedding because Anglicans did not preach the truth, and Nwamgba would silently carve designs on her pottery while Mgbeke cried, uncertain of how to handle a woman crying about things that did not deserve tears.

Mgbeke was called "missus" by everyone, even the non-Christians, all of whom respected the catechist's wife, but on the day she went to the Oyi stream and refused to remove her clothes because she was a Christian, the women of the clan, outraged that she dared to disrespect the goddess, beat her and dumped her at the grove. The news spread quickly. Missus had been harassed. Anikwenwa threatened to lock up all the elders if his wife was treated that way again, but Father O'Donnell, on his next trek from his station in Onicha, visited the elders and apologized on Mgbeke's behalf and asked whether perhaps Christian women could be allowed to fetch water fully clothed. The elders refused—if one wanted Oyi's waters, then one had to follow Oyi's rules—but they were courteous to Father O'Donnell, who listened to them and did not behave like their own son Anikwenwa.

Nwamgba was ashamed of her son, irritated with his wife, upset by their rarefied life in which they treated non-Christians as if they had smallpox, but she held out her hope for a grandchild; she prayed and sacrificed for Mgbeke to have a boy, because it would be Obierika come back and would bring a semblance of sense back into her world. She did not know of Mgbeke's first or second miscarriage, it was only after the third that Mgbeke, sniffling and blowing her nose, told her. They had to consult the oracle, as this was a family misfortune, Nwamgba said, but Mgbeke's eyes widened with fear. Michael would be very angry if he ever heard of this oracle suggestion. Nwamgba, who still found it difficult to remember that Michael was Anikwenwa, went to the oracle herself, and afterwards thought it ludicrous how even the gods had changed and no longer asked for palm wine but for gin. Had they converted, too?

A few months later, Mgbeke visited, smiling, bringing a covered bowl of one of those concoctions that Nwamgba found inedible, and Nwamgba knew that her chi was still wide awake and that her daughter-in-law was pregnant. Anikwenwa had decreed that Mgbeke would have the baby at the mission in Onicha, but the gods had different plans and she went into early labor on a rainy afternoon; somebody ran in the drenching rain to Nwamgba's hut to call her. It was a boy. Father O'Donnell baptized him Peter, but Nwamgba called him Nnamdi, because she believed he was Obierika come back. She sang to him, and when he cried she pushed her dried-up nipple into his mouth, but try as she might, she did not feel the spirit of her magnificent husband Obierika. Mgbeke had three more miscarriages and Nwamgba went to the oracle many times until a pregnancy stayed and the second baby was born, this time at the mission in Onicha.

A girl. From the moment Nwamgba held her, the baby's bright eyes delightfully focused on her, she knew that it was the spirit of Obierika that had returned; odd, to have come in a girl, but who could predict the ways of the ancestors? Father O'Donnell baptized her Grace, but Nwamgba called her Afamefuna, "My Name Will Not Be Lost," and was thrilled by the child's solemn interest in her poetry and her stories, the teenager's keen watchfulness as Nwamgba struggled to make pottery with newly shaky hands. But Nwamgba was not thrilled that Afamefuna was to go away to secondary school (Peter was already living with the priest in Onicha), because she feared that, at boarding school, the new ways would dissolve her granddaughter's fighting spirit and replace it either with an incurious rigidity, like Anikwenwa's, or a limp helplessness, like Mgbeke's.

The year that Afamefuna left for secondary school in Onicha, Nwamgba felt as if a lamp had been blown out on a moonless night. It was a strange year, the year that darkness suddenly descended on the land in the middle of the afternoon, and when Nwamgba felt the deep-seated ache in her joints, she knew her end was near. She lay on her bed gasping for breath, while Anikwenwa pleaded with her to be baptized and anointed so that he could hold a Christian funeral for her, as he could not participate in a heathen ceremony. Nwamgba told him that if he dared to bring anybody to rub some filthy oil on her, she would slap that person with her last strength. All she wanted was to see Afamefuna before she joined the ancestors, but Anikwenwa said that Grace was taking exams in school and could not come home. But she came. Nwamgba heard the squeaky swing of her door and there was Afamefuna, her granddaughter who had come on her own from Onicha because she had been unable to sleep for days, her restless spirit urging her home. Grace put down her schoolbag, inside of which was her textbook with a chapter called "The Pacification of the Primitive Tribes of Southern Nigeria," by an administrator from Worcestershire[8] who had lived among them for seven years.

It was Grace who would read about these savages, titillated by their curious and meaningless customs, not connecting them to herself until her teacher, Sister Maureen, told her she could not refer to the call-and-response her grandmother had taught her as poetry because primitive tribes did not have poetry. It was Grace who would laugh loudly until Sister Maureen took her to detention and then summoned her father, who slapped Grace in front of the teachers to show them how well he disciplined his children. It was Grace who would nurse a deep scorn for her father for years, spending holidays working as a maid in Onicha so as to avoid the sanctimonies, the dour certainties, of her parents and brother. It was Grace who, after graduating from secondary school, would teach elementary school in Agueke, where people told stories of the destruction of their village years before by the white men's guns, stories she was not sure she believed, because they also told stories of mermaids appearing from the River Niger holding wads of crisp cash. It was Grace who, as one of the few women at the University College in Ibadan[9] in 1950, would change her degree from chemistry to history after she heard, while drinking tea at the home of a friend, the story of Mr. Gboyega. The eminent Mr. Gboyega, a chocolate-skinned Nigerian,

8. County in England.
9. Oldest and most prestigious Nigerian university.

educated in London, distinguished expert on the history of the British Empire, had resigned in disgust when the West African Examinations Council began talking of adding African history to the curriculum, because he was appalled that African history would even be considered a subject. Grace would ponder this story for a long time, with great sadness, and it would cause her to make a clear link between education and dignity, between the hard, obvious things that are printed in books and the soft, subtle things that lodge themselves into the soul. It was Grace who would begin to rethink her own schooling—how lustily she had sung, on Empire Day, "God bless our Gracious King. Send him victorious, happy and glorious. Long to reign over us," how she had puzzled over words like "wallpaper" and "dandelions" in her textbooks, unable to picture those things; how she had struggled with arithmetic problems that had to do with mixtures, because what was coffee and what was chicory[1] and why did they have to be mixed? It was Grace who would begin to rethink her father's schooling and then hurry home to see him, his eyes watery with age, telling him she had not received all the letters she had ignored, saying amen when he prayed, pressing her lips against his forehead. It was Grace who, driving past Agueke on her way back, would become haunted by the image of a destroyed village and would go to London and to Paris and to Onicha, sifting through moldy files in archives, reimagining the lives and smells of her grandmother's world, for the book she would write called *Pacifying with Bullets: A Reclaimed History of Southern Nigeria*. It was Grace who, in a conversation about the early manuscript with her fiancé, George Chikadibia—stylish graduate of Kings College, Lagos;[2] engineer-to-be; wearer of three-piece suits; expert ballroom dancer who often said that a grammar school without Latin was like a cup of tea without sugar—knew that the marriage would not last when George told her she was misguided to write about primitive culture instead of a worthwhile topic like African Alliances in the American-Soviet Tension. They would divorce in 1972, not because of the four miscarriages Grace had suffered but because she woke up sweating one night and realized that she would strangle him to death if she had to listen to one more rapturous monologue about his Cambridge days. It was Grace who, as she received faculty prizes, as she spoke to solemn-faced people at conferences about the Ijaw and Ibibio and Igbo and Efik peoples of Southern Nigeria, as she wrote reports for international organizations about commonsense things for which she nevertheless received generous pay, would imagine her grandmother looking on and chuckling with great amusement. It was Grace who, feeling an odd rootlessness in the later years of her life, surrounded by her awards, her friends, her garden of peerless roses, would go to the courthouse in Lagos and officially change her first name from Grace to Afamefuna.

But on that day as she sat at her grandmother's bedside in the fading evening light, Grace was not contemplating her future. She simply held her grandmother's hand, the palm thickened from years of making pottery.

2008

---

1. Herbaceous root substituted for coffee during wartime in England.   2. Elite Nigerian secondary school for boys.

Selected Bibliographies

I. Literatures of Early Modern East Asia

EARLY MODERN CHINESE LITERATURE

For an introduction to Chinese vernacular literature, including drama, stories, and novels, see the relevant chapters in Victor H. Mair's *The Columbia History of Chinese Literature* (2001) and Stephen Owen and Kang-i Sun Chang's *The Cambridge History of Chinese Literature* (2010). To further explore women's writing in the early modern period, the second half of Wilt Idema and Beata Grant's *The Red Brush: Writing Women of Imperial China* (2004) and the relevant parts of Kang-i Sun Chang and Haun Saussy's *Women Writers of Traditional China: An Anthology of Poetry and Criticism* (1999) are a treasure trove with introductions to major female authors and sample works.

A basic survey of the history of Chinese drama can be found in William Dolby, *A History of Chinese Drama* (1976). For a comprehensive history of Japanese literature, see Haruo Shirane, Tomi Suzuki, and David Lurie's *Cambridge History of Japanese Literature* (2016). C. T. Hsia's *The Classic Chinese Novel: A Critical Introduction* (1968) remains one of the most readable introductions to the major novels. Patrick Hanan, *The Chinese Vernacular Story* (1981) provides an insightful study of the cultural background of vernacular fiction. To explore how writers of China's literary revolution during the first half of the twentieth century discovered vernacular literature and elevated it to its central place in the Chinese literary canon, see the tremendously popular *A Brief History of Chinese Fiction* (1959, originally published 1925) by Lu Xun, one of China's first and foremost modern writers.

Wu Cheng'en

Arthur Waley's translation *Monkey* (1943) is an abridged adaptation of thirty of the original hundred chapters, but Waley's gifts as a translator and the nature of his abridgement make this version still a delight to read. There is a complete translation in four volumes by Anthony C. Yu, *The Journey to the West* (1977). The translation of the selections here comes from Anthony C. Yu's abridged version *Monkey & the Monk: A Revised Abridgment of The Journey to the West* (2006). There is an excellent chapter on the novel in C. T. Hsia, *The Classic Chinese Novel: A Critical Introduction* (1968).

Glen Dudbridge's *The Hsi-yu-chi: A Study of the Antecedents to the Sixteenth-Century Chinese Novel* (1970) examines the development of Xuanzang's story before the novel. For comparisons of the pursuit of enlightenment and the role of magic stones in *The Journey to the West* and *The Story of the Stone*, see Li Qiancheng's *Fictions of Enlightenment: Journey to the West, Tower of Myriad Mirrors, and Dream of the Red Chamber* (2004) and Jing Wang's *Story of Stone: Intertextuality, Ancient Chinese Stone Lore, and the Stone Symbolism in Dream of the Red Chamber, Water Margin, and The Journey to the West* (1992).

EARLY MODERN JAPANESE POPULAR LITERATURE

For a close-up of Tokugawa culture and society see Andrew C. Gerstle's *Eighteenth-Century Japan: Culture and Society* (1989), Matsunosuke Nishiyama's *Edo Culture: Daily Life and Diversions in Urban Japan 1600–1868* (1997), and Chie Nakane and Shinzaburō Ōishi's *Tokugawa Japan: The Social and Economic Antecedents of Modern Japan* (1991).

To read more of early modern Japanese literature, Haruo Shirane's *Early Modern Japanese Literature: An Anthology 1600–1900* (2002) is a treasure trove of texts with excellent introductions. On Tokugawa wood prints and urban culture see Christine Guth's *Art of Edo Japan: The Artist and the City, 1615–1868* (1996). On the Japanese printing revolution in the context of the development of book culture Peter Kornicki's *The Book in Japan: A Cultural History from the Beginnings to the Nineteenth Century* (1998) is highly recommended. To further explore the pleasure quarters there is Cecilia Segawa's *Yoshiwara: The Glittering World of the Japanese Courtesan* (1993) and Elizabeth Swinton's *The Women of the Pleasure Quarter: Japanese Paintings and Prints of the Floating World* (1995).

Bashō and the World of Haiku

For compelling introductions into the world of Japanese haiku see Haruo Shirane, *Traces of Dreams: Landscape, Cultural Memory, and the Poetry of Bashō* (1998); Kenneth Yasuda, *The Japanese Haiku: Its Essential Nature, History, and Possibilities in English* (1957); Harold G. Henderson, *An Introduction to Haiku* (1958); Koji Kawamoto's *The Poetics of Japanese Verse: Imagery, Structure, Meter* (2000); Stephen Addiss, Fumiko Yamamoto, and Akira Yamamoto, *Haiku: An Anthology of Japanese Poems* (2009); and Michael F. Marra's *Seasons and Landscapes in Japanese Poetry: An Introduction to Haiku and Waka* (2009). Nippon Gakujutsu Shinkokai, ed., *Haikai and Haiku* (1958) is a basic reference.

To explore haiku movements beyond Japan, see Bruce Ross's *Haiku Moment: An Anthology of Contemporary North American Haiku* (1993); John Brandi and Dennis Maloney, *The Unswept Path: Contemporary American Haiku* (2005); and Hiroaki Sato's *One Hundred Frogs: From Renga to Haiku in English* (1983). Yoshinobu Hakutani's *Haiku and Modernist Poetics* (2009) explores the impact of haiku on modernist literature in the West.

For Bashō's poetry see Jane Reichhold, *Bashō: The Complete Haiku* (2008); Sam Hamill, *The Essential Bashō* (1999). All five of Bashō's travel journals are found in Nobuyuki Yuasa's *The Narrow Road to the Deep North and Other Travel Sketches* (1966). For Bashō's linked verse see Earl Miner and Hiroko Odagiri, *The Monkey's Straw Raincoat* (1981) and, more generally, Earl Miner's *Japanese Linked Poetry* (1979). The following translations of *Narrow Road of the Interior* are recommended: Cid Corman and Kamaike Susumu, *Back Roads to Far Towns* (1986); Donald Keene, *The Narrow Road to Oku* (1996); Dorothy Britton, *A Haiku Journey: Bashō's "Narrow Road to a Far Province"* (1980). There are two interesting studies of Bashō, both by Makoto Ueda: *Matsuo Bashō* (1982) and *Bashō and His Interpreters* (1991).

On the painter literatus and haiku poet Yosa Buson, see Makoto Ueda's study *The Path of Flowering Thorn: The Life and Poetry of Yosa Buson* (1998) and Yuki Sawa and Eith M. Shiffert's *Haiku Master Buson* (1978).

Chikamatsu Monzaemon

To explore the world of Japanese puppet theater, Barbara Curtis Adachi's *Backstage at Bunraku: A Behind the Scenes Look at Japan's Traditional Puppet Theater* (1985), Adachi's *The Voices and Hands of Bunraku* (1978), Donald Keene's *Bunraku: The Art of the Japanese Puppet Theatre* (1965), and C. U. Dunn's *The Early Japanese Puppet Drama* (1966) are recommended.

To read other plays by Chikamatsu, see Andrew C. Gerstle's *Chikamatsu: Five Late Plays* (2001), Donald Keene's *Four Major Plays of Chikamatsu* (1969) and his *Major Plays of Chikamatsu* (1961). Gerstle's *Circles of Fantasy: Convention in the Plays of Chikamatsu* (1986) discusses Chikamatsu's art and craft as a playwright.

To read some of the greatest puppet plays by authors other than Chikamatsu, consult

Stanleigh H. Jones's *Sugawara and the Secrets of Calligraphy* (1985) (a puppet play revolving around the tenth-century poet-official Sugawara no Michizane), Stanleigh H. Jones's *Yoshitsune and the Thousand Cherry Trees: A Masterpiece of the Eighteenth-Century Japanese Puppet Theater* (1993), and Donald Keene's *Chûshingura: The Treasury of Loyal Retainers* (1971), a play about the forty-seven samurai who avenged the humiliation of their lord and then committed ritual suicide.

II. The Enlightenment in Europe and the Americas

Peter Gay, *Age of Enlightenment* (1966) is the classic work on the subject. Two other good historical introductions are Dorinda Outram, *The Enlightenment* (1995; 2nd ed. 2005) and Roy Porter, *The Enlightenment* (2001). See also Porter's *Creation of the Modern World: The Untold Story of the British Enlightenment* (2001). Studies of women in the period include Carla Hesse, *The Other Enlightenment: How French Women Became Modern* (2003), Karen O'Brien, *Women and Enlightenment in Eighteenth-Century Britain* (2009), and M. Williamson, *Raising Their Voices, 1650–1750* (1990). For excellent studies of Enlightenment philosophical thinking, see F. C. Beiser, *The Sovereignty of Reason: The Defense of Rationality in the Early English Enlightenment* (1996); L. Crocker, *An Age of Crisis: Man and World in Eighteenth-Century French Thought* (1959); Knud Haakonssen, *Natural Law and Moral Philosophy: From Grotius to the Scottish Enlightenment* (1996); and Jonathan Israel, *Enlightenment Contested: Philosophy, Modernity, and the Emancipation of Man* (2006). A brilliant survey of literature, art, and history can be found in John Brewer, *The Pleasures of the Imagination: English Culture in the Eighteenth Century* (1998). Useful works for considering the literature of the period include M. Price, *To the Palace of Wisdom: Studies in Order and Energy from Dryden to Blake* (1964); L. Gossman, *French Society and Culture: Background for Eighteenth-Century Literature* (1972); S. Gearhart, *The Open Boundary of History and Fiction: A Critical Approach to the French Enlightenment* (1984); J. Sambrook, *The Eighteenth Century: The Intellectual and Cultural Context of English Literature, 1700–1789* (1986); and T. M. Kavanaugh, *Esthetics of the Moment: Literature and Art in the French Enlightenment* (1996).

Aphra Behn
Janet Todd, *The Secret Life of Aphra Behn* (1996) delves into the contradictions of Behn's biography. *Rereading Aphra Behn: History, Theory and Criticism* (1993), a collection of essays edited by Heidi Hutner, locates Behn in the larger literary culture of the Restoration. Laura Brown's *Ends of Empire: Women and Ideology in Early Eighteenth-Century English Literature* (1993) discusses *Oroonoko*, gender, and the slave trade. Recent years have seen an explosion of new work on race and colonialism in *Oroonoko*. Important essays include Srinivas Aravamudan, "Petting Oroonoko," *Tropicopolitans* (1999) and Elliott Visconsi, "A Degenerate Race: English Barbarism in Behn's *Oroonoko* and *The Widow Ranter*," *ELH* (2002). Thomas Southerne's theatrical adaptation of Behn's novella, first performed in 1695, is also available in print.

Sor Juana Inés de la Cruz
Gerard Flynn's *Sor Juana Inés de la Cruz* (1971) provides a biographical, critical, and bibliographical introduction. Octavio Paz's *Sor Juana; Or, The Traps of Faith* (1988) is a famous study by the Mexican writer and Nobel Prize winner. Other important studies include Pamela Kirk, *Sor Juana Inés de la Cruz: Religion, Art, and Feminism* (1998); Stephanie Merrim, *Early Modern Women's Writing and Sor Juana Inés de la Cruz* (1999); and Frederick Luciani, *Literary Self-Fashioning in Sor Juana Inés de la Cruz* (2004). *Feminist Perspectives on Sor Juana Inés de la Cruz*, edited by Stephanie Merrim (1991), is a useful collection of essays.

Molière

H. Walker, *Molière* (1990), provides a general biographical and critical introduction to the playwright. Useful critical studies include L. Gossman, *Men and Masks: A Study of Molière* (1963); Jacques Guicharnaud, ed., *Molière: A Collection of Critical Essays* (1964); N. Gross, *From Gesture to Idea: Esthetics and Ethics in Molière's Comedy* (1982); J. F. Gaines, *Social Structures in Molière's Theater* (1984); and L. F. Norman, *The Public Mirror: Molière and the Social Commerce of Depiction* (1999). An excellent treatment of Molière in his historical context is W. D. Howarth, *Molière: A Playwright and His Audience* (1984). Harold C. Knutson, *The Triumph of Wit* (1988) examines Molière in relation to Shakespeare and Ben Jonson.

Martin Turnell, *The Classical Moment: Studies of Corneille, Molière, and Racine* (1975) offers useful insight into the French dramatic tradition.

Voltaire

Roger Pearson has a lively biography called *Voltaire Almighty: A Life in Pursuit of Freedom* (2005). Theodore Besterman's *Voltaire* (1969) is longer and more detailed. Nicholas Cronk's collection of essays in *The Cambridge Companion to Voltaire* (2009) provides both excellent readings and helpful contextual material. Haydn Mason's *Candide, Optimism Demolished* (1992) considers the ideas, the reception, and the form of the text. For a series of competing interpretations of the Eldorado section of *Candide*, see Thomas Walsh, ed., *Readings on* Candide (2001).

III. An Age of Revolutions

The excellent, classic resource for the industrial and political revolutions of the period is E. J. Hobsbawm, *The Age of Revolution, 1789–1848* (1962). Another fine introduction to the upheavals of the period is Charles Breunig, *Age of Revolution and Reaction, 1789–1850* (1977). For the global implications of the industrial revolution, see E. J. Hobsbawm, *Industry and Empire* (1990) and Peter N. Stearns, *The Industrial Revolution in World History* (3rd ed. 2007). Gavin Weightman tells absorbing stories about particular inventors, entrepreneurs, and industrial breakthroughs in *The Industrial Revolutionaries* (2010). Good scholarly works on the French Revolution include William Doyle, *The Oxford History of the French Revolution* (2003) and Simon Schama, *Citizens* (1990). Alan Schom's *Napoleon Bonaparte: A Life* (1998) is a lively biography; see also J. Christopher Herold, *The Age of Napoleon* (2002). *Latin American Independence: An Anthology of Sources*, ed. John Chasteen and Sarah C. Chambers (2010), contains fascinating source materials; for a historical overview, see Michael Eakin, *The History of Latin America* (2007). A detailed account of the upheavals of 1848 can be found in Mike Rapport, *1848: Year of Revolution* (2009).

Charles Baudelaire

There have been many English translations of Baudelaire's poetry, including those by the well-known poets included here. The most comprehensive collection is Walter Martin's *Charles Baudelaire: Complete Poems* (2002), which includes juvenilia and poems that have been ascribed to Baudelaire; Keith Waldrop's prose translation of *Flowers of Evil*, with French and English on facing pages, is widely respected (2006). Baudelaire's essays on painting and the other arts, including his studies of Delacroix, Poe, and Wagner, have been considered the beginning of modern criticism: see *The Painter of Modern Life and Other Essays*, trans. Jonathan Mayne (1964). The definitive biography is Claude Pichois and Jean Ziegler, *Charles Baudelaire*, trans. G. Robb (1991). The most famous essays on Baudelaire as a modern writer are Walter Benjamin's *Charles Baudelaire*, trans. Harry Zohn (1973). For useful introductions, see Lois Boe Hyslop, *Charles Baudelaire Revisited* (1992); Laurence Porter, ed., *Approaches to Teaching Baudelaire's Flowers of Evil* (2000); and Rosemary Lloyd, *Baudelaire's World* (2002). Strong readings of individual works include Barbara Johnson's classic deconstructive approach, "Poetry and Its Double: Two *Invitations au voyage*," in *The Critical Difference* (1980), 23–51; Jonathan

Culler's introduction to *Charles Baudelaire: The Flowers of Evil* (1993); and the collection of readings in William J. Thompson, ed., *Understanding Les Fleurs du Mal* (1997). For more on the city, see Ross Chambers, "Baudelaire's Paris," in *The Cambridge Companion to Baudelaire*, ed. Rosemary Lloyd (2005), 101–16.

William Blake
The standard edition of the works is David V. Erdman's *The Complete Poetry and Prose of William Blake* (rev. 1988). Peter Ackroyd's marvelously well-written biography *William Blake: A Life* (1996) is to be recommended, as is the more scholarly, detailed life by G. E. Bentley Jr., *The Stranger from Paradise* (2003). Martin K. Nurmi's *William Blake* (1976) is a helpful introduction to the man and his work. For excellent critical and contextual readings, see *The Cambridge Companion to William Blake*, ed. Morris Eaves (2003), which suggests a range of approaches to reading and teaching Blake, including serious attention to Blake's images and processes of image-making. Also helpful are Jacob Brunowski, *William Blake and the Age of Revolution* (1965); W. J. T. Mitchell, *Blake's Composite Art: A Study of the Illuminated Poetry* (1978); and Saree Makdisi, *William Blake and the Impossible History of the 1790s* (2003).

Emily Dickinson
R. W. Franklin's three-volume edition of Emily Dickinson's work is carefully comprehensive and preserves as much as possible her spelling and punctuation: *The Poems of Emily Dickinson: The Variorum Edition* (1998). Franklin has also put together a more accessible, one-volume version: *The Poems of Emily Dickinson: Reading Edition* (2005) and a facsimile edition, which allows readers to see her handwritten pages (1981). The classic biography is the award-winning *Life of Emily Dickinson* by Richard B. Sewall (1974). Alfred Habegger has added fresh material and perspectives in *My Wars Are Laid Away in Books: The Life of Emily Dickinson* (2001). The poet Adrienne Rich has a wonderful essay on Dickinson's sense of her own genius in *Critical Essays on Emily Dickinson*, ed. Paul J. Ferlazzo (1984), 175–95. For critical readings, see Sharon Cameron, *Lyric Time: Dickinson and the Limits of Genre* (1979); J. Dobson, *Dickinson and the Strategies of Reticence* (1989); E. Phillips, *Emily Dickinson: Personae and Performance* (1996); Elizabeth A. Petrino, *Emily Dickinson and Her Contemporaries: Women's Verse in America, 1820–85*

(1998); and Virginia Jackson, *Dickinson's Misery: A Theory of Lyric Reading* (2005). For Dickinson in context, see *The Emily Dickinson Handbook*, ed. Gudrun Grabher, Roland Hagenbüchle, and Cristanne Miller (1998); Paula Bernat Bennett, "Emily Dickinson and her American Women Poet Peers," in *The Cambridge Companion to Emily Dickinson* (2002), 215–35; and *A Historical Guide to Emily Dickinson*, ed. Vivian R. Pollak (2004).

Frederick Douglass
Douglass himself wrote three autobiographies: not only the *Narrative*, but also *My Bondage and My Freedom* (1855) and *The Life and Times of Frederick Douglass, Written by Himself* (1892). For a more recent scholarly account, see William S. McFeely's *Frederick Douglass* (1991). Excellent critical and historical studies include *The Cambridge Companion to Frederick Douglass*, ed. Maurice S. Lee (2009); William L. Andrews, *To Tell a Free Story* (1986); Houston A. Baker, *Blues, Ideology, and Afro-American Literature* (1991); Audrey A. Fisch, *American Slaves in Victorian England* (2000); Dwight A. McBride, *Impossible Witnesses: Truth, Abolitionism, and Slave Testimony* (2001); and John Stauffer, *Giants: The Parallel Lives of Frederick Douglass and Abraham Lincoln* (2008). On the question of gender in the narrative, see Deborah E. McDowell, "In the First Place: Making Frederick Douglass and the Afro-American Narrative Tradition," in *Critical Essays on Frederick Douglass*, ed. William L. Andrews (1991), 192–211.

Johann Wolfgang von Goethe
Nicholas Boyle's two-volume biography, *Goethe: The Poet and the Age* (1991), is the most recent and one of the most extensive, informative biographies of Goethe and his work. More compact is John R. Williams's *The Life of Goethe: A Critical Biography* (1998), which is divided by genre and thus allows for a good, concise overview of Goethe's dramatic work. A classic study of *Faust* in English is Stuart Atkins's *Goethe's* Faust: *A Literary Analysis* (1964), a close textual analysis of the play in the tradition of the New Critics. John R. Williams's *Goethe's* Faust (1987) is more varied in its method and includes a useful discussion of the different sources, versions, and revisions that led to the final text. Most attuned to literary form is Benjamin Bennett's *Goethe's Theory of Poetry* (1986), which discusses Goethe's use and interruption of the traditional tragic plot as

well as other stylistic devices. Focusing on Goethe's theater practice is Marvin Carlson's *Goethe and the Weimar Theatre* (1978). Goethe's *Faust* has also attracted the attention of philosophers and cultural critics. An early example was the Marxist critic Georg Lukács, whose *Goethe and His Age* (1940, 1969) places Goethe within the history of political and social upheaval. This line of interpretation was later taken up by Marshall Berman, whose powerful *All That Is Sold Melts into Air* (1982) reads *Faust* alongside Marx and Engels's *Communist Manifesto*, written some fifteen years after Goethe's death, as an expression of modernist upheaval and productivity.

Jean-Jacques Rousseau
Leo Damrosch has written an excellent, lively biography, *Jean-Jacques Rousseau: Restless Genius* (2005). For a study of Rousseau's impact, see Thomas McFarland, *Romanticism and the Heritage of Rousseau* (1995). An appealing and readable account of the relationship between Hume and Rousseau, including a meditation on the ideas of both, can be found in David Edmonds and John Eidinow, *Rousseau's Dog: Two Great Thinkers at War in the Age of Enlightenment* (2006). For classic readings of *The Confessions*, see Jean Starobinski, *Jean-Jacques Rousseau: Transparency and Obstruction*, trans. Arthur Goldhammer (1988); Huntington Williams, *Rousseau and Romantic Autobiography* (1983); and Christopher Kelly, *Rousseau's Exem-*

plary Life: The Confessions as Political Philosophy (1987). One of the most important works of contemporary French philosophy is Jacques Derrida's reading of *The Confessions* in *Of Grammatology*, trans. Gayatri Chakravorty Spivak (1976). James Olney reads Rousseau as part of the history of autobiography

William Wordsworth
The best editions of Wordsworth's poetry are the volumes in "The Cornell Wordsworth" series, ed. Stephen Parrish (1974–2008). A good serious biography of the poet is Stephen Gill's *William Wordsworth: A Life* (1989); for a stunningly sensitive and intelligent reading of Wordsworth's poetry with his politics, see David Bromwich's *Disowned by Memory: Wordsworth's Poetry of the 1790s* (1998). Other fine studies include Geoffrey Hartman's *Wordsworth's Poetry* (1964), Alan Liu's *Wordsworth: A Sense of History* (1989), and Theresa M. Kelley's *Wordsworth's Revisionary Aesthetics* (1988). For a study of Wordsworth's ecological consciousness, see Jonathan Bate, *Romantic Ecology* (1991) and *The Song of the Earth* (2000); for a general look at audiences of Wordsworth's historical moment, see Richard Altick's classic study, *The English Common Reader* (1957), and William St. Clair, *The Reading Nation in the Romantic Period* (2004).

IV. At the Crossroads of Empire

Oscar Chapuis has written a two-part historical account of Vietnam in English: *A History of Vietnam: From Hong Bang to Tu Duc* (1995) and *The Last Emperors of Vietnam: From Tu Duc to Bao Dai* (2000). D. R. SarDesai's *India: The Definitive History* (2007) is a well-written overview. For a look at European imperial power in Asia in the period, see H. L. Wesseling, *The European Colonial Empires: 1815– 1919* (2004) and Andrew Porter, *The Oxford History of the British Empire: The Nineteenth Century* (1999).

Ghalib
Ghalib's poetry and prose have been translated and discussed widely in English. New poetic translations, with a comprehensive introduction and notes, are found in Vinay Dharwadker, *Ghalib: Ghazals* (2011); Aijaz Ahmad, *Ghazals of Ghalib* (1971) includes translations by American poets, with commentary on individual poems.

For historical context, biographical interpretation, and analysis of the Urdu and Persian writings, see Ralph Russell and Khurshidul Islam, *Ghalib: Life and Letters* (1994); and Ralph Russell, *Ghalib: The Poet and His Age* (1997). Daud Rahbar, *Urdu Letters of Mirza Asadu'llah Khan Ghalib* (1987) is a large translated selection; Pavan K. Verma, *Ghalib: The Man, the*

Times (1988) is an informative popular biography. Agha Shahid Ali's *Ravishing Disunities: Real Ghazals in English* (2000) collects recent experiments in the form by a large number of British, American, South Asian, and diasporic poets.

Nguyễn Du
There have been a number of recent translations of *The Tale of Kiều*, the best of which is Huỳnh Sanh Thông's revised bilingual edition (1983). This includes an excellent introduction by Alexander B. Woodside, which offers both historical and literary contexts for the poem. Nathalie Huynh Chau Nguyen's *Vietnamese Voices* (2003) explores the femininity of the central character and tracks the powerful influence of *Kiều* on modern Vietnamese literature. The 2007 film *Saigon Eclipse*, directed by Othello Khanh, is a contemporary retelling of the story.

Rabindranath Tagore
Amiya Chakravarty, ed., *A Tagore Reader* (1961) and Krishna Dutta and Andrew Robinson, *Rabindranath Tagore: An Anthology* (1997) provide the best overviews of Tagore's career and work in many genres. Dutta and Robinson's *Rabindranath Tagore: The Myriad-Minded Man* (1995) and Krishna Kripalani's *Rabindranath Tagore: A Biography* (1962) offer informative accounts in English of the artist's life. Older translations, prepared under Tagore's own supervision, are still available in *Collected Poems and Plays* (1936). Among important recent translations and accounts of Tagore's work are William Radice's *Rabindranath Tagore: Selected Poems* (1985) and *Rabindranath Tagore: Selected Short Stories* (1991); Ketaki Kushari Dyson's *I Won't Let You Go* (1993), a selection of poetry; and Anand Lal's *Rabindranath Tagore: Three Plays* (2001). Some of the best new translations and critical introductions are contained in the Oxford Tagore Translations series edited by Shukanta Chaudhuri and others, which includes *Selected Short Stories* (2000) and *Selected Writings on Literature and Language* (2001).

V. Realism across the Globe

Erich Auerbach's beautiful classic work of criticism, *Mimesis* (1946), explores a number of different attempts to capture reality in the Western tradition, including nineteenth-century realism. Pam Morris's *Realism* (2003) is a fine introduction to the concept, focusing exclusively on French and British literary examples. For a historical understanding of the rise of realism, with a special focus on the visual arts, see Linda Nochlin, *Realism* (1972). György Lukács has been one of the most influential theorists of the realist novel: see his *Theory of the Novel* (1920) and *Studies in European Realism* (1948). For the roots of British realism in eighteenth-century thought and social experience, Ian Watt's *Rise of the Novel* (1957) is a landmark study. An overview of Russian realism can be found in Dmitrij Cizevskij and Dmitrij Tschižewskij, *The History of Nineteenth-Century Russian Literature: The Age of Realism* (1974).

Anton Chekhov
Donald Rayfield's detailed biography *Anton Chekhov: A Life* (2000) is the most substantial in English. Rayfield's *Understanding Chekhov: A Critical Study of Chekhov's Prose and Drama* (1999) brings together biography and criticism. A more popular book on Chekhov is Janet Malcolm's *Reading Chekhov: A Critical Journey* (2001), which combines travel writing, biography, and criticism in a lively and intelligent—though not scholarly—combination. Dana Gioia's short essay on "Anton Chekhov's 'The Lady with the Pet Dog,'" in *Eclectic Literary Review* (Fall/Winter 1998) is concise and illuminating. See also Vladimir Nabokov's wonderful essay on Chekhov in his *Lectures on Russian Literature* (1981). Three fine collections of essays offer an array of good historical and critical responses to Chekhov's drama: *A Chekhov Companion*, ed. Toby W. Clyman (1985); the second *Critical Essays on Anton Chekhov*, ed. Thomas A. Eekman (1989); and *The Cambridge*

Companion to Chekhov, ed. Vera Gottlieb and Paul Allain (2000). Jean-Louis Barrault's poetic essay "Why *The Cherry Orchard?*" explores the musical structure of the play (included in *Anton Chekhov's Selected Plays*, ed. Laurence Senelick [2005], pp. 620–28).

Fyodor Dostoyevsky

Written over the course of three decades, Joseph Frank's magisterial five-volume biography of Dostoyevsky is widely hailed as a great achievement (1976–2002). There is a helpfully condensed one-volume version of this, called *Dostoevsky: A Writer in His Time*, ed. Mary Petrusewicz (2009), that focuses mostly on the impact of events on the author's ideas. Mikhail Bakhtin makes his influential argument that Dostoyevsky's work is always multi-voiced—"polyphonic"—in *Problems of Dostoyevsky's Poetics*, trans. Caryl Emerson (1984). The Norton Critical Edition of the text contains many useful critical commentaries, including Joseph Frank's, which considers the two parts of the text as responding to two different historical contexts, the first part concerned with the mid-1860s, the second part looking back to the idealist moment of the 1840s. This edition also includes parodies and imitations of the text by Woody Allen, Ralph Ellison, and Jean-Paul Sartre. See Fyodor Dostoevsky, *Notes from Underground*, ed. Michael Katz (2000).

Gustave Flaubert

Frederick Brown's *Flaubert: A Biography* (2006) is rich in historical detail; Geoffrey Wall's *Flaubert: A Life* (2002) is more psychological in focus. Flaubert's *Selected Letters*, ed. Geoffrey Wall (1998), give access to the writer's feelings and opinions in a way that his literary texts deliberately do not. Victor Brombert offers a classic reading of *A Simple Heart* in *The Novels of Flaubert* (1966). Winifred Woodhull investigates the relationship between private experience and public, historical events in "Configurations of the Family in *Un Coeur Simple*," *Comparative Literature* 39 (1987): 139–61.

Henrik Ibsen

Overall, the best book on Ibsen is Toril Moi's *Henrik Ibsen and the Birth of Modernism* (2006). Among the early reactions to Ibsen was George Bernard Shaw's *The Quintessence of Ibsenism* (1891), which emphasizes Ibsen's concern with pressing social and political issues, while William Archer's essays, collected by Thomas Postlewait in *William Archer on Ibsen: The Major Essays, 1889–1919* (1984), foreground Ibsen's poetic choices and techniques. Charles Lyons's compilation, *Critical Essays on Henrik Ibsen* (1987), includes landmark essays by Ibsen's modernist admirers, including James Joyce, E. M. Forster, and Georg Lukàcs. The wider cultural context of Ibsen's European success, as well as a wealth of personal detail, is captured in Michael Meyer's *Ibsen: A Biography* (1971). Michael Goldman's *Ibsen: The Dramaturgy of Fear* (1999) focuses on subtexts and psychologies. In *Ibsen and Early Modernist Theatre, 1890–1900*, Kirsten Shepherd-Barr situates Ibsen in the context of theater history, and Joan Templeton's *Ibsen's Women* is the first in-depth analysis of Ibsen's construction of female characters, including Hedda Gabler. *The Cambridge Companion to Ibsen*, ed. James McFarlane (1994), provides a good introduction into recent scholarship and contemporary approaches.

Leo Tolstoy

A. N. Wilson's *Tolstoy* (1988) is an entertaining and readable biography. Gary R. Jahn's *Tolstoy's The Death of Ivan Il'ich* (1999) contains a number of fine interpretive essays and an excellent introduction. It also includes a set of notes on connotations of phrases in the original Russian text. For other good critical essays, see R. F. Christian, *Tolstoy: A Critical Introduction* (1969); Edward Wasiolek, ed., *Critical Essays on Tolstoy* (1986); Harold Bloom, ed., *Leo Tolstoy* (1986); *Tolstoy* by John Bayley (1997); and David Holbrook's *Tolstoy, Woman and Death* (1997). The fascinating correspondence between Tolstoy and Gandhi can be found in B. Srinivasa Murthy, ed., *Mahatma Gandhi and Leo Tolstoy: Letters* (1987).

VI. Modernity and Modernism, 1900–1945

Pericles Lewis, *The Cambridge Introduction to Modernism* (2007), offers an overview of developments in England and Europe. Ástráður Eysteinsson and Vivian Lisca, eds., *Modernism*, 2 vols. (2007) provides detailed studies of particular national contexts. Harry Levin, "What Was Modernism?" (1962, repr. in *Refractions*, 1966) is a survey of modernist writers as humanists and inheritors of the Enlightenment. Many of the original critical writings on modern literature and art are collected in Vassiliki Kolocotroni, Jane Goldman, and Olga Taxidoe, eds., *Modernism: An Anthology of Sources and Documents* (1998). Richard Gilman, *The Making of Modern Drama* (1974) treats developments in drama, while Martin Puchner, *Stage Fright: Modernism, Anti-Theatricality, and Drama* (2002) explores the modernists' ambivalence toward theater. H. H. Arnason and Elizabeth Mansfield, *History of Modern Art: Painting, Sculpture, Architecture* (6th ed., 2009, illus.) follows the evolution of the arts in the West, from the nineteenth century to the 1960s. Matei Calinescu, *Five Faces of Modernity* (1987) is an informative collection of essays on the aesthetics of modernism, avant-garde, decadence, and kitsch. Peter Gay, *Modernism: The Lure of Heresy* (2007) places the movement in historical context.

Anna Akhmatova

Eileen Feinstein, *Anna of All the Russias: A Life of Anna Akhmatova* (2007) is a good recent biography. Roberta Reeder, *Anna Akhmatova: Poet and Prophet* (1994) is thorough. David Wells, *Anna Akhmatova: Her Poetry* (1996) is a readable, well-documented study that discusses works in chronological order. Amanda Haight, *Anna Akhmatova: A Poetic Pilgrimage* (1976) and Susan Amert, *In a Shattered Mirror: The Later Poetry of Anna Akhmatova* (1992) are perceptive book-length studies. Ronald Hingley, *Nightingale Fever: Russian Poets in Revolution* (1981) discusses Akhmatova, Pasternak, Tsvetaeva, and Mandelstam in the context of Russian literary history and Soviet politics up to the early years of World War II. Anna Akhmatova, *My Half Century: Selected Prose*, ed. Ronald Meyer (1992), includes autobiographical material, correspondence, short pieces on other writers, and an essay on Akhmatova's prose.

Jorge Luis Borges

Useful biographies include James Woodall, *The Man in the Mirror of the Book: A Life of Jorge Luis Borges* (1996); James Woodall, *Borges: A Life* (1996); and Jason Wilson, *Jorge Luis Borges* (2006). George R. McMurray, *Jorge Luis Borges* (1980) and Martin S. Stabb, *Borges Revisited* (1991) are general introductions to the man and his work. Jaime Alazraki,

ed., *Critical Essays on Jorge Luis Borges* (1987) assembles articles and reviews (including the 1970 *Autobiographical Essay*), four comparative essays, and a general introduction that offer valuable perspectives on Borges's writing as well as his impact on writers and critics in the United States. Edna Aizenberg, ed., *Borges and His Successors: The Borgesian Impact on Literature and the Arts* (1990) is a wide-ranging collection of essays describing Borges as the precursor of postmodern fiction and criticism. Anna Maria Barrenechea, *Borges the Labyrinth Maker* (1965) discusses the writer's intricate style, while Daniel Balderston, *Out of Context: Historical Reference and the Representation of Reality in Borges* (1993) focuses on the texts' manipulation of fictional and historical reality. Fernando Sorrentino, *Seven Conversations with Jorge Luis Borges* (1981) is a series of informal, widely ranging interviews from 1972, with a list of the topics of each conversation. Recent translations into English include *Collected Fictions*, trans. Andrew Hurley (1998) and *Selected Non-Fictions*, ed. Eliot Weinberger (2000).

Joseph Conrad

Among the many sources of biographical information are Conrad's *The Mirror of the Sea* (1906) and *A Personal Record* (1912) and Jocelyn Baines, *Joseph Conrad: A Critical Biography* (1960). The best general biography is Zdzislaw

Najder, *Joseph Conrad: A Life* (2007). Albert J. Guérard's critical study, *Conrad the Novelist* (1958), is also recommended. The best general critical study, Ian Watt's *Conrad in the Nine-teenth Century* (1979), discusses Conrad's impressionist and symbolist techniques. Chinua Achebe's essay "An Image of Africa: Racism in Conrad's *Heart of Darkness*" is published in his *Hopes and Impediments* (1988). J. H. Stape, ed., *The Cambridge Companion to Joseph Conrad* (1996) offers a wide variety of perspectives on Conrad's work, including *Heart of Darkness*; Allan Simmons, *Heart of Darkness: A Reader's Guide* (2007) provides an introduction to the critical themes of the novella. Adam Hochs-child, *King Leopold's Ghost: A Story of Greed, Terror, and Heroism in Colonial Africa* (1998) is a detailed and informative study of the Congo setting of Conrad's novella.

T. S. Eliot

Peter Ackroyd, *T. S. Eliot* (1984) and Tony Sharpe, *T. S. Eliot: A Literary Life* (1991) are brief, readable introductions to Eliot's life and works. Lyndall Gordon, *T. S. Eliot: An Imperfect Life* (1998) is a fuller biography. Several volumes of Eliot's correspondence are being published in Valerie Eliot and Hugh Haughton, ed., *The Letters of T. S. Eliot* (2009–). The influence of Eliot's life on his poems is the subject of Ronald Schuchard, *Eliot's Dark Angel: Intersections of Life and Art* (1999). Martin Scofield, *T. S. Eliot: The Poems* (1988) offers a concise, balanced discussion of the evolution of Eliot's poetry. A fine study is Denis Donogue, *Words Alone: The Poet T. S. Eliot* (2000). Useful general collections are Linda Wagner, ed., *T. S. Eliot: A Collection of Criticism* (1974); Ronald Bush, ed., *T. S. Eliot: The Modernist in History* (1991); A. David Moody, ed., *The Cambridge Companion to T. S. Eliot* (1995); and Harold Bloom, ed., *T. S. Eliot* (1999).

James Joyce

Harry Levin, *James Joyce: A Critical Introduction* (1941) is an excellent, readable general introduction. The standard, detailed biography, with illustrations, is Richard Ellmann, *James Joyce* (1982). Morris Beja, *James Joyce: A Literary Life* (1992) includes recent scholarship. Derek Attridge, ed., *The Cambridge Companion to James Joyce* (1990) and Mary T. Reynolds, ed., *James Joyce: A Collection of Critical Essays* (1993) treat various aspects of the work. Daniel R. Schwarz, ed., *The Dead* (1994) is a useful short book that contains the

text and contextual material, an account of *Dubliners'* history and criticism from the 1950s, and analyses by several authors using five critical perspectives. John Wyse Jackson and Bernard McGinley, eds., *Joyce's* Dubliners: *An Illustrated Edition with Annotations* (1995) is a fascinating, copiously illustrated and documented edition that includes allusions to other works and a capsule essay after each story. A valuable recent introduction is David Pierce, *Reading Joyce* (2008). Pierce's earlier *James Joyce's Ireland* (1992) provides contemporary photographs by Dan Harper and uses documents, photographs, and quotations to reconstruct Joyce's biography in historical context.

Franz Kafka

Kafka's life has been the subject of many studies, starting with Max Brod, *Franz Kafka: A Biography* (English trans., 1960). One of the best recent works is Nicholas Murray, *Kafka: A Biography* (2004). Readable introductions to the author's life and work include Klaus Wagenbach, *Kafka* (2003) and Louis Begley, *The Tremendous World I Have Inside My Head: Franz Kafka: A Biographical Essay* (2008). Heinz Politzer, *Franz Kafka: Parable and Paradox* (1962) is an interesting early study concerned with Kafka's symbolism. *Kafka: A Collection of Critical Essays*, ed. Ronald Gray (1962), introduces the main themes of Kafka criticism, while more recent essays, specifically on the selection here, are collected in Harold Bloom, ed., *Franz Kafka's The Metamorphosis* (1988) and Stanley Corngold, ed., *The Metamorphosis* (1996). Kafka's religious background is the subject of Sander Gilman, *Franz Kafka: The Jewish Patient* (1995), while the Czech context is discussed by Scott Spector, *Prague Territories* (2000).

Lu Xun

A valuable and readable biography is David Pollard, *The True Story of Lu Xun* (2002). Leo Ou-fan Lee, *Voices from the Iron House: A Study of Lu Xun* (1987) is an excellent introduction to Lu Xun's work, placing it in the context of his life and Chinese cultural history; and Lee, *Lu Xun and His Legacy* (1985) is a collection of scholarly articles treating Lu's literary work, his politics, and his influence. William A. Lyell, *Lu Hsün's Vision of Reality* (1976) is also useful.

Pablo Neruda

Pablo Neruda, *Memoirs*, trans. Hardie St. Martin (1977) contains much biographical information.

A good recent biography in English is Adam Feinstein, *Pablo Neruda: A Passion for Life* (2004). Manuel Duran and Margery Safir, *Earth Tones: The Poetry of Pablo Neruda* (1981) is an excellent thematic study that includes a short biography. *Pablo Neruda*, ed. Harold Bloom (1989), contains nineteen valuable essays and reminiscences by scholars, translators, and those who knew Neruda. John Felstiner, *Translating Neruda: The Way to Macchu Picchu* (1980) describes in detail the process of translating *The Heights of Macchu Picchu* in terms of Neruda's life and perspectives. Louis Poirot, *Pablo Neruda: Absence and Presence* (1990) matches photographs of Neruda, his friends, and his homes with related passages from the poet, his wife, and friends. A recent work is *The Poetry of Pablo Neruda*, trans. Ilan Stavans (2005).

Luigi Pirandello

Gaspare Guidice's *Pirandello: A Biography* (1975), trans. Alastair Hamilton provides a good overview of the artist's life. The best essay on Pirandello and metatheater is by Maurizio Grande, "Pirandello and the Theatre-within-the-Theatre: Thresholds and Frames in *Cascuno a suo modo*" (in *Luigi Pirandello: Contemporary Perspectives* [1999]). Roger W. Oliver's *Dreams of Passion: The Theater of Luigi Pirandello* (1979) focuses on Pirandello's theory of humor and applies it to his best-known plays, including *Six Characters*. Ann Hallamore Caesar's *Characters and Authors in Luigi Pirandello* (1998) offers a wide-ranging discussion of Pirandello through the diversity of genres in which he worked, from novels and poetry to drama and film. Pirandello's work in the theater is captured in *Luigi Pirandello in the Theatre: A Documentary Record* (1993), ed. Susan Bassnett and Jennifer Lorch, and in A. Richard Sogliuzzo's *Luigi Pirandello, Director: The Playwright in the Theatre* (1982).

Rainer Maria Rilke

J. F. Hendry, *The Sacred Threshold: A Life of Rainer Maria Rilke* (1983) and Patricia Pollock Brodsky, *Rainer Maria Rilke* (1988) are brief, readable biographies with numerous citations from Rilke's letters and work. A more recent, comprehensive biography is Ralph Freedman's *Life of a Poet: Rainer Maria Rilke* (1998). Heinz F. Peters, *Rainer Maria Rilke: Masks and the Man* (1977) is a biographical and thematic study of the poet's work and influence. William H. Gass, *Reading Rilke: Reflections on the Problems of Translation* (1999) combines biography, philosophy, and commentary on specific translation problems in the *Duino Elegies*. Judith Ryan, *Rilke, Modernism and Poetic Tradition* (1999) places his work in its literary-historical context.

Virginia Woolf

Hermione Lee's biography, *Virginia Woolf* (1996) is now, and surely for a while to come, the definitive work on Woolf's life. Julia Briggs has also produced a detailed recent biography that pays close attention to the author's works and their creation, *Virginia Woolf: An Inner Life* (2005). Alison Light's study, *Mrs. Woolf and the Servants* (2007), examines Woolf's place amid the shifting social and economic issues of the era through the lens of her relationships with the domestic help. Two valuable collections of essays on Woolf's writing and her position in the modernist tradition are Patricia Clements and Isobel Grundy, eds., *Virginia Woolf: New Critical Essays* (1983) and Margaret Homans, ed., *Virginia Woolf: A Collection of Critical Essays* (1993). S. P. Rosenbaum, ed., *Virginia Woolf: Women and Fiction* (1992) transcribes and edits two draft manuscripts that are the basis for *A Room of One's Own*. Gillian Beer, *Virginia Woolf: The Common Ground* (1996) offers four useful general essays and four discussions of specific novels.

William Butler Yeats

Edward Malins presents a brief introduction with biography, illustrations, and maps in *A Preface to Yeats* (1994). Richard Ellmann, *The Identity of Yeats* (1964) is an excellent discussion of the poet's work as a whole. Norman A. Jeffares has revised his major study, *A New Commentary on the Collected Poems of W. B. Yeats* (1983); a useful reference work is Lester I. Conner, *A Yeats Dictionary: Persons and Places in the Poetry of William Butler Yeats* (1998). The most thorough and balanced biographical study is R. F. Foster, *W. B. Yeats: A Life*, 2 vols. (1997–2003). A major account of Yeats's use of poetic form is Helen Vendler, *Our Secret Discipline: Yeats and Lyric Form* (2007). Essay collections include Harold Bloom, ed., *William Butler Yeats* (1986); Richard J. Finneran, ed., *Critical Essays on W. B. Yeats* (1986); and Marjorie Howes and John Kelly, eds., *Cambridge Companion to W. B. Yeats* (2006).

VII. Postwar and Postcolonial Literature, 1945–68

Ihab and Sally Hassan, eds., *Essays in Innovation/Renovation: New Perspectives on the Humanities* (1983) explores change in Western culture in the second half of the twentieth century. Tony Judt, *Postwar: A History of Europe Since 1945* (2005) explores the historical context in Europe, while Michael Howard and William Roger Louis, eds., *The Oxford History of the Twentieth Century* (1998) includes informative essays on other parts of the world. Janheinz Jahn, *Muntu: African Culture and the Western World*, trans. Marjorie Grene (1990, orig. 1961) is an influential discussion of the interface of two cultures. Anthony Appiah, *In My Father's House: Africa in the Philosophy of Culture* (1992) explores similar issues in a postcolonial context. Marjorie Perloff, ed., *Postmodern Genres* (1989) collects essays on postmodernism in art and literature. Linda Hutcheon, *A Poetics of Postmodernism* (1988) analyzes the movement's literary forms.

Chinua Achebe

A good reference is Ezenwa Ohaeto, *Chinua Achebe: A Biography* (1997). Achebe has written a series of memoirs of his early life, collected as *The Education of a British-Protected Child* (2009). C. L. Innes, *Chinua Achebe* (1990) is a comprehensive study of the writer's work through 1988 that emphasizes his literary techniques and Africanization of the novel. Simon Gikandi, *Reading Chinua Achebe: Language and Ideology in Fiction* (1991) is also recommended. Also of interest is *Conversations with Chinua Achebe* (1997), ed. Bernth Lindfors. Jago Morrison, *The Fiction of Chinua Achebe* (2007) is a guide to criticism that includes discussions of his short fiction.

James Baldwin

David Leeming, who served as Baldwin's personal secretary, later recollected his friend and employer in *James Baldwin: A Biography* (1995). Also recommended is James Campbell, *Talking at the Gates: A Life of James Baldwin* (1991). A collection of essays published near the end of Baldwin's life, Harold Bloom, ed., *James Baldwin: Modern Critical Views* (1986) represents a range of views by Baldwin's contemporaries. A more recent collection, Dwight A. McBride, ed., *James Baldwin Now* (1999) includes a number of essays on race and sexuality.

Tadeusz Borowski

Brief discussions of Borowski are found in Czeslaw Milosz, *The History of Polish Literature* (1969); and from a different perspective, Sidra DeKoven Ezrahi, *By Words Alone: The Holocaust in Literature* (1980) and James Hatley, *Suffering Witness: The Quandary of Responsibility after the Irreparable* (2000). Jan Kott, "Introduction," *This Way for the Gas, Ladies and Gentlemen* (1976), and Jan Walc, "When the Earth Is No Longer a Dream and Cannot Be Dreamed through to the End," *Polish Review* (1987), combine biography and literary analysis, while Czeslaw Milosz, *The Captive Mind* (1953) analyzes Borowski's later communism in relation to his generation. Selections from the poetry are available in *Selected Poems* (1990), trans. Tadeusz Pióro with Larry Rafferty. Tadeusz Drewnowski, ed., *Postal Indiscretions: The Correspondence of Tadeusz Borowski* (2007), trans. Alicia Nitecki, includes letters written to his family from Auschwitz.

Albert Camus

Germaine Brée, *Albert Camus* (1964) is an excellent general study. Catherine Savage Brosman, *Albert Camus* (2001) is a short introduction and biography. Herbert Lottman, *Albert Camus: A Biography* (1979) and Oliver Todd, *Albert Camus: A Life* (1997) are detailed accounts. English Showalter, *Exiles and Strangers: A Reading of Camus's* Exile and the Kingdom (1984) offers essays on the six stories in Camus's collection and separate comments on translations. For a collection of recent essays on Camus, see Edward J. Hughes, ed., *The Cambridge Companion to Camus* (2007), which contains a bibliography.

Doris Lessing

The most comprehensive biography is Carol Klein, *Doris Lessing* (2000). Ruth Whittaker, *Doris Lessing* (1988) is a concise, informative discussion of the writer's fiction to 1985; it includes biographical contexts and selective bibliography. Two volumes of Lessing's autobiography are published as *Under My Skin* (1995) and *Walking in the Shade* (1997). A good critical study of the novels is Roberta Rubenstein, *The Novelistic Vision of Doris Lessing* (1979). Perspectives on women and literature are the focus of Gayle Greene, *Doris Lessing: The Poetics of Change* (1994).

Naguib Mahfouz

Roger M. A. Allen, *The Arabic Novel: An Historical and Critical Introduction* (1982) is an authoritative introduction that situates Mahfouz in the context of modern Arabic literature and includes a bibliography of works in Arabic and Western languages. The author's own perspective is given in Najib Mahfuz, *Echoes of an Autobiography*, trans. Denys Johnson-Davies (1997). Sasson Somekh, *"Za 'balawi"—Author, Theme and Technique,"* in *Journal of Arabic Literature* (1970), examines the story as a "double-layered" structure governed by references to Sufi mysticism. Michael Beard and Adnan Haydar, eds., *Naguib Mahfouz: From Regional Fame to Global Recognition* (1993) assembles eleven original essays on themes, individual works, and cultural contexts in Mahfouz's work. Trevor le Gassick, ed., *Critical Perspectives on Naguib Mahfouz* (1991) reprints articles on the writer's work up to the 1970s. Rasheed El-Enany, ed., *Naguib Mahfouz: The Pursuit of Meaning* (1993) is an excellent study that offers biography; analyses of novels, short stories, and plays; and a guide for further reading. Comparative studies include Mona Mikhail, *Studies in the Short Fiction of Mahfouz and Idris* (1992), an introductory work juxtaposing themes in Hemingway, Yusuf Idris, Mahfouz, and Camus, and Samia Mehrez, *Egyptian Writers Between History and Fiction: Essays on Naguib Mahfouz, Sonallah Ibrahim, and Gamal al-Ghitani* (1994). Rasheed El-Enany discusses the place of religion in Mahfouz's work in "The Dichotomy of Islam and Modernity in the Fiction of Naguib Mahfouz," in John C. Hawley, ed., *The Postcolonial Crescent: Islam's Impact on Contemporary Literature* (1998).

VIII. Contemporary World Literature

Lois Parkinson Zamora and Wendy B. Faris, eds., *Magical Realism: Theory, History, Community* (1997) examines the theoretical and cultural implications of the style in Latin America and elsewhere. Nancy K. Miller, ed., *The Poetics of Gender* (1986) presents essays on various aspects of feminist criticism. Sarah Lawall, ed., *Reading World Literature: Theory, History, Practice* (1994) includes a theoretical introduction to the subject of world literature and twelve essays on specific topics. David Damrosch, *What Is World Literature?* (2003) explores a range of issues in the study of world literature, while Pascale Casanova, *The World Republic of Letters* (2004) offers a sociological view of the development of literary reputations. Accounts of crucial moments in contemporary history include Jeremi Suri, ed., *The Global Revolutions of 1968* (2007); Timothy Garton Ash, *The Magic Lantern: The Revolution of '89 Witnessed in Warsaw, Budapest, Berlin, and Prague* (1993); and Thomas L. Friedman, *The World Is Flat 3.0: A Brief History of the Twenty-First Century* (2007).

Chimamanda Ngozi Adichie

Adichie gives expression to some of her political and social views in *We Should All be Feminists* (2017). She outlines her views on literary representation in her Commonwealth Lecture, "To Instruct and Delight: A Case for Realist Literature" (2012). Ernest N. Emenyonu, ed., *A Companion to Chimamanda Ngozi Adichie*, includes essays on various facets of Adichie's work. Her earlier works are studied in Allwell

Abalogu Onukaogu, *Chimamanda Ngozi Adichie: The Aesthetics of Commitment and Narrative* (2010).

Hanan al-Shaykh

Several of al-Shaykh's novels, and her memoir, *The Locust and the Bird: My Mother's Story* (2010), have been translated into English. A lengthy interview by Paula W. Sunderman was published in *Literary Review* in 1997 as "Between Two Worlds: An Interview with Hanan al-Shaykh."

Nawal El Saadawi

Several articles in journals and collective volumes offer views and assessments of Nawal El Saadawi's work, but Fedwa Malti-Douglas, *Men, Women and God(s): Nawal El Saadawi and Arab Feminist Poetics* (1995) is the only study so far devoted to a systematic account and critical interpretation of the corpus in the light of its social and cultural background. El Saadawi has published two volumes of autobiography, translated by Sherif Hetata as *Daughter of Isis* (1999) and *Walking Through Fire* (2002). A recent collection of essays is Ernest N. Emenyonu and Maureen N. Eke, eds., *Emerging Perspectives on Nawal El Saadawi* (2010).

Gabriel García Márquez

The best biography is Gerald Martin, *Gabriel García Márquez* (2008). A shorter overview is Rubén Pelayo, *Gabriel García Márquez: A Biography* (2009). García Márquez has himself published a remarkable autobiography, *Living to Tell the Tale* (2003). Regina Janes, *Gabriel García Márquez, Revolutions in Wonderland* (1981) is an excellent early study on the author in a Latin American context. Other useful introductions to the writer and his work are George P. McMurray, *Gabriel García Márquez* (1977); Robin W. Fiddian, *García Márquez* (1995); and Joan Mellen, *Gabriel García Márquez* (2000). See also Julio Ortega, ed., *Gabriel García Márquez and the Powers of Fiction* (1988) and Isabel Rodriguez-Vergara, *Haunting Demons: Critical Essays on the Works of Gabriel García Márquez* (1998). Harley D. Oberhelman, ed., *Gabriel García Márquez: A Study of the Short Fiction* (1991) includes a bibliography.

Seamus Heaney

Michael Parker, *Seamus Heaney: The Making of a Poet* (1993) combines biography with literary criticism, while the best overall critical study is Helen Vendler, *Seamus Heaney* (1998), which focuses on Heaney's intellectual and aesthetic experiments. Bernard O'Donoghue, ed., *The Cambridge Companion to Seamus Heaney* (2009) includes several essays on Heaney's relationship to other poets. A number of the poet's interviews are collected in Dennis O'Driscoll, ed., *Stepping Stones: Interviews with Seamus Heaney* (2008).

Jamaica Kincaid

Diane Simmons provides an overview of Kincaid's work, with biographical information, in *Jamaica Kincaid* (1994). Elizabeth Paravisini-Gebert, *Jamaica Kincaid: A Critical Companion* (1999) focuses on the early short stories and the first three novels. A more recent overview is Justin Edwards, *Understanding Jamaica Kincaid* (2007).

Mo Yan

The Roots literary movement, to which Mo Yan belongs, is discussed in Xueping Zhong, *Masculinity Besieged: Issues of Modernity and Male Subjectivity in Chinese Literature of the Late Twentieth Century* (2000). David Der-Wei Wang's essay, "The Literary World of Mo Yan," in *World Literature Today* (2000), offers a general introduction to the work of Mo Yan, with a focus on his novels and their complex narration.

Orhan Pamuk

Pamuk's melancholic memoir, *Istanbul: Memories and the City*, trans. Maureen Freely (2004), intersperses autobiographical reflections with historical analysis of Turkey and descriptions of literary figures associated with the country. Michael D. McGaha, *Autobiographies of Orhan Pamuk: The Writer in His Novels* (2008) explores the relationship between Pamuk's life and his work. Nilgun Anadolu-Okur, ed., *Essays Interpreting the Writings of Novelist Orhan Pamuk: The Turkish Winner of the Nobel Prize* (2009) explores Pamuk's stature as a global writer.

Salman Rushdie

Midnight's Children (1980) has been in print since its first publication. Among the many books about Rushdie and his work, particularly helpful and informative are Damian Grant, *Salman Rushdie* (1999), for an overview of much of his career; Jaina C. Sanga, *Salman Rushdie's Postcolonial Metaphors* (2001) and Sabrina Hassumani, *Salman Rushdie* (2002), for analyses of his style and major themes. Discussions of the writer's work in wider literary contexts appear in Timothy Brennan, *Salman Rushdie and the Third World* (1989) and Fawzia Afzal-Khan, *Cultural Imperialism and the Indo-English Novel* (1993). Important documentary sources include Lisa Appignanesi and Sara Maitland, *The Rushdie File* (1990); Michael R. Reder, *Conversations with Salman Rushdie* (2000); and Pradyumna S. Chauhan, *Salman Rushdie Interviews* (2001).

Leslie Marmon Silko

Gregory Salyer, *Leslie Marmon Silko* (1997) is a brief introduction to the author and her work; Brewster E. Fitz offers an updated view of the author's career in *Silko: Writing Storyteller and Medicine Woman* (2004). Helen Jaskoski, *Leslie Marmon Silko: A Study of the Short Fiction* (1998) focuses on the stories. Leslie Marmon Silko, *Sacred Water: Narratives and Pictures* (1994) is an autobiographical narrative. Melody Graulich, ed., *"Yellow Woman": Leslie Marmon Silko* (1993) collects pertinent critical essays. "Yellow Woman" and other works are treated in Louise K. Barnett and James L. Thorson, eds., *Leslie Marmon Silko: A Collection of Critical Essays* (1999). For traditional texts on Yellow Woman and other figures in Laguna mythology, the best source is Franz Boas, *Keresan Texts* (1928); the stories in Boas's volume were obtained in 1919–1921 from several Laguna informants, including Leslie Silko's great-grandfather, Robert Marmon.

Wole Soyinka

For an authoritative text and extensive background readings on *Death and the King's Horseman*, consult the Norton Critical Edition of that play (2003). Derek Wright, *Wole Soyinka Revisited* (1993) provides a nuanced analysis of the dramatic oeuvre, focusing on theatrical categories, such as ritual, tragedy, and satire, that are central to an understanding of Soyinka's work. Ketu H. Katrak, *Wole Soyinka and Modern Tragedy* (1986) focuses on the author's attempt to create a Yoruba tragedy. By far the best of the critical literature on the playwright is Biodun Jeyifo, *Wole Soyinka: Politics, Poetics and Postcoloniality* (2004), which analyzes the complex relations among colonial culture, independence, and literature that mark this playwright's oeuvre. See also a collection of interviews, *Conversations with Wole Soyinka*, ed. Biodun Jeyifo (2001). The philosopher K. Anthony Appiah has devoted attention to Soyinka in his work *In My Father's House: Africa in the Philosophy of Culture* (1992). There are several useful collections of essays on Soyinka, including James Gibbs, ed., *Critical Perspectives on Wole Soyinka* (1980) and Biodun Jeyifo, ed., *Perspectives on Wole Syoinka*.

Derek Walcott

Derek Walcott, *Another Life* (1973), an autobiography in verse, traces the poet's artistic development. A full biography is Bruce King, *Derek Walcott: A Caribbean Life* (2000). Walcott's collection of essays, *What the Twilight Says* (1998), is an indispensable compendium of his social and aesthetic ideas. Robert Hamner, *Derek Walcott* (1978, rev. 1993), is a comprehensive and accessible full-length study of the writer's work; John Thieme, *Derek Walcott* (1999) is more up-to-date and provides commentaries on the key poems in Walcott's various collections and on the dramatic works. Robert Hamner, *Epic of the Dispossessed* (1997) offers a detailed discussion of *Omeros* that considers its adaptation of epic idiom to the experience and life dilemmas of the common folk. *The Art of Derek Walcott*, ed. Stewart Brown (1991), and *Critical Perspectives on Derek Walcott*, ed. Robert Hamner (1993), are collective volumes that cover Walcott's work up to the dates of their publication.

Permissions Acknowledgments

Luigi Pirandello: "Six Characters in Search of an Author" from PIRANDELLO'S MAJOR PLAYS, trans. by Eric Bentley. Reprinted with permission of the publisher, Northwestern University Press.

Rainer Maria Rilke: "Archaic Torso of Apollo," "The Panther," "The Swan," and "Spanish Dancer," trans. by M. D. Herter Norton. Copyright 1938 by W. W. Norton & Co., Inc. Renewed © 1966 by M. D. Herter Norton. Used by permission of W. W. Norton & Company, Inc.

Jean-Jacques Rousseau: From CONFESSIONS, trans. by Angela Scholar, ed. by Patrick Coleman (2000). By permission of Oxford University Press.

Salman Rushdie: "The Perforated Sheet" from MIDNIGHT'S CHILDREN is reprinted with permission of The Wylie Agency LLC. Copyright © 1981 by Salman Rushdie.

Nawal el Saadawi: "In Camera" from DEATH OF AN EX-MINISTER, trans. by Shirley Eber. First published by Methuen in 1987. Copyright © 1987. Reprinted by permission of the author.

Leslie Marmon Silko: "Yellow Woman" from STORYTELLER. Copyright © 1981, 2012 by Leslie Marmon Silko. Used with permission of Viking Books, an imprint of Penguin Publishing Group, a division of Penguin Random House LLC. All rights reserved. Any third-party use of this material, outside of this publication, is prohibited. Interested parties must apply directly to Penguin Random House LLC for permission

Wole Soyinka: DEATH AND THE KING'S HORSEMAN. Copyright © 1975, 2003 by Wole Soyinka. Used by permission of W. W. Norton & Company, Inc. and Melanie Jackson Agency, LLC.

Rabindranath Tagore: "Punishment" from RABINDRANATH TAGORE: SELECTED SHORT STORIES (Penguin Books Ltd. 1991), trans. by William Radice. Copyright © 1991 by William Radice. Reprinted with permission of John Johnson, Author's Agent, Ltd. "Kabuliwala," trans. by Madhuchchhanda Karlekar) from SELECTED SHORT STORIES. Reproduced with permission of Oxford University Press India. Copyright © 2000 by Oxford University Press.

Voltaire: CANDIDE: A NORTON CRITICAL EDITION, second ed., trans. by Robert M. Adams. Copyright © 1991, 1966 by W. W. Norton & Company, Inc. Used by permission of W. W. Norton & Company, Inc.

Derek Walcott: Excerpts from OMEROS. Copyright © 1990 by Derek Walcott. Reprinted by permission of Farrar, Straus and Giroux.

Virginia Woolf: Excerpts from A ROOM OF ONE'S OWN by Virginia Woolf, copyright 1929 by Houghton Mifflin Harcourt Publishing Company and renewed 1957 by Leonard Woolf. Reprinted by permission Houghton Mifflin Harcourt Publishing Company. All rights reserved.

Wu Cheng'en: From THE MONKEY AND THE MONK: A REVISED ABRIDGMENT OF JOURNEY TO THE WEST, trans. by Anthony Yu. Copyright © 2006 by The University of Chicago. Reprinted by permission of the University of Chicago Press.

W. B. Yeats: "Leda and the Swan," "Sailing to Byzantium," "Byzantium," and "Among School Children from THE COLLECTED WORKS OF W.B. YEATS, Vol. 1: THE POEMS: REVISED, ed. by Richard J. Finneran. Copyright © 1928 by the Macmillan Company, renewed 1956 by Georgie Yeats. Copyright © 1933 by The Macmillan Company, renewed 1961 by Bertha Georgie Yeats. Reprinted with the permission of Scribner, a division of Simon & Schuster, Inc. All rights reserved.

IMAGES

2–3 The Metropolitan Museum of Art, Rogers Fund, 1922 (JP1398); 6 Wikimedia Commons, public domain; 9 © RMN-Grand Palais/Art Resource, NY; 100 Werner Forman/Art Resource, NY; 126–7 Erich Lessing/Art Resource, NY; 129 Courtesy of Historical Collections & Services, Claude Moore Health Sciences Library, University of VA; 130 Erich Lessing/Art Resource, NY; 132 © RMN-Grand Palais/Art Resource, NY; 320–1 © RMN-Grand Palais/Art Resource, NY; 322 HIP/Art Resource, NY; 325 © RMN-Grand Palais/Art Resource, NY; 328 National Army Museum, London/Bridgeman Images; 332 © The Trustees of the British Museum/Art Resource, NY; 576–7 SSPL/Getty Images; 579 Adoc-photos/Art Resource, NY; 582 © Hulton-Deutsch Collection/CORBIS/Corbis via Getty Images; 654-5 bpk, Berlin/Tretyakov Gallery/Roman Beniaminson/Art Resource, NY; 656 bpk, Berlin/Galerie Neue Meister, Staatliche Kunstsammlungen/Art Resource, NY; 658 The New York Public Library/Art Resource, NY; 885 Rodchenko, Alexander (1891–1956) © VAGA, NY Advertisement: "Books!", 1925. Scala/Art Resource, NY. Art © Estate of Alexander Rodchenko/RAO, Moscow/VAGA, New York; 886 Wikimedia Commons, public domain; 887 Bettmann/Getty Images; 890 United States Holocaust Memorial Museum; 892 Picasso, Pablo (1881–1973) Guernica. 1937. Photo: John Bigelow Taylor/Art Resource, NY. © 2017 Estate of Pablo Picasso/Artists Rights Society (ARS), New York; 1194–5 Margaret Bourke-White/The LIFE Picture Collection/Getty Images; 1197 Photo by Loomis Dean/The LIFE Picture Collection/Getty Images; 1198 ©Bettmann/Getty Images; 1270–1 © Marc Riboud/Magnum Photos; 1272 Jean-Claude LABBE/Gamma-Rapho via Getty Images; 1273 Gallo Images/Oryx Media Archive/Getty Images; 1276 Shirin Neshat/Gladstone Gallery

COLOR INSERT

Index